George Eliot: Four Novels

George Eliot

Four Novels

Adam Bede, Middlemarch,
The Mill on the Floss &
Silas Marner

Wordsworth Editions

Readers who are interested in other titles from
Wordsworth Editions are invited to visit our website at
www.wordsworth-editions.com

For our latest list and a full mail-order service contact
Bibliophile Books, 5 Thomas Road, London E14 7BN
Tel: +44 0207 515 9222   Fax: +44 0207 538 4115
e-mail: orders@bibliophilebooks.com

This edition published 2005 by Wordsworth Editions Limited
8B East Street, Ware, Hertfordshire SG12 9HJ

ISBN 1 84022 062 7

Typeset by Antony Gray
Printed in Great Britain by
Mackays of Chatham, Chatham, Kent

CONTENTS

ADAM BEDE

Adam Bede

A novel by
GEORGE ELIOT
first published in 1859

Contents

BOOK FOURTH

BOOK FIFTH

BOOK SIXTH

So that ye may have
Clear images before your gladden'd eyes
Of nature's unambitious underwood
And flowers that prosper in the shade. And when
I speak of such among the flock as swerved
Or fell, those only shall be singled out
Upon whose lapse, or error, something more
Than brotherly forgiveness may attend.

WILLIAM WORDSWORTH

BOOK FIRST

I

The Workshop

With a single drop of ink for a mirror, the Egyptian sorcerer undertakes to reveal to any chance comer far-reaching visions of the past. This is what I undertake to do for you, reader. With this drop of ink at the end of my pen, I will show you the roomy workshop of Mr Jonathan Burge, carpenter and builder, in the village of Hayslope, as it appeared on the eighteenth of June, in the year of our Lord 1799.

The afternoon sun was warm on the five workmen there, busy upon doors and window-frames and wainscoting. A scent of pine-wood from a tent-like pile of planks outside the open door mingled itself with the scent of the elder-bushes which were spreading their summer snow close to the open window opposite; the slanting sunbeams shone through the transparent shavings that flew before the steady plane, and lit up the fine grain of the oak panelling which stood propped against the wall. On a heap of those soft shavings a rough grey shepherd-dog had made himself a pleasant bed, and was lying with his nose between his forepaws, occasionally wrinkling his brows to cast a glance at the tallest of the five workmen, who was carving a shield in the centre of a wooden mantelpiece. It was to this workman that the strong baritone belonged which was heard above the sound of plane and hammer singing –

> 'Awake, my soul, and with the sun
> Thy daily stage of duty run;
> Shake off dull sloth . . . '

Here some measurement was to be taken which required more concentrated attention, and the sonorous voice subsided into a low whistle; but it presently broke out again with renewed vigour –

> 'Let all thy converse be sincere,
> Thy conscience as the noonday clear.'

Such a voice could only come from a broad chest, and the broad chest belonged to a large-boned muscular man nearly six feet high, with a back so flat and a head so well poised that when he drew himself up to take a more distant survey of his work, he had the air of a soldier standing at ease. The sleeve rolled up above the elbow showed an arm that was likely to win the prize for feats of strength; yet the long supple hand, with its broad fingertips, looked ready for works of skill. In his tall stalwartness Adam Bede was a Saxon, and justified his name; but the jet-black hair, made the more noticeable by its contrast with the light paper cap, and the keen glance of the dark eyes that shone from under strongly marked, prominent and mobile eyebrows, indicated a mixture of Celtic blood. The face was large and roughly hewn, and when in repose had no other beauty than such as belongs to an expression of good-humoured honest intelligence.

It is clear at a glance that the next workman is Adam's brother. He is nearly as tall; he has the same type of features, the same hue of hair and complexion; but the strength of the family likeness seems only to render more conspicuous the remarkable difference of expression both in form and face. Seth's broad shoulders have a slight stoop; his eyes are grey; his eyebrows have less prominence and more repose than his brother's; and his glance, instead of being keen, is confiding and benignant. He has thrown off his paper cap, and you see that his hair is not thick and straight, like Adam's, but thin and wavy, allowing you to discern the exact contour of a coronal arch that predominates very decidedly over the brow.

The idle tramps always felt sure they could get a copper from Seth; they scarcely ever spoke to Adam.

The concert of the tools and Adam's voice was at last broken by Seth, who, lifting the door at which he had been working intently, placed it against the wall, and said – 'There! I've finished my door today, anyhow.'

The workmen all looked up; Jim Salt, a burly red-haired man, known as Sandy Jim, paused from his planing, and Adam said to Seth, with a sharp glance of surprise – 'What! dost think thee'st finished the door?'

'Ay, sure,' said Seth, with answering surprise; 'what's a-wanting to't?'

A loud roar of laughter from the other three workmen made Seth look round confusedly. Adam did not join in the laughter, but there was a slight smile on his face as he said, in a gentler tone than before – 'Why, thee'st forgot the panels.'

The laughter burst out afresh as Seth clapped his hands to his head, and coloured over brow and crown.

'Hoorray!' shouted a small lithe fellow, called Wiry Ben, running forward and seizing the door. 'We'll hang up th' door at fur end o' th' shop an' write on't "Seth Bede, the Methody, his work". Here, Jim, lend's hould o' th' red-pot.'

'Nonsense!' said Adam. 'Let it alone, Ben Cranage. You'll mayhap be making such a slip yourself someday; you'll laugh o' th' other side o' your mouth then.'

'Catch me at it, Adam. It'll be a good while afore my head's full o' th' Methodies,' said Ben.

'Nay, but it's often full o' drink, and that's worse.'

Ben, however, had now got the 'red-pot', in his hand, and was about to begin writing his inscription, making, by way of preliminary, an imaginary S in the air.

'Let it alone, will you?' Adam called out, laying down his tools, striding up to Ben, and seizing his right shoulder. 'Let it alone, or I'll shake the soul out o' your body.'

Ben shook in Adam's iron grasp, but, like a plucky small man as he was, he didn't mean to give in. With his left hand he snatched the brush from his powerless right, and made a movement as if he would perform the feat of writing with his left. In a moment Adam turned him round, seized his other shoulder, and, pushing him along, pinned him against the wall. But now Seth spoke.

'Let be, Addy, let be. Ben will be joking. Why, he's i' the right to laugh at me – I canna help laughing at myself.'

'I shan't loose him, till he promises to let the door alone,' said Adam.

'Come, Ben, lad,' said Seth, in a persuasive tone, 'don't let's have a quarrel about it. You know Adam will have his way. You may's well try to turn a waggon in a narrow lane. Say you'll leave the door alone, and make an end on't.'

'I binna frighted at Adam,' said Ben, 'but I donna mind sayin' as I'll let 't alone at your askin', Seth.'

'Come, that's wise of you, Ben,' said Adam, laughing and relaxing his grasp.

They all returned to their work now; but Wiry Ben, having had the worst in the bodily contest, was bent on retrieving that humiliation by a success in sarcasm.

'Which was ye thinkin' on, Seth,' he began – 'the pretty parson's face or her sarmunt, when ye forgot the panels?'

'Come and hear her, Ben,' said Seth, good-humouredly; 'she's going to preach on the Green tonight; happen ye'd get something to think on yourself then, instead o' those wicked songs you're so fond on. Ye might get religion, and that 'ud be the best day's earnings y' ever made.'

'All i' good time for that, Seth; I'll think about that when I'm agoin' to settle i' life; bachelors doesn't want such heavy earnins. Happen I shall do the coortin' an' the religion both together, as ye do, Seth; but ye wouldna ha' me get converted an' chop in atween ye an' the pretty preacher, an' carry her aff?'

'No fear o' that, Ben; she's neither for you nor for me to win, I doubt. Only you come and hear her, and you won't speak lightly on her again.'

'Well, I'n half a mind t' ha' a look at her tonight, if there isn't good company at th' Holly Bush. What'll she take for her text? Happen ye can tell me, Seth, if so be as I shouldna come up i' time for't. Will't be – What come ye out for to see? A prophetess? Yea, I say unto you, and more than a prophetess – a uncommon pretty young woman.'

'Come, Ben,' said Adam, rather sternly, 'you let the words o' the Bible alone; you're going too far now.'

'What! are ye a-turnin' roun', Adam? I thought ye war dead again th' women preachin', a while agoo?'

'Nay, I'm not turnin' noway. I said nought about the women preachin': I said, You let the Bible alone: you've got a jest-book, han't you, as you're rare and proud on? Keep your dirty fingers to that.'

'Why, y' are gettin' as big a saint as Seth. Y' are goin' to th' preachin' tonight, I should think. Ye'll do finely t' lead the singin'. But I don' know what Parson Irwine 'ull say at his gran' favright Adam Bede a-turnin' Methody.'

'Never do you bother yourself about me, Ben. I'm not a-going to turn Methodist any more nor you are – though it's like enough you'll turn to something worse. Mester Irwine's got more sense nor to meddle wi' people's doing as they like in religion. That's between themselves and God, as he's said to me many a time.'

'Ay, ay; but he's none so fond o' your dissenters, for all that.'

'Maybe; I'm none so fond o' Josh Tod's thick ale, but I don't hinder you from making a fool o' yourself wi't.'

There was a laugh at this thrust of Adam's, but Seth said, very seriously –
'Nay, nay, Addy, thee mustna say as anybody's religion's like thick ale. Thee
dostna believe but what the dissenters and the Methodists have got the root o'
the matter as well as the church folks.'

'Nay, Seth, lad; I'm not for laughing at no man's religion. Let em follow their
consciences, that's all. Only I think it 'ud be better if their consciences 'ud let 'em
stay quiet i' the church – there's a deal to be learnt there. And there's such a thing
as being over-speritial; we must have something beside Gospel i' this world.
Look at the canals, an' th' aqueducs, an' th' coal-pit engines, and Arkwright's
mills there at Cromford; a man must learn summat beside Gospel to make them
things, I reckon. But t' hear some o' them preachers, you'd think as a man must
be doing nothing all 's life but shutting's eyes and looking what's a-going on
inside him. I know a man must have the love o' God in his soul, and the Bible's
God's word. But what does the Bible say? Why, it says as God put his sperrit into
the workman as built the tabernacle, to make him do all the carved work and
things as wanted a nice hand. And this is my way o' looking at it: there's the
sperrit o' God in all things and all times – weekday as well as Sunday – and i' the
great works and inventions, and i' the figuring and the mechanics. And God
helps us with our headpieces and our hands as well as with our souls; and if a man
does bits o' jobs out o' working hours – builds a oven for 's wife to save her from
going to the bakehouse, or scrats at his bit o' garden and makes two potatoes
grow istead o' one, he's doing more good, and he's just as near to God, as if he
was running after some preacher and a-praying and a-groaning.'

'Well done, Adam!' said Sandy Jim, who had paused from his planing to shift
his planks while Adam was speaking; 'that's the best sarmunt I've heared this
long while. By th' same token, my wife's been a-plaguin' on me to build her a
oven this twelvemont.'

'There's reason in what thee say'st, Adam,' observed Seth, gravely. 'But thee
know'st thyself as it's hearing the preachers thee find'st so much fault with has
turned many an idle fellow into an industrious un. It's the preacher as empties th'
alehouse; and if a man gets religion, he'll do his work none the worse for that.'

'On'y he'll lave the panels out o' th' doors sometimes, eh, Seth?' said Wiry
Ben.

'Ah, Ben, you've got a joke again' me as 'll last you your life. But it isna
religion as was i' fault there; it was Seth Bede, as was allays a wool-gathering
chap, and religion hasna cured him, the more's the pity.'

'Ne'er heed me, Seth,' said Wiry Ben, 'y' are a downright good-hearted chap,
panels or no panels; an' ye donna set up your bristles at every bit o' fun, like
some o' your kin, as is mayhap cliverer.'

'Seth, lad,' said Adam, taking no notice of the sarcasm against himself, 'thee
mustna take me unkind. I wasna driving at thee in what I said just now. Some's
got one way o' looking at things and some 's got another.'

'Nay, nay, Addy, thee mean'st me no unkindness,' said Seth, 'I know that well
enough. Thee't like thy dog Gyp – thee bark'st at me sometimes, but thee allays
lick'st my hand after.'

All hands worked on in silence for some minutes, until the church clock began to strike six. Before the first stroke had died away, Sandy Jim had loosed his plane and was reaching his jacket; Wiry Ben had left a screw half driven in, and thrown his screwdriver into his tool-basket; Mum Taft, who, true to his name, had kept silence throughout the previous conversation, had flung down his hammer as he was in the act of lifting it; and Seth, too, had straightened his back, and was putting out his hand towards his paper cap. Adam alone had gone on with his work as if nothing had happened. But observing the cessation of the tools, he looked up, and said, in a tone of indignation – 'Look there, now! I can't abide to see men throw away their tools i' that way, the minute the clock begins to strike, as if they took no pleasure i' their work, and was afraid o' doing a stroke too much.'

Seth looked a little conscious, and began to be slower in his preparations for going, but Mum Taft broke silence, and said – 'Ay, ay, Adam lad, ye talk like a young un. When y' are six-an'-forty like me, istid o' six-an'-twenty, ye wonna be so flush o' workin, for nought.'

'Nonsense,' said Adam, still wrathful; 'what's age got to do with it, I wonder? Ye arena getting stiff yet, I reckon. I hate to see a man's arms drop down as if he was shot, before the clock's fairly struck, just as if he'd never a bit o' pride and delight in's work. The very grindstone 'ull go on turning a bit after you loose it.'

'Bodderation, Adam!' exclaimed Wiry Ben; 'lave a chap aloon, will 'ee? Ye war a-finding faut wi' preachers a while agoo – y' are fond enough o' preachin' yoursen. Ye may like work better nor play, but I like play better nor work; that'll 'commodate ye – it laves ye th' more to do.'

With this exit speech, which he considered effective, Wiry Ben shouldered his basket and left the workshop, quickly followed by Mum Taft and Sandy Jim. Seth lingered, and looked wistfully at Adam, as if he expected him to say something.

'Shalt go home before thee go'st to the preaching?' Adam asked, looking up.

'Nay; I've got my hat and things at Will Maskery's. I shan't be home before going for ten. I'll happen see Dinah Morris safe home, if she's willing. There's nobody comes with her from Poyser's, thee know'st.'

'Then I'll tell mother not to look for thee,' said Adam.

'Thee artna going to Poyser's thyself tonight?' said Seth, rather timidly, as he turned to leave the workshop.

'Nay, I'm going to th' school.'

Hitherto Gyp had kept his comfortable bed, only lifting up his head and watching Adam more closely as he noticed the other workmen departing. But no sooner did Adam put his ruler in his pocket, and begin to twist his apron round his waist, than Gyp ran forward and looked up in his master's face with patient expectation. If Gyp had had a tail he would doubtless have wagged it, but being destitute of that vehicle for his emotions, he was like many other worthy personages, destined to appear more phlegmatic than nature had made him.

'What! art ready for the basket, eh, Gyp?' said Adam, with the same gentle modulation of voice as when he spoke to Seth.

Gyp jumped and gave a short bark, as much as to say, 'Of course.' Poor fellow, he had not a great range of expression.

The basket was the one which on workdays held Adam's and Seth's dinner; and no official, walking in procession, could look more resolutely unconscious of all acquaintances than Gyp with his basket, trotting at his master's heels.

On leaving the workshop Adam locked the door, took the key out, and carried it to the house on the other side of the woodyard. It was a low house, with smooth grey thatch and buff walls, looking pleasant and mellow in the evening light. The leaded windows were bright and speckless, and the door-stone was as clean as a white boulder at ebb tide. On the door-stone stood a clean old woman, in a dark-stripped linen gown, a red kerchief, and a linen cap, talking to some speckled fowls which appeared to have been drawn towards her by an illusory expectation of cold potatoes or barley. The old woman's sight seemed to be dim, for she did not recognise Adam till he said – 'Here's the key, Dolly; lay it down for me in the house, will you?'

'Ay, sure; but wunna ye come in, Adam? Miss Mary's i' th' house, an' Mester Burge 'ull be back anon; he'd be glad t' ha' ye to supper wi'm, I'll be's warrand.'

'No, Dolly, thank you; I'm off home. Good-evening.'

Adam hastened with long strides, Gyp close to his heels, out of the workyard, and along the highroad leading away from the village and down to the valley. As he reached the foot of the slope, an elderly horseman, with his portmanteau strapped behind him, stopped his horse when Adam had passed him, and turned round to have another long look at the stalwart workman in paper cap, leather breeches, and dark-blue worsted stockings.

Adam, unconscious of the admiration he was exciting, presently struck across the fields, and now broke out into the tune which had all day long been running in his head –

> Let all thy converse be sincere,
> Thy conscience as the noonday clear;
> For God's all-seeing eye surveys
> Thy secret thoughts, thy works and ways.

2

The Preaching

About a quarter to seven there was an unusual appearance of excitement in the village of Hayslope, and through the whole length of its little street, from the Donnithorne Arms to the churchyard gate, the inhabitants had evidently been drawn out of their houses by something more than the pleasure of lounging in the evening sunshine. The Donnithorne Arms stood at the entrance of the village, and a small farmyard and stackyard which flanked it, indicating that there was a pretty take of land attached to the inn, gave the traveller a promise of good feed for himself and his horse, which might well console him for the ignorance in which the weather-beaten sign left him as to the heraldic bearings of that ancient family, the Donnithornes. Mr Casson, the landlord, had been for some time standing at the door with his hands in his pockets, balancing himself on his heels and toes, and looking towards a piece of unenclosed ground, with a maple in the middle of it, which he knew to be the destination of certain grave-looking men and women whom he had observed passing at intervals.

Mr Casson's person was by no means of that common type which can be allowed to pass without description. On a front view it appeared to consist principally of two spheres, bearing about the same relation to each other as the earth and the moon: that is to say, the lower sphere might be said, at a rough guess, to be thirteen times larger than the upper, which naturally performed the function of a mere satellite and tributary. But here the resemblance ceased, for Mr Casson's head was not at all a melancholy-looking satellite, nor was it a 'spotty globe', as Milton has irreverently called the moon; on the contrary, no head and face could look more sleek and healthy, and its expression, which was chiefly confined to a pair of round and ruddy cheeks, the slight knot and interruptions forming the nose and eyes being scarcely worth mention, was one of jolly contentment, only tempered by that sense of personal dignity which usually made itself felt in his attitude and bearing. This sense of dignity could hardly be considered excessive in a man who had been butler to 'the family', for fifteen years, and who, in his present high position, was necessarily very much in contact with his inferiors. How to reconcile his dignity with the satisfaction of his curiosity by walking towards the Green, was the problem that Mr Casson had been revolving in his mind for the last five minutes; but when he had partly solved it by taking his hands out of his pockets, and thrusting them into the armholes of his waistcoat, by throwing his head on one side, and providing himself with an air of contemptuous indifference to whatever might fall under his notice, his thoughts were diverted by the approach of the horseman whom we lately saw pausing to have another look at our friend Adam, and who now pulled up at the door of the Donnithorne Arms.

'Take off the bridle and give him a drink, ostler,' said the traveller to the lad in a smock-frock, who had come out of the yard at the sound of the horse's hoofs.

'Why, what's up in your pretty village, landlord?' he continued, getting down. 'There seems to be quite a stir.'

'It's a Methodis preaching, sir; it's been gev hout as a young woman's a-going to preach on the Green,' answered Mr Casson, in a treble and wheezy voice, with a slightly mincing accent. 'Will you please to step in, sir, an' tek some-think?'

'No, I must be getting on to Rosseter. I only want a drink for my horse. And what does your parson say, I wonder, to a young woman preaching just under his nose?'

'Parson Irwine, sir, doesn't live here; he lives at Brox'on, over the hill there. The parsonage here's a tumbledown place, sir, not fit for gentry to live in. He comes here to preach of a Sunday afternoon, sir, an' puts up his hoss here. It's a grey cob, sir, an' he sets great store by't. He's allays put up his hoss here, sir, iver since before I hed the Donnithorne Arms. I'm not this countryman, you may tell by my tongue, sir. They're cur'ous talkers i' this country, sir; the gentry's hard work to hunderstand 'em. I was brought hup among the gentry, sir, an' got the turn o' their tongue when I was a bye. Why, what do you think the folks here says for 'hevn't you?' – the gentry, you know, says, "hevn't you" – well, the people about here says "hanna yey." It's what they call the dileck as is spoke hereabout, sir. That's what I've heard Squire Donnithorne say many a time; it's the dileck, says he.'

'Ay, ay,' said the stranger, smiling. 'I know it very well. But you've not got many Methodists about here, surely – in this agricultural spot? I should have thought there would hardly be such a thing as a Methodist to be found about here. You're all farmers, aren't you? The Methodists can seldom lay much hold on them.'

'Why, sir, there's a pretty lot o' workmen round about, sir. There's Mester Burge as owns the timberyard over there, he underteks a good bit o' building an' repairs. An' there's the stone-pits not far off. There's plenty of emply i' this countryside, sir. An' there's a fine batch o' Methodisses at Treddles'on – that's the market-town about three mile off – you'll maybe ha' come through it, sir. There's pretty nigh a score of 'em on the Green now, as come from there. That's where our people gets it from, though there's only two men of 'em in all Hayslope: that's Will Maskery, the wheelwright, and Seth Bede, a young man as works at the carpenterin'.'

'The preacher comes from Treddleston, then, does she?'

'Nay, sir, she comes out o' Stonyshire, pretty nigh thirty mile off. But she's a-visitin' hereabout at Mester Poyser's at the Hall Farm – it's them barns an' big walnut trees, right away to the left, sir. She's own niece to Poyser's wife an' they'll be fine an' vexed at her for making a fool of herself i' that way. But I've heared as there's no holding these Methodisses when the maggit's once got i' their head: many of 'em goes stark starin' mad wi' their religion. Though this young woman's quiet enough to look at, by what I can make out; I've not seen her myself.'

'Well, I wish I had time to wait and see her, but I must get on. I've been out of my way for the last twenty minutes, to have a look at that place in the valley. It's Squire Donnithorne's, I suppose?'

'Yes, sir, that's Donnithorne Chase, that is. Fine hoaks there, isn't there, sir? I should know what it is, sir, for I've lived butler there a-going i' fifteen year. It's Captain Donnithorne as is th' heir, sir – Squire Donnithorne's grandson. He'll be comin' of hage this 'ay-'arvest, sir, an' we shall hev fine doins. He owns all the land about here, sir, Squire Donnithorne does.'

'Well, it's a pretty spot, whoever may own it,' said the traveller, mounting his horse; 'and one meets some fine strapping fellows about too. I met as fine a young fellow as ever I saw in my life, about half an hour ago, before I came up the hill – a carpenter, a tall broad-shouldered fellow with black hair and black eyes, marching along like a soldier. We want such fellows as he to lick the French.'

'Ay, sir, that's Adam Bede, that is, I'll be bound – Thias Bede's son – everybody knows him hereabout. He's an uncommon clever stiddy fellow, an' wonderful strong. Lord bless you, sir – if you'll hexcuse me for saying so – he can walk forty mile a day, an' lift a matter o' sixty ston'. He's an uncommon

favourite wi' the gentry, sir: Captain Donnithorne and Parson Irwine meks a
fine fuss wi' him. But he's a little lifted up an' peppery-like.'

'Well, good-evening to you, landlord; I must get on.'

'Your servant, sir; good evenin'.'

The traveller put his horse into a quick walk up the village, but when he
approached the Green, the beauty of the view that lay on his right hand, the
singular contrast presented by the groups of villagers with the knot of Methodists
near the maple, and perhaps yet more, curiosity to see the young female preacher,
proved too much for his anxiety to get to the end of his journey, and he paused.

The Green lay at the extremity of the village, and from it the road branched
off in two directions, one leading farther up the hill by the church, and the other
winding gently down towards the valley. On the side of the Green that led
towards the church, the broken line of thatched cottages was continued nearly
to the churchyard gate; but on the opposite, northwestern side, there was
nothing to obstruct the view of gently-swelling meadow, and wooded valley,
and dark masses of distant hill. That rich undulating district of Loamshire to
which Hayslope belonged, lies close to a grim outskirt of Stonyshire, overlooked
by its barren hills as a pretty blooming sister may sometimes be seen linked in
the arm of a rugged, tall swarthy brother; and in two or three hours' ride the
traveller might exchange a bleak treeless region, intersected by lines of cold grey
stone, for one where his road wound under the shelter of woods, or up swelling
hills, muffled with hedgerows and long meadow-grass and thick corn; and
where at every turn he came upon some fine old country-seat nestled in the
valley or crowning the slope, some homestead with its long length of barn and
its cluster of golden ricks, some grey steeple looking out from a pretty confusion
of trees and thatch and dark-red tiles. It was just such a picture as this last that
Hayslope Church had made to the traveller as he began to mount the gentle
slope leading to its pleasant uplands, and now from his station near the Green he
had before him in one view nearly all the other typical features of this pleasant
land. High up against the horizon were the huge conical masses of hill, like giant
mounds intended to fortify this region of corn and grass against the keen and
hungry winds of the north; not distant enough to be clothed in purple mystery,
but with sombre greenish sides visibly specked with sheep, whose motion was
only revealed by memory, not detected by sight; wooed from day to day by the
changing hours, but responding with no change in themselves – left for ever
grim and sullen after the flush of morning, the winged gleams of the April
noonday, the parting crimson glory of the ripening summer sun. And directly
below them the eye rested on a more advanced line of hanging woods, divided
by bright patches of pasture or furrowed crops, and not yet deepened into the
uniform leafy curtains of high summer, but still showing the warm tints of the
young oak and the tender green of the ash and lime. Then came the valley,
where the woods grew thicker, as if they had rolled down and hurried together
from the patches left smooth on the slope, that they might take the better care of
the tall mansion which lifted its parapets and sent its faint blue summer smoke
among them. Doubtless there was a large sweep of park and a broad glassy pool
in front of that mansion, but the swelling slope of meadow would not let our

traveller see them from the village green. He saw instead a foreground which was just as lovely – the level sunlight lying like transparent gold among the gently-curving stems of the feathered grass and the tall red sorrel, and the white umbels of the hemlocks lining the bushy hedgerows. It was that moment in summer when the sound of the scythe being whetted makes us cast more lingering looks at the flower-sprinkled tresses of the meadows.

He might have seen other beauties in the landscape if he had turned a little in his saddle and looked eastward, beyond Jonathan Burge's pasture and woodyard towards the green cornfields and walnut trees of the Hall Farm; but apparently there was more interest for him in the living groups close at hand. Every generation in the village was there, from old 'Feyther Taft' in his brown worsted nightcap, who was bent nearly double, but seemed tough enough to keep on his legs a long while, leaning on his short stick, down to the babies with their little round heads lolling forward in quilted linen caps. Now and then there was a new arrival; perhaps a slouching labourer, who, having eaten his supper, came out to look at the unusual scene with a slow bovine gaze, willing to hear what anyone had to say in explanation of it, but by no means excited enough to ask a question. But all took care not to join the Methodists on the Green, and identify themselves in that way with the expectant audience, for there was not one of them that would not have disclaimed the imputation of having come out to hear the 'preacher-woman' – they had only come out to see 'what war a-goin, on, like'. The men were chiefly gathered in the neighbourhood of the blacksmith's shop. But do not imagine them gathered in a knot. Villagers never swarm: a whisper is unknown among them, and they seem almost as incapable of an undertone as a cow or a stag. Your true rustic turns his back on his interlocutor, throwing a question over his shoulder as if he meant to run away from the answer, and walking a step or two farther off when the interest of the dialogue culminates. So the group in the vicinity of the blacksmith's door was by no means a close one, and formed no screen in front of Chad Cranage, the blacksmith himself, who stood with his black brawny arms folded, leaning against the doorpost, and occasionally sending forth a bellowing laugh at his own jokes, giving them a marked preference over the sarcasms of Wiry Ben, who had renounced the pleasures of the Holly Bush for the sake of seeing life under a new form. But both styles of wit were treated with equal contempt by Mr Joshua Rann. Mr Rann's leathern apron and subdued griminess can leave no one in any doubt that he is the village shoemaker; the thrusting out of his chin and stomach, and the twirling of his thumbs, are more subtle indications, intended to prepare unwary strangers for the discovery that they are in the presence of the parish clerk. 'Old Joshway', as he is irreverently called by his neighbours, is in a state of simmering indignation; but he has not yet opened his lips except to say, in a resounding bass undertone, like the tuning of a violoncello, 'Sehon, King of the Amorites: for His mercy endureth for ever; and Og the King of Basan: for His mercy endureth for ever' – a quotation which may seem to have slight bearing on the present occasion, but, as with every other anomaly, adequate knowledge will show it to be a natural sequence. Mr Rann was inwardly maintaining the dignity of the Church in the face of this scandalous irruption of Methodism, and as that dignity was bound up with his own sonorous utterance of the responses, his argument naturally suggested a quotation from the psalm he had read the last Sunday afternoon.

The stronger curiosity of the women had drawn them quite to the edge of the Green, where they could examine more closely the Quaker-like costume and odd deportment of the female Methodists. Underneath the maple there was a small cart which had been brought from the wheelwright's to serve as a pulpit, and round this a couple of benches and a few chairs had been placed. Some of the Methodists were resting on these, with their eyes closed, as if wrapped in prayer or meditation. Others chose to continue standing, and had turned their faces towards the villagers with a look of melancholy compassion, which was highly amusing to Bessy Cranage, the blacksmith's buxom daughter, known to her neighbours as Chad's Bess, who wondered 'why the folks war a-makin' faces a that'ns.' Chad's Bess was the object of peculiar compassion, because her hair, being turned back under a cap which was set at the top of her head, exposed to view an ornament of which she was much prouder than of her red cheeks, namely, a pair of large round ear-rings with false garnets in them, ornaments contemned not only by the Methodists, but by her own cousin and namesake Timothy's Bess, who, with much cousinly feeling, often wished 'them ear-rings' might come to no good.

Timothy's Bess, though retaining her maiden appellation among her familiars, had long been the wife of Sandy Jim, and possessed a handsome set of matronly jewels, of which it is enough to mention the heavy baby she was rocking in her arms, and the sturdy fellow of five in knee-breeches, and red legs, who had a rusty milk-can round his neck by way of drum, and was very carefully avoided by Chad's small terrier. This young olive-branch, notorious under the name of Timothy's Bess's Ben, being of an enquiring disposition, unchecked by any false modesty, had advanced beyond the group of women and children, and was walking round the Methodists, looking up in their faces with his mouth wide open, and beating his stick against the milk-can by way of musical accompaniment. But one of the elderly women bending down to take him by the shoulder, with an air of grave remonstrance, Timothy's Bess's Ben first kicked out vigorously, then took to his heels and sought refuge behind his father's legs.

'Ye gallows young dog,' said Sandy Jim, with some paternal pride, 'if ye donna keep that stick quiet, I'll tek it from ye. What d'ye mane by kickin' foulks?'

'Here! gie him here to me, Jim,' said Chad Cranage; 'I'll tie him up an' shoe him as I do th' hosses. Well, Mester Casson,' he continued, as that personage sauntered up towards the group of men, 'how are ye t' naight? Are ye coom t' help groon? They say folks allays groon when they're hearkenin' to th' Methodys, as if they war bad i' th' inside. I mane to groon as loud as your cow did th' other naight, an' then the praicher 'ull think I'm i' th' raight way.'

'I'd advise you not to be up to no nonsense, Chad,' said Mr Casson, with some dignity; 'Poyser wouldn't like to hear as his wife's niece was treated any ways disrespectful, for all he mayn't be fond of her taking on herself to preach.'

'Ay, an' she's a pleasant-looked un too,' said Wiry Ben. 'I'll stick up for the pretty women preachin'; I know they'd persuade me over a deal sooner nor th' ugly men. I shouldna wonder if I turn Methody afore the night's out, an' begin to coort the preacher, like Seth Bede.'

'Why, Seth's looking rether too high, I should think,' said Mr Casson. 'This woman's kin wouldn't like her to demean herself to a common carpenter.'

'Tchu!' said Ben, with a long treble intonation, 'what's folks's kin got to do wi't? – Not a chip. Poyser's wife may turn her nose up an' forget bygones, but this Dinah Morris, they tell me, 's as poor as iver she was – works at a mill, an's much ado to keep hersen. A strappin' young carpenter as is a ready-made Methody, like Seth, wouldna be a bad match for her. Why, Poysers make as big a fuss wi' Adam Bede as if he war a nevvy o' their own.'

'Idle talk! idle talk!' said Mr Joshua Rann. 'Adam an' Seth's two men; you wunna fit them two wi' the same last.'

'Maybe,' said Wiry Ben, contemptuously, 'but Seth's the lad for me, though he war a Methody twice o'er. I'm fair beat wi' Seth, for I've been teazin' him iver sin' we've been workin' together, an' he bears me no more malice nor a lamb. An' he's a stout-hearted feller too, for when we saw the old tree all a-fire a-comin' across the fields one night, an' we thought as it war a boguy, Seth made no more ado, but he up to't as bold as a constable. Why, there he comes out o' Will Maskery's; an' there's Will hisself, lookin' as meek as if he couldna knock a nail o' the head for fear o' hurtin't. An' there's the pretty preacher-woman! My eye, she's got her bonnet off. I mun go a bit nearer.'

Several of the men followed Ben's lead, and the traveller pushed his horse on to the Green, as Dinah walked rather quickly, and in advance of her companions, towards the cart under the maple tree. While she was near Seth's tall figure, she looked short, but when she had mounted the cart, and was away from all comparison, she seemed above the middle height of woman, though in reality she did not exceed it – an effect which was due to the slimness of her figure, and the simple line of her black stuff dress. The stranger was struck with surprise as he saw her approach and mount the cart – surprise, not so much at the feminine delicacy of her appearance, as at the total absence of self-consciousness in her demeanour. He had made up his mind to see her advance with a measured step, and a demure solemnity of countenance; he had felt sure that her face would be mantled with the smile of conscious saintship, or else charged with denunciatory bitterness. He knew but two types of Methodist – the ecstatic and the bilious. But Dinah walked as simply as if she were going to market, and seemed as unconscious of her outward appearance as a little boy: there was no blush, no tremulousness, which said, 'I know you think me a pretty woman, too young to preach;' no casting up or down of the eyelids, no compression of the lips, no attitude of the arms, that said, 'But you must think of me as a saint.' She held no book in her ungloved hands, but let them hang down lightly crossed before her, as she stood and turned her grey eyes on the people. There was no keenness in the eyes; they seemed rather to be shedding love than making observations; they had the liquid look which tells that the mind is full of what it has to give out, rather than impressed by external objects. She stood with her left hand towards the descending sun, and leafy boughs screened her from its rays; but in this sober light the delicate colouring of her face seemed to gather a calm vividness, like flowers at evening. It was a small oval face, of a uniform transparent whiteness, with an egg-like line of cheek and chin, a full but firm mouth, a delicate nostril, and a low perpendicular brow, surmounted by a rising arch of parting between smooth locks of pale reddish hair. The hair was drawn straight back behind the ears, and covered, except for an inch or two, above the brow, by a net Quaker cap. The eyebrows, of the same colour as the hair, were perfectly horizontal and firmly pencilled; the eyelashes, though no darker, were long and abundant; nothing was left blurred or unfinished. It was one of those faces that make one think of white flowers with light touches of colour on their pure petals. The eyes had no peculiar beauty, beyond that of expression; they looked so simple, so candid, so gravely loving, that no accusing scowl, no light sneer could help melting away before their glance. Joshua Rann gave a long cough, as if he were clearing his throat in order to come to a new understanding with himself; Chad Cranage lifted up his leather skull-cap and scratched his head; and Wiry Ben wondered how Seth had the pluck to think of courting her.

'A sweet woman,' the stranger said to himself, 'but surely nature never meant her for a preacher.'

Perhaps he was one of those who think that nature has theatrical properties, and, with the considerate view of facilitating art and psychology, 'makes up' her characters, so that there may be no mistake about them. But Dinah began to speak.

'Dear friends,' she said, in a clear but not loud voice, 'let us pray for a blessing.'

She closed her eyes, and hanging her head down a little, continued in the same moderate tone, as if speaking to someone quite near her – 'Saviour of sinners! when a poor woman, laden with sins, went out to the well to draw water, she found Thee sitting at the well. She knew Thee not; she had not sought Thee; her mind was dark; her life was unholy. But Thou didst speak to her, Thou didst teach her, Thou didst show her that her life lay open before Thee, and yet Thou wast ready to give her that blessing which she had never sought. Jesus! Thou art in the midst of us, and Thou knowest all men: if there is any here like that poor woman – if their minds are dark, their lives unholy – if they have come out not seeking Thee, not desiring to be taught; deal with them according to the free mercy which Thou didst show to her. Speak to them, Lord; open their ears to my message; bring their sins to their minds, and make them thirst for that salvation which Thou art ready to give.

'Lord! Thou art with Thy people still: they see Thee in the night-watches, and their hearts burn within them as Thou talkest with them by the way. And Thou art near to those who have not known Thee: open their eyes that they may see Thee – see Thee weeping over them, and saying "Ye will not come unto me that ye might have life" – see Thee hanging on the cross and saying, 'Father, forgive them, for they know not what they do" – see Thee as Thou wilt come again in Thy glory to judge them at the last. Amen.'

Dinah opened her eyes again and paused, looking at the group of villagers, who were now gathered rather more closely on her right hand.

'Dear friends,' she began, raising her voice a little, 'you have all of you been to church, and I think you must have heard the clergyman read these words: "The spirit of the Lord is upon me, because he hath anointed me to preach the gospel to the poor." Jesus Christ spoke those words – he said he came to preach the Gospel to the poor: I don't know whether you ever thought about those words much; but I will tell you when I remember first hearing them. It was on just such a sort of evening as this, when I was a little girl, and my aunt as brought me up, took me to hear a good man preach out of doors, just as we are here. I remember his face well: he was a very old man, and had very long white hair; his voice was very soft and beautiful, not like any voice I had ever heard before. I was a little girl, and scarcely knew anything, and this old man seemed to me such a different sort of a man from anybody I had ever seen before, that I thought he had perhaps come down from the sky to preach to us, and I said, "Aunt, will he go back to the sky tonight, like the picture in the Bible?"

'That man of God was Mr Wesley, who spent his life in doing what our blessed Lord did – preaching the Gospel to the poor – and he entered into his rest eight years ago. I came to know more about him years after, but I was a foolish thoughtless child then, and I remembered only one thing he told us in his sermon. He told us as "Gospel" meant "good news." The Gospel, you know, is what the Bible tells us about God.

'Think of that now! Jesus Christ did really come down from heaven, as I, like a silly child, thought Mr Wesley did; and what he came down for, was to tell good news about God to the poor. Why, you and me, dear friends, are poor. We have been brought up in poor cottages, and have been reared on oatcake, and lived coarse; and we haven't been to school much, nor read books, and we don't know much about anything but what happens just round us. We are just the sort of people that want to hear good news. For when anybody's well off, they don't much mind about hearing news from distant parts; but if a poor man or woman's in trouble and has hard work to make out a living, they like to have a letter to tell 'em they've got a friend as will help 'em. To be sure, we can't help knowing something about God, even if we've never heard the Gospel, the good news that our saviour brought us. For we know everything comes from God: don't you say almost every day, "This and that will happen, please God;" and "We shall begin to cut the grass soon, please God to send us a little more sunshine"? We know very well we are altogether in the hands of God: we didn't bring ourselves into the world, we can't keep ourselves alive while we're sleeping; the daylight, and the wind, and the corn, and the cows to give us milk – everything we have comes from God. And he gave us our souls, and put love between parents and children, and husband and wife. But is that as much as we want to know about God? We see he is great and mighty, and can do what he will: we are lost, as if we was struggling in great waters, when we try to think of him.

'But perhaps doubts come into your mind like this: Can God take much notice of us poor people? Perhaps he only made the world for the great and the wise and the rich. It doesn't cost him much to give us our little handful of victual and bit of clothing ; but how do we know he cares for us any more than we care for the worms and things in the garden, so as we rear our carrots and onions? Will God take care of us when we die? and has he any comfort for us when we

are lame and sick and helpless? Perhaps, too, he is angry with us; else why does
the blight come, and the bad harvests, and the fever, and all sorts of pain and
trouble? For our life is full of trouble, and if God sends us good, he seems to
send bad too. How is it? how is it?

'Ah! dear friends, we are in sad want of good news about God; and what does
other good news signify if we haven't that? For everything else comes to an end,
and when we die we leave it all. But God lasts when everything else is gone.
What shall we do if he is not our friend?'

Then Dinah told how the good news had been brought, and how the mind of
God towards the poor had been made manifest in the life of Jesus, dwelling on
its lowliness and its acts of mercy.

'So you see, dear friends,' she went on, 'Jesus spent his time almost all in doing
good to poor people; he preached out of doors to them, and he made friends of
poor workmen, and taught them and took pains with them. Not but what he did
good to the rich too, for he was full of love to all men, only he saw as the poor
were more in want of his help. So he cured the lame and the sick and the blind,
and he worked miracles, to feed the hungry, because, he said, he was sorry for
them; and he was very kind to the little children, and comforted those who had
lost their friends: and he spoke very tenderly to poor sinners that were sorry for
their sins.

'Ah! wouldn't you love such a man if you saw him – if he was here in this
village? What a kind heart he must have! What a friend he would be to go to in
trouble! How pleasant it must be to be taught by him.

'Well, dear friends, who was this man? Was he only a good man – a very good
man, and no more – like our dear Mr Wesley, who has been taken from us? . . .
He was the son of God – "in the image of the Father" the Bible says; that means,
just like God, who is the beginning and end of all things – the God we want to
know about. So then, all the love that Jesus showed to the poor is the same love
that God has for us. We can understand what Jesus felt, because he came in a
body like ours, and spoke words such as we speak to each other. We were afraid
to think what God was before – the God who made the world and the sky and
the thunder and lightning. We could never see him; we could only see the
things he had made; and some of these things was very terrible, so as we might
well tremble when we thought of him. But our blessed Saviour has showed us
what God is in a way us poor ignorant people can understand; he has showed us
what God's heart is, what are his feelings towards us.

'But let us see a little more about what Jesus came on earth for. Another time
he said, "I came to seek and to save that which was lost;" and another time, "I
came not to call the righteous but sinners to repentance."

'The lost! . . . Sinners! . . . Ah! dear friends, does that mean you and me?'

Hitherto the traveller had been chained to the spot against his will by the
charm of Dinah's mellow treble tones, which had a variety of modulation like
that of a fine instrument touched with the unconscious skill of musical instinct.
The simple things she said seemed like novelties, as a melody strikes us with a
new feeling when we hear it sung by the pure voice of a boyish chorister; the
quiet depth of conviction with which she spoke seemed in itself an evidence for

the truth of her message. He saw that she had thoroughly arrested her hearers. The villagers had pressed nearer to her, and there was no longer anything but grave attention on all faces. She spoke slowly, though quite fluently, often pausing after a question, or before any transition of ideas. There was no change of attitude, no gesture; the effect of her speech was produced entirely by the inflections of her voice, and when she came to the question, 'Will God take care of us when we die?' she uttered it in such a tone of plaintive appeal that the tears came into some of the hardest eyes. The stranger had ceased to doubt, as he had done at the first glance, that she could fix the attention of her rougher hearers, but still he wondered whether she could have that power of rousing their more violent emotions, which must surely be a necessary seal of her vocation as a Methodist preacher, until she came to the words, 'Lost! – Sinners!' when there was a great change in her voice and manner. She had made a long pause before the exclamation, and the pause seemed to be filled by agitating thoughts that showed themselves in her features. Her pale face became paler; the circles under her eyes deepened, as they do when tears half gather without falling; and the mild loving eyes took an expression of appalled pity, as if she had suddenly discerned a destroying angel hovering over the heads of the people. Her voice became deep and muffled, but there was still no gesture. Nothing could be less like the ordinary type of the Ranter than Dinah. She was not preaching as she heard others preach, but speaking directly from her own emotions, and under the inspiration of her own simple faith.

But now she had entered into a new current of feeling. Her manner became less calm, her utterance more rapid and agitated, as she tried to bring home to the people their guilt, their wilful darkness, their state of disobedience to God – as she dwelt on the hatefulness of sin, the Divine holiness, and the sufferings of the Saviour, by which a way had been opened for their salvation. At last it seemed as if, in her yearning desire to reclaim the lost sheep, she could not be satisfied by addressing her hearers as a body. She appealed first to one and then to another, beseeching them with tears to turn to God while there was yet time; painting to them the desolation of their souls, lost in sin, feeding on the husks of this miserable world, far away from God their Father; and then the love of the Saviour, who was waiting and watching for their return.

There was many a responsive sigh and groan from her fellow Methodists, but the village mind does not easily take fire, and a little smouldering vague anxiety, that might easily die out again, was the utmost effect Dinah's preaching had wrought in them at present. Yet no one had retired, except the children and 'old Feyther Taft', who being too deaf to catch many words, had some time ago gone back to his inglenook. Wiry Ben was feeling very uncomfortable, and almost wishing he had not come to hear Dinah; he thought what she said would haunt him somehow. Yet he couldn't help liking to look at her and listen to her, though he dreaded every moment that she would fix her eyes on him, and address him in particular. She had already addressed Sandy Jim, who was now holding the baby to relieve his wife, and the big soft-hearted man had rubbed away some tears with his fist, with a confused intention of being a better fellow, going less to the Holly Bush down by the stone-pits, and cleaning himself more regularly of a Sunday.

In front of Sandy Jim stood Chad's Bess, who had shown an unwonted quietude and fixity of attention ever since Dinah had begun to speak. Not that the matter of the discourse had arrested her at once, for she was lost in a puzzling speculation as to what pleasure and satisfaction there could be in life to a young woman who wore a cap like Dinah's. Giving up this enquiry in despair, she took to studying Dinah's nose, eyes, mouth, and hair, and wondering whether it was better to have such a sort of pale face as that, or fat red cheeks and round black eyes like her own. But gradually the influence of the general gravity told upon her, and she became conscious of what Dinah was saying. The gentle tones, the loving persuasion, did not touch her, but when the more severe appeals came she began to be frightened. Poor Bessy had always been considered a naughty girl; she was conscious of it; if it was necessary to be very good, it was clear she must be in a bad way. She couldn't find her places at church as Sally Rann could; she had often been tittering when she 'curcheyed' to Mr Irwine; and these religious deficiencies were accompanied by a corresponding slackness in the minor morals, for Bessy belonged unquestionably to that unsoaped, lazy class of feminine characters with whom you may venture to 'eat an egg, an apple, or a nut.' All this she was generally conscious of, and hitherto had not been greatly ashamed of it. But now she began to feel very much as if the constable had come to take her up and carry her before the justice for some undefined offence. She had a terrified sense that God, whom she had always thought of as very far off, was very near to her, and that Jesus was close by looking at her, though she could not see him. For Dinah had that belief in visible manifestations of Jesus, which is common among the Methodists, and she communicated it irresistibly to her hearers: she made them feel that he was among them bodily, and might at any moment show himself to them in some way that would strike anguish and penitence into their hearts.

'See!' she exclaimed, turning to the left, with her eyes fixed on a point above the heads of the people – 'see where our blessed Lord stands and weeps, and stretches out his arms towards you. Hear what he says: "How often would I have gathered you as a hen gathereth her chickens under her wings, and ye would not!" . . . and ye would not,' she repeated, in a tone of pleading reproach, turning her eyes on the people again. 'See the print of the nails on his dear hands and feet. It is your sins that made them! Ah! how pale and worn he looks! He has gone through all that great agony in the garden, when his soul was exceeding sorrowful even unto death, and the great drops of sweat fell like blood to the ground. They spat upon him and buffeted him, they scourged him, they mocked him, they laid the heavy cross on his bruised shoulders. Then they nailed him up. Ah! what pain! His lips are parched with thirst, and they mock him still in this great agony; yet with those parched lips he prays for them, "Father, forgive them, for they know not what they do." Then a horror of great darkness fell upon him, and he felt what sinners feel when they are for ever shut out from God. That was the last drop in the cup of bitterness. "My God, my God!" he cries, "why hast Thou forsaken me?"

'All this he bore for you! For you – and you never think of him; for you – and you turn your backs on him; you don't care what he has gone through for you.

Yet he is not weary of toiling for you: he has risen from the dead, he is praying for you at the right hand of God – "Father, forgive them, for they know not what they do." And he is upon this earth too; he is among us; he is there close to you now; I see his wounded body and his look of love.'

Here Dinah turned to Bessy Cranage, whose bonny youth and evident vanity had touched her with pity.

'Poor child! poor child! He is beseeching you, and you don't listen to him. You think of earrings and fine gowns and caps, and you never think of the Saviour who died to save your precious soul. Your cheeks will be shrivelled one day, your hair will be grey, your poor body will be thin and tottering! Then you will begin to feel that your soul is not saved; then you will have to stand before God dressed in your sins, in your evil tempers and vain thoughts. And Jesus, who stands ready to help you now, won't help you then: because you won't have him to be your Saviour, he will be your judge. Now he looks at you with love and mercy, and says, "Come to me that you may have life;" then he will turn away from you, and say, "Depart from me into everlasting fire!" '

Poor Bessy's wide-open black eyes began to fill with tears, her great red cheeks and lips became quite pale, and her face was distorted like a little child's before a burst of crying.

'Ah! poor blind child!' Dinah went on, 'think if it should happen to you as it once happened to a servant of God in the days of her vanity. She thought of her lace caps, and saved all her money to buy 'em; she thought nothing about how she might get a clean heart and a right spirit, she only wanted to have better lace than other girls. And one day when she put her new cap on and looked in the glass, she saw a bleeding Face crowned with thorns. That face is looking at you now' – here Dinah pointed to a spot close in front of Bessy. – 'Ah! tear off those follies! cast them away from you, as if they were stinging adders. They *are* stinging you – they are poisoning your soul – they are dragging you down into a dark bottomless pit, where you will sink for ever, and for ever, and for ever, further away from light and God.'

Bessy could bear it no longer: a great terror was upon her, and wrenching her earrings from her ears, she threw them down before her, sobbing aloud. Her father, Chad, frightened lest he should be 'laid hold on' too, this impression on the rebellious Bess striking him as nothing less than a miracle, walked hastily away, and began to work at his anvil by way of reassuring himself. 'Folks mun ha' hoss-shoes, praichin' or no praichin': the divil canna lay hould o' me for that,' he muttered to himself.

But now Dinah began to tell of the joys that were in store for the penitent, and to describe in her simple way the divine peace and love with which the soul of the believer is filled – how the sense of God's love turns poverty into riches, and satisfies the soul, so that no uneasy desire vexes it, no fear alarms it: how, at last, the very temptation to sin is extinguished, and heaven is begun upon earth, because no cloud passes between the soul and God, who is its eternal sun.

'Dear friends,' she said at last, 'brothers and sisters, whom I love as those for whom my Lord has died, believe me, I know what this great blessedness is; and because I know it, I want you to have it too. I am poor, like you: I have to get my living with my hands; but no lord nor lady can be so happy as me, if they haven't got the love of God in their souls. Think what it is – not to hate anything but sin; to be full of love to every creature; to be frightened at nothing; to be sure that all things will turn to good; not to mind pain, because it is our Father's will; to know that nothing – no, not if the earth was to be burnt up, or the waters come and drown us – nothing could part us from God who loves us, and who fills our souls with peace and joy, because we are sure that whatever he wills is holy, just, and good.

'Dear friends, come and take this blessedness; it is offered to you; it is the good news that Jesus came to preach to the poor. It is not like the riches of this world, so that the more one gets the less the rest can have. God is without end; his love is without end –

> 'Its streams the whole creation reach,
> So plenteous is the store;
> Enough for all, enough for each,
> Enough for evermore.'

Dinah had been speaking at least an hour, and the reddening light of the parting day seemed to give a solemn emphasis to her closing words. The stranger, who had been interested in the course of her sermon, as if it had been the development of a drama – for there is this sort of fascination in all sincere unpremeditated eloquence, which opens to one the inward drama of the speaker's emotions – now turned his horse aside, and pursued his way, while Dinah said, 'Let us sing a little, dear friends;' and as he was still winding down the slope, the voices of the Methodists reached him, rising and falling in that strange blending of exultation and sadness which belongs to the cadence of a hymn.

3

After the Preaching

In less than an hour from that time Seth Bede was walking by Dinah's side along the hedgerow-path that skirted the pastures and green cornfields which lay between the village and the Hall Farm. Dinah had taken off her little Quaker bonnet again, and was holding it in her hands that she might have a freer enjoyment of the cool evening twilight, and Seth could see the expression of her face quite clearly as he walked by her side, timidly revolving something he wanted to say to her. It was an expression of unconscious placid gravity – of absorption in thoughts that had no connection with the present moment or with her own personality: an expression that is most of all discouraging to a lover. Her very walk was discouraging: it had that quiet elasticity that asks for no support. Seth felt this dimly; he said to himself, 'She's too good and holy for any man, let alone me,' and the words he had been summoning rushed back again before they had reached his lips. But another thought gave him courage: 'There's no man could love her better, and leave her freer to follow the Lord's work.'

They had been silent for many minutes now, since they had done talking about Bessy Cranage; Dinah seemed almost to have forgotten Seth's presence, and her pace was becoming so much quicker, that the sense of their being only a few minutes' walk from the yard-gates of the Hall Farm at last gave Seth courage to speak.

'You've quite made up your mind to go back to Snowfield o' Saturday, Dinah?'

'Yes,' said Dinah, quietly. 'I'm called there. It was borne in upon my mind while I was meditating on Sunday night, as sister Allen, who's in a decline, is in need of me. I saw her as plain as we see that bit of thin white cloud, lifting up her poor thin hand and beckoning to me. And this morning when I opened the Bible for direction, the first words my eyes fell on were, 'And after we had seen the vision, immediately we endeavoured to go into Macedonia.' If it wasn't for that clear showing of the Lord's will I should be loth to go, for my heart yearns over my aunt and her little ones, and that poor wandering lamb Hetty Sorrel. I've been much drawn out in prayer for her of late, and I look on it as a token that there may be mercy in store for her.'

'God grant it,' said Seth. 'For I doubt Adam's heart is so set on her, he'll never turn to anybody else; and yet it 'ud go to my heart if he was to marry her, for I canna think as she'd make him happy. It's a deep mystery – the way the heart of man turns to one woman out of all the rest he's seen i' the world, and makes it easier for him to work seven year for her, like Jacob did for Rachel; sooner than have any other woman for th' asking. I often think of them words, "And Jacob served seven years for Rachel; and they seemed to him but a few days for the love he had to her." I know those words 'ud come true with me, Dinah, if so be you'd give me hope as I might win you after seven years was over. I know you think a husband 'ud be taking up too much o' your thoughts, because St Paul says, "She that's married careth for the things of the world how she may please her husband;" and may happen you'll think me over-bold to speak to you about it again, after what you told me o' your mind last Saturday. But I've been thinking it over again by night and by day, and I've prayed not to be blinded by my own desires, to think what's only good for me must be good for you too. And it seems to me there's more texts for your marrying than ever you can find against it. For St Paul says as plain as can be in another place, "I will that the younger women marry, bear children, guide the house, give none occasion to the adversary to speak reproachfully;" and then "two are better than one;" and that holds good with marriage as well as with other things. For we should be o' one heart and o' one mind, Dinah. We both serve the same Master, and are striving after the same gifts; and I'd never be the husband to make a claim on you as could interfere with your doing the work God has fitted you for. I'd make a shift, and fend indoor and out, to give you more liberty – more than you can have now, for you've got to get your own living now, and I'm strong enough to work for us both.'

When Seth had once begun to urge his suit, he went on earnestly, and almost hurriedly, lest Dinah should speak some decisive word before he had poured forth all the arguments he had prepared. His cheeks became flushed as he went on, his mild grey eyes filled with tears, and his voice trembled as he spoke the last sentence. They had reached one of those very narrow passes between two tall stones, which performed the office of a stile in Loamshire, and Dinah paused as she turned towards Seth and said, in her tender but calm treble notes – 'Seth Bede, I thank you for your love towards me, and if I could think of any man as more than a Christian brother, I think it would be you. But my heart is not free to marry. That is good for other women, and it is a great and a blessed thing to be a wife and mother; but "as God has distributed to every man, as the Lord hath called every man, so let him walk." God has called me to minister to others, not to have any joys or sorrows of my own, but to rejoice with them that do rejoice, and to weep with those that weep. He has called me to speak his word, and he has greatly owned my work. It could only be on a very clear showing that I could leave the brethren and sisters at Snowfield, who are favoured with very little of this world's good; where the trees are few, so that a child might count them, and there's very hard living for the poor in the winter. It has been given me to help, to comfort, and strengthen the little flock there, and to call in many wanderers; and my soul is filled with these things from my rising up till my lying down. My life is too short, and God's work is too great for me to think of making a home for myself in this world. I've not turned a deaf ear to your words, Seth, for when I saw as your love was given to me, I thought it might be a leading of Providence for me to change my way of life, and that we should be fellow-helpers; and I spread the matter before the Lord. But whenever I tried to fix my mind on marriage, and our living together, other thoughts always came in – the times when I've prayed by the sick and dying, and the happy hours I've had preaching, when my heart was filled with love, and the Word was given to me abundantly. And when I've opened the Bible for direction, I've always lighted on some clear word to tell me where my work lay. I believe what you say, Seth, that you would try to be a help and not a hindrance to my work; but I see that our marriage is not God's will – He draws my heart another way. I desire to live and die without husband or children. I seem to have no room in my soul for wants and fears of my own, it has pleased God to fill my heart so full with the wants and sufferings of his poor people.'

Seth was unable to reply, and they walked on in silence. At last, as they were nearly at the yard-gate, he said – 'Well, Dinah, I must seek for strength to bear it, and to endure as seeing Him who is invisible. But I feel now how weak my faith is. It seems as if, when you are gone, I could never joy in anything any more. I think it's something passing the love of women as I feel for you, for I could be content without your marrying me if I could go and live at Snowfield, and be near you. I trusted as the strong love God had given me towards you was a leading for us both; but it seems it was only meant for my trial. Perhaps I feel more for you than I ought to feel for any creature, for I often can't help saying of you what the hymn says –

> In darkest shades if she appear,
> My dawning is begun;
> She is my soul's bright morning-star,
> And she my rising sun.

That may be wrong, and I am to be taught better. But you wouldn't be displeased with me if things turned out so as I could leave this country and go to live at Snowfield?'

'No, Seth; but I counsel you to wait patiently, and not lightly to leave your own country and kindred. Do nothing without the Lord's clear bidding. It's a bleak and barren country there, not like this land of Goshen you've been used to. We mustn't be in a hurry to fix and choose our own lot; we must wait to be guided.'

'But you'd let me write you a letter, Dinah, if there was anything I wanted to tell you?'

'Yes, sure; let me know if you're in any trouble. You'll be continually in my prayers.'

They had now reached the yard-gate, and Seth said, 'I won't go in, Dinah; so farewell.' He paused and hesitated after she had given him her hand, and then said, 'There's no knowing but what you may see things different after a while. There may be a new leading.'

'Let us leave that, Seth. It's good to live only a moment at a time, as I've read in one of Mr Wesley's books. It isn't for you and me to lay plans; we've nothing to do but to obey and to trust. Farewell.'

Dinah pressed his hand with rather a sad look in her loving eyes and then passed through the gate, while Seth turned away to walk lingeringly home. But instead of taking the direct road, he chose to turn back along the fields through which he and Dinah had already passed; and I think his blue linen handkerchief was very wet with tears long before he had made up his mind that it was time for him to set his face steadily homewards. He was but three-and-twenty, and had only just learned what it is to love – to love with that adoration which a young man gives to a woman whom he feels to be greater and better than himself. Love of this sort is hardly distinguishable from religious feeling. What deep and worthy love is so? whether of woman or child, or art or music. Our caresses, our tender words, our still rapture under the influence of autumn sunsets, or pillared vistas, or calm majestic statues, or Beethoven symphonies, all bring with them the consciousness that they are mere waves and ripples in an unfathomable ocean of love and beauty; our emotion in its keenest moment passes from expression into silence, our love at its highest flood rushes beyond its object, and loses itself in the sense of divine mystery. And this blessed gift of venerating love has been given to too many humble craftsmen since the world began, for us to feel any surprise that it should have existed in the soul of a Methodist carpenter half a century ago while there was yet a lingering afterglow from the time when Wesley and his fellow-labourer fed on the hips and haws of the Cornwall hedges, after exhausting limbs and lungs in carrying a divine message to the poor.

That afterglow has long faded away; and the picture we are apt to make of Methodism in our imagination is not an amphitheatre of green hills, or the deep shade of broad-leaved sycamores, where a crowd of rough men and weary-hearted women drank in a faith which was a rudimentary culture, which linked their thoughts with the past, lifted their imagination above the sordid details of their own narrow lives, and suffused their souls with the sense of a pitying, loving, infinite Presence, sweet as summer to the houseless needy. It is too possible that to some of my readers Methodism may mean nothing more than low-pitched gables up dingy streets, sleek grocers, sponging preachers, and hypocritical jargon - elements which are regarded as an exhaustive analysis of Methodism in many fashionable quarters.

That would be a pity; for I cannot pretend that Seth and Dinah were anything else than Methodists – not indeed of that modern type which reads quarterly reviews and attends in chapels with pillared porticoes; but of a very old-fashioned kind. They believed in present miracles, in instantaneous conversions, in revelations by dreams and visions; they drew lots, and sought for Divine guidance by opening the Bible at hazard; having a literal way of interpreting the Scripture, which is not at all sanctioned by approved commentators; and it is impossible for me to represent their diction as correct, or their instruction as liberal. Still – if I have read religious history aright – faith, hope, and charity have not always been found in a direct ratio with a sensibility to the three concords; and it is possible, thank Heaven! to have very erroneous theories and very sublime feelings. The raw bacon which clumsy Molly spares from her own scanty store, that she may carry it to her neighbour's child to 'stop the fits,' may be a piteously inefficacious remedy; but the generous stirring of neighbourly kindness that prompted the deed has a beneficent radiation that is not lost.

Considering these things, we can hardly think Dinah and Seth beneath our sympathy, accustomed as we may be to weep over the loftier sorrows of heroines in satin boots and crinoline, and of heroes riding fiery horses, themselves ridden by still more fiery passions.

Poor Seth! he was never on horseback in his life except once, when he was a little lad, and Mr Jonathan Burge took him up behind, telling him to 'hold on tight;' and instead of bursting out into wild accusing apostrophes to God and destiny, he is resolving, as he now walks homeward under the solemn starlight, to repress his sadness, to be less bent on having his own will, and to live more for others, as Dinah does.

4

Home and its Sorrows

A green valley with a brook running through it, full almost to overflowing with the late rains; overhung by low stooping willows. Across this brook a plank is thrown, and over this plank Adam Bede is passing with his undoubting step, followed close by Gyp with the basket; evidently making his way to the thatched house, with a stack of timber by the side of it, about twenty yards up the opposite slope.

The door of the house is open, and an elderly woman is looking out; but she is not placidly contemplating the evening sunshine; she has been watching with dim eyes the gradually enlarging speck which for the last few minutes she has been quite sure is her darling son Adam. Lisbeth Bede loves her son with the love of a woman to whom her first-born has come late in life. She is an anxious, spare, yet vigorous old woman, clean as a snowdrop. Her grey hair is turned neatly back under a pure linen cap with a black band round it; her broad chest is covered with a buff neckerchief, and below this you see a sort of short bed-gown made of blue-checkered linen, tied round the waist and descending to the hips, from whence there is a considerable length of linsey-wolsey petticoat. For Lisbeth is tall, and in other points too there is a strong likeness between her and her son Adam. Her dark eyes are somewhat dim now – perhaps from too much crying – but her broadly-marked eyebrows are still black, her teeth are sound, and as she stands knitting rapidly and unconsciously with her work- hardened hands, she has as firmly-upright an attitude as when she is carrying a pail of water on her head from the spring. There is the same type of frame and the same keen activity of temperament in mother and son, but it was not from her that Adam got his well-filled brow and his expression of large-hearted intelligence.

Family likeness has often a deep sadness in it. Nature, that great tragic dramatist, knits us together by bone and muscle, and divides us by the subtler web of our brains; blends yearning and repulsion; and ties us by our heart-strings to the beings that jar us at every movement. We hear a voice with the very cadence of our own uttering the thoughts we despise; we see eyes – ah! so like our mother's – averted from us in cold alienation; and our last darling child startles us with the air and gestures of the sister we parted from in bitterness long years ago. The father to whom we owe our best heritage – the mechanical instinct, the keen sensibility to harmony, the unconscious skill of the modelling hand – galls us, and puts us to shame by his daily errors; the long-lost mother, whose face we begin to see in the glass as our own wrinkles come, once fretted our young souls with her anxious humours and irrational persistence.

It is such a fond anxious mother's voice that you hear, as Lisbeth says – 'Well, my lad, it's gone seven by th' clock. Thee't allays stay till the last child's born. Thee wants thy supper, I'll warrand. Where's Seth? gone arter some o's chapellin', I reckon?'

'Ay, ay, Seth's at no harm, mother, thee mayst be sure. But where's father?' said Adam quickly, as he entered the house and glanced into the room on the left hand, which was used as a workshop. 'Hasn't he done the coffin for Tholer? There's the stuff standing just as I left it this morning.'

'Done the coffin?' said Lisbeth, following him, and knitting uninterruptedly, though she looked at her son very anxiously. 'Eh, my lad, he went aff to Treddles'on this forenoon, an's niver come back. I doubt he's got to th' Waggin Overthrow again.'

A deep flush of anger passed rapidly over Adam's face. He said nothing, but threw off his jacket, and began to roll up his shirt-sleeves again.

'What art goin' to do, Adam?' said the mother, with a tone and look of alarm. 'Thee wouldstna go to work again, wi'out ha'in thy bit o' supper?'

Adam, too angry to speak, walked into the workshop. But his mother threw down her knitting, and, hurrying after him, took hold of his arm, and said in a tone of plaintive remonstrance – 'Nay, my lad, my lad, thee munna go wi'out thy supper; there's the taters wi' the gravy in 'em, just as thee lik'st 'em. I saved 'em o' purpose for thee. Come an' ha' thy supper, come.'

'Let be!' said Adam impetuously, shaking her off, and seizing one of the planks that stood against the wall. 'It's fine talking about having supper when here's a coffin promised to be ready at Brox'on by seven o'clock tomorrow morning, and ought to ha' been there now, and not a nail struck yet. My throat's too full to swallow victuals.'

'Why, thee canstna get the coffin ready,' said Lisbeth. 'Thee't work thyself to death. It 'ud take thee all night to do't.'

'What signifies how long it takes me? Isn't the coffin promised? Can they bury the man without a coffin? I'd work my right hand off sooner than deceive people with lies i' that way. It makes me mad to think on't. I shall overrun these doings before long. I've stood enough of 'em.'

Poor Lisbeth did not hear this threat for the first time, and if she had been wise she would have gone away quietly, and said nothing for the next hour. But one of the lessons a woman most rarely learns, is never to talk to an angry or a drunken man. Lisbeth sat down on the chopping bench and began to cry, and by the time she had cried enough to make her voice very piteous, she burst out into words.

'Nay, my lad, my lad, thee wouldstna go away an' break thy mother's heart, an' leave thy feyther to ruin. Thee wouldstna ha' 'em carry me to th' church-yard, an' thee not to follow me. I shanna rest i' my grave if I donna see thee at th' last; an' how's they to let thee know as I'm a-dyin', if thee't gone a-workin' i' distant parts, an' Seth belike gone arter thee, and thy feyther not able to hold a pen for's hand shakin', besides not knowin' where thee art? Thee mun forgie thy feyther – thee munna be so bitter again' him. He war a good feyther to thee afore he took to th' drink. He's a clever workman, an' taught thee thy trade, remember, an's niver gen me a blow nor so much as an ill word – no, not even in's drink. Thee wouldstna ha'm go to the workhus – thy own feyther – an' him as was a fine-growed man an' handy at everythin' amost as thee art thysen, five-an'-twenty 'ear ago, when thee wast a baby at the breast.'

Lisbeth's voice became louder and choked with sobs: a sort of wail, the most irritating of all sounds where real sorrows are to be borne, and real work to be done. Adam broke in impatiently.

'Now, mother, don't cry and talk so. Haven't I got enough to vex me without that? What's th' use o' telling me things as I only think too much on every day? If I didna think on 'em why should I do as I do, for the sake o' keeping things together here? But I hate to be talking where it's no use: I like to keep my breath for doing istead o' talking.'

'I know thee dost things as nobody else 'ud do, my lad. But thee't allays so hard upo' thy feyther, Adam. Thee think'st nothing too much to do for Seth: thee snapp'st me up if iver I find faut wi' th' lad. But thee't so angered wi' thy feyther, more nor wi' anybody else.'

'That's better than speaking soft, and letting things go the wrong way, I reckon, isn't it? If I wasn't sharp with him, he'd sell every bit o' stuff i' th' yard, and spend it on drink. I know there's a duty to be done by my father, but it isn't my duty to encourage him in running headlong to ruin. And what has Seth got to do with it? The lad does no harm as I know of. But leave me alone, mother, and let me get on with the work.'

Lisbeth dared not say any more; but she got up and called Gyp, thinking to console herself somewhat for Adam's refusal of the supper she had spread out in the loving expectation of looking at him while he ate it, by feeding Adam's dog with extra liberality. But Gyp was watching his master with wrinkled brow and ears erect, puzzled at this unusual course of things; and though he glanced at Lisbeth when she called him, and moved his fore-paws uneasily, well knowing that she was inviting him to supper, he was in a divided state of mind, and remained seated on his haunches, again fixing his eyes anxiously on his master. Adam noticed Gyp's mental conflict, and though his anger had made him less tender than usual to his mother, it did not prevent him from caring as much as usual for his dog. We are apt to be kinder to the brutes that love us than to the women that love us. Is it because the brutes are dumb?

'Go, Gyp; go, lad!' Adam said, in a tone of encouraging command; and Gyp, apparently satisfied that duty and pleasure were one, followed Lisbeth into the house-place.

But no sooner had he licked up his supper than he went back to his master, while Lisbeth sat down alone to cry over her knitting. Women who are never bitter and resentful are often the most querulous; and if Solomon was as wise as he is reputed to be, I feel sure that when he compared a contentious woman to a continual dropping on a very rainy day, he had not a vixen in his eye – a fury with long nails, acrid and selfish. Depend upon it, he meant a good creature, who had no joy but in the happiness of the loved ones whom she contributed to make uncomfortable, putting by all the tid-bits for them, and spending nothing on herself. Such a woman as Lisbeth, for example – at once patient and complaining, self-renouncing and exacting, brooding the livelong day over what happened yesterday, and what is likely to happen tomorrow, and crying very readily both at the good and the evil. But a certain awe mingled itself with her idolatrous love of Adam, and when he said, 'Leave me alone,' she was always silenced.

So the hours passed, to the loud ticking of the old day-clock and the sound of Adam's tools. At last he called for a light and a draught of water (beer was a thing only to be drunk on holidays), and Lisbeth ventured to say as she took it in, 'Thy supper stans ready for thee, when thee lik'st.'

'Donna thee sit up, mother,' said Adam, in a gentle tone. He had worked off his anger now, and whenever he wished to be especially kind to his mother, he fell into his strongest native accent and dialect, with which at other times his speech was less deeply tinged. 'I'll see to father when he comes home; maybe he wonna come at all tonight. I shall be easier if thee't i' bed.'

'Nay, I'll bide till Seth comes. He wonna be long now, reckon.'

It was then past nine by the clock, which was always in advance of the day, and before it had struck ten the latch was lifted and Seth entered. He had heard the sound of the tools as he was approaching.

'Why, mother,' he said, 'how is it as father's working so late?'

'It's none o' thy feyther as is a-workin' – thee might know that well anoof if thy head warna full o' chapellin' – it's thy brother as does iverything, for there's niver nobody else i' th' way to do nothin'.'

Lisbeth was going on, for she was not at all afraid of Seth, and usually poured into his ears all the querulousness which was repressed by her awe of Adam. Seth had never in his life spoken a harsh word to his mother, and timid people always wreak their peevishness on the gentle. But Seth, with an anxious look, had passed into the workshop and said – 'Addy, how's this? What! father's forgot the coffin?'

'Ay, lad, th' old tale; but I shall get it done,' said Adam, looking up, and casting one of his bright keen glances at his brother. 'Why, what's the matter with thee? Thee't in trouble.'

Seth's eyes were red, and there was a look of deep depression on his mild face.

'Yes, Addy, but it's what must be borne, and can't be helped. Why, thee'st never been to the school, then?'

'School? no; that screw can wait,' said Adam, hammering away again.

'Let me take my turn now, and do thee go to bed,' said Seth.

'No, lad, I'd rather go on, now I'm in harness. Thee't help me to carry it to Brox'on when it's done. I'll call thee up at sunrise. Go and eat thy supper, and shut the door, so as I mayn't hear mother's talk.'

Seth knew that Adam always meant what he said, and was not to be persuaded into meaning anything else. So he turned, with rather a heavy heart, into the house-place.

'Adam's niver touched a bit o' victual sin' home he's come,' said Lisbeth. 'I reckon thee'st hed thy supper at some o' thy Methody folks.'

'Nay, mother,' said Seth, 'I've had no supper yet.'

'Come, then,' said Lisbeth, 'but donna thee ate the taters, for Adam 'ull happen ate 'em if I leave 'em stannin'. He loves a bit o' taters an' gravy. But he's been so sore an' angered, he wouldn't ate 'em, for all I'd putten 'em by o' purpose for him. An' he's been a-threatenin' to go away again,' she went on, whimpering, 'an' I'm fast sure he'll go some dawnin' afore I'm up, an' niver let me know aforehand, an' he'll niver come back again when once he's gone. An' I'd better niver ha' had a son, as is like no other body's son for the deftness an' th' handiness, an' so looked on by th' grit folks, an' tall an' upright like a poplar tree, an' me to be parted from him, an' niver see 'm no more.'

'Come, mother, donna grieve thyself in vain,' said Seth, in a soothing voice. 'Thee'st not half so good reason to think as Adam 'ull go away as to think he'll stay with thee. He may say such a thing when he's in wrath – and he's got excuse for being wrathful sometimes – but his heart 'ud never let him go. Think how he's stood by us all when it's been none so easy – paying his savings to free me from going for a soldier, an' turnin' his earnins into wood for father, when he's got plenty o' uses for his money, and many a young man like him 'ud ha' been married and settled before now. He'll never turn round and knock down his own work, and forsake them as it's been the labour of his life to stand by.'

'Donna talk to me about's marr'in',' said Lisbeth, crying afresh. 'He's set's heart on that Hetty Sorrel, as 'ull niver save a penny, an' 'ull toss up her head at's old mother. An' to think as he might ha' Mary Burge, an' be took partners, an' be a big man wi' workmen under him, like Mester Burge – Dolly's told me so o'er an' o'er again – if it warna as he's set's heart on that bit of a wench, as is o' no more use nor the gillyflower on the wall. An' he so wise at bookin' an' figurin', an' not to know no better nor that!'

'But, mother, thee know'st we canna love just where other folks 'ud have us. There's nobody but God can control the heart of man. I could ha' wished myself as Adam could ha' made another choice, but I wouldn't reproach him for what he can't help. And I'm not sure but what he tries to o'ercome it. But it's a matter as he doesn't like to be spoke to about, and I can only pray to the Lord to bless and direct him.'

'Ay, thee't allays ready enough at prayin', but I donna see as thee gets much wi' thy prayin'. Thee wotna get double earnins o' this side Yule. Th' Methodies 'll niver make thee half the man thy brother is, for all they're a-makin' a preacher on thee.'

'It's partly truth thee speak'st there, mother,' said Seth, mildly; 'Adam's far before me, an's done more for me than I can ever do for him. God distributes talents to every man according as He sees good. But thee mustna undervally prayer. Prayer mayna bring money, but it brings us what no money can buy – a power to keep from sin, and be content with God's will, whatever He may please to send. If thee wouldst pray to God to help thee, and trust in His goodness, thee wouldstna be so uneasy about things.'

'Unaisy? I'm i' th' right on't to be unaisy. It's well seen on thee what it is niver to be unaisy. Thee't gi' away all thy earnins, an' niver be unaisy as thee'st nothin' laid up again' a rainy day. If Adam had been as aisy as thee, he'd niver ha' had no money to pay for thee. Take no thought for the morrow – take no thought – that's what thee't allays sayin'; an' what comes on't? Why, as Adam has to take thought for thee.'

'Those are the words o' the Bible, mother,' said Seth. 'They don't mean as we should be idle. They mean we shouldn't be over anxious and worreting our-selves about what'll happen tomorrow, but do our duty, and leave the rest to God's will.'

'Ay, ay, that's the way wi' thee: thee allays makes a peck o' thy own words out o' a pint o' the Bible's. I donna see how thee't to know as "take no thought for the morrow" means all that. An' when the Bible's such a big book, an' thee canst read all thro't, an' ha' the pick o' the texes, I canna think why thee dostna pick better words as donna mean so much more nor they say. Adam doesna pick a that'n; I can understan' the tex as he's allays a sayin', "God helps them as helps their sens."'

'Nay, mother,' said Seth, 'that's no text o' the Bible. It comes out of a book as Adam picked up at the stall at Treddles'on. It was wrote by a knowing man, but over-worldly, I doubt. However, that saying's partly true; for the Bible tells us we must be workers together with God.'

'Well, how'm I to know? It sounds like a tex. But what's th' matter wi' th' lad? Thee't hardly atin' a bit o' supper. Dostna mean to ha' no more nor that bit o' oatcake? An' thee lookst as white as a flick o' new bacon. What's th' matter wi' thee?'

'Nothing to mind about, mother; I'm not hungry. I'll just look in at Adam again, and see if he'll let me go on with the coffin.'

'Ha' a drop o' warm broth?' said Lisbeth, whose motherly feeling now got the better of her 'nattering' habit. 'I'll set two-three sticks alight in a minute.'

'Nay, mother, thank thee; thee't very good,' said Seth, gratefully; and encouraged by this touch of tenderness, he went on: 'Let me pray a bit with thee for father, and Adam, and all of us – it'll comfort thee, happen, more than thee thinkst.'

'Well, I've nothin' to say again' it.'

Lisbeth, though disposed always to take the negative side in her conversations with Seth, had a vague sense that there was some comfort and safety in the fact of his piety, and that it somehow relieved her from the trouble of any spiritual transactions on her own behalf.

So the mother and son knelt down together, and Seth prayed for the poor wandering father, and for those who were sorrowing for him at home. And when he came to the petition that Adam might never be called to set up his tent in a far country, but that his mother might be cheered and comforted by his presence all the days of her pilgrimage, Lisbeth's ready tears flowed again, and she wept aloud.

When they rose from their knees, Seth went to Adam again, and said, 'Wilt only lie down for an hour or two, and let me go on the while?'

'No, Seth, no. Make mother go to bed, and go thyself.'

Meantime Lisbeth had dried her eyes, and now followed Seth, holding something in her hands. It was the brown-and-yellow platter containing the baked potatoes with the gravy in them and bits of meat which she had cut and mixed among them. Those were dear times, when wheaten bread and fresh meat were delicacies to working people. She set the dish down rather timidly on the bench by Adam's side, and said, 'Thee canst pick a bit while thee't workin'. I'll bring thee another drop o' water.'

'Ay, mother, do,' said Adam, kindly; 'I'm getting very thirsty.'

In half an hour all was quiet; no sound was to be heard in the house but the loud ticking of the old day-clock, and the ringing of Adam's tools. The night was very still: when Adam opened the door to look out at twelve o'clock, the only motion seemed to be in the glowing, twinkling stars: every blade of grass was asleep.

Bodily haste and exertion usually leave our thoughts very much at the mercy of our feelings and imagination; and it was so tonight with Adam. While his muscles were working lustily, his mind seemed as passive as a spectator at a diorama: scenes of the sad past, and probably sad future, floating before him, and giving place one to the other in swift succession.

He saw how it would be tomorrow morning, when he had carried the coffin to Broxton and was at home again, having his breakfast: his father perhaps would come in ashamed to meet his son's glance – would sit down, looking older and more tottering than he had done the morning before, and hang down his head, examining the floor-quarries; while Lisbeth would ask him how he supposed the coffin had been got ready, that he had slinked off and left undone – for Lisbeth was always the first to utter the word of reproach, although she cried at Adam's severity towards his father.

'So it will go on, worsening and worsening,' thought Adam; 'there's no slipping uphill again, and no standing still when once you've begun to slip down.' And then the day came back to him when he was a little fellow and used to run by his father's side, proud to be taken out to work, and prouder still to hear his father boasting to his fellow-workmen how 'the little chap had an uncommon notion o' carpentering.' What a fine active fellow his father was then! When people asked Adam whose little lad he was, he had a sense of distinction as he answered, 'I'm Thias Bede's lad' – he was quite sure everybody knew Thias Bede: didn't he make the wonderful pigeon-house at Broxton parsonage? Those were happy days, especially when Seth, who was three years the younger, began to go out working too, and Adam began to be a teacher as well as a learner. But then came the days of sadness, when Adam was some way on in his teens, and Thias began to loiter at the public-houses, and Lisbeth began to cry at home, and to pour forth her plaints in the hearing of her sons. Adam remembered well the night of shame and anguish when he first saw his father quite wild and foolish, shouting a song out fitfully among his drunken companions at the Waggon Overthrown. He had run away once when he was only eighteen, making his escape in the morning twilight with a little blue bundle over his shoulder, and his 'mensuration book' in his pocket, and saying to himself very decidedly that he could bear the vexations of home no longer – he would go and seek his fortune, setting up his stick at the crossways and bending his steps the way it fell. But by the time he got to Stoniton, the thought of his mother and Seth, left behind to endure everything without him, became too importunate, and his resolution failed him. He came back the next day, but the misery and terror his mother had gone through in those two days had haunted her ever since.

'No!' Adam said to himself tonight, 'that must never happen again. It 'ud make a poor balance when my doings are cast up at the last, if my poor old mother stood o' the wrong side. My back's broad enough and strong enough; I should be no better than a coward to go away and leave the troubles to be borne by them as aren't half so able. "They that are strong ought to bear the infirmities of those that are weak, and not to please themselves." There's a text wants no candle to show't; it shines by its own light. It's plain enough you get into the wrong road i' this life if you run after this and that only for the sake o' making things easy and pleasant to yourself. A pig may poke his nose into the trough and think o' nothing outside it; but if you've got a man's heart and soul in you, you can't be easy a-making your own bed an' leaving the rest to lie on the stones. Nay, nay, I'll never slip my neck out o' the yoke, and leave the load to be drawn by the weak uns. Father's a sore cross to me, an's likely to be for many a long year to come. What then? I've got th' health, and the limbs, and the sperrit to bear it.'

At this moment a smart rap, as if with a willow wand, was given at the house door, and Gyp, instead of barking, as might have been expected, gave a loud howl. Adam, very much startled, went at once to the door and opened it.

Nothing was there; all was still, as when he opened it an hour before; the leaves were motionless, and the light of the stars showed the placid fields on both sides of the brook quite empty of visible life. Adam walked round the house, and still saw nothing except a rat which darted into the woodshed as he passed. He went in again, wondering; the sound was so peculiar, that the moment he heard it, it called up the image of the willow wand striking the door. He could not help a little shudder, as he remembered how often his mother had told him of just such a sound coming as a sign when someone was dying. Adam was not a man to be gratuitously superstitious; but he had the blood of the peasant in him as well as of the artisan, and a peasant can no more help believing in a traditional superstition than a horse can help trembling when he sees a camel. Besides, he had that mental combination which is at once humble in the region of mystery, and keen in the region of knowledge: it was the depth of his reverence quite as much as his hard common sense, which gave him his disinclination to doctrinal religion, and he often checked Seth's argumentative spiritualism by saying, 'Eh, it's a big mystery; thee know'st but little about it.' And so it happened that Adam was at once penetrating and credulous. If a new building had fallen down and he had been told that this was a divine judgement, he would have said, 'May be; but the bearing o' the roof and walls wasn't right, else it wouldn't ha' come down;' yet he believed in dreams and prognostics, and to his dying day he bated his breath a little when he told the story of the stroke with the willow wand. I tell it as he told it, not attempting to reduce it to its natural elements: in our eagerness to explain impressions, we often lose our hold of the sympathy that comprehends them.

But he had the best antidote against imaginative dread in the necessity for getting on with the coffin, and for the next ten minutes his hammer was ringing so uninterruptedly, that other sounds, if there were any, might well be over-powered. A pause came, however, when he had to take up his ruler, and now again came the strange rap, and again Gyp howled. Adam was at the door without the loss of a moment; but again all was still, and the starlight showed there was nothing but the dew-laden grass in front of the cottage.

Adam for a moment thought uncomfortably about his father; but of late years he had never come home at dark hours from Treddleston, and there was every reason for believing that he was then sleeping off his drunkenness at the Waggon Overthrown. Besides, to Adam, the conception of the future was so inseparable from the painful image of his father, that the fear of any fatal accident to him was excluded by the deeply-infixed fear of his continual degradation. The next thought that occurred to him was one that made him slip off his shoes and tread lightly upstairs, to listen at the bedroom doors. But both Seth and his mother were breathing regularly.

Adam came down and set to work again, saying to himself, 'I won't open the door again. It's no use staring about to catch sight of a sound. Maybe there's a world about us as we can't see, but th' ear's quicker than the eye, and catches a sound from't now and then. Some people think they get a sight on't too, but they're mostly folks whose eyes are not much use to 'em at anything else. For my part, I think it's better to see when your perpendicular's true, than to see a ghost.'

Such thoughts as these are apt to grow stronger and stronger as daylight quenches the candles and the birds begin to sing. By the time the red sunlight shone on the brass nails that formed the initials on the lid of the coffin, any lingering foreboding from the sound of the willow wand was merged in satisfaction that the work was done and the promise redeemed. There was no need to call Seth, for he was already moving overhead, and presently came downstairs.

'Now, lad,' said Adam, as Seth made his appearance, 'the coffin's done, and we can take it over to Brox'on, and be back again before half after six. I'll take a mouthful o' oat cake, and then we'll be off.'

The coffin was soon propped on the tall shoulders of the two brothers, and they were making their way, followed close by Gyp, out of the little woodyard into the lane at the back of the house. It was but about a mile and a half to Broxton over the opposite slope, and their road wound very pleasantly along lanes and across fields, where the pale woodbines and the dog-roses were scenting the hedgerows, and the birds were twittering and trilling in the tall leafy boughs of oak and elm. It was a strangely-mingled picture – the fresh youth of the summer morning, with its Eden-like peace and loveliness, the stalwart strength of the two brothers in their rusty working clothes, and the long coffin on their shoulders. They paused for the last time before a small farmhouse outside the village of Broxton. By six o'clock the task was done, the coffin nailed down, and Adam and Seth were on their way home. They chose a shorter way homeward, which would take them across the fields and the brook in front of the house. Adam had not mentioned to Seth what had happened in the night, but he still retained sufficient impression from it himself to say – 'Seth, lad, if father isn't come home by the time we've had our breakfast, I think it'll be as well for thee to go over to Treddles'on and look after him, and thee canst get me the brass wire I want. Never mind about losing an hour at thy work; we can make that up. What dost say?'

'I'm willing,' said Seth. 'But see what clouds have gathered since we set out. I'm thinking we shall have more rain. It'll be a sore time for th' haymaking if the meadows are flooded again. The brook's fine and full now: another day's rain 'ud cover the plank, and we should have to go round by the road.'

They were coming across the valley now, and had entered the pasture through which the brook ran.

'Why, what's that sticking against the willow?' continued Seth, beginning to walk faster. Adam's heart rose to his mouth: the vague anxiety about his father was changed into a great dread. He made no answer to Seth, but ran forward, preceded by Gyp, who began to bark uneasily; and in two moments he was at the bridge.

This was what the omen meant, then! And the grey-haired father, of whom he had thought with a sort of hardness a few hours ago, as certain to live to be a thorn in his side, was perhaps even then struggling with that watery death! This was the first thought that flashed through Adam's conscience, before he had time to seize the coat and drag out the tall heavy body. Seth was already by his side, helping him, and when they had it on the bank, the two sons in the first moments knelt and looked with mute awe at the glazed eyes, forgetting that there was need for action – forgetting everything but that their father lay dead before them. Adam was the first to speak.

'I'll run to mother,' he said, in a loud whisper. 'I'll be back to thee in a minute.'

Poor Lisbeth was busy preparing her sons' breakfast, and their porridge was already steaming on the fire. Her kitchen always looked the pink of cleanliness, but this morning she was more than usually bent on making her hearth and breakfast-table look comfortable and inviting.

'The lads 'ull be fine an' hungry,' she said, half aloud, as she stirred the porridge. 'It's a good step to Brox'on, an' it's hungry air o'er the hill – wi' that heavy coffin too. Eh! it's heavier now, wi' poor Bob Tholer in't. Howiver, I've made a drap more porridge nor common this mornin'. The feyther 'ull happen come in arter a bit. Not as he'll ate much porridge. He swallers sixpenn'orth o' ale, an' saves a hap'orth o' porridge – that's his way o' layin' by money, as I've told him many a time, an' am likely to tell him again afore the day's out. Eh! poor mon, he takes it quiet enough; there's no denyin' that.'

But now Lisbeth heard the heavy 'thud' of a running footstep on the turf, and, turning quickly towards the door, she saw Adam enter, looking so pale and overwhelmed that she screamed aloud and rushed towards him before he had time to speak.

'Hush, mother,' Adam said, rather hoarsely, 'don't be frightened. Father's tumbled into the water. Belike we may bring him round again. Seth and me are going to carry him in. Get a blanket and make it hot at the fire.'

In reality Adam was convinced that his father was dead, but he knew there was no other way of repressing his mother's impetuous wailing grief than by occupying her with some active task which had hope in it.

He ran back to Seth, and the two sons lifted the sad burden in heart-stricken silence. The wide-open glazed eyes were grey, like Seth's, and had once looked with mild pride on the boys before whom Thias had lived to hang his head in shame. Seth's chief feeling was awe and distress at this sudden snatching away of his father's soul; but Adam's mind rushed back over the past in a flood of relenting and pity. When death, the great Reconciler, has come, it is never our tenderness that we repent of, but our severity.

5

The Rector

Before twelve o'clock there had been some heavy storms of rain, and the water lay in deep gutters on the sides of the gravel-walks in the garden of Broxton Parsonage; the great Provence roses had been cruelly tossed by the wind and beaten by the rain, and all the delicate-stemmed border flowers had been dashed down and stained with the wet soil. A melancholy morning – because it was nearly time hay-harvest should begin, and instead of that the meadows were likely to be flooded.

But people who have pleasant homes get indoor enjoyments that they would never think of but for the rain. If it had not been a wet morning, Mr Irwine would not have been in the dining-room playing at chess with his mother, and he loves both his mother and chess quite well enough to pass some cloudy hours very easily by their help. Let me take you into that dining-room, and show you the Rev Adolphus Irwine, Rector of Broxton, vicar of Hayslope, and vicar of Blythe, a pluralist at whom the severest church-reformer would have found it difficult to look sour. We will enter very softly and stand still in the open doorway, without awaking the glossy brown setter who is stretched across the hearth, with her two puppies beside her; or the pug, who is dozing, with his black muzzle aloft, like a sleepy president.

The room is a large and lofty one, with an ample mullioned oriel window at one end; the walls, you see, are new, and not yet painted; but the furniture, though originally of an expensive sort, is old and scanty, and there is no drapery about the window. The crimson cloth over the large dining-table is very thread-bare, though it contrasts pleasantly enough with the dead hue of the plaster on the walls; but on this cloth there is a massive silver waiter with a decanter of water on it, of the same pattern as two larger ones that are propped up on the sideboard with a coat of arms conspicuous in their centre. You suspect at once that the inhabitants of this room have inherited more blood than wealth, and would not be surprised to find that Mr Irwine had a finely-cut nostril and upper lip; but at present we can only see that he has a broad flat back and an abundance of powdered hair, all thrown backward and tied behind with a black ribbon – a bit of conservatism in costume which tells you that he is not a young man. He will perhaps turn round by and by, and in the meantime we can look at that stately old lady, his mother, a beautiful aged brunette, whose rich-toned complexion is well set off by the complex wrappings of pure white cambric and lace about her head and neck. She is as erect in her comely embonpoint as a statue of Ceres; and her dark face, with its delicate aquiline nose, firm proud mouth, and small intense black eye, is so keen and sarcastic in its expression that you instinctively substitute a pack of cards for the chessmen, and imagine her telling your fortune. The small brown hand with which she is lifting her queen is laden with pearls, diamonds, and turquoises; and a large black veil is very carefully adjusted over the crown of her cap, and falls in sharp contrast on the white folds about her neck. It must take a long time to dress that old lady in the morning! But it seems a law of nature that she should be dressed so: she is clearly one of those children of royalty who have never doubted their right divine, and never met with anyone so absurd as to question it.

'There, Dauphin, tell me what that is!' says this magnificent old lady, as she deposits her queen very quietly and folds her arms. 'I should be sorry to utter a word disagreeable to your feelings.'

'Ah! you witch-mother, you sorceress! How is a Christian man to win a game off you? I should have sprinkled the board with holy water before we began. You've not won that game by fair means, now, so don't pretend it.'

'Yes, yes, that's what the beaten have always said of great conquerors. But see, there's the sunshine falling on the board, to show you more clearly what a foolish move you made with that pawn. Come, shall I give you another chance?'

'No, mother, I shall leave you to your own conscience, now it's clearing up. We must go and plash up the mud a little, mustn't we, Juno?' This was addressed to the brown setter, who had jumped up at the sound of the voices and laid her nose in an insinuating way on her master's leg. 'But I must go upstairs first and see Anne. I was called away to Tholer's funeral just when I was going before.'

'It's of no use, child; she can't speak to you. Kate says she has one of her worst headaches this morning.'

'Oh, she likes me to go and see her just the same; she's never too ill to care about that.'

If you know how much of human speech is mere purposeless impulse or habit, you will not wonder when I tell you that this identical objection had been made, and had received the same kind of answer, many hundred times in the course of the fifteen years that Mr Irwine's sister Anne had been an invalid. Splendid old ladies, who take a long time to dress in the morning, have often slight sympathy with sickly daughters.

But while Mr Irwine was still seated, leaning back in his chair and stroking Juno's head, the servant came to the door and said, 'If you please, sir, Joshua Rann wishes to speak with you, if you're at liberty.'

'Let him be shown in here,' said Mrs Irwine, taking up her knitting. 'I always like to hear what Mr Rann has got to say. His shoes will be dirty, but see that he wipes them, Carroll.'

In two minutes Mr Rann appeared at the door with very deferential bows, which, however, were far from conciliating Pug, who gave a sharp bark, and ran across the room to reconnoitre the stranger's legs; while the two puppies, regarding Mr Rann's prominent calf and ribbed worsted stockings from a more sensuous point of view, plunged and growled over them in great enjoyment. Meantime, Mr Irwine turned round his chair and said – 'Well, Joshua, anything the matter at Hayslope, that you've come over this damp morning? Sit down, sit down. Never mind the dogs; give them a friendly kick. Here, Pug, you rascal!'

It is very pleasant to see some men turn round; pleasant as a sudden rush of warm air in winter, or the flash of firelight in the chill dusk. Mr Irwine was one of those men. He bore the same sort of resemblance to his mother that our loving memory of a friend's face often bears to the face itself: the lines were all more generous, the smile brighter, the expression heartier. If the outline had been less finely cut, his face might have been called jolly; but that was not the right word for its mixture of *bonhomie* and distinction.

'Thank your reverence,' answered Mr Rann, endeavouring to look unconcerned about his legs, but shaking them alternately to keep off the puppies; 'I'll stand, if you please, as more becoming. I hope I see you and Mrs Irwine well, an' Miss Irwine – an' Miss Anne, I hope's as well as usual.'

'Yes, Joshua, thank you. You see how blooming my mother looks. She beats us younger people hollow. But what's the matter?'

'Why, sir, I had to come to Brox'on to deliver some work, and I thought it but right to call and let you know the goins-on as there's been i' the village, such as I hanna seen i' my time, and I've lived in it man and boy sixty year come St Thomas, and collected th' Easter dues for Mr Blick before your reverence come into the parish, and been at the ringin' o' every bell, and the diggin' o' every grave, and sung i' the quire long afore Bartle Massey come from nobody knows where, wi' his counter-singin' and fine anthems, as puts everybody out but himself – one takin' it up after another like sheep a-bleatin' i' th' fold. I know what belongs to bein' a parish clerk, and I know as I should be wantin' i' respect to your reverence, an' church, an' king, if I was t' allow such goins-on wi'out speakin'. I was took by surprise, an' knowed nothin' on it beforehand, an' I was so flustered, I was clean as if I'd lost my tools. I hanna slep more nor four hour this night as is past an' gone; an' then it was nothin' but nightmare, as tired me worse nor wakin'.'

'Why, what in the world is the matter, Joshua? Have the thieves been at the church lead again?'

'Thieves! no, sir – an' yet, as I may say, it is thieves, an' athievin' the church, too. It's the Methodisses as is like to get th' upper hand i' th' parish, if your reverence an' his honour, squire Donnithorne, doesna think well to say the word an' forbid it. Not as I'm a-dictatin' to you, sir; I'm not forgettin' myself so far as to be wise above my betters. Howiver, whether I'm wise or no, that's neither here nor there, but what I've got to say I say – as the young Methodis woman, as is at Mester Poyser's, was a-preachin' an' a-praying on the Green last night, as sure as I'm a-stannin' afore your reverence now.'

'Preaching on the Green!' said Mr Irwine, looking surprised but quite serene. 'What, that pale pretty young woman I've seen at Poyser's? I saw she was a Methodist, or Quaker, or something of that sort, by her dress, but I didn't know she was a preacher.'

'It's a true word as I say, sir,' rejoined Mr Rann, compressing his mouth into a semicircular form, and pausing long enough to indicate three notes of exclamation. 'She preached on the Green last night; an' she's laid hold of Chad's Bess, as the girl's been i' fits welly iver sin'.'

'Well, Bessy Cranage is a hearty-looking lass; I dare say she'll come round again, Joshua. Did anybody else go into fits?'

'No, sir, I canna say as they did. But there's no knowin' what'll come, if we're t' have such preachins as that agoin' on ivery week – there'll be no livin' i' th' village. For them Methodisses make folks believe as if they take a mug o' drink extry, an' make theirselves a bit comfortable, they'll have to go to hell for't as sure as they're born. I'm not a tipplin' man nor a drunkard – nobody can say it on me – but I like a extry quart at Easter or Christmas time, as is nat'ral when we're goin' the rounds a-singin', an' folks offer't you for nothin'; or when I'm a-collectin' the dues; an' I like a pint wi' my pipe, an' a neighbourly chat at Mester Casson's now an' then, for I was brought up i' the Church, thank God, an' ha' been a parish clerk this two-an'-thirty year: I should know what the church religion is.'

'Well, what's your advice, Joshua? What do you think should be done?'

'Well, your reverence, I'm not for takin' any measures again the young woman. She's well enough if she'd let alone preachin'; an' I hear as she's a-goin' away back to her own country soon. She's Mr Poyser's own niece, an' I donna wish to say what's anyways disrespectful o' th' family at th' Hall Farm, as I've measured for shoes, little an' big, welly iver sin' I've been a shoemaker. But there's that Will Maskery, sir, as is the rampageousest Methodis as can be, an' I make no doubt it was him as stirred up th' young woman to preach last night, an' he'll be a-bringin' other folks to preach from Treddles'on, if his comb isn't cut a bit; an' I think as he should be let know as he isna t' have the makin' an' mendin' o' church carts an' implemens, let alone stayin' i' that house an' yard as is Squire Donnithorne's.'

'Well, but you say yourself, Joshua, that you never knew anyone come to preach on the Green before; why should you think they'll come again? The Methodists don't come to preach in little villages like Hayslope, where there's only a handful of labourers, too tired to listen to them. They might almost as well go and preach on the Binton Hills. Will Maskery is no preacher himself, I think.'

'Nay, sir, he's no gift at stringin' the words together wi'out book; he'd be stuck fast like a cow i' wet clay. But he's got tongue enough to speak disrespectful about's neebors, for he said as I was a blind Pharisee – a-usin' the Bible i' that way to find nicknames for folks as are his elders an' betters! – and what's worse, he's been heard to say very unbecomin' words about your reverence; for I could bring them as 'ud swear as he called you a "dumb dog", an' a "idle shepherd". You'll forgi'e me for sayin' such things over again.'

'Better not, better not, Joshua. Let evil words die as soon as they're spoken. Will Maskery might be a great deal worse fellow than he is. He used to be a wild drunken rascal, neglecting his work and beating his wife, they told me; now he's thrifty and decent, and he and his wife look comfortable together. If you can bring me any proof that he interferes with his neighbours, and creates any disturbance, I shall think it my duty as a clergyman and a magistrate to interfere. But it wouldn't become wise people, like you and me, to be making a fuss about trifles, as if we thought the church was in danger because Will Maskery lets his tongue wag rather foolishly, or a young woman talks in a serious way to a handful of people on the Green. We must "live and let live," Joshua, in religion as well as in other things. You go on doing your duty, as parish clerk and sexton, as well as you've always done it, and making those capital thick boots for your neighbours, and things won't go far wrong in Hayslope, depend upon it.'

'Your reverence is very good to say so; an' I'm sensable as, you not livin' i' the parish, there's more upo' my shoulders.'

'To be sure; and you must mind and not lower the church in people's eyes by seeming to be frightened about it for a little thing, Joshua. I shall trust to your good sense, now, to take no notice at all of what Will Maskery says, either about you or me. You and your neighbours can go on taking your pot of beer soberly, when you've done your day's work, like good churchmen; and if Will Maskery doesn't like to join you, but to go to a prayer-meeting at Treddleston instead, let him ; that's no business of yours, so long as he doesn't hinder you from doing what you like. And as to people saying a few idle words about us, we must not mind that, any more than the old church-steeple minds the rooks cawing about it. Will Maskery comes to church every Sunday afternoon, and does his wheelwright's business steadily in the weekdays, and as long as he does that he must be let alone.'

'Ah, sir, but when he comes to church, he sits an' shakes his head, an' looks as sour an' as coxy when we're a-singin', as I should like to fetch him a rap across the jowl – God forgi'e me – an' Mrs Irwine, an' your reverence, too, for speakin' so afore you. An' he said as our Christmas singin' was no better nor the cracklin' o' thorns under a pot.'

'Well, he's got a bad ear for music, Joshua. When people have wooden heads, you know, it can't be helped. He won't bring the other people in Hayslope round to his opinion, while you go on singing as well as you do.'

'Yes, sir, but it turns a man's stomach t' hear the scripture misused i' that way. I know as much o' the words o' the Bible as he does, an' could say the Psalms right through i' my sleep if you was to pinch me; but I know better nor to take 'em to say my own say wi'. I might as well take the sacriment-cup home and use it at meals.'

'That's a very sensible remark of yours, Joshua; but, as I said before – '

While Mr Irwine was speaking, the sound of a booted step, and the clink of a spur, were heard on the stone floor of the entrance-hall, and Joshua Rann moved hastily aside from the doorway to make room for someone who paused there, and said, in a ringing tenor voice, 'Godson Arthur – may he come in?'

'Come in, come in, godson!' Mrs Irwine answered, in the deep half-masculine tone which belongs to the vigorous old woman, and there entered a young gentleman in a riding-dress, with his right arm in a sling; whereupon followed that pleasant confusion of laughing interjections, and hand-shakings, and 'How are you's?' mingled with joyous short barks and wagging of tails on the part of the canine members of the family, which tells that the visitor is on the best terms with the visited. The young gentleman was Arthur Donni-thorne, known in Hayslope, variously, as 'the young squire,' 'the heir,' and 'the captain.' He was only a captain in the Loamshire Militia; but to the Hayslope tenants he was more intensely a captain than all the young gentlemen of the same rank in his Majesty's regulars – he outshone them as the planet Jupiter outshines the Milky Way. If you want to know more particularly how he looked, call to your remembrance some tawny-whiskered, brown-locked, clear-complexioned young Englishman whom you have met with in a foreign town, and been proud of as a fellow-countryman – well-washed, high-bred, white-handed, yet looking as if he could deliver well from the left shoulder, and floor his man: I will not be so much of a tailor as to trouble your imagination with the difference of costume, and insist on the striped waistcoat, long-tailed coat, and low top-boots.

Turning round to take a chair, Captain Donnithorne said, 'But don't let me interrupt Joshua's business – he has something to say.'

'Humbly begging your honour's pardon,' said Joshua, bowing low, 'there was one thing I had to say to his reverence as other things had drove out o' my head.'

'Out with it, Joshua, quickly!' said Mr Irwine.

'Belike, sir, you havena heared as Thias Bede's dead-drownded this morning, or more like overnight, i' the Willow Brook, again' the bridge right i' front o' the house.'

'Ah!' exclaimed both the gentlemen at once, as if they were a good deal interested in the information.

'An' Seth Bede's been to me this morning to say he wished me to tell your reverence as his brother Adam begged of you particular t' allow his father's grave to be dug by the whitethorn, because his mother's set her heart on it, on account of a dream as she had; an' they'd ha' come theirselves to ask you, but they've so much to see after with the crowner, an' that; an' their mother's took on so, an' wants 'em to make sure o' the spot for fear somebody else should take it. An' if your reverence sees well and good, I'll send my boy to tell 'em as soon as I get home; an' that's why I make bold to trouble you wi' it, his honour being present.'

'To be sure, Joshua, to be sure, they shall have it. I'll ride round to Adam myself, and see him. Send your boy, however, to say they shall have the grave, lest anything should happen to detain me. And now, good-morning, Joshua; go into the kitchen and have some ale.'

'Poor old Thias!' said Mr Irwine, when Joshua was gone, 'I'm afraid the drink helped the brook to drown him. I should have been glad for the load to have been taken off my friend Adam's shoulders in a less painful way. That fine fellow has been propping up his father from ruin for the last five or six years.'

'He's a regular trump, is Adam,' said Captain Donnithorne. 'When I was a little fellow, and Adam was a strapping lad of fifteen, and taught me carpentering, I used to think if ever I was a rich sultan, I would make Adam my grand-vizier. And I believe now, he would bear the exaltation as well as any poor wise man in an Eastern story. If ever I live to be a large-acred man instead of a poor devil with a mortgaged allowance of pocket-money, I'll have Adam for my right-hand. He shall manage my woods for me, for he seems to have a better notion of those things than any man I ever met with; and I know he would make twice the money of them that my grandfather does, with that miserable old Satchell to manage, who understands no more about timber than an old carp. I've mentioned the subject to my grandfather once or twice, but for some reason or other he has a dislike to Adam, and I can do nothing. But come, your reverence, are you for a ride with me? It's splendid out of doors now. We can go to Adam's together, if you like; but I want to call at the Hall Farm on my way, to look at the whelps Poyser is keeping for me.'

'You must stay and have lunch first, Arthur,' said Mrs Irwine. 'It's nearly two. Carroll will bring it in directly.'

'I want to go to the Hall Farm too,' said Mr Irwine, 'to have another look at the little Methodist who is staying there. Joshua tells me she was preaching on the Green last night.'

'Oh, by Jove!' said Captain Donnithorne, laughing. 'Why, she looks as quiet as a mouse. There's something rather striking about her, though. I positively felt quite bashful the first time I saw her: she was sitting stooping over her sewing in the sunshine outside the house, when I rode up and called out, without noticing that she was a stranger, "Is Martin Poyser at home?" I declare, when she got up and looked at me, and just said, "He's in the house, I believe: I'll go and call him," I felt quite ashamed of having spoken so abruptly to her. She looked like St Catherine in a Quaker dress. It's a type of face one rarely sees among our common people.'

'I should like to see the young woman, Dauphin,' said Mrs Irwine. 'Make her come here on some pretext or other.'

'I don't know how I can manage that, mother; it will hardly do for me to patronise a Methodist preacher, even if she would consent to be patronised by an idle shepherd, as Will Maskery calls me. You should have come in a little sooner, Arthur, to hear Joshua's denunciation of his neighbour Will Maskery. The old fellow wants me to excommunicate the wheelwright, and then deliver him over to the civil arm – that is to say, to your grandfather – to be turned out of house and yard. If I chose to interfere in this business, now, I might get up as pretty a story of hatred and persecution as the Methodists need desire to publish in the next number of their magazine. It wouldn't take me much trouble to persuade Chad Cranage and half a dozen other bull-headed fellows, that they would be doing an acceptable service to the church by hunting Will Maskery out of the village with rope-ends and pitchforks; and then, when I had furnished them with half a sovereign to get gloriously drunk after their exertions, I should have put the climax to as pretty a farce as any of my brother clergy have set going in their parishes for the last thirty years.'

'It is really insolent of the man, though, to call you an "idle shepherd", and a "dumb dog", "said Mrs Irwine: 'I should be inclined to check him a little there. You are too easy-tempered Dauphin.'

'Why, mother, you don't think it would be a good way of sustaining my dignity to set about vindicating myself from the aspersions of Will Maskery? Besides, I'm not so sure that they are aspersions. I am a lazy fellow, and get terribly heavy in my saddle; not to mention that I'm always spending more than I can afford in bricks and mortar, so that I get savage at a lame beggar when he asks me for sixpence. Those poor lean cobblers, who think they can help to regenerate mankind by setting out to preach in the morning twilight before they begin their day's work, may well have a poor opinion of me. But come, let us have our luncheon. Isn't Kate coming to lunch?'

'Miss Irwine told Bridget to take her lunch upstairs,' said Carroll; 'she can't leave Miss Anne.'

'Oh, very well. Tell Bridget to say I'll go up and see Miss Anne presently. You can use your right arm quite well, now, Arthur,' Mr Irwine continued, observing that Captain Donnithorne had taken his arm out of the sling.

'Yes, pretty well; but Godwin insists on my keeping it up constantly for some time to come. I hope I shall be able to get away to the regiment, though, in the beginning of August. It's a desperately dull business being shut up at the Chase in the summer months, when one can neither hunt nor shoot, so as to make one self pleasantly sleepy in the evening. However, we are to astonish the echoes on the 30th of July. My grandfather has given me *carte blanche* for once, and I promise you the entertainment shall be worthy of the occasion. The world will not see the grand epoch of my majority twice. I think I shall have a lofty throne for you, godmamma, or rather two, one on the lawn and another in the ball-room, that you may sit and look down upon us like an Olympian goddess.'

'I mean to bring out my best brocade, that I wore at your christening twenty years ago,' said Mrs Irwine. 'Ah, I think I shall see your poor mother flitting about in her white dress, which looked to me almost like a shroud that very day; and it was her shroud only three months after; and your little cap and christening dress were buried with her too. She had set her heart on that, sweet soul! Thank God you take after your mother's family, Arthur. If you had been a puny, wiry, yellow baby, I wouldn't have stood godmother to you. I should have been sure you would turn out a Donnithorne. But you were such a broad-faced, broad-chested, loud-screaming rascal, I knew you were every inch of you a Tradgett.'

'But you might have been a little too hasty there, mother,' said Mr Irwine, smiling. 'Don't you remember how it was with Juno's last pups? One of them was the very image of its mother, but it had two or three of its father's tricks notwithstanding. Nature is clever enough to cheat even you, mother.'

'Nonsense, child! Nature never makes a ferret in the shape of a mastiff. You'll never persuade me that I can't tell what men are by their outsides. If I don't like a man's looks, depend upon it I shall never like him. I don't want to know people that look ugly and disagreeable, any more than I want to taste dishes that look disagreeable. If they make me shudder at the first glance, I say, take them away. An ugly, piggish, or fishy eye, now, makes me feel quite ill; it's like a bad smell.'

'Talking of eyes,' said Captain Donnithorne, 'that reminds me that I've got a book I meant to bring you, godmamma. It came down in a parcel from London the other day. I know you are fond of queer, wizard-like stories. It's a volume of poems, *Lyrical Ballads*: most of them seem to be twaddling stuff; but the first is in a different style – *The Ancient Mariner* is the title. I can hardly make head or tail of it as a story, but it's a strange, striking thing. I'll send it over to you; and there are some other books that you may like to see, Irwine – pamphlets about Antinomianism and Evangelicalism, whatever they may be. I can't think what the fellow means by sending such things to me. I've written to him, to desire that from henceforth he will send me no book or pamphlet on anything that ends in *ism*.'

'Well, I don't know that I'm very fond of *isms* myself; but I may as well look at the pamphlets; they let one see what is going on. I've a little matter to attend to, Arthur,' continued Mr Irwine, rising to leave the room, 'and then I shall be ready to set out with you.'

The little matter that Mr Irwine had to attend to took him up the old stone staircase (part of the house was very old), and made him pause before a door at which he knocked gently. 'Come in,' said a woman's voice, and he entered a room so darkened by blinds and curtains that Miss Kate, the thin middle-aged lady standing by the bedside, would not have had light enough for any other sort of work than the knitting which lay on the little table near her. But at present she was doing what required only the dimmest light – sponging the aching head that lay on the pillow with fresh vinegar. It was a small face, that of the poor sufferer; perhaps it had once been pretty, but now it was worn and sallow. Miss Kate came towards her brother and whispered, "Don't speak to her; she can't bear to be spoken to today." Anne's eyes were closed, and her brow contracted as if from intense pain. Mr Irwine went to the bedside, and took up one of the delicate hands and kissed it; a slight pressure from the small fingers told him that it was worth while to have come upstairs for the sake of doing that. He lingered a moment, looking at her, and then turned away and left the room, treading very gently – he had taken off his boots and put on slippers before he came upstairs. Whoever remembers how many things he has declined to do even for himself, rather than have the trouble of putting on or taking off his boots, will not think this last detail insignificant.

And Mr Irwine's sisters, as any person of family within ten miles of Broxton could have testified, were such stupid, uninteresting women! It was quite a pity handsome, clever Mrs Irwine should have had such commonplace daughters. That fine old lady herself was worth driving ten miles to see, any day; her beauty, her well-preserved facilities, and her old-fashioned dignity, made her a graceful subject for conversation in turn with the King's health, the sweet new patterns in cotton dresses, the news from Egypt, and Lord Dacey's lawsuit, which was fretting poor Lady Dacey to death. But no one ever thought of mentioning the Miss Irwines, except the poor people in Broxton village, who regarded them as deep in the science of medicine, and spoke of them vaguely as 'the gentlefolks.' If anyone had asked old Job Dummilow who gave him his flannel jacket, he would have answered, 'the gentlefolks, last winter;' and widow Steene dwelt much on the virtues of the 'stuff' the gentlefolks gave her for her cough. Under this name, too, they were used with great effect as a means of taming refractory children, so that at the sight of poor Miss Anne's sallow face, several small urchins had a terrified sense that she was cognisant of all their worst misdemeanours, and knew the precise number of stones with which they had intended to hit farmer Britton's ducks. But for all who saw them through a less mythical medium, the Miss Irwines were quite superfluous existences; inartistic figures crowding the canvas of life without adequate effect. Miss Anne, indeed, if her chronic headaches could have been accounted for by a pathetic story of disappointed love, might have had some romantic interest attached to her; but no such story had either been known or invented concerning her, and the general impression was quite in accordance with the fact, that both the sisters were old maids for the prosaic reason that they had never received an eligible offer.

Nevertheless, to speak paradoxically, the existence of insignificant people has very important consequences in the world. It can be shown to affect the price of bread and the rate of wages, to call forth many evil tempers from the selfish, and many heroisms from the sympathetic, and, in other ways, to play no small part in the tragedy of life. And if that handsome, generous-blooded clergyman, the Rev Adolphus Irwine, had not had these two hopelessly-maiden sisters, his lot would have been shaped quite differently: he would very likely have taken a comely wife in his youth, and now, when his hair was getting grey under the powder, would have had tall sons and blooming daughters – such possessions, in short, as men commonly think will repay them for all the labour they take under the sun. As it was – having with all his three livings no more than seven hundred a year, and seeing no way of keeping his splendid mother and his sickly sister, not to reckon a second sister, who was usually spoken of without any adjective, in such ladylike ease as became their birth and habits, and at the same time providing for a family of his own – he remained, you see, at the age of eight-

and-forty, a bachelor, not making any merit of that renunciation, but saying laughingly, if anyone alluded to it, that he made it an excuse for many indulgences which a wife would never have allowed him. And perhaps he was the only person in the world who did not think his sisters uninteresting and superfluous; for his was one of those large-hearted, sweet-blooded natures that never know a narrow or a grudging thought; epicurean, if you will, with no enthusiasm, no self-scourging sense of duty; but yet, as you have seen, of a sufficiently subtle moral fibre to have an unwearying tenderness for obscure and monotonous suffering. It was his large-hearted indulgence that made him ignore his mother's hardness towards her daughters, which was the more striking from its contrast with her doting fondness towards himself: he held it no virtue to frown at irremediable faults.

See the difference between the impression a man makes on you when you walk by his side in familiar talk, or look at him in his home, and the figure he makes when seen from a lofty historical level, or even in the eyes of a critical neighbour who thinks of him as an embodied system or opinion rather than as a man. Mr Roe, the 'travelling preacher' stationed at Treddleston, had included Mr Irwine in a general statement concerning the church clergy in the surrounding district, whom he described as men given up to the lusts of the flesh and the pride of life; hunting and shooting, and adorning their own houses; asking what shall we eat, and what shall we drink, and wherewithal shall we be clothed? – careless of dispensing the bread of life to their flocks, preaching at best but a carnal and soul-benumbing morality, and trafficking in the souls of men by receiving money for discharging the pastoral office in parishes where they did not so much as look on the faces of the people more than once a year. The ecclesiastical historian, too, looking into parliamentary reports of that period, finds honourable members zealous for the Church, and untainted with any sympathy for the 'tribe of canting Methodists,' making statements scarcely less melancholy than that of Mr Roe. And it is impossible for me to say that Mr Irwine was altogether belied by the generic classification assigned him. He really had no very lofty aims, no theological enthusiasm: if I were closely questioned, I should be obliged to confess that he felt no serious alarms about the souls of his parishioners, and would have thought it a mere loss of time to talk in a doctrinal and awakening manner to old 'Feyther Taft,' or even to Chad Cranage the blacksmith. If he had been in the habit of speaking theoretically, he would perhaps have said that the only healthy form religion could take in such minds was that of certain dim but strong emotions, suffusing themselves as a hallowing influence over the family affections and neighbourly duties. He thought the custom of baptism more important than its doctrine, and that the religious benefits the peasant drew from the church where his fathers worshipped and the sacred piece of turf where they lay buried, were but slightly dependent on a clear understanding of the Liturgy or the sermon. Clearly the Rector was not what is called in these days an 'earnest' man: he was fonder of church history than of divinity, and had much more insight into men's characters than interest in their opinions; he was neither laborious, nor obviously self-denying, nor very copious in almsgiving, and his theology, you perceive, was lax. His mental palate, indeed, was rather pagan, and found a savouriness in a quotation from Sophocles or Theocritus that was quite absent from any text in Isaiah or Amos. But if you feed your young setter on raw flesh, how can you wonder at its retaining a relish for uncooked partridge in afterlife? and Mr Irwine's recollections of young enthusiasm and ambition were all associated with poetry and ethics that lay aloof from the Bible.

On the other hand, I must plead, for I have an affectionate partiality towards the Rector's memory, that he was not vindictive – and some philanthropists have been so; that he was not intolerant – and there is a rumour that some zealous theologians have not been altogether free from that blemish; that although he would probably have declined to give his body to be burned in any public cause, and was far from bestowing all his goods to feed the poor, he had that charity which has sometimes been lacking to very illustrious virtue – he was tender to other men's failings, and unwilling to impute evil. He was one of those men, and they are not the commonest, of whom we can know the best only by following them away from the market-place, the platform, and the pulpit, entering with them into their own homes, hearing the voice with which they speak to the young and aged about their own hearthstone, and witnessing their thoughtful care for the everyday wants of everyday companions, who take all their kindness as a matter of course, and not as a subject for panegyric.

Such men, happily, have lived in times when great abuses flourished, and have sometimes even been the living representatives of the abuses. That is a thought which might comfort us a little under the opposite fact that it is better sometimes not to follow great reformers of abuses beyond the threshold of their homes.

But whatever you may think of Mr Irwine now, if you had met him that June afternoon riding on his grey cob, with his dogs running beside him – portly, upright, manly, with a good-natured smile on his finely-turned lips as he talked to his dashing young companion on the bay mare, you must have felt that, however ill he harmonised with sound theories of the clerical office, he some-how harmonised extremely well with that peaceful landscape.

See them in the bright sunlight, interrupted every now and then by rolling masses of cloud, ascending the slope from the Broxton side, where the tall gables and elms of the rectory predominate over the tiny whitewashed church. They will soon be in the parish of Hayslope; the grey church-tower and village roofs lie before them to the left, and farther on, to the right, they can just see the chimneys of the Hall Farm.

6

The Hall Farm

Evidently that gate is never opened: for the long grass and the great hemlocks grow close against it; and if it were opened, it is so rusty, that the force necessary to turn it on its hinges would be likely to pull down the square stone-built pillars, to the detriment of the two stone lionesses which grin with a doubtful carnivorous affability above a coat of arms, surmounting each of the pillars. It would be easy enough, by the aid of the nicks in the stone pillars, to climb over the brick wall with its smooth stone coping; but by putting our eyes close to the rusty bars of the gate, we can see the house well enough, and all but the very corners of the grassy enclosure.

It is a very fine old place, of red brick, softened by a pale powdery lichen, which has dispersed itself with happy irregularity, so as to bring the red brick into terms of friendly companionship with the limestone ornaments surrounding the three gables, the windows, and the door-place. But the windows are patched with wooden panes, and the door, I think, is like the gate – it is never opened: how it would groan and grate against the stone floor if it were! For it is a solid, heavy, handsome door, and must once have been in the habit of shutting with a sonorous bang behind a liveried lackey, who had just seen his master and mistress off the grounds in a carriage and pair.

But at present one might fancy the house in the early stage of a chancery suit, and that the fruit from that grand double row of walnut trees on the right hand of the enclosure would fall and rot among the grass, if it were not that we heard the booming bark of dogs echoing from great buildings at the back. And now the half-weaned calves that have been sheltering themselves in a gorse-built hovel against the left-hand wall, come out and set up a silly answer to that terrible bark, doubtless supposing that it has reference to buckets of milk.

Yes, the house must be inhabited, and we will see by whom; for imagination is a licensed trespasser: it has no fear of dogs, but may climb over walls and peep in at windows with impunity. Put your face to one of the glass panes in the right hand window: what do you see? A large open fireplace, with rusty dogs in it, and a bare-boarded floor; at the far end, fleeces of wool stacked up; in the middle of the floor, some empty corn bags. That is the furniture of the dining-room. And what through the left-hand window? Several clothes-horses, a pillion, a spinning-wheel, and an old box wide open, and stuffed full of coloured rags. At the edge of this box there lies a great wooden doll, which, so far as mutilation is concerned, bears a strong resemblance to the finest Greek sculpture, and especially in the total loss of its nose. Near it there is a little chair, and the butt-end of a boy's leather long-lashed whip.

The history of the house is plain now. It was once the residence of a country squire, whose family, probably dwindling down to mere spinsterhood, got merged in the more territorial name of Donnithorne. It was once the Hall; it is now the Hall Farm. Like the life in some coast-town that was once a watering-place, and is now a port, where the genteel streets are silent and grass-grown, and the docks and warehouses busy and resonant, the life at the Hall has changed its focus, and no longer radiates from the parlour, but from the kitchen and the farmyard.

Plenty of life there! though this is the drowsiest time of the year, just before hay-harvest; and it is the drowsiest time of the day too, for it is close upon three by the sun, and it is half-past three by Mrs Poyser's handsome eight-day clock. But there is always a stronger sense of life when the sun is brilliant after rain; and now he is pouring down his beams, and making sparkles among the wet straw, and lighting up every patch of vivid green moss on the red tiles of the cowshed, and turning even the muddy water that is hurrying along the channel to the drain into a mirror for the yellow-billed ducks, who are seizing the opportunity of getting a drink with as much body in it as possible. There is quite a concert of noises: the great bulldog, chained against the stables, is thrown into furious exasperation by the unwary approach of a cock too near the mouth of his kennel, and sends forth a thundering bark, which is answered by two foxhounds shut up in the opposite cow-house; the old top-knotted hens, scratching with their chicks among the straw, set up a sympathetic croaking as the discomfited cock joins them; a sow with her brood, all very muddy as to the legs, and curled as to the tail, throws in some deep staccato notes; our friends the calves are bleating from the home croft; and, under all, a fine ear discerns the continuous hum of human voices.

For the great barn-doors are thrown wide open, and men are busy there mending the harness, under the superintendence of Mr Goby the 'whittaw,' otherwise saddler, who entertains them with the latest Treddleston gossip. It is certainly rather an unfortunate day that Alick, the shepherd, has chosen for having the whittaws, since the morning turned out so wet; and Mrs Poyser has spoken her mind pretty strongly as to the dirt which the extra number of men's shoes brought into the house at dinner-time. Indeed, she has not yet recovered her equanimity on the subject, though it is now nearly three hours since dinner, and the house-floor is perfectly clean again; as clean as everything else in that wonderful house-place, where the only chance of collecting a few grains of dust would be to climb on the salt-coffer, and put your finger on the high mantelshelf on which the glittering brass candlesticks are enjoying their summer sinecure; for at this time of year, of course, everyone goes to bed while it is yet light, or at least light enough to discern the outline of objects after you have bruised your shins against them. Surely nowhere else could an oak clock-case and an oak table have got to such a polish by the hand: genuine 'elbow polish,' as Mrs Poyser called it, for she thanked God she never had any of your varnished rubbish in her house. Hetty Sorrel often took the opportunity, when her aunt's back was turned, of looking at the pleasing reflection of herself in those polished surfaces, for the oak table was usually turned up like a screen, and was more for ornament than for use; and she could see herself sometimes in the great round pewter dishes that were ranged on the shelves above the long deal dinner-table, or in the hobs of the grate, which always shone like jasper.

Everything was looking at its brightest at this moment, for the sun shone right on the pewter dishes, and from their reflecting surfaces pleasant jets of light were thrown on mellow oak and bright brass – and on a still pleasanter object than these; for some of the rays fell on Dinah's finely moulded cheek, and lit up her pale red hair to auburn, as she bent over the heavy household linen which she was mending for her aunt. No scene could have been more peaceful, if Mrs Poyser, who was ironing a few things that still remained from the Monday's wash, had not been making a frequent clinking with her iron, and moving to and fro whenever she wanted it to cool; carrying the keen glance of her blue-grey eye from the kitchen to the dairy, where Hetty was making up the butter, and from the dairy to the back-kitchen, where Nancy was taking the pies out of the oven. Do not suppose, however, that Mrs Poyser was elderly or shrewish in her appearance; she was a good-looking woman, not more than eight-and-thirty, of fair complexion and sandy hair, well-shapen, light-footed: the most conspicuous article in her attire was an ample checkered linen apron, which almost covered her skirt; and nothing could be plainer or less noticeable than her cap and gown, for there was no weakness of which she was less tolerant than feminine vanity, and the preference of ornament to utility. The family likeness between her and her niece Dinah Morris, with the contrast between her keenness and Dinah's seraphic gentleness of expression, might have served a painter as an excellent suggestion for a Martha and Mary. Their eyes were just of the same colour, but a striking test of the difference in their operation was seen in the demeanour of Trip, the black-and-tan terrier, whenever that much-suspected dog unwarily exposed himself to the freezing arctic ray of Mrs Poyser's glance. Her tongue was not less keen than her eye, and, whenever a damsel came within earshot, seemed to take up an unfinished lecture, as a barrel-organ takes up a tune, precisely at the point where it had left off.

The fact that it was churning-day was another reason why it was inconvenient to have the 'whittaws,' and why, consequently, Mrs Poyser should scold Molly the housemaid with unusual severity. To all appearance Molly had got through her after-dinner work in an exemplary manner, had 'cleaned herself' with great despatch, and now came to ask, submissively, if she should sit down to her spinning till milking-time. But this blameless conduct, according to Mrs Poyser, shrouded a secret indulgence of unbecoming wishes, which she now dragged forth and held up to Molly's view with cutting eloquence.

'Spinning, indeed! It isn't spinning as you'd be at, I'll be bound, and let you have your own way. I never knew your equals for gallowsness. To think of a gell o' your age wanting to go and sit with half a dozen men! I'd ha' been ashamed to let the words pass over my lips if I'd been you. And you, as have been here ever since last Michaelmas, and I hired you at Treddles'on stattits, without a bit o' character – as I say, you might be grateful to be hired in that way to a respectable place; and you knew no more o' what belongs to work when you come here than the mawkin i' the field. As poor a two-fisted thing as ever I saw, you know you was. Who taught you to scrub a floor, I should like to know? Why, you'd leave the dirt in heaps i' the corners – anybody 'ud think you'd never been brought up among Christians. And as for spinning, why, you've wasted as much as your wage i' the flax you've spoiled learning to spin. And you've a right to feel that, and not to go about as gaping and as thoughtless as if you was beholding to nobody. Comb the wool for the whittaws, indeed! That's what you'd like to be doing, is it? That's the way with you – that's the road you'd all like to go, headlongs to ruin. You're never easy till you've got some sweetheart as is as big a fool as yourself: you think you'll be finely off when you're married, I dare say, and have got a three-legged stool to sit on, and never a blanket to cover you and a bit o' oatcake for your dinner, as three children are a-snatching at.'

'I'm sure I donna want t' go wi' the whittaws,' said Molly, whimpering, and quite overcome by this Dantean picture of her future, 'on'y we allays used to comb the wool for'n at Mester Ottley's; an' so I just axed ye. I donna want to set eyes on the whittaws again; I wish I may never stir if I do.'

'Mr Ottley's, indeed! It's fine talking o' what you did at Mr Ottley's. Your missis there might like her floors dirted wi' whittaws for what I know. There's no knowing what people wonna like – such ways as I've heard of! I never had a gell come into my house as seemed to know what cleaning was; I think people live like pigs, for my part. And as to that Betty as was dairymaid at Trent's before she come to me, she'd ha' left the cheeses without turning from week's end to week's end, and the dairy thralls, I might ha' wrote my name on 'em when I come downstairs after my illness, as the doctor said it was inflammation – it was a mercy I got well of it. And to think o' your knowing no better, Molly, and been here a-going i' nine months, and not for want o' talking to, neither – and what are you stanning there for, like a jack as is run down, istead o' getting your wheel out? You're a rare un for sitting down to your work a little while after it's time to put by.'

'Munny, my iron's twite told; pease put it down to warm.'

The small chirruping voice that uttered this request came from a little sunny-haired girl between three and four, who, seated on a high chair at the end of the ironing-table, was arduously clutching the handle of a miniature iron with her tiny fat fist, and ironing rags with an assiduity that required her to put her little red tongue out as far as anatomy would allow.

'Cold, is it, my darling? Bless your sweet face!' said Mrs Poyser, who was remarkable for the facility with which she could relapse from her official objurgatory tone to one of fondness or of friendly converse. 'Never mind! Mother's done her ironing now. She's going to put the ironing things away.'

'Munny, I tould 'ike to do into de barn to Tommy, to see de whittawd.'

'No, no, no; Totty 'ud get her feet wet,' said Mrs Poyser, carrying away her iron. 'Run into the dairy, and see cousin Hetty make the butter.'

'I tould 'ike a bit o' pum-take,' rejoined Totty, who seemed to be provided with several relays of requests; at the same time, taking the opportunity of her momentary leisure, to put her fingers into a bowl of starch, and drag it down, so as to empty the contents with tolerable completeness on to the ironing-sheet.

'Did ever anybody see the like?' screamed Mrs Poyser, running towards the table when her eye had fallen on the blue stream. 'The child's allays i' mischief if your back's turned a minute. What shall I do to you, you naughty, naughty gell?'

Totty, however, had descended from her chair with great swiftness, and was already in retreat towards the dairy with a sort of waddling run, and an amount of fat on the nape of her neck, which made her look like the metamorphosis of a white sucking-pig.

The starch having been wiped up by Molly's help, and the ironing apparatus put by, Mrs Poyser took up her knitting, which always lay ready at hand, and was the work she liked best, because she could carry it on automatically as she walked to and fro. But now she came and sat down opposite Dinah, whom she looked at in a meditative way, as she knitted her grey worsted stocking.

'You look th' image o' your aunt Judith, Dinah, when you sit a-sewing. I could almost fancy it was thirty years back, and I was a little gell at home, looking at Judith as she sat at her work, after she'd done th' house up; only it was a little cottage, father's was, and not a big rambling house as gets dirty i' one corner as fast as you clean it in another; but for all that, I could fancy you was your aunt Judith, only her hair was a deal darker than yours, and she was stouter and broader i' the shoulders. Judith and me allays hung together, though she had such queer ways, but your mother and her never could agree. Ah! your mother little thought as she'd have a daughter just cut out after the very pattern o' Judith, and leave her an orphan, too, for Judith to take care on, and bring up with a spoon when she was in the graveyard at Stoniton. I allays said that o' Judith, as she'd bear a pound weight any day, to save anybody else carrying a ounce. And she was just the same from the first o' my remembering her; it made no difference in her, as I could see, when she took to the Methodists, only she talked a bit different, and wore a different sort o' cap; but she'd never in her life spent a penny on herself more than keeping herself decent.'

'She was a blessed woman,' said Dinah; 'God had given her a loving, self-forgetting nature, and He perfected it by grace. And she was very fond of you too, aunt Rachel. I've often heard her talk of you in the same sort of way. When she had that bad illness, and I was only eleven years old, she used to say, "You'll have a friend on earth in your aunt Rachel, if I'm taken from you; for she has a kind heart;" and I'm sure I've found it so.'

'I don't know how, child; anybody 'ud be cunning to do anything for you, I think; you're like the birds o' th' air, and live nobody knows how. I'd ha' been glad to behave to you like a mother's sister, if you'd come and live i' this country, where there's some shelter and victual for man and beast, and folks don't live on the naked hills, like poultry a-scratching on a gravel bank. And then you might get married to some decent man, and there'd be plenty ready to have you, if you'd only leave off that preaching, as is ten times worse than anything your aunt Judith ever did. And even if you'd marry Seth Bede, as is a poor wool-gathering Methodist, and's never like to have a penny beforehand, I know your uncle 'ud help you with a pig, and very like a cow, for he's allays been good-natur'd to my kin, for all they're poor, and made 'em welcome to the house; and 'ud do for you, I'll be bound, as much as ever he'd do for Hetty, though she's his own niece. And there's linen in the house as I could well spare you, for I've got lots o' sheeting and tableclothing, and towelling, as isn't made up. There's a piece o' sheeting I could give you as that squinting Kitty spun – she was a rare girl to spin, for all she squinted, and the children couldn't abide her; and, you know, the spinning's going on constant, and there's new linen wove twice as fast as the old wears out. But where's the use o' talking, if ye wonna be persuaded, and settle down like any other woman in her senses, istead o' wearing yourself out with walking and preaching, and giving away every penny you get, so as you've nothing saved against sickness; and all the things you've got i' the world, I verily believe, 'ud go into a bundle no bigger nor a double cheese. And all because you've got notions i' your head about religion more nor what's i' the Catechism and the Prayer-book.'

'But not more than what's in the Bible, aunt,' said Dinah.

'Yes, and the Bible too, for that matter,' Mrs Poyser rejoined, rather sharply; 'else why shouldn't them as know best what's in the Bible – the parsons and people as have got nothing to do but learn it – do the same as you do? But, for the matter o' that, if everybody was to do like you, the world must come to a standstill; for if everybody tried to do without house and home, and with poor eating and drinking, and was allays talking as we must despise the things o' the world, as you say, I should like to know where the pick o' the stock, and the corn, and the best new-milk cheeses 'ud have to go. Everybody 'ud be wanting bread made o' tail-ends, and everybody 'ud be running after everybody else to preach to 'em, istead o' bringing up their families, and laying by against a bad harvest. It stands to sense as that can't be the right religion.'

'Nay, dear aunt, you never heard me say that all people are called to forsake their work and their families. It's quite right the land should be ploughed and sowed, and the precious corn stored, and the things of this life cared for, and right that people should rejoice in their families, and provide for them, so that this is done in the fear of the Lord, and that they are not unmindful of the soul's wants while they are caring for the body. We can all be servants of God wherever our lot is cast, but He gives us different sorts of work, according as He fits us for it and calls us to it. I can no more help spending my life in trying to do what I can for the souls of others, than you could help running if you heard little Totty crying at the other end of the house; the voice would go to your heart, you would think the dear child was in trouble or in danger, and you couldn't rest without running to help her and comfort her.'

'Ah,' said Mrs Poyser, rising and walking towards the door, 'I know it 'ud be just the same if I was to talk to you for hours. You'd make me the same answer at th' end. I might as well talk to the running brook, and tell it to stan' still.'

The causeway outside the kitchen door was dry enough now for Mrs Poyser to stand there quite pleasantly and see what was going on in the yard, the grey worsted stocking making a steady progress in her hands all the while. But she had not been standing there more than five minutes before she came in again, and said to Dinah, in rather a flurried, awe-stricken tone – 'If there isn't Captain Donnithorne and Mr Irwine a coming into the yard! I'll lay my life they're come to speak about your preaching on the Green, Dinah; it's you must answer 'em, for I'm dumb. I've said enough a'ready about your bringing such disgrace upo' your uncle's family. I wouldn't ha' minded if you'd been Mr Poyser's own niece – folks must put up wi' their own kin, as they put up wi' their own noses – it's their own flesh and blood. But to think of a niece o' mine being cause o' my husband's being turned out of his farm, and me brought him no fortin but my savin's – '

'Nay, dear aunt Rachel,' said Dinah gently, 'you've no cause for such fears. I've strong assurance that no evil will happen to you and my uncle and the children from anything I've done. I didn't preach without direction.'

'Direction! I know very well what you mean by direction,' said Mrs Poyser, knitting in a rapid and agitated manner. 'When there's a bigger maggot than usual in your head you call it 'direction;' and then nothing can stir you – you look like the statty o' the outside o' Treddles'on church, a starin' and a smilin' whether it's fair weather or foul. I hanna common patience with you.'

By this time the two gentlemen had reached the palings, and had got down from their horses: it was plain they meant to come in. Mrs Poyser advanced to the door to meet them curtsying low, and trembling between anger with Dinah and anxiety to conduct herself with perfect propriety on the occasion. For in those days the keenest of bucolic minds felt a whispering awe at the sight of the gentry, such as of old men felt when they stood on tiptoe to watch the gods passing by in tall human shape.

'Well, Mrs Poyser, how are you after this stormy morning?' said Mr Irwine, with his stately cordiality. 'Our feet are quite dry; we shall not soil your beautiful floor.'

'Oh, sir, don't mention it,' said Mrs Poyser. 'Will you and the Captain please to walk into the parlour?'

'No, indeed, thank you, Mrs Poyser,' said the Captain, looking eagerly round the kitchen, as if his eye were seeking something it could not find. 'I delight in your kitchen. I think it is the most charming room I know. I should like every farmer's wife to come and look at it for a pattern.'

'Oh, you're pleased to say so, sir. Pray take a seat,' said Mrs Poyser, relieved a little by this compliment and the Captain's evident good-humour, but still glancing anxiously at Mr Irwine, who, she saw, was looking at Dinah and advancing towards her!

'Poyser is not at home, is he?' said Captain Donnithorne, seating himself where he could see along the short passage to the open dairy-door.

'No, sir, he isn't; he's gone to Rosseter to see Mr West, the factor, about the wool. But there's father i' the barn, sir, if he'd be of any use.'

'No, thank you; I'll just look at the whelps and leave a message about them with your shepherd. I must come another day and see your husband; I want to have a consultation with him about horses. Do you know when he's likely to be at liberty?'

'Why, sir, you can hardly miss him, except it's o' Treddles'on market-day – that's of a Friday, you know. For if he's anywhere on the farm we can send for him in a minute. If we'd got rid o' the Scantlands we should have no outlying fields; and I should be glad of it, for if ever anything happens he's sure to be gone to the Scantlands. Things allays happen so contrairy, if they've a chance; and it's an unnat'ral thing to have one bit o' your farm in one county and all the rest in another.'

'Ah, the Scantlands would go much better with Choyce's farm, especially as he wants dairy-land and you've got plenty. I think yours is the prettiest farm on the estate, though; and do you know, Mrs Poyser, if I were going to marry and settle, I should be tempted to turn you out, and do up this fine old house, and turn farmer myself.'

'Oh, sir,' said Mrs Poyser, rather alarmed, 'you wouldn't like it at all. As for farming, it's putting money into your pocket wi' your right hand and fetching it out wi' your left. As fur as I can see, it's raising victual for other folks, and just getting a mouthful for yourself and your children as you go along. Not as you'd be like a poor man as wants to get his bread: you could afford to lose as much money as you liked i' farming; but it's poor fun losing money, I should think, though I understan' it's what the great folks i' London play at more than anything. For my husband heard at market as Lord Dacey's eldest son had lost thousands upo' thousands to the Prince o' Wales, and they said my lady was going to pawn her jewels to pay for him. But you know more about that than I do, sir. But, as for farming, sir, I canna think as you'd like it; and this house – the draughts in it are enough to cut you through, and it's my opinion the floors upstairs are very rotten, and the rats i' the cellar are beyond anything.'

'Why, that's a terrible picture, Mrs Poyser. I think I should be doing you a service to turn you out of such a place. But there's no chance of that. I'm not likely to settle for the next twenty years, till I'm a stout gentleman of forty; and my grandfather would never consent to part with such good tenants as you.'

'Well, sir, if he thinks so well o' Mr Poyser for a tenant, I wish you could put in a word for him to allow us some new gates for the Five closes, for my husband's been asking and asking till he's tired, and to think o' what he's done for the farm, and's never had a penny allowed him, be the times bad or good. And as I've said to my husband often and often, I'm sure if the Captain had anything to do with it, it wouldn't be so. Not as I wish to speak disrespectful o' them as have got the power i' their hands, but it's more than flesh and blood 'ull bear sometimes, to be toiling and striving, and up early and down late, and hardly sleeping a wink when you lie down for thinking as the cheese may swell, or the cows may slip their calf, or the wheat may grow green again i' the sheaf – and after all, at th' end o' the year, it's like as if you'd been cooking a feast and had got the smell of it for your pains.'

Mrs Poyser, once launched into conversation, always sailed along without any check from her preliminary awe of the gentry. The confidence she felt in her own powers of exposition was a motive force that overcame all resistance.

'I'm afraid I should only do harm instead of good, if I were to speak about the gates, Mrs Poyser,' said the Captain, 'though I assure you there's no man on the estate I would sooner say a word for than your husband. I know his farm is in better order than any other within ten miles of us; and as for the kitchen,' he added, smiling, 'I don't believe there's one in the kingdom to beat it. By the by, I've never seen your dairy: I must see your dairy, Mrs Poyser.'

'Indeed, sir, it's not fit for you to go in, for Hetty's in the middle o' making the butter, for the churning was thrown late, and I'm quite ashamed.' This Mrs Poyser said blushing, and believing that the Captain was really interested in her milk-pans, and would adjust his opinion of her to the appearance of her dairy.

'Oh, I've no doubt it's in capital order. Take me in,' said the Captain, himself leading the way, while Mrs Poyser followed.

7

The Dairy

The dairy was certainly worth looking at: it was a scene to sicken for with a sort of calenture in hot and dusty streets – such coolness, such purity, such fresh fragrance of new-pressed cheese, of firm butter, of wooden vessels perpetually bathed in pure water; such soft colouring of red earthenware and creamy surfaces, brown wood and polished tin, grey limestone and rich orange-red rust on the iron weights and hooks and hinges. But one gets only a confused notion of these details when they surround a distractingly pretty girl of seventeen, standing on little pattens and rounding her dimpled arm to lift a pound of butter out of the scale.

Hetty blushed a deep rose-colour when Captain Donnithorne entered the dairy and spoke to her; but it was not at all a distressed blush, for it was enwreathed with smiles and dimples, and with sparkles from under long curled dark eyelashes; and while her aunt was discoursing to him about the limited amount of milk that was to be spared for butter and cheese so long as the calves were not all weaned, and a large quantity but inferior quality of milk yielded by the short horn, which had been bought on experiment, together with other matters which must be interesting to a young gentleman who would one day be a landlord, Hetty tossed and patted her pound of butter with quite a self-possessed, coquettish air, slily conscious that no turn of her head was lost.

There are various orders of beauty, causing men to make fools of themselves in various styles, from the desperate to the sheepish; but there is one order of beauty which seems made to turn the heads not only of men, but of all intelligent mammals, even of women. It is a beauty like that of kittens, or very small downy ducks making gentle rippling noises with their soft bills, or babies just beginning to toddle and to engage in conscious mischief – a beauty with which you can never be angry, but that you feel ready to crush for inability to comprehend the state of mind into which it throws you. Hetty Sorrel's was that sort of beauty. Her aunt, Mrs Poyser, who professed to despise all personal attractions, and intended to be the severest of mentors, continually gazed at Hetty's charms by the sly, fascinated in spite of herself; and after administering such a scolding as naturally flowed from her anxiety to do well by her husband's niece – who had no mother of her own to scold her, poor thing! – she would often confess to her husband, when they were safe out of hearing, that she firmly believed 'the naughtier the little huzzy behaved, the prettier she looked.'

It is of little use for me to tell you that Hetty's cheek was like a rose-petal, that dimples played about her pouting lips, that her large dark eyes hid a soft roguishness under their long lashes, and that her curly hair, though all pushed back under her round cap while she was at work, stole back in dark delicate rings on her forehead, and about her white shell-like ears; it is of little use for me to say how lovely was the contour of her pink-and-white neckerchief, tucked into her low plum-coloured stuff bodice, or how the linen butter-making apron, with its bib, seemed a thing to be imitated in silk by duchesses, since it fell in such charming lines, or how her brown stockings and thick-soled buckled shoes lost all that clumsiness which they must certainly have had when empty of her foot and ankle – of little use, unless you have seen a woman who affected you as Hetty affected her beholders, for otherwise, though you might conjure up the image of a lovely woman, she would not in the least resemble that distracting kittenlike maiden. I might mention all the divine charms of a bright spring day, but if you had never in your life utterly forgotten yourself in straining your eyes after the mounting lark, or in wandering through the still lanes when the fresh-opened blossoms fill them with a sacred silent beauty like that of fretted aisles, where would be the use of my descriptive catalogue? I could never make you know what I meant by a bright spring day. Hetty's was a spring-tide beauty; it was the beauty of young frisking things, round-limbed, gambolling, circumventing you by a false air of innocence – the innocence of a young star-browed calf, for example, that, being inclined for a promenade out of bounds, leads you a severe steeplechase over hedge and ditch, and only comes to a stand in the middle of a bog.

And they are the prettiest attitudes and movements into which a pretty girl is thrown in making up butter – tossing movements that give a charming curve to the arm, and a sideward inclination of the round white neck; little patting and rolling movements with the palm of the hand, and nice adaptations and finishings which cannot at all be effected without a great play of the pouting mouth and the dark eyes. And then the butter itself seems to communicate a fresh charm – it is so pure, so sweet-scented; it is turned off the mould with such a beautiful firm surface, like marble in a pale yellow light! Moreover, Hetty was particularly clever at making up the butter; it was the one performance of hers that her aunt allowed to pass without severe criticism; so she handled it with all the grace that belongs to mastery.

'I hope you will be ready for a great holiday on the thirtieth of July, Mrs Poyser,' said Captain Donnithorne, when he had sufficiently admired the dairy, and given several improvised opinions on swede turnips and short horns. 'You know what is to happen then, and I shall expect you to be one of the guests who come earliest and leave latest. Will you promise me your hand for two dances, Miss Hetty? If I don't get your promise now, I know I shall hardly have a chance, for all the smart young farmers will take care to secure you.'

Hetty smiled and blushed, but before she could answer, Mrs Poyser interposed, scandalised at the mere suggestion that the young squire could be excluded by any meaner partners.

'Indeed, sir, you are very kind to take that notice of her. And I'm sure, whenever you're pleased to dance with her, she'll be proud and thankful, if she stood still all the rest o' th' evening.'

'Oh no, no, that would be too cruel to all the other young fellows who can dance. But you will promise me two dances, won't you?' the Captain continued, determined to make Hetty look at him and speak to him.

Hetty dropped the prettiest little curtsy, and stole a half-shy, half-coquettish glance at him as she said – 'Yes, thank you, sir.'

'And you must bring all your children, you know, Mrs Poyser; your little Totty, as well as the boys. I want all the youngest children on the estate to be there – all those who will be fine young men and women when I'm a bald old fellow.'

'Oh dear, sir, that 'ull be a long time first,' said Mrs Poyser, quite overcome at the young squire's speaking so lightly of himself, and thinking how her husband would be interested in hearing her recount this remarkable specimen of high-born humour. The Captain was thought to be 'very full of his jokes,' and was a great favourite throughout the estate on account of his free manners. Every tenant was quite sure things would be different when the reins got into his hands – there was to be a millennial abundance of new gates, allowances of lime, and returns of ten per cent.

'But where is Totty today?' he said. 'I want to see her.'

'Where *is* the little un, Hetty?' said Mrs Poyser. 'She came in here not long ago.'

'I don't know. She went into the brew-house to Nancy, I think.'

The proud mother, unable to resist the temptation to show her Totty, passed at once into the back-kitchen, in search of her, not, however, without misgivings lest something should have happened to render her person and attire unfit for presentation.

'And do you carry the butter to market when you've made it?' said the Captain to Hetty, meanwhile.

'Oh no, sir; not when it's so heavy: I'm not strong enough to carry it. Alick takes it on horseback.'

'No, I'm sure your pretty arms were never meant for such heavy weights. But you go out a walk sometimes these pleasant evenings, don't you? Why don't you have a walk in the Chase sometimes, now it's so green and pleasant? I hardly ever see you anywhere except at home and at church.'

'Aunt doesn't like me to go a-walking only when I'm going somewhere,' said Hetty. 'But I go through the Chase sometimes.'

'And don't you ever go to see Mrs Best, the housekeeper? I think I saw you once in the housekeeper's room.'

'It isn't Mrs Best, it's Mrs Pomfret, the lady's maid, as I go to see. She's teaching me tent stitch and the lace-mending. I'm going to tea with her to morrow afternoon.'

The reason why there had been space for this tête-à-tête can only be known by looking into the back-kitchen, where Totty had been discovered rubbing a stray blue-bag against her nose, and in the same moment allowing some liberal indigo drops to fall on her afternoon pinafore. But now she appeared holding her mother's hand – the end of her round nose rather shiny from a recent and hurried application of soap and water.

'Here she is!' said the Captain, lifting her up and setting her on the low stone shelf. 'Here's Totty! By the by, what's her other name? She wasn't christened Totty.'

'Oh, sir, we call her sadly out of her name. Charlotte's her christened name. It's a name i' Mr Poyser's family: his grandmother was named Charlotte. But we began with calling her Lotty, and now it's got to Totty. To be sure it's more like a name for a dog than a Christian child.'

'Totty's a capital name. Why, she looks like a Totty. Has she got a pocket on?' said the Captain, feeling in his own waistcoat pockets.

Totty immediately with great gravity lifted up her frock, and showed a tiny pink pocket at present in a state of collapse.

'It dot notin in it,' she said, as she looked down at it very earnestly.

'No! what a pity! such a pretty pocket. Well, I think I've got some things in mine that will make a pretty jingle in it. Yes! I declare I've got five little round silver things, and hear what a pretty noise they make in Totty's pink pocket.'

Here he shook the pocket with the five sixpences in it, and Totty showed her teeth and wrinkled her nose in great glee; but, divining that there was nothing more to be got by staying, she jumped off the shelf and ran away to jingle her pocket in the hearing of Nancy, while her mother called after her, 'Oh for shame, you naughty gell! not to thank the Captain for what he's given you. I'm sure, sir, it's very kind of you; but she's spoiled shameful; her father won't have her said nay in anything, and there's no managing her. It's being the youngest, and th' only gell.'

'Oh, she's a funny little fatty; I wouldn't have her different. But I must be going now, for I suppose the Rector is waiting for me.'

With a 'goodbye', a bright glance, and a bow to Hetty, Arthur left the dairy. But he was mistaken in imagining himself waited for. The Rector had been so much interested in his conversation with Dinah, that he would not have chosen to close it earlier; and you shall hear now what they had been saying to each other.

8

A Vocation

Dinah, who had risen when the gentlemen came in, but still kept hold of the sheet she was mending, curtsied respectfully when she saw Mr Irwine looking at her and advancing towards her. He had never yet spoken to her, or stood face to face with her, and her first thought, as her eyes met his, was, 'What a well-favoured countenance! Oh that the good seed might fall on that soil, for it would surely flourish.' The agreeable impression must have been mutual, for Mr Irwine bowed to her with a benignant deference, which would have been equally in place if she had been the most dignified lady of his acquaintance.

'You are only a visitor in this neighbourhood, I think?' were his first words, as he seated himself opposite to her.

'No, sir, I come from Snowfield, in Stonyshire. But my aunt was very kind, wanting me to have rest from my work there, because I'd been ill, and she invited me to come and stay with her for a while.'

'Ah, I remember Snowfield very well; I once had occasion to go there. It's a dreary bleak place. They were building a cotton-mill there; but that's many years ago now: I suppose the place is a good deal changed by the employment that mill must have brought.'

'It *is* changed so far as the mill has brought people there, who get a livelihood for themselves by working in it, and make it better for the tradesfolks. I work in it myself, and have reason to be grateful, for thereby I have enough and to spare. But it's still a bleak place, as you say, sir – very different from this country.'

'You have relations living there probably, so that you are attached to the place as your home?'

'I had an aunt there once, she brought me up, for I was an orphan. But she was taken away seven years ago, and I have no other kindred that I know of, besides my aunt Poyser, who is very good to me, and would have me come and live in this country, which to be sure is a good land, wherein they eat bread without scarceness. But I'm not free to leave Snowfield, where I was first planted, and have grown deep into it, like the small grass on the hilltop.'

'Ah, I dare say you have many religious friends and companions there; you are a Methodist – a Wesleyan, I think?'

'Yes, my aunt at Snowfield belonged to the society, and I have cause to be thankful for the privileges I have had thereby from my earliest childhood.'

'And have you been long in the habit of preaching? – for I understand you preached at Hayslope last night.'

'I first took to the work four years since, when I was twenty-one.'

'Your society sanctions women's preaching, then?'

'It doesn't forbid them, sir, when they've a clear call to the work, and when their ministry is owned by the conversion of sinners, and the strengthening of God's people. Mrs Fletcher, as you may have heard about, was the first woman to preach in the society, I believe, before she was married, when she was Miss Bosanquet; and Mr Wesley approved of her undertaking the work. She had a great gift, and there are many others now living who are precious fellow-helpers in the work of the ministry. I understand there's been voices raised against it in the Society of late, but I cannot but think their counsel will come to nought. It isn't for men to make channels for God's spirit, as they make channels for the watercourses, and say, 'Flow here, but flow not there.''

'But don't you find some danger among your people – I don't mean to say that it is so with you, far from it – but don't you find sometimes that both men and women fancy themselves channels for God's spirit, and are quite mistaken, so that they set about a work for which they are unfit, and bring holy things into contempt?'

'Doubtless it is so sometimes; for there have been evil-doers among us who have sought to deceive the brethren, and some there are who deceive their own selves. But we are not without discipline and correction to put a check upon these things. There's a very strict order kept among us, and the brethren and sisters watch for each other's souls as they that must give account. They don't go everyone his own way and say, "Am I my brother's keeper?"'

'But tell me – if I may ask, and I am really interested in knowing it – how you first came to think of preaching?'

'Indeed, sir, I didn't think of it at all – I'd been used from the time I was sixteen to talk to the little children and teach them, and sometimes I had had my heart enlarged to speak in class, and was much drawn out in prayer with the sick. But I had felt no call to preach; for when I'm not greatly wrought upon, I'm too much given to sit still and keep by myself: it seems as if I could sit silent all day long with the thought of God overflowing my soul – as the pebbles lie bathed in the Willow Brook. For thoughts are so great aren't they, sir? They seem to lie upon us like a deep flood; and it's my besetment to forget where I am and everything about me, and lose myself in thoughts that I could give no account of, for I could neither make a beginning nor ending of them in words. That was my way as long as I can remember; but sometimes it seemed as if speech came to me without any will of my own, and words were given to me that came out as the tears come, because our hearts are full and we can't help it. And those were always times of great blessing, though I had never thought it could be so with me before a congregation of people. But, sir, we are led on, like the little children, by a way that we know not. I was called to preach quite suddenly, and since then I have never been left in doubt about the work that was laid upon me.'

'But tell me the circumstances – just how it was, the very day you began to preach.'

'It was one Sunday I walked with brother Marlowe, who was an aged man, one of the local preachers, all the way to Hetton-Deeps – that's a village where the people get their living by working in the lead-mines, and where there's no church nor preacher, but they live like sheep without a shepherd. It's better than twelve miles from Snowfield, so we set out early in the morning, for it was summertime; and I had a wonderful sense of the Divine love as we walked over the hills, where there's no trees, you know, sir, as there is here, to make the sky look smaller, but you see the heavens stretched out like a tent, and you feel the everlasting arms around you. But before we got to Hetton, brother Marlowe was seized with a dizziness that made him afraid of falling, for he overworked himself sadly, at his years, in watching and praying, and walking so many miles to speak the Word, as well as carrying on his trade of linen-weaving. And when we got to the village, the people were expecting him, for he'd appointed the time and the place when he was there before, and such of them as cared to hear the Word of Life were assembled on a spot where the cottages was thickest, so as others might be drawn to come. But he felt as he couldn't stand up to preach, and he was forced to lie down in the first of the cottages we came to. So I went to tell the people, thinking we'd go into one of the houses, and I would read and pray with them. But as I passed along by the cottages and saw the aged and trembling women at the doors, and the hard looks of the men, who seemed to have their eyes no more filled with the sight of the Sabbath morning than if they had been dumb oxen that never looked up to the sky, I felt a great movement in my soul, and I trembled as if I was shaken by a strong spirit entering into my weak body. And I went to where the little flock of people was gathered together, and stepped on the low wall that was built against the green hillside, and I spoke the words that were given to me abundantly. And they all came round me out of all the cottages, and many wept over their sins, and have since been joined to the Lord. That was the beginning of my preaching, sir, and I've preached ever since.'

Dinah had let her work fall during this narrative, which she uttered in her usual simple way, but with that sincere, articulate, thrilling treble, by which she always mastered her audience. She stooped now to gather up her sewing, and then went on with it as before. Mr Irwine was deeply interested. He said to himself, 'He must be a miserable prig who would act the pedagogue here: one might as well go and lecture the trees for growing in their own shape.'

'And you never feel any embarrassment from the sense of your youth – that you are a lovely young woman on whom men's eyes are fixed?' he said aloud.

'No, I've no room for such feelings, and I don't believe the people ever take notice about that. I think, sir, when God makes His presence felt through us, we are like the burning bush: Moses never took any heed what sort of bush it was – he only saw the brightness of the Lord. I've preached to as rough ignorant people as can be in the villages about Snowfield – men that looked very hard and wild: but they never said an uncivil word to me, and often thanked me kindly as they made way for me to pass through the midst of them.'

'*That* I can believe – that I can well believe,' said Mr Irwine, emphatically. 'And what did you think of your hearers last night, now? Did you find them quiet and attentive?'

'Very quiet, sir; but I saw no signs of any great work upon them, except in a young girl named Bessy Cranage, towards whom my heart yearned greatly, when my eyes first fell on her blooming youth, given up to folly and vanity. I had some private talk and prayer with her afterwards, and I trust her heart is touched. But I've noticed, that in these villages where the people lead a quiet life among the green pastures and the still waters, tilling the ground and tending the cattle, there's a strange deadness to the Word, as different as can be from the great towns, like Leeds, where I once went to visit a holy woman who preaches there. It's wonderful how rich is the harvest of souls up those high-walled streets, where you seemed to walk as in a prison-yard, and the ear is deafened with the sounds of worldly toil. I think maybe it is because the promise is sweeter when this life is so dark and weary, and the soul gets more hungry when the body is ill at ease.'

'Why, yes, our farm-labourers are not easily roused. They take life almost as slowly as the sheep and cows. But we have some intelligent workmen about here. I dare say you know the Bedes, Seth Bede, by the by, is a Methodist.'

'Yes, I know Seth well, and his brother Adam a little. Seth is a gracious young man – sincere and without offence; and Adam is like the patriarch Joseph, for his great skill and knowledge, and the kindness he shows to his brother and his parents.'

'Perhaps you don't know the trouble that has just happened to them? Their father, Matthias Bede, was drowned in the Willow Brook last night, not far from his own door. I'm going now to see Adam.'

'Ah, their poor aged mother!' said Dinah, dropping her hands, and looking before her with pitying eyes, as if she saw the object of her sympathy. 'She will mourn heavily; for Seth has told me she's of an anxious troubled heart. I must go and see if I can give her any help.'

As she rose and was beginning to fold up her work, Captain Donnithorne, having exhausted all plausible pretexts for remaining among the milk-pans, came out of the dairy, followed by Mrs Poyser. Mr Irwine now rose also, and, advancing towards Dinah, held out his hand, and said – 'Goodbye. I hear you are going away soon; but this will not be the last visit you will pay your aunt – so we shall meet again, I hope.' His cordiality towards Dinah set all Mrs Poyser's anxieties at rest, and her face was brighter than usual, as she said – 'I've never asked after Mrs Irwine and the Miss Irwines, sir; I hope they're as well as usual.'

'Yes, thank you, Mrs Poyser, except that Miss Anne has one of her bad headaches to day. By the by, we all liked that nice cream-cheese you sent us – my mother especially.'

'I'm very glad, indeed, sir. It is but seldom I make one, but I remembered Mrs Irwine was fond of 'em. Please to give my duty to her, and to Miss Kate and Miss Anne. They've never been to look at my poultry this long while, and I've got some beautiful speckled chickens, black and white, as Miss Kate might like to have some of amongst hers.'

'Well, I'll tell her; she must come and see them. Goodbye,' said the Rector, mounting his horse.

'Just ride slowly on, Irwine,' said Captain Donnithorne, mounting also. 'I'll overtake you in three minutes. I'm only going to speak to the shepherd about the whelps. Goodbye, Mrs Poyser; tell your husband I shall come and have a long talk with him soon.'

Mrs Poyser curtsied duly, and watched the two horses until they had disappeared from the yard, amidst great excitement on the part of the pigs and the poultry, and under the furious indignation of the bulldog, who performed a Pyrrhic dance, that every moment seemed to threaten the breaking of his chain. Mrs Poyser delighted in this noisy exit; it was a fresh assurance to her that the farmyard was well guarded, and that no loiterers could enter unobserved; and it was not until the gate had closed behind the Captain that she turned into the kitchen again, where Dinah stood with her bonnet in her hand, waiting to speak to her aunt, before she set out for Lisbeth Bede's cottage.

Mrs Poyser, however, though she noticed the bonnet, deferred remarking on it until she had disburdened herself of her surprise at Mr Irwine's behaviour.

'Why, Mr Irwine wasn't angry, then? What did he say to you, Dinah? Didn't he scold you for preaching?'

'No, he was not at all angry; he was very friendly to me. I was quite drawn out to speak to him; I hardly know how, for I had always thought of him as a worldly Sadducee. But his countenance is as pleasant as the morning sunshine.'

'Pleasant! and what else did y' expect to find him but pleasant?' said Mrs Poyser, impatiently, resuming her knitting. 'I should think his countenance is pleasant indeed! and him a gentleman born, and's got a mother like a picter. You may go the country round, and not find such another woman turned sixty-six. It's summat-like to see such a man as that i' the desk of a Sunday! As I say to Poyser, it's like looking at a full crop o' wheat, or a pasture with a fine dairy o' cows in it; it makes you think the world's comfortable-like. But as for such creaturs as you Methodisses run after, I'd as soon go to look at a lot o' bare-ribbed runts on a common. Fine folks they are to tell you what's right, as look as if they'd never tasted nothing better than bacon-sword and sour-cake i' their lives. But what did Mr Irwine say to you about that fool's trick o' preaching on the Green?'

'He only said he'd heard of it; he didn't seem to feel any displeasure about it. But, dear aunt, don't think any more about that. He told me something that I'm sure will cause you sorrow, as it does me. Thias Bede was drowned last night in the Willow Brook, and I'm thinking that the aged mother will be greatly in need of comfort. Perhaps I can be of use to her, so I have fetched my bonnet and am going to set out.'

'Dear heart, dear heart! But you must have a cup o' tea first, child,' said Mrs

Poyser, falling at once from the key of B with five sharps to the frank and genial C. 'The kettle's boiling – we'll have it ready in a minute; and the young uns 'ull be in and wanting theirs directly. I'm quite willing you should go and see th' old woman, for you're one as is allays welcome in trouble, Methodist or no Methodist; but, for the matter o' that, it's the flesh and blood folks are made on as makes the difference. Some cheeses are made o' skimmed milk and some o' new milk, and it's no matter what you call 'em, you may tell which is which by the look and the smell. But as to Thias Bede, he's better out o' the way nor in – God forgi' me for saying so – for he's done little this ten year but make trouble for them as belonged to him; and I think it 'ud be well for you to take a little bottle o' rum for th' old woman, for I dare say she's got never a drop o' nothing to comfort her inside. Sit down, child, and be easy, for you shan't stir out till you've had a cup o' tea, and so I tell you.'

During the latter part of this speech, Mrs Poyser had been reaching down the tea-things from the shelves, and was on her way towards the pantry for the loaf (followed close by Totty, who had made her appearance on the rattling of the tea cups), when Hetty came out of the dairy relieving her tired arms by lifting them up, and clasping her hands at the back of her head.

'Molly,' she said, rather languidly, 'just run out and get me a bunch of dock-leaves: the butter's ready to pack up now.'

'D'you hear what's happened, Hetty?' said her aunt.

'No; how should I hear anything?' was the answer, in a pettish tone.

'Not as you'd care much, I dare say, if you did hear; for you're too feather-headed to mind if everybody was dead, so as you could stay upstairs a dressing yourself for two hours by the clock. But anybody besides yourself 'ud mind about such things happening to them as think a deal more of you than you deserve. But Adam Bede and all his kin might be drownded for what you'd care – you'd be perking at the glass the next minute.'

'Adam Bede – drowned?' said Hetty, letting her arms fall, and looking rather bewildered, but suspecting that her aunt was as usual exaggerating with a didactic purpose.

'No, my dear, no,' said Dinah, kindly, for Mrs Poyser had passed on to the pantry without deigning more precise information. 'Not Adam. Adam's father, the old man, is drowned. He was drowned last night in the Willow Brook. Mr Irwine has just told me about it.'

'Oh, how dreadful!' said Hetty, looking serious, but not deeply affected; and as Molly now entered with the dock-leaves, she took them silently and returned to the dairy without asking further questions.

Hetty's World

While she adjusted the broad leaves that set off the pale fragrant butter as the primrose is set off by its nest of green, I am afraid Hetty was thinking a great deal more of the looks Captain Donnithorne had cast at her than of Adam and his troubles. Bright, admiring glances from a handsome young gentleman, with white hands, a gold chain, occasional regimentals, and wealth and grandeur immeasurable – those were the warm rays that set poor Hetty's heart vibrating, and playing its little foolish tunes over and over again. We do not hear that Memnon's statue gave forth its melody at all under the rushing of the mightiest wind, or in response to any other influence divine or human than certain short-lived sunbeams of morning; and we must learn to accommodate ourselves to the discovery that some of those cunningly-fashioned instruments called human souls have only a very limited range of music, and will not vibrate in the least under a touch that fills others with tremulous rapture or quivering agony.

Hetty was quite used to the thought that people liked to look at her. She was not blind to the fact that young Luke Britton of Broxton came to Hayslope Church on a Sunday afternoon on purpose that he might see her; and that he would have made much more decided advances if her uncle Poyser, thinking but lightly of a young man whose father's land was so foul as old Luke Britton's, had not forbidden her aunt to encourage him by any civilities. She was aware, too, that Mr Craig, the gardener at the Chase, was over head and ears in love with her, and had lately made unmistakable avowals in luscious strawberries and hyperbolical peas. She knew still better, that Adam Bede – tall, upright, clever, brave Adam Bede – who carried such authority with all the people round about, and whom her uncle was always delighted to see of an evening, saying that 'Adam knew a fine sight more o' the natur o' things than those as thought themselves his betters' – she knew that this Adam, who was often rather stern to other people, and not much given to run after the lasses, could be made to turn pale or red any day by a word or a look from her. Hetty's sphere of comparison was not large, but she couldn't help perceiving that Adam was 'something like' a man; always knew what to say about things, could tell her uncle how to prop the hovel, and had mended the churn in no time; knew, with only looking at it, the value of the chestnut tree that was blown down, and why the damp came in the walls, and what they must do to stop the rats; and wrote a beautiful hand that you could read off, and could do figures in his head – a degree of accomplishment totally unknown among the richest farmers of that countryside. Not at all like that slouching Luke Britton, who, when she once walked with him all the way from Broxton to Hayslope, had only broken silence to remark that the grey goose had begun to lay. And as for Mr Craig the gardener, he was a sensible man enough, to be sure, but he was knock-kneed, and had a queer sort of singsong in his talk; moreover, on the most charitable supposition, he must be far on the way to forty.

Hetty was quite certain her uncle wanted her to encourage Adam, and would be pleased for her to marry him. For those were times when there was no rigid demarcation of rank between the farmer and the respectable artisan, and on the home hearth, as well as in the public-house, they might be seen taking their jug of ale together; the farmer having a latent sense of capital, and of weight in parish affairs, which sustained him under his conspicuous inferiority in conversation. Martin Poyser was not a frequenter of public-houses, but he liked a friendly chat over his own home-brewed; and though it was pleasant to lay down the law to a stupid neighbour who had no notion how to make the best of his farm, it was also an agreeable variety to learn something from a clever fellow like Adam Bede. Accordingly, for the last three years – ever since he had superintended the building of the new barn – Adam had always been made welcome at the Hall Farm, especially of a winter evening when the whole family, in patriarchal fashion, master and mistress, children and servants, were assembled in that glorious kitchen, at well-graduated distances from the blazing fire. And for the last two years, at least, Hetty had been in the habit of hearing her uncle say, 'Adam Bede may be working for wage now, but he'll be a master-man someday, as sure as I sit in this chair. Mester Burge is in the right on't to want him to go partners and marry his daughter, if it's true what they say; the woman as marries him 'ull have a good take, be't Lady-day or Michaelmas' – a remark which Mrs Poyser always followed up with her cordial assent. 'Ah!' she would say, 'it's all very fine having a ready-made rich man, but may-happen he'll be a ready-made fool; and it's no use filling your pocket full of money if you've got a hole in the corner. It'll do you no good to sit in a spring-cart o' your own, if you've got a soft to drive you: he'll soon turn you over into the ditch. I allays said I'd never marry a man as had got no brains; for where's the use of a woman having brains of her own if she's tackled to a geck as everybody's a-laughing at? She might as well dress herself fine to sit back'ards on a donkey.'

These expressions, though figurative, sufficiently indicated the bent of Mrs Poyser's mind with regard to Adam; and though she and her husband might have viewed the subject differently if Hetty had been a daughter of their own, it was clear that they would have welcomed the match with Adam for a penniless niece. For what could Hetty have been but a servant elsewhere, if her uncle had not taken her in and brought her up as a domestic help to her aunt, whose health since the birth of Totty had not been equal to more positive labour than the superintendence of servants and children? But Hetty had never given Adam any steady encouragement. Even in the moments when she was most thoroughly conscious of his superiority to her other admirers, she had never brought herself to think of accepting him. She liked to feel that this strong, skilful, keen-eyed man was in her power, and would have been indignant if he had shown the least sign of slipping from under the yoke of her coquettish tyranny, and attaching himself to the gentle Mary Burge, who would have been grateful enough for the most trifling notice from him. 'Mary Burge, indeed! such a sallow-faced girl: if she put on a bit of pink ribbon, she looked as yellow as a crow-flower, and her hair was as straight as a hank of cotton.' And always when Adam stayed away for several weeks from the Hall Farm, and otherwise made some show of resistance to his passion as a foolish one, Hetty took care to entice him back into the net by little airs of meekness and timidity, as if she were in trouble at his neglect. But as to marrying Adam, that was a very different affair! There was nothing in the world to tempt her to do that. Her cheeks never grew a shade deeper when his name was mentioned; she felt no thrill when she saw him passing along the causeway by the window, or advancing towards her unexpectedly in the footpath across the meadow; she felt nothing when his eyes rested on her, but the cold triumph of knowing that he loved her, and would not care to look at Mary Burge: he could no more stir in her the emotions that make the sweet intoxication of young love, than the mere picture of a sun can stir the spring sap in the subtle fibres of the plant. She saw him as he was – a poor man, with old parents to keep, who would not be able, for a long while to come, to give her even such luxuries as she shared in her uncle's house. And Hetty's dreams were all of luxuries: to sit in a carpeted parlour, and always wear white stockings; to have some large beautiful earrings such as were all the fashion; to have Nottingham lace round the top of her gown, and something to make her handkerchief smell nice, like Miss Lydia Donnithorne's when she drew it out at church; and not to be obliged to get up early or be scolded by anybody. She thought, if Adam had been rich and could have given her these things, she loved him well enough to marry him.

But for the last few weeks a new influence had come over Hetty – vague, atmospheric, shaping itself into no self-confessed hopes or prospects, but producing a pleasant narcotic effect, making her tread the ground and go about her work in a sort of dream, unconscious of weight or effort, and showing her all things through a soft, liquid veil, as if she were living not in this solid world of brick and stone, but in a beatified world, such as the sun lights up for us in the waters. Hetty had become aware that Mr Arthur Donnithorne would take a good deal of trouble for the chance of seeing her; that he always placed himself at church so as to have the fullest view of her both sitting and standing; that he was constantly finding reasons for calling at the Hall Farm, and always would contrive to say something for the sake of making her speak to him and look at him. The poor child no more conceived at present the idea that the young squire could ever be her lover, than a baker's pretty daughter in the crowd, whom a young emperor distinguishes by an imperial but admiring smile, conceives that she shall be made empress. But the baker's daughter goes home and dreams of the handsome young emperor, and perhaps weighs the flour amiss while she is thinking what a heavenly lot it must be to have him for a husband: and so poor Hetty had got a face and a presence haunting her waking and sleeping dreams; bright, soft glances had penetrated her, and suffused her life with a strange, happy languor. The eyes that shed those glances were really not half so fine as Adam's, which sometimes looked at her with a sad, beseeching tenderness; but they had found a ready medium in Hetty's little silly imagination, whereas Adam's could get no entrance through that atmosphere. For three weeks, at least, her inward life had consisted of little else than living through in memory the looks and words Arthur had directed towards her – of little else than recalling the sensations with which she heard his voice outside the house, and saw him enter, and became conscious that his eyes were fixed on her, and then became conscious that a tall figure, looking down on her with eyes that seemed to touch her, was coming nearer in clothes of beautiful texture, with an odour like that of a flower-garden borne on the evening breeze. Foolish thoughts! but all this happened, you must remember, nearly sixty years ago, and Hetty was quite uneducated – a simple farmer's girl, to whom a gentleman with a white hand was dazzling as an Olympian god. Until today, she had never looked farther into the future than to the next time Captain Donnithorne would come to the Farm, or the next Sunday when she should see him at church; but now she thought, perhaps he would try to meet her when she went to the Chase tomorrow – and if he should speak to her, and walk a little way, when nobody was by! That had never happened yet; and now her imagination, instead of retracing the past, was busy fashioning what would happen tomorrow – whereabout in the Chase she should see him coming towards her, how she should put her new rose-coloured ribbon on, which he had never seen, and what he would say to her to make her return his glance – a glance which she would be living through in her memory, over and over again, all the rest of the day.

In this state of mind, how could Hetty give any feeling to Adam's troubles, or think much about poor old Thias being drowned? Young souls, in such pleasant delirium as hers, are as unsympathetic as butterflies sipping nectar; they are isolated from all appeals by a barrier of dreams – by invisible looks and impalpable arms.

While Hetty's hands were busy packing up the butter, and her head filled with these pictures of the morrow, Arthur Donnithorne, riding by Mr Irwine's side towards the valley of the Willow Brook, had also certain indistinct anticipations, running as an undercurrent in his mind while he was listening to Mr Irwine's account of Dinah – indistinct, yet strong enough to make him feel rather conscious when Mr Irwine suddenly said – 'What fascinated you so in Mrs Poyser's dairy, Arthur? Have you become an amateur of damp quarries and skimming-dishes?'

Arthur knew the Rector too well to suppose that a clever invention would be of any use, so he said, with his accustomed frankness – 'No, I went to look at the pretty butter-maker, Hetty Sorrel. She's a perfect Hebe; and if I were an artist, I would paint her. It's amazing what pretty girls one sees among the farmers' daughters, when the men are such clowns. That common round red face one sees sometimes in the men – all cheek and no features, like Martin Poyser's – comes out in the women of the family as the most charming phiz imaginable.'

'Well, I have no objection to your contemplating Hetty in an artistic light, but I must not have you feeding her vanity, and filling her little noddle with the notion that she's a great beauty, attractive to fine gentlemen, or you will spoil her for a poor man's wife – honest Craig's, for example, whom I have seen bestowing soft glances on her. The little puss seems already to have airs enough to make a husband as miserable as it's a law of nature for a quiet man to be when he marries a beauty. Apropos of marrying, I hope our friend Adam will get settled, now the poor old man's gone. He will only have his mother to keep in future, and I've a notion that there's a kindness between him and that nice modest girl, Mary

Burge, from something that fell from old Jonathan one day when I was talking to him. But when I mentioned the subject to Adam he looked uneasy, and turned the conversation. I suppose the love-making doesn't run smooth, or perhaps Adam hangs back till he's in a better position. He has independence of spirit enough for two men – rather an excess of pride if anything.'

'That would be a capital match for Adam. He would slip into old Burge's shoes, and make a fine thing of that building business, I'll answer for him. I should like to see him well settled in this parish; he would be ready then to act as my grand-vizier when I wanted one. We could plan no end of repairs and improvements together. I've never seen the girl, though, I think – at least I've never looked at her.'

'Look at her next Sunday at church – she sits with her father on the left of the reading-desk. You needn't look quite so much at Hetty Sorrel then. When I've made up my mind that I can't afford to buy a tempting dog, I take no notice of him, because if he took a strong fancy to me, and looked lovingly at me, the struggle between arithmetic and inclination might become unpleasantly severe. I pique myself on my wisdom there, Arthur, and as an old fellow to whom wisdom has become cheap, I bestow it upon you.'

'Thank you. It may stand me in good stead someday, though I don't know that I have any present use for it. Bless me! how the brook has overflowed. Suppose we have a canter, now we're at the bottom of the hill.'

That is the great advantage of dialogue on horseback; it can be merged any minute into a trot or canter, and one might have escaped from Socrates himself in the saddle. The two friends were free from the necessity of further conversation till they pulled up in the lane behind Adam's cottage.

10

Dinah Visits Lisbeth

At five o'clock Lisbeth came downstairs with a large key in her hand: it was the key of the chamber where her husband lay dead. Throughout the day, except in her occasional outbursts of wailing grief, she had been in incessant movement, performing the initial duties to her dead with the awe and exactitude that belong to religious rites. She had brought out her little store of bleached linen, which she had for long years kept in reserve for this supreme use. It seemed but yesterday – that time so many midsummers ago, when she had told Thias where this linen lay, that he might be sure and reach it out for her when she died, for she was the elder of the two. Then there had been the work of cleansing to the strictest purity every object in the sacred chamber, and of removing from it every trace of common daily occupation. The small window which had hitherto freely let in the frosty moonlight or the warm summer sunrise on the working-man's slumber, must now be darkened with a fair white sheet, for this was the sleep which is as sacred under the bare rafters as in ceiled houses. Lisbeth had even mended a long-neglected and unnoticeable rent in the checkered bit of bed-curtain; for the moments were few and precious now in which she would be able to do the smallest office of respect or love for the still corpse, to which in all her thoughts she attributed some consciousness. Our dead are never dead to us until we have forgotten them: they can be injured by us, they can be wounded; they know all our penitence, all our aching sense that their place is empty, all the kisses we bestow on the smallest relic of their presence. And the aged peasant-woman most of all believes that her dead are conscious. Decent burial was what Lisbeth had been thinking of for herself through years of thrift, with an indistinct expectation that she should know when she was being carried to the churchyard, followed by her husband and her sons; and now she felt as if the greatest work of her life were to be done in seeing that Thias was buried decently before her – under the whitethorn, where once, in a dream, she had thought she lay in the coffin, yet all the while saw the sunshine above, and smelt the white blossoms that were so thick upon the thorn the Sunday she went to be churched after Adam was born.

But now she had done everything that could be done today in the chamber of death – had done it all herself, with some aid from her sons in lifting, for she would let no one be fetched to help her from the village, not being fond of female neighbours generally; and her favourite Dolly, the old housekeeper at Mr Burge's, who had come to condole with her in the morning as soon as she heard of Thias's death, was too dim-sighted to be of much use. She had locked the door, and now held the key in her hand, as she threw herself wearily into a chair that stood out of its place in the middle of the house floor, where in ordinary times she would never have consented to sit. The kitchen had had none of her attention that day; it was soiled with the tread of muddy shoes, and untidy with clothes and other objects out of place. But what at another time would have been intolerable to Lisbeth's habits of order and cleanliness, seemed to her now just what should be: it was right that things should look strange and disordered and wretched, now the old man had come to his end in that sad way: the kitchen ought not to look as if nothing had happened. Adam, overcome with the agitations and exertions of the day after his night of hard work, had fallen asleep on a bench in the workshop; and Seth was in the back kitchen making a fire of sticks that he might get the kettle to boil, and persuade his mother to have a cup of tea, an indulgence which she rarely allowed herself.

There was no one in the kitchen when Lisbeth entered and threw herself into the chair. She looked round with blank eyes at the dirt and confusion on which the bright afternoon's sun shone dismally; it was all of a piece with the sad confusion of her mind – that confusion which belongs to the first hours of a sudden sorrow, when the poor human soul is like one who has been deposited sleeping among the ruins of a vast city, and wakes up in dreary amazement, not knowing whether it is the growing or the dying day – not knowing why and whence came this illimitable scene of desolation, or why he too finds himself desolate in the midst of it.

At another time Lisbeth's first thought would have been, 'Where is Adam?' but the sudden death of her husband had restored him in these hours to that first place in her affections which he had held six-and-twenty years ago: she had forgotten his faults as we forget the sorrows of our departed childhood, and thought of nothing but the young husband's kindness and the old man's patience. Her eyes continued to wander blankly until Seth came in and began to remove some of the scattered things, and clear the small round deal table that he might set out his mother's tea upon it.

'What art goin' to do?' she said, rather peevishly.

'I want thee to have a cup of tea, mother,' answered Seth, tenderly. 'It'll do thee good; and I'll put two or three of these things away, and make the house look more comfortable.'

'Comfortable! How canst talk o' ma'in' things comfortable? Let a-be, let a-be. There's no comfort for me no more,' she went on, the tears coming when she began to speak, 'now thy poor feyther's gone, as I'n washed for and mended, an' got's victual for him for thirty 'ear, an' him allays so pleased wi' iverything I done for him, an' used to be so handy an' do the jobs for me when I war ill an' cumbered wi' th' babby, an' made me the posset an' brought it upstairs as proud as could be, an' carried the lad as war as heavy as two children for five mile an' ne'er grumbled, all the way to Warson Wake, 'cause I wanted to go an' see my sister, as war dead an' gone the very next Christmas as e'er come. An' him to be drownded in the brook as we passed o'er the day we war married an' come home together, an' he'd made them lots o' shelves for me to put my plates an' things on, an' showed 'em me as proud as could be, 'cause he know'd I should be pleased. An' he war to die an' me not to know, but to be a-sleepin' i' my bed, as if I caredna nought about it. Eh! an' me to live to see that! An' us as war young folks once, an' thought we should do rarely when we war married. Let a-be, lad, let a-be! I wonna ha' no tay: I carena if I ne'er ate nor drink no more. When one end o' th' bridge tumbles down, where's th' use o' th' other stannin'? I may's well die, an' foller my old man. There's no knowin' but he'll want me.'

Here Lisbeth broke from words into moans, swaying herself backwards and forwards on her chair. Seth, always timid in his behaviour towards his mother, from the sense that he had no influence over her, felt it was useless to attempt to persuade or soothe her, till this passion was past; so he contented himself with tending the back-kitchen fire, and folding up his father's clothes, which had been hanging out to dry since morning; afraid to move about in the room where his mother was, lest he should irritate her further.

But after Lisbeth had been rocking herself and moaning for some minutes, she suddenly paused, and said aloud to herself – 'I'll go an' see arter Adam, for I canna think where he's gotten; an' I want him to go upstairs wi' me afore it's dark, for the minutes to look at the corpse is like the meltin' snow.'

Seth overheard this, and coming into the kitchen again, as his mother rose from her chair, he said – 'Adam's asleep in the workshop, mother. Thee'dst better not wake him. He was o'erwrought with work and trouble.'

'Wake him? Who's a-goin' to wake him? I shanna wake him wi' lookin' at him. I hanna seen the lad this two hour – I'd welly forgot as he'd e'er growed up from a babby when's feyther carried him.'

Adam was seated on a rough bench, his head supported by his arm, which rested from the shoulder to the elbow on the long planing-table in the middle of the workshop. It seemed as if he had sat down for a few minutes' rest, and had fallen asleep without slipping from his first attitude of sad, fatigued thought. His face, unwashed since yesterday, looked pallid and clammy; his hair was tossed shaggily about his forehead, and his closed eyes had the sunken look which follows upon watching and sorrow. His brow was knit, and his whole face had an expression of weariness and pain. Gyp was evidently uneasy, for he sat on his haunches resting his nose on his master's stretched-out leg, and dividing the time between licking the hand that hung listlessly down, and glancing with a listening air towards the door. The poor dog was hungry and restless, but would not leave his master, and was waiting impatiently for some change in the scene. It was owing to this feeling on Gyp's part, that when Lisbeth came into the workshop, and advanced towards Adam as noiselessly as she could, her intention not to awake him was immediately defeated; for Gyp's excitement was too great to find vent in anything short of a sharp bark, and in a moment Adam opened his eyes and saw his mother standing before him. It was not very unlike his dream, for his sleep had been little more than living through again, in a fevered delirious way, all that had happened since daybreak, and his mother with her fretful grief was present to him through it all. The chief difference between the reality and the vision was, that in his dream Hetty was continually coming before him in bodily presence – strangely mingling herself as an actor in scenes with which she had nothing to do. She was even by the Willow Brook; she made his mother angry by coming into the house; and he met her with her smart clothes quite wet through, as he walked in the rain to Treddleston, to tell the coroner. But wherever Hetty came, his mother was sure to follow soon; and when he opened his eyes, it was not at all startling to see her standing near him.

'Eh, my lad, my lad!' Lisbeth burst out immediately, her wailing impulse returning, for grief in its freshness feels the need of associating its loss and its lament with every change of scene and incident, 'thee'st got nobody now but thy old mother to torment thee and be a burden to thee: thy poor feyther 'ull ne'er anger thee no more; an' thy mother may's well go arter him – the sooner the better – for I'm no good to nobody now. One old coat 'ull do to patch another, but it's good for nought else. Thee'dst like to ha' a wife to mend thy clothes an' get thy victual, better nor thy old mother. An' I shall be nought but cumber, a-sittin' i' th' chimney-corner. '(Adam winced and moved uneasily; he dreaded, of all things, to hear his mother speak of Hetty.) 'But if thy feyther had lived, he'd ne'er ha' wanted me to go to make room for another, for he could no more ha' done wi'out me nor one side o' the scissars can do wi'out th' other. Eh, we should ha' been both flung away together, an' then I shouldna ha' seen this day, an' one buryin' 'ud ha' done for us both.'

Here Lisbeth paused, but Adam sat in pained silence: he could not speak otherwise than tenderly to his mother today but he could not help being irritated by this plaint. It was not possible for poor Lisbeth to know how it affected Adam, any more than it is possible for a wounded dog to know how his moans affect the nerves of his master. Like all complaining women, she complained in the expectation of being soothed, and when Adam said nothing, she was only prompted to complain more bitterly.

'I know thee couldst do better wi'out me, for thee couldst go where thee likedst, an' marry them as thee likedst. But I donna want to say thee nay, let thee bring home who thee wut; I'd ne'er open my lips to find faut, for when folks is old an' o' no use, they may think theirsens well off to get the bit an' the sup, though they'n to swallow ill words wi't. An' if thee'st set thy heart on a lass as'll bring thee nought and waste all, when thee mightst ha' them as 'ud make a man on thee, I'll say nought, now thy feyther's dead an' drownded, for I'm no better nor an old haft when the blade's gone.'

Adam, unable to bear this any longer, rose silently from the bench, and walked out of the workshop into the kitchen. But Lisbeth followed him.

'Thee wutna go upstairs an' see thy feyther, then? I'n done everythin' now, an' he'd like thee to go an' look at him, for he war allays so pleased when thee wast mild to him.'

Adam turned round at once, and said, 'Yes, mother; let us go upstairs. Come, Seth, let us go together.'

They went upstairs, and for five minutes all was silence. Then the key was turned again, and there was a sound of footsteps on the stairs. But Adam did not come down again; he was too weary and worn-out to encounter more of his mother's querulous grief, and he went to rest on his bed. Lisbeth no sooner entered the kitchen and sat down than she threw her apron over her head, and began to cry and moan, and rock herself as before. Seth thought, 'she will be quieter by and by, now we have been upstairs;' and he went into the back-kitchen again, to tend his little fire, hoping that he should presently induce her to have some tea.

Lisbeth had been rocking herself in this way for more than five minutes, giving a low moan with every forward movement of her body, when she suddenly felt a hand placed gently on hers, and a sweet treble voice said to her, 'Dear sister, the Lord has sent me to see if I can be a comfort to you.'

Lisbeth paused, in a listening attitude, without removing her apron from her face. The voice was strange to her. Could it be her sister's spirit come back to her from the dead after all those years? she trembled, and dared not look.

Dinah, believing that this pause of wonder was in itself a relief for the sorrowing woman, said no more just yet, but quietly took off her bonnet, and then, motioning silence to Seth, who, on hearing her voice, had come in with a beating heart, laid one hand on the back of Lisbeth's chair, and leaned over her, that she might be aware of a friendly presence.

Slowly Lisbeth drew down her apron, and timidly she opened her dim dark eyes. She saw nothing at first but a face – a pure, pale face, with loving grey eyes, and it was quite unknown to her. Her wonder increased; perhaps it was an angel. But in the same instant Dinah had laid her hand on Lisbeth's again, and the old woman looked down at it. It was a much smaller hand than her own, but it was not white and delicate, for Dinah had never worn a glove in her life, and her hand bore the traces of labour from her childhood upwards. Lisbeth looked earnestly at the hand for a moment, and then, fixing her eyes again on Dinah's face, said, with something of restored courage, but in a tone of surprise – 'Why, ye're a workin' woman!'

'Yes, I am Dinah Morris, and I work in the cotton-mill when I am at home.'

'Ah!' said Lisbeth slowly, still wondering; 'ye comed in so light, like the shadow on the wall, an' spoke i' my ear, as I thought ye might be a sperrit. Ye've got a'most the face o' one as is a-sittin' on the grave i' Adam's new Bible.'

'I come from the Hall Farm now. You know Mrs Poyser – she's my aunt, and she has heard of your great affliction, and is very sorry; and I'm come to see if I can be any help to you in your trouble; for I know your sons Adam and Seth, and I know you have no daughter; and when the clergyman told me how the hand of God was heavy upon you, my heart went out towards you, and I felt a command to come and be to you in the place of a daughter in this grief, if you will let me.'

'Ah! I know who y' are now; y' are a Methody, like Seth; he's told me on you,' said Lisbeth, fretfully, her overpowering sense of pain returning, now her wonder was gone. 'Ye'll make it out as trouble's a good thing, like he allays does. But where's the use o' talkin' to me a-that'n? Ye canna make the smart less wi' talkin'. Ye'll ne'er make me believe as it's better for me not to ha' my old man die in's bed, if he must die, an' ha' the parson to pray by him, an' me to sit by him, an' tell him ne'er to mind th' ill words I've gi'en him sometimes when I war angered, an' to gi' him a bit an' a sup, as long as a bit an' a sup he'd swallow. But eh! to die i' the cold water, an' us close to him an' ne'er to know; an' me a-sleepin', as if I ne'er belonged to him no more nor if he'd been a journeyman tramp from nobody knows where!'

Here Lisbeth began to cry and rock herself again; and Dinah said 'Yes, dear friend, your affliction is great. It would be hardness of heart to say that your trouble was not heavy to bear. God didn't send me to you to make light of your sorrow, but to mourn with you, if you will let me. If you had a table spread for a feast, and was making merry with your friends, you would think it was kind to let me come and sit down and rejoice with you, because you'd think I should like to share those good things; but I should like better to share in your trouble and your labour, and it would seem harder to me if you denied me that. You won't send me away? You're not angry with me for coming?'

'Nay, nay; angered! who said I war angered? It war good on you to come. An' Seth, why donna ye get her some tay? Ye war in a hurry to get some for me, as had no need, but ye donna think o' gettin' 't for them as wants it. Sit ye down; sit ye down. I thank you kindly for comin', for it's little wage ye get by walkin' through the wet fields to see an old woman like me . . . Nay, I'n got no daughter o' my own – ne'er had one – an' I warna sorry, for they're poor queechy things, gells is; I allays wanted to ha' lads, as could fend for theirsens. An' the lads 'ull be marryin' – I shall ha' daughters eno', an' too many. But now, do ye make the tay as ye like it, for I'n got no taste i' my mouth this day – it's all one what I swaller – it's all got the taste o' sorrow wi't.'

Dinah took care not to betray that she had had her tea, and accepted Lisbeth's invitation very readily, for the sake of persuading the old woman herself to take the food and drink she so much needed after a day of hard work and fasting.

Seth was so happy now Dinah was in the house that he could not help thinking her presence was worth purchasing with a life in which grief incessantly followed upon grief; but the next moment he reproached himself – it was almost as if he were rejoicing in his father's sad death. Nevertheless the joy of being with Dinah *would* triumph: it was like the influence of climate, which no resistance can overcome. And the feeling even suffused itself over his face so as to attract his mother's notice, while she was drinking her tea.

'Thee may'st well talk o' trouble bein' a good thing, Seth, for thee thriv'st on't. Thee look'st as if thee know'dst no more o' care an' cumber nor when thee wast a babby a-lyin' awake i' th' cradle. For thee'dst allays lie still wi' thy eyes open, an' Adam ne'er 'ud lie still a minute when he wakened. Thee wast allays like a bag o' meal as can ne'er be bruised – though, for the matter o' that, thy poor feyther war just such another. But ye've got the same look too' (here Lisbeth turned to Dinah). 'I reckon it's wi' bein' a Methody. Not as I'm a-findin' faut wi' ye for't, for ye've no call to be frettin', an' somehow ye looken sorry too. Eh! well, if the Methodies are fond o' trouble, they're like to thrive: it's a pity they canna ha't all, an' take it away from them as donna like it. I could ha' gi'en 'em plenty; for when I'd gotten my old man I war worreted from morn till night; and now's he's gone, I'd be glad for the worst o'er again.'

'Yes,' said Dinah, careful not to oppose any feeling of Lisbeth's, for her reliance, in her smallest words and deeds, on a divine guidance, always issued in that finest woman's tact which proceeds from acute and ready sympathy – 'yes; I remember, too, when my dear aunt died, I longed for the sound of her bad cough in the nights, instead of the silence that came when she was gone. But now, dear friend, drink this other cup of tea and eat a little more.'

'What!' said Lisbeth, taking the cup, and speaking in a less querulous tone, 'had ye got no feyther and mother, then, as ye war so sorry about your aunt?'

'No, I never knew a father or mother; my aunt brought me up from a baby. She had no children, for she was never married, and she brought me up as tenderly as if I'd been her own child.'

'Eh, she'd fine work wi' ye, I'll warrant, bringin' ye up from a babby, an' her a lone woman – it's ill bringin' up a cade lamb. But I dare say ye warna franzy, for ye look as if ye'd ne'er been angered i' your life. But what did ye do when your aunt died, an' why didna ye come to live in this country, bein' as Mrs Poyser's your aunt too?'

Dinah, seeing that Lisbeth's attention was attracted, told her the story of her early life – how she had been brought up to work hard, and what sort of place Snowfield was, and how many people had a hard life there – all the details that she thought likely to interest Lisbeth. The old woman listened, and forgot to be fretful, unconsciously subject to the soothing influence of Dinah's face and voice. After a while she was persuaded to let the kitchen be made tidy; for Dinah was bent on this, believing that the sense of order and quietude around her would help in disposing Lisbeth to join in the prayer she longed to pour forth at her side. Seth, meanwhile, went out to chop wood; for he surmised that Dinah would like to be left alone with his mother.

Lisbeth sat watching her as she moved about in her still quick way, and said at last, 'Ye've got a notion o' cleanin' up. I wouldna mind ha'in ye for a daughter, for ye wouldna spend the lad's wage i' fine clothes an' waste. Ye're not like the lasses o' this countryside. I reckon folks is different at Snowfield from what they are here.'

'They have a different sort of life, many of 'em,' said Dinah; 'they work at different things – some in the mill, and many in the mines, in the villages round about. But the heart of man is the same everywhere, and there are the children of this world and the children of light there as well as elsewhere. But we've many more Methodists there than in this country.'

'Well, I didna know as the Methody women war like ye; for there's Will Maskery's wife, as they say's a big Methody, isna pleasant to look at, at all. I'd as lief look at a tooad. An' I'm thinkin' I wouldna mind if ye'd stay an' sleep here, for I should like to see ye i' th' house i' th' mornin'. But may-happen they'll be lookin' for ye at Mester Poyser's.'

'No,' said Dinah, 'they don't expect me, and I should like to stay, if you'll let me.'

'Well, there's room; I'n got my bed laid i' th' little room o'er the back-kitchen, an' ye can lie beside me. I'd be glad to ha' ye wi' me to speak to i' th' night, for ye've got a nice way o' talkin'. It puts me i' mind o' the swallows as was under the thack last 'ear, when they fust begun to sing low an' soft-like i' th' mornin'. Eh, but my old man war fond o' them birds! an' so war Adam, but they'n ne'er comed again this 'ear. Happen they're dead too.'

'There,' said Dinah, 'now the kitchen looks tidy, and now, dear mother – for I'm your daughter tonight, you know – I should like you to wash your face and have a clean cap on. Do you remember what David did, when God took away his child from him? While the child was yet alive he fasted and prayed to God to spare it, and he would neither eat nor drink, but lay on the ground all night, beseeching God for the child. But when he knew it was dead, he rose up from the ground and washed and anointed himself, and changed his clothes, and ate and drank; and when they asked him how it was that he seemed to have left off grieving now the child was dead, he said, "While the child was yet alive, I fasted and wept; for I said, Who can tell whether God will be gracious to me, that the child may live? But now he is dead, wherefore should I fast? can I bring him back again? I shall go to him, but he shall not return to me."

'Eh, that's a true word,' said Lisbeth. 'Yea, my old man wonna come back to me, but I shall go to him – the sooner the better. Well, ye may do as ye like wi' me: there's a clean cap i' that drawer, an' I'll go i' the back-kitchen an' wash my face. An' Seth, thee may'st reach down Adam's new Bible wi' th' picters in, an' she shall read us a chapter. Eh, I like them words – "I shall go to him, but he wonna come back to me."

Dinah and Seth were both inwardly offering thanks for the greater quietness of spirit that had come over Lisbeth. This was what Dinah had been trying to bring about, through all her still sympathy and absence from exhortation. From her girlhood upwards she had had experience among the sick and the mourning, among minds hardened and shrivelled through poverty and ignorance, and had gained the subtlest perception of the mode in which they could best be touched, and softened into willingness to receive words of spiritual consolation or warning. As Dinah expressed it, 'she was never left to herself; but it was always given her when to keep silence and when to speak.' And do we not all agree to call rapid thought and noble impulse by the name of inspiration? After our subtlest analysis of the mental process, we must still say, as Dinah did, that our highest thoughts and our best deeds are all given to us.

And so there was earnest prayer – there was faith, love, and hope pouring itself forth that evening in the little kitchen. And poor aged fretful Lisbeth, without grasping any distinct idea, without going through any course of religious emotions, felt a vague sense of goodness and love, and of something right lying underneath and beyond all this sorrowing life. She couldn't understand the sorrow; but, for these moments, under the subduing influence of Dinah's spirit, she felt that she must be patient and still.

II

In the Cottage

It was but half-past four the next morning, when Dinah, tired of lying awake listening to the birds, and watching the growing light through the little window in the garret roof, rose and began to dress herself very quietly, lest she should disturb Lisbeth. But already someone else was astir in the house, and had gone downstairs, preceded by Gyp. The dog's pattering step was a sure sign that it was Adam who went down; but Dinah was not aware of this, and she thought it was more likely to be Seth, for he had told her how Adam had stayed up working the night before. Seth, however, had only just awakened at the sound of the opening door. The exciting influence of the previous day, heightened at last by Dinah's unexpected presence, had not been counteracted by any bodily weariness, for he had not done his ordinary amount of hard work; and so when he went to bed, it was not till he had tired himself with hours of tossing wakefulness that drowsiness came, and led on a heavier morning sleep than was usual with him.

But Adam had been refreshed by his long rest, and, with his habitual impatience of mere passivity, he was eager to begin the new day, and subdue sadness by his strong will and strong arm. The white mist lay in the valley; it was going to be a bright, warm day, and he would start to work again when he had had his breakfast.

'There's nothing but what's bearable as long as a man can work,' he said to himself: 'the natur o' things doesn't change, though it seems as if one's own life was nothing but change. The square o' four is sixteen, and you must lengthen your lever in proportion to your weight, is as true when a man's miserable as when he's happy; and the best o' working is, it gives you a grip hold o' things outside your own lot.'

As he dashed the cold water over his head and face, he felt completely himself again, and with his black eyes as keen as ever, and his thick black hair all glistening with the fresh moisture, he went into the workshop to look out the wood for his father's coffin, intending that he and Seth should carry it with them to Jonathan Burge's, and have the coffin made by one of the workmen there, so that his mother might not see and hear the sad task going forward at home.

He had just gone into the workshop, when his quick ear detected a light rapid foot on the stairs – certainly not his mother's. He had been in bed and asleep when Dinah had come in, in the evening, and now he wondered whose step this could be. A foolish thought came, and moved him strangely. As if it could be Hetty! she was the last person likely to be in the house. And yet he felt reluctant to go and look, and have the clear proof that it was someone else. He stood leaning on a plank he had taken hold of, listening to sounds which his imagination interpreted for him so pleasantly, that the keen strong face became suffused with a timid tenderness. The light footstep moved about the kitchen, followed by the sound of the sweeping brush, hardly making so much noise as the lightest breeze that chases the autumn leaves along the dusty path; and Adam's imagination saw a dimpled face, with dark bright eyes and roguish smiles, looking backward at this brush, and a rounded figure just leaning a little to clasp the handle. A very foolish thought – it could not be Hetty; but the only way of dismissing such nonsense from his head was to go and see who it was, for his fancy only got nearer and nearer to belief while he stood there listening. He loosed the plank, and went to the kitchen door.

'How do you do, Adam Bede?' said Dinah, in her calm treble, pausing from her sweeping, and fixing her mild grave eyes upon him. 'I trust you feel rested and strengthened again to bear the burthen and heat of the day.'

It was like dreaming of the sunshine, and awaking in the moonlight. Adam had seen Dinah several times, but always at the Hall Farm, where he was not very vividly conscious of any woman's presence except Hetty's, and he had only in the last day or two begun to suspect that Seth was in love with her, so that his attention had not hitherto been drawn towards her for his brother's sake. But now her slim figure, her plain black gown, and her pale serene face, impressed him with all the force that belongs to a reality contrasted with a preoccupying fancy. For the first moment or two he made no answer, but looked at her with the concentrated, examining glance which a man gives to an object in which he has suddenly begun to be interested. Dinah, for the first time in her life, felt a painful self-consciousness; there was something in the dark penetrating glance of this strong man so different from the mildness and timidity of his brother Seth. A faint blush came, which deepened as she wondered at it. This blush recalled Adam from his forgetfulness.

'I was quite taken by surprise; it was very good of you to come and see my mother in her trouble,' he said, in a gentle grateful tone, for his quick mind told him at once how she came to be there. 'I hope my mother was thankful to have you,' he added, wondering rather anxiously what had been Dinah's reception.

'Yes,' said Dinah, resuming her work, 'she seemed greatly comforted after a while, and she's had a good deal of rest in the night, by times. She was fast asleep when I left her.'

'Who was it took the news to the Hall Farm?' said Adam, his thoughts reverting to someone there; he wondered whether she had felt anything about it.

'It was Mr Irwine, the clergyman, told me, and my aunt was grieved for your mother when she heard it, and wanted me to come; and so is my uncle, I'm sure, now he's heard it, but he was gone out to Rosseter all yesterday. They'll look for you there as soon as you've got time to go, for there's nobody round that hearth but what's glad to see you.'

Dinah, with her sympathetic divination, knew quite well that Adam was longing to hear if Hetty had said anything about their trouble; she was too rigorously truthful for benevolent invention, but she had contrived to say something in which Hetty was tacitly included. Love has a way of cheating itself consciously, like a child who plays at solitary-hide and-seek; it is pleased with assurances that it all the while disbelieves. Adam liked what Dinah had said so much that his mind was directly full of the next visit he should pay to the Hall Farm, when Hetty would perhaps behave more kindly to him than she had ever done before.

'But you won't be there yourself any longer?' he said to Dinah.

'No, I go back to Snowfield on Saturday, and I shall have to set out to Treddleston early, to be in time for the Oakbourne carrier. So I must go back to the farm tonight, that I may have the last day with my aunt and her children. But I can stay here all today, if your mother would like me; and her heart seemed inclined towards me last night.'

'Ah, then, she's sure to want you today. If mother takes to people at the beginning, she's sure to get fond of 'em; but she's a strange way of not liking young women. Though, to be sure,' Adam went on, smiling, 'her not liking other young women is no reason why she shouldn't like you.'

Hitherto Gyp had been assisting at this conversation in motionless silence, seated on his haunches, and alternately looking up in his master's face to watch its expression, and observing Dinah's movements about the kitchen. The kind smile with which Adam uttered the last words was apparently decisive with Gyp of the light in which the stranger was to be regarded, and as she turned round after putting aside her sweeping-brush, he trotted towards her, and put up his muzzle against her hand in a friendly way.

'You see Gyp bids you welcome,' said Adam, 'and he's very slow to welcome strangers.'

'Poor dog!' said Dinah, patting the rough grey coat, 'I've a strange feeling about the dumb things as if they wanted to speak, and it was a trouble to 'em because they couldn't. I can't help being sorry for the dogs always, though perhaps there's no need. But they may well have more in them than they know how to make us understand, for we can't say half what we feel; with all our words.'

Seth came down now, and was pleased to find Adam talking with Dinah; he wanted Adam to know how much better she was than all other women. But after a few words of greeting, Adam drew him into the workshop to consult about the coffin, and Dinah went on with her cleaning.

By six o'clock they were all at breakfast with Lisbeth in a kitchen as clean as she could have made it herself. The window and door were open, and the morning air brought with it a mingled scent of southernwood, thyme, and sweetbriar from the patch of garden by the side of the cottage. Dinah did not sit down at first, but moved about, serving the others with the warm porridge and the toasted oatcake, which she had got ready in the usual way, for she had asked Seth to tell her just what his mother gave them for breakfast. Lisbeth had been unusually silent since she came downstairs, apparently requiring some time to adjust her ideas to a state of things in which she came down like a lady to find all the work done, and sat still to be waited on. Her new sensations seemed to exclude the remembrance of her grief. At last, after tasting the porridge, she broke silence – 'Ye might ha' made the parridge worse,' she said to Dinah; 'I can ate it wi'out it's turnin' my stomach. It might ha' been a trifle thicker an' no harm, an' I allays putten a sprig o' mint in mysen; but how's ye t' know that? The lads arena like to get folks as'll make their parridge as I'n made it for 'em; it's well if they get onybody as'll make parridge at all. But ye might do, wi' a bit o' showin'; for ye're a stirrin' body in a mornin', an' ye've a light heel, an' ye've cleaned th' house well enough for a ma'-shift.'

'Makeshift, mother?' said Adam. 'Why, I think the house looks beautiful. I don't know how it could look better.'

'Thee dostna know? – nay; how's thee to know? Th' men ne'er know whether the floor's clean or cat-licked. But thee'lt know when thee gets thy parridge burnt, as it's like enough to be when I'n gi'en o'er makin' it. Thee'lt think thy mother war good for summat then.'

'Dinah,' said Seth, 'do come and sit down now and have your breakfast. We're all served now.'

'Ay, come an' sit ye down – do,' said Lisbeth, 'an' ate a morsel; ye'd need, arter bein' upo' your legs this hour an' half a'ready. Come, then,' she added, in a tone of complaining affection, as Dinah sat down by her side, 'I'll be loath for ye t' go' but ye canna stay much longer, I doubt. I could put up wi' ye i' th' house better nor wi' most folks.'

'I'll stay till tonight if you're willing,' said Dinah. 'I'd stay longer, only I'm going back to Snowfield on Saturday, and I must be with my aunt tomorrow.'

'Eh, I'd ne'er go back to that country. My old man come from that Stonyshire side, but he left it when he war a young un, an' i' the right on't too; for he said as there war no wood there, an' it 'ud ha' been a bad country for a carpenter.'

'Ah,' said Adam, 'I remember father telling me when I was a little lad, that he made up his mind if ever he moved it should be south'ard. But I'm not so sure about it. Bartle Massey says – and he knows the south – as the northern men are a finer breed than the southern, harder-headed and stronger-bodied, and a deal taller. And then he says, in some o' those counties it's as flat as the back o' your hand, and you can see nothing of a distance, without climbing up the highest trees. I couldn't abide that: I like to go to work by a road that'll take me up a bit of a hill, and see the fields for miles round me, and a bridge, or a town, or a bit of a steeple here and there. It makes you feel the world's a big place, and there's other men working in it with their heads and hands besides yourself.'

'I like th' hills best,' said Seth, 'when the clouds are over your head, and you see the sun shining ever so far off, over the Loamford way, as I've often done o' late, on the stormy days: it seems to me as if that was heaven where there's always joy and sunshine, though this life's dark and cloudy.'

'Oh, I love the Stonyshire side,' said Dinah; 'I shouldn't like to set my face towards the countries where they're rich in corn and cattle, and the ground so level and easy to tread; and to turn my back on the hills where the poor people have to live such a hard life, and the men spend their days in the mines away from the sunlight. It's very blessed on a bleak cold day, when the sky is hanging dark over the hill, to feel the love of God in one's soul, and carry it to the lonely, bare, stone houses, where there's nothing else to give comfort.'

'Eh!' said Lisbeth, 'that's very well for ye to talk, as looks welly like the snowdrop-flowers as ha' lived for days an' days when I'n gethered 'em, wi' nothin' but a drop o' water an' a peep o' daylight; but the hungry foulks had better leave th' hungry country. It makes less mouths for the scant cake. But,' she went on, looking at Adam, 'donna thee talk o' goin' south'ard or north'ard, an' leavin' thy feyther and mother i' the churchyard, an' goin' to a country as they know nothin' on. I'll ne'er rest i' my grave if I donna see thee i' the churchyard of a Sunday.'

'Donna fear, mother,' said Adam. 'If I hadna made up my mind not to go, I should ha' been gone before now.'

He had finished his breakfast now, and rose as he was speaking.

'What art goin' to do?' asked Lisbeth 'set about thy feyther's coffin?'

'No, mother,' said Adam; 'we're going to take the wood to the village, and have it made there.'

'Nay, my lad, nay,' Lisbeth burst out in an eager, wailing tone; 'thee wotna let nobody make thy feyther's coffin but thysen? Who'd make it so well? An' him as know'd what good work war, an's got a son as is the head o' the village, an' all Treddles'on too, for cleverness.'

'Very well, mother, if that's thy wish, I'll make the coffin at home; but I thought thee wouldstna like to hear the work going on.'

'An' why shouldna I like't? It's the right thing to be done. An' what's liking got to do wi't? It's choice o' mislikings is all I'n got i' this world. One morsel's as good as another when your mouth's out o' taste. Thee mun set about it now this mornin' fust thing. I wonna ha' nobody to touch the coffin but thee.'

Adam's eyes met Seth's, which looked from Dinah to him rather wistfully.

'No, mother,' he said, ' I'll not consent but Seth shall have a hand in it too, if it's to be done at home. I'll go to the village this forenoon, because Mr Burge 'ull want to see me, and Seth shall stay at home and begin the coffin. I can come back at noon, and then he can go.'

'Nay, nay,' persisted Lisbeth, beginning to cry, ' I'n set my heart on't as thee shalt ma' thy feyther's coffin. Thee't so stiff an' masterful, thee't ne'er do as thy mother wants thee. Thee wast often angered wi' thy feyther when he war alive; thee must be the better to him now he's gone. He'd ha' thought nothin' on't for Seth to ma's coffin.'

'Say no more, Adam, say no more,' said Seth, gently, though his voice told that he spoke with some effort; 'mother's in the right. I'll go to work, and do thee stay at home.'

He passed into the workshop immediately, followed by Adam; while Lisbeth, automatically obeying her old habits, began to put away the breakfast things, as if she did not mean Dinah to take her place any longer. Dinah said nothing, but presently used the opportunity of quietly joining the brothers in the workshop.

They had already got on their aprons and paper-caps, and Adam was standing with his left hand on Seth's shoulder, while he pointed with the hammer in his right to some boards which they were looking at. Their backs were turned towards the door by which Dinah entered, and she came in so gently that they were not aware of her presence till they heard her voice saying, 'Seth Bede!' Seth started, and they both turned round. Dinah looked as if she did not see Adam, and fixed her eyes on Seth's face, saying with calm kindness – 'I won't say farewell. I shall see you again when you come from work. So as I'm at the farm before dark, it will be quite soon enough.'

'Thank you, Dinah; I should like to walk home with you once more. It'll perhaps be the last time.'

There was a little tremor in Seth's voice. Dinah put out her hand and said, 'You'll have sweet peace in your mind today, Seth, for your tenderness and long-suffering towards your aged mother.'

She turned round and left the workshop as quickly and quietly as she had entered it. Adam had been observing her closely all the while, but she had not looked at him. As soon as she was gone, he said – 'I don't wonder at thee for loving her, Seth. She's got a face like a lily.'

Seth's soul rushed to his eyes and lips: he had never yet confessed his secret to Adam, but now he felt a delicious sense of disburthenment, as he answered – 'Ay, Addy, I do love her – too much, I doubt. But she doesna love me, lad, only as one child o' God loves another. She'll never love any man as a husband – that's my belief.'

'Nay, lad, there's no telling; thee mustna lose heart. She's made out o' stuff with a finer grain than most o' the women; I can see that clear enough. But if she's better than they are in other things, I canna think she'll fall short of 'em in loving.'

No more was said. Seth set out to the village, and Adam began his work on the coffin.

'God help the lad, and me too,' he thought, as he lifted the board. 'We're like enough to find life a tough job – hard work inside and out. It's a strange thing to think of a man as can lift a chair with his teeth, and walk fifty mile on end, trembling and turning hot and cold at only a look from one woman out of all the rest i' the world. It's a mystery we can give no account of; but no more we can of the sprouting o' the seed, for that matter.'

12

In the Wood

That same Thursday morning, as Arthur Donnithorne was moving about in his dressing-room seeing his well-looking British person reflected in the old-fashioned mirrors, and stared at, from a dingy olive-green piece of tapestry, by Pharaoh's daughter and her maidens, who ought to have been minding the infant Moses, he was holding a discussion with himself, which, by the time his valet was tying the black silk sling over his shoulder, had issued in a distinct practical resolution.

'I mean to go to Eagledale and fish for a week or so,' he said aloud. 'I shall take you with me, Pym, and set off this morning; so be ready by half-past eleven.'

The low whistle, which had assisted him in arriving at this resolution, here broke out into his loudest ringing tenor, and the corridor, as he hurried along it, echoed to his favourite song from the *Beggar's Opera*, 'When the heart of a man is oppressed with care'. Not an heroic strain; nevertheless Arthur felt himself very heroic as he strode towards the stables to give his orders about the horses. His own approbation was necessary to him, and it was not an approbation to be enjoyed quite gratuitously; it must be won by a fair amount of merit. He had never yet forfeited that approbation, and he had considerable reliance on his own virtues. No young man could confess his faults more candidly; candour was one of his favourite virtues; and how can a man's candour be seen in all its lustre unless he has a few failings to talk of? But he had an agreeable confidence that his faults were all of a generous kind – impetuous, warm-blooded, leonine; never crawling, crafty, reptilian. It was not possible for Arthur Donnithorne to do anything mean, dastardly, or cruel. 'No! I'm a devil of a fellow for getting myself into a hobble, but I always take care the load shall fall on my own shoulders.' Unhappily there is no inherent poetical justice in hobbles, and they will some-times obstinately refuse to inflict their worst consequences on the prime offender, in spite of his loudly expressed wish. It was entirely owing to this deficiency in the scheme of things that Arthur had ever brought anyone into trouble besides himself. He was nothing, if not good-natured; and all his pictures of the future, when he should come into the estate, were made up of a pros-perous, contented tenantry, adoring their landlord, who would be the model of an English gentleman – mansion in first-rate order, all elegance and high taste – jolly housekeeping, finest stud in Loamshire – purse open to all public objects – in short, everything as different as possible from what was now associated with the name of Donnithorne. And one of the first good actions he would perform in that future should be to increase Irwine's income for the vicarage of Hayslope, so that he might keep a carriage for his mother and sisters. His hearty affection for the Rector dated from the age of frocks and trousers. It was an affection partly filial, partly fraternal – fraternal enough to make him like Irwine's company better than that of most younger men, and filial enough to make him shrink strongly from incurring Irwine's disapprobation.

You perceive that Arthur Donnithorne was 'a good fellow' – all his college friends thought him such: he couldn't bear to see anyone uncomfortable; he would have been sorry even in his angriest moods for any harm to happen to his grandfather; and his aunt Lydia herself had the benefit of that soft-heartedness which he bore towards the whole sex. Whether he would have self-mastery enough to be always as harmless and purely beneficent as his good nature led him to desire, was a question that no one had yet decided against him: he was but twenty-one, you remember; and we don't enquire too closely into character in the case of a handsome generous young fellow, who will have property enough to support numerous peccadilloes – who, if he should unfortunately break a man's legs in his rash driving, will be able to pension him handsomely; or if he should happen to spoil a woman's existence for her, will make it up to her with expensive bon-bons, packed up and directed by his own hand. It would be ridiculous to be prying and analytic in such cases, as if one were enquiring into the character of a confidential clerk. We use round, general, gentlemanly epithets about a young man of birth and fortune; and ladies, with that fine intuition which is the distinguishing attribute of their sex, see at once that he is 'nice.' The chances are that he will go through life without scandalising anyone; a seaworthy vessel that no one would refuse to insure. Ships, certainly, are liable to casualties, which sometimes make terribly evident some flaw in their construction, that would never have been discoverable in smooth water; and many a 'good fellow,' through a disastrous combination of circumstances, has undergone a like betrayal.

But we have no fair ground for entertaining unfavourable auguries concerning Arthur Donnithorne, who this morning proves himself capable of a prudent resolution founded on conscience. One thing is clear: Nature has taken care that he shall never go far astray with perfect comfort and satisfaction to himself; he will never get beyond that borderland of sin, where he will be perpetually harassed by assaults from the other side of the boundary. He will never be a courtier of vice, and wear her orders in his buttonhole.

It was about ten o'clock, and the sun was shining brilliantly; everything was looking lovelier for the yesterday's rain. It is a pleasant thing on such a morning to walk along the well-rolled gravel on one's way to the stables, meditating an excursion. But the scent of the stables, which, in a natural state of things, ought to be among the soothing influences of a man's life, always brought with it some irritation to Arthur. There was no having his own way in the stables; everything was managed in the stingiest fashion. His grandfather persisted in retaining as head groom an old dolt whom no sort of lever could move out of his old habits, and who was allowed to hire a succession of raw Loamshire lads as his sub-ordinates, one of whom had lately tested a new pair of shears by clipping an oblong patch on Arthur's bay mare. This state of things is naturally embittering; one can put up with annoyances in the house, but to have the stable made a scene of vexation and disgust, is a point beyond what human flesh and blood can be expected to endure long together without danger of misanthropy.

Old John's wooden, deep-wrinkled face was the first object that met Arthur's eyes as he entered the stable yard, and it quite poisoned for him the bark of the two bloodhounds that kept watch there. He could never speak quite patiently to the old blockhead.

'You must have Meg saddled for me and brought to the door at half-past eleven, and I shall want Rattler saddled for Pym at the same time. Do you hear?'

'Yes, I hear, I hear, Cap'n,' said old John, very deliberately, following the young master into the stable. John considered a young master as the natural enemy of an old servant, and young people in general as a poor contrivance for carrying on the world.

Arthur went in for the sake of patting Meg, declining as far as possible to see anything in the stables, lest he should lose his temper before breakfast. The pretty creature was in one of the inner stables, and turned her mild head as her master came beside her. Little Trot, a tiny spaniel, her inseparable companion in the stable, was comfortably curled up on her back.

'Well, Meg, my pretty girl,' said Arthur, patting her neck, 'we'll have a glorious canter this morning.'

'Nay, your honour, I donna see as that can be,' said John.

'Not be? Why not?'

'Why, she's got lamed.'

'Lamed, confound you! what do you mean?'

'Why, th' lad took her too close to Dalton's hosses, an' one on 'em flung out at her, an' she's got her shank bruised o' the near fore-leg.'

The judicious historian abstains from narrating precisely what ensued. You understand that there was a great deal of strong language, mingled with soothing 'who-ho's' while the leg was examined; that John stood by with quite as much emotion as if he had been a cunningly carved crab-tree walking-stick, and that Arthur Donnithorne presently repassed the iron gates of the pleasure-ground without singing as he went.

He considered himself thoroughly disappointed and annoyed. There was not another mount in the stable for himself and his servant besides Meg and Rattler. It was vexatious; just when he wanted to get out of the way for a week or two. It seemed culpable in Providence to allow such a combination of circumstances. To be shut up at the Chase with a broken arm, when every other fellow in his regiment was enjoying himself at Windsor – shut up with his grandfather, who had the same sort of affection for him as for his parchment deeds! And to be disgusted at every turn with the management of the house and the estate! In such circumstances a man necessarily gets in an ill humour, and works off the irritation by some excess or other. 'Salkeld would have drunk a bottle of port every day,' he muttered to himself; 'but I'm not well seasoned enough for that. Well, since I can't go to Eagledale, I'll have a gallop on Rattler to Norburne this morning, and lunch with Gawaine.'

Behind this explicit resolution there lay an implicit one. If he lunched with Gawaine and lingered chatting, he should not reach the Chase again till nearly five, when Hetty would be safe out of his sight in the housekeeper's room; and when she set out to go home, it would be his lazy time after dinner, so he should keep out of her way altogether. There really would have been no harm in being kind to the little thing, and it was worth dancing with a dozen ballroom belles only to look at Hetty for half an hour. But perhaps he had better not take any more notice of her; it might put notions into her head, as Irwine had hinted; though Arthur, for his part, thought girls were not by any means so soft and easily bruised; indeed, he had generally found them twice as cool and cunning as he was himself. As for any real harm in Hetty's case, it was out of the question: Arthur Donnithorne accepted his own bond for himself with perfect confidence.

So the twelve o'clock sun saw him galloping towards Norburne; and by good fortune Halsell Common lay in his road, and gave him some fine leaps for Rattler. Nothing like 'taking' a few bushes and ditches for exorcising a demon; and it is really astonishing that the Centaurs, with their immense advantages in this way, have left so bad a reputation in history.

After this, you will perhaps be surprised to hear, that although Gawaine was at home, the hand of the dial in the courtyard had scarcely cleared the last stroke of three, when Arthur returned through the entrance-gates, got down from the panting Rattler, and went into the house to take a hasty luncheon. But I believe there have been men since his day who have ridden a long way to avoid a *rencontre*, and then galloped hastily back lest they should miss it. It is the favourite stratagem of our passions to sham a retreat, and to turn sharp round upon us at the moment we have made up our minds that the day is our own.

'The Cap'n's been ridin' the devil's own pace,' said Dalton the coachman, whose person stood out in high relief as he smoked his pipe against the stable wall, when John brought up Rattler.

'An' I wish he'd get the devil to do's grooming for'n,' growled John.

'Ay; he'd hev a deal haimabler groom nor what he has now,' observed Dalton; and the joke appeared to him so good, that, being left alone upon the scene, he continued at intervals to take his pipe from his mouth in order to wink at an imaginary audience, and shake luxuriously with a silent, ventral laughter; mentally rehearsing the dialogue from the beginning, that he might recite it with effect in the servants' hall.

When Arthur went up to his dressing-room again after luncheon, it was inevitable that the debate he had had with himself there earlier in the day should flash across his mind; but it was impossible for him now to dwell on the remembrance – impossible to recall the feelings and reflections which had been decisive with him then, any more than to recall the peculiar scent of the air that had freshened him when he first opened his window. The desire to see Hetty had rushed back like an ill-stemmed current; he was amazed himself at the force with which this trivial fancy seemed to grasp him: he was even rather tremulous as he brushed his hair – pooh! it was riding in that breakneck way. It was because he had made a serious affair of an idle matter, by thinking of it as if it were of any consequence. He would amuse himself by seeing Hetty today, and get rid of the whole thing from his mind. It was all Irwine's fault. 'If Irwine had said nothing, I shouldn't have thought half so much of Hetty as of Meg's lameness.' However, it was just the sort of day for lolling in the Hermitage, and he would go and finish Dr Moore's *Zeluco* there before dinner. The Hermitage stood in Fir Tree Grove – the way Hetty was sure to come in walking from the Hall Farm. So nothing could be simpler and more natural: meeting Hetty was a mere circumstance of his walk, not its object.

Arthur's shadow flitted rather faster among the sturdy oaks of the Chase than might have been expected from the shadow of a tired man on a warm afternoon, and it was still scarcely four o'clock when he stood before the tall narrow gate leading into the delicious labyrinthine wood which skirted one side of the Chase, and which was called Fir Tree Grove, not because the firs were many, but because they were few. It was a wood of beeches and limes, with here and there a light, silver-stemmed birch – just the sort of wood most haunted by the nymphs: you see their white sunlit limbs gleaming athwart the boughs, or peeping from behind the smooth-sweeping outline of a tall lime; you hear their soft liquid laughter – but if you look with a too curious sacrilegious eye, they vanish behind the silvery beeches, they make you believe that their voice was only a running brooklet, perhaps they metamorphose themselves into a tawny squirrel that scampers away and mocks you from the topmost bough. It was not a grove with measured grass or rolled gravel for you to tread upon, but with narrow, hollow-shaped, earthy paths, edged with faint dashes of delicate moss-paths which look as if they were made by the free-will of the trees and under-wood, moving reverently aside to look at the tall queen of the white-footed nymphs.

It was along the broadest of these paths that Arthur Donnithorne passed, under an avenue of limes and beeches. It was a still afternoon – the golden light was lingering languidly among the upper boughs, only glancing down here and there on the purple pathway and its edge of faintly sprinkled moss: an afternoon in which destiny disguises her cold awful face behind a hazy radiant veil, encloses us in warm downy wings, and poisons us with violet-scented breath. Arthur strolled along carelessly, with a book under his arm, but not looking on the ground as meditative men are apt to do; his eyes would fix themselves on the distant bend in the road, round which a little figure must surely appear before long. Ah! there she comes: first a bright patch of colour, like a tropic bird among the boughs, then a tripping figure, with a round hat on, and a small basket under her arm; then a deep-blushing, almost frightened, but bright-smiling girl, making her curtsy with a fluttered yet happy glance, as Arthur came up to her. If Arthur had had time to think at all, he would have thought it strange that he should feel fluttered too, be conscious of blushing too – in fact, look and feel as foolish as if he had been taken by surprise instead of meeting just what he expected. Poor things! It was a pity they were not in that golden age of child-hood when they would have stood face to face, eyeing each other with timid liking, then given each other a little butterfly kiss, and toddled off to play together. Arthur would have gone home to his silk-curtained cot, and Hetty to her home-spun pillow, and both would have slept without dreams, and tomorrow would have been a life hardly conscious of a yesterday.

Arthur turned round and walked by Hetty's side without giving a reason. They were alone together for the first time. What an overpowering presence that first privacy is! He actually dared not look at this little butter-maker for the first minute or two. As for Hetty, her feet rested on a cloud, and she was borne along by warm zephyrs; she had forgotten her rose-coloured ribbons; she was no more conscious of her limbs than if her childish soul had passed into a water-lily, resting on a liquid bed, and warmed by the midsummer sunbeams. It may seem a contradiction, but Arthur gathered a certain carelessness and confidence from his timidity: it was an entirely different state of mind from what he had expected in such a meeting with Hetty; and full as he was of vague feeling, there was room, in those moments of silence, for the thought that his previous debates and scruples were needless.

'You are quite right to choose this way of coming to the Chase,' he said at last, looking down at Hetty, 'it is so much prettier as well as shorter than coming by either of the lodges.'

'Yes, sir,' Hetty answered, with a tremulous, almost whispering voice. She didn't know one bit how to speak to a gentleman like Mr Arthur, and her very vanity made her more coy of speech.

'Do you come every week to see Mrs Pomfret?'

'Yes, sir, every Thursday, only when she's got to go out with Miss Donnithorne.'

'And she's teaching you something, is she?'

'Yes, sir, the lace-mending as she learnt abroad, and the stocking-mending – it looks just like the stocking, you can't tell it's been mended; and she teaches me cutting-out too.'

'What, are you going to be a lady's-maid?'

'I should like to be one very much indeed.' Hetty spoke more audibly now, but still rather tremulously; she thought, perhaps she seemed as stupid to Captain Donnithorne as Luke Britton did to her.

'I suppose Mrs Pomfret always expects you at this time?'

'She expects me at four o'clock. I'm rather late today, because my aunt couldn't spare me; but the regular time is four, because that gives us time before Miss Donnithorne's bell rings.'

'Ah, then, I must not keep you now, else I should like to show you the Hermitage. Did you ever see it?'

'No, sir.'

'This is the walk where we turn up to it. But we must not go now. I'll show it you some other time, if you'd like to see it?'

'Yes, please, sir.'

'Do you always come back this way in the evening, or are you afraid to come so lonely a road?'

'Oh no, sir, it's never late; I always set out by eight o'clock, and it's so light now in the evening. My aunt would be angry with me if I didn't get home before nine.'

'Perhaps Craig, the gardener, comes to take care of you?'

A deep blush overspread Hetty's face and neck. 'I'm sure he doesn't; I'm sure he never did; I wouldn't let him; I don't like him,' she said hastily, and the tears of vexation had come so fast, that before she had done speaking a bright drop rolled down her hot cheek. Then she felt ashamed to death that she was crying, and for one long instant her happiness was all gone, But in the next she felt an arm steal round her, and a gentle voice said – 'Why, Hetty, what makes you cry? I didn't mean to vex you. I wouldn't vex you for the world, you little blossom. Come, don't cry; look at me, else I shall think you won't forgive me.'

Arthur had laid his hand on the soft arm that was nearest to him, and was stooping towards Hetty with a look of coaxing entreaty. Hetty lifted her long dewy lashes, and met the eyes that were bent towards her with a sweet, timid, beseeching look. What a space of time those three moments were, while their eyes met and his arms touched her! Love is such a simple thing when we have only one-and-twenty summers and a sweet girl of seventeen trembles under our glance, as if she were a bud first opening her heart with wondering rapture to the morning. Such young unfurrowed souls roll to meet each other like two velvet peaches that touch softly and are at rest; they mingle as easily as two brooklets that ask for nothing but to entwine themselves and ripple with ever-interlacing curves in the leafiest hiding-places. While Arthur gazed into Hetty's dark beseeching eyes, it made no difference to him what sort of English she spoke; and even if hoops and powder had been in fashion, he would very likely not have been sensible just then that Hetty wanted those signs of high breeding.

But they started asunder with beating hearts: something had fallen on the ground with a rattling noise; it was Hetty's basket; all her little workwoman's matters were scattered on the path, some of them showing a capability of rolling to great lengths. There was much to be done in picking up, and not a word was spoken; but when Arthur hung the basket over her arm again the poor child felt a strange difference in his look and manner. He just pressed her hand, and said, with a look and tone that were almost chilling to her – 'I have been hindering you; I must not keep you any longer now. You will be expected at the house. Goodbye.'

Without waiting for her to speak, he turned away from her and hurried back towards the road that led to the Hermitage, leaving Hetty to pursue her way in a strange dream, that seemed to have begun in bewildering delight, and was now passing into contrarieties and sadness. Would he meet her again as she came home? Why had he spoken almost as if he were displeased with her? and then run away so suddenly? She cried, hardly knowing why.

Arthur too was very uneasy, but his feelings were lit up for him by a more distinct conciousness. He hurried to the Hermitage, which stood in the heart of the wood, unlocked the door with a hasty wrench, slammed it after him, pitched *Zeluco* into the most distant corner, and, thrusting his right hand into his pocket, first walked four or five times up and down the scanty length of the little room, and then seated himself on the ottoman in an uncomfortable stiff way, as we often do when we wish not to abandon ourselves to feeling.

He was getting in love with Hetty – that was quite plain. He was ready to pitch everything else – no matter where – for the sake of surrendering himself to this delicious feeling which had just disclosed itself. It was no use blinking the fact now – they would get too fond of each other, if he went on taking notice of her – and what would come of it? He should have to go away in a few weeks, and the poor little thing would be miserable. He *must not* see her alone again; he must keep out of her way. What a fool he was for coming back from Gawaine's!

He got up and threw open the windows to let in the soft breath of the afternoon, and the healthy scent of the firs that made a belt round the Hermitage. The soft air did not help his resolutions, as he leaned out and looked into the leafy distance. But he considered his resolution sufficiently fixed: there was no need to debate with himself any longer. He had made up his mind not to meet Hetty again; and now he might give himself up to thinking how immensely agreeable it would be if circumstances were different – how pleasant it would have been to meet her this evening as she came back, and put his arm round her again and look into her sweet face. He wondered if the dear little thing were thinking of him too – twenty to one she was. How beautiful her eyes were with the tear on their lashes! He would like to satisfy his soul for a day with looking at them, and he must see her again – he must see her, simply to remove any false impression from her mind about his manner to her just now. He would behave in a quiet, kind way to her – just to prevent her from going home with her head full of wrong fancies. Yes, that would be the best thing to do after all.

It was a long while – more than an hour – before Arthur had brought his meditations to this point; but once arrived there, he could stay no longer at the Hermitage. The time must be filled up with movement until he should see Hetty again. And it was already late enough to go and dress for dinner, for his grandfather's dinner hour was six.

13

Evening in the Wood

It happened that Mrs Pomfret had had a slight quarrel with Mrs Best, the housekeeper, on this Thursday morning – a fact which had two consequences highly convenient to Hetty. It caused Mrs Pomfret to have tea sent up to her own room, and it inspired that exemplary lady's-maid with so lively a recollection of former passages in Mrs Best's conduct, and of dialogues in which Mrs Best had decidedly the inferiority as an interlocutor with Mrs Pomfret, that Hetty required no more presence of mind than was demanded for using her needle, and throwing in an occasional 'yes' or 'no.' She would have wanted to put on her hat earlier than usual: only she had told Captain Donnithorne that she usually set out about eight o'clock, and if he should go to the Grove again expecting to see her, and she should be gone! Would he come? Her little butterfly-soul fluttered incessantly between memory and dubious expectation. At last the minute-hand of the old-fashioned brazen-faced timepiece was on the last quarter to eight, and there was every reason for its being time to get ready for departure. Even Mrs Pomfret's preoccupied mind did not prevent her from noticing what looked like a new flush of beauty in the little thing as she tied on her hat before the looking-glass.

'That child gets prettier and prettier every day, I do believe,' was her inward comment. 'The more's the pity. She'll get neither a place nor a husband any the sooner for it. Sober well-to-do men don't like such pretty wives. When I was a girl, I was more admired than if I had been so very pretty. However, she's reason to be grateful to me for teaching her something to get her bread with, better than farmhouse work. They always told me I was good-natured – and that's the truth, and to my hurt, too, else there's them in this house that wouldn't be here now to lord it over me in the housekeeper's room.'

Hetty walked hastily across the short space of pleasure-ground which she had to traverse, dreading to meet Mr Craig, to whom she could hardly have spoken civilly. How relieved she was when she had got safely under the oaks and among the fern of the Chase! Even then she was as ready to be startled as the deer that leaped away at her approach. She thought nothing of the evening light that lay gently in the grassy alleys between the fern, and made the beauty of their living green more visible than it had been in the overpowering flood of noon: she thought of nothing that was present. She only saw something that was possible: Mr Arthur Donnithorne coming to meet her again along the Fir Tree Grove. That was the foreground of Hetty's picture; behind it lay a bright hazy something – days that were not to be as the other days of her life had been. It was as if she had been wooed by a river-god, who might any time take her to his wondrous halls below a watery heaven. There was no knowing what would come, since this strange entrancing delight had come. If a chest full of lace and satin and jewels had been sent her from some unknown source, how could she but have thought that her whole lot was going to change, and that tomorrow some still more bewildering joy would befall her? Hetty had never read a novel; if she had ever seen one, I think the words would have been too hard for her; how then could she find a shape for her expectations? They were as formless as the sweet languid odours of the garden at the Chase, which had floated past her as she walked by the gate.

She is at another gate now – that leading into Fir Tree Grove. She enters the wood, where it is already twilight, and at every step she takes, the fear at her heart becomes colder. If he should not come! Oh how dreary it was – the thought of going out at the other end of the wood, into the unsheltered road, without having seen him. She reaches the first turning towards the Hermitage, walking slowly – he is not there. She hates the leveret that runs across the path: she hates everything that is not what she longs for. She walks on, happy whenever she is coming to a bend in the road, for perhaps he is behind it. No. She is beginning to cry: her heart has swelled so, the tears stand in her eyes; she gives one great sob, while the corners of her mouth quiver, and the tears roll down.

She doesn't know that there is another turning to the Hermitage, that she is close against it, and that Arthur Donnithorne is only a few yards from her, full of one thought, and a thought of which she only is the object. He is going to see Hetty again: that is the longing which has been growing through the last three hours to a feverish thirst. Not, of course, to speak in the caressing way into which he had unguardedly fallen before dinner, but to set things right with her by a kindness which would have the air of friendly civility, and prevent her from running away with wrong notions about their mutual relation.

If Hetty had known he was there, she would not have cried; and it would have been better, for then Arthur would perhaps have behaved as wisely as he had intended. As it was, she started when he appeared at the end of the side-alley, and looked up at him with two great drops rolling down her cheeks. What else could he do but speak to her in a soft, soothing tone, as if she were a bright-eyed spaniel with a thorn in her foot?

'Has something frightened you, Hetty? Have you seen anything in the wood? Don't be frightened – I'll take care of you now.'

Hetty was blushing so, she didn't know whether she was happy or miserable. To be crying again – what did gentlemen think of girls who cried in that way? She felt unable even to say 'no,' but could only look away from him, and wipe the tears from her cheek. Not before a great drop had fallen on her rose-coloured strings: she knew that quite well.

'Come, be cheerful again. Smile at me, and tell me what's the matter. Come, tell me.'

Hetty turned her head towards him, whispered, 'I thought you wouldn't come,' and slowly got courage to lift her eyes to him. That look was too much: he must have had eyes of Egyptian granite not to look too lovingly in return.

'You little frightened bird! little tearful rose! silly pet! You won't cry again, now I'm with you, will you?'

Ah, he doesn't know in the least what he is saying. This is not what he meant to say. His arm is stealing round the waist again, it is tightening its clasp; he is bending his face nearer and nearer to the round cheek, his lips are meeting those pouting child-lips, and for a long moment time has vanished. He may be a shepherd in Arcadia for aught he knows, he may be the first youth kissing the first maiden, he may be Eros himself, sipping the lips of Psyche – it is all one.

There was no speaking for minutes after. They walked along with beating hearts till they came within sight of the gate at the end of the wood. Then they looked at each other, not quite as they had looked before, for in their eyes there was the memory of a kiss.

But already something bitter had begun to mingle itself with the fountain of sweets: already Arthur was uncomfortable. He took his arm from Hetty's waist, and said – 'Here we are, almost at the end of the Grove. I wonder how late it is,' he added, pulling out his watch. 'Twenty minutes past eight – but my watch is too fast. However, I'd better not go any further now. Trot along quickly with your little feet, and get home safely. Goodbye.'

He took her hand, and looked at her half sadly, half with a constrained smile. Hetty's eyes seemed to beseech him not to go away yet; but he patted her cheek and said 'Goodbye' again. She was obliged to turn away from him, and go on.

As for Arthur, he rushed back through the wood, as if he wanted to put a wide space between himself and Hetty. He would not go to the Hermitage again, he remembered how he had debated with himself there before dinner, and it had all come to nothing – worse than nothing. He walked right on into the Chase, glad to get out of the Grove, which surely was haunted by his evil genius. Those beeches and smooth limes – there was something enervating in the very sight of them; but the strong knotted old oaks had no bending languor in them – the sight of them would give a man some energy. Arthur lost himself among the narrow openings in the fern, winding about without seeking any issue, till the twilight deepened almost to night under the great boughs, and the hare looked black as it darted across his path.

He was feeling much more strongly than he had done in the morning: it was as if his horse had wheeled round from a leap, and dared to dispute his mastery. He was dissatisfied with himself, irritated, mortified. He no sooner fixed his mind on the probable consequences of giving way to the emotions which had stolen over him today – of continuing to notice Hetty, of allowing himself any opportunity for such slight caresses as he had been betrayed into already – than he refused to believe such a future possible for himself. To flirt with Hetty was a very different affair from flirting with a pretty girl of his own station: that was understood to be an amusement on both sides; or, if it became serious, there was no obstacle to marriage. But this little thing would be spoken ill of directly, if she happened to be seen walking with him; and then those excellent people, the Poysers, to whom a good name was as precious as if they had the best blood in the land in their veins – he should hate himself if he made a scandal of that sort, on the estate that was to be his own someday, and among tenants by whom he liked, above all, to be respected. He could no more believe that he should so fall in his own esteem than that he should break both his legs and go on crutches all the rest of his life. He couldn't imagine himself in that position; it was too odious, too unlike him.

And even if no one knew anything about it, they might get too fond of each other, and then there could be nothing but the misery of parting, after all. No gentleman, out of a ballad, could marry a farmer's niece. There must be an end to the whole thing at once. It was too foolish.

And yet he had been so determined this morning, before he went to Gawaine's; and while he was there something had taken hold of him and made him gallop back. It seemed, he couldn't quite depend on his own resolution, as he had thought he could: he almost wished his arm would get painful again, and then he should think of nothing but the comfort it would be to get rid of the pain. There was no knowing what impulse might seize him tomorrow, in this confounded place, where there was nothing to occupy him imperiously through the live-long day. What could he do to secure himself from any more of this folly?

There was but one resource. He would go and tell Irwine – tell him every-thing. The mere act of telling it would make it seem trivial; the temptation would vanish, as the charm of fond words vanishes when one repeats them to the indifferent. In every way it would help him, to tell Irwine. He would ride to Broxton Rectory the first thing after breakfast tomorrow.

Arthur had no sooner come to this determination than he began to think which of the paths would lead him home, and made as short a walk thither as he could. He felt sure he should sleep now: he had had enough to tire him, and there was no more need for him to think.

14

The Return Home

While that parting in the wood was happening, there was a parting in the cottage too, and Lisbeth had stood with Adam at the door, straining her aged eyes to get the last glimpse of Seth and Dinah, as they mounted the opposite slope.

'Eh, I'm loath to see the last on her,' she said to Adam, as they turned into the house again. 'I'd ha' been willin' t' ha' her about me till I died and went to lie by my old man. She'd make it easier dyin' – she spakes so gentle an' moves about so still. I could be fast sure that pictur was drawed for her i' thy new Bible – th' angel a sittin' on the big stone by the grave. Eh, I wouldna mind ha'in' a daughter like that; but nobody ne'er marries them as is good for aught.'

'Well, mother, I hope thee wilt have her for a daughter; for Seth's got a liking for her, and I hope she'll get a liking for Seth in time.'

'Where's th' use o' talkin' a-that'n? She caresna for Seth. She's goin' away twenty mile aff. How's she to get a likin' for him, I'd like to know? No more nor the cake 'ull come wi'out the leaven. Thy figurin' books might ha' told thee better nor that, I should think, else thee mightst as well read the commin print, as Seth allays does.'

'Nay, mother,' said Adam, laughing, 'the figures tell us a fine deal, and we couldn't go far without 'em, but they don't tell us about folks's feelings. It's a nicer job to calculate them. But Seth's as good-hearted a lad as ever handled a tool, and plenty o' sense, and good-looking too; and he's got the same way o' thinking as Dinah. He deserves to win her, though there's no denying she's a rare bit o' workmanship. You don't see such women turned off the wheel every day.'

'Eh, thee't allays stick up for thy brother. Thee'st been just the same, e'er sin' ye war little uns together. Thee wart allays for halving iverything wi' him. But what's Seth got to do with marryin', as is on'y three-an'-twenty? He'd more need to learn an' lay by sixpence. An' as for his desarving her – she's two 'ear older nor Seth: she's pretty near as old as thee. But that's the way; folks mun allays choose by contrairies, as if they must be sorted like the pork – a bit o' good meat wi' a bit o' offal.'

To the feminine mind in some of its moods, all things that might be, receive a temporary charm from comparison with what is; and since Adam did not want to marry Dinah himself, Lisbeth felt rather peevish on that score – as peevish as she would have been if he *had* wanted to marry her, and so shut himself out from Mary Burge and the partnership as effectually as by marrying Hetty.

It was more than half-past eight when Adam and his mother were talking in this way, so that when, about ten minutes later, Hetty reached the turning of the lane that led to the farmyard gate, she saw Dinah and Seth approaching it from the opposite direction, and waited for them to come up to her. They, too, like Hetty, had lingered a little in their walk, for Dinah was trying to speak words of comfort and strength to Seth in these parting moments. But when they saw Hetty, they paused and shook hands: Seth turned homewards, and Dinah came on alone.

'Seth Bede would have come and spoken to you, my dear,' she said, as she reached Hetty, "but he's very full of trouble tonight.'

Hetty answered with a dimpled smile, as if she did not quite know what had been said; and it made a strange contrast to see that sparkling self-engrossed loveliness looked at by Dinah's calm pitying face, with its open glance which told that her heart lived in no cherished secrets of its own, but in feelings which it longed to share with all the world. Hetty liked Dinah as well as she had ever liked any woman; how was it possible to feel otherwise towards one who always put in a kind word for her when her aunt was finding fault, and who was always ready to take Totty off her hands – little tiresome Totty, that was made such a pet of by everyone, and that Hetty could see no interest in at all? Dinah had never said anything disapproving or reproachful to Hetty during her whole visit to the Hall Farm; she had talked to her a great deal in a serious way, but Hetty didn't mind that much, for she never listened: whatever Dinah might say, she almost always stroked Hetty's cheek after it, and wanted to do some mending for her. Dinah was a riddle to her; Hetty looked at her much in the same way as one might imagine a little perching bird that could only flutter from bough to bough, to look at the swoop of the swallow or the mounting of the lark; but she did not care to solve such riddles, any more than she cared to know what was meant by the pictures in the *Pilgrim's Progress*, or in the old folio Bible that Marty and Tommy always plagued her about on a Sunday.

Dinah took her hand now and drew it under her own arm.

'You look very happy tonight, dear child,' she said. 'I shall think of you often when I'm at Snowfield, and see your face before me as it is now. It's a strange thing – sometimes when I'm quite alone, sitting in my room with my eyes closed, or walking over the hills, the people I've seen and known, if it's only been for a few days, are brought before me, and I hear their voices and see them look and move almost plainer than I ever did when they were really with me so as I could touch them. And then my heart is drawn out towards them, and I feel their lot as if it was my own, and I take comfort in spreading it before the Lord and resting in His love, on their behalf as well as my own. And so I feel sure you will come before me.'

She paused a moment, but Hetty said nothing.

'It has been a very precious time to me,' Dinah went on, 'last night and today – seeing two such good sons as Adam and Seth Bede. They are so tender and thoughtful for their aged mother. And she has been telling me what Adam has done, for these many years, to help his father and his brother; it's wonderful what a spirit of wisdom and knowledge he has, and how he's ready to use it all in behalf of them that are feeble. And I'm sure he has a loving spirit too. I've noticed it often among my own people around Snowfield, that the strong, skilful men are often the gentlest to the women and children; and it's pretty to see 'em carrying the little babies as if they were no heavier than little birds. And the babies always seem to like the strong arm best. I feel sure it would be so with Adam Bede. Don't you think so, Hetty?'

'Yes,' said Hetty, abstractedly, for her mind had been all the while in the wood, and she would have found it difficult to say what she was assenting to. Dinah saw she was not inclined to talk, but there would not have been time to say much more, for they were now at the yard-gate.

The still twilight, with its dying western red, and its few faint struggling stars, rested on the farmyard, where there was not a sound to be heard but the stamping of the cart-horses in the stable. It was about twenty minutes after sunset: the fowls were all gone to roost, and the bulldog lay stretched on the straw outside his kennel, with the black-and-tan terrier by his side, when the falling-to of the gate disturbed them, and set them barking, like good officials, before they had any distinct knowledge of the reason.

The barking had its effect in the house, for, as Dinah and Hetty approached, the doorway was filled by a portly figure, with a ruddy black-eyed face, which bore in it the possibility of looking extremely acute, and occasionally contemptuous, on market-days, but had now a predominant after-supper expression of hearty good nature. It is well known that great scholars who have shown the most pitiless acerbity in their criticism of other men's scholarship, have yet been of a relenting and indulgent temper in private life; and I have heard of a learned man meekly rocking the twins in the cradle with his left hand, while with his right he inflicted the most lacerating sarcasms on an opponent who had betrayed a brutal ignorance of Hebrew. Weaknesses and errors must be forgiven – alas! they are not alien to us – but the man who takes the wrong side on the momentous subject of the Hebrew points must be treated as the enemy of his race. There was the same sort of antithetic mixture in Martin Poyser: he was of so excellent a disposition that he had been kinder and more respectful than ever to his old father since he had made a deed of gift of all his property, and no man judged his neighbours more charitably on all personal matters; but for a farmer, like Luke Britton, for example, whose fallows were not well cleaned, who didn't know the rudiments of hedging and ditching, and showed but a small share of judgement in the purchase of winter stock, Martin Poyser was as hard and implacable as the north-east wind. Luke Britton could not make a remark, even on the weather, but Martin Poyser detected in it a taint of that unsoundness and general ignorance which was palpable in all his farming operations. He hated to see the fellow lift the pewter pint to his mouth in the bar of the Royal George on market-day, and the mere sight of him on the other side of the road brought a severe and critical expression into his black eyes, as different as possible from the fatherly glance he bent on his two nieces as they approached the door. Mr Poyser had smoked his evening pipe, and now held his hands in his pockets, as the only resource of a man who continues to sit up after the day's business is done.

'Why, lasses, ye're rather late tonight,' he said, when they reached the little gate leading into the causeway. 'The mother's begun to fidget about you, an' she's got the little un ill. An' how did you leave the old woman Bede, Dinah? Is she much down about the old man? He'd been but a poor bargain to her this five year.'

'She's been greatly distressed for the loss of him,' said Dinah; 'but she's seemed more comforted today. Her son Adam's been at home all day, working at his father's coffin, and she loves to have him at home. She's been talking about him to me almost all the day. She has a loving heart, though she's sorely given to fret and be fearful. I wish she had a surer trust to comfort her in her old age.'

'Adam's sure enough,' said Mr Poyser, misunderstanding Dinah's wish. 'There's no fear but he'll yield well i' the threshing. He's not one o' them as is all straw and no grain. I'll be bond for him any day, as he'll be a good son to the last. Did he say he'd be coming to see us soon? But come in, come in,' he added, making way for them; 'I hadn't need keep y' out any longer.'

The tall buildings round the yard shut out a good deal of the sky, but the large window let in abundant light to show every corner of the house-place.

Mrs Poyser, seated in the rocking-chair, which had been brought out of the 'right-hand parlour,' was trying to soothe Totty to sleep. But Totty was not disposed to sleep; and when her cousins entered, she raised herself up, and showed a pair of flushed cheeks, which looked fatter than ever now they were defined by the edge of her linen nightcap.

In the large wicker-bottomed armchair in the left-hand chimney-nook sat old Martin Poyser, a hale but shrunken and bleached image of his portly black-haired son – his head hanging forward a little, and his elbows pushed backwards so as to allow the whole of his forearm to rest on the arm of the chair. His blue hand kerchief was spread over his knees, as was usual indoors, when it was not hanging over his head; and he sat watching what went forward with the quiet outward glance of healthy old age, which, disengaged from any interest in an inward drama, spies out pins upon the floor, follows one's minutest motions with an unexpectant purposeless tenacity, watches the flickering of the flame or the sun-gleams on the wall, counts the quarries on the floor, watches even the hand of the clock, and pleases itself with detecting a rhythm in the tick.

'What a time o' night this is to come home, Hetty,' said Mrs Poyser. 'Look at the clock, do; why, it's going on for half-past nine, and I've sent the gells to bed this half-hour, and late enough too; when they've got to get up at half after four, and the mowers' bottles to fill, and the baking; and here's this blessed child wi' the fever for what I know, and as wakeful as if it was dinner-time, and nobody to help me to give her the physic but your uncle, and fine work there's been, and half of it spilt on her nightgown – it's well if she's swallowed more nor 'ull make her worse istead o' better. But folks as have no mind to be o' use have allays the luck to be out o' the road when there's anything to be done.'

'I did set out before eight, aunt,' said Hetty, in a pettish tone, with a slight toss of her head. 'But this clock's so much before the clock at the Chase, there's no telling what time it'll be when I get here.'

'What! you'd be wanting the clock set by gentlefolk's time, would you? an' sit up burnin' candle, an' lie a-bed wi' the sun a-bakin' you like a cowcumber i' the frame? The clock hasn't been put forrard for the first time today, I reckon.'

The fact was, Hetty had really forgotten the difference of the clocks when she told Captain Donnithorne that she set out at eight, and this, with her lingering pace, had made her nearly half an hour later than usual. But here her aunt's attention was diverted from this tender subject by Totty, who, perceiving at length that the arrival of her cousins was not likely to bring anything satisfactory to her in particular, began to cry, 'Munny, munny,' in an explosive manner.

'Well, then, my pet, mother's got her, mother won't leave her; Totty be a good dilling, and go to sleep now,' said Mrs Poyser, leaning back and rocking the chair, while she tried to make Totty nestle against her. But Totty only cried louder, and said 'Don't yock!' so the mother, with that wondrous patience which love gives to the quickest temperament, sat up again, and pressed her cheek against the linen nightcap and kissed it, and forgot to scold Hetty any longer.

'Come, Hetty,' said Martin Poyser, in a conciliatory tone, 'go and get your supper i' the pantry, as the things are all put away; an' then you can come an' take the little un while your aunt undresses herself, for she won't lie down in bed without her mother. An' I reckon you could eat a bit, Dinah, for they don't keep much of a house down there.'

'No, thank you, uncle,' said Dinah; 'I ate a good meal before I came away, for Mrs Bede would make a kettle-cake for me.'

'I don't want any supper,' said Hetty, taking off her hat. 'I can hold Totty now, if aunt wants me.'

'Why, what nonsense that is to talk!' said Mrs Poyser. 'Do you think you can live wi'out eatin', an' nourish your inside wi' stickin' red ribbons on your head? Go an' get your supper this minute, child; there's a nice bit o' cold pudding i' the safe – just what you're fond of.'

Hetty complied silently by going towards the pantry, and Mrs Poyser went on speaking to Dinah.

'Sit down, my dear, an' look as if you knowed what it was to make yourself a bit comfortable i' the world. I warrant the old woman was glad to see you, since you stayed so long.'

'She seemed to like having me there at last; but her sons say she doesn't like young women about her commonly; and I thought just at first she was almost angry with me for going.'

'Eh, it's a poor look-out when th' ould foulks doesna like the young uns,' said old Martin, bending his head down lower, and seeming to trace the pattern of the quarries with his eye.

'Ay, it's ill livin' in a hen-roost for them as doesn't like fleas,' said Mrs Poyser. 'We've all had our turn at bein' young, I reckon, be't good luck or ill.'

'But she must learn to 'commodate herself to young women,' said Mr Poyser, 'for it isn't to be counted on as Adam and Seth 'ull keep bachelors for the next ten year to please their mother. That 'ud be unreasonable. It isn't right for old nor young nayther to make a bargain all o' their own side. What's good for one's good all round i' the long-run. I'm no friend to young fellows a-marrying afore they know the difference atween a crab an' a apple; but they may wait o'er long.'

'To be sure,' said Mrs Poyser; 'if you go past your dinnertime, there'll be little relish o' your meat. You turn it o'er an' o'er wi' your fork, an' don't eat it after all. You find faut wi' your meat, an' the faut's all i' your own stomach.'

Hetty now came back from the pantry, and said, 'I can take Totty now, aunt, if you like.'

'Come, Rachel,' said Mr Poyser, as his wife seemed to hesitate, seeing that Totty was at last nestling quietly, 'thee'dst better let Hetty carry her upstairs, while thee tak'st thy things off. Thee't tired. It's time thee wast in bed. Thee't bring on the pain in thy side again.'

'Well, she may hold her if the child 'ull go to her,' said Mrs Poyser.

Hetty went close to the rocking-chair, and stood without her usual smile, and without any attempt to entice Totty, simply waiting for her aunt to give the child into her hands.

'Wilt go to cousin Hetty, my dilling, while mother gets ready to go to bed? Then Totty shall go into mother's bed, and sleep there all night.'

Before her mother had done speaking, Totty had given her answer in an unmistakable manner, by knitting her brow, setting her tiny teeth against her under-lip, and leaning forward to slap Hetty on the arm with her utmost force. Then, without speaking, she nestled to her mother again.

'Hey, hey,' said Mr Poyser, while Hetty stood without moving, 'not go to cousin Hetty? That's like a babby: Totty's a little woman, an' not a babby.'

'It's no use trying to persuade her,' said Mrs Poyser 'she allays takes against Hetty when she isn't well. Happen she'll go to Dinah.'

Dinah, having taken off her bonnet and shawl, had hitherto kept quietly seated in the background, not liking to thrust herself between Hetty and what was considered Hetty's proper work. But now she came forward, and, putting out her arms, said, 'Come, Totty, come and let Dinah carry her upstairs along with mother: poor, poor mother! she's so tired – she wants to go to bed.'

Totty turned her face towards Dinah, and looked at her an instant, then lifted herself up, put out her little arms, and let Dinah lift her from her mother's lap. Hetty turned away without any sign of ill-humour, and taking her hat from the table, stood waiting with an air of indifference, to see if she should be told to do anything else.

'You may make the door fast now, Poyser; Alick's been come in this long while,' said Mrs Poyser, rising with an appearance of relief from her low chair. 'Get me the matches down, Hetty, for I must have the rush light burning i' my room. Come, father.'

The heavy wooden bolts began to roll in the house doors, and old Martin prepared to move, by gathering up his blue handkerchief, and reaching his bright knobbed walnut-tree stick from the corner. Mrs Poyser then led the way out of the kitchen, followed by the grandfather, and Dinah with Totty in her arms – all going to bed by twilight, like the birds. Mrs Poyser, on her way, peeped into the room where her two boys lay, just to see their ruddy round cheeks on the pillow, and to hear for a moment their light regular breathing.

'Come, Hetty, get to bed,' said Mr Poyser, in a soothing tone, as he himself turned to go upstairs. 'You didna mean to be late, I'll be bound, but your aunt's been worried today. Good-night, my wench, good-night.'

15

The Two Bedchambers

Hetty and Dinah both slept in the second storey, in rooms adjoining each other, meagrely-furnished rooms, with no blinds to shut out the light, which was now beginning to gather new strength from the rising of the moon – more than enough strength to enable Hetty to move about and undress with perfect comfort. She could see quite well the pegs in the old painted linen-press on which she hung her hat and gown; she could see the head of every pin on her red cloth pincushion; she could see a reflection of herself in the old-fashioned looking-glass, quite as distinct as was needful, considering that she had only to brush her hair and put on her nightcap. A queer old looking-glass! Hetty got into an ill-temper with it almost every time she dressed. It had been considered a handsome glass in its day, and had probably been bought into the Poyser family a quarter of a century before, at a sale of genteel household furniture. Even now an auctioneer could say something for it: it had a great deal of tarnished gilding about it; it had a firm mahogany base, well supplied with drawers, which opened with a decided jerk, and sent the contents leaping out from the farthest corners, without giving you the trouble of reaching them; above all, it had a brass candle-socket on each side, which would give it an aristocratic air to the very last. But Hetty objected to it because it had numerous dim blotches sprinkled over the mirror, which no rubbing would remove, and because, instead of swinging backwards and forwards, it was fixed in an upright position, so that she could only get one good view of her head and neck, and that was to be had only by sitting down on a low chair before her dressing-table. And the dressing-table was no dressing-table at all, but a small old chest of drawers, the most awkward thing in the world to sit down before, for the big brass handles quite hurt her knees, and she couldn't get near the glass at all comfortably. But devout worshippers never allow inconveniences to prevent them from performing their religious rites, and Hetty this evening was more bent on her peculiar form of worship than usual.

Having taken off her gown and white kerchief, she drew a key from the large pocket that hung outside her petticoat, and, unlocking one of the lower drawers in the chest, reached from it two short bits of wax candle – secretly bought at Treddleston – and stuck them in the two brass sockets. Then she drew forth a bundle of matches, and lighted the candles; and last of all, a small red-framed shilling looking-glass, without blotches. It was into this small glass that she chose to look first after seating herself. She looked into it, smiling, and turning her head on one side, for a minute, then laid it down and took out her brush and comb from an upper drawer. She was going to let down her hair, and make herself look like that picture of a lady in Miss Lydia Donnithorne's dressing-room. It was soon done, and the dark hyacinthine curves fell on her neck. It was not heavy, massive, merely rippling hair, but soft and silken, running at every opportunity into delicate rings. But she pushed it all backward to look like the picture, and form a dark curtain, throwing into relief her round white neck. Then she put down her brush and comb, and looked at herself, folding her arms before her, still like the picture. Even the old mottled glass couldn't help sending back a lovely image, none the less lovely because Hetty's stays were not of white satin – such as I feel sure heroines must generally wear – but of a dark greenish cotton texture.

O yes! she was very pretty: Captain Donnithorne thought so. Prettier than anybody about Hayslope – prettier than any of the ladies she had ever seen visiting at the Chase – indeed it seemed fine ladies were rather old and ugly – and prettier than Miss Bacon, the miller's daughter, who was called the beauty of Treddleston. And Hetty looked at herself tonight with quite a different sensation from what she had ever felt before; there was an invisible spectator whose eye rested on her like morning on the flowers. His soft voice was saying over and over again those pretty things she had heard in the wood; his arm was round her, and the delicate rose-scent of his hair was with her still. The vainest woman is never thoroughly conscious of her own beauty till she is loved by the man who sets her own passion vibrating in return.

But Hetty seemed to have made up her mind that something was wanting, for she got up and reached an old black lace scarf out of the linen-press, and a pair of large earrings out of the sacred drawer from which she had taken her candles. It was an old old scarf, full of rents, but it would make a becoming border round her shoulders, and set off the whiteness of her upper arm. And she would take out the little earrings she had in her ears – oh, how her aunt had scolded her for having her ears bored! – and put in those large ones: they were but coloured glass and gilding; but if you didn't know what they were made of, they looked just as well as what the ladies wore. And so she sat down again, with the large earrings in her ears, and the black lace scarf adjusted round her shoulders. She looked down at her arms: no arms could be prettier down to a little way below the elbow – they were white and plump, and dimpled to match her cheeks; but towards the wrist, she thought with vexation that they were coarsened by butter-making, and other work that ladies never did.

Captain Donnithorne couldn't like her to go on doing work: he would like to see her in nice clothes, and thin shoes and white stockings, perhaps with silk clocks to them; for he must love her very much – no one else had ever put his arm round her and kissed her in that way. He would want to marry her, and make a lady of her; she could hardly dare to shape the thought – yet how else could it be? Marry her quite secretly, as Mr James, the doctor's assistant, married the doctor's niece, and nobody ever found it out for a long while after, and then it was of no use to be angry. The doctor had told her aunt all about it in Hetty's hearing. She didn't know how it would be, but it was quite plain the old squire could never be told anything about it, for Hetty was ready to faint with awe and fright if she came across him at the Chase. He might have been earth-born, for what she knew: it had never entered her mind that he had been young like other men; he had always been the old squire at whom everybody was frightened. Oh, it was impossible to think how it would be! But Captain Donnithorne would know; he was a great gentleman, and could have his way in everything, and could buy everything he liked. And nothing could be as it had been again: perhaps someday she should be a grand lady, and ride in her coach, and dress for dinner in a brocaded silk, with feathers in her hair, and her dress sweeping the ground, like Miss Lydia and Lady Dacey, when she saw them going into the dining-room one evening, as she peeped through the little round window in the lobby; only she should not be old and ugly like Miss Lydia, or all the same thickness like Lady Dacey, but very pretty, with her hair done in a great many different ways, and sometimes in a pink dress, and sometimes in a white one – she didn't know which she liked best; and Mary Burge and everybody would perhaps see her going out in her carriage – or rather, they would hear of it: it was impossible to imagine these things happening at Hayslope in sight of her aunt. At the thought of all this splendour, Hetty got up from her chair, and in doing so caught the little red-framed glass with the edge of her scarf, so that it fell with a bang on the floor; but she was too eagerly occupied with her vision to care about picking it up; and after a momentary start, began to pace with a pigeon-like stateliness backwards and forwards along her room, in her coloured stays and coloured skirt, and the old black lace scarf round her shoulders, and the great glass earrings in her ears.

How pretty the little puss looks in that odd dress! It would be the easiest folly in the world to fall in love with her: there is such a sweet baby-like roundness about her face and figure; the delicate dark rings of hair lie so charmingly about her ears and neck; her great dark eyes with their long eyelashes touch one so strangely, as if an imprisoned frisky sprite looked out of them.

Ah, what a prize the man gets who wins a sweet bride like Hetty! How the men envy him who come to the wedding breakfast, and see her hanging on his arm in her white lace and orange blossoms. The dear, young, round, soft, flexible thing! Her heart must be just as soft, her temper just as free from angles, her character just as pliant. If anything ever goes wrong, it must be the husband's fault there: he can make her what he likes – that is plain. And the lover himself thinks so too: the little darling is so fond of him, her little vanities are so bewitching, he wouldn't consent to her being a bit wiser; those kittenlike glances and movements are just what one wants to make one's hearth a paradise. Every man under such circumstances is conscious of being a great physiognomist. Nature, he knows, has a language of her own, which she uses with strict veracity, and he considers himself an adept in the language. Nature has written out his bride's character for him in those exquisite lines of cheek and lip and chin, in those eyelids delicate as petals, in those long lashes curled like the stamen of a flower, in the dark liquid depths of those wonderful eyes. How she will dote on her children! She is almost a child herself, and the little pink round things will hang about her like florets round the central flower; and the husband will look on, smiling benignly, able, whenever he chooses, to withdraw into the sanctuary of his wisdom, towards which his sweet wife will look reverently, and never lift the curtain. It is a marriage such as they made in the golden age, when the men were all wise and majestic, and the women all lovely and loving.

It was very much in this way that our friend Adam Bede thought about Hetty; only he put his thoughts into different words. If ever she behaved with cold vanity towards him, he said to himself, it is only because she doesn't love me well enough; and he was sure that her love, whenever she gave it, would be the most precious thing a man could possess on earth. Before you despise Adam as deficient in penetration, pray ask yourself if you were ever predisposed to believe evil of any pretty woman – if you ever *could*, without hard head-breaking demonstration, believe evil of the one supremely pretty woman who has bewitched you. No: people who love downy peaches are apt not to think of the stone, and sometimes jar their teeth terribly against it.

Arthur Donnithorne, too, had the same sort of notion about Hetty, so far as he had thought of her nature at all. He felt sure she was a dear, affectionate, good little thing. The man who awakes the wondering tremulous passion of a young girl always thinks her affectionate; and if he chances to look forward to future years, probably imagines himself being virtuously tender to her, because the poor thing is so clingingly fond of him. God made these dear women so – and it is a convenient arrangement in case of sickness.

After all, I believe the wisest of us must be beguiled in this way sometimes, and must think both better and worse of people than they deserve. Nature has her language, and she is not unveracious; but we don't know all the intricacies of her syntax just yet, and in a hasty reading we may happen to extract the very opposite of her real meaning. Long dark eyelashes, now: what can be more exquisite? I find it impossible not to expect some depth of soul behind a deep grey eye with a long dark eyelash, in spite of an experience which has shown me that they may go along with deceit, peculation, and stupidity. But if, in the reaction of disgust, I have betaken myself to a fishy eye, there has been a surprising similarity of result. One begins to suspect at length that there is no direct correlation between eyelashes and morals; or else, that the eyelashes express the disposition of the fair one's grandmother, which is on the whole less important to us.

No eyelashes could be more beautiful than Hetty's; and now, while she walks with her pigeon-like stateliness along the room and looks down on her shoulders bordered by the old black lace the dark fringe shows to perfection on her pink cheek. They are but dim ill-defined pictures that her narrow bit of an imagination can make of the future; but of every picture she is the central figure in fine clothes; Captain Donnithorne is very close to her, putting his arm round her, perhaps kissing her, and everybody else is admiring and envying her – especially Mary Burge, whose new print dress looks very contemptible by the side of Hetty's resplendent toilette. Does any sweet or sad memory mingle with this dream of the future – any loving thought of her second parents – of the children she had helped to tend – of any youthful companion, any pet animal, any relic of her own childhood even? Not one. There are some plants that have hardly any roots: you may tear them from their native nook of rock or wall, and just lay them over your ornamental flowerpot, and they blossom none the worse. Hetty could have cast all her past life behind her, and never cared to be reminded of it again. I think she had no feeling at all towards the old house, and did not like the Jacob's Ladder and the long row of hollyhocks in the garden better than other flowers – perhaps not so well. It was wonderful how little she seemed to care about waiting on her uncle, who had been a good father to her: she hardly ever remembered to reach him his pipe at the right time without being told, unless a visitor happened to be there, who would have a better opportunity of seeing her as she walked across the hearth. Hetty did not understand how anybody could be very fond of middle-aged people. And as for those tiresome children, Marty and Tommy and Totty, they had been the very nuisance of her life – as bad as buzzing insects that will come teasing you on a hot day when you want to be quiet. Marty, the eldest, was a baby when she first came to the farm, for the children born before him had died, and so Hetty had had them all three, one after the other, toddling by her side in the meadow, or playing about her on wet days in the half-empty rooms of the large old house. The boys were out of hand now, but Totty was still a day-long plague, worse than either of the others had been, because there was more fuss made about her. And there was no end to the making and mending of clothes. Hetty would have been glad to hear that she should never see a child again; they were worse than the nasty little lambs that the shepherd was always bringing in to be taken special care of in lambing time; for the lambs were got rid of sooner or later. As for the young chickens and turkeys, Hetty would have hated the very word 'hatching,' if her aunt had not bribed her to attend to the young poultry by promising her the proceeds of one out of every brood. The round downy chicks peeping out from under their mother's wing never touched Hetty with any pleasure; that was not the sort of prettiness she cared about, but she did care about the prettiness of the new things she would buy for herself at Treddleston fair with the money they fetched. And yet she looked so dimpled, so charming, as she stooped down to put the soaked bread under the hencoop, that you must have been a very acute personage indeed to suspect her of that hardness. Molly, the housemaid, with a turn-up nose and a protuberant jaw, was really a tender-hearted girl, and, as Mrs Poyser said, a jewel to look after the poultry; but her stolid face showed nothing of this maternal delight, any more than a brown earthenware pitcher will show the light of the lamp within it.

It is generally a feminine eye that first detects the moral deficiencies hidden under the 'dear deceit' of beauty: so it is not surprising that Mrs Poyser, with her keenness and abundant opportunity for observation, should have formed a tolerably fair estimate of what might be expected from Hetty in the way of feeling, and in moments of indignation she had sometimes spoken with great openness on the subject to her husband.

'She's no better than a peacock, as 'ud strut about on the wall, and spread its tail when the sun shone if all the folks i' the parish was dying: there's nothing seems to give her a turn i' th' inside, not even when we thought Totty had tumbled into the pit. To think o' that dear cherub! And we found her wi' her little shoes stuck i' the mud and crying fit to break her heart by the far horse-pit. But Hetty niver minded it, I could see, though she's been at the nussin' o' the child ever since it was a babby. It's my belief her heart's as hard as a pebble.'

'Nay, nay,' said Mr Poyser, 'thee mustn't judge Hetty too hard. Them young gells are like th' unripe grain; they'll make good meal by and by, but they're squashy as yet. Thee't see Hetty'll be all right when she's got a good husband and children of her own.'

'I don't want to be hard upo' the gell. She's got cliver fingers of her own, and can be useful enough when she likes, and I should miss her wi' the butter, for she's got a cool hand. An' let be what may, I'd strive to do my part by a niece o' yours, an' *that* I've done: for I've taught her everything as belongs to a house, an' I've told her her duty often enough, though, God knows, I've no breath to spare, an' that catchin' pain comes on dreadful by times. Wi' them three gells in the house I'd need have twice the strength, to keep 'em up to their work. It's like having roast-meat at three fires; as soon as you've basted one, another's burnin'.'

Hetty stood sufficiently in awe of her aunt to be anxious to conceal from her so much of her vanity as could be hidden without too great a sacrifice. She could not resist spending her money in bits of finery which Mrs Poyser disapproved; but she would have been ready to die with shame, vexation, and fright, if her aunt had this moment opened the door, and seen her with her bits of candle lighted, and strutting about decked in her scarf and earrings. To prevent such a surprise, she always bolted her door, and she had not forgotten to do so tonight. It was well: for there now came a light tap, and Hetty, with a leaping heart, rushed to blow out the candles and throw them into the drawer. She dared not stay to take out her earrings, but she threw off her scarf, and let it fall on the floor, before the light tap came again. We shall know how it was that the light tap came, if we leave Hetty for a short time, and return to Dinah, at the moment when she had delivered Totty to her mother's arms, and was come upstairs to her bedroom, adjoining Hetty's.

Dinah delighted in her bedroom window. Being on the second storey of that tall house, it gave her a wide view over the fields. The thickness of the wall formed a broad step about a yard below the window, where she could place her chair.

And now the first thing she did, on entering her room, was to seat herself in this chair, and look out on the peaceful fields beyond which the large moon was rising, just above the hedgerow elms. She liked the pasture best where the milch cows were lying, and next to that the meadow where the grass was half mown, and lay in silvered sweeping lines. Her heart was very full, for there was to be only one more night on which she would look out on those fields for a long time to come; but she thought little of leaving the mere scene, for, to her, bleak Snowfield had just as many charms: she thought of all the dear people whom she had learned to care for among these peaceful fields, and who would now have a place in her loving remembrance for ever. She thought of the struggles and the weariness that might lie before them in the rest of their life's journey, when she would be away from them, and know nothing of what was befalling them; and the pressure of this thought soon became too strong for her to enjoy the unresponding stillness of the moonlit fields. She closed her eyes, that she might feel more intensely the presence of a Love and Sympathy deeper and more tender than was breathed from the earth and sky. That was often Dinah's mode of praying in solitude. Simply to close her eyes, and to feel herself enclosed by the Divine Presence; then gradually her fears, her yearning anxieties for others, melted away like ice-crystals in a warm ocean. She had sat in this way perfectly still, with her hands crossed on her lap, and the pale light resting on her calm face, for at least ten minutes, when she was startled by a loud sound, apparently of something falling in Hetty's room. But like all sounds that fall on our ears in a state of abstraction, it had no distinct character, but was simply loud and startling, so that she felt uncertain whether she had interpreted it rightly. She rose and listened, but all was quiet afterwards, and she reflected that Hetty might merely have knocked something down in getting into bed. She began slowly to undress; but now, owing to the suggestions of this sound, her thoughts became concentrated on Hetty: that sweet young thing, with life and all its trials before her – the solemn daily duties of the wife and mother – and her mind so unprepared for them all; bent merely on little foolish selfish pleasures, like a child hugging its toys in the beginning of a long toilsome journey, in which it will have to bear hunger and cold and unsheltered darkness. Dinah felt a double care for Hetty, because she shared Seth's anxious interest in his brother's lot, and she had not come to the conclusion that Hetty did not love Adam well enough to marry him. She saw too clearly the absence of any warm, self-devoting love in Hetty's nature, to regard the coldness of her behaviour towards Adam as any indication that he was not the man she would like to have for a husband. And this blank in Hetty's nature, instead of exciting Dinah's dislike, only touched her with a deeper pity: the lovely face and form affected her as beauty always affects a pure and tender mind, free from selfish jealousies: it was an excellent divine gift, that gave a deeper pathos to the need, the sin, the sorrow with which it was mingled, as the canker in a lily-white bud is more grievous to behold than in a common pot-herb.

By the time Dinah had undressed and put on her nightgown, this feeling about Hetty had gathered a painful intensity; her imagination had created a thorny thicket of sin and sorrow, in which she saw the poor thing struggling torn and bleeding, looking with tears for rescue and finding none. It was in this way that Dinah's imagination and sympathy acted and reacted habitually, each heightening the other. She felt a deep longing to go now and pour into Hetty's ear all the words of tender warning and appeal that rushed into her mind. But perhaps Hetty was already asleep. Dinah put her ear to the partition, and heard still some slight noises, which convinced her that Hetty was not yet in bed. Still she hesitated; she was not quite certain of a divine direction; the voice that told her to go to Hetty seemed no stronger than the other voice which said that Hetty was weary, and that going to her now in an unseasonable moment would only tend to close her heart more obstinately. Dinah was not satisfied without a more unmistakable guidance than those inward voices. There was light enough for her, if she opened her Bible, to discern the text sufficiently to know what it would say to her. She knew the physiognomy of every page, and could tell on what book she opened, sometimes on what chapter, without seeing title or number. It was a small thick Bible, worn quite round at the edges. Dinah laid it sideways on the window ledge, where the light was strongest, and then opened it with her forefinger. The first words she looked at were those at the top of the left-hand page: 'And they all wept sore, and fell on Paul's neck and kissed him.' That was enough for Dinah; she had opened on that memorable parting at Ephesus, when Paul had felt bound to open his heart in a last exhortation and warning. She hesitated no longer, but, opening her own door gently, went and tapped at Hetty's. We know she had to tap twice, because Hetty had to put out her candles and throw off her black lace scarf; but after the second tap the door was opened immediately. Dinah said, 'Will you let me come in, Hetty?' and Hetty, without speaking, for she was confused and vexed, opened the door wider and let her in.

What a strange contrast the two figures made! Visible enough in that mingled twilight and moonlight. Hetty, her cheeks flushed and her eyes glistening from her imaginary drama, her beautiful neck and arms bare, her hair hanging in a curly tangle down her back, and the baubles in her ears. Dinah, covered with her long white dress, her pale face full of subdued emotion, almost like a lovely corpse into which the soul has returned charged with sublimer secrets and a sublimer love. They were nearly of the same height; Dinah evidently a little the taller as she put her arm round Hetty's waist, and kissed her forehead.

'I knew you were not in bed, my dear,' she said, in her sweet clear voice, which was irritating to Hetty, mingling with her own peevish vexation like music with jangling chains, 'for I heard you moving; and I longed to speak to you again tonight, for it is the last but one that I shall be here, and we don't know what may happen tomorrow to keep us apart. Shall I sit down with you while you do up your hair?'

'Oh yes,' said Hetty, hastily turning round and reaching the second chair in the room, glad that Dinah looked as if she did not notice her earrings.

Dinah sat down, and Hetty began to brush together her hair before twisting it up, doing it with that air of excessive indifference which belongs to confused self-consciousness. But the expression of Dinah's eyes gradually relieved her; they seemed unobservant of all details.

'Dear Hetty,' she said, 'it has been borne in upon my mind tonight that you may someday be in trouble – trouble is appointed for us all here below, and there comes a time when we need more comfort and help than the things of this life can give. I want to tell you that if ever you are in trouble, and need a friend that will always feel for you and love you, you have got that friend in Dinah Morris at Snowfield; and if you come to her, or send for her, she'll never forget this night and the words she is speaking to you now. Will you remember it, Hetty?'

'Yes,' said Hetty, rather frightened. 'But why should you think I shall be in trouble? Do you know of anything?'

Hetty had seated herself as she tied on her cap, and now Dinah leaned forwards and took her hands as she answered – 'Because, dear, trouble comes to us all in this life: we set our hearts on things which it isn't God's will for us to have, and then we go sorrowing; the people we love are taken from us, and we can joy in nothing because they are not with us; sickness comes, and we faint under the burden of our feeble bodies; we go astray and do wrong, and bring ourselves into trouble with our fellow-men. There is no man or woman born into this world to whom some of these trials do not fall, and so I feel that some of them must happen to you; and I desire for you, that while you are young you should seek for strength from your Heavenly Father, that you may have a support which will not fail you in the evil day.'

Dinah paused and released Hetty's hands, that she might not hinder her. Hetty sat quite still; she felt no response within herself to Dinah's anxious affection; but Dinah's words, uttered with solemn pathetic distinctness, affected her with a chill fear. Her flush had died away almost to paleness; she had the timidity of a luxurious pleasure-seeking nature; which shrinks from the hint of pain. Dinah saw the effect, and her tender anxious pleading became the more earnest, till Hetty, full of a vague fear that something evil was sometime to befall her, began to cry.

It is our habit to say that while the lower nature can never understand the higher, the higher nature commands a complete view of the lower. But I think the higher nature has to learn this comprehension, as we learn the art of vision, by a good deal of hard experience, often with bruises and gashes incurred in taking things up by the wrong end, and fancying our space wider than it is. Dinah had never seen Hetty affected in this way before, and, with her usual benignant hopefulness, she trusted it was the stirring of a divine impulse. She kissed the sobbing thing, and began to cry with her for grateful joy. But Hetty was simply in that excitable state of mind in which there is no calculating what turn the feelings may take from one moment to another, and for the first time she became irritated under Dinah's caress. She pushed her away impatiently, and said, with a childish sobbing voice – 'Don't talk to me so, Dinah. Why do you come to frighten me? I've never done anything to you. Why can't you let me be?'

Poor Dinah felt a pang. She was too wise to persist, and only said mildly, 'Yes, my dear, you're tired; I won't hinder you any longer. Make haste and get into bed. Good-night.'

She went out of the room almost as quietly and quickly as if she had been a ghost; but once by the side of her own bed, she threw herself on her knees, and poured out in deep silence all the passionate pity that filled her heart.

As for Hetty, she was soon in the wood again – her waking dreams being merged in a sleeping life scarcely more fragmentary and confused.

16

Links

Arthur Donnithorne, you remember, is under an engagement with himself to go and see Mr Irwine this Friday morning, and he is awake and dressing so early, that he determines to go before breakfast, instead of after. The Rector, he knows, breakfasts alone at half-past nine, the ladies of the family having a different breakfast-hour; Arthur will have an early ride over the hill and breakfast with him. One can say everything best over a meal.

The progress of civilisation has made a breakfast or a dinner an easy and cheerful substitute for more troublesome and disagreeable ceremonies. We take a less gloomy view of our errors now our father confessor listens to us over his egg and coffee. We are more distinctly conscious that rude penances are out of the question for gentlemen in an enlightened age, and that mortal sin is not incompatible with an appetite for muffins. An assault on our pockets, which in more barbarous times would have been made in the brusque form of a pistol-shot, is quite a well-bred and smiling procedure now it has become a request for a loan thrown in as an easy parenthesis between the second and third glasses of claret.

Still, there was this advantage in the old rigid forms, that they committed you to the fulfilment of a resolution by some outward deed: when you have put your mouth to one end of a hole in a stone wall, and are aware that there is an expectant ear at the other end, you are more likely to say what you came out with the intention of saying, than if you were seated with your legs in an easy attitude under the mahogany, with a companion who will have no reason to be surprised if you have nothing particular to say.

However, Arthur Donnithorne, as he winds among the pleasant lanes on horseback in the morning sunshine, has a sincere determination to open his heart to the Rector, and the swirling sound of the scythe as he passes by the meadow is all the pleasanter to him because of this honest purpose. He is glad to see the promise of settled weather now, for getting in the hay, about which the farmers have been fearful; and there is something so healthful in the sharing of a joy that is general and not merely personal, that this thought about the hay-harvest reacts on his state of mind, and makes his resolution seem an easier matter. A man about town might perhaps consider that these influences were not to be felt out of a child's storybook; but when you are among the fields and hedgerows, it is impossible to maintain a consistent superiority to simple natural pleasures.

Arthur had passed the village of Hayslope, and was approaching the Broxton side of the hill, when, at a turning in the road, he saw a figure about a hundred yards before him which it was impossible to mistake for anyone else than Adam Bede, even if there had been no grey, tailless shepherd-dog at his heels. He was striding along at his usual rapid pace; and Arthur pushed on his horse to over-take him for he retained too much of his boyish feeling for Adam to miss an opportunity of chatting with him. I will not say that his love for that good fellow did not owe some of its force to the love of patronage: our friend Arthur liked to do everything that was handsome, and to have his handsome deeds recognised.

Adam looked round as he heard the quickening clatter of the horse's heels, and waited for the horseman, lifting his paper cap from his head with a bright smile of recognition. Next to his own brother Seth, Adam would have done more for Arthur Donnithorne than for any other young man in the world. There was hardly anything he would not rather have lost than the two-feet ruler which he always carried in his pocket; it was Arthur's present, bought with his pocket money when he was a fair-haired lad of eleven, and when he had profited so well by Adam's lessons in carpentering and turning, as to embarrass every female in the house with gifts of superfluous thread-reels and round boxes. Adam had quite a pride in the little squire in those early days, and the feeling had only become slightly modified as the fair-haired lad had grown into the whiskered young man. Adam, I confess, was very susceptible to the influence of rank, and quite ready to give an extra amount of respect to everyone who had more advantages than himself, not being a philosopher, or a proletaire with democratic ideas, but simply a stout-limbed clever carpenter with a large fund of reverence in his nature, which inclined him to admit all established claims unless he saw very clear grounds for questioning them. He had no theories about setting the world to rights, but he saw there was a great deal of damage done by building with ill-seasoned timber – by ignorant men in fine clothes making plans for outhouses and workshops and the like, without knowing the bearings of things – by slovenly joiners' work, and by hasty contracts that could never be fulfilled without ruining somebody; and he resolved, for his part, to set his face against such doings. On these points he would have maintained his opinion against the largest landed proprietor in Loamshire or Stonyshire either; but he felt that beyond these it would be better for him to defer to people who were more knowing than himself. He saw as plainly as possible how ill the woods on the estate were managed, and the shameful state of the farm-buildings; and if old squire Donnithorne had asked him the effect of this mis-management, he would have spoken his opinion without flinching, but the impulse to a respectful demeanour towards a 'gentleman' would have been strong within him all the while. The word 'gentleman' had a spell for Adam, and, as he often said, he 'couldn't abide a fellow who thought he made himself fine by being coxy to's betters.' I must remind you again that Adam had the blood of the peasant in his veins, and that since he was in his prime half a century ago, you must expect some of his characteristics to be obsolete.

Towards the young squire this instinctive reverence of Adam's was assisted by boyish memories and personal regard; so you may imagine that he thought far more of Arthur's good qualities, and attached far more value to very slight actions of his, than if they had been the qualities and actions of a common workman like himself. He felt sure it would be a fine day for everybody about Hayslope when the young squire came into the estate – such a generous open-hearted disposition as he had, and an 'uncommon' notion about improvements and repairs, considering he was only just coming of age. Thus there was both respect and affection in the smile with which he raised his paper cap as Arthur Donnithorne rode up.

'Well, Adam, how are you?' said Arthur, holding out his hand. He never shook hands with any of the farmers, and Adam felt the honour keenly. 'I could swear to your back a long way off. It's just the same back, only broader, as when you used to carry me on it. Do you remember?'

'Ay, sir, I remember. It 'ud be a poor look-out if folks didn't remember what they did and said when they were lads. We should think no more about old friends than we do about new uns, then.'

'You're going to Broxton, I suppose?' said Arthur, putting his horse on at a slow pace while Adam walked by his side. 'Are you going to the Rectory?'

'No, sir, I'm going to see about Bradwell's barn. They're afraid of the roof pushing the walls out; and I'm going to see what can be done with it before we send the stuff and the workmen.'

'Why, Burge trusts almost everything to you now, Adam, doesn't he? I should think he will make you his partner soon. He will, if he's wise.'

'Nay, sir, I don't see as he'd be much the better off for that. A foreman, if he's got a conscience, and delights in his work, will do his business as well as if he was a partner. I wouldn't give a penny for a man as 'ud drive a nail in slack because he didn't get extra pay for it.'

'I know that, Adam; I know you work for him as well as if you were working for yourself. But you would have more power than you have now, and could turn the business to better account perhaps. The old man must give up his business some time, and he has no son; I suppose he'll want a son-in-law who can take to it. But he has rather grasping fingers of his own, I fancy: I dare say he wants a man who can put some money into the business. If I were not as poor as a rat, I would gladly invest some money in that way, for the sake of having you settled on the estate. I'm sure I should profit by it in the end. And perhaps I shall be better off in a year or two. I shall have a larger allowance now I'm of age; and when I've paid off a debt or two, I shall be able to look about me.'

'You're very good to say so, sir, and I'm not unthankful. But' – Adam continued, in a decided tone – 'I shouldn't like to make any offers to Mr Burge, or t' have any made for me. I see no clear road to a partnership. If he should ever want to dispose of the business, that 'ud be a different matter. I should be glad of some money at a fair interest then, for I feel sure I conld pay it off in time.'

'Very well, Adam,' said Arthur, remembering what Mr Irwine had said about a probable hitch in the love-making between Adam and Mary Burge, 'we'll say no more about it at present. When is your father to be buried?'

'On Sunday, sir; Mr Irwine's coming earlier on purpose. I shall be glad when it's over, for I think my mother 'ull perhaps get easier then. It cuts one sadly to see the grief of old people; they've no way o' working it off; and the new spring brings no new shoots out on the withered tree.'

'Ah, you've had a good deal of trouble and vexation in your life, Adam. I don't think you've ever been harebrained and light-hearted, like other youngsters. You've always had some care on your mind.'

'Why, yes, sir; but that's nothing to make a fuss about. If we're men, and have men's feelings, I reckon we must have men's troubles. We can't be like the birds, as fly from their nest as soon as they've got their wings, and never know their kin when they see 'em, and get a fresh lot every year. I've had enough to be thankful for: I've allays had health and strength and brains to give me a delight in my work; and I count it a great thing as I've had Bartle Massey's night-school to go to. He's helped me to knowledge I could never ha' got by myself.'

'What a rare fellow you are, Adam!' said Arthur, after a pause, in which he had looked musingly at the big fellow walking by his side. 'I could hit out better than most men at Oxford, and yet I believe you would knock me into next week if I were to have a battle with you.'

'God forbid I should ever do that, sir,' said Adam, looking round at Arthur, and smiling. 'I used to fight for fun; but I've never done that since I was the cause o' poor Gil Tranter being laid up for a fortnight. I'll never fight any man again, only when he behaves like a scoundrel. If you get hold of a chap that's got no shame nor conscience to stop him, you must try what you can do by bunging his eyes up.'

Arthur did not laugh, for he was preoccupied with some thought that made him say presently – 'I should think now, Adam, you never have any struggles within yourself. I fancy you would master a wish that you had made up your mind it was not quite right to indulge, as easily as you would knock down a drunken fellow who was quarrelsome with you. I mean, you are never shilly-shally, first making up your mind that you won't do a thing, and then doing it after all?'

'Well,' said Adam, slowly, after a moment's hesitation – 'no. I don't remember ever being see-saw in that way, when I'd made my mind up, as you say, that a thing was wrong. It takes the taste out o' my mouth for things, when I know I should have a heavy conscience after 'em. I've seen pretty clear, ever since I could cast up a sum, as you can never do what's wrong without breeding sin and trouble more than you can ever see. It's like a bit o' bad workmanship – you never see th' end o' the mischief it'll do. And it's a poor look-out to come into the world to make your fellow-creatures worse off instead o' better. But there's a difference between the things folks call wrong. I'm not for making a sin of every little fool's trick, or bit o' nonsense anybody may be let into, like some o' them dissenters. And a man may have two minds whether it isn't worth while to get a bruise or two for the sake of a bit o' fun. But it isn't my way to be see-saw about anything: I think my fault lies th' other way. When I've said a thing, if it's only to myself, it's hard for me to go back.'

'Yes, that's just what I expected of you,' said Arthur. 'You've got an iron will, as well as an iron arm. But however strong a man's resolution may be, it costs him something to carry it out, now and then. We may determine not to gather any cherries, and keep our hands sturdily in our pockets, but we can't prevent our mouths from watering.'

'That's true, sir; but there's nothing like settling with ourselves as there's a deal we must do without i' this life. It's no use looking on life as if it was Treddles'on fair, where folks only go to see shows and get fairings. If we do, we shall find it different. But where's the use o' me talking to you, sir? You know better than I do.'

'I'm not so sure of that, Adam. You've had four or five years of experience more than I've had, and I think your life has been a better school to you than college has been to me.'

'Why, sir, you seem to think o' college something like what Bartle Massey does. He says college mostly makes people like bladders – just good for nothing but t' hold the stuff as is poured into 'em. But he's got a tongue like a sharp blade, Bartle has: it never touches anything but it cuts. Here's the turning, sir. I must bid you good-morning, as you're going to the Rectory.'

'Goodbye, Adam, goodbye.'

Arthur gave his horse to the groom at the Rectory gate, and walked along the gravel towards the door which opened on the garden. He knew that the Rector always breakfasted in his study, and the study lay on the left hand of this door, opposite the dining-room. It was a small low room, belonging to the old part of the house – dark with the sombre covers of the books that lined the walls; yet it looked very cheery this morning as Arthur reached the open window. For the morning sun fell aslant on the great glass globe with goldfish in it, which stood on a scagliola pillar in front of the ready-spread bachelor breakfast-table, and by the side of this breakfast-table was a group which would have made any room enticing. In the crimson damask easy-chair sat Mr Irwine, with that radiant freshness which he always had when he came from his morning toilet; his finely-formed plump white hand was playing along Juno's brown curly back; and close to Juno's tail, which was wagging with calm matronly pleasure, the two brown pups were rolling over each other in an ecstatic duet of worrying noises. On a cushion a little removed sat Pug, with the air of a maiden lady, who looked on these familiarities as animal weaknesses, which she made as little show as possible of observing. On the table, at Mr Irwine's elbow, lay the first volume of the Foulis Aeschylus, which Arthur knew well by sight; and the silver coffee-pot, which Carroll was bringing in, sent forth a fragrant steam which completed the delights of a bachelor breakfast.

'Hallo, Arthur, that's a good fellow! You're just in time,' said Mr Irwine, as Arthur paused and stepped in over the low window-sill. 'Carroll, we shall want more coffee and eggs and haven't you got some cold fowl for us to eat with that ham? Why, this is like old days, Arthur; you haven't been to breakfast with me these five years.'

'It was a tempting morning for a ride before breakfast,' said Arthur; 'and I used to like breakfasting with you so when I was reading with you. My grandfather is always a few degrees colder at breakfast than at any other hour in the day. I think his morning bath doesn't agree with him.'

Arthur was anxious not to imply that he came with any special purpose. He had no sooner found himself in Mr Irwine's presence than the confidence which he had thought quite easy before, suddenly appeared the most difficult thing in the world to him, and at the very moment of shaking hands he saw his purpose in quite a new light. How could he make Irwine understand his position unless he told him those little scenes in the wood; and how could he tell them without looking like a fool? And then his weakness in coming back from Gawaine's, and doing the very opposite of what he intended! Irwine would think him a shilly-shally fellow ever after. However, it must come out in an unpremeditated way; the conversation might lead up to it.

'I like breakfast-time better than any other moment in the day,' said Mr Irwine. 'No dust has settled on one's mind then, and it presents a clear mirror to the rays of things. I always have a favourite book by me at breakfast, and I enjoy the bits I pick up then so much, that regularly every morning it seems to me as if I should certainly become studious again. But presently Dent brings up a poor fellow who has killed a hare, and when I've got through my 'justicing,' as Carroll calls it, I'm inclined for a ride round the glebe, and on my way back I meet with the master of the workhouse, who has got a long story of a mutinous pauper to tell me; and so the day goes on, and I'm always the same lazy fellow before evening sets in. Besides, one wants the stimulus of sympathy, and I have never had that since poor D'Oyley left Treddleston. If you had stuck to your books well, you rascal, I should have had a pleasanter prospect before me. But scholar-ship doesn't run in your family blood.'

'No indeed. It's well if I can remember a little inapplicable Latin to adorn my maiden speech in Parliament six or seven years hence. *Cras ingens iterabimus aequor*, and a few shreds of that sort, will perhaps stick to me, and I shall arrange my opinions so as to introduce them. But I don't think a knowledge of the classics is a pressing want to a country gentleman; as far as I can see, he'd much better have a knowledge of manures. I've been reading your friend Arthur Young's books lately, and there's nothing I should like better than to carry out some of his ideas in putting the farmers on a better management of their land; and, as he says, making what was a wild country, all of the same dark hue, bright and variegated with corn and cattle. My grandfather will never let me have any power while he lives; but there's nothing I should like better than to undertake the Stonyshire side of the estate – it's in a dismal condition – and set improvements on foot, and gallop about from one place to another and overlook them. I should like to know all the labourers, and see them touching their hats to me with a look of goodwill.'

'Bravo, Arthur! a man who has no feeling for the classics couldn't make a better apology for coming into the world than by increasing the quantity of food to maintain scholars – and rectors who appreciate scholars. And whenever you enter on your career of model landlord may I be there to see. You'll want a portly rector to complete the picture, and take his tithe of all the respect and honour you get by your hard work. Only don't set your heart too strongly on the goodwill you are to get in consequence. I'm not sure that men are the fondest of those who try to be useful to them. You know Gawaine has got the curses of the whole neighbourhood upon him about that enclosure. You must make it quite clear to your mind which you are most bent upon, old boy – popularity or usefulness – else you may happen to miss both.'

'Oh! Gawaine is harsh in his manners; he doesn't make himself personally agreeable to his tenants, I don't believe there's anything you can't prevail on people to do with kindness. For my part, I couldn't live in a neighbourhood where I was not respected and beloved; and it's very pleasant to go among the tenants here, they seem all so well inclined to me. I suppose it seems only the other day to them since I was a little lad, riding on a pony about as big as a sheep. And if fair allowances were made to them, and their buildings attended to, one could persuade them to farm on a better plan, stupid as they are.'

'Then mind you fall in love in the right place, and don't get a wife who will drain your purse and make you niggardly in spite of yourself. My mother and I have a little discussion about you sometimes: she says, "I'll never risk a single prophecy on Arthur until I see the woman he falls in love with." She thinks your lady-love will rule you as the moon rules the tides. But I feel bound to stand up for you, as my pupil, you know; and I maintain that you're not of that watery quality. So mind you don't disgrace my judgement.'

Arthur winced under this speech, for keen old Mrs Irwine's opinion about him had the disagreeable effect of a sinister omen. This, to be sure, was only another reason for persevering in his intention, and getting an additional security against himself. Nevertheless, at this point in the conversation, he was conscious of increased disinclination to tell his story about Hetty. He was of an impressible nature, and lived a great deal in other people's opinions and feelings concerning himself; and the mere fact that he was in the presence of an intimate friend, who had not the slightest notion that he had had any such serious internal struggle as he came to confide, rather shook his own belief in the seriousness of the struggle. It was not, after all, a thing to make a fuss about; and what could Irwine do for him that he could not do for himself? He would go to Eagledale in spite of Meg's lameness – go on Rattler, and let Pym follow as well as he could on the old hack. That was his thought as he sugared his coffee; but the next minute, as he was lifting the cup to his lips, he remembered how thoroughly he had made up his mind last night to tell Irwine. No! he would not be vacillating again – he would do what he had meant to do, this time. So it would be well not to let the personal tone of the conversation altogether drop. If they went to quite indifferent topics, his difficulty would be heightened. It had required no noticeable pause for this rush and rebound of feeling, before he answered – 'But I think it is hardly an argument against a man's general strength of character, that he should be apt to be mastered by love. A fine constitution doesn't insure one against smallpox or any other of those inevitable diseases. A man may be very firm in other matters, and yet be under a sort of witchery from a woman.'

'Yes; but there's this difference between love and smallpox, or bewitchment either – that if you detect the disease at an early stage and try change of air, there is every chance of complete escape without any further development of symptoms. And there are certain alternative doses which a man may administer to himself by keeping unpleasant consequences before his mind: this gives you a sort of smoked glass through which you may look at the resplendent fair one and discern her true outline; though I'm afraid, by the by, the smoked glass is apt to be missing just at the moment it is most wanted. I dare say, now, even a man fortified with a knowledge of the classics might be lured into an imprudent marriage, in spite of the warning given him by the chorus in the Prometheus.'

The smile that flitted across Arthur's face was a faint one, and instead of following Mr Irwine's playful lead, he said, quite seriously – 'Yes, that's the worst of it. It's a desperately vexatious thing, that after all one's reflections and quiet determinations, we should be ruled by moods that one can't calculate on beforehand. I don't think a man ought to be blamed so much if he is betrayed into doing things in that way, in spite of his resolutions.'

'Ah, but the moods lie in his nature, my boy, just as much as his reflections did, and more. A man can never do anything at variance with his own nature. He carries within him the germ of his most exceptional action; and if we wise people make eminent fools of ourselves on any particular occasion, we must endure the legitimate conclusion that we carry a few grains of folly to our ounce of wisdom.'

'Well, but one may be betrayed into doing things by a combination of circumstances, which one might never have done otherwise.'

'Why, yes, a man can't very well steal a banknote unless the banknote lies within convenient reach; but he won't make us think him an honest man because he begins to howl at the banknote for falling in his way.'

'But surely you don't think a man who struggles against a temptation into which he falls at last, as bad as the man who never struggles at all?'

'No, certainly; I pity him in proportion to his struggles, for they foreshadow the inward suffering which is the worst form of Nemesis. Consequences are unpitying. Our deeds carry their terrible consequences, quite apart from any fluctuations that went before – consequences that are hardly ever confined to ourselves. And it is best to fix our minds on that certainty, instead of considering what may be the elements of excuse for us. But I never knew you so inclined for moral discussion, Arthur? Is it some danger of your own that you are considering in this philosophical, general way?'

In asking this question, Mr Irwine pushed his plate away, threw himself back in his chair, and looked straight at Arthur. He really suspected that Arthur wanted to tell him something, and thought of smoothing the way for him by this direct question. But he was mistaken. Brought suddenly and involuntarily to the brink of confession, Arthur shrank back, and felt less disposed towards it than ever. The conversation had taken a more serious tone than he had intended – it would quite mislead Irwine – he would imagine there was a deep passion for Hetty, while there was no such thing. He was conscious of colouring, and was annoyed at his boyishness.

'Oh no, no danger,' he said as indifferently as he could. 'I don't know that I am more liable to irresolution than other people; only there are little incidents now and then that set one speculating on what might happen in the future.'

Was there a motive at work under this strange reluctance of Arthur's which had a sort of backstairs influence, not admitted to himself? Our mental business is carried on much in the same way as the business of the state: a great deal of hard work is done by agents who are not acknowledged. In a piece of machinery, too, I believe there is often a small unnoticeable wheel which has a great deal to do with the motion of the large obvious ones. Possibly there was some such unrecognised agent secretly busy in Arthur's mind at this moment – possibly it was the fear lest he might hereafter find the fact of having made a confession to the Rector a serious annoyance, in case he should *not* be able quite to carry out his good resolutions? I dare not assert that it was not so. The human soul is a very complex thing.

The idea of Hetty had just crossed Mr Irwine's mind as he looked enquiringly at Arthur, but his disclaiming, indifferent answer confirmed the thought which had quickly followed – that there could be nothing serious in that direction. There was no probability that Arthur ever saw her except at church, and at her own home under the eye of Mrs Poyser; and the hint he had given Arthur about her the other day had no more serious meaning than to prevent him from noticing her so as to rouse the little chit's vanity, and in this way perturb the rustic drama of her life. Arthur would soon join his regiment, and be far away: no, there could be no danger in that quarter, even if Arthur's character had not been a strong security against it. His honest, patronising pride in the goodwill and respect of everybody about him was a safeguard even against foolish romance, still more against a lower kind of folly. If there had been anything special on Arthur's mind in the previous conversation, it was clear he was not inclined to enter into details, and Mr Irwine was too delicate to imply even a friendly curiosity. He perceived a change of subject would be welcome, and said – 'By the way, Arthur, at your colonel's birthday fête there were some transparencies that made a great effect in honour of Britannia, and Pitt, and the Loamshire Militia, and, above all, the "generous youth', the hero of the day. Don't you think you should get up something of the same sort to astonish our weak minds?'

The opportunity was gone. While Arthur was hesitating, the rope to which he might have clung had drifted away – he must trust now to his own swimming.

In ten minutes from that time, Mr Irwine was called for on business, and Arthur, bidding him goodbye, mounted his horse again with a sense of dissatisfaction, which he tried to quell by determining to set off for Eagledale without an hour's delay.

BOOK SECOND

17

In Which the Story Pauses a Little

'This Rector of Broxton is little better than a pagan!' I hear one of my readers exclaim. 'How much more edifying it would have been if you had made him give Arthur some truly spiritual advice. You might have put into his mouth the most beautiful things – quite as good as reading a sermon.'

Certainly I could, if I held it the highest vocation of the novelist to represent things as they never have been and never will be. Then, of course, I might refashion life and character entirely after my own liking; I might select the most unexceptionable type of clergyman, and put my own admirable opinions into his mouth on all occasions. But it happens, on the contrary, that my strongest effort is to avoid any such arbitrary picture, and to give a faithful account of men and things as they have mirrored themselves in my mind. The mirror is doubtless defective; the outlines will sometimes be disturbed, the reflection faint or confused; but I feel as much bound to tell you as precisely as I can what that reflection is, as if I were in the witness-box narrating my experience on oath.

Sixty years ago – it is a long time, so no wonder things have changed – all clergymen were not zealous; indeed there is reason to believe that the number of zealous clergymen was small, and it is probable that if one among the small minority had owned the livings of Broxton and Hayslope in the year 1799, you would have liked him no better than you like Mr Irwine. Ten to one, you would have thought him a tasteless, indiscreet, methodistical man. It is so very rarely that facts hit that nice medium required by our own enlightened opinions and refined taste! Perhaps you will say, 'Do improve the facts a little, then; make them more accordant with those correct views which it is our privilege to possess. The world is not just what we like; do touch it up with a tasteful pencil, and make believe it is not quite such a mixed entangled affair. Let all people who hold unexceptionable opinions act unexceptionably. Let your most faulty characters always be on the wrong side, and your virtuous ones on the right. Then we shall see at a glance whom we are to condemn, and whom we are to approve. Then we shall be able to admire, without the slightest disturbance of our prepossessions: we shall hate and despise with that true ruminant relish which belongs to undoubting confidence.'

But, my good friend, what will you do then with your fellow-parishioner who opposes your husband in the vestry? – with your newly-appointed vicar, whose style of preaching you find painfully below that of his regretted predecessor? – with the honest servant who worries your soul with her one failing? – with your neighbour, Mrs Green, who was really kind to you in your last illness, but has said several ill-natured things about you since your convalescence? – nay, with your excellent husband himself, who has other irritating habits besides that of not wiping his shoes? These fellow-mortals, every one, must be accepted as they are: you can neither straighten their noses, nor brighten their wit, nor rectify their dispositions; and it is these people – amongst whom your life is passed – that it is needful you should tolerate, pity, and love: it is these more or less ugly, stupid, inconsistent people, whose movements of goodness you should be able to admire – for whom you should cherish all possible hopes, all possible patience. And I would not, even if I had the choice, be the clever novelist who could create a world so much better than this, in which we get up in the morning to do our daily work, that you would be likely to turn a harder, colder eye on the dusty streets and the common green fields – on the real breathing men and women, who can be chilled by your indifference or injured by your prejudice; who can be cheered and helped onward by your fellow-feeling, your forbearance, your outspoken, brave justice.

So I am content to tell my simple story, without trying to make things seem better than they were; dreading nothing, indeed, but falsity, which, in spite of one's best efforts, there is reason to dread. Falsehood is so easy, truth so difficult. The pencil is conscious of a delightful facility in drawing a griffin – the longer the claws, and the larger the wings, the better; but that marvellous facility which we mistook for genius is apt to forsake us when we want to draw a real unexaggerated lion. Examine your words well, and you will find that even when you have no motive to be false, it is a very hard thing to say the exact truth, even about your own immediate feelings – much harder than to say something fine about them which is *not* the exact truth.

It is for this rare, precious quality of truthfulness that I delight in many Dutch paintings, which lofty-minded people despise. I find a source of delicious sympathy in these faithful pictures of a monotonous homely existence, which has been the fate of so many more among my fellow-mortals than a life of pomp or of absolute indigence, of tragic suffering or of world-stirring actions. I turn, without shrinking, from cloud-borne angels, from prophets, sibyls, and heroic warriors, to an old woman bending over her flowerpot, or eating her solitary dinner, while the noonday light, softened perhaps by a screen of leaves, falls on her mob-cap, and just touches the rim of her spinning-wheel, and her stone jug, and all those cheap common things which are the precious necessaries of life to her – or I turn to that village wedding, kept between four brown walls, where an awkward bridegroom opens the dance with a high-shouldered, broad-faced bride, while elderly and middle-aged friends look on, with very irregular noses and lips, and probably with quart pots in their hands, but with an expression of unmistakable contentment and goodwill. 'Foh!' says my idealistic friend, 'what vulgar details! What good is there in taking all these pains to give an exact likeness of old women and clowns? What a low phase of life! – what clumsy, ugly people!'

But bless us, things may be lovable that are not altogether handsome, I hope? I am not at all sure that the majority of the human race have not been ugly, and even among those 'lords of their kind,' the British, squat figures, ill-shapen nostrils, and dingy complexions are not startling exceptions. Yet there is a great deal of family love amongst us. I have a friend or two whose class of features is such that the Apollo curl on the summit of their brows would be decidedly trying; yet to my certain knowledge tender hearts have beaten for them, and their miniatures – flattering, but still not lovely – are kissed in secret by motherly lips. I have seen many an excellent matron, who could never in her best days have been handsome, and yet she had a packet of yellow love-letters in a private drawer, and sweet children showered kisses on her sallow cheeks. And I believe there have been plenty of young heroes, of middle stature and feeble beards, who have felt quite sure they could never love anything more insignificant than a Diana, and yet have found themselves in middle life happily settled with a wife who waddles. Yes! thank God; human feeling is like the mighty rivers that bless the earth: it does not wait for beauty – it flows with resistless force and brings beauty with it.

All honour and reverence to the divine beauty of form! Let us cultivate it to the utmost in men, women, and children – in our gardens and in our houses. But let us love that other beauty too, which lies in no secret of proportion, but in the secret of deep human sympathy. Paint us an angel, if you can, with a floating violet robe, and a face paled by the celestial light; paint us yet oftener a Madonna, turning her mild face upward and opening her arms to welcome the divine glory; but do not impose on us any aesthetic rules which shall banish from the region of Art those old women scraping carrots with their work-worn hands, those heavy clowns taking holiday in a dingy pot-house, those rounded backs and stupid weather-beaten faces that have bent over the spade and done the rough work of the world – those homes with their tin pans, their brown pitchers, their rough curs, and their clusters of onions. In this world there are so many of these common coarse people, who have no picturesque sentimental wretchedness! It is so needful we should remember their existence, else we may happen to leave them quite out of our religion and philosophy, and frame lofty theories which only fit a world of extremes. Therefore let Art always remind us of them; therefore let us always have men ready to give the loving pains of a life to the faithful representing of commonplace things – men who see beauty in these commonplace things, and delight in showing how kindly the light of heaven falls on them. There are few prophets in the world; few sublimely beautiful women; few heroes. I can't afford to give all my love and reverence to such rarities: I want a great deal of those feelings for my everyday fellow-men, especially for the few in the foreground of the great multitude, whose faces I know, whose hands I touch, for whom I have to make way with kindly courtesy. Neither are picturesque lazzaroni or romantic criminals half so frequent as your common labourer, who gets his own bread, and eats it vulgarly but creditably with his own pocket knife. It is more needful that I should have a fibre of sympathy connecting me with that vulgar citizen who weighs out my sugar in a vilely-assorted cravat and waistcoat, than with the handsomest rascal in red scarf and green feathers – more needful that my heart should swell with loving admiration at some trait of gentle goodness in the faulty people who sit at the same hearth with me, or in the clergyman of my own parish, who is perhaps rather too corpulent, and in other respects is not an Oberlin or a

Tillotson, than at the deeds of heroes whom I shall never know except by hearsay, or at the sublimest abstract of all clerical graces that was ever conceived by an able novelist.

And so I come back to Mr Irwine, with whom I desire you to be in perfect charity, far as he may be from satisfying your demands on the clerical character. Perhaps you think he was not – as he ought to have been – a living demonstration of the benefits attached to a national church? But I am not sure of that; at least I know that the people in Broxton and Hayslope would have been very sorry to part with their clergyman, and that most faces brightened at his approach; and until it can be proved that hatred is a better thing for the soul than love, I must believe that Mr Irwine's influence in his parish was a more wholesome one than that of the zealous Mr Ryde, who came there twenty years afterwards, when Mr Irwine had been gathered to his fathers. It is true, Mr Ryde insisted strongly on the doctrines of the Reformation, visited his flock a great deal in their own homes, and was severe in rebuking the aberrations of the flesh – put a stop, indeed, to the Christmas rounds of the church singers, as promoting drunkenness, and too light a handling of sacred things. But I gathered from Adam Bede, to whom I talked of these matters in his old age, that few clergymen could be less successful in winning the hearts of their parishioners than Mr Ryde. They learned a great many notions about doctrine from him, so that almost every churchgoer under fifty began to distinguish as well between the genuine gospel and what did not come precisely up to that standard, as if he had been born and bred a Dissenter; and for some time after his arrival there seemed to be quite a religious movement in that quiet rural district. 'But,' said Adam, 'I've seen pretty clear, ever since I was a young un, as religion's something else besides notions. It isn't notions sets people doing the right thing – it's feelings. It's the same with the notions in religion as it is with math'matics – a man may be able to work problems straight off in's head as he sits by the fire and smokes his pipe; but if he has to make a machine or a building, he must have a will and a resolution, and love something else better than his own ease. Somehow, the congregation began to fall off, and people began to speak light o' Mr Ryde. I believe he meant right at bottom; but, you see, he was sourish-tempered, and was for beating down prices with the people as worked for him; and his preaching wouldn't go down well with that sauce. And he wanted to be like my lord judge i'the parish, punishing folks for doing wrong; and he scolded 'em from the pulpit as if he'd been a Ranter, and yet he couldn't abide the Dissenters, and was a deal more set against 'em than Mr Irwine was. And then he didn't keep within his income, for he seemed to think at first go-off that six hundred a year was to make him as big a man as Mr Donnithorne: that's a sore mischief I've often seen with the poor curates jumping into a bit of a living all of a sudden. Mr Ryde was a deal thought on at a distance, I believe, and he wrote books; but as for math'matics and the natur o' things, he was as ignorant as a woman. He was very knowing about doctrines, and used to call 'em the bulwarks of the Reformation; but I've always mistrusted that sort o' learning as leaves folks foolish and unreasonable about business. Now Mester Irwine was as different as could be: as quick! – he understood what you meant in a minute; and he knew all about building, and could see when you'd made a good job. And he behaved as much like a gentleman to the farmers, and th' old women and the labourers, as he did to the gentry. You never saw him interfering and scolding, and trying to play th' emperor. Ah! he was a fine man as ever you set eyes on; and so kind to's mother and sisters. That poor sickly Miss Anne – he seemed to think more of her than of anybody else in the world. There wasn't a soul in the parish had a word to say against him; and his servants stayed with him till they were so old and pottering, he had to hire other folks to do their work.'

'Well,' I said, 'that was an excellent way of preaching in the week days; but I dare say, if your old friend Mr Irwine were to come to life again, and get into the pulpit next Sunday, you would be rather ashamed that he didn't preach better after all your praise of him.'

'Nay, nay,' said Adam, broadening his chest and throwing himself back in his chair, as if he were ready to meet all inferences, 'nobody has ever heard me say Mr Irwine was much of a preacher. He didn't go into deep speritial experience; and I know there's a deal in a man's inward life as you can't measure by the square, and say, "Do this and that'll follow," and, "Do that and this'll follow." There's things go on in the soul, and times when feelings come into you like a rushing mighty wind, as the scripture says, and part your life in two a'most, so as you look back on yourself as if you was somebody else. Those are things as you can't bottle up in a "do this" and "do that"; and I'll go so far with the strongest Methodist ever you'll find. That shows me there's deep speritial things in religion. You can't make much out wi' talking about it, but you feel it. Mr Irwine didn't go into those things: he preached short moral sermons, and that was all. But then he acted pretty much up to what he said; he didn't set up for being so different from other folks one day, and then be as like 'em as two peas the next. And he made folks love him and respect him, and that was better nor stirring up their gall wi' being over-busy. Mrs Poyser used to say – you know she would have her word about everything – she said, Mr Irwine was like a good meal o' victual, you were the better for him without thinking on it, and Mr Ryde was like a dose o' physic, he gripped you and worreted you, and after all he left you much the same.'

'But didn't Mr Ryde preach a great deal more about that spiritual part of religion than you talk of, Adam? Couldn't you get more out of his sermons than out of Mr Irwine's?'

'Eh, I knowna. He preached a deal about doctrines. But I've seen pretty clear ever since I was a young un, as religion's something else besides doctrines and notions. I look at it as if the doctrines was like finding names for your feelings, so as you can talk of 'em when you've never known 'em, just as a man may talk o' tools when he knows their names, though he's never so much as seen 'em, still less handled 'em. I've heard a deal o' doctrine i' my time, for I used to go after the Dissenting preachers along wi' Seth, when I was a lad o' seventeen, and got puzzling myself a deal about th' Arminians and the Calvinists. The Wesleyans, you know, are strong Arminians; and Seth, who could never abide anything harsh, and was always for hoping the best, held fast by the Wesleyans from the very first; but I thought I could pick a hole or two in their notions, and I got disputing wi' one o' the class leaders down at Treddles'on, and harassed him so, first o' this side and then o' that, till at last he said, "Young man, it's the devil making use o' your pride and conceit as a weapon to war against the simplicity o' the truth." I couldn't help laughing then, but as I was going home, I thought the man wasn't far wrong. I began to see as all this weighing and sifting what this text means and that text means, and whether folks are saved all by God's grace, or whether there goes an ounce o' their own will to 't, was no part o' real religion at all. You may talk o' these things for hours on end, and you'll only be all the more coxy and conceited for't. So I took to going nowhere but to church, and hearing nobody but Mr Irwine, for he said nothing but what was good, and what you'd be the wiser for remembering. And I found it better for my soul to be humble before the mysteries o' God's dealings, and not be making a clatter about what I could never understand. And they're poor foolish questions after all; for what have we got either inside or outside of us but what comes from God? If we've got a resolution to do right, He gave it us, I reckon, first or last; but I see plain enough we shall never do it without a resolution, and that's enough for me.'

Adam, you perceive, was a warm admirer, perhaps a partial judge, of Mr Irwine, as, happily, some of us still are of the people we have known familiarly. Doubtless it will be despised as a weakness by that lofty order of minds who pant after the ideal, and are oppressed by a general sense that their emotions are of too exquisite a character to find fit objects among their everyday fellow-men. I have often been favoured with the confidence of these select natures, and find them concur in the experience that great men are over-estimated and small men are insupportable; that if you would love a woman without ever looking back on your love as a folly, she must die while you are courting her; and if you would maintain the slightest belief in human heroism, you must never make a pilgrimage to see the hero. I confess I have often meanly shrunk from confessing to these accomplished and acute gentlemen what my own experience has been. I am afraid I have often smiled with hypocritical assent, and gratified the with an epigram on the fleeting nature of our illusions, which anyone moderately acquainted with French literature can command at a moment's notice. Human converse, I think some wise man has remarked, is not rigidly sincere. But I herewith discharge my conscience, and declare, that I have had quite enthusiastic movements of admiration towards old gentlemen who spoke the worst English, who were occasionally fretful in their temper, and who had never moved in a higher sphere of influence than that of parish overseer; and that the way in which I have come to the conclusion that human nature is lovable – the way I have learnt something of its deep pathos, its sublime mysteries – has been by living a great deal among people more or less commonplace and vulgar, of whom you would perhaps hear nothing very surprising if you were to enquire about them in the neighbourhoods where they dwelt. Ten to one most of the small shopkeepers in their vicinity saw nothing at all in them. For I have observed this remarkable coincidence, that the select natures who pant after the ideal, and find nothing in pantaloons or petticoats great enough to command their reverence and love, are curiously in unison with the narrowest and pettiest.

For example, I have often heard Mr Gedge, the landlord of the Royal Oak, who used to turn a bloodshot eye on his neighbours in the village of Shepperton, sum up his opinion of the people in his own parish – and they were all the people he knew – in these emphatic words: 'Ay, sir, I've said it often, and I'll say it again, they're a poor lot i' this parish – a poor lot, sir, big and little.' I think he had a dim idea that if he could migrate to a distant parish, he might find neighbours worthy of him; and indeed he did subsequently transfer himself to the Saracen's Head, which was doing a thriving business in the back street of a neighbouring market-town. But, oddly enough, he has found the people up that back street of precisely the same stamp as the inhabitants of Shepperton – 'a poor lot, sir, big and little, and them as comes for a go o' gin are no better than them as comes for a pint o' twopenny – a poor lot.'

18

Church

'Hetty, Hetty, don't you know church begins at two, and it's gone half after one a'ready? Have you got nothing better to think on this good Sunday, as poor old Thias Bede's to be put into the ground, and him drownded i' th' dead o' the night, as it's enough to make one's back run cold, but you must be 'disening yourself as if there was a wedding istid of a funeral?'

'Well, aunt,' said Hetty, 'I can't be ready so soon as everybody else, when I've got Totty's things to put on. And I'd ever such work to make her stand still.'

Hetty was coming downstairs, and Mrs Poyser, in her plain bonnet and shawl, was standing below. If ever a girl looked as if she had been made of roses, that girl was Hetty in her Sunday hat and frock. For her hat was trimmed with pink, and her frock had pink spots, sprinkled on a white ground. There was nothing but pink and white about her, except in her dark hair and eyes and her little buckled shoes. Mrs Poyser was provoked at herself, for she could hardly keep from smiling, as any mortal is inclined to do at the sight of pretty round things. So she turned without speaking, and joined the group outside the house door, followed by Hetty, whose heart was fluttering so at the thought of someone she expected to see at church, that she hardly felt the ground she trod on.

And now the little procession set off. Mr Poyser was in his Sunday suit of drab, with a red and green waistcoat, and a green watch-ribbon having a large cornelian seal attached, pendant like a plumb-line from that promontory where his watch-pocket was situated; a silk handkerchief of a yellow tone round his neck; and excellent grey ribbed stockings, knitted by Mrs Poyser's own hand, setting off the proportions of his leg. Mr Poyser had no reason to be ashamed of his leg, and suspected that the growing abuse of top-boots and other fashions tending to disguise the nether limbs, had their origin in a pitiable degeneracy of the human calf. Still less had he reason to be ashamed of his round jolly face, which was good-humour itself as he said, 'Come, Hetty – come, little uns!' and, giving his arm to his wife, led the way through the causeway gate into the yard.

The 'little uns' addressed were Marty and Tommy, boys of nine and seven, in little fustian tailed coats and knee-breeches, relieved by rosy cheeks and black eyes; looking as much like their father as a very small elephant is like a very large one. Hetty walked between them, and behind came patient Molly, whose task it was to carry Totty through the yard, and over all the wet places on the road; for Totty, having speedily recovered from her threatened fever, had insisted on going to church today, and especially on wearing her red-and-black necklace outside her tippet. And there were many wet places for her to be carried over this afternoon, for there had been heavy showers in the morning, though now the clouds had rolled off and lay in towering silvery masses on the horizon.

You might have known it was Sunday if you had only waked up in the farmyard. The cocks and hens seemed to know it, and made only crooning subdued noises; the very bulldog looked less savage, as if he would have been satisfied with a smaller bite than usual. The sunshine seemed to call all things to rest and not to labour; it was asleep itself on the moss-grown cowshed; on the group of white ducks nestling together with their bills tucked under their wings; on the old black sow stretched languidly on the straw, while her largest young one found an excellent spring-bed on his mother's fat ribs; on Alick, the shepherd, in his new smock-frock, taking an uneasy siesta half-sitting half-standing on the granary steps. Alick was of opinion that church, like other luxuries, was not to be indulged in often by a foreman who had the weather and the ewes on his mind. 'Church! nay – I'n gotten summat else to think on,' was an answer which he often uttered in a tone of bitter significance that silenced further question. I feel sure Alick meant no irreverence; indeed, I know that his mind was not of a speculative negative cast, and he would on no account have missed going to church on Christmas Day, Easter Sunday, and 'Whissuntide'. But he had a general impression that public worship and religious ceremonies, like other non-productive employments, were intended for people who had leisure.

'There's father a-standing at the yard-gate,' said Martin Poyser. 'I reckon he wants to watch us down the field. It's wonderful what sight he has, and him turned seventy-five.'

'Ah, I often think it's wi' th' old folks as it is wi' the babbies,' said Mrs Poyser; 'they're satisfied wi' looking, no matter what they're looking at. It's God A'mighty's way o' quietening 'em, I reckon, afore they go to sleep.'

Old Martin opened the gate as he saw the family procession approaching, and held it wide open, leaning on his stick – pleased to do this bit of work; for, like all old men whose life has been spent in labour, he liked to feel that he was still useful – that there was a better crop of onions in the garden because he was by at the sowing – and that the cows would be milked the better if he stayed at home on a Sunday afternoon to look on. He always went to church on Sacrament Sundays, but not very regularly at other times; on wet Sundays, or whenever he had a touch of rheumatism, he used to read the three first chapters of Genesis instead.

'They'll ha' putten Thias Bede i' the ground afore ye get to the churchyard,' he said, as his son came up. 'It 'ud ha' been better luck if they'd ha' buried him i' the forenoon when the rain was fallin'; there's no likelihoods of a drop now; an' the moon lies like a boat there, dost see? That's a sure sign o' fair weather – there's a many as is false, but that's sure.'

'Ay, ay,' said the son, 'I'm in hopes it'll hold up now.'

'Mind what the parson says, mind what the parson says, my lads,' said Grandfather to the black-eyed youngsters in knee-breeches, conscious of a marble or two in their pockets, which they looked forward to handling a little, secretly, during the sermon.

'Doodbye, dandad,' said Totty. 'Me doin to church. Me dot my netlace on. Dive me a peppermint.'

Grandad, shaking with laughter at this 'deep little wench,' slowly transferred his stick to his left hand, which held the gate open, and slowly thrust his finger into the waistcoat-pocket on which Tótty had fixed her eyes with a confident look of expectation.

And when they were all gone, the old man leaned on the gate again, watching them across the lane along the Home Close, and through the far gate, till they disappeared behind a bend in the hedge. For the hedgerows in those days shut out one's view, even on the better-managed farms; and this afternoon, the dog-roses were tossing out their pink wreaths, the nightshade was in its yellow and purple glory, the pale honeysuckle grew out of reach, peeping high up out of a holly bush, and over all an ash or a sycamore every now and then threw its shadow across the path.

There were acquaintances at other gates who had to move aside and let them pass: at the gate of the Home Close there was half the dairy of cows standing one behind the other, extremely slow to understand that their large bodies might be in the way; at the far gate there was the mare holding her head over the bars, and beside her the liver-coloured foal with its head towards its mother's flank, apparently still much embarrassed by its own straddling existence. The way lay entirely through Mr Poyser's own fields till they reached the main road leading to the village, and he turned a keen eye on the stock and the crops as they went along, while Mrs Poyser was ready to supply a running commentary on them all. The woman who manages a dairy has a large share in making the rent, so she may well be allowed to have her opinion on stock and their 'keep' – an exercise which strengthens her understanding so much that she finds herself able to give her husband advice on most other subjects.

'There's that short-horned Sally,' she said, as they entered the Home Close, and she caught sight of the meek beast that lay chewing the cud, and looking at her with a sleepy eye. 'I begin to hate the sight o' the cow; and I say now what I said three weeks ago, the sooner we get rid of her the better, for there's that little yellow cow as doesn't give half the milk, and yet I've twice as much butter from her.'

'Why, thee't not like the women in general,' said Mr Poyser; 'they like the short-horns, as give such a lot o' milk. There's Chowne's wife wants him to buy no other sort.'

'What's it sinnify what Chowne's wife likes? – a poor soft thing, wi' no more head-piece nor a sparrow. She'd take a big colander to strain her lard wi', and then wonder as the scratchins run through. I've seen enough of her to know as I'll niver take a servant from her house again – all hugger-mugger – and you'd niver know, when you went in, whether it was Monday or Friday, the wash draggin' on to th' end o' the week; and as for her cheese, I know well enough it rose like a loaf in a tin last year. And then she talks o' the weather bein' i' fault, as there's folks 'ud stand on their heads and then say the fault was i' their boots.'

'Well, Chowne's been wanting to buy Sally, so we can get rid of her if thee lik'st,' said Mr Poyser, secretly proud of his wife's superior power of putting two and two together; indeed, on recent market-days he had more than once boasted of her discernment in this very matter of short-horns.

'Ay, them as choose a soft for a wife may's well buy up the short-horns, for if you get your head stuck in a bog your legs may's well go after it. Eh! talk o' legs, there's legs for you,' Mrs Poyser continued, as Totty, who had been set down now the road was dry, toddled on in front of her father and mother. 'There's shapes! An' she's got such a long foot, she'll be her father's own child.'

'Ay, she'll be welly such a one as Hetty i' ten years' time, on'y she's got thy coloured eyes. I niver remember a blue eye i' my family; my mother had eyes as black as sloes, just like Hetty's."

'The child 'ull be none the worse for having summat as isn't like Hetty. An' I'm none for having her so over pretty. Though, for the matter o' that, there's people wi' light hair an' blue eyes as pretty as them wi' black. If Dinah had got a bit o' colour in her cheeks, an' didn't stick that Methodist cap on her head, enough to frighten the cows, folks 'ud think her as pretty as Hetty.'

'Nay, nay,' said Mr Poyser, with rather a contemptuous emphasis, 'thee dostna know the pints of a woman. The men 'ud niver run after Dinah as they would after Hetty.'

'What care I what the men 'ud run after? It's well seen what choice the most of 'em know how to make, by the poor draggle-tails o' wives you see, like bits o' gauze ribbin, good for nothing when the colour's gone.'

'Well, well, thee canstna say but what I knowed how to make a choice when I married thee,' said Mr Poyser, who usually settled little conjugal disputes by a compliment of this sort; 'and thee wast twice as buxom as Dinah ten year ago.'

'I niver said as a woman had need to be ugly to make a good missis of a house. There's Chowne's wife ugly enough to turn the milk an' save the rennet, but she'll niver save nothing any other way. But as for Dinah, poor child, she's niver likely to be buxom as long as she'll make her dinner o' cake and water, for the sake o' giving to them as want. She provoked me past bearing sometimes; and, as I told her, she went clean again' the Scriptur', for that says, "Love your neighbour as yourself"; but I said, "if you loved your neighbour no better nor you do yourself, Dinah, it's little enough you'd do for him. You'd be thinking he might do well enough on a half-empty stomach." Eh, I wonder where she is this blessed Sunday! – sitting by that sick woman, I dare say, as she'd set her heart on going to all of a sudden.'

'Ah, it was a pity she should take such megrims into her head, when she might ha' stayed wi' us all summer, and eaten twice as much as she wanted, and it 'ud niver ha' been missed. She made no odds in th' house at all, for she sat as still at her sewing as a bird on the nest, and was uncommon nimble at running to fetch anything. If Hetty gets married, theed'st like to ha' Dinah wi' thee constant.'

'It's no use thinking o' that,' said Mrs Poyser. 'You might as well beckon to the flying swallow, as ask Dinah to come an' live here comfortable, like other folks. If anything could turn her, I should ha' turned her, for I've talked to her for a hour on end, and scolded her too; for she's my own sister's child, and it behoves me to do what I can for her. But eh, poor thing, as soon as she'd said us goodbye, an got into the cart, an' looked back at me with her pale face, as is welly like her aunt Judith come back from heaven, I begun to be frightened to think o' the set-downs I had given her; for it comes over you sometimes as if she'd a way o' knowing the rights o' things more nor other folks have. But I'll niver give in as that's 'cause she's a Methodist, no more nor a white calf's white 'cause it eats out o' the same bucket wi' a black un.'

'Nay,' said Mr Poyser, with as near an approach to a snarl as his good nature would allow; 'I'n no opinion o' the Methodists. It's on'y tradesfolks as turn Methodists; you niver knew a farmer bitten wi' them maggots. There's maybe a workman now an' then, as isn't over clever at's work, takes to preachin' an' that, like Seth Bede. But you see Adam, as has got one o' the best head-pieces hereabout, knows better; he's a good churchman, else I'd never encourage him for a sweetheart for Hetty.'

'Why, goodness me,' said Mrs Poyser, who had looked back while her husband was speaking, 'look where Molly is with them lads. They're the field's length behind us. How could you let 'em do so, Hetty? Anybody might as well set a pictur to watch the children as you. Run back, and tell 'em to come on.'

Mr and Mrs Poyser were now at the end of the second field, so they set Totty on the top of one of the large stones forming the true Loamshire stile, and awaited the loiterers; Totty observing with complacency, 'Dey naughty, naughty boys – me dood.'

The fact was that this Sunday walk through the fields was fraught with great excitement to Marty and Tommy, who saw a perpetual drama going on in the hedgerows, and could no more refrain from stopping and peeping than if they had been a couple of spaniels or terriers. Marty was quite sure he saw a yellowhammer on the boughs of the great ash, and while he was peeping, he missed the sight of a white-throated stoat, which had run across the path and was described with much fervour by the junior Tommy. Then there was a little greenfinch, just fledged, fluttering along the ground, and it seemed quite possible to catch it, till it managed to flutter under the blackberry bush. Hetty could not be got to give any heed to these things, so Molly was called on for her ready sympathy, and peeped with open mouth wherever she was told, and said 'Lawks!' whenever she was expected to wonder.

Molly hastened on with some alarm when Hetty had come back and called to them that her aunt was angry; but Marty ran on first, shouting, 'We've found the speckled turkey's nest, mother!' with the instinctive confidence that people who bring good news are never in fault.

'Ah,' said Mrs Poyser, really forgetting all discipline in this pleasant surprise, 'that's a good lad; why, where is it?'

'Down in ever such a hole, under the hedge. I saw it first, looking after the greenfinch, and she sat on the nest.'

'You didn't frighten her, I hope,' said the mother, 'else she'll forsake it.'

'No, I went away as still as still, and whispered to Molly – didn't I, Molly?'

'Well, well, now come on,' said Mrs Poyser, 'and walk before father and mother, and take your little sister by the hand. We must go straight on now. Good boys don't look after the birds of a Sunday.'

'But, mother,' said Marty, 'you said you'd give half a crown to find the speckled turkey's nest. Mayn't I have the half-crown put into my money-box?'

'We'll see about that, my lad, if you walk along now like a good boy.'

The father and mother exchanged a significant glance of amusement at their eldest-born's acuteness; but on Tommy's round face there was a cloud.

'Mother,' he said, half crying, 'Marty's got ever so much more money in his box nor I've got in mine.'

'Munny, me want half a toun in my bots,' said Totty.

'Hush, hush, hush,' said Mrs Poyser, 'did ever anybody hear such naughty children? Nobody shall ever see their money-boxes any more, if they don't make haste and go on to church.'

This dreadful threat had the desired effect, and through the two remaining fields the three pair of small legs trotted on without any serious interruption, notwithstanding a small pond full of tadpoles, alias 'bullheads,' which the lads looked at wistfully.

The damp hay that must be scattered and turned afresh tomorrow was not a cheering sight to Mr Poyser, who during hay and corn harvest had often some mental struggles as to the benefits of a day of rest; but no temptation would have induced him to carry on any fieldwork, however early in the morning on a Sunday; for had not Michael Holdsworth had a pair of oxen 'sweltered' while he was ploughing on Good Friday? That was a demonstration that work on sacred days was a wicked thing; and with wickedness of any sort Martin Poyser was quite clear that he would have nothing to do, since money got by such means would never prosper.

'It a'most makes your fingers itch to be at the hay now the sun shines so,' he observed, as they passed through the 'Big Meadow.' 'But it's poor foolishness to think o' saving by going against your conscience. There's that Jim Wakefield, as they used to call 'Gentleman Wakefield,' used to do the same of a Sunday as o' weekdays, and took no heed to right or wrong, as if there was nayther God nor devil. An' what's he come to? Why, I saw him myself last market-day a-carrying a basket wi' oranges in't.'

'Ah, to be sure,' said Mrs Poyser, emphatically, 'you make but a poor trap to catch luck if you go and bait it wi' wickedness. The money as is got so's like to burn holes i' your pocket. I'd niver wish us to leave our lads a sixpence but what was got i' the rightful way. And as for the weather, there's one above makes it, and we must put up wi't: it's nothing of a plague to what the wenches are.'

Notwithstanding the interruption in their walk, the excellent habit which Mrs Poyser's clock had of taking time by the forelock, had secured their arrival at the village while it was still a quarter to two, though almost everyone who meant to go to church was already within the churchyard gates. Those who stayed at home were chiefly mothers, like Timothy's Bess, who stood at her own door nursing her baby, and feeling as women feel in that position – that nothing else can be expected of them.

It was not entirely to see Thias Bede's funeral that the people were standing about the churchyard so long before service began; that was their common practice. The women, indeed, usually entered the church at once, and the farmers' wives talked in an undertone to each other, over the tall pews, about their illnesses and the total failure of doctor's stuff, recommending dandelion-tea, and other home-made specifics, as far preferable – about the servants, and their growing exorbitance as to wages, whereas the quality of their services declined from year to year, and there was no girl nowadays to be trusted any further than you could see her – about the bad price Mr Dingall, the Treddleston grocer, was giving for butter, and the reasonable doubts that might be held as to his solvency, notwithstanding that Mrs Dingall was a sensible woman, and they were all sorry for her, for she had very good kin. Meantime the men lingered outside, and hardly any of them except the singers, who had a humming and fragmentary rehearsal to go through, entered the church until Mr Irwine was in the desk. They saw no reason for that premature entrance, – what could they do in church, if they were there before service began? – and they did not conceive that any power in the universe could take it ill of them if they stayed out and talked a little about 'bus'ness.'

Chad Cranage looks like quite a new acquaintance today, for he has got his clean Sunday face, which always makes his little granddaughter cry at him as a stranger. But an experienced eye would have fixed on him at once as the village blacksmith, after seeing the humble deference with which the big saucy fellow took off his hat and stroked his hair to the farmers; for Chad was accustomed to say that a working man must hold a candle to a personage understood to be as black as he was himself on weekdays; by which evil-sounding rule of conduct he meant what was, after all, rather virtuous than otherwise, namely, that men who had horses to be shod must be treated with respect. Chad and the rougher sort of workmen kept aloof from the grave under the whitethorn, where the burial was going forward; but Sandy Jim, and several of the farm-labourers, made a group round it, and stood with their hats off, as fellow mourners with the mother and sons. Others held a midway position, sometimes watching the group at the grave, sometimes listening to the conversation of the farmers, who stood in a knot near the church door, and were now joined by Martin Poyser, while his family passed into the church. On the outside of this knot stood Mr Casson, the landlord of the Donnithorne Arms, in his most striking attitude – that is to say, with the forefinger of his right hand thrust between the buttons of his waistcoat, his left hand in his breeches-pocket, and his head very much on one side; looking, on the whole, like an actor who has only a monosyllabic part intrusted to him, but feels sure that the audience discern his fitness for the leading business; curiously in contrast with old Jonathan Burge, who held his hands behind him, and leaned forward coughing asthmatically, with an inward scorn of all knowingness that could not be turned into cash. The talk was in rather a lower tone than usual today, hushed a little by the sound of Mr Irwine's voice reading the final prayers of the burial-service. They had all had their word of pity for poor Thias, but now they had got upon the nearer subject of their own grievances against Satchell, the Squire's bailiff, who played the part of steward so far as it was not performed by old Mr Donnithorne himself, for that gentleman had the meanness to receive his own rents and make bargains about his own timber. This subject of conversation was an additional reason for not being loud, since Satchell himself might presently be walking up the paved road to the church door. And soon they became suddenly silent; for Mr Irwine's voice had ceased, and the group round the whitethorn was dispersing itself towards the church.

They all moved aside, and stood with their hats off, while Mr Irwine passed. Adam and Seth were coming next with their mother between them; for Joshua Rann officiated as head sexton as well as clerk, and was not yet ready to follow the rector into the vestry. But there was a pause before the three mourners came on: Lisbeth had turned round to look again towards the grave! Ah! there was nothing now but the brown earth under the whitethorn. Yet she cried less today than she had done any day since her husband's death: along with all her grief there was mixed an unusual sense of her own importance in having a 'burial,' and in Mr Irwine's reading a special service for her husband; and besides, she knew the funeral psalm was going to be sung for him. She felt this counter-excitement to her sorrow still more strongly as she walked with her sons towards the church door, and saw the friendly sympathetic nods of their fellow-parishioners.

The mother and sons passed into the church, and one by one the loiterers followed, though some still lingered without; the sight of Mr Donnithorne's carriage, which was winding slowly up the hill, perhaps helping to make them feel that there was no need for haste.

But presently the sound of the bassoon and the key-bugles burst forth; the evening hymn, which always opened the service, had begun, and everyone must now enter and take his place.

I cannot say that the interior of Hayslope Church was remarkable for anything except for the grey age of its oaken pews – great square pews mostly, ranged on each side of a narrow aisle. It was free, indeed, from the modern blemish of galleries. The choir had two narrow pews to themselves in the middle of the right-hand row, so that it was a short process for Joshua Rann to take his place among them as principal bass, and return to his desk after the singing was over. The pulpit and desk, grey and old as the pews, stood on one side of the arch leading into the chancel, which also had its grey square pews for Mr Donnithorne's family and servants. Yet I assure you these grey pews, with the buff-washed walls, gave a very pleasing tone to this shabby interior, and agreed extremely well with the ruddy faces and bright waistcoats. And there were liberal touches of crimson toward the chancel, for the pulpit and Mr Donnithorne's own pew had handsome crimson cloth cushions; and, to close the vista, there was a crimson altar-cloth, embroidered with golden rays by Miss Lydia's own hand.

But even without the crimson cloth, the effect must have been warm and cheering when Mr Irwine was in the desk, looking benignly round on that simple congregation – on the hardy old men, with bent knees and shoulders, perhaps, but with vigour left for much hedge-clipping and thatching; on the tall stalwart frames and roughly-cut bronzed faces of the stonecutters and carpenters; on the half-dozen well-to-do farmers, with their apple-cheeked families; and on the clean old women, mostly farm-labourers' wives, with their bit of snow-white cap-border under their black bonnets, and with their withered arms, bare from the elbow, folded passively over their chests. For none of the old people held books – why should they? not one of them could read. But they knew a few 'good words' by heart, and their withered lips now and then moved silently, following the service without any very clear comprehension indeed, but with a simple faith in its efficacy to ward off harm and bring blessing. And now all faces were visible, for all were standing up – the little children on the seats, peeping over the edge of the grey pews, while good Bishop Ken's evening hymn was being sung to one of those lively psalm-tunes which died out with the last generation of rectors and choral parish-clerks. Melodies die out, like the pipe of Pan, with the ears that love them and listen for them. Adam was not in his usual place among the singers today, for he sat with his mother and Seth, and he noticed with surprise that Bartle Massey was absent too: all the more agreeable for Mr Joshua Rann, who gave out his bass notes with unusual complacency, and threw an extra ray of severity into the glances he sent over his spectacles at the recusant Will Maskery.

I beseech you to imagine Mr Irwine looking round on this scene, in his ample white surplice, that became him so well, with his powdered hair thrown back, his rich brown complexion, and his finely-cut nostril and upper lip; for there was a certain virtue in that benignant yet keen countenance, as there is in all human faces from which a generous soul beams out. And over all streamed the delicious June sunshine through the old windows, with their desultory patches of yellow, red, and blue, that threw pleasant touches of colour on the opposite wall.

I think, as Mr Irwine looked round today, his eyes rested an instant longer than usual on the square pew occupied by Martin Poyser and his family. And there was another pair of dark eyes that found it impossible not to wander thither, and rest on that round pink-and-white figure. But Hetty was at that moment quite careless of any glances – she was absorbed in the thought that Arthur Donnithorne would soon be coming into church, for the carriage must surely be at the church gate by this time. She had never seen him since she parted with him in the wood on Thursday evening, and oh! how long the time had seemed! Things had gone on just the same as ever since that evening; the wonders that had happened then had brought no changes after them; they were already like a dream. When she heard the church door swinging, her heart beat so, she dared not look up. She felt that her aunt was curtsying; she curtsied herself. That must be old Mr Donnithorne – he always came first, the wrinkled small old man, peering round with short-sighted glances at the bowing and curtsying congregation; then she knew Miss Lydia was passing, and though Hetty liked so much to look at her fashionable little coal-scuttle bonnet, with the wreath of small roses round it, she didn't mind it today. But there were no more curtsies – no, he was not come; she felt sure there was nothing else passing the pew door but the housekeeper's black bonnet, and the lady's-maid's beautiful straw that had once been Miss Lydia's, and then the powdered heads of the butler and footman. No, he was not there; yet she would look now – she might be mistaken – for, after all, she had not looked. So she lifted up her eyelids and glanced timidly at the cushioned pew in the chancel: – there was no one but old Mr Donnithorne rubbing his spectacles with his white handkerchief, and Miss Lydia opening the large gilt-edged prayer-book. The chill disappointment was too hard to bear: she felt herself turning pale, her lips trembling; she was ready to cry. Oh, what should she do? Everybody would know the reason; they would know she was crying because Arthur was not there. And Mr Craig, with the wonderful hot-house plant in his buttonhole, was staring at her, she knew. It was dreadfully long before the General Confession began, so that she could kneel down. Two great drops would fall then, but no one saw them except good-natured Molly, for her aunt and uncle knelt with their backs towards her. Molly, unable to imagine any cause for tears in church except faintness, of which she had a vague traditional knowledge, drew out of her pocket a queer little flat blue smelling-bottle, and after much labour in pulling the cork out, thrust the narrow neck against Hetty's nostrils. 'It donna smell,' she whispered, thinking this was a great advantage which old salts had over fresh ones: they did you good without biting your nose. Hetty pushed it away peevishly; but this little flash of temper did what the salts could not have done – it roused her to wipe away the traces of her tears, and try with all her might not to shed any more. Hetty had a certain strength in her vain little nature: she would have borne anything rather than be laughed at, or pointed at with any other feeling than admiration; she would have pressed her own nails into her tender flesh rather than people should know a secret she did not want them to know.

What fluctuations there were in her busy thoughts and feelings, while Mr Irwine was pronouncing the solemn 'Absolution' in her deaf ears, and through all the tones of petition that followed! Anger lay very close to disappointment, and soon won the victory over the conjectures her small ingenuity could devise to account for Arthur's absence on the supposition that he really wanted to come, really wanted to see her again. And by the time she rose from her knees mechanically, because all the rest were rising, the colour had returned to her cheeks even with a heightened glow, for she was framing little indignant speeches to herself, saying she hated Arthur for giving her this pain – she would like him to suffer too. Yet while this selfish tumult was going on in her soul, her eyes were bent down on her prayer-book, and the eyelids with their dark fringe looked as lovely as ever. Adam Bede thought so, as he glanced at her for a moment on rising from his knees.

But Adam's thoughts of Hetty did not deafen him to the service; they rather blended with all the other deep feelings for which the church service was a channel to him this afternoon, as a certain consciousness of our entire past and our imagined future blends itself with all our moments of keen sensibility. And to Adam the church service was the best channel he could have found for his mingled regret, yearning, and resignation; its interchange of beseeching cries for help, with outbursts of faith and praise – its recurrent responses and the familiar rhythm of its collects, seemed to speak for him as no other form of worship could have done; as, to those early Christians who had worshipped from their childhood upward in catacombs, the torchlight and shadows must have seemed nearer the Divine presence than the heathenish daylight of the street. The secret of our emotions never lies in the bare object, but in its subtle relations to our own past: no wonder the secret escapes the unsympathising observer, who might as well put on his spectacles to discern odours.

But there was one reason why even a chance comer would have found the service in Hayslope Church more impressive than in most other village nooks in the kingdom – a reason, of which I am sure you have not the slightest suspicion. It was the reading of our friend Joshua Rann. Where that good shoemaker got his notion of reading from, remained a mystery even to his most intimate acquaintances. I believe, after all, he got it chiefly from Nature, who had poured some of her music into this honest conceited soul, as she had been known to do into other narrow souls before his. She had given him, at least, a fine bass voice and a musical ear; but I cannot positively say whether these alone had sufficed to inspire him with the rich chant in which he delivered the responses. The way he rolled from a rich deep forte into a melancholy cadence, subsiding, at the end of the last word, into a sort of faint resonance, like the lingering vibrations of a fine violoncello, I can compare to nothing for its strong calm melancholy but the rush and cadence of the wind among the autumn boughs. This may seem a strange mode of speaking about the reading of a parish clerk – a man in rusty spectacles, with stubbly hair, a large occiput, and a prominent crown. But that is Nature's way: she will allow a gentleman of splendid physiognomy and poetic aspirations to sing woefully out of tune, and not give him the slightest hint of it; and takes care that some narrow-browed fellow, trolling a ballad in the corner of a pot-house, shall be as true to his intervals as a bird.

Joshua himself was less proud of his reading than of his singing, and it was always with a sense of heightened importance that he passed from the desk to the choir. Still more today: it was a special occasion; for an old man, familiar to all the parish, had died a sad death – not in his bed, a circumstance the most painful to the mind of the peasant – and now the funeral psalm was to be sung in memory of his sudden departure. Moreover, Bartle Massey was not at church, and Joshua's importance in the choir suffered no eclipse. It was a solemn minor strain they sang. The old psalm-tunes have many a wail among them and the words: 'Thou sweep'st us off as with a flood; we vanish hence like dreams', seemed to have a closer application than usual, in the death of poor Thias. The mother and sons listened, each with peculiar feelings. Lisbeth had a vague belief that the psalm was doing her husband good; it was part of that decent burial which she would have thought it a greater wrong to withhold from him than to have caused him many unhappy days while he was living. The more there was said about her husband, the more there was done for him, surely the safer he would be. It was poor Lisbeth's blind way of feeling that human love and pity are a ground of faith in some other love. Seth, who was easily touched, shed tears, and tried to recall, as he had done continually since his father's death, all that he had heard of the possibility that a single moment of consciousness at the last might be a moment of pardon and reconcilement; for was it not written in the very psalm they were singing, that the divine dealings were not measured and circumscribed by time? Adam had never been unable to join in a psalm before. He had known plenty of trouble and vexation since he had been a lad; but this was the first sorrow that had hemmed in his voice, and strangely enough it was sorrow because the chief source of his past trouble and vexation was for ever gone out of his reach. He had not been able to press his father's hand before their parting, and say, 'Father, you know it was all right between us; I never forgot what I owed you when I was a lad; you forgive me if I have been too hot and hasty now and then!' Adam thought but little today of the hard work and the earnings he had spent on his father: his thoughts ran constantly on what the old man's feelings had been in moments of humiliation, when he had held down his head before the rebukes of his son. When our indignation is borne in submissive silence, we are apt to feel twinges of doubt afterwards as to our own generosity, if not justice; how much more when the object of our anger has gone into everlasting silence, and we have seen his face for the last time in the meekness of death!

'Ah! I was always too hard,' Adam said to himself. 'It's a sore fault in me as I'm so hot and out o' patience with people when they do wrong, and my heart gets shut up against 'em, so as I can't bring myself to forgive 'em. I see clear enough there's more pride nor love in my soul, for I could sooner make a thousand strokes with th' hammer for my father than bring myself to say a kind word to him. And there went plenty o' pride and temper to the strokes, as the devil will be having his finger in what we call our duties as well as our sins. Mayhap the best thing I ever did in my life was only doing what was easiest for myself. It's allays been easier for me to work nor to sit still, but the real tough job for me 'ud be to master my own will and temper, and go right against my own pride. It seems to me now, if I was to find father at home tonight, I should behave different; but there's no knowing – perhaps nothing 'ud be a lesson to us if it didn't come too late. It's well we should feel as life's a reckoning we can't make twice over; there's no real making amends in this world, any more nor you can mend a wrong subtraction by doing your addition right.'

This was the keynote to which Adam's thoughts had perpetually returned since his father's death, and the solemn wail of the funeral psalm was only an influence that brought back the old thoughts with stronger emphasis. So was the sermon, which Mr Irwine had chosen with reference to Thias's funeral. It spoke briefly and simply of the words, 'In the midst of life we are in death' – how the present moment is all we can call our own for works of mercy, of righteous dealing, and of family tenderness. All very old truths – but what we thought the oldest truth becomes the most startling to us in the week when we have looked on the dead face of one who has made a part of our own lives. For when men want to impress us with the effect of a new and wonderfully vivid light, do they not let it fall on the most familiar objects, that we may measure its intensity by remembering the former dimness?

Then came the moment of the final blessing, when the forever sublime words, 'The peace of God, which passeth all understanding,' seemed to blend with the calm afternoon sunshine that fell on the bowed heads of the congregation; and then the quiet rising, the mothers tying on the bonnets of the little maidens who had slept through the sermon, the fathers collecting the prayer-books, until all streamed out through the old archway into the green churchyard, and began their neighbourly talk, their simple civilities, and their invitations to tea; for on a Sunday everyone was ready to receive a guest – it was the day when all must be in their best clothes and their best humour.

Mr and Mrs Poyser paused a minute at the church gate: they were waiting for Adam to come up, not being contented to go away without saying a kind word to the widow and her sons.

'Well, Mrs Bede,' said Mrs Poyser, as they walked on together, 'you must keep up your heart; husbands and wives must be content when they've lived to rear their children and see one another's hair grey.'

'Ay, ay,' said Mr Poyser; 'they wonna have long to wait for one another then, anyhow. And ye've got two o' the strapping'st sons i' th' country; and well you may, for I remember poor Thias as fine a broad-shouldered fellow as need to be; and as for you, Mrs Bede, why you're straighter i' the back nor half the young women now.'

'Eh,' said Lisbeth, 'it's poor luck for the platter to wear well when it's broke i' two. The sooner I'm laid under the thorn the better. I'm no good to nobody now.'

Adam never took notice of his mother's little unjust plaints; but Seth said, 'Nay, mother, thee mustna say so. Thy sons ull never get another mother.'

'That's true, lad, that's true,' said Mr Poyser; 'and it's wrong on us to give way to grief, Mrs Bede; for it's like the children cryin' when the fathers and mothers take things from 'em. There's one above knows better nor us.'

'Ah,' said Mrs Poyser, 'an' it's poor work allays settin' the dead above the livin'. We shall all on us be dead some time I reckon – it 'ud be better if folks 'ud make much on us beforehand, istid o' beginnin' when we're gone. It's but little good you'll do a-watering the last year's crop.'

'Well, Adam,' said Mr Poyser, feeling that his wife's words were, as usual, rather incisive than soothing, and that it would be well to change the subject, 'you'll come and see us again now, I hope. I hanna had a talk with you this long while, and the missis here wants you to see what can be done with her best spinning-wheel, for it's got broke, and it'll be a nice job to mend it – there'll want a bit o' turning. You'll come as soon as you can now, will you?'

Mr Poyser paused and looked round while he was speaking, as if to see where Hetty was; for the children were running on before. Hetty was not without a companion, and she had, besides, more pink and white about her than ever; for she held in her hand the wonderful pink-and-white hot-house plant, with a very long name – a Scotch name, she supposed, since people said Mr Craig the gardener was Scotch. Adam took the opportunity of looking round too; and I am sure you will not require of him that he should feel any vexation in observing a pouting expression on Hetty's face as she listened to the gardener's small-talk. Yet in her secret heart she was glad to have him by her side, for she would perhaps learn from him how it was Arthur had not come to church. Not that she cared to ask him the question, but she hoped the information would be given spontaneously; for Mr Craig, like a superior man, was very fond of giving information.

Mr Craig was never aware that his conversation and advances were received coldly, for to shift one's point of view beyond certain limits is impossible to the most liberal and expansive mind; we are none of us aware of the impression we produce on Brazilian monkeys of feeble understanding – it is possible they see hardly anything in us. Moreover, Mr Craig was a man of sober passions, and was already in his tenth year of hesitation as to the relative advantages of matrimony and bachelorhood. It is true that, now and then, when he had been a little heated by an extra glass of grog, he had been heard to say of Hetty that the 'lass was well enough,' and that 'a man might do worse;' but on convivial occasions men are apt to express themselves strongly.

Martin Poyser held Mr Craig in honour, as a man who 'knew his business,' and who had great lights concerning soils and compost; but he was less of a favourite with Mrs Poyser, who had more than once said in confidence to her husband, 'You're mighty fond o' Craig; but for my part, I think he's welly like a cock as thinks the sun's rose o' purpose to hear him crow.' For the rest, Mr Craig was an estimable gardener, and was not without reasons for having a high opinion of himself. He had also high shoulders and high cheek-bones, and hung his head forward a little, as he walked along with his hands in his breeches-pockets. I think it was his pedigree only that had the advantage of being Scotch, and not his 'bringing up;' for except that he had a stronger burr in his accent, his speech differed little from that of the Loamshire people about him. But a gardener is Scotch, as a French teacher is Parisian.

'Well, Mr Poyser,' he said, before the good slow farmer had time to speak, 'ye'll not be carrying your hay tomorrow, I'm thinking: the glass sticks at "change," and ye may rely upo' my word as we'll ha' more downfall afore twenty-four hours is past. Ye see that darkish blue cloud there upo' the 'rizon – ye know what I mean by the 'rizon, where the land and sky seems to meet?'

'Ay, ay, I see the cloud,' said Mr Poyser, 'rizon or no 'rizon. It's right o'er Mike Holdsworth's fallow, and a foul fallow it is.'

'Well, you mark my words, as that cloud 'ull spread o'er the sky pretty nigh as quick as you'd spread a tarpaulin over one o' your hay-ricks. It's a great thing to ha' studied the look o' the clouds. Lord bless you! th' met'orological almanecks can learn me nothing, but there's a pretty sight o' things I could let them up to, if they'd just come to me. And how are you, Mrs Poyser? – thinking o' getherin' the red currants soon, I reckon. You'd a deal better gether 'em afore they're o'er-ripe, wi' such weather as we've got to look forward to. How do ye do, Mistress Bede?' Mr Craig continued, without a pause, nodding by the way to Adam and Seth. 'I hope y' enjoyed them spinach and gooseberries as I sent Chester with th' other day. If ye want vegetables while ye're in trouble, ye know where to come to. It's well known I'm not giving other folks' things away; for when I've supplied the house, the garden's my own spekilation, and it isna every man th' old squire could get as 'ud be equil to the undertaking, let alone asking whether he'd be willing. I've got to run my calkilation fine, I can tell you, to make sure o' getting back the money as I pay the squire. I should like to see some o' them fellows as make the almanecks looking as far before their noses as I've got to do every year as comes.'

'They look pretty fur, though,' said Mr Poyser, turning his head on one side, and speaking in rather a subdued reverential tone. 'Why, what could come truer nor that pictur o' the cock wi' the big spurs, as has got its head knocked down wi' th' anchor, an' th' firin', an' the ships behind? Why, that pictur was made afore Christmas, and yit it's come as true as th' Bible. Why, th' cock's France, an' th' anchor's Nelson – an' they told us that beforehand.'

'Pee–ee–eh!' said Mr Craig. 'A man doesna want to see fur to know as th' English 'ull beat the French. Why, I know upo' good authority as it's a big Frenchman as reaches five foot high, an' they live upo' spoon-meat mostly. I knew a man as his father had a particular knowledge o' the French. I should like to know what them grasshoppers are to do against such fine fellows as our young Captain Arthur. Why, it 'ud astonish a Frenchman only to look at him; his arm's thicker nor a Frenchman's body, I'll be bound, for they pinch theirsells in wi' stays; and it's easy enough, for they've got nothing i' their insides.'

'Where is the Captain, as he wasna at church today?' said Adam. 'I was talking to him o' Friday, and he said nothing about his going away.'

'Oh, he's only gone to Eagledale for a bit o' fishing; I reckon he'll be back again afore many days are o'er, for he's to be at all th' arranging and preparing o' things for the comin' o' age o' the 30th o' July. But he's fond o' getting away for a bit, now and then. Him and th' old squire fit one another like frost and flowers.'

Mr Craig smiled and winked slowly as he made this last observation, but the subject was not developed farther, for now they had reached the turning in the road where Adam and his companions must say 'goodbye.' The gardener, too, would have had to turn off in the same direction if he had not accepted Mr Poyser's invitation to tea. Mrs Poyser duly seconded the invitation, for she would have held it a deep disgrace not to make her neighbours welcome to her house: personal likes and dislikes must not interfere with that sacred custom. Moreover, Mr Craig had always been full of civilities to the family at the Hall Farm, and Mrs Poyser was scrupulous in declaring that she had 'nothing to say again' him, on'y it was a pity he couldna be hatched o'er again, an' hatched different.'

So Adam and Seth, with their mother between them, wound their way down to the valley and up again to the old house, where a saddened memory had taken the place of a long, long anxiety – where Adam would never have to ask again as he entered, 'Where's father?'

And the other family party, with Mr Craig for company, went back to the pleasant bright house-place at the Hall Farm – all with quiet minds, except Hetty, who knew now where Arthur was gone, but was only the more puzzled and uneasy. For it appeared that his absence was quite voluntary; he need not have gone – he would not have gone if he had wanted to see her. She had a sickening sense that no lot could ever be pleasant to her again if her Thursday night's vision was not to be fulfilled; and in this moment of chill, bare, wintry disappointment and doubt, she looked towards the possibility of being with Arthur again, of meeting his loving glance, and hearing his soft words, with that eager yearning which one may call the 'growing pain' of passion.

Adam on a Working Day

Not with standing Mr Craig's prophecy, the dark-blue cloud dispersed itself without having produced the threatened consequences. 'The weather,' as he observed the next morning – 'the weather, you see, 's a ticklish thing, an' a fool 'ull hit on't sometimes when a wise man misses; that's why the almanecks get so much credit. It's one o' them chancy things as fools thrive on.'

This unreasonable behaviour of the weather, however, could displease no one else in Hayslope beside Mr Craig. All hands were to be out in the meadows this morning as soon as the dew had risen; the wives and daughters did double work in every farmhouse, that the maids might give their help in tossing the hay; and when Adam was marching along the lanes, with his basket of tools over his shoulder, he caught the sound of jocose talk and ringing laughter from behind the hedges. The jocose talk of haymakers is best at a distance; like those clumsy bells round the cows' necks, it has rather a coarse sound when it comes close, and may even grate on your ears painfully, but heard from far off, it mingles very prettily with the other joyous sounds of nature. Men's muscles move better when their souls are making merry music, though their merriment is of a poor blundering sort, not at all like the merriment of birds.

And perhaps there is no time in a summer's day more cheering, than when the warmth of the sun is just beginning to triumph over the freshness of the morning – when there is just a lingering hint of early coolness to keep off languor under the delicious influence of warmth. The reason Adam was walking along the lanes at this time was because his work for the rest of the day lay at a country house about three miles off, which was being put in repair for the son of a neighbouring squire; and he had been busy since early morning with the packing of panels, doors, and chimney-pieces, in a waggon which was now gone on before him, while Jonathan Burge himself had ridden to the spot on horseback, to await its arrival and direct the workmen.

This little walk was a rest to Adam, and he was unconsciously under the charm of the moment. It was summer morning in his heart, and he saw Hetty in the sunshine: a sunshine without glare – with slanting rays that tremble between the delicate shadows of the leaves. He thought, yesterday, when he put out his hand to her as they came out of church, that there was a touch of melancholy kindness in her face, such as he had not seen before, and he took it as a sign that she had some sympathy with his family trouble. Poor fellow! that touch of melancholy came from quite another source; but how was he to know? We look at the one little woman's face we love, as we look at the face of our mother earth, and see all sorts of answers to our own yearnings. It was impossible for Adam not to feel that what had happened in the last week had brought the prospect of marriage nearer to him. Hitherto he had felt keenly the danger that some other man might step in and get possession of Hetty's heart and hand, while he himself was still in a position that made him shrink from asking her to accept him. Even if he had had a strong hope that she was fond of him – and his hope was far from being strong – he had been too heavily burthened with other claims to provide a home for himself and Hetty – a home such as he could expect her to be content with after the comfort and plenty of the Farm. Like all strong natures, Adam had confidence in his ability to achieve something in the future; he felt sure he should someday, if he lived, be able to maintain a family, and make a good broad path for himself; but he had too cool a head not to estimate to the full the obstacles that were to be overcome. And the time would be so long! And there was Hetty, like a bright-cheeked apple hanging over the orchard wall, within sight of everybody, and everybody must long for her! To be sure, if she loved him very much, she would be content to wait for him: but did she love him? His hopes had never risen so high that he had dared to ask her. He was clear-sighted enough to be aware that her uncle and aunt would have looked kindly on his suit, and indeed without this encouragement he would never have persevered in going to the Farm; but it was impossible to come to any but fluctuating conclusions about Hetty's feelings. She was like a kitten, and had the same distractingly pretty looks, that meant nothing, for everybody that came near her.

But now he could not help saying to himself that the heaviest part of his burden was removed, and that even before the end of another year his circumstances might be brought into a shape that would allow him to think of marrying. It would always be a hard struggle with his mother, he knew: she would be jealous of any wife he might choose, and she had set her mind especially against Hetty – perhaps for no other reason than that she suspected Hetty to be the woman he had chosen. It would never do, he feared, for his mother to live in the same house with him when he was married; and yet how hard she would think it if he asked her to leave him! Yes, there was a great deal of pain to be gone through with his mother, but it was a case in which he must make her feel that his will was strong – it would be better for her in the end. For himself, he would have liked that they should all live together till Seth was married, and they might have built a bit themselves to the old house, and made more room. He did not like 'to part wi' th' lad': they had hardly ever been separated for more than a day since they were born.

But Adam had no sooner caught his imagination leaping forward in this way – making arrangements for an uncertain future – than he checked himself 'A pretty building I'm making, without either bricks or timber. I'm up i' the garret a'ready, and haven't so much as dug the foundation.' Whenever Adam was strongly convinced of any proposition, it took the form of a principle in his mind: it was knowledge to be acted on, as much as the knowledge that damp will cause rust. Perhaps here lay the secret of the hardness he had accused himself of: he had too little fellow-feeling with the weakness that errs in spite of foreseen consequences. Without this fellow-feeling, how are we to get enough patience and charity towards our stumbling, falling companions in the long and changeful journey? And there is but one way in which a strong determined soul can learn it – by getting his heart-strings bound round the weak and erring, so that he must share not only the outward consequence of their error, but their inward suffering.

That is a long and hard lesson and Adam had at present only learned the alphabet of it in his father's sudden death, which, by annihilating in an instant all that had stimulated his indignation, had sent a sudden rush of thought and memory over what had claimed his pity and tenderness.

But it was Adam's strength, not its correlative hardness, that influenced his meditations this morning. He had long made up his mind that it would be wrong as well as foolish for him to marry a blooming young girl, so long as he had no other prospect than that of growing poverty with a growing family. And his savings had been so constantly drawn upon (besides the terrible sweep of paying for Seth's substitute in the militia), that he had not enough money beforehand to furnish even a small cottage, and keep something in reserve against a rainy day. He had good hope that he should be 'firmer on his legs' by and by; but he could not be satisfied with a vague confidence in his arm and brain; he must have definite plans, and set about them at once. The partnership with Jonathan Burge was not to be thought of at present – there were things implicitly tacked to it that he could not accept; but Adam thought that he and Seth might carry on a little business for themselves in addition to their journeyman's work, by buying a small stock of superior wood and making articles of household furniture, for which Adam had no end of contrivances. Seth might gain more by working at separate jobs under Adam's direction than by his journeyman's work, and Adam, in his over-hours, could do all the 'nice' work, that required peculiar skill. The money gained in this way, with the good wages he received as foreman, would soon enable them to get beforehand with the world so sparingly as they would all live now. No sooner had this little plan shaped itself in his mind than he began to be busy with exact calculations about the wood to be bought, and the particular article of furniture that should be undertaken first – a kitchen cupboard of his own contrivance, with such an ingenious arrangement of sliding-doors and bolts, such convenient nooks for stowing household provender, and such a symmetrical result to the eye, that every good housewife would be in raptures with it, and fall through all the gradations of melancholy longing till her husband promised to buy it for her. Adam pictured to himself Mrs Poyser examining it with her keen eye, and trying in vain to find out a deficiency; and, of course, close to Mrs Poyser stood Hetty, and Adam was again beguiled from calculations and contrivances into dreams and hopes. Yes, he would go and see her this evening – it was so long since he had been at the Hall Farm. He would have liked to go to the night-school, to see why Bartle Massey had not been at church yesterday, for he feared his old friend was ill; but, unless he could manage both visits, this last must be put off till tomorrow – the desire to be near Hetty, and to speak to her again, was too strong.

As he made up his mind to this, he was coming very near to the end of his walk, within the sound of the hammers at work on the refitting of the old house. The sound of tools to a clever workman who loves his work is like the tentative sounds of the orchestra to the violinist who has to bear his part in the overture: the strong fibres begin their accustomed thrill, and what was a moment before joy, vexation, or ambition, begins its change into energy. All passion becomes strength when it has an outlet from the narrow limits of our personal lot in the labour of our right arm, the cunning of our right hand, or the still, creative activity of our thought. Look at Adam through the rest of the day, as he stands on the scaffolding with the two-feet ruler in his hand, whistling low while he considers how a difficulty about a floor-joist or a window-frame is to be over-come; or as he pushes one of the younger workmen aside, and takes his place in upheaving a weight of timber, saying, 'Let alone, lad! thee'st got too much gristle i' thy bones yet;' or as he fixes his keen black eyes on the motions of a workman on the other side of the room, and warns him that his distances are not right. Look at this broad-shouldered man with the bare muscular arms, and the thick firm black hair tossed about like trodden meadow-grass whenever he takes off his paper cap, and with the strong baritone voice bursting every now and then into loud and solemn psalm-tunes, as if seeking an outlet for superfluous strength, yet presently checking himself, apparently crossed by some thought which jars with the singing. Perhaps, if you had not been already in the secret, you might not have guessed what sad memories, what warm affection, what tender fluttering hopes, had their home in this athletic body with the broken fingernails – in this rough man, who knew no better lyrics than he could find in the Old and New version and an occasional hymn; who knew the smallest possible amount of profane history; and for whom the motion and shape of the earth, the course of the sun, and the changes of the seasons, lay in the region of mystery just made visible by fragmentary knowledge. It had cost Adam a great deal of trouble, and work in over-hours, to know what he knew over and above the secrets of his handicraft, and that acquaintance with mechanics and figures, and the nature of the materials he worked with, which was made easy to him by inborn inherited faculty – to get the mastery of his pen, and write a plain hand, to spell without any other mistakes than must in fairness be attributed to the unreasonable character of orthography rather than to any deficiency in the speller, and, moreover, to learn his musical notes and part-singing. Besides all this, he had read his Bible, including the apocryphal books; *Poor Richard's Almanac*, Taylor's *Holy Living and Dying*, *The Pilgrim's Progress*, with Bunyan's Life and *Holy War*, a great deal of Bailey's Dictionary, *Valentine and Orson*, and part of a *History of Babylon*, which Bartle Massey had lent him. He might have had many more books from Bartle Massey, but he had no time for reading 'the commin print,' as Lisbeth called it, so busy as he was with figures in all the leisure moments which he did not fill up with extra carpentry.

Adam, you perceive, was by no means a marvellous man, nor, properly speaking, a genius, yet I will not pretend that his was an ordinary character among workmen; and it would not be at all a safe conclusion that the next best man you may happen to see with a basket of tools over his shoulder and a paper cap on his head has the strong conscience and the strong sense, the blended susceptibility and self-command, of our friend Adam. He was not an average man. Yet such men as he are reared here and there in every generation of our peasant artisans – with an inheritance of affections nurtured by a simple family life of common need and common industry, and an inheritance of faculties trained in skilful courageous labour: they make their way upward, rarely as geniuses, most commonly as painstaking honest men, with the skill and conscience to do well the tasks that lie before them. Their lives have no discernible echo beyond the neighbourhood where they dwelt, but you are almost sure to find there some good piece of road, some building, some application of mineral produce, some improvement in farming practice, some reform of parish abuses, with which their names are associated by one or two generations after them. Their employers were the richer for them, the work of their hands has worn well, and the work of their brains has guided well the hands of other men. They went about in their youth in flannel or paper caps, in coats black with coal-dust or streaked with lime and red paint; in old age their white hairs are seen in a place of honour at church and at market, and they tell their well-dressed sons and daughters, seated round the bright hearth on winter evenings, how pleased they were when they first earned their twopence a day. Others there are who die poor, and never put off the workman's coat on week days: they have not had the art of getting rich; but they are men of trust, and when they die before the work is all out of them, it is as if some main screw had got loose in a machine; the master who employed them says, 'Where shall I find their like?'

20

Adam Visits the Hall Farm

Adam came back from his work in the empty waggon; that was why he had changed his clothes, and was ready to set out to the Hall Farm when it still wanted a quarter to seven.

'What's thee got thy Sunday cloose on for?' said Lisbeth, complainingly, as he came downstairs. 'Thee artna goin' to th' school i' thy best coat?'

'No, mother,' said Adam, quietly. 'I'm going to the Hall Farm, but mayhap I may go to the school after, so thee mustna wonder if I'm a bit late. Seth 'ull be at home in half an hour – he's only gone to the village; so thee wutna mind.'

'Eh, an' what's thee got thy best cloose on for to go to th' Hall Farm? The Poyser folks see'd thee in 'em yesterday, I warrand. What dost mean by turnin' worki'day into Sunday a-that'n? It's poor keepin' company wi' folks as donna like to see thee i' thy workin' jacket.'

'Goodbye, mother, I can't stay,' said Adam, putting on his hat and going out.

But he had no sooner gone a few paces beyond the door than Lisbeth became uneasy at the thought that she had vexed him. Of course, the secret of her objection to the best clothes was her suspicion that they were put on for Hetty's sake; but deeper than all her peevishness lay the need that her son should love her. She hurried after him, and laid hold of his arm before he had got halfway down to the brook, and said, 'Nay, my lad, thee wutna go away angered wi' thy mother, an' her got nought to do but to sit by hersen an' think on thee?'

'Nay, nay, mother,' said Adam, gravely, and standing still while he put his arm on her shoulder, 'I'm not angered. But I wish, for thy own sake, thee'dst be more contented to let me do what I've made up my mind to do. I'll never be no other than a good son to thee as long as we live. But a man has other feelings besides what he owes to's father and mother; and thee oughtna to want to rule over me body and soul. And thee must make up thy mind, as I'll not give way to thee where I've a right to do what I like. So let us have no more words about it.'

'Eh,' said Lisbeth, not willing to show that she felt the real bearing of Adam's words, 'an' who likes to see thee i' thy best cloose better nor thy mother? An' when thee'st got thy face washed as clean as the smooth white pibble, an' thy hair combed so nice, and thy eyes a-sparklin – what else is there as thy old mother should like to look at half so well? An' thee sha't put on thy Sunday cloose when thee lik'st for me – I'll ne'er plague thee no moor about'n.'

'Well, well; goodbye, mother,' said Adam, kissing her, and hurrying away. He saw there was no other means of putting an end to the dialogue. Lisbeth stood still on the spot, shading her eyes and looking after him till he was quite out of sight. She felt to the full all the meaning that had lain in Adam's words, and, as she lost sight of him and turned back slowly into the house, she said aloud to herself – for it was her way to speak her thoughts aloud in the long days when her husband and sons were at their work – 'Eh, he'll be tellin' me as he's goin' to bring her home one o' these days; an' she'll be missis o'er me, and I mun look on, belike, while she uses the blue-edged platters, and breaks 'em, mayhap, though there's ne'er been one broke sin' my old man an' me bought 'em at the fair twenty 'ear come next Whissuntide. Eh!' she went on, still louder, as she caught up her knitting from the table, 'but she'll ne'er knit the lads' stockins, nor foot 'em nayther, while I live; an' when I'm gone, he'll bethink him as nobody 'ull ne'er fit's leg an' foot as his old mother did. She'll know nothin' o' narrowin' an' heelin', I warrand, an' she'll make a long toe as he canna get's boot on. That's what comes o' marr'in' young wenches. I war gone thirty, an' th' feyther too, afore we war married; an' young enough too. She'll be a poor dratchell by then *she's* thirty, a-marr'in' a-that'n, afore her teeth's all come.'

Adam walked so fast that he was at the yard gate before seven. Martin Poyser and the grandfather were not yet come in from the meadow: everyone was in the meadow, even to the black-and-tan terrier – no one kept watch in the yard but the bulldog; and when Adam reached the house-door, which stood wide open, he saw there was no one in the bright clean house-place. But he guessed where Mrs Poyser and someone else would be, quite within hearing; so he knocked on the door and said in his strong voice, 'Mrs Poyser within?'

'Come in, Mr Bede, come in,' Mrs Poyser called out from the dairy. She always gave Adam this title when she received him in her own house. 'You may come into the dairy if you will, for I canna justly leave the cheese.'

Adam walked into the dairy, where Mrs Poyser and Nancy were crushing the first evening cheese.

'Why, you might think you war come to a dead-house,' said Mrs Poyser, as he stood in the open doorway; 'they're all i' the meadow; but Martin's sure to be in afore long, for they're leaving the hay cocked tonight, ready for carrying first thing tomorrow. I've been forced t' have Nancy in' upo' 'count as Hetty must gether the red currans tonight; the fruit allays ripens so contrairy, just when every hand's wanted. An' there's no trustin' the children to gether it, for they put more into their own mouths nor into the basket; you might as well set the wasps to gether the fruit.'

Adam longed to say he would go into the garden till Mr Poyser came in, but he was not quite courageous enough, so he said, 'I could be looking at your spinning-wheel, then, and see what wants doing to it. Perhaps it stands in the house, where I can find it?'

'No, I've put it away in the right-hand parlour; but let it be till I can fetch it and show it you. I'd be glad now, if you'd go into the garden, and tell Hetty to send Totty in. The child 'ull run in if she's told, an' I know Hetty's lettin' her eat too many currans. I'll be much obliged to you, Mr Bede, if you'll go and send her in; an' there's the York and Lankester roses beautiful in the garden now – you'll like to see 'em. But you'd like a drink o' whey first, p'r'aps; I know you're fond o' whey, as most folks is when they hanna got to crush it out.'

'Thank you, Mrs Poyser,' said Adam; 'a drink o' whey's allays a treat to me. I'd rather have it than beer any day.'

'Ay, ay,' said Mrs Poyser, reaching a small white basin that stood on the shelf, and dipping it into the whey-tub, 'the smell o' bread's sweet t' everybody but the baker. The Miss Irwines allays say, "Oh, Mrs Poyser, I envy you your dairy; and I envy you your chickens; and what a beautiful thing a farmhouse is, to be sure!" An' I say, "Yes; a farmhouse is a fine thing for them as look on, an' don't know the liftin', an' the stannin', an' the worritin' o' th' inside, as belongs to't." '

'Why, Mrs Poyser, you wouldn't like to live anywhere else but in a farmhouse, so well as you manage it,' said Adam, taking the basin; 'and there can be nothing to look at pleasanter nor a fine milch cow, standing up to'ts knees in pasture, and the new milk frothing in the pail, and the fresh butter ready for market, and the calves, and the poultry. Here's to your health, and may you allays have strength to look after your own dairy, and set a pattern t' all the farmers' wives in the country.'

Mrs Poyser was not to be caught in the weakness of smiling at a compliment, but a quiet complacency overspread her face like a stealing sunbeam, and gave a milder glance than usual to her blue-grey eyes, as she looked at Adam drinking the whey. Ah! I think I taste that whey now – with a flavour so delicate that one can hardly distinguish it from an odour, and with that soft gliding warmth that fills one's imagination with a still, happy dreaminess. And the light music of the dropping whey is in my ears, mingling with the twittering of a bird outside the wire network window – the window overlooking the garden, and shaded by tall Gueldres roses.

'Have a little more, Mr Bede?' said Mrs Poyser, as Adam set down the basin.

'No, thank you; I'll go into the garden now, and send in the little lass.'

'Ay, do; and tell her to come to her mother in the dairy.'

Adam walked round by the rick-yard, at present empty of ricks, to the little wooden gate leading into the garden – once the well-tended kitchen-garden of a manor-house; now, but for the handsome brick wall with stone coping that ran along one side of it, a true farmhouse garden, with hardy perennial flowers, unpruned fruit trees, and kitchen vegetables growing together in careless, half-neglected abundance. In that leafy, flowery, bushy time, to look for anyone in this garden was like playing at 'hide-and-seek'. There were the tall hollyhocks beginning to flower, and dazzle the eye with their pink, white, and yellow; there were the syringas and Gueldres roses, all large and disorderly for want of trimming, there were leafy walls of scarlet beans and late peas; there was a row of bushy filberts in one direction, and in another a huge apple tree making a barren circle under its low-spreading boughs. But what signified a barren patch or two? The garden was so large. There was always a superfluity of broad beans – it took nine or ten of Adam's strides to get to the end of the uncut grass walk that ran by the side of them; and as for other vegetables, there was so much more room than was necessary for them, that in the rotation of crops a large flourishing bed of groundsel was of yearly occurrence on one spot or other. The very rose trees, at which Adam stopped to pluck one, looked as if they grew wild; they were all huddled together in bushy masses, now flaunting with wide open petals, almost all of them of the streaked pink-and-white kind, which doubtless dated from the union of the houses of York and Lancaster. Adam was wise enough to choose a compact Provence rose that peeped out half-smothered by its flaunting scentless neighbours, and held it in his hand – he thought he should be more at ease holding something in his hand – as he walked on to the far end of the garden, where he remembered there was the largest row of currant trees, not far off from the great yew-tree arbour.

But he had not gone many steps beyond the roses, when he heard the shaking of a bough, and a boy's voice saying – 'Now, then, Totty, hold out your pinny – there's a duck.'

The voice came from the boughs of a tall cherry tree, where Adam had no difficulty in discerning a small blue-pinafored figure perched in a commodious position where the fruit was thickest. Doubtless Totty was below, behind the screen of peas. Yes – with her bonnet hanging down her back, and her fat face, dreadfully smeared with red juice, turned up towards the cherry tree, while she held her little round hole of a mouth and her red-stained pinafore to receive the promised downfall. I am sorry to say, more than half the cherries that fell were hard and yellow instead of juicy and red; but Totty spent no time in useless regrets, and she was already sucking the third juiciest when Adam said, 'There now, Totty, you've got your cherries. Run into the house with 'em to mother – she wants you – she's in the dairy. Run in this minute – there's a good little girl.'

He lifted her up in his strong arms and kissed her as he spoke, a ceremony which Totty regarded as a tiresome interruption to cherry-eating; and when he set her down she trotted off quite silently towards the house, sucking her cherries as she went along.

'Tommy, my lad, take care you're not shot for a little thieving bird,' said Adam, as he walked on towards the currant trees.

He could see there was a large basket at the end of the row: Hetty would not be far off, and Adam already felt as if she were looking at him. Yet when he turned the corner she was standing with her back towards him, and stooping to gather the low-hanging fruit. Strange that she had not heard him coming! perhaps it was because she was making the leaves rustle. She started when she became conscious that someone was near – started so violently that she dropped the basin with the currants in it, and then, when she saw it was Adam, she turned from pale to deep red. That blush made his heart beat with a new happiness. Hetty had never blushed at seeing him before.

'I frightened you,' he said, with a delicious sense that it didn't signify what he said, since Hetty seemed to feel as much as he did; 'let me pick the currants up.'

That was soon done, for they had only fallen in a tangled mass on the grass-plot, and Adam, as he rose and gave her the basin again, looked straight into her eyes with the subdued tenderness that belongs to the first moments of hopeful love.

Hetty did not turn away her eyes; her blush had subsided, and she met his glance with a quiet sadness, which contented Adam, because it was so unlike anything he had seen in her before.

'There's not many more currants to get,' she said; 'I shall soon ha' done now.'

'I'll help you,' said Adam; and he fetched the large basket which was nearly full of currants, and set it close to them.

Not a word more was spoken as they gathered the currants. Adam's heart was too full to speak, and he thought Hetty knew all that was in it. She was not indifferent to his presence after all; she had blushed when she saw him, and then there was that touch of sadness about her which must surely mean love, since it was the opposite of her usual manner, which had often impressed him as indifference. And he could glance at her continually as she bent over the fruit, while the level evening sunbeams stole through the thick apple-tree boughs, and rested on her round cheek and neck as if they too were in love with her. It was to Adam the time that a man can least forget in afterlife – the time when he believes that the first woman he has ever loved betrays by a slight something – a word, a tone, a glance, the quivering of a lip or an eyelid – that she is at least beginning to love him in return. The sign is so slight, it is scarcely perceptible to the ear or eye – he could describe it to no one – it is a mere feather-touch, yet it seems to have changed his whole being, to have merged an uneasy yearning into a delicious unconsciousness of everything but the present moment. So much of our early gladness vanishes utterly from our memory: we can never recall the joy with which we laid our heads on our mother's bosom or rode on our father's back in childhood; doubtless that joy is wrought up into our nature, as the sunlight of long-past mornings is wrought up in the soft mellowness of the apricot, but it is gone for ever from our imagination, and we can only *believe* in the joy of childhood. But the first glad moment in our first love is a vision which returns to us to the last, and brings with it a thrill of feeling intense and special as the recurrent sensation of a sweet odour breathed in a far-off hour of happiness. It is a memory that gives a more exquisite touch to tenderness, that feeds the madness of jealousy, and adds the last keenness to the agony of despair.

Hetty bending over the red bunches, the level rays piercing the screen of apple-tree boughs, the length of bushy garden beyond, his own emotion as he looked at her and believed that she was thinking of him, and that there was no need for them to talk – Adam remembered it all to the last moment of his life.

And Hetty? You know quite well that Adam was mistaken about her. Like many other men, he thought the signs of love for another were signs of love towards himself. When Adam was approaching unseen by her, she was absorbed as usual in thinking and wondering about Arthur's possible return: the sound of any man's footstep would have affected her just in the same way – she would have *felt* it might be Arthur before she had time to see, and the blood that forsook her cheek in the agitation of that momentary feeling would have rushed back again at the sight of anyone else just as much as at the sight of Adam. He was not wrong in thinking that a change had come over Hetty: the anxieties and fears of a first passion, with which she was trembling, had become stronger than vanity, had given her for the first time that sense of helpless dependence on another's feeling which awakens the clinging deprecating womanhood even in the shallowest girl that can ever experience it, and creates in her a sensibility to kindness which found her quite hard before. For the first time Hetty felt that there was something soothing to her in Adam's timid yet manly tenderness: she wanted to be treated lovingly – oh, it was very hard to bear this blank of absence, silence, apparent indifference, after those moments of glowing love! she was not afraid that Adam would tease her with love-making and flattering speeches like her other admirers: he had always been so reserved to her: she could enjoy without any fear the sense that this strong brave man loved her, and was near her. It never entered into her mind that Adam was pitiable too – that Adam, too, must suffer one day.

Hetty, we know, was not the first woman that had behaved more gently to the man who loved her in vain, because she had herself begun to love another. It was a very old story; but Adam knew nothing about it, so he drank in the sweet delusion.

'That'll do,' said Hetty, after a little while. 'Aunt wants me to leave some on the trees. I'll take 'em in now.'

'It's very well I came to carry the basket,' said Adam, 'for it 'ud ha' been too heavy for your little arms.'

'No; I could ha' carried it with both hands.'

'Oh, I dare say,' said Adam, smiling, 'and been as long getting into the house as a little ant carrying a caterpillar. Have you ever seen those tiny fellows carrying things four times as big as themselves?'

'No,' said Hetty, indifferently, not caring to know the difficulties of ant-life.

'Oh, I used to watch 'em often when I was a lad. But now, you see, I can carry the basket with one arm, as if it was an empty nutshell, and give you th' other arm to lean on. Won't you? Such big arms as mine were made for little arms like yours to lean on.'

Hetty smiled faintly, and put her arm within his. Adam looked down at her, but her eyes were turned dreamily towards another corner of the garden.

'Have you ever been to Eagledale?' she said, as they walked slowly along.

'Yes,' said Adam, pleased to have her ask a question about himself; 'ten years ago, when I was a lad, I went with father to see about some work there. It's a wonderful sight – rocks and caves such as you never saw in your life. I never had a right notion o' rocks till I went there.'

'How long did it take to get there?'

'Why, it took us the best part o' two days' walking. But it's nothing of a day's journey for anybody as has got a first-rate nag. The Captain 'ud get there in nine or ten hours, I'll be bound, he's such a rider. And I shouldn't wonder if he's back again tomorrow; he's too active to rest long in that lonely place, all by himself, for there's nothing but a bit of a inn i' that part where he's gone to fish. I wish he'd got th' estate in his hands; that 'ud be the right thing for him, for it 'ud give him plenty to do, and he'd do't well too, for all he's so young; he's got better notions o' things than many a man twice his age. He spoke very handsome to me th' other day about lending me money to set up i' business; and if things came round that way, I'd rather be beholding to him nor to any man i' the world.'

Poor Adam was led on to speak about Arthur because he thought Hetty would be pleased to know that the young squire was so ready to befriend him; the fact entered into his future prospects, which he would like to seem promising in her eyes. And it was true that Hetty listened with an interest which brought a new light into her eyes and a half smile upon her lips.

'How pretty the roses are now!' Adam continued, pausing to look at them. 'See! I stole the prettiest, but I didna mean to keep it myself. I think these as are all pink, and have got a finer sort o' green leaves, are prettier than the striped uns, don't you?'

He set down the basket, and took the rose from his button hole.

'It smells very sweet,' he said; 'those striped uns have no smell. Stick it in your frock, and then you can put it in water after. It 'ud be a pity to let it fade.'

Hetty took the rose, smiling as she did so at the pleasant thought that Arthur could so soon get back if he liked. There was a flash of hope and happiness in her mind, and with a sudden impulse of gaiety she did what she had very often done before – stuck the rose in her hair a little above the left ear. The tender admiration in Adam's face was slightly shadowed by reluctant disapproval. Hetty's love of finery was just the thing that would most provoke his mother, and he himself disliked it as much as it was possible for him to dislike anything that belonged to her.

'Ah,' he said, 'that's like the ladies in the pictures at the Chase; they've mostly got flowers or feathers or gold things i' their hair, but somehow I don't like to see 'em: they allays put me i' mind o' the painted women outside the shows at Treddles'on fair. What can a woman have to set her off better than her own hair, when it curls so, like yours? If a woman's young and pretty, I think you can see her good looks all the better for her being plain dressed. Why, Dinah Morris looks very nice, for all she wears such a plain cap and gown. It seems to me as a woman's face doesna want flowers; it's almost like a flower itself. I'm sure yours is.'

'Oh, very well,' said Hetty, with a little playful pout, taking the rose out of her hair. 'I'll put one o' Dinah's caps on when we go in, and you'll see if I look better in it. She left one behind, so I can take the pattern.'

'Nay, nay, I don't want you to wear a Methodist cap like Dinah's. I dare say it's a very ugly cap, and I used to think when I saw her here, as it was nonsense for her to dress different t' other people; but I never rightly noticed her till she came to see mother last week, and then I thought the cap seemed to fit her face somehow as th' acorn cup fits th' acorn, and I shouldn't like to see her so well without it. But you've got another sort o' face; I'd have you just as you are now, without anything t' interfere with your own looks. It's like when a man's singing a good tune, you don't want t' hear bells tinkling and interfering wi' the sound.'

He took her arm and put it within his again, looking down on her fondly. He was afraid she should think he had lectured her; imagining, as we are apt to do, that she had perceived all the thoughts he had only half expressed. And the thing he dreaded most was lest any cloud should come over this evening's happiness. For the world he would not have spoken of his love to Hetty yet, till this commencing kindness towards him should have grown into unmistakable love. In his imagination he saw long years of his future life stretching before him, blest with the right to call Hetty his own: he could be content with very little at present. So he took up the basket of currants once more, and they went on towards the house.

The scene had quite changed in the half-hour that Adam had been in the garden. The yard was full of life now: Marty was letting the screaming geese through the gate, and wickedly provoking the gander by hissing at him; the granary-door was groaning on its hinges as Alick shut it, after dealing out the corn; the horses were being led out to watering, amidst much barking of all the three dogs, and many 'whups', from Tim the ploughman, as if the heavy animals who held down their meek, intelligent heads, and lifted their shaggy feet so deliberately, were likely to rush wildly in every direction but the right. Everybody was come back from the meadow; and when Hetty and Adam entered the house-place, Mr Poyser was seated in the three-cornered chair, and the grandfather in the large armchair opposite, looking on with pleasant expectation while the supper was being laid on the oak table. Mrs Poyser had laid the cloth herself – a cloth made of homespun linen, with a shining checkered pattern on it, and of an agreeable whitey-brown hue, such as all sensible housewives like to see – none of your bleached 'shop-rag' that would wear into holes in no time, but good home-spun that would last for two generations. The cold veal, the fresh lettuces, and the stuffed chine, might well look tempting to hungry men who had dined at half-past twelve o'clock. On the large deal table against the wall there were bright pewter plates and spoons and cans, ready for Alick and his companions; for the master and servants ate their supper not far off each other; which was all the pleasanter, because if a remark about tomorrow morning's work occurred to Mr Poyser, Alick was at hand to hear it.

'Well, Adam, I'm glad to see ye,' said Mr Poyser. 'What! ye've been helping Hetty to gether the currans, eh? Come, sit ye down, sit ye down. Why, it's pretty near a three-week since y' had your supper with us; and the missis has got one of her rare stuffed chines. I'm glad ye're come.'

'Hetty,' said Mrs Poyser, as she looked into the basket of currants to see if the fruit was fine, 'run upstairs, and send Molly down. She's putting Totty to bed, and I want her to draw th' ale, for Nancy's busy yet i' the dairy. You can see to the child. But whativer did you let her run away from you along wi' Tommy for, and stuff herself wi' fruit as she can't eat a bit o' good victual?'

This was said in a lower tone than usual, while her husband was talking to Adam; for Mrs Poyser was strict in adherence to her own rules of propriety, and she considered that a young girl was not to be treated sharply in the presence of a respectable man who was courting her. That would not be fair play: every woman was young in her turn, and had her chances of matrimony, which it was a point of honour for other women not to spoil – just as one market-woman who has sold her own eggs must not try to balk another of a customer.

Hetty made haste to run away upstairs, not easily finding an answer to her aunt's question, and Mrs Poyser went out to see after Marty and Tommy, and bring them in to supper.

Soon they were all seated – the two rosy lads, one on each side, by the pale mother, a place being left for Hetty between Adam and her uncle. Alick too was come in, and was seated in his far corner, eating cold broad beans out of a large dish with his pocket-knife, and finding a flavour in them which he would not have exchanged for the finest pineapple.

'What a time that gell is drawing th' ale, to be sure!' said Mrs Poyser, when she was dispensing her slices of stuffed chine. 'I think she sets the jug under and forgets to turn the tap, as there's nothing you can't believe o' them wenches: they'll set the empty kettle o' the fire, and then come an hour after to see if the water boils.'

'She's drawin' for the men too,' said Mr Poyser. 'Thee shouldst ha' told her to bring our jug up first.'

'Told her?' said Mrs Poyser: 'yes, I might spend all the wind i' my body, an' take the bellows too, if I was to tell them gells everything as their own sharpness wonna tell 'em. Mr Bede, will you take some vinegar with your lettuce? Ay, you're i' the right not. It spoils the flavour o' the chine, to my thinking. It's poor eating where the flavour o' the meat lies i' the cruets. There's folks as make bad butter, and trusten to the salt t' hide it.'

Mrs Poyser's attention was here diverted by the appearance of Molly, carrying a large jug, two small mugs, and four drinking-cans, all full of ale or small beer – an interesting example of the prehensile power possessed by the human hand. Poor Molly's mouth was rather wider open than usual, as she walked along with her eyes fixed on the double cluster of vessels in her hands, quite innocent of the expression in her mistress's eye.

'Molly, I niver knew your equils – to think o' your poor mother as is a widow, an' I took you wi' as good as no character, an' the times an' times I've told you.'

Molly had not seen the lightning, and the thunder shook her nerves the more for the want of that preparation. With a vague alarmed sense that she must somehow comport herself differently, she hastened her step a little towards the far deal table, where she might set down her cans – caught her foot in her apron, which had become untied, and fell with a crash and a splash into a pool of beer; whereupon a tittering explosion from Marty and Tommy, and a serious 'Ello!' from Mr Poyser, who saw his draught of ale unpleasantly deferred.

'There you go!' resumed Mrs Poyser, in a cutting tone, as she rose and went towards the cupboard while Molly began dolefully to pick up the fragments of pottery. 'It's what I told you 'ud come, over and over again; and there's your month's wage gone, and more, to pay for that jug as I've had i' the house this ten year, and nothing ever happened to't before; but the crockery you've broke sin' here in th' house you've been 'ud make a parson swear – God forgi' me for saying

so; an' if it had been boiling wort out o' the copper, it 'ud ha' been the same, and
you'd ha' been scalded, and very like lamed for life, as there's no knowing but
what you will be someday if you go on; for anybody 'ud think you'd got the St
Vitus's Dance, to see the things you've throwed down. It's a pity but what the
bits was stacked up for you to see, though it's neither seeing nor hearing as 'ull
make much odds to you – anybody 'ud think you war case-hardened.'

Poor Molly's tears were dropping fast by this time, and in her desperation at
the lively movement of the beer-stream towards Alick's legs, she was converting her apron into a mop, while Mrs Poyser, opening the cupboard, turned
a blighting eye upon her.

'Ah,' she went on, 'you'll do no good wi' crying an' making more wet to wipe
up. It's all your own wilfulness, as I tell you, for there's nobody no call to break
anything if they'll only go the right way to work. But wooden folks had need ha'
wooden things t' handle. And here must I take the brown-and-white jug, as it's
niver been used three times this year, and go down i' the cellar myself, and
belike catch my death, and be laid up wi' inflammation.'

Mrs Poyser had turned round from the cupboard with the brown-and-white
jug in her hand, when she caught sight of something at the other end of the
kitchen; perhaps it was because she was already trembling and nervous that the
apparition had so strong an effect on her; perhaps jug-breaking, like other
crimes, has a contagious influence. However it was, she stared and started like a
ghost seer, and the precious brown-and-white jug fell to the ground, parting for
ever with its spout and handle.

'Did ever anybody see the like?' she said, with a suddenly lowered tone, after a
moment's bewildered glance round the room. 'The jugs are bewitched, I think.
It's them nasty glazed handles – they slip o'er the finger like a snail.'

'Why, thee'st let thy own whip fly i' thy face,' said her husband, who had now
joined in the laugh of the young ones.

'It's all very fine to look on and grin,' rejoined Mrs Poyser; 'but there's times
when the crockery seems alive, an' flies out o' your hand like a bird. It's like the
glass, sometimes, 'ull crack as it stands. What is to be broke will be broke, for I
never dropped a thing i' my life for want o' holding it, else I should never ha'
kept the crockery all these 'ears as I bought at my own wedding. And Hetty, are
you mad? Whativer do you mean by coming down i' that way, and making one
think as there's a ghost a-walking i' th' house?'

A new outbreak of laughter, while Mrs Poyser was speaking, was caused, less
by her sudden conversion to a fatalistic view of jug-breaking, than by that
strange appearance of Hetty, which had startled her aunt. The little minx had
found a black gown of her aunt's, and pinned it close round her neck to look like
Dinah's, had made her hair as flat as she could, and had tied on one of Dinah's
high-crowned borderless net-caps. The thought of Dinah's pale grave face and
mild grey eyes, which the sight of the gown and cap brought with it, made it a
laughable surprise enough to see them replaced by Hetty's round rosy cheeks
and coquettish dark eyes. The boys got off their chairs and jumped round her,
clapping their hands, and even Alick gave a low ventral laugh as he looked up
from his beans. Under cover of the noise, Mrs Poyser went into the back kitchen

to send Nancy into the cellar with the great pewter measure, which had some chance of being free from bewitchment.

'Why, Hetty, lass, are ye turned Methodist?' said Mr Poyser, with that comfortable slow enjoyment of a laugh which one only sees in stout people. 'You must pull your face a deal longer before you'll do for one; mustna she, Adam? How come you to put them things on, eh?'

'Adam said he liked Dinah's cap and gown better nor my clothes,' said Hetty, sitting down demurely. 'He says folks look better in ugly clothes.'

'Nay, nay,' said Adam, looking at her admiringly; 'I only said they seemed to suit Dinah. But if I'd said you'd look pretty in 'em, I should ha' said nothing but what was true.'

'Why, thee thought'st Hetty war a ghost, didstna?' said Mr Poyser to his wife, who now came back and took her seat again. 'Thee look'dst as scared as scared.'

'It little sinnifies how I looked,' said Mrs Poyser; 'looks 'ull mend no jugs, nor laughing neither, as I see. Mr Bede, I'm sorry you've to wait so long for your ale, but it's coming in a minute. Make yourself at home wi' th' cold potatoes: I know you like 'em. Tommy, I'll send you to bed this minute, if you don't give over laughing. What is there to laugh at, I should like to know? I'd sooner cry nor laugh at the sight o' that poor thing's cap; and there's them as 'ud be better if they could make theirselves like her i' more ways nor putting on her cap. It little becomes anybody i' this house to make fun o' my sister's child, an' her just gone away from us, as it went to my heart to part wi' her: an' I know one thing, as if trouble was to come, an' I was to be laid up i' my bed, an' the children was to die – as there's no knowing but what they will – an' the murrain was to come among the cattle again, an' everything went to rack an' ruin – I say we might be glad to get sight o' Dinah's cap again, wi' her own face under it, border or no border. For she's one o' them things as looks the brightest on a rainy day, and loves you the best when you're most i' need on't.'

Mrs Poyser, you perceive, was aware that nothing would be so likely to expel the comic as the terrible. Tommy, who was of a susceptible disposition, and very fond of his mother, and who had, besides, eaten so many cherries as to have his feelings less under command than usual, was so affected by the dreadful picture she had made of the possible future, that he began to cry; and the good-natured father, indulgent to all weaknesses but those of negligent farmers, said to Hetty –

'You'd better take the things off again, my lass; it hurts your aunt to see 'em.'

Hetty went upstairs again, and the arrival of the ale made an agreeable diversion; for Adam had to give his opinion of the new tap, which could not be otherwise than complimentary to Mrs Poyser; and then followed a discussion on the secrets of good brewing, the folly of stinginess in 'hopping', and the doubtful economy of a farmer's making his own malt. Mrs Poyser had so many opportunities of expressing herself with weight on these subjects, that by the time supper was ended, the ale jug refilled, and Mr Poyser's pipe alight, she was once more in high good-humour, and ready, at Adam's request, to fetch the broken spinning-wheel for his inspection.

'Ah,' said Adam, looking at it carefully, 'here's a nice bit o' turning wanted. It's a pretty wheel. I must have it up at the turning-shop in the village, and do it there, for I've no convenence for turning at home. If you'll send it to Mr Burge's shop i' the morning, I'll get it done for you by Wednesday. I've been turning it over in my mind,' he continued, looking at Mr Poyser, 'to make a bit more convenence at home for nice jobs o' cabinet-making. I've always done a deal at such little things in odd hours, and they're profitable, for there's more workman-ship nor material in 'em. I look for me and Seth to get a little business for ourselves i' that way, for I know a man at Rosseter as 'ull take as many things as we should make, besides what we could get orders for round about.'

Mr Poyser entered with interest into a project which seemed a step towards Adam's becoming a 'master-man;' and Mrs Poyser gave her approbation to the scheme of the movable kitchen cupboard, which was to be capable of containing grocery, pickles, crockery, and house-linen, in the utmost compactness, without confusion. Hetty, once more in her own dress, with her neckerchief pushed a little backwards on this warm evening, was seated picking currants near the window, where Adam could see her quite well. And so the time passed pleasantly till Adam got up to go. He was pressed to come again soon, but not to stay longer, for at this busy time sensible people would not run the risk of being sleepy at five o'clock in the morning.

'I shall take a step farther,' said Adam, 'and go on to see Mester Massey, for he wasn't at church yesterday, and I've not seen him for a week past. I've never hardly known him to miss church before.'

'Ay,' said Mr Poyser, 'we've heared nothing about him, for it's the boys' hollodays now, so we can give you no account.'

'But you'll niver think o' going there at this hour o' the night?' said Mrs Poyser, folding up her knitting.

'Oh, Mester Massey sits up late,' said Adam. 'An' the night-school's not over yet. Some o' the men don't come till late – they've got so far to walk. And Bartle himself's never in bed till it's gone eleven.'

'I wouldna have him to live wi' me, then,' said Mrs Poyser, 'a-dropping candle-grease about, as you're like to tumble down o' the floor the first thing i' the morning.'

'Ay, eleven o'clock's late – it's late,' said old Martin. 'I ne'er sot up so i' my life, not to say as it warna a marr'in', or a christenin', or a wake, or th' harvest-supper. Eleven o'clock's late.'

'Why, I sit up till after twelve often,' said Adam, laughing, 'but it isn't t' eat and drink extry, it's to work extry. Good-night, Mrs Poyser; good-night, Hetty.'

Hetty could only smile and not shake hands, for hers were dyed and damp with currant juice; but all the rest gave a hearty shake to the large palm that was held out to them, and said, 'Come again, come again!'

'Ay, think o' that now,' said Mr Poyser, when Adam was out on the causeway. 'Sitting up till past twelve to do extry work! Ye'll not find many men o' six-an'-twenty as 'ull do to put i' the shafts wi' him. If you can catch Adam for a husband, Hetty, you'll ride i' your own spring-cart someday, I'll be your warrant.'

Hetty was moving across the kitchen with the currants, so her uncle did not see the little toss of the head with which she answered him. To ride in a spring-cart seemed a very miserable lot indeed to her now.

The Night-School and the Schoolmaster

Bartle Massey's was one of a few scattered houses on the edge of a common, which was divided by the road to Treddleston. Adam reached it in a quarter of an hour after leaving the Hall Farm; and when he had his hand on the door-latch, he could see, through the curtainless window, that there were eight or nine heads bending over the desks, lighted by thin dips.

When he entered, a reading lesson was going forward, and Bartle Massey merely nodded, leaving him to take his place where he pleased. He had not come for the sake of a lesson tonight, and his mind was too full of personal matters, too full of the last two hours he had passed in Hetty's presence, for him to amuse himself with a book till school was over; so he sat down in a corner, and looked on with an absent mind. It was a sort of scene which Adam had beheld almost weekly for years; he knew by heart every arabesque flourish in the framed specimen of Bartle Massey's handwriting which hung over the schoolmaster's head, by way of keeping a lofty ideal before the minds of his pupils; he knew the backs of all the books on the shelf running along the whitewashed wall above the pegs for the slates; he knew exactly how many grains were gone out of the ear of Indian-corn that hung from one of the rafters; he had long ago exhausted the resources of his imagination in trying to think how the bunch of leathery seaweed had looked and grown in its native element; and from the place where he sat, he could make nothing of the old map of England that hung against the opposite wall, for age had turned it of a fine yellow brown, something like that of a well-seasoned meerschaum. The drama that was going on was almost as familiar as the scene, nevertheless habit had not made him indifferent to it, and even in his present self-absorbed mood, Adam felt a momentary stirring of the old fellow-feeling, as he looked at the rough men painfully holding pen or pencil with their cramped hands, or humbly labouring through their reading lesson.

The reading class now seated on the form in front of the schoolmaster's desk, consisted of the three most backward pupils. Adam would have known it, only by seeing Bartle Massey's face as he looked over his spectacles, which he had shifted to the ridge of his nose, not requiring them for present purposes. The face wore its mildest expression: the grizzled bushy eyebrows had taken their more acute angle of compassionate kindness, and the mouth, habitually compressed with a pout of the lower lip, was relaxed so as to be ready to speak a helpful word or syllable in a moment. This gentle expression was the more interesting because the schoolmaster's nose, an irregular aquiline twisted a little on one side, had rather a formidable character; and his brow, moreover, had that peculiar tension which always impresses one as a sign of a keen impatient temperament: the blue veins stood out like cords under the transparent yellow skin, and this intimidating brow was softened by no tendency to baldness, for the grey bristly hair, cut down to about an inch in length, stood round it in as close ranks as ever.

'Nay, Bill, nay,' Bartle was saying in a kind tone, as he nodded to Adam, 'begin that again, and then perhaps, it'll come to you what d, r, y, spells. It's the same lesson you read last week, you know.'

'Bill' was a sturdy fellow, aged four-and-twenty, an excellent stone-sawyer, who could get as good wages as any man in the trade of his years, but he found a reading lesson in words of one syllable a harder matter to deal with than the hardest stone he had ever had to saw. The letters, he complained, were so 'uncommon alike, there was no tellin' 'em one from another,' the sawyer's business not being concerned with minute differences such as exist between a letter with its tail turned up and a letter with its tail turned down. But Bill had a firm determination that he would learn to read, founded chiefly on two reasons: first, that Tom Hazelow, his cousin, could read anything 'right off,' whether it was print or writing, and Tom had sent him a letter from twenty miles off, saying how he was prospering in the world, and had got an overlooker's place; secondly, that Sam Phillips, who sawed with him, had learned to read when he was turned twenty; and what could be done by a little fellow like Sam Phillips, Bill considered, could be done by himself, seeing that he could pound Sam into wet clay if circumstances required it. So here he was, pointing his big finger towards three words at once, and turning his head on one side that he might keep better hold with his eye of the one word which was to be discriminated out of the group. The amount of knowledge Bartle Massey must possess was something so dim and vast that Bill's imagination recoiled before it: he would hardly have ventured to deny that the schoolmaster might have something to do in bringing about the regular return of daylight and the changes in the weather.

The man seated next to Bill was of a very different type: he was a Methodist brickmaker, who, after spending thirty years of his life in perfect satisfaction with his ignorance, had lately 'got religion,' and along with it the desire to read the Bible. But with him, too, learning was a heavy business, and on his way out tonight he had offered as usual a special prayer for help, seeing that he had undertaken this hard task with a single eye to the nourishment of his soul – that he might have a greater abundance of texts and hymns wherewith to banish evil memories and the temptations of old habit; or, in brief language, the devil. For the brickmaker had been a notorious poacher, and was suspected, though there was no good evidence against him, of being the man who had shot a neighbouring gamekeeper in the leg. However that might be, it is certain that shortly after the accident referred to, which was coincident with the arrival of an awakening Methodist preacher at Treddleston, a great change had been observed in the brickmaker; and though he was still known in the neighbourhood by his old sobriquet of 'Brimstone,' there was nothing he held in so much horror as any farther transactions with that evil-smelling element. He was a broad-chested fellow, with a fervid temperament, which helped him better in imbibing religious ideas than in the dry process of acquiring the mere human knowledge of the alphabet. Indeed, he had been already a little shaken in his resolution by a brother Methodist, who assured him that the letter was a mere obstruction to the spirit, and expressed a fear that Brimstone was too eager for the knowledge that puffeth up.

The third beginner was a much more promising pupil. He was a tall but thin and wiry man, nearly as old as Brimstone, with a very pale face, and hands stained a deep blue. He was a dyer, who, in the course of dipping homespun wool and old women's petticoats, had got fired with the ambition to learn a great deal more about the strange secrets of colour. He had already a high reputation in the district for his dyes, and he was bent on discovering some method by which he could reduce the expense of crimsons and scarlets. The druggist at Treddleston had given him a notion that he might save himself a great deal of labour and expense if he could learn to read, and so he had begun to give his spare hours to the night-school, resolving that his 'little chap' should lose no time in coming to Mr Massey's day-school as soon as he was old enough.

It was touching to see these three big men, with the marks of their hard labour about them, anxiously bending over the worn books, and painfully making out, 'The grass is green,' 'The sticks are dry,' 'The corn is ripe' – a very hard lesson to pass to after columns of single words all alike except in the first letter. It was almost as if three rough animals were making humble efforts to learn how they might become human. And it touched the tenderest fibre in Bartle Massey's nature, for such full-grown children as these were the only pupils for whom he had no severe epithets, and no impatient tones. He was not gifted with an imperturbable temper, and on music-nights it was apparent that patience could never be an easy virtue to him; but this evening, as he glances over his spectacles at Bill Downes, the sawyer, who is turning his head on one side with a desperate sense of blankness before the letters d, r, y, his eyes shed their mildest and most encouraging light.

After the reading class, two youths, between sixteen and nineteen, came up with imaginary bills of parcels, which they had been writing out on their slates, and were now required to calculate 'off-hand' – a test which they stood with such imperfect success that Bartle Massey, whose eyes had been glaring at them ominously through his spectacles for some minutes, at length burst out in a bitter, high-pitched tone, pausing between every sentence to rap the floor with a knobbed stick which rested between his legs.

'Now, you see, you don't do this thing a bit better than you did a fortnight ago; and I'll tell you what's the reason. You want to learn accounts; that's well and good. But you think all you need do to learn accounts is to come to me and do sums for an hour or so, two or three times a week; and no sooner do you get your caps on and turn out of doors again, than you sweep the whole thing clean out of your mind. You go whistling about, and take no more care what you're thinking of than if your heads were gutters for any rubbish to swill through that happened to be in the way, and if you get a good notion in 'em, it's pretty soon washed out again. You think knowledge is to be got cheap – you'll come and pay Bartle Massey sixpence a week, and he'll make you clever at figures without your taking any trouble. But knowledge isn't to be got with paying sixpence, let me tell you: if you're to know figures, you must turn 'em over in your own heads, and keep your thoughts fixed on 'em. There's nothing you can't turn into a sum, for there's nothing but what's got number in it – even a fool. You may say to yourselves, "I'm one fool, and Jack's another; if my fool's head weighed four pound, and Jack's three pound three ounces and three quarters, how many pennyweights heavier would my head be than Jack's?" A man that had got his heart in learning figures would make sums for himself, and work 'em in his head: when he sat at his shoemaking, he'd count his stitches by fives, and then put a price on his stitches, say half a farthing, and then see how much money he could get in an hour; and then ask himself how much money he'd get in a day at that rate; and then how much ten workmen would get working three, or twenty, or a hundred years at that rate – and all the while his needle would be going just as fast as if he left his head empty for the devil to dance in. But the long and the short of it is – I'll have nobody in my night-school that doesn't strive to learn what he comes to learn, as hard as if he was striving to get out of a dark hole into broad daylight. I'll send no man away because he's stupid: if Billy Taft, the idiot, wanted to learn anything, I'd not refuse to teach him. But I'll not throw away good knowledge on people who think they can get it by the sixpenn'orth, and carry it away with 'em as they would an ounce of snuff. So never come to me again, if you can't show that you've been working with your own heads, instead of thinking you can pay for mine to work for you. That's the last word I've got to say to you.'

With this final sentence, Bartle Massey gave a sharper rap than ever with his knobbed stick, and the discomfited lads got up to go with a sulky look. The other pupils had happily only their writing-books to show, in various stages of progress from pot-hooks to round text; and mere pen-strokes, however perverse, were less exasperating to Bartle than false arithmetic. He was a little more severe than usual on Jacob Storey's Zs, of which poor Jacob had written a pageful, all with their tops turned the wrong way, with a puzzled sense that they were not right 'somehow.' But he observed in apology, that it was a letter you never wanted hardly, and he thought it had only been put there 'to finish off th' alphabet, like, though ampus-and (&) would ha' done as well, for what he could see.'

At last the pupils had all taken their hats and said their 'Good-nights,' and Adam, knowing his old master's habits, rose and said, 'Shall I put the candles out, Mr Massey?'

'Yes, my boy, yes, all but this, which I'll carry into the house; and just lock the outer door, now you're near it,' said Bartle, getting his stick in the fitting angle to help him in descending from his stool. He was no sooner on the ground than it became obvious why the stick was necessary – the left leg was much shorter than the right. But the schoolmaster was so active with his lameness, that it was hardly thought of as a misfortune; and if you had seen him make his way along the schoolroom floor, and up the step into his kitchen, you would perhaps have understood why the naughty boys sometimes felt that his pace might be indefinitely quickened, and that he and his stick might overtake them even in their swiftest run.

The moment he appeared at the kitchen door with the candle in his hand, a faint whimpering began in the chimney-corner, and a brown-and-tan-coloured bitch, of that wise-looking breed with short legs and long body, known to an unmechanical generation as turnspits, came creeping along the floor, wagging her tail, and hesitating at every other step, as if her affections were painfully divided between the hamper in the chimney-corner and the master, whom she could not leave without a greeting.

'Well, Vixen, well then, how are the babbies?' said the schoolmaster, making haste towards the chimney-corner, and holding the candle over the low hamper, where two extremely blind puppies lifted up their heads towards the light, from a nest of flannel and wool. Vixen could not even see her master look at them without painful excitement: she got into the hamper and got out again the next moment, and behaved with true feminine folly, though looking all the while as wise as a dwarf with a large old-fashioned head and body on the most abbreviated legs.

'Why, you've got a family, I see, Mr Massey?' said Adam, smiling, as he came into the kitchen. 'How's that? I thought it was against the law here.'

'Law? What's the use o' law when a man's once such a fool as to let a woman into his house?' said Bartle, turning away from the hamper with some bitterness. He always called Vixen a woman, and seemed to have lost all consciousness that he was using a figure of speech. 'If I'd known Vixen was a woman, I'd never have held the boys from drowning her; but when I'd got her into my hand, I was forced to take to her. And now you see what she's brought me to – the sly, hypocritical wench' – Bartle spoke these last words in a rasping tone of reproach, and looked at Vixen, who poked down her head and turned up her eyes towards him with a keen sense of opprobrium – 'and contrived to be brought to bed on a Sunday at church-time. I've wished again and again I'd been a bloody-minded man, that I could have strangled the mother and the brats with one cord.'

'I'm glad it was no worse a cause kept you from church,' said Adam. 'I was afraid you must be ill for the first time i' your life. And I was particular sorry not to have you at church yesterday.'

'Ah, my boy, I know why, I know why,' said Bartle, kindly, going up to Adam, and raising his hand up to the shoulder that was almost on a level with his own head. 'You've had a rough bit o' road to get over since I saw you – a rough bit o' road. But I'm in hopes there are better times coming for you. I've got some news to tell you. But I must get my supper first, for I'm hungry, I'm hungry. Sit down, sit down.'

Bartle went into his little pantry, and brought out an excellent home-baked loaf; for it was his one extravagance in these dear times to eat bread once a day instead of oatcake; and he justified it by observing, that what a schoolmaster wanted was brains, and oatcake ran too much to bone instead of brains. Then came a piece of cheese and a quart jug with a crown of foam upon it. He placed them all on the round deal table which stood against his large armchair in the chimney-corner with Vixen's hamper on one side of it, and a window-shelf with a few books piled up in it on the other. The table was as clean as if Vixen had been an excellent housewife in a checkered apron; so was the quarry floor; and the old carved oaken press, table, and chairs, which in these days would be bought at a high price in aristocratic houses, though, in that period of spider-legs and inlaid cupids, Bartle had got them for an old song, were as free from dust as things could be at the end of a summer's day.

'Now, then, my boy, draw up, draw up. We'll not talk about business till we've had our supper. No man can be wise on an empty stomach. But,' said Bartle, rising from his chair again, 'I must give Vixen her supper too, confound her! though she'll do nothing with it but nourish those unnecessary babbies. That's the way with these women, they've got no head-pieces to nourish, and so their food all runs either to fat or to brats.'

He brought out of the pantry a dish of scraps, which Vixen at once fixed her eyes on, and jumped out of her hamper to lick up with the utmost despatch.

'I've had my supper, Mr Massey,' said Adam, 'so I'll look on while you eat yours. I've been at the Hall Farm, and they always have their supper betimes, you know: they don't keep your late hours.'

'I know little about their hours,' said Bartle, dryly, cutting his bread and not shrinking from the crust. 'It's a house I seldom go into, though I'm fond of the boys, and Martin Poyser's a good fellow. There's too many women in the house for me: I hate the sound of women's voices; they're always either a-buzz or a-squeak always either a-buzz or a-squeak. Mrs Poyser keeps at the top o' the talk like a fife; and as for the young lasses, I'd as soon look at water-grubs – I know what they'll turn to – stinging gnats, stinging gnats. Here, take some ale, my boy: it's been drawn for you – it's been drawn for you.'

'Nay, Mr Massey,' said Adam, who took his old friend's whim more seriously than usual tonight, 'don't be so hard on the creaturs God has made to be companions for us. A working man 'ud be badly off without a wife to see to th' house and the victual, and make things clean and comfortable.'

'Nonsense! It's the silliest lie a sensible man like you ever believed, to say a woman makes a house comfortable. It's a story got up, because the women are there, and something must be found for 'em to do. I tell you there isn't a thing under the sun that needs to be done at all, but what a man can do better than a woman, unless it's bearing children, and they do that in a poor makeshift way; it had better ha' been left to the men – it had better ha' been left to the men. I tell you, a woman 'ull bake you a pie every week of her life, and never come to see that the hotter th' oven the shorter the time. I tell you, a woman 'ull make your porridge every day for twenty years, and never think of measuring the proportion between the meal and the milk – a little more or less, she'll think, doesn't signify: the porridge will be awk'ard now and then: if it's wrong, it's summat in the meal, or it's summat in the milk, or it's summat in the water. Look at me! I make my own bread, and there's no difference between one batch and another from year's end to year's end; but if I'd got any other woman besides Vixen in the house, I must pray to the Lord every baking to give me patience if the bread turned out heavy. And as for cleanliness, my house is cleaner than any other house on the Common, though the half of 'em swarm with women. Will Baker's lad comes to help me in a morning, and we get as much cleaning done in one hour without any fuss, as a woman 'ud get done in three, and all the while be sending buckets o' water after your ankles, and let the fender and the fire-irons stand in the middle o' the floor half the day, for you to break your shins against 'em. Don't tell me about God having made such creatures to be companions for us! I don't say but He might make Eve to be a companion to Adam in Paradise – there was no cooking to be spoilt there, and no other woman to cackle with and make mischief; though you see what mischief she did as soon as she'd an opportunity. But it's an impious, unscriptural opinion to say a woman's a blessing to a man now; you might as well say adders and wasps, and foxes and wild beasts, are a blessing, when they're only the evils that belong to this state o' probation, which it's lawful for a man to keep as clear of as he can in this life, hoping to get quit of 'em for ever in another – hoping to get quit of 'em for ever in another.'

Bartle had become so excited and angry in the course of his invective that he had forgotten his supper, and only used the knife for the purpose of rapping the table with the haft. But towards the close, the raps became so sharp and frequent, and his voice so quarrelsome, that Vixen felt it incumbent on her to jump out of the hamper and bark vaguely.

'Quiet, Vixen!' snarled Bartle, turning round upon her. 'You're like the rest o' the women – always putting in your word before you know why.'

Vixen returned to her hamper again in humiliation, and her master continued his supper in a silence which Adam did not choose to interrupt; he knew the old man would be in a better humour when he had had his supper and lighted his pipe. Adam was used to hear him talk in this way, but had never learned so much of Bartle's past life as to know whether his view of married comfort was founded on experience. On that point Bartle was mute; and it was even a secret where he had lived previous to the twenty years in which, happily for the peasants and artisans of this neighbourhood, he had been settled among them as their only schoolmaster. If anything like a question was ventured on this subject, Bartle always replied, 'Oh, I've seen many places – I've been a deal in the south' – and the Loamshire men would as soon have thought of asking for a particular town or village in Africa as in 'the south.'

'Now then, my boy,' said Bartle, at last, when he had poured out his second mug of ale and lighted his pipe – 'now then, we'll have a little talk. But tell me first, have you heard any particular news today?'

'No,' said Adam, 'not as I remember.'

'Ah, they'll keep it close, they'll keep it close, I dare say. But I found it out by chance; and it's news that may concern you, Adam, else I'm a man that don't know a superficial square foot from a solid.'

Here Bartle gave a series of fierce and rapid puffs, looking earnestly the while at Adam. Your impatient loquacious man has never any notion of keeping his pipe alight by gentle measured puffs; he is always letting it go nearly out, and then punishing it for that negligence. At last he said – 'Satchell's got a paralytic stroke. I found it out from the lad they sent to Treddleston for the doctor, before seven o'clock this morning. He's a good way beyond sixty, you know; it's much if he gets over it.'

'Well,' said Adam, 'I dare say there'd be more rejoicing than sorrow in the parish at his being laid up. He's been a selfish, tale-bearing, mischievous fellow; but, after all, there's nobody he's done so much harm to as to th' old squire. Though it's the squire himself as is to blame – making a stupid fellow like that a sort o' man-of-all-work, just to save th' expense of having a proper steward to look after th' estate. And he's lost more by ill-management o' the woods, I'll be bound, than 'ud pay for two stewards. If he's laid on the shelf, it's to be hoped he'll make way for a better man, but I don't see how it's like to make any difference to me.'

'But I see it, but I see it,' said Bartle; 'and others besides me. The Captain's coming of age now – you know that as well as I do – and it's to be expected he'll have a little more voice in things. And I know, and you know too, what 'ud be the Captain's wish about the woods, if there was a fair opportunity for making a change. He's said in plenty of people's hearing that he'd make you manager of the woods tomorrow, if he'd the power. Why, Carroll, Mr Irwine's butler, heard him say so to the parson not many days ago. Carroll looked in when we were smoking our pipes o' Saturday night at Casson's, and he told us about it; and whenever anybody says a good word for you, the parson's ready to back it, that I'll answer for. It was pretty well talked over, I can tell you, at Casson's, and one and another had their fling at you: for if donkeys set to work to sing, you're pretty sure what the tune 'ull be.'

'Why, did they talk it over before Mr Burge?' said Adam 'or wasn't he there o' Saturday?'

'Oh, he went away before Carroll came; and Casson – he's always for setting other folks right, you know – would have it Burge was the man to have the management of the woods. "A substantial man," says he, "with pretty near sixty years' experience o' timber: it 'ud be all very well for Adam Bede to act under him, but it isn't to be supposed the squire 'ud appoint a young fellow like Adam, when there's his elders and betters at hand!" But I said, "That's a pretty notion o' yours, Casson. Why, Burge is the man to buy timber; would you put the woods into his hands, and let him make his own bargains? I think you don't leave your customers to score their own drink, do you? And as for age, what that's worth depends on the quality o' the liquor. It's pretty well known who's the backbone of Jonathan Burge's business".'

'I thank you for your good word, Mr Massey,' said Adam. 'But, for all that, Casson was partly i' the right for once. There's not much likelihood that th' old squire 'ud ever consent t' employ me: I offended him about two years ago, and he's never forgiven me.'

'Why, how was that? You never told me about it,' said Bartle.

'Oh, it was a bit o' nonsense. I'd made a frame for a screen for Miss Lyddy – she's allays making something with her worsted-work, you know – and she'd given me particular orders about this screen, and there was as much talking and measuring as if we'd been planning a house. However, it was a nice bit o' work, and I liked doing it for her. But, you know, those little friggling things take a deal o' time. I only worked at it in over-hours often late at night – and I had to go to Treddleston over an' over again, about little bits o' brass nails and such gear; and I turned the little knobs and the legs, and carved th' open work, after a pattern, as nice as could be. And I was uncommon pleased with it when it was done. And when I took it home, Miss Lyddy sent for me to bring it into her drawing-room, so as she might give me directions about fastening on the work – very fine needlework, Jacob and Rachel a-kissing one another among the sheep, like a picture – and th' old squire was sitting there, for he mostly sits with her. Well, she was mighty pleased with the screen, and then she wanted to know what pay she was to give me. I didn't speak at random – you know it's not my way; I'd calculated pretty close, though I hadn't made out a bill, and I said, one pound thirteen. That was paying for the mater'als and paying me, but none too much, for my work. Th' old squire looked up at this, and peered in his way at the screen, and said, "One pound thirteen for a gimcrack like that! Lydia, my dear, if you must spend money on these things, why don't you get them at Rosseter, instead of paying double price for clumsy work here? Such things are not work for a carpenter like Adam. Give him a guinea, and no more." Well, Miss Lyddy, I reckon, believed what he told her, and she's not over-fond o' parting with the money herself – she's not a bad woman at bottom, but she's been brought up under his thumb; so she began fidgeting with her purse, and turned as red as her ribbon. But I made a bow, and said, "No, thank you, madam; I'll make you a present o' the screen, if you please. I've charged the regular price for my work, and I know it's done well; and I know, begging his honour's pardon, that you couldn't get such a screen at Rosseter under two guineas. I'm willing to give you my work – it's been done in my own time, and nobody's got anything to do with it but me; but if I'm paid, I can't take a smaller price than I asked, because that 'ud be like saying, I'd asked more than was just. With your leave, madam, I'll bid you good-morning." I made my bow and went out before she'd time to say any more, for she stood with the purse in her hand, looking almost foolish. I didn't mean to be disrespectful, and I spoke as polite as I could; but I can give in to no man, if he wants to make it out as I'm trying t' overreach him. And in the evening the footman brought me the one pound thirteen wrapped in paper. But since then I've seen pretty clear as th' old squire can't abide me.'

'That's likely enough, that's likely enough,' said Bartle, meditatively. 'The only way to bring him round would be to show him what was for his own interest, and that the Captain may do – that the Captain may do.'

'Nay, I don't know,' said Adam; 'the squire's 'cute enough, but it takes something else besides 'cuteness to make folks see what'll be their interest in the long run. It takes some conscience and belief in right and wrong, I see that pretty clear. You'd hardly ever bring round th' old squire to believe he'd gain as much in a straightfor'ard way as by tricks and turns. And, besides, I've not much mind to work under him: I don't want to quarrel with any gentleman, more particular an old gentleman turned eighty, and I know we couldn't agree long. If the Captain was master o' th' estate, it 'ud be different: he's got a conscience and a will to do right, and I'd sooner work for him nor for any man living.'

'Well, well, my boy, if good luck knocks at your door, don't you put your head out at window and tell it to be gone about its business, that's all. You must learn to deal with odd and even in life, as well as in figures. I tell you now, as I told you ten years ago, when you pommelled young Mike Holdsworth for wanting to pass a bad shilling, before you knew whether he was in jest or earnest – you're over-hasty and proud, and apt to set your teeth against folks that don't square to your notions. It's no harm for me to be a bit fiery and stiff-backed: I'm an old schoolmaster, and shall never want to get on to a higher perch. But where's the use of all the time I've spent in teaching you writing and mapping and mensuration, if you're not to get for'ard in the world, and show folks there's some advantage in having a head on your shoulders, instead of a turnip? Do you mean to go on turning up your nose at every opportunity, because it's got a bit of a smell about it that nobody finds out but yourself? It's as foolish as that notion o' yours that a wife is to make a working man comfortable. Stuff and nonsense! – stuff and nonsense! Leave that to fools that never got beyond a sum in simple addition. Simple addition enough! Add one fool to another fool, and in six years' time six fools more – they're all of the same denomination, big and little's nothing to do with the sum!'

During this rather heated exhortation to coolness and discretion the pipe had gone out, and Bartle gave the climax to his speech by striking a light furiously, after which he puffed with fierce resolution, fixing his eye still on Adam, who was trying not to laugh.

'There's a good deal o' sense in what you say, Mr Massey,' Adam began, as soon as he felt quite serious, 'as there always is. But you'll give in that it's no business o' mine to be building on chances that may never happen. What I've got to do is to work as well as I can with the tools and mater'als I've got in my hands. If a good chance comes to me, I'll think o' what you've been saying; but till then, I've got nothing to do but to trust to my own hands and my own head-piece. I'm turning over a little plan for Seth and me to go into the cabinet-making a bit by ourselves, and win a extra pound or two in that way. But it's getting late now – it'll be pretty near eleven before I'm at home, and mother may happen to lie awake; she's more fidgety nor usual now. So I'll bid you good-night.'

'Well, well, we'll go to the gate with you – it's a fine night,' said Bartle, taking up his stick. Vixen was at once on her legs, and without further words the three walked out into the starlight, by the side of Bartle's potato-beds, to the little gate.

'Come to the music o' Friday night, if you can, my boy,' said the old man, as he closed the gate after Adam, and leaned against it.

'Ay, ay,' said Adam, striding along towards the streak of pale road. He was the only object moving on the wide common. The two grey donkeys, just visible in front of the gorse bushes, stood as still as limestone images – as still as the grey-thatched roof of the mud cottage a little farther on. Bartle kept his eye on the moving figure till it passed into the darkness, while Vixen, in a state of divided affection, had twice run back to the house to bestow a parenthetic lick on her puppies.

'Ay, ay,' muttered the schoolmaster, as Adam disappeared; 'there you go, stalking along – stalking along; but you wouldn't have been what you are if you hadn't had a bit of old lame Bartle inside you. The strongest calf must have something to suck at. There's plenty of these big, lumbering fellows 'ud never have known their ABC, if it hadn't been for Bartle Massey. Well, well, Vixen, you foolish wench, what is it, what is it? I must go in, must I? Ay, ay, I'm never to have a will o' my own any more. And those pups, what do you think I'm to do with 'em, when they're twice as big as you? – for I'm pretty sure the father was that hulking bull-terrier of Will Baker's – wasn't he now, eh, you sly hussey?' (Here Vixen tucked her tail between her legs, and ran forward into the house. Subjects are sometimes broached which a well-bred female will ignore.)

'But where's the use of talking to a woman with babbies?' continued Bartle: 'she's got no conscience – no conscience; it's all run to milk.'

BOOK THIRD

2 2

Going to the Birthday Feast

The thirtieth of July was come, and it was one of those half-dozen warm days which sometimes occur in the middle of a rainy English summer. No rain had fallen for the last three or four days, and the weather was perfect for that time of the year: there was less dust than usual on the dark-green hedgerows, and on the wild camomile that starred the roadside, yet the grass was dry enough for the little children to roll on it, and there was no cloud but a long dash of light, downy ripple, high, high up in the far-off blue sky. Perfect weather for an outdoor July merrymaking, yet surely not the best time of year to be in. Nature seems to make a hot pause just then – all the loveliest flowers are gone; the sweet time of early growth and vague hopes is past; and yet the time of harvest and ingathering is not come, and we tremble at the possible storms that may ruin the precious fruit in the moment of its ripeness. The woods are all one dark monotonous green; the waggon-loads of hay no longer creep along the lanes, scattering their sweet-smelling fragments on the blackberry branches; the pastures are often a little tanned, yet the corn has not got its last splendour of red and gold; the lambs and calves have lost all traces of their innocent frisky prettiness, and have become stupid young sheep and cows. But it is a time of leisure on the farm – that pause between hay and corn harvest, and so the farmers and labourers in Hayslope and Broxton thought the Captain did well to come of age just then, when they could give their undivided minds to the flavour of the great cask of ale which had been brewed the autumn after 'the heir' was born, and was to be tapped on his twenty-first birthday. The air had been merry with the ringing of church bells very early this morning, and everyone had made haste to get through the needful work before twelve, when it would be time to think of getting ready to go to the Chase.

The midday sun was streaming into Hetty's bedchamber, and there was no blind to temper the heat with which it fell on her head as she looked at herself in the old specked glass. Still, that was the only glass she had in which she could see her neck and arms, for the small hanging glass she had fetched out of the next room – the room that had been Dinah's – would show her nothing below her little chin, and that beautiful bit of neck where the roundness of her cheek melted into another roundness shadowed by dark delicate curls. And today she thought more than usual about her neck and arms; for at the dance this evening she was not to wear any neckerchief, and she had been busy yesterday with her spotted pink-and-white frock, that she might make the sleeves either long or short at will. She was dressed now just as she was to be in the evening, with a tucker made of 'real' lace, which her aunt had lent her for this unparalleled occasion, but with no ornaments besides; she had even taken out her small round earrings which she wore every day. But there was something more to be done, apparently, before she put on her neckerchief and long sleeves, which she was to wear in the daytime, for now she unlocked the drawer that held her private treasures. It is more than a month since we saw her unlock that drawer before, and now it holds new treasures, so much more precious than the old ones that these are thrust into the corner. Hetty would not care to put the large coloured glass earrings into her ears now; for see! she has got a beautiful pair of gold and pearls and garnet, lying snugly in a pretty little box lined with white satin. Oh the delight of taking out that little box and looking at the earrings! Do not reason about it, my philosophical reader, and say that Hetty, being very pretty, must have known that it did not signify whether she had on any ornaments or not; and that, moreover, to look at earrings which she could not possibly wear out of her bedroom could hardly be a satisfaction, the essence of vanity being a reference to the impressions produced on others; you will never understand women's natures if you are so excessively rational. Try rather to divest yourself of all your rational prejudices, as much as if you were studying the psychology of a canary bird, and only watch the movements of this pretty round creature as she turns her head on one side with an unconscious smile at the earrings nestled in the little box. Ah, you think, it is for the sake of the person who has given them to her, and her thoughts are gone back now to the moment when they were put into her hands. No; else why should she have cared to have earrings rather than anything else? and I know that she had longed for earrings from among all the ornaments she could imagine.

'Little, little ears!' Arthur had said, pretending to pinch them one evening, as Hetty sat beside him on the grass without her hat. 'I wish I had some pretty earrings!' she said in a moment, almost before she knew what she was saying – the wish lay so close to her lips, it would flutter past them at the slightest breath. And the next day – it was only last week – Arthur had ridden over to Rosseter on purpose to buy them. That little wish so naïvely uttered, seemed to him the prettiest bit of childishness; he had never heard anything like it before; and he had wrapped the box up in a great many covers, that he might see Hetty unwrapping it with growing curiosity, till at last her eyes flashed back their new delight into his.

No, she was not thinking most of the giver when she smiled at the earrings, for now she is taking them out of the box, not to press them to her lips, but to fasten them in her ears – only for one moment, to see how pretty they look, as she peeps at them in the glass against the wall, with first one position of the head and then another, like a listening bird. It is impossible to be wise on the subject of earrings as one looks at her; what should those delicate pearls and crystals be made for, if not for such ears? One cannot even find fault with the tiny round hole which they leave when they are taken out; perhaps water-nixies, and such lovely things without souls, have these little round holes in their ears by nature, ready to hang jewels in. And Hetty must be one of them: it is too painful to think that she is a woman, with a woman's destiny before her – a woman spinning in young ignorance a light web of folly and vain hopes which may one day close round her and press upon her, a rancorous poisoned garment, changing all at once her fluttering, trivial butterfly sensations into a life of deep human anguish.

But she cannot keep in the earrings long, else she may make her uncle and aunt wait. She puts them quickly into the box again, and shuts them up. Some-day she will be able to wear any earrings she likes, and already she lives in an invisible world of brilliant costumes, shimmering gauze, soft satin, and velvet, such as the lady's-maid at the Chase has shown her in Miss Lydia's wardrobe: she feels the bracelets on her arms, and treads on a soft carpet in front of a tall mirror. But she has one thing in the drawer which she can venture to wear today, because she can hang it on the chain of dark-brown berries which she has been used to wear on grand days, with a tiny flat scent-bottle at the end of it tucked inside her frock; and she must put on her brown berries – her neck would look so unfinished without it. Hetty was not quite as fond of the locket as of the earrings, though it was a handsome large locket, with enamelled flowers at the back and a beautiful gold border round the glass, which showed a light-brown slightly waving lock, forming a background for two little dark rings. She must keep it under her clothes, and no one would see it. But Hetty had another passion, only a little less strong than her love of finery; and that other passion made her like to wear the locket even hidden in her bosom. She would always have worn it, if she had dared to encounter her aunt's questions about a ribbon round her neck. So now she slipped it on along her chain of dark-brown berries, and snapped the chain round her neck. It was not a very long chain, only allowing the locket to hang a little way below the edge of her frock. And now she had nothing to do but to put on her long sleeves, her new white gauze neckerchief, and her straw hat trimmed with white today instead of the pink, which had become rather faded under the July sun. That hat made the drop of bitterness in Hetty's cup today, for it was not quite new – everybody would see that it was a little tanned against the white ribbon – and Mary Burge, she felt sure, would have a new hat or bonnet on. She looked for consolation at her fine white cotton stockings: they really were very nice indeed, and she had given almost all her spare money for them. Hetty's dream of the future could not make her insensible to triumph in the present: to be sure, Captain Donnithorne loved her so, that he would never care about looking at other people, but then those other people didn't know how he loved her, and she was not satisfied to appear shabby and insignificant in their eyes even for a short space.

The whole party was assembled in the house-place when Hetty went down, all of course in their Sunday clothes; and the bells had been ringing so this morning in honour of the Captain's twenty-first birthday, and the work had all been got done so early, that Marty and Tommy were not quite easy in their minds until their mother had assured them that going to church was not part of the day's festivities. Mr Poyser had once suggested that the house should be shut up, and left to take care of itself; 'for,' said he, 'there's no danger of anybody's breaking in – everybody 'll be at the Chase, thieves an' all. If we lock th' house up, all the men can go: it's a day they wonna see twice i' their lives.' But Mrs Poyser answered with great decision: 'I never left th' house to take care of itself since I was a missis' and I never will. There's been ill-looking tramps enoo' about the place this last week, to carry off every ham an' every spoon we'n got; and they all collogue together, them tramps, as it's a mercy they hanna come and pisoned the dogs and murdered us all in our beds afore we knowed, some Friday night when we'n got the money in th' house to pay the men. And it's like enough the tramps know where we're going as well as we do oursens; for if Old Harry wants any work done, you may be sure he'll find the means.'

'Nonsense about murdering us in our beds,' said Mr Poyser; 'I've got a gun i' our room, hanna I? and thee'st got ears as 'ud find it out if a mouse was gnawing the bacon. Howiver, if thee wouldstna be easy, Alick can stay at home i' the forepart o' the day, and Tim can come back tow'rds five o'clock, and let Alick have his turn. They may let Growler loose if anybody offers to do mischief, and there's Alick's dog, too, ready enough to set his tooth in a tramp if Alick gives him a wink.'

Mrs Poyser accepted this compromise, but thought it advisable to bar and bolt to the utmost; and now, at the last moment before starting, Nancy, the dairymaid, was closing the shutters of the house-place, although the window, lying under the immediate observation of Alick and the dogs, might have been supposed the least likely to be selected for a burglarious attempt.

The covered cart, without springs, was standing ready to carry the whole family except the menservants: Mr Poyser and the grandfather sat on the seat in front, and within there was room for all the women and children; the fuller the cart the better, because then the jolting would not hurt so much, and Nancy's broad person and thick arms were an excellent cushion to be pitched on. But Mr Poyser drove at no more than a walking pace, that there might be as little risk of jolting as possible on this warm day; and there was time to exchange greetings and remarks with the foot-passengers who were going the same way, specking the paths between the green meadows and the golden cornfields with bits of movable bright colour – a scarlet waistcoat to match the poppies that nodded a little too thickly among the corn, or a dark-blue neckerchief with ends flaunting across a bran-new white smock-frock. All Broxton and all Hayslope were to be at the Chase, and make merry there in honour of 'th' heir;' and the old men and women, who had never been so far down this side of the hill for the last twenty years, were being brought from Broxton and Hayslope in one of the farmer's waggons, at Mr Irwine's suggestion. The church bells had struck up again now – a last tune, before the ringers came down the hill to have their share in the festival; and before the bells had finished, other music was heard approaching, so that even old Brown, the sober horse that was drawing Mr Poyser's cart, began to prick up his ears. It was the band of the Benefit Club, which had mustered in all its glory; that is to say, in bright-blue scarfs and blue favours, and carrying its banner with the motto, 'Let brotherly love continue,' encircling a picture of a stone-pit.

The carts, of course, were not to enter the Chase. Everyone must get down at the lodges, and the vehicles must be sent back.

'Why, the Chase is like a fair a'ready,' said Mrs Poyser, as she got down from the cart, and saw the groups scattered under the great oaks, and the boys running about in the hot sunshine to survey the tall poles surmounted by the fluttering garments that were to be the prize of the successful climbers. 'I should ha' thought there wasna so many people i' the two parishes. Mercy on us! how hot it is out o' the shade! Come here, Totty, else your little face 'ull be burnt to a scratchin'! They might ha' cooked the dinners i' that open space, an' saved the fires. I shall go to Mrs Best's room an' sit down.'

'Stop a bit, stop a bit,' said Mr Poyser. 'There's th' waggin coming wi' th' old folks in't; it'll be such a sight as wonna come o'er again, to see 'em get down an' walk along all together. You remember some on 'em i' their prime, eh, father?'

'Ay, ay,' said old Martin, walking slowly under the shade of the lodge porch, from which he could see the aged party descend. 'I remember Jacob Taft walking fifty mile after the Scotch raybels, when they turned back from Stoniton.'

He felt himself quite a youngster, with a long life before him, as he saw the Hayslope patriarch, old Feyther Taft, descend from the waggon and walk towards him, in his brown nightcap, and leaning on his two sticks.

'Well, Mester Taft,' shouted old Martin, at the utmost stretch of his voice – for though he knew the old man was stone deaf, he could not omit the propriety of a greeting – 'you're hearty yet. You can enjoy yoursen today, for all you're ninety an' better.'

'Your sarvant, mesters, your sarvant,' said Feyther Taft in a treble tone, perceiving that he was in company.

The aged group, under care of sons or daughters, themselves worn and grey, passed on along the least winding carriage-road towards the house, where a special table was prepared for them; while the Poyser party wisely struck across the grass under the shade of the great trees, but not out of view of the house-front, with its sloping lawn and flower-beds, or of the pretty striped marquee at the edge of the lawn, standing at right angles with two larger marquees on each side of the open green space where the games were to be played. The house would have been nothing but a plain square mansion of Queen Anne's time, but for the remnant of an old abbey to which it was united at one end, in much the same way as one may sometimes see a new farmhouse rising high and prim at the end of older and lower farm-offices. The fine old remnant stood a little backward and under the shadow of tall beeches, but the sun was now on the taller and more advanced front, the blinds were all down, and the house seemed asleep in the hot midday: it made Hetty quite sad to look at it: Arthur must be somewhere in the back rooms, with the grand company, where he could not possibly know that she was come, and she should not see him for a long, long while – not till after dinner, when they said he was to come up and make a speech.

But Hetty was wrong in part of her conjecture. No grand company was come except the Irwines, for whom the carriage had been sent early, and Arthur was at that moment not in a back room, but walking with the Rector into the broad stone cloisters of the old abbey, where the long tables were laid for all the cottage tenants and the farm-servants. A very handsome young Briton he looked today, in high spirits and a bright-blue frock-coat, the highest mode – his arm no longer in a sling. So open-looking and candid, too; but candid people have their secrets, and secrets leave no lines in young faces.

'Upon my word,' he said, as they entered the cool cloisters, 'I think the cottagers have the best of it: these cloisters make a delightful dining-room on a hot day. That was capital advice of yours, Irwine, about the dinners – to let them be as orderly and comfortable as possible, and only for the tenants: especially as I had only a limited sum after all; for though my grandfather talked of a carte blanche, he couldn't make up his mind to trust me, when it came to the point.'

'Never mind, you'll give more pleasure in this quiet way,' said Mr Irwine. 'In this sort of thing people are constantly confounding liberality with riot and disorder. It sounds very grand to say that so many sheep and oxen were roasted whole, and everybody ate who liked to come; but in the end it generally happens that no one has had an enjoyable meal. If the people get a good dinner and a moderate quantity of ale in the middle of the day, they'll be able to enjoy the games as the day cools. You can't hinder some of them from getting too much towards evening, but drunkenness and darkness go better together than drunkenness and daylight.'

'Well, I hope there won't be much of it. I've kept the Treddleston people away, by having a feast for them in the town; and I've got Casson and Adam Bede, and some other good fellows, to look to the giving out of ale in the booths, and to take care things don't go too far. Come, let us go up above now, and see the dinner-tables for the large tenants.'

They went up the stone staircase leading simply to the long gallery above the cloisters, a gallery where all the dusty worthless old pictures had been banished for the last three generations – mouldy portraits of Queen Elizabeth and her ladies, General Monk with his eye knocked out, Daniel very much in the dark among the lions, and Julius Caesar on horseback, with a high nose and laurel crown, holding his Commentaries in his hand.

'What a capital thing it is that they saved this piece of the old abbey!' said Arthur. 'If I'm ever master here, I shall do up the gallery in first-rate style: we've got no room in the house a third as large as this. That second table is for the farmers' wives and children: Mrs Best said it would be more comfortable for the mothers and children to be by themselves. I was determined to have the children, and make a regular family thing of it. I shall be the 'old squire' to those little lads and lasses someday, and they'll tell their children what a much finer young fellow I was than my own son. There's a table for the women and children below as well. But you will see them all – you will come up with me after dinner, I hope?'

'Yes, to be sure,' said Mr Irwine. 'I wouldn't miss your maiden speech to the tenantry.'

'And there will be something else you'll like to hear,' said Arthur. 'Let us go into the library and I'll tell you all about it while my grandfather is in the drawing-room with the ladies. Something that will surprise you,' he continued, as they sat down. 'My grandfather has come round after all.'

'What, about Adam?'

'Yes; I should have ridden over to tell you about it, only I was so busy. You know I told you I had quite given up arguing the matter with him – I thought it was hopeless; but yesterday morning he asked me to come in here to him before I went out, and astonished me by saying that he had decided on all the new arrangements he should make in consequence of old Satchell being obliged to lay by work, and that he intended to employ Adam in superintending the woods at a salary of a guinea a week, and the use of a pony to be kept here. I believe the secret of it is, he saw from the first it would be a profitable plan, but he had some particular dislike of Adam to get over – and besides, the fact that I propose a thing is generally a reason with him for rejecting it. There's the most curious contradiction in my grandfather: I know he means to leave me all the money he has saved, and he is likely enough to have cut off poor aunt Lydia, who has been a slave to him all her life, with only five hundred a year, for the sake of giving me all the more; and yet I sometimes think he positively hates me because I'm his heir. I believe if I were to break my neck, he would feel it the greatest misfortune that could befall him, and yet it seems a pleasure to him to make my life a series of petty annoyances.'

'Ah, my boy, it is not only woman's love that is ἀπέρωτος ἔρως, as old Aeschylus calls it. There's plenty of 'unloving love' in the world of a masculine kind. But tell me about Adam. Has he accepted the post? I don't see that it can be much more profitable than his present work, though, to be sure, it will leave him a good deal of time on his own hands.'

'Well, I felt some doubt about it when I spoke to him, and he seemed to hesitate at first. His objection was, that he thought he should not be able to satisfy my grandfather. But I begged him as a personal favour to me not to let any reason prevent him from accepting the place, if he really liked the employment, and would not be giving up anything that was more profitable to him. And he assured me he should like it of all things – it would be a great step forward for him in business, and it would enable him to do what he had long wished to do – to give up working for Burge. He says he shall have plenty of time to superintend a little business of his own, which he and Seth will carry on, and will perhaps be able to enlarge by degrees. So he has agreed at last, and I have arranged that he shall dine with the large tenants to day; and I mean to announce the appointment to them, and ask them to drink Adam's health. It's a little drama I've got up in honour of my friend Adam. He's a fine fellow, and I like the opportunity of letting people know that I think so.'

'A drama in which friend Arthur piques himself on having a pretty part to play,' said Mr Irwine, smiling. But when he saw Arthur colour, he went on relentingly, 'My part, you know, is always that of the old Fogy who sees nothing to admire in the young folks. I don't like to admit that I'm proud of my pupil when he does graceful things. But I must play the amiable old gentleman for once, and second your toast in honour of Adam. Has your grandfather yielded on the other point too, and agreed to have a respectable man as steward?'

'Oh, no,' said Arthur, rising from his chair with an air of impatience, and walking along the room with his hands in his pockets. 'He's got some project or other about letting the Chase Farm, and bargaining for a supply of milk and butter for the house. But I ask no questions about it – it makes me too angry. I believe he means to do all the business himself, and have nothing in the shape of a steward. It's amazing what energy he has, though.'

'Well, we'll go to the ladies now,' said Mr Irwine, rising too. 'I want to tell my mother what a splendid throne you've prepared for her under the marquee.'

'Yes, and we must be going to luncheon too,' said Arthur. 'It must be two o'clock, for there is the gong beginning to sound for the tenants' dinners.'

Dinner-Time

When Adam heard that he was to dine upstairs with the large tenants, he felt rather uncomfortable at the idea of being exalted in this way above his mother and Seth, who were to dine in the cloisters below. But Mr Mills, the butler, assured him that Captain Donnithorne had given particular orders about it, and would be very angry if Adam was not there.

Adam nodded, and went up to Seth, who was standing a few yards off. 'Seth, lad,' he said, 'the Captain has sent to say I'm to dine upstairs he wishes it particular, Mr Mills says, so I suppose it 'ud be behaving ill for me not to go. But I don't like sitting up above thee and mother, as if I was better than my own flesh and blood. Thee't not take it unkind, I hope?'

'Nay, nay, lad,' said Seth, 'thy honour's our honour; and if thee get'st respect, thee'st won it by thy own deserts. The further I see thee above me, the better, so long as thee feel'st like a brother to me. It's because o' thy being appointed over the woods, and it's nothing but what's right. That's a place o' trust, and thee't above a common workman now.'

'Ay,' said Adam, 'but nobody knows a word about it yet. I haven't given notice to Mr Burge about leaving him, and I don't like to tell anybody else about it before he knows, for he'll be a good bit hurt, I doubt. People 'ull be wondering to see me there, and they'll like enough be guessing the reason, and asking questions, for there's been so much talk up and down about my having the place, this last three weeks.'

'Well, thee canst say thee wast ordered to come without being told the reason. That's the truth. And mother 'ull be fine and joyful about it. Let's go and tell her.'

Adam was not the only guest invited to come upstairs on other grounds than the amount he contributed to the rent-roll. There were other people in the two parishes who derived dignity from their functions rather than from their pocket, and of these Bartle Massey was one. His lame walk was rather slower than usual on this warm day, so Adam lingered behind when the bell rang for dinner, that he might walk up with his old friend; for he was a little too shy to join the Poyser party on this public occasion. Opportunities of getting to Hetty's side would be sure to turn up in the course of the day, and Adam contented himself with that, for he disliked any risk of being 'joked' about Hetty – the big, outspoken, fearless man was very shy and diffident as to his love-making.

'Well, Mester Massey,' said Adam, as Bartle came up, 'I'm going to dine upstairs with you today: the Captain's sent me orders.'

'Ah!' said Bartle, pausing, with one hand on his back. 'Then there's something in the wind – there's something in the wind. Have you heard anything about what the old squire means to do?'

'Why, yes,' said Adam; 'I'll tell you what I know, because I believe you can keep a still tongue in your head if you like; and I hope you'll not let drop a word till it's common talk, for I've particular reasons against its being known.'

'Trust to me, my boy, trust to me. I've got no wife to worm it out of me and then run out and cackle it in everybody's hearing. If you trust a man, let him be a bachelor – let him be a bachelor.'

'Well, then, it was so far settled yesterday, that I'm to take the management o' the woods. The Captain sent for me, t' offer it me, when I was seeing to the poles and things here, and I've agreed to't. But if anybody asks any questions upstairs, just you take no notice, and turn the talk to something else, and I'll be obliged to you. Now, let us go on, for we're pretty nigh the last, I think.'

'I know what to do, never fear,' said Bartle, moving on. 'The news will be good sauce to my dinner. Ay, ay, my boy, you'll get on. I'll back you for an eye at measuring, and a head-piece for figures, against any man in this county; and you've had good teaching – you've had good teaching.'

When they got upstairs, the question which Arthur had left unsettled, as to who was to be president, and who vice, was still under discussion, so that Adam's entrance passed without remark.

'It stands to sense,' Mr Casson was saying, 'as old Mr Poyser, as is th' oldest man i' the room, should sit at top o' the table. I wasn't butler fifteen year without learning the rights and the wrongs about dinner.'

'Nay, nay,' said old Martin, 'I'n gi'en up to my son; I'm no tenant now: let my son take my place. Th' ould folks ha' had their turn: they mun make way for the young uns.'

'I should ha' thought the biggest tenant had the best right, more nor th' oldest,' said Luke Britton, who was not fond of the critical Mr Poyser; 'there's Mester Holdsworth has more land nor anybody else on th' estate.'

'Well,' said Mr Poyser, 'suppose we say th' man wi' the foulest land shall sit at top, then whoever gets th' honour, there'll be no envying on him.'

'Eh, here's Mester Massey,' said Mr Craig, who, being a neutral in the dispute, had no interest but in conciliation; 'the schoolmaster ought to be able to tell you what's right. Who's to sit at top o' the table, Mr Massey?'

'Why, the broadest man,' said Bartle; 'and then he won't take up other folks' room, and the next broadest must sit at bottom.'

This happy mode of settling the dispute produced much laughter – a smaller joke would have sufficed for that. Mr Casson, however, did not feel it compatible with his dignity and superior knowledge to join in the laugh, until it turned out that he was fixed on as the second broadest man. Martin Poyser, the younger, as the broadest, was to be president, and Mr Casson, as next broadest, was to be vice.

Owing to this arrangement, Adam, being, of course, at the bottom of the table, fell under the immediate observation of Mr Casson, who, too much occupied with the question of precedence, had not hitherto noticed his entrance. Mr Casson, we have seen, considered Adam 'rather lifted up and peppery-like:' he thought the gentry made more fuss about this young carpenter than was necessary; they made no fuss about Mr Casson, although he had been an excellent butler for fifteen years.

'Well, Mr Bede, you're one o' them as mounts hup'ards apace,' he said, when Adam sat down. 'You've niver dined here before, as I remember.'

'No, Mr Casson,' said Adam, in his strong voice, that could be heard along the table; 'I've never dined here before, but I come by Captain Donnithorne's wish, and I hope it's not disagreeable to anybody here.'

'Nay, nay,' said several voices at once, 'we're glad ye're come. Who's got anything to say again' it?'

'And ye'll sing us 'Over the hills and far away' after dinner, wonna ye?' said Mr Chowne. 'That's a song I'm uncommon fond on.'

'Peeh!' said Mr Craig; 'it's not to be named by side o' the Scotch tunes. I've never cared about singing myself; I've had something better to do. A man that's got the names and the natur o' plants in's head isna likely to keep a hollow place t' hold tunes in. But a second cousin o' mine, a drovier, was a rare hand at remembering the Scotch tunes. He'd got nothing else to think on.'

'The Scotch tunes!' said Bartle Massey, contemptuously; 'I've heard enough o' the Scotch tunes to last me while I live. They're fit for nothing but to frighten the birds with – that's to say, the English birds, for the Scotch birds may sing Scotch for what I know. Give the lads a bagpipes instead of a rattle, and I'll answer for it the corn'll be safe.'

'Yes, there's folks as find a pleasure in undervallying what they know but little about,' said Mr Craig.

'Why, the Scotch tunes are just like a scolding, nagging woman,' Bartle went on, without deigning to notice Mr Craig's remark. 'They go on with the same thing over and over again, and never come to a reasonable end. Anybody'ud think the Scotch tunes had always been asking a question of somebody as deaf as old Taft, and had never got an answer yet.'

Adam minded the less about sitting by Mr Casson, because this position enabled him to see Hetty, who was not far off him at the next table. Hetty, however, had not even noticed his presence yet, for she was giving angry attention to Totty, who insisted on drawing up her feet on to the bench in antique fashion, and thereby threatened to make dusty marks on Hetty's pink-and-white frock. No sooner were the little fat legs pushed down than up they came again, for Totty's eyes were too busy in staring at the large dishes to see where the plum-pudding was, for her to retain any consciousness of her legs. Hetty got quite out of patience, and at last, with a frown and pout, and gathering tears, she said – 'Oh dear, aunt, I wish you'd speak to Totty; she keeps putting her legs up so, and messing my frock.'

'What's the matter wi' the child? She can niver please you,' said the mother. 'Let her come by the side o' me, then: I can put up wi' her.'

Adam was looking at Hetty, and saw the frown and pout, and the dark eyes seeming to grow larger with pettish half-gathered tears. Quiet Mary Burge, who sat near enough to see that Hetty was cross, and that Adam's eyes were fixed on her, thought that so sensible a man as Adam must be reflecting on the small value of beauty in a woman whose temper was bad. Mary was a good girl, not given to indulge in evil feelings, but she said to herself, that, since Hetty had a bad temper, it was better Adam should know it. And it was quite true, that if

Hetty had been plain she would have looked very ugly and unamiable at that moment, and no one's moral judgement upon her would have been in the least beguiled. But really there was something quite charming in her pettishness: it looked so much more like innocent distress than ill-humour; and the severe Adam felt no movement of disapprobation; he only felt a sort of amused pity, as if he had seen a kitten setting up its back, or a little bird with its feathers ruffled. He could not gather what was vexing her, but it was impossible to him to feel otherwise than that she was the prettiest thing in the world, and that if he could have his way, nothing should ever vex her any more. And presently, when Totty was gone, she caught his eye, and her face broke into one of its brightest smiles, as she nodded to him. It was a bit of flirtation: she knew Mary Burge was looking at them. But the smile was like wine to Adam.

24

The Health-Drinking

When the dinner was over, and the first draughts from the great cask of birthday ale were brought up, room was made for the broad Mr Poyser at the side of the table, and two chairs were placed at the head. It had been settled very definitely what Mr Poyser was to do when the young squire should appear, and for the last five minutes he had been in a state of abstraction, with his eyes fixed on the dark picture opposite, and his hands busy with the loose cash and other articles in his breeches-pockets.

When the young squire entered, with Mr Irwine by his side, everyone stood up, and this moment of homage was very agreeable to Arthur. He liked to feel his own importance, and besides that, he cared a great deal for the goodwill of these people: he was fond of thinking that they had a hearty, special regard for him. The pleasure he felt was in his face as he said – 'My grandfather and I hope all our friends here have enjoyed their dinner, and find my birthday ale good. Mr Irwine and I are come to taste it with you, and I am sure we shall all like anything the better that the Rector shares with us.'

All eyes were now turned on Mr Poyser, who, with his hands still busy in his pockets, began with the deliberateness of a slow-striking clock. 'Captain, my neighbours have put it upo' me to speak for 'em today, for where folks think pretty much alike, one spokesman's as good as a score. And though we've mayhappen got contrary ways o' thinking about a many things – one man lays down his land one way, an' another another – an' I'll not take it upon me to speak to no man's farming, but my own – this I'll say, as we're all o' one mind about our young squire. We've pretty nigh all on us known you when you war a little un, an' we've niver known anything on you but what was good an' honourable. You speak fair an' y' act fair, an' we're joyful when we look forrard to your being our landlord, for we b'lieve you mean to do right by everybody, an' 'ull make no man's bread bitter to him if you can help it. That's what I mean, an' that's what we all mean; and when a man's said what he means, he'd better stop, for th' ale 'ull be none the better for stannin'. An' I'll not say how we like th' ale yet, for we couldna well taste it till we'd drunk your health in it; but the dinner was good, an' if there's anybody hasna enjoyed it, it must be the fault of his own inside. An' as for the Rector's company, it's well known as that's welcome t' all the parish wherever he may be; an' I hope, an' we all hope, as he'll live to see us old folks, an' our children grown to men an' women, an' your honour a family man. I've no more to say as concerns the present time, an' so we'll drink our young Squire's health – three times three.'

Hereupon a glorious shouting, a rapping, a jingling, a clattering, and a shouting, with plentiful *da capo*, pleasanter than a strain of sublimest music in the ears that receive such a tribute for the first time. Arthur had felt a twinge of conscience during Mr Poyser's speech, but it was too feeble to nullify the pleasure he felt in being praised. Did he not deserve what was said of him on the whole? If there was something in his conduct that Poyser wouldn't have liked if he had known it, why, no man's conduct will bear too close an inspection; and Poyser was not likely to know it; and, after all, what had he done? Gone a little too far, perhaps, in flirtation, but another man in his place would have acted much worse; and no harm could come – no harm should come, for the next time he was alone with Hetty, he would explain to her that she must not think seriously of him or of what had passed. It was necessary to Arthur, you perceive, to be satisfied with himself: uncomfortable thoughts must be got rid of by good intentions for the future, which can be formed so rapidly, that he had time to be uncomfortable and to become easy again before Mr Poyser's slow speech was finished, and when it was time for him to speak he was quite light-hearted.

'I thank you all, my good friends and neighbours,' Arthur said, 'for the good opinion of me, and the kind feelings towards me which Mr Poyser has been expressing on your behalf and on his own, and it will always be my heartiest wish to deserve them. In the course of things we may expect that, if I live, I shall one day or other be your landlord; indeed it is on the ground of that expectation that my grandfather has wished me to celebrate this day and to come among you now; and I look forward to this position, not merely as one of power and pleasure for myself, but as a means of benefiting my neighbours. It hardly becomes so young a man as I am, to talk much about farming to you, who are most of you so much older, and are men of experience; still, I have interested myself a good deal in such matters, and learned as much about them as my opportunities have allowed; and when the course of events shall place the estate in my hands, it will be my first desire to afford my tenants all the encouragement a landlord can give them, in improving their land, and trying to bring about a better practice of husbandry. It will be my wish to be looked on by all my deserving tenants as their best friend, and nothing would make me so happy as to be able to respect every man on the estate, and to be respected by him in return. It is not my place at present to enter into particulars; I only meet your good hopes concerning me by telling you that my own hopes correspond to them – that what you expect from me I desire to fulfil; and I am quite of Mr Poyser's opinion, that when a man has said what he means, he had better stop. But the pleasure I feel in having my own health drunk by you would not be perfect if we did not drink the health of my grandfather, who has filled the place of both parents to me. I will say no more, until you have joined me in drinking his health on a day when he has wished me to appear among you as the future representative of his name and family.'

Perhaps there was no one present except Mr Irwine who thoroughly understood and approved Arthur's graceful mode of proposing his grandfather's health. The farmers thought the young Squire knew well enough that they hated the old Squire, and Mrs Poyser said, 'he'd better not ha' stirred a kettle o' sour broth.' The bucolic mind does not readily apprehend the refinements of good taste. But the toast could not be rejected, and when it had been drunk, Arthur said – 'I thank you, both for my grandfather and myself; and now there is one more thing I wish to tell you, that you may share my pleasure about it, as I hope and believe you will. I think there can be no man here who has not a respect, and some of you, I am sure, have a very high regard, for my friend Adam Bede. It is well known to everyone in this neighbourhood that there is no man whose word can be more depended on than his; that whatever he undertakes to do, he does well, and is as careful for the interests of those who employ him as for his own. I'm proud to say that I was very fond of Adam when I was a little boy, and I have never lost my old feeling for him – I think that shows that I know a good fellow when I find him. It has long been my wish that he should have the management of the woods on the estate, which happen to be very valuable; not only because I think so highly of his character, but because he has the knowledge and the skill which fit him for the place. And I am happy to tell you that it is my grandfather's wish too, and it is now settled that Adam shall manage the woods – a change which I am sure will be very much for the advantage of the estate; and I hope you will by and by join me in drinking his health, and in wishing him all the prosperity in life that he deserves. But there is a still older friend of mine than Adam Bede present, and I need not tell you that it is Mr Irwine. I'm sure you will agree with me that we must drink no other person's health until we have drunk his. I know you have all reason to love him, but no one of his parishioners has so much reason as I. Come, charge your glasses, and let us drink to our excellent Rector – three times three!'

This toast was drunk with all the enthusiasm that was wanting to the last, and it certainly was the most picturesque moment in the scene when Mr Irwine got up to speak, and all the faces in the room were turned towards him. The superior refinement of his face was much more striking than that of Arthur's when seen in comparison with the people round them. Arthur's was a much commoner British face, and the splendour of his new-fashioned clothes was more akin to the young farmer's taste in costume than Mr Irwine's powder, and the well-brushed but well-worn black, which seemed to be his chosen suit for great occasions; for he had the mysterious secret of never wearing a new-looking coat.

'This is not the first time, by a great many,' he said, 'that I have had to thank my parishioners for giving me tokens of their goodwill, but neighbourly kindness is among those things that are the more precious the older they get. Indeed, our pleasant meeting today is a proof that when what is good comes of age and is likely to live, there is reason for rejoicing, and the relation between us as clergy-man and parishioners came of age two years ago, for it is three-and-twenty years since I first came among you, and I see some tall fine-looking young men here, as well as some blooming young women, that were far from looking as pleasantly at me when I christened them, as I am happy to see them looking now. But I'm sure you will not wonder when I say, that among all those young men, the one in whom I have the strongest interest is my friend Mr Arthur Donnithorne, for whom you have just expressed your regard. I had the pleasure of being his tutor for several years, and have naturally had opportunities of knowing him intimately which cannot have occurred to anyone else who is present; and I have some pride as well as pleasure in assuring you that I share your high hopes concerning him, and your confidence in his possession of those qualities which will make him an excellent landlord when the time shall come for him to take that important position among you. We feel alike on most matters on which a man who is getting towards fifty can feel in common with a young man of one-and-twenty, and he has just been expressing a feeling which I share very heartily, and I would not willingly omit the opportunity of saying so. That feeling is his value and respect for Adam Bede. People in a high station are of course more thought of and talked about, and have their virtues more praised, than those whose lives are passed in humble everyday work; but every sensible man knows how necessary that humble everyday work is, and how important it is to us that it should be done well. And I agree with my friend Mr Arthur Donnithorne in feeling that when a man whose duty lies in that sort of work shows a character which would make him an example in any station, his merit should be acknowledged. He is one of those to whom honour is due, and his friends should delight to honour him. I know Adam Bede well – I know what he is as a workman, and what he has been as a son and brother – and I am saying the simplest truth when I say that I respect him as much as I respect any man living. But I am not speaking to you about a stranger; some of you are his intimate friends, and I believe there is not one here who does not know enough of him to join heartily in drinking his health.'

As Mr Irwine paused, Arthur jumped up, and, filling his glass, said, 'A bumper to Adam Bede, and may he live to have sons as faithful and clever as himself!'

No hearer, not even Bartle Massey, was so delighted with this toast as Mr Poyser: 'tough work' as his first speech had been, he would have started up to make another if he had not known the extreme irregularity of such a course. As it was he found an outlet for his feeling in drinking his ale unusually fast, and setting down his glass with a swing of his arm, and a determined rap. If Jonathan Burge and a few others felt less comfortable on the occasion, they tried their best to look contented, and so the toast was drunk with a goodwill apparently unanimous.

Adam was rather paler than usual when he got up to thank his friends. He was a good deal moved by this public tribute – very naturally, for he was in the presence of all his little world, and it was uniting to do him honour. But he felt no shyness about speaking, not being troubled with small vanity or lack of words; he looked neither awkward nor embarrassed, but stood in his usual firm upright attitude, with his head thrown a little backward and his hands perfectly still, in that rough dignity which is peculiar to intelligent, honest, well-built workmen, who are never wondering what is their business in the world.

'I'm quite taken by surprise,' he said. 'I didn't expect anything o' this sort, for it's a good deal more than my wages. But I've the more reason to be grateful to you, Captain, and to you, Mr Irwine, and to all my friends here, who've drunk my health and wished me well. It 'ud be nonsense for me to be saying, I don't at all deserve th' opinion you have of me; that 'ud be poor thanks to you, to say that you've known me all these years, and yet haven't sense enough to find out a great deal o' the truth about me. You think, if I undertake to do a bit o' work, I'll do it well, be my pay big or little – and that's true. I'd be ashamed to stand before you here if it wasna true. But it seems to me, that's a man's plain duty, and nothing to be conceited about, and it's pretty clear to me as I've never done more than my duty; for let us do what we will, it's only making use o' the sperrit and the powers that ha' been given to us. And so this kindness o' yours, I'm sure, is no debt you owe me, but a free gift, and as such I accept it and am thankful. And as to this new employment I've taken in hand, I'll only say that I took it at Captain Donnithorne's desire, and that I'll try to fulfil his expectations. I'd wish for no better lot than to work under him, and to know that while I was getting my own bread I was taking care of his int'rests. For I believe he's one o' those gentlemen as wishes to do the right thing, and to leave the world a bit better than he found it, which it's my belief every man may do, whether he's gentle or simple, whether he sets a good bit o' work going and finds the money, or whether he does the work with his own hands. There's no occasion for me to say any more about what I feel towards him: I hope to show it through the rest o' my life in my actions.'

There were various opinions about Adam's speech: some of the women whispered that he didn't show himself thankful enough, and seemed to speak as proud as could be; but most of the men were of opinion that nobody could speak more straightfor'ard, and that Adam was as fine a chap as need to be. While such observations were being buzzed about, mingled with wonderings as to what the old Squire meant to do for a bailiff, and whether he was going to have a steward, the two gentlemen had risen, and were walking round to the table where the wives and children sat. There was none of the strong ale here, of course, but wine and dessert-sparkling gooseberry for the young ones, and some good sherry for the mothers. Mrs Poyser was at the head of this table, and Totty was now seated in her lap, bending her small nose deep down into a wineglass in search of the nuts floating there.

'How do you do, Mrs Poyser?' said Arthur. 'Weren't you pleased to hear your husband make such a good speech today?'

'Oh, sir, the men are mostly so tongue-tied – you're forced partly to guess what they mean, as you do wi' the dumb creaturs.'

'What! you think you could have made it better for him?' said Mr Irwine, laughing.

'Well, sir, when I want to say anything, I can mostly find words to say it in, thank God. Not as I'm a-finding faut wi' my husband, for if he's a man o' few words, what he says he'll stand to.'

'I'm sure I never saw a prettier party than this,' Arthur said, looking round at the apple-cheeked children. 'My aunt and the Miss Irwines will come up and see you presently. They were afraid of the noise of the toasts, but it would be a shame for them not to see you at table.'

He walked on, speaking to the mothers and patting the children, while Mr Irwine satisfied himself with standing still, and nodding at a distance, that no one's attention might be disturbed from the young Squire, the hero of the day. Arthur did not venture to stop near Hetty, but merely bowed to her as he passed along the opposite side. The foolish child felt her heart swelling with discontent; for what woman was ever satisfied with apparent neglect, even when she knows it to be the mask of love? Hetty thought this was going to be the most miserable day she had had for a long while; a moment of chill daylight and reality came across her dream: Arthur, who had seemed so near to her only a few hours before, was separated from her, as the hero of a great procession is separated from a small outsider in the crowd.

25

The Games

The great dance was not to begin until eight o'clock; but for any lads and lasses who liked to dance on the shady grass before then, there was music always at hand; for was not the band of the Benefit Club capable of playing excellent jigs, reels, and hornpipes? And, besides this, there was a grand band hired from Rosseter, who, with their wonderful wind-instruments and puffed-out cheeks, were themselves a delightful show to the small boys and girls. To say nothing of Joshua Rann's fiddle, which, by an act of generous forethought, he had provided himself with, in case anyone should be of sufficiently pure taste to prefer dancing to a solo on that instrument.

Meantime, when the sun had moved off the great open space in front of the house, the games began. There were of course well-soaped poles to be climbed by the boys and youths, races to be run by the old women, races to be run in sacks, heavy weights to be lifted by the strong men, and a long list of challenges to such ambitious attempts as that of walking as many yards as possible on one leg – feats in which it was generally remarked that Wiry Ben, being 'the lissom'st, springest fellow i' the country,' was sure to be pre-eminent. To crown all, there was to be a donkey-race – that sublimest of all races, con-ducted on the grand socialistic idea of everybody encouraging everybody else's donkey, and the sorriest donkey winning.

And soon after four o'clock, splendid old Mrs Irwine, in her damask satin and jewels and black lace, was led out by Arthur, followed by the whole family party, to her raised seat under the striped marquee, where she was to give out the prizes to the victors. Staid, formal Miss Lydia had requested to resign that queenly office to the royal old lady, and Arthur was pleased with this opportunity of gratifying his godmother's taste for stateliness. Old Mr Donnithorne, the delicately-clean, finely-scented, withered old man, led out Miss Irwine, with his air of punctilious, acid politeness; Mr Gawaine brought Miss Lydia, looking neutral and stiff in an elegant peach-blossom silk; and Mr Irwine came last with his pale sister Anne. No other friend of the family, besides Mr Gawaine, was invited today; there was to be a grand dinner for the neighbouring gentry on the morrow, but today all the forces were required for the entertainment of the tenants.

There was a sunk fence in front of the marquee, dividing the lawn from the park, but a temporary bridge had been made for the passage of the victors, and the groups of people standing, or seated here and there on benches, stretched on each side of the open space from the white marquees up to the sunk fence.

'Upon my word it's a pretty sight,' said the old lady, in her deep voice, when she was seated, and looked round on the bright scene with its dark-green background; 'and it's the last fête-day I'm likely to see, unless you make haste and get married, Arthur. But take care you get a charming bride, else I would rather die without seeing her.'

'You're so terribly fastidious, godmother,' said Arthur, 'I'm afraid I should never satisfy you with my choice.'

'Well, I won't forgive you if she's not handsome. I can't be put off with amiability, which is always the excuse people are making for the existence of plain people. And she must not be silly; that will never do, because you'll want managing, and a silly woman can't manage you. Who is that tall young man, Dauphin, with the mild face? There, standing without his hat, and taking such care of that tall old woman by the side of him – his mother, of course. I like to see that.'

'What, don't you know him, mother?' said Mr Irwine. 'That is Seth Bede, Adam's brother – a Methodist, but a very good fellow. Poor Seth has looked rather down hearted of late; I thought it was because of his father's dying in that sad way; but Joshua Rann tells me he wanted to marry that sweet little Methodist preacher who was here about a month ago, and I suppose she refused him.'

'Ah, I remember hearing about her: but there are no end of people here that I don't know, for they're grown up and altered so since I used to go about.'

'What excellent sight you have!' said old Mr Donnithorne, who was holding a double glass up to his eyes, 'to see the expression of that young man's face so far off. His face is nothing but a pale blurred spot to me. But I fancy I have the advantage of you when we come to look close. I can read small print without spectacles.'

'Ah, my dear sir, you began with being very near-sighted, and those near-sighted eyes always wear the best. I want very strong spectacles to read with, but then I think my eyes get better and better for things at a distance. I suppose if I could live another fifty years, I should be blind to everything that wasn't out of other people's sight, like a man who stands in a well, and sees nothing but the stars.'

'See,' said Arthur, 'the old women are ready to set out on their race now. Which do you bet on, Gawaine?'

'The long-legged one, unless they're going to have several heats, and then the little wiry one may win.'

'There are the Poysers mother, not far off on the right hand,' said Miss Irwine. 'Mrs Poyser is looking at you. Do take notice of her.'

'To be sure I will,' said the old lady, giving a gracious bow to Mrs Poyser. 'A woman who sends me such excellent cream-cheese is not to be neglected. Bless me! what a fat child that is she is holding on her knee! But who is that pretty girl with dark eyes?'

'That is Hetty Sorrel,' said Miss Lydia Donnithorne, 'Martin Poyser's niece – a very likely young person, and well-looking too. My maid has taught her fine needlework, and she has mended some lace of mine very respectably indeed – very respectably.'

'Why, she has lived with the Poysers six or seven years, mother; you must have seen her,' said Miss Irwine.

'No, I've never seen her, child; at least not as she is now,' said Mrs Irwine, continuing to look at Hetty. 'Well-looking, indeed! she's a perfect beauty! I've never seen anything so pretty since my young days. What a pity such beauty as that should be thrown away among the farmers, when it's wanted so terribly among the good families without fortune! I dare say, now, she'll marry a man who would have thought her just as pretty if she had had round eyes and red hair.'

Arthur dared not turn his eyes towards Hetty while Mrs Irwine was speaking of her. He feigned not to hear, and to be occupied with something on the opposite side. But he saw her plainly enough without looking; saw her in heightened beauty, because he heard her beauty praised – for other men's opinion, you know, was like a native climate to Arthur's feelings: it was the air on which they thrived the best, and grew strong. Yes! she was enough to turn any man's head: any man in his place would have done and felt the same. And to give her up after all, as he was determined to do, would be an act that he should always look back upon with pride.

'No, mother,' said Mr Irwine, replying to her last words; 'I can't agree with you there. The common people are not quite so stupid as you imagine. The commonest man, who has his ounce of sense and feeling, is conscious of the difference between a lovely, delicate woman, and a coarse one. Even a dog feels a difference in their presence. The man may be no better able than the dog to explain the influence the more refined beauty has on him, but he feels it.'

'Bless me, Dauphin, what does an old bachelor like you know about it?'

'Oh, that is one of the matters in which old bachelors are wiser than married men, because they have time for more general contemplation. Your fine critic of women must never shackle his judgement by calling one woman his own. But, as an example of what I was saying, that pretty Methodist preacher I mentioned just now, told me that she had preached to the roughest miners, and had never been treated with anything but the utmost respect and kindness by them. The reason is – though she doesn't know it – that there's so much tenderness, refinement, and purity about her. Such a woman as that brings with her "airs from heaven" that the coarsest fellow is not insensible to.'

'Here's a delicate bit of womanhood, or girlhood, coming to receive a prize, I suppose,' said Mr Gawaine. 'She must be one of the racers in the sacks, who had set off before we came.'

The 'bit of womanhood' was our old acquaintance Bessy Cranage, otherwise Chad's Bess, whose large red cheeks and blowsy person had undergone an exaggeration of colour, which, if she had happened to be a heavenly body, would have made her sublime. Bessy, I am sorry to say, had taken to her earrings again since Dinah's departure, and was otherwise decked out in such small finery as she could muster. Anyone who could have looked into poor Bessy's heart would have seen a striking resemblance between her little hopes and anxieties and Hetty's. The advantage, perhaps, would have been on Bessy's side in the matter of feeling. But then, you see, they were so very different outside! You would have been inclined to box Bessy's ears, and you would have longed to kiss Hetty.

Bessy had been tempted to run the arduous race, partly from mere hoidenish gaiety, partly because of the prize. Someone had said there were to be cloaks and other nice clothes for prizes, and she approached the marquee, fanning herself with her handkerchief, but with exultation sparkling in her round eyes.

'Here is the prize for the first sack-race,' said Miss Lydia, taking a large parcel from the table where the prizes were laid, and giving it to Mrs Irwine before Bessy came up; 'an excellent grogram gown and a piece of flannel.'

'You didn't think the winner was to be so young, I suppose, aunt?' said Arthur. 'Couldn't you find something else for this girl, and save that grim-looking gown for one of the older women?'

'I have bought nothing but what is useful and substantial,' said Miss Lydia, adjusting her own lace; 'I should not think of encouraging a love of finery in young women of that class. I have a scarlet cloak, but that is for the old woman who wins.'

This speech of Miss Lydia's produced rather a mocking expression in Mrs Irwine's face as she looked at Arthur, while Bessy came up and dropped a series of curtsies.

'This is Bessy Cranage, mother,' said Mr Irwine, kindly, 'Chad Cranage's daughter. You remember Chad Cranage, the blacksmith?'

'Yes, to be sure,' said Mrs Irwine. 'Well, Bessy, here is your prize – excellent warm things for winter. I'm sure you have had hard work to win them this warm day.'

Bessy's lip fell as she saw the ugly, heavy gown – which felt so hot and disagreeable, too, on this July day, and was such a great ugly thing to carry. She dropped her curtsies again, without looking up, and with a growing tremulousness about the corners of her mouth, and then turned away.

'Poor girl,' said Arthur; 'I think she's disappointed. I wish it had been something more to her taste.'

'She's a bold-looking young person,' observed Miss Lydia. 'Not at all one I should like to encourage.'

Arthur silently resolved that he would make Bessy a present of money before the day was over, that she might buy something more to her mind; but she, not aware of the consolation in store for her, turned out of the open space, where she was visible from the marquee, and throwing down the odious bundle under a tree, began to cry – very much tittered at the while by the small boys. In this situation she was descried by her discreet matronly cousin, who lost no time in coming up, having just given the baby into her husband's charge.

'What's the matter wi' ye?' said Bess the matron, taking up the bundle and examining it. 'Ye'n sweltered yoursen, I reckon, running that fool's race. An' here, they'n gi'en you lots o' good grogram and flannel, as should ha' been gi'en by good rights to them as had the sense to keep away from such foolery. Ye might spare me a bit o' this grogram to make clothes for the lad – ye war ne'er ill-natured, Bess; I ne'er said that on ye.'

'Ye may take it all, for what I care,' said Bess the maiden with a pettish movement, beginning to wipe away her tears and recover herself.

'Well, I could do wi't, if so be ye want to get rid on't,' said the disinterested cousin, walking quickly away with the bundle, lest Chad's Bess should change her mind.

But that bonny-cheeked lass was blest with an elasticity of spirits that secured her from any rankling grief; and by the time the grand climax of the donkey-race came on, her disappointment was entirely lost in the delightful excitement of attempting to stimulate the last donkey by hisses, while the boys applied the argument of sticks. But the strength of the donkey mind lies in adopting a course inversely as the arguments urged, which, well considered, requires as great a mental force as the direct sequence; and the present donkey proved the first-rate order of his intelligence by coming to a dead standstill just when the blows were thickest. Great was the shouting of the crowd, radiant the grinning of Bill Downes the stone-sawyer and the fortunate rider of this superior beast, which stood calm and stiff-legged in the midst of its triumph.

Arthur himself had provided the prizes for the men, and Bill was made happy with a splendid pocket-knife, supplied with blades and gimlets enough to make a man at home on a desert island. He had hardly returned from the marquee with the prize in his hand, when it began to be understood that Wiry Ben proposed to amuse the company, before the gentry went to dinner, with an impromptu and gratuitous performance – namely, a hornpipe, the main idea of which was doubtless borrowed; but this was to be developed by the dancer in so peculiar and complex a manner that no one could deny him the praise of originality. Wiry Ben's pride in his dancing – an accomplishment productive of great effect at the yearly Wake – had needed only slightly elevating by an extra quantity of good ale, to convince him that the gentry would be very much struck with his performance of the hornpipe; and he had been decidedly encouraged in this idea by Joshua Rann, who observed that it was nothing but right to do something to please the young Squire, in return for what he had done for them. You will be the less surprised at this opinion in so grave a personage when you learn that Ben had requested Mr Rann to accompany him on the fiddle, and Joshua felt quite sure that though there might not be much in the dancing, the music would make up for it. Adam Bede, who was present in one of the large marquees, where the plan was being discussed, told Ben he had better not make a fool of himself – a remark which at once fixed Ben's determination: he was not going to let anything alone because Adam Bede turned up his nose at it.

'What's this, what's this?' said old Mr Donnithorne. 'Is it something you've arranged, Arthur? Here's the clerk coming with his fiddle, and a smart fellow with a nosegay in his buttonhole.'

'No,' said Arthur; 'I know nothing about it. By Jove, he's going to dance! It's one of the carpenters – I forget his name at this moment.'

'It's Ben Cranage – wiry Ben, they call him,' said Mr Irwine; 'rather a loose fish, I think. Anne, my dear, I see that fiddle-scraping is too much for you: you're getting tired. Let me take you in now, that you may rest till dinner.'

Miss Anne rose assentingly, and the good brother took her away, while Joshua's preliminary scrapings burst into the 'White Cockade', from which he intended to pass to a variety of tunes, by a series of transitions which his good ear really taught him to execute with some skill. It would have been an exasperating fact to him, if he had known it, that the general attention was too thoroughly absorbed by Ben's dancing for anyone to give much heed to the music.

Have you ever seen a real English rustic perform a solo dance? Perhaps you have only seen a ballet rustic, smiling like a merry countryman in crockery, with graceful turns of the haunch and insinuating movements of the head. That is as much like the real thing as the 'Bird Waltz' is like the song of birds. Wiry Ben never smiled: he looked as serious as a dancing monkey – as serious as if he had been an experimental philosopher ascertaining in his own person the amount of shaking and the varieties of angularity that could be given to the human limbs.

To make amends for the abundant laughter in the striped marquee, Arthur clapped his hands continually and cried 'Bravo!' But Ben had one admirer whose eyes followed his movements with a fervid gravity that equalled his own. It was Martin Poyser, who was seated on a bench, with Tommy between his legs.

'What dost think o' that?' he said to his wife. 'He goes as pat to the music as if he was made o' clockwork. I used to be a pretty good un at dancing myself when I was lighter, but I could niver ha' hit it just to th' hair like that.'

'It's little matter what his limbs are, to my thinking,' returned Mrs Poyser. 'He's empty enough i' the upper storey, or he'd niver come jigging an' stamping i' that way, like a mad grasshopper, for the gentry to look at him. They're fit to die wi' laughing, I can see.'

'Well, well, so much the better, it amuses 'em,' said Mr Poyser, who did not easily take an irritable view of things. 'But they're going away now, t' have their dinner, I reckon. We'll move about a bit, shall we? and see what Adam Bede's doing. He's got to look after the drinking and things: I doubt he hasna had much fun.'

26

The Dance

Arthur had chosen the entrance-hall for the ballroom: very wisely, for no other room could have been so airy, or would have had the advantage of the wide doors opening into the garden, as well as a ready entrance into the other rooms. To be sure, a stone floor was not the pleasantest to dance on, but then, most of the dancers had known what it was to enjoy a Christmas dance on kitchen quarries. It was one of those entrance-halls which make the surrounding rooms look like closets – with stucco angels, trumpets, and flower wreaths on the lofty ceiling, and great medallions of miscellaneous heroes on the walls, alternating with statues in niches. Just the sort of place to be ornamented well with green boughs, and Mr Craig had been proud to show his taste and his hot-house plants on the occasion. The broad steps of the stone staircase were covered with cushions to serve as seats for the children, who were to stay till half-past nine with the servant-maids, to see the dancing; and as this dance was confined to the chief tenants, there was abundant room for everyone. The lights were charmingly disposed in coloured-paper lamps, high up among green boughs, and the farmers' wives and daughters, as they peeped in, believed no scene could be more splendid; they knew now quite well in what sort of rooms the king and queen lived, and their thoughts glanced with some pity towards cousins and acquaintances who had not this fine opportunity of knowing how things went on in the great world. The lamps were already lit, though the sun had not long set, and there was that calm light out of doors in which we seem to see all objects more distinctly than in the broad day.

It was a pretty scene outside the house: the farmers and their families were moving about the lawn, among the flowers and shrubs, or along the broad straight road leading from the east front, where a carpet of mossy grass spread on each side, studded here and there with a dark flat-boughed cedar, or a grand pyramidal fir sweeping the ground with its branches, all tipped with a fringe of paler green. The groups of cottagers in the park were gradually diminishing, the young ones being attracted towards the lights that were beginning to gleam from the windows of the gallery in the abbey, which was to be their dancing-room, and some of the sober elder ones thinking it time to go home quietly. One of these was Lisbeth Bede, and Seth went with her – not from filial attention only, for his conscience would not let him join in dancing. It had been rather a melancholy day to Seth: Dinah had never been more constantly present with him than in this scene, where everything was so unlike her. He saw her all the more vividly after looking at the thoughtless faces and gay-coloured dresses of the young women – just as one feels the beauty and the greatness of a pictured Madonna the more, when it has been for a moment screened from us by a vulgar head in a bonnet. But this presence of Dinah in his mind only helped him to bear the better with his mother's mood, which had been becoming more and more querulous for the last hour. Poor Lisbeth was suffering from a strange conflict of feelings. Her joy and pride in the honour paid to her darling son Adam was beginning to be worsted in the conflict with the jealousy and fretfulness which had revived when Adam came to tell her that Captain Donnithorne desired him to join the dancers in the hall. Adam was getting more and more out of her reach; she wished all the old troubles back again, for then it mattered more to Adam what his mother said and did.

'Eh, it's fine talkin' o' dancin',' she said, 'an' thy father not a five week in's grave. An' I wish I war there too, istid o' bein' left to take up merrier folks's room above ground.'

'Nay, don't look at it i' that way, mother,' said Adam, who was determined to be gentle to her today. 'I don't mean to dance – I shall only look on. And since the Captain wishes me to be there, it 'ud look as if I thought I knew better than him to say as I'd rather not stay. And thee know'st how he's behaved to me today.'

'Eh, thee't do as thee lik'st, for thy old mother's got no right t' hinder thee. She's nought but th' old husk, and thee'st slipped away from her, like the ripe nut.'

'Well, mother,' said Adam, 'I'll go and tell the Captain as it hurts thy feelings for me to stay, and I'd rather go home upo' that account: he won't take it ill then, I dare say, and I'm willing.' He said this with some effort, for he really longed to be near Hetty this evening.

'Nay, nay, I wonna ha' thee do that – the young Squire 'ull be angered. Go an' do what thee't ordered to do, an' me and Seth 'ull go whome. I know it's a grit honour for thee to be so looked on – an' who's to be prouder on it nor thy mother? Hadna she the cumber o' rearin' thee an' doin' for thee all these 'ears?'

'Well, goodbye, then, mother – goodbye, lad – remember Gyp when you get home,' said Adam, turning away towards the gate of the pleasure-grounds, where he hoped he might be able to join the Poysers, for he had been so occupied throughout the afternoon that he had had no time to speak to Hetty. His eye soon detected a distant group, which he knew to be the right one, returning to the house along the broad gravel road, and he hastened on to meet them.

'Why, Adam, I'm glad to get sight on y' again,' said Mr Poyser, who was carrying Totty on his arm. 'You're going t' have a bit o' fun, I hope, now your work's all done. And here's Hetty has promised no end o' partners, an' I've just been askin' her if she'd agreed to dance wi' you, an' she says no.'

'Well, I didn't think o' dancing tonight,' said Adam, already tempted to change his mind, as he looked at Hetty.

'Nonsense!' said Mr Poyser. 'Why, everybody's goin' to dance tonight, all but the old Squire and Mrs Irwine. Mrs Best's been tellin' us as Miss Lyddy and Miss Irwine 'ull dance, an' the young Squire 'ull pick my wife for his first partner, t' open the ball: so she'll be forced to dance, though she's laid by ever sin' the Christmas afore the little un was born. You canna for shame stand still, Adam, an' you a fine young fellow, and can dance as well as anybody.'

'Nay, nay,' said Mrs Poyser, 'it 'ud be unbecomin'. I know the dancin's nonsense; but if you stick at everything because it's nonsense, you wonna go far i' this life. When your broth's ready-made for you, you mun swallow the thickenin' or else let the broth alone.'

'Then if Hetty 'ull dance with me,' said Adam, yielding either to Mrs Poyser's argument or to something else, 'I'll dance whichever dance she's free.'

'I've got no partner for the fourth dance,' said Hetty; 'I'll dance that with you, if you like.'

'Ah,' said Mr Poyser, 'but you mun dance the first dance, Adam, else it'll look partic'ler. There's plenty o' nice partners to pick an' choose from, an' it's hard for the gells when the men stan' by and don't ask 'em.'

Adam felt the justice of Mr Poyser's observation: it would not do for him to dance with no one besides Hetty; and remembering that Jonathan Burge had some reason to feel hurt today, he resolved to ask Miss Mary to dance with him the first dance, if she had no other partner.

'There's the big clock strikin' eight,' said Mr Poyser; 'we must make haste in now, else the Squire and the ladies 'ull be in afore us, an' that wouldna look well.'

When they had entered the hall, and the three children under Molly's charge had been seated on the stairs, the folding-doors of the drawing-room were thrown open, and Arthur entered in his regimentals, leading Mrs Irwine to a carpet-covered dais ornamented with hothouse plants, where she and Miss Anne were to be seated with old Mr Donnithorne, that they might look on at the dancing, like the kings and queens in the plays. Arthur had put on his uniform to please the tenants, he said, who thought as much of his militia dignity as if it had been an elevation to the premiership. He had not the least objection to gratify them in that way: his uniform was very advantageous to his figure.

The old Squire, before sitting down, walked round the hall to greet the tenants and make polite speeches to the wives: he was always polite; but the farmers had found out, after long puzzling, that this polish was one of the signs of hardness. It was observed that he gave his most elaborate civility to Mrs Poyser tonight, enquiring particularly about her health, recommending her to strengthen herself with cold water as he did, and avoid all drugs. Mrs Poyser curtsied and thanked him with great self-command, but when he had passed on, she whispered to her husband, 'I'll lay my life he's brewin' some nasty turn against us. Old Harry doesna wag his tail so for nothin'.' Mr Poyser had no time to answer, for now Arthur came up and said, 'Mrs Poyser, I'm come to request the favour of your hand for the first dance; and, Mr Poyser, you must let me take you to my aunt, for she claims you as her partner.'

The wife's pale cheek flushed with a nervous sense of unwonted honour as Arthur led her to the top of the room; but Mr Poyser, to whom an extra glass had restored his youthful confidence in his good looks and good dancing, walked along with them quite proudly, secretly flattering himself that Miss Lydia had never had a partner in her life who could lift her off the ground as he would. In order to balance the honours given to the two parishes, Miss Irwine danced with Luke Britton, the largest Broxton farmer, and Mr Gawine led out Mrs Britton. Mr Irwine, after seating his sister Anne, had gone to the abbey gallery, as he had agreed with Arthur beforehand, to see how the merriment of the cottagers was prospering. Meanwhile, all the less distinguished couples had taken their places: Hetty was led out by the inevitable Mr Craig, and Mary Burge by Adam; and now the music struck up, and the glorious country-dance, best of all dances, began.

Pity it was not a boarded floor! Then the rhythmic stamping of the thick shoes would have been better than any drums. That merry stamping, that gracious nodding of the head, that waving bestowal of the hand – where can we see them now? That simple dancing of well-covered matrons, laying aside for an hour the cares of house and dairy, remembering but not affecting youth, not jealous but proud of the young maidens by their side – that holiday sprightliness of portly husbands paying little compliments to their wives, as if their courting days were come again – those lads and lasses a little confused and awkward with their partners, having nothing to say – it would be a pleasant variety to see all that sometimes, instead of low dresses and large skirts, and scanning glances exploring costumes, and languid men in lackered boots smiling with double meaning.

There was but one thing to mar Martin Poyser's pleasure in this dance: it was, that he was always in close contact with Luke Britton, that slovenly farmer. He thought of throwing a little glazed coldness into his eye in the crossing of hands; but then, as Miss Irwine was opposite to him instead of the offensive Luke, he might freeze the wrong person. So he gave his face up to hilarity, unchilled by moral judgements.

How Hetty's heart beat as Arthur approached her! He had hardly looked at her today: now he must take her hand. Would he press it? would he look at her? She thought she would cry if he gave her no sign of feeling. Now he was there – he had taken her hand – yes, he was pressing it. Hetty turned pale as she looked up at him for an instant and met his eyes, before the dance carried him away. That pale look came upon Arthur like the beginning of a dull pain, which clung to him, though he must dance and smile and joke all the same. Hetty would look so, when he told her what he had to tell her; and he should never be able to bear it – he should be a fool and give way again. Hetty's look did not really mean so much as he thought: it was only the sign of a struggle between the desire for him to notice her, and the dread lest she should betray the desire to others. But Hetty's face had a language that transcended her feelings. There are faces which nature charges with a meaning and pathos not belonging to the single human soul that flutters beneath them, but speaking the joys and sorrows of foregone generations – eyes that tell of deep love which doubtless has been and is somewhere, but not paired with these eyes – perhaps paired with pale eyes that can say nothing; just as a national language may be instinct with poetry unfelt by the lips that use it. That look of Hetty's oppressed Arthur with a dread which yet had something of a terrible unconfessed delight in it, that she loved him too well. There was a hard task before him, for at that moment he felt he would have given up three years of his youth for the happiness of abandoning himself without remorse to his passion for Hetty.

These were the incongruous thoughts in his mind, as he led Mrs Poyser, who was panting with fatigue, and secretly resolving that neither judge nor jury should force her to dance another dance, to take a quiet rest in the dining-room, where supper was laid out for the guests to come and take it as they chose.

'I've desired Hetty to remember as she's got to dance wi' you, sir,' said the good innocent woman; 'for she's so thoughtless, she'd be like enough to go an' engage herself for ivery dance. So I told her not to promise too many.'

'Thank you, Mrs Poyser,' said Arthur, not without a twinge. 'Now, sit down in this comfortable chair, and here is Mills ready to give you what you would like best.'

He hurried away to seek another matronly partner, for due honour must be paid to the married women before he asked any of the young ones; and the country-dances, and the stamping, and the gracious nodding, and the waving of the hands, went on joyously.

At last the time had come for the fourth dance – longed for by the strong, grave Adam, as if he had been a delicate-handed youth of eighteen; for we are all very much alike when we are in our first love; and Adam had hardly ever touched Hetty's hand for more than a transient greeting – had never danced with her but once before. His eyes had followed her eagerly tonight in spite of himself, and had taken in deeper draughts of love. He thought she behaved so prettily, so quietly; she did not seem to be flirting at all, she smiled less than usual; there was almost a sweet sadness about her. 'God bless her!' he said inwardly; 'I'd make her life a happy un, if a strong arm to work for her, and a heart to love her, could do it.'

And then there stole over him delicious thoughts of coming home from work, and drawing Hetty to his side, and feeling her cheek softly pressed against his, till he forgot where he was, and the music and the tread of feet might have been the falling of rain and the roaring of the wind, for what he knew.

But now the third dance was ended, and he might go up to her and claim her hand. She was at the far end of the hall near the staircase, whispering with Molly, who had just given the sleeping Totty into her arms, before running to fetch shawls and bonnets from the landing. Mrs Poyser had taken the two boys away into the dining-room to give them some cake before they went home in the cart with grandfather, and Molly was to follow as fast as possible.

'Let me hold her,' said Adam, as Molly turned upstairs: 'the children are so heavy when they're asleep.'

Hetty was glad of the relief, for to hold Totty in her arms, standing, was not at all a pleasant variety to her. But this second transfer had the unfortunate effect of rousing Totty, who was not behind any child of her age in peevishness at an unseasonable awaking. While Hetty was in the act of placing her in Adam's arms, and had not yet withdrawn her own, Totty opened her eyes, and forthwith fought out with her left fist at Adam's arm, and with her right caught at the string of brown beads round Hetty's neck. The locket leaped out from her frock, and the next moment the string was broken, and Hetty, helpless, saw beads and locket scattered wide on the floor.

'My locket, my locket!' she said, in a loud frightened whisper to Adam; 'never mind the beads.'

Adam had already seen where the locket fell, for it had attracted his glance as it leaped out of her frock. It had fallen on the raised wooden dais where the band sat, not on the stone floor; and as Adam picked it up, he saw the glass with the dark and light locks of hair under it. It had fallen that side upwards, so the glass was not broken. He turned it over on his hand, and saw the enamelled gold back.

'It isn't hurt,' he said, as he held it towards Hetty, who was unable to take it because both her hands were occupied with Totty.

'Oh, it doesn't matter, I don't mind about it,' said Hetty, who had been pale and was now red.

'Not matter?' said Adam, gravely. 'You seemed very frightened about it. I'll hold it till you're ready to take it,' he added, quietly closing his hand over it, that she might not think he wanted to look at it again.

By this time Molly had come with bonnet and shawl, and as soon as she had taken Totty, Adam placed the locket in Hetty's hand. She took it with an air of indifference, and put it in her pocket; in her heart vexed and angry with Adam, because he had seen it, but determined now that she would show no more signs of agitation.

'See,' she said, 'they're taking their places to dance; let us go.'

Adam assented silently. A puzzled alarm had taken possession of him. Had Hetty a lover he didn't know of? – for none of her relations, he was sure, would give her a locket like that; and none of her admirers, with whom he was acquainted, was in the position of an accepted lover, as the giver of that locket must be. Adam was lost in the utter impossibility of finding any person for his fears to alight on: he could only feel with a terrible pang that there was something in Hetty's life unknown to him; that while he had been rocking himself in the hope that she would come to love him, she was already loving another. The pleasure of the dance with Hetty was gone; his eyes, when they rested on her, had an uneasy questioning expression in them; he could think of nothing to say to her; and she, too, was out of temper and disinclined to speak. They were both glad when the dance was ended.

Adam was determined to stay no longer; no one wanted him, and no one would notice if he slipped away. As soon as he got out of doors, he began to walk at his habitual rapid pace, hurrying along without knowing why, busy with the painful thought that the memory of this day, so full of honour and promise to him, was poisoned for ever. Suddenly, when he was far on through the Chase, he stopped, startled by a flash of reviving hope. After all, he might be a fool, making a great misery out of a trifle. Hetty, fond of finery as she was, might have bought the thing herself. It looked too expensive for that – it looked like the things on white satin in the great jeweller's shop at Rosseter. But Adam had very imperfect notions of the value of such things, and he thought it could certainly not cost more than a guinea. Perhaps Hetty had had as much as that in Christmas boxes, and there was no knowing but she might have been childish enough to spend it in that way; she was such a young thing, and she couldn't help loving finery! But then, why had she been so frightened about it at first, and changed colour so, and afterwards pretended not to care? Oh, that was because she was ashamed of his seeing that she had such a smart thing – she was conscious that it was wrong for her to spend her money on it, and she knew that Adam disapproved of finery. It was a proof she cared about what he liked and disliked. She must have thought from his silence and gravity afterwards that he was very much displeased with her, that he was inclined to be harsh and severe towards her foibles. And as he walked on more quietly, chewing the cud of this new hope, his only uneasiness was that he had behaved in a way which might chill Hetty's feeling towards him. For this last view of the matter must be the true one. How could Hetty have an accepted lover, quite unknown to him? She was never away from her uncle's house for more than a day; she could have no acquaintances that did not come there, and no intimacies unknown to her uncle and aunt. It would be folly to believe that the locket was given to her by a lover. The little ring of dark hair he felt sure was her own; he could form no guess about the light hair under it, for he had not seen it very distinctly. It might be a bit of her father's or mother's, who had died when she was a child, and she would naturally put a bit of her own along with it.

And so Adam went to bed comforted, having woven for himself an ingenious web of probabilities – the surest screen a wise man can place between himself and the truth. His last waking thoughts melted into a dream that he was with Hetty again at the Hall Farm, and that he was asking her to forgive him for being so cold and silent.

And while he was dreaming this, Arthur was leading Hetty to the dance, and saying to her in low hurried tones, 'I shall be in the wood the day after tomorrow at seven; come as early as you can.' And Hetty's foolish joys and hopes, which had flown away for a little space, scared by a mere nothing, now all came fluttering back, unconscious of the real peril. She was happy for the first time this long day, and wished that dance would last for hours. Arthur wished it too; it was the last weakness he meant to indulge in; and a man never lies with more delicious languor under the influence of a passion, than when he has persuaded himself that he shall subdue it tomorrow.

But Mrs Poyser's wishes were quite the reverse of this, for her mind was filled with dreary forebodings as to the retardation of tomorrow morning's cheese in consequence of these late hours. Now that Hetty had done her duty and danced one dance with the young Squire, Mr Poyser must go out and see if the cart was come back to fetch them, for it was half-past ten o'clock, and notwithstanding a mild suggestion on his part that it would be bad manners for them to be the first to go, Mrs Poyser was resolute on the point, 'manners or no manners.'

'What! going already, Mrs Poyser?' said old Mr Donnithorne, as she came to curtsy and take leave; 'I thought we should not part with any of our guests till eleven: Mrs Irwine and I, who are elderly people, think of sitting out the dance till then.'

'Oh, your honour, it's all right and proper for gentlefolks to stay up by candlelight – they've got no cheese on their minds. We're late enough as it is, an' there's no lettin' the cows know as they mustn't want to be milked so early tomorrow mornin'. So, if you'll please t' excuse us, we'll take our leave.'

'Eh!' she said to her husband, as they set off in the cart, 'I'd sooner ha' brewin' day and washin' day together than one o' these pleasurin' days. There's no work so tirin' as danglin' about an' starin' an' not rightly knowin' what you're goin' to do next; and keepin' your face i' smilin' order like a grocer o' market-day for fear people shouldna think you civil enough. An' you've nothing to show for't when it's done, if it isn't a yallow face wi' eatin' things as disagree.'

'Nay, nay,' said Mr Poyser, who was in his merriest mood, and felt that he had had a great day, 'a bit o' pleasuring's good for thee sometimes. An' thee danc'st as well as any of 'em, for I'll back thee against all the wives i' the parish for a light foot an' ankle. An' it was a great honour for the young Squire to ask thee first – I reckon it was because I sat at th' head o' the table an' made the speech. An' Hetty too – she never had such a partner before – a fine young gentleman in reg'mentals. It'll serve you to talk on, Hetty, when you're an old woman – how you danced wi' th' young Squire the day he come o' age.'

BOOK FOURTH

27

A Crisis

It was beyond the middle of August – nearly three weeks after the birthday feast. The reaping of the wheat had begun in our north midland county of Loamshire, but the harvest was likely still to be retarded by the heavy rains, which were causing inundations and much damage throughout the country. From this last trouble the Broxton and Hayslope farmers, on their pleasant uplands, and in their brook-watered valleys, had not suffered, and as I cannot pretend that they were such exceptional farmers as to love the general good better than their own, you will infer that they were not in very low spirits about the rapid rise in the price of bread, so long as there was hope of gathering in their own corn undamaged; and occasional days of sunshine and drying winds flattered this hope.

The eighteenth of August was one of these days, when the sunshine looked brighter in all eyes for the gloom that went before. Grand masses of cloud were hurried across the blue, and the great round hills behind the Chase seemed alive with their flying shadows; the sun was hidden for a moment, and then shone out warm again like a recovered joy; the leaves, still green, were tossed off the hedgerow trees by the wind; around the farmhouses there was a sound of clapping doors: the apples fell in the orchards; and the stray horses on the green sides of the lanes and on the common had their manes blown about their faces. And yet the wind seemed only part of the general gladness because the sun was shining. A merry day for the children, who ran and shouted to see if they could top the wind with their voices; and the grown-up people, too, were in good spirits, inclined to believe in yet finer days, when the wind had fallen. If only the corn were not ripe enough to be blown out of the husk and scattered as untimely seed!

And yet a day on which a blighting sorrow may fall upon a man. For if it be true that Nature at certain moments seems charged with a presentiment of one individual lot, must it not also be true that she seems unmindful, unconscious of another? For there is no hour that has not its births of gladness and despair, no morning brightness that does not bring new sickness to desolation as well as new forces to genius and love. There are so many of us, and our lots are so different: what wonder that Nature's mood is often in harsh contrast with the great crisis of our lives? We are children of a large family, and must learn, as such children do, not to expect that our hurts will be made much of – to be content with little nurture and caressing, and help each other the more.

It was a busy day with Adam, who of late had done almost double work; for he was continuing to act as foreman for Jonathan Burge, until some satisfactory person could be found to supply his place, and Jonathan was slow to find that person. But he had done the extra work cheerfully, for his hopes were buoyant again about Hetty. Every time she had seen him since the birthday, she had seemed to make an effort to behave all the more kindly to him, that she might make him understand she had forgiven his silence and coldness during the dance. He had never mentioned the locket to her again; too happy that she smiled at him – still happier because he observed in her a more subdued air, something that he interpreted as the growth of womanly tenderness and seriousness. 'Ah!' he thought, again and again, 'she's only seventeen; she'll be thoughtful enough after a while. And her aunt allays says how clever she is at the work. She'll make a wife as mother'll have no occasion to grumble at, after all.' To be sure, he had only seen her at home twice since the birthday; for one Sunday, when he was intending to go from church to the Hall Farm, Hetty had joined the party of upper servants from the Chase, and had gone home with them – almost as if she were inclined to encourage Mr Craig. 'She's takin' too much likin' to them folks i' the housekeeper's room,' Mrs Poyser remarked. 'For my part, I was never over-fond o' gentlefolks's servants – they're mostly like the fine ladies' fat dogs, nayther good for barking nor butcher's meat, but on'y for show.' And another evening she was gone to Treddleston to buy some things; though, to his great surprise, as he was returning home, he saw her at a distance getting over a stile quite out of the Treddleston road. But when he hastened to her, she was very kind, and asked him to go in again when he had taken her to the yard gate. She had gone a little farther into the fields after coming from Treddleston, because she didn't want to go in, she said: it was so nice to be out of doors, and her aunt always made such a fuss about it if she wanted to go out. 'Oh, do come in with me!' she said, as he was going to shake hands with her at the gate, and he could not resist that. So he went in, and Mrs Poyser was contented with only a slight remark on Hetty's being later than was expected; while Hetty, who had looked out of spirits when he met her, smiled and talked, and waited on them all with unusual promptitude.

That was the last time he had seen her; but he meant to make leisure for going to the Farm tomorrow. Today, he knew, was her day for going to the Chase to sew with the lady's-maid, so he would get as much work done as possible this evening, that the next might be clear.

One piece of work that Adam was superintending was some slight repairs at the Chase Farm, which had been hitherto occupied by Satchell, as bailiff, but which it was now rumoured that the old Squire was going to let to a smart man in top-boots, who had been seen to ride over it one day. Nothing but the desire to get a tenant could account for the Squire's undertaking repairs, though the Saturday–evening party at Mr Casson's agreed over their pipes that no man in his senses would take the Chase Farm unless there was a bit more ploughland laid to it. However that might be, the repairs were ordered to be executed with all despatch; and Adam, acting for Mr Burge, was carrying out the order with his usual energy. But today, having been occupied elsewhere, he had not been able to arrive at the Chase Farm till late in the afternoon; and he then discovered that some old roofing, which he had calculated on preserving, had given way. There was clearly no good to be done with this part of the building without pulling it all down; and Adam immediately saw in his mind a plan for building it up again, so as to make the most convenient of cowsheds and calf-pens, with a hovel for implements; and all without any great expense for materials. So, when the workmen were gone, he sat down, took out his pocket-book, and busied himself with sketching a plan, and making a specification of the expenses, that he might show it to Burge the next morning, and set him on persuading the Squire to consent. To 'make a good job' of anything, however small, was always a pleasure to Adam; and he sat on a block, with his book resting on a planing-table, whistling low every now and then, and turning his head on one side with a just perceptible smile of gratification – of pride, too, for if Adam loved a bit of good work, he loved also to think, 'I did it!' And I believe the only people who are free from that weakness are those who have no work to call their own. It was nearly seven before he had finished and put on his jacket again; and on giving a last look round, he observed that Seth, who had been working here today, had left his basket of tools behind him. 'Why, th' lad's forgot his tools,' thought Adam, 'and he's got to work up at the shop tomorrow. There never was such a chap for wool-gathering; he'd leave his head behind him, if it was loose. However, it's lucky I've seen 'em; I'll carry 'em home.'

The buildings of the Chase Farm lay at one extremity of the Chase, at about ten minutes' walking distance from the Abbey. Adam had come thither on his pony, intending to ride to the stables, and put up his nag on his way home. At the stables he encountered Mr Craig, who had come to look at the Captain's new horse, on which he was to ride away the day after tomorrow; and Mr Craig detained him to tell how all the servants were to collect at the gate of the courtyard to wish the young Squire luck as he rode out; so that, by the time Adam had got into the Chase, and was striding along with the basket of tools over his shoulder, the sun was on the point of setting, and was sending level crimson rays among the great trunks of the old oaks, and touching every bare patch of ground with a transient glory, that made it look like a jewel dropped upon the grass. The wind had fallen now, and there was only enough breeze to stir the delicate-stemmed leaves. Anyone who had been sitting in the house all day would have been glad to walk now; but Adam had been quite enough in the open air to wish to shorten his way home; and he bethought himself that he might do so by striking across the Chase and going through the Grove, where he had never been for years. He hurried on across the Chase, stalking along the narrow paths between the fern, with Gyp at his heels, not lingering to watch the magnificent changes of the light – hardly once thinking of it – yet feeling its presence in a certain calm happy awe which mingled itself with his busy working-day thoughts. How could he help feeling it? The very deer felt it, and were more timid.

Presently Adam's thoughts recurred to what Mr Craig had said about Arthur Donnithorne, and pictured his going away, and the changes that might take place before he came back: then they travelled back affectionately over the old scenes of boyish companionship, and dwelt on Arthur's good qualities, which Adam had a pride in, as we all have in the virtues of the superior who honours us. A nature like Adam's, with a great need of love and reverence in it, depends for so much of its happiness on what it can believe and feel about others! And he had no ideal world of dead heroes; he knew little of the life of men in the past; he must find the beings to whom he could cling with loving admiration among those who came within speech of him. These pleasant thoughts about Arthur brought a milder expression than usual into his keen rough face: perhaps they were the reason why, when he opened the old green gate leading into the Grove, he paused to pat Gyp, and say a kind word to him.

After that pause, he strode on again along the broad winding path through the Grove. What grand beeches! Adam delighted in a fine tree of all things; as the fisherman's sight is keenest on the sea, so Adam's perceptions were more at home with trees than with other objects. He kept them in his memory, as a painter does, with all the flecks and knots in their bark, all the curves and angles of their boughs; and had often calculated the height and contents of a trunk to a nicety, as he stood looking at it. No wonder that, notwithstanding his desire to get on, he could not help pausing to look at a curious large beech which he had seen standing before him at a turning in the road, and convince himself that it was not two trees wedded together, but only one. For the rest of his life he remembered that moment when he was calmly examining the beech, as a man remembers his last glimpse of the home where his youth was passed, before the road turned, and he saw it no more. The beech stood at the last turning before the Grove ended in an archway of boughs that let in the eastern light; and as Adam stepped away from the tree to continue his walk, his eyes fell on two figures about twenty yards before him.

He remained as motionless as a statue, and turned almost as pale. The two figures were standing opposite to each other, with clasped hands, about to part; and while they were bending to kiss, Gyp, who had been running among the brushwood, came out, caught sight of them, and gave a sharp bark. They separated with a start – one hurried through the gate out of the Grove, and the other, turning round, walked slowly, with a sort of saunter towards Adam, who still stood transfixed and pale, clutching tighter the stick with which he held the basket of tools over his shoulder, and looking at the approaching figure with eyes in which amazement was fast turning to fierceness.

Arthur Donnithorne looked flushed and excited; he had tried to make unpleasant feelings more bearable by drinking a little more wine than usual at dinner today, and was still enough under its flattering influence to think more lightly of this unwished-for rencontre with Adam than he would otherwise have done. After all, Adam was the best person who could have happened to see him and Hetty together: he was a sensible fellow, and would not babble about it to other people. Arthur felt confident that he could laugh the thing off, and explain it away. And so he sauntered forward with elaborate carelessness – his flushed face, his evening dress of fine cloth and fine linen, his hands half thrust into his waistcoat-pockets, all shone upon by the strange evening light which the light clouds had caught up even to the zenith, and were now shedding down between the topmost branches above him.

Adam was still motionless, looking at him as he came up. He understood it all now – the locket, and everything else that had been doubtful to him: a terrible scorching light showed him the hidden letters that changed the meaning of the past. If he had moved a muscle, he must inevitably have sprung upon Arthur like a tiger; and in the conflicting emotions that filled those long moments, he had told himself that he would not give loose to passion, he would only speak the right thing. He stood as if petrified by an unseen force, but the force was his own strong will.

'Well, Adam,' said Arthur, 'you've been looking at the fine old beeches, eh? They're not to be come near by the hatchet, though; this is a sacred grove. I overtook pretty little Hetty Sorrel as I was coming to my den – the Hermitage, there. She ought not to come home this way so late. So I took care of her to the gate, and asked for a kiss for my pains. But I must get back now, for this road is confoundedly damp. Good-night, Adam: I shall see you tomorrow – to say goodbye you know.'

Arthur was too much preoccupied with the part he was playing himself to be thoroughly aware of the expression in Adam's face. He did not look directly at Adam, but glanced carelessly round at the trees, and then lifted up one foot to look at the sole of his boot. He cared to say no more; he had thrown quite dust enough into honest Adam's eyes; and as he spoke the last words, he walked on.

'Stop a bit, sir,' said Adam, in a hard peremptory voice, without turning round. 'I've got a word to say to you.'

Arthur paused in surprise. Susceptible persons are more affected by a change of tone than by unexpected words, and Arthur had the susceptibility of a nature at once affectionate and vain. He was still more surprised when he saw that Adam had not moved, but stood with his back to him, as if summoning him to return. What did he mean? He was going to make a serious business of this affair. Arthur felt his temper rising. A patronising disposition always has its meaner side, and in the confusion of his irritation and alarm there entered the feeling that a man to whom he had shown so much favour as to Adam, was not in a position to criticise his conduct. And yet he was dominated, as one who feels himself in the wrong always is, by the man whose good opinion he cares for. In spite of pride and temper, there was as much deprecation as anger in his voice when he said – 'What do you mean, Adam?'

'I mean, sir,' answered Adam, in the same harsh voice, still without turning round – 'I mean, sir, that you don't deceive me by your light words. This is not the first time you've met Hetty Sorrel in this grove, and this is not the first time you've kissed her.'

Arthur felt a startled uncertainty how far Adam was speaking from knowledge, and how far from mere inference. And this uncertainty, which prevented him from contriving a prudent answer, heightened his irritation. He said in a high sharp tone – 'Well, sir, what then?'

'Why, then, instead of acting like th' upright, honourable man we've all believed you to be, you've been acting the part of a selfish light-minded scoundrel. You know, as well as I do, what it's to lead to, when a gentleman like you kisses and makes love to a young woman like Hetty, and gives her presents as she's frightened for other folks to see. And I say it again, you're acting the part of a selfish, light-minded scoundrel, though it cuts me to th' heart to say so, and I'd rather ha' lost my right hand.'

'Let me tell you, Adam,' said Arthur, bridling his growing anger, and trying to recur to his careless tone, 'you're not only devilishly impertinent, but you're talking nonsense. Every pretty girl is not such a fool as you, to suppose that when a gentleman admires her beauty, and pays her a little attention, he must mean something particular. Every man likes to flirt with a pretty girl, and every pretty girl likes to be flirted with. The wider the distance between them the less harm there is, for then she's not likely to deceive herself.'

'I don't know what you mean by flirting,' said Adam, 'but if you mean behaving to a woman as if you loved her, and yet not loving her all the while, I say that's not the action of an honest man, and what isn't honest does come t' harm. I'm not a fool, and you're not a fool, and you know better than what you're saying. You know it couldn't be made public as you've behaved to Hetty as y' have done without her losing her character, and bringing shame and trouble on her and her relations. What if you meant nothing by your kissing and your presents? Other folks won't believe as you've meant nothing; and don't tell me about her not deceiving herself. I tell you as you've filled her mind so with the thought of you as it'll mayhap poison her life; and she'll never love another man as 'ud make her a good husband.'

Arthur had felt a sudden relief while Adam was speaking; he perceived that Adam had no positive knowledge of the past, and that there was no irrevocable damage done by this evening's unfortunate rencontre. Adam could still be deceived. The candid Arthur had brought himself into a position in which successful lying was his only hope. The hope allayed his anger a little.

'Well, Adam,' he said, in a tone of friendly concession, 'you're perhaps right. Perhaps I've gone a little too far in taking notice of the pretty little thing, and stealing a kiss now and then. You're such a grave, steady fellow, you don't understand the temptation to such trifling. I'm sure I wouldn't bring any trouble or annoyance on her and the good Poysers on any account if I could help it. But I think you look a little too seriously at it. You know I'm going away immediately, so I shan't make any more mistakes of the kind. But let us say good-night' – Arthur here turned round to walk on – 'and talk no more about the matter. The whole thing will soon be forgotten.'

'No, by God!' Adam burst out with rage that could be controlled no longer, throwing down the basket of tools, and striding forward till he was right in front of Arthur. All his jealousy and sense of personal injury, which he had been hitherto trying to keep under, had leaped up and mastered him. What man of us, in the first moments of a sharp agony, could ever feel that the fellow-man who has been the medium of inflicting it, did not mean to hurt us? In our instinctive rebellion against pain, we are children again, and demand an active will to wreak our vengeance on. Adam at this moment could only feel that he had been robbed of Hetty – robbed treacherously by the man in whom he had trusted, and he stood close in front of Arthur, with fierce eyes glaring at him, with pale lips and clenched hands, the hard tones in which he had hitherto been constraining himself to express no more than a just indignation, giving way to a deep agitated voice that seemed to shake him as he spoke.

'No, it'll not be soon forgot, as you've come in between her and me, when she might ha' loved me – it'll not soon be forgot as you've robbed me o' my happiness, while I thought you was my best friend, and a noble-minded man, as I was proud to work for. And you've been kissing her, and meaning nothing, have you? And I never kissed her i' my life – but I'd ha' worked hard for years for the right to kiss her. And you make light of it. You think little o' doing what may damage other folks, so as you get your bit o' trifling, as means nothing. I throw back your favours, for you're not the man I took you for. I'll never count you my friend any more. I'd rather you'd act as my enemy, and fight me where I stand – it's all th' amends you can make me.'

Poor Adam, possessed by rage that could find no other vent, began to throw off his coat and his cap, too blind with passion to notice the change that had taken place in Arthur while he was speaking. Arthur's lips were now as pale as Adam's; his heart was beating violently. The discovery that Adam loved Hetty was a shock which made him for the moment see himself in the light of Adam's indignation, and regard Adam's suffering as not merely a consequence, but an element of his error. The words of hatred and contempt – the first he had ever heard in his life – seemed like scorching missiles that were making ineffaceable scars on him. All screening self-excuse, which rarely falls quite away while others respect us, forsook him for an instant, and he stood face to face with the first great irrevocable evil he had ever committed. He was only twenty-one – and three months ago – nay, much later – he had thought proudly that no man should ever be able to reproach him justly. His first impulse, if there had been time for it, would perhaps have been to utter words of propitiation; but Adam had no sooner thrown off his coat and cap, than he became aware that Arthur was standing pale and motionless, with his hands still thrust in his waistcoat-pockets.

'What!' he said, 'won't you fight me like a man? You know I won't strike you while you stand so.'

'Go away, Adam,' said Arthur, 'I don't want to fight you.'

'No,' said Adam, bitterly; 'you don't want to fight me – you think I'm a common man, as you can injure without answering for it.'

'I never meant to injure you,' said Arthur, with returning anger. 'I didn't know you loved her.'

'But you've made her love you,' said Adam. 'You're a double-faced man – I'll never believe a word you say again.'

'Go away, I tell you,' said Arthur, angrily, 'or we shall both repent.'

'No,' said Adam, with a convulsed voice, 'I swear I won't go away without fighting you. Do you want provoking any more? I tell you you're a coward and a scoundrel, and I despise you.'

The colour had all rushed back to Arthur's face: in a moment his right hand was clenched, and dealt a blow like lightning, which sent Adam staggering backward. His blood was as thoroughly up as Adam's now, and the two men, forgetting the emotions that had gone before, fought with the instinctive fierceness of panthers in the deepening twilight darkened by the trees. The delicate-handed gentleman was a match for the workman in everything but strength, and Arthur's skill enabled him to protract the struggle for some long moments. But between unarmed men the battle is to the strong, where the strong is no blunderer, and

Arthur must sink under a well planted blow of Adam's, as a steel rod is broken by an iron bar. The blow soon came, and Arthur fell, his head lying concealed in a tuft of fern, so that Adam could only discern his darkly-clad body.

He stood still in the dim light waiting for Arthur to rise.

The blow had been given now, towards which he had been straining all the force of nerve and muscle – and what was the good of it? What had he done by fighting? Only satisfied his own passion, only wreaked his own vengeance. He had not rescued Hetty, nor changed the past – there it was just as it had been, and he sickened at the vanity of his own rage.

But why did not Arthur rise? He was perfectly motionless and the time seemed long to Adam . . . Good God! had the blow been too much for him? Adam shuddered at the thought of his own strength, as with the oncoming of this dread he knelt down by Arthur's side and lifted his head from among the fern. There was no sign of life: the eyes and teeth were set. The horror that rushed over Adam completely mastered him, and forced upon him its own belief. He could feel nothing but that death was in Arthur's face, and that he was helpless before it. He made not a single movement, but knelt like an image of despair gazing at an image of death.

28

A Dilemma

It was only a few minutes measured by the clock – though Adam always thought it had been a long while – before he perceived a gleam of consciousness in Arthur's face and a slight shiver through his frame. The intense joy that flooded his soul brought back some of the old affection with it.

'Do you feel any pain, sir?' he said, tenderly, loosening Arthur's cravat.

Arthur turned his eyes on Adam with a vague stare which gave way to a slightly startled motion as if from the shock of returning memory. But he only shivered again and said nothing.

'Do you feel any hurt, sir?' Adam said again, with a trembling in his voice.

Arthur put his hand up to his waistcoat buttons, and when Adam had unbuttoned it, he took a longer breath. 'Lay my head down,' he said, faintly, 'and get me some water if you can.'

Adam laid the head down gently on the fern again, and emptying the tools out of the flag-basket, hurried through the trees to the edge of the Grove bordering on the Chase, where a brook ran below the bank.

When he returned with his basket leaking, but still half full, Arthur looked at him with a more thoroughly reawakened consciousness.

'Can you drink a drop out o' your hand, sir?' said Adam, kneeling down again to lift up Arthur's head.

'No,' said Arthur, 'dip my cravat in and souse it on my head.'

The water seemed to do him some good, for he presently raised himself a little higher, resting on Adam's arm.

'Do you feel any hurt inside, sir?' Adam asked again.

'No – no hurt,' said Arthur, still faintly, 'but rather done up.' After a while he said, 'I suppose I fainted away when you knocked me down.'

'Yes, sir, thank God,' said Adam. 'I thought it was worse.'

'What! you thought you'd done for me, eh? come, help me on my legs.'

'I feel terribly shaky and dizzy,' Arthur said, as he stood leaning on Adam's arm; 'that blow of yours must have come against me like a battering-ram. I don't believe I can walk alone.'

'Lean on me, sir; I'll get you along,' said Adam. 'Or, will you sit down a bit longer, on my coat here? and I'll prop y' up. You'll perhaps be better in a minute or two.'

'No,' said Arthur. 'I'll go to the Hermitage – I think I've got some brandy there. There's a short road to it a little further on, near the gate. If you'll just help me on.'

They walked slowly, with frequent pauses, but without speaking again. In both of them, the concentration in the present which had attended the first moments of Arthur's revival, had now given way to a vivid recollection of the previous scene. It was nearly dark in the narrow path among the trees, but within the circle of fir trees round the Hermitage there was room for the growing moonlight to enter in at the windows. Their steps were noiseless on the thick carpet of fir needles, and the outward stillness seemed to heighten their inward consciousness, as Arthur took the key out of his pocket and placed it in Adam's hand, for him to open the door. Adam had not known before that Arthur had furnished the old Hermitage and made it a retreat for himself, and it was a surprise to him when he opened the door to see a snug room with all the signs of frequent habitation.

Arthur loosed Adam's arm and threw himself on the ottoman. 'You'll see my hunting-bottle somewhere,' he said. 'A leather case with a bottle and glass in.'

Adam was not long in finding the case. 'There's very little brandy in it, sir,' he said, turning it downwards over the glass, as he held it before the window, 'hardly this little glassful.'

'Well, give me that,' said Arthur, with the peevishness of physical depression. When he had taken some sips, Adam said, 'Hadn't I better run to th' house, sir, and get some more brandy? I can be there and back pretty soon. It'll be a stiff walk home for you, if you don't have something to revive you.'

'Yes – go. But don't say I'm ill. Ask for my man Pym, and tell him to get it from Mills, and not to say I'm at the Hermitage. Get some water too.'

Adam was relieved to have an active task – both of them were relieved to be apart from each other for a short time. But Adam's swift pace could not still the eager pain of thinking – of living again with concentrated suffering through the last wretched hour, and looking out from it over all the new, sad future.

Arthur lay still for some minutes after Adam was gone, but presently he rose feebly from the ottoman and peered about slowly in the broken moonlight, seeking something. It was a short bit of wax candle that stood amongst a confusion of writing and drawing materials. There was more searching for the means of lighting the candle, and when that was done, he went cautiously round the room as if wishing to assure himself of the presence or absence of some-thing. At last he had found a slight thing, which he put first in his pocket, and then, on a second thought, took out again, and thrust deep down into a waste-paper basket. It was a woman's little pink silk neckerchief. He set the candle on the table, and threw himself down on the ottoman again, exhausted with the effort.

When Adam came back with his supplies, his entrance awoke Arthur from a dose.

'That's right,' Arthur said; 'I'm tremendously in want of some brandy-vigour.'

'I'm glad to see you've got a light, sir,' said Adam. 'I've been thinking I'd better have asked for a lanthorn.'

'No, no; the candle will last long enough – I shall soon be up to walking home now.'

'I can't go before I've seen you safe home, sir,' said Adam, hesitatingly.

'No: it will be better for you to stay – sit down.'

Adam sat down, and they remained opposite to each other in uneasy silence, while Arthur slowly drank brandy-and-water, with visibly renovating effect. He began to lie in a more voluntary position, and looked as if he were less over-powered by bodily sensations. Adam was keenly alive to these indications, and as his anxiety about Arthur's condition began to be allayed, he felt more of that impatience which everyone knows who has had his just indignation suspended by the physical state of the culprit. Yet there was one thing on his mind to be done before he could recur to remonstrance: it was to confess what had been unjust in his own words. Perhaps he longed all the more to make this confession, that his indignation might be free again; and as he saw the signs of returning ease in Arthur, the words again and again came to his lips and went back, checked by the thought that it would be better to leave everything till tomorrow. As long as they were silent they did not look at each other, and a foreboding came across Adam that if they began to speak as though they remembered the past – if they looked at each with full recognition – they must take fire again. So they sat in silence till the bit of wax candle flickered low in the socket; the silence all the while becoming more irksome to Adam. Arthur had just poured out some more brandy-and-water, and he threw one arm behind his head and drew up one leg in an attitude of recovered ease, which was an irresistible temptation to Adam to speak what was on his mind.

'You begin to feel more yourself again, sir,' he said, as the candle went out, and they were half-hidden from each other in the faint moonlight.

'Yes: I don't feel good for much – very lazy, and not inclined to move; but I'll go home when I've taken this dose.'

There was a slight pause before Adam said – 'My temper got the better of me, and I said things as wasn't true. I'd no right to speak as if you'd known you was doing me an injury: you'd no grounds for knowing it; I've always kept what I felt for her as secret as I could.'

He paused again before he went on.

'And perhaps I judged you too harsh – I'm apt to be harsh; and you may have acted out o' thoughtlessness more than I should ha' believed was possible for a man with a heart and a conscience. We're not all put together alike, and we may misjudge one another. God knows, it's all the joy I could have now, to think the best of you.'

Arthur wanted to go home without saying any more – he was too painfully embarrassed in mind, as well as too weak in body, to wish for any further explanation tonight. And yet it was a relief to him that Adam reopened the subject in a way the least difficult for him to answer. Arthur was in the wretched position of an open, generous man, who has committed an error which makes deception seem a necessity. The native impulse to give truth in return for truth, to meet trust with frank confession, must be suppressed, and duty was become a question of tactics. His deed was reacting upon him – was already governing him tyrannously, and forcing him into a course that jarred with his habitual feelings. The only aim that seemed admissible to him now was to deceive Adam to the utmost: to make Adam think better of him than he deserved. And when he heard the words of honest retraction – when he heard the sad appeal with which Adam ended – he was obliged to rejoice in the remains of ignorant confidence it implied. He did not answer immediately, for he had to be judicious, and not truthful.

'Say no more about our anger, Adam,' he said, at last, very languidly, for the labour of speech was unwelcome to him; 'I forgive your momentary injustice – it was quite natural, with the exaggerated notions you had in your mind. We shall be none the worse friends in future, I hope, because we've fought: you had the best of it, and that was as it should be, for I believe I've been most in the wrong of the two. Come, let us shake hands.'

Arthur held out his hand, but Adam sat still.

'I don't like to say "No" to that, sir,' he said, 'but I can't shake hands till it's clear what we mean by't. I was wrong when I spoke as if you'd done me an injury knowingly, but I wasn't wrong in what I said before, about your behaviour t' Hetty, and I can't shake hands with you as if I held you my friend the same as ever, till you've cleared that up better.'

Arthur swallowed his pride and resentment as he drew back his hand. He was silent for some moments, and then said, as indifferently as he could – 'I don't know what you mean by clearing up, Adam. I've told you already that you think too seriously of a little flirtation. But if you are right in supposing there is any danger in it – I'm going away on Saturday, and there will be an end of it. As for the pain it has given you, I'm heartily sorry for it. I can say no more.'

Adam said nothing, but rose from his chair, and stood with his face towards one of the windows, as if looking at the blackness of the moonlit fir trees; but he was in reality conscious of nothing but the conflict within him. It was of no use now – his resolution not to speak till tomorrow: he must speak there and then. But it was several minutes before he turned round and stepped nearer to Arthur, standing and looking down on him as he lay.

'It'll be better for me to speak plain,' he said, with evident effort, 'though it's hard work. You see, sir, this isn't a trifle to me, whatever it may be to you. I'm none o' them men as can go making love first to one woman and then t' another, and don't think it much odds which of 'em I take. What I feel for Hetty's a different sort o' love, such as I believe nobody can know much about but them as feel it, and God as has given it to 'em. She's more nor everything else to me, all but my conscience and my good name. And if it's true what you've been saying all along – and if it's only been trifling and flirting as you call it, as'll be put an end to by your going away – why, then, I'd wait, and hope her heart 'ud turn to me after all. I'm loath to think you'd speak false to me, and I'll believe your word, however things may look.'

'You would be wronging Hetty more than me not to believe it,' said Arthur, almost violently, starting up from the ottoman, and moving away. But he threw himself into a chair again directly, saying, more feebly, 'You seem to forget that, in suspecting me, you are casting imputations upon her.'

'Nay, sir,' Adam said, in a calmer voice, as if he were half relieved – for he was too straightforward to make a distinction between a direct falsehood and an indirect one – 'Nay, sir, things don't lie level between Hetty and you. You're acting with your eyes open, whatever you may do; but how do you know what's been in her mind? She's all but a child – as any man with a conscience in him ought to feel bound to take care on. And whatever you may think, I know you've disturbed her mind. I know she's been fixing her heart on you; for there's a many things clear to me now as I didn't understand before. But you seem to make light o' what she may feel – you don't think o' that.'

'Good God, Adam, let me alone!' Arthur burst out impetuously; 'I feel it enough without your worrying me.'

He was aware of his indiscretion as soon as the words had escaped him.

'Well, then, if you feel it,' Adam rejoined eagerly; 'if you feel as you may ha' put false notions into her mind, and made her believe as you loved her, when all the while you meant nothing, I've this demand to make of you – I'm not speaking for myself, but for her. I ask you t' undeceive her before you go away. Y'aren't going away for ever; and if you leave her behind with a notion in her head o' your feeling about her the same as she feels about you, she'll be hankering after you, and the mischief may get worse. It may be a smart to her now, but it'll save her pain i' th' end. I ask you to write a letter – you may trust to my seeing as she gets it: tell her the truth, and take blame to yourself for behaving as you'd no right to do to a young woman as isn't your equal. I speak plain, sir. But I can't speak any other way. There's nobody can take care o' Hetty in this thing but me.'

'I can do what I think needful in the matter,' said Arthur, more and more irritated by mingled distress and perplexity, 'without giving promises to you. I shall take what measures I think proper.'

'No,' said Adam, in an abrupt decided tone, 'that won't do. I must know what ground I'm treading on. I must be safe as you've put an end to what ought never to ha' been begun. I don't forget what's owing to you as a gentleman; but in this thing we're man and man, and I can't give up.'

There was no answer for some moments. Then Arthur said, 'I'll see you tomorrow. I can bear no more now; I'm ill.' He rose as he spoke, and reached his cap, as if intending to go.

'You won't see her again!' Adam exclaimed, with a flash of recurring anger and suspicion, moving towards the door and placing his back against it. 'Either tell me she can never be my wife – tell me you've been lying – or else promise me what I've said.'

Adam, uttering this alternative, stood like a terrible fate before Arthur, who had moved forward a step or two, and now stopped, faint, shaken, sick in mind and body. It seemed long to both of them – that inward struggle of Arthur's – before he said, feebly, 'I promise; let me go.'

Adam moved away from the door and opened it, but when Arthur reached the step, he stopped again and leaned against the doorpost.

'You're not well enough to walk alone, sir,' said Adam. 'Take my arm again.'

Arthur made no answer, and presently walked on, Adam following. But, after a few steps, he stood still again, and said coldly, 'I believe I must trouble you. It's getting late now, and there may be an alarm set up about me at home.'

Adam gave his arm, and they walked on without uttering a word, till they came where the basket and the tools lay.

'I must pick up the tools, sir,' Adam said. 'They're my brother's. I doubt they'll be rusted. If you'll please to wait a minute.'

Arthur stood still without speaking, and no other word passed between them till they were at the side entrance, where he hoped to get in without being seen by anyone. He said then, 'Thank you; I needn't trouble you any further.'

'What time will it be conven'ent for me to see you tomorrow, sir?' said Adam.

'You may send me word that you're here at five o'clock,' said Arthur; 'not before.'

'Good-night, sir,' said Adam. But he heard no reply; Arthur had turned into the house.

29

The Next Morning

Arthur did not pass a sleepless night, he slept long and well. For sleep comes to the perplexed – if the perplexed are only weary enough. But at seven he rang his bell and astonished Pym by declaring he was going to get up, and must have breakfast brought to him at eight.

'And see that my mare is saddled at half-past eight, and tell my grandfather when he's down that I'm better this morning, and am gone for a ride.'

He had been awake an hour, and could rest in bed no longer. In bed our yesterdays are too oppressive: if a man can only get up, though it be but to whistle or to smoke, he has a present which offers some resistance to the past – sensations which assert themselves against tyrannous memories. And if there were such a thing as taking averages of feeling, it would certainly be found that in the hunting and shooting seasons regret, self-reproach, and mortified pride, weigh lighter on country gentlemen than in late spring and summer. Arthur felt that he should be more of a man on horseback. Even the presence of Pym, waiting on him with the usual deference, was a reassurance to him after the scenes of yesterday. For, with Arthur's sensitiveness to opinion, the loss of Adam's respect was a shock to his self-contentment which suffused his imagination with the sense that he had sunk in all eyes; as a sudden shock of fear from some real peril makes a nervous woman afraid even to step, because all her perceptions are suffused with a sense of danger.

Arthur's, as you know, was a loving nature. Deeds of kindness were as easy to him as a bad habit: they were the common issue of his weaknesses and good qualities, of his egoism and his sympathy. He didn't like to witness pain, and he liked to have grateful eyes beaming on him as the giver of pleasure. When he was a lad of seven, he one day kicked down an old gardener's pitcher of broth, from no motive but a kicking impulse, not reflecting that it was the old man's dinner; but on learning that sad fact, he took his favourite pencil-case and a silver-hafted knife out of his pocket and offered them as compensation. He had been the same Arthur ever since, trying to make all offences forgotten in benefits. If there were any bitterness in his nature, it could only show itself against the man who refused to be conciliated by him. And perhaps the time was come for some of that bitterness to rise. At the first moment, Arthur had felt pure distress and self-reproach at discovering that Adam's happiness was involved in his relation to Hetty: if there had been a possibility of making Adam tenfold amends – if deeds of gift, or any other deeds, could have restored Adam's contentment and regard for him as a benefactor, Arthur would not only have executed them without hesitation, but would have felt bound all the more closely to Adam, and would never have been weary of making retribution. But Adam could receive no amends; his suffering could not be cancelled; his respect and affection could not be recovered by any prompt deeds of atonement. He stood like an immovable obstacle against which no pressure could avail; an embodiment of what Arthur most shrank from believing in – the irrevocableness of his own wrong-doing. The words of scorn, the refusal to shake hands, the mastery asserted over him in their last conversation in the Hermitage – above all, the sense of having been knocked down, to which a man does not very well reconcile himself, even under the most heroic circumstances – pressed on him with a galling pain which was stronger than compunction. Arthur would so gladly have persuaded himself that he had done no harm! And if no one had told him the contrary, he could have persuaded himself so much better. Nemesis can seldom forge a sword for herself out of our consciences – out of the suffering we feel in the suffering we may have caused: there is rarely metal enough there to make an effective weapon. Our moral sense learns the manners of good society, and smiles when others smile; but when some rude person gives rough names to our actions, she is apt to take part against us. And so it was with Arthur: Adam's judgement of him, Adam's grating words, disturbed his self-soothing arguments.

Not that Arthur had been at ease before Adam's discovery. Struggles and resolves had transformed themselves into compunction and anxiety. He was distressed for Hetty's sake, and distressed for his own, that he must leave her behind. He had always, both in making and breaking resolutions, looked beyond his passion, and seen that it must speedily end in separation; but his nature was too ardent and tender for him not to suffer at this parting; and on Hetty's account he was filled with uneasiness. He had found out the dream in which she was living – that she was to be a lady in silks and satins; and when he had first talked to her about his going away, she had asked him tremblingly to let her go with him and be married. It was his painful knowledge of this which had given the most exasperating sting to Adam's reproaches. He had said no word with the purpose of deceiving her, her vision was all spun by her own childish fancy; but he was obliged to confess to himself that it was spun half out of his own actions. And to increase the mischief, on this last evening he had not dared to hint the truth to Hetty: he had been obliged to soothe her with tender, hopeful words, lest he should throw her into violent distress. He felt the situation acutely; felt the sorrow of the dear thing in the present and thought with a darker anxiety of the tenacity which her feelings might have in the future. That was the one sharp point which pressed against him; every other he could evade by hopeful self-persuasion. The whole thing had been secret; the Poysers had not the shadow of a suspicion. No one, except Adam, knew anything of what had passed – no one else was likely to know; for Arthur had impressed on Hetty that it would be fatal to betray, by word or look, that there had been the least intimacy between them; and Adam, who knew half their secret, would rather help them to keep it than betray it. It was an unfortunate business altogether, but there was no use in making it worse than it was, by imaginary exaggerations and forebodings of evil that might never come. The temporary sadness for Hetty was the worst consequence; he resolutely turned away his eyes from any bad consequence that was not demonstrably inevitable. But – but Hetty might have had the trouble in some other way if not in this. And perhaps hereafter he might be able to do a great deal for her, and make up to her for all the tears she would shed about him. She would owe the advantage of his care for her in future years to the sorrow she had incurred now. *So* good comes out of evil. Such is the beautiful arrangement of things!

Are you inclined to ask whether this can be the same Arthur who, two months ago, had that freshness of feeling, that delicate honour which shrinks from wounding even a sentiment, and does not contemplate any more positive offence as possible for it? – who thought that his own self-respect was a higher tribunal than any external opinion? The same, I assure you, only under different conditions. Our deeds determine us, as much as we determine our deeds; and until we know what has been or will be the peculiar combination of outward with inward facts, which constitutes a man's critical actions, it will be better not to think ourselves wise about his character. There is a terrible coercion in our deeds which may first turn the honest man into a deceiver, and then reconcile him to the change; for this reason – that the second wrong presents itself to him in the guise of the only practicable right. The action which before commission has been seen with that blended common-sense and fresh untarnished feeling which is the healthy eye of the soul, is looked at afterwards with the lens of apologetic ingenuity, through which all things that men call beautiful and ugly are seen to be made up of textures very much alike. Europe adjusts itself to a *fait accompli*, and so does an individual character – until the placid adjustment is disturbed by a convulsive retribution.

No man can escape this vitiating effect of an offence against his own sentiment of right, and the effect was the stronger in Arthur because of that very need of self-respect which, while his conscience was still at ease, was one of his best safeguards. Self-accusation was too painful to him – he could not face it. He must persuade himself that he had not been very much to blame; he began even to pity himself for the necessity he was under of deceiving Adam: it was a course so opposed to the honesty of his own nature. But then, it was the only right thing to do.

Well, whatever had been amiss in him, he was miserable enough in consequence: miserable about Hetty: miserable about this letter that he had promised to write, and that seemed at one moment to be a gross barbarity, at another perhaps the greatest kindness he could do to her. And across all this reflection would dart every now and then a sudden impulse of passionate defiance towards all consequences: he would carry Hetty away, and all other considerations might go to . . .

In this state of mind the four walls of his room made an intolerable prison to him; they seemed to hem in and press down upon him all the crowd of contra-dictory thoughts and conflicting feelings, some of which would fly away in the open air. He had only an hour or two to make up his mind in, and he must get clear and calm. Once on Meg's back, in the fresh air of that fine morning, he should be more master of the situation.

The pretty creature arched her bay neck in the sunshine, and pawed the gravel, and trembled with pleasure when her master stroked her nose, and patted her, and talked to her even in a more caressing tone than usual. He loved her the better because she knew nothing of his secrets. But Meg was quite as well acquainted with her master's mental state as many others of her sex with the mental condition of the nice young gentlemen towards whom their hearts are in a state of fluttering expectation.

Arthur cantered for five miles beyond the Chase, till he was at the foot of a hill where there were no hedges or trees to hem in the road. Then he threw the bridle on Meg's neck, and prepared to make up his mind.

Hetty knew that their meeting yesterday must be the last before Arthur went away; there was no possibility of their contriving another without exciting suspicion; and she was like a frightened child, unable to think of anything, only able to cry at the mention of parting, and then put her face up to have the tears kissed away. He could do nothing but comfort her, and lull her into dreaming on. A letter would be a dreadfully abrupt way of awakening her! Yet there was truth in what Adam said – that it would save her from a lengthened delusion, which might be worse than a sharp immediate pain. And it was the only way of satisfying Adam, who must be satisfied, for more reasons than one. If he could have seen her again! But that was impossible; there was such a thorny hedge of hindrances between them, and an imprudence would be fatal. And yet, if he could see her again, what good would it do? Only cause him to suffer more from the sight of her distress and the remembrance of it. Away from him, she was surrounded by all the motives to self-control.

A sudden dread here fell like a shadow across his imagination – the dread lest she should do something violent in her grief; and close upon that dread came another, which deepened the shadow. But he shook them off with the force of youth and hope. What was the ground for painting the future in that dark way? It was just as likely to be the reverse. Arthur told himself, he did not deserve that things should turn out badly – he had never meant beforehand to do anything his conscience disapproved – he had been led on by circumstances. There was a sort of implicit confidence in him that he was really such a good fellow at bottom, Providence would not treat him harshly.

At all events, he couldn't help what would come now: all he could do was to take what seemed the best course at the present moment. And he persuaded himself that that course was to make the way open between Adam and Hetty. Her heart might really turn to Adam, as he said, after a while; and in that case there would have been no great harm done, since it was still Adam's ardent wish to make her his wife. To be sure, Adam was deceived – deceived in a way that Arthur would have resented as a deep wrong if it had been practised on himself. That was a reflection that marred the consoling prospect. Arthur's cheeks even burned in mingled shame and irritation at the thought. But what could a man do in such a dilemma? He was bound in honour to say no word that could injure Hetty: his first duty was to guard *her*. He would never have told or acted a lie on his own account. Good God! what a miserable fool he was to have brought himself into such a dilemma; and yet, if ever a man had excuses, he had. (Pity that consequences are determined not by excuses but by actions!)

Well, the letter must be written; it was the only means that promised a solution of the difficulty. The tears came into Arthur's eyes as he thought of Hetty reading it; but it would be almost as hard for him to write it: he was not doing anything easy to himself; and this last thought helped him to arrive at a conclusion. He could never deliberately have taken a step which inflicted pain on another and left himself at ease. Even a movement of jealousy at the thought of giving up Hetty to Adam, went to convince him that he was making a sacrifice.

When once he had come to this conclusion, he turned Meg round, and set off home again in a canter. The letter should be written the first thing, and the rest of the day would be filled up with other business: he should have no time to look behind him. Happily Irwine and Gawaine were coming to dinner, and by twelve o'clock the next day he should have left the Chase miles behind him. There was some security in this constant occupation against an uncontrollable impulse seizing him to rush to Hetty, and thrust into her hand some mad proposition that would undo everything. Faster and faster went the sensitive Meg, at every slight sign from her rider, till the canter had passed into a swift gallop.

'I thought they said th' young mester war took ill last night,' said sour old John, the groom, at dinner-time in the servants' hall. 'He's been ridin' fit to split the mare i' two this forenoon.'

'That's happen one o' the symptoms, John,' said the facetious coachman.

'Then I wish he war let blood for 't, that's all,' said John, grimly.

Adam had been early at the Chase to know how Arthur was, and had been relieved from all anxiety about the effects of his blow by learning that he was gone out for a ride. At five o'clock he was punctually there again, and sent up word of his arrival. In a few minutes Pym came down with a letter in his hand,

and gave it to Adam, saying that the Captain was too busy to see him, and had written everything he had to say. The letter was directed to Adam, but he went out of doors again before opening it. It contained a sealed enclosure directed to Hetty. On the inside of the cover Adam read:

> In the enclosed letter I have written everything you wish. I leave it to you to decide whether you will be doing best to deliver it to Hetty or to return it to me. Ask yourself once more whether you are not taking a measure which may pain her more than mere silence.
>
> There is no need for our seeing each other again now. We shall meet with better feelings some months hence.   A. D.

'Perhaps he's i' th' right on't not to see me,' thought Adam. 'It's no use meeting to say more hard words, and it's no use meeting to shake hands and say we're friends again. We're not friends, an' it's better not to pretend it. I know forgiveness is a man's duty, but, to my thinking, that can only mean as you're to give up all thoughts o' taking revenge: it can never mean as you're t' have your old feelings back again, for that's not possible. He's not the same man to me, and I can't feel the same towards him. God help me! I don't know whether I feel the same towards anybody: I seem as if I'd been measuring my work from a false line, and had got it all to measure over again.'

But the question about delivering the letter to Hetty soon absorbed Adam's thoughts. Arthur had procured some relief to himself by throwing the decision on Adam with a warning; and Adam, who was not given to hesitation, hesitated here. He determined to feel his way – to ascertain as well as he could what was Hetty's state of mind before he decided on delivering the letter.

30

The Delivery of the Letter

The next Sunday Adam joined the Poysers on their way out of church, hoping for an invitation to go home with them. He had the letter in his pocket, and was anxious to have an opportunity of talking to Hetty alone. He could not see her face at church, for she had changed her seat, and when he came up to her to shake hands, her manner was doubtful and constrained. He expected this, for it was the first time she had met him since she had been aware that he had seen her with Arthur in the Grove.

'Come, you'll go on with us, Adam,' Mr Poyser said when they reached the turning; and as soon as they were in the fields Adam ventured to offer his arm to Hetty. The children soon gave them an opportunity of lingering behind a little, and then Adam said – 'Will you contrive for me to walk out in the garden a bit with you this evening, if it keeps fine, Hetty? I've something partic'lar to talk to you about.'

Hetty said, 'Very well.' She was really as anxious as Adam was that she should have some private talk with him: she wondered what he thought of her and

Arthur: he must have seen them kissing, she knew, but she had no conception of the scene that had taken place between Arthur and Adam. Her first feeling had been that Adam would be very angry with her, and perhaps would tell her aunt and uncle; but it never entered her mind that he would dare to say anything to Captain Donnithorne. It was a relief to her that he behaved so kindly to her today, and wanted to speak to her alone; for she had trembled when she found he was going home with them lest he should mean 'to tell.' But, now he wanted to talk to her by herself, she should learn what he thought, and what he meant to do. She felt a certain confidence that she could persuade him not to do anything she did not want him to do; she could perhaps even make him believe that she didn't care for Arthur; and as long as Adam thought there was any hope of her having him, he would do just what she liked, she knew. Besides, she must go on seeming to encourage Adam, lest her uncle and aunt should be angry, and suspect her of having some secret lover.

Hetty's little brain was busy with this combination, as she hung on Adam's arm, and said 'yes' or 'no' to some slight observations of his about the many hawthorn-berries there would be for the birds this next winter, and the low-hanging clouds that would hardly hold up till morning. And when they rejoined her aunt and uncle, she could pursue her thoughts without interruption, for Mr Poyser held that though a young man might like to have the woman he was courting on his arm, he would nevertheless be glad of a little reasonable talk about business the while; and, for his own part, he was curious to hear the most recent news about the Chase Farm. So, through the rest of the walk, he claimed Adam's conversation for himself; and Hetty laid her small plots, and imagined her little scenes of cunning blandishment, as she walked along by the hedgerows on honest Adam's arm, quite as well as if she had been an elegantly clad coquette alone in her boudoir. For if a country beauty in clumsy shoes be only shallow-hearted enough, it is astonishing how closely her mental processes may resemble those of a lady in society and crinoline, who applies her refined intellect to the problem of committing indiscretions without compromising herself. Perhaps the resemblance was not much the less because Hetty felt very unhappy all the while. The parting with Arthur was a double pain to her; mingling with the tumult of passion and vanity, there was a dim undefined fear that the future might shape itself in some way quite unlike her dream. She clung to the comforting hopeful words Arthur had uttered in their last meeting – 'I shall come again at Christmas, and then we will see what can be done.' She clung to the belief that he was so fond of her, he would never be happy without her; and she still hugged her secret – that a great gentleman loved her – with gratified pride, as a superiority over all the girls she knew. But the uncertainty of the future, the possibilities to which she could give no shape, began to press upon her like the invisible weight of air; she was alone on her little island of dreams, and all around her was the dark unknown water where Arthur was gone. She could gather no elation of spirits now by looking forward, but only by looking backward to build confidence on past words and caresses. But occasionally, since Thursday evening, her dim anxieties had been almost lost behind the more definite fear that Adam might betray what he knew to her uncle and aunt, and his sudden proposition to talk with her alone had set her thoughts to work in a new way. She was eager not to lose this evening's opportunity; and after tea, when the boys were going into the garden, and Totty begged to go with them, Hetty said, with an alacrity that surprised Mrs Poyser – 'I'll go with her, aunt.'

It did not seem at all surprising that Adam said he would go too; and soon he and Hetty were left alone together on the walk by the filbert trees, while the boys were busy elsewhere gathering the large unripe nuts to play at 'cob-nut' with, and Totty was watching them with a puppylike air of contemplation. It was but a short time – hardly two months – since Adam had had his mind filled with delicious hopes, as he stood by Hetty's side in this garden. The remembrance of that scene had often been with him since Thursday evening: the sunlight through the apple-tree boughs, the red bunches, Hetty's sweet blush. It came importunately now, on this sad evening, with the low-hanging clouds; but he tried to suppress it, lest some emotion should impel him to say more than was needful for Hetty's sake.

'After what I saw on Thursday night, Hetty,' he began, 'you won't think me making too free in what I'm going to say. If you was being courted by any man as 'ud make you his wife, and I'd known you was fond of him, and meant to have him, I should have no right to speak a word to you about it; but when I see you're being made love to by a gentleman as can never marry you, and doesna think o' marrying you, I feel bound t' interfere for you. I can't speak about it to them as are i' the place o' your parents, for that might bring worse trouble than's needful.'

Adam's words relieved one of Hetty's fears, but they also carried a meaning which sickened her with a strengthened foreboding. She was pale and trembling, and yet she would have angrily contradicted Adam, if she had dared to betray her feelings. But she was silent.

'You're so young, you know, Hetty,' he went on, almost tenderly, 'and y' haven't seen much o' what goes on in the world. It's right for me to do what I can to save you from getting into trouble for want o' your knowing where you're being led to. If anybody besides me knew what I know about your meeting a gentleman, and having fine presents from him, they'd speak light on you, and you'd lose your character. And besides that, you'll have to suffer in your feelings, wi' giving your love to a man as can never marry you, so as he might take care of you all your life.'

Adam paused, and looked at Hetty, who was plucking the leaves from the filbert trees, and tearing them up in her hand. Her little plans and preconcerted speeches had all forsaken her, like an ill-learnt lesson, under the terrible agitation produced by Adam's words. There was a cruel force in their calm certainty which threatened to grapple and crush her flimsy hopes and fancies. She wanted to resist them – she wanted to throw them off with angry contradiction; but the determination to conceal what she felt still governed her. It was nothing more than a blind prompting now, for she was unable to calculate the effect of her words.

'You've no right to say as I love him,' she said, faintly, but impetuously, plucking another rough leaf and tearing it up. She was very beautiful in her paleness and agitation, with her dark childish eyes dilated, and her breath shorter than usual. Adam's heart yearned over her as he looked at her. Ah, if he could but comfort her, and soothe her, and save her from this pain; if he had but some sort of strength that would enable him to rescue her poor troubled mind, as he would have rescued her body in the face of all danger!

'I doubt it must be so, Hetty,' he said, tenderly; 'for I canna believe you'd let any man kiss you by yourselves, and give you a gold box with his hair, and go a-walking i' the Grove to meet him, if you didna love him. I'm not blaming you, for I know it 'ud begin by little and little, till at last you'd not be able to throw it off. It's him I blame for stealing your love i' that way, when he knew he could never make you the right amends. He's been trifling with you, and making a plaything of you, and caring nothing about you as a man ought to care.'

'Yes, he does care for me; I know better nor you,' Hetty burst out. Everything was forgotten but the pain and anger she felt at Adam's words.

'Nay, Hetty,' said Adam, 'if he'd cared for you rightly he'd never ha' behaved so. He told me himself he meant nothing by his kissing and presents, and he wanted to make me believe as you thought light of 'em too. But I know better nor that. I can't help thinking as you've been trusting to his loving you well enough to marry you, for all he's a gentleman. And that's why I must speak to you about it, Hetty – for fear you should be deceiving yourself. It's never entered his head the thought o' marrying you.'

'How do you know? How durst you say so?' said Hetty, pausing in her walk and trembling. The terrible decision of Adam's tone shook her with fear. She had no presence of mind left for the reflection that Arthur would have his reasons for not telling the truth to Adam. Her words and look were enough to determine Adam: he must give her the letter.

'Perhaps you can't believe me, Hetty; because you think too well of him – because you think he loves you better than he does. But I've got a letter i' my pocket, as he wrote himself for me to give you. I've not read the letter, but he says he's told you the truth in it. But before I give you the letter, consider, Hetty, and don't let it take too much hold on you. It wouldna ha' been good for you if he'd wanted to do such a mad thing as marry you: it 'ud ha' led to no happiness i'th' end.'

Hetty said nothing: she felt a revival of hope at the mention of a letter which Adam had not read. There would be something quite different in it from what he thought.

Adam took out the letter, but he held it in his hand still, while he said, in a tone of tender entreaty – 'Don't you bear me ill-will, Hetty, because I'm the means o' bringing you this pain. God knows I'd ha' borne a good deal worse for the sake o' sparing it you. And think – there's nobody but me knows about this; and I'll take care of you as if I was your brother. You're the same as ever to me, for I don't believe you've done any wrong knowingly.'

Hetty had laid her hand on the letter, but Adam did not loose it till he had done speaking. She took no notice of what he said – she had not listened; but when he loosed the letter, she put it into her pocket, without opening it, and then began to walk more quickly, as if she wanted to go in.

'You're in the right not to read it just yet,' said Adam. 'Read it when you're by yourself. But stay out a little bit longer, and let us call the children: you look so white and ill; your aunt may take notice of it.'

Hetty heard the warning. It recalled to her the necessity of rallying her native powers of concealment, which had half given way under the shock of Adam's words. And she had the letter in her pocket: she was sure there was comfort in that letter, in spite of Adam. She ran to find Totty, and soon reappeared with recovered colour, leading Totty, who was making a sour face, because she had been obliged to throw away an unripe apple that she had set her small teeth in.

'Hegh, Totty,' said Adam, 'come and ride on my shoulder – ever so high – you'll touch the tops o' the trees.'

What little child ever refused to be comforted by that glorious sense of being seized strongly and swung upward? I don't believe Ganymede cried when the eagle carried him away, and perhaps deposited him on Jove's shoulder at the end. Totty smiled down complacently from her secure height, and pleasant was the sight to the mother's eyes, as she stood at the house door and saw Adam coming with his small burthen.

'Bless your sweet face, my pet,' she said, the mother's strong love filling her keen eyes with mildness, as Totty leaned forward and put out her arms. She had no eyes for Hetty at that moment, and only said, without looking at her, 'You go and draw some ale, Hetty: the gells are both at the cheese.'

After the ale had been drawn and her uncle's pipe lighted, there was Totty to be taken to bed, and brought down again in her nightgown, because she would cry instead of going to sleep. Then there was supper to be got ready, and Hetty must be continually in the way to give help. Adam stayed till he knew Mrs Poyser expected him to go, engaging her and her husband in talk as constantly as he could, for the sake of leaving Hetty more at ease. He lingered, because he wanted to see her safely through that evening, and he was delighted to find how much self-command she showed. He knew she had not had time to read the letter, but he did not know she was buoyed up by a secret hope that the letter would contradict everything he had said. It was hard work for him to leave her – hard to think that he should not know for days how she was bearing her trouble. But he must go at last, and all he could do was to press her hand gently as he said 'Goodbye,' and hope she would take that as a sign that if his love could ever be a refuge for her, it was there the same as ever. How busy his thoughts were, as he walked home, in devising pitying excuses for her folly; in referring all her weakness to the sweet lovingness of her nature; in blaming Arthur, with less and less inclination to admit that his conduct might be extenuated too! His exasperation at Hetty's suffering – and also at the sense that she was possibly thrust for ever out of his own reach – deafened him to any plea for the miscalled friend who had wrought this misery. Adam was a clear-sighted, fair-minded man – a fine fellow, indeed, morally as well as physically. But if Aristides the Just was ever in love and jealous, he was at that moment not perfectly magnanimous. And I cannot pretend that Adam, in these painful days, felt nothing but righteous indignation and loving pity. He was bitterly jealous; and in proportion as his love made him indulgent in his judgement of Hetty, the bitterness found a vent in his feeling towards Arthur.

'Her head was allays likely to be turned,' he thought, 'when a gentleman, with his fine manners, and fine clothes, and his white hands, and that way o' talking gentlefolks have, came about her, making up to her in a bold way, as a man couldn't do that was only her equal; and it's much if she'll ever like a common man now.' He could not help drawing his own hands out of his pocket, and looking at them – at the hard palms and the broken fingernails. 'I'm a roughish fellow, altogether: I don't know, now I come to think on't, what there is much for a woman to like about me; and yet I might ha' got another wife easy enough, if I hadn't set my heart on her. But it's little matter what other women think about me, if she can't love me. She might ha' loved me, perhaps, as likely as any other man – there's nobody hereabouts as I'm afraid of, if he hadn't come between us; but now I shall belike be hateful to her because I'm so different to him. And yet there's no telling – she may turn round the other way, when she finds he's made light of her all the while. She may come to feel the vally of a man as 'ud be thankful to be bound to her all his life. But I must put up with it whichever way it is – I've only to be thankful it's been no worse: I am not th' only man that's got to do without much happiness i' this life. There's many a good bit o' work done with a sad heart. It's God's will, and that's enough for us: we shouldn't know better how things ought to be than He does, I reckon, if we was to spend our lives i' puzzling. But it 'ud ha' gone near to spoil my work for me, if I'd seen her brought to sorrow and shame, and through the man as I've always been proud to think on. Since I've been spared that, I've no right to grumble. When a man's got his limbs whole, he can bear a smart cut or two.'

As Adam was getting over a stile at this point in his reflections, he perceived a man walking along the field before him. He knew it was Seth, returning from an evening preaching, and made haste to overtake him.

'I thought thee'dst be at home before me,' he said, as Seth turned round to wait for him, 'for I'm later than usual tonight.'

'Well, I'm later too, for I got into talk, after meeting, with John Barnes, who has lately professed himself in a state of perfection, and I'd a question to ask him about his experience. It's one o' them subjects that lead you further than y' expect – they don't lie along the straight road.'

They walked along together in silence two or three minutes. Adam was not inclined to enter into the subtleties of religious experience, but he was inclined to interchange a word or two of brotherly affection and confidence with Seth. That was a rare impulse in him, much as the brothers loved each other. They hardly ever spoke of personal matters, or uttered more than an allusion to their family troubles. Adam was by nature reserved in all matters of feeling, and Seth felt a certain timidity towards his more practical brother.

'Seth, lad,' Adam said, putting his arm on his brother's shoulder, 'hast heard anything from Dinah Morris since she went away?'

'Yes,' said Seth. 'She told me I might write her word after a while, how we went on, and how mother bore up under her trouble. So I wrote to her a fortnight ago, and told her about thee having a new employment, and how mother was more contented; and last Wednesday, when I called at the post at Treddles'on I found a letter from her. I think thee'dst perhaps like to read it; but

I didna say anything about it, because thee'st seemed so full of other things. It's quite easy t' read – she writes wonderful for a woman.'

Seth had drawn the letter from his pocket and held it out to Adam, who said, as he took it – 'Ay, lad, I've got a tough load to carry just now – thee mustna take it ill if I'm a bit silenter and crustier nor usual. Trouble doesna make me care the less for thee. I know we shall stick together to the last.'

'I take nought ill o' thee, Adam: I know well enough what it means if thee't a bit short wi' me now and then.'

'There's mother opening the door to look out for us,' said Adam, as they mounted the slope. 'She's been sitting i' the dark as usual. Well, Gyp, well! art glad to see me?'

Lisbeth went in again quickly and lighted a candle, for she had heard the welcome rustling of footsteps on the grass, before Gyp's joyful bark.

'Eh, my lads! th' hours war ne'er so long sin' I war born as they'n been this blessed Sunday night. What can ye both ha' been doin' till this time?'

'Thee shouldstna sit i' the dark, mother,' said Adam; 'that makes the time seem longer.'

'Eh, what am I to do wi' burnin' candle of a Sunday, when there's on'y me, an' it's sin to do a bit o' knittin'? The daylight's long enough for me to stare i' th' booke as I canna read. It 'ud be a fine way o' shortenin' the time, to make it waste the good candle. But which on you's for ha'in' supper? Ye mun ayther be clemmed or full, I should think, seein' what time o' night it is.'

'I'm hungry, mother,' said Seth, seating himself at the little table, which had been spread ever since it was light.

'I've had my supper,' said Adam. 'Here, Gyp,' he added, taking some cold potato from the table, and rubbing the rough grey head that looked up towards him.

'Thee needstna be gi'in' th' dog,' said Lisbeth: 'I'n fed him well a'ready. I'm not like to forget him, I reckon, when he's all o' thee I can get sight on.'

'Come, then, Gyp,' said Adam, 'we'll go to bed. Good-night, mother; I'm very tired.'

'What ails him, dost know?' Lisbeth said to Seth, when Adam was gone upstairs. 'He's like as if he was struck for death this day or two – he's so cast down. I found him i' the shop this forenoon, arter thee wast gone, a-sittin' an' doin' nothin' – not so much as a booke afore him.'

'He's a deal o' work upon him just now, mother,' said Seth, 'and I think he's a bit troubled in his mind. Don't you take notice of it, because it hurts him when you do. Be as kind to him as you can, mother, and don't say anything to vex him.'

'Eh, what dost talk o' my vexin' him? an' what am I like to be but kind? I'll ma' him a kettle-cake for breakfast i' the mornin'.'

Adam, meanwhile, was reading Dinah's letter by the light of his dip candle.

DEAR BROTHER SETH – Your letter lay three days beyond my knowing of it at the Post, for I had not money enough by me to pay the carriage, this being a time of great need and sickness here, with the rains that have fallen, as if the windows of heaven were opened again; and to lay by money, from day to day, in such a time, when there are so many in present need of all things, would be a want of trust like the laying up of the manna. I speak of this, because I would not have you think me slow to answer, or that I had small joy in your rejoicing at the worldly good that has befallen your brother Adam. The honour and love you bear him is nothing but meet, for God has given him great gifts, and he uses them as the patriarch Joseph did, who, when he was exalted to a place of power and trust, yet yearned with tenderness towards his parent and his younger brother.

My heart is knit to your aged mother since it was granted me to be near her in the day of trouble. Speak to her of me, and tell her I often bear her in my thoughts at evening time, when I am sitting in the dim light as I did with her, and we held one another's hands, and I spoke the words of comfort that were given to me. Ah, that is a blessed time, isn't it, Seth, when the outward light is fading, and the body is a little wearied with its work and its labour. Then the inward light shines the brighter, and we have a deeper sense of resting on the Divine strength. I sit on my chair in the dark room and close my eyes, and it is as if I was out of the body and could feel no want for evermore. For then, the very hardship, and the sorrow, and the blindness, and the sin, I have beheld and been ready to weep over – yea, all the anguish of the children of men, which sometimes wraps me round like sudden darkness – I can bear with a willing pain, as if I was sharing the Redeemer's cross. For I feel it, I feel it – infinite love is suffering too – yea, in the fullness of knowledge it suffers, it yearns, it mourns; and that is a blind self-seeking which wants to be freed from the sorrow wherewith the whole creation groaneth and travaileth. Surely it is not true blessedness to be free from sorrow, while there is sorrow and sin in the world: sorrow is then a part of love, and love does not seek to throw it off. It is not the spirit only that tells me this – I see it in the whole work and word of the gospel. Is there not pleading in heaven? Is not the Man of Sorrows there in that crucified body wherewith he ascended? And is He not one with the Infinite Love itself – as our love is one with our sorrow?

These thoughts have been much borne in on me of late, and I have seen with new clearness the meaning of those words, "If any man love me, let him take up my cross". I have heard this enlarged on as if it meant the troubles and persecutions we bring on ourselves by confessing Jesus. But surely that is a narrow thought. The true cross of the Redeemer was the sin and sorrow of this world – that was what lay heavy on his heart – and that is the cross we shall share with him, that is the cup we must drink of with him, if we would have any part in that Divine Love which is one with his sorrow.

In my outward lot, which you ask about, I have all things and abound. I have had constant work in the mill, though some of the other hands have been turned off for a time; and my body is greatly strengthened, so that I feel little weariness after long walking and speaking. What you say about staying in your own country with your mother and brother shows me that you have a true guidance: your lot is appointed there by a clear showing, and to seek a greater blessing elsewhere would be like laying a false offering on the altar and expecting the fire from heaven to kindle it. My work and my joy are here among the hills, and I sometimes think I cling too much to my life among the people here, and should be rebellious if I was called away.

I was thankful for your tidings about the dear friends at the Hall Farm; for though I sent them a letter, by my aunt's desire, after I came back from my sojourn among them, I have had no word from them. My aunt has not the pen of a ready writer, and the work of the house is sufficient for the day, for she is weak in body. My heart cleaves to her and her children as the nearest of all to me in the flesh; yea, and to all in that house. I am carried away to them continually in my sleep, and often in the midst of work, and even of speech, the thought of them is borne in on me as if they were in need and trouble, which yet is dark to me. There may be some leading here; but I wait to be taught. You say they are all well.

We shall see each other again in the body, I trust – though, it may be, not for a long while; for the brethren and sisters at Leeds are desirous to have me for a short space among them, when I have a door opened me again to leave Snowfield.

Farewell, dear brother – and yet not farewell. For those children of God whom it has been granted to see each other face to face and to hold communion together, and to feel the same spirit working in both, can never more be sundered, though the hills may lie between. For their souls are enlarged for evermore by that union, and they bear one another about in their thoughts continually as it were a new strength – Your faithful sister and fellow-worker in Christ,

DINAH MORRIS

I have not skill to write the words so small as you do, and my pen moves slow. And so I am straitened, and say but little of what is in my mind. Greet your mother for me with a kiss. She asked me to kiss her twice when we parted.

Adam had refolded the letter, and was sitting meditatively with his head resting on his arm at the head of the bed, when Seth came upstairs.

'Hast read the letter?' said Seth.

'Yes,' said Adam. 'I don't know what I should ha' thought of her and her letter if I'd never seen her: I dare say I should ha' thought a preaching woman hateful. But she's one as makes everything seem right she says and does, and I seemed to see her and hear her speaking when I read the letter. It's wonderful how I remember her looks and her voice. She'd make thee rare and happy, Seth; she's just the woman for thee.'

'It's no use thinking o' that,' said Seth, despondingly. 'She spoke so firm, and she's not the woman to say one thing and mean another.'

'Nay, but her feelings may grow different. A woman may get to love by degrees – the best fire doesna flare up the soonest. I'd have thee go and see her by and by: I'd make it convenient for thee to be away three or four days, and it 'ud be no walk for thee – only between twenty and thirty mile.'

'I should like to see her again, whether or no, if she wouldna be displeased with me for going,' said Seth.

'She'll be none displeased,' said Adam, emphatically, getting up and throwing off his coat. 'It might be a great happiness to us all, if she'd have thee, for mother took to her so wonderful, and seemed so contented to be with her.'

'Ay,' said Seth, rather timidly, 'and Dinah's fond o' Hetty too; she thinks a deal about her.'

Adam made no reply to that, and no other word but 'good-night' passed between them.

31

Hetty's Bedchamber

It was no longer light enough to go to bed without a candle, even in Mrs Poyser's early household, and Hetty carried one with her as she went up at last to her bedroom soon after Adam was gone and bolted the door behind her.

Now she would read her letter. It must – it must have comfort in it. How was Adam to know the truth? It was always likely he should say what he did say.

She set down the candle, and took out the letter. It had a faint scent of roses, which made her feel as if Arthur were close to her. She put it to her lips, and a rush of remembered sensations for a moment or two swept away all fear. But her heart began to flutter strangely, and her hands to tremble as she broke the seal. She read slowly; it was not easy for her to read a gentleman's handwriting, though Arthur had taken pains to write plainly.

DEAREST HETTY – I have spoken truly when I have said that I loved you, and. I shall never forget our love. I shall be your true friend as long as life lasts, and I hope to prove this to you in many ways. If I say anything to pain you in this letter, do not believe it is for want of love and tenderness towards you, for there is nothing I would not do for you, if I knew it to be really for your happiness. I cannot bear to think of my little Hetty shedding tears when I am not there to kiss them away; and if I followed only my own inclinations, I should be with her at this moment instead of writing. It is very hard for me to part from her – harder still for me to write words which may seem unkind, though they spring from the truest kindness.

Dear, dear Hetty, sweet as our love has been to me, sweet as it would be to me for you to love me always, I feel that it would have been better for us both if we had never had that happiness, and that it is my duty to ask you to love me and care for me as little as you can. The fault has all been mine, for though I have been unable to resist the longing to be near you, I have felt all the while that your affection for me might cause you grief. I ought to have resisted my feelings. I should have done so, if I had been a better fellow than I am; but now, since the past cannot be altered, I am bound to save you from any evil that I have power to prevent. And I feel it would be a great evil for you if your affections continued so fixed on me that you could think of no other man who might be able to make you happier by his love than I ever can, and if you continued to look towards something in the future which cannot possibly happen. For, dear Hetty, if I were to do what you one day spoke of, and make you my wife, I should do what you yourself would come to feel was for your misery instead of your welfare. I know you can never be happy except by marrying a man in your own station; and if I were to marry you now, I should only be adding to any wrong I have done, besides offending against my duty in the other relations of life. You know nothing, dear Hetty, of the world in which I must always live, and you would soon begin to dislike me, because there would be so little in which we should be alike.

And since I cannot marry you, we must part – we must try not to feel like lovers any more. I am miserable while I say this, but nothing else can be. Be angry with me, my sweet one, I deserve it; but do not believe that I shall not always care for you – always be grateful to you – always remember my Hetty; and if any trouble should come that we do not now foresee, trust in me to do everything that lies in my power.

I have told you where you are to direct a letter to, if you want to write, but I put it down below lest you should have forgotten. Do not write unless there is something I can really do for you; for, dear Hetty, we must try to think of each other as little as we can. Forgive me, and try to forget everything about me, except that I shall be, as long as I live, your affectionate friend,

ARTHUR DONNITHORNE

Slowly Hetty had read this letter; and when she looked up from it there was the reflection of a blanched face in the old dim glass – a white marble face with rounded childish forms, but with something sadder than a child's pain in it. Hetty did not see the face – she saw nothing – she only felt that she was cold and sick and trembling. The letter shook and rustled in her hand. She laid it down. It was a horrible sensation – this cold and trembling: it swept away the very ideas that produced it, and Hetty got up to reach a warm cloak from her clothes-press, wrapped it round her, and sat as if she were thinking of nothing but getting warm. Presently she took up the letter with a firmer hand, and began to read it through again. The tears came this time – great rushing tears, that blinded her and blotched the paper. She felt nothing but that Arthur was cruel – cruel to write so, cruel not to marry her. Reasons why he could not marry her had no existence for her mind; how could she believe in any misery that could come to her from the fulfilment of all she had been longing for and dreaming of? She had not the ideas that could make up the notion of that misery.

As she threw down the letter again, she caught sight of her face in the glass; it was reddened now, and wet with tears; it was almost like a companion that she might complain to – that would pity her. She leaned forward on her elbows, and looked into those dark overflooding eyes, and at that quivering mouth, and saw how the tears came thicker and thicker, and how the mouth became convulsed with sobs.

The shattering of all her little dream-world, the crushing blow on her new-born passion, afflicted her pleasure-craving nature with an overpowering pain that annihilated all impulse to resistance, and suspended her anger. She sat sobbing till the candle went out, and then, wearied, aching, stupefied with crying, threw herself on the bed without undressing, and went to sleep.

There was a feeble dawn in the room when Hetty awoke, a little after four o'clock, with a sense of dull misery, the cause of which broke upon her gradually, as she began to discern the objects round her in the dim light. And then came the frightening thought that she had to conceal her misery, as well as to bear it, in this dreary daylight that was coming. She could lie no longer: she got up and went towards the table: there lay the letter; she opened her treasure-drawer: there lay the earrings and the locket – the signs of all her short happiness – the signs of the lifelong dreariness that was to follow it. Looking at the little trinkets which she had once eyed and fingered so fondly as the earnest of her future paradise of finery, she lived back in the moments when they had been given to her with such tender caresses, such strangely pretty words, such glowing looks, which filled her with a bewildering delicious surprise – they were so much sweeter than she had thought anything could be. And the Arthur who had spoken to her and looked at her in this way, who was present with her now – whose arm she felt round her, his cheek against hers, his very breath upon her – was the cruel, cruel Arthur who had written that letter: – that letter which she snatched and crushed and then opened again, that she might read it once more. The half-benumbed mental condition which was the effect of the last night's violent crying, made it necessary to her to look again and see if her wretched thoughts were actually true – if the letter was really so cruel. She had to hold it close to the window, else she could not have read it by the faint light. Yes! it was worse – it was more cruel. She crushed it up again in anger. She hated the writer of that letter – hated him for the very reason that she hung upon him with all her love – all the girlish passion and vanity that made up her love.

She had no tears this morning. She had wept them all away last night, and now she felt that dry-eyed morning misery, which is worse than the first shock, because it has the future in it as well as the present. Every morning to come, as far as her imagination could stretch, she would have to get up and feel that the day would have no joy for her. For there is no despair so absolute as that which comes with the first moments of our first great sorrow, when we have not yet known what it is to have suffered and be healed, to have despaired and to have recovered hope. As Hetty began languidly to take off the clothes she had worn all the night, that she might wash herself and brush her hair, she had a sickening sense that her life would go on in this way: she should always be doing things she had no pleasure in, getting up to the old tasks of work, seeing people she cared nothing about, going to church, and to Treddleston, and to tea with Mrs Best, and carrying no happy thought with her. For her short poisonous delights had spoiled for ever all the little joys that had once made the sweetness of her life – the new frock ready for Treddleston fair, the party at Mr Britton's at Broxton wake, the beaux that she would say 'No' to for a long while, and the prospect of the wedding that was to come at last when she would have a silk gown and a great many clothes all at once. These things were all flat and dreary to her now: everything would be a weariness: and she would carry about for ever a hopeless thirst and longing.

She paused in the midst of her languid undressing, and leaned against the dark old clothes-press. Her neck and arms were bare, her hair hung down in delicate rings; and they were just as beautiful as they were that night two months ago, when she walked up and down this bedchamber glowing with vanity and hope. She was not thinking of her neck and arms now; even her own beauty was indifferent to her. Her eyes wandered sadly over the dull old chamber, and then looked out vacantly towards the growing dawn. Did a remembrance of Dinah come across her mind? – of her foreboding words, which had made her angry? – of Dinah's affectionate entreaty to think of her as a friend in trouble? No, the impression had been too slight to recur. Any affection or comfort Dinah could have given her would have been as indifferent to Hetty this morning as every-thing else was except her bruised passion. She was only thinking she could never stay here and go on with the old life – she could better bear something quite new than sinking back into the old everyday round. She would like to run away that very morning, and never see any of the old faces again. But Hetty's was not a nature to face difficulties – to dare to loose her hold on the familiar, and rush blindly on some unknown condition. Hers was a luxurious and vain nature, not a passionate one; and if she were ever to take any violent measure, she must be urged to it by the desperation of terror. There was not much room for her thoughts to travel in the narrow circle of her imagination, and she soon fixed on the one thing she would do to get away from her old life: she would ask her uncle to let her go to be a lady's-maid. Miss Lydia's maid would help her to get a situation, if she knew Hetty had her uncle's leave.

When she had thought of this, she fastened up her hair and began to wash: it seemed more possible to her to go downstairs and try to behave as usual. She would ask her uncle this very day. On Hetty's blooming health it would take a great deal of such mental suffering as hers to leave any deep impress; and when she was dressed as neatly as usual in her working-dress, with her hair tucked up under her little cap, an indifferent observer would have been more struck with the young roundness of her cheek and neck, and the darkness of her eyes and eyelashes, than with any signs of sadness about her. But when she took up the crushed letter and put it in her drawer, that she might lock it out of sight, hard smarting tears, having no relief in them as the great drops had that fell last night, forced their way into her eyes. She wiped them away quickly: she must not cry in the daytime: nobody should find out how miserable she was, nobody should know she was disappointed about anything; and the thought that the eyes of her aunt and uncle would be upon her, gave her the self-command which often accompanied a great dread. For Hetty looked out from her secret misery towards the possibility of their ever knowing what had happened, as the sick and weary prisoner might think of the possible pillory. They would think her conduct shameful; and shame was torture. That was poor little Hetty's conscience.

So she locked up her drawer and went away to her early work.

In the evening, when Mr Poyser was smoking his pipe, and his good nature was therefore at its superlative moment, Hetty seized the opportunity of her aunt's absence to say – 'Uncle, I wish you'd let me go for a lady's-maid.'

Mr Poyser took the pipe from his mouth, and looked at Hetty in mild surprise for some moments. She was sewing, and went on with her work industriously.

'Why, what's put that into your head, my wench?' he said at last, after he had given one conservative puff.

'I should like it – I should like it better than farmwork.'

'Nay, nay; you fancy so because you donna know it, my wench. It wouldn't be half so good for your health, nor for your luck i' life. I'd like you to stay wi' us till you've got a good husband: you're my own niece, and I wouldn't have you go to service, though it was a gentleman's house, as long as I've got a home for you.'

Mr Poyser paused, and puffed away at his pipe.

'I like the needlework,' said Hetty, 'and I should get good wages.'

'Has your aunt been a bit sharp wi' you?' said Mr Poyser, not noticing Hetty's further argument. 'You mustna mind that, my wench – she does it for your good. She wishes you well; an' there isn't many aunts as are no kin to you 'ud ha' done by you as she has.'

'No, it isn't my aunt,' said Hetty, 'but I should like the work better.'

'It was all very well for you to learn the work a bit – an' I gev my consent to that fast enough, sin' Mrs Pomfret was willing to teach you. For if anything was t' happen, it's well to know how to turn your hand to different sorts o' things. But I niver meant you to go to service, my wench; my family's ate their own bread and cheese as fur back as anybody knows, hanna they, father? You wouldna like your grandchild to take wage?'

'Na–a–y,' said old Martin, with an elongation of the word, meant to make it bitter as well as negative, while he leaned forward and looked down on the floor. 'But the wench takes arter her mother. I'd hard work t' hould *her* in, an' she married i' spite o' me – a feller wi' on'y two head o' stock when there should ha' been ten on's farm – she might well die o' th' inflammation afore she war thirty.'

It was seldom the old man made so long a speech; but his son's question had fallen like a bit of dry fuel on the embers of a long unextinguished resentment, which had always made the grandfather more indifferent to Hetty than to his son's children. Her mother's fortune had been spent by that good-for-nought Sorrel, and Hetty had Sorrel's blood in her veins.

'Poor thing, poor thing!' said Martin the younger, who was sorry to have provoked this retrospective harshness. 'She'd but bad luck. But Hetty's got as good a chanche o' getting a solid, sober husband as any gell i' this country.'

After throwing out this pregnant hint, Mr Poyser recurred to his pipe and his silence, looking at Hetty to see if she did not give some sign of having renounced her ill-advised wish. But instead of that, Hetty, in spite of herself, began to cry, half out of ill-temper at the denial, half out of the day's repressed sadness.

'Hegh, hegh!' said Mr Poyser, meaning to check her playfully, 'don't let's have any crying. Crying's for them as ha' got no home, not for them as want to get rid o' one. What dost think?' he continued to his wife, who now came back into the house-place, knitting with fierce rapidity, as if that movement were a necessary function, like the twittering of a crab's antenne.

'Think? – why, I think we shall have the fowl stole before we are much older, wi' that gell forgetting to lock the pens up o' nights. What's the matter now, Hetty? What are you crying at?'

'Why, she's been wanting to go for a lady's-maid,' said Mr Poyser, 'I tell her we can do better for her nor that.'

'I thought she'd got some maggot in her head, she's gone about wi' her mouth buttoned up so all day. It's all wi' going so among them servants at the Chase, as we war fools for letting her. She thinks it 'ud be a finer life than being wi' them as are akin to her, and ha' brought her up sin' she war no bigger nor Marty. She thinks there's nothing belongs to being a lady's-maid, but wearing finer clothes nor she was born to, I'll be bound. It's what rag she can get to stick on her as she's thinking on from morning till night; as I often ask her if she wouldn't like to be the mawkin i' the field, for then she'd be made o' rags inside and out. I'll never gi' my consent to her going for a lady's-maid, while she's got good friends to take care on her till she's married to somebody better nor one o' them valets, as is neither a common man nor a gentleman, an' must live on the fat o' the land, an's like enough to stick his hand under his coat tails and expect his wife to work for him.'

'Ay, ay,' said Mr Poyser, 'we must have a better husband for her nor that, and there's better at hand. Come, my wench, give over crying, and get to bed. I'll do better for you nor letting you go for a lady's-maid. Let's hear no more on't.'

When Hetty was gone upstairs he said – 'I canna make it out as she should want to go away, for I thought she'd got a mind t' Adam Bede. She's looked like it o' late.'

'Eh, there's no knowing what she's got a liking to, for things take no more hold on her than if she was a dried pea. I believe that gell Molly – as is aggravatin' enough, for the matter o' that – but I believe she'd care more about leaving us and the children, for all she's been here but a year come Michaelmas, nor Hetty would. But she's got this notion o' being a lady's-maid wi' going among them servants – we might ha' known what it 'ud lead to when we let her go to learn the fine work. But I'll put a stop to it pretty quick.'

'Thee'dst be sorry to part wi' her, if it wasn't for her good,' said Mr Poyser. 'She's useful to thee i' the work.'

'Sorry? yes; I'm fonder on her nor she deserves – a little hard-hearted hussy, wanting to leave us i' that way. I can't ha' had her about me these seven year, I reckon, and done for her, and taught her everything, wi'out caring about her. An' here I'm having linen spun, an' thinking all the while it'll make sheeting and table-clothing for her when she's married, an' she'll live i' the parish wi' us, and never go out of our sights – like a fool as I am for thinking aught about her, as is no better nor a cherry wi' a hard stone inside it.'

'Nay, nay, thee mustna make much of a trifle,' said Mr Poyser, soothingly. 'She's fond on us, I'll be bound; but she's young, an' gets things in her head as she can't rightly give account on. Them young fillies 'ull run away often wi'out knowing why.'

Her uncle's answers, however, had had another effect on Hetty besides that of disappointing her and making her cry. She knew quite well whom he had in his mind in his allusions to marriage, and to a sober, solid husband; and when she was in her bedroom again, the possibility of her marrying Adam presented itself to her in a new light. In a mind where no strong sympathies are at work, where there is no supreme sense of right to which the agitated nature can cling and steady itself to quiet endurance, one of the first results of sorrow is a desperate vague clutching after any deed that will change the actual condition. Poor Hetty's vision of consequences, at no time more than a narrow fantastic calculation of her own probable pleasures and pains, was now quite shut out by reckless irritation under present suffering, and she was ready for one of those convulsive, motiveless actions by which wretched men and women leap from a temporary sorrow into a lifelong misery.

Why should she not marry Adam? She did not care what she did, so that it made some change in her life. She felt confident that he would still want to marry her, and any further thought about Adam's happiness in the matter had never yet visited her.

'Strange!' perhaps you will say, 'this rush of impulse towards a course that might have seemed the most repugnant to her present state of mind, and in only the second night of her sadness!'

Yes, the actions of a little trivial soul like Hetty's, struggling amidst the serious, sad destinies of a human being are strange. So are the motions of a little vessel without ballast tossed about on a stormy sea. How pretty it looked with its particoloured sail in the sunlight, moored in the quiet bay!

'Let that man bear the loss who loosed it from its moorings.'

But that will not save the vessel – the pretty thing that might have been a lasting joy.

32

Mrs Poyser 'Has Her Say Out'

The next Saturday evening there was much excited discussion at the Donnithorne Arms concerning an incident which had occurred that very day – no less than a second appearance of the smart man in top boots, said by some to be a mere farmer in treaty for the Chase Farm, by others to be the future steward; but by Mr Casson himself, the personal witness to the stranger's visit, pronounced contemptuously to be nothing better than a bailiff, such as Satchell had been before him. No one had thought of denying Mr Casson's testimony to the fact that he had seen the stranger, nevertheless he proffered various corroborating circumstances.

'I see him myself,' he said; 'I see him coming along by the crab-tree meadow on a bald-faced hoss. I'd just been t' hev a pint – it was half after ten i' the forenoon, when I hev my pint as reg'lar as the clock – and I says to Knowles, as druv up with his waggon, "You'll get a bit o' barley today, Knowles," I says, "if you look about you;" and then I went round by the rick-yard, and towart the Treddles'on road; and just as I come up by the big ash tree, I see the man i' top-boots coming along on a bald-faced hoss – I wish I may never stir if I didn't. And I stood still till he come up, and I says, "Good-morning, sir," I says, for I wanted to hear the turn of his tongue, as I might know whether he was a this-countryman; so I says, "Good-morning, sir: it'll 'old hup for the barley this morning, I think. There'll be a bit got hin, if we've good luck." And he says, 'Eh, ye may be raight, there's no tallin," he says; and I knowed by that' – here Mr Casson gave a wink – 'as he didn't come from a hundred mile off. I dare say he'd think me a hodd talker, as you Loamshire folks allays does hanyone as talks the right language.'

'The right language!' said Bartle Massey, contemptuously. 'You're about as near the right language as a pig's squeaking is like a tune played on a key-bugle.'

'Well, I don't know,' answered Mr Casson, with an angry smile. 'I should think a man as has lived among the gentry from a by, is likely to know what's the right language pretty nigh as well as a schoolmaster.'

'Ay, ay, man,' said Bartle, with a tone of sarcastic consolation, 'you talk the right language for you. When Mike Holdsworth's goat says ba–a–a, it's all right – it 'ud be unnatural for it to make any other noise.'

The rest of the party being Loamshire men, Mr Casson had the laugh strongly against him, and wisely fell back on the previous question, which, far from being exhausted in a single evening, was renewed in the churchyard, before service, the next day, with the fresh interest conferred on all news when there is a fresh person to hear it; and that fresh hearer was Martin Poyser, who, as his wife said, 'never went boozin' with that set at Casson's, a-sittin' soakin'-in drink, and looking as wise as a lot o' codfish wi' red faces.'

It was probably owing to the conversation she had had with her husband on their way from church, concerning this problematic stranger, that Mrs Poyser's thoughts immediately reverted to him when, a day or two afterwards, as she was standing at the house-door with her knitting, in that eager leisure which came to her when the afternoon cleaning was done, she saw the old Squire enter the yard on his black pony, followed by John the groom. She always cited it afterwards as a case of prevision, which really had something more in it than her own remarkable penetration, that the moment she set eyes on the Squire, she said to herself, 'I shouldna wonder if he's come about that man as is a-going to take the Chase Farm, wanting Poyser to do something for him without pay. But Poyser's a fool if he does.'

Something unwonted must clearly be in the wind, for the old Squire's visits to his tenantry were rare; and though Mrs Poyser had during the last twelvemonth recited many imaginary speeches, meaning even more than met the ear, which she was quite determined to make to him the next time he appeared within the gates of the Hall Farm, the speeches had always remained imaginary.

'Good-day, Mrs Poyser,' said the old Squire, peering at her with his short-sighted eyes – a mode of looking at her which, as Mrs Poyser observed, 'allays aggravated her: it was as if you was a insect, and he was going to dab his fingernail on you.'

However, she said, 'Your servant, sir,' and curtsied with an air of perfect deference as she advanced towards him: she was not the woman to misbehave towards her betters, and fly in the face of the catechism, without severe provocation.

'Is your husband at home, Mrs Poyser?'

'Yes, sir; he's only i' the rick-yard. I'll send for him in a minute, if you'll please to get down and step in.'

'Thank you; I will do so. I want to consult him about a little matter; but you are quite as much concerned in it, if not more. I must have your opinion too.'

'Hetty, run and tell your uncle to come in,' said Mrs Poyser, as they entered the house, and the old gentleman bowed low in answer to Hetty's curtsy; while Totty, conscious of a pinafore stained with gooseberry jam, stood hiding her face against the clock, and peeping round furtively.

'What a fine old kitchen this is!' said Mr Donnithorne, looking round admiringly. He always spoke in the same deliberate, well-chiselled, polite way, whether his words were sugary or venomous. 'And you keep it so exquisitely clean, Mrs Poyser. I like these premises, do you know, beyond any on the estate.'

'Well, sir, since you're fond of 'em, I should be glad if you'd let a bit o' repairs be done to 'em, for the boarding's i' that state, as we're like to be eaten up wi' rats and mice; and the cellar, you may stan' up to your knees i' water in't, if you like to go down; but perhaps you'd rather believe my words. Won't you please to sit down, sir?'

'Not yet; I must see your dairy. I have not seen it for years, and I hear on all hands about your fine cheese and butter,' said the Squire, looking politely unconscious that there could be any question on which he and Mrs Poyser might happen to disagree. 'I think I see the door open, there: you must not be surprised if I cast a covetous eye on your cream and butter. I don't expect that Mrs Satchell's cream and butter will bear comparison with yours.'

'I can't say, sir, I'm sure. It's seldom I see other folks's butter, though there's some on it as one's no need to see – the smell's enough.'

'Ah, now this I like,' said Mr Donnithorne, looking round at the damp temple of cleanliness, but keeping near the door. 'I'm sure I should like my breakfast better if I knew the butter and cream came from this dairy. Thank you, that really is a pleasant sight. Unfortunately, my slight tendency to rheumatism makes me afraid of damp: I'll sit down in your comfortable kitchen. Ah, Poyser, how do you do? In the midst of business, I see, as usual. I've been looking at your wife's beautiful dairy – the best manager in the parish, is she not?'

Mr Poyser had just entered in shirt-sleeves and open waistcoat, with a face a shade redder than usual, from the exertion of 'pitching'. As he stood, red, rotund, and radiant, before the small, wiry, cool, old gentleman, he looked like a prize apple by the side of a withered crab.

'Will you please to take this chair, sir?' he said, lifting his father's armchair forward a little: 'you'll find it easy.'

'No, thank you, I never sit in easy-chairs,' said the old gentleman, seating himself on a small chair near the door. 'Do you know, Mrs Poyser – sit down, pray, both of you – I've been far from contented, for some time, with Mrs Satchell's dairy management. I think she has not a good method, as you have.'

'Indeed, sir, I can't speak to that" said Mrs Poyser, in a hard voice, rolling and unrolling her knitting, and looking icily out of the window, as she continued to stand opposite the Squire. Poyser might sit down if he liked, she thought: she wasn't going to sit down, as if she'd give in to any such smooth-tongued palaver. Mr Poyser, who looked and felt the reverse of icy, did sit down in his three-cornered chair.

'And now, Poyser, as Satchell is laid up, I am intending to let the Chase Farm to a respectable tenant. I'm tired of having a farm on my own hands – nothing is made the best of in such cases, as you know. A satisfactory bailiff is hard to find; and I think you and I, Poyser, and your excellent wife here, can enter into a little arrangement in consequence, which will be to our mutual advantage.'

'Oh,' said Mr Poyser, with a good-natured blankness of imagination as to the nature of the arrangement.

'If I'm called upon to speak, sir,' said Mrs Poyser, after glancing at her husband with pity at his softness, 'you know better than me; but I don't see what the Chase Farm is t' us – we've cumber enough wi' our own farm. Not but what I'm glad to hear o' anybody respectable coming into the parish: there's some as ha' been brought in as hasn't been looked on i' that character.'

'You're likely to find Mr Thurle an excellent neighbour, I assure you: such a one as you will feel glad to have accommodated by the little plan I'm going to mention; especially as I hope you will find it as much to your own advantage as his.'

'Indeed, sir, if it's anything to our advantage, it'll be the first offer o' the sort I've heared on. It's them as take advantage that get advantage i' this world, I think: folks have to wait long enough afore it's brought to 'em.'

'The fact is, Poyser,' said the Squire, ignoring Mrs Poyser's theory of worldly prosperity, 'there is too much dairy land, and too little plough land, on the Chase Farm, to suit Thurle's purpose – indeed, he will only take the farm on condition of some change in it: his wife, it appears, is not a clever dairy-woman, like yours. Now, the plan I'm thinking of is to effect a little exchange. If you were to have the Hollow Pastures, you might increase your dairy, which must be so profitable under your wife's management; and I should request you, Mrs Poyser, to supply my house with milk, cream, and butter at the market prices. On the other hand, Poyser, you might let Thurle have the Lower and Upper Ridges, which really, with our wet seasons, would be a good riddance for you. There is much less risk in dairy land than corn land.'

Mr Poyser was leaning forward, with his elbows on his knees, his head on one side, and his mouth screwed up – apparently absorbed in making the tips of his fingers meet so as to represent with perfect accuracy the ribs of a ship. He was much too acute a man not to see through the whole business, and to foresee perfectly what would be his wife's view of the subject; but he disliked giving unpleasant answers: unless it was on a point of farming practice, he would rather give up than have a quarrel, any day; and, after all, it mattered more to his wife than to him. So, after a few moments, silence, he looked up at her and said mildly. 'What dost say?'

Mrs Poyser had had her eyes fixed on her husband with cold severity during his silence, but now she turned away her head with a toss, looked icily at the opposite roof of the cowshed, and spearing her knitting together with the loose pin, held it firmly between her clasped hands.

'Say? Why, I say you may do as you like about giving up any o' your corn land afore your lease is up, which it won't be for a year come next Michaelmas, but I'll not consent to take more dairy work into my hands, either for love or money; and there's nayther love nor money here, as I can see, on'y other folks's love o' theirselves, and the money as is to go into other folks's pockets. I know there's them as is born t' own the land, and them as is born to sweat on't' – here Mrs Poyser paused to gasp a little – 'and I know it's christened folks's duty to submit to their betters as fur as flesh and blood 'ull bear it; but I'll not make a martyr o' myself, and wear myself to skin and bone, and worret myself as if I was a churn wi' butter a coming in't, for no landlord in England, not if he was King George himself.

'No, no, my dear Mrs Poyser, certainly not,' said the Squire, still confident in his own powers of persuasion, 'you must not overwork yourself; but don't you think your work will rather be lessened than increased in this way? There is so much milk required at the Abbey, that you will have little increase of cheese and butter making from the addition to your dairy; and I believe selling the milk is the most profitable way of disposing of dairy produce, is it not?'

'Ay, that's true,' said Mr Poyser, unable to repress an opinion on a question of farming profits, and forgetting that it was not in this case a purely abstract question.

'I dare say,' said Mrs Poyser bitterly, turning her head halfway towards her husband, and looking at the vacant armchair – ' I dare say it's true for men as sit i' th' chimney-corner and make believe as everything's cut wi' ins an' outs to fit int' everything else. If you could make a pudding wi' thinking o' the batter, it 'ud be easy getting dinner. How do I know whether the milk 'ull be wanted constant? What's to make me sure as the house won't be put o' board-wage afore we're many months older, and then I may have to lie awake o' nights wi' twenty gallons o' milk on my mind – and Dingall 'ull take no more butter, let alone paying for it; and we must fat pigs till we're obliged to beg the butcher on our knees to buy 'em, and lose half of 'em wi' the measles. And there's the fetching and carrying, as 'ud be welly half a day's work for a man an' hoss – that's to be took out o' the profits, I reckon? But there's folks 'ud hold a sieve under the pump and expect to carry away the water.'

'That difficulty – about the fetching and carrying – you will not have, Mrs Poyser,' said the Squire, who thought that this entrance into particulars indicated a distant inclination to compromise on Mrs Poyser's part – 'Bethell will do that regularly with the cart and pony.'

'Oh, sir, begging your pardon, I've never been used t' having gentlefolks's servants coming about my back places, a-making love to both the gells at once, and keeping 'em with their hands on their hips listening to all manner o' gossip when they should be down on their knees a-scouring. If we're to go to ruin it shanna be wi' having our back kitchen turned into a public.'

'Well, Poyser,' said the Squire, shifting his tactics, and looking as if he thought Mrs Poyser had suddenly withdrawn from the proceedings and left the room, 'you can turn the Hollows into feeding-land. I can easily make another arrangement about supplying my house. And I shall not forget your readiness to accommodate your landlord as well as a neighbour. I know you will be glad to have your lease renewed for three years when the present one expires; otherwise, I dare say Thurle, who is a man of some capital, would be glad to take both the farms, as they could be worked so well together. But I don't want to part with an old tenant like you.'

To be thrust out of the discussion in this way would have been enough to complete Mrs Poyser's exasperation, even without the final threat. Her husband, really alarmed at the possibility of their leaving the old place where he had been bred and born – for he believed the old Squire had small spite enough for anything – was beginning a mild remonstrance explanatory of the inconvenience he should find in having to buy and sell more stock, with – 'Well, sir, I think as it's rether hard' . . . when Mrs Poyser burst in with the desperate determination to have her say out this once, though it were to rain notices to quit, and the only shelter were the workhouse.

'Then, sir, if I may speak – as, for all I'm a woman, and there's folks as thinks a woman's fool enough to stan' by an' look on while the men sign her soul away, I've a right to speak, for I make one quarter o' the rent, and save th' other quarter – I say, if Mr Thurle's so ready to take farms under you, it's a pity but what he should take this, and see if he likes to live in a house wi' all the plagues o' Egypt in't – wi' the cellar full o' water, and frogs and toads hoppin' up the steps by dozens – and the floors rotten, and the rats and mice gnawing every bit o' cheese, and runnin' over our heads as we lie i' bed till we expect 'em to eat us up alive – as it's a mercy they hanna eat the children long ago. I should like to see if there's another tenant besides Poyser as 'ud put up wi' never having a bit o' repairs done till a place tumbles down – and not then, on'y wi' begging and praying, and having to pay half – and being strung up wi' the rent as it's much if he gets enough out o' the land to pay, for all he's put his own money into the ground beforehand. See if you'll get a stranger to lead such a life here as that: a maggot must be born i' the rotten cheese to like it, I reckon. You may run away from my words, sir,' continued Mrs Poyser, following the old Squire beyond the door – for after the first moments of stunned surprise he had got up, and, waving his hand towards her with a smile, had walked out towards his pony. But it was impossible for him to get away immediately, for John was walking the pony up and down the yard, and was some distance from the causeway when his master beckoned.

'You may run away from my words, sir, and you may go spinnin' underhand ways o' doing us a mischief, for you've got Old Harry to your friend, though nobody else is, but I tell you for once as we're not dumb creatures to be abused and made money on by them as ha' got the lash i' their hands, for want o' knowing how t' undo the tackle. An' if I'm the only one as speaks my mind, there's plenty o' the same way o' thinking i' this parish and the next to 't, for your name's no better than a brimstone match in everybody's nose – if it isna two-three old folks as you think o' saving your soul by giving 'em a bit o' flannel and a drop o' porridge. An' you may be right i' thinking it'll take but little to save your soul, for it'll be the smallest savin' y' iver made, wi' all your scrapin'.'

There are occasions on which two servant-girls and a waggoner may be a formidable audience, and as the Squire rode away on his black pony, even the gift of short-sightedness did not prevent him from being aware that Molly and

Nancy and Tim were grinning not far from him. Perhaps he suspected that sour old John was grinning behind him – which was also the fact. Meanwhile the bulldog, the black-and-tan terrier, Alick's sheepdog, and the gander hissing at a safe distance from the pony's heels, carried out the idea of Mrs Poyser's solo in an impressive quartet.

Mrs Poyser, however, had no sooner seen the pony move off than she turned round, gave the two hilarious damsels a look which drove them into the back kitchen, and, unspearing her knitting, began to knit again with her usual rapidity, as she re-entered the house.

'Thee'st done it now,' said Mr Poyser, a little alarmed and uneasy, but not without some triumphant amusement at his wife's outbreak.

'Yes, I know I've done it,' said Mrs Poyser; 'but I've had my say out, and I shall be th' easier for't all my life. There's no pleasure i' living, if you're to be corked up for ever, and only dribble your mind out by the sly, like a leaky barrel. I shan't repent saying what I think, if I like to be as old as th' old Squire; and there's little likelihoods – for it seems as if them as aren't wanted here are th' only folks as aren't wanted i' th' other world.'

'But thee wutna like moving from th' old place this Michaelmas twelve-month,' said Mr Poyser, 'and going into a strange parish, where thee know'st nobody. It'll be hard upon us both, and upo' father too.'

'Eh, it's no use worreting; there's plenty o' things may happen between this and Michaelmas twelvemonth. The Captain may be master afore then, for what we know,' said Mrs Poyser, inclined to take an unusually hopeful view of an embarrassment which had been brought about by her own merit, and not by other people's fault.

'I'm none for worreting,' said Mr Poyser, rising from his three-cornered chair, and walking slowly towards the door; 'but I should be loath to leave the old place, and the parish where I was bred and born, and father afore me. We should leave our roots behind us, I doubt, and niver thrive again.'

33

More Links

The barley was all carried at last, and the harvest suppers went by without waiting for the dismal black crop of beans. The apples and nuts were gathered and stored; the scent of whey departed from the farmhouses, and the scent of brewing came in its stead. The woods behind the Chase, and all the hedgerow trees, took on a solemn splendour under the dark low-hanging skies. Michaelmas was come, with its fragrant basketfuls of purple damsons, and its paler purple daisies, and its lads and lasses leaving or seeking service, and winding along between the yellow hedges, with their bundles under their arms. But though Michaelmas was come, Mr Thurle, that desirable tenant, did not come to the Chase Farm, and the old Squire, after all, had been obliged to put in a new bailiff. It was known throughout the two parishes that the Squire's plan had been frustrated because the Poysers had refused to be 'put upon', and Mrs Poyser's outbreak was discussed in all the farmhouses with a zest which was only heightened by frequent repetition. The news that 'Bony' was come back from Egypt was comparatively insipid, and the repulse of the French in Italy was nothing to Mrs Poyser's repulse of the old Squire. Mr Irwine had heard a version of it in every parishioner's house, with the one exception of the Chase. But since he had always, with marvellous skill, avoided any quarrel with Mr Donnithorne, he could not allow himself the pleasure of laughing at the old gentleman's discomfiture with anyone besides his mother, who declared that if she were rich she should like to allow Mrs Poyser a pension for life, and wanted to invite her to the parsonage, that she might hear an account of the scene from Mrs Poyser's own lips.

'No, no, mother,' said Mr Irwine; 'it was a little bit of irregular justice on Mrs Poyser's part, but a magistrate like me must not countenance irregular justice. There must be no report spread that I have taken notice of the quarrel, else I shall lose the little good influence I have over the old man.'

'Well, I like that woman even better than her cream-cheeses,' said Mrs Irwine. 'She has the spirit of three men, with that pale face of hers; and she says such sharp things too.'

'Sharp! yes, her tongue is like a new-set razor. She's quite original in her talk, too; one of those untaught wits that help to stock a country with proverbs. I told you that capital thing I heard her say about Craig – that he was like a cock who thought the sun had risen to hear him crow. Now that's an Aesop's fable in a sentence.'

'But it will be a bad business if the old gentleman turns them out of the farm next Michaelmas, eh?' said Mrs Irwine.

'Oh, that must not be; and Poyser is such a good tenant, that Donnithorne is likely to think twice, and digest his spleen rather than turn them out. But if he should give them notice at Lady-day, Arthur and I must move heaven and earth to mollify him. Such old parishioners as they are must not go.'

'Ah, there's no knowing what may happen before Lady Day,' said Mrs Irwine. 'It struck me on Arthur's birthday that the old man was a little shaken: he's eighty-three, you know. It's really an unconscionable age. It's only women who have a right to live as long as that.'

'When they've got old-bachelor sons who would be forlorn without them,' said Mr Irwine, laughing, and kissing his mother's hand.

Mrs Poyser, too, met her husband's occasional forebodings of a notice to quit with, 'There's no knowing what may happen before Lady-day:' – one of those undeniable general propositions which are usually intended to convey a particular meaning very far from undeniable. But it is really too hard upon human nature that it should be held a criminal offence to imagine the death even of the king when he is turned eighty-three. It is not to be believed that any but the dullest Britons can be good subjects under that hard condition.

Apart from this foreboding, things went on much as usual in the Poyser household. Mrs Poyser thought she noticed a surprising improvement in Hetty. To be sure, the girl got 'closer tempered, and sometimes she seemed as if there'd be no drawing a word from her with cart-ropes;' but she thought much less about her dress, and went after the work quite eagerly, without any telling. And it was wonderful how she never wanted to go out now – indeed, could hardly be persuaded to go; and she bore her aunt's putting a stop to her weekly lesson in fine-work at the Chase, without the least grumbling or pouting. It must be, after all, that she had set her heart on Adam at last, and her sudden freak of wanting to be a lady's-maid must have been caused by some little pique or misunderstanding between them, which had passed by. For whenever Adam came to the Hall Farm, Hetty seemed to be in better spirits, and to talk more than at other times, though she was almost sullen when Mr Craig or any other admirer happened to pay a visit there.

Adam himself watched her at first with trembling anxiety, which gave way to surprise and delicious hope. Five days after delivering Arthur's letter, he had ventured to go to the Hall Farm again – not without dread lest the sight of him might be painful to her. She was not in the house-place when he entered, and he sat talking to Mr and Mrs Poyser for a few minutes with a heavy fear on his heart that they might presently tell him Hetty was ill. But by and by there came a light step that he knew, and when Mrs Poyser said, 'Come, Hetty, where have you been?' Adam was obliged to turn round, though he was afraid to see the changed look there must be in her face. He almost started when he saw her smiling as if she were pleased to see him – looking the same as ever at a first glance, only that she had her cap on, which he had never seen her in before when he came of an evening. Still, when he looked at her again and again as she moved about or sat at her work, there was a change: the cheeks were as pink as ever, and she smiled as much as she had ever done of late, but there was something different in her eyes, in the expression of her face, in all her movements, Adam thought – something harder, older, less childlike. 'Poor thing!' he said to himself, 'that's allays likely. It's because she's had her first heartache. But she's got a spirit to bear up under it. Thank God for that.'

As the weeks went by, and he saw her always looking pleased to see him – turning up her lovely face towards him as if she meant him to understand that she was glad for him to come – and going about her work in the same equable way, making no sign of sorrow, he began to believe that her feeling towards Arthur must have been much slighter than he had imagined in his first indignation and alarm, and that she had been able to think of her girlish fancy that Arthur was in love with her and would marry her, as a folly of which she was timely cured. And it perhaps was, as he had sometimes in his more cheerful moments hoped it would be – her heart was really turning with all the more warmth towards the man she knew to have a serious love for her.

Possibly you think that Adam was not at all sagacious in his interpretations, and that it was altogether extremely unbecoming in a sensible man to behave as he did – falling in love with a girl who really had nothing more than her beauty to recommend her, attributing imaginary virtues to her, and even condescending to cleave to her after she had fallen in love with another man, waiting for her kind looks as a patient trembling dog waits for his master's eye to be turned upon him. But in so complex a thing as human nature, we must consider, it is hard to find rules without exceptions. Of course, I know that, as a rule, sensible men fall in love with the most sensible women of their acquaintance, see through all the pretty deceits of coquettish beauty, never imagine themselves loved when they are not loved, cease loving on all proper occasions, and marry the woman most fitted for them in every respect – indeed, so as to compel the approbation of all the maiden ladies in their neighbourhood. But even to this rule an exception will occur now and then in the lapse of centuries, and my friend Adam was one. For my own part, however, I respect him none the less: nay, I think the deep love he had for that sweet, rounded, blossom-like, dark-eyed Hetty, of whose inward self he was really very ignorant, came out of the very strength of his nature, and not out of any inconsistent weakness. Is it any weakness, pray, to be wrought on by exquisite music? – to feel its wondrous harmonies searching the subtlest windings of your soul, the delicate fibres of life where no memory can penetrate, and binding together your whole being past and present in one unspeakable vibration: melting you in one moment with all the tenderness, all the love that has been scattered through the toilsome years, concentrating in one emotion of heroic courage or resignation all the hard-learnt lessons of self-renouncing sympathy, blending your present joy with past sorrow, and your present sorrow with all your past joy? If not, then neither is it a weakness to be so wrought upon by the exquisite curves of a woman's cheek and neck and arms, by the liquid depths of her beseeching eyes, or the sweet childish pout of her lips. For the beauty of a lovely woman is like music: what can one say more? Beauty has an expression beyond and far above the one woman's soul that it clothes, as the words of genius have a wider meaning than the thought that prompted them: it is more than a woman's love that moves us in a woman's eyes – it seems to be a far-off mighty love that has come near to us, and made speech for itself there; the rounded neck, the dimpled arm, move us by something more than their prettiness – by their close kinship with all we have known of tenderness and peace. The noblest nature sees the most of this *impersonal* expression in beauty (it is needless to say that there are gentlemen with whiskers dyed and undyed who see none of it whatever), and for this reason, the noblest nature is often the most blinded to the character of the one woman's soul that the beauty clothes. Whence, I fear, the tragedy of human life is likely to continue for a long time to come, in spite of mental philosophers who are ready with the best receipts for avoiding all mistakes of the kind.

Our good Adam had no fine words into which he could put his feeling for Hetty: he could not disguise mystery in this way with the appearance of know-ledge; he called his love frankly a mystery, as you have heard him. He only knew that the sight and memory of her moved him deeply, touching the spring of all love and tenderness, all faith and courage within him. How could he imagine narrowness, selfishness, hardness in her? He created the mind he believed in out of his own, which was large, unselfish, tender.

The hopes he felt about Hetty softened a little his feeling towards Arthur. Surely his attentions to Hetty must have been of a slight kind; they were altogether wrong, and such as no man in Arthur's position ought to have allowed himself, but they must have had an air of playfulness about them, which had probably blinded him to their danger, and had prevented them from laying any strong hold on Hetty's heart. As the new promise of happiness rose for Adam, his indignation and jealousy began to die out: Hetty was not made unhappy; he almost believed that she liked him best; and the thought sometimes crossed his mind that the friendship which had once seemed dead for ever might revive in the days to come, and he would not have to say 'goodbye' to the grand old woods, but would like them better because they were Arthur's. For this new promise of happiness, following so quickly on the shock of pain, had an intoxicating effect on the sober Adam, who had all his life been used to much hardship and moderate hope. Was he really going to have an easy lot after all? It seemed so; for at the beginning of November, Jonathan Burge, finding it impossible to replace Adam, had at last made up his mind to offer him a share in the business, without further condition than that he should continue to give his energies to it, and renounce all thought of having a separate business of his own. Son-in-law or no son-in-law, Adam had made himself too necessary to be parted with, and his headwork was so much more important to Burge than his skill in handicraft, that his having the management of the woods made little difference in the value of his services; and as to the bargains about the Squire's timber, it would be easy to call in a third person. Adam saw here an opening into a broadening path of prosperous work, such as he had thought of with ambitious longing ever since he was a lad: he might come to build a bridge, or a town-hall, or a factory, for he had always said to himself that Jonathan Burge's building business was like an acorn, which might be the mother of a great tree. So he gave his hand to Burge on that bargain, and went home with his mind full of happy visions, in which (my refined reader will perhaps be shocked when I say it) the image of Hetty hovered, and smiled over plans for seasoning timber at a trifling expense, calculations as to the cheapening of bricks per thousand by water-carriage, and a favourite scheme for the strengthening of roofs and walls with a peculiar form of iron girder. What then? Adam's enthusiasm lay in these things; and our love is inwrought in our enthusiasm as electricity is inwrought in the air, exalting its power by a subtle presence.

Adam would be able to take a separate house now, and provide for his mother in the old one; his prospects would justify his marrying very soon, and if Dinah consented to have Seth, their mother would perhaps be more contented to live apart from Adam. But he told himself that he would not be hasty – he would not try Hetty's feeling for him until it had had time to grow strong and firm. However, tomorrow, after church, he would go to the Hall Farm, and tell them the news. Mr Poyser, he knew, would like it better than a five pound note, and he should see if Hetty's eyes brightened at it. The months would be short with all he had to fill his mind, and this foolish eagerness which had come over him of late must not hurry him into any premature words. Yet when he got home and told his mother the good news, and ate his supper, while she sat by almost crying for joy, and wanting him to eat twice as much as usual because of his good luck, he could not help preparing her gently for the coming change, by talking of the old house being too small for them all to go on living in it always.

The Betrothal

It was a dry Sunday, and really a pleasant day for the second of November. There was no sunshine, but the clouds were high, and the wind was so still that the yellow leaves which fluttered down from the hedgerow elms must have fallen from pure decay. Nevertheless, Mrs Poyser did not go to church, for she had taken a cold too serious to be neglected; only two winters ago she had been laid up for weeks with a cold; and since his wife did not go to church, Mr Poyser considered that on the whole it would be as well for him to stay away too and 'keep her company.' He could perhaps have given no precise form to the reasons that determined this conclusion; but it is well known to all experienced minds that our firmest convictions are often dependent on subtle impressions for which words are quite too coarse a medium. However it was, no one from the Poyser family went to church that afternoon except Hetty and the boys – yet Adam was bold enough to join them after church, and say that he would walk home with them, though all the way through the village he appeared to be chiefly occupied with Marty and Tommy, telling them about the squirrels in Binton Coppice, and promising to take them there someday. But when they came to the fields he said to the boys, 'Now, then, which is the stoutest walker? Him as gets to th' home-gate first shall be the first to go with me to Binton Coppice on the donkey. But Tommy must have the start up to the next stile, because he's the smallest.'

Adam had never behaved so much like a determined lover before. As soon as the boys had both set off, he looked down at Hetty, and said, 'Won't you hang on my arm, Hetty?' in a pleading tone, as if he had already asked her and she had refused. Hetty looked up at him smilingly and put her round arm through his in a moment. It was nothing to her – putting her arm through Adam's; but she knew he cared a great deal about having her arm through his, and she wished him to care. Her heart beat no faster, and she looked at the half-bare hedgerows and the ploughed field with the same sense of oppressive dulness as before. But Adam scarcely felt that he was walking; he thought Hetty must know that he was pressing her arm a little – a very little; words rushed to his lips that he dared not utter – that he had made up his mind not to utter yet; and so he was silent for the length of that field. The calm patience with which he had once waited for Hetty's love, content only with her presence and the thought of the future, had forsaken him since that terrible shock nearly three months ago. The agitations of jealousy had given a new restlessness to his passion – had made fear and uncertainty too hard almost to bear. But though he might not speak to Hetty of his love, he would tell her about his new prospects, and see if she would be pleased. So when he was enough master of himself to talk, he said – 'I'm going to tell your uncle some news that'll surprise him, Hetty; and I think he'll be glad to hear it too.'

'What's that?' Hetty said, indifferently.

'Why, Mr Burge has offered me a share in his business, and I'm going to take it.'

There was a change in Hetty's face, certainly not produced by any agreeable impression from this news. In fact she felt a momentary annoyance and alarm; for she had so often heard it hinted by her uncle that Adam might have Mary Burge and a share in the business any day if he liked, that she associated the two objects now, and the thought immediately occurred that perhaps Adam had given her up because of what had happened lately, and had turned towards Mary Burge. With that thought, and before she had time to remember any reasons why it could not be true, came a new sense of forsakenness and disappointment: the one thing – the one person – her mind had rested on in its dull weariness, had slipped away from her, and peevish misery filled her eyes with tears. She was looking on the ground, but Adam saw her face, saw the tears, and before he had finished saying, 'Hetty, dear Hetty, what are you crying for?' his eager rapid thought had flown through all the causes conceivable to him, and had at last alighted on half the true one. Hetty thought he was going to marry Mary Burge – she didn't like him to marry – perhaps she didn't like him to marry anyone but herself? All caution was swept away – all reason for it was gone, and Adam could feel nothing but trembling joy. He leaned towards her and took her hand, as he said – 'I could afford to be married now, Hetty – I could make a wife comfortable; but I shall never want to be married if you won't have me.'

Hetty looked up at him, and smiled through her tears as she had done to Arthur that first evening in the wood when she had thought he was not coming, and yet he came. It was a feebler relief, a feebler triumph she felt now, but the great dark eyes and the sweet lips were as beautiful as ever, perhaps more beautiful, for there was a more luxuriant womanliness about Hetty of late. Adam could hardly believe in the happiness of that moment. His right hand held her left, and he pressed her arm close against his heart as he leaned down towards her.

'Do you really love me, Hetty? Will you be my own wife, to love and take care of as long as I live?'

Hetty did not speak, but Adam's face was very close to hers, and she put up her round cheek against his, like a kitten. She wanted to be caressed – she wanted to feel as if Arthur were with her again.

Adam cared for no words after that, and they hardly spoke through the rest of the walk. He only said, 'I may tell your uncle and aunt, mayn't I, Hetty?' and she said, 'Yes.'

The red firelight on the hearth at the Hall Farm shone on joyful faces that evening, when Hetty was gone upstairs and Adam took the opportunity of telling Mr and Mrs Poyser and the grandfather that he saw his way to maintaining a wife now, and that Hetty had consented to have him.

'I hope you have no objections against me for her husband,' said Adam; 'I'm a poor man as yet, but she shall want nothing as I can work for.'

'Objections?' said Mr Poyser, while the grandfather leaned forward and brought out his long 'Nay, nay.' 'What objections can we ha' to you, lad? Never mind your being poorish as yet; there's money in your head-piece as there's money i' the sown field, but it must ha' time. You'n got enough to begin on, and we can do a deal tow'rt the bit o' furniture you'll want. Thee'st got feathers and linen to spare – plenty, eh?'

This question was of course addressed to Mrs Poyser, who was wrapped up in a warm shawl, and was too hoarse to speak with her usual facility. At first she only nodded emphatically, but she was presently unable to resist the temptation to be more explicit.

'It 'ud be a poor tale if I hadna feathers and linen,' she said, hoarsely, 'when I never sell a fowl but what's plucked, and the wheel's a-going every day o' the week.'

'Come, my wench,' said Mr Poyser, when Hetty came down, 'come and kiss us, and let us wish you luck.'

Hetty went very quietly and kissed the big good-natured man.

'There!' he said, patting her on the back, 'go and kiss your aunt and your grandfather. I'm as wishful t' have you settled well as if you was my own daughter; and so's your aunt, I'll be bound, for she's done by you this seven 'ear, Hetty, as if you'd been her own. Come, come, now,' he went on, becoming jocose, as soon as Hetty had kissed her aunt and the old man, 'Adam wants a kiss too, I'll warrant, and he's a right to one now.'

Hetty turned away, smiling, towards her empty chair.

'Come, Adam, then, take one,' persisted Mr Poyser, 'else y' arena half a man.'

Adam got up, blushing like a small maiden – great strong fellow as he was – and, putting his arm round Hetty, stooped down and gently kissed her lips.

It was a pretty scene in the red firelight: for there were no candles; why should there be, when the fire was so bright, and was reflected from all the pewter and the polished oak? No one wanted to work on a Sunday evening. Even Hetty felt something like contentment in the midst of all this love. Adam's attachment to her, Adam's caress, stirred no passion in her, were no longer enough to satisfy her vanity; but they were the best her life offered her now – they promised her some change.

There was a great deal of discussion before Adam went away, about the possibility of his finding a house that would do for him to settle in. No house was empty except the one next to Will Maskery's in the village, and that was too small for Adam now. Mr Poyser insisted that the best plan would be for Seth and his mother to move, and leave Adam in the old home, which might be enlarged after a while, for there was plenty of space in the woodyard and garden; but Adam objected to turning his mother out.

'Well, well,' said Mr Poyser at last, 'we needna fix everything tonight. We must take time to consider. You canna think o' getting married afore Easter. I'm not for long courtships, but there must be a bit o' time to make things comfortable.'

'Ay, to be sure,' said Mrs Poyser, in a hoarse whisper; 'Christian folks can't be married like cuckoos, I reckon.'

'I'm a bit daunted, though,' said Mr Poyser, 'when I think as we may have notice to quit, and belike be forced to take a farm twenty mile off.'

'Eh,' said the old man, staring at the floor, and lifting his hands up and down, while his arms rested on the elbows of his chair, 'it's a poor tale if I mun leave th' ould spot, an' be buried in a strange parish. An' you'll happen ha' double rates to pay,' he added, looking up at his son.

'Well, thee mustna fret beforehand, father,' said Martin the younger. 'Happen the Captain 'ull come home and make our peace wi' th' old Squire. I build upo' that, for I know the Captain 'll see folk righted if he can.'

35

The Hidden Dread

It was a busy time for Adam – the time between the beginning of November and the beginning of February, and he could see little of Hetty, except on Sundays. But a happy time, nevertheless; for it was taking him nearer and nearer to March, when they were to be married; and all the little preparations for their new housekeeping marked the progress towards the longed-for day. Two new rooms had been 'run up' to the old house, for his mother and Seth were to live with them after all. Lisbeth had cried so piteously at the thought of leaving Adam, that he had gone to Hetty and asked her if, for the love of him, she would put up with his mother's ways, and consent to live with her. To his great delight, Hetty said, 'Yes; I'd as soon she lived with us as not.' Hetty's mind was oppressed at that moment with a worse difficulty than poor Lisbeth's ways, she could not care about them. So Adam was consoled for the disappointment he had felt when Seth had come back from his visit to Snowfield and said 'it was no use – Dinah's heart wasna turned towards marrying.' For when he told his mother that Hetty was willing they should all live together, and there was no more need of them to think of parting, she said, in a more contented tone than he had heard her speak in since it had been settled that he was to be married, 'Eh, my lad, I'll be as still as th' ould tabby, an' ne'er want to do aught but the offal work, as she wonna like t' do. An' then, we needna part the platters an' things, as ha' stood on the shelf together sin' afore thee wast born.'

There was only one cloud that now and then came across Adam's sunshine: Hetty seemed unhappy sometimes. But to all his anxious, tender questions, she replied with an assurance that she was quite contented and wished nothing different; and the next time he saw her she was more lively than usual. It might be that she was a little overdone with work and anxiety now, for soon after Christmas Mrs Poyser had taken another cold, which had brought on inflammation, and this illness had confined her to her room all through January. Hetty had to manage everything downstairs, and half supply Molly's place too, while that good damsel waited on her mistress; and she seemed to throw herself so entirely into her new functions, working with a grave steadiness which was new in her, that Mr Poyser often told Adam she was wanting to show him what a good housekeeper he would have; but he 'doubted the lass was o'er-doing it – she must have a bit o' rest when her aunt could come downstairs.'

This desirable event of Mrs Poyser's coming downstairs happened in the early part of February, when some mild weather thawed the last patch of snow on the

Binton Hills. On one of these days, soon after her aunt came down, Hetty went to Treddleston to buy some of the wedding things which were wanting, and which Mrs Poyser had scolded her for neglecting, observing that she supposed 'it was because they were not for th' outside, else she'd ha' bought 'em fast enough.'

It was about ten o'clock when Hetty set off, and the slight hoar-frost that had whitened the hedges in the early morning had disappeared as the sun mounted the cloudless sky. Bright February days have a stronger charm of hope about them than any other days in the year. One likes to pause in the mild rays of the sun, and look over the gates at the patient plough-horses turning at the end of the furrow, and think that the beautiful year is all before one. The birds seem to feel just the same: their notes are as clear as the clear air. There are no leaves on the trees and hedgerows, but how green all the grassy fields are! and the dark purplish brown of the ploughed earth and of the bare branches is beautiful too. What a glad world this looks like, as one drives or rides along the valleys and over the hills! I have often thought so when, in foreign countries, where the fields and woods have looked to me like our English Loamshire – the rich land tilled with just as much care, the woods rolling down the gentle slopes to the green meadows – I have come on something by the roadside which has reminded me that I am not in Loamshire: an image of a great agony – the agony of the Cross. It has stood perhaps by the clustering apple-blossoms, or in the broad sunshine by the corn-field, or at a turning by the wood where a clear brook was gurgling below; and surely, if there came a traveller to this world who knew nothing of the story of man's life upon it, this image of agony would seem to him strangely out of place in the midst of this joyous nature. He would not know that hidden behind the apple-blossoms, or among the golden corn, or under the shrouding boughs of the wood, there might be a human heart beating heavily with anguish; perhaps a young blooming girl, not knowing where to turn for refuge from swift-advancing shame; understanding no more of this life of ours than a foolish lost lamb wandering farther and farther in the nightfall on the lonely heath; yet tasting the bitterest of life's bitterness.

Such things are sometimes hidden among the sunny fields and behind the blossoming orchards; and the sound of the gurgling brook, if you came close to one spot behind a small bush, would be mingled for your ear with a despairing human sob. No wonder man's religion has much sorrow in it: no wonder he needs a suffering God.

Hetty, in her red cloak and warm bonnet, with her basket in her hand, is turning towards a gate by the side of the Treddleston road, but not that she may have a more lingering enjoyment of the sunshine, and think with hope of the long unfolding year. She hardly knows that the sun is shining; and for weeks, now, when she has hoped at all, it has been for something at which she herself trembles and shudders. She only wants to be out of the highroad, that she may walk slowly, and not care how her face looks, as she dwells on wretched thoughts; and through this gate she can get into a field-path behind the wide thick hedgerows. Her great dark eyes wander blankly over the fields like the eyes of one who is desolate, homeless, unloved, not the promised bride of a brave, tender man. But there are no tears in them: her tears were all wept away in the weary night, before she went to sleep. At the next stile the pathway branches off: there are two roads before her – one along by the hedgerow, which will by and by lead her into the road again; the other across the fields, which will take her much farther out of the way into the Scantlands, low shrouded pastures where she will see nobody. She chooses this, and begins to walk a little faster, as if she had suddenly thought of an object towards which it was worth while to hasten. Soon she is in the Scantlands, where the grassy land slopes gradually downwards, and she leaves the level ground to follow the slope. Farther on there is a clump of trees on the low ground, and she is making her way towards it. No, it is not a clump of trees, but a dark shrouded pool, so full with the wintry rains that the under boughs of the elder-bushes lie low beneath the water. She sits down on the grassy bank, against the stooping stem of the great oak that hangs over the dark pool. She has thought of this pool often in the nights of the month that has just gone by, and now at last she is come to see it. She clasps her hands round her knees and leans forward, and looks earnestly at it, as if trying to guess what sort of bed it would make for her young round limbs.

No, she has not courage to jump into that cold watery bed, and if she had, they might find her – they might find out why she had drowned herself. There is but one thing left to her: she must go away, go where they can't find her.

After the first oncoming of her great dread, some weeks after her betrothal to Adam, she had waited and waited, in the blind vague hope that something would happen to set her free from her terror; but she could wait no longer. All the force of her nature had been concentrated on the one effort of concealment, and she had shrunk with irresistible dread from every course that could tend towards a betrayal of her miserable secret. Whenever the thought of writing to Arthur had occurred to her, she had rejected it: he could do nothing for her that would shelter her from discovery and scorn among the relatives and neighbours who once more made all her world, now her airy dream had vanished. Her imagination no longer saw happiness with Arthur, for he could do nothing that would satisfy or soothe her pride. No, something else would happen – something must happen – to set her free from this dread. In young, childish, ignorant souls there is constantly this blind trust in some unshapen chance: it is as hard to a boy or girl to believe that a great wretchedness will actually befall them, as to believe that they will die.

But now necessity was pressing hard upon her – now the time of her marriage was close at hand – she could no longer rest in this blind trust. She must run away; she must hide herself where no familiar eyes could detect her; and then the terror of wandering out into the world, of which she knew nothing, made the possibility of going to Arthur a thought which brought some comfort with it. She felt so helpless now, so unable to fashion the future for herself, that the prospect of throwing herself on him had a relief in it which was stronger than her pride. As she sat by the pool, and shuddered at the dark cold water, the hope that he would receive her tenderly – that he would care for her and think for her – was like a sense of lulling warmth, that made her for the moment indifferent to everything else; and she began now to think of nothing but the scheme by which she should get away.

She had had a letter from Dinah lately, full of kind words about the coming marriage, which she had heard of from Seth; and when Hetty had read this letter aloud to her uncle, he had said, 'I wish Dinah 'ud come again now, for she'd be a comfort to your aunt when you're gone. What do you think, my wench, o' going to see her as soon as you can be spared, and persuading her to come back wi' you? You might happen persuade her wi' telling her as her aunt wants her, for all she writes o' not being able to come.' Hetty had not liked the thought of going to Snowfield, and felt no longing to see Dinah, so she only said, 'It's so far off, uncle.' But now she thought this proposed visit would serve as a pretext for going away. She would tell her aunt when she got home again, that she should like the change of going to Snowfield for a week or ten days. And then, when she got to Stoniton, where nobody knew her, she would ask for the coach that would take her on the way to Windsor. Arthur was at Windsor, and she would go to him.

As soon as Hetty had determined on this scheme, she rose from the grassy bank of the pool, took up her basket, and went on her way to Treddleston, for she must buy the wedding things she had come out for, though she would never want them. She must be careful not to raise any suspicion that she was going to run away.

Mrs Poyser was quite agreeably surprised that Hetty wished to go and see Dinah, and try to bring her back to stay over the wedding. The sooner she went the better, since the weather was pleasant now; and Adam, when he came in the evening, said, if Hetty could set off tomorrow, he would make time to go with her to Treddleston, and see her safe into the Stoniton coach.

'I wish I could go with you and take care of you, Hetty,' he said, the next morning, leaning in at the coach door; 'but you won't stay much beyond a week – the time'll seem long.'

He was looking at her fondly, and his strong hand held hers in its grasp. Hetty felt a sense of protection in his presence – she was used to it now: if she could have had the past undone, and known no other love than her quiet liking for Adam! The tears rose as she gave him the last look.

'God bless her for loving me,' said Adam, as he went on his way to work again, with Gyp at his heels.

But Hetty's tears were not for Adam – not for the anguish that would come upon him when he found she was gone from him for ever. They were for the misery of her own lot, which took her away from this brave tender man who offered up his whole life to her, and threw her, a poor helpless suppliant, on the man who would think it a misfortune that she was obliged to cling to him.

At three o'clock that day, when Hetty was on the coach that was to take her, they said, to Leicester – part of the long, long way to Windsor – she felt dimly that she might be travelling all this weary journey towards the beginning of new misery.

Yet Arthur was at Windsor; he would surely not be angry with her. If he did not mind about her as he used to do, he had promised to be good to her.

BOOK FIFTH

36

The Journey in Hope

A long, lonely journey, with sadness in the heart; away from the familiar to the strange: that is a hard and dreary thing even to the rich, the strong, the instructed: a hard thing, even when we are called by duty, not urged by dread.

What was it then to Hetty? With her poor narrow thoughts, no longer melting into vague hopes, but pressed upon by the chill of definite fear; repeating again and again the same small round of memories – shaping again and again the same childish, doubtful images of what was to come – seeing nothing in this wide world but the little history of her own pleasures and pains; with so little money in her pocket, and the way so long and difficult. Unless she could afford always to go in the coaches – and she felt sure she could not, for the journey to Stoniton was more expensive than she had expected – it was plain that she must trust to carriers, carts or slow waggons; and what a time it would be before she could get to the end of her journey! The burly old coachman from Oakbourne, seeing such a pretty young woman among the outside passengers, had invited her to come and sit beside him; and feeling that it became him as a man and a coachman to open the dialogue with a joke, he applied himself as soon as they were off the stones to the elaboration of one suitable in all respects. After many cuts with his whip and glances at Hetty out of the corner of his eye, he lifted his lips above the edge of his wrapper and said – 'He's pretty nigh six foot, I'll be bound, isna he, now?'

'Who?' said Hetty, rather startled

'Why, the sweetheart as you've left behind, or else him as you're goin' arter – which is it?'

Hetty felt her face flushing and then turning pale. She thought this coachman must know something about her. He must know Adam, and might tell him where she was gone, for it is difficult to country people to believe that those who make a figure in their own parish are not known everywhere else, and it was equally difficult to Hetty to understand that chance words could happen to apply closely to her circumstances. She was too frightened to speak.

'Hegh, hegh!' said the coachman, seeing that his joke was not so gratifying as he had expected, 'you munna take it too ser'ous; if he's behaved ill, get another. Such a pretty lass as you can get a sweetheart any day.'

Hetty's fear was allayed by and by, when she found that the coachman made no further allusion to her personal concerns; but it still had the effect of preventing her from asking him what were the places on the road to Windsor. She told him she was only going a little way out of Stoniton, and when she got down at the inn

where the coach stopped, she hastened away with her basket to another part of
the town. When she had formed her plan of going to Windsor, she had not
foreseen any difficulties except that of getting away; and after she had overcome
this by proposing the visit to Dinah, her thoughts flew to the meeting with
Arthur, and the question how he would behave to her – not resting on any
probable incidents of the journey. She was too entirely ignorant of travelling to
imagine any of its details, and with all her store of money – her three guineas – in
her pocket, she thought herself amply provided. It was not until she found how
much it cost her to get to Stoniton that she began to be alarmed about the
journey, and then, for the first time, she felt her ignorance as to the places that
must be passed on her way. Oppressed with this new alarm, she walked along the
grim Stoniton streets, and at last turned into a shabby little inn, where she hoped
to get a cheap lodging for the night. Here she asked the landlord if he could tell
her what places she must go to, to get to Windsor.

'Well, I can't rightly say. Windsor must be pretty nigh London, for it's where
the king lives,' was the answer. 'Anyhow, you'd best go t' Ashby next – that's
south'ard. But there's as many places from here to London as there's houses in
Stoniton, by what I can make out. I've never been no traveller myself. But how
comes a lone young woman like you, to be thinking o' taking such a journey as
that?'

'I'm going to my brother – he's a soldier at Windsor,' said Hetty, frightened at
the landlord's questioning look. 'I can't afford to go by the coach; do you think
there's a cart goes toward Ashby in the morning?'

'Yes, there may be carts if anybody knowed where they started from; but you
might run over the town before you found out. You'd best set off and walk, and
trust to summat overtaking you.'

Every word sank like lead on Hetty's spirits; she saw the journey stretch bit by
bit before her now; even to get to Ashby seemed a hard thing: it might take the
day, for what she knew, and that was nothing to the rest of the journey. But it
must be done – she must get to Arthur: oh, how she yearned to be again with
somebody who would care for her! She who had never got up in the morning
without the certainty of seeing familiar faces, people on whom she had an
acknowledged claim; whose farthest journey had been to Rosseter on the pillion
with her uncle; whose thoughts had always been taking holiday in dreams of
pleasure, because all the business of her life was managed for her: this kittenlike
Hetty, who till a few months ago had never felt any other grief than that of
envying Mary Burge a new ribbon, or being girded at by her aunt for neglecting
Totty, must now make her toilsome way in loneliness, her peaceful home left
behind for ever, and nothing but a tremulous hope of distant refuge before her.
Now for the first time, as she lay down tonight in the strange hard bed, she felt
that her home had been a happy one, that her uncle had been very good to her,
that her quiet lot at Hayslope among the things and people she knew, with her
little pride in her one best gown and bonnet, and nothing to hide from anyone,
was what she would like to wake up to as a reality, and find that all the feverish
life she had known besides was a short nightmare. She thought of all she had left
behind with yearning regret for her own sake: her own misery filled her heart:

there was no room in it for other people's sorrow. And yet, before the cruel letter, Arthur had been so tender and loving: the memory of that had still a charm for her, though it was no more than a soothing draught that just made pain bearable. For Hetty could conceive no other existence for herself in future than a hidden one and a hidden life, even with love, would have had no delights for her; still less a life mingled with shame. She knew no romances, and had only a feeble share in the feelings which are the source of romance, so that well-read ladies may find it difficult to understand her state of mind. She was too ignorant of everything beyond the simple notions and habits in which she had been brought up, to have any more definite idea of her probable future than that Arthur would take care of her somehow, and shelter her from anger and scorn. He would not marry her and make her a lady; and apart from that she could think of nothing he could give towards which she looked with longing and ambition.

The next morning she rose early, and taking only some milk and bread for her breakfast, set out to walk on the road towards Ashby, under a leaden-coloured sky, with a narrowing streak of yellow, like a departing hope, on the edge of the horizon. Now in her faintness of heart at the length and difficulty of her journey, she was most of all afraid of spending her money, and becoming so destitute that she would have to ask people's charity; for Hetty had the pride not only of a proud nature but of a proud class – the class that pays the most poor-rates, and most shudders at the idea of profiting by a poor-rate. It had not yet occurred to her that she might get money for her locket and earrings which she carried with her, and she applied all her small arithmetic and knowledge of prices to calculating how many meals and how many rides were contained in her two guineas, and the odd shillings, which had a melancholy look, as if they were the pale ashes of the other bright-flaming coin.

For the first few miles out of Stoniton she walked on bravely, always fixing on some tree or gate or projecting bush at the most distant visible point in the road as a goal, and feeling a faint joy when she had reached it. But when she came to the fourth milestone, the first she had happened to notice among the long grass by the roadside, and read that she was still only four miles beyond Stoniton, her courage sank. She had come only this little way, and yet felt tired, and almost hungry again in the keen morning air; for though Hetty was accustomed to much movement and exertion indoors, she was not used to long walks, which produce quite a different sort of fatigue from that of household activity. As she was looking at the milestone she felt some drops falling on her face – it was beginning to rain. Here was a new trouble which had not entered into her sad thoughts before; and quite weighed down by this sudden addition to her burden, she sat down on the step of a stile and began to sob hysterically. The beginning of hardship is like the first taste of bitter food – it seems for a moment unbearable; yet, if there is nothing else to satisfy our hunger, we take another bite and find it possible to go on. When Hetty recovered from her burst of weeping, she rallied her fainting courage: it was raining, and she must try to get on to a village where she might find rest and shelter.

Presently, as she walked on wearily, she heard the rumbling of heavy wheels behind her; a covered waggon was coming creeping slowly along with a slouching driver cracking his whip beside the horses. She waited for it, thinking that if the waggoner were not a very sour-looking man, she would ask him to take her up. As the waggon approached her, the driver had fallen behind, but there was something in the front of the big vehicle which encouraged her. At any previous moment in her life she would not have noticed it; but now, the new susceptibility that suffering had awakened in her caused this object to impress her strongly. It was only a small white-and-liver-coloured spaniel which sat on the front ledge of the waggon, with large timid eyes, and an incessant trembling in the body, such as you may have seen in some of these small creatures. Hetty cared little for animals, as you know, but at this moment she felt as if the helpless timid creature had some fellowship with her, and without being quite aware of the reason, she was less doubtful about speaking to the driver, who now came forward – a large ruddy man, with a sack over his shoulders by way of scarf or mantle.

'Could you take me up in your waggon, if you're going towards Ashby?' said Hetty. 'I'll pay you for it.'

'Aw,' said the big fellow, with that slowly dawning smile which belongs to heavy faces, 'I can take y' up fawst enough wi'out bein' paid for't if you dooant mind lyin' a bit closish a-top o' the woolpacks. Where do you coom from? and what do you want at Ashby?'

'I come from Stoniton. I'm going a long way – to Windsor.'

'What! arter some service, or what?'

'Going to my brother – he's a soldier there.'

'Well, I'm going no furder nor Leicester – and fur enough too – but I'll take you, if you dooant mind being a bit long on the road. Th' hosses wooant feel *your* weight no more nor they feel the little doog there, as I puck up on the road a fortni't agoo. He war lost, I b'lieve, an's been all of a tremble iver sin'. Come, gi' us your basket, an' come behind and let me put y' in.'

To lie on the wool packs, with a cranny left between the curtains of the awning to let in the air, was luxury to Hetty now, and she half slept away the hours till the driver came to ask her if she wanted to get down and have 'some victual;' he himself was going to eat his dinner at this 'public.' Late at night they reached Leicester, and so this second day of Hetty's journey was past. She had spent no money except what she had paid for her food, but she felt that this slow journeying would be intolerable for her another day, and in the morning she found her way to a coach-office to ask about the road to Windsor, and see if it would cost her too much to go part of the distance by coach again. Yes! the distance was too great – the coaches were too dear – she must give them up; but the elderly clerk at the office, touched by her pretty anxious face, wrote down for her the names of the chief places she must pass through. This was the only comfort she got in Leicester, for the men stared at her as she went along the street, and for the first time in her life Hetty wished no one would look at her. She set out walking again; but this day she was fortunate, for she was soon overtaken by a carrier's cart which carried her to Hinckley, and by the help of a return chaise, with a drunken postilion – who frightened her by driving like Jehu the son of Nimshi, and shouting hilarious remarks at her, twisting himself backwards on his saddle – she was before night in the heart of woody Warwickshire: but still almost a hundred miles from Windsor, they told her. Oh what a large world it was, and what hard work for her to find her way in it! She went by mistake to Stratford-on-Avon, finding Stratford set down in her list of places, and then she was told she had come a long way out of the right road. It was not till the fifth day that she got to Stony Stratford. That seems but a slight journey as you look at the map, or remember your own pleasant travels to and from the meadowy banks of the Avon. But how wearily long it was to Hetty! It seemed to her as if this country of flat fields and hedgerows, and dotted houses, and villages, and market-towns – all so much alike to her indifferent eyes – must have no end, and she must go on wandering among them for ever, waiting tired at toll-gates for some cart to come, and then finding the cart went only a little way – a very little way – to the miller's a mile off perhaps; and she hated going into the public-houses, where she must go to get food and ask questions, because there were always men lounging there, who stared at her and joked her rudely. Her body was very weary too with these days of new fatigue and anxiety; they had made her look more pale and worn than all the time of hidden dread she had gone through at home. When at last she reached Stony Stratford, her impatience and weariness had become too strong for her economical caution; she determined to take the coach for the rest of the way, though it should cost her all her remaining money. She would need nothing at Windsor but to find Arthur. When she had paid the fare for the last coach, she had only a shilling; and as she got down at the sign of the Green Man in Windsor at twelve o'clock in the middle of the seventh day, hungry and faint, the coachman came up, and begged her to 'remember him'. She put her hand in her pocket, and took out the shilling, but the tears came with the sense of exhaustion and the thought that she was giving away her last means of getting food, which she really required before she could go in search of Arthur. As she held out the shilling, she lifted up her dark tear-filled eyes to the coachman's face and said, 'Can you give me back sixpence?'

'No, no,' he said, gruffly, 'never mind – put the shilling up again.'

The landlord of the Green Man had stood near enough to witness this scene, and he was a man whose abundant feeding served to keep his good nature, as well as his person, in high condition. And that lovely tearful face of Hetty's would have found out the sensitive fibre in most men.

'Come, young woman, come in,' he said, 'and have a drop o' something; you're pretty well knocked up: I can see that.'

He took her into the bar and said to his wife, 'Here, missis, take this young woman into the parlour; she's a little overcome' – for Hetty's tears were falling fast. They were merely hysterical tears: she thought she had no reason for weeping now, and was vexed that she was too weak and tired to help it. She was at Windsor at last, not far from Arthur.

She looked with eager, hungry eyes at the bread and meat and beer that the landlady brought her, and for some minutes she forgot everything else in the delicious sensations of satisfying hunger and recovering from exhaustion. The landlady sat opposite to her as she ate, and looked at her earnestly. No wonder: Hetty had thrown off her bonnet, and her curls had fallen down: her face was all the more touching in its youth and beauty because of its weary look; and the good woman's eyes presently wandered to her figure, which in her hurried dressing on her journey she had taken no pains to conceal; moreover, the stranger's eye detects what the familiar unsuspecting eye leaves unnoticed.

'Why, you're not very fit for travelling,' she said, glancing while she spoke at Hetty's ringless hand. 'Have you come far?'

'Yes,' said Hetty, roused by this question to exert more self-command, and feeling the better for the food she had taken. 'I've come a good long way, and it's very tiring. But I'm better now. Could you tell me which way to go to this place?'

Here Hetty took from her pocket a bit of paper: it was the end of Arthur's letter on which he had written his address.

While she was speaking, the landlord had come in, and had begun to look at her as earnestly as his wife had done. He took up the piece of paper which Hetty handed across the table, and read the address.

'Why, what do you want at this house?' he said. It is in the nature of inn-keepers, and all men who have no pressing business of their own, to ask as many questions as possible before giving any information.

'I want to see a gentleman as is there,' said Hetty.

'But there's no gentleman there,' returned the landlord. 'It's shut up – been shut up this fortnight. What gentleman is it you want? Perhaps I can let you know where to find him.'

'It's Captain Donnithorne,' said Hetty, tremulously, her heart beginning to beat painfully at this disappointment of her hope that she should find Arthur at once.

'Captain Donnithorne? Stop a bit,' said the landlord, slowly. 'Was he in the Loamshire Militia? A tall young officer with a fairish skin and reddish whiskers – and had a servant by the name o' Pym?'

'Oh yes,' said Hetty; 'you know him – where is he?'

'A fine sight o' miles away from here: the Loamshire Militia's gone to Ireland; it's been gone this fortnight.'

'Look there! she's fainting,' said the landlady, hastening to support Hetty, who had lost her miserable consciousness and looked like a beautiful corpse. They carried her to the sofa and loosened her dress.

'Here's a bad business, I suspect,' said the landlord, as he brought in some water.

'Ah, it's plain enough what sort of business it is,' said the wife. 'She's not a common flaunting dratchell, I can see that. She looks like a respectable country girl, and she comes from a good way off, to judge by her tongue. She talks something like that ostler we had that come from the north: he was as honest a fellow as we ever had about the house – they're all honest folks in the north.'

'I never saw a prettier young woman in my life,' said the husband. 'She's like a pictur in a shop-winder. It goes to one's 'eart to look at her.'

'It 'ud have been a good deal better for her if she'd been uglier and had more conduct,' said the landlady, who on any charitable construction must have been supposed to have more 'conduct' than beauty. 'But she's coming to again. Fetch a drop more water.'

The Journey in Despair

Hetty was too ill through the rest of that day for any questions to be addressed to her – too ill even to think with any distinctness of the evils that were to come. She only felt that all her hope was crushed, and that instead of having found a refuge she had only reached the borders of a new wilderness where no goal lay before her. The sensations of bodily sickness, in a comfortable bed, and with the tendance of the good-natured landlady, made a sort of respite for her; such a respite as there is in the faint weariness which obliges a man to throw himself on the sand, instead of toiling onward under the scorching sun.

But when sleep and rest had brought back the strength necessary for the keenness of mental suffering – when she lay the next morning looking at the growing light which was like a cruel taskmaster returning to urge from her a fresh round of hated hopeless labour,– she began to think what course she must take, to remember that all her money was gone, to look at the prospect of further wandering among strangers with the new clearness shed on it by the experience of her journey to Windsor. But which way could she turn? It was impossible for her to enter into any service, even if she could obtain it: there was nothing but immediate beggary before her. She thought of a young woman who had been found against the church wall at Hayslope one Sunday, nearly dead with cold and hunger – a tiny infant in her arms: the woman was rescued and taken to the parish. 'The parish!' You can perhaps hardly understand the effect of that word on a mind like Hetty's, brought up among people who were somewhat hard in their feelings even towards poverty, who lived among the fields, and had little pity for want and rags as a cruel inevitable fate such as they sometimes seem in cities, but held them a mark of idleness and vice – and it was idleness and vice that brought burthens on the parish. To Hetty the 'parish' was next to the prison in obloquy; and to ask anything of strangers – to beg – lay in the same far-off hideous region of intolerable shame that Hetty had all her life thought it impossible she could ever come near. But now the remembrance of that wretched woman whom she had seen herself, on her way from church, being carried into Joshua Rann's, came back upon her with the new terrible sense that there was very little now to divide *her* from the same lot. And the dread of bodily hardship mingled with the dread of shame; for Hetty had the luxurious nature of a round, soft-coated pet animal.

How she yearned to be back in her safe home again, cherished and cared for as she had always been! Her aunt's scolding about trifles would have been music to her ears now: she longed for it: she used to hear it in a time when she had only trifles to hide. Could she be the same Hetty that used to make up the butter in the dairy with the Gueldres roses peeping in at the window – she, a runaway whom her friends would not open their doors to again, lying in this strange bed, with the knowledge that she had no money to pay for what she received, and must offer those strangers some of the clothes in her basket? It was then she thought of her locket and earrings, and seeing her pocket lie near, she reached it and spread the contents on the bed before her. There were the locket and earrings in the little velvet-lined boxes, and with them there was a beautiful silver thimble which Adam had bought her, the words 'Remember me' making the ornament of the border; a steel purse, with her one shilling in it, and a small red-leather case, fastening with a strap. Those beautiful little earrings, with their delicate pearls and garnet, that she had tried in her ears with such longing in the bright sunshine on the 30th of July! She had no longing to put them in her ears now: her head with its dark rings of hair lay back languidly on the pillow, and the sadness that rested about her brow and eyes was something too hard for regretful memory. Yet she put her hands up to her ears: it was because there were some thin gold rings in them, which were also worth a little money. Yes, she could surely get some money for her ornaments: those Arthur had given her must have cost a great deal of money. The landlord and landlady had been good to her; perhaps they would help her to get the money for these things.

But this money would not keep her long: what should she do when it was gone? Where should she go? The horrible thought of want and beggary drove her once to think she would go back to her uncle and aunt, and ask them to forgive her and have pity on her. But she shrank from that idea again, as she might have shrunk from scorching metal: she could never endure that shame before her uncle and aunt, before Mary Burge, and the servants at the Chase, and the people at Broxton, and everybody who knew her. They should never know what had happened to her. What *could* she do? She would go away from Windsor – travel again as she had done the last week, and get among the flat green fields with the high hedges round them, where nobody could see her or know her: and there, perhaps, when there was nothing else she could do, she should get courage to drown herself in some pond like that in the Scantlands. Yes, she would get away from Windsor as soon as possible: she didn't like these people at the inn to know about her, to know that she had come to look for Captain Donnithorne: she must think of some reason to tell them why she had asked for him.

With this thought she began to put the things back into her pocket, meaning to get up and dress before the landlady came to her. She had her hand on the red-leather case, when it occurred to her that there might be something in this case which she had forgotten – something worth selling; for without knowing what she should do with her life, she craved the means of living as long as possible; and when we desire eagerly to find something, we are apt to search for it in hopeless places. No, there was nothing but common needles and pins, and dried tulip-petals between the paper leaves where she had written down her little money-accounts. But on one of these leaves there was a name, which, often as she had seen it before, now flashed on Hetty's mind like a newly-discovered message. The name was – *Dinah Morris, Snowfield*. There was a text above it, written, as well as the name, by Dinah's own hand with a little pencil, one evening that they were sitting together and Hetty happened to have the red case lying open before her. Hetty did not read the text now: she was only arrested by the name. Now, for the first time she remembered without indifference the affectionate kindness Dinah had shown her, and those words of Dinah in the bedchamber – that Hetty must think of her as a friend in trouble. Suppose she were to go to Dinah, and ask her to help her? Dinah did not think about things as other people did: she was a mystery to Hetty, but Hetty knew she was always kind. She couldn't imagine Dinah's face turning away from her in dark reproof or scorn, Dinah's voice willingly speaking ill of her, or rejoicing in her misery, as a punishment. Dinah did not seem to belong to that world of Hetty's, whose glance she dreaded like scorching fire. But even to her Hetty shrank from beseeching and confession: she could not prevail on herself to say, 'I will go to Dinah;' she only thought of that as a possible alternative, if she had not courage for death.

The good landlady was amazed when she saw Hetty come downstairs soon after herself, neatly dressed, and looking resolutely self-possessed. Hetty told her she was quite well this morning: she had only been very tired and overcome with her journey, for she had come a long way to ask about her brother, who had run away, and they thought he was gone for a soldier, and Captain Donnithorne might know, for he had been very kind to her brother once. It was a lame story, and the landlady looked doubtfully at Hetty as she told it; but there was a resolute air of self-reliance about her this morning, so different from the helpless prostration of yesterday, that the landlady hardly knew how to make a remark that might seem like prying into other people's affairs. She only invited her to sit down to breakfast with them, and in the course of it Hetty brought out her earrings and locket, and asked the landlord if he could help her to get money for them: her journey, she said, had cost her much more than she expected, and now she had no money to get back to her friends, which she wanted to do at once.

It was not the first time the landlady had seen the ornaments, for she had examined the contents of Hetty's pocket yesterday, and she and her husband had discussed the fact of a country girl having these beautiful things, with a stronger conviction than ever that Hetty had been miserably deluded by the fine young officer.

'Well,' said the landlord, when Hetty had spread the precious trifles before him, 'we might take 'em to the jeweller's shop, for there's one not far off; but Lord bless you, they wouldn't give you a quarter o' what the things are worth. And you wouldn't like to part with 'em?' he added, looking at her enquiringly.

'Oh, I don't mind,' said Hetty, hastily, 'so as I can get money to go back.'

'And they might think the things were stolen, as you wanted to sell 'em,' he went on, 'for it isn't usual for a young woman like you to have fine jewellery like that.'

The blood rushed to Hetty's face with anger. 'I belong to respectable folks,' she said; 'I'm not a thief.'

'No, that you aren't, I'll be bound,' said the landlady; 'and you'd no call to say that,' looking indignantly at her husband. 'The things were gev to her: that's plain enough to be seen.'

'I didn't mean as I thought so,' said the husband, apologetically, 'but I said it was what the jeweller might think, and so he wouldn't be offering much money for 'em.'

'Well,' said the wife, 'suppose you were to advance some money on the things yourself, and then if she liked to redeem 'em when she got home, she could. But if we heard nothing from her after two months, we might do as we liked with 'em.'

I will not say that in this accommodating proposition the landlady had no regard whatever to the possible reward of her good-nature in the ultimate possession of the locket and earrings: indeed, the effect they would have in that case on the mind of the grocer's wife had presented itself with remarkable vividness to her rapid imagination. The landlord took up the ornaments and pushed out his lips in a meditative manner. He wished Hetty well, doubtless; but pray, how many of your well-wishers would decline to make a little gain out of you? Your landlady is sincerely affected at parting with you, respects you highly, and will really rejoice if anyone else is generous to you; but at the same time she hands you a bill by which she gains as high a percentage as possible.

'How much money do you want to get home with, young woman?' said the well-wisher, at length.

'Three guineas,' answered Hetty, fixing on the sum she set out with, for want of any other standard, and afraid of asking too much.

'Well, I've no objections to advance you three guineas,' said the landlord; 'and if you like to send it me back and get the jewellery again, you can, you know: the Green Man isn't going to run away.'

'Oh yes, I'll be very glad if you'll give me that,' said Hetty, relieved at the thought that she would not have to go to the jeweller's, and be stared at and questioned.

'But if you want the things again, you'll write before long,' said the landlady, 'because when two months are up, we shall make up our minds as you don't want 'em.'

'Yes,' said Hetty, indifferently.

The husband and wife were equally content with this arrangement. The husband thought, if the ornaments were not redeemed, he could make a good thing of it by taking them to London and selling them: the wife thought she would coax the good man into letting her keep them. And they were accommodating Hetty, poor thing: – a pretty, respectable-looking young woman, apparently in a sad case. They declined to take anything for her food and bed: she was quite welcome. And at eleven o'clock Hetty said 'Goodbye' to them, with the same quiet, resolute air she had worn all the morning, mounting the coach that was to take her twenty miles back along the way she had come.

There is a strength of self-possession which is the sign that the last hope has departed. Despair no more leans on others than perfect contentment, and in despair pride ceases to be counteracted by the sense of dependence.

Hetty felt that no one could deliver her from the evils that would make life hateful to her; and no one, she said to herself, should ever know her misery and humiliation. No; she would not confess even to Dinah: she would wander out of sight, and drown herself where her body would never be found, and no one should know what had become of her.

When she got off this coach, she began to walk again, and take cheap rides in carts, and get cheap meals, going on and on without distinct purpose, yet strangely, by some fascination, taking the way she had come, though she was determined not to go back to her own country. Perhaps it was because she had fixed her mind on the grassy Warwickshire fields, with the bushy tree-studded hedgerows that made a hiding-place even in this leafless season. She went more slowly than she came, often getting over the stiles, and sitting for hours under the hedgerows, looking before her with blank, beautiful eyes; fancying herself at the edge of a hidden pool, low down, like that in the Scantlands; wondering if it were very painful to be drowned, and if there would be anything worse after death than what she dreaded in life. Religious doctrines had taken no hold on Hetty's mind: she was one of those numerous people who have had godfathers and godmothers, learned their catechism, been confirmed, and gone to church every Sunday, and yet, for any practical result of strength in life, or trust in death, have never appropriated a single Christian idea or Christian feeling. You would misunderstand her thoughts during these wretched days, if you imagined that they were influenced either by religious fears or religious hopes.

She chose to go to Stratford-on-Avon again, where she had gone before by mistake; for she remembered some grassy fields on her former way towards it – fields among which she thought she might find just the sort of pool she had in her mind. Yet she took care of her money still; she carried her basket: death seemed still a long way off, and life was so strong in her! She craved food and rest – she hastened towards them at the very moment she was picturing to herself the bank from which she would leap towards death. It was already five days since she had left Windsor, for she had wandered about, always avoiding speech or questioning looks, and recovering her air of proud self-dependence whenever she was under observation, choosing her decent lodging at night, and dressing herself neatly in the morning, and setting off on her way steadily, or remaining under shelter if it rained, as if she had a happy life to cherish.

And yet, even in her most self-conscious moments, the face was sadly different from that which had smiled at itself in the old specked glass, or smiled at others when they glanced at it admiringly. A hard and even fierce look had come in the eyes, though their lashes were as long as ever, and they had all their dark brightness. And the cheek was never dimpled with smiles now. It was the same rounded, pouting, childish prettiness, but with all love and belief in love departed from it – the sadder for its beauty, like that wondrous Medusa-face, with the passionate, passionless lips.

At last she was among the fields she had been dreaming of, on a long narrow pathway leading towards a wood. If there should be a pool in that wood! It would be better hidden than one in the fields. No, it was not a wood, only a wild brake, where there had once been gravel-pits, leaving mounds and hollows studded with brushwood and small trees. She roamed up and down, thinking there was perhaps a pool in every hollow before she came to it, till her limbs were weary, and she sat down to rest. The afternoon was far advanced, and the leaden sky was darkening, as if the sun were setting behind it. After a little while Hetty started up again, feeling that darkness would soon come on; and she must put off finding the pool till tomorrow, and make her way to some shelter for the night. She had quite lost her way in the fields, and might as well go in one direction as another, for aught she knew. She walked through field after field, and no village, no house was in sight; but there, at the corner of this pasture, there was a break in the hedges; the land seemed to dip down a little, and two trees leaned towards each other across the opening. Hetty's heart gave a great beat as she thought there must be a pool there. She walked towards it heavily over the tufted grass, with pale lips and a sense of trembling: it was as if the thing were come in spite of herself, instead of being the object of her search.

There it was, black under the darkening sky: no motion, no sound near. She set down her basket, and then sank down herself on the grass, trembling. The pool had its wintry depth now: by the time it got shallow, as she remembered the pools did at Hayslope, in the summer, no one could find out that it was her body. But then there was her basket – she must hide that too: she must throw it into the water – make it heavy with stones first, and then throw it in. She got up to look about for stones, and soon brought five or six, which she laid down beside her basket, and then sat down again. There was no need to hurry – there was all the night to drown herself in. She sat leaning her elbow on the basket. She was weary, hungry. There were some buns in her basket – three, which she had supplied herself with at the place where she ate her dinner. She took them out now, and ate them eagerly, and then sat still again, looking at the pool. The soothed sensation that came over her from the satisfaction of her hunger, and this fixed dreamy attitude, brought on drowsiness, and presently her head sank down on her knees. She was fast asleep.

When she awoke it was deep night, and she felt chill. She was frightened at this darkness – frightened at the long night before her. If she could but throw herself into the water! No, not yet. She began to walk about that she might get warm again, as if she would have more resolution then. Oh how long the time was in that darkness! The bright hearth and the warmth and the voices of home – the secure uprising and lying down – the familiar fields, the familiar people, the Sundays and holidays with their simple joys of dress and feasting – all the sweets of her young life rushed before her now, and she seemed to be stretching her arms towards them across a great gulf. She set her teeth when she thought of Arthur: she cursed him, without knowing what her cursing would do: she wished he too might know desolation, and cold, and a life of shame that he dared not end by death.

The horror of this cold, and darkness, and solitude—out of all human reach – became greater every long minute: it was almost as if she were dead already, and knew that she was dead, and longed to get back to life again. But no: she was alive still; she had not taken the dreadful leap. She felt a strange contradictory wretchedness and exultation: wretchedness, that she did not dare to face death; exultation, that she was still in life – that she might yet know light and warmth again. She walked backwards and forwards to warm herself, beginning to discern something of the objects around her, as her eyes became accustomed to the night: the darker line of the hedge, the rapid motion of some living creature – perhaps a fieldmouse rushing across the grass. She no longer felt as if the darkness hedged her in: she thought she could walk back across the field, and get over the stile; and then, in the very next field, she thought she remembered there was a hovel of furze near a sheepfold. If she could get into that hovel, she would be warmer; she could pass the night there, for that was what Alick did at Hayslope in lambing-time. The thought of this hovel brought the energy of a new hope: she took up her basket and walked across the field, but it was some time before she got in the right direction for the stile. The exercise and the occupation of finding the stile were a stimulus to her, however, and lightened the horror of the darkness and solitude. There were sheep in the next field, and she startled a group as she set down her basket and got over the stile; and the sound of their movement comforted her, for it assured her that her impression was right: this was the field where she had seen the hovel, for it was the field where the sheep were. Right on along the path, and she would get to it. She reached the opposite gate, and felt her way along its rails, and the rails of the sheepfold, till her hand encountered the pricking of the gorsy wall. Delicious sensation! She had found the shelter: she groped her way, touching the prickly gorse, to the door, and pushed it open. It was an ill-smelling close place, but warm, and there was straw on the ground: Hetty sank down on the straw with a sense of escape. Tears came – she had never shed tears before since she left Windsor – tears and sobs of hysterical joy that she had still hold of life, that she was still on the familiar earth, with the sheep near her. The very consciousness of her own limbs was a delight to her: she turned up her sleeves, and kissed her arms with the passionate love of life. Soon warmth and weariness lulled her in the midst of her sobs, and she fell continually into dozing, fancying herself at the brink of the pool again – fancying that she had jumped into the water, and then awaking with a start, and wondering where she was. But at last deep dreamless sleep came; her head, guarded by her bonnet, found a pillow against the gorsy wall; and the poor soul, driven to and fro between two equal terrors, found the one relief that was possible to it – the relief of unconsciousness.

Alas! that relief seems to end the moment it has begun. It seemed to Hetty as if those dozing dreams had only passed into another dream – that she was in the hovel, and her aunt was standing over her with a candle in her hand. She trembled under her aunt's glance, and opened her eyes. There was no candle, but there was light in the hovel – the light of early morning through the open door. And there was a face looking down on her; but it was an unknown face, belonging to an elderly man in a smock-frock.

'Why, what do you do here, young woman?' the man said, roughly.

Hetty trembled still worse under this real fear and shame than she had done in her momentary dream under her aunt's glance. She felt that she was like a beggar already – found sleeping in that place. But in spite of her trembling, she was so eager to account to the man for her presence here, that she found words at once.

'I lost my way,' she said. 'I'm travelling – north'ard, and I got away from the road into the fields, and was overtaken by the dark. Will you tell me the way to the nearest village?

She got up as she was speaking, and put her hands to her bonnet to adjust it, and then laid hold of her basket.

The man looked at her with a slow bovine gaze, without giving her any answer, for some seconds. Then he turned away and walked towards the door of the hovel, but it was not till he got there that he stood still, and, turning his shoulder half round towards her, said, 'Aw, I can show you the way to Norton, if you like. But what do you do gettin' out o' the highroad?' he added, with a tone of gruff reproof. 'Y'ull be gettin' into mischief, if you dooant mind.'

'Yes,' said Hetty, 'I won't do it again. I'll keep in the road, if you'll be so good as show me how to get to it.'

'Why dooant you keep where there's finger-poasses an' folks to ax the way on?' the man said, still more gruffly. 'Anybody 'ud think you was a wild woman, an' look at yer.'

Hetty was frightened at this gruff old man, and still more at this last suggestion that she looked like a wild woman. As she followed him out of the hovel she thought she would give him a sixpence for telling her the way, and then he would not suppose she was wild. As he stopped to point out the road to her, she put her hand in her pocket to get the sixpence ready, and when he was turning away, without saying good-morning, she held it out to him and said, 'Thank you; will you please to take something for your trouble?'

He looked slowly at the sixpence, and then said, 'I want none o' your money. You'd better take care on't, else you'll get it stool from yer, if you go trapesin' about the fields like a mad woman a-that-way.'

The man left her without further speech, and Hetty held on her way. Another day had risen, and she must wander on. It was no use to think of drowning herself – she could not do it, at least while she had money left to buy food, and strength to journey on. But the incident on her waking this morning heightened her dread of that time when her money would be all gone; she would have to sell her basket and clothes then, and she would really look like a beggar or a wild woman, as the man had said. The passionate joy in life she had felt in the night, after escaping from the brink of the black cold death in the pool, was gone now. Life now, by the morning light, with the impression of that man's hard wondering look at her, was as full of dread as death – it was worse; it was a dread to which she felt chained, from which she shrank and shrank as she did from the black pool, and yet could find no refuge from it.

She took out her money from her purse, and looked at it; she had still two-and-twenty shillings; it would serve her for many days more, or it would help her to get on faster to Stonyshire, within reach of Dinah. The thought of Dinah urged itself more strongly now, since the experience of the night had driven her shuddering imagination away from the pool. If it had been only going to Dinah – if nobody besides Dinah would ever know – Hetty could have made up her mind to go to her. The soft voice, the pitying eyes, would have drawn her. But afterwards the other people must know, and she could no more rush on that shame than she could rush on death.

She must wander on and on, and wait for a lower depth of despair to give her courage. Perhaps death would come to her, for she was getting less and less able to bear the day's weariness. And yet – such is the strange action of our souls, drawing us by a lurking desire towards the very ends we dread – Hetty, when she set out again from Norton, asked the straightest road northward towards Stonyshire, and kept it all that day.

Poor wandering Hetty, with the rounded childish face, and the hard unloving despairing soul looking out of it – with the narrow heart and narrow thoughts, no room in them for any sorrows but her own, and tasting that sorrow with the more intense bitterness! My heart bleeds for her as I see her toiling along on her weary feet, or seated in a cart, with her eyes fixed vacantly on the road before her, never thinking or caring whither it tends, till hunger comes and makes her desire that a village may be near.

What will be the end? – the end of her objectless wandering, apart from all love, caring for human beings only through her pride, clinging to life only as the hunted wounded brute clings to it?

God preserve you and me from being the beginners of such misery!

38

The Quest

The first ten days after Hetty's departure passed as quietly as any other days with the family at the Hall Farm, and with Adam at his daily work. They had expected Hetty to stay away a week or ten days at least, perhaps a little longer if Dinah came back with her, because there might then be something to detain them at Snowfield. But when a fortnight had passed they began to feel a little surprise that Hetty did not return; she must surely have found it pleasanter to be with Dinah than anyone could have supposed. Adam, for his part, was getting very impatient to see her, and he resolved that, if she did not appear the next day (Saturday), he would set out on Sunday morning to fetch her. There was no coach on a Sunday; but by setting out before it was light, and perhaps getting a lift in a cart by the way, he would arrive pretty early at Snowfield, and bring back Hetty the next day – Dinah too, if she were coming. It was quite time Hetty came home, and he would afford to lose his Monday for the sake of bringing her.

His project was quite approved at the Farm when he went there on Saturday evening. Mrs Poyser desired him emphatically not to come back without Hetty, for she had been quite too long away, considering the things she had to get ready by the middle of March, and a week was surely enough for anyone to go out for their health. As for Dinah, Mrs Poyser had small hope of their bringing her, unless they could make her believe the folks at Hayslope were twice as miserable as the folks at Snowfield. 'Though,' said Mrs Poyser, by way of conclusion, 'you might tell her she's got but one aunt left, and she's wasted pretty nigh to a shadder; and we shall p'rhaps all be gone twenty mile further off her next Michaelmas, and shall die o' broken hearts among strange folks, and leave the children fatherless and motherless.'

'Nay, nay,' said Mr Poyser, who certainly had the air of a man perfectly heart-whole, 'it isna so bad as that. Thee't looking rarely now, and getting flesh every day. But I'd be glad for Dinah t' come, for she'd help thee wi' the little uns: they took t' her wonderful.'

So at daybreak, on Sunday, Adam set off. Seth went with him the first mile or two, for the thought of Snowfield, and the possibility that Dinah might come again, made him restless, and the walk with Adam in the cold morning air, both in their best clothes, helped to give him a sense of Sunday calm. It was the last morning in February, with a low grey sky, and a slight hoar-frost on the green border of the road and on the black hedges. They heard the gurgling of the full brooklet hurrying down the hill, and the faint twittering of the early birds. For they walked in silence, though with a pleased sense of companionship.

'Goodbye, lad,' said Adam, laying his hand on Seth's shoulder, and looking at him affectionately as they were about to part, 'I wish thee wast going all the way wi' me, and as happy as I am.'

'I'm content, Addy, I'm content,' said Seth, cheerfully. 'I'll be an old bachelor, belike, and make a fuss wi' thy children.'

They turned away from each other, and Seth walked leisurely homeward, mentally repeating one of his favourite hymns – he was very fond of hymns:

> Dark and cheerless is the morn
> Unaccompanied by thee:
> Joyless is the day's return
> Till thy mercy's beams I see:
> Till thou inward light impart,
> Glad my eyes and warm my heart.
>
> Visit, then, this soul of mine,
> Pierce the gloom of sin and grief,
> Fill me, Radiancy Divine,
> Scatter all my unbelief.
> More and more thyself display,
> Shining to the perfect day.

Adam walked much faster, and anyone coming along the Oakbourne road at sunrise that morning must have had a pleasant sight in this tall broad-chested man, striding along with a carriage as upright and firm as any soldier's, glancing with keen glad eyes at the dark-blue hills as they began to show themselves on his way. Seldom in Adam's life had his face been so free from any cloud of anxiety as it was this morning; and this freedom from care, as is usual with constructive practical minds like his, made him all the more observant of the objects round him, and all the more ready to gather suggestions from them towards his own favourite plans and ingenious contrivances. His happy love – the knowledge that his steps were carrying him nearer and nearer to Hetty, who was so soon to be his – was to his thoughts what the sweet morning air was to his sensations: it gave him a consciousness of wellbeing that made activity delightful. Every now and then there was a rush of more intense feeling towards her, which chased away other images than Hetty; and along with that would come a wondering thankfulness that all this happiness was given to him – that this life of ours had such sweetness in it. For Adam had a devout mind, though he was perhaps rather impatient of devout words; and his tenderness lay very close to his reverence, so that the one could hardly be stirred without the other. But after feeling had welled up and poured itself out in this way, busy thought would come back with the greater vigour; and this morning it was intent on schemes by which the roads might be improved that were so imperfect all through the country, and on picturing all the benefits that might come from the exertions of a single country gentleman, if he would set himself to getting the roads made good in his own district.

It seemed a very short walk, the ten miles to Oakbourne, that pretty town within sight of the blue hills, where he breakfasted. After this, the country grew barer and barer: no more rolling woods, no more wide–branching trees near frequent homesteads, no more bushy hedgerows; but grey stone walls intersecting the meagre pastures, and dismal wide-scattered grey stone houses on broken lands where mines had been and were no longer. 'A hungry land,' said Adam to himself 'I'd rather go south'ard, where they say it's as flat as a table, than come to live here; though if Dinah likes to live in a country where she can be the most comfort to folks, she's i' the right to live o' this side; for she must look as if she'd come straight from heaven, like th' angels in the desert, to strengthen them as ha' got nothing t' eat.' And when at last he came in sight of Snowfield, he thought it looked like a town that was 'fellow to the country,' though the stream through the valley where the great mill stood gave a pleasant greenness to the lower fields. The town lay, grim, stony, and unsheltered, up the side of a steep hill, and Adam did not go forward to it at present, for Seth had told him where to find Dinah. It was at a thatched cottage outside the town, a little way from the mill – an old cottage, standing sideways towards the road, with a little bit of potato-ground before it. Here Dinah lodged with an elderly couple; and if she and Hetty happened to be out, Adam could learn where they were gone, or when they would be at home again. Dinah might be out on some preaching errand, and perhaps she would have left Hetty at home. Adam could not help hoping this, and as he recognised the cottage by the roadside before him, there shone out in his face that involuntary smile which belongs to the expectation of a near joy.

He hurried his step along the narrow causeway, and rapped at the door. It was opened by a very clean old woman, with a slow palsied shake of the head.

'Is Dinah Morris at home?' said Adam.

'Eh? . . . no,' said the old woman, looking up at this tall stranger with a wonder that made her slower of speeeh than usual. 'Will you please to come in?' she added, retiring from the door, as if recollecting herself 'Why, ye're brother to the young man as come afore, arena ye?'

'Yes,' said Adam, entering. 'That was Seth Bede. I'm his brother Adam. He told me to give his respects to you and your good master.'

'Ay, the same t' him: he was a gracious young man. An' ye feature him, on'y ye're darker. Sit ye down i' th' armchair. My man isna come home from meeting.'

Adam sat down patiently, not liking to hurry the shaking old woman with questions, but looking eagerly towards the narrow twisting stairs in one corner, for he thought it was possible Hetty might have heard his voice, and would come down them.

'So you're come to see Dinah Morris?' said the old woman, standing opposite to him. 'An' you didna know she was away from home, then?'

'No,' said Adam, 'but I thought it likely she might be away, seeing as it's Sunday. But the other young woman – is she at home, or gone along with Dinah? '

The old woman looked at Adam with a bewildered air.

'Gone along wi' her?' she said. 'Eh, Dinah's gone to Leeds, a big town ye may ha' heared on, where there's a many o' the Lord's people. She's been gone sin' Friday was a fortnight: they sent her the money for her journey. You may see her room here,' she went on, opening a door, and not noticing the effect of her words on Adam. He rose and followed her, and darted an eager glance into the little room, with its narrow bed, the portrait of Wesley on the wall, and the few books lying on the large Bible. He had had an irrational hope that Hetty might be there. He could not speak in the first moment after seeing that the room was empty; an undefined fear had seized him – something had happened to Hetty on the journey. Still the old woman was so slow of speech and apprehension, that Hetty might be at Snowfield after all.

'It's a pity ye didna know,' she said. 'Have ye come from your own country o' purpose to see her?'

'But Hetty - Hetty Sorrel,' said Adam, abruptly; 'where is *she*?'

'I know nobody by that name,' said the old woman, wonderingly. 'Is it anybody ye've heared on at Snowfield?'

'Did there come no young woman here – very young and pretty – Friday was a fortnight, to see Dinah Morris?'

'Nay; I'n seen no young woman.'

'Think; are you quite sure? A girl, eighteen years old, with dark eyes and dark curly hair, and a red cloak on, and a basket on her arm? You couldn't forget her if you saw her.'

'Nay; Friday was a fortnight – it was the day as Dinah went away – there come nobody. There's ne'er been nobody asking for her till you come, for the folks about know as she's gone. Eh dear, eh dear, is there summat the matter?'

The old woman had seen the ghastly look of fear in Adam's face. But he was not stunned or confounded: he was thinking eagerly where he could enquire about Hetty.

'Yes; a young woman started from our country to see Dinah, Friday was a fortnight. I came to fetch her back. I'm afraid something has happened to her. I can't stop. Goodbye.'

He hastened out of the cottage, and the old woman followed him to the gate, watching him sadly with her shaking head, as he almost ran towards the town. He was going to enquire at the place where the Oakbourne coach stopped.

No! no young woman like Hetty had been seen there. Had any accident happened to the coach a fortnight ago? No. And there was no coach to take him back to Oakbourne that day. Well, he would walk: he couldn't stay here, in wretched inaction. But the innkeeper, seeing that Adam was in great anxiety, and entering into this new incident with the eagerness of a man who passes a great deal of time with his hands in his pockets looking into an obstinately monotonous street, offered to take him back to Oakbourne in his own 'taxed cart' this very evening. It was not five o'clock; there was plenty of time for Adam to take a meal, and yet to get to Oakbourne before ten o'clock. The innkeeper declared that he really wanted to go to Oakbourne, and might as well go tonight; he should have all Monday before him then. Adam, after making an ineffectual attempt to eat, put the food in his pocket, and, drinking a draught of ale, declared himself ready to set off. As they approached the cottage, it occurred to him that he would do well to learn from the old woman where Dinah was to be found in Leeds: if there was trouble at the Hall Farm – he only half admitted the foreboding that there would be – the Poysers might like to send for Dinah. But Dinah had not left any address, and the old woman, whose memory for names was infirm, could not recall the name of the 'blessed woman,' who was Dinah's chief friend in the society at Leeds.

During that long, long journey in the taxed cart, there was time for all the conjectures of importunate fear and struggling hope. In the very first shock of discovering that Hetty had not been to Snowfield, the thought of Arthur had darted through Adam like a sharp pang: but he tried for some time to ward off its return by busying himself with modes of accounting for the alarming fact, quite apart from that intolerable thought. Some accident had happened. Hetty had, by some strange chance, got into a wrong vehicle from Oakbourne: she had been taken ill, and did not want to frighten them by letting them know. But this frail fence of vague improbabilities was soon hurled down by a rush of distinct agonising fears. Hetty had been deceiving herself in thinking that she could love and marry him: she had been loving Arthur all the while: and now, in her desperation at the nearness of their marriage, she had run away. And she was gone to him. The old indignation and jealousy rose again, and prompted the suspicion that Arthur had been dealing falsely – had written to Hetty – had tempted her to come to him – being unwilling, after all, that she should belong to another man besides himself. Perhaps the whole thing had been contrived by him, and he had given her directions how to follow him to Ireland: for Adam knew that Arthur had been gone thither three weeks ago, having recently learnt it at the Chase. Every sad look of Hetty's, since she had been engaged to Adam, returned upon him now with all the exaggeration of painful retrospect. He had been foolishly sanguine and confident. The poor thing hadn't perhaps known her own mind for a long while; had thought that she could forget Arthur; had been momentarily drawn towards the man who offered her a protecting, faithful love. He couldn't bear to blame her: she never meant to cause him this dreadful pain. The blame lay with that man who had selfishly played with her heart – had perhaps even deliberately lured her away.

At Oakbourne, the ostler at the Royal Oak remembered such a young woman as Adam described getting out of the Treddleston coach more than a fortnight ago – wasn't likely to forget such a pretty lass as that in a hurry – was sure she had not gone on by the Buxton coach that went through Snowfield, but had lost sight of her while he went away with the horses, and had never set eyes on her again. Adam then went straight to the house from which the Stoniton coach started: Stoniton was the most obvious place for Hetty to go to first, whatever might be her destination, for she would hardly venture on any but the chief coach-roads. She had been noticed here too, and was remembered to have sat on the box by the coachman; but the coachman could not be seen, for another man had been driving on that road in his stead the last three or four days: he could probably be seen at Stoniton, through enquiry at the inn where the coach put up. So the anxious, heart-stricken Adam must of necessity wait and try to rest till morning – nay, till eleven o'clock, when the coach started.

At Stoniton another delay occurred, for the old coachman who had driven Hetty would not be in the town again till night. When he did come he remembered Hetty well, and remembered his own joke addressed to her, quoting it many times to Adam, and observing with equal frequency that he thought there was something more than common, because Hetty had not laughed when he joked her. But he declared, as the people had done at the inn, that he had lost sight of Hetty directly she got down. Part of the next morning was consumed in enquiries at every house in the town from which a coach started (all in vain; for you know Hetty did not start from Stoniton by coach, but on foot in the grey morning) and then in walking out to the first toll-gates on the different lines of road, in the forlorn hope of finding some recollection of her there. No, she was not to be traced any farther; and the next hard task for Adam was to go home, and carry the wretched tidings to the Hall Farm. As to what he should do beyond that, he had come to two distinct resolutions amidst the tumult of thought and feeling which was going on within him while he went to and fro. He would not mention what he knew of Arthur Donnithorne's behaviour to Hetty till there was a clear necessity for it: it was still possible Hetty might come back, and the disclosure might be an injury or an offence to her. And as soon as he had been home, and done what was necessary there to prepare for his further absence, he would start off to Ireland: if he found no trace of Hetty on the road, he would go straight to Arthur Donnithorne, and make himself certain how far he was acquainted with her movements. Several times the thought occurred to him that he would consult Mr Irwine; but that would be useless unless he told him all, and so betrayed the secret about Arthur. It seems strange that Adam, in the incessant occupation of his mind about Hetty, should never have alighted on the probability that she had gone to Windsor, ignorant that Arthur was no longer there. Perhaps the reason was, that he could not conceive Hetty's throwing herself on Arthur uncalled; he imagined no cause that could have driven her to such a step, after that letter written in August. There were but two alternatives in his mind: either Arthur had written to her again and enticed her away, or she had simply fled from her approaching marriage with himself, because she found, after all, she could not love him well enough, and yet was afraid of her friends' anger if she retracted.

With this last determination on his mind, of going straight to Arthur, the thought that he had spent two days in enquiries which had proved to be almost useless, was torturing to Adam; and yet, since he would not tell the Poysers his conviction as to where Hetty was gone, or his intention to follow her thither, he must be able to say to them that he had traced her as far as possible.

It was after twelve o'clock on Tuesday night when Adam reached Treddleston; and, unwilling to disturb his mother and Seth, and also to encounter their questions at that hour, he threw himself without undressing on a bed at the Waggon Overthrown, and slept hard from pure weariness. Not more than four hours, however; for before five o'clock he set out on his way home in the faint morning twilight. He always kept a key of the workshop door in his pocket, so that he could let himself in; and he wished to enter without awaking his mother, for he was anxious to avoid telling her the new trouble himself by seeing Seth first, and asking him to tell her when it should be necessary. He walked gently along the yard, and turned the key gently in the door; but, as he expected, Gyp, who lay in the workshop, gave a sharp bark. It subsided when he saw Adam, holding up his finger at him to impose silence; and in his dumb, tailless joy he must content himself with rubbing his body against his master's legs.

Adam was too heart-sick to take notice of Gyp's fondling. He threw himself on the bench, and stared dully at the wood and the signs of work around him, wondering if he should ever come to feel pleasure in them again; while Gyp, dimly aware that there was something wrong with his master, laid his rough grey head on Adam's knee, and wrinkled his brows to look up at him. Hitherto, since Sunday afternoon, Adam had been constantly among strange people and in strange places, having no associations with the details of his daily life; and now that by the light of this new morning he was come back to his home, and surrounded by the familiar objects that seemed for ever robbed of their charm, the reality – the hard, inevitable reality – of his troubles pressed upon him with a new weight. Right before him was an unfinished chest of drawers, which he had been making in spare moments for Hetty's use, when his home should be hers.

Seth had not heard Adam's entrance, but he had been roused by Gyp's bark, and Adam heard him moving about in the room above, dressing himself. Seth's first thoughts were about his brother: he would come home today, surely, for the business would be wanting him sadly by tomorrow, but it was pleasant to think he had had a longer holiday than he had expected. And would Dinah come too? Seth felt that that was the greatest happiness he could look forward to for himself, though he had no hope left that she would ever love him well enough to marry him; but he had often said to himself, it was better to be Dinah's friend and brother than any other woman's husband. If he could but be always near her, instead of living so far off!

He came downstairs and opened the inner door leading from the kitchen into the workshop, intending to let out Gyp; but he stood still in the doorway, smitten with a sudden shock at the sight of Adam seated listlessly on the bench, pale, unwashed, with sunken blank eyes, almost like a drunkard in the morning. But Seth felt in an instant what the marks meant: not drunkenness, but some great calamity. Adam looked up at him without speaking, and Seth moved forward towards the bench, himself trembling so that speech did not come readily.

'God have mercy on us, Addy,' he said, in a low voice, sitting down on the bench beside Adam, 'what is it?'

Adam was unable to speak: the strong man, accustomed to suppress the signs of sorrow, had felt his heart swell like a child's at this first approach of sympathy. He fell on Seth's neck and sobbed.

Seth was prepared for the worst now, for, even in his recollections of their boyhood, Adam had never sobbed before.

'Is it death, Adam? Is she dead?' he asked, in a low tone, when Adam raised his head and was recovering himself.

'No, lad; but she's gone – gone away from us. She's never been to Snowfield. Dinah's been gone to Leeds ever since last Friday was a fortnight, the very day Hetty set out. I can't find out where she went after she got to Stoniton.'

Seth was silent from utter astonishment: he knew nothing that could suggest to him a reason for Hetty's going away.

'Hast any notion what she's done it for?' he said, at last.

'She can't ha' loved me: she didn't like our marriage when it came nigh – that must be it,' said Adam. He had determined to mention no further reason.

'I hear mother stirring,' said Seth. 'Must we tell her?'

'No, not yet,' said Adam, rising from the bench, and pushing the hair from his face, as if he wanted to rouse himself.

'I can't have her told yet; and I must set out on another journey directly, after I've been to the village and th' Hall Farm. I can't tell thee where I'm going, and thee must say to her I'm gone on business as nobody is to know anything about. I'll go and wash myself now.' Adam moved towards the door of the workshop, but after a step or two he turned round, and, meeting Seth's eyes with a calm sad glance, he said, 'I must take all the money out o' the tin box, lad; but if anything happens to me, all the rest'll be thine, to take care o' mother with.'

Seth was pale and trembling: he felt there was some terrible secret under all this. 'Brother,' he said, faintly – he never called Adam 'brother' except in solemn moments – 'I don't believe you'll do anything as you can't ask God's blessing on.'

'Nay, lad,' said Adam, 'don't be afraid. I'm for doing nought but what's a man's duty.'

The thought that if he betrayed his trouble to his mother, she would only distress him by words, half of blundering affection, half of irrepressible triumph that Hetty proved as unfit to be his wife as she had always foreseen, brought back some of his habitual firmness and self-command. He had felt ill on his journey home – he told her when she came down – had stayed all night at Treddleston for that reason; and a bad headache, that still hung about him this morning, accounted for his paleness and heavy eyes.

He determined to go to the village, in the first place; attend to his business for an hour, and give notice to Burge of his being obliged to go on a journey, which he must beg him not to mention to anyone; for he wished to avoid going to the Hall Farm near breakfast-time, when the children and servants would be in the house-place, and there must be exclamations in their hearing about his having returned without Hetty. He waited until the clock struck nine before he left the work-yard at the village, and set off, through the fields towards the Farm. It was an immense relief to him, as he came near the Home Close, to see Mr Poyser advancing towards him, for this would spare him the pain of going to the house. Mr Poyser was walking briskly this March morning, with a sense of spring business on his mind: he was going to cast the master's eye on the shoeing of a new cart-horse, carrying his spud as a useful companion by the way. His surprise was great when he caught sight of Adam, but he was not a man given to presentiments of evil.

'Why, Adam, lad, is't you? Have ye been all this time away, and not brought the lasses back, after all? Where are they?'

'No, I've not brought 'em,' said Adam, turning round, to indicate that he wished to walk back with Mr Poyser.

'Why,' said Martin, looking with sharper attention at Adam, 'ye look bad. Is there anything happened?'

'Yes,' said Adam, heavily. 'A sad thing's happened. I didna find Hetty at Snowfield.'

Mr Poyser's good–natured face showed signs of troubled astonishment. 'Not find her? What's happened to her?' he said, his thoughts flying at once to bodily accident.

'That I can't tell, whether anything's happened to her. She never went to Snowfield – she took the coach to Stoniton, but I can't learn nothing of her after she got down from the Stoniton coach.'

'Why, you donna mean she's run away?' said Martin, standing still, so puzzled and bewildered that the fact did not yet make itself felt as a trouble by him.

'She must ha' done,' said Adam. 'She didn't like our marriage when it came to the point – that must be it. She'd mistook her feelings.'

Martin was silent for a minute or two, looking on the ground and rooting up the grass with his spud, without knowing what he was doing. His usual slowness was always trebled when the subject of speech was painful. At last he looked up, right in Adam's face, saying – 'Then she didna deserve t' ha' ye, my lad. An' I feel i' fault myself, for she was my niece, and I was allays hot for her marr'ing ye. There's no amends I can make ye, lad – the more's the pity: it's a sad cut-up for ye, I doubt.'

Adam could say nothing; and Mr Poyser, after pursuing his walk for a little while, went on: 'I'll be bound she's gone after trying to get a lady's-maid's place, for she'd got that in her head half a year ago, and wanted me to gi' my consent. But I'd thought better on her,' he added, shaking his head slowly and sadly – 'I'd thought better on her, nor to look for this, after she'd gi'en y' her word, an' everything been got ready.'

Adam had the strongest motives for encouraging this supposition in Mr Poyser, and he even tried to believe that it might possibly be true. He had no warrant for the certainty that she was gone to Arthur.

'It was better it should be so,' he said, as quietly as he could, 'if she felt she couldn't like me for a husband. Better run away before than repent after. I hope you won't look harshly on her if she comes back, as she may do if she finds it hard to get on away from home.'

'I canna look on her as I've done before,' said Martin decisively. 'She's acted bad by you, and by all of us. But I'll not turn my back on her: she's but a young un' and it's the first harm I've knowed on her. It'll be a hard job for me to tell her aunt. Why didna Dinah come back wi' ye? – she'd ha' helped to pacify her aunt a bit.'

'Dinah wasn't at Snowfield. She's been gone to Leeds this fortnight; and I couldn't learn from th' old woman any direction where she is at Leeds, else I should ha' brought it you.'

'She'd a deal better be staying wi' her own kin,' said Mr Poyser, indignantly, 'than going preaching among strange folks a-that'n.'

'I must leave you now Mr Poyser,' said Adam, 'for I've a deal to see to.'

'Ay, you'd best be after your business, and I must tell the missis when I go home. It's a hard job.'

'But,' said Adam, 'I beg particular, you'll keep what's happened quiet for a week or two. I've not told my mother yet, and there's no knowing how things may turn out.'

'Ay, ay; least said, soonest mended. We'n no need to say why the match is broke off, an' we may hear of her after a bit. Shake hands wi' me, lad: I wish I could make thee amends.'

There was something in Martin Poyser's throat at that moment which caused him to bring out those scanty words in rather a broken fashion. Yet Adam knew what they meant all the better; and the two honest men grasped each other's hard hands in mutual understanding.

There was nothing now to hinder Adam from setting off. He had told Seth to go to the Chase, and leave a message for the Squire, saying that Adam Bede had been obliged to start off suddenly on a journey – and to say as much, and no more, to anyone else who made enquiries about him. If the Poysers learned that he was gone away again, Adam knew they would infer that he was gone in search of Hetty.

He had intended to go right on his way from the Hall Farm; but now the impulse which had frequently visited him before – to go to Mr Irwine, and make a confidant of him – recurred with the new force which belongs to a last opportunity. He was about to start on a long journey – a difficult one – by sea – and no soul would know where he was gone. If anything happened to him? or, if he absolutely needed help in any matter concerning Hetty? Mr Irwine was to be trusted; and the feeling which made Adam shrink from telling anything which was *her* secret, must give way before the need there was that she should have someone else besides himself, who would be prepared to defend her in the worst extremity. Towards Arthur, even though he might have incurred no new guilt, Adam felt that he was not bound to keep silence when Hetty's interest called on him to speak.

'I must do it,' said Adam, when these thoughts, which had spread themselves through hours of his sad journeying, now rushed upon him in an instant, like a wave that had been slowly gathering; 'it's the right thing. I can't stand alone in this way any longer.'

39

The Tidings

Adam turned his face towards Broxton and walked with his swiftest stride, looking at his watch with the fear that Mr Irwine might be gone out – hunting, perhaps. The fear and haste together produced a state of strong excitement before he reached the Rectory gate; and outside it he saw the deep marks of a recent hoof on the gravel.

But the hoofs were turned towards the gate, not away from it; and though there was a horse against the stable door, it was not Mr Irwine's: it had evidently had a journey this morning, and must belong to someone who had come on business. Mr Irwine was at home, then; but Adam could hardly find breath and calmness to tell Carroll that he wanted to speak to the Rector. The double suffering of certain and uncertain sorrow had begun to shake the strong man. The butler looked at him wonderingly, as he threw himself on a bench in the passage and stared absently at the clock on the opposite wall: the master had somebody with him, he said, but he heard the study door open – the stranger seemed to be coming out, and as Adam was in a hurry, he would let the master know at once.

Adam sat looking at the clock: the minute-hand was hurrying along the last five minutes to ten, with a loud hard indifferent tick, and Adam watched the movement and listened to the sound as if he had had some reason for doing so. In our times of bitter suffering, there are almost always these pauses, when our consciousness is benumbed to everything but some trivial perception or sensation. It is as if semi-idiocy came to give us rest from the memory and the dread which refuse to leave us in our sleep.

Carroll, coming back, recalled Adam to the sense of his burthen. He was to go into the study immediately. 'I can't think what that strange person's come about,' the butler added, from mere incontinence of remark, as he preceded Adam to the door, 'he's gone i' the dining-room. And master looks unaccountable – as if he was frightened.' Adam took no notice of the words: he could not care about other people's business. But when he entered the study and looked in Mr Irwine's face, he felt in an instant that there was a new expression in it, strangely different from the warm friendliness it had always worn for him before. A letter lay open on the table, and Mr Irwine's hand was on it; but the changed glance he cast on Adam could not be owing entirely to preoccupation with some disagreeable business, for he was looking eagerly towards the door, as if Adam's entrance were a matter of poignant anxiety to him.

'You want to speak to me, Adam,' he said, in that low constrainedly quiet tone which a man uses when he is determined to suppress agitation. 'Sit down here.' He pointed to a chair just opposite to him, at no more than a yard's distance from his own, and Adam sat down with a sense that this cold manner of Mr Irwine's gave an additional unexpected difficulty to his disclosure. But when

Adam had made up his mind to a measure, he was not the man to renounce it for any but imperative reasons.

'I come to you, sir,' he said, 'as the gentleman I look up to most of anybody. I've something very painful to tell you – something as it'll pain you to hear, as well as me to tell. But if I speak o' the wrong other people have done, you'll see I didn't speak till I'd good reason.'

Mr Irwine nodded slowly, and Adam went on rather tremulously.

'You was t' ha' married me and Hetty Sorrel, you know, sir, o' the fifteenth o' this month. I thought she loved me, and I was th' happiest man i' the parish. But a dreadful blow's come upon me.'

Mr Irwine started up from his chair, as if involuntarily, but then, determined to control himself, walked to the window and looked out.

'She's gone away, sir, and we don't know where. She said she was going to Snowfield o' Friday was a fortnight – and I went last Sunday to fetch her back; but she'd never been there, and she took the coach to Stoniton, and beyond that I can't trace her. But now I'm going a long journey to look for her, and I can't trust t' anybody but you where I'm going.'

Mr Irwine came back from the window and sat down.

'Have you no idea of the reason why she went away?' he said.

'It's plain enough she didn't want to marry me, sir,' said Adam. 'She didn't like it when it came so near. But that isn't all, I doubt. There's something else I must tell you, sir. There's somebody else concerned besides me.'

A gleam of something – it was almost like relief or joy came across the eager anxiety of Mr Irwine's face at that moment. Adam was looking on the ground, and paused a little: the next words were hard to speak. But when he went on, he lifted up his head and looked straight at Mr Irwine. He would do the thing he had resolved to do, without flinching.

'You know who's the man I've reckoned my greatest friend,' he said, 'and used to be proud to think as I should pass my life i' working for him, and had felt so ever since we were lads.'

Mr Irwine, as if all self-control had forsaken him, grasped Adam's arm, which lay on the table, and, clutching it tightly like a man in pain, said, with pale lips and a low hurried voice – 'No, Adam, no – don't say it, for God's sake!'

Adam, surprised at the violence of Mr Irwine's feeling, repented of the words that had passed his lips, and sat in distressed silence. The grasp on his arm gradually relaxed, and Mr Irwine threw himself back in his chair, saying, 'Go on – I must know it.'

'That man played with Hetty's feelings, and behaved to her as he'd no right to do to a girl in her station o' life – made her presents, and used to go and meet her out a-walking: I found it out only two days before he went away – found him a-kissing her as they were parting in the Grove. There'd been nothing said between me and Hetty then, though I'd loved her for a long while, and she knew it. But I reproached him with his wrong actions, and words and blows passed between us; and he said solemnly to me, after that, as it had been all nonsense, and no more than a bit o' flirting. But I made him write a letter to tell Hetty he'd meant nothing; for I saw clear enough, sir, by several things as I hadn't understood at the time, as he'd got hold of her heart, and I thought she'd belike go on thinking of him, and never come to love another man as wanted to marry her. And I gave her the letter, and she seemed to bear it all after a while better than I'd expected . . . and she behaved kinder and kinder to me . . . I dare say she didn't know her own feelings then, poor thing, and they came back upon her when it was too late . . . I don't want to blame her . . . I can't think as she meant to deceive me. But I was encouraged to think she loved me, and – you know the rest, sir. But it's on my mind as he's been false to me, and 'ticed her away, and she's gone to him – and I'm going now to see; for I can never go to work again till I know what's become of her.'

During Adam's narrative, Mr Irwine had had time to recover his self-mastery in spite of the painful thoughts that crowded upon him. It was a bitter remembrance to him now – that morning when Arthur breakfasted with him, and seemed as if he were on the verge of a confession. It was plain enough now what he had wanted to confess. And if their words had taken another turn . . . if he himself had been less fastidious about intruding on another man's secrets . . . it was cruel to think how thin a film had shut out rescue from all this guilt and misery. He saw the whole history now by that terrible illumination which the present sheds back upon the past. But every other feeling as it rushed upon him was thrown into abeyance by pity, deep respectful pity, for the man who sat before him – already so bruised, going forth with sad blind resignedness to an unreal sorrow, while a real one was close upon him, too far beyond the range of common trial for him ever to have feared it. His own agitation was quelled by a certain awe that comes over us in the presence of a great anguish; for the anguish he must inflict on Adam was already present to him. Again he put his hand on the arm that lay on the table, but very gently this time, as he said solemnly – 'Adam, my dear friend, you have had some hard trials in your life. You can bear sorrow manfully, as well as act manfully: God requires both tasks at our hands. And there is a heavier sorrow coming upon you than any you have yet known. But you are not guilty – you have not the worst of all sorrows. God help him who has!'

The two pale faces looked at each other; in Adam's there was trembling suspense, in Mr Irwine's hesitating, shrinking pity. But he went on.

'I have had news of Hetty this morning. She is not gone to him. She is in Stonyshire – at Stoniton.'

Adam started up from his chair, as if he thought he could have leaped to her that moment. But Mr Irwine laid hold of his arm again, and said, persuasively, 'Wait, Adam, wait,' so he sat down.

'She is in a very unhappy position – one which will make it worse for you to find her, my poor friend, than to have lost her for ever.'

Adam's lips moved tremulously, but no sound came. They moved again, and he whispered, 'Tell me.'

'She has been arrested . . . she is in prison.'

It was as if an insulting blow had brought back the spirit of resistance into Adam. The blood rushed to his face, and he said, loudly and sharply – 'For what?'

'For a great crime – the murder of her child.'

'It *can't be!*' Adam almost shouted, starting up from his chair, and making a stride towards the door; but he turned round again, setting his back against the bookcase, and looking fiercely at Mr Irwine. 'It isn't possible. She never had a child. She can't be guilty. *Who* says it?'

'God grant she may be innocent, Adam. We can still hope she is.'

'But who says she is guilty?' said Adam, violently. 'Tell me everything.'

'Here is a letter from the magistrate before whom she was taken, and the constable who arrested her is in the dining-room. She will not confess her name or where she comes from; but I fear, I fear, there can be no doubt it is Hetty. The description of her person corresponds, only that she is said to look very pale and ill. She had a small red-leather pocket-book in her pocket with two names written in it – one at the beginning, 'Hetty Sorrel, Hayslope' and the other near the end, ' Dinah Morris, Snowfield.' She will not say which is her own name – she denies everything and will answer no questions; and application has been made to me, as a magistrate, that I may take measures for identifying her, for it was thought probable that the name which stands first is her own name.'

'But what proof have they got against her, if it *is* Hetty?' said Adam, still violently, with an effort that seemed to shake his whole frame. 'I'll not believe it. It couldn't ha' been and none of us know it.'

'Terrible proof that she was under the temptation to commit the crime; but we have room to hope that she did not really commit it. Try and read that letter, Adam.'

Adam took the letter between his shaking hands, and tried to fix his eyes steadily on it. Mr Irwine meanwhile went out to give some orders. When he came back, Adam's eyes were still on the first page – he couldn't read – he could not put the words together, and make out what they meant. He threw it down at last, and clenched his fist.

'It's *his* doing,' he said; 'if there's been any crime, it's at his door, not at hers. *He* taught her to deceive – *he* deceived me first. Let 'em put *him* on his trial – let him stand in court beside her, and I'll tell 'em how he got hold of her heart, and 'ticed her t' evil, and then lied to me. Is *he* to go free, while they lay all the punishment on her . . . So weak and young?'

The image called up by these last words gave a new direction to poor Adam's maddened feelings. He was silent, looking at the corner of the room as if he saw something there. Then he burst out again, in a tone of appealing anguish – 'I *can't* bear it . . . O God, it's too hard to lay upon me – it's too hard to think she's wicked.'

Mr Irwine had sat down again in silence: he was too wise to utter soothing words at present, and indeed the sight of Adam before him, with that look of sudden age which sometimes comes over a young face in moments of terrible emotion – the hard bloodless look of the skin, the deep lines about the quivering mouth, the furrows in the brow – the sight of this strong firm man shattered by the invisible stroke of sorrow, moved him so deeply that speech was not easy. Adam stood motionless, with his eyes vacantly fixed in this way for a minute or two; in that short space he was living through all his love again.

'She can't ha' done it,' he said, still without moving his eyes, as if he were only talking to himself: 'it was fear made her hide it . . . I forgive her for deceiving me . . . I forgive thee, Hetty . . . thee wast deceived too . . . it's gone hard wi' thee, my poor Hetty . . . but they'll never make me believe it.'

He was silent again for a few moments, and then he said, with fierce abruptness – 'I'll go to him – I'll bring him back – I'll make him go and look at her in her misery – he shall look at her till he can't forget it – it shall follow him night and day – as long as he lives it shall follow him – he shan't escape wi' lies this time – I'll fetch him, I'll drag him myself.'

In the act of going towards the door, Adam paused automatically and looked about for his hat, quite unconscious where he was, or who was present with him. Mr Irwine had followed him, and now took him by the arm, saying, in a quiet but decided tone – 'No, Adam, no; I'm sure you will wish to stay and see what good can be done for *her*, instead of going on a useless errand of vengeance. The punishment will surely fall without your aid. Besides, he is no longer in Ireland: he must be on his way home – or would be, long before you arrived; for his grandfather, I know, wrote for him to come at least ten days ago. I want you now to go with me to Stoniton. I have ordered a horse for you to ride with us, as soon as you can compose yourself.'

While Mr Irwine was speaking, Adam recovered his consciousness of the actual scene: he rubbed his hair off his forehead and listened.

'Remember,' Mr Irwine went on, 'there are others to think of, and act for, besides yourself, Adam: there are Hetty's friends, the good Poysers, on whom this stroke will fall more heavily than I can bear to think. I expect it from your strength of mind, Adam – from your sense of duty to God and man – that you will try to act as long as action can be of any use.'

In reality, Mr Irwine proposed this journey to Stoniton for Adam's own sake. Movement, with some object before him, was the best means of counteracting the violence of suffering in these first hours.

'You will go with me to Stoniton, Adam?' he said again, after a moment's pause. 'We have to see if it is really Hetty who is there, you know.'

'Yes, sir,' said Adam, 'I'll do what you think right. But the folks at th' Hall Farm?'

'I wish them not to know till I return to tell them myself. I shall have ascertained things then which I am uncertain about now, and I shall return as soon as possible. Come now, the horses are ready.'

40

The Bitter Waters Spread

Mr Irwine returned from Stoniton in a post-chaise that night, and the first words Carroll said to him, as he entered the house, were, that Squire Donnithorne was dead – found dead in his bed at ten o'clock that morning – and that Mrs Irwine desired him to say she should be awake when Mr Irwine came home, and she begged him not to go to bed without seeing her.

'Well, Dauphin,' Mrs Irwine said, as her son entered her room, 'you're come at last. So the old gentleman's fidgetiness and low spirits, which made him send for Arthur in that sudden way, really meant something. I suppose Carroll has told you that Donnithorne was found dead in his bed this morning. You will believe my prognostications another time, though I dare say I shan't live to prognosticate anything but my own death.'

'What have they done about Arthur?' said Mr Irwine. 'Sent a messenger to await him at Liverpool?'

'Yes, Ralph was gone before the news was brought to us. Dear Arthur, I shall live now to see him master at the Chase, and making good times on the estate, like a generous-hearted fellow as he is. He'll be as happy as a king now.'

Mr Irwine could not help giving a slight groan: he was worn with anxiety and exertion, and his mother's light words were almost intolerable.

'What are you so dismal about, Dauphin? Is there any bad news? Or are you thinking of the danger for Arthur in crossing that frightful Irish Channel at this time of year?'

'No, mother, I'm not thinking of that; but I'm not prepared to rejoice just now.'

'You've been worried by this law business that you've been to Stoniton about. What in the world is it, that you can't tell me?'

'You will know by and by, mother. It would not be right for me to tell you at present. Good-night: you'll sleep now you have no longer anything to listen for.'

Mr Irwine gave up his intention of sending a letter to meet Arthur, since it would not now hasten his return: the news of his grandfather's death would bring him as soon as he could possibly come. He could go to bed now and get some needful rest, before the time came for the morning's heavy duty of carrying his sickening news to the Hall Farm and to Adam's home.

Adam himself was not come back from Stoniton, for though he shrank from seeing Hetty, he could not bear to go to a distance from her again.

'It's no use, sir,' he said to the Rector – 'it's no use for me to go back. I can't go to work again while she's here; and I couldn't bear the sight o' the things and folks round home. I'll take a bit of a room here, where I can see the prison walls, and perhaps I shall get, in time, to bear seeing *her*.'

Adam had not been shaken in his belief that Hetty was innocent of the crime she was charged with, for Mr Irwine, feeling that the belief in her guilt would be a crushing addition to Adam's load, had kept from him the facts which left no hope in his own mind. There was not any reason for thrusting the whole burthen on Adam at once, and Mr Irwine, at parting, only said, 'If the evidence should tell too strongly against her, Adam, we may still hope for a pardon. Her youth and other circumstances will be a plea for her.'

'Ah, and it's right people should know how she was tempted into the wrong way,' said Adam, with bitter earnestness. 'It's right they should know it was a fine gentleman made love to her, and turned her head wi' notions. You'll remember, sir, you've promised to tell my mother, and Seth, and the people at the Farm, who it was as led her wrong, else they'll think harder of her than she deserves. You'll be doing her a hurt by sparing him, and I hold him the guiltiest before God, let her ha' done what she may. If you spare him, I'll expose him!'

'I think your demand is just, Adam,' said Mr Irwine, 'but when you are calmer, you will judge Arthur more mercifully. I say nothing now, only that his punishment is in other hands than ours.'

Mr Irwine felt it hard upon him that he should have to tell of Arthur's sad part in the story of sin and sorrow – he who cared for Arthur with fatherly affection – who had cared for him with fatherly pride. But he saw clearly that the secret must be known before long, even apart from Adam's determination, since it was scarcely to be supposed that Hetty would persist to the end in her obstinate silence. He made up his mind to withhold nothing from the Poysers, but to tell them the worst at once, for there was no time to rob the tidings of their suddenness. Hetty's trial must come on at the Lent assizes, and they were to be held at Stoniton the next week. It was scarcely to be hoped that Martin Poyser could escape the pain of being called as a witness, and it was better he should know everything as long beforehand as possible.

Before ten o'clock on Thursday morning the home at the Hall Farm was a house of mourning for a misfortune felt to be worse than death. The sense of family dishonour was too keen even in the kind-hearted Martin Poyser the younger, to leave room for any compassion towards Hetty. He and his father were simple-minded farmers, proud of their untarnished character, proud that they came of a family which had held up its head and paid its way as far back as its name was in the parish register; and Hetty had brought disgrace on them all – disgrace that could never be wiped out. That was the all-conquering feeling in the mind both of father and son – the scorching sense of disgrace, which neutralised all other sensibility; and Mr Irwine was struck with surprise to observe that Mrs Poyser was less severe than her husband. We are often startled by the severity of mild people on exceptional occasions; the reason is, that mild people are most liable to be under the yoke of traditional impressions.

'I'm willing to pay any money as is wanted towards trying to bring her off,' said Martin the younger when Mr Irwine was gone, while the old grandfather was crying in the opposite chair, 'but I'll not go nigh her, nor ever see her again, by my own will. She's made our bread bitter to us, for all our lives to come, an' we shall ne'er hold up our heads i' this parish nor i' any other. The parson talks o' folks pitying us; it's poor amends pity 'ull make us.'

'Pity?' said the grandfather, sharply. 'I ne'er wanted folks's pity i' my life afore . . . an' I mun begin to be looked down on now, an' me turned seventy-two last St Thomas's, an' all th' under-bearers and pallbearers as I'n picked for my funeral are i' this parish and the next to't . . . It's o' no use now . . . I mun be ta'en to the grave by strangers.'

'Don't fret so, father,' said Mrs Poyser, who had spoken very little, being almost overawed by her husband's unusual hardness and decision. 'You'll have your children wi' you; an' there's the lads and the little un 'ull grow up in a new parish as well as i' th' old un.'

'Ah, there's no staying i' this country for us now,' said Mr Poyser, and the hard tears trickled slowly down his round cheeks. 'We thought it 'ud be bad luck if the old Squire gave us notice this Lady Day, but I must gi' notice myself now, an' see if there can anybody be got to come an' take to the crops as I'n put i' the ground; for I wonna stay upo' that man's land a day longer nor I'm forced to't.

An' me as thought him such a good upright young man, as I should be glad when
he come to be our landlord. I'll ne'er lift my hat to him again, nor sit i' the same
church wi' him . . . a man as has brought shame on respectable folks . . . an'
pretended to be such a friend t' everybody. . . Poor Adam there . . . a fine friend
he's been t' Adam, making speeches an' talking so fine, an' all the while poisoning
the lad's life, as it's much if he can stay i' this country any more nor we can.'

'An' you t' ha' to go into court, and own you're akin t' her,' said the old man.
'Why, they'll cast it up to the little un' as isn't four 'ear old, someday – they'll
cast it up t' her as she'd a cousin tried at the 'sizes for murder.'

'It'll be their own wickedness, then,' said Mrs Poyser, with a sob in her voice.
'But there's One above 'ull take care o' the innicent child, else it's but little truth
they tell us at church. It'll be harder nor ever to die an' leave the little uns, an'
nobody to be a mother to 'em.'

'We'd better ha' sent for Dinah, if we'd known where she is,' said Mr Poyser;
'but Adam said she'd left no direction where she'd be at Leeds.'

'Why, she'd be wi' that woman as was a friend t' her aunt Judith,' said Mrs
Poyser, comforted a little by this suggestion of her husband's. 'I've often heard
Dinah talk of her, but I can't remember what name she called her by. But there's
Seth Bede; he's like enough to know, for she's a preaching woman as the
Methodists think a deal on.'

'I'll send to Seth,' said Mr Poyser. 'I'll send Alick to tell him to come, or else to
send us word o' the woman's name, an' thee canst write a letter ready to send off
to Treddles'on as soon as we can make out a direction.'

'It's poor work writing letters when you want folks to come to you i' trouble,'
said Mrs Poyser. 'Happen it'll be ever so long on the road, an' never reach her
at last.'

Before Alick arrived with the message, Lisbeth's thoughts too had already
flown to Dinah, and she had said to Seth – 'Eh, there's no comfort for us i' this
world any more, wi'out thee couldst get Dinah Morris to come to us, as she did
when my old man died. I'd like her to come in an' take me by th' hand again, an'
talk to me: she'd tell me the rights on't, belike – she'd happen know some good i'
all this trouble an' heartbreak comin' upo' that poor lad, as ne'er done a bit o'
wrong in's life, but war better nor anybody else's son, pick the country round.
Eh, my lad . . . Adam, my poor lad!'

'Thee wouldstna like me to leave thee, to go and fetch Dinah?' said Seth, as
his mother sobbed, and rocked herself to and fro.

'Fetch her?' said Lisbeth, looking up, and pausing from her grief, like a crying
child, who hears some promise of consolation. 'Why, what place is't she's at, do
they say?'

'It's a good way off, mother – Leeds, a big town. But I could be back in three
days, if thee couldst spare me.'

'Nay, nay, I canna spare thee. Thee must go an' see thy brother, an' bring me
word what he's a-doin'. Mester Irwine said he'd come an' tell me, but I canna
make out so well what it means when he tells me. Thee must go thysen, sin'
Adam wonna let me go to him. Write a letter to Dinah, canstna? Thee't fond
enough o' writin' when nobody wants thee.'

'I'm not sure where she'd be i' that big town,' said Seth. 'If I'd gone myself, I could ha' found out by asking the members o' the society. But perhaps, if I put Sarah Williamson, Methodist preacher, Leeds, o' th' outside, it might get to her; for most like she'd be wi' Sarah Williamson.'

Alick came now with the message, and Seth, finding that Mrs Poyser was writing to Dinah, gave up the intention of writing himself; but he went to the Hall Farm to tell them all he could suggest about the address of the letter, and warn them that there might be some delay in the delivery, from his not knowing an exact direction.

On leaving Lisbeth, Mr Irwine had gone to Jonathan Burge, who had also a claim to be acquainted with what was likely to keep Adam away from business for some time; and before six o'clock that evening there were few people in Broxton and Hayslope who had not heard the sad news. Mr Irwine had not mentioned Arthur's name to Burge, and yet the story of his conduct towards Hetty, with all the dark shadows cast upon it by its terrible consequences, was presently as well known as that his grandfather was dead, and that he was come into the estate. For Martin Poyser felt no motive to keep silence towards the one or two neighbours who ventured to come and shake him sorrowfully by the hand on the first day of his trouble; and Carroll, who kept his ears open to all that passed at the Rectory, had framed an inferential version of the story, and found early opportunities of communicating it.

One of those neighbours who came to Martin Poyser and shook him by the hand without speaking for some minutes, was Bartle Massey. He had shut up his school, and was on his way to the Rectory, where he arrived about half-past seven in the evening, and, sending his duty to Mr Irwine, begged pardon for troubling him at that hour, but had something particular on his mind. He was shown into the study, where Mr Irwine soon joined him.

'Well, Bartle?' said Mr Irwine, putting out his hand. That was not his usual way of saluting the schoolmaster, but trouble makes us treat all who feel with us very much alike. 'Sit down.'

'You know what I'm come about as well as I do, sir, I dare say,' said Bartle.

'You wish to know the truth about the sad news that has reached you . . . about Hetty Sorrel?'

'Nay, sir, what I wish to know is about Adam Bede. I understand you left him at Stoniton, and I beg the favour of you to tell me what's the state of the poor lad's mind, and what he means to do. For as for that bit o' pink-and-white they've taken the trouble to put in jail, I don't value her a rotten nut – not a rotten nut – only for the harm or good that may come out of her to an honest man – a lad I've set such store by – trusted to, that he'd make my bit o' knowledge go a good way in the world . . . Why, sir, he's the only scholar I've had in this stupid country that ever had the will or the headpiece for mathematics. If he hadn't had so much hard work to do, poor fellow, he might have gone into the higher branches, and then this might never have happened – might never have happened.'

Bartle was heated by the exertion of walking fast in an agitated frame of mind, and was not able to check himself on this first occasion of venting his feelings. But he paused now to rub his moist forehead, and probably his moist eyes also.

'You'll excuse me, sir,' he said, when this pause had given him time to reflect, 'for running on in this way about my own feelings, like that foolish dog of mine, howling in a storm, when there's nobody wants to listen to me. I came to hear you speak, not to talk myself; if you'll take the trouble to tell me what the poor lad's doing.'

'Don't put yourself under any restraint, Bartle,' said Mr Irwine. 'The fact is, I'm very much in the same condition as you just now; I've a great deal that's painful on my mind, and I find it hard work to be quite silent about my own feelings and only attend to others. I share your concern for Adam, though he is not the only one whose sufferings I care for in this affair. He intends to remain at Stoniton till after the trial: it will come on probably a week tomorrow. He has taken a room there, and I encouraged him to do so, because I think it better he should be away from his own home at present; and, poor fellow, he still believes Hetty is innocent – he wants to summon up courage to see her if he can; he is unwilling to leave the spot where she is.'

'Do you think the creatur's guilty, then?' said Bartle. 'Do you think they'll hang her?'

'I'm afraid it will go hard with her: the evidence is very strong. And one bad symptom is that she denies everything – denies that she has had a child, in the face of the most positive evidence. I saw her myself, and she was obstinately silent to me; she shrank up like a frightened animal when she saw me. I was never so shocked in my life as at the change in her. But I trust that, in the worst case, we may obtain a pardon for the sake of the innocent who are involved.'

'Stuff and nonsense!' said Bartle, forgetting in his irritation to whom he was speaking – 'I beg your pardon, sir, I mean it's stuff and nonsense for the innocent to care about her being hanged. For my own part, I think the sooner such women are put out o' the world the better; and the men that help 'em to do mischief had better go along with 'em for that matter. What good will you do by keeping such vermin alive? eating the victual that 'ud feed rational beings. But if Adam's fool enough to care about it, I don't want him to suffer more than's needful . . . Is he very much cut up, poor fellow?' Bartle added, taking out his spectacles and putting them on, as if they would assist his imagination.

'Yes, I'm afraid the grief cuts very deep,' said Mr Irwine. 'He looks terribly shattered, and a certain violence came over him now and then yesterday, which made me wish I could have remained near him. But I shall go to Stoniton again tomorrow, and I have confidence enough in the strength of Adam's principle to trust that he will be able to endure the worst without being driven to anything rash.'

Mr Irwine, who was involuntarily uttering his own thoughts rather than addressing Bartle Massey in the last sentence, had in his mind the possibility that the spirit of vengeance towards Arthur, which was the form Adam's anguish was continually taking, might make him seek an encounter that was likely to end more fatally than the one in the Grove. This possibility heightened the anxiety with which he looked forward to Arthur's arrival. But Bartle thought Mr Irwine was referring to suicide, and his face wore a new alarm.

'I'll tell you what I have in my head, sir,' he said, 'and I hope you'll approve of it. I'm going to shut up my school: if the scholars come, they must go back again, that's all: and I shall go to Stoniton and look after Adam till this business is over. I'll pretend I'm come to look on at the assizes; he can't object to that. What do you think about it, sir?'

'Well,' said Mr Irwine, rather hesitatingly, 'there would be some real advantages in that ... and I honour you for your friendship towards him, Bartle. But ... you must be careful what you say to him, you know. I'm afraid you have too little fellow-feeling in what you consider his weakness about Hetty.'

'Trust to me, sir – trust to me. I know what you mean. I've been a fool myself in my time, but that's between you and me. I shan't thrust myself on him – only keep my eye on him, and see that he gets some good food, and put in a word here and there.'

'Then,' said Mr Irwine, reassured a little as to Bartle's discretion, 'I think you'll be doing a good deed; and it will be well for you to let Adam's mother and brother know that you're going.'

'Yes, sir, yes,' said Bartle, rising, and taking off his spectacles, 'I'll do that, I'll do that; though the mother's a whimpering thing – I don't like to come within earshot of her; however, she's a straight-backed, clean woman, none of your slatterns. I wish you Goodbye, sir, and thank you for the time you've spared me. You're everybody's friend in this business – everybody's friend. It's a heavy weight you've got on your shoulders.'

'Goodbye, Bartle, till we meet at Stoniton, as I dare say we shall.'

Bartle hurried away from the Rectory, evading Carroll's conversational advances, and saying in an exasperated tone to Vixen, whose short legs pattered beside him on the gravel – 'Now, I shall be obliged to take you with me, you good-for-nothing woman. You'd go fretting yourself to death if I left you – you know you would, and perhaps get snapped up by some tramp; and you'll be running into bad company, I expect, putting your nose in every hole and corner where you've no business! but if you do anything disgraceful, I'll disown you – mind that, madam, mind that!'

41

The Eve of the Trial

An upper room in a dull Stoniton street, with two beds in it – one laid on the floor. It is ten o'clock on Thursday night, and the dark wall opposite the window shuts out the moonlight that might have struggled with the light of the one dip candle by which Bartle Massey is pretending to read, while he is really looking over his spectacles at Adam Bede, seated near the dark window.

You would hardly have known it was Adam without being told. His face has got thinner this last week: he has the sunken eyes, the neglected beard of a man just risen from a sick-bed. His heavy black hair hangs over his forehead, and there is no active impulse in him which inclines him to push it off, that he may be more awake to what is around him. He has one arm over the back of the chair, and he seems to be looking down at his clasped hands. He is roused by a knock at the door.

'There he is,' said Bartle Massey, rising hastily and unfastening the door. It was Mr Irwine.

Adam rose from his chair with instinctive respect, as Mr Irwine approached him and took his hand.

'I'm late, Adam,' he said, sitting down on the chair which Bartle placed for him; 'but I was later in setting off from Broxton than I intended to be, and I have been incessantly occupied since I arrived. I have done everything now, however – everything that can be done tonight, at least. Let us all sit down.'

Adam took his chair again mechanically, and Bartle, for whom there was no chair remaining, sat on the bed in the background.

'Have you seen her, sir?' said Adam, tremulously.

'Yes, Adam; I and the chaplain have both been with her this evening.'

'Did you ask her, sir . . . did you say anything about me?'

'Yes,' said Mr Irwine, with some hesitation, 'I spoke of you. I said you wished to see her before the trial, if she consented.'

As Mr Irwine paused, Adam looked at him with eager, questioning eyes.

'You know she shrinks from seeing anyone, Adam. It is not only you – some fatal influence seems to have shut up her heart against her fellow-creatures. She has scarcely said anything more than "No," either to me or the chaplain. Three or four days ago, before you were mentioned to her, when I asked her if there was anyone of her family whom she would like to see – to whom she could open her mind, she said, with a violent shudder, "Tell them not to come near me – I won't see any of them." '

Adam's head was hanging down again, and he did not speak. There was silence for a few minutes, and then Mr Irwine said – 'I don't like to advise you against your own feelings, Adam, if they now urge you strongly to go and see her tomorrow morning, even without her consent. It is just possible, notwithstanding appearances to the contrary, that the interview might affect her favourably. But I grieve to say I have scarcely any hope of that. She didn't seem agitated when I mentioned your name; she only said "No," in the same cold, obstinate way as usual. And if the meeting had no good effect on her, it would be pure, useless suffering to you – severe suffering, I fear. She is very much changed . . .'

Adam started up from his chair, and seized his hat which lay on the table. But he stood still then, and looked at Mr Irwine, as if he had a question to ask, which it was yet difficult to utter. Bartle Massey rose quietly, turned the key in the door, and put it in his pocket.

'Is he come back?' said Adam at last.

'No, he is not,' said Mr Irwine, quietly. 'Lay down your hat, Adam, unless you like to walk out with me for a little fresh air. I fear you have not been out again today.'

'You needn't deceive me, sir,' said Adam, looking hard at Mr Irwine, and speaking in a tone of angry suspicion. 'You needn't be afraid of me. I only want justice. I want him to feel what she feels. It's his work . . . She was a child as it 'ud ha' gone t' anybody's heart to look at . . . I don't care what she's done . . . it was him brought her to it. And he shall know it . . . he shall feel it . . . if there's a just God, he shall feel what it is t' ha' brought a child like her to sin and misery.'

'I'm not deceiving you, Adam,' said Mr Irwine. 'Arthur Donnithorne is not come back – was not come back when I left. I have left a letter for him: he will know all as soon as he arrives.'

'But you don't mind about it,' said Adam, indignantly. 'You think it doesn't matter as she lies there in shame and misery, and he knows nothing about it – he suffers nothing.'

'Adam, he will know – he will suffer, long and bitterly. He has a heart and a conscience: I can't be entirely deceived in his character. I am convinced – I am sure he didn't fall under temptation without a struggle. He may be weak, but he is not callous, not coldly selfish. I am persuaded that this will be a shock of which he will feel the effects all his life. Why do you crave vengeance in this way? No amount of torture that you could inflict on him could benefit her.'

'No–o God, no,' Adam groaned out, sinking on his chair again; 'but then, that's the deepest curse of all . . . that's what makes the blackness of it . . . *it can never be undone*. My poor Hetty . . . she can never be my sweet Hetty again . . . the prettiest thing God had made – smiling up at me . . . I thought she loved me . . . and was good . . .'

Adam's voice had been gradually sinking into a hoarse undertone, as if he were only talking to himself; but now he said abruptly, looking at Mr Irwine – 'But she isn't as guilty as they say? You don't think she is, sir? She can't ha' done it.'

'That perhaps can never be known with certainty, Adam,' Mr Irwine answered, gently. 'In these cases we sometimes form our judgement on what seems to us strong evidence, and yet, for want of knowing some small fact, our judgement is wrong. But suppose the worst: you have no right to say that the guilt of her crime lies with him, and that he ought to bear the punishment. It is not for us men to apportion the shares of moral guilt and retribution. We find it impossible to avoid mistakes even in determining who has committed a single criminal act, and the problem how far a man is to be held responsible for the unforeseen consequences of his own deed, is one that might well make us tremble to look into it. The evil consequences that may lie folded in a single act of selfish indulgence, is a thought so awful that it ought surely to awaken some feeling less presumptuous than a rash desire to punish. You have a mind that can understand this fully, Adam, when you are calm. Don't suppose I can't enter into the anguish that drives you into this state of revengeful hatred; but think of this: if you were to obey your passion – for it is passion, and you deceive yourself in calling it justice – it might be with you precisely as it has been with Arthur; nay, worse; your passion might lead you yourself into a horrible crime.'

'No, not worse,' said Adam, bitterly; 'I don't believe it's worse – I'd sooner do it – I'd sooner do a wickedness as I could suffer for by myself, than ha' brought her to do wickedness and then stand by and see 'em punish her while they let me alone; and all for a bit o' pleasure, as, if he'd had a man's heart in him, he'd ha' cut his hand off sooner than he'd ha' taken it. What if he didn't foresee what's happened? He foresaw enough: he'd no right to expect anything but harm and shame to her. And then he wanted to smooth it off wi' lies. No – there's plenty o' things folks are hanged for, not half so hateful as that: let a man do what he will, if he knows he's to bear the punishment himself, he isn't half so bad as a mean selfish coward as makes things easy t' himself, and knows all the while the punishment 'ull fall on somebody else.'

'There again you partly deceive yourself, Adam. There is no sort of wrong deed of which a man can bear the punishment alone; you can't isolate yourself, and say that the evil which is in you shall not spread. Men's lives are as thoroughly blended with each other as the air they breathe: evil spreads as necessarily as disease. I know, I feel the terrible extent of suffering this sin of Arthur's has caused to others; but so does every sin cause suffering to others besides those who commit it. An act of vengeance on your part against Arthur would simply be another evil added to those we are suffering under: you could not bear the punishment alone; you would entail the worst sorrows on every one who loves you. You would have committed an act of blind fury, that would leave all the present evils just as they were, and add worse evils to them. You may tell me that you meditate no fatal act of vengeance: but the feeling in your mind is what gives birth to such actions, and as long as you indulge it, as long as you do not see that to fix your mind on Arthur's punishment is revenge, and not justice, you are in danger of being led on to the commission of some great wrong. Remember what you told me about your feelings after you had given that blow to Arthur in the Grove.'

Adam was silent: the last words had called up a vivid image of the past, and Mr Irwine left him to his thoughts, while he spoke to Bartle Massey about old Mr Donnithorne's funeral and other matters of an indifferent kind. But at length Adam turned round and said, in a more subdued tone – 'I've not asked about 'em at th' Hall Farm, sir. Is Mr Poyser coming?'

'He is come; he is in Stoniton tonight. But I could not advise him to see you, Adam. His own mind is in a very perturbed state, and it is best he should not see you till you are calmer.'

'Is Dinah Morris come to 'em, sir? Seth said they'd sent for her.'

'No. Mr Poyser tells me she was not come when he left. They're afraid the letter has not reached her. It seems they had no exact address.'

Adam sat ruminating a little while, and then said – 'I wonder if Dinah 'ud ha' gone to see her. But perhaps the Poysers would ha' been sorely against it, since they won't come nigh her themselves. But I think she would, for the Methodists are great folks for going into the prisons; and Seth said he thought she would. She'd a very tender way with her, Dinah had; I wonder if she could ha' done any good. You never saw her, sir, did you?'

'Yes, I did: I had a conversation with her – she pleased me a good deal. And now you mention it, I wish she would come; for it is possible that a gentle, mild woman like her might move Hetty to open her heart. The jail chaplain is rather harsh in his manner.'

'But it's o' no use if she doesn't come,' said Adam, sadly.

'If I'd thought of it earlier, I would have taken some measures for finding her out,' said Mr Irwine, 'but it's too late now, I fear . . . Well, Adam, I must go now. Try to get some rest tonight. God bless you. I'll see you early tomorrow morning.'

42

The Morning of the Trial

At one o'clock the next day, Adam was alone in his dull upper room; his watch lay before him on the table, as if he were counting the long minutes. He had no knowledge of what was likely to be said by the witnesses on the trial, for he had shrunk from all the particulars connected with Hetty's arrest and accusation. This brave active man, who would have hastened towards any danger or toil to rescue Hetty from an apprehended wrong or misfortune, felt himself powerless to contemplate irremediable evil and suffering. The susceptibility which would have been an impelling force where there was any possibility of action, became helpless anguish when he was obliged to be passive, or else sought an active outlet in the thought of inflicting justice on Arthur. Energetic natures, strong for all strenuous deeds, will often rush away from a hopeless sufferer, as if they were hard-hearted. It is the overmastering sense of pain that drives them. They shrink by an ungovernable instinct, as they would shrink from laceration. Adam had brought himself to think of seeing Hetty, if she would consent to see him, because he thought the meeting might possibly be a good to her – might help to melt away this terrible hardness they told him of. If she saw he bore her no ill-will for what she had done to him, she might open her heart to him. But this resolution had been an immense effort; he trembled at the thought of seeing her changed face, as a timid woman trembles at the thought of the surgeon's knife; and he chose now to bear the long hours of suspense, rather than encounter what seemed to him the more intolerable agony of witnessing her trial.

Deep, unspeakable suffering may well be called a baptism, a regeneration, the initiation into a new state. The yearning memories, the bitter regret, the agonised sympathy, the struggling appeals to the Invisible Right – all the intense emotions which had filled the days and nights of the past week, and were compressing themselves again like an eager crowd into the hours of this single morning, made Adam look back on all the previous years as if they had been a dim sleepy existence, and he had only now awaked to full consciousness. It seemed to him as if he had always before thought it a light thing that men should suffer; as if all that he had himself endured and called sorrow before, was only a moment's stroke that had never left a bruise. Doubtless a great anguish may do the work of years, and we may come out from that baptism of fire with a soul full of new awe and new pity.

'O God,' Adam groaned, as he leaned on the table, and looked blankly at the face of the watch, 'and men have suffered like this before . . . and poor helpless young things have suffered like her . . . Such a little while ago looking so happy and so pretty . . . kissing 'em all, her grandfather and all of 'em, and they wishing her luck . . . Oh my poor, poor Hetty . . . dost think on it now?'

Adam started and looked round towards the door. Vixen had begun to whimper, and there was a sound of a stick and a lame walk on the stairs. It was Bartle Massey come back. Could it be all over?

Bartle entered quietly, and, going up to Adam, grasped his hand and said, 'I'm just come to look at you, my boy, for the folks are gone out of court for a bit.'

Adam's heart beat so violently, he was unable to speak – he could only return the pressure of his friend's hand; and Bartle, drawing up the other chair, came and sat in front of him, taking off his hat and his spectacles.

'That's a thing never happened to me before,' he observed – 'to go out o' door with my spectacles on. I clean forgot to take 'em off.'

The old man made this trivial remark, thinking it better not to respond at all to Adam's agitation: he would gather, in an indirect way, that there was nothing decisive to communicate at present.

'And now,' he said, rising again, 'I must see to your having a bit of the loaf, and some of that wine Mr Irwine sent this morning. He'll be angry with me if you don't have it. Come, now,' he went on, bringing forward the bottle and the loaf, and pouring some wine into a cup, 'I must have a bit and a sup myself. Drink a drop with me, my lad – drink with me.'

Adam pushed the cup gently away, and said, entreatingly, 'Tell me about it, Mr Massey – tell me all about it. Was she there? Have they begun?'

'Yes, my boy, yes – it's taken all the time since I first went; but they're slow, they're slow; and there's the counsel they've got for her puts a spoke in the wheel whenever he can, and makes a deal to do with cross-examining the witnesses, and quarrelling with the other lawyers. That's all he can do for the money they give him; and it's a big sum – it's a big sum. But he's a 'cute fellow, with an eye that 'ud pick the needles out of the hay in no time. If a man had got no feelings, it 'ud be as good as a demonstration to listen to what goes on in court; but a tender heart makes one stupid. I'd have given up figures for ever only to have had some good news to bring to you, my poor lad.'

'But does it seem to be going against her?' said Adam. 'Tell me what they've said. I must know it now-I must know what they have to bring against her.'

'Why, the chief evidence yet has been the doctors; all but Martin Poyser – poor Martin. Everybody in court felt for him – it was like one sob, the sound they made when he came down again. The worst was, when they told him to look at the prisoner at the bar. It was hard work, poor fellow – it was hard work. Adam, my boy, the blow falls heavily on him as well as you: you must help poor Martin; you must show courage. Drink some wine now, and show me you mean to bear it like a man.'

Bartle had made the right sort of appeal. Adam, with an air of quiet obedience, took up the cup, and drank a little.

'Tell me how she looked,' he said, presently.

'Frightened, very frightened, when they first brought her in; it was the first sight of the crowd and the judge, poor creatur. And there's a lot o' foolish women in fine clothes, with gewgaws all up their arms and feathers on their heads, sitting near the judge: they've dressed themselves out in that way, one 'ud think, to be scarecrows and warnings against any man ever meddling with a woman again; they put up their glasses, and stared and whispered. But after that she stood like a white image, staring down at her hands, and seeming neither to hear nor see anything. And she's as white as a sheet. She didn't speak when they asked her if she'd plead "guilty", or "not guilty", and they pled "not guilty" for her. But when she heard her uncle's name, there seemed to go a shiver right through her; and when they told him to look at her, she hung her head down, and cowered, and hid her face in her hands. He'd much ado to speak, poor man, his voice trembled so. And the counsellors – who look as hard as nails mostly – I saw, spared him as much as they could. Mr Irwine put himself near him, and went with him out o' court. Ah, it's a great thing in a man's life to be able to stand by a neighbour, and uphold him in such trouble as that.'

'God bless him, and you too, Mr Massey,' said Adam, in a low voice, laying his hand on Bartle's arm.

'Ay, ay, he's good metal: he gives the right ring when you try him, our parson does. A man o' sense – says no more than's needful. He's not one of those that think they can comfort you with chattering, as if folks who stand by and look on knew a deal better what the trouble was than those who have to bear it. I've had to do with such folks in my time – in the south, when I was in trouble myself. Mr Irwine is to be a witness himself, by and by, on her side, you know, to speak to her character and bringing up.'

'But the other evidence . . . does it go hard against her?' said Adam. 'What do you think, Mr Massey? Tell me the truth.'

'Yes, my lad, yes: the truth is the best thing to tell. It must come at last. The doctor's evidence is heavy on her – is heavy. But she's gone on denying she's had a child from first to last: these poor silly women-things – they've not the sense to know it's no use denying what's proved. It'll make against her with the jury, I doubt, her being so obstinate: they may be less for recommending her to mercy, if the verdict's against her. But Mr Irwine'll leave no stone unturned with the judge – you may rely upon that, Adam.'

'Is there nobody to stand by her, and seem to care for her in the court?' said Adam.

'There's the chaplain o' the jail sits near her, but he's a sharp ferrety-faced man – another sort o' flesh and blood to Mr Irwine. They say the jail chaplains are mostly the fag-end o' the clergy.'

'There's one man as ought to be there,' said Adam, bitterly. Presently he drew himself up, and looked fixedly out of the window, apparently turning over some new idea in his mind.

'Mr Massey,' he said at last, pushing the hair off his forehead, 'I'll go back with you. I'll go into court. It's cowardly of me to keep away. I'll stand by her – I'll own her – for all she's been deceitful. They oughtn't to cast her off – her own flesh and blood. We hand folks over to God's mercy, and show none ourselves. I used to be hard sometimes: I'll never be hard again. I'll go, Mr Massey – I'll go with you.'

There was a decision in Adam's manner which would have prevented Bartle from opposing him, even if he had wished to do so. He only said – 'Take a bit, then, and another sup, Adam, for the love of me. See, I must stop and eat a morsel. Now, you take some.'

Nerved by an active resolution, Adam took a morsel of bread and drank some wine. He was haggard and unshaven, as he had been yesterday, but he stood upright again, and looked more like the Adam Bede of former days.

43

The Verdict

The place fitted up that day as a court of justice was a grand old hall, now destroyed by fire. The midday light that fell on the close pavement of human heads, was shed through a line of high pointed windows, variegated with the mellow tints of old painted glass. Grim dusty armour hung in high relief in front of the dark oaken gallery at the farther end; and under the broad arch of the great mullioned window opposite was spread a curtain of old tapestry, covered with dim melancholy figures, like a dozing indistinct dream of the past. It was a place that through the rest of the year was haunted with the shadowy memories of old kings and queens, unhappy, discrowned, imprisoned; but today all those shadows had fled, and not a soul in the vast hall felt the presence of any but a living sorrow, which was quivering in warm hearts.

But that sorrow seemed to have made itself feebly felt hitherto, now when Adam Bede's tall figure was suddenly seen, being ushered to the side of the prisoner's dock. In the broad sunlight of the great hall, among the sleek shaven faces of other men, the marks of suffering in his face were startling even to Mr Irwine, who had last seen him in the dim light of his small room; and the neighbours from Hayslope who were present, and who told Hetty Sorrel's story by their firesides in their old age, never forgot to say how it moved them when Adam Bede, poor fellow, taller by the head than most of the people round him, came into court, and took his place by her side.

But Hetty did not see him. She was standing in the same position Bartle Massey had described, her hands crossed over each other, and her eyes fixed on them. Adam had not dared to look at her in the first moments, but at last, when the attention of the court was withdrawn by the proceedings, he turned his face towards her with a resolution not to shrink.

Why did they say she was so changed? In the corpse we love, it is the *likeness* we see – it is the likeness, which makes itself felt the more keenly because something else *was* and is *not*. There they were – the sweet face and neck, with the dark tendrils of hair, the long dark lashes, the rounded cheek and the pouting lips: pale and thin – yes – but like Hetty, and only Hetty. Others thought she looked as if some demon had cast a blighting glance upon her, withered up the woman's soul in her, and left only a hard despairing obstinacy. But the mother's yearning, that completest type of the life in another life which is the essence of real human love, feels the presence of the cherished child even in the debased, degraded man; and to Adam, this pale, hard-looking culprit was the Hetty who had smiled at him in the garden under the apple-tree boughs – she was that Hetty's corpse, which he had trembled to look at the first time, and then was unwilling to turn away his eyes from.

But presently he heard something that compelled him to listen, and made the sense of sight less absorbing. A woman was in the witness-box, a middle-aged woman, who spoke in a firm distinct voice. She said – 'My name is Sarah Stone. I am a widow, and keep a small shop licensed to sell tobacco, snuff, and tea, in Church Lane, Stoniton. The prisoner at the bar is the same young woman who came, looking ill and tired, with a basket on her arm, and asked for a lodging at my house on Saturday evening, the 27th of February. She had taken the house for a public, because there was a figure against the door. And when I said I didn't take in lodgers, the prisoner began to cry, and said she was too tired to go anywhere else, and she only wanted a bed for one night. And her prettiness, and her condition, and something respectable about her clothes and looks, and the trouble she seemed to be in, made me as I couldn't find in my heart to send her away at once. I asked her to sit down, and gave her some tea, and asked her where she was going, and where her friends were. She said she was going home to her friends: they were farming folks a good way off, and she'd had a long journey that had cost her more money than she expected, so as she'd hardly any money left in her pocket, and was afraid of going where it would cost her much. She had been obliged to sell most of the things out of her basket; but she'd thankfully give a shilling for a bed. I saw no reason why I shouldn't take the young woman in for the night. I had only one room, but there were two beds in it, and I told her she might stay with me. I thought she'd been led wrong, and got into trouble, but if she was going to her friends, it would be a good work to keep her out of further harm.'

The witness then stated that in the night a child was born, and she identified the baby-clothes then shown to her as those in which she had herself dressed the child.

'Those are the clothes. I made them myself, and had kept them by me ever since my last child was born. I took a deal of trouble both for the child and the mother. I couldn't help taking to the little thing and being anxious about it. I didn't send for a doctor, for there seemed no need. I told the mother in the daytime she must tell me the name of her friends, and where they lived, and let me write to them. She said, by and by she would write herself, but not today. She would have no nay, but she would get up and be dressed, in spite of everything I could say. She said she felt quite strong enough; and it was wonderful what spirit she showed. But I wasn't quite easy what I should do about her, and towards evening I made up my mind I'd go, after Meeting was over, and speak to our minister about it. I left the house about half-past eight o'clock. I didn't go out at the shop door, but at the back door, which opens into a narrow alley. I've only got the ground-floor of the house, and the kitchen and bedroom both look into the alley. I left the prisoner sitting up by the fire in the kitchen with the baby on her lap. She hadn't cried or seemed low at all, as she did the night before. I thought she had a strange look with her eyes, and she got a bit flushed towards evening. I was afraid of the fever, and I thought I'd call and ask an acquaintance of mine, an experienced woman, to come back with me when I went out. It was a very dark night. I didn't fasten the door behind me: there was no lock: it was a latch with a bolt inside, and when there was nobody in the house I always went out at the shop door. But I thought there was no danger in leaving it unfastened that little while. I was longer than I meant to be, for I had to wait for the woman that came back with me. It was an hour and a half before we got back, and when we went in, the candle was standing burning just as I left it, but the prisoner and the baby were both gone. She'd taken her cloak and bonnet, but she'd left the basket and the things in it . . . I was dreadful frightened, and angry with her for going. I didn't go to give information, because I'd no thought she meant to do any harm, and I knew she had money in her pocket to buy her food and lodging. I didn't like to set the constable after her, for she'd a right to go from me if she liked.'

The effect of this evidence on Adam was electrical; it gave him new force. Hetty could not be guilty of the crime – her heart must have clung to her baby – else why should she have taken it with her? She might have left it behind. The little creature had died naturally, and then she had hidden it: babies were so liable to death – and there might be the strongest suspicions without any proof of guilt. His mind was so occupied with imaginary arguments against such suspicions, that he could not listen to the cross-examination by Hetty's counsel, who tried, without result, to elicit evidence that the prisoner had shown some movements of maternal affection towards the child. The whole time this witness was being examined, Hetty had stood as motionless as before: no word seemed to arrest her ear. But the sound of the next witness's voice touched a chord that was still sensitive; she gave a start and a frightened look towards him, but immediately turned away her head and looked down at her hands as before. This witness was a man, a rough peasant. He said – 'My name is John Olding. I am a labourer, and live at Tedd's Hole, two miles out of Stoniton. A week last Monday, towards one o'clock in the afternoon, I was going towards Hetton Coppice, and about a quarter of a mile from the coppice I saw the prisoner, in a red cloak, sitting under a bit of a haystack not far off the stile. She got up when she saw me, and seemed as if she'd be walking on the other way. It was a regular road through the fields, and nothing very uncommon to see a young woman there, but I took notice of her because she looked white and scared. I should have thought she was a beggar-woman, only for her good clothes. I thought she looked a bit crazy, but it was no business of mine. I stood and looked back after her, but she went right on while she was in sight. I had to go to the other side of the coppice to look after some stakes. There's a road right through it, and bits of openings here and there, where the trees have been cut down, and some of 'em not carried away. I didn't go straight along the road, but turned on towards the middle, and took a shorter way towards the spot I wanted to get to. I hadn't got far out of the road into one of the open places, before I heard a strange cry. I thought it didn't come from any animal I knew, but I wasn't for stopping to look about just then. But it went on, and seemed so strange to me in that place, I couldn't help stopping to look. I began to think I might make some money of it, if it was a new thing. But I had hard work to tell which way it came from, and for a good while I kept looking up at the boughs. And then I thought it came from the ground; and there was a lot of timber-choppings lying about, and loose pieces of turf, and a trunk or two. And I looked about among them, but could find nothing; and at last the cry stopped. So I was for giving it up, and I went on about my business. But when I came back the same way pretty nigh an hour after, I couldn't help laying down my stakes to have another look. And just as I was stooping and laying down the stakes, I saw something odd and round and whitish lying on the ground under a nut-bush by the side of me. And I stooped down on hands and knees to pick it up. And I saw it was a little baby's hand.'

At these words a thrill ran through the court. Hetty was visibly trembling: now, for the first time, she seemed to be listening to what a witness said.

'There was a lot of timber-choppings put together just where the ground went hollow, like, under the bush, and the hand came out from among them. But there was a hole left in one place, and I could see down it, and see the child's head; and I made haste and did away the turf and the choppings, and took out the child. It had got comfortable clothes on, but its body was cold, and I thought it must be dead. I made haste back with it out of the wood, and took it home to my wife. She said it was dead, and I'd better take it to the parish and tell the constable. And I said, 'I'll lay my life it's that young woman's child as I met going to the coppice.' But she seemed to be gone clean out of sight. And I took the child on to Hetton parish and told the constable, and we went on to Justice Hardy. And then we went looking after the young woman till dark at night, and we went and gave information at Stoniton, as they might stop her. And the next morning another constable came to me, to go with him to the spot where I found the child. And when we got there, there was the prisoner a-sitting against the bush where I found the child; and she cried out when she saw us, but she never offered to move. She'd got a big piece of bread on her lap.'

Adam had given a faint groan of despair while this witness was speaking. He had hidden his face on his arm, which rested on the boarding in front of him. It was the supreme moment of his suffering: Hetty was guilty: and he was silently calling to God for help. He heard no more of the evidence, and was unconscious when the case for the prosecution had closed – unconscious that Mr Irwine was in the witness-box, telling of Hetty's unblemished character in her own parish, and of the virtuous habits in which she had been brought up. This testimony could have no influence on the verdict, but it was given as part of that plea for mercy which her own counsel would have made if he had been allowed to speak for her – a favour not granted to criminals in those stern times.

At last Adam lifted up his head, for there was a general movement round him. The judge had addressed the jury, and they were retiring. The decisive moment was not far off. Adam felt a shuddering horror that would not let him look at Hetty, but she had long relapsed into her blank hard indifference. All eyes were strained to look at her, but she stood like a statue of dull despair.

There was a mingled rustling, whispering, and low buzzing throughout the court during this interval. The desire to listen was suspended, and everyone had some feeling or opinion to express in undertones. Adam sat looking blankly

before him, but he did not see the objects that were right in front of his eyes –
the counsel and attorneys talking with an air of cool business, and Mr Irwine in
low earnest conversation with the judge: did not see Mr Irwine sit down again in
agitation, and shake his head mournfully when somebody whispered to him.
The inward action was too intense for Adam to take in outward objects until
some strong sensation roused him.

It was not very long, hardly more than a quarter of an hour, before the knock
which told that the jury had come to their decision, fell as a signal for silence on
every ear. It is sublime – that sudden pause of a great multitude, which tells that
one soul moves in them all. Deeper and deeper the silence seemed to become,
like the deepening night, while the jurymen's names were called over, and the
prisoner was made to hold up her hand, and the jury were asked for their verdict.
 'Guilty.'

It was the verdict everyone expected, but there was a sigh of disappointment
from some hearts, that it was followed by no recommendation to mercy. Still
the sympathy of the court was not with the prisoner: the unnaturalness of her
crime stood out the more harshly by the side of her hard immovability and
obstinate silence. Even the verdict, to distant eyes, had not appeared to move
her; but those who were near saw her trembling.

The stillness was less intense until the judge put on his black cap, and the
chaplain in his canonicals was observed behind him. Then it deepened again,
before the crier had had time to command silence. If any sound were heard, it must
have been the sound of beating hearts. The judge spoke – 'Hester Sorrel . . .'

The blood rushed to Hetty's face, and then fled back again, as she looked up
at the judge, and kept her wide-open eyes fixed on him, as if fascinated by fear.
Adam had not yet turned towards her: there was a deep horror, like a great gulf,
between them. But at the words – 'and then to be hanged by the neck till you be
dead,' a piercing shriek rang through the hall. It was Hetty's shriek. Adam
started to his feet and stretched out his arms towards her, but the arms could not
reach her: she had fallen down in a fainting-fit, and was carried out of court.

44

Arthur's Return

When Arthur Donnithorne landed at Liverpool, and read the letter from his
aunt Lydia, briefly announcing his grandfather's death, his first feeling was,
'Poor grandfather! I wish I could have got to him to be with him when he died.
He might have felt or wished something at the last that I shall never know now.
It was a lonely death.'

It is impossible to say that his grief was deeper than that. Pity and softened
memory took place of the old antagonism, and in his busy thoughts about the
future, as the chaise carried him rapidly along towards the home where he was
now to be master, there was a continually recurring effort to remember anything by which he could show a regard for his grandfather's wishes, without

counteracting his own cherished aims for the good of the tenants and the estate. But it is not in human nature – only in human pretence – for a young man like Arthur, with a fine constitution and fine spirits, thinking well of himself, believing that others think well of him, and having a very ardent intention to give them more and more reason for that good opinion – it is not possible for such a young man, just coming into a splendid estate through the death of a very old man whom he was not fond of, to feel anything very different from exultant joy. Now his real life was beginning; now he would have room and opportunity for action, and he would use them. He would show the Loamshire people what a fine country gentleman was; he would not exchange that career for any other under the sun. He felt himself riding over the hills in the breezy autumn days, looking after favourite plans of drainage and enclosure; then admired on sombre mornings as the best rider on the best horse in the hunt; spoken well of on market-days as a first-rate landlord; by and by making speeches at election dinners, and showing a wonderful knowledge of agriculture; the patron of new ploughs and drills, the severe upbraider of negligent landowners, and withal a jolly fellow that everybody must like – happy faces greeting him everywhere on his own estate, and the neighbouring families on the best terms with him. The Irwines should dine with him every week, and have their own carriage to come in, for in some very delicate way that Arthur would devise, the lay-impropriator of the Hayslope tithes would insist on paying a couple of hundreds more to the Vicar; and his aunt should be as comfortable as possible, and go on living at the Chase, if she liked, in spite of her old-maidish ways – at least until he was married; and that event lay in the indistinct background, for Arthur had not yet seen the woman who would play the lady-wife to the first-rate country gentleman.

These were Arthur's chief thoughts, so far as a man's thoughts through hours of travelling can be compressed into a few sentences, which are only like the list of names telling you what are the scenes in a long, long panorama, full of colour, of detail, and of life. The happy faces Arthur saw greeting him were not pale abstractions, but real ruddy faces, long familiar to him: Martin Poyser was there – the whole Poyser family.

What – Hetty?

Yes; for Arthur was at ease about Hetty: not quite at ease about the past, for a certain burning of the ears would come whenever he thought of the scenes with Adam last August – but at ease about her present lot. Mr Irwine, who had been a regular correspondent, telling him all the news about the old places and people, had sent him word nearly three months ago that Adam Bede was not to marry Mary Burge, as he had thought, but pretty Hetty Sorrel. Martin Poyser and Adam himself had both told Mr Irwine all about it – that Adam had been deeply in love with Hetty these two years, and that now it was agreed they were to be married in March. That stalwart rogue Adam was more susceptible than the Rector had thought; it was really quite an idyllic love affair; and if it had not been too long to tell in a letter, he would have liked to describe to Arthur the blushing looks and the simple strong words with which the fine honest fellow told his secret. He knew Arthur would like to hear that Adam had this sort of happiness in prospect.

Yes, indeed! Arthur felt there was not air enough in the room to satisfy his renovated life, when he had read that passage in the letter. He threw up the windows, he rushed out of doors into the December air, and greeted everyone who spoke to him with an eager gaiety, as if there had been news of a fresh Nelson victory. For the first time that day since he had come to Windsor, he was in true boyish spirits: the load that had been pressing upon him was gone; the haunting fear had vanished. He thought he could conquer his bitterness towards Adam now – could offer him his hand, and ask to be his friend again, in spite of that painful memory which would still make his ears burn. He had been knocked down, and he had been forced to tell a lie: such things make a scar, do what we will. But if Adam were the same again as in the old days, Arthur wished to be the same too, and to have Adam mixed up with his business and his future, as he had always desired before that accursed meeting in August. Nay, he would do a great deal more for Adam than he should otherwise have done, when he came into the estate; Hetty's husband had a special claim on him – Hetty herself should feel that any pain she had suffered through Arthur in the past, was compensated to her a hundredfold. For really she could not have felt much, since she had so soon made up her mind to marry Adam.

You perceive clearly what sort of picture Adam and Hetty made in the panorama of Arthur's thoughts on his journey homeward. It was March now; they were soon to be married: perhaps they were already married. And *now* it was actually in his power to do a great deal for them. Sweet – sweet little Hetty! The little puss hadn't cared for him half as much as he cared for her; for he was a great fool about her still – was almost afraid of seeing her – indeed, had not cared much to look at any other woman since he parted from her. That little figure coming towards him in the Grove, those dark-fringed childish eyes, the lovely lips put up to kiss him – that picture had got no fainter with the lapse of months. And she would look just the same. It was impossible to think how he could meet her: he should certainly tremble. Strange, how long this sort of influence lasts; for he was certainly not in love with Hetty now: he had been earnestly desiring, for months, that she should marry Adam, and there was nothing that contributed more to his happiness in these moments than the thought of their marriage. It was the exaggerating effect of imagination that made his heart still beat a little more quickly at the thought of her. When he saw the little thing again, as she really was, as Adam's wife, at work quite prosaically in her new home, he should perhaps wonder at the possibility of his past feelings. Thank heaven it had turned out so well! He should have plenty of affairs and interests to fill his life now, and not be in danger of playing the fool again.

Pleasant the crack of the postboy's whip! Pleasant the sense of being hurried along in swift ease through English scenes, so like those round his own home, only not quite so charming. Here was a market-town – very much like Treddleston – where the arms of the neighbouring lord of the manor were borne on the sign of the principal inn: then mere fields and hedges, their vicinity to a market-town carrying an agreeable suggestion of high rent, till the land began to assume a trimmer look, the woods were more frequent, and at length a white or red mansion looked down from a moderate eminence, or allowed him to be aware of its parapet and chimneys among the dense-looking masses of oaks and elms – masses reddened now with early buds. And close at hand came the village: the small church, with its red-tiled roof, looking humble even among the faded half-timbered houses; the old green gravestones with nettles round them; nothing fresh and bright but the children, opening round eyes at the swift post-chaise; nothing noisy and busy but the gaping curs of mysterious pedigree. What a much prettier village Hayslope was! And it should not be neglected like this place: vigorous repairs should go on everywhere among farm-buildings and cottages, and travellers in post-chaises, coming along the Rosseter road, should do nothing but admire as they went. And Adam Bede should superintend all the repairs, for he had a share in Burge's business now, and, if he liked, Arthur would put some money into the concern, and buy the old man out in another year or two. That was an ugly fault in Arthur's life, that affair last summer; but the future should make amends. Many men would have retained a feeling of vindictiveness towards Adam; but *he* would not – he would resolutely overcome all littleness of that kind, for he had certainly been very much in the wrong; and though Adam had been harsh and violent, and had thrust on him a painful dilemma, the poor fellow was in love, and had real provocation. No; Arthur had not an evil feeling in his mind towards any human being: he was happy, and would make everyone else happy that came within his reach.

And here was dear old Hayslope at last, sleeping on the hill, like a quiet old place as it was, in the late afternoon sunlight; and opposite to it the great shoulders of the Binton Hills, below them the purplish blackness of the hanging woods, and at last the pale front of the Abbey, looking out from among the oaks of the Chase, as if anxious for the heir's return. 'Poor grandfather! and he lies dead there. *He* was a young fellow once, coming into the estate, and making his plans. So the world goes round! Aunt Lydia must feel very desolate, poor thing; but she shall be indulged as much as she indulges her fat Fido.'

The wheels of Arthur's chaise had been anxiously listened for at the Chase, for today was Friday, and the funeral had already been deferred two days. Before it drew up on the gravel of the courtyard, all the servants in the house were assembled to receive him with a grave, decent welcome, befitting a house of death. A month ago, perhaps, it would have been difficult for them to have maintained a suitable sadness in their faces, when Mr Arthur was come to take possession; but the hearts of the head-servants were heavy that day for another cause than the death of the old Squire, and more than one of them was longing to be twenty miles away, as Mr Craig was, knowing what was to become of Hetty Sorrel – pretty Hetty Sorrel – whom they used to see every week. They had the partisanship of household servants who like their places, and were not inclined to go the full length of the severe indignation felt against him by the farming tenants, but rather to make excuses for him; nevertheless, the upper servants, who had been on terms of neighbourly intercourse with the Poysers for many years, could not help feeling that the longed-for event of the young Squire's coming into the estate had been robbed of all its pleasantness.

To Arthur it was nothing surprising that the servants looked grave and sad: he himself was very much touched on seeing them all again, and feeling that he was in a new relation to them. It was that sort of pathetic emotion which has more pleasure than pain in it – which is perhaps one of the most delicious of all states to a good-natured man, conscious of the power to satisfy his good-nature. His heart swelled agreeably as he said – 'Well, Mills, how is my aunt?'

But now Mr Bygate, the lawyer, who had been in the house ever since the death, came forward to give deferential greetings and answer all questions, and Arthur walked with him towards the library, where his aunt Lydia was expecting him. Aunt Lydia was the only person in the house who knew nothing about Hetty: her sorrow as a maiden daughter was unmixed with any other thoughts than those of anxiety about funeral arrangements and her own future lot; and, after the manner of women, she mourned for the father who had made her life important, all the more because she had a secret sense that there was little mourning for him in other hearts.

But Arthur kissed her tearful face more tenderly than he had ever done in his life before.

'Dear aunt,' he said affectionately, as he held her hand, '*your* loss is the greatest of all, but you must tell me how to try and make it up to you all the rest of your life.'

'It was so sudden and so dreadful, Arthur,' poor Miss Lydia began, pouring out her little plaints; and Arthur sat down to listen with impatient patience. When a pause came, he said – 'Now, aunt, I'll leave you for a quarter of an hour just to go to my own room, and then I shall come and give full attention to everything.'

'My room is all ready for me, I suppose, Mills?' he said to the butler, who seemed to be lingering uneasily about the entrance-hall.

'Yes, sir, and there are letters for you; they are all laid on the writing-table in your dressing-room.'

On entering the small anteroom which was called a dressing-room, but which Arthur really used only to lounge and write in, he just cast his eyes on the writing-table, and saw that there were several letters and packets lying there; but he was in the uncomfortable dusty condition of a man who has had a long hurried journey, and he must really refresh himself by attending to his toilette a little, before he read his letters. Pym was there, making everything ready for him and soon, with a delightful freshness about him, as if he were prepared to begin a new day, he went back into his dressing-room to open his letters. The level rays of the low afternoon sun entered directly at the window, and as Arthur seated himself in his velvet chair with their pleasant warmth upon him, he was conscious of that quiet wellbeing which perhaps you and I have felt on a sunny afternoon, when, in our brightest youth and health, life has opened a new vista for us, and long tomorrows of activity have stretched before us like a lovely plain which there was no need for hurrying to look at, because it was all our own.

The top letter was placed with its address upwards: it was in Mr Irwine's handwriting, Arthur saw at once; and below the address was written, 'To be delivered as soon as he arrives'. Nothing could have been less surprising to him than a letter from Mr Irwine at that moment: of course there was something he wished Arthur to know earlier than it was possible for them to see each other. At such a time as that it was quite natural that Irwine should have something pressing to say. Arthur broke the seal with an agreeable anticipation of soon seeing the writer:

I send this letter to meet you on your arrival, Arthur, because I may then be at Stoniton, whither I am called by the most painful duty it has ever been given me to perform, and it is right that you should know what I have to tell you without delay.

I will not attempt to add by one word of reproach to the retribution that is now falling on you: any other words that I could write at this moment must be weak and unmeaning by the side of those in which I must tell you the simple fact.

Hetty Sorrel is in prison, and will be tried on Friday for the crime of child-murder . . .'

Arthur read no more. He started up from his chair, and stood for a single minute with a sense of violent convulsion in his whole frame, as if the life were going out of him with horrible throbs; but the next minute he had rushed out of the room, still clutching the letter – he was hurrying along the corridor, and down the stairs into the hall. Mills was still there, but Arthur did not see him, as he passed like a hunted man across the hall and out along the gravel. The butler hurried out after him as fast as his elderly limbs could run: he guessed, he knew, where the young Squire was going.

When Mills got to the stables, a horse was being saddled, and Arthur was forcing himself to read the remaining words of the letter. He thrust it into his pocket as the horse was led up to him, and at that moment caught sight of Mills's anxious face in front of him.

'Tell them I'm gone – gone to Stoniton,' he said, in a muffled tone of agitation – sprang into the saddle, and set off at a gallop.

45

In the Prison

Near sunset that evening an elderly gentleman was standing with his back against the smaller entrance-door of Stoniton jail, saying a few last words to the departing chaplain. The chaplain walked away, but the elderly gentleman stood still, looking down on the pavement, and stroking his chin with a ruminating air, when he was roused by a sweet clear woman's voice, saying – 'Can I get into the prison, if you please?'

He turned his head, and looked fixedly at the speaker for a few moments without answering.

'I have seen you before,' he said at last. 'Do you remember preaching on the village green at Hayslope in Loamshire?'

'Yes, sir, surely. Are you the gentleman that stayed to listen on horseback?'

'Yes. Why do you want to go into the prison?'

'I want to go to Hetty Sorrel, the young woman who has been condemned to death – and to stay with her, if I may be permitted. Have you power in the prison, sir?'

'Yes; I am a magistrate, and can get admittance for you. But did you know this criminal, Hetty Sorrel?'

'Yes, we are kin: my own aunt married her uncle, Martin Poyser. But I was away at Leeds, and didn't know of this great trouble in time to get here before today. I entreat you, sir, for the love of our heavenly Father, to let me go to her and stay with her.'

'How did you know she was condemned to death, if you are only just come from Leeds?'

'I have seen my uncle since the trial, sir. He is gone back to his home now, and the poor sinner is forsaken of all. I beseech you to get leave for me to be with her.'

'What! have you courage to stay all night in the prison? She is very sullen, and will scarcely make answer when she is spoken to.'

'Oh, sir, it may please God to open her heart still. Don't let us delay.'

'Come, then,' said the elderly gentleman, ringing and gaining admission; 'I know you have a key to unlock hearts.'

Dinah mechanically took off her bonnet and shawl as soon as they were within the prison court, from the habit she had of throwing them off when she preached or prayed, or visited the sick; and when they entered the jailer's room, she laid them down on a chair unthinkingly. There was no agitation visible in her, but a deep concentrated calmness, as if, even when she was speaking, her soul was in prayer reposing on an unseen support.

After speaking to the jailer, the magistrate turned to her and said, 'The turnkey will take you to the prisoner's cell, and leave you there for the night, if you desire it; but you can't have a light during the night – it is contrary to rules. My name is Colonel Townley: if I can help you in anything, ask the jailer for my address, and come to me. I take some interest in this Hetty Sorrel, for the sake of that fine fellow, Adam Bede: I happened to see him at Hayslope the same evening I heard you preach, and recognised him in court today, ill as he looked.'

'Ah, sir, can you tell me anything about him? Can you tell me where he lodges? For my poor uncle was too much weighed down with trouble to remember.'

'Close by here. I enquired all about him of Mr Irwine. He lodges over a tinman's shop, in the street on the right hand as you entered the prison. There is an old schoolmaster with him. Now, Goodbye: I wish you success.'

'Farewell, sir. I am grateful to you.'

As Dinah crossed the prison court with the turnkey, the solemn evening light seemed to make the walls higher than they were by day, and the sweet pale face in the cap was more than ever like a white flower on this background of gloom. The turnkey looked askance at her all the while, but never spoke: he somehow felt that the sound of his own rude voice would be grating just then. He struck a light as they entered the dark corridor leading to the condemned cell, and then said in his most civil tone, 'It'll be pretty nigh dark in the cell a'ready; but I can stop with my light a bit, if you like.'

'Nay, friend, thank you,' said Dinah. 'I wish to go in alone.'

'As you like,' said the jailer, turning the harsh key in the lock, and opening the door wide enough to admit Dinah. A jet of light from his lantern fell on the opposite corner of the cell, where Hetty was sitting on her straw pallet with her face buried in her knees. It seemed as if she were asleep, and yet the grating of the lock would have been likely to waken her.

The door closed again, and the only light in the cell was that of the evening sky, through the small high grating – enough to discern human faces by. Dinah stood still for a minute, hesitating to speak, because Hetty might be asleep; and looking at the motionless heap with a yearning heart. Then she said, softly – 'Hetty!'

There was a slight movement perceptible in Hetty's frame – a start such as might have been produced by a feeble electrical shock; but she did not look up. Dinah spoke again, in a tone made stronger by irrepressible emotion – 'Hetty . . . it's Dinah.'

Again there was a slight, startled movement through Hetty's frame, and without uncovering her face, she raised her head a little, as if listening.

'Hetty . . . Dinah is come to you.'

After a moment's pause, Hetty lifted her head slowly and timidly from her knees, and raised her eyes. The two pale faces were looking at each other: one with a wild hard despair in it, the other full of sad, yearning love. Dinah unconsciously opened her arms and stretched them out.

'Don't you know me, Hetty? Don't you remember Dinah? Did you think I wouldn't come to you in trouble?'

Hetty kept her eyes fixed on Dinah's face – at first like an animal that gazes, and gazes, and keeps aloof.

'I'm come to be with you, Hetty – not to leave you – to stay with you – to be your sister to the last.'

Slowly, while Dinah was speaking, Hetty rose, took a step forward, and was clasped in Dinah's arms.

They stood so a long while, for neither of them felt the impulse to move apart again. Hetty, without any distinct thought of it, hung on this something that was come to clasp her now, while she was sinking helpless in a dark gulf; and Dinah felt a deep joy in the first sign that her love was welcomed by the wretched lost one. The light got fainter as they stood, and when at last they sat down on the straw pallet together, their faces had become indistinct.

Not a word was spoken. Dinah waited, hoping for a spontaneous word from Hetty; but she sat in the same dull despair, only clutching the hand that held hers, and leaning her cheek against Dinah's. It was the human contact she clung to, but she was not the less sinking into the dark gulf.

Dinah began to doubt whether Hetty was conscious who it was that sat beside her. She thought suffering and fear might have driven the poor sinner out of her mind. But it was borne in upon her, as she afterwards said, that she must not hurry God's work: we are over-hasty to speak – as if God did not manifest himself by our silent feeling, and make his love felt through ours. She did not know how long they sat in that way, but it got darker and darker, till there was only a pale patch of light on the opposite wall: all the rest was darkness. But she felt the Divine presence more and more, – nay, as if she herself were a part of it, and it was the Divine pity that was beating in her heart, and was willing the rescue of this helpless one. At last she was prompted to speak, and find out how far Hetty was conscious of the present.

'Hetty,' she said, gently, 'do you know who it is that sits by your side?'

'Yes,' Hetty answered, slowly, 'it's Dinah.'

'And do you remember the time when we were at the Hall Farm together, and that night when I told you to be sure and think of me as a friend in trouble?'

'Yes,' said Hetty. Then, after a pause, she added, 'But you can do nothing for me. You can't make 'em do anything. They'll hang me o' Monday – it's Friday now.'

As Hetty said the last words, she clung closer to Dinah, shuddering.

'No, Hetty, I can't save you from that death. But isn't the suffering less hard when you have somebody with you, that feels for you – that you can speak to, and say what's in your heart? . . . Yes, Hetty: you lean on me: you are glad to have me with you.'

'You won't leave me, Dinah? You'll keep close to me?'

'No, Hetty, I won't leave you. I'll stay with you to the last . . . But, Hetty, there is someone else in this cell besides me, someone close to you.'

Hetty said, in a frightened whisper, 'Who?'

'Someone who has been with you through all your hours of sin and trouble – who has known every thought you have had – has seen where you went, where you lay down and rose up again, and all the deeds you have tried to hide in darkness. And on Monday, when I can't follow you – when my arms can't reach you – when death has parted us – He who is with us now, and knows all, will be with you then. It makes no difference – whether we live or die, we are in the presence of God.'

'O Dinah, won't nobody do anything for me? *Will* they hang me for certain? . . . I wouldn't mind if they'd let me live.'

'My poor Hetty, death is very dreadful to you. I know it's dreadful. But if you had a friend to take care of you after death – in that other world – someone whose love is greater than mine – who can do everything? . . . If God our Father was your friend, and was willing to save you from sin and suffering, so as you should neither know wicked feelings nor pain again? If you could believe he loved you and would help you, as you believe I love you and will help you, it wouldn't be so hard to die on Monday, would it?'

'But I can't know anything about it,' Hetty said, with sullen sadness.

'Because, Hetty, you are shutting up your soul against him, by trying to hide the truth. God's love and mercy can overcome all things – our ignorance, and weakness, and all the burthen of our past wickedness – all things but our wilful sin; sin that we cling to, and will not give up. You believe in my love and pity for you, Hetty; but if you had not let me come near you, if you wouldn't have looked at me or spoken to me, you'd have shut me out from helping you: I couldn't have made you feel my love; I couldn't have told you what I felt for you. Don't shut God's love out in that way, by clinging to sin . . . He can't bless you while you have one falsehood in your soul; his pardoning mercy can't reach you until you open your heart to him, and say, "I have done this great wickedness; O God, save me, make me pure from sin." While you cling to one sin and will not part with it, it must drag you down to misery after death, as it has dragged you to misery here in this world, my poor, poor Hetty. It is sin that brings dread, and darkness, and despair: there is light and blessedness for us as soon as we cast it off: God enters our souls then, and teaches us, and brings us strength and peace. Cast it off now, Hetty – now: confess the wickedness you have done – the sin you have been guilty of against your heavenly Father. Let us kneel down together, for we are in the presence of God.'

Hetty obeyed Dinah's movement, and sank on her knees. They still held each other's hands, and there was long silence. Then Dinah said – 'Hetty, we are before God: he is waiting for you to tell the truth.'

Still there was silence. At last Hetty spoke, in a tone of beseeching – 'Dinah . . . help me . . . I can't feel anything like you . . . my heart is hard.'

Dinah held the clinging hand, and all her soul went forth in her voice: 'Jesus, thou present Saviour! Thou hast known the depths of all sorrow: thou hast entered that black darkness where God is not, and hast uttered the cry of the forsaken. Come, Lord, and gather of the fruits of thy travail and thy pleading: stretch forth thy hand, thou who art mighty to save to the uttermost, and rescue this lost one. She is clothed round with thick darkness: the fetters of her sin are upon her, and she cannot stir to come to thee: she can only feel her heart is hard, and she is helpless. She cries to me, thy weak creature . . . Saviour! it is a blind cry to thee. Hear it! Pierce the darkness! Look upon her with thy face of love and sorrow that thou didst turn on him who denied thee; and melt her hard heart.

'See, Lord – I bring her, as they of old brought the sick and helpless, and thou didst heal them: I bear her on my arms and carry her before thee. Fear and trembling have taken hold on her; but she trembles only at the pain and death of the body: breathe upon her thy life-giving Spirit, and put a new fear within her – the fear of her sin. Make her dread to keep the accursed thing within her soul: make her feel the presence of the living God, who beholds all the past, to whom the darkness is as noonday; who is waiting now, at the eleventh hour, for her to turn to him, and confess her sin, and cry for mercy – now, before the night of death comes, and the moment of pardon is for ever fled, like yesterday that returneth not.

'Saviour! it is yet time – time to snatch this poor soul from everlasting darkness. I believe – I believe in thy infinite love. What is *my* love or *my* pleading? It is quenched in thine. I can only clasp her in my weak arms, and urge her with my weak pity. Thou – thou wilt breathe on the dead soul, and it shall arise from the unanswering sleep of death.

'Yea, Lord, I see thee, coming through the darkness, coming, like the morning, with healing on thy wings. The marks of thy agony are upon thee – I see, I see thou art able and willing to save – thou wilt not let her perish for ever.

'Come, mighty Saviour! let the dead hear thy voice; let the eyes of the blind be opened: let her see that God encompasses her; let her tremble at nothing but at the sin that cuts her off from him. Melt the hard heart; unseal the closed lips: make her cry with her whole soul, "Father, I have sinned . . . " '

'Dinah,' Hetty sobbed out, throwing her arms round Dinah's neck, 'I will speak . . . I will tell . . . I won't hide it any more.'

But the tears and sobs were too violent. Dinah raised her gently from her knees, and seated her on the pallet again, sitting down by her side. It was a long time before the convulsed throat was quiet, and even then they sat some time in stillness and darkness, holding each other's hands. At last Hetty whispered – 'I did do it, Dinah . . . I buried it in the wood . . . the little baby . . . and it cried . . . I heard it cry . . . ever such a way off . . . all night . . . and I went back because it cried.'

She paused, and then spoke hurriedly in a louder, pleading tone.

'But I thought perhaps it wouldn't die – there might somebody find it. I didn't kill it – I didn't kill it myself. I put it down there and covered it up, and when I came back it was gone . . . It was because I was so very miserable, Dinah . . . I didn't know where to go . . . and I tried to kill myself before, and I couldn't. Oh, I tried so to drown myself in the pool, and I couldn't. I went to Windsor – I ran away – did you know? I went to find him, as he might take care of me; and he was gone; and then I didn't know what to do. I daredn't go back home again – I couldn't bear it. I couldn't have bore to look at anybody, for they'd have scorned me. I thought o' you sometimes, and thought I'd come to you, for I didn't think you'd be cross with me, and cry shame on me: I thought I could tell you. But then the other folks 'ud come to know it at last, and I couldn't bear that. It was partly thinking o' you made me come toward Stoniton; and, besides, I was so frightened at going wandering about till I was a beggar-woman, and had nothing; and sometimes it seemed as if I must go back to the Farm sooner than that. Oh, it was so dreadful, Dinah . . . I was so miserable . . . I wished I'd never been born into this world. I should never like to go into the green fields again – I hated 'em so in my misery.'

Hetty paused again, as if the sense of the past were too strong upon her for words.

'And then I got to Stoniton, and I began to feel frightened that night, because I was so near home. And then the little baby was born, when I didn't expect it; and the thought came into my mind that I might get rid of it, and go home again. The thought came all of a sudden, as I was lying in the bed, and it got stronger and stronger . . . I longed so to go back again . . . I couldn't bear being so lonely, and coming to beg for want. And it gave me strength and resolution to get up and dress myself. I felt I must do it . . . I didn't know how . . . I thought I'd find a pool, if I could, like that other, in the corner of the field, in the dark. And when the woman went out, I felt as if I was strong enough to do anything . . . I thought I should get rid of all my misery, and go back home, and never let 'em know why I ran away. I put on my bonnet and shawl, and went out into the dark street, with the baby under my cloak; and I walked fast till I got into a street a good way off, and there was a public, and I got some warm stuff to drink and some bread. And I walked on and on, and I hardly felt the ground I trod on; and it got lighter, for there came the moon – O Dinah, it frightened me when it first looked at me out o' the clouds – it never looked so before; and I turned out of the road into the fields, for I was afraid o' meeting anybody with the moon shining on me. And I came to a haystack, where I thought I could lie down and keep myself warm all night. There was a place cut into it, where I could make me a bed; and I lay comfortable, and the baby was warm against me; and I must have gone to sleep for a good while, for when I woke it was morning, but not very light, and the baby was crying. And I saw a wood a little way off . . . I thought there'd perhaps be a ditch or a pond there . . . and it was so early I thought I could hide the child there, and get a long way off before folks was up. And then I thought I'd go home – I'd get rides in carts and go home, and tell 'em I'd been to try and see for a place, and couldn't get one. I longed so for it, Dinah, I longed so to be safe at home. I don't know how I felt about the baby. I seemed to hate it – it was like a heavy weight hanging round my neck; and yet its crying went through me, and I daredn't look at its little hands and face. But I went on to the wood, and I walked about, but there was no water' . . .

Hetty shuddered. She was silent for some moments, and when she began again, it was in a whisper.

'I came to a place where there was lots of chips and turf, and I sat down on the trunk of a tree to think what I should do. And all of a sudden I saw a hole under the nut tree, like a little grave. And it darted into me like lightning – I'd lay the baby there, and cover it with the grass and the chips. I couldn't kill it any other way. And I'd done it in a minute; and, oh, it cried so, Dinah – I couldn't cover it quite up – I thought perhaps somebody 'ud come and take care of it, and then it wouldn't die. And I made haste out of the wood, but I could hear it crying all the while; and when I got out into the fields, it was as if I was held fast – I couldn't go away, for all I wanted so to go. And I sat against the haystack to watch if anybody 'ud come: I was very hungry, and I'd only a bit of bread left; but I couldn't go away. And after ever such a while – hours and hours – the man came – him in a smock-frock, and he looked at me so, I was frightened, and I made haste and went on. I thought he was going to the wood, and would perhaps find the baby. And I went right on, till I came to a village, a long way off from the wood; and I was very sick, and faint, and hungry. I got something to eat there, and bought a loaf. But I was frightened to stay. I heard the baby crying, and thought the other folks heard it too – and I went on. But I was so tired, and it was getting towards dark. And at last, by the roadside there was a barn – ever such a way off any house – like the barn in Abbot's Close; and I thought I could go in there and hide myself among the hay and straw, and nobody 'ud be likely to come. I went in, and it was half full o' trusses of straw, and there was some hay, too. And I made myself a bed, ever so far behind, where nobody could find me; and I was so tired and weak, I went to sleep . . . But oh, the baby's crying kept waking me; and I thought that man as looked at me so was come and laying hold of me. But I must have slept a long while at last, though I didn't know; for when I got up and went out of the barn, I didn't know whether it was night or morning. But it was morning, for it kept getting lighter; and I turned back the way I'd come. I couldn't help it, Dinah; it was the baby's crying made me go: and yet I was frightened to death. I thought that man in the smock-frock 'ud see me, and know I put the baby there. But I went on, for all that: I'd left off thinking about going home – it had gone out o' my mind. I saw nothing but that place in the wood where I'd buried the baby . . . I see it now. O Dinah! shall I allays see it?'

Hetty clung round Dinah, and shuddered again, The silence seemed long before she went on.

'I met nobody, for it was very early, and I got into the wood . . . I knew the way to the place . . . the place against the nut tree; and I could hear it crying at every step . . . I thought it was alive . . . I don't know whether I was frightened or glad . . . I don't know what I felt. I only know I was in the wood, and heard the cry. I don't know what I felt till I saw the baby was gone. And when I'd put it there, I thought I should like somebody to find it, and save it from dying; but when I saw it was gone, I was struck like a stone, with fear. I never thought o' stirring, I felt so weak. I knew I couldn't run away, and everybody as saw me 'ud know about the baby. My heart went like a stone: I couldn't wish or try for anything; it seemed like as if I should stay there for ever, and nothing 'ud ever change. But they came and took me away.'

Hetty was silent, but she shuddered again, as if there were still something behind; and Dinah waited, for her heart was so full, that tears must come before words. At last Hetty burst out, with a sob – 'Dinah, do you think God will take away that crying and the place in the wood, now I've told everything?'

'Let us pray, poor sinner: let us fall on our knees again, and pray to the God of all mercy.'

46

The Hours of Suspense

On Sunday morning, when the church bells in Stoniton were ringing for morning service, Bartle Massey re-entered Adam's room, after a short absence, and said – 'Adam, here's a visitor wants to see you.'

Adam was seated with his back towards the door, but he started up and turned round instantly, with a flushed face and an eager look. His face was even thinner and more worn than we have seen it before, but he was washed and shaven this Sunday morning.

'Is it any news ?' he said.

'Keep yourself quiet, my lad,' said Bartle; 'keep quiet. It's not what you're thinking of: it's the young Methodist woman come from the prison. She's at the bottom o' the stairs and wants to know if you think well to see her, for she has something to say to you about that poor castaway; but she wouldn't come in without your leave, she said. She thought you'd perhaps like to go out and speak to her. These preaching women are not so back'ard commonly,' Bartle muttered to himself.

'Ask her to come in,' said Adam.

He was standing with his face towards the door, and as Dinah entered, lifting up her mild grey eyes towards him, she saw at once the great change that had come since the day when she had looked up at the tall man in the cottage. There was a trembling in her clear voice as she put her hand into his, and said – 'Be comforted, Adam Bede: the Lord has not forsaken her.'

'Bless you for coming to her,' Adam said. 'Mr Massey brought me word yesterday as you was come.'

They could neither of them say any more just yet, but stood before each other in silence; and Bartle Massey, too, who had put on his spectacles, seemed transfixed, examining Dinah's face. But he recovered himself first, and said, 'Sit down, young woman, sit down,' placing the chair for her, and retiring to his old seat on the bed.

'Thank you, friend; I won't sit down,' said Dinah, 'for I must hasten back: she entreated me not to stay long away. What I came for, Adam Bede, was to pray you to go and see the poor sinner, and bid her farewell. She desires to ask your forgiveness, and it is meet you should see her today, rather than in the early morning, when the time will be short.'

Adam stood trembling, and at last sank down on his chair again.

'It won't be,' he said: 'it'll be put off – there'll perhaps come a pardon. Mr Irwine said there was hope: he said, I needn't quite give it up.'

'That's a blessed thought to me,' said Dinah, her eyes filling with tears. 'It's a fearful thing hurrying her soul away so fast.'

'But let what will be,' she added, presently, 'you will surely come, and let her speak the words that are in her heart. Although her poor soul is very dark, and discerns little beyond the things of the flesh, she is no longer hard: she is contrite – she has confessed all to me. The pride of her heart has given way, and she leans on me for help, and desires to be taught. This fills me with trust; for I cannot but think that the brethren sometimes err in measuring the Divine love by the sinner's knowledge. She is going to write a letter to the friends at the Hall Farm for me to give them when she is gone; and when I told her you were here, she said, "I should like to say Goodbye to Adam, and ask him to forgive me." You will come, Adam? – perhaps you will even now come back with me.'

'I can't,' Adam said: 'I can't say Goodbye, while there's any hope. I'm listening, and listening – I can't think o' nothing but that. It can't be as she'll die that shameful death – I can't bring my mind to it.'

He got up from his chair again, and looked away out of the window, while Dinah stood with compassionate patience. In a minute or two he turned round and said – 'I will come, Dinah . . . tomorrow morning . . . if it must be. I may have more strength to bear it, if I know it must be. Tell her, I forgive her; tell her I will come – at the very last.'

'I will not urge you against the voice of your own heart,' said Dinah. 'I must hasten back to her, for it is wonderful how she clings now, and was not willing to let me out of her sight. She used never to make any return to my affection before, but now tribulation has opened her heart. Farewell, Adam: our heavenly Father comfort you, and strengthen you to bear all things.' Dinah put out her hand, and Adam pressed it in silence.

Bartle Massey was getting up to lift the stiff latch of the door for her, but before he could reach it, she had said, gently, 'Farewell, friend,' and was gone, with her light step, down the stairs.

'Well,' said Bartle, taking off his spectacles, and putting them into his pocket, 'if there must be women to make trouble in the world, it's but fair there should be women to be comforters under it; and she's one – she's one. It's a pity she's a Methodist; but there's no getting a woman without some foolishness or other.'

Adam never went to bed that night: the excitement of suspense, heightening with every hour that brought him nearer the fatal moment, was too great; and in spite of his entreaties, in spite of his promises that he would be perfectly quiet, the schoolmaster watched too.

'What does it matter to me, lad?' Bartle said: 'a night's sleep more or less? I shall sleep long enough, by and by, underground. Let me keep thee company in trouble while I can.'

It was a long and dreary night in that small chamber. Adam would sometimes get up, and tread backwards and forwards along the short space from wall to wall; then he would sit down and hide his face, and no sound would be heard but the ticking of the watch on the table, or the falling of a cinder from the fire which the schoolmaster carefully tended. Sometimes he would burst out into vehement speech – 'If I could ha' done anything to save her – if my bearing anything would ha' done any good . . . but t' have to sit still, and know it, and do nothing . . . it's hard for a man to bear . . . and to think o' what might ha' been now, if it hadn't been for *him* . . . O God, it's the very day we should ha' been married.'

'Ay, my lad,' said Bartle, tenderly, 'it's heavy – it's heavy. But you must remember this: when you thought of marrying her, you'd a notion she'd got another sort of a nature inside her. You didn't think she could have got hardened in that little while to do what she's done.'

'I know – I know that,' said Adam. 'I thought she was loving and tender-hearted, and wouldn't tell a lie, or act deceitful. How could I think any other way? And if he'd never come near her, and I'd married her, and been loving to her, and took care of her, she might never ha' done anything bad. What would it ha' signified – my having a bit o' trouble with her? It 'ud ha' been nothing to this.'

'There's no knowing, my lad – there's no knowing what might have come. The smart's bad for you to bear now: you must have time – you must have time. But I've that opinion of you, that you'll rise above it all, and be a man again; and there may good come out of this that we don't see.'

'Good come out of it!' said Adam, passionately. 'That doesn't alter th' evil: her ruin can't be undone. I hate that talk o' people, as if there was a way o' making amends for everything. They'd more need be brought to see as the wrong they do can never be altered. When a man's spoiled his fellow creatur's life, he's no right to comfort himself with thinking good may come out of it: somebody else's good doesn't alter her shame and misery.'

'Well, lad, well,' said Bartle, in a gentle tone, strangely in contrast with his usual peremptoriness and impatience of contradiction, 'it's likely enough I talk foolishness: I'm an old fellow, and it's a good many years since I was in trouble myself. It's easy finding reasons why other folks should be patient.'

'Mr Massey,' said Adam, penitently, 'I'm very hot and hasty. I owe you something different, but you mustn't take it ill of me.'

'Not I, lad – not I.'

So the night wore on in agitation, till the chill dawn and the growing light brought the tremulous quiet that comes on the brink of despair. There would soon be no more suspense.

'Let us go to the prison now, Mr Massey,' said Adam, when he saw the hand of his watch at six. 'If there's any news come, we shall hear about it.'

The people were astir already, moving rapidly, in one direction, through the streets. Adam tried not to think where they were going, as they hurried past him in that short space between his lodging and the prison gates. He was thankful when the gates shut him in from seeing those eager people.

No; there was no news come – no pardon – no reprieve.

Adam lingered in the court half an hour before he could bring himself to send word to Dinah that he was come. But a voice caught his ear: he could not shut out the words.

'The cart is to set off at half-past seven.'

It must be said – the last Goodbye: there was no help.

In ten minutes from that time, Adam was at the door of the cell. Dinah had sent him word that she could not come to him, she could not leave Hetty one moment; but Hetty was prepared for the meeting.

He could not see her when he entered, for agitation deadened his senses, and the dim cell was almost dark to him. He stood a moment after the door closed behind him, trembling and stupefied.

But he began to see through the dimness – to see the dark eyes lifted up to him once more, but with no smile in them. O God, how sad they looked! The last time they had met his was when he parted from her with his heart full of joyous, hopeful love, and they looked out with a tearful smile from a pink, dimpled, childish face. The face was marble now; the sweet lips were pallid and half-open, and quivering; the dimples were all gone – all but one, that never went; and the eyes – Oh! the worst of all was the likeness they had to Hetty's. They were Hetty's eyes looking at him with that mournful gaze, as if she had come back to him from the dead to tell him of her misery.

She was clinging close to Dinah; her cheek was against Dinah's. It seemed as if her last faint strength and hope lay in that contact; and the pitying love that shone out from Dinah's face looked like a visible pledge of the Invisible Mercy.

When the sad eyes met – when Hetty and Adam looked at each other, she felt the change in *him* too, and it seemed to strike her with fresh fear. It was the first time she had seen any being whose face seemed to reflect the change in herself: Adam was a new image of the dreadful past and the dreadful present. She trembled more as she looked at him.

'Speak to him, Hetty,' Dinah said; 'tell him what is in your heart.'

Hetty obeyed her, like a little child.

'Adam . . . I'm very sorry . . . I behaved very wrong to you . . . will you forgive me . . . before I die?'

Adam answered with a half-sob: 'Yes, I forgive thee, Hetty: I forgave thee long ago.'

It had seemed to Adam as if his brain would burst with the anguish of meeting

Hetty's eyes in the first moments; but the sound of her voice uttering these penitent words touched a chord which had been less strained: there was a sense of relief from what was becoming unbearable, and the rare tears came – they had never come before, since he had hung on Seth's neck in the beginning of his sorrow.

Hetty made an involuntary movement towards him; some of the love that she had once lived in the midst of was come near her again. She kept hold of Dinah's hand, but she went up to Adam and said, timidly – 'Will you kiss me again, Adam, for all I've been so wicked?'

Adam took the blanched wasted hand she put out to him, and they gave each other the solemn unspeakable kiss of a lifelong parting.

'And tell him,' Hetty said, in rather a stronger voice, 'tell him . . . for there's nobody else to tell him . . . as I went after him and couldn't find him . . . and I hated him and cursed him once . . . but Dinah says, I should forgive him . . . and I try . . . for else God won't forgive me.'

There was a noise at the door of the cell now – the key was being turned in the lock, and when the door opened, Adam saw indistinctly that there were several faces there: he was too agitated to see more – even to see that Mr Irwine's face was one of them. He felt that the last preparations were beginning, and he could stay no longer. Room was silently made for him to depart, and he went to his chamber in loneliness, leaving Bartle Massey to watch and see the end.

47

The Last Moment

It was a sight that some people remembered better even than their own sorrows – the sight in that grey clear morning, when the fatal cart with the two young women in it was descried by the waiting watching multitude, cleaving its way towards the hideous symbol of a deliberately-inflicted sudden death.

All Stoniton had heard of Dinah Morris, the young Methodist woman who had brought the obstinate criminal to confess, and there was as much eagerness to see her as to see the wretched Hetty.

But Dinah was hardly conscious of the multitude. When Hetty had caught sight of the vast crowd in the distance, she had clutched Dinah convulsively.

'Close your eyes, Hetty,' Dinah said, 'and let us pray without ceasing to God.'

And in a low voice, as the cart went slowly along through the midst of the gazing crowd, she poured forth her soul with the wrestling intensity of a last pleading, for the trembling creature that clung to her and clutched her as the only visible sign of love and pity.

Dinah did not know that the crowd was silent, gazing at her with a sort of awe – she did not even know how near they were to the fatal spot, when the cart stopped, and she shrank appalled at a loud shout hideous to her ear, like a vast yell of demons. Hetty's shriek mingled with the sound, and they clasped each other in mutual horror.

But it was not a shout of execration – not a yell of exultant cruelty.

It was a shout of sudden excitement at the appearance of a horseman cleaving the crowd at full gallop. The horse is hot and distressed, but answers to the desperate spurring; the rider looks as if his eyes were glazed by madness, and he saw nothing but what was unseen by others. See, he has something in his hand – he is holding it up as if it were a signal.

The sheriff knows him: it is Arthur Donnithorne, carrying in his hand a hard-won release from death.

48

Another Meeting in the Wood

The next day, at evening, two men were walking from opposite points towards the same scene, drawn thither by a common memory. The scene was the Grove by Donnithorne Chase: you know who the men were.

The old Squire's funeral had taken place that morning, the will had been read, and now in the first breathing-space, Arthur Donnithorne had come out for a lonely walk, that he might look fixedly at the new future before him, and confirm himself in a sad resolution. He thought he could do that best in the Grove.

Adam, too, had come from Stoniton on Monday evening, and today he had not left home, except to go to the family at the Hall Farm, and tell them everything that Mr Irwine had left untold. He had agreed with the Poysers that he would follow them to their new neighbourhood, wherever that might be; for he meant to give up the management of the woods, and, as soon as it was practicable, he would wind up his business with Jonathan Burge, and settle with his mother and Seth in a home within reach of the friends to whom he felt bound by a mutual sorrow.

'Seth and me are sure to find work,' he said. 'A man that's got our trade at his finger ends is at home everywhere; and we must make a new start. My mother won't stand in the way, for she's told me, since I came home, she'd made up her mind to being buried in another parish, if I wished it, and if I'd be more comfortable elsewhere. It's wonderful how quiet she's been ever since I came back. It seems as if the very greatness o' the trouble had quieted and calmed her. We shall all be better in a new country; though there's some I shall be loth to leave behind. But I won't part from you and yours, if I can help it, Mr Poyser. Trouble's made us kin.'

'Ay, lad,' said Martin. 'We'll go out o' hearing o' that man's name. But I doubt we shall ne'er go far enough for folks not to find out as we've got them belonging to us as are transported o'er the seas, and were like to be hanged. We shall have that flyin' up in our faces, and our children's after us.'

That was a long visit to the Hall Farm, and drew too strongly on Adam's energies for him to think of seeing others, or re-entering on his old occupations till the morrow. 'But tomorrow,' he said to himself, 'I'll go to work again. I shall learn to like it again some time, maybe; and it's right, whether I like it or not.'

This evening was the last he would allow to be absorbed by sorrow: suspense was gone now, and he must bear the unalterable. He was resolved not to see Arthur Donnithorne again, if it were possible to avoid him. He had no message to deliver from Hetty now, for Hetty had seen Arthur; and Adam distrusted himself: he had learned to dread the violence of his own feeling. That word of Mr Irwine's – that he must remember what he had felt after giving the last blow to Arthur in the Grove – had remained with him.

These thoughts about Arthur, like all thoughts that are charged with strong feeling, were continually recurring, and they always called up the image of the Grove – of that spot under the overarching boughs where he had caught sight of the two bending figures, and had been possessed by sudden rage.

'I'll go and see it again tonight for the last time,' he said; 'it'll do me good; it'll make me feel over again what I felt when I'd knocked him down. I felt what poor empty work it was, as soon as I'd done it, before I began to think he might be dead.'

In this way it happened that Arthur and Adam were walking towards the same spot at the same time.

Adam had on his working-dress again, now – for he had thrown off the other with a sense of relief as soon as he came home; and if he had had the basket of tools over his shoulder, he might have been taken, with his pale wasted face, for the spectre of the Adam Bede who entered the Grove on that August evening eight months ago. But he had no basket of tools, and he was not walking with the old erectness, looking keenly round him; his hands were thrust in his side pockets and his eyes rested chiefly on the ground. He had not long entered the Grove, and now he paused before a beech. He knew that tree well; it was the boundary mark of his youth – the sign, to him, of the time when some of his earliest, strongest feelings had left him. He felt sure they would never return. And yet, at this moment, there was a stirring of affection at the remembrance of that Arthur Donnithorne whom he had believed in before he had come up to this beech eight months ago. It was affection for the dead: that Arthur existed no longer.

He was disturbed by the sound of approaching footsteps, but the beech stood at a turning in the road, and he could not see who was coming, until the tall slim figure in deep mourning suddenly stood before him at only two yards distance. They both started, and looked at each other in silence. Often, in the last fortnight, Adam had imagined himself as close to Arthur as this, assailing him with words that should be as harrowing as the voice of remorse, forcing upon him a just share in the misery he had caused; and often, too, he had told himself that such a meeting had better not be. But in imagining the meeting he had always seen Arthur, as he had met him on that evening in the Grove, florid, careless, light of speech; and the figure before him touched him with the signs of suffering. Adam knew what suffering was – he could not lay a cruel finger on a bruised man. He felt no impulse that he needed to resist: silence was more just than reproach. Arthur was the first to speak.

'Adam,' he said, quietly, 'it may be a good thing that we have met here, for I wished to see you. I should have asked to see you tomorrow.'

He paused, but Adam said nothing.

'I know it is painful to you to meet me,' Arthur went on, 'but it is not likely to happen again for years to come.'

'No, sir,' said Adam, coldly, 'that was what I meant to write to you tomorrow, as it would be better all dealings should be at an end between us, and somebody else put in my place.'

Arthur felt the answer keenly, and it was not without an effort that he spoke again.

'It was partly on that subject I wished to speak to you. I don't want to lessen your indignation against me, or ask you to do anything for my sake. I only wish to ask you if you will help me to lessen the evil consequences of the past, which is unchangeable. I don't mean consequences to myself, but to others. It is but little I can do, I know. I know the worst consequences will remain; but something may be done, and you can help me. Will you listen to me patiently?'

'Yes, sir,' said Adam, after some hesitation; 'I'll hear what it is. If I can help to mend anything, I will. Anger 'ull mend nothing, I know. We've had enough o' that.'

'I was going to the Hermitage,' said Arthur. 'Will you go there with me and sit down? We can talk better there.'

The Hermitage had never been entered since they left it together, for Arthur had locked up the key in his desk. And now, when he opened the door, there was the candle burnt out in the socket; there was the chair in the same place where Adam remembered sitting; there was the waste-paper basket full of scraps, and deep down in it, Arthur felt in an instant, there was the little pink silk handkerchief. It would have been painful to enter this place if their previous thoughts had been less painful.

They sat down opposite each other in the old places, and Arthur said, 'I'm going away, Adam; I'm going into the army.'

Poor Arthur felt that Adam ought to be affected by this announcement – ought to have a movement of sympathy towards him. But Adam's lips remained firmly closed, and the expression of his face unchanged.

'What I want to say to you,' Arthur continued, 'is this: one of my reasons for going away is, that no one else may leave Hayslope – may leave their home on my account. I would do anything, there is no sacrifice I would not make, to prevent any further injury to others through my – through what has happened.'

Arthur's words had precisely the opposite effect to that he had anticipated. Adam thought he perceived in them that notion of compensation for irretrievable wrong, that self-soothing attempt to make evil bear the same fruits as good, which most of all roused his indignation. He was as strongly impelled to look painful facts right in the face as Arthur was to turn away his eyes from them. Moreover, he had the wakeful suspicious pride of a poor man in the presence of a rich man. He felt his old severity returning as he said – 'The time's past for that, sir. A man should make sacrifices to keep clear of doing a wrong; sacrifices won't undo it when it's done. When people's feelings have got a deadly wound, they can't be cured with favours.'

'Favours!' said Arthur, passionately; 'no; how can you suppose I meant that?

But the Poysers – Mr Irwine tells me the Poysers mean to leave the place where they have lived so many years – for generations. Don't you see, as Mr Irwine does, that if they could be persuaded to overcome the feeling that drives them away, it would be much better for them in the end to remain on the old spot, among the friends and neighbours who know them?'

'That's true,' said Adam, coldly. 'But then, sir, folks's feelings are not so easily overcome. It'll be hard for Martin Poyser to go to a strange place, among strange faces, when he's been bred up on the Hall Farm, and his father before him; but then it 'ud be harder for a man with his feelings to stay. I don't see how the thing's to be made any other than hard. There's a sort o' damage, sir, that can't be made up for.'

Arthur was silent some moments. In spite of other feelings, dominant in him this evening, his pride winced under Adam's mode of treating him. Wasn't he himself suffering? Was not he too obliged to renounce his most cherished hopes? It was now as it had been eight months ago – Adam was forcing Arthur to feel more intensely the irrevocableness of his own wrong-doing: he was presenting the sort of resistance that was the most irritating to Arthur's eager, ardent nature. But his anger was subdued by the same influence that had subdued Adam's when they first confronted each other – by the marks of suffering in a long familiar face. The momentary struggle ended in the feeling that he could bear a great deal from Adam, to whom he had been the occasion of bearing so much; but there was a touch of pleading, boyish vexation in his tone as he said – 'But people may make injuries worse by unreasonable conduct – by giving way to anger and satisfying that for the moment, instead of thinking what will be the effect in the future.

'If I were going to stay here and act as landlord,' he added, presently, with still more eagerness – 'if I were careless about what I've done – what I've been the cause of, you would have some excuse, Adam, for going away and encouraging others to go. You would have some excuse then for trying to make the evil worse. But when I tell you I'm going away for years – when you know what that means for me, how it cuts off every plan of happiness I've ever formed – it is impossible for a sensible man like you to believe that there is any real ground for the Poysers refusing to remain. I know their feeling about disgrace – Mr Irwine has told me all; but he is of opinion that they might be persuaded out of this idea that they are disgraced in the eyes of their neighbours, and that they can't remain on my estate, if you would join him in his efforts – if you would stay yourself, and go on managing the old woods.'

Arthur paused a moment, and then added, pleadingly, 'You know that's a good work to do for the sake of other people, besides the owner. And you don't know but that they may have a better owner soon, whom you will like to work for. If I die, my cousin Tradgett will have the estate, and take my name. He is a good fellow.'

Adam could not help being moved: it was impossible for him not to feel that this was the voice of the honest, warm-hearted Arthur whom he had loved and been proud of in old days; but nearer memories would not be thrust away. He was silent; yet Arthur saw an answer in his face that induced him to go on, with growing earnestness.

'And then, if you would talk to the Poysers – if you would talk the matter over with Mr Irwine – he means to see you tomorrow – and then if you would join your arguments to his to prevail on them not to go . . . I know, of course, that they would not accept any favour from me: I mean nothing of that kind: but I'm sure they would suffer less in the end. Irwine thinks so too; and Mr Irwine is to have the chief authority on the estate – he has consented to undertake that. They will really be under no man but one whom they respect and like. It would be the same with you, Adam; and it could be nothing but a desire to give me worse pain that could incline you to go.'

Arthur was silent again for a little while, and then said, with some agitation in his voice – 'I wouldn't act so towards you, I know. If you were in my place and I in yours, I should try to help you to do the best.'

Adam made a hasty movement on his chair, and looked on the ground. Arthur went on – 'Perhaps you've never done anything you've had bitterly to repent of in your life, Adam; if you had, you would be more generous. You would know then that it's worse for me than for you.'

Arthur rose from his seat with the last words, and went to one of the windows, looking out and turning his back on Adam, as he continued, passionately – 'Haven't I loved her too? Didn't I see her yesterday? Shan't I carry the thought of her about with me as much as you will? And don't you think you would suffer more if you'd been in fault?'

There was silence for several minutes, for the struggle in Adam's mind was not easily decided. Facile natures, whose emotions have little permanence, can hardly understand how much inward resistance he overcame before he rose from his seat and turned towards Arthur. Arthur heard the movement, and, turning round, met the sad but softened look with which Adam said – 'It's true what you say, sir: I'm hard – it's in my nature. I was too hard with my father, for doing wrong. I've been a bit hard t' everybody but *her*. I felt as if nobody pitied her enough – her suffering cut into me so; and when I thought the folks at the Farm were too hard with her, I said I'd never be hard to anybody myself again. But feeling overmuch about her has perhaps made me unfair to you. I've known what it is in my life to repent and feel it's too late: I felt I'd been too harsh to my father when he was gone from me – I feel it now, when I think of him. I've no right to be hard towards them as have done wrong and repent.'

Adam spoke these words with the firm distinctness of a man who is resolved to leave nothing unsaid that he is bound to say; but he went on with more hesitation.

'I wouldn't shake hands with you once, sir, when you asked me – but if you're willing to do it now, for all I refused then . . . '

Arthur's white hand was in Adam's large grasp in an instant, and with that action there was a strong rush, on both sides, of the old, boyish affection.

'Adam,' Arthur said, impelled to full confession now, 'it would never have happened if I'd known you loved her. That would have helped to save me from it. And I *did* struggle: I never meant to injure her. I deceived you afterwards – and that led on to worse; but I thought it was forced upon me, I thought it was the best thing I could do. And in that letter I told her to let me know if she were in any trouble: don't think I would not have done everything I could. But I was all wrong from the very first, and horrible wrong has come of it. God knows, I'd give my life if I could undo it.'

They sat down again opposite each other, and Adam said, tremulously – 'How did she seem when you left her, sir?'

'Don't ask me, Adam,' Arthur said; 'I feel sometimes as if I should go mad with thinking of her looks and what she said to me, and then, that I couldn't get a full pardon – that I couldn't save her from that wretched fate of being transported – that I can do nothing for her all those years; and she may die under it, and never know comfort any more.'

'Ah, sir,' said Adam, for the first time feeling his own pain merged in sympathy for Arthur, 'you and me'll often be thinking o' the same thing, when we're a long way off one another. I'll pray God to help you, as I pray him to help me.'

'But there's that sweet woman – that Dinah Morris,' Arthur said, pursuing his own thoughts, and not knowing what had been the sense of Adam's words, 'she says she shall stay with her to the very last moment – till she goes; and the poor thing clings to her as if she found some comfort in her. I could worship that woman; I don't know what I should do if she were not there. Adam, you will see her when she comes back: I could say nothing to her yesterday – nothing of what I felt towards her. Tell her,' Arthur went on hurriedly, as if he wanted to hide the emotion with which he spoke, while he took off his chain and watch – 'tell her I asked you to give her this in remembrance of me – of the man to whom she is the one source of comfort, when he thinks of . . . I know she doesn't care about such things - or anything else I can give her for its own sake. But she will use the watch – I shall like to think of her using it.'

'I'll give it to her, sir,' Adam said, 'and tell her your words. She told me she should come back to the people at the Hall Farm.'

'And you will persuade the Poysers to stay, Adam?' said Arthur, reminded of the subject which both of them had forgotten in the first interchange of revived friendship. 'You will stay yourself, and help Mr Irwine to carry out the repairs and improvements on the estate?'

'There's one thing, sir, that perhaps you don't take account of,' said Adam, with hesitating gentleness, 'and that was what made me hang back longer. You see, it's the same with both me and the Poysers: if we stay, it's for our own worldly interest, and it looks as if we'd put up with anything for the sake o' that. I know that's what they'll feel, and I can't help feeling a little of it myself. When folks have got an honourable, independent spirit, they don't like to do anything that might make 'em seem base-minded.'

'But no one who knows you will think that, Adam: that is not a reason strong enough against a course that is really more generous, more unselfish than the other. And it will be known – it shall be made known, that both you and the Poysers stayed at my entreaty. Adam, don't try to make things worse for me; I'm punished enough without that.'

'No, sir, no,' Adam said, looking at Arthur with mournful affection. 'God forbid I should make things worse for you. I used to wish I could do it, in my passion – but that was when I thought you didn't feel enough. I'll stay, sir: I'll do the best I can. It's all I've got to think of now – to do my work well, and make the world a bit better place for them as can enjoy it.'

'Then we'll part now, Adam. You will see Mr Irwine tomorrow, and consult with him about everything.'

'Are you going soon, sir?' said Adam.

'As soon as possible – after I've made the necessary arrangements. Goodbye, Adam. I shall think of you going about the old place.'

'Goodbye, sir. God bless you.'

The hands were clasped once more, and Adam left the Hermitage, feeling that sorrow was more bearable now hatred was gone.

As soon as the door was closed behind him, Arthur went to the waste-paper basket and took out the little pink silk handkerchief.

BOOK SIXTH

49

At the Hall Farm

The first autumnal afternoon sunshine of 1801 – more than eighteen months after that parting of Adam and Arthur in the Hermitage – was on the yard at the Hall Farm, and the bulldog was in one of his most excited moments; for it was that hour of the day when the cows were being driven into the yard for their afternoon milking. No wonder the patient beasts ran confusedly into the wrong places, for the alarming din of the bulldog was mingled with more distant sounds which the timid feminine creatures, with pardonable superstition, imagined also to have some relation to their own movements – with the tremendous crack of the waggoner's whip, the roar of his voice, and the booming thunder of the waggon, as it left the rickyard empty of its golden load.

The milking of the cows was a sight Mrs Poyser loved, and at this hour on mild days she was usually standing at the house door, with her knitting in her hands, in quiet contemplation, only heightened to a keener interest when the vicious yellow cow, who had once kicked over a pailful of precious milk, was about to undergo the preventive punishment of having her hinder-legs strapped.

Today, however, Mrs Poyser gave but a divided attention to the arrival of the cows, for she was in eager discussion with Dinah, who was stitching Mr Poyser's shirt-collars, and had borne patiently to have her thread broken three times by Totty pulling at her arm with a sudden insistance that she should look at 'Baby', that is, at a large wooden doll with no legs and a long skirt, whose bald head Totty, seated in her small chair at Dinah's side, was caressing and pressing to her fat cheek with much fervour. Totty is larger by more than two years' growth than when you first saw her, and she has on a black frock under her pinafore: Mrs Poyser too has on a black gown, which seems to heighten the family likeness between her and Dinah. In other respects there is little outward change now discernible in our old friends, or in the pleasant house-place, bright with polished oak and pewter.

'I never saw the like to you, Dinah,' Mrs Poyser was saying, 'when you've once took anything into your head: there's no more moving you than the rooted tree. You may say what you like, but I don't believe *that's* religion; for what's the Sermon on the Mount about, as you're so fond o' reading to the boys, but doing what other folks 'ud have you do? But if it was anything unreasonable they wanted you to do, like taking your cloak off and giving it to 'em, or letting 'em slap you i' the face, I dare say you'd be ready enough: it's only when one 'ud have you do what's plain common-sense and good for yourself, as you're obstinate th' other way.'

'Nay, dear aunt,' said Dinah, smiling slightly as she went on with her work. 'I'm sure your wish 'ud be a reason for me to do anything that I didn't feel it was wrong to do.'

'Wrong! You drive me past bearing. What is there wrong, I should like to know, i' staying along wi' your own friends, as are th' happier for having you with 'em, an' are willing to provide for you, even if your work didn't more nor pay 'em for the bit o' sparrow's victual y' eat, and the bit o' rag you put on? An' who is it, I should like to know, as you're bound t' help and comfort i' the world more nor your own flesh and blood – an' me th' only aunt you've got above-ground, an' am brought to the brink o' the grave welly every winter as comes, an' there's the child as sits beside you 'ull break her little heart when you go, an' the grandfather not been dead a twelvemonth, an' your uncle 'ull miss you so as never was – a-lighting his pipe an' waiting on him, an' now I can trust you wi' the butter, an' have had all the trouble o' teaching you, and there's all the sewing to be done, an' I must have a strange gell out o' Treddles'on to do it – an' all because you must go back to that bare heap o' stones as the very crows fly over an' won't stop at.'

'Dear aunt Rachel,' said Dinah, looking up in Mrs Poyser's face, 'it's your kindness makes you say I'm useful to you. You don't really want me now; for Nancy and Molly are clever at their work, and you're in good health now, by the blessing of God, and my uncle is of a cheerful countenance again, and you have neighbours and friends not a few – some of them come to sit with my uncle almost daily. Indeed, you will not miss me; and at Snowfield there are brethren and sisters in great need, who have none of those comforts you have around you. I feel that I am called back to those amongst whom my lot was first cast: I feel drawn again towards the hills where I used to be blessed in carrying the word of life to the sinful and desolate.'

'You feel! yes,' said Mrs Poyser, returning from a parenthetic glance at the cows. 'That's allays the reason I'm to sit down wi', when you've a mind to do anything contrairy. What do you want to be preaching for more than you're preaching now? Don't you go off, the Lord knows where, every Sunday a-preaching and praying? an' haven't you got Methodists enow at Treddles'on to go and look at, if church folks's faces are too handsome to please you? an' isn't there them i' this parish as you've got under hand, and they're like enough to make friends wi' Old Harry again as soon as your back's turned? There's that Bessy Cranage – she'll be flaunting i' new finery three weeks after you're gone, I'll be bound: she'll no more go on in her new ways without you, than a dog 'ull stand on its hindlegs when there's nobody looking. But I suppose it doesna matter so much about folks's souls i' this country, else you'd be for staying with your own aunt, for she's none so good but what you might help her to be better.'

There was a certain something in Mrs Poyser's voice just then, which she did not wish to be noticed, so she turned round hastily to look at the clock and said: 'See there! It's teatime; an' if Martin's i' the rickyard, he'll like a cup. Here, Totty, my chicken, let mother put your bonnet on, and then you go out into the rickyard, and see if father's there, and tell him he mustn't go away again without coming t' have a cup o' tea; and tell your brothers to come in too.'

Totty trotted off in her flapping bonnet, while Mrs Poyser set out the bright
oak table, and reached down the teacups.

'You talk o' them gells Nancy and Molly being clever i' their work,' she began
again – 'it's fine talking. They're all the same, clever or stupid – one can't trust
'em out o' one's sight a minute. They want somebody's eye on 'em constant if
they're to be kept to their work. An' suppose I'm ill again this winter, as I was
the winter before last, who's to look after 'em then, if you're gone? An' there's
that blessed child – something's sure t' happen to her – they'll let her tumble
into the fire, or get at the kettle wi' the boiling lard in't, or some mischief as 'ull
lame her for life; an' it'll be all your fault, Dinah.'

'Aunt,' said Dinah, 'I promise to come back to you in the winter if you're ill.
Don't think I will ever stay away from you if you're in real want of me. But
indeed it is needful for my own soul that I should go away from this life of ease
and luxury, in which I have all things too richly to enjoy – at least that I should
go away for a short space. No one can know but myself what are my inward
needs, and the besetments I am most in danger from. Your wish for me to stay is
not a call of duty which I refuse to hearken to because it is against my own
desires; it is a temptation that I must resist, lest the love of the creature should
become like a mist in my soul shutting out the heavenly light.'

'It passes my cunning to know what you mean by ease and luxury,' said Mrs
Poyser, as she cut the bread and butter. 'It's true there's good victual enough
about you, as nobody shall ever say I don't provide enough and to spare, but if
there's ever a bit o' odds and ends as nobody else 'ud eat, you're sure to pick it
out . . . but look there! there's Adam Bede a carrying the little un in. I wonder
how it is he's come so early.'

Mrs Poyser hastened to the door for the pleasure of looking at her darling in a
new position, with love in her eyes but reproof on her tongue.

'Oh for shame, Totty! Little gells o' five year old should be ashamed to be
carried. Why, Adam, she'll break your arm, such a big gell as that; set her
down – for shame!'

'Nay, nay,' said Adam, 'I can lift her with my hand, I've no need to take my
arm to it.'

Totty, looking as serenely unconscious of remark as a fat white puppy, was set
down at the door-place, and the mother enforced her reproof with a shower of
kisses.

'You're surprised to see me at this hour o' the day,' said Adam.

'Yes, but come in,' said Mrs Poyser, making way for him; 'there's no bad news,
I hope?'

'No, nothing bad,' Adam answered, as he went up to Dinah and put out his
hand to her. She had laid down her work and stood up, instinctively, as he
approached her. A faint blush died away from her pale cheek as she put her hand
in his, and looked up at him timidly.

'It's an errand to you brought me, Dinah,' said Adam, apparently unconscious
that he was holding her hand all the while; 'mother's a bit ailing, and she's set
her heart on your coming to stay the night with her, if you'll be so kind. I told
her I'd call and ask you as I came from the village. She overworks herself, and I

can't persuade her to have a little girl t' help her. I don't know what's to be done.'

Adam released Dinah's hand as he ceased speaking, and was expecting an answer; but before she had opened her lips Mrs Poyser said – 'Look there now! I told you there was folks enow t' help i' this parish, wi'out going further off. There's Mrs Bede getting as old and cas'alty as can be, and she won't let anybody but you go a-nigh her hardly. The folks at Snowfield have learnt by this time to do better wi'out you nor she can.'

'I'll put my bonnet on and set off directly, if you don't want anything done first, aunt,' said Dinah, folding up her work.

'Yes, I do want something done. I want you t' have your tea, child; it's all ready; and you'll have a cup, Adam, if y' arena in too big a hurry.'

'Yes, I'll have a cup, please; and then I'll walk with Dinah. I'm going straight home, for I've got a lot o' timber valuations to write out.'

'Why, Adam lad, are you here?' said Mr Poyser, entering warm and coatless, with the two black-eyed boys behind him still looking as much like him as two small elephants are like a large one. 'How is it we've got sight o' you so long before foddering-time?'

'I came on an errand for mother,' said Adam. 'She's got a touch of her old complaint, and she wants Dinah to go and stay with her a bit.'

'Well, we'll spare her for your mother a little while,' said Mr Poyser. 'But we wonna spare her for anybody else, on'y her husband.'

'Husband!' said Marty, who was at the most prosaic and literal period of the boyish mind. 'Why, Dinah hasn't got a husband.'

'Spare her?' said Mrs Poyser, placing a seed-cake on the table, and then seating herself to pour out the tea. 'But we must spare her, it seems, and not for a husband neither, but for her own megrims. Tommy, what are you doing to your little sister's doll? making the child naughty, when she'd be good if you'd let her. You shanna have a morsel o' cake if you behave so.'

Tommy, with true brotherly sympathy, was amusing himself by turning Dolly's skirt over her bald head, and exhibiting her truncated body to the general scorn - an indignity which cut Totty to the heart.

'What do you think Dinah's been a-telling me since dinnertime?' Mrs Poyser continued, looking at her husband.

'Eh! I'm a poor un at guessing,' said Mr Poyser.

'Why, she means to go back to Snowfield again, and work i' the mill, and starve herself, as she used to do, like a creatur as has got no friends.'

Mr Poyser did not readily find words to express his unpleasant astonishment; he only looked from his wife to Dinah, who had now seated herself beside Totty, as a bulwark against brotherly playfulness, and was busying herself with the children's tea. If he had been given to making general reflections, it would have occurred to him that there was certainly a change come over Dinah, for she never used to change colour; but, as it was, he merely observed that her face was flushed at that moment. Mr Poyser thought she looked the prettier for it: it was a flush no deeper than the petal of a monthly rose. Perhaps it came because her uncle was looking at her so fixedly; but there is no knowing; for just then Adam was saying, with quiet surprise – 'Why, I hoped Dinah was settled among us for life. I thought she'd given up the notion o' going back to her old country.'

'Thought! yes,' said Mrs Poyser; 'and so would anybody else ha' thought, as had got their right end up'ards. But I suppose you must be a Methodist to know what a Methodist 'ull do. It's ill guessing what the bats are flying after.'

'Why, what have we done to you, Dinah, as you must go away from us?' said Mr Poyser, still pausing over his teacup. 'It's like breaking your word, welly; for your aunt never had no thought but you'd make this your home.'

'Nay, uncle,' said Dinah, trying to be quite calm. 'When I first came, I said it was only for a time, as long as I could be of any comfort to my aunt.'

'Well, an' who said you'd ever left off being a comfort to me?' said Mrs Poyser. 'If you didna mean to stay wi' me, you'd better never ha' come. Them as ha' never had a cushion don't miss it.'

'Nay, nay,' said Mr Poyser, who objected to exaggerated views. 'Thee mustna say so; we should ha' been ill off wi'out her, Lady Day was a twelvemont': we mun be thankful for that, whether she stays or no. But I canna think what she mun leave a good home for, to go back int' a country where the land, most on't, isna worth ten shillings an acre, rent and profits.'

'Why, that's just the reason she wants to go, as fur as she can give a reason,' said Mrs Poyser; 'she says this country's too comfortable, an' there's too much t' eat' an' folks arena miserable enough. And she's going next week: I canna turn her, say what I will. It's allays the way wi' them meekfaced people; you may's well pelt a bag o' feathers as talk to 'em. But I say it isna religion, to be so obstinate – is it now, Adam?'

Adam saw that Dinah was more disturbed than he had ever seen her by any matter relating to herself, and, anxious to relieve her, if possible, he said, looking at her affectionately – 'Nay, I can't find fault with anything Dinah does. I believe her thoughts are better than our guesses, let 'em be what they may. I should ha' been thankful for her to stay among us; but if she thinks well to go, I wouldn't cross her, or make it hard to her by objecting. We owe her something different to that.'

As it often happens, the words intended to relieve her were just too much for Dinah's susceptible feelings at this moment. The tears came into the grey eyes too fast to be hidden; and she got up hurriedly, meaning it to be understood that she was going to put on her bonnet.

'Mother, what's Dinah crying for?' said Totty. 'She isn't a naughty dell.'

'Thee'st gone a bit too fur,' said Mr Poyser. 'We've no right t' interfere with her doing as she likes. An' thee'dst be as angry as could be wi' me, if I said a word against anything she did.'

'Because you'd very like be finding fault wi'out reason,' said Mrs Poyser. 'But there's reason i' what I say, else I shouldna say it. It's easy talking for them as can't love her so well as her own aunt does. An' me got so used to her! I shall feel as uneasy as a new sheared sheep when she's gone from me. An' to think of her leaving a parish where she's so looked on. There's Mr Irwine makes as much of her as if she was a lady, for all her being a Methodist, an' wi' that maggot o' preaching in her head – God forgi'e me if I'm i' the wrong to call it so.'

'Ay,' said Mr Poyser, looking jocose; 'but thee dostna tell Adam what he said to thee about it one day. The missis was saying, Adam, as the preaching was th' only fault to be found wi' Dinah, and Mr Irwine says, "But you mustn't find fault with her for that, Mrs Poyser; you forget she's got no husband to preach to. I'll answer for it, you give Poyser many a good sermon." The parson had thee there,' Mr Poyser added, laughing unctuously. 'I told Bartle Massey on it, an' he laughed too.'

'Yes, it's a small joke sets men laughing when they sit a staring at one another with a pipe i' their mouths,' said Mrs Poyser. 'Give Bartle Massey his way, and he'd have all the sharpness to himself. If the chaff-cutter had the making of us, we should all be straw, I reckon. Totty, my chicken, go upstairs to cousin Dinah, and see what she's doing, and give her a pretty kiss.'

This errand was devised for Totty as a means of checking certain threatening symptoms about the corners of the mouth; for Tommy, no longer expectant of cake, was lifting up his eyelids with his forefingers, and turning his eyeballs towards Totty, in a way that she felt to be disagreeably personal.

'You're rare and busy now – eh, Adam?' said Mr Poyser. 'Burge's getting so bad wi' his asthmy, it's well if he'll ever do much riding about again.'

'Yes, we've got a pretty bit o' building on hand now,' said Adam: 'what with the repairs on th' estate, and the new houses at Treddles'on.'

'I'll bet a penny that new house Burge is building on his own bit o' land is for him and Mary to go to,' said Mr Poyser. 'He'll be for laying by business soon, I'll warrant, and be wanting you to take to it all, and pay him so much by th' 'ear. We shall see you living on th' hill before another twelvemont's over.'

'Well,' said Adam, 'I should like t' have the business in my own hands. It isn't as I mind much about getting any more money: we've enough and to spare now, with only our two selves and mother; but I should like t' have my own way about things: I could try plans then, as I can't do now.'

'You get on pretty well wi' the new steward, I reckon?' said Mr Poyser.

'Yes, yes; he's a sensible man enough: understands farming – he's carrying on the draining, and all that, capital. You must go someday towards the Stonyshire side, and see what alterations they're making. But he's got no notion about buildings: you can so seldom get hold of a man as can turn his brains to more nor one thing; it's just as if they wore blinkers like th' horses, and could see nothing o' one side of 'em. Now, there's Mr Irwine has got notions o' building more nor most architects; for as for th' architects, they set up to be fine fellows, but the most of 'em don't know where to set a chimney so as it shan't be quarrelling with a door. My notion is, a practical builder, that's got a bit o' taste, makes the best architect for common things; and I've ten times the pleasure i' seeing after the work when I've made the plan myself.'

Mr Poyser listened with an admiring interest to Adam's discourse on building; but perhaps it suggested to him that the building of his corn-rick had been proceeding a little too long without the control of the master's eye; for when Adam had done speaking, he got up and said – 'Well, lad, I'll bid you Goodbye now, for I'm off to the rickyard again.'

Adam rose too, for he saw Dinah entering, with her bonnet on, and a little basket in her hand, preceded by Totty.

'You're ready, I see, Dinah,' Adam said; 'so we'll set off, for the sooner I'm at home the better.'

'Mother,' said Totty, with her treble pipe, 'Dinah was saying her prayers and crying ever so.'

'Hush, hush,' said the mother: 'little gells mustn't chatter.'

Whereupon the father, shaking with silent laughter, set Totty on the white deal table, and desired her to kiss him. Mr and Mrs Poyser, you perceive, had no correct principles of education.

'Come back tomorrow if Mrs Bede doesn't want you, Dinah,' said Mrs Poyser: 'but you can stay, you know, if she's ill.'

So, when the Goodbyes had been said, Dinah and Adam left the Hall Farm together.

50

In the Cottage

Adam did not ask Dinah to take his arm when they got out into the lane. He had never yet done so, often as they had walked together; for he had observed that she never walked arm-in-arm with Seth, and he thought, perhaps, that kind of support was not agreeable to her. So they walked apart, though side by side, and the close poke of her little black bonnet hid her face from him.

'You can't be happy, then, to make the Hall Farm your home, Dinah?' Adam said, with the quiet interest of a brother who has no anxiety for himself in the matter. 'It's a pity, seeing they're so fond of you.'

'You know, Adam, my heart is as their heart, so far as love for them and care for their welfare goes; but they are in no present need, their sorrows are healed, and I feel that I am called back to my old work, in which I found a blessing that I have missed of late in the midst of too abundant worldly good. I know it is a vain thought to flee from the work that God appoints us, for the sake of finding a greater blessing to our own souls, as if we could choose for ourselves where we shall find the fulness of the Divine Presence, instead of seeking it where alone it is to be found, in loving obedience. But now, I believe, I have a clear showing that my work lies elsewhere – at least for a time. In the years to come, if my aunt's health should fail, or she should otherwise need me, I shall return.'

'You know best, Dinah,' said Adam. 'I don't believe you'd go against the wishes of them that love you, and are akin to you, without a good and sufficient reason in your own conscience. I've no right to say anything about my being sorry: you know well enough what cause I have to put you above every other friend I've got; and if it had been ordered so that you could ha' been my sister, and lived with us all our lives, I should ha' counted it the greatest blessing as could happen to us now; but Seth tells me there's no hope o' that: your feelings are different; and perhaps I'm taking too much upon me to speak about it.'

Dinah made no answer, and they walked on in silence for some yards, till they came to the stone stile; where, as Adam had passed through first, and turned round to give her his hand while she mounted the unusually high step, she could not prevent him from seeing her face. It struck him with surprise; for the grey eyes, usually so mild and grave, had the bright uneasy glance which accompanied suppressed agitation, and the slight flush in her cheeks, with which she had come downstairs, was heightened to a deep rose-colour. She looked as if she were only sister to Dinah. Adam was silent with surprise and conjecture for some moments, and then he said – 'I hope I've not hurt or displeased you, by what I've said, Dinah: perhaps I was making too free. I've no wish different from what you see to be best; and I'm satisfied for you to live thirty mile off, if you think it right. I shall think of you just as much as I do now; for you're bound up with what I can no more help remembering, than I can help my heart beating.'

Poor Adam! Thus do men blunder. Dinah made no answer, but she presently said – 'Have you heard any news from that poor young man, since we last spoke of him?'

Dinah always called Arthur so; she had never lost the image of him as she had seen him in the prison.

'Yes,' said Adam. 'Mr Irwine read me part of a letter from him yesterday. It's pretty certain, they say, that there'll be a peace soon, though nobody believes it'll last long; but he says he doesn't mean to come home. He's no heart for it yet; and it's better for others that he should keep away. Mr Irwine thinks he's in the right not to come: – it's a sorrowful letter. He asks about you and the Poysers, as he always does. There's one thing in the letter cut me a good deal: "You can't think what an old fellow I feel" he says; "I make no schemes now. I'm the best when I've a good day's march or fighting before me."'

'He's of a rash, warm-hearted nature, like Esau, for whom I have always felt great pity,' said Dinah. 'That meeting between the brothers, where Esau is so loving and generous, and Jacob so timid and distrustful, notwithstanding his sense of the Divine favour, has always touched me greatly. Truly I have been tempted sometimes to say that Jacob was of a mean spirit. But that is our trial – we must learn to see the good in the midst of much that is unlovely.'

'Ah,' said Adam, 'I like to read about Moses best, in th' old Testament. He carried a hard business well through, and died when other folks were going to reap the fruits: a man must have courage to look at his life so, and think what'll come of it after he's dead and gone. A good solid bit o' work lasts: if it's only laying a floor down, somebody's the better for it being done well, besides the man as does it.'

They were both glad to talk of subjects that were not personal, and in this way they went on till they passed the bridge across the Willow Brook, when Adam turned round and said – 'Ah, here's Seth. I thought he'd be home soon. Does he know of your going, Dinah?'

'Yes, I told him last Sabbath.'

Adam remembered now that Seth had come home much depressed on Sunday evening, a circumstance which had been very unusual with him of late, for the happiness he had in seeing Dinah every week seemed long to have outweighed the pain of knowing she would never marry him. This evening he had his habitual air of dreamy benignant contentment, until he came quite close to Dinah, and saw the traces of tears on her delicate eyelids and eyelashes. He gave

one rapid glance at his brother; but Adam was evidently quite outside the current of emotion that had shaken Dinah: he wore his everyday look of unexpectant calm. Seth tried not to let Dinah see that he had noticed her face, and only said –
'I'm thankful you're come, Dinah, for mother's been hungering after the sight of you all day. She began to talk of you the first thing in the morning.'

When they entered the cottage, Lisbeth was seated in her armchair, too tired with setting out the evening meal, a task she always performed a long time beforehand, to go and meet them at the door as usual, when she heard the approaching footsteps.

'Coom, child, thee't coom at last,' she said, when Dinah went towards her. 'What dost mane by lavin' me a week, an' ne'er coomin, a-nigh me?'

'Dear friend,' said Dinah, taking her hand, 'you're not well. If I'd known it sooner, I'd have come.'

'An' how's thee t' know if thee dostna coom? Th' lads on'y know what I tell 'em: as long as ye can stir hand and foot the men think ye're hearty. But I'm none so bad, on'y a bit of a cold sets me achin'. An' th' lads tease me so t' ha' somebody wi' me t' do the work – they make me ache worse wi' talkin'. If thee'dst come and stay wi' me, they'd let me alone. The Poysers canna want thee so bad as I do. But take thy bonnet off, an' let me look at thee.'

Dinah was moving away, but Lisbeth held her fast while she was taking off her bonnet, and looked at her face, as one looks into a newly-gathered snowdrop, to renew the old impressions of purity and gentleness.

'What's the matter wi' thee?' said Lisbeth, in astonishment; 'thee'st been a-cryin'.'

'It's only a grief that'll pass away,' said Dinah, who did not wish just now to call forth Lisbeth's remonstrances by disclosing her intention to leave Hayslope. 'You shall know about it shortly – we'll talk of it tonight. I shall stay with you tonight.'

Lisbeth was pacified by this prospect; and she had the whole evening to talk with Dinah alone; for there was a new room in the cottage, you remember, built nearly two years ago, in the expectation of a new inmate; and here Adam always sat when he had writing to do, or plans to make. Seth sat there too this evening, for he knew his mother would like to have Dinah all to herself.

There were two pretty pictures on the two sides of the wall in the cottage. On one side there was the broad-shouldered large-featured, hardy old woman, in her blue jacket and buff kerchief, with her dim-eyed anxious looks turned continually on the lily face and the slight form in the black dress that were either moving lightly about in helpful activity, or seated close by the old woman's armchair, holding her withered hand, with eyes lifted up towards her to speak a language which Lisbeth understood far better than the Bible or the hymn-book. She would scarcely listen to reading at all tonight. 'Nay, nay, shut the book,' she said. 'We mun talk. I want t' know what thee wast cryin' about. Hast got troubles o' thy own, like other folks?'

On the other side of the wall there were the two brothers, so like each other in the midst of their unlikeness: Adam, with knit brows, shaggy hair, and dark vigorous colour, absorbed in his 'figuring;' Seth, with large rugged features, the close copy of his brother's, but with thin wavy brown hair and blue dreamy eyes, as often as not looking vaguely out of the window instead of at his book although it was a newly-bought book – Wesley's abridgment of Madame Guyon's Life, which was full of wonder and interest for him. Seth had said to Adam, 'Can I help thee with anything in here tonight? I don't want to make a noise in the shop.'

'No, lad,' Adam answered, 'there's nothing but what I must do myself. Thee'st got thy new book to read.'

And often, when Seth was quite unconscious, Adam, as he paused after drawing a line with his ruler, looked at his brother with a kind smile dawning in his eyes. He knew 'th' lad liked to sit full o' thoughts he could give no account of; they'd never come t' anything, but they made him happy;' and in the last year or so, Adam had been getting more and more indulgent to Seth. It was part of that growing tenderness which came from the sorrow at work within him.

For Adam, though you see him quite master of himself, working hard and delighting in his work after his inborn inalienable nature, had not outlived his sorrow – had not felt it slip from him as a temporary burthen, and leave him the same man again. Do any of us? God forbid. It would be a poor result of all our anguish and our wrestling, if we won nothing but our old selves at the end of it – if we could return to the same blind loves, the same self-confident blame, the same light thoughts of human suffering, the same frivolous gossip over blighted human lives, the same feeble sense of that Unknown towards which we have sent forth irrepressible cries in our loneliness. Let us rather be thankful that our sorrow lives in us as an indestructible force, only changing its form, as forces do, and passing from pain into sympathy – the one poor word which includes all our best insight and our best love. Not that this transformation of pain into sympathy had completely taken place in Adam yet: there was still a great remnant of pain, and this he felt would subsist as long as *her* pain was not a memory, but an existing thing, which he must think of as renewed with the light of every new morning. But we get accustomed to mental as well as bodily pain, without, for all that, losing our sensibility to it: it becomes a habit of our lives, and we cease to imagine a condition of perfect ease as possible for us. Desire is chastened into submission; and we are contented with our day when we have been able to bear our grief in silence, and act as if we were not suffering. For it is at such periods that the sense of our lives having visible and invisible relations beyond any of which either our present or prospective self is the centre, grows like a muscle that we are obliged to lean on and exert.

That was Adam's state of mind in this second autumn of his sorrow. His work, as you know, had always been part of his religion, and from very early days he saw clearly that good carpentry was God's will – was that form of God's will that most immediately concerned him; but now there was no margin of dreams for him beyond this daylight reality, no holidaytime in the working-day world: no moment in the distance when duty would take off her iron glove and breastplate, and clasp him gently into rest. He conceived no picture of the future but one made up of hard-working days such as he lived through, with growing contentment and intensity of interest, every fresh week: love, he thought, could never be anything to him, but a living memory – a limb lopped off, but not gone from consciousness. He did not know that the power of loving was all the while gaining new force within him; that the new sensibilities bought by a deep experience were so many new fibres by which it was possible, nay, necessary to him, that his nature should intertwine with another. Yet he was aware that common affection and friendship were more precious to him than they used to be – that he clung more to his mother and Seth, and had an unspeakable satisfaction in the sight or imagination of any small addition to their happiness. The Poysers, too – hardly three or four days passed but he felt the need of seeing them, and interchanging words and looks of friendliness with them: he would have felt this, probably, even if Dinah had not been with them; but he had only said the simplest truth in telling Dinah that he put her above all other friends in the world. Could anything be more natural? For in the darkest moments of memory the thought of her always came as the first ray of returning comfort: the early days of gloom at the Hall Farm had been gradually turned into soft moonlight by her presence; and in the cottage, too – for she had come at every spare moment to soothe and cheer poor Lisbeth, who had been stricken with a fear that subdued even her querulousness, at the sight of her darling Adam's grief-worn face. He had become used to watching her light quiet movements, her pretty loving ways to the children, when he went to the Hall Farm; to listen for her voice as for a recurrent music; to think everything she said and did was just right, and could not have been better. In spite of his wisdom, he could not find fault with her for her over-indulgence of the children, who had managed to convert Dinah the preacher, before whom a circle of rough men had often trembled a little, into a convenient household slave; though Dinah herself was rather ashamed of this weakness, and had some inward conflict as to her departure from the precepts of Solomon. Yes, there was one thing that might have been better; she might have loved Seth, and consented to marry him. He felt a little vexed, for his brother's sake; and he could not help thinking regretfully how Dinah, as Seth's wife, would have made their home as happy as it could be for them all – how she was the one being that would have soothed their mother's last days into peacefulness and rest.

'It's wonderful she doesn't love th' lad,' Adam had said sometimes to himself; 'for anybody 'ud think he was just cut out for her. But her heart's so taken up with other things. She's one o' those women that feel no drawing towards having a husband and children o' their own. She thinks she should be filled up with her own life then; and she's been used so to living in other folks's cares, she can't bear the thought of her heart being shut up from 'em. I see how it is, well enough. She's cut out o' different stuff from most women: I saw that long ago. She's never easy but when she's helping somebody, and marriage 'ud interfere with her ways' – that's true. I've no right to be contriving and thinking it 'ud be better if she'd have Seth, as if I was wiser than she is – or than God either, for He made her what she is, and that's one o' the greatest blessings I've ever had from His hands, and others besides me.'

This self-reproof had recurred strongly to Adam's mind, when he gathered from Dinah's face that he had wounded her by referring to his wish that she had accepted Seth, and so he had endeavoured to put into the strongest words his confidence in her decision as right – his resignation even to her going away from them, and ceasing to make part of their life otherwise than by living in their thoughts, if that separation were chosen by herself. He felt sure she knew quite well enough how much he cared to see her continually – to talk to her with the silent consciousness of a mutual great remembrance. It was not possible she should hear anything but self-renouncing affection and respect in his assurance that he was contented for her to go away; and yet there remained an uneasy feeling in his mind that he had not said quite the right thing – that, somehow, Dinah had not understood him.

Dinah must have risen a little before the sun the next morning, for she was downstairs about five o'clock. So was Seth; for, through Lisbeth's obstinate refusal to have any woman-helper in the house, he had learned to make himself, as Adam said, 'very handy in the housework,' that he might save his mother from too great weariness; on which ground I hope you will not think him unmanly, any more than you can have thought the gallant Colonel Bath unmanly when he made the gruel for his invalid sister. Adam, who had sat up late at his writing, was still asleep, and was not likely, Seth said, to be down till breakfast-time. Often as Dinah had visited Lisbeth during the last eighteen months, she had never slept in the cottage since that night after Thias's death, when, you remember, Lisbeth praised her deft movements, and even gave a modified approval to her porridge. But in that long interval Dinah had made great advances in household cleverness: and this morning, since Seth was there to help, she was bent on bringing everything to a pitch of cleanliness and order that would have satisfied her aunt Poyser. The cottage was far from that standard at present, for Lisbeth's rheumatism had forced her to give up her old habits of dilettante scouring and polishing. When the kitchen was to her mind, Dinah went into the new room, where Adam had been writing the night before, to see what sweeping and dusting were needed there. She opened the window and let in the fresh morning air, and the smell of the sweetbrier, and the bright low-slanting rays of the early sun, which made a glory about her pale face and pale auburn hair as she held the long brush, and swept, singing to herself in a very low tone – like a sweet summer murmur that you have to listen for very closely – one of Charles Wesley's hymns:

'Eternal Beam of Light Divine,
Fountain of unexhausted love,
In whom the Father's glories shine,
Through earth beneath and heaven above;

Jesus! the weary wanderer's rest,
Give me thy easy yoke to bear;
With steadfast patience arm my breast,
With spotless love and holy fear.

Speak to my warring passions, "Peace!"
Say to my trembling heart, "Be still!"
Thy power my strength and fortress is,
For all things serve thy sovereign will.'

She laid by the brush and took up the duster; and if you had ever lived in Mrs Poyser's household, you would know how the duster behaved in Dinah's hand – how it went into every small corner, and on every ledge in and out of sight – how it went again and again round every bar of the chairs, and every leg, and under and over everything that lay on the table, till it came to Adam's papers and rulers, and the open desk near them. Dinah dusted up to the very edge of these, and then hesitated, looking at them with a longing but timid eye. It was painful to see how much dust there was among them. As she was looking in this way, she heard Seth's step just outside the open door, towards which her back was turned, and said, raising her clear treble – 'Seth, is your brother wrathful when his papers are stirred?'

'Yes, very, when they are not put back in the right places,' said a deep strong voice, not Seth's.

It was as if Dinah had put her hands unawares on a vibrating chord; she was shaken with an intense thrill, and for the instant felt nothing else; then she knew her cheeks were glowing, and dared not look round, but stood still, distressed because she could not say good-morning in a friendly way. Adam, finding that she did not look round so as to see the smile on his face, was afraid she had thought him serious about his wrathfulness, and went up to her, so that she was obliged to look at him.

'What! you think I'm a cross fellow at home, Dinah?' he said, smilingly.

'Nay,' said Dinah, looking up with timid eyes, 'not so. But you might be put about by finding things meddled with; and even the man Moses, the meekest of men, was wrathful sometimes.'

'Come, then,' said Adam, looking at her affectionately, 'I'll help you move the things, and put 'em back again, and then they can't get wrong. You're getting to be your aunt's own niece, I see, for particularness.'

They began their little task together, but Dinah had not recovered herself sufficiently to think of any remark, and Adam looked at her uneasily. Dinah, he thought, had seemed to disapprove him somehow lately; she had not been so kind and open to him as she used to be. He wanted her to look at him and be as pleased as he was himself with doing this bit of playful work. But Dinah did not look at him – it was easy for her to avoid looking at the tall man; and when at last there was no more dusting to be done, and no further excuse for him to linger near her, he could bear it no longer, and said, in rather a pleading tone – 'Dinah, you're not displeased with me for anything, are you? I've not said or done anything to make you think ill of me?'

The question surprised her, and relieved her by giving a new course to her feeling. She looked up at him now, quite earnestly, almost with the tears coming, and said – 'Oh, no, Adam! how could you think so?'

'I couldn't bear you not to feel as much a friend to me as I do to you,' said Adam. 'And you don't know the value I set on the very thought of you, Dinah. That was what I meant yesterday, when I said I'd be content for you to go, if you thought right. I meant, the thought of you was worth so much to me, I should feel I ought to be thankful, and not grumble, if you see right to go away. You know I do mind parting with you, Dinah?'

'Yes, dear friend,' said Dinah, trembling, but trying to speak calmly, 'I know you have a brother's heart towards me, and we shall often be with one another in spirit; but at this season I am in heaviness through manifold temptations; you must not mark me. I feel called to leave my kindred for a while; but it is a trial: the flesh is weak.'

Adam saw that it pained her to be obliged to answer.

'I hurt you by talking about it, Dinah,' he said: 'I'll say no more. Let's see if Seth's ready with breakfast now.'

That is a simple scene, reader. But it is almost certain that you, too, have been in love – perhaps, even, more than once, though you may not choose to say so to all your feminine friends. If so, you will no more think the slight words, the timid looks, the tremulous touches, by which two human souls approach each other gradually, like two little quivering rain-streams, before they mingle into one – you will no more think these things trivial than you will think the first-detected signs of coming spring trivial, though they be but a faint, indescribable something in the air and in the song of the birds, and the tiniest perceptible budding on the hedgerow branches. Those slight words and looks and touches are part of the soul's language; and the finest language, I believe, is chiefly made up of unimposing words, such as 'light, 'sound', 'stars', 'music' – words really not worth looking at, or hearing, in themselves, any more than 'chips' or 'sawdust': it is only that they happen to be the signs of something unspeakably great and beautiful. I am of opinion that love is a great and beautiful thing too; and if you agree with me, the smallest signs of it will not be chips and sawdust to you: they will rather be like those little words, 'light' and 'music', stirring the long-winding fibres of your memory, and enriching your present with your most precious past.

51

Sunday Morning

Lisbeth's touch of rheumatism could not be made to appear serious enough to detain Dinah another night from the Hall Farm, now she had made up her mind to leave her aunt so soon: and at evening the friends must part. 'For a long while,' Dinah had said; for she had told Lisbeth of her resolve.

'Then it'll be for all my life, an' I shall ne'er see thee again,' said Lisbeth. 'Long while! I'n got no long while t' live. An' I shall be took bad an' die, an' thee canst ne'er come a-nigh me, an' I shall die a-longing for thee.'

That had been the keynote of her wailing talk all day; for Adam was not in the house, and so she put no restraint on her complaining. She had tried poor Dinah by returning again and again to the question, why she must go away; and refusing to accept reasons, which seemed to her nothing but whim and 'contrairiness'; and still more, by regretting that she 'couldna ha' one o' the lads', and be her daughter.

'Thee couldstna put up wi' Seth,' she said: 'he isna cliver enough for thee, happen; but he'd ha' been very good t' thee – he's as handy as can be at doin' things for me when I'm bad; an' he's as fond o' the Bible an' chapellin' as thee art thysen. But happen, thee'dst like a husband better as isna just the cut o' thysen: the runnin' brook isna a-thirst for th' rain. Adam 'ud ha' done for thee – I know he would; an' he might come t' like thee well enough, if thee'dst stop. But he's as stubborn as th' iron bar – there's no bending him no way but's own. But he'd be a fine husband for anybody, be they who they will, so looked-on an' so cliver as he is. And he'd be rare an' lovin': it does me good on'y a look o' the lad's eye, when he means kind tow'rt me.'

Dinah tried to escape from Lisbeth's closest looks and questions by finding little tasks of housework, that kept her moving about; and as soon as Seth came home in the evening she put on her bonnet to go. It touched Dinah keenly to say the last Goodbye, and still more to look round on her way across the fields, and see the old woman still standing at the door, gazing after her till she must have been the faintest speck in the dim aged eyes. 'The God of love and peace be with them,' Dinah prayed, as she looked back from the last stile. 'Make them glad according to the days wherein thou hast afflicted them, and the years wherein they have seen evil. It is thy will that I should part from them; let me have no will but thine.'

Lisbeth turned into the house at last, and sat down in the workshop near Seth, who was busying himself there with fitting some bits of turned wood he had brought from the village, into a small workbox which he meant to give to Dinah before she went away.

'Thee't see her again o' Sunday afore she goes,' were her first words. 'If thee wast good for anything, thee'dst make her come in again o' Sunday night wi' thee, an' see me once more.'

'Nay, mother,' said Seth, 'Dinah 'ud be sure to come again if she saw right to come. I should have no need to persuade her. She only thinks it 'ud be troubling thee for nought, just to come in to say Goodbye over again.'

'She'd ne'er go away, I know, if Adam 'ud be fond on her an' marry her; but everything's so contrairy,' said Lisbeth, with a burst of vexation.

Seth paused a moment, and looked up, with a slight blush, at his mother's face. 'What! has she said anything o' that sort to thee, mother?' he said, in a lower tone.

'Said? nay, she'll say nothin'. It's on'y the men as have to wait till folks say things afore they find 'em out.'

'Well, but what makes thee think so, mother? What's put it into thy head?'

'It's no matter what's put it into my head: my head's none so hollow as it must get in, an' nought to put it there. I know she's fond on him, as I know th' wind's comin' in at the door an' that's anoof. An' he might be willin' to marry her if he know'd she's fond on him, but he'll ne'er think on't if somebody doesna put it into's head.'

His mother's suggestion about Dinah's feeling towards Adam was not quite a new thought to Seth, but her last words alarmed him, lest she should herself undertake to open Adam's eyes. He was not sure about Dinah's feeling, and he thought he was sure about Adam's.

'Nay, mother, nay,' he said, earnestly, 'thee mustna think o' speaking o' such things to Adam. Thee'st no right to say what Dinah's feelings are if she hasna told thee; and it 'ud do nothing but mischief to say such things to Adam: he feels very grateful and affectionate toward Dinah, but he's no thoughts towards her that 'ud incline him to make her his wife; and I don't believe Dinah 'ud marry him either. I don't think she'll marry at all.'

'Eh,' said Lisbeth, impatiently. 'Thee think'st so 'cause she wouldna ha' thee. She'll ne'er marry thee; thee mightst as well like her t' ha' thy brother.'

Seth was hurt. 'Mother,' he said, in a remonstrating tone, 'don't think that of me. I should be as thankful t' have her for a sister as thee wouldst t' have her for a daughter. I've no more thoughts about myself in that thing, and I shall take it hard if ever thee say'st it again.'

'Well, well, then thee shouldstna cross me wi' sayin' things arena as I say they are.'

'But, mother,' said Seth, 'thee'dst be doing Dinah a wrong by telling Adam what thee think'st about her. It 'ud do nothing but mischief; for it 'ud make Adam uneasy if he doesna feel the same to her. And I'm pretty sure he feels nothing o' the sort.'

'Eh, donna tell me what thee't sure on; thee know'st nought about it. What's he allays goin' to the Poysers' for, if he didna want t' see her? He goes twice where he used t' go once. Happen he knowsna as he wants t' see her; he knowsna as I put salt in's broth, but he'd miss it pretty quick if it warna there. He'll ne'er think o' marrying if it isna put into's head; an' if thee'dst any love for thy mother, thee'dst put him up to't, an' not let her go away out o' my sight, when I might ha' her to make a bit o' comfort for me afore I go to bed to my old man under the whitethorn.'

'Nay, mother,' said Seth, 'thee mustna think me unkind; but I should be going against my conscience if I took upon me to say what Dinah's feelings are. And besides that, I think I should give offence to Adam by speaking to him at all about marrying; and I counsel thee not to do't. Thee may'st be quite deceived about Dinah; nay, I'm pretty sure, by words she said to me last Sabbath, as she's no mind to marry.'

'Eh, thee't as contrairy as the rest on 'em. If it war summat I didna want, it 'ud be done fast enough.'

Lisbeth rose from the bench at this, and went out of the workshop, leaving Seth in much anxiety lest she should disturb Adam's mind about Dinah. He consoled himself after a time with reflecting that, since Adam's trouble, Lisbeth had been very timid about speaking to him on matters of feeling, and that she would hardly dare to approach this tenderest of all subjects. Even if she did, he hoped Adam would not take much notice of what she said.

Seth was right in believing that Lisbeth would be held in restraint by timidity; and during the next three days, the intervals in which she had an opportunity of speaking to Adam were too rare and short to cause her any strong temptation.

But in her long solitary hours she brooded over her regretful thoughts about Dinah, till they had grown very near that point of unmanageable strength when thoughts are apt to take wing out of their secret nest in a startling manner. And on

Sunday morning, when Seth went away to chapel at Treddleston, the dangerous opportunity came.

Sunday morning was the happiest time in all the week to Lisbeth; for as there was no service at Hayslope church till the afternoon, Adam was always at home, doing nothing but reading, an occupation in which she could venture to interrupt him. Moreover, she had always a better dinner than usual to prepare for her sons – very frequently for Adam and herself alone, Seth being often away the entire day; and the smell of the roast meat before the clear fire in the clean kitchen, the clock ticking in a peaceful Sunday manner, her darling Adam seated near her in his best clothes, doing nothing very important, so that she could go and stroke her hand across his hair if she liked, and see him look up at her and smile, while Gyp, rather jealous, poked his muzzle up between them – all these things made poor Lisbeth's earthly paradise.

The book Adam most often read on a Sunday morning was his large pictured Bible, and this morning it lay open before him on the round white deal table in the kitchen; for he sat there in spite of the fire, because he knew his mother liked to have him with her, and it was the only day in the week when he could indulge her in that way. You would have liked to see Adam reading his Bible: he never opened it on a weekday, and so he came to it as a holiday book, serving him for history, biography, and poetry. He held one hand thrust between his waistcoat buttons, and the other ready to turn the pages; and in the course of the morning you would have seen many changes in his face. Sometimes his lips moved in semi-articulation – it was when he came to a speech that he could fancy himself uttering, such as Samuel's dying speech to the people; then his eyebrows would be raised, and the corners of his mouth would quiver a little with sad sympathy – something, perhaps old Isaac's meeting with his son, touched him closely; at other times, over the New Testament, a very solemn look would come upon his face, and he would every now and then shake his head in serious assent, or just lift up his hand and let it fall again; and on some mornings, when he read in the Apocrypha, of which he was very fond, the son of Sirach's keen-edged words would bring a delighted smile, though he also enjoyed the freedom of occasionally differing from an Apocryphal writer. For Adam knew the Articles quite well, as became a good churchman.

Lisbeth, in the pauses of attending to her dinner, always sat opposite to him and watched him, till she could rest no longer without going up to him and giving him a caress, to call his attention to her. This morning he was reading the Gospel according to St Matthew, and Lisbeth had been standing close by him for some minutes, stroking his hair, which was smoother than usual this morning, and looking down at the large page with silent wonderment at the mystery of letters. She was encouraged to continue this caress, because when she first went up to him, he had thrown himself back in his chair to look at her affectionately and say, 'Why, mother, thee look'st rare and hearty this morning. Eh, Gyp wants me t' look at him: he can't abide to think I love thee the best.' Lisbeth said nothing because she wanted to say so many things. And now there was a new leaf to be turned over, and it was a picture – that of the angel seated on the great stone that has been rolled away from the sepulchre. This picture had one strong association in Lisbeth's memory, for she had been reminded of it when she first saw Dinah; and Adam had no sooner turned the page, and lifted the book sideways that they might look at the angel, than she said, 'That's her – that's Dinah.'

Adam smiled, and, looking more intently at the angel's face, said – 'It's a bit like her; but Dinah's prettier, I think.'

'Well, then, if thee think'st her so pretty, why arn't fond on her?'

Adam looked up in surprise. 'Why, mother, dost think I don't set store by Dinah?'

'Nay,' said Lisbeth, frightened at her own courage, yet feeling that she had broken the ice, and the waters must flow, whatever mischief they might do. 'What's th' use o' settin' store by things as are thirty mile off? If thee wast fond enough on her thee wouldstna let her go away.'

'But I've no right t' hinder her, if she thinks well,' said Adam, looking at his book as if he wanted to go on reading. He foresaw a series of complaints tending to nothing. Lisbeth sat down again in the chair opposite to him, as she said – 'But she wouldna think well if thee wastna so contrairy.' Lisbeth dared not venture beyond a vague phrase yet.

'Contrairy, mother?' Adam said, looking up again in some anxiety. 'What have I done? What dost mean?'

'Why, thee't never look at nothin' nor think o' nothin', but thy figurin' an' thy work,' said Lisbeth, half crying 'An' dost think thee canst go on so all thy life, as if thee wast a man cut out o' timber? An' what wut do when thy mother's gone, an' nobody to take care on thee as thee gett'st a bit o' victual comfortable i' the mornin'?'

'What hast got i' thy mind, mother?' said Adam, vexed at this whimpering 'I canna see what thee't driving at. Is there anything I could do for thee as I don't do?'

'Ay, an' that there is. Thee might'st do as I should ha' somebody wi' me to comfort me a bit, an' wait on me when I'm bad, an' be good to me.'

'Well, mother, whose fault is it there isna some tidy body i' th' house t' help thee? It isna by my wish as thee hast a stroke o' work to do. We can afford it – I've told thee often enough. It 'ud be a deal better for us.'

'Eh, what's the use o' talkin' o' tidy bodies, when thee mean'st one o' th' wenches out o' th' village, or somebody from Treddles'on as I ne'er set eyes on i' my life? I'd sooner make a shift an' get into my own coffin afore I die, nor ha' them folks to put me in.'

Adam was silent, and tried to go on reading. That was the utmost severity he could show towards his mother on a Sunday morning. But Lisbeth had gone too far now to check herself, and after scarcely a minute's quietness she began again.

'Thee mightst know well enough who 'tis I'd like t' ha' wi' me. It isna many folks I send for t' come an' see me, I reckon. An' thee'st had the fetchin' on her times enow.'

'Thee mean'st Dinah, mother, I know,' said Adam. 'But it's no use setting thy mind on what can't be. If Dinah 'ud be willing to stay at Hayslope, it isn't likely she can come away from her aunt's house, where they hold her like a daughter,

and where she's more bound than she is to us. If it had been so that she could ha'
married Seth, that 'ud ha' been a great blessing to us, but we can't have things just
as we like in this life. Thee must try and make up thy mind to do without her.'

'Nay, but I canna ma' up my mind, when she's just cut out for thee; an' nought
shall ma' me believe as God didna make her an' send her there o' purpose for
thee. What's it sinnify about her being a Methody? It 'ud happen wear out on
her wi' marryin'.'

Adam threw himself back in his chair and looked at his mother. He understood now what she had been aiming at from the beginning of the conversation.
It was as unreasonable, impracticable a wish as she had ever urged, but he could
not help being moved by so entirely new an idea. The chief point, however, was
to chase away the notion from his mother's mind as quickly as possible.

'Mother,' he said, gravely, 'thee't talking wild. Don't let me hear thee say such
things again. It's no good talking o' what can never be. Dinah's not for marrying;
she's fixed her heart on a different sort o' life.'

'Very like,' said Lisbeth, impatiently, 'very like she's none for marr'ing, when
them as she'd be willin' t' marry wonna ax her. I shouldna ha' been for marr'ing
thy feyther if he'd ne'er axed me; an' she's as fond o' thee as e'er I war o' Thias,
poor fellow.'

The blood rushed to Adam's face, and for a few moments he was not quite
conscious where he was: his mother and the kitchen had vanished for him, and
he saw nothing but Dinah's face turned up towards his. It seemed as if there
were a resurrection of his dead joy. But he woke up very speedily from that
dream (the waking was chill and sad); for it would have been very foolish in him
to believe his mother's words; she could have no ground for them. He was
prompted to express his disbelief very strongly – perhaps that he might call forth
the proofs, if there were any to be offered.

'What dost say such things for, mother, when thee'st got no foundation for
'em? Thee know'st nothing as gives thee a right to say that.'

'Then I knowna nought as gi'es me a right to say as the year's turned, for all I
feel it fust thing when I get up i' th' mornin'. She isna fond o' Seth, I reckon, is
she? She doesna want to marry *him?* But I can see as she doesna behave tow'rt
thee as she does tow'rt Seth. She makes no more o' Seth's coming a-nigh her
nor if he war Gyp, but she's all of a tremble when thee't a-sittin' down by her at
breakfast, an' a looking at her. Thee think'st thy mother knows nought, but she
war alive afore thee wast born.'

'But thee canstna be sure as the trembling means love?' said Adam, anxiously.

'Eh, what else should it mane? It isna hate, I reckon. An' what should she do
but love thee? Thee't made to be loved – for where's there a straighter, cliverer
man? An' what's it sinnify her bein' a Methody? It's on'y the marigold i' th'
parridge.'

Adam had thrust his hands in his pockets, and was looking down at the book
on the table, without seeing any of the letters. He was trembling like a gold-
seeker, who sees the strong promise of gold, but sees in the same moment a
sickening vision of disappointment. He could not trust his mother's insight; she
had seen what she wished to see. And yet – and yet, now the suggestion had

been made to him, he remembered so many things, very slight things, like the stirring of the water by an imperceptible breeze, which seemed to him some confirmation of his mother's words.

Lisbeth noticed that he was moved. She went on – 'An' thee't find out as thee't poorly aff when she's gone. Thee't fonder on her nor thee know'st. Thy eyes follow her about, welly as Gyp's follow thee.'

Adam could sit still no longer. He rose, took down his hat, and went out into the fields.

The sunshine was on them: that early autumn sunshine which we should know was not summer's, even if there were not the touches of yellow on the lime and chestnut: the Sunday sunshine, too, which has more than autumnal calmness for the working man: the morning sunshine, which still leaves the dew-crystals on the fine gossamer webs in the shadow of the bushy hedgerows.

Adam needed the calm influence; he was amazed at the way in which this new thought of Dinah's love had taken possession of him, with an overmastering power that made all other feelings give way before the impetuous desire to know that the thought was true. Strange that till that moment the possibility of their ever being lovers had never crossed his mind, and yet now, all his longing suddenly went out towards that possibility; he had no more doubt or hesitation as to his own wishes than the bird that flies towards the opening through which the daylight gleams and the breath of heaven enters.

The autumnal Sunday sunshine soothed him; but not by preparing him with resignation to the disappointment if his mother – if he himself - proved to be mistaken about Dinah: it soothed him by gentle encouragement of his hopes. Her love was so like that calm sunshine that they seemed to make one presence to him, and he believed in them both alike. And Dinah was so bound up with the sad memories of his first passion, that he was not forsaking them, but rather giving them a new sacredness by loving her. Nay, his love for her had grown out of that past: it was the noon of that morning.

But Seth? Would the lad be hurt? Hardly; for he had seemed quite contented of late, and there was no selfish jealousy in him; he had never been jealous of his mother's fondness for Adam. But had he seen anything of what their mother talked about? Adam longed to know this, for he thought he could trust Seth's observation better than his mother's. He must talk to Seth before he went to see Dinah; and, with this intention in his mind, he walked back to the cottage and said to his mother – 'Did Seth say anything to thee about when he was coming home? Will he be back to dinner?'

'Ay, lad, he'll be back for a wonder. He isna gone to Treddles'on. He's gone somewhere else a-preachin, and a-prayin'.'

'Hast any notion which way he's gone?' said Adam.

'Nay, but he aften goes to th' Common. Thee know'st more o's goings nor I do.'

Adam wanted to go and meet Seth, but he must content himself with walking about the near fields and getting sight of him as soon as possible. That would not be for more than an hour to come, for Seth would scarcely be at home much before their dinner-time, which was twelve o'clock. But Adam could not sit

FOUR NOVELS OF GEORGE ELIOT

down to his reading again, and he sauntered along by the brook and stood leaning against the stiles, with eager, intense eyes, which looked as if they saw something very vividly; but it was not the brook or the willows, not the fields or the sky. Again and again his vision was interrupted by wonder at the strength of his own feeling, at the strength and sweetness of this new love – almost like the wonder a man feels at the added power he finds in himself for an art which he had laid aside for a space. How is it that the poets have said so many fine things about our first love, so few about our later love? Are their first poems their best? or are not those the best which come from their fuller thought, their larger experience, their deeper-rooted affections? The boy's flutelike voice has its own spring charm; but the man should yield a richer, deeper music.

At last, there was Seth, visible at the farthest stile, and Adam hastened to meet him. Seth was surprised, and thought something unusual must have happened: but when Adam came up, his face said plainly enough that it was nothing alarming.

'Where hast been?" said Adam, when they were side by side.

'I've been to the Common,' said Seth. 'Dinah's been speaking the Word to a little company of hearers at Brimstone's, as they call him. They're folks as never go to church hardly – them on the Common – but they'll go and hear Dinah a bit. She's been speaking with power this forenoon from the words, "I came not to call the righteous, but sinners to repentance." And there was a little thing happened as was pretty to see. The women mostly bring their children with 'em, but today there was one stout curly-headed fellow about three or four year old, that I never saw there before. He was as naughty as could be at the beginning while I was praying, and while we was singing, but when we all sat down and Dinah began to speak, th' young un stood stock-still all at once, and began to look at her with's mouth open, and presently he ran away from's mother and went up to Dinah, and pulled at her, like a little dog, for her to take notice of him. So Dinah lifted him up and held th' lad on her lap, while she went on speaking; and he was as good as could be till he went to sleep – and the mother cried to see him.'

'It's a pity she shouldna be a mother herself,' said Adam, 'so fond as the children are of her. Dost think she's quite fixed against marrying, Seth? Dost think nothing 'ud turn her?'

There was something peculiar in his brother's tone, which made Seth steal a glance at his face before he answered.

'It 'ud be wrong of me to say nothing 'ud turn her,' he answered. 'But if thee mean'st it about myself, I've given up all thoughts as she can ever be my wife. She calls me her brother, and that's enough.'

'But dost think she might ever get fond enough of anybody else to be willing to marry 'em?' said Adam, rather shyly.

'Well,' said Seth, after some hesitation, 'it's crossed my mind sometimes o' late as she might; but Dinah 'ud let no fondness for the creature draw her out o' the path as she believed God had marked out for her. If she thought the leading was not from Him, she's not one to be brought under the power of it. And she's allays seemed clear about that – as her work was to minister t' others, and make no home for herself i' this world.'

'But suppose,' said Adam, earnestly, 'suppose there was a man as 'ud let her do just the same and not interfere with her – she might do a good deal o' what she does now, just as well when she was married as when she was single. Other women of her sort have married – that's to say, not just like her, but women as preached and attended on the sick and needy. There's Mrs Fletcher as she talks of.'

A new light had broken in on Seth. He turned round, and laying his hand on Adam's shoulder, said, 'Why, wouldst like her to marry *thee*, brother?'

Adam looked doubtfully at Seth's enquiring eyes, and said, 'Wouldst be hurt if she was to be fonder o' me than o' thee?'

'Nay,' said Seth, warmly, 'how canst think it? Have I felt thy trouble so little, that I shouldna feel thy joy?'

There was silence a few moments as they walked on, and then Seth said – 'I'd no notion as thee'dst ever think of her for a wife.'

'But is it o' any use to think of her?' said Adam – 'what dost say? Mother's made me as I hardly know where I am, with what she's been saying to me this forenoon. She says she's sure Dinah feels for me more than common, and 'ud be willing t' have me. But I'm afraid she speaks without book. I want to know if thee'st seen anything.'

'It's a nice point to speak about,' said Seth, 'and I'm afraid o' being wrong; besides, we've no right t' intermeddle with people's feelings when they wouldn't tell 'em themselves.'

Seth paused.

'But thee mightst ask her,' he said, presently. 'She took no offence at me for asking, and thee'st more right than I had, only thee't not in the society. But Dinah doesn't hold wi' them as are for keeping the society so strict to themselves. She doesn't mind about making folks enter the society, so as they're fit t' enter the kingdom o' God. Some o' the brethren at Treddles'on are displeased with her for that.'

'Where will she be the rest o' the day?' said Adam.

'She said she shouldn't leave the Farm again today,' said Seth, 'because it's her last Sabbath there, and she's going t' read out o' the big Bible wi' the children.'

Adam thought – but did not say – 'Then I'll go this afternoon; for if I go to church my thoughts 'ull be with her all the while. They must sing th' anthem without me today.'

52

Adam and Dinah

It was about three o'clock when Adam entered the farmyard and roused Alick and the dogs from their Sunday dozing. Alick said everybody was gone to church 'but th' young missis' – so he called Dinah; but this did not disappoint Adam, although the 'everybody' was so liberal as to include Nancy the dairymaid, whose works of necessity were not unfrequently incompatible with church-going.

There was perfect stillness about the house: the doors were all closed, and the very stones and tubs seemed quieter than usual. Adam heard the water gently dripping from the pump – that was the only sound; and he knocked at the house door rather softly, as was suitable in that stillness.

The door opened, and Dinah stood before him, colouring deeply with the great surprise of seeing Adam at this hour, when she knew it was his regular practice to be at church. Yesterday he would have said to her without any difficulty, 'I came to see you, Dinah: I knew the rest were not at home.' But today something prevented him from saying that, and he put out his hand to her in silence. Neither of them spoke, and yet both wished they could speak, as Adam entered, and they sat down. Dinah took the chair she had just left; it was at the corner of the table near the window, and there was a book lying on the table, but it was not open: she had been sitting perfectly still, looking at the small bit of clear fire in the bright grate. Adam sat down opposite her, in Mr Poyser's three-cornered chair.

'Your mother is not ill again, I hope, Adam?' Dinah said, recovering herself. 'Seth said she was well this morning.'

'No, she's very hearty today,' said Adam, happy in the signs of Dinah's feeling at the sight of him, but shy.

'There's nobody at home, you see,' Dinah said; 'but you'll wait. You've been hindered from going to church today, doubtless.'

'Yes,' Adam said, and then paused, before he added, 'I was thinking about you: that was the reason.'

This confession was very awkward and sudden, Adam felt; for he thought Dinah must understand all he meant. But the frankness of the words caused her immediately to interpret them into a renewal of his brotherly regrets that she was going away, and she answered calmly – 'Do not be careful and troubled for me, Adam. I have all things and abound at Snowfield. And my mind is at rest, for I am not seeking my own will in going.'

'But if things were different, Dinah,' said Adam, hesitatingly – 'if you knew things that perhaps you don't know now . . .'

Dinah looked at him enquiringly, but instead of going on, he reached a chair and brought it near the corner of the table where she was sitting. She wondered and was afraid – and the next moment her thoughts flew to the past: was it something about those distant unhappy ones that she didn't know?

Adam looked at her: it was so sweet to look at her eyes, which had now a self-forgetful questioning in them – for a moment he forgot that he wanted to say anything, or that it was necessary to tell her what he meant.

'Dinah,' he said suddenly, taking both her hands between his, 'I love you with my whole heart and soul. I love you next to God who made me.'

Dinah's lips became pale, like her cheeks, and she trembled violently under the shock of painful joy. Her hands were cold as death between Adam's. She could not draw them away, because he held them fast.

'Don't tell me you can't love me, Dinah. Don't tell me we must part, and pass our lives away from one another.'

The tears were trembling in Dinah's eyes, and they fell before she could answer. But she spoke in a quiet low voice.

'Yes, dear Adam, we must submit to another Will. We must part.'

'Not if you love me, Dinah – not if you love me,' Adam said passionately. 'Tell me – tell me if you can love me better than a brother?'

Dinah was too entirely reliant on the Supreme guidance to attempt to achieve any end by a deceptive concealment. She was recovering now from the first shock of emotion, and she looked at Adam with simple sincere eyes as she said –

'Yes, Adam, my heart is drawn strongly towards you; and of my own will, if I had no clear showing to the contrary, I could find my happiness in being near you, and ministering to you continually. I fear I should forget to rejoice and weep with others; nay, I fear I should forget the Divine presence, and seek no love but yours.'

Adam did not speak immediately. They sat looking at each other in delicious silence – for the first sense of mutual love excludes other feelings; it will have the soul all to itself.

'Then, Dinah,' Adam said at last, 'how can there be anything contrary to what's right in our belonging to one another, and spending our lives together? Who put this great love into our hearts? Can anything be holier than that? For we can help one another in everything as is good. I'd never think o' putting myself between you and God, and saying you oughtn't to do this, and you oughtn't to do that. You'd follow your conscience as much as you do now.'

'Yes, Adam,' Dinah said, 'I know marriage is a holy state for those who are truly called to it, and have no other drawing; but from my childhood upward I have been led towards another path; all my peace and my joy have come from having no life of my own, no wants, no wishes for myself, and living only in God and those of his creatures whose sorrows and joys he has given me to know. Those have been very blessed years to me, and I feel that if I was to listen to any voice that would draw me aside from that path, I should be turning my back on the light that has shone upon me, and darkness and doubt would take hold of me. We could not bless each other, Adam, if there were doubts in my soul, and if I yearned, when it was too late, after that better part which had once been given me and I had put away from me.'

'But if a new feeling has come into your mind, Dinah, and if you love me so as to be willing to be nearer to me than to other people, isn't that a sign that it's right for you to change your life? Doesn't the love make it right when nothing else would?'

'Adam, my mind is full of questionings about that; for now, since you tell me of your strong love towards me, what was clear to me has become dark again. I felt before that my heart was too strongly drawn towards you, and that your heart was not as mine; and the thought of you had taken hold of me, so that my soul had lost its freedom, and was becoming enslaved to an earthly affection, which made me anxious and careful about what should befall myself. For in all other affection I had been content with any small return, or with none; but my heart was beginning to hunger after an equal love from you. And I had no doubt that I must wrestle against that as a great temptation; and the command was clear that I must go away.'

'But now, dear, dear Dinah, now you know I love you better than you love me . . . it's all different now. You won't think o' going: you'll stay, and be my dear wife, and I shall thank God for giving me my life as I never thanked him before.'

'Adam, it's hard to me to turn a deaf ear . . . you know it's hard; but a great fear is upon me. It seems to me as if you were stretching out your arms to me, and beckoning me to come and take my ease, and live for my own delight, and Jesus, the Man of Sorrows, was standing looking towards me, and pointing to the sinful, and suffering, and afflicted. I have seen that again and again when I have been sitting in stillness and darkness, and a great terror has come upon me lest I should become hard, and a lover of self, and no more bear willingly the Redeemer's cross.'

Dinah had closed her eyes, and a faint shudder went through her. 'Adam,' she went on, 'you wouldn't desire that we should seek a good through any unfaithfulness to the light that is in us; you wouldn't believe that could be a good. We are of one mind in that.'

'Yes, Dinah,' said Adam, sadly, 'I'll never be the man t' urge you against your conscience. But I can't give up the hope that you may come to see different. I don't believe your loving me could shut up your heart; it's only adding to what you've been before, not taking away from it; for it seems to me it's the same with love and happiness as with sorrow – the more we know of it the better we can feel what other people's lives are or might be, and so we shall only be more tender to 'em, and wishful to help 'em. The more knowledge a man has, the better he'll do's work; and feeling's a sort o' knowledge.'

Dinah was silent; her eyes were fixed in contemplation of something visible only to herself. Adam went on presently with his pleading – 'And you can do almost as much as you do now. I won't ask you to go to church with me of a Sunday; you shall go where you like among the people, and teach 'em; for though I like church best, I don't put my soul above yours, as if my words was better for you to follow than your own conscience. And you can help the sick just as much, and you'll have more means o' making 'em a bit comfortable; and you'll be among all your own friends as love you, and can help 'em and be a blessing to 'em till their dying day. Surely, Dinah, you'd be as near to God as if you was living lonely and away from me.'

Dinah made no answer for some time. Adam was still holding her hands, and looking at her with almost trembling anxiety, when she turned her grave loving eyes on his, and said, in rather a sad voice – 'Adam, there is truth in what you say, and there's many of the brethren and sisters who have greater strength than I have, and find their hearts enlarged by the cares of husband and kindred. But I have not faith that it would be so with me, for since my affections have been set above measure on you, I have had less peace and joy in God; I have felt as it were a division in my heart. And think how it is with me, Adam: – that life I have led is like a land I have trodden in blessedness since my childhood; and if I long for a moment to follow the voice which calls me to another land that I know not, I cannot but fear that my soul might hereafter yearn for that early blessedness which I had forsaken; and where doubt enters, there is not perfect love. I must wait for clearer guidance: I must go from you, and we must submit ourselves entirely to the Divine Will. We are sometimes required to lay our natural, lawful affections on the altar.'

Adam dared not plead again, for Dinah's was not the voice of caprice or insincerity. But it was very hard for him; his eyes got dim as he looked at her.

'But you may come to feel satisfied . . . to feel that you may come to me again, and we may never part, Dinah?'

'We must submit ourselves, Adam. With time, our duty will be made clear. It may be, when I have entered on my former life, I shall find all these new thoughts and wishes vanish, and become as things that were not. Then I shall know that my calling is not towards marriage. But we must wait.'

'Dinah,' said Adam, mournfully, 'you can't love me so well as I love you, else you'd have no doubts. But it's natural you shouldn't; for I'm not so good as you. I can't doubt it's right for me to love the best thing God's ever given me to know.'

'Nay, Adam; it seems to me that my love for you is not weak; for my heart waits on your words and looks, almost as a little child waits on the help and tenderness of the strong on whom it depends. If the thought of you took slight hold of me, I should not fear that it would be an idol in the temple. But you will strengthen me – you will not hinder me in seeking to obey to the uttermost.'

'Let us go out into the sunshine, Dinah, and walk together. I'll speak no word to disturb you.'

They went out and walked towards the fields, where they would meet the family coming from church. Adam said, 'Take my arm, Dinah,' and she took it. That was the only change in their manner to each other since they were last walking together. But no sadness in the prospect of her going away – in the uncertainty of the issue – could rob the sweetness from Adam's sense that Dinah loved him. He thought he would stay at the Hall Farm all that evening. He would be near her as long as he could.

'Heyday! there's Adam along wi' Dinah,' said Mr Poyser, as he opened the far gate into the Home Close. 'I couldna think how he happened away from church. Why,' added good Martin, after a moment's pause, 'what dost think has just jumped into my head?'

'Summat as hadna far to jump, for it's just under our nose. You mean as Adam's fond o' Dinah.'

'Ay! hast ever had any notion of it before?'

'To be sure I have,' said Mrs Poyser, who always declined, if possible, to be taken by surprise. 'I'm not one o' those as can see the cat i' the dairy, an' wonder what she's come after.'

'Thee never saidst a word to me about it.'

'Well, I aren't like a bird-clapper, forced to make a rattle when the wind blows on me. I can keep my own counsel when there's no good i' speaking.'

'But Dinah 'ull ha' none o' him; dost think she will?'

'Nay,' said Mrs Poyser, not sufficiently on her guard against a possible surprise; 'she'll never marry anybody, if he isn't a Methodist and a cripple.'

'It 'ud ha' been a pretty thing though for 'em t' marry,' said Martin, turning his head on one side, as if in pleased contemplation of his new idea. 'Thee'dst ha' liked it too wouldstna?'

'Ah! I should. I should ha' been sure of her then, as she wouldn't go away from me to Snowfield, welly thirty mile off, and me not got a creatur to look to, only neighbours, as are no kin to me, an' most of 'em women as I'd be ashamed to show my face, if my dairy things war like their'n. There may well be streaky butter i' the market. An' I should be glad to see the poor thing settled like a Christian woman, with a house of her own over her head; and we'd stock her well wi' linen and feathers; for I love her next to my own children. An' she makes one feel safer when she's i' the house; for she's like the driven snow: anybody might sin for two as had her at their elbow.'

'Dinah,' said Tommy, running forward to meet her, 'mother says you'll never marry anybody but a Methodist cripple. What a silly you must be!' a comment which Tommy followed up by seizing Dinah with both arms, and dancing along by her side with incommodious fondness.

'Why, Adam, we missed you i' the singing today,' said Mr Poyser. 'How was it?'

'I wanted to see Dinah: she's going away so soon,' said Adam.

'Ah, lad! can you persuade her to stop somehow? Find her a good husband somewhere i' the parish. If you'll do that, we'll forgive you for missing church. But, anyway, she isna going before the harvest-supper o' Wednesday, and you must come then. There's Bartle Massey comin', an' happen Craig. You'll be sure an' come, now, at seven? The missus wunna have it a bit later.'

'Ay,' said Adam, 'I'll come if I can. But I can't often say what I'll do before-hand, for the work often holds me longer than I expect. You'll stay till the end o' the week, Dinah?'

'Yes, yes!' said Mr Poyser; 'we'll have no nay.'

'She's no call to be in a hurry,' observed Mrs Poyser; 'scarceness o' victual 'ull keep: there's no need to be hasty wi' the cooking. An' scarceness is what there's the biggest stock of i' that country.'

Dinah smiled, but gave no promise to stay, and they talked of other things through the rest of the walk, lingering in the sunshine to look at the great flock of geese grazing, at the near corn-ricks, and at the surprising abundance of fruit on the old pear tree; Nancy and Molly having already hastened home, side by side, each holding, carefully wrapped in her pocket-handkerchief, a prayer-book, in which she could read little beyond the large letters and the Amens.

Surely all other leisure is hurry compared with a sunny walk through the fields from 'afternoon church' – as such walks used to be in those old leisurely times, when the boat, gliding sleepily along the canal, was the newest locomotive wonder; when Sunday books had most of them old brown-leather covers, and opened with remarkable precision always in one place. Leisure is gone – gone where the spinning-wheels are gone, and the packhorses, and the slow waggons, and the pedlars, who brought bargains to the door on sunny afternoons. Ingenious philosophers tell you, perhaps, that the great work of the steam-engine is to create leisure for mankind. Do not believe them: it only creates a vacuum for eager thought to rush in. Even idleness is eager now – eager for amusement: prone to excursion-trains, art-museums, periodical literature, and exciting novels: prone even to scientific theorising, and cursory peeps through microscopes. Old Leisure was quite a different personage: he only read one newspaper, innocent of leaders, and was free from that periodicity of sensations which we call post-time. He was a contemplative, rather stout gentleman, of excellent digestion – of quiet perceptions, undiseased by hypothesis: happy in his inability to know the causes of things, preferring the things themselves. He lived chiefly in the country, among pleasant seats and homesteads, and was fond of sauntering by the fruit-tree wall, and scenting the apricots when they were warmed by the morning sunshine, or of sheltering himself under the orchard boughs at noon, when the summer pears were falling. He knew nothing of weekday services, and thought none the worse of the Sunday sermon if it allowed him to sleep from the text to the blessing – liking the afternoon service best, because the prayers were the shortest, and not ashamed to say so; for he had an easy, jolly conscience, broad-backed like himself, and able to carry a great deal of beer or port-wine – not being made squeamish by doubts and qualms and lofty aspirations. Life was not a task to him, but a sinecure: he fingered the guineas in his pocket, and ate his dinners, and slept the sleep of the irresponsible; for had he not kept up his charter by going to church on the Sunday afternoons?

Fine old Leisure! Do not be severe upon him, and judge him by our modern standard: he never went to Exeter Hall, or heard a popular preacher, or read *Tracts for the Times* or *Sartor Resartus*.

53

The Harvest Supper

As Adam was going homewards, on Wednesday evening, in the six o'clock sunlight, he saw in the distance the last load of barley winding its way towards the yard-gate of the Hall Farm, and heard the chant of 'Harvest Home!' rising and sinking like a wave. Fainter and fainter, and more musical through the growing distance, the falling dying sound still reached him, as he neared the Willow Brook. The low westering sun shone right on the shoulders of the old Binton Hills, turning the unconscious sheep into bright spots of light; shone on the windows of the cottage too, and made them aflame with a glory beyond that of amber or amethyst. It was enough to make Adam feel that he was in a great temple, and that the distant chant was a sacred song.

'It's wonderful,' he thought, 'how that sound goes to one's heart almost like a funeral-bell, for all it tells one o' the joyfullest time o' the year, and the time when men are mostly the thankfullest. I suppose it's a bit hard to us to think anything's over and gone in our lives; and there's a parting at the root of all our joys. It's like what I feel about Dinah: I should never ha' come to know that her love 'ud be the greatest o' blessings to me, if what I counted a blessing hadn't been wrenched and torn away from me, and left me with a greater need, so as I could crave and hunger for a greater and a better comfort.'

He expected to see Dinah again this evening, and get leave to accompany her as far as Oakbourne; and then he would ask her to fix some time when he might go to Snowfield, and learn whether the last best hope that had been born to him must be resigned like the rest. The work he had to do at home, besides putting on his best clothes, made it seven before he was on his way again to the Hall Farm, and it was questionable whether, with his longest and quickest strides, he should be there in time even for the roast-beef, which came after the plum-pudding; for Mrs Poyser's supper would be punctual.

Great was the clatter of knives and pewter plates and tin cans when Adam entered the house, but there was no hum of voices to this accompaniment: the eating of excellent roast-beef, provided free of expense, was too serious a business to those good farm-labourers to be performed with a divided attention, even if they had had anything to say to each other – which they had not; and Mr Poyser, at the head of the table, was too busy with his carving to listen to Bartle Massey's or Mr Craig's ready talk.

'Here, Adam,' said Mrs Poyser, who was standing and looking on to see that Molly and Nancy did their duty as waiters, 'here's a place kept for you between Mr Massey and the boys. It's a poor tale you couldn't come to see the pudding when it was whole.'

Adam looked anxiously round for a fourth woman's figure; but Dinah was not there. He was almost afraid of asking about her; besides, his attention was claimed by greetings, and there remained the hope that Dinah was in the house, though perhaps disinclined to festivities on the eve of her departure.

It was a goodly sight – that table with Martin Poyser's round good-humoured face and large person at the head of it, helping his servants to the fragrant roast-beef, and pleased when the empty plates came again. Martin, though usually blest with a good appetite, really forgot to finish his own beef tonight – it was so pleasant to him to look on in the intervals of carving, and see how the others enjoyed their supper; for were they not men who, on all the days of the year except Christmas Day and Sundays, ate their cold dinner, in a makeshift manner, under the hedgerows, and drank their beer out of wooden bottles – with relish certainly, but with their mouths towards the zenith, after a fashion more endurable to ducks than to human bipeds. Martin Poyser had some faint conception of the flavour such men must find in hot roast-beef and fresh-drawn ale. He held his head on one side, and screwed up his mouth, as he nudged Bartle Massey, and watched half-witted Tom Tholer, otherwise known as 'Tom Saft,' receiving his second plateful of beef. A grin of delight broke over Tom's face as the plate was set down before him between his knife and fork, which he held erect, as if they had been sacred tapers; but the delight was too strong to continue smouldering in a grin – it burst out the next instant in a long-drawn 'haw, haw!' followed by a sudden collapse into utter gravity, as the knife and fork darted down on the prey. Martin Poyser's large person shook with his silent unctuous laugh: he turned towards Mrs Poyser to see if she, too, had been observant of Tom, and the eyes of husband and wife met in a glance of good-natured amusement.

'Tom Saft' was a great favourite on the farm, where he played the part of the old jester, and made up for his practical deficiencies by his success in repartee.

His hits, I imagine, were those of the flail, which falls quite at random, but nevertheless smashes an insect now and then. They were much quoted at sheep shearing and haymaking times; but I refrain from recording them here, lest Tom's wit should prove to be like that of many other bygone jesters eminent in their day – rather of a temporary nature, not dealing with the deeper and more lasting relations of things.

Tom excepted, Martin Poyser had some pride in his servants and labourers, thinking with satisfaction that they were the best worth their pay of any set on the estate. There was Kester Bale, for example (Beale, probably, if the truth were known, but he was called Bale, and was not conscious of any claim to a fifth letter) – the old man with the close leather cap, and the network of wrinkles on his sun-browned face. Was there any man in Loamshire who knew better the 'natur' of all farming work? He was one of those invaluable labourers who can not only turn their hand to everything, but excel in everything they turn their hand to. It is true Kester's knees were much bent outward by this time, and he walked with a perpetual curtsy, as if he were among the most reverent of men. And so he was; but I am obliged to admit that the object of his reverence was his own skill, towards which he performed some rather affecting acts of worship. He always thatched the ricks; for if anything were his forte more than another, it was thatching; and when the last touch had been put to the last beehive rick, Kester, whose home lay at some distance from the farm, would take a walk to the rickyard in his best clothes on a Sunday morning, and stand in the lane, at a due distance, to contemplate his own thatching – walking about to get each rick from the proper point of view. As he curtsied along, with his eyes upturned to the straw knobs imitative of golden globes at the summits of the beehive ricks, which indeed were gold of the best sort, you might have imagined him to be engaged in some pagan act of adoration. Kester was an old bachelor, and reputed to have stockings full of coin, concerning which his master cracked a joke with him every pay-night: not a new, unseasoned joke, but a good old one, that had been tried many times before, and had worn well. 'Th' young measter's a merry mon,' Kester frequently remarked; for having begun his career by frightening away the crows under the last Martin Poyser but one, he could never cease to account the reigning Martin a young master. I am not ashamed of commemorating old Kester: you and I are indebted to the hard hands of such men – hands that have long ago mingled with the soil they tilled so faithfully, thriftily making the best they could of the earth's fruits, and receiving the smallest share as their own wages.

Then, at the end of the table, opposite his master, there was Alick, the shepherd and head man, with the ruddy face and broad shoulders, not on the best terms with old Kester; indeed, their intercourse was confined to an occasional snarl, for though they probably differed little concerning hedging and ditching and the treatment of ewes, there was a profound difference of opinion between them as to their own respective merits. When Tityrus and Meliboeus happen to be on the same farm, they are not sentimentally polite to each other. Alick, indeed, was not by any means a honeyed man: his speech had usually something of a snarl in it, and his broad-shouldered aspect something of the bulldog expression – 'Don't you meddle with me, and I won't meddle with you;' but he was honest even to the splitting of an oat-grain rather than he would take beyond his acknowledged share, and as 'close-fisted' with his master's property as if it had been his own – throwing very small handfuls of damaged barley to the chickens, because a large handful affected his imagination painfully with a sense of profusion. Good-tempered Tim, the waggoner, who loved his horses, had his grudge against Alick in the matter of corn: they rarely spoke to each other, and never looked at each other, even over their dish of cold potatoes; but then, as this was their usual mode of behaviour towards all mankind, it would be an unsafe conclusion that they had more than transient fits of unfriendliness. The bucolic character at Hayslope, you perceive, was not of that entirely genial, merry, broad-grinning sort, apparently observed in most districts visited by artists. The mild radiance of a smile was a rare sight on a field labourer's face, and there was seldom any gradation between bovine gravity and a laugh. Nor was every labourer so honest as our friend Alick. At this very table, among Mr Poyser's men, there is that big Ben Tholoway, a very powerful thresher, but detected more than once in carrying away his master's corn in his pockets: an action which, as Ben was not a philosopher, could hardly be ascribed to absence of mind. However, his master had forgiven him, and continued to employ him; for the Tholoways had lived on the Common, time out of mind, and had always worked for the Poysers. And on the whole, I dare say, society was not much the worse because Ben had not six months of it at the treadmill; for his views of depredation were narrow, and the House of Correction might have enlarged them. As it was, Ben ate his roast-beef tonight with a serene sense of having stolen nothing more than a few peas and beans as seed for his garden, since the last harvest-supper, and felt warranted in thinking that Alick's suspicious eye, for ever upon him, was an injury to his innocence.

But *now* the roast-beef was finished, and the cloth was drawn, leaving a fair large deal table for the bright drinking-cans, and the foaming brown jugs, and the bright brass candlesticks, pleasant to behold. *Now*, the great ceremony of the evening was to begin – the harvest-song, in which every man must join: he might be in tune, if he liked to be singular, but he must not sit with closed lips. The movement was obliged to be in triple time; the rest was *ad libitum*.

As to the origin of this song – whether it came in its actual state from the brain of a single rhapsodist, or was gradually perfected by a school or succession of rhapsodists, I am ignorant. There is a stamp of unity, of individual genius, upon it, which inclines me to the former hypothesis, though I am not blind to the consideration that this unity may rather have arisen from that consensus of many minds which was a condition of primitive thought, foreign to our modern consciousness. Some will perhaps think that they detect in the first quatrain an indication of a lost line, which later rhapsodists, failing in imaginative vigour, have supplied by the feeble device of iteration: others, however, may rather maintain that this very iteration is an original felicity, to which none but the most prosaic minds can be insensible.

The ceremony connected with the song was a drinking ceremony. (That is perhaps a painful fact, but then, you know, we cannot reform our forefathers.) During the first and second quatrain, sung decidedly *forte*, no can was filled.

'Here's a health unto our master,
The founder of the feast:
Here's a health unto our master
And to our mistress!

And may his doings prosper,
Whate'er he takes in hand,
For we are all his servants,
And are at his command.'

But now, immediately before the third quatrain or chorus, sung *fortissimo*, with emphatic raps of the table, which gave the effect of cymbals and drum together, Alick's can was filled, and he was bound to empty it before the chorus ceased.

'Then drink, boys, drink!
And see ye do not spill,
For if ye do, ye shall drink two,
For 'tis our master's will.'

When Alick had gone successfully through this test of steady-handed manliness, it was the turn of old Kester, at his right hand – and so on, till every man had drunk his initiatory pint under the stimulus of the chorus. Tom Saft – the rogue – took care to spill a little by accident; but Mrs Poyser (too officiously, Tom thought) interfered to prevent the exaction of the penalty.

To any listener outside the door it would have been the reverse of obvious why the 'Drink, boys, drink!' should have such an immediate and often-repeated encore; but once entered, he would have seen that all faces were at present sober, and most of them serious: it was the regular and respectable thing for those excellent farm-labourers to do, as much as for elegant ladies and gentlemen to smirk and bow over their wine-glasses. Bartle Massey, whose ears were rather sensitive, had gone out to see what sort of evening it was, at an early stage in the ceremony; and had not finished his contemplation until a silence of five minutes declared that 'Drink, boys, drink!' was not likely to begin again for the next twelvemonth. Much to the regret of the boys and Totty: on them the stillness fell rather flat, after that glorious thumping of the table, towards which Totty, seated on her father's knee, contributed with her small might and small fist.

When Bartle re-entered, however, there appeared to be a general desire for solo music after the choral. Nancy declared that Tim the waggoner knew a song and was 'allays singing like a lark i' the stable;' whereupon Mr Poyser said encouragingly, 'Come, Tim, lad, let's hear it.' Tim looked sheepish, tucked down his head, and said he couldn't sing; but this encouraging invitation of the master's was echoed all round the table. It was a conversational opportunity: everybody could say 'Come, Tim' – except Alick, who never relaxed into the frivolity of unnecessary speech. At last, Tim's next neighbour, Ben Tholoway, began to give emphasis to his speech by nudges, at which Tim, growing rather savage, said, 'Let me alooan, will ye? else I'll ma' ye sing a toon ye wonna like.' A good-tempered waggoner's patience has limits, and Tim was not to be urged further.

'Well, then, David, ye're the lad to sing,' said Ben, willing to show that he was not discomfited by this check. 'Sing "My loove's a roos wi'out a thorn." '

The amatory David was a young man of an unconscious abstracted expression, which was due probably to a squint of superior intensity rather than to any mental characteristic; for he was not indifferent to Ben's invitation, but blushed and laughed and rubbed his sleeve over his mouth in a way that was regarded as a symptom of yielding. And for some time the company appeared to be much in earnest about the desire to hear David's song. But in vain. The lyrism of the evening was in the cellar at present, and was not to be drawn from that retreat just yet.

Meanwhile the conversation at the head of the table had taken a political turn. Mr Craig was not above talking politics occasionally, though he piqued himself rather on a wise insight than on specific information. He saw so far beyond the mere facts of a case, that really it was superfluous to know them.

'I'm no reader o' the paper myself,' he observed tonight as he filled his pipe, 'though I might read it fast enough if I liked, for there's Miss Lyddy has 'em, and 's done with 'em i' no time; but there's Mills, now, sits i' the chimney-corner and reads the paper pretty nigh from morning to night, and when he's got to th' end on't he's more addleheaded than he was at the beginning. He's full o' this peace now, as they talk on; he's been reading and reading, and thinks he's got to the bottom on't. "Why, Lor, bless you, Mills," says I, "you see no more into this thing nor you can see into the middle of a potato. I'll tell you what it is: you think it'll be a fine thing for the country; and I'm not again' it – mark my words – I'm not again' it. But it's my opinion as there's them at th' head o' this country as are worse enemies to us nor Bony and all the mounseers he's got at 's back; for as for the mounseers, you may skewer half a dozen of 'em at once as if they war frogs." '

'Ay, ay,' said Martin Poyser, listening with an air of much intelligence and edification, 'they ne'er ate a bit o' beef i' their lives. Mostly sallet, I reckon.'

'And says I to Mills,' continued Mr Craig, '"Will *you* try to make me believe as furriners like them can do us half th' harm them ministers do with their bad government? If King George 'ud turn 'em all away and govern by himself, he'd see everything righted. He might take on Billy Pitt again if he liked; but I don't see myself what we want wi' anybody besides King and Parliament. It's that nest o' ministers does the mischief, I tell you." '

'Ah, it's fine talking,' observed Mrs Poyser, who was now seated near her husband, with Totty on her lap – 'it's fine talking. It's hard work to tell which is Old Harry when everybody's got boots on.'

'As for this peace,' said Mr Poyser, turning his head on one side in a dubitative manner, and giving a precautionary puff to his pipe between each sentence, 'I don't know. Th' war's a fine thing for the country, an' how'll you keep up prices wi'out it? An' them French are a wicked sort o' folks, by what I can make out; what can you do better nor fight 'em?'

'Ye're partly right there, Poyser,' said Mr Craig, 'but I'm not again' the peace – to make a holiday for a bit. We can break it when we like, an' I'm in no fear o' Bony, for all they talk so much o' his cliverness. That's what I says to Mills this morning. Lor, bless you, he sees no more through Bony! ... why, I put him up to more in three minutes than he gets from 's paper all the year round. Says I, "Am I a gardener as knows his business, or aren't I, Mills? answer me that." "To be sure y' are, Craig," says he – he's not a bad fellow, Mills isn't, for a butler, but weak i' the head. "Well," says I, "you talk o' Bony's cliverness; would it be any use my being a first-rate gardener if I'd got nought but a quagmire to work on?" "No" says he. "Well," I says, "that's just what it is wi' Bony. I'll not deny but he may be a bit cliver - he's no Frenchman born, as I understand; but what's he got at's back but mounseers?" '

Mr Craig paused a moment with an emphatic stare after this triumphant specimen of Socratic argument, and then added, thumping the table rather fiercely – 'Why, it's a sure thing – and there's them 'ull bear witness to't – as i' one regiment where there was one man a-missing, they put the regimentals on a big monkey, and they fit him as the shell fits the walnut, and you couldn't tell the monkey from the mounseers!'

'Ah! think o' that now!' said Mr Poyser, impressed at once with the political bearings of the fact, and with its striking interest as an anecdote in natural history.

'Come, Craig,' said Adam, 'that's a little too strong. You don't believe that. It's all nonsense about the French being such poor sticks. Mr Irwine's seen 'em in their own country, and he says they've plenty o' fine fellows among 'em. And as for knowledge, and contrivances, and manufactures, there's a many things as we're a fine sight behind 'em in. It's poor foolishness to run down your enemies. Why, Nelson and the rest of 'em 'ud have no merit i' beating 'em, if they were such offal as folks pretend.'

Mr Poyser looked doubtfully at Mr Craig, puzzled by this opposition of authorities. Mr Irwine's testimony was not to be disputed; but, on the other hand, Craig was a knowing fellow, and his view was less startling. Martin had never 'heard tell' of the French being good for much. Mr Craig had found no answer but such as was implied in taking a long draught of ale, and then looking down fixedly at the proportions of his own leg, which he turned a little outward for that purpose, when Bartle Massey returned from the fireplace, where he had been smoking his first pipe in quiet, and broke the silence by saying, as he thrust his forefinger into the canister – 'Why, Adam, how happened you not to be at church on Sunday? answer me that, you rascal. The anthem went limping without you. Are you going to disgrace your schoolmaster in his old age?'

'No, Mr Massey,' said Adam. 'Mr and Mrs Poyser can tell you where I was. I was in no bad company.'

'She's gone, Adam – gone to Snowfield,' said Mr Poyser, reminded of Dinah for the first time this evening. 'I thought you'd ha' persuaded her better. Nought 'ud hold her, but she must go yesterday forenoon. The missis has hardly got over it. I thought she'd ha' no sperrit for the harvest supper.'

Mrs Poyser had thought of Dinah several times since Adam had come in, but she had had 'no heart' to mention the bad news.

'What!' said Bartle, with an air of disgust. 'Was there a woman concerned? Then I give you up, Adam.'

'But it's a woman you'n spoke well on, Bartle,' said Mr Poyser. 'Come, now, you canna draw back; you said once as women wouldna ha' been a bad invention if they'd all been like Dinah.'

'I meant her voice, man – I meant her voice, that was all,' said Bartle. 'I can bear to hear her speak without wanting to put wool in my ears. As for other things, I dare say she's like the rest o' the women – thinks two and two 'ull come to make five, if she cries and bothers enough about it.'

'Ay, ay!' said Mrs Poyser; 'one 'ud think, an' hear some folks talk, as the men war 'cute enough to count the corns in a bag o' wheat wi' only smelling at it. They can see through a barn-door, they can. Perhaps that's the reason they can see so little o' this side on't.'

Martin Poyser shook with delighted laughter, and winked at Adam, as much as to say the schoolmaster was in for it now.

'Ah!' said Bartle, sneeringly, 'the women are quick enough – they're quick enough. They know the rights of a story before they hear it, and can tell a man what his thoughts are before he knows 'em himself.'

'Like enough,' said Mrs Poyser; 'for the men are mostly so slow, their thoughts overrun 'em, an' they can only catch 'em by the tail. I can count a stocking-top while a man's getting's tongue ready; an' when he outs wi' his speech at last, there's little broth to be made on't. It's your dead chicks take the longest hatchin'. Howiver, I'm not denyin' the women are foolish: God Almighty made 'em to match the men.'

'Match!' said Bartle; 'ay, as vinegar matches one's teeth. If a man says a word, his wife'll match it with a contradiction; if he's a mind for hot meat, his wife'll match it with cold bacon; if he laughs, she'll match him with whimpering. She's such a match as the horse-fly is to th' horse: she's got the right venom to sting him with – the right venom to sting him with.'

'Yes,' said Mrs Poyser, 'I know what the men like – a poor soft, as 'ud simper at 'em like the pictur o' the sun, whether they did right or wrong, an' say thank you for a kick, an' pretend she didna know which end she stood uppermost, till her husband told her. That's what a man wants in a wife, mostly; he wants to make sure o' one fool as 'ull tell him he's wise. But there's some men can do wi'out that – they think so much o' themselves a'ready; an' that's how it is there's old bachelors.'

'Come, Craig,' said Mr Poyser, jocosely, 'you mun get married pretty quick, else you'll be set down for an old bachelor; an' you see what the women 'ull think on you.'

'Well,' said Mr Craig, willing to conciliate Mrs Poyser, and setting a high value on his own compliments, 'I like a cleverish woman – a woman o' sperrit – a managing woman.'

'You're out there, Craig,' said Bartle, dryly; 'you're out there. You judge o' your garden-stuff on a better plan than that: you pick the things for what they can excel in – for what they can excel in. You don't value your peas for their roots, or your carrots for their flowers. Now, that's the way you should choose women: their cleverness'll never come to much – never come to much; but they make excellent simpletons, ripe and strong-flavoured.'

'What dost say to that?' said Mr Poyser, throwing himself back and looking merrily at his wife.

'Say!' answered Mrs Poyser, with dangerous fire kindling in her eye; 'why, I say as some folks' tongues are like the clocks as run on strikin', not to tell you the time o' the day, but because there's summat wrong i' their own inside . . . '

Mrs Poyser would probably have brought her rejoinder to a further climax, if every one's attention had not at this moment been called to the other end of the table, where the lyrism, which had at first only manifested itself by David's *sotto voce* performance of 'My love's a rose without a thorn,' had gradually assumed a rather deafening and complex character. Tim, thinking slightly of David's vocalisation, was impelled to supersede that feeble buzz by a spirited commencement of 'Three Merry Mowers;' but David was not to be put down so easily, and showed himself capable of a copious crescendo, which was rendering it doubtful whether the rose would not predominate over the mowers, when old Kester, with an entirely unmoved and immovable aspect, suddenly set up a quavering treble – as if he had been an alarum, and the time was come for him to go off.

The company at Alick's end of the table took this form of vocal entertainment very much as a matter of course, being free from musical prejudices; but Bartle Massey laid down his pipe and put his fingers in his ears; and Adam, who had been longing to go, ever since he had heard Dinah was not in the house, rose and said he must bid good-night.

'I'll go with you, lad,' said Bartle; 'I'll go with you before my ears are split.'

'I'll go round by the Common, and see you home, if you like, Mr Massey,' said Adam.

'Ay, ay!' said Bartle; 'then we can have a bit o' talk together. I never get hold of you now.'

'Eh! it's a pity but you'd sit it out,' said Martin Poyser. 'They'll all go soon; for th' missus niver lets 'em stay past ten.'

But Adam was resolute, so the good-nights were said, and the two friends turned out on their starlight walk together.

'There's that poor fool, Vixen, whimpering for me at home,' said Bartle. 'I can never bring her here with me for fear she should be struck with Mrs Poyser's eye, and the poor bitch might go limping for ever after.'

'I've never any need to drive Gyp back,' said Adam, laughing. 'He always turns back of his own head when he finds out I'm coming here.'

'Ay, ay,' said Bartle. 'A terrible woman! – made of needles – made of needles. But I stick to Martin – I shall always stick to Martin. And he likes the needles, God help him! He's a cushion made on purpose for 'em.'

'But she's a downright good-natur'd woman, for all that,' said Adam, 'and as true as the daylight. She's a bit cross wi' the dogs when they offer to come in th' house, but if they depended on her, she'd take care and have 'em well fed. If her tongue's keen her heart's tender: I've seen that in times o' trouble. She's one o' those women as are better than their word.'

'Well, well,' said Bartle, 'I don't say th' apple isn't sound at the core; but it sets my teeth on edge – it sets my teeth on edge.'

The Meeting on the Hill

Adam understood Dinah's haste to go away, and drew hope rather than discouragement from it. She was fearful lest the strength of her feeling towards him should hinder her from waiting and listening faithfully for the ultimate guiding voice from within.

'I wish I'd asked her to write to me, though,' he thought. 'And yet even that might disturb her a bit, perhaps. She wants to be quite quiet in her old way for a while. And I've no right to be impatient and interrupting her with my wishes. She's told me what her mind is; and she's not a woman to say one thing and mean another. I'll wait patiently.'

That was Adam's wise resolution, and it throve excellently for the first two or three weeks on the nourishment it got from the remembrance of Dinah's confession that Sunday afternoon. There is a wonderful amount of sustenance in the first few words of love. But towards the middle of October the resolution began to dwindle perceptibly, and showed dangerous symptoms of exhaustion. The weeks were unusually long: Dinah must surely have had more than enough time to make up her mind. Let a woman say what she will after she has once told a man that she loves him, he is a little too flushed and exalted with that first draught she offers him to care much about the taste of the second: he treads the earth with a very elastic step as he walks away from her, and makes light of all difficulties. But that sort of glow dies out: memory gets sadly diluted with time, and is not strong enough to revive us. Adam was no longer so confident as he had been: he began to fear that perhaps Dinah's old life would have too strong a grasp upon her for any new feeling to triumph. If she had not felt this, she would surely have written to him to give him some comfort; but it appeared that she held it right to discourage him. As Adam's confidence waned, his patience waned with it, and he thought he must write himself; he must ask Dinah not to leave him in painful doubt longer than was needful. He sat up late one night to write her a letter, but the next morning he burnt it, afraid of its effect. It would be worse to have a discouraging answer by letter than from her own lips, for her presence reconciled him to her will.

You perceive how it was: Adam was hungering for the sight of Dinah; and when that sort of hunger reaches a certain stage, a lover is likely to still it though he may have to put his future in pawn.

But what harm could he do by going to Snowfield? Dinah could not be displeased with him for it: she had not forbidden him to go: she must surely expect that he would go before long. By the second Sunday in October this view of the case had become so clear to Adam, that he was already on his way to Snowfield; on horseback this time, for his hours were precious now, and he had borrowed Jonathan Burge's good nag for the journey.

What keen memories went along the road with him! He had often been to

Oakbourne and back since that first journey to Snowfield, but beyond Oakbourne the grey stone walls, the broken country, the meagre trees, seemed to be telling him afresh the story of that painful past which he knew so well by heart. But no story is the same to us after a lapse of time; or rather, we who read it are no longer the same interpreters: and Adam this morning brought with him new thoughts through that grey country – thoughts which gave an altered significance to its story of the past.

That is a base and selfish, even a blasphemous, spirit, which rejoices and is thankful over the past evil that has blighted or crushed another, because it has been made a source of unforeseen good to ourselves: Adam could never cease to mourn over that mystery of human sorrow which had been brought so close to him: he could never thank God for another's misery. And if I were capable of that narrow-sighted joy in Adam's behalf, I should still know he was not the man to feel it for himself: he would have shaken his head at such a sentiment, and said, 'Evil's evil, and sorrow's sorrow, and you can't alter its natur by wrapping it up in other words. Other folks were not created for my sake, that I should think all square when things turn out well for me.'

But it is not ignoble to feel that the fuller life which a sad experience has brought us is worth our own personal share of pain: surely it is not possible to feel otherwise, any more than it would be possible for a man with cataract to regret the painful process by which his dim blurred sight of men as trees walking had been exchanged for clear outline and effulgent day. The growth of higher feeling within us is like the growth of faculty, bringing with it a sense of added strength: we can no more wish to return to a narrower sympathy, than a painter or a musician can wish to return to his cruder manner, or a philosopher to his less complete formula.

Something like this sense of enlarged being was in Adam's mind this Sunday morning as he rode along in vivid recollection of the past. His feeling towards Dinah, the hope of passing his life with her, had been the distant unseen point towards which that hard journey from Snowfield eighteen months ago had been leading him. Tender and deep as his love for Hetty had been – so deep that the roots of it would never be torn away – his love for Dinah was better and more precious to him; for it was the outgrowth of that fuller life which had come to him from his acquaintance with deep sorrow. 'It's like as if it was a new strength to me,' he said to himself, 'to love her, and know as she loves me. I shall look t' her to help me to see things right. For she's better than I am – there's less o' self in her, and pride. And it's a feeling as gives you a sort o' liberty, as if you could walk more fearless, when you've more trust in another than y' have in yourself. I've always been thinking I knew better than them as belonged to me, and that's a poor sort o' life, when you can't look to them nearest to you t' help you with a bit better thought than what you've got inside you a'ready.'

It was more than two o'clock in the afternoon when Adam came in sight of the grey town on the hillside, and looked searchingly towards the green valley below, for the first glimpse of the old thatched roof near the ugly red mill. The scene looked less harsh in the soft October sunshine than it had done in the eager time of early spring; and the one grand charm it possessed in common

with all wide-stretching woodless regions – that it filled you with a new consciousness of the overarching sky – had a milder, more soothing influence than
usual, on this almost cloudless day. Adam's doubts and fears melted under this
influence as the delicate weblike clouds had gradually melted away into the clear
blue above him. He seemed to see Dinah's gentle face assuring him, with its
looks alone, of all he longed to know.

He did not expect Dinah to be at home at this hour, but he got down from his
horse and tied it at the little gate, that he might ask where she was gone today.
He had set his mind on following her and bringing her home. She was gone to
Sloman's End, a hamlet about three miles off, over the hill, the old woman told
him: had set off directly after morning chapel, to preach in a cottage there, as
her habit was. Anybody at the town would tell him the way to Sloman's End. So
Adam got on his horse again and rode to the town, putting up at the old inn, and
taking a hasty dinner there in the company of the too chatty landlord, from
whose friendly questions and reminiscences he was glad to escape as soon as
possible, and set out towards Sloman's End. With all his haste, it was nearly four
o'clock before he could set off, and he thought that as Dinah had gone so early,
she would perhaps already be near returning. The little, grey, desolate-looking
hamlet, unscreened by sheltering trees, lay in sight long before he reached it;
and as he came near he could hear the sound of voices singing a hymn. 'Perhaps
that's the last hymn before they come away,' Adam thought: 'I'll walk back a bit,
and turn again to meet her, further off the village.' He walked back till he got
nearly to the top of the hill again, and seated himself on a loose stone, against
the low wall, to watch till he should see the little black figure leaving the hamlet
and winding up the hill. He chose this spot, almost at the top of the hill, because
it was away from all eyes – no house, no cattle, not even a nibbling sheep near –
no presence but the still lights and shadows, and the great embracing sky.

She was much longer coming than he expected: he waited an hour at least
watching for her and thinking of her, while the afternoon shadows lengthened,
and the light grew softer. At last he saw the little black figure coming from
between the grey houses, and gradually approaching the foot of the hill. Slowly,
Adam thought; but Dinah was really walking at her usual pace, with a light quiet
step. Now she was beginning to wind along the path up the hill, but Adam
would not move yet: he would not meet her too soon; he had set his heart on
meeting her in this assured loneliness. And now he began to fear lest he should
startle her too much: 'Yet,' he thought, 'she's not one to be overstartled; she's
always so calm and quiet, as if she was prepared for anything.'

What was she thinking of as she wound up the hill? Perhaps she had found
complete repose without him, and had ceased to feel any need of his love. On
the verge of a decision we all tremble: hope pauses with fluttering wings.

But now at last she was very near, and Adam rose from the stone wall. It
happened that just as he walked forward, Dinah had paused and turned round to
look back at the village: who does not pause and look back in mounting a hill?
Adam was glad; for, with the fine instinct of a lover, he felt that it would be best
for her to hear his voice before she saw him. He came within three paces of her
and then said, 'Dinah!' She started without looking round, as if she connected

the sound with no place. 'Dinah!' Adam said again. He knew quite well what was in her mind. She was so accustomed to think of impressions as purely spiritual monitions, that she looked for no material visible accompaniment of the voice.

But this second time she looked round. What a look of yearning love it was that the mild grey eyes turned on the strong dark-eyed man! She did not start again at the sight of him; she said nothing, but moved towards him so that his arm could clasp her round.

And they walked on so in silence, while the warm tears fell. Adam was content, and said nothing. It was Dinah who spoke first.

'Adam,' she said, 'it is the Divine Will. My soul is so knit to yours that it is but a divided life I live without you. And this moment, now you are with me, and I feel that our hearts are filled with the same love, I have a fullness of strength to bear and do our heavenly Father's Will, that I had lost before.'

Adam paused and looked into her sincere eyes.

'Then we'll never part any more, Dinah, till death parts us.'

And they kissed each other with a deep joy.

What greater thing is there for two human souls, than to feel that they are joined for life – to strengthen each other in all labour, to rest on each other in all sorrow, to minister to each other in all pain, to be one with each other in silent unspeakable memories at the moment of the last parting?

55

Marriage Bells

In little more than a month after that meeting on the hill – on a rimy morning in departing November – Adam and Dinah were married.

It was an event much thought of in the village. All Mr Burge's men had a holiday, and all Mr Poyser's; and most of those who had a holiday appeared in their best clothes at the wedding. I think there was hardly an inhabitant of Hayslope specially mentioned in this history and still resident in the parish on this November morning, who was not either in church to see Adam and Dinah married, or near the church door to greet them as they came forth. Mrs Irwine and her daughters were waiting at the churchyard gates in their carriage (for they had a carriage now) to shake hands with the bride and bridegroom, and wish them well; and in the absence of Miss Lydia Donnithorne at Bath, Mrs Best, Mr Mills, and Mr Craig had felt it incumbent on them to represent 'the family' at the Chase on the occasion. The churchyard walk was quite lined with familiar faces, many of them faces that had first looked at Dinah when she preached on the Green; and no wonder they showed this eager interest on her marriage morning, for nothing like Dinah and the history which had brought her and Adam Bede together had been known at Hayslope within the memory of man.

Bessy Cranage, in her neatest cap and frock, was crying, though she did not exactly know why; for, as her cousin Wiry Ben, who stood near her, judiciously suggested, Dinah was not going away, and if Bessy was in low spirits, the best thing for her to do was to follow Dinah's example, and marry an honest fellow who was ready to have her. Next to Bessy, just within the church door, there were the Poyser children, peeping round the corner of the pews to get a sight of the mysterious ceremony; Totty's face wearing an unusual air of anxiety at the idea of seeing cousin Dinah come back looking rather old, for in Totty's experience no married people were young.

I envy them all the sight they had when the marriage was fairly ended and Adam led Dinah out of church. She was not in black this morning; for her aunt Poyser would by no means allow such a risk of incurring bad luck, and had herself made a present of the wedding dress, made all of grey, though in the usual Quaker form, for on this point Dinah could not give way. So the lily face looked out with sweet gravity from under a grey Quaker bonnet, neither smiling nor blushing, but with lips trembling a little under the weight of solemn feelings. Adam, as he pressed her arm to his side, walked with his old erectness and his head thrown rather backward as if to face all the world better; but it was not because he was particularly proud this morning, as is the wont of bridegrooms, for his happiness was of a kind that had little reference to men's opinion of it. There was a tinge of sadness in his deep joy; Dinah knew it, and did not feel aggrieved.

There were three other couples, following the bride and bridegroom: first, Martin Poyser, looking as cheery as a bright fire on this rimy morning, led quiet Mary Burge, the bridesmaid; then came Seth, serenely happy, with Mrs Poyser on his arm; and last of all Bartle Massey, with Lisbeth – Lisbeth in a new gown and bonnet, too busy with her pride in her son, and her delight in possessing the one daughter she had desired, to devise a single pretext for complaint.

Bartle Massey had consented to attend the wedding at Adam's earnest request, under protest against marriage in general, and the marriage of a sensible man in particular. Nevertheless, Mr Poyser had a joke against him after the wedding dinner, to the effect that in the vestry he had given the bride one more kiss than was necessary.

Behind this last couple came Mr Irwine, glad at heart over this good morning's work of joining Adam and Dinah. For he had seen Adam in the worst moments of his sorrow; and what better harvest from that painful seed-time could there be than this? The love that had brought hope and comfort in the hour of despair, the love that had found its way to the dark prison cell and to poor Hetty's darker soul – this strong, gentle love was to be Adam's companion and helper till death.

There was much shaking of hands mingled with 'God bless yous,' and other good wishes to the four couples, at the churchyard gate, Mr Poyser answering for the rest with unwonted vivacity of tongue, for he had all the appropriate wedding-day jokes at his command. And the women, he observed, could never do anything but put finger in eye at a wedding. Even Mrs Poyser could not trust herself to speak as the neighbours shook hands with her; and Lisbeth began to cry in the face of the very first person who told her she was getting young again.

Mr Joshua Rann, having a slight touch of rheumatism, did not join in the ringing of the bells this morning, and, looking on with some contempt at these informal greetings which required no official co-operation from the clerk, began to hum in his musical bass, 'O what a joyful thing it is', by way of preluding a little to the effect he intended to produce in the wedding psalm next Sunday.

'That's a bit of good news to cheer Arthur,' said Mr Irwine to his mother, as they drove off. 'I shall write to him the first thing when we get home.'

EPILOGUE

It is near the end of June, in 1807. The workshops have been shut up half an hour or more in Adam Bede's timberyard, which used to be Jonathan Burge's, and the mellow evening light is falling on the pleasant house with the buff walls and the soft grey thatch, very much as it did when we saw Adam bringing in the keys on that June evening nine years ago.

There is a figure we know well, just come out of the house, and shading her eyes with her hands as she looks for something in the distance; for the rays that fall on her white borderless cap and her pale auburn hair are very dazzling. But now she turns away from the sunlight and looks towards the door. We can see the sweet pale face quite well now: it is scarcely at all altered – only a little fuller, to correspond to her more matronly figure, which still seems light and active enough in the plain black dress.

'I see him, Seth,' Dinah said, as she looked into the house. 'Let us go and meet him. Come, Lisbeth, come with mother.'

The last call was answered immediately by a small fair creature with pale auburn hair and grey eyes, little more than four years old, who ran out silently and put her hand into her mother's.

'Come, Uncle Seth,' said Dinah.

'Ay, ay, we're coming,' Seth answered from within, and presently appeared stooping under the doorway, being taller than usual by the black head of a sturdy two-year-old nephew, who had caused some delay by demanding to be carried on uncle's shoulder.

'Better take him on thy arm, Seth,' said Dinah, looking fondly at the stout black-eyed fellow. 'He's troublesome to thee so.'

'Nay, nay: Addy likes a ride on my shoulder. I can carry him so for a bit.' A kindness which young Addy acknowledged by drumming his heels with promising force against Uncle Seth's chest. But to walk by Dinah's side, and be tyrannised over by Dinah's and Adam's children, was uncle Seth's earthly happiness.

'Where didst see him?' asked Seth, as they walked on into the adjoining field. 'I can't catch sight of him anywhere.'

'Between the hedges by the roadside,' said Dinah. 'I saw his hat and his shoulder. There he is again.'

'Trust thee for catching sight of him if he's anywhere to be seen,' said Seth, smiling. 'Thee't like poor mother used to be. She was always on the look-out for Adam, and could see him sooner than other folks, for all her eyes got dim.'

'He's been longer than he expected,' said Dinah, taking Arthur's watch from a small side-pocket and looking at it; 'it's nigh upon seven now.'

'Ay, they'd have a deal to say to one another,' said Seth, 'and the meeting 'ud touch 'em both pretty closish. Why, it's getting on towards eight years since they parted.'

'Yes,' said Dinah, 'Adam was greatly moved this morning at the thought of the change he should see in the poor young man, from the sickness he has undergone, as well as the years which have changed us all. And the death of the poor wanderer, when she was coming back to us, has been sorrow upon sorrow.'

'See, Addy,' said Seth, lowering the young one to his arm now, and pointing, 'there's father coming – at the far stile.'

Dinah hastened her steps, and little Lisbeth ran on at her utmost speed till she clasped her father's leg. Adam patted her head and lifted her up to kiss her, but Dinah could see the marks of agitation on his face as she approached him, and he put her arm within his in silence.

'Well, youngster, must I take you?' he said, trying to smile, when Addy stretched out his arms – ready, with the usual baseness of infancy, to give up his uncle Seth at once, now there was some rarer patronage at hand.

'It's cut me a good deal, Dinah,' Adam said at last, when they were walking on.

'Didst find him greatly altered?' said Dinah.

'Why, he's altered and yet not altered. I should ha' known him anywhere. But his colour's changed, and he looks sadly. However, the doctors say he'll soon be set right in his own country air. He's all sound in th' inside; it's only the fever shattered him so. But he speaks just the same, and smiles at me just as he did when he was a lad. It's wonderful how he's always had just the same sort o' look when he smiles.'

'I've never seen him smile, poor young man,' said Dinah.

'But thee wilt see him smile, tomorrow,' said Adam. 'He asked after thee the first thing when he began to come round, and we could talk to one another. "I hope she isn't altered" he said, "I remember her face so well." I told him, "no",' Adam continued, looking fondly at the eyes that were turned up towards his, 'only a bit plumper, as thee'dst a right to be after seven year. "I may come and see her tomorrow, mayn't I?" he said; 'I long to tell her how I've thought of her all these years".'

'Didst tell him I'd always used the watch?' said Dinah.

'Ay; and we talked a deal about thee, for he says he never saw a woman a bit like thee. "I shall turn Methodist someday" he said, "when she preaches out of doors, and go to hear her." And I said, "Nay, sir, you can't do that, for Conference has forbid the women preaching, and she's given it up, all but talking to the people a bit in their houses." '

'Ah,' said Seth, who could not repress a comment on this point, 'and a sore pity it was o' Conference; and if Dinah had seen as I did, we'd ha' left the Wesleyans and joined a body that 'ud put no bonds on Christian liberty.'

'Nay, lad, nay,' said Adam, 'she was right and thee wast wrong. There's no rule so wise but what it's a pity for somebody or other. Most o' the women do more harm nor good with their preaching – they've not got Dinah's gift nor her sperrit; and she's seen that, and she thought it right to set th' example o' submitting, for she's not held from other sorts o' teaching. And I agree with her, and approve o' what she did.'

Seth was silent. This was a standing subject of difference rarely alluded to, and Dinah, wishing to quit it at once, said – 'Didst remember, Adam, to speak to Colonel Donnithorne the words my uncle and aunt intrusted to thee?'

'Yes, and he's going to the Hall Farm with Mr Irwine the day after tomorrow. Mr Irwine came in while we were talking about it, and he would have it as the Colonel must see nobody but thee tomorrow: he said – and he's in the right of it – as it'll be bad for him t' have his feelings stirred with seeing many people one after another. "We must get you strong and hearty" he said, "that's the first thing to be done, Arthur, and then you shall have your own way. But I shall keep you under your old tutor's thumb till then." Mr Irwine's fine and joyful at having him home again.'

Adam was silent a little while, and then said – 'It was very cutting when we first saw one another. He'd never heard about poor Hetty till Mr Irwine met him in London, for the letters missed him on his journey. The first thing he said to me, when we'd got hold o' one another's hands, was, "I could never do anything for her, Adam – she lived long enough for all the suffering – and I'd thought so of the time when I might do something for her. But you told me the truth when you said to me once, "There's a sort of wrong that can never be made up for." '

'Why, there's Mr and Mrs Poyser coming in at the yard gate,' said Seth.

'So there is,' said Dinah. 'Run, Lisbeth, run to meet Aunt Poyser. Come in, Adam, and rest; it has been a hard day for thee.'

MIDDLEMARCH

Middlemarch

A novel by
GEORGE ELIOT
first published in 1871–2

Contents

Prelude

Who that cares much to know the history of man, and how the mysterious mixture behaves under the varying experiments of Time, has not dwelt, at least briefly, on the life of Saint Theresa, has not smiled with some gentleness at the thought of the little girl walking forth one morning hand-in-hand with her still smaller brother, to go and seek martyrdom in the country of the Moors? Out they toddled from rugged Avila, wide-eyed and helpless-looking as two fawns, but with human hearts, already beating to a national idea; until domestic reality met them in the shape of uncles, and turned them back from their great resolve. That child-pilgrimage was a fit beginning. Theresa's passionate, ideal nature demanded an epic life: what were many-volumed romances of chivalry and the social conquests of a brilliant girl to her? Her flame quickly burned up that light fuel; and, fed from within, soared after some illimitable satisfaction, some object which would never justify weariness, which would reconcile self-despair with the rapturous consciousness of life beyond self. She found her epos in the reform of a religious order.

That Spanish woman who lived three hundred years ago was certainly not the last of her kind. Many Theresas have been born who found for themselves no epic life wherein there was a constant unfolding of far-resonant action; perhaps only a life of mistakes, the offspring of a certain spiritual grandeur ill-matched with the meanness of opportunity; perhaps a tragic failure which found no sacred poet and sank unwept into oblivion. With dim lights and tangled circumstance they tried to shape their thought and deed in noble agreement; but after all, to common eyes their struggles seemed mere inconsistency and formlessness; for these later-born Theresas were helped by no coherent social faith and order which could perform the function of knowledge for the ardently willing soul. Their ardour alternated between a vague ideal and the common yearning of womanhood; so that the one was disapproved as extravagance, and the other condemned as a lapse.

Some have felt that these blundering lives are due to the inconvenient indefiniteness with which the Supreme Power has fashioned the natures of women: if there were one level of feminine incompetence as strict as the ability to count three and no more, the social lot of women might be treated with scientific certitude. Meanwhile the indefiniteness remains, and the limits of variation are really much wider than anyone would imagine from the sameness of women's coiffure and the favourite love-stories in prose and verse. Here and there a cygnet is reared uneasily among the ducklings in the brown pond, and never finds the living stream in fellowship with its own oary-footed kind. Here and there is born a Saint Theresa, foundress of nothing, whose loving heart-beats and sobs after an unattained goodness tremble off and are dispersed among hindrances, instead of centring in some long-recognisable deed.

BOOK ONE

Miss Brooke

Chapter 1

Since I can do no good because a woman,
Reach constantly at something that is near it.
BEAUMONT AND FLETCHER, *The Maid's Tragedy*

Miss Brooke had that kind of beauty which seems to be thrown into relief by poor dress. Her hand and wrist were so finely formed that she could wear sleeves not less bare of style than those in which the Blessed Virgin appeared to Italian painters; and her profile as well as her stature and bearing seemed to gain the more dignity from her plain garments, which by the side of provincial fashion gave her the impressiveness of a fine quotation from the Bible, – or from one of our elder poets, – in a paragraph of today's newspaper. She was usually spoken of as being remarkably clever, but with the addition that her sister Celia had more common-sense. Nevertheless, Celia wore scarcely more trimmings; and it was only to close observers that her dress differed from her sister's, and had a shade of coquetry in its arrangements; for Miss Brooke's plain dressing was due to mixed conditions, in most of which her sister shared. The pride of being ladies had something to do with it: the Brooke connections, though not exactly aristocratic, were unquestionably 'good': if you enquired backward for a generation or two, you would not find any yard-measuring or parcel-tying forefathers – anything lower than an admiral or a clergyman; and there was even an ancestor discernible as a Puritan gentleman who served under Cromwell, but afterwards conformed, and managed to come out of all political troubles as the proprietor of a respectable family estate. Young women of such birth, living in a quiet country-house, and attending a village church hardly larger than a parlour, naturally regarded frippery as the ambition of a huckster's daughter. Then there was well-bred economy, which in those days made show in dress the first item to be deducted from, when any margin was required for expenses more distinctive of rank. Such reasons would have been enough to account for plain dress, quite apart from religious feeling; but in Miss Brooke's case, religion alone would have determined it; and Celia mildly acquiesced in all her sister's sentiments, only infusing them with that common-sense which is able to accept momentous doctrines without any eccentric agitation. Dorothea knew many passages of Pascal's *Pensées* and of Jeremy Taylor by heart; and to her the destinies of mankind, seen by the light of Christianity, made the solicitudes of feminine fashion appear an occupation for Bedlam. She could not reconcile the anxieties of a spiritual life involving eternal consequences, with a keen interest in guimp and artificial protrusions of drapery. Her mind was theoretic, and yearned by its nature after some lofty conception of the world which might frankly include the parish of Tipton and her own rule of conduct there; she was enamoured of intensity and greatness, and rash in embracing whatever seemed to her to have those aspects; likely to seek martyrdom, to make retractions, and then to incur martyrdom after all in a quarter where she had not sought it. Certainly such elements in the character of a marriageable girl tended to interfere with her lot, and hinder it from being decided according to custom, by good looks, vanity, and merely canine affection. With all this, she, the elder of the sisters, was not yet twenty, and they had both been educated, since they were about twelve years old and had lost their parents, on plans at once narrow and promiscuous, first in an English family and afterwards in a Swiss family at Lausanne, their bachelor uncle and guardian trying in this way to remedy the disadvantages of their orphaned condition.

It was hardly a year since they had come to live at Tipton Grange with their uncle, a man nearly sixty, of acquiescent temper, miscellaneous opinions, and uncertain vote. He had travelled in his younger years, and was held in this part of the county to have contracted a too rambling habit of mind. Mr Brooke's conclusions were as difficult to predict as the weather: it was only safe to say that he would act with benevolent intentions, and that he would spend as little money as possible in carrying them out. For the most glutinously indefinite minds enclose some hard grains of habit; and a man has been seen lax about all his own interests except the retention of his snuff-box, concerning which he was watchful, suspicious, and greedy of clutch.

In Mr Brooke the hereditary strain of Puritan energy was clearly in abeyance: but in his niece Dorothea it glowed alike through faults and virtues, turning sometimes into impatience of her uncle's talk or his way of 'letting things be' on his estate, and making her long all the more for the time when she would be of age and have some command of money for generous schemes. She was regarded as an heiress, for not only had the sisters seven hundred a year each from their parents, but if Dorothea married and had a son, that son would inherit Mr Brooke's estate, presumably worth about three thousand a year – a rental which seemed wealth to provincial families, still discussing Mr Peel's late conduct on the Catholic Question, innocent of future gold-fields, and of that gorgeous plutocracy which has so nobly exalted the necessities of genteel life.

And how should Dorothea not marry? – a girl so handsome and with such prospects? Nothing could hinder it but her love of extremes, and her insistence on regulating life according to notions which might cause a wary man to hesitate before he made her an offer, or even might lead her at last to refuse all offers. A young lady of some birth and fortune, who knelt suddenly down on a brick floor by the side of a sick labourer and prayed fervidly as if she thought herself living in the time of the Apostles – who had strange whims of fasting like a Papist, and of sitting up at night to read old theological books! Such a wife might awaken you some fine morning with a new scheme for the application of her income which would interfere with political economy and the keeping of saddle-horses: a man would naturally think twice before he risked himself in such fellowship.

Women were expected to have weak opinions; but the great safeguard of society and of domestic life was, that opinions were not acted on. Sane people did what their neighbours did, so that if any lunatics were at large, one might know and avoid them.

The rural opinion about the new young ladies, even among the cottagers, was generally in favour of Celia, as being so amiable and innocent-looking, while Miss Brooke's large eyes seemed, like her religion, too unusual and striking. Poor Dorothea! compared with her, the innocent-looking Celia was knowing and worldly-wise; so much subtler is a human mind than the outside tissues which make a sort of blazonry or clock-face for it.

Yet those who approached Dorothea, though prejudiced against her by this alarming hearsay, found that she had a charm unaccountably reconcilable with it. Most men thought her bewitching when she was on horseback. She loved the fresh air and the various aspects of the country, and when her eyes and cheeks glowed with mingled pleasure she looked very little like a devotee. Riding was an indulgence which she allowed herself in spite of conscientious qualms; she felt that she enjoyed it in a pagan sensuous way, and always looked forward to renouncing it.

She was open, ardent, and not in the least self-admiring; indeed, it was pretty to see how her imagination adorned her sister Celia with attractions altogether superior to her own, and if any gentleman appeared to come to the Grange from some other motive than that of seeing Mr Brooke, she concluded that he must be in love with Celia: Sir James Chettam, for example, whom she constantly considered from Celia's point of view, inwardly debating whether it would be good for Celia to accept him. That he should be regarded as a suitor to herself would have seemed to her a ridiculous irrelevance. Dorothea, with all her eagerness to know the truths of life, retained very childlike ideas about marriage. She felt sure that she would have accepted the judicious Hooker, if she had been born in time to save him from that wretched mistake he made in matrimony; or John Milton when his blindness had come on; or any of the other great men whose odd habits it would have been glorious piety to endure; but an amiable handsome baronet, who said 'Exactly' to her remarks even when she expressed uncertainty, – how could he affect her as a lover? The really delightful marriage must be that where your husband was a sort of father, and could teach you even Hebrew, if you wished it.

These peculiarities of Dorothea's character caused Mr Brooke to be all the more blamed in neighbouring families for not securing some middle-aged lady as guide and companion to his nieces. But he himself dreaded so much the sort of superior woman likely to be available for such a position, that he allowed himself to be dissuaded by Dorothea's objections, and was in this case brave enough to defy the world – that is to say, Mrs Cadwallader the Rector's wife, and the small group of gentry with whom he visited in the north-east corner of Loamshire. So Miss Brooke presided in her uncle's household, and did not at all dislike her new authority, with the homage that belonged to it.

Sir James Chettam was going to dine at the Grange today with another gentleman whom the girls had never seen, and about whom Dorothea felt some venerating expectation. This was the Reverend Edward Casaubon, noted in the county as a man of profound learning, understood for many years to be engaged on a great work concerning religious history; also as a man of wealth enough to give lustre to his piety, and having views of his own which were to be more clearly ascertained on the publication of his book. His very name carried an impressiveness hardly to be measured without a precise chronology of scholarship.

Early in the day Dorothea had returned from the infant school which she had set going in the village, and was taking her usual place in the pretty sitting-room which divided the bedrooms of the sisters, bent on finishing a plan for some buildings (a kind of work which she delighted in), when Celia, who had been watching her with a hesitating desire to propose something, said: 'Dorothea dear, if you don't mind – if you are not very busy suppose we looked at mamma's jewels today, and divided them? It is exactly six months today since uncle gave them to you, and you have not looked at them yet.'

Celia's face had the shadow of a pouting expression in it, the full presence of the pout being kept back by a habitual awe of Dorothea and principle; two associated facts which might show a mysterious electricity if you touched them incautiously. To her relief, Dorothea's eyes were full of laughter as she looked up.

'What a wonderful little almanac you are, Celia! Is it six calendar or six lunar months?'

'It is the last day of September now, and it was the first of April when uncle gave them to you. You know, he said that he had forgotten them till then. I believe you have never thought of them since you locked them up in the cabinet here.'

'Well, dear, we should never wear them, you know.' Dorothea spoke in a full cordial tone, half-caressing, half-explanatory. She had her pencil in her hand, and was making tiny side-plans on a margin.

Celia coloured, and looked very grave. 'I think, dear, we are wanting in respect to mamma's memory, to put them by and take no notice of them. And,' she added, after hesitating a little, with a rising sob of mortification, 'necklaces are quite usual now; and Madame Poinçon, who was stricter in some things even than you are, used to wear ornaments. And Christians generally – surely there are women in heaven now who wore jewels.' Celia was conscious of some mental strength when she really applied herself to argument.

'You would like to wear them?' exclaimed Dorothea, an air of astonished discovery animating her whole person with a dramatic action which she had caught from that very Madame Poinçon who wore the ornaments. 'Of course, then, let us have them out. Why did you not tell me before? But the keys, the keys!' She pressed her hands against the sides of her head and seemed to despair of her memory.

'They are here,' said Celia, with whom this explanation had been long-meditated and prearranged.

'Pray open the large drawer of the cabinet and get out the jewel-box.'

The casket was soon open before them, and the various jewels spread out, making a bright parterre on the table. It was no great collection, but a few of the ornaments were really of remarkable beauty, the finest that was obvious at first being a necklace of purple amethysts set in exquisite gold-work, and a pearl cross with five brilliants in it. Dorothea immediately took up the necklace and fastened it round her sister's neck, where it fitted almost as closely as a bracelet; but the circle suited the Henrietta-Maria style of Celia's head and neck, and she could see that it did, in the pier-glass opposite.

'There, Celia! you can wear that with your Indian muslin. But this cross you must wear with your dark dresses.'

Celia was trying not to smile with pleasure. 'O Dodo, you must keep the cross yourself.'

'No, no, dear, no,' said Dorothea, putting up her hand with careless deprecation.

'Yes, indeed you must; it would suit you – in your black dress, now,' said Celia, insistingly. 'You *might* wear that.'

'Not for the world, not for the world. A cross is the last thing I would wear as a trinket.' Dorothea shuddered slightly.

'Then you will think it wicked in me to wear it,' said Celia, uneasily.

'No, dear, no,' said Dorothea, stroking her sister's cheek. 'Souls have complexions too: what will suit one will not suit another.'

'But you might like to keep it for mamma's sake.'

'No, I have other things of mamma's – her sandalwood box, which I am so fond of – plenty of things. In fact, they are all yours, dear. We need discuss them no longer. There – take away your property.'

Celia felt a little hurt. There was a strong assumption of superiority in this Puritanic toleration, hardly less trying to the blond flesh of an unenthusiastic sister than a Puritanic persecution.

'But how can I wear ornaments if you, who are the elder sister, will never wear them?'

'Nay, Celia, that is too much to ask, that I should wear trinkets to keep you in countenance. If I were to put on such a necklace as that, I should feel as if I had been pirouetting. The world would go round with me, and I should not know how to walk.'

Celia had unclasped the necklace and drawn it off. 'It would be a little tight for your neck; something to lie down and hang would suit you better,' she said, with some satisfaction. The complete unfitness of the necklace from all points of view for Dorothea, made Celia happier in taking it. She was opening some ring-boxes, which disclosed a fine emerald with diamonds, and just then the sun passing beyond a cloud sent a bright gleam over the table.

'How very beautiful these gems are!' said Dorothea, under a new current of feeling, as sudden as the gleam. 'It is strange how deeply colours seem to penetrate one, like scent. I suppose that is the reason why gems are used as spiritual emblems in the Revelation of St John. They look like fragments of heaven. I think that emerald is more beautiful than any of them.'

'And there is a bracelet to match it,' said Celia. 'We did not notice this at first.'

'They are lovely,' said Dorothea, slipping the ring and bracelet on her finely-turned finger and wrist, and holding them towards the window on a level with her eyes. All the while her thought was trying to justify her delight in the colours by merging them in her mystic religious joy.

'You *would* like those, Dorothea,' said Celia, rather falteringly, beginning to think with wonder that her sister showed some weakness, and also that emeralds would suit her own complexion even better than purple amethysts. 'You must keep that ring and bracelet – if nothing else. But see, these agates are very pretty – and quiet.'

'Yes! I will keep these – this ring and bracelet,' said Dorothea. Then, letting her hand fall on the table, she said in another tone – 'Yet what miserable men find such things, and work at them, and sell them!' She paused again, and Celia thought that her sister was going to renounce the ornaments, as in consistency she ought to do.

'Yes, dear, I will keep these,' said Dorothea, decidedly. 'But take all the rest away, and the casket.'

She took up her pencil without removing the jewels, and still looking at them. She thought of often having them by her, to feed her eye at these little fountains of pure colour.

'Shall you wear them in company?' said Celia, who was watching her with real curiosity as to what she would do.

Dorothea glanced quickly at her sister. Across all her imaginative adornment of those whom she loved, there darted now and then a keen discernment, which was not without a scorching quality. If Miss Brooke ever attained perfect meekness, it would not be for lack of inward fire.

'Perhaps,' she said, rather haughtily. 'I cannot tell to what level I may sink.'

Celia blushed, and was unhappy; she saw that she had offended her sister, and dared not say even anything pretty about the gift of the ornaments which she put back into the box and carried away. Dorothea too was unhappy, as she went on with her plan-drawing, questioning the purity of her own feeling and speech in the scene which had ended with that little explosion.

Celia's consciousness told her that she had not been at all in the wrong: it was quite natural and justifiable that she should have asked that question, and she repeated to herself that Dorothea was inconsistent: either she should have taken her full share of the jewels, or, after what she had said, she should have renounced them altogether.

'I am sure – at least, I trust,' thought Celia, 'that the wearing of a necklace will not interfere with my prayers. And I do not see that I should be bound by Dorothea's opinions now we are going into society, though of course she herself ought to be bound by them. But Dorothea is not always consistent.'

Thus Celia, mutely bending over her tapestry, until she heard her sister calling her.

'Here, Kitty, come and look at my plan; I shall think I am a great architect, if I have not got incompatible stairs and fireplaces.'

As Celia bent over the paper, Dorothea put her cheek against her sister's arm caressingly. Celia understood the action. Dorothea saw that she had been in the wrong, and Celia pardoned her. Since they could remember, there had been a mixture of criticism and awe in the attitude of Celia's mind towards her elder sister. The younger had always worn a yoke; but is there any yoked creature without its private opinions?

Chapter 2

'Dime; no ves aquel caballero que hácia nostros viene sobre un caballo rucio rodado que trae puesto en la cabeza un yelmo de oro?' 'Lo que veo y columbro,' respondió Sancho, 'no es sino un hombre sobre un asno pardo como el mío, que trae sobre la cabeza una cosa que relumbra.' 'Pues ése es el yelmo de Mambrino,' dijo Don Quijote.   CERVANTES

'Seest thou not yon cavalier who cometh toward us on a dapple-grey steed, and weareth a golden helmet?' 'What I see,' answered Sancho, 'is nothing but a man on a grey ass like my own, who carries something shiny on his head.' 'Just so,' answered Don Quixote: 'and that resplendent object is the helmet of Mambrino.'

'Sir Humphry Davy?' said Mr Brooke, over the soup, in his easy smiling way, taking up Sir James Chettam's remark that he was studying Davy's *Agricultural Chemistry*. 'Well, now, Sir Humphry Davy: I dined with him years ago at Cartwright's, and Wordsworth was there too – the poet Wordsworth, you know. Now there was something singular. I was at Cambridge when Wordsworth was there, and I never met him – and I dined with him twenty years afterwards at Cartwright's. There's an oddity in things, now. But Davy was there: he was a poet too. Or, as I may say, Wordsworth was poet one, and Davy was poet two. That was true in every sense, you know.'

Dorothea felt a little more uneasy than usual. In the beginning of dinner, the party being small and the room still, these motes from the mass of a magistrate's mind fell too noticeably. She wondered how a man like Mr Casaubon would support such triviality. His manners, she thought, were very dignified; the set of his iron-grey hair and his deep eye-sockets made him resemble the portrait of Locke. He had the spare form and the pale complexion which became a student; as different as possible from the blooming Englishman of the red-whiskered type represented by Sir James Chettam.

'I am reading the *Agricultural Chemistry*,' said this excellent baronet, 'because I am going to take one of the farms into my own hands, and see if something cannot be done in setting a good pattern of farming among my tenants. Do you approve of that, Miss Brooke?'

'A great mistake, Chettam,' interposed Mr Brooke, 'going into electrifying your land and that kind of thing, and making a parlour of your cow-house. It won't do. I went into science a great deal myself at one time; but I saw it would not do. It leads to everything; you can let nothing alone. No, no – see that your tenants don't sell their straw, and that kind of thing; and give them draining-tiles, you know. But your fancy-farming will not do – the most expensive sort of whistle you can buy; you may as well keep a pack of hounds.'

'Surely,' said Dorothea, 'it is better to spend money in finding out how men can make the most of the land which supports them all, than in keeping dogs and horses only to gallop over it. It is not a sin to make yourself poor in performing experiments for the good of all.'

She spoke with more energy than is expected of so young a lady, but Sir James had appealed to her. He was accustomed to do so, and she had often thought that she could urge him to many good actions when he was her brother-in-law.

Mr Casaubon turned his eyes very markedly on Dorothea while she was speaking, and seemed to observe her newly.

'Young ladies don't understand political economy, you know,' said Mr Brooke, smiling towards Mr Casaubon. 'I remember when we were all reading Adam Smith. *There* is a book, now. I took in all the new ideas at one time – human perfectibility, now. But some say, history moves in circles; and that may be very well argued; I have argued it myself. The fact is, human reason may carry you a little too far – over the hedge, in fact. It carried me a good way at one time; but I saw it would not do. I pulled up; I pulled up in time. But not too hard. I have always been in favour of a little theory: we must have Thought; else we shall be landed back in the dark ages. But talking of books, there is Southey's *Peninsular War*. I am reading that of a morning. You know Southey?'

'No,' said Mr Casaubon, not keeping pace with Mr Brooke's impetuous reason, and thinking of the book only. 'I have little leisure for such literature just now. I have been using up my eyesight on old characters lately; the fact is, I want a reader for my evenings; but I am fastidious in voices, and I cannot endure listening to an imperfect reader. It is a misfortune, in some senses: I feed too much on the inward sources; I live too much with the dead. My mind is something like the ghost of an ancient, wandering about the world and trying mentally to construct it as it used to be, in spite of ruin and confusing changes. But I find it necessary to use the utmost caution about my eyesight.'

This was the first time that Mr Casaubon had spoken at any length. He delivered himself with precision, as if he had been called upon to make a public statement; and the balanced singsong neatness of his speech, occasionally corresponded to by a movement of his head, was the more conspicuous from its contrast with good Mr Brooke's scrappy slovenliness. Dorothea said to herself that Mr Casaubon was the most interesting man she had ever seen, not excepting even Monsieur Liret, the Vaudois clergyman who had given conferences on the history of the Waldenses. To reconstruct a past world, doubtless with a view to the highest purposes of truth – what a work to be in any way present at, to assist in, though only as a lamp-holder! This elevating thought lifted her above her annoyance at being twitted with her ignorance of political economy, that never-explained science which was thrust as an extinguisher over all her lights.

'But you are fond of riding, Miss Brooke,' Sir James presently took an opportunity of saying. 'I should have thought you would enter a little into the pleasures of hunting. I wish you would let me send over a chestnut horse for you to try. It has been trained for a lady. I saw you on Saturday cantering over the hill on a nag not worthy of you. My groom shall bring Corydon for you every day, if you will only mention the time.'

'Thank you, you are very good. I mean to give up riding. I shall not ride any more,' said Dorothea, urged to this brusque resolution by a little annoyance that Sir James would be soliciting her attention when she wanted to give it all to Mr Casaubon.

'No, that is too hard,' said Sir James, in a tone of reproach that showed strong interest. 'Your sister is given to self-mortification, is she not?' he continued, turning to Celia, who sat at his right hand.

'I think she is,' said Celia, feeling afraid lest she should say something that would not please her sister, and blushing as prettily as possible above her necklace. 'She likes giving up.'

'If that were true, Celia, my giving up would be self-indulgence, not self-mortification. But there may be good reasons for choosing not to do what is very agreeable,' said Dorothea.

Mr Brooke was speaking at the same time, but it was evident that Mr Casaubon was observing Dorothea, and she was aware of it.

'Exactly,' said Sir James. 'You give up from some high, generous motive.'

'No, indeed, not exactly. I did not say that of myself,' answered Dorothea, reddening. Unlike Celia, she rarely blushed, and only from high delight or anger. At this moment she felt angry with the perverse Sir James. Why did he not pay attention to Celia, and leave her to listen to Mr Casaubon? – if that learned man would only talk, instead of allowing himself to be talked to by Mr Brooke, who was just then informing him that the Reformation either meant something or it did not, that he himself was a Protestant to the core, but that Catholicism was a fact; and as to refusing an acre of your ground for a Romanist chapel, all men needed the bridle of religion, which, properly speaking, was the dread of a Hereafter.

'I made a great study of theology at one time,' said Mr Brooke, as if to explain the insight just manifested. 'I know something of all schools. I knew Wilberforce in his best days. Do you know Wilberforce?'

Mr Casaubon said, 'No.'

'Well, Wilberforce was perhaps not enough of a thinker; but if I went into Parliament, as I have been asked to do, I should sit on the independent bench, as Wilberforce did, and work at philanthropy.'

Mr Casaubon bowed, and observed that it was a wide field.

'Yes,' said Mr Brooke, with an easy smile, 'but I have documents. I began a long while ago to collect documents. They want arranging, but when a question has struck me, I have written to somebody and got an answer. I have documents at my back. But now, how do you arrange your documents?'

'In pigeon-holes partly,' said Mr Casaubon, with rather a startled air of effort.

'Ah, pigeon-holes will not do. I have tried pigeon-holes, but everything gets mixed in pigeon-holes: I never know whether a paper is in A or Z.'

'I wish you would let me sort your papers for you, uncle,' said Dorothea. 'I would letter them all, and then make a list of subjects under each letter.'

Mr Casaubon gravely smiled approval, and said to Mr Brooke, 'You have an excellent secretary at hand, you perceive.'

'No, no,' said Mr Brooke, shaking his head; 'I cannot let young ladies meddle with my documents. Young ladies are too flighty.'

Dorothea felt hurt. Mr Casaubon would think that her uncle had some special reason for delivering this opinion, whereas the remark lay in his mind as lightly as the broken wing of an insect among all the other fragments there, and a chance current had sent it alighting on *her*.

When the two girls were in the drawing-room alone, Celia said: 'How very ugly Mr Casaubon is!'

'Celia! He is one of the most distinguished-looking men I ever saw. He is remarkably like the portrait of Locke. He has the same deep eye-sockets.'

'Had Locke those two white moles with hairs on them?'

'Oh, I dare say! when people of a certain sort looked at him,' said Dorothea, walking away a little.

'Mr Casaubon is so sallow.'

'All the better. I suppose you admire a man with the complexion of a *cochon de lait*.'

'Dodo!' exclaimed Celia, looking after her in surprise. 'I never heard you make such a comparison before.'

'Why should I make it before the occasion came? It is a good comparison: the match is perfect.'

Miss Brooke was clearly forgetting herself, and Celia thought so.

'I wonder you show temper, Dorothea.'

'It is so painful in you, Celia, that you will look at human beings as if they were merely animals with a toilette, and never see the great soul in a man's face.'

'Has Mr Casaubon a great soul?' Celia was not without a touch of naïve malice.

'Yes, I believe he has,' said Dorothea, with the full voice of decision. 'Everything I see in him corresponds to his pamphlet on Biblical Cosmology.'

'He talks very little,' said Celia.

'There is no one for him to talk to.'

Celia thought privately, 'Dorothea quite despises Sir James Chettam; I believe she would not accept him.' Celia felt that this was a pity. She had never been deceived as to the object of the baronet's interest. Sometimes, indeed, she had reflected that Dodo would perhaps not make a husband happy who had not her way of looking at things; and stifled in the depths of her heart was the feeling that her sister was too religious for family comfort. Notions and scruples were like spilt needles, making one afraid of treading, or sitting down, or even eating.

When Miss Brooke was at the tea-table, Sir James came to sit down by her, not having felt her mode of answering him at all offensive. Why should he? He thought it probable that Miss Brooke liked him, and manners must be very marked indeed before they cease to be interpreted by preconceptions either confident or distrustful. She was thoroughly charming to him, but of course he theorised a little about his attachment. He was made of excellent human dough, and had the rare merit of knowing that his talents, even if let loose, would not set the smallest stream in the county on fire: hence he liked the prospect of a wife to whom he could say, 'What shall we do?' about this or that; who could help her husband out with reasons, and would also have the property qualification for doing so. As to the excessive religiousness alleged against Miss Brooke, he had a very indefinite notion of what it consisted in, and thought that it would die out with marriage. In short, he felt himself to be in love in the right place, and was ready to endure a great deal of predominance, which, after all, a man could always put down when he liked. Sir James had no idea that he should ever like to put down the predominance of this handsome girl, in whose cleverness he delighted. Why not? A man's mind – what there is of it – has always the advantage of being masculine – as the smallest birch tree is of a higher kind than the most soaring palm – and even his ignorance is of a sounder quality. Sir James might not have originated this estimate; but a kind Providence furnishes the limpest personality with a little gum or starch in the form of tradition.

'Let me hope that you will rescind that resolution about the horse, Miss Brooke,' said the persevering admirer. 'I assure you, riding is the most healthy of exercises.'

'I am aware of it,' said Dorothea, coldly. 'I think it would do Celia good – if she would take to it.'

'But you are such a perfect horsewoman.'

'Excuse me; I have had very little practice, and I should be easily thrown.'

'Then that is a reason for more practice. Every lady ought to be a perfect horsewoman, that she may accompany her husband.'

'You see how widely we differ, Sir James. I have made up my mind that I ought not to be a perfect horsewoman, and so I should never correspond to your pattern of a lady.' Dorothea looked straight before her, and spoke with cold brusquerie, very much with the air of a handsome boy, in amusing contrast with the solicitous amiability of her admirer.

'I should like to know your reasons for this cruel resolution. It is not possible that you should think horsemanship wrong.'

'It is quite possible that I should think it wrong for me.'

'Oh, why?' said Sir James, in a tender tone of remonstrance.

Mr Casaubon had come up to the table, teacup in hand, and was listening.

'We must not enquire too curiously into motives,' he interposed, in his measured way. 'Miss Brooke knows that they are apt to become feeble in the utterance: the aroma is mixed with the grosser air. We must keep the germinating grain away from the light.'

Dorothea coloured with pleasure, and looked up gratefully to the speaker. Here was a man who could understand the higher inward life, and with whom there could be some spiritual communion; nay, who could illuminate principle with the widest knowledge: a man whose learning almost amounted to a proof of whatever he believed!

Dorothea's inferences may seem large but really life could never have gone on at any period but for this liberal allowance of conclusion, which has facilitated marriage under the difficulties of civilisation. Has anyone ever pinched into its pilulous smallness the cobweb of pre-matrimonial acquaintanceship?

'Certainly,' said good Sir James. 'Miss Brooke shall not be urged to tell reasons she would rather be silent upon. I am sure her reasons would do her honour.'

He was not in the least jealous of the interest with which Dorothea had looked up at Mr Casaubon: it never occurred to him that a girl to whom he was meditating an offer of marriage could care for a dried bookworm towards fifty, except, indeed, in a religious sort of way, as for a clergyman of some distinction.

However, since Miss Brooke had become engaged in a conversation with Mr Casaubon about the Vaudois clergy, Sir James betook himself to Celia, and talked to her about her sister; spoke of a house in town, and asked whether Miss Brooke disliked London. Away from her sister, Celia talked quite easily, and Sir James said to himself that the second Miss Brooke was certainly very agreeable as well as pretty, though not, as some people pretended, more clever and sensible than the elder sister. He felt that he had chosen the one who was in all respects the superior; and a man naturally likes to look forward to having the best. He would be the very Mawworm of bachelors who pretended not to expect it.

Chapter 3

> Say, goddess, what ensued, when Raphaël,
> The affable archangel . . .
>   Eve
> The story heard attentive, and was filled
> With admiration, and deep muse, to hear
> Of things so high and strange.
>
>   MILTON, *Paradise Lost*

If it had really occurred to Mr Casaubon to think of Miss Brooke as a suitable wife for him, the reasons that might induce her to accept him were already planted in her mind, and by the evening of the next day the reasons had budded and bloomed. For they had had a long conversation in the morning, while Celia, who did not like the company of Mr Casaubon's moles and sallowness, had escaped to the vicarage to play with the curate's ill-shod but merry children.

Dorothea by this time had looked deep into the ungauged reservoir of Mr Casaubon's mind, seeing reflected there in vague labyrinthine extension every quality she herself brought; had opened much of her own experience to him, and had understood from him the scope of his great work, also of attractively labyrinthine extent. For he had been as instructive as Milton's 'affable arch-angel'; and with something of the archangelic manner he told her how he had undertaken to show (what indeed had been attempted before, but not with that thoroughness, justice of comparison, and effectiveness of arrangement at which Mr Casaubon aimed) that all the mythical systems or erratic mythical fragments in the world were corruptions of a tradition originally revealed. Having once mastered the true position and taken a firm footing there, the vast field of mythical constructions became intelligible, nay, luminous with the reflected light of correspondences. But to gather in this great harvest of truth was no light or speedy work. His notes already made a formidable range of volumes, but the crowning task would be to condense these voluminous still-accumulating results and bring them, like the earlier vintage of Hippocratic books, to fit a little shelf. In explaining this to Dorothea, Mr Casaubon expressed himself nearly as he would have done to a fellow-student, for he had not two styles of talking at command: it is true that when he used a Greek or Latin phrase he always gave the English with scrupulous care, but he would probably have done this in any case. A learned provincial clergyman is accustomed to think of his acquaintances as of 'lords, knyghtes, and other noble and worthi men, that conne Latyn but lytille'.

Dorothea was altogether captivated by the wide embrace of this conception. Here was something beyond the shallows of ladies'-school literature: here was a living Bossuet, whose work would reconcile complete knowledge with devoted piety; here was a modern Augustine who united the glories of doctor and saint.

The sanctity seemed no less clearly marked than the learning, for when Dorothea was impelled to open her mind on certain themes which she could speak of to no one whom she had before seen at Tipton, especially on the secondary importance of ecclesiastical forms and articles of belief compared with that spiritual religion, that submergence of self in communion with Divine perfection which seemed to her to be expressed in the best Christian books of widely-distant ages, she found in Mr Casaubon a listener who understood her at once, who could assure her of his own agreement with that view when duly tempered with wise conformity, and could mention historical examples before unknown to her.

'He thinks with me,' said Dorothea to herself, 'or rather, he thinks a whole world of which my thought is but a poor twopenny mirror. And his feelings too, his whole experience – what a lake compared with my little pool!'

Miss Brooke argued from words and dispositions not less unhesitatingly than other young ladies of her age. Signs are small measurable things, but interpretations are illimitable, and in girls of sweet, ardent nature, every sign is apt to conjure up wonder, hope, belief, vast as a sky, and coloured by a diffused thimbleful of matter in the shape of knowledge. They are not always too grossly deceived; for Sinbad himself may have fallen by good luck on a true description, and wrong reasoning sometimes lands poor mortals in right conclusions: starting a long way off the true point, and proceeding by loops and zig-zags, we now and then arrive just where we ought to be. Because Miss Brooke was hasty in her trust, it is not therefore clear that Mr Casaubon was unworthy of it.

He stayed a little longer than he had intended, on a slight pressure of invitation from Mr Brooke, who offered no bait except his own documents on machine-breaking and rick-burning. Mr Casaubon was called into the library to look at these in a heap, while his host picked up first one and then the other to read aloud from in a skipping and uncertain way, passing from one unfinished passage to another with a 'Yes, now, but here!' and finally pushing them all aside to open the journal of his youthful Continental travels.

'Look here – here is all about Greece, Rhamnus, the ruins of Rhamnus – you are a great Grecian, now. I don't know whether you have given much study to the topography. I spent no end of time in making out these things – Helicon, now. Here, now I – "We started the next morning for Parnassus, the double-peaked Parnassus." All this volume is about Greece, you know,' Mr Brooke wound up, rubbing his thumb transversely along the edges of the leaves as he held the book forward.

Mr Casaubon made a dignified though somewhat sad audience; bowed in the right place, and avoided looking at anything documentary as far as possible, without showing disregard or impatience; mindful that this desultoriness was associated with the institutions of the country, and that the man who took him on this severe mental scamper was not only an amiable host, but a landholder and *custos rotulorum*. Was his endurance aided also by the reflection that Mr Brooke was the uncle of Dorothea?

Certainly he seemed more and more bent on making her talk to him, on drawing her out, as Celia remarked to herself; and in looking at her, his face was often lit up by a smile like pale wintry sunshine. Before he left the next morning, while taking a pleasant walk with Miss Brooke along the gravelled terrace, he had mentioned to her that he felt the disadvantage of loneliness, the need of that cheerful companionship with which the presence of youth can lighten or vary the serious toils of maturity. And he delivered this statement with as much careful precision as if he had been a diplomatic envoy whose words would be attended with results. Indeed, Mr Casaubon was not used to expect that he should have to repeat or revise his communications of a practical or personal kind. The inclinations which he had deliberately stated on the 2d of October he would think it enough to refer to by the mention of that date; judging by the standard of his own memory, which was a volume where a *vide supra* could serve instead of repetitions, and not the ordinary long-used blotting-book which only tells of forgotten writing. But in this case Mr Casaubon's confidence was not likely to be falsified, for Dorothea heard and retained what he said with the eager interest of a fresh young nature to which every variety in experience is an epoch.

It was three o'clock in the beautiful breezy autumn day when Mr Casaubon drove off to his Rectory at Lowick, only five miles from Tipton; and Dorothea, who had on her bonnet and shawl, hurried along the shrubbery and across the park that she might wander through the bordering wood with no other visible companionship than that of Monk, the Great St Bernard dog, who always took care of the young ladies in their walks. There had risen before her the girl's vision of a possible future for herself to which she looked forward with trembling hope, and she wanted to wander on in that visionary future without interruption. She walked briskly in the brisk air, the colour rose in her cheeks, and her straw-bonnet (which our contemporaries might look at with conjectural curiosity as at an obsolete form of basket) fell a little backward. She would perhaps be hardly characterised enough if it were omitted that she wore her brown hair flatly braided and coiled behind so as to expose the outline of her head in a daring manner at a time when public feeling required the meagreness of nature to be dissimulated by tall barricades of frizzed curls and bows, never surpassed by any great race except the Feejeean. This was a trait of Miss Brooke's asceticism. But there was nothing of an ascetic's expression in her bright full eyes, as she looked before her, not consciously seeing, but absorbing into the intensity of her mood, the solemn glory of the afternoon with its long swathes of light between the far-off rows of limes, whose shadows touched each other.

All people, young or old (that is, all people in those ante-reform times), would have thought her an interesting object if they had referred the glow in her eyes and cheeks to the newly awakened ordinary images of young love: the illusions of Chloe about Strephon have been sufficiently consecrated in poetry, as the pathetic loveliness of all spontaneous trust ought to be. Miss Pippin adoring young Pumpkin and dreaming along endless vistas of unwearying companionship, was a little drama which never tired our fathers and mothers, and had been put into all costumes. Let but Pumpkin have a figure which would sustain the disadvantages of the short-waisted swallow-tail, and everybody felt it not only natural but necessary to the perfection of womanhood, that a sweet girl should be at once convinced of his virtue, his exceptional ability, and above all, his perfect sincerity. But perhaps no persons then living – certainly none in the neighbourhood of Tipton – would have had a sympathetic understanding for the dreams of a girl whose notions about marriage took their colour entirely from an exalted enthusiasm about the ends of life, an enthusiasm which was lit chiefly by its own fire, and included neither the niceties of the *trousseau*, the pattern of plate, nor even the honours and sweet joys of the blooming matron.

It had now entered Dorothea's mind that Mr Casaubon might wish to make her his wife, and the idea that he would do so touched her with a sort of reverential gratitude. How good of him – nay, it would be almost as if a winged messenger had suddenly stood beside her path and held out his hand towards her! For a long while she had been oppressed by the indefiniteness which hung in her mind, like a thick summer haze, over all her desire to make her life greatly effective. What could she do, what ought she to do? – she, hardly more than a budding woman, but yet with an active conscience and a great mental need, not to be satisfied by a girlish instruction comparable to the nibblings and judgements of a discursive mouse. With some endowment of stupidity and conceit, she might have thought that a Christian young lady of fortune should find her ideal of life in village charities, patronage of the humbler clergy, the perusal of *Female Scripture Characters*, unfolding the private experience of Sara under the Old Dispensation, and Dorcas under the New, and the care of her soul over her embroidery in her own boudoir – with a background of prospective marriage to a man who, if less strict than herself as being involved in affairs religiously inexplicable, might be prayed for and seasonably exhorted. From such contentment poor Dorothea was shut out. The intensity of her religious disposition, the coercion it exercised over her life, was but one aspect of a nature altogether ardent, theoretic, and intellectually consequent: and with such a nature, struggling in the bands of a narrow teaching, hemmed in by a social life which seemed nothing but a labyrinth of petty courses, a walled-in maze of small paths that led no whither, the outcome was sure to strike others as at once exaggeration and inconsistency. The thing which seemed to her best, she wanted to justify by the completest knowledge; and not to live in a pretended admission of rules which were never acted on. Into this soul-hunger as yet all her youthful passion was poured; the union which attracted her was one that would deliver her from her girlish subjection to her own ignorance, and give her the freedom of voluntary submission to a guide who would take her along the grandest path.

'I should learn everything then,' she said to herself, still walking quickly along the bridle road through the wood. 'It would be my duty to study that I might help him the better in his great works. There would be nothing trivial about our lives. Everyday-things with us would mean the greatest things. It would be like marrying Pascal. I should learn to see the truth by the same light as great men have seen it by. And then I should know what to do, when I got older: I should see how it was possible to lead a grand life here – now – in England. I don't feel sure about doing good in any way now: everything seems like going on a mission to a people whose language I don't know; – unless it were building good cottages – there can be no doubt about that. Oh, I hope I should be able to get the people well housed in Lowick! I will draw plenty of plans while I have time.'

Dorothea checked herself suddenly with self-rebuke for the presumptuous way in which she was reckoning on uncertain events, but she was spared any inward effort to change the direction of her thoughts by the appearance of a cantering horseman round a turning of the road. The well-groomed chestnut horse and two beautiful setters could leave no doubt that the rider was Sir James Chettam. He discerned Dorothea, jumped off his horse at once, and, having delivered it to his groom, advanced towards her with something white on his arm, at which the two setters were barking in an excited manner.

'How delightful to meet you, Miss Brooke,' he said, raising his hat and showing his sleekly-waving blond hair. 'It has hastened the pleasure I was looking forward to.'

Miss Brooke was annoyed at the interruption. This amiable baronet, really a suitable husband for Celia, exaggerated the necessity of making himself agreeable to the elder sister. Even a prospective brother-in-law may be an oppression if he will always be presupposing too good an understanding with you, and agreeing with you even when you contradict him. The thought that he had made the mistake of paying his addresses to herself could not take shape: all her mental activity was used up in persuasions of another kind. But he was positively obtrusive at this moment, and his dimpled hands were quite disagreeable. Her roused temper made her colour deeply, as she returned his greeting with some haughtiness.

Sir James interpreted the heightened colour in the way most gratifying to himself, and thought he never saw Miss Brooke looking so handsome.

'I have brought a little petitioner,' he said, 'or rather I have brought him to see if he will be approved before his petition is offered.' He showed the white object under his arm, which was a tiny Maltese puppy, one of nature's most naïve toys.

'It is painful to me to see these creatures that are bred merely as pets,' said Dorothea, whose opinion was forming itself that very moment (as opinions will) under the heat of irritation.

'Oh, why?' said Sir James, as they walked forward.

'I believe all the petting that is given them does not make them happy. They are too helpless: their lives are too frail. A weasel or a mouse that gets its own living is more interesting. I like to think that the animals about us have souls something like our own, and either carry on their own little affairs or can be companions to us, like Monk here. Those creatures are parasitic.'

'I am so glad I know that you do not like them,' said good Sir James, 'I should never keep them for myself, but ladies usually are fond of these Maltese dogs. Here, John, take this dog, will you?'

The objectionable puppy, whose nose and eyes were equally black and expressive, was thus got rid of, since Miss Brooke decided that it had better not have been born. But she felt it necessary to explain.

'You must not judge of Celia's feeling from mine. I think she likes these small pets. She had a tiny terrier once, which she was very fond of. It made me unhappy, because I was afraid of treading on it. I am rather short-sighted.'

'You have your own opinion about everything, Miss Brooke, and it is always a good opinion.'

What answer was possible to such stupid complimenting?

'Do you know, I envy you that,' Sir James said, as they continued walking at the rather brisk pace set by Dorothea.

'I don't quite understand what you mean.'

'Your power of forming an opinion. I can form an opinion of persons. I know when I like people. But about other matters, do you know, I have often a difficulty in deciding. One hears very sensible things said on opposite sides.'

'Or that seem sensible. Perhaps we don't always discriminate between sense and nonsense.'

Dorothea felt that she was rather rude.

'Exactly,' said Sir James. 'But you seem to have the power of discrimination.'

'On the contrary, I am often unable to decide. But that is from ignorance. The right conclusion is there all the same, though I am unable to see it.'

'I think there are few who would see it more readily. Do you know, Lovegood was telling me yesterday that you had the best notion in the world of a plan for cottages – quite wonderful for a young lady, he thought. You had a real *genus*, to use his expression. He said you wanted Mr Brooke to build a new set of cottages, but he seemed to think it hardly probable that your uncle would consent. Do you know, that is one of the things I wish to do – I mean, on my own estate? I should be so glad to carry out that plan of yours, if you would let me see it. Of course, it is sinking money; that is why people object to it. Labourers can never pay rent to make it answer. But, after all, it is worth doing.'

'Worth doing! yes, indeed,' said Dorothea, energetically, forgetting her previous small vexations. 'I think we deserve to be beaten out of our beautiful houses with a scourge of small cords – all of us who let tenants live in such sties as we see round us. Life in cottages might be happier than ours, if they were real houses fit for human beings from whom we expect duties and affections.'

'Will you show me your plan?'

'Yes, certainly. I dare say it is very faulty. But I have been examining all the plans for cottages in Loudon's book, and picked out what seem the best things. Oh what a happiness it would be to set the pattern about here! I think, instead of Lazarus at the gate, we should put the pigsty cottages outside the park gate.'

Dorothea was in the best temper now. Sir James, as brother-in-law, building model cottages on his estate, and then, perhaps, others being built at Lowick, and more and more elsewhere in imitation – it would be as if the spirit of Oberlin had passed over the parishes to make the life of poverty beautiful!

Sir James saw all the plans, and took one away to consult upon with Love-good. He also took away a complacent sense that he was making great progress in Miss Brooke's good opinion. The Maltese puppy was not offered to Celia; an omission which Dorothea afterwards thought of with surprise; but she blamed herself for it. She had been engrossing Sir James. After all, it was a relief that there was no puppy to tread upon.

Celia was present while the plans were being examined, and observed Sir James's illusion. 'He thinks that Dodo cares about him, and she only cares about her plans. Yet I am not certain that she would refuse him if she thought he would let her manage everything and carry out all her notions. And how very uncomfortable Sir James would be! I cannot bear notions.'

It was Celia's private luxury to indulge in this dislike. She dared not confess it to her sister in any direct statement, for that would be laying herself open to a demonstration that she was somehow or other at war with all goodness. But on safe opportunities, she had an indirect mode of making her negative wisdom tell upon Dorothea, and calling her down from her rhapsodic mood by reminding her that people were staring, not listening. Celia was not impulsive: what she had to say could wait, and came from her always with the same quiet, staccato evenness. When people talked with energy and emphasis she watched their faces and features merely. She never could understand how well-bred persons consented to sing and open their mouths in the ridiculous manner requisite for that vocal exercise.

It was not many days before Mr Casaubon paid a morning visit, on which he was invited again for the following week to dine and stay the night. Thus Dorothea had three more conversations with him, and was convinced that her first impressions had been just. He was all she had at first imagined him to be: almost everything he had said seemed like a specimen from a mine, or the inscription on the door of a museum which might open on the treasures of past ages; and this trust in his mental wealth was all the deeper and more effective on her inclination because it was now obvious that his visits were made for her sake. This accomplished man condescended to think of a young girl, and take the pains to talk to her, not with absurd compliment, but with an appeal to her understanding, and sometimes with instructive correction. What delightful companionship. Mr Casaubon seemed even unconscious that trivialities existed, and never handed round that small-talk of heavy men which is as acceptable as stale bride-cake brought forth with an odour of cupboard. He talked of what he was interested in, or else he was silent and bowed with sad civility. To Dorothea this was adorable genuineness, and religious abstinence from that artificiality which uses up the soul in the efforts of pretence. For she looked as reverently at Mr Casaubon's religious elevation above herself as she did at his intellect and learning. He assented to her expressions of devout feeling, and usually with an appropriate quotation; he allowed himself to say that he had gone through some spiritual conflicts in his youth; in short, Dorothea saw that here she might reckon on understanding sympathy and guidance. On one – only one – of her favourite themes she was disappointed. Mr Casaubon apparently did not care about building cottages, and diverted the talk to the extremely narrow accommodation which was to be had in the dwellings of the ancient Egyptians, as if to check a too high standard. After he was gone, Dorothea dwelt with some agitation on this indifference of his; and her mind was much exercised with arguments drawn from the varying conditions of climate which modify human needs, and from the admitted wickedness of pagan despots. Should she not urge these arguments on Mr Casaubon when he came again? But further reflection told her that she was presumptuous in demanding his attention to such a subject; he would not disapprove of her occupying herself with it in leisure moments, as other women expected to occupy themselves with their dress and embroidery – would not forbid it when – Dorothea felt rather ashamed as she detected herself in these speculations. But her uncle had been invited to go to Lowick to stay a couple of days: was it reasonable to suppose that Mr Casaubon delighted in Mr Brooke's society for its own sake, either with or without documents?

Meanwhile that little disappointment made her delight the more in Sir James Chettam's readiness to set on foot the desired improvements. He came much oftener than Mr Casaubon, and Dorothea ceased to find him disagreeable since he showed himself so entirely in earnest; for he had already entered with much practical ability into Lovegood's estimates, and was charmingly docile. She proposed to build a couple of cottages, and transfer two families from their old cabins, which could then be pulled down, so that new ones could be built on the old sites. Sir James said, 'Exactly,' and she bore the word remarkably well.

Certainly these men who had so few spontaneous ideas might be very useful members of society under good feminine direction, if they were fortunate in choosing their sisters-in-law! It is difficult to say whether there was or was not a little wilfulness in her continuing blind to the possibility that another sort of choice was in question in relation to her. But her life was just now full of hope and action: she was not only thinking of her plans, but getting down learned books from the library and reading many things hastily (that she might be a little less ignorant in talking to Mr Casaubon), all the while being visited with con-scientious questionings whether she were not exalting these poor doings above measure and contemplating them with that self-satisfaction which was the last doom of ignorance and folly.

Chapter 4

1st Gent.	Our deeds are fetters that we forge ourselves.
2nd Gent.	Ay, truly: but I think it is the world
	That brings the iron.

'Sir James seems determined to do everything you wish,' said Celia, as they were driving home from an inspection of the new building-site.

'He is a good creature, and more sensible than anyone would imagine,' said Dorothea, inconsiderately.

'You mean that he appears silly.'

'No, no,' said Dorothea, recollecting herself, and laying her hand on her sister's a moment, 'but he does not talk equally well on all subjects.'

'I should think none but disagreeable people do,' said Celia, in her usual purring way. 'They must be very dreadful to live with. Only think! at breakfast, and always.'

Dorothea laughed. 'O Kitty, you are a wonderful creature!' She pinched Celia's chin, being in the mood now to think her very winning and lovely – fit hereafter to be an eternal cherub, and if it were not doctrinally wrong to say so, hardly more in need of salvation than a squirrel. 'Of course people need not be always talking well. Only one tells the quality of their minds when they try to talk well.'

'You mean that Sir James tries and fails.'

'I was speaking generally. Why do you catechise me about Sir James? It is not the object of his life to please me.'

'Now, Dodo, can you really believe that?'

'Certainly. He thinks of me as a future sister – that is all.' Dorothea had never hinted this before, waiting, from a certain shyness on such subjects which was mutual between the sisters, until it should be introduced by some decisive event. Celia blushed, but said at once; 'Pray do not make that mistake any longer, Dodo. When Tantripp was brushing my hair the other day, she said that Sir James's man knew from Mrs Cadwallader's maid that Sir James was to marry the eldest Miss Brooke.'

'How can you let Tantripp talk such gossip to you, Celia?' said Dorothea, indignantly, not the less angry because details asleep in her memory were now awakened to confirm the unwelcome revelation. 'You must have asked her questions. It is degrading.'

'I see no harm at all in Tantripp's talking to me. It is better to hear what people say. You see what mistakes you make by taking up notions. I am quite sure that Sir James means to make you an offer; and he believes that you will accept him, especially since you have been so pleased with him about the plans. And uncle too – I know he expects it. Everyone can see that Sir James is very much in love with you.'

The revulsion was so strong and painful in Dorothea's mind that the tears welled up and flowed abundantly. All her dear plans were embittered, and she thought with disgust of Sir James's conceiving that she recognised him as her lover. There was vexation too on account of Celia.

'How could he expect it?' she burst forth in her most impetuous manner. 'I have never agreed with him about anything but the cottages: I was barely polite to him before.'

'But you have been so pleased with him since then; he has begun to feel quite sure that you are fond of him.'

'Fond of him, Celia! How can you choose such odious expressions?' said Dorothea, passionately.

'Dear me, Dorothea, I suppose it would be right for you to be fond of a man whom you accepted for a husband.'

'It is offensive to me to say that Sir James could think I was fond of him. Besides, it is not the right word for the feeling I must have towards the man I would accept as a husband.'

'Well, I am sorry for Sir James. I thought it right to tell you, because you went on as you always do, never looking just where you are, and treading in the wrong place. You always see what nobody else sees; it is impossible to satisfy you; yet you never see what is quite plain. That's your way, Dodo.' Something certainly gave Celia unusual courage; and she was not sparing the sister of whom she was occasionally in awe. Who can tell what just criticisms Murr the Cat may be passing on us beings of wider speculation?

'It is very painful,' said Dorothea, feeling scourged. 'I can have no more to do with the cottages. I must be uncivil to him. I must tell him I will have nothing to do with them. It is very painful.' Her eyes filled again with tears.

'Wait a little. Think about it. You know he is going away for a day or two to see his sister. There will be nobody besides Lovegood.' Celia could not help relenting. 'Poor Dodo,' she went on, in an amiable staccato. 'It is very hard: it is your favourite *fad* to draw plans.'

'*Fad* to draw plans; Do you think I only care about my fellow-creatures' houses in that childish way? I may well make mistakes. How can one ever do anything nobly Christian, living among people with such petty thoughts?'

No more was said: Dorothea was too much jarred to recover her temper and behave so as to show that she admitted any error in herself. She was disposed rather to accuse the intolerable narrowness and the purblind conscience of the society around her: and Celia was no longer the eternal cherub, but a thorn in her spirit, a pink-and-white nullifidian, worse than any discouraging presence in the *Pilgrim's Progress*. The *fad* of drawing plans! What was life worth – what great faith was possible when the whole effect of one's actions could be withered up into such parched rubbish as that? When she got out of the carriage, her cheeks were pale and her eyelids red. She was an image of sorrow, and her uncle, who met her in the hall, would have been alarmed, if Celia had not been close to her looking so pretty and composed, that he at once concluded Dorothea's tears to have their origin in her excessive religiousness. He had returned, during their absence, from a journey to the county town, about a petition for the pardon of some criminal.

'Well, my dears,' he said, kindly, as they went up to kiss him, 'I hope nothing disagreeable has happened while I have been away.'

'No, uncle,' said Celia, 'we have been to Freshitt to look at the cottages. We thought you would have been at home by lunch.'

'I came by Lowick to lunch – you didn't know I came by Lowick. And I have brought a couple of pamphlets for you, Dorothea – in the library, you know; they lie on the table in the library.'

It seemed as if an electric stream went through Dorothea, thrilling her from despair into expectation. They were pamphlets about the early Church. The oppression of Celia, Tantripp, and Sir James was shaken off, and she walked straight to the library. Celia went upstairs. Mr Brooke was detained by a message, but when he re-entered the library, he found Dorothea seated and already deep in one of the pamphlets, which had some marginal manuscript of Mr Casaubon's, – taking it in as eagerly as she might have taken in the scent of a fresh bouquet after a dry, hot, dreary walk.

She was getting away from Tipton and Freshitt, and her own sad liability to tread in the wrong places on her way to the New Jerusalem.

Mr Brooke sat down in his armchair, stretched his legs towards the wood-fire, which had fallen into a wondrous mass of glowing dice between the dogs, and rubbed his hands gently, looking very mildly towards Dorothea, but with a neutral leisurely air, as if he had nothing particular to say. Dorothea closed her pamphlet, as soon as she was aware of her uncle's presence, and rose as if to go. Usually she would have been interested about her uncle's merciful errand on behalf of the criminal, but her late agitation had made her absent-minded.

'I came back by Lowick, you know,' said Mr Brooke, not as if with any intention to arrest her departure, but apparently from his usual tendency to say what he had said before. This fundamental principle of human speech was markedly exhibited in Mr Brooke. 'I lunched there and saw Casaubon's library, and that kind of thing. There's a sharp air, driving. Won't you sit down, my dear? You look cold.'

Dorothea felt quite inclined to accept the invitation. Sometimes, when her uncle's easy way of taking things did not happen to be exasperating, it was rather soothing. She threw off her mantle and bonnet, and sat down opposite to him, enjoying the glow, but lifting up her beautiful hands for a screen. They were not thin hands, or small hands; but powerful, feminine, maternal hands. She seemed to be holding them up in propitiation for her passionate desire to know and to think, which in the unfriendly mediums of Tipton and Freshitt had issued in crying and red eyelids.

She bethought herself now of the condemned criminal. 'What news have you brought about the sheep-stealer, uncle?'

'What, poor Bunch? – well, it seems we can't get him off – he is to be hanged.'

Dorothea's brow took an expression of reprobation and pity.

'Hanged, you know,' said Mr Brooke, with a quiet nod. 'Poor Romilly! he would have helped us. I knew Romilly. Casaubon didn't know Romilly. He is a little buried in books, you know, Casaubon is.'

'When a man has great studies and is writing a great work, he must of course give up seeing much of the world. How can he go about making acquaintances?'

'That's true. But a man mopes, you know. I have always been a bachelor too, but I have that sort of disposition that I never moped; it was my way to go about everywhere and take in everything. I never moped: but I can see that Casaubon does, you know. He wants a companion – a companion, you know.'

'It would be a great honour to anyone to be his companion,' said Dorothea, energetically.

'You like him, eh?' said Mr Brooke, without showing any surprise, or other emotion. 'Well, now, I've known Casaubon ten years, ever since he came to Lowick. But I never got anything out of him – any ideas, you know. However, he is a tiptop man and may be a bishop – that kind of thing, you know, if Peel stays in. And he has a very high opinion of you, my dear.'

Dorothea could not speak.

'The fact is, he has a very high opinion indeed of you. And he speaks uncommonly well – does Casaubon. He has deferred to me, you not being of age. In short, I have promised to speak to you, though I told him I thought there was not much chance. I was bound to tell him that. I said, my niece is very young, and that kind of thing. But I didn't think it necessary to go into everything. However, the long and the short of it is, that he has asked my permission to make you an offer of marriage – of marriage, you know,' said Mr Brooke, with his explanatory nod. 'I thought it better to tell you, my dear.'

No one could have detected any anxiety in Mr Brooke's manner, but he did really wish to know something of his niece's mind, that, if there were any need for advice, he might give it in time. What feeling he, as a magistrate who had taken in so many ideas, could make room for, was unmixedly kind. Since Dorothea did not speak immediately, he repeated, 'I thought it better to tell you, my dear.'

'Thank you, uncle,' said Dorothea, in a clear unwavering tone. 'I am very grateful to Mr Casaubon. If he makes me an offer, I shall accept him. I admire and honour him more than any man I ever saw.'

Mr Brooke paused a little, and then said in a lingering low tone. 'Ah? . . . Well! He is a good match in some respects. But now, Chettam is a good match. And our land lies together. I shall never interfere against your wishes, my dear. People should have their own way in marriage, and that sort of thing – up to a certain point, you know. I have always said that, up to a certain point. I wish you to marry well; and I have good reason to believe that Chettam wishes to marry you. I mention it, you know.'

'It is impossible that I should ever marry Sir James Chettam,' said Dorothea. 'If he thinks of marrying me, he has made a great mistake.'

'That is it, you see. One never knows. I should have thought Chettam was just the sort of man a woman would like, now.'

'Pray do not mention him in that light again, uncle,' said Dorothea, feeling some of her late irritation revive.

Mr Brooke wondered, and felt that women were an inexhaustible subject of study, since even he at his age was not in a perfect state of scientific prediction about them! Here was a fellow like Chettam with no chance at all.

'Well, but Casaubon, now. There is no hurry – I mean for you. It's true, every year will tell upon him. He is over five-and-forty, you know. I should say a good seven-and-twenty years older than you. To be sure, – if you like learning and standing, and that sort of thing, we can't have everything. And his income is good – he has a handsome property independent of the Church – his income is good. Still he is not young, and I must not conceal from you, my dear, that I think his health is not over-strong. I know nothing else against him.'

'I should not wish to have a husband very near my own age,' said Dorothea, with grave decision. 'I should wish to have a husband who was above me in judgement and in all knowledge.'

Mr Brooke repeated his subdued, 'Ah? – I thought you had more of your own opinion than most girls. I thought you liked your own opinion – liked it, you know.'

'I cannot imagine myself living without some opinions, but I should wish to have good reasons for them, and a wise man could help me to see which opinions had the best foundation, and would help me to live according to them.'

'Very true. You couldn't put the thing better – couldn't put it better, before-hand, you know. But there are oddities in things,' continued Mr Brooke, whose conscience was really roused to do the best he could for his niece on this occasion. 'Life isn't cast in a mould – not cut out by rule and line, and that sort of thing. I never married myself, and it will be the better for you and yours. The fact is, I never loved anyone well enough to put myself into a noose for them. It is a noose, you know. Temper, now. There is temper. And a husband likes to be master.'

'I know that I must expect trials, uncle. Marriage is a state of higher duties. I never thought of it as mere personal ease,' said poor Dorothea.

'Well, you are not fond of show, a great establishment, balls, dinners, that kind of thing. I can see that Casaubon's ways might suit you better than Chettam's. And you shall do as you like, my dear. I would not hinder Casaubon; I said so at once; for there is no knowing how anything may turn out. You have not the same tastes as every young lady; and a clergyman and scholar – who may be a bishop – that kind of thing – may suit you better than Chettam. Chettam is a good fellow, a good sound-hearted fellow, you know; but he doesn't go much into ideas. I did, when I was his age. But Casaubon's eyes, now. I think he has hurt them a little with too much reading.'

'I should be all the happier, uncle, the more room there was for me to help him,' said Dorothea, ardently.

'You have quite made up your mind, I see. Well, my dear, the fact is, I have a letter for you in my pocket.' Mr Brooke handed the letter to Dorothea, but as she rose to go away, he added, 'There is not too much hurry, my dear. Think about it, you know.'

When Dorothea had left him, he reflected that he had certainly spoken strongly: he had put the risks of marriage before her in a striking manner. It was his duty to do so. But as to pretending to be wise for young people, – no uncle, however much he had travelled in his youth, absorbed the new ideas, and dined with celebrities now deceased, could pretend to judge what sort of marriage would turn out well for a young girl who preferred Casaubon to Chettam. In short, woman was a problem which, since Mr Brooke's mind felt blank before it, could be hardly less complicated than the revolutions of an irregular solid.

Chapter 5

Hard students are commonly troubled with gowts, catarrhs, rheums, cachexia, bradypepsia, bad eyes, stone, and collick, crudities, oppilations, vertigo, winds, consumptions, and all such diseases as come by overmuch sitting: they are most part lean, dry, ill coloured . . . and all through immoderate pains and extraordinary studies. If you will not believe the truth of this, look upon great Tostatus and Thomas Aquinas' works; and tell me whether those men took pains.

BURTON's *Anatomy of Melancholy*

This was Mr Casaubon's letter.

MY DEAR MISS BROOKE – I have your guardian's permission to address you on a subject than which I have none more at heart. I am not, I trust, mistaken in the recognition of some deeper correspondence than that of date in the fact that a consciousness of need in my own life had arisen contemporaneously with the possibility of my becoming acquainted with you. For in the first hour of meeting you, I had an impression of your eminent and perhaps exclusive fitness to supply that need (connected, I may say, with such activity of the affections as even the preoccupations of a work too special to be abdicated could not uninterruptedly dissimulate); and each succeeding opportunity for observation has given the impression an added depth by convincing me more emphatically of that fitness which I had preconceived, and thus evoking more decisively those affections to which I have but now referred. Our conversations have, I think, made sufficiently clear to you the tenor of my life and purposes: a tenor unsuited, I am aware, to the commoner order of minds. But I have discerned in you an elevation of thought and a capability of devotedness, which I had hitherto not conceived to be compatible either with the early bloom of youth or with those graces of sex that may be said at once to win and to confer distinction when combined, as they notably are in you, with the mental qualities above indicated. It was, I confess, beyond my hope to meet with this rare combination of elements both solid and attractive, adapted to supply aid in graver labours and to cast a charm over vacant hours; and but for the event of my introduction to you (which, let me again say, I trust not to be superficially coincident with foreshadowing needs, but providentially related thereto as stages towards the completion of a life's plan), I should presumably have gone on to the last without any attempt to lighten my solitariness by a matrimonial union.

Such, my dear Miss Brooke, is the accurate statement of my feelings; and I rely on your kind indulgence in venturing now to ask you how far your own are of a nature to confirm my happy presentiment. To be accepted by you as your husband and the earthly guardian of your welfare, I should regard as the highest of providential gifts. In return I can at least offer you an affection hitherto unwasted, and the faithful consecration of a life which, however short in the sequel, has no backward pages whereon, if you choose to turn them, you will find records such as might justly cause you either bitterness or shame. I await the expression of your sentiments with an anxiety which it would be the part of wisdom (were it possible) to divert by a more arduous labour than usual. But in this order of experience I am still young, and in looking forward to an unfavourable possibility I cannot but feel that resignation to solitude will be more difficult after the temporary illumination of hope. In any case, I shall remain, yours with sincere devotion,

EDWARD CASAUBON

Dorothea trembled while she read this letter; then she fell on her knees, buried her face, and sobbed. She could not pray under the rush of solemn emotion in which thoughts became vague and images floated uncertainly, she could but cast herself, with a childlike sense of reclining in the lap of a divine consciousness which sustained her own. She remained in that attitude till it was time to dress for dinner.

How could it occur to her to examine the letter, to look at it critically as a profession of love? Her whole soul was possessed by the fact that a fuller life was opening before her: she was a neophyte about to enter on a higher grade of initiation. She was going to have room for the energies which stirred uneasily under the dimness and pressure of her own ignorance and the petty per-emptoriness of the world's habits.

Now she would be able to devote herself to large yet definite duties; now she would be allowed to live continually in the light of a mind that she could reverence. This hope was not unmixed with the glow of proud delight – the joyous maiden surprise that she was chosen by the man whom her admiration had chosen. All Dorothea's passion was transfused through a mind struggling towards an ideal life; the radiance of her transfigured girlhood fell on the first object that came within its level. The impetus with which inclination became resolution was heightened by those little events of the day which had roused her discontent with the actual conditions of her life.

After dinner, when Celia was playing an 'air, with variations', a small kind of tinkling which symbolised the aesthetic part of the young ladies' education, Dorothea went up to her room to answer Mr Casaubon's letter. Why should she defer the answer? She wrote it over three times, not because she wished to change the wording, but because her hand was unusually uncertain, and she could not bear that Mr Casaubon should think her handwriting bad and illegible. She piqued herself on writing a hand in which each letter was distinguishable without any large range of conjecture, and she meant to make much use of this accomplishment, to save Mr Casaubon's eyes. Three times she wrote.

MY DEAR MR CASAUBON – I am very grateful to you for loving me, and thinking me worthy to be your wife. I can look forward to no better happiness than that which would be one with yours. If I said more, it would only be the same thing written out at greater length, for I cannot now dwell on any other thought than that I may be through life, yours devotedly

DOROTHEA BROOKE

Later in the evening she followed her uncle into the library to give him the letter, that he might send it in the morning. He was surprised, but his surprise only issued in a few moments' silence, during which he pushed about various objects on his writing-table, and finally stood with his back to the fire, his glasses on his nose, looking at the address of Dorothea's letter.

'Have you thought enough about this, my dear?' he said at last.

'There was no need to think long, uncle. I know of nothing to make me vacillate. If I changed my mind, it must be because of something important and entirely new to me.'

'Ah! – then you have accepted him? Then Chettam has no chance? Has Chettam offended you – offended you, you know? What is it you don't like in Chettam?'

'There is nothing that I like in him,' said Dorothea, rather impetuously.

Mr Brooke threw his head and shoulders backward as if someone had thrown a light missile at him. Dorothea immediately felt some self-rebuke, and said: 'I mean in the light of a husband. He is very kind, I think – really very good about the cottages. A well-meaning man.'

'But you must have a scholar, and that sort of thing? Well, it lies a little in our family. I had it myself – that love of knowledge, and going into everything – a little too much – it took me too far; though that sort of thing doesn't often run in the female line; or it runs underground like the rivers in Greece, you know – it comes out in the sons. Clever sons, clever mothers. I went a good deal into that, at one time. However, my dear, I have always said that people should do as they like in these things up to a certain point. I couldn't, as your guardian, have consented to a bad match. But Casaubon stands well: his position is good. I am afraid Chettam will be hurt, though, and Mrs Cadwallader will blame me.'

That evening, of course, Celia knew nothing of what had happened. She attributed Dorothea's abstracted manner, and the evidence of further crying since they had got home, to the temper she had been in about Sir James Chettam and the buildings, and was careful not to give further offence: having once said what she wanted to say, Celia had no disposition to recur to disagreeable subjects. It had been her nature when a child never to quarrel with anyone – only to observe with wonder that they quarrelled with her, and looked like turkey-cocks; whereupon she was ready to play at cat's cradle with them whenever they recovered themselves. And as to Dorothea, it had always been her way to find something wrong in her sister's words, though Celia inwardly protested that she always said just how things were, and nothing else: she never did and never could put words together out of her own head. But the best of Dodo was, that she did not keep angry for long together. Now, though they had hardly spoken to each other all the evening, yet when Celia put by her work, intending to go to bed, a proceeding in which she was always much the earlier, Dorothea, who was seated on a low stool, unable to occupy herself except in meditation, said, with the musical intonation which in moments of deep but quiet feeling made her speech like a fine bit of recitative: 'Celia, dear, come and kiss me,' holding her arms open as she spoke.

Celia knelt down to get the right level and gave her little butterfly kiss, while

Dorothea encircled her with gentle arms and pressed her lips gravely on each cheek in turn.

'Don't sit up, Dodo, you are so pale tonight: go to bed soon,' said Celia, in a comfortable way, without any touch of pathos.

'No, dear, I am very, very happy,' said Dorothea, fervently.

'So much the better,' thought Celia. 'But how strangely Dodo goes from one extreme to the other.'

The next day, at luncheon, the butler, handing something to Mr Brooke, said, 'Jonas is come back, sir, and has brought this letter.'

Mr Brooke read the letter, and then, nodding toward Dorothea, said, 'Casaubon, my dear: he will be here to dinner; he didn't wait to write more – didn't wait, you know.'

It could not seem remarkable to Celia that a dinner guest should be announced to her sister beforehand, but her eyes following the same direction as her uncle's, she was struck with the peculiar effect of the announcement on Dorothea. It seemed as if something like the reflection of a white sunlit wing had passed across her features, ending in one of her rare blushes. For the first time it entered into Celia's mind that there might be something more between Mr Casaubon and her sister than his delight in bookish talk and her delight in listening. Hitherto she had classed the admiration for this 'ugly' and learned acquaintance with the admiration for Monsieur Liret at Lausanne, also ugly and learned. Dorothea had never been tired of listening to old Monsieur Liret when Celia's feet were as cold as possible, and when it had really become dreadful to see the skin of his bald head moving about. Why then should her enthusiasm not extend to Mr Casaubon simply in the same way as to Monsieur Liret? And it seemed probable that all learned men had a sort of schoolmaster's view of young people.

But now Celia was really startled at the suspicion which had darted into her mind. She was seldom taken by surprise in this way, her marvellous quickness in observing a certain order of signs generally preparing her to expect such outward events as she had an interest in. Not that she now imagined Mr Casaubon to be already an accepted lover: she had only begun to feel disgust at the possibility that anything in Dorothea's mind could tend toward such an issue. Here was something really to vex her about Dodo: it was all very well not to accept Sir James Chettam, but the idea of marrying Mr Casaubon! Celia felt a sort of shame mingled with a sense of the ludicrous. But perhaps Dodo, if she were really bordering on such an extravagance, might be turned away from it: experience had often shown that her impressibility might be calculated on. The day was damp, and they were not going to walk out, so they both went up to their sitting-room; and there Celia observed that Dorothea, instead of settling down with her usual diligent interest to some occupation, simply leaned her elbow on an open book and looked out of the window at the great cedar silvered with the damp. She herself had taken up the making of a toy for the curate's children, and was not going to enter on any subject too precipitately.

Dorothea was in fact thinking that it was desirable for Celia to know of the momentous change in Mr Casaubon's position since he had last been in the house: it did not seem fair to leave her in ignorance of what would necessarily affect her attitude towards him; but it was impossible not to shrink from telling her. Dorothea accused herself of some meanness in this timidity: it was always odious to her to have any small fears or contrivances about her actions, but at this moment she was seeking the highest aid possible that she might not dread the corrosiveness of Celia's pretty carnally minded prose. Her reverie was broken, and the difficulty of decision banished, by Celia's small and rather guttural voice speaking in its usual tone, of a remark aside or a 'by the by'.

'Is anyone else coming to dine besides Mr Casaubon?'

'Not that I know of.'

'I hope there is someone else. Then I shall not hear him eat his soup so.'

'What is there remarkable about his soup-eating?'

'Really, Dodo, can't you hear how he scrapes his spoon? And he always blinks before he speaks. I don't know whether Locke blinked, but I'm sure I am sorry for those who sat opposite to him, if he did.'

'Celia,' said Dorothea, with emphatic gravity, 'pray don't make any more observations of that kind.'

'Why not? They are quite true,' returned Celia, who had her reasons for persevering, though she was beginning to be a little afraid.

'Many things are true which only the commonest minds observe.'

'Then I think the commonest minds must be rather useful. I think it is a pity Mr Casaubon's mother had not a commoner mind: she might have taught him better.' Celia was inwardly frightened, and ready to run away, now she had hurled this light javelin.

Dorothea's feelings had gathered to an avalanche, and there could be no further preparation.

'It is right to tell you, Celia, that I am engaged to marry Mr Casaubon.'

Perhaps Celia had never turned so pale before. The paper man she was making would have had his leg injured, but for her habitual care of whatever she held in her hands. She laid the fragile figure down at once, and sat perfectly still for a few moments. When she spoke there was a tear gathering.

'O Dodo, I hope you will be happy.' Her sisterly tenderness could not but surmount other feelings at this moment, and her fears were the fears of affection.

Dorothea was still hurt and agitated.

'It is quite decided, then?' said Celia, in an awed undertone. 'And uncle knows?'

'I have accepted Mr Casaubon's offer. My uncle brought me the letter that contained it; he knew about it beforehand.'

'I beg your pardon, if I have said anything to hurt you, Dodo,' said Celia, with a slight sob. She never could have thought that she should feel as she did. There was something funereal in the whole affair, and Mr Casaubon seemed to be the officiating clergyman, about whom it would be indecent to make remarks.

'Never mind, Kitty, do not grieve. We should never admire the same people. I often offend in something of the same way; I am apt to speak too strongly of those who don't please me.'

In spite of this magnanimity Dorothea was still smarting: perhaps as much from Celia's subdued astonishment as from her small criticisms. Of course all the world round Tipton would be out of sympathy with this marriage. Dorothea knew of no one who thought as she did about life and its best objects.

Nevertheless before the evening was at an end she was very happy. In an hour's tête-à-tête with Mr Casaubon she talked to him with more freedom than she had ever felt before, even pouring out her joy at the thought of devoting herself to him, and of learning how she might best share and further all his great ends. Mr Casaubon was touched with an unknown delight (what man would not have been?) at this childlike unrestrained ardour: he was not surprised (what lover would have been?) that he should be the object of it.

'My dear young lady – Miss Brooke – Dorothea!' he said, pressing her hand between his hands, 'this is a happiness greater than I had ever imagined to be in reserve for me. That I should ever meet with a mind and person so rich in the mingled graces which could render marriage desirable, was far indeed from my conception. You have all – nay, more than all – those qualities which I have ever regarded as the characteristic excellences of womanhood. The great charm of your sex is its capability of an ardent self-sacrificing affection, and herein we see its fitness to round and complete the existence of our own. Hitherto I have known few pleasures save of the severer kind: my satisfactions have been those of the solitary student. I have been little disposed to gather flowers that would wither in my hand, but now I shall pluck them with eagerness, to place them in your bosom.'

No speech could have been more thoroughly honest in its intention: the frigid rhetoric at the end was as sincere as the bark of a dog, or the cawing of an amorous rook. Would it not be rash to conclude that there was no passion behind those sonnets to Delia which strike us as the thin music of a mandolin?

Dorothea's faith supplied all that Mr Casaubon's words seemed to leave unsaid: what believer sees a disturbing omission or infelicity? The text, whether of prophet or of poet, expands for whatever we can put into it, and even his bad grammar is sublime.

'I am very ignorant – you will quite wonder at my ignorance,' said Dorothea. 'I have so many thoughts that may be quite mistaken; and now I shall be able to tell them all to you, and ask you about them. But,' she added, with rapid imagination of Mr Casaubon's probable feeling, 'I will not trouble you too much; only when you are inclined to listen to me. You must often be weary with the pursuit of subjects in your own track. I shall gain enough if you will take me with you there.'

'How should I be able now to persevere in any path without your companion-ship?' said Mr Casaubon, kissing her candid brow, and feeling that heaven had vouchsafed him a blessing in every way suited to his peculiar wants. He was being unconsciously wrought upon by the charms of a nature which was entirely without hidden calculations either for immediate effects or for remoter ends. It was this which made Dorothea so childlike, and according to some judges, so stupid, with all her reputed cleverness; as, for example, in the present case of throwing herself, metaphorically speaking, at Mr Casaubon's feet, and kissing his unfashionable shoe-ties as if he were a Protestant Pope. She was not in the least teaching Mr Casaubon to ask if he were good enough for her, but merely asking herself anxiously how she could be good enough for Mr Casaubon. Before he left the next day it had been decided that the marriage should take place within six weeks. Why not? Mr Casaubon's house was ready. It was not a parsonage, but a considerable mansion, with much land attached to it. The parsonage was inhabited by the curate, who did all the duty except preaching the morning sermon.

Chapter 6

> My lady's tongue is like the meadow blades,
> That cut you stroking them with idle hand.
> Nice cutting is her function: she divides
> With spiritual edge the millet-seed,
> And makes intangible savings.

As Mr Casaubon's carriage was passing out of the gateway, it arrested the entrance of a pony phaeton driven by a lady with a servant seated behind. It was doubtful whether the recognition had been mutual, for Mr Casaubon was looking absently before him; but the lady was quick-eyed, and threw a nod and a 'how do you do?' in the nick of time. In spite of her shabby bonnet and very old Indian shawl, it was plain that the lodge-keeper regarded her as an important personage, from the low curtsey which was dropped on the entrance of the small phaeton.

'Well, Mrs Fitchett, how are your fowls laying now?' said the high-coloured, dark-eyed lady, with the clearest chiselled utterance.

'Pretty well for laying, madam, but they've ta'en to eating their eggs: I've no peace o' mind with 'em at all.'

'O the cannibals! Better sell them cheap at once. What will you sell them a couple? One can't eat fowls of a bad character at a high price.'

'Well, madam, half a crown: I couldn't let 'em go, not under.'

'Half a crown, these times! Come now – for the Rector's chicken-broth on a Sunday. He has consumed all ours that I can spare. You are half-paid with the sermon, Mrs Fitchett, remember that. Take a pair of tumbler-pigeons for them – little beauties. You must come and see them. You have no tumblers among your pigeons.'

'Well, madam, Master Fitchett shall go and see 'em after work. He's very hot on new sorts; to oblige *you*.'

'Oblige me! It will be the best bargain he ever made. A pair of church pigeons for a couple of wicked Spanish fowls that eat their own eggs! Don't you and Fitchett boast too much, that is all!'

The phaeton was driven onwards with the last words, leaving Mrs Fitchett laughing and shaking her head slowly, with an interjectional 'Surely, surely!' – from which it might be inferred that she would have found the countryside somewhat duller if the Rector's lady had been less free-spoken and less of a skinflint. Indeed, both the farmers and labourers in the parishes of Freshitt and Tipton would have felt a sad lack of conversation but for the stories about what Mrs Cadwallader said and did: a lady of immeasurably high birth, descended, as it were, from unknown earls, dim as the crowd of heroic shades – who pleaded poverty, pared down prices, and cut jokes in the most companionable manner, though with a turn of tongue that let you know who she was. Such a lady gave a neighbourliness to both rank and religion, and mitigated the bitterness of uncommuted tithe. A much more exemplary character with an infusion of sour dignity would not have furthered their comprehension of the Thirty-nine Articles, and would have been less socially uniting.

Mr Brooke, seeing Mrs Cadwallader's merits from a different point of view, winced a little when her name was announced in the library, where he was sitting alone.

'I see you have had our Lowick Cicero here,' she said, seating herself comfortably, throwing back her wraps, and showing a thin but well-built figure. 'I suspect you and he are brewing some bad politics, else you would not be seeing so much of the lively man. I shall inform against you: remember you are both suspicious characters since you took Peel's side about the Catholic Bill. I shall tell everybody that you are going to put up for Middlemarch on the Whig side when old Pinkerton resigns, and that Casaubon is going to help you in an underhand manner: going to bribe the voters with pamphlets, and throw open the public-houses to distribute them. Come, confess!'

'Nothing of the sort,' said Mr Brooke, smiling and rubbing his eye-glasses, but really blushing a little at the impeachment. 'Casaubon and I don't talk politics much. He doesn't care much about the philanthropic side of things; punishments, and that kind of thing. He only cares about Church questions. That is not my line of action, you know.'

'Ra–a–ther too much, my friend. *I* have heard of your doings. Who was it that sold his bit of land to the Papists at Middlemarch? I believe you bought it on purpose. You are a perfect Guy Faux. See if you are not burnt in effigy this 5th of November coming. Humphrey would not come to quarrel with you about it, so I am come.'

'Very good. I was prepared to be persecuted for not persecuting – not persecuting, you know.'

'There you go! That is a piece of claptrap you have got ready for the hustings. Now, *do not* let them lure you to the hustings, my dear Mr Brooke. A man always makes a fool of himself, speechifying: there's no excuse but being on the right side, so that you can ask a blessing on your humming and hawing. You will lose yourself, I forewarn you. You will make a Saturday pie of all parties' opinions, and be pelted by everybody.'

'That is what I expect, you know,' said Mr Brooke, not wishing to betray how little he enjoyed this prophetic sketch, 'what I expect as an independent man. As to the Whigs, a man who goes with the thinkers is not likely to be hooked on by any party. He may go with them up to a certain point – up to a certain point, you know. But that is what you ladies never understand.'

'Where your certain point is? No. I should like to be told how a man can have any certain point when he belongs to no party – leading a roving life, and never letting his friends know his address. "Nobody knows where Brooke will be – there's no counting on Brooke" – that is what people say of you, to be quite frank. Now, do turn respectable. How will you like going to Sessions with everybody looking shy on you, and you with a bad conscience and an empty pocket?'

'I don't pretend to argue with a lady on politics,' said Mr Brooke, with an air of smiling indifference, but feeling rather unpleasantly conscious that this attack of Mrs Cadwallader's had opened the defensive campaign to which certain rash steps had exposed him. 'Your sex are not thinkers, you know – varium et mutabile semper – that kind of thing. You don't know Virgil. I knew' – Mr Brooke reflected in time that he had not had the personal acquaintance of the Augustan poet – 'I was going to say, poor Stoddart, you know. That was what *he* said. You ladies are always against an independent attitude – a man's caring for nothing but truth, and that sort of thing. And there is no part of the county where opinion is narrower than it is here – I don't mean to throw stones, you know, but somebody is wanted to take the independent line; and if I don't take it, who will?'

'Who? Why, any upstart who has got neither blood nor position. People of standing should consume their independent nonsense at home, not hawk it about. And you! who are going to marry your niece, as good as your daughter, to one of our best men. Sir James would be cruelly annoyed: it will be too hard on him if you turn round now and make yourself a Whig signboard.'

Mr Brooke again winced inwardly, for Dorothea's engagement had no sooner been decided, than he had thought of Mrs Cadwallader's prospective taunts. It might have been easy for ignorant observers to say, 'Quarrel with Mrs Cadwallader'; but where is a country gentleman to go who quarrels with his oldest neighbours? Who could taste the fine flavour in the name of Brooke if it were delivered casually, like wine without a seal? Certainly a man can only be cosmopolitan up to a certain point.

'I hope Chettam and I shall always be good friends; but I am sorry to say there is no prospect of his marrying my niece,' said Mr Brooke, much relieved to see through the window that Celia was coming in.

'Why not?' said Mrs Cadwallader, with a sharp note of surprise. 'It is hardly a fortnight since you and I were talking about it.'

'My niece has chosen another suitor – has chosen him, you know. I have had nothing to do with it. I should have preferred Chettam; and I should have said Chettam was the man any girl would have chosen. But there is no accounting for these things. Your sex is capricious, you know.'

'Why, whom do you mean to say that you are going to let her marry?' Mrs Cadwallader's mind was rapidly surveying the possibilities of choice for Dorothea.

But here Celia entered, blooming from a walk in the garden, and the greeting with her delivered Mr Brooke from the necessity of answering immediately. He got up hastily, and saying, 'By the way, I must speak to Wright about the horses,' shuffled quickly out of the room.

'My dear child, what is this? – this about your sister's engagement?' said Mrs Cadwallader.

'She is engaged to marry Mr Casaubon,' said Celia, resorting, as usual, to the simplest statement of fact, and enjoying this opportunity of speaking to the Rector's wife alone.

'This is frightful. How long has it been going on?'

'I only knew of it yesterday. They are to be married in six weeks.'

'Well, my dear, I wish you joy of your brother-in-law.'

'I am so sorry for Dorothea.'

'Sorry! It is her doing, I suppose.'

'Yes: she says Mr Casaubon has a great soul.'

'With all my heart.'

'O Mrs Cadwallader, I don't think it can be nice to marry a man with a great soul.'

'Well, my dear, take warning. You know the look of one now; when the next comes and wants to marry you, don't you accept him.'

'I'm sure I never should.'

'No; one such in a family is enough. So your sister never cared about Sir James Chettam? What would you have said to *him* for a brother-in-law?'

'I should have liked that very much. I am sure he would have been a good husband. Only,' Celia added, with a slight blush (she sometimes seemed to blush as she breathed), 'I don't think he would have suited Dorothea.'

'Not high-flown enough?'

'Dodo is very strict. She thinks so much about everything, and is so particular about what one says. Sir James never seemed to please her.'

'She must have encouraged him, I am sure. That is not very creditable.'

'Please don't be angry with Dodo; she does not see things. She thought so much about the cottages, and she *was* rude to Sir James sometimes; but he is so kind, he never noticed it.'

'Well,' said Mrs Cadwallader, putting on her shawl, and rising, as if in haste, 'I must go straight to Sir James and break this to him. He will have brought his mother back by this time, and I must call. Your uncle will never tell him. We a re all disappointed, my dear. Young people should think of their families in marrying. I set a bad example – married a poor clergyman, and made myself a pitiable object among the De Bracys – obliged to get my coals by stratagem, and pray to heaven for my salad oil. However, Casaubon has money enough; I must do him that justice. As to his blood, I suppose the family quarterings are three cuttlefish sable, and a commentator rampant. By the by, before I go, my dear, I must speak to your Mrs Carter about pastry. I want to send my young cook to learn of her. Poor people with four children, like us, you know, can't afford to keep a good cook. I have no doubt Mrs Carter will oblige me. Sir James's cook is a perfect dragon.'

In less than an hour, Mrs Cadwallader had circumvented Mrs Carter and driven to Freshitt Hall, which was not far from her own parsonage, her husband being resident in Freshitt and keeping a curate in Tipton.

Sir James Chettam had returned from the short journey which had kept him absent for a couple of days, and had changed his dress, intending to ride over to Tipton Grange. His horse was standing at the door when Mrs Cadwallader drove up, and he immediately appeared there himself, whip in hand. Lady Chettam had not yet returned, but Mrs Cadwallader's errand could not be despatched in the presence of grooms, so she asked to be taken into the conservatory close by, to look at the new plants; and on coming to a contemplative stand, she said, 'I have a great shock for you; I hope you are not so far gone in love as you pretended to be.'

It was of no use protesting against Mrs Cadwallader's way of putting things. But Sir James's countenance changed a little. He felt a vague alarm.

'I do believe Brooke is going to expose himself after all. I accused him of meaning to stand for Middlemarch on the Liberal side, and he looked silly and never denied it – talked about the independent line, and the usual nonsense.'

'Is that all?' said Sir James, much relieved.

'Why,' rejoined Mrs Cadwallader, with a sharper note, 'you don't mean to say that you would like him to turn public man in that way – making a sort of political Cheap Jack of himself?'

'He might be dissuaded, I should think. He would not like the expense.'

'That is what I told him. He is vulnerable to reason there, always a few grains of common-sense in an ounce of miserliness. Miserliness is a capital quality to run in families; it's the safe side for madness to dip on. And there must be a little crack in the Brooke family, else we should not see what we are to see.'

'What? Brooke standing for Middlemarch?'

'Worse than that. I really feel a little responsible. I always told you Miss Brooke would be such a fine match. I knew there was a great deal of nonsense in her – a flighty sort of Methodistical stuff. But these things wear out of girls. However, I am taken by surprise for once.'

'What do you mean, Mrs Cadwallader?' said Sir James. His fear lest Miss Brooke should have run away to join the Moravian Brethren, or some preposterous sect unknown to good society, was a little allayed by the knowledge that Mrs Cadwallader always made the worst of things. 'What has happened to Miss Brooke? Pray speak out.'

'Very well. She is engaged to be married.' Mrs Cadwallader paused a few moments, observing the deeply-hurt expression in her friend's face, which he was trying to conceal by a nervous smile, while he whipped his boot; but she soon added, 'Engaged to Casaubon.'

Sir James let his whip fall and stooped to pick it up. Perhaps his face had never before gathered so much concentrated disgust as when he turned to Mrs Cadawallader and repeated, 'Casaubon?'

'Even so. You know my errand now.'

'Good God! It is horrible! He is no better than a mummy!' (The point of view has to be allowed for, as that of a blooming and disappointed rival.)

'She says, he is a great soul. – A great bladder for dried peas to rattle in!' said Mrs Cadwallader.

'What business has an old bachelor like that to marry?' said Sir James. 'He has one foot in the grave.'

'He means to draw it out again, I suppose.'

'Brooke ought not to allow it: he should insist on its being put off till she is of age. She would think better of it then. What is a guardian for?'

'As if you could ever squeeze a resolution out of Brooke!'

'Cadwallader might talk to him.'

'Not he! Humphrey finds everybody charming. I never can get him to abuse Casaubon. He will even speak well of the bishop, though I tell him it is unnatural in a beneficed clergyman: what can one do with a husband who attends so little to the decencies? I hide it as well as I can by abusing everybody myself. Come, come, cheer up! you are well rid of Miss Brooke, a girl who would have been requiring you to see the stars by daylight. Between ourselves, little Celia is worth two of her, and likely after all to be the better match. For this marriage to Casaubon is as good as going to a nunnery.'

'Oh, on my own account – it is for Miss Brooke's sake I think her friends should try to use their influence.'

'Well, Humphrey doesn't know yet. But when I tell him, you may depend on it he will say, "Why not? Casaubon is a good fellow – and young – young enough." These charitable people never know vinegar from wine till they have swallowed it and got the colic. However, if I were a man I should prefer Celia, especially when Dorothea was gone. The truth is, you have been courting one and have won the other. I can see that she admires you almost as much as a man expects to be admired. If it were anyone but me who said so, you might think it exaggeration. Goodbye!'

Sir James handed Mrs Cadwallader to the phaeton, and then jumped on his horse. He was not going to renounce his ride because of his friend's unpleasant news – only to ride the faster in some other direction than that of Tipton Grange.

Now, why on earth should Mrs Cadwallader have been at all busy about Miss Brooke's marriage; and why, when one match that she liked to think she had a hand in was frustrated, should she have straightway contrived the preliminaries of another? Was there any ingenious plot, any hide-and-seek course of action, which might be detected by a careful telescopic watch? Not at all: a telescope might have swept the parishes of Tipton and Freshitt, the whole area visited by Mrs Cadwallader in her phaeton, without witnessing any interview that could excite suspicion, or any scene from which she did not return with the same unperturbed keenness of eye and the same high natural colour. In fact, if that convenient vehicle had existed in the days of the Seven Sages, one of them would doubtless have remarked, that you can know little of women by following them about in their pony phaetons. Even with a microscope directed on a water-drop we find ourselves making interpretations which turn out to be rather coarse; for whereas under a weak lens you may seem to see a creature exhibiting an active voracity into which other smaller creatures actively play as if they were so many animated tax-pennies, a stronger lens reveals to you certain tiniest hairlets which make vortices for these victims while the swallower waits passively at his receipt of custom. In this way, metaphorically speaking, a strong lens applied to Mrs Cadwallader's matchmaking will show a play of minute causes producing what may be called thought and speech vortices to bring her the sort of food she needed.

Her life was rurally simple, quite free from secrets either foul, dangerous, or otherwise important, and not consciously affected by the great affairs of the world. All the more did the affairs of the great world interest her, when communicated in the letters of highborn relations: the way in which fascinating younger sons had gone to the dogs by marrying their mistresses; the fine old-blooded idiocy of young Lord Tapir, and the furious gouty humours of old Lord Megatherium; the exact crossing of genealogies which had brought a coronet into a new branch and widened the relations of scandal, – these were topics of which she retained details with the utmost accuracy, and reproduced them in an excellent pickle of epigrams, which she herself enjoyed the more because she believed as unquestioningly in birth and no-birth as she did in game and vermin. She would never have disowned anyone on the ground of poverty: a De Bracy reduced to take his dinner in a basin would have seemed to her an example of pathos worth exaggerating, and I fear his aristocratic vices would not have horrified her. But her feeling towards the vulgar rich was a sort of religious hatred: they had probably made all their money out of high retail prices, and Mrs Cadwallader detested high prices for everything that was not paid in kind at the Rectory: such people were no part of God's design in making the world; and their accent was an affliction to the ears. A town where such monsters abounded was hardly more than a sort of low comedy, which could not be taken account of in a well-bred scheme of the universe. Let any lady who is inclined to be hard on Mrs Cadwallader enquire into the comprehensiveness of her own beautiful views, and be quite sure that they afford accommodation for all the lives which have the honour to coexist with hers.

With such a mind, active as phosphorus, biting everything that came near into the form that suited it, how could Mrs Cadwallader feel that the Miss Brookes and their matrimonial prospects were alien to her? especially as it had been the habit of years for her to scold Mr Brooke with the friendliest frankness, and let him know in confidence that she thought him a poor creature. From the first arrival of the young ladies in Tipton she had prearranged Dorothea's marriage with Sir James, and if it had taken place would have been quite sure that it was her doing: that it should not take place after she had preconceived it, caused her an irritation which every thinker will sympathise with. She was the diplomatist of Tipton and Freshitt, and for anything to happen in spite of her was an offensive irregularity. As to freaks like this of Miss Brooke's, Mrs Cadwallader had no patience with them, and now saw that her opinion of this girl had been infected with some of her husband's weak charitableness: those Methodistical whims, that air of being more religious than the rector and curate together, came from a deeper and more constitutional disease than she had been willing to believe.

'However,' said Mrs Cadwallader, first to herself and afterwards to her husband, 'I throw her over: there was a chance, if she had married Sir James, of her becoming a sane, sensible woman. He would never have contradicted her, and when a woman is not contradicted, she has no motive for obstinacy in her absurdities. But now I wish her joy of her hair shirt.'

It followed that Mrs Cadwallader must decide on another match for Sir

James, and having made up her mind that it was to be the younger Miss Brooke, there could not have been a more skilful move toward the success of her plan than her hint to the baronet that he had made an impression on Celia's heart. For he was not one of those gentlemen who languish after the unattainable Sappho's apple that laughs from the topmost bough – the charms which

> Smile like the knot of cowslips on the cliff,
> Not to be come at by the willing hand.

He had no sonnets to write, and it could not strike him agreeably that he was not an object of preference to the woman whom he had preferred. Already the knowledge that Dorothea had chosen Mr Casaubon had bruised his attachment and relaxed its hold. Although Sir James was a sportsman, he had some other feelings towards women than towards grouse and foxes, and did not regard his future wife in the light of prey, valuable chiefly for the excitements of the chase. Neither was he so well acquainted with the habits of primitive races as to feel that an ideal combat for her, tomahawk in hand, so to speak, was necessary to the historical continuity of the marriage-tie. On the contrary, having the amiable vanity which knits us to those who are fond of us, and disinclines us to those who are indifferent, and also a good grateful nature, the mere idea that a woman had a kindness towards him spun little threads of tenderness from out his heart towards hers.

Thus it happened, that after Sir James had ridden rather fast for half an hour in a direction away from Tipton Grange, he slackened his pace, and at last turned into a road which would lead him back by a shorter cut. Various feelings wrought in him the determination after all to go to the Grange today as if nothing new had happened. He could not help rejoicing that he had never made the offer and been rejected; mere friendly politeness required that he should call to see Dorothea about the cottages, and now happily Mrs Cadwallader had prepared him to offer his congratulations, if necessary, without showing too much awkwardness. He really did not like it: giving up Dorothea was very painful to him; but there was something in the resolve to make this visit forthwith and conquer all show of feeling, which was a sort of file-biting and counter-irritant. And without his distinctly recognising the impulse, there certainly was present in him the sense that Celia would be there, and that he should pay her more attention than he had done before.

We mortals, men and women, devour many a disappointment between breakfast and dinner-time; keep back the tears and look a little pale about the lips, and in answer to enquiries say, 'Oh, nothing!' Pride helps us; and pride is not a bad thing when it only urges us to hide our own hurts – not to hurt others.

Chapter 7

Piacer e popone
Vuol la sua stagione.   Italian proverb

Mr Casaubon, as might be expected, spent a great deal of his time at the Grange
in these weeks, and the hindrance which courtship occasioned to the progress of
his great work – the *Key to all Mythologies* – naturally made him look forward the
more eagerly to the happy termination of courtship. But he had deliberately
incurred the hindrance, having made up his mind that it was now time for him
to adorn his life with the graces of female companionship, to irradiate the gloom
which fatigue was apt to hang over the intervals of studious labour with the play
of female fancy, and to secure in this, his culminating age, the solace of female
tendance for his declining years. Hence he determined to abandon himself to
the stream of feeling, and perhaps was surprised to find what an exceedingly
shallow rill it was. As in droughty regions baptism by immersion could only be
performed symbolically, so Mr Casaubon found that sprinkling was the utmost
approach to a plunge which his stream would afford him; and he concluded that
the poets had much exaggerated the force of masculine passion. Nevertheless,
he observed with pleasure that Miss Brooke showed an ardent submissive
affection which promised to fulfil his most agreeable previsions of marriage. It
had once or twice crossed his mind that possibly there was some deficiency in
Dorothea to account for the moderation of his abandonment; but he was unable
to discern the deficiency, or to figure to himself a woman who would have
pleased him better: so that there was clearly no reason to fall back upon but the
exaggerations of human tradition.

'Could I not be preparing myself now to be more useful?' said Dorothea to
him, one morning, early in the time of courtship; 'could I not learn to read Latin
and Greek aloud to you, as Milton's daughters did to their father, without
understanding what they read?'

'I fear that would be wearisome to you,' said Mr Casaubon, smiling; 'and,
indeed, if I remember rightly, the young women you have mentioned regarded
that exercise in unknown tongues as a ground for rebellion against the poet.'

'Yes; but in the first place they were very naughty girls, else they would have
been proud to minister to such a father; and in the second place they might
have studied privately and taught themselves to understand what they read, and
then it would have been interesting. I hope you don't expect me to be naughty
and stupid?'

'I expect you to be all that an exquisite young lady can be in every possible
relation of life. Certainly it might be a great advantage if you were able to copy
the Greek character, and to that end it were well to begin with a little reading.'

Dorothea seized this as a precious permission. She would not have asked Mr
Casaubon at once to teach her the languages, dreading of all things to be
tiresome instead of helpful; but it was not entirely out of devotion to her future

husband that she wished to know Latin and Greek. Those provinces of masculine knowledge seemed to her a standing-ground from which all truth could be seen more truly. As it was, she constantly doubted her own con-clusions, because she felt her own ignorance: how could she be confident that one-roomed cottages were not for the glory of God, when men who knew the classics appeared to conciliate indifference to the cottages with zeal for the glory? Perhaps even Hebrew might be necessary – at least the alphabet and a few roots – in order to arrive at the core of things, and judge soundly on the social duties of the Christian. And she had not reached that point of renunciation at which she would have been satisfied with having a wise husband; she wished, poor child, to be wise herself. Miss Brooke was certainly very naïve with all her alleged cleverness. Celia, whose mind had never been thought too powerful, saw the emptiness of other people's pretensions much more readily. To have in general but little feeling, seems to be the only security against feeling too much on any particular occasion.

However, Mr Casaubon consented to listen and teach for an hour together, like a schoolmaster of little boys, or rather like a lover, to whom a mistress's elementary ignorance and difficulties have a touching fitness. Few scholars would have disliked teaching the alphabet under such circumstances. But Dorothea herself was a little shocked and discouraged at her own stupidity, and the answers she got to some timid questions about the value of the Greek accents gave her a painful suspicion that here indeed there might be secrets not capable of explanation to a woman's reason.

Mr Brooke had no doubt on that point, and expressed himself with his usual strength upon it one day that he came into the library while the reading was going forward.

'Well, but now, Casaubon, such deep studies, classics, mathematics, that kind of thing, are too taxing for a woman – too taxing, you know.'

'Dorothea is learning to read the characters simply,' said Mr Casaubon, evading the question. 'She had the very considerate thought of saving my eyes.'

'Ah, well, without understanding, you know – that may not be so bad. But there is a lightness about the feminine mind – a touch and go – music, the fine arts, that kind of thing – they should study those up to a certain point, women should; but in a light way, you know. A woman should be able to sit down and play you or sing you a good old English tune. That is what I like; though I have heard most things – been at the opera in Vienna: Gluck, Mozart, everything of that sort. But I'm a conservative in music – it's not like ideas, you know. I stick to the good old tunes.'

'Mr Casaubon is not fond of the piano, and I am very glad he is not,' said Dorothea, whose slight regard for domestic music and feminine fine art must be forgiven her, considering the small tinkling and smearing in which they chiefly consisted at that dark period. She smiled and looked up at her betrothed with grateful eyes. If he had always been asking her to play the 'Last Rose of Summer,' she would have required much resignation. 'He says there is only an old harpsichord at Lowick, and it is covered with books.'

'Ah, there you are behind Celia, my dear. Celia, now, plays very prettily, and is always ready to play. However, since Casaubon does not like it, you are all right. But it's a pity you should not have little recreations of that sort, Casaubon: the bow always strung – that kind of thing, you know – will not do.'

'I never could look on it in the light of a recreation to have my ears teased with measured noises,' said Mr Casaubon. 'A tune much iterated has the ridiculous effect of making the words in my mind perform a sort of minuet to keep time – an effect hardly tolerable, I imagine, after boyhood. As to the grander forms of music, worthy to accompany solemn celebrations, and even to serve as an educating influence according to the ancient conception, I say nothing, for with these we are not immediately concerned.'

'No; but music of that sort I should enjoy,' said Dorothea. 'When we were coming home from Lausanne my uncle took us to hear the great organ at Freiberg, and it made me sob.'

'That kind of thing is not healthy, my dear,' said Mr Brooke. 'Casaubon, she will be in your hands now: you must teach my niece to take things more quietly, eh, Dorothea?'

He ended with a smile, not wishing to hurt his niece, but really thinking that it was perhaps better for her to be early married to so sober a fellow as Casaubon, since she would not hear of Chettam.

'It is wonderful, though,' he said to himself as he shuffled out of the room – 'it is wonderful that she should have liked him. However, the match is good. I should have been travelling out of my brief to have hindered it, let Mrs Cadwallader say what she will. He is pretty certain to be a bishop, is Casaubon. That was a very seasonable pamphlet of his on the Catholic Question: – a deanery at least. They owe him a deanery.'

And here I must vindicate a claim to philosophical reflectiveness, by remarking that Mr Brooke on this occasion little thought of the Radical speech which, at a later period, he was led to make on the incomes of the bishops. What elegant historian would neglect a striking opportunity for pointing out that his heroes did not foresee the history of the world, or even their own actions? – For example, that Henry of Navarre, when a Protestant baby, little thought of being a Catholic monarch; or that Alfred the Great, when he measured his laborious nights with burning candles, had no idea of future gentlemen measuring their idle days with watches. Here is a mine of truth, which, however vigorously it may be worked, is likely to outlast our coal.

But of Mr Brooke I make a further remark perhaps less warranted by precedent – namely, that if he had foreknown his speech, it might not have made any great difference. To think with pleasure of his niece's husband having a large ecclesiastical income was one thing – to make a Liberal speech was another thing; and it is a narrow mind which cannot look at a subject from various points of view.

Chapter 8

Oh, rescue her! I am her brother now,
And you her father. Every gentle maid
Should have a guardian in each gentleman.

It was wonderful to Sir James Chettam how well he continued to like going to
the Grange after he had once encountered the difficulty of seeing Dorothea for
the first time in the light of a woman who was engaged to another man. Of
course the forked lightning seemed to pass through him when he first
approached her, and he remained conscious throughout the interview of hiding
uneasiness; but, good as he was, it must be owned that his uneasiness was less
than it would have been if he had thought his rival a brilliant and desirable
match. He had no sense of being eclipsed by Mr Casaubon; he was only shocked
that Dorothea was under a melancholy illusion, and his mortification lost some
of its bitterness by being mingled with compassion.

Nevertheless, while Sir James said to himself that he had completely resigned
her, since with the perversity of a Desdemona she had not affected a proposed
match that was clearly suitable and according to nature; he could not yet be quite
passive under the idea of her engagement to Mr Casaubon. On the day when he
first saw them together in the light of his present knowledge, it seemed to him
that he had not taken the affair seriously enough. Brooke was really culpable; he
ought to have hindered it. Who could speak to him? Something might be done
perhaps even now, at least to defer the marriage. On his way home he turned into
the Rectory and asked for Mr Cadwallader. Happily, the Rector was at home,
and his visitor was shown into the study, where all the fishing-tackle hung. But
he himself was in a little room adjoining, at work with his turning apparatus, and
he called to the baronet to join him there. The two were better friends than any
other landholder and clergyman in the county – a significant fact which was in
agreement with the amiable expression of their faces.

Mr Cadwallader was a large man, with full lips and a sweet smile; very plain
and rough in his exterior, but with that solid imperturbable ease and good-
humour which is infectious, and like great grassy hills in the sunshine, quiets
even an irritated egoism, and makes it rather ashamed of itself. 'Well, how are
you?' he said, showing a hand not quite fit to be grasped. 'Sorry I missed you
before. Is there anything particular? You look vexed.'

Sir James's brow had a little crease in it, a little depression of the eyebrow,
which he seemed purposely to exaggerate as he answered.

'It is only this conduct of Brooke's. I really think somebody should speak to
him.'

'What? meaning to stand?' said Mr Cadwallader, going on with the arrangement of the reels which he had just been turning. 'I hardly think he means
it. But where's the harm, if he likes it? Anyone who objects to Whiggery
should be glad when the Whigs don't put up the strongest fellow. They won't

overturn the Constitution with our friend Brooke's head for a battering ram.'

'Oh, I don't mean that,' said Sir James, who, after putting down his hat and throwing himself into a chair, had begun to nurse his leg and examine the sole of his boot with much bitterness. 'I mean this marriage. I mean his letting that blooming young girl marry Casaubon.'

'What is the matter with Casaubon? I see no harm in him if the girl likes him.'

'She is too young to know what she likes. Her guardian ought to interfere. He ought not to allow the thing to be done in this headlong manner. I wonder a man like you, Cadwallader – a man with daughters, can look at the affair with indifference: and with such a heart as yours! Do think seriously about it.'

'I am not joking; I am as serious as possible,' said the Rector, with a provoking little inward laugh. 'You are as bad as Elinor. She has been wanting me to go and lecture Brooke; and I have reminded her that her friends had a very poor opinion of the match she made when she married me.'

'But look at Casaubon,' said Sir James, indignantly. 'He must be fifty, and I don't believe he could ever have been much more than the shadow of a man. Look at his legs !'

'Confound you handsome young fellows! you think of having it all your own way in the world. You don't understand women. They don't admire you half so much as you admire yourselves. Elinor used to tell her sisters that she married me for my ugliness – it was so various and amusing that it had quite conquered her prudence.'

'You! it was easy enough for a woman to love you. But this is no question of beauty. I don't *like* Casaubon.' This was Sir James's strongest way of implying that he thought ill of a man's character.

'Why? what do you know against him?' said the Rector, laying down his reels, and putting his thumbs into his armholes with an air of attention.

Sir James paused. He did not usually find it easy to give his reasons: it seemed to him strange that people should not know them without being told, since he only felt what was reasonable. At last he said: 'Now, Cadwallader, has he got any heart?'

'Well, yes. I don't mean of the melting sort, but a sound kernel, *that* you may be sure of. He is very good to his poor relations; pensions several of the women, and is educating a young fellow at a good deal of expense. Casaubon acts up to his sense of justice. His mother's sister made a bad match – a Pole, I think – lost herself – at any rate was disowned by her family. If it had not been for that, Casaubon would not have had so much money by half. I believe he went himself to find out his cousins, and see what he could do for them. Every man would not ring so well as that, if you tried his metal. You would, Chettam; but not every man.'

'I don't know,' said Sir James, colouring. 'I am not so sure of myself.' He paused a moment, and then added, 'That was a right thing for Casaubon to do. But a man may wish to do what is right, and yet be a sort of parchment code. A woman may not be happy with him. And I think when a girl is so young as Miss Brooke is, her friends ought to interfere a little to hinder her from doing anything foolish. You laugh, because you fancy I have some feeling on my own account. But upon my honour, it is not that. I should feel just the same if I were Miss Brooke's brother or uncle.'

'Well, but what should you do?'

'I should say that the marriage must not be decided on until she was of age. And depend upon it, in that case, it would never come off. I wish you saw it as I do – I wish you would talk to Brooke about it.'

Sir James rose as he was finishing his sentence, for he saw Mrs Cadwallader entering from the study. She held by the hand her youngest girl, about five years old, who immediately ran to papa, and was made comfortable on his knee.

'I hear what you are talking about,' said the wife. 'But you will make no impression on Humphrey. As long as the fish rise to his bait, everybody is what he ought to be. Bless you, Casaubon has got a trout stream, and does not care about fishing in it himself: could there be a better fellow?'

'Well, there is something in that,' said the Rector, with his quiet, inward laugh. 'It is a very good quality in a man to have a trout stream.'

'But seriously,' said Sir James, whose vexation had not yet spent itself, 'don't you think the Rector might do some good by speaking?'

'Oh, I told you beforehand what he would say,' answered Mrs Cadwallader, lifting up her eyebrows. 'I have done what I could: I wash my hands of the marriage.'

'In the first place,' said the Rector, looking rather grave. 'it would be non-sensical to expect that I could convince Brooke, and make him act accordingly. Brooke is a very good fellow, but pulpy; he will run into any mould, but he won't keep shape.'

'He might keep shape long enough to defer the marriage,' said Sir James.

'But, my dear Chettam, why should I use my influence to Casaubon's dis-advantage, unless I were much surer than I am that I should be acting for the advantage of Miss Brooke? I know no harm of Casaubon. I don't care about his Xisuthrus and Fee-fo-fum and the rest; but then he doesn't care about my fishing-tackle. As to the line he took on the Catholic Question, that was unexpected; but he has always been civil to me, and I don't see why I should spoil his sport. For anything I can tell, Miss Brooke may be happier with him than she would be with any other man.'

'Humphrey! I have no patience with you. You know you would rather dine under the hedge than with Casaubon alone. You have nothing to say to each other.'

'What has that to do with Miss Brooke's marrying him? She does not do it for my amusement.'

'He has got no good red blood in his body,' said Sir James.

'No. Somebody put a drop under a magnifying-glass, and it was all semicolons and parentheses,' said Mrs Cadwallader.

'Why does he not bring out his book, instead of marrying?' said Sir James, with a disgust which he held warranted by the sound feeling of an English layman.

'Oh, he dreams footnotes, and they run away with all his brains. They say, when he was a little boy, he made an abstract of "Hop o' my Thumb", and he has been making abstracts ever since. Ugh! And that is the man Humphrey goes on saying that a woman may be happy with.'

'Well, he is what Miss Brooke likes,' said the Rector. 'I don't profess to understand every young lady's taste.'

'But if she were your own daughter?' said Sir James.

'That would be a different affair. She is not my daughter, and I don't feel called upon to interfere. Casaubon is as good as most of us. He is a scholarly clergyman, and creditable to the cloth. Some Radical fellow speechifying at Middlemarch said Casaubon was the learned straw-chopping incumbent, and Freke was the brick-and-mortar incumbent, and I was the angling incumbent. And upon my word, I don't see that one is worse or better than the other.' The Rector ended with his silent laugh. He always saw the joke of any satire against himself. His conscience was large and easy, like the rest of him: it did only what it could do without any trouble.

Clearly, there would be no interference with Miss Brooke's marriage through Mr Cadwallader; and Sir James felt with some sadness that she was to have perfect liberty of misjudgement. It was a sign of his good disposition that he did not slacken at all in his intention of carrying out Dorothea's design of the cottages. Doubtless this persistence was the best course for his own dignity: but pride only helps us to be generous; it never makes us so, any more than vanity makes us witty. She was now enough aware of Sir James's position with regard to her, to appreciate the rectitude of his perseverance in a landlord's duty, to which he had at first been urged by a lover's complaisance, and her pleasure in it was great enough to count for something even in her present happiness. Perhaps she gave to Sir James Chettam's cottages all the interest she could spare from Mr Casaubon, or rather from the symphony of hopeful dreams, admiring trust, and passionate self-devotion which that learned gentleman had set playing in her soul. Hence it happened that in the good baronet's succeeding visits, while he was beginning to pay small attentions to Celia, he found himself talking with more and more pleasure to Dorothea. She was perfectly unconstrained and without irritation towards him now, and he was gradually discovering the delight there is in frank kindness and companionship between a man and a woman who have no passion to hide or confess.

Chapter 9

> *1st Gent.* An ancient land in ancient oracles
> Is called 'law-thirsty': all the struggle there
> Was after order and a perfect rule.
> Pray, where lie such lands now? . . .
> *2nd Gent.* Why, where they lay of old – in human souls.

Mr Casaubon's behaviour about settlements was highly satisfactory to Mr Brooke, and the preliminaries of marriage rolled smoothly along, shortening the weeks of courtship. The betrothed bride must see her future home, and dictate any changes that she would like to have made there. A woman dictates before marriage in order that she may have an appetite for submission afterwards. And certainly, the mistakes that we male and female mortals make when we have our own way might fairly raise some wonder that we are so fond of it.

On a grey but dry November morning Dorothea drove to Lowick in company with her uncle and Celia. Mr Casaubon's home was the manor-house. Close by, visible from some parts of the garden, was the little church, with the old parsonage opposite. In the beginning of his career, Mr Casaubon had only held the living, but the death of his brother had put him in possession of the manor also. It had a small park, with a fine old oak here and there, and an avenue of limes towards the south-west front, with a sunk fence between park and pleasure-ground, so that from the drawing-room windows the glance swept uninter-ruptedly along a slope of greensward till the limes ended in a level of corn and pastures, which often seemed to melt into a lake under the setting sun. This was the happy side of the house, for the south and east looked rather melancholy even under the brightest morning. The grounds here were more confined, the flower-beds showed no very careful tendance, and large clumps of trees, chiefly of sombre yews, had risen high, not ten yards from the windows. The building, of greenish stone, was in the old English style, not ugly, but small-windowed and melancholy-looking: the sort of house that must have children, many flowers, open windows, and little vistas of bright things, to make it seem a joyous home. In this latter end of autumn, with a sparse remnant of yellow leaves falling slowly athwart the dark evergreens in a stillness without sunshine, the house too had an air of autumnal decline, and Mr Casaubon, when he presented himself, had no bloom that could be thrown into relief by that background.

'Oh dear!' Celia said to herself, 'I am sure Freshitt Hall would have been pleasanter than this.' She thought of the white freestone, the pillared portico, and the terrace full of flowers, Sir James smiling above them like a prince issuing from his enchantment in a rose-bush, with a handkerchief swiftly metamor-phosed from the most delicately-odorous petals – Sir James, who talked so agreeably, always about things which had common-sense in them, and not about learning! Celia had those light young feminine tastes which grave and weather-worn gentlemen sometimes prefer in a wife; but happily Mr Casaubon's bias had been different, for he would have had no chance with Celia.

Dorothea, on the contrary, found the house and grounds all that she could wish: the dark bookshelves in the long library, the carpets and curtains with colours subdued by time, the curious old maps and bird's-eye views on the walls of the corridor, with here and there an old vase below, had no oppression for her, and seemed more cheerful than the casts and pictures at the Grange, which her uncle had long ago brought home from his travels – they being probably among the ideas he had taken in at one time. To poor Dorothea these severe classical nudities and smirking Renaissance-Correggiosities were painfully inexplicable, staring into the midst of her Puritanic conceptions: she had never been taught how she could bring them into any sort of relevance with her life. But the owners of Lowick apparently had not been travellers, and Mr Casaubon's studies of the past were not carried on by means of such aids.

Dorothea walked about the house with delightful emotion. Everything seemed hallowed to her: this was to be the home of her wife-hood, and she looked up with eyes full of confidence to Mr Casaubon when he drew her attention specially to some actual arrangement and asked her if she would like an alteration.

All appeals to her taste she met gratefully but saw nothing to alter. His efforts at exact courtesy and formal tenderness had no defect for her. She filled up all blanks with unmanifested perfections, interpreting him as she interpreted the works of Providence, and accounting for seeming discords by her own deafness to the higher harmonies. And there are many blanks left in the weeks of court-ship, which a loving faith fills with happy assurance.

'Now, my dear Dorothea, I wish you to favour me by pointing out which room you would like to have as your boudoir,' said Mr Casaubon, showing that his views of the womanly nature were sufficiently large to include that requirement.

'It is very kind of you to think of that,' said Dorothea, 'but I assure you I would rather have all those matters decided for me. I shall be much happier to take everything as it is – just as you have been used to have it, or as you will yourself choose it to be. I have no motive for wishing anything else.'

'O Dodo,' said Celia, 'will you not have the bow-windowed room upstairs?'

Mr Casaubon led the way thither. The bow-window looked down the avenue of limes; the furniture was all of a faded blue, and there were miniatures of ladies and gentlemen with powdered hair hanging in a group. A piece of tapestry over a door also showed a blue-green world with a pale stag in it. The chairs and tables were thin-legged and easy to upset. It was a room where one might fancy the ghost of a tight-laced lady revisiting the scene of her embroidery. A light bookcase contained duodecimo volumes of polite literature in calf, completing the furniture.

'Yes,' said Mr Brooke, 'this would be a pretty room with some new hangings, sofas, and that sort of thing. A little bare now.'

'No, uncle,' said Dorothea, eagerly. 'Pray do not speak of altering anything. There are so many other things in the world that want altering – I like to take these things as they are. And you like them as they are, don't you?' she added, looking at Mr Casaubon. 'Perhaps this was your mother's room when she was young.'

'It was,' he said, with his slow bend of the head.

'This is your mother,' said Dorothea, who had turned to examine the group of miniatures. 'It is like the tiny one you brought me; only, I should think a better portrait. And this one opposite, who is this?'

'Her elder sister. They were, like you and your sister, the only two children of their parents, who hang above them, you see.'

'The sister is pretty,' said Celia, implying that she thought less favourably of Mr Casaubon's mother. It was a new opening to Celia's imagination, that he came of a family who had all been young in their time – the ladies wearing necklaces.

'It is a peculiar face,' said Dorothea, looking closely. 'Those deep grey eyes rather near together – and the delicate irregular nose with a sort of ripple in it – and all the powdered curls hanging backward. Altogether it seems to me peculiar rather than pretty. There is not even a family likeness between her and your mother.'

'No. And they were not alike in their lot.'

'You did not mention her to me,' said Dorothea.

'My aunt made an unfortunate marriage. I never saw her.'

Dorothea wondered a little, but felt that it would be indelicate just then to ask for any information which Mr Casaubon did not proffer, and she turned to the window to admire the view. The sun had lately pierced the grey, and the avenue of limes cast shadows.

'Shall we not walk in the garden now?' said Dorothea.

'And you would like to see the church, you know,' said Mr Brooke. 'It is a droll little church. And the village. It all lies in a nutshell. By the way, it will suit you, Dorothea; for the cottages are like a row of alms-houses – little gardens, gillyflowers, that sort of thing.'

'Yes, please,' said Dorothea, looking at Mr Casaubon, 'I should like to see all that.' She had got nothing from him more graphic about the Lowick cottages than that they were 'not bad'.

They were soon on a gravel walk which led chiefly between grassy borders and clumps of trees, this being the nearest way to the church, Mr Casaubon said. At the little gate leading into the churchyard there was a pause while Mr Casaubon went to the parsonage close by to fetch a key. Celia, who had been hanging a little in the rear, came up presently, when she saw that Mr Casaubon was gone away, and said in her easy staccato, which always seemed to contradict the suspicion of any malicious intent: 'Do you know, Dorothea, I saw someone quite young coming up one of the walks.'

'Is that astonishing, Celia?'

'There may be a young gardener, you know – why not?' said Mr Brooke. 'I told Casaubon he should change his gardener.'

'No, not a gardener,' said Celia; 'a gentleman with a sketchbook. He had light-brown curls. I only saw his back. But he was quite young.'

'The curate's son, perhaps,' said Mr Brooke. 'Ah, there is Casaubon again, and Tucker with him. He is going to introduce Tucker. You don't know Tucker yet.'

Mr Tucker was the middle-aged curate, one of the 'inferior clergy', who are usually not wanting in sons. But after the introduction, the conversation did not lead to any question about his family, and the startling apparition of youthfulness was forgotten by everyone but Celia. She inwardly declined to believe that the light-brown curls and slim figure could have any relationship to Mr Tucker, who was just as old and musty-looking as she would have expected Mr Casaubon's curate to be; doubtless an excellent man who would go to heaven (for Celia wished not to be unprincipled), but the corners of his mouth were so unpleasant. Celia thought with some dismalness of the time she should have to spend as bridesmaid at Lowick, where the curate had probably no pretty little children whom she could like, irrespective of principle.

Mr Tucker was invaluable in their walk; and perhaps Mr Casaubon had not been without foresight on this head, the curate being able to answer all Dorothea's questions about the villagers and the other parishioners. Everybody, he assured her, was well off in Lowick: not a cottager in those double cottages at a low rent but kept a pig, and the strips of garden at the back were well tended.

The small boys wore excellent corduroy, the girls went out as tidy servants, or did a little straw-plaiting at home: no looms here, no Dissent; and though the public disposition was rather towards laying by money than towards spirituality, there was not much vice. The speckled fowls were so numerous that Mr Brooke observed, 'Your farmers leave some barley for the women to glean, I see. The poor folks here might have a fowl in their pot, as the good French king used to wish for all his people. The French eat a good many fowls – skinny fowls, you know.'

'I think it was a very cheap wish of his,' said Dorothea, indignantly. 'Are kings such monsters that a wish like that must be reckoned a royal virtue?'

'And if he wished them a skinny fowl,' said Celia, 'that would not be nice. But perhaps he wished them to have fat fowls.'

'Yes, but the word has dropped out of the text, or perhaps was *subauditum*; that is, present in the king's mind, but not uttered,' said Mr Casaubon, smiling and bending his head to wards Celia, who immediately dropped backward a little, because she could not bear Mr Casaubon to blink at her.

Dorothea sank into silence on the way back to the house. She felt some disappointment, of which she was yet ashamed, that there was nothing for her to do in Lowick; and in the next few minutes her mind had glanced over the possibility, which she would have preferred, of finding that her home would be in a parish which had a larger share of the world's misery, so that she might have had more active duties in it. Then, recurring to the future actually before her, she made a picture of more complete devotion to Mr Casaubon's aims, in which she would await new duties. Many such might reveal themselves to the higher knowledge gained by her in that companionship.

Mr Tucker soon left them, having some clerical work which would not allow him to lunch at the Hall; and as they were re-entering the garden through the little gate, Mr Casaubon said: 'You seem a little sad, Dorothea. I trust you are pleased with what you have seen.'

'I am feeling something which is perhaps foolish and wrong,' answered Dorothea, with her usual openness – 'almost wishing that the people wanted more to be done for them here. I have known so few ways of making my life good for anything. Of course, my notions of usefulness must be narrow. I must learn new ways of helping people.'

'Doubtless,' said Mr Casaubon. 'Each position has its corresponding duties. Yours, I trust, as the mistress of Lowick, will not leave any yearning unfulfilled.'

'Indeed, I believe that,' said Dorothea, earnestly. 'Do not suppose that I am sad.'

'That is well. But, if you are not tired, we will take another way to the house than that by which we came.'

Dorothea was not at all tired, and a little circuit was made towards a fine yew tree, the chief hereditary glory of the grounds on this side of the house. As they approached it, a figure, conspicuous on a dark background of evergreens, was seated on a bench, sketching the old tree. Mr Brooke, who was walking in front with Celia, turned his head, and said: 'Who is that youngster, Casaubon?'

They had come very near when Mr Casaubon answered: 'That is a young relative of mine, a second cousin: the grandson, in fact,' he added, looking at Dorothea, 'of the lady whose portrait you have been noticing, my aunt Julia.'

The younger man had laid down his sketchbook and risen. His bushy light-brown curls, as well as his youthfulness, identified him at once with Celia's apparition.

'Dorothea, let me introduce to you my cousin, Mr Ladislaw. Will, this is Miss Brooke.'

The cousin was so close now, that, when he lifted his hat, Dorothea could see a pair of grey eyes rather near together, a delicate irregular nose with a little ripple in it, and hair falling backward; but there was a mouth and chin of a more prominent, threatening aspect than belonged to the type of the grandmother's miniature. Young Ladislaw did not feel it necessary to smile, as if he were charmed with this introduction to his future second cousin and her relatives; but wore rather a pouting air of discontent.

'You are an artist, I see,' said Mr Brooke, taking up the sketchbook and turning it over in his unceremonious fashion.

'No, I only sketch a little. There is nothing fit to be seen there,' said young Ladislaw, colouring, perhaps with temper rather than modesty.

'Oh, come, this is a nice bit, now. I did a little in this way myself at one time, you know. Look here, now; this is what I call a nice thing, done with what we used to call *brio*.' Mr Brooke held out towards the two girls a large coloured sketch of stony ground and trees, with a pool.

'I am no judge of these things,' said Dorothea, not coldly, but with an eager deprecation of the appeal to her. 'You know, uncle, I never see the beauty of those pictures which you say are so much praised. They are a language I do not understand. I suppose there is some relation between pictures and nature which I am too ignorant to feel – just as you see what a Greek sentence stands for which means nothing to me.' Dorothea looked up at Mr Casaubon, who bowed his head towards her while Mr Brooke said, smiling nonchalantly: 'Bless me, now, how different people are! But you had a bad style of teaching, you know – else this is just the thing for girls – sketching, fine art and so on. But you took to drawing plans; you don't understand *morbidezza*, and that kind of thing. You will come to my house, I hope, and I will show you what I did in this way,' he continued, turning to young Ladislaw, who had to be recalled from his pre-occupation in observing Dorothea. Ladislaw had made up his mind that she must be an unpleasant girl, since she was going to marry Casaubon, and what she said of her stupidity about pictures would have confirmed that opinion even if he had believed her. As it was, he took her words for a covert judgement, and was certain that she thought his sketch detestable. There was too much clever-ness in her apology: she was laughing both at her uncle and himself. But what a voice! It was like the voice of a soul that had once lived in an Aeolian harp. This must be one of Nature's inconsistencies. There could be no sort of passion in a girl who would marry Casaubon. But he turned from her, and bowed his thanks for Mr Brooke's invitation.

'We will turn over my Italian engravings together,' continued that good-natured man. 'I have no end of those things, that I have laid by for years. One gets rusty in this part of the country, you know. Not you, Casaubon; you stick to your studies; but my best ideas get undermost – out of use, you know. You clever young men must guard against indolence. I was too indolent, you know: else I might have been anywhere at one time.'

'That is a seasonable admonition,' said Mr Casaubon; 'but now we will pass on to the house, lest the young ladies should be tired of standing.'

When their backs were turned, young Ladislaw sat down to go on with his sketching, and as he did so his face broke into an expression of amusement which increased as he went on drawing, till at last he threw back his head and laughed aloud. Partly it was the reception of his own artistic production that tickled him; partly the notion of his grave cousin as the lover of that girl; and partly Mr Brooke's definition of the place he might have held but for the impediment of indolence. Mr Will Ladislaw's sense of the ludicrous lit up his features very agreeably: it was the pure enjoyment of comicality, and had no mixture of sneering and self-exaltation.

'What is your nephew going to do with himself, Casaubon?' said Mr Brooke, as they went on.

'My cousin, you mean – not my nephew.'

'Yes, yes, cousin. But in the way of a career, you know.'

'The answer to that question is painfully doubtful. On leaving Rugby he declined to go to an English university, where I would gladly have placed him, and chose what I must consider the anomalous course of studying at Heidelberg. And now he wants to go abroad again, without any special object, save the vague purpose of what he calls culture, preparation for he knows not what. He declines to choose a profession.'

'He has no means but what you furnish, I suppose.'

'I have always given him and his friends reason to understand that I would furnish in moderation what was necessary for providing him with a scholarly education, and launching him respectably. I am therefore bound to fulfil the expectation so raised,' said Mr Casaubon, putting his conduct in the light of mere rectitude: a trait of delicacy which Dorothea noticed with admiration.

'He has a thirst for travelling; perhaps he may turn out a Bruce or a Mungo Park,' said Mr Brooke. 'I had a notion of that myself at one time.'

'No, he has no bent towards exploration, or the enlargement of our geognosis: that would be a special purpose which I could recognise with some approbation, though without felicitating him on a career which so often ends in premature and violent death. But so far is he from having any desire for a more accurate knowledge of the earth's surface, that he said he should prefer not to know the sources of the Nile, and that there should be some unknown regions preserved as hunting-grounds for the poetic imagination.'

'Well, there is something in that, you know,' said Mr Brooke, who had certainly an impartial mind.

'It is, I fear, nothing more than a part of his general inaccuracy and indisposition to thoroughness of all kinds, which would be a bad augury for him in any profession, civil or sacred, even were he so far submissive to ordinary rule as to choose one.'

'Perhaps he has conscientious scruples founded on his own unfitness,' said Dorothea, who was interesting herself in finding a favourable explanation. 'Because the law and medicine should be very serious professions to undertake, should they not? People's lives and fortunes depend on them.'

'Doubtless; but I fear that my young relative Will Ladislaw is chiefly determined in his aversion to these callings by a dislike to steady application, and to that kind of acquirement which is needful instrumentally, but is not charming or immediately inviting to self-indulgent taste. I have insisted to him on what Aristotle has stated with admirable brevity, that for the achievement of any work regarded as an end there must be a prior exercise of many energies or acquired facilities of a secondary order, demanding patience. I have pointed to my own manuscript volumes, which represent the toil of years preparatory to a work not yet accomplished. But in vain. To careful reasoning of this kind he replies by calling himself Pegasus, and every form of prescribed work "harness".'

Celia laughed. She was surprised to find that Mr Casaubon could say something quite amusing.

'Well, you know, he may turn out a Byron, a Chatterton, a Churchill – that sort of thing – there's no telling,' said Mr Brooke. 'Shall you let him go to Italy, or wherever else he wants to go?'

'Yes; I have agreed to furnish him with moderate supplies for a year or so; he asks no more. I shall let him be tried by the test of freedom.'

'That is very kind of you,' said Dorothea, looking up at Mr Casaubon with delight. 'It is noble. After all, people may really have in them some vocation which is not quite plain to themselves, may they not? They may seem idle and weak because they are growing. We should be very patient with each other, I think.'

'I suppose it is being engaged to be married that has made you think patience good,' said Celia, as soon as she and Dorothea were alone together, taking off their wrappings.

'You mean that I am very impatient, Celia.'

'Yes; when people don't do and say just what you like.' Celia had become less afraid of 'saying things' to Dorothea since this engagement; cleverness seemed to her more pitiable than ever.

Chapter 10

He had catched a great cold, had he had no other clothes
to wear than the skin of a bear not yet killed.

FULLER

Young Ladislaw did not pay that visit to which Mr Brooke had invited him, and only six days afterwards Mr Casaubon mentioned that his young relative had started for the Continent, seeming by this cold vagueness to waive enquiry. Indeed, Will had declined to fix on any more precise destination than the entire area of Europe. Genius, he held, is necessarily intolerant of fetters: on the one hand it must have the utmost play for its spontaneity; on the other, it may confidently await those messages from the universe which summon it to its peculiar work, only placing itself in an attitude of receptivity towards all sublime chances. The attitudes of receptivity are various, and Will had sincerely tried many of them. He was not excessively fond of wine, but he had several times taken too much, simply as an experiment in that form of ecstasy; he had fasted till he was faint, and then supped on lobster; he had made himself ill with doses of opium. Nothing greatly original had resulted from these measures; and the effects of the opium had convinced him that there was an entire dissimilarity between his constitution and De Quincey's. The super-added circumstance which would evolve the genius had not yet come; the universe had not yet beckoned. Even Caesar's fortune at one time was but a grand presentiment. We know what a masquerade all development is, and what effective shapes may be disguised in helpless embryos. In fact, the world is full of hopeful analogies and handsome dubious eggs called possibilities. Will saw clearly enough the pitiable instances of long incubation producing no chick, and but for gratitude would have laughed at Casaubon, whose plodding application, rows of notebooks, and small taper of learned theory exploring the tossed ruins of the world, seemed to enforce a moral entirely encouraging to Will's generous reliance on the intentions of the universe with regard to himself. He held that reliance to be a mark of genius; and certainly it is no mark to the contrary; genius consisting neither in self-conceit nor in humility, but in a power to make or do, not anything in general, but something in particular. Let him start for the Continent, then, without our pronouncing on his future. Among all forms of mistake, prophecy is the most gratuitous.

But at present this caution against a too hasty judgement interests me more in relation to Mr Casaubon than to his young cousin. If to Dorothea Mr Casaubon had been the mere occasion which had set alight the fine inflammable material of her youthful illusions, does it follow that he was fairly represented in the minds of those less impassioned personages who have hitherto delivered their judgements concerning him? I protest against any absolute conclusion, any prejudice derived from Mrs Cadwallader's contempt for a neighbouring clergyman's alleged greatness of soul, of Sir James Chettam's poor opinion of his rival's legs, from Mr Brooke's failure to elicit a companion's ideas, or from Celia's criticism of a middle-aged scholar's personal appearance. I am not sure that the greatest man of his age, if ever that solitary superlative existed, could escape these unfavourable reflections of himself in various small mirrors; and even Milton, looking for his portrait in a spoon, must submit to have the facial angle of a bumpkin. Moreover, if Mr Casaubon, speaking for himself, has rather chilling rhetoric, it is not therefore certain that there is no good work or fine feeling in him. Did not an immortal physicist and interpreter of hieroglyphs write detestable verses? Has the theory of the solar system been advanced by graceful manners and conversational tact? Suppose we turn from outside estimates of a man, to wonder, with keener interest, what is the report of his own consciousness about his doings or capacity: with what hindrances he is carrying on his daily labours; what fading of hopes, or what deeper fixity of self-delusion the years are marking off within him; and with what spirit he wrestles against universal pressure, which will one day be too heavy for him, and bring his heart to its final pause. Doubtless his lot is important in his own eyes; and the chief reason that we think he asks too large a place in our consideration must be our want of room for him, since we refer him to the Divine regard with perfect confidence; nay, it is even held sublime for our neighbour to expect the utmost there, however little he may have got from us. Mr Casaubon, too, was the centre of his own world; if he was liable to think that others were providentially made for him, and especially to consider them in the light of their fitness for the author of a *Key to all Mythologies*, this trait is not quite alien to us, and, like the other mendicant hopes of mortals, claims some of our pity.

Certainly this affair of his marriage with Miss Brooke touched him more nearly than it did any one of the persons who have hitherto shown their dis- approval of it, and in the present stage of things I feel more tenderly towards his experience of success than towards the disappointment of the amiable Sir James. For in truth, as the day fixed for his marriage came nearer, Mr Casaubon did not find his spirits rising; nor did the contemplation of that matrimonial garden- scene, where, as all experience showed, the path was to be bordered with flowers, prove persistently more enchanting to him than the accustomed vaults where he walked taper in hand. He did not confess to himself, still less could he have breathed to another, his surprise that though he had won a lovely and noble- hearted girl he had not won delight, – which he had also regarded as an object to be found by search. It is true that he knew all the classical passages implying the contrary; but knowing classical passages, we find, is a mode of motion, which explains why they leave so little extra force for their personal application.

Poor Mr Casaubon had imagined that his long studious bachelorhood had stored up for him a compound interest of enjoyment, and that large drafts on his affections would not fail to be honoured; for we all of us, grave or light, get our thoughts entangled in metaphors, and act fatally on the strength of them. And now he was in danger of being saddened by the very conviction that his circum- stances were unusually happy: there was nothing external by which he could account for a certain blankness of sensibility which came over him just when his expectant gladness should have been most lively, just when he exchanged the accustomed dulness of his Lowick library for his visits to the Grange. Here was a weary experience in which he was as utterly condemned to loneliness as in the despair which sometimes threatened him while toiling in the morass of author- ship without seeming nearer to the goal. And his was that worst loneliness which would shrink from sympathy. He could not but wish that Dorothea should think him not less happy than the world would expect her successful suitor to be; and in relation to his authorship he leaned on her young trust and veneration, he liked to draw forth her fresh interest in listening, as a means of encouragement to himself: in talking to her he presented all his performance and intention with the reflected confidence of the pedagogue, and rid himself for the time of that chilling ideal audience which crowded his laborious uncreative hours with the vaporous pressure of Tartarean shades.

For to Dorothea, after that toy-box history of the world adapted to young ladies which had made the chief part of her education, Mr Casaubon's talk about his great book was full of new vistas; and this sense of revelation, this surprise of a nearer introduction to Stoics and Alexandrians, as people who had ideas not totally unlike her own, kept in abeyance for the time her usual eagerness for a binding theory which could bring her own life and doctrine into strict connection with that amazing past, and give the remotest sources of knowledge some bearing on her actions. That more complete teaching would come – Mr Casaubon would tell her all that: she was looking forward to higher initiation in ideas, as she was looking forward to marriage, and blending her dim conceptions of both. It would be a great mistake to suppose that Dorothea would have cared about any share in Mr Casaubon's learning as mere accomplishment; for though opinion in the neighbourhood of Freshitt and Tipton had pronounced her clever, that epithet would not have described her to circles in whose more precise vocabulary cleverness implies mere aptitude for knowing and doing, apart from character. All her eagerness for acquirement lay within that full current of sympathetic motive in which her ideas and impulses were habitually swept along. She did not want to deck herself with knowledge – to wear it loose from the nerves and blood that fed her action; and if she had written a book she must have done it as Saint Theresa did, under the command of an authority that constrained her conscience. But something she yearned for by which her life might be filled with action at once rational and ardent; and since the time was gone by for guiding visions and spiritual directors, since prayer heightened yearning but not instruction, what lamp was there but knowledge? Surely learned men kept the only oil; and who more learned than Mr Casaubon?

Thus in these brief weeks Dorothea's joyous grateful expectation was unbroken, and however her lover might occasionally be conscious of flatness, he could never refer it to any slackening of her affectionate interest.

The season was mild enough to encourage the project of extending the wedding journey as far as Rome, and Mr Casaubon was anxious for this because he wished to inspect some manuscripts in the Vatican.

'I still regret that your sister is not to accompany us,' he said one morning, some time after it had been ascertained that Celia objected to go, and that Dorothea did not wish for her companionship. 'You will have many lonely hours, Dorothea, for I shall be constrained to make the utmost use of my time during our stay in Rome, and I should feel more at liberty if you had a companion.'

The words 'I should feel more at liberty' grated on Dorothea. For the first time in speaking to Mr Casaubon she coloured from annoyance.

'You must have misunderstood me very much,' she said, 'if you think I should not enter into the value of your time – if you think that I should not willingly give up whatever interfered with your using it to the best purpose.'

'That is very amiable in you, my dear Dorothea,' said Mr Casaubon, not in the least noticing that she was hurt 'but if you had a lady as your companion, I could put you both under the care of a cicerone, and we could thus achieve two purposes in the same space of time.'

'I beg you will not refer to this again,' said Dorothea, rather haughtily. But immediately she feared that she was wrong, and turning toward him she laid her hand on his, adding in a different tone, 'Pray do not be anxious about me. I shall have so much to think of when I am alone. And Tantripp will be a sufficient companion, just to take care of me. I could not bear to have Celia: she would be miserable.'

It was time to dress. There was to be a dinner-party that day, the last of the parties which were held at the Grange as proper preliminaries to the wedding, and Dorothea was glad of a reason for moving away at once on the sound of the bell, as if she needed more than her usual amount of preparation. She was ashamed of being irritated from some cause she could not define even to herself; for though she had no intention to be untruthful, her reply had not touched the real hurt within her. Mr Casaubon's words had been quite reasonable, yet they had brought a vague instantaneous sense of aloofness on his part.

'Surely I am in a strangely selfish weak state of mind,' she said to herself. 'How can I have a husband who is so much above me without knowing that he needs me less than I need him?'

Having convinced herself that Mr Casaubon was altogether right, she recovered her equanimity, and was an agreeable image of serene dignity when she came into the drawing-room in her silver-grey dress – the simple lines of her dark-brown hair parted over her brow and coiled massively behind, in keeping with the entire absence from her manner and expression of all search after mere effect. Sometimes when Dorothea was in company, there seemed to be as complete an air of repose about her as if she had been a picture of Santa Barbara looking out from her tower into the clear air; but these intervals of quietude made the energy of her speech and emotion the more remarked when some outward appeal had touched her.

She was naturally the subject of many observations this evening, for the dinner-party was large and rather more miscellaneous as to the male portion than any which had been held at the Grange since Mr Brooke's nieces had resided with him, so that the talking was done in duos and trios more or less inharmonious. There was the newly-elected mayor of Middlemarch, who happened to be a manufacturer; the philanthropic banker his brother-in-law, who predominated so much in the town that some called him a Methodist, others a hypocrite, according to the resources of their vocabulary; and there were various professional men. In fact Mrs Cadwallader said that Brooke was beginning to treat the Middle-marchers, and that she preferred the farmers at the tithe-dinner, who drank her health unpretentiously, and were not ashamed of their grandfathers' furniture. For in that part of the country, before Reform had done its notable part in developing the political consciousness, there was a clearer distinction of ranks and a dimmer distinction of parties; so that Mr Brooke's miscellaneous invitations seemed to belong to that general laxity which came from his inordinate travel and habit of taking too much in the form of ideas.

Already, as Miss Brooke passed out of the dining-room, opportunity was found for some interjectional 'asides'.

'A fine woman, Miss Brooke! an uncommonly fine woman, by God !' said Mr Standish, the old lawyer, who had been so long concerned with the landed gentry that he had become landed himself, and used that oath in a deep-mouthed manner as a sort of armorial bearings, stamping the speech of a man who held a good position.

Mr Bulstrode, the banker, seemed to be addressed, but that gentleman disliked coarseness and profanity, and merely bowed. The remark was taken up by Mr Chichely, a middle-aged bachelor and coursing celebrity, who had a complexion something like an Easter egg, a few hairs carefully arranged, and a carriage implying the consciousness of a distinguished appearance.

'Yes, but not my style of woman: I like a woman who lays herself out a little more to please us. There should be a little filigree about a woman – something of the coquette. A man likes a sort of challenge. The more of a dead set she makes at you the better.'

'There's some truth in that,' said Mr Standish, disposed to be genial. 'And, by God, it's usually the way with them. I suppose it answers some wise ends: Providence made them so, eh, Bulstrode?'

'I should be disposed to refer coquetry to another source,' said Mr Bulstrode. 'I should rather refer it to the devil.'

'Ay, to be sure, there should be a little devil in a woman,' said Mr Chichely, whose study of the fair sex seemed to have been detrimental to his theology. 'And I like them blond, with a certain gait, and a swan neck. Between ourselves, the mayor's daughter is more to my taste than Miss Brooke or Miss Celia either. If I were a marrying man I should choose Miss Vincy before either of them.'

'Well, make up, make up,' said Mr Standish, jocosely; 'you see the middle-aged fellows carry the day.'

Mr Chichely shook his head with much meaning: he was not going to incur the certainty of being accepted by the woman he would choose.

The Miss Vincy who had the honour of being Mr Chichely's ideal was of course not present; for Mr Brooke, always objecting to go too far, would not have chosen that his nieces should meet the daughter of a Middlemarch manufacturer, unless it were on a public occasion. The feminine part of the company included none whom Lady Chettam or Mrs Cadwallader could object to; for Mrs Renfrew, the colonel's widow, was not only unexceptionable in point of breeding, but also interesting on the ground of her complaint, which puzzled the doctors, and seemed clearly a case wherein the fullness of professional knowledge might need the supplement of quackery. Lady Chettam, who attributed her own remarkable health to home-made bitters united with constant medical attendance, entered with much exercise of the imagination into Mrs Renfrew's account of symptoms, and into the amazing futility in her case of all strengthening medicines.

'Where can all the strength of those medicines go, my dear?' said the mild but stately dowager, turning to Mrs Cadwallader reflectively, when Mrs Renfrew's attention was called away.

'It strengthens the disease,' said the Rector's wife, much too well – born not to be an amateur in medicine. 'Everything depends on the constitution: some people make fat, some blood, and some bile – that's my view of the matter; and whatever they take is a sort of grist to the mill.'

'Then she ought to take medicines that would reduce – reduce the disease, you know, if you are right, my dear. And I think what you say is reasonable.'

'Certainly it is reasonable. You have two sorts of potatoes, fed on the same soil. One of them grows more and more watery – '

'Ah! like this poor Mrs Renfrew – that is what I think. Dropsy! There is no swelling yet – it is inward. I should say she ought to take drying medicines, shouldn't you? – or a dry hot-air bath. Many things might be tried, of a drying nature.'

'Let her try a certain person's pamphlets,' said Mrs Cadwallader in an under-tone, seeing the gentlemen enter. 'He does not want drying.'

'Who, my dear?' said Lady Chettam, a charming woman, not so quick as to nullify the pleasure of explanation.

'The bridegroom – Casaubon. He has certainly been drying up faster since the engagement: the flame of passion, I suppose.'

'I should think he is far from having a good constitution,' said Lady Chettam, with a still deeper undertone. 'And then his studies – so very dry, as you say.'

'Really, by the side of Sir James, he looks like a death's head skinned over for the occasion. Mark my words: in a year from this time that girl will hate him. She looks up to him as an oracle now, and by and by she will be at the other extreme. All flightiness!'

'How very shocking! I fear she is headstrong. But tell me you know all about him – is there anything very bad? What is the truth?'

'The truth? he is as bad as the wrong physic – nasty to take, and sure to disagree.'

'There could not be anything worse than that,' said Lady Chettam, with so vivid a conception of the physic that she seemed to have learned something exact about Mr Casaubon's disadvantages. 'However, James will hear nothing about Miss Brooke. He says she is the mirror of women still.'

'That is a generous make-believe of his. Depend upon it, he likes little Celia better, and she appreciates him. I hope you like my little Celia?'

'Certainly; she is fonder of geraniums, and seems more docile, though not so fine a figure. But we were talking of physic: tell me about this new young surgeon, Mr Lydgate. I am told he is wonderfully clever: he certainly looks it – a fine brow indeed.'

'He is a gentleman. I heard him talking to Humphrey. He talks well.'

'Yes. Mr Brooke says he is one of the Lydgates of Northumberland, really well connected. One does not expect it in a practitioner of that kind. For my own part, I like a medical man more on a footing with the servants; they are often all the cleverer. I assure you I found poor Hicks's judgement unfailing; I never knew him wrong. He was coarse and butcher-like, but he knew my constitution. It was a loss to me his going off so suddenly. Dear me, what a very animated conversation Miss Brooke seems to be having with this Mr Lydgate !'

'She is talking cottages and hospitals with him,' said Mrs Cadwallader, whose ears and power of interpretation were quick. 'I believe he is a sort of philan-thropist, so Brooke is sure to take him up.'

'James,' said Lady Chettam when her son came near, 'bring Mr Lydgate and introduce him to me. I want to test him.'

The affable dowager declared herself delighted with this opportunity of making Mr Lydgate's acquaintance, having heard of his success in treating fever on a new plan.

Mr Lydgate had the medical accomplishment of looking perfectly grave whatever nonsense was talked to him, and his dark steady eyes gave him impressiveness as a listener. He was as little as possible like the lamented Hicks, especially in a certain careless refinement about his toilette and utterance. Yet Lady Chettam gathered much confidence in him. He confirmed her view of her own constitution as being peculiar, by admitting that all constitutions might be called peculiar, and he did not deny that hers might be more peculiar than others. He did not approve of a too lowering system, including reckless cupping, nor, on the other hand, of incessant port wine and bark. He said 'I think so' with an air of so much deference accompanying the insight of agreement, that she formed the most cordial opinion of his talents.

'I am quite pleased with your *protégé*,' she said to Mr Brooke before going away.

'My *protégé* ? – dear me! – who is that?' said Mr Brooke.

'This young Lydgate, the new doctor. He seems to me to understand his profession admirably.'

'Oh, Lydgate! he is not my *protégé*, you know; only I knew an uncle of his who sent me a letter about him. However, I think he is likely to be first-rate – has studied in Paris, knew Broussais; has ideas, you know – wants to raise the profession.'

'Lydgate has lots of ideas, quite new, about ventilation and diet, that sort of thing,' resumed Mr Brooke, after he had handed out Lady Chettam, and had returned to be civil to a group of Middlemarchers.

'Hang it, do you think that is quite sound? – upsetting the old treatment, which has made Englishmen what they are?' said Mr Standish.

'Medical knowledge is at a low ebb among us,' said Mr Bulstrode, who spoke in a subdued tone, and had rather a sickly air. 'I, for my part, hail the advent of Mr Lydgate. I hope to find good reason for confiding the new hospital to his management.'

'That is all very fine,' replied Mr Standish, who was not fond of Mr Bulstrode; 'if you like him to try experiments on your hospital patients, and kill a few people for charity, I have no objection. But I am not going to hand money out of my purse to have experiments tried on me. I like treatment that has been tested a little.'

'Well, you know, Standish, every dose you take is an experiment – an experiment, you know,' said Mr Brooke, nodding towards the lawyer.

'Oh, if you talk in that sense!' said Mr Standish, with as much disgust at such non-legal quibbling as a man can well betray towards a valuable client.

'I should be glad of any treatment that would cure me without reducing me to a skeleton, like poor Grainger,' said Mr Vincy, the mayor, a florid man, who would have served for a study of flesh in striking contrast with the Franciscan tints of Mr Bulstrode. 'It's an uncommonly dangerous thing to be left without any padding against the shafts of disease, as somebody said – and I think it a very good expression myself.'

Mr Lydgate, of course, was out of hearing. He had quitted the party early, and would have thought it altogether tedious but for the novelty of certain introductions, especially the introduction to Miss Brooke, whose youthful bloom, with her approaching marriage to that faded scholar, and her interest in matters socially useful, gave her the piquancy of an unusual combination.

'She is a good creature – that fine girl – but a little too earnest,' he thought. 'It is troublesome to talk to such women. They are always wanting reasons, yet they are too ignorant to understand the merits of any question, and usually fall back on their moral sense to settle things after their own taste.'

Evidently Miss Brooke was not Mr Lydgate's style of woman any more than Mr Chichely's. Considered, indeed, in relation to the latter, whose mind was matured, she was altogether a mistake, and calculated to shock his trust in final causes, including the adaptation of fine young women to purple-faced bachelors. But Lydgate was less ripe, and might possibly have experience before him which would modify his opinion as to the most excellent things in woman.

Miss Brooke, however, was not again seen by either of these gentlemen under her maiden name. Not long after that dinner-party she had become Mrs Casaubon, and was on her way to Rome.

Chapter 11

> But deeds and language such as men do use,
> And persons such as comedy would choose,
> When she would show an image of the times,
> And sport with human follies, not with crimes.
>
> BEN JONSON

Lydgate, in fact, was already conscious of being fascinated by a woman strikingly different from Miss Brooke: he did not in the least suppose that he had lost his balance and fallen in love but he had said of that particular woman, 'She is grace itself; she is perfectly lovely and accomplished. That is what a woman ought to be: she ought to produce the effect of exquisite music.' Plain women he regarded as he did the other severe facts of life, to be faced with philosophy and investigated by science. But Rosamond Vincy seemed to have the true melodic charm; and when a man has seen the woman whom he would have chosen if he had intended to marry speedily, his remaining a bachelor will usually depend on her resolution rather than on his. Lydgate believed that he should not marry for several years: not marry until he had trodden out a good clear path for himself away from the broad road which was quite ready made. He had seen Miss Vincy above his horizon almost as long as it had taken Mr Casaubon to become engaged and married: but this learned gentleman was possessed of a fortune; he had assembled his voluminous notes, and had made that sort of reputation which precedes performance, – often the larger part of a man's fame. He took a wife, as we have seen, to adorn the remaining quadrant of his course, and be a little moon that would cause hardly a calculable perturbation. But Lydgate was young, poor, ambitious. He had his half-century before him instead of behind him, and he had come to Middlemarch bent on doing many things that were not directly fitted to make his fortune or even secure him a good income. To a man under such circumstances, taking a wife is something more than a question of adornment, however highly he may rate this; and Lydgate was disposed to give it the first place among wifely functions. To his taste, guided by a single conversation, here was the point on which Miss Brooke would be found wanting, notwithstanding her undeniable beauty. She did not look at things from the proper feminine angle. The society of such women was about as relaxing as going from your work to teach the second form, instead of reclining in a paradise with sweet laughs for bird-notes, and blue eyes for a heaven.

Certainly nothing at present could seem much less important to Lydgate than the turn of Miss Brooke's mind, or to Miss Brooke than the qualities of the woman who had attracted this young surgeon. But anyone watching keenly the stealthy convergence of human lots, sees a slow preparation of effects from one life on another, which tells like a calculated irony on the indifference or the frozen stare with which we look at our unintroduced neighbour. Destiny stands by sarcastic with our *dramatis personae* folded in her hand.

Old provincial society had its share of this subtle movement: had not only its striking downfalls, its brilliant young professional dandies who ended by living up an entry with a drab and six children for their establishment, but also those less marked vicissitudes which are constantly shifting the boundaries of social intercourse, and begetting new consciousness of interdependence. Some slipped a little downward, some got higher footing: people denied aspirates, gained wealth, and fastidious gentlemen stood for boroughs; some were caught in political currents, some in ecclesiastical, and perhaps found themselves surprisingly grouped in consequence; while a few personages or families that stood with rock firmness amid all this fluctuation, were slowly presenting new aspects in spite of solidity, and altering with the double change of self and beholder. Municipal town and rural parish gradually made fresh threads of connection – gradually, as the old stocking gave way to the savings-bank, and the worship of the solar guinea became extinct, while squires and baronets, and even lords who had once lived blamelessly afar from the civic mind, gathered the faultiness of closer acquaintanceship. Settlers, too, came from distant counties, some with an alarming novelty of skill, others with an offensive advantage in cunning. In fact, much the same we find in older Herodotus, who also, in telling what had been, thought it well to take a woman's lot for his starting-point; though Io, as a maiden apparently beguiled by attractive merchandise, was the reverse of Miss Brooke, and in this respect perhaps bore more resemblance to Rosamond Vincy, who had excellent taste in costume, with that nymphlike figure and pure blondness which gave the largest range to choice in the flow and colour of drapery. But these things made only part of her charm. She was admitted to be the flower of Mrs Lemon's school, the chief school in the county, where the teaching included all that was demanded in the accomplished female – even to extras, such as the getting in and out of a carriage. Mrs Lemon herself had always held up Miss Vincy as an example: no pupil, she said, exceeded that young lady for mental acquisition and propriety of speech, while her musical execution was quite exceptional. We cannot help the way in which people speak of us, and probably if Mrs Lemon had undertaken to describe Juliet or Imogen, these heroines would not have seemed poetical. The first vision of Rosamond would have been enough with most judges to dispel any prejudice excited by Mrs Lemon's praise.

Lydgate could not be long in Middlemarch without having that agreeable vision, or even without making the acquaintance of the Vincy family; for though Mr Peacock whose practice he had paid something to enter on, had not been their doctor (Mrs Vincy not liking the lowering system adopted by him), he had many patients among their connections and acquaintances. For who of any consequence in Middlemarch was not connected or at least acquainted with the Vincys? They were old manufacturers, and had kept a good house for three generations, in which there had naturally been much intermarrying with neighbours more or less decidedly genteel. Mr Vincy's sister had made a wealthy match in accepting Mr Bulstrode, who, however, as a man not born in the town, and altogether of dimly known origin, was considered to have done well in uniting himself with a real Middlemarch family; on the other hand, Mr Vincy had descended a little, having taken an innkeeper's daughter. But on this side too there was a cheering sense of money; for Mrs Vincy's sister had been second wife to rich old Mr Featherstone, and had died childless years ago, so that her nephews and nieces might be supposed to touch the affections of the widower. And it happened that Mr Bulstrode and Mr Featherstone, two of Peacock's most important patients, had, from different causes, given an especially good reception to his successor, who had raised some partisanship as well as discussion. Mr Wrench, medical attendant to the Vincy family, very early had grounds for thinking lightly of Lydgate's professional discretion, and there was no report about him which was not retailed at the Vincy's, where visitors were frequent. Mr Vincy was more inclined to general good-fellowship than to taking sides, but there was no need for him to be hasty in making any new man's acquaintance. Rosamond silently wished that her father would invite Mr Lydgate. She was tired of the faces and figures she had always been used to – the various irregular profiles and gaits and turns of phrase distinguishing those Middlemarch young men whom she had known as boys. She had been at school with girls of higher position, whose brothers, she felt sure, it would have been possible for her to be more interested in, than in these inevitable Middlemarch companions. But she would not have chosen to mention her wish to her father; and he, for his part, was in no hurry on the subject. An alderman about to be mayor must by and by enlarge his dinner-parties, but at present there were plenty of guests at his well-spread table.

That table often remained covered with the relics of the family breakfast long after Mr Vincy had gone with his second son to the warehouse, and when Miss Morgan was already far on in morning lessons with the younger girls in the schoolroom. It awaited the family laggard, who found any sort of inconvenience (to others) less disagreeable than getting up when he was called. This was the case one morning of the October in which we have lately seen Mr Casaubon visiting the Grange; and though the room was a little overheated with the fire, which had sent the spaniel panting to a remote corner, Rosamond, for some reason, continued to sit at her embroidery longer than usual, now and then giving herself a little shake, and laying her work on her knee to contemplate it with an air of hesitating weariness. Her mamma, who had returned from an excursion to the kitchen, sat on the other side of the small work-table with an air of more entire placidity, until, the clock again giving notice that it was going to strike, she looked up from the lace-mending which was occupying her plump fingers and rang the bell.

'Knock at Mr Fred's door again, Pritchard, and tell him it has struck half-past ten.'

This was said without any change in the radiant good-humour of Mrs Vincy's face, in which forty-five years had delved neither angles nor parallels; and pushing back her pink cap-strings, she let her work rest on her lap, while she looked admiringly at her daughter.

'Mamma,' said Rosamond, 'when Fred comes down I wish you would not let him have red herrings. I cannot bear the smell of them all over the house at this hour of the morning.'

'Oh, my dear, you are so hard on your brothers! It is the only fault I have to find with you. You are the sweetest temper in the world, but are so tetchy with your brothers.'

'Not tetchy, mamma; you never hear me speak in an unladylike way.'

'Well, but you want to deny them things.'

'Brothers are so unpleasant.'

'Oh, my dear, you must allow for young men. Be thankful if they have good hearts. A woman must learn to put up with little things. You will be married someday.'

'Not to anyone who is like Fred.'

'Don't decry your own brother, my dear. Few young men have less against them, although he couldn't take his degree. I'm sure I can't understand why, for he seems to me most clever. And you know yourself he was thought equal to the best society at college. So particular as you are, my dear, I wonder you are not glad to have such a gentlemanly young man for a brother. You are always finding fault with Bob because he is not Fred.'

'Oh no, mamma, only because he is Bob.'

'Well, my dear, you will not find any Middlemarch young man who has not something against him.'

'But' – here Rosamond's face broke into a smile which suddenly revealed two dimples. She herself thought unfavourably of these dimples and smiled little in general society. 'But I shall not marry any Middlemarch young man.'

'So it seems, my love, for you have as good as refused the pick of them; and if there's better to be had, I'm sure there's no girl better deserves it.'

'Excuse me, mamma – I wish you would not say, "the pick of them".'

'Why, what else are they?'

'I mean, mamma, it is rather a vulgar expression.'

'Very likely, my dear; I never was a good speaker. What should I say?'

'The best of them.'

'Why, that seems just as plain and common. If I had had time to think, I should have said, "the most superior young men". But with your education you must know.'

'What must Rosy know, mother?' said Mr Fred, who had slid in unobserved through the half-open door while the ladies were bending over their work, and now going up to the fire stood with his back towards it, warming the soles of his slippers.

'Whether it's right to say "superior young men",' said Mrs Vincy ringing the bell.

'Oh, there are so many superior teas and sugars now. Superior is getting to be shopkeepers' slang.'

'Are you beginning to dislike slang, then?' said Rosamond, with mild gravity.

'Only the wrong sort. All choice of words is slang. It marks a class.'

'There is correct English: that is not slang.'

'I beg your pardon: correct English is the slang of prigs who write history and essays. And the strongest slang of all is the slang of poets.'

'You will say anything, Fred, to gain your point.'

'Well, tell me whether it is slang or poetry to call an ox a *leg-plaiter*.'

'Of course you can call it poetry if you like.'

'Aha, Miss Rosy, you don't know Homer from slang. I shall invent a new game; I shall write bits of slang and poetry on slips, and give them to you to separate.'

'Dear me, how amusing it is to hear young people talk !' said Mrs Vincy, with cheerful admiration.

'Have you got nothing else for my breakfast, Pritchard?' said Fred, to the servant who brought in coffee and buttered toast; while he walked round the table surveying the ham, potted beef, and other cold remnants, with an air of silent rejection, and polite forbearance from signs of disgust.

'Should you like eggs, sir?'

'Eggs, no! Bring me a grilled bone.'

'Really, Fred,' said Rosamond, when the servant had left the room, 'if you must have hot things for breakfast, I wish you would come down earlier. You can get up at six o'clock to go out hunting; I cannot understand why you find it so difficult to get up on other mornings.'

'That is your want of understanding, Rosy. I can get up to go hunting because I like it.'

'What would you think of me if I came down two hours after everyone else and ordered grilled bone?'

'I should think you were an uncommonly fast young lady,' said Fred, eating his toast with the utmost composure.

'I cannot see why brothers are to make themselves disagreeable, any more than sisters.'

'I don't make myself disagreeable; it is you who find me so. Disagreeable is a word that describes your feelings and not my actions.'

'I think it describes the smell of grilled bone.'

'Not at all. It describes a sensation in your little nose associated with certain finicking notions which are the classics of Mrs Lemon's school. Look at my mother: you don't see her objecting to everything except what she does herself. She is my notion of a pleasant woman.'

'Bless you both, my dears, and don't quarrel,' said Mrs Vincy, with motherly cordiality. 'Come, Fred, tell us all about the new doctor. How is your uncle pleased with him?'

'Pretty well, I think. He asks Lydgate all sorts of questions and then screws up his face while he hears the answers, as if they were pinching his toes. That's his way. Ah, here comes my grilled bone.'

'But how came you to stay out so late, my dear? You only said you were going to your uncle's.'

'Oh, I dined at Plymdale's. We had whist. Lydgate was there too.'

'And what do you think of him? He is very gentlemanly, I suppose. They say he is of excellent family – his relations quite county people.'

'Yes,' said Fred. 'There was a Lydgate at John's who spent no end of money. I find this man is a second cousin of his. But rich men may have very poor devils for second cousins.'

'It always makes a difference, though, to be of good family,' said Rosamond, with a tone of decision which showed that she had thought on this subject. Rosamond felt that she might have been happier if she had not been the daughter of a Middlemarch manufacturer. She disliked anything which reminded her that her mother's father had been an innkeeper. Certainly anyone remembering the fact might think that Mrs Vincy had the air of a very handsome good-humoured landlady, accustomed to the most capricious orders of gentlemen.

'I thought it was odd his name was Tertius,' said the bright-faced matron, 'but of course it's a name in the family. But now, tell us exactly what sort of man he is.'

'Oh, tallish, dark, clever – talks well – rather a prig, I think.'

'I never can make out what you mean by a prig,' said Rosamond.

'A fellow who wants to show that he has opinions.'

'Why, my dear, doctors must have opinions,' said Mrs Vincy. 'What are they there for else?'

'Yes, mother, the opinions are paid for. But a prig is a fellow who is always making you a present of his opinions.'

'I suppose Mary Garth admires Mr Lydgate,' said Rosamond, not without a touch of innuendo.

'Really, I can't say,' said Fred, rather glumly, as he left the table, and taking up a novel which he had brought down with him, threw himself into an armchair. 'If you are jealous of her, go oftener to Stone Court yourself and eclipse her.'

'I wish you would not be so vulgar. Fred. If you have finished, pray ring the bell.'

'It is true, though – what your brother says, Rosamond,' Mrs Vincy began, when the servant had cleared the table. 'It is a thousand pities you haven't patience to go and see your uncle more, so proud of you as he is, and wanted you to live with him. There's no knowing what he might have done for you as well as for Fred. God knows, I'm fond of having you at home with me, but I can part with my children for their good. And now it stands to reason that your uncle Featherstone will do something for Mary Garth.'

'Mary Garth can bear being at Stone Court, because she likes that better than being a governess,' said Rosamond, folding up her work. 'I would rather not have anything left to me if I must earn it by enduring much of my uncle's cough and his ugly relations.'

'He can't be long for this world, my dear; I wouldn't hasten his end, but what with asthma and that inward complaint, let us hope there is something better for him in another. And I have no ill-will towards Mary Garth, but there's justice to be thought of. And Mr Featherstone's first wife brought him no money, as my sister did. Her nieces and nephews can't have so much claim as my sister's. And I must say I think Mary Garth a dreadful plain girl – more fit for a governess.'

'Everyone would not agree with you there, mother,' said Fred, who seemed to be able to read and listen too.

'Well, my dear,' said Mrs Vincy, wheeling skilfully, 'if she *had* some fortune left her, – a man marries his wife's relations, and the Garths are so poor, and live in such a small way. But I shall leave you to your studies, my dear; for I must go and do some shopping.'

'Fred's studies are not very deep,' said Rosamond, rising with her mamma, 'he is only reading a novel.'

'Well, well, by and by he'll go to his Latin and things,' said Mrs Vincy, soothingly, stroking her son's head. 'There's a fire in the smoking-room on purpose. It's your father's wish, you know – Fred, my dear – and I always tell him you will be good, and go to college again to take your degree.'

Fred drew his mother's hand down to his lips, but said nothing.

'I suppose you are not going out riding today?' said Rosamond, lingering a little after her mamma was gone.

'No; why?'

'Papa says I may have the chestnut to ride now.'

'You can go with me tomorrow, if you like. Only I am going to Stone Court, remember.'

'I want the ride so much, it is indifferent to me where we go.' Rosamond really wished to go to Stone Court, of all other places.

'Oh, I say, Rosy,' said Fred, as she was passing out of the room, 'if you are going to the piano, let me come and play some airs with you.'

'Pray do not ask me this morning.'

'Why not this morning?'

'Really, Fred, I wish you would leave off playing the flute. A man looks very silly playing the flute. And you play so out of tune.'

'When next anyone makes love to you, Miss Rosamond, I will tell him how obliging you are.'

'Why should you expect me to oblige you by hearing you play the flute, any more than I should expect you to oblige me by not playing it.'

'And why should you expect me to take you out riding?'

This question led to an adjustment, for Rosamond had set her mind on that particular ride.

So Fred was gratified with nearly an hour's practice of 'Ar hyd y nos', 'Ye banks and braes', and other favourite airs from his 'Instructor on the Flute'; a wheezy performance, into which he threw much ambition and an irrepressible hopefulness.

Chapter 12

> He had more tow on his distaffe
> Than Gerveis knew.
>   CHAUCER

The ride to Stone Court, which Fred and Rosamond took the next morning, lay through a pretty bit of midland landscape, almost all meadows and pastures, with hedgerows still allowed to grow in bushy beauty and to spread out coral fruit for the birds. Little details gave each field a particular physiognomy, dear to the eyes that have looked on them from childhood: the pool in the corner where the grasses were dank and trees leaned whisperingly; the great oak shadowing a bare place in mid-pasture; the high bank where the ash trees grew; the sudden slope of the old marl-pit making a red background for the burdock; the huddled roofs and ricks of the homestead without a traceable way of approach; the grey gate and fences against the depths of the bordering wood; and the stray hovel, its old, old thatch full of mossy hills and valleys with wondrous modulations of light and shadow such as we travel far to see in later life, and see larger, but not more beautiful. These are the things that make the gamut of joy in landscape to midland-bred souls – the things they toddled among, or perhaps learned by heart standing between their father's knees while he drove leisurely.

But the road, even the byroad, was excellent; for Lowick, as we have seen, was not a parish of muddy lanes and poor tenants; and it was into Lowick parish that Fred and Rosamond entered after a couple of miles' riding. Another mile would bring them to Stone Court, and at the end of the first half, the house was already visible, looking as if it had been arrested in its growth toward a stone mansion by an unexpected budding of farm-buildings on its left flank, which had hindered it from becoming anything more than the substantial dwelling of a gentleman farmer. It was not the less agreeable an object in the distance for the cluster of pinnacled corn-ricks which balanced the fine row of walnuts on the right.

Presently it was possible to discern something that might be a gig on the circular drive before the front door.

'Dear me,' said Rosamond, 'I hope none of my uncle's horrible relations are there.'

'They are, though. That is Mrs Waule's gig – the last yellow gig left, I should think. When I see Mrs Waule in it, I understand how yellow can have been worn for mourning. That gig seems to me more funereal than a hearse. But then Mrs Waule always has black crape on. How does she manage it, Rosy? Her friends can't always be dying.'

'I don't know at all. And she is not in the least evangelical,' said Rosamond, reflectively, as if that religious point of view would have fully accounted for perpetual crape. 'And not poor,' she added, after a moment's pause.

'No, by George! They are as rich as Jews, those Waules and Featherstones; I mean, for people like them, who don't want to spend anything. And yet they hang about my uncle like vultures, and are afraid of a farthing going away from their side of the family. But I believe he hates them all.'

The Mrs Waule who was so far from being admirable in the eyes of these distant connections, had happened to say this very morning (not at all with a defiant air, but in a low, muffled, neutral tone, as of a voice heard through cotton wool) that she did not wish 'to enjoy their good opinion'. She was seated, as she observed, on her own brother's hearth, and had been Jane Featherstone five-and-twenty years before she had been Jane Waule, which entitled her to speak when her own brother's name had been made free with by those who had no right to it.

'What are you driving at there?' said Mr Featherstone, holding his stick between his knees and settling his wig, while he gave her a momentary sharp glance, which seemed to react on him like a draught of cold air and set him coughing.

Mrs Waule had to defer her answer till he was quiet again, till Mary Garth had supplied him with fresh syrup, and he had begun to rub the gold knob of his stick, looking bitterly at the fire. It was a bright fire, but it made no difference to the chill-looking purplish tint of Mrs Waule's face, which was as neutral as her voice; having mere chinks for eyes, and lips that hardly moved in speaking.

'The doctors can't master that cough, brother. It's just like what I have; for I'm your own sister, constitution and everything. But, as I was saying, it's a pity Mrs Vincy's family can't be better conducted.'

'Tchah! you said nothing o' the sort. You said somebody had made free with my name.'

'And no more than can be proved, if what everybody says is true. My brother Solomon tells me it's the talk up and down in Middlemarch how unsteady young Vincy is, and has been forever gambling at billiards since home he came.'

'Nonsense! What's a game at billiards? It's a good gentlemanly game; and young Vincy is not a clodhopper. If your son John took to billiards, now, he'd make a fool of himself.'

'Your nephew John never took to billiards or any other game, brother, and is far from losing hundreds of pounds, which, if what everybody says is true, must be found somewhere else than out of Mr Vincy the father's pocket. For they say he's been losing money for years, though nobody would think so, to see him go coursing and keeping open house as they do. And I've heard say Mr Bulstrode condemns Mrs Vincy beyond anything for her flightiness, and spoiling her children so.'

'What's Bulstrode to me? I don't bank with him.'

'Well, Mrs Bulstrode is Mr Vincy's own sister, and they do say that Mr Vincy mostly trades on the Bank money; and you may see yourself, brother, when a woman past forty has pink strings always flying, and that light way of laughing at everything, it's very unbecoming. But indulging your children is one thing, and finding money to pay their debts is another. And it's openly said that young Vincy has raised money on his expectations. I don't say what expectations. Miss Garth hears me, and is welcome to tell again. I know young people hang together.'

'No, thank you, Mrs Waule,' said Mary Garth. 'I dislike hearing scandal too much to wish to repeat it.'

Mr Featherstone rubbed the knob of his stick and made a brief convulsive show of laughter, which had much the same genuineness as an old whist-player's chuckle over a bad hand. Still looking at the fire, he said: 'And who pretends to say Fred Vincy hasn't got expectations? Such a fine, spirited fellow is like enough to have 'em.'

There was a slight pause before Mrs Waule replied, and when she did so, her voice seemed to be slightly moistened with tears, though her face was still dry.

'Whether or no, brother, it is naturally painful to me and my brother Solomon to hear your name made free with, and your complaint being such as may carry you off sudden, and people who are no more Featherstones than the Merry-Andrew at the fair, openly reckoning on your property coming to *them*. And me your own sister, and Solomon your own brother! And if that's to be it, what has it pleased the Almighty to make families for?' Here Mrs Waule's tears fell, but with moderation.

'Come, out with it, Jane!' said Mr Featherstone, looking at her. 'You mean to say, Fred Vincy has been getting somebody to advance him money on what he says he knows about my will, eh?'

'I never said so, brother' (Mrs Waule's voice had again become dry and unshaken). 'It was told me by my brother Solomon last night when he called coming from market to give me advice about the old wheat, me being a widow, and my son John only three-and-twenty, though steady beyond anything. And he had it from most undeniable authority, and not one, but many.'

'Stuff and nonsense! I don't believe a word of it. It's all a got-up story. Go to the window, Missy; I thought I heard a horse. See if the doctor's coming.'

'Not got up by me, brother, nor yet by Solomon, who, whatever else he may be – and I don't deny he has oddities – has made his will and parted his property equal between such kin as he's friends with; though, for my part, I think there are times when some should be considered more than others. But Solomon makes it no secret what he means to do.'

'The more fool he!' said Mr Featherstone, with some difficulty; breaking into a severe fit of coughing that required Mary Garth to stand near him, so that she did not find out whose horses they were which presently paused stamping on the gravel before the door.

Before Mr Featherstone's cough was quiet, Rosamond entered, bearing up her riding-habit with much grace. She bowed ceremoniously to Mrs Waule, who said stiffly, 'How do you do, miss?', smiled and nodded silently to Mary, and remained standing till the coughing should cease and allow her uncle to notice her.

'Heyday, Miss,' he said at last, 'you have a fine colour. Where's Fred?'

'Seeing about the horses. He will be in presently.'

'Sit down, sit down. Mrs Waule, you'd better go.'

Even those neighbours who had called Peter Featherstone an old fox, had never accused him of being insincerely polite, and his sister was quite used to the peculiar absence of ceremony with which he marked his sense of blood-relationship. Indeed, she herself was accustomed to think that entire freedom from the necessity of behaving agreeably was included in the Almighty's intentions about families. She rose slowly without any sign of resentment, and said in her usual muffled monotone, 'Brother, I hope the new doctor will be able to do something for you. Solomon says there's great talk of his cleverness. I'm sure it's my wish you should be spared. And there's none more ready to nurse you than your own sister and your own nieces, if you'd only say the word. There's Rebecca, and Joanna, and Elizabeth, you know.'

'Ay, ay, I remember – you'll see I've remembered 'em all all dark and ugly. They'd need some money, eh? There never was any beauty in the women of our family; but the Featherstones have always had some money, and the Waules too. Waule had money too. A warm man was Waule. Ay, ay; money's a good egg; and if you've got money to leave behind you, lay it in a warm nest. Goodbye, Mrs Waule.'

Here Mr Featherstone pulled at both sides of his wig as if he wanted to deafen himself, and his sister went away ruminating on this oracular speech of his. Notwithstanding her jealousy of the Vincys and of Mary Garth, there remained as the nethermost sediment in her mental shallows a persuasion that her brother Peter Featherstone could never leave his chief property away from his blood-relations: – else, why had the Almighty carried off his two wives both childless, after he had gained so much by manganese and things, turning up when nobody expected it? – and why was there a Lowick parish church, and the Waules and Powderells all sitting in the same pew for generations, and the Featherstone pew next to them, if, the Sunday after her brother Peter's death, everybody was to know that the property was gone out of the family? The human mind has at no period accepted a moral chaos; and so preposterous a result was not strictly conceivable. But we are frightened at much that is not strictly conceivable.

When Fred came in the old man eyed him with a peculiar twinkle, which the younger had often had reason to interpret as pride in the satisfactory details of his appearance.

'You two misses go away,' said Mr Featherstone. 'I want to speak to Fred.'

'Come into my room, Rosamond, you will not mind the cold for a little while,' said Mary. The two girls had not only known each other in childhood, but had been at the same provincial school together (Mary as an articled pupil), so that they had many memories in common, and liked very well to talk in private. Indeed, this tête-à-tête was one of Rosamond's objects in coming to Stone Court.

Old Featherstone would not begin the dialogue till the door had been closed. He continued to look at Fred with the same twinkle and with one of his habitual grimaces, alternately screwing and widening his mouth; and when he spoke, it was in a low tone, which might be taken for that of an informer ready to be bought off, rather than for the tone of an offended senior. He was not a man to feel any strong moral indignation even on account of trespasses against himself.

It was natural that others should want to get an advantage over him, but then, he was a little too cunning for them.

'So, sir, you've been paying ten per cent for money which you've promised to pay off by mortgaging my land when I'm dead and gone, eh? You put my life at a twelvemonth, say. But I can alter my will yet.'

Fred blushed. He had not borrowed money in that way, for excellent reasons. But he was conscious of having spoken with some confidence (perhaps with more than he exactly remembered) about his prospect of getting Featherstone's land as a future means of paying present debts.

'I don't know what you refer to, sir. I have certainly never borrowed any money on such an insecurity. Please to explain.'

'No, sir, it's you must explain. I can alter my will yet, let me tell you. I'm of sound mind – can reckon compound interest in my head, and remember every fool's name as well as I could twenty years ago. What the deuce? I'm under eighty. I say, you must contradict this story.'

'I have contradicted it, sir,' Fred answered, with a touch of impatience, not remembering that his uncle did not verbally discriminate contradicting from disproving, though no one was further from confounding the two ideas than old Featherstone, who often wondered that so many fools took his own assertions for proofs. 'But I contradict it again. The story is a silly lie.'

'Nonsense! you must bring dockiments. It comes from authority.'

'Name the authority, and make him name the man of whom I borrowed the money, and then I can disprove the story.'

'It's pretty good authority, I think – a man who knows most of what goes on in Middlemarch. It's that fine, religious, charitable uncle o' yours. Come now!' Here Mr Featherstone had his peculiar inward shake which signified merriment.

'Mr Bulstrode?'

'Who else, eh?'

'Then the story has grown into this lie out of some sermonising words he may have let fall about me. Do they pretend that he named the man who lent me the money?'

'If there is such a man, depend upon it Bulstrode knows him. But, supposing you only tried to get the money lent, and didn't get it – Bulstrode 'ud know that too. You bring me a writing from Bulstrode to say he doesn't believe you've ever promised to pay your debts out o' my land. Come now !'

Mr Featherstone's face required its whole scale of grimaces as a muscular outlet to his silent triumph in the soundness of his faculties.

Fred felt himself to be in a disgusting dilemma.

'You must be joking, sir. Mr Bulstrode, like other men, believes scores of things that are not true, and he has a prejudice against me. I could easily get him to write that he knew no facts in proof of the report you speak of, though it might lead to unpleasantness. But I could hardly ask him to write down what he believes or does not believe about me.' Fred paused an instant, and then added, in politic appeal to his uncle's vanity, 'That is hardly a thing for a gentleman to ask.'

But he was disappointed in the result.

'Ay, I know what you mean. You'd sooner offend me than Bulstrode. And what's he? – he's got no land hereabout that ever I heard tell of. A speckilating fellow! He may come down any day, when the devil leaves off backing him. And that's what his religion means: he wants God A'mighty to come in. That's nonsense! There's one thing I made out pretty clear when I used to go to church – and it's this: God A'mighty sticks to the land. He promises land, and He gives land, and He makes chaps rich with corn and cattle. But you take the other side. You like Bulstrode and speckilation better than Featherstone and land.'

'I beg your pardon, sir,' said Fred, rising, standing with his back to the fire and beating his boot with his whip. 'I like neither Bulstrode nor speculation.' He spoke rather sulkily, feeling himself stalemated.

'Well, well, you can do without *me*, that's pretty clear,' said old Feather-stone, secretly disliking the possibility that Fred would show himself at all independent. 'You neither want a bit of land to make a squire of you instead of a starving parson, nor a lift of a hundred pound by the way. It's all one to me. I can make five codicils if I like, and I shall keep my bank-notes for a nest-egg. It's all one to me.'

Fred coloured again. Featherstone had rarely given him presents of money, and at this moment it seemed almost harder to part with the immediate prospect of bank-notes than with the more distant prospect of the land.

'I am not ungrateful, sir. I never meant to show disregard for any kind intentions you might have towards me. On the contrary.'

'Very good. Then prove it. You bring me a letter from Bulstrode saying he doesn't believe you've been cracking and promising to pay your debts out o' my land, and then, if there's any scrape you've got into, we'll see if I can back you a bit. Come now! That's a bargain. Here, give me your arm. I'll try and walk round the room.'

Fred, in spite of his irritation, had kindness enough in him to be a little sorry for the unloved, unvenerated old man, who with his dropsical legs looked more than usually pitiable in walking. While giving his arm, he thought that he should not himself like to be an old fellow with his constitution breaking up; and he waited good-temperedly, first before the window to hear the wonted remarks about the guinea-fowls and the weathercock, and then before the scanty book-shelves, of which the chief glories in dark calf were Josephus, Culpepper, Klop-stock's *Messiah*, and several volumes of the *Gentleman's Magazine*.

'Read me the names o' the books. Come now! you're a college man.'

Fred gave him the titles.

'What did Missy want with more books? What must you be bringing her more books for?'

'They amuse her, sir. She is very fond of reading.'

'A little too fond,' said Mr Featherstone, captiously. 'She was for reading when she sat with me. But I put a stop to that. She's got the newspaper to read out loud. That's enough for one day, I should think. I can't abide to see her reading to herself. You mind and not bring her any more books, do you hear?'

'Yes, sir, I hear.' Fred had received this order before, and had secretly dis-obeyed it. He intended to disobey it again.

'Ring the bell,' said Mr Featherstone; 'I want Missy to come down.'

Rosamond and Mary had been talking faster than their male friends. They did not think of sitting down, but stood at the toilette-table near the window while Rosamond took off her hat, adjusted her veil, and applied little touches of her fingertips to her hair – hair of infantile fairness, neither flaxen nor yellow. Mary Garth seemed all the plainer standing at an angle between the two nymphs – the one in the glass, and the one out of it, who looked at each other with eyes of heavenly blue, deep enough to hold the most exquisite meanings an ingenious beholder could put into them, and deep enough to hide the meanings of the owner if these should happen to be less exquisite. Only a few children in Middlemarch looked blond by the side of Rosamond, and the slim figure displayed by her riding-habit had delicate undulations. In fact, most men in Middlemarch, except her brothers, held that Miss Vincy was the best girl in the world, and some called her an angel. Mary Garth, on the contrary, had the aspect of an ordinary sinner: she was brown; her curly dark hair was rough and stubborn; her stature was low; and it would not be true to declare, in satisfactory antithesis, that she had all the virtues. Plainness has its peculiar temptations and vices quite as much as beauty; it is apt either to feign amiability, or, not feigning it, to show all the repulsiveness of discontent: at any rate, to be called an ugly thing in contrast with that lovely creature your companion, is apt to produce some effect beyond a sense of fine veracity and fitness in the phrase. At the age of two-and-twenty Mary had certainly not attained that perfect good sense and good principle which are usually recommended to the less fortunate girl, as if they were to be obtained in quantities ready mixed, with a flavour of resignation as required. Her shrewdness had a streak of satiric bitterness continually renewed and never carried utterly out of sight, except by a strong current of gratitude towards those who, instead of telling her that she ought to be contented, did something to make her so. Advancing womanhood had tempered her plainness, which was of a good human sort, such as the mothers of our race have very commonly worn in all latitudes under a more or less becoming headgear. Rembrandt would have painted her with pleasure, and would have made her broad features look out of the canvas with intelligent honesty. For honesty, truth telling fairness, was Mary's reigning virtue: she neither tried to create illusions, nor indulged in them for her own behoof, and when she was in a good mood she had humour enough in her to laugh at herself. When she and Rosamond happened both to be reflected in the glass, she said laughingly: 'What a brown patch I am by the side of you, Rosy ! You are the most unbecoming companion.'

'Oh no! No one thinks of your appearance, you are so sensible and useful, Mary. Beauty is of very little consequence in reality,' said Rosamond, turning her head towards Mary, but with eyes swerving towards the new view of her neck in the glass.

'You mean *my* beauty,' said Mary, rather sardonically.

Rosamond thought, 'Poor Mary, she takes the kindest things ill.' Aloud she said, 'What have you been doing lately?'

'I? Oh, minding the house – pouring out syrup – pretending to be amiable and contented – learning to have a bad opinion of everybody.'

'It is a wretched life for you.'

'No,' said Mary, curtly, with a little toss of her head. 'I think my life is pleasanter than your Miss Morgan's.'

'Yes; but Miss Morgan is so uninteresting, and not young.'

'She is interesting to herself, I suppose; and I am not at all sure that everything gets easier as one gets older.'

'No,' said Rosamond, reflectively; 'one wonders what such people do, without any prospect. To be sure, there is religion as a support. But,' she added, dimpling, 'it is very different with you, Mary. You may have an offer.'

'Has anyone told you he means to make me one?'

'Of course not. I mean, there is a gentleman who may fall in love with you, seeing you almost every day.'

A certain change in Mary's face was chiefly determined by the resolve not to show any change.

'Does that always make people fall in love?' she answered, carelessly; 'it seems to me quite as often a reason for detesting each other.'

'Not when they are interesting and agreeable. I hear that Mr Lydgate is both.'

'Oh, Mr Lydgate!' said Mary, with an unmistakable lapse into indifference. 'You want to know something about him,' she added, not choosing to indulge Rosamond's indirectness.

'Merely, how you like him.'

'There is no question of liking at present. My liking always wants some little kindness to kindle it. I am not magnanimous enough to like people who speak to me without seeming to see me.'

'Is he so haughty?' said Rosamond, with heightened satisfaction. 'You know that he is of good family?'

'No; he did not give that as a reason.'

'Mary! you are the oddest girl. But what sort of looking man is he? Describe him to me.'

'How can one describe a man? I can give you an inventory: heavy eyebrows, dark eyes, a straight nose, thick dark hair, large solid white hands – and – let me see – oh, an exquisite cambric pocket handkerchief. But you will see him. You know this is about the time of his visits.'

Rosamond blushed a little, but said, meditatively, 'I rather like a haughty manner. I cannot endure a rattling young man.'

'I did not tell you that Mr Lydgate was haughty; but *il y en a pour tous les goûts*, as little Mamselle used to say, and if any girl can choose the particular sort of conceit she would like, I should think it is you, Rosy.'

'Haughtiness is not conceit; I call Fred conceited.'

'I wish no one said any worse of him. He should be more careful. Mrs Waule has been telling uncle that Fred is very unsteady.' Mary spoke from a girlish impulse which got the better of her judgement. There was a vague uneasiness associated with the word 'unsteady' which she hoped Rosamond might say something to dissipate. But she purposely abstained from mentioning Mrs Waule's more special insinuation.

'Oh, Fred is horrid!' said Rosamond. She would not have allowed herself so unsuitable a word to anyone but Mary.

'What do you mean by horrid?'

'He is so idle, and makes papa so angry, and says he will not take orders.'

'I think Fred is quite right.'

'How can you say he is quite right, Mary? I thought you had more sense of religion.'

'He is not fit to be a clergyman.'

'But he ought to be fit.'

'Well, then, he is not what he ought to be. I know some other people who are in the same case.'

'But no one approves of them. I should not like to marry a clergyman; but there must be clergymen.'

'It does not follow that Fred must be one.'

'But when papa has been at the expense of educating him for it! And only suppose, if he should have no fortune left him?'

'I can suppose that very well,' said Mary, dryly.

'Then I wonder you can defend Fred,' said Rosamond, inclined to push this point.

'I don't defend him,' said Mary, laughing; 'I would defend any parish from having him for a clergyman.'

'But of course if he were a clergyman, he must be different.'

'Yes, he would be a great hypocrite; and he is not that yet.'

'It is of no use saying anything to you, Mary. You always take Fred's part.'

'Why should I not take his part?' said Mary, lighting up. 'He would take mine. He is the only person who takes the least trouble to oblige me.'

'You make me feel very uncomfortable, Mary,' said Rosamond, with her gravest mildness; 'I would not tell mamma for the world.'

'What would you not tell her?' said Mary, angrily.

'Pray do not go into a rage, Mary,' said Rosamond, mildly as ever.

'If your mamma is afraid that Fred will make me an offer, tell her that I would not marry him if he asked me. But he is not going to do so, that I am aware. He certainly never has asked me.'

'Mary, you are always so violent.'

'And you are always so exasperating.'

'I? What can you blame me for?'

'Oh, blameless people are always the most exasperating. There is the bell – I think we must go down.'

'I did not mean to quarrel,' said Rosamond, putting on her hat.

'Quarrel? Nonsense; we have not quarrelled. If one is not to get into a rage sometimes, what is the good of being friends?'

'Am I to repeat what you have said?'

'Just as you please. I never say what I am afraid of having repeated. But let us go down.'

Mr Lydgate was rather late this morning, but the visitors stayed long enough to see him; for Mr Featherstone asked Rosamond to sing to him, and she herself was so kind as to propose a second favourite song of his – 'Flow on, thou shining river' after she had sung 'Home, sweet home' (which she detested). This hard-headed old Overreach approved of the sentimental song, as the suitable garnish for girls, and also as fundamentally fine, sentiment being the right thing for a song.

Mr Featherstone was still applauding the last performance, and assuring Missy that her voice was as clear as a blackbird's, when Mr Lydgate's horse passed the window.

His dull expectation of the usual disagreeable routine with an aged patient – who can hardly believe that medicine would not 'set him up' if the doctor were only clever enough – added to his general disbelief in Middlemarch charms, made a doubly effective background to this vision of Rosamond, whom old Featherstone made haste ostentatiously to introduce as his niece, though he had never thought it worth while to speak of Mary Garth in that light. Nothing escaped Lydgate in Rosamond's graceful behaviour: how delicately she waived the notice which the old man's want of taste had thrust upon her by a quiet gravity, not showing her dimples on the wrong occasion, but showing them afterwards in speaking to Mary, to whom she addressed herself with so much good-natured interest, that Lydgate, after quickly examining Mary more fully than he had done before, saw an adorable kindness in Rosamond's eyes. But Mary from some cause looked rather out of temper.

'Miss Rosy has been singing me a song – you've nothing to say against that, eh, doctor?' said Mr Featherstone. 'I like it better than your physic.'

'That has made me forget how the time was going,' said Rosamond, rising to reach her hat, which she had laid aside before singing, so that her flower-like head on its white stem was seen in perfection above her riding-habit. 'Fred, we must really go.'

'Very good,' said Fred, who had his own reasons for not being in the best spirits, and wanted to get away.

'Miss Vincy is a musician?' said Lydgate, following her with his eyes. (Every nerve and muscle in Rosamond was adjusted to the consciousness that she was being looked at. She was by nature an actress of parts that entered into her *physique:* she even acted her own character, and so well, that she did not know it to be precisely her own.)

'The best in Middlemarch, I'll be bound,' said Mr Featherstone, 'let the next be who she will. Eh, Fred? Speak up for your sister.'

'I'm afraid I'm out of court, sir. My evidence would be good for nothing.'

'Middlemarch has not a very high standard, uncle,' said Rosamond, with a pretty lightness, going towards her whip, which lay at a distance.

Lydgate was quick in anticipating her. He reached the whip before she did, and turned to present it to her. She bowed and looked at him: he of course was looking at her, and their eyes met with that peculiar meeting which is never arrived at by effort, but seems like a sudden divine clearance of haze. I think Lydgate turned a little paler than usual, but Rosamond blushed deeply and felt a certain astonishment. After that, she was really anxious to go, and did not know what sort of stupidity her uncle was talking of when she went to shake hands with him.

Yet this result, which she took to be a mutual impression, called falling in love, was just what Rosamond had contemplated beforehand. Ever since that important new arrival in Middlemarch she had woven a little future, of which something like this scene was the necessary beginning. Strangers, whether wrecked and clinging to a raft, or duly escorted and accompanied by portmanteaus, have always had a circumstantial fascination for the virgin mind, against which native merit has urged itself in vain. And a stranger was absolutely necessary to Rosamond's social romance, which had always turned on a lover and bridegroom who was not a Middlemarcher, and who had no connections at all like her own: of late, indeed, the construction seemed to demand that he should somehow be related to a baronet. Now that she and the stranger had met, reality proved much more moving than anticipation, and Rosamond could not doubt that this was the great epoch of her life. She judged of her own symptoms as those of awakening love, and she held it still more natural that Mr Lydgate should have fallen in love at first sight of her. These things happened so often at balls, and why not by the morning light, when the complexion showed all the better for it? Rosamond, though no older than Mary, was rather used to being fallen in love with; but she, for her part, had remained indifferent and fastidiously critical towards both fresh sprig and faded bachelor. And here was Mr Lydgate suddenly corresponding to her ideal, being altogether foreign to Middlemarch, carrying a certain air of distinction congruous with good family, and possessing connections which offered vistas of that middle-class heaven, rank; a man of talent, also, whom it would be especially delightful to enslave: in fact, a man who had touched her nature quite newly, and brought a vivid interest into her life which was better than any fancied 'might-be' such as she was in the habit of opposing to the actual.

Thus, in riding home, both the brother and the sister were preoccupied and inclined to be silent. Rosamond, whose basis for her structure had the usual airy slightness, was of remarkably detailed and realistic imagination when the foundation had been once presupposed; and before they had ridden a mile she was far on in the costume and introductions of her wedded life, having determined on her house in Middlemarch, and foreseen the visits she would pay to her husband's high-bred relatives at a distance, whose finished manners she could appropriate as thoroughly as she had done her school accomplishments, preparing herself thus for vaguer elevations which might ultimately come. There was nothing financial, still less sordid, in her previsions: she cared about what were considered refinements, and not about the money that was to pay for them.

Fred's mind, on the other hand, was busy with an anxiety which even his ready hopefulness could not immediately quell. He saw no way of eluding Featherstone's stupid demand without incurring consequences which he liked less even than the task of fulfilling it. His father was already out of humour with him, and would be still more so if he were the occasion of any additional coolness between his own family and the Bulstrodes. Then, he himself hated having to go and speak to his uncle Bulstrode, and perhaps after drinking wine he had said many foolish things about Featherstone's property, and these had been magnified by report. Fred felt that he made a wretched figure as a fellow who bragged about expectations from a queer old miser like Featherstone, and went to beg for certificates at his bidding. But – those expectations! He really had them, and he saw no agreeable alternative if he gave them up: besides, he had lately made a debt which galled him extremely, and old Featherstone had almost bargained to pay it off. The whole affair was miserably small: his debts were small, even his expectations were not anything so very magnificent. Fred had known men to whom he would have been ashamed of confessing the smallness of his scrapes. Such ruminations naturally produced a streak of misanthropic bitterness. To be born the son of a Middlemarch manufacturer, and inevitable heir to nothing in particular, while such men as Mainwaring and Vyan – certainly life was a poor business, when a spirited young fellow, with a good appetite for the best of everything, had so poor an outlook.

It had not occurred to Fred that the introduction of Bulstrode's name in the matter was a fiction of old Featherstone's; nor could this have made any difference to his position. He saw plainly enough that the old man wanted to exercise his power by tormenting him a little, and also probably to get some satisfaction out of seeing him on unpleasant terms with Bulstrode. Fred fancied that he saw to the bottom of his uncle Featherstone's soul, though in reality half what he saw there was no more than the reflex of his own inclinations. The difficult task of knowing another soul is not for young gentlemen whose consciousness is chiefly made up of their own wishes.

Fred's main point of debate with himself was, whether he should tell his father, or try to get through the affair without his father's knowledge. It was probably Mrs Waule who had been talking about him; and if Mary Garth had repeated Mrs Waule's report to Rosamond, it would be sure to reach his father, who would as surely question him about it. He said to Rosamond, as they slackened their pace: 'Rosy, did Mary tell you that Mrs Waule had said anything about me?'

'Yes, indeed, she did.'

'What?'

'That you were very unsteady.'

'Was that all?'

'I should think that was enough, Fred.'

'You are sure she said no more?'

'Mary mentioned nothing else. But really, Fred, I think you ought to be ashamed.'

'Oh, fudge! don't lecture me. What did Mary say about it?'

'I am not obliged to tell you. You care so very much what Mary says, and you are too rude to allow me to speak.'

'Of course I care what Mary says. She is the best girl I know.'

'I should never have thought she was a girl to fall in love with.'

'How do you know what men would fall in love with? Girls never know.'

'At least, Fred, let me advise you not to fall in love with her, for she says she would not marry you if you asked her.'

'She might have waited till I did ask her.'

'I knew it would nettle you, Fred.'

'Not at all. She would not have said so if you had not provoked her.'

Before reaching home, Fred concluded that he would tell the whole affair as simply as possible to his father, who might perhaps take on himself the unpleasant business of speaking to Bulstrode.

BOOK TWO

Old and Young

Chapter 13

1st Gent.	How class your man? – as better than the most,
	Or, seeming better, worse beneath that cloak?
	As saint or knave, pilgrim or hypocrite?
2nd Gent.	Nay, tell me how you class your wealth of books,
	The drifted relics of all time. As well
	Sort them at once by size and livery:
	Vellum, tall copies, and the common calf
	Will hardly cover more diversity
	Than all your labels cunningly devised
	To class your unread authors.

In consequence of what he had heard from Fred, Mr Vincy determined to speak with Mr Bulstrode in his private room at the Bank at half-past one, when he was usually free from other callers. But a visitor had come in at one o'clock, and Mr Bulstrode had so much to say to him, that there was little chance of the interview being over in half an hour. The banker's speech was fluent, but it was also copious, and he used up an appreciable amount of time in brief meditative pauses. Do not imagine his sickly aspect to have been of the yellow, black-haired sort: he had a pale blond skin, thin grey-besprinkled brown hair, light-grey eyes, and a large forehead. Loud men called his subdued tone an undertone, and sometimes implied that it was inconsistent with openness; though there seems to be no reason why a loud man should not be given to concealment of anything except his own voice, unless it can be shown that Holy Writ has placed the seat of candour in the lungs. Mr Bulstrode had also a deferential bending attitude in listening, and an apparently fixed attentiveness in his eyes which made those persons who thought themselves worth hearing infer that he was seeking the utmost improvement from their discourse. Others, who expected to make no great figure, disliked this kind of moral lantern turned on them. If you are not proud of your cellar, there is no thrill of satisfaction in seeing your guest hold up his wineglass to the light and look judicial. Such joys are reserved for conscious merit. Hence Mr Bulstrode's close attention was not agreeable to the publicans and sinners in Middlemarch; it was attributed by some to his being a Pharisee, and by others to his being Evangelical. Less superficial reasoners among them wished to know who his father and grandfather were, observing that five-and-twenty years ago nobody had ever heard of a Bulstrode in Middlemarch. To his present visitor, Lydgate, the scrutinising look was a matter of indifference: he simply formed an unfavourable opinion of the banker's constitution, and concluded that he had an eager inward life with little enjoyment of tangible things.

'I shall be exceedingly obliged if you will look in on me here occasionally, Mr Lydgate,' the banker observed, after a brief pause. 'If, as I dare to hope, I have the privilege of finding you a valuable co-adjutor in the interesting matter of hospital management, there will be many questions which we shall need to discuss in private. As to the new hospital, which is nearly finished, I shall consider what you have said about the advantages of the special destination for fevers. The decision will rest with me, for though Lord Medlicote has given the land and timber for the building, he is not disposed to give his personal attention to the object.'

'There are few things better worth the pains in a provincial town like this,' said Lydgate. 'A fine fever hospital in addition to the old infirmary might be the nucleus of a medical school here, when once we get our medical reforms; and what would do more for medical education than the spread of such schools over the country? A born provincial man who has a grain of public spirit as well as a few ideas, should do what he can to resist the rush of everything that is a little better than common towards London. Any valid professional aims may often find a freer, if not a richer field, in the provinces.'

One of Lydgate's gifts was a voice habitually deep and sonorous, yet capable of becoming very low and gentle at the right moment. About his ordinary bearing there was a certain fling, a fearless expectation of success, a confidence in his own powers and integrity much fortified by contempt for petty obstacles or seductions of which he had had no experience. But this proud openness was made lovable by an expression of unaffected goodwill. Mr Bulstrode perhaps liked him the better for the difference between them in pitch and manners; he certainly liked him the better, as Rosamond did, for being a stranger in Middlemarch. One can begin so many things with a new person! – even begin to be a better man.

'I shall rejoice to furnish your zeal with fuller opportunities,' Mr Bulstrode answered; 'I mean, by confiding to you the superintendence of my new hospital, should a maturer knowledge favour that issue, for I am determined that so great an object shall not be shackled by our two physicians. Indeed, I am encouraged to consider your advent to this town as a gracious indication that a more manifest blessing is now to be awarded to my efforts, which have hitherto been much withstood. With regard to the old infirmary, we have gained the initial point; I mean your election. And now I hope you will not shrink from incurring a certain amount of jealousy and dislike from your professional brethren by presenting yourself as a reformer.'

'I will not profess bravery,' said Lydgate, smiling, 'but I acknowledge a good deal of pleasure in fighting, and I should not care for my profession, if I did not believe that better methods were to be found and enforced there as well as everywhere else.'

'The standard of that profession is low in Middlemarch, my dear sir,' said the banker. 'I mean in knowledge and skill; not in social status, for our medical men are most of them connected with respectable townspeople here. My own imperfect health has induced me to give some attention to those palliative resources which the divine mercy has placed within our reach. I have consulted eminent men in the metropolis, and I am painfully aware of the backwardness under which medical treatment labours in our provincial districts.'

'Yes; – with our present medical rules and education, one must be satisfied now and then to meet with a fair practitioner. As to all the higher questions which determine the starting-point of a diagnosis – as to the philosophy of medical evidence any glimmering of these can only come from a scientific culture of which country practitioners have usually no more notion than the man in the moon.'

Mr Bulstrode, bending and looking intently, found the form which Lydgate had given to his agreement not quite suited to his comprehension. Under such circumstances a judicious man changes the topic and enters on ground where his own gifts may be more useful.

'I am aware,' he said, 'that the peculiar bias of medical ability is towards material means. Nevertheless, Mr Lydgate, I hope we shall not vary in sentiment as to a measure in which you are not likely to be actively concerned, but in which your sympathetic concurrence may be an aid to me. You recognise, I hope, the existence of spiritual interests in your patients?'

'Certainly I do. But those words are apt to cover different meanings to different minds.'

'Precisely. And on such subjects wrong teaching is as fatal as no teaching. Now a point which I have much at heart to secure is a new regulation as to clerical attendance at the old infirmary. The building stands in Mr Farebrother's parish. You know Mr Farebrother?'

'I have seen him. He gave me his vote. I must call to thank him. He seems a very bright pleasant little fellow. And I understand he is a naturalist.'

'Mr Farebrother, my dear sir, is a man deeply painful to contemplate. I suppose there is not a clergyman in this country who has greater talents.' Mr Bulstrode paused and looked meditative.

'I have not yet been pained by finding any excessive talent in Middlemarch,' said Lydgate, bluntly.

'What I desire,' Mr Bulstrode continued, looking still more serious, 'is that Mr Farebrother's attendance at the hospital should be superseded by the appoint-ment of a chaplain – of Mr Tyke, in fact – and that no other spiritual aid should be called in.'

'As a medical man I could have no opinion on such a point unless I knew Mr Tyke, and even then I should require to know the cases in which he was applied.' Lydgate smiled, but he was bent on being circumspect.

'Of course you cannot enter fully into the merits of this measure at present. But' – here Mr Bulstrode began to speak with a more chiselled emphasis – 'the subject is likely to be referred to the medical board of the infirmary, and what I trust I may ask of you is, that in virtue of the co-operation between us which I now look forward to, you will not, so far as you are concerned, be influenced by my opponents in this matter.'

'I hope I shall have nothing to do with clerical disputes,' said Lydgate. 'The path I have chosen is to work well in my own profession.'

'My responsibility, Mr Lydgate, is of a broader kind. With me, indeed, this question is one of sacred accountableness; whereas with my opponents, I have good reason to say that it is an occasion for gratifying a spirit of worldly opposition. But I shall not therefore drop one iota of my convictions, or cease to identify myself with that truth which an evil generation hates. I have devoted myself to this object of hospital improvement, but I will boldly confess to you, Mr Lydgate, that I should have no interest in hospitals if I believed that nothing more was concerned therein than the cure of mortal diseases. I have another ground of action, and in the face of persecution I will not conceal it.'

Mr Bulstrode's voice had become a loud and agitated whisper as he said the last words.

'There we certainly differ,' said Lydgate. But he was not sorry that the door was now opened, and Mr Vincy was announced. That florid sociable personage was become more interesting to him since he had seen Rosamond. Not that, like her, he had been weaving any future in which their lots were united; but a man naturally remembers a charming girl with pleasure, and is willing to dine where he may see her again. Before he took leave, Mr Vincy had given that invitation which he had been 'in no hurry about', for Rosamond at breakfast had mentioned that she thought her uncle Featherstone had taken the new doctor into great favour.

Mr Bulstrode, alone with his brother-in-law, poured himself out a glass of water, and opened a sandwich-box.

'I cannot persuade you to adopt my regimen, Vincy?'

'No, no; I've no opinion of that system. Life wants padding,' said Mr Vincy, unable to omit his portable theory. 'However,' he went on, accenting the word, as if to dismiss all irrelevance, 'what I came here to talk about was a little affair of my young scapegrace, Fred's.'

'That is a subject on which you and I are likely to take quite as different views as on diet, Vincy.'

'I hope not this time.' (Mr Vincy was resolved to be good humoured.) 'The fact is, it's about a whim of old Featherstone's. Somebody has been cooking up a story out of spite, and telling it to the old man, to try to set him against Fred. He's very fond of Fred, and is likely to do something handsome for him; indeed, he has as good as told Fred that he means to leave him his land, and that makes other people jealous.'

'Vincy, I must repeat, that you will not get any concurrence from me as to the course you have pursued with your eldest son. It was entirely from worldly vanity that you destined him for the Church: with a family of three sons and four daughters, you were not warranted in devoting money to an expensive education which has succeeded in nothing but in giving him extravagant idle habits. You are now reaping the consequences.'

To point out other people's errors was a duty that Mr Bulstrode rarely shrank from, but Mr Vincy was not equally prepared to be patient. When a man has the immediate prospect of being mayor, and is ready, in the interests of commerce, to take up a firm attitude on politics generally, he has naturally a sense of his importance to the framework of things which seems to throw questions of private conduct into the background. And this particular reproof irritated him more than any other. It was eminently superfluous to him to be told that he was reaping the consequences. But he felt his neck under Bulstrode's yoke; and though he usually enjoyed kicking, he was anxious to refrain from that relief.

'As to that, Bulstrode, it's no use going back. I'm not one of your pattern men, and I don't pretend to be. I couldn't foresee everything in the trade; there wasn't a finer business in Middlemarch than ours, and the lad was clever. My poor brother was in the Church, and would have done well – had got preferment already, but that stomach fever took him off: else he might have been a dean by this time. I think I was justified in what I tried to do for Fred. If you come to religion, it seems to me a man shouldn't want to carve out his meat to an ounce beforehand: – one must trust a little to Providence and be generous. It's a good British feeling to try and raise your family a little: in my opinion, it's a father's duty to give his sons a fine chance.'

'I don't wish to act otherwise than as your best friend, Vincy, when I say that what you have been uttering just now is one mass of worldliness and inconsistent folly.'

'Very well,' said Mr Vincy, kicking in spite of resolutions, 'I never profess to be anything but worldly; and, what's more, I don't see anybody else who is not worldly. I suppose you don't conduct business on what you call unworldly principles. The only difference I see is that one worldliness is a little bit honester than another.'

'This kind of discussion is unfruitful, Vincy,' said Mr Bulstrode, who, finishing his sandwich, had thrown himself back in his chair, and shaded his eyes as if weary. 'You had some more particular business.'

'Yes, yes. The long and short of it is, somebody has told old Featherstone, giving you as the authority, that Fred has been borrowing or trying to borrow money on the prospect of his land. Of course you never said any such nonsense. But the old fellow will insist on it that Fred should bring him a denial in your handwriting: that is, just a bit of a note saying you don't believe a word of such stuff, either of his having borrowed or tried to borrow in such a fool's way. I suppose you can have no objection to do that.'

'Pardon me. I have an objection. I am by no means sure that your son, in his recklessness and ignorance – I will use no severer word – has not tried to raise money by holding out his future prospects, or even that someone may not have been foolish enough to supply him on so vague a presumption: there is plenty of such lax moneylending as of other folly in the world.'

'But Fred gives me his honour that he has never borrowed money on the pretence of any understanding about his uncle's land. He is not a liar. I don't want to make him better than he is. I have blown him up well – nobody can say I wink at what he does. But he is not a liar. And I should have thought – but I may be wrong – that there was no religion to hinder a man from believing the best of a young fellow, when you don't know worse. It seems to me it would be a poor sort of religion to put a spoke in his wheel by refusing to say you don't believe such harm of him as you've got no good reason to believe.'

'I am not at all sure that I should be befriending your son by smoothing his way to the future possession of Featherstone's property. I cannot regard wealth as a blessing to those who use it simply as a harvest for this world. You do not like to hear these things, Vincy, but on this occasion I feel called upon to tell you that I have no motive for furthering such a disposition of property as that which you refer to. I do not shrink from saying that it will not tend to your son's eternal welfare or to the glory of God. Why then should you expect me to pen this kind of affidavit, which has no object but to keep up a foolish partiality and secure a foolish bequest?'

'If you mean to hinder everybody from having money but saints and evangelists, you must give up some profitable partnerships, that's all I can say,' Mr Vincy burst out very bluntly. 'It may be for the glory of God, but it is not for the glory of the Middlemarch trade, that Plymdale's house uses those blue and green dyes it gets from the Brassing manufactory; they rot the silk, that's all I know about it. Perhaps if other people knew so much of the profit went to the glory of God, they might like it better. But I don't mind so much about that – I could get up a pretty row, if I chose.'

Mr Bulstrode paused a little before he answered. 'You pain me very much by speaking in this way, Vincy. I do not expect you to understand my grounds of action – it is not an easy thing even to thread a path for principles in the intricacies of the world – still less to make the thread clear for the careless and the scoffing. You must remember, if you please, that I stretch my tolerance towards you as my wife's brother, and that it little becomes you to complain of me as withholding material help towards the worldly position of your family. I must remind you that it is not your own prudence or judgement that has enabled you to keep your place in the trade.'

'Very likely not; but you have been no loser by my trade yet,' said Mr Vincy, thoroughly nettled (a result which was seldom much retarded by previous resolutions). 'And when you married Harriet, I don't see how you could expect that our families should not hang by the same nail. If you've changed your mind, and want my family to come down in the world, you'd better say so. I've never changed: I'm a plain Churchman now, just as I used to be before doctrines came up. I take the world as I find it, in trade and everything else. I'm contented to be no worse than my neighbours. But if you want us to come down in the world, say so. I shall know better what to do then.'

'You talk unreasonably. Shall you come down in the world for want of this letter about your son?'

'Well, whether or not, I consider it very unhandsome of you to refuse it. Such doings may be lined with religion, but outside they have a nasty, dog-in-the-manger look. You might as well slander Fred: it comes pretty near to it when you refuse to say you didn't set a slander going. It's this sort of thing – this tyrannical spirit, wanting to play bishop and banker everywhere – it's this sort of thing makes a man's name stink.'

'Vincy, if you insist on quarrelling with me, it will be exceedingly painful to Harriet as well as myself,' said Mr Bulstrode, with a trifle more eagerness and paleness than usual.

'I don't want to quarrel. It's for my interest – and perhaps for yours too – that we should be friends. I bear you no grudge; I think no worse of you than I do of other people. A man who half-starves himself, and goes the length of family prayers, and so on, that you do, believes in his religion whatever it may be: you could turn over your capital just as fast with cursing and swearing: – plenty of fellows do. You like to be master, there's no denying that; you must be first chop in heaven, else you won't like it much. But you're my sister's husband, and we ought to stick together; and if I know Harriet, she'll consider it your fault if we quarrel because you strain at a gnat in this way, and refuse to do Fred a good turn. And I don't mean to say I shall bear it well. I consider it unhandsome.'

Mr Vincy rose, began to button his greatcoat, and looked steadily at his brother-in-law, meaning to imply a demand for a decisive answer.

This was not the first time that Mr Bulstrode had begun by admonishing Mr Vincy, and had ended by seeing a very unsatisfactory reflection of himself in the coarse unflattering mirror which that manufacturer's mind presented to the subtler lights and shadows of his fellow-men; and perhaps his experience full-fed fountain will be generous with its waters even in the rain, when they are worse than useless; and a fine fount of admonition is apt to be equally irrepressible.

It was not in Mr Bulstrode's nature to comply directly in consequence of uncomfortable suggestions. Before changing his course, he always needed to shape his motives and bring them into accordance with his habitual standard. He said, at last: 'I will reflect a little, Vincy. I will mention the subject to Harriet. I shall probably send you a letter.'

'Very well. As soon as you can, please. I hope it will all be settled before I see you tomorrow.'

Chapter 14

> Follows here the strict receipt
> For that sauce to dainty meat,
> Named Idleness, which many eat
> By preference, and call it sweet:
>
> First watch for morsels, like a hound,
> Mix well with buffets, stir them round
> With good thick oil of flatteries,
> And froth with mean self-lauding lies.
> Serve warm: the vessels you must choose
> To keep it in are dead men's shoes.

Mr Bulstrode's consultation of Harriet seemed to have had the effect desired by Mr Vincy, for early the next morning a letter came which Fred could carry to Mr Featherstone as the required testimony.

The old gentleman was staying in bed on account of the cold weather, and as Mary Garth was not to be seen in the sitting-room Fred went upstairs immediately and presented the letter to his uncle, who, propped up comfortably on a bed-rest, was not less able than usual to enjoy his consciousness of wisdom in distrusting and frustrating mankind. He put on his spectacles to read the letter, pursing up his lips and drawing down their corners.

'*Under the circumstances I will not decline to state my conviction* – tchah! what fine words the fellow puts! He's as fine as an auctioneer – *that your son Frederic has not obtained any advance of money on bequests promised by Mr Featherstone* – promised? who said I had ever promised? I promise nothing – I shall make codicils as long as I like – *and that considering the nature of such a proceedings, it is unreasonable to presume that a young man of sense and character would attempt it* – ah, but the gentleman doesn't say you *are* a young man of sense and character, mark you that, sir! – *as to my own concern with any report of such a nature, I distinctly affirm that I never made any statement to the effect that your son had borrowed money on any property that might accrue to him on Mr Featherstone's demise* – bless my heart! "property – accrue – demise!" Lawyer Standish is nothing to him. He couldn't speak finer if he wanted to borrow. Well,' Mr Featherstone here looked over his spectacles at Fred, while he handed back the letter to him with a contemptuous gesture, 'you don't suppose I believe a thing because Bulstrode writes it out fine, eh?'

Fred coloured. 'You wished to have the letter, sir. I should think it very likely that Mr Bulstrode's denial is as good as the authority which told you what he denies.'

'Every bit. I never said I believed either one or the other. And now what d'you expect?' said Mr Featherstone, curtly, keeping on his spectacles, but withdrawing his hands under his wraps.

'I expect nothing, sir.' Fred with difficulty restrained himself from venting his irritation. 'I came to bring you the letter. If you like, I will bid you good-morning.'

'Not yet, not yet. Ring the bell; I want Missy to come.'

It was a servant who came in answer to the bell.

'Tell Missy to come!' said Mr Featherstone, impatiently. 'What business had she to go away?' He spoke in the same tone when Mary came.

'Why couldn't you sit still here till I told you to go? I want my waistcoat now. I told you always to put it on the bed.'

Mary's eyes looked rather red, as if she had been crying. It was clear that Mr Featherstone was in one of his most snappish humours this morning, and though Fred had now the prospect of receiving the much-needed present of money, he would have preferred being free to turn round on the old tyrant and tell him that Mary Garth was too good to be at his beck. Though Fred had risen as she entered the room, she had barely noticed him, and looked as if her nerves were quivering with the expectation that something would be thrown at her. But she never had anything worse than words to dread. When she went to reach the waistcoat from a peg, Fred went up to her and said, 'Allow me.'

'Let it alone! You bring it, Missy, and lay it down here,' said Mr Featherstone. 'Now you go away again till I call you,' he added, when the waistcoat was laid down by him. It was usual with him to season his pleasure in showing favour to one person by being especially disagreeable to another, and Mary was always at hand to furnish the condiment. When his own relatives came she was treated better. Slowly he took out a bunch of keys from the waistcoat-pocket, and slowly he drew forth a tin box which was under the bedclothes.

'You expect I'm going to give you a little fortune, eh?' he said, looking above his spectacles and pausing in the act of opening the lid.

'Not at all, sir. You were good enough to speak of making me a present the other day, else, of course, I should not have thought of the matter.' But Fred was of a hopeful disposition, and a vision had presented itself of a sum just large enough to deliver him from a certain anxiety. When Fred got into debt, it always seemed to him highly probable that something or other – he did not necessarily conceive what – would come to pass enabling him to pay in due time. And now that the providential occurrence was apparently close at hand, it would have been sheer absurdity to think that the supply would be short of the need: as absurd as a faith that believed in half a miracle for want of strength to believe in a whole one.

The deep-veined hands fingered many bank-notes one after the other, laying them down flat again, while Fred leaned back in his chair, scorning to look eager. He held himself to be a gentleman at heart, and did not like courting an old fellow for his money. At last, Mr Featherstone eyed him again over his spectacles and presented him with a little sheaf of notes; Fred could see distinctly that there were but five, as the less significant edges gaped towards him. But then, each might mean fifty pounds. He took them, saying: 'I am very much obliged to you, sir,' and was going to roll them up without seeming to think of their value. But this did not suit Mr Featherstone, who was eyeing him intently.

'Come, don't you think it worth your while to count 'em? You take money like a lord; I suppose you lose it like one.'

'I thought I was not to look a gift-horse in the mouth, sir. But I shall be very happy to count them.'

Fred was not so happy, however, after he had counted them. For they actually presented the absurdity of being less than his hopefulness had decided that they must be. What can the fitness of things mean, if not their fitness to a man's expectations? Failing this, absurdity and atheism gape behind him. The collapse for Fred was severe when he found that he held no more than five twenties, and his share in the higher education of this country did not seem to help him. Nevertheless he said, with rapid changes in his fair complexion: 'It is very handsome of you, sir.'

'I should think it is,' said Mr Featherstone, locking his box and replacing it, then taking off his spectacles deliberately, and at length, as if his inward meditation had more deeply convinced him, repeating, 'I should think it is handsome.'

'I assure you, sir, I am very grateful,' said Fred, who had had time to recover his cheerful air.

'So you ought to be. You want to cut a figure in the world, and I reckon Peter Featherstone is the only one you've got to trust to.' Here the old man's eyes gleamed with a curiously-mingled satisfaction in the consciousness that this smart young fellow relied upon him, and that the smart young fellow was rather a fool for doing so.

'Yes, indeed; I was not born to very splendid chances. Few men have been more cramped than I have been,' said Fred, with some sense of surprise at his own virtue, considering how hardly he was dealt with. 'It really seems a little too bad to have to ride a broken-winded hunter, and see men, who are not half such good judges as yourself, able to throw away any amount of money on buying bad bargains.'

'Well, you can buy yourself a fine hunter now. Eighty pounds is enough for that, I reckon – and you'll have twenty pound over to get yourself out of any little scrape,' said Mr Featherstone, chuckling slightly.

'You are very good, sir,' said Fred, with a fine sense of contrast between the words and his feeling.

'Ay, rather a better uncle than your fine uncle Bulstrode. You won't get much out of his spekilations, I think. He's got a pretty strong string round your father's leg, by what I hear, eh?'

'My father never tells me anything about his affairs, sir.'

'Well, he shows some sense there. But other people find 'em out without his telling. *He'll* never have much to leave you: he'll most-like die without a will – he's the sort of man to do it – let 'em make him mayor of Middlemarch as much as they like. But you won't get much by his dying without a will, though you are the eldest son.'

Fred thought that Mr Featherstone had never been so disagreeable before. True, he had never before given him quite so much money at once.

'Shall I destroy this letter of Mr Bulstrode's, sir?' said Fred, rising with the letter as if he would put it in the fire.

'Ay, ay, I don't want it. It's worth no money to me.'

Fred carried the letter to the fire, and thrust the poker through it with much zest. He longed to get out of the room, but he was a little ashamed before his inner self, as well as before his uncle, to run away immediately after pocketing the money. Presently, the farm bailiff came up to give his master a report, and Fred, to his unspeakable relief, was dismissed with the injunction to come again soon.

He had longed not only to be set free from his uncle, but also to find Mary Garth. She was now in her usual place by the fire, with sewing in her hands and a book open on the little table by her side. Her eyelids had lost some of their redness now, and she had her usual air of self-command.

'Am I wanted upstairs?' she said, half-rising as Fred entered.

'No; I am only dismissed, because Simmons is gone up.'

Mary sat down again, and resumed her work. She was certainly treating him with more indifference than usual: she did not know how affectionately indignant he had felt on her behalf upstairs.

'May I stay here a little, Mary, or shall I bore you?'

'Pray sit down,' said Mary; 'you will not be so heavy a bore as Mr John Waule, who was here yesterday, and he sat down without asking my leave.'

'Poor fellow! I think he is in love with you.'

'I am not aware of it. And to me it is one of the most odious things in a girl's life, that there must always be some supposition of falling in love coming between her and any man who is kind to her, and to whom she is grateful. I should have thought that I, at least, might have been safe from all that. I have no ground for the nonsensical vanity of fancying everybody who comes near me is in love with me.'

Mary did not mean to betray a feeling, but in spite of herself she ended in a tremulous tone of vexation.

'Confound John Waule! I did not mean to make you angry. I didn't know you had any reason for being grateful to him. I forgot what a great service you think it if anyone snuffs a candle for you.' Fred also had his pride, and was not going to show that he knew what had called forth this outburst of Mary's.

'Oh, I am not angry, except with the ways of the world. I do like to be spoken to as if I had common-sense. I really often feel as if I could understand a little more than I ever hear even from young gentlemen who have been to college.' Mary had recovered, and she spoke with a suppressed rippling undercurrent of laughter pleasant to hear.

'I don't care how merry you are at my expense this morning,' said Fred. 'I thought you looked so sad when you came upstairs. It is a shame you should stay here to be bullied in that way.'

'Oh, I have an easy life – by comparison. I have tried being a teacher, but I am not fit for that: my mind is too fond of wandering on its own way. I think any hardship is better than pretending to do what one is paid for, and never really doing it. Everything here I can do as well as anyone else could; perhaps better than some – Rosy, for example. Though she is just the sort of beautiful creature that is imprisoned with ogres in fairy tales.'

'*Rosy!*' cried Fred, in a tone of profound brotherly scepticism.

'Come, Fred!' said Mary, emphatically; 'you have no right to be so critical.'

'Do you mean anything particular – just now?'

'No, I mean something general – always.'

'Oh, that I am idle and extravagant. Well, I am not fit to be a poor man. I should not have made a bad fellow if I had been rich.'

'You would have done your duty in that state of life to which it has not pleased God to call you,' said Mary, laughing.

'Well, I couldn't do my duty as a clergyman, any more than you could do yours as a governess. You ought to have a little fellow-feeling there, Mary.'

'I never said you ought to be a clergyman. There are other sorts of work. It seems to me very miserable not to resolve on some course and act accordingly,'

'So I could, if – ' Fred broke off, and stood up, leaning against the mantelpiece.

'If you were sure you should not have a fortune?'

'I did not say that. You want to quarrel with me. It is too bad of you to be guided by what other people say about me.'

'How can I want to quarrel with you! I should be quarrelling with all my new books,' said Mary, lifting the volume on the table. 'However naughty you may be to other people, you are good to me.'

'Because I like you better than anyone else. But I know you despise me.'

'Yes, I do – a little,' said Mary, nodding, with a smile.

'You would admire a stupendous fellow, who would have wise opinions about everything.'

'Yes, I should.' Mary was sewing swiftly, and seemed provokingly mistress of the situation. When a conversation has taken a wrong turn for us, we only get farther and farther into the swamp of awkwardness. This was what Fred Vincy felt.

'I suppose a women is never in love with anyone she has always known – ever since she can remember; as a man often is. It is always some new fellow who strikes a girl.'

'Let me see,' said Mary, the corners of her mouth curling archly; 'I must go back on my experience. There is Juliet – she seems an example of what you say. But then Ophelia had probably known Hamlet a long while; and Brenda Troil – she had known Mordaunt Merton ever since they were children; but then he seems to have been an estimable young man; and Minna was still more deeply in love with Cleveland, who was a stranger. Waverley was new to Flora MacIvor; but then she did not fall in love with him. And there are Olivia and Sophia Primrose, and Corinne – they may be said to have fallen in love with new men. Altogether, my experience is rather mixed.'

Mary looked up with some roguishness at Fred, and that look of hers was very dear to him, though the eyes were nothing more than clear windows where observation sat laughingly. He was certainly an affectionate fellow, and as he had grown from boy to man, he had grown in love with his old playmate, notwithstanding that share in the higher education of the country which had exalted his views of rank and income.

'When a man is not loved, it is no use for him to say that he could be a better fellow – could do anything – I mean, if he were sure of being loved in return.'

'Not of the least use in the world for him to say he *could* be better. Might, could, would – they are contemptible auxiliaries.'

'I don't see how a man is to be good for much unless he has some one woman to love him dearly.'

'I think the goodness should come before he expects that.'

'You know better, Mary. Women don't love their men for their goodness.'

'Perhaps not. But if they love them, they never think them bad.'

'It is hardly fair to say I am bad.'

'I said nothing at all about you.'

'I never shall be good for anything, Mary, if you will not say that you love me – if you will not promise to marry me – I mean, when I am able to marry.'

'If I did love you, I would not marry you: I would certainly not promise ever to marry you.'

'I think that is quite wicked, Mary. If you love me, you ought to promise to marry me.'

'On the contrary, I think it would be wicked in me to marry you even if I did love you.'

'You mean, just as I am, without any means of maintaining a wife. Of course: I am but three-and-twenty.'

'In that last point you will alter. But I am not so sure of any other alteration. My father says an idle man ought not to exist, much less be married.'

'Then I am to blow my brains out?'

'No; on the whole I should think you would do better to pass your examination. I have heard Mr Farebrother say it is disgracefully easy.'

'That is all very fine. Anything is easy to him. Not that cleverness has anything to do with it. I am ten times cleverer than many men who pass.'

'Dear me!' said Mary, unable to repress her sarcasm. 'That accounts for the curates like Mr Crowse. Divide your cleverness by ten, and the quotient – dear me! – is able to take a degree. But that only shows you are ten times more idle than the others.'

'Well, if I did pass, you would not want me to go into the Church?'

'That is not the question – what I want you to do. You have a conscience of your own, I suppose. There! there is Mr Lydgate. I must go and tell my uncle.'

'Mary,' said Fred, seizing her hand as she rose; 'if you will not give me some encouragement, I shall get worse instead of better.'

'I will not give you any encouragement,' said Mary, reddening. 'Your friends would dislike it, and so would mine. My father would think it a disgrace to me if I accepted a man who got into debt, and would not work!'

Fred was stung, and released her hand. She walked to the door, but there she turned and said: 'Fred, you have always been so good, so generous to me. I am not ungrateful. But never speak to me in that way again.'

'Very well,' said Fred, sulkily, taking up his hat and whip. His complexion showed patches of pale pink and dead white. Like many a plucked idle young gentleman, he was thoroughly in love, and with a plain girl, who had no money! But having Mr Featherstone's land in the background, and a persuasion that, let Mary say what she would, she really did care for him, Fred was not utterly in despair.

When he got home, he gave four of the twenties to his mother, asking her to keep them for him. 'I don't want to spend that money, mother. I want it to pay a debt with. So keep it safe away from my fingers.'

'Bless you, my dear' said Mrs Vincy. She doted on her eldest son and her youngest girl (a child of six), whom others thought her two naughtiest children. The mother's eyes are not always deceived in their partiality: she at least can best judge who is the tender, filial-hearted child. And Fred was certainly very fond of his mother. Perhaps it was his fondness for another person also that made him particularly anxious to take some security against his own liability to spend the hundred pounds. For the creditor to whom he owed a hundred and sixty held a firmer security in the shape of a bill signed by Mary's father.

Chapter 15

Black eyes you have left, you say
  Blue eyes fail to draw you;
Yet you seem more rapt today,
  Than of old we saw you.

Oh I track the fairest fair
  Through new haunts of pleasure;
Footprints here and echoes there
  Guide me to my treasure:

Lo! She turns – immortal youth
  Wrought to mortal stature,
Fresh as starlight's aged truth –
  Many-namèd Nature!

A great historian, as he insisted on calling himself, who had the happiness to be dead a hundred and twenty years ago, and so to take his place among the colossi whose huge legs our living pettiness is observed to walk under, glories in his copious remarks and digressions as the least imitable part of his work, and especially in those initial chapters to the successive books of his history, where he seems to bring his armchair to the proscenium and chat with us in all the lusty ease of his fine English. But Fielding lived when the days were longer (for time, like money, is measured by our needs), when summer afternoons were spacious, and the clock ticked slowly in the winter evenings. We belated historians must not linger after his example; and if we did so, it is probable that our chat would be thin and eager, as if delivered from a camp-stool in a parrot-house. I at least have so much to do in unravelling certain human lots, and seeing how they were woven and interwoven, that all the light I can command must be concentrated on this particular web, and not dispersed over that tempting range of relevancies called the universe.

At present I have to make the new settler Lydgate better known to anyone interested in him than he could possibly be even to those who had seen the most of him since his arrival in Middlemarch. For surely all must admit that a man may be puffed and belauded, envied, ridiculed, counted upon as a tool and fallen in love with, or at least selected as a future husband, and yet remain virtually unknown – known merely as a cluster of signs for his neighbours' false suppositions. There was a general impression, however, that Lydgate was not altogether a common country doctor, and in Middlemarch at that time such an impression was significant of great things being expected from him. For everybody's family doctor was remarkably clever, and was understood to have immeasurable skill in the management and training of the most skittish or vicious diseases. The evidence of his cleverness was of the higher intuitive order, lying in his lady patients' immovable conviction, and was unassailable by any objection except that their intuitions were opposed by others equally strong; each lady who saw medical truth in Wrench and 'the strengthening treatment' regarding Toller and 'the lowering system' as medical perdition. For the heroic times of copious bleeding and blistering had not yet departed, still less the times of thoroughgoing theory, when disease in general was called by some bad name, and treated accordingly without shilly-shally – as if, for example, it were to be called insurrection, which must not be fired on with blank-cartridge, but have its blood drawn at once. The strengtheners and the lowerers were all 'clever' men in somebody's opinion, which is really as much as can be said for any living talents. Nobody's imagination had gone so far as to conjecture that Mr Lydgate could know as much as Dr Sprague and Dr Minchin, the two physicians, who alone could offer any hope when danger was extreme, and when the smallest hope was worth a guinea. Still, I repeat, there was a general impression that Lydgate was something rather more uncommon than any general practitioner in Middlemarch. And this was true. He was but seven-and-twenty, an age at which many men are not quite common – at which they are hopeful of achievement, resolute in avoidance, thinking that Mammon shall never put a bit in their mouths and get astride their backs, but rather that Mammon, if they have anything to do with him, shall draw their chariot.

He had been left an orphan when he was fresh from a public school. His father, a military man, had made but little provision for three children, and when the boy Tertius asked to have a medical education, it seemed easier to his guardians to grant his request by apprenticing him to a country practitioner than to make any objections on the score of family dignity. He was one of the rarer lads who early get a decided bent and make up their minds that there is something particular in life which they would like to do for its own sake, and not because their fathers did it. Most of us who turn to any subject we love remember some morning or evening hour when we got on a high stool to reach down an untried volume, or sat with parted lips listening to a new talker, or for very lack of books began to listen to the voices within, as the first traceable beginning of our love. Something of that sort happened to Lydgate. He was a quick fellow, and when hot from play, would toss himself in a corner, and in five minutes be deep in any sort of book that he could lay his hands on: if it were Rasselas or Gulliver, so much the better, but Bailey's Dictionary would do, or the Bible with the Apocrypha in it. Something he must read, when he was not riding the pony, or running and hunting, or listening to the talk of men. All this was true of him at ten years of age; he had then read through *Chrysal, or the Adventures of a Guinea*, which was neither milk for babes, nor any chalky mixture meant to pass for milk, and it had already occurred to him that books were stuff, and that life was stupid. His school studies had not much modified that opinion, for though he 'did' his classics and mathematics, he was not pre-eminent in them. It was said of him, that Lydgate could do anything he liked, but he had certainly not yet liked to do anything remarkable. He was a vigorous animal with a ready understanding, but no spark had yet kindled in him an intellectual passion; knowledge seemed to him a very superficial affair, easily mastered: judging from the conversation of his elders, he had apparently got already more than was necessary for mature life. Probably this was not an exceptional result of expensive teaching at that period of short-waisted coats, and other fashions which have not yet recurred. But, one vacation, a wet day sent him to the small home library to hunt once more for a book which might have some freshness for him: in vain! unless, indeed, he took down a dusty row of volumes with grey-paper backs and dingy labels – the volumes of an old Cyclopaedia which he had never disturbed. It would at least be a novelty to disturb them. They were on the highest shelf, and he stood on a chair to get them down. But he opened the volume which he first took from the shelf: somehow, one is apt to read in a makeshift attitude, just where it might seem inconvenient to do so. The page he opened on was under the heading of Anatomy, and the first passage that drew his eyes was on the valves of the heart. He was not much acquainted with valves of any sort, but he knew that *valvae* were folding doors, and through this crevice came a sudden light startling him with his first vivid notion of finely adjusted mechanism in the human frame. A liberal education had of course left him free to read the indecent passages in the school classics, but beyond a general sense of secrecy and obscenity in connection with his internal structure, had left his imagination quite unbiassed, so that for anything he knew his brains lay in small bags at his temples, and he had no more thought of representing to himself how his blood circulated than how paper served instead of gold. But the moment of vocation had come, and before he got down from his chair, the world was made new to him by a presentiment of endless processes filling the vast spaces planked out of his sight by that wordy ignorance which he had supposed to be know-ledge. From that hour Lydgate felt the growth of an intellectual passion.

We are not afraid of telling over and over again how a man comes to fall in love with a woman and be wedded to her, or else be fatally parted from her. Is it due to excess of poetry or of stupidity that we are never weary of describing what King James called a woman's 'makdom and her fairnesse', never weary of listening to the twanging of the old Troubadour strings, and are comparatively uninterested in that other kind of 'makdom and fairnesse' which must be wooed with industrious thought and patient renunciation of small desires? In the story of this passion, too, the development varies: sometimes it is the glorious marriage, sometimes frustration and final parting. And not seldom the catastrophe is bound up with the other passion, sung by the Troubadours. For in the multitude of middle-aged men who go about their vocations in a daily course determined for them much in the same way as the tie of their cravats, there is always a good number who once meant to shape their own deeds and alter the world a little. The story of their coming to be shapen after the average and fit to be packed by the gross, is hardly ever told even in their conscious-ness; for perhaps their ardour in generous unpaid toil cooled as imperceptibly as the ardour of other youthful loves, till one day their earlier self walked like a ghost in its old home and made the new furniture ghastly. Nothing in the world more subtle than the process of their gradual change! In the beginning they inhaled it unknowingly; you and I may have sent some of our breath towards infecting them, when we uttered our conforming falsities or drew our silly conclusions: or perhaps it came with the vibrations from a woman's glance.

Lydgate did not mean to be one of those failures, and there was the better hope of him because his scientific interest soon took the form of a professional enthusiasm: he had a youthful belief in his bread-winning work, not to be stifled by that initiation in makeshift called his 'prentice days; and he carried to his studies in London, Edinburgh, and Paris, the conviction that the medical profession as it might be was the finest in the world; presenting the most perfect interchange between science and art; offering the most direct alliance between intellectual conquest and the social good. Lydgate's nature demanded this combination: he was an emotional creature, with a flesh-and-blood sense of fellowship which withstood all the abstractions of special study. He cared not only for 'cases', but for John and Elizabeth, especially Elizabeth.

There was another attraction in this profession: it wanted reform, and gave a man an opportunity for some indignant resolve to reject its venal decorations and other humbug, and to be the possessor of genuine though undemanded qualifications. He went to study in Paris with the determination that when he came home again he would settle in some provincial town as a general prac- titioner, and resist the irrational severance between medical and surgical know- ledge in the interest of his own scientific pursuits, as well as of the general advance: he would keep away from the range of London intrigues, jealousies, and social truckling, and win celebrity, however slowly, as Jenner had done, by the independent value of his work. For it must be remembered that this was a dark period; and in spite of venerable colleges which used great efforts to secure purity of knowledge by making it scarce, and to exclude error by a rigid exclusiveness in relation to fees and appointments, it happened that very ignorant young gentlemen were promoted in town, and many more got a legal right to practise over large areas in the country. Also, the high standard held up to the public mind by the College of Physicians, which gave its peculiar sanction to the expensive and highly-rarified medical instruction obtained by graduates of Oxford and Cambridge, did not hinder quackery from having an excellent time of it; for since professional practice chiefly consisted in giving a great many drugs, the public inferred that it might be better off with more drugs still if they could only be got cheaply, and hence swallowed large cubic measures of physic prescribed by unscrupulous ignorance which had taken no degrees. Considering that statistics had not yet embraced a calculation as to the number of ignorant or canting doctors which absolutely must exist in the teeth of all changes, it seemed to Lydgate that a change in the units was the most direct mode of changing the numbers. He meant to be a unit who would make a certain amount of difference towards that spreading change which would one day tell appreciably upon the averages, and in the meantime have the pleasure of making an advantageous difference to the viscera of his own patients. But he did not simply aim at a more genuine kind of practice than was common. He was ambitious of a wider effect: he was fired with the possibility that he might work out the proof of an anatomical conception and make a link in the chain of discovery.

Does it seem incongruous to you that a Middlemarch surgeon should dream of himself as a discoverer? Most of us, indeed, know little of the great originators until they have been lifted up among the constellations and already rule our fates. But that Herschel, for example, who 'broke the barriers of the heavens' – did he not once play a provincial church-organ, and give music-lessons to stumbling pianists? Each of those Shining Ones had to walk on the earth among neighbours who perhaps thought much more of his gait and his garments than of anything which was to give him a title to everlasting fame: each of them had his little local personal history sprinkled with small temptations and sordid cares, which made the retarding friction of his course towards final companionship with the immortals. Lydgate was not blind to the dangers of such friction, but he had plenty of confidence in his resolution to avoid it as far as possible: being seven-and-twenty, he felt himself experienced. And he was not going to have his vanities provoked by contact with the showy worldly successes of the capital, but to live among people who could hold no rivalry with that pursuit of a great idea which was to be a twin object with the assiduous practice of his profession. There was fascination in the hope that the two purposes would illuminate each other: the careful observation and inference which was his daily work, the use of the lens to further his judgement in special cases, would further his thought as an instrument of larger enquiry. Was not this the typical pre-eminence of his profession? He would be a good Middlemarch doctor, and by that very means keep himself in the track of far-reaching investigation. On one point he may fairly claim approval at this particular stage of his career; he did not mean to imitate those philanthropic models who make a profit out of poisonous pickles to support themselves while they are exposing adulteration, or hold shares in a gambling-hell that they may have leisure to represent the cause of public morality. He intended to begin in his own case some particular reforms which were quite certainly within his reach, and much less of a problem than the demonstrating of an anatomical conception. One of these reforms was to act stoutly on the strength of a recent legal decision, and simply prescribe, without dispensing drugs or taking percentage from druggists. This was an innovation for one who had chosen to adopt the style of general practitioner in a country town, and would be felt as offensive criticism by his professional brethren. But Lydgate meant to innovate in his treatment also, and he was wise enough to see that the best security for his practising honestly according to his belief was to get rid of systematic temptations to the contrary.

Perhaps that was a more cheerful time for observers and theorisers than the present; we are apt to think it the finest era of the world when America was beginning to be discovered, when a bold sailor, even if he were wrecked, might alight on a new kingdom; and about 1829 the dark territories of Pathology were a fine America for a spirited young adventurer. Lydgate was ambitious above all to contribute towards enlarging the scientific, rational basis of his profession. The more he became interested in special questions of disease, such as the nature of fever or fevers, the more keenly he felt the need for that fundamental knowledge of structure which just at the beginning of the century had been illuminated by the brief and glorious career of Bichat, who died when he was only one-and-thirty, but, like another Alexander, left a realm large enough for many heirs. That great Frenchman first carried out the conception that living bodies, fundamentally considered, are not associations of organs which can be understood by studying them first apart, and then as it were federally; but must be regarded as consisting of certain primary webs or tissues, out of which the various organs – brain, heart, lungs, and so on – are compacted, as the various accommodations of a house are built up in various proportions of wood, iron, stone, brick, zinc, and the rest, each material having its peculiar composition and proportions. No man, one sees, can understand and estimate the entire structure or its parts – what are its frailties and what its repairs, without knowing the nature of the materials. And the conception wrought out by Bichat, with his detailed study of the different tissues, acted necessarily on medical questions as the turning of gaslight would act on a dim, oil-lit street, showing new connections and hitherto hidden facts of structure which must be taken into account in considering the symptoms of maladies and the action of medicaments. But results which depend on human conscience and intelligence work slowly, and now at the end of 1829, most medical practice was still strutting or shambling along the old paths, and there was still scientific work to be done which might have seemed to be a direct sequence of Bichat's. This great seer did not go beyond the consideration of the tissues as ultimate facts in the living organism, marking the limit of anatomical analysis; but it was open to another mind to say, have not these structures some common basis from which they have all started, as your sarsnet, gauze, net, satin and velvet from the raw cocoon? Here would be another light, as of oxy-hydrogen, showing the very grain of things, and revising all former explanations. Of this sequence to Bichat's work, already vibrating along many currents of the European mind, Lydgate was enamoured; he longed to demonstrate the more intimate relations of living structure and help to define men's thought more accurately after the true order. The work had not yet been done, but only prepared for those who knew how to use the preparation. What was the primitive tissue? In that way Lydgate put the question – not quite in the way required by the awaiting answer; but such missing of the right word befalls many seekers. And he counted on quiet intervals to be watchfully seized, for taking up the threads of investigation – on many hints to be won from diligent application, not only of the scalpel, but of the microscope, which research had begun to use again with new enthusiasm of reliance. Such was Lydgate's plan of his future: to do good small work for Middlemarch, and great work for the world.

He was certainly a happy fellow at this time: to be seven-and-twenty, without any fixed vices, with a generous resolution that his action should be beneficent, and with ideas in his brain that made life interesting quite apart from the *cultus* of horseflesh and other mystic rites of costly observance, which the eight hundred pounds left him after buying his practice would certainly not have gone far in paying for. He was at a starting-point which makes many a man's career a fine subject for betting, if there were any gentlemen given to that amusement who could appreciate the complicated probabilities of an arduous purpose, with all the possible thwartings and furtherings of circumstance, all the niceties of inward balance, by which a man swims and makes his point or else is carried headlong. The risk would remain, even with close knowledge of Lydgate's character; for character too is a process and an unfolding. The man was still in the making, as much as the Middlemarch doctor and immortal discoverer, and there were both virtues and faults capable of shrinking or expanding. The faults will not, I hope, be a reason for the withdrawal of your interest in him. Among our valued friends is there not someone or other who is a little too self-confident and disdainful; whose distinguished mind is a little spotted with commonness; who is a little pinched here and protuberant there with native prejudices; or whose better energies are liable to lapse down the wrong channel under the influence of transient solicitations? All these things might be alleged against Lydgate, but then, they are the periphrases of a polite preacher, who talks of Adam, and would not like to mention anything painful to the pew-renters. The particular faults from which these delicate generalities are distilled have distinguishable physiognomies, diction, accent, and grimaces; filling up parts in very various dramas. Our vanities differ as our noses do: all conceit is not the same conceit, but varies in correspondence with the minutiae of mental make in which one of us differs from another. Lydgate's conceit was of the arrogant sort, never simpering, never impertinent, but massive in its claims and benevolently contemptuous. He would do a great deal for noodles, being sorry for them, and feeling quite sure that they could have no power over him: he had thought of joining the Saint Simonians when he was in Paris, in order to turn them against some of their own doctrines. All his faults were marked by kindred traits, and were those of a man who had a fine baritone, whose clothes hung well upon him, and who even in his ordinary gestures had an air of inbred distinction. Where then lay the spots of commonness? says a young lady enamoured of that careless grace. How could there be any commonness in a man so well-bred, so ambitious of social distinction, so generous and unusual in his views of social duty? As easily as there may be stupidity in a man of genius if you take him unawares on the wrong subject, or as many a man who has the best will to advance the social millennium might be ill-inspired in imagining its lighter pleasures; unable to go beyond Offenbach's music, or the brilliant punning in the last burlesque. Lydgate's spots of commonness lay in the complexion of his prejudices, which, in spite of noble intentions and sympathy, were half of them such as are found in ordinary men of the world: that distinction of mind which belonged to his intellectual ardour, did not penetrate his feeling and judgement about furniture, or women, or the desirability of its being known (without his telling) that he was better born than other country surgeons. He did not mean to think of furniture at present; but whenever he did so, it was to be feared that neither biology nor schemes of reform would lift him above the vulgarity of feeling that there would be an incompatibility in his furniture not being of the best.

As to women, he had once already been drawn headlong by impetuous folly, which he meant to be final, since marriage at some distant period would of course not be impetuous. For those who want to be acquainted with Lydgate it will be good to know what was that case of impetuous folly, for it may stand as an example of the fitful swerving of passion to which he was prone, together with the chivalrous kindness which helped to make him morally lovable. The story can be told without many words. It happened when he was studying in Paris, and just at the time when, over and above his other work, he was occupied with some galvanic experiments. One evening, tired with his experimenting, and not being able to elicit the facts he needed, he left his frogs and rabbits to some repose under their trying and mysterious dispensation of unexplained shocks, and went to finish his evening at the theatre of the Porte Saint Martin, where there was a melodrama which he had already seen several times: attracted, not by the ingenious work of the collaborating authors, but by an actress whose part it was to stab her lover, mistaking him for the evil-designing duke of the piece. Lydgate was in love with this actress, as a man is in love with a woman whom he never expects to speak to. She was a Provençale, with dark eyes, a Greek profile, and rounded majestic form, having that sort of beauty which carries a sweet matronliness even in youth, and her voice was a soft cooing. She had but lately come to Paris, and bore a virtuous reputation, her husband acting with her as the unfortunate lover. It was her acting which was 'no better than it should be', but the public was satisfied. Lydgate's only relaxation now was to go and look at this woman, just as he might have thrown himself under the breath of the sweet south on a bank of violets for a while, without prejudice to his galvanism, to which he would presently return. But this evening the old drama had a new catastrophe. At the moment when the heroine was to act the stabbing of her lover, and he was to fall gracefully, the wife veritably stabbed her husband, who fell as death willed. A wild shriek pierced the house, and the Provençale fell swooning: a shriek and a swoon were demanded by the play, but the swooning too was real this time. Lydgate leaped and climbed, he hardly knew how, on to the stage, and was active in help, making the acquaintance of his heroine by finding a contusion on her head and lifting her gently in his arms. Paris rang with the story of this death: – was it a murder? Some of the actress's warmest admirers were inclined to believe in her guilt, and liked her the better for it (such was the taste of those times); but Lydgate was not one of these. He vehemently contended for her innocence, and the remote impersonal passion for her beauty which he had felt before, had passed now into personal devotion, and tender thought of her lot. The notion of murder was absurd; no motive was discoverable, the young couple being understood to dote on each other; and it was not unprecedented that an accidental slip of the foot should have brought these grave consequences. The legal investigation ended in Madame Laure's release. Lydgate by this time had had many interviews with her, and found her more and more adorable. She talked little; but that was an additional charm. She was melancholy, and seemed grateful; her presence was enough, like that of the evening light. Lydgate was madly anxious about her affection, and jealous lest any other man than himself should win it and ask her to marry him. But instead of re-opening her engagement at the Porte Saint Martin, where she would have been all the more popular for the fatal episode, she left Paris without warning, forsaking her little court of admirers. Perhaps no one carried enquiry far except Lydgate, who felt that all science had come to a standstill while he imagined the unhappy Laure, stricken by ever-wandering sorrow, herself wandering, and finding no faithful comforter. Hidden actresses, however, are not so difficult to find as some other hidden facts, and it was not long before Lydgate gathered indications that Laure had taken the route to Lyons. He found her at last acting with great success at Avignon under the same name, looking more majestic than ever as a forsaken wife carrying her child in her arms. He spoke to her after the play, was received with the usual quietude which seemed to him beautiful as clear depths of water, and obtained leave to visit her the next day; when he was bent on telling her that he adored her, and on asking her to marry him. He knew that this was like the sudden impulse of a madman – incongruous even with his habitual foibles. No matter! It was the one thing which he was resolved to do. He had two selves within him apparently, and they must learn to accommodate each other and bear reciprocal impediments. Strange, that some of us, with quick alternate vision see beyond our infatuations, and even while we rave on the heights behold the wide plain where our persistent self pauses and awaits us.

To have approached Laure with any suit that was not reverentially tender would have been simply a contradiction of his whole feeling towards her.

'You have come all the way from Paris to find me?' she said to him the next day, sitting before him with folded arms, and looking at him with eyes that seemed to wonder as an untamed ruminating animal wonders. 'Are all Englishmen like that?'

'I came because I could not live without trying to see you. You are lonely; I love you; I want you to consent to be my wife: I will wait, but I want you to promise that you will marry me – no one else.'

Laure looked at him in silence with a melancholy radiance from under her grand eyelids, until he was full of rapturous certainty, and knelt close to her knees.

'I will tell you something,' she said, in her cooing way, keeping her arms folded. 'My foot really slipped.'

'I know, I know,' said Lydgate, deprecatingly. 'It was a fatal accident – a dreadful stroke of calamity that bound me to you the more.'

Again Laure paused a little and then said, slowly, '*I meant to do it.*'

Lydgate, strong man as he was, turned pale and trembled: moments seemed to pass before he rose and stood at a distance from her.

'There was a secret, then,' he said at last, even vehemently. 'He was brutal to you: you hated him.'

'No! he wearied me; he was too fond: he would live in Paris and not in my country; that was not agreeable to me.'

'Great God!' said Lydgate, in a groan of horror. 'And you planned to murder him?'

'I did not plan: it came to me in the play – *I meant to do it.*'

Lydgate stood mute, and unconsciously pressed his hat on while he looked at her. He saw this woman – the first to whom he had given his young adoration – amid the throng of stupid criminals.

'You are a good young man,' she said. 'But I do not like husbands. I will never have another.'

Three days afterwards Lydgate was at his galvanism again in his Paris chambers, believing that illusions were at an end for him. He was saved from hardening effects by the abundant kindness of his heart and his belief that human life might be made better. But he had more reason than ever for trusting his judgement, now that it was so experienced; and henceforth he would take a strictly scientific view of woman, entertaining no expectations, but such as were justified beforehand.

No one in Middlemarch was likely to have such a notion of Lydgate's past as has here been faintly shadowed, and indeed the respectable townsfolk there were not more given than mortals generally to any eager attempt at exactness in the representation to themselves of what did not come under their own senses. Not only young virgins of that town, but grey-bearded men also, were often in haste to conjecture how a new acquaintance might be wrought into their purposes, contented with very vague knowledge as to the way in which life had been shaping him for that instrumentality. Middlemarch, in fact, counted on swallowing Lydgate and assimilating him very comfortably.

Chapter 16

All that in woman is adored
In thy fair self I find –
For the whole sex can but afford
The handsome and the kind.

SIR CHARLES SEDLEY

The question whether Mr Tyke should be appointed as salaried chaplain to the hospital was an exciting topic to the Middlemarchers; and Lydgate heard it discussed in a way that threw much light on the power exercised in the town by Mr Bulstrode. The banker was evidently a ruler, but there was an opposition party, and even among his supporters there were some who allowed it to be seen that their support was a compromise, and who frankly stated their impression that the general scheme of things, and especially the casualties of trade, required you to hold a candle to the devil.

Mr Bulstrode's power was not due simply to his being a country banker, who knew the financial secrets of most traders in the town and could touch the springs of their credit; it was fortified by a beneficence that was at once ready and severe – ready to confer obligations, and severe in watching the result. He had gathered, as an industrious man always at his post, a chief share in administering the town charities, and his private charities were both minute and abundant. He would take a great deal of pains about apprenticing Tegg the shoemaker's son, and he would watch over Tegg's churchgoing; he would defend Mrs Strype the washerwoman against Stubb's unjust exaction on the score of her drying-ground, and he would himself scrutinise a calumny against Mrs Strype. His private minor loans were numerous, but he would enquire strictly into the circumstances both before and after. In this way a man gathers a domain in his neighbours' hope and fear as well as gratitude; and power, when once it has got into that subtle region, propagates itself, spreading out of all proportion to its external means. It was a principle with Mr Bulstrode to gain as much power as possible, that he might use it for the glory of God. He went through a great deal of spiritual conflict and inward argument in order to adjust his motives, and make clear to himself what

God's glory required. But, as we have seen, his motives were not always rightly appreciated. There were many crass minds in Middlemarch whose reflective scales could only weigh things in the lump; and they had a strong suspicion that since Mr Bulstrode could not enjoy life in their fashion, eating and drinking so little as he did, and worreting himself about everything, he must have a sort of vampire's feast in the sense of mastery.

The subject of the chaplaincy came up at Mr Vincy's table when Lydgate was dining there, and the family connection with Mr Bulstrode did not, he observed, prevent some freedom of remark even on the part of the host himself, though his reasons against the proposed arrangement turned entirely on his objection to Mr Tyke's sermons, which were all doctrine, and his preference for Mr Farebrother, whose sermons were free from that taint. Mr Vincy liked well enough the notion of the chaplain's having a salary, supposing it were given to Farebrother, who was as good a little fellow as ever breathed, and the best preacher anywhere, and companionable too.

'What line shall you take, then?' said Mr Chichely, the coroner, a great coursing comrade of Mr Vincy's.

'Oh, I'm precious glad I'm not one of the Directors now. I shall vote for referring the matter to the Directors and the Medical Board together. I shall roll some of my responsibility on your shoulders, doctor,' said Mr Vincy, glancing first at Dr Sprague, the senior physician of the town, and then at Lydgate, who sat opposite. 'You medical gentlemen must consult which sort of black draught you will prescribe, eh, Mr Lydgate?'

'I know little of either,' said Lydgate; 'but in general, appointments are apt to be made too much a question of personal liking. The fittest man for a particular post is not always the best fellow or the most agreeable. Sometimes, if you wanted to get a reform, your only way would be to pension off the good fellows whom everybody is fond of, and put them out of the question.'

Dr Sprague, who was considered the physician of most 'weight', though Dr Minchin was usually said to have more 'penetration', divested his large heavy face of all expression, and looked at his wineglass while Lydgate was speaking. Whatever was not problematical and suspected about this young man – for example, a certain showiness as to foreign ideas, and a disposition to unsettle what had been settled and forgotten by his elders – was positively unwelcome to a physician whose standing had been fixed thirty years before by a treatise on Meningitis, of which at least one copy marked 'own' was bound in calf. For my part I have some fellow-feeling with Dr Sprague: one's self-satisfaction is an untaxed kind of property which it is very unpleasant to find depreciated.

Lydgate's remark, however, did not meet the sense of the company. Mr Vincy said, that if he could have *his* way, he would not put disagreeable fellows anywhere.

'Hang your reforms!' said Mr Chichely. 'There's no greater humbug in the world. You never hear of a reform, but it means some trick to put in new men. I hope you are not one of the *Lancet*'s men, Mr Lydgate – wanting to take the coronership out of the hands of the legal profession: your words appear to point that way.'

'I disapprove of Wakley,' interposed Dr Sprague, 'no man more: he is an ill-intentioned fellow, who would sacrifice the respectability of the profession, which everybody knows depends on the London Colleges, for the sake of getting some notoriety for himself. There are men who don't mind about being kicked blue if they can only get talked about. But Wakley is right sometimes,' the doctor added, judicially. 'I could mention one or two points in which Wakley is in the right.'

'Oh, well,' said Mr Chichely, 'I blame no man for standing up in favour of his own cloth; but, coming to argument, I should like to know how a coroner is to judge of evidence if he has not had a legal training?'

'In my opinion,' said Lydgate, 'legal training only makes a man more incompetent in questions that require knowledge of another kind. People talk about evidence as if it could really be weighed in scales by a blind Justice. No man can judge what is good evidence on any particular subject, unless he knows that subject well. A lawyer is no better than an old woman at a post-mortem examination. How is he to know the action of a poison? You might as well say that scanning verse will teach you to scan the potato crops.'

'You are aware, I suppose, that it is not the coroner's business to conduct the post-mortem, but only to take the evidence of the medical witness?' said Mr Chichely, with some scorn.

'Who is often almost as ignorant as the coroner himself,' said Lydgate. 'Questions of medical jurisprudence ought not to be left to the chance of decent knowledge in a medical witness, and the coroner ought not to be a man who will believe that strychnine will destroy the coats of the stomach if an ignorant practitioner happens to tell him so.'

Lydgate had really lost sight of the fact that Mr Chichely was his Majesty's coroner, and ended innocently with the question, 'Don't you agree with me, Dr Sprague?'

'To a certain extent – with regard to populous districts, and in the metropolis,' said the doctor. 'But I hope it will be long before this part of the country loses the services of my friend Chichely, even though it might get the best man in our profession to succeed him. I am sure Vincy will agree with me.'

'Yes, yes, give me a coroner who is a good coursing man,' said Mr Vincy, jovially. 'And in my opinion, you're safest with a lawyer. Nobody can know everything. Most things are "visitation of God". And as to poisoning, why, what you want to know is the law. Come, shall we join the ladies?'

Lydgate's private opinion was that Mr Chichely might be the very coroner without bias as to the coats of the stomach, but he had not meant to be personal. This was one of the difficulties of moving in good Middlemarch society: it was dangerous to insist on knowledge as a qualification for any salaried office. Fred Vincy had called Lydgate a prig, and now Mr Chichely was inclined to call him prick-eared, especially when, in the drawing-room, he seemed to be making himself eminently agreeable to Rosamond, whom he had easily monopolised in a tête-à-tête, since Mrs Vincy herself sat at the tea-table. She resigned no domestic function to her daughter; and the matron's blooming good-natured face, with the too volatile pink strings floating from her fine throat, and her cheery manners to husband and children, were certainly among the great attractions of the Vincy house – attractions which made it all the easier to fall in love with the daughter. The tinge of unpretentious, inoffensive vulgarity in Mrs Vincy gave more effect to Rosamond's refinement, which was beyond what Lydgate had expected.

Certainly, small feet and perfectly turned shoulders aid the impression of refined manners, and the right thing said seems quite astonishingly right when it is accompanied with exquisite curves of lip and eyelid. And Rosamond could say the right thing; for she was clever with that sort of cleverness which catches every tone except the humorous. Happily she never attempted to joke, and this perhaps was the most decisive mark of her cleverness.

She and Lydgate readily got into conversation. He regretted that he had not heard her sing the other day at Stone Court. The only pleasure he allowed himself during the latter part of his stay in Paris was to go and hear music.

'You have studied music, probably?' said Rosamond.

'No, I know the notes of many birds, and I know many melodies by ear; but the music that I don't know at all, and have no notion about, delights me – affects me. How stupid the world is that it does not make more use of such a pleasure within its reach!'

'Yes, and you will find Middlemarch very tuneless. There are hardly any good musicians. I only know two gentlemen who sing at all well.'

'I suppose it is the fashion to sing comic songs in a rhythmic way, leaving you to fancy the tune – very much as if it were tapped on a drum?'

'Ah, you have heard Mr Bowyer,' said Rosamond, with one of her rare smiles. 'But we are speaking very ill of our neighbours.'

Lydgate was almost forgetting that he must carry on the conversation, in thinking how lovely this creature was, her garment seeming to be made out of the faintest blue sky, herself so immaculately blond, as if the petals of some gigantic flower had just opened and disclosed her; and yet with this infantile blondness showing so much ready, self-possessed grace. Since he had had the memory of Laure, Lydgate had lost all taste for large-eyed silence: the divine cow no longer attracted him, and Rosamond was her very opposite. But he recalled himself.

'You will let me hear some music tonight, I hope.'

'I will let you hear my attempts, if you like,' said Rosamond. 'Papa is sure to insist on my singing. But I shall tremble before you, who have heard the best singers in Paris. I have heard very little: I have only once been to London. But our organist at St Peter's is a good musician, and I go on studying with him.'

'Tell me what you saw in London.'

'Very little.' (A more naïve girl would have said, 'Oh, everything!' But Rosamond knew better.) 'A few of the ordinary sights, such as raw country girls are always taken to.'

'Do you call yourself a raw country girl?' said Lydgate, looking at her with an involuntary emphasis of admiration, which made Rosamond blush with pleasure. But she remained simply serious, turned her long neck a little, and put up her hand to touch her wondrous hair-plaits – a habitual gesture with her as pretty as any movements of a kitten's paw. Not that Rosamond was in the least like a kitten: she was a sylph caught young and educated at Mrs Lemon's.

'I assure you my mind is raw,' she said immediately; 'I pass at Middlemarch. I am not afraid of talking to our old neighbours. But I am really afraid of you.'

'An accomplished woman almost always knows more than we men, though her knowledge is of a different sort. I am sure you could teach me a thousand things – as an exquisite bird could teach a bear if there were any common language between them. Happily, there is a common language between women and men, and so the bears can get taught.'

'Ah, there is Fred beginning to strum! I must go and hinder him from jarring all your nerves,' said Rosamond, moving to the other side of the room, where Fred having opened the piano, at his father's desire, that Rosamond might give them some music, was parenthetically performing 'Cherry Ripe!' with one hand. Able men who have passed their examinations will do these things sometimes, not less than the plucked Fred.

'Fred, pray defer your practising till tomorrow; you will make Mr Lydgate ill,' said Rosamond. 'He has an ear.'

Fred laughed, and went on with his tune to the end.

Rosamond turned to Lydgate, smiling gently, and said, 'You perceive, the bears will not always be taught.'

'Now then, Rosy!' said Fred, springing from the stool and twisting it upward for her, with a hearty expectation of enjoyment. 'Some good rousing tunes first.'

Rosamond played admirably. Her master at Mrs Lemon's school (close to a county town with a memorable history that had its relics in church and castle) was one of those excellent musicians here and there to be found in our provinces, worthy to compare with many a noted Kapellmeister in a country which offers more plentiful conditions of musical celebrity. Rosamond, with the executant's instinct, had seized his manner of playing, and gave forth his large rendering of noble music with the precision of an echo. It was almost startling, heard for the first time. A hidden soul seemed to be flowing forth from Rosamond's fingers; and so indeed it was, since souls live on in perpetual echoes, and to all fine expression there goes somewhere an originating activity, if it be only that of an interpreter. Lydgate was taken possession of, and began to believe in her as something exceptional. After all, he thought, one need not be surprised to find the rare conjunctions of nature under circumstances apparently unfavourable: come where they may, they always depend on conditions that are not obvious. He sat looking at her, and did not rise to pay her any compliments, leaving that to others, now that his admiration was deepened.

Her singing was less remarkable, but also well trained, and sweet to hear as a chime perfectly in tune. It is true she sang 'Meet me by the moonlight' and 'I've been roaming'; for mortals must share the fashions of their time, and none but the ancients can be always classical. But Rosamond could also sing 'Black-eyed Susan' with effect, or Haydn's canzonets, or *'Voi, che sapete'*, or *'Batti, batti'* – she only wanted to know what her audience liked.

Her father looked round at the company, delighting in their admiration. Her mother sat, like a Niobe before her troubles, with her youngest little girl on her lap, softly beating the child's hand up and down in time to the music. And Fred, notwithstanding his general scepticism about Rosy, listened to her music with perfect allegiance, wishing he could do the same thing on his flute. It was the pleasantest family party that Lydgate had seen since he came to Middlemarch. The Vincys had the readiness to enjoy, the rejection of all anxiety, and the belief in life as a merry lot, which made a house exceptional in most county towns at that time, when Evangelicalism had cast a certain suspicion as of plague-infection over the few amusements which survived in the provinces. At the Vincys' there was always whist, and the card-tables stood ready now, making some of the company secretly impatient of the music. Before it ceased Mr Farebrother came in – a handsome, broad-chested but otherwise small man, about forty, whose black was very threadbare: the brilliancy was all in his quick grey eyes. He came like a pleasant change in the light, arresting little Louisa with fatherly nonsense as she was being led out of the room by Miss Morgan, greeting everybody with some special word, and seeming to condense more talk into ten minutes than had been held all through the evening. He claimed from Lydgate the fulfilment of a promise to come and see him. 'I can't let you off, you know, because I have some beetles to show you. We collectors feel an interest in every new man till he has seen all we have to show him.'

But soon he swerved to the whist-table, rubbing his hands and saying, 'Come now, let us be serious! Mr Lydgate? not play? Ah! you are too young and light for this kind of thing.'

Lydgate said to himself that the clergyman whose abilities were so painful to Mr Bulstrode appeared to have found an agreeable resort in this certainly not erudite household. He could half understand it: the good-humour, the good looks of elder and younger, and the provision for passing the time with out any labour of intelligence, might make the house beguiling to people who had no particular use for their odd hours.

Everything looked blooming and joyous except Miss Morgan, who was brown, dull, and resigned, and altogether, as Mrs Vincy often said, just the sort of person for a governess. Lydgate did not mean to pay many such visits himself. They were a wretched waste of the evenings; and now, when he had talked a little more to Rosamond, he meant to excuse himself and go.

'You will not like us at Middlemarch, I feel sure,' she said, when the whist-players were settled. 'We are very stupid, and you have been used to something quite different.'

'I suppose all country towns are pretty much alike,' said Lydgate. 'But I have noticed that one always believes one's own town to be more stupid than any other. I have made up my mind to take Middlemarch as it comes, and shall be much obliged if the town will take me in the same way. I have certainly found some charms in it which are much greater than I had expected.'

'You mean the rides towards Tipton and Lowick: everyone is pleased with those,' said Rosamond, with simplicity.

'No, I mean something much nearer to me.'

Rosamond rose and reached her netting, and then said, 'Do you care about dancing at all? I am not quite sure whether clever men ever dance.'

'I would dance with you, if you would allow me.'

'Oh!' said Rosamond, with a slight deprecatory laugh. 'I was only going to say that we sometimes have dancing, and I wanted to know whether you would feel insulted if you were asked to come.'

'Not on the condition I mentioned.'

After this chat Lydgate thought that he was going, but on moving towards the whist-tables, he got interested in watching Mr Farebrother's play, which was masterly, and also his face, which was a striking mixture of the shrewd and the mild. At ten o'clock supper was brought in (such were the customs of Middlemarch), and there was punch-drinking; but Mr Farebrother had only a glass of water. He was winning, but there seemed to be no reason why the renewal of rubbers should end, and Lydgate at last took his leave.

But as it was not eleven o'clock, he chose to walk in the brisk air towards the tower of St Botolph's, Mr Farebrother's church, which stood out dark, square, and massive against the starlight. It was the oldest church in Middlemarch; the living, however, was but a vicarage worth barely four hundred a year. Lydgate had heard that, and he wondered now whether Mr Farebrother cared about the money he won at cards; thinking 'He seems a very pleasant fellow, but Bulstrode may have his good reasons.' Many things would be easier to Lydgate if it should turn out that Mr Bulstrode was generally justifiable. 'What is his religious doctrine to me, if he carries some good notions along with it? One must use such brains as are to be found.'

These were actually Lydgate's first meditations as he walked away from Mr Vincy's, and on this ground I fear that many ladies will consider him hardly worthy of their attention. He thought of Rosamond and her music only in the second place; and though, when her turn came, he dwelt on the image of her for the rest of his walk, he felt no agitation, and had no sense that any new current had set into his life. He could not marry yet; he wished not to marry for several years; and therefore he was not ready to entertain the notion of being in love with a girl whom he happened to admire. He did admire Rosamond exceedingly; but that madness which had once beset him about Laure was not, he thought, likely to recur in relation to any other woman. Certainly, if falling in love had been at all in question, it would have been quite safe with a creature like this Miss Vincy, who had just the kind of intelligence one would desire in a woman – polished, refined, docile, lending itself to finish in all the delicacies of life, and enshrined in a body which expressed this with a force of demonstration that excluded the need for other evidence. Lydgate felt sure that if ever he married, his wife would have that feminine radiance, that distinctive womanhood which must be classed with flowers and music, that sort of beauty which by its very nature was virtuous, being moulded only for pure and delicate joys.

But since he did not mean to marry for the next five years his more pressing business was to look into Louis' new book on Fever, which he was specially interested in, because he had known Louis in Paris, and had followed many anatomical demonstrations in order to ascertain the specific differences of typhus and typhoid. He went home and read far into the smallest hour, bringing a much more testing vision of details and relations into this pathological study than he had ever thought it necessary to apply to the complexities of love and marriage, these being subjects on which he felt himself amply informed by literature, and that traditional wisdom which is handed down in the genial conversation of men. Whereas Fever had obscure conditions, and gave him that delightful labour of the imagination which is not mere arbitrariness, but the exercise of disciplined power combining and constructing with the clearest eye for probabilities and the fullest obedience to knowledge; and then, in yet more energetic alliance with impartial Nature, standing aloof to invent tests by which to try its own work.

Many men have been praised as vividly imaginative on the strength of their profuseness in indifferent drawing or cheap narration: – reports of very poor talk going on in distant orbs; or portraits of Lucifer coming down on his bad errands as a large ugly man with bat's wings and spurts of phosphorescence; or exaggerations of wantonness that seem to reflect life in a diseased dream. But these kinds of inspiration Lydgate regarded as rather vulgar and vinous compared with the imagination that reveals subtle actions inaccessible by any sort of lens, but tracked in that outer darkness through long pathways of necessary sequence by the inward light which is the last refinement of Energy, capable of bathing even the ethereal atoms in its ideally illuminated space. He for his part had tossed away all cheap inventions where ignorance finds itself able and at ease: he was enamoured of that arduous invention which is the very eye of research, provisionally framing its object and correcting it to more and more exactness of relation; he wanted to pierce the obscurity of those minute processes which prepare human misery and joy, those invisible thoroughfares which are the first lurking-places of anguish, mania, and crime, that delicate poise and transition which determine the growth of happy or unhappy consciousness.

As he threw down his book, stretched his legs towards the embers in the grate, and clasped his hands at the back of his head, in that agreeable afterglow of excitement when thought lapses from examination of a specific object into a suffusive sense of its connections with all the rest of our existence seems, as it were, to throw itself on its back after vigorous swimming and float with the repose of unexhausted strength – Lydgate felt a triumphant delight in his studies, and something like pity for those less lucky men who were not of his profession.

'If I had not taken that turn when I was a lad,' he thought, 'I might have got into some stupid draught-horse work or other, and lived always in blinkers. I should never have been happy in any profession that did not call forth the highest intellectual strain, and yet keep me in good warm contact with my neighbours. There is nothing like the medical profession for that: one can have the exclusive scientific life that touches the distance and befriend the old fogies in the parish too. It is rather harder for a clergyman: Farebrother seems to be an anomaly.'

This last thought brought back the Vincys and all the pictures of the evening. They floated in his mind agreeably enough, and as he took up his bed-candle his lips were curled with that incipient smile which is apt to accompany agreeable recollections. He was an ardent fellow, but at present his ardour was absorbed in love of his work and in the ambition of making his life recognised as a factor in the better life of mankind – like other heroes of science who had nothing but an obscure country practice to begin with.

Poor Lydgate! or shall I say, Poor Rosamond! Each lived in a world of which the other knew nothing. It had not occurred to Lydgate that he had been a subject of eager meditation to Rosamond, who had neither any reason for throwing her marriage into distant perspective, nor any pathological studies to divert her mind from that ruminating habit, that inward repetition of looks, words, and phrases, which makes a large part of the lives of most girls. He had not meant to look at her or speak to her with more than the inevitable amount of admiration and compliment which a man must give to a beautiful girl; indeed, it seemed to him that his enjoyment of her music had remained almost silent, for he feared falling into the rudeness of telling her his great surprise at her possession of such accomplishment. But Rosamond had registered every look and word, and estimated them as the opening incidents of a preconceived romance – incidents which gather value from the foreseen development and climax. In Rosamond's romance it was not necessary to imagine much about the inward life of the hero, or of his serious business in the world: of course, he had a profession and was clever, as well as sufficiently handsome; but the piquant fact about Lydgate was his good birth, which distinguished him from all Middle-march admirers, and presented marriage as a prospect of rising in rank and getting a little nearer to that celestial condition on earth in which she would have nothing to do with vulgar people, and perhaps at last associate with relatives quite equal to the county people who looked down on the Middlemarchers. It was part of Rosamond's cleverness to discern very subtly the faintest aroma of rank, and once when she had seen the Miss Brookes accompanying their uncle at the county assizes, and seated among the aristocracy, she had envied them, notwithstanding their plain dress.

If you think it incredible that to imagine Lydgate as a man of family could cause thrills of satisfaction which had anything to do with the sense that she was in love with him, I will ask you to use your power of comparison a little more effectively, and consider whether red cloth and epaulets have never had an influence of that sort. Our passions do not live apart in locked chambers, but, dressed in their small wardrobe of notions, bring their provisions to a common table and mess together, feeding out of the common store according to their appetite.

Rosamond, in fact, was entirely occupied not exactly with Tertius Lydgate as he was in himself, but with his relation to her; and it was excusable in a girl who was accustomed to hear that all young men might, could, would be, or actually were in love with her, to believe at once that Lydgate could be no exception. His looks and words meant more to her than other men's, because she cared more for them: she thought of them diligently, and diligently attended to that perfection of appearance, behaviour, sentiments, and all other elegancies, which would find in Lydgate a more adequate admirer than she had yet been conscious of.

For Rosamond, though she would never do anything that was disagreeable to her, was industrious; and now more than ever she was active in sketching her landscapes and market-carts and portraits of friends, in practising her music, and in being from morning till night her own standard of a perfect lady, having always an audience in her own consciousness, with sometimes the not unwelcome addition of a more variable external audience in the numerous visitors of the house. She found time also to read the best novels, and even the second best, and she knew much poetry by heart. Her favourite poem was 'Lalla Rookh'.

'The best girl in the world! He will be a happy fellow who gets her!' was the sentiment of the elderly gentlemen who visited the Vincys; and the rejected young men thought of trying again, as is the fashion in country towns where the horizon is not thick with coming rivals. But Mrs Plymdale thought that Rosamond had been educated to a ridiculous pitch, for what was the use of accomplishments which would be all laid aside as soon as she was married? While her aunt Bulstrode, who had a sisterly faithfulness towards her brother's family, had two sincere wishes for Rosamond – that she might show a more serious turn of mind, and that she might meet with a husband whose wealth corresponded to her habits.

Chapter 17

The clerkly person smiled and said,
Promise was a pretty maid,
But being poor she died unwed.

The Revd Camden Farebrother, whom Lydgate went to see the next evening, lived in an old parsonage, built of stone, venerable enough to match the church which it looked out upon. All the furniture too in the house was old, but with another grade of age – that of Mr Farebrother's father and grandfather. There were painted white chairs, with gilding and wreaths on them, and some lingering red silk damask with slits in it. There were engraved portraits of Lord Chancellors and other celebrated lawyers of the last century; and there were old pier-glasses to reflect them, as well as the little satinwood tables and the sofas resembling a prolongation of uneasy chairs, all standing in relief against the dark wainscot. This was the physiognomy of the drawing-room into which Lydgate was shown; and there were three ladies to receive him, who were also old-fashioned, and of a faded but genuine respectability: Mrs Farebrother, the Vicar's white-haired mother, befrilled and kerchiefed with dainty cleanliness, upright, quick-eyed and still under seventy; Miss Noble, her sister, a tiny old lady of meeker aspect, with frills and kerchief decidedly more worn and mended; and, Miss Winifred Farebrother, the Vicar's elder sister, well-looking like himself, but nipped and subdued as single women are apt to be who spend their lives in uninterrupted subjection to their elders. Lydgate had not expected to see so quaint a group: knowing simply that Mr Farebrother was a bachelor, he had thought of being ushered into a snuggery where the chief furniture would probably be books and collections of natural objects. The Vicar himself seemed to wear rather a changed aspect, as most men do when acquaintances made elsewhere see them for the first time in their own homes; some indeed showing like an actor of genial parts disadvantageously cast for the curmudgeon in a new piece. This was not the case with Mr Farebrother: he seemed a trifle milder and more silent, the chief talker being his mother, while he only put in a good-humoured moderating remark here and there. The old lady was evidently accustomed to tell her company what they ought to think, and to regard no subject as quite safe without her steering. She was afforded leisure for this function by having all her little wants attended to by Miss Winifred. Meanwhile tiny Miss Noble carried on her arm a small basket, into which she diverted a bit of sugar, which she had first dropped in her saucer as if by mistake; looking round furtively afterwards, and reverting to her teacup with a small innocent noise as of a tiny timid quadruped. Pray think no ill of Miss Noble. That basket held small savings from her more portable food, destined for the children of her poor friends among whom she trotted on fine mornings; fostering and petting all needy creatures being so spontaneous a delight to her, that she regarded it much as if it had been a pleasant vice that she was addicted to. Perhaps she was conscious of being tempted to steal from those who had much that she might give to those who had nothing, and carried in her conscience the guilt of that repressed desire. One must be poor to know the luxury of giving!

Mrs Farebrother welcomed the guest with a lively formality and precision. She presently informed him that they were not often in want of medical aid in that house. She had brought up her children to wear flannel and not to overeat themselves, which last habit she considered the chief reason why people needed doctors. Lydgate pleaded for those whose fathers and mothers had over-eaten themselves, but Mrs Farebrother held that view of things dangerous: Nature was more just than that; it would be easy for any felon to say that his ancestors ought to have been hanged instead of him. If those who had bad fathers and mothers were bad themselves, they were hanged for that. There was no need to go back on what you couldn't see.

'My mother is like old George the Third,' said the Vicar, 'she objects to metaphysics.'

'I object to what is wrong, Camden. I say, keep hold of a few plain truths, and make everything square with them. When I was young, Mr Lydgate, there never was any question about right and wrong. We knew our catechism, and that was enough; we learned our creed and our duty. Every respectable Church person had the same opinions. But, now if you speak out of the Prayer-book itself, you are liable to be contradicted.'

'That makes rather a pleasant time of it for those who like to maintain their own point,' said Lydgate.

'But my mother always gives way,' said the Vicar, slyly.

'No, no, Camden, you must not lead Mr Lydgate into a mistake about *me*. I shall never show that disrespect to my parents, to give up what they taught me. Anyone may see what comes of turning. If you change once, why not twenty times?'

'A man might see good arguments for changing once, and not see them for changing again,' said Lydgate, amused with the decisive old lady.

'Excuse me there. If you go upon arguments, they are never wanting, when a man has no constancy of mind. My father never changed, and he preached plain moral sermons without argument, and was a good man – few better. When you get me a good man made out of arguments, I will get you a good dinner with reading you the cookery-book. That's my opinion, and I think anybody's stomach will bear me out.'

'About the dinner certainly, mother,' said Mr Farebrother.

'It is the same thing, the dinner or the man. I am nearly seventy, Mr Lydgate, and I go upon experience. I am not likely to follow new lights, though there are plenty of them here as elsewhere. I say, they came in with the mixed stuffs that will neither wash nor wear. It was not so in my youth: a Churchman was a Churchman, and a clergyman, you might be pretty sure, was a gentleman, if nothing else. But now he may be no better than a Dissenter, and want to push aside my son on pretence of doctrine. But whoever may wish to push him aside, I am proud to say, Mr Lydgate, that he will compare with any preacher in this kingdom, not to speak of this town, which is but a low standard to go by; at least, to my thinking, for I was born and bred at Exeter.'

'A mother is never partial,' said Mr Farebrother, smiling. 'What do you think Tyke's mother says about him?'

'Ah, poor creature! what indeed?' said Mrs Farebrother, her sharpness blunted for the moment by her confidence in maternal judgements. 'She says the truth to herself, depend upon it.'

'And what is the truth?' said Lydgate. 'I am curious to know.'

'Oh, nothing bad at all,' said Mr Farebrother. 'He is a zealous fellow: not very learned, and not very wise, I think – because I don't agree with him.'

'Why, Camden!' said Miss Winifred, 'Griffin and his wife told me only today, that Mr Tyke said they should have no more coals if they came to hear you preach.'

Mrs Farebrother laid down her knitting, which she had resumed after her small allowance of tea and toast, and looked at her son as if to say 'You hear that?' Miss Noble said, 'Oh, poor things! poor things!' in reference, probably, to the double loss of preaching and coal. But the Vicar answered quietly: 'That is because they are not my parishioners. And I don't think my sermons are worth a load of coals to them.'

'Mr Lydgate,' said Mrs Farebrother, who could not let this pass, 'you don't know my son: he always undervalues himself. I tell him he is undervaluing the God who made him, and made him a most excellent preacher.'

'That must be a hint for me to take Mr Lydgate away to my study, mother,' said the Vicar, laughing. 'I promised to show you my collection,' he added, turning to Lydgate; 'shall we go?'

All three ladies remonstrated. Mr Lydgate ought not to be hurried away without being allowed to accept another cup of tea: Miss Winifred had abundance of good tea in the pot. Why was Camden in such haste to take a visitor to his den? There was nothing but pickled vermin, and drawers full of bluebottles and moths, with no carpet on the floor. Mr Lydgate must excuse it. A game at cribbage would be far better. In short, it was plain that a vicar might be adored by his womankind as the king of men and preachers, and yet be held by them to stand in much need of their direction. Lydgate, with the usual shallowness of a young bachelor, wondered that Mr Farebrother had not taught them better.

'My mother is not used to my having visitors who can take any interest in my hobbies,' said the Vicar, as he opened the door of his study, which was indeed as bare of luxuries for the body as the ladies had implied, unless a short porcelain pipe and a tobacco-box were to be excepted.

'Men of your profession don't generally smoke,' he said. Lydgate smiled and shook his head. 'Nor of mine either, properly, I suppose. You will hear that pipe alleged against me by Bulstrode and Company. They don't know how pleased the devil would be if I gave it up.'

'I understand. You are of an excitable temper, and want a sedative. I am heavier, and should get idle with it. I should rush into idleness, and stagnate there with all my might.'

'And you mean to give it all to your work. I am some ten or twelve years older than you, and have come to a compromise. I feed a weakness or two lest they should get clamorous. See,' continued the Vicar, opening several small drawers, 'I fancy I have made an exhaustive study of the entomology of this district. I am going on both with the fauna and flora; but I have at least done my insects well. We are singularly rich in orthoptera: I don't know whether – Ah! you have got hold of that glass jar – you are looking into that instead of my drawers. You don't really care about these things?'

'Not by the side of this lovely anencephalous monster. I have never had time to give myself much to natural history. I was early bitten with an interest in structure, and it is what lies most directly in my profession. I have no hobby besides. I have the sea to swim in there.'

'Ah! you are a happy fellow,' said Mr Farebrother, turning on his heel and beginning to fill his pipe. 'You don't know what it is to want spiritual tobacco— bad emendations of old texts, or small items about a variety of *Aphis brassicae*, with the well-known signature of Philomicron, for the *Twaddler's Magazine*; or a learned treatise on the entomology of the Pentateuch, including all the insects not mentioned, but probably met with by the Israelites in their passage through the desert; with a monograph on the Ant, as treated by Solomon, showing the harmony of the Book of Proverbs with the results of modern research. You don't mind my fumigating you?'

Lydgate was more surprised at the openness of this talk than at its implied meaning – that the Vicar felt himself not altogether in the right vocation, The neat fitting-up of drawers and shelves, and the bookcase filled with expensive illustrated books on Natural History, made him think again of the winnings at cards and their destination. But he was beginning to wish that the very best construction of everything that Mr Farebrother did should be the true one. The Vicar's frankness seemed not of the repulsive sort that comes from an uneasy consciousness seeking to forestall the judgement of others, but simply the relief of a desire to do with as little pretence as possible. Apparently he was not without a sense that his freedom of speech might seem premature, for he presently said; 'I have not yet told you that I have the advantage of you, Mr Lydgate, and know you better than you know me. You remember Trawley, who shared your apartment at Paris for some time? I was a correspondent of his, and he told a good deal about you. I was not quite sure when you first came that you were the same man. I was very glad when I found that you were. Only I don't forget that you have not had the like prologue about me.'

Lydgate divined some delicacy of feeling here, but did not half understand it. 'By the way,' he said, 'what has become of Trawley? I have quite lost sight of him. He was hot on the French social systems, and talked of going to the Backwoods to found a sort of Pythagorean community. Is he gone?'

'Not at all. He is practising at a German bath, and has married a rich patient.'

'Then my notions wear the best, so far,' said Lydgate, with a short scornful laugh. 'He would have it, the medical profession was an inevitable system of humbug. I said, the fault was in the men – men who truckle to lies and folly. Instead of preaching against humbug outside the walls, it might be better to set up a disinfecting apparatus within. In short – I am reporting my own conversation – you may be sure I had all the good sense on my side.'

'Your scheme is a good deal more difficult to carry out than the Pythagorean community, though. You have not only got the old Adam in yourself against you, but you have got all those descendants of the original Adam who form the society around you. You see, I have paid twelve or thirteen years more than you for my knowledge of difficulties. But' – Mr Farebrother broke off a moment, and then added, 'you are eyeing that glass vase again. Do you want to make an exchange? You shall not have it without a fair barter.'

'I have some sea-mice – fine specimens – in spirits. And I will throw in Robert Brown's new thing – *Microscopic Observations on the Pollen of Plants* – if you don't happen to have it already.'

'Why, seeing how you long for the monster, I might ask a higher price. Suppose I ask you to look through my drawers and agree with me about all my new species?' The Vicar, while he talked in this way, alternately moved about with his pipe in his mouth, and returned to hang rather fondly over his drawers. 'That would be good discipline, you know, for a young doctor who has to please his patients in Middlemarch. You must learn to be bored, remember. However, you shall have the monster on your own terms.'

'Don't you think men overrate the necessity for humouring everybody's nonsense, till they get despised by the very fools they humour?' said Lydgate, moving to Mr Farebrother's side, and looking rather absently at the insects ranged in fine gradation, with names subscribed in exquisite writing: 'The shortest way is to make your value felt, so that people must put up with you whether you flatter them or not.'

'With all my heart. But then you must be sure of having the value, and you must keep yourself independent. Very few men can do that. Either you slip out of service altogether, and become good for nothing, or you wear the harness and draw a good deal where your yoke-fellows pull you. But do look at these delicate orthoptera!'

Lydgate had after all to give some scrutiny to each drawer, the Vicar laughing at himself, and yet persisting in the exhibition.

'Apropos of what you said about wearing harness,' Lydgate began, after they had sat down, 'I made up my mind some time ago to do with as little of it as possible. That was why I determined not to try anything in London, for a good many years at least. I didn't like what I saw when I was studying there – so much empty big-wiggism, and obstructive trickery. In the country, people have less pretension to knowledge, and are less of companions, but for that reason they affect one's *amour propre* less: one makes less bad blood, and can follow one's own course more quietly.'

'Yes – well – you have got a good start; you are in the right profession, the work you feel yourself most fit for. Some people miss that, and repent too late. But you must not be too sure of keeping your independence.'

'You mean of family ties?' said Lydgate, conceiving that these might press rather tightly on Mr Farebrother.

'Not altogether. Of course they make many things more difficult. But a good wife – a good unworldly woman – may really help a man, and keep him more independent. There's a parishioner of mine – a fine fellow, but who would hardly have pulled through as he has done without his wife. Do you know the Garths? I think they were not Peacock's patients.'

'No; but there is a Miss Garth at old Featherstone's, at Lowick.'

'Their daughter: an excellent girl.'

'She is very quiet – I have hardly noticed her.'

'She has taken notice of you, though, depend upon it.'

'I don't understand,' said Lydgate; he could hardly say 'Of course.'

'Oh, she gauges everybody. I prepared her for confirmation – she is a favourite of mine.'

Mr Farebrother puffed a few moments in silence, Lydgate not caring to know more about the Garths. At last the Vicar laid down his pipe, stretched out his legs, and turned his bright eyes with a smile towards Lydgate, saying: 'But we Middlemarchers are not so tame as you take us to be. We have our intrigues and our parties. I am a party man, for example, and Bulstrode is another. If you vote for me you will offend Bulstrode.'

'What is there against Bulstrode?' said Lydgate, emphatically

'I did not say there was anything against him except that. If you vote against him you will make him your enemy.'

'I don't know that I need mind about that,' said Lydgate, rather proudly; 'but he seems to have good ideas about hospitals, and he spends large sums on useful public objects. He might help me a good deal in carrying out my ideas. As to his religious notions – why, as Voltaire said, incantations will destroy a flock of sheep if administered with a certain quantity of arsenic. I look for the man who will bring the arsenic, and don't mind about his incantations.'

'Very good. But then you must not offend your arsenic-man. You will not offend me, you know,' said Mr Farebrother, quite unaffectedly. 'I don't translate my own convenience into other people's duties. I am opposed to Bulstrode in many ways. I don't like the set he belongs to: they are a narrow ignorant set, and do more to make their neighbours uncomfortable than to make them better. Their system is a sort of worldly-spiritual cliqueism: they really look on the rest of mankind as a doomed carcase which is to nourish them for heaven. But,' he added, smilingly, 'I don't say that Bulstrode's new hospital is a bad thing; and as to his wanting to oust me from the old one – why, if he thinks me a mischievous

fellow, he is only returning a compliment. And I am not a model clergyman –
only a decent makeshift.'

Lydgate was not all sure that the Vicar maligned himself. A model clergyman,
like a model doctor, ought to think his own profession the finest in the world,
and take all knowledge as mere nourishment to his moral pathology and thera-
peutics. He only said, 'What reason does Bulstrode give for superseding you?'

'That I don't teach his opinions – which he calls spiritual religion; and that I
have no time to spare. Both statements are true. But then I could make time, and
I should be glad of the forty pounds. That is the plain fact of the case. But let us
dismiss it. I only wanted to tell you that if you vote for your arsenic-man, you are
not to cut me in consequence. I can't spare you. You are a sort of circum-
navigator come to settle among us, and will keep up my belief in the antipodes.
Now tell me all about them in Paris.'

Chapter 18

> Oh, sir, the loftiest hopes on earth
> Draw lots with meaner hopes: heroic breasts,
> Breathing bad air, run risk of pestilence;
> Or, lacking lime-juice when they cross the Line,
> May languish with the scurvy.

Some weeks passed after this conversation before the question of the chaplaincy
gathered any practical import for Lydgate, and without telling himself the reason,
he deferred the predetermination on which side he should give his vote. It would
really have been a matter of total indifference to him – that is to say, he would
have taken the more convenient side, and given his vote for the appointment of
Tyke without any hesitation if he had not cared personally for Mr Farebrother.

But his liking for the Vicar of St Botolph's grew with growing acquaintanceship. That, entering into Lydgate's position as a newcomer who had his
own professional objects to secure, Mr Farebrother should have taken pains
rather to warn off than to obtain his interest, showed an unusual delicacy and
generosity which Lydgate's nature was keenly alive to. It went along with other
points of conduct in Mr Farebrother which were exceptionally fine, and made
his character resemble those southern landscapes which seem divided between
natural grandeur and social slovenliness. Very few men could have been as filial
and chivalrous as he was to the mother, aunt, and sister, whose dependence on
him had in many ways shaped his life rather uneasily for himself; few men who
feel the pressure of small needs are so nobly resolute not to dress up their
inevitably self-interested desires in a pretext of better motives. In these matters
he was conscious that his life would bear the closest scrutiny; and perhaps the
consciousness encouraged a little defiance towards the critical strictness of
persons whose celestial intimacies seemed not to improve their domestic
manners, and whose lofty aims were not needed to account for their actions.
Then, his preaching was ingenious and pithy, like the preaching of the English

Church in its robust age, and his sermons were delivered without book. People outside his parish went to hear him; and, since to fill the church was always the most difficult part of a clergyman's function, here was another ground for a careless sense of superiority. Besides, he was a likeable man: sweet-tempered, ready-witted, frank, without grins of suppressed bitterness or other conversational flavours which make half of us an affliction to our friends. Lydgate liked him heartily, and wished for his friendship.

With this feeling uppermost, he continued to waive the question of the chaplaincy, and to persuade himself that it was not only no proper business of his, but likely enough never to vex him with a demand for his vote. Lydgate, at Mr Bulstrode's request, was laying down plans for the internal arrangements of the new hospital, and the two were often in consultation. The banker was always presupposing that he could count in general on Lydgate as a co-adjutor, but made no special recurrence to the coming decision between Tyke and Farebrother. When the General Board of the Infirmary had met, however, and Lydgate had notice that the question of the chaplaincy was thrown on a council of the directors and medical men, to meet on the following Friday, he had a vexed sense that he must make up his mind on this trivial Middlemarch business. He could not help hearing within him the distinct declaration that Bulstrode was prime minister, and that the Tyke affair was a question of office or no office; and he could not help an equally pronounced dislike to giving up the prospect of office. For his observation was constantly confirming Mr Farebrother's assurance that the banker would not overlook opposition. 'Confound their petty politics!' was one of his thoughts for three mornings in the meditative process of shaving, when he had begun to feel that he must really hold a court of conscience on this matter. Certainly there were valid things to be said against the election of Mr Farebrother: he had too much on his hands already, especially considering how much time he spent on non-clerical occupations. Then again it was a continually repeated shock, disturbing Lydgate's esteem, that the Vicar should obviously play for the sake of money, liking the play indeed, but evidently liking some end which it served. Mr Farebrother contended on theory for the desirability of all games, and said that Englishmen's wit was stagnant for want of them; but Lydgate felt certain that he would have played very much less but for the money. There was a billiard-room at the Green Dragon, which some anxious mothers and wives regarded as the chief temptation in Middlemarch. The Vicar was a first-rate billiard-player, and though he did not frequent the Green Dragon, there were reports that he had sometimes been there in the daytime and had won money. And as to the chaplaincy, he did not pretend that he cared for it, except for the sake of the forty pounds. Lydgate was no Puritan, but he did not care to play, and winning money at it had always seemed a meanness to him; besides, he had an ideal of life which made this subservience of conduct to the gaining of small sums thoroughly hateful to him. Hitherto in his own life his wants had been supplied without any trouble to himself, and his first impulse was always to be liberal with half-crowns as matters of no importance to a gentleman; it had never occurred to him to devise a plan for getting half-crowns. He had always known in a general way that he was not rich, but he had never felt poor, and he had no power of imagining the part which the want of money plays in determining the actions of men. Money had never been a motive to him. Hence he was not ready to frame excuses for this deliberate pursuit of small gains. It was altogether repulsive to him, and he never entered into any calculation of the ratio between the Vicar's income and his more or less necessary expenditure. It was possible that he would not have made such a calculation in his own case.

And now, when the question of voting had come, this repulsive fact told more strongly against Mr Farebrother than it had done before. One would know much better what to do if men's characters were more consistent, and especially if one's friends were invariably fit for any function they desired to undertake! Lydgate was convinced that if there had been no valid objection to Mr Farebrother, he would have voted for him whatever Bulstrode might have felt on the subject: he did not intend to be a vassal of Bulstrode's. On the other hand, there was Tyke, a man entirely given to his clerical office, who was simply curate at a chapel of ease in St Peter's parish, and had time for extra duty. Nobody had anything to say against Mr Tyke, except that they could not bear him, and suspected him of cant. Really, from his point of view, Bulstrode was thoroughly justified.

But whichever way Lydgate began to incline, there was something to make him wince; and being a proud man, he was a little exasperated at being obliged to wince. He did not like frustrating his own best purposes by getting on bad terms with Bulstrode; he did not like voting against Farebrother, and helping to deprive him of function and salary; and the question occurred whether the additional forty pounds might not leave the Vicar free from that ignoble care about winning at cards. Moreover, Lydgate did not like the consciousness that in voting for Tyke he should be voting on the side obviously convenient for himself. But would the end really be his own convenience? Other people would say so, and would allege that he was currying favour with Bulstrode for the sake of making himself important and getting on in the world. What then? He for his own part knew that if his personal prospects simply had been concerned, he would not have cared a rotten nut for the banker's friendship or enmity. What he really cared for was a medium for his work, a vehicle for his ideas; and after all, was he not bound to prefer the object of getting a good hospital, where he could demonstrate the specific distinctions of fever and test therapeutic results, before anything else connected with this chaplaincy? For the first time Lydgate was feeling the hampering threadlike pressure of small social conditions, and their frustrating complexity. At the end of his inward debate, when he set out for the hospital, his hope was really in the chance that discussion might somehow give a new aspect to the question, and make the scale dip so as to exclude the necessity for voting. I think he trusted a little also to the energy which is begotten by circumstances – some feeling rushing warmly and making resolve easy, while debate in cool blood had only made it more difficult. However it was, he did not distinctly say to himself on which side he would vote; and all the while he was inwardly resenting the subjection which had been forced upon him. It would have seemed beforehand like a ridiculous piece of bad logic that he, with his unmixed resolutions of independence and his select purpose, would find himself at the very outset in the grasp of petty alternatives, each of which was repugnant to him. In his student's chambers, he had prearranged his social action quite differently.

Lydgate was late in setting out, but Dr Sprague, the two other surgeons, and several of the directors had arrived early; Mr Bulstrode, treasurer and chairman, being among those who were still absent. The conversation seemed to imply that the issue was problematical, and that a majority for Tyke was not so certain as had been generally supposed. The two physicians, for a wonder, turned out to be unanimous, or rather, though of different minds, they concurred in action. Dr Sprague, the rugged and weighty, was, as everyone had foreseen, an adherent of Mr Farebrother. The doctor was more than suspected of having no religion, but somehow Middlemarch tolerated this deficiency in him as if he had been a Lord Chancellor; indeed it is probable that his professional weight was the more believed in, the world-old association of cleverness with the evil principle being still potent in the minds even of lady-patients who had the strictest ideas of frilling and sentiment. It was perhaps this negation in the doctor which made his neighbours call him hard-headed and dry-witted; conditions of texture which were also held favourable to the storing of judgements connected with drugs. At all events, it is certain that if any medical man had come to Middlemarch with the reputation of having very definite religious views, of being given to prayer, and of otherwise showing an active piety, there would have been a general presumption against his medical skill.

On this ground it was (professionally speaking) fortunate for Dr Minchin that his religious sympathies were of a general kind, and such as gave a distant medical sanction to all serious sentiment, whether of Church or Dissent, rather than any adhesion to particular tenets. If Mr Bulstrode insisted, as he was apt to do, on the Lutheran doctrine of justification, as that by which a church must stand or fall, Dr Minchin in return was quite sure that man was not a mere machine or a fortuitous conjunction of atoms; if Mrs Wimple insisted on a particular providence in relation to her stomach complaint, Dr Minchin for his part liked to keep the mental windows open and objected to fixed limits; if the Unitarian brewer jested about the Athanasian Creed, Dr Minchin quoted Pope's *Essay on Man*. He objected to the rather free style of anecdote in which Dr Sprague indulged, preferring well-sanctioned quotations, and liking refinement of all kinds: it was generally known that he had some kinship to a bishop, and sometimes spent his holidays at the 'palace'.

Dr Minchin was soft-handed, pale-complexioned, and of rounded outline, not to be distinguished from a mild clergyman in appearance: whereas Dr Sprague was superfluously tall: his trousers got creased at the knees, and showed an excess of boot at a time when straps seemed necessary to any dignity of bearing; you heard him go in and out, and up and down, as if he had come to see after the roofing. In short, he had weight, and might be expected to grapple with a disease and throw it; while Dr Minchin might be better able to detect it lurking and to circumvent it. They enjoyed about equally the mysterious privilege of medical reputation, and concealed with much etiquette their contempt for each other's skill. Regarding themselves as Middlemarch institutions, they were ready to combine against all innovators, and against non-professionals given to interference. On this ground they were both in their hearts equally averse to Mr Bulstrode, though Dr Minchin had never been in open hostility with him, and never differed from him without elaborate explanation to Mrs Bulstrode, who had found that Dr Minchin alone understood her constitution. A layman who pried into the professional conduct of medical men, and was always obtruding his reforms, – though he was less directly embarrassing to the two physicians than to the surgeon-apothecaries who attended paupers by contract, was nevertheless offensive to the professional nostril as such; and Dr Minchin shared fully in the new pique against Bulstrode, excited by his apparent determination to patronise Lydgate. The long-established practitioners, Mr Wrench and Mr Toller, were just now standing apart and having a friendly colloquy, in which they agreed that Lydgate was a jackanapes, just made to serve Bulstrode's purpose. To non-medical friends they had already concurred in praising the other young practitioner, who had come into the town on Mr Peacock's retirement without further recommendation than his own merits and such argument for solid professional acquirement as might be gathered from his having apparently wasted no time on other branches of knowledge. It was clear that Lydgate, by not dispensing drugs, intended to cast imputations on his equals, and also to obscure the limit between his own rank as a general practitioner and that of the physicians, who, in the interest of the profession, felt bound to maintain its various grades. Especially against a man who had not been to either of the English universities and enjoyed the absence of anatomical and bedside study there, but came with a libellous pretension to experience in Edinburgh and Paris, where observation might be abundant indeed, but hardly sound.

Thus it happened that on this occasion Bulstrode became identified with Lydgate, and Lydgate with Tyke; and owing to this variety of interchangeable names for the chaplaincy question, diverse minds were enabled to form the same judgement concerning it.

Dr Sprague said at once bluntly to the group assembled when he entered, 'I go for Farebrother. A salary, with all my heart. But why take it from the Vicar? He has none too much – has to insure his life, besides keeping house, and doing a vicar's charities. Put forty pounds in his pocket and you'll do no harm. He's a good fellow, is Farebrother, with as little of the parson about him as will serve to carry orders.'

'Ho, ho! doctor,' said old Mr Powderell, a retired ironmonger of some standing – his interjection being something between a laugh and a Parliamentary disapproval. 'We must let you have your say. But what we have to consider is not anybody's income – it's the souls of the poor sick people' – here Mr Powderell's voice and face had a sincere pathos in them. 'He is a real Gospel preacher, is Mr Tyke. I should vote against my conscience if I voted against Mr Tyke – I should indeed.'

'Mr Tyke's opponents have not asked anyone to vote against his conscience, I believe,' said Mr Hackbutt, a rich tanner of fluent speech, whose glittering spectacles and erect hair were turned with some severity towards innocent Mr Powderell. 'But in my judgement it behoves us, as Directors, to consider whether we will regard it as our whole business to carry out propositions emanating from a single quarter. Will any member of the committee aver that he would have entertained the idea of displacing the gentleman who has always discharged the function of chaplain here, if it had not been suggested to him by parties whose disposition it is to regard every institution of this town as a machinery for carrying out their own views? I tax no man's motives: let them lie between himself and a higher Power: but I do say, that there are influences at work here which are incompatible with genuine independence, and that a crawling servility is usually dictated by circumstances which gentlemen so conducting themselves could not afford either morally or financially to avow. I myself am a layman, but I have given no inconsiderable attention to the divisions in the Church and . . . '

'Oh, damn the divisions!' burst in Mr Frank Hawley, lawyer and town-clerk, who rarely presented himself at the board, but now looked in hurriedly, whip in hand. 'We have nothing to do with them here. Farebrother has been doing the work – what there was – without pay, and if pay is to be given, it should be given to him. I call it a confounded job to take the thing away from Farebrother.'

'I think it would be as well for gentlemen not to give their remarks a personal bearing,' said Mr Plymdale. 'I shall vote for the appointment of Mr Tyke, but I should not have known, if Mr Hackbutt hadn't hinted it, that I was a Servile Crawler.'

'I disclaim any personalities. I expressly said, if I may be allowed to repeat, or even to conclude what I was about to say – '

'Ah, here's Minchin!' said Mr Frank Hawley; at which everybody turned away from Mr Hackbutt, leaving him to feel the uselessness of superior gifts in Middlemarch. 'Come, doctor, I must have you on the right side, eh?'

'I hope so,' said Dr Minchin, nodding and shaking hands here and there. 'At whatever cost to my feelings.'

'If there's any feeling here, it should be feeling for the man who is turned out, I think,' said Mr Frank Hawley.

'I confess I have feelings on the other side also. I have a divided esteem,' said Dr Minchin, rubbing his hands. 'I consider Mr Tyke an exemplary man – none more so – and I believe him to be proposed from unimpeachable motives. I, for my part, wish that I could give him my vote. But I am constrained to take a view of the case which gives the preponderance to Mr Farebrother's claims. He is an amiable man, an able preacher, and has been longer among us.'

Old Mr Powderell looked on, sad and silent. Mr Plymdale settled his cravat, uneasily.

'You don't set up Farebrother as a pattern of what a clergyman ought to be, I hope,' said Mr Larcher, the eminent carrier, who had just come in. 'I have no ill-will towards him, but I think we owe something to the public, not to speak of anything higher, in these appointments. In my opinion Farebrother is too lax for a clergyman. I don't wish to bring up particulars against him; but he will make a little attendance here go as far as he can.'

'And a devilish deal better than too much,' said Mr Hawley, whose bad language was notorious in that part of the county. 'Sick people can't bear so much praying and preaching. And that methodistical sort of religion is bad for the spirits – bad for the inside, eh!' he added, turning quickly round to the four medical men who were assembled.

But any answer was dispensed with by the entrance of three gentlemen, with whom there were greetings more or less cordial. These were the Revd Edward Thesiger, Rector of St Peter's, Mr Bulstrode and our friend Mr Brooke of Tipton, who had lately allowed himself to be put on the board of directors in his turn, but had never before attended, his attendance now being due to Mr Bulstrode's exertions. Lydgate was the only person still expected.

Everyone now sat down, Mr Bulstrode presiding, pale and self-restrained as usual. Mr Thesiger, a moderate evangelical, wished for the appointment of his friend Mr Tyke, a zealous, able man, who, officiating at a chapel of ease, had not a cure of souls too extensive to leave him ample time for the new duty. It was desirable that chaplaincies of this kind should be entered on with a fervent intention: they were peculiar opportunities for spiritual influence; and while it was good that a salary should be allotted, there was the more need for scrupulous watching lest the office should be perverted into a mere question of salary. Mr Thesiger's manner had so much quiet propriety that objectors could only simmer in silence.

Mr Brooke believed that everybody meant well in the matter. He had not himself attended to the affairs of the Infirmary, though he had a strong interest in whatever was for the benefit of Middlemarch, and was most happy to meet the gentlemen present on any public question – 'any public question, you know,' Mr Brooke repeated, with his nod of perfect understanding. 'I am a good deal occupied as a magistrate, and in the collection of documentary evidence, but I regard my time as being at the disposal of the public – and, in short, my friends have convinced me that a chaplain with a salary – a salary, you know – is a very good thing, and I am happy to be able to come here and vote for the appointment of Mr Tyke, who, I understand, is an unexceptionable man, apostolic and eloquent and everything of that kind – and I am the last man to withhold my vote – under the circumstances, you know.'

'It seems to me that you have been crammed with one side of the question, Mr Brooke,' said Mr Frank Hawley, who was afraid of nobody, and was a Tory suspicious of electioneering intentions. 'You don't seem to know that one of the worthiest men we have has been doing duty as chaplain here for years without pay, and that Mr Tyke is proposed to supersede him.'

'Excuse me, Mr Hawley,' said Mr Bulstrode. 'Mr Brooke has been fully informed of Mr Farebrother's character and position.'

'By his enemies,' flashed out Mr Hawley.

'I trust there is no personal hostility concerned here,' said Mr Thesiger.

'I'll swear there is, though,' retorted Mr Hawley.

'Gentlemen,' said Mr Bulstrode, in a subdued tone, 'the merits of the question may be very briefly stated, and if anyone present doubts that every gentleman who is about to give his vote has not been fully informed, I can now recapitulate the considerations that should weigh on either side.'

'I don't see the good of that,' said Mr Hawley. 'I suppose we all know whom we mean to vote for. Any man who wants to do justice does not wait till the last minute to hear both sides of the question. I have no time to lose, and I propose that the matter be put to the vote at once.'

A brief but still hot discussion followed before each person wrote 'Tyke' or 'Farebrother' on a piece of paper and slipped it into a glass tumbler; and in the meantime Mr Bulstrode saw Lydgate enter.

'I perceive that the votes are equally divided at present,' said Mr Bulstrode, in a clear biting voice. Then, looking up at Lydgate; 'There is a casting-vote still to be given. It is yours, Mr Lydgate: will you be good enough to write?'

'The thing is settled now,' said Mr Wrench, rising. 'We all know how Mr Lydgate will vote.'

'You seem to speak with some peculiar meaning, sir,' said Lydgate, rather defiantly, and keeping his pencil suspended.

'I merely mean that you are expected to vote with Mr Bulstrode. Do you regard that meaning as offensive?'

'It may be offensive to others. But I shall not desist from voting with him on that account.'

Lydgate immediately wrote down 'Tyke'.

So the Revd Walter Tyke became chaplain to the Infirmary, and Lydgate continued to work with Mr Bulstrode. He was really uncertain whether Tyke were not the more suitable candidate, and yet his consciousness told him that if he had been quite free from indirect bias he should have voted for Mr Farebrother. The affair of the chaplaincy remained a sore point in his memory as a case in which this petty medium of Middlemarch had been too strong for him. How could a man be satisfied with a decision between such alternatives and under such circumstances? No more than he can be satisfied with his hat, which he has chosen from among such shapes as the resources of the age offer him, wearing it at best with a resignation which is chiefly supported by comparison.

But Mr Farebrother met him with the same friendliness as before. The character of the publican and sinner is not always practically incompatible with that of the modern Pharisee, for the majority of us scarcely see more distinctly the faultiness of our own conduct than the faultiness of our own arguments, or the dulness of our own jokes. But the Vicar of St Botolph's had certainly escaped the slightest tincture of the Pharisee, and by dint of admitting to himself that he was too much as other men were, he had become remarkably unlike them in this – that he could excuse others for thinking slightly of him, and could judge impartially of their conduct even when it told against him.

'The world has been too strong for *me*, I know,' he said one day to Lydgate. 'But then I am not a mighty man – I shall never be a man of renown. The choice of Hercules is a pretty fable; but Prodicus makes it easy work for the hero, as if the first resolves were enough. Another story says that he came to hold the distaff, and at last wore the Nessus shirt. I suppose one good resolve might keep a man right if everybody else's resolve helped him.'

The Vicar's talk was not always inspiriting: he had escaped being a Pharisee, but he had not escaped that low estimate of possibilities which we rather hastily arrive at as an inference from our own failure. Lydgate thought that there was a pitiable infirmity of will in Mr Farebrother.

Chapter 19

L'altra vedete ch'ha fatto alla guancia
Della sua palma, sospirando, letto.

Purga

When George the Fourth was still reigning over the privacies of Windsor, when the Duke of Wellington was Prime Minister, and Mr Vincy was mayor of the old corporation in Middlemarch, Mrs Casaubon, born Dorothea Brooke, had taken her wedding journey to Rome. In those days the world in general was more ignorant of good and evil by forty years than it is at present. Travellers did not often carry full information on Christian art either in their heads or their pockets; and even the most brilliant English critic of the day mistook the flower-flushed tomb of the ascended Virgin for an ornamental vase due to the painter's fancy. Romanticism, which has helped to fill some dull blanks with love and knowledge, had not yet penetrated the times with its leaven and entered into everybody's food; it was fermenting still as a distinguishable vigorous enthusiasm in certain long-haired German artists at Rome, and the youth of other nations who worked or idled near them were sometimes caught in the spreading movement.

One fine morning a young man whose hair was not immoderately long, but abundant and curly, and who was otherwise English in his equipment, had just turned his back on the Belvedere Torso in the Vatican and was looking out on the magnificent view of the mountains from the adjoining round vestibule. He was sufficiently absorbed not to notice the approach of a dark-eyed, animated German who came up to him and placing a hand on his shoulder, said with a strong accent, 'Come here, quick! else she will have changed her pose.'

Quickness was ready at the call, and the two figures passed lightly along by the Meleager towards the hall where the reclining Ariadne, then called the Cleopatra, lies in the marble voluptuousness of her beauty, the drapery folding around her with a petal-like ease and tenderness. They were just in time to see another figure standing against a pedestal near the reclining marble: a breathing blooming girl, whose form, not shamed by the Ariadne, was clad in Quakerish grey drapery; her long cloak, fastened at the neck, was thrown backward from her arms, and one beautiful ungloved hand pillowed her cheek, pushing somewhat backward the white beaver bonnet which made a sort of halo to her face around the simply braided dark-brown hair. She was not looking at the sculpture, probably not thinking of it: her large eyes were fixed dreamily on a streak of sunlight which fell across the floor. But she became conscious of the two strangers who suddenly paused as if to contemplate the Cleopatra, and, without looking at them, immediately turned away to join a maidservant and courier who were loitering along the hall at a little distance off.

'What do you think of that for a fine bit of antithesis?' said the German, searching in his friend's face for responding admiration, but going on volubly without waiting for any other answer. 'There lies antique beauty, not corpse-like even in death, but arrested in the complete contentment of its sensuous perfection: and here stands beauty in its breathing life, with the consciousness of Christian centuries in its bosom. But she should be dressed as a nun; I think she looks almost what you call a Quaker; I would dress her as a nun in my picture. However, she is married! I saw her wedding-ring on that wonderful left hand, otherwise I should have thought the sallow *Geistlicher* was her father. I saw him parting from her a good while ago, and just now I found her in that magnificent pose. Only think! he is perhaps rich, and would like to have her portrait taken. Ah! it is no use looking after her – there she goes! Let us follow her home!'

'No, no,' said his companion, with a little frown.

'You are singular, Ladislaw. You look struck together. Do you know her?'

'I know that she is married to my cousin,' said Will Ladislaw, sauntering down the hall with a preoccupied air, while his German friend kept at his side and watched him eagerly.

'What, the *Geistlicher*? He looks more like an uncle – a more useful sort of relation.'

'He is not my uncle. I tell you he is my second cousin,' said Ladislaw, with some irritation.

'*Schön, Schön.* Don't be snappish. You are not angry with me for thinking Mrs Second-Cousin the most perfect young Madonna I ever saw?'

'Angry? nonsense. I have only seen her once before, for a couple of minutes, when my cousin introduced her to me, just before I left England. They were not married then. I didn't know they were coming to Rome.'

'But you will go to see them now – you will find out what they have for an address – since you know the name. Shall we go to the post? And you could speak about the portrait.'

'Confound you, Naumann! I don't know what I shall do. I am not so brazen as you.'

'Bah! that is because you are dilettantish and amateurish. If you were an artist, you would think of Mistress Second-Cousin as antique form animated by Christian sentiment – a sort of Christian Antigone – sensuous force controlled by spiritual passion.'

'Yes, and that your painting her was the chief outcome of her existence – the divinity passing into higher completeness and all but exhausted in the act of covering your bit of canvas. I am amateurish if you like: I do *not* think that all the universe is straining towards the obscure significance of your pictures.'

'But it is, my dear! – so far as it is straining through me, Adolf Naumann: that stands firm,' said the good-natured painter, putting a hand on Ladislaw's shoulder, and not in the least disturbed by the unaccountable touch of ill-humour in his tone. 'See now! My existence presupposes the existence of the whole universe – does it *not*? and my function is to paint – and as a painter I have a conception which is altogether *genialisch*, of your great-aunt or second grandmother as a subject for a picture; therefore, the universe is straining towards that picture through that particular hook or claw which is put forth in the shape of me not true?'

'But how if another claw in the shape of me is straining to thwart it? – the case is a little less simple then.'

'Not at all: the result of the struggle is the same thing – picture or no picture – logically.' Will could not resist this imperturbable temper, and the cloud in his face broke into sunshiny laughter.

'Come now, my friend – you will help?' said Naumann, in a hopeful tone.

'No; nonsense, Naumann! English ladies are not at everybody's service as models. And you want to express too much with your painting. You would only have made a better or worse portrait with a background which every connoisseur would give a different reason for or against. And what is a portrait of a woman? Your painting and Plastik are poor stuff after all. They perturb and dull conceptions instead of raising them. Language is a finer medium.'

'Yes, for those who can't paint,' said Naumann. 'There you have perfect right. I did not recommend you to paint, my friend.'

The amiable artist carried his sting, but Ladislaw did not choose to appear stung. He went on as if he had not heard.

'Language gives a fuller image, which is all the better for being vague. After all, the true seeing is within; and painting stares at you with an insistent imperfection. I feel that especially about representations of women. As if a woman were a mere coloured superficies! You must wait for movement and tone. There is a difference in their very breathing: they change from moment to moment. – This woman whom you have just seen, for example: how would you paint her voice, pray? But her voice is much diviner than anything you have seen of her.'

'I see, I see. You are jealous. No man must presume to think that he can paint your ideal. This is serious, my friend! Your great-aunt! "*Der Neffe als Onkel*" in a tragic sense – *ungeheuer!*'

'You and I shall quarrel, Naumann, if you call that lady my aunt again.'

'How is she to be called then?'

'Mrs Casaubon.'

'Good. Suppose I get acquainted with her in spite of you, and find that she very much wishes to be painted?'

'Yes, suppose!' said Will Ladislaw, in a contemptuous undertone, intended to dismiss the subject. He was conscious of being irritated by ridiculously small causes, which were half of his own creation. Why was he making any fuss about Mrs Casaubon? And yet he felt as if something had happened to him with regard to her. There are characters which are continually creating collisions and nodes for themselves in dramas which nobody is prepared to act with them. Their susceptibilities will clash against objects that remain innocently quiet.

Chapter 20

A child forsaken, waking suddenly,
Whose gaze afear'd on all things round doth rove,
And seeth only that it cannot see
    The meeting eyes of love.

Two hours later, Dorothea was seated in an inner room or boudoir of a hand-some apartment in the Via Sistina.

I am sorry to add that she was sobbing bitterly, with such abandonment to this relief of an oppressed heart as a woman habitually controlled by pride on her own account and thoughtfulness for others will sometimes allow herself when she feels securely alone. And Mr Casaubon was certain to remain away for some time at the Vatican.

Yet Dorothea had no distinctly shapen grievance that she could state even to herself; and in the midst of her confused thought and passion, the mental act that was struggling forth into clearness was a self-accusing cry that her feeling of desolation was the fault of her own spiritual poverty. She had married the man of her choice, and with the advantage over most girls that she had contemplated her marriage chiefly as the beginning of new duties: from the very first she had thought of Mr Casaubon as having a mind so much above her own, that he must often be claimed by studies which she could not entirely share; moreover, after the brief narrow experience of her girlhood she was beholding Rome, the city of visible history, where the past of a whole hemisphere seems moving in funeral procession with strange ancestral images and trophies gathered from afar.

But this stupendous fragmentariness heightened the dreamlike strangeness of her bridal life. Dorothea had now been five weeks in Rome, and in the kindly mornings when autumn and winter seemed to go hand in hand like a happy aged couple one of whom would presently survive in chiller loneliness, she had driven about at first with Mr Casaubon, but of late chiefly with Tantripp and their experienced courier. She had been led through the best galleries, had been taken to the chief points of view, had been shown the greatest ruins and the most glorious churches, and she had ended by oftenest choosing to drive out to the Campagna where she could feel alone with the earth and sky, away from the oppressive masquerade of ages, in which her own life too seemed to become a masque with enigmatical costumes.

To those who have looked at Rome with the quickening power of a know-ledge which breathes a growing soul into all historic shapes, and traces out the suppressed transitions which unite all contrasts, Rome may still be the spiritual centre and interpreter of the world. But let them conceive one more historical contrast: the gigantic broken revelations of that Imperial and Papal city thrust abruptly on the notions of a girl who had been brought up in English and Swiss Puritanism, fed on meagre Protestant histories and on art chiefly of the hand-screen sort a girl whose ardent nature turned all her small allowance of knowledge into principles, fusing her actions into their mould, and whose quick emotions gave the most abstract things the quality of a pleasure or a pain; a girl who had lately become a wife, and from the enthusiastic acceptance of untried duty found herself plunged in tumultuous preoccupation with her personal lot. The weight of unintelligible Rome might lie easily on bright nymphs to whom it formed a background for the brilliant picnic of Anglo-foreign society; but Dorothea had no such defence against deep impressions. Ruins and basilicas, palaces and colossi, set in the midst of a sordid present, where all that was living and warm-blooded seemed sunk in the deep degeneracy of a superstition divorced from reverence; the dimmer but yet eager Titanic life gazing and struggling on walls and ceilings; the long vistas of white forms whose marble eyes seemed to hold the monotonous light of an alien world: all this vast wreck of ambitious ideals, sensuous and spiritual, mixed confusedly with the signs of breathing forgetfulness and degradation, at first jarred her as with an electric shock, and then urged themselves on her with that ache belonging to a glut of confused ideas which check the flow of emotion. Forms both pale and glowing took possession of her young sense, and fixed themselves in her memory even when she was not thinking of them, preparing strange associations which remained through her after-years. Our moods are apt to bring with them images which succeed each other like the magic-lantern pictures of a doze; and in certain states of dull forlornness Dorothea all her life continued to see the vastness of St Peter's, the huge bronze canopy, the excited intention in the attitudes and garments of the prophets and evangelists in the mosaics above, and the red drapery which was being hung for Christmas spreading itself everywhere like a disease of the retina.

Not that this inward amazement of Dorothea's was anything very exceptional: many souls in their young nudity are tumbled out among incongruities and left to 'find their feet' among them, while their elders go about their business. Nor can I suppose that when Mrs Casaubon is discovered in a fit of weeping six weeks after her wedding, the situation will be regarded as tragic. Some discouragement, some faintness of heart at the new real future which replaces the imaginary, is not unusual, and we do not expect people to be deeply moved by what is not unusual. That element of tragedy which lies in the very fact of frequency, has not yet wrought itself into the coarse emotion of mankind; and perhaps our frames could hardly bear much of it. If we had a keen vision and feeling of all ordinary human life, it would be like hearing the grass grow and the squirrel's heart beat, and we should die of that roar which lies on the other side of silence. As it is, the quickest of us walk about well wadded with stupidity.

However, Dorothea was crying, and if she had been required to state the cause, she could only have done so in some such general words as I have already used: to have been driven to be more particular would have been like trying to give a history of the lights and shadows; for that new real future which was replacing the imaginary drew its material from the endless minutiae by which her view of Mr Casaubon and her wifely relation, now that she was married to him, was gradually changing with the secret motion of a watch-hand from what it had been in her maiden dream. It was too early yet for her fully to recognise or at least admit the change, still more for her to have readjusted that devotedness which was so necessary a part of her mental life that she was almost sure sooner or later to recover it. Permanent rebellion, the disorder of a life without some loving reverent resolve, was not possible to her; but she was now in an interval when the very force of her nature heightened its confusion. In this way, the early months of marriage often are times of critical tumult – whether that of a shrimp-pool or of deeper waters – which afterwards subsides into cheerful peace.

But was not Mr Casaubon just as learned as before? Had his forms of expression changed, or his sentiments become less laudable? O waywardness of womanhood! did his chronology fail him, or his ability to state not only a theory but the names of those who held it; or his provision for giving the heads of any subject on demand? And was not Rome the place in all the world to give free play to such accomplishments? Besides, had not Dorothea's enthusiasm especially dwelt on the prospect of relieving the weight and perhaps the sadness with which great tasks lie on him who has to achieve them? – And that such weight pressed on Mr Casaubon was only plainer than before.

All these are crushing questions; but whatever else remained the same, the light had changed, and you cannot find the pearly dawn at noonday. The fact is unalterable, that a fellow-mortal with whose nature you are acquainted solely through the brief entrances and exits of a few imaginative weeks called courtship, may, when seen in the continuity of married companionship, be disclosed as something better or worse than what you have preconceived, but will certainly not appear altogether the same. And it would be astonishing to find how soon the change is felt if we had no kindred changes to compare with it. To share lodgings with a brilliant dinner-companion, or to see your favourite politician in the Ministry, may bring about changes quite as rapid: in these cases too we begin by knowing little and believing much, and we sometimes end by inverting the quantities.

Still, such comparisons might mislead, for no man was more incapable of flashy make-believe than Mr Casaubon: he was as genuine a character as any ruminant animal, and he had not actively assisted in creating any illusions about himself. How was it that in the weeks since her marriage, Dorothea had not distinctly observed but felt with a stifling depression, that the large vistas and wide fresh air which she had dreamed of finding in her husband's mind were replaced by ante-rooms and winding passages which seemed to lead nowhither? I suppose it was that in courtship everything is regarded as provisional and preliminary, and the smallest sample of virtue or accomplishment is taken to guarantee delightful stores which the broad leisure of marriage will reveal. But the door-sill of marriage once crossed, expectation is concentrated on the present. Having once embarked on your marital voyage, it is impossible not to be aware that you make no way and that the sea is not within sight – that, in fact, you are exploring an enclosed basin.

In their conversation before marriage, Mr Casaubon had often dwelt on some explanation or questionable detail of which Dorothea did not see the bearing; but such imperfect coherence seemed due to the brokenness of their inter-course, and, supported by her faith in their future, she had listened with fervid patience to a recitation of possible arguments to be brought against Mr Casaubon's entirely new view of the Philistine god Dagon and other fish-deities, thinking that hereafter she should see this subject which touched him so nearly from the same high ground whence doubtless it had become so important to him. Again, the matter-of-course statement and tone of dismissal with which he treated what to her were the most stirring thoughts, was easily accounted for as belonging to the sense of haste and preoccupation in which she herself shared during their engagement. But now, since they had been in Rome, with all the depths of her emotion roused to tumultuous activity, and with life made a new problem by new elements, she had been becoming more and more aware, with a certain terror, that her mind was continually sliding into inward fits of anger or repulsion, or else into forlorn weariness. How far the judicious Hooker or any other hero of erudition would have been the same at Mr Casaubon's time of life, she had no means of knowing, so that he could not have the advantage of comparison; but her husband's way of commenting on the strangely impressive objects around them had begun to affect her with a sort of mental shiver: he had perhaps the best intention of acquitting himself worthily, but only of acquitting himself. What was fresh to her mind was worn out to his; and such capacity of thought and feeling as had ever been stimulated in him by the general life of mankind had long shrunk to a sort of dried preparation, a lifeless embalmment of knowledge.

When he said, 'Does this interest you, Dorothea? Shall we stay a little longer? I am ready to stay if you wish it,' – it seemed to her as if going or staying were alike dreary. Or, 'Should you like to go to the Farnesina, Dorothea? It contains celebrated frescoes designed or painted by Raphael, which most persons think it worth while to visit.'

'But do you care about them?' was always Dorothea's question.

'They are, I believe, highly esteemed. Some of them represent the fable of Cupid and Psyche, which is probably the romantic invention of a literary period, and cannot, I think, be reckoned as a genuine mythical product. But if you like these wall-paintings we can easily drive thither; and you will then, I think, have seen the chief works of Raphael, any of which it were a pity to omit in a visit to Rome. He is the painter who has been held to combine the most complete grace of form with sublimity of expression. Such at least I have gathered to be the opinion of cognoscenti.'

This kind of answer given in a measured official tone, as of a clergyman reading according to the rubric, did not help to justify the glories of the Eternal City, or to give her the hope that if she knew more about them the world would be joyously illuminated for her. There is hardly any contact more depressing to a young ardent creature than that of a mind in which years full of knowledge seem to have issued in a blank absence of interest or sympathy.

On other subjects indeed Mr Casaubon showed a tenacity of occupation and an eagerness which are usually regarded as the effect of enthusiasm, and Dorothea was anxious to follow this spontaneous direction of his thoughts, instead of being made to feel that she dragged him away from it. But she was gradually ceasing to expect with her former delightful confidence that she should see any wide opening where she followed him. Poor Mr Casaubon himself was lost among small closets and winding stairs, and in an agitated dimness about the Cabeiri, or in an exposure of other mythologists' ill-considered parallels, easily lost sight of any purpose which had prompted him to these labours. With his taper stuck before him he forgot the absence of windows, and in bitter manuscript remarks on other men's notions about the solar deities, he had become indifferent to the sunlight.

These characteristics, fixed and unchangeable as bone in Mr Casaubon, might have remained longer unfelt by Dorothea if she had been encouraged to pour forth her girlish and womanly feeling – if he would have held her hands between his and listened with the delight of tenderness and understanding to all the little histories which made up her experience, and would have given her the same sort of intimacy in return, so that the past life of each could be included in their mutual knowledge and affection – or if she could have fed her affection with those childlike caresses which are the bent of every sweet woman, who has begun by showering kisses on the hard pate of her bald doll, creating a happy soul within that woodenness from the wealth of her own love. That was Dorothea's bent. With all her yearning to know what was afar from her and to be widely benignant, she had ardour enough for what was near, to have kissed Mr Casaubon's coat-sleeve, or to have caressed his shoe-latchet, if he would have made any other sign of acceptance than pronouncing her, with his unfailing propriety, to be of a most affectionate and truly feminine nature, indicating at the same time by politely reaching a chair for her that he regarded these manifestations as rather crude and startling. Having made his clerical toilette with due care in the morning, he was prepared only for those amenities of life which were suited to the well-adjusted stiff cravat of the period, and to a mind weighted with unpublished matter.

And by a sad contradiction Dorothea's ideas and resolves seemed like melting ice floating and lost in the warm flood of which they had been but another form. She was humiliated to find herself a mere victim of feeling, as if she could know nothing except through that medium: all her strength was scattered in fits of agitation, of struggle, of despondency, and then again in visions of more complete renunciation, transforming all hard conditions into duty. Poor Dorothea! she was certainly troublesome – to herself chiefly; but this morning for the first time she had been troublesome to Mr Casaubon.

She had begun, while they were taking coffee, with a determination to shake off what she inwardly called her selfishness, and turned a face all cheerful attention to her husband when he said, 'My dear Dorothea, we must now think of all that is yet left undone, as a preliminary to our departure. I would fain have returned home earlier that we might have been at Lowick for the Christmas; but my enquiries here have been protracted beyond their anticipated period. I trust, however, that the time here has not been passed unpleasantly to you. Among the sights of Europe, that of Rome has ever been held one of the most striking and in some respects edifying. I well remember that I considered it an epoch in my life when I visited it for the first time; after the fall of Napoleon, an event which opened the Continent to travellers. Indeed I think it is one among several cities to which an extreme hyperbole has been applied – "See Rome and die": but in your case I would propose an emendation and say, See Rome as a bride, and live thenceforth as a happy wife.'

Mr Casaubon pronounced this little speech with the most conscientious intention, blinking a little and swaying his head up and down, and concluding with a smile. He had not found marriage a rapturous state, but he had no idea of being anything else than an irreproachable husband, who would make a charming young woman as happy as she deserved to be.

'I hope you are thoroughly satisfied with our stay – I mean, with the result so far as your studies are concerned,' said Dorothea, trying to keep her mind fixed on what most affected her husband.

'Yes,' said Mr Casaubon, with that peculiar pitch of voice which makes the word half a negative. 'I have been led farther than I had foreseen, and various subjects for annotation have presented themselves which, though I have no direct need of them, I could not pretermit. The task, notwithstanding the assistance of my amanuensis, has been a somewhat laborious one, but your society has happily prevented me from that too continuous prosecution of thought beyond the hours of study which has been the snare of my solitary life.'

'I am very glad that my presence has made any difference to you,' said Dorothea, who had a vivid memory of evenings in which she had supposed that Mr Casaubon's mind had gone too deep during the day to be able to get to the surface again. I fear there was a little temper in her reply. 'I hope when we get to Lowick, I shall be more useful to you, and be able to enter a little more into what interests you.'

'Doubtless, my dear,' said Mr Casaubon, with a slight bow. 'The notes I have here made will want sifting, and you can, if you please, extract them under my direction.'

'And all your notes,' said Dorothea, whose heart had already burned within her on this subject so that now she could not help speaking with her tongue. 'All those rows of volumes will you not now do what you used to speak of? – will you not make up your mind what part of them you will use, and begin to write the book which will make your vast knowledge useful to the world? I will write to your dictation, or I will copy and extract what you tell me: I can be of no other use.' Dorothea, in a most unaccountable, darkly-feminine manner, ended with a slight sob and eyes full of tears.

The excessive feeling manifested would alone have been highly disturbing to Mr Casaubon, but there were other reasons why Dorothea's words were among the most cutting and irritating to him that she could have been impelled to use. She was as blind to his inward troubles as he to hers; she had not yet learned those hidden conflicts in her husband which claim our pity. She had not yet listened patiently to his heartbeats, but only felt that her own was beating violently. In Mr Casaubon's ear, Dorothea's voice gave loud emphatic iteration to those muffled suggestions of consciousness which it was possible to explain as mere fancy, the illusion of exaggerated sensitiveness: always when such suggestions are unmistakably repeated from without, they are resisted as cruel and unjust. We are angered even by the full acceptance of our humiliating confessions how much more by hearing in hard distinct syllables from the lips of a near observer, those confused murmurs which we try to call morbid, and strive against as if they were the oncoming of numbness! And this cruel outward accuser was there in the shape of a wife – nay, of a young bride, who, instead of observing his abundant pen scratches and amplitude of paper with the uncritical awe of an elegant-minded canary-bird, seemed to present herself as a spy watching everything with a malign power of inference. Here, towards this particular point of the compass, Mr Casaubon had a sensitiveness to match Dorothea's, and an equal quickness to imagine more than the fact. He had formerly observed with approbation her capacity for worshipping the right object; he now foresaw with sudden terror that this capacity might be replaced by presumption, this worship by the most exasperating of all criticism, – that which sees vaguely a great many fine ends and has not the least notion what it costs to reach them.

For the first time since Dorothea had known him, Mr Casaubon's face had a quick angry flush upon it.

'My love,' he said, with irritation reined in by propriety, 'you may rely upon me for knowing the times and the seasons, adapted to the different stages of a work which is not to be measured by the facile conjectures of ignorant onlookers. It had been easy for me to gain a temporary effect by a mirage of baseless opinion; but it is ever the trial of the scrupulous explorer to be saluted with the impatient scorn of chatterers who attempt only the smallest achievements, being indeed equipped for no other. And it were well if all such could be admonished to discriminate judgements of which the true subject-matter lies entirely beyond their reach, from those of which the elements may be compassed by a narrow and superficial survey.'

This speech was delivered with an energy and readiness quite unusual with Mr Casaubon. It was not indeed entirely an improvisation, but had taken shape in inward colloquy, and rushed out like the round grains from a fruit when sudden heat cracks it. Dorothea was not only his wife: she was a personification of that shallow world which surrounds the ill-appreciated or desponding author.

Dorothea was indignant in her turn. Had she not been repressing everything in her except the desire to enter into some fellowship with her husband's chief interests?

'My judgement *was* a very superficial one – such as I am capable of forming,' she answered, with a prompt resentment, that needed no rehearsal. 'You showed me the rows of notebooks, you have often spoken of them – you have often said that they wanted digesting. But I never heard you speak of the writing that is to be published. Those were very simple facts, and my judgement went no farther. I only begged you to let me be of some good to you.'

Dorothea rose to leave the table and Mr Casaubon made no reply, taking up a letter which lay beside him as if to re-peruse it. Both were shocked at their mutual situation – that each should have betrayed anger towards the other. If they had been at home, settled at Lowick in ordinary life among their neighbours, the clash would have been less embarrassing: but on a wedding journey, the express object of which is to isolate two people on the ground that they are all the world to each other, the sense of disagreement is, to say the least, confounding and stultifying.

To have changed your longitude extensively, and placed yourselves in a moral solitude in order to have small explosions, to find conversation difficult and to hand a glass of water without looking, can hardly be regarded as satisfactory fulfilment even to the toughest minds. To Dorothea's inexperienced sensitiveness, it seemed like a catastrophe, changing all prospects; and to Mr Casaubon it was a new pain, he never having been on a wedding journey before, or found himself in that close union which was more of a subjection than he had been able to imagine, since this charming young bride not only obliged him to much consideration on her behalf (which he had sedulously given), but turned out to be capable of agitating him cruelly just where he most needed soothing. Instead of getting a soft fence against the cold, shadowy, unapplausive audience of his life, had he only given it a more substantial presence?

Neither of them felt it possible to speak again at present. To have reversed a previous arrangement and declined to go out would have been a show of persistent anger which Dorothea's conscience shrank from, seeing that she already began to feel herself guilty. However just her indignation might be, her ideal was not to claim justice, but to give tenderness. So when the carriage came to the door, she drove with Mr Casaubon to the Vatican, walked with him through the stony avenue of inscriptions, and when she parted with him at the entrance to the Library, went on through the Museum out of mere listlessness as to what was around her. She had not spirit to turn round and say that she would drive anywhere. It was when Mr Casaubon was quitting her that Naumann had first seen her, and he had entered the long gallery of sculpture at the same time with her; but here Naumann had to await Ladislaw, with whom he was to settle a bet of champagne about an enigmatical mediaeval-looking figure there. After they had examined the figure, and had walked on finishing their dispute, they had parted, Ladislaw lingering behind while Naumann had gone into the Hall of Statues, where he again saw Dorothea, and saw her in that brooding abstraction which made her pose remarkable. She did not really see the streak of sunlight on the floor more than she saw the statues: she was inwardly seeing the light of years to come in her own home and over the English fields and elms and hedge-bordered high-roads: and feeling that the way in which they might be filled with joyful devotedness was not so clear to her as it had been. But in Dorothea's mind there was a current into which all thought and feeling were apt sooner or later to flow – the reaching forward of the whole consciousness towards the fullest truth, the least partial good. There was clearly something better than anger and despondency.

Chapter 21

Hire facounde eke full womanly and plain,
No contrefeted termes had she
To semen wise.
                                                CHAUCER

It was in that way Dorothea came to be sobbing as soon as she was securely alone. But she was presently roused by a knock at the door, which made her hastily dry her eyes before saying, 'Come in.' Tantripp had brought a card, and said that there was a gentleman waiting in the lobby. The courier had told him that only Mrs Casaubon was at home, but he said he was a relation of Mr Casaubon's: would she see him?

'Yes,' said Dorothea, without pause: 'show him into the salon.' Her chief impressions about young Ladislaw were that when she had seen him at Lowick she had been made aware of Mr Casaubon's generosity towards him, and also that she had been interested in his own hesitation about his career. She was alive to anything that gave her an opportunity for active sympathy, and at this moment it seemed as if the visit had come to shake her out of her self-absorbed discontent – to remind her of her husband's goodness, and make her feel that she had now the right to be his helpmate in all kind deeds. She waited a minute or two, but when she passed into the next room there were just signs enough that she had been crying to make her open face look more youthful and appealing than usual. She met Ladislaw with that exquisite smile of goodwill which is unmixed with vanity, and held out her hand to him. He was the elder by several years, but at that moment he looked much the younger, for his transparent complexion flushed suddenly, and he spoke with a shyness extremely unlike the ready indifference of his manner with his male companion, while Dorothea became all the calmer with a wondering desire to put him at ease.

'I was not aware that you and Mr Casaubon were in Rome, until this morning, when I saw you in the Vatican Museum,' he said. 'I knew you at once – but – I mean, that I concluded Mr Casaubon's address would be found at the Poste Restante, and I was anxious to pay my respects to him and you as early as possible.'

'Pray sit down. He is not here now, but he will be glad to hear of you, I am sure,' said Dorothea, seating herself unthinkingly between the fire and the light of the tall window, and pointing to a chair opposite, with the quietude of a benignant matron. The signs of girlish sorrow in her face were only the more striking. 'Mr Casaubon is much engaged: but you will leave your address – will you not? – and he will write to you.'

'You are very good,' said Ladislaw, beginning to lose his diffidence in the interest with which he was observing the signs of weeping which had altered her face. 'My address is on my card. But if you will allow me I will call again tomorrow at an hour when Mr Casaubon is likely to be at home.'

'He goes to read in the Library of the Vatican every day, and you can hardly see him except by an appointment. Especially now. We are about to leave Rome, and he is very busy. He is usually away almost from breakfast till dinner. But I am sure he will wish you to dine with us.'

Will Ladislaw was struck mute for a few moments. He had never been fond of Mr Casaubon, and if it had not been for the sense of obligation, would have laughed at him as a Bat of erudition. But the idea of this dried-up pedant, this elaborator of small explanations about as important as the surplus stock of false antiquities kept in a vendor's back chamber, having first got this adorable young creature to marry him, and then passing his honeymoon away from her, groping after his mouldy futilities (Will was given to hyperbole) – this sudden picture stirred him with a sort of comic disgust: he was divided between the impulse to laugh aloud and the equally unseasonable impulse to burst into scornful invective. For an instant he felt that the struggle was causing a queer contortion of his mobile features, but with a good effort he resolved it into nothing more offensive than a merry smile.

Dorothea wondered; but the smile was irresistible, and shone back from her face too. Will Ladislaw's smile was delightful, unless you were angry with him beforehand: it was a gush of inward light illuminating the transparent skin as well as the eyes, and playing about every curve and line as if some Ariel were touching them with a new charm, and banishing for ever the traces of moodiness. The reflection of that smile could not but have a little merriment in it too, even under dark eyelashes still moist, as Dorothea said enquiringly, 'Something amuses you?'

'Yes,' said Will, quick in finding resources. 'I am thinking of the sort of figure I cut the first time I saw you, when you annihilated my poor sketch with your criticism.'

'My criticism?' said Dorothea, wondering still more. 'Surely not. I always feel particularly ignorant about painting.'

'I suspected you of knowing so much, that you knew how to say just what was most cutting. You said – I dare say you don't remember it as I do – that the relation of my sketch to nature was quite hidden from you. At least, you implied that.' Will could laugh now as well as smile.

'That was really my ignorance,' said Dorothea, admiring Will's good humour. 'I must have said so only because I never could see any beauty in the pictures which my uncle told me all judges thought very fine. And I have gone about with just the same ignorance in Rome. There are comparatively few paintings that I can really enjoy. At first when I enter a room where the walls are covered with frescoes, or with rare pictures, I feel a kind of awe – like a child present at great ceremonies where there are grand robes and processions; I feel myself in the presence of some higher life than my own. But when I begin to examine the pictures one by one, the life goes out of them, or else is something violent and strange to me. It must be my own dulness. I am seeing so much all at once, and not understanding half of it. That always makes one feel stupid. It is painful to be told that anything is very fine and not be able to feel that it is fine – something like being blind, while people talk of the sky.'

'Oh, there is a great deal in the feeling for art which must be acquired,' said

Will. (It was impossible now to doubt the directness of Dorothea's confession.) 'Art is an old language with a great many artificial affected styles, and sometimes the chief pleasure one gets out of knowing them is the mere sense of knowing. I enjoy the art of all sorts here immensely; but I suppose if I could pick my enjoyment to pieces I should find it made up of many different threads. There is something in daubing a little one's self, and having an idea of the process.'

'You mean perhaps to be a painter?' said Dorothea, with a new direction of interest. 'You mean to make painting your profession. Mr Casaubon will like to hear that you have chosen a profession.'

'No, oh no,' said Will, with some coldness. 'I have quite made up my mind against it. It is too one-sided a life. I have been seeing a great deal of the German artists here: I travelled from Frankfort with one of them. Some are fine, even brilliant fellows – but I should not like to get into their way of looking at the world entirely from the studio point of view.'

'That I can understand,' said Dorothea, cordially. 'And in Rome it seems as if there were so many things which are more wanted in the world than pictures. But if you have a genius for painting, would it not be right to take that as a guide? Perhaps you might do better things than these – or different, so that there might not be so many pictures almost all alike in the same place.'

There was no mistaking this simplicity, and Will was won by it into frankness. 'A man must have a very rare genius to make changes of that sort. I am afraid mine would not carry me even to the pitch of doing well what has been done already, at least not so well as to make it worth while. And I should never succeed in anything by dint of drudgery. If things don't come easily to me I never get them.'

'I have heard Mr Casaubon say that he regrets your want of patience,' said Dorothea, gently. She was rather shocked at this mode of taking all life as a holiday.

'Yes, I know Mr Casaubon's opinion. He and I differ.'

The slight streak of contempt in his hasty reply offended Dorothea. She was all the more susceptible about Mr Casaubon because of her morning's trouble.

'Certainly you differ,' she said, rather proudly. 'I did not think of comparing you: such power of persevering devoted labour as Mr Casaubon's is not common.'

Will saw that she was offended, but this only gave an additional impulse to the new irritation of his latent dislike towards Mr Casaubon. It was too intolerable that Dorothea should be worshipping this husband: such weakness in a woman is pleasant to no man but the husband in question. Mortals are easily tempted to pinch the life out of their neighbour's buzzing glory, and think that such killing is no murder.

'No, indeed,' he answered, promptly. 'And therefore it is a pity that it should be thrown away, as so much English scholarship is, for want of knowing what is being done by the rest of the world. If Mr Casaubon read German he would save himself a great deal of trouble.'

'I do not understand you,' said Dorothea, startled and anxious.

'I merely mean,' said Will, in an offhand way, 'that the Germans have taken the lead in historical enquiries, and they laugh at results which are got by groping about in the woods with a pocket-compass while they have made good roads. When I was with Mr Casaubon I saw that he deafened himself in that direction: it was almost against his will that he read a Latin treatise written by a German. I was very sorry.'

Will only thought of giving a good pinch that would annihilate that vaunted laboriousness, and was unable to imagine the mode in which Dorothea would be wounded. Young Mr Ladislaw was not at all deep himself in German writers; but very little achievement is required in order to pity another man's short-comings.

Poor Dorothea felt a pang at the thought that the labour of her husband's life might be void, which left her no energy to spare for the question whether this young relative who was so much obliged to him ought not to have repressed his observation. She did not even speak, but sat looking at her hands, absorbed in the piteousness of that thought.

Will, however, having given that annihilating pinch, was rather ashamed, imagining from Dorothea's silence that he had offended her still more; and having also a conscience about plucking the tail-feathers from a benefactor.

'I regretted it especially,' he resumed, taking the usual course from detraction to insincere eulogy, 'because of my gratitude and respect towards my cousin. It would not signify so much in a man whose talents and character were less distinguished.'

Dorothea raised her eyes, brighter than usual with excited feeling, and said, in her saddest recitative, 'How I wish I had learned German when I was at Lausanne! There were plenty of German teachers. But now I can be of no use.'

There was a new light, but still a mysterious light, for Will in Dorothea's last words. The question how she had come to accept Mr Casaubon – which he had dismissed when he first saw her by saying that she must be disagreeable in spite of appearances – was not now to be answered on any such short and easy method. Whatever else she might be, she was not disagreeable. She was not coldly clever and indirectly satirical, but adorably simple and full of feeling. She was an angel beguiled. It would be a unique delight to wait and watch for the melodious fragments in which her heart and soul came forth so directly and ingenuously. The Aeolian harp again came into his mind.

She must have made some original romance for herself in this marriage. And if Mr Casaubon had been a dragon who had carried her off to his lair with his talons simply and without legal forms, it would have been an unavoidable feat of heroism to release her and fall at her feet. But he was something more unmanageable than a dragon: he was a benefactor with collective society at his back, and he was at that moment entering the room in all the unimpeachable correctness of his demeanour, while Dorothea was looking animated with a newly aroused alarm and regret, and Will was looking animated with his admiring speculation about her feelings.

Mr Casaubon felt a surprise which was quite unmixed with pleasure, but he did not swerve from his usual politeness of greeting, when Will rose and explained his presence. Mr Casaubon was less happy than usual, and this perhaps made him look all the dimmer and more faded; else, the effect might easily have been produced by the contrast of his young cousin's appearance. The first impression on seeing Will was one of sunny brightness, which added to the uncertainty of his changing expression. Surely, his very features changed their form; his jaw looked sometimes large and sometimes small; and the little ripple in his nose was a preparation for metamorphosis. When he turned his head quickly his hair seemed to shake out light, and some persons thought they saw decided genius in this coruscation. Mr Casaubon, on the contrary, stood rayless.

As Dorothea's eyes were turned anxiously on her husband she was perhaps not insensible to the contrast, but it was only mingled with other causes in making her more conscious of that new alarm on his behalf which was the first stirring of a pitying tenderness fed by the realities of his lot and not by her own dreams. Yet it was a source of greater freedom to her that Will was there; his young equality was agreeable, and also perhaps his openness to conviction. She felt an immense need of someone to speak to, and she had never before seen anyone who seemed so quick and pliable, so likely to understand everything.

Mr Casaubon gravely hoped that Will was passing his time profitably as well as pleasantly in Rome – had thought his intention was to remain in South Germany – but begged him to come and dine tomorrow, when he would converse more at large: at present he was somewhat weary. Ladislaw understood, and accepting the invitation immediately took his leave.

Dorothea's eyes followed her husband anxiously, while he sank down wearily at the end of a sofa, and resting his elbow supported his head and looked on the floor. A little flushed, and with bright eyes, she seated herself beside him, and said, 'Forgive me for speaking so hastily to you this morning. I was wrong. I fear I hurt you and made the day more burdensome.'

'I am glad that you feel that, my dear,' said Mr Casaubon. He spoke quietly and bowed his head a little, but there was still an uneasy feeling in his eyes as he looked at her.

'But you do forgive me?' said Dorothea, with a quick sob. In her need for some manifestation of feeling she was ready to exaggerate her own fault. Would not love see returning penitence afar off, and fall on its neck and kiss it?

'My dear Dorothea – "who with repentance is not satisfied, is not of heaven nor earth". – you do not think me worthy to be banished by that severe sentence,' said Mr Casaubon, exerting himself to make a strong statement, and also to smile faintly.

Dorothea was silent, but a tear which had come up with the sob would insist on falling.

'You are excited, my dear. And I also am feeling some unpleasant consequences of too much mental disturbance,' said Mr Casaubon. In fact, he had it in his thought to tell her that she ought not to have received young Ladislaw in his absence; but he abstained, partly from the sense that it would be ungracious to bring a new complaint in the moment of her penitent acknowledgment, partly because he wanted to avoid further agitation of himself by speech, and partly because he was too proud to betray that jealousy of disposition which was not so exhausted on his scholarly compeers that there was none to spare in other directions. There is a sort of jealousy which needs very little fire; it is hardly a passion, but a blight bred in the cloudy, damp despondency of uneasy egoism.

'I think it is time for us to dress,' he added, looking at his watch. They both rose, and there was never any further allusion between them to what had passed on this day.

But Dorothea remembered it to the last with the vividness with which we all remember epochs in our experience when some dear expectation dies, or some new motive is born. Today she had begun to see that she had been under a wild illusion in expecting a response to her feeling from Mr Casaubon, and she had felt the waking of a presentiment that there might be a sad consciousness in his life which made as great a need on his side as on her own.

We are all of us born in moral stupidity, taking the world as an udder to feed our supreme selves: Dorothea had early begun to emerge from that stupidity, but yet it had been easier to her to imagine how she would devote herself to Mr Casaubon, and become wise and strong in his strength and wisdom, than to conceive with that distinctness which is no longer reflection but feeling – an idea wrought back to the directness of sense, like the solidity of objects – that he had an equivalent centre of self, whence the lights and shadows must always fall with a certain difference.

Chapter 22

> Nous causâmes longtemps; elle était simple et bonne.
> Ne sachant pas le mal, elle faisait le bien;
> Des richesses du coeur elle me fit l'aumône,
> Et tout en écoutant comme le coeur se donne,
> Sans oser y penser, je lui donnai le mien;
> Elle emporta ma vie, et n'en sut jamais rien.
>
> ALFRED DE MUSSET

Will Ladislaw was delightfully agreeable at dinner the next day, and gave no opportunity for Mr Casaubon to show disapprobation. On the contrary it seemed to Dorothea that Will had a happier way of drawing her husband into conversation and of deferentially listening to him than she had ever observed in anyone before. To be sure, the listeners about Tipton were not highly gifted! Will talked a good deal himself, but what he said was thrown in with such rapidity, and with such an unimportant air of saying something by the way, that it seemed a gay little chime after the great bell. If Will was not always perfect, this was certainly one of his good days. He described touches of incident among the poor people in Rome, only to be seen by one who could move about freely; he found himself in agreement with Mr Casaubon as to the unsound opinions of Middleton concerning the relations of Judaism and Catholicism; and passed easily to a half-enthusiastic half-playful picture of the enjoyment he got out of the very miscellaneousness of Rome, which made the mind flexible with constant comparison, and saved you from seeing the world's ages as a set of boxlike partitions without vital connection. Mr Casaubon's studies, Will observed, had always been of too broad a kind for that, and he had perhaps never felt any such sudden effect, but for himself he confessed that Rome had given him quite a new sense of history as a whole; the fragments stimulated his imagination and made him constructive. Then occasionally, but not too often, he appealed to Dorothea, and discussed what she said, as if her sentiment were an item to be considered in the final judgement even of the Madonna di Foligno or the Laocoon. A sense of contributing to form the world's opinion makes conversation particularly cheerful; and Mr Casaubon too was not without his pride in his young wife, who spoke better than most women, as indeed he had perceived in choosing her.

Since things were going on so pleasantly, Mr Casaubon's statement that his labours in the Library would be suspended for a couple of days, and that after a brief renewal he should have no further reason for staying in Rome, encouraged Will to urge that Mrs Casaubon should not go away without seeing a studio or two. Would not Mr Casaubon take her? That sort of thing ought not to be missed; it was quite special: it was a form of life that grew like a small fresh vegetation with its population of insects on huge fossils. Will would be happy to conduct them – not to anything wearisome, only to a few examples.

Mr Casaubon, seeing Dorothea look earnestly towards him, could not but ask her if she would be interested in such visits: he was now at her service during the whole day; and it was agreed that Will should come on the morrow and drive with them.

Will could not omit Thorwaldsen, a living celebrity about whom even Mr Casaubon enquired, but before the day was far advanced he led the way to the studio of his friend Adolf Naumann, whom he mentioned as one of the chief renovators of Christian art, one of those who had not only revived but expanded that grand conception of supreme events as mysteries at which the successive ages were spectators, and in relation to which the great souls of all periods became as it were contemporaries. Will added that he had made himself Naumann's pupil for the nonce.

'I have been making some oil-sketches under him,' said Will. 'I hate copying. I must put something of my own in. Naumann has been painting the Saints drawing the Car of the Church, and I have been making a sketch of Marlowe's Tamburlaine Driving the Conquered Kings in his Chariot. I am not so ecclesiastical as Naumann, and I sometimes twit him with his excess of meaning. But this time I mean to outdo him in breadth of intention. I take Tamburlaine in his chariot for the tremendous course of the world's physical history lashing on the harnessed dynasties. In my opinion, that is a good mythical interpretation.' Will here looked at Mr Casaubon, who received this offhand treatment of symbolism very uneasily, and bowed with a neutral air.

'The sketch must be very grand, if it conveys so much,' said Dorothea. 'I should need some explanation even of the meaning you give. Do you intend Tamburlaine to represent earthquakes and volcanoes?'

'O yes,' said Will, laughing, 'and migrations of races and clearings of forests – and America and the steam-engine. Everything you can imagine!'

'What a difficult kind of shorthand!' said Dorothea, smiling towards her husband. 'It would require all your knowledge to be able to read it.'

Mr Casaubon blinked furtively at Will. He had a suspicion that he was being laughed at. But it was not possible to include Dorothea in the suspicion.

They found Naumann painting industriously, but no model was present; his pictures were advantageously arranged, and his own plain vivacious person set off by a dove-coloured blouse and a maroon velvet cap, so that everything was as fortunate as if he had expected the beautiful young English lady exactly at that time.

The painter in his confident English gave little dissertations on his finished and unfinished subjects, seeming to observe Mr Casaubon as much as he did Dorothea. Will burst in here and there with ardent words of praise, marking out particular merits in his friend's work; and Dorothea felt that she was getting quite new notions as to the significance of Madonnas seated under inexplicable canopied thrones with the simple country as a background, and of saints with architectural models in their hands, or knives accidentally wedged in their skulls. Some things which had seemed monstrous to her were gathering intelligibility and even a natural meaning; but all this was apparently a branch of knowledge in which Mr Casaubon had not interested himself.

'I think I would rather feel that painting is beautiful than have to read it as an enigma; but I should learn to understand these pictures sooner than yours with the very wide meaning,' said Dorothea, speaking to Will.

'Don't speak of my painting before Naumann,' said Will. 'He will tell you, it is all *pfuscherei*, which is his most opprobrious word!'

'Is that true?' said Dorothea, turning her sincere eyes on Naumann, who made a slight grimace and said, 'Oh, he does not mean it seriously with painting. His walk must be *belles-lettres*. That is wi–ide.'

Naumann's pronunciation of the vowel seemed to stretch the word satirically. Will did not half like it, but managed to laugh; and Mr Casaubon, while he felt some disgust at the artist's German accent, began to entertain a little respect for his judicious severity.

The respect was not diminished when Naumann, after drawing Will aside for a moment and looking, first at a large canvas, then at Mr Casaubon, came forward again and said, 'My friend Ladislaw thinks you will pardon me, sir, if I say that a sketch of your head would be invaluable to me for the St Thomas Aquinas in my picture there. It is too much to ask; but I so seldom see just what I want – the idealistic in the real.'

'You astonish me greatly, sir,' said Mr Casaubon, his looks improved with a glow of delight; 'but if my poor physiognomy, which I have been accustomed to regard as of the commonest order, can be of any use to you in furnishing some traits for the angelical doctor, I shall feel honoured. That is to say, if the operation will not be a lengthy one; and if Mrs Casaubon will not object to the delay.'

As for Dorothea, nothing could have pleased her more, unless it had been a miraculous voice pronouncing Mr Casaubon the wisest and worthiest among the sons of men. In that case her tottering faith would have become firm again.

Naumann's apparatus was at hand in wonderful completeness, and the sketch went on at once as well as the conversation. Dorothea sat down and subsided into calm silence, feeling happier than she had done for a long while before. Everyone about her seemed good, and she said to herself that Rome, if she had only been less ignorant, would have been full of beauty; its sadness would have been winged with hope. No nature could be less suspicious than hers; when she was a child she believed in the gratitude of wasps and the honourable susceptibility of sparrows, and was proportionately indignant when their baseness was made manifest.

The adroit artist was asking Mr Casaubon questions about English politics, which brought long answers, and Will meanwhile had perched himself on some steps in the background overlooking all.

Presently Naumann said – 'Now if I could lay this by for half an hour and take it up again – come and look, Ladislaw – I think it is perfect so far.'

Will vented those adjuring interjections which imply that admiration is too strong for syntax; and Naumann said in a tone of piteous regret: 'Ah – now – if I could but have had more – but you have other engagements – I could not ask it – or even to come again tomorrow.'

'O let us stay!' said Dorothea. 'We have nothing to do today except to go about, have we?' she added, looking entreatingly at Mr Casaubon. 'It would be a pity not to make the head as good as possible.'

'I am at your service, sir, in the matter,' said Mr Casaubon, with polite condescension. 'Having given up the interior of my head to idleness, it is as well that the exterior should work in this way.'

'You are unspeakably good – now I am happy!' said Naumann, and then went on in German to Will, pointing here and there to the sketch as if he were considering that. Putting it aside for a moment, he looked round vaguely, as if seeking some occupation for his visitors, and afterwards turning to Mr Casaubon said, 'Perhaps the beautiful bride, the gracious lady, would not be unwilling to let me fill up the time by trying to make a slight sketch of her – not, of course, as you see, for that picture only as a single study.'

Mr Casaubon, bowing, doubted not that Mrs Casaubon would oblige him, and Dorothea said, at once, 'Where shall I put myself?'

Naumann was all apologies in asking her to stand, and allow him to adjust her attitude to which she submitted without any of the affected airs and laughs frequently thought necessary on such occasions, when the painter said, 'It is as Santa Clara that I want you to stand – leaning so, with your cheek against your hand – so – looking at that stool, please, so!'

Will was divided between the inclination to fall at the Saint's feet and kiss her robe, and the temptation to knock Naumann down while he was adjusting her arm. All this was impudence and desecration, and he repented that he had brought her.

The artist was diligent, and Will recovering himself moved about and occupied Mr Casaubon as ingeniously as he could; but he did not in the end prevent the time from seeming long to that gentleman, as was clear from his expressing a fear that Mrs Casaubon would be tired. Naumann took the hint and said: 'Now, sir, if you can oblige me again, I will release the lady-wife.'

So Mr Casaubon's patience held out further, and when after all it turned out that the head of Saint Thomas Aquinas would be more perfect if another sitting could be had, it was granted for the morrow. On the morrow Santa Clara too was retouched more than once. The result of all was so far from displeasing to Mr Casaubon that he arranged for the purchase of the picture in which Saint Thomas Aquinas sat among the doctors of the Church in a disputation too abstract to be represented, but listened to with more or less attention by an audience above. The Santa Clara, which was spoken of in the second place, Naumann declared himself to be dissatisfied with – he could not, in conscience, engage to make a worthy picture of it; so about the Santa Clara the arrangement was conditional.

I will not dwell on Naumann's jokes at the expense of Mr Casaubon that evening, or on his dithyrambs about Dorothea's charm, in all which Will joined, but with a difference. No sooner did Naumann mention any detail of Dorothea's beauty, than Will got exasperated at his presumption: there was grossness in his choice of the most ordinary words, and what business had he to talk of her lips? She was not a woman to be spoken of as other women were. Will could not say just what he thought, but he became irritable. And yet, when after some resistance he had consented to take the Casaubons to his friend's studio, he had been allured by the gratification of his pride in being the person who could grant Naumann such an opportunity of studying her loveliness – or rather her divineness, for the ordinary phrases which might apply to mere bodily prettiness were not applicable to her. (Certainly all Tipton and its neighbourhood, as well as Dorothea herself, would have been surprised at her beauty being made so much of. In that part of the world Miss Brooke had been only a 'fine young woman'.)

'Oblige me by letting the subject drop, Naumann. Mrs Casaubon is not to be talked of as if she were a model,' said Will. Naumann stared at him.

'*Schön*! I will talk of my Aquinas. The head is not a bad type, after all. I dare say the great scholastic himself would have been flattered to have his portrait asked for. Nothing like these starchy doctors for vanity! It was as I thought: he cared much less for her portrait than his own.'

'He's a cursed white-blooded pedantic coxcomb,' said Will, with gnashing impetuosity. His obligations to Mr Casaubon were not known to his hearer, but Will himself was thinking of them, and wishing that he could discharge them all by a cheque.

Naumann gave a shrug and said, 'It is good they go away soon, my dear. They are spoiling your fine temper.'

All Will's hope and contrivance were now concentrated on seeing Dorothea when she was alone. He only wanted her to take more emphatic notice of him: he only wanted to be something more special in her remembrance than he could yet believe himself likely to be. He was rather impatient under that open ardent goodwill, which he saw was her usual state of feeling. The remote worship of a woman throned out of their reach plays a great part in men's lives, but in most cases the worshipper longs for some queenly recognition, some approving sign by which his soul's sovereign may cheer him without descending from her high

place. That was precisely what Will wanted. But there were plenty of contradictions in his imaginative demands. It was beautiful to see how Dorothea's eyes
turned with wifely anxiety and beseeching to Mr Casaubon: she would have lost
some of her halo if she had been without that duteous preoccupation: and yet
at the next moment the husband's sandy absorption of such nectar was too
intolerable; and Will's longing to say damaging things about him was perhaps
not the less tormenting because he felt the strongest reasons for restraining it.

Will had not been invited to dine the next day. Hence he persuaded himself
that he was bound to call, and that the only eligible time was the middle of the
day, when Mr Casaubon would not be at home.

Dorothea, who had not been made aware that her former reception of Will
had displeased her husband, had no hesitation about seeing him, especially as he
might be come to pay a farewell visit. When he entered she was looking at some
cameos which she had been buying for Celia. She greeted Will as if his visit were
quite a matter of course, and said at once, having a cameo bracelet in her hand, 'I
am so glad you are come. Perhaps you understand all about cameos, and can tell
me if these are really good. I wished to have you with us in choosing them, but
Mr Casaubon objected; he thought there was not time. He will finish his work
tomorrow, and we shall go away in three days. I have been uneasy about these
cameos. Pray sit down and look at them.'

'I am not particularly knowing, but there can be no great mistake about these
little Homeric bits: they are exquisitely neat. And the colour is fine: it will just
suit you.'

'O, they are for my sister, who has quite a different complexion. You saw her
with me at Lowick: she is light-haired and very pretty – at least I think so. We
were never so long away from each other in our lives before. She is a great pet,
and never was naughty in her life. I found out before I came away that she
wanted me to buy her some cameos, and I should be sorry for them not to be
good – after their kind.' Dorothea added the last words with a smile.

'You seem not to care about cameos,' said Will, seating himself at some
distance from her, and observing her while she closed the cases.

'No, frankly, I don't think them a great object in life,' said Dorothea.

'I fear you are a heretic about art generally. How is that? I should have
expected you to be very sensitive to the beautiful everywhere.'

'I suppose I am dull about many things,' said Dorothea, simply. 'I should like
to make life beautiful – I mean everybody's life. And then all this immense
expense of art, that seems somehow to lie outside life and make it no better for
the world, pains one. It spoils my enjoyment of anything when I am made to
think that most people are shut out from it.'

'I call that the fanaticism of sympathy,' said Will, impetuously. 'You might say
the same of landscape, of poetry, of all refinement. If you carried it out you
ought to be miserable in your own goodness, and turn evil that you might have
no advantage over others. The best piety is to enjoy – when you can. You are
doing the most then to save the earth's character as an agreeable planet. And
enjoyment radiates. It is of no use to try and take care of all the world; that is
being taken care of when you feel delight – in art or in anything else. Would you

turn all the youth of the world into a tragic chorus, wailing and moralising over misery? I suspect that you have some false belief in the virtues of misery, and want to make your life a martyrdom.' Will had gone further than he intended, and checked himself. But Dorothea's thought was not taking just the same direction as his own, and she answered without any special emotion: 'Indeed you mistake me. I am not a sad, melancholy creature. I am never unhappy long together. I am angry and naughty not like Celia: I have a great outburst, and then all seems glorious again. I cannot help believing in glorious things in a blind sort of way. I should be quite willing to enjoy the art here, but there is so much that I don't know the reason of – so much that seems to me a consecration of ugliness rather than beauty. The painting and sculpture may be wonderful, but the feeling is often low and brutal, and sometimes even ridiculous. Here and there I see what takes me at once as noble – something that I might compare with the Alban Mountains or the sunset from the Pincian Hill; but that makes it the greater pity that there is so little of the best kind among all that mass of things over which men have toiled so.'

'Of course there is always a great deal of poor work: the rarer things want that soil to grow in.'

'O dear,' said Dorothea, taking up that thought into the chief current of anxiety, 'I see it must be very difficult to do anything good. I have often felt since I have been in Rome that most of our lives would look much uglier and more bungling than the pictures, if they could be put on the wall.'

Dorothea parted her lips again as if she were going to say more, but changed her mind and paused.

'You are too young – it is an anachronism for you to have such thoughts,' said Will energetically, with a quick shake of the head, habitual to him. 'You talk as if you had never known any youth. It is monstrous – as if you had had a vision of Hades in your childhood, like the boy in the legend. You have been brought up in some of those horrible notions that choose the sweetest women to devour – like Minotaurs. And now you will go and be shut up in that stone prison at Lowick: you will be buried alive. It makes me savage to think of it! I would rather never have seen you than think of you with such a prospect.'

Will again feared that he had gone too far; but the meaning we attach to words depends on our feeling, and his tone of angry regret had so much kindness in it for Dorothea's heart, which had always been giving out ardour and had never been fed with much from the living beings around her, that she felt a new sense of gratitude and answered with a gentle smile.

'It is very good of you to be anxious about me. It is because you did not like Lowick yourself: you had set your heart on another kind of life. But Lowick is my chosen home.'

The last sentence was spoken with an almost solemn cadence, and Will did not know what to say, since it would not be useful for him to embrace her slippers, and tell her that he would die for her: it was clear that she required nothing of the sort; and they were both silent for a moment or two, when Dorothea began again with an air of saying at last what had been in her mind beforehand.

'I wanted to ask you again about something you said the other day. Perhaps it was half of it your lively way of speaking: I notice that you like to put things strongly; I myself often exaggerate when I speak hastily.'

'What was it?' said Will, observing that she spoke with a timidity quite new in her. 'I have a hyperbolical tongue: it catches fire as it goes. I dare say I shall have to retract.'

'I mean what you said about the necessity of knowing German – I mean, for the subjects that Mr Casaubon is engaged in. I have been thinking about it; and it seems to me that with Mr Casaubon's learning he must have before him the same materials as German scholars – has he not?' Dorothea's timidity was due to an indistinct consciousness that she was in the strange situation of consulting a third person about the adequacy of Mr Casaubon's learning.

'Not exactly the same materials,' said Will, thinking that he would be duly reserved. 'He is not an Orientalist, you know. He does not profess to have more than second-hand knowledge there.'

'But there are very valuable books about antiquities which were written a long while ago by scholars who knew nothing about these modern things; and they are still used. Why should Mr Casaubon's not be valuable, like theirs?' said Dorothea, with more remonstrant energy. She was impelled to have the argument aloud, which she had been having in her own mind.

'That depends on the line of study taken,' said Will, also getting a tone of rejoinder. 'The subject Mr Casaubon has chosen is as changing as chemistry: new discoveries are constantly making new points of view. Who wants a system on the basis of the four elements, or a book to refute Paracelsus? Do you not see that it is no use now to be crawling a little way after men of the last century – men like Bryant – and correcting their mistakes? – living in a lumber-room and furbishing up broken-legged theories about Chus and Mizraim?'

'How can you bear to speak so lightly?' said Dorothea, with a look between sorrow and anger. 'If it were as you say, what could be sadder than so much ardent labour all in vain? I wonder it does not affect you more painfully, if you really think that a man like Mr Casaubon, of so much goodness, power, and learning, should in any way fail in what has been the labour of his best years.' She was beginning to be shocked that she had got to such a point of supposition, and indignant with Will for having led her to it.

'You questioned me about the matter of fact, not of feeling,' said Will. 'But if you wish to punish me for the fact, I submit. I am not in a position to express my feeling toward Mr Casaubon: it would be at best a pensioner's eulogy.'

'Pray excuse me,' said Dorothea, colouring deeply. 'I am aware, as you say, that I am in fault, in having introduced the subject. Indeed, I am wrong altogether. Failure after long perseverance is much grander than never to have a striving good enough to be called a failure.'

'I quite agree with you,' said Will, determined to change the situation – 'so much so that I have made up my mind not to run that risk of never attaining a failure. Mr Casaubon's generosity has perhaps been dangerous to me, and I mean to renounce the liberty it has given me. I mean to go back to England shortly and work my own way – depend on nobody else than myself.'

'That is fine – I respect that feeling,' said Dorothea, with returning kindness.

'But Mr Casaubon, I am sure, has never thought of anything in the matter except what was most for your welfare.'

'She has obstinacy and pride enough to serve instead of love, now she has married him,' said Will to himself. Aloud he said, rising, 'I shall not see you again.'

'O stay till Mr Casaubon comes,' said Dorothea, earnestly. 'I am so glad we met in Rome. I wanted to know you.'

'And I have made you angry,' said Will. 'I have made you think ill of me.'

'Oh no! My sister tells me I am always angry with people who do not say just what I like. But I hope I am not given to think ill of them. In the end I am usually obliged to think ill of myself, for being so impatient.'

'Still, you don't like me; I have made myself an unpleasant thought to you.'

'Not at all,' said Dorothea, with the most open kindness. 'I like you very much.'

Will was not quite contented, thinking that he would apparently have been of more importance if he had been disliked. He said nothing, but looked dull, not to say sulky.

'And I am quite interested to see what you will do,' Dorothea went on cheerfully. 'I believe devoutly in a natural difference of vocation. If it were not for that belief, I suppose I should be very narrow – there are so many things, besides painting, that I am quite ignorant of. You would hardly believe how little I have taken in of music and literature, which you know so much of. I wonder what your vocation will turn out to be: perhaps you will be a poet?'

'That depends. To be a poet is to have a soul so quick to discern, that no shade of quality escapes it, and so quick to feel, that discernment is but a hand playing with finely ordered variety on the chords of emotion – a soul in which knowledge passes instantaneously into feeling, and feeling flashes back as a new organ of knowledge. One may have that condition by fits only.'

'But you leave out the poems,' said Dorothea. 'I think they are wanted to complete the poet. I understand what you mean about knowledge passing into feeling, for that seems to be just what I experience. But I am sure I could never produce a poem.'

'You *are* a poem – and that is to be the best part of a poet what makes up the poet's consciousness in his best moods,' said Will, showing such originality as we all share with the morning and the springtime and other endless renewals.

'I am very glad to hear it,' said Dorothea, laughing out her words in a birdlike modulation, and looking at Will with playful gratitude in her eyes. 'What very kind things you say to me!'

'I wish I could ever do anything that would be what you call kind – that I could ever be of the slightest service to you. I fear I shall never have the opportunity.' Will spoke with fervour.

'Oh yes!' said Dorothea, cordially. 'It will come; and I shall remember how well you wish me. I quite hoped that we should be friends when I first saw you – because of your relationship to Mr Casaubon.' There was a certain liquid brightness in her eyes, and Will was conscious that his own were obeying a law of nature and filling too. The allusion to Mr Casaubon would have spoiled all if anything at that moment could have spoiled the subduing power, the sweet dignity, of her noble unsuspicious inexperience.

'And there is one thing even now that you can do,' said Dorothea, rising and walking a little way under the strength of a recurring impulse. 'Promise me that you will not again, to anyone, speak of that subject – I mean, about Mr Casaubon's writings – I mean in that kind of way. It was I who led to it. It was my fault. But promise me.'

She had returned from her brief pacing and stood opposite Will, looking gravely at him.

'Certainly, I will promise you,' said Will, reddening however. If he never said a cutting word about Mr Casaubon again and left off receiving favours from him, it would clearly be permissible to hate him the more. The poet must know how to hate, says Goethe; and Will was at least ready with that accomplishment. He said that he must go now without waiting for Mr Casaubon, whom he would come to take leave of at the last moment. Dorothea gave him her hand, and they exchanged a simple 'Goodbye.'

But going out of the *porte cochère* he met Mr Casaubon, and that gentleman, expressing the best wishes for his cousin, politely waived the pleasure of any further leave-taking on the morrow, which would be sufficiently crowded with the preparations for departure.

'I have something to tell you about our cousin, Mr Ladislaw, which I think will heighten your opinion of him,' said Dorothea to her husband in the course of the evening. She had mentioned immediately on his entering that Will had just gone away, and would come again, but Mr Casaubon had said, 'I met him outside, and we made our final adieux, I believe,' saying this with the air and tone by which we imply that any subject, whether private or public, does not interest us enough to wish for a further remark upon it. So Dorothea had waited.

'What is that, my love?' said Mr Casaubon (he always said 'my love', when his manner was the coldest).

'He has made up his mind to leave off wandering at once, and to give up his dependence on your generosity. He means soon to go back to England, and work his own way. I thought you would consider that a good sign,' said Dorothea, with an appealing look into her husband's neutral face.

'Did he mention the precise order of occupation to which he would addict himself?'

'No. But he said that he felt the danger which lay for him in your generosity. Of course he will write to you about it. Do you not think better of him for his resolve?'

'I shall await his communication on the subject,' said Mr Casaubon.

'I told him I was sure that the thing you considered in all you did for him was his own welfare. I remembered your goodness in what you said about him when I first saw him at Lowick,' said Dorothea, putting her hand on her husband's.

'I had a duty towards him,' said Mr Casaubon, laying his other hand on Dorothea's in conscientious acceptance of her caress, but with a glance which he could not hinder from being uneasy. 'The young man, I confess, is not otherwise an object of interest to me, nor need we, I think, discuss his future course, which it is not ours to determine beyond the limits which I have sufficiently indicated.'

Dorothea did not mention Will again.

BOOK THREE

Waiting for Death

Chapter 23

> 'Your horses of the Sun,' he said,
> 'And first-rate whip Apollo!
> Whate'er they be, I'll eat my head,
> But I will beat them hollow.'

Fred Vincy, we have seen, had a debt on his mind, and though no such immaterial burthen could depress that buoyant-hearted young gentleman for many hours together, there were circumstances connected with this debt which made the thought of it unusually importunate. The creditor was Mr Bambridge, a horse-dealer of the neighbourhood, whose company was much sought in Middlemarch by young men understood to be 'addicted to pleasure'. During the vacations Fred had naturally required more amusements than he had ready money for, and Mr Bambridge had been accommodating enough not only to trust him for the hire of horses and the accidental expense of ruining a fine hunter, but also to make a small advance by which he might be able to meet some losses at billiards. The total debt was a hundred and sixty pounds. Bambridge was in no alarm about his money, being sure that young Vincy had backers; but he had required something to show for it, and Fred had at first given a bill with his own signature. Three months later he had renewed this bill with the signature of Caleb Garth. On both occasions Fred had felt confident that he should meet the bill himself, having ample funds at disposal in his own hopefulness. You will hardly demand that his confidence should have a basis in external facts; such confidence, we know, is something less coarse and material-istic: it is a comfortable disposition leading us to expect that the wisdom of providence or the folly of our friends, the mysteries of luck or the still greater mystery of our high individual value in the universe, will bring about agreeable issues, such as are consistent with our good taste in costume, and our general preference for the best style of thing. Fred felt sure that he should have a present from his uncle, that he should have a run of luck, that by dint of 'swapping' he should gradually metamorphose a horse worth forty pounds into a horse that would fetch a hundred at any moment – 'judgement' being always equivalent to an unspecified sum in hard cash. And in any case, even supposing negations which only a morbid distrust could imagine, Fred had always (at that time) his father's pocket as a last resource, so that his assets of hopefulness had a sort of gorgeous superfluity about them. Of what might be the capacity of his father's pocket, Fred had only a vague notion: was not trade elastic? And would not the deficiencies of one year be made up for by the surplus of another? The Vincys lived in an easy profuse way, not with any new ostentation, but according to the family habits and traditions, so that the children had no standard of economy, and the elder ones retained some of their infantine notion that their father might pay for anything if he would. Mr Vincy himself had expensive Middlemarch habits – spent money on coursing, on his cellar, and on dinner-giving, while mamma had those running accounts with tradespeople, which give a cheerful sense of getting everything one wants without any question of payment. But it was in the nature of fathers, Fred knew, to bully one about expenses: there was always a little storm over his extravagance if he had to disclose a debt, and Fred disliked bad weather within doors. He was too filial to be disrespectful to his father, and he bore the thunder with the certainty that it was transient; but in the meantime it was disagreeable to see his mother cry, and also to be obliged to look sulky instead of having fun; for Fred was so good-tempered that if he looked glum under scolding, it was chiefly for propriety's sake. The easier course, plainly was to renew the bill with a friend's signature. Why not? With the superfluous securities of hope at his command, there was no reason why he should not have increased other people's liabilities to any extent, but for the fact that men whose names were good for anything were usually pessimists, indisposed to believe that the universal order of things would necessarily be agreeable to an agreeable young gentleman.

With a favour to ask we review our list of friends, do justice to their more amiable qualities, forgive their little offences, and concerning each in turn, try to arrive at the conclusion that he will be eager to oblige us, our own eagerness to be obliged being as communicable as other warmth. Still there is always a certain number who are dismissed as but moderately eager until the others have refused; and it happened that Fred checked off all his friends but one, on the ground that applying to them would be disagreeable; being implicitly convinced that he at least (whatever might be maintained about mankind generally) had a right to be free from anything disagreeable. That he should ever fall into a thoroughly unpleasant position – wear trousers shrunk with washing, eat cold mutton, have to walk for want of a horse, or to 'duck under' in any sort of way – was an absurdity irreconcilable with those cheerful intuitions implanted in him by nature. And Fred winced under the idea of being looked down upon as wanting funds for small debts. Thus it came to pass that the friend whom he chose to apply to was at once the poorest and the kindest – namely, Caleb Garth.

The Garths were very fond of Fred, as he was of them; for when he and Rosamond were little ones, and the Garths were better off, the slight connection between the two families through Mr Featherstone's double marriage (the first to Mr Garth's sister, and the second to Mrs Vincy's) had led to an acquaintance which was carried on between the children rather than the parents: the children drank tea together out of their toy teacups, and spent whole days together in play. Mary was a little hoyden, and Fred at six years old thought her the nicest girl in the world, making her his wife with a brass ring which he had cut from an umbrella. Through all the stages of his education he had kept his affection for the Garths, and his habit of going to their house as a second home, though any intercourse between them and the elders of his family had long ceased. Even when Caleb Garth was prosperous, the Vincys were on condescending terms with him and his wife, for there were nice distinctions of rank in Middlemarch; and though old manufacturers could not any more than dukes be connected with none but equals, they were conscious of an inherent social superiority which was defined with great nicety in practice, though hardly expressible theoretically. Since then Mr Garth had failed in the building business, which he had unfortunately added to his other avocations of surveyor, valuer, and agent, had conducted that business for a time entirely for the benefit of his assignees, and had been living narrowly, exerting himself to the utmost that he might after all pay twenty shillings in the pound. He had now achieved this, and from all who did not think it a bad precedent, his honourable exertions had won him due esteem; but in no part of the world is genteel visiting founded on esteem, in the absence of suitable furniture and complete dinner-service. Mrs Vincy had never been at her ease with Mrs Garth, and frequently spoke of her as a woman who had had to work for her bread – meaning that Mrs Garth had been a teacher before her marriage; in which case an intimacy with Lindley Murray and Mangnall's *Questions* was something like a draper's discrimination of calico trademarks, or a courier's acquaintance with foreign countries: no woman who was better off needed that sort of thing. And since Mary had been keeping Mr Featherstone's house, Mrs Vincy's want of liking for the Garths had been converted into something more positive, by alarm lest Fred should engage himself to this plain girl, whose parents 'lived in such a small way'. Fred, being aware of this, never spoke at home of his visits to Mrs Garth, which had of late become more frequent, the increasing ardour of his affection for Mary inclining him the more towards those who belonged to her.

Mr Garth had a small office in the town, and to this Fred went with his request. He obtained it without much difficulty, for a large amount of painful experience had not sufficed to make Caleb Garth cautious about his own affairs, or distrustful of his fellow-men when they had not proved themselves untrust-worthy; and he had the highest opinion of Fred, was 'sure the lad would turn out well – an open affectionate fellow, with a good bottom to his character – you might trust him for anything'. Such was Caleb's psychological argument. He was one of those rare men who are rigid to themselves and indulgent to others. He had a certain shame about his neighbours' errors, and never spoke of them willingly; hence he was not likely to divert his mind from the best mode of hardening timber and other ingenious devices in order to preconceive those errors. If he had to blame anyone, it was necessary for him to move all the papers within his reach, or describe various diagrams with his stick, or make calculations with the odd money in his pocket, before he could begin; and he would rather do other men's work than find fault with their doing. I fear he was a bad disciplinarian.

When Fred stated the circumstances of his debt, his wish to meet it without troubling his father, and the certainty that the money would be forthcoming so as to cause no one any inconvenience, Caleb pushed his spectacles upward, listened, looked into his favourite's clear young eyes, and believed him, not distinguishing confidence about the future from veracity about the past; but he felt that it was an occasion for a friendly hint as to conduct, and that before giving his signature he must give a rather strong admonition. Accordingly, he took the paper and lowered his spectacles, measured the space at his command, reached his pen and examined it, dipped it in the ink and examined it again, then pushed the paper a little way from him, lifted up his spectacles again, showed a deepened depression in the outer angle of his bushy eyebrows, which gave his face a peculiar mildness (pardon these details for once – you would have learned to love them if you had known Caleb Garth), and said in a comfortable tone; 'It was a misfortune, eh, that breaking the horse's knees? And then, these exchanges, they don't answer when you have 'cute jockies to deal with. You'll be wiser another time, my boy.'

Whereupon Caleb drew down his spectacles, and proceeded to write his signature with the care which he always gave to that performance; for whatever he did in the way of business he did well. He contemplated the large well-proportioned letters and final flourish, with his head a trifle on one side for an instant, then handed it to Fred, said 'Goodbye,' and returned forthwith to his absorption in a plan for Sir James Chettam's new farm-buildings.

Either because his interest in this work thrust the incident of the signature from his memory, or for some reason of which Caleb was more conscious, Mrs Garth remained ignorant of the affair.

Since it occurred, a change had come over Fred's sky, which altered his view of the distance, and was the reason why his uncle Featherstone's present of money was of importance enough to make his colour come and go, first with a too definite expectation, and afterwards with a proportionate disappointment. His failure in passing his examination had made his accumulation of college debts the more unpardonable by his father, and there had been an unprecedented storm at home. Mr Vincy had sworn that if he had anything more of that sort to put up with, Fred should turn out and get his living how he could; and he had never yet quite recovered his good-humoured tone to his son, who had especially enraged him by saying at this stage of things that he did not want to be a clergyman, and would rather not 'go on with that'. Fred was conscious that he would have been yet more severely dealt with if his family as well as himself had not secretly regarded him as Mr Featherstone's heir; that old gentleman's pride in him, and apparent fondness for him, serving in the stead of more exemplary conduct – just as when a youthful nobleman steals jewellery we call the act kleptomania, speak of it with a philosophical smile, and never think of his being sent to the house of correction as if he were a ragged boy who had stolen turnips. In fact, tacit expectations of what would be done for him by Uncle Featherstone determined the angle at which most people viewed Fred Vincy in Middlemarch; and in his own consciousness, what Uncle Featherstone would do for him in an emergency or what he would do simply as an incorporated luck, formed always an im-measurable depth of aërial perspective. But that present of bank-notes, once made, was measurable, and being applied to the amount of the debt, showed a deficit which had still to be filled up either by Fred's 'judgement' or by luck in some other shape. For that little episode of the alleged borrowing, in which he had made his father the agent in getting the Bulstrode certificate, was a new reason against going to his father for money towards meeting his actual debt. Fred was keen enough to foresee that anger would confuse distinctions, and that his denial of having borrowed expressly on the strength of his uncle's will would be taken as a falsehood. He had gone to his father and told him one vexatious affair, and he had left another untold: in such cases the complete revelation always produces the impression of a previous duplicity. Now Fred piqued himself on keeping clear of lies, and even fibs; he often shrugged his shoulders and made a significant grimace at what he called Rosamond's fibs (it is only brothers who can associate such ideas with a lovely girl); and rather than incur the accusation of falsehood he would even incur some trouble and self-restraint. It was under strong inward pressure of this kind that Fred had taken the wise step of depositing the eighty pounds with his mother. It was a pity that he had not at once given them to Mr Garth; but he meant to make the sum complete with another sixty, and with a view to this, he had kept twenty pounds in his own pocket as a sort of seed-corn, which, planted by judgement, and watered by luck, might yield more than threefold – a very poor rate of multiplication when the field is a young gentleman's infinite soul, with all the numerals at command.

Fred was not a gambler: he had not that specific disease in which the suspension of the whole nervous energy on a chance or risk becomes as necessary as the dram to the drunkard; he had only the tendency to that diffusive form of gambling which has no alcoholic intensity, but is carried on with the healthiest chyle-fed blood, keeping up a joyous imaginative activity which fashions events according to desire, and having no fears about its own weather, only sees the advantage there must be to others in going aboard with it. Hopefulness has a pleasure in making a throw of any kind, because the prospect of success is certain; and only a more generous pleasure in offering as many as possible a share in the stake. Fred liked play, especially billiards, as he liked hunting or riding a steeplechase; and he only liked it the better because he wanted money and hoped to win. But the twenty pounds' worth of seed-corn had been planted in vain in the seductive green plot – all of it at least which had not been dispersed by the roadside – and Fred found himself close upon the term of payment with no money at command beyond the eighty pounds which he had deposited with his mother. The broken-winded horse which he rode represented a present which had been made to him a long while ago by his uncle Featherstone: his father always allowed him to keep a horse, Mr Vincy's own habits making him regard this as a reasonable demand even for a son who was rather exasperating. This horse, then, was Fred's property, and in his anxiety to meet the imminent bill he determined to sacrifice a possession without which life would certainly be worth little. He made the resolution with a sense of heroism – heroism forced on him by the dread of breaking his word to Mr Garth, by his love for Mary and awe of her opinion. He would start for Houndsley horse-fair which was to be held the next morning, and – simply sell his horse, bringing back the money by coach? – Well, the horse would hardly fetch more than thirty pounds, and there was no knowing what might happen: it would be folly to balk himself of luck beforehand. It was a hundred to one that some good chance would fall in his way: the longer he thought of it, the less possible it seemed that he should not have a good chance, and the less reasonable that he should not equip himself with the powder and shot for bringing it down. He would ride to Houndsley with Bambridge and with Horrock 'the vet', and without asking them anything expressly, he should virtually get the benefit of their opinion. Before he set out, Fred got the eighty pounds from his mother.

Most of those who saw Fred riding out of Middlemarch in company with Bambridge and Horrock, on his way of course to Houndsley horse-fair, thought that young Vincy was pleasure-seeking as usual; and but for an unwonted consciousness of grave matters on hand, he himself would have had a sense of dissipation, and of doing what might be expected of a gay young fellow. Considering that Fred was not at all coarse, that he rather looked down on the manners and speech of young men who had not been to the university, and that he had written stanzas as pastoral and unvoluptuous as his flute-playing, his attraction towards Bambridge and Horrock was an interesting fact which even the love of horseflesh would not wholly account for without that mysterious influence of Naming which determinates so much of mortal choice. Under any other name than 'pleasure' the society of Messieurs Bambridge and Horrock must certainly have been regarded as monotonous; and to arrive with them at Houndsley on a drizzling afternoon, to get down at the Red Lion in a street shaded with coal-dust, and dine in a room furnished with a dirt-enamelled map of the county, a bad portrait of an anonymous horse in a stable, His Majesty George the Fourth with legs and cravat, and various leaden spittoons, might have seemed a hard business, but for the sustaining power of nomenclature which determined that the pursuit of these things was 'gay'.

In Mr Horrock there was certainly an apparent unfathomableness which offered play to the imagination. Costume, at a glance, gave him a thrilling association with horses (enough to specify the hat-brim, which took the slightest upward angle just to escape the suspicion of bending downwards), and nature had given him a face which by dint of Mongolian eyes, and a nose, mouth, and chin, seeming to follow his hat-brim in a moderate inclination upwards, gave the effect of a subdued unchangeable sceptical smile, of all expressions the most tyrannous over a susceptible mind, and, when accompanied by adequate silence, likely to create the reputation of an invincible understanding, an infinite fund of humour – too dry to flow, and probably in a state of immovable crust – and a critical judgement which, if you could ever be fortunate enough to know it, would be the thing and no other. It is a physiognomy seen in all vocations, but perhaps it has never been more powerful over the youth of England than in a judge of horses.

Mr Horrock, at a question from Fred about his horse's fetlock, turned sideways in his saddle, and watched the horse's action for the space of three minutes, then turned forward, twitched his own bridle, and remained silent with a profile neither more nor less sceptical than it had been.

The part thus played in dialogue by Mr Horrock was terribly effective. A mixture of passions was excited in Fred – a mad desire to thrash Horrock's opinion into utterance, restrained by anxiety to retain the advantage of his friendship. There was always the chance that Horrock might say something quite invaluable at the right moment.

Mr Bambridge had more open manners, and appeared to give forth his ideas without economy. He was loud, robust, and was sometimes spoken of as being 'given to indulgence' – chiefly in swearing, drinking, and beating his wife. Some people who had lost by him called him a vicious man; but he regarded horse-dealing as the finest of the arts, and might have argued plausibly that it had nothing to do with morality. He was undeniably a prosperous man, bore his drinking better than others bore their moderation, and, on the whole, flourished like the green bay tree. But his range of conversation was limited, and like the fine old tune, 'Drops of Brandy', gave you after a while a sense of returning upon itself in a way that might make weak heads dizzy. But a slight infusion of Mr Bambridge was felt to give tone and character to several circles in Middlemarch; and he was a distinguished figure in the bar and billiard-room at the Green Dragon. He knew some anecdotes about the heroes of the turf, and various clever tricks of Marquesses and Viscounts which seemed to prove that blood asserted its pre-eminence even among blacklegs, but the minute retentiveness of his memory was chiefly shown about the horses he had himself bought and sold; the number of miles they would trot you in no time without turning a hair being, after the lapse of years, still a subject of passionate asseveration, in which he would assist the imagination of his hearers by solemnly swearing that they never saw anything like it. In short, Mr Bambridge was a man of pleasure and a gay companion.

Fred was subtle, and did not tell his friends that he was going to Houndsley bent on selling his horse: he wished to get indirectly at their genuine opinion of its value, not being aware that a genuine opinion was the last thing likely to be extracted from such eminent critics. It was not Mr Bambridge's weakness to be a gratuitous flatterer. He had never before been so much struck with the fact that this unfortunate bay was a roarer to a degree which required the roundest word for perdition to give you any idea of it.

'You made a bad hand at swapping when you went to anybody but me, Vincy! Why, you never threw your leg across a finer horse than that chestnut, and you gave him for this brute. If you set him cantering, he goes on like twenty sawyers. I never heard but one worse roarer in my life, and that was a roan: it belonged to Pegwell, the corn-factor; he used to drive him in his gig seven years ago, and he wanted me to take him, but I said, "Thank you, Peg, I don't deal in wind-instruments." That was what I said. It went the round of the country, that joke did. But, what the hell! the horse was a penny trumpet to that roarer of yours.'

'Why, you said just now his was worse than mine,' said Fred, more irritable than usual.

'I said a lie, then,' said Mr Bambridge, emphatically. 'There wasn't a penny to choose between 'em.'

Fred spurred his horse, and they trotted on a little way. When they slackened again, Mr Bambridge said: 'Not but what the roan was a better trotter than yours.'

'I'm quite satisfied with his paces, I know,' said Fred, who required all the consciousness of being in gay company to support him: 'I say, his trot is an uncommonly clean one, eh, Horrock?'

Mr Horrock looked before him with as complete a neutrality as if he had been a portrait by a great master.

Fred gave up the fallacious hope of getting a genuine opinion; but on reflection he saw that Bambridge's depreciation and Horrock's silence were both virtually encouraging, and indicated that they thought better of the horse than they chose to say.

That very evening, indeed, before the fair had set in, Fred thought he saw a favourable opening for disposing advantageously of his horse, but an opening which made him congratulate himself on his foresight in bringing with him his eighty pounds. A young farmer, acquainted with Mr Bambridge, came into the Red Lion, and entered into conversation about parting with a hunter, which he introduced at once as Diamond, implying that it was a public character. For himself he only wanted a useful hack, which would draw upon occasion; being about to marry and to give up hunting. The hunter was in a friend's stable at some little distance; there was still time for gentlemen to see it before dark. The friend's stable had to be reached through a back street where you might as easily have been poisoned without expense of drugs as in any grim street of that unsanitary period. Fred was not fortified against disgust by brandy, as his companions were, but the hope of having at last seen the horse that would enable him to make money was exhilarating enough to lead him over the same ground again the first thing in the morning. He felt sure that if he did not come to a bargain with the farmer, Bambridge would; for the stress of circumstances, Fred felt, was sharpening his acuteness and endowing him with all the constructive power of suspicion. Bambridge had run down Diamond in a way that he never would have done (the horse being a friend's) if he had not thought of buying it; everyone who looked at the animal – even Horrock – was evidently impressed with its merit. To get all the advantage of being with men of this sort, you must know how to draw your inferences, and not be a spoon who takes things literally. The colour of the horse was a dappled grey, and Fred happened to know that Lord Medlicote's man was on the look-out for just such a horse. After all his running down, Bambridge let it out in the course of the evening, when the farmer was absent, that he had seen worse horses go for eighty pounds. Of course he contradicted himself twenty times over, but when you know what is likely to be true you can test a man's admissions. And Fred could not but reckon his own judgement of a horse was worth something. The farmer had paused over Fred's respectable though broken-winded steed long enough to show that he thought it worth consideration, and it seemed probable that he would take it, with five-and-twenty pounds in addition, as the equivalent of Diamond. In that case Fred, when he had parted with his new horse for at least eighty pounds, would be fifty-five pounds in pocket by the transaction, and would have a hundred and thirty-five pounds towards meeting the bill; so that the deficit temporarily thrown on Mr Garth would at the utmost be twenty-five pounds. By the time he was hurrying on his clothes in the morning, he saw so clearly the importance of not losing this rare chance, that if Bambridge and Horrock had both dissuaded him, he would not have been deluded into a direct interpretation of their purpose: he would have been aware that those deep hands held something else than a young fellow's interest. With regard to horses, distrust was your only clue. But scepticism, as we know, can never be thoroughly applied, else life would come to a standstill: something we must believe in and do, and whatever that something may be called, it is virtually our own judgement, even when it seems like the most slavish reliance on another. Fred believed in the excellence of his bargain, and even before the fair had well set in, had got possession of the dappled grey, at the price of his old horse and thirty pounds in addition – only five pounds more than he had expected to give.

But he felt a little worried and wearied, perhaps with mental debate, and without waiting for the further gaieties of the horse-fair, he set out alone on his fourteen miles' journey, meaning to take it very quietly and keep his horse fresh.

Chapter 24

The offender's sorrow brings but small relief
To him who wears the strong offence's cross.
SHAKESPEARE, *Sonnets*

I am sorry to say that only the third day after the propitious events at Houndsley Fred Vincy had fallen into worse spirits than he had known in his life before. Not that he had been disappointed as to the possible market for his horse, but that before the bargain could be concluded with Lord Medlicote's man, this Diamond, in which hope to the amount of eighty pounds had been invested, had without the slightest warning exhibited in the stable a most vicious energy in kicking, had just missed killing the groom, and had ended in laming himself severely by catching his leg in a rope that overhung the stable-board. There was no more redress for this than for the discovery of bad temper after marriage – which of course old companions were aware of before the ceremony. For some reason or other, Fred had none of his usual elasticity under this stroke of ill-fortune: he was simply aware that he had only fifty pounds, that there was no chance of his getting any more at present, and that the bill for a hundred and sixty would be presented in five days. Even if he had applied to his father on the plea that Mr Garth should be saved from loss, Fred felt smartingly that his father would angrily refuse to rescue Mr Garth from the consequence of what he would call encouraging extravagance and deceit. He was so utterly downcast that he could frame no other project than to go straight to Mr Garth and tell him the sad truth, carrying with him the fifty pounds, and getting that sum at least safely out of his own hands. His father, being at the warehouse, did not yet know of the accident: when he did, he would storm about the vicious brute being brought into his stable; and before meeting that lesser annoyance Fred wanted to get away with all his courage to face the greater. He took his father's nag, for he had made up his mind that when he had told Mr Garth, he would ride to Stone Court and confess all to Mary. In fact, it is probable that but for Mary's existence and Fred's love for her, his conscience would have been much less active both in previously urging the debt on his thought and in impelling him not to spare himself after his usual fashion by deferring an unpleasant task, but to act as directly and simply as he could. Even much stronger mortals than Fred Vincy hold half their rectitude in the mind of the being they love best. 'The theatre of all my actions is fallen,' said an antique personage when his chief friend was dead; and they are fortunate who get a theatre where the audience demands their best. Certainly it would have made a considerable difference to Fred at that time if Mary Garth had had no decided notions as to what was admirable in character.

Mr Garth was not at the office, and Fred rode on to his house, which was a little way outside the town – a homely place with an orchard in front of it, a rambling, old-fashioned, half-timbered building, which before the town had spread had been a farmhouse, but was now surrounded with the private gardens of the townsmen. We get the fonder of our houses if they have a physiognomy of their own, as our friends have. The Garth family, which was rather a large one, for Mary had four brothers and one sister, were very fond of their old house, from which all the best furniture had long been sold. Fred liked it too, knowing it by heart even to the attic which smelt deliciously of apples and quinces, and until today he had never come to it without pleasant expectations; but his heart beat uneasily now with the sense that he should probably have to make his confession before Mrs Garth, of whom he was rather more in awe than of her husband. Not that she was inclined to sarcasm and to impulsive sallies, as Mary was. In her present matronly age at least, Mrs Garth never committed herself by over-hasty speech; having, as she said, borne the yoke in her youth, and learned self-control. She had that rare sense which discerns what is un-alterable, and submits to it without murmuring. Adoring her husband's virtues, she had very early made up her mind to his incapacity of minding his own interests, and had met the consequences cheerfully. She had been magnanimous enough to renounce all pride in teapots or children's frilling, and had never poured any pathetic confidences into the ears of her feminine neighbours con-cerning Mr Garth's want of prudence and the sums he might have had if he had been like other men. Hence these fair neighbours thought her either proud or eccentric, and sometimes spoke of her to their husbands as 'your fine Mrs Garth'. She was not without her criticism of them in return, being more accurately instructed than most matrons in Middlemarch, and – where is the blameless woman? – apt to be a little severe towards her own sex, which in her opinion was framed to be entirely subordinate. On the other hand, she was disproportion-ately indulgent towards the failings of men, and was often heard to say that these were natural. Also, it must be admitted that Mrs Garth was a trifle too emphatic in her resistance to what she held to be follies: the passage from governess into housewife had wrought itself a little too strongly into her consciousness, and she rarely forgot that while her grammar and accent were above the town standard, she wore a plain cap, cooked the family dinner, and darned all the stockings. She had sometimes taken pupils in a peripatetic fashion, making them follow her about in the kitchen with their book or slate. She thought it good for them to see that she could make an excellent lather while she corrected their blunders 'without looking', that a woman with her sleeves tucked up above her elbows might know all about the Subjunctive Mood or the Torrid Zone – that, in short, she might possess 'education' and other good things ending in 'tion', and worthy to be pronounced emphatically, without being a useless doll. When she made remarks to this edifying effect, she had a firm little frown on her brow, which yet did not hinder her face from looking benevolent, and her words which came forth like a procession were uttered in a fervid agreeable contralto. Certainly, the exemplary Mrs Garth had her droll aspects, but her character sustained her oddities, as a very fine wine sustains a flavour of skin.

Towards Fred Vincy she had a motherly feeling, and had always been disposed to excuse his errors, though she would probably not have excused Mary for engaging herself to him, her daughter being included in that more rigorous judgement which she applied to her own sex. But this very fact of her exceptional indulgence towards him made it the harder to Fred that he must now inevitably sink in her opinion. And the circumstances of his visit turned out to be still more unpleasant than he had expected; for Caleb Garth had gone out early to look at some repairs not far off. Mrs Garth at certain hours was always in the kitchen, and this morning she was carrying on several occupations at once there – making her pies at the well-scoured deal table on one side of that airy room, observing Sally's movements at the oven and dough-tub through an open door, and giving lessons to her youngest boy and girl, who were standing opposite to her at the table with their books and slates before them. A tub and a clothes-horse at the other end of the kitchen indicated an intermittent wash of small things also going on.

Mrs Garth, with her sleeves turned above her elbows, deftly handling her pastry – applying her rolling-pin and giving ornamental pinches, while she expounded with grammatical fervour what were the right views about the con-cord of verbs and pronouns with 'nouns of multitude or signifying many', was a sight agreeably amusing. She was of the same curly-haired, square-faced type as Mary, but handsomer, with more delicacy of feature, a pale skin, a solid matronly figure, and a remarkable firmness of glance. In her snowy-frilled cap she reminded one of that delightful Frenchwoman whom we have all seen marketing, basket on arm. Looking at the mother, you might hope that the daughter would become like her, which is a prospective advantage equal to a dowry – the mother too often standing behind the daughter like a malignant prophecy – 'Such as I am, she will shortly be.'

'Now let us go through that once more,' said Mrs Garth, pinching an apple-puff which seemed to distract Ben, an energetic young male with a heavy brow, from due attention to the lesson. ' "Not without regard to the import of the word as conveying unity or plurality of idea" – tell me again what that means, Ben.'

(Mrs Garth, like more celebrated educators, had her favourite ancient paths, and in a general wreck of society would have tried to hold her 'Lindley Murray' above the waves.)

'Oh – it means – you must think what you mean,' said Ben, rather peevishly. 'I hate grammar. What's the use of it?'

'To teach you to speak and write correctly, so that you can be understood,' said Mrs Garth, with severe precision. 'Should you like to speak as old Job does?'

'Yes,' said Ben, stoutly; 'it's funnier. He says, "Yo goo" – that's just as good as "You go".'

'But he says, "A ship's in the garden", instead of "a sheep",' said Letty, with an air of superiority. 'You might think he meant a ship off the sea.'

'No, you mightn't, if you weren't silly,' said Ben. 'How could a ship off the sea come there?'

'These things belong only to pronunciation, which is the least part of grammar,' said Mrs Garth. 'That apple peel is to be eaten by the pigs, Ben; if you eat it, I must give them your piece of pastry. Job has only to speak about very plain things. How do you think you would write or speak about anything more difficult, if you knew no more of grammar than he does? You would use wrong words, and put words in the wrong places, and instead of making people understand you, they would turn away from you as a tiresome person. What would you do then?'

'I shouldn't care, I should leave off,' said Ben, with a sense that this was an agreeable issue where grammar was concerned.

'I see you are getting tired and stupid, Ben,' said Mrs Garth, accustomed to these obstructive arguments from her male offspring. Having finished her pies, she moved towards the clothes horse, and said, 'Come here and tell me the story I told you on Wednesday, about Cincinnatus.'

'I know! he was a farmer,' said Ben.

'Now, Ben, he was a Roman – let *me* tell,' said Letty, using her elbow contentiously.

'You silly thing, he was a Roman farmer, and he was ploughing.'

'Yes, but before that – that didn't come first – people wanted him,' said Letty.

'Well, but you must say what sort of a man he was first,' insisted Ben. 'He was a wise man, like my father, and that made the people want his advice. And he was a brave man, and could fight. And so could my father – couldn't he, mother?'

'Now, Ben, let me tell the story straight on, as mother told it us,' said Letty, frowning. 'Please, mother, tell Ben not to speak.'

'Letty, I am ashamed of you,' said her mother, wringing out the caps from the tub. 'When your brother began, you ought to have waited to see if he could not tell the story. How rude you look, pushing and frowning, as if you wanted to conquer with your elbows! Cincinnatus, I am sure, would have been sorry to see his daughter behave so.' (Mrs Garth delivered this awful sentence with much majesty of enunciation, and Letty felt that between repressed volubility and general dis-esteem, that of the Romans inclusive, life was already a painful affair.) 'Now, Ben.'

'Well – oh – well – why, there was a great deal of fighting, and they were all blockheads, and – I can't tell it just how you told it – but they wanted a man to be captain and king and everything – '

'Dictator, now,' said Letty, with injured looks, and not without a wish to make her mother repent.

'Very well, dictator!' said Ben, contemptuously. 'But that isn't a good word: he didn't tell them to write on slates.'

'Come, come, Ben, you are not so ignorant as that,' said Mrs Garth, carefully serious. 'Hark, there is a knock at the door! Run, Letty, and open it.'

The knock was Fred's; and when Letty said that her father was not in yet, but that her mother was in the kitchen, Fred had no alternative. He could not depart from his usual practice of going to see Mrs Garth in the kitchen if she happened to be at work there. He put his arm round Letty's neck silently, and led her into the kitchen without his usual jokes and caresses.

Mrs Garth was surprised to see Fred at this hour, but surprise was not a feeling that she was given to express, and she only said, quietly continuing her work: 'You, Fred, so early in the day? You look quite pale. Has anything happened?'

'I want to speak to Mr Garth,' said Fred, not yet ready to say more – 'and to you also,' he added, after a little pause, for he had no doubt that Mrs Garth knew everything about the bill, and he must in the end speak of it before her, if not to her solely.

'Caleb will be in again in a few minutes,' said Mrs Garth, who imagined some trouble between Fred and his father. 'He is sure not to be long, because he has some work at his desk that must be done this morning. Do you mind staying with me, while I finish my matters here?'

'But we needn't go on about Cincinnatus, need we?' said Ben, who had taken Fred's whip out of his hand, and was trying its efficiency on the cat.

'No, go out now. But put that whip down. How very mean of you to whip poor old Tortoise! Pray take the whip from him, Fred.'

'Come, old boy, give it me,' said Fred, putting out his hand.

'Will you let me ride on your horse today?' said Ben, rendering up the whip, with an air of not being obliged to do it.

'Not today – another time. I am not riding my own horse.'

'Shall you see Mary today?'

'Yes, I think so,' said Fred, with an unpleasant twinge.

'Tell her to come home soon, and play at forfeits, and make fun.'

'Enough, enough, Ben! run away,' said Mrs Garth, seeing that Fred was teased.

'Are Letty and Ben your only pupils now, Mrs Garth?' said Fred, when the children were gone and it was needful to say something that would pass the time. He was not yet sure whether he should wait for Mr Garth, or use any good opportunity in conversation to confess to Mrs Garth herself, give her the money and ride away.

'One – only one. Fanny Hackbutt comes at half-past eleven. I am not getting a great income now,' said Mrs Garth, smiling. 'I am at a low ebb with pupils. But I have saved my little purse for Alfred's premium: I have ninety-two pounds. He can go to Mr Hanmer's now; he is just at the right age.'

This did not lead well towards the news that Mr Garth was on the brink of losing ninety-two pounds and more. Fred was silent. 'Young gentlemen who go to college are rather more costly than that,' Mrs Garth innocently continued, pulling out the edging on a cap border. 'And Caleb thinks that Alfred will turn out a distinguished engineer: he wants to give the boy a good chance. There he is! I hear him coming in. We will go to him in the parlour, shall we?'

When they entered the parlour Caleb had thrown down his hat and was seated at his desk.

'What, Fred, my boy? ' he said in a tone of mild surprise, holding his pen still undipped. 'You are here betimes.' But missing the usual expression of cheerful greeting in Fred's face, he immediately added, 'Is there anything up at home? – anything the matter?'

'Yes, Mr Garth, I am come to tell something that I am afraid will give you a bad opinion of me. I am come to tell you and Mrs Garth that I can't keep my word. I can't find the money to meet the bill after all. I have been unfortunate; I have only got these fifty pounds towards the hundred and sixty.'

While Fred was speaking, he had taken out the notes and laid them on the desk before Mr Garth. He had burst forth at once with the plain fact, feeling boyishly miserable and without verbal resources. Mrs Garth was mutely astonished, and looked at her husband for an explanation. Caleb blushed, and after a little pause said: 'Oh, I didn't tell you, Susan: I put my name to a bill for Fred; it was for a hundred and sixty pounds. He made sure he could meet it himself.'

There was an evident change in Mrs Garth's face, but it was like a change below the surface of water which remains smooth. She fixed her eyes on Fred, saying: 'I suppose you have asked your father for the rest of the money and he has refused you.'

'No,' said Fred, biting his lip, and speaking with more difficulty; 'but I know it will be of no use to ask him; and unless it were of use, I should not like to mention Mr Garth's name in the matter.'

'It has come at an unfortunate time,' said Caleb, in his hesitating way, looking down at the notes and nervously fingering the paper, 'Christmas upon us – I'm rather hard up just now. You see, I have to cut out everything like a tailor with short measure. What can we do, Susan? I shall want every farthing we have in the bank. It's a hundred and ten pounds, the deuce take it!'

'I must give you the ninety-two pounds that I have put by for Alfred's premium,' said Mrs Garth, gravely and decisively, though a nice ear might have discerned a slight tremor in some of the words. 'And I have no doubt that Mary has twenty pounds saved from her salary by this time. She will advance it.'

Mrs Garth had not again looked at Fred, and was not in the least calculating what words she should use to cut him the most effectively. Like the eccentric woman she was, she was at present absorbed in considering what was to be done, and did not fancy that the end could be better achieved by bitter remarks or explosions. But she had made Fred feel for the first time something like the tooth of remorse. Curiously enough, his pain in the affair beforehand had consisted almost entirely in the sense that he must seem dishonourable, and sink in the opinion of the Garths: he had not occupied himself with the incon-venience and possible injury that his breach might occasion them, for this exercise of the imagination on other people's needs is not common with hopeful young gentlemen. Indeed we are most of us brought up in the notion that the highest motive for not doing a wrong is something irrespective of the beings who would suffer the wrong. But at this moment he suddenly saw himself as a pitiful rascal who was robbing two women of their savings.

'I shall certainly pay it all, Mrs Garth – ultimately,' he stammered out.

'Yes, ultimately,' said Mrs Garth, who having a special dislike to fine words on ugly occasions, could not now repress an epigram. 'But boys cannot well be apprenticed ultimately: they should be apprenticed at fifteen.' She had never been so little inclined to make excuses for Fred.

'I was the most in the wrong, Susan,' said Caleb. 'Fred made sure of finding the money. But I'd no business to be fingering bills. I suppose you have looked all round and tried all honest means?' he added fixing his merciful grey eyes on Fred. Caleb was too delicate to specify Mr Featherstone.

'Yes, I have tried everything – I really have. I should have had a hundred and thirty pounds ready but for a misfortune with a horse which I was about to sell. My uncle had given me eighty pounds, and I paid away thirty with my old horse in order to get another which I was going to sell for eighty or more – I meant to go without a horse – but now it has turned out vicious and lamed itself. I wish I and the horses too had been at the devil, before I had brought this on you. There's no one else I care so much for: you and Mrs Garth have always been so kind to me. However, it's no use saying that. You will always think me a rascal now.'

Fred turned round and hurried out of the room, conscious that he was getting rather womanish, and feeling confusedly that his being sorry was not of much use to the Garths. They could see him mount, and quickly pass through the gate.

'I am disappointed in Fred Vincy,' said Mrs Garth. 'I would not have believed beforehand that he would have drawn you into his debts. I knew he was extravagant, but I did not think that he would be so mean as to hang his risks on his oldest friend, who could the least afford to lose.'

'I was a fool, Susan.'

'That you were,' said the wife, nodding and smiling. 'But I should not have gone to publish it in the marketplace. Why should you keep such things from me? It is just so with your buttons; you let them burst off without telling me, and go out with your wristband hanging. If I had only known I might have been ready with some better plan.'

'You are sadly cut up, I know, Susan,' said Caleb, looking feelingly at her. 'I can't abide your losing the money you've scraped together for Alfred.'

'It is very well that I *had* scraped it together; and it is you who will have to suffer, for you must teach the boy yourself. You must give up your bad habits. Some men take to drinking, and you have taken to working without pay. You must indulge yourself a little less in that. And you must ride over to Mary, and ask the child what money she has.'

Caleb had pushed his chair back, and was leaning forward, shaking his head slowly, and fitting his fingertips together with much nicety.

'Poor Mary!' he said. 'Susan,' he went on in a lowered tone, 'I'm afraid she may be fond of Fred.'

'Oh no! She always laughs at him; and he is not likely to think of her in any other than a brotherly way.'

Caleb made no rejoinder, but presently lowered his spectacles, drew up his chair to the desk, and said, 'Deuce take the bill – I wish it was at Hanover! These things are a sad interruption to business!'

The first part of this speech comprised his whole store of maledictory expression, and was uttered with a slight snarl easy to imagine. But it would be difficult to convey to those who never heard him utter the word 'business', the peculiar tone of fervid veneration, of religious regard, in which he wrapped it, as a consecrated symbol is wrapped in its gold-fringed linen.

Caleb Garth often shook his head in meditation on the value, the indispensable might of that myriad-headed, myriad-handed labour by which the social body is fed, clothed, and housed. It had laid hold of his imagination in boyhood. The echoes of the great hammer where roof or keel were a-making, the signal shouts of the workmen, the roar of the furnace, the thunder and plash of the engine, were a sublime music to him; the felling and lading of timber, and the huge trunk vibrating starlike in the distance along the highway, the crane at work on the wharf, the piled-up produce in warehouses, the precision and variety of muscular effort wherever exact work had to be turned out, – all these sights of his youth had acted on him as poetry without the aid of the poets, had made a philosophy for him without the aid of philosophers, a religion without the aid of theology. His early ambition had been to have as effective a share as possible in this sublime labour, which was peculiarly dignified by him with the name of 'business'; and though he had only been a short time under a surveyor, and had been chiefly his own teacher, he knew more of land, building, and mining than most of the special men in the county.

His classification of human employments was rather crude, and, like the categories of more celebrated men, would not be acceptable in these advanced times. He divided them into 'business, politics, preaching, learning, and amusement'. He had nothing to say against the last four; but he regarded them as a reverential pagan regarded other gods than his own. In the same way, he thought very well of all ranks, but he would not himself have liked to be of any rank in which he had not such close contact with 'business' as to get often honourably decorated with marks of dust and mortar, the damp of the engine, or the sweet soil of the woods and fields. Though he had never regarded himself as other than an orthodox Christian, and would argue on prevenient grace if the subject were proposed to him, I think his virtual divinities were good practical schemes, accurate work, and the faithful completion of undertakings: his prince of darkness was a slack workman. But there was no spirit of denial in Caleb, and the world seemed so wondrous to him that he was ready to accept any number of systems, like any number of firmaments, if they did not obviously interfere with the best land-drainage, solid building, correct measuring, and judicious boring (for coal). In fact, he had a reverential soul with a strong practical intelligence. But he could not manage finance: he knew values well, but he had no keenness of imagination for monetary results in the shape of profit and loss: and having ascertained this to his cost, he determined to give up all forms of his beloved 'business' which required that talent. He gave himself up entirely to the many kinds of work which he could do without handling capital, and was one of those precious men within his own district whom everybody would choose to work for them, because he did his work well, charged very little, and often declined to charge at all. It is no wonder, then, that the Garths were poor, and 'lived in a small way'. However, they did not mind it.

Chapter 25

> Love seeketh not itself to please,
>   Nor for itself hath any care,
> But for another gives its ease,
>   And builds a heaven in hell's despair.
>
> Love seeketh only self to please,
>   To bind another to its delight,
> Joys in another's loss of ease,
>   And builds a hell in heaven's despite.
>   WILLIAM BLAKE, *Songs of Experience*

Fred Vincy wanted to arrive at Stone Court when Mary could not expect him, and when his uncle was not downstairs: in that case she might be sitting alone in the wainscoted parlour. He left his horse in the yard to avoid making a noise on the gravel in front, and entered the parlour without other notice than the noise on the door-handle. Mary was in her usual corner, laughing over Mrs Piozzi's recollections of Johnson, and looked up with the fun still in her face. It gradually faded as she saw Fred approach her without speaking, and stand before her with his elbow on the mantelpiece, looking ill. She too was silent, only raising her eyes to him enquiringly.

'Mary,' he began, 'I am a good-for-nothing blackguard.'

'I should think one of those epithets would do at a time,' said Mary, trying to smile, but feeling alarmed.

'I know you will never think well of me any more. You will think me a liar. You will think me dishonest. You will think I didn't care for you, or your father and mother. You always do make the worst of me, I know.'

'I cannot deny that I shall think all that of you, Fred, if you give me good reasons. But please to tell me at once what you have done. I would rather know the painful truth than imagine it.'

'I owed money – a hundred and sixty pounds. I asked your father to put his name to a bill. I thought it would not signify to him. I made sure of paying the money myself, and I have tried as hard as I could. And now, I have been so unlucky – a horse has turned out badly – I can only pay fifty pounds. And I can't ask my father for the money: he would not give me a farthing. And my uncle gave me a hundred a little while ago. So what can I do? And now your father has no ready money to spare, and your mother will have to pay away her ninety-two pounds that she has saved, and she says your savings must go too. You see what a – '

'Oh, poor mother, poor father!' said Mary, her eyes filling with tears, and a little sob rising which she tried to repress. She looked straight before her and took no notice of Fred, all the consequences at home becoming present to her. He too remained silent for some moments, feeling more miserable than ever.

'I wouldn't have hurt you so for the world, Mary,' he said at last. 'You can never forgive me.'

'What does it matter whether I forgive you?' said Mary passionately. 'Would that make it any better for my mother to lose the money she has been earning by lessons for four years, that she might send Alfred to Mr Hanmer's? Should you think all that pleasant enough if I forgave you?'

'Say what you like, Mary. I deserve it all.'

'I don't want to say anything,' said Mary, more quietly; 'my anger is of no use.' She dried her eyes, threw aside her book, rose and fetched her sewing.

Fred followed her with his eyes, hoping that they would meet hers, and in that way find access for his imploring penitence. But no! Mary could easily avoid looking upward.

'I do care about your mother's money going,' he said, when she was seated again and sewing quickly. 'I wanted to ask you, Mary – don't you think that Mr Featherstone – if you were to tell him – tell him, I mean, about apprenticing Alfred – would advance the money?'

'My family is not fond of begging, Fred. We would rather work for our money. Besides, you say that Mr Featherstone has lately given you a hundred pounds. He rarely makes presents; he has never made presents to us, I am sure my father will not ask him for anything; and even if I chose to beg of him, it would be of no use.'

'I am so miserable, Mary – if you knew how miserable I am, you would be sorry for me.'

'There are other things to be more sorry for than that. But selfish people always think their own discomfort of more importance than anything else in the world: I see enough of that every day.'

'It is hardly fair to call me selfish. If you knew what things other young men do, you would think me a good way off the worst.'

'I know that people who spend a great deal of money on themselves without knowing how they shall pay, must be selfish. They are always thinking of what they can get for themselves, and not of what other people may lose.'

'Any man may be unfortunate, Mary, and find himself unable to pay when he meant it. There is not a better man in the world than your father, and yet he got into trouble.'

'How dare you make any comparison between my father and you, Fred?' said Mary, in a deep tone of indignation. 'He never got into trouble by thinking of his own idle pleasures, but because he was always thinking of the work he was doing for other people. And he has fared hard, and worked hard to make good everybody's loss.'

'And you think that I shall never try to make good anything, Mary. It is not generous to believe the worst of a man. When you have got any power over him, I think you might try and use it to make him better; but that is what you never do. However, I'm going,' Fred ended, languidly. 'I shall never speak to you about anything again. I'm very sorry for all the trouble I've caused – that's all.'

Mary had dropped her work out of her hand and looked up. There is often something maternal even in a girlish love, and Mary's hard experience had wrought her nature to an impressibility very different from that hard slight thing which we call girlishness. At Fred's last words she felt an instantaneous pang, something like what a mother feels at the imagined sobs or cries of her naughty truant child, which may lose itself and get harm, and when, looking up, her eyes met his dull despairing glance, her pity for him surmounted her anger and all her other anxieties.

'Oh, Fred, how ill you look? Sit down a moment. Don't go yet. Let me tell uncle that you are here. He has been wondering that he has not seen you for a whole week.' Mary spoke hurriedly, saying the words that came first without knowing very well what they were, but saying them in a half-soothing, half-beseeching tone, and rising as if to go away to Mr Featherstone. Of course Fred felt as if the clouds had parted and a gleam had come: he moved and stood in her way.

'Say one word, Mary, and I will do anything. Say you will not think the worst of me – will not give me up altogether.'

'As if it were any pleasure to me to think ill of you,' said Mary, in a mournful tone. 'As if it were not very painful to me to see you an idle frivolous creature. How can you bear to be so contemptible, when others are working and striving, and there are so many things to be done – how can you bear to be fit for nothing in the world that is useful? And with so much good in your disposition, Fred, – you might be worth a great deal.'

'I will try to be anything you like, Mary, if you will say that you love me.'

'I should be ashamed to say that I loved a man who must always be hanging on others, and reckoning on what they would do for him. What will you be when you are forty? Like Mr Bowyer, I suppose – just as idle, living in Mrs Beck's front parlour – fat and shabby, hoping somebody will invite you to dinner – spending your morning in learning a comic song – oh no! learning a tune on the flute.'

Mary's lips had begun to curl with a smile as soon as she had asked that question about Fred's future (young souls are mobile), and before she ended, her face had its full illumination of fun. To him it was like the cessation of an ache that Mary could laugh at him, and with a passive sort of smile he tried to reach her hand; but she slipped away quickly towards the door and said, 'I shall tell uncle. You *must* see him for a moment or two.'

Fred secretly felt that his future was guaranteed against the fulfilment of Mary's sarcastic prophecies, apart from that 'anything' which he was ready to do if she would define it. He never dared in Mary's presence to approach the subject of his expectations from Mr Featherstone, and she always ignored them, as if everything depended on himself. But if ever he actually came into the property, she must recognise the change in his position. All this passed through his mind somewhat languidly, before he went up to see his uncle. He stayed but a little while, excusing himself on the ground that he had a cold; and Mary did not reappear before he left the house. But as he rode home, he began to be more conscious of being ill, than of being melancholy.

When Caleb Garth arrived at Stone Court soon after dusk, Mary was not surprised, although he seldom had leisure for paying her a visit, and was not at all fond of having to talk with Mr Featherstone. The old man, on the other hand, felt himself ill at ease with a brother-in-law whom he could not annoy, who did not mind about being considered poor, had nothing to ask of him, and understood all kinds of farming and mining business better than he did. But Mary had felt sure that her parents would want to see her, and if her father had not come, she would have obtained leave to go home for an hour or two the next day. After discussing prices during tea with Mr Featherstone, Caleb rose to bid him goodbye, and said, 'I want to speak to you, Mary.'

She took a candle into another large parlour, where there was no fire, and setting down the feeble light on the dark mahogany table, turned round to her father, and putting her arms round his neck kissed him with childish kisses which he delighted in, the expression of his large brows softening as the expression of a great beautiful dog softens when it is caressed. Mary was his favourite child, and whatever Susan might say, and right as she was on all other subjects, Caleb thought it natural that Fred or anyone else should think Mary more lovable than other girls.

'I've got something to tell you, my dear,' said Caleb in his hesitating way. 'No very good news; but then it might be worse.'

'About money, father? I think I know what it is.'

'Ay? how can that be? You see, I've been a bit of a fool again, and put my name to a bill, and now it comes to paying; and your mother has got to part with her savings, that's the worst of it, and even they won't quite make things even. We wanted a hundred and ten pounds: your mother has ninety-two, and I have none to spare in the bank; and she thinks that you will have some savings.'

'Oh yes; I have more than four-and-twenty pounds. I thought you would come, father, so I put it in my bag. See! beautiful white notes and gold.'

Mary took out the folded money from her reticule and put it into her father's hand.

'Well, but how – we only want eighteen – here, put the rest back, child, – but how did you know about it?' said Caleb, who, in his unconquerable indifference to money, was beginning to be chiefly concerned about the relation the affair might have to Mary's affections.

'Fred told me this morning.'

'Ah! Did he come on purpose?'

'Yes, I think so. He was a good deal distressed.'

'I'm afraid Fred is not to be trusted, Mary,' said the father, with hesitating tenderness. 'He means better than he acts, perhaps. But I should think it a pity for anybody's happiness to be wrapped up in him, and so would your mother.'

'And so should I, father,' said Mary, not looking up, but putting the back of her father's hand against her cheek.

'I don't want to pry, my dear. But I was afraid there might be something between you and Fred, and I wanted to caution you. You see, Mary' – here

Caleb's voice became more tender; he had been pushing his hat about on the table and looking at it, but finally he turned his eyes on his daughter – 'a woman, let her be as good as she may, has got to put up with the life her husband makes for her. Your mother has had to put up with a good deal because of me.'

Mary turned the back of her father's hand to her lips and smiled at him.

'Well, well, nobody's perfect, but' – here Mr Garth shook his head to help out the inadequacy of words – 'what I am thinking of is – what it must be for a wife when she's never sure of her husband, when he hasn't got a principle in him to make him more afraid of doing the wrong thing by others than of getting his own toes pinched. That's the long and the short of it, Mary. Young folks may get fond of each other before they know what life is, and they may think it all holiday if they can only get together; but it soon turns into working day, my dear. However, you have more sense than most, and you haven't been kept in cotton-wool: there may be no occasion for me to say this, but a father trembles for his daughter, and you are all by yourself here.'

'Don't fear for me, father,' said Mary, gravely meeting her father's eyes; 'Fred has always been very good to me; he is kind-hearted and affectionate, and not false, I think, with all his self-indulgence. But I will never engage myself to one who has no manly independence, and who goes on loitering away his time on the chance that others will provide for him. You and my mother have taught me too much pride for that.'

'That's right – that's right. Then I am easy,' said Mr Garth, taking up his hat. 'But it's hard to run away with your earnings, child.'

'Father!' said Mary, in her deepest tone of remonstrance. 'Take pocketfuls of love besides to them all at home,' was her last word before he closed the outer door on himself.

'I suppose your father wanted your earnings,' said old Mr Featherstone, with his usual power of unpleasant surmise, when Mary returned to him. 'He makes but a tight fit, I reckon. You're of age now; you ought to be saving for yourself.'

'I consider my father and mother the best part of myself, sir,' said Mary, coldly.

Mr Featherstone grunted: he could not deny that an ordinary sort of girl like her might be expected to be useful, so he thought of another rejoinder, dis- agreeable enough to be always apropos. 'If Fred Vincy comes tomorrow, now, don't you keep him chattering: let him come up to me.'

Chapter 26

He beats me and I rail at him: O worthy satisfaction! would it
were otherwise – that I could beat him while he railed at me.
                                        Troilus and Cressida

But Fred did not go to Stone Court the next day, for reasons that were quite
peremptory. From those visits to unsanitary Houndsley streets in search of
Diamond, he had brought back not only a bad bargain in horseflesh, but the
further misfortune of some ailment which for a day or two had seemed mere
depression and headache, but which got so much worse when he returned from
his visit to Stone Court that, going into the dining-room, he threw himself on
the sofa, and in answer to his mother's anxious question, said, 'I feel very ill: I
think you must send for Wrench.'

Wrench came but did not apprehend anything serious, spoke of a 'slight
derangement', and did not speak of coming again on the morrow. He had a due
value for the Vincys' house, but the wariest men are apt to be a little dulled by
routine, and on worried mornings will sometimes go through their business with
the zest of the daily bell-ringer. Mr Wrench was a small, neat, bilious man, with a
well-dressed wig: he had a laborious practice, an irascible temper, a lymphatic
wife, and seven children; and he was already rather late before setting out on a
four-miles' drive to meet Dr Minchin on the other side of Tipton, the decease of
Hicks, a rural practitioner, having increased Middlemarch practice in that
direction. Great statesmen err, and why not small medical men? Mr Wrench did
not neglect sending the usual white parcels, which this time had black and drastic
contents. Their effect was not alleviating to poor Fred, who, however, unwilling
as he said to believe that he was 'in for an illness', rose at his usual hour the next
morning and went downstairs meaning to breakfast, but succeeded in nothing
but in sitting and shivering by the fire. Mr Wrench was again sent for, but was
gone on his rounds, and Mrs Vincy, seeing her darling's changed looks and
general misery, began to cry and said she would send for Dr Sprague.

'Oh nonsense, mother! It's nothing,' said Fred, putting out his hot dry hand to
her, 'I shall soon be all right. I must have taken cold in that nasty damp ride.'

'Mamma!' said Rosamond, who was seated near the window (the dining-room
windows looked on that highly respectable street called Lowick Gate), 'there is
Mr Lydgate, stopping to speak to someone. If I were you I would call him in. He
has cured Ellen Bulstrode. They say he cures every one.'

Mrs Vincy sprang to the window and opened it in an instant, thinking only of
Fred and not of medical etiquette. Lydgate was only two yards off on the other
side of some iron palisading, and turned round at the sudden sound of the sash,
before she called to him. In two minutes he was in the room, and Rosamond
went out, after waiting just long enough to show a pretty anxiety conflicting
with her sense of what was becoming.

Lydgate had to hear a narrative in which Mrs Vincy's mind insisted with remarkable instinct on every point of minor importance, especially on what Mr Wrench had said and had not said about coming again. That there might be an awkward affair with Wrench, Lydgate saw at once; but the case was serious enough to make him dismiss that consideration: he was convinced that Fred was in the pink-skinned stage of typhoid fever, and that he had taken just the wrong medicines. He must go to bed immediately, must have a regular nurse, and various appliances and precautions must be used, about which Lydgate was particular. Poor Mrs Vincy's terror at these indications of danger found vent in such words as came most easily. She thought it 'very ill usage on the part of Mr Wrench, who had attended their house so many years in preference to Mr Peacock, though Mr Peacock was equally a friend. Why Mr Wrench should neglect her children more than others, she could not for the life of her understand. He had not neglected Mrs Larcher's when they had the measles, nor indeed would Mrs Vincy have wished that he should. And if anything should happen . . . '

Here poor Mrs Vincy's spirit quite broke down, and her Niobe-throat and good-humoured face were sadly convulsed. This was in the hall out of Fred's hearing, but Rosamond had opened the drawing-room door, and now came forward anxiously. Lydgate apologised for Mr Wrench, said that the symptoms yesterday might have been disguising, and that this form of fever was very equivocal in its beginnings: he would go immediately to the druggists and have a prescription made up in order to lose no time, but he would write to Mr Wrench and tell him what had been done.

'But you must come again – you must go on attending Fred. I can't have my boy left to anybody who may come or not. I bear nobody ill-will, thank God, and Mr Wrench saved me in the pleurisy, but he'd better have let me die – if – if – '

'I will meet Mr Wrench here, then, shall I?' said Lydgate, really believing that Wrench was not well prepared to deal wisely with a case of this kind.

'Pray make that arrangement, Mr Lydgate,' said Rosamond, coming to her mother's aid, and supporting her arm to lead her away.

When Mr Vincy came home he was very angry with Wrench, and did not care if he never came into his house again. Lydgate should go on now, whether Wrench liked it or not. It was no joke to have fever in the house. Everybody must be sent to now, not to come to dinner on Thursday. And Pritchard needn't get up any wine: brandy was the best thing against infection. 'I shall drink brandy,' added Mr Vincy emphatically – as much as to say, this was not an occasion for firing with blank-cartridges. 'He's an uncommonly unfortunate lad, is Fred. He'd need have some luck by and by to make up for all this – else I don't know who'd have an eldest son.'

'Don't say so, Vincy,' said the mother, with a quivering lip, 'if you don't want him to be taken from me.'

'It will worret you to death, Lucy; *that* I can see,' said Mr Vincy, more mildly. 'However, Wrench shall know what I think of the matter.' (What Mr Vincy thought confusedly was, that the fever might somehow have been hindered if Wrench had shown the proper solicitude about his – the Mayor's – family.) 'I'm the last man to give in to the cry about new doctors or new parsons, either –

whether they're Bulstrode's men or not. But Wrench shall know what I think, take it as he will.'

Wrench did not take it at all well. Lydgate was as polite as he could be in his offhand way, but politeness in a man who has placed you at a disadvantage is only an additional exasperation, especially if he happens to have been an object of dislike beforehand. Country practitioners used to be an irritable species, susceptible on the point of honour; and Mr Wrench was one of the most irritable among them. He did not refuse to meet Lydgate in the evening, but his temper was somewhat tried on the occasion. He had to hear Mrs Vincy say: 'Oh, Mr Wrench, what have I ever done that you should use me so? – To go away, and never to come again! And my boy might have been stretched a corpse!'

Mr Vincy, who had been keeping up a sharp fire on the enemy Infection, and was a good deal heated in consequence, started up when he heard Wrench come in, and went into the hall to let him know what he thought.

'I'll tell you what, Wrench, this is beyond a joke,' said the Mayor, who of late had had to rebuke offenders with an official air, and now broadened himself by putting his thumbs in his armholes. – 'To let fever get unawares into a house like this. There are some things that ought to be actionable, and are not so – that's my opinion.'

But irrational reproaches were easier to bear than the sense of being instructed, or rather the sense that a younger man, like Lydgate, inwardly considered him in need of instruction, for 'in point of fact', Mr Wrench afterwards said, Lydgate paraded flighty, foreign notions, which would not wear. He swallowed his ire for the moment, but he afterwards wrote to decline further attendance in the case. The house might be a good one, but Mr Wrench was not going to truckle to anybody on a professional matter. He reflected, with much probability on his side, that Lydgate would by and by be caught tripping too, and that his ungentlemanly attempts to discredit the sale of drugs by his professional brethren would by and by recoil on himself. He threw out biting remarks on Lydgate's tricks, worthy only of a quack, to get himself a factitious reputation with credulous people. That cant about cures was never got up by sound practitioners.

This was a point on which Lydgate smarted as much as Wrench could desire. To be puffed by ignorance was not only humiliating, but perilous, and not more enviable than the reputation of the weather-prophet. He was impatient of the foolish expectations amidst which all work must be carried on, and likely enough to damage himself as much as Mr Wrench could wish, by an unprofessional openness.

However, Lydgate was installed as medical attendant on the Vincys, and the event was a subject of general conversation in Middlemarch. Some said, that the Vincys had behaved scandalously, that Mr Vincy had threatened Wrench, and that Mrs Vincy had accused him of poisoning her son. Others were of opinion that Mr Lydgate's passing by was providential, that he was wonderfully clever in fevers, and that Bulstrode was in the right to bring him forward. Many people believed that Lydgate's coming to the town at all was really due to Bulstrode; and Mrs Taft, who was always counting stitches and gathered her information in misleading fragments caught between the rows of her knitting, had got it into her head that Mr Lydgate was a natural son of Bulstrode's, a fact which seemed to justify her suspicions of evangelical laymen.

She one day communicated this piece of knowledge to Mrs Farebrother, who did not fail to tell her son of it, observing: 'I should not be surprised at anything in Bulstrode, but I should be sorry to think it of Mr Lydgate.'

'Why, mother,' said Mr Farebrother, after an explosive laugh, 'you know very well that Lydgate is of a good family in the North. He never heard of Bulstrode before he came here.'

'That is satisfactory so far as Mr Lydgate is concerned, Camden,' said the old lady, with an air of precision. 'But as to Bulstrode – the report may be true of some other son.'

Chapter 27

Let the high Muse chant loves Olympian:
We are but mortals, and must sing of man.

An eminent philosopher among my friends, who can dignify even your ugly furniture by lifting it into the serene light of science, has shown me this pregnant little fact. Your pier-glass or extensive surface of polished steel made to be rubbed by a housemaid, will be minutely and multitudinously scratched in all directions; but place now against it a lighted candle as a centre of illumination, and lo! the scratches will seem to arrange themselves in a fine series of concentric circles round that little sun. It is demonstrable that the scratches are going everywhere impartially, and it is only your candle which produces the flattering illusion of a concentric arrangement, its light falling with an exclusive optical selection. These things are a parable. The scratches are events, and the candle is the egoism of any person now absent – of Miss Vincy, for example. Rosamond had a Providence of her own who had kindly made her more charming than other girls, and who seemed to have arranged Fred's illness and Mr Wrench's mistake in order to bring her and Lydgate within effective proximity. It would have been to contravene these arrangements if Rosamond had consented to go away to Stone Court or elsewhere, as her parents wished her to do, especially since Mr Lydgate thought the precaution needless. Therefore, while Miss Morgan and the children were sent away to a farmhouse the morning after Fred's illness had declared itself, Rosamond refused to leave papa and mamma.

Poor mamma indeed was an object to touch any creature born of woman; and Mr Vincy, who doted on his wife, was more alarmed on her account than on Fred's. But for his insistence she would have taken no rest: her brightness was all bedimmed; unconscious of her costume which had always been so fresh and gay, she was like a sick bird with languid eye and plumage ruffled, her senses dulled to the sights and sounds that used most to interest her. Fred's delirium, in which he seemed to be wandering out of her reach, tore her heart. After her first outburst against Mr Wrench she went about very quietly: her one low cry was to

Lydgate. She would follow him out of the room and put her hand on his arm moaning out, 'Save my boy.' Once she pleaded, 'He has always been good to me, Mr Lydgate: he never had a hard word for his mother,' – as if poor Fred's suffering were an accusation against him, all the deepest fibres of the mother's memory were stirred, and the young man whose voice took a gentler tone when he spoke to her, was one with the babe whom she had loved, with a love new to her, before he was born.

'I have good hope, Mrs Vincy,' Lydgate would say. 'Come down with me and let us talk about the food.' In that way he led her to the parlour where Rosamond was, and made a change for her, surprising her into taking some tea or broth which had been prepared for her. There was a constant understanding between him and Rosamond on these matters. He almost always saw her before going to the sickroom, and she appealed to him as to what she could do for mamma. Her presence of mind and adroitness in carrying out his hints were admirable, and it is not wonderful that the idea of seeing Rosamond began to mingle itself with his interest in the case. Especially when the critical stage was passed, and he began to feel confident of Fred's recovery. In the more doubtful time, he had advised calling in Dr Sprague (who, if he could, would rather have remained neutral on Wrench's account); but after two consultations, the conduct of the case was left to Lydgate, and there was every reason to make him assiduous. Morning and evening he was at Mr Vincy's, and gradually the visits became cheerful as Fred became simply feeble, and lay not only in need of the utmost petting but conscious of it, so that Mrs Vincy felt as if after all the illness had made a festival for her tenderness.

Both father and mother held it an added reason for good spirits, when old Mr Featherstone sent messages by Lydgate, saying that Fred must make haste and get well, as he, Peter Featherstone, could not do without him, and missed his visits sadly. The old man himself was getting bedridden, Mrs Vincy told these messages to Fred when he could listen, and he turned towards her his delicate, pinched face, from which all the thick blond hair had been cut away, and in which the eyes seemed to have got larger, yearning for some word about Mary – wondering what she felt about his illness. No word passed his lips: but 'to hear with eyes belongs to love's rare wit', and the mother in the fullness of her heart not only divined Fred's longing, but felt ready for any sacrifice in order to satisfy him.

'If I can only see my boy strong again,' she said, in her loving folly; 'and who knows? – perhaps master of Stone Court! and he can marry anybody he likes then.'

'Not if they won't have me, mother,' said Fred. The illness had made him childish, and tears came as he spoke.

'Oh, take a bit of jelly, my dear,' said Mrs Vincy, secretly incredulous of any such refusal.

She never left Fred's side when her husband was not in the house, and thus Rosamond was in the unusual position of being much alone. Lydgate, naturally, never thought of staying long with her, yet it seemed that the brief impersonal conversations they had together were creating that peculiar intimacy which consists in shyness. They were obliged to look at each other in speaking, and somehow the looking could not be carried through as the matter of course which it really was. Lydgate began to feel this sort of consciousness unpleasant, and one day looked down, or anywhere, like an ill-worked puppet. But this turned out badly: the next day, Rosamond looked down, and the consequence was that when their eyes met again, both were more conscious than before. There was no help for this in science, and as Lydgate did not want to flirt, there seemed to be no help for it in folly. It was therefore a relief when neighbours no longer considered the house in quarantine, and when the chances of seeing Rosamond alone were very much reduced.

But that intimacy of mutual embarrassment, in which each feels that the other is feeling something, having once existed, its effect is not to be done away with. Talk about the weather and other well-bred topics is apt to seem a hollow device, and behaviour can hardly become easy unless it frankly recognises a mutual fascination – which of course need not mean anything deep or serious. This was the way in which Rosamond and Lydgate slid gracefully into ease, and made their intercourse lively again. Visitors came and went as usual, there was once more music in the drawing-room, and all the extra hospitality of Mr Vincy's mayoralty returned. Lydgate, whenever he could, took his seat by Rosamond's side, and lingered to hear her music, calling himself her captive – meaning, all the while, not to be her captive. The preposterousness of the notion that he could at once set up a satisfactory establishment as a married man was a sufficient guarantee against danger. This play at being a little in love was agreeable, and did not interfere with graver pursuits. Flirtation, after all, was not necessarily a singeing process. Rosamond, for her part, had never enjoyed the days so much in her life before: she was sure of being admired by someone worth captivating, and she did not distinguish flirtation from love, either in herself or in another. She seemed to be sailing with a fair wind just whither she would go, and her thoughts were much occupied with a handsome house in Lowick Gate which she hoped would by and by be vacant, She was quite determined, when she was married, to rid herself adroitly of all the visitors who were not agreeable to her at her father's; and she imagined the drawing-room in her favourite house with various styles of furniture.

Certainly her thoughts were much occupied with Lydgate himself; he seemed to her almost perfect: if he had known his notes so that his enchantment under her music had been less like an emotional elephant's, and if he had been able to discriminate better the refinements of her taste in dress, she could hardly have mentioned a deficiency in him. How different he was from young Plymdale or Mr Caius Larcher! Those young men had not a notion of French, and could speak on no subject with striking knowledge, except perhaps the dyeing and carrying trades, which of course they were ashamed to mention; they were Middlemarch gentry, elated with their silver-headed whips and satin stocks, but embarrassed in their manners, and timidly jocose: even Fred was above them, having at least the accent and manner of a university man. Whereas Lydgate was always listened to, bore himself with the careless politeness of conscious superiority, and seemed to have the right clothes on by a certain natural affinity, without ever having to think about them. Rosamond was proud when he entered the room, and when he approached her with a distinguishing smile, she had a delicious sense that she was the object of enviable homage. If Lydgate had been aware of all the pride he excited in that delicate bosom, he might have been just as well pleased as any other man, even the most densely ignorant of humoral pathology or fibrous tissue: he held it one of the prettiest attitudes of the feminine mind to adore a man's pre-eminence without too precise a knowledge of what it consisted in.

But Rosamond was not one of those helpless girls who betray themselves unawares, and whose behaviour is awkwardly driven by their impulses, instead of being steered by wary grace and propriety. Do you imagine that her rapid fore-cast and rumination concerning house-furniture and society were ever discernible in her conversation, even with her mamma? On the contrary, she would have expressed the prettiest surprise and disapprobation if she had heard that another young lady had been detected in that immodest prematureness – indeed, would probably have disbelieved in its possibility. For Rosamond never showed any unbecoming knowledge, and was always that combination of correct sentiments, music, dancing, drawing, elegant note-writing, private album for extracted verse, and perfect blond loveliness, which made the irresistible woman for the doomed man of that date. Think no unfair evil of her, pray: she had no wicked plots, nothing sordid or mercenary: in fact, she never thought of money except as something necessary which other people would always provide. She was not in the habit of devising falsehoods, and if her statements were no direct clue to fact, why, they were not intended in that light – they were among her elegant accomplishments, intended to please. Nature had inspired many arts in finishing Mrs Lemon's favourite pupil, who by general consent (Fred's excepted) was a rare compound of beauty, cleverness, and amiability.

Lydgate found it more and more agreeable to be with her, and there was no constraint now, there was a delightful interchange of influence in their eyes, and what they said had that superfluity of meaning for them, which is observable with some sense of flatness by a third person; still they had no interviews or asides from which a third person need have been excluded. In fact, they flirted; and Lydgate was secure in the belief that they did nothing else. If a man could not love and be wise, surely he could flirt and be wise at the same time? Really, the men in Middlemarch, except Mr Farebrother, were great bores, and Lyd-gate did not care about commercial politics or cards: what was he to do for relaxation? He was often invited to the Bulstrodes'; but the girls there were hardly out of the schoolroom; and Mrs Bulstrode's naïve way of conciliating piety and worldliness, the nothingness of this life and the desirability of cut glass, the consciousness at once of filthy rags and the best damask, was not a sufficient relief from the weight of her husband's invariable seriousness. The Vincys' house, with all its faults, was the pleasanter by contrast; besides, it nourished Rosamond, sweet to look at as a half-opened blush-rose, and adorned with accomplishments for the refined amusement of man.

But he made some enemies, other than medical, by his success with Miss Vincy. One evening he came into the drawing-room rather late, when several other visitors were there. The card-table had drawn off the elders, and Mr Ned Plymdale (one of the good matches in Middlemarch, though not one of its leading minds) was in tête-à-tête with Rosamond. He had brought the last *Keepsake*, the gorgeous watered-silk publication which marked modern progress at that time; and he considered himself very fortunate that he could be the first to look over it with her, dwelling on the ladies and gentlemen with shiny copperplate cheeks and copperplate smiles, and pointing to comic verses as capital and sentimental stories as interesting. Rosamond was gracious, and Mr Ned was satisfied that he had the very best thing in art and literature as a medium for 'paying addresses', the very thing to please a nice girl. He had also reasons, deep rather than ostensible, for being satisfied with his own appearance. To superficial observers his chin had too vanishing an aspect, looking as if it were being gradually re-absorbed. And it did indeed cause him some difficulty about the fit of his satin stocks, for which chins were at that time useful.

'I think the Honourable Mrs S. is something like you,' said Mr Ned. He kept the book open at the bewitching portrait, and looked at it rather languishingly.

'Her back is very large; she seems to have sat for that,' said Rosamond, not meaning any satire, but thinking how red young Plymdale's hands were, and wondering why Lydgate did not come. She went on with her tatting all the while.

'I did not say she was as beautiful as you are,' said Mr Ned, venturing to look from the portrait to its rival.

'I suspect you of being an adroit flatterer,' said Rosamond, feeling sure that she should have to reject this young gentleman a second time.

But now Lydgate came in; the book was closed before he reached Rosamond's corner, and as he took his seat with easy confidence on the other side of her, young Plymdale's jaw fell like a barometer towards the cheerless side of change. Rosamond enjoyed not only Lydgate's presence but its effect: she liked to excite jealousy.

'What a late comer you are!' she said, as they shook hands. 'Mamma had given you up a little while ago. How do you find Fred?'

'As usual; going on well, but slowly. I want him to go away to Stone Court, for example. But your mamma seems to have some objection.'

'Poor fellow! ' said Rosamond, prettily. 'You will see Fred so changed,' she added, turning to the other suitor; 'we have looked to Mr Lydgate as our guardian angel during his illness.'

Mr Ned smiled nervously, while Lydgate, drawing the *Keepsake* towards him and opening it, gave a short scornful laugh and tossed up his chin, as if in wonderment at human folly.

'What are you laughing at so profanely?' said Rosamond, with bland neutrality.

'I wonder which would turn out to be the silliest – the engravings or the writing here,' said Lydgate, in his most convinced tone, while he turned over the pages quickly, seeming to see all through the book in no time, and showing his large white hands to much advantage, as Rosamond thought. 'Do look at this bridegroom coming out of church: did you ever see such a "sugared invention" – as the Elizabethans used to say? Did any haberdasher ever look so smirking? Yet I will answer for it the story makes him one of the first gentlemen in the land.'

'You are so severe, I am frightened at you,' said Rosamond, keeping her amusement duly moderate. Poor young Plymdale had lingered with admiration over this very engraving, and his spirit was stirred.

'There are a great many celebrated people writing in the *Keepsake*, at all events,' he said, in a tone at once piqued and timid. 'This is the first time I have heard it called silly.'

'I think I shall turn round on you and accuse you of being a Goth,' said Rosamond, looking at Lydgate with a smile. 'I suspect you know nothing about Lady Blessington and L. E. L.' Rosamond herself was not without relish for these writers, but she did not readily commit herself by admiration, and was alive to the slightest hint that anything was not, according to Lydgate, in the very highest taste.

'But Sir Walter Scott – I suppose Mr Lydgate knows him,' said young Plymdale, a little cheered by this advantage.

'Oh, I read no literature now,' said Lydgate, shutting the book, and pushing it away. 'I read so much when I was a lad, that I suppose it will last me all my life. I used to know Scott's poems by heart.'

'I should like to know when you left off,' said Rosamond, 'because then I might be sure that I knew something which you did not know.'

'Mr Lydgate would say that was not worth knowing,' said Mr Ned, purposely caustic.

'On the contrary,' said Lydgate, showing no smart, but smiling with exasperating confidence at Rosamond. 'It would be worth knowing by the fact that Miss Vincy could tell it me.'

Young Plymdale soon went to look at the whist-playing, thinking that Lydgate was one of the most conceited, unpleasant fellows it had ever been his ill-fortune to meet.

'How rash you are!' said Rosamond, inwardly delighted. 'Do you see that you have given offence?'

'What – is it Mr Plymdale's book? I am sorry. I didn't think about it.'

'I shall begin to admit what you said of yourself when you first came here – that you are a bear, and want teaching by the birds.'

'Well, there is a bird who can teach me what she will. Don't I listen to her willingly?'

To Rosamond it seemed as if she and Lydgate were as good as engaged. That they were some time to be engaged had long been an idea in her mind; and ideas, we know, tend to a more solid kind of existence, the necessary materials being at hand. It is true, Lydgate had the counter idea of remaining unengaged; but this was a mere negative, a shadow cast by other resolves which themselves were capable of shrinking. Circumstance was almost sure to be on the side of Rosamond's idea, which had a shaping activity and looked through watchful blue eyes, whereas Lydgate's lay blind and unconcerned as a jellyfish which gets melted without knowing it.

That evening when he went home, he looked at his phials to see how a process of maceration was going on, with undisturbed interest; and he wrote out his daily notes with as much precision as usual. The reveries from which it was difficult for him to detach himself were ideal constructions of something else than Rosamond's virtues, and the primitive tissue was still his fair unknown. Moreover, he was beginning to feel some zest for the growing though half-suppressed feud between him and the other medical men, which was likely to become more manifest, now that Bulstrode's method of managing the new hospital was about to be declared; and there were various inspiriting signs that his non-acceptance by some of Peacock's patients might be counter-balanced by the impression he had produced in other quarters. Only a few days later, when he had happened to overtake Rosamond on the Lowick road and had got down from his horse to walk by her side until he had quite protected her from a passing drove, he had been stopped by a servant on horseback with a message calling him in to a house of some importance where Peacock had never attended; and it was the second instance of this kind. The servant was Sir James Chettam's, and the house was Lowick Manor.

Chapter 28

1st Gent.	All times are good to seek your wedded home
	Bringing a mutual delight.
2nd Gent.	Why, true.
	The calendar hath not an evil day
	For souls made one by love, and even death
	Were sweetness, if it came like rolling waves
	While they two clasped each other, and foresaw
	No life apart.

Mr and Mrs Casaubon, returning from their wedding journey, arrived at Lowick Manor in the middle of January. A light snow was falling as they descended at the door, and in the morning, when Dorothea passed from her dressing-room into the blue-green boudoir that we know of, she saw the long avenue of limes lifting their trunks from a white earth, and spreading white branches against the dun and motionless sky. The distant flat shrank in uniform whiteness and low-hanging uniformity of cloud. The very furniture in the room seemed to have shrunk since she saw it before: the stag in the tapestry looked more like a ghost in his ghostly blue-green world; the volumes of polite literature in the bookcase looked more like immovable imitations of books. The bright fire of dry oak-boughs burning on the dogs seemed an incongruous renewal of life and glow – like the figure of Dorothea herself as she entered carrying the red-leather cases containing the cameos for Celia.

She was glowing from her morning toilette as only healthful youth can glow; there was gemlike brightness on her coiled hair and in her hazel eyes; there was warm red life in her lips; her throat had a breathing whiteness above the differing white of the fur which itself seemed to wind about her neck and cling down her blue-grey pelisse with a tenderness gathered from her own, a sentient commingled innocence which kept its loveliness against the crystalline purity of the outdoor snow. As she laid the cameo-cases on the table in the bow-window, she unconsciously kept her hands on them, immediately absorbed in looking out on the still, white enclosure which made her visible world.

Mr Casaubon, who had risen early complaining of palpitation, was in the library giving audience to his curate Mr Tucker. By and by Celia would come in her quality of bridesmaid as well as sister, and through the next weeks there would be wedding visits received and given; all in continuance of that transitional life understood to correspond with the excitement of bridal felicity, and keeping up the sense of busy ineffectiveness, as of a dream which the dreamer begins to suspect. The duties of her married life, contemplated as so great beforehand, seemed to be shrinking with the furniture and the white vapour-walled landscape. The clear heights where she expected to walk in full communion had become difficult to see even in her imagination; the delicious repose of the soul on a complete superior had been shaken into uneasy effort and alarmed with dim presentiment. When would the days begin of that active wifely devotion which was to strengthen her husband's life and exalt her own? Never perhaps, as she had preconceived them; but somehow still somehow. In this solemnly pledged union of her life, duty would present itself in some new form of inspiration and give a new meaning to wifely love.

Meanwhile there was the snow and the low arch of dun vapour – there was the stifling oppression of that gentlewoman's world, where everything was done for her and none asked for her aid – where the sense of connection with a manifold pregnant existence had to be kept up painfully as an inward vision, instead of coming from without in claims that would have shaped her energies. – 'What shall I do?' 'Whatever you please, my dear': that had been her brief history since she had left off learning morning lessons and practising silly rhythms on the hated piano. Marriage, which was to bring guidance into worthy and imperative occupation, had not yet freed her from the gentlewoman's oppressive liberty: it had not even filled her leisure with the ruminant joy of unchecked tenderness. Her blooming full-pulsed youth stood there in a moral imprisonment which made itself one with the chill, colourless, narrowed landscape, with the shrunken furniture, the never-read books, and the ghostly stag in a pale fantastic world that seemed to be vanishing from the daylight.

In the first minutes when Dorothea looked out she felt nothing but the dreary oppression; then came a keen remembrance, and turning away from the window she walked round the room. The ideas and hopes which were living in her mind when she first saw this room nearly three months before were present now only as memories: she judged them as we judge transient and departed things. All existence seemed to beat with a lower pulse than her own, and her religious faith was a solitary cry, the struggle out of a nightmare in which every object was withering and shrinking away from her. Each remembered thing in the room was disenchanted, was deadened as an unlit transparency, till her wandering gaze came to the group of miniatures, and there at last she saw something which had gathered new breath and meaning: it was the miniature of Mr Casaubon's aunt Julia, who had made the unfortunate marriage – of Will Ladislaw's grandmother. Dorothea could fancy that it was alive now – the delicate woman's face which yet had a head-strong look, a peculiarity difficult to interpret. Was it only her friends who thought her marriage unfortunate? or did she herself find it out to be a mistake, and taste the salt bitterness of her tears in the merciful silence of the night? What breadths of experience Dorothea seemed to have passed over since she first looked at this miniature! She felt a new companionship with it, as if it had an ear for her and could see how she was looking at it. Here was a woman who had known some difficulty about marriage. Nay, the colours deepened, the lips and chin seemed to get larger, the hair and eyes seemed to be sending out light, the face was masculine and beamed on her with that full gaze which tells her on whom it falls that she is too interesting for the slightest movement of her eyelid to pass unnoticed and uninterpreted. The vivid presentation came like a pleasant glow to Dorothea: she felt herself smiling, and turning from the miniature sat down and looked up as if she were again talking to a figure in front of her. But the smile disappeared as she went on meditating, and at last she said aloud: 'Oh, it was cruel to speak so! How sad – how dreadful!'

She rose quickly and went out of the room, hurrying along the corridor, with the irresistible impulse to go and see her husband and enquire if she could do anything for him. Perhaps Mr Tucker was gone and Mr Casaubon was alone in the library. She felt as if all her morning's gloom would vanish if she could see her husband glad because of her presence.

But when she reached the head of the dark oak staircase, there was Celia coming up, and below there was Mr Brooke, exchanging welcomes and congratulations with Mr Casaubon.

'Dodo!' said Celia, in her quiet staccato; then kissed her sister, whose arms encircled her, and said no more. I think they both cried a little in a furtive manner, while Dorothea ran downstairs to greet her uncle.

'I need not ask how you are, my dear,' said Mr Brooke, after kissing her forehead. 'Rome has agreed with you, I see – happiness, frescoes, the antique – that sort of thing. Well, it's very pleasant to have you back again, and you understand all about art now, eh? But Casaubon is a little pale, I tell him – a little pale, you know. Studying hard in his holidays is carrying it rather too far. I overdid it at one time' – Mr Brooke still held Dorothea's hand, but had turned his face to Mr Casaubon 'about topography, ruins, temples – I thought I had a clue, but I saw it would carry me too far, and nothing might have come of it. You may go any length in that sort of thing, and nothing may come of it, you know.'

Dorothea's eyes also were turned up to her husband's face with some anxiety at the idea that those who saw him afresh after absence might be aware of signs which she had not noticed.

'Nothing to alarm you, my dear,' said Mr Brooke, observing her expression. 'A little English beef and mutton will soon make a difference. It was all very well to look pale, sitting for the portrait of Aquinas, you know – we got your letter just in time. But Aquinas, now – he was a little too subtle, wasn't he? Does anybody read Aquinas?'

'He is not indeed an author adapted to superficial minds,' said Mr Casaubon, meeting these timely questions with dignified patience.

'You would like coffee in your own room, uncle?' said Dorothea, coming to the rescue.

'Yes; and you must go to Celia: she has great news to tell you, you know. I leave it all to her.'

The blue-green boudoir looked much more cheerful when Celia was seated there in a pelisse exactly like her sister's, surveying the cameos with a placid satisfaction, while the conversation passed on to other topics.

'Do you think it nice to go to Rome on a wedding journey?' said Celia, with her ready delicate blush which Dorothea was used to on the smallest occasion.

'It would not suit all – not you, dear, for example,' said Dorothea, quietly. No one would ever know what she thought of a wedding journey to Rome.

'Mrs Cadwallader says it is nonsense, people going a long journey when they are married. She says they get tired to death of each other, and can't quarrel comfortably, as they would at home. And Lady Chettam says she went to Bath.' Celia's colour changed again and again – seemed

> To come and go with tidings from the heart,
> As it a running messenger had been.

It must mean more than Celia's blushing usually did.

'Celia! has something happened?' said Dorothea, in a tone full of sisterly feeling. 'Have you really any great news to tell me?'

'It was because you went away, Dodo. Then there was nobody but me for Sir James to talk to,' said Celia, with a certain roguishness in her eyes.

'I understand. It is as I used to hope and believe,' said Dorothea, taking her sister's face between her hands, and looking at her half anxiously. Celia's marriage seemed more serious than it used to do.

'It was only three days ago,' said Celia. 'And Lady Chettam is very kind.'

'And you are very happy?'

'Yes. We are not going to be married yet. Because everything is to be got ready. And I don't want to be married so very soon, because I think it is nice to be engaged. And we shall be married all our lives after.'

'I do believe you could not marry better, Kitty. Sir James is a good, honourable man,' said Dorothea, warmly.

'He has gone on with the cottages, Dodo. He will tell you about them when he comes. Shall you be glad to see him?'

'Of course I shall. How can you ask me?'

'Only I was afraid you would be getting so learned,' said Celia, regarding Mr Casaubon's learning as a kind of damp which might in due time saturate a neighbouring body.

Chapter 29

I found that no genius in another could please me. My unfortunate
paradoxes had entirely dried up that source of comfort.

GOLDSMITH

One morning, some weeks after her arrival at Lowick, Dorothea – but why
always Dorothea? Was her point of view the only possible one with regard to
this marriage? I protest against all our interest, all our effort at understanding
being given to the young skins that look blooming in spite of trouble; for these
too will get faded, and will know the older and more eating griefs which we are
helping to neglect. In spite of the blinking eyes and white moles objectionable to
Celia, and the want of muscular curve which was morally painful to Sir James,
Mr Casaubon had an intense consciousness within him, and was spiritually a-
hungered like the rest of us. He had done nothing exceptional in marrying –
nothing but what society sanctions, and considers an occasion for wreaths and
bouquets. It had occurred to him that he must not any longer defer his intention
of matrimony, and he had reflected that in taking a wife, a man of good position
should expect and carefully choose a blooming young lady – the younger the
better, because more educable and submissive – of a rank equal to his own, of
religious principles, virtuous disposition, and good understanding. On such a
young lady he would make handsome settlements, and he would neglect no
arrangement for her happiness: in return, he should receive family pleasures and
leave behind him that copy of himself which seemed so urgently required of a
man – to the sonneteers of the sixteenth century. Times had altered since then,
and no sonneteer had insisted on Mr Casaubon's leaving a copy of himself;
moreover, he had not yet succeeded in issuing copies of his mythological key;
but he had always intended to acquit himself by marriage, and the sense that he
was fast leaving the years behind him, that the world was getting dimmer and
that he felt lonely, was a reason to him for losing no more time in overtaking
domestic delights before they too were left behind by the years.

And when he had seen Dorothea he believed that he had found even more
than he demanded: she might really be such a helpmate to him as would enable
him to dispense with a hired secretary, an aid which Mr Casaubon had never yet
employed and had a suspicious dread of. (Mr Casaubon was nervously conscious
that he was expected to manifest a powerful mind.) Providence, in its kindness,
had supplied him with the wife he needed. A wife, a modest young lady, with the
purely appreciative, unambitious abilities of her sex, is sure to think her husband's
mind powerful. Whether Providence had taken equal care of Miss Brooke in
presenting her with Mr Casaubon was an idea which could hardly occur to him.
Society never made the preposterous demand that a man should think as much
about his own qualifications for making a charming girl happy as he thinks of
hers for making himself happy. As if a man could choose not only his wife but
his wife's husband! Or as if he were bound to provide charms for his posterity in

his own person! – When Dorothea accepted him with effusion, that was only natural; and Mr Casaubon believed that his happiness was going to begin.

He had not had much foretaste of happiness in his previous life. To know intense joy without a strong bodily frame, one must have an enthusiastic soul. Mr Casaubon had never had a strong bodily frame, and his soul was sensitive without being enthusiastic: it was too languid to thrill out of self-consciousness into passionate delight; it went on fluttering in the swampy ground where it was hatched, thinking of its wings and never flying. His experience was of that pitiable kind which shrinks from pity, and fears most of all that it should be known: it was that proud narrow sensitiveness which has not mass enough to spare for transformation into sympathy, and quivers threadlike in small currents of self-preoccupation or at best of an egoistic scrupulosity. And Mr Casaubon had many scruples: he was capable of a severe self-restraint; he was resolute in being a man of honour according to the code; he would be unimpeachable by any recognised opinion. In conduct these ends had been attained; but the difficulty of making his *Key to all Mythologies* unimpeachable weighed like lead upon his mind; and the pamphlets – or 'Parerga' as he called them – by which he tested his public and deposited small monumental records of his march, were far from having been seen in all their significance. He suspected the Archdeacon of not having read them: he was in painful doubt as to what was really thought of them by the leading minds of Brasenose, and bitterly convinced that his old acquaintance Carp had been the writer of that depreciatory recension which was kept locked in a small drawer of Mr Casaubon's desk, and also in a dark closet of his verbal memory. These were heavy impressions to struggle against, and brought that melancholy embitterment which is the consequence of all excessive claim: even his religious faith wavered with his wavering trust in his own authorship, and the consolations of the Christian hope in immortality seemed to lean on the immortality of the still unwritten *Key to all Mythologies*. For my part I am very sorry for him. It is an uneasy lot at best, to be what we call highly taught and yet not to enjoy: to be present at this great spectacle of life and never to be liberated from a small hungry shivering self – never to be fully possessed by the glory we behold, never to have our consciousness rapturously transformed into the vividness of a thought, the ardour of a passion, the energy of an action, but always to be scholarly and uninspired, ambitious and timid, scrupulous and dim-sighted. Becoming a dean or even a bishop would make little difference, I fear, to Mr Casaubon's uneasiness. Doubtless some ancient Greek has observed that behind the big mask and the speaking-trumpet, there must always be our poor little eyes peeping as usual and our timorous lips more or less under anxious control.

To this mental estate mapped out a quarter of a century before, to sensibilities thus fenced in, Mr Casaubon had thought of annexing happiness with a lovely young bride, but even before marriage, as we have seen, he found himself under a new depression in the consciousness that the new bliss was not blissful to him. Inclination yearned back to its old, easier custom. And the deeper he went in domesticity the more did the sense of acquitting himself and acting with propriety predominate over any other satisfaction. Marriage, like religion and erudition, nay, like authorship itself, was fated to become an outward requirement, and

Edward Casaubon was bent on fulfilling unimpeachably all requirements. Even drawing Dorothea into use in his study, according to his own intention before marriage, was an effort which he was always tempted to defer, and but for her pleading insistence it might never have begun. But she had succeeded in making it a matter of course that she should take her place at an early hour in the library and have work either of reading aloud or copying assigned her. The work had been easier to define because Mr Casaubon had adopted an immediate intention: there was to be a new Parergon, a small monograph on some lately traced indications concerning the Egyptian mysteries whereby certain assertions of Warburton's could be corrected. References were extensive even here, but not altogether shoreless; and sentences were actually to be written in the shape wherein they would be scanned by Brasenose and a less formidable posterity. These minor monumental productions were always exciting to Mr Casaubon: digestion was made difficult by the interference of citations, or by the rivalry of dialectical phrases ringing against each other in his brain. And from the first there was to be a Latin dedication about which everything was uncertain except that it was not to be addressed to Carp: it was a poisonous regret to Mr Casaubon that he had once addressed a dedication to Carp in which he had numbered that member of the animal kingdom among the *viros nullo aevo perituros*, a mistake which would infallibly lay the dedicator open to ridicule in the next age, and might even be chuckled over by Pike and Tench in the present.

Thus Mr Casaubon was in one of his busiest epochs, and as I began to say a little while ago, Dorothea joined him early in the library where he had breakfasted alone. Celia at this time was on a second visit to Lowick, probably the last before her marriage, and was in the drawing-room expecting Sir James.

Dorothea had learned to read the signs of her husband's mood, and she saw that the morning had become more foggy there during the last hour. She was going silently to her desk when he said, in that distant tone which implied that he was discharging a disagreeable duty: 'Dorothea, here is a letter for you, which was enclosed in one addressed to me.'

It was a letter of two pages, and she immediately looked at the signature.

'Mr Ladislaw! What can he have to say to me?' she exclaimed, in a tone of pleased surprise. 'But,' she added, looking at Mr Casaubon, 'I can imagine what he has written to you about.'

'You can, if you please, read the letter,' said Mr Casaubon, severely pointing to it with his pen, and not looking at her. 'But I may as well say beforehand, that I must decline the proposal it contains to pay a visit here. I trust I may be excused for desiring an interval of complete freedom from such distractions as have been hitherto inevitable, and especially from guests whose desultory vivacity makes their presence a fatigue.'

There had been no clashing of temper between Dorothea and her husband since that little explosion in Rome, which had left such strong traces in her mind that it had been easier ever since to quell emotion than to incur the consequence of venting it. But this ill-tempered anticipation that she could desire visits which might be disagreeable to her husband, this gratuitous defence of himself against selfish complaint on her part, was too sharp a sting to be meditated on until after it had been resented. Dorothea had thought that she could have been patient with John Milton, but she had never imagined him behaving in this way; and for a moment Mr Casaubon seemed to be stupidly undiscerning and odiously unjust. Pity, that 'newborn babe' which was by and by to rule many a storm within her, did not 'stride the blast' on this occasion. With her first words, uttered in a tone that shook him, she startled Mr Casaubon into looking at her, and meeting the flash of her eyes.

'Why do you attribute to me a wish for anything that would annoy you? You speak to me as if I were something you had to contend against. Wait at least till I appear to consult my own pleasure apart from yours.'

'Dorothea, you are hasty,' answered Mr Casaubon, nervously.

Decidedly, this woman was too young to be on the formidable level of wifehood – unless she had been pale and featureless and taken everything for granted.

'I think it was you who were first hasty in your false suppositions about my feeling,' said Dorothea, in the same tone. The fire was not dissipated yet, and she thought it was ignoble in her husband not to apologise to her.

'We will, if you please, say no more on this subject, Dorothea. I have neither leisure nor energy for this kind of debate.'

Here Mr Casaubon dipped his pen and made as if he would return to his writing, though his hand trembled so much that the words seemed to be written in an unknown character. There are answers which, in turning away wrath, only send it to the other end of the room, and to have a discussion coolly waived when you feel that justice is all on your own side is even more exasperating in marriage than in philosophy.

Dorothea left Ladislaw's two letters unread on her husband's writing-table and went to her own place, the scorn and indignation within her rejecting the reading of these letters, just as we hurl away any trash towards which we seem to have been suspected of mean cupidity. She did not in the least divine the subtle sources of her husband's bad temper about these letters; she only knew that they had caused him to offend her. She began to work at once, and her hand did not tremble; on the contrary, in writing out the quotations which had been given to her the day before, she felt that she was forming her letters beautifully, and it seemed to her that she saw the construction of the Latin she was copying, and which she was beginning to understand, more clearly than usual. In her indignation there was a sense of superiority, but it went out for the present in firmness of stroke, and did not compress itself into an inward articulate voice pronouncing the once 'affable archangel' a poor creature.

There had been this apparent quiet for half an hour, and Dorothea had not looked away from her own table, when she heard the loud bang of a book on the floor, and turning quickly saw Mr Casaubon on the library-steps clinging forward as if he were in some bodily distress. She started up and bounded towards him in an instant: he was evidently in great straits for breath. Jumping on a stool she got close to his elbow and said with her whole soul melted into tender alarm: 'Can you lean on me, dear?'

He was still for two or three minutes, which seemed endless to her, unable to speak or move, gasping for breath. When at last he descended the three steps and fell backwards in the large chair which Dorothea had drawn close to the foot of the ladder, he no longer gasped but seemed helpless and about to faint. Dorothea rang the bell violently, and presently Mr Casaubon was helped to the couch: he did not faint, and was gradually reviving, when Sir James Chettam came in, having been met in the hall with the news that Mr Casaubon had 'had a fit in the library'.

'Good God! this is just what might have been expected,' was his immediate thought. If his prophetic soul had been urged to particularise, it seemed to him that 'fits' would have been the definite expression alighted upon. He asked his informant, the butler, whether the doctor had been sent for. The butler never knew his master want the doctor before; but would it not be right to send for a physician?

When Sir James entered the library, however, Mr Casaubon could make some signs of his usual politeness, and Dorothea, who in the reaction from her first terror had been kneeling and sobbing by his side, now rose and herself proposed that someone should ride off for a medical man.

'I recommend you to send for Lydgate,' said Sir James. 'My mother has called him in, and she has found him uncommonly clever. She has had a poor opinion of the physicians since my father's death.'

Dorothea appealed to her husband, and he made a silent sign of approval. So Mr Lydgate was sent for and he came wonderfully soon, for the messenger, who was Sir James Chettam's man and knew Mr Lydgate, met him leading his horse along the Lowick road and giving his arm to Miss Vincy.

Celia, in the drawing-room, had known nothing of the trouble till Sir James told her of it. After Dorothea's account, he no longer considered the illness a fit, but still something 'of that nature'.

'Poor dear Dodo – how dreadful!' said Celia, feeling as much grieved as her own perfect happiness would allow. Her little hands were clasped, and enclosed by Sir James's as a bud is enfolded by a liberal calyx. 'It is very shocking that Mr Casaubon should be ill; but I never did like him. And I think he is not half fond enough of Dorothea; and he ought to be, for I am sure no one else would have had him – do you think they would?'

'I always thought it a horrible sacrifice of your sister,' said Sir James.

'Yes. But poor Dodo never did do what other people do, and I think she never will.'

'She is a noble creature,' said the loyal-hearted Sir James. He had just had a fresh impression of this kind, as he had seen Dorothea stretching her tender arm under her husband's neck and looking at him with unspeakable sorrow. He did not know how much penitence there was in the sorrow.

'Yes,' said Celia, thinking it was very well for Sir James to say so, but *he* would not have been comfortable with Dodo. 'Shall I go to her? Could I help her, do you think?'

'I think it would be well for you just to go and see her before Lydgate comes,' said Sir James, magnanimously. 'Only don't stay long.'

While Celia was gone, he walked up and down remembering what he had originally felt about Dorothea's engagement, and feeling a revival of his disgust at Mr Brooke's indifference. If Cadwallader – if everyone else had regarded the affair as he, Sir James, had done, the marriage might have been hindered. It was wicked to let a young girl blindly decide her fate in that way, without any effort to save her. Sir James had long ceased to have any regrets on his own account: his heart was satisfied with his engagement to Celia. But he had a chivalrous nature (was not the disinterested service of woman among the ideal glories of old chivalry?): his disregarded love had not turned to bitterness; its death had made sweet odours – floating memories that clung with a consecrating effect to Dorothea. He could remain her brotherly friend, interpreting her actions with generous trustfulness.

Chapter 30

Qui veut délasser hors de propos, lasse.
                                                    PASCAL

Mr Casaubon had no second attack of equal severity with the first, and in a few days began to recover his usual condition. But Lydgate seemed to think the case worth a great deal of attention. He not only used his stethoscope (which had not become a matter of course in practice at that time), but sat quietly by his patient and watched him. To Mr Casaubon's questions about himself, he replied that the source of the illness was the common error of intellectual men – a too eager and monotonous application: the remedy was, to be satisfied with moderate work, and to seek variety of relaxation. Mr Brooke, who sat by on one occasion, suggested that Mr Casaubon should go fishing, as Cadwallader did, and have a turning-room, make toys, table-legs, and that kind of thing.

'In short you recommend me to anticipate the arrival of my second childhood,' said poor Mr Casaubon, with some bitterness. 'These things,' he added, looking at Lydgate, 'would be to me such relaxation as tow-picking is to prisoners in a house of correction.'

'I confess,' said Lydgate, smiling, 'amusement is rather an unsatisfactory prescription. It is something like telling people to keep up their spirits. Perhaps I had better say, that you must submit to be mildly bored rather than to go on working.'

'Yes, yes,' said Mr Brooke. 'Get Dorothea to play backgammon with you in the evenings. And shuttlecock, now – I don't know a finer game than shuttlecock for the daytime. I remember it all the fashion. To be sure, your eyes might not stand that, Casaubon. But you must unbend, you know. Why, you might take to some light study: conchology, now: I always think that must be a light study. Or get Dorothea to read you light things, Smollett – *Roderick Random, Humphry Clinker*: they are a little broad, but she may read anything now she's married, you know. I remember they made me laugh uncommonly – there's a droll bit about a postilion's breeches. We have no such humour now. I have gone through all these things, but they might be rather new to you.'

'As new as eating thistles,' would have been an answer to represent Mr Casaubon's feelings. But he only bowed resignedly, with due respect to his wife's uncle, and observed that doubtless the works he mentioned had 'served as a resource to a certain order of mind'.

'You see,' said the able magistrate to Lydgate, when they were outside the door, 'Casaubon has been a little narrow: it leaves him rather at a loss when you forbid him his particular work, which I believe is something very deep indeed – in the line of research, you know. I would never give way to that; I was always versatile. But a clergyman is tied a little tight. If they would make him a bishop, now! – he did a very good pamphlet for Peel. He would have more movement then, more show; he might get a little flesh. But I recommend you to talk to Mrs Casaubon. She is clever enough for anything, is my niece. Tell her, her husband wants liveliness, diversion: put her on amusing tactics.'

Without Mr Brooke's advice, Lydgate had determined on speaking to Dorothea. She had not been present while her uncle was throwing out his pleasant suggestions as to the mode in which life at Lowick might be enlivened, but she was usually by her husband's side, and the unaffected signs of intense anxiety in her face and voice about whatever touched his mind or health, made a drama which Lydgate was inclined to watch. He said to himself that he was only doing right in telling her the truth about her husband's probable future, but he certainly thought also that it would be interesting to talk confidentially with her. A medical man likes to make psychological observations, and sometimes in the pursuit of such studies is too easily tempted into momentous prophecy which life and death easily set at nought. Lydgate had often been satirical on this gratuitous prediction, and he meant now to be guarded.

He asked for Mrs Casaubon, but being told that she was out walking, he was going away, when Dorothea and Celia appeared, both glowing from their struggle with the March wind.

When Lydgate begged to speak with her alone, Dorothea opened the library door which happened to be the nearest, thinking of nothing at the moment but what he might have to say about Mr Casaubon. It was the first time she had entered this room since her husband had been taken ill, and the servant had chosen not to open the shutters. But there was light enough to read by from the narrow upper panes of the windows.

'You will not mind this sombre light,' said Dorothea, standing in the middle of the room. 'Since you forbade books, the library has been out of the question. But Mr Casaubon will soon be here again, I hope. Is he not making progress?'

'Yes, much more rapid progress than I at first expected. Indeed, he is already nearly in his usual state of health.'

'You do not fear that the illness will return?' said Dorothea, whose quick ear had detected some significance in Lydgate's tone.

'Such cases are peculiarly difficult to pronounce upon,' said Lydgate. 'The only point on which I can be confident is that it will be desirable to be very watchful on Mr Casaubon's account lest he should in any way strain his nervous power.'

'I beseech you to speak quite plainly,' said Dorothea, in an imploring tone. 'I cannot bear to think that there might be something which I did not know, and which, if I had known it, would have made me act differently.' The words came out like a cry: it was evident that they were the voice of some mental experience which lay not very far off.

'Sit down,' she added, placing herself on the nearest chair, and throwing off her bonnet and gloves, with an instinctive discarding of formality where a great question of destiny was concerned.

'What you say now justifies my own view,' said Lydgate 'I think it is one's function as a medical man to hinder regrets of that sort as far as possible. But I beg you to observe that Mr Casaubon's case is precisely of the kind in which the issue is most difficult to pronounce upon. He may possibly live for fifteen years or more, without much worse health than he has had hitherto.'

Dorothea had turned very pale, and when Lydgate paused she said in a low voice, 'You mean if we are very careful.'

'Yes – careful against mental agitation of all kinds, and against excessive application.'

'He would be miserable, if he had to give up his work,' said Dorothea, with a quick prevision of that wretchedness.

'I am aware of that. The only course is to try by all means, direct and indirect, to moderate and vary his occupations. With a happy concurrence of circumstances, there is, as I said, no immediate danger from that affection of the heart which I believe to have been the cause of his late attack. On the other hand, it is possible that the disease may develop itself more rapidly: it is one of those cases in which death is sometimes sudden. Nothing should be neglected which might be affected by such an issue.'

There was silence for a few moments, while Dorothea sat as if she had been turned to marble, though the life within her was so intense that her mind had never before swept in brief time over an equal range of scenes and motives.

'Help me, pray,' she said, at last, in the same low voice as before. 'Tell me what I can do.'

'What do you think of foreign travel? You have been lately in Rome, I think.'

The memories which made this resource utterly hopeless were a new current that shook Dorothea out of her pallid immobility.

'Oh, that would not do – that would be worse than anything,' she said with a more childlike despondency, while the tears rolled down. 'Nothing will be of any use that he does not enjoy.'

'I wish that I could have spared you this pain,' said Lydgate, deeply touched, yet wondering about her marriage. Women just like Dorothea had not entered into his traditions.

'It was right of you to tell me. I thank you for telling me the truth.'

'I wish you to understand that I shall not say anything to enlighten Mr Casaubon himself. I think it desirable for him to know nothing more than that he must not overwork himself, and must observe certain rules. Anxiety of any kind would be precisely the most unfavourable condition for him.'

Lydgate rose, and Dorothea mechanically rose at the same time, unclasping her cloak and throwing it off as if it stifled her. He was bowing and quitting her, when an impulse which if she had been alone would have turned into a prayer, made her say with a sob in her voice: 'Oh, you are a wise man, are you not? You know all about life and death. Advise me. Think what I can do. He has been labouring all his life and looking forward. He minds about nothing else. And I mind about nothing else – '

For years after Lydgate remembered the impression produced in him by this involuntary appeal – this cry from soul to soul, without other consciousness than their moving with kindred natures in the same embroiled medium, the same troublous fitfully-illuminated life. But what could he say now except that he should see Mr Casaubon again tomorrow?

When he was gone, Dorothea's tears gushed forth, and relieved her stifling oppression. Then she dried her eyes, reminded that her distress must not be betrayed to her husband; and looked round the room thinking that she must order the servant to attend to it as usual, since Mr Casaubon might now at any moment wish to enter. On his writing-table there were letters which had lain untouched since the morning when he was taken ill, and among them, as Dorothea well remembered, there were young Ladislaw's letters, the one addressed to her still unopened. The associations of these letters had been made the more painful by that sudden attack of illness which she felt that the agitation caused by her anger might have helped to bring on: it would be time enough to read them when they were again thrust upon her, and she had had no inclination to fetch them from the library, but now it occurred to her that they should be put out of her husband's sight: whatever might have been the sources of his annoyance about them, he must, if possible, not be annoyed again; and she ran her eyes first over the letter addressed to him to assure herself whether or not it would be necessary to write in order to hinder the offensive visit.

Will wrote from Rome, and began by saying that his obligations to Mr Casaubon were too deep for all thanks not to seem impertinent. It was plain that if he were not grateful, he must be the poorest-spirited rascal who had ever found a generous friend. To expand in wordy thanks would be like saying, 'I am honest'. But Will had come to perceive that his defects – defects which Mr Casaubon had himself often pointed to – needed for their correction that more strenuous position which his relative's generosity had hitherto prevented from being inevitable. He trusted that he should make the best return, if return were possible, by showing the effectiveness of the education for which he was indebted, and by ceasing in future to need any diversion towards himself of funds on which others might have a better claim. He was coming to England to try his fortune, as many other young men were obliged to do whose only capital was in their brains. His friend Naumann had desired him to take charge of the 'Dispute' – the picture painted for Mr Casaubon, with whose permission, and Mrs Casaubon's, Will would convey it to Lowick in person. A letter addressed to the Poste Restante in Paris within the fortnight would hinder him, if necessary, from arriving at an inconvenient moment. He enclosed a letter to Mrs Casaubon in which he continued a discussion about art, begun with her in Rome.

Opening her own letter Dorothea saw that it was a lively continuance of his remonstrance with her fanatical sympathy and her want of sturdy neutral delight in things as they were an outpouring of his young vivacity which it was impossible to read just now. She had immediately to consider what was to be done about the other letter: there was still time perhaps to prevent Will from coming to Lowick, Dorothea ended by giving the letter to her uncle, who was still in the house, and begging him to let Will know that Mr Casaubon had been ill, and that his health would not allow the reception of any visitors.

No one more ready than Mr Brooke to write a letter: his only difficulty was to write a short one, and his ideas in this case expanded over the three large pages and the inward foldings. He had simply said to Dorothea: 'To be sure, I will write, my dear. He's a very clever young fellow – this young Ladislaw – I dare say will be a rising young man. It's a good letter – marks his sense of things, you know. However, I will tell him about Casaubon.'

But the end of Mr Brooke's pen was a thinking organ, evolving sentences, especially of a benevolent kind, before the rest of his mind could well overtake them. It expressed regrets and proposed remedies, which, when Mr Brooke read them, seemed felicitously worded – surprisingly the right thing, and determined a sequel which he had never before thought of. In this case, his pen found it such a pity that young Ladislaw should not have come into the neighbourhood just at that time, in order that Mr Brooke might make his acquaintance more fully, and that they might go over the long-neglected Italian drawings together – it also felt such an interest in a young man who was starting in life with a stock of ideas – that by the end of the second page it had persuaded Mr Brooke to invite young Ladislaw, since he could not be received at Lowick, to come to Tipton Grange. Why not? They could find a great many things to do together, and this was a period of peculiar growth – the political horizon was expanding, and – in short, Mr Brooke's pen went off into a little speech which it had lately reported for that imperfectly-edited organ the *Middlemarch Pioneer*. While Mr Brooke was sealing this letter, he felt elated with an influx of dim projects: – a young man capable of putting ideas into form, the *Pioneer* purchased to clear the pathway for a new candidate, documents utilised – who knew what might come of it all? Since Celia was going to marry immediately, it would be very pleasant to have a young fellow at table with him, at least for a time.

But he went away without telling Dorothea what he had put into the letter, for she was engaged with her husband, and – in fact, these things were of no importance to her.

Chapter 31

How will you know the pitch of that great bell
Too large for you to stir? Let but a flute
Play 'neath the fine-mixed metal: listen close
Till the right note flows forth, a silvery rill:
Then shall the huge bell tremble – then the mass
With myriad waves concurrent shall respond
In low soft unison.

Lydgate that evening spoke to Miss Vincy of Mrs Casaubon, and laid some emphasis on the strong feeling she appeared to have for that formal studious man thirty years older than herself.

'Of course she is devoted to her husband,' said Rosamond, implying a notion of necessary sequence which the scientific man regarded as the prettiest possible for a woman; but she was thinking at the same time that it was not so very melancholy to be mistress of Lowick Manor with a husband likely to die soon. 'Do you think her very handsome?'

'She certainly is handsome, but I have not thought about it,' said Lydgate.

'I suppose it would be unprofessional,' said Rosamond, dimpling. 'But how your practice is spreading! You were called in before to the Chettams, I think; and now, the Casaubons.'

'Yes,' said Lydgate, in a tone of compulsory admission. 'But I don't really like attending such people so well as the poor. The cases are more monotonous, and one has to go through more fuss and listen more deferentially to nonsense.'

'Not more than in Middlemarch,' said Rosamond. 'And at least you go through wide corridors and have the scent of rose-leaves everywhere.'

'That is true, Mademoiselle de Montmorenci,' said Lydgate, just bending his head to the table and lifting with his fourth finger her delicate handkerchief which lay at the mouth of her reticule, as if to enjoy its scent, while he looked at her with a smile.

But this agreeable holiday freedom with which Lydgate hovered about the flower of Middlemarch, could not continue indefinitely. It was not more possible to find social isolation in that town than elsewhere, and two people persistently flirting could by no means escape from 'the various entanglements, weights, blows, clashings, motions, by which things severally go on'. Whatever Miss Vincy did must be remarked, and she was perhaps the more conspicuous to admirers and critics because just now Mrs Vincy, after some struggle, had gone with Fred to stay a little while at Stone Court, there being no other way of at once gratifying old Featherstone and keeping watch against Mary Garth, who appeared a less tolerable daughter-in-law in proportion as Fred's illness disappeared.

Aunt Bulstrode, for example, came a little oftener into Lowick Gate to see Rosamond, now she was alone. For Mrs Bulstrode had a true sisterly feeling for her brother; always thinking that he might have married better, but wishing well to the children. Now Mrs Bulstrode had a long-standing intimacy with Mrs Plymdale. They had nearly the same preferences in silks, patterns for under-clothing, china-ware, and clergymen; they confided their little troubles of health and household management to each other, and various little points of superiority on Mrs Bulstrode's side, namely, more decided seriousness, more admiration for mind, and a house outside the town, sometimes served to give colour to their conversation without dividing them: well-meaning women both, knowing very little of their own motives.

Mrs Bulstrode, paying a morning visit to Mrs Plymdale, happened to say that she could not stay longer, because she was going to see poor Rosamond.

'Why do you say "poor Rosamond"?' said Mrs Plymdale, a round-eyed sharp little woman, like a tamed falcon.

'She is so pretty, and has been brought up in such thoughtlessness. The mother, you know, had always that levity about her which makes me anxious for the children.'

'Well, Harriet, if I am to speak my mind,' said Mrs Plymdale, with emphasis, 'I must say, anybody would suppose you and Mr Bulstrode would be delighted with what has happened, for you have done everything to put Mr Lydgate forward.'

'Selina, what do you mean?' said Mrs Bulstrode in genuine surprise.

'Not but what I am truly thankful for Ned's sake,' said Mrs Plymdale. 'He could certainly better afford to keep such a wife than some people can; but I should wish him to look elsewhere. Still a mother has anxieties, and some young men would take to a bad life in consequence. Besides, if I was obliged to speak, I should say I was not fond of strangers coming into a town.'

'I don't know, Selina,' said Mrs Bulstrode, with a little emphasis in her turn. 'Mr Bulstrode was a stranger here at one time. Abraham and Moses were strangers in the land, and we are told to entertain strangers. And especially,' she added, after a slight pause, 'when they are unexceptionable.'

'I was not speaking in a religious sense, Harriet. I spoke as a mother.'

'Selina, I am sure you have never heard me say anything against a niece of mine marrying your son.'

'Oh, it is pride in Miss Vincy – I am sure it is nothing else,' said Mrs Plymdale, who had never before given all her confidence to 'Harriet' on this subject. 'No young man in Middlemarch was good enough for her: I have heard her mother say as much. That is not a Christian spirit, I think. But now, from all I hear, she has found a man as proud as herself.'

'You don't mean that there is anything between Rosamond and Mr Lydgate?' said Mrs Bulstrode, rather mortified at finding out her own ignorance.

'Is it possible you don't know, Harriet?'

'Oh, I go about so little; and I am not fond of gossip; I really never hear any. You see so many people that I don't see. Your circle is rather different from ours.'

'Well, but your own niece and Mr Bulstrode's great favourite – and yours too, I am sure, Harriet! I thought, at one time, you meant him for Kate, when she is a little older.'

'I don't believe there can be anything serious at present,' said Mrs Bulstrode. 'My brother would certainly have told me.'

'Well, people have different ways, but I understand that nobody can see Miss Vincy and Mr Lydgate together without taking them to be engaged. However, it is not my business. Shall I put up the pattern of mittens?'

After this Mrs Bulstrode drove to her niece with a mind newly weighted. She was herself handsomely dressed, but she noticed with a little more regret than usual that Rosamond, who was just come in and met her in walking-dress, was almost as expensively equipped. Mrs Bulstrode was a feminine, smaller edition of her brother, and had none of her husband's low-toned pallor. She had a good honest glance and used no circumlocution.

'You are alone, I see, my dear,' she said, as they entered the drawing-room together, looking round gravely. Rosamond felt sure that her aunt had something particular to say, and they sat down near each other. Nevertheless, the quilling inside Rosamond's bonnet was so charming that it was impossible not to desire the same kind of thing for Kate, and Mrs Bulstrode's eyes, which were rather fine, rolled round that ample quilled circuit, while she spoke.

'I have just heard something about you that has surprised me very much, Rosamond.'

'What is that, aunt?' Rosamond's eyes also were roaming over her aunt's large embroidered collar.

'I can hardly believe it – that you should be engaged without my knowing it – without your father's telling me.'

Here Mrs Bulstrode's eyes finally rested on Rosamond's, who blushed deeply, and said: 'I am not engaged, aunt.'

'How is it that everyone says so, then – that it is the town's talk?'

'The town's talk is of very little consequence, I think,' said Rosamond, inwardly gratified.

'Oh, my dear, be more thoughtful: don't despise your neighbours so. Remember you are turned twenty-two now, and you will have no fortune: your father, I am sure, will not be able to spare you anything. Mr Lydgate is very intellectual and clever; I know there is an attraction in that. I like talking to such men myself; and your uncle finds him very useful. But the profession is a poor one here. To be sure, this life is not everything; but it is seldom a medical man has true religious views, there is too much pride of intellect. And you are not fit to marry a poor man.'

'Mr Lydgate is not a poor man, aunt. He has very high connections.'

'He told me himself he was poor.'

'That is because he is used to people who have a high style of living.'

'My dear Rosamond, you must not think of living in high style.'

Rosamond looked down and played with her reticule. She was not a fiery young lady and had no sharp answers, but she meant to live as she pleased.

'Then it is really true?' said Mrs Bulstrode, looking very earnestly at her niece. 'You are thinking of Mr Lydgate: there is some understanding between you, though your father doesn't know. Be open, my dear Rosamond: Mr Lydgate has really made you an offer?'

Poor Rosamond's feelings were very unpleasant. She had been quite easy as to Lydgate's feeling and intention, but now when her aunt put this question she did not like being unable to say Yes. Her pride was hurt, but her habitual control of manner helped her.

'Pray excuse me, aunt. I would rather not speak on the subject.'

'You would not give your heart to a man without a decided prospect, I trust, my dear. And think of the two excellent offers I know of that you have refused! – and one still within your reach, if you will not throw it away. I knew a very great beauty who married badly at last, by doing so. Mr Ned Plymdale is a nice young man – some might think good looking; and an only son; and a large business of that kind is better than a profession. Not that marrying is everything. I would have you seek first the kingdom of God. But a girl should keep her heart within her own power.'

'I should never give it to Mr Ned Plymdale, if it were. I have already refused him. If I loved, I should love at once and without change,' said Rosamond, with a great sense of being a romantic heroine, and playing the part prettily.

'I see how it is, my dear,' said Mrs Bulstrode, in a melancholy voice, rising to go. 'You have allowed your affections to be engaged without return.'

'No, indeed, aunt,' said Rosamond, with emphasis.

'Then you are quite confident that Mr Lydgate has a serious attachment to you?'

Rosamond's cheeks by this time were persistently burning, and she felt much mortification. She chose to be silent, and her aunt went away all the more convinced.

Mr Bulstrode in things worldly and indifferent was disposed to do what his wife bade him, and she now, without telling her reasons, desired him on the next opportunity to find out in conversation with Mr Lydgate whether he had any intention of marrying soon. The result was a decided negative. Mr Bulstrode, on being cross-questioned, showed that Lydgate had spoken as no man would who had any attachment that could issue in matrimony. Mrs Bulstrode now felt that she had a serious duty before her, and she soon managed to arrange a tête-à-tête with Lydgate, in which she passed from enquiries about Fred Vincy's health, and expressions of her sincere anxiety for her brother's large family, to general remarks on the dangers which lay before young people with regard to their settlement in life. Young men were often wild and disappointing, making little return for the money spent on them, and a girl was exposed to many circumstances which might interfere with her prospects.

'Especially when she has great attractions, and her parents see much company,' said Mrs Bulstrode. 'Gentlemen pay her attention, and engross her all to themselves, for the mere pleasure of the moment, and that drives off others. I think it is a heavy responsibility, Mr Lydgate, to interfere with the prospects of any girl.' Here Mrs Bulstrode fixed her eyes on him, with an unmistakable purpose of warning, if not of rebuke.

'Clearly,' said Lydgate, looking at her – perhaps even staring a little in return. 'On the other hand, a man must be a great coxcomb to go about with a notion that he must not pay attention to a young lady lest she should fall in love with him, or lest others should think she must.'

'Oh, Mr Lydgate, you know well what your advantages are. You know that our young men here cannot cope with you. Where you frequent a house it may militate very much against a girl's making a desirable settlement in life, and prevent her from accepting offers even if they are made.'

Lydgate was less flattered by his advantage over the Middlemarch Orlandos than he was annoyed by the perception of Mrs Bulstrode's meaning. She felt that she had spoken as impressively as it was necessary to do, and that in using the superior word 'militate' she had thrown a noble drapery over a mass of particulars which were still evident enough.

Lydgate was fuming a little, pushed his hair back with one hand, felt curiously in his waistcoat-pocket with the other, and then stooped to beckon the tiny black spaniel, which had the insight to decline his hollow caresses. It would not have been decent to go away, because he had been dining with other guests, and had just taken tea. But Mrs Bulstrode, having no doubt that she had been understood, turned the conversation.

Solomon's Proverbs, I think, have omitted to say, that as the sore palate findeth grit, so an uneasy consciousness heareth innuendoes. The next day Mr Farebrother, parting from Lydgate in the street, supposed that they should meet at Vincy's in the evening. Lydgate answered curtly, no – he had work to do – he must give up going out in the evening.

'What, you are going to get lashed to the mast, eh, and are stopping your ears?' said the Vicar. 'Well, if you don't mean to be won by the sirens, you are right to take precautions in time.'

A few days before, Lydgate would have taken no notice of these words as anything more than the Vicar's usual way of putting things. They seemed now to convey an innuendo which confirmed the impression that he had been making a fool of himself and behaving so as to be misunderstood: not, he believed, by Rosamond herself; she, he felt sure, took everything as lightly as he intended it. She had an exquisite tact and insight in relation to all points of manners; but the people she lived among were blunderers and busybodies. However, the mistake should go no farther. He resolved – and kept his resolution – that he would not go to Mr Vincy's except on business.

Rosamond became very unhappy. The uneasiness first stirred by her aunt's questions grew and grew till at the end of ten days that she had not seen Lydgate, it grew into terror at the blank that might possibly come – into fore-boding of that ready, fatal sponge which so cheaply wipes out the hopes of mortals. The world would have a new dreariness for her, as a wilderness that a magician's spells had turned for a little while into a garden. She felt that she was beginning to know the pang of disappointed love, and that no other man could be the occasion of such delightful aerial building as she had been enjoying for the last six months, Poor Rosamond lost her appetite and felt as forlorn as Ariadne – as a charming stage Ariadne left behind with all her boxes full of costumes and no hope of a coach.

There are many wonderful mixtures in the world which are all alike called love, and claim the privileges of a sublime rage which is an apology for every-thing (in literature and the drama). Happily Rosamond did not think of committing any desperate act: she plaited her fair hair as beautifully as usual, and kept herself proudly calm. Her most cheerful supposition was that her aunt Bulstrode had interfered in some way to hinder Lydgate's visits: everything was better than a spontaneous indifference in him. Anyone who imagines ten days too short a time – not for falling into leanness, lightness, or other measurable effects of passion, but – for the whole spiritual circuit of alarmed conjecture and disappointment, is ignorant of what can go on in the elegant leisure of a young lady's mind.

On the eleventh day, however, Lydgate when leaving Stone Court was requested by Mrs Vincy to let her husband know that there was a marked change in Mr Featherstone's health, and that she wished him to come to Stone Court on that day. Now Lydgate might have called at the warehouse, or might have written a message on a leaf of his pocketbook and left it at the door. Yet these simple devices apparently did not occur to him, from which we may conclude that he had no strong objection to calling at the house at an hour when Mr Vincy was not at home, and leaving the message with Miss Vincy. A man may, from various motives, decline to give his company, but perhaps not even a sage would be gratified that nobody missed him. It would be a graceful, easy way of piecing on the new habits to the old, to have a few playful words with Rosamond about his resistance to dissipation, and his firm resolve to take long fasts even from sweet sounds. It must be confessed, also, that momentary speculations as to all the possible grounds for Mrs Bulstrode's hints had managed to get woven like slight clinging hairs into the more substantial web of his thoughts.

Miss Vincy was alone, and blushed so deeply when Lydgate came in that he felt a corresponding embarrassment, and instead of any playfulness, he began at once to speak of his reason for calling, and to beg her, almost formally, to deliver the message to her father. Rosamond, who at the first moment felt as if her happiness were returning, was keenly hurt by Lydgate's manner; her blush had departed, and she assented coldly, without adding an unnecessary word, some trivial chain-work which she had in her hands enabling her to avoid looking at Lydgate higher than his chin. In all failures, the beginning is certainly the half of the whole. After sitting two long moments while he moved his whip and could say nothing, Lydgate rose to go, and Rosamond, made nervous by her struggle between mortification and the wish not to betray it, dropped her chain as if startled, and rose too, mechanically. Lydgate instantaneously stooped to pick up the chain. When he rose he was very near to a lovely little face set on a fair long neck which he had been used to see turning about under the most perfect management of self-contented grace. But as he raised his eyes now he saw a certain helpless quivering which touched him quite newly, and made him look at Rosamond with a questioning flash. At this moment she was as natural as she had ever been when she was five years old: she felt that her tears had risen, and it was no use to try to do anything else than let them stay like water on a blue flower or let them fall over her cheeks, even as they would.

That moment of naturalness was the crystallising feather-touch: it shook flirtation into love. Remember that the ambitious man who was looking at those Forget-me-nots under the water was very warm-hearted and rash. He did not know where the chain went; an idea had thrilled through the recesses within him which had a miraculous effect in raising the power of passionate love lying buried there in no sealed sepulchre, but under the lightest, easily pierced mould. His words were quite abrupt and awkward; but the tone made them sound like an ardent, appealing avowal.

'What is the matter? you are distressed. Tell me – pray.'

Rosamond had never been spoken to in such tones before. I am not sure that she knew what the words were; but she looked at Lydgate and the tears fell over her cheeks. There could have been no more complete answer than that silence, and Lydgate, forgetting everything else, completely mastered by the outrush of tenderness at the sudden belief that this sweet young creature depended on him for her joy, actually put his arms round her, folding her gently and protectingly – he was used to being gentle with the weak and suffering – and kissed each of the two large tears. This was a strange way of arriving at an understanding, but it was a short way. Rosamond was not angry, but she moved backward a little in timid happiness, and Lydgate could now sit near her and speak less incompletely. Rosamond had to make her little confession, and he poured out words of gratitude and tenderness with impulsive lavishment. In half an hour he left the house an engaged man, whose soul was not his own, but the woman's to whom he had bound himself.

He came again in the evening to speak with Mr Vincy, who, just returned from Stone Court, was feeling sure that it would not be long before he heard of Mr Featherstone's demise. The felicitous word 'demise', which had seasonably occurred to him, had raised his spirits even above their usual evening pitch. The right word is always a power, and communicates its definiteness to our action. Considered as a demise, old Featherstone's death assumed a merely legal aspect, so that Mr Vincy could tap his snuffbox over it and be jovial, without even an intermittent affectation of solemnity; and Mr Vincy hated both solemnity and affectation. Who was ever awestruck about a testator, or sang a hymn on the title to real property? Mr Vincy was inclined to take a jovial view of all things that evening: he even observed to Lydgate that Fred had got the family constitution after all, and would soon be as fine a fellow as ever again; and when his approbation of Rosamond's engagement was asked for, he gave it with astonishing facility, passing at once to general remarks on the desirableness of matrimony for young men and maidens, and apparently deducing from the whole the appropriateness of a little more punch.

Chapter 32

They'll take suggestion as a cat laps milk.

SHAKESPEARE, *The Tempest*

The triumphant confidence of the Mayor founded on Mr Featherstone's insistent demand that Fred and his mother should not leave him, was a feeble emotion compared with all that was agitating the breasts of the old man's blood-relations, who naturally manifested more their sense of the family tie and were more visibly numerous now that he had become bedridden. Naturally: for when 'poor Peter' had occupied his armchair in the wainscoted parlour, no assiduous beetles for whom the cook prepares boiling water could have been less welcome on a hearth which they had reasons for preferring, than those persons whose Featherstone blood was ill-nourished, not from penuriousness on their part, but from poverty. Brother Solomon and Sister Jane were rich, and the family candour and total abstinence from false politeness with which they were always received seemed to them no argument that their brother in the solemn act of making his will would overlook the superior claims of wealth. Themselves at least he had never been unnatural enough to banish from his house, and it seemed hardly eccentric that he should have kept away Brother Jonah, Sister Martha, and the rest, who had no shadow of such claims. They knew Peter's maxim, that money was a good egg, and should be laid in a warm nest.

But Brother Jonah, Sister Martha, and all the needy exiles, held a different point of view. Probabilities are as various as the faces to be seen at will in fretwork or paperhangings: every form is there, from Jupiter to Judy, if you only look with creative inclination. To the poorer and least favoured it seemed likely that since Peter had done nothing for them in his life, he would remember them at the last. Jonah argued that men like to make a surprise of their wills, while Martha said that nobody need be surprised if he left the best part of his money to those who least expected it. Also it was not to be thought but that an own brother 'lying there' with dropsy in his legs must come to feel that blood was thicker than water, and if he didn't alter his will, he might have money by him. At any rate some blood-relations should be on the premises and on the watch against those who were hardly relations at all. Such things had been known as forged wills and disputed wills, which seemed to have the golden-hazy advantage of somehow enabling non-legatees to live out of them. Again, those who were no blood-relations might be caught making away with things – and poor Peter 'lying there' helpless! Somebody should be on the watch. But in this conclusion they were at one with Solomon and Jane; also some nephews, nieces, and cousins, arguing with still greater subtilty as to what might be done by a man able to 'will away' his property and give himself large treats of oddity, felt in a handsome sort of way that there was a family interest to be attended to, and thought of Stone Court as a place which it would be nothing but right for them to visit. Sister Martha, otherwise Mrs Cranch, living with some wheeziness in the Chalky Flats, could not undertake the journey; but her son, as being poor Peter's own nephew, could represent her advantageously, and watch lest his uncle Jonah should make an unfair use of the improbable things which seemed likely to happen. In fact there was a general sense running in the Featherstone blood that everybody must watch everybody else, and that it would be well for everybody else to reflect that the Almighty was watching him.

Thus Stone Court continually saw one or other blood-relation alighting or departing, and Mary Garth had the unpleasant task of carrying their messages to Mr Featherstone, who would see none of them, and sent her down with the still more unpleasant task of telling them so. As manager of the household she felt bound to ask them in good provincial fashion to stay and eat; but she chose to consult Mrs Vincy on the point of extra downstairs consumption now that Mr Featherstone was laid up.

'Oh, my dear, you must do things handsomely where there's last illness and a property. God knows, I don't grudge them every ham in the house – only, save the best for the funeral. Have some stuffed veal always, and a fine cheese in cut. You must expect to keep open house in these last illnesses,' said liberal Mrs Vincy, once more of cheerful note and bright plumage.

But some of the visitors alighted and did not depart after the handsome treating to veal and ham. Brother Jonah, for example (there are such unpleasant people in most families; perhaps even in the highest aristocracy there are Brobdingnag specimens, gigantically in debt and bloated at greater expense) – Brother Jonah, I say, having come down in the world, was mainly supported by a calling which he was modest enough not to boast of, though it was much better than swindling either on exchange or turf, but which did not require his presence at Brassing so long as he had a good corner to sit in and a supply of food. He chose the kitchen-corner, partly because he liked it best, and partly because he did not want to sit with Solomon, concerning whom he had a strong brotherly opinion. Seated in a famous armchair and in his best suit, constantly within sight of good cheer, he had a comfortable consciousness of being on the premises, mingled with fleeting suggestions of Sunday and the bar at the Green Man; and he informed Mary Garth that he should not go out of reach of his brother Peter while that poor fellow was above ground. The troublesome ones in a family are usually either the wits or the idiots. Jonah was the wit among the Featherstones, and joked with the maidservants when they came about the hearth, but seemed to consider Miss Garth a suspicious character, and followed her with cold eyes.

Mary would have borne this one pair of eyes with comparative ease, but unfortunately there was young Cranch, who, having come all the way from the Chalky Flats to represent his mother and watch his uncle Jonah, also felt it his duty to stay and to sit chiefly in the kitchen to give his uncle company. Young Cranch was not exactly the balancing point between the wit and the idiot, – verging slightly towards the latter type, and squinting so as to leave everything in doubt about his sentiments except that they were not of a forcible character. When Mary Garth entered the kitchen and Mr Jonah Featherstone began to follow her with his cold detective eyes, young Cranch turning his head in the same direction seemed to insist on it that she should remark how he was squinting, as if he did it with design, like the gypsies when Borrow read the New Testament to them. This was rather too much for poor Mary; sometimes it made her bilious, sometimes it upset her gravity. One day that she had an opportunity she could not resist describing the kitchen scene to Fred, who would not be hindered from immediately going to see it, affecting simply to pass through. But no sooner did he face the four eyes than he had to rush through the nearest door, which happened to lead to the dairy, and there under the high roof and among the pans he gave way to laughter which made a hollow resonance perfectly audible in the kitchen. He fled by another doorway, but Mr Jonah, who had not before seen Fred's white complexion, long legs, and pinched delicacy of face, prepared many sarcasms in which these points of appearance were wittily combined with the lowest moral attributes.

'Why, Tom, *you* don't wear such gentlemanly trousers – you haven't got half such fine long legs,' said Jonah to his nephew, winking at the same time, to imply that there was something more in these statements than their undeniableness. Tom looked at his legs, but left it uncertain whether he preferred his moral advantages to a more vicious length of limb and reprehensible gentility of trouser.

In the large wainscoted parlour too there were constantly pairs of eyes on the watch, and own relatives eager to be 'sitters-up'. Many came, lunched, and departed, but Brother Solomon and the lady who had been Jane Featherstone for twenty-five years before she was Mrs Waule found it good to be there every day for hours, without other calculable occupation than that of observing the cunning Mary Garth (who was so deep that she could be found out in nothing) and giving occasional dry wrinkly indications of crying – as if capable of torrents in a wetter season – at the thought that they were not allowed to go into Mr Featherstone's room. For the old man's dislike of his own family seemed to get stronger as he got less able to amuse himself by saying biting things to them. Too languid to sting, he had the more venom refluent in his blood.

Not fully believing the message sent through Mary Garth, they had presented themselves together within the door of the bedroom, both in black – Mrs Waule having a white handkerchief partially unfolded in her hand – and both with faces in a sort of half-mourning purple; while Mrs Vincy with her pink cheeks and pink ribbons flying was actually administering a cordial to their own brother, and the light-complexioned Fred, his short hair curling as might be expected in a gambler's, was lolling at his ease in a large chair.

Old Featherstone no sooner caught sight of these funereal figures appearing in spite of his orders than rage came to strengthen him more successfully than the cordial. He was propped up on a bed-rest, and always had his gold-headed stick lying by him. He seized it now and swept it backwards and forwards in as large an area as he could, apparently to ban these ugly spectres, crying in a hoarse sort of screech: 'Back, back, Mrs Waule! Back, Solomon!'

'Oh, Brother Peter,' Mrs Waule began – but Solomon put his hand before her repressingly. He was a large-cheeked man, nearly seventy, with small furtive eyes, and was not only of much blander temper but thought himself much deeper than his brother Peter; indeed not likely to be deceived in any of his fellow-men, inasmuch as they could not well be more greedy and deceitful than he suspected them of being. Even the invisible powers, he thought, were likely to be soothed by a bland parenthesis here and there – coming from a man of property, who might have been as impious as others.

'Brother Peter,' he said, in a wheedling yet gravely official tone, 'it's nothing but right I should speak to you about the Three Crofts and the Manganese. The Almighty knows what I've got on my mind . . .'

'Then He knows more than I want to know,' said Peter, laying down his stick with a show of truce which had a threat in it too, for he reversed the stick so as to make the gold handle a club in case of closer fighting, and looked hard at Solomon's bald head.

'There's things you might repent of, Brother, for want of speaking to me,' said Solomon, not advancing, however. 'I could sit up with you tonight, and Jane with me, willingly, and you might take your own time to speak, or let me speak.'

'Yes, I shall take my own time – you needn't offer me yours,' said Peter.

'But you can't take your own time to die in, Brother,' began Mrs Waule, with her usual woolly tone. 'And when you lie speechless you may be tired of having strangers about you, and you may think of me and my children – ' but here her voice broke under the touching thought which she was attributing to her speechless brother; the mention of ourselves being naturally affecting.

'No, I shan't', said old Featherstone, contradictiously. 'I shan't think of any of you. I've made my will, I tell you, I've made my will.' Here he turned his head towards Mrs Vincy, and swallowed some more of his cordial.

'Some people would be ashamed to fill up a place belonging by rights to others,' said Mrs Waule, turning her narrow eyes in the same direction.

'Oh, Sister,' said Solomon, with ironical softness, 'you and me are not fine, and handsome, and clever enough: we must be humble and let smart people push themselves before us.'

Fred's spirit could not bear this: rising and looking at Mr Featherstone, he said, 'Shall my mother and I leave the room, sir, that you may be alone with your friends?'

'Sit down, I tell you,' said old Featherstone, snappishly. 'Stop where you are. Goodbye, Solomon,' he added, trying to wield his stick again, but failing now that he had reversed the handle. 'Goodbye, Mrs Waule. Don't you come again.'

'I shall be downstairs, Brother, whether or no,' said Solomon. 'I shall do my duty, and it remains to be seen what the Almighty will allow.'

'Yes, in property going out of families,' said Mrs Waule, in continuation, – 'and where there's steady young men to carry on. But I pity them who are not such, and I pity their mothers. Goodbye, Brother Peter.'

'Remember, I'm the eldest after you, Brother, and prospered from the first, just as you did, and have got land already by the name of Featherstone,' said Solomon, relying much on that reflection, as one which might be suggested in the watches of the night. 'But I bid you goodbye for the present.'

Their exit was hastened by their seeing old Mr Featherstone pull his wig on each side and shut his eyes with his mouth-widening grimace, as if he were determined to be deaf and blind.

None the less they came to Stone Court daily and sat below at the post of duty, sometimes carrying on a slow dialogue in an undertone in which the observation and response were so far apart, that anyone hearing them might have imagined himself listening to speaking automata, in some doubt whether the ingenious mechanism would really work, or wind itself up for a long time in order to stick and be silent. Solomon and Jane would have been sorry to be quick: what that led to might be seen on the other side of the wall in the person of Brother Jonah.

But their watch in the wainscoted parlour was sometimes varied by the presence of other guests from far or near. Now that Peter Featherstone was upstairs, his property could be discussed with all that local enlightenment to be found on the spot: some rural and Middlemarch neighbours expressed much agreement with the family and sympathy with their interest against the Vincys, and feminine visitors were even moved to tears, in conversation with Mrs Waule, when they recalled the fact that they themselves had been disappointed in times past by codicils and marriages for spite on the part of ungrateful elderly gentlemen, who, it might have supposed, had been spared for something better. Such conversation paused suddenly, like an organ when the bellows are let drop, if Mary Garth came into the room; and all eyes were turned on her as a possible legatee, or one who might get access to iron chests.

But the younger men who were relatives or connections of the family, were disposed to admire her in this problematic light, as a girl who showed much conduct, and who among all the chances that were flying might turn out to be at least a moderate prize. Hence she had her share of compliments and polite attentions.

Especially from Mr Borthrop Trumbull, a distinguished bachelor and auctioneer of those parts, much concerned in the sale of land and cattle: a public character, indeed, whose name was seen on widely distributed placards, and who might reasonably be sorry for those who did not know of him. He was second cousin to Peter Featherstone, and had been treated by him with more amenity than any other relative, being useful in matters of business; and in that programme of his funeral which the old man had himself dictated, he had been named as a Bearer. There was no odious cupidity in Mr Borthrop Trumbull – nothing more than a sincere sense of his own merit, which, he was aware, in case of rivalry might tell against competitors; so that if Peter Featherstone, who so far as he, Trumbull, was concerned, had behaved like as good a soul as ever breathed, should have done anything handsome by him, all he could say was, that he had never fished and fawned, but had advised him to the best of his experience, which now extended over twenty years from the time of his apprenticeship at fifteen, and was likely to yield a knowledge of no surreptitious kind. His admiration was far from being confined to himself, but was accustomed professionally as well as privately to delight in estimating things at a high rate. He was an amateur of superior phrases, and never used poor language without immediately correcting himself, which was fortunate, as he was rather loud, and given to predominate, standing or walking about frequently, pulling down his waistcoat with the air of a man who is very much of his own opinion, trimming himself rapidly with his forefinger, and marking each new series in these movements by a busy play with his large seals. There was occasionally a little fierceness in his demeanour, but it was directed chiefly against false opinion, of which there is so much to correct in the world that a man of some reading and experience necessarily has his patience tried. He felt that the Featherstone family generally was of limited understanding, but being a man of the world and a public character, took everything as a matter of course, and even went to converse with Mr Jonah and young Cranch in the kitchen, not doubting that he had impressed the latter greatly by his leading questions concerning the Chalky Flats. If anybody had observed that Mr Borthrop Trumbull, being an auctioneer, was bound to know the nature of everything, he would have smiled and trimmed himself silently with the sense that he came pretty near that. On the whole, in an auctioneering way, he was an honourable man, not ashamed of his business, and feeling that 'the celebrated Peel, now Sir Robert', if introduced to him, would not fail to recognise his importance.

'I don't mind if I have a slice of that ham, and a glass of that ale, Miss Garth, if you will allow me,' he said, coming into the parlour at half-past eleven, after having had the exceptional privilege of seeing old Featherstone, and standing with his back to the fire between Mrs Waule and Solomon. 'It's not necessary for you to go out; – let me ring the bell.'

'Thank you,' said Mary, 'I have an errand.'

'Well, Mr Trumbull, you're highly favoured,' said Mrs Waule.

'What, seeing the old man?' said the auctioneer, playing with his seals dispassionately. 'Ah, you see he has relied on me considerably,' Here he pressed his lips together, and frowned meditatively.

'Might anybody ask what their brother has been saying?' said Solomon, in a soft tone of humility, in which he had a sense of luxurious cunning, he being a rich man and not in need of it.

'Oh yes, anybody may ask,' said Mr Trumbull, with loud and good-humoured though cutting sarcasm. 'Anybody may interrogate. Anyone may give their remarks an interrogative turn,' he continued, his sonorousness rising with his style. 'This is constantly done by good speakers, even when they anticipate no answer. It is what we call a figure of speech – speech at a high figure, as one may say.' The eloquent auctioneer smiled at his own ingenuity.

'I shouldn't be sorry to hear he'd remembered *you*, Mr Trumbull,' said Solomon. 'I never was against the deserving. It's the undeserving I'm against.'

'Ah, there it is, you see, there it is,' said Mr Trumbull, significantly. 'It can't be denied that undeserving people have been legatees, and even residuary legatees. It is so, with testamentary dispositions.' Again he pursed up his lips and frowned a little.

'Do you mean to say for certain, Mr Trumbull, that my brother has left his land away from our family?' said Mrs Waule, on whom, as an unhopeful woman, those long words had a depressing effect.

'A man might as well turn his land into charity land at once as leave it to some people,' observed Solomon, his sister's question having drawn no answer.

'What, Blue-Coat land?' said Mrs Waule, again. 'Oh, Mr Trumbull, you never can mean to say that. It would be flying in the face of the Almighty that's prospered him.'

While Mrs Waule was speaking, Mr Borthrop Trumbull walked away from the fireplace towards the window, patrolling with his forefinger round the inside of his stock, then along his whiskers and the curves of his hair. He now walked to Miss Garth's work-table, opened a book which lay there, and read the title aloud with pompous emphasis as if he were offering it for sale: 'Anne of Geierstein' (pronounced Jeersteen) 'or the Maiden of the Mist, by the Author of Waverley.' Then turning the page, he began sonorously – 'The course of four centuries has well-nigh elapsed since the series of events which are related in the following chapters took place on the Continent.' He pronounced the last truly admirable word with the accent on the last syllable, not as unaware of vulgar usage, but feeling that this novel delivery enhanced the sonorous beauty which his reading had given to the whole.

And now the servant came in with the tray, so that the moments for answering Mrs Waule's question had gone by safely, while she and Solomon, watching Mr Trumbull's movements, were thinking that high learning interfered sadly with serious affairs. Mr Borthrop Trumbull really knew nothing about old Feather-stone's will; but he could hardly have been brought to declare any ignorance unless he had been arrested for misprision of treason.

'I shall take a mere mouthful of ham and a glass of ale,' he said, reassuringly. 'As a man with public business, I take a snack when I can. I will back this ham,' he added, after swallowing some morsels with alarming haste, 'against any ham in the three kingdoms. In my opinion it is better than the hams at Freshitt Hall – and I think I am a tolerable judge.'

'Some don't like so much sugar in their hams,' said Mrs Waule. 'But my poor brother would always have sugar.'

'If any person demands better, he is at liberty to do so; but, God bless me, what an aroma! I should be glad to buy-in that quality, I know. There is some gratification to a gentleman' here Mr Trumbull's voice conveyed an emotional remonstrance – 'in having this kind of ham set on his table.'

He pushed aside his plate, poured out his glass of ale and drew his chair a little forward, profiting by the occasion to look at the inner side of his legs, which he stroked approvingly – Mr Trumbull having all those less frivolous airs and gestures which distinguish the predominant races of the north.

'You have an interesting work there, I see, Miss Garth,' he observed, when Mary re-entered. 'It is by the author of Waverley: that is Sir Walter Scott. I have bought one of his works myself – a very nice thing, a very superior publication, entitled Ivanhoe. You will not get any writer to beat him in a hurry, I think – he will not, in my opinion, be speedily surpassed. I have just been reading a portion at the commencement of Anne of Jeersteen. It commences well.' (Things never began with Mr Borthrop Trumbull: they always commenced, both in private life and on his handbills.) 'You are a reader, I see. Do you subscribe to our Middlemarch library?'

'No,' said Mary. 'Mr Fred Vincy brought this book.'

'I am a great bookman myself,' returned Mr Trumbull. 'I have no less than two hundred volumes in calf, and I flatter myself they are well selected. Also pictures by Murillo, Rubens, Teniers, Titian, Vandyck, and others. I shall be happy to lend you any work you like to mention, Miss Garth.'

'I am much obliged,' said Mary, hastening away again, 'but I have little time for reading.'

'I should say my brother has done something for *her* in his will,' said Mr Solomon, in a very low undertone, when she had shut the door behind her, pointing with his head towards the absent Mary.

'His first wife was a poor match for him, though,' said Mrs Waule. 'She brought him nothing: and this young woman is only her niece. And very proud. And my brother has always paid her wage.'

'A sensible girl though, in my opinion,' said Mr Trumbull, finishing his ale and starting up with an emphatic adjustment of his waistcoat. 'I have observed her when she has been mixing medicine in drops. She minds what she is doing, sir. That is a great point in a woman, and a great point for our friend upstairs, poor dear old soul. A man whose life is of any value should think of his wife as a nurse: that is what I should do, if I married; and I believe I have lived single long enough not to make a mistake in that line. Some men must marry to elevate themselves a little, but when I am in need of that, I hope someone will tell me so – I hope some individual will apprise me of the fact. I wish you good-morning, Mrs Waule. Good-morning, Mr Solomon. I trust we shall meet under less melancholy auspices.'

When Mr Trumbull had departed with a fine bow, Solomon, leaning forward, observed to his sister, 'You may depend, Jane, my brother has left that girl a lumping sum.'

'Anybody would think so, from the way Mr Trumbull talks,' said Jane. Then, after a pause, 'He talks as if my daughters wasn't to be trusted to give drops.'

'Auctioneers talk wild,' said Solomon, 'Not but what Trumbull has made money.'

Chapter 33

Close up his eyes and draw the curtain close;
And let us all to meditation.
SHAKESPEARE, *Henry VI, Part 2*

That night after twelve o'clock Mary Garth relieved the watch in Mr Feather-stone's room, and sat there alone through the small hours. She often chose this task, in which she found some pleasure, notwithstanding the old man's testiness whenever he demanded her attentions. There were intervals in which she could sit perfectly still, enjoying the outer stillness and the subdued light. The red fire with its gently audible movement seemed like a solemn existence calmly independent of the petty passions, the imbecile desires, the straining after worthless uncertainties, which were daily moving her contempt. Mary was fond of her own thoughts, and could amuse herself well sitting in twilight with her hands in her lap; for, having early had strong reason to believe that things were not likely to be arranged for her peculiar satisfaction, she wasted no time in astonishment and annoyance at that fact. And she had already come to take life very much as a comedy in which she had a proud, nay, a generous resolution not to act the mean or treacherous part. Mary might have become cynical if she had not had parents whom she honoured, and a well of affectionate gratitude within her, which was all the fuller because she had learned to make no unreasonable claims.

She sat tonight revolving, as she was wont, the scenes of the day, her lips often curling with amusement at the oddities to which her fancy added fresh drollery: people were so ridiculous with their illusions, carrying their fools' caps unawares, thinking their own lies opaque while everybody else's were transparent, making themselves exceptions to everything, as if when all the world looked yellow under a lamp they alone were rosy. Yet there were some illusions under Mary's eyes which were not quite comic to her. She was secretly convinced, though she had no other grounds than her close observation of old Featherstone's nature, that in spite of his fondness for having the Vincys about him, they were as likely to be disappointed as any of the relations whom he kept at a distance. She had a good deal of disdain for Mrs Vincy's evident alarm lest she and Fred should be alone together, but it did not hinder her from thinking anxiously of the way in which Fred would be affected, if it should turn out that his uncle had left him as poor as ever. She could make a butt of Fred when he was present, but she did not enjoy his follies when he was absent.

Yet she liked her thoughts: a vigorous young mind not overbalanced by passion, finds a good in making acquaintance with life, and watches its own powers with interest. Mary had plenty of merriment within.

Her thought was not veined by any solemnity or pathos about the old man on the bed: such sentiments are easier to affect than to feel about an aged creature whose life is not visibly anything but a remnant of vices. She had always seen the most disagreeable side of Mr Featherstone: he was not proud of her, and she was only useful to him. To be anxious about a soul that is always snapping at you must be left to the saints of the earth; and Mary was not one of them. She had never returned him a harsh word, and had waited on him faithfully: that was her utmost. Old Featherstone himself was not in the least anxious about his soul, and had declined to see Mr Tucker on the subject.

Tonight he had not once snapped, and for the first hour or two he lay remarkably still, until at last Mary heard him rattling his bunch of keys against the tin box which he always kept in the bed beside him. About three o'clock he said, with remarkable distinctness, 'Missy, come here!'

Mary obeyed and found that he had already drawn the tin box from under the clothes, though he usually asked to have this done for him; and he had selected the key. He now unlocked the box, and, drawing from it another key, looked straight at her with eyes that seemed to have recovered all their sharpness and said, 'How many of 'em are in the house?'

'You mean of your own relations, sir,' said Mary, well used to the old man's way of speech. He nodded slightly and she went on.

'Mr Jonah Featherstone and young Cranch are sleeping here.'

'Oh ay, they stick, do they? and the rest – they come every day, I'll warrant – Solomon and Jane, and all the young uns? They come peeping, and counting and casting up?'

'Not all of them every day. Mr Solomon and Mrs Waule are here every day, and the others come often.'

The old man listened with a grimace while she spoke, and then said, relaxing his face, 'The more fools they. You hearken, Missy. It's three o'clock in the morning, and I've got all my faculties as well as ever I had in my life. I know all my property, and where the money's put out, and everything. And I've made everything ready to change my mind, and do as I like at the last. Do you hear, Missy? I've got my faculties.'

'Well, sir?' said Mary, quietly.

He now lowered his tone with an air of deeper cunning. 'I've made two wills, and I'm going to burn one. Now you do as I tell you. This is the key of my iron chest, in the closet there. You push well at the side of the brass plate at the top, till it goes like a bolt: then you can put the key in the front lock and turn it. See and do that; and take out the topmost paper – Last Will and Testament – big printed.'

'No, sir,' said Mary, in a firm voice, 'I cannot do that.'

'Not do it? I tell you, you must,' said the old man, his voice beginning to shake under the shock of this resistance.

'I cannot touch your iron chest or your will. I must refuse to do anything that might lay me open to suspicion.'

'I tell you, I'm in my right mind. Shan't I do as I like at the last? I made two wills on purpose. Take the key, I say.'

'No, sir, I will not,' said Mary, more resolutely still. Her repulsion was getting stronger.

'I tell you, there's no time to lose.'

'I cannot help that, sir. I will not let the close of your life soil the beginning of mine. I will not touch your iron chest or your will.' She moved to a little distance from the bedside.

The old man paused with a blank stare for a little while, holding the one key erect on the ring; then with an agitated jerk he began to work with his bony left hand at emptying the tin box before him.

'Missy,' he began to say, hurriedly, 'look here! take the money – the notes and gold – look here – take it – you shall have it all – do as I tell you.'

He made an effort to stretch out the key towards her as far as possible, and Mary again retreated.

'I will not touch your key or your money, sir. Pray don't ask me to do it again. If you do, I must go and call your brother,'

He let his hand fall, and for the first time in her life Mary saw old Peter Featherstone begin to cry childishly. She said, in as gentle a tone as she could command, 'Pray put up your money, sir'; and then went away to her seat by the fire, hoping this would help to convince him that it was useless to say more. Presently he rallied and said eagerly; 'Look here, then. Call the young chap. Call Fred Vincy.'

Mary's heart began to beat more quickly. Various ideas rushed through her mind as to what the burning of a second will might imply. She had to make a difficult decision in a hurry.

'I will call him, if you will let me call Mr Jonah and others with him.'

'Nobody else, I say. The young chap. I shall do as I like.'

'Wait till broad daylight, sir, when everyone is stirring. Or let me call Simmons now, to go and fetch the lawyer. He can be here in less than two hours.'

'Lawyer? What do I want with the lawyer? Nobody shall know – I say, nobody shall know. I shall do as I like.'

'Let me call someone else, sir,' said Mary, persuasively. She did not like her position – alone with the old man, who seemed to show a strange flaring of nervous energy which enabled him to speak again and again without falling into his usual cough; yet she desired not to push unnecessarily the contradiction which agitated him. 'Let me, pray, call someone else.'

'You let me alone, I say. Look here, Missy. Take the money. You'll never have the chance again. It's pretty nigh two hundred – there's more in the box, and nobody knows how much there was. Take it and do as I tell you.'

Mary, standing by the fire, saw its red light falling on the old man, propped up on his pillows and bed-rest, with his bony hand holding out the key, and the money lying on the quilt before him. She never forgot that vision of a man wanting to do as he liked at the last. But the way in which he had put the offer of the money urged her to speak with harder resolution than ever.

'It is of no use, sir. I will not do it. Put up your money. I will not touch your money. I will do anything else I can to comfort you; but I will not touch your keys or your money.'

'Anything else – anything else!' said old Featherstone, with hoarse rage, which, as if in a nightmare, tried to be loud, and yet was only just audible. 'I want nothing else. You come here, you come here.'

Mary approached him cautiously, knowing him too well. She saw him dropping his keys and trying to grasp his stick, while he looked at her like an aged hyena, the muscles of his face getting distorted with the effort of his hand. She paused at a safe distance.

'Let me give you some cordial,' she said, quietly, 'and try to compose yourself. You will perhaps go to sleep. And tomorrow by daylight you can do as you like.'

He lifted the stick, in spite of her being beyond his reach, and threw it with a hard effort which was but impotence. It fell, slipping over the foot of the bed. Mary let it lie, and retreated to her chair by the fire. By and by she would go to him with the cordial. Fatigue would make him passive. It was getting towards the chillest moment of the morning, the fire had got low, and she could see through the chink between the moreen window-curtains the light whitened by the blind. Having put some wood on the fire and thrown a shawl over her, she sat down, hoping that Mr Featherstone might now fall asleep. If she went near him the irritation might be kept up. He had said nothing after throwing the stick, but she had seen him taking his keys again and laying his right hand on the money. He did not put it up, however, and she thought that he was dropping off to sleep.

But Mary herself began to be more agitated by the remembrance of what she had gone through, than she had been by the reality – questioning those acts of hers which had come imperatively and excluded all question in the critical moment.

Presently the dry wood sent out a flame which illuminated every crevice, and Mary saw that the old man was lying quietly with his head turned a little on one side. She went towards him with inaudible steps, and thought that his face looked strangely motionless; but the next moment the movement of the flame communicating itself to all objects made her uncertain. The violent beating of her heart rendered her perceptions so doubtful that even when she touched him and listened for his breathing, she could not trust her conclusions. She went to the window and gently propped aside the curtain and blind, so that the still light of the sky fell on the bed.

The next moment she ran to the bell and rang it energetically. In a very little while there was no longer any doubt that Peter Featherstone was dead, with his right hand clasping the keys, and his left hand lying on the heap of notes and gold.

BOOK FOUR

Three Love Problems

Chapter 34

1st Gent.	Such men as this are feathers, chips, and straws,
	Carry no weight, no force.
2nd Gent.	But levity
	Is casual too, and makes the sum of weight.
	For power finds its place in lack of power;
	Advance is cession, and the driven ship
	May run aground because the helmsman's thought
	Lacked force to balance opposites.

It was on a morning of May that Peter Featherstone was buried. In the prosaic neighbourhood of Middlemarch, May was not always warm and sunny, and on this particular morning a chill wind was blowing the blossoms from the surrounding gardens on to the green mounds of Lowick churchyard. Swiftly moving clouds only now and then allowed a gleam to light up any object, whether ugly or beautiful, that happened to stand within its golden shower. In the churchyard the objects were remarkably various, for there was a little country crowd waiting to see the funeral. The news had spread that it was to be a 'big burying'; the old gentleman had left written directions about everything, and meant to have a funeral 'beyond his betters'. This was true; for old Featherstone had not been a Harpagon whose passions had all been devoured by the ever-lean and ever-hungry passion of saving, and who would drive a bargain with his undertaker beforehand. He loved money, but he also loved to spend it in gratifying his peculiar tastes, and perhaps he loved it best of all as a means of making others feel his power more or less uncomfortably. If anyone will here contend that there must have been traits of goodness in old Featherstone, I will not presume to deny this; but I must observe that goodness is of a modest nature, easily discouraged, and when much elbowed in early life by unabashed vices, is apt to retire into extreme privacy, so that it is more easily believed in by those who construct a selfish old gentleman theoretically, than by those who form the narrower judgements based on his personal acquaintance. In any case, he had been bent on having a handsome funeral, and on having persons 'bid' to it who would rather have stayed at home. He had even desired that female relatives should follow him to the grave, and poor sister Martha had taken a difficult journey for this purpose from the Chalky Flats. She and Jane would have been altogether cheered (in a tearful manner) by this sign that a brother who disliked seeing them while he was living had been prospectively fond of their presence when he should have become a testator, if the sign had not been made equivocal by being extended to Mrs Vincy, whose expense in handsome crape seemed to imply the most presumptuous hopes, aggravated by a bloom of complexion which told pretty plainly that she was not a blood-relation, but of that generally objectionable class called wife's kin.

We are all of us imaginative in some form or other, for images are the brood of desire; and poor old Featherstone, who laughed much at the way in which others cajoled themselves, did not escape the fellowship of illusion. In writing the programme for his burial he certainly did not make clear to himself that his pleasure in the little drama of which it formed a part was confined to anticipation. In chuckling over the vexations he could inflict by the rigid clutch of his dead hand, he inevitably mingled his consciousness with that livid stagnant presence, and so far as he was preoccupied with a future life, it was with one of gratification inside his coffin. Thus old Featherstone was imaginative, after his fashion.

However, the three mourning-coaches were filled according to the written orders of the deceased. There were pallbearers on horseback, with the richest scarves and hatbands, and even the under-bearers had trappings of woe which were of a good well-priced quality. The black procession, when dismounted, looked the larger for the smallness of the churchyard; the heavy human faces and the black draperies shivering in the wind seemed to tell of a world strangely incongruous with the lightly-dropping blossoms and the gleams of sunshine on the daisies. The clergyman who met the procession was Mr Cadwallader – also according to the request of Peter Featherstone, prompted as usual by peculiar reasons. Having a contempt for curates, whom he always called under-strappers, he was resolved to be buried by a beneficed clergyman. Mr Casaubon was out of the question, not merely because he declined duty of this sort, but because Featherstone had an especial dislike to him as the rector of his own parish, who had a lien on the land in the shape of tithe, also as the deliverer of morning sermons, which the old man, being in his pew and not at all sleepy, had been obliged to sit through with an inward snarl. He had an objection to a parson stuck up above his head preaching to him. But his relations with Mr Cadwallader had been of a different kind: the trout-stream which ran through Mr Casaubon's land took its course through Featherstone's also, so that Mr Cadwallader was a parson who had had to ask a favour instead of preaching. Moreover, he was one of the high gentry living four miles away from Lowick, and was thus exalted to an equal sky with the sheriff of the county and other dignities vaguely regarded as necessary to the system of things. There would be a satisfaction in being buried by Mr Cadwallader, whose very name offered a fine opportunity for pronouncing wrongly if you liked.

This distinction conferred on the Rector of Tipton and Freshitt was the reason why Mrs Cadwallader made one of the group that watched old Featherstone's funeral from an upper window of the manor. She was not fond of visiting that house, but she liked, as she said, to see collections of strange animals such as there would be at this funeral; and she had persuaded Sir James and the young Lady Chettam to drive the Rector and herself to Lowick in order that the visit might be altogether pleasant.

'I will go anywhere with you, Mrs Cadwallader,' Celia had said; 'but I don't like funerals.'

'Oh, my dear, when you have a clergyman in your family you must accommodate your tastes: I did that very early. When I married Humphrey I made up my mind to like sermons, and I set out by liking the end very much. That soon spread to the middle and the beginning, because I couldn't have the end without them.'

'No, to be sure not,' said the Dowager Lady Chettam, with stately emphasis.

The upper window from which the funeral could be well seen was in the room occupied by Mr Casaubon when he had been forbidden to work; but he had resumed nearly his habitual style of life now in spite of warnings and prescriptions, and after politely welcoming Mrs Cadwallader had slipped again into the library to chew a cud of erudite mistake about Cush and Mizraim.

But for her visitors Dorothea too might have been shut up in the library, and would not have witnessed this scene of old Featherstone's funeral, which, aloof as it seemed to be from the tenor of her life, always afterwards came back to her at the touch of certain sensitive points in memory, just as the vision of St Peter's at Rome was enwoven with moods of despondency. Scenes which make vital changes in our neighbours' lot are but the background of our own, yet, like a particular aspect of the fields and trees, they become associated for us with the epochs of our own history, and make a part of that unity which lies in the selection of our keenest consciousness.

The dreamlike association of something alien and ill-understood with the deepest secrets of her experience seemed to mirror that sense of loneliness which was due to the very ardour of Dorothea's nature. The country gentry of old time lived in a rarefied social air: dotted apart on their stations up the mountain they looked down with imperfect discrimination on the belts of thicker life below. And Dorothea was not at ease in the perspective and chilliness of that height.

'I shall not look any more,' said Celia, after the train had entered the church, placing herself behind her husband's elbow so that she could slyly touch his coat with her cheek. 'I dare say Dodo likes it: she is fond of melancholy things and ugly people.'

'I am fond of knowing something about the people I live among,' said Dorothea, who had been watching everything with the interest of a monk on his holiday tour. 'It seems to me we know nothing of our neighbours, unless they are cottagers. One is constantly wondering what sort of lives other people lead, and how they take things. I am quite obliged to Mrs Cadwallader for coming and calling me out of the library.'

'Quite right to feel obliged to me,' said Mrs Cadwallader. 'Your rich Lowick farmers are as curious as any buffaloes or bisons, and I dare say you don't half see them at church. They are quite different from your uncle's tenants or Sir James's – monsters – farmers without landlords – one can't tell how to class them.'

'Most of these followers are not Lowick people,' said Sir James; 'I suppose they are legatees from a distance, or from Middlemarch. Lovegood tells me the old fellow has left a good deal of money as well as land.'

'Think of that now! when so many younger sons can't dine at their own expense,' said Mrs Cadwallader. 'Ah,' turning round at the sound of the opening door, 'here is Mr Brooke. I felt that we were incomplete before, and here is the explanation. You are come to see this odd funeral, of course?'

'No, I came to look after Casaubon – to see how he goes on, you know. And to bring a little news – a little news, my dear,' said Mr Brooke, nodding at Dorothea as she came towards him. 'I looked into the library, and I saw Casaubon over his books. I told him it wouldn't do: I said, "This will never do, you know: think of your wife, Casaubon." And he promised me to come up. I didn't tell him my news: I said, he must come up.'

'Ah, now they are coming out of church,' Mrs Cadwallader exclaimed. 'Dear me, what a wonderfully mixed set! Mr Lydgate as doctor, I suppose. But that is really a good-looking woman, and the fair young man must be her son. Who are they, Sir James, do you know?'

'I see Vincy, the mayor of Middlemarch; they are probably his wife and son,' said Sir James, looking interrogatively at Mr Brooke, who nodded and said; 'Yes, a very decent family – a very good fellow is Vincy; a credit to the manufacturing interest. You have seen him at my house, you know.'

'Ah, yes: one of your secret committee,' said Mrs Cadwallader, provokingly.

'A coursing fellow, though,' said Sir James, with a fox-hunter's disgust.

'And one of those who suck the life out of the wretched hand-loom weavers in Tipton and Freshitt. That is how his family look so fair and sleek,' said Mrs Cadwallader. 'Those dark, purple-faced people are an excellent foil. Dear me, they are like a set of jugs! Do look at Humphrey: one might fancy him an ugly archangel towering above them in his white surplice.'

'It's a solemn thing, though, a funeral,' said Mr Brooke, 'if you take it in that light, you know.'

'But I am not taking it in that light. I can't wear my solemnity too often, else it will go to rags. It was time the old man died, and none of these people are sorry.'

'How piteous!' said Dorothea. 'This funeral seems to me the most dismal thing I ever saw. It is a blot on the morning. I cannot bear to think that anyone should die and leave no love behind.'

She was going to say more, but she saw her husband enter and seat himself a little in the background. The difference his presence made to her was not always a happy one: she felt that he often inwardly objected to her speech.

'Positively,' exclaimed Mrs Cadwallader, 'there is a new face come out from behind that broad man queerer than any of them: a little round head with bulging eyes – a sort of frog-face – do look. He must be of another blood, I think.'

'Let me see!' said Celia, with awakened curiosity, standing behind Mrs Cadwallader and leaning forward over her head. 'Oh, what an odd face!' Then with a quick change to another sort of surprised expression, she added, 'Why, Dodo, you never told me that Mr Ladislaw was come again!'

Dorothea felt a shock of alarm: everyone noticed her sudden paleness as she looked up immediately at her uncle, while Mr Casaubon looked at her.

'He came with me, you know; he is my guest – puts up with me at the

Grange,' said Mr Brooke, in his easiest tone, nodding at Dorothea, as if the announcement were just what she might have expected. 'And we have brought the picture at the top of the carriage. I knew you would be pleased with the surprise, Casaubon. There you are to the very life – as Aquinas, you know. Quite the right sort of thing. And you will hear young Ladislaw talk about it. He talks uncommonly well – points out this, that, and the other – knows art and everything of that kind – companionable, you know – is up with you in any track – what I've been wanting a long while.'

Mr Casaubon bowed with cold politeness, mastering his irritation, but only so far as to be silent. He remembered Will's letter quite as well as Dorothea did; he had noticed that it was not among the letters which had been reserved for him on his recovery, and secretly concluding that Dorothea had sent word to Will not to come to Lowick, he had shrunk with proud sensitiveness from ever recurring to the subject. He now inferred that she had asked her uncle to invite Will to the Grange; and she felt it impossible at that moment to enter into any explanation.

Mrs Cadwallader's eyes diverted from the churchyard, saw a good deal of dumb show which was not so intelligible to her as she could have desired, and could not repress the question, 'Who is Mr Ladislaw?'

'A young relative of Mr Casaubon's,' said Sir James, promptly. His good-nature often made him quick and clear-seeing in personal matters, and he had divined from Dorothea's glance at her husband that there was some alarm in her mind.

'A very nice young fellow – Casaubon has done everything for him,' explained Mr Brooke. 'He repays your expense in him, Casaubon,' he went on, nodding encouragingly. 'I hope he will stay with me a long while and we shall make something of my documents. I have plenty of ideas and facts, you know, and I can see he is just the man to put them into shape – remembers what the right quotations are, *omne tulit punctum*, and that sort of thing – gives subjects a kind of turn. I invited him some time ago when you were ill, Casaubon: Dorothea said you couldn't have anybody in the house, you know, and she asked me to write.'

Poor Dorothea felt that every word of her uncle's was about as pleasant as a grain of sand in the eye of Mr Casaubon. It would be altogether unfitting now to explain that she had not wished her uncle to invite Will Ladislaw. She could not in the least make clear to herself the reasons for her husband's dislike to his presence – a dislike painfully impressed on her by the scene in the library; but she felt the unbecomingness of saying anything that might convey a notion of it to others. Mr Casaubon, indeed, had not thoroughly represented those mixed reasons to himself; irritated feeling with him, as with all of us, seeking rather for justification than for self-knowledge. But he wished to repress outward signs, and only Dorothea could discern the changes in her husband's face before he observed with more of dignified bending and singsong than usual: 'You are exceedingly hospitable, my dear sir; and I owe you acknowledgments for exercising your hospitality towards a relative of mine.'

The funeral was ended now, and the churchyard was being cleared.

'Now you can see him, Mrs Cadwallader,' said Celia. 'He is just like a miniature of Mr Casaubon's aunt that hangs in Dorothea's boudoir – quite nice-looking.'

'A very pretty sprig,' said Mrs Cadwallader, dryly. 'What is your nephew to be, Mr Casaubon?'

'Pardon me, he is not my nephew. He is my cousin.'

'Well, you know,' interposed Mr Brooke, 'he is trying his wings. He is just the sort of young fellow to rise. I should be glad to give him an opportunity. He would make a good secretary, now, like Hobbes, Milton, Swift – that sort of man.'

'I understand,' said Mrs Cadwallader. 'One who can write speeches.'

'I'll fetch him in now, eh, Casaubon?' said Mr Brooke. 'He wouldn't come in till I had announced him, you know. And we'll go down and look at the picture. There you are to the life: a deep subtle sort of thinker with his forefinger on the page, while Saint Bonaventure or somebody else, rather fat and florid, is looking up at the Trinity. Everything is symbolical, you know – the higher style of art: I like that up to a certain point but not too far – it's rather straining to keep up with, you know. But you are at home in that, Casaubon. And your painter's flesh is good – solidity, transparency, everything of that sort. I went into that a great deal at one time. However, I'll go and fetch Ladislaw.'

Chapter 35

Non, je ne comprends pas de plus charmant plaisir
Que de voir d'héritiers une troupe affligée,
Le maintien interdit, et la mine allongée,
Lire un long testament où pales, étonnés,
On leur laisse un bonsoir avec un pied de nez.
Pour voir au natural leur tristesse profonde,
Je reviendrais, je crois, exprès de l'autre monde.
REGNARD, *Le Légataire Universel*

When the animals entered the Ark in pairs, one may imagine that allied species made much private remark on each other, and were tempted to think that so many forms feeding on the same store of fodder were eminently superfluous, as tending to diminish the rations. (I fear the part played by the vultures on that occasion would be too painful for art to represent, those birds being disadvantageously naked about the gullet, and apparently without rites and ceremonies.)

The same sort of temptation befell the Christian Carnivora who formed Peter Featherstone's funeral procession; most of them having minds bent on a limited store which each would have liked to get the most of. The long-recognised blood-relations and connections by marriage made already a goodly number, which, multiplied by possibilities, presented a fine range for jealous conjecture and pathetic hopefulness. Jealousy of the Vincys had created a fellowship in hostility among all persons of the Featherstone blood, so that in the absence of any decided indication that one of themselves was to have more than the rest, the dread lest that long-legged Fred Vincy should have the land was necessarily dominant, though it left abundant feeling and leisure for vaguer jealousies, such as were entertained towards Mary Garth. Solomon found time to reflect that Jonah was undeserving, and Jonah to abuse Solomon as greedy; Jane, the elder sister, held that Martha's children ought not to expect so much as the young Waules; and Martha, more lax on the subject of primogeniture, was sorry to think that Jane was so 'having'. These nearest of kin were naturally impressed with the unreasonableness of expectations in cousins and second cousins, and used their arithmetic in reckoning the large sums that small legacies might mount to, if there were too many of them. Two cousins were present to hear the will, and a second cousin besides Mr Trumbull. This second cousin was a Middlemarch mercer of polite manners and superfluous aspirates. The two cousins were elderly men from Brassing, one of them conscious of claims on the score of inconvenient expense sustained by him in presents of oysters and other eatables to his rich cousin Peter; the other entirely saturnine, leaning his hands and chin on a stick, and conscious of claims based on no narrow performance but on merit generally: both blameless citizens of Brassing, who wished that Jonah Featherstone did not live there. The wit of a family is usually best received among strangers.

'Why, Trumbull himself is pretty sure of five hundred – *that* you may depend, – I shouldn't wonder if my brother promised him,' said Solomon, musing aloud with his sisters, the evening before the funeral.

'Dear, dear!' said poor Sister Martha, whose imagination of hundreds had been habitually narrowed to the amount of her unpaid rent.

But in the morning all the ordinary currents of conjecture were disturbed by the presence of a strange mourner who had plashed among them as if from the moon. This was the stranger described by Mrs Cadwallader as frog-face: a man perhaps about two- or three-and-thirty, whose prominent eyes, thin-lipped, downward-curved mouth, and hair sleekly brushed away from a forehead that sank suddenly above the ridge of the eyebrows, certainly gave his face a batrachian unchangeableness of expression. Here, clearly, was a new legatee; else why was he bidden as a mourner? Here were new possibilities, raising a new uncertainty, which almost checked remark in the mourning-coaches. We are all humiliated by the sudden discovery of a fact which has existed very comfortably and perhaps been staring at us in private while we have been making up our world entirely without it. No one had seen this questionable stranger before except Mary Garth, and she knew nothing more of him than that he had twice been to Stone Court when Mr Featherstone was downstairs, and had sat alone with him for several hours. She had found an opportunity of mentioning this to her father, and perhaps Caleb's were the only eyes, except the lawyer's, which examined the stranger with more of enquiry than of disgust or suspicion. Caleb Garth, having little expectation and less cupidity, was interested in the verification of his own guesses, and the calmness with which he half-smilingly rubbed his chin and shot intelligent glances much as if he were valuing a tree, made a fine contrast with the alarm or scorn visible in other faces when the unknown mourner, whose name was understood to be Rigg, entered the wainscoted parlour and took his seat near the door to make part of the audience when the will should be read. Just then Mr Solomon and Mr Jonah were gone upstairs with the lawyer to search for the will; and Mrs Waule, seeing two vacant seats between herself and Mr Borthrop Trumbull, had the spirit to move next to that great authority, who was handling his watch-seals and trimming his outlines with a determination not to show anything so compromising to a man of ability as wonder or surprise.

'I suppose you know everything about what my poor brother's done, Mr Trumbull,' said Mrs Waule, in the lowest of her woolly tones, while she turned her crape-shadowed bonnet towards Mr Trumbull's ear.

'My good lady, whatever was told me was told in confidence,' said the auctioneer, putting his hand up to screen that secret.

'Them who've made sure of their good-luck may be disappointed yet,' Mrs Waule continued, finding some relief in this communication.

'Hopes are often delusive,' said Mr Trumbull, still in confidence.

'Ah!' said Mrs Waule, looking across at the Vincys, and then moving back to the side of her sister Martha.

'It's wonderful how close poor Peter was,' she said, in the same undertones. 'We none of us know what he might have had on his mind. I only hope and trust he wasn't a worse liver than we think of, Martha.'

Poor Mrs Cranch was bulky, and, breathing asthmatically, had the additional motive for making her remarks unexceptionable and giving them a general bearing, that even her whispers were loud and liable to sudden bursts like those of a deranged barrel organ.

'I never *was* covetous, Jane,' she replied; 'but I have six children and have buried three, and I didn't marry into money. The eldest, that sits there, is but nineteen – so I leave you to guess. And stock always short, and land most awkward. But if ever I've begged and prayed, it's been to God above; though where there's one brother a bachelor and the other childless after twice marrying – anybody might think!'

Meanwhile, Mr Vincy had glanced at the passive face of Mr Rigg, and had taken out his snuffbox and tapped it, but had put it back again unopened as an indulgence which, however clarifying to the judgement, was unsuited to the occasion. 'I shouldn't wonder if Featherstone had better feelings than any of us gave him credit for,' he observed, in the ear of his wife. 'This funeral shows a thought about everybody: it looks well when a man wants to be followed by his friends, and if they are humble, not to be ashamed of them. I should be all the better pleased if he'd left lots of small legacies. They may be uncommonly useful to fellows in a small way.'

'Everything is as handsome as could be, crape and silk and everything,' said Mrs Vincy, contentedly.

But I am sorry to say that Fred was under some difficulty in repressing a laugh, which would have been more unsuitable than his father's snuffbox. Fred had overheard Mr Jonah suggesting something about a 'love-child', and with this thought in his mind, the stranger's face, which happened to be opposite him, affected him too ludicrously. Mary Garth, discerning his distress in the twitchings of his mouth, and his recourse to a cough, came cleverly to his rescue by asking him to change seats with her, so that he got into a shadowy corner. Fred was feeling as good-naturedly as possible towards everybody, including Rigg; and having some relenting towards all these people who were less lucky than he was aware of being himself, he would not for the world have behaved amiss; still, it was particularly easy to laugh.

But the entrance of the lawyer and the two brothers drew everyone's attention.

The lawyer was Mr Standish, and he had come to Stone Court this morning believing that he knew thoroughly well who would be pleased and who disappointed before the day was over. The will he expected to read was the last of three which he had drawn up for Mr Featherstone. Mr Standish was not a man who varied his manners: he behaved with the same deep-voiced, offhand-civility to everybody, as if he saw no difference in them, and talked chiefly of the hay crop, which would be 'very fine, by God!', of the last bulletins concerning the King, and of the Duke of Clarence, who was a sailor every inch of him, and just the man to rule over an island like Britain.

Old Featherstone had often reflected as he sat looking at the fire that Standish would be surprised someday: it is true that if he had done as he liked at the last, and burnt the will drawn up by another lawyer, he would not have secured that minor end; still he had had his pleasure in ruminating on it. And certainly Mr Standish was surprised, but not at all sorry; on the contrary, he rather enjoyed the zest of a little curiosity in his own mind, which the discovery of a second will added to the prospective amazement on the part of the Featherstone family.

As to the sentiments of Solomon and Jonah, they were held in utter suspense: it seemed to them that the old will would have a certain validity, and that there might be such an interlacement of poor Peter's former and latter intentions as to create endless 'lawing' before anybody came by their own – an inconvenience which would have at least the advantage of going all round. Hence the brothers showed a thoroughly neutral gravity as they re-entered with Mr Standish; but Solomon took out his white handkerchief again with a sense that in any case there would be affecting passages, and crying at funerals, however dry, was customarily served up in lawn.

Perhaps the person who felt the most throbbing excitement at this moment was Mary Garth, in the consciousness that it was she who had virtually determined the production of this second will, which might have momentous effects on the lot of some persons present. No soul except herself knew what had passed on that final night.

'The will I hold in my hand,' said Mr Standish, who, seated at the table in the middle of the room, took his time about everything, including the coughs with which he showed a disposition to clear his voice, 'was drawn up by myself and executed by our deceased friend on the 9th of August 1825. But I find that there is a subsequent instrument hitherto unknown to me, bearing date the 20th of July 1826, hardly a year later than the previous one. And there is farther, I see' – Mr Standish was cautiously travelling over the document with his spectacles – 'a codicil to this latter will, bearing date March the first, 1828.'

'Dear, dear!' said Sister Martha, not meaning to be audible, but driven to some articulation under this pressure of dates.

'I shall begin by reading the earlier will,' continued Mr Standish, 'since such, as appears by his not having destroyed the document, was the intention of deceased.'

The preamble was felt to be rather long, and several besides Solomon shook their heads pathetically, looking on the ground: all eyes avoided meeting other eyes, and were chiefly fixed either on the spots in the tablecloth or on Mr Standish's bald head; excepting Mary Garth's. When all the rest were trying to look nowhere in particular, it was safe for her to look at them. And at the sound of the first 'give and bequeath' she could see all complexions changing subtly, as if some faint vibration were passing through them, save that of Mr Rigg. He sat in unaltered calm, and, in fact, the company, preoccupied with more important problems, and with the complication of listening to bequests which might or might not be revoked, had ceased to think of him. Fred blushed, and Mr Vincy found it impossible to do without his snuffbox in his hand, though he kept it closed.

The small bequests came first, and even the recollection that there was another will and that poor Peter might have thought better of it, could not quell the rising disgust and indignation. One likes to be done well by in every tense, past, present, and future. And here was Peter capable five years ago of leaving only two hundred apiece to his own brothers and sisters, and only a hundred apiece to his own nephews and nieces: the Garths were not mentioned, but Mrs Vincy and Rosamond were each to have a hundred. Mr Trumbull was to have the gold-headed cane and fifty pounds; the other second cousins and the cousins present were each to have the like handsome sum, which, as the saturnine cousin observed, was a sort of legacy that left a man nowhere; and there was much more of such offensive dribbling in favour of persons not present – problematical, and, it was to be feared, low connections. Altogether, reckoning hastily, here were about three thousand disposed of. Where then had Peter meant the rest of the money to go – and where the land? and what was revoked and what not revoked – and was the revocation for better or for worse? All emotion must be conditional, and might turn out to be the wrong thing. The men were strong enough to bear up and keep quiet under this confused suspense: some letting their lower lip fall, others pursing it up, according to the habit of their muscles. But Jane and Martha sank under the rush of questions, and began to cry; poor Mrs Cranch being half moved with the consolation of getting any hundreds at all without working for them, and half aware that her share was scanty; whereas Mrs Waule's mind was entirely flooded with the sense of being an own sister and getting little, while somebody else was to have much. The general expectation now was that the 'much' would fall to Fred Vincy, but the Vincys themselves were surprised when ten thousand pounds in specified investments were declared to be bequeathed to him: – was the land coming too? Fred bit his lips: it was difficult to help smiling, and Mrs Vincy felt herself the happiest of women, possible revocation shrinking out of sight in this dazzling vision.

There was still a residue of personal property as well as the land, but the whole was left to one person, and that person was – O possibilities! O expectations founded on the favour of 'close' old gentlemen! O endless vocatives that would still leave expression slipping helpless from the measurement of mortal folly! –

that residuary legatee was Joshua Rigg, who was also sole executor, and who was to take thenceforth the name of Featherstone.

There was a rustling which seemed like a shudder running round the room. Everyone stared afresh at Mr Rigg, who apparently experienced no surprise.

'A most singular testamentary disposition!' exclaimed Mr Trumbull, preferring for once that he should be considered ignorant in the past. 'But there is a second will – there is a further document. We have not yet heard the final wishes of the deceased.'

Mary Garth was feeling that what they had yet to hear were not the final wishes. The second will revoked everything except the legacies to the low persons before mentioned (some alterations in these being the occasion of the codicil), and the bequest of all the land lying in Lowick parish, with all the stock and household furniture, to Joshua Rigg. The residue of the property was to be devoted to the erection and endowment of almshouses for old men, to be called Featherstone's Alms-houses, and to be built on a piece of land near Middlemarch already bought for the purpose by the testator, he wishing – so the document declared – to please God Almighty. Nobody present had a farthing; but Mr Trumbull had the gold-headed cane. It took some time for the company to recover the power of expression. Mary dared not look at Fred.

Mr Vincy was the first to speak – after using his snuffbox energetically – and he spoke with loud indignation. 'The most unaccountable will I ever heard! I should say he was not in his right mind when he made it. I should say this last will was void,' added Mr Vincy, feeling that this expression put the thing in the true light. 'Eh, Standish?'

'Our deceased friend always knew what he was about, I think,' said Mr Standish. 'Everything is quite regular. Here is a letter from Clemmens of Brassing tied with the will. He drew it up. A very respectable solicitor.'

'I never noticed any alienation of mind – any aberration of intellect in the late Mr Featherstone,' said Borthrop Trumbull, 'but I call this will eccentric. I was always willingly of service to the old soul; and he intimated pretty plainly a sense of obligation which would show itself in his will. The gold-headed cane is farcical considered as an acknowledgment to me; but happily I am above mercenary considerations.'

'There's nothing very surprising in the matter that I can see,' said Caleb Garth. 'Anybody might have had more reason for wondering if the will had been what you might expect from an open-minded straightforward man. For my part, I wish there was no such thing as a will.'

'That's a strange sentiment to come from a Christian man, by God!' said the lawyer. 'I should like to know how you will back that up, Garth!'

'Oh,' said Caleb, leaning forward, adjusting his fingertips with nicety and looking meditatively on the ground. It always seemed to him that words were the hardest part of 'business'.

But here Mr Jonah Featherstone made himself heard. 'Well, he always was a fine hypocrite, was my brother Peter. But this will cuts out everything. If I'd known, a waggon and six horses shouldn't have drawn me from Brassing. I'll put a white hat and drab coat on tomorrow.'

'Dear, dear,' wept Mrs Cranch, 'and we've been at the expense of travelling, and that poor lad sitting idle here so long! It's the first time I ever heard my brother Peter was so wishful to please God Almighty; but if I was to be struck helpless I must say it's hard – I can think no other.'

'It'll do him no good where he's gone, that's my belief,' said Solomon, with a bitterness which was remarkably genuine, though his tone could not help being sly. 'Peter was a bad liver, and almshouses won't cover it, when he's had the impudence to show it at the last.'

'And all the while had got his own lawful family – brothers and sisters and nephews and nieces – and has sat in church with 'em whenever he thought well to come,' said Mrs Waule. 'And might have left his property so respectable, to them that's never been used to extravagance or unsteadiness in no manner of way – and not so poor but what they could have saved every penny and made more of it. And me – the trouble I've been at, times and times, to come here and be sisterly – and him with things on his mind all the while that might make anybody's flesh creep. But if the Almighty's allowed it, He means to punish him for it. Brother Solomon, I shall be going, if you'll drive me.'

'I've no desire to put my foot on the premises again,' said Solomon. 'I've got land of my own and property of my own to will away.'

'It's a poor tale how luck goes in the world,' said Jonah. 'It never answers to have a bit of spirit in you. You'd better be a dog in the manger. But those above ground might learn a lesson. One fool's will is enough in a family.'

'There's more ways than one of being a fool,' said Solomon. 'I shan't leave my money to be poured down the sink, and I shan't leave it to fondlings from Africay. I like Featherstones that were brewed such, and not turned Featherstones with sticking the name on 'em.'

Solomon addressed these remarks in a loud aside to Mrs Waule as he rose to accompany her. Brother Jonah felt himself capable of much more stinging wit than this, but he reflected that there was no use in offending the new proprietor of Stone Court, until you were certain that he was quite without intentions of hospitality towards witty men whose name he was about to bear.

Mr Joshua Rigg, in fact, appeared to trouble himself little about any innuendoes, but showed a notable change of manner, walking coolly up to Mr Standish and putting business questions with much coolness. He had a high chirping voice and a vile accent. Fred, whom he no longer moved to laughter, thought him the lowest monster he had ever seen. But Fred was feeling rather sick. The Middlemarch mercer waited for an opportunity of engaging Mr Rigg in conversation: there was no knowing how many pairs of legs the new proprietor might require hose for, and profits were more to be relied on than legacies. Also, the mercer, as a second cousin, was dispassionate enough to feel curiosity.

Mr Vincy, after his one outburst, had remained proudly silent, though too much preoccupied with unpleasant feelings to think of moving, till he observed that his wife had gone to Fred's side and was crying silently while she held her darling's hand. He rose immediately, and turning his back on the company while he said to her in an undertone – 'Don't give way, Lucy; don't make a fool of yourself, my dear, before these people,' he added in his usual loud voice – 'Go and order the phaeton, Fred; I have no time to waste.'

Mary Garth had before this been getting ready to go home with her father. She met Fred in the hall, and now for the first time had the courage to look at him. He had that withered sort of paleness which will sometimes come on young faces, and his hand was very cold when she shook it. Mary too was agitated: she was conscious that fatally, without will of her own, she had perhaps made a great difference to Fred's lot.

'Goodbye,' she said, with affectionate sadness. 'Be brave, Fred. I do believe you are better without the money. What was the good of it to Mr Feather-stone?'

'That's all very fine,' said Fred, pettishly. 'What is a fellow to do? I must go into the Church now.' (He knew that this would vex Mary: very well; then she must tell him what else he could do.) 'And I thought I should be able to pay your father at once and make everything right. And you have not even a hundred pounds left you. What shall you do now, Mary?'

'Take another situation, of course, as soon as I can get one. My father has enough to do to keep the rest, without me. Goodbye.'

In a very short time Stone Court was cleared of well-brewed Featherstones and other long-accustomed visitors. Another stranger had been brought to settle in the neighbourhood of Middlemarch, but in the case of Mr Rigg Featherstone there was more discontent with immediate visible consequence than speculation as to the effect which his presence might have in the future. No soul was prophetic enough to have any foreboding as to what might appear on the trail of Joshua Rigg.

And here I am naturally led to reflect on the means of elevating a low subject. Historical parallels are remarkably efficient in this way. The chief objection to them is, that the diligent narrator may lack space, or (what is often the same thing) may not be able to think of them with any degree of particularity, though he may have a philosophical confidence that if known they would be illustrative. It seems an easier and shorter way to dignity, to observe that – since there never was a true story which could not be told in parables where you might put a monkey for a margrave, and *vice versa* – whatever has been or is to be narrated by me about low people, may be ennobled by being considered a parable; so that if any bad habits and ugly consequences are brought into view, the reader may have the relief of regarding them as not more than figuratively ungenteel, and may feel himself virtually in company with persons of some style. Thus while I tell the truth about loobies, my reader's imagination need not be entirely excluded from an occupation with lords; and the petty sums which any bankrupt of high standing would be sorry to retire upon, may be lifted to the level of high commercial transactions by the inexpensive addition of proportional ciphers.

As to any provincial history in which the agents are all of high moral rank, that must be of a date long posterior to the first Reform Bill, and Peter Featherstone, you perceive, was dead and buried some months before Lord Grey came into office.

Chapter 36

'Tis strange to see the humours of these men,
These great aspiring spirits, that should be wise:

For being the nature of great spirits to love
To be where they may be most eminent;
They, rating of themselves so farre above
Us in conceit, with whom they do frequent,
Imagine how we wonder and esteeme
All that they do or say; which makes them strive
To make our admiration more extreme,
Which they suppose they cannot, 'less they give
Notice of their extreme and highest thoughts.

DANIEL, *Tragedy of Philotas*

Mr Vincy went home from the reading of the will with his point of view considerably changed in relation to many subjects. He was an open-minded man, but given to indirect modes of expressing himself: when he was disappointed in a market for his silk braids, he swore at the groom; when his brother-in-law Bulstrode had vexed him, he made cutting remarks on Methodism; and it was now apparent that he regarded Fred's idleness with a sudden increase of severity, by his throwing an embroidered cap out of the smoking-room on to the hall-floor.

'Well, sir,' he observed, when that young gentleman was moving off to bed, 'I hope you've made up your mind now to go up next term and pass your examination. I've taken my resolution, so I advise you to lose no time in taking yours.'

Fred made no answer: he was too utterly depressed. Twenty-four hours ago he had thought that instead of needing to know what he should do, he should by this time know that he needed to do nothing: that he should hunt in pink, have a first-rate hunter, ride to cover on a fine hack, and be generally respected for doing so; moreover, that he should be able at once to pay Mr Garth, and that Mary could not longer have any reason for not marrying him. And all this was to have come without study or other inconvenience, purely by the favour of providence in the shape of an old gentleman's caprice. But now, at the end of twenty-four hours, all those firm expectations were upset. It was 'rather hard lines' that while he was smarting under this disappointment he should be treated as if he could have helped it. But he went away silently and his mother pleaded for him.

'Don't be hard on the poor boy, Vincy. He'll turn out well yet, though that wicked man has deceived him. I feel as sure as I sit here, Fred will turn out well – else why was he brought back from the brink of the grave? And I call it a robbery: it was like giving him the land, to promise it; and what is promising, if making everybody believe is not promising? And you see he did leave him ten thousand pounds, and then took it away again.'

'Took it away again!' said Mr Vincy, pettishly. 'I tell you the lad's an unlucky lad, Lucy. And you've always spoiled him.'

'Well, Vincy, he was my first, and you made a fine fuss with him when he came. You were as proud as proud,' said Mrs Vincy, easily recovering her cheerful smile.

'Who knows what babies will turn to? I was fool enough, I dare say,' said the husband – more mildly, however.

'But who has handsomer, better children than ours? Fred is far beyond other people's sons: you may hear it in his speech, that he has kept college company. And Rosamond – where is there a girl like her? She might stand beside any lady in the land, and only look the better for it. You see – Mr Lydgate has kept the highest company and been everywhere, and he fell in love with her at once. Not but what I could have wished Rosamond had not engaged herself. She might have met somebody on a visit who would have been a far better match; I mean at her schoolfellow Miss Willoughby's. There are relations in that family quite as high as Mr Lydgate's.'

'Damn relations!' said Mr Vincy; 'I've had enough of them. I don't want a son-in-law who has got nothing but his relations to recommend him.'

'Why, my dear,' said Mrs Vincy, 'you seemed as pleased as could be about it. It's true, I wasn't at home; but Rosamond told me you hadn't a word to say against the engagement. And she has begun to buy in the best linen and cambric for her underclothing.'

'Not by my will,' said Mr Vincy. 'I shall have enough to do this year, with an idle scamp of a son, without paying for wedding-clothes. The times are as tight as can be; everybody is being ruined; and I don't believe Lydgate has got a farthing. I shan't give my consent to their marrying. Let 'em wait, as their elders have done before 'em.'

'Rosamond will take it hard, Vincy, and you know you never could bear to cross her.'

'Yes, I could. The sooner the engagement's off, the better. I don't believe he'll ever make an income, the way he goes on. He makes enemies; that's all I hear of his making.'

'But he stands very high with Mr Bulstrode, my dear. The marriage would please *him*, I should think.'

'Please the deuce!' said Mr Vincy. 'Bulstrode won't pay for their keep. And if Lydgate thinks I'm going to give money for them to set up housekeeping, he's mistaken, that's all. I expect I shall have to put down my horses soon. You'd better tell Rosy what I say.'

This was a not infrequent procedure with Mr Vincy – to be rash in jovial assent, and on becoming subsequently conscious that he had been rash, to employ others in making the offensive retractation. However, Mrs Vincy, who never willingly opposed her husband, lost no time the next morning in letting Rosamond know what he had said. Rosamond, examining some muslin-work, listened in silence, and at the end gave a certain turn of her graceful neck, of which only long experience could teach you that it meant perfect obstinacy.

'What do you say, my dear?' said her mother, with affectionate deference.

'Papa does not mean anything of the kind,' said Rosamond, quite calmly. 'He has always said that he wished me to marry the man I loved. And I shall marry Mr Lydgate. It is seven weeks now since papa gave his consent. And I hope we shall have Mrs Bretton's house.'

'Well, my dear, I shall leave you to manage your papa. You always do manage everybody. But if we ever do go and get damask, Sadler's is the place – far better than Hopkins's. Mrs Bretton's is very large though: I should love you to have such a house; but it will take a great deal of furniture – carpeting and everything, besides plate and glass. Do you think Mr Lydgate expects it?'

'You cannot imagine that I should ask him, mamma. Of course he understands his own affairs.'

'But he may have been looking for money, my dear, and we all thought of your having a pretty legacy as well as Fred; – and now everything is so dreadful – there's no pleasure in thinking of anything, with that poor boy disappointed as he is.'

'That has nothing to do with my marriage, mamma. Fred must leave off being idle. I am going upstairs to take this work to Miss Morgan: she does the open-hemming very well. Mary Garth might do some work for me now, I should think. Her sewing is exquisite; it is the nicest thing I know about Mary. I should so like to have all my cambric frilling double-hemmed. And it takes a long time.'

Mrs Vincy's belief that Rosamond could manage her papa was well founded. Apart from his dinners and his coursing, Mr Vincy, blustering as he was, had as little of his own way as if he had been a prime minister: the force of circumstances was easily too much for him, as it is for most pleasure-loving florid men; and the circumstance called Rosamond was particularly forcible by means of that mild persistence which, as we know, enables a white soft living substance to make its way in spite of opposing rock. Papa was not a rock: he had no other fixity than that fixity of alternating impulses sometimes called habit, and this was altogether unfavourable to his taking the only decisive line of conduct in relation to his daughter's engagement – namely, to enquire thoroughly into Lydgate's circumstances, declare his own inability to furnish money, and forbid alike either a speedy marriage or an engagement which must be too lengthy. That seems very simple and easy in the statement; but a disagreeable resolve formed in the chill hours of the morning had as many conditions against it as the early frost, and rarely persisted under the warming influences of the day. The indirect though emphatic expression of opinion to which Mr Vincy was prone suffered much restraint in this case: Lydgate was a proud man towards whom innuendoes were obviously unsafe, and throwing his hat on the floor was out of the question. Mr Vincy was a little in awe of him, a little vain that he wanted to marry Rosamond, a little indisposed to raise a question of money in which his own position was not advantageous, a little afraid of being worsted in dialogue with a man better educated and more highly bred than himself, and a little afraid of doing what his daughter would not like. The part Mr Vincy preferred playing was that of the generous host whom nobody criticises. In the earlier half of the day there was business to hinder any formal communication of an adverse resolve; in the later there was dinner, wine, whist, and general satisfaction. And in the meanwhile the hours were each leaving their little deposit and gradually forming the final reason for inaction, namely, that action was too late.

The accepted lover spent most of his evenings in Lowick Gate, and a love-making not at all dependent on money-advances from fathers-in-law, or prospective income from a profession, went on flourishingly under Mr Vincy's own eyes. Young love-making – that gossamer web! Even the points it clings to – the things whence its subtle interlacings are swung – are scarcely perceptible; momentary touches of fingertips, meetings of rays from blue and dark orbs, unfinished phrases, lightest changes of cheek and lip, faintest tremors. The web itself is made of spontaneous beliefs and indefinable joys, yearnings of one life towards another, visions of completeness, indefinite trust. And Lydgate fell to spinning that web from his inward self with wonderful rapidity, in spite of experience supposed to be finished off with the drama of Laure – in spite too of medicine and biology; for the inspection of macerated muscle or of eyes presented in a dish (like Santa Lucia's), and other incidents of scientific enquiry, are observed to be less incompatible with poetic love than a native dulness or a lively addiction to the lowest prose. As for Rosamond, she was in the water-lily's expanding wonderment at its own fuller life, and she too was spinning industriously at the mutual web. All this went on in the corner of the drawing-room where the piano stood, and subtle as it was, the light made it a sort of rainbow visible to many observers besides Mr Farebrother. The certainty that Miss Vincy and Mr Lydgate were engaged became general in Middlemarch without the aid of formal announcement.

Aunt Bulstrode was again stirred to anxiety; but this time she addressed herself to her brother, going to the warehouse expressly to avoid Mrs Vincy's volatility. His replies were not satisfactory.

'Walter, you never mean to tell me that you have allowed all this to go on without enquiry into Mr Lydgate's prospects?' said Mrs Bulstrode, opening her eyes with wider gravity at her brother, who was in his peevish warehouse humour. 'Think of this girl brought up in luxury – in too worldly a way, I am sorry to say – what will she do on a small income?'

'Oh, confound it, Harriet! what can I do when men come into the town without any asking of mine? Did you shut your house up against Lydgate? Bulstrode has pushed him forward more than anybody. I never made any fuss about the young fellow. You should go and talk to your husband about it, not me.'

'Well, really, Walter, how can Mr Bulstrode be to blame? I am sure he did not wish for the engagement.'

'Oh, if Bulstrode had not taken him by the hand, I should never have invited him.'

'But you called him in to attend on Fred, and I am sure that was a mercy,' said Mrs Bulstrode, losing her clue in the intricacies of the subject.

'I don't know about mercy,' said Mr Vincy, testily. 'I know I am worried more than I like with my family. I was a good brother to you, Harriet, before you married Bulstrode, and I must say he doesn't always show that friendly spirit towards your family that might have been expected of him.' Mr Vincy was very little like a Jesuit, but no accomplished Jesuit could have turned a question more adroitly. Harriet had to defend her husband instead of blaming her brother, and the conversation ended at a point as far from the beginning as some recent sparring between the brothers-in-law at a vestry meeting.

Mrs Bulstrode did not repeat her brother's complaints to her husband, but in the evening she spoke to him of Lydgate and Rosamond. He did not share her warm interest, however; and only spoke with resignation of the risks attendant on the beginning of medical practice and the desirability of prudence.

'I am sure we are bound to pray for that thoughtless girl – brought up as she has been,' said Mrs Bulstrode, wishing to rouse her husband's feelings.

'Truly, my dear,' said Mr Bulstrode, assentingly. 'Those who are not of this world can do little else to arrest the errors of the obstinately worldly. That is what we must accustom ourselves to recognise with regard to your brother's family. I could have wished that Mr Lydgate had not entered into such a union; but my relations with him are limited to that use of his gifts for God's purposes which is taught us by the divine government under each dispensation.'

Mrs Bulstrode said no more, attributing some dissatisfaction which she felt to her own want of spirituality. She believed that her husband was one of those men whose memoirs should be written when they died.

As to Lydgate himself, having been accepted, he was prepared to accept all the consequences which he believed himself to foresee with perfect clearness. Of course he must be married in a year – perhaps even in half a year. This was not what he had intended; but other schemes would not be hindered: they would simply adjust themselves anew. Marriage, of course, must be prepared for in the usual way. A house must be taken instead of the rooms he at present occupied; and Lydgate, having heard Rosamond speak with admiration of old Mrs Bretton's house (situated in Lowick Gate), took notice when it fell vacant after the old lady's death, and immediately entered into treaty for it.

He did this in an episodic way, very much as he gave orders to his tailor for every requisite of perfect dress, without any notion of being extravagant. On the contrary, he would have despised any ostentation of expense; his profession had familiarised him with all grades of poverty, and he cared much for those who suffered hardships. He would have behaved perfectly at a table where the sauce was served in a jug with the handle off, and he would have remembered nothing about a grand dinner except that a man was there who talked well. But it had never occurred to him that he should live in any other than what he would have called an ordinary way, with green glasses for hock, and excellent waiting at table. In warming himself at French social theories he had brought away no smell of scorching. We may handle even extreme opinions with impunity while our furniture, our dinner-giving, and preference for armorial bearings in our own case, link us indissolubly with the established order. And Lydgate's tendency was not towards extreme opinions: he would have liked no barefooted doctrines, being particular about his boots: he was no radical in relation to anything but medical reform and the prosecution of discovery. In the rest of practical life he walked by hereditary habit; half from that personal pride and unreflecting egoism which I have already called commonness, and half from that naïveté which belonged to preoccupation with favourite ideas.

Any inward debate Lydgate had as to the consequence of this engagement which had stolen upon him, turned on the paucity of time rather than of money. Certainly, being in love and being expected continually by someone who always turned out to be prettier than memory could represent her to be, did interfere with the diligent use of spare hours which might serve some 'plodding fellow of a German' to make the great, imminent discovery. This was really an argument for not deferring the marriage too long, as he implied to Mr Farebrother, one day that the Vicar came to his room with some pond-products which he wanted to examine under a better microscope than his own, and, finding Lydgate's tableful of apparatus and specimens in confusion, said sarcastically, 'Eros has degenerated; he began by introducing order and harmony, and now he brings back chaos.'

'Yes, at some stages,' said Lydgate, lifting his brows and smiling, while he began to arrange his microscope. 'But a better order will begin after.'

'Soon?' said the Vicar.

'I hope so, really. This unsettled state of affairs uses up the time, and when one has notions in science, every moment is an opportunity. I feel sure that marriage must be the best thing for a man who wants to work steadily. He has everything at home then – no teasing with personal speculations. He can get calmness and freedom.'

'You are an enviable dog,' said the Vicar, 'to have such a prospect – Rosamond, calmness and freedom, all to your share. Here am I with nothing but my pipe and pond animalcules. Now, are you ready?'

Lydgate did not mention to the Vicar another reason he had for wishing to shorten the period of courtship. It was rather irritating to him, even with the wine of love in his veins, to be obliged to mingle so often with the family part at the Vincys', and to enter so much into Middlemarch gossip, protracted good cheer, whist-playing, and general futility. He had to be deferential when Mr Vincy decided questions with trenchant ignorance, especially as to those liquors which were the best inward pickle, preserving you from the effects of bad air. Mrs Vincy's openness and simplicity were quite unstreaked with suspicion as to the subtle offence she might give to the taste of her intended son-in-law; and altogether Lydgate had to confess to himself that he was descending a little in relation to Rosamond's family. But that exquisite creature herself suffered in the same sort of way: – it was at least one delightful thought that in marrying her, he could give her a much-needed transplantation.

'Dear!' he said to her one evening, in his gentlest tone, as he sat down by her and looked closely at her face; But I must first say that he had found her alone in the drawing-room where the great old-fashioned window, almost as large as the side of the room, was opened to the summer scents of the garden at the back of the house. Her father and mother were gone to a party, and the rest were all out with the butterflies.

'Dear! your eyelids are red.'

'Are they?' said Rosamond. 'I wonder why.' It was not in her nature to pour forth wishes or grievances. They only came forth gracefully on solicitation.

'As if you could hide it from me!' said Lydgate, laying his hand tenderly on both of hers. 'Don't I see a tiny drop on one of the lashes? Things trouble you, and you don't tell me. That is unloving.'

'Why should I tell you what you cannot alter? They are everyday things: – perhaps they have been a little worse lately.'

'Family annoyances. Don't fear speaking. I guess them.'

'Papa has been more irritable lately. Fred makes him angry, and this morning there was a fresh quarrel because Fred threatens to throw his whole education away, and do something quite beneath him. And besides – '

Rosamond hesitated, and her cheeks were gathering a slight flush. Lydgate had never seen her in trouble since the morning of their engagement, and he had never felt so passionately towards her as at this moment. He kissed the hesitating lips gently, as if to encourage them.

'I feel that papa is not quite pleased about our engagement,' Rosamond continued, almost in a whisper; 'and he said last night that he should certainly speak to you and say it must be given up.'

'Will you give it up?' said Lydgate, with quick energy almost angrily.

'I never give up anything that I choose to do,' said Rosamond, recovering her calmness at the touching of this cord.

'God bless you!' said Lydgate, kissing her again. This constancy of purpose in the right place was adorable. He went on; 'It is too late now for your father to say that our engagement must be given up. You are of age, and I claim you as mine. If anything is done to make you unhappy, – that is a reason for hastening our marriage.'

An unmistakable delight shone forth from the blue eyes that met his, and the radiance seemed to light up all his future with mild sunshine. Ideal happiness (of the kind known in the Arabian Nights, in which you are invited to step from the labour and discord of the street into a paradise where everything is given to you and nothing claimed) seemed to be an affair of a few weeks' waiting, more or less.

'Why should we defer it?' he said, with ardent insistence. 'I have taken the house now: everything else can soon be got ready – can it not? You will not mind about new clothes. Those can be bought afterwards.'

'What original notions you clever men have!' said Rosamond, dimpling with more thorough laughter than usual at this humorous incongruity. 'This is the first time I ever heard of wedding-clothes being bought after marriage.'

'But you don't mean to say you would insist on my waiting months for the sake of clothes?' said Lydgate, half thinking that Rosamond was tormenting him prettily, and half fearing that she really shrank from speedy marriage. 'Remember, we are looking forward to a better sort of happiness than this – being continually together, independent of others, and ordering our lives as we will. Come, dear, tell me how soon you can be altogether mine.'

There was a serious pleading in Lydgate's tone, as if he felt that she would be injuring him by any fantastic delays. Rosamond became serious too, and slightly meditative; in fact, she was going through many intricacies of lace-edging and hosiery and petticoat-tucking, in order to give an answer that would at least be approximate.

'Six weeks would be ample – say so, Rosamond,' insisted Lydgate, releasing her hands to put his arm gently round her.

One little hand immediately went to pat her hair, while she gave her neck a meditative turn, and then said seriously: 'There would be the house-linen and the furniture to be prepared. Still mamma could see to those while we were away.'

'Yes, to be sure. We must be away a week or so.'

'Oh, more than that!' said Rosamond, earnestly. She was thinking of her evening dresses for the visit to Sir Godwin Lydgate's, which she had long been secretly hoping for as a delightful employment of at least one quarter of the honeymoon, even if she deferred her introduction to the uncle who was a doctor of divinity (also a pleasing though sober kind of rank, when sustained by blood). She looked at her lover with some wondering remonstrance as she spoke, and he readily understood that she might wish to lengthen the sweet time of double solitude.

'Whatever you wish, my darling, when the day is fixed. But let us take a decided course, and put an end to any discomfort you may be suffering. Six weeks! – I am sure they would be ample.'

'I could certainly hasten the work,' said Rosamond. 'Will you, then, mention it to papa? – I think it would be better to write to him.' She blushed and looked at him as the garden flowers look at us when we walk forth happily among them in the transcendent evening light: is there not a soul beyond utterance, half-nymph, half-child, in those delicate petals which glow and breathe about the centres of deep colour?

He touched her ear and a little bit of neck under it with his lips, and they sat quite still for many minutes which flowed by them like a small gurgling brook with the kisses of the sun upon it. Rosamond thought that no one could be more in love than she was; and Lydgate thought that after all his wild mistakes and absurd credulity, he had found perfect womanhood – felt as if already breathed upon by exquisite wedded affection such as would be bestowed by an accomplished creature who venerated his high musings and momentous labours and would never interfere with them; who would create order in the home and accounts with still magic, yet keep her fingers ready to touch the lute and transform life into romance at any moment; who was instructed to the true womanly limit and not a hair's-breadth beyond – docile, therefore, and ready to carry out behests which came from beyond that limit. It was plainer now than ever that his notion of remaining much longer a bachelor had been a mistake: marriage would not be an obstruction but a furtherance. And happening the next day to accompany a patient to Brassing, he saw a dinner-service there which struck him as so exactly the right thing that he bought it at once. It saved time to do these things just when you thought of them, and Lydgate hated ugly crockery. The dinner-service in question was expensive, but that might be in the nature of dinner-services. Furnishing was necessarily expensive; but then it had to be done only once.

'It must be lovely,' said Mrs Vincy, when Lydgate mentioned his purchase with some descriptive touches. 'Just what Rosy ought to have. I trust in heaven it won't be broken!'

'One must hire servants who will not break things,' said Lydgate. (Certainly, this was reasoning with an imperfect vision of sequences. But at that period there was no sort of reasoning which was not more or less sanctioned by men of science.)

Of course it was unnecessary to defer the mention of anything to mamma, who did not readily take views that were not cheerful, and being a happy wife herself, had hardly any feeling but pride in her daughter's marriage. But Rosamond had good reasons for suggesting to Lydgate that papa should be appealed to in writing. She prepared for the arrival of the letter by walking with her papa to the warehouse the next morning, and telling him on the way that Mr Lydgate wished to be married soon.

'Nonsense, my dear,' said Mr Vincy. 'What has he got to marry on? You'd much better give up the engagement. I've told you so pretty plainly before this. What have you had such an education for, if you are to go and marry a poor man? It's a cruel thing for a father to see.'

'Mr Lydgate is not poor, papa. He bought Mr Peacock's practice, which, they say, is worth eight or nine hundred a year.'

'Stuff and nonsense! What's buying a practice? He might as well buy next year's swallows. It'll all slip through his fingers.'

'On the contrary, papa, he will increase the practice. See how he has been called in by the Chettams and Casaubons.'

'I hope he knows I shan't give anything – with this disappointment about Fred, and Parliament going to be dissolved, and machine-breaking everywhere, and an election coming on – '

'Dear papa! what can that have to do with my marriage?'

'A pretty deal to do with it! We may all be ruined for what I know – the country's in that state! Some say it's the end of the world, and be hanged if I don't think it looks like it. Anyhow, it's not a time for me to be drawing money out of my business, and I should wish Lydgate to know that.'

'I am sure he expects nothing, papa. And he has such very high connections: he is sure to rise in one way or another. He is engaged in making scientific discoveries.'

Mr Vincy was silent.

'I cannot give up my only prospect of happiness, papa. Mr Lydgate is a gentleman. I could never love anyone who was not a perfect gentleman. You would not like me to go into a consumption, as Arabella Hawley did. And you know that I never change my mind.'

Again papa was silent.

'Promise me, papa, that you will consent to what we wish. We shall never give each other up; and you know that you have always objected to long courtships and late marriages.'

There was a little more urgency of this kind, till Mr Vincy said, 'Well, well, child, he must write to me first before I can answer him,' – and Rosamond was certain that she had gained her point.

Mr Vincy's answer consisted chiefly in a demand that Lydgate should insure his life – a demand immediately conceded. This was a delightfully reassuring idea supposing that Lydgate died, but in the meantime not a self-supporting idea. However, it seemed to make everything comfortable about Rosamond's marriage; and the necessary purchases went on with much spirit. Not without prudential considerations, however. A bride (who is going to visit at a baronet's) must have a few first-rate pocket handkerchiefs; but beyond the absolutely necessary half-dozen, Rosamond contented herself without the very highest style of embroidery and Valenciennes. Lydgate also, finding that his sum of eight hundred pounds had been considerably reduced since he had come to Middlemarch, restrained his inclination for some plate of an old pattern which was shown to him when he went into Kibble's establishment at Brassing to buy forks and spoons. He was too proud to act as if he presupposed that Mr Vincy would advance money to provide furniture; and though, since it would not be necessary to pay for everything at once, some bills would be left standing over, he did not waste time in conjecturing how much his father-in-law would give in the form of dowry, to make payment easy. He was not going to do anything extravagant, but the requisite things must be bought, and it would be bad economy to buy them of a poor quality. All these matters were by the by. Lydgate foresaw that science and his profession were the objects he should alone pursue enthusiastically; but he could not imagine himself pursuing them in such a home as Wrench had – the doors all open, the oilcloth worn, the children in soiled pinafores, and lunch lingering in the form of bones, black-handled knives, and willow-pattern. But Wrench had a wretched lymphatic wife who made a mummy of herself indoors in a large shawl; and he must have altogether begun with an ill-chosen domestic apparatus.

Rosamond, however, was on her side much occupied with conjectures, though her quick imitative perception warned her against betraying them too crudely.

'I shall like so much to know your family,' she said one day, when the wedding-journey was being discussed. 'We might perhaps take a direction that would allow us to see them as we returned. Which of your uncles do you like best?'

'Oh, – my uncle Godwin, I think. He is a good-natured old fellow.'

'You were constantly at his house at Quallingham, when you were a boy, were you not? I should so like to see the old spot and everything you were used to. Does he know you are going to be married?'

'No,' said Lydgate, carelessly, turning in his chair and rubbing his hair up.

'Do send him word of it, you naughty undutiful nephew. He will perhaps ask you to take me to Quallingham: and then you could show me about the grounds, and I could imagine you there when you were a boy. Remember, you see me in my home, just as it has been since I was a child. It is not fair that I should be so ignorant of yours. But perhaps you would be a little ashamed of me. I forgot that.'

Lydgate smiled at her tenderly, and really accepted the suggestion that the proud pleasure of showing so charming a bride was worth some trouble. And now he came to think of it, he would like to see the old spots with Rosamond.

'I will write to him, then. But my cousins are bores.'

It seemed magnificent to Rosamond to be able to speak so slightingly of a baronet's family, and she felt much contentment in the prospect of being able to estimate them contemptuously on her own account.

But mamma was near spoiling all, a day or two later, by saying, 'I hope your uncle Sir Godwin will not look down on Rosy, Mr Lydgate. I should think he would do something handsome. A thousand or two can be nothing to a baronet.'

'Mamma!' said Rosamond, blushing deeply; and Lydgate pitied her so much that he remained silent and went to the other end of the room to examine a print curiously, as if he had been absent-minded. Mamma had a little filial lecture afterwards, and was docile as usual. But Rosamond reflected that if any of those high-bred cousins who were bores, should be induced to visit Middlemarch, they would see many things in her own family which might shock them. Hence it seemed desirable that Lydgate should by and by get some first-rate position elsewhere than in Middlemarch; and this could hardly be difficult in the case of a man who had a titled uncle and could make discoveries. Lydgate, you perceive, had talked fervidly to Rosamond of his hopes as to the highest uses of his life, and had found it delightful to be listened to by a creature who would bring him the sweet furtherance of satisfying affection – beauty – repose such help as our thoughts get from the summer sky and the flower-fringed meadows.

Lydgate relied much on the psychological difference between what for the sake of variety I will call goose and gander: especially on the innate submissiveness of the goose as beautifully corresponding to the strength of the gander.

Chapter 37

Thrice happy she that is so well assured
Unto herself, and settled so in heart,
That neither will for better be allured
Ne fears to worse with any chance to start,
But like a steddy ship doth strongly part
The raging waves, and keeps her course aright:
Ne aught for tempest doth from it depart,
Ne aught for fairer weather's false delight.
Such self-assurance need not fear the spight
Of grudging foes; ne favour seek of friends;
But in the stay of her own stedfast might
Neither to one herself nor other bends.
   Most happy she that most assured doth rest,
   But he most happy who such one loves best.

SPENSER

The doubt hinted by Mr Vincy whether it were only the general election or the end of the world that was coming on, now that George the Fourth was dead, Parliament dissolved, Wellington and Peel generally depreciated and the new King apologetic, was a feeble type of the uncertainties in provincial opinion at that time. With the glowworm lights of country places, how could men see which were their own thoughts in the confusion of a Tory Ministry passing Liberal measures, of Tory nobles and electors being anxious to return Liberals rather than friends of the recreant Ministers, and of outcries for remedies which seemed to have a mysteriously remote bearing on private interest and were made suspicious by the advocacy of disagreeable neighbours? Buyers of the Middlemarch newspapers found themselves in an anomalous position: during the agitation on the Catholic Question many had given up the *Pioneer* – which had a motto from Charles James Fox and was in the van of progress – because it had taken Peel's side about the Papists, and had thus blotted its Liberalism with a toleration of Jesuitry and Baal; but they were ill-satisfied with the *Trumpet*, which – since its blasts against Rome, and in the general flaccidity of the public mind (nobody knowing who would support whom) – had become feeble in its blowing.

It was a time, according to a noticeable article in the *Pioneer*, when the crying needs of the country might well counteract a reluctance to public action on the part of men whose minds had from long experience acquired breadth as well as concentration, decision of judgement as well as tolerance, dispassionateness as well as energy – in fact, all those qualities which in the melancholy experience of mankind have been the least disposed to share lodgings.

Mr Hackbutt, whose fluent speech was at that time floating more widely than usual, and leaving much uncertainty as to its ultimate channel, was heard to say in Mr Hawley's office that the article in question 'emanated' from Brooke of Tipton, and that Brooke had secretly bought the *Pioneer* some months ago.

'That means mischief, eh?' said Mr Hawley. 'He's got the freak of being a popular man now, after dangling about like a stray tortoise. So much the worse for him. I've had my eye on him for some time. He shall be prettily pumped upon. He's a damned bad landlord. What business has an old county man to come currying favour with a low set of dark-blue freemen? As to his paper, I only hope he may do the writing himself. It would be worth our paying for.'

'I understand he has got a very brilliant young fellow to edit it, who can write the highest style of leading article, quite equal to anything in the London papers. And he means to take very high ground on Reform.'

'Let Brooke reform his rent-roll. He's a cursed old screw, and the buildings all over his estate are going to rack. I suppose this young fellow is some loose fish from London.'

'His name is Ladislaw. He is said to be of foreign extraction.'

'I know the sort,' said Mr Hawley; 'some emissary. He'll begin with flourish about the Rights of Man and end with murdering a wench. That's the style.'

'You must concede that there are abuses, Hawley,' said Mr Hackbutt, foreseeing some political disagreement with his family lawyer. 'I myself should never favour immoderate views – in fact I take my stand with Huskisson – but I cannot blind myself to the consideration that the non-representation of large towns – '

'Large towns be damned!' said Mr Hawley, impatient of exposition. 'I know a little too much about Middlemarch elections. Let 'em quash every pocket borough tomorrow, and bring in every mushroom town in the kingdom – they'll only increase the expense of getting into Parliament. I go upon facts.'

Mr Hawley's disgust at the notion of the *Pioneer* being edited by an emissary, and of Brooke becoming actively political – as if a tortoise of desultory pursuits should protrude its small head ambitiously and become rampant – was hardly equal to the annoyance felt by some members of Mr Brooke's own family. The result had oozed forth gradually, like the discovery that your neighbour has set up an unpleasant kind of manufacture which will be permanently under your nostrils without legal remedy. The *Pioneer* had been secretly bought even before Will Ladislaw's arrival, the expected opportunity having offered itself in the readiness of the proprietor to part with valuable property which did not pay; and in the interval since Mr Brooke had written his invitation, those germinal ideas of making his mind tell upon the world at large which had been present in him from his younger years, but had hitherto lain in some obstruction, had been sprouting under cover.

The development was much furthered by a delight in his guest which proved greater even than he had anticipated. For it seemed Will was not only at home in all those artistic and literary subjects which Mr Brooke had gone into at one time, but that he was strikingly ready at seizing the points of the political situation, and dealing with them in that large spirit which, aided by adequate memory, lends itself to quotation and general effectiveness of treatment.

'He seems to me a kind of Shelley, you know,' Mr Brooke took an opportunity of saying, for the gratification of Mr Casaubon. 'I don't mean as to anything objectionable – laxities or atheism, or anything of that kind, you know –

Ladislaw's sentiments in every way I am sure are good – indeed, we were talking a great deal together last night. But he has the same sort of enthusiasm for liberty, freedom, emancipation – a fine thing under guidance – under guidance, you know. I think I shall be able to put him on the right tack; and I am the more pleased because he is a relation of yours, Casaubon.'

If the right tack implied anything more precise than the rest of Mr Brooke's speech, Mr Casaubon silently hoped that it referred to some occupation at a great distance from Lowick. He had disliked Will while he helped him, but he had begun to dislike him still more now that Will had declined his help. That is the way with us when we have any uneasy jealousy in our disposition: if our talents are chiefly of the burrowing kind, our honey-sipping cousin (whom we have grave reasons for objecting to) is likely to have a secret contempt for us, and anyone who admires him passes an oblique criticism on ourselves. Having the scruples of rectitude in our souls, we are above the meanness of injuring him – rather we meet all his claims on us by active benefits; and the drawing of cheques for him, being a superiority which he must recognise, gives our bitterness a milder infusion. Now Mr Casaubon had been deprived of that superiority (as anything more than a remembrance) in a sudden, capricious manner. His antipathy to Will did not spring from the common jealousy of a winter-worn husband: it was something deeper, bred by his lifelong claims and discontents; but Dorothea, now that she was present – Dorothea, as a young wife who herself had shown an offensive capability of criticism, necessarily gave concentration to the uneasiness which had before been vague.

Will Ladislaw on his side felt that his dislike was flourishing at the expense of his gratitude, and spent much inward discourse in justifying the dislike. Casaubon hated him – he knew that very well; on his first entrance he could discern a bitterness in the mouth and a venom in the glance which would almost justify declaring war in spite of past benefits. He was much obliged to Casaubon in the past, but really the act of marrying this wife was a set-off against the obligation. It was a question whether gratitude which refers to what is done for one's self ought not to give way to indignation at what is done against another. And Casaubon had done a wrong to Dorothea in marrying her. A man was bound to know himself better than that, and if he chose to grow grey crunching bones in a cavern, he had no business to be luring a girl into his companionship. 'It is the most horrible of virgin sacrifices,' said Will; and he painted to himself what were Dorothea's inward sorrows as if he had been writing a choric wail. But he would never lose sight of her: he would watch over her – if he gave up everything else in life he would watch over her, and she should know that she had one slave in the world. Will had – to use Sir Thomas Browne's phrase – a 'passionate prodigality' of statement both to himself and others. The simple truth was that nothing then invited him so strongly as the presence of Dorothea.

Invitations of the formal kind had been wanting, however, for Will had never been asked to go to Lowick. Mr Brooke, indeed, confident of doing everything agreeable which Casaubon, poor fellow, was too much absorbed to think of, had arranged to bring Ladislaw to Lowick several times (not neglecting meanwhile to introduce him elsewhere on every opportunity as 'a young relative of

Casaubon's'). And though Will had not seen Dorothea alone, their interviews had been enough to restore her former sense of young companionship with one who was cleverer than herself, yet seemed ready to be swayed by her. Poor Dorothea before her marriage had never found much room in other minds for what she cared most to say; and she had not, as we know, enjoyed her husband's superior instruction so much as she had expected. If she spoke with any keenness of interest to Mr Casaubon, he heard her with an air of patience as if she had given a quotation from the Delectus familiar to him from his tender years, and sometimes mentioned curtly what ancient sects or personages had held similar ideas, as if there were too much of that sort in stock already; at other times he would inform her that she was mistaken, and reassert what her remark had questioned.

But Will Ladislaw always seemed to see more in what she said than she herself saw. Dorothea had little vanity, but she had the ardent woman's need to rule beneficently by making the joy of another soul. Hence the mere chance of seeing Will occasionally was like a lunette opened in the wall of her prison, giving her a glimpse of the sunny air; and this pleasure began to nullify her original alarm at what her husband might think about the introduction of Will as her uncle's guest. On this subject Mr Casaubon had remained dumb.

But Will wanted to talk with Dorothea alone, and was impatient of slow circumstances. However slight the terrestrial intercourse between Dante and Beatrice or Petrarch and Laura, time changes the proportion of things, and in later days it is preferable to have fewer sonnets and more conversation. Necessity excused stratagem, but stratagem was limited by the dread of offending Dorothea. He found out at last that he wanted to take a particular sketch at Lowick; and one morning when Mr Brooke had to drive along the Lowick road on his way to the county town, Will asked to be set down with his sketchbook and camp-stool at Lowick, and without announcing himself at the Manor settled himself to sketch in a position where he must see Dorothea if she came out to walk – and he knew that she usually walked an hour in the morning.

But the stratagem was defeated by the weather. Clouds gathered with treacherous quickness, the rain came down, and Will was obliged to take shelter in the house. He intended, on the strength of relationship, to go into the drawing-room and wait there without being announced; and seeing his old acquaintance the butler in the hall, he said, 'Don't mention that I am here, Pratt; I will wait till luncheon; I know Mr Casaubon does not like to be disturbed when he is in the library.'

'Master is out, sir; there's only Mrs Casaubon in the library. I'd better tell her you're here sir,' said Pratt, a red-cheeked man given to lively converse with Tantripp, and often agreeing with her that it must be dull for Madam.

'Oh, very well; this confounded rain has hindered me from sketching,' said Will, feeling so happy that he affected indifference with delightful ease.

In another minute he was in the library, and Dorothea was meeting him with her sweet unconstrained smile.

'Mr Casaubon has gone to the Archdeacon's,' she said, at once. 'I don't know whether he will be at home again long before dinner. He was uncertain how long he should be. Did you want to say anything particular to him?'

'No; I came to sketch, but the rain drove me in. Else I would not have disturbed you yet. I supposed that Mr Casaubon was here and I know he dislikes interruption at this hour.'

'I am indebted to the rain, then. I am so glad to see you.' Dorothea uttered these common words with the simple sincerity of an unhappy child, visited at school.

'I really came for the chance of seeing you alone,' said Will, mysteriously forced to be just as simple as she was. He could not stay to ask himself, why not? 'I wanted to talk about things, as we did in Rome. It always makes a difference when other people are present.'

'Yes,' said Dorothea, in her clear full tone of assent. 'Sit down.' She seated herself on a dark ottoman with the brown books behind her, looking in her plain dress of some thin woollen-white material, without a single ornament on her besides her wedding-ring, as if she were under a vow to be different from all other women; and Will sat down opposite her at two yards' distance, the light falling on his bright curls and delicate but rather petulant profile, with its defiant curves of lip and chin. Each looked at the other as if they had been two flowers which had opened then and there. Dorothea for the moment forgot her husband's mysterious irritation against Will: it seemed fresh water at her thirsty lips to speak without fear to the one person whom she had found receptive; for in looking backward through sadness she exaggerated a past solace.

'I have often thought that I should like to talk to you again,' she said, immediately. 'It seems strange to me how many things I said to you.'

'I remember them all,' said Will, with the unspeakable content in his soul of feeling that he was in the presence of a creature worthy to be perfectly loved. I think his own feelings at that moment were perfect, for we mortals have our divine moments, when love is satisfied in the completeness of the beloved object.

'I have tried to learn a great deal since we were in Rome,' said Dorothea. 'I can read Latin a little, and I am beginning to understand just a little Greek. I can help Mr Casaubon better now. I can find out references for him and save his eyes in many ways. But it is very difficult to be learned; it seems as if people were worn out on the way to great thoughts, and can never enjoy them because they are too tired.'

'If a man has a capacity for great thoughts, he is likely to overtake them before he is decrepit,' said Will, with irrepressible quickness. But through certain sensibilities Dorothea was as quick as he, and seeing her face change, he added, immediately, 'But it is quite true that the best minds have been sometimes over-strained in working out their ideas.'

'You correct me,' said Dorothea. 'I expressed myself ill. I should have said that those who have great thoughts get too much worn in working them out. I used to feel about that, even when I was a little girl; and it always seemed to me that the use I should like to make of my life would be to help someone who did great works, so that his burthen might be lighter.'

Dorothea was led on to this bit of autobiography without any sense of making a revelation. But she had never before said anything to Will which threw so strong a light on her marriage. He did not shrug his shoulders; and for want of that muscular outlet he thought the more irritably of beautiful lips kissing holy skulls and other emptinesses ecclesiastically enshrined. Also he had to take care that his speech should not betray that thought.

'But you may easily carry the help too far,' he said, 'and get overwrought yourself. You are not too much shut up? You already look paler. It would be better for Mr Casaubon to have a secretary; he could easily get a man who would do half his work for him. It would save him more effectually, and you need only help him in lighter ways.'

'How can you think of that?' said Dorothea, in a tone of earnest remonstrance. 'I should have no happiness if I did not help him in his work. What could I do? There is no good to be done in Lowick. The only thing I desire is to help him more. And he objects to a secretary: please not to mention that again.'

'Certainly not, now I know your feeling. But I have heard both Mr Brooke and Sir James Chettam express the same wish.'

'Yes,' said Dorothea, 'but they don't understand – they want me to be a great deal on horseback, and have the garden altered and new conservatories, to fill up my days. I thought you could understand that one's mind has other wants,' she added, rather impatiently – 'besides, Mr Casaubon cannot bear to hear of a secretary.'

'My mistake is excusable,' said Will. 'In old days I used to hear Mr Casaubon speak as if he looked forward to having a secretary. Indeed he held out the prospect of that office to me. But I turned out to be – not good enough for it.'

Dorothea was trying to extract out of this an excuse for her husband's evident repulsion, as she said, with a playful smile, 'You were not a steady worker enough.'

'No,' said Will, shaking his head backward somewhat after the manner of a spirited horse. And then, the old irritable demon prompting him to give another good pinch at the moth-wings of poor Mr Casaubon's glory, he went on, 'And I have seen since that Mr Casaubon does not like anyone to overlook his work and know thoroughly what he is doing. He is too doubtful – too uncertain of himself. I may not be good for much, but he dislikes me because I disagree with him.'

Will was not without his intentions to be always generous, but our tongues are little triggers which have usually been pulled before general intentions can be brought to bear. And it was too intolerable that Casaubon's dislike of him should not be fairly accounted for to Dorothea. Yet when he had spoken he was rather uneasy as to the effect on her.

But Dorothea was strangely quiet – not immediately indignant as she had been on a like occasion in Rome. And the cause lay deep. She was no longer struggling against the perception of facts, but adjusting herself to their clearest perception; and now when she looked steadily at her husband's failure, still more at his possible consciousness of failure, she seemed to be looking along the one track where duty became tenderness. Will's want of reticence might have been met with more severity, if he had not already been recommended to her mercy by her husband's dislike, which must seem hard to her till she saw better reason for it.

She did not answer at once, but after looking down ruminatingly she said, with some earnestness, 'Mr Casaubon must have overcome his dislike of you so far as his actions were concerned: and that is admirable.'

'Yes; he has shown a sense of justice in family matters. It was an abominable thing that my grandmother should have been disinherited because she made what they called a *mésalliance*, though there was nothing to be said against her husband except that he was a Polish refugee who gave lessons for his bread.'

'I wish I knew all about her!' said Dorothea. 'I wonder how she bore the change from wealth to poverty: I wonder whether she was happy with her husband! Do you know much about them?'

'No: only that my grandfather was a patriot – a bright fellow – could speak many languages – musical – got his bread by teaching all sorts of things. They both died rather early. And I never knew much of my father, beyond what my mother told me; but he inherited the musical talents. I remember his slow walk and his long thin hands; and one day remains with me when he was lying ill, and I was very hungry, and had only a little bit of bread.'

'Ah, what a different life from mine !' said Dorothea, with keen interest, clasping her hands on her lap. 'I have always had too much of everything. But tell me how it was – Mr Casaubon could not have known about you then.'

'No; but my father had made himself known to Mr Casaubon, and that was my last hungry day. My father died soon after, and my mother and I were well taken care of. Mr Casaubon always expressly recognised it as his duty to take care of us because of the harsh injustice which had been shown to his mother's sister. But now I am telling you what is not new to you.'

In his inmost soul Will was conscious of wishing to tell Dorothea what was rather new even in his own construction of things – namely, that Mr Casaubon had never done more than pay a debt towards him. Will was much too good a fellow to be easy under the sense of being ungrateful. And when gratitude has become a matter of reasoning there are many ways of escaping from its bonds.

'No,' answered Dorothea: 'Mr Casaubon has always avoided dwelling on his honourable actions.' She did not feel that her husband's conduct was depreciated; but this notion of what justice had required in his relations with Will Ladislaw took strong hold on her mind. After a moment's pause, she added, 'He had never told me that he supported your mother. Is she still living?'

'No; she died by an accident – a fall – four years ago. It is curious that my mother, too, ran away from her family, but not for the sake of a husband. She never would tell me anything about her family, except that she forsook them to get her own living – went on the stage, in fact. She was a dark eyed creature, with crisp ringlets, and never seemed to be getting old. You see I come of rebellious blood on both sides,' Will ended, smiling brightly at Dorothea, while she was still looking with serious intentness before her, like a child seeing a drama for the first time.

But her face, too, broke into a smile as she said, 'That is your apology, I suppose, for having yourself been rather rebellious; I mean, to Mr Casaubon's wishes. You must remember that you have not done what he thought best for you. And if he dislikes you – you were speaking of dislike a little while ago – but

I should rather say, if he has shown any painful feelings towards you, you must consider how sensitive he has become from the wearing effect of study. Perhaps,' she continued, getting into a pleading tone, 'my uncle has not told you how serious Mr Casaubon's illness was. It would be petty of us who are well and can bear things, to think much of small offences from those who carry a weight of trial.'

'You teach me better,' said Will. 'I will never grumble on that subject again.' There was a gentleness in his tone which came from the unutterable contentment of perceiving – what Dorothea was hardly conscious of – that she was travelling into the remoteness of pure pity and loyalty towards her husband. Will was ready to adore her pity and loyalty, if she would associate himself with her in manifesting them 'I have really sometimes been a perverse fellow,' he went on, 'but I will never again, if I can help it, do or say what you would disapprove.'

'That is very good of you,' said Dorothea, with another open smile. 'I shall have a little kingdom then, where I shall give laws. But you will soon go away, out of my rule, I imagine. You will soon be tired of staying at the Grange.'

'That is a point I wanted to mention to you – one of the reasons why I wished to speak to you alone. Mr Brooke proposes that I should stay in this neighbourhood. He has bought one of the Middlemarch newspapers, and he wishes me to conduct that, and also to help him in other ways.'

'Would not that be a sacrifice of higher prospects for you?' said Dorothea.

'Perhaps; but I have always been blamed for thinking of prospects, and not settling to anything. And here is something offered to me. If you would not like me to accept it, I will give it up. Otherwise I would rather stay in this part of the country than go away. I belong to nobody anywhere else.'

'I should like you to stay very much,' said Dorothea, at once, as simply and readily as she had spoken at Rome. There was not the shadow of a reason in her mind at the moment why she should not say so.

'Then I *will* stay,' said Ladislaw, shaking his head backward, rising and going towards the window, as if to see whether the rain had ceased.

But the next moment, Dorothea, according to a habit which was getting continually stronger, began to reflect that her husband felt differently from herself, and she coloured deeply under the double embarrassment of having expressed what might be in opposition to her husband's feeling, and of having to suggest this opposition to Will. His face was not turned towards her, and this made it easier to say: 'But my opinion is of little consequence on such a subject. I think you should be guided by Mr Casaubon. I spoke without thinking of anything else than my own feeling, which has nothing to do with the real question. But it now occurs to me perhaps Mr Casaubon might see that the proposal was not wise. Can you not wait now and mention it to him?'

'I can't wait today,' said Will, inwardly scared by the possibility that Mr Casaubon would enter. 'The rain is quite over now. I told Mr Brooke not to call for me: I would rather walk the five miles. I shall strike across Halsell Common, and see the gleams on the wet grass. I like that.'

He approached her to shake hands quite hurriedly, longing but not daring to say, 'Don't mention the subject to Mr Casaubon.' No, he dared not, could not say it. To ask her to be less simple and direct would be like breathing on the crystal that you want to see the light through. And there was always the other great dread – of himself becoming dimmed and for ever ray-shorn in her eyes.

'I wish you could have stayed,' said Dorothea, with a touch of mournfulness, as she rose and put out her hand. She also had her thought which she did not like to express: – Will certainly ought to lose no time in consulting Mr Casaubon's wishes, but for her to urge this might seem an undue dictation.

So they only said 'Goodbye', and Will quitted the house, striking across the fields so as not to run any risk of encountering Mr Casaubon's carriage, which, however, did not appear at the gate until four o'clock. That was an unpropitious hour for coming home: it was too early to gain the moral support under *ennui* of dressing his person for dinner, and too late to undress his mind of the day's frivolous ceremony and affairs, so as to be prepared for a good plunge into the serious business of study. On such occasions he usually threw himself into an easy-chair in the library, and allowed Dorothea to read the London papers to him, closing his eyes the while. Today, however, he declined that relief, observing that he had already had too many public details urged upon him; but he spoke more cheerfully than usual, when Dorothea asked about his fatigue, and added with that air of formal effort which never forsook him even when he spoke without his waistcoat and cravat, 'I have had the gratification of meeting my former acquaintance, Dr Spanning, today, and of being praised by one who is himself a worthy recipient of praise. He spoke very handsomely of my late tractate on the Egyptian Mysteries – using, in fact, terms which it would not become me to repeat.'

In uttering the last clause, Mr Casaubon leaned over the elbow of his chair, and swayed his head up and down, apparently as a muscular outlet instead of that recapitulation which would not have been becoming.

'I am very glad you have had that pleasure,' said Dorothea, delighted to see her husband less weary than usual at this hour. 'Before you came I had been regretting that you happened to be out today.'

'Why so, my dear?' said Mr Casaubon, throwing himself backward again.

'Because Mr Ladislaw has been here; and he has mentioned a proposal of my uncle's which I should like to know your opinion of.' Her husband she felt was really concerned in this question. Even with her ignorance of the world she had a vague impression that the position offered to Will was out of keeping with his family connections, and certainly Mr Casaubon had a claim to be consulted. He did not speak, but merely bowed.

'Dear uncle, you know, has many projects. It appears that he has bought one of the Middlemarch newspapers, and he has asked Mr Ladislaw to stay in this neighbourhood and conduct the paper for him, besides helping him in other ways.'

Dorothea looked at her husband while she spoke, but he had at first blinked and finally closed his eyes, as if to save them: while his lips became more tense. 'What is your opinion?' she added, rather timidly, after a slight pause.

'Did Mr Ladislaw come on purpose to ask my opinion?' said Mr Casaubon, opening his eyes narrowly with a knife-edge look at Dorothea. She was really uncomfortable on the point he enquired about, but she only became a little more serious, and her eyes did not swerve.

'No,' she answered, immediately, 'he did not say that he came to ask your opinion. But when he mentioned the proposal, he of course expected me to tell you of it.'

Mr Casaubon was silent.

'I feared that you might feel some objection. But certainly a young man with so much talent might be very useful to my uncle – might help him to do good in a better way. And Mr Ladislaw wishes to have some fixed occupation. He has been blamed, he says, for not seeking something of that kind, and he would like to stay in this neighbourhood because no one cares for him elsewhere.'

Dorothea felt that this was a consideration to soften her husband. However, he did not speak, and she presently recurred to Dr Spanning and the Arch-deacon's breakfast. But there was no longer sunshine on these subjects.

The next morning, without Dorothea's knowledge, Mr Casaubon dis-patched the following letter, beginning 'Dear Mr Ladislaw' (he had always before addressed him as 'Will'):

Mrs Casaubon informs me that a proposal has been made to you, and (according to an inference by no means stretched) has on your part been in some degree entertained, which involves your residence in this neighbourhood in a capacity which I am justified in saying touches my own position in such a way as renders it not only natural and warrantable in me when that effect is viewed under the influence of legitimate feeling, but incumbent on me when the same effect is considered in the light of my responsibilities, to state at once that your acceptance of the proposal above indicated would be highly offensive to me. That I have some claim to the exercise of a veto here, would not, I believe, be denied by any reasonable person cognisant of the relations between us: relations which, though thrown into the past by your recent procedure, are not thereby annulled in their character of determining antecedents. I will not here make reflections on any person's judgement. It is enough for me to point out to yourself that there are certain social fitnesses and proprieties which should hinder a somewhat near relative of mine from becoming in anywise conspicuous in this vicinity in a status not only much beneath my own, but associated at best with the sciolism of literary or political adventurers. At any rate, the contrary issue must exclude you from further reception at my house. – Yours faithfully,   EDWARD CASAUBON

Meanwhile Dorothea's mind was innocently at work towards the further embitterment of her husband; dwelling, with a sympathy that grew to agitation, on what Will had told her about his parents and grandparents. Any private hours in her day were usually spent in her blue-green boudoir, and she had come to be very fond of its pallid quaintness. Nothing had been outwardly altered there; but while the summer had gradually advanced over the western fields beyond the avenue of elms, the bare room had gathered within it those memories of an inward life which fill the air as with a cloud of good or bad angels, the invisible yet active forms of our spiritual triumphs or our spiritual falls. She had been so used to struggle for and to find resolve in looking along the avenue towards the arch of western light that the vision itself had gained a communicating power. Even the pale stag seemed to have reminding glances and to mean mutely, 'Yes, we know.' And the group of delicately touched miniatures had made an audience as of beings no longer disturbed about their own earthly lot, but still humanly interested. Especially the mysterious 'Aunt Julia' about whom Dorothea had never found it easy to question her husband.

And now, since her conversation with Will, many fresh images had gathered round that Aunt Julia who was Will's grandmother: the presence of that delicate miniature, so like a living face that she knew, helping to concentrate her feelings. What a wrong, to cut off the girl from the family protection and inheritance only because she had chosen a man who was poor! Dorothea, early troubling her elders with questions about the facts around her, had wrought herself into some independent clearness as to the historical, political reasons why eldest sons had superior rights, and why land should be entailed: those reasons, impressing her with a certain awe, might be weightier than she knew, but here was a question of ties which left them uninfringed. Here was a daughter whose child – even according to the ordinary aping of aristocratic institutions by people who are no more aristocratic than retired grocers, and who have no more land to 'keep together' than a lawn and a paddock – would have a prior claim. Was inheritance a question of liking or of responsibility? All the energy of Dorothea's nature went on the side of responsibility – the fulfilment of claims founded on our own deeds, such as marriage and parentage.

It was true, she said to herself, that Mr Casaubon had a debt to the Ladislaws – that he had to pay back what the Ladislaws had been wronged of. And now she began to think of her husband's will which had been made at the time of their marriage, leaving the bulk of his property to her, with proviso in case of her having children. That ought to be altered; and no time ought to be lost. This very question which had just arisen about Will Ladislaw's occupation, was the occasion for placing things on a new, right footing. Her husband, she felt sure, according to all his previous conduct, would be ready to take the just view, if she proposed it – she, in whose interest an unfair concentration of the property had been urged. His sense of right had surmounted and would continue to surmount anything that might be called antipathy. She suspected that her uncle's scheme was disapproved by Mr Casaubon, and this made it seem all the more opportune that a fresh understanding should be begun, so that instead of Will's starting penniless and accepting the first function that offered itself, he should find himself in possession of a rightful income which should be paid by her husband during his life, and, by an immediate alteration of the will, should be secured at his death. The vision of all this as what ought to be done seemed to Dorothea like a sudden letting in of daylight, waking her from her previous stupidity and incurious self-absorbed ignorance about her husband's relation to others. Will Ladislaw had refused Mr Casaubon's future aid on a ground that no longer appeared right to her; and Mr Casaubon had never himself seen fully what was the claim upon him. 'But he will!' said Dorothea. 'The great strength of his character lies here. And what are we doing with our money? We make no use of half of our income. My own money buys me nothing but an uneasy conscience.'

There was a peculiar fascination for Dorothea in this division of property intended for herself, and always regarded by her as excessive. She was blind, you see, to many things obvious to others – likely to tread in the wrong places, as Celia had warned her; yet her blindness to whatever did not lie in her own pure purpose carried her safely by the side of precipices where vision would have been perilous with fear.

The thoughts which had gathered vividness in the solitude of her boudoir occupied her incessantly through the day on which Mr Casaubon had sent his letter to Will. Everything seemed hindrance to her till she could find an opportunity of opening her heart to her husband. To his preoccupied mind all subjects were to be approached gently, and she had never since his illness lost from her consciousness the dread of agitating him. But when young ardour is set brooding over the conception of a prompt deed, the deed itself seems to start forth with independent life, mastering ideal obstacles. The day passed in a sombre fashion, not unusual, though Mr Casaubon was perhaps unusually silent; but there were hours of the night which might be counted on as opportunities of conversation; for Dorothea, when aware of her husband's sleeplessness, had established the habit of rising, lighting a candle, and reading him to sleep again. And this night she was from the beginning sleepless, excited by resolves. He slept as usual for a few hours, but she had risen softly and had sat in the darkness for nearly an hour before he said: 'Dorothea, since you are up, will you light a candle?'

'Do you feel ill, dear?' was her first question, as she obeyed him.

'No, not at all; but I shall be obliged, since you are up, if you will read me a few pages of Lowth.'

'May I talk to you a little, instead?' said Dorothea.

'Certainly.'

'I have been thinking about money all day – that I have always had too much, and especially the prospect of too much.'

'These, my dear Dorothea, are providential arrangements.'

'But if one has too much in consequence of others being wronged, it seems to me that the divine voice which tells us to set that wrong right must be obeyed.'

'What, my love, is the bearing of your remark?'

'That you have been too liberal in arrangements for me – I mean, with regard to property; and that makes me unhappy.'

'How so? I have none but comparatively distant connections.'

'I have been led to think about your aunt Julia, and how she was left in poverty only because she married a poor man, an act which was not disgraceful, since he was not unworthy. It was on that ground, I know, that you educated Mr Ladislaw and provided for his mother.'

Dorothea waited a few moments for some answer that would help her onward. None came, and her next words seemed the more forcible to her, falling clear upon the dark silence.

'But surely we should regard his claim as a much greater one, even to the half of that property which I know that you have destined for me. And I think he ought at once to be provided for on that understanding. It is not right that he should be in the dependence of poverty while we are rich. And if there is any objection to the proposal he mentioned, the giving him his true place and his true share would set aside any motive for his accepting it.'

'Mr Ladislaw has probably been speaking to you on this subject?' said Mr Casaubon, with a certain biting quickness not habitual to him.

'Indeed, no!' said Dorothea, earnestly. 'How can you imagine it, since he has so lately declined everything from you? I fear you think too hardly of him, dear. He only told me a little about his parents and grandparents, and almost all in answer to my questions. You are so good, so just – you have done everything you thought to be right. But it seems to me clear that more than that is right; and I must speak about it, since I am the person who would get what is called benefit by that "more" not being done.'

There was a perceptible pause before Mr Casaubon replied, not quickly as before, but with a still more biting emphasis.

'Dorothea, my love, this is not the first occasion, but it were well that it should be the last, on which you have assumed a judgement on subjects beyond your scope. Into the question how far conduct, especially in the matter of alliances, constitutes a forfeiture of family claims, I do not now enter. Suffice it, that you are not here qualified to discriminate. What I now wish you to understand is, that I accept no revision, still less dictation within that range of affairs which I have deliberated upon as distinctly and properly mine. It is not for you to interfere between me and Mr Ladislaw, and still less to encourage communications from him to you which constitute a criticism on my procedure.'

Poor Dorothea, shrouded in the darkness, was in a tumult of conflicting emotions. Alarm at the possible effect on himself of her husband's strongly-manifested anger, would have checked any expression of her own resentment, even if she had been quite free from doubt and compunction under the consciousness that there might be some justice in his last insinuation. Hearing him breathe quickly after he had spoken, she sat listening, frightened, wretched – with a dumb inward cry for help to bear this nightmare of a life in which every energy was arrested by dread. But nothing else happened, except that they both remained a long while sleepless, without speaking again.

The next day, Mr Casaubon received the following answer from Will Ladislaw:

DEAR MR CASAUBON – I have given all due consideration to your letter of yesterday, but I am unable to take precisely your view of our mutual position. With the fullest acknowledgment of your generous conduct to me in the past, I must still maintain that an obligation of this kind cannot fairly fetter me as you appear to expect that it should. Granted that a benefactor's wishes may constitute a claim: there must always be a reservation as to the quality of those wishes. They may possibly clash with more imperative considerations. Or a benefactor's veto might impose such a negation on a man's life that the consequent blank might be more cruel than the benefaction was generous. I am merely using strong illustrations. In the present case I am unable to take your view of the bearing which my acceptance of occupation – not enriching certainly, but not dishonourable – will have on your own position, which seems to me too substantial to be affected in that shadowy manner. And though I do not believe that any change in our relations will occur (certainly none has yet occurred) which can nullify the obligations imposed on me by the past, pardon me for not seeing that those obligations should restrain me from using the ordinary freedom of living where I choose, and maintaining myself by any lawful occupation I may choose. Regretting that there exists this difference between us as to a relation in which the conferring of benefits has been entirely on your side – I remain, yours with persistent obligation,

WILL LADISLAW

Poor Mr Casaubon felt (and must not we, being impartial, feel with him a little?) that no man had juster cause for disgust and suspicion than he. Young Ladislaw, he was sure, meant to defy and annoy him, meant to win Dorothea's confidence and sow her mind with disrespect, and perhaps aversion, towards her husband. Some motive beneath the surface had been needed to account for Will's sudden change of course in rejecting Mr Casaubon's aid and quitting his travels; and this defiant determination to fix himself in the neighbourhood by taking up something so much at variance with his former choice as Mr Brooke's Middlemarch projects, revealed clearly enough that the undeclared motive had relation to Dorothea. Not for one moment did Mr Casaubon suspect Dorothea of any doubleness: he had no suspicions of her, but he had (what was little less uncomfortable) the positive knowledge that her tendency to form opinions about her husband's conduct was accompanied with a disposition to regard Will Ladislaw favourably and be influenced by what he said. His own proud reticence had prevented him from ever being undeceived in the supposition that Dorothea had originally asked her uncle to invite Will to his house.

And now, on receiving Will's letter, Mr Casaubon had to consider his duty. It would never have been easy to call his action anything else than duty; but in this case, contending motives thrust him back into negations.

Should he apply directly to Mr Brooke, and demand of that troublesome gentleman to revoke his proposal? Or should he consult Sir James Chettam, and get him to concur in remonstrance against a step which touched the whole family? In either case Mr Casaubon was aware that failure was just as probable as success. It was impossible for him to mention Dorothea's name in the matter, and without some alarming urgency Mr Brooke was as likely as not, after meeting all representations with apparent assent, to wind up by saying, 'Never fear, Casaubon! Depend upon it, young Ladislaw will do you credit. Depend upon it, I have put my finger on the right thing.' And Mr Casaubon shrank nervously from communicating on the subject with Sir James Chettam, between whom and himself there had never been cordiality, and who would immediately think of Dorothea without any mention of her.

Poor Mr Casaubon was distrustful of everybody's feeling towards him, especially as a husband. To let anyone suppose that he was jealous would be to admit their (suspected) view of his disadvantages: to let them know that he did not find marriage particularly blissful would imply his conversion to their (probably) earlier disapproval. It would be as bad as letting Carp, and Brasenose generally, know how backward he was in organising the matter for his *Key to all Mythologies*. All through his life Mr Casaubon had been trying not to admit even to himself the inward sores of self-doubt and jealousy. And on the most delicate of all personal subjects, the habit of proud suspicious reticence told doubly.

Thus Mr Casaubon remained proudly, bitterly silent. But he had forbidden Will to come to Lowick Manor, and he was mentally preparing other means of frustration.

Chapter 38

C'est beaucoup que le jugement des hommes sur les
actions humaines; tôt ou tard il devient efficace.
                                                    GUIZOT

Sir James Chettam could not look with any satisfaction on Mr Brooke's new courses; but it was easier to object than to hinder. Sir James accounted for his having come in alone one day to lunch with the Cadwalladers by saying: 'I can't talk to you as I want, before Celia: it might hurt her. Indeed, it would not be right.'

'I know what you mean – the *Pioneer* at the Grange!' darted in Mrs Cadwallader, almost before the word was off her friend's tongue. 'It is frightful – this taking to buying whistles and blowing them in everybody's hearing. Lying in bed all day and playing at dominoes, like poor Lord Plessy, would be more private and bearable.'

'I see they are beginning to attack our friend Brooke in the *Trumpet*,' said the Rector, lounging back and smiling easily, as he would have done if he had been attacked himself. 'There are tremendous sarcasms against a Landlord not a hundred miles from Middlemarch, who receives his own rents, and makes no returns.'

'I do wish Brooke would leave that off,' said Sir James, with his little frown of annoyance.

'Is he really going to be put in nomination, though?' said Mr Cadwallader. 'I saw Farebrother yesterday – he's Whiggish himself, hoists Brougham and Useful Knowledge, that's the worst I know of him – and he says that Brooke is getting up a pretty strong party. Bulstrode, the banker, is his foremost man. But he thinks Brooke would come off badly at a nomination.'

'Exactly,' said Sir James, with earnestness. 'I have been enquiring into the thing, for I've never known anything about Middlemarch politics before – the county being my business. What Brooke trusts to, is that they are going to turn out Oliver because he is a Peelite. But Hawley tells me that if they send up a Whig at all it is sure to be Bagster, one of those candidates who come from heaven knows where, but dead against Ministers, and an experienced Parliamentary man. Hawley's rather rough: he forgot that he was speaking to me. He said if Brooke wanted a pelting, he could get it cheaper than by going to the hustings.'

'I warned you all of it,' said Mrs Cadwallader, waving her hands outward. 'I said to Humphrey long ago, Mr Brooke is going to make a splash in the mud. And now he has done it.'

'Well, he might have taken it into his head to marry,' said the Rector. 'That would have been a graver mess than a little flirtation with politics.'

'He may do that afterwards,' said Mrs Cadwallader – 'when he has come out on the other side of the mud with an ague.'

'What I care for most is his own dignity,' said Sir James. 'Of course I care the more because of the family. But he's getting on in life now, and I don't like to think of his exposing himself. They will be raking up everything against him.'

'I suppose it's no use trying any persuasion,' said the Rector. 'There's such an odd mixture of obstinacy and changeableness in Brooke. Have you tried him on the subject?'

'Well, no,' said Sir James; 'I feel a delicacy in appearing to dictate. But I have been talking to this young Ladislaw that Brooke is making a factotum of. Ladislaw seems clever enough for anything. I thought it as well to hear what he had to say; and he is against Brooke's standing this time. I think he'll turn him round: I think the nomination may be staved off.'

'I know,' said Mrs Cadwallader, nodding. 'The independent member hasn't got his speeches well enough by heart.'

'But this Ladislaw – there again is a vexatious business,' said Sir James. 'We have had him two or three times to dine at the Hall (you have met him, by the by) as Brooke's guest and a relation of Casaubon's, thinking he was only on a flying visit. And now I find he's in everybody's mouth in Middlemarch as the editor of the *Pioneer*. There are stories going about him as a quill-driving alien, a foreign emissary, and what not.'

'Casaubon won't like that,' said the Rector.

'There is some foreign blood in Ladislaw,' returned Sir James. 'I hope he won't go into extreme opinions and carry Brooke on.'

'Oh, he's a dangerous young sprig, that Mr Ladislaw,' said Mrs Cadwallader, 'with his opera songs and his ready tongue. A sort of Byronic hero – an amorous conspirator, it strikes me. And Thomas Aquinas is not fond of him. I could see that, the day the picture was brought.'

'I don't like to begin on the subject with Casaubon,' said Sir James. 'He has more right to interfere than I. But it's a disagreeable affair all round. What a character for anybody with decent connections to show himself in! – one of those newspaper fellows! You have only to look at Keck, who manages the *Trumpet*. I saw him the other day with Hawley. His writing is sound enough, I believe, but he's such a low fellow, that I wished he had been on the wrong side.'

'What can you expect with these peddling Middlemarch papers?' said the Rector. 'I don't suppose you could get a high style of man anywhere to be writing up interests he doesn't really care about, and for pay that hardly keeps him in at elbows.'

'Exactly: that makes it so annoying that Brooke should have put a man who has a sort of connection with the family in a position of that kind. For my part, I think Ladislaw is rather a fool for accepting.'

'It is Aquinas's fault,' said Mrs Cadwallader. 'Why didn't he use his interest to get Ladislaw made an *attaché* or sent to India? That is how families get rid of troublesome sprigs.'

'There is no knowing to what lengths the mischief may go,' said Sir James, anxiously. 'But if Casaubon says nothing, what can I do?'

'Oh, my dear Sir James,' said the Rector, 'don't let us make too much of all this. It is likely enough to end in mere smoke. After a month or two Brooke and this Master Ladislaw will get tired of each other; Ladislaw will take wing; Brooke will sell the *Pioneer*, and everything will settle down again as usual.'

'There is one good chance – that he will not like to feel his money oozing away,' said Mrs Cadwallader. 'If I knew the items of election expenses I could scare him. It's no use plying him with wide words like Expenditure: I wouldn't talk of phlebotomy, I would empty a pot of leeches upon him. What we good stingy people don't like, is having our sixpences sucked away from us.'

'And he will not like having things raked up against him,' said Sir James. 'There is the management of his estate. They have begun upon that already. And it really is painful for me to see. It is a nuisance under one's very nose. I do think one is bound to do the best for one's land and tenants, especially in these hard times.'

'Perhaps the *Trumpet* may rouse him to make a change, and some good may come of it all,' said the Rector. 'I know I should be glad. I should hear less grumbling when my tithe is paid. I don't know what I should do if there were not a modus in Tipton.'

'I want him to have a proper man to look after things – I want him to take on Garth again,' said Sir James. 'He got rid of Garth twelve years ago, and every-thing has been going wrong since. I think of getting Garth to manage for me – he has made such a capital plan for my buildings; and Lovegood is hardly up to the mark. But Garth would not undertake the Tipton estate again unless Brooke left it entirely to him.'

'In the right of it too,' said the Rector. 'Garth is an independent fellow: an original, simple-minded fellow. One day, when he was doing some valuation for me, he told me point-blank that clergymen seldom understood anything about business, and did mischief when they meddled; but he said it as quietly and respectfully as if he had been talking to me about sailors. He would make a different parish of Tipton, if Brooke would let him manage. I wish, by the help of the *Trumpet*, you could bring that round.'

'If Dorothea had kept near her uncle, there would have been some chance,' said Sir James. 'She might have got some power over him in time, and she was always uneasy about the estate. She had wonderfully good notions about such things. But now Casaubon takes her up entirely. Celia complains a good deal. We can hardly get her to dine with us since he had that fit.' Sir James ended with a look of pitying disgust, and Mrs Cadwallader shrugged her shoulders as much as to say that *she* was not likely to see anything new in that direction.

'Poor Casaubon!' the Rector said. 'That was a nasty attack. I thought he looked shattered the other day at the Archdeacon's.'

'In point of fact,' resumed Sir James, not choosing to dwell on 'fits', 'Brooke doesn't mean badly by his tenants or anyone else, but he has got that way of paring and clipping at expenses.'

'Come, that's a blessing,' said Mrs Cadwallader. 'That helps him to find himself in the morning. He may not know his own opinions, but he does know his own pocket.'

'I don't believe a man is in pocket by stinginess on his land,' said Sir James.

'Oh, stinginess may be abused like other virtues: it will not do to keep one's own pigs lean,' said Mrs Cadwallader, who had risen to look out of the window. 'But talk of an independent politician and he will appear.'

'What, Brooke?' said her husband.

'Yes. Now, you ply him with the *Trumpet*, Humphrey and I will put the leeches on him. What will you do, Sir James?'

'The fact is, I don't like to begin about it with Brooke, in our mutual position; the whole thing is so unpleasant. I do wish people would behave like gentlemen,' said the good baronet, feeling that this was a simple and comprehensive programme for social well-being.

'Here you all are, eh?' said Mr Brooke, shuffling round and shaking hands. 'I was going up to the Hall by and by, Chettam. But it's pleasant to find everybody, you know. Well, what do you think of things? – going on a little fast! It was true enough, what Lafitte said – "Since yesterday, a century has passed away": – they're in the next century, you know, on the other side of the water. Going on faster than we are.'

'Why, yes,' said the Rector, taking up the newspaper. 'Here is the *Trumpet* accusing you of lagging behind – did you see?'

'Eh? no,' said Mr Brooke, dropping his gloves into his hat and hastily adjusting his eye-glass. But Mr Cadwallader kept the paper in his hand, saying, with a smile in his eyes; 'Look here! all this is about a landlord not a hundred miles from Middlemarch, who receives his own rents. They say he is the most retrogressive man in the county. I think you must have taught them that word in the *Pioneer*.

'Oh, that is Keck – an illiterate fellow, you know. Retrogressive, now! Come, that's capital. He thinks it means destructive: they want to make me out a destructive, you know,' said Mr Brooke, with that cheerfulness which is usually sustained by an adversary's ignorance.

'I think he knows the meaning of the word. Here is a sharp stroke or two.

If we had to describe a man who is retrogressive in the most evil sense of the word – we should say, he is one who would dub himself a reformer of our constitution, while every interest for which he is immediately responsible is going to decay: a philanthropist who cannot bear one rogue to be hanged, but does not mind five honest tenants being half-starved: a man who shrieks at corruption, and keeps his farms at rack-rent: who roars himself red at rotten boroughs, and does not mind if every field on his farms has a rotten gate: a man very open-hearted to Leeds and Manchester, no doubt; he would give any number of representatives who will pay for their seats out of their own pockets: what he objects to giving, is a little return on rent-days to help a tenant to buy stock, or an outlay on repairs to keep the weather out at a tenant's barn-door or make his house look a little less like an Irish cottier's. But we all know the wag's definition of a philanthropist: a man whose charity increases directly as the square of the distance.

And so on. All the rest is to show what sort of legislator a philanthropist is likely to make,' ended the Rector, throwing down the paper, and clasping his hands at the back of his head, while he looked at Mr Brooke with an air of amused neutrality.

'Come, that's rather good you know,' said Mr Brooke, taking up the paper and trying to bear the attack as easily as his neighbour did, but colouring and smiling rather nervously; 'that about roaring himself red at rotten boroughs – I never made a speech about rotten boroughs in my life. And as to roaring myself red and that kind of thing – these men never understand what is good satire. Satire, you know, should be true up to a certain point. I recollect they said that in *The Edinburgh* somewhere – it must be true up to a certain point.'

'Well, that is really a hit about the gates,' said Sir James, anxious to tread carefully. 'Dagley complained to me the other day that he hadn't got a decent gate on his farm. Garth has invented a new pattern of gate – I wish you would try it. One ought to use some of one's timber in that way.'

'You go in for fancy farming, you know, Chettam,' said Mr Brooke, appearing to glance over the columns of the *Trumpet*. 'That's your hobby, and you don't mind the expense.'

'I thought the most expensive hobby in the world was standing for Parliament,' said Mrs Cadwallader. 'They said the last unsuccessful candidate at Middlemarch – Giles, wasn't his name? – spent ten thousand pounds and failed because he did not bribe enough. What a bitter reflection for a man!'

'Somebody was saying,' said the Rector, laughingly, 'that East Retford was nothing to Middlemarch, for bribery.'

'Nothing of the kind,' said Mr Brooke. 'The Tories bribe, you know: Hawley and his set bribe with treating, hot codlings, and that sort of thing; and they bring the voters drunk to the poll. But they are not going to have it their own way in future – not in future, you know. Middlemarch is a little backward, I admit the freemen are a little backward. But we shall educate them we shall bring them on, you know. The best people there are on our side.'

'Hawley says you have men on your side who will do you harm,' remarked Sir James. 'He says Bulstrode the banker will do you harm.'

'And that if you got pelted,' interposed Mrs Cadwallader, 'half the rotten eggs would mean hatred of your committee-man. Good heavens! Think what it must be to be pelted for wrong opinions. And I seem to remember a story of a man they pretended to chair and let him fall into a dust-heap on purpose!'

'Pelting is nothing to their finding holes in one's coat,' said the Rector. 'I confess that's what I should be afraid of, if we parsons had to stand at the hustings for preferment. I should be afraid of their reckoning up all my fishing days. Upon my word, I think the truth is the hardest missile one can be pelted with.'

'The fact is,' said Sir James, 'if a man goes into public life he must be prepared for the consequences. He must make himself proof against calumny.'

'My dear Chettam, that is all very fine, you know,' said Mr Brooke. 'But how will you make yourself proof against calumny? You should read history – look at ostracism, persecution, martyrdom, and that kind of thing. They always happen to the best men, you know. But what is that in Horace? – *fiat justitia, ruat* . . . something or other.'

'Exactly,' said Sir James, with a little more heat than usual. 'What I mean by being proof against calumny is being able to point to the fact as a contradiction.'

'And it is not martyrdom to pay bills that one has run into one's self,' said Mrs Cadwallader.

But it was Sir James's evident annoyance that most stirred Mr Brooke. 'Well, you know, Chettam,' he said, rising, taking up his hat and leaning on his stick, 'you and I have a different system. You are all for outlay with your farms. I don't want to make out that my system is good under all circumstances – under all circumstances, you know.'

'There ought to be a new valuation made from time to time,' said Sir James. 'Returns are very well occasionally, but I like a fair valuation. What do you say, Cadwallader?'

'I agree with you. If I were Brooke, I would choke the *Trumpet* at once by getting Garth to make a new valuation of the farms, and giving him *carte blanche* about gates and repairs: that's my view of the political situation,' said the Rector, broadening himself by sticking his thumbs in his armholes, and laughing towards Mr Brooke.

'That's a showy sort of thing to do, you know,' said Mr Brooke. 'But I should like you to tell me of another landlord who has distressed his tenants for arrears as little as I have. I let the old tenants stay on. I'm uncommonly easy, let me tell you uncommonly easy. I have my own ideas, and I take my stand on them, you know. A man who does that is always charged with eccentricity, inconsistency, and that kind of thing. When I change my line of action, I shall follow my own ideas.'

After that, Mr Brooke remembered that there was a packet which he had omitted to send off from the Grange, and he bade everybody hurriedly goodbye.

'I didn't want to take a liberty with Brooke,' said Sir James; 'I see he is nettled. But as to what he says about old tenants, in point of fact no new tenant would take the farms on the present terms.'

'I have a notion that he will be brought round in time,' said the Rector. 'But you were pulling one way, Elinor, and we were pulling another. You wanted to frighten him away from expense, and we want to frighten him into it. Better let him try to be popular and see that his character as a landlord stands in his way. I don't think it signifies two straws about the *Pioneer*, or Ladislaw, or Brooke's speechifying to the Middlemarchers. But it does signify about the parishioners in Tipton being comfortable.'

'Excuse me, it is you two who are on the wrong tack,' said Mrs Cadwallader. 'You should have proved to him that he loses money by bad management, and then we all should have pulled together. If you put him a-horseback on politics, I warn you of the consequences. It was all very well to ride on sticks at home and call them ideas.'

Chapter 39

If, as I have, you also doe,
  Vertue attired in woman see,
And dare love that, and say so too,
  And forget the He and She;

And if this love, though placed so,
  From prophane men you hide,
Which will no faith on this bestow,
  Or, if they doe, deride:

Then you have done a braver thing
  Than all the Worthies did,
And a braver thence will spring,
  Which is, to keep that hid.
                              DR DONNE

Sir James Chettam's mind was not fruitful in devices, but his growing anxiety to 'act on Brooke', once brought close to his constant belief in Dorothea's capacity for influence, became formative and issued in a little plan; namely, to plead Celia's indisposition as a reason for fetching Dorothea by herself to the Hall, and to leave her at the Grange with the carriage on the way, after making her fully aware of the situation concerning the management of the estate.

In this way it happened that one day near four o'clock, when Mr Brooke and Ladislaw were seated in the library, the door opened and Mrs Casaubon was announced.

Will, the moment before, had been low in the depths of boredom, and, obliged to help Mr Brooke in arranging 'documents' about hanging sheep-stealers, was exemplifying the power our minds have of riding several horses at once by inwardly arranging measures towards getting a lodging for himself in Middlemarch and cutting short his constant residence at the Grange; while there flitted through all these steadier images a tickling vision of a sheep-stealing epic written with Homeric particularity. When Mrs Casaubon was announced he started up as from an electric shock, and felt a tingling at his finger-ends. Anyone observing him would have seen a change in his complexion, in the adjustment of his facial muscles, in the vividness of his glance, which might have made them imagine that every molecule in his body had passed the message of a magic touch. And so it had. For effective magic is transcendent nature; and who shall measure the subtlety of those touches which convey the quality of soul as well as body, and make a man's passion for one woman differ from his passion for another as joy in the morning light over valley and river and white mountain-top differs from joy among Chinese lanterns and glass panels? Will, too, was made of very impressible stuff. The bow of a violin drawn near him cleverly, would at one stroke change the aspect of the world for him, and his point of view shifted as easily as his mood. Dorothea's entrance was the freshness of morning.

'Well, my dear, this is pleasant, now,' said Mr Brooke, meeting and kissing her. 'You have left Casaubon with his books, I suppose. That's right. We must not have you getting too learned for a woman, you know.'

'There is no fear of that, uncle,' said Dorothea, turning to Will and shaking hands with open cheerfulness, while she made no other form of greeting, but went on answering her uncle. 'I am very slow. When I want to be busy with books, I am often playing truant among my thoughts. I find it is not so easy to be learned as to plan cottages.'

She seated herself beside her uncle opposite to Will, and was evidently pre-occupied with something that made her almost unmindful of him. He was ridiculously disappointed, as if he had imagined that her coming had anything to do with him.

'Why, yes, my dear, it was quite your hobby to draw plans. But it was good to break that off a little. Hobbies are apt to run away with us, you know; it doesn't do to be run away with. We must keep the reins. I have never let myself be run away with; I always pulled up. That is what I tell Ladislaw. He and I are alike, you know: he likes to go into everything. We are working at capital punishment. We shall do a great deal together, Ladislaw and I.'

'Yes,' said Dorothea, with characteristic directness, 'Sir James has been telling me that he is in hope of seeing a great change made soon in your management of the estate – that you are thinking of having the farms valued, and repairs made, and the cottages improved, so that Tipton may look quite another place. Oh, how happy!' – she went on, clasping her hands, with a return to that more childlike impetuous manner which had been subdued since her marriage. 'If I were at home still, I should take to riding again, that I might go about with you and see all that! And you are going to engage Mr Garth, who praised my cottages, Sir James says.'

'Chettam is a little hasty, my dear,' said Mr Brooke, colouring slightly. 'A little hasty, you know. I never said I should do anything of the kind. I never said I should not do it, you know.'

'He only feels confident that you will do it,' said Dorothea, in a voice as clear and unhesitating as that of a young chorister chanting a *credo*, 'because you mean to enter Parliament as a member who cares for the improvement of the people, and one of the first things to be made better is the state of the land and the labourers. Think of Kit Downes, uncle, who lives with his wife and seven children in a house with one sitting-room and one bedroom hardly larger than this table! – and those poor Dagleys, in their tumbledown farmhouse, where they live in the back kitchen and leave the other rooms to the rats! That is one reason why I did not like the pictures here, dear uncle which you think me stupid about. I used to come from the village with all that dirt and coarse ugliness like a pain within me, and the simpering pictures in the drawing-room seemed to me like a wicked attempt to find delight in what is false, while we don't mind how hard the truth is for the neighbours outside our walls. I think we have no right to come forward and urge wider changes for good, until we have tried to alter the evils which lie under our own hands.'

Dorothea had gathered emotion as she went on, and had forgotten everything except the relief of pouring forth her feelings, unchecked: an experience once habitual with her, but hardly ever present since her marriage, which had been a perpetual struggle of energy with fear. For the moment, Will's admiration was accompanied with a chilling sense of remoteness. A man is seldom ashamed of feeling that he cannot love a woman so well when he sees a certain greatness in her: nature having intended greatness for men. But nature has sometimes made sad oversights in carrying out her intentions; as in the case of good Mr Brooke, whose masculine consciousness was at this moment in rather a stammering condition under the eloquence of his niece. He could not immediately find any other mode of expressing himself than that of rising, fixing his eye-glass, and fingering the papers before him. At last he said: 'There is something in what you say, my dear, something in what you say – but not everything – eh, Ladislaw. You and I don't like our pictures and statues being found fault with. Young ladies are a little ardent, you know – a little one-sided, my dear. Fine art, poetry, that kind of thing, elevates a nation – *emollit mores* – you understand a little Latin now. But – eh, what?'

These interrogatives were addressed to the footman who had come in to say that the keeper had found one of Dagley's boys with a leveret in his hand, just killed.

'I'll come, I'll come. I shall let him off easily, you know,' said Mr Brooke aside to Dorothea, shuffling away very cheerfully.

'I hope you feel how right this change is that I – that Sir James wishes for,' said Dorothea to Will, as soon as her uncle was gone.

'I do, now I have heard you speak about it. I shall not forget what you have said. But can you think of something else at this moment? I may not have another opportunity of speaking to you about what has occurred,' said Will, rising with a movement of impatience, and holding the back of his chair with both hands.

'Pray tell me what it is,' said Dorothea, anxiously, also rising and going to the open window, where Monk was looking in, panting and wagging his tail. She leaned her back against the window-frame, and laid her hand on the dog's head; for though, as we know, she was not fond of pets that must be held in the hands or trodden on, she was always attentive to the feelings of dogs, and very polite if she had to decline their advances.

Will followed her only with his eyes and said, 'I presume you know that Mr Casaubon has forbidden me to go to his house.'

'No, I did not,' said Dorothea, after a moment's pause. She was evidently much moved. 'I am very, very sorry,' she added, mournfully. She was thinking of what Will had no knowledge of – the conversation between her and her husband in the darkness; and she was anew smitten with hopelessness that she could influence Mr Casaubon's action. But the marked expression of her sorrow convinced Will that it was not all given to him personally, and that Dorothea had not been visited by the idea that Mr Casaubon's dislike and jealousy of him turned upon herself. He felt an odd mixture of delight and vexation: of delight that he could dwell and be cherished in her thought as in a pure home, without suspicion and without stint – of vexation because he was of too little account with her, was not formidable enough, was treated with an unhesitating benevolence which did not flatter him. But his dread of any change in Dorothea was stronger than his discontent, and he began to speak again in a tone of mere explanation.

'Mr Casaubon's reason is, his displeasure at my taking a position here which he considers unsuited to my rank as his cousin. I have told him that I cannot give way on this point. It is a little too hard on me to expect that my course in life is to be hampered by prejudices which I think ridiculous. Obligation may be stretched till it is no better than a brand of slavery stamped on us when we were too young to know its meaning. I would not have accepted the position if I had not meant to make it useful and honourable. I am not bound to regard family dignity in any other light.'

Dorothea felt wretched. She thought her husband altogether in the wrong, on more grounds than Will had mentioned.

'It is better for us not to speak on the subject,' she said, with a tremulousness not common in her voice, 'since you and Mr Casaubon disagree. You intend to remain?' She was looking out on the lawn, with melancholy meditation.

'Yes; but I shall hardly ever see you now,' said Will, in a tone of almost boyish complaint.

'No,' said Dorothea, turning her eyes full upon him, 'hardly ever. But I shall hear of you. I shall know what you are doing for my uncle.'

'I shall know hardly anything about you,' said Will. 'No one will tell me anything.'

'Oh, my life is very simple,' said Dorothea, her lips curling with an exquisite smile, which irradiated her melancholy. 'I am always at Lowick.'

'That is a dreadful imprisonment,' said Will, impetuously.

'No, don't think that,' said Dorothea. 'I have no longings.'

He did not speak, but she replied to some change in his expression. 'I mean, for myself. Except that I should like not to have so much more than my share without doing anything for others. But I have a belief of my own, and it comforts me.'

'What is that?' said Will, rather jealous of the belief.

'That by desiring what is perfectly good, even when we don't quite know what it is and cannot do what we would, we are part of the divine power against evil – widening the skirts of light and making the struggle with darkness narrower.'

'That is a beautiful mysticism – it is a –'

'Please not to call it by any name,' said Dorothea, putting out her hands entreatingly. 'You will say it is Persian, or something else geographical. It is my life. I have found it out, and cannot part with it. I have always been finding out my religion since I was a little girl. I used to pray so much – now I hardly ever pray. I try not to have desires merely for myself, because they may not be good for others, and I have too much already. I only told you, that you might know quite well how my days go at Lowick.'

'God bless you for telling me!' said Will, ardently, and rather wondering at himself. They were looking at each other like two fond children who were talking confidentially of birds.

'What is your religion?' said Dorothea. 'I mean – not what you know about religion, but the belief that helps you most?'

'To love what is good and beautiful when I see it,' said Will. 'But I am a rebel: I don't feel bound, as you do, to submit to what I don't like.'

'But if you like what is good, that comes to the same thing,' said Dorothea, smiling.

'Now you are subtle,' said Will.

'Yes; Mr Casaubon often says I am too subtle. I don't feel as if I were subtle,' said Dorothea, playfully. 'But how long my uncle is! I must go and look for him. I must really go on to the Hall. Celia is expecting me.'

Will offered to tell Mr Brooke, who presently came and said that he would step into the carriage and go with Dorothea as far as Dagley's, to speak about the small delinquent who had been caught with the leveret. Dorothea renewed the subject of the estate as they drove along, but Mr Brooke, not being taken unawares, got the talk under his own control.

'Chettam, now,' he replied; 'he finds fault with me, my dear; but I should not preserve my game if it were not for Chettam, and he can't say that that expense is for the sake of the tenants, you know. It's a little against my feeling: – poaching, now, if you come to look into it – I have often thought of getting up the subject. Not long ago, Flavell, the Methodist preacher, was brought up for knocking down a hare that came across his path when he and his wife were walking out together. He was pretty quick, and knocked it on the neck.'

'That was very brutal, I think,' said Dorothea.

'Well, now, it seemed rather black to me, I confess, in a Methodist preacher, you know. And Johnson said, "You may judge what a hypocrite he is." And upon my word, I thought Flavell looked very little like "the highest style of man" – as somebody calls the Christian – Young, the poet Young, I think you know Young? Well, now, Flavell in his shabby black gaiters, pleading that he thought the Lord had sent him and his wife a good dinner, and he had a right to knock it down, though not a mighty hunter before the Lord, as Nimrod was – I assure you it was rather comic: Fielding would have made something of it – or Scott, now – Scott might have worked it up. But really, when I came to think of it, I couldn't help liking that the fellow should have a bit of hare to say grace over. It's all a matter of prejudice – prejudice with the law on its side, you know – about the stick and the gaiters, and so on. However, it doesn't do to reason about things; and law is law. But I got Johnson to be quiet, and I hushed the matter up. I doubt whether Chettam would not have been more severe, and yet he comes down on me as if I were the hardest man in the county. But we are here at Dagley's.'

Mr Brooke got down at the farmyard-gate, and Dorothea drove on. It is wonderful how much uglier things will look when we only suspect that we are blamed for them. Even our own persons in the glass are apt to change their aspect for us after we have heard some frank remark on their less admirable points; and on the other hand it is astonishing how pleasantly conscience takes our encroachments on those who never complain or have nobody to complain for them. Dagley's homestead never looked before so dismal to Mr Brooke as it did today, with his mind thus sore about the fault-finding of the *Trumpet*, echoed by Sir James.

It is true that an observer, under that softening influence of the fine arts which makes other people's hardships picturesque, might have been delighted with this homestead called Freeman's End: the old house had dormer-windows in the dark-red roof, two of the chimneys were choked with ivy, the large porch was blocked up with bundles of sticks, and half the windows were closed with grey worm-eaten shutters about which the jasmine-boughs grew in wild luxuriance; the mouldering garden wall with hollyhocks peeping over it was a perfect study of highly-mingled subdued colour, and there was an aged goat (kept doubtless on interesting superstitious grounds) lying against the open back-kitchen door. The mossy thatch of the cowshed, the broken grey barn-doors, the pauper labourers in ragged breeches who had nearly finished un-loading a waggon of corn into the barn ready for early thrashing; the scanty dairy of cows being tethered for milking and leaving one half of the shed in brown emptiness; the very pigs and white ducks seeming to wander about the uneven neglected yard as if in low spirits from feeding on a too meagre quality of rinsings – all these objects under the quiet light of a sky marbled with high clouds would have made a sort of picture which we have all paused over as a 'charming bit', touching other sensibilities than those which are stirred by the depression of the agricultural interest, with the sad lack of farming capital, as seen constantly in the newspapers of that time. But these troublesome associations were just now strongly present to Mr Brooke, and spoiled the scene for him. Mr Dagley himself made a figure in the landscape, carrying a pitchfork and wearing his milking-hat – a very old beaver flattened in front. His coat and breeches were the best he had, and he would not have been wearing them on this weekday occasion if he had not been to market and returned later than usual, having given himself the rare treat of dining at the public table of the Blue Bull. How he came to fall into this extravagance would perhaps be matter of wonderment to himself on the morrow; but before dinner something in the state of the country, a slight pause in the harvest before the Far Dips were cut, the stories about the new King and the numerous handbills on the walls, had seemed to warrant a little recklessness. It was a maxim about Middlemarch, and regarded as self-evident, that good meat should have good drink, which last Dagley interpreted as plenty of table ale well followed up by rum-and-water. These liquors have so far truth in them that they were not false enough to make poor Dagley seem merry: they only made his discontent less tongue-tied than usual. He had also taken too much in the shape of muddy political talk, a stimulant dangerously disturbing to his farming conservatism, which consisted in holding that whatever is, is bad, and any change is likely to be worse. He was flushed, and his eyes had a decidedly quarrelsome stare as he stood still grasping his pitchfork, while the landlord approached with his easy shuffling walk, one hand in his trouser-pocket and the other swinging round a thin walking-stick.

'Dagley, my good fellow,' began Mr Brooke, conscious that he was going to be very friendly about the boy.

'Oh, ay I'm a good feller, am I? Thank ye, sir, thank ye,' said Dagley, with a loud snarling irony which made Fag the sheepdog stir from his seat and prick his ears; but seeing Monk enter the yard after some outside loitering, Fag seated himself again in an attitude of observation. 'I'm glad to hear I'm a good feller.'

Mr Brooke reflected that it was market-day, and that his worthy tenant had probably been dining, but saw no reason why he should not go on, since he could take the precaution of repeating what he had to say to Mrs Dagley.

'Your little lad Jacob has been caught killing a leveret, Dagley: I have told Johnson to lock him up in the empty stable an hour or two, just to frighten him, you know. But he will be brought home by and by, before night: and you'll just look after him, will you, and give him a reprimand, you know?'

'No, I woon't: I'll be dee'd if I'll leather my boy to please you or anybody else, not if you was twenty landlords istid o' one, and that a bad un.'

Dagley's words were loud enough to summon his wife to the back-kitchen door – the only entrance ever used, and one always open except in bad weather – and Mr Brooke, saying soothingly, 'Well, well, I'll speak to your wife – I didn't mean beating, you know,' turned to walk to the house. But Dagley, only the more inclined to 'have his say' with a gentleman who walked away from him, followed at once, with Fag slouching at his heels and sullenly evading some small and probably charitable advances on the part of Monk.

'How do you do, Mrs Dagley?' said Mr Brooke, making some haste. 'I came to tell you about your boy: I don't want you to give him the stick, you know.' He was careful to speak quite plainly this time.

Overworked Mrs Dagley – a thin, worn woman, from whose life pleasure had so entirely vanished that she had not even any Sunday clothes which could give her satisfaction in preparing for church – had already had a misunderstanding with her husband since he had come home, and was in low spirits, expecting the worst. But her husband was beforehand in answering.

'No, nor he woon't hev the stick, whether you want it or no,' pursued Dagley, throwing out his voice, as if he wanted it to hit hard. 'You've got no call to come an' talk about sticks o' these primises, as you woon't give a stick tow'rt mending. Go to Middlemarch to ax for *your* charrickter.'

'You'd far better hold your tongue, Dagley,' said the wife, 'and not kick your own trough over. When a man as is father of a family has been an' spent money at market and made himself the worse for liquor, he's done enough mischief for one day. But I should like to know what my boy's done, sir.'

'Niver do you mind what he's done,' said Dagley, more fiercely, 'it's my business to speak, an' not yourn. An' I wull speak, too. I'll hev my say – supper or no. An' what I say is, as I've lived upo' your ground from my father and grand-father afore me, an' hev dropped our money into't, an' me an' my children might lie an' rot on the ground for top-dressin' as we can't find the money to buy, if the King wasn't to put a stop.'

'My good fellow, you're drunk, you know,' said Mr Brooke, confidentially, but not judiciously. 'Another day, another day,' he added, turning as if to go.

But Dagley immediately fronted him, and Fag at his heels growled low, as his master's voice grew louder and more insulting, while Monk also drew close in silent dignified watch. The labourers on the waggon were pausing to listen, and it seemed wiser to be quite passive than to attempt a ridiculous flight pursued by a bawling man.

'I'm no more drunk nor you are, nor so much,' said Dagley. 'I can carry my liquor, an' I know what I mean. An' I meean as the King 'ull put a stop to't, for them say it as knows it, as there's to be a Rinform, and them landlords as never done the right thing by their tenants 'ull be treated i' that way as they'll hev to scuttle off. An' there's them i' Middlemarch knows what the Rinform is – an' as knows who'll hev to scuttle. Says they, "I know who your landlord is." An' says I, "I hope you're the better for knowin' him, I arn't." Says they, "He's a close-fisted un." "Ay, ay," says I. "He's a man for the Rinform," says they. That's what they says. An' I made out what the Rinform were – an' it were to send you an' your likes a-scuttlin'; an' wi' pretty strong-smellin' things too. An' you may do as you like now, for I'm none afeard on you. An' you'd better let my boy aloan, an' look to yoursen, afore the Rinform has got upo' your back. That's what I'n got to say,' concluded Mr Dagley, striking his fork into the ground with a firmness which proved inconvenient as he tried to draw it up again.

At this last action Monk began to bark loudly, and it was a moment for Mr Brooke to escape. He walked out of the yard as quickly as he could, in some amazement at the novelty of his situation. He had never been insulted on his own land before, and had been inclined to regard himself as a general favourite (we are all apt to do so, when we think of our own amiability more than of what other people are likely to want of us). When he had quarrelled with Caleb Garth twelve years before he had thought that the tenants would be pleased at the landlord's taking everything into his own hands.

Some who follow the narrative of his experience may wonder at the midnight darkness of Mr Dagley; but nothing was easier in those times than for a hereditary farmer of his grade to be ignorant, in spite somehow of having a rector in the twin parish who was a gentleman to the backbone, a curate nearer at hand who preached more learnedly than the rector, a landlord who had gone into everything, especially fine art and social improvement, and all the lights of Middlemarch only three miles off. As to the facility with which mortals escape knowledge, try an average acquaintance in the intellectual blaze of London, and consider what that eligible person for a dinner-party would have been if he had learned scant skill in 'summing' from the parish-clerk of Tipton, and read a chapter in the Bible with immense difficulty, because such names as Isaiah or Apollos remained unmanageable after twice spelling. Poor Dagley read a few verses sometimes on a Sunday evening, and the world was at least not darker to him than it had been before. Some things he knew thoroughly, namely, the slovenly habits of farming, and the awkwardness of weather, stock, and crops, at Freeman's End – so called apparently by way of sarcasm, to imply that a man was free to quit it if he chose, but that there was no earthly 'beyond' open to him.

Chapter 40

Wise in his daily work was he:
    To fruits of diligence,
And not to faiths or polity,
    He plied his utmost sense.
These perfect in their little parts,
    Whose work is all their prize –
Without them how could laws, or arts,
    Or towered cities rise?

In watching effects, if only of an electric battery, it is often necessary to change our place and examine a particular mixture or group at some distance from the point where the movement we are interested in was set up. The group I am moving towards is at Caleb Garth's breakfast-table in the large parlour where the maps and desk were: father, mother, and five of the children. Mary was just now at home waiting for a situation, while Christy, the boy next to her, was getting cheap learning and cheap fare in Scotland, having to his father's disappointment taken to books instead of that sacred calling 'business'.

The letters had come – nine costly letters, for which the postman had been paid three and twopence, and Mr Garth was forgetting his tea and toast while he read his letters and laid them open one above the other, sometimes swaying his head slowly, sometimes screwing up his mouth in inward debate, but not forgetting to cut off a large red seal unbroken, which Letty snatched up like an eager terrier.

The talk among the rest went on unrestrainedly, for nothing disturbed Caleb's absorption except shaking the table when he was writing.

Two letters of the nine had been for Mary. After reading them, she had passed them to her mother, and sat playing with her teaspoon absently, till with a sudden recollection she returned to her sewing, which she had kept on her lap during breakfast.

'Oh, don't sew, Mary!' said Ben, pulling her arm down. 'Make me a peacock with this bread-crumb.' He had been kneading a small mass for the purpose.

'No, no, Mischief!' said Mary, good-humouredly, while she pricked his hand lightly with her needle. 'Try and mould it yourself: you have seen me do it often enough. I must get this sewing done. It is for Rosamond Vincy: she is to be married next week, and she can't be married without this handkerchief.' Mary ended merrily, amused with the last notion.

'Why can't she, Mary?' said Letty, seriously interested in this mystery, and pushing her head so close to her sister that Mary now turned the threatening needle towards Letty's nose.

'Because this is one of a dozen, and without it there would only be eleven,' said Mary, with a grave air of explanation, so that Letty sank back with a sense of knowledge.

'Have you made up your mind, my dear,' said Mrs Garth, laying the letters down.

'I shall go to the school at York,' said Mary. 'I am less unfit to teach in a school than in a family. I like to teach classes best. And, you see, I must teach: there is nothing else to be done.'

'Teaching seems to me the most delightful work in the world,' said Mrs Garth, with a touch of rebuke in her tone. 'I could understand your objection to it if you had not knowledge enough, Mary, or if you disliked children.'

'I suppose we never quite understand why another dislikes what we like, mother,' said Mary, rather curtly. 'I am not fond of a schoolroom: I like the outside world better. It is a very inconvenient fault of mine.'

'It must be very stupid to be always in a girls' school,' said Alfred, 'Such a set of nincompoops, like Mrs Ballard's pupils walking two and two.'

'And they have no games worth playing at,' said Jim. 'They can neither throw nor leap. I don't wonder at Mary's not liking it.'

'What is that Mary doesn't like, eh?' said the father, looking over his spectacles and pausing before he opened his next letter.

'Being among a lot of nincompoop girls,' said Alfred.

'Is it the situation you had heard of, Mary?' said Caleb, gently, looking at his daughter.

'Yes, father: the school at York. I have determined to take it. It is quite the best. Thirty-five pounds a year, and extra pay for teaching the smallest strummers at the piano.'

'Poor child! I wish she could stay at home with us, Susan,' said Caleb, looking plaintively at his wife.

'Mary would not be happy without doing her duty,' said Mrs Garth, magisterially, conscious of having done her own.

'It wouldn't make me happy to do such a nasty duty as that,' said Alfred – at which Mary and her father laughed silently, but Mrs Garth said, gravely; 'Do find a fitter word than nasty, my dear Alfred, for everything that you think disagreeable. And suppose that Mary could help you to go to Mr Hanmer's with the money she gets?'

'That seems to me a great shame. But she's an old brick,' said Alfred, rising from his chair, and pulling Mary's head backward to kiss her.

Mary coloured and laughed, but could not conceal that the tears were coming. Caleb, looking on over his spectacles, with the angles of his eyebrows falling, had an expression of mingled delight and sorrow as he returned to the opening of his letter; and even Mrs Garth, her lips curling with a calm contentment, allowed that inappropriate language to pass without correction, although Ben immediately took it up, and sang, 'She's an old brick, old brick, old brick!' to a cantering measure, which he beat out with his fist on Mary's arm.

But Mrs Garth's eyes were now drawn towards her husband, who was already deep in the letter he was reading. His face had an expression of grave surprise, which alarmed her a little, but he did not like to be questioned while he was reading, and she remained anxiously watching till she saw him suddenly shaken by a little joyous laugh as he turned back to the beginning of the letter, and looking at her above his spectacles, said, in a low tone, 'What do you think, Susan?'

She went and stood behind him, putting her hand on his shoulder, while they read the letter together. It was from Sir James Chettam, offering to Mr Garth the management of the family estates at Freshitt and elsewhere, and adding that Sir James had been requested by Mr Brooke of Tipton to ascertain whether Mr Garth would be disposed at the same time to resume the agency of the Tipton property. The Baronet added in very obliging words that he himself was particularly desirous of seeing the Freshitt and Tipton estates under the same management, and he hoped to be able to show that the double agency might be held on terms agreeable to Mr Garth, whom he would be glad to see at the Hall at twelve o'clock on the following day.

'He writes handsomely, doesn't he, Susan?' said Caleb, turning his eyes upward to his wife, who raised her hand from his shoulder to his ear, while she rested her chin on his head. 'Brooke didn't like to ask me himself, I can see,' he continued, laughing silently.

'Here is an honour to your father, children,' said Mrs Garth, looking round at the five pairs of eyes, all fixed on the parents. 'He is asked to take a post again by those who dismissed him long ago. That shows that he did his work well, so that they feel the want of him.'

'Like Cincinnatus – hooray!' said Ben, riding on his chair, with a pleasant confidence that discipline was relaxed.

'Will they come to fetch him, mother?' said Letty, thinking of the Mayor and Corporation in their robes.

Mrs Garth patted Letty's head and smiled, but seeing that her husband was gathering up his letters and likely soon to be out of reach in that sanctuary 'business', she pressed his shoulder and said emphatically.

'Now, mind you ask fair pay, Caleb.'

'Oh, yes,' said Caleb, in a deep voice of assent, as if it would be unreasonable to suppose anything else of him. 'It'll come to between four and five hundred, the two together.' Then with a little start of remembrance he said, 'Mary, write and give up that school. Stay and help your mother. I'm as pleased as Punch, now I've thought of that.'

No manner could have been less like that of Punch triumphant than Caleb's, but his talents did not lie in finding phrases, though he was very particular about his letter-writing, and regarded his wife as a treasury of correct language.

There was almost an uproar among the children now, and Mary held up the cambric embroidery towards her mother entreatingly, that it might be put out of reach while the boys dragged her into a dance. Mrs Garth, in placid joy, began to put the cups and plates together, while Caleb pushing his chair from the table, as if he were going to move to the desk, still sat holding his letters in his hand and looking on the ground meditatively, stretching out the fingers of his left hand, according to a mute language of his own. At last he said: 'It's a thousand pities Christy didn't take to business, Susan. I shall want help by and by. And Alfred must go off to the engineering – I've made up my mind to that.' He fell into meditation and finger rhetoric again for a little while, and then continued: – 'I shall make Brooke have new agreements with the tenants, and I shall draw up a rotation of crops. And I'll lay a wager we can get fine bricks out of the clay at Bott's corner. I must look into that: it would cheapen the repairs. It's a fine bit of work, Susan! A man without a family would be glad to do it for nothing.'

'Mind you don't, though,' said his wife, lifting up her finger.

'No, no; but it's a fine thing to come to a man when he's seen into the nature of business; to have a chance of getting a bit of the country into good fettle, as they say, and putting men into the right way with their farming, and getting a bit of good contriving and solid building done – that those who are living and those who come after will be the better for. I'd sooner have it than a fortune. I hold it the most honourable work that is.' Here Caleb laid down his letters, thrust his fingers between the buttons of his waistcoat, and sat upright, but presently proceeded with some awe in his voice and moving his head slowly aside – 'It's a great gift of God, Susan.'

'That it is, Caleb,' said his wife, with answering fervour. 'And it will be a blessing to your children to have had a father who did such work: a father whose good work remains though his name may be forgotten.' She could not say any more to him then about the pay.

In the evening, when Caleb, rather tired with his day's work, was seated in silence with his pocketbook open on his knee, while Mrs Garth and Mary were at their sewing, and Letty in a corner was whispering a dialogue with her doll, Mr Farebrother came up the orchard walk, dividing the bright August lights and shadows with the tufted grass and the apple-tree boughs. We know that he was fond of his parishioners the Garths, and had thought Mary worth mentioning to Lydgate. He used to the full the clergyman's privilege of disregarding the Middlemarch discrimination of ranks, and always told his mother that Mrs Garth was more of a lady than any matron in the town. Still, you see, he spent his evenings at the Vincys', where the matron, though less of a lady, presided over a well-lit drawing-room and whist. In those days human intercourse was not determined solely by respect. But the Vicar did heartily respect the Garths, and a visit from him was no surprise to that family. Nevertheless he accounted for it even while he was shaking hands, by saying, 'I come as an envoy, Mrs Garth: I have something to say to you and Garth on behalf of Fred Vincy. The fact is, poor fellow,' he continued, as he seated himself and looked round with his bright glance at the three who were listening to him, 'he has taken me into his confidence.'

Mary's heart beat rather quickly: she wondered how far Fred's confidence had gone.

'We haven't seen the lad for months,' said Caleb. 'I couldn't think what was become of him.'

'He has been away on a visit,' said the Vicar, 'because home was a little too hot for him, and Lydgate told his mother that the poor fellow must not begin to study yet. But yesterday he came and poured himself out to me. I am very glad he did, because I have seen him grow up from a youngster of fourteen, and I am so much at home in the house that the children are like nephews and nieces to me. But it is a difficult case to advise upon. However, he has asked me to come and tell you that he is going away, and that he is so miserable about his debt to you, and his inability to pay, that he can't bear to come himself even to bid you goodbye.'

'Tell him it doesn't signify a farthing,' said Caleb, waving his hand. 'We've had the pinch and have got over it. And now I'm going to be as rich as a Jew.'

'Which means,' said Mrs Garth, smiling at the Vicar, 'that we are going to have enough to bring up the boys well and to keep Mary at home.'

'What is the treasure-trove?' said Mr Farebrother.

'I'm going to be agent for two estates, Freshitt and Tipton; and perhaps for a pretty little bit of land in Lowick besides: it's all the same family connection, and employment spreads like water if it's once set going. It makes me very happy, Mr Farebrother' – here Caleb threw back his head a little, and spread his arms on the elbows of his chair – 'that I've got an opportunity again with the letting of the land, and carrying out a notion or two with improvements. It's a most uncommonly cramping thing, as I've often told Susan, to sit on horseback and look over the hedges at the wrong thing, and not be able to put your hand to it to make it right. What people do who go into politics I can't think: it drives me almost mad to see mismanagement over only a few hundred acres.'

It was seldom that Caleb volunteered so long a speech, but his happiness had the effect of mountain air: his eyes were bright, and the words came without effort.

'I congratulate you heartily, Garth,' said the Vicar. 'This is the best sort of news I could have had to carry to Fred Vincy, for he dwelt a good deal on the injury he had done you in causing you to part with money – robbing you of it, he said – which you wanted for other purposes. I wish Fred was not such an idle dog; he has some very good points, and his father is a little hard upon him.'

'Where is he going?' said Mrs Garth, rather coldly.

'He means to try again for his degree, and he is going up to study before term. I have advised him to do that. I don't urge him to enter the Church – on the contrary. But if he will go and work so as to pass, that will be some guarantee that he has energy and a will; and he is quite at sea; he doesn't know what else to do. So far he will please his father, and I have promised in the meantime to try and reconcile Vincy to his son's adopting some other line of life. Fred says frankly he is not fit for a clergyman, and I would do anything I could to hinder a man from the fatal step of choosing the wrong profession. He quoted to me what you said, Miss Garth – do you remember it?' (Mr Farebrother used to say 'Mary' instead of 'Miss Garth', but it was part of his delicacy to treat her with the more deference because, according to Mrs Vincy's phrase, she worked for her bread.)

Mary felt uncomfortable, but, determined to take the matter lightly, answered at once, 'I have said so many impertinent things to Fred – we are such old playfellows.'

'You said, according to him, that he would be one of those ridiculous clergymen who help to make the whole clergy ridiculous. Really, that was so cutting that I felt a little cut myself.'

Caleb laughed. 'She gets her tongue from you, Susan,' he said, with some enjoyment.

'Not its flippancy, father,' said Mary, quickly, fearing that her mother would be displeased. 'It is rather too bad of Fred to repeat my flippant speeches to Mr Farebrother.'

'It was certainly a hasty speech, my dear,' said Mrs Garth, with whom speaking evil of dignities was a high misdemeanour. 'We should not value our Vicar the less because there was a ridiculous curate in the next parish.'

'There's something in what she says, though,' said Caleb, not disposed to have Mary's sharpness undervalued. 'A bad workman of any sort makes his fellows mistrusted. Things hang together,' he added, looking on the floor and moving his feet uneasily with a sense that words were scantier than thoughts.

'Clearly,' said the Vicar, amused. 'By being contemptible we set men's minds to the tune of contempt. I certainly agree with Miss Garth's view of the matter, whether I am condemned by it or not. But as to Fred Vincy, it is only fair he should be excused a little: old Featherstone's delusive behaviour did help to spoil him. There was something quite diabolical in not leaving him a farthing after all. But Fred has the good taste not to dwell on that. And what he cares most about is having offended you, Mrs Garth; he supposes you will never think well of him again.'

'I have been disappointed in Fred,' said Mrs Garth, with decision. 'But I shall be ready to think well of him again when he gives me good reason to do so.'

At this point Mary went out of the room, taking Letty with her.

'Oh, we must forgive young people when they're sorry,' said Caleb, watching Mary close the door. 'And as you say, Mr Farebrother, there was the very devil in that old man. Now Mary's gone out, I must tell you a thing – it's only known to Susan and me, and you'll not tell it again. The old scoundrel wanted Mary to burn one of the wills the very night he died, when she was sitting up with him by herself, and he offered her a sum of money that he had in the box by him if she would do it. But Mary, you understand, could do no such thing – would not be handling his iron chest, and so on. Now, you see, the will he wanted burnt was this last, so that if Mary had done what he wanted, Fred Vincy would have had ten thousand pounds. The old man did turn to him at the last. That touches poor Mary close; she couldn't help it – she was in the right to do what she did, but she feels, as she says, much as if she had knocked down somebody's property and broken it against her will, when she was rightfully defending herself. I feel with her, somehow, and if I could make any amends to the poor lad, instead of bearing him a grudge for the harm he did us, I should be glad to do it. Now, what is your opinion, sir? Susan doesn't agree with me. She says – tell what you say, Susan.'

'Mary could not have acted otherwise, even if she had known what would be the effect on Fred,' said Mrs Garth, pausing from her work, and looking at Mr Farebrother. 'And she was quite ignorant of it. It seems to me, a loss which falls on another because we have done right is not to lie upon our conscience.'

The Vicar did not answer immediately, and Caleb said, 'It's the feeling. The child feels in that way, and I feel with her. You don't mean your horse to tread on a dog when you're backing out of the way; but it goes through you, when it's done.'

'I am sure Mrs Garth would agree with you there,' said Mr Farebrother, who for some reason seemed more inclined to ruminate than to speak. 'One could hardly say that the feeling you mention about Fred is wrong – or rather, mistaken – though no man ought to make a claim on such feeling.'

'Well, well,' said Caleb; 'it's a secret. You will not tell Fred.'

'Certainly not. But I shall carry the other good news – that you can afford the loss he caused you.'

Mr Farebrother left the house soon after, and seeing Mary in the orchard with Letty, went to say goodbye to her. They made a pretty picture in the western light which brought out the brightness of the apples on the old scant-leaved boughs – Mary in her lavender gingham and black ribbons holding a basket, while Letty in her well-worn nankin picked up the fallen apples. If you want to know more particularly how Mary looked, ten to one you will see a face like hers in the crowded street tomorrow, if you are there on the watch: she will not be among those daughters of Zion who are haughty, and walk with stretched-out necks and wanton eyes, mincing as they go: let all those pass, and fix your eyes on some small plump brownish person of firm but quiet carriage, who looks about her, but does not suppose that anybody is looking at her. If she has a broad face and square brow, well-marked eyebrows and curly dark hair, a certain expression of amusement in her glance which her mouth keeps the secret of, and for the rest features entirely insignificant – take that ordinary but not dis-agreeable person for a portrait of Mary Garth. If you made her smile she would show you perfect little teeth; if you made her angry, she would not raise her voice, but would probably say one of the bitterest things you have ever tasted the flavour of; if you did her a kindness, she would never forget it. Mary admired the keen-faced handsome little Vicar in his well-brushed threadbare clothes more than any man she had had the opportunity of knowing. She had never heard him say a foolish thing, though she knew that he did unwise ones; and perhaps foolish sayings were more objectionable to her than any of Mr Farebrother's unwise doings. At least, it was remarkable that the actual imperfections of the Vicar's clerical character never seemed to call forth the same scorn and dislike which she showed beforehand for the predicted imperfections of the clerical character sustained by Fred Vincy. These irregularities of judgement, I imagine, are found even in riper minds than Mary Garth's: our impartiality is kept for abstract merit and demerit, which none of us ever saw. Will anyone guess towards which of these widely different men Mary had the peculiar woman's tenderness? – the one she was most inclined to be severe on, or the contrary?

'Have you any message for your old playfellow, Miss Garth?' said the Vicar, as he took a fragrant apple from the basket which she held towards him, and put it in his pocket. 'Something to soften down that harsh judgement? I am going straight to see him.'

'No,' said Mary, shaking her head, and smiling. 'If I were to say that he would not be ridiculous as a clergyman, I must say that he would be something worse than ridiculous. But I am very glad to hear that he is going away to work.'

'On the other hand, I am very glad to hear that *you* are not going away to work. My mother, I am sure, will be all the happier if you will come to see her at the vicarage: you know she is fond of having young people to talk to, and she has a great deal to tell about old times. You will really be doing a kindness.'

'I should like it very much, if I may,' said Mary. 'Everything seems too happy for me all at once. I thought it would always be part of my life to long for home, and losing that grievance makes me feel rather empty: I suppose it served instead of sense to fill up my mind?'

'May I go with you, Mary?' whispered Letty – a most inconvenient child, who listened to everything. But she was made exultant by having her chin pinched and her cheek kissed by Mr Farebrother – an incident which she narrated to her mother and father.

As the Vicar walked to Lowick, anyone watching him closely might have seen him twice shrug his shoulders. I think that the rare Englishmen who have this gesture are never of the heavy type – for fear of any lumbering instance to the contrary, I will say, hardly ever; they have usually a fine temperament and much tolerance towards the smaller errors of men (themselves inclusive). The Vicar was holding an inward dialogue in which he told himself that there was probably something more between Fred and Mary Garth than the regard of old play-fellows, and replied with a question whether that bit of womanhood were not a great deal too choice for that crude young gentleman. The rejoinder to this was the first shrug. Then he laughed at himself for being likely to have felt jealous, as if he had been a man able to marry, which, added he, it is as clear as any balance-sheet that I am not. Whereupon followed the second shrug.

What could two men, so different from each other, see in this 'brown patch', as Mary called herself? It was certainly not her plainness that attracted them (and let all plain young ladies be warned against the dangerous encouragement given them by Society to confide in their want of beauty). A human being in this aged nation of ours is a very wonderful whole, the slow creation of long inter-changing influences; and charm is a result of two such wholes, the one loving and the one loved.

When Mr and Mrs Garth were sitting alone, Caleb said, 'Susan, guess what I'm thinking of.'

'The rotation of crops,' said Mrs Garth, smiling at him, above her knitting, 'or else the backdoors of the Tipton cottages.'

'No,' said Caleb, gravely; 'I am thinking that I could do a great turn for Fred Vincy. Christy's gone, Alfred will be gone soon, and it will be five years before Jim is ready to take to business. I shall want help, and Fred might come in and learn the nature of things and act under me, and it might be the making of him into a useful man, if he gives up being a parson. What do you think?'

'I think, there is hardly anything honest that his family would object to more,' said Mrs Garth, decidedly.

'What care I about their objecting?' said Caleb, with a sturdiness which he was apt to show when he had an opinion. 'The lad is of age and must get his bread. He has sense enough and quickness enough; he likes being on the land, and it's my belief that he could learn business well if he gave his mind to it.'

'But would he? His father and mother wanted him to be a fine gentleman, and I think he has the same sort of feeling himself. They all think us beneath them. And if the proposal came from you, I am sure Mrs Vincy would say that we wanted Fred for Mary.'

'Life is a poor tale, if it is to be settled by nonsense of that sort,' said Caleb, with disgust.

'Yes, but there is a certain pride which is proper, Caleb.'

'I call it improper pride to let fools' notions hinder you from doing a good action. There's no sort of work,' said Caleb, with fervour, putting out his hand and moving it up and down to mark his emphasis, 'that could ever be done well, if you minded what fools say. You must have it inside you that your plan is right, and that plan you must follow.'

'I will not oppose any plan you have set your mind on, Caleb,' said Mrs Garth, who was a firm woman, but knew that there were some points on which her mild husband was yet firmer. 'Still, it seems to be fixed that Fred is to go back to college: will it not be better to wait and see what he will choose to do after that? It is not easy to keep people against their will. And you are not yet quite sure enough of your own position, or what you will want.'

'Well, it may be better to wait a bit. But as to my getting plenty of work for two, I'm pretty sure of that. I've always had my hands full with scattered things, and there's always something fresh turning up. Why, only yesterday – bless me, I don't think I told you! – it was rather odd that two men should have been at me on different sides to do the same bit of valuing. And who do you think they were?' said Caleb, taking a pinch of snuff and holding it up between his fingers, as if it were a part of his exposition. He was fond of a pinch when it occurred to him, but he usually forgot that this indulgence was at his command.

His wife held down her knitting and looked attentive.

'Why, that Rigg, or Rigg Featherstone, was one. But Bulstrode was before him, so I'm going to do it for Bulstrode. Whether it's mortgage or purchase they're going for, I can't tell yet.'

'Can that man be going to sell the land just left him – which he has taken the name for?' said Mrs Garth.

'Deuce knows,' said Caleb, who never referred the knowledge of discreditable doings to any higher power than the deuce. 'But Bulstrode has long been wanting to get a handsome bit of land under his fingers – that I know. And it's a difficult matter to get, in this part of the country.'

Caleb scattered his snuff carefully instead of taking it, and then added, 'The ins and outs of things are curious. Here is the land they've been all along expecting for Fred, which it seems the old man never meant to leave him a foot of, but left it to this side-slip of a son that he kept in the dark, and thought of his sticking there and vexing everybody as well as he could have vexed 'em himself if he could have kept alive. I say, it would be curious if it got into Bulstrode's hands after all. The old man hated him, and never would bank with him.'

'What reason could the miserable creature have for hating a man whom he had nothing to do with?' said Mrs Garth.

'Pooh! where's the use of asking for such fellows' reasons? The soul of man,' said Caleb, with the deep tone and grave shake of the head which always came when he used this phrase – 'the soul of man, when it gets fairly rotten, will bear you all sorts of poisonous toadstools, and no eye can see whence came the seed thereof.'

It was one of Caleb's quaintnesses, that in his difficulty of finding speech for his thought, he caught, as it were, snatches of diction which he associated with various points of view or states of mind; and whenever he had a feeling of awe, he was haunted by a sense of Biblical phraseology, though he could hardly have given a strict quotation.

Chapter 41

> By swaggering could I never thrive,
> For the rain it raineth every day.
> SHAKESPEARE, *Twelfth Night*

The transactions referred to by Caleb Garth, as having gone forward between Mr Bulstrode and Mr Joshua Rigg Featherstone concerning the land attached to Stone Court, had occasioned the interchange of a letter or two between these personages.

Who shall tell what may be the effect of writing? If it happens to have been cut in stone, though it lie face downmost for ages on a forsaken beach, or 'rest quietly under the drums and tramplings of many conquests', it may end by letting us into the secret of usurpations and other scandals gossiped about long empires ago: – this world being apparently a huge whispering-gallery. Such conditions are often minutely represented in our petty lifetime. As the stone which has been kicked by generations of clowns may come by curious little links of effect under the eyes of a scholar, through whose labours it may at last fix the date of invasions and unlock religions, so a bit of ink and paper which has long been an innocent wrapping or stopgap may at last be laid open under the one pair of eyes which have knowledge enough to turn it into the opening of a catastrophe. To Uriel watching the progress of planetary history from the Sun, the one result would be just as much of a coincidence as the other.

Having made this rather lofty comparison I am less uneasy in calling attention to the existence of low people by whose interference, however little we may like it, the course of the world is very much determined. It would be well, certainly, if we could help to reduce their number, and something might perhaps be done by not lightly giving occasion to their existence. Socially speaking, Joshua Rigg would have been generally pronounced a superfluity. But those who like Peter Featherstone never had a copy of themselves demanded, are the very last to wait for such a request either in prose or verse. The copy in this case bore more of outside resemblance to the mother, in whose sex frog-features, accompanied with fresh-coloured cheeks and a well-rounded figure, are compatible with much charm for a certain order of admirers. The result is sometimes a frog-faced male, desirable, surely, to no order of intelligent beings. Especially when he is suddenly brought into evidence to frustrate other people's expectations – the very lowest aspect in which a social superfluity can present himself.

But Mr Rigg Featherstone's low characteristics were all of the sober, water-drinking kind. From the earliest to the latest hour of the day he was always as sleek, neat, and cool as the frog he resembled, and old Peter had secretly chuckled over an offshoot almost more calculating, and far more imperturbable, than himself. I will add that his fingernails were scrupulously attended to, and that he meant to marry a well-educated young lady (as yet unspecified) whose person was good, and whose connections, in a solid middle-class way, were undeniable. Thus his nails and modesty were comparable to those of most gentlemen; though his ambition had been educated only by the opportunities of a clerk and accountant in the smaller commercial houses of a seaport. He thought the rural Featherstones very simple absurd people, and they in their turn regarded his 'bringing up' in a seaport town as an exaggeration of the monstrosity that their brother Peter, and still more Peter's property, should have had such belongings.

The garden and gravel approach, as seen from the two windows of the wainscoted parlour at Stone Court, were never in better trim than now, when Mr Rigg Featherstone stood, with his hands behind him, looking out on these grounds as their master. But it seemed doubtful whether he looked out for the sake of contemplation or of turning his back to a person who stood in the middle of the room, with his legs considerably apart and his hands in his trouser-pockets: a person in all respects a contrast to the sleek and cool Rigg. He was a man obviously on the way towards sixty, very florid and hairy, with much grey in his bushy whiskers and thick curly hair, a stoutish body which showed to disadvantage the somewhat worn joinings of his clothes, and the air of a swaggerer, who would aim at being noticeable even at a show of fireworks, regarding his own remarks on any other person's performance as likely to be more interesting than the performance itself.

His name was John Raffles, and he sometimes wrote jocosely W. A. G. after his signature, observing when he did so, that he was once taught by Leonard Lamb, of Finsbury, who wrote B.A. after his name, and that he, Raffles, originated the witticism of calling that celebrated principal Ba-Lamb. Such were the appearance and mental flavour of Mr Raffles, both of which seemed to have a stale odour of traveller's rooms in the commercial hotels of that period.

'Come, now, Josh,' he was saying, in a full rumbling tone, 'look at it in this light: here is your poor mother going into the vale of years, and you could afford something handsome now to make her comfortable.'

'Not while you live. Nothing would make her comfortable while you live,' returned Rigg, in his cool high voice. 'What I give her, you'll take.'

'You bear me a grudge, Josh, that l know. But come now, as between man and man – without humbug – a little capital might enable me to make a first-rate thing of the shop. The tobacco trade is growing. I should cut my own nose off in not doing the best I could at it. I should stick to it like a flea to a fleece for my own sake. I should always be on the spot. And nothing would make your poor mother so happy. I've pretty well done with my wild oats – turned fifty-five. I want to settle down in my chimney-corner. And if I once buckled to the tobacco trade, I could bring an amount of brains and experience to bear on it that would not be found elsewhere in a hurry. I don't want to be bothering you one time after another, but to get things once for all into the right channel. Consider that, Josh – as between man and man – and with your poor mother to be made easy for her life. I was always fond of the old woman, by Jove.'

'Have you done?' said Mr Rigg, quietly, without looking away from the window. 'Yes, *I've* done,' said Raffles, taking hold of his hat, which stood before him on the table, and giving it a sort of oratorical push.

'Then just listen to me. The more you say anything, the less I shall believe it. The more you want me to do a thing, the more reason I shall have for never doing it. Do you think I mean to forget your kicking me when I was a lad, and eating all the best victual away from me and my mother? Do you think I forget your always coming home to sell and pocket everything and going off again leaving us in the lurch? I should be glad to see you whipped at the cart-tail. My mother was a fool to you: she'd no right to give me a father-in-law, and she's been punished for it. She shall have her weekly allowance paid and no more: and that shall be stopped if you dare to come on to these premises again, or to come into this country after me again. The next time you show yourself inside the gates here, you shall be driven off with the dogs and the waggoner's whip.'

As Rigg pronounced the last words he turned round and looked at Raffles with his prominent frozen eyes. The contrast was as striking as it could have been eighteen years before, when Rigg was a most unengaging kickable boy, and Raffles was the rather thickset Adonis of bar-rooms and back-parlours. But the advantage now was on the side of Rigg, and auditors of this conversation might probably have expected that Raffles would retire with the air of a defeated dog. Not at all. He made a grimace which was habitual with him whenever he was 'out' in a game; then subsided into a laugh, and drew a brandy-flask from his pocket.

'Come, Josh,' he said, in a cajoling tone, 'give us a spoonful of brandy, and a sovereign to pay the way back, and I'll go. Honour bright! I'll go like a bullet, by Jove!'

'Mind,' said Rigg, drawing out a bunch of keys, 'if I ever see you again, I shan't speak to you. I don't own you any more than if I saw a crow; and if you want to own me you'll get nothing by it but a character for being what you are – a spiteful, brassy, bullying rogue.'

'That's a pity, now, Josh,' said Raffles, affecting to scratch his head and wrinkle his brows upwards as if he were nonplussed.

'I'm very fond of you; *by* Jove, I am! There's nothing I like better than plaguing you – you're so like your mother; and I must do without it. But the brandy and the sovereign's a bargain.'

He jerked forward the flask and Rigg went to a fine old oaken bureau with his keys. But Raffles had reminded himself by his movement with the flask that it had become dangerously loose from its leather covering, and catching sight of a folded paper which had fallen within the fender, he took it up and shoved it under the leather so as to make the glass firm.

By that time Rigg came forward with a brandy-bottle, filled the flask, and handed Raffles a sovereign, neither looking at him nor speaking to him. After locking up the bureau again, he walked to the window and gazed out as impassibly as he had done at the beginning of the interview, while Raffles took a small allowance from the flask, screwed it up, and deposited it in his side-pocket, with provoking slowness, making a grimace at his stepson's back.

'Farewell, Josh – and if for ever!' said Raffles, turning back his head as he opened the door.

Rigg saw him leave the grounds and enter the lane. The grey day had turned to a light drizzling rain, which freshened the hedgerows and the grassy borders of the byroads, and hastened the labourers who were loading the last shocks of corn. Raffles, walking with the uneasy gait of a town loiterer obliged to do a bit of country journeying on foot, looked as incongruous amid this moist rural quiet and industry as if he had been a baboon escaped from a menagerie. But there were none to stare at him except the long-weaned calves, and none to show dislike of his appearance except the little water-rats which rustled away at his approach.

He was fortunate enough when he got on to the highroad to be overtaken by the stagecoach, which carried him to Brassing; and there he took the new-made railway, observing to his fellow-passengers that he considered it pretty well seasoned now it had done for Huskisson. Mr Raffles on most occasions kept up the sense of having been educated at an academy, and being able, when he chose, to pass well everywhere; indeed, there was not one of his fellow-men whom he did not feel himself in a position to ridicule and torment, confident of the entertainment which he thus gave to all the rest of the company.

He played this part now with as much spirit as if his journey had been entirely successful, resorting at frequent intervals to his flask. The paper with which he had wedged it was a letter signed *Nicholas Bulstrode*, but Raffles was not likely to disturb it from its present useful position.

Chapter 42

> How much, methinks, I could despise this man,
> Were I not bound in charity against it!
>
> SHAKESPEARE, *Henry VIII*

One of the professional calls made by Lydgate soon after his return from his wedding-journey was to Lowick Manor, in consequence of a letter which had requested him to fix a time for his visit.

Mr Casaubon had never put any question concerning the nature of his illness to Lydgate, nor had he even to Dorothea betrayed any anxiety as to how far it might be likely to cut short his labours or his life. On this point, as on all others, he shrank from pity; and if the suspicion of being pitied for anything in his lot surmised or known in spite of himself was embittering, the idea of calling forth a show of compassion by frankly admitting an alarm or a sorrow was necessarily intolerable to him. Every proud mind knows something of this experience, and perhaps it is only to be overcome by a sense of fellowship deep enough to make all efforts at isolation seem mean and petty instead of exalting.

But Mr Casaubon was now brooding over something through which the question of his health and life haunted his silence with a more harassing importunity even than through the autumnal unripeness of his authorship. It is true that this last might be called his central ambition; but there are some kinds of authorship in which by far the largest result is the uneasy susceptibility accumulated in the consciousness of the author one knows of the river by a few streaks amid a long-gathered deposit of uncomfortable mud. That was the way with Mr Casaubon's hard intellectual labours. Their most characteristic result was not the *Key to all Mythologies*, but a morbid consciousness that others did not give him the place which he had not demonstrably merited – a perpetual suspicious conjecture that the views entertained of him were not to his advantage – a melancholy absence of passion in his efforts at achievement, and a passionate resistance to the confession that he had achieved nothing.

Thus his intellectual ambition which seemed to others to have absorbed and dried him, was really no security against wounds, least of all against those which came from Dorothea. And he had begun now to frame possibilities for the future which were somehow more embittering to him than anything his mind had dwelt on before.

Against certain facts he was helpless: against Will Ladislaw's existence, his defiant stay in the neighbourhood of Lowick, and his flippant state of mind with regard to the possessor of authentic, well-stamped erudition: against Dorothea's nature, always taking on some new shape of ardent activity, and even in submission and silence covering fervid reasons which it was an irritation to think of: against certain notions and likings which had taken possession of her mind in relation to subjects that he could not possibly discuss with her. There was no denying that Dorothea was as virtuous and lovely a young lady as he could have obtained for a wife; but a young lady turned out to be something more troublesome than he had conceived. She nursed him, she read to him, she anticipated his wants, and was solicitous about his feelings; but there had entered into the husband's mind the certainty that she judged him, and that her wifely devotedness was like a penitential expiation of unbelieving thoughts – was accompanied with a power of comparison by which himself and his doings were seen too luminously as a part of things in general. His discontent passed vapour-like through all her gentle loving manifestations, and clung to that inappreciative world which she had only brought nearer to him.

Poor Mr Casaubon! This suffering was the harder to bear because it seemed like a betrayal: the young creature who had worshipped him with perfect trust had quickly turned into the critical wife; and early instances of criticism and resentment had made an impression which no tenderness and submission afterwards could remove. To his suspicious interpretation Dorothea's silence now was a suppressed rebellion; a remark from her which he had not in any way anticipated was an assertion of conscious superiority; her gentle answers had an irritating cautiousness in them; and when she acquiesced it was a self-approved effort of forbearance. The tenacity with which he strove to hide this inward drama made it the more vivid for him; as we hear with the more keenness what we wish others not to hear.

Instead of wondering at this result of misery in Mr Casaubon, I think it quite ordinary. Will not a tiny speck very close to our vision blot out the glory of the world, and leave only a margin by which we see the blot? I know no speck so troublesome as self. And who, if Mr Casaubon had chosen to expound his discontents – his suspicions that he was not any longer adored without criticism – could have denied that they were founded on good reasons? On the contrary, there was a strong reason to be added, which he had not himself taken explicitly into account – namely, that he was not unmixedly adorable. He suspected this, however, as he suspected other things, without confessing it, and like the rest of us, felt how soothing it would have been to have a companion who would never find it out.

This sore susceptibility in relation to Dorothea was thoroughly prepared before Will Ladislaw had returned to Lowick, and what had occurred since then had brought Mr Casaubon's power of suspicious construction into exasperated activity. To all the facts which he knew, he added imaginary facts both present and future which became more real to him than those, because they called up a stronger dislike, a more predominating bitterness. Suspicion and jealousy of Will Ladislaw's intentions, suspicion and jealousy of Dorothea's impressions, were constantly at their weaving work. It would be quite unjust to him to suppose that he could have entered into any coarse misinterpretation of Dorothea: his own habits of mind and conduct, quite as much as the open elevation of her nature, saved him from any such mistake. What he was jealous of was her opinion, the sway that might be given to her ardent mind in its judgements, and the future possibilities to which these might lead her. As to Will, though until his last defiant letter he had nothing definite which he would choose formally to allege against him, he felt himself warranted in believing that he was capable of any design which could fascinate a rebellious temper and an undisciplined impulsiveness. He was quite sure that Dorothea was the cause of Will's return from Rome, and his determination to settle in the neighbourhood; and he was penetrating enough to imagine that Dorothea had innocently encouraged this course. It was as clear as possible that she was ready to be attached to Will and to be pliant to his suggestions: they had never had a tête-à-tête without her bringing away from it some new troublesome impression, and the last interview that Mr Casaubon was aware of (Dorothea, on returning from Freshitt Hall, had for the first time been silent about having seen Will) had led to a scene which roused an angrier feeling against them both than he had ever known before. Dorothea's outpouring of her notions about money, in the darkness of the night, had done nothing but bring a mixture of more odious foreboding into her husband's mind.

And there was the shock lately given to his health always sadly present with him. He was certainly much revived; he had recovered all his usual power of work: the illness might have been mere fatigue, and there might still be twenty

years of achievement before him, which would justify the thirty years of preparation. That prospect was made the sweeter by a flavour of vengeance against
the hasty sneers of Carp & Company; for even when Mr Casaubon was carrying
his taper among the tombs of the past, those modern figures came athwart the
dim light, and interrupted his diligent exploration. To convince Carp of his
mistake, so that he would have to eat his own words with a good deal of
indigestion, would be an agreeable accident of triumphant authorship, which
the prospect of living to future ages on earth and to all eternity in heaven could
not exclude from contemplation. Since, thus, the prevision of his own unending
bliss could not nullify the bitter savours of irritated jealousy and vindictiveness,
it is the less surprising that the probability of a transient earthly bliss for other
persons, when he himself should have entered into glory, had not a potently
sweetening effect. If the truth should be that some undermining disease was at
work within him, there might be large opportunity for some people to be the
happier when he was gone; and if one of those people should be Will Ladislaw,
Mr Casaubon objected so strongly that it seemed as if the annoyance would
make part of his disembodied existence.

This is a very bare and therefore a very incomplete way of putting the case.
The human soul moves in many channels, and Mr Casaubon, we know, had a
sense of rectitude and an honourable pride in satisfying the requirements of
honour, which compelled him to find other reasons for his conduct than those
of jealousy and vindictiveness.

The way in which Mr Casaubon put the case was this: 'In marrying Dorothea
Brooke I had to care for her wellbeing in case of my death. But wellbeing is not
to be secured by ample, independent possession of property; on the contrary,
occasions might arise in which such possession might expose her to the more
danger. She is ready prey to any man who knows how to play adroitly either on her
affectionate ardour or her Quixotic enthusiasm; and a man stands by with that very
intention in his mind – a man with no other principle than transient caprice, and
who has a personal animosity towards me – I am sure of it – an animosity which is
fed by the consciousness of his ingratitude, and which he has constantly vented in
ridicule of which I am as well assured as if I had heard it. Even if I live I shall not be
without uneasiness as to what he may attempt through indirect influence. This
man has gained Dorothea's ear: he has fascinated her attention; he has evidently
tried to impress her mind with the notion that he has claims beyond anything I
have done for him. If I die – and he is waiting here on the watch for that – he will
persuade her to marry him. That would be calamity for her and success for him.
She would not think it calamity: he would make her believe anything; she has a
tendency to immoderate attachment which she inwardly reproaches me for not
responding to, and already her mind is occupied with his fortunes. He thinks of an
easy conquest and of entering into my nest. That I will hinder! Such a marriage
would be fatal to Dorothea. Has he ever persisted in anything except from contradiction? In knowledge, he has always tried to be showy at small cost. In religion he
could be, as long as it suited him, the facile echo of Dorothea's vagaries. When was
sciolism ever dissociated from laxity? I utterly distrust his morals, and it is my duty
to hinder to the utmost the fulfilment of his designs.'

The arrangements made by Mr Casaubon on his marriage left strong measures open to him, but in ruminating on them his mind inevitably dwelt so much on the probabilities of his own life that the longing to get the nearest possible calculation had at last overcome his proud reticence, and had determined him to ask Lydgate's opinion as to the nature of his illness.

He had mentioned to Dorothea that Lydgate was coming by appointment at half-past three, and in answer to her anxious question, whether he had felt ill, replied, – 'No, I merely wish to have his opinion concerning some habitual symptoms. You need not see him, my dear. I shall give orders that he may be sent to me in the yew-tree walk, where I shall be taking my usual exercise.'

When Lydgate entered the yew-tree walk he saw Mr Casaubon slowly receding with his hands behind him according to his habit, and his head bent forward. It was a lovely afternoon; the leaves from the lofty limes were falling silently across the sombre evergreens, while the lights and shadows slept side by side: there was no sound but the cawing of the rooks, which to the accustomed ear is a lullaby, or that last solemn lullaby, a dirge. Lydgate, conscious of an energetic frame in its prime, felt some compassion when the figure which he was likely soon to overtake turned round, and in advancing towards him showed more markedly than ever the signs of premature age – the student's bent shoulders, the emaciated limbs, and the melancholy lines of the mouth. 'Poor fellow,' he thought, 'some men with his years are like lions; one can tell nothing of their age except that they are full grown.'

'Mr Lydgate,' said Mr Casaubon, with his invariably polite air, 'I am exceedingly obliged to you for your punctuality. We will, if you please, carry on our conversation in walking to and fro.'

'I hope your wish to see me is not due to the return of unpleasant symptoms,' said Lydgate, filling up a pause.

'Not immediately – no. In order to account for that wish I must mention – what it were otherwise needless to refer to that my life, on all collateral accounts insignificant, derives a possible importance from the incompleteness of labours which have extended through all its best years. In short, I have long had on hand a work which I would fain leave behind me in such a state, at least, that it might be committed to the press by – others. Were I assured that this is the utmost I can reasonably expect, that assurance would be a useful circumscription of my attempts, and a guide in both the positive and negative determination of my course.'

Here Mr Casaubon paused, removed one hand from his back and thrust it between the buttons of his single-breasted coat. To a mind largely instructed in the human destiny hardly anything could be more interesting than the inward conflict implied in his formal measured address, delivered with the usual sing-song and motion of the head. Nay, are there many situations more sublimely tragic than the struggle of the soul with the demand to renounce a work which has been all the significance of its life – a significance which is to vanish as the waters which come and go where no man has need of them? But there was nothing to strike others as sublime about Mr Casaubon, and Lydgate, who had some contempt at hand for futile scholarship, felt a little amusement mingling with his pity. He was at present too ill acquainted with disaster to enter into the pathos of a lot where everything is below the level of tragedy except the passionate egoism of the sufferer.

'You refer to the possible hindrances from want of health?' he said, wishing to help forward Mr Casaubon's purpose, which seemed to be clogged by some hesitation.

'I do. You have not implied to me that the symptoms which I am bound to testify – you watched with scrupulous care, were those of a fatal disease. But were it so, Mr Lydgate, I should desire to know the truth without reservation, and I appeal to you for an exact statement of your conclusions: I request it as a friendly service. If you can tell me that my life is not threatened by anything else than ordinary casualties, I shall rejoice, on grounds which I have already indicated. If not, knowledge of the truth is even more important to me.'

'Then I can no longer hesitate as to my course,' said Lydgate; 'but the first thing I must impress on you is that my conclusions are doubly uncertain – uncertain not only because of my fallibility, but because diseases of the heart are eminently difficult to found predictions on. In any case, one can hardly increase appreciably the tremendous uncertainty of life.'

Mr Casaubon winced perceptibly, but bowed.

'I believe that you are suffering from what is called fatty degeneration of the heart, a disease which was first divined and explored by Laennec, the man who gave us the stethoscope, not so very many years ago. A good deal of experience – a more lengthened observation – is wanted on the subject. But after what you have said, it is my duty to tell you that death from this disease is often sudden. At the same time, no such result can be predicted. Your condition may be consistent with a tolerably comfortable life for another fifteen years, or even more. I could add no information to this, beyond anatomical or medical details, which would leave expectation at precisely the same point.'

Lydgate's instinct was fine enough to tell him that plain speech, quite free from ostentatious caution, would be felt by Mr Casaubon as a tribute of respect.

'I thank you, Mr Lydgate,' said Mr Casaubon, after a moment's pause. 'One thing more I have still to ask: did you communicate what you have now told me to Mrs Casaubon?'

'Partly – I mean, as to the possible issues.' Lydgate was going to explain why he had told Dorothea, but Mr Casaubon, with an unmistakable desire to end the conversation, waved his hand slightly, and said again, 'I thank you,' proceeding to remark on the rare beauty of the day.

Lydgate, certain that his patient wished to be alone, soon left him; and the black figure with hands behind and head bent forward continued to pace the walk where the dark yew trees gave him a mute companionship in melancholy, and the little shadows of bird or leaf that fleeted across the isles of sunlight, stole along in silence as in the presence of a sorrow. Here was a man who now for the first time found himself looking into the eyes of death – who was passing through one of those rare moments of experience when we feel the truth of a commonplace, which is as different from what we call knowing it, as the vision of waters upon the earth is different from the delirious vision of the water which cannot be had to cool the burning tongue. When the commonplace 'We must all die' transforms itself suddenly into the acute consciousness 'I must die – and soon', then death grapples us, and his fingers are cruel; afterwards, he may come to fold us in his arms as our mother did, and our last moment of dim earthly discerning may be like the first. To Mr Casaubon now, it was as if he suddenly found himself on the dark river-brink and heard the plash of the oncoming oar, not discerning the forms, but expecting the summons. In such an hour the mind does not change its lifelong bias, but carries it onwards in imagination to the other side of death, gazing backward – perhaps with the divine calm of beneficence, perhaps with the petty anxieties of self-assertion. What was Mr Casaubon's bias his acts will give us a clue to. He held himself to be, with some private scholarly reservations, a believing Christian, as to estimates of the present and hopes of the future. But what we strive to gratify, though we may call it a distant hope, is an immediate desire; the future estate for which men drudge up city alleys exists already in their imagination and love. And Mr Casaubon's immediate desire was not for divine communion and light divested of earthly conditions; his passionate longings, poor man, clung low and mist-like in very shady places.

Dorothea had been aware when Lydgate had ridden away, and she had stepped into the garden, with the impulse to go at once to her husband. But she hesitated, fearing to offend him by obtruding herself; for her ardour, continually repulsed, served, with her intense memory, to heighten her dread, as thwarted energy subsides into a shudder; and she wandered slowly round the nearer clumps of trees until she saw him advancing. Then she went towards him, and might have represented a heaven-sent angel coming with a promise that the short hours remaining should yet be filled with that faithful love which clings the closer to a comprehended grief. His glance in reply to hers was so chill that she felt her timidity increased; yet she turned and passed her hand through his arm.

Mr Casaubon kept his hands behind him and allowed her pliant arm to cling with difficulty against his rigid arm.

There was something horrible to Dorothea in the sensation which this unresponsive hardness inflicted on her. That is a strong word, but not too strong: it is in these acts called trivialities that the seeds of joy are for ever wasted, until men and women look round with haggard faces at the devastation their own waste has made, and say, the earth bears no harvest of sweetness – calling their denial knowledge. You may ask why, in the name of manliness, Mr Casaubon should have behaved in that way. Consider that his was a mind which shrank from pity: have you ever watched in such a mind the effect of a suspicion that what is pressing it as a grief may be really a source of con- tentment, either actual or future, to the being who already offends by pitying? Besides, he knew little of Dorothea's sensations, and had not reflected that on such an occasion as the present they were comparable in strength to his own sensibilities about Carp's criticisms.

Dorothea did not withdraw her arm, but she could not venture to speak. Mr Casaubon did not say, 'I wish to be alone', but he directed his steps in silence towards the house, and as they entered by the glass door on this eastern side,

Dorothea withdrew her arm and lingered on the matting, that she might leave her husband quite free. He entered the library and shut himself in, alone with his sorrow.

She went up to her boudoir. The open bow-window let in the serene glory of the afternoon lying in the avenue, where the lime trees cast long shadows. But Dorothea knew nothing of the scene. She threw herself on a chair, not heeding that she was in the dazzling sun-rays: if there were discomfort in that, how could she tell that it was not part of her inward misery?

She was in the reaction of a rebellious anger stronger than any she had felt since her marriage. Instead of tears there came words: 'What have I done – what am I – that he should treat me so? He never knows what is in my mind – he never cares. What is the use of anything I do? He wishes he had never married me.'

She began to hear herself, and was checked into stillness. Like one who has lost his way and is weary, she sat and saw as in one glance all the paths of her young hope which she should never find again. And just as clearly in the miserable light she saw her own and her husband's solitude – how they walked apart so that she was obliged to survey him. If he had drawn her towards him, she would never have surveyed him – never have said, 'Is he worth living for?' but would have felt him simply a part of her own life. Now she said bitterly, 'It is his fault, not mine.' In the jar of her whole being, Pity was overthrown. Was it her fault that she had believed in him – had believed in his worthiness? – And what, exactly, was he? – She was able enough to estimate him – she who waited on his glances with trembling, and shut her best soul in prison, paying it only hidden visits, that she might be petty enough to please him. In such a crisis as this, some women begin to hate.

The sun was low when Dorothea was thinking that she would not go down again, but would send a message to her husband saying that she was not well and preferred remaining upstairs. She had never deliberately allowed her resentment to govern her in this way before, but she believed now that she could not see him again without telling him the truth about her feeling, and she must wait till she could do it without interruption. He might wonder and be hurt at her message. It was good that he should wonder and be hurt. Her anger said, as anger is apt to say, that God was with her – that all heaven, though it were crowded with spirits watching them, must be on her side. She had determined to ring her bell, when there came a rap at the door.

Mr Casaubon had sent to say that he would have his dinner in the library. He wished to be quite alone this evening, being much occupied.

'I shall not dine, then, Tantripp.'

'Oh, madam, let me bring you a little something?'

'No; I am not well. Get everything ready in my dressing-room, but pray do not disturb me again.'

Dorothea sat almost motionless in her meditative struggle, while the evening slowly deepened into night. But the struggle changed continually, as that of a man who begins with a movement towards striking and ends with conquering his desire to strike. The energy that would animate a crime is not more than is

wanted to inspire a resolved submission, when the noble habit of the soul reasserts
itself. That thought with which Dorothea had gone out to meet her husband –
her conviction that he had been asking about the possible arrest of all his work,
and that the answer must have wrung his heart, could not be long with out rising
beside the image of him, like a shadowy monitor looking at her anger with sad
remonstrance. It cost her a litany of pictured sorrows and of silent cries that she
might be the mercy for those sorrows – but the resolved submission did come;
and when the house was still, and she knew that it was near the time when Mr
Casaubon habitually went to rest, she opened her door gently and stood outside
in the darkness waiting for his coming upstairs with a light in his hand. If he did
not come soon she thought that she would go down and even risk incurring
another pang. She would never again expect anything else. But she did hear the
library door open, and slowly the light advanced up the staircase without noise
from the footsteps on the carpet. When her husband stood opposite to her, she
saw that his face was more haggard. He started slightly on seeing her, and she
looked up at him beseechingly, without speaking.

'Dorothea!' he said, with a gentle surprise in his tone. 'Were you waiting
for me?'

'Yes, I did not like to disturb you.'

'Come, my dear, come. You are young, and need not to extend your life by
watching.'

When the kind quiet melancholy of that speech fell on Dorothea's ears, she
felt something like the thankfulness that might well up in us if we had narrowly
escaped hurting a lamed creature. She put her hand into her husband's, and they
went along the broad corridor together.

BOOK FIVE

The Dead Hand

Chapter 43

This figure hath high price: 'twas wrought with love
Ages ago in finest ivory:
Nought modish in it, pure and noble lines
Of generous womanhood that fits all time.
That too is costly ware; majolica
Of deft design, to please a lordly eye:
The smile, you see, is perfect – wonderful
As mere Faience! a table ornament
To suit the richest mounting.

Dorothea seldom left home without her husband, but she did occasionally drive into Middlemarch alone, on little errands of shopping or charity such as occur to every lady of any wealth when she lives within three miles of a town. Two days after that scene in the yew-tree walk, she determined to use such an opportunity in order if possible to see Lydgate and learn from him whether her husband had really felt any depressing change of symptoms which he was concealing from her, and whether he had insisted on knowing the utmost about himself. She felt almost guilty in asking for knowledge about him from another, but the dread of being without it – the dread of that ignorance which would make her unjust or hard – overcame every scruple. That there had been some crisis in her husband's mind she was certain: he had the very next day begun a new method of arranging his notes, and had associated her quite newly in carrying out his plan. Poor Dorothea needed to lay up stores of patience.

It was about four o'clock when she drove to Lydgate's house in Lowick Gate, wishing, in her immediate doubt of finding him at home, that she had written beforehand. And he was not at home.

'Is Mrs Lydgate at home?' said Dorothea, who had never, that she knew of, seen Rosamond, but now remembered the fact of the marriage. Yes, Mrs Lydgate was at home.

'I will go in and speak to her, if she will allow me. Will you ask her if she can see me – see Mrs Casaubon, for a few minutes?'

When the servant had gone to deliver that message, Dorothea could hear sounds of music through an open window – a few notes from a man's voice and then a piano bursting into roulades. But the roulades broke off suddenly, and then the servant came back saying that Mrs Lydgate would be happy to see Mrs Casaubon.

When the drawing-room door opened and Dorothea entered, there was a sort of contrast not infrequent in country life when the habits of the different ranks were less blended than now. Let those who know, tell us exactly what stuff it was that Dorothea wore in those days of mild autumn – that thin white woollen stuff soft to the touch and soft to the eye. It always seemed to have been lately washed, and to smell of the sweet hedges, was always in the shape of a pelisse with sleeves hanging all out of the fashion. Yet if she had entered before a still audience as Imogen or Cato's daughter, the dress might have seemed right enough: the grace and dignity were in her limbs and neck; and about her simply parted hair and candid eyes the large round poke which was then in the fate of women, seemed no more odd as a headdress than the gold trencher we call a halo. By the present audience of two persons, no dramatic heroine could have been expected with more interest than Mrs Casaubon. To Rosamond she was one of those county divinities not mixing with Middlemarch mortality, whose slightest marks of manner or appearance were worthy of her study; moreover, Rosamond was not without satisfaction that Mrs Casaubon should have an opportunity of studying *her*. What is the use of being exquisite if you are not seen by the best judges? and since Rosamond had received the highest compliments at Sir Godwin Lydgate's, she felt quite confident of the impression she must make on people of good birth. Dorothea put out her hand with her usual simple kindness, and looked admiringly at Lydgate's lovely bride, aware that there was a gentleman standing at a distance, but seeing him merely as a coated figure at a wide angle. The gentleman was too much occupied with the presence of the one woman to reflect on the contrast between the two – a contrast that would certainly have been striking to a calm observer. They were both tall, and their eyes were on a level; but imagine Rosamond's infantine blondness and wondrous crown of hair-plaits, with her pale-blue dress of a fit and fashion so perfect that no dressmaker could look at it without emotion, a large embroidered collar which it was to be hoped all beholders would know the price of, her small hands duly set off with rings, and that controlled self-consciousness of manner which is the expensive substitute for simplicity.

'Thank you very much for allowing me to interrupt you,' said Dorothea, immediately. 'I am anxious to see Mr Lydgate, if possible, before I go home, and I hoped that you might possibly tell me where I could find him, or even allow me to wait for him, if you expect him soon.'

'He is at the New Hospital,' said Rosamond; 'I am not sure how soon he will come home. But I can send for him.'

'Will you let me go and fetch him?' said Will Ladislaw, coming forward. He had already taken up his hat before Dorothea entered. She coloured with surprise, but put out her hand with a smile of unmistakable pleasure, saying: 'I did not know it was you: I had no thought of seeing you here.'

'May I go to the Hospital and tell Mr Lydgate that you wish to see him?' said Will.

'It would be quicker to send the carriage for him,' said Dorothea, 'if you will be kind enough to give the message to the coachman.'

Will was moving to the door when Dorothea, whose mind had flashed in an instant over many connected memories, turned quickly and said, 'I will go myself, thank you. I wish to lose no time before getting home again. I will drive to the Hospital and see Mr Lydgate there. Pray excuse me, Mrs Lydgate. I am very much obliged to you.'

Her mind was evidently arrested by some sudden thought, and she left the room hardly conscious of what was immediately around her – hardly conscious that Will opened the door for her and offered her his arm to lead her to the carriage. She took the arm but said nothing. Will was feeling rather vexed and miserable, and found nothing to say on his side. He handed her into the carriage in silence, they said goodbye, and Dorothea drove away.

In the five minutes' drive to the Hospital she had time for some reflections that were quite new to her. Her decision to go, and her preoccupation in leaving the room, had come from the sudden sense that there would be a sort of deception in her voluntarily allowing any further intercourse between herself and Will which she was unable to mention to her husband, and already her errand in seeking Lydgate was a matter of concealment. That was all that had been explicitly in her mind; but she had been urged also by a vague discomfort. Now that she was alone in her drive, she heard the notes of the man's voice and the accompanying piano, which she had not noted much at the time, returning on her inward sense; and she found herself thinking with some wonder that Will Ladislaw was passing his time with Mrs Lydgate in her husband's absence. And then she could not help remembering that he had passed some time with her under like circumstances, so why should there be any unfitness in the fact? But Will was Mr Casaubon's relative, and one towards whom she was bound to show kindness. Still there had been signs which perhaps she ought to have understood as implying that Mr Casaubon did not like his cousin's visits during his own absence. 'Perhaps I have been mistaken in many things,' said poor Dorothea to herself, while the tears came rolling and she had to dry them quickly. She felt confusedly unhappy, and the image of Will which had been so clear to her before was mysteriously spoiled. But the carriage stopped at the gate of the Hospital. She was soon walking round the grass plots with Lydgate, and her feelings recovered the strong bent which had made her seek for this interview.

Will Ladislaw, meanwhile, was mortified, and knew the reason of it clearly enough. His chances of meeting Dorothea were rare; and here for the first time there had come a chance which had set him at a disadvantage. It was not only, as it had been hitherto, that she was not supremely occupied with him, but that she had seen him under circumstances in which he might appear not to be supremely occupied with her. He felt thrust to a new distance from her, amongst the circles of Middlemarchers who made no part of her life. But that was not his fault: of course, since he had taken his lodgings in the town, he had been making as many acquaintances as he could, his position requiring that he should know everybody and everything. Lydgate was really better worth knowing than anyone else in the neighbourhood, and he happened to have a wife who was musical and altogether worth calling upon. Here was the whole history of the situation in which Diana had descended too unexpectedly on her worshipper. It was mortifying. Will was conscious that he should not have been at Middlemarch but for Dorothea; and yet his position there was threatening to divide him from her with those barriers of habitual sentiment which are more fatal to the persistence of mutual interest than all the distance between Rome and Britain. Prejudices about rank and status were easy enough to defy in the form of a tyrannical letter from Mr Casaubon; but prejudices, like odorous bodies, have a double existence both solid and subtle – solid as the pyramids, subtle as the twentieth echo of an echo, or as the memory of hyacinths which once scented the darkness. And Will was of a temperament to feel keenly the presence of subtleties: a man of clumsier perceptions would not have felt, as he did, that for the first time some sense of unfitness in perfect freedom with him had sprung up in Dorothea's mind, and that their silence, as he conducted her to the carriage, had had a chill in it. Perhaps Casaubon, in his hatred and jealousy, had been insisting to Dorothea that Will had slid below her socially. Confound Casaubon!

Will re-entered the drawing-room, took up his hat, and looking irritated as he advanced towards Mrs Lydgate, who had seated herself at her work-table, said: 'It is always fatal to have music or poetry interrupted. May I come another day and just finish about the rendering of "Lungi dal caro bene"?'

'I shall be happy to be taught,' said Rosamond. 'But I am sure you admit that the interruption was a very beautiful one. I quite envy your acquaintance with Mrs Casaubon. Is she very clever? She looks as if she were.'

'Really, I never thought about it,' said Will, sulkily.

'That is just the answer Tertius gave me, when I first asked him if she were handsome. What is it that you gentlemen are thinking of when you are with Mrs Casaubon?'

'Herself,' said Will, not indisposed to provoke the charming Mrs Lydgate. 'When one sees a perfect woman one never thinks of her attributes – one is conscious of her presence.'

'I shall be jealous when Tertius goes to Lowick,' said Rosamond, dimpling, and speaking with aëry lightness. 'He will come back and think nothing of me.'

'That does not seem to have been the effect on Lydgate hitherto. Mrs Casaubon is too unlike other women for them to be compared with her.'

'You are a devout worshipper, I perceive. You often see her, I suppose.'

'No,' said Will, almost pettishly. 'Worship is usually a matter of theory rather than of practice. But I am practising it to excess just at this moment – I must really tear myself away.'

'Pray come again some evening: Mr Lydgate will like to hear the music, and I cannot enjoy it so well without him.'

When her husband was at home again, Rosamond said, standing in front of him and holding his coat-collar with both her hands, 'Mr Ladislaw was here singing with me when Mrs Casaubon came in. He seemed vexed. Do you think he disliked her seeing him at our house? Surely your position is more than equal to his – whatever may be his relation to the Casaubons.'

'No, no; it must be something else if he were really vexed. Ladislaw is a sort of gypsy; he thinks nothing of leather and prunella.'

'Music apart, he is not always very agreeable. Do you like him?'

'Yes: I think he is a good fellow: rather miscellaneous and bric-à-brac, but likable.'

'Do you know, I think he adores Mrs Casaubon.'

'Poor devil!' said Lydgate, smiling and pinching his wife's ears.

Rosamond felt herself beginning to know a great deal of the world, especially in discovering – what when she was in her unmarried girlhood had been inconceivable to her except as a dim tragedy in bygone costumes – that women, even after marriage, might make conquests and enslave men. At that time young ladies in the country, even when educated at Mrs Lemon's, read little French literature later than Racine, and public prints had not cast their present magnificent illumination over the scandals of life. Still, vanity, with a woman's whole mind and day to work in, can construct abundantly on slight hints, especially on such a hint as the possibility of indefinite conquests. How delightful to make captives from the throne of marriage with a husband as crown-prince by your side – himself in fact a subject – while the captives look up for ever hopeless, losing their rest probably, and if their appetite too, so much the better! But Rosamond's romance turned at present chiefly on her crown-prince, and it was enough to enjoy his assured subjection. When he said, 'Poor devil!' she asked, with playful curiosity; 'Why so?'

'Why, what can a man do when he takes to adoring one of you mermaids? He only neglects his work and runs up bills.'

'I am sure you do not neglect your work. You are always at the Hospital, or seeing poor patients, or thinking about some doctor's quarrel; and then at home you always want to pore over your microscope and phials. Confess you like those things better than me.'

'Haven't you ambition enough to wish that your husband should be something better than a Middlemarch doctor?' said Lydgate, letting his hands fall on to his wife's shoulders, and looking at her with affectionate gravity. 'I shall make you learn my favourite bit from an old poet –

> Why should our pride make such a stir to be
> And be forgot? What good is like to this,
> To do worthy the writing, and to write
> Worthy the reading and the world's delight?

What I want, Rosy, is to do worthy the writing, – and to write out myself what I have done. A man must work, to do that, my pet.'

'Of course, I wish you to make discoveries: no one could more wish you to attain a high position in some better place than Middlemarch. You cannot say that I have ever tried to hinder you from working. But we cannot live like hermits. You are not discontented with me, Tertius?'

'No, dear, no. I am too entirely contented.'

'But what did Mrs Casaubon want to say to you?'

'Merely to ask about her husband's health. But I think she is going to be splendid to our New Hospital: I think she will give us two hundred a year.'

Chapter 44

I would not creep along the coast, but steer
Out in mid-sea, by guidance of the stars.

When Dorothea, walking round the laurel-planted plots of the New Hospital with Lydgate, had learned from him that there were no signs of change in Mr Casaubon's bodily condition beyond the mental sign of anxiety to know the truth about his illness, she was silent for a few moments, wondering whether she had said or done anything to rouse this new anxiety. Lydgate, not willing to let slip an opportunity of furthering a favourite purpose, ventured to say: 'I don't know whether your or Mr Casaubon's attention has been drawn to the needs of our New Hospital. Circumstances have made it seem rather egotistic in me to urge the subject; but that is not my fault; it is because there is a fight being made against it by the other medical men. I think you are generally interested in such things, for I remember that when I first had the pleasure of seeing you at Tipton Grange before your marriage you were asking me some questions about the way in which the health of the poor was affected by their miserable housing.'

'Yes, indeed,' said Dorothea, brightening. 'I shall be quite grateful to you if you will tell me how I can help to make things a little better. Everything of that sort has slipped away from me since I have been married. I mean,' she said, after a moment's hesitation, 'that the people in our village are tolerably comfortable, and my mind has been too much taken up for me to enquire further. But here – in such a place as Middlemarch there must be a great deal to be done.'

'There is everything to be done,' said Lydgate, with abrupt energy. 'And this Hospital is a capital piece of work, due entirely to Mr Bulstrode's exertions, and in a great degree to his money. But one man can't do everything in a scheme of this sort. Of course he looked forward to help. And now there's a mean, petty feud set up against the thing in the town, by certain persons who want to make it a failure.'

'What can be their reasons?' said Dorothea, with naïve surprise.

'Chiefly Mr Bulstrode's unpopularity, to begin with. Half the town would almost take trouble for the sake of thwarting him. In this stupid world most people never consider that a thing is good to be done unless it is done by their own set. I had no connection with Bulstrode before I came here. I look at him quite impartially, and I see that he has some notions – that he has set things on foot – which I can turn to good public purpose. If a fair number of the better educated men went to work with the belief that their observations might contribute to the reform of medical doctrine and practice, we should soon see a change for the better. That's my point of view. I hold that by refusing to work with Mr Bulstrode I should be turning my back on an opportunity of making my profession more generally serviceable.'

'I quite agree with you,' said Dorothea, at once fascinated by the situation sketched in Lydgate's words. 'But what is there against Mr Bulstrode? I know that my uncle is friendly with him.'

'People don't like his religious tone,' said Lydgate, breaking off there.

'That is all the stronger reason for despising such an opposition,' said Dorothea, looking at the affairs of Middlemarch by the light of the great persecutions.

'To put the matter quite fairly, they have other objections to him: – he is masterful and rather unsociable, and he is concerned with trade, which has complaints of its own that I know nothing about. But what has that to do with the question whether it would not be a fine thing to establish here a more valuable hospital than any they have in the county? The immediate motive to the opposition, however, is the fact that Bulstrode has put the medical direction into my hands. Of course I am glad of that. It gives me an opportunity of doing some good work, – and I am aware that I have to justify his choice of me. But the consequence is, that the whole profession in Middlemarch have set themselves tooth and nail against the Hospital, and not only refuse to co-operate themselves, but try to blacken the whole affair and hinder subscriptions.'

'How very petty!' exclaimed Dorothea, indignantly.

'I suppose one must expect to fight one's way: there is hardly anything to be done without it. And the ignorance of people about here is stupendous. I don't lay claim to anything else than having used some opportunities which have not come within everybody's reach; but there is no stifling the offence of being young, and a new-comer, and happening to know something more than the old inhabitants. Still, if I believe that I can set going a better method of treatment – if I believe that I can pursue certain observations and enquiries which may be a lasting benefit to medical practice, I should be a base truckler if I allowed any consideration of personal comfort to hinder me. And the course is all the clearer from there being no salary in question to put my persistence in an equivocal light.'

'I am glad you have told me this, Mr Lydgate,' said Dorothea, cordially. 'I feel sure I can help a little. I have some money, and don't know what to do with it – that is often an uncomfortable thought to me. I am sure I can spare two hundred a year for a grand purpose like this. How happy you must be, to know things that you feel sure will do great good! I wish I could awake with that knowledge every morning. There seems to be so much trouble taken that one can hardly see the good of!'

There was a melancholy cadence in Dorothea's voice as she spoke these last words. But she presently added, more cheerfully, 'Pray come to Lowick and tell us more of this. I will mention the subject to Mr Casaubon. I must hasten home now.'

She did mention it that evening, and said that she should like to subscribe two hundred a year – she had seven hundred a year as the equivalent of her own fortune, settled on her at her marriage. Mr Casaubon made no objection beyond a passing remark that the sum might be disproportionate in relation to other good objects, but when Dorothea in her ignorance resisted that suggestion, he acquiesced. He did not care himself about spending money, and was not reluctant to give it. If he ever felt keenly any question of money it was through the medium of another passion than the love of material property.

Dorothea told him that she had seen Lydgate, and recited the gist of her conversation with him about the Hospital. Mr Casaubon did not question her further, but he felt sure that she had wished to know what had passed between Lydgate and himself. 'She knows that I know,' said the ever-restless voice within; but that increase of tacit knowledge only thrust further off any confidence between them. He distrusted her affection; and what loneliness is more lonely than distrust?

Chapter 45

It is the humour of many heads to extol the days of their forefathers, and declaim against the wickedness of times present. Which notwithstanding they cannot handsomely do, without the borrowed help and satire of times past; condemning the vices of their own times, by the expressions of vices in times which they commend, which cannot but argue the community of vice in both. Horace, therefore, Juvenal, and Persius, were no prophets, although their lines did seem to indigitate and point at our times.

SIR THOMAS BROWNE, *Pseudodoxia Epidemica*

That opposition to the New Fever Hospital which Lydgate had sketched to Dorothea was, like other oppositions, to be viewed in many different lights. He regarded it as a mixture of jealousy and dunder-headed prejudice. Mr Bulstrode saw in it not only medical jealousy but a determination to thwart himself, prompted mainly by a hatred of that vital religion of which he had striven to be an effectual lay representative – a hatred which certainly found pretexts apart from religion such as were only too easy to find in the entanglements of human action. These might be called the ministerial views. But oppositions have the illimitable range of objections at command, which need never stop short at the boundary of knowledge, but can draw for ever on the vasts of ignorance. What the opposition in Middlemarch said about the New Hospital and its administration had certainly a great deal of echo in it, for heaven has taken care that everybody shall not be an originator; but there were differences which represented every social shade between the polished moderation of Dr Minchin and the trenchant assertion of Mrs Dollop, the landlady of the Tankard in Slaughter Lane.

Mrs Dollop became more and more convinced by her own asseveration, that Dr Lydgate meant to let the people die in the Hospital, if not to poison them, for the sake of cutting them up without saying by your leave or with your leave; for it was a known 'fac' that he had wanted to cut up Mrs Goby, as respectable a woman as any in Parley Street, who had money in trust before her marriage – a poor tale for a doctor, who if he was good for anything should know what was the matter with you before you died, and not want to pry into your inside after you were gone. If that was not reason, Mrs Dollop wished to know what was; but there was a prevalent feeling in her audience that her opinion was a bulwark, and that if it were overthrown there would be no limits to the cutting-up of bodies, as had been well seen in Burke and Hare with their pitch-plaisters – such a hanging business as that was not wanted in Middlemarch!

And let it not be supposed that opinion at the Tankard in Slaughter Lane was unimportant to the medical profession: that old authentic public-house – the original Tankard known by the name of Dollop's – was the resort of a great Benefit Club, which had some months before put to the vote whether its long-standing medical man, 'Dr Gambit', should not be cashiered in favour of 'this Dr Lydgate', who was capable of performing the most astonishing cures, and rescuing people altogether given up by other practitioners. But the balance had been turned against Lydgate by two members, who for some private reasons held that this power of resuscitating persons as good as dead was an equivocal recommendation, and might interfere with providential favours. In the course of the year, however, there had been a change in the public sentiment, of which the unanimity at Dollop's was an index.

A good deal more than a year ago, before anything was known of Lydgate's skill, the judgements on it had naturally been divided, depending on a sense of likelihood, situated perhaps in the pit of the stomach or in the pineal gland, and differing in its verdicts, but not the less valuable as a guide in the total deficit of evidence. Patients who had chronic diseases or whose lives had long been worn threadbare, like old Featherstone's, had been at once inclined to try him; also, many who did not like paying their doctor's bills, thought agreeably of opening an account with a new doctor and sending for him without stint if the children's temper wanted a dose, occasions when the old practitioners were often crusty; and all persons thus inclined to employ Lydgate held it likely that he was clever. Some considered that he might do more than others 'where there was liver'; – at least there would be no harm in getting a few bottles of 'stuff' from him, since if these proved useless it would still be possible to return to the Purifying Pills, which kept you alive, if they did not remove the yellowness. But these were people of minor importance. Good Middlemarch families were of course not going to change their doctor without reason shown; and everybody who had employed Mr Peacock did not feel obliged to accept a new man merely in the character of his successor, objecting that he was 'not likely to be equal to Peacock'.

But Lydgate had not been long in the town before there were particulars enough reported of him to breed much more specific expectations and to intensify differences into partisanship; some of the particulars being of that impressive order of which the significance is entirely hidden, like a statistical amount without a standard of comparison, but with a note of exclamation at the end. The cubic feet of oxygen yearly swallowed by a full-grown man – what a shudder they might have created in some Middlemarch circles! 'Oxygen! nobody knows what that may be – is it any wonder the cholera has got to Dantzic? And yet there are people who say quarantine is no good!'

One of the facts quickly rumoured was that Lydgate did not dispense drugs. This was offensive both to the physicians whose exclusive distinction seemed infringed on, and to the surgeon-apothecaries with whom he ranged himself; and only a little while before, they might have counted on having the law on their side against a man who without calling himself a London-made M.D. dared to ask for pay except as a charge on drugs. But Lydgate had not been experienced enough to foresee that his new course would be even more offensive to the laity; and to Mr Mawmsey, an important grocer in the Top Market, who, though not one of his patients, questioned him in an affable manner on the subject, he was injudicious enough to give a hasty popular explanation of his reasons, pointing out to Mr Mawmsey that it must lower the character of practitioners, and be a constant injury to the public, if their only mode of getting paid for their work was by their making out long bills for draughts, boluses, and mixtures.

'It is in that way that hard-working medical men may come to be almost as mischievous as quacks,' said Lydgate, rather thoughtlessly. 'To get their own bread they must overdose the kings lieges; and that's a bad sort of treason, Mr Mawmsey – undermines the constitution in a fatal way.'

Mr Mawmsey was not only an overseer (it was about a question of outdoor pay that he was having an interview with Lydgate), he was also asthmatic and had an increasing family: thus, from a medical point of view, as well as from his own, he was an important man indeed, an exceptional grocer, whose hair was arranged in a flamelike pyramid, and whose retail deference was of the cordial, encouraging kind – jocosely complimentary, and with a certain considerate abstinence from letting out the full force of his mind. It was Mr Mawmsey's friendly jocoseness in questioning him which had set the tone of Lydgate's reply. But let the wise be warned against too great readiness at explanation: it multiplies the sources of mistake, lengthening the sum for reckoners sure to go wrong.

Lydgate smiled as he ended his speech, putting his foot into the stirrup, and Mr Mawmsey laughed more than he would have done if he had known who the king's lieges were, giving his 'Good-morning, sir, good-morning, sir' with the air of one who saw everything clearly enough. But in truth his views were perturbed. For years he had been paying bills with strictly-made items, so that for every half-crown and eighteenpence he was certain something measurable had been delivered. He had done this with satisfaction, including it among his responsibilities as a husband and father, and regarding a longer bill than usual as a dignity worth mentioning. Moreover, in addition to the massive benefit of the drugs to 'self and family', he had enjoyed the pleasure of forming an acute judgement as to their immediate effects, so as to give an intelligent statement for the guidance of Mr Gambit – a practitioner just a little lower in status than Wrench or Toller, and especially esteemed as an accoucheur, of whose ability Mr Mawmsey had the poorest opinion on all other points, but in doctoring, he was wont to say in an undertone, he placed Gambit above any of them.

Here were deeper reasons than the superficial talk of a new man, which appeared still flimsier in the drawing-room over the shop, when they were recited to Mrs Mawmsey, a woman accustomed to be made much of as a fertile mother, – generally under attendance more or less frequent from Mr Gambit, and occasionally having attacks which required Dr Minchin.

'Does this Mr Lydgate mean to say there is no use in taking medicine?' said Mrs Mawmsey, who was slightly given to drawling. 'I should like him to tell me how I could bear up at Fair time, if I didn't take strengthening medicine for a month beforehand. Think of what I have to provide for calling customers, my dear!' – here Mrs Mawmsey turned to an intimate female friend who sat by – 'a large veal pie – a stuffed fillet, a round of beef – ham, tongue, *et* cetera, *et* cetera! But what keeps me up best is the pink mixture, not the brown. I wonder, Mr Mawmsey, with your experience, you could have patience to listen. *I* should have told him at once that I knew a little better than that.'

'No, no, no,' said Mr Mawmsey; 'I was not going to tell him my opinion. Hear everything and judge for yourself is my motto. But he didn't know who he was talking to. I was not to be turned on *his* finger. People often pretend to tell me things, when they might as well say, "Mawmsey, you're a fool." But I smile at it: I humour everybody's weak place. If physic had done harm to self and family, I should have found it out by this time.'

The next day Mr Gambit was told that Lydgate went about saying physic was of no use.

'Indeed!' said he, lifting his eyebrows with cautious surprise. (He was a stout husky man with a large ring on his fourth finger.) 'How will he cure his patients then?'

'That is what I say,' returned Mrs Mawmsey, who habitually gave weight to her speech by loading her pronouns. 'Does *he* suppose that people will pay him only to come and sit with them and go away again?'

Mrs Mawmsey had had a great deal of sitting from Mr Gambit, including very full accounts of his own habits of body and other affairs; but of course he knew there was no innuendo in her remark, since his spare time and personal narrative had never been charged for. So he replied, humorously: 'Well, Lydgate is a good-looking young fellow, you know.'

'Not one that *I* would employ,' said Mrs Mawmsey. '*Others* may do as they please.'

Hence Mr Gambit could go away from the chief grocer's without fear of rivalry, but not without a sense that Lydgate was one of those hypocrites who try to discredit others by advertising their own honesty, and that it might be worth some people's while to show him up. Mr Gambit, however, had a satisfactory practice, much pervaded by the smells of retail trading which suggested the reduction of cash payments to a balance. And he did not think it worth his while to show Lydgate up until he knew how. He had not indeed great resources of education, and had to work his own way against a good deal of professional contempt; but he made none the worse accoucheur for calling the breathing apparatus 'longs'.

Other medical men felt themselves more capable. Mr Toller shared the highest practice in the town and belonged to an old Middlemarch family: there were Tollers in the law and everything else above the line of retail trade. Unlike our irascible friend Wrench, he had the easiest way in the world of taking things which might be supposed to annoy him, being a well bred, quietly facetious man, who kept a good house, was very fond of a little sporting when he could get it, very friendly with Mr Hawley, and hostile to Mr Bulstrode. It may seem odd that with such pleasant habits he should have been given to the heroic treatment, bleeding and blistering and starving his patients, with a dispassionate disregard to his personal example; but the incongruity favoured the opinion of his ability among his patients, who commonly observed that Mr Toller had lazy manners, but his treatment was as active as you could desire: – no man, said they, carried more seriousness into his profession: he was a little slow in coming, but when he came he *did* something. He was a great favourite in his own circle, and whatever he implied to anyone's disadvantage told doubly from his careless ironical tone.

He naturally got tired of smiling and saying, 'Ah!' when he was told that Mr Peacock's successor did not mean to dispense medicines; and Mr Hackbutt one day mentioning it over the wine at a dinner-party, Mr Toller said, laughingly, 'Dibbitts will get rid of his stale drugs, then. I'm fond of little Dibbitts – I'm glad he's in luck.'

'I see your meaning, Toller,' said Mr Hackbutt, 'and I am entirely of your opinion. I shall take an opportunity of expressing myself to that effect. A medical man should be responsible for the quality of the drugs consumed by his patients. That is the *rationale* of the system of charging which has hitherto obtained; and nothing is more offensive than this ostentation of reform, where there is no real amelioration.'

'Ostentation, Hackbutt? ' said Mr Toller, ironically. 'I don't see that. A man can't very well be ostentatious of what nobody believes in. There's no reform in the matter: the question is, whether the profit on the drugs is paid to the medical man by the druggist or by the patient, and whether there shall be extra pay under the name of attendance.'

'Ah, to be sure; one of your damned new versions of old humbug,' said Mr Hawley, passing the decanter to Mr Wrench.

Mr Wrench, generally abstemious, often drank wine rather freely at a party, getting the more irritable in consequence.

'As to humbug, Hawley,' he said, 'that's a word easy to fling about. But what I contend against is the way medical men are fouling their own nest, and setting up a cry about the country as if a general practitioner who dispenses drugs couldn't be a gentleman. I throw back the imputation with scorn. I say, the most ungentlemanly trick a man can be guilty of is to come among the members of his profession with innovations which are a libel on their time-honoured procedure. That is my opinion, and I am ready to maintain it against anyone who contradicts me.' Mr Wrench's voice had become exceedingly sharp.

'I can't oblige you there, Wrench,' said Mr Hawley, thrusting his hands into his trouser-pockets.

'My dear fellow,' said Mr Toller, striking in pacifically, and looking at Mr Wrench, 'the physicians have their toes trodden on more than we have. If you come to dignity it is a question for Minchin and Sprague.'

'Does medical jurisprudence provide nothing against these infringements?' said Mr Hackbutt, with a disinterested desire to offer his lights. 'How does the law stand, eh, Hawley?'

'Nothing to be done there,' said Mr Hawley. 'I looked into it for Sprague. You'd only break your nose against a damned judge's decision.'

'Pooh! no need of law,' said Mr Toller. 'So far as practice is concerned the attempt is an absurdity. No patient will like it – certainly not Peacock's, who have been used to depletion. Pass the wine.'

Mr Toller's prediction was partly verified. If Mr and Mrs Mawmsey, who had no idea of employing Lydgate, were made uneasy by his supposed declaration against drugs, it was inevitable that those who called him in should watch a little anxiously to see whether he did 'use all the means he might use' in the case. Even good Mr Powderell, who in his constant charity of interpretation was inclined to esteem Lydgate the more for what seemed a conscientious pursuit of a better plan, had his mind disturbed with doubts during his wife's attack of erysipelas, and could not abstain from mentioning to Lydgate that Mr Peacock on a similar occasion had administered a series of boluses which were not otherwise definable than by their remarkable effect in bringing Mrs Powderell round before Michaelmas from an illness which had begun in a remarkably hot August. At last, indeed, in the conflict between his desire not to hurt Lydgate and his anxiety that no 'means' should be lacking, he induced his wife privately to take Widgeon's Purifying Pills, an esteemed Middlemarch medicine, which arrested every disease at the fountain by setting to work at once upon the blood. This co-operative measure was not to be mentioned to Lydgate, and Mr Powderell himself had no certain reliance on it, only hoping that it might be attended with a blessing.

But in this doubtful stage of Lydgate's introduction he was helped by what we mortals rashly call good fortune. I suppose no doctor ever came newly to a place without making cures that surprised somebody – cures which may be called fortune's testimonials, and deserve as much credit as the written or printed kind. Various patients got well while Lydgate was attending them, some even of dangerous illnesses; and it was remarked that the new doctor with his new ways had at least the merit of bringing people back from the brink of death. The trash talked on such occasions was the more vexatious to Lydgate, because it gave precisely the sort of prestige which an incompetent and unscrupulous man would desire, and was sure to be imputed to him by the simmering dislike of the other medical men as an encouragement on his own part of ignorant puffing. But even his proud outspokenness was checked by the discernment that it was as useless to fight against the interpretations of ignorance as to whip the fog; and 'good fortune' insisted on using those interpretations.

Mrs Larcher having just become charitably concerned about alarming symptoms in her charwoman, when Dr Minchin called, asked him to see her then and there, and to give her a certificate for the Infirmary; whereupon after examination he wrote a statement of the case as one of tumour, and recommended the bearer Nancy Nash as an out-patient. Nancy, calling at home on her way to the Infirmary, allowed the stay-maker and his wife, in whose attic she lodged, to read Dr Minchin's paper, and by this means became a subject of compassionate conversation in the neighbouring shops of Churchyard Lane as being afflicted with a tumour at first declared to be as large and hard as a duck's egg, but later in the day to be about the size of 'your fist'. Most hearers agreed that it would have to be cut out, but one had known of oil and another of 'squitchineal' as adequate to soften and reduce any lump in the body when taken enough of into the inside – the oil by gradually 'soopling', the squitchineal by eating away.

Meanwhile when Nancy presented herself at the Infirmary it happened to be one of Lydgate's days there. After questioning and examining her, Lydgate said to the house-surgeon in an undertone, 'It's not tumour: it's cramp.' He ordered her a blister and some steel mixture, and told her to go home and rest, giving her at the same time a note to Mrs Larcher, who, she said, was her best employer, to testify that she was in need of good food.

But by and by Nancy, in her attic, became portentously worse, the supposed tumour having indeed given way to the blister, but only wandered to another region with angrier pain. The stay-maker's wife went to fetch Lydgate, and he continued for a fortnight to attend Nancy in her own home, until under his treatment she got quite well and went to work again. But the case continued to be described as one of tumour in Churchyard Lane and other streets – nay, by Mrs Larcher also; for when Lydgate's remarkable cure was mentioned to Dr Minchin, he naturally did not like to say, 'The case was not one of tumour, and I was mistaken in describing it as such,' but answered, 'Indeed! ah! I saw it was a surgical case, not of a fatal kind.' He had been inwardly annoyed, however, when he had asked at the Infirmary about the woman he had recommended two days before, to hear from the house-surgeon, a youngster who was not sorry to vex Minchin with impunity, exactly what had occurred: he privately pronounced that it was indecent in a general practitioner to contradict a physician's diagnosis in that open manner, and afterwards agreed with Wrench that Lydgate was disagreeably inattentive to etiquette. Lydgate did not make the affair a ground for valuing himself or (very particularly) despising Minchin, such rectification of misjudgements often happening among men of equal qualifications. But report took up this amazing case of tumour, not clearly distinguished from cancer, and considered the more awful for being of the wandering sort; till much prejudice against Lydgate's method as to drugs was overcome by the proof of his marvellous skill in the speedy restoration of Nancy Nash after she had been rolling and rolling in agonies from the presence of a tumour both hard and obstinate, but nevertheless compelled to yield.

How could Lydgate help himself? It is offensive to tell a lady when she is expressing her amazement at your skill, that she is altogether mistaken and rather foolish in her amazement. And to have entered into the nature of diseases would only have added to his breaches of medical propriety. Thus he had to wince under a promise of success given by that ignorant praise which misses every valid quality.

In the case of a more conspicuous patient, Mr Borthrop Trumbull, Lydgate was conscious of having shown himself something better than an everyday doctor, though here too it was an equivocal advantage that he won. The eloquent auctioneer was seized with pneumonia, and having been a patient of Mr Peacock's, sent for Lydgate, whom he had expressed his intention to patronise. Mr Trumbull was a robust man, a good subject for trying the expectant theory upon – watching the course of an interesting disease when left as much as possible to itself, so that the stages might be noted for future guidance; and from the air with which he described his sensations Lydgate surmised that he would like to be taken into his medical man's confidence, and be represented as a partner in his own cure. The auctioneer heard, without much surprise, that his was a constitution which (always with due watching) might be left to itself, so as to offer a beautiful example of a disease with all its phases seen in clear delineation, and that he probably had the rare strength of mind voluntarily to become the test of a rational procedure, and thus make the disorder of his pulmonary functions a general benefit to society.

Mr Trumbull acquiesced at once, and entered strongly into the view that an illness of his was no ordinary occasion for medical science.

'Never fear, sir; you are not speaking to one who is altogether ignorant of the *vis medicatrix*,' said he, with his usual superiority of expression, made rather pathetic by difficulty of breathing. And he went without shrinking through his abstinence from drugs, much sustained by application of the thermometer which implied the importance of his temperature, by the sense that he furnished objects for the microscope, and by learning many new words which seemed suited to the dignity of his secretions. For Lydgate was acute enough to indulge him with a little technical talk.

It may be imagined that Mr Trumbull rose from his couch with a disposition to speak of an illness in which he had manifested the strength of his mind as well as constitution; and he was not backward in awarding credit to the medical man who had discerned the quality of patient he had to deal with. The auctioneer was not an ungenerous man, and liked to give others their due, feeling that he could afford it. He had caught the words 'expectant method', and rang chimes on this and other learned phrases to accompany the assurance that Lydgate 'knew a thing or two more than the rest of the doctors – was far better versed in the secrets of his profession than the majority of his compeers'.

This had happened before the affair of Fred Vincy's illness had given to Mr Wrench's enmity towards Lydgate more definite personal ground. The new-comer already threatened to be a nuisance in the shape of rivalry, and was certainly a nuisance in the shape of practical criticism or reflections on his hard-driven elders, who had had something else to do than to busy themselves with untried notions. His practice had spread in one or two quarters, and from the first the report of his high family had led to his being pretty generally invited, so that the other medical men had to meet him at dinner in the best houses; and having to meet a man whom you dislike is not observed always to end in mutual attachment. There was hardly ever so much unanimity among them as in the opinion that Lydgate was an arrogant young fellow, and yet ready for the sake of ultimately predominating to show a crawling subservience to Bulstrode. That Mr Farebrother, whose name was a chief flag of the anti-Bulstrode party, always defended Lydgate and made a friend of him, was referred to Farebrother's unaccountable way of fighting on both sides.

Here was plenty of preparation for the outburst of professional disgust at the announcement of the laws Mr Bulstrode was laying down for the direction of the New Hospital, which were the more exasperating because there was no present possibility of interfering with his will and pleasure, everybody except

Lord Medlicote having refused help towards the building, on the ground that they preferred giving to the Old Infirmary. Mr Bulstrode met all the expenses, and had ceased to be sorry that he was purchasing the right to carry out his notions of improvement without hindrance from prejudiced coadjutors; but he had had to spend large sums and the building had lingered. Caleb Garth had undertaken it, had failed during its progress, and before the interior fittings were begun had retired from the management of the business; and when referring to the Hospital he often said that however Bulstrode might ring if you tried him, he liked good solid carpentry and masonry, and had a notion both of drains and chimneys. In fact, the Hospital had become an object of intense interest to Bulstrode, and he would willingly have continued to spare a large yearly sum that he might rule it dictatorially without any Board; but he had another favourite object which also required money for its accomplishment: he wished to buy some land in the neighbourhood of Middlemarch, and therefore he wished to get considerable contributions towards maintaining the Hospital. Meanwhile he framed his plan of management. The Hospital was to be reserved for fever in all its forms; Lydgate was to be chief medical superintendent, that he might have free authority to pursue all comparative investigations which his studies, particularly in Paris, had shown him the importance of, the other medical visitors having a consultative influence, but no power to contravene Lydgate's ultimate decisions; and the general management was to be lodged exclusively in the hands of five directors associated with Mr Bulstrode, who were to have votes in the ratio of their contributions, the Board itself filling up any vacancy in its numbers, and no mob of small contributors being admitted to a share of government.

There was an immediate refusal on the part of every medical man in the town to become a visitor at the Fever Hospital.

'Very well,' said Lydgate to Mr Bulstrode, 'we have a capital house-surgeon and dispenser, a clear-headed, neat-handed fellow; we'll get Webb from Crabsley, as good a country practitioner as any of them, to come over twice a week, and in case of any exceptional operation, Protheroe will come from Brassing. I must work the harder, that's all, and I have given up my post at the Infirmary. The plan will flourish in spite of them, and then they'll be glad to come in. Things can't last as they are: there must be all sorts of reform soon, and then young fellows may be glad to come and study here.' Lydgate was in high spirits.

'I shall not flinch, you may depend upon it, Mr Lydgate,' said Mr Bulstrode. 'While I see you carrying out high intentions with vigour, you shall have my unfailing support. And I have humble confidence that the blessing which has hitherto attended my efforts against the spirit of evil in this town will not be withdrawn. Suitable directors to assist me I have no doubt of securing. Mr Brooke of Tipton has already given me his concurrence, and a pledge to contribute yearly: he has not specified the sum – probably not a great one. But he will be a useful member of the Board.'

A useful member was perhaps to be defined as one who would originate nothing, and always vote with Mr Bulstrode.

The medical aversion to Lydgate was hardly disguised now. Neither Dr

Sprague nor Dr Minchin said that he disliked Lydgate's knowledge, or his disposition to improve treatment: what they disliked was his arrogance, which nobody felt to be altogether deniable. They implied that he was insolent, pretentious, and given to that reckless innovation for the sake of noise and show which was the essence of the charlatan.

The word charlatan once thrown on the air could not be let drop. In those days the world was agitated about the wondrous doings of Mr St John Long, 'noblemen and gentlemen' attesting his extraction of a fluid like mercury from the temples of a patient.

Mr Toller remarked one day, smilingly, to Mrs Taft, that 'Bulstrode had found a man to suit him in Lydgate; a charlatan in religion is sure to like other sorts of charlatans.'

'Yes, indeed, I can imagine,' said Mrs Taft, keeping the number of thirty stitches carefully in her mind all the while; 'there are so many of that sort. I remember Mr Cheshire, with his irons, trying to make people straight when the Almighty had made them crooked.'

'No, no,' said Mr Toller, 'Cheshire was all right – all fair and above board. But there's St John Long – that's the kind of fellow we call a charlatan, advertising cures in ways nobody knows anything about; a fellow who wants to make a noise by pretending to go deeper than other people. The other day he was pretending to tap a man's brain and get quicksilver out of it.'

'Good gracious! what dreadful trifling with people's constitutions!' said Mrs Taft.

After this it came to be held in various quarters that Lydgate played even with respectable constitutions for his own purposes, and how much more likely that in his flighty experimenting he should make sixes and sevens of hospital patients. Especially it was to be expected, as the landlady of the Tankard had said, that he would recklessly cut up their dead bodies. For Lydgate having attended Mrs Goby, who died apparently of a heart-disease not very clearly expressed in the symptoms, too daringly asked leave of her relatives to open the body, and thus gave an offence quickly spreading beyond Parley Street, where that lady had long resided on an income such as made this association of her body with the victims of Burke and Hare a flagrant insult to her memory.

Affairs were in this stage when Lydgate opened the subject of the Hospital to Dorothea. We see that he was bearing enmity and silly misconception with much spirit, aware that they were partly created by his good share of success.

'They will not drive me away,' he said, talking confidentially in Mr Farebrother's study. 'I have got a good opportunity here, for the ends I most care about: and I am pretty sure to get income enough for our wants. By and by I shall go on as quietly as possible: I have no seductions now away from home and work. And I am more and more convinced that it will be possible to demonstrate the homogeneous origin of all the tissues. Raspail and others are on the same track, and I have been losing time.'

'I have no power of prophecy there,' said Mr Farebrother, who had been puffing at his pipe thoughtfully while Lydgate talked; 'but as to the hostility in the town, you'll weather it if you are prudent.'

'How am I to be prudent?' said Lydgate, 'I just do what comes before me to do. I can't help people's ignorance and spite, any more than Vesalius could. It isn't possible to square one's conduct to silly conclusions which nobody can foresee.'

'Quite true; I didn't mean that. I meant only two things. One is, keep yourself as separable from Bulstrode as you can: of course, you can go on doing good work of your own by his help; but don't get tied. Perhaps it seems like personal feeling in me to say so – and there's a good deal of that, I own – but personal feeling is not always in the wrong if you boil it down to the impressions which make it simply an opinion.'

'Bulstrode is nothing to me,' said Lydgate, carelessly, 'except on public grounds. As to getting very closely united to him, I am not fond enough of him for that. But what was the other thing you meant?' said Lydgate, who was nursing his leg as comfortably as possible, and feeling in no great need of advice.

'Why, this. Take care – *experto crede* – take care not to get hampered about money matters. I know, by a word you let fall one day, that you don't like my playing at cards so much for money. You are right enough there. But try and keep clear of wanting small sums that you haven't got. I am perhaps talking rather superfluously; but a man likes to assume superiority over himself, by holding up his bad example and sermonising on it.'

Lydgate took Mr Farebrother's hints very cordially, though he would hardly have borne them from another man. He could not help remembering that he had lately made some debts, but these had seemed inevitable, and he had no intention now to do more than keep house in a simple way. The furniture for which he owed would not want renewing; nor even the stock of wine for a long while.

Many thoughts cheered him at that time – and justly. A man conscious of enthusiasm for worthy aims is sustained under petty hostilities by the memory of great workers who had to fight their way not without wounds, and who hover in his mind as patron saints, invisibly helping. At home, that same evening when he had been chatting with Mr Farebrother, he had his long legs stretched on the sofa, his head thrown back, and his hands clasped behind it according to his favourite ruminating attitude, while Rosamond sat at the piano, and played one tune after another, of which her husband only knew (like the emotional elephant he was!) that they fell in with his mood as if they had been melodious sea-breezes.

There was something very fine in Lydgate's look just then, and anyone might have been encouraged to bet on his achievement. In his dark eyes and on his mouth and brow there was that placidity which comes from the fullness of contemplative thought – the mind not searching, but beholding, and the glance seeming to be filled with what is behind it.

Presently Rosamond left the piano and seated herself on a chair close to the sofa and opposite her husband's face.

'Is that enough music for you, my lord?' she said, folding her hands before her and putting on a little air of meekness.

'Yes, dear, if you are tired,' said Lydgate, gently, turning his eyes and resting them on her, but not otherwise moving. Rosamond's presence at that moment was perhaps no more than a spoonful brought to the lake, and her woman's instinct in this matter was not dull.

'What is absorbing you?' she said, leaning forward and bringing her face nearer to his.

He moved his hands and placed them gently behind her shoulders.

'I am thinking of a great fellow, who was about as old as I am three hundred years ago, and had already begun a new era in anatomy.'

'I can't guess,' said Rosamond, shaking her head. 'We used to play at guessing historical characters at Mrs Lemon's, but not anatomists.'

'I'll tell you. His name was Vesalius. And the only way he could get to know anatomy as he did, was by going to snatch bodies at night, from graveyards and places of execution.'

'Oh!' said Rosamond, with a look of disgust on her pretty face, 'I am very glad you are not Vesalius. I should have thought he might find some less horrible way than that.'

'No, he couldn't,' said Lydgate, going on too earnestly to take much notice of her answer. 'He could only get a complete skeleton by snatching the whitened bones of a criminal from the gallows, and burying them, and fetching them away by bits secretly, in the dead of night.'

'I hope he is not one of your great heroes,' said Rosamond, half-playfully, half-anxiously, 'else I shall have you getting up in the night to go to St Peter's churchyard. You know how angry you told me the people were about Mrs Goby. You have enemies enough already.'

'So had Vesalius, Rosy. No wonder the medical fogies in Middlemarch are jealous, when some of the greatest doctors living were fierce upon Vesalius because they had believed in Galen, and he showed that Galen was wrong. They called him a liar and a poisonous monster. But the facts of the human frame were on his side; and so he got the better of them.'

'And what happened to him afterwards?' said Rosamond, with some interest.

'Oh, he had a good deal of fighting to the last. And they did exasperate him enough at one time to make him burn a good deal of his work. Then he got shipwrecked just as he was coming from Jerusalem to take a great chair at Padua. He died rather miserably.'

There was a moment's pause before Rosamond said, 'Do you know, Tertius, I often wish you had not been a medical man.'

'Nay, Rosy, don't say that,' said Lydgate, drawing her closer to him. 'That is like saying you wish you had married another man.'

'Not at all; you are clever enough for anything: you might easily have been something else. And your cousins at Quallingham all think that you have sunk below them in your choice of a profession.'

'The cousins at Quallingham may go to the devil!' said Lydgate with scorn. 'It was like their impudence if they said anything of the sort to you.'

'Still,' said Rosamond, 'I do not think it is a nice profession, dear.' We know that she had much quiet perseverance in her opinion.

'It is the grandest profession in the world, Rosamond,' said Lydgate, gravely. 'And to say that you love me without loving the medical man in me, is the same sort of thing as to say that you like eating a peach but don't like its flavour. Don't say that again, dear, it pains me.'

'Very well, Dr Grave-face,' said Rosy, dimpling, 'I will declare in future that I dote on skeletons, and body-snatchers, and bits of things in phials, and quarrels with everybody, that end in your dying miserably.'

'No, no, not so bad as that,' said Lydgate, giving up remonstrance and petting her resignedly.

Chapter 46

Pues no podemos haber aquello que queremos,
queramos aquello que podremos.

Since we cannot get what we like, let us like what we can get.
Spanish proverb

While Lydgate, safely married and with the Hospital under his command, felt himself struggling for Medical Reform against Middlemarch, Middlemarch was becoming more and more conscious of the national struggle for another kind of Reform.

By the time that Lord John Russell's measure was being debated in the House of Commons, there was a new political animation in Middlemarch, and a new definition of parties which might show a decided change of balance if a new election came. And there were some who already predicted this event, declaring that a Reform Bill would never be carried by the actual Parliament. This was what Will Ladislaw dwelt on to Mr Brooke as a reason for congratulation that he had not yet tried his strength at the hustings.

'Things will grow and ripen as if it were a comet year,' said Will. 'The public temper will soon get to a cometary heat, now the question of Reform has set in. There is likely to be another election before long, and by that time Middlemarch will have got more ideas into its head. What we have to work at now is the *Pioneer* and political meetings.'

'Quite right, Ladislaw; we shall make a new thing of opinion here,' said Mr Brooke. 'Only I want to keep myself independent about Reform, you know: I don't want to go too far. I want to take up Wilberforce's and Romilly's line, you know, and work at Negro Emancipation, Criminal Law – that kind of thing. But of course I should support Grey.'

'If you go in for the principle of Reform, you must be prepared to take what the situation offers,' said Will. 'If everybody pulled for his own bit against everybody else, the whole question would go to tatters.'

'Yes, yes, I agree with you – I quite take that point of view. I should put it in that light. I should support Grey, you know. But I don't want to change the balance of the constitution, and I don't think Grey would.'

'But that is what the country wants,' said Will. 'Else there would be no meaning in political unions or any other movement that knows what it's about. It wants to have a House of Commons which is not weighted with nominees of the landed class, but with representatives of the other interests. And as to contending for a reform short of that, it is like asking for a bit of an avalanche which has already begun to thunder.'

'That is fine, Ladislaw: that is the way to put it. Write that down, now. We must begin to get documents about the feeling of the country, as well as the machine-breaking and general distress.'

'As to documents,' said Will, 'a two-inch card will hold plenty. A few rows of figures are enough to deduce misery from, and a few more will show the rate at which the political determination of the people is growing.'

'Good: draw that out a little more at length, Ladislaw. That is an idea, now: write it out in the *Pioneer*. Put the figures and deduce the misery, you know; and put the other figures and deduce – and so on. You have a way of putting things. Burke, now: – when I think of Burke, I can't help wishing somebody had a pocket-borough to give you, Ladislaw. You'd never get elected, you know. And we shall always want talent in the House: reform as we will, we shall always want talent. That avalanche and the thunder, now, was really a little like Burke. I want that sort of thing – not ideas, you know, but a way of putting them.'

'Pocket-boroughs would be a fine thing,' said Ladislaw, 'if they were always in the right pocket, and there were always a Burke at hand.'

Will was not displeased with that complimentary comparison, even from Mr Brooke; for it is a little too trying to human flesh to be conscious of expressing one's self better than others and never to have it noticed, and in the general dearth of admiration for the right thing, even a chance bray of applause falling exactly in time is rather fortifying. Will felt that his literary refinements were usually beyond the limits of Middlemarch perception; nevertheless, he was beginning thoroughly to like the work of which when he began he had said to himself rather languidly, 'Why not?' – and he studied the political situation with as ardent an interest as he had ever given to poetic metres or mediaevalism. It is undeniable that but for the desire to be where Dorothea was, and perhaps the want of knowing what else to do, Will would not at this time have been meditating on the needs of the English people or criticising English statesmanship: he would probably have been rambling in Italy sketching plans for several dramas, trying prose and finding it too jejune, trying verse and finding it too artificial, beginning to copy 'bits' from old pictures, leaving off because they were 'no good', and observing that, after all, self-culture was the principal point; while in politics he would have been sympathising warmly with liberty and progress in general. Our sense of duty must often wait for some work which shall take the place of dilettantism and make us feel that the quality of our action is not a matter of indifference.

Ladislaw had now accepted his bit of work, though it was not that indeterminate loftiest thing which he had once dreamed of as alone worthy of continuous effort. His nature warmed easily in the presence of subjects which were visibly mixed with life and action, and the easily-stirred rebellion in him helped the glow of public spirit. In spite of Mr Casaubon and the banishment from

Lowick, he was rather happy; getting a great deal of fresh knowledge in a vivid way and for practical purposes, and making the *Pioneer* celebrated as far as Brassing (never mind the smallness of the area; the writing was not worse than much that reaches the four corners of the earth).

Mr Brooke was occasionally irritating; but Will's impatience was relieved by the division of his time between visits to the Grange and retreats to his Middlemarch lodgings, which gave variety to his life.

'Shift the pegs a little,' he said to himself, 'and Mr Brooke might be in the Cabinet, while I was Under-Secretary. That is the common order of things: the little waves make the large ones and are of the same pattern. I am better here than in the sort of life Mr Casaubon would have trained me for, where the doing would be all laid down by a precedent too rigid for me to react upon. I don't care for prestige or high pay.'

As Lydgate had said of him, he was a sort of gypsy, rather enjoying the sense of belonging to no class; he had a feeling of romance in his position, and a pleasant consciousness of creating a little surprise wherever he went. That sort of enjoyment had been disturbed when he had felt some new distance between himself and Dorothea in their accidental meeting at Lydgate's, and his irritation had gone out towards Mr Casaubon, who had declared beforehand that Will would lose caste. 'I never had any caste,' he would have said, if that prophecy had been uttered to him, and the quick blood would have come and gone like breath in his transparent skin. But it is one thing to like defiance, and another thing to like its consequences.

Meanwhile, the town opinion about the new editor of the *Pioneer* was tending to confirm Mr Casaubon's view. Will's relationship in that distinguished quarter did not, like Lydgate's high connections, serve as an advantageous introduction: if it was rumoured that young Ladislaw was Mr Casaubon's nephew or cousin, it was also rumoured that 'Mr Casaubon would have nothing to do with him'.

'Brooke has taken him up,' said Mr Hawley, 'because that is what no man in his senses could have expected. Casaubon has devilish good reasons, you may be sure, for turning the cold shoulder on a young fellow whose bringing-up he paid for. Just like Brooke – one of those fellows who would praise a cat to sell a horse.'

And some oddities of Will's, more or less poetical, appeared to support Mr Keck, the editor of the *Trumpet*, in asserting that Ladislaw if the truth were known, was not only a Polish emissary but crack-brained, which accounted for the preternatural quickness and glibness of his speech when he got on to a platform – as he did whenever he had an opportunity, speaking with a facility which cast reflections on solid Englishmen generally. It was disgusting to Keck to see a strip of a fellow, with light curls round his head, get up and speechify by the hour against institutions 'which had existed when he was in his cradle'. And in a leading article of the *Trumpet*, Keck characterised Ladislaw's speech at a Reform meeting as 'the violence of an energumen – a miserable effort to shroud in the brilliancy of fireworks the daring of irresponsible statements and the poverty of a knowledge which was of the cheapest and most recent description'.

'That was a rattling article yesterday, Keck,' said Dr Sprague, with sarcastic intentions. 'But what is an energumen?'

'Oh, a term that came up in the French Revolution,' said Keck.

This dangerous aspect of Ladislaw was strangely contrasted with other habits which became matter of remark. He had a fondness, half artistic, half affectionate, for little children – the smaller they were on tolerably active legs, and the funnier their clothing, the better Will liked to surprise and please them. We know that in Rome he was given to ramble about among the poor people, and the taste did not quit him in Middlemarch.

He had somehow picked up a troop of droll children, little hatless boys with their galligaskins much worn and scant shirting to hang out, little girls who tossed their hair out of their eyes to look at him, and guardian brothers at the mature age of seven. This troop he had led out on gypsy excursions to Halsell Wood at nutting-time, and since the cold weather had set in he had taken them on a clear day to gather sticks for a bonfire in the hollow of a hillside, where he drew out a small feast of gingerbread for them, and improvised a Punch-and-Judy drama with some private home-made puppets. Here was one oddity. Another was, that in houses where he got friendly, he was given to stretch himself at full length on the rug while he talked, and was apt to be discovered in this attitude by occasional callers for whom such an irregularity was likely to confirm the notions of his dangerously mixed blood and general laxity.

But Will's articles and speeches naturally recommended him in families which the new strictness of party division had marked off on the side of Reform. He was invited to Mr Bulstrode's; but here he could not lie down on the rug, and Mrs Bulstrode felt that his mode of talking abut Catholic countries, as if there were any truce with Antichrist, illustrated the usual tendency to unsoundness in intellectual men.

At Mr Farebrother's, however, whom the irony of events had brought on the same side with Bulstrode in the national movement, Will became a favourite with the ladies, especially with little Miss Noble, whom it was one of his oddities to escort when he met her in the street with her little basket, giving her his arm in the eyes of the town, and insisting on going with her to pay some call where she distributed her small filchings from her own share of sweet things.

But the house where he visited oftenest and lay most on the rug was Lydgate's. The two men were not at all alike, but they agreed none the worse. Lydgate was abrupt but not irritable, taking little notice of megrims in healthy people: and Ladislaw did not usually throw away his susceptibilities on those who took no notice of them. With Rosamond, on the other hand, he pouted and was wayward – nay, often uncomplimentary, much to her inward surprise: nevertheless he was gradually becoming necessary to her entertainment by his companionship in her music, his varied talk, and his freedom from the grave preoccupation which, with all her husband's tenderness and indulgence, often made his manners unsatisfactory to her, and confirmed her dislike of the medical profession.

Lydgate, inclined to be sarcastic on the superstitious faith of the people in the efficacy of 'the bill', while nobody cared about the low state of pathology, sometimes assailed Will with troublesome questions. One evening in March, Rosamond in her cherry-coloured dress with swan's-down trimming about the throat sat at the tea-table; Lydgate, lately come in tired from his outdoor work, was seated sideways on an easy-chair by the fire with one leg over the elbow, his brow looking a little troubled as his eyes rambled over the columns of the *Pioneer*, while Rosamond, having noticed that he was perturbed, avoided looking at him, and inwardly thanked heaven that she herself had not a moody disposition. Will Ladislaw was stretched on the rug contemplating the curtain-pole abstractedly, and humming very low the notes of 'When first I saw thy face'; while the house spaniel, also stretched out with small choice of room, looked from between his paws at the usurper of the rug with silent but strong objection.

Rosamond bringing Lydgate his cup of tea, he threw down the paper, and said to Will, who had started up and gone to the table: 'It's no use your puffing Brooke as a reforming landlord, Ladislaw: they only pick the more holes in his coat in the *Trumpet*.'

'No matter; those who read the *Pioneer* don't read the *Trumpet*,' said Will, swallowing his tea and walking about. 'Do you suppose the public reads with a view to its own conversion? We should have a witches' brewing with a vengeance then "Mingle, mingle, mingle, mingle. You that mingle may" – and nobody would know which side he was going to take.'

'Farebrother says, he doesn't believe Brooke would get elected if the opportunity came: the very men who profess to be for him would bring another member out of the bag at the right moment.'

'There's no harm in trying. It's good to have resident members.'

'Why?' said Lydgate, who was much given to use that inconvenient word in a curt tone.

'They represent the local stupidity better,' said Will, laughing, and shaking his curls; 'and they are kept on their best behaviour in the neighbourhood. Brooke is not a bad fellow, but he has done some good things on his estate that he never would have done but for this Parliamentary bite.'

'He's not fitted to be a public man,' said Lydgate, with contemptuous decision. 'He would disappoint everybody who counted on him: I can see that at the Hospital. Only, there Bulstrode holds the reins and drives him.'

'That depends on how you fix your standard of public men,' said Will. 'He's good enough for the occasion: when the people have made up their mind as they are making it up now, they don't want a man – they only want a vote.'

'That is the way with you political writers, Ladislaw – crying up a measure as if it were a universal cure, and crying up men who are a part of the very disease that wants curing.'

'Why not? Men may help to cure themselves off the face of the land without knowing it,' said Will, who could find reasons impromptu, when he had not thought of a question beforehand.

'That is no excuse for encouraging the superstitious exaggeration of hopes about this particular measure, helping the cry to swallow it whole and to send up voting popinjays who are good for nothing but to carry it. You go against rottenness, and there is nothing more thoroughly rotten than making people believe that society can be cured by a political hocus-pocus.'

'That's very fine, my dear fellow. But your cure must begin somewhere, and put it that a thousand things which debase a population can never be reformed without this particular reform to begin with. Look what Stanley said the other day – that the House had been tinkering long enough at small questions of bribery, enquiring whether this or that voter has had a guinea when everybody knows that the seats have been sold wholesale. Wait for wisdom and conscience in public agents – fiddlestick! The only conscience we can trust to is the massive sense of wrong in a class, and the best wisdom that will work is the wisdom of balancing claims. That's my text – which side is injured? I support the man who supports their claims; not the virtuous upholder of the wrong.'

'That general talk about a particular case is mere question-begging, Ladislaw. When I say, I go in for the dose that cures, it doesn't follow that I go in for opium in a given case of gout.'

'I am not begging the question we are upon – whether we are to try for nothing till we find immaculate men to work with. Should you go on that plan? If there were one man who would carry you a medical reform and another who would oppose it, should you enquire which had the better motives or even the better brains?'

'Oh, of course,' said Lydgate, seeing himself checkmated by a move which he had often used himself, 'if one did not work with such men as are at hand, things must come to a deadlock. Suppose the worst opinion in the town about Bulstrode were a true one, that would not make it less true that he has the sense and the resolution to do what I think ought to be done in the matters I know and care most about; but that is the only ground on which I go with him,' Lydgate added rather proudly, bearing in mind Mr Farebrother's remarks. 'He is nothing to me otherwise; I would not cry him up on any personal ground – I would keep clear of that.'

'Do you mean that I cry up Brooke on any personal ground?' said Will Ladislaw, nettled, and turning sharp round. For the first time he felt offended with Lydgate; not the less so, perhaps, because he would have declined any close enquiry into the growth of his relation to Mr Brooke.

'Not at all,' said Lydgate, 'I was simply explaining my own action. I meant that a man may work for a special end with others whose motives and general course are equivocal, if he is quite sure of his personal independence, and that he is not working for his private interest – either place or money.'

'Then, why don't you extend your liberality to others?' said Will, still nettled. 'My personal independence is as important to me as yours is to you. You have no more reason to imagine that I have personal expectations from Brooke, than I have to imagine that you have personal expectations from Bulstrode. Motives are points of honour, I suppose – nobody can prove them. But as to money and place in the world,' Will ended, tossing back his head, 'I think it is pretty clear that I am not determined by considerations of that sort.'

'You quite mistake me, Ladislaw,' said Lydgate, surpassed. He had been pre-occupied with his own vindication, and had been blind to what Ladislaw might infer on his own account. 'I beg your pardon for unintentionally annoying you. In fact, I should rather attribute to you a romantic disregard of your own worldly interests. On the political question, I referred simply to intellectual bias.'

'How very unpleasant you both are this evening! ' said Rosamond. 'I cannot conceive why money should have been referred to. Politics and medicine are sufficiently disagreeable to quarrel upon. You can both of you go on quarrelling with all the world and with each other on those two topics.'

Rosamond looked mildly neutral as she said this, rising to ring the bell, and then crossing to her work-table.

'Poor Rosy!' said Lydgate, putting out his hand to her as she was passing him. 'Disputation is not amusing to cherubs. Have some music. Ask Ladislaw to sing with you.'

When Will was gone Rosamond said to her husband, 'What put you out of temper this evening, Tertius?'

'Me? It was Ladislaw who was out of temper. He is like a bit of tinder.'

'But I mean, before that. Something had vexed you before you came in, you looked cross. And that made you begin to dispute with Mr Ladislaw. You hurt me very much when you look so, Tertius.'

'Do I? Then I am a brute,' said Lydgate, caressing her penitently.

'What vexed you?'

'Oh, outdoor things – business.'

It was really a letter insisting on the payment of a bill for furniture. But Rosamond was expecting to have a baby, and Lydgate wished to save her from any perturbation.

Chapter 47

> Was never true love loved in vain,
> For truest love is highest gain.
> No art can make it: it must spring
> Where elements are fostering.
> So in heaven's spot and hour
> Springs the little native flower,
> Downward root and upward eye,
> Shapen by the earth and sky.

It happened to be on a Saturday evening that Will Ladislaw had that little discussion with Lydgate. Its effect when he went to his own rooms was to make him sit up half the night, thinking over again, under a new irritation, all that he had before thought of his having settled in Middlemarch and harnessed himself with Mr Brooke. Hesitations before he had taken the step had since turned into susceptibility to every hint that he would have been wiser not to take it; and hence came his heat towards Lydgate – a heat which still kept him restless. Was he not making a fool of himself? – and at a time when he was more than ever conscious of being something better than a fool? And for what end?

Well, for no definite end. True, he had dreamy visions of possibilities: there is no human being who having both passions, and thoughts does not think in consequence of his passions does not find images rising in his mind which soothe the passion with hope or sting it with dread. But this, which happens to us all, happens to some with a wide difference; and Will was not one of those whose wit 'keeps the roadway': he had his bypaths where there were little joys of his own choosing, such as gentlemen cantering on the highroad might have thought rather idiotic. The way in which he made a sort of happiness for himself out of his feeling for Dorothea was an example of this. It may seem strange, but it is the fact, that the ordinary vulgar vision of which Mr Casaubon suspected him – namely, that Dorothea might become a widow, and that the interest he had established in her mind might turn into acceptance of him as a husband – had no tempting, arresting power over him: he did not live in the scenery of such an event, and follow it out, as we all do with that imagined 'otherwise' which is our practical heaven. It was not only that he was unwilling to entertain thoughts which could be accused of baseness, and was already uneasy in the sense that he had to justify himself from the charge of ingratitude – the latent consciousness of many other barriers between himself and Dorothea besides the existence of her husband, had helped to turn away his imagination from speculating on what might befall Mr Casaubon. And there were yet other reasons. Will, we know, could not bear the thought of any flaw appearing in his crystal: he was at once exasperated and delighted by the calm freedom with which Dorothea looked at him and spoke to him, and there was something so exquisite in thinking of her just as she was, that he could not long for a change which must somehow change her. Do we not shun the street version of a fine melody? – or shrink from the news that the rarity – some bit of chiselling or engraving perhaps – which we have dwelt on even with exultation in the trouble it has cost us to snatch glimpses of it, is really not an uncommon thing, and may be obtained as an everyday possession? Our good depends on the quality and breadth of our emotion; and to Will, a creature who cared little for what are called the solid things of life and greatly for its subtler influences, to have within him such a feeling as he had towards Dorothea, was like the inheritance of a fortune. What others might have called the futility of his passion, made an additional delight for his imagination: he was conscious of a generous movement, and of verifying in his own experience that higher love-poetry which had charmed his fancy. Dorothea, he said to himself, was for ever enthroned in his soul: no other woman could sit higher than her footstool; and if he could have written out in immortal syllables the effect she wrought within him, he might have boasted after the example of old Drayton, that –

> Queens hereafter might be glad to live
> Upon the alms of her superfluous praise.

But this result was questionable. And what else could he do for Dorothea? What was his devotion worth to her? It was impossible to tell. He would not go out of her reach. He saw no creature among her friends to whom he could believe that she spoke with the same simple confidence as to him. She had once said that she would like him to stay; and stay he would, whatever fire-breathing dragons might hiss around her.

This had always been the conclusion of Will's hesitations. But he was not without contradictoriness and rebellion even towards his own resolve. He had often got irritated, as he was on this particular night, by some outside demonstration that his public exertions with Mr Brooke as a chief could not seem as heroic as he would like them to be, and this was always associated with the other ground of irritation – that notwithstanding his sacrifice of dignity for Dorothea's sake, he could hardly ever see her. Whereupon, not being able to contradict these unpleasant facts, he contradicted his own strongest bias and said, 'I am a fool.'

Nevertheless, since the inward debate necessarily turned on Dorothea, he ended, as he had done before, only by getting a livelier sense of what her presence would be to him: and suddenly reflecting that the morrow would be Sunday, he determined to go to Lowick Church and see her. He slept upon that idea, but when he was dressing in the rational morning light, Objection said: 'That will be a virtual defiance of Mr Casaubon's prohibition to visit Lowick, and Dorothea will be displeased.'

'Nonsense!' argued Inclination, 'it would be too monstrous for him to hinder me from going out to a pretty country church on a spring morning. And Dorothea will be glad.'

'It will be clear to Mr Casaubon that you have come either to annoy him or to see Dorothea.'

'It is not true that I go to annoy him, and why should I not go to see Dorothea? Is he to have everything to himself and be always comfortable? Let him smart a little, as other people are obliged to do. I have always liked the quaintness of the church and congregation; besides, I know the Tuckers: I shall go into their pew.'

Having silenced Objection by force of unreason, Will walked to Lowick as if he had been on the way to Paradise, crossing Halsell Common and skirting the woods, where the sunlight fell broadly under the budding boughs, bringing out the beauties of moss and lichen, and fresh green growths piercing the brown. Everything seemed to know that it was Sunday, and to approve of his going to Lowick Church. Will easily felt happy when nothing crossed his humour, and by this time the thought of vexing Mr Casaubon had become rather amusing to him, making his face break into its merry smile, pleasant to see as the breaking of sunshine on the water – though the occasion was not exemplary. But most of us are apt to settle within ourselves that the man who blocks our way is odious, and not to mind causing him a little of the disgust which his personality excites in ourselves. Will went along with a small book under his arm and a hand in each side-pocket, never reading, but chanting a little, as he made scenes of what would happen in church and coming out. He was experimenting in tunes to suit some words of his own, sometimes trying a ready-made melody, sometimes improvising. The words were not exactly a hymn, but they certainly fitted his Sunday experience:

> O me, O me, what frugal cheer
>   My love doth feed upon!
> A touch, a ray, that is not here,
>   A shadow that is gone:

A dream of breath that might be near,
  An inly-echoed tone,
The thought that one may think me dear,
  The place where one was known,

The tremor of a banished fear,
  An ill that was not done –
O me, O me, what frugal cheer
  My love doth feed upon!

Sometimes, when he took off his hat, shaking his head backward, and showing his delicate throat as he sang, he looked like an incarnation of the spring whose spirit filled the air – a bright creature, abundant in uncertain promises.

The bells were still ringing when he got to Lowick, and he went into the curate's pew before anyone else arrived there. But he was still left alone in it when the congregation had assembled. The curate's pew was opposite the rector's at the entrance of the small chancel, and Will had time to fear that Dorothea might not come while he looked round at the group of rural faces which made the congregation from year to year within the whitewashed walls and dark old pews, hardly with more change than we see in the boughs of a tree which breaks here and there with age, but yet has young shoots. Mr Rigg's frog-face was something alien and unaccountable, but notwithstanding this shock to the order of things, there were still the Waules and the rural stock of the Powderells in their pews side by side; Brother Samuel's cheek had the same purple round as ever, and the three generations of decent cottagers came as of old with a sense of duty to their betters generally – the smaller children regarding Mr Casaubon, who wore the black gown and mounted to the highest box, as probably the chief of all betters, and the one most awful if offended. Even in 1831 Lowick was at peace, not more agitated by Reform than by the solemn tenor of the Sunday sermon. The congregation had been used to seeing Will at church in former days, and no one took much note of him except the quire, who expected him to make a figure in the singing.

Dorothea did at last appear in this quaint background, walking up the short aisle in her white beaver bonnet and grey cloak – the same she had worn in the Vatican. Her face being, from her entrance, towards the chancel, even her short-sighted eyes soon discerned Will, but there was no outward show of her feeling except a slight paleness and a grave bow as she passed him. To his own surprise Will felt suddenly uncomfortable, and dared not look at her after they had bowed to each other. Two minutes later, when Mr Casaubon came out of the vestry, and, entering the pew, seated himself in face of Dorothea, Will felt his paralysis more complete. He could look nowhere except at the quire in the little gallery over the vestry-door: Dorothea was perhaps pained, and he had made a wretched blunder. It was no longer amusing to vex Mr Casaubon, who had the advantage probably of watching him and seeing that he dared not turn his head. Why had he not imagined this beforehand? – but he could not expect that he should sit in that square pew alone, unrelieved by any Tuckers, who had apparently departed from Lowick altogether, for a new clergyman was in the desk. Still he called himself stupid now for not foreseeing that it would be

impossible for him to look towards Dorothea – nay, that she might feel
his coming an impertinence. There was no delivering himself from his cage,
however; and Will found his places and looked at his book as if he had been a
schoolmistress, feeling that the morning service had never been so immeasurably
long before, that he was utterly ridiculous, out of temper, and miserable. This
was what a man got by worshipping the sight of a woman! The clerk observed
with surprise that Mr Ladislaw did not join in the tune of Hanover, and reflected
that he might have a cold.

Mr Casaubon did not preach that morning, and there was no change in Will's
situation until the blessing had been pronounced and everyone rose. It was the
fashion at Lowick for 'the betters' to go out first. With a sudden determination
to break the spell that was upon him, Will looked straight at Mr Casaubon. But
that gentleman's eyes were on the button of the pew-door, which he opened,
allowing Dorothea to pass, and following her immediately without raising his
eyelids. Will's glance had caught Dorothea's as she turned out of the pew, and
again she bowed, but this time with a look of agitation, as if she were repressing
tears. Will walked out after them, but they went on towards the little gate
leading out of the churchyard into the shrubbery, never looking round.

It was impossible for him to follow them, and he could only walk back sadly at
midday along the same road which he had trodden hopefully in the morning.
The lights were all changed for him both without and within.

Chapter 48

> Surely the golden hours are turning grey
> And dance no more, and vainly strive to run:
> I see their white locks streaming in the wind –
> Each face is haggard as it looks at me,
> Slow turning in the constant clasping round
> Storm-driven.

Dorothea's distress when she was leaving the church came chiefly from the
perception that Mr Casaubon was determined not to speak to his cousin, and
that Will's presence at church had served to mark more strongly the alienation
between them. Will's coming seemed to her quite excusable, nay, she thought
it an amiable movement in him towards a reconciliation which she herself had
been constantly wishing for. He had probably imagined, as she had, that if
Mr Casaubon and he could meet easily, they would shake hands and friendly
intercourse might return. But now Dorothea felt quite robbed of that hope.
Will was banished further than ever, for Mr Casaubon must have been newly
embittered by this thrusting upon him of a presence which he refused to
recognise.

He had not been very well that morning, suffering from some difficulty in
breathing, and had not preached in consequence; she was not surprised, therefore, that he was nearly silent at luncheon, still less that he made no allusion to

Will Ladislaw. For her own part she felt that she could never again introduce that subject. They usually spent apart the hours between luncheon and dinner on a Sunday; Mr Casaubon in the library dozing chiefly, and Dorothea in her boudoir, where she was wont to occupy herself with some of her favourite books. There was a little heap of them on the table in the bow-window of various sorts, from Herodotus, which she was learning to read with Mr Casaubon, to her old companion Pascal, and Keble's Christian Year. But today she opened one after another, and could read none of them. Everything seemed dreary: the portents before the birth of Cyrus – Jewish antiquities – oh dear! – devout epigrams – the sacred chime of favourite hymns – all alike were as flat as tunes beaten on wood: even the spring flowers and the grass had a dull shiver in them under the afternoon clouds that hid the sun fitfully: even the sustaining thoughts which had become habits seemed to have in them the weariness of long future days in which she would still live with them for her sole companions. It was another or rather a fuller sort of companionship that poor Dorothea was hungering for, and the hunger had grown from the perpetual effort demanded by her married life. She was always trying to be what her husband wished, and never able to repose on his delight in what she was. The thing that she liked, that she spontaneously cared to have, seemed to be always excluded from her life; for if it was only granted and not shared by her husband it might as well have been denied. About Will Ladislaw there had been a difference between them from the first, and it had ended, since Mr Casaubon had so severely repulsed Dorothea's strong feeling about his claims on the family property, by her being convinced that she was in the right and her husband in the wrong, but that she was helpless. This afternoon the helplessness was more wretchedly benumbing than ever: she longed for objects who could be dear to her, and to whom she could be dear. She longed for work which would be directly beneficent like the sunshine and the rain, and now it appeared that she was to live more and more in a virtual tomb, where there was the apparatus of a ghastly labour producing what would never see the light. Today she had stood at the door of the tomb and seen Will Ladislaw receding into the distant world of warm activity and fellowship – turning his face towards her as he went.

Books were of no use. Thinking was of no use. It was Sunday, and she could not have the carriage to go to Celia, who had lately had a baby. There was no refuge now from spiritual emptiness and discontent, and Dorothea had to bear her bad mood, as she would have borne a headache.

After dinner, at the hour when she usually began to read aloud, Mr Casaubon proposed that they should go into the library, where, he said, he had ordered a fire and lights. He seemed to have revived and to be thinking intently.

In the library Dorothea observed that he had newly arranged a row of his notebooks on a table, and now he took up and put into her hand a well-known volume, which was a table of contents to all the others.

'You will oblige me, my dear,' he said, seating himself, 'if instead of other reading this evening, you will go through this aloud, pencil in hand, and at each point where I say 'mark', will make a cross with your pencil. This is the first step in a sifting process which I have long had in view, and as we go on I shall be able to indicate to you certain principles of selection whereby you will, I trust, have an intelligent participation in my purpose.'

This proposal was only one more sign added to many since his memorable interview with Lydgate, that Mr Casaubon's original reluctance to let Dorothea work with him had given place to the contrary disposition, namely, to demand much interest and labour from her.

After she had read and marked for two hours, he said, 'We will take the volume upstairs – and the pencil, if you please and in case of reading in the night, we can pursue this task. It is not wearisome to you, I trust, Dorothea?'

'I prefer always reading what you like best to hear,' said Dorothea, who told the simple truth; for what she dreaded was to exert herself in reading or anything else which left him as joyless as ever.

It was a proof of the force with which certain characteristics in Dorothea impressed those around her, that her husband, with all his jealousy and suspicion, had gathered implicit trust in the integrity of her promises, and her power of devoting herself to her idea of the right and best. Of late he had begun to feel that these qualities were a peculiar possession for himself, and he wanted to engross them.

The reading in the night did come. Dorothea in her young weariness had slept soon and fast: she was awakened by a sense of light, which seemed to her at first like a sudden vision of sunset after she had climbed a steep hill: she opened her eyes and saw her husband wrapped in his warm gown seating himself in the armchair near the fireplace where the embers were still glowing. He had lit two candles, expecting that Dorothea would awake, but not liking to rouse her by more direct means.

'Are you ill, Edward?' she said, rising immediately.

'I felt some uneasiness in a reclining posture. I will sit here for a time.' She threw wood on the fire, wrapped herself up, and said, 'You would like me to read to you?'

'You would oblige me greatly by doing so, Dorothea,' said Mr Casaubon, with a shade more meekness than usual in his polite manner. 'I am wakeful: my mind is remarkably lucid.'

'I fear that the excitement may be too great for you,' said Dorothea, remembering Lydgate's cautions.

'No, I am not conscious of undue excitement. Thought is easy.' Dorothea dared not insist, and she read for an hour or more on the same plan as she had done in the evening, but getting over the pages with more quickness. Mr Casaubon's mind was more alert, and he seemed to anticipate what was coming after a very slight verbal indication, saying, 'That will do – mark that' or 'Pass on to the next head – I omit the second excursus on Crete.' Dorothea was amazed to think of the birdlike speed with which his mind was surveying the ground where it had been creeping for years. At last he said: 'Close the book now, my dear. We will resume our work tomorrow. I have deferred it too long, and would gladly see it completed. But you observe that the principle on which my selection is made, is to give adequate, and not disproportionate illustration to each of the theses enumerated in my introduction, as at present sketched.

You have perceived that distinctly, Dorothea?'

'Yes,' said Dorothea, rather tremulously. She felt sick at heart.

'And now I think that I can take some repose,' said Mr Casaubon. He lay down again and begged her to put out the lights. When she had lain down too, and there was a darkness only broken by a dull glow on the hearth, he said; 'Before I sleep, I have a request to make, Dorothea.'

'What is it?' said Dorothea, with a dread in her mind.

'It is that you will let me know, deliberately, whether, in case of my death, you will carry out my wishes: whether you will avoid doing what I should deprecate, and apply yourself to do what I should desire.'

Dorothea was not taken by surprise: many incidents had been leading her to the conjecture of some intention on her husband's part which might make a new yoke for her. She did not answer immediately.

'You refuse?' said Mr Casaubon, with more edge in his tone.

'No, I do not yet refuse,' said Dorothea, in a clear voice, the need of freedom asserting itself within her; 'but it is too solemn – I think it is not right – to make a promise when I am ignorant what it will bind me to. Whatever affection prompted I would do without promising.'

'But you would use your own judgement: I ask you to obey mine; you refuse.'

'No, dear, no!' said Dorothea, beseechingly, crushed by opposing fears. 'But may I wait and reflect a little while? I desire with my whole soul to do what will comfort you; but I cannot give any pledge suddenly – still less a pledge to do I know not what.'

'You cannot then confide in the nature of my wishes?'

'Grant me till tomorrow,' said Dorothea beseechingly.

'Till tomorrow then,' said Mr Casaubon.

Soon she could hear that he was sleeping, but there was no more sleep for her. While she constrained herself to lie still lest she should disturb him, her mind was carrying on a conflict in which imagination ranged its forces first on one side and then on the other. She had no presentiment that the power which her husband wished to establish over her future action had relation to anything else than his work. But it was clear enough to her that he would expect her to devote herself to sifting those mixed heaps of material, which were to be the doubtful illustration of principles still more doubtful. The poor child had become altogether unbelieving as to the trustworthiness of that Key which had made the ambition and the labour of her husband's life. It was not wonderful that, in spite of her small instruction, her judgement in this matter was truer than his: for she looked with unbiassed comparison and healthy sense at probabilities on which he had risked all his egoism. And now she pictured to herself the days, and months, and years which she must spend in sorting what might be called shattered mummies, and fragments of a tradition which was itself a mosaic wrought from crushed ruins – sorting them as food for a theory which was already withered in the birth like an elfin child. Doubtless a vigorous error vigorously pursued has kept the embryos of truth a-breathing: the quest of gold being at the same time a questioning of substances, the body of chemistry is prepared for its soul, and Lavoisier is born. But Mr Casaubon's theory of the elements which made the seed of all tradition was not likely to bruise itself unawares against discoveries: it floated among flexible conjectures no more solid than those etymologies which seemed strong because of likeness in sound, until it was shown that likeness in sound made them impossible: it was a method of interpretation which was not tested by the necessity of forming anything which had sharper collisions than an elaborate notion of Gog and Magog: it was as free from interruption as a plan for threading the stars together. And Dorothea had so often had to check her weariness and impatience over this questionable riddle-guessing, as it revealed itself to her instead of the fellowship in high knowledge which was to make life worthier. She could understand well enough now why her husband had come to cling to her, as possibly the only hope left that his labours would ever take a shape in which they could be given to the world. At first it had seemed that he wished to keep even her aloof from any close knowledge of what he was doing; but gradually the terrible stringency of human need – the prospect of a too speedy death; And here Dorothea's pity turned from her own future to her husband's past – nay, to his present hard struggle with a lot which had grown out of that past: the lonely labour, the ambition breathing hardly under the pressure of self-distrust; the goal receding, and the heavier limbs; and now at last the sword visibly trembling above him! And had she not wished to marry him that she might help him in his life's labour? – But she had thought the work was to be something greater, which she could serve in devoutly for its own sake. Was it right, even to soothe his grief – would it be possible, even if she promised to work as in a treadmill fruitlessly?

And yet, could she deny him? Could she say, 'I refuse to content this pining hunger?' It would be refusing to do for him dead, what she was almost sure to do for him living. If he lived, as Lydgate had said he might, for fifteen years or more, her life would certainly be spent in helping him and obeying him.

Still, there was a deep difference between that devotion to the living, and that indefinite promise of devotion to the dead. While he lived, he could claim nothing that she would not still be free to remonstrate against, and even to refuse. But – the thought passed through her mind more than once, though she could not believe in it – might he not mean to demand something more from her than she had been able to imagine, since he wanted her pledge to carry out his wishes without telling her exactly what they were? No; his heart was bound up in his work only: that was the end for which his failing life was to be eked out by hers.

And now, if she were to say, 'No! if you die, I will put no finger to your work' – it seemed as if she would be crushing that bruised heart.

For four hours Dorothea lay in this conflict, till she felt ill and bewildered, unable to resolve, praying mutely. Helpless as a child which has sobbed and sought too long, she fell into a late morning sleep, and when she waked Mr Casaubon was already up. Tantripp told her that he had read prayers, breakfasted, and was in the library.

'I never saw you look so pale, madam,' said Tantripp, a solid-figured woman who had been with the sisters at Lausanne.

'Was I ever high-coloured, Tantripp?' said Dorothea, smiling faintly.

'Well, not to say high-coloured, but with a bloom like a Chiny rose. But always smelling those leather books, what can be expected? Do rest a little this morning, madam. Let me say you are ill and not able to go into that close library.'

'Oh no, no! let me make haste,' said Dorothea. 'Mr Casaubon wants me particularly.'

When she went down she felt sure that she should promise to fulfil his wishes; but that would be later in the day – not yet.

As Dorothea entered the library, Mr Casaubon turned round from the table where he had been placing some books, and said: 'I was waiting for your appearance, my dear. I had hoped to set to work at once this morning, but I find myself under some indisposition, probably from too much excitement yesterday. I am going now to take a turn in the shrubbery, since the air is milder.'

'I am glad to hear that,' said Dorothea. 'Your mind, I feared, was too active last night.'

'I would fain have it set at rest on the point I last spoke of, Dorothea. You can now, I hope, give me an answer.'

'May I come out to you in the garden presently?' said Dorothea, winning a little breathing space in that way.

'I shall be in the yew-tree walk for the next half-hour,' said Mr Casaubon, and then he left her.

Dorothea, feeling very weary, rang and asked Tantripp to bring her some wraps. She had been sitting still for a few minutes, but not in any renewal of the former conflict: she simply felt that she was going to say 'Yes' to her own doom: she was too weak, too full of dread at the thought of inflicting a keen-edged blow on her husband, to do anything but submit completely. She sat still and let Tantripp put on her bonnet and shawl, a passivity which was unusual with her, for she liked to wait on herself.

'God bless you, madam!' said Tantripp, with an irrepressible movement of love towards the beautiful, gentle creature for whom she felt unable to do anything more, now that she had finished tying the bonnet.

This was too much for Dorothea's highly-strung feeling, and she burst into tears, sobbing against Tantripp's arm. But soon she checked herself, dried her eyes, and went out at the glass door into the shrubbery.

'I wish every book in that library was built into a caticom for your master,' said Tantripp to Pratt, the butler, finding him in the breakfast-room. She had been at Rome, and visited the antiquities, as we know; and she always declined to call Mr Casaubon anything but 'your master', when speaking to the other servants.

Pratt laughed. He liked his master very well, but he liked Tantripp better.

When Dorothea was out on the gravel walks, she lingered among the nearer clumps of trees, hesitating, as she had done once before, though from a different cause. Then she had feared lest her effort at fellowship should be unwelcome; now she dreaded going to the spot where she foresaw that she must bind herself to a fellowship from which she shrank. Neither law nor the world's opinion compelled her to this – only her husband's nature and her own compassion, only the ideal and not the real yoke of marriage. She saw clearly enough the whole situation, yet she was fettered: she could not smite the stricken soul that entreated hers. If that were weakness, Dorothea was weak. But the half-hour was passing, and she must not delay longer. When she entered the yew-tree walk she could not see her husband; but the walk had bends, and she went, expecting to catch sight of his figure wrapped in a blue cloak, which, with a warm velvet cap, was his outer garment on chill days for the garden. It occurred to her that he might be resting in the summerhouse, towards which the path diverged a little. Turning the angle, she could see him seated on the bench, close to a stone table. His arms were resting on the table, and his brow was bowed down on them, the blue cloak being dragged forward and screening his face on each side.

'He exhausted himself last night,' Dorothea said to herself, thinking at first that he was asleep, and that the summerhouse was too damp a place to rest in. But then she remembered that of late she had seen him take that attitude when she was reading to him, as if he found it easier than any other; and that he would sometimes speak, as well as listen, with his face down in that way. She went into the summerhouse and said, 'I am come, Edward; I am ready.'

He took no notice, and she thought that he must be fast asleep. She laid her hand on his shoulder, and repeated, 'I am ready!' Still he was motionless; and with a sudden confused fear, she leaned down to him, took off his velvet cap, and leaned her cheek close to his head, crying in a distressed tone, 'Wake, dear, wake! Listen to me. I am come to answer.'

But Dorothea never gave her answer.

Later in the day, Lydgate was seated by her bedside, and she was talking deliriously, thinking aloud, and recalling what had gone through her mind the night before. She knew him, and called him by his name, but appeared to think it right that she should explain everything to him; and again, and again, begged him to explain everything to her husband.

'Tell him I shall go to him soon: I am ready to promise. Only, thinking about it was so dreadful – it has made me ill. Not very ill. I shall soon be better. Go and tell him.'

But the silence in her husband's ear was never more to be broken.

Chapter 49

> A task too strong for wizard spells
> This squire had brought about;
> 'Tis easy dropping stones in wells,
> But who shall get them out?

'I wish to God we could hinder Dorothea from knowing this,' said Sir James Chettam, with the little frown on his brow, and an expression of intense disgust about his mouth.

He was standing on the hearthrug in the library at Lowick Grange, and speaking to Mr Brooke. It was the day after Mr Casaubon had been buried, and Dorothea was not yet able to leave her room.

'That would be difficult, you know, Chettam, as she is an executrix, and she likes to go into these things – property, land, that kind of thing. She has her notions, you know,' said Mr Brooke, sticking his eye-glasses on nervously, and exploring the edges of a folded paper which he held in his hand; 'and she would like to act – depend upon it, as an executrix Dorothea would want to act. And she was twenty-one last December, you know. I can hinder nothing.'

Sir James looked at the carpet for a minute in silence, and then lifting his eyes suddenly fixed them on Mr Brooke, saying, 'I will tell you what we can do. Until Dorothea is well, all business must be kept from her, and as soon as she is able to be moved she must come to us. Being with Celia and the baby will be the best thing in the world for her, and will pass away the time. And meanwhile you must get rid of Ladislaw: you must send him out of the country.' Here Sir James's look of disgust returned in all its intensity.

Mr Brooke put his hands behind him, walked to the window and straightened his back with a little shake before he replied: 'That is easily said, Chettam, easily said, you know.'

'My dear sir,' persisted Sir James, restraining his indignation within respectful forms, 'it was you who brought him here, and you who keep him here – I mean by the occupation you give him.'

'Yes, but I can't dismiss him in an instant without assigning reasons, my dear Chettam. Ladislaw has been invaluable, most satisfactory. I consider that I have done this part of the country a service by bringing him – by bringing him, you know.' Mr Brooke ended with a nod, turning round to give it.

'It's a pity this part of the country didn't do without him, that's all I have to say about it. At any rate, as Dorothea's brother-in-law, I feel warranted in objecting strongly to his being kept here by any action on the part of her friends. You admit, I hope, that I have a right to speak about what concerns the dignity of my wife's sister?'

Sir James was getting warm.

'Of course, my dear Chettam, of course. But you and I have different ideas – different – '

'Not about this action of Casaubon's, I should hope,' interrupted Sir James. 'I say that he has most unfairly compromised Dorothea. I say that there never was a meaner, more ungentlemanly action than this – a codicil of this sort to a will which he made at the time of his marriage with the knowledge and reliance of her family – a positive insult to Dorothea!'

'Well, you know, Casaubon was a little twisted about Ladislaw. Ladislaw has told me the reason – dislike of the bent he took, you know – Ladislaw didn't think much of Casaubon's notions, Thoth and Dagon – that sort of thing: and I fancy that Casaubon didn't like the independent position Ladislaw had taken up. I saw the letters between them, you know. Poor Casaubon was a little buried in books – he didn't know the world.'

'It's all very well for Ladislaw to put that colour on it,' said Sir James. 'But I believe Casaubon was only jealous of him on Dorothea's account, and the world will suppose that she gave him some reason; and that is what makes it so abominable coupling her name with this young fellow's.'

'My dear Chettam, it won't lead to anything, you know,' said Mr Brooke, seating himself and sticking on his eye-glass again. 'It's all of a piece with Casaubon's oddity. This paper, now, "Synoptical Tabulation" and so on, "for the use of Mrs Casaubon", it was locked up in the desk with the will. I suppose he meant Dorothea to publish his researches, eh? and she'll do it, you know; she has gone into his studies uncommonly.'

'My dear sir,' said Sir James, impatiently, 'that is neither here nor there. The question is, whether you don't see with me the propriety of sending young Ladislaw away?'

'Well, no, not the urgency of the thing. By and by, perhaps, it may come round. As to gossip, you know, sending him away won't hinder gossip. People say what they like to say, not what they have chapter and verse for,' said Mr Brooke, becoming acute about the truths that lay on the side of his own wishes. 'I might get rid of Ladislaw up to a certain point – take away the *Pioneer* from him, and that sort of thing; but I couldn't send him out of the country if he didn't choose to go – didn't choose, you know.'

Mr Brooke, persisting as quietly as if he were only discussing the nature of last year's weather, and nodding at the end with his usual amenity, was an exasperating form of obstinacy.

'Good God!' said Sir James, with as much passion as he ever showed, 'let us get him a post; let us spend money on him. If he could go in the suite of some Colonial Governor! Grampus might take him – and I could write to Fulke about it.'

'But Ladislaw won't be shipped off like a head of cattle, my dear fellow; Ladislaw has his ideas. It's my opinion that if he were to part from me tomorrow, you'd only hear the more of him in the country. With his talent for speaking and drawing up documents, there are few men who could come up to him as an agitator – an agitator, you know.'

'Agitator!' said Sir James, with bitter emphasis, feeling that the syllables of this word properly repeated were a sufficient exposure of its hatefulness.

'But be reasonable, Chettam. Dorothea, now. As you say, she had better go to Celia as soon as possible. She can stay under your roof, and in the meantime things may come round quietly. Don't let us be firing off our guns in a hurry, you know. Standish will keep our counsel, and the news will be old before it's known. Twenty things may happen to carry off Ladislaw – without my doing anything, you know.'

'Then I am to conclude that you decline to do anything?'

'Decline, Chettam? – no – I don't say decline. But I really don't see what I could do. Ladislaw is a gentleman.'

'I am glad to hear it!' said Sir James, his irritation making him forget himself a little. 'I am sure Casaubon was not.'

'Well, it would have been worse if he had made the codicil to hinder her from marrying again at all, you know.'

'I don't know that,' said Sir James. 'It would have been less indelicate.'

'One of poor Casaubon's freaks! That attack upset his brain a little. It all goes for nothing. She doesn't want to marry Ladislaw.'

'But this codicil is framed so as to make everybody believe that she did. I don't believe anything of the sort about Dorothea,' said Sir James – then frowningly, 'but I suspect Ladislaw. I tell you frankly, I suspect Ladislaw.'

'I couldn't take any immediate action on that ground, Chettam. In fact, if it were possible to pack him off – send him to Norfolk Island – that sort of thing – it would look all the worse for Dorothea to those who knew about it. It would seem as if we distrusted her – distrusted her, you know.'

That Mr Brooke had hit on an undeniable argument, did not tend to soothe Sir James. He put out his hand to reach his hat, implying that he did not mean to contend further, and said, still with some heat: 'Well, I can only say that I think Dorothea was sacrificed once, because her friends were too careless. I shall do what I can, as her brother, to protect her now.'

'You can't do better than get her to Freshitt as soon as possible, Chettam. I approve that plan altogether,' said Mr Brooke, well pleased that he had won the argument. It would have been highly inconvenient to him to part with Ladislaw at that time, when a dissolution might happen any day, and electors were to be convinced of the course by which the interests of the country would be best served. Mr Brooke sincerely believed that this end could be secured by his own return to Parliament: he offered the forces of his mind honestly to the nation.

Chapter 50

'This Loller here wol prechen us somewhat.'
'Nay by my father's soule! that schal he nat,'
Sayde the Schipman, 'here schal he not preche,
He schal no gospel glosen here ne teche.
We leven all in the gret God,' quod he.
He wolden sowen some diffcultee.

CHAUCER, Canterbury Tales

Dorothea had been safe at Freshitt Hall nearly a week before she had asked any dangerous questions. Every morning now she sat with Celia in the prettiest of upstairs sitting-rooms, opening into a small conservatory – Celia all in white and lavender like a bunch of mixed violets, watching the remarkable acts of the baby, which were so dubious to her inexperienced mind that all conversation was interrupted by appeals for their interpretation made to the oracular nurse. Dorothea sat by in her widow's dress, with an expression which rather provoked Celia, as being much too sad; for not only was baby quite well, but really when a husband had been so dull and troublesome while he lived, and besides that had – well, well! Sir James, of course, had told Celia everything, with a strong representation how important it was that Dorothea should not know it sooner than was inevitable.

But Mr Brooke had been right in predicting that Dorothea would not long remain passive where action had been assigned to her; she knew the purport of her husband's will made at the time of their marriage, and her mind, as soon as she was clearly conscious of her position, was silently occupied with what she ought to do as the owner of Lowick Manor with the patronage of the living attached to it.

One morning when her uncle paid his usual visit, though with an unusual alacrity in his manner which he accounted for by saying that it was now pretty certain Parliament would be dissolved forthwith, Dorothea said: 'Uncle, it is right now that I should consider who is to have the living at Lowick. After Mr Tucker had been provided for, I never heard my husband say that he had any clergyman in his mind as a successor to himself. I think I ought to have the keys now and go to Lowick to examine all my husband's papers. There may be something that would throw light on his wishes.'

'No hurry, my dear,' said Mr Brooke, quietly. 'By and by, you know, you can go, if you like. But I cast my eyes over things in the desks and drawers – there was nothing – nothing but deep subjects, you know – besides the will. Everything can be done by and by. As to the living, I have had an application for interest already – I should say rather good. Mr Tyke has been strongly recommended to me – I had something to do with getting him an appointment before. An apostolic man, I believe – the sort of thing that would suit you, my dear.'

'I should like to have fuller knowledge about him, uncle, and judge for myself, if Mr Casaubon has not left any expression of his wishes. He has perhaps made some addition to his will, there may be some instructions for me,' said Dorothea, who had all the while had this conjecture in her mind with relation to her husband's work.

'Nothing about the rectory, my dear – nothing,' said Mr Brooke, rising to go away, and putting out his hand to his nieces: 'nor about his researches, you know. Nothing in the will.'

Dorothea's lip quivered.

'Come, you must not think of these things yet, my dear. By and by, you know.'

'I am quite well now, uncle: I wish to exert myself.'

'Well, well, we shall see. But I must run away now – I have no end of work now – it's a crisis – a political crisis, you know. And here is Celia and her little man – you are an aunt, you know, now, and I am a sort of grandfather,' said Mr Brooke, with placid hurry, anxious to get away and tell Chettam that it would not be his (Mr Brooke's) fault if Dorothea insisted on looking into everything.

Dorothea sank back in her chair when her uncle had left the room, and cast her eyes down meditatively on her crossed hands.

'Look, Dodo! look at him! Did you ever see anything like that?' said Celia in her comfortable staccato.

'What, Kitty?' said Dorothea, lifting her eyes rather absently. 'What? why, his upper lip; see how he is drawing it down, as if he meant to make a face. Isn't it wonderful! He may have his little thoughts. I wish nurse were here. Do look at him.'

A large tear, which had been for some time gathering, rolled down Dorothea's cheek as she looked up and tried to smile.

'Don't be sad, Dodo; kiss baby. What are you brooding over so? I am sure you did everything, and a great deal too much. You should be happy now.'

'I wonder if Sir James would drive me to Lowick. I want to look over every-thing – to see if there were any words written for me.'

'You are not to go till Mr Lydgate says you may go. And he has not said so yet (here you are, nurse; take baby and walk up and down the gallery). Besides, you have got a wrong notion in your head as usual, Dodo – I can see that: it vexes me.'

'Where am I wrong, Kitty?' said Dorothea, quite meekly. She was almost ready now to think Celia wiser than herself, and was really wondering with some fear what her wrong notion was. Celia felt her advantage, and was determined to use it. None of them knew Dodo as well as she did, or knew how to manage her. Since Celia's baby was born, she had had a new sense of her mental solidity and calm wisdom. It seemed clear that where there was a baby, things were right enough, and that error, in general, was a mere lack of that central poising force.

'I can see what you are thinking of as well as can be, Dodo,' said Celia. 'You are wanting to find out if there is anything uncomfortable for you to do now, only because Mr Casaubon wished it. As if you had not been uncomfortable enough before. And he doesn't deserve it, and you will find that out. He has behaved very badly. James is as angry with him as can be. And I had better tell you, to prepare you.'

'Celia,' said Dorothea, entreatingly, 'you distress me. Tell me at once what you mean.' It glanced through her mind that Mr Casaubon had left the property away from her – which would not be so very distressing.

'Why, he has made a codicil to his will, to say the property was all to go away from you if you married – I mean – '

'That is of no consequence,' said Dorothea, breaking in impetuously.

'But if you married Mr Ladislaw, not anybody else,' Celia went on with persevering quietude. 'Of course that is of no consequence in one way – you never *would* marry Mr Ladislaw; but that only makes it worse of Mr Casaubon.'

The blood rushed to Dorothea's face and neck painfully. But Celia was administering what she thought a sobering dose of fact. It was taking up notions that had done Dodo's health so much harm. So she went on in her neutral tone, as if she had been remarking on baby's robes.

'James says so. He says it is abominable, and not like a gentleman. And there never was a better judge than James. It is as if Mr Casaubon wanted to make people believe that you would wish to marry Mr Ladislaw – which is ridiculous. Only James says it was to hinder Mr Ladislaw from wanting to marry you for your money – just as if he ever would think of making you an offer. Mrs Cadwallader said you might as well marry an Italian with white mice! But I must just go and look at baby,' Celia added, without the least change of tone, throwing a light shawl over her, and tripping away.

Dorothea by this time had turned cold again, and now threw herself back helplessly in her chair. She might have compared her experience at that moment to the vague, alarmed consciousness that her life was taking on a new form, that she was undergoing a metamorphosis in which memory would not adjust itself to the stirring of new organs. Everything was changing its aspect: her husband's conduct, her own duteous feeling towards him, every struggle between them – and yet more, her whole relation to Will Ladislaw. Her world was in a state of convulsive change; the only thing she could say distinctly to herself was, that she must wait and think anew. One change terrified her as if it had been a sin; it was a violent shock of repulsion from her departed husband, who had had hidden thoughts, perhaps perverting everything she said and did. Then again she was conscious of another change which also made her tremulous; it was a sudden strange yearning of heart towards Will Ladislaw. It had never before entered her mind that he could, under any circumstances, be her lover: conceive the effect of the sudden revelation that another had thought of him in that light – that perhaps he himself had been conscious of such a possibility, – and this with the hurrying, crowding vision of unfitting conditions, and questions not soon to be solved.

It seemed a long while – she did not know how long – before she heard Celia saying, 'That will do, nurse; he will be quiet on my lap now. You can go to lunch, and let Garratt stay in the next room.' 'What I think, Dodo,' Celia went on, observing nothing more than that Dorothea was leaning back in her chair, and likely to be passive, 'is that Mr Casaubon was spiteful. I never did like him, and James never did. I think the corners of his mouth were dreadfully spiteful. And now he has behaved in this way, I am sure religion does not require you to make yourself uncomfortable about him. If he has been taken away, that is a mercy, and you ought to be grateful. We should not grieve, should we, baby?' said Celia confidentially to that unconscious centre and poise of the world, who had the most remarkable fists all complete even to the nails, and hair enough, really, when you took his cap off, to make – you didn't know what: – in short, he was Buddha in a Western form.

At this crisis Lydgate was announced, and one of the first things he said was, 'I fear you are not so well as you were, Mrs Casaubon; have you been agitated? allow me to feel your pulse.' Dorothea's hand was of a marble coldness.

'She wants to go to Lowick, to look over papers,' said Celia. 'She ought not, ought she?'

Lydgate did not speak for a few moments. Then he said, looking at Dorothea, 'I hardly know. In my opinion Mrs Casaubon should do what would give her the most repose of mind. That repose will not always come from being forbidden to act.'

'Thank you,' said Dorothea, exerting herself, 'I am sure that is wise. There are so many things which I ought to attend to. Why should I sit here idle?' Then, with an effort to recall subjects not connected with her agitation, she added, abruptly, 'You know everyone in Middlemarch, I think, Mr Lydgate. I shall ask you to tell me a great deal. I have serious things to do now. I have a living to give away. You know Mr Tyke and all the – ' But Dorothea's effort was too much for her; she broke off and burst into sobs.

Lydgate made her drink a dose of sal-volatile.

'Let Mrs Casaubon do as she likes,' he said to Sir James, whom he asked to see before quitting the house. 'She wants perfect freedom, I think, more than any other prescription.'

His attendance on Dorothea while her brain was excited, had enabled him to form some true conclusions concerning the trials of her life. He felt sure that she had been suffering from the strain and conflict of self-repression; and that she was likely now to feel herself only in another sort of pinfold than that from which she had been released.

Lydgate's advice was all the easier for Sir James to follow when he found that Celia had already told Dorothea the unpleasant fact about the will. There was no help for it now – no reason for any further delay in the execution of necessary business. And the next day Sir James complied at once with her request that he would drive her to Lowick.

'I have no wish to stay there at present,' said Dorothea; 'I could hardly bear it. I am much happier at Freshitt with Celia. I shall be able to think better about what should be done at Lowick by looking at it from a distance. And I should like to be at the Grange a little while with my uncle, and go about in all the old walks and among the people in the village.'

'Not yet, I think. Your uncle is having political company, and you are better out of the way of such doings,' said Sir James, who at that moment thought of the Grange chiefly as a haunt of young Ladislaw's. But no word passed between him and Dorothea about the objectionable part of the will; indeed, both of them felt that the mention of it between them would be impossible. Sir James was shy, even with men, about disagreeable subjects; and the one thing that Dorothea would have chosen to say, if she had spoken on the matter at all, was forbidden to her at present because it seemed to be a further exposure of her husband's injustice. Yet she did wish that Sir James could know what had passed between her and her husband about Will Ladislaw's moral claim on the property: it would then, she thought, be apparent to him as it was to her, that her husband's strange indelicate proviso had been chiefly urged by his bitter resistance to that idea of claim, and not merely by personal feelings more difficult to talk about. Also, it must be admitted, Dorothea wished that this could be known for Will's sake, since her friends seemed to think of him as simply an object of Mr Casaubon's charity. Why should he be compared with an Italian carrying white mice? That word quoted from Mrs Cadwallader seemed like a mocking travesty wrought in the dark by an impish finger.

At Lowick Dorothea searched desk and drawer – searched all her husband's places of deposit for private writing, but found no paper addressed especially to her, except that 'Synoptical Tabulation' which was probably only the beginning of many intended directions for her guidance. In carrying out this bequest of labour to Dorothea, as in all else, Mr Casaubon had been slow and hesitating, oppressed in the plan of transmitting his work, as he had been in executing it, by the sense of moving heavily in a dim and clogging medium: distrust of Dorothea's competence to arrange what he had prepared was subdued only by distrust of any other redactor. But he had come at last to create a trust for himself out of Dorothea's nature: she could do what she resolved to do: and he willingly imagined her toiling under the fetters of a promise to erect a tomb with his name upon it. (Not that Mr Casaubon called the future volumes a tomb: he called them the *Key to all Mythologies*.) But the months gained on him and left his plans belated: he had only had time to ask for that promise by which he sought to keep his cold grasp on Dorothea's life.

The grasp had slipped away. Bound by a pledge given from the depths of her pity, she would have been capable of undertaking a toil which her judgement whispered was vain for all uses except that consecration of faithfulness which is a supreme use. But now her judgement, instead of being controlled by duteous devotion, was made active by the embittering discovery that in her past union there had lurked the hidden alienation of secrecy and suspicion. The living, suffering man was no longer before her to awaken her pity: there remained only the retrospect of painful subjection to a husband whose thoughts had been lower than she had believed, whose exorbitant claims for himself had even blinded his scrupulous care for his own character, and made him defeat his own pride by shocking men of ordinary honour. As for the property which was the sign of that broken tie, she would have been glad to be free from it and have nothing more than her original fortune which had been settled on her, if there had not been duties attached to ownership, which she ought not to flinch from. About this property many troublous questions insisted on rising: had she not been right in thinking that the half of it ought to go to Will Ladislaw – but was it not impossible now for her to do that act of justice? Mr Casaubon had taken a cruelly effective means of hindering her: even with indignation against him in her heart, any act that seemed a triumphant eluding of his purpose revolted her.

After collecting papers of business which she wished to examine she locked up again the desks and drawers – all empty of personal words for her – empty of any sign that in her husband's lonely brooding his heart had gone out to her in excuse or explanation; and she went back to Freshitt with the sense that around his last hard demand and his last injurious assertion of his power, the silence was unbroken.

Dorothea tried now to turn her thoughts towards immediate duties, and one of these was of a kind which others were determined to remind her of. Lydgate's ear had caught eagerly her mention of the living, and as soon as he could, he reopened the subject, seeing here a possibility of making amends for the casting-vote he had once given with an ill-satisfied conscience.

'Instead of telling you anything about Mr Tyke,' he said, 'I should like to speak of another man – Mr Farebrother, the Vicar of St Botolph's. His living is a poor one, and gives him a stinted provision for himself and his family. His mother, aunt, and sister all live with him, and depend upon him. I believe he has never married because of them. I never heard such good preaching as his – such plain, easy eloquence. He would have done to preach at St Paul's Cross after old Latimer. His talk is just as good about all subjects: original, simple, clear. I think him a remarkable fellow; he ought to have done more than he has done.'

'Why has he not done more?' said Dorothea, interested now in all who had slipped below their own intention.

'That's a hard question,' said Lydgate. 'I find myself that it's uncommonly difficult to make the right thing work: there are so many strings pulling at once. Farebrother often hints that he has got into the wrong profession; he wants a wider range than that of a poor clergyman, and I suppose he has no interest to help him on. He is very fond of Natural History and various scientific matters, and he is hampered in reconciling these tastes with his position. He has no money to spare – hardly enough to use; and that has led him into card-playing – Middlemarch is a great place for whist. He does play for money, and wins a good deal. Of course that takes him into company a little beneath him, and makes him slack about some things; and yet, with all that, looking at him as a whole, I think he is one of the most blameless men I ever knew. He has neither venom nor doubleness in him, and those often go with a more correct outside.'

'I wonder whether he suffers in his conscience because of that habit,' said Dorothea: 'I wonder whether he wishes he could leave it off.'

'I have no doubt he would leave it off, if he were transplanted into plenty: he would be glad of the time for other things.'

'My uncle says that Mr Tyke is spoken of as an apostolic man,' said Dorothea, meditatively. She was wishing it were possible to restore the times of primitive zeal, and yet thinking of Mr Farebrother with a strong desire to rescue him from his chance-gotten money.

'I don't pretend to say that Farebrother is apostolic,' said Lydgate. 'His position is not quite like that of the Apostles: he is only a parson among parishioners whose lives he has to try and make better. Practically I find that what is called being apostolic now, is an impatience of everything in which the parson doesn't cut the principal figure. I see something of that in Mr Tyke at the Hospital: a good deal of his doctrine is a sort of pinching hard to make people uncomfortably aware of him. Besides, an apostolic man at Lowick! – he ought to think, as St Francis did, that it is needful to preach to the birds.'

'True,' said Dorothea. 'It is hard to imagine what sort of notions our farmers and labourers get from their teaching. I have been looking into a volume of sermons by Mr Tyke: such sermons would be of no use at Lowick – I mean, about imputed righteousness and the prophecies in the Apocalypse. I have always been thinking of the different ways in which Christianity is taught, and whenever I find one way that makes it a wider blessing than any other, I cling to that as the truest – I mean that which takes in the most good of all kinds, and brings in the most people as sharers in it. It is surely better to pardon too much, than to condemn too much. But I should like to see Mr Farebrother and hear him preach.'

'Do,' said Lydgate; 'I trust to the effect of that. He is very much beloved, but he has his enemies too: there are always people who can't forgive an able man for differing from them. And that money-winning business is really a blot. You don't, of course, see many Middlemarch people: but Mr Ladislaw, who is constantly seeing Mr Brooke, is a great friend of Mr Farebrother's old ladies, and would be glad to sing the Vicar's praises. One of the old ladies – Miss Noble, the aunt – is a wonderfully quaint picture of self-forgetful goodness, and Ladislaw gallants her about sometimes. I met them one day in a back street: you know Ladislaw's look – a sort of Daphnis in coat and waistcoat; and this little old maid reaching up to his arm they looked like a couple dropped out of a romantic comedy. But the best evidence about Farebrother is to see him and hear him.'

Happily Dorothea was in her private sitting-room when this conversation occurred, and there was no one present to make Lydgate's innocent introduction of Ladislaw painful to her. As was usual with him in matters of personal gossip, Lydgate had quite forgotten Rosamond's remark that she thought Will adored Mrs Casaubon. At that moment he was only caring for what would recommend the Farebrother family; and he had purposely given emphasis to the worst that could be said about the Vicar, in order to forestall objections. In the weeks since Mr Casaubon's death he had hardly seen Ladislaw, and he had heard no rumour to warn him that Mr Brooke's confidential secretary was a dangerous subject with Mrs Casaubon. When he was gone, his picture of Ladislaw lingered in her mind and disputed the ground with that question of the Lowick living. What was Will Ladislaw thinking about her? Would he hear of that fact which made her cheeks burn as they never used to do? And how would he feel when he heard it? – But she could see as well as possible how he smiled down at the little old maid. An Italian with white mice! – on the contrary, he was a creature who entered into everyone's feelings, and could take the pressure of their thought instead of urging his own with iron resistance.

Chapter 51

> Party is Nature too, and you shall see
> By force of Logic how they both agree:
> The Many in the One, the One in Many;
> All is not Some, nor Some the same as Any:
> Genus holds species, both are great or small;
> One genus highest, one not high at all;
> Each species has its differentia too,
> This is not That, and He was never You,
> Though this and that are ayes, and you and he
> Are like as one to one, or three to three.

No gossip about Mr Casaubon's will had yet reached Ladislaw: the air seemed to be filled with the dissolution of Parliament and the coming election, as the old wakes and fairs were filled with the rival clatter of itinerant shows; and more private noises were taken little notice of. The famous 'dry election' was at hand, in which the depths of public feeling might be measured by the low flood-mark of drink. Will Ladislaw was one of the busiest at this time; and though Dorothea's widowhood was continually in his thought, he was so far from wishing to be spoken to on the subject, that when Lydgate sought him out to tell him what had passed about the Lowick living, he answered rather waspishly: 'Why should you bring me into the matter? I never see Mrs Casaubon, and am not likely to see her, since she is at Freshitt. I never go there. It is Tory ground, where I and the *Pioneer* are no more welcome than a poacher and his gun.'

The fact was that Will had been made the more susceptible by observing that Mr Brooke, instead of wishing him, as before, to come to the Grange oftener than was quite agreeable to himself, seemed now to contrive that he should go there as little as possible. This was a shuffling concession of Mr Brooke's to Sir James Chettam's indignant remonstrance; and Will, awake to the slightest hint in this direction, concluded that he was to be kept away from the Grange on Dorothea's account. Her friends, then, regarded him with some suspicion? Their fears were quite superfluous: they were very much mistaken if they imagined that he would put himself forward as a needy adventurer trying to win the favour of a rich woman.

Until now Will had never fully seen the chasm between himself and Dorothea – until now that he was come to the brink of it, and saw her on the other side. He began, not without some inward rage, to think of going away from the neighbourhood: it would be impossible for him to show any further interest in Dorothea without subjecting himself to disagreeable imputations – perhaps even in her mind, which others might try to poison.

'We are for ever divided,' said Will. 'I might as well be at Rome; she would be no farther from me.' But what we call our despair is often only the painful eagerness of unfed hope. There were plenty of reasons why he should not go – public reasons why he should not quit his post at this crisis, leaving Mr Brooke in the lurch when he needed 'coaching' for the election, and when there was so much canvassing, direct and indirect, to be carried on. Will could not like to leave his own chessmen in the heat of a game; and any candidate on the right side, even if his brain and marrow had been as soft as was consistent with a gentlemanly bearing, might help to turn a majority. To coach Mr Brooke and keep him steadily to the idea that he must pledge himself to vote for the actual Reform Bill, instead of insisting on his independence and power of pulling up in time, was not an easy task. Mr Farebrother's prophecy of a fourth candidate 'in the bag' had not yet been fulfilled, neither the Parliamentary Candidate Society nor any other power on the watch to secure a reforming majority seeing a worthy nodus for interference while there was a second reforming candidate like Mr Brooke, who might be returned at his own expense; and the fight lay entirely between Pinkerton the old Tory member, Bagster, the new Whig member returned at the last election, and Brooke the future independent member, who was to fetter himself for this occasion only. Mr Hawley and his party would bend all their forces to the return of Pinkerton, and Mr Brooke's success must depend either on plumpers which would leave Bagster in the rear, or on the new minting of Tory votes into reforming votes. The latter means, of course, would be preferable.

This prospect of converting votes was a dangerous distraction to Mr Brooke: his impression that waverers were likely to be allured by wavering statements, and also the liability of his mind to stick afresh at opposing arguments as they turned up in his memory, gave Will Ladislaw much trouble.

'You know there are tactics in these things,' said Mr Brooke; 'meeting people half way – tempering your ideas – saying, "Well now, there's something in that", and so on. I agree with you that this is a peculiar occasion – the country with a will of its own – political unions – that sort of thing – but we sometimes cut with rather too sharp a knife, Ladislaw. These ten-pound householders, now: why ten? Draw the line somewhere yes: but why just at ten? That's a difficult question, now, if you go into it.'

'Of course it is,' said Will, impatiently. 'But if you are to wait till we get a logical Bill, you must put yourself forward as a revolutionist, and then

Middlemarch would not elect you, I fancy. As for trimming, this is not a time for trimming.'

Mr Brooke always ended by agreeing with Ladislaw, who still appeared to him a sort of Burke with a leaven of Shelley; but after an interval the wisdom of his own methods reasserted itself, and he was again drawn into using them with much hopefulness. At this stage of affairs he was in excellent spirits, which even supported him under large advances of money; for his powers of convincing and persuading had not yet been tested by anything more difficult than a chairman's speech, introducing other orators, or a dialogue with a Middlemarch voter, from which he came away with a sense that he was a tactician by nature, and that it was a pity he had not gone earlier into this kind of thing. He was a little conscious of defeat, however, with Mr Mawmsey, a chief representative in Middlemarch of that great social power, the retail trader, and naturally one of the most doubtful voters in the borough – willing for his own part to supply an equal quality of teas and sugars to reformer and anti-reformer, as well as to agree impartially with both, and feeling like the burgesses of old that this necessity of electing members was a great burthen to a town; for even if there were no danger in holding out hopes to all parties beforehand, there would be the painful necessity at last of disappointing respectable people whose names were on his books. He was accustomed to receive large orders from Mr Brooke of Tipton; but then, there were many of Pinkerton's committee whose opinions had a great weight of grocery on their side. Mr Mawmsey thinking that Mr Brooke, as not too 'clever in his intellects', was the more likely to forgive a grocer who gave a hostile vote under pressure, had become confidential in his back parlour.

'As to Reform, sir, put it in a family light,' he said, rattling the small silver in his pocket, and smiling affably. 'Will it support Mrs Mawmsey, and enable her to bring up six children when I am no more? I put the question *fictiously*, knowing what must be the answer. Very well, sir. I ask you what, as a husband and a father, I am to do when gentlemen come to me and say, "Do as you like, Mawmsey; but if you vote against us, I shall get my groceries elsewhere; when I sugar my liquor I like to feel that I am benefiting the country by maintaining tradesmen of the right colour." Those very words have been spoken to me, sir, in the very chair where you are now sitting. I don't mean by your honourable self, Mr Brooke.'

'No, no, no – that's narrow, you know. Until my butler complains to me of your goods, Mr Mawmsey,' said Mr Brooke, soothingly, 'until I hear that you send bad sugars, spices – that sort of thing – I shall never order him to go elsewhere.'

'Sir, I am your humble servant and greatly obliged,' said Mr Mawmsey, feeling that politics were clearing up a little. 'There would be some pleasure in voting for a gentleman who speaks in that honourable manner.'

'Well, you know, Mr Mawmsey, you would find it the right thing to put yourself on our side. This Reform will touch everybody by and by – a thoroughly popular measure – a sort of A, B, C, you know, that must come first before the rest can follow. I quite agree with you that you've got to look at the thing in a family light: but public spirit, now. We're all one family, you know – it's all one cupboard. Such a thing as a vote, now: why, it may help to make men's fortunes at the Cape – there's no knowing what may be the effect of a vote,' Mr Brooke ended, with a sense of being a little out at sea, though finding it still enjoyable. But Mr Mawmsey answered in a tone of decisive check.

'I beg your pardon, sir, but I can't afford that. When I give a vote I must know what I'm doing; I must look to what will be the effects on my till and ledger, speaking respectfully. Prices, I'll admit, are what nobody can know the merits of; and the sudden falls after you've bought in currants, which are a goods that will not keep – I've never myself seen into the ins and outs there; which is a rebuke to human pride. But as to one family, there's debtor and creditor, I hope; they're not going to reform that away; else I should vote for things staying as they are. Few men have less need to cry for change than I have, personally speaking – that is, for self and family. I am not one of those who have nothing to lose; I mean as to respectability both in parish and private business, and no ways in respect of your honourable self and custom, which you was good enough to say you would not withdraw from me, vote or no vote, while the article sent in was satisfactory.'

After this conversation Mr Mawmsey went up and boasted to his wife that he had been rather too many for Brooke of Tipton, and that he didn't mind so much now about going to the poll.

Mr Brooke on this occasion abstained from boasting of his tactics to Ladislaw, who for his part was glad enough to persuade himself that he had no concern with any canvassing except the purely argumentative sort, and that he worked no meaner engine than knowledge. Mr Brooke, necessarily, had his agents, who understood the nature of the Middlemarch voter and the means of enlisting his ignorance on the side of the Bill which were remarkably similar to the means of enlisting it on the side against the Bill. Will stopped his ears. Occasionally Parliament, like the rest of our lives, even to our eating and apparel, could hardly go on if our imaginations were too active about processes. There were plenty of dirty-handed men in the world to do dirty business; and Will protested to himself that his share in bringing Mr Brooke through would be quite innocent.

But whether he should succeed in that mode of contributing to the majority on the right side was very doubtful to him. He had written out various speeches and memoranda for speeches, but he had begun to perceive that Mr Brooke's mind, if it had the burthen of remembering any train of thought, would let it drop, run away in search of it, and not easily come back again. To collect documents is one mode of serving your country, and to remember the contents of a document is another. No! the only way in which Mr Brooke could be coerced into thinking of the right arguments at the right time was to be well plied with them till they took up all the room in his brain. But here there was the difficulty of finding room, so many things having been taken in beforehand. Mr Brooke himself observed that his ideas stood rather in his way when he was speaking.

However, Ladislaw's coaching was forthwith to be put to the test, for before the day of nomination Mr Brooke was to explain himself to the worthy electors of Middlemarch from the balcony of the White Hart, which looked out advantageously at an angle of the market-place, commanding a large area in front and two converging streets. It was a fine May morning and everything seemed hopeful: there was some prospect of an understanding between Bagster's committee and Brooke's, to which Mr Bulstrode, Mr Standish as a Liberal lawyer, and such manufacturers as Mr Plymdale and Mr Vincy, gave a solidity which almost counterbalanced Mr Hawley and his associates who sat for Pinkerton at the Green Dragon. Mr Brooke, conscious of having weakened the blasts of the *Trumpet* against him, by his reforms as a landlord in the last half year, and hearing himself cheered a little as he drove into the town, felt his heart tolerably light under his buff-coloured waistcoat. But with regard to critical occasions, it often happens that all moments seem comfortably remote until the last.

'This looks well, eh?' said Mr Brooke as the crowd gathered. 'I shall have a good audience, at any rate. I like this, now – this kind of public made up of one's own neighbours, you know.'

The weavers and tanners of Middlemarch, unlike Mr Mawmsey, had never thought of Mr Brooke as a neighbour, and were not more attached to him than if he had been sent in a box from London. But they listened without much disturbance to the speakers who introduced the candidate, though one of them – a political personage from Brassing, who came to tell Middlemarch its duty – spoke so fully, that it was alarming to think what the candidate could find to say after him. Meanwhile the crowd became denser, and as the political personage neared the end of his speech, Mr Brooke felt a remarkable change in his sensations while he still handled his eye-glass, trifled with documents before him, and exchanged remarks with his committee, as a man to whom the moment of summons was indifferent.

'I'll take another glass of sherry, Ladislaw,' he said, with an easy air, to Will, who was close behind him, and presently handed him the supposed fortifier. It was ill-chosen; for Mr Brooke was an abstemious man, and to drink a second glass of sherry quickly at no great interval from the first was a surprise to his system which tended to scatter his energies instead of collecting them. Pray pity him: so many English gentlemen make themselves miserable by speechifying on entirely private grounds! whereas Mr Brooke wished to serve his country by standing for Parliament – which, indeed, may also be done on private grounds, but being once undertaken does absolutely demand some speechifying.

It was not about the beginning of his speech that Mr Brooke was at all anxious; this, he felt sure, would be all right; he should have it quite pat, cut out as neatly as a set of couplets from Pope. Embarking would be easy, but the vision of open sea that might come after was alarming. 'And questions, now,' hinted the demon just waking up in his stomach, 'somebody may put questions about the schedules – Ladislaw,' he continued, aloud, 'just hand me the memorandum of the schedules.'

When Mr Brooke presented himself on the balcony, the cheers were quite loud enough to counterbalance the yells, groans, brayings, and other expressions of adverse theory, which were so moderate that Mr Standish (decidedly an old bird) observed in the ear next to him, 'This looks dangerous, by God! Hawley has got some deeper plan than this.' Still, the cheers were exhilarating, and no candidate could look more amiable than Mr Brooke, with the memorandum in his breast-pocket, his left hand on the rail of the balcony, and his right trifling with his eyeglass. The striking points in his appearance were his buff waistcoat, short-clipped blond hair, and neutral physiognomy. He began with some confidence.

'Gentlemen – Electors of Middlemarch!'

This was so much the right thing that a little pause after it seemed natural.

'I'm uncommonly glad to be here – I was never so proud and happy in my life – never so happy, you know.'

This was a bold figure of speech, but not exactly the right thing; for, unhappily, the pat opening had slipped away – even couplets from Pope may be but 'fallings from us, vanishings', when fear clutches us, and a glass of sherry is hurrying like smoke among our ideas. Ladislaw, who stood at the window behind the speaker, thought, 'It's all up now. The only chance is that, since the best thing won't always do, floundering may answer for once.' Mr Brooke, meanwhile, having lost other clues, fell back on himself and his qualifications – always an appropriate graceful subject for a candidate.

'I am a close neighbour of yours, my good friends – you've known me on the bench a good while – I've always gone a good deal into public questions – machinery, now, and machine-breaking – you're many of you concerned with machinery, and I've been going into that lately. It won't do, you know, breaking machines: everything must go on – trade, manufactures, commerce, interchange of staples – that kind of thing – since Adam Smith, that must go on. We must look all over the globe: – "Observation with extensive view", must look everywhere "from China to Peru", as somebody says – Johnson, I think, *The Rambler*, you know. That is what I have done up to a certain point – not as far as Peru; but I've not always stayed at home I saw it wouldn't do. I've been in the Levant, where some of your Middlemarch goods go – and then, again, in the Baltic. The Baltic, now.'

Plying among his recollections in this way, Mr Brooke might have got along, easily to himself, and would have come back from the remotest seas without trouble; but a diabolical procedure had been set up by the enemy. At one and the same moment there had risen above the shoulders of the crowd, nearly opposite Mr Brooke, and within ten yards of him, the effigy of himself; buff-coloured waistcoat, eye-glass, and neutral physiognomy, painted on rag; and there had arisen apparently in the air, like the note of the cuckoo, a parrotlike, Punch-voiced echo of his words. Everybody looked up at the open windows in the houses at the opposite angles of the converging streets; but they were either blank, or filled by laughing listeners. The most innocent echo has an impish mockery in it when it follows a gravely persistent speaker, and this echo was not at all innocent; if it did not follow with the precision of a natural echo, it had a wicked choice of the words it overtook. By the time it said, 'The Baltic, now', the laugh which had been running through the audience became a general shout, and but for the sobering effects of party and that great public cause which the entanglement of things had identified with 'Brooke of Tipton', the laugh might have caught his committee. Mr Bulstrode asked, reprehensively, what the new police was doing; but a voice could not well be collared, and an attack on the effigy of the candidate would have been too equivocal, since Hawley probably meant it to be pelted.

Mr Brooke himself was not in a position to be quickly conscious of anything except a general slipping away of ideas within himself: he had even a little singing in the ears, and he was the only person who had not yet taken distinct account of the echo or discerned the image of himself. Few things hold the perceptions more thoroughly captive than anxiety about what we have got to say. Mr Brooke heard the laughter; but he had expected some Tory efforts at disturbance, and he was at this moment additionally excited by the tickling, stinging sense that his lost exordium was coming back to fetch him from the Baltic.

'That reminds me,' he went on, thrusting a hand into his side-pocket, with an easy air, 'if I wanted a precedent, you know – but we never want a precedent for the right thing – but there is Chatham, now; I can't say I should have supported Chatham, or Pitt, the younger Pitt – he was not a man of ideas, and we want ideas, you know.'

'Blast your ideas! we want the Bill,' said a loud rough voice from the crowd below.

Immediately the invisible Punch, who had hitherto followed Mr Brooke, repeated, 'Blast your ideas! we want the Bill.' The laugh was louder than ever, and for the first time Mr Brooke, being himself silent, heard distinctly the mocking echo. But it seemed to ridicule his interrupter, and in that light was encouraging; so he replied with amenity: 'There is something in what you say, my good friend, and what do we meet for but to speak our minds – freedom of opinion, freedom of the press, liberty – that kind of thing? The Bill, now – you shall have the Bill' – here Mr Brooke paused a moment to fix on his eye-glass and take the paper from his breast-pocket, with a sense of being practical and coming to particulars. The invisible Punch followed: 'You shall have the Bill, Mr Brooke, per electioneering contest, and a seat outside Parliament as delivered, five thousand pounds, seven shillings, and fourpence.'

Mr Brooke, amid the roars of laughter, turned red, let his eye-glass fall, and looking about him confusedly, saw the image of himself, which had come nearer. The next moment he saw it dolorously bespattered with eggs. His spirit rose a little, and his voice too.

'Buffoonery, tricks, ridicule the test of truth – all that is very well' – here an unpleasant egg broke on Mr Brooke's shoulder, as the echo said, 'All that is very well'; then came a hail of eggs, chiefly aimed at the image, but occasionally hitting the original, as if by chance. There was a stream of new men pushing among the crowd; whistles, yells, bellowings, and fifes made all the greater hubbub because there was shouting and struggling to put them down. No voice would have had wing enough to rise above the uproar, and Mr Brooke, disagreeably anointed, stood his ground no longer. The frustration would have been less exasperating if it had been less gamesome and boyish: a serious assault of which the newspaper reporter 'can aver that it endangered the learned gentleman's ribs', or can respectfully bear witness to 'the soles of that gentle-man's boots having been visible above the railing,' has perhaps more con-solations attached to it.

Mr Brooke re-entered the committee-room, saying, as carelessly as he could, 'This is a little too bad, you know. I should have got the ear of the people by and by – but they didn't give me time. I should have gone into the Bill by and by, you know,' he added, glancing at Ladislaw. 'However, things will come all right at the nomination.'

But it was not resolved unanimously that things would come right; on the contrary, the committee looked rather grim, and the political personage from Brassing was writing busily, as if he were brewing new devices.

'It was Bowyer who did it,' said Mr Standish, evasively. 'I know it as well as if he had been advertised. He's uncommonly good at ventriloquism, and he did it uncommonly well, by God! Hawley has been having him to dinner lately: there's a fund of talent in Bowyer.'

'Well, you know, you never mentioned him to me, Standish, else I would have invited him to dine,' said poor Mr Brooke, who had gone through a great deal of inviting for the good of his country.

'There's not a more paltry fellow in Middlemarch than Bowyer,' said Ladislaw, indignantly, 'but it seems as if the paltry fellows were always to turn the scale.'

Will was thoroughly out of temper with himself as well as with his 'principal', and he went to shut himself in his rooms with a half-formed resolve to throw up the *Pioneer* and Mr Brooke together. Why should he stay? If the impassable gulf between himself and Dorothea were ever to be filled up, it must rather be by his going away and getting into a thoroughly different position than by staying here and slipping into deserved contempt as an under-strapper of Brooke's. Then came the young dream of wonders that he might do – in five years, for example: political writing, political speaking, would get a higher value now public life was going to be wider and more national, and they might give him such distinction that he would not seem to be asking Dorothea to step down to him. Five years: – if he could only be sure that she cared for him more than for others; if he could only make her aware that he stood aloof until he could tell his love without lowering himself – then he could go away easily, and begin a career which at five-and-twenty seemed probable enough in the inward order of things, where talent brings fame, and fame everything else which is delightful. He could speak and he could write; he could master any subject if he chose, and he meant always to take the side of reason and justice, on which he would carry all his ardour. Why should he not one day be lifted above the shoulders of the crowd, and feel that he had won that eminence well? Without doubt he would leave Middle-march, go to town, and make himself fit for celebrity by 'eating his dinners'.

But not immediately: not until some kind of sign had passed between him and Dorothea. He could not be satisfied until she knew why, even if he were the man she would choose to marry, he would not marry her. Hence he must keep his post and bear with Mr Brooke a little longer.

But he soon had reason to suspect that Mr Brooke had anticipated him in the wish to break up their connection. Deputations without and voices within had concurred in inducing that philanthropist to take a stronger measure than usual for the good of mankind; namely, to withdraw in favour of another candidate, to whom he left the advantages of his canvassing machinery. He himself called this a strong measure, but observed that his health was less capable of sustaining excitement than he had imagined.

'I have felt uneasy about the chest – it won't do to carry that too far,' he said to Ladislaw in explaining the affair. 'I must pull up. Poor Casaubon was a warning, you know. I've made some heavy advances, but I've dug a channel. It's rather coarse work – this electioneering, eh, Ladislaw? I dare say you are tired of it. However, we have dug a channel with the *Pioneer* – put things in a track, and so on. A more ordinary man than you might carry it on now – more ordinary, you know.'

'Do you wish me to give it up?' said Will, the quick colour coming in his face, as he rose from the writing-table, and took a turn of three steps with his hands in his pockets. 'I am ready to do so whenever you wish it.'

'As to wishing, my dear Ladislaw, I have the highest opinion of your powers, you know. But about the *Pioneer*, I have been consulting a little with some of the men on our side, and they are inclined to take it into their hands – indemnify me to a certain extent – carry it on, in fact. And under the circumstances, you might like to give up – might find a better field. These people might not take that high view of you which I have always taken, as an *alter ego*, a right hand – though I always looked forward to your doing something else. I think of having a run into France. But I'll write you any letters, you know – to Althorpe and people of that kind. I've met Althorpe.'

'I am exceedingly obliged to you,' said Ladislaw proudly. 'Since you are going to part with the *Pioneer*, I need not trouble you about the steps I shall take. I may choose to continue here for the present.'

After Mr Brooke had left him Will said to himself, 'The rest of the family have been urging him to get rid of me, and he doesn't care now about my going. I shall stay as long as I like. I shall go of my own movement, and not because they are afraid of me.'

Chapter 52

His heart
The lowliest duties on itself did lay.
WORDSWORTH

On that June evening when Mr Farebrother knew that he was to have the Lowick living, there was joy in the old-fashioned parlour, and even the portraits of the great lawyers seemed to look on with satisfaction. His mother left her tea and toast untouched, but sat with her usual pretty primness, only showing her emotion by that flush in the cheeks and brightness in the eyes which give an old woman a touching momentary identity with her far-off youthful self, and saying decisively: 'The greatest comfort, Camden, is that you have deserved it.'

'When a man gets a good berth, mother, half the deserving must come after,' said the son, brimful of pleasure, and not trying to conceal it. The gladness in his face was of that active kind which seems to have energy enough not only to flash outwardly, but to light up busy vision within: one seemed to see thoughts, as well as delight, in his glances.

'Now, aunt,' he went on, rubbing his hands and looking at Miss Noble, who was making tender little beaverlike noises, 'there shall be sugar-candy always on the table for you to steal and give to the children, and you shall have a great many new stockings to make presents of, and you shall darn your own more than ever!'

Miss Noble nodded at her nephew with a subdued half-frightened laugh, conscious of having already dropped an additional lump of sugar into her basket on the strength of the new preferment.

'As for you, Winny' – the Vicar went on – 'I shall make no difficulty about your marrying any Lowick bachelor – Mr Solomon Featherstone, for example, as soon as I find you are in love with him.'

Miss Winifred, who had been looking at her brother all the while and crying heartily, which was her way of rejoicing, smiled through her tears and said, 'You must set me the example, Cam: you must marry now.'

'With all my heart. But who is in love with me? I am a seedy old fellow,' said the Vicar, rising, pushing his chair away and looking down at himself. 'What do you say, mother?'

'You are a handsome man, Camden: though not so fine a figure of a man as your father,' said the old lady.

'I wish you would marry Miss Garth, brother,' said Miss Winifred. 'She would make us so lively at Lowick.'

'Very fine! You talk as if young women were tied up to be chosen, like poultry at market; as if I had only to ask and everybody would have me,' said the Vicar, not caring to specify.

'We don't want everybody,' said Miss Winifred. 'But you would like Miss Garth, mother, shouldn't you?'

'My son's choice shall be mine,' said Mrs Farebrother, with majestic discretion, 'and a wife would be most welcome, Camden. You will want your whist at home when we go to Lowick, and Henrietta Noble never was a whist-player.' (Mrs Farebrother always called her tiny old sister by that magnificent name.)

'I shall do without whist now, mother.'

'Why so, Camden? In my time whist was thought an undeniable amusement for a good churchman,' said Mrs Farebrother, innocent of the meaning that whist had for her son, and speaking rather sharply, as at some dangerous countenancing of new doctrine.

'I shall be too busy for whist; I shall have two parishes,' said the Vicar, preferring not to discuss the virtues of that game.

He had already said to Dorothea, 'I don't feel bound to give up St Botolph's. It is protest enough against the pluralism they want to reform if I give somebody else most of the money. The stronger thing is not to give up power, but to use it well.'

'I have thought of that,' said Dorothea. 'So far as self is concerned. I think it would be easier to give up power and money than to keep them. It seems very unfitting that I should have this patronage, yet I felt that I ought not to let it be used by someone else instead of me.'

'It is I who am bound to act so that you will not regret your power,' said Mr Farebrother.

His was one of the natures in which conscience gets the more active when the yoke of life ceases to gall them. He made no display of humility on the subject, but in his heart he felt rather ashamed that his conduct had shown laches which others who did not get benefices were free from.

'I used often to wish I had been something else than a clergyman,' he said to Lydgate, 'but perhaps it will be better to try and make as good a clergyman out of myself as I can. That is the well-beneficed point of view, you perceive, from which difficulties are much simplified,' he ended, smiling.

The Vicar did feel then as if his share of duties would be easy. But Duty has a trick of behaving unexpectedly – something like a heavy friend whom we have amiably asked to visit us, and who breaks his leg within our gates.

Hardly a week later, Duty presented itself in his study under the disguise of Fred Vincy, now returned from Omnibus College with his bachelor's degree.

'I am ashamed to trouble you, Mr Farebrother,' said Fred, whose fair open face was propitiating, 'but you are the only friend I can consult. I told you everything once before, and you were so good that I can't help coming to you again.'

'Sit down, Fred, I'm ready to hear and do anything I can,' said the Vicar, who was busy packing some small objects for removal, and went on with his work.

'I wanted to tell you – ' Fred hesitated an instant and then went on plungingly, 'I might go into the Church now; and really, look where I may, I can't see anything else to do. I don't like it, but I know it's uncommonly hard on my father to say so, after he has spent a good deal of money in educating me for it.' Fred paused again an instant, and then repeated, 'and I can't see anything else to do.'

'I did talk to your father about it, Fred, but I made little way with him. He said it was too late. But you have got over one bridge now: what are your other difficulties?'

'Merely that I don't like it. I don't like divinity, and preaching, and feeling obliged to look serious. I like riding across country, and doing as other men do. I don't mean that I want to be a bad fellow in any way; but I've no taste for the sort of thing people expect of a clergyman. And yet what else am I to do? My father can't spare me any capital, else I might go into farming. And he has no room for me in his trade. And of course I can't begin to study for law or physic now, when my father wants me to earn something. It's all very well to say I'm wrong to go into the Church; but those who say so might as well tell me to go into the backwoods.'

Fred's voice had taken a tone of grumbling remonstrance, and Mr Farebrother might have been inclined to smile if his mind had not been too busy in imagining more than Fred told him.

'Have you any difficulties about doctrines – about the Articles?' he said, trying hard to think of the question simply for Fred's sake.

'No, I suppose the Articles are right. I am not prepared with any arguments to disprove them, and much better, cleverer fellows than I am go in for them entirely. I think it would be rather ridiculous in me to urge scruples of that sort, as if I were a judge,' said Fred, quite simply.

'I suppose, then, it has occurred to you that you might be a fair parish priest without being much of a divine?'

'Of course, if I am obliged to be a clergyman, I shall try and do my duty, though I mayn't like it. Do you think anybody ought to blame me?'

'For going into the Church under the circumstances? That depends on your conscience, Fred – how far you have counted the cost, and seen what your position will require of you. I can only tell you about myself, that I have always been too lax, and have been uneasy in consequence.'

'But there is another hindrance,' said Fred, colouring. 'I did not tell you before, though perhaps I may have said things that made you guess it. There is somebody I am very fond of: I have loved her ever since we were children.'

'Miss Garth, I suppose?' said the Vicar, examining some labels very closely.

'Yes. I shouldn't mind anything if she would have me. And I know I could be a good fellow then.'

'And you think she returns the feeling?'

'She never will say so; and a good while ago she made me promise not to speak to her about it again. And she has set her mind especially against my being a clergyman; I know that. But I can't give her up. I do think she cares about me. I saw Mrs Garth last night and she said that Mary was staying at Lowick Rectory with Miss Farebrother.'

'Yes, she is very kindly helping my sister. Do you wish to go there?'

'No, I want to ask a great favour of you. I am ashamed to bother you in this way; but Mary might listen to what you said, if you mentioned the subject to her – I mean about my going into the Church.'

'That is rather a delicate task, my dear Fred. I shall have to presuppose your attachment to her; and to enter on the subject as you wish me to do, will be asking her to tell me whether she returns it.'

'That is what I want her to tell you,' said Fred, bluntly. 'I don't know what to do, unless I can get at her feeling.'

'You mean that you would be guided by that as to your going into the Church?'

'If Mary said she would never have me I might as well go wrong in one way as another.'

'That is nonsense, Fred. Men outlive their love, but they don't outlive the consequences of their recklessness.'

'Not my sort of love: I have never been without loving Mary. If I had to give her up, it would be like beginning to live on wooden legs.'

'Will she not be hurt at my intrusion?'

'No, I feel sure she will not. She respects you more than anyone, and she would not put you off with fun as she does me. Of course I could not have told anyone else, or asked anyone else to speak to her, but you. There is no one else who could be such a friend to both of us.' Fred paused a moment, and then said, rather complainingly, 'And she ought to acknowledge that I have worked in order to pass. She ought to believe that I would exert myself for her sake.'

There was a moment's silence before Mr Farebrother laid down his work, and putting out his hand to Fred said: 'Very well, my boy. I will do what you wish.'

That very day Mr Farebrother went to Lowick parsonage on the nag which he had just set up. 'Decidedly I am an old stalk,' he thought, 'the young growths are pushing me aside.'

He found Mary in the garden gathering roses and sprinkling the petals on a sheet. The sun was low, and tall trees sent their shadows across the grassy walks where Mary was moving without bonnet or parasol. She did not observe Mr Farebrother's approach along the grass, and had just stooped down to lecture a small black-and-tan terrier, which would persist in walking on the sheet and smelling at the rose-leaves as Mary sprinkled them. She took his forepaws in one hand, and lifted up the forefinger of the other, while the dog wrinkled his brows and looked embarrassed. 'Fly, I am ashamed of you,' Mary was saying in a grave contralto. 'This is not becoming in a sensible dog; anybody would think you were a silly young gentleman.'

'You are unmerciful to young gentlemen, Miss Garth,' said the Vicar, within two yards of her.

Mary started up and blushed. 'It always answers to reason with Fly,' she said, laughingly.

'But not with young gentlemen?'

'Oh, with some, I suppose; since some of them turn into excellent men.'

'I am glad of that admission, because I want at this very moment to interest you in a young gentleman.'

'Not a silly one, I hope,' said Mary, beginning to pluck the roses again, and feeling her heart beat uncomfortably.

'No; though perhaps wisdom is not his strong point, but rather affection and sincerity. However, wisdom lies more in those two qualities than people are apt to imagine. I hope you know by those marks what young gentleman I mean.'

'Yes, I think I do,' said Mary, bravely, her face getting more serious, and her hands cold; 'it must be Fred Vincy.'

'He has asked me to consult you about his going into the Church. I hope you will not think that I consented to take a liberty in promising to do so.'

'On the contrary, Mr Farebrother,' said Mary, giving up the roses, and folding her arms, but unable to look up, 'whenever you have anything to say to me I feel honoured.'

'But before I enter on that question, let me just touch a point on which your father took me into confidence; by the way, it was that very evening on which I once before fulfilled a mission from Fred, just after he had gone to college. Mr Garth told me what happened on the night of Featherstone's death – how you refused to burn the will; and he said that you had some heart-prickings on that subject, because you had been the innocent means of hindering Fred from getting his ten thousand pounds. I have kept that in mind, and I have heard something that may relieve you on that score – may show you that no sin-offering is demanded from you there.'

Mr Farebrother paused a moment and looked at Mary. He meant to give Fred his full advantage, but it would be well, he thought, to clear her mind of any superstitions, such as women sometimes follow when they do a man the wrong of marrying him as an act of atonement. Mary's cheeks had begun to burn a little, and she was mute.

'I mean, that your action made no real difference to Fred's lot. I find that the first will would not have been legally good after the burning of the last; it would not have stood if it had been disputed, and you may be sure it would have been disputed. So, on that score, you may feel your mind free.'

'Thank you, Mr Farebrother,' said Mary, earnestly. 'I am grateful to you for remembering my feelings.'

'Well, now I may go on. Fred, you know, has taken his degree. He has worked his way so far, and now the question is, what is he to do? That question is so difficult that he is inclined to follow his father's wishes and enter the Church, though you know better than I do that he was quite set against that formerly. I have questioned him on the subject and I confess I see no insuperable objection to his being a clergyman, as things go. He says that he could turn his mind to doing his best in that vocation, on one condition. If that condition were fulfilled I would do my utmost in helping Fred on. After a time – not, of course, at first – he might be with me as my curate, and he would have so much to do that his stipend would be nearly what I used to get as vicar. But I repeat that there is a condition without which all this cannot come to pass. He has opened his heart to me, Miss Garth, and asked me to plead for him. The condition lies entirely in your feeling.'

Mary looked so much moved, that he said after a moment, 'Let us walk a little'; and when they were walking he added. 'To speak quite plainly, Fred will not take any course which would lessen the chance that you would consent to be his wife; but with that prospect, he will try his best at anything you approve.'

'I cannot possibly say that I will ever be his wife, Mr Farebrother: but I certainly never will be his wife if he becomes a clergyman. What you say is most generous and kind; I don't mean for a moment to correct your judgement. It is only that I have my girlish, mocking way of looking at things,' said Mary, with a returning sparkle of playfulness in her answer which only made its modesty more charming.

'He wishes me to report exactly what you think,' said Mr Farebrother.

'I could not love a man who is ridiculous,' said Mary, not choosing to go deeper. 'Fred has sense and knowledge enough to make him respectable, if he likes, in some good worldly business, but I can never imagine him preaching and exhorting and pronouncing blessings, and praying by the sick, without feeling as if I were looking at a caricature. His being a clergyman would be only for gentility's sake, and I think there is nothing more contemptible than such imbecile gentility. I used to think that of Mr Crowse, with his empty face and neat umbrella, and mincing little speeches. What right have such men to represent Christianity – as if it were an institution for getting up idiots genteelly – as if – ' Mary checked herself. She had been carried along as if she had been speaking to Fred instead of Mr Farebrother.

'Young women are severe; they don't feel the stress of action as men do, though perhaps I ought to make you an exception there. But you don't put Fred

Vincy on so low a level as that?'

'No, indeed; he has plenty of sense, but I think he would not show it as a clergyman. He would be a piece of professional affectation.'

'Then the answer is quite decided. As a clergyman he could have no hope?'

Mary shook her head.

'But if he braved all the difficulties of getting his bread in some other way – will you give him the support of hope? May he count on winning you?'

'I think Fred ought not to need telling again what I have already said to him,' Mary answered, with a slight resentment in her manner. 'I mean that he ought not to put such questions until he has done something worthy, instead of saying that he could do it.'

Mr Farebrother was silent for a minute or more, and then, as they turned and paused under the shadow of a maple at the end of a grassy walk, said, 'I understand that you resist any attempt to fetter you, but either your feeling for Fred Vincy excludes your entertaining another attachment, or it does not: either he may count on your remaining single until he shall have earned your hand, or he may in any case be disappointed. Pardon me, Mary – you know I used to catechise you under that name – but when the state of a woman's affections touches the happiness of another life – of more lives than one – I think it would be the nobler course for her to be perfectly direct and open.'

Mary in her turn was silent, wondering not at Mr Farebrother's manner but at his tone, which had a grave restrained emotion in it. When the strange idea flashed across her that his words had reference to himself, she was incredulous and ashamed of entertaining it. She had never thought that any man could love her except Fred, who had espoused her with the umbrella ring, when she wore socks and little strapped shoes; still less that she could be of any importance to Mr Farebrother, the cleverest man in her narrow circle. She had only time to feel that all this was hazy and perhaps illusory; but one thing was clear and determined – her answer.

'Since you think it my duty, Mr Farebrother, I will tell you that I have too strong a feeling for Fred to give him up for anyone else. I should never be quite happy if I thought he was unhappy for the loss of me. It has taken such deep root in me – my gratitude to him for always loving me best, and minding so much if I hurt myself, from the time when we were very little. I cannot imagine any new feeling coming to make that weaker. I should like better than anything to see him worthy of everyone's respect. But please tell him I will not promise to marry him till then; I should shame and grieve my father and mother. He is free to choose someone else.'

'Then I have fulfilled my commission thoroughly,' said Mr Farebrother, putting out his hand to Mary, 'and I shall ride back to Middlemarch forthwith. With this prospect before him, we shall get Fred into the right niche somehow, and I hope I shall live to join your hands. God bless you!'

'Oh, please stay, and let me give you some tea,' said Mary. Her eyes filled with tears, for something indefinable, something like the resolute suppression of a pain in Mr Farebrother's manner, made her feel suddenly miserable, as she had once felt when she saw her father's hands trembling in a moment of trouble.

'No, my dear, no. I must get back.'

In three minutes the Vicar was on horseback again, having gone magnanimously through a duty much harder than the renunciation of whist, or even than the writing of penitential meditations.

Chapter 53

It is but a shallow haste which concludeth insincerity from what outsiders
call inconsistency – putting a dead mechanism of 'ifs' and 'therefores' for
the living myriad of hidden suckers whereby the belief and the conduct
are wrought into mutual sustainment.

Mr Bulstrode, when he was hoping to acquire a new interest in Lowick, had naturally had an especial wish that the new clergyman should be one whom he thoroughly approved; and he believed it to be a chastisement and admonition directed to his own shortcomings and those of the nation at large, that just about the time when he came in possession of the deeds which made him the proprietor of Stone Court, Mr Farebrother 'read himself' into the quaint little church and preached his first sermon to the congregation of farmers, labourers, and village artisans. It was not that Mr Bulstrode intended to frequent Lowick Church or to reside at Stone Court for a good while to come: he had bought the excellent farm and fine homestead simply as a retreat which he might gradually enlarge as to the land and beautify as to the dwelling, until it should be conducive to the divine glory that he should enter on it as a residence, partially withdrawing from his present exertions in the administration of business, and throwing more conspicuously on the side of Gospel truth the weight of local landed proprietorship, which Providence might increase by unforeseen occasions of purchase. A strong leading in this direction seemed to have been given in the surprising facility of getting Stone Court, when everyone had expected that Mr Rigg Featherstone would have clung to it as the Garden of Eden. That was what poor old Peter himself had expected; having often, in imagination, looked up through the sods above him, and, unobstructed by perspective, seen his frog-faced legatee enjoying the fine old place to the perpetual surprise and disappointment of other survivors.

But how little we know what would make paradise for our neighbours! We judge from our own desires, and our neighbours themselves are not always open enough even to throw out a hint of theirs. The cool and judicious Joshua Rigg had not allowed his parent to perceive that Stone Court was anything less than the chief good in his estimation, and he had certainly wished to call it his own. But as Warren Hastings looked at gold and thought of buying Daylesford, so Joshua Rigg looked at Stone Court and thought of buying gold. He had a very distinct and intense vision of his chief good, the vigorous greed which he had inherited having taken a special form by dint of circumstance: and his chief good was to be a money-changer. From his earliest employment as an errand-boy in a seaport, he had looked though the windows of the money-changers as other boys look through the windows of the pastry-cooks; the fascination had wrought itself gradually into a deep special passion: he meant, when he had property, to do many things, one of them being to marry a genteel young person; but these were all accidents and joys that imagination could dispense with. The one joy after which his soul thirsted was to have a money-changer's shop on a much-frequented quay, to have locks all round him of which he held the keys, and to look sublimely cool as he handled the breeding coins of all nations, while helpless Cupidity looked at him enviously from the other side of an iron lattice. The strength of that passion had been a power enabling him to master all the knowledge necessary to gratify it. And when others were thinking that he had settled at Stone Court for life, Joshua himself was thinking that the moment now was not far off when he should settle on the North Quay with the best appointments in safes and locks.

Enough. We are concerned with looking at Joshua Rigg's sale of his land from Mr Bulstrode's point of view, and he interpreted it as a cheering dispensation conveying perhaps a sanction to a purpose which he had for some time entertained without external encouragement; he interpreted it thus, but not too confidently, offering up his thanksgiving in guarded phraseology. His doubts did not arise from the possible relations of the event to Joshua Rigg's destiny, which belonged to the unmapped regions not taken under the providential government, except perhaps in an imperfect colonial way; but they arose from reflecting that this dispensation too might be a chastisement for himself, as Mr Farebrother's induction to the living clearly was.

This was not what Mr Bulstrode said to any man for the sake of deceiving him: it was what he said to himself – it was as genuinely his mode of explaining events as any theory of yours may be, if you happen to disagree with him. For the egoism which enters into our theories does not affect their sincerity; rather, the more our egoism is satisfied, the more robust is our belief.

However, whether for sanction or for chastisement, Mr Bulstrode, hardly fifteen months after the death of Peter Featherstone, had become the proprietor of Stone Court, and what Peter would say 'if he were worthy to know', had become an inexhaustible and consolatory subject of conversation to his disappointed relatives. The tables were now turned on that dear brother departed, and to contemplate the frustration of his cunning by the superior cunning of things in general was a cud of delight to Solomon. Mrs Waule had a melancholy triumph in the proof that it did not answer to make false Featherstones and cut off the genuine; and Sister Martha receiving the news in the Chalky Flats said, 'Dear, dear! then the Almighty could have been none so pleased with the almshouses after all.'

Affectionate Mrs Bulstrode was particularly glad of the advantage which her husband's health was likely to get from the purchase of Stone Court. Few days passed without his riding thither and looking over some part of the farm with the bailiff, and the evenings were delicious in that quiet spot, when the new hayricks lately set up were sending forth odours to mingle with the breath of the rich old garden. One evening, while the sun was still above the horizon and burning in golden lamps among the great walnut boughs, Mr Bulstrode was pausing on horseback outside the front gate waiting for Caleb Garth, who had met him by appointment to give an opinion on a question of stable drainage, and was now advising the bailiff in the rick-yard.

Mr Bulstrode was conscious of being in a good spiritual frame and more than usually serene, under the influence of his innocent recreation. He was doctrinally convinced that there was a total absence of merit in himself; but that doctrinal conviction may be held without pain when the sense of demerit does not take a distinct shape in memory and revive the tingling of shame or the pang of remorse. Nay, it may be held with intense satisfaction when the depth of our sinning is but a measure for the depth of forgiveness, and clenching proof that we are peculiar instruments of the divine intention. The memory has as many moods as the temper, and shifts its scenery like a diorama. At this moment Mr Bulstrode felt as if the sunshine were all one with that of far-off evenings when he was a very young man and used to go out preaching beyond Highbury. And he would willingly have had that service of exhortation in prospect now. The texts were there still, and so was his own facility in expounding them. His brief reverie was interrupted by the return of Caleb Garth, who also was on horseback, and was just shaking his bridle before starting, when he exclaimed: 'Bless my heart! what's this fellow in black coming along the lane? He's like one of those men one sees about after the races.' Mr Bulstrode turned his horse and looked along the lane, but made no reply. The comer was our slight acquaintance Mr Raffles, whose appearance presented no other change than such as was due to a suit of black and a crape hat-band. He was within three yards of the horsemen now, and they could see the flash of recognition in his face as he whirled his stick upward, looking all the while at Mr Bulstrode, and at last exclaiming:: 'By Jove, Nick, it's you! I couldn't be mistaken, though the five-and-twenty years have played old Bogey with us both! How are you, eh? you didn't expect to see me here. Come, shake us by the hand.'

To say that Mr Raffles's manner was rather excited would be only one mode of saying that it was evening. Caleb Garth could see that there was a moment of struggle and hesitation in Mr Bulstrode, but it ended in his putting out his hand coldly to Raffles and saying: 'I did not indeed expect to see you in this remote country place.'

'Well, it belongs to a stepson of mine,' said Raffles, adjusting himself in a swaggering attitude. 'I came to see him here before. I'm not so surprised at seeing you, old fellow, because I picked up a letter – what you may call a providential thing. It's uncommonly fortunate I met you, though; for I don't care about seeing my stepson: he's not affectionate, and his poor mother's gone now. To tell the truth, I came out of love to you, Nick: I came to get your address, for – look here!' Raffles drew a crumpled paper from his pocket.

Almost any other man than Caleb Garth might have been tempted to linger on the spot for the sake of hearing all he could about a man whose acquaintance with Bulstrode seemed to imply passages in the banker's life so unlike anything that was known of him in Middlemarch that they must have the nature of a secret to pique curiosity. But Caleb was peculiar: certain human tendencies which are commonly strong were almost absent from his mind; and one of these was curiosity about personal affairs. Especially if there was anything discreditable to be found out concerning another man, Caleb preferred not to know it: and if he had to tell anybody under him that his evil doings were discovered, he was more embarrassed than the culprit. He now spurred his horse, and saying, 'I wish you good-evening, Mr Bulstrode; I must be getting home,' set off at a trot.

'You didn't put your full address to this letter,' Raffles continued. 'That was not like the first-rate man of business you used to be. "The Shrubs", – they may be anywhere: you live near at hand, eh? – have cut the London concern altogether perhaps turned country squire – have a rural mansion to invite me to. Lord, how many years it is ago! The old lady must have been dead a pretty long while – gone to glory without the pain of knowing how poor her daughter was, eh? But, by Jove! you're very pale and pasty, Nick. Come, if you're going home, I'll walk by your side.'

Mr Bulstrode's usual paleness had in fact taken an almost deathly hue. Five minutes before, the expanse of his life had been submerged in its evening sunshine which shone backward to its remembered morning: sin seemed to be a question of doctrine and inward penitence, humiliation an exercise of the closet, the bearing of his deeds a matter of private vision adjusted solely by spiritual relations and conceptions of the divine purposes. And now, as if by some hideous magic, this loud red figure had risen before him in unmanageable solidity, an incorporate past which had not entered into his imagination of chastisements. But Mr Bulstrode's thought was busy, and he was not a man to act or speak rashly.

'I was going home,' he said, 'but I can defer my ride a little. And you can, if you please, rest here.'

'Thank you,' said Raffles, making a grimace. 'I don't care now about seeing my stepson. I'd rather go home with you.'

'Your stepson, if Mr Rigg Featherstone was he, is here no longer. I am master here now.'

Raffles opened wide eyes, and gave a long whistle of surprise, before he said, 'Well, then, I've no objection. I've had enough walking from the coach-road. I never was much of a walker, or rider either. What I like is a smart vehicle and a spirited cob. I was always a little heavy in the saddle. What a pleasant surprise it must be to you to see me, old fellow!' he continued, as they turned towards the house. 'You don't say so; but you never took your luck heartily – you were always thinking of improving the occasion – you'd such a gift for improving your luck.'

Mr Raffles seemed greatly to enjoy his own wit, and swung his leg in a swaggering manner which was rather too much for his companion's judicious patience.

'If I remember rightly,' Mr Bulstrode observed, with chill anger, 'our acquaintance many years ago had not the sort of intimacy which you are now assuming, Mr Raffles. Any services you desire of me will be the more readily rendered if you will avoid a tone of familiarity which did not lie in our former intercourse, and can hardly be warranted by more than twenty years of separation.'

'You don't like being called Nick? Why, I always called you Nick in my heart, and though lost to sight, to memory dear. By Jove! my feelings have ripened for you like fine old cognac. I hope you've got some in the house now. Josh filled my flask well the last time.'

Mr Bulstrode had not yet fully learned that even the desire for cognac was not stronger in Raffles than the desire to torment, and that a hint of annoyance always served him as a fresh cue. But it was at least clear that further objection was useless, and Mr Bulstrode, in giving orders to the housekeeper for the accommodation to the guest, had a resolute air of quietude.

There was the comfort of thinking that this housekeeper had been in the service of Rigg also, and might accept the idea that Mr Bulstrode entertained Raffles merely as a friend of her former master. When there was food and drink spread before his visitor in the wainscoted parlour, and no witness in the room, Mr Bulstrode said: 'Your habits and mine are so different, Mr Raffles, that we can hardly enjoy each other's society. The wisest plan for both of us will there-fore be to part as soon as possible. Since you say that you wished to meet me, you probably considered that you had some business to transact with me. But under the circumstances I will invite you to remain here for the night, and I will myself ride over here early tomorrow morning – before breakfast, in fact, when I can receive any communication you have to make to me.'

'With all my heart,' said Raffles, 'this is a comfortable place, a little dull for a continuance, but I can put up with it for a night, with this good liquor and the prospect of seeing you again in the morning. You're a much better host than my stepson was; but Josh owed me a bit of a grudge for marrying his mother; and between you and me there was never anything but kindness.'

Mr Bulstrode, hoping that the peculiar mixture of joviality and sneering in Raffles's manner was a good deal the effect of drink, had determined to wait till he was quite sober before he spent more words upon him. But he rode home with a terribly lucid vision of the difficulty there would be in arranging any result that could be permanently counted on with this man. It was inevitable that he should wish to get rid of John Raffles, though his reappearance could not be regarded as lying outside the divine plan. The spirit of evil might have sent him to threaten Mr Bulstrode's subversion as an instrument of good; but the threat must have been permitted, and was a chastisement of a new kind. It was an hour of anguish for him very different from the hours in which his struggle had been securely private, and which had ended with a sense that his secret misdeeds were pardoned and his services accepted. Those misdeeds, even when committed – had they not been half sanctified by the singleness of his desire to devote himself and all he possessed to the furtherance of the divine scheme? And was he after all to become a mere stone of stumbling and a rock of offence? For who would understand the work within him? Who would not, when there was the pretext of casting disgrace upon him, confound his whole life and the truths he had espoused in one heap of obloquy?

In his closest meditations the lifelong habit of Mr Bulstrode's mind clad his most egoistic terrors in doctrinal references to superhuman ends. But even while we are talking and meditating about the earth's orbit and the solar system, what we feel and adjust our movements to is the stable earth and the changing day. And now within all the automatic succession of theoretic phrases – distinct and inmost as the shiver and the ache of oncoming fever when we are discussing abstract pain – was the forecast of disgrace in the presence of his neighbours and of his own wife. For the pain, as well as the public estimate of disgrace, depends on the amount of previous profession. To men who only aim at escaping felony, nothing short of the prisoner's dock is disgrace. But Mr Bulstrode had aimed at being an eminent Christian.

It was not more than half-past seven in the morning when he again reached Stone Court. The fine old place never looked more like a delightful home than at that moment; the great white lilies were in flower, the nasturtiums, their pretty leaves all silvered with dew, were running away over the low stone wall; the very noises all around had a heart of peace within them. But everything was spoiled for the owner as he walked on the gravel in front and awaited the descent of Mr Raffles, with whom he was condemned to breakfast.

It was not long before they were seated together in the wainscoted parlour over their tea and toast, which was as much as Raffles cared to take at that early hour. The difference between his morning and evening self was not so great as his companion had imagined that it might be; the delight in tormenting was perhaps even the stronger because his spirits were rather less highly pitched. Certainly his manners seemed more disagreeable by the morning light.

'As I have little time to spare, Mr Raffles,' said the banker, who could hardly do more than sip his tea and break his toast without eating it, 'I shall be obliged if you will mention at once the ground on which you wished to meet with me. I presume that you have a home elsewhere and will be glad to return to it.'

'Why, if a man has got any heart, doesn't he want to see an old friend, Nick? – I must call you Nick – we always did call you young Nick when we knew you meant to marry the old widow. Some said you had a handsome family likeness to old Nick, but that was your mother's fault, calling you Nicholas. Aren't you glad to see me again? I expected an invite to stay with you at some pretty place. My own establishment is broken up now my wife's dead. I've no particular attachment to any spot; I would as soon settle hereabout as anywhere.'

'May I ask why you returned from America? I considered that the strong wish you expressed to go there, when an adequate sum was furnished, was tantamount to an engagement that you would remain there for life.'

'Never knew that a wish to go to a place was the same thing as a wish to stay. But I did stay a matter of ten years; it didn't suit me to stay any longer. And I'm not going again, Nick.' Here Mr Raffles winked slowly as he looked at Mr Bulstrode.

'Do you wish to be settled in any business? What is your calling now?'

'Thank you, my calling is to enjoy myself as much as I can. I don't care about working any more. If I did anything it would be a little travelling in the tobacco line – or something of that sort, which takes a man into agreeable company. But not without an independence to fall back upon. That's what I want: I'm not so strong as I was, Nick, though I've got more colour than you. I want an independence.'

'That could be supplied to you, if you would engage to keep at a distance,' said Mr Bulstrode, perhaps with a little too much eagerness in his undertone.

'That must be as it suits my convenience,' said Raffles, coolly. 'I see no reason why I shouldn't make a few acquaintances hereabout. I'm not ashamed of myself as company for anybody. I dropped my portmanteau at the turnpike when I got down – change of linen – genuine – honour bright! – more than fronts and wristbands; and with this suit of mourning, straps and everything, I should do you credit among the nobs here.' Mr Raffles had pushed away his chair and looked down at himself, particularly at his straps. His chief intention was to annoy Bulstrode, but he really thought that his appearance now would produce a good effect, and that he was not only handsome and witty, but clad in a mourning style which implied solid connections.

'If you intend to rely on me in any way, Mr Raffles,' said Bulstrode, after a moment's pause, 'you will expect to meet my wishes.'

'Ah, to be sure,' said Raffles, with a mocking cordiality. 'Didn't I always do it? Lord, you made a pretty thing out of me, and I got but little. I've often thought since, I might have done better by telling the old woman that I'd found her daughter and her grandchild: it would have suited my feelings better; I've got a soft place in my heart. But you've buried the old lady by this time, I suppose – it's all one to her now. And you've got your fortune out of that profitable business which had such a blessing on it. You've taken to being a nob, buying land, being a country bashaw. Still in the Dissenting line, eh? Still godly? Or taken to the Church as more genteel?'

This time Mr Raffles's slow wink and slight protrusion of his tongue was worse than a nightmare, because it held the certitude that it was not a nightmare, but a waking misery. Mr Bulstrode felt a shuddering nausea, and did not speak, but was considering diligently whether he should not leave Raffles to do as he would, and simply defy him as a slanderer. The man would soon show himself disreputable enough to make people disbelieve him. 'But not when he tells any ugly-looking truth about you,' said discerning consciousness. And again: it seemed no wrong to keep Raffles at a distance, but Mr Bulstrode shrank from the direct falsehood of denying true statements. It was one thing to look back on forgiven sins, nay, to explain questionable conformity to lax customs, and another to enter deliberately on the necessity of falsehood.

But since Bulstrode did not speak, Raffles ran on, by way of using time to the utmost.

'I've not had such fine luck as you, by Jove! Things went confoundedly with me in New York; those Yankees are cool hands, and a man of gentlemanly feelings has no chance with them. I married when I came back – a nice woman in the tobacco trade – very fond of me – but the trade was restricted, as we say. She had been settled there a good many years by a friend; but there was a son too much in the case. Josh and I never hit it off. However, I made the most of the position, and I've always taken my glass in good company. It's been all on the square with me; I'm as open as the day. You won't take it ill of me that I didn't look you up before; I've got a complaint that makes me a little dilatory. I thought you were trading and praying away in London still, and didn't find you there. But you see I was sent to you, Nick – perhaps for a blessing to both of us.'

Mr Raffles ended with a jocose snuffle: no man felt his intellect more superior to religious cant. And if the cunning which calculates on the meanest feelings in men could be called intellect, he had his share, for under the blurting rallying tone with which he spoke to Bulstrode, there was an evident selection of state-ments, as if they had been so many moves at chess. Meanwhile Bulstrode had determined on his move, and he said, with gathered resolution: 'You will do well to reflect, Mr Raffles, that it is possible for a man to overreach himself in the effort to secure undue advantage. Although I am not in any way bound to you, I am willing to supply you with a regular annuity – in quarterly payments so long as you fulfil a promise to remain at a distance from this neighbourhood. It is in your power to choose. If you insist on remaining here, even for a short time, you will get nothing from me. I shall decline to know you.'

'Ha ha!' said Raffles, with an affected explosion, 'that reminds me of a droll dog of a thief who declined to know the constable.'

'Your allusions are lost on me, sir,' said Bulstrode, with white heat; 'the law has no hold on me either through your agency or any other.'

'You can't understand a joke, my good fellow. I only meant that I should never decline to know you. But let us be serious. Your quarterly payment won't quite suit me. I like my freedom.'

Here Raffles rose and stalked once or twice up and down the room, swinging his leg, and assuming an air of masterly meditation. At last he stopped opposite Bulstrode, and said, 'I'll tell you what! Give us a couple of hundreds – come, that's modest – and I'll go away – honour bright! – pick up my portmanteau and go away. But I shall not give up my liberty for a dirty annuity. I shall come and go where I like. Perhaps it may suit me to stay away, and correspond with a friend; perhaps not. Have you the money with you?'

'No, I have one hundred,' said Bulstrode, feeling the immediate riddance too great a relief to be rejected on the ground of future uncertainties. 'I will forward you the other if you will mention an address.'

'No, I'll wait here till you bring it,' said Raffles. 'I'll take a stroll, and have a snack, and you'll be back by that time.'

Mr Bulstrode's sickly body, shattered by the agitations he had gone through since the last evening, made him feel abjectly in the power of this loud invulner-able man. At that moment he snatched at a temporary repose to be won on any terms. He was rising to do what Raffles suggested, when the latter said, lifting up his finger as if with a sudden recollection: 'I did have another look after Sarah again, though I didn't tell you; I'd a tender conscience about that pretty young woman. I didn't find her, but I found out her husband's name, and I made a note of it. But hang it, I lost my pocketbook. However, if I heard it, I should know it again. I've got my faculties as if I was in my prime, but names wear out, by Jove! Sometimes I'm no better than a confounded tax-paper before the names are filled in. However, if I hear of her and her family, you shall know, Nick. You'd like to do something for her, now she's your stepdaughter.'

'Doubtless,' said Mr Bulstrode, with the usual steady look of his light-grey eyes; 'though that might reduce my power of assisting you.'

As he walked out of the room, Raffles winked slowly at his back, and then turned towards the window to watch the banker riding away – virtually at his command. His lips first curled with a smile and then opened with a short triumphant laugh.

'But what the deuce was the name?' he presently said, half aloud, scratching his head, and wrinkling his brows horizontally. He had not really cared or thought about this point of forgetfulness until it occurred to him in his invention of annoyances for Bulstrode.

'It began with L; it was almost all l's, I fancy,' he went on, with a sense that he was getting hold of the slippery name. But the hold was too slight, and he soon got tired of this mental chase; for few men were more impatient of private occupation or more in need of making themselves continually heard than Mr Raffles. He preferred using his time in pleasant conversation with the bailiff and the housekeeper, from whom he gathered as much as he wanted to know about Mr Bulstrode's position in Middlemarch.

After all, however, there was a dull space of time which needed relieving with bread and cheese and ale, and when he was seated alone with these resources in the wainscoted parlour, he suddenly slapped his knee, and exclaimed, 'Ladislaw!' That action of memory which he had tried to set going, and had abandoned in despair, had suddenly completed itself without conscious effort – a common experience, agreeable as a completed sneeze, even if the name remembered is of no value. Raffles immediately took out his pocketbook and wrote down the name, not because he expected to use it, but merely for the sake of not being at a loss if he ever did happen to want it. He was not going to tell Bulstrode: there was no actual good in telling, and to a mind like that of Mr Raffles there is always probable good in a secret.

He was satisfied with his present success, and by three o'clock that day he had taken up his portmanteau at the turnpike and mounted the coach, relieving Mr Bulstrode's eyes of an ugly black spot on the landscape at Stone Court, but not relieving him of the dread that the black spot might reappear and become inseparable even from the vision of his hearth.

BOOK SIX

The Widow and the Wife

Chapter 54

Negli occhi porta la mia donna Amore;
　Per che si fa gentil ciò ch'ella mira:
　Ov' ella passa, ogni uom ver lei si gira,
　E cui saluta fa tremar lo core.
Sicchè, bassando il viso, tutto smore,
　E d'ogni suo difetto allor sospira:
　Fuggon dinanzi a lei Superbia ed Ira:
　Aiutatemi, donne, a farle onore.
Ogni dolcezza, ogni pensiero umile
　Nasce nel core a chi parlar la sente;
　Ond' è beato chi prima la vide.
Quel ch'ella par quand' un poco sorride,
　Non si può dicer, nè tener a mente,
　Si è nuovo miracolo gentile.

DANTE, La Vita Nuova

By that delightful morning when the hayricks at Stone Court were scenting the air quite impartially, as if Mr Raffles had been a guest worthy of finest incense, Dorothea had again taken up her abode at Lowick Manor. After three months Freshitt had become rather oppressive: to sit like a model for St Catherine looking rapturously at Celia's baby would not do for many hours in the day, and to remain in that momentous babe's presence with persistent disregard was a course that could not have been tolerated in a childless sister. Dorothea would have been capable of carrying baby joyfully for a mile if there had been need, and of loving it the more tenderly for that labour; but to an aunt who does not recognise her infant nephew as Buddha, and has nothing to do for him but to admire, his behaviour is apt to appear monotonous, and the interest of watching him exhaustible.

This possibility was quite hidden from Celia, who felt that Dorothea's childless widowhood fell in quite prettily with the birth of little Arthur (baby was named after Mr Brooke).

'Dodo is just the creature not to mind about having anything of her own – children or anything!' said Celia to her husband. 'And if she had had a baby, it never could have been such a dear as Arthur. Could it, James?'

'Not if it had been like Casaubon,' said Sir James, conscious of some indirectness in his answer, and of holding a strictly private opinion as to the perfections of his first-born.

'No! just imagine? Really it was a mercy,' said Celia; 'and I think it is very nice for Dodo to be a widow. She can be just as fond of our baby as if it were her own, and she can have as many notions of her own as she likes.'

'It is a pity she was not a queen.' said the devout Sir James.

'But what should we have been then? We must have been something else,' said Celia, objecting to so laborious a flight of imagination. 'I like her better as she is.'

Hence, when she found that Dorothea was making arrangements for her final departure to Lowick, Celia raised her eyebrows with disappointment, and in her quiet unemphatic way shot a needle-arrow of sarcasm.

'What will you do at Lowick, Dodo? You say yourself there is nothing to be done there: everybody is so clean and well off, it makes you quite melancholy. And here you have been so happy going all about Tipton with Mr Garth into the worst backyards. And now uncle is abroad, you and Mr Garth can have it all your own way; and I am sure James does everything you tell him.'

'I shall often come here, and I shall see how baby grows all the better,' said Dorothea.

'But you will never see him washed,' said Celia: 'and that is quite the best part of the day.' She was almost pouting: it did seem to her very hard in Dodo to go away from the baby when she might stay.

'Dear Kitty, I will come and stay all night on purpose,' said Dorothea: 'but I want to be alone now, and in my own home. I wish to know the Farebrothers better, and to talk to Mr Farebrother about what there is to be done in Middle-march.'

Dorothea's native strength of will was no longer all converted into resolute submission. She had a great yearning to be at Lowick, and was simply deter-mined to go, not feeling bound to tell all her reasons. But everyone around her disapproved. Sir James was much pained, and offered that they should all migrate to Cheltenham for a few months with the sacred ark, otherwise called a cradle: at that period a man could hardly know what to propose if Cheltenham were rejected.

The Dowager Lady Chettam, just returned from a visit to her daughter in town, wished, at least, that Mrs Vigo should be written to, and invited to accept the office of companion to Mrs Casaubon: it was not credible that Dorothea as a young widow would think of living alone in the house at Lowick. Mrs Vigo had been reader and secretary to royal personages, and in point of knowledge and sentiments even Dorothea could have nothing to object to her.

Mrs Cadwallader said, privately, 'You will certainly go mad in that house alone, my dear. You will see visions. We have all got to exert ourselves a little to keep sane, and call things by the same names as other people call them by. To be sure, for younger sons and women who have no money, it is a sort of provision to go mad: they are taken care of then. But you must not run into that. I dare say you are a little bored here with our good dowager; but think what a bore you might become yourself to your fellow-creatures if you were always playing tragedy queen and taking things sublimely. Sitting alone in that library at Lowick you may fancy yourself ruling the weather; you must get a few people round you who wouldn't believe you if you told them. That is a good lowering medicine.'

'I never called everything by the same name that all the people about me did,' said Dorothea, stoutly.

'But I suppose you have found out your mistake, my dear,' said Mrs Cadwallader, 'and that is a proof of sanity.'

Dorothea was aware of the sting, but it did not hurt her. 'No,' she said, 'I still think that the greater part of the world is mistaken about many things. Surely one may be sane and yet think so, since the greater part of the world has often had to come round from its opinion.'

Mrs Cadwallader said no more on that point to Dorothea, but to her husband she remarked, 'It will be well for her to marry again as soon as it is proper, if one could get her among the right people. Of course the Chettams would not wish it. But I see clearly a husband is the best thing to keep her in order. If we were not so poor I would invite Lord Triton. He will be marquis someday, and there is no denying that she would make a good marchioness: she looks handsomer than ever in her mourning.'

'My dear Elinor, do let the poor woman alone. Such contrivances are of no use,' said the easy Rector.

'No use? How are matches made, except by bringing men and women together? And it is a shame that his uncle should have run away and shut up the Grange just now. There ought to be plenty of eligible matches invited to Freshitt and the Grange. Lord Triton is precisely the man: full of plans for making the people happy in a soft-headed sort of way. That would just suit Mrs Casaubon.'

'Let Mrs Casaubon choose for herself, Elinor.'

'That is the nonsense you wise men talk! How can she choose if she has no variety to choose from? A woman's choice usually means taking the only man she can get. Mark my words, Humphrey. If her friends don't exert themselves, there will be a worse business than the Casaubon business yet.'

'For heaven's sake don't touch on that topic, Elinor! It is a very sore point with Sir James. He would be deeply offended if you entered on it to him unnecessarily.'

'I have never entered on it,' said Mrs Cadwallader, opening her hands. 'Celia told me all about the will at the beginning, without any asking of mine.'

'Yes, yes; but they want the thing hushed up, and I understand that the young fellow is going out of the neighbourhood.'

Mrs Cadwallader said nothing, but gave her husband three significant nods, with a very sarcastic expression in her dark eyes.

Dorothea quietly persisted in spite of remonstrance and persuasion. So by the end of June the shutters were all opened at Lowick Manor, and the morning gazed calmly into the library, shining on the rows of notebooks as it shines on the weary waste planted with huge stones, the mute memorial of a forgotten faith; and the evening laden with roses entered silently into the blue-green boudoir where Dorothea chose oftenest to sit. At first she walked into every room, questioning the eighteen months of her married life, and carrying on her thoughts as if they were a speech to be heard by her husband. Then, she lingered in the library and could not be at rest till she had carefully ranged all the notebooks as she imagined that he would wish to see them, in orderly sequence. The pity which had been the restraining compelling motive in her life with him still clung about his image, even while she remonstrated with him in indignant thought and told him that he was unjust. One little act of hers may perhaps be smiled at as superstitious. The 'Synoptical Tabulation for the use of Mrs Casaubon', she carefully enclosed and sealed, writing within the envelope:

I could not use it. Do you not see now that I could not submit my soul to yours, by working hopelessly at what I have no belief in?

DOROTHEA

Then she deposited the paper in her own desk.

That silent colloquy was perhaps only the more earnest because underneath and through it all there was always the deep longing which had really determined her to come to Lowick. The longing was to see Will Ladislaw. She did not know any good that could come of their meeting: she was helpless; her hands had been tied from making up to him for any unfairness in his lot. But her soul thirsted to see him. How could it be otherwise? If a princess in the days of enchantment had seen a four-footed creature from among those which live in herds come to her once and again with a human gaze which rested upon her with choice and beseeching, what would she think of in her journeying, what would she look for when the herds passed her? Surely for the gaze which had found her, and which she would know again. Life would be no better than candlelight tinsel and daylight rubbish if our spirits were not touched by what has been, to issues of longing and constancy. It was true that Dorothea wanted to know the Farebrothers better, and especially to talk to the new rector, but also true that remembering what Lydgate had told her about Will Ladislaw and little Miss Noble, she counted on Will's coming to Lowick to see the Farebrother family. The very first Sunday, *before* she entered the church, she saw him as she had seen him the last time she was there, alone in the clergyman's pew; but *when* she entered his figure was gone.

In the weekdays when she went to see the ladies at the Rectory, she listened in vain for some word that might fall about Will; but it seemed to her that Mrs Farebrother talked of everyone else in the neighbourhood and out of it.

'Probably some of Mr Farebrother's Middlemarch hearers may follow him to Lowick sometimes. Do you not think so?' said Dorothea, rather despising herself for having a secret motive in asking the question.

'If they are wise they will, Mrs Casaubon,' said the old lady. 'I see that you set a right value on my son's preaching. His grandfather on my side was an excellent clergyman, but his father was in the law – most exemplary and honest nevertheless, which is a reason for our never being rich. They say Fortune is a woman and capricious. But sometimes she is a good woman and gives to those who merit, which has been the case with you, Mrs Casaubon, who have given a living to my son.'

Mrs Farebrother recurred to her knitting with a dignified satisfaction in her neat little effort at oratory, but this was not what Dorothea wanted to hear. Poor thing! she did not even know whether Will Ladislaw was still at Middlemarch, and there was no one whom she dared to ask, unless it were Lydgate. But just now she could not see Lydgate without sending for him or going to seek him. Perhaps Will Ladislaw, having heard of that strange ban against him left by Mr Casaubon, had felt it better that he and she should not meet again, and perhaps she was wrong to wish for a meeting that others might find many good reasons against. Still 'I do wish it' came at the end of those wise reflections as naturally as a sob after holding the breath. And the meeting did happen, but in a formal way quite unexpected by her.

One morning, about eleven, Dorothea was seated in her boudoir with a map of the land attached to the manor and other papers before her, which were to help her in making an exact statement for herself of her income and affairs. She had not yet applied herself to her work, but was seated with her hands folded on her lap, looking out along the avenue of limes to the distant fields. Every leaf was at rest in the sunshine, the familiar scene was changeless, and seemed to represent the prospect of her life, full of motiveless ease – motiveless, if her own energy could not seek out reasons for ardent action. The widow's cap of those times made an oval frame for the face, and had a crown standing up; the dress was an experiment in the utmost laying on of crape; but this heavy solemnity of clothing made her face look all the younger, with its recovered bloom, and the sweet, enquiring candour of her eyes.

Her reverie was broken by Tantripp, who came to say that Mr Ladislaw was below, and begged permission to see Madam if it were not too early.

'I will see him,' said Dorothea, rising immediately. 'Let him be shown into the drawing-room.'

The drawing-room was the most neutral room in the house to her – the one least associated with the trials of her married life: the damask matched the woodwork, which was all white and gold; there were two tall mirrors and tables with nothing on them – in brief, it was a room where you had no reason for sitting in one place rather than in another. It was below the boudoir, and had also a bow-window looking out on the avenue. But when Pratt showed Will Ladislaw into it the window was open; and a winged visitor, buzzing in and out now and then without minding the furniture, made the room look less formal and uninhabited.

'Glad to see you here again, sir,' said Pratt, lingering to adjust a blind.

'I am only come to say goodbye, Pratt,' said Will, who wished even the butler to know that he was too proud to hang about Mrs Casaubon now she was a rich widow.

'Very sorry to hear it, sir,' said Pratt, retiring. Of course, as a servant who was to be told nothing, he knew the fact of which Ladislaw was still ignorant, and had drawn his inferences indeed, had not differed from his betrothed Tantripp when she said, 'Your master was as jealous as a fiend – and no reason. Madam would look higher than Mr Ladislaw, else I don't know her. Mrs Cadwallader's maid says there's a lord coming who is to marry her when the mourning's over.'

There were not many moments for Will to walk about with his hat in his hand before Dorothea entered. The meeting was very different from that first meeting in Rome when Will had been embarrassed and Dorothea calm. This time he felt miserable but determined, while she was in a state of agitation which could not be hidden. Just outside the door she had felt that this longed-for meeting was after all too difficult, and when she saw Will advancing towards her, the deep blush which was rare in her came with painful suddenness. Neither of them knew how it was, but neither of them spoke. She gave her hand for a moment, and then they went to sit down near the window, she on one settee and he on another opposite. Will was peculiarly uneasy: it seemed to him not like Dorothea that the mere fact of her being a widow should cause such a change in her manner of receiving him; and he knew of no other condition which could have affected their previous relation to each other except that, as his imagination at once told him, her friends might have been poisoning her mind with their suspicions of him.

'I hope I have not presumed too much in calling,' said Will; 'I could not bear to leave the neighbourhood and begin a new life without seeing you to say goodbye.'

'Presumed? Surely not. I should have thought it unkind if you had not wished to see me,' said Dorothea, her habit of speaking with perfect genuineness asserting itself through all her uncertainty and agitation. 'Are you going away immediately?'

'Very soon, I think. I intend to go to town and eat my dinners as a barrister, since, they say, that is the preparation for all public business. There will be a great deal of political work to be done by and by, and I mean to try and do some of it. Other men have managed to win an honourable position for themselves without family or money.'

'And that will make it all the more honourable,' said Dorothea, ardently. 'Besides, you have so many talents. I have heard from my uncle how well you speak in public, so that everyone is sorry when you leave off, and how clearly you can explain things. And you care that justice should be done to everyone. I am so glad. When we were in Rome, I thought you only cared for poetry and art, and the things that adorn life for us who are well off. But now I know you think about the rest of the world.'

While she was speaking Dorothea had lost her personal embarrassment and had become like her former self. She looked at Will with a direct glance, full of delighted confidence.

'You approve of my going away for years, then, and never coming here again till I have made myself of some mark in the world?' said Will, trying hard to reconcile the utmost pride with the utmost effort to get an expression of strong feeling from Dorothea.

She was not aware how long it was before she answered. She had turned her head and was looking out of the window on the rose-bushes, which seemed to have in them the summers of all the years when Will would be away. This was not judicious behaviour. But Dorothea never thought of studying her manners: she thought only of bowing to a sad necessity which divided her from Will. Those first words of his about his intentions had seemed to make everything clear to her: he knew, she supposed, all about Mr Casaubon's final conduct in relation to him, and it had come to him with the same sort of shock as to herself. He had never felt more than friendship for her – had never had anything in his mind to justify what she felt to be her husband's outrage on the feelings of both: and that friendship he still felt. Something which may be called an inward silent sob had gone on in Dorothea before she said with a pure voice, just trembling in the last words as if only from its liquid flexibility: 'Yes, it must be right for you to do as you say. I shall be very happy when I hear that you have made your value felt. But you must have patience. It will perhaps be a long while.'

Will never quite knew how it was that he saved himself from falling down at her feet, when the 'long while' came forth with its gentle tremor. He used to say that the horrible hue and surface of her crape dress was most likely the sufficient controlling force. He sat still, however, and only said: 'I shall never hear from you. And you will forget all about me.'

'No,' said Dorothea, 'I shall never forget you. I have never forgotten anyone whom I once knew. My life has never been crowded, and seems not likely to be so. And I have a great deal of space for memory at Lowick, haven't I?' She smiled.

'Good God!' Will burst out passionately, rising with his hat still in his hand, and walking to a marble table, where he suddenly turned and leaned his back against it. The blood had mounted to his face and neck, and he looked almost angry. It had seemed to him as if they were like two creatures slowly turning to marble in each other's presence, while their hearts were conscious and their eyes were yearning. But there was no help for it. It should never be true of him that in this meeting to which he had come with bitter resolution he had ended by a confession which might be interpreted into asking for her fortune. Moreover, it was actually true that he was fearful of the effect which such confessions might have on Dorothea herself.

She looked at him from that distance in some trouble, imagining that there might have been an offence in her words. But all the while there was a current of thought in her about his probable want of money, and the impossibility of her helping him. If her uncle had been at home, something might have been done through him! It was this preoccupation with the hardship of Will's wanting money, while she had what ought to have been his share, which led her to say, seeing that he remained silent and looked away from her: 'I wonder whether you would like to have that miniature which hangs upstairs – I mean that beautiful miniature of your grandmother. I think it is not right for me to keep it, if you would wish to have it. It is wonderfully like you.'

'You are very good,' said Will, irritably. 'No; I don't mind about it. It is not very consoling to have one's own likeness. It would be more consoling if others wanted to have it.'

'I thought you would like to cherish her memory – I thought – ' Dorothea broke off in an instant, her imagination suddenly warning her away from Aunt Julia's history – 'you would surely like to have the miniature as a family memorial.'

'Why should I have that, when I have nothing else! A man with only a portmanteau for his stowage must keep his memorials in his head.'

Will spoke at random: he was merely venting his petulance: it was a little too exasperating to have his grandmother's portrait offered him at that moment. But to Dorothea's feeling his words had a peculiar sting. She rose and said with a touch of indignation as well as hauteur: 'You are much the happier of us two, Mr Ladislaw, to have nothing.'

Will was startled. Whatever the words might be, the tone seemed like a dismissal; and quitting his leaning posture, he walked a little way towards her. Their eyes met, but with a strange questioning gravity. Something was keeping their minds aloof, and each was left to conjecture what was in the other. Will had really never thought of himself as having a claim of inheritance on the property which was held by Dorothea, and would have required a narrative to make him understand her present feeling.

'I never felt it a misfortune to have nothing till now,' he said. 'But poverty may be as bad as leprosy, if it divides us from what we most care for.'

The words cut Dorothea to the heart, and made her relent. She answered in a tone of sad fellowship.

'Sorrow comes in so many ways. Two years ago I had no notion of that – I mean of the unexpected way in which trouble comes, and ties our hands, and makes us silent when we long to speak. I used to despise women a little for not shaping their lives more, and doing better things. I was very fond of doing as I liked, but I have almost given it up,' she ended, smiling playfully.

'I have not given up doing as I like, but I can very seldom do it,' said Will. He was standing two yards from her with his mind full of contradictory desires and resolves – desiring some unmistakable proof that she loved him, and yet dreading the position into which such a proof might bring him. 'The thing one most longs for may be surrounded with conditions that would be intolerable.'

At this moment Pratt entered and said, 'Sir James Chettam is in the library, madam.'

'Ask Sir James to come in here,' said Dorothea, immediately. It was as if the same electric shock had passed through her and Will. Each of them felt proudly resistant, and neither looked at the other, while they awaited Sir James's entrance.

After shaking hands with Dorothea, he bowed as slightly as possible to Ladislaw, who repaid the slightness exactly, and then going towards Dorothea, said: 'I must say goodbye, Mrs Casaubon; and probably for a long while.'

Dorothea put out her hand and said her goodbye cordially. The sense that Sir James was depreciating Will, and behaving rudely to him, roused her resolution and dignity: there was no touch of confusion in her manner. And when Will had left the room, she looked with such calm self-possession at Sir James, saying, 'How is Celia?' that he was obliged to behave as if nothing had annoyed him. And what would be the use of behaving otherwise! Indeed, Sir James shrank with so much dislike from the association even in thought of Dorothea with Ladislaw as her possible lover, that he would himself have wished to avoid an outward show of displeasure which would have recognised the disagreeable possibility. If anyone had asked him why he shrank in that way, I am not sure that he would at first have said anything fuller or more precise than 'that Ladislaw!' – though on reflection he might have urged that Mr Casaubon's codicil, barring Dorothea's marriage with Will, except under a penalty, was enough to cast unfitness over any relation at all between them. His aversion was all the stronger because he felt himself unable to interfere.

But Sir James was a power in a way unguessed by himself. Entering at that moment, he was an incorporation of the strongest reasons through which Will's pride became a repellent force, keeping him asunder from Dorothea.

Chapter 55

> Hath she her faults? I would you had them too.
> They are the fruity must of soundest wine
> Or say, they are regenerating fire
> Such as hath turned the dense black element
> Into a crystal pathway for the sun.

If youth is the season of hope, it is often so only in the sense that our elders are hopeful about us; for no age is so apt as youth to think its emotions, partings, and resolves are the last of their kind. Each crisis seems final, simply because it is new. We are told that the oldest inhabitants in Peru do not cease to be agitated by the earthquakes, but they probably see beyond each shock, and reflect that there are plenty more to come.

To Dorothea, still in that time of youth when the eyes with their long full lashes look out after their rain of tears unsoiled and unwearied as a freshly-opened passionflower, that morning's parting with Will Ladislaw seemed to be the close of their personal relations. He was going away into the distance of unknown years, and if ever he came back he would be another man. The actual state of his mind – his proud resolve to give the lie beforehand to any suspicion that he would play the needy adventurer seeking a rich woman – lay quite out of her imagination, and she had interpreted all his behaviour easily enough by her supposition that Mr Casaubon's codicil seemed to him, as it did to her, a gross and cruel interdict on any active friendship between them. Their young delight in speaking to each other, and saying what no one else would care to hear, was for ever ended, and become a treasure of the past. For this very reason she dwelt on it without inward check. That unique happiness too was dead, and in its shadowed silent chamber she might vent the passionate grief which she herself wondered at. For the first time she took down the miniature from the wall and kept it before her, liking to blend the woman who had been too hardly judged with the grandson whom her own heart and judgement defended. Can anyone who has rejoiced in woman's tenderness think it a reproach to her that she took the little oval picture in her palm and made a bed for it there, and leaned her cheek upon it, as if that would soothe the creature who had suffered unjust condemnation? She did not know then that it was Love who had come to her briefly as in a dream before awaking, with the hues of morning on his wings – that it was Love to whom she was sobbing her farewell as his image was banished by the blameless rigour of irresistible day. She only felt that there was something irrevocably amiss and lost in her lot, and her thoughts about the future were the more readily shapen into resolve. Ardent souls, ready to construct their coming lives, are apt to commit themselves to the fulfilment of their own visions.

One day that she went to Freshitt to fulfil her promise of staying all night and seeing baby washed, Mrs Cadwallader came to dine, the Rector being gone on a fishing excursion. It was a warm evening, and even in the delightful drawing-room, where the fine old turf sloped from the open window towards a lilied pool and well-planted mounds, the heat was enough to make Celia in her white muslin and light curls reflect with pity on what Dodo must feel in her black dress and close cap. But this was not until some episodes with baby were over, and had left her mind at leisure. She had seated herself and taken up a fan for some time before she said, in her quiet guttural: 'Dear Dodo, do throw off that cap. I am sure your dress must make you feel ill.'

'I am so used to the cap – it has become a sort of shell,' said Dorothea, smiling. 'I feel rather bare and exposed when it is off.'

'I *must* see you without it; it makes us all warm,' said Celia, throwing down her fan, and going to Dorothea. It was a pretty picture to see this little lady in white muslin unfastening the widow's cap from her more majestic sister, and tossing it on to a chair. Just as the coils and braids of dark-brown hair had been set free, Sir James entered the room. He looked at the released head, and said, 'Ah!' in a tone of satisfaction.

'It was I who did it, James,' said Celia. 'Dodo need not make such a slavery of her mourning; she need not wear that cap any more among her friends.'

'My dear Celia,' said Lady Chettam, 'a widow must wear her mourning at least a year.'

'Not if she marries again before the end of it,' said Mrs Cadwallader, who had some pleasure in startling her good friend the Dowager. Sir James was annoyed, and leaned forward to play with Celia's Maltese dog.

'That is very rare, I hope,' said Lady Chettam, in a tone intended to guard against such events. 'No friend of ours ever committed herself in that way except Mrs Beevor, and it was very painful to Lord Grinsell when she did so. Her first husband was objectionable, which made it the greater wonder. And severely she was punished for it. They said Captain Beevor dragged her about by the hair, and held up loaded pistols at her.'

'Oh, if she took the wrong man!' said Mrs Cadwallader, who was in a decidedly wicked mood. 'Marriage is always bad then, first or second. Priority is a poor recommendation in a husband if he has got no other. I would rather have a good second husband than an indifferent first.'

'My dear, your clever tongue runs away with you,' said Lady Chettam. 'I am sure you would be the last woman to marry again prematurely, if our dear Rector were taken away.'

'Oh, I make no vows; it might be a necessary economy. It is lawful to marry again, I suppose; else we might as well be Hindus instead of Christians. Of course if a woman accepts the wrong man, she must take the consequences, and one who does it twice over deserves her fate. But if she can marry blood, beauty, and bravery – the sooner the better.'

'I think the subject of our conversation is very ill-chosen,' said Sir James, with a look of disgust. 'Suppose we change it.'

'Not on my account, Sir James,' said Dorothea, determined not to lose the opportunity of freeing herself from certain oblique references to excellent matches. 'If you are speaking on my behalf, I can assure you that no question can be more indifferent and impersonal to me than second marriage. It is no more to me than if you talked of women going fox-hunting: whether it is admirable in them or not, I shall not follow them. Pray let Mrs Cadwallader amuse herself on that subject as much as on any other.'

'My dear Mrs Casaubon,' said Lady Chettam, in her stateliest way, 'you do not, I hope, think there was any allusion to you in my mentioning Mrs Beevor. It was only an instance that occurred to me. She was stepdaughter to Lord Grinsell: he married Mrs Teveroy for his second wife. There could be no possible allusion to you.'

'Oh no,' said Celia. 'Nobody chose the subject; it all came out of Dodo's cap. Mrs Cadwallader only said what was quite true. A woman could not be married in a widow's cap, James.'

'Hush, my dear!' said Mrs Cadwallader. 'I will not offend again. I will not even refer to Dido or Zenobia. Only what are we to talk about? I, for my part, object to the discussion of Human Nature, because that is the nature of rectors' wives.'

Later in the evening, after Mrs Cadwallader was gone, Celia said privately to Dorothea, 'Really, Dodo, taking your cap off made you like yourself again in more ways than one. You spoke up just as you used to do, when anything was said to displease you. But I could hardly make out whether it was James that you thought wrong, or Mrs Cadwallader.'

'Neither,' said Dorothea. 'James spoke out of delicacy to me, but he was mistaken in supposing that I minded what Mrs Cadwallader said. I should only mind if there were a law obliging me to take any piece of blood and beauty that she or anybody else recommended.'

'But you know, Dodo, if you ever did marry, it would be all the better to have blood and beauty,' said Celia, reflecting that Mr Casaubon had not been richly endowed with those gifts, and that it would be well to caution Dorothea in time.

'Don't be anxious, Kitty; I have quite other thoughts about my life. I shall never marry again,' said Dorothea, touching her sister's chin, and looking at her with indulgent affection. Celia was nursing her baby, and Dorothea had come to say good-night to her.

'Really – quite?' said Celia. 'Not anybody at all – if he were very wonderful indeed?'

Dorothea shook her head slowly. 'Not anybody at all. I have delightful plans. I should like to take a great deal of land, and drain it, and make a little colony, where everybody should work, and all the work should be done well. I should know every one of the people and be their friend. I am going to have great consultations with Mr Garth: he can tell me almost everything I want to know.'

'Then you *will* be happy, if you have a plan, Dodo,' said Celia. 'Perhaps little Arthur will like plans when he grows up, and then he can help you.'

Sir James was informed that same night that Dorothea was really quite set against marrying anybody at all, and was going to take to 'all sorts of plans', just like what she used to have. Sir James made no remark. To his secret feeling, there was something repulsive in a woman's second marriage, and no match would prevent him from feeling it a sort of desecration for Dorothea. He was aware that the world would regard such a sentiment as preposterous, especially in relation to a woman of one-and-twenty; the practice of 'the world' being to treat of a young widow's second marriage as certain and probably near, and to smile with meaning if the widow acts accordingly. But if Dorothea did choose to espouse her solitude, he felt that the resolution would well become her.

Chapter 56

How happy is he born and taught,
That serveth not another's will?
Whose armour is his honest thought,
And simple truth his only skill?

This man is freed from servile bands
Of hope to rise, or fear to fall:
Lord of himself, though not of lands,
And having nothing, yet hath all.

SIR HENRY WOTTON

Dorothea's confidence in Caleb Garth's knowledge, which had begun on her hearing that he approved of her cottages, had grown fast during her stay at Freshitt, Sir James having induced her to take rides over the two estates in company with himself and Caleb, who quite returned her admiration, and told his wife that Mrs Casaubon had a head for business most uncommon in a woman. It must be remembered that by 'business' Caleb never meant money transactions, but the skilful application of labour.

'Most uncommon!' repeated Caleb. 'She said a thing I often used to think myself when I was a lad: – "Mr Garth, I should like to feel, if I lived to be old, that I had improved a great piece of land and built a great many good cottages, because the work is of a healthy kind while it is being done, and after it is done, men are the better for it." Those were the very words: she sees into things in that way.'

'But womanly, I hope,' said Mrs Garth, half suspecting that Mrs Casaubon might not hold the true principle of subordination.

'Oh, you can't think!' said Caleb, shaking his head. 'You would like to hear her speak, Susan. She speaks in such plain words, and a voice like music. Bless me! it reminds me of bits in the *Messiah* – "and straightway there appeared a multitude of the heavenly host, praising God and saying"; it has a tone with it that satisfies your ear.'

Caleb was very fond of music, and when he could afford it went to hear an oratorio that came within his reach, returning from it with a profound reverence for this mighty structure of tones, which made him sit meditatively, looking on the floor and throwing much unutterable language into his outstretched hands.

With this good understanding between them, it was natural that Dorothea asked Mr Garth to undertake any business connected with the three farms and the numerous tenements attached to Lowick Manor; indeed, his expectation of getting work for two was being fast fulfilled. As he said, 'Business breeds'. And one form of business which was beginning to breed just then was the construction of railways. A projected line was to run through Lowick parish where the cattle had hitherto grazed in a peace unbroken by astonishment; and thus it happened that the infant struggles of the railway system entered into the affairs of Caleb Garth, and determined the course of this history with regard to two persons who were dear to him.

The submarine railway may have its difficulties; but the bed of the sea is not divided among various landed proprietors with claims for damages not only measurable but sentimental. In the hundred to which Middlemarch belonged railways were as exciting a topic as the Reform Bill or the imminent horrors of Cholera, and those who held the most decided views on the subject were women and landholders. Women both old and young regarded travelling by steam as presumptuous and dangerous, and argued against it by saying that nothing should induce them to get into a railway carriage; while proprietors, differing from each other in their arguments as much as Mr Solomon Featherstone differed from Lord Medlicote, were yet unanimous in the opinion that in selling land, whether to the Enemy of mankind or to a company obliged to purchase, these pernicious agencies must be made to pay a very high price to landowners for permission to injure mankind.

But the slower wits, such as Mr Solomon and Mrs Waule, who both occupied land of their own, took a long time to arrive at this conclusion, their minds halting at the vivid conception of what it would be to cut the Big Pasture in two, and turn it into three-cornered bits, which would be 'nohow'; while accommodation-bridges and high payments were remote and incredible.

'The cows will all cast their calves, Brother,' said Mrs Waule, in a tone of deep melancholy, 'if the railway comes across the Near Close; and I shouldn't wonder at the mare too, if she was in foal. It's a poor tale if a widow's property is to be spaded away, and the law say nothing to it. What's to hinder 'em from cutting right and left if they begin? It's well known, I can't fight.'

'The best way would be to say nothing, and set somebody on to send 'em away with a flea in their ear, when they came spying and measuring,' said Solomon. 'Folks did that about Brassing, by what I can understand. It's all a pretence, if the truth was known, about their being forced to take one way. Let 'em go cutting in another parish. And I don't believe in any pay to make amends for bringing a lot of ruffians to trample your crops. Where's a company's pocket?'

'Brother Peter, God forgive him, got money out of a company,' said Mrs Waule. 'But that was for the manganese. That wasn't for railways to blow you to pieces right and left.'

'Well, there's this to be said, Jane,' Mr Solomon concluded, lowering his voice in a cautious manner – 'the more spokes we put in their wheel, the more they'll pay us to let 'em go on, if they must come whether or not.'

This reasoning of Mr Solomon's was perhaps less thorough than he imagined, his cunning bearing about the same relation to the course of railways as the cunning of a diplomatist bears to the general chill or catarrh of the solar system. But he set about acting on his views in a thoroughly diplomatic manner, by stimulating suspicion. His side of Lowick was the most remote from the village, and the houses of the labouring people were either lone cottages or were collected in a hamlet called Frick, where a water-mill and some stone-pits made a little centre of slow, heavy-shouldered industry.

In the absence of any precise idea as to what railways were, public opinion in Frick was against them; for the human mind in that grassy corner had not the proverbial tendency to admire the unknown, holding rather that it was likely to be against the poor man, and that suspicion was the only wise attitude with regard to it. Even the rumour of Reform had not yet excited any millennial expectations in Frick, there being no definite promise in it, as of gratuitous grains to fatten Hiram Ford's pig, or of a publican at the 'Weights and Scales' who would brew beer for nothing, or of an offer on the part of the three neighbouring farmers to raise wages during winter. And without distinct good of this kind in its promises, Reform seemed on a footing with the bragging of pedlars, which was a hint for distrust to every knowing person. The men of Frick were not ill-fed, and were less given to fanaticism than to a strong muscular suspicion; less inclined to believe that they were peculiarly cared for by heaven, than to regard heaven itself as rather disposed to take them in – a disposition observable in the weather.

Thus the mind of Frick was exactly of the sort for Mr Solomon Featherstone to work upon, he having more plenteous ideas of the same order, with a suspicion of heaven and earth which was better fed and more entirely at leisure. Solomon was overseer of the roads at that time, and on his slow-paced cob often took his rounds by Frick to look at the workmen getting the stones there, pausing with a mysterious deliberation, which might have misled you into supposing that he had some other reason for staying than the mere want of impulse to move. After looking for a long while at any work that was going on, he would raise his eyes a little and look at the horizon; finally he would shake his bridle, touch his horse with the whip, and get it to move slowly onward. The hour-hand of a clock was quick by comparison with Mr Solomon, who had an agreeable sense that he could afford to be slow. He was in the habit of pausing for a cautious, vaguely-designing chat with every hedger or ditcher on his way, and was especially willing to listen even to news which he had heard before, feeling himself at an advantage over all narrators in partially disbelieving them. One day, however, he got into a dialogue with Hiram Ford, a waggoner, in which he himself contributed information. He wished to know whether Hiram had seen fellows with staves and instruments spying about: they called themselves railroad people, but there was no telling what they were, or what they meant to do. The least they pretended was that they were going to cut Lowick Parish into sixes and sevens.

'Why, there'll be no stirrin' from one pla–ace to another,' said Hiram, thinking of his waggon and horses.

'Not a bit,' said Mr Solomon. 'And cutting up fine land such as this parish! Let 'em go into Tipton, say I. But there's no knowing what there is at the bottom of it. Traffick is what they put for'ard; but it's to do harm to the land and the poor man in the long-run.'

'Why, they're Lunnon chaps, I reckon,' said Hiram, who had a dim notion of London as a centre of hostility to the country.

'Ay, to be sure. And in some parts against Brassing, by what I've heard say, the folks fell on 'em when they were spying and broke their peep-holes as they carry, and drove 'em away, so as they knew better than come again.'

'It war good foon, I'd be bound,' said Hiram, whose fun was much restricted by circumstances.

'Well, I wouldn't meddle with 'em myself,' said Solomon. 'But some say this country's seen its best days, and the sign is, as it's being overrun with these fellows trampling right and left, and wanting to cut it up into railways: and all for the big traffic to swallow up the little, so as there shan't be a team left on the land, nor a whip to crack.'

'I'll crack *my* whip about their ear'n, afore they bring it to that, though,' said Hiram, while Mr Solomon, shaking his bridle, moved onward.

Nettle-seed needs no digging. The ruin of this countryside by railroads was discussed, not only at the 'Weights and Scales', but in the hayfield, where the muster of working hands gave opportunities for talk such as were rarely had through the rural year.

One morning, not long after that interview between Mr Farebrother and Mary Garth, in which she confessed to him her feeling for Fred Vincy, it happened that her father had some business which took him to Yoddrell's farm in the direction of Frick: it was to measure and value an outlying piece of land belonging to Lowick Manor, which Caleb expected to dispose of advantageously for Dorothea (it must be confessed that his bias was towards getting the best possible terms from railroad companies). He put up his gig at Yoddrell's, and in walking with his assistant and measuring-chain to the scene of his work, he encountered the party of the company's agents, who were adjusting their spirit-level. After a little chat he left them, observing that by and by they would reach him again where he was going to measure. It was one of those grey mornings after light rains, which become delicious about twelve o'clock, when the clouds part a little, and the scent of the earth is sweet along the lanes and by the hedgerows.

The scent would have been sweeter to Fred Vincy, who was coming along the lanes on horseback, if his mind had not been worried by unsuccessful efforts to imagine what he was to do, with his father on one side expecting him straight-way to enter the Church, with Mary on the other threatening to forsake him if he did enter it, and with the working-day world showing no eager need what-ever of a young gentleman without capital and generally unskilled. It was the harder to Fred's disposition because his father, satisfied that he was no longer rebellious, was in good humour with him, and had sent him on this pleasant ride to see after some greyhounds. Even when he had fixed on what he should do, there would be the task of telling his father. But it must be admitted that the fixing, which had to come first, was the more difficult task: – what secular avocation on earth was there for a young man (whose friends could not get him an 'appointment') which was at once gentlemanly, lucrative, and to be followed without special knowledge? Riding along the lanes by Frick in this mood, and slackening his pace while he reflected whether he should venture to go round by Lowick Parsonage to call on Mary, he could see over the hedges from one field to another. Suddenly a noise roused his attention, and on the far side of a field on his left hand he could see six or seven men in smock-frocks with hay-forks in their hands making an offensive approach towards the four railway agents who were facing them, while Caleb Garth and his assistant were hastening across the field to join the threatened group. Fred, delayed a few moments by having to find the gate, could not gallop up to the spot before the party in smock-frocks, whose work of turning the hay had not been too pressing after swallowing their midday beer, were driving the men in coats before them with their hay-forks; while Caleb Garth's assistant, a lad of seventeen, who had snatched up the spirit-level at Caleb's order, had been knocked down and seemed to be lying helpless. The coated men had the advantage as runners, and Fred covered their retreat by getting in front of the smock-frocks and charging them suddenly enough to throw their chase into confusion. 'What do you confounded fools mean?' shouted Fred, pursuing the divided group in a zig-zag, and cutting right and left with his whip. 'I'll swear to every one of you before the magistrate. You've knocked the lad down and killed him, for what I know. You'll everyone of you be hanged at the next assizes, if you don't mind,' said Fred, who afterwards laughed heartily as he remembered his own phrases.

The labourers had been driven through the gateway into their hayfield, and Fred had checked his horse, when Hiram Ford, observing himself at a safe challenging distance, turned back and shouted a defiance which he did not know to be Homeric.

'Yo're a coward, yo are. Yo git off your horse, young measter, and I'll have a round wi' ye, I wull. Yo daredn't come on wi'out your hoss an' whip. I'd soon knock the breath out on ye, I would.'

'Wait a minute, and I'll come back presently, and have a round with you all in turn, if you like,' said Fred, who felt confidence in his power of boxing with his dearly-beloved brethren. But just now he wanted to hasten back to Caleb and the prostrate youth.

The lad's ankle was strained, and he was in much pain from it, but he was no further hurt, and Fred placed him on the horse that he might ride to Yoddrell's and be taken care of there.

'Let them put the horse in the stable, and tell the surveyors they can come back for their traps,' said Fred. 'The ground is clear now.'

'No, no,' said Caleb, 'here's a breakage. They'll have to give up for today, and it will be as well. Here, take the things before you on the horse, Tom. They'll see you coming, and they'll turn back.'

'I'm glad I happened to be here at the right moment, Mr Garth,' said Fred, as Tom rode away. 'No knowing what might have happened if the cavalry had not come up in time.'

'Ay, ay, it was lucky,' said Caleb, speaking rather absently, and looking towards the spot where he had been at work at the moment of interruption. 'But – deuce take it – this is what comes of men being fools – I'm hindered of my day's work. I can't get along without somebody to help me with the measuring chain. However!' He was beginning to move towards the spot with a look of vexation, as if he had forgotten Fred's presence, but suddenly he turned round and said quickly, 'What have you got to do today, young fellow?'

'Nothing, Mr Garth. I'll help you with pleasure – can I?' said Fred, with a sense that he should be courting Mary when he was helping her father.

'Well, you mustn't mind stooping and getting hot.'

'I don't mind anything. Only I want to go first and have a round with that hulky fellow who turned to challenge me. It would be a good lesson for him. I shall not be five minutes.'

'Nonsense!' said Caleb, with his most peremptory intonation. 'I shall go and speak to the men myself. It's all ignorance. Somebody has been telling them lies. The poor fools don't know any better.'

'I shall go with you, then,' said Fred.

'No, no; stay where you are. I don't want your young blood. I can take care of myself.'

Caleb was a powerful man and knew little of any fear except the fear of hurting others and the fear of having to speechify. But he felt it his duty at this moment to try and give a little harangue. There was a striking mixture in him – which came from his having always been a hard-working man himself – of rigorous notions about workmen and practical indulgence towards them. To do a good day's work and to do it well, he held to be part of their welfare, as it was the chief part of his own happiness; but he had a strong sense of fellowship with them. When he advanced towards the labourers they had not gone to work again, but were standing in that form of rural grouping which consists in each turning a shoulder towards the other, at a distance of two or three yards. They looked rather sulkily at Caleb, who walked quickly with one hand in his pocket and the other thrust between the buttons of his waistcoat, and had his everyday mild air when he paused among them.

'Why, my lads, how's this?' he began, taking as usual to brief phrases, which seemed pregnant to himself, because he had many thoughts lying under them, like the abundant roots of a plant that just manages to peep above the water. 'How came you to make such a mistake as this! Somebody has been telling you lies. You thought those men up there wanted to do mischief.'

'Aw!' was the answer, dropped at intervals by each according to his degree of unreadiness.

'Nonsense! No such thing! They're looking out to see which way the railroad is to take. Now, my lads, you can't hinder the railroad: it will be made whether you like it or not. And if you go fighting against it, you'll get yourselves into trouble. The law gives those men leave to come here on the land. The owner has nothing to say against it, and if you meddle with them you'll have to do with the constable and Justice Blakesley, and with the handcuffs and Middlemarch jail. And you might be in for it now, if anybody informed against you.'

Caleb paused here, and perhaps the greatest orator could not have chosen either his pause or his images better for the occasion.

'But come, you didn't mean any harm. Somebody told you the railroad was a bad thing. That was a lie. It may do a bit of harm here and there, to this and to that; and so does the sun in heaven. But the railway's a good thing.'

'Aw! good for the big folks to make money out on,' said old Timothy Cooper, who had stayed behind turning his hay while the others had been gone on their spree; – 'I'n seen lots o' things turn up sin' I war a young un – the war an' the peace, and the canells, an' the oald King George, an' the Regen', an' the new King George, an' the new un as has got a new ne-ame – an' it's been all aloike to the poor mon. What's the canells been t' him? They'n brought him neyther me-at nor be-acon, nor wage to lay by, if he didn't save it wi' clemmin' his own inside. Times ha' got wusser for him sin' I war a young un. An' so it'll be wi' the railroads. They'll on'y leave the poor mon furder behind. But them are fools as meddle, and so I told the chaps here. This is the big folks's world, this is. But yo're for the big folks, Muster Garth, yo are.'

Timothy was a wiry old labourer, of a type lingering in those times – who had his savings in a stocking-foot, lived in a lone cottage, and was not to be wrought on by any oratory, having as little of the feudal spirit, and believing as little, as if he had not been totally unacquainted with the *Age of Reason* and the *Rights of Man*. Caleb was in a difficulty known to any person attempting in dark times and unassisted by miracle to reason with rustics who are in possession of an undeniable truth which they know through a hard process of feeling, and can let it fall like a giant's club on your neatly-carved argument for a social benefit which they do not feel. Caleb had no cant at command, even if he could have chosen to use it; and he had been accustomed to meet all such difficulties in no other way than by doing his 'business' faithfully. He answered: 'If you don't think well of me, Tim, never mind; that's neither here nor there now. Things may be bad for the poor man – bad they are; but I want the lads here not to do what will make things worse for themselves. The cattle may have a heavy load, but it won't help 'em to throw it over into the roadside pit, when it's partly their own fodder.'

'We war on'y for a bit o' foon,' said Hiram, who was beginning to see consequences. 'That war all we war arter.'

'Well, promise me not to meddle again, and I'll see that nobody informs against you.'

'I'n ne'er meddled, an' I'n no call to promise,' said Timothy.

'No, but the rest. Come, I'm as hard at work as any of you today, and I can't spare much time. Say you'll be quiet without the constable.'

'Aw, we wooant meddle – they may do as they loike for oos' – were the forms in which Caleb got his pledges; and then he hastened back to Fred, who had followed him, and watched him in the gateway.

They went to work, and Fred helped vigorously. His spirits had risen, and he heartily enjoyed a good slip in the moist earth under the hedgerow, which soiled his perfect summer trousers. Was it his successful onset which had elated him, or the satisfaction of helping Mary's father? Something more. The accidents of the morning had helped his frustrated imagination to shape an employment for himself which had several attractions. I am not sure that certain fibres in

Mr Garth's mind had not resumed their old vibration towards the very end which now revealed itself to Fred. For the effective accident is but the touch of fire where there is oil and tow; and it always appeared to Fred that the railway brought the needed touch. But they went on in silence except when their business demanded speech. At last, when they had finished and were walking away, Mr Garth said: 'A young fellow needn't be a B.A. to do this sort of work, eh, Fred?'

'I wish I had taken to it before I had thought of being a B.A.,' said Fred. He paused a moment, and then added, more hesitatingly, 'Do you think I am too old to learn your business, Mr Garth?'

'My business is of many sorts, my boy,' said Mr Garth, smiling. 'A good deal of what I know can only come from experience: you can't learn it off as you learn things out of a book. But you are young enough to lay a foundation yet.' Caleb pronounced the last sentence emphatically, but paused in some uncertainty. He had been under the impression lately that Fred had made up his mind to enter the Church.

'You do think I could do some good at it, if I were to try?' said Fred, more eagerly.

'That depends,' said Caleb, turning his head on one side and lowering his voice, with the air of a man who felt himself to be saying something deeply religious. 'You must be sure of two things: you must love your work, and not be always looking over the edge of it, wanting your play to begin. And the other is, you must not be ashamed of your work, and think it would be more honourable to you to be doing something else. You must have a pride in your own work and in learning to do it well, and not be always saying, There's this and there's that – if I had this or that to do, I might make something of it. No matter what a man is – I wouldn't give twopence for him' – here Caleb's mouth looked bitter, and he snapped his fingers – 'whether he was the prime minister or the rick-thatcher, if he didn't do well what he undertook to do.'

'I can never feel that I should do that in being a clergyman,' said Fred, meaning to take a step in argument.

'Then let it alone, my boy,' said Caleb, abruptly, 'else you'll never be easy. Or, if you *are* easy, you'll be a poor stick.'

'That is very nearly what Mary thinks about it,' said Fred, colouring. 'I think you must know what I feel for Mary, Mr Garth: I hope it does not displease you that I have always loved her better than anyone else, and that I shall never love anyone as I love her.'

The expression of Caleb's face was visibly softening while Fred spoke. But he swung his head with a solemn slowness, and said: 'That makes things more serious, Fred, if you want to take Mary's happiness into your keeping.'

'I know that, Mr Garth,' said Fred, eagerly, 'and I would do anything for *her*. She says she will never have me if I go into the Church; and I shall be the most miserable devil in the world if I lose all hope of Mary. Really, if I could get some other profession, business – anything that I am at all fit for, I would work hard, I would deserve your good opinion. I should like to have to do with outdoor things. I know a good deal about land and cattle already. I used to believe, you know – though you will think me rather foolish for it – that I should have land of my own. I am sure knowledge of that sort would come easily to me, especially if I could be under you in any way.'

'Softly, my boy,' said Caleb, having the image of 'Susan' before his eyes. 'What have you said to your father about all this?'

'Nothing, yet: but I must tell him. I am only waiting to know what I can do instead of entering the Church. I am very sorry to disappoint him, but a man ought to be allowed to judge for himself when he is four-and-twenty. How could I know when I was fifteen, what it would be right for me to do now? My education was a mistake.'

'But hearken to this, Fred,' said Caleb. 'Are you sure Mary is fond of you, or would ever have you?'

'I asked Mr Farebrother to talk to her, because she had forbidden me – I didn't know what else to do,' said Fred, apologetically. 'And he says that I have every reason to hope, if I can put myself in an honourable position – I mean, out of the Church. I dare say you think it unwarrantable in me, Mr Garth, to be troubling you and obtruding my own wishes about Mary, before I have done anything at all for myself. Of course I have not the least claim – indeed, I have already a debt to you which will never be discharged, even when I have been able to pay it in the shape of money.'

'Yes, my boy, you have a claim,' said Caleb, with much feeling in his voice. 'The young ones have always a claim on the old to help them forward. I was young myself once and had to do without much help; but help would have been welcome to me, if it had been only for the fellow-feeling's sake. But I must consider. Come to me tomorrow at the office, at nine o'clock. At the office, mind.'

Mr Garth would take no important step without consulting Susan, but it must be confessed that before he reached home he had taken his resolution. With regard to a large number of matters about which other men are decided or obstinate, he was the most easily manageable man in the world. He never knew what meat he would choose, and if Susan had said that they ought to live in a four-roomed cottage, in order to save, he would have said, 'Let us go', without enquiring into details. But where Caleb's feeling and judgement strongly pronounced, he was a ruler; and in spite of his mildness and timidity in reproving, everyone about him knew that on the exceptional occasions when he chose, he was absolute. He never, indeed, chose to be absolute except on someone else's behalf. On ninety-nine points Mrs Garth decided, but on the hundredth she was often aware that she would have to perform the singularly difficult task of carrying out her own principle, and to make herself subordinate.

'It is come round as I thought, Susan,' said Caleb, when they were seated alone in the evening. He had already narrated the adventure which had brought about Fred's sharing in his work, but had kept back the further result. 'The children *are* fond of each other – I mean, Fred and Mary.'

Mrs Garth laid her work on her knee, and fixed her penetrating eyes anxiously on her husband.

'After we'd done our work, Fred poured it all out to me. He can't bear to be a clergyman, and Mary says she won't have him if he is one; and the lad would like to be under me and give his mind to business. And I've determined to take him and make a man of him.'

'Caleb!' said Mrs Garth, in a deep contralto, expressive of resigned astonishment.

'It's a fine thing to do,' said Mr Garth, settling himself firmly against the back of his chair, and grasping the elbows. 'I shall have trouble with him, but I think I shall carry it through. The lad loves Mary, and a true love for a good woman is a great thing, Susan. It shapes many a rough fellow.'

'Has Mary spoken to you on the subject?' said Mrs Garth, secretly a little hurt that she had to be informed on it herself.

'Not a word. I asked her about Fred once; I gave her a bit of a warning. But she assured me she would never marry an idle, self-indulgent man – nothing since. But it seems Fred set on Mr Farebrother to talk to her, because she had forbidden him to speak himself, and Mr Farebrother has found out that she is fond of Fred, but says he must not be a clergyman. Fred's heart is fixed on Mary, that I can see: it gives me a good opinion of the lad – and we always liked him, Susan.'

'It is a pity for Mary, I think,' said Mrs Garth.

'Why – a pity?'

'Because, Caleb, she might have had a man who is worth twenty Fred Vincys.'

'Ah?' said Caleb, with surprise.

'I firmly believe that Mr Farebrother is attached to her, and meant to make her an offer; but of course now that Fred has used him as an envoy, there is an end to that better prospect.' There was a severe precision in Mrs Garth's utterance. She was vexed and disappointed, but she was bent on abstaining from useless words.

Caleb was silent for a few moments under a conflict of feelings. He looked at the floor and moved his head and hands in accompaniment to some inward argumentation. At last he said: 'That would have made me very proud and happy, Susan, and I should have been glad for your sake. I've always felt that your belongings have never been on a level with you. But you took me, though I was a plain man.'

'I took the best and cleverest man I had ever known,' said Mrs Garth, convinced that *she* would never have loved anyone who came short of that mark.

'Well, perhaps others thought you might have done better. But it would have been worse for me. And that is what touches me close about Fred. The lad is good at bottom, and clever enough to do, if he's put in the right way; and he loves and honours my daughter beyond anything, and she has given him a sort of promise according to what he turns out. I say, that young man's soul is in my hand; and I'll do the best I can for him, so help me God! It's my duty, Susan.'

Mrs Garth was not given to tears, but there was a large one rolling down her face before her husband had finished. It came from the pressure of various feelings, in which there was much affection and some vexation. She wiped it away quickly, saying: 'Few men besides you would think it a duty to add to their anxieties in that way, Caleb.'

'That signifies nothing – what other men would think. I've got a clear feeling inside me, and that I shall follow; and I hope your heart will go with me, Susan, in making everything as light as can be to Mary, poor child.'

Caleb, leaning back in his chair, looked with anxious appeal towards his wife. She rose and kissed him, saying, 'God bless you, Caleb! Our children have a good father.'

But she went out and had a hearty cry to make up for the suppression of her words. She felt sure that her husband's conduct would be misunderstood, and about Fred she was rational and unhopeful. Which would turn out to have the more foresight in it – her rationality or Caleb's ardent generosity?

When Fred went to the office the next morning, there was a test to be gone through which he was not prepared for.

'Now, Fred,' said Caleb, 'you will have some desk-work. I have always done a good deal of writing myself, but I can't do without help, and as I want you to understand the accounts and get the values into your head, I mean to do without another clerk. So you must buckle to. How are you at writing and arithmetic?'

Fred felt an awkward movement of the heart; he had not thought of desk-work; but he was in a resolute mood, and not going to shrink. 'I'm not afraid of arithmetic, Mr Garth: it always came easily to me. I think you know my writing.'

'Let us see,' said Caleb, taking up a pen, examining it carefully and handing it, well dipped, to Fred with a sheet of ruled paper. 'Copy me a line or two of that valuation, with the figures at the end.'

At that time the opinion existed that it was beneath a gentleman to write legibly, or with a hand in the least suitable to a clerk. Fred wrote the lines demanded in a hand as gentlemanly as that of any viscount or bishop of the day: the vowels were all alike and the consonants only distinguishable as turning up or down, the strokes had a blotted solidity and the letters disdained to keep the line – in short, it was a manuscript of that venerable kind easy to interpret when you know beforehand what the writer means.

As Caleb looked on, his visage showed a growing depression, but when Fred handed him the paper he gave something like a snarl, and rapped the paper passionately with the back of his hand. Bad work like this dispelled all Caleb's mildness.

'The deuce!' he exclaimed, snarlingly. 'To think that this is a country where a man's education may cost hundreds and hundreds, and it turns you out this!' Then in a more pathetic tone, pushing up his spectacles and looking at the unfortunate scribe, 'The Lord have mercy on us, Fred, I can't put up with this!'

'What can I do, Mr Garth?' said Fred, whose spirits had sunk very low, not only at the estimate of his handwriting, but at the vision of himself as liable to be ranked with office-clerks.

'Do? Why, you must learn to form your letters and keep the line. What's the use of writing at all if nobody can understand it?' asked Caleb, energetically, quite preoccupied with the bad quality of the work. 'Is there so little business in the world that you must be sending puzzles over the country? But that's the way people are brought up. I should lose no end of time with the letters some people send me, if Susan did not make them out for me. It's disgusting.' Here Caleb tossed the paper from him.

Any stranger peeping into the office at that moment might have wondered what was the drama between the indignant man of business, and the fine-looking young fellow whose blond complexion was getting rather patchy as he bit his lip with mortification. Fred was struggling with many thoughts. Mr Garth had been so kind and encouraging at the beginning of their interview, that gratitude and hopefulness had been at a high pitch, and the downfall was proportionate. He had not thought of desk-work – in fact, like the majority of young gentlemen, he wanted an occupation which should be free from dis-agreeables. I cannot tell what might have been the consequences if he had not distinctly promised himself that he would go to Lowick to see Mary and tell her that he was engaged to work under her father. He did not like to disappoint himself there.

'I am very sorry,' were all the words that he could muster. But Mr Garth was already relenting.

'We must make the best of it, Fred,' he began, with a return to his usual quiet tone. 'Every man can learn to write. I taught myself. Go at it with a will, and sit up at night if the daytime isn't enough. We'll be patient, my boy. Callum shall go on with the books for a bit, while you are learning. But now I must be off,' said Caleb, rising. 'You must let your father know our agreement. You'll save me Callum's salary, you know, when you can write; and I can afford to give you eighty pounds for the first year, and more after.'

When Fred made the necessary disclosure to his parents, the relative effect on the two was a surprise which entered very deeply into his memory. He went straight from Mr Garth's office to the warehouse, rightly feeling that the most respectful way in which he could behave to his father, was to make the painful communication as gravely and formally as possible. Moreover, the decision would be more certainly understood to be final, if the interview took place in his father's gravest hours, which were always those spent in his private room at the warehouse.

Fred entered on the subject directly, and declared briefly what he had done and was resolved to do, expressing at the end his regret that he should be the cause of disappointment to his father, and taking the blame on his own deficiencies. The regret was genuine, and inspired Fred with strong, simple words.

Mr Vincy listened in profound surprise without uttering even an exclamation, a silence which in his impatient temperament was a sign of unusual emotion. He had not been in good spirits about trade that morning, and the slight bitterness in his lips grew intense as he listened. When Fred had ended, there was a pause of nearly a minute, during which Mr Vincy replaced a book in his desk and turned the key emphatically. Then he looked at his son steadily, and said: 'So you've made up your mind at last, sir?'

'Yes, father.'

'Very well; stick to it. I've no more to say. You've thrown away your education, and gone down a step in life, when I had given you the means of rising, that's all.'

'I am very sorry that we differ, father. I think I can be quite as much of a gentleman at the work I have undertaken, as if I had been a curate. But I am grateful to you for wishing to do the best for me.'

'Very well; I have no more to say. I wash my hands of you. I only hope, when you have a son of your own he will make a better return for the pains you spend on him.'

This was very cutting to Fred. His father was using that unfair advantage possessed by us all when we are in a pathetic situation and see our own past as if it were simply part of the pathos. In reality, Mr Vincy's wishes about his son had had a great deal of pride, inconsiderateness, and egoistic folly in them. But still the disappointed father held a strong lever; and Fred felt as if he were being banished with a malediction.

'I hope you will not object to my remaining at home, sir?' he said, after rising to go; 'I shall have a sufficient salary to pay for my board, as of course I should wish to do.'

'Board, be hanged!' said Mr Vincy, recovering himself in his disgust at the notion that Fred's keep would be missed at his table. 'Of course your mother will want you to stay. But I shall keep no horse for you, you understand; and you will pay your own tailor. You will do with a suit or two less, I fancy, when you have to pay for 'em.'

Fred lingered; there was still something to be said. At last it came.

'I hope you will shake hands with me, father, and forgive me the vexation I have caused you.'

Mr Vincy from his chair threw a quick glance upward at his son, who had advanced near to him, and then gave his hand, saying hurriedly, 'Yes, yes, let us say no more.'

Fred went through much more narrative and explanation with his mother, but she was inconsolable, having before her eyes what perhaps her husband had never thought of, the certainty that Fred would marry Mary Garth, that her life would henceforth be spoiled by a perpetual infusion of Garths and their ways, and that her darling boy, with his beautiful face and stylish air 'beyond anybody else's son in Middlemarch', would be sure to get like that family in plainness of appearance and carelessness about his clothes. To her it seemed that there was a Garth conspiracy to get possession of the desirable Fred, but she dared not enlarge on this opinion, because a slight hint of it had made him 'fly out' at her as he had never done before. Her temper was too sweet for her to show any anger; but she felt that her happiness had received a bruise, and for several days merely to look at Fred made her cry a little as if he were the subject of some baleful prophecy. Perhaps she was the slower to recover her usual cheerfulness because Fred had warned her that she must not reopen the sore question with his father, who had accepted his decision and forgiven him. If her husband had been vehement against Fred, she would have been urged into defence of her darling. It was the end of the fourth day when Mr Vincy said to her: 'Come, Lucy, my dear, don't be so down-hearted. You have always spoiled the boy, and you must go on spoiling him.'

'Nothing ever did cut me so before, Vincy,' said the wife, her fair throat and chin beginning to tremble again, 'only his illness.'

'Pooh, pooh, never mind! We must expect to have trouble with our children. Don't make it worse by letting me see you out of spirits.'

'Well, I won't,' said Mrs Vincy, roused by this appeal and adjusting herself with a little shake as of a bird which lays down its ruffled plumage.

'It won't do to begin making a fuss about one,' said Mr Vincy, wishing to combine a little grumbling with domestic cheerfulness. 'There's Rosamond as well as Fred.'

'Yes, poor thing. I'm sure I felt for her being disappointed of her baby; but she got over it nicely.'

'Baby, pooh! I can see Lydgate is making a mess of his practice, and getting into debt too, by what I hear. I shall have Rosamond coming to me with a pretty tale one of these days. But they'll get no money from me, I know. Let *his* family help him. I never did like that marriage. But it's no use talking. Ring the bell for lemons, and don't look dull any more, Lucy. I'll drive you and Louisa to Riverston tomorrow.'

Chapter 57

> They numbered scarce eight summers when a name
>   Rose on their souls and stirred such motions there
> As thrill the buds and shape their hidden frame
>   At penetration of the quickening air:
> His name who told of loyal Evan Dhu,
>   Of quaint Bradwardine, and Vich Ian Vor,
> Making the little world their childhood knew
>   Large with a land of mountain, lake, and scaur,
> And larger yet with wonder, love, belief
>   Toward Walter Scott, who living far away
> Sent them this wealth of joy and noble grief.
>   The book and they must part, but day by day,
>   In lines that thwart like portly spiders ran,
>   They wrote the tale, from Tully Veolan.

The evening that Fred Vincy walked to Lowick Parsonage (he had begun to see that this was a world in which even a spirited young man must sometimes walk for want of a horse to carry him) he set out at five o'clock and called on Mrs Garth by the way, wishing to assure himself that she accepted their new relations willingly.

He found the family group, dogs and cats included, under the great apple tree in the orchard. It was a festival with Mrs Garth, for her eldest son, Christy, her peculiar joy and pride, had come home for a short holiday – Christy, who held it the most desirable thing in the world to be a tutor, to study all literatures and be a regenerate Porson, and who was an incorporate criticism on poor Fred, a sort of object-lesson given to him by the educational mother. Christy himself, a square-browed, broad-shouldered masculine edition of his mother not much higher than Fred's shoulder – which made it the harder that he should be held superior – was always as simple as possible, and thought no more of Fred's disinclination to scholarship than of a giraffe's' wishing that he himself were more of the same height. He was lying on the ground now by his mother's chair, with his straw-hat laid flat over his eyes, while Jim on the other side was reading aloud from that beloved writer who has made a chief part in the happiness of many young lives. The volume was *Ivanhoe*, and Jim was in the great archery scene at the tournament, but suffered much interruption from Ben, who had fetched his own old bow and arrows, and was making himself dreadfully dis-agreeable, Letty thought, by begging all present to observe his random shots, which no one wished to do except Brownie, the active-minded but probably shallow mongrel, while the grizzled Newfoundland lying in the sun looked on with the dull-eyed neutrality of extreme old age. Letty herself, showing as to her mouth and pinafore some slight signs that she had been assisting at the gathering of the cherries which stood in a coral-heap on the tea-table, was now seated on the grass, listening open-eyed to the reading.

But the centre of interest was changed for all by the arrival of Fred Vincy. When, seating himself on a garden-stool, he said that he was on his way to Lowick Parsonage, Ben, who had thrown down his bow, and snatched up a reluctant half-grown kitten instead, strode across Fred's outstretched leg and said, 'Take me!'

'Oh, and me too,' said Letty.

'You can't keep up with Fred and me,' said Ben.

'Yes, I can. Mother, please say that I am to go,' urged Letty, whose life was much checkered by resistance to her depreciation as a girl.

'*I* shall stay with Christy,' observed Jim; as much as to say that he had the advantage of these simpletons; whereupon Letty put her hand up to her head and looked with jealous indecision from the one to the other.

'Let us all go and see Mary,' said Christy, opening his arms.

'No, my dear child, we must not go in a swarm to the parsonage. And that old Glasgow suit of yours would never do. Besides, your father will come home. We must let Fred go alone. He can tell Mary that you are here, and she will come back tomorrow.'

Christy glanced at his own threadbare knees, and then Fred's beautiful white trousers. Certainly Fred's tailoring suggested the advantage of an English university, and he had a graceful way even of looking warm and of pushing his hair back with his handkerchief.

'Children, run away,' said Mrs Garth; 'it is too warm to hang about your friends. Take your brother and show him the rabbits.'

The eldest understood, and led off the children immediately. Fred felt that Mrs Garth wished to give him an opportunity of saying anything that he had to say, but he could only begin by observing: 'How glad you must be to have Christy here!'

'Yes; he has come sooner than I expected. He got down from the coach at nine o'clock, just after his father went out. I am longing for Caleb to come and hear what wonderful progress Christy is making. He has paid his expenses for the last year by giving lessons, carrying on hard study at the same time. He hopes soon to get a private tutorship and go abroad.'

'He is a great fellow,' said Fred, to whom these cheerful truths had a medicinal taste, 'and no trouble to anybody.' After a slight pause, he added, 'But I fear you will think that I am going to be a great deal of trouble to Mr Garth.'

'Caleb likes taking trouble: he is one of those men who always do more than anyone would have thought of asking them to do,' answered Mrs Garth. She was knitting, and could either look at Fred or not, as she chose – always an advantage when one is bent on loading speech with salutary meaning; and though Mrs Garth intended to be duly reserved, she did wish to say something that Fred might be the better for.

'I know you think me very undeserving, Mrs Garth, and with good reason,' said Fred, his spirit rising a little at the perception of something like a disposition to lecture him. 'I happen to have behaved just the worst to the people I can't help wishing for the most from. But while two men like Mr Garth and Mr Farebrother have not given me up, I don't see why I should give myself up.' Fred thought it might be well to suggest these masculine examples to Mrs Garth.

'Assuredly,' said she, with gathering emphasis. 'A young man for whom two such elders had devoted themselves would indeed be culpable if he threw himself away and made their sacrifices vain.'

Fred wondered a little at this strong language, but only said, 'I hope it will not be so with me, Mrs Garth, since I have some encouragement to believe that I may win Mary. Mr Garth has told you about that? You were not surprised, I dare say?' Fred ended, innocently referring only to his own love as probably evident enough.

'Not surprised that Mary has given you encouragement?' returned Mrs Garth, who thought it would be well for Fred to be more alive to the fact that Mary's friends could not possibly have wished this beforehand, whatever the Vincys might suppose. 'Yes, I confess I *was* surprised.'

'She never did give me any – not the least in the world, when I talked to her myself,' said Fred, eager to vindicate Mary. 'But when I asked Mr Farebrother to speak for me, she allowed him to tell me there was a hope.'

The power of admonition which had begun to stir in Mrs Garth had not yet discharged itself. It was a little too provoking even for *her* self-control that this blooming youngster should flourish on the disappointments of sadder and wiser people making a meal of a nightingale and never knowing it – and that all the while his family should suppose that hers was in eager need of this sprig; and her vexation had fermented the more actively because of its total repression towards her husband. Exemplary wives will sometimes find scapegoats in this way. She now said with energetic decision. 'You made a great mistake, Fred, in asking Mr Farebrother to speak for you.'

'Did I?' said Fred, reddening instantaneously. He was alarmed, but at a loss to know what Mrs Garth meant, and added, in an apologetic tone, 'Mr Farebrother has always been such a friend of ours; and Mary, I knew, would listen to him gravely; and he took it on himself quite readily.'

'Yes, young people are usually blind to everything but their own wishes, and seldom imagine how much those wishes cost others,' said Mrs Garth. She did not mean to go beyond this salutary general doctrine, and threw her indignation into a needless unwinding of her worsted, knitting her brow at it with a grand air.

'I cannot conceive how it could be any pain to Mr Farebrother,' said Fred, who nevertheless felt that surprising conceptions were beginning to form themselves.

'Precisely; you cannot conceive,' said Mrs Garth, cutting her words as neatly as possible.

For a moment Fred looked at the horizon with a dismayed anxiety, and then turning with a quick movement said almost sharply: 'Do you mean to say, Mrs Garth, that Mr Farebrother is in love with Mary?'

'And if it were so, Fred, I think you are the last person who ought to be surprised,' returned Mrs Garth, laying her knitting down beside her and folding her arms. It was an unwonted sign of emotion in her that she should put her work out of her hands. In fact her feelings were divided between the satisfaction of giving Fred his discipline and the sense of having gone a little too far. Fred took his hat and stick and rose quickly.

'Then you think I am standing in his way, and in Mary's too?' he said, in a tone which seemed to demand an answer.

Mrs Garth could not speak immediately. She had brought herself into the unpleasant position of being called on to say what she really felt, yet what she knew there were strong reasons for concealing. And to her the consciousness of having exceeded in words was peculiarly mortifying. Besides, Fred had given out unexpected electricity, and he now added, 'Mr Garth seemed pleased that Mary should be attached to me. He could not have known anything of this.'

Mrs Garth felt a severe twinge at this mention of her husband, the fear that Caleb might think her in the wrong not being easily endurable. She answered, wanting to check unintended consequences: 'I spoke from inference only. I am not aware that Mary knows anything of the matter.'

But she hesitated to beg that he would keep entire silence on a subject which she had herself unnecessarily mentioned, not being used to stoop in that way; and while she was hesitating there was already a rush of unintended consequences under the apple tree where the tea-things stood. Ben, bouncing across the grass with Brownie at his heels, and seeing the kitten dragging the knitting by a lengthening line of wool, shouted and clapped his hands; Brownie barked, the kitten, desperate, jumped on the tea-table and upset the milk, then jumped down again and swept half the cherries with it; and Ben, snatching up the half-knitted sock-top, fitted it over the kitten's head as a new source of madness, while Letty arriving cried out to her mother against this cruelty – it was a history as full of sensation as 'This is the house that Jack built'. Mrs Garth was obliged to interfere, the other young ones came up and the tête-à-tête with Fred was ended. He got away as soon as he could, and Mrs Garth could only imply some retraction of her severity by saying 'God bless you' when she shook hands with him.

She was unpleasantly conscious that she had been on the verge of speaking as 'one of the foolish women speaketh' telling first and entreating silence after. But she had not entreated silence, and to prevent Caleb's blame she determined to blame herself and confess all to him that very night. It was curious what an awful tribunal the mild Caleb's was to her, whenever he set it up. But she meant to point out to him that the revelation might do Fred Vincy a great deal of good.

No doubt it was having a strong effect on him as he walked to Lowick. Fred's light hopeful nature had perhaps never had so much of a bruise as from this suggestion that if he had been out of the way Mary might have made a thoroughly good match. Also he was piqued that he had been what he called such a stupid lout as to ask that intervention from Mr Farebrother. But it was not in a lover's nature – it was not in Fred's that the new anxiety raised about Mary's feeling should not surmount every other. Notwithstanding his trust in Mr Farebrother's generosity, notwithstanding what Mary had said to him, Fred could not help feeling he had a rival: it was a new consciousness, and he objected to it extremely, not being in the least ready to give up Mary for her good, being ready rather to fight for her with any man whatsoever. But the fighting with Mr Farebrother must be of a metaphorical kind, which was much more difficult to Fred than the muscular. Certainly this experience was a discipline for Fred hardly less sharp than his disappointment about his uncle's will. The iron had not entered his soul, but he had begun to imagine what the sharp edge would be. It did not once occur to Fred that Mrs Garth might be mistaken about Mr Farebrother, but he suspected that she might be wrong about Mary. Mary had been staying at the parsonage lately, and her mother might know very little of what had been passing in her mind.

He did not feel easier when he found her looking cheerful with the three ladies in the drawing-room. They were in animated discussion on some subject which was dropped when he entered, and Mary was copying the labels from a heap of shallow cabinet drawers, in a minute handwriting which she was skilled in. Mr Farebrother was somewhere in the village, and the three ladies knew nothing of Fred's peculiar relation to Mary: it was impossible for either of them to propose that they should walk round the garden, and Fred predicted to himself that he should have to go away without saying a word to her in private. He told her first of Christy's arrival and then of his own engagement with her father; and he was comforted by seeing that this latter news touched her keenly. She said hurriedly, 'I am so glad,' and then bent over her writing to hinder anyone from noticing her face. But here was a subject which Mrs Farebrother could not let pass.

'You don't mean, my dear Miss Garth, that you are glad of a young man giving up the Church for which he was educated: you only mean that things being so, you are glad that he should be under an excellent man like your father.'

'No, really, Mrs Farebrother, I am glad of both, I fear,' said Mary, cleverly getting rid of one rebellious tear. 'I have a dreadfully secular mind. I never liked any clergyman except the Vicar of Wakefield and Mr Farebrother.'

'Now why, my dear?' said Mrs Farebrother, pausing on her large wooden knitting-needles and looking at Mary. 'You have always a good reason for your opinions, but this astonishes me. Of course I put out of the question those who preach new doctrine. But why should you dislike clergymen?'

'Oh dear,' said Mary, her face breaking into merriment as she seemed to consider a moment. 'I don't like their neckcloths.'

'Why, you don't like Camden's, then,' said Miss Winifred, in some anxiety.

'Yes, I do,' said Mary. 'I don't like the other clergymen's neckcloths, because it is they who wear them.'

'How very puzzling!' said Miss Noble, feeling that her own intellect was probably deficient.

'My dear, you are joking. You would have better reasons than these for slighting so respectable a class of men,' said Mrs Farebrother, majestically.

'Miss Garth has such severe notions of what people should be that it is difficult to satisfy her,' said Fred.

'Well, I am glad at least that she makes an exception in favour of my son,' said the old lady.

Mary was wondering at Fred's piqued tone, when Mr Farebrother came in and had to hear the news about the engagement under Mr Garth. At the end he said with quiet satisfaction, '*That* is right;' and then bent to look at Mary's labels and praise her handwriting. Fred felt horribly jealous – was glad, of course, that Mr Farebrother was so estimable, but wished that he had been ugly and fat as men at forty sometimes are. It was clear what the end would be, since Mary openly placed Farebrother above everybody; and these women were all evidently encouraging the affair. He was feeling sure that he should have no chance of speaking to Mary, when Mr Farebrother said: 'Fred, help me to carry these drawers back into my study, you have never seen my fine new study. Pray come too, Miss Garth. I want you to see a stupendous spider I found this morning.'

Mary at once saw the Vicar's intention. He had never since the memorable evening deviated from his old pastoral kindness towards her, and her momentary wonder and doubt had quite gone to sleep. Mary was accustomed to think rather rigorously of what was probable, and if a belief flattered her vanity she felt warned to dismiss it as ridiculous, having early had much exercise in such dismissals. It was as she had foreseen: when Fred had been asked to admire the fittings of the study, and she had been asked to admire the spider, Mr Farebrother said: 'Wait here a minute or two. I am going to look out an engraving which Fred is tall enough to hang for me. I shall be back in a few minutes.' And then he went out. Nevertheless, the first word Fred said to Mary was: 'It is of no use, whatever I do, Mary. You are sure to marry Farebrother at last.' There was some rage in his tone.

'What do you mean, Fred?' Mary exclaimed indignantly, blushing deeply, and surprised out of all her readiness in reply.

'It is impossible that you should not see it all clearly enough – you who see everything.'

'I only see that you are behaving very ill, Fred, in speaking so of Mr Farebrother after he has pleaded your cause in every way. How can you have taken up such an idea?'

Fred was rather deep, in spite of his irritation. If Mary had really been unsuspicious, there was no good in telling her what Mrs Garth had said.

'It follows as a matter of course,' he replied. 'When you are continually seeing a man who beats me in everything, and whom you set up above everybody, I can have no fair chance.'

'You are very ungrateful, Fred,' said Mary. 'I wish I had never told Mr Farebrother that I cared for you in the least.'

'No, I am not ungrateful; I should be the happiest fellow in the world if it were not for this. I told your father everything, and he was very kind; he treated me as if I were his son. I could go at the work with a will, writing and everything, if it were not for this.'

'For this? for what?' said Mary, imagining now that something specific must have been said or done.

'This dreadful certainty that I shall be bowled out by Farebrother.' Mary was appeased by her inclination to laugh.

'Fred,' she said, peeping round to catch his eyes, which were sulkily turned away from her, 'you are too delightfully ridiculous. If you were not such a charming simpleton, what a temptation this would be to play the wicked coquette, and let you suppose that somebody besides you made love to me.'

'Do you really like me best, Mary?' said Fred, turning eyes full of affection on her, and trying to take her hand.

'I don't like you at all at this moment,' said Mary, retreating, and putting her hands behind her. 'I only said that no mortal ever made love to me besides you. And that is no argument that a very wise man ever will,' she ended, merrily.

'I wish you would tell me that you could not possibly ever think of him,' said Fred.

'Never dare to mention this anymore to me, Fred,' said Mary, getting serious again. 'I don't know whether it is more stupid or ungenerous in you not to see that Mr Farebrother has left us together on purpose that we might speak freely. I am disappointed that you should be so blind to his delicate feeling.'

There was no time to say anymore before Mr Farebrother came back with the engraving; and Fred had to return to the drawing-room still with a jealous dread in his heart, but yet with comforting arguments from Mary's words and manner. The result of the conversation was on the whole more painful to Mary: inevitably her attention had taken a new attitude, and she saw the possibility of new interpretations. She was in a position in which she seemed to herself to be slighting Mr Farebrother, and this, in relation to a man who is much honoured, is always dangerous to the firmness of a grateful woman. To have a reason for going home the next day was a relief, for Mary earnestly desired to be always clear that she loved Fred best. When a tender affection has been storing itself in us through many of our years, the idea that we could accept any exchange for it seems to be a cheapening of our lives. And we can set a watch over our affections and our constancy as we can over other treasures.

'Fred has lost all his other expectations; he must keep this,' Mary said to herself, with a smile curling her lips. It was impossible to help fleeting visions of another kind – new dignities and an acknowledged value of which she had often felt the absence. But these things with Fred outside them, Fred forsaken and looking sad for the want of her, could never tempt her deliberate thought.

Chapter 58

For there can live no hatred in thine eye,
Therefore in that I cannot know thy change:
In many's looks the false heart's history
Is writ in moods and frowns and wrinkles strange;
But Heaven in thy creation did decree
That in thy face sweet love should ever dwell;
Whate'er thy thoughts or thy heart's workings be,
Thy looks should nothing thence but sweetness tell.

SHAKESPEARE, *Sonnets*

At the time when Mr Vincy uttered that presentiment about Rosamond, she herself had never had the idea that she should be driven to make the sort of appeal which he foresaw. She had not yet had any anxiety about ways and means, although her domestic life had been expensive as well as eventful. Her baby had been born prematurely, and all the embroidered robes and caps had to be laid by in darkness. This misfortune was attributed entirely to her having persisted in going out on horseback one day when her husband had desired her not to do so; but it must not be supposed that she had shown temper on the occasion, or rudely told him that she would do as she liked.

What led her particularly to desire horse-exercise was a visit from Captain Lydgate, the baronet's third son, who, I am sorry to say, was detested by our Tertius of that name as a vapid fop 'parting his hair from brow to nape in a despicable fashion' (not followed by Tertius himself), and showing an ignorant security that he knew the proper thing to say on every topic. Lydgate inwardly cursed his own folly that he had drawn down this visit by consenting to go to his uncle's on the wedding-tour, and he made himself rather disagreeable to Rosamond by saying so in private. For to Rosamond this visit was a source of unprecedented but gracefully-concealed exultation. She was so intensely conscious of having a cousin who was a baronet's son staying in the house, that she imagined the knowledge of what was implied by his presence to be diffused through all other minds; and when she introduced Captain Lydgate to her guests, she had a placid sense that his rank penetrated them as if it had been an odour. The satisfaction was enough for the time to melt away some disappointment in the conditions of marriage with a medical man even of good birth: it seemed now that her marriage was visibly as well as ideally floating her above the Middlemarch level, and the future looked bright with letters and visits to and from Quallingham, and vague advancement in consequence for Tertius. Especially as, probably at the Captain's suggestion, his married sister, Mrs Mengan, had come with her maid, and stayed two nights on her way from town. Hence it was clearly worth while for Rosamond to take pains with her music and the careful selection of her lace.

As to Captain Lydgate himself, his low brow, his aquiline nose bent on one side, and his rather heavy utterance, might have been disadvantageous in any young gentleman who had not a military bearing and moustache to give him what is doted on by some flower-like blond heads as 'style'. He had, moreover, that sort of high-breeding which consists in being free from the petty solicitudes of middle-class gentility, and he was a great critic of feminine charms. Rosamond delighted in his admiration now even more than she had done at Quallingham, and he found it easy to spend several hours of the day in flirting with her. The visit altogether was one of the pleasantest larks he had ever had, not the less so perhaps because he suspected that his queer cousin Tertius wished him away: though Lydgate, who would rather (hyperbolically speaking) have died than have failed in polite hospitality, suppressed his dislike, and only pretended generally not to hear what the gallant officer said, consigning the task of answering him to Rosamond. For he was not at all a jealous husband, and preferred leaving a feather-headed young gentleman alone with his wife to bearing him company.

'I wish you would talk more to the Captain at dinner, Tertius,' said Rosamond, one evening when the important guest was gone to Loamford to see some brother officers stationed there. 'You really look so absent sometimes – you seem to be seeing through his head into something behind it, instead of looking at him.'

'My dear Rosy, you don't expect me to talk much to such a conceited ass as that, I hope,' said Lydgate, brusquely. 'If he got his head broken, I might look at it with interest, not before.'

'I cannot conceive why you should speak of your cousin so contemptuously,' said Rosamond, her fingers moving at her work while she spoke with a mild gravity which had a touch of disdain in it.

'Ask Ladislaw if he doesn't think your Captain the greatest bore he ever met with. Ladislaw has almost forsaken the house since he came.'

Rosamond thought she knew perfectly well why Mr Ladislaw disliked the Captain: he was jealous, and she liked his being jealous.

'It is impossible to say what will suit eccentric persons,' she answered, 'but in my opinion Captain Lydgate is a thorough gentleman, and I think you ought not, out of respect to Sir Godwin, to treat him with neglect.'

'No, dear; but we have had dinners for him. And he comes in and goes out as he likes. He doesn't want me.'

'Still, when he is in the room, you might show him more attention. He may not be a phoenix of cleverness in your sense; his profession is different; but it would be all the better for you to talk a little on his subjects. I think his conversation is quite agreeable. And he is anything but an unprincipled man.'

'The fact is, you would wish me to be a little more like him, Rosy,' said Lydgate, in a sort of resigned murmur, with a smile which was not exactly tender, and certainly not merry. Rosamond was silent and did not smile again; but the lovely curves of her face looked good-tempered enough without smiling.

Those words of Lydgate's were like a sad milestone marking how far he had travelled from his old dreamland, in which Rosamond Vincy appeared to be that perfect piece of womanhood who would reverence her husband's mind after the fashion of an accomplished mermaid, using her comb and looking-glass and singing her song for the relaxation of his adored wisdom alone. He had begun to distinguish between that imagined adoration and the attraction towards a man's talent because it gives him prestige, and is like an order in his buttonhole or an Honourable before his name.

It might have been supposed that Rosamond had travelled too, since she had found the pointless conversation of Mr Ned Plymdale perfectly wearisome; but to most mortals there is a stupidity which is unendurable and a stupidity which is altogether acceptable – else, indeed, what would become of social bonds? Captain Lydgate's stupidity was delicately scented, carried itself with 'style', talked with a good accent, and was closely related to Sir Godwin. Rosamond found it quite agreeable and caught many of its phrases.

Therefore, since Rosamond, as we know, was fond of horseback, there were plenty of reasons why she should be tempted to resume her riding when Captain Lydgate, who had ordered his man with two horses to follow him and put up at the Green Dragon, begged her to go out on the grey which he warranted to be gentle and trained to carry a lady – indeed he had bought it for his sister, and was taking it to Quallingham. Rosamond went out the first time without telling her husband, and came back before his return; but the ride had been so thorough a success, and she declared herself so much the better in consequence, that he was informed of it with full reliance on his consent that she should go riding again.

On the contrary Lydgate was more than hurt – he was utterly confounded that she had risked herself on a strange horse with out referring the matter to his wish. After the first almost thundering exclamations of astonishment which sufficiently warned Rosamond of what was coming, he was silent for some moments.

'However, you have come back safely,' he said, at last, in a decisive tone. 'You will not go again, Rosy; that is understood. If it were the quietest, most familiar horse in the world, there would always be the chance of accident. And you know very well that I wished you to give up riding the roan on that account.'

'But there is the chance of accident indoors, Tertius.'

'My darling, don't talk nonsense,' said Lydgate, in an imploring tone; 'surely I am the person to judge for you. I think it is enough that I say you are not to go again.'

Rosamond was arranging her hair before dinner, and the reflection of her head in the glass showed no change in its loveliness except a little turning aside of the long neck. Lydgate had been moving about with his hands in his pockets, and now paused near her, as if he awaited some assurance.

'I wish you would fasten up my plaits, dear,' said Rosamond, letting her arms fall with a little sigh, so as to make a husband ashamed of standing there like a brute. Lydgate had often fastened the plaits before, being among the deftest of men with his large finely-formed fingers. He swept up the soft festoons of plaits and fastened in the tall comb (to such uses do men come!); and what could he do then but kiss the exquisite nape which was shown in all its delicate curves? But when we do what we have done before, it is often with a difference. Lydgate was still angry, and had not forgotten his point.

'I shall tell the Captain that he ought to have known better than offer you his horse,' he said, as he moved away.

'I beg you will not do anything of the kind, Tertius,' said Rosamond, looking at him with something more marked than usual in her speech. 'It will be treating me as if I were a child. Promise that you will leave the subject to me.'

There did seem to be some truth in her objection. Lydgate said, 'Very well,' with a surly obedience, and thus the discussion ended with his promising Rosamond, and not with her promising him.

In fact, she had been determined not to promise. Rosamond had that victorious obstinacy which never wastes its energy in impetuous resistance. What she liked to do was to her the right thing and all her cleverness was directed to getting the means of doing it. She meant to go out riding again on the grey, and she did go on the next opportunity of her husband's absence, not intending that he should know until it was late enough not to signify to her. The temptation was certainly great: she was very fond of the exercise, and the gratification of riding on a fine horse, with Captain Lydgate, Sir Godwin's son, on another fine horse by her side, and of being met in this position by anyone but her husband, was something as good as her dreams before marriage: moreover, she was riveting the connection with the family at Quallingham, which must be a wise thing to do.

But the gentle grey, unprepared for the crash of a tree that was being felled on the edge of Halsell Wood, took fright, and caused a worse fright to Rosamond, leading finally to the loss of her baby. Lydgate could not show his anger towards her, but he was rather bearish to the Captain, whose visit naturally soon came to an end.

In all future conversations on the subject, Rosamond was mildly certain that the ride had made no difference, and that if she had stayed at home the same symptoms would have come on and would have ended in the same way, because she had felt something like them before.

Lydgate could only say, 'Poor, poor darling!' but he secretly wondered over the terrible tenacity of this mild creature. There was gathering within him an amazed sense of his powerlessness over Rosamond. His superior knowledge and mental force, instead of being, as he had imagined, a shrine to consult on all occasions, was simply set aside on every practical question. He had regarded Rosamond's cleverness as precisely of the receptive kind which became a woman. He was now beginning to find out what that cleverness was – what was the shape into which it had run as into a close network aloof and independent. No one quicker than Rosamond to see causes and effects which lay within the track of her own tastes and interests: she had seen clearly Lydgate's pre-eminence in Middle-march society, and could go on imaginatively tracing still more agreeable social effects when his talent should have advanced him; but for her, his professional and scientific ambition had no other relation to these desirable effects than if they had been the fortunate discovery of an ill-smelling oil. And that oil apart, with which she had nothing to do, of course she believed in her own opinion more than she did in his. Lydgate was astounded to find in numberless trifling matters, as well as in this last serious case of the riding, that affection did not make her compliant. He had no doubt that the affection was there, and had no presentiment that he had done anything to repel it. For his own part he said to himself that he loved her as tenderly as ever, and could make up his mind to her negations; but – well! Lydgate was much worried, and conscious of new elements in his life as noxious to him as an inlet of mud to a creature that has been used to breathe and bathe and dart after its illuminated prey in the clearest of waters.

Rosamond was soon looking lovelier than ever at her work-table, enjoying drives in her father's phaeton and thinking it likely that she might be invited to Quallingham. She knew that she was a much more exquisite ornament to the drawing-room there than any daughter of the family, and in reflecting that the gentlemen were aware of that, did not perhaps sufficiently consider whether the ladies would be eager to see themselves surpassed.

Lydgate, relieved from anxiety about her, relapsed into what she inwardly called his moodiness – a name which to her covered his thoughtful preoccupation with other subjects than herself, as well as that uneasy look of the brow and distaste for all ordinary things as if they were mixed with bitter herbs, which really made a sort of weather-glass to his vexation and foreboding. These latter states of mind had one cause amongst others, which he had generously but mistakenly avoided mentioning to Rosamond, lest it should affect her health and spirits. Between him and her indeed there was that total missing of each other's mental track, which is too evidently possible even between persons who are continually thinking of each other. To Lydgate it seemed that he had been spending month after month in sacrificing more than half of his best intent and best power to his tenderness for Rosamond; bearing her little claims and interruptions without impatience, and above all, bearing without betrayal of bitterness to look through less and less of interfering illusion at the blank unreflecting surface her mind presented to his ardour for the more impersonal ends of his profession and his scientific study, an ardour which he had fancied that the ideal wife must somehow worship as sublime, though not in the least knowing why. But his endurance was mingled with a self-discontent which, if we know how to be candid, we shall confess to make more than half our bitterness under grievances, wife or husband included. It always remains true that if we had been greater, circumstance would have been less strong against us. Lydgate was aware that his concessions to Rosamond were often little more than the lapse of slackening resolution, the creeping paralysis apt to seize an enthusiasm which is out of adjustment to a constant portion of our lives. And on Lydgate's enthusiasm there was constantly pressing not a simple weight of sorrow, but the biting presence of a petty degrading care, such as casts the blight of irony over all higher effort.

This was the care which he had hitherto abstained from mentioning to Rosamond; and he believed, with some wonder, that it had never entered her mind, though certainly no difficulty could be less mysterious. It was an inference with a conspicuous handle to it, and had been easily drawn by indifferent observers, that Lydgate was in debt; and he could not succeed in keeping out of his mind for long together that he was every day getting deeper into that swamp, which tempts men towards it with such a pretty covering of flowers and verdure. It is wonderful how soon a man gets up to his chin there – in a condition in which, in spite of himself, he is forced to think chiefly of release, though he had a scheme of the universe in his soul.

Eighteen months ago Lydgate was poor, but had never known the eager want of small sums, and felt rather a burning contempt for any who descended a step in order to gain them. He was now experiencing something worse than a simple deficit; he was assailed by the vulgar hateful trials of a man who has bought and used a great many things which might have been done without, and which he is unable to pay for, though the demand for payment has become pressing.

How this came about may be easily seen without much arithmetic or knowledge of prices. When a man in setting up a house and preparing for marriage finds that his furniture and other initial expenses come to between four and five hundred pounds more than he has capital to pay for; when at the end of a year it appears that his household expenses, horses and *et caeteras*, amount to nearly a thousand, while the proceeds of the practice reckoned from the old books to be worth eight hundred per annum have sunk like a summer pond and make hardly five hundred chiefly in unpaid entries, the plain inference is that, whether he minds it or not, he is in debt. Those were less expensive times than our own, and provincial life was comparatively modest; but the ease with which a medical man who had lately bought a practice, who thought that he was obliged to keep two horses, whose table was supplied without stint, and who paid an insurance on his life and a high rent for house and garden, might find his expenses doubling his receipts, can be conceived by anyone who does not think these details beneath his consideration. Rosamond, accustomed from her childhood to an extravagant household, thought that good housekeeping consisted simply in ordering the best of everything – nothing else 'answered'; and Lydgate supposed that 'if things were done at all, they must be done properly' – he did not see how they were to live otherwise. If each head of household expenditure had been mentioned to him beforehand, he would have probably observed that 'it could hardly come to much', and if anyone had suggested a saving on a particular article – for example, the substitution of cheap fish for dear – it would have appeared to him simply a penny-wise, mean notion. Rosamond, even without such an occasion as Captain Lydgate's visit, was fond of giving invitations, and Lydgate, though he often thought the guests tiresome, did not interfere. The sociability seemed a necessary part of professional prudence, and the entertainment must be suitable. It is true Lydgate was constantly visiting the homes of the poor and adjusting his prescriptions of diet to their small means; but, dear me! has it not by this time ceased to be remarkable – is it not rather what we expect in men, that they should have numerous strands of experience lying side by side and never compare them with each other? Expenditure – like ugliness and errors – becomes a totally new thing when we attach our own personality to it, and measure it by that wide difference which is manifest (in our own sensations) between ourselves and others. Lydgate believed himself to be careless about his dress, and he despised a man who calculated the effects of his costume; it seemed to him only a matter of course that he had abundance of fresh garments – such things were naturally ordered in sheaves. It must be remembered that he had never hitherto felt the check of importunate debt, and he walked by habit, not by self-criticism. But the check had come.

Its novelty made it the more irritating. He was amazed, disgusted that conditions so foreign to all his purposes, so hatefully disconnected with the objects he cared to occupy himself with, should have lain in ambush and clutched him when he was unaware. And there was not only the actual debt; there was the certainty that in his present position he must go on deepening it. Two furnishing tradesmen at Brassing, whose bills had been incurred before his marriage, and whom uncalculated current expenses had ever since prevented him from paying, had repeatedly sent him unpleasant letters which had forced themselves on his attention, This could hardly have been more galling to any disposition than to Lydgate's, with his intense pride – his dislike of asking a favour or being under an obligation to anyone. He had scorned even to form conjectures about Mr Vincy's intentions on money matters, and nothing but extremity could have induced him to apply to his father-in-law, even if he had not been made aware in various indirect ways since his marriage that Mr Vincy's own affairs were not flourishing, and that the expectation of help from him would be resented. Some men easily trust in the readiness of friends; it had never in the former part of his life occurred to Lydgate that he should need to do so: he had never thought what borrowing would be to him; but now that the idea had entered his mind, he felt that he would rather incur any other hardship. In the meantime he had no money or prospects of money; and his practice was not getting more lucrative.

No wonder that Lydgate had been unable to suppress all signs of inward trouble during the last few months, and now that Rosamond was regaining brilliant health, he meditated taking her entirely into confidence on his difficulties. New conversance with tradesmen's bills had forced his reasoning into a new channel of comparison: he had begun to consider from a new point of view what was necessary and unnecessary in goods ordered, and to see that there must be some change of habits. How could such a change be made without Rosamond's concurrence? The immediate occasion of opening the disagreeable fact on her was forced upon him.

Having no money, and having privately sought advice as to what security could possibly be given by a man in his position, Lydgate had offered the one good security in his power to the less peremptory creditor, who was a silversmith and jeweller, and who consented to take on himself the upholsterer's credit also, accepting interest for a given term. The security necessary was a bill of sale on the furniture of his house, which might make a creditor easy for a reasonable time about a debt amounting to less than four hundred pounds: and the silversmith, Mr Dover, was willing to reduce it by taking back a portion of the plate and any other article which was as good as new. 'Any other article' was a phrase delicately implying jewellery, and more particularly some purple amethysts costing thirty pounds, which Lydgate had bought as a bridal present.

Opinions may be divided as to his wisdom in making this present: some may think that it was a graceful attention to be expected from a man like Lydgate, and that the fault of any troublesome consequences lay in the pinched narrowness of provincial life at that time, which offered no conveniences for professional people whose fortune was not proportioned to their tastes; also, in Lydgate's ridiculous fastidiousness about asking his friends for money.

However, it had seemed a question of no moment to him on that fine morning when he went to give a final order for plate: in the presence of other jewels enormously expensive, and as an addition to orders of which the amount had not been exactly calculated, thirty pounds for ornaments so exquisitely suited to Rosamond's neck and arms could hardly appear excessive when there was no ready cash for it to exceed. But at this crisis Lydgate's imagination could not help dwelling on the possibility of letting the amethysts take their place again among Mr Dover's stock, though he shrank from the idea of proposing this to Rosamond. Having been roused to discern consequences which he had never been in the habit of tracing, he was preparing to act on this discernment with some of the rigour (by no means all) that he would have applied in pursuing experiment. He was nerving himself to this rigour as he rode from Brassing, and meditated on the representations he must make to Rosamond.

It was evening when he got home. He was intensely miserable, this strong man of nine-and-twenty and of many gifts. He was not saying angrily within himself that he had made a profound mistake; but the mistake was at work in him like a recognised chronic disease, mingling its uneasy importunities with every prospect, and enfeebling every thought. As he went along the passage to the drawing-room, he heard the piano and singing. Of course, Ladislaw was there. It was some weeks since Will had parted from Dorothea, yet he was still at the old post in Middlemarch. Lydgate had no objection in general to Ladislaw's coming, but just now he was annoyed that he could not find his hearth free. When he opened the door the two singers went on towards the keynote, raising their eyes and looking at him indeed, but not regarding his entrance as an interruption. To a man galled with his harness as poor Lydgate was, it is not soothing to see two people warbling at him, as he comes in with the sense that the painful day has still pains in store. His face, already paler than usual, took on a scowl as he walked across the room and flung himself into a chair.

The singers, feeling themselves excused by the fact that they had had only three bars to sing, now turned round.

'How are you, Lydgate?' said Will, coming forward to shake hands.

Lydgate took his hand, but did not think it necessary to speak.

'Have you dined, Tertius? I expected you much earlier,' said Rosamond, who had already seen that her husband was in a 'horrible humour'. She seated herself in her usual place as she spoke.

'I have dined. I should like some tea, please,' said Lydgate, curtly, still scowling and looking markedly at his legs stretched out before him.

Will was too quick to need more. 'I shall be off,' he said reaching his hat.

'Tea is coming,' said Rosamond; 'pray don't go.'

'Yes, Lydgate is bored,' said Will, who had more comprehension of Lydgate than Rosamond had, and was not offended by his manner, easily imagining outdoor causes of annoyance.

'There is the more need for you to stay,' said Rosamond, playfully, and in her lightest accent; 'he will not speak to me all the evening.'

'Yes, Rosamond, I shall,' said Lydgate, in his strong baritone. 'I have some serious business to speak to you about.'

No introduction of the business could have been less like that which Lydgate had intended; but her indifferent manner had been too provoking.

'There! you see,' said Will. 'I'm going to the meeting about the Mechanics' Institute. Goodbye;' and he went quickly out of the room.

Rosamond did not look at her husband, but presently rose and took her place before the tea-tray. She was thinking that she had never seen him so disagreeable. Lydgate turned his dark eyes on her and watched her as she delicately handled the tea-service with her taper fingers, and looked at the objects immediately before her with no curve in her face disturbed, and yet with an ineffable protest in her air against all people with unpleasant manners. For the moment he lost the sense of his wound in a sudden speculation about this new form of feminine impassibility revealing itself in the sylphlike frame which he had once interpreted as the sign of a ready intelligent sensitiveness. His mind glancing back to Laure while he looked at Rosamond, he said inwardly, 'Would *she* kill me because I wearied her?' and then, 'It is the way with all women.' But this power of generalising which gives men so much the superiority in mistake over the dumb animals, was immediately thwarted by Lydgate's memory of wondering impressions from the behaviour of another woman – from Dorothea's looks and tones of emotion about her husband when Lydgate began to attend him from her passionate cry to be taught what would best comfort that man for whose sake it seemed as if she must quell every impulse in her except the yearnings of faithfulness and compassion. These revived impressions succeeded each other quickly and dreamily in Lydgate's mind while the tea was being brewed. He had shut his eyes in the last instant of reverie while he heard Dorothea saying, 'Advise me – think what I can do – he has been all his life labouring and looking forward. He minds about nothing else – and I mind about nothing else.'

That voice of deep-souled womanhood had remained within him as the enkindling conceptions of dead and sceptred genius had remained within him (is there not a genius for feeling nobly which also reigns over human spirits and their conclusions?): the tones were a music from which he was falling away – he had really fallen into a momentary doze, when Rosamond said in her silvery neutral way, 'Here is your tea, Tertius,' setting it on the small table by his side, and then moved back to her place without looking at him. Lydgate was too hasty in attributing insensibility to her; after her own fashion, she was sensitive enough, and took lasting impressions. Her impression now was one of offence and repulsion. But then, Rosamond had no scowls and had never raised her voice: she was quite sure that no one could justly find fault with her.

Perhaps Lydgate and she had never felt so far off each other before; but there were strong reasons for not deferring his revelation, even if he had not already begun it by that abrupt announcement; indeed some of the angry desire to rouse her into more sensibility on his account which had prompted him to speak prematurely, still mingled with his pain in the prospect of her pain. But he waited till the tray was gone, the candles were lit, and the evening quiet might be counted on: the interval had left time for repelled tenderness to return into the old course. He spoke kindly.

'Dear Rosy, lay down your work and come and sit by me,' he said, gently, pushing away the table, and stretching out his arm to draw a chair near his own.

Rosamond obeyed. As she came towards him in her drapery of transparent faintly-tinted muslin, her slim yet round figure never looked more graceful; as she sat down by him and laid one hand on the elbow of his chair, at last looking at him and meeting his eyes, her delicate neck and cheek and purely-cut lips never had more of that untarnished beauty which touches us in springtime and infancy and all sweet freshness. It touched Lydgate now, and mingled the early moments of his love for her with all the other memories which were stirred in this crisis of deep trouble. He laid his ample hand softly on hers, saying: 'Dear!' with the lingering utterance which affection gives to the word. Rosamond too was still under the power of that same past, and her husband was still in part the Lydgate whose approval had stirred delight. She put his hair lightly away from his forehead, then laid her other hand on his, and was conscious of forgiving him.

'I am obliged to tell you what will hurt you, Rosy. But there are things which husband and wife must think of together. I dare say it has occurred to you already that I am short of money.'

Lydgate paused; but Rosamond turned her neck and looked at a vase on the mantelpiece.

'I was not able to pay for all the things we had to get before we were married, and there have been expenses since which I have been obliged to meet. The consequence is, there is a large debt at Brassing – three hundred and eighty pounds – which has been pressing on me a good while, and in fact we are getting deeper every day, for people don't pay me the faster because others want the money. I took pains to keep it from you while you were not well; but now we must think together about it, and you must help me.'

'What can *I* do, Tertius?' said Rosamond, turning her eyes on him again. That little speech of four words, like so many others in all languages, is capable by varied vocal inflexions of expressing all states of mind from helpless dimness to exhaustive argumentative perception, from the completest self-devoting fellow-ship to the most neutral aloofness. Rosamond's thin utterance threw into the words 'What can I do!' as much neutrality as they could hold. They fell like a mortal chill on Lydgate's roused tenderness. He did not storm in indignation – he felt too sad a sinking of the heart. And when he spoke again it was more in the tone of a man who forces himself to fulfil a task.

'It is necessary for you to know, because I have to give security for a time, and a man must come to make an inventory of the furniture.'

Rosamond coloured deeply. 'Have you not asked papa for money?' she said, as soon as she could speak.

'No.'

'Then I must ask him!' she said, releasing her hands from Lydgate's and rising to stand at two yards distance from him.

'No, Rosy,' said Lydgate, decisively. 'It is too late to do that. The inventory will be begun tomorrow. Remember it is a mere security: it will make no difference: it is a temporary affair. I insist upon it that your father shall not know, unless I choose to tell him,' added Lydgate, with a more peremptory emphasis.

This certainly was unkind, but Rosamond had thrown him back on evil expectation as to what she would do in the way of quiet steady disobedience. The unkindness seemed unpardonable to her: she was not given to weeping and disliked it, but now her chin and lips began to tremble and the tears welled up. Perhaps it was not possible for Lydgate, under the double stress of outward material difficulty and of his own proud resistance to humiliating consequences, to imagine fully what this sudden trial was to a young creature who had known nothing but indulgence, and whose dreams had all been of new indulgence, more exactly to her taste. But he did wish to spare her as much as he could, and her tears cut him to the heart. He could not speak again immediately; but Rosamond did not go on sobbing: she tried to conquer her agitation and wiped away her tears, continuing to look before her at the mantelpiece.

'Try not to grieve, darling,' said Lydgate, turning his eyes up towards her. That she had chosen to move away from him in this moment of her trouble made everything harder to say, but he must absolutely go on. 'We must brace ourselves to do what is necessary. It is I who have been in fault: I ought to have seen that I could not afford to live in this way. But many things have told against me in my practice, and it really just now has ebbed to a low point. I may recover it, but in the meantime we must pull up – we must change our way of living. We shall weather it. When I have given this security I shall have time to look about me; and you are so clever that if you turn your mind to managing you will school me into carefulness. I have been a thoughtless rascal about squaring prices – but come, dear, sit down and forgive me.'

Lydgate was bowing his neck under the yoke like a creature who had talons, but who had Reason too, which often reduces us to meekness. When he had spoken the last words in an imploring tone, Rosamond returned to the chair by his side. His self-blame gave her some hope that he would attend to her opinion, and she said: 'Why can you not put off having the inventory made? You can send the men away tomorrow when they come.'

'I shall not send them away,' said Lydgate, the peremptoriness rising again. Was it of any use to explain?

'If we left Middlemarch, there would of course be a sale, and that would do as well.'

'But we are not going to leave Middlemarch.'

'I am sure, Tertius, it would be much better to do so. Why can we not go to London? Or near Durham, where your family is known?'

'We can go nowhere without money, Rosamond.'

'Your friends would not wish you to be without money. And surely these odious tradesmen might be made to understand that, and to wait, if you would make proper representations to them.'

'This is idle, Rosamond,' said Lydgate angrily. 'You must learn to take my judgement on questions you don't understand. I have made necessary arrangements, and they must be carried out. As to friends, I have no expectations whatever from them, and shall not ask them for anything.'

Rosamond sat perfectly still. The thought in her mind was that if she had known how Lydgate would behave, she would never have married him.

'We have no time to waste now on unnecessary words, dear,' said Lydgate, trying to be gentle again. 'There are some details that I want to consider with you. Dover says he will take a good deal of the plate back again, and any of the jewellery we like. He really behaves very well.'

'Are we to go without spoons and forks then?' said Rosamond, whose very lips seemed to get thinner with the thinness of her utterance. She was determined to make no further resistance or suggestions.

'Oh no, dear!' said Lydgate. 'But look here,' he continued, drawing a paper from his pocket and opening it; 'here is Dover's account. See, I have marked a number of articles, which if we returned them would reduce the amount by thirty pounds and more. I have not marked any of the jewellery.' Lydgate had really felt this point of the jewellery very bitter to himself; but he had overcome the feeling by severe argument. He could not propose to Rosamond that she return any particular present of his, but he had told himself that he was bound to put Dover's offer before her, and her inward prompting might make the affair easy.

'It is useless for me to look, Tertius,' said Rosamond, calmly; 'you will return what you please.' She would not turn her eyes on the paper, and Lydgate, flushing up to the roots of his hair, drew it back and let it fall on his knee. Meanwhile Rosamond quietly went out of the room, leaving Lydgate helpless and wondering. Was she not coming back? It seemed that she had no more identified herself with him than if they had been creatures of different species and opposing interests. He tossed his head and thrust his hands deep into his pockets with a sort of vengeance. There was still science – there were still good objects to work for. He must give a tug still – all the stronger because other satisfactions were going.

But the door opened and Rosamond re-entered. She carried the leather box containing the amethysts, and a tiny ornamental basket which contained other boxes, and laying them on the chair where she had been sitting, she said, with perfect propriety in her air: 'This is all the jewellery you ever gave me. You can return what you like of it, and of the plate also. You will not, of course, expect me to stay at home tomorrow. I shall go to papa's.'

To many women the look Lydgate cast at her would have been more terrible than one of anger: it had in it a despairing acceptance of the distance she was placing between them.

'And when shall you come back again?' he said, with a bitter edge on his accent.

'Oh, in the evening. Of course I shall not mention the subject to mamma.' Rosamond was convinced that no woman could behave more irreproachably than she was behaving and she went to sit down at her work-table. Lydgate sat meditating a minute or two, and the result was that he said, with some of the old emotion in his tone: 'Now we have been united, Rosy, you should not leave me to myself in the first trouble that has come.'

'Certainly not,' said Rosamond; 'I shall do everything it becomes me to do.'

'It is not right that the thing should be left to servants, or that I should have to speak to them about it. And I shall be obliged to go out – I don't know how early. I understand your shrinking from the humiliation of these money affairs. But, my dear Rosamond, as a question of pride, which I feel just as much as you can, it is surely better to manage the thing ourselves, and let the servants see as little of it as possible; and since you are my wife, there is no hindering your share in my disgraces – if there were disgraces.'

Rosamond did not answer immediately, but at last she said, 'Very well, I will stay at home.'

'I shall not touch these jewels Rosy. Take them away again. But I will write out a list of plate that we may return, and that can be packed up and sent at once.'

'The servants will know *that*,' said Rosamond, with the slightest touch of sarcasm.

'Well, we must meet some disagreeables as necessities. Where is the ink, I wonder?' said Lydgate, rising, and throwing the account on the larger table where he meant to write.

Rosamond went to reach the inkstand, and after setting it on the table was going to turn away, when Lydgate, who was standing close by, put his arm round her and drew her towards him, saying, 'Come, darling, let us make the best of things. It will only be for a time, I hope, that we shall have to be stingy and particular. Kiss me.'

His native warm-heartedness took a great deal of quenching, and it *is* a part of manliness for a husband to feel keenly the fact that an inexperienced girl has got into trouble by marrying him. She received his kiss and returned it faintly, and in this way an appearance of accord was recovered for the time. But Lydgate could not help looking forward with dread to the inevitable future discussions about expenditure and the necessity for a complete change in their way of living.

Chapter 59

> They said of old the Soul had human shape,
> But smaller, subtler than the fleshly self,
> So wandered forth for airing when it pleased.
> And see! beside her cherub-face there floats
> A pale-lipped form aerial whispering
> Its promptings in that little shell her ear.

News is often dispersed as thoughtlessly and effectively as that pollen which the bees carry off (having no idea how powdery they are) when they are buzzing in search of their particular nectar. This fine comparison has reference to Fred Vincy, who on that evening at Lowick Parsonage heard a lively discussion among the ladies on the news which their old servant had got from Tantripp concerning Mr Casaubon's strange mention of Mr Ladislaw in a codicil to his will made not long before his death. Miss Winifred was astounded to find that her brother had known the fact before, and observed that Camden was the most wonderful man for knowing things and not telling them; whereupon Mary

Garth said that the codicil had perhaps got mixed up with the habits of spiders, which Miss Winifred never would listen to. Mrs Farebrother considered that the news had something to do with their having only once seen Mr Ladislaw at Lowick, and Miss Noble made many small compassionate mewings.

Fred knew little and cared less about Ladislaw and the Casaubons, and his mind never recurred to that discussion till one day calling on Rosamond at his mother's request to deliver a message as he passed, he happened to see Ladislaw going away. Fred and Rosamond had little to say to each other now that marriage had removed her from collision with the unpleasantness of brothers, and especially now that he had taken what she held the stupid and even reprehensible step of giving up the Church to take to such a business as Mr Garth's. Hence Fred talked by preference of what he considered indifferent news, and 'apropos of that young Ladislaw' mentioned what he had heard at Lowick Parsonage.

Now Lydgate, like Mr Farebrother, knew a great deal more than he told, and when he had once been set thinking about the relation between Will and Dorothea his conjectures had gone beyond the fact. He imagined that there was a passionate attachment on both sides, and this struck him as much too serious to gossip about. He remembered Will's irritability when he had mentioned Mrs Casaubon, and was the more circumspect. On the whole his surmises, in addition to what he knew of the fact, increased his friendliness and tolerance towards Ladislaw, and made him understand the vacillation which kept him at Middlemarch after he had said that he should go away. It was significant of the separateness between Lydgate's mind and Rosamond's that he had no impulse to speak to her on the subject; indeed, he did not quite trust her reticence towards Will. And he was right there; though he had no vision of the way in which her mind would act in urging her to speak.

When she had repeated Fred's news to Lydgate, he said, 'Take care you don't drop the faintest hint to Ladislaw, Rosy. He is likely to fly out as if you insulted him. Of course it is a painful affair.'

Rosamond turned her neck and patted her hair, looking the image of placid indifference. But the next time Will came when Lydgate was away, she spoke archly about his not going to London as he had threatened.

'I know all about it. I have a confidential little bird,' said she, showing very pretty airs of her head over the bit of work held high between her active fingers. 'There is a powerful magnet in this neighbourhood.'

'To be sure there is. Nobody knows that better than you,' said Will, with light gallantry, but inwardly prepared to be angry.

'It is really the most charming romance: Mr Casaubon jealous, and foreseeing that there was no one else whom Mrs Casaubon would like so much to marry, and no one who would so much like to marry her as a certain gentleman and then laying a plan to spoil all by making her forfeit her property if she did marry that gentleman – and then – and then – and then – oh, I have no doubt the end will be thoroughly romantic.'

'Great God! what do you mean?' said Will, flushing over face and ears, his features seeming to change as if he had had a violent shake. 'Don't joke; tell me what you mean.'

'You don't really know?' said Rosamond, no longer playful, and desiring nothing better than to tell in order that she might evoke effects.

'No!' he returned, impatiently.

'Don't know that Mr Casaubon has left it in his will that if Mrs Casaubon marries you she is to forfeit all her property?'

'How do you know that it is true?' said Will, eagerly.

'My brother Fred heard it from the Farebrothers.'

Will started up from his chair and reached his hat.

'I dare say she likes you better than the property,' said Rosamond, looking at him from a distance.

'Pray don't say any more about it,' said Will, in a hoarse undertone extremely unlike his usual light voice. 'It is a foul insult to her and to me.' Then he sat down absently, looking before him, but seeing nothing.

'Now you are angry with me,' said Rosamond. 'It is too bad to bear *me* malice. You ought to be obliged to me for telling you.'

'So I am,' said Will, abruptly, speaking with that kind of double soul which belongs to dreamers who answer questions.

'I expect to hear of the marriage,' said Rosamond, playfully.

'Never! You will never hear of the marriage!'

With those words uttered impetuously, Will rose, put out his hand to Rosamond, still with the air of a somnambulist, and went away.

When he was gone, Rosamond left her chair and walked to the other end of the room, leaning when she got there against a chiffonnier, and looking out of the window wearily. She was oppressed by ennui, and by that dissatisfaction which in women's minds is continually turning into a trivial jealousy, referring to no real claims, springing from no deeper passion than the vague exactingness of egoism, and yet capable of impelling action as well as speech. 'There really is nothing to care for much,' said poor Rosamond inwardly, thinking of the family at Quallingham, who did not write to her; and that perhaps Tertius when he came home would tease her about expenses. She had already secretly disobeyed him by asking her father to help them, and he had ended decisively by saying, 'I am more likely to want help myself.'

Chapter 60

> Good phrases are surely, and ever were,
> very commendable.
>
> JUSTICE SHALLOW

A few days afterwards – it was already the end of August – there was an occasion which caused some excitement in Middlemarch: the public, if it chose, was to have the advantage of buying, under the distinguished auspices of Mr Borthrop Trumbull, the furniture, books, and pictures, which anybody might see by the handbills to be the best in every kind, belonging to Edwin Larcher, Esq. This was not one of the sales indicating the depression of trade; on the contrary, it was due to Mr Larcher's great success in the carrying business, which warranted his purchase of a mansion near Riverston already furnished in high style by an illustrious Spa physician – furnished indeed with such large framefuls of expensive flesh-painting in the dining-room, that Mrs Larcher was nervous until reassured by finding the subjects to be Scriptural. Hence the fine opportunity to purchasers which was well pointed out in the handbills of Mr Borthrop Trumbull, whose acquaintance with the history of art enabled him to state that the hall furniture, to be sold without reserve, comprised a piece of carving by a contemporary of Gibbons.

At Middlemarch in those times a large sale was regarded as a kind of festival. There was a table spread with the best cold eatables, as at a superior funeral; and facilities were offered for that generous drinking of cheerful glasses which might lead to generous and cheerful bidding for undesirable articles. Mr Larcher's sale was the more attractive in the fine weather because the house stood just at the end of the town, with a garden and stables attached, in that pleasant issue from Middlemarch called the London Road, which was also the road to the New Hospital and to Mr Bulstrode's retired residence, known as The Shrubs. In short, the auction was as good as a fair, and drew all classes with leisure at command: to some, who risked making bids in order simply to raise prices, it was almost equal to betting at the races. The second day, when the best furniture was to be sold, 'everybody' was there; even Mr Thesiger, the rector of St Peter's, had looked in for a short time, wishing to buy the carved table, and had rubbed elbows with Mr Bambridge and Mr Horrock. There was a wreath of Middlemarch ladies accommodated with seats round the large table in the dining-room, where Mr Borthrop Trumbull was mounted with desk and hammer; but the rows chiefly of masculine faces behind were often varied by incomings and outgoings both from the door and the large bow-window opening on to the lawn.

'Everybody' that day did not include Mr Bulstrode, whose health could not well endure crowds and draughts. But Mrs Bulstrode had particularly wished to have a certain picture – a *Supper at Emmaus*, attributed in the catalogue to Guido, and at the last moment before the day of the sale Mr Bulstrode had called at the office of the *Pioneer*, of which he was now one of the proprietors, to beg of Mr Ladislaw as a great favour that he would obligingly use his remarkable knowledge of pictures on behalf of Mrs Bulstrode, and judge of the value of this particular painting – 'if,' added the scrupulously polite banker, 'attendance at the sale would not interfere with the arrangements for your departure, which I know is imminent.'

This proviso might have sounded rather satirically in Will's ear if he had been in a mood to care about such satire. It referred to an understanding entered into many weeks before with the proprietors of the paper, that he should be at liberty any day he pleased to hand over the management to the sub-editor whom he had been training; since he wished finally to quit Middlemarch. But indefinite visions of ambition are weak against the ease of doing what is habitual or beguilingly agreeable; and we all know the difficulty of carrying out a resolve when we secretly long that it may turn out to be unnecessary. In such states of mind the most incredulous person has a private leaning towards miracle:

impossible to conceive how our wish could be fulfilled, still – very wonderful things have happened! Will did not confess this weakness to himself, but he lingered. What was the use of going to London at that time of the year? The Rugby men who would remember him were not there; and so far as political writing was concerned, he would rather for a few weeks go on with the *Pioneer*. At the present moment, however, when Mr Bulstrode was speaking to him, he had both a strengthened resolve to go and an equally strong resolve not to go till he had once more seen Dorothea. Hence he replied that he had reasons for deferring his departure a little, and would be happy to go to the sale.

Will was in a defiant mood, his consciousness being deeply stung with the thought that the people who looked at him probably knew a fact tantamount to an accusation against him as a fellow with low designs which were to be frustrated by a disposal of property. Like most people who assert their freedom with regard to conventional distinction, he was prepared to be sudden and quick at quarrel with anyone who might hint that he had personal reasons for that assertion – that there was anything in his blood, his bearing, or his character to which he gave the mask of an opinion. When he was under an irritating impression of this kind he would go about for days with a defiant look, the colour changing in his transparent skin as if he were on the *qui vive*, watching for something which he had to dart upon.

This expression was peculiarly noticeable in him at the sale, and those who had only seen him in his moods of gentle oddity or of bright enjoyment would have been struck with a contrast. He was not sorry to have this occasion for appearing in public before the Middlemarch tribes of Toller, Hackbutt, and the rest, who looked down on him as an adventurer, and were in a state of brutal ignorance about Dante – who sneered at his Polish blood, and were themselves of a breed very much in need of crossing. He stood in a conspicuous place not far from the auctioneer, with a forefinger in each side-pocket and his head thrown backward, not caring to speak to anybody, though he had been cordially welcomed as a connoiss*ure* by Mr Trumbull, who was enjoying the utmost activity of his great faculties.

And surely among all men whose vocation requires them to exhibit their powers of speech, the happiest is a prosperous provincial auctioneer keenly alive to his own jokes and sensible of his encyclopaedic knowledge. Some saturnine, sour-blooded persons might object to be constantly insisting on the merits of all articles from bootjacks to 'Berghems'; but Mr Borthrop Trumbull had a kindly liquid in his veins; he was an admirer by nature, and would have liked to have the universe under his hammer, feeling that it would go at a higher figure for his recommendation.

Meanwhile Mrs Larcher's drawing-room furniture was enough for him. When Will Ladislaw had come in, a second fender, said to have been forgotten in its right place, suddenly claimed the auctioneer's enthusiasm, which he distributed on the equitable principle of praising those things most which were most in need of praise. The fender was of polished steel, with much lancet-shaped open-work and a sharp edge.

'Now, ladies,' said he, 'I shall appeal to you. Here is a fender, which at any other sale would hardly be offered without reserve, being, as I may say, for quality of steel and quaintness of design, a kind of thing' – here Mr Trumbull dropped his voice and became slightly nasal, trimming his outlines with his left finger – 'that might not fall in with ordinary tastes. Allow me to tell you that by and by this style of workmanship will be the only one in vogue – half a crown, you said? thank you – going at half a crown, this characteristic fender; and I have particular information that the antique style is very much sought after in high quarters. Three shillings – three-and-sixpence – hold it well up, Joseph. Look, ladies, at the chastity of the design – I have no doubt myself that it was turned out in the last century! Four shillings, Mr Mawmsey? – four shillings.'

'It's not a thing I would put in *my* drawing-room,' said Mrs Mawmsey, audibly, for the warning of the rash husband. 'I wonder *at* Mrs Larcher. Every blessed child's head that fell against it would be cut in two. The edge is like a knife.'

'Quite true,' rejoined Mr Trumbull, quickly, 'and most uncommonly useful to have a fender at hand that will cut, if you have a leather shoetie or a bit of string that wants cutting and no knife at hand: many a man has been left hanging because there was no knife to cut him down. Gentlemen, here's a fender that if you had the misfortune to hang yourselves would cut you down in no time – with astonishing celerity – four-and-sixpence – five – five-and-sixpence – an appropriate thing for a spare bedroom where there was a four-poster and a guest a little out of his mind – six shillings – thank you, Mr Clintup – going at six shillings – going – gone!' The auctioneer's glance, which had been searching round him with a preternatural susceptibility to all signs of bidding, here dropped on the paper before him, and his voice too dropped into a tone of indifferent despatch as he said, 'Mr Clintup. Be handy, Joseph.'

'It was worth six shillings to have a fender you could always tell that joke on,' said Mr Clintup, laughing low and apologetically to his next neighbour. He was a diffident though distinguished nurseryman, and feared that the audience might regard his bid as a foolish one.

Meanwhile Joseph had brought a trayful of small articles. 'Now, ladies,' said Mr Trumbull, taking up one of the articles, 'this tray contains a very recherchy lot – a collection of trifles for the drawing-room table – and trifles make the sum of human things – nothing more important than trifles – (yes, Mr Ladislaw, yes, by and by) – but pass the tray round, Joseph – these bijoux must be examined, ladies. This I have in my hand is an ingenious contrivance – a sort of practical rebus I may call it: here, you see, it looks like an elegant heart-shaped box, portable – for the pocket; there, again, it becomes like a splendid double flower – an ornament for the table; and now' – Mr Trumbull allowed the flower to fall alarmingly into strings of heart-shaped leaves – 'a book of riddles! No less than five hundred printed in a beautiful red. Gentlemen, if I had less of a conscience, I should not wish you to bid high for this lot – I have a longing for it myself. What can promote innocent mirth, and I may say virtue, more than a good riddle? – it hinders profane language, and attaches a man to the society of refined females. This ingenious article itself, without the elegant domino-box, card-basket, &c., ought alone to give a high price to the lot. Carried in the pocket it might make an individual welcome in any society. Four shillings, sir? – four shillings for this remarkable collection of riddles with the *et caeteras*. Here is a sample: "How must you spell honey to make it catch ladybirds? Answer – money." You hear? – ladybirds – honey – money. This is an amusement to sharpen the intellect; it has a sting, it has what we call satire, and wit without indecency. Four-and-sixpence – five shillings.'

The bidding ran on with warming rivalry. Mr Bowyer was a bidder, and this was too exasperating. Bowyer couldn't afford it, and only wanted to hinder every other man from making a figure. The current carried even Mr Horrock with it, but this committal of himself to an opinion fell from him with so little sacrifice of his neutral expression, that the bid might not have been detected as his but for the friendly oaths of Mr Bambridge, who wanted to know what Horrock would do with the blasted stuff only fit for haberdashers given over to that state of perdition which the horse-dealer so cordially recognised in the majority of earthly existences. The lot was finally knocked down at a guinea to Mr Spilkins, a young Slender of the neighbourhood, who was reckless with his pocket-money and felt his want of memory for riddles.

'Come, Trumbull, this is too bad – you've been putting some old maid's rubbish into the sale,' murmured Mr Toller, getting close to the auctioneer. 'I want to see how the prints go, and I must be off soon.'

'Immediately, Mr Toller. It was only an act of benevolence which your noble heart would approve. Joseph! quick with the prints – Lot 235. Now, gentlemen, you who are connoiss*ures*, you are going to have a treat. Here is an engraving of the Duke of Wellington surrounded by his staff on the Field of Waterloo; and notwithstanding recent events which have, as it were, enveloped our great Hero in a cloud, I will be bold to say – for a man in my line must not be blown about by political winds – that a finer subject – of the modern order, belonging to our own time and epoch – the understanding of man could hardly conceive: angels might, perhaps, but not men, sirs, not men.'

'Who painted it?' said Mr Powderell, much impressed.

'It is a proof before the letter, Mr Powderell – the painter is not known,' answered Trumbull, with a certain gaspingness in his last words, after which he pursed up his lips and stared round him.

'I'll bid a pound!' said Mr Powderell, in a tone of resolved emotion, as of a man ready to put himself in the breach. Whether from awe or pity, nobody raised the price on him.

Next came two Dutch prints which Mr Toller had been eager for, and after he had secured them he went away. Other prints, and afterwards some paintings, were sold to leading Middlemarchers who had come with a special desire for them, and there was a more active movement of the audience in and out; some who had bought what they wanted, going away, others coming in either quite newly or from a temporary visit to the refreshments which were spread under the marquee on the lawn. It was this marquee that Mr Bambridge was bent on buying, and he appeared to like looking inside it frequently, as a foretaste of its possession. On the last occasion of his return from it he was observed to bring with him a new companion, a stranger to Mr Trumbull and everyone else, whose appearance, however, led to the supposition that he might be a relative of the horse-dealer's – also 'given to indulgence'. His large whiskers, imposing swagger, and swing of the leg, made him a striking figure; but his suit of black, rather shabby at the edges, caused the prejudicial inference that he was not able to afford himself as much indulgence as he liked.

'Who is it you've picked up, Bam?' said Mr Horrock, aside.

'Ask him yourself,' returned Mr Bambridge. 'He said he'd just turned in from the road.'

Mr Horrock eyed the stranger, who was leaning back against his stick with one hand, using his toothpick with the other, and looking about him with a certain restlessness apparently under the silence imposed on him by circumstances.

At length the *Supper at Emmaus* was brought forward, to Will's immense relief, for he was getting so tired of the proceedings that he had drawn back a little and leaned his shoulder against the wall just behind the auctioneer. He now came forward again, and his eye caught the conspicuous stranger, who, rather to his surprise, was staring at him markedly. But Will was immediately appealed to by Mr Trumbull.

'Yes, Mr Ladislaw, yes; this interests you as a connoiss*ure*, I think. It is some pleasure,' the auctioneer went on with a rising fervour, 'to have a picture like this to show to a company of ladies and gentlemen – a picture worth any sum to an individual whose means were on a level with his judgement. It is a painting of the Italian school – by the celebrated *Guydo*, the greatest painter in the world, the chief of the Old Masters, as they are called – I take it, because they were up to a thing or two beyond most of us – in possession of secrets now lost to the bulk of mankind. Let me tell you, gentlemen, I have seen a great many pictures by the Old Masters, and they are not all up to this mark – some of them are darker than you might like, and not family subjects. But here is a *Guydo* – the frame alone is worth pounds – which any lady might be proud to hang up – a suitable thing for what we call a refectory in a charitable institution, if any gentleman of the Corporation wished to show his munificence. Turn it a little, sir? yes. Joseph, turn it a little to Mr Ladislaw. Mr Ladislaw, having been abroad, understands the merit of these things, you observe.'

All eyes were for a moment turned towards Will, who said, coolly, 'Five pounds.' The auctioneer burst out in deep remonstrance: 'Ah! Mr Ladislaw! the frame alone is worth that. Ladies and gentlemen, for the credit of the town! Suppose it should be discovered hereafter that a gem of art has been amongst us in this town, and nobody in Middlemarch awake to it. Five guineas – five seven-six – five ten. Still, ladies, still! It is a gem, and "Full many a gem", as the poet says, has been allowed to go at a nominal price because the public knew no better, because it was offered in circles where there was – I was going to say a low feeling, but no! – Six pounds – six guineas – a *Guydo* of the first order going at six guineas – it is an insult to religion, ladies; it touches us all as Christians, gentlemen, that a subject like this should go at such a low figure – six pounds ten – seven –'

The bidding was brisk, and Will continued to share in it, remembering that

Mrs Bulstrode had a strong wish for the picture, and thinking that he might stretch the price to twelve pounds. But it was knocked down to him at ten guineas, whereupon he pushed his way towards the bow-window and went out. He chose to go under the marquee to get a glass of water, being hot and thirsty: it was empty of other visitors, and he asked the woman in attendance to fetch him some fresh water; but before she was well gone he was annoyed to see entering the florid stranger who had stared at him. It struck Will at this moment that the man might be one of those political parasitic insects of the bloated kind who had once or twice claimed acquaintance with him as having heard him speak on the Reform question, and who might think of getting a shilling by news. In this light his person, already rather heating to behold on a summer's day appeared the more disagreeable, and Will, half-seated on the elbow of a garden-chair, turned his eyes carefully away from the corner. But this signified little to our acquaintance Mr Raffles, who never hesitated to thrust himself on unwilling observation, if it suited his purpose to do so. He moved a step or two till he was in front of Will, and said with full-mouthed haste, 'Excuse me, Mr Ladislaw – was your mother's name Sarah Dunkirk?'

Will, starting to his feet, moved backward a step, frowning and saying with some fierceness, 'Yes, sir, it was. And what is that to you?'

It was in Will's nature that the first spark it threw out was a direct answer of the question and a challenge of the consequences. To have said, 'What is that to you?' in the first instance, would have seemed like shuffling – as if he minded who knew anything about his origin.

Raffles on his side had not the same eagerness for a collision which was implied in Ladislaw's threatening air. The slim young fellow with his girl's complexion looked like a tiger-cat ready to spring on him. Under such circumstances Mr Raffles's pleasure in annoying his company was kept in abeyance.

'No offence, my good sir, no offence; I only remember your mother – knew her when she was a girl. But it is your father that you feature, sir. I had the pleasure of seeing your father too. Parents alive, Mr Ladislaw?'

'No!' thundered Will, in the same attitude as before.

'Should be glad to do you a service, Mr Ladislaw – by Jove, I should! Hope to meet again.'

Hereupon Raffles, who had lifted his hat with the last words, turned himself round with a swing of his leg and walked away. Will looked after him a moment, and could see that he did not re-enter the auction room, but appeared to be walking towards the road. For an instant he thought that he had been foolish not to let the man go on talking; – but no! on the whole he preferred doing without knowledge from that source.

Later in the evening, however, Raffles overtook him in the street, and appearing either to have forgotten the roughness of his former reception or to intend avenging it by a forgiving familiarity, greeted him jovially and walked by his side, remarking at first on the pleasantness of the town and neighbourhood. Will at first suspected that the man had been drinking and was considering how to shake him off when Raffles said: 'I've been abroad myself, Mr Ladislaw – I've seen the world, used to parley-vous a little. It was at Boulogne I saw your father – a most uncommon likeness you are of him, by Jove! mouth – nose – eyes – hair turned off your brow just like this a little in the foreign style. John Bull doesn't do much of that. But your father was very ill when I saw him. Lord, lord! hands you might see through. You were a small youngster, then. Did he get well?'

'No,' said Will, curtly.

'Ah! Well! I've often wondered what became of your mother. She ran away from her friends when she was a young lass – a proud-spirited lass, and pretty, by Jove. *I* knew the reason why she ran away,' said Raffles, winking slowly as he looked sideways at Will.

'You know nothing dishonourable of her, sir,' said Will, turning on him rather savagely. But Mr Raffles just now was not sensitive to shades of manner.

'Not a bit!' said he, tossing his head decisively. 'She was a little too honourable to like her friends – that was it!' Here Raffles again winked slowly. 'Lord bless you, I knew all about 'em – a little in what you may call the respectable thieving line, the high style of receiving-house – none of your holes and corners – first-rate. Slap-up shop, high profits and no mistake. But Lord! Sarah would have known nothing about it – a dashing young lady she was – fine boarding-school – fit for a lord's wife, only Archie Duncan threw it at her out of spite, because she would have nothing to do with him. And so she ran away from the whole concern. I travelled for 'em, sir, in a gentlemanly way – at a high salary. They didn't mind her running away at first – godly folk, sir, very godly – and she was for the stage. The son was alive then, and the daughter was at a discount. Hallo! here we are at the Blue Bull. What do you say, Mr Ladislaw? shall we turn in and have a glass?'

'No, I must say good-evening,' said Will; dashing up a passage which led to Lowick Gate, and almost running to get out of Raffles's reach.

He walked a long while on the Lowick Road away from the town, glad of the starlit darkness when it came. He felt as if he had had dirt cast on him amidst shouts of scorn. There was this to confirm the fellow's statement – that his mother never would tell him the reason why she had run away from her family.

Well! what was he, Will Ladislaw, the worse, supposing the truth about that family to be the ugliest? His mother had braved hardship in order to separate herself from it. But if Dorothea's friends had known this story – if the Chettams had known it they would have had a fine colour to give their suspicions, a welcome ground for thinking him unfit to come near her. However, let them suspect what they pleased, they would find themselves in the wrong. They would find out that the blood in his veins was as free from the taint of meanness as theirs.

Chapter 61

'Inconsistencies,' answered Imlac, 'cannot both be
right, but imputed to man they may both be true.'

SAMUEL JOHNSON, *Rasselas*

The same night, when Mr Bulstrode returned from a journey to Brassing on
business, his good wife met him in the entrance-hall and drew him into his
private sitting-room.

'Nicholas,' she said, fixing her honest eyes upon him anxiously, 'there has
been such a disagreeable man here asking for you – it has made me quite
uncomfortable.'

'What kind of man, my dear?' said Mr Bulstrode, dreadfully certain of the
answer.

'A red-faced man with large whiskers, and most impudent in his manner. He
declared he was an old friend of yours, and said you would be sorry not to see
him. He wanted to wait for you here, but I told him he could see you at the Bank
tomorrow. Most impudent he was! – stared at me, and said his friend Nick had
luck in wives. I don't believe he would have gone away if Blucher had not
happened to break his chain and come running round on the gravel – for I was
in the garden; so I said, "You'd better go away – the dog is very fierce, and I can't
hold him." Do you really know anything of such a man?'

'I believe I know who he is, my dear,' said Bulstrode, in his usual subdued
voice, 'an unfortunate, dissolute wretch, whom I helped too much in days gone
by. However, I presume you will not be troubled by him again. He will probably
come to the Bank – to beg, doubtless.'

No more was said on the subject until the next day, when Mr Bulstrode had
returned from the town and was dressing for dinner. His wife, not sure that he
was come home, looked into his dressing-room and saw him with his coat and
cravat off, leaning one arm on a chest of drawers and staring absently at the
ground. He started nervously and looked up as she entered.

'You look very ill, Nicholas. Is there anything the matter?'

'I have a good deal of pain in my head,' said Mr Bulstrode, who was so
frequently ailing that his wife was always ready to believe in this cause of
depression.

'Sit down and let me sponge it with vinegar.'

Physically Mr Bulstrode did not want the vinegar, but morally the affectionate
attention soothed him. Though always polite, it was his habit to receive such
services with marital coolness, as his wife's duty. But today, while she was
bending over him, he said, 'You are very good, Harriet,' in a tone which had
something new in it to her ear; she did not know exactly what the novelty was,
but her woman's solicitude shaped itself into a darting thought that he might be
going to have an illness.

'Has anything worried you?' she said. 'Did that man come to you at the Bank?'

'Yes; it was as I had supposed. He is a man who at one time might have done better. But he has sunk into a drunken debauched creature.'

'Is he quite gone away?' said Mrs Bulstrode, anxiously; but for certain reasons she refrained from adding, 'it was very disagreeable to hear him calling himself a friend of yours.' At that moment she would not have liked to say anything which implied her habitual consciousness that her husband's earlier connections were not quite on a level with her own. Not that she knew much about them. That her husband had at first been employed in a bank, that he had afterwards entered into what he called city business and gained a fortune before he was three-and-thirty, that he had married a widow who was much older than himself – a Dissenter, and in other ways probably of that disadvantageous quality usually perceptible in a first wife if enquired into with the dispassionate judgement of a second – was almost as much as she had cared to learn beyond the glimpses which Mr Bulstrode's narrative occasionally gave of his early bent towards religion, his inclination to be a preacher, and his association with missionary and philanthropic efforts. She believed in him as an excellent man whose piety carried a peculiar eminence in belonging to a layman, whose influence had turned her own mind towards seriousness, and whose share of perishable good had been the means of raising her own position. But she also liked to think that it was well in every sense for Mr Bulstrode to have won the hand of Harriet Vincy; whose family was undeniable in a Middlemarch light – a better light surely than any thrown in London thoroughfares or dissenting chapel-yards. The unreformed provincial mind distrusted London; and while true religion was everywhere saving, honest Mrs Bulstrode was convinced that to be saved in the Church was more respectable. She so much wished to ignore towards others that her husband had ever been a London Dissenter, that she liked to keep it out of sight even in talking to him. He was quite aware of this; indeed in some respects he was rather afraid of this ingenuous wife, whose imitative piety and native worldliness were equally sincere, who had nothing to be ashamed of, and whom he had married out of a thorough inclination still subsisting. But his fears were such as belong to a man who cares to maintain his recognised supremacy: the loss of high consideration from his wife as from everyone else who did not clearly hate him out of enmity to the truth, would be as the beginning of death to him. When she said: 'Is he quite gone away?'

'Oh, I trust so,' he answered, with an effort to throw as much sober unconcern into his tone as possible.

But in truth Mr Bulstrode was very far from a state of quiet trust. In the interview at the Bank, Raffles had made it evident that his eagerness to torment was almost as strong in him as any other greed. He had frankly said that he had turned out of the way to come to Middlemarch, just to look about him and see whether the neighbourhood would suit him to live in. He had certainly had a few debts to pay more than he expected, but the two hundred pounds were not gone yet: a cool five-and-twenty would suffice him to go away with for the present. What he had wanted chiefly was to see his friend Nick and family, and know all about the prosperity of a man to whom he was so much attached. By and by he might come back for a longer stay. This time Raffles declined to be 'seen off the premises', as he expressed it – declined to quit Middlemarch under Bulstrode's eyes. He meant to go by coach the next day – if he chose.

Bulstrode felt himself helpless. Neither threats nor coaxing could avail: he could not count on any persistent fear nor on any promise. On the contrary, he felt a cold certainty at his heart that Raffles – unless providence sent death to hinder him – would come back to Middlemarch before long. And that certainty was a terror.

It was not that he was in danger of legal punishment or of beggary: he was in danger only of seeing disclosed to the judgement of his neighbours and the mournful perception of his wife certain facts of his past life which would render him an object of scorn and an opprobrium of the religion with which he had diligently associated himself. The terror of being judged sharpens the memory: it sends an inevitable glare over that long-unvisited past which has been habitually recalled only in general phrases. Even without memory, the life is bound into one by a zone of dependence in growth and decay: but intense memory forces a man to own his blameworthy past. With memory set smarting like a reopened wound, a man's past is not simply a dead history, an outworn preparation of the present: it is not a repented error shaken loose from the life: it is a still quivering part of himself, bringing shudders and bitter flavours and the tinglings of a merited shame.

Into this second life Bulstrode's past had now risen, only the pleasures of it seeming to have lost their quality. Night and day, without interruption save of brief sleep which only wove retrospect and fear into a fantastic present, he felt the scenes of his earlier life coming between him and everything else, as obstinately as when we look through the window from a lighted room, the objects we turn our backs on are still before us, instead of the grass and the trees. The successive events inward and outward were there in one view: though each might be dwelt on in turn, the rest still kept their hold in the consciousness.

Once more he saw himself the young banker's clerk, with an agreeable person, as clever in figures as he was fluent in speech and fond of theological definition: an eminent though young member of a Calvinistic dissenting church at Highbury, having had striking experience in conviction of sin and sense of pardon. Again he heard himself called for as Brother Bulstrode in prayer meetings, speaking on religious platforms, preaching in private houses. Again he felt himself thinking of the ministry as possibly his vocation, and inclined towards missionary labour. That was the happiest time of his life: that was the spot he would have chosen now to awake in and find the rest a dream. The people among whom Brother Bulstrode was distinguished were very few, but they were very near to him, and stirred his satisfaction the more; his power stretched through a narrow space, but he felt its effect the more intensely. He believed without effort in the peculiar work of grace within him, and in the signs that God intended him for special instrumentality.

Then came the moment of transition; it was with the sense of promotion he had when he, an orphan educated at a commercial charity-school, was invited to a fine villa belonging to Mr Dunkirk, the richest man in the congregation. Soon he became an intimate there, honoured for his piety by the wife, marked out for his ability by the husband, whose wealth was due to a flourishing city and west-end trade. That was the setting-in of a new current for his ambition, directing his prospects of 'instrumentality' towards the uniting of distinguished religious gifts with successful business.

By and by came a decided external leading: a confidential subordinate partner died, and nobody seemed to the principal so well fitted to fill the severely-felt vacancy as his young friend Bulstrode, if he would become confidential accountant. The offer was accepted. The business was a pawnbroker's, of the most magnificent sort both in extent and profits; and on a short acquaintance with it Bulstrode became aware that one source of magnificent profit was the easy reception of any goods offered without strict enquiry as to where they came from. But there was a branch house at the west end, and no pettiness or dinginess to give suggestions of shame.

He remembered his first moments of shrinking. They were private, and were filled with arguments; some of these taking the form of prayer. The business was established and had old roots; is it not one thing to set up a new gin-palace and another to accept an investment in an old one? The profits made out of lost souls – where can the line be drawn at which they begin in human transactions? Was it not even God's way of saving His chosen? 'Thou knowest,' – the young Bulstrode had said then, as the older Bulstrode was saying now – 'Thou knowest how loose my soul sits from these things – how I view them all as implements for tilling Thy garden rescued here and there from the wilderness.'

Metaphors and precedents were not wantin, peculiar spiritual experiences were not wanting, which at last made the retention of his position seem a service demanded of him: the vista of a fortune had already opened itself, and Bulstrode's shrinking remained private. Mr Dunkirk had never expected that there would be any shrinking at all: he had never conceived that trade had anything to do with the scheme of salvation. And it was true that Bulstrode found himself carrying on two distinct lives; his religious activity could not be incompatible with his business as soon as he had argued himself into not feeling it incompatible.

Mentally surrounded with that past again, Bulstrode had the same pleas – indeed, the years had been perpetually spinning them into intricate thickness, like masses of spider-web, padding the moral sensibility; nay, as age made egoism more eager but less enjoying, his soul had become more saturated with the belief that he did everything for God's sake, being indifferent to it for his own. And yet – if he could be back in that far-off spot with his youthful poverty – why, then he would choose to be a missionary.

But the train of causes in which he had locked himself went on. There was trouble in the fine villa at Highbury. Years before, the only daughter had run away, defied her parents, and gone on the stage; and now the only boy died, and after a short time Mr Dunkirk died also. The wife, a simple pious woman, left with all the wealth in and out of the magnificent trade, of which she never knew the precise nature, had come to believe in Bulstrode, and innocently adore him as women often adore their priest or 'man-made' minister. It was natural that after a time marriage should have been thought of between them. But Mrs Dunkirk had qualms and yearnings about her daughter, who had long been regarded as lost both to God and her parents. It was known that the daughter had married, but she was utterly gone out of sight. The mother, having lost her boy, imagined a grandson, and wished in a double sense to reclaim her daughter. If she were found, there would be a channel for property – perhaps a wide one, in the provision for several grandchildren. Efforts to find her must be made before Mrs Dunkirk would marry again. Bulstrode concurred; but after advertisement as well as other modes of enquiry had been tried, the mother believed that her daughter was not to be found, and consented to marry without reservation of property.

The daughter had been found; but only one man besides Bulstrode knew it, and he was paid for keeping silence and carrying himself away.

That was the bare fact which Bulstrode was now forced to see in the rigid outline with which acts present themselves to onlookers. But for himself at that distant time, and even now in burning memory, the fact was broken into little sequences, each justified as it came by reasonings which seemed to prove it righteous. Bulstrode's course up to that time had, he thought, been sanctioned by remarkable providences, appearing to point the way for him to be the agent in making the best use of a large property and withdrawing it from perversion. Death and other striking dispositions, such as feminine trustfulness, had come, and Bulstrode would have adopted Cromwell's words 'Do you call these bare events? The Lord pity you!' The events were comparatively small, but the essential condition was there – namely, that they were in favour of his own ends. It was easy for him to settle what was due from him to others by enquiring what were God's intentions with regard to himself. Could it be for God's service that this fortune should in any considerable proportion go to a young woman and her husband who were given up to the lightest pursuits, and might scatter it abroad in triviality – people who seemed to lie outside the path of remarkable providences? Bulstrode had never said to himself beforehand, 'The daughter shall not be found' – nevertheless when the moment came he kept her existence hidden; and when other moments followed, he soothed the mother with consolation in the probability that the unhappy young woman might be no more.

There were hours in which Bulstrode felt that his action was unrighteous; but how could he go back? He had mental exercises, called himself nought, laid hold on redemption, and went on in his course of instrumentality. And after five years Death again came to widen his path, by taking away his wife. He did gradually withdraw his capital, but he did not make the sacrifices requisite to put an end to the business, which was carried on for thirteen years afterwards before it finally collapsed. Meanwhile Nicholas Bulstrode had used his hundred thousand discreetly, and was becoming provincially, solidly important – a banker, a Churchman, a public benefactor; also a sleeping partner in trading concerns, in which his ability was directed to economy in the raw material, as in the case of the dyes which rotted Mr Vincy's silk. And now, when this respectability had lasted undisturbed for nearly thirty years – when all that preceded it had long lain benumbed in the consciousness – that past had risen and immersed his thoughts as if with the terrible irruption of a new sense overburthening the feeble being.

Meanwhile, in his conversation with Raffles, he had learned something momentous, something which entered actively into the struggle of his longings and terrors. There, he thought, lay an opening towards spiritual, perhaps towards material rescue.

The spiritual kind of rescue was a genuine need with him. There may be coarse hypocrites, who consciously affect beliefs and emotions for the sake of gulling the world, but Bulstrode was not one of them. He was simply a man whose desires had been stronger than his theoretic beliefs, and who had gradually explained the gratification of his desires into satisfactory agreement with those beliefs. If this be hypocrisy, it is a process which shows itself occasionally in us all, to whatever confession we belong, and whether we believe in the future perfection of our race or in the nearest date fixed for the end of the world; whether we regard the earth as a putrefying nidus for a saved remnant, including ourselves, or have a passionate belief in the solidarity of mankind.

The service he could do to the cause of religion had been through life the ground he alleged to himself for his choice of action: it had been the motive which he had poured out in his prayers. Who would use money and position better than he meant to use them? Who could surpass him in self-abhorrence and exaltation of God's cause? And to Mr Bulstrode God's cause was something distinct from his own rectitude of conduct: it enforced a discrimination of God's enemies, who were to be used merely as instruments, and whom it would be well if possible to keep out of money and consequent influence. Also, profitable investments in trades where the power of the prince of this world showed its most active devices, became sanctified by a right application of the profits in the hands of God's servant.

This implicit reasoning is essentially no more peculiar to evangelical belief than the use of wide phrases for narrow motives is peculiar to Englishmen. There is no general doctrine which is not capable of eating out our morality if unchecked by the deep-seated habit of direct fellow-feeling with individual fellow-men.

But a man who believes in something else than his own greed, has necessarily a conscience or standard to which he more or less adapts himself. Bulstrode's standard had been his serviceableness to God's cause: 'I am sinful and nought – a vessel to be consecrated by use – but use me!' – had been the mould into which he had constrained his immense need of being something important and pre-dominating. And now had come a moment in which that mould seemed in danger of being broken and utterly cast away.

What if the acts he had reconciled himself to, because they made him a stronger instrument of the divine glory, were to become the pretext of the scoffer, and a darkening of that glory? If this were to be the ruling of Providence, he was cast out from the temple as one who had brought unclean offerings.

He had long poured out utterances of repentance. But today a repentance had come which was of a bitterer flavour, and a threatening Providence urged him to a kind of propitiation which was not simply a doctrinal transaction. The divine tribunal had changed its aspect for him; self-prostration was no longer enough, and he must bring restitution in his hand. It was really before his God that Bulstrode was about to attempt such restitution as seemed possible: a great dread had seized his susceptible frame, and the scorching approach of shame wrought in him a new spiritual need. Night and day, while the resurgent threatening past was making a conscience within him, he was thinking by what means he could recover peace and trust – by what sacrifice he could stay the rod. His belief in these moments of dread was, that if he spontaneously did something right, God would save him from the consequences of wrong-doing. For religion can only change when the emotions which fill it are changed; and the religion of personal fear remains nearly at the level of the savage.

He had seen Raffles actually going away on the Brassing coach, and this was a temporary relief; it removed the pressure of an immediate dread, but did not put an end to the spiritual conflict and the need to win protection. At last he came to a difficult resolve, and wrote a letter to Will Ladislaw, begging him to be at The Shrubs that evening for a private interview at nine o'clock. Will had felt no particular surprise at the request, and connected it with some new notions about the *Pioneer*; but when he was shown into Mr Bulstrode's private room, he was struck with the painfully worn look on the banker's face, and was going to say, 'Are you ill?' when, checking himself in that abruptness, he only enquired after Mrs Bulstrode, and her satisfaction with the picture bought for her.

'Thank you, she is quite satisfied; she has gone out with her daughters this evening. I begged you to come, Mr Ladislaw, because I have a communication of a very private – indeed, I will say, of a sacredly confidential nature, which I desire to make to you. Nothing, I dare say, has been farther from your thoughts than that there had been important ties in the past which could connect your history with mine.'

Will felt something like an electric shock. He was already in a state of keen sensitiveness and hardly allayed agitation on the subject of ties in the past, and his presentiments were not agreeable. It seemed like the fluctuations of a dream – as if the action begun by that loud bloated stranger were being carried on by this pale-eyed sickly-looking piece of respectability, whose subdued tone and glib formality of speech were at this moment almost as repulsive to him as their remembered contrast. He answered, with a marked change of colour: 'No, indeed, nothing.'

'You see before you, Mr Ladislaw, a man who is deeply stricken. But for the urgency of conscience and the knowledge that I am before the bar of One who seeth not as man seeth, I should be under no compulsion to make the disclosure which has been my object in asking you to come here tonight. So far as human laws go, you have no claim on me whatever.'

Will was even more uncomfortable than wondering. Mr Bulstrode had paused, leaning his head on his hand, and looking at the floor. But he now fixed his examining glance on Will and said: 'I am told that your mother's name was Sarah Dunkirk, and that she ran away from her friends to go on the stage. Also, that your father was at one time much emaciated by illness. May I ask if you can confirm these statements?'

'Yes, they are all true,' said Will, struck with the order in which an enquiry had come, that might have been expected to be preliminary to the banker's hints. But Mr Bulstrode had tonight followed the order of his emotions; he entertained no doubt that the opportunity for restitution had come, and he had an overpowering impulse towards the penitential expression by which he was deprecating chastisement.

'Do you know any particulars of your mother's family?' he continued.

'No; she never liked to speak of them. She was a very generous, honourable woman,' said Will, almost angrily.

'I do not wish to allege anything against her. Did she never mention her mother to you at all?'

'I have heard her say that she thought her mother did not know the reason of her running away. She said "poor mother" in a pitying tone.'

'That mother became my wife,' said Bulstrode, and then paused a moment before he added, 'you have a claim on me, Mr Ladislaw: as I said before, not a legal claim, but one which my conscience recognises. I was enriched by that marriage – a result which would probably not have taken place – certainly not to the same extent – if your grandmother could have discovered her daughter. That daughter, I gather, is no longer living!'

'No,' said Will, feeling suspicion and repugnance rising so strongly within him, that without quite knowing what he did, he took his hat from the floor and stood up. The impulse within him was to reject the disclosed connection.

'Pray be seated, Mr Ladislaw,' said Bulstrode, anxiously. 'Doubtless you are startled by the suddenness of this discovery. But I entreat your patience with one who is already bowed down by inward trial.'

Will reseated himself, feeling some pity which was half contempt for this voluntary self-abasement of an elderly man.

'It is my wish, Mr Ladislaw, to make amends for the deprivation which befell your mother. I know that you are without fortune, and I wish to supply you adequately from a store which would have probably already been yours had your grandmother been certain of your mother's existence and been able to find her.'

Mr Bulstrode paused. He felt that he was performing a striking piece of scrupulosity in the judgement of his auditor, and a penitential act in the eyes of God. He had no clue to the state of Will Ladislaw's mind, smarting as it was from the clear hint of Raffles, and with its natural quickness in construction stimulated by the expectation of discoveries which he would have been glad to conjure back into darkness. Will made no answer for several moments, till Mr Bulstrode, who at the end of his speech had cast his eyes on the floor, now raised them with an examining glance, which Will met fully, saying: 'I suppose you did know of my mother's existence, and knew where she might have been found.'

Bulstrode shrank – there was a visible quivering in his face and hands. He was totally unprepared to have his advances met in this way, or to find himself urged into more revelation than he had beforehand set down as needful. But at that moment he dared not tell a lie, and he felt suddenly uncertain of his ground which he had trodden with some confidence before.

'I will not deny that you conjecture rightly,' he answered, with a faltering in his tone. 'And I wish to make atonement to you as the one still remaining who has suffered a loss through me. You enter, I trust, into my purpose, Mr Ladislaw, which has a reference to higher than merely human claims, and as I have already said, is entirely independent of any legal compulsion. I am ready to narrow my own resources and the prospects of my family by binding myself to allow you five hundred pounds yearly during my life, and to leave you a proportional capital at my death – nay, to do still more, if more should be definitely necessary to any laudable project on your part.' Mr Bulstrode had gone on to particulars in the expectation that these would work strongly on Ladislaw, and merge other feelings in grateful acceptance.

But Will was looking as stubborn as possible, with his lip pouting and his fingers in his side-pockets. He was not in the least touched, and said firmly: 'Before I make any reply to your proposition, Mr Bulstrode, I must beg you to answer a question or two. Were you connected with the business by which that fortune you speak of was originally made?'

Mr Bulstrode's thought was, 'Raffles has told him.' How could he refuse to answer when he had volunteered what drew forth the question? He answered, 'Yes.'

'And was that business – or was it not – a thoroughly dishonourable one – nay, one that, if its nature had been made public, might have ranked those concerned in it with thieves and convicts?'

Will's tone had a cutting bitterness: he was moved to put his question as nakedly as he could.

Bulstrode reddened with irrepressible anger. He had been prepared for a scene of self-abasement, but his intense pride and his habit of supremacy over-powered penitence, and even dread, when this young man, whom he had meant to benefit, turned on him with the air of a judge.

'The business was established before I became acquainted with it, sir; nor is it for you to institute an enquiry of that kind,' he answered, not raising his voice, but speaking with quick defiantness.

'Yes, it is,' said Will, starting up again with his hat in his hand. 'It is eminently mine to ask such questions, when I have to decide whether I will have trans-actions with you and accept your money. My unblemished honour is important to me. It is important to me to have no stain on my birth and connections. And now I find there is a stain which I can't help. My mother felt it, and tried to keep as clear of it as she could, and so will I. You shall keep your ill-gotten money. If I had any fortune of my own, I would willingly pay it to anyone who could disprove what you have told me. What I have to thank you for is that you kept the money till now, when I can refuse it. It ought to lie with a man's self that he is a gentleman. Good-night, sir.'

Bulstrode was going to speak, but Will with determined quickness was out of the room in an instant, and in another the hall-door had closed behind him. He was too strongly possessed with passionate rebellion against this inherited blot which had been thrust on his knowledge to reflect at present whether he had not been too hard on Bulstrode – too arrogantly merciless towards a man of sixty, who was making efforts at retrieval when time had rendered them in vain.

No third person listening could have thoroughly understood the impetuosity of Will's repulse or the bitterness of his words. No one but himself then knew how everything connected with the sentiment of his own dignity had an immediate bearing for him on his relation to Dorothea and to Mr Casaubon's treatment of him. And in the rush of impulses by which he flung back that offer of Bulstrode's, there was mingled the sense that it would have been impossible for him ever to tell Dorothea that he had accepted it.

As for Bulstrode – when Will was gone he suffered a violent reaction, and wept like a woman. It was the first time he had encountered an open expression of scorn from any man higher than Raffles; and with that scorn hurrying like venom through his system, there was no sensibility left to consolations. But the relief of weeping had to be checked. His wife and daughters soon came home from hearing the address of an Oriental missionary, and were full of regret that papa had not heard, in the first instance, the interesting things which they tried to repeat to him.

Perhaps, through all other hidden thoughts, the one that breathed most comfort, was that Will Ladislaw at least was not likely to publish what had taken place that evening.

Chapter 62

He was a squyer of lowe degre,
That loved the king's daughter of Hungrie.

Old romance

Will Ladislaw's mind was now wholly bent on seeing Dorothea again, and forthwith quitting Middlemarch. The morning after his agitating scene with Bulstrode he wrote a brief letter to her, saying that various causes had detained him in the neighbourhood longer than he had expected, and asking her permission to call again at Lowick at some hour which she would mention on the earliest possible day, he being anxious to depart, but unwilling to do so until she had granted him an interview. He left the letter at the office, ordering the messenger to carry it to Lowick Manor, and wait for an answer.

Ladislaw felt the awkwardness of asking for more last words. His former farewell had been made in the hearing of Sir James Chettam, and had been announced as final even to the butler. It is certainly trying to a man's dignity to reappear when he is not expected to do so: a first farewell has pathos in it, but to come back for a second lends an opening to comedy, and it was possible even that there might be bitter sneers afloat about Will's motives for lingering. Still it was on the whole more satisfactory to his feeling to take the directest means of seeing Dorothea, than to use any device which might give an air of chance to a meeting of which he wished her to understand that it was what he earnestly sought. When he had parted from her before, he had been in ignorance of facts which gave a new aspect to the relation between them, and made a more absolute severance than he had then believed in. He knew nothing of Dorothea's private fortune, and being little used to reflect on such matters, took it for granted that according to Mr Casaubon's arrangement marriage to him, Will Ladislaw, would mean that she consented to be penniless. That was not what he could wish for even in his secret heart, or even if she had been ready to meet such hard contrast for his sake. And then, too, there was the fresh smart of that disclosure about his mother's family, which if known would be an added reason why Dorothea's friends should look down upon him as utterly below her. The secret hope that after some years he might come back with the sense that he had at least a personal value equal to her wealth, seemed now the dreamy continuation of a dream. This change would surely justify him in asking Dorothea to receive him once more.

But Dorothea on that morning was not at home to receive Will's note. In consequence of a letter from her uncle announcing his intention to be at home in a week, she had driven first to Freshitt to carry the news, meaning to go on to the Grange to deliver some orders with which her uncle had intrusted her – thinking, as he said, 'a little mental occupation of this sort good for a widow'.

If Will Ladislaw could have overheard some of the talk at Freshitt that morning, he would have felt all his suppositions confirmed as to the readiness of certain people to sneer at his lingering in the neighbourhood. Sir James, indeed, though much relieved concerning Dorothea, had been on the watch to learn Ladislaw's movements, and had an instructed informant in Mr Standish, who was necessarily in his confidence on this matter. That Ladislaw had stayed in Middlemarch nearly two months after he had declared that he was going immediately, was a fact to embitter Sir James's suspicions, or at least to justify his aversion to a 'young fellow' whom he represented to himself as slight, volatile, and likely to show such recklessness as naturally went along with a position unriveted by family ties or a strict profession. But he had just heard something from Standish which, while it justified these surmises about Will, offered a means of nullifying all danger with regard to Dorothea.

Unwonted circumstances may make us all rather unlike ourselves: there are conditions under which the most majestic person is obliged to sneeze, and our emotions are liable to be acted on in the same incongruous manner. Good Sir James was this morning so far unlike himself that he was irritably anxious to say something to Dorothea on a subject which he usually avoided as if it had been a matter of shame to them both. He could not use Celia as a medium, because he did not choose that she should know the kind of gossip he had in his mind; and before Dorothea happened to arrive he had been trying to imagine how, with his shyness and unready tongue, he could ever manage to introduce his communication. Her unexpected presence brought him to utter hopelessness in his own power of saying anything unpleasant; but desperation suggested a resource; he sent the groom on an unsaddled horse across the park with a pencilled note to Mrs Cadwallader, who already knew the gossip, and would think it no compromise of herself to repeat it as often as required.

Dorothea was detained on the good pretext that Mr Garth, whom she wanted to see, was expected at the Hall within the hour, and she was still talking to Caleb on the gravel when Sir James, on the watch for the rector's wife, saw her coming and met her with the needful hints.

'Enough! I understand,' said Mrs Cadwallader. 'You shall be innocent. I am such a blackamoor that I cannot smirch myself.'

'I don't mean that it's of any consequence,' said Sir James, disliking that Mrs Cadwallader should understand too much. 'Only it is desirable that Dorothea should know there are reasons why she should not receive him again; and I really can't say so to her. It will come lightly from you.'

It came very lightly indeed. When Dorothea quitted Caleb and turned to meet them, it appeared that Mrs Cadwallader had stepped across the park by the merest chance in the world, just to chat with Celia in a matronly way about the baby. And so Mr Brooke was coming back? Delightful – coming back, it was to be hoped, quite cured of Parliamentary fever and pioneering. *Apropos* of the *Pioneer* – somebody had prophesied that it would soon be like a dying dolphin, and turn all colours for want of knowing how to help itself, because Mr Brooke's *protégé*, the brilliant young Ladislaw, was gone or going. Had Sir James heard that?

The three were walking along the gravel slowly, and Sir James, turning aside to whip a shrub, said he had heard something of that sort.

'All false!' said Mrs Cadwallader. 'He is not gone, or going, apparently; the *Pioneer* keeps its colour, and Mr Orlando Ladislaw is making a sad dark-blue scandal by warbling continually with your Mr Lydgate's wife, who they tell me is as pretty as pretty can be. It seems nobody ever goes into the house without finding this young gentleman lying on the rug or warbling at the piano. But the people in manufacturing towns are always disreputable.'

'You began by saying that one report was false, Mrs Cadwallader, and I believe this is false too,' said Dorothea, with indignant energy: 'at least, I feel sure it is a misrepresentation. I will not hear any evil spoken of Mr Ladislaw: he has already suffered too much injustice.'

Dorothea when thoroughly moved cared little what anyone thought of her feelings: and even if she had been able to reflect, she would have held it petty to keep silence at injurious words about Will from fear of being herself misunderstood. Her face was flushed and her lip trembled.

Sir James, glancing at her, repented of his stratagem; but Mrs Cadwallader, equal to all occasions, spread the palms of her hands outward and said, 'Heaven grant it, my dear! – I mean that all bad tales about anybody may be false. But it is a pity that young Lydgate should have married one of these Middlemarch girls. Considering he's a son of somebody, he might have got a woman with good blood in her veins, and not too young, who would have put up with his profession. There's Clara Harfager, for instance, whose friends don't know what to do with her and she has a portion. Then we might have had her among us. However! – it's no use being wise for other people. Where is Celia? Pray let us go in.'

'I am going on immediately to Tipton,' said Dorothea rather haughtily. 'Goodbye.'

Sir James could say nothing as he accompanied her to the carriage. He was altogether discontented with the result of a contrivance which had cost him some secret humiliation beforehand.

Dorothea drove along between the berried hedgerows and the shorn cornfields, not seeing or hearing anything around. The tears came and rolled down her cheeks, but she did not know it. The world, it seemed, was turning ugly and hateful, and there was no place for her trustfulness. 'It is not true – it is not true!' was the voice within her that she listened to; but all the while a remembrance to which there had always clung a vague uneasiness would thrust itself on her attention – the remembrance of that day when she had found Will Ladislaw with Mrs Lydgate, and had heard his voice accompanied by the piano.

'He said he would never do anything that I disapproved – I wish I could have told him that I disapproved of that,' said poor Dorothea, inwardly, feeling a strange alternation between anger with Will and the passionate defence of him. 'They all try to blacken him before me; but I will care for no pain, if he is not to blame. I always believed he was good.' – These were her last thoughts before she felt that the carriage was passing under the archway of the lodge-gate at the Grange, when she hurriedly pressed her handkerchief to her face and began to think of her errands. The coachman begged leave to take out the horses for half an hour as there was something wrong with a shoe; and Dorothea, having the sense that she was going to rest, took off her gloves and bonnet, while she was leaning against a statue in the entrance-hall, and talking to the housekeeper. At last she said: 'I must stay here a little, Mrs Kell. I will go into the library and write you some memoranda from my uncle's letter, if you will open the shutters for me.'

'The shutters are open, madam,' said Mrs Kell, following Dorothea, who had walked along as she spoke. 'Mr Ladislaw is there, looking for something.'

(Will had come to fetch a portfolio of his own sketches which he had missed in the act of packing his movables, and did not choose to leave behind.)

Dorothea's heart seemed to turn over as if it had had a blow, but she was not perceptibly checked: in truth, the sense that Will was there was for the moment all-satisfying to her, like the sight of something precious that one has lost. When she reached the door she said to Mrs Kell: 'Go in first, and tell him that I am here.'

Will had found his portfolio, and had laid it on the table at the far end of the room, to turn over the sketches and please himself by looking at the memorable piece of art which had a relation to nature too mysterious for Dorothea. He was smiling at it still, and shaking the sketches into order with the thought that he might find a letter from her awaiting him at Middlemarch, when Mrs Kell close to his elbow said: 'Mrs Casaubon is coming in, sir.'

Will turned round quickly, and the next moment Dorothea was entering. As Mrs Kell closed the door behind her they met: each was looking at the other, and consciousness was overflowed by something that suppressed utterance. It was not confusion that kept them silent, for they both felt that parting was near, and there is no shamefacedness in a sad parting.

She moved automatically towards her uncle's chair against the writing-table, and Will, after drawing it out a little for her, went a few paces off and stood opposite her.

'Pray sit down,' said Dorothea, crossing her hands on her lap; 'I am very glad you were here.' Will thought that her face looked just as it did when she first shook hands with him in Rome; for her widow's cap, fixed in her bonnet, had gone off with it, and he could see that she had lately been shedding tears. But the mixture of anger in her agitation had vanished at the sight of him; she had been used, when they were face to face, always to feel confidence and the happy freedom which comes with mutual understanding, and how could other people's words hinder that effect on a sudden? Let the music which can take possession of our frame and fill the air with joy for us, sound once more – what does it signify that we heard it found fault with in its absence?

'I have sent a letter to Lowick Manor today, asking leave to see you,' said Will, seating himself opposite to her. 'I am going away immediately, and I could not go without speaking to you again.'

'I thought we had parted when you came to Lowick many weeks ago – you thought you were going then,' said Dorothea, her voice trembling a little.

'Yes; but I was in ignorance then of things which I know now – things which have altered my feelings about the future. When I saw you before, I was dreaming that I might come back someday. I don't think I ever shall – now.' Will paused here.

'You wished me to know the reasons?' said Dorothea, timidly.

'Yes,' said Will, impetuously, shaking his head backward, and looking away from her with irritation in his face. 'Of course I must wish it. I have been grossly insulted in your eyes and in the eyes of others. There has been a mean implication against my character. I wish you to know that under no circumstances would I have lowered myself by – under no circumstances would I have given men the chance of saying that I sought money under the pretext of seeking – something else. There was no need of other safeguard against me – the safeguard of wealth was enough.'

Will rose from his chair with the last word and went – he hardly knew where; but it was to the projecting window nearest him, which had been open as now about the same season a year ago, when he and Dorothea had stood within it and talked together. Her whole heart was going out at this moment in sympathy with Will's indignation: she only wanted to convince him that she had never done him injustice, and he seemed to have turned away from her as if she too had been part of the unfriendly world.

'It would be very unkind of you to suppose that I ever attributed any meanness to you,' she began. Then in her ardent way, wanting to plead with him, she moved from her chair and went in front of him to her old place in the window, saying, 'Do you suppose that I ever disbelieved in you?'

When Will saw her there, he gave a start and moved backward out of the window, without meeting her glance. Dorothea was hurt by this movement following up the previous anger of his tone. She was ready to say that it was as hard on her as on him, and that she was helpless but those strange particulars of their relation which neither of them could explicitly mention kept her always in dread of saying too much. At this moment she had no belief that Will would in any case have wanted to marry her, and she feared using words which might imply such a belief. She only said earnestly, recurring to his last word: 'I am sure no safeguard was ever needed against you.'

Will did not answer. In the stormy fluctuation of his feelings these words of hers seemed to him cruelly neutral, and he looked pale and miserable after his angry outburst. He went to the table and fastened up his portfolio, while Dorothea looked at him from the distance. They were wasting these last moments together in wretched silence. What could he say, since what had got obstinately uppermost in his mind was the passionate love for her which he forbade himself to utter? What could she say, since she might offer him no help – since she was forced to keep the money that ought to have been his? – since today he seemed not to respond as he used to do to her thorough trust and liking?

But Will at last turned away from his portfolio and approached the window again.

'I must go,' he said, with that peculiar look of the eyes which sometimes accompanies bitter feeling, as if they had been tired and burned with gazing too close at a light.

'What shall you do in life?' said Dorothea, timidly. 'Have your intentions remained just the same as when we said goodbye before?'

'Yes,' said Will, in a tone that seemed to waive the subject as uninteresting. 'I shall work away at the first thing that offers. I suppose one gets a habit of doing without happiness or hope.'

'Oh, what sad words!' said Dorothea, with a dangerous tendency to sob. Then trying to smile, she added, 'We used to agree that we were alike in speaking too strongly.'

'I have not spoken too strongly now,' said Will, leaning back against the angle of the wall. 'There are certain things which a man can only go through once in his life; and he must know sometime or other that the best is over with him. This experience has happened to me while I am very young – that is all. What I care more for than I can ever care for anything else is absolutely forbidden to me – I don't mean merely by being out of my reach, but forbidden me, even if it were within my reach, by my own pride and honour – by everything I respect myself for. Of course I shall go on living as a man might do who had seen heaven in a trance.'

Will paused, imagining that it would be impossible for Dorothea to misunderstand this; indeed he felt that he was contradicting himself and offending against his self-approval in speaking to her so plainly; but still – it could not be fairly called wooing a woman to tell her that he would never woo her. It must be admitted to be a ghostly kind of wooing.

But Dorothea's mind was rapidly going over the past with quite another vision than his. The thought that she herself might be what Will most cared for did throb through her an instant, but then came doubt: the memory of the little they had lived through together turned pale and shrank before the memory which suggested how much fuller might have been the intercourse between Will and someone else with whom he had had constant companionship. Everything he had said might refer to that other relation, and whatever had passed between him and herself was thoroughly explained by what she had always regarded as their simple friendship and the cruel obstruction thrust upon it by her husband's injurious act. Dorothea stood silent, with her eyes cast down dreamily, while images crowded upon her which left the sickening certainty that Will was referring to Mrs Lydgate. But why sickening? He wanted her to know that here too his conduct should be above suspicion.

Will was not surprised at her silence. His mind also was tumultuously busy while he watched her, and he was feeling rather wildly that something must happen to hinder their parting – some miracle, clearly nothing in their own deliberate speech. Yet, after all, had she any love for him? – he could not pretend to himself that he would rather believe her to be without that pain. He could not deny that a secret longing for the assurance that she loved him was at the root of all his words.

Neither of them knew how long they stood in that way. Dorothea was raising her eyes, and was about to speak, when the door opened and her footman came to say: 'The horses are ready, madam, whenever you like to start.'

'Presently,' said Dorothea. Then turning to Will, she said, 'I have some memoranda to write for the housekeeper.'

'I must go,' said Will, when the door had closed again – advancing towards her. 'The day after tomorrow I shall leave Middlemarch.'

'You have acted in every way rightly,' said Dorothea, in a low tone, feeling a pressure at her heart which made it difficult to speak.

She put out her hand, and Will took it for an instant without speaking, for her words had seemed to him cruelly cold and unlike herself. Their eyes met, but there was discontent in his, and in hers there was only sadness. He turned away and took his portfolio under his arm.

'I have never done you injustice. Please remember me,' said Dorothea, repressing a rising sob.

'Why should you say that?' said Will, with irritation. 'As if I were not in danger of forgetting everything else.'

He had really a movement of anger against her at that moment, and it impelled him to go away without pause. It was all one flash to Dorothea – his last words – his distant bow to her as he reached the door – the sense that he was no longer there. She sank into the chair, and for a few moments sat there like a statue, while images and emotions were hurrying upon her. Joy came first, in spite of the threatening train behind it – joy in the impression that it was really herself whom Will loved and was renouncing, that there was really no other love less permissible, more blameworthy, which honour was hurrying him away from. They were parted all the same, but – Dorothea drew a deep breath and felt her strength return – she could think of him unrestrainedly. At that moment the parting was easy to bear: the first sense of loving and being loved excluded sorrow. It was as if some hard icy pressure had melted, and her consciousness had room to expand; her past was come back to her with larger interpretation. The joy was not the less – perhaps it was the more complete just then – because of the irrevocable parting; for there was no reproach, no contemptuous wonder to imagine in any eye or from any lips. He had acted so as to defy reproach, and make wonder respectful.

Anyone watching her might have seen that there was a fortifying thought within her. Just as when inventive power is working with glad ease some small claim on the attention is fully met as if it were only a cranny opened to the sunlight, it was easy now for Dorothea to write her memoranda. She spoke her last words to the housekeeper in cheerful tones, and when she seated herself in the carriage her eyes were bright and her cheeks blooming under the dismal bonnet. She threw back the heavy 'weepers', and looked before her, wondering which road Will had taken. It was in her nature to be proud that he was blameless, and through all her feelings there ran this vein – 'I was right to defend him.'

The coachman was used to drive his greys at a good pace, Mr Casaubon being unenjoying and impatient in everything away from his desk, and wanting to get to the end of all journeys; and Dorothea was now bowled along quickly. Driving was pleasant, for rain in the night had laid the dust, and the blue sky looked far off, away from the region of the great clouds that sailed in masses. The earth looked like a happy place under the vast heavens, and Dorothea was wishing that she might overtake Will and see him once more.

After a turn of the road, there he was with the portfolio under his arm; but the next moment she was passing him while he raised his hat, and she felt a pang at being seated there in a sort of exaltation, leaving him behind. She could not look back at him. It was as if a crowd of indifferent objects had thrust them asunder, and forced them along different paths, taking them farther and farther away from each other, and making it useless to look back. She could no more make any sign that would seem to say, 'Need we part?' than she could stop the carriage to wait for him. Nay, what a world of reasons crowded upon her against any movement of her thought towards a future that might reverse the decision of this day!

'I only wish I had known before – I wish he knew – then we could be quite happy in thinking of each other, though we are for ever parted. And if I could but have given him the money, and made things easier for him!' – were the longings that came back the most persistently. And yet, so heavily did the world weigh on her in spite of her independent energy, that with this idea of Will as in need of such help and at a disadvantage with the world, there came always the vision of that unfittingness of any closer relation between them which lay in the opinion of everyone connected with her. She felt to the full all the imperativeness of the motives which urged Will's conduct. How could he dream of her defying the barrier that her husband had placed between them? – how could she ever say to herself that she would defy it?

Will's certainty, as the carriage grew smaller in the distance, had much more bitterness in it. Very slight matters were enough to gall him in his sensitive mood, and the sight of Dorothea driving past him while he felt himself plodding along as a poor devil seeking a position in a world which in his present temper offered him little that he coveted, made his conduct seem a mere matter of necessity, and took away the sustainment of resolve. After all, he had no assurance that she loved him: could any man pretend that he was simply glad in such a case to have the suffering all on his own side?

That evening Will spent with the Lydgates; the next evening he was gone.

BOOK SEVEN

Two Temptations

Chapter 63

These little things are great to little man.

OLIVER GOLDSMITH

'Have you seen much of your scientific phoenix, Lydgate, lately?' said Mr Toller at one of his Christmas dinner-parties, speaking to Mr Farebrother on his right hand.

'Not much I am sorry to say,' answered the Vicar, accustomed to parry Mr Toller's banter about his belief in the new medical light. 'I am out of the way, and he is too busy.'

'Is he? I am glad to hear it,' said Dr Minchin, with mingled suavity and surprise.

'He gives a great deal of time to the New Hospital,' said Mr Farebrother, who had his reasons for continuing the subject: 'I hear of that from my neighbour, Mrs Casaubon, who goes there often. She says Lydgate is indefatigable, and is making a fine thing of Bulstrode's institution. He is preparing a new ward in case of the cholera coming to us.'

'And preparing theories of treatment to try on the patients, I suppose,' said Mr Toller.

'Come, Toller, be candid,' said Mr Farebrother. 'You are too clever not to see the good of a bold fresh mind in medicine, as well as in everything else; and as to cholera, I fancy, none of you are very sure what you ought to do. If a man goes a little too far along a new road, it is usually himself that he harms more than anyone else.'

'I am sure you and Wrench ought to be obliged to him,' said Dr Minchin, looking towards Toller, 'for he has sent you the cream of Peacock's patients.'

'Lydgate has been living at a great rate for a young beginner,' said Mr Harry Toller, the brewer. 'I suppose his relations in the North back him up.'

'I hope so,' said Mr Chichely, 'else he ought not to have married that nice girl we were all so fond of. Hang it, one has a grudge against a man who carries off the prettiest girl in the town.'

'Ay, by God! and the best too,' said Mr Standish.

'My friend Vincy didn't half like the marriage, I know that,' said Mr Chichely. '*He* wouldn't do much. How the relations on the other side may have come down I can't say.' There was an emphatic kind of reticence in Mr Chichely's manner of speaking.

'Oh, I shouldn't think Lydgate ever looked to practice for a living,' said Mr Toller, with a slight touch of sarcasm; and there the subject was dropped.

This was not the first time that Mr Farebrother had heard hints of Lydgate's expenses being obviously too great to be met by his practice, but he thought it not unlikely that there were resources of expectations which excused the large outlay at the time of Lydgate's marriage, and which might hinder any bad consequences from the disappointment in his practice. One evening, when he took the pains to go to Middlemarch on purpose to have a chat with Lydgate as of old, he noticed in him an air of excited effort quite unlike his usual easy way of keeping silence or breaking it with abrupt energy whenever he had anything to say. Lydgate talked persistently when they were in his workroom, putting arguments for and against the probability of certain biological views; but he had none of those definite things to say or to show which give the way-marks of a patient uninterrupted pursuit, such as he used himself to insist on, saying that 'there must be a systole and diastole in all enquiry', and that 'a man's mind must be continually expanding and shrinking between the whole human horizon and the horizon of an object-glass'. That evening he seemed to be talking widely for the sake of resisting any personal bearing; and before long they went into the drawing-room, where Lydgate, having asked Rosamond to give them music, sank back in his chair in silence, but with a strange light in his eyes. 'He may have been taking an opiate,' was a thought that crossed Mr Farebrother's mind 'tic-douloureux perhaps – or medical worries.'

It did not occur to him that Lydgate's marriage was not delightful: he believed, as the rest did, that Rosamond was an amiable, docile creature, though he had always thought her rather uninteresting – a little too much the pattern-card of the finishing-school; and his mother could not forgive Rosamond because she never seemed to see that Henrietta Noble was in the room. 'However, Lydgate fell in love with her,' said the Vicar to himself, 'and she must be to his taste.'

Mr Farebrother was aware that Lydgate was a proud man, but having very little corresponding fibre in himself, and perhaps too little care about personal dignity, except the dignity of not being mean or foolish, he could hardly allow enough for the way in which Lydgate shrank, as from a burn, from the utterance of any word about his private affairs. And soon after that conversation at Mr Toller's, the Vicar learned something which made him watch the more eagerly for an opportunity of indirectly letting Lydgate know that if he wanted to open himself about any difficulty there was a friendly ear ready.

The opportunity came at Mr Vincy's, where, on New Year's Day, there was a party, to which Mr Farebrother was irresistibly invited, on the plea that he must not forsake his old friends on the first new year of his being a greater man, and Rector as well as Vicar. And this party was thoroughly friendly: all the ladies of the Farebrother family were present; the Vincy children all dined at the table, and Fred had persuaded his mother that if she did not invite Mary Garth, the Farebrothers would regard it as a slight to themselves, Mary being their particular friend. Mary came and Fred was in high spirits, though his enjoyment was of a checkered kind – triumph that his mother should see Mary's importance with the chief personages in the party being much streaked with jealousy when Mr Farebrother sat down by her. Fred used to be much more easy about his own accomplishments in the days when he had not begun to dread being 'bowled out by Farebrother', and this terror was still before him. Mrs Vincy, in her fullest matronly bloom, looked at Mary's little figure, rough wavy hair, and visage quite without lilies and roses, and wondered; trying unsuccessfully to fancy herself caring about Mary's appearance in wedding clothes, or feeling complacency in grandchildren who would 'feature' the Garths. However, the party was a merry one, and Mary was particularly bright; being glad, for Fred's sake, that his friends were getting kinder to her, and being also quite willing that they should see how much she was valued by others whom they must admit to be the judges.

Mr Farebrother noticed that Lydgate seemed bored, and that Mr Vincy spoke as little as possible to his son-in-law. Rosamond was perfectly graceful and calm, and only a subtle observation such as the Vicar had not been roused to bestow on her would have perceived the total absence of that interest in her husband's presence which a loving wife is sure to betray, even if etiquette keeps her aloof from him. When Lydgate was taking part in the conversation, she never looked towards him any more than if she had been a sculptured Psyche modelled to look another way: and when, after being called out for an hour or two, he re-entered the room, she seemed unconscious of the fact, which eighteen months before would have had the effect of a numeral before cyphers. In reality, how-ever, she was intensely aware of Lydgate's voice and movements; and her pretty good-tempered air of unconsciousness was a studied negation by which she satisfied her inward opposition to him without compromise of propriety. When the ladies were in the drawing-room after Lydgate had been called away from the dessert, Mrs Farebrother, when Rosamond happened to be near her, said – 'You have to give up a great deal of your husband's society, Mrs Lydgate.'

'Yes, the life of a medical man is very arduous; especially when he is so devoted to his profession as Mr Lydgate is,' said Rosamond, who was standing, and moved easily away at the end of this correct little speech.

'It is dreadfully dull for her when there is no company,' said Mrs Vincy, who was seated at the old lady's side. 'I am sure I thought so when Rosamond was ill, and I was staying with her. You know, Mrs Farebrother, ours is a cheerful house. I am of a cheerful disposition myself, and Mr Vincy always likes some-thing to be going on. That is what Rosamond has been used to. Very different from a husband out at odd hours, and never knowing when he will come home, and of a close, proud disposition, I think' – indiscreet Mrs Vincy did lower her tone slightly with this parenthesis. 'But Rosamond always had an angel of a temper; her brothers used very often not to please her, but she was never the girl to show temper; from a baby she was always as good as good, and with a complexion beyond anything. But my children are all good-tempered, thank God.'

This was easily credible to anyone looking at Mrs Vincy as she threw back her broad cap-strings, and smiled towards her three little girls, aged from seven to eleven. But in that smiling glance she was obliged to include Mary Garth, whom the three girls had got into a corner to make her tell them stories. Mary was just finishing the delicious tale of Rumpelstiltskin, which she had well by heart, because Letty was never tired of communicating it to her ignorant elders from a favourite red volume. Louisa, Mrs Vincy's darling, now ran to her with wide-eyed serious excitement, crying, 'O mamma, mamma, the little man stamped so hard on the floor he couldn't get his leg out again!'

'Bless you, my cherub!' said mamma; 'you shall tell me all about it tomorrow. Go and listen!' and then, as her eyes followed Louisa back towards the attractive corner, she thought that if Fred wished her to invite Mary again she would make no objection, the children being so pleased with her.

But presently the corner became still more animated, for Mr Farebrother came in, and seating himself behind Louisa, took her on his lap: whereupon the girls insisted that he must hear Rumpelstiltskin, and Mary must tell it over again. He insisted too, and Mary, without fuss, began in her neat fashion, with precisely the same words as before. Fred, who had also seated himself near, would have felt unmixed triumph in Mary's effectiveness if Mr Farebrother had not been looking at her with evident admiration, while he dramatised an intense interest in the tale to please the children.

'You will never care any more about my one-eyed giant, Loo,' said Fred at the end.

'Yes, I shall. Tell about him now,' said Louisa.

'Oh, I dare say; I am quite cut out. Ask Mr Farebrother.'

'Yes,' added Mary; 'ask Mr Farebrother to tell you about the ants whose beautiful house was knocked down by a giant named Tom, and he thought they didn't mind because he couldn't hear them cry, or see them use their pocket-handkerchiefs.'

'Please,' said Louisa, looking up at the Vicar.

'No, no, I am a grave old parson. If I try to draw a story out of my bag a sermon comes instead. Shall I preach you a sermon? ' said he, putting on his short-sighted glasses, and pursing up his lips.

'Yes,' said Louisa, falteringly.

'Let me see, then. Against cakes: how cakes are bad things, especially if they are sweet and have plums in them.'

Louisa took the affair rather seriously, and got down from the Vicar's knee to go to Fred.

'Ah, I see it will not do to preach on New Year's Day,' said Mr Farebrother, rising and walking away. He had discovered of late that Fred had become jealous of him, and also that he himself was not losing his preference for Mary above all other women.

'A delightful young person is Miss Garth,' said Mrs Farebrother, who had been watching her son's movements.

'Yes,' said Mrs Vincy, obliged to reply, as the old lady turned to her expectantly. 'It is a pity she is not better-looking.'

'I cannot say that,' said Mrs Farebrother, decisively. 'I like her countenance. We must not always ask for beauty, when a good God has seen fit to make an excellent young woman without it. I put good manners first, and Miss Garth will know how to conduct herself in any station.'

The old lady was a little sharp in her tone, having a prospective reference to Mary's becoming her daughter-in-law; for there was this inconvenience in Mary's position with regard to Fred, that it was not suitable to be made public, and hence the three ladies at Lowick Parsonage were still hoping that Camden would choose Miss Garth.

New visitors entered, and the drawing-room was given up to music and games, while whist-tables were prepared in the quiet room on the other side of the hall. Mr Farebrother played a rubber to satisfy his mother, who regarded her occasional whist as a protest against scandal and novelty of opinion, in which light even a revoke had its dignity. But at the end he got Mr Chichely to take his place, and left the room. As he crossed the hall, Lydgate had just come in and was taking off his greatcoat.

'You are the man I was going to look for,' said the Vicar, and instead of entering the drawing-room, they walked along the hall and stood against the fireplace, where the frosty air helped to make a glowing bank. 'You see, I can leave the whist-table easily enough,' he went on, smiling at Lydgate, 'now I don't play for money. I owe that to you, Mrs Casaubon says.'

'How?' said Lydgate, coldly.

'Ah, you didn't mean me to know it; I call that ungenerous reticence. You should let a man have the pleasure of feeling that you have done him a good turn. I don't enter into some people's dislike of being under an obligation; upon my word, I prefer being under an obligation to everybody for behaving well to me.'

'I can't tell what you mean,' said Lydgate, 'unless it is that I once spoke of you to Mrs Casaubon. But I did not think that she would break her promise not to mention that I had done so,' said Lydgate, leaning his back against the corner of the mantelpiece, and showing no radiance in his face.

'It was Brooke who let it out, only the other day. He paid me the compliment of saying that he was very glad I had the living, though you had come across his tactics, and had praised me up as a Ken and a Tillotson, and that sort of thing, till Mrs Casaubon would hear of no one else.'

'Oh, Brooke is such a leaky-minded fool,' said Lydgate contemptuously.

'Well, I was glad of the leakiness then. I don't see why you shouldn't like me to know that you have wished to do me a service, my dear fellow. And you certainly have done me one. It's rather a strong check to one's self-complacency to find how much of one's right doing depends on not being in want of money. A man will not be tempted to say the Lord's Prayer backward to please the devil, if he doesn't want the devil's services. I have no need to hang on the smiles of chance now.'

'I don't see that there's any money-getting without chance,' said Lydgate; 'if a man gets it in a profession, it's pretty sure to come by chance.'

Mr Farebrother thought he could account for this speech, in striking contrast with Lydgate's former way of talking, as the perversity which will often spring from the moodiness of a man ill at ease in his affairs. He answered in a tone of good-humoured admission: 'Ah, there's enormous patience wanted with the way of the world. But it is easier for a man to wait patiently when he has friends who love him, and ask for nothing better than to help him through, so far as it lies in their power.'

'Oh yes,' said Lydgate, in a careless tone, changing his attitude and looking at his watch. 'People make much more of their difficulties than they need to do.'

He knew as distinctly as possible that this was an offer of help to himself from Mr Farebrother, and he could not bear it. So strangely determined are we mortals, that, after having been long gratified with the sense that he had privately done the Vicar a service, the suggestion that the Vicar discerned his need of a service in return made him shrink into unconquerable reticence. Besides, behind all making of such offers what else must come? – that he should 'mention his case', imply that he wanted specific things. At that moment, suicide seemed easier.

Mr Farebrother was too keen a man not to know the meaning of that reply, and there was a certain massiveness in Lydgate's manner and tone, corresponding with his physique, which if he repelled your advances in the first instance seemed to put persuasive devices out of question.

'What time are you?' said the Vicar, devouring his wounded feeling.

'After eleven,' said Lydgate. And they went into the drawing-room.

Chapter 64

1st Gent.	Where lies the power, there let the blame lie too.
2nd Gent.	Nay, power is relative: you cannot fright
	The coming pest with border fortresses,
	Or catch your carp with subtle argument.
	All force is twain in one: cause is not cause
	Unless effect be there; and action's self
	Must needs contain a passive. So command
	Exists but with obedience.

Even if Lydgate had been inclined to be quite open about his affairs, he knew that it would hardly have been in Mr Farebrother's power to give him the help he immediately wanted. With the year's bills coming in from his tradesmen, with Dover's threatening hold on his furniture, and with nothing to depend on but slow dribbling payments from patients who must not be offended – for the handsome fees he had had from Freshitt Hall and Lowick Manor had been easily absorbed – nothing less than a thousand pounds would have freed him from actual embarrassment, and left a residue which, according to the favourite phrase of hopefulness in such circumstances, would have given him 'time to look about him'.

Naturally the merry Christmas bringing the happy New Year, when fellow-citizens expect to be paid for the trouble and goods they have smilingly bestowed on their neighbours, had so tightened the pressure of sordid cares on Lydgate's mind that it was hardly possible for him to think unbrokenly of any other subject, even the most habitual and soliciting. He was not an ill-tempered man; his intellectual activity, the ardent kindness of his heart, as well as his strong frame, would always, under tolerably easy conditions, have kept him above the petty uncontrolled susceptibilities which make bad temper. But he was now a prey to that worst irritation which arises not simply from annoyance, but from the second consciousness underlying those annoyances, of wasted energy and a degrading preoccupation, which was the reverse of all his former purposes. 'This is what I am thinking of; and *that* is what I might have been thinking of', was the bitter incessant murmur within him, making every difficulty a double goad to impatience.

Some gentlemen have made an amazing figure in literature by general discontent with the universe as a trap of dulness into which their great souls have fallen by mistake; but the sense of a stupendous self and an insignificant world may have its consolations. Lydgate's discontent was much harder to bear; it was the sense that there was a grand existence in thought and effective action lying around him, while his self was being narrowed into the miserable isolation of egoistic fears, and vulgar anxieties for events that might allay such fears. His troubles will perhaps appear miserably sordid, and beneath the attention of lofty persons who can know nothing of debt except on a magnificent scale. Doubtless they were sordid; and for the majority, who are not lofty, there is no escape from sordidness but by being free from money-craving, with all its base hopes and temptations, its watching for death, its hinted requests, its horse-dealer's desire to make bad work pass for good, its seeking for function which ought to be another's, its compulsion often to long for Luck in the shape of a wide calamity.

It was because Lydgate writhed under the idea of getting his neck beneath this vile yoke that he had fallen into a bitter moody state which was continually widening Rosamond's alienation from him. After the first disclosure about the bill of sale, he had made many efforts to draw her into sympathy with him about possible measures for narrowing their expenses, and with the threatening approach of Christmas his propositions grew more and more definite. 'We can do with only one servant, and live on very little,' he said, 'and I shall manage with one horse.' For Lydgate, as we have seen, had begun to reason, with a more distinct vision, about the expenses of living, and any share of pride he had given to appearances of that sort was meagre compared with the pride which made him revolt from exposure as a debtor, or from asking men to help him with their money.

'Of course you can dismiss the other two servants, if you like,' said Rosamond; 'but I should have thought it would be very injurious to your position for us to live in a poor way. You must expect your practice to be lowered.'

'My dear Rosamond, it is not a question of choice. We have begun too expensively. Peacock, you know, lived in a much smaller house than this. It is my fault: I ought to have known better, and I deserve a thrashing – if there were anybody who had a right to give it me – for bringing you into the necessity of living in a poorer way than you have been used to. But we married because we loved each other, I suppose. And that may help us to pull along till things get better. Come dear, put down that work and come to me.'

He was really in chill gloom about her at that moment, but he dreaded a future without affection, and was determined to resist the oncoming of division between them. Rosamond obeyed him, and he took her on his knee, but in her secret soul she was utterly aloof from him. The poor thing saw only that the world was not ordered to her liking, and Lydgate was part of that world. But he held her waist with one hand and laid the other gently on both of hers; for this rather abrupt man had much tenderness in his manners towards women, seeming to have always present in his imagination the weakness of their frames and the delicate poise of their health both in body and mind. And he began again to speak persuasively.

'I find, now I look into things a little, Rosy, that it is wonderful what an amount of money slips away in our housekeeping. I suppose the servants are careless, and we have had a great many people coming. But there must be many in our rank who manage with much less: they must do with commoner things, I suppose, and look after the scraps. It seems, money goes but a little way in these matters, for Wrench has everything as plain as possible, and he has a very large practice.'

'Oh, if you think of living as the Wrenches do!' said Rosamond, with a little turn of her neck. 'But I have heard you express your disgust at that way of living.'

'Yes, they have very bad taste in everything – they make economy look ugly. We needn't do that. I only meant that they avoid expenses, although Wrench has a capital practice.'

'Why should not you have a good practice, Tertius? Mr Peacock had. You should be more careful not to offend people, and you should send out medicines as the others do. I am sure you began well, and you got several good houses. It cannot answer to be eccentric; you should think what will be generally liked,' said Rosamond, in a decided little tone of admonition.

Lydgate's anger rose; he was prepared to be indulgent towards feminine weakness, but not towards feminine dictation. The shallowness of a waternixie's soul may have a charm until she becomes didactic. But he controlled himself, and only said, with a touch of despotic firmness: 'What I am to do in my practice, Rosy, it is for me to judge. That is not the question between us. It is enough for you to know that our income is likely to be a very narrow one – hardly four hundred, perhaps less, for a long time to come, and we must try to rearrange our lives in accordance with that fact.'

Rosamond was silent for a moment or two, looking before her, and then said, 'My uncle Bulstrode ought to allow you a salary for the time you give to the Hospital: it is not right that you should work for nothing.'

'It was understood from the beginning that my services would be gratuitous. That, again, need not enter into our discussion. I have pointed out what is the only probability,' said Lydgate, impatiently. Then checking himself, he went on more quietly; 'I think I see one resource which would free us from a good deal of the present difficulty. I hear that young Ned Plymdale is going to be married to Miss Sophy Toller. They are rich, and it is not often that a good house is vacant in Middlemarch. I feel sure that they would be glad to take this house from us with most of our furniture, and they would be willing to pay handsomely for the lease. I can employ Trumbull to speak to Plymdale about it.'

Rosamond left her husband's knee and walked slowly to the other end of the room; when she turned round and walked towards him it was evident that the tears had come, and that she was biting her underlip and clasping her hands to keep herself from crying. Lydgate was wretched – shaken with anger and yet feeling that it would be unmanly to vent the anger just now.

'I am very sorry, Rosamond; I know this is painful.'

'I thought, at least, when I had borne to send the plate back and have that man taking an inventory of the furniture – I should have thought *that* would suffice.'

'I explained it to you at the time, dear. That was only a security and behind that security there is a debt. And that debt must be paid within the next few months, else we shall have our furniture sold. If young Plymdale will take our house and most of our furniture, we shall be able to pay that debt and some others too, and we shall be quit of a place too expensive for us. We might take a smaller house: Trumbull, I know, has a very decent one to let at thirty pounds a year, and this is ninety.' Lydgate uttered this speech in the curt hammering way with which we usually try to nail down a vague mind to imperative facts. Tears rolled silently down Rosamond's cheeks; she just pressed her handkerchief against them, and stood looking at the large vase on the mantelpiece. It was a moment of more intense bitterness than she had ever felt before. At last she said, without hurry and with careful emphasis: 'I could never have believed that you would like to act in that way.'

'Like it?' burst out Lydgate, rising from his chair, thrusting his hands in his pockets and stalking away from the hearth; 'it's not a question of liking. Of course, I don't like it; it's the only thing I can do.' He wheeled round there, and turned towards her.

'I should have thought there were many other means than that,' said Rosamond. 'Let us have a sale and leave Middlemarch altogether.'

'To do what? What is the use of my leaving my work in Middlemarch to go where I have none? We should be just as penniless elsewhere as we are here,' said Lydgate still more angrily.

'If we are to be in that position it will be entirely your own doing, Tertius,' said Rosamond, turning round to speak with the fullest conviction. 'You will not behave as you ought to do to your own family. You offended Captain Lydgate. Sir Godwin was very kind to me when we were at Quallingham, and I am sure if you showed proper regard to him and told him your affairs, he would do anything for you. But rather than that, you like giving up our house and furniture to Mr Ned Plymdale.'

There was something like fierceness in Lydgate's eyes, as he answered with new violence, 'Well then, if you will have it so I do like it. I admit that I like it better than making a fool of myself by going to beg where it's of no use. Understand then, that it is what *I like to do.*'

There was a tone in the last sentence which was equivalent to the clutch of his strong hand on Rosamond's delicate arm. But for all that, his will was not a whit stronger than hers. She immediately walked out of the room in silence, but with an intense determination to hinder what Lydgate liked to do.

He went out of the house, but as his blood cooled he felt that the chief result of the discussion was a deposit of dread within him at the idea of opening with his wife in future subjects which might again urge him to violent speech. It was as if a fracture in delicate crystal had begun, and he was afraid of any movement that might make it fatal. His marriage would be a mere piece of bitter irony if they could not go on loving each other. He had long ago made up his mind to what he thought was her negative character – her want of sensibility, which showed itself in disregard both of his specific wishes and of his general aims. The first great disappointment had been borne: the tender devotedness and docile adoration of the ideal wife must be renounced, and life must be taken up on a lower stage of expectation, as it is by men who have lost their limbs. But the real wife had not only her claims, she had still a hold on his heart, and it was his intense desire that the hold should remain strong. In marriage, the certainty, 'She will never love me much', is easier to bear than the fear, 'I shall love her no more'. Hence, after that outburst, his inward effort was entirely to excuse her, and to blame the hard circumstances which were partly his fault. He tried that evening, by petting her, to heal the wound he had made in the morning, and it was not in Rosamond's nature to be repellent or sulky; indeed, she welcomed the signs that her husband loved her and was under control. But this was something quite distinct from loving *him*.

Lydgate would not have chosen soon to recur to the plan of parting with the house: he was resolved to carry it out, and say as little more about it as possible. But Rosamond herself touched on it at breakfast by saying, mildly: 'Have you spoken to Trumbull yet?'

'No,' said Lydgate, 'but I shall call on him as I go by this morning. No time must be lost.' He took Rosamond's question as a sign that she withdrew her inward opposition, and kissed her head caressingly when he got up to go away.

As soon as it was late enough to make a call, Rosamond went to Mrs Plymdale, Mr Ned's mother, and entered with pretty congratulations into the subject of the coming marriage. Mrs Plymdale's maternal view was, that Rosamond might possibly now have retrospective glimpses of her own folly; and feeling the advantages to be at present all on the side of her son, was too kind a woman not to behave graciously.

'Yes, Ned is most happy, I must say. And Sophy Toller is all I could desire in a daughter-in-law. Of course her father is able to do something handsome for her – that is only what would be expected with a brewery like his. And the connection is everything we should desire. But that is not what I look at. She is a very nice girl – no airs, no pretensions, though on a level with the first. I don't mean with the titled aristocracy. I see very little good in people aiming out of their own sphere. I mean that Sophy is equal to the best in the town, and she is contented with that.'

'I have always thought her very agreeable,' said Rosamond.

'I look upon it as a reward for Ned, who never held his head too high, that he should have got into the very best connection,' continued Mrs Plymdale, her native sharpness softened by a fervid sense that she was taking a correct view. 'And such particular people as the Tollers are, they might have objected because some of our friends are not theirs. It is well known that your aunt Bulstrode and I have been intimate from our youth, and Mr Plymdale has always been on Mr Bulstrode's side. And I myself prefer serious opinions. But the Tollers have welcomed Ned all the same.'

'I am sure he is very deserving, well-principled young man,' said Rosamond, with a neat air of patronage, in return for Mrs Plymdale's wholesome corrections.

'Oh, he has not the style of a captain in the army, or that sort of carriage as if everybody was beneath him, or that showy kind of talking, and singing, and intellectual talent. But I am thankful he has not. It is a poor preparation both for here and Hereafter.'

'Oh dear, yes; appearances have very little to do with happiness,' said Rosamond. 'I think there is every prospect of their being a happy couple. What house will they take?'

'Oh, as for that, they must put up with what they can get. They have been looking at the house in St Peter's Place, next to Mr Hackbutt's; it belongs to him, and he is putting it nicely in repair. I suppose they are not likely to hear of a better. Indeed, I think Ned will decide the matter today.'

'I should think it is a nice house; I like St Peter's Place.'

'Well, it is near the Church, and a genteel situation. But the windows are narrow, and it is all ups and downs. You don't happen to know of any other that would be at liberty?' said Mrs Plymdale, fixing her round black eyes on Rosamond with the animation of a sudden thought in them.

'Oh no; I hear so little of those things.'

Rosamond had not foreseen that question and answer in setting out to pay her visit; she had simply meant to gather any information which would help her to avert the parting with her own house under circumstances thoroughly disagreeable to her. As to the untruth in her reply, she no more reflected on it than she did on the untruth there was in her saying that appearances had very little to do with happiness. Her object, she was convinced, was thoroughly justifiable: it was Lydgate whose intention was inexcusable: and there was a plan in her mind which, when she had carried it out fully, would prove how very false a step it would have been for him to have descended from his position.

She returned home by Mr Borthrop Trumbull's office, meaning to call there. It was the first time in her life that Rosamond had thought of doing anything in the form of business, but she felt equal to the occasion. That she should be obliged to do what she intensely disliked, was an idea which turned her quiet tenacity into active invention. Here was a case in which it could not be enough simply to disobey and be serenely, placidly obstinate: she must act according to her judgement, and she said to herself that her judgement was right – 'indeed, if it had not been, she would not have wished to act on it.'

Mr Trumbull was in the back-room of his office, and received Rosamond with his finest manners, not only because he had much sensibility to her charms, but because the good-natured fibre in him was stirred by his certainty that Lydgate was in difficulties, and that this uncommonly pretty woman – this young lady with the highest personal attractions – was likely to feel the pinch of trouble – to find herself involved in circumstances beyond her control. He begged her to do him the honour to take a seat, and stood before her trimming and comporting himself with an eager solicitude, which was chiefly benevolent. Rosamond's first question was, whether her husband had called on Mr Trumbull that morning, to speak about disposing of their house.

'Yes, ma'am, yes, he did; he did so,' said the good auctioneer, trying to throw something soothing into his iteration. 'I was about to fulfil his order if possible, this afternoon. He wished me not to procrastinate.'

'I called to tell you not to go any further, Mr Trumbull; and I beg of you not to mention what has been said on the subject. Will you oblige me?'

'Certainly I will, Mrs Lydgate, certainly. Confidence is sacred with me on business or any other topic. I am then to consider the commission withdrawn?' said Mr Trumbull, adjusting the long ends of his blue cravat with both hands, and looking at Rosamond deferentially.

'Yes, if you please. I find that Mr Ned Plymdale has taken a house – the one in St Peter's Place next to Mr Hackbutt's. Mr Lydgate would be annoyed that his orders should be fulfilled uselessly. And besides that, there are other circumstances which render the proposal unnecessary.'

'Very good, Mrs Lydgate, very good. I am at your commands, whenever you require any service of me,' said Mr Trumbull, who felt pleasure in conjecturing that some new resources had been opened. 'Rely on me, I beg. The affair shall go no further.'

That evening Lydgate was a little comforted by observing that Rosamond was more lively than she had usually been of late, and even seemed interested in doing what would please him without being asked. He thought, 'If she will be happy and I can rub through, what does it all signify? It is only a narrow swamp that we have to pass in a long journey. If I can get my mind clear again, I shall do.'

He was so much cheered that he began to search for an account of experiments which he had long ago meant to look up, and had neglected out of that creeping self-despair which comes in the train of petty anxieties. He felt again some of the old delightful absorption in a far-reaching enquiry, while Rosamond played the quiet music which was as helpful to his meditation as the plash of an oar on the evening lake. It was rather late, he had pushed away all the books, and was looking at the fire with his hands clasped behind his head in forgetfulness of everything except the construction of a new controlling experiment, when Rosamond, who had left the piano and was leaning back in her chair watching him, said: 'Mr Ned Plymdale has taken a house already.'

Lydgate, startled and jarred, looked up in silence for a moment, like a man who has been disturbed in his sleep. Then flushing with an unpleasant consciousness, he asked: 'How do you know?'

'I called at Mrs Plymdale's this morning, and she told me that he had taken the house in St Peter's Place next to Mr Hackbutt's.'

Lydgate was silent. He drew his hands from behind his head and pressed them against the hair which was hanging, as it was apt to do, in a mass on his forehead, while he rested his elbow on his knees. He was feeling bitter disappointment, as if he had opened a door out of a suffocating place and had found it walled up; but he also felt sure that Rosamond was pleased with the cause of his disappointment. He preferred not looking at her and not speaking, until he had got over the first spasm of vexation. After all, he said in his bitterness, what can a woman care about so much as house and furniture? a husband without them is an absurdity. When he looked up and pushed his hair aside, his dark eyes had a miserable blank non-expectance of sympathy in them, but he only said coolly: 'Perhaps someone else may turn up. I told Trumbull to be on the look-out if he failed with Plymdale.'

Rosamond made no remark. She trusted to the chance that nothing more would pass between her husband and the auctioneer until some issue should have justified her interference; at any rate, she had hindered the event which she immediately dreaded. After a pause, she said: 'How much money is it that those disagreeable people want?'

'What disagreeable people?'

'Those who took the list – and the others. I mean, how much money would satisfy them so that you need not be troubled any more?'

Lydgate surveyed her for a moment, as if he were looking for symptoms, and then said, 'Oh, if I could have got six hundred from Plymdale for furniture and as premium, I might have managed. I could have paid off Dover, and given enough on account to the others to make them wait patiently, if we contracted our expenses.'

'But I mean how much should you want if we stayed in this house?'

'More than I am likely to get anywhere,' said Lydgate, with rather a grating sarcasm in his tone. It angered him to perceive that Rosamond's mind was wandering over impracticable wishes instead of facing possible efforts.

'Why should you not mention the sum?' said Rosamond, with a mild indication that she did not like his manners.

'Well,' said Lydgate, in a guessing tone, 'it would take at least a thousand to set me at ease. But,' he added incisively, 'I have to consider what I shall do without it, not with it.'

Rosamond said no more.

But the next day she carried out her plan of writing to Sir Godwin Lydgate. Since the Captain's visit, she had received a letter from him, and also one from Mrs Mengan, his married sister, condoling with her on the loss of her baby, and expressing vaguely the hope that they should see her again at Quallingham. Lydgate had told her that this politeness meant nothing: but she was secretly convinced that any backwardness in Lydgate's family towards him was due to his cold and contemptuous behaviour, and she answered the letters in her most charming manner, feeling some confidence that a specific invitation would follow. But there had been total silence. The Captain evidently was not a great penman, and Rosamond reflected that the sisters might have been abroad. However, the season was come for thinking of friends at home, and at any rate Sir Godwin, who had chucked her under the chin, and pronounced her to be like the celebrated beauty, Mrs Croly, who had made a conquest of him in 1790, would be touched by any appeal from her, and would find it pleasant for her sake to behave as he ought to do towards his nephew. Rosamond was naïvely convinced of what an old gentleman ought to do to prevent her from suffering annoyance. And she wrote what she considered the most judicious letter possible – one which would strike Sir Godwin as a proof of her excellent sense – pointing out how desirable it was that Tertius should quit such a place as Middlemarch for one more fitted to his talents, how the unpleasant character of the inhabitants had hindered his professional success, and how in consequence he was in money difficulties, from which it would require a thousand pounds thoroughly to extricate him. She did not say that Tertius was unaware of her intention to write; for she had the idea that his supposed sanction of her letter would be in accordance with what she did say of his great regard for his uncle Godwin as the relative who had always been his best friend. Such was the force of poor Rosamond's tactics now she applied them to affairs.

This had happened before the party on New Year's Day, and no answer had yet come from Sir Godwin. But on the morning of that day Lydgate had to learn that Rosamond had revoked his order to Borthrop Trumbull. Feeling it necessary that she should be gradually accustomed to the idea of their quitting the house in Lowick Gate, he overcame his reluctance to speak to her again on the subject, and when they were breakfasting, said: 'I shall try to see Trumbull this morning, and tell him to advertise the house in the *Pioneer* and the *Trumpet*. If the thing were advertised, someone might be inclined to take it who would not otherwise have thought of a change. In these country places many people go on in their old houses when their families are too large for them, for want of knowing where they can find another. And Trumbull seems to have got no bite at all.'

Rosamond knew that the inevitable moment was come. 'I ordered Trumbull not to enquire further,' she said, with a careful calmness which was evidently defensive.

Lydgate stared at her in mute amazement. Only half an hour before he had been fastening up her plaits for her, and talking the 'little language' of affection, which Rosamond, though not returning it, accepted, as if she had been a serene and lovely image, now and then miraculously dimpling towards her votary. With such fibres still astir in him, the shock he received could not at once be distinctly anger; it was confused pain. He laid down the knife and fork with which he was carving, and throwing himself back in his chair, said at last, with a cool irony in his tone: 'May I ask when and why you did so?'

'When I knew that the Plymdales had taken a house, I called to tell him not to mention ours to them; and at the same time I told him not to let the affair go on any further. I knew that it would be very injurious to you if it were known that you wished to part with your house and furniture, and I had a very strong objection to it. I think that was reason enough.'

'It was of no consequence then that I had told you imperative reasons of another kind; of no consequence that I had come to a different conclusion, and given an order accordingly?' said Lydgate, bitingly, the thunder and lightning gathering about his brow and eyes.

The effect of anyone's anger on Rosamond had always been to make her shrink in cold dislike, and to become all the more calmly correct, in the conviction that she was not the person to misbehave, whatever others might do. She replied: 'I think I had a perfect right to speak on a subject which concerns me at least as much as you.'

'Clearly – you had a right to speak, but only to me. You had no right to contradict my orders secretly, and treat me as if I were a fool,' said Lydgate, in the same tone as before. Then with some added scorn, 'Is it possible to make you understand what the consequences will be? Is it of any use for me to tell you again why we must try to part with the house?'

'It is not necessary for you to tell me again,' said Rosamond, in a voice that fell and trickled like cold water-drops. 'I remembered what you said. You spoke just as violently as you do now. But that does not alter my opinion that you ought to try every other means rather than take a step which is so painful to me. And as to advertising the house, I think it would be perfectly degrading to you.'

'And suppose I disregard your opinion as you disregard mine?'

'You can do do so, of course. But I think you ought to have told me before we were married that you would place me in the worst position, rather than give up your own will.'

Lydgate did not speak, but tossed his head on one side, and twitched the corners of his mouth in despair. Rosamond, seeing that he was not looking at her, rose and set his cup of coffee before him; but he took no notice of it, and went on with an inward drama and argument, occasionally moving in his seat, resting one arm on the table, and rubbing his hand against his hair. There was a conflux of emotions and thoughts in him that would not let him either give thorough way to his anger or persevere with simple rigidity of resolve. Rosamond took advantage of his silence.

'When we were married everyone felt that your position was very high. I could not have imagined then that you would want to sell our furniture, and take a house in Bride Street, where the rooms are like cages. If we are to live in that way let us at least leave Middlemarch.'

'These would be very strong considerations,' said Lydgate, half ironically – still there was a withered paleness about his lips as he looked at his coffee, and did not drink – 'these would be very strong considerations if I did not happen to be in debt.'

'Many persons must have been in debt in the same way, but if they are respectable, people trust them. I am sure I have heard papa say that the Torbits were in debt, and they went on very well. It cannot be good to act rashly,' said Rosamond, with serene wisdom.

Lydgate sat paralysed by opposing impulses: since no reasoning he could apply to Rosamond seemed likely to conquer her assent, he wanted to smash and grind some object on which he could at least produce an impression, or else to tell her brutally that he was master, and she must obey. But he not only dreaded the effect of such extremities on their mutual life – he had a growing dread of Rosamond's quiet elusive obstinacy, which would not allow any assertion of power to be final; and again, she had touched him in a spot of keenest feeling by implying that she had been deluded with a false vision of happiness in marrying him. As to saying that he was master, it was not the fact. The very resolution to which he had wrought himself by dint of logic and honourable pride was beginning to relax under her torpedo contact. He swallowed half his cup of coffee, and then rose to go.

'I may at least request that you will not go to Trumbull at present – until it has been seen that there are no other means,' said Rosamond. Although she was not subject to much fear, she felt it safer not to betray that she had written to Sir Godwin. 'Promise me that you will not go to him for a few weeks, or without telling me.'

Lydgate gave a short laugh. 'I think it is I who should exact a promise that you will do nothing without telling me,' he said, turning his eyes sharply upon her, and then moving to the door.

'You remember that we are going to dine at papa's,' said Rosamond, wishing that he should turn and make a more thorough concession to her. But he only said, 'Oh yes,' impatiently, and went away. She held it to be very odious in him that he did not think the painful propositions he had had to make to her were enough, without showing so unpleasant a temper. And when she put the moderate request that he would defer going to Trumbull again, it was cruel in him not to assure her of what he meant to do. She was convinced of her having acted in every way for the best; and each grating or angry speech of Lydgate's served only as an addition to the register of offences in her mind. Poor Rosamond for months had begun to associate her husband with feelings of disappointment, and the terribly inflexible relation of marriage had lost its charm of encouraging delightful dreams. It had freed her from the disagreeables of her father's house, but it had not given her everything that she had wished and hoped. The Lydgate with whom she had been in love had been a group of airy conditions for her, most of which had disappeared, while their place had been taken by everyday details which must be lived through slowly from hour to hour, not floated through with a rapid selection of favourable aspects. The habits of Lydgate's profession, his home preoccupation with scientific subjects, which seemed to her almost like a morbid vampire's taste, his peculiar views of things which had never entered into the dialogue of courtship – all these continually-alienating influences, even without the fact of his having placed himself at a disadvantage in the town, and without that first shock of revelation about Dover's debt, would have made his presence dull to her. There was another presence which ever since the early days of her marriage, until four months ago, had been an agreeable excitement, but that was gone: Rosamond would not confess to herself how much the consequent blank had to do with her utter ennui; and it seemed to her (perhaps she was right) that an invitation to Quallingham, and an opening for Lydgate to settle elsewhere than in Middlemarch – in London, or somewhere likely to be free from unpleasantness – would satisfy her quite well, and make her indifferent to the absence of Will Ladislaw, towards whom she felt some resentment for his exaltation of Mrs Casaubon.

That was the state of things with Lydgate and Rosamond on the New Year's Day when they dined at her father's, she looking mildly neutral towards him in remembrance of his ill-tempered behaviour at breakfast, and he carrying a much deeper effect from the inward conflict in which that morning scene was only one of many epochs. His flushed effort while talking to Mr Farebrother – his effort after the cynical pretence that all ways of getting money are essentially the same, and that chance has an empire which reduces choice to a fool's illusion – was but the symptom of a wavering resolve, a benumbed response to the old stimuli of enthusiasm.

What was he to do? He saw even more keenly than Rosamond did the dreariness of taking her into the small house in Bride Street, where she would have scanty furniture around her and discontent within: a life of privation and life with Rosamond were two images which had become more and more irreconcilable ever since the threat of privation had disclosed itself. But even if his resolves had forced the two images into combination, the useful preliminaries to that hard change were not visibly within reach. And though he had not given the promise which his wife had asked for, he did not go again to Trumbull. He even began to think of taking a rapid journey to the North and seeing Sir Godwin. He had once believed that nothing would urge him into making an application for money to his uncle, but he had not then known the full pressure of alternatives yet more disagreeable. He could not depend on the effect of a letter; it was only in an interview, however disagreeable this might be to himself, that he could give a thorough explanation and could test the effectiveness of kinship. No sooner had Lydgate begun to represent this step to himself as the easiest than there was a reaction of anger that he – he who had long ago determined to live aloof from such abject calculations, such self-interested anxiety about the inclinations and the pockets of men with whom he had been proud to have no aims in common should have fallen not simply to their level, but to the level of soliciting them.

Chapter 65

> One of us two must bowen douteless,
> And, sith a man is more reasonable
> Than woman is, ye [men] moste be suffrable.
>
> CHAUCER, *Canterbury Tales*

The bias of human nature to be slow in correspondence triumphs even over the present quickening in the general pace of things: what wonder then that in 1832 old Sir Godwin Lydgate was slow to write a letter which was of consequence to others rather than to himself? Nearly three weeks of the new year were gone, and Rosamond, awaiting an answer to her winning appeal, was every day disappointed. Lydgate, in total ignorance of her expectations, was seeing the bills come in, and feeling that Dover's use of his advantage over other creditors was imminent. He had never mentioned to Rosamond his brooding purpose of going to Quallingham: he did not want to admit what would appear to her a concession to her wishes after indignant refusal, until the last moment; but he was really expecting to set off soon. A slice of the railway would enable him to manage the whole journey and back in four days.

But one morning after Lydgate had gone out, a letter came addressed to him, which Rosamond saw clearly to be from Sir Godwin. She was full of hope. Perhaps there might be a particular note to her enclosed; but Lydgate was naturally addressed on the question of money or other aid, and the fact that he was written to, nay, the very delay in writing at all, seemed to certify that the answer was thoroughly compliant. She was too much excited by these thoughts to do anything but light stitching in a warm corner of the dining-room, with the outside of this momentous letter lying on the table before her. About twelve she heard her husband's step in the passage, and tripping to open the door, she said in her lightest tones, 'Tertius, come in here – here is a letter for you.'

'Ah?' he said, not taking off his hat, but just turning her round within his arm to walk towards the spot where the letter lay. 'My uncle Godwin!' he exclaimed, while Rosamond reseated herself, and watched him as he opened the letter. She had expected him to be surprised.

While Lydgate's eyes glanced rapidly over the brief letter, she saw his face, usually of a pale brown, taking on a dry whiteness; with nostrils and lips quivering he tossed down the letter before her and said violently: 'It will be impossible to endure life with you, if you will be always acting secretly – acting in opposition to me and hiding your actions.'

He checked his speech and turned his back on her – then wheeled round and walked about, sat down, and got up again restlessly, grasping hard objects deep down in his pockets. He was afraid of saying something irremediably cruel.

Rosamond too had changed colour as she read. The letter ran this way –

DEAR TERTIUS – Don't set your wife to write to me when you have anything to ask. It is a roundabout wheedling sort of thing which I should not have credited you with. I never choose to write to a woman on matters of business. As to my supplying you with a thousand pounds, or only half that sum, I can do nothing of the sort. My own family drains me to the last penny. With two younger sons and three daughters, I am not likely to have cash to spare. You seem to have got through your own money pretty quickly, and to have made a mess where you are: the sooner you go somewhere else the better. But I have nothing to do with men of your profession, and can't help you there. I did the best I could for you as guardian, and let you have your own way in taking to medicine. You might have gone into the army or the Church. Your money would have held out for that, and there would have been a surer ladder before you. Your uncle Charles has had a grudge against you for not going into his profession, but not I. I have always wished you well, but you must consider yourself on your own legs entirely now. – Your affectionate uncle,

GODWIN LYDGATE

When Rosamond had finished reading the letter she sat quite still, with her hands folded before her, restraining any show of her keen disappointment, and intrenching herself in quiet passivity under her husband's wrath. Lydgate paused in his movements, looked at her again, and said, with biting severity: 'Will this be enough to convince you of the harm you may do by secret meddling? Have you sense enough to recognise now your incompetence to judge and act for me – to interfere with your ignorance in affairs which it belongs to me to decide on?'

The words were hard; but this was not the first time that Lydgate had been frustrated by her. She did not look at him, and made no reply.

'I had nearly resolved on going to Quallingham. It would have cost me pain enough to do it, yet it might have been of some use. But it has been of no use for me to think of anything. You have always been counteracting me secretly. You delude me with a false assent, and then I am at the mercy of your devices. If you mean to resist every wish I express, say so and defy me. I shall at least know what I am doing then.'

It is a terrible moment in young lives when the closeness of love's bond has turned to this power of galling. In spite of Rosamond's self-control a tear fell silently and rolled over her lips. She still said nothing; but under that quietude was hidden an intense effect: she was in such entire disgust with her husband that she wished that she had never seen him. Sir Godwin's rudeness towards her and utter want of feeling ranged him with Dover and all other creditors – disagreeable people who only thought of themselves, and did not mind how annoying they were to her. Even her father was unkind, and might have done more for them. In fact there was but one person in Rosamond's world whom she did not regard as blameworthy, and that was the graceful creature with blond plaits and with little hands crossed before her, who had never expressed herself unbecomingly, and had always acted for the best – the best naturally being what she best liked.

Lydgate pausing and looking at her again began to feel that half-maddening sense of helplessness which comes over passionate people when their passion is met by an innocent-looking silence whose meek victimised air seems to put them in the wrong, and at last infects even the justest indignation with a doubt of its justice. He needed to recover the full sense that he was in the right by moderating his words.

'Can you not see, Rosamond,' he began again, trying to be simply grave and not bitter, 'that nothing can be so fatal as a want of openness and confidence between us? It has happened again and again that I have expressed a decided wish, and you have seemed to assent, yet after that you have secretly disobeyed my wish. In that way I can never know what I have to trust to. There would be some hope for us if you would admit this. Am I such an unreasonable, furious brute? Why should you not be open with me?'

Still silence.

'Will you only say that you have been mistaken, and that I may depend on your not acting secretly in future?' said Lydgate, urgently, but with something of request in his tone which Rosamond was quick to perceive. She spoke with coolness.

'I cannot possibly make admissions or promises in answer to such words as you have used towards me. I have not been accustomed to language of that kind. You have spoken of my "secret meddling", and my "interfering ignorance", and my "false assent". I have never expressed myself in that way to you, and I think that you ought to apologise. You spoke of its being impossible to live with me. Certainly you have not made my life pleasant to me of late. I think it was to be expected that I should try to avert some of the hardships which our marriage has brought on me.' Another tear fell as Rosamond ceased speaking, and she pressed it away as quietly as the first.

Lydgate flung himself into a chair, feeling checkmated. What place was there in her mind for a remonstrance to lodge in? He laid down his hat, flung an arm over the back of his chair, and looked down for some moments without speaking. Rosamond had the double purchase over him of insensibility to the point of justice in his reproach, and of sensibility to the undeniable hardships now present in her married life. Although her duplicity in the affair of the house had exceeded what he knew, and had really hindered the Plymdales from knowing of it, she had no consciousness that her action could rightly be called false. We are not obliged to identify our own acts according to a strict classification, any more than the materials of our grocery and clothes. Rosamond felt that she was aggrieved, and that this was what Lydgate had to recognise.

As for him, the need of accommodating himself to her nature, which was inflexible in proportion to its negations, held him as with pincers. He had begun to have an alarmed foresight of her irrevocable loss of love for him, and the consequent dreariness of their life. The ready fullness of his emotions made this dread alternate quickly with the first violent movements of his anger. It would assuredly have been a vain boast in him to say that he was her master.

'You have not made my life pleasant to me of late' – 'the hardships which our marriage has brought on me' – these words were stinging his imagination as a pain makes an exaggerated dream. If he were not only to sink from his highest resolve, but to sink into the hideous fettering of domestic hate?

'Rosamond,' he said, turning his eyes on her with a melancholy look, 'you should allow for a man's words when he is disappointed and provoked. You and I cannot have opposite interests. I cannot part my happiness from yours. If I am angry with you, it is that you seem not to see how any concealment divides us. How could I wish to make anything hard to you either by my words or conduct? When I hurt you, I hurt part of my own life. I should never be angry with you if you would be quite open with me.'

'I have only wished to prevent you from hurrying us into wretchedness without any necessity,' said Rosamond, the tears coming again from a softened feeling now that her husband had softened. 'It is so very hard to be disgraced here among all the people we know, and to live in such a miserable way. I wish I had died with the baby.'

She spoke and wept with that gentleness which makes such words and tears omnipotent over a loving-hearted man. Lydgate drew his chair near to hers and pressed her delicate head against his cheek with his powerful tender hand. He only caressed her; he did not say anything; for what was there to say? He could not promise to shield her from the dreaded wretchedness, for he could see no sure means of doing so. When he left her to go out again, he told himself that it was ten times harder for her than for him: he had a life away from home, and constant appeals to his activity on behalf of others. He wished to excuse every-thing in her if he could – but it was inevitable that in that excusing mood he should think of her as if she were an animal of another and feebler species. Nevertheless she had mastered him.

Chapter 66

'Tis one thing to be tempted, Escalus,
Another thing to fall.
SHAKESPEARE, *Measure for Measure*

Lydgate certainly had good reason to reflect on the service his practice did him in counteracting his personal cares. He had no longer free energy enough for spontaneous research and speculative thinking, but by the bedside of patients the direct external calls on his judgement and sympathies brought the added impulse needed to draw him out of himself. It was not simply that beneficient harness of routine which enables silly men to live respectably and unhappy men to live calmly – it was a perpetual claim on the immediate fresh application of thought, and on the consideration of another's need and trial. Many of us looking back through life would say that the kindest man we have ever known has been a medical man, or perhaps that surgeon whose fine tact, directed by deeply-informed perception, has come to us in our need with a more sublime beneficence than that of miracle-workers. Some of that twice-blessed mercy was always with Lydgate in his work at the Hospital or in private houses, serving better than any opiate to quiet and sustain him under anxieties and his sense of mental degeneracy.

Mr Farebrother's suspicion as to the opiate was true, however. Under the first galling pressure of foreseen difficulties, and the first perception that his marriage, if it were not to be a yoked loneliness, must be a state of effort to go on loving without too much care about being loved, he had once or twice tried a dose of opium. But he had no hereditary constitutional craving after such transient escapes from the hauntings of misery. He was strong, could drink a great deal of wine, but did not care about it; and when the men round him were drinking spirits, he took sugar and water, having a contemptuous pity even for the earliest stages of excitement from drink. It was the same with gambling. He had looked on at a great deal of gambling in Paris, watching it as if it had been a disease. He was no more tempted by such winning than he was by drink. He had said to himself that the only winning he cared for must be attained by a conscious process of high, difficult combination tending towards a beneficent result. The power he longed for could not be represented by agitated fingers, clutching a heap of coin, or by the half-barbarous, half-idiotic triumph in the eyes of a man who sweeps within his arms the ventures of twenty chapfallen companions.

But just as he had tried opium, so his thought now began to turn upon gambling – not with appetite for its excitement, but with a sort of wistful inward gaze after that easy way of getting money, which implied no asking and brought no responsibility. If he had been in London or Paris at that time, it is probable that such thoughts, seconded by opportunity, would have taken him into a gambling-house, no longer to watch the gamblers, but to watch them in kindred eagerness. Repugnance would have been surmounted by the immense need to win, if chance would be kind enough to let him. An incident which happened not very long after that airy notion of getting aid from his uncle had been excluded, was a strong sign of the effect that might have followed any extant opportunity of gambling.

The billiard-room at the Green Dragon was the constant resort of a certain set, most of whom, like our acquaintance Mr Bambridge, were regarded as men of pleasure. It was here that poor Fred Vincy had made part of his memorable debt, having lost money in betting, and had been obliged to borrow of that gay companion. It was generally known in Middlemarch that a good deal of money was lost and won in this way; and the consequent repute of the Green Dragon as a place of dissipation naturally heightened in some quarters the temptation to go there. Probably its regular visitants, like the initiates of freemasonry, wished that there were something a little more tremendous to keep to themselves concerning it; but they were not a closed community, and many decent seniors as well as juniors occasionally turned into the billiard-room to see what was going on. Lydgate, who had the muscular aptitude for billiards, and was fond of the game, had once or twice in the early days after his arrival in Middlemarch taken his turn with the cue at the Green Dragon; but afterwards he had no leisure for the game, and no inclination for the socialities there. One evening, however, he had occasion to seek Mr Bambridge at that resort. The horse-dealer had engaged to get him a customer for his remaining good horse, for which Lydgate had determined to substitute a cheap hack, hoping by this reduction of style to get perhaps twenty pounds; and he cared now for every small sum, as a help towards feeding the patience of his tradesmen. To run up to the billiard-room, as he was passing, would save time.

Mr Bambridge was not yet come, but he would be sure to arrive by and by, said his friend Mr Horrock; and Lydgate stayed, playing a game for the sake of passing the time. That evening he had the peculiar light in the eyes and the unusual vivacity which had been once noticed in him by Mr Farebrother. The exceptional fact of his presence was much noticed in the room, where there was a good deal of Middlemarch company; and several lookers-on, as well as some of the players, were betting with animation. Lydgate was playing well, and felt confident; the bets were dropping round him, and with a swift glancing thought of the probable gain which might double the sum he was saving from his horse, he began to bet on his own play, and won again and again. Mr Bambridge had come in, but Lydgate did not notice him. He was not only excited with his play, but visions were gleaming on him of going the next day to Brassing, where there was gambling on a grander scale to be had, and where, by one powerful snatch at the devil's bait, he might carry it off without the hook, and buy his rescue from his daily solicitings.

He was still winning when two new visitors entered. One of them was a young Hawley, just come from his law studies in town, and the other was Fred Vincy, who had spent several evenings of late at this old haunt of his. Young Hawley, an accomplished billiard-player, brought a cool fresh hand to the cue. But Fred Vincy, startled at seeing Lydgate, and astonished to see him betting with an excited air, stood aside, and kept out of the circle round the table.

Fred had been rewarding resolution by a little laxity of late. He had been working heartily for six months at all outdoor occupations under Mr Garth, and by dint of severe practice had nearly mastered the defects of his hand-writing, this practice being, perhaps, a little the less severe that it was often carried on in the evening at Mr Garth's under the eyes of Mary. But the last fortnight Mary had been staying at Lowick Parsonage with the ladies there, during Mr Farebrother's residence in Middlemarch, where he was carrying out some parochial plans; and Fred, not seeing anything more agreeable to do, had turned into the Green Dragon, partly to play at billiards, partly to taste the old flavour of discourse about horses, sport, and things in general, considered from a point of view which was not strenuously correct. He had not been out hunting once this season, had had no horse of his own to ride, and had gone from place to place chiefly with Mr Garth in his gig, or on the sober cob which Mr Garth could lend him. It was a little too bad, Fred began to think, that he should be kept in the traces with more severity than if he had been a clergyman. 'I will tell you what, Mistress Mary – it will be rather harder work to learn surveying and drawing plans than it would have been to write sermons,' he had said, wishing her to appreciate what he went through for her sake; 'and as to Hercules and Theseus, they were nothing to me. They had sport, and never learned to write a bookkeeping hand.' And now, Mary being out of the way for a little while, Fred, like any other strong dog who cannot slip his collar, had pulled up the staple of his chain and made a small escape, not of course meaning to go fast or far. There could be no reason why he should not play at billiards, but he was determined not to bet. As to money just now, Fred had in his mind the heroic project of saving almost all of the eighty pounds that Mr Garth offered him, and returning it, which he could easily do by giving up all futile money-spending, since he had a superfluous stock of clothes, and no expense in his board. In that way he could, in one year, go a good way towards repaying the ninety pounds of which he had deprived Mrs Garth, unhappily at a time when she needed that sum more than she did now. Nevertheless, it must be acknowledged that on this evening, which was the fifth of his recent visits to the billiard-room, Fred had not in his pocket, but in his mind, the ten pounds which he meant to reserve for himself from his half-year's salary (having before him the pleasure of carrying thirty to Mrs Garth when Mary was likely to be come home again) – he had those ten pounds in his mind as a fund from which he might risk something, if there were a chance of a good bet. Why? Well, when sovereigns were flying about, why shouldn't he catch a few? He would never go far along that road again; but a man likes to assure himself, and men of pleasure generally, what he could do in the way of mischief if he chose, and that if he abstains from making himself ill, or beggaring himself, or talking with the utmost looseness which the narrow limits of human capacity will allow, it is not because he is a spooney. Fred did not enter into formal reasons, which are a very artificial, inexact way of representing the tingling returns of old habit, and the caprices of young blood: but there was lurking in him a prophetic sense that evening, that when he began to play he should also begin to bet – that he should enjoy some punch-drinking, and in general prepare himself for feeling 'rather seedy' in the morning. It is in such indefinable movements that action often begins.

But the last thing likely to have entered Fred's expectation was that he should see his brother-in-law Lydgate – of whom he had never quite dropped the old opinion that he was a prig, and tremendously conscious of his superiority – looking excited and betting, just as he himself might have done. Fred felt a shock greater than he could quite account for by the vague knowledge that Lydgate was in debt, and that his father had refused to help him; and his own inclination to enter into the play was suddenly checked. It was a strange reversal of attitudes: Fred's blond face and blue eyes, usually bright and careless, ready to give attention to anything that held out a promise of amusement, looking involuntarily grave and almost embarrassed as if by the sight of something unfitting: while Lydgate, who had habitually an air of self-possessed strength, and a certain meditativeness that seemed to lie behind his most observant attention, was acting, watching, speaking with that excited narrow consciousness which reminds one of an animal with fierce eyes and retractile claws.

Lydgate, by betting on his own strokes, had won sixteen pounds; but young Hawley's arrival had changed the poise of things. He made first-rate strokes himself, and began to bet against Lydgate's strokes, the strain of whose nerves was thus changed from simple confidence in his own movements to defying another person's doubt in them. The defiance was more exciting than the confidence, but it was less sure. He continued to bet on his own play, but began often to fail. Still he went on, for his mind was as utterly narrowed into that precipitous crevice of play as if he had been the most ignorant lounger there. Fred observed that Lydgate was losing fast, and found himself in the new situation of puzzling his brains to think of some device by which, without being offensive, he could withdraw Lydgate's attention, and perhaps suggest to him a reason for quitting the room. He saw that others were observing Lydgate's strange unlikeness to himself, and it occurred to him that merely to touch his elbow and call him aside for a moment might rouse him from his absorption. He could think of nothing cleverer that the daring improbability of saying that he wanted to see Rosy, and wished to know if she were at home this evening; and he was going desperately to carry out this weak device, when a waiter came up to him with a message, saying that Mr Farebrother was below, and begged to speak with him.

Fred was surprised, not quite comfortably, but sending word that he would be down immediately, he went with a new impulse up to Lydgate, said, 'Can I speak to you a moment?' and drew him aside.

'Farebrother has just sent up a message to say he wants to speak to me. He is below. I thought you might like to know he was there, if you had anything to say to him.'

Fred had simply snatched up this pretext for speaking, because he could not say, 'You are losing confoundedly, and are making everybody stare at you; you had better come away.' But inspiration could hardly have served him better. Lydgate had not before seen that Fred was present, and his sudden appearance with an announcement of Mr Farebrother had the effect of a sharp concussion.

'No, no,' said Lydgate; 'I have nothing particular to say to him. But – the game is up – I must be going – I came in just to see Bambridge.'

'Bambridge is over there, but he is making a row – I don't think he's ready for business. Come down with me to Farebrother. I expect he is going to blow me up, and you will shield,' said Fred, with some adroitness.

Lydgate felt shame, but could not bear to act as if he felt it, by refusing to see Mr Farebrother; and he went down. They merely shook hands, however, and spoke of the frost; and when all three had turned into the street, the Vicar seemed quite willing to say goodbye to Lydgate. His present purpose was clearly to talk with Fred alone, and he said, kindly, 'I disturbed you, young gentleman, because I have some pressing business with you. Walk with me to St Botolph's, will you?'

It was a fine night, the sky was thick with stars, and Mr Farebrother proposed that they should make a circuit to the old church by the London road. The next thing he said was: 'I thought Lydgate never went to the Green Dragon?'

'So did I,' said Fred. 'But he said that he went to see Bambridge.'

'He was not playing then?'

Fred had not meant to tell this, but he was obliged now to say, 'Yes, he was. But I suppose it was an accidental thing. I have never seen him there before.'

'You have been going often yourself, then, lately?'

'Oh, about five or six times.'

'I think you had some good reason for giving up the habit of going there?'

'Yes. You know all about it,' said Fred, not liking to be catechised in this way. 'I made a clean breast to you.'

'I suppose that gives me a warrant to speak about the matter now. It is understood between us – is it not? – that we are on a footing of open friendship: I have listened to you, and you will be willing to listen to me. I may take my turn in talking a little about myself?'

'I am under the deepest obligation to you, Mr Farebrother,' said Fred, in a state of uncomfortable surmise.

'I will not affect to deny that you are under some obligation to me. But I am going to confess to you, Fred, that I have been tempted to reserve all that by keeping silence with you just now. When somebody said to me, "Young Vincy has taken to being at the billiard-table every night again – he won't bear the curb long": I was tempted to do the opposite of what I am doing – to hold my tongue and wait while you went down the ladder again, – betting first and then –'

'I have not made any bets,' said Fred hastily.

'Glad to hear it. But I say, my prompting was to look on and see you take the wrong turning, wear out Garth's patience, and lose the best opportunity of your life – the opportunity which you made some rather difficult effort to secure. You can guess the feeling which raised that temptation in me – I am sure you know it. I am sure you know that the satisfaction of your affections stands in the way of mine.'

There was a pause. Mr Farebrother seemed to wait for a recognition of the fact; and the emotion perceptible in the tones of his fine voice gave solemnity to his words. But no feeling could quell Fred's alarm.

'I could not be expected to give her up,' he said, after a moment's hesitation: it was not a case for any pretence of generosity.

'Clearly not, when her affection met yours. But relations of this sort, even when they are of long standing, are always liable to change. I can easily conceive that you might act in a way to loosen the tie she feels towards you – it must be remembered that she is only conditionally bound to you – and that in that case, another man, who may flatter himself that he has a hold on her regard, might succeed in winning that firm place in her love as well as respect which you had let slip. I can easily conceive such a result,' repeated Mr Farebrother, emphatically. 'There is a companionship of ready sympathy, which might get the advantage even over the longest associations.'

It seemed to Fred that if Mr Farebrother had had a beak and talons instead of his very capable tongue, his mode of attack could hardly be more cruel. He had a horrible conviction that behind all this hypothetic statement there was know-ledge of some actual change in Mary's feeling.

'Of course I know it might easily be all up with me,' he said, in a troubled voice. 'If she is beginning to compare – ' He broke off, not liking to betray all he felt, and then said, by the help of a little bitterness, 'But I thought you were friendly to me.'

'So I am; that is why we are here. But I have had a strong disposition to be otherwise. I have said to myself, "If there is a likelihood of that youngster doing himself harm, why should you interfere? Aren't you worth as much as he is, and don't your sixteen years over and above his, in which you have gone rather hungry, give you more right to satisfaction than he has? If there's a chance of his going to the dogs, let him – perhaps you could nohow hinder it – and do you take the benefit." '

There was a pause, in which Fred was seized by a most uncomfortable chill. What was coming next? He dreaded to hear that something had been said to Mary – he felt as if he were listening to a threat rather than a warning. When the Vicar began again there was a change in his tone like the encouraging transition to a major key.

'But I had once meant better than that, and I am come back to my old intention. I thought that I could hardly *secure myself* in it better, Fred, than by telling you just what had been going on in me. And now, do you understand me? I want you to make the happiness of her life and your own, and if there is any chance that a word of warning from me may turn aside any risk to the contrary – well, I have uttered it.'

There was a drop in the Vicar's voice when he spoke the last words. He paused – they were standing on a patch of green where the road diverged towards St Botolph's, and he put out his hand, as if to imply that the con-versation was closed. Fred was moved quite newly. Someone highly susceptible to the contemplation of a fine act has said, that it produces a sort of regenerating shudder through the frame, and makes one feel ready to begin a new life. A good degree of that effect was just then present in Fred Vincy.

'I will try to be worthy,' he said, breaking off before he could say 'of you as well as of her'. And meanwhile Mr Farebrother had gathered the impulse to say something more.

'You must not imagine that I believe there is at present any decline in her preference of you, Fred. Set your heart at rest, that if you keep right, other things will keep right.'

'I shall never forget what you have done,' Fred answered. 'I can't say anything that seems worth saying – only I will try that your goodness shall not be thrown away.'

'That's enough. Goodbye, and God bless you.'

In that way they parted. But both of them walked about a long while before they went out of the starlight. Much of Fred's rumination might be summed up in the words, 'It certainly would have been a fine thing for her to marry Fare-brother but if she loves me best and I am a good husband?'

Perhaps Mr Farebrother's might be concentrated into a single shrug and one little speech. 'To think of the part one little woman can play in the life of a man, so that to renounce her may be a very good imitation of heroism, and to win her may be a discipline!'

Chapter 67

> Now is there civil war within the soul;
> Resolve is thrust from off the sacred throne
> By clamorous Needs, and Pride the grand-vizier
> Makes humble compact, plays the supple part
> Of envoy and deft-tongued apologist
> For hungry rebels.

Happily Lydgate had ended by losing in the billiard-room, and brought away no encouragement to make a raid on luck. On the contrary, he felt unmixed disgust with himself the next day when he had to pay four or five pounds over and above his gains, and he carried about with him a most unpleasant vision of the figure he had made, not only rubbing elbows with the men at the Green Dragon but behaving just as they did. A philosopher fallen to betting is hardly distinguishable from a Philistine under the same circumstances: the difference will chiefly be found in his subsequent reflections, and Lydgate chewed a very disagreeable cud in that way. His reason told him how the affair might have been magnified into ruin by a slight change of scenery – if it had been a gambling-house that he had turned into, where chance could be clutched with both hands instead of being picked up with thumb and forefinger. Nevertheless, though reason strangled the desire to gamble, there remained the feeling that, with an assurance of luck to the needful amount, he would have liked to gamble, rather than take the alternative which was beginning to urge itself as inevitable.

That alternative was to apply to Mr Bulstrode. Lydgate had so many times boasted both to himself and others that he was totally independent of Bulstrode, to whose plans he had lent himself solely because they enabled him to carry out his own ideas of professional work and public benefit – he had so constantly in their personal intercourse had his pride sustained by the sense that he was making a good social use of this predominating banker, whose opinions he thought contemptible and whose motives often seemed to him an absurd mixture of contradictory impressions – that he had been creating for himself strong ideal obstacles to the proffering of any considerable request to him on his own account.

Still, early in March his affairs were at that pass in which men begin to say that their oaths were delivered in ignorance, and to perceive that the act which they had called impossible to them is becoming manifestly possible. With Dover's ugly security soon to be put in force, with the proceeds of his practice immediately absorbed in paying back-debts, and with the chance, if the worst were known, of daily supplies being refused on credit, above all with the vision of Rosamond's hopeless discontent continually haunting him, Lydgate had begun to see that he should inevitably bend himself to ask help from somebody or other. At first he had considered whether he should write to Mr Vincy: but on questioning Rosamond he found that, as he had suspected, she had already applied twice to her father, the last time being since the disappointment from Sir Godwin and papa had said that Lydgate must look for himself. 'Papa said he had come, with one bad year after another, to trade more and more on borrowed capital, and had had to give up many indulgences: he could not spare a single hundred from the charges of his family. He said, let Lydgate ask Bulstrode: they have always been hand in glove.'

Indeed, Lydgate himself had come to the conclusion that if he must end by asking for a free loan, his relations with Bulstrode, more at least than with any other man, might take the shape of a claim which was not purely personal. Bulstrode had indirectly helped to cause the failure of his practice, and had also been highly gratified by getting a medical partner in his plans: – but who among us ever reduced himself to the sort of dependence in which Lydgate now stood, without trying to believe that he had claims which diminished the humiliation of asking? It was true that of late there had seemed to be a new languor of interest in Bulstrode about the Hospital; but his health had got worse, and showed signs of a deep-seated nervous affection. In other respects he did not appear to be changed: he had always been highly polite, but Lydgate had observed in him from the first a marked coldness about his marriage and other private circum- stances, a coldness which he had hitherto preferred to any warmth of familiarity between them. He deferred the intention from day to day, his habit of acting on his conclusions being made infirm by his repugnance to every possible con- clusion and its subsequent act. He saw Mr Bulstrode often, but he did not try to use any occasion for his private purpose. At one moment he thought, 'I will write a letter: I prefer that to any circuitous talk'; at another he thought, 'No; if I were talking to him, I could make a retreat before any signs of disinclination'.

Still the days passed and no letter was written, no special interview sought. In his shrinking from the humiliation of a dependent attitude towards Bulstrode, he began to familiarise his imagination with another step even more unlike his remembered self. He began spontaneously to consider whether it would be possible to carry out that puerile notion of Rosamond's, which had often made him angry, namely, that they should quit Middlemarch without seeing anything beyond that preface. The question came – 'Would any man buy the practice of me even now, for as little as it is worth? Then the sale might happen as a necessary preparation for going away.'

But against his taking this step, which he still felt to be a contemptible relinquishment of present work, a guilty turning aside from what was a real and might be a widening channel for worthy activity, to start again without any justified destination, there was this obstacle, that the purchaser, if procurable at all, might not be quickly forthcoming. And afterwards? Rosamond in a poor lodging, though in the largest city or most distant town, would not find the life that could save her from gloom, and save him from the reproach of having plunged her into it. For when a man is at the foot of the hill in his fortunes, he may stay a long while there in spite of professional accomplishment. In the British climate there is no incompatibility between scientific insight and furnished lodgings: the incompatibility is chiefly between scientific ambition and a wife who objects to that kind of residence.

But in the midst of his hesitation, opportunity came to decide him. A note from Mr Bulstrode requested Lydgate to call on him at the Bank. A hypochondriacal tendency had shown itself in the banker's constitution of late; and a lack of sleep, which was really only a slight exaggeration of an habitual dyspeptic symptom, had been dwelt on by him as a sign of threatening insanity. He wanted to consult Lydgate without delay on that particular morning, although he had nothing to tell beyond what he had told before. He listened eagerly to what Lydgate had to say in dissipation of his fears, though this too was only repetition; and this moment, in which Bulstrode was receiving a medical opinion with a sense of comfort, seemed to make the communication of a personal need to him easier than it had been in Lydgate's contemplation beforehand. He had been insisting that it would be well for Mr Bulstrode to relax his attention to business.

'One sees how any mental strain, however slight, may affect a delicate frame,' said Lydgate at that stage of the consultation when the remarks tend to pass from the personal to the general, 'by the deep stamp which anxiety will make for a time even on the young and vigorous. I am naturally very strong; yet I have been thoroughly shaken lately by an accumulation of trouble.'

'I presume that a constitution in the susceptible state in which mine at present is, would be especially liable to fall a victim to cholera, if it visited our district. And since its appearance near London, we may well besiege the Mercy-seat for our protection,' said Mr Bulstrode, not intending to evade Lydgate's allusion, but really preoccupied with alarms about himself.

'You have at all events taken your share in using good practical precautions for the town, and that is the best mode of asking for protection,' said Lydgate, with a strong distaste for the broken metaphor and bad logic of the banker's religion, somewhat increased by the apparent deafness of his sympathy. But his mind had taken up its long-prepared movement towards getting help, and was not yet arrested. He added, 'The town has done well in the way of cleansing, and finding appliances; and I think that if the cholera should come, even our enemies will admit that the arrangements in the Hospital are a public good.'

'Truly,' said Mr Bulstrode, with some coldness. 'With regard to what you say, Mr Lydgate, about the relaxation of my mental labour, I have for some-time been entertaining a purpose to that effect – a purpose of a very decided character. I contemplate at least a temporary withdrawal from the management of much business, whether benevolent or commercial. Also I think of changing my residence for a time: probably I shall close or let The Shrubs, and take some place near the coast – under advice, of course, as to salubrity. That would be a measure which you would recommend?'

'Oh yes,' said Lydgate, falling backward in his chair, with ill-repressed impatience under the banker's pale earnest eyes and intense preoccupation with himself.

'I have for sometime felt that I should open this subject with you in relation to our Hospital,' continued Bulstrode. 'Under the circumstances I have indicated, of course, I must cease to have any personal share in the management, and it is contrary to my views of responsibility to continue a large application of means to an institution which I cannot watch over and to some extent regulate. I shall therefore, in case of my ultimate decision to leave Middlemarch, consider that I withdraw other support to the New Hospital than that which will subsist in the fact that I chiefly supplied the expenses of building it, and have contributed further large sums to its successful working.'

Lydgate's thought, when Bulstrode paused according to his wont, was, 'He has perhaps been losing a good deal of money.' This was the most plausible explanation of a speech which had caused rather a startling change in his expectations. He said in reply; 'The loss to the Hospital can hardly be made up, I fear.'

'Hardly,' returned Bulstrode, in the same deliberate, silvery tone; 'except by some changes of plan. The only person who may be certainly counted on as willing to increase her contributions is Mrs Casaubon. I have had an interview with her on the subject, and I have pointed out to her, as I am about to do to you, that it will be desirable to win a more general support to the New Hospital by a change of system.'

Another pause, but Lydgate did not speak.

'The change I mean is an amalgamation with the Infirmary, so that the New Hospital shall be regarded as a special addition to the elder institution, having the same directing board. It will be necessary, also, that the medical management of the two shall be combined. In this way any difficulty as to the adequate maintenance of our new establishment will be removed; the benevolent interests of the town will cease to be divided.'

Mr Bulstrode had lowered his eyes from Lydgate's face to the buttons of his coat as he again paused.

'No doubt that is a good device as to ways and means,' said Lydgate, with an edge of irony in his tone. 'But I can't be expected to rejoice in it at once, since one of the first results will be that the other medical men will upset or interrupt my methods, if it were only because they are mine.'

'I myself, as you know, Mr Lydgate, highly value the opportunity of new and independent procedure which you have diligently employed: the original plan, I confess, was one which I had much at heart, under submission to the Divine Will. But since providential indications demand a renunciation from me, I renounce.'

Bulstrode showed a rather exasperating ability in this conversation. The broken metaphor and bad logic of motive which had stirred his hearer's contempt were quite consistent with a mode of putting the facts which made it difficult for Lydgate to vent his own indignation and disappointment. After some rapid reflection, he only asked, 'What did Mrs Casaubon say?'

'That was the further statement which I wished to make to you,' said Bulstrode, who had thoroughly prepared his ministerial explanation. 'She is, you are aware, a woman of most munificent disposition, and happily in possession – not I presume of great wealth, but of funds which she can well spare. She has informed me that though she had destined the chief part of those funds to another purpose, she is willing to consider whether she cannot fully take my place in relation to the Hospital. But she wishes for ample time to mature her thoughts on the subject, and I have told her that there is no need for haste – that, in fact, my own plans are not yet absolute.'

Lydgate was ready to say, 'If Mrs Casaubon would take your place, there would be gain, instead of loss.' But there was still a weight on his mind which arrested this cheerful candour. He replied, 'I suppose, then, that I may enter into the subject with Mrs Casaubon.'

'Precisely; that is what she expressly desires. Her decision, she says, will much depend on what you can tell her. But not at present: she is, I believe, just setting out on a journey. I have her letter here,' said Mr Bulstrode, drawing it out, and reading from it. ' "I am immediately otherwise engaged," she says. "I am going into Yorkshire with Sir James and Lady Chettam; and the conclusions I come to about some land which I am to see there may affect my power of contributing to the Hospital." Thus Mr Lydgate, there is no haste necessary in this matter; but I wished to apprise you beforehand of what may possibly occur.'

Mr Bulstrode returned the letter to his side-pocket, and changed his attitude as if his business were closed. Lydgate, whose renewed hope about the Hospital only made him more conscious of the facts which poisoned his hope, felt that his effort after help, if made at all, must be made now and vigorously.

'I am much obliged to you for giving me full notice,' he said, with a firm intention in his tone, yet with an interruptedness in his delivery which showed that he spoke unwillingly. 'The highest object to me is my profession, and I had identified the Hospital with the best use I can at present make of my profession. But the best use is not always the same with monetary success. Everything which has made the Hospital unpopular has helped with other causes – I think they are all connected with my professional zeal – to make me unpopular as a practitioner. I get chiefly patients who can't pay me. I should like them best, if I had nobody to pay on my own side.' Lydgate waited a little, but Bulstrode only bowed, looking at him fixedly, and he went on with the same interrupted enunciation – as if he were biting an objectionable leek.

'I have slipped into money difficulties which I can see no way out of, unless someone who trusts me and my future will advance me a sum without other security. I had very little fortune left when I came here. I have no prospects of money from my own family. My expenses, in consequence of my marriage, have been very much greater than I had expected. The result at this moment is that it would take a thousand pounds to clear me. I mean, to free me from the risk of having all my goods sold in security of my largest debt – as well as to pay other debts – and leave anything to keep us a little beforehand with our small income. I find that it is out of the question that my wife's father should make such an advance. That is why I mention my position to – to the only other man who may be held to have some personal connection with my prosperity or ruin.'

Lydgate hated to hear himself. But he had spoken now, and had spoken with unmistakable directness. Mr Bulstrode replied without haste, but also without hesitation.

'I am grieved, though, I confess, not surprised by this information, Mr Lydgate. For my own part, I regretted your alliance with my brother-in-law's family, which has always been of prodigal habits, and which has already been much indebted to me for sustainment in its present position. My advice to you, Mr Lydgate, would be, that instead of involving yourself in further obligations, and continuing a doubtful struggle, you should simply become a bankrupt.'

'That would not improve my prospect,' said Lydgate, rising, and speaking bitterly, 'even if it were a more agreeable thing in itself.'

'It is always a trial,' said Mr Bulstrode; 'but trial, my dear sir, is our portion here, and is a needed corrective. I recommend you to weigh the advice I have given.'

'Thank you,' said Lydgate, not quite knowing what he said. 'I have occupied you too long. Good-day.'

Chapter 68

What suit of grace hath Virtue to put on
If Vice shall wear as good, and do as well?
If Wrong, if Craft, if Indiscretion
Act as fair parts with ends as laudable?
Which all this mighty volume of events
The world, the universal map of deeds,
Strongly controls, and proves from all descents,
That the directest course still best succeeds.
For should not grave and learn'd Experience
That looks with the eyes of all the world beside,
And with all ages holds intelligence,
Go safer than Deceit without a guide!

DANIEL, *Musophilus*

That change of plan and shifting of interest which Bulstrode stated or betrayed in his conversation with Lydgate, had been determined in him by some severe experience which he had gone through since the epoch of Mr Larcher's sale, when Raffles had recognised Will Ladislaw, and when the banker had in vain attempted an act of restitution which might move Divine Providence to arrest painful consequences.

His certainty that Raffles, unless he were dead, would return to Middlemarch before long, had been justified. On Christmas Eve he had reappeared at The Shrubs. Bulstrode was at home to receive him, and hinder his communication with the rest of the family, but he could not altogether hinder the circumstances of the visit from compromising himself and alarming his wife. Raffles proved more unmanageable than he had shown himself to be in his former appearances, his chronic state of mental restlessness, the growing effect of habitual intemperance, quickly shaking off every impression from what was said to him. He insisted on staying in the house, and Bulstrode, weighing two sets of evils, felt that this was at least not a worse alternative than his going into the town. He kept him in his own room for the evening and saw him to bed, Raffles all the while amusing himself with the annoyance he was causing this decent and highly prosperous fellow-sinner, an amusement which he facetiously expressed as sympathy with his friend's pleasure in entertaining a man who had been serviceable to him, and who had not had all his earnings. There was a cunning calculation under this noisy joking – a cool resolve to extract something the handsomer from Bulstrode as payment for release from this new application of torture. But his cunning had a little overcast its mark.

Bulstrode was indeed more tortured than the coarse fibre of Raffles could enable him to imagine. He had told his wife that he was simply taking care of this wretched creature, the victim of vice, who might otherwise injure himself; he implied, without the direct form of falsehood, that there was a family tie which bound him to this care, and that there were signs of mental alienation in

Raffles which urged caution. He would himself drive the unfortunate being away the next morning. In these hints he felt that he was supplying Mrs Bulstrode with precautionary information for his daughters and servants, and accounting for his allowing no one but himself to enter the room even with food and drink. But he sat in an agony of fear lest Raffles should be overheard in his loud and plain references to past facts – lest Mrs Bulstrode should be even tempted to listen at the door. How could he hinder her, how betray his terror by opening the door to detect her? She was a woman of honest direct habits, and little likely to take so low a course in order to arrive at painful knowledge; but fear was stronger than the calculation of probabilities.

In this way Raffles had pushed the torture too far, and produced an effect which had not been in his plan. By showing himself hopelessly unmanageable he had made Bulstrode feel that a strong defiance was the only resource left. After taking Raffles to bed that night the banker ordered his closed carriage to be ready at half-past seven the next morning. At six o'clock he had already been long dressed, and had spent some of his wretchedness in prayer, pleading his motives for averting the worst evil if in anything he had used falsity and spoken what was not true before God. For Bulstrode shrank from a direct lie with an intensity disproportionate to the number of his more indirect misdeeds. But many of these misdeeds were like the subtle muscular movements which are not taken account of in the consciousness, though they bring about the end that we fix our mind on and desire. And it is only what we are vividly conscious of that we can vividly imagine to be seen by Omniscience.

Bulstrode carried his candle to the bedside of Raffles, who was apparently in a painful dream. He stood silent, hoping that the presence of the light would serve to waken the sleeper gradually and gently, for he feared some noise as the consequence of a too sudden awakening. He had watched for a couple of minutes or more the shudderings and pantings which seemed likely to end in waking, when Raffles, with a long half-stifled moan, started up and stared round him in terror, trembling and gasping. But he made no further noise, and Bulstrode, setting down the candle, awaited his recovery.

It was a quarter of an hour later before Bulstrode, with a cold peremptoriness of manner which he had not before shown, said, 'I came to call you thus early, Mr Raffles, because I have ordered the carriage to be ready at half-past seven, and intend myself to conduct you as far as Ilsely, where you can either take the railway or await a coach.'

Raffles was about to speak, but Bulstrode anticipated him imperiously, with the words, 'Be silent, sir, and hear what I have to say. I shall supply you with money now, and I will furnish you with a reasonable sum from time to time, on your application to me by letter; but if you choose to present yourself here again, if you return to Middlemarch, if you use your tongue in a manner injurious to me, you will have to live on such fruits as your malice can bring you, without help from me. Nobody will pay you well for blasting my name: I know the worst you can do against me, and I shall brave it if you dare to thrust yourself upon me again. Get up, sir, and do as I order you, without noise, or I will send for a policeman to take you off my premises, and you may carry your stories into every pot-house in the town, but you shall have no sixpence from me to pay your expenses there.'

Bulstrode had rarely in his life spoken with such nervous energy: he had been deliberating on this speech and its probable effects through a large part of the night; and though he did not trust to its ultimately saving him from any return of Raffles, he had concluded that it was the best throw he could make. It succeeded in enforcing submission from the jaded man this morning: his empoisoned system at this moment quailed before Bulstrode's cold, resolute bearing, and he was taken off quietly in the carriage before the family breakfast-time. The servants imagined him to be a poor relation and were not surprised that a strict man like their master, who held his head high in the world, should be ashamed of such a cousin and want to get rid of him. The banker's drive of ten miles with his hated companion was a dreary beginning of the Christmas day; but at the end of the drive, Raffles had recovered his spirits, and parted in a contentment for which there was the good reason that the banker had given him a hundred pounds. Various motives urged Bulstrode to this open-handedness, but he did not himself enquire closely into all of them. As he had stood watching Raffles in his uneasy sleep, it had certainly entered his mind that the man had been much shattered since the first gift of two hundred pounds.

He had taken care to repeat the incisive statement of his resolve not to be played on any more; and had tried to penetrate Raffles with the fact that he had shown the risks of bribing him to be quite equal to the risks of defying him. But when, freed from his repulsive presence, Bulstrode returned to his quiet home, he brought with him no confidence that he had secured more than a respite. It was as if he had had a loathsome dream, and could not shake off its images with their hateful kindred of sensations – as if on all the pleasant surroundings of his life a dangerous reptile had left his slimy traces.

Who can know how much of his most inward life is made up of the thoughts he believes other men to have about him, until that fabric of opinion is threatened with ruin?

Bulstrode was only the more conscious that there was a deposit of uneasy presentiment in his wife's mind, because she carefully avoided any allusion to it. He had been used every day to taste the flavour of supremacy and the tribute of complete deference; and the certainty that he was watched or measured with a hidden suspicion of his having some discreditable secret, made his voice totter when he was speaking to edification. Foreseeing, to men of Bulstrode's anxious temperament, is often worse than seeing; and his imagination continually heightened the anguish of an imminent disgrace. Yes, imminent; for if his defiance of Raffles did not keep the man away – and though he prayed for this result he hardly hoped for it – the disgrace was certain. In vain he said to himself that, if permitted, it would be a divine visitation, a chastisement, a preparation; he recoiled from the imagined burning; and he judged that it must be more for the Divine glory that he should escape dishonour. That recoil had at last urged him to make preparations for quitting Middlemarch. If evil truth must be reported of him, he would then be at a less scorching distance from the contempt of his old neighbours; and in a new scene, where his life would not have gathered the same wide sensibility, the tormentor, if he pursued him, would be less formidable. To leave the place finally would, he knew, be extremely painful to his wife, and on other grounds he would have preferred to stay where he had struck root. Hence he made his preparations at first in a conditional way, wishing to leave on all sides an opening for his return after a brief absence, if any favourable inter-vention of Providence should dissipate his fears. He was preparing to transfer his management of the Bank, and to give up any active control of other commercial affairs in the neighbourhood, on the ground of his failing health, but without excluding his future resumption of such work. The measure would cause him some added expense and some diminution of income beyond what, he had already undergone from the general depression of trade; and the Hospital presented itself as a principal object of outlay on which he could fairly economise.

This was the experience which had determined his conversation with Lydgate. But at this time his arrangements had most of them gone no farther than a stage at which he could recall them if they proved to be unnecessary. He continually deferred the final steps; in the midst of his fears, like many a man who is in danger of shipwreck or of being dashed from his carriage by runaway horses, he had a clinging impression that something would happen to hinder the worst, and that to spoil his life by a later transplantation might be over-hasty – especially since it was difficult to account satisfactorily to his wife for the project of their indefinite exile from the only place where she would like to live.

Among the affairs Bulstrode had to care for, was the management of the farm at Stone Court in case of his absence; and on this as well as on all other matters connected with any houses and land he possessed in or about Middlemarch, he had consulted Caleb Garth. Like everyone else who had business of that sort, he wanted to get the agent who was more anxious for his employer's interests than his own. With regard to Stone Court, since Bulstrode wished to retain his hold on the stock, and to have an arrangement by which he himself could, if he chose, resume his favourite recreation of superintendence, Caleb had advised him not to trust a mere bailiff, but to let the land, stock, and implements yearly, and take a proportionate share of the proceeds.

'May I trust to you to find me a tenant on these terms, Mr Garth?' said Bulstrode. 'And will you mention to me the yearly sum which would repay you for managing these affairs which we have discussed together?'

'I'll think about it,' said Caleb, in his blunt way. 'I'll see how I can make it out.'

If it had not been that he had to consider Fred Vincy's future, Mr Garth would not probably have been glad of any addition to his work, of which his wife was always fearing an excess for him as he grew older. But on quitting Bulstrode after that conversation, a very alluring idea occurred to him about this said letting of Stone Court. What if Bulstrode would agree to his placing Fred Vincy there on the understanding that he, Caleb Garth, should be responsible for the management? It would be an excellent schooling for Fred; he might make a modest income there, and still have time left to get knowledge by helping in other business. He mentioned his notion to Mrs Garth with such evident delight that she could not bear to chill his pleasure by expressing her constant fear of his undertaking too much.

'The lad would be as happy as two,' he said, throwing himself back in his chair, and looking radiant, 'if I could tell him it was all settled. Think, Susan! His mind had been running on that place for years before old Featherstone died. And it would be as pretty a turn of things as could be that he should hold the place in a good industrious way after all – by his taking to business. For it's likely enough Bulstrode might let him go on, and gradually buy the stock. He hasn't made up his mind, I can see, whether or not he shall settle somewhere else as a lasting thing. I never was better pleased with a notion in my life. And then the children might be married by and by, Susan.'

'You will not give any hint of the plan to Fred, until you are sure that Bulstrode would agree to the plan?' said Mrs Garth, in a tone of gentle caution. 'And as to marriage, Caleb, we old people need not help to hasten it.'

'Oh, I don't know,' said Caleb, swinging his head aside. 'Marriage is a taming thing. Fred would want less of my bit and bridle. However, I shall say nothing till I know the ground I'm treading on. I shall speak to Bulstrode again.'

He took his earliest opportunity of doing so. Bulstrode had anything but a warm interest in his nephew Fred Vincy, but he had a strong wish to secure Mr Garth's services on many scattered points of business at which he was sure to be a considerable loser, if they were under less conscientious management. On that ground he made no objection to Mr Garth's proposal; and there was also another reason why he was not sorry to give a consent which was to benefit one of the Vincy family. It was that Mrs Bulstrode, having heard of Lydgate's debts, had been anxious to know whether her husband could not do something for poor Rosamond, and had been much troubled on learning from him that Lydgate's affairs were not easily remediable, and that the wisest plan was to let them 'take their course'. Mrs Bulstrode had then said for the first time, 'I think you are always a little hard towards my family, Nicholas. And I am sure I have no reason to deny any of my relatives. Too worldly they may be, but no one ever had to say that they were not respectable.'

'My dear Harriet,' said Mr Bulstrode, wincing under his wife's eyes, which were filling with tears, 'I have supplied your brother with a great deal of capital. I cannot be expected to take care of his married children.'

That seemed to be true, and Mrs Bulstrode's remonstrance subsided into pity for poor Rosamond, whose extravagant education she had always foreseen the fruits of.

But remembering that dialogue, Mr Bulstrode felt that when he had to talk to his wife fully about his plan of quitting Middlemarch, he should be glad to tell her that he had made an arrangement which might be for the good of her nephew Fred. At present he had merely mentioned to her that he thought of shutting up The Shrubs for a few months, and taking a house on the Southern Coast.

Hence Mr Garth got the assurance he desired, namely, that in case of Bulstrode's departure from Middlemarch for an indefinite time, Fred Vincy should be allowed to have the tenancy of Stone Court on the terms proposed.

Caleb was so elated with his hope of this 'neat turn' being given to things, that if his self-control had not been braced by a little affectionate wifely scolding, he would have betrayed everything to Mary, wanting 'to give the child comfort'. However, he restrained himself, and kept in strict privacy from Fred certain visits which he was making to Stone Court, in order to look more thoroughly into the state of the land and stock, and take a preliminary estimate. He was certainly more eager in these visits than the probable speed of events required him to be; but he was stimulated by a fatherly delight in occupying his mind with this bit of probable happiness which he held in store like a hidden birthday gift for Fred and Mary.

'But suppose the whole scheme should turn out to be a castle in the air?' said Mrs Garth.

'Well, well,' replied Caleb; 'the castle will tumble about nobody's head.'

Chapter 69

If thou hast heard a word, let it die with thee.

Ecclesiasticus

Mr Bulstrode was still seated in his manager's room at the Bank, about three o'clock of the same day on which he had received Lydgate there, when the clerk entered to say that his horse was waiting, and also that Mr Garth was outside and begged to speak with him.

'By all means,' said Bulstrode; and Caleb entered. 'Pray sit down, Mr Garth,' continued the banker, in his suavest tone. 'I am glad that you arrived just in time to find me here. I know you count your minutes.'

'Oh,' said Caleb, gently, with a slow swing of his head on one side, as he seated himself and laid his hat on the floor. He looked at the ground, leaning forward and letting his long fingers droop between his legs, while each finger moved in succession, as if it were sharing some thought which filled his large quiet brow.

Mr Bulstrode, like everyone else who knew Caleb, was used to his slowness in beginning to speak on any topic which he felt to be important, and rather expected that he was about to recur to the buying of some houses in Blindman's Court, for the sake of pulling them down, as a sacrifice of property which would be well repaid by the influx of air and light on that spot. It was by propositions of this kind that Caleb was sometimes troublesome to his employers; but he had usually found Bulstrode ready to meet him in projects of improvement, and they had got on well together. When he spoke again, however, it was to say, in rather a subdued voice: 'I have just come away from Stone Court, Mr Bulstrode.'

'You found nothing wrong there, I hope,' said the banker; 'I was there myself yesterday. Abel has done well with the lambs this year.'

'Why, yes,' said Caleb, looking up gravely, 'there *is* something wrong – a stranger, who is very ill, I think. He wants a doctor, and I came to tell you of that. His name is Raffles.'

He saw the shock of his words passing through Bulstrode's frame. On this subject the banker had thought that his fears were too constantly on the watch to be taken by surprise; but he had been mistaken.

'Poor wretch!' he said in a compassionate tone, though his lips trembled a little. 'Do you know how he came there?'

'I took him myself,' said Caleb, quietly – 'took him up in my gig. He had got down from the coach, and was walking a little beyond the turning from the toll-house, and I overtook him. He remembered seeing me with you once before, at Stone Court, and he asked me to take him on. I saw he was ill: it seemed to me the right thing to do, to carry him under shelter. And now I think you should lose no time in getting advice for him.' Caleb took up his hat from the floor as he ended, and rose slowly from his seat.

'Certainly,' said Bulstrode, whose mind was very active at this moment. 'Perhaps you will yourself oblige me, Mr Garth, by calling at Mr Lydgate's as you pass – or stay! he may at this hour probably be at the Hospital. I will first send my man on the horse there with a note this instant, and then I will myself ride to Stone Court.'

Bulstrode quickly wrote a note, and went out himself to give the commission to his man. When he returned, Caleb was standing as before with one hand on the back of the chair, holding his hat with the other. In Bulstrode's mind the dominant thought was, 'Perhaps Raffles only spoke to Garth of his illness. Garth may wonder, as he must have done before, at this disreputable fellow's claiming intimacy with me; but he will know nothing. And he is friendly to me – I can be of use to him.'

He longed for some information of this hopeful conjecture, but to have asked any question as to what Raffles had said or done would have been to betray fear.

'I am exceedingly obliged to you, Mr Garth,' he said, in his usual tone of politeness. 'My servant will be back in a few minutes, and I shall then go myself to see what can be done for this unfortunate man. Perhaps you had some other business with me? If so, pray be seated.'

'Thank you,' said Caleb, making a slight gesture with his right hand to waive the invitation. 'I wish to say, Mr Bulstrode, that I must request you to put your business into some other hands than mine. I am obliged to you for your handsome way of meeting me – about the letting of Stone Court, and all other business. But I must give it up.'

A sharp certainty entered like a stab into Bulstrode's soul.

'This is sudden, Mr Garth,' was all he could say at first.

'It is,' said Caleb; 'but it is quite fixed. I must give it up.'

He spoke with a firmness which was very gentle, and yet he could see that Bulstrode seemed to cower under that gentleness, his face looking dried and his eyes swerving away from the glance which rested on him. Caleb felt a deep pity for him, but he could have used no pretexts to account for his resolve, even if they would have been of any use.

'You have been led to this, I apprehend, by some slanders concerning me uttered by that unhappy creature,' said Bulstrode, anxious now to know the utmost.

'That is true. I can't deny that I act upon what I heard from him.'

'You are a conscientious man, Mr Garth – a man, I trust, who feels himself accountable to God. You would not wish to injure me by being too ready to believe a slander,' said Bulstrode, casting about for pleas that might be adapted to his hearer's mind. 'That is a poor reason for giving up a connection which I think I may say will be mutually beneficial.'

'I would injure no man if I could help it,' said Caleb; 'even if I thought God winked at it. I hope I should have a feeling for my fellow-creature. But, sir – I am obliged to believe that this Raffles has told me the truth. And I can't be happy in working with you, or profiting by you. It hurts my mind. I must beg you to seek another agent.'

'Very well, Mr Garth. But I must at least claim to know the worst that he has told you. I must know what is the foul speech that I am liable to be the victim of,' said Bulstrode, a certain amount of anger beginning to mingle with his humiliation before this quiet man who renounced his benefits.

'That's needless,' said Caleb, waving his hand, bowing his head slightly, and not swerving from the tone which had in it the merciful intention to spare this pitiable man. 'What he has said to me will never pass from my lips, unless something now unknown forces it from me. If you led a harmful life for gain, and kept others out of their rights by deceit, to get the more for yourself, I dare say you repent – you would like to go back, and can't: that must be a bitter thing' – Caleb paused a moment and shook his head – 'it is not for me to make your life harder to you.'

'But you do – you do make it harder to me,' said Bulstrode, constrained into a genuine, pleading cry. 'You make it harder to me by turning your back on me.'

'That I'm forced to do,' said Caleb, still more gently, lifting up his hand. 'I am sorry. I don't judge you and say, he is wicked, and I am righteous. God forbid. I don't know everything. A man may do wrong, and his will may rise clear out of it, though he can't get his life clear. That's a bad punishment. If it is so with you – well, I'm very sorry for you. But I have that feeling inside me, that I can't go on working with you. That's all, Mr Bulstrode. Everything else is buried, so far as my will goes. And I wish you good-day.'

'One moment, Mr Garth!' said Bulstrode, hurriedly. 'I may trust then to your solemn assurance that you will not repeat either to man or woman what – even if it had any degree of truth in it – is yet a malicious representation?'

Caleb's wrath was stirred, and he said, indignantly: 'Why should I have said it if I didn't mean it? I am in no fear of you. Such tales as that will never tempt my tongue.'

'Excuse me – I am agitated – I am the victim of this abandoned man.'

'Stop a bit! you have got to consider whether you didn't help to make him worse, when you profited by his vices.'

'You are wronging me by too readily believing him,' said Bulstrode, oppressed, as by a nightmare, with the inability to deny flatly what Raffles might have said; and yet feeling it an escape that Caleb had not so stated it to him as to ask for that flat denial.

'No,' said Caleb, lifting his hand deprecatingly; 'I am ready to believe better, when better is proved. I rob you of no good chance. As to speaking, I hold it a crime to expose a man's sin unless I'm clear it must be done to save the innocent.

That is my way of thinking, Mr Bulstrode, and what I say, I've no need to swear. I wish you good-day.'

Some hours later, when he was at home, Caleb said to his wife, incidentally, that he had had some little differences with Bulstrode, and that in consequence, he had given up all notion of taking Stone Court, and had indeed resigned doing further business for him.

'He was disposed to interfere too much, was he?' said Mrs Garth, imagining that her husband had been touched on his sensitive point, and not been allowed to do what he thought right as to materials and modes of work.

'Oh,' said Caleb, bowing his head and waving his hand gravely. And Mrs Garth knew that this was a sign of his not intending to speak further on the subject.

As for Bulstrode, he had almost immediately mounted his horse and set off for Stone Court, being anxious to arrive there before Lydgate.

His mind was crowded with images and conjectures, which were a language to his hopes and fears, just as we hear tones from the vibrations which shake our whole system. The deep humiliation with which he had winced under Caleb Garth's knowledge of his past and rejection of his patronage, alternated with and almost gave way to the sense of safety in the fact that Garth, and no other, had been the man to whom Raffles had spoken. It seemed to him a sort of earnest that Providence intended his rescue from worse consequences; the way being thus left open for the hope of secrecy. That Raffles should be afflicted with illness, that he should have been led to Stone Court rather than elsewhere – Bulstrode's heart fluttered at the vision of probabilities which these events conjured up. If it should turn out that he was freed from all danger of disgrace, if he could breathe in perfect liberty – his life should be more consecrated than it had ever been before. He mentally lifted up this vow as if it would urge the result he longed for – he tried to believe in the potency of that prayerful resolution – its potency to determine death. He knew that he ought to say, 'Thy will be done', and he said it often. But the intense desire remained that the will of God might be the death of that hated man.

Yet when he arrived at Stone Court he could not see the change in Raffles without a shock. But for his pallor and feebleness, Bulstrode would have called the change in him entirely mental. Instead of his loud tormenting mood, he showed an intense, vague terror, and seemed to deprecate Bulstrode's anger, because the money was all gone – he had been robbed – it had half of it been taken from him. He had only come here because he was ill and somebody was hunting him – somebody was after him: he had told nobody anything, he had kept his mouth shut. Bulstrode, not knowing the significance of these symptoms, interpreted this new nervous susceptibility into a means of alarming Raffles into true confessions, and taxed him with falsehood in saying that he had not told anything, since he had just told the man who took him up in his gig and brought him to Stone Court. Raffles denied this with solemn adjurations; the fact being that the links of consciousness were interrupted in him, and that his minute terror-stricken narrative to Caleb Garth had been delivered under a set of visionary impulses which had dropped back into darkness.

Bulstrode's heart sank again at this sign that he could get no grasp over the wretched man's mind, and that no word of Raffles could be trusted as to the fact which he most wanted to know, namely, whether or not he had really kept silence to everyone in the neighbourhood except Caleb Garth. The house-keeper had told him without the least constraint of manner that since Mr Garth left, Raffles had asked her for beer, and after that had not spoken, seeming very ill. On that side it might be concluded that there had been no betrayal. Mrs Abel thought, like the servants at The Shrubs, that the strange man belonged to the unpleasant 'kin' who are among the troubles of the rich; she had at first referred the kinship to Mr Rigg, and where there was property left, the buzzing presence of such large bluebottles seemed natural enough. How he could be 'kin' to Bulstrode as well was not so clear, but Mrs Abel agreed with her husband that there was 'no knowing', a proposition which had a great deal of mental food for her, so that she shook her head over it without further speculation.

In less than an hour Lydgate arrived. Bulstrode met him outside the wainscoted parlour, where Raffles was, and said: 'I have called you in, Mr Lydgate, to an unfortunate man who was once in my employment many years ago. Afterwards he went to America, and returned I fear to an idle dissolute life. Being destitute, he has a claim on me. He was slightly connected with Rigg, the former owner of this place, and in consequence found his way here. I believe he is seriously ill: apparently his mind is affected, I feel bound to do the utmost for him.'

Lydgate, who had the remembrance of his last conversation with Bulstrode strongly upon him, was not disposed to say an unnecessary word to him, and bowed slightly in answer to this account; but just before entering the room he turned automatically and said, 'What is his name?' – to know names being as much a part of the medical man's accomplishment as of the practical politician's.

'Raffles, John Raffles,' said Bulstrode, who hoped that whatever became of Raffles, Lydgate would never know any more of him.

When he had thoroughly examined and considered the patient, Lydgate ordered that he should go to bed, and be kept there in as complete quiet as possible, and then went with Bulstrode into another room.

'It is a serious case, I apprehend,' said the banker, before Lydgate began to speak.

'No – and yes,' said Lydgate, half dubiously. 'It is difficult to decide as to the possible effect of long-standing complications; but the man had a robust con-stitution to begin with. I should not expect this attack to be fatal, though of course the system is in a ticklish state. He should be well watched and attended to.'

'I will remain here myself,' said Bulstrode. 'Mrs Abel and her husband are inexperienced. I can easily remain here for the night, if you will oblige me by taking a note for Mrs Bulstrode.'

'I should think that is hardly necessary,' said Lydgate. 'He seems tame and terrified enough. He might become more unmanageable. But there is a man here – is there not?'

'I have more than once stayed here a few nights for the sake of seclusion,' said Bulstrode, indifferently: 'I am quite disposed to do so now. Mrs Abel and her husband can relieve or aid me, if necessary.'

'Very well. Then I need give my directions only to you,' said Lydgate, not feeling surprised at a little peculiarity in Bulstrode.

'You think, then, that the case is hopeful?' said Bulstrode, when Lydgate had ended giving his orders.

'Unless there turn out to be further complications, such as I have not at present detected – yes,' said Lydgate. 'He may pass on to a worse stage; but I should not wonder if he got better in a few days, by adhering to the treatment I have prescribed. There must be firmness. Remember, if he calls for liquors of any sort, not to give them to him. In my opinion, men in his condition are oftener killed by treatment than by the disease. Still, new symptoms may arise. I shall come again tomorrow morning.'

After waiting for the note to be carried to Mrs Bulstrode, Lydgate rode away, forming no conjectures, in the first instance, about the history of Raffles, but rehearsing the whole argument which had lately been much stirred by the publication of Dr Ware's abundant experience in America, as to the right way of treating cases of alcoholic poisoning such as this. Lydgate, when abroad, had already been interested in this question: he was strongly convinced against the prevalent practice of allowing alcohol and persistently administering large doses of opium; and he had repeatedly acted on this conviction with a favourable result.

'The man is in a diseased state,' he thought, 'but there's a good deal of wear in him still. I suppose he is an object of charity to Bulstrode. It is curious what patches of hardness and tenderness lie side by side in men's dispositions. Bulstrode seems the most unsympathetic fellow I ever saw about some people, and yet he has taken no end of trouble, and spent a great deal of money, on benevolent objects. I suppose he has some test by which he finds out whom Heaven cares for – he has made up his mind that it doesn't care for me.'

This streak of bitterness came from a plenteous source, and kept widening in the current of his thought as he neared Lowick Gate. He had not been there since his first interview with Bulstrode in the morning, having been found at the Hospital by the banker's messenger; and for the first time he was returning to his home without the vision of any expedient in the background which left him a hope of raising money enough to deliver him from the coming destitution of everything which made his married life tolerable – everything which saved him and Rosamond from that bare isolation in which they would be forced to recognise how little of a comfort they could be to each other. It was more bearable to do without tenderness for himself than to see that his own tenderness could make no amends for the lack of other things to her. The sufferings of his own pride from humiliations past and to come were keen enough, yet they were hardly distinguishable to himself from that more acute pain which dominated them – the pain of foreseeing that Rosamond would come to regard him chiefly as the cause of disappointment and unhappiness to her. He had never liked the make-shifts of poverty, and they had never before entered into his prospects for himself; but he was beginning now to imagine how two creatures who loved each other, and had a stock of thoughts in common, might laugh over their shabby furniture, and their calculations how far they could afford butter and eggs. But the glimpse of that poetry seemed as far off from him as the carelessness of the golden age; in poor Rosamond's mind there was not room enough for luxuries to look small in. He got down from his horse in a very sad mood, and went into the house, not expecting to be cheered except by his dinner, and reflecting that before the evening closed it would be wise to tell Rosamond of his application to Bulstrode and his failure. It would be well not to lose time in preparing her for the worst.

But his dinner waited long for him before he was able to eat it. For on entering he found that Dover's agent had already put a man in the house, and when he asked where Mrs Lydgate was, he was told that she was in her bed-room. He went up and found her stretched on the bed pale and silent, without an answer even in her face to any word or look of his. He sat down by the bed and leaning over her said with almost a cry of prayer: 'Forgive me for this misery, my poor Rosamond! Let us only love one another.'

She looked at him silently, still with the blank despair on her face; but the tears began to fill her blue eyes, and her lip trembled. The strong man had had too much to bear that day. He let his head fall beside hers and sobbed.

He did not hinder her from going to her father early in the morning – it seemed now that he ought not to hinder her from doing as she pleased. In half an hour she came back, and said that papa and mamma wished her to go and stay with them while things were in this miserable state. Papa said he could do nothing about the debt – if he paid this, there would be half a dozen more. She had better come back home again till Lydgate had got a comfortable home for her. 'Do you object, Tertius?'

'Do as you like,' said Lydgate. 'But things are not coming to a crisis immediately. There is no hurry.'

'I should not go till tomorrow,' said Rosamond; 'I shall want to pack my clothes.'

'Oh, I would wait a little longer than tomorrow – there is no knowing what may happen,' said Lydgate, with bitter irony. 'I may get my neck broken, and that may make things easier to you.'

It was Lydgate's misfortune and Rosamond's too, that his tenderness towards her, which was both an emotional prompting and a well-considered resolve, was inevitably interrupted by these outbursts of indignation either ironical or remonstrant. She thought them totally unwarranted, and the repulsion which this exceptional severity excited in her was in danger of making the more persistent tenderness unacceptable.

'I see you do not wish me to go,' she said, with chill mildness; 'why can you not say so, without that kind of violence? I shall stay until you request me to do otherwise.'

Lydgate said no more, but went out on his rounds. He felt bruised and shattered, and there was a dark line under his eyes which Rosamond had not seen before. She could not bear to look at him. Tertius had a way of taking things which made them a great deal worse for her.

Chapter 70

Our deeds still travel with us from afar,
And what we have been makes us what we are.

Bulstrode's first object after Lydgate had left Stone Court was to examine Raffles's pockets, which he imagined were sure to carry signs in the shape of hotel-bills of the places he had stopped in, if he had not told the truth in saying that he had come straight from Liverpool because he was ill and had no money. There were various bills crammed into his pocketbook, but none of a later date than Christmas at any other place, except one, which bore date that morning. This was crumpled up with a handbill about a horse-fair in one of his tail-pockets and represented the cost of three days' stay at an inn at Bilkley, where the fair was held – a town at least forty miles from Middlemarch. The bill was heavy, and since Raffles had no luggage with him, it seemed probable that he had left his portmanteau behind in payment, in order to save money for his travelling fare; for his purse was empty, and he had only a couple of sixpences and some loose pence in his pockets.

Bulstrode gathered a sense of safety from these indications that Raffles had really kept at a distance from Middlemarch since his memorable visit at Christmas. At a distance and among people who were strangers to Bulstrode, what satisfaction could there be to Raffles's tormenting, self-magnifying vein in telling old scandalous stories about a Middlemarch banker? And what harm if he did talk? The chief point now was to keep watch over him as long as there was any danger of that intelligible raving, that unaccountable impulse to tell, which seemed to have acted towards Caleb Garth; and Bulstrode felt much anxiety lest some such impulse should come over him at the sight of Lydgate. He sat up alone with him through the night, only ordering the housekeeper to lie down in her clothes, so as to be ready when he called her, alleging his own indisposition to sleep, and his anxiety to carry out the doctor's orders. He did carry them out faithfully, although Raffles was incessantly asking for brandy, and declaring that he was sinking away – that the earth was sinking away from under him. He was restless and sleepless, but still quailing and manageable. On the offer of the food ordered by Lydgate, which he refused, and the denial of other things which he demanded, he seemed to concentrate all his terror on Bulstrode, imploringly deprecating his anger, his revenge on him by starvation, and declaring with strong oaths that he had never told any mortal a word against him. Even this Bulstrode felt that he would not have liked Lydgate to hear; but a more alarming sign of fitful alternation in his delirium was, that in the morning twilight Raffles suddenly seemed to imagine a doctor present, addressing him and declaring that Bulstrode wanted to starve him to death out of revenge for telling, when he never had told.

Bulstrode's native imperiousness and strength of determination served him well. This delicate-looking man, himself nervously perturbed, found the needed stimulus in his strenuous circumstances, and through that difficult night and morning, while he had the air of an animated corpse returned to movement without warmth, holding the mastery by its chill impassibility, his mind was intensely at work thinking of what he had to guard against and what would win him security. Whatever prayers he might lift up, whatever statements he might inwardly make of this man's wretched spiritual condition, and the duty he himself was under to submit to the punishment divinely appointed for him rather than to wish for evil to another through all this effort to condense words into a solid mental state, there pierced and spread with irresistible vividness the images of the events he desired. And in the train of those images came their apology. He could not but see the death of Raffles, and see in it his own deliverance. What was the removal of this wretched creature? He was impenitent – but were not public criminals impenitent? – yet the law decided on their fate. Should Providence in this case award death, there was no sin in contemplating death as the desirable issue – if he kept his hands from hastening it – if he scrupulously did what was prescribed. Even here there might be a mistake; human prescriptions were fallible things: Lydgate had said that treatment had hastened death, – why not his own method of treatment? But of course intention was everything in the question of right and wrong.

And Bulstrode set himself to keep his intention separate from his desire. He inwardly declared that he intended to obey orders. Why should he have got into any argument about the validity of these orders? It was only the common trick of desire – which avails itself of any irrelevant scepticism, finding larger room for itself in all uncertainty about effects, in every obscurity that looks like the absence of law. Still, he did obey the orders.

His anxieties continually glanced towards Lydgate, and his remembrance of what had taken place between them the morning before was accompanied with sensibilities which had not been roused at all during the actual scene. He had then cared but little about Lydgate's painful impressions with regard to the suggested change in the Hospital, or about the disposition towards himself which what he held to be his justifiable refusal of a rather exorbitant request might call forth. He recurred to the scene now with a perception that he had probably made Lydgate his enemy, and with an awakened desire to propitiate him, or rather to create in him a strong sense of personal obligation. He regretted that he had not at once made even an unreasonable money-sacrifice. For in case of unpleasant suspicions or even knowledge gathered from the raving of Raffles, Bulstrode would have felt that he had a defence in Lydgate's mind by having conferred a momentous benefit on him. But the regret had perhaps come too late.

Strange, piteous conflict in the soul of this unhappy man, who had longed for years to be better than he was – who had taken his selfish passions into discipline and clad them in severe robes, so that he had walked with them as a devout quire, till now that a terror had risen among them, and they could chant no longer, but threw out their common cries for safety.

It was nearly the middle of the day before Lydgate arrived: he had meant to come earlier, but had been detained, he said; and his shattered looks were noticed by Bulstrode. But he immediately threw himself into the consideration of the patient, and enquired strictly into all that had occurred. Raffles was worse, would take hardly any food, was persistently wakeful and restlessly raving; but still not violent. Contrary to Bulstrode's alarmed expectation, he took little notice of Lydgate's presence, and continued to talk or murmur incoherently.

'What do you think of him?' said Bulstrode, in private.

'The symptoms are worse.'

'You are less hopeful?'

'No; I still think he may come round. Are you going to stay here yourself?' said Lydgate, looking at Bulstrode with an abrupt question, which made him uneasy, though in reality it was not due to any suspicious conjecture.

'Yes, I think so,' said Bulstrode, governing himself and speaking with deliberation. 'Mrs Bulstrode is advised of the reasons which detain me. Mrs Abel and her husband are not experienced enough to be left quite alone, and this kind of responsibility is scarcely included in their service of me. You have some fresh instructions, I presume.'

The chief new instruction that Lydgate had to give was on the administration of extremely moderate doses of opium, in case of the sleeplessness continuing after several hours. He had taken the precaution of bringing opium in his pocket, and he gave minute directions to Bulstrode as to the doses, and the point at which they should cease. He insisted on the risk of not ceasing; and repeated his order that no alcohol should be given.

'From what I see of the case,' he ended, 'narcotism is the only thing I should be much afraid of. He may wear through even without much food. There's a good deal of strength in him.'

'You look ill yourself, Mr Lydgate – a most unusual, I may say unprecedented thing in my knowledge of you,' said Bulstrode, showing a solicitude as unlike his indifference the day before, as his present recklessness about his own fatigue was unlike his habitual self-cherishing anxiety. 'I fear you are harassed.'

'Yes, I am,' said Lydgate, brusquely, holding his hat, and ready to go.

'Something new, I fear,' said Bulstrode, enquiringly. 'Pray be seated.'

'No, thank you,' said Lydgate, with some *hauteur*. 'I mentioned to you yesterday what was the state of my affairs. There is nothing to add, except that the execution has since then been actually put into my house. One can tell a good deal of trouble in a short sentence. I will say good-morning.'

'Stay, Mr Lydgate, stay,' said Bulstrode; 'I have been reconsidering this subject. I was yesterday taken by surprise and saw it superficially. Mrs Bulstrode is anxious for her niece, and I myself should grieve at a calamitous change in your position. Claims on me are numerous, but on reconsideration, I esteem it right that I should incur a small sacrifice rather than leave you unaided. You said, I think, that a thousand pounds would suffice entirely to free you from your burthens, and enable you to recover a firm stand?'

'Yes,' said Lydgate, a great leap of joy within him surmounting every other feeling; 'that would pay all my debts, and leave me a little on hand. I could set about economising in our way of living. And by and by my practice might look up.'

'If you will wait a moment, Mr Lydgate, I will draw a cheque to that amount. I am aware that help, to be effectual in these cases, should be thorough.'

While Bulstrode wrote, Lydgate turned to the window thinking of his home – thinking of his life with its good start saved from frustration, its good purposes still unbroken.

'You can give me a note of hand for this, Mr Lydgate,' said the banker, advancing towards him with the cheque. 'And by and by, I hope, you may be in circumstances gradually to repay me. Meanwhile, I have great pleasure in thinking that you will be released from further difficulty.'

'I am deeply obliged to you,' said Lydgate. 'You have restored to me the prospect of working with some happiness and some chance of good.'

It appeared to him a very natural movement in Bulstrode that he should have reconsidered his refusal: it corresponded with the more munificent side of his character. But as he put his hack into a canter, that he might get the sooner home, and tell the good news to Rosamond, and get cash at the bank to pay over to Dover's agent, there crossed his mind, with an unpleasant impression, as from a dark-winged flight of evil augury across his vision, the thought of that contrast in himself which a few months had brought – that he should be over-joyed at being under a strong personal obligation – that he should be overjoyed at getting money for himself from Bulstrode.

The banker felt that he had done something to nullify one cause of uneasiness, and yet he was scarcely the easier. He did not measure the quantity of diseased motive which had made him wish for Lydgate's goodwill, but the quantity was none the less actively there, like an irritating agent in his blood. A man vows, and yet will not cast away the means of breaking his vow. Is it that he distinctly means to break it? Not at all; but the desires which tend to break it are at work in him dimly, and make their way into his imagination, and relax his muscles in the very moments when he is telling himself over again the reasons for his vow. Raffles, recovering quickly, returning to the free use of his odious powers – how could Bulstrode wish for that? Raffles dead was the image that brought release, and indirectly he prayed for that way of release, beseeching that, if it were possible, the rest of his days here below might be freed from the threat of an ignominy which would break him utterly as an instrument of God's service. Lydgate's opinion was not on the side of promise that this prayer would be fulfilled: and as the day advanced, Bulstrode felt himself getting irritated at the persistent life in this man, whom he would fain have seen sinking in to the silence of death: imperious will stirred murderous impulses towards this brute life, over which will, by itself, had no power. He said inwardly that he was getting too much worn; he would not sit up with the patient tonight, but leave him to Mrs Abel, who, if necessary, could call her husband.

At six o'clock, Raffles, having had only fitful perturbed snatches of sleep, from which he waked with fresh restlessness and perpetual cries that he was sinking away, Bulstrode began to administer the opium according to Lydgate's directions. At the end of half an hour or more he called Mrs Abel and told her that he found himself unfit for further watching. He must now consign the patient to her care; and he proceeded to repeat to her Lydgate's directions as to the quantity of each dose. Mrs Abel had not before known anything of Lydgate's prescriptions; she had simply prepared and brought whatever Bulstrode ordered, and had done what he pointed out to her. She began now to ask what else she should do besides administering the opium.

'Nothing at present, except the offer of the soup or the soda-water: you can come to me for further directions. Unless there is any important change, I shall not come into the room again tonight. You will ask your husband for help, if necessary. I must go to bed early.'

'You've much need, sir, I'm sure,' said Mrs Abel, 'and to take something more strengthening than what you've done.'

Bulstrode went away now without anxiety as to what Raffles might say in his raving, which had taken on a muttering incoherence not likely to create any dangerous belief. At any rate he must risk this. He went down into the wainscoted parlour first, and began to consider whether he would not have his horse saddled and go home by the moonlight, and give up caring for earthly consequences. Then, he wished that he had begged Lydgate to come again that evening. Perhaps he might deliver a different opinion, and think that Raffles was getting into a less hopeful state. Should he send for Lydgate? If Raffles were really getting worse, and slowly dying, Bulstrode felt that he could go to bed and sleep in gratitude to Providence. But was he worse? Lydgate might come and simply say that he was going on as he expected, and predict that he would by and by fall into a good sleep, and get well. What was the use of sending for him? Bulstrode shrank from that result. No ideas or opinions could hinder him from seeing the one probability to be, that Raffles recovered would be just the same man as before, with his strength as a tormentor renewed, obliging him to drag away his wife to spend her years apart from her friends and native place, carrying an alienating suspicion against him in her heart.

He had sat an hour and a half in this conflict by the firelight only, when a sudden thought made him rise and light the bed-candle, which he had brought down with him. The thought was, that he had not told Mrs Abel when the doses of opium must cease.

He took hold of the candlestick, but stood motionless for a long while. She might already have given him more than Lydgate had prescribed. But it was excusable in him, that he should forget part of an order, in his present wearied condition. He walked upstairs, candle in hand, not knowing whether he should straightway enter his own room and go to bed, or turn to the patient's room and rectify his omission. He paused in the passage, with his face turned towards Raffles's room, and he could hear him moaning and murmuring. He was not asleep, then. Who could know that Lydgate's prescription would not be better disobeyed than followed, since there was still no sleep?

He turned into his own room. Before he had quite undressed, Mrs Abel rapped at the door; he opened it an inch, so that he could hear her speak low.

'If you please, sir, should I have no brandy nor nothing to give the poor creetur? He feels sinking away, and nothing else will he swaller – and but little strength in it, if he did – only the opium. And he says more and more he's sinking down through the earth.'

To her surprise, Mr Bulstrode did not answer. A struggle was going on within him.

'I think he must die for want o' support, if he goes on in that way. When I nursed my poor master, Mr Robisson, I had to give him port-wine and brandy constant, and a big glass at a time,' added Mrs Abel with a touch of remonstrance in her tone.

But again Mr Bulstrode did not answer immediately, and she continued, 'It's not a time to spare when people are at death's door, nor would you wish it, sir, I'm sure. Else I should give him our own bottle o' rum as we keep by us. But a sitter-up so as you've been, and doing everything as laid in your power – '

Here a key was thrust through the inch of doorway, and Mr Bulstrode said huskily, 'That is the key of the wine-cooler. You will find plenty of brandy there.'

Early in the morning – about six – Mr Bulstrode rose and spent sometime in prayer. Does anyone suppose that private prayer is necessarily candid – necessarily goes to the roots of action! Private prayer is inaudible speech, and speech is representative: who can represent himself just as he is, even in his own reflections? Bulstrode had not yet unravelled in his thought the confused promptings of the last four-and-twenty hours.

He listened in the passage, and could hear hard stertorous breathing. Then he walked out in the garden, and looked at the early rime on the grass and fresh spring leaves. When he re-entered the house, he felt startled at the sight of Mrs Abel.

'How is your patient – asleep, I think?' he said, with an attempt at cheerfulness in his tone.

'He's gone very deep, sir,' said Mrs Abel. 'He went off gradual between three and four o'clock. Would you please to go and look at him? I thought it no harm to leave him. My man's gone afield, and the little girl's seeing to the kettles.'

Bulstrode went up. At a glance he knew that Raffles was not in the sleep which brings revival, but in the sleep which streams deeper and deeper into the gulf of death.

He looked round the room and saw a bottle with some brandy in it, and the almost empty opium phial. He put the phial out of sight, and carried the brandy-bottle downstairs with him, locking it again in the wine-cooler.

While breakfasting he considered whether he should ride to Middlemarch at once, or wait for Lydgate's arrival. He decided to wait, and told Mrs Abel that she might go about her work, he could watch in the bedchamber.

As he sat there and beheld the enemy of his peace going irrevocably into silence, he felt more at rest than he had done for many months. His conscience was soothed by the enfolding wing of secrecy, which seemed just then like an angel sent down for his relief. He drew out his pocketbook to review various memoranda there as to the arrangements he had projected and partly carried out in the prospect of quitting Middlemarch, and considered how far he would let them stand or recall them, now that his absence would be brief. Some economies which he felt desirable might still find a suitable occasion in his temporary withdrawal from management, and he hoped still that Mrs Casaubon would take a large share in the expenses of the Hospital. In that way the moments passed, until a change in the stertorous breathing was marked enough to draw his attention wholly to the bed, and forced him to think of the departing life, which had once been subservient to his own – which he had once been glad to find base enough for him to act as he would. It was his gladness then which impelled him now to be glad that the life was at an end.

And who could say that the death of Raffles had been hastened? Who knew what would have saved him?

Lydgate arrived at half-past ten, in time to witness the final pause of the breath. When he entered the room Bulstrode observed a sudden expression in his face, which was not so much surprise as a recognition that he had not judged correctly. He stood by the bed in silence for sometime, with his eyes turned on the dying man, but with that subdued activity of expression which showed that he was carrying on an inward debate.

'When did this change begin?' said he, looking at Bulstrode.

'I did not watch by him last night,' said Bulstrode. 'I was over-worn, and left him under Mrs Abel's care. She said that he sank into sleep between three and four o'clock. When I came in before eight he was nearly in this condition.'

Lydgate did not ask another question, but watched in silence until he said, 'It's all over.'

This morning Lydgate was in a state of recovered hope and freedom. He had set out on his work with all his old animation, and felt strong enough to bear all the deficiencies of his married life. And he was conscious that Bulstrode had been a benefactor to him. But he was uneasy about this case. He had not expected it to terminate as it had done. Yet he hardly knew how to put a question on the subject to Bulstrode without appearing to insult him; and if he examined the housekeeper – why, the man was dead. There seemed to be no use in implying that somebody's ignorance or imprudence had killed him. And after all, he himself might be wrong.

He and Bulstrode rode back to Middlemarch together, talking of many things – chiefly cholera and the chances of the Reform Bill in the House of Lords, and the firm resolve of the Political Unions. Nothing was said about Raffles, except that Bulstrode mentioned the necessity of having a grave for him in Lowick churchyard and observed that, so far as he knew, the poor man had no connections, except Rigg, whom he had stated to be unfriendly towards him.

On returning home Lydgate had a visit from Mr Farebrother. The Vicar had not been in town the day before, but the news that there was an execution in Lydgate's house had got to Lowick by the evening, having been carried by Mr Spicer, shoemaker and parish-clerk, who had it from his brother, the respectable bell-hanger in Lowick Gate. Since that evening when Lydgate had come down from the billiard-room with Fred Vincy, Mr Farebrother's thoughts about him had been rather gloomy. Playing at the Green Dragon once or oftener might have been a trifle in another man; but in Lydgate it was one of several signs that he was getting unlike his former self. He was beginning to do things for which he had formerly even an excessive scorn. Whatever certain dissatisfactions in marriage, which some silly tinklings of gossip had given him hints of, might have to do with this change, Mr Farebrother felt that it was chiefly connected with the debts which were being more and more distinctly reported, and he began to fear that any notion of Lydgate's having resources or friends in the background must be quite illusory. The rebuff he had met with in his first attempt to win Lydgate's confidence, disinclined him to a second; but this news of the execution being actually in the house, determined the Vicar to overcome his reluctance.

Lydgate had just dismissed a poor patient, in whom he was much interested, and he came forward to put out his hand with an open cheerfulness which surprised Mr Farebrother. Could this too be a proud rejection of sympathy and help? Never mind; the sympathy and help should be offered.

'How are you, Lydgate? I came to see you because I had heard something which made me anxious about you,' said the Vicar, in the tone of a good brother, only that there was no reproach in it. They were both seated by this time, and Lydgate answered immediately; 'I think I know what you mean. You had heard that there was an execution in the house?'

'Yes; is it true?'

'It was true,' said Lydgate, with an air of freedom, as if he did not mind talking about the affair now. 'But the danger is over; the debt is paid. I am out of my difficulties now: I shall be freed from debts, and able, I hope, to start afresh on a better plan.'

'I am very thankful to hear it,' said the Vicar, falling back in his chair, and speaking with that low-toned quickness which often follows the removal of a load. 'I like that better than all the news in the *Times*. I confess I came to you with a heavy heart.'

'Thank you for coming,' said Lydgate, cordially. 'I can enjoy the kindness all the more because I am happier. I have certainly been a good deal crushed. I'm afraid I shall find the bruises still painful by and by,' he added, smiling rather sadly; 'but just now I can only feel that the torture-screw is off.'

Mr Farebrother was silent for a moment, and then said earnestly, 'My dear fellow, let me ask you one question. Forgive me if I take a liberty.'

'I don't believe you will ask anything that ought to offend me.'

'Then – this is necessary to set my heart quite at rest – you have not – have you? – in order to pay your debts, incurred another debt which may harass you worse hereafter?'

'No,' said Lydgate, colouring slightly. 'There is no reason why I should not tell you – since the fact is so – that the person to whom I am indebted is Bulstrode. He has made me a very handsome advance – a thousand pounds – and he can afford to wait for repayment.'

'Well, that is generous,' said Mr Farebrother, compelling himself to approve of the man whom he disliked. His delicate feeling shrank from dwelling even in his thought on the fact that he had always urged Lydgate to avoid any personal entanglement with Bulstrode. He added immediately, 'And Bulstrode must naturally feel an interest in your welfare, after you have worked with him in a way which has probably reduced your income instead of adding to it. I am glad to think that he has acted accordingly.'

Lydgate felt uncomfortable under these kindly suppositions. They made more distinct within him the uneasy consciousness which had shown its first dim stirrings only a few hours before, that Bulstrode's motives for his sudden beneficence following close upon the chillest indifference might be merely selfish. He let the kindly suppositions pass. He could not tell the history of the loan, but it was more vividly present with him than ever, as well as the fact which the Vicar delicately ignored – that this relation of personal indebtedness to Bulstrode was what he had once been most resolved to avoid.

He began, instead of answering, to speak of his projected economies, and of his having come to look at his life from a different point of view.

'I shall set up a surgery,' he said. 'I really think I made a mistaken effort in that respect. And if Rosamond will not mind, I shall take an apprentice. I don't like these things, but if one carries them out faithfully they are not really lowering. I have had a severe galling to begin with: that will make the small rubs seem easy.'

Poor Lydgate! the 'if Rosamond will not mind', which had fallen from him involuntarily as part of his thought, was a significant mark of the yoke he bore. But Mr Farebrother, whose hopes entered strongly into the same current with Lydgate's, and who knew nothing about him that could now raise a melancholy presentiment, left him with affectionate congratulation.

Chapter 71

> CLOWN   . . . 'Twas in the Bunch of Grapes, where, indeed,
> you have a delight to sit, have you not?
> FROTH   I have so; because it is an open room, and good for
> winter.
> CLOWN   Why, very well then: I hope here be truths.
>   SHAKESPEARE, *Measure for Measure*

Five days after the death of Raffles, Mr Bambridge was standing at his leisure under the large archway leading into the yard of the Green Dragon. He was not fond of solitary contemplation, but he had only just come out of the house, and any human figure standing at ease under the archway in the early afternoon was as certain to attract companionship as a pigeon which has found something worth pecking at. In this case there was no material object to feed upon, but the eye of reason saw a probability of mental sustenance in the shape of gossip. Mr Hopkins, the meek-mannered draper opposite, was the first to act on this inward vision, being the more ambitious of a little masculine talk because his customers were chiefly women. Mr Bambridge was rather curt to the draper, feeling that Hopkins was of course glad to talk to *him*, but that he was not going to waste much of his talk on Hopkins. Soon, however, there was a small cluster of more important listeners, who were either deposited from the passers-by, or had sauntered to the spot expressly to see if there were anything going on at the Green Dragon; and Mr Bambridge was finding it worth his while to say many impressive things about the fine studs he had been seeing and the purchases he had made on a journey in the north from which he had just returned. Gentlemen present were assured that when they could show him anything to cut out a blood mare, a bay, rising four, which was to be seen at Doncaster if they chose to go and look at it, Mr Bambridge would gratify them by being shot 'from here to Hereford'. Also, a pair of blacks which he was going to put into the break recalled vividly to his mind a pair which he had sold to Faulkner in '19, for a hundred guineas, and which Faulkner had sold for a hundred and sixty two months later – any agent who could disprove this statement being offered the privilege of calling Mr Bambridge by a very ugly name until the exercise made his throat dry.

When the discourse was at this point of animation, came up Mr Frank Hawley. He was not a man to compromise his dignity by lounging at the Green Dragon, but happening to pass along the High Street and seeing Bambridge on the other side, he took some of his long strides to ask the horse-dealer whether he had found the first-rate gig-horse which he had engaged to look for. Mr Hawley was requested to wait until he had seen a grey selected at Bilkley: if that did not meet his wishes to a hair, Bambridge did not know a horse when he saw it, which seemed to be the highest conceivable unlikelihood. Mr Hawley, standing with his back to the street, was fixing a time for looking at the grey and seeing it tried, when a horseman passed slowly by.

'Bulstrode!' said two or three voices at once in a low tone, one of them, which was the draper's, respectfully fixing the Mr' but nobody having more intention in this interjectional naming than if they had said 'the Riverston coach' when that vehicle appeared in the distance. Mr Hawley gave a careless glance round at Bulstrode's back, but as Bambridge's eyes followed it he made a sarcastic grimace.

'By jingo! that reminds me,' he began, lowering his voice a little, 'I picked up something else at Bilkley besides your gig-horse, Mr Hawley. I picked up a fine story about Bulstrode. Do you know how he came by his fortune? Any gentleman wanting a bit of curious information, I can give it him free of expense. If everybody got their deserts, Bulstrode might have had to say his prayers at Botany Bay.'

'What do you mean?' said Mr Hawley, thrusting his hands into his pockets, and pushing a little forward under the archway. If Bulstrode should turn out to be a rascal, Frank Hawley had a prophetic soul.

'I had it from a party who was an old chum of Bulstrode's. I'll tell you where I first picked him up,' said Bambridge, with a sudden gesture of his forefinger. 'He was at Larcher's sale, but I knew nothing of him then – he slipped through my fingers – was after Bulstrode, no doubt. He tells me he can tap Bulstrode to any amount, knows all his secrets. However, he blabbed to me at Bilkley: he takes a stiff glass. Damme if I think he meant to turn king's evidence; but he's that sort of bragging fellow, the bragging runs over hedge and ditch with him, till he'd brag of a spavin as if it 'ud fetch money. A man should know when to pull up.' Mr Bambridge made this remark with an air of disgust, satisfied that his own bragging showed a fine sense of the marketable.

'What's the man's name? Where can he be found?' said Mr Hawley.

'As to where he is to be found, I left him to it at the Saracen's Head; but his name is Raffles.'

'Raffles!' exclaimed Mr Hopkins. 'I furnished his funeral yesterday. He was buried at Lowick. Mr Bulstrode followed him. A very decent funeral.'

There was a strong sensation among the listeners. Mr Bambridge gave an ejaculation in which 'brimstone' was the mildest word, and Mr Hawley, knitting his brows and bending his head forward, exclaimed, 'What? – where did the man die?'

'At Stone Court,' said the draper. 'The housekeeper said he was a relation of the master's. He came there ill on Friday.'

'Why, it was on Wednesday I took a glass with him,' interposed Bambridge.

'Did any doctor attend him?' said Mr Hawley.

'Yes, Mr Lydgate. Mr Bulstrode sat up with him one night. He died the third morning.'

'Go on, Bambridge,' said Mr Hawley, insistently. 'What did this fellow say about Bulstrode?'

The group had already become larger, the town-clerk's presence being a guarantee that something worth listening to was going on there; and Mr Bambridge delivered his narrative in the hearing of seven. It was mainly what we know, including the fact about Will Ladislaw, with some local colour and circumstance added: it was what Bulstrode had dreaded the betrayal of – and hoped to have buried for ever with the corpse of Raffles – it was that haunting ghost of his earlier life which as he rode past the archway of the Green Dragon he was trusting that Providence had delivered him from. Yes, Providence. He had not confessed to himself yet that he had done anything in the way of contrivance to this end; he had accepted what seemed to have been offered. It was impossible to prove that he had done anything which hastened the departure of that man's soul.

But this gossip about Bulstrode spread through Middlemarch like the smell of fire. Mr Frank Hawley followed up his information by sending a clerk whom he could trust to Stone Court on a pretext of enquiring about hay, but really to gather all that could be learned about Raffles and his illness from Mrs Abel. In this way it came to his knowledge that Mr Garth had carried the man to Stone Court in his gig; and Mr Hawley in consequence took an opportunity of seeing Caleb, calling at his office to ask whether he had time to undertake an arbitration if it were required, and then asking him incidentally about Raffles. Caleb was betrayed into no word injurious to Bulstrode beyond the fact which he was forced to admit, that he had given up acting for him within the last week. Mr Hawley drew his inferences, and feeling convinced that Raffles had told his story to Garth, and that Garth had given up Bulstrode's affairs in consequence, said so a few hours later to Mr Toller. The statement was passed on until it had quite lost the stamp of an inference, and was taken as information coming straight from Garth, so that even a diligent historian might have concluded Caleb to be the chief publisher of Bulstrode's misdemeanours.

Mr Hawley was not slow to perceive that there was no handle for the law either in the revelations made by Raffles or in the circumstances of his death. He had himself ridden to Lowick village that he might look at the register and talk over the whole matter with Mr Farebrother, who was not more surprised than the lawyer that an ugly secret should have come to light about Bulstrode, though he had always had justice enough in him to hinder his antipathy from turning into conclusions. But while they were talking another combination was silently going forward in Mr Farebrother's mind, which foreshadowed what was soon to be loudly spoken of in Middlemarch as a necessary 'putting of two and two together'. With the reasons which kept Bulstrode in dread of Raffles there flashed the thought that the dread might have something to do with his munificence towards his medical man; and though he resisted the suggestion that it had been consciously accepted in any way as a bribe, he had a foreboding that this complication of things might be of malignant effect on Lydgate's reputation. He perceived that Mr Hawley knew nothing at present of the sudden relief from debt, and he himself was careful to glide away from all approaches towards the subject.

'Well,' he said, with a deep breath, wanting to wind up the illimitable discussion of what might have been, though nothing could be legally proven, 'it is a strange story. So our mercurial Ladislaw has a queer genealogy! A high-spirited young lady and a musical Polish patriot made a likely enough stock for him to spring from, but I should never have suspected a grafting of the Jew pawnbroker. However, there's no knowing what a mixture will turn out beforehand. Some sorts of dirt serve to clarify.'

'It's just what I should have expected,' said Mr Hawley, mounting his horse. 'Any cursed alien blood, Jew, Corsican, or Gypsy.'

'I know he's one of your black sheep, Hawley. But he is really a disinterested unworldly fellow,' said Mr Farebrother, smiling.

'Ay, ay, that is your Whiggish twist,' said Mr Hawley, who had been in the habit of saying apologetically that Farebrother was such a damned pleasant good-hearted fellow you would mistake him for a Tory.

Mr Hawley rode home without thinking of Lydgate's attendance on Raffles in any other light than as a piece of evidence on the side of Bulstrode. But the news that Lydgate had all at once become able not only to get rid of the execution in his house but to pay all his debts in Middlemarch was spreading fast, gathering round it conjectures and comments which gave it new body and impetus, and soon filling the ears of other persons besides Mr Hawley, who were not slow to see a significant relation between this sudden command of money and Bulstrode's desire to stifle the scandal of Raffles. That the money came from Bulstrode would infallibly have been guessed even if there had been no direct evidence of it; for it had beforehand entered into the gossip about Lydgate's affairs, that neither his father-in-law nor his own family would do anything for him, and direct evidence was furnished not only by a clerk at the Bank, but by innocent Mrs Bulstrode herself, who mentioned the loan to Mrs Plymdale, who mentioned it to her daughter-in-law of the house of Toller, who mentioned it generally. The business was felt to be so public and important that it required dinners to feed it, and many invitations were just then issued and accepted on the strength of this scandal concerning Bulstrode and Lydgate; wives, widows, and single ladies took their work and went out to tea oftener than usual; and all public conviviality, from the Green Dragon to Dollop's, gathered a zest which could not be won from the question whether the Lords would throw out the Reform Bill.

For hardly anybody doubted that some scandalous reason or other was at the bottom of Bulstrode's liberality to Lydgate. Mr Hawley, indeed, in the first instance, invited a select party, including the two physicians, with Mr Toller and Mr Wrench, expressly to hold a close discussion as to the probabilities of Raffles's illness, reciting to them all the particulars which had been gathered from Mrs Abel in connection with Lydgate's certificate, that the death was due to *delirium tremens;* and the medical gentlemen, who all stood undisturbedly on the old paths in relation to this disease, declared that they could see nothing in these particulars which could be transformed into a positive ground of suspicion. But the moral grounds of suspicion remained; the strong motives Bulstrode clearly had for wishing to be rid of Raffles, and the fact that at this critical moment he had given Lydgate the help which he must for sometime have known the need for; the disposition, moreover, to believe that Bulstrode would be unscrupulous, and the absence of any indisposition to believe that Lydgate might be as easily bribed as other haughty-minded men when they have found themselves in want of money. Even if the money had been given merely to make him hold his tongue about the scandal of Bulstrode's earlier life, the fact threw an odious light on Lydgate, who had long been sneered at as making himself subservient to the banker for the sake of working himself into predominance, and discrediting the older members of his profession. Hence, in spite of the negative as to any direct sign of guilt, in relation to the death at Stone Court, Mr Hawley's select party broke up with the sense that the affair had 'an ugly look'.

But this vague conviction of indeterminable guilt, which was enough to keep up much head-shaking and biting innuendo even among substantial professional seniors, had for the general mind all the superior power of mystery over fact. Everybody liked better to conjecture how the thing was, than simply to know it; for conjecture soon became more confident than knowledge, and had a more liberal allowance for the incompatible. Even the more definite scandal concerning Bulstrode's earlier life was, for some minds, melted into the mass of mystery, as so much lively metal to be poured out in dialogue, and to take such fantastic shapes as heaven pleased.

This was the tone of thought chiefly sanctioned by Mrs Dollop, the spirited landlady of the Tankard in Slaughter Lane, who had often to resist the shallow pragmatism of customers disposed to think that their reports from the outer world were of equal force with what had 'come up' in her mind. How it had been brought to her she didn't know, but it was there before her as if it had been scored with the chalk on the chimney-board – 'as Bulstrode should say, his inside was *that black* as if the hairs of his head knowed the thoughts of his heart, he'd tear 'em up by the roots.'

'That's odd,' said Mr Limp, a meditative shoemaker, with weak eyes and a piping voice. 'Why, I read in the *Trumpet* that was what the Duke of Wellington said when he turned his coat and went over to the Romans.'

'Very like,' said Mrs Dollop. 'If one raskill said it, it's more reason why another should. But hypo*crite* as he's been, and holding things with that high hand, as there was no parson i' the country good enough for him, he was forced to take Old Harry into his counsel, and Old Harry's been too many for him.'

'Ay, ay, he's a 'complice you can't send out o' the country,' said Mr Crabbe the glazier, who gathered much news and groped among it dimly. 'But by what I can make out, there's them says Bulstrode was for running away, for fear o' being found out, before now.'

'He'll be drove away, whether or no,' said Mr Dill, the barber, who had just dropped in. 'I shaved Fletcher, Hawley's clerk, this morning – he's got a bad finger – and he says they're all of one mind to get rid of Bulstrode. Mr Thesiger is turned against him, and wants him out o' the parish. And there's gentlemen in this town says they'd as soon dine with a fellow from the hulks. "And a deal sooner I would," says Fletcher; "for what's more against one's stomach than a man coming and making himself bad company with his religion, and giving out as the Ten Commandments are not enough for him, and all the while he's worse than half the men at the treadmill?" Fletcher said so himself.'

'It'll be a bad thing for the town though, if Bulstrode's money goes out of it,' said Mr Limp, quaveringly.

'Ah, there's better folk spend their money worse,' said a firm-voiced dyer, whose crimson hands looked out of keeping with his good-natured face.

'But he won't keep his money, by what I can make out,' said the glazier. 'Don't they say as there's somebody can strip it off him? By what I can understan', they could take every penny off him, if they went to lawing.'

'No such thing!' said the barber, who felt himself a little above his company at Dollop's, but liked it none the worse. 'Fletcher says it's no such thing. He says they might prove over and over again whose child this young Ladislaw was, and they'd do no more than if they proved I came out of the Fens – he couldn't touch a penny.'

'Look you there now!' said Mrs Dollop, indignantly. 'I thank the Lord he took my children to Himself, if that's all the law can do for the motherless. Then by that, it's o' no use who your father and mother is. But as to listening to what one lawyer says without asking another – I wonder at a man o' your cleverness, Mr Dill. It's well known there's always two sides, if no more; else who'd go to law, I should like to know? It's a poor tale, with all the law as there is up and down, if it's no use proving whose child you are. Fletcher may say that if he likes, but I say, don't Fletcher *me*!'

Mr Dill affected to laugh in a complimentary way at Mrs Dollop, as a woman who was more than a match for the lawyers; being disposed to submit to much twitting from a landlady who had a long score against him.

'If they come to lawing, and it's all true as folks say, there's more to be looked to nor money,' said the glazier. 'There's this poor creetur as is dead and gone: by what I can make out, he'd seen the day when he was a deal finer gentleman nor Bulstrode.'

'Finer gentleman! I'll warrant him,' said Mrs Dollop, 'and a far personabler man, by what I can hear. As I said when Mr Baldwin, the tax-gatherer, comes in, a-standing where you sit, and says, "Bulstrode got all his money as he brought into this town by thieving and swindling," – I said, "You don't make me no wiser, Mr Baldwin: it's set my blood a-creeping to look at him ever sin' here he came into Slaughter Lane a-wanting to buy the house over my head: folks don't look the colour o' the dough-tub and stare at you as if they wanted to see into your backbone for nothingk." That was what I said, and Mr Baldwin can bear me witness.'

'And in the rights of it too,' said Mr Crabbe. 'For by what I can make out, this Raffles, as they call him, was a lusty, fresh-coloured man as you'd wish to see, and the best o' company though dead he lies in Lowick churchyard sure enough and by what I can understan', there's them knows more than they *should* know about how he got there.'

'I'll believe you!' said Mrs Dollop, with a touch of scorn at Mr Crabbe's apparent dimness. 'When a man's been 'ticed to a lone house, and there's them can pay for hospitals and nurses for half the countryside choose to be sitters-up night and day, and nobody to come near but a doctor as is known to stick at nothingk, and as poor as he can hang together, and after that so flushed o' money as he can pay off Mr Byles the butcher as his bill has been running on for the best o' joints since last Michaelmas was a twelvemonth – I don't want anybody to come and tell me as there's been more going on nor the Prayer-book's got a service for – I don't want to stand winking and blinking and thinking.'

Mrs Dollop looked round with the air of a landlady accustomed to dominate her company. There was a chorus of adhesion from the more courageous; but Mr Limp, after taking a draught, placed his flat hands together and pressed them hard between his knees, looking down at them with blear-eyed contemplation, as if the scorching power of Mrs Dollop's speech had quite dried up and nullified his wits until they could be brought round again by further moisture.

'Why shouldn't they dig the man up and have the Crowner?' said the dyer. 'It's been done many and many's the time. If there's been foul play they might find it out.'

'Not they, Mr Jonas!' said Mrs Dollop, emphatically. 'I know what doctors are. They're a deal too cunning to be found out. And this Dr Lydgate that's been for cutting up everybody before the breath was well out o' their body – it's plain enough what use he wanted to make o' looking into respectable people's insides. He knows drugs, you may be sure, as you can neither smell nor see, neither before they're swallowed nor after. Why, I've seen drops myself ordered by Dr Gambit, as is our club doctor and a good charikter, and has brought more live children into the world nor ever another i' Middlemarch – I say I've seen drops myself as made no difference whether they was in the glass or out, and yet have griped you the next day. So I'll leave your own sense to judge. Don't tell me! All I say is, it's a mercy they didn't take this Dr Lydgate on to our club. There's many a mother's child might ha' rued it.'

The heads of this discussion at 'Dollop's' had been the common theme among all classes in the town, had been carried to Lowick Parsonage on one side and to Tipton Grange on the other, had come fully to the ears of the Vincy family, and had been discussed with sad reference to 'poor Harriet' by all Mrs Bulstrode's friends, before Lydgate knew distinctly why people were looking strangely at him, and before Bulstrode himself suspected the betrayal of his secrets. He had not been accustomed to very cordial relations with his neighbours, and hence he could not miss the signs of cordiality; moreover, he had been taking journeys on business of various kinds, having now made up his mind that he need not quit Middlemarch, and feeling able consequently to determine on matters which he had before left in suspense.

'We will make a journey to Cheltenham in the course of a month or two,' he had said to his wife. 'There are great spiritual advantages to be had in that town along with the air and the waters, and six weeks there will be eminently refreshing to us.'

He really believed in the spiritual advantages, and meant that his life henceforth should be the more devoted because of those later sins which he represented to himself as hypothetic, praying hypothetically for their pardon: – 'if I have herein trangressed.'

As to the Hospital, he avoided saying anything further to Lydgate, fearing to manifest a too sudden change of plans immediately on the death of Raffles. In his secret soul he believed that Lydgate suspected his orders to have been intentionally disobeyed, and suspecting this he must also suspect a motive. But nothing had been betrayed to him as to the history of Raffles, and Bulstrode was anxious not to do anything which would give emphasis to his undefined suspicions. As to any certainty that a particular method of treatment would either save or kill, Lydgate himself was constantly arguing against such dogmatism; he had no right to speak, and he had every motive for being silent. Hence Bulstrode felt himself providentially secured. The only incident he had strongly winced under had been an occasional encounter with Caleb Garth, who, however, had raised his hat with mild gravity.

Meanwhile, on the part of the principal townsmen a strong determination was growing against him.

A meeting was to be held in the Town Hall on a sanitary question which had risen into pressing importance by the occurrence of a cholera case in the town. Since the Act of Parliament, which had been hurriedly passed, authorising assessments for sanitary measures, there had been a Board for the super-intendence of such measures appointed in Middlemarch, and much cleansing and preparation had been concurred in by Whigs and Tories. The question now was, whether a piece of ground outside the town should be secured as a burial-ground by means of assessment or by private subscription. The meeting was to be open, and almost everybody of importance in the town was expected to be there.

Mr Bulstrode was a member of the Board, and just before twelve o'clock he started from the Bank with the intention of urging the plan of private sub-scription. Under the hesitation of his projects, he had for sometime kept himself in the background, and he felt that he should this morning resume his old position as a man of action and influence in the public affairs of the town where he expected to end his days. Among the various persons going in the same direction, he saw Lydgate; they joined, talked over the object of the meeting, and entered it together.

It seemed that everybody of mark had been earlier than they. But there were still spaces left near the head of the large central table, and they made their way thither. Mr Farebrother sat opposite, not far from Mr Hawley; all the medical men were there; Mr Thesiger was in the chair, and Mr Brooke of Tipton was on his right hand.

Lydgate noticed a peculiar interchange of glances when he and Bulstrode took their seats.

After the business had been fully opened by the chairman, who pointed out the advantages of purchasing by subscription a piece of ground large enough to be ultimately used as a general cemetery, Mr Bulstrode, whose rather high-pitched but subdued and fluent voice the town was used to at meetings of this sort, rose and asked leave to deliver his opinion. Lydgate could see again the peculiar interchange of glances before Mr Hawley started up, and said in his firm resonant voice, 'Mr Chairman, I request that before anyone delivers his opinion on this point I may be permitted to speak on a question of public feeling, which not only by myself, but by many gentlemen present, is regarded as preliminary.'

Mr Hawley's mode of speech, even when public decorums repressed his 'awful language', was formidable in its curtness and self-possession. Mr Thesiger sanctioned the request, Mr Bulstrode sat down, and Mr Hawley continued.

'In what I have to say, Mr Chairman, I am not speaking simply on my own behalf: I am speaking with the concurrence and at the express request of no fewer than eight of my fellow-townsmen, who are immediately around us. It is our united sentiment that Mr Bulstrode should be called upon – and I do now call upon him – to resign public positions which he holds not simply as a tax-payer, but as a gentleman among gentlemen. There are practices and there are acts which, owing to circumstances, the law cannot visit, though they may be worse than many things which are legally punishable. Honest men and gentle-men, if they don't want the company of people who perpetrate such acts, have got to defend themselves as they best can, and that is what I and the friends whom I may call my clients in this affair are determined to do. I don't say that Mr Bulstrode has been guilty of shameful acts, but I call upon him either publicly to deny and confute the scandalous statements made against him by a man now dead, and who died in his house – the statement that he was for many years engaged in nefarious practices, and that he won his fortune by dishonest procedures – or else to withdraw from positions which could only have been allowed him as a gentleman among gentlemen.'

All eyes in the room were turned on Mr Bulstrode, who, since the first mention of his name, had been going through a crisis of feeling almost too violent for his delicate frame to support. Lydgate, who himself was undergoing a shock as from the terrible practical interpretation of some faint augury, felt, nevertheless, that his own movement of resentful hatred was checked by that instinct of the Healer which thinks first of bringing rescue or relief to the sufferer, when he looked at the shrunken misery of Bulstrode's livid face.

The quick vision that his life was after all a failure, that he was a dishonoured man, and must quail before the glance of those towards whom he had habitually assumed the attitude of a reprover – that God had disowned him before men and left him unscreened to the triumphant scorn of those who were glad to have their hatred justified – the sense of utter futility in that equivocation with his conscience in dealing with the life of his accomplice, an equivocation which now turned venomously upon him with the full-grown fang of a discovered lie: – all this rushed through him like the agony of terror which fails to kill, and leaves the ears still open to the returning wave of execration. The sudden sense of exposure after the re-established sense of safety came – not to the coarse organisation of a criminal but – to the susceptible nerve of a man whose intensest being lay in such mastery and predominance as the conditions of his life had shaped for him.

But in that intense being lay the strength of reaction. Through all his bodily infirmity there ran a tenacious nerve of ambitious self-preserving will, which had continually leaped out like a flame, scattering all doctrinal fears, and which, even while he sat an object of compassion for the merciful, was beginning to stir and glow under his ashy paleness. Before the last words were out of Mr Hawley's mouth, Bulstrode felt that he should answer, and that his answer would be a retort. He dared not get up and say, 'I am not guilty, the whole story is false' – even if he had dared this, it would have seemed to him, under his present keen sense of betrayal, as vain as to pull, for covering to his nakedness, a frail rag which would rend at every little strain.

For a few moments there was total silence, while every man in the room was looking at Bulstrode. He sat perfectly still, leaning hard against the back of his chair: he could not venture to rise, and when he began to speak he pressed his hands upon the seat on each side of him. But his voice was perfectly audible, though hoarser than usual, and his words were distinctly pronounced, though he paused between each sentence as if short of breath. He said, turning first towards Mr Thesiger, and then looking at Mr Hawley: 'I protest before you, sir, as a Christian minister, against the sanction of proceedings towards me which are dictated by virulent hatred. Those who are hostile to me are glad to believe any libel uttered by a loose tongue against me. And their consciences become strict against me. Say that the evil-speaking of which I am to be made the victim accuses me of malpractices – ' here Bulstrode's voice rose and took on a more biting accent, till it seemed a low cry – 'who shall be my accuser? Not men whose own lives are unchristian, nay, scandalous – not men who themselves use low instruments to carry out their ends – whose profession is a tissue of chicanery – who have been spending their income on their own sensual enjoyments, while I have been devoting mine to advance the best objects with regard to this life and the next.'

After the word chicanery there was a growing noise, half of murmurs and half of hisses, while four persons started up at once – Mr Hawley, Mr Toller, Mr Chichely, and Mr Hackbutt; but Mr Hawley's outburst was instantaneous, and left the others behind in silence.

'If you mean me, sir, I call upon you and everyone else to the inspection of my professional life. As to Christian or unchristian, I repudiate your canting palavering Christianity; and as to the way in which I spend my income, it is not my principle to maintain thieves and cheat offspring of their due inheritance in order to support religion and set myself up as a saintly Kill-joy. I affect no niceness of conscience – I have not found any nice standards necessary yet to measure your actions by, sir. And I again call upon you to enter into satisfactory explanations concerning the scandals against you, or else to withdraw from posts in which we at any rate decline you as a colleague. I say, sir, we decline to co-operate with a man whose character is not cleared from infamous lights cast upon it, not only by reports but by recent actions.'

'Allow me, Mr Hawley,' said the chairman; and Mr Hawley, still fuming, bowed half impatiently, and sat down with his hands thrust deep in his pockets.

'Mr Bulstrode, it is not desirable, I think, to prolong the present discussion,' said Mr Thesiger, turning to the pallid trembling man: 'I must so far concur with what has fallen from Mr Hawley in expression of a general feeling, as to think it due to your Christian profession that you should clear yourself, if possible, from unhappy aspersions. I for my part should be willing to give you full opportunity and hearing. But I must say that your present attitude is painfully inconsistent with those principles which you have sought to identify yourself with, and for the honour of which I am bound to care. I recommend you at present as your clergyman, and one who hopes for your reinstatement in respect, to quit the room, and avoid further hindrance to business.'

Bulstrode, after a moment's hesitation, took his hat from the floor and slowly rose, but he grasped the corner of the chair so totteringly that Lydgate felt sure there was not strength enough in him to walk away without support. What could he do? He could not see a man sink close to him for want of help. He rose and gave his arm to Bulstrode, and in that way led him out of the room; yet this act, which might have been one of gentle duty and pure compassion, was at this moment unspeakably bitter to him. It seemed as if he were putting his sign-manual to that association of himself with Bulstrode, of which he now saw the full meaning as it must have presented itself to other minds. He now felt the conviction that this man who was leaning tremblingly on his arm, had given him the thousand pounds as a bribe, and that somehow the treatment of Raffles had been tampered with from an evil motive. The inferences were closely linked enough: the town knew of the loan, believed it to be a bribe, and believed that he took it as a bribe.

Poor Lydgate, his mind struggling under the terrible clutch of this revelation, was all the while morally forced to take Mr Bulstrode to the Bank, send a man off for his carriage, and wait to accompany him home.

Meanwhile the business of the meeting was despatched, and fringed off into eager discussion among various groups concerning this affair of Bulstrode – and Lydgate.

Mr Brooke, who had before heard only imperfect hints of it, and was very uneasy that he had 'gone a little too far' in countenancing Bulstrode, now got himself fully informed, and felt some benevolent sadness in talking to Mr Fare-brother about the ugly light in which Lydgate had come to be regarded. Mr Farebrother was going to walk back to Lowick.

'Step into my carriage,' said Mr Brooke. 'I am going round to see Mrs Casaubon. She was to come back from Yorkshire last night. She will like to see me, you know.'

So they drove along, Mr Brooke chatting with good-natured hope that there had not really been anything black in Lydgate's behaviour – a young fellow whom he had seen to be quite above the common mark, when he brought a letter from his uncle, Sir Godwin. Mr Farebrother said little: he was deeply mournful: with a keen perception of human weakness, he could not be confident that under the pressure of humiliating needs Lydgate had not fallen below himself.

When the carriage drove up to the gate of the manor, Dorothea was out on the gravel, and came to greet them.

'Well, my dear,' said Mr Brooke, 'we have just come from a meeting – a sanitary meeting, you know.'

'Was Mr Lydgate there?' said Dorothea, who looked full of health and animation, and stood with her head bare under the gleaming April lights. 'I want to see him and have a great consultation with him about the Hospital. I have engaged with Mr Bulstrode to do so.'

'Oh, my dear,' said Mr Brooke, 'we have been hearing bad news – bad news, you know.'

They walked through the garden towards the churchyard gate, Mr Farebrother wanting to go on to the parsonage; and Dorothea heard the whole sad story.

She listened with deep interest, and begged to hear twice over the facts and impressions concerning Lydgate. After a short silence, pausing at the churchyard gate, and addressing Mr Farebrother, she said energetically: 'You don't believe that Mr Lydgate is guilty of anything base? I will not believe it. Let us find out the truth and clear him!'

BOOK EIGHT

Sunset and Sunrise

Chapter 72

Full souls are double mirrors, making still
An endless vista of fair things before,
Repeating things behind.

Dorothea's impetuous generosity, which would have leaped at once to the vindication of Lydgate from the suspicion of having accepted money as a bribe, underwent a melancholy check when she came to consider all the circumstances of the case by the light of Mr Farebrother's experience.

'It is a delicate matter to touch,' he said. 'How can we begin to enquire into it? It must be either publicly by setting the magistrate and coroner to work, or privately by questioning Lydgate. As to the first proceeding there is no solid ground to go upon, else Hawley would have adopted it; and as to opening the subject with Lydgate, I confess I should shrink from it. He would probably take it as a deadly insult. I have more than once experienced the difficulty of speaking to him on personal matters. And – one should know the truth about his conduct beforehand, to feel very confident of a good result.'

'I feel convinced that his conduct has not been guilty: I believe that people are almost always better than their neighbours think they are,' said Dorothea. Some of her intensest experience in the last two years had set her mind strongly in opposition to any unfavourable construction of others; and for the first time she felt rather discontented with Mr Farebrother. She disliked this cautious weighing of consequences, instead of an ardent faith in efforts of justice and mercy, which would conquer by their emotional force. Two days afterwards, he was dining at the Manor with her uncle and the Chettams, and when the dessert was standing uneaten, the servants were out of the room, and Mr Brooke was nodding in a nap, she returned to the subject with renewed vivacity.

'Mr Lydgate would understand that if his friends hear a calumny about him their first wish must be to justify. What do we live for, if it is not to make life less difficult to each other? I cannot be indifferent to the troubles of a man who advised me in *my* trouble, and attended me in my illness.'

Dorothea's tone and manner were not more energetic than they had been when she was at the head of her uncle's table nearly three years before, and her experience since had given her more right to express a decided opinion. But Sir James Chettam was no longer the diffident and acquiescent suitor: he was the anxious brother-in-law, with a devout admiration for his sister, but with a constant alarm lest she should fall under some new illusion almost as bad as marrying Casaubon. He smiled much less; when he said 'Exactly' it was more often an introduction to a dissentient opinion than in those submissive bachelor days: and Dorothea found to her surprise that she had to resolve not to be afraid of him – all the more because he was really her best friend. He disagreed with her now.

'But, Dorothea,' he said, remonstrantly, 'you can't undertake to manage a man's life for him in that way. Lydgate must know – at least he will soon come to know how he stands. If he can clear himself, he will. He must act for himself.'

'I think his friends must wait till they find an opportunity,' added Mr Farebrother. 'It is possible – I have often felt so much weakness in myself that I can conceive even a man of honourable disposition, such as I have always believed Lydgate to be, succumbing to such a temptation as that of accepting money which was offered more or less indirectly as a bribe to insure his silence about scandalous facts long gone by. I say, I can conceive this, if he were under the pressure of hard circumstances – if he had been harassed as I feel sure Lydgate has been. I would not believe anything worse of him except under stringent proof. But there is the terrible Nemesis following on some errors, that it is always possible for those who like it to interpret them into a crime: there is no proof in favour of the man outside his own consciousness and assertion.'

'Oh, how cruel!' said Dorothea, clasping her hands. 'And would you not like to be the one person who believed in that man's innocence, if the rest of the world belied him? Besides, there is a man's character beforehand to speak for him.'

'But, my dear Mrs Casaubon,' said Mr Farebrother, smiling gently at her ardour, 'character is not cut in marble – it is not something solid and unalterable. It is something living and changing, and may become diseased as our bodies do.'

'Then it may be rescued and healed,' said Dorothea. 'I should not be afraid of asking Mr Lydgate to tell me the truth, that I might help him. Why should I be afraid? Now that I am not to have the land, James, I might do as Mr Bulstrode proposed, and take his place in providing for the hospital: and I have to consult Mr Lydgate, to know thoroughly what are the prospects of doing good by keeping up the present plans. There is the best opportunity in the world for me to ask for his confidence; and he would be able to tell me things which might make all the circumstances clear. Then we would all stand by him and bring him out of his trouble. People glorify all sorts of bravery except the bravery they might show on behalf of their nearest neighbours.' Dorothea's eyes had a moist brightness in them, and the changed tones of her voice roused her uncle, who began to listen.

'It is true that a woman may venture on some efforts of sympathy which would hardly succeed if we men undertook them,' said Mr Farebrother, almost converted by Dorothea's ardour.

'Surely, a woman is bound to be cautious and listen to those who know the world better than she does,' said Sir James, with his little frown. 'Whatever you do in the end, Dorothea, you should really keep back at present, and not volunteer any meddling with this Bulstrode business. We don't know yet what may turn up. You must agree with me?' he ended, looking at Mr Farebrother.

'I do think it would be better to wait,' said the latter.

'Yes, yes, my dear,' said Mr Brooke, not quite knowing at what point the discussion had arrived, but coming up to it with a contribution which was generally appropriate. 'It is easy to go too far, you know. You must not let your ideas run away with you. And as to being in a hurry to put money into schemes – it won't do, you know. Garth has drawn me in uncommonly with repairs, draining, that sort of thing: I'm uncommonly out of pocket with one thing or another. I must pull up. As for you, Chettam, you are spending a fortune on those oak fences round your demesne.'

Dorothea, submitting uneasily to this discouragement, went with Celia into the library, which was her usual drawing-room.

'Now, Dodo, do listen to what James says,' said Celia, 'else you will be getting into a scrape. You always did, and you always will, when you set about doing as you please. And I think it is a mercy now after all that you have got James to think for you. He lets you have your plans, only he hinders you from being taken in. And that is the good of having a brother instead of a husband. A husband would not let you have your plans.'

'As if I wanted a husband!' said Dorothea. 'I only want not to have my feelings checked at every turn.' Mrs Casaubon was still undisciplined enough to burst into angry tears.

'Now, really, Dodo,' said Celia, with rather a deeper guttural than usual, 'you *are* contradictory: first one thing and then another. You used to submit to Mr Casaubon quite shamefully: I think you would have given up ever coming to see me if he had asked you.'

'Of course I submitted to him, because it was my duty; it was my feeling for him,' said Dorothea, looking through the prism of her tears.

'Then why can't you think it your duty to submit a little to what James wishes?' said Celia, with a sense of stringency in her argument. 'Because he only wishes what is for your own good. And, of course men know best about everything, except what women know better.'

Dorothea laughed and forgot her tears.

'Well, I mean about babies and those things,' explained Celia. 'I should not give up to James when I knew he was wrong, as you used to do to Mr Casaubon.'

Chapter 73

Pity the laden one: this wandering woe
May visit you and me.

When Lydgate had allayed Mrs Bulstrode's anxiety by telling her that her husband had been seized with faintness at the meeting, but that he trusted to see him better and would call again the next day, unless she sent for him earlier, he went directly home, got on his horse, and rode three miles out of the town for the sake of being out of reach.

He felt himself becoming violent and unreasonable as if raging under the pain of stings: he was ready to curse the day on which he had come to Middlemarch. Everything that had happened to him there seemed a mere preparation for this hateful fatality, which had come as a blight on his honourable ambition, and must make even people who had only vulgar standards regard his reputation as irrevocably damaged. In such moments a man can hardly escape being unloving. Lydgate thought of himself as the sufferer, and of others as the agents who had injured his lot. He had meant everything to turn out differently; and others had thrust themselves into his life and thwarted his purposes. His marriage seemed an unmitigated calamity; and he was afraid of going to Rosamond before he had vented himself in this solitary rage, lest the mere sight of her should exasperate him and make him behave unwarrantably. There are episodes in most men's lives in which their highest qualities can only cast a deterring shadow over the objects that fill their inward vision: Lydgate's tender-heartedness was present just then only as a dread lest he should offend against it, not as an emotion that swayed him to tenderness. For he was very miserable. Only those who know the supremacy of the intellectual life – the life which has a seed of ennobling thought and purpose within it – can understand the grief of one who falls from that serene activity into the absorbing soul-wasting struggle with worldly annoyances.

How was he to live on without vindicating himself among people who suspected him of baseness? How could he go silently away from Middlemarch as if he were retreating before a just condemnation? And yet how was he to set about vindicating himself?

For that scene at the meeting, which he had just witnessed, although it had told him no particulars, had been enough to make his own situation thoroughly clear to him. Bulstrode had been in dread of scandalous disclosures on the part of Raffles. Lydgate could now construct all the probabilities of the case. 'He was afraid of some betrayal in my hearing: all he wanted was to bind me to him by a strong obligation: that was why he passed on a sudden from hardness to liberality. And he may have tampered with the patient – he may have disobeyed my orders. I fear he did. But whether he did or not, the world believes that he somehow or other poisoned the man and that I winked at the crime, if I didn't help in it. And yet – and yet he may not be guilty of the last offence; and it is just possible that the change towards me may have been a genuine relenting – the effect of second thoughts such as he alleged. What we call the "just possible" is sometimes true and the thing we find it easier to believe is grossly false. In his last dealings with this man Bulstrode may have kept his hands pure, in spite of my suspicion to the contrary.'

There was a benumbing cruelty in his position. Even if he renounced every other consideration than that of justifying himself – if he met shrugs, cold glances, and avoidance as an accusation, and made a public statement of all the facts as he knew them, who would be convinced? It would be playing the part of a fool to offer his own testimony on behalf of himself, and say, 'I did not take the money as a bribe.' The circumstances would always be stronger than his assertion. And besides, to come forward and tell everything about himself must include declarations about Bulstrode which would darken the suspicions of others against him. He must tell that he had not known of Raffles's existence when he first mentioned his pressing need of money to Bulstrode, and that he took the money innocently as a result of that communication, not knowing that a new motive for the loan might have arisen on his being called in to this man. And after all, the suspicion of Bulstrode's motives might be unjust.

But then came the question whether he should have acted in precisely the same way if he had not taken the money? Certainly, if Raffles had continued alive and susceptible of further treatment when he arrived, and he had then imagined any disobedience to his orders on the part of Bulstrode, he would have made a strict enquiry, and if his conjecture had been verified he would have thrown up the case, in spite of his recent heavy obligation. But if he had not received any money – if Bulstrode had never revoked his cold recommendation of bankruptcy would he, Lydgate, have abstained from all enquiry even on finding the man dead? – would the shrinking from an insult to Bulstrode – would the dubiousness of all medical treatment and the argument that his own treatment would pass for the wrong with most members of his profession – have had just the same force or significance with him?

That was the uneasy corner of Lydgate's consciousness while he was reviewing the facts and resisting all reproach. If he had been independent, this matter of a patient's treatment and the distinct rule that he must do or see done that which he believed best for the life committed to him, would have been the point on which he would have been the sturdiest. As it was, he had rested in the consideration that disobedience to his orders, however it might have arisen, could not be considered a crime, that in the dominant opinion obedience to his orders was just as likely to be fatal, and that the affair was simply one of etiquette. Whereas, again and again, in his time of freedom, he had denounced the perversion of pathological doubt into moral doubt and had said – 'the purest experiment in treatment may still be conscientious: my business is to take care of life, and to do the best I can think of for it. Science is properly more scrupulous than dogma. Dogma gives a charter to mistake, but the very breath of science is a contest with mistake, and must keep the conscience alive.' Alas! the scientific conscience had got into the debasing company of money obligation and selfish respects.

'Is there a medical man of them all in Middlemarch who would question himself as I do?' said poor Lydgate, with a renewed outburst of rebellion against the oppression of his lot. 'And yet they will all feel warranted in making a wide space between me and them, as if I were a leper! My practice and my reputation are utterly damned – I can see that. Even if I could be cleared by valid evidence, it would make little difference to the blessed world here. I have been set down as tainted and should be cheapened to them all the same.'

Already there had been abundant signs which had hitherto puzzled him, that just when he had been paying off his debts and getting cheerfully on his feet, the townsmen were avoiding him or looking strangely at him, and in two instances it came to his knowledge that patients of his had called in another practitioner. The reasons were too plain now. The general blackballing had begun.

No wonder that in Lydgate's energetic nature the sense of a hopeless miscon-struction easily turned into a dogged resistance. The scowl which occasionally showed itself on his square brow was not a meaningless accident. Already when he was re-entering the town after that ride taken in the first hours of stinging pain, he was setting his mind on remaining in Middlemarch in spite of the worst that could be done against him. He would not retreat before calumny, as if he submitted to it. He would face it to the utmost, and no act of his should show that he was afraid. It belonged to the generosity as well as defiant force of his nature that he resolved not to shrink from showing to the full his sense of obligation to Bulstrode. It was true that the association with this man had been fatal to him – true that if he had the thousand pounds still in his hands with all his debts unpaid he would have returned the money to Bulstrode, and taken beggary rather than the rescue which had been sullied with the suspicion of a bribe (for, remember, he was one of the proudest among the sons of men) – nevertheless, he would not turn away from this crushed fellow-mortal whose aid he had used, and make a pitiful effort to get acquittal for himself by howling against another. 'I shall do as I think right, and explain to nobody. They will try to starve me out, but – ' he was going on with an obstinate resolve, but he was getting near home, and the thought of Rosamond urged itself again into that chief place from which it had been thrust by the agonised struggles of wounded honour and pride.

How would Rosamond take it all? Here was another weight of chain to drag, and poor Lydgate was in a bad mood for bearing her dumb mastery. He had no impulse to tell her the trouble which must soon be common to them both. He preferred waiting for the incidental disclosure which events must soon bring about.

Chapter 74

Mercifully grant that we may grow aged together.
                              'Marriage Prayer', *Book of Tobit*

In Middlemarch a wife could not long remain ignorant that the town held a bad opinion of her husband. No feminine intimate might carry her friendship so far as to make a plain statement to the wife of the unpleasant fact known or believed about her husband: but when a woman with her thoughts much at leisure got them suddenly employed on something grievously disadvantageous to her neighbours, various moral impulses were called into play which tended to stimulate utterance. Candour was one. To be candid, in Middlemarch phraseology, meant, to use an early opportunity of letting your friends know that you did not take a cheerful view of their capacity, their conduct, or their position; and a robust candour never waited to be asked for its opinion. Then, again, there was the love of truth – a wide phrase, but meaning in this relation, a lively objection to seeing a wife look happier than her husband's character warranted, or manifest too much satisfaction in her lot: the poor thing should have some hint given her that if she knew the truth she would have less complacency in her bonnet, and in light dishes for a supper-party. Stronger than all, there was the regard for a friend's moral improvement, sometimes called her soul, which was likely to be benefited by remarks tending to gloom, uttered with the accompaniment of pensive staring at the furniture and a manner implying that the speaker would not tell what was on her mind, from regard to the feelings of her hearer. On the whole, one might say that an ardent charity was at work setting the virtuous mind to make a neighbour unhappy for her good.

There were hardly any wives in Middlemarch whose matrimonial misfortunes would in different ways be likely to call forth more of this moral activity than Rosamond and her aunt Bulstrode. Mrs Bulstrode was not an object of dislike, and had never consciously injured any human being. Men had always thought her a handsome comfortable woman, and had reckoned it among the signs of Bulstrode's hypocrisy that he had chosen a red-blooded Vincy, instead of a ghastly and melancholy person suited to his low esteem for earthly pleasure. When the scandal about her husband was disclosed they remarked of her 'Ah, poor woman! She's as honest as the day – *she* never suspected anything wrong in him, you may depend on it.' Women, who were intimate with her, talked together much of 'poor Harriet', imagined what her feelings must be when she came to know everything, and conjectured how much she had already come to know. There was no spiteful disposition towards her; rather, there was a busy benevolence anxious to ascertain what it would be well for her to feel and do under the circumstances, which of course kept the imagination occupied with her character and history from the time when she was Harriet Vincy till now. With the review of Mrs Bulstrode and her position it was inevitable to associate Rosamond, whose prospects were under the same blight with her aunt's. Rosamond was more severely criticised and less pitied, though she too, as one of the good old Vincy family who had always been known in Middlemarch, was regarded as a victim to marriage with an interloper. The Vincys had their weaknesses, but then they lay on the surface: there was never anything bad to be 'found out' concerning them. Mrs Bulstrode was vindicated from any resemblance to her husband. Harriet's faults were her own.

'She has always been showy,' said Mrs Hackbutt, making tea for a small party, 'though she has got into the way of putting her religion forward, to conform to her husband; she has tried to hold her head up above Middlemarch by making it known that she invites clergymen and heaven-knows-who from Riverston and those places.'

'We can hardly blame her for that,' said Mrs Sprague; 'because few of the best people in the town cared to associate with Bulstrode, and she must have somebody to sit down at her table.'

'Mr Thesiger has always countenanced him,' said Mrs Hackbutt. 'I think he must be sorry now.'

'But he was never fond of him in his heart – that everyone knows,' said Mrs Toller. 'Mr Thesiger never goes into extremes. He keeps to the truth in what is evangelical. It is only clergymen like Mr Tyke, who want to use Dissenting hymn-books and that low kind of religion who ever found Bulstrode to their taste.'

'I understand Mr Tyke is in great distress about him,' said Mrs Hackbutt.

'And well he may be: they say the Bulstrodes have half kept the Tyke family.'

'And of course it is a discredit to his doctrines,' said Mrs Sprague, who was elderly and old-fashioned in her opinions. 'People will not make a boast of being methodistical in Middlemarch for a good while to come.'

'I think we must not set down people's bad actions to their religion,' said falcon-faced Mrs Plymdale, who had been listening hitherto.

'Oh, my dear, we are forgetting,' said Mrs Sprague. 'We ought not to be talking of this before you.'

'I am sure I have no reason to be partial,' said Mrs Plymdale, colouring. 'It's true Mr Plymdale has always been on good terms with Mr Bulstrode, and Harriet Vincy was my friend long before she married him. But I have always kept my own opinions and told her where she was wrong, poor thing. Still, in point of religion, I must say, Mr Bulstrode might have done what he has, and worse, and yet have been a man of no religion. I don't say that there has not been a little too much of that – I like moderation myself. But truth is truth. The men tried at the assizes are not all over-religious, I suppose.'

'Well,' said Mrs Hackbutt, wheeling adroitly, 'all I can say is, that I think she ought to separate from him.'

'I can't say that,' said Mrs Sprague. 'She took him for better or worse, you know.'

'But "worse" can never mean finding out that your husband is fit for Newgate,' said Mrs Hackbutt. 'Fancy living with such a man! I should expect to be poisoned.'

'Yes, I think myself it is an encouragement to crime if such men are to be taken care of and waited on by good wives,' said Mrs Tom Toller.

'And a good wife poor Harriet has been,' said Mrs Plymdale. 'She thinks her husband the first of men. It's true he has never denied her anything.'

'Well, we shall see what she will do,' said Mrs Hackbutt. 'I suppose she knows nothing yet, poor creature. I do hope and trust I shall not see her, for I should be frightened to death lest I should say anything about her husband. Do you think any hint has reached her?'

'I should hardly think so,' said Mrs Tom Toller. 'We hear that *he* is ill, and has never stirred out of the house since the meeting on Thursday; but she was with her girls at church yesterday, and they had new Tuscan bonnets. Her own had a feather in it. I have never seen that her religion made any difference in her dress.'

'She wears very neat patterns always,' said Mrs Plymdale, a little stung. 'And that feather I know she got dyed a pale lavender on purpose to be consistent. I must say it of Harriet that she wishes to do right.'

'As to her knowing what has happened, it can't be kept from her long,' said Mrs Hackbutt. 'The Vincys know, for Mr Vincy was at the meeting. It will be a great blow to him. There is his daughter as well as his sister.'

'Yes, indeed,' said Mrs Sprague. 'Nobody supposes that Mr Lydgate can go on holding up his head in Middlemarch, things look so black about the thousand pounds he took just at that man's death. It really makes one shudder.'

'Pride must have a fall,' said Mrs Hackbutt.

'I am not so sorry for Rosamond Vincy that was as I am for her aunt,' said Mrs Plymdale. 'She needed a lesson.'

'I suppose the Bulstrodes will go and live abroad somewhere,' said Mrs Sprague. 'That is what is generally done when there is anything disgraceful in a family.'

'And a most dreadful blow it will be to Harriet,' said Mrs Plymdale. 'If ever a woman was crushed, she will be. I pity her from my heart. And with all her faults, few women are better. From a girl she had the neatest ways, and was always good-hearted, and as open as the day. You might look into her drawers when you would – always the same. And so she has brought up Kate and Ellen. You may think how hard it will be for her to go among foreigners.'

'The doctor says that is what he should recommend the Lydgates to do,' said Mrs Sprague. 'He says Lydgate ought to have kept among the French.'

'That would suit her well enough, I dare say,' said Mrs Plymdale; 'there is that kind of lightness about her. But she got that from her mother; she never got it from her aunt Bulstrode, who always gave her good advice, and to my knowledge would rather have had her marry elsewhere.'

Mrs Plymdale was in a situation which caused her some complication of feeling. There had been not only her intimacy with Mrs Bulstrode, but also a profitable business relation of the great Plymdale dyeing house with Mr Bulstrode, which on the one hand would have inclined her to desire that the mildest view of his character should be the true one, but on the other, made her the more afraid of seeming to palliate his culpability. Again, the late alliance of her family with the Tollers had brought her in connection with the best circle, which gratified her in every direction except in the inclination to those serious views which she believed to be the best in another sense. The sharp little woman's conscience was somewhat troubled in the adjustment of these opposing 'bests' and of her griefs and satisfactions under late events, which were likely to humble those who needed humbling, but also to fall heavily on her old friend whose faults she would have preferred seeing on a background of prosperity.

Poor Mrs Bulstrode, meanwhile, had been no further shaken by the oncoming tread of calamity than in the busier stirring of that secret uneasiness which had always been present in her since the last visit of Raffles to The Shrubs. That the hateful man had come ill to Stone Court, and that her husband had chosen to remain there and watch over him, she allowed to be explained by the fact that Raffles had been employed and aided in earlier days, and that this made a tie of benevolence towards him in his degraded helplessness; and she had been since then innocently cheered by her husband's more hopeful speech about his own health and ability to continue his attention to business. The calm was disturbed when Lydgate had brought him home ill from the meeting, and in spite of comforting assurances during the next few days, she cried in private from the conviction that her husband was not suffering from bodily illness merely, but from something that afflicted his mind. He would not allow her to read to him, and scarcely to sit with him, alleging nervous susceptibility to sounds and movements; yet she suspected that in shutting himself up in his private room he wanted to be busy with his papers. Something, she felt sure, had happened. Perhaps it was some great loss of money; and she was kept in the dark. Not daring to question her husband, she said to Lydgate, on the fifth day after the meeting, when she had not left home except to go to church: 'Mr Lydgate, pray be open with me: I like to know the truth. Has anything happened to Mr Bulstrode?'

'Some little nervous shock,' said Lydgate, evasively. He felt that it was not for him to make the painful revelation.

'But what brought it on?' said Mrs Bulstrode, looking directly at him with her large dark eyes.

'There is often something poisonous in the air of public rooms,' said Lydgate. 'Strong men can stand it, but it tells on people in proportion to the delicacy of their systems. It is often impossible to account for the precise moment of an attack or rather, to say why the strength gives way at a particular moment.'

Mrs Bulstrode was not satisfied with his answer. There remained in her the belief that some calamity had befallen her husband, of which she was to be kept in ignorance; and it was in her nature strongly to object to such concealment. She begged leave for her daughters to sit with their father, and drove into the town to pay some visits, conjecturing that if anything were known to have gone wrong in Mr Bulstrode's affairs, she should see or hear some sign of it.

She called on Mrs Thesiger, who was not at home, and then drove to Mrs Hackbutt's on the other side of the churchyard. Mrs Hackbutt saw her coming from an upstairs window, and remembering her former alarm lest she should meet Mrs Bulstrode, felt almost bound in consistency to send word that she was not at home; but against that, there was a sudden strong desire within her for the excitement of an interview in which she was quite determined not to make the slightest allusion to what was in her mind.

Hence Mrs Bulstrode was shown into the drawing-room, and Mrs Hackbutt went to her, with more tightness of lip and rubbing of her hands than was usually observable in her, these being precautions adopted against freedom of speech. She was resolved not to ask how Mr Bulstrode was.

'I have not been anywhere except to church for nearly a week,' said Mrs Bulstrode, after a few introductory remarks. 'But Mr Bulstrode was taken so ill at the meeting on Thursday that I have not liked to leave the house.'

Mrs Hackbutt rubbed the back of one hand with the palm of the other held against her chest, and let her eyes ramble over the pattern on the rug.

'Was Mr Hackbutt at the meeting?' persevered Mrs Bulstrode.

'Yes, he was,' said Mrs Hackbutt, with the same attitude. 'The land is to be bought by subscription, I believe.'

'Let us hope that there will be no more cases of cholera to be buried in it,' said Mrs Bulstrode. 'It is an awful visitation. But I always think Middlemarch a very healthy spot. I suppose it is being used to it from a child; but I never saw the town I should like to live at better, and especially our end.'

'I am sure I should be glad that you always should live at Middlemarch, Mrs Bulstrode,' said Mrs Hackbutt, with a slight sigh. 'Still, we must learn to resign ourselves, wherever our lot may be cast. Though I am sure there will always be people in this town who will wish you well.'

Mrs Hackbutt longed to say, 'if you take my advice you will part from your husband', but it seemed clear to her that the poor woman knew nothing of the thunder ready to bolt on her head, and she herself could do no more than prepare her a little. Mrs Bulstrode felt suddenly rather chill and trembling: there was evidently something unusual behind this speech of Mrs Hackbutt's; but though she had set out with the desire to be fully informed, she found herself unable now to pursue her brave purpose, and turning the conversation by an enquiry about the young Hackbutts, she soon took her leave saying that she was going to see Mrs Plymdale. On her way thither she tried to imagine that there might have been some unusually warm sparring at the meeting between Mr Bulstrode and some of his frequent opponents – perhaps Mr Hackbutt might have been one of them. That would account for everything.

But when she was in conversation with Mrs Plymdale that comforting explanation seemed no longer tenable. 'Selina' received her with a pathetic affectionateness and a disposition to give edifying answers on the commonest topics, which could hardly have reference to an ordinary quarrel of which the most important consequence was a perturbation of Mr Bulstrode's health. Beforehand Mrs Bulstrode had thought that she would sooner question Mrs Plymdale than anyone else; but she found to her surprise that an old friend is not always the person whom it is easiest to make a confidant of: there was the barrier of remembered communication under other circumstances – there was the dislike of being pitied and informed by one who had been long wont to allow her the superiority. For certain words of mysterious appropriateness that Mrs Plymdale let fall about her resolution never to turn her back on her friends, convinced Mrs Bulstrode that what had happened must be some kind of misfortune, and instead of being able to say with her native directness, 'What is it that you have in your mind?' she found herself anxious to get away before she had heard anything more explicit. She began to have an agitating certainty that the misfortune was something more than the mere loss of money, being keenly sensitive to the fact that Selina now, just as Mrs Hackbutt had done before avoided noticing what she said about her husband, as they would have avoided noticing a personal blemish.

She said goodbye with nervous haste, and told the coachman to drive to Mr Vincy's warehouse. In that short drive her dread gathered so much force from the sense of darkness, that when she entered the private counting-house where her brother sat at his desk, her knees trembled and her usually florid face was deathly pale. Something of the same effect was produced in him by the sight of her: he rose from his seat to meet her, took her by the hand, and said, with his impulsive rashness: 'God help you, Harriet! you know all.'

That moment was perhaps worse than any which came after. It contained that concentrated experience which in great crises of emotion reveals the bias of a nature, and is prophetic of the ultimate act which will end an intermediate struggle. Without that memory of Raffles she might still have thought only of monetary ruin, but now along with her brother's look and words there darted into her mind the idea of some guilt in her husband – then, under the working of terror came the image of her husband exposed to disgrace – and then, after an instant of scorching shame in which she felt only the eyes of the world, with one leap of her heart she was at his side in mournful but unreproaching fellowship with shame and isolation. All this went on within her in a mere flash of time –

while she sank into the chair, and raised her eyes to her brother, who stood over her. 'I know nothing, Walter. What is it?' she said, faintly.

He told her everything, very inartificially, in slow fragments, making her aware that the scandal went much beyond proof, especially as to the end of Raffles.

'People will talk,' he said. 'Even if a man has been acquitted by a jury, they'll talk, and nod and wink – and as far as the world goes, a man might often as well be guilty as not. It's a breakdown blow, and it damages Lydgate as much as Bulstrode. I don't pretend to say what is the truth. I only wish we had never heard the name of either Bulstrode or Lydgate. You'd better have been a Vincy all your life, and so had Rosamond.'

Mrs Bulstrode made no reply.

'But you must bear up as well as you can, Harriet. People don't blame you. And I'll stand by you whatever you make up your mind to do,' said the brother, with rough but well-meaning affectionateness.

'Give me your arm to the carriage, Walter,' said Mrs Bulstrode. 'I feel very weak.'

And when she got home she was obliged to say to her daughter, 'I am not well, my dear; I must go and lie down. Attend to your papa. Leave me in quiet. I shall take no dinner.'

She locked herself in her room. She needed time to get used to her maimed consciousness, her poor lopped life, before she could walk steadily to the place allotted her. A new searching light had fallen on her husband's character, and she could not judge him leniently: the twenty years in which she had believed in him and venerated him by virtue of his concealments came back with particulars that made them seem an odious deceit. He had married her with that bad past life hidden behind him and she had no faith left to protest his innocence of the worst that was imputed to him. Her honest ostentatious nature made the sharing of a merited dishonour as bitter as it could be to any mortal.

But this imperfectly-taught woman, whose phrases and habits were an odd patchwork, had a loyal spirit within her. The man whose prosperity she had shared through nearly half a life, and who had unvaryingly cherished her – now that punishment had befallen him it was not possible to her in any sense to forsake him. There is a forsaking which still sits at the same board and lies on the same couch with the forsaken soul, withering it the more by unloving proximity. She knew, when she locked her door, that she should unlock it ready to go down to her unhappy husband and espouse his sorrow, and say of his guilt, I will mourn and not reproach. But she needed time to gather up her strength; she needed to sob out her farewell to all the gladness and pride of her life. When she had resolved to go down, she prepared herself by some little acts which might seem mere folly to a hard onlooker; they were her way of expressing to all spectators visible or invisible that she had begun a new life in which she embraced humiliation. She took off all her ornaments and put on a plain black gown, and instead of wearing her much adorned cap and large bows of hair, she brushed her hair down and put on a plain bonnet-cap, which made her look suddenly like an early Methodist.

Bulstrode, who knew that his wife had been out and had come in saying that she was not well, had spent the time in an agitation equal to hers. He had looked forward to her learning the truth from others, and had acquiesced in that probability, as something easier to him than any confession. But now that he imagined the moment of her knowledge come, he awaited the result in anguish. His daughters had been obliged to consent to leave him, and though he had allowed some food to be brought to him, he had not touched it. He felt himself perishing slowly in unpitied misery. Perhaps he should never see his wife's face with affection in it again. And if he turned to God there seemed to be no answer but the pressure of retribution.

It was eight o'clock in the evening before the door opened and his wife entered. He dared not look up at her. He sat with his eyes bent down, and as she went towards him she thought he looked smaller – he seemed so withered and shrunken. A movement of new compassion and old tenderness went through her like a great wave, and putting one hand on his which rested on the arm of the chair, and the other on his shoulder, she said, solemnly but kindly: 'Look up, Nicholas.'

He raised his eyes with a little start and looked at her half amazed for a moment: her pale face, her changed, mourning dress, the trembling about her mouth, all said, 'I know': and her hands and eyes rested gently on him. He burst out crying and they cried together, she sitting at his side. They could not yet speak to each other of the shame which she was bearing with him, or of the acts which had brought it down on them. His confession was silent, and her promise of faithfulness was silent. Open-minded as she was, she nevertheless shrank from the words which would have expressed their mutual consciousness as she would have shrunk from flakes of fire. She could not say, 'How much is only slander and false suspicion?' and he did not say, 'I am innocent.'

Chapter 75

Le sentiment de la fausseté des plaisirs présents, et l'ignorance
de la vanité des plaisirs absents, causent l'inconstance.

PASCAL

Rosamond had a gleam of returning cheerfulness when the house was freed from the threatening figure, and when all the disagreeable creditors were paid. But she was not joyous: her married life had fulfilled none of her hopes, and had been quite spoiled for her imagination. In this brief interval of calm, Lydgate, remembering that he had often been stormy in his hours of perturbation, and mindful of the pain Rosamond had had to bear, was carefully gentle towards her; but he, too, had lost some of his old spirit, and he still felt it necessary to refer to an economical change in their way of living as a matter of course, trying to reconcile her to it gradually, and repressing his anger when she answered by wishing that he would go to live in London. When she did not make this answer, she listened languidly, and wondered what she had that was worth living for. The hard and contemptuous words which had fallen from her husband in his anger had deeply offended that vanity which he had at first called into active enjoyment; and what she regarded as his perverse way of looking at things, kept up a secret repulsion, which made her receive all his tenderness as a poor substitute for the happiness he had failed to give her. They were at a disadvantage with their neighbours, and there was no longer any outlook towards Quallingham – there was no outlook anywhere except in an occasional letter from Will Ladislaw. She had felt stung and disappointed by Will's resolution to quit Middlemarch, for in spite of what she knew and guessed about his admiration for Dorothea, she secretly cherished the belief that he had, or would necessarily come to have, much more admiration for herself; Rosamond being one of those women who live much in the idea that each man they meet would have preferred them if the preference had not been hopeless. Mrs Casaubon was all very well; but Will's interest in her dated before he knew Mrs Lydgate. Rosamond took his way of talking to herself, which was a mixture of playful fault-finding and hyperbolical gallantry, as the disguise of a deeper feeling; and in his presence she felt that agreeable titillation of vanity and sense of romantic drama which Lydgate's presence had no longer the magic to create. She even fancied – what will not men and women fancy in these matters? – that Will exaggerated his admiration for Mrs Casaubon in order to pique herself. In this way poor Rosamond's brain had been busy before Will's departure. He would have made, she thought, a much more suitable husband for her than she had found in Lydgate. No notion could have been falser than this, for Rosamond's discontent in her marriage was due to the conditions of marriage itself, to its demand for self-suppression and tolerance, and not to the nature of her husband; but the easy conception of an unreal Better had a sentimental charm which diverted her ennui. She constructed a little romance which was to vary the flatness of her life: Will Ladislaw was always to be a bachelor and live near her, always to be at her command, and have an understood though never fully expressed passion for her, which would be sending out lambent flames every now and then in interesting scenes. His departure had been a proportionate disappointment, and had sadly increased her weariness of Middlemarch; but at first she had the alternative dream of pleasure in store from her intercourse with the family at Quallingham. Since then the troubles of her married life had deepened, and the absence of other relief encouraged her regretful rumination over that thin romance which she had once fed on. Men and women make sad mistakes about their own symptoms, taking their vague uneasy longings, sometimes for genius, sometimes for religion, and oftener still for a mighty love. Will Ladislaw had written chatty letters, half to her, and half to Lydgate, and she had replied: their separation, she felt, was not likely to be final, and the change she now most longed for was that Lydgate should go to live in London; everything would be agreeable in London; and she had set to work with quiet determination to win this result, when there came a sudden, delightful promise which inspirited her.

It came shortly before the memorable meeting at the town-hall, and was nothing less than a letter from Will Ladislaw to Lydgate, which turned chiefly on his new interest in plans of colonisation, but mentioned incidentally, that he might find it necessary to pay a visit to Middlemarch within the next few weeks – a very pleasant necessity, he said, almost as good as holidays to a schoolboy. He hoped there was his old place on the rug, and a great deal of music in store for him. But he was quite uncertain as to the time. While Lydgate was reading the letter to Rosamond, her face looked like a reviving flower – it grew prettier and more blooming. There was nothing unendurable now: the debts were paid, Mr Ladislaw was coming, and Lydgate would be persuaded to leave Middlemarch and settle in London, which was 'so different from a provincial town'.

That was a bright bit of morning. But soon the sky became black over poor Rosamond. The presence of a new gloom in her husband, about which he was entirely reserved towards her for he dreaded to expose his lacerated feeling to her neutrality and misconception – soon received a painfully strange explanation, alien to all her previous notions of what could affect her happiness. In the new gaiety of her spirits, thinking that Lydgate had merely a worse fit of moodiness than usual, causing him to leave her remarks unanswered, and evidently to keep out of her way as much as possible, she chose, a few days after the meeting, and without speaking to him on the subject, to send out notes of invitation for a small evening party, feeling convinced that this was a judicious step, since people seemed to have been keeping aloof from them, and wanted restoring to the old habit of intercourse. When the invitations had been accepted, she would tell Lydgate, and give him a wise admonition as to how a medical man should behave to his neighbours; for Rosamond had the gravest little airs possible about other people's duties. But all the invitations were declined, and the last answer came into Lydgate's hands.

'This is Chichely's scratch. What is he writing to you about?' said Lydgate, wonderingly, as he handed the note to her. She was obliged to let him see it, and, looking at her severely, he said, 'Why on earth have you been sending out invitations without telling me, Rosamond? I beg, I insist that you will not invite anyone to this house. I suppose you have been inviting others, and they have refused too.'

She said nothing.

'Do you hear me?' thundered Lydgate.

'Yes, certainly I hear you,' said Rosamond, turning her head aside with the movement of a graceful long-necked bird.

Lydgate tossed his head without any grace and walked out of the room, feeling himself dangerous. Rosamond's thought was, that he was getting more and more unbearable – not that there was any new special reason for this peremptoriness. His indisposition to tell her anything in which he was sure beforehand that she would not be interested was growing into an unreflecting habit, and she was in ignorance of everything connected with the thousand pounds, except that the loan had come from her uncle Bulstrode. Lydgate's odious humours and their neighbours' apparent avoidance of them had an unaccountable date for her in their relief from money difficulties. If the invitations had been accepted she would have gone to invite her mamma and the rest, whom she had seen nothing of for several days; and she now put on her bonnet to go and enquire what had become of them all, suddenly feeling as if there were a conspiracy to leave her in isolation with a husband disposed to offend everybody. It was after the dinner hour, and she found her father and mother seated together alone in the drawing-room. They greeted her with sad looks, saying, 'Well, my dear!' and no more. She had never seen her father look so downcast; and seating herself near him she said, 'Is there anything the matter, papa?'

He did not answer, but Mrs Vincy, said, 'Oh, my dear, have you heard nothing? It won't be long before it reaches you.'

'Is it anything about Tertius?' said Rosamond, turning pale. The idea of trouble immediately connected itself with what had been unaccountable to her in him.

'Oh my dear, yes. To think of your marrying into this trouble. Debt was bad enough, but this will be worse.'

'Stay, stay, Lucy,' said Mr Vincy. 'Have you heard nothing about your uncle Bulstrode, Rosamond?'

'No, papa,' said the poor thing, feeling as if trouble were not anything she had before experienced, but some invisible power with an iron grasp that made her soul faint within her.

Her father told her everything, saying at the end, 'It's better for you to know, my dear. I think Lydgate must leave the town. Things have gone against him. I dare say he couldn't help it. I don't accuse him of any harm,' said Mr Vincy. He had always before been disposed to find the utmost fault with Lydgate.

The shock to Rosamond was terrible. It seemed to her that no lot could be so cruelly hard as hers – to have married a man who had become the centre of infamous suspicions. In many cases it is inevitable that the shame is felt to be the worst part of crime; and it would have required a great deal of disentangling reflection, such as had never entered into Rosamond's life, for her in these moments to feel that her trouble was less than if her husband had been certainly known to have done something criminal. All the shame seemed to be there. And she had innocently married this man with the belief that he and his family were a glory to her! She showed her usual reticence to her parents, and only said, that if Lydgate had done as she wished he would have left Middlemarch long ago.

'She bears it beyond anything,' said her mother when she was gone.

'Ah, thank God!' said Mr Vincy, who was much broken down.

But Rosamond went home with a sense of justified repugnance towards her husband. What had he really done – how had he really acted? She did not know. Why had he not told her everything? He did not speak to her on the subject, and of course she could not speak to him. It came into her mind once that she would ask her father to let her go home again; but dwelling on that prospect made it seem utter dreariness to her: a married woman gone back to live with her parents – life seemed to have no meaning for her in such a position: she could not contemplate herself in it.

The next two days Lydgate observed a change in her, and believed that she had heard the bad news. Would she speak to him about it, or would she go on for ever in the silence which seemed to imply that she believed him guilty? We must remember that he was in a morbid state of mind, in which almost all contact was pain. Certainly Rosamond in this case had equal reason to complain of reserve and want of confidence on his part; but in the bitterness of his soul he excused himself; – was he not justified in shrinking from the task of telling her, since now she knew the truth she had no impulse to speak to him? But a deeper-lying consciousness that he was in fault made him restless, and the silence between them became intolerable to him; it was as if they were both adrift on one piece of wreck and looked away from each other.

He thought, 'I am a fool. Haven't I given up expecting anything? I have married care, not help.' And that evening he said, 'Rosamond, have you heard anything that distresses you?'

'Yes,' she answered, laying down her work, which she had been carrying on with a languid semi-consciousness, most unlike her usual self.

'What have you heard?'

'Everything, I suppose. Papa told me.'

'That people think me disgraced?'

'Yes,' said Rosamond, faintly, beginning to sew again automatically.

There was silence, Lydgate thought, 'If she has any trust in me – any notion of what I am, she ought to speak now and say that she does not believe I have deserved disgrace.'

But Rosamond on her side went on moving her fingers languidly. Whatever was to be said on the subject she expected to come from Tertius. What did she know? And if he were innocent of any wrong, why did he not do something to clear himself?

This silence of hers brought a new rush of gall to that bitter mood in which Lydgate had been saying to himself that nobody believed in him – even Fare-brother had not come forward. He had begun to question her with the intent that their conversation should disperse the chill fog which had gathered between them, but he felt his resolution checked by despairing resentment. Even this trouble, like the rest, she seemed to regard as if it were hers alone. He was always to her a being apart, doing what she objected to. He started from his chair with an angry impulse, and thrusting his hands in his pockets, walked up and down the room. There was an underlying consciousness all the while that he should have to master this anger, and tell her everything, and convince her of the facts. For he had almost learned the lesson that he must bend himself to her nature, and that because she came short in her sympathy, he must give the more. Soon he recurred to his intention of opening himself: the occasion must not be lost. If he could bring her to feel with some solemnity that here was a slander which must be met and not run away from, and that the whole trouble had come out of his desperate want of money, it would be a moment for urging powerfully on her that they should be one in the resolve to do with as little money as possible, so that they might weather the bad time and keep themselves independent. He would mention the definite measures which he desired to take, and win her to a willing spirit. He was bound to try this – and what else was there for him to do?

He did not know how long he had been walking uneasily backwards and forwards, but Rosamond felt that it was long, and wished that he would sit down. She too had begun to think this an opportunity for urging on Tertius what he ought to do. Whatever might be the truth about all this misery, there was one dread which asserted itself.

Lydgate at last seated himself, not in his usual chair, but in one nearer to Rosamond, leaning aside in it towards her, and looking at her gravely before he reopened the sad subject. He had conquered himself so far, and was about to speak with a sense of solemnity, as on an occasion which was not to be repeated. He had even opened his lips, when Rosamond, letting her hands fall, looked at him and said, 'Surely, Tertius – '

'Well?'

'Surely now at last you have given up the idea of staying in Middlemarch. I cannot go on living here. Let us go to London. Papa, and everyone else, says you had better go. Whatever misery I have to put up with, it will be easier away from here.'

Lydgate felt miserably jarred. Instead of that critical outpouring for which he had prepared himself with effort, here was the old round to be gone through again. He could not bear it. With a quick change of countenance he rose and went out of the room.

Perhaps if he had been strong enough to persist in his determination to be the more because she was less, that evening might have had a better issue. If his energy could have borne down that check, he might still have wrought on Rosamond's vision and will. We cannot be sure that any natures, however inflexible or peculiar, will resist this effect from a more massive being than their own. They may be taken by storm and for the moment converted, becoming part of the soul which enwraps them in the ardour of its movement. But poor Lydgate had a throbbing pain within him, and his energy had fallen short of its task.

The beginning of mutual understanding and resolve seemed as far off as ever; nay, it seemed blocked out by the sense of unsuccessful effort. They lived on from day to day with their thoughts still apart, Lydgate going about what work he had in a mood of despair, and Rosamond feeling, with some justification, that he was behaving cruelly. It was of no use to say anything to Tertius; but when Will Ladislaw came, she was determined to tell him everything. In spite of her general reticence, she needed someone who would recognise her wrongs.

Chapter 76

To mercy, pity, peace, and love
  All pray in their distress,
And to these virtues of delight,
  Return their thankfulness.

For Mercy has a human heart,
  Pity a human face;
And Love, the human form divine;
  And Peace, the human dress.

WILLIAM BLAKE, *Songs of Innocence*

Some days later, Lydgate was riding to Lowick Manor, in consequence of a summons from Dorothea. The summons had not been unexpected, since it had followed a letter from Mr Bulstrode, in which he stated that he had resumed his arrangements for quitting Middlemarch, and must remind Lydgate of his previous communications about the Hospital, to the purport of which he still adhered. It had been his duty, before taking further steps, to reopen the subject with Mrs Casaubon, who now wished, as before, to discuss the question with Lydgate. 'Your views may possibly have undergone some change,' wrote Mr Bulstrode; 'but, in that case also, it is desirable that you should lay them before her.'

Dorothea awaited his arrival with eager interest. Though, in deference to her masculine advisers, she had refrained from what Sir James had called 'interfering in this Bulstrode business', the hardship of Lydgate's position was continually in her mind, and when Bulstrode applied to her again about the Hospital, she felt that the opportunity was come to her which she had been hindered from hastening. In her luxurious home, wandering under the boughs of her own great trees, her thought was going out over the lot of others, and her emotions were imprisoned. The idea of some active good within her reach, 'haunted her like a passion', and another's need having once come to her as a distinct image, preoccupied her desire with the yearning to give relief, and made her own ease tasteless. She was full of confident hope about this interview with Lydgate, never heeding what was said of his personal reserve; never heeding that she was a very young woman. Nothing could have seemed more irrelevant to Dorothea than insistence on her youth and sex when she was moved to show her human fellowship.

As she sat waiting in the library, she could do nothing but live through again all the past scenes which had brought Lydgate into her memories. They all owed their significance to her marriage and its troubles – but no; there were two occasions in which the image of Lydgate had come painfully in connection with his wife and someone else. The pain had been allayed for Dorothea, but it had left in her an awakening conjecture as to what Lydgate's marriage might be to him, a susceptibility to the slightest hint about Mrs Lydgate. These thoughts were like a drama to her, and made her eyes bright, and gave an attitude of suspense to her whole frame, though she was only looking out from the brown library on to the turf and the bright green buds which stood in relief against the dark evergreens.

When Lydgate came in, she was almost shocked at the change in his face, which was strikingly perceptible to her who had not seen him for two months. It was not the change of emaciation, but that effect which even young faces will very soon show from the persistent presence of resentment and despondency. Her cordial look, when she put out her hand to him, softened his expression, but only with melancholy.

'I have wished very much to see you for a long while, Mr Lydgate,' said Dorothea when they were seated opposite each other; 'but I put off asking you to come until Mr Bulstrode applied to me again about the Hospital. I know that the advantage of keeping the management of it separate from that of the Infirmary depends on you, or, at least, on the good which you are encouraged to hope for from having it under your control. And I am sure you will not refuse to tell me exactly what you think.'

'You want to decide whether you should give a generous support to the Hospital,' said Lydgate. 'I cannot conscientiously advise you to do it in dependence on any activity of mine. I may be obliged to leave the town.'

He spoke curtly, feeling the ache of despair as to his being able to carry out any purpose that Rosamond had set her mind against.

'Not because there is no one to believe in you?' said Dorothea, pouring out her words in clearness from a full heart. 'I know the unhappy mistakes about you. I knew them from the first moment to be mistakes. You have never done anything vile. You would not do anything dishonourable.'

It was the first assurance of belief in him that had fallen on Lydgate's ears. He drew a deep breath, and said 'Thank you.' He could say no more: it was something very new and strange in his life that these few words of trust from a woman should be so much to him.

'I beseech you to tell me how everything was,' said Dorothea, fearlessly. 'I am sure that the truth would clear you.'

Lydgate started up from his chair and went towards the window, forgetting where he was. He had so often gone over in his mind the possibility of explaining everything without aggravating appearances that would tell, perhaps, unfairly, against Bulstrode, and had so often decided against it – he had so often said to himself that his assertions would not change people's impressions – that Dorothea's words sounded like a temptation to do something which in his soberness he had pronounced to be unreasonable.

'Tell me, pray,' said Dorothea, with simple earnestness; 'then we can consult together. It is wicked to let people think evil of anyone falsely, when it can be hindered.'

Lydgate turned, remembering where he was, and saw Dorothea's face looking up at him with a sweet trustful gravity. The presence of a noble nature, generous in its wishes, ardent in its charity, changes the lights for us: we begin to see things again in their larger, quieter masses, and to believe that we too can be seen and judged in the wholeness of our character. That influence was beginning to act on

Lydgate, who had for many days been seeing all life as one who is dragged and struggling amid the throng. He sat down again, and felt that he was recovering his old self in the consciousness that he was with one who believed in it.

'I don't want,' he said, 'to bear hard on Bulstrode, who has lent me money of which I was in need – though I would rather have gone without it now. He is hunted down and miserable, and has only a poor thread of life in him. But I should like to tell you everything. It will be a comfort to me to speak where belief has gone beforehand, and where I shall not seem to be offering assertions of my own honesty. You will feel what is fair to another, as you feel what is fair to me.'

'Do trust me,' said Dorothea; 'I will not repeat anything without your leave. But at the very least, I could say that you have made all the circumstances clear to me, and that I know you are not in any way guilty. Mr Farebrother would believe me, and my uncle, and Sir James Chettam. Nay, there are persons in Middlemarch to whom I could go; although they don't know much of me, they would believe me. They would know that I could have no other motive than truth and justice. I would take any pains to clear you. I have very little to do. There is nothing better that I can do in the world.'

Dorothea's voice, as she made this childlike picture of what she would do, might have been almost taken as a proof that she could do it effectively. The searching tenderness of her woman's tones seemed made for a defence against ready accusers. Lydgate did not stay to think that she was Quixotic; he gave himself up, for the first time in his life, to the exquisite sense of leaning entirely on a generous sympathy, without any check of proud reserve. And he told her everything, from the time when, under the pressure of his difficulties, he unwillingly made his first application to Bulstrode; gradually, in the relief of speaking, getting into a more thorough utterance of what had gone on in his mind – entering fully into the fact that his treatment of the patient was opposed to the dominant practice, into his doubts at the last, his ideal of medical duty, and his uneasy consciousness that the acceptance of the money had made some difference in his private inclination and professional behaviour, though not in his fulfilment of any publicly recognised obligation.

'It has come to my knowledge since,' he added, 'that Hawley sent someone to examine the housekeeper at Stone Court, and she said that she gave the patient all the opium in the phial I left, as well as a good deal of brandy. But that would not have been opposed to ordinary prescriptions, even of first-rate men. The suspicions against me had no hold there: they are grounded on the knowledge that I took money, that Bulstrode had strong motives for wishing the man to die, and that he gave me the money as a bribe to concur in some malpractices or other against the patient – that in any case I accepted a bribe to hold my tongue. They are just the suspicions that cling the most obstinately, because they lie in people's inclination and can never be disproved. How my orders came to be disobeyed is a question to which I don't know the answer. It is still possible that Bulstrode was innocent of any criminal intention – even possible that he had nothing to do with the disobedience, and merely abstained from mentioning it. But all that has nothing to do with the public belief. It is one of those cases on which a man is condemned on the ground of his character – it is believed that he has committed a crime in some undefined way, because he had the motive for doing it; and Bulstrode's character has enveloped me, because I took his money. I am simply blighted – like a damaged ear of corn – the business is done and can't be undone.'

'Oh, it is hard!' said Dorothea. 'I understand the difficulty there is in your vindicating yourself. And that all this should have come to you who had meant to lead a higher life than the common, and to find out better ways – I cannot bear to rest in this as unchangeable. I know you meant that. I remember what you said to me when you first spoke to me about the Hospital. There is no sorrow I have thought more about than that – to love what is great, and try to reach it, and yet to fail.'

'Yes,' said Lydgate, feeling that here he had found room for the full meaning of his grief. 'I had some ambition. I meant everything to be different with me. I thought I had more strength and mastery. But the most terrible obstacles are such as nobody can see except oneself.'

'Suppose,' said Dorothea, meditatively. 'Suppose we kept on the Hospital according to the present plan, and you stayed here though only with the friendship and support of a few, the evil feeling towards you would gradually die out; there would come opportunities in which people would be forced to acknowledge that they had been unjust to you, because they would see that your purposes were pure. You may still win a great fame like the Louis and Laennec I have heard you speak of, and we shall all be proud of you,' she ended, with a smile.

'That might do if I had my old trust in myself,' said Lydgate, mournfully. 'Nothing galls me more than the notion of turning round and running away before this slander, leaving it unchecked behind me. Still, I can't ask anyone to put a great deal of money into a plan which depends on me.'

'It would be quite worth my while,' said Dorothea, simply. 'Only think. I am very uncomfortable with my money, because they tell me I have too little for any great scheme of the sort I like best, and yet I have too much. I don't know what to do. I have seven hundred a-year of my own fortune, and nineteen hundred a-year that Mr Casaubon left me, and between three and four thousand of ready money in the bank. I wished to raise money and pay it off gradually out of my income which I don't want, to buy land with and found a village which should be a school of industry; but Sir James and my uncle have convinced me that the risk would be too great. So you see that what I should most rejoice at would be to have something good to do with my money: I should like it to make other people's lives better to them. It makes me very uneasy – coming all to me who don't want it.'

A smile broke through the gloom of Lydgate's face. The childlike grave-eyed earnestness with which Dorothea said all this was irresistible – blent into an adorable whole with her ready understanding of high experience. (Of lower experience such as plays a great part in the world, poor Mrs Casaubon had a very blurred shortsighted knowledge, little helped by her imagination.) But she took the smile as encouragement of her plan.

'I think you see now that you spoke too scrupulously,' she said, in a tone of persuasion. 'The Hospital would be one good; and making your life quite whole and well again would be another.'

Lydgate's smile had died away. 'You have the goodness as well as the money to do all that; if it could be done,' he said. 'But-'

He hesitated a little while, looking vaguely towards the window; and she sat in silent expectation. At last he turned towards her and said impetuously, 'Why should I not tell you? – you know what sort of bond marriage is. You will understand everything.'

Dorothea felt her heart beginning to beat faster. Had he that sorrow too? But she feared to say any word, and he went on immediately.

'It is impossible for me now to do anything – to take any step without considering my wife's happiness. The thing that I might like to do if I were alone, is become impossible to me. I can't see her miserable. She married me without knowing what she was going into, and it might have been better for her if she had not married me.'

'I know, I know – you could not give her pain, if you were not obliged to do it,' said Dorothea, with keen memory of her own life.

'And she has set her mind against staying. She wishes to go. The troubles she has had here have wearied her,' said Lydgate, breaking off again, lest he should say too much.

'But when she saw the good that might come of staying-' said Dorothea, remonstrantly, looking at Lydgate as if he had forgotten the reasons which had just been considered. He did not speak immediately.

'She would not see it,' he said at last, curtly, feeling at first that this statement must do without explanation. 'And, indeed, I have lost all spirit about carrying on my life here.' He paused a moment and then, following the impulse to let Dorothea see deeper into the difficulty of his life, he said, 'The fact is, this trouble has come upon her confusedly. We have not been able to speak to each other about it. I am not sure what is in her mind about it: she may fear that I have really done something base. It is my fault; I ought to be more open. But I have been suffering cruelly.'

'May I go and see her?' said Dorothea, eagerly. 'Would she accept my sympathy? I would tell her that you have not been blamable before anyone's judgement but your own. I would tell her that you shall be cleared in every fair mind. I would cheer her heart. Will you ask her if I may go to see her? I did see her once.'

'I am sure you may,' said Lydgate, seizing the proposition with some hope. 'She would feel honoured – cheered, I think, by the proof that you at least have some respect for me. I will not speak to her about your coming – that she may not connect it with my wishes at all. I know very well that I ought not to have left anything to be told her by others, but – '

He broke off, and there was a moment's silence. Dorothea refrained from saying what was in her mind – how well she knew that there might be invisible barriers to speech between husband and wife. This was a point on which even sympathy might make a wound. She returned to the more outward aspect of

Lydgate's position, saying cheerfully, 'And if Mrs Lydgate knew that there were friends who would believe in you and support you, she might then be glad that you should stay in your place and recover your hopes – and do what you meant to do. Perhaps then you would see that it was right to agree with what I proposed about your continuing at the Hospital. Surely you would, if you still have faith in it as a means of making your knowledge useful?'

Lydgate did not answer, and she saw that he was debating with himself.

'You need not decide immediately,' she said, gently. 'A few days hence it will be early enough for me to send my answer to Mr Bulstrode.'

Lydgate still waited, but at last turned to speak in his most decisive tones.

'No; I prefer that there should be no interval left for wavering. I am no longer sure enough of myself – I mean of what it would be possible for me to do under the changed circumstances of my life. It would be dishonourable to let others engage themselves to anything serious in dependence on me. I might be obliged to go away after all; I see little chance of anything else. The whole thing is too problematic; I cannot consent to be the cause of your goodness being wasted. No, let the New Hospital be joined with the Old Infirmary, and everything go on as it might have done if I had never come. I have kept a valuable register since I have been there; I shall send it to a man who will make use of it,' he ended bitterly. 'I can think of nothing for a long while but getting an income.'

'It hurts me very much to hear you speak so hopelessly,' said Dorothea. 'It would be a happiness to your friends, who believe in your future, in your power to do great things, if you would let them save you from that. Think how much money I have; it would be like taking a burden from me if you took some of it every year till you got free from this fettering want of income. Why should not people do these things? It is so difficult to make shares at all even. This is one way.'

'God bless you, Mrs Casaubon!' said Lydgate, rising as if with the same impulse that made his words energetic, and resting his arm on the back of the great leather chair he had been sitting in. 'It is good that you should have such feelings. But I am not the man who ought to allow himself to benefit by them. I have not given guarantees enough. I must not at least sink into the degradation of being pensioned for work that I never achieved. It is very clear to me that I must not count on anything else than getting away from Middlemarch as soon as I can manage it. I should not be able for a long while, at the very best, to get an income here, and – it is easier to make the necessary changes in a new place. I must do as other men do, and think what will please the world and bring in money; look for a little opening in the London crowd, and push myself; set up in a watering-place, or go to some southern town where there are plenty of idle English, and get myself puffed, – that is the sort of shell I must creep into and try to keep my soul alive in.'

'Now that is not brave,' said Dorothea, – 'to give up the fight.'

'No, it is not brave,' said Lydgate, 'but if a man is afraid of creeping paralysis?' Then, in another tone, 'Yet you have made a great difference in my courage by believing in me. Everything seems more bearable since I have talked to you; and if you can clear me in a few other minds, especially in Farebrother's, I shall be deeply grateful. The point I wish you not to mention is the fact of disobedience to my orders. That would soon get distorted. After all, there is no evidence for me but people's opinion of me beforehand. You can only repeat my own report of myself.'

'Mr Farebrother will believe – others will believe,' said Dorothea. 'I can say of you what will make it stupidity to suppose that you would be bribed to do a wickedness.'

'I don't know,' said Lydgate, with something like a groan in his voice. 'I have not taken a bribe yet. But there is a pale shade of bribery which is sometimes called prosperity. You will do me another great kindness, then, and come to see my wife?'

'Yes, I will. I remember how pretty she is,' said Dorothea, into whose mind every impression about Rosamond had cut deep. 'I hope she will like me.'

As Lydgate rode away, he thought, 'This young creature has a heart large enough for the Virgin Mary. She evidently thinks nothing of her own future, and would pledge away half her income at once, as if she wanted nothing for herself but a chair to sit in from which she can look down with those clear eyes at the poor mortals who pray to her. She seems to have what I never saw in any woman before – a fountain of friendship towards men – a man can make a friend of her. Casaubon must have raised some heroic hallucination in her. I wonder if she could have any other sort of passion for a man? Ladislaw? – there was certainly an unusual feeling between them. And Casaubon must have had a notion of it. Well – her love might help a man more than her money.'

Dorothea on her side had immediately formed a plan of relieving Lydgate from his obligation to Bulstrode, which she felt sure was a part, though small, of the galling pressure he had to bear. She sat down at once under the inspiration of their interview, and wrote a brief note, in which she pleaded that she had more claim than Mr Bulstrode had to the satisfaction of providing the money which had been serviceable to Lydgate – that it would be unkind in Lydgate not to grant her the position of being his helper in this small matter, the favour being entirely to her who had so little that was plainly marked out for her to do with her superfluous money. He might call her a creditor or by any other name if it did but imply that he granted her request. She enclosed a cheque for a thousand pounds, and determined to take the letter with her the next day when she went to see Rosamond.

Chapter 77

And thus thy fall hath left a kind of blot,
To mark the full-fraught man and best indued
With some suspicion.

SHAKESPEARE, *Henry V*

The next day Lydgate had to go to Brassing, and told Rosamond that he should be away until the evening. Of late she had never gone beyond her own house and garden, except to church, and once to see her papa, to whom she said, 'If Tertius goes away, you will help us to move, will you not, papa? I suppose we shall have very little money. I am sure I hope someone will help us.' And Mr Vincy had said, 'Yes, child, I don't mind a hundred or two. I can see the end of that.' With these exceptions she had sat at home in languid melancholy and suspense, fixing her mind on Will Ladislaw's coming as the one point of hope and interest, and associating this with some new urgency on Lydgate to make immediate arrangements for leaving Middlemarch and going to London, till she felt assured that the coming would be a potent cause of the going, without at all seeing how. This way of establishing sequences is too common to be fairly regarded as a peculiar folly in Rosamond. And it is precisely this sort of sequence which causes the greatest shock when it is sundered: for to see how an effect may be produced is often to see possible missings and checks; but to see nothing except the desirable cause, and close upon it the desirable effect, rids us of doubt and makes our minds strongly intuitive. That was the process going on in poor Rosamond, while she arranged all objects around her with the same nicety as ever, only with more slowness – or sat down to the piano, meaning to play, and then desisting, yet lingering on the music stool with her white fingers suspended on the wooden front, and looking before her in dreamy ennui. Her melancholy had become so marked that Lydgate felt a strange timidity before it, as a perpetual silent reproach, and the strong man, mastered by his keen sensibilities towards this fair fragile creature whose life he seemed somehow to have bruised, shrank from her look, and sometimes started at her approach, fear of her and fear for her rushing in only the more forcibly after it had been momentarily expelled by exasperation.

But this morning Rosamond descended from her room upstairs – where she sometimes sat the whole day when Lydgate was out – equipped for a walk in the town. She had a letter to post – a letter addressed to Mr Ladislaw and written with charming discretion, but intended to hasten his arrival by a hint of trouble. The servant-maid, their sole house-servant now, noticed her coming downstairs in her walking dress, and thought 'there never did anybody look so pretty in a bonnet, poor thing'.

Meanwhile Dorothea's mind was filled with her project of going to Rosamond, and with the many thoughts, both of the past and the probable future, which gathered round the idea of that visit. Until yesterday when Lydgate had opened to her a glimpse of some trouble in his married life, the image of Mrs Lydgate had always been associated for her with that of Will Ladislaw. Even in her most uneasy moments – even when she had been agitated by Mrs Cadwallader's painfully graphic report of gossip – her effort, nay, her strongest impulsive prompting, had been towards the vindication of Will from any sullying surmises; and when, in her meeting with him afterwards, she had at first interpreted his words as a probable allusion to a feeling towards Mrs Lydgate which he was determined to cut himself off from indulging, she had had a quick, sad, excusing vision of the charm there might be in his constant opportunities of companionship with that fair creature, who most likely shared his other tastes as she evidently did his delight in music. But there had followed his parting words – the few passionate words in which he had implied that she herself was the object of whom his love held him in dread, that it was his love for her only which he was resolved not to declare but to carry away into banishment. From the time of that parting, Dorothea, believing in Will's love for her, believing with a proud delight in his delicate sense of honour and his determination that no one should impeach him justly, felt her heart quite at rest as to the regard he might have for Mrs Lydgate. She was sure that the regard was blameless.

There are natures in which, if they love us, we are conscious of having a sort of baptism and consecration: they bind us over to rectitude and purity by their pure belief about us; and our sins become that worst kind of sacrilege which tears down the invisible altar of trust. 'If you are not good, none is good'; those little words may give a terrific meaning to responsibility, may hold a vitriolic intensity for remorse.

Dorothea's nature was of that kind: her own passionate faults lay along the easily-counted open channels of her ardent character; and while she was full of pity for the visible mistakes of others, she had not yet any material within her experience for subtle constructions and suspicions of hidden wrong. But that simplicity of hers, holding up an ideal for others in her believing conception of them, was one of the great powers of her womanhood. And it had from the first acted strongly on Will Ladislaw. He felt, when he parted from her, that the brief words by which he had tried to convey to her his feeling about herself and the division which her fortune made between them, would only profit by their brevity when Dorothea had to interpret them: he felt that in her mind he found his highest estimate.

And he was right there. In the months since their parting Dorothea had felt a delicious sad repose in their relation to each other, as one which was inwardly whole and without blemish. She had an active force of antagonism within her, when the antagonism turned on the defence either of plans or persons that she believed in; and the wrongs which she felt that Will had received from her husband, and the external conditions which to others were grounds for slighting him, only gave the more tenacity to her affection and admiring judgement. And now with the disclosures about Bulstrode had come another fact affecting Will's social position, which roused afresh Dorothea's inward resistance to what was said about him in that part of her world which lay within park palings.

'Young Ladislaw the grandson of a thieving Jew pawnbroker' was a phrase which had entered emphatically into the dialogues about the Bulstrode business, at Lowick, Tipton and Freshitt, and was a worse kind of placard on poor Will's back than the 'Italian with white mice'. Upright Sir James Chettam was convinced that his own satisfaction was righteous when he thought with some complacency that here was an added league to that mountainous distance between Ladislaw and Dorothea, which enabled him to dismiss any anxiety in that direction as too absurd. And perhaps there had been some pleasure in pointing Mr Brooke's attention to this ugly bit of Ladislaw's genealogy, as a fresh candle for him to see his own folly by. Dorothea had observed the animus with which Will's part in the painful story had been recalled more than once; but she had uttered no word, being checked now, as she had not been formerly in speaking of Will, by the consciousness of a deeper relation between them which must always remain in consecrated secrecy. But her silence shrouded her resistant emotion into a more thorough glow; and this misfortune in Will's lot which, it seemed, others were wishing to fling at his back as an opprobrium, only gave something more of enthusiasm to her clinging thought.

She entertained no visions of their ever coming into nearer union, and yet she had taken no posture of renunciation. She had accepted her whole relation to Will very simply as part of her marriage sorrows, and would have thought it very sinful in her to keep up an inward wail because she was not completely happy, being rather disposed to dwell on the superfluities of her lot. She could bear that the chief pleasures of her tenderness should lie in memory, and the idea of marriage came to her solely as a repulsive proposition from some suitor of whom she at present knew nothing, but whose merits, as seen by her friends, would be a source of torment to her: – 'somebody who will manage your property for you, my dear,' was Mr Brooke's attractive suggestion of suitable characteristics. 'I should like to manage it myself, if I knew what to do with it,' said Dorothea. No – she adhered to her declaration that she would never be married again, and in the long valley of her life, which looked so flat and empty of way-marks, guidance would come as she walked along the road, and saw her fellow-passengers by the way.

This habitual state of feeling about Will Ladislaw had been strong in all her waking hours since she had proposed to pay a visit to Mrs Lydgate, making a sort of background against which she saw Rosamond's figure presented to her without hindrances to her interest and compassion. There was evidently some mental separation, some barrier to complete confidence which had arisen between this wife and the husband who had yet made her happiness a law to him. That was a trouble which no third person must directly touch. But Dorothea thought with deep pity of the loneliness which must have come upon Rosamond from the suspicions cast on her husband; and there would surely be help in the manifestation of respect for Lydgate and sympathy with her.

'I shall talk to her about her husband,' thought Dorothea, as she was being driven towards the town. The clear spring morning, the scent of the moist earth, the fresh leaves just showing their creased-up wealth of greenery from out their half-opened sheaths, seemed part of the cheerfulness she was feeling from a long conversation with Mr Farebrother, who had joyfully accepted the justifying explanation of Lydgate's conduct. 'I shall take Mrs Lydgate good news, and perhaps she will like to talk to me and make a friend of me.'

Dorothea had another errand in Lowick Gate: it was about a new fine-toned bell for the school-house, and as she had to get out of her carriage very near to Lydgate's, she walked thither across the street, having told the coachman to wait for some packages. The street door was open, and the servant was taking the opportunity of looking out at the carriage which was pausing within sight when it became apparent to her that the lady who 'belonged to it' was coming towards her.

'Is Mrs Lydgate at home?' said Dorothea.

'I'm not sure, my lady; I'll see, if you'll please walk in,' said Martha, a little confused on the score of her kitchen apron, but collected enough to be sure that 'mum' was not the right title for this queenly young widow with a carriage and pair. 'Will you please to walk in, and I'll go and see.'

'Say that I am Mrs Casaubon,' said Dorothea, as Martha moved forward intending to show her into the drawing-room and then to go upstairs to see if Rosamond had returned from her walk.

They crossed the broader part of the entrance hall, and turned up the passage which led to the garden. The drawing-room door was unlatched, and Martha, pushing it without looking into the room, waited for Mrs Casaubon to enter and then turned away, the door having swung open and swung back again without noise. Dorothea had less of outward vision than usual this morning, being filled with images of things as they had been and were going to be. She found herself on the other side of the door without seeing anything remarkable, but immediately she heard a voice speaking in low tones which startled her as with a sense of dreaming in daylight, and advancing unconsciously a step or two beyond the projecting slab of a bookcase, she saw, in the terrible illumination of a certainty which filled up all outlines, something which made her pause motionless, without self-possession enough to speak.

Seated with his back towards her on a sofa which stood against the wall on a line with the door by which she had entered she saw Will Ladislaw: close by him and turned towards him with a flushed tearfulness which gave a new brilliancy to her face sat Rosamond, her bonnet hanging back, while Will leaning towards her clasped both her upraised hands in his and spoke with low-toned fervour.

Rosamond in her agitated absorption had not noticed the silently advancing figure; but when Dorothea, after the first immeasurable instant of this vision, moved confusedly backward and found herself impeded by some piece of furniture, Rosamond was suddenly aware of her presence, and with a spasmodic movement snatched away her hands and rose, looking at Dorothea who was necessarily arrested. Will Ladislaw, starting up, looked round also, and meeting Dorothea's eyes with a new lightning in them, seemed changing to marble. But she immediately turned them away from him to Rosamond and said in a firm voice, 'Excuse me, Mrs Lydgate, the servant did not know that you were here. I called to deliver an important letter for Mr Lydgate, which I wished to put into your own hands.'

She laid down the letter on the small table which had checked her retreat, and then including Rosamond and Will in one distant glance and bow, she went quickly out of the room, meeting in the passage the surprised Martha, who said she was sorry the mistress was not at home, and then showed the strange lady out with an inward reflection that grand people were probably more impatient than others.

Dorothea walked across the street with her most elastic step and was quickly in her carriage again.

'Drive on to Freshitt Hall,' she said to the coachman, and anyone looking at her might have thought that though she was paler than usual she was never animated by a more self-possessed energy. And that was really her experience. It was as if she had drunk a great draught of scorn that stimulated her beyond the susceptibility to other feelings. She had seen something so far below her belief, that her emotions rushed back from it and made an excited throng without an object. She needed something active to turn her excitement out upon. She felt power to walk and work for a day, without meat or drink. And she would carry out the purpose with which she had started in the morning, of going to Freshitt and Tipton to tell Sir James and her uncle all that she wished them to know about Lydgate, whose married loneliness under his trial now presented itself to her with new significance, and made her more ardent in readiness to be his champion. She had never felt anything like this triumphant power of indignation in the struggle of her married life, in which there had always been a quickly subduing pang; and she took it as a sign of new strength.

'Dodo, how very bright your eyes are!' said Celia, when Sir James was gone out of the room. 'And you don't see anything you look at, Arthur or anything. You are going to do something uncomfortable, I know. Is it all about Mr Lydgate, or has something else happened?' Celia had been used to watch her sister with expectation.

'Yes, dear, a great many things have happened,' said Dodo, in her full tones.

'I wonder what,' said Celia, folding her arms cozily and leaning forward upon them.

'Oh, all the troubles of all people on the face of the earth,' said Dorothea, lifting her arms to the back of her head.

'Dear me, Dodo, are you going to have a scheme for them?' said Celia, a little uneasy at this Hamlet-like raving.

But Sir James came in again, ready to accompany Dorothea to the Grange, and she finished her expedition well, not swerving in her resolution until she descended at her own door.

Chapter 78

Would it were yesterday and I i' the grave,
With her sweet faith above for monument.

Rosamond and Will stood motionless – they did not know how long – he looking
towards the spot where Dorothea had stood, and she looking towards him with
doubt. It seemed an endless time to Rosamond, in whose inmost soul there was
hardly so much annoyance as gratification from what had just happened. Shallow
natures dream of an easy sway over the emotions of others, trusting implicitly in
their own petty magic to turn the deepest streams, and confident, by pretty
gestures and remarks, of making the thing that is not as though it were. She knew
that Will had received a severe blow, but she had been little used to imagining
other people's states of mind except as a material cut into shape by her own
wishes; and she believed in her own power to soothe or subdue. Even Tertius,
that most perverse of men, was always subdued in the long-run: events had
been obstinate, but still Rosamond would have said now, as she did before her
marriage, that she never gave up what she had set her mind on.

She put out her arm and laid the tips of her fingers on Will's coat-sleeve.

'Don't touch me!' he said, with an utterance like the cut of a lash, darting from
her, and changing from pink to white and back again, as if his whole frame were
tingling with the pain of the sting. He wheeled round to the other side of the
room and stood opposite to her, with the tips of his fingers in his pockets and his
head thrown back, looking fiercely not at Rosamond but at a point a few inches
away from her.

She was keenly offended, but the signs she made of this were such as only
Lydgate was used to interpret. She became suddenly quiet and seated herself,
untying her hanging bonnet and laying it down with her shawl. Her little hands
which she folded before her were very cold.

It would have been safer for Will in the first instance to have taken up his hat
and gone away; but he had felt no impulse to do this; on the contrary, he had a
horrible inclination to stay and shatter Rosamond with his anger. It seemed as
impossible to bear the fatality she had drawn down on him without venting his
fury as it would be to a panther to bear the javelin-wound without springing and
biting. And yet – how could he tell a woman that he was ready to curse her? He
was fuming under a repressive law which he was forced to acknowledge: he was
dangerously poised, and Rosamond's voice now brought the decisive vibration.
In flute-like tones of sarcasm she said,

'You can easily go after Mrs Casaubon and explain your preference.'

'Go after her!' he burst out, with a sharp edge in his voice. 'Do you think she
would turn to look at me, or value any word I ever uttered to her again at more
than a dirty feather? – Explain! How can a man explain at the expense of a
woman!'

'You can tell her what you please,' said Rosamond, with more tremor.

'Do you suppose she would like me better for sacrificing you? She is not a woman to be flattered because I made myself despicable – to believe that I must be true to her because I was a dastard to you.'

He began to move about with the restlessness of a wild animal that sees prey but cannot reach it. Presently he burst out again, 'I had no hope before – not much – of anything better to come. But I had one certainty – that she believed in me. Whatever people had said or done about me, she believed in me. That's gone! She'll never again think me anything but a paltry pretence – too nice to take heaven except upon flattering conditions, and yet selling myself for any devil's change by the sly. She'll think of me as an incarnate insult to her, from the first moment we . . .'

Will stopped as if he had found himself grasping something that must not be thrown and shattered. He found another vent for his rage by snatching up Rosamond's words again, as if they were reptiles to be throttled and flung off.

'Explain! Tell a man to explain how he dropped into hell! Explain my preference! I never had a *preference* for her, any more than I have a preference for breathing. No other woman exists by the side of her. I would rather touch her hand if it were dead, than I would touch any other woman's living.'

Rosamond, while these poisoned weapons were being hurled at her, was almost losing the sense of her identity, and seemed to be waking into some new terrible existence. She had no sense of chill resolute repulsion, of reticent self-justification such as she had known under Lydgate's most stormy displeasure; all her sensibility was turned into a bewildering novelty of pain; she felt a new terrified recoil under a lash never experienced before. What another nature felt in opposition to her own was being burnt and bitten into her consciousness. When Will had ceased to speak she had become a image of sickened misery: her lips were pale, and her eyes had a tearless dismay in them. If it had been Tertius who stood opposite to her, that look of misery would have been a pang to him, and he would have sunk by her side to comfort her, with that strong-armed comfort which she had often held very cheap.

Let it be forgiven to Will that he had no such movement of pity. He had felt no bond beforehand to this woman who had spoiled the ideal treasure of his life, and he held himself blameless. He knew that he was cruel, but he had no relenting in him yet.

After he had done speaking, he still moved about, half in absence of mind, and Rosamond sat perfectly still. At length Will, seeming to bethink himself, took up his hat, yet stood some moments irresolute. He had spoken to her in a way that made a phrase of common politeness difficult to utter; and yet, now that he had come to the point of going away from her without further speech, he shrank from it as a brutality; he felt checked and stultified in his anger. He walked towards the mantelpiece and leaned his arm on it, and waited in silence for – he hardly knew what. The vindictive fire was still burning in him, and he could utter no word of retraction; but it was nevertheless in his mind that having come back to this hearth where he had enjoyed a caressing friendship he had found calamity seated there – he had had suddenly revealed to him a trouble that lay outside the home as well as within it. And what seemed a foreboding was pressing upon him as with slow pincers: that his life might come to be enslaved by this helpless woman who had thrown herself upon him in the dreary sadness of her heart. But he was in gloomy rebellion against the fact that his quick apprehensiveness foreshadowed to him, and when his eyes fell on Rosamond's blighted face it seemed to him that he was the more pitiable of the two: for pain must enter into its glorified life of memory before it can turn into compassion.

And so they remained for many minutes, opposite each other, far apart, in silence; Will's face still possessed by a mute rage, and Rosamond's by a mute misery. The poor thing had no force to fling out any passion in return; the terrible collapse of the illusion towards which all her hope had been strained was a stroke which had too thoroughly shaken her: her little world was in ruins, and she felt herself tottering in the midst as a lonely bewildered consciousness.

Will wished that she would speak and bring some mitigating shadow across his own cruel speech, which seemed to stand staring at them both in mockery of any attempt at revived fellowship. But she said nothing, and at last with a desperate effort over himself, he asked, 'Shall I come in and see Lydgate this evening?'

'If you like,' Rosamond answered, just audibly.

And then Will went out of the house, Martha never knowing that he had been in.

After he was gone, Rosamond tried to get up from her seat, but fell back fainting. When she came to herself again, she felt too ill to make the exertion of rising to ring the bell, and she remained helpless until the girl, surprised at her long absence, thought for the first time of looking for her in all the downstairs rooms. Rosamond said that she had felt suddenly sick and faint, and wanted to be helped upstairs. When there she threw herself on the bed with her clothes on, and lay in apparent torpor, as she had done once before on a memorable day of grief.

Lydgate came home earlier than he had expected, about half-past five, and found her there. The perception that she was ill threw every other thought into the background. When he felt her pulse, her eyes rested on him with more persistence than they had done for a long while, as if she felt some content that he was there. He perceived the difference in a moment, and seating himself by her put his arm gently under her, and bending over her said, 'My poor Rosamond! has something agitated you?' Clinging to him she fell into hysterical sobbings and cries, and for the next hour he did nothing but soothe and tend her. He imagined that Dorothea had been to see her, and that all this effect on her nervous system, which evidently involved some new turning towards himself, was due to the excitement of the new impressions which that visit had raised.

Chapter 79

> Now, I saw in my dream, that just as they had ended their talk,
> they drew nigh to a very miry slough, that was in the midst of
> the plain: and they, being heedless, did both fall suddenly into
> the bog. The name of the slough was Despond.
>
> JOHN BUNYAN, *Pilgrim's Progress*

When Rosamond was quiet, and Lydgate had left her, hoping that she might soon sleep under the effect of an anodyne, he went into the drawing-room to fetch a book which he had left there, meaning to spend the evening in his work-room, and he saw on the table Dorothea's letter addressed to him. He had not ventured to ask Rosamond if Mrs Casaubon had called, but the reading of this letter assured him of the fact, for Dorothea mentioned that it was to be carried by herself.

When Will Ladislaw came in a little later, Lydgate met him with a surprise which made it clear that he had not been told of the earlier visit, and Will could not say, 'Did not Mrs Lydgate tell you that I came this morning?'

'Poor Rosamond is ill,' Lydgate added immediately on his greeting.

'Not seriously, I hope,' said Will.

'No – only a slight nervous shock – the effect of some agitation. She has been overwrought lately. The truth is, Ladislaw, I am an unlucky devil. We have gone through several rounds of purgatory since you left, and I have lately got on to a worse ledge of it than ever. I suppose you are only just come down – you look rather battered – you have not been long enough in the town to hear anything?'

'I travelled all night and got to the White Hart at eight o'clock this morning. I have been shutting myself up and resting,' said Will, feeling himself a sneak, but seeing no alternative to this evasion.

And then he heard Lydgate's account of the troubles which Rosamond had already depicted to him in her way. She had not mentioned the fact of Will's name being connected with the public story – this detail not immediately affecting her – and he now heard it for the first time.

'I thought it better to tell you that your name is mixed up with the disclosures,' said Lydgate, who could understand better than most men how Ladislaw might be stung by the revelation. 'You will be sure to hear it as soon as you turn out into the town. I suppose it is true that Raffles spoke to you.'

'Yes,' said Will, sardonically. 'I shall be fortunate if gossip does not make me the most disreputable person in the whole affair. I should think the latest version must be, that I plotted with Raffles to murder Bulstrode, and ran away from Middlemarch for the purpose.'

He was thinking 'Here is a new ring in the sound of my name to recommend it in her hearing; however – what does it signify now?'

But he said nothing of Bulstrode's offer to him. Will was very open and careless about his personal affairs, but it was among the more exquisite touches in nature's modelling of him that he had a delicate generosity which warned him into reticence here. He shrank from saying that he had rejected Bulstrode's money, in the moment when he was learning that it was Lydgate's misfortune to have accepted it.

Lydgate too was reticent in the midst of his confidence. He made no allusion to Rosamond's feeling under their trouble, and of Dorothea he only said, 'Mrs Casaubon has been the one person to come forward and say that she had no belief in any of the suspicions against me.' Observing a change in Will's face, he avoided any further mention of her, feeling himself too ignorant of their relation to each other not to fear that his words might have some hidden painful bearing on it. And it occurred to him that Dorothea was the real cause of the present visit to Middlemarch.

The two men were pitying each other, but it was only Will who guessed the extent of his companion's trouble. When Lydgate spoke with desperate resignation of going to settle in London, and said with a faint smile, 'We shall have you again, old fellow', Will felt inexpressibly mournful, and said nothing. Rosamond had that morning entreated him to urge this step on Lydgate; and it seemed to him as if he were beholding in a magic panorama a future where he himself was sliding into that pleasureless yielding to the small solicitations of circumstance, which is a commoner history of perdition than any single momentous bargain.

We are on a perilous margin when we begin to look passively at our future selves, and see our own figures led with dull consent into insipid misdoing and shabby achievement. Poor Lydgate was inwardly groaning on that margin, and Will was arriving at it. It seemed to him this evening as if the cruelty of his outburst to Rosamond had made an obligation for him, and he dreaded the obligation: he dreaded Lydgate's unsuspecting goodwill: he dreaded his own distaste for his spoiled life, which would leave him in motiveless levity.

Chapter 80

> Stern lawgiver! yet thou dost wear
> The Godhead's most benignant grace:
> Nor know we anything so fair
> As is the smile upon thy face;
> Flowers laugh before thee on their beds,
> And fragrance in thy footing treads;
> Thou dost preserve the Stars from wrong;
> And the most ancient Heavens, through thee, are fresh and strong.
>
> WORDSWORTH, *Ode to Duty*

When Dorothea had seen Mr Farebrother in the morning, she had promised to go and dine at the parsonage on her return from Freshitt. There was a frequent interchange of visits between her and the Farebrother family, which enabled her to say that she was not at all lonely at the Manor, and to resist for the present the severe prescription of a lady companion. When she reached

home and remembered her engagement, she was glad of it; and finding that she
had still an hour before she could dress for dinner, she walked straight to the
schoolhouse and entered into a conversation with the master and mistress
about the new bell, giving eager attention to their small details and repetitions,
and getting up a dramatic sense that her life was very busy. She paused on her
way back to talk to old Master Bunney who was putting in some garden-seeds,
and discoursed wisely with that rural sage about the crops that would make the
most return on a perch of ground, and the result of sixty years' experience as to
soils – namely, that if your soil was pretty mellow it would do, but if there came
wet, wet, wet to make it all of a mummy, why then –

Finding that the social spirit had beguiled her into being rather late, she
dressed hastily and went over to the parsonage rather earlier than was necessary.
That house was never dull, Mr Farebrother, like another White of Selborne,
having continually something new to tell of his inarticulate guests and *protégés*,
whom he was teaching the boys not to torment; and he had just set up a pair of
beautiful goats to be pets of the village in general, and to walk at large as sacred
animals. The evening went by cheerfully till after tea, Dorothea talking more
than usual and dilating with Mr Farebrother on the possible histories of creatures
that converse compendiously with their antennæ, and for aught we know may
hold reformed parliaments; when suddenly some inarticulate little sounds were
heard which called everybody's attention.

'Henrietta Noble,' said Mrs Farebrother, seeing her small sister moving about
the furniture-legs distressfully, 'what is the matter?'

'I have lost my tortoise-shell lozenge-box. I fear the kitten has rolled it away,'
said the tiny old lady, involuntarily continuing her beaver-like notes.

'Is it a great treasure, aunt?' said Mr Farebrother, putting up his glasses and
looking at the carpet.

'Mr Ladislaw gave it me,' said Miss Noble. 'A German box very pretty; but if
it falls it always spins away as far as it can.'

'Oh, if it is Ladislaw's present,' said Mr Farebrother, in a deep tone of comprehension, getting up and hunting. The box was found at last under a chiffonier,
and Miss Noble grasped it with delight, saying, 'It was under a fender the last
time.'

'That is an affair of the heart with my aunt,' said Mr Farebrother, smiling at
Dorothea, as he reseated himself.

'If Henrietta Noble forms an attachment to anyone, Mrs Casaubon,' said his
mother, emphatically, – 'she is like a dog, she would take their shoes for a pillow
and sleep the better.'

'Mr Ladislaw's shoes, I would,' said Henrietta Noble.

Dorothea made an attempt at smiling in return. She was surprised and
annoyed to find that her heart was palpitating violently, and that it was quite
useless to try after a recovery of her former animation. Alarmed at herself –
fearing some further betrayal of a change so marked in its occasion, she rose
and said in a low voice with undisguised anxiety, 'I must go; I have overtired
myself.'

Mr Farebrother, quick in perception, rose and said, 'It is true you must have half-exhausted yourself in talking about Lydgate. That sort of work tells upon one after the excitement is over.'

He gave her his arm back to the Manor, but Dorothea did not attempt to speak, even when he said good-night.

The limit of resistance was reached, and she had sunk back helpless within the clutch of inescapable anguish. Dismissing Tantripp with a few faint words, she locked her door, and turning away from it towards the vacant room she pressed her hands hard on the top of her head, and moaned out, 'Oh, I did love him!'

Then came the hour in which the waves of suffering shook her too thoroughly to leave any power of thought. She could only cry in loud whispers, between her sobs, after her lost belief which she had planted and kept alive from a very little seed since the days in Rome – after her lost joy of clinging with silent love and faith to one who, misprized by others, was worthy in her thought – after her lost woman's pride of reigning in his memory – after her sweet dim perspective of hope, that along some pathway they should meet with unchanged recognition and take up the backward years as a yesterday.

In that hour she repeated what the merciful eyes of solitude have looked on for ages in the spiritual struggles of man – she besought hardness and coldness and aching weariness to bring her relief from the mysterious incorporeal might of her anguish: she lay on the bare floor and let the night grow cold around her; while her grand woman's frame was shaken by sobs as if she had been a despairing child.

There were two images – two living forms that tore her heart in two, as if it had been the heart of a mother who seems to see her child divided by the sword, and presses one bleeding half to her breast while her gaze goes forth in agony towards the half which is carried away by the lying woman that has never known the mother's pang.

Here, with the nearness of an answering smile, here within the vibrating bond of mutual speech, was the bright creature whom she had trusted – who had come to her like the spirit of morning visiting the dim vault where she sat as the bride of a worn-out life; and now, with a full consciousness which had never awakened before, she stretched out her arms towards him and cried with bitter cries that their nearness was a parting vision: she discovered her passion to herself in the unshrinking utterance of despair.

And there, aloof, yet persistently with her, moving wherever she moved, was the Will Ladislaw who was a changed belief exhausted of hope, a detected illusion – no, a living man towards whom there could not yet struggle any wail of regretful pity, from the midst of scorn and indignation and jealous offended pride. The fire of Dorothea's anger was not easily spent, and it flamed out in fitful returns of spurning reproach. Why had he come obtruding his life into hers, hers that might have been whole enough without him? Why had he brought his cheap regard and his lip-born words to her who had nothing paltry to give in exchange? He knew that he was deluding her – wished, in the very moment of farewell, to make her believe that he gave her the whole price of her heart, and knew that he had spent it half before. Why had he not stayed among the crowd of whom she asked nothing – but only prayed that they might be less contemptible?

But she lost energy at last even for her loud-whispered cries and moans: she subsided into helpless sobs, and on the cold floor she sobbed herself to sleep.

In the chill hours of the morning twilight, when all was dim around her, she awoke – not with any amazed wondering where she was or what had happened, but with the clearest consciousness that she was looking into the eyes of sorrow. She rose, and wrapped warm things around her, and seated herself in a great chair where she had often watched before. She was vigorous enough to have borne that hard night without feeling ill in body, beyond some aching and fatigue: but she had waked to a new condition: she felt as if her soul had been liberated from its terrible conflict; she was no longer wrestling with her grief, but could sit down with it as a lasting companion and make it a sharer in her thoughts. For now the thoughts came thickly. It was not in Dorothea's nature, for longer than the duration of a paroxysm, to sit in the narrow cell of her calamity, in the besotted misery of a consciousness that only sees another's lot as an accident of its own.

She began now to live through that yesterday morning deliberately again, forcing herself to dwell on every detail and its possible meaning. Was she alone in that scene? Was it her event only? She forced herself to think of it as bound up with another woman's life – a woman towards whom she had set out with a longing to carry some clearness and comfort into her beclouded youth. In her first outleap of jealous indignation and disgust, when quitting the hateful room, she had flung away all the mercy with which she had undertaken that visit. She had enveloped both Will and Rosamond in her burning scorn, and it seemed to her as if Rosamond were burned out of her sight for ever. But that base prompting which makes a woman more cruel to a rival than to a faithless lover, could have no strength of recurrence in Dorothea when the dominant spirit of justice within her had once overcome the tumult and had once shown her the truer measure of things. All the active thought with which she had before been representing to herself the trials of Lydgate's lot, and this young marriage union which, like her own, seemed to have its hidden as well as evident troubles – all this vivid sympathetic experience returned to her now as a power: it asserted itself as acquired knowledge asserts itself and will not let us see as we saw in the day of our ignorance. She said to her own irremediable grief, that it should make her more helpful, instead of driving her back from effort.

And what sort of crisis might not this be in three lives whose contact with hers laid an obligation on her as if they had been suppliants bearing the sacred branch? The objects of her rescue were not to be sought out by her fancy: they were chosen for her. She yearned towards the perfect Right, that it might make a throne within her, and rule her errant will. 'What should I do – how should I act now, this very day if I could clutch my own pain, and compel it to silence, and think of those three!'

It had taken long for her to come to that question, and there was light piercing into the room. She opened her curtains, and looked out towards the bit of road that lay in view, with fields beyond, outside the entrance-gates. On the road there was a man with a bundle on his back and a woman carrying her baby; in the field she could see figures moving – perhaps the shepherd with his dog. Far off in the bending sky was the pearly light; and she felt the largeness of the world and the manifold wakings of men to labour and endurance. She was a part of that involuntary, palpitating life, and could neither look out on it from her luxurious shelter as a mere spectator, nor hide her eyes in selfish complaining.

What she would resolve to do that day did not yet seem quite clear, but something that she could achieve stirred her as with an approaching murmur which would soon gather distinctness. She took off the clothes which seemed to have some of the weariness of a hard watching in them, and began to make her toilet. Presently she rang for Tantripp, who came in her dressing-gown.

'Why, madam, you've never been in bed this blessed night,' burst out Tantripp, looking first at the bed and then at Dorothea's face, which in spite of bathing had the pale cheeks and pink eyelids of a *mater dolorosa*. 'You'll kill yourself, you *will*. Anybody might think now you had a right to give yourself a little comfort.'

'Don't be alarmed, Tantripp,' said Dorothea, smiling. 'I have slept; I am not ill. I shall be glad of a cup of coffee as soon as possible. And I want you to bring me my new dress; and most likely I shall want my new bonnet today.'

'They've lain there a month and more ready for you, madam, and most thankful I shall be to see you with a couple o' pounds' worth less of crape,' said Tantripp, stooping to light the fire. 'There's a reason in mourning, as I've always said; and three folds at the bottom of your skirt and a plain quilling in your bonnet – and if ever anybody looked like an angel, it's you in a net quilling – is what's consistent for a second year. At least, that's my thinking,' ended Tantripp, looking anxiously at the fire; 'and if anybody was to marry me flattering himself I should wear those hijeous weepers two years for him, he'd be deceived by his own vanity, that's all.'

'The fire will do, my good Tan,' said Dorothea, speaking as she used to do in the old Lausanne days, only with a very low voice; 'get me the coffee.'

She folded herself in the large chair, and leaned her head against it in fatigued quiescence, while Tantripp went away wondering at this strange contrariness in her young mistress that just the morning when she had more of a widow's face than ever, she should have asked for her lighter mourning which she had waived before. Tantripp would never have found the clue to this mystery. Dorothea wished to acknowledge that she had not the less an active life before her because she had buried a private joy; and the tradition that fresh garments belonged to all initiation, haunting her mind, made her grasp after even that slight outward help towards calm resolve. For the resolve was not easy.

Nevertheless at eleven o'clock she was walking towards Middlemarch, having made up her mind that she would make as quietly and unnoticeably as possible her second attempt to see and save Rosamond.

Chapter 81

Du Erde warst auch diese Nacht beständig,
Und athmest neu erquickt zu meinen Füssen,
Beginnest schon mit Lust mich zu umgeben,
Du regst und rührst ein kräftiges Beschliessen
Zum hochsten Dasein immerfort zu streben.

GOETHE, *Faust*

When Dorothea was again at Lydgate's door speaking to Martha, he was in the room close by with the door ajar, preparing to go out. He heard her voice, and immediately came to her.

'Do you think that Mrs Lydgate can receive me this morning?' she said, having reflected that it would be better to leave out all allusion to her previous visit.

'I have no doubt she will,' said Lydgate, suppressing his thought about Dorothea's looks, which were as much changed as Rosamond's, 'if you will be kind enough to come in and let me tell her that you are here. She has not been very well since you were here yesterday, but she is better this morning, and I think it is very likely that she will be cheered by seeing you again.'

It was plain that Lydgate, as Dorothea had expected, knew nothing about the circumstances of her yesterday's visit; nay, he appeared to imagine that she had carried it out according to her intention. She had prepared a little note asking Rosamond to see her, which she would have given to the servant if he had not been in the way, but now she was in much anxiety as to the result of his announcement.

After leading her into the drawing-room, he paused to take a letter from his pocket and put it into her hands, saying, 'I wrote this last night, and was going to carry it to Lowick in my ride. When one is grateful for something too good for common thanks, writing is less unsatisfactory than speech – one does not at least *hear* how inadequate the words are.'

Dorothea's face brightened. 'It is I who have most to thank for, since you have let me take that place. You *have* consented?' she said, suddenly doubting.

'Yes, the cheque is going to Bulstrode today.'

He said no more, but went upstairs to Rosamond, who had but lately finished dressing herself, and sat languidly wondering what she should do next, her habitual industry in small things, even in the days of her sadness, prompting her to begin some kind of occupation, which she dragged through slowly or paused in from lack of interest. She looked ill, but had recovered her usual quietude of manner, and Lydgate had feared to disturb her by any questions. He had told her of Dorothea's letter containing the cheque, and afterwards he had said, 'Ladislaw is come, Rosy; he sat with me last night; I dare say he will be here again today. I thought he looked rather battered and depressed.' And Rosamond had made no reply.

Now, when he came up, he said to her very gently, 'Rosy, dear, Mrs Casaubon is come to see you again; you would like to see her, would you not?' That she coloured and gave rather a startled movement did not surprise him after the agitation produced by the interview yesterday – a beneficent agitation, he thought, since it seemed to have made her turn to him again.

Rosamond dared not say no. She dared not with a tone of her voice touch the facts of yesterday. Why had Mrs Casaubon come again? The answer was a blank which Rosamond could only fill up with dread, for Will Ladislaw's lacerating words had made every thought of Dorothea a fresh smart to her. Nevertheless, in her new humiliating uncertainty she dared do nothing but comply. She did not say yes, but she rose and let Lydgate put a light shawl over her shoulders, while he said, 'I am going out immediately.' Then something crossed her mind which prompted her to say, 'Pray tell Martha not to bring anyone else into the drawing-room.' And Lydgate assented, thinking that he fully understood this wish. He led her down to the drawing-room door, and then turned away, observing to himself that he was rather a blundering husband to be dependent for his wife's trust in him on the influence of another woman.

Rosamond, wrapping her soft shawl around her as she walked towards Dorothea, was inwardly wrapping her soul in cold reserve. Had Mrs Casaubon come to say anything to her about Will? If so, it was a liberty that Rosamond resented; and she prepared herself to meet every word with polite impassibility. Will had bruised her pride too sorely for her to feel any compunction towards him and Dorothea: her own injury seemed much the greater. Dorothea was not only the 'preferred' woman, but had also a formidable advantage in being Lydgate's benefactor; and to poor Rosamond's pained confused vision it seemed that this Mrs Casaubon – this woman who predominated in all things concerning her – must have come now with the sense of having the advantage, and with animosity prompting her to use it. Indeed, not Rosamond only, but anyone else, knowing the outer facts of the case, and not the simple inspiration on which Dorothea acted, might well have wondered why she came.

Looking like the lovely ghost of herself, her graceful slimness wrapped in her soft white shawl, the rounded infantine mouth and cheek inevitably suggesting mildness and innocence, Rosamond paused at three yards' distance from her visitor and bowed. But Dorothea, who had taken off her gloves, from an impulse which she could never resist when she wanted a sense of freedom, came forward, and with her face full of a sad yet sweet openness, put out her hand. Rosamond could not avoid meeting her glance, could not avoid putting her small hand into Dorothea's which clasped it with gentle motherliness; and immediately a doubt of her own prepossessions began to stir within her. Rosamond's eye was quick for faces; she saw that Mrs Casaubon's face looked pale and changed since yesterday, yet gentle, and like the firm softness of her hand. But Dorothea had counted a little too much on her own strength: the clearness and intensity of her mental action this morning were the continuance of a nervous exaltation which made her frame as dangerously responsive as a bit of finest Venetian crystal; and in looking at Rosamond, she suddenly found her heart swelling, and was unable to speak – all her effort was required to keep back tears. She succeeded in that, and the emotion only passed over her face like the spirit of a sob; but it added to Rosamond's impression that Mrs Casaubon's state of mind must be something quite different from what she had imagined.

So they sat down without a word of preface on the two chairs that happened to be nearest, and happened also to be close together; though Rosamond's notion when she first bowed was that she should stay a long way off from Mrs Casaubon. But she ceased thinking how anything would turn out – merely wondering what would come. And Dorothea began to speak quite simply, gathering firmness as she went on.

'I had an errand yesterday which I did not finish; that is why I am here again so soon. You will not think me too troublesome, when I tell you that I came to talk to you about the injustice that has been shown towards Mr Lydgate. It will cheer you will it not? – to know a great deal about him, that he may not like to speak about himself just because it is in his own vindication and to his own honour. You will like to know that your husband has warm friends, who have not left off believing in his high character? You will let me speak of this without thinking that I take a liberty?'

The cordial, pleading tones which seemed to flow with generous heedlessness above all the facts which had filled Rosamond's mind as grounds of obstruction and hatred between her and this woman, came as soothingly as a warm stream over her shrinking fears. Of course Mrs Casaubon had the facts in her mind, but she was not going to speak of anything connected with them. That relief was too great for Rosamond to feel much else at the moment. She answered prettily, in the new ease of her soul, 'I know you have been very good. I shall like to hear anything you will say to me about Tertius.'

'The day before yesterday,' said Dorothea, 'when I had asked him to come to Lowick to give me his opinion on the affairs of the Hospital, he told me everything about his conduct and feelings in this sad event which has made ignorant people cast suspicions on him. The reason he told me was because I was very bold and asked him. I believed that he had never acted dishonourably, and I begged him to tell me the history. He confessed to me that he had never told it before, not even to you, because he had a great dislike to say, "I was not wrong", as if that were proof, when there are guilty people who will say so. The truth is, he knew nothing of this man Raffles, or that there were any bad secrets about him; and he thought that Mr Bulstrode offered him the money because he repented, out of kindness, of having refused it before. All his anxiety about his patient was to treat him rightly, and he was a little uncomfortable that the case did not end as he had expected; but he thought then and still thinks that there may have been no wrong in it on anyone's part. And I have told Mr Farebrother, and Mr Brooke, and Sir James Chettam: they all believe in your husband. That will cheer you, will it not? That will give you courage?'

Dorothea's face had become animated, and as it beamed on Rosamond very close to her, she felt something like bashful timidity before a superior, in the presence of this self-forgetful ardour. She said, with blushing embarrassment, 'Thank you: you are very kind.'

'And he felt that he had been so wrong not to pour out everything about this to you. But you will forgive him. It was because he feels so much more about your happiness than anything else – he feels his life bound into one with yours, and it hurts him more than anything, that his misfortunes must hurt you. He could speak to me because I am an indifferent person. And then I asked him if I might come to see you; because I felt so much for his trouble and yours. That is why I came yesterday, and why I am come today. Trouble is so hard to bear, is it not? How can we live and think that anyone has trouble – piercing trouble – and we could help them, and never try?'

Dorothea, completely swayed by the feeling that she was uttering, forgot everything but that she was speaking from out the heart of her own trial to Rosamond's. The emotion had wrought itself more and more into her utterance, till the tones might have gone to one's very marrow, like a low cry from some suffering creature in the darkness. And she had unconsciously laid her hand again on the little hand that she had pressed before.

Rosamond, with an overmastering pang, as if a wound within her had been probed, burst into hysterical crying as she had done the day before when she clung to her husband. Poor Dorothea was feeling a great wave of her own sorrow returning over her – her thought being drawn to the possible share that Will Ladislaw might have in Rosamond's mental tumult. She was beginning to fear that she should not be able to suppress herself enough to the end of this meeting, and while her hand was still resting on Rosamond's lap, though the hand underneath it was withdrawn, she was struggling against her own rising sobs. She tried to master herself with the thought that this might be a turning-point in three lives – not in her own: no, there the irrevocable had happened, but – in those three lives which were touching hers with the solemn neighbour-hood of danger and distress. The fragile creature who was crying close to her – there might still be time to rescue her from the misery of false incompatible bonds and this moment was unlike any other: she and Rosamond could never be together again with the same thrilling consciousness of yesterday within them both. She felt the relation between them to be peculiar enough to give her a peculiar influence, though she had no conception that the way in which her own feelings were involved was fully known to Mrs Lydgate.

It was a newer crisis in Rosamond's experience than even Dorothea could imagine: she was under the first great shock that had shattered her dream-world in which she had been easily confident of herself and critical of others; and this strange unexpected manifestation of feeling in a woman whom she had approached with a shrinking aversion and dread, as one who must necessarily have a jealous hatred towards her, made her soul totter all the more with a sense that she had been walking in an unknown world which had just broken in upon her.

When Rosamond's convulsed throat was subsiding into calm, and she with-drew the handkerchief with which she had been hiding her face, her eyes met Dorothea's as helplessly as if they had been blue flowers. What was the use of thinking about behaviour after this crying? And Dorothea looked almost as childish, with the neglected trace of a silent tear. Pride was broken down between these two.

'We were talking about your husband,' Dorothea said, with some timidity. 'I thought his looks were sadly changed with suffering the other day. I had not seen him for many weeks before. He said he had been feeling very lonely in his trial; but I think he would have borne it all better if he had been able to be quite open with you.'

'Tertius is so angry and impatient if I say anything,' said Rosamond, imagining that he had been complaining of her to Dorothea. 'He ought not to wonder that I object to speak to him on painful subjects.'

'It was himself he blamed for not speaking,' said Dorothea. 'What he said of you was, that he could not be happy in doing anything which made you unhappy – that his marriage was of course a bond which must affect his choice about everything; and for that reason he refused my proposal that he should keep his position at the Hospital, because that would bind him to stay in Middlemarch, and he would not undertake to do anything which would be painful to you. He could say that to me, because he knows that I had much trial in my marriage, from my husband's illness, which hindered his plans and saddened him; and he knows that I have felt how hard it is to walk always in fear of hurting another who is tied to us.'

Dorothea waited a little; she had discerned a faint pleasure stealing over Rosamond's face. But there was no answer, and she went on, with a gathering tremor, 'Marriage is so unlike everything else. There is something even awful in the nearness it brings. Even if we loved someone else better than – than those we were married to, it would be no use' – poor Dorothea, in her palpitating anxiety, could only seize her language brokenly – 'I mean, marriage drinks up all our power of giving or getting any blessedness in that sort of love. I know it may be very dear but it murders our marriage – and then the marriage stays with us like a murder – and everything else is gone. And then our husband – if he loved and trusted us, and we have not helped him, but made a curse in his life . . .'

Her voice had sunk very low: there was a dread upon her of presuming too far, and of speaking as if she herself were perfection addressing error. She was too much preoccupied with her own anxiety, to be aware that Rosamond was trembling too; and filled with the need to express pitying fellowship rather than rebuke, she put her hands on Rosamond's, and said with more agitated rapidity, – 'I know, I know that the feeling may be very dear – it has taken hold of us unawares – it is so hard, it may seem like death to part with it – and we are weak – I am weak –'

The waves of her own sorrow, from out of which she was struggling to save another, rushed over Dorothea with conquering force. She stopped in speechless agitation, not crying, but feeling as if she were being inwardly grappled. Her face had become of a deathlier paleness, her lips trembled, and she pressed her hands helplessly on the hands that lay under them.

Rosamond, taken hold of by an emotion stronger than her own – hurried along in a new movement which gave all things some new, awful, undefined aspect – could find no words, but involuntarily she put her lips to Dorothea's forehead which was very near her, and then for a minute the two women clasped each other as if they had been in a shipwreck.

'You are thinking what is not true,' said Rosamond, in an eager half-whisper, while she was still feeling Dorothea's arms round her – urged by a mysterious necessity to free herself from something that oppressed her as if it were blood-guiltiness.

They moved apart, looking at each other.

'When you came in yesterday – it was not as you thought,' said Rosamond in the same tone.

There was a movement of surprised attention in Dorothea. She expected a vindication of Rosamond herself.

'He was telling me how he loved another woman, that I might know he could never love me,' said Rosamond, getting more and more hurried as she went on. 'And now I think he hates me because – because you mistook him yesterday. He says it is through me that you will think ill of him – think that he is a false person. But it shall not be through me. He has never had any love for me – I know he has not – he has always thought slightly of me. He said yesterday that no other woman existed for him besides you. The blame of what happened is entirely mine. He said he could never explain to you – because of me. He said you could never think well of him again. But now I have told you, and he cannot reproach me any more.'

Rosamond had delivered her soul under impulses which she had not known before. She had begun her confession under the subduing influence of Dorothea's emotion; and as she went on she had gathered the sense that she was repelling Will's reproaches, which were still like a knife-wound within her.

The revulsion of feeling in Dorothea was too strong to be called joy. It was a tumult in which the terrible strain of the night and morning made a resistant pain: – she could only perceive that this would be joy when she had recovered her power of feeling it. Her immediate consciousness was one of immense sympathy without check; she cared for Rosamond without struggle now, and responded earnestly to her last words:

'No, he cannot reproach you any more.'

With her usual tendency to over-estimate the good in others, she felt a great outgoing of her heart towards Rosamond for the generous effort which had redeemed her from suffering, not counting that the effort was a reflex of her own energy.

After they had been silent a little, she said, 'You are not sorry that I came this morning?'

'No, you have been very good to me,' said Rosamond. 'I did not think that you would be so good. I was very unhappy. I am not happy now. Everything is so sad.'

'But better days will come. Your husband will be rightly valued. And he depends on you for comfort. He loves you best. The worst loss would be to lose that – and you have not lost it,' said Dorothea.

She tried to thrust away the too overpowering thought of her own relief, lest she should fail to win some sign that Rosamond's affection was yearning back towards her husband.

'Tertius did not find fault with me, then?' said Rosamond, understanding now that Lydgate might have said anything to Mrs Casaubon, and that she certainly was different from other women. Perhaps there was a faint taste of jealousy in the question. A smile began to play over Dorothea's face as she said, 'No, indeed! How could you imagine it?' But here the door opened, and Lydgate entered.

'I am come back in my quality of doctor,' he said. 'After I went away, I was haunted by two pale faces: Mrs Casaubon looked as much in need of care as you, Rosy. And I thought that I had not done my duty in leaving you together: so when I had been to Coleman's I came home again. I noticed that you were walking, Mrs Casaubon, and the sky has changed – I think we may have rain. May I send someone to order your carriage to come for you?'

'Oh no! I am strong: I need the walk,' said Dorothea, rising with animation in her face. 'Mrs Lydgate and I have chatted a great deal, and it is time for me to go. I have always been accused of being immoderate and saying too much.'

She put out her hand to Rosamond, and they said an earnest, quiet goodbye without kiss or other show of effusion: there had been between them too much serious emotion for them to use the signs of it superficially.

As Lydgate took her to the door she said nothing of Rosamond, but told him of Mr Farebrother and the other friends who had listened with belief to his story.

When he came back to Rosamond, she had already thrown herself on the sofa, in resigned fatigue.

'Well, Rosy,' he said, standing over her, and touching her hair, 'what do you think of Mrs Casaubon now you have seen so much of her?'

'I think she must be better than anyone,' said Rosamond, 'and she is very beautiful. If you go to talk to her so often, you will be more discontented with me than ever!'

Lydgate laughed at the 'so often'. 'But has she made you any less discontented with me?'

'I think she has,' said Rosamond, looking up in his face. 'How heavy your eyes are, Tertius – and do push your hair back.' He lifted up his large white hand to obey her, and felt thankful for this little mark of interest in him. Poor Rosamond's vagrant fancy had come back terribly scourged – meek enough to nestle under the old despised shelter. And the shelter was still there: Lydgate had accepted his narrowed lot with sad resignation. He had chosen this fragile creature, and had taken the burthen of her life upon his arms. He must walk as he could, carrying that burthen pitifully.

Chapter 82

My grief lies onward and my joy behind.
SHAKESPEARE, *Sonnets*

Exiles notoriously feed much on hopes, and are unlikely to stay in banishment unless they are obliged. When Will Ladislaw exiled himself from Middlemarch he had placed no stronger obstacle to his return than his own resolve, which was by no means an iron barrier, but simply a state of mind liable to melt into a minuet with other states of mind, and to find itself bowing, smiling, and giving place with polite facility. As the months went on, it had seemed more and more difficult to him to say why he should not run down to Middlemarch – merely for the sake of hearing something about Dorothea; and if on such a flying visit he should chance by some strange coincidence to meet with her, there was no reason for him to be ashamed of having taken an innocent journey which he had beforehand supposed that he should not take. Since he was hopelessly divided from her, he might surely venture into her neighbourhood; and as to the suspicious friends who kept a dragon-watch over her – their opinions seemed less and less important with time and change of air.

And there had come a reason quite irrespective of Dorothea, which seemed to make a journey to Middlemarch a sort of philanthropic duty. Will had given a disinterested attention to an intended settlement on a new plan in the Far West, and the need for funds in order to carry out a good design had set him on debating with himself whether it would not be a laudable use to make of his claim on Bulstrode, to urge the application of that money which had been offered to himself as a means of carrying out a scheme likely to be largely beneficial. The question seemed a very dubious one to Will, and his repugnance to again entering into any relation with the banker might have made him dismiss it quickly, if there had not arisen in his imagination the probability that his judgement might be more safely determined by a visit to Middlemarch.

That was the object which Will stated to himself as a reason for coming down. He had meant to confide in Lydgate, and discuss the money question with him, and he had meant to amuse himself for the few evenings of his stay by having a great deal of music and badinage with fair Rosamond, without neglecting his friends at Lowick Parsonage: – if the Parsonage was close to the Manor, that was no fault of his. He had neglected the Farebrothers before his departure, from a proud resistance to the possible accusation of indirectly seeking interviews with Dorothea; but hunger tames us, and Will had become very hungry for the vision of a certain form and the sound of a certain voice. Nothing had done instead – not the opera, or the converse of zealous politicians, or the flattering reception (in dim corners) of his new hand in leading articles.

Thus he had come down, foreseeing with confidence how almost everything would be in his familiar little world; fearing, indeed, that there would be no surprises in his visit. But he had found that humdrum world in a terribly dynamic condition, in which even badinage and lyrism had turned explosive; and the first day of this visit had become the most fatal epoch of his life. The next morning he felt so harassed with the nightmare of consequences – he dreaded so much the immediate issues before him – that seeing while he breakfasted the arrival of the Riverston coach, he went out hurriedly and took his place on it, that he might be relieved, at least for a day, from the necessity of doing or saying anything in Middlemarch. Will Ladislaw was in one of those tangled crises which are commoner in experience than one might imagine, from the shallow absoluteness of men's judgements. He had found Lydgate, for whom he had the sincerest respect, under circumstances which claimed his thorough and frankly-declared sympathy; and the reason why, in spite of that claim, it would have been better for Will to have avoided all further intimacy, or even contact, with Lydgate, was precisely of the kind to make such a course appear impossible. To a creature of Will's susceptible temperament without any neutral region of indifference in his nature, ready to turn everything that befell him into the collisions of a passionate drama – the revelation that Rosamond had made her happiness in any way dependent on him was a difficulty which his outburst of rage towards her had immeasurably increased for him. He hated his own cruelty, and yet he dreaded to show the fullness of his relenting: he must go to her again; the friendship could not be put to a sudden end; and her unhappiness was a power which he dreaded. And all the while there was no more foretaste of enjoyment in the life before him than if his limbs had been lopped off and he was making his fresh start on crutches. In the night he had debated whether he should not get on the coach, not for Riverston, but for London, leaving a note to Lydgate which would give a makeshift reason for his retreat. But there were strong cords pulling him back from that abrupt departure: the blight on his happiness in thinking of Dorothea, the crushing of that chief hope which had remained in spite of the acknowledged necessity for renunciation, was too fresh a misery for him to resign himself to it, and go straightway into a distance which was also despair.

Thus he did nothing more decided than take the Riverston coach. He came back again by it while it was still daylight, having made up his mind that he must go to Lydgate's that evening. The Rubicon, we know, was a very insignificant stream to look at; its significance lay entirely in certain invisible conditions. Will felt as if he were forced to cross his small boundary ditch, and what he saw beyond it was not empire but discontented subjection.

But it is given to us sometimes even in our everyday life to witness the saving influence of a noble nature, the divine efficacy of rescue that may lie in a self-subduing act of fellowship. If Dorothea, after her night's anguish, had not taken that walk to Rosamond – why, she perhaps would have been a woman who gained a higher character for discretion, but it would certainly not have been as well for those three who were on one hearth in Lydgate's house at half-past seven that evening.

Rosamond had been prepared for Will's visit, and she received him with a languid coldness which Lydgate accounted for by her nervous exhaustion, of which he could not suppose that it had any relation to Will. And when she sat in silence bending over a bit of work, he innocently apologised for her in an indirect way by begging her to lean backward and rest. Will was miserable in the necessity for playing the part of a friend who was making his first appearance and greeting to Rosamond, while his thoughts were busy about her feeling since that scene of yesterday, which seemed still inexorably to enclose them both, like the painful vision of a double madness. It happened that nothing called Lydgate out of the room; but when Rosamond poured out the tea, and Will came near to fetch it, she placed a tiny bit of folded paper in his saucer. He saw it and secured it quickly, but as he went back to his inn he had no eagerness to unfold the paper. What Rosamond had written to him would probably deepen the painful impressions of the evening. Still, he opened and read it by his bed-candle. There were only these few words in her neatly-flowing hand:

I have told Mrs Casaubon. She is not under any mistake about you. I told her because she came to see me and was very kind. You will have nothing to reproach me with now. I shall not have made any difference to you.

The effect of these words was not quite all gladness. As Will dwelt on them with excited imagination, he felt his cheeks and ears burning at the thought of what had occurred between Dorothea and Rosamond – at the uncertainty how far Dorothea might still feel her dignity wounded in having an explanation of his conduct offered to her. There might still remain in her mind a changed association with him which made an irremediable difference – a lasting flaw. With active fancy he wrought himself into a state of doubt little more easy than that of the man who has escaped from wreck by night and stands on unknown ground in the darkness. Until that wretched yesterday except the moment of vexation long ago in the very same room and in the very same presence – all their vision, all their thought of each other, had been as in a world apart, where the sunshine fell on tall white lilies, where no evil lurked, and no other soul entered. But now – would Dorothea meet him in that world again?

Chapter 83

And now good-morrow to our waking souls
Which watch not one another out of fear;
For love all love of other sights controls,
And makes one little room, an everywhere.

DR DONNE

On the second morning after Dorothea's visit to Rosamond, she had had two nights of sound sleep, and had not only lost all trace of fatigue, but felt as if she had a great deal of superfluous strength – that is to say, more strength than she could manage to concentrate on any occupation. The day before, she had taken long walks outside the grounds, and had paid two visits to the Parsonage; but she never in her life told anyone the reason why she spent her time in that fruitless manner, and this morning she was rather angry with herself for her childish restlessness. Today was to be spent quite differently. What was there to be done in the village? Oh dear! nothing. Everybody was well and had flannel; nobody's pig had died; and it was Saturday morning, when there was a general scrubbing of floors and door-stones, and when it was useless to go into the school. But there were various subjects that Dorothea was trying to get clear upon, and she resolved to throw herself energetically into the gravest of all. She sat down in the library before her particular little heap of books on political economy and kindred matters, out of which she was trying to get light as to the best way of spending money so as not to injure one's neighbours, or – what comes to the same thing – so as to do them the most good. Here was a weighty subject which, if she could but lay hold of it, would certainly keep her mind steady. Unhappily her mind slipped off it for a whole hour; and at the end she found herself reading sentences twice over with an intense consciousness of many things, but not of any one thing contained in the text. This was hopeless. Should she order the carriage and drive to Tipton? No; for some reason or other she preferred staying at Lowick. But her vagrant mind must be reduced to order: there was an art in self-discipline; and she walked round and round the brown library considering by what sort of manoeuvre she could arrest her wandering thoughts. Perhaps a mere task was the best means – something to which she must go doggedly. Was there not the geography of Asia Minor, in which her slackness had often been rebuked by Mr Casaubon? She went to the cabinet of maps and unrolled one: this morning she might make herself finally sure that Paphlagonia was not on the Levantine coast, and fix her total darkness about the Chalybes firmly on the shores of the Euxine. A map was a fine thing to study when you were disposed to think of something else, being made up of names that would turn into a chime if you went back upon them. Dorothea set earnestly to work, bending close to her map, and uttering the names in an audible, subdued tone, which often got into a chime. She looked amusingly girlish after all her deep experience – nodding her head and marking the names off on her fingers, with a little pursing of her lip, and now and then breaking off to put her hands on each side of her face and say, 'Oh dear! oh dear!'

There was no reason why this should end any more than a merry-go-round; but it was at last interrupted by the opening of the door and the announcement of Miss Noble.

The little old lady, whose bonnet hardly reached Dorothea's shoulder was warmly welcomed, but while her hand was being pressed she made many of her beaver-like noises, as if she had something difficult to say.

'Do sit down,' said Dorothea, rolling a chair forward. 'Am I wanted for anything? I shall be so glad if I can do anything.'

'I will not stay,' said Miss Noble, putting her hand into her small basket, and holding some article inside it nervously; 'I have left a friend in the churchyard.' She lapsed into her inarticulate sounds, and unconsciously drew forth the article which she was fingering. It was the tortoiseshell lozenge-box, and Dorothea felt the colour mounting to her cheeks.

'Mr Ladislaw,' continued the timid little woman. 'He fears he has offended you, and has begged me to ask if you will see him for a few minutes.'

Dorothea did not answer on the instant: it was crossing her mind that she could not receive him in this library, where her husband's prohibition seemed to dwell. She looked towards the window. Could she go out and meet him in the grounds? The sky was heavy, and the trees had begun to shiver as at a coming storm. Besides, she shrank from going out to him.

'Do see him, Mrs Casaubon,' said Miss Noble, pathetically; 'else I must go back and say no, and that will hurt him.'

'Yes, I will see him,' said Dorothea. 'Pray tell him to come.'

What else was there to be done? There was nothing that she longed for at the moment except to see Will: the possibility of seeing him had thrust itself insistently between her and every other object; and yet she had a throbbing excitement like an alarm upon her – a sense that she was doing something daringly defiant for his sake.

When the little lady had trotted away on her mission, Dorothea stood in the middle of the library with her hands falling clasped before her, making no attempt to compose herself in an attitude of dignified unconsciousness. What she was least conscious of just then was her own body: she was thinking of what was likely to be in Will's mind, and of the hard feelings that others had had about him. How could any duty bind her to hardness? Resistance to unjust dispraise had mingled with her feeling for him from the very first, and now in the rebound of her heart after her anguish the resistance was stronger than ever. 'If I love him too much it is because he has been used so ill': there was a voice within her saying this to some imagined audience in the library, when the door was opened, and she saw Will before her.

She did not move, and he came towards her with more doubt and timidity in his face than she had ever seen before. He was in a state of uncertainty which made him afraid lest some look or word of his should condemn him to a new distance from her; and Dorothea was afraid of her own emotion. She looked as if there were a spell upon her, keeping her motionless and hindering her from unclasping her hands, while some intense, grave yearning was imprisoned within her eyes. Seeing that she did not put out her hand as usual, Will paused a yard from her and said with embarrassment, 'I am so grateful to you for seeing me.'

'I wanted to see you,' said Dorothea, having no other words at command. It did not occur to her to sit down, and Will did not give a cheerful interpretation to this queenly way of receiving him; but he went on to say what he had made up his mind to say.

'I fear you think me foolish and perhaps wrong for coming back so soon. I have been punished for my impatience. You know – everyone knows now – a painful story about my parentage. I knew of it before I went away, and I always meant to tell you of it if – if we ever met again.'

There was a slight movement in Dorothea, and she unclasped her hands, but immediately folded them over each other.

'But the affair is matter of gossip now,' Will continued. 'I wished you to know that something connected with it – something which happened before I went away – helped to bring me down here again. At least I thought it excused my coming. It was the idea of getting Bulstrode to apply some money to a public purpose – some money which he had thought of giving me. Perhaps it is rather to Bulstrode's credit that he privately offered me compensation for an old injury: he offered to give me a good income to make amends; but I suppose you know the disagreeable story?'

Will looked doubtfully at Dorothea, but his manner was gathering some of the defiant courage with which he always thought of this fact in his destiny. He added, 'You know that it must be altogether painful to me.'

'Yes – yes – I know,' said Dorothea, hastily.

'I did not choose to accept an income from such a source. I was sure that you would not think well of me if I did so,' said Will. Why should he mind saying anything of that sort to her now? She knew that he had avowed his love for her. 'I felt that' – he broke off, nevertheless.

'You acted as I should have expected you to act,' said Dorothea, her face brightening and her head becoming a little more erect on its beautiful stem.

'I did not believe that you would let any circumstance of my birth create a prejudice in you against me, though it was sure to do so in others,' said Will, shaking his head backward in his old way, and looking with a grave appeal into her eyes.

'If it were a new hardship it would be a new reason for me to cling to you,' said Dorothea, fervidly. 'Nothing could have changed me but – ' her heart was swelling, and it was difficult to go on; she made a great effort over herself to say in a low tremulous voice, 'but thinking that you were different – not so good as I had believed you to be.'

'You are sure to believe me better than I am in everything but one,' said Will, giving way to his own feeling in the evidence of hers. 'I mean, in my truth to you. When I thought you doubted of that, I didn't care about anything that was left. I thought it was all over with me, and there was nothing to try for – only things to endure.'

'I don't doubt you any longer,' said Dorothea, putting out her hand; a vague fear for him impelling her unutterable affection.

He took her hand and raised it to his lips with something like a sob. But he stood with his hat and gloves in the other hand, and might have done for the portrait of a Royalist. Still it was difficult to loose the hand, and Dorothea, withdrawing it in a confusion that distressed her, looked and moved away.

'See how dark the clouds have become, and how the trees are tossed,' she said, walking towards the window, yet speaking and moving with only a dim sense of what she was doing.

Will followed her at a little distance, and leaned against the tall back of a leather chair, on which he ventured now to lay his hat and gloves, and free himself from the intolerable durance of formality to which he had been for the first time condemned in Dorothea's presence. It must be confessed that he felt very happy at that moment leaning on the chair. He was not much afraid of anything that she might feel now.

They stood silent, not looking at each other, but looking at the evergreens which were being tossed, and were showing the pale underside of their leaves against the blackening sky. Will never enjoyed the prospect of a storm so much: it delivered him from the necessity of going away. Leaves and little branches were hurled about, and the thunder was getting nearer. The light was more and more sombre, but there came a flash of lightning which made them start and look at each other, and then smile. Dorothea began to say what she had been thinking of.

'That was a wrong thing for you to say, that you would have had nothing to try for. If we had lost our own chief good, other people's good would remain, and that is worth trying for. Some can be happy. I seemed to see that more clearly than ever, when I was the most wretched. I can hardly think how I could have borne the trouble, if that feeling had not come to me to make strength.'

'You have never felt the sort of misery I felt,' said Will; 'the misery of knowing that you must despise me.'

'But I have felt worse – it was worse to think ill – ' Dorothea had begun impetuously, but broke off.

Will coloured. He had the sense that whatever she said was uttered in the vision of a fatality that kept them apart. He was silent a moment, and then said passionately, 'We may at least have the comfort of speaking to each other without disguise. Since I must go away – since we must always be divided – you may think of me as one on the brink of the grave.'

While he was speaking there came a vivid flash of lightning which lit each of them up for the other – and the light seemed to be the terror of a hopeless love. Dorothea darted instantaneously from the window; Will followed her, seizing her hand with a spasmodic movement; and so they stood, with their hands clasped, like two children, looking out on the storm, while the thunder gave a tremendous crack and roll above them, and the rain began to pour down. Then they turned their faces towards each other, with the memory of his last words in them, and they did not loose each other's hands.

'There is no hope for me,' said Will. 'Even if you loved me as well as I love you – even if I were everything to you – I shall most likely always be very poor: on a sober calculation, one can count on nothing but a creeping lot. It is impossible for us ever to belong to each other. It is perhaps base of me to have asked for a word from you. I meant to go away into silence, but I have not been able to do what I meant.'

'Don't be sorry,' said Dorothea, in her clear tender tones. 'I would rather share all the trouble of our parting.'

Her lips trembled, and so did his. It was never known which lips were the first to move towards the other lips; but they kissed tremblingly, and then they moved apart.

The rain was dashing against the window-panes as if an angry spirit were within it, and behind it was the great swoop of the wind; it was one of those moments in which both the busy and the idle pause with a certain awe.

Dorothea sat down on the seat nearest to her, a long low ottoman in the middle of the room, and with her hands folded over each other on her lap, looked at the drear outer world. Will stood still an instant looking at her, then seated himself beside her, and laid his hand on hers, which turned itself upward to be clasped. They sat in that way without looking at each other, until the rain abated and began to fall in stillness. Each had been full of thoughts which neither of them could begin to utter.

But when the rain was quiet, Dorothea turned to look at Will. With passionate exclamation, as if some torture-screw were threatening him, he started up and said, 'It is impossible!'

He went and leaned on the back of the chair again, and seemed to be battling with his own anger, while she looked towards him sadly.

'It is as fatal as a murder or any other horror that divides people,' he burst out again; 'it is more intolerable – to have our life maimed by petty accidents.'

'No – don't say that – your life need not be maimed,' said Dorothea, gently.

'Yes, it must,' said Will, angrily. 'It is cruel of you to speak in that way – as if there were any comfort. You may see beyond the misery of it, but I don't. It is unkind – it is throwing back my love for you as if it were a trifle, to speak in that way in the face of the fact. We shall never be married.'

'Sometime – we might,' said Dorothea, in a trembling voice.

'When?' said Will, bitterly. 'What is the use of counting on any success of mine? It is a mere toss up whether I shall ever do more than keep myself decently, unless I choose to sell myself as a mere pen and a mouthpiece. I can see that clearly enough. I could not offer myself to any woman, even if she had no luxuries to renounce.'

There was silence. Dorothea's heart was full of something that she wanted to say, and yet the words were too difficult. She was wholly possessed by them: at that moment debate was mute within her. And it was very hard that she could not say what she wanted to say. Will was looking out of the window angrily. If he would have looked at her and not gone away from her side, she thought everything would have been easier. At last he turned, still resting against the chair, and stretching his hand automatically towards his hat, said with a sort of exasperation, 'Goodbye.'

'Oh, I cannot bear it – my heart will break,' said Dorothea, starting from her seat, the flood of her young passion bearing down all the obstructions which had kept her silent – the great tears rising and falling in an instant: 'I don't mind about poverty – I hate my wealth.'

In an instant Will was close to her and had his arms round her, but she drew her head back and held his away gently that she might go on speaking, her large tear-filled eyes looking at his very simply, while she said in a sobbing childlike way, 'We could live quite well on my own fortune – it is too much – seven hundred a year – I want so little – no new clothes – and I will learn what everything costs.'

Chapter 84

Though it be songe of old and yonge,
    That I sholde be to blame,
Theyrs be the charge, that spoke so large
    In hurtynge of my name.

                                    The Nut-Browne Mayde

It was just after the Lords had thrown out the Reform Bill: that explains how Mr Cadwallader came to be walking on the slope of the lawn near the great conservatory at Freshitt Hall, holding *The Times* in his hands behind him, while he talked with a trout-fisher's dispassionateness about the prospects of the country to Sir James Chettam. Mrs Cadwallader, the Dowager Lady Chettam, and Celia were sometimes seated on garden-chairs, sometimes walking to meet little Arthur, who was being drawn in his chariot, and, as became the infantine Buddha, was sheltered by his sacred umbrella with handsome silken fringe.

The ladies also talked politics, though more fitfully. Mrs Cadwallader was strong on the intended creation of peers: she had it for certain from her cousin that Truberry had gone over to the other side entirely at the instigation of his wife, who had scented peerages in the air from the very first introduction of the Reform question, and would sign her soul away to take precedence of her younger sister, who had married a baronet. Lady Chettam thought that such conduct was very reprehensible, and remembered that Mrs Truberry's mother was a Miss Walsingham of Melspring. Celia confessed it was nicer to be 'Lady' than 'Mrs', and that Dodo never minded about precedence if she could have her own way. Mrs Cadwallader held that it was a poor satisfaction to take precedence when everybody about you knew that you had not a drop of good blood in your veins; and Celia again, stopping to look at Arthur, said, 'It would be nice, though, if he were a Viscount – and his lordship's little tooth coming through! He might have been, if James had been an Earl.'

'My dear Celia,' said the Dowager, 'James's title is worth far more than any new earldom. I never wished his father to be anything else than Sir James.'

'Oh, I only meant about Arthur's little tooth,' said Celia, comfortably. 'But see, here is my uncle coming.'

She tripped off to meet her uncle, while Sir James and Mr Cadwallader came forward to make one group with the ladies. Celia had slipped her arm through her uncle's, and he patted her hand with a rather melancholy 'Well, my dear!' As they approached, it was evident that Mr Brooke was looking dejected, but this was fully accounted for by the state of politics; and as he was shaking hands all round without more greeting than a 'Well, you're all here, you know,' the Rector said, laughingly, 'Don't take the throwing out of the Bill so much to heart, Brooke; you've got all the riff-raff of the country on your side.'

'The Bill, eh? ah!' said Mr Brooke, with a mild distractedness of manner. 'Thrown out, you know, eh? The Lords are going too far, though. They'll have to pull up. Sad news, you know. I mean, here at home – sad news. But you must not blame me, Chettam.'

'What is the matter?' said Sir James. 'Not another gamekeeper shot, I hope? It's what I should expect, when a fellow like Trapping Bass is let off so easily.'

'Gamekeeper? No. Let us go in; I can tell you all in the house, you know,' said Mr Brooke, nodding at the Cadwalladers, to show that he included them in his confidence. 'As to poachers like Trapping Bass, you know, Chettam,' he continued, as they were entering, 'when you are a magistrate, you'll not find it so easy to commit. Severity is all very well, but it's a great deal easier when you've got somebody to do it for you. You have a soft place in your heart yourself, you know – you're not a Draco, a Jeffreys, that sort of thing.'

Mr Brooke was evidently in a state of nervous perturbation. When he had something painful to tell, it was usually his way to introduce it among a number of disjointed particulars, as if it were a medicine that would get a milder flavour by mixing. He continued his chat with Sir James about the poachers until they were all seated, and Mrs Cadwallader, impatient of this drivelling, said, 'I'm dying to know the sad news. The gamekeeper is not shot; that is settled. What is it, then?'

'Well, it's a very trying thing, you know,' said Mr Brooke. 'I'm glad you and the Rector are here; it's a family matter – but you will help us all to bear it, Cadwallader. I've got to break it to you, my dear.' Here Mr Brooke looked at Celia – 'You've no notion what it is, you know. And, Chettam, it will annoy you uncommonly – but you see you have not been able to hinder it, any more than I have. There's something singular in things: they came round, you know.'

'It must be about Dodo,' said Celia, who had been used to think of her sister as the dangerous part of the family machinery. She had seated herself on a low stool against her husband's knee.

'For God's sake let us hear what it is!' said Sir James.

'Well, you know, Chettam, I couldn't help Casaubon's will: it was a sort of will to make things worse.'

'Exactly,' said Sir James, hastily. 'But *what* is worse?'

'Dorothea is going to be married again, you know,' said Mr Brooke, nodding towards Celia, who immediately looked up at her husband with a frightened glance, and put her hand on his knee.

Sir James was almost white with anger, but he did not speak.

'Merciful heaven!' said Mrs Cadwallader. 'Not to young Ladislaw?'

Mr Brooke nodded, saying, 'Yes; to Ladislaw,' and then fell into a prudential silence.

'You see, Humphrey!' said Mrs Cadwallader, waving her arm towards her husband. 'Another time you will admit that I have some foresight; or rather you will contradict me and be just as blind as ever. You supposed that the young gentleman was gone out of the country.'

'So he might be, and yet come back,' said the Rector, quietly.

'When did you learn this?' said Sir James, not liking to hear anyone else speak, though finding it difficult to speak himself.

'Yesterday,' said Mr Brooke, meekly, 'I went to Lowick. Dorothea sent for me, you know. It had come about quite suddenly – neither of them had any idea two days ago – not any idea, you know. There's something singular in things. But Dorothea is quite determined – it is no use opposing. I put it strongly to her. I did my duty, Chettam. But she can act as she likes, you know.'

'It would have been better if I had called him out and shot him a year ago,' said Sir James, not from bloody-mindedness, but because he needed something strong to say.

'Really, James, that would have been very disagreeable,' said Celia.

'Be reasonable, Chettam. Look at the affair more quietly,' said Mr Cadwallader, sorry to see his good-natured friend so over-mastered by anger.

'That is not so very easy for a man of any dignity – with any sense of right – when the affair happens to be in his own family,' said Sir James, still in his white indignation. 'It is perfectly scandalous. If Ladislaw had had a spark of honour he would have gone out of the country at once, and never shown his face in it again. However, I am not surprised. The day after Casaubon's funeral I said what ought to be done. But I was not listened to.'

'You wanted what was impossible, you know, Chettam,' said Mr Brooke. 'You wanted him shipped off. I told you Ladislaw was not to be done as we liked with: he had his ideas. He was a remarkable fellow – I always said he was a remarkable fellow.'

'Yes,' said Sir James, unable to repress a retort, 'it is rather a pity you formed that high opinion of him. We are indebted to that for him being lodged in this neighbourhood. We are indebted to that for seeing a woman like Dorothea degrading herself by marrying him.' Sir James made little stoppages between his clauses, the words not coming easily. 'A man so marked out by her husband's will, that delicacy ought to have forbidden her from seeing him again – who takes her out of her proper rank – into poverty – has the meanness to accept such a sacrifice – has always had an objectionable position – a bad origin and, I *believe*, is a man of little principle and light character. That is my opinion,' Sir James ended emphatically, turning aside and crossing his leg.

'I pointed everything out to her,' said Mr Brooke, apologetically – 'I mean the poverty, and abandoning her position. I said, "My dear, you don't know what it is to live on seven hundred a-year, and have no carriage, and that kind of thing, and go amongst people who don't know who you are." I put it strongly to her. But I advise you to talk to Dorothea herself. The fact is, she has a dislike to Casaubon's property. You will hear what she says, you know.'

'No – excuse me – I shall not,' said Sir James, with more coolness. 'I cannot bear to see her again; it is too painful. It hurts me too much that a woman like Dorothea should have done what is wrong.'

'Be just, Chettam,' said the easy, large-lipped Rector, who objected to all this unnecessary discomfort. 'Mrs Casaubon may be acting imprudently: she is giving up a fortune for the sake of a man, and we men have so poor an opinion of each other that we can hardly call a woman wise who does that. But I think you should not condemn it as a wrong action, in the strict sense of the word.'

'Yes, I do,' answered Sir James. 'I think that Dorothea commits a wrong action in marrying Ladislaw.'

'My dear fellow, we are rather apt to consider an act wrong because it is unpleasant to us,' said the Rector, quietly. Like many men who take life easily, he had the knack of saying a home truth occasionally to those who felt themselves virtuously out of temper. Sir James took out his handkerchief and began to bite the corner.

'It is very dreadful of Dodo, though,' said Celia, wishing to justify her husband. 'She said she *never would* marry again – not anybody at all.'

'I heard her say the same thing myself,' said Lady Chettam, majestically, as if this were royal evidence.

'Oh, there is usually a silent exception in such cases,' said Mrs Cadwallader. 'The only wonder to me is, that any of you are surprised. You did nothing to hinder it. If you would have had Lord Triton down here to woo her with his philanthropy, he might have carried her off before the year was over. There was no safety in anything else. Mr Casaubon had prepared all this as beautifully as possible. He made himself disagreeable or it pleased God to make him so – and then he dared her to contradict him. It's the way to make any trumpery tempting, to ticket it at a high price in that way.'

'I don't know what you mean by wrong, Cadwallader,' said Sir James, still feeling a little stung, and turning round in his chair towards the Rector. 'He's not a man we can take into the family. At least I must speak for myself,' he continued, carefully keeping his eyes off Mr Brooke. 'I suppose others will find his society too pleasant to care about the propriety of the thing.'

'Well, you know, Chettam,' said Mr Brooke, good-humouredly, nursing his leg, 'I can't turn my back on Dorothea. I must be a father to her up to a certain point. I said, "My dear, I won't refuse to give you away." I had spoken strongly before. But I can cut off the entail, you know. It will cost money and be trouble-some; but I can do it, you know.'

Mr Brooke nodded at Sir James, and felt that he was both showing his own force of resolution and propitiating what was just in the Baronet's vexation. He had hit on a more ingenious mode of parrying than he was aware of. He had touched a motive of which Sir James was ashamed. The mass of his feeling about Dorothea's marriage to Ladislaw was due partly to excusable prejudice, or even justifiable opinion, partly to a jealous repugnance hardly less in Ladislaw's case than in Casaubon's. He was convinced that the marriage was a fatal one for Dorothea. But amid that mass ran a vein of which he was too good and honourable a man to like the avowal even to himself: it was undeniable that the union of the two estates – Tipton and Freshitt – lying charmingly within a ring-fence, was a prospect that flattered him for his son and heir. Hence when Mr Brooke noddingly appealed to that motive, Sir James felt a sudden embarrassment; there was a stoppage in his throat; he even blushed. He had found more words than usual in the first jet of his anger, but Mr Brooke's propitiation was more clogging to his tongue than Mr Cadwallader's caustic hint.

But Celia was glad to have room for speech after her uncle's suggestion of the marriage ceremony, and she said, though with as little eagerness of manner as if the question had turned on an invitation to dinner, 'Do you mean that Dodo is going to be married directly, uncle?'

'In three weeks, you know,' said Mr Brooke, helplessly. 'I can do nothing to hinder it, Cadwallader,' he added, turning for a little countenance towards the Rector, who said, 'I should not make any fuss about it. If she likes to be poor, that is her affair. Nobody would have said anything if she had married the young fellow because he was rich. Plenty of beneficed clergy are poorer than they will be. Here is Elinor,' continued the provoking husband; 'she vexed her friends by marrying me: I had hardly a thousand a-year – I was a lout – nobody could see anything in me – my shoes were not the right cut – all the men wondered how a woman could like me. Upon my word, I must take Ladislaw's part until I hear more harm of him.'

'Humphrey, that is all sophistry, and you know it,' said his wife. 'Everything is all one – that is the beginning and end with you. As if you had not been a Cadwallader! Does anyone suppose that I would have taken such a monster as you by any other name?'

'And a clergyman too,' observed Lady Chettam with approbation. 'Elinor cannot be said to have descended below her rank. It is difficult to say what Mr Ladislaw is, eh, James?'

Sir James gave a small grunt, which was less respectful than his usual mode of answering his mother. Celia looked up at him like a thoughtful kitten.

'It must be admitted that his blood is a frightful mixture!' said Mrs Cadwallader. 'The Casaubon cuttlefish fluid to begin with, and then a rebellious Polish fiddler or dancing-master, was it? and then an old clo – '

'Nonsense, Elinor,' said the Rector, rising. 'It is time for us to go.'

'After all, he is a pretty sprig,' said Mrs Cadwallader, rising too, and wishing to make amends. 'He is like the fine old Crichley portraits before the idiots came in.'

'I'll go with you,' said Mr Brooke, starting up with alacrity. 'You must all come and dine with me tomorrow, you know eh, Celia, my dear?'

'You will, James – won't you?' said Celia, taking her husband's hand.

'Oh, of course, if you like,' said Sir James, pulling down his waistcoat, but unable yet to adjust his face good-humouredly. 'That is to say, if it is not to meet anybody else.'

'No, no, no,' said Mr Brooke, understanding the condition.

'Dorothea would not come, you know, unless you had been to see her.'

When Sir James and Celia were alone, she said, 'Do you mind about my having the carriage to go to Lowick, James?'

'What, now, directly?' he answered, with some surprise.

'Yes, it is very important,' said Celia.

'Remember, Celia, I cannot see her,' said Sir James.

'Not if she gave up marrying?'

'What is the use of saying that? – however, I'm going to the stables. I'll tell Briggs to bring the carriage round.'

Celia thought it was of great use, if not to say that, at least to take a journey to Lowick in order to influence Dorothea's mind. All through their girlhood she had felt that she could act on her sister by a word judiciously placed – by opening a little window for the daylight of her own understanding to enter among the strange coloured lamps by which Dodo habitually saw. And Celia the matron naturally felt more able to advise her childless sister. How could anyone understand Dodo so well as Celia did, or love her so tenderly?

Dorothea, busy in her boudoir, felt a glow of pleasure at the sight of her sister so soon after the revelation of her intended marriage. She had prefigured to herself, even with exaggeration, the disgust of her friends, and she had even feared that Celia might be kept aloof from her.

'O Kitty, I am delighted to see you!' said Dorothea, putting her hands on Celia's shoulder, and beaming on her. 'I almost thought you would not come to me.'

'I have not brought Arthur, because I was in a hurry,' said Celia, and they sat down on two small chairs opposite each other, with their knees touching.

'You know, Dodo, it is very bad,' said Celia, in her placid guttural, looking as prettily free from humours as possible. 'You have disappointed us all so. And I can't think that it ever will be – you never can go and live in that way. And then there are all your plans! You never can have thought of that. James would have taken any trouble for you, and you might have gone on all your life doing what you liked.'

'On the contrary, dear,' said Dorothea, 'I never could do anything that I liked. I have never carried out any plan yet.'

'Because you always wanted things that wouldn't do. But other plans would have come. And how *can* you marry Mr Ladislaw, that we none of us ever thought you *could* marry? It shocks James so dreadfully. And then it is all so different from what you have always been. You would have Mr Casaubon because he had such a great soul, and was so old and dismal and learned; and now, to think of marrying Mr Ladislaw, who has got no estate or anything. I suppose it is because you must be making yourself uncomfortable in some way or other.'

Dorothea laughed.

'Well, it is very serious, Dodo,' said Celia, becoming more impressive. 'How will you live? and you will go away among queer people. And I shall never see you – and you won't mind about little Arthur – and I thought you always would –'

Celia's rare tears had got into her eyes, and the corners of her mouth were agitated.

'Dear Celia,' said Dorothea, with tender gravity, 'if you don't ever see me, it will not be my fault.'

'Yes, it will,' said Celia, with the same touching distortion of her small features. 'How can I come to you or have you with me when James can't bear it? – that is because he thinks it is not right – he thinks you are so wrong, Dodo. But you always were wrong; only I can't help loving you. And nobody can think where you will live: where can you go?'

'I am going to London,' said Dorothea.

'How can you always live in a street? And you will be so poor. I could give you half my things, only how can I, when I never see you?'

'Bless you, Kitty,' said Dorothea, with gentle warmth. 'Take comfort: perhaps James will forgive me sometime.'

'But it would be much better if you would not be married,' said Celia, drying her eyes, and returning to her argument; 'then there would be nothing uncomfortable. And you would not do what nobody thought you could do. James always said you ought to be a queen; but this is not at all being like a queen. You know what mistakes you have always been making, Dodo, and this is another. Nobody thinks Mr Ladislaw a proper husband for you. And you *said* you would never be married again.'

'It is quite true that I might be a wiser person, Celia,' said Dorothea, 'and that I might have done something better, if I had been better. But this is what I am going to do. I have promised to marry Mr Ladislaw; and I am going to marry him.'

The tone in which Dorothea said this was a note that Celia had long learned to recognise. She was silent, a few moments, and then said, as if she had dismissed all contest, 'Is he very fond of you, Dodo?'

'I hope so. I am very fond of him.'

'That is nice,' said Celia, comfortably. 'Only I would rather you had such a sort of husband as James is, with a place very near, that I could drive to.'

Dorothea smiled, and Celia looked rather meditative. Presently she said, 'I cannot think how it all came about.' Celia thought it would be pleasant to hear the story.

'I dare say not,' said Dorothea, pinching her sister's chin. 'If you knew how it came about, it would not seem wonderful to you.'

'Can't you tell me?' said Celia, settling her arms cozily.

'No, dear, you would have to feel with me, else you would never know.'

Chapter 85

Then went the jury out, whose names were Mr Blindman, Mr No-good, Mr Malice, Mr Love-lust, Mr Live-loose, Mr Heady, Mr Highmind, Mr Enmity, Mr Liar, Mr Cruelty, Mr Hate-light, Mr Implacable, who everyone gave in his private verdict against him among themselves, and afterwards unanimously concluded to bring him in guilty before the judge. And first among themselves, Mr Blindman, the foreman, said, I see clearly that this man is a heretic. Then said Mr No-good, Away with such a fellow from the earth! Ay, said Mr Malice, for I hate the very look of him. Then said Mr Love-lust, I could never endure him. Nor I, said Mr Live-loose; for he would be always condemning my way. Hang him, hang him, said Mr Heady. A sorry scrub, said Mr Highmind. My heart riseth against him, said Mr Enmity. He is a rogue, said Mr Liar. Hanging is too good for him, said Mr Cruelty. Let us despatch him out of the way, said Mr Hate-light. Then said Mr Implacable, Might I have all the world given me, I could not be reconciled to him: therefore let us forthwith bring him in guilty of death.

JOHN BUNYAN, *Pilgrim's Progress*

When immortal Bunyan makes his picture of the persecuting passions bringing in their verdict of guilty, who pities Faithful? That is a rare and blessed lot which some greatest men have not attained, to know ourselves guiltless before a condemning crowd – to be sure that what we are denounced for is solely the good in us. The pitiable lot is that of the man who could not call himself a martyr even though he were to persuade himself that the men who stoned him were but ugly passions incarnate – who knows that he is stoned, not for professing the Right, but for not being the man he professed to be.

This was the consciousness that Bulstrode was withering under while he made his preparations for departing from Middlemarch, and going to end his stricken life in that sad refuge, the indifference of new faces. The duteous merciful constancy of his wife had delivered him from one dread, but it could not hinder her presence from being still a tribunal before which he shrank from confession and desired advocacy. His equivocations with himself about the death of Raffles had sustained the conception of an Omniscience whom he prayed to, yet he had a terror upon him which would not let him expose them to judgement by a full confession to his wife: the acts which he had washed and diluted with inward argument and motive, and for which it seemed comparatively easy to win invisible pardon – what name would she call them by? That she should ever silently call his acts Murder was what he could not bear. He felt shrouded by her doubt: he got strength to face her from the sense that she could not yet feel warranted in pronouncing that worst condemnation on him. Sometime, perhaps – when he was dying – he would tell her all: in the deep shadow of that time, when she held his hand in the gathering darkness, she might listen without recoiling from his touch. Perhaps: but concealment had been the habit of his life, and the impulse to confession had no power against the dread of a deeper humiliation.

He was full of timid care for his wife, not only because he deprecated any harshness of judgement from her, but because he felt a deep distress at the sight of her suffering. She had sent her daughters away to board at a school on the coast, that his crisis might be hidden from them as far as possible. Set free by their absence from the intolerable necessity of accounting for her grief or of beholding their frightened wonder, she could live unconstrainedly with the sorrow that was every day streaking her hair with whiteness and making her eyelids languid.

'Tell me anything that you would like to have me do, Harriet,' Bulstrode had said to her; 'I mean with regard to arrangements of property. It is my intention not to sell the land I possess in this neighbourhood, but to leave it to you as a safe provision. If you have any wish on such subjects, do not conceal it from me.'

A few days afterwards, when she had returned from a visit to her brother's, she began to speak to her husband on a subject which had for some time been in her mind.

'I *should* like to do something for my brother's family, Nicholas; and I think we are bound to make some amends to Rosamond and her husband. Walter says Mr Lydgate must leave the town, and his practice is almost good for nothing, and they have very little left to settle anywhere with. I would rather do without something for ourselves, to make some amends to my poor brother's family.'

Mrs Bulstrode did not wish to go nearer to the facts than in the phrase 'make some amends'; knowing that her husband must understand her. He had a particular reason, which she was not aware of, for wincing under her suggestion. He hesitated before he said, 'It is not possible to carry out your wish in the way you propose, my dear. Mr Lydgate has virtually rejected any further service from me. He has returned the thousand pounds which I lent him. Mrs Casaubon advanced him the sum for that purpose. Here is his letter.'

The letter seemed to cut Mrs Bulstrode severely. The mention of Mrs Casaubon's loan seemed a reflection of that public feeling which held it a matter of course that everyone would avoid a connection with her husband. She was silent for some time; and the tears fell one after the other, her chin trembling as she wiped them away. Bulstrode, sitting opposite her, ached at the sight of that grief-worn face, which two months before had been bright and blooming. It had aged to keep sad company with his own withered features. Urged into some effort at comforting her, he said, 'There is another means, Harriet, by which I might do a service to your brother's family, if you like to act in it. And it would, I think, be beneficial to you: it would be an advantageous way of managing the land which I mean to be yours.'

She looked attentive.

'Garth once thought of undertaking the management of Stone Court in order to place your nephew Fred there. The stock was to remain as it is, and they were to pay a certain share of the profits instead of an ordinary rent. That would be a desirable beginning for the young man, in conjunction with his employment under Garth. Would it be a satisfaction to you?'

'Yes, it would,' said Mrs Bulstrode, with some return of energy. 'Poor Walter is so cast down: I would try anything in my power to do him some good before I go away. We have always been brother and sister.'

'You must make the proposal to Garth yourself, Harriet,' said Mr Bulstrode, not liking what he had to say, but desiring the end he had in view, for other reasons besides the consolation of his wife. 'You must state to him that the land is virtually yours, and that he need have no transactions with me. Communications can be made through Standish. I mention this, because Garth gave up being my agent. I can put into your hands a paper which he himself drew up, stating conditions; and you can propose his renewed acceptance of them. I think it is not unlikely that he will accept when you propose the thing for the sake of your nephew.'

Chapter 86

Le coeur se sature d'amour comme d'un sel divin qui le conserve; de là l'incorruptible adhérence de ceux qui se sont aimés dès l'aube de la vie, et la fraîcheur des vieilles amours prolongés. Il existe un embaumement d'amour. C'est de Daphnis et Chlöe que sont faits Philémon et Baucis. Cette vieillesse-là, ressemblance du soir avec l'aurore.

VICTOR HUGO, *L'Homme qui rit*

Mrs Garth, hearing Caleb enter the passage about teatime, opened the parlour-door and said, 'There you are, Caleb. Have you had your dinner?' (Mr Garth's meals were much subordinated to 'business'.)

'Oh yes, a good dinner – cold mutton and I don't know what. Where is Mary?'

'In the garden with Letty, I think.'

'Fred is not come yet?'

'No. Are you going out again without taking tea, Caleb?' said Mrs Garth, seeing that her absent-minded husband was putting on again the hat which he had just taken off.

'No, no; I'm only going to Mary a minute.'

Mary was in a grassy corner of the garden, where there was a swing loftily hung between two pear trees. She had a pink kerchief tied over her head, making a little poke to shade her eyes from the level sunbeams, while she was giving a glorious swing to Letty, who laughed and screamed wildly.

Seeing her father, Mary left the swing and went to meet him, pushing back the pink kerchief and smiling afar off at him with the involuntary smile of loving pleasure.

'I came to look for you, Mary,' said Mr Garth. 'Let us walk about a bit.'

Mary knew quite well that her father had something particular to say: his eyebrows made their pathetic angle, and there was a tender gravity in his voice: these things had been signs to her when she was Letty's age. She put her arm within his, and they turned by the row of nut trees.

'It will be a sad while before you can be married, Mary,' said her father, not looking at her, but at the end of the stick which he held in his other hand.

'Not a sad while, father – I mean to be merry,' said Mary, laughingly. 'I have been single and merry for four-and-twenty years and more: I suppose it will not be quite as long again as that.' Then, after a little pause, she said, more gravely, bending her face before her father's, 'If you are contented with Fred?'

Caleb screwed up his mouth and turned his head aside wisely.

'Now, father, you did praise him last Wednesday. You said he had an uncommon notion of stock, and a good eye for things.'

'Did I?' said Caleb, rather slyly.

'Yes, I put it all down, and the date, *anno Domini*, and everything,' said Mary. 'You like things to be neatly booked. And then his behaviour to you, father, is really good; he has a deep respect for you; and it is impossible to have a better temper than Fred has.'

'Ay, ay; you want to coax me into thinking him a fine match.'

'No, indeed, father. I don't love him because he is a fine match.'

'What for, then?'

'Oh, dear, because I have always loved him. I should never like scolding anyone else so well; and that is a point to be thought of in a husband.'

'Your mind is quite settled, then, Mary?' said Caleb, returning to his first tone. 'There's no other wish come into it since things have been going on as they have been of late?' (Caleb meant a great deal in that vague phrase;) 'because, better late than never. A woman must not force her heart – she'll do a man no good by that.'

'My feelings have not changed, father,' said Mary, calmly. 'I shall be constant to Fred as long as he is constant to me. I don't think either of us could spare the other, or like anyone else better, however much we might admire them. It would make too great a difference to us – like seeing all the old places altered, and changing the name for everything. We must wait for each other a long while; but Fred knows that.'

Instead of speaking immediately, Caleb stood still and screwed his stick on the grassy walk. Then he said, with emotion in his voice, 'Well, I've got a bit of news. What do you think of Fred going to live at Stone Court, and managing the land there?'

'How can that ever be, father?' said Mary, wonderingly.

'He would manage it for his aunt Bulstrode. The poor woman has been to me begging and praying. She wants to do the lad good, and it might be a fine thing for him. With saving, he might gradually buy the stock, and he has a turn for farming.'

'Oh Fred would be so happy? It is too good to believe.'

'Ah, but mind you,' said Caleb, turning his head warningly, 'I must take it on *my* shoulders, and be responsible, and see after everything; and that will grieve your mother a bit, though she mayn't say so. Fred had need be careful.'

'Perhaps it is too much, father,' said Mary, checked in her joy. 'There would be no happiness in bringing you any fresh trouble.'

'Nay, nay; work is my delight, child, when it doesn't vex your mother. And then, if you and Fred get married,' here Caleb's voice shook just perceptibly, 'he'll be steady and saving; and you've got your mother's cleverness, and mine too, in a woman's sort of way; and you'll keep him in order. He'll be coming by and by, so I wanted to tell you first, because I think you'd like to tell *him* by yourselves. After that, I could talk it well over with him, and we could go into business and the nature of things.'

'Oh, you dear good father!' cried Mary, putting her hands round her father's neck, while he bent his head placidly, willing to be caressed. 'I wonder if any other girl thinks her father the best man in the world!'

'Nonsense, child; you'll think your husband better.'

'Impossible,' said Mary, relapsing into her usual tone; 'husbands are an inferior class of men, who require keeping in order.'

When they were entering the house with Letty, who had run to join them, Mary saw Fred at the orchard-gate, and went to meet him.

'What fine clothes you wear, you extravagant youth!' said Mary, as Fred stood still and raised his hat to her with playful formality. 'You are not learning economy.'

'Now that is too bad, Mary,' said Fred. 'Just look at the edges of these coat-cuffs! It is only by dint of good brushing that I look respectable. I am saving up three suits – one for a wedding-suit.'

'How very droll you will look! – like a gentleman in an old fashion-book.'

'Oh no. They will keep two years.'

'Two years! be reasonable, Fred,' said Mary, turning to walk. 'Don't encourage flattering expectations.'

'Why not? One lives on them better than on unflattering ones. If we can't be married in two years, the truth will be quite bad enough when it comes.'

'I have heard a story of a young gentleman who once encouraged flattering expectations, and they did him harm.'

'Mary, if you've got something discouraging to tell me, I shall bolt; I shall go into the house to Mr Garth. I am out of spirits. My father is so cut up – home is not like itself. I can't bear any more bad news.'

'Should you call it bad news to be told that you were to live at Stone Court, and manage the farm, and be remarkably prudent, and save money every year till all the stock and furniture were your own, and you were a distinguished agricultural character, as Mr Borthrop Trumbull says – rather stout, I fear, and with the Greek and Latin sadly weather-worn?'

'You don't mean anything except nonsense, Mary?' said Fred, colouring slightly nevertheless.

'That is what my father has just told me of as what may happen, and he never talks nonsense,' said Mary, looking up at Fred now, while he grasped her hand as they walked, till it rather hurt her; but she would not complain.

'Oh, I could be a tremendously good fellow then, Mary, and we could be married directly.'

'Not so fast, sir; how do you know that I would not rather defer our marriage for some years? That would leave you time to misbehave, and then if I liked someone else better, I should have an excuse for jilting you.'

'Pray don't joke, Mary,' said Fred, with strong feeling. 'Tell me seriously that all this is true, and that you are happy because of it – because you love me best.'

'It is all true, Fred, and I am happy because of it – because I love you best,' said Mary, in a tone of obedient recitation.

They lingered on the doorstep under the steep-roofed porch, and Fred almost in a whisper said,, 'When we were first engaged, with the umbrella-ring, Mary, you used to – '

The spirit of joy began to laugh more decidedly in Mary's eyes, but the fatal Ben came running to the door with Brownie yapping behind him, and, bouncing against them, said, 'Fred and Mary! are you ever coming in? – or may I eat your cake?'

Finale

Every limit is a beginning as well as an ending. Who can quit young lives after being long in company with them, and not desire to know what befell them in their after-years? For the fragment of a life, however typical, is not the sample of an even web: promises may not be kept, and an ardent outset may be followed by declension; latent powers may find their long-waited opportunity; a past error may urge a grand retrieval.

Marriage, which has been the bourne of so many narratives, is still a great beginning, as it was to Adam and Eve, who kept their honeymoon in Eden, but had their first little one among the thorns and thistles of the wilderness. It is still the beginning of the home epic; the gradual conquest or irremediable loss of that complete union which makes the advancing years a climax, and age the harvest of sweet memories in common.

Some set out, like Crusaders of old, with a glorious equipment of hope and enthusiasm, and get broken by the way, wanting patience with each other and the world.

All who have cared for Fred Vincy and Mary Garth will like to know that these two made no such failure, but achieved a solid mutual happiness. Fred surprised his neighbours in various ways. He became rather distinguished in his side of the county as a theoretic and practical farmer, and produced a work on the *Cultivation of Green Crops and the Economy of Cattle-Feeding* which won him high congratulations at agricultural meetings. In Middlemarch admiration was more reserved: most persons there were inclined to believe that the merit of Fred's authorship was due to his wife, since they had never expected Fred Vincy to write on turnips and mangelwurzel.

But when Mary wrote a little book for her boys, called *Stories of Great Men, taken from Plutarch*, and had it printed and published by Gripp & Co., Middlemarch, everyone in the town was willing to give the credit of this work to Fred, observing that he had been to the University, 'where the ancients were studied', and might have been a clergyman if he had chosen.

In this way it was made clear that Middlemarch had never been deceived, and that there was no need to praise anybody for writing a book, since it was always done by somebody else.

Moreover, Fred remained unswervingly steady. Some years after his marriage he told Mary that his happiness was half owing to Farebrother, who gave him a strong pull-up at the right moment. I cannot say that he was never again misled by his hopefulness: the yield of crops or the profits of a cattle sale usually fell below his estimate; and he was always prone to believe that he could make money by the purchase of a horse which turned out badly – though this, Mary observed, was of course the fault of the horse, not of Fred's judgement. He kept his love of horsemanship, but he rarely allowed himself a day's hunting; and when he did so, it was remarkable that he submitted to be laughed at for cowardliness at the fences, seeming to see Mary and the boys sitting on the five-barred gate, or showing their curly heads between hedge and ditch.

There were three boys: Mary was not discontented that she brought forth men-children only; and when Fred wished to have a girl like her, she said, laughingly, 'That would be too great a trial to your mother.' Mrs Vincy in her declining years, and in the diminished lustre of her housekeeping, was much comforted by her perception that two at least of Fred's boys were real Vincys, and did not 'feature the Garths'. But Mary secretly rejoiced that the youngest of the three was very much what her father must have been when he wore a round jacket, and showed a marvellous nicety of aim in playing at marbles, or in throwing stones to bring down the mellow pears.

Ben and Letty Garth, who were uncle and aunt before they were well in their teens, disputed much as to whether nephews or nieces were more desirable; Ben contending that it was clear girls were good for less than boys, else they would not be always in petticoats, which showed how little they were meant for: whereupon Letty, who argued much from books, got angry in replying that God made coats of skins for both Adam and Eve alike – also it occurred to her that in the East the men too wore petticoats. But this latter argument, obscuring the majesty of the former, was one too many, for Ben answered contempt-uously, 'The more spooneys they!' and immediately appealed to his mother whether boys were not better than girls. Mrs Garth pronounced that both were alike naughty, but that boys were undoubtedly stronger, could run faster, and throw with more precision to a greater distance. With this oracular sentence Ben was well satisfied, not minding the naughtiness; but Letty took it ill, her feeling of superiority being stronger than her muscles.

Fred never became rich – his hopefulness had not led him to expect that; but he gradually saved enough to become owner of the stock and furniture at Stone Court, and the work which Mr Garth put into his hands carried him in plenty through those 'bad times' which are always present with farmers. Mary, in her matronly days, became as solid in figure as her mother; but, unlike her, gave the boys little formal teaching, so that Mrs Garth was alarmed lest they should never be well grounded in grammar and geography. Nevertheless, they were found quite forward enough when they went to school; perhaps, because they had liked nothing so well as being with their mother. When Fred was riding home on winter evenings he had a pleasant vision beforehand of the bright hearth in the wainscoted parlour, and was sorry for other men who could not have Mary for their wife; especially for Mr Farebrother. 'He was ten times worthier of you than I was,' Fred could now say to her, magnanimously. 'To be sure he was,' Mary answered; 'and for that reason he could do better without me. But you – I shudder to think what you would have been – a curate in debt for horse-hire and cambric pocket-handkerchiefs!'

On enquiry it might possibly be found that Fred and Mary still inhabit Stone Court – that the creeping plants still cast the foam of their blossoms over the fine stone walls into the field where the walnut trees stand in stately row – and that on sunny days the two lovers who were first engaged with the umbrella-ring may be seen in white-haired placidity at the open window from which Mary Garth, in the days of old Peter Featherstone, had often been ordered to look out for Mr Lydgate.

Lydgate's hair never became white. He died when he was only fifty, leaving his wife and children provided for by a heavy insurance on his life. He had gained an excellent practice, alternating, according to the season, between London and a Continental bathing-place; having written a treatise on Gout, a disease which has a good deal of wealth on its side. His skill was relied on by many paying patients, but he always regarded himself as a failure: he had not done what he once meant to do. His acquaintances thought him enviable to have so charming a wife, and nothing happened to shake their opinion. Rosamond never committed a second compromising indiscretion. She simply continued to be mild in her temper, inflexible in her judgement, disposed to admonish her husband, and able to frustrate him by stratagem. As the years went on he opposed her less and less, whence Rosamond concluded that he had learned the value of her opinion; on the other hand, she had a more thorough conviction of his talents now that he gained a good income, and instead of the threatened cage in Bride Street provided one all flowers and gilding, fit for the bird of paradise that she resembled. In brief, Lydgate was what is called a successful man. But he died prematurely of diphtheria, and Rosamond afterwards married an elderly and wealthy physician, who took kindly to her four children. She made a very pretty show with her daughters, driving out in her carriage, and often spoke of her happiness as 'a reward' – she did not say for what, but probably she meant that it was a reward for her patience with Tertius, whose temper never became faultless, and to the last occasionally let slip a bitter speech which was more memorable than the signs he made of his repentance. He once called her his basil plant; and when she asked for an explanation, said that basil was a plant which had flourished wonderfully on a murdered man's brains. Rosamond had a placid but strong answer to such speeches. Why then had he chosen her? It was a pity he had not had Mrs Ladislaw, whom he was always praising and placing above her. And thus the conversation ended with the advantage on Rosamond's side. But it would be unjust not to tell, that she never uttered a word in depreciation of Dorothea, keeping in religious remembrance the generosity which had come to her aid in the sharpest crisis of her life.

Dorothea herself had no dreams of being praised above other women, feeling that there was always something better which she might have done, if she had only been better and known better. Still, she never repented that she had given up position and fortune to marry Will Ladislaw, and he would have held it the greatest shame as well as sorrow to him if she had repented. They were bound to each other by a love stronger than any impulses which could have marred it. No life would have been possible to Dorothea which was not filled with emotion, and she had now a life filled also with a beneficent activity which she had not the doubtful pains of discovering and marking out for herself. Will became an ardent public man, working well in those times when reforms were begun with a young hopefulness of immediate good which has been much checked in our days, and getting at last returned to Parliament by a constituency who paid his expenses. Dorothea could have liked nothing better, since wrongs existed, than that her husband should be in the thick of a struggle against them, and that she should give him wifely help. Many who knew her, thought it a pity that so substantive and rare a creature should have been absorbed into the life of another, and be only known in a certain circle as a wife and mother. But no one stated exactly what else that was in her power she ought rather to have done – not even Sir James Chettam, who went no further than the negative prescription that she ought not to have married Will Ladislaw.

But this opinion of his did not cause a lasting alienation; and the way in which the family was made whole again was characteristic of all concerned. Mr Brooke could not resist the pleasure of corresponding with Will and Dorothea; and one morning when his pen had been remarkably fluent on the prospects of Municipal Reform, it ran off into an invitation to the Grange, which, once written, could not be done away with at less cost than the sacrifice (hardly to be conceived) of the whole valuable letter. During the months of this correspondence Mr Brooke had continually, in his talk with Sir James Chettam, been presupposing or hinting that the intention of cutting off the entail was still maintained; and the day on which his pen gave the daring invitation, he went to Freshitt expressly to intimate that he had a stronger sense than ever of the reasons for taking that energetic step as a precaution against any mixture of low blood in the heir of the Brookes.

But that morning something exciting had happened at the Hall. A letter had come to Celia which made her cry silently as she read it; and when Sir James, unused to see her in tears, asked anxiously what was the matter, she burst out in a wail such as he had never heard from her before.

'Dorothea has a little boy. And you will not let me go and see her. And I am sure she wants to see me. And she will not know what to do with the baby – she will do wrong things with it. And they thought she would die. It is very dreadful! Suppose it had been me and little Arthur, and Dodo had been hindered from coming to see me! I wish you would be less unkind, James!'

'Good heavens, Celia!' said Sir James, much wrought upon, 'what do you wish? I will do anything you like. I will take you to town tomorrow if you wish it.' And Celia did wish it.

It was after this that Mr Brooke came, and meeting the Baronet in the grounds, began to chat with him in ignorance of the news, which Sir James for some reason did not care to tell him immediately. But when the entail was touched on in the usual way, he said, 'My dear sir, it is not for me to dictate to you, but for my part I would let that alone. I would let things remain as they are.'

Mr Brooke felt so much surprise that he did not at once find out how much he was relieved by the sense that he was not expected to do anything in particular.

Such being the bent of Celia's heart, it was inevitable that Sir James should consent to a reconciliation with Dorothea and her husband. Where women love each other, men learn to smother their mutual dislike. Sir James never liked Ladislaw, and Will always preferred to have Sir James's company mixed with another kind: they were on a footing of reciprocal tolerance which was made quite easy only when Dorothea and Celia were present.

It became an understood thing that Mr and Mrs Ladislaw should pay at least two visits during the year to the Grange, and there came gradually a small row of cousins at Freshitt who enjoyed playing with the two cousins visiting Tipton as much as if the blood of these cousins had been less dubiously mixed.

Mr Brooke lived to a good old age, and his estate was inherited by Dorothea's son, who might have represented Middlemarch, but declined, thinking that his opinions had less chance of being stifled if he remained out of doors.

Sir James never ceased to regard Dorothea's second marriage as a mistake; and indeed this remained the tradition concerning it in Middlemarch, where she was spoken of to a younger generation as a fine girl who married a sickly clergyman, old enough to be her father, and in little more than a year after his death gave up her estate to marry his cousin – young enough to have been his son, with no property, and not well-born. Those who had not seen anything of Dorothea usually observed that she could not have been 'a nice woman', else she would not have married either the one or the other.

Certainly those determining acts of her life were not ideally beautiful. They were the mixed result of a young and noble impulse struggling amidst the conditions of an imperfect social state, in which great feelings will often take the aspect of error, and great faith the aspect of illusion. For there is no creature whose inward being is so strong that it is not greatly determined by what lies outside it. A new Theresa will hardly have the opportunity of reforming a conventual life, any more than a new Antigone will spend her heroic piety in daring all for the sake of a brother's burial: the medium in which their ardent deeds took shape is forever gone. But we insignificant people with our daily words and acts are preparing the lives of many Dorotheas, some of which may present a far sadder sacrifice than that of the Dorothea whose story we know.

Her finely-touched spirit had still its fine issues, though they were not widely visible. Her full nature, like that river of which Cyrus broke the strength, spent itself in channels which had no great name on the earth. But the effect of her being on those around her was incalculably diffusive: for the growing good of the world is partly dependent on unhistoric acts; and that things are not so ill with you and me as they might have been, is half owing to the number who lived faithfully a hidden life, and rest in unvisited tombs.

THE MILL ON THE FLOSS

The Mill on the Floss

A novel by
GEORGE ELIOT
first published in 1860

Contents

BOOK FIRST

Boy and Girl

CHAPTER I

Outside Dorlcote Mill

A wide plain, where the broadening Floss hurries on between its green banks to the sea, and the loving tide, rushing to meet it, checks its passage with an impetuous embrace. On this mighty tide the black ships – laden with the fresh-scented fir-planks, with rounded sacks of oil-bearing seed, or with the dark glitter of coal – are borne along to the town of St Ogg's, which shows its aged, fluted red roofs and the broad gables of its wharves between the low wooded hill and the river brink, tinging the water with a soft purple hue under the transient glance of this February sun. Far away on each hand stretch the rich pastures, and the patches of dark earth, made ready for the seed of broad-leaved green crops, or touched already with the tint of the tender-bladed autumn-sown corn. There is a remnant still of the last year's golden clusters of beehive ricks rising at intervals beyond the hedgerows; and everywhere the hedgerows are studded with trees: the distant ships seem to be lifting their masts and stretching their red-brown sails close among the branches of the spreading ash. Just by the red-roofed town the tributary Ripple flows with a lively current into the Floss. How lovely the little river is, with its dark, changing wavelets! It seems to me like a living companion while I wander along the bank and listen to its low placid voice, as to the voice of one who is deaf and loving. I remember those large dipping willows. I remember the stone bridge.

And this is Dorlcote Mill. I must stand a minute or two here on the bridge and look at it, though the clouds are threatening, and it is far on in the afternoon. Even in this leafless time of departing February it is pleasant to look at – perhaps the chill damp season adds a charm to the trimly-kept, comfortable dwelling-house, as old as the elms and chestnuts that shelter it from the northern blast. The stream is brimful now, and lies high in this little withy plantation, and half drowns the grassy fringe of the croft in front of the house. As I look at the full stream, the vivid grass, the delicate bright-green powder softening the outline of the great trunks and branches that gleam from under the bare purple boughs, I am in love with moistness, and envy the white ducks that are dipping their heads far into the water here among the withes, unmindful of the awkward appearance they make in the drier world above.

The rush of the water, and the booming of the mill, bring a dreamy deafness, which seems to heighten the peacefulness of the scene. They are like a great curtain of sound, shutting one out from the world beyond. And now there is the thunder of the huge covered waggon coming home with sacks of grain. That honest waggoner is thinking of his dinner, getting sadly dry in the oven at this late hour; but he will not touch it till he has fed his horses, – the strong, submissive, meek-eyed beasts, who, I fancy, are looking mild reproach at him from between their blinkers, that he should crack his whip at them in that awful manner, as if they needed that hint! See how they stretch their shoulders up the slope towards the bridge, with all the more energy because they are so near home. Look at their grand shaggy feet that seem to grasp the firm earth, at the patient strength of their necks, bowed under the heavy collar, at the mighty muscles of their struggling haunches! I should like well to hear them neigh over their hardly-earned feed of corn, and see them, with their moist necks freed from the harness, dipping their eager nostrils into the muddy pond. Now they are on the bridge, and down they go again at a swifter pace, and the arch of the covered waggon disappears at the turning behind the trees.

Now I can turn my eyes towards the mill again, and watch the unresting wheel sending out its diamond jets of water. That little girl is watching it too: she has been standing on just the same spot at the edge of the water ever since I paused on the bridge. And that queer white cur with the brown ear seems to be leaping and barking in ineffectual remonstrance with the wheel; perhaps he is jealous, because his playfellow in the beaver bonnet is so rapt in its movement. It is time the little playfellow went in, I think; and there is a very bright fire to tempt her: the red light shines out under the deepening grey of the sky. It is time, too, for me to leave off resting my arms on the cold stone of this bridge . . .

Ah, my arms are really benumbed. I have been pressing my elbows on the arms of my chair, and dreaming that I was standing on the bridge in front of Dorlcote Mill, as it looked one February afternoon many years ago. Before I dozed off, I was going to tell you what Mr and Mrs Tulliver were talking about, as they sat by the bright fire in the left-hand parlour, on that very afternoon I have been dreaming of.

CHAPTER 2

Mr Tulliver, of Dorlcote Mill, Declares his Resolution about Tom

'What I want, you know,' said Mr Tulliver – 'what I want is to give Tom a good eddication; an eddication as'll be a bread to him. That was what I was thinking of when I gave notice for him to leave th' academy at Ladyday. I mean to put him to a downright good school at Midsummer. The two years at th' academy 'ud ha' done well enough, if I'd meant to make a miller and farmer of him, for he's had a fine sight more schoolin' nor I ever got: all the learnin' *my* father ever paid for was a bit o' birch at one end and the alphabet at th' other. But I should like Tom to be a bit of a scholard, so as he might be up to the tricks o' these fellows as talk fine and write with a flourish. It 'ud be a help to me wi' these lawsuits, and arbitrations, and things. I wouldn't make a downright lawyer o' the lad – I should be sorry for him to be a raskill – but a sort o' engineer, or a surveyor, or an auctioneer and vallyer, like Riley, or one o' them smartish businesses as are all profits and no outlay, only for a big watch-chain and a high stool. They're pretty nigh all one, and they're not far off being even wi' the law, I believe; for Riley looks Lawyer Wakem i' the face as hard as one cat looks another. *He's* none frightened at him.'

Mr Tulliver was speaking to his wife, a blond comely woman in a fan-shaped cap (I am afraid to think how long it is since fan-shaped caps were worn – they must be so near coming in again. At that time, when Mrs Tulliver was nearly forty, they were new at St Ogg's, and considered sweet things).

'Well, Mr Tulliver, you know best: *I've* no objections. But hadn't I better kill a couple o' fowl and have th' aunts and uncles to dinner next week, so as you may hear what sister Glegg and sister Pullet have got to say about it? There's a couple o' fowl *wants* killing!'

'You may kill every fowl i' the yard, if you like, Bessy; but I shall ask neither aunt nor uncle what I'm to do wi' my own lad,' said Mr Tulliver, defiantly.

'Dear heart!' said Mrs Tulliver, shocked at this sanguinary rhetoric, 'how can you talk so, Mr Tulliver? But it's your way to speak disrespectful o' my family; and sister Glegg throws all the blame upo' me, though I'm sure I'm as innocent as the babe unborn. For nobody's ever heard *me* say as it wasn't lucky for my children to have aunts and uncles as can live independent. Howiver, if Tom's to go to a new school, I should like him to go where I can wash him and mend him; else he might as well have calico as linen, for they'd be one as yallow as th' other before they'd been washed half a dozen times. And then, when the box is goin' backards and forrards, I could send the lad a cake, or a pork-pie, or an apple; for he can do with an extry bit, bless him, whether they stint him at his meals or no. My children can eat as much victuals as most, thank God.'

'Well, well, we won't send him out o' reach o' the carrier's cart, if other things fit in,' said Mr Tulliver. 'But you mustn't put a spoke i' the wheel about the washin', if we can't get a school near enough, That's the fault I have to find wi' you, Bessy; if you see a stick i' the road, you're allays thinkin' you can't step over it. You'd want me not to hire a good waggoner, 'cause he'd got a mole on his face.'

'Dear heart!' said Mrs Tulliver, in mild surprise, 'when did I iver make objections to a man because he'd got a mole on his face? I'm sure I'm rether fond o' the moles; for my brother, as is dead an' gone, had a mole on his brow. But I can't remember your iver offering to hire a waggoner with a mole, Mr Tulliver. There was John Gibbs hadn't a mole on his face no more nor you have, an' I was all for having you hire *him*; an' so you did hire him, an' if he hadn't died o' th' inflammation, as we paid Dr Turnbull for attending him, he'd very like ha' been driving the waggon now. He might have a mole somewhere out o' sight, but how was I to know that, Mr Tulliver?'

'No, no, Bessy; I didn't mean justly the mole; I meant it to stand for summat else; but niver mind – it's puzzling work, talking is. What I'm thinking on, is how to find the right sort o' school to send Tom to, for I might be ta'en in again, as I've been wi' th' academy. I'll have nothing to do wi' a academy again: whativer school I send Tom to, it shan't be a academy; it shall be a place where the lads spend their time i' summat else besides blacking the family's shoes, and getting up the potatoes. it's an uncommon puzzling thing to know what school to pick.'

Mr Tulliver paused a minute or two, and dived with both hands into his breeches pockets as if he hoped to find some suggestion there. Apparently he was not disappointed, for he presently said, 'I know what I'll do – I'll talk it over wi' Riley: he's coming tomorrow, t' arbitrate about the dam.'

'Well, Mr Tulliver, I've put the sheets out for the best bed, and Kezia's got 'em hanging at the fire. They aren't the best sheets, but they're good enough for anybody to sleep in, be he who he will; for as for them best Holland sheets, I should repent buying 'em, only they'll do to lay us out in. An' if you was to die tomorrow, Mr Tulliver, they're mangled beautiful, an' all ready, an' smell o' lavender as it 'ud be a pleasure to lay 'em out; an' they lie at the left-hand corner o' the big oak linen-chest at the back: not as I should trust anybody to look 'em out but myself.'

As Mrs Tulliver uttered the last sentence, she drew a bright bunch of keys from her pocket, and singled out one, rubbing her thumb and finger up and down it with a placid smile while she looked at the clear fire. If Mr Tulliver had been a susceptible man in his conjugal relation, he might have supposed that she drew out the key to aid her imagination in anticipating the moment when he would be in a state to justify the production of the best Holland sheets. Happily he was not so; he was only susceptible in respect of his right to water-power; moreover, he had the marital habit of not listening very closely, and since his mention of Mr Riley, had been apparently occupied in a tactile examination of his woollen stockings.

'I think I've hit it, Bessy,' was his first remark after a short silence. 'Riley's as likely a man as any to know o' some school; he's had schooling himself, an' goes about to all sorts o' places – arbitratin' and vallyin' and that. And we shall have time to talk it over tomorrow night when the business is done. I want Tom to be such a sort o' man as Riley, you know – as can talk pretty nigh as well as if it was all wrote out for him, and knows a good lot o' words as don't mean much, so as you can't lay hold of 'em i' law; and a good solid knowledge o' business too.'

'Well,' said Mrs Tulliver, 'so far as talking proper, and knowing everything, and walking with a bend in his back, and setting his hair up, I shouldn't mind the lad being brought up to that. But them fine-talking men from the big towns mostly wear false shirt-fronts; they wear a frill till it's all a mess, and then hide it with a bib; I know Riley does. And then, if Tom's to go and live at Mudport, like Riley, he'll have a house with a kitchen hardly big enough to turn in, an' niver get a fresh egg for his breakfast, an' sleep up three pair o' stairs – or four, for what I know – an' be burnt to death before he can get down.'

'No, no,' said Mr Tulliver, 'I've no thoughts of his going to Mudport: I mean him to set up his office at St Ogg's, close by us, an' live at home. But,' continued Mr Tulliver after a pause, 'what I'm a bit afraid on is, as Tom hasn't got the right sort o' brains for a smart fellow. I doubt he's a bit slowish. He takes after your family, Bessy.'

'Yes, that he does,' said Mrs Tulliver, accepting the last proposition entirely on its own merits; 'he's wonderful for liking a deal o' salt in his broth. That was my brother's way, and my father's before him.'

'It seems a bit of a pity, though,' said Mr Tulliver, 'as the lad should take after the mother's side instead o' the little wench. That's the worst on't wi' the crossing o' breeds: you can never justly calkilate what'll come on't. The little un takes after my side, now: she's twice as 'cute as Tom. Too 'cute for a woman, I'm afraid,' continued Mr Tulliver, turning his head dubiously first on one side and then on the other. 'It's no mischief much while she's a little un, but an over-'cute woman's no better nor a long-tailed sheep – she'll fetch none the bigger price for that.'

'Yes, it *is* a mischief while she's a little un, Mr Tulliver, for it all runs to naughtiness. How to keep her in a clean pinafore two hours together passes my cunning. An' now you put me i' mind,' continued Mrs Tulliver, rising and going to the window, 'I don't know where she is now, an' it's pretty nigh teatime. Ah, I thought so – wanderin' up an' down by the water, like a wild thing: she'll tumble in someday.'

Mrs Tulliver rapped the window sharply, beckoned, and shook her head – a process which she repeated more than once before she returned to her chair.

'You talk o' 'cuteness, Mr Tulliver,' she observed as she sat down, 'but I'm sure the child's half an idiot i' some things; for if I send her upstairs to fetch anything, she forgets what she's gone for, an' perhaps 'ull sit down on the floor i' the sunshine an' plait her hair an' sing to herself like a Bedlam creatur', all the while I'm waiting for her downstairs. That niver run i' my family, thank God, no more nor a brown skin as makes her look like a mulatter. I don't like to fly i' the face o' Providence, but it seems hard as I should have but one gell, an' her so comical.'

'Pooh, nonsense!' said Mr Tulliver, 'she's a straight black-eyed wench as anybody need wish to see. I don't know i' what she's behind other folks's children; and she can read almost as well as the parson.'

'But her hair won't curl all I can do with it, and she's so franzy about having it put i' paper, and I've such work as never was to make her stand and have it pinched with th' irons.'

'Cut it off – cut it off short,' said the father, rashly.

'How can you talk so, Mr Tulliver? She's too big a gell, gone nine, and tall of her age, to have her hair cut short; an' there's her cousin Lucy's got a row o' curls round her head, an' not a hair out o' place. It seems hard as my sister Deane should have that pretty child; I'm sure Lucy takes more after me nor my own child does. Maggie, Maggie,' continued the mother, in a tone of half-coaxing fretfulness, as this small mistake of nature entered the room, 'where's the use o' my telling you to keep away from the water? You'll tumble in and be drownded someday, an' then you'll be sorry you didn't do as mother told you.'

Maggie's hair, as she threw off her bonnet, painfully confirmed her mother's accusation: Mrs Tulliver, desiring her daughter to have a curled crop, 'like other folks's children', had had it cut too short in front to be pushed behind the ears; and as it was usually straight an hour after it had been taken out of paper, Maggie was incessantly tossing her head to keep the dark heavy locks out of her gleaming black eyes – an action which gave her very much the air of a small Shetland pony.

'Oh, dear, Oh, dear, Maggie, what are you thinkin' of, to throw your bonnet down there? Take it upstairs, there's a good gell, an' let your hair be brushed, an' put your other pinafore on, an' change your shoes – do, for shame; an' come an' go on with your patchwork, like a little lady.'

'Oh, mother', said Maggie, in a vehemently cross tone, 'I don't *want* to do my patchwork.'

'What! not your pretty patchwork, to make a counterpane for your aunt Glegg?'

'It's foolish work,' said Maggie, with a toss of her mane – 'tearing things to pieces to sew 'em together again. And I don't want to do anything for my aunt Glegg – I don't like her.'

Exit Maggie, dragging her bonnet by the string, while Mr Tulliver laughs audibly.

'I wonder at you, as you'll laugh at her, Mr Tulliver,' said the mother, with feeble fretfulness in her tone. 'You encourage her i' naughtiness. An' her aunts will have it as it's me spoils her.'

Mrs Tulliver was what is called a good-tempered person – never cried, when she was a baby, on any slighter ground than hunger and pins; and from the cradle upwards had been healthy, fair, plump, and dull-witted; in short, the flower of her family for beauty and amiability. But milk and mildness are not the best things for keeping, and when they turn only a little sour, they may disagree with young stomachs seriously. I have often wondered whether those early Madonnas of Raphael, with the blond faces and somewhat stupid expression, kept their placidity undisturbed when their strong-limbed, strong-willed boys got a little too old to do without clothing. I think they must have been given to feeble remonstrance, getting more and more peevish as it became more and more ineffectual.

CHAPTER 3

Mr Riley Gives his Advice Concerning a School for Tom

The gentleman in the ample white cravat and shirt-frill, taking his brandy-and-water so pleasantly with his good friend Tulliver, is Mr Riley, a gentleman with a waxen complexion and fat hands, rather highly educated for an auctioneer and appraiser, but large-hearted enough to show a great deal of *bonhommie* towards simple country acquaintances of hospitable habits. Mr Riley spoke of such acquaintances kindly as 'people of the old school'.

The conversation had come to a pause. Mr Tulliver, not without a particular reason, had abstained from a seventh recital of the cool retort by which Riley had shown himself too many for Dix, and how Wakem had had his comb cut for once in his life, now the business of the dam had been settled by arbitration, and how there never would have been any dispute at all about the height of water if everybody was what they should be, and Old Harry hadn't made the lawyers. Mr Tulliver was, on the whole, a man of safe traditional opinions; but on one or two points he had trusted to his unassisted intellect, and had arrived at several questionable conclusions; among the rest, that rats, weevils, and lawyers were created by Old Harry. Unhappily he had no one to tell him that this was rampant Manichaeism, else he might have seen his error. But today it was clear that the good principle was triumphant: this affair of the water-power had been a tangled business somehow, for all it seemed – look at it one way – as plain as water's water; but, big a puzzle as it was, it hadn't got the better of Riley. Mr Tulliver took his brandy-and-water a little stronger than usual, and, for a man who might be supposed to have a few hundreds lying idle at his banker's, was rather incautiously open in expressing his high estimate of his friend's business talents.

But the dam was a subject of conversation that would keep; it could always be taken up again at the same point, and exactly in the same condition; and there was another subject, as you know, on which Mr Tulliver was in pressing want of Mr Riley's advice. This was his particular reason for remaining silent for a short space after his last draught, and rubbing his knees in a meditative manner. He was not a man to make an abrupt transition. This was a puzzling world, as he often said, and if you drive your waggon in a hurry, you may light on an awkward corner. Mr Riley, meanwhile, was not impatient. Why should he be? Even Hotspur, one would think, must have been patient in his slippers on a warm hearth, taking copious snuff, and sipping gratuitous brandy-and-water.

'There's a thing I've got i' my head,' said Mr Tulliver at last, in rather a lower tone than usual, as he turned his head and looked steadfastly at his companion.

'Ah!' said Mr Riley, in a tone of mild interest. He was a man with heavy waxen eyelids and high-arched eyebrows, looking exactly the same under all circumstances. This immovability of face, and the habit of taking a pinch of snuff before he gave an answer, made him trebly oracular to Mr Tulliver.

'It's a very particular thing,' he went on; 'it's about my boy Tom.'

At the sound of this name, Maggie, who was seated on a low stool close by the fire, with a large book open on her lap, shook her heavy hair back and looked up eagerly. There were few sounds that roused Maggie when she was dreaming over her book, but Tom's name served as well as the shrillest whistle: in an instant she was on the watch, with gleaming eyes, like a Skye terrier suspecting mischief, or at all events determined to fly at anyone who threatened it towards Tom.

'You see, I want to put him to a new school at Midsummer,' said Mr Tulliver; 'he's comin' away from th' academy at Ladyday, an' I shall let him run loose for a quarter; but after that I want to send him to a downright good school, where they'll make a scholard of him.'

'Well,' said Mr Riley, 'there's no greater advantage you can give him than a good education. Not,' he added, with polite significance – 'not that a man can't be an excellent miller and farmer, and a shrewd sensible fellow into the bargain, without much help from the schoolmaster.'

'I believe you,' said Mr Tulliver, winking, and turning his head on one side, 'but that's where it is. I don't *mean* Tom to be a miller and farmer. I see no fun i' that: why, if I made him a miller an' farmer, he'd be expectin' to take to the mill an' the land, an' a-hinting at me as it was time for me to lay by an' think o' my latter end. Nay, nay, I've seen enough o' that wi' sons. I'll never pull my coat off before I go to bed. I shall give Tom an eddication an' put him to a business, as he may make a nest for himself, an' not want to push me out o' mine. Pretty well if he gets it when I'm dead an' gone. I shan't be put off wi' spoon-meat afore I've lost my teeth.'

This was evidently a point on which Mr Tulliver felt strongly, and the impetus which had given unusual rapidity and emphasis to his speech, showed itself still unexhausted for some minutes afterwards, in a defiant motion of the head from side to side, and an occasional 'Nay, nay,' like a subsiding growl.

These angry symptoms were keenly observed by Maggie, and cut her to the quick. Tom, it appeared, was supposed capable of turning his father out of doors, and of making the future in some way tragic by his wickedness. This was not to be borne; and Maggie jumped up from her stool, forgetting all about her heavy book, which fell with a bang within the fender; and going up between her father's knees, said, in a half-crying, half-indignant voice, 'Father, Tom wouldn't be naughty to you ever; I know he wouldn't.'

Mrs Tulliver was out of the room superintending a choice supper-dish, and Mr Tulliver's heart was touched; so Maggie was not scolded about the book. Mr Riley quietly picked it up and looked at it, while the father laughed with a certain tenderness in his hard-lined face, and patted his little girl on the back, and then held her hands and kept her between his knees.

'What! they mustn't say any harm o' Tom, eh?' said Mr Tulliver, looking at Maggie with a twinkling eye. Then, in a lower voice, turning to Mr Riley, as though Maggie couldn't hear, 'She understands what one's talking about so as never was. And you should hear her read – straight off, as if she knowed it all beforehand. And allays at her book! But it's bad – it's bad,' Mr Tulliver added, sadly, checking this blamable exultation; 'a woman's no business wi' being so clever; it'll turn to trouble, I doubt. But, bless you!' – here the exultation was clearly recovering the mastery – 'she'll read the books and understand 'em better nor half the folks as are growed up.'

Maggie's cheeks began to flush with triumphant excitement: she thought Mr Riley would have a respect for her now; it had been evident that he thought nothing of her before.

Mr Riley was turning over the leaves of the book, and she could make nothing of his face, with its high-arched eyebrows; but he presently looked at her and said,

'Come, come and tell me something about this book; here are some pictures – I want to know what they mean.'

Maggie with deepening colour went without hesitation to Mr Riley's elbow and looked over the book, eagerly seizing one corner, and tossing back her mane, while she said,

'Oh, I'll tell you what that means. It's a dreadful picture, isn't it? But I can't help looking at it. That old woman in the water's a witch – they've put her in to find out whether she's a witch or no, and if she swims she's a witch, and if she's drowned – and killed, you know – she's innocent, and not a witch, but only a poor silly old woman. But what good would it do her then, you know, when she was drowned? Only, I suppose, she'd go to heaven, and God would make it up to her. And this dreadful blacksmith with his arms akimbo, laughing – oh, isn't he ugly? – I'll tell you what he is. He's the devil *really*' (here Maggie's voice became louder and more emphatic), 'and not a right blacksmith; for the devil takes the shape of wicked men, and walks about and sets people doing wicked things, and he's oftener in the shape of a bad man than any other, because, you know, if people saw he was the devil, and he roared at 'em, they'd run away, and he couldn't make 'em do what he pleased.'

Mr Tulliver had listened to this exposition of Maggie's with petrifying wonder. 'Why, what book is it the wench has got hold on?' he burst out at last.

'*The History of the Devil*, by Daniel Defoe; not quite the right book for a little girl,' said Mr Riley. 'How came it among your books, Tulliver?'

Maggie looked hurt and discouraged, while her father said,

'Why, it's one o' the books I bought at Partridge's sale. They was all bound alike – it's a good binding, you see – and I thought they'd be all good books. There's Jeremy Taylor's *Holy Living and Dying* among 'em; I read in it often of a Sunday' (Mr Tulliver felt somehow a familiarity with that great writer because his name was Jeremy); 'and there's a lot more of 'em, sermons mostly, I think; but they've all got the same covers, and I thought they were all o' one sample, as you may say. But it seems one mustn't judge by th' outside. This is a puzzlin' world.'

'Well,' said Mr Riley, in an admonitory patronising tone, as he parted Maggie on the head, 'I advise you to put by *The History of the Devil*, and read some prettier book. Have you no prettier books?'

'O yes,' said Maggie, reviving a little in the desire to vindicate the variety of her reading, 'I know the reading in this book isn't pretty – but I like the pictures, and I make stories to the pictures out of my own head, you know. But I've got *Aesop's Fables*, and a book about Kangaroos and things, and the *Pilgrim's Progress*.' . . .

'Ah, a beautiful book,' said Mr Riley; 'you can't read a better.'

'Well, but there's a great deal about the devil in that,' said Maggie, triumphantly, 'and I'll show you the picture of him in his true shape, as he fought with Christian.'

Maggie ran in an instant to the corner of the room, jumped on a chair, and reached down from the small bookcase a shabby old copy of Bunyan, which opened at once, without the least trouble of search, at the picture she wanted.

'Here he is,' she said, running back to Mr Riley, 'and Tom coloured him for me with his paints when he was at home last holidays – the body all black, you know, and the eyes red, like fire, because he's all fire inside, and it shines out at his eyes.'

'Go, go!' said Mr Tulliver, peremptorily, beginning to feel rather uncomfortable at these free remarks on the personal appearance of a being powerful enough to create lawyers; 'shut up the book, and let's hear no more o' such talk.

It is as I thought – the child 'ull learn more mischief nor good wi' the books. Go, go and see after your mother.'

Maggie shut up the book at once, with a sense of disgrace, but not being inclined to see after her mother, she compromised the matter by going into a dark corner behind her father's chair, and nursing her doll, towards which she had an occasional fit of fondness in Tom's absence, neglecting its toilet, but lavishing so many warm kisses on it that the waxen cheeks had a wasted unhealthy appearance.

'Did you ever hear the like on't?' said Mr Tulliver, as Maggie retired. 'It's a pity but what she'd been the lad – she'd ha' been a match for the lawyers, *she* would. It's the wonderful'st thing' – here he lowered his voice – 'as I picked the mother because she wasn't o'er 'cute – bein' a good-looking woman too, an' come of a rare family for managing; but I picked her from her sisters o' purpose, 'cause she was a bit weak, like; for I wasn't agoin' to be told the rights o' things by my own fireside. But you see, when a man's got brains himself, there's no knowing where they'll run to; an' a pleasant sort o' soft woman may go on breeding you stupid lads and 'cute wenches, till it's like as if the world was turned topsy-turvy. It's an uncommon puzzlin' thing.'

Mr Riley's gravity gave way, and he shook a little under the application of his pinch of snuff, before he said, 'But your lad's not stupid, is he? I saw him, when I was here last, busy making fishing-tackle; he seemed quite up to it.'

'Well, he isn't not to say stupid – he's got a notion o' things out o' door, an' a sort o' common-sense, as he'd lay hold o' things by the right handle. But he's slow with his tongue, you see, and he reads but poorly, and can't abide the books, and spells all wrong, they tell me, an' as shy as can be wi' strangers, an' you never hear him say 'cute things like the little wench. Now, what I want is to send him to a school where they'll make him a bit nimble with his tongue and his pen, and make a smart chap of him. I want my son to be even wi' these fellows as have got the start o' me with having better schooling. Not but what, if the world had been left as God made it, I could ha' seen my way, and held my own wi' the best of 'em; but things have got so twisted round and wrapped up i' unreasonable words, as aren't a bit like 'em, as I'm clean at fault, often an' often. Everything winds about so – the more straightforrard you are, the more you're puzzled.'

Mr Tulliver took a draught, swallowed it slowly, and shook his head in a melancholy manner, conscious of exemplifying the truth that a perfectly sane intellect is hardly at home in this insane world.

'You're quite in the right of it, Tulliver,' observed Mr Riley. 'Better spend an extra hundred or two on your son's education, than leave it him in your will. I know I should have tried to do so by a son of mine, if I'd had one, though, God knows, I haven't your ready-money to play with, Tulliver; and I have a houseful of daughters into the bargain.'

'I dare say, now, you know of a school as 'ud be just the thing for Tom,' said Mr Tulliver, not diverted from his purpose by any sympathy with Mr Riley's deficiency of ready cash.

Mr Riley took a pinch of snuff, and kept Mr Tulliver in suspense by a silence that seemed deliberative, before he said, 'I know of a very fine chance for anyone that's got the necessary money, and that's what you have, Tulliver. The fact is, I wouldn't recommend any friend of mine to send a boy to a regular school, if he could afford to do better. But if anyone wanted his boy to get superior instruction and training, where he would be the companion of his master, and that master a first-rate fellow – I know his man. I wouldn't mention the chance to everybody, because I don't think everybody would succeed in getting it, if he were to try, but I mention it to you, Tulliver – between ourselves.'

The fixed enquiring glance with which Mr Tulliver had been watching his friend's oracular face became quite eager.

'Ay, now, let's hear,' he said adjusting himself in his chair with the complacency of a person who is thought worthy of important communications.

'He's an Oxford man,' said Mr Riley, sententiously, shutting his mouth close, and looking at Mr Tulliver to observe the effect of this stimulating information.

'What! a parson?' said Mr Tulliver, rather doubtfully.

'Yes – and an M.A. The bishop, I understand, thinks very highly of him: why, it was the bishop who got him his present curacy.'

'Ah!' said Mr Tulliver, to whom one thing was as wonderful as another concerning these unfamiliar phenomena. 'But what can he want wi' Tom, then?'

'Why, the fact is, he's fond of teaching, and wishes to keep up his studies, and a clergyman has but little opportunity for that in his parochial duties. He's willing to take one or two boys as pupils to fill up his time profitably. The boys would be quite of the family – the finest thing in the world for them; under Stelling's eye continually.'

'But do you think they'd give the poor lad twice o' pudding?' said Mrs Tulliver, who was now in her place again. 'He's such a boy for pudding as never was; an' a growing boy like that – it's dreadful to think o' their stintin' him.'

'And what money 'ud he want?' said Mr Tulliver, whose instinct told him that the services of this admirable M.A. would bear a high price.

'Why, I know of a clergyman who asks a hundred and fifty with his youngest pupils, and he's not to be mentioned with Stelling, the man I speak of. I know, on good authority, that one of the chief people at Oxford said, 'Stelling might get the highest honours if he chose." But he didn't care about university honours. He's a quiet man – not noisy.'

'Ah, a deal better – a deal better,' said Mr Tulliver; 'but a hundred and fifty's an uncommon price. I never thought o' payin' so much as that.'

'A good education, let me tell you, Tulliver – a good education is cheap at the money. But Stelling is moderate in his terms – he's not a grasping man. I've no doubt he'd take your boy at a hundred, and that's what you wouldn't get many other clergymen to do. I'll write to him about it, if you like.'

Mr Tulliver rubbed his knees, and looked at the carpet in a meditative manner.

'But belike he's a bachelor,' observed Mrs Tulliver in the interval, 'an' I've no opinion o' housekeepers. There was my brother, as is dead an' gone, had a housekeeper once, an' she took half the feathers out o' the best bed an' packed 'em a up an' sent 'em away. An' it's unknown the linen she made away with – Stott her name was. It 'ud break my heart to send Tom where there's a house-keeper, an' I hope you won't think of it, Mr Tulliver.'

'You may set your mind at rest on that score, Mrs Tulliver,' said Mr Riley, 'for Stelling is married to as nice a little woman as any man need wish for a wife. There isn't a kinder little soul in the world; I know her family well. She has very much your complexion – light curly hair. She comes of a good Mudport family, and it's not every offer that would have been acceptable in that quarter. But Stelling's not an everyday man. Rather a particular fellow as to the people he chooses to be connected with. But I *think* he would have no objection to take your son – *I think* he would not, on my representation.'

'I don't know what he could have *against* the lad,' said Mrs Tulliver, with a slight touch of motherly indignation, 'a nice fresh-skinned lad as anybody need wish to see.'

'But there's one thing I'm thinking on,' said Mr Tulliver, turning his head on one side and looking at Mr Riley, after a long perusal of the carpet. 'Wouldn't a parson be almost too high-learnt to bring up a lad to be a man o' business? My notion o' the parsons was as they'd got a sort o' learning as lay mostly out o' sight. And that isn't what I want for Tom. I want him to know figures, and write like print, and see into things quick, and know what folks mean, and how to wrap things up in words as aren't actionable. It's an uncommon fine thing, that is,' concluded Mr Tulliver, shaking his head, 'when you can let a man know what you think of him without paying for it.'

'O my dear Tulliver,' said Mr Riley, 'you're quite under a mistake about the clergy; all the best schoolmasters are of the clergy. The schoolmasters who are not clergymen, are a very low set of men generally' . . .

'Ay, that Jacobs is, at th' academy,' interposed Mr Tulliver.

'To be sure – men who have failed in other trades, most likely. Now a clergyman is a gentleman by profession and education, and besides that, he has the knowledge that will ground a boy, and prepare him for entering on any career with credit. There may be some clergymen who are mere book-men; but you may depend upon it, Stelling is not one of them – a man that's wide awake, let me tell you. Drop him a hint, and that's enough. You talk of figures, now; you have only to say to Stelling, "I want my son to be a thorough arithmetician," and you may leave the rest to him.'

Mr Riley paused a moment, while Mr Tulliver, somewhat reassured as to clerical tutorship, was inwardly rehearsing to an imaginary Mr Stelling the statement, 'I want my son to know 'rethmetic.'

'You see, my dear Tulliver,' Mr Riley continued, 'when you get a thoroughly educated man, like Stelling, he's at no loss to take up any branch of instruction. When a workman knows the use of his tools, he can make a door as well as a window.'

'Ay, that's true,' said Mr Tulliver, almost convinced now that the clergy must be the best of schoolmasters.

'Well, I'll tell you what I'll do for you,' said Mr Riley, 'and I wouldn't do it for everybody. I'll see Stelling's father-in-law, or drop him a line when I get back to Mudport, to say that you wish to place your boy with his son-in-law, and I dare say Stelling will write to you, and send you his terms.'

'But there's no hurry, is there?' said Mrs Tulliver; 'for I hope, Mr Tulliver, you won't let Tom begin at his new school before Midsummer. He began at th' academy at the Ladyday quarter, and you see what good's come of it.'

'Ay, ay, Bessy, never brew wi' bad malt upo' Michaelmas day, else you'll have a poor tap,' said Mr Tulliver, winking and smiling at Mr Riley with the natural pride of a man who has a buxom wife conspicuously his inferior in intellect. 'But it's true there's no hurry – you've hit it there, Bessy.'

'It might be as well not to defer the arrangement too long,' said Mr Riley, quietly, 'for Stelling may have propositions from other parties, and I know he would not take more than two or three boarders, if so many. If I were you, I think I would enter on the subject with Stelling at once: there's no necessity for sending the boy before Midsummer, but I would be on the safe side, and make sure that nobody forestalls you.'

'Ay, there's summat in that,' said Mr Tulliver.

'Father,' broke in Maggie, who had stolen unperceived to her father's elbow again, listening with parted lips, while she held her doll topsy-turvey, and crushed its nose against the wood of the chair – 'Father, is it a long way off where Tom is to go? shan't we ever go to see him?'

'I don't know, my wench,' said the father, tenderly. 'Ask Mr Riley; he knows.'

Maggie came round promptly in front of Mr Riley, and said, 'How far is it, please, sir.'

'Oh, a long long way off,' that gentleman answered, being of opinion that children, when they are not naughty, should always be spoken to jocosely. 'You must borrow the seven-leagued boots to get to him.'

'That's nonsense!' said Maggie, tossing her head haughtily, and turning away, with the tears springing in her eyes. She began to dislike Mr Riley: it was evident he thought her silly and of no consequence.

'Hush Maggie, for shame of you, asking questions and chattering,' said her mother. 'Come and sit down on your little stool and hold your tongue, do. But,' added Mrs Tulliver, who had her own alarm awakened, 'is it so far off as I couldn't wash him and mend him?'

'About fifteen miles, that's all,' said Mr Riley. 'You can drive there and back in a day quite comfortably. Or – Stelling is a hospitable, pleasant man – he'd be glad to have you stay.'

'But it's too far off for the linen, I doubt,' said Mrs Tulliver, sadly.

The entrance of supper opportunely adjourned this difficulty, and relieved Mr Riley from the labour of suggesting some solution or compromise – a labour which he would otherwise doubtless have undertaken; for, as you perceive, he was a man of very obliging manners. And he had really given himself the trouble of recommending Mr Stelling to his friend Tulliver without any positive expectation of a solid, definite advantage resulting to himself, notwithstanding the subtle indications to the contrary which might have misled a too sagacious observer. For there is nothing more widely misleading than sagacity if it happens to get on a wrong scent; and sagacity, persuaded that men usually act and speak from distinct motives, with a consciously proposed end in view, is certain to waste its energies on imaginary game. Plotting covetousness, and deliberate contrivance, in order to compass a selfish end, are nowhere abundant but in the world of the dramatist:

they demand too intense a mental action for many of our fellow-parishioners to be guilty of them. It is easy enough to spoil the lives of our neighbours without taking so much trouble: we can do it by lazy acquiescence and lazy omission, by trivial falsities for which we hardly know a reason, by small frauds neutralised by small extravagances, by maladroit flatteries, and clumsily improvised insinuations. We live from hand to mouth, most of us, with a small family of immediate desires – we do little else than snatch a morsel to satisfy the hungry brood, rarely thinking of seed-corn or the next year's crop.

Mr Riley was a man of business, and not cold towards his own interest, yet even he was more under the influence of small promptings than of far-sighted designs. He had no private understanding with the Revd Walter Stelling; on the contrary he knew very little of that M.A. and his acquirements – not quite enough perhaps to warrant so strong a recommendation of him as he had given to his friend Tulliver. But he believed Mr Stelling to be an excellent classic, for Gadsby had said so, and Gadsby's first cousin was an Oxford tutor; which was better ground for the belief even than his own immediate observation would have been, for though Mr Riley had received a tincture of the classics at the great Mudport Free School, and had a sense of understanding Latin generally, his comprehension of any particular Latin was not ready. Doubtless there remained a subtle aroma from his juvenile contact with the *De Senectute* and the Fourth Book of the *Aeneid*, but it had ceased to be distinctly recognisable as classical, and was only perceived in the higher finish and force of his auctioneering style. Then, Stelling was an Oxford man, and the Oxford men were always – no, no, it was the Cambridge men who were always good mathematicians. But a man who had had a university education could teach anything he liked; especially a man like Stelling who had made a speech at a Mudport dinner on a political occasion, and had acquitted himself so well that it was generally remarked, this son-in-law of Timpson's was a sharp fellow. It was to be expected of a Mudport man, from the parish of St Ursula, that he would not omit to do a good turn to a son-in-law of Timpson's, for Timpson was one of the most useful and influential men in the parish, and had a good deal of business, which he knew how to put into the right hands. Mr Riley liked such men, quite apart from any money which might be diverted, through their good judgement, from less worthy pockets into his own; and it would be a satisfaction to him to say to Timpson on his return home, 'I've secured a good pupil for your son-in-law.' Timpson had a large family of daughters; Mr Riley felt for him; besides, Louisa Timpson's face, with its light curls, had been a familiar object to him over the pew wainscot on a Sunday for nearly fifteen years; – it was natural her husband should be a commendable tutor. Moreover, Mr Riley knew of no other schoolmaster whom he had any ground for recommending in preference: why then should he not recommend Stelling? His friend Tulliver had asked him for an opinion: it is always chilling in friendly intercourse, to say you have no opinion to give. And if you deliver an opinion at all, it is mere stupidity not to do it with an air of conviction and well-founded knowledge. You make it your own in uttering it, and naturally get fond of it. Thus, Mr Riley, knowing no harm of Stelling to begin with, and wishing him well, so far as he had any wishes at all concerning him, had no sooner recommended him than he began to think with admiration of a man recommended on such high authority, and would soon have gathered so warm an interest on the subject, that if Mr Tulliver had in the end declined to send Tom to Stelling, Mr Riley would have thought his friend of the old school a thoroughly pig-headed fellow.

If you blame Mr Riley very severely for giving a recommendation on such slight grounds, I must say you are rather hard upon him. Why should an auctioneer and appraiser thirty years ago, who had as good as forgotten his free-school Latin, be expected to manifest a delicate scrupulosity which is not always exhibited by gentlemen of the learned professions, even in our present advanced state of morality?

Besides, a man with the milk of human kindness in him can scarcely abstain from doing a good-natured action, and one cannot be good-natured all round. Nature herself occasionally quarters an inconvenient parasite on an animal towards whom she has otherwise no ill-will. What then? We admire her care for the parasite. If Mr Riley had shrunk from giving a recommendation that was not based on valid evidence, he would not have helped Mr Stelling to a paying pupil, and that would not have been so well for the reverend gentleman. Consider, too, that all the pleasant little dim ideas and complacencies – of standing well with Timpson, of dispensing advice when he was asked for it, of impressing his friend Tulliver with additional respect, of saying something, and saying it emphatically, with other inappreciably minute ingredients that went along with the warm hearth and the brandy-and-water to make up Mr Riley's consciousness on this occasion – would have been a mere blank.

CHAPTER 4

Tom is Expected

It was a heavy disappointment to Maggie that she was not allowed to go with her father in the gig when he went to fetch Tom home from the academy; but the morning was too wet, Mrs Tulliver said, for a little girl to go out in her best bonnet. Maggie took the opposite view very strongly, and it was a direct consequence of this difference of opinion that when her mother was in the act of brushing out the reluctant black crop, Maggie suddenly rushed from under her hands and dipped her head in a basin of water standing near – in the vindictive determination that there should be no more chance of curls that day.

'Maggie, Maggie,' exclaimed Mrs Tulliver, sitting stout and helpless with the brushes on her lap, 'what is to become of you if you're so naughty? I'll tell your aunt Glegg and your aunt Pullet when they come next week, and they'll never love you any more. Oh dear, Oh dear! look at your clean pinafore, wet from top to bottom. Folks 'ull think it's a judgement on me as I've got such a child – they'll think I've done summat wicked.'

Before this remonstrance was finished, Maggie was already out of hearing, making her way towards the great attic that ran under the old high-pitched roof, shaking the water from her black locks as she ran, like a Skye terrier escaped from his bath. This attic was Maggie's favourite retreat on a wet day, when the weather was not too cold; here she fretted out all her ill-humours, and talked aloud to the worm-eaten floors, and the worm-eaten shelves, and the dark rafters festooned with cobwebs; and here she kept a Fetish which she punished for all her misfortunes. This was the trunk of a large wooden doll, which once stared with the roundest of eyes above the reddest of cheeks; but was now entirely defaced by a long career of vicarious suffering. Three nails driven into the head commemorated as many crises in Maggie's nine years of earthly struggle; that luxury of vengeance having been suggested to her by the picture of Jael destroying Sisera in the old Bible. The last nail had been driven in with a fiercer stroke than usual, for the Fetish on that occasion represented aunt Glegg. But immediately afterwards Maggie had reflected that if she drove many nails in, she would not be so well able to fancy that the head was hurt when she knocked it against the wall, nor to comfort it, and make believe to poultice it, when her fury was abated; for even aunt Glegg would be pitiable when she had been hurt very much, and thoroughly humiliated, so as to beg her niece's pardon. Since then she had driven no more nails in, but had soothed herself by alternately grinding and beating the wooden head against the rough brick of the great chimneys that made two square pillars supporting the roof. That was what she did this morning on reaching the attic, sobbing all the while with a passion that expelled every other form of consciousness – even the memory of the grievance that had caused it. As at last the sobs were getting quieter, and the grinding less fierce, a sudden beam of sunshine, falling through the wire lattice across the worm-eaten shelves, made her throw away the Fetish and run to the window. The sun was really breaking out; the sound of the mill seemed cheerful again; the granary doors were open; and there was Yap, the queer white-and-brown terrier, with one ear turned back, trotting about and sniffing vaguely, as if he were in search of a companion. It was irresistible. Maggie tossed her hair back and ran downstairs, seized her bonnet without putting it on, peeped, and then dashed along the passage lest she should encounter her mother, and was quickly out in the yard, whirling round like a Pythoness, and singing as she whirled, 'Yap, Yap, Tom's coming home!' while Yap danced and barked round her, as much as to say, if there was any noise wanted he was the dog for it.

'Hegh, hegh, miss, you'll make yourself giddy, an' tumble down i' the dirt,' said Luke, the head miller, a tall broad-shouldered man of forty, black-eyed and black-haired, subdued by a general mealiness, like an auricula.

Maggie paused in her whirling and said, staggering a little, 'Oh, no, it doesn't make me giddy, Luke; may I go into the mill with you?'

Maggie loved to linger in the great spaces of the mill, and often came out with her black hair powdered to a soft whiteness that made her dark eyes flash out with new fire. The resolute din, the unresting motion of the great stones, giving her a dim delicious awe as at the presence of an uncontrollable force – the meal for ever pouring, pouring – the fine white powder softening all surfaces, and making the very spider-nets look like a faery lace-work – the sweet pure scent of the meal – all helped to make Maggie feel that the mill was a little world apart from her outside everyday life. The spiders were especially a subject of speculation with her. She wondered if they had any relations outside the mill, for in that case there must be a painful difficulty in their family intercourse – a fat and floury spider, accustomed to take his fly well dusted with meal, must suffer a little at a cousin's table where the fly was *au naturel*, and the lady-spiders must be mutually shocked at each other's appearance. But the part of the mill she liked best was the topmost storey – the corn-hutch, where there were the great heaps of grain, which she could sit on and slide down continually. She was in the habit of taking this recreation as she conversed with Luke, to whom she was very communicative, wishing him to think well of her understanding, as her father did.

Perhaps she felt it necessary to recover her position with him on the present occasion, for, as she sat sliding on the heap of grain near which he was busying himself, she said, at that shrill pitch which was requisite in mill-society, 'I think you never read any book but the Bible – did you, Luke?'

'Nay, Miss – an' not much o' that,' said Luke, with great frankness. 'I'm no reader, I aren't.'

'But if I lent you one of my books, Luke? I've not got any *very* pretty books that would be easy for you to read; but there's 'Pug's Tour of Europe' – that would tell you all about the different sorts of people in the world, and if you didn't understand the reading, the pictures would help you – they show the looks and ways of the people, and what they do. There are the Dutchmen, very fat, and smoking, you know – and one sitting on a barrel.'

'Nay, Miss, I'n no opinion o' Dutchmen. There ben't much good i' knowin' about *them*.'

'But they're our fellow-creatures, Luke – we ought to know about our fellow-creatures.'

'Not much o' fellow-creaturs, I think, Miss; all I know – my old master, as war a knowin' man, used to say, says he, "If e'er I sow my wheat wi'out brinin', I'm a Dutchman," says he; an' that war as much as to say as a Dutchman war a fool, or next door. Nay, nay, I aren't goin' to bother mysen about Dutchmen. There's fools enoo – an' rogues enoo – wi'out lookin' i' books for 'em.'

'Oh, well,' said Maggie, rather foiled by Luke's unexpectedly decided views about Dutchmen, 'perhaps you would like 'Animated Nature' better – that's not Dutchmen, you know, but elephants, and kangaroos, and the civet cat, and the sun-fish, and a bird sitting on its tail – I forget its name. There are countries full of those creatures, instead of horses and cows, you know. Shouldn't you like to know about them, Luke?'

'Nay, Miss, I'n got to keep count o' the flour an' corn – I can't do wi' knowin' so many things besides my work. That's what brings folks to the gallows – knowin' everything but what they'n got to get their bread by. An' they're mostly lies, I think, what's printed i' the books: them printed sheets are, anyhow, as the men cry i' the streets.'

'Why, you're like my brother Tom, Luke,' said Maggie, wishing to turn the conversation agreeably; 'Tom's not fond of reading. I love Tom so dearly, Luke – better than anybody else in the world. When he grows up, I shall keep his house, and we shall always live together. I can tell him everything he doesn't know. But I think Tom's clever, for all he doesn't like books: he makes beautiful whipcord and rabbit-pens.'

'Ah,' said Luke, 'but he'll be fine an' vexed, as the rabbits are all dead.'

'Dead!' screamed Maggie, jumping up from her sliding seat on the corn. 'Oh dear, Luke! What! the lop-eared one, and the spotted doe that Tom spent all his money to buy?'

'As dead as moles,' said Luke, fetching his comparison from the unmistakable corpses nailed to the stable-wall.

'O dear, Luke,' said Maggie, in a piteous tone, while the big tears rolled down her cheek; 'Tom told me to take care of 'em, and I forgot. What shall I do?'

'Well, you see, Miss, they were in that far tool-house, an' it was nobody's business to see to 'em. I reckon Master Tom told Harry to feed 'em, but there's no countin' on Harry – *he's* an offal creatur as iver come about the primises, he is. He remembers nothing but his own inside – an' I wish it 'ud gripe him.'

'O, Luke, Tom told me to be sure and remember the rabbits every day; but how could I, when they didn't come into my head, you know? O, he will be so angry with me, I know he will, and so sorry about his rabbits – and so am I sorry. O, what shall I do?'

'Don't you fret, Miss,' said Luke, soothingly, 'they're nash things, them lop-eared rabbits – they'd happen ha' died, if they'd been fed. Things out o' natur niver thrive: God A'mighty doesn't like 'em. He made the rabbits' ears to lie back, an' it's nothin' but contrariness to make 'em hing down like a mastiff dog's. Master Tom 'ull know better nor buy such things another time. Don't you fret, Miss. Will you come along home wi' me, and see my wife? I'm a-goin' this minute.'

The invitation offered an agreeable distraction to Maggie's grief, and her tears gradually subsided as she trotted along by Luke's side to his pleasant cottage, which stood with its apple and pear trees, and with the added dignity of a lean-to pigsty, close to the brink of the Ripple. Mrs Moggs, Luke's wife, was a decidedly agreeable acquaintance. She exhibited her hospitality in bread and treacle, and possessed various works of art. Maggie actually forgot that she had any special cause of sadness this morning, as she stood on a chair to look at a remarkable series of pictures representing the Prodigal Son, in the costume of Sir Charles Grandison, except that, as might have been expected from his defective moral character, he had not, like that accomplished hero, the taste and strength of mind to dispense with a wig. But the indefinable weight the dead rabbits had left on her mind caused her to feel more than usual pity for the career of this weak young man, particularly when she looked at the picture where he leaned against a tree with a flaccid appearance, his knee-breeches unbuttoned and his wig awry, while the swine, apparently of some foreign breed, seemed to insult him by their good spirits over their feast of husks.

'I'm very glad his father took him back again – aren't you, Luke?' she said. 'For he was very sorry, you know, and wouldn't do wrong again.'

'Eh, Miss,' said Luke, 'he'd be no great shakes, I doubt, let's feyther do what he would for him.'

That was a painful thought to Maggie, and she wished much that the subsequent history of the young man had not been left a blank.

CHAPTER 5

Tom Comes Home

Tom was to arrive early in the afternoon, and there was another fluttering heart besides Maggie's when it was late enough for the sound of the gig-wheels to be expected; for if Mrs Tulliver had a strong feeling, it was fondness for her boy. At last the sound came – that quick light bowling of the gig-wheels – and in spite of the wind, which was blowing the clouds about, and was not likely to respect Mrs Tulliver's curls and cap-strings, she came outside the door, and even held her hand on Maggie's offending head, forgetting all the griefs of the morning.

'There he is, my sweet lad! But, Lord ha' mercy! he's got never a collar on; it's been lost on the road, I'll be bound, and spoilt the set.'

Mrs Tulliver stood with her arms open; Maggie jumped first on one leg and then on the other; while Tom descended from the gig, and said, with masculine reticence as to the tender emotions, 'Hallo! Yap – what! are you there?'

Nevertheless he submitted to be kissed willingly enough, though Maggie hung on his neck in rather a strangling fashion, while his blue-grey eyes wandered towards the croft and the lambs and the river, where he promised himself that he would begin to fish the first thing tomorrow morning. He was one of those lads that grow everywhere in England, and, at twelve or thirteen years of age, look as much alike as goslings: – a lad with light-brown hair, cheeks of cream and roses, full lips, indeterminate nose and eyebrows – a physiognomy in which it seems impossible to discern anything but the generic character of boyhood; as different as possible from poor Maggie' phiz, which Nature seemed to have moulded and coloured with the most decided intention. But that same Nature has the deep cunning which hides itself under the appearance of openness, so that simple people think they can see through her quite well, and all the while she is secretly preparing a refutation of their confident prophecies. Under these average boyish physiognomies that she seems to turn off by the gross, she conceals some of her most rigid, inflexible purposes, some of her most un-modifiable characters; and the dark-eyed, demonstrative, rebellious girl may after all turn out to be a passive being compared with this pink-and-white bit of masculinity with the indeterminate features.

'Maggie,' said Tom, confidentially, taking her into a corner, as soon as his mother was gone out to examine his box, and the warm parlour had taken off the chill he had felt from the long drive, 'you don't know what I've got in *my* pockets,' nodding his head up and down as a means of rousing her sense of mystery.

'No,' said Maggie. 'How stodgy they look, Tom! Is it marls [marbles] or cobnuts?' Maggie's heart sank a little, because Tom always said it was 'no good' playing with *her* at those games – she played so badly.

'Marls! no, I've swopped all my marls with the little fellows, and cobnuts are no fun, you silly, only when the nuts are green. But see here!' He drew something half out of his right-hand pocket.

'What is it?' said Maggie, in a whisper. 'I can see nothing but a bit of yellow.'

'Why it's . . . a . . . new . . . guess, Maggie?'

'Oh, I *can't* guess, Tom,' said Maggie, impatiently.

'Don't be a spitfire, else I won't tell you,' said Tom, thrusting his hand back into his pocket, and looking determined.

'No, Tom,' said Maggie, imploringly, laying hold of the arm that was held stiffly in the pocket. 'I'm not cross, Tom; it was only because I can't bear guessing. *Please* be good to me.'

Tom's arm slowly relaxed, and he said, 'Well, then it's a new fish-line – two new uns – one for you, Maggie, all to yourself. I wouldn't go halves in the toffee and gingerbread on purpose to save the money; and Gibson and Spouncer fought with me because I wouldn't. And here's hooks; see here! . . . I say, *won't* we go and fish tomorrow down by the Round Pool? And you shall catch your own fish, Maggie, and put the worms on, and everything – won't it be fun?'

Maggie's answer was to throw her arms round Tom's neck and hug him, and hold her cheek against his without speaking, while he slowly unwound some of the line, saying, after a pause,

'Wasn't I a good brother, now, to buy you a line all to yourself? You know, I needn't have bought it, if I hadn't liked.' 'Yes, very, very good . . . I *do* love you, Tom.'

Tom had put the line back in his pocket, and was looking at the hooks one by one, before he spoke again.

'And the fellows fought me, because I wouldn't give in about the toffee.'

'Oh dear! wish they wouldn't fight at your school, Tom. Didn't it hurt you?'

'Hurt me? no,' said Tom, putting up the hooks again, taking out a large pocket-knife, and slowly opening the largest blade, which he looked at meditatively as he rubbed his finger along it. Then he added, 'I gave Spouncer a black eye, I know – that's what he got by wanting to leather *me;* I wasn't going to go halves because anybody leathered me.'

'Oh, how brave you are, Tom! I think you're like Samson. If there came a lion roaring at me, I think you'd fight him – wouldn't you, Tom?'

'How can a lion come roaring at you, you silly thing? There's no lions, only in the shows.'

'No; but if we were in the lion countries – I mean in Africa, where it's very hot – the lions eat people there. I can show it you in the book where I read it.'

'Well, I should get a gun and shoot him.'

'But if you hadn't got a gun – we might have gone out, you know, not thinking – just as we go fishing; and then a great lion might run towards us roaring, and we couldn't get away from him. What should you do, Tom?'

Tom paused, and at last turned away contemptuously, saying, 'But the lion isn't coming. What's the use of talking?'

'But I like to fancy how it would be,' said Maggie, following him. 'Just think what you would do, Tom.'

'O don't bother, Maggie! you're such a silly – I shall go and see my rabbits.'

Maggie's heart began to flutter with fear.

She dared not tell the sad truth at once, but she walked after Tom in trembling silence as he went out, thinking how she could tell him the news so as to soften at once his sorrow and his anger; for Maggie dreaded Tom's anger of all things – it was quite a different anger from her own.

'Tom,' she said, timidly, when they were out of doors, 'how much money did you give for your rabbits?'

'Two half-crowns and a sixpence,' said Tom, promptly.

'I think I've got a great deal more than that in my steel purse upstairs. I'll ask mother to give it you.'

'What for?' said Tom 'I don't want *your* money, you silly thing. I've got a great deal more money than you, because I'm a boy. I always have half-sovereigns and sovereigns for my Christmas boxes, because I shall be a man, and you only have five-shilling pieces, because you're only a girl.'

'Well, but, Tom – if mother would let me give you two half-crowns and a sixpence out of my purse to put into your pocket and spend, you know; and buy some more rabbits with it?'

'More rabbits? I don't want any more.'

'Oh, but Tom, they're all dead.'

Tom stopped immediately in his walk and turned round towards Maggie. 'You forgot to feed 'em, then, and Harry forgot?' he said, his colour heightening for a moment, but soon subsiding. 'I'll pitch into Harry – I'll have him turned away. And I don't love you, Maggie. You shan't go fishing with me tomorrow. I told you to go and see the rabbits every day.' He walked on again.

'Yes, but I forgot – and I couldn't help it, indeed, Tom. I'm so very sorry,' said Maggie, while the tears rushed fast.

'You're a naughty girl,' said Tom severely, 'and I'm sorry I bought you the fish-line. I don't love you.'

'Oh, Tom, it's very cruel,' sobbed Maggie. 'I'd forgive you, if *you* forgot anything – I wouldn't mind what you did – I'd forgive you and love you.'

'Yes, you're a silly – but I never *do* forget things – *I* don't.'

'O, please forgive me, Tom; my heart will break,' said Maggie, shaking with sobs, clinging to Tom's arm, and laying her wet cheek on his shoulder.

Tom shook her off, and stopped again, saying in a peremptory tone, 'Now, Maggie, you just listen. Aren't I a good brother to you?'

'Ye-ye-es,' sobbed Maggie, her chin rising and falling convulsedly.

'Didn't I think about your fish-line all this quarter, and mean to buy it, and saved my money o' purpose, and wouldn't go halves in the toffee, and Spouncer fought me because I wouldn't?'

'Ye-ye-es . . . and I . . . lo-lo-love you so, Tom.'

'But you're a naughty girl. Last holidays you licked the paint off my lozenge box, and the holidays before that you let the boat drag my fish-line down when I'd set you to watch it, and you pushed your head through my kite, all for nothing.'

'But I didn't mean,' said Maggie; 'I couldn't help it.'

'Yes, you could,' said Tom, 'if you'd minded what you were doing. And you're a naughty girl, and you shan't go fishing with me tomorrow.'

With this terrible conclusion, Tom ran away from Maggie towards the mill, meaning to greet Luke there, and complain to him of Harry.

Maggie stood motionless, except from her sobs, for a minute or two; then she turned round and ran into the house, and up to her attic, where she sat on the floor, and laid her head against the worm-eaten shelf, with a crushing sense of misery. Tom was come home, and she had thought how happy she should be – and now he was cruel to her. What use was anything, if Tom didn't love her? O, he was very cruel! Hadn't she wanted to give him the money, and said how very sorry she was? She knew she was naughty to her mother, but she had never been naughty to Tom – had never *meant* to be naughty to him.

'O, he is cruel!' Maggie sobbed aloud, finding a wretched pleasure in the hollow resonance that came through the long empty space of the attic. She never thought of beating or grinding her Fetish; she was too miserable to be angry.

These bitter sorrows of childhood! when sorrow is all new and strange, when hope has not yet got wings to fly beyond the days and weeks, and the space from summer to summer seems measureless.

Maggie soon thought she had been hours in the attic, and it must be teatime, and they were all having their tea, and not thinking of her. Well, then, she would stay up there and starve herself – hide herself behind the tub, and stay there all night; and then they would all be frightened, and Tom would be sorry. Thus Maggie thought in the pride of her heart, as she crept behind the tub; but presently she began to cry again at the idea that they didn't mind her being there. If she went down again to Tom now – would he forgive her? – perhaps her father would be there, and he would take her part. But, then, she wanted Tom to forgive her because he loved her, not because his father told him. No, she would never go down if Tom didn't come to fetch her. This resolution lasted in great intensity for five dark minutes behind the tub; but then the need of being loved, the strongest need in poor Maggie's nature, began to wrestle with her pride, and soon threw it. She crept from behind her tub into the twilight of the long attic, but just then she heard a quick footstep on the stairs.

Tom had been too much interested in his talk with Luke, in going the round of the premises, walking in and out where he pleased, and whittling sticks without any particular reason, except that he didn't whittle sticks at school, to think of Maggie and the effect his anger had produced on her. He meant to punish her, and that business having been performed, he occupied himself with other matters, like a practical person. But when he had been called in to tea, his father said, 'Why, where's the little wench?' and Mrs Tulliver, almost at the same moment, said, 'Where's your little sister?' – both of them having supposed that Maggie and Tom had been together all the afternoon.

'I don't know,' said Tom. He didn't want to 'tell' of Maggie, though he was angry with her; for Tom Tulliver was a lad of honour.

'What! hasn't she been playing with you all this while?' said the father. 'She'd been thinking o' nothing but your coming home.'

'I haven't seen her this two hours,' says Tom, commencing on the plumcake.

'Goodness heart! she's got drownded,' exclaimed Mrs Tulliver, rising from her seat and running to the window. 'How could you let her do so?' she added, as became a fearful woman, accusing she didn't know whom of she didn't know what.

'Nay, nay, she's none drownded,' said Mr Tulliver. 'You've been naughty to her, I doubt, Tom?'

'I'm sure I haven't, father,' said Tom, indignantly. 'I think she's in the house.'

'Perhaps up in that attic,' said Mrs Tulliver, 'a-singing and talking to herself, and forgetting all about meal-times.'

'You go and fetch her down, Tom,' said Mr Tulliver, rather sharply, his perspicacity or his fatherly fondness for Maggie making him suspect that the lad had been hard upon 'the little un,' else she would never have left his side. 'And be good to her, do you hear? Else I'll let you know better.'

Tom never disobeyed his father, for Mr Tulliver was a peremptory man, and, as he said, would never let anybody get hold of his whip-hand; but he went out rather sullenly, carrying his piece of plumcake, and not intending to reprieve Maggie's punishment, which was no more than she deserved. Tom was only thirteen, and had no decided views in grammar and arithmetic, regarding them for the most part as open questions, but he was particularly clear and positive on one point – namely, that he would punish everybody who deserved it: why, he wouldn't have minded being punished himself, if he deserved it; but, then, he never *did* deserve it.

It was Tom's step, then, that Maggie heard on the stairs, when her need of love had triumphed over her pride, and she was going down with her swollen eyes and dishevelled hair to beg for pity. At least her father would stroke her head and say, 'Never mind, my wench.' It is a wonderful subduer, this need of love – this hunger of the heart – as peremptory as that other hunger by which Nature forces us to submit to the yoke, and change the face of the world.

But she knew Tom's step, and her heart began to beat violently with the sudden shock of hope. He only stood still at the top of the stairs and said, 'Maggie, you're to come down.' But she rushed to him and clung round his neck, sobbing, 'Oh, Tom, please forgive me – I can't bear it – I will always be good – always remember things – do love me – please, dear Tom!'

We learn to restrain ourselves as we get older. We keep apart when we have quarrelled, express ourselves in well-bred phrases, and in this way preserve a dignified alienation, showing much firmness on one side, and swallowing much grief on the other. We no longer approximate in our behaviour to the mere impulsiveness of the lower animals, but conduct ourselves in every respect like members of a highly civilised society. Maggie and Tom were still very much like young animals, and so she could rub her cheek against his, and kiss his ear in a random, sobbing way; and there were tender fibres in the lad that had been used to answer to Maggie's fondling; so that he behaved with a weakness quite inconsistent with his resolution to punish her as much as she deserved: he actually began to kiss her in return, and say, 'Don't cry, then, Magsie – here, eat a bit o' cake.'

Maggie's sobs began to subside, and she put out her mouth for the cake and bit a piece: and then Tom bit a piece, just for company, and they ate together and rubbed each other's cheeks and brows and noses together, while they ate, with a humiliating resemblance to two friendly ponies.

'Come along, Magsie, and have tea,' said Tom at last, when there was no more cake except what was downstairs.

So ended the sorrows of this day, and the next morning Maggie was trotting with her own fishing-rod in one hand and a handle of the basket in the other, stepping always, by a peculiar gift, in the muddiest places, and looking darkly radiant from under her beaver-bonnet because Tom was good to her. She had told Tom, however, that she should like him to put the worms on the hook for her, although she accepted his word when he assured her that worms couldn't feel (it was Tom's private opinion that it didn't much matter if they did). He knew all about worms, and fish, and those things; and what birds were mischievous, and how padlocks opened, and which way the handles of the gates were to be lifted. Maggie thought this sort of knowledge was very wonderful – much more difficult than remembering what was in the books; and she was rather in awe of Tom's superiority, for he was the only person who called her knowledge 'stuff,' and did not feel surprised at her cleverness. Tom, indeed, was of opinion that Maggie was a silly little thing; all girls were silly – they couldn't throw a stone so as to hit anything, couldn't do anything with a pocketknife, and were frightened at frogs. Still he was very fond of his sister, and meant always to take care of her, make her his housekeeper, and punish her when she did wrong.

They were on their way to the Round Pool – that wonderful pool, which the floods had made a long while ago: no one knew how deep it was; and it was mysterious, too, that it should be almost a perfect round, framed in with willows and tall reeds, so that the water was only to be seen when you got close to the brink. The sight of the old favourite spot always heightened Tom's good-humour, and he spoke to Maggie in the most amicable whispers, as he opened the precious basket, and prepared their tackle. He threw her line for her, and put the rod into her hand. Maggie thought it probable that the small fish would come to her hook, and the large ones to Tom's. But she had forgotten all about the fish, and was looking dreamily at the glassy water, when Tom said, in a loud whisper, 'Look, look, Maggie!' and came running to prevent her from snatching her line away.

Maggie was frightened lest she had been doing something wrong, as usual, but presently Tom drew out her line and brought a large tench bouncing on the grass.

Tom was excited.

'O Magsie! you little duck! Empty the basket.'

Maggie was not conscious of unusual merit, but it was enough that Tom called her Magsie, and was pleased with her. There was nothing to mar her delight in the whispers and the dreamy silences, when she listened to the light dipping sounds of the rising fish, and the gentle rustling, as if the willows and the reeds and the water had their happy whisperings also. Maggie thought it would make a very nice heaven to sit by the pool in that way, and never be scolded. She never knew she had a bite till Tom told her; but she liked fishing very much.

It was one of their happy mornings. They trotted along and sat down together, with no thought that life would ever change much for them: they would only get bigger and not go to school, and it would always be like the holidays; they would always live together and be fond of each other. And the mill with its booming –

the great chestnut tree under which they played at houses – their own little river, the Ripple, where the banks seemed like home, and Tom was always seeing the water-rats, while Maggie gathered the purple plumy tops of the reeds, which she forgot and dropped afterwards – above all, the great Floss, along which they wandered with a sense of travel, to see the rushing spring-tide, the awful Eagre, come up like a hungry monster, or to see the Great Ash which had once wailed and groaned like a man – these things would always be just the same to them. Tom thought people were at a disadvantage who lived on any other spot of the globe; and Maggie, when she read about Christiana passing 'the river over which there is no bridge,' always saw the Floss between the green pastures by the Great Ash.

Life did change for Tom and Maggie; and yet they were not wrong in believing that the thoughts and loves of these first years would always make part of their lives. We could never have loved the earth so well if we had had no childhood in it – if it were not the earth where the same flowers come up again every spring that we used to gather with our tiny fingers as we sat lisping to ourselves on the grass – the same hips and haws on the autumn hedgerows – the same redbreasts that we used to call 'God's birds', because they did no harm to the precious crops. What novelty is worth that sweet monotony where everything is known, and *loved* because it is known?

The wood I walk in on this mild May day, with the young yellow-brown foliage of the oaks between me and the blue sky, the white star-flowers and the blue-eyed speedwell and the ground ivy at my feet – what grove of tropic palms, what strange ferns or splendid broad-petalled blossoms, could ever thrill such deep and delicate fibres within me as this home-scene? These familiar flowers, these well-remembered bird-notes, this sky, with its fitful brightness, these furrowed and grassy fields, each with a sort of personality given to it by the capricious hedgerows – such things as these are the mother tongue of our imagination, the language that is laden with all the subtle inextricable associations the fleeting hours of our childhood left behind them. Our delight in the sunshine on the deep-bladed grass today, might be no more than the faint perception of wearied souls, if it were not for the sunshine and the grass in the far-off years, which still live in us, and transform our perception into love.

CHAPTER 6

The Aunts and Uncles are Coming

It was Easter week, and Mrs Tulliver's cheesecakes were more exquisitely light than usual: 'a puff o' wind 'ud make 'em blow about like feathers,' Kezia the housemaid said – feeling proud to live under a mistress who could make such pastry; so that no season or circumstances could have been more propitious for a family party, even if it had not been advisable to consult sister Glegg and sister Pullet about Tom's going to school.

'I'd as lief not invite sister Deane this time,' said Mrs Tulliver, 'for she's as jealous and 'having' as can be, and 's allays trying to make the worst o' my poor children to their aunts and uncles.'

'Yes, yes,' said Mr Tulliver, 'ask her to come. I never hardly get a bit o' talk with Deane now: we haven't had him this six months. What's it matter what she says? – my children need be beholding to nobody.'

'That's what you allays say, Mr Tulliver; but I'm sure there's nobody o' your side, neither aunt nor uncle, to leave 'em so much as a five-pound note for a leggicy. And there's sister Glegg, and sister Pullet too, saving money unknown – for they put by all their own interest and butter-money too; their husbands buy 'em everything.' Mrs Tulliver was a mild woman, but even a sheep will face about a little when she has lambs.

'Tchuh!' said Mr Tulliver. 'It takes a big loaf when there's many to breakfast. What signifies your sisters' bits o' money when they've got half a dozen nevvies and nieces to divide it among? And your sister Deane won't get 'em to leave all to one, I reckon, and make the country cry shame on 'em when they are dead?'

'I don't know what she won't get 'em to do,' said Mrs Tulliver, 'for my children are so awk'ard wi' their aunts and uncles. Maggie's ten times naughtier when they come than she is other days, and Tom doesn't like 'em, bless him – though it's more nat'ral in a boy than a gell. And there's Lucy Deane's such a good child – you may set her on a stool, and there she'll sit for an hour together, and never offer to get off. I can't help loving the child as if she was my own; and I'm sure she's more like *my* child than sister Deane's, for she'd allays a very poor colour for one of our family, sister Deane had.'

'Well, well, if you're fond o' the child, ask her father and mother to bring her with 'em. And won't you ask their aunt and uncle Moss too? and some o' *their* children?'

'Oh dear, Mr Tulliver, why, there'd be eight people besides the children, and I must put two more leaves i' the table, besides reaching down more o' the dinner-service; and you know as well as I do, as *my* sisters and *your* sister don't suit well together.'

'Well, well, do as you like, Bessy,' said Mr Tulliver, taking up his hat and walking out to the mill. Few wives were more submissive than Mrs Tulliver on all points unconnected with her family relations; but she had been a Miss Dodson, and the Dodsons were a very respectable family indeed – as much looked up to as any in their own parish, or the next to it. The Miss Dodsons had always been thought to hold up their heads very high, and no one was surprised the two eldest had married so well – not at an early age, for that was not the practice of the Dodson family. There were particular ways of doing everything in that family: particular ways of bleaching the linen, of making the cowslip wine, curing the hams, and keeping the bottled gooseberries; so that no daughter of that house could be indifferent to the privilege of having been born a Dodson, rather than a Gibson or a Watson. Funerals were always conducted with peculiar propriety in the Dodson family: the hatbands were never of a blue shade, the gloves never split at the thumb, everybody was a mourner who ought to be, and there were always scarfs for the bearers. When one of the family was in trouble or sickness, all the rest went to visit the unfortunate member, usually at the same time, and did not shrink from uttering the most disagreeable truths that correct family feeling dictated: if the illness or trouble was the sufferer's own fault, it was not in the practice of the Dodson family to shrink from saying so. In short, here was in this family a peculiar tradition as to what was the right thing in household management and social demeanour, and the only bitter circumstance attending this superiority was a painful inability to approve the condiments or the conduct of families ungoverned by the Dodson tradition. A female Dodson, when in 'strange houses,' always ate dry bread with her tea, and declined any sort of preserves, having no confidence in the butter, and thinking that the preserves had probably begun to ferment from want of due sugar and boiling. There were some Dodsons less like the family than others – that was admitted; but in so far as they were 'kin,' they were of necessity better than those who were 'no kin.' And it is remarkable that while no individual Dodson was satisfied with any other individual Dodson, each was satisfied, not only with him or her self, but with the Dodsons collectively. The feeblest member of a family – the one who has the least character – is often the merest epitome of the family habits and traditions; and Mrs Tulliver was a thorough Dodson, though a mild one, as small-beer, so long as it is anything, is only describable as very weak ale: and though she had groaned a little in her youth under the yoke of her elder sisters, and still shed occasional tears at their sisterly reproaches, it was not in Mrs Tulliver to be an innovator on the family ideas. She was thankful to have been a Dodson, and to have one child who took after her own family, at least in his features and complexion, in liking salt and in eating beans, which a Tulliver never did.

In other respects the true Dodson was partly latent in Tom, and he was as far from appreciating his 'kin' on the mother's side as Maggie herself, generally absconding for the day with a large supply of the most portable food, when he received timely warning that his aunts and uncles were coming: a moral symptom from which his aunt Glegg deduced the gloomiest views of his future. It was rather hard on Maggie that Tom always absconded without letting her into the secret, but the weaker sex are acknowledged to be serious *impedimenta* in cases of flight.

On Wednesday, the day before the aunts and uncles were coming, there were such various and suggestive scents, as of plumcakes in the oven and jellies in the hot state, mingled with the aroma of gravy, that it was impossible to feel altogether gloomy: there was hope in the air. Tom and Maggie made several inroads into the kitchen, and, like other marauders, were induced to keep aloof for a time only by being allowed to carry away a sufficient load of booty.

'Tom,' said Maggie, as they sat on the boughs of the elder tree, eating their jam puffs, 'shall you run away tomorrow?'

'No,' said Tom, slowly, when he had finished his puff, and was eyeing the third, which was to be divided between them, 'no, I shan't.'

'Why, Tom? Because Lucy's coming?'

'No,' said Tom, opening his pocketknife and holding it over the puff, with his head on one side in a dubitative manner. (It was a difficult problem to divide that very irregular polygon into two equal parts.) 'What do *I* care about Lucy? She's only a girl – *she* can't play at bandy.'

'Is it the tipsy-cake, then?' said Maggie, exerting her hypothetic powers, while she leaned forward towards Tom with her eyes fixed on the hovering knife.

'No, you silly, that'll be good the day after. It's the pudden. I know what the pudden's to be – apricot roll-up – oh my buttons!'

With this interjection, the knife descended on the puff and it was in two, but the result was not satisfactory to Tom, for he still eyed the halves doubtfully. At last he said, 'Shut your eyes, Maggie.'

'What for?'

'You never mind what for. Shut 'em, when I tell you.'

Maggie obeyed.

'Now, which'll you have, Maggie – right hand or left?'

'I'll have that with the jam run out,' said Maggie, keeping her eyes shut to please Tom.

'Why, you don't like that, you silly. You may have it if it comes to you fair, but I shan't give it you without. Right or left – you choose, now. Ha-a-a!' said Tom, in a tone of exasperation, as Maggie peeped. 'You keep your eyes shut, now, else you shan't have any.'

Maggie's power of sacrifice did not extend so far; indeed, I fear she cared less that Tom should enjoy the utmost possible amount of puff, than that he should be pleased with her for giving him the best bit. So she shut her eyes quite close, till Tom bid her to 'say which,' and then she said, 'Left-hand.'

'You've got it,' said Tom, in rather a bitter tone.

'What! the bit with the jam run out?'

'No; here take it,' said Tom, firmly, handing decidedly the best piece to Maggie.

'Oh, please, Tom, have it: I don't mind – I like the other: please take this.'

'No, I shan't,' said Tom, almost crossly, beginning on his own inferior piece.

Maggie, thinking it was no use to contend further, began too, and ate up her half puff with considerable relish as well as rapidity. But Tom had finished first, and had to look on while Maggie ate her last morsel or two, feeling in himself a capacity for more. Maggie didn't know Tom was looking at her; she was see-sawing on the elder bough, lost to almost everything but a vague sense of jam and idleness.

'Oh, you greedy thing!' said Tom, when she had swallowed the last morsel. He was conscious of having acted very fairly, and thought she ought to have considered this, and made up to him for it. He would have refused a bit of hers beforehand, but one is naturally at a different point of view before and after one's own share of puff is swallowed.

Maggie turned quite pale. 'O, Tom, why didn't you ask me?'

'*I* wasn't going to ask you for a bit, you greedy. You might have thought of it without, when you knew I gave you the best bit.'

'But I wanted you to have it – you know I did,' said Maggie, in an injured tone.

'Yes, but I wasn't going to do what wasn't fair, like Spouncer. He always takes the best bit, if you don't punch him for it; and if you choose the best with your eyes shut, he changes his hands. But if I go halves, I'll go 'em fair – only I wouldn't be a greedy.'

With this cutting innuendo, Tom jumped down from his bough, and threw a stone with a 'hoigh!' as a friendly attention to Yap, who had also been looking on while the eatables vanished, with an agitation of his ears and feelings which could hardly have been without bitterness. Yet the excellent dog accepted Tom's attention with as much alacrity as if he had been treated quite generously.

But Maggie, gifted with that superior power of misery which distinguishes the human being, and places him at a proud distance from the most melancholy chimpanzee, sat still on her bough, and gave herself up to the keen sense of unmerited reproach. She would have given the world not to have eaten all her puff, and to have saved some of it for Tom. Not but that the puff was very nice, for Maggie's palate was not at all obtuse, but she would have gone without it many times over, sooner than Tom should call her greedy and be cross with her. And he had said he wouldn't have it – and she ate it without thinking – how could she help it? The tears flowed so plentifully that Maggie saw nothing around her for the next ten minutes; but by that time resentment began to give way to the desire of reconciliation, and she jumped from her bough to look for Tom. He was no longer in the paddock behind the rickyard – where was he likely to be gone, and Yap with him? Maggie ran to the high bank against the great holly tree, where she could see far away towards the Floss. There was Tom; but her heart sank again as she saw how far off he was on his way to the great river, and that he had another companion besides Yap – naughty Bob Jakin, whose official, if not natural function, of frightening the birds, was just now at a standstill. Maggie felt sure that Bob was wicked, without very distinctly knowing why; unless it was because Bob's mother was a dreadfully large fat woman, who lived at a queer round house down the river; and once, when Maggie and Tom had wandered thither, there rushed out a brindled dog that wouldn't stop barking; and when Bob's mother came out after it, and screamed above the barking to tell them not to be frightened, Maggie thought she was scolding them fiercely, and her heart beat with terror. Maggie thought it very likely that the round house had snakes on the floor, and bats in the bedroom: for she had seen Bob take off his cap to show Tom a little snake that was inside it, and another time he had a handful of young bats: altogether, he was an irregular character, perhaps even slightly diabolical, judging from his intimacy with snakes and bats; and to crown all, when Tom had Bob for a companion, he didn't mind about Maggie, and would never let her go with him.

It must be owned that Tom was fond of Bob's company. How could it be otherwise? Bob knew, directly he saw a bird's egg, whether it was a swallow's, or a tomtit's, or a yellowhammers; he found out all the wasps' nests, and could set all sorts of traps; he could climb the trees like a squirrel, and had quite a magical power of detecting hedgehogs and stoats; and he had courage to do things that were rather naughty, such as making gaps in the hedgerows, throwing stones after the sheep, and killing a cat that was wandering *incognito*. Such qualities in an inferior, who could always be treated with authority, in spite of his superior knowingness, had necessarily, a fatal fascination for Tom; and every, holiday-time Maggie was sure to have days of grief because he had gone off with Bob.

Well! there was no hope for it: he was gone now, and Maggie could think of no comfort but to sit down by the holly, or wander by the hedgerow, and fancy it was all different, refashioning her little world into just what she should like it to be.

Maggie's was a troublous life, and this was the form in which she took her opium.

Meanwhile Tom, forgetting all about Maggie and the sting of reproach which he had left in her heart, was hurrying along with Bob, whom he had met accidentally, to the scene of a great rat-catching in a neighbouring barn. Bob knew all about this particular affair, and spoke of the sport with an enthusiasm which no one who is not either divested of all manly feeling, or pitiably ignorant of rat-catching, can fail to imagine. For a person suspected of preternatural wickedness, Bob was really not so very villainous-looking; there was even something agreeable in his snub-nosed face, with its close-curled border of red hair. But then his trousers were always rolled up at the knee, for the convenience of wading on the slightest notice; and his virtue, supposing it to exist, was undeniably 'virtue in rags', which, on the authority even of bilious philosophers, who think all well-dressed merit overpaid, is notoriously likely to remain unrecognised (perhaps because it is seen so seldom).

'I know the chap as owns the ferrets,' said Bob, in a hoarse treble voice, as he shuffled along, keeping his blue eyes fixed on the river, like an amphibious animal who foresaw occasion for darting in. 'He lives up the Kennel Yard at Sut Ogg's – he does. He's the biggest rot-catcher anywhere – he is. I'd sooner be a rot-catcher nor anything – I would. The moles is nothing to the rots. But Lors! you mun ha' ferrets. Dogs is no good. Why, there's that dog, now!' Bob continued, pointing with an air of disgust towards Yap, 'he's no more good wi' a rot nor nothin'. I see it myself – I did – at the rot-catchin' i' your feyther's barn.'

Yap, feeling the withering influence of this scorn, tucked his tail in and shrank close to Tom's leg, who felt a little hurt for him, but had not the superhuman courage to seem behindhand with Bob in contempt for a dog who made so poor a figure.

'No, no,' he said, 'Yap's no good at sport. I'll have regular good dogs for rats and everything, when I've done school.'

'Hev ferrets, Measter Tom,' said Bob, eagerly, 'them white ferrets wi' pink eyes; Lors, you might catch your own rots, an' you might put a rot in a cage wi' a ferret, an' see 'em fight – you might. That's what I'd do, I know, an' it 'ud be better fun a'most nor seein' two chaps fight – if it wasn't them chaps as sell cakes an' oranges at the Fair, as the things flew out o' their baskets, an' some o' the cakes was smashed . . . But they tasted just as good,' added Bob, by way of note or addendum, after a moment's pause.

'But, I say, Bob,' said Tom, in a tone of deliberation, 'ferrets are nasty biting things – they'll bite a fellow without being set on.'

'Lors! why, that's the beauty on 'em. If a chap lays hold o' your ferret, he won't be long before he hollows out a good un – *he* won't.'

At this moment a striking incident made the boys pause suddenly in their walk. It was the plunging of some small body in the water from among the neighbouring bulrushes: if it was not a water-rat, Bob intimated that he was ready to undergo the most unpleasant consequences.

'Hoigh! Yap – hoigh! there he is,' said Tom, clapping his hands, as the little black snout made its arrowy course to the opposite bank. 'Seize him, lad, seize him!'

Yap agitated his ears and wrinkled his brows, but declined to plunge, trying whether barking would not answer the purpose just as well.

'Ugh! you coward!' said Tom, and kicked him over, feeling humiliated as a sportsman to possess so poor-spirited an animal. Bob abstained from remark and passed on, choosing, however, to walk in the shallow edge of the over-flowing river by way of change.

'He's none so full now, the Floss isn't,' said Bob, as he kicked the water up before him, with an agreeable sense of being insolent to it. 'Why, last 'ear, the meadows was all one sheet o' water, they was.'

'Ay, but,' said Tom, whose mind was prone to see an opposition between statements that were really quite accordant, 'but there was a big flood once, when the Round Pool was 'made. *I* know there was, 'cause father says so. And the sheep and cows were all drowned, and the boats went all over the fields ever such a way.'

'*I* don't care about a flood comin',' said Bob; 'I don't mind the water, no more nor the land. I'd swim – *I* would.'

'Ah, but if you got nothing to eat for ever so long?' said Tom, his imagination becoming quite active under the stimulus of that dread. 'When I'm a man, I shall make a boat with a wooden house on the top of it, like Noah's ark, and keep plenty to eat in it – rabbits and things – all ready. And then if the flood came, you know, Bob, I shouldn't mind . . . . And I'd take you in, if I saw you swimming,' he added, in the tone of a benevolent patron.

'I aren't frighted,' said Bob, to whom hunger did not appear so appalling. 'But I'd get in an' knock the rabbits on th' head when you wanted to eat 'em.'

'Ah, and I should have halfpence, and we'd play at heads-and-tails,' said Tom, not contemplating the possibility that this recreation might have fewer charms for his mature age. 'I'd divide fair to begin with, and then we'd see who'd win.'

'I've got a halfpenny o' my own,' said Bob, proudly, coming out of the water and tossing his halfpenny in the air. 'Yeads or tails?'

'Tails,' said Tom, instantly fired with the desire to win.

'It's yeads,' said Bob, hastily, snatching up the halfpenny as it fell.

'It wasn't,' said Tom, loudly and peremptorily. 'You give me the halfpenny – I've won it fair.'

'I shan't,' said Bob, holding it tight in his pocket.

'Then I'll make you – see if I don't,' said Tom.

'You can't make me do nothing, you can't,' said Bob.

'Yes, I can.'

'No, you can't.'

'I'm master.'

'I don't care for you.'

'But I'll make you care, you cheat,' said Tom, collaring Bob and shaking him.

'You get out wi' you,' said Bob, giving Tom a kick.

Tom's blood was thoroughly up: he went at Bob with a lunge and threw him

FOUR NOVELS OF GEORGE ELIOT

down, but Bob seized hold and kept it like a cat, and pulled Tom down after him. They struggled fiercely on the ground for a moment or two, till Tom, pinning Bob down by the shoulders, thought he had the mastery.

'*You* say you'll give me the halfpenny now,' he said, with difficulty, while he exerted himself to keep the command of Bob's arms.

But at this moment, Yap, who had been running on before, returned barking to the scene of action, and saw a favourable opportunity for biting Bob's bare leg not only with impunity but with honour. The pain from Yap's teeth, instead of surprising Bob into a relaxation of his hold, gave it a fiercer tenacity, and, with a new exertion of his force, he pushed Tom backward and got uppermost. But now Yap, who could get no sufficient purchase before, set his teeth in a new place, so that Bob, harassed in this way, let go his hold of Tom, and, almost throttling Yap, flung him into the river. By this time Tom was up again, and before Bob had quite recovered his balance after the act of swinging Yap, Tom fell upon him, threw him down, and got his knees firmly on Bob's chest.

'You give me the halfpenny now,' said Tom.

'Take it,' said Bob, sulkily.

'No, I shan't take it; you give it me.'

Bob took the halfpenny out of his pocket, and threw it away from him on the ground.

Tom loosed his hold, and left Bob to rise.

'There the halfpenny lies,' he said. 'I don't want your halfpenny; I wouldn't have kept it. But you wanted to cheat: I hate a cheat. I shan't go along with you any more,' he added, turning round homeward, not without casting a regret towards the rat-catching and other pleasures which he must relinquish along with Bob's society.

'You may let it alone, then,' Bob called out after him. 'I shall cheat if I like; there's no fun i' playing else; and I know where there's a goldfinch's nest, but I'll take care *you* don't . . . An' you're a nasty fightin' turkey-cock, you are . . . '

Tom walked on without looking round, and Yap followed his example, the cold bath having moderated his passions.

'Go along wi' you, then, wi' your drownded dog; I wouldn't own such a dog – *I* wouldn't,' said Bob, getting louder, in a last effort to sustain his defiance. But Tom was not to be provoked into turning round, and Bob's voice began to falter a little as he said,

'An' I'n gi'en you everything, an' showed you everything, an' niver wanted nothin' from you . . . An' there's your hornhanded knife, then, as you gi'en me' . . . Here Bob flung the knife as far as he could after Tom's retreating footsteps. But it produced no effect, except the sense in Bob's mind that there was a terrible void in his lot, now that knife was gone.

He stood still till Tom had passed through the gate and disappeared behind the hedge. The knife would do no good on the ground there – it wouldn't vex Tom, and pride or resentment was a feeble passion in Bob's mind compared with the love of a pocketknife. His very fingers sent entreating thrills that he would go and clutch that familiar rough buck's-horn handle, which they had so often grasped for mere affection as it lay idle in his pocket. And there were two blades, and they had just been sharpened! What is life without a pocketknife to him who has once tasted a higher existence? No: to throw the handle after the hatchet is a comprehensible act of desperation, but to throw one's pocketknife after an implacable friend is clearly in every sense a hyperbole, or throwing beyond the mark. So Bob shuffled back to the spot where the beloved knife lay in the dirt, and felt quite a new pleasure in clutching it again after the temporary separation, in opening one blade after the other, and feeling their edge with his well-hardened thumb. Poor Bob! he was not sensitive on the point of honour – not a chivalrous character. That fine moral aroma would not have been thought much of by the public opinion of Kennel Yard, which was the very focus or heart of Bob's world, even if it could have made itself perceptible there; yet, for all that, he was not utterly a sneak and a thief, as our friend Tom had hastily decided.

But Tom, you perceive, was rather a Rhadamanthine personage, having more than the usual share of boy's justice in him – the justice that desires to hurt culprits as much as they deserve to be hurt, and is troubled with no doubts concerning the exact amount of their deserts. Maggie saw a cloud on his brow when he came home, which checked her joy at his coming so much sooner than she had expected, and she dared hardly speak to him as he stood silently throwing small gravel-stones into the mill-dam. It is not pleasant to give up a rat-catching when you have set your mind on it. But if Tom had told his strongest feeling at that moment, he would have said, 'I'd do just the same again.' That was his usual mode of viewing his past actions; whereas Maggie was always wishing she had done something different.

CHAPTER 7

Enter the Aunts and Uncles

The Dodsons were certainly a handsome family, and Mrs Glegg was not the least handsome of the sisters. As she sat in Mrs Tulliver's armchair, no impartial observer could have denied that for a woman of fifty she had a very comely face and figure, though Tom and Maggie considered their aunt Glegg as the type of ugliness. It is true she despised the advantages of costume, for though, as she often observed, no woman had better clothes, it was not her way to wear her new things out before her old ones. Other women, if they liked, might have their best thread-lace in every wash; but when Mrs Glegg died, it would be found that she had better lace laid by in the right-hand drawer of her wardrobe, in the Spotted Chamber, than ever Mrs Wooll of St Ogg's had bought in her life, although Mrs Wooll wore her lace before it was paid for. So of her curled fronts: Mrs Glegg had doubtless the glossiest and crispest brown curls in her drawers, as well as curls in various degrees of fuzzy laxness; but to look out on the weekday world from under a crisp and glossy front, would be to introduce a most dreamlike and unpleasant confusion between the sacred and the secular. Occasionally, indeed, Mrs Glegg wore one of her third-best fronts on a weekday visit, but not at a sister's house; especially not at Mrs Tulliver's, who, since her marriage, had hurt her sisters' feelings greatly by wearing her own hair, though, as Mrs Glegg observed to Mrs Deane, a mother of a family, like Bessy, with a husband always going to law, might have been expected to know better. But Bessy was always weak!

So if Mrs Glegg's front today was more fuzzy and lax than usual, she had a design under it: she intended the most pointed and cutting allusion to Mrs Tulliver's bunches of blond curls, separated from each other by a due wave of smoothness on each side of the parting. Mrs Tulliver had shed tears several times at sister Glegg's unkindness on the subject of these unmatronly curls, but the consciousness of looking the handsomer for them, naturally administered support. Mrs Glegg chose to wear her bonnet in the house today – untied and tilted slightly, of course – a frequent practice of hers when she was on a visit, and happened to be in a severe humour: she didn't know what draughts there might be in strange houses. For the same reason she wore a small sable tippet, which reached just to her shoulders, and was very far from meeting across her well-formed chest, while her long neck was protected by a *chevaux-de-frise* of miscellaneous frilling. One would need to be learned in the fashions of those times to know how far in the rear of them Mrs Glegg's slate-coloured silk-gown must have been; but from certain constellations of small yellow spots upon it, and a mouldy odour about it suggestive of a damp clothes-chest, it was probable that it belonged to a stratum of garments just old enough to have come recently into wear.

Mrs Glegg held her large gold watch in her hand, with the many-doubled chain round her fingers, and observed to Mrs Tulliver, who had just returned from a visit to the kitchen, that whatever it might be by other people's clocks and watches, it was gone half-past twelve by hers.

'I don't know what ails sister Pullet,' she continued. 'It used to be the way in our family for one to be as early as another – I'm sure it was so in my poor father's time – and not for one sister to sit half an hour before the others came. But if the ways o' the family are altered, it shan't be *my* fault – *I'll* never be the one to come into a house when all the rest are going away. I wonder *at* sister Deane – she used to be more like me. But if you'll take my advice, Bessy, you'll put the dinner forrard a bit, sooner than put it back because folks are late as ought to ha' known better.'

'Oh dear, there's no fear but what they'll be all here in time, sister,' said Mrs Tulliver, in her mild-peevish tone. 'The dinner won't be ready till half-past one. But if it's long for you to wait, let me fetch you a cheesecake and a glass o' wine.'

'Well, Bessy!' said Mrs Glegg, with a bitter smile, and, a scarcely perceptible toss of her head. 'I should ha' thought you'd known your own sister better. I never *did* eat between meals, and I'm not going to begin. Not but what I hate that nonsense of having your dinner at half-past one, when you might have it at one. You was never brought up in that way, Bessy.'

'Why, Jane, what can I do? Mr Tulliver doesn't like his dinner before two o'clock, but I put it half an hour earlier because o' you.'

'Yes, yes, I know how it is with husbands – they're for putting everything off –

they'll put the dinner off till after tea, if they've got wives as are weak enough to give in to such work; but it's a pity for you, Bessy, as you haven't got more strength o' mind. It'll be well if your children don't suffer for it. And I hope you've not gone and got a great dinner for us – going to expense for your sisters, as 'ud sooner eat a crust o' dry bread nor help to ruin you with extravagance. I wonder you don't take pattern by your sister Deane – she's far more sensible. And here you've got two children to provide for and your husband's spent your fortin i' going to law, and 's likely to spend his own too. A boiled joint, as you could make broth of for the kitchen,' Mrs Glegg added, in a tone of emphatic protest, 'and a plain pudding, with a spoonful o' sugar, and no spice, 'ud be far more becoming.'

With sister Glegg in this humour, there was a cheerful prospect for the day. Mrs Tulliver never went the length of quarrelling with her, any more than a water-fowl that puts out its leg in a deprecating manner can be said to quarrel with a boy who throws stones. But this point of the dinner was a tender one, and not at all new, so that Mrs Tulliver could make the same answer she had often made before.

'Mr Tulliver says he always *will* have a good dinner for his friends while he can pay for it,' she said, 'and he's a right to do as he likes in his own house, sister.'

'Well, Bessy, *I* can't leave your children enough, out o' my savings, to keep 'em from ruin. And you mustn't look to having any o' Mr Glegg's money, for it's well if I don't go first – he comes of a long-lived family; and if he was to die and leave me well for my life, he'd tie all the money up to go back to his own kin.'

The sound of wheels while Mrs Glegg was speaking was an interruption highly welcome to Mrs Tulliver, who hastened out to receive sister Pullet – it must be sister Pullet, because the sound was that of a four-wheel.

Mrs Glegg tossed her head and looked rather sour about the mouth at the thought of the 'four-wheel.' She had a strong opinion on that subject.

Sister Pullet was in tears when the one-horse chaise stopped before Mrs Tulliver's door, and it was apparently requisite that she should shed a few more before getting out, for though her husband and Mrs Tulliver stood ready to support her, she sat still and shook her head sadly, as she looked through her tears at the vague distance.

'Why, whativer is the matter, sister?' said Mrs Tulliver. She was not an imaginative woman, but it occurred to her that the large toilet-glass in sister Pullet's best bedroom was possibly broken for the second time.

There was no reply but a further shake of the head, as Mrs Pullet slowly rose and got down from the chaise, not without casting a glance at Mr Pullet to see that he was guarding her handsome silk dress from injury. Mr Pullet was a small man with a high nose, small twinkling eyes, and thin lips, in a fresh-looking suit of black, and a white cravat, that seemed to have been tied very tight on some higher principle than that of mere personal ease. He bore about the same relation to his tall, good-looking wife, with her balloon sleeves, abundant mantle, and large be-feathered and be-ribboned bonnet, as a small fishing-smack bears to a brig with all its sails spread.

It is a pathetic sight, and a striking example of the complexity introduced into the emotions by a high state of civilisation – the sight of a fashionably-dressed female in grief. From the sorrow of a Hottentot to that of a woman in large buckram sleeves, with several bracelets on each arm, an architectural bonnet, and delicate ribbon-strings – what a long series of gradations! In the enlightened child of civilisation the abandonment characteristic of grief is checked and varied in the subtlest manner, so as to present an interesting problem to the analytic mind. If, with a crushed heart and eyes half-blinded by the mist of tears, she were to walk with a too devious step through a door-place, she might crush her buckram sleeves too, and the deep consciousness of this possibility produces a composition of forces by which she takes a line that just clears the doorpost. Perceiving that the tears are hurrying fast, she unpins her strings and throws them languidly backward – a touching gesture, indicative, even in the deepest gloom, of the hope in future dry moments when cap-strings will once more have a charm. As the tears subside a little, and with her head leaning backward at the angle that will not injure her bonnet, she endures that terrible moment when grief, which has made all things else a weariness, has itself become weary; she looks down pensively at her bracelets, and adjusts their clasps with that pretty studied fortuity which would be gratifying to her mind if it were once more in a calm and healthy state.

Mrs Pullet brushed each doorpost with great nicety, about the latitude of her shoulders (at that period a woman was truly ridiculous to an instructed eye if she did not measure a yard and a half across the shoulders), and having done that, sent the muscles of her face in quest of fresh tears as she advanced into the parlour where Mrs Glegg was seated.

'Well, sister, you're late; what's the matter?' said Mrs Glegg, rather sharply, as they shook hands.

Mrs Pullet sat down – lifting up her mantle carefully behind, before she answered, 'She's gone,' unconsciously using an impressive figure of rhetoric.

'It isn't the glass this time, then,' thought Mrs Tulliver.

'Died the day before yesterday,' continued Mrs Pullet; 'an' her legs was as thick as my body,' she added, with deep sadness, after a pause. 'They'd tapped her no end o' times, and the water – they say you might ha' swum in it, if you'd liked.'

'Well, Sophy, it's a mercy she's gone, then, whoever she may be,' said Mrs Glegg, with the promptitude and emphasis of a mind naturally clear and decided; 'but I can't think who you're talking of, for my part.'

'But I know,' said Mrs Pullet, sighing and shaking her head; 'and there isn't another such a dropsy in the parish. I know as it's old Mrs Sutton o' the Twenty-lands.'

'Well, she's no kin o' yours, nor much acquaintance as I've ever heared of,' said Mrs Glegg, who always cried just as much as was proper when anything happened to her own 'kin,' but not on other occasions.

'She's so much acquaintance as I've seen her legs when they was like bladders . . . And an old lady as had doubled her money over and over again, and kept it all in her own management to the last, and had her pocket with her keys in under her pillow constant. There isn't many old parish'ners like her, I doubt.'

'And they say she'd took as much physic as 'ud fill a waggon,' observed Mr Pullet.

'Ah!' sighed Mrs Pullet, 'she'd another complaint ever so many years before she had the dropsy, and the doctors couldn't make out what it was. And she said to me, when I went to see her last Christmas, she said, "Mrs Pullet, if ever you have the dropsy, you'll think o' me." She *did* say so,' added Mrs Pullet, beginning to cry bitterly again; 'those were her very words. And she's to be buried o' Saturday, and Pullet's bid to the funeral.'

'Sophy,' said Mrs Glegg, unable any longer to contain her spirit of rational remonstrance – 'Sophy, I wonder *at* you, fretting and injuring your health about people as don't belong to you. Your poor father never did so, nor your Aunt Frances neither, nor any o' the family as I ever heared of. You couldn't fret no more than this, if we'd heared as our cousin Abbott had died sudden without making his will.'

Mrs Pullet was silent, having to finish her crying, and rather flattered than indignant at being upbraided for crying too much. It was not everybody who could afford to cry so much about their neighbours who had left them nothing; but Mrs Pullet had married a gentleman farmer, and had leisure and money to carry her crying and everything else to the highest pitch of respectability.

'Mrs Sutton didn't die without making her will, though,' said Mr Pullet, with a confused sense that he was saying something to sanction his wife's tears; 'ours is a rich parish, but they say there's nobody else to leave as many thousands behind 'em as Mrs Sutton. And she's left no leggicies, to speak on – left it all in a lump to her husband's nevvy.'

'There wasn't much good i' being so rich, then,' said Mrs Glegg, 'if she'd got none but husband's kin to leave it to. It's poor work when that's all you've got to pinch yourself for – not as I'm one o' those as 'ud like to die without leaving more money out at interest than other folks had reckoned. But it's a poor tale when it must go out o' your own family.'

'I'm sure, sister,' said Mrs Pullet, who had recovered sufficiently to take off her veil and fold it carefully, 'it's a nice sort o' man as Mrs Sutton has left her money to, for he's troubled with the asthmy, and goes to bed every night at eight o'clock. He told me about it himself – as free as could be – one Sunday when he came to our church. He wears a hare-skin on his chest, and has a trembling in his talk – quite a gentleman sort o' man. I told him there wasn't many months in the year as I wasn't under the doctor's hands. And he said, "Mrs Pullet, I can feel for you." That was what he said – the very words. Ah!' sighed Mrs Pullet, shaking her head at the idea that there were but few who could enter fully into her experiences in pink mixture and white mixture, strong stuff in small bottles, and weak stuff in large bottles, damp boluses at a shilling, and draughts at eighteen-pence. 'Sister, I may as well go and take my bonnet off now. Did you see as the cap-box was put out?' she added, turning to her husband.

Mr Pullet, by an unaccountable lapse of memory, had forgotten it, and hastened out, with a stricken conscience, to remedy the omission.

'They'll bring it upstairs, sister,' said Mrs Tulliver, wishing to go at once, lest

Mrs Glegg should begin to explain her feelings about Sophy's being the first Dodson who ever ruined her constitution with doctor's stuff.

Mrs Tulliver was fond of going upstairs with her sister Pullet, and looking thoroughly at her cap before she put it on her head, and discussing millinery in general. This was part of Bessy's weakness, that stirred Mrs Glegg's sisterly compassion: Bessy went far too well dressed, considering; and she was too proud to dress her child in the good clothing her sister Glegg gave her from the primeval strata of her wardrobe; it was a sin and a shame to buy anything to dress that child, if it wasn't a pair of shoes. In this particular, however, Mrs Glegg did her sister Bessy some injustice, for Mrs Tulliver had really made great efforts to induce Maggie to wear a Leghorn bonnet and a dyed silk frock made out of her aunt Glegg's, but the results had been such that Mrs Tulliver was obliged to bury them in her maternal bosom; for Maggie, declaring that the frock smelt of nasty dye, had taken an opportunity of basting it together with the roast-beef the first Sunday she wore it, and, finding this scheme answer, she had subsequently pumped on the bonnet with its green ribbons, so as to give it a general resemblance to a sage cheese garnished with withered lettuces. I must urge in excuse for Maggie, that Tom had laughed at her in the bonnet, and said she looked like an old Judy. Aunt Pullet, too, made presents of clothes, but these were always pretty enough to please Maggie as well as her mother. Of all her sisters, Mrs Tulliver certainly preferred her sister Pullet, not without a return of preference; but Mrs Pullet was sorry Bessy had those naughty awkward children; she would do the best she could by them, but it was a pity they weren't as good and as pretty as sister Deane's child. Maggie and Tom, on their part, thought their aunt Pullet tolerable, chiefly because she was not their aunt Glegg. Tom always declined to go more than once, during his holidays, to see either of them: both his uncles tipped him that once, of course; but at his aunt Pullet's there were a great many toads to pelt in the cellar-area, so that he preferred the visit to her. Maggie shuddered at the toads, and dreamed of them horribly, but she liked her uncle Pullet's musical snuffbox. Still, it was agreed by the sisters, in Mrs Tulliver's absence, that the Tulliver blood did not mix well with the Dodson blood; that, in fact, poor Bessy's children were Tullivers, and that Tom, notwithstanding he had the Dodson complexion, was likely to be as 'contrairy' as his father. As for Maggie, she was the picture of her aunt Moss, Mr Tulliver's sister – a large-boned woman, who had married as poorly as could be, had no china, and had a husband who had much ado to pay his rent. But when Mrs Pullet was alone with Mrs Tulliver upstairs, the remarks were naturally to the disadvantage of Mrs Glegg, and they agreed, in confidence, that there was no knowing what sort of fright sister Jane would come out next. But their tête-à-tête was curtailed by the appearance of Mrs Deane with little Lucy; and Mrs Tulliver had to look with a silent pang while Lucy's blond curls were adjusted. It was quite unaccountable that Mrs Deane, the thinnest and sallowest of all the Miss Dodsons, should have had this child, who might have been taken for Mrs Tulliver's any day. And Maggie always looked twice as dark as usual when she was by the side of Lucy.

She did today, when she and Tom came in from the garden with their father and their uncle Glegg. Maggie had thrown her bonnet off very carelessly, and, coming in with her hair rough as well as out of curl, rushed at once to Lucy, who was standing by her mother's knee. Certainly the contrast between the cousins was conspicuous, and, to superficial eyes, was very much to the disadvantage of Maggie, though a connoisseur might have seen 'points' in her which had a higher promise for maturity than Lucy's natty completeness. It was like the contrast between a rough, dark, overgrown puppy and a white kitten. Lucy put up the neatest little rosebud mouth to be kissed: everything about her was neat – her little round neck with the row of coral beads, her little straight nose, not at all snubby, her little clear eyebrows, rather darker than her curls, to match her hazel eyes, which looked up with shy pleasure at Maggie, taller by the head, though scarcely a year older. Maggie always looked at Lucy with delight. She was fond of fancying a world where the people never got any larger than children of their own age, and she made the queen of it just like Lucy, with a little crown on her head, and a little sceptre in her hand'. . . only the queen was Maggie herself in Lucy's form.

'Oh, Lucy,' she burst out, after kissing her, 'you'll stay with Tom and me, won't you? Oh, kiss her, Tom.'

Tom, too, had come up to Lucy, but he was not going to kiss her – no; he came up to her with Maggie, because it seemed easier, on the whole, than saying, 'How do you do?' to all those aunts and uncles: he stood looking at nothing in particular, with the blushing, awkward air and semi-smile which are common to shy boys when in company – very much as if they had come into the world by mistake, and found it in a degree of undress that was quite embarrassing.

'Heyday!' said aunt Glegg, with loud emphasis. 'Do little boys and gells come into a room without taking notice o' their uncles and aunts? That wasn't the way when *I* was a little gell.'

'Go and speak to your aunts and uncles, my dears,' said Mrs Tulliver, looking anxious and melancholy. She wanted to whisper to Maggie a command to go and have her hair brushed.

'Well, and how do you do? And I hope you're good children, are you?' said aunt Glegg, in the same loud emphatic way, as she took their hands, hurting them with her large rings, and kissing their cheeks much against their desire. 'Look up, Tom, look up. Boys as go to boarding-schools should hold their heads up. Look at me now.' Tom declined that pleasure apparently, for he tried to draw his hand away. 'Put your hair behind your ears, Maggie, and keep your frock on your shoulder.'

Aunt Glegg always spoke to them in this loud emphatic way, as if she considered them deaf, or perhaps rather idiotic: it was a means, she thought, of making them feel that they were accountable creatures, and might be a salutary check on naughty tendencies. Bessy's children were so spoiled – they'd need have somebody to make them feel their duty.

'Well, my dears,' said aunt Pullet, in a compassionate voice, 'you grow wonderful fast. I doubt they'll outgrow their strength,' she added, looking over their heads with a melancholy expression, at their mother. 'I think the gell has too much hair. I'd have it thinned and cut shorter, sister, if I was you: it isn't good for her health. It's that as makes her skin so brown, I shouldn't wonder. Don't you think so, sister Deane?'

'I can't say, I'm sure, sister,' said Mrs Deane, shutting her lips close again, and looking at Maggie with a critical eye.

'No, no,' said Mr Tulliver, 'the child's healthy enough – there's nothing ails her. There's red wheat as well as white, for that matter, and some like the dark grain best. But it 'ud be as well if Bessy 'ud have the child's hair cut, so as it 'ud lie smooth.'

A dreadful resolve was gathering in Maggie's breast, but it was arrested by the desire to know from her aunt Deane whether she would leave Lucy behind: aunt Deane would hardly ever let Lucy come to see them. After various reasons for refusal, Mrs Deane appealed to Lucy herself.

'You wouldn't like to stay behind without mother, should you, Lucy?'

'Yes, please, mother,' said Lucy, timidly, blushing very pink all over her little neck.

'Well done, Lucy! Let her stay, Mrs Deane, let her stay,' said Mr Deane, a large but alert-looking man, with a type of physique to be seen in all ranks of English society – bald crown, red whiskers, full forehead, and general solidity without heaviness. You may see noblemen like Mr Deane, and you may see grocers or day-labourers like him; but the keenness of his brown eyes was less common than his contour. He held a silver snuffbox very tightly in his hand, and now and then exchanged a pinch with Mr Tulliver, whose box was only silver-mounted, so that it was naturally a joke between them that Mr Tulliver wanted to exchange snuffboxes also. Mr Deane's box had been given him by the superior partners in the firm to which he belonged, at the same time that they gave him a share in the business, in acknowledgment of his valuable services as manager. No man was thought more highly of in St Ogg's than Mr Deane, and some persons were even of opinion that Miss Susan Dodson, who was held to have made the worst match of all the Dodson sisters, might one day ride in a better carriage, and live in a better house, even than her sister Pullet. There was no knowing where a man would stop, who had got his foot into a great mill-owning, ship-owning business like that of Guest & Co., with a banking concern attached. And Mrs Deane, as her intimate female friends observed, was proud and 'having' enough: *she* wouldn't let her husband stand still in the world for want of spurring.

'Maggie,' said Mrs Tulliver, beckoning Maggie to her, and whispering in her ear, as soon as this point of Lucy's staying was settled, 'go and get your hair brushed – do, for shame. I told you not to come in without going to Martha first; you know I did.'

'Tom, come out with me,' whispered Maggie, pulling his sleeve as she passed him; and Tom followed willingly enough.

'Come upstairs with me, Tom,' she whispered, when they were outside the door. 'There's something I want to do before dinner.'

'There's no time to play at anything before dinner,' said Tom, whose imagination was impatient of any intermediate prospect.

'O, yes, there is time for this – *do* come, Tom.'

Tom followed Maggie upstairs into her mother's room, and saw her go at once to a drawer, from which she took out a large pair of scissors.

'What are they for, Maggie?' said Tom, feeling his curiosity awakened.

Maggie answered by seizing her front locks and cutting them straight across the middle of her forehead.

'O, my buttons, Maggie, you'll catch it!' exclaimed Tom; 'you'd better not cut any more off.'

Snip! went the great scissors again while Tom was speaking, and he couldn't help feeling it was rather good fun: Maggie would look so queer.

'Here, Tom, cut it behind for me,' said Maggie, excited by her own daring, and anxious to finish the deed.

'You'll catch it, you know,' said Tom, nodding his head in an 'admonitory manner, and hesitating a little as he took the scissors.

'Never mind – make haste!' said Maggie, giving a little stamp with her foot. Her cheeks were quite flushed.

The black locks were so thick – nothing could be more tempting to a lad who had already tasted the forbidden pleasure of cutting the pony's mane. I speak to those who know the satisfaction of making a pair of shears meet through a duly resisting mass of hair. One delicious grinding snip, and then another and another, and the hinderlocks fell heavily on the floor, and Maggie stood cropped in a jagged, uneven manner, but with a sense of clearness and freedom, as if she had emerged from a wood into the open plain.

'Oh, Maggie,' said Tom, jumping round her, and slapping his knees as he laughed, 'oh my buttons, what a queer thing you look! Look at yourself in the glass – you look like the idiot we throw our nutshells to at school.'

Maggie felt an unexpected pang. She had thought beforehand chiefly of her own deliverance from her teasing hair and teasing remarks about it, and something also of the triumph she should have over her mother and her aunts by this very decided course of action: she didn't want her hair to look pretty – that was out of the question – she only wanted people to think her a clever little girl, and not to find fault with her. But now, when Tom began to laugh at her, and say she was like the idiot, the affair had quite a new aspect. She looked in the glass, and still Tom laughed and clapped his hands, and Maggie's flushed cheeks began to pale, and her lips to tremble a little.

'O Maggie, you'll have to go down to dinner directly,' said Tom. 'O my!'

'Don't laugh at me, Tom,' said Maggie, in a passionate tone, with an outburst of angry tears, stamping, and giving him a push.

'Now, then, spitfire!' said Tom. 'What did you cut it off for, then? I shall go down: I can smell the dinner going in.'

He hurried downstairs and left poor Maggie to that bitter sense of the irrevocable which was almost an everyday experience of her small soul. She could see clearly enough, now the thing was done, that it was very foolish, and that she should have to hear and think more about her hair than ever; for Maggie rushed to her deeds with passionate impulse, and then saw not only their consequences, but what would have happened if they had not been done, with all the detail and exaggerated circumstance of an active imagination. Tom never did the same sort of foolish things as Maggie, having a wonderful instinctive discernment of what would turn to his advantage or disadvantage; and so it happened, that though he was much more wilful and inflexible than Maggie, his mother hardly ever called him naughty. But if Tom did make a mistake of that sort, he espoused it, and stood by it: he 'didn't mind'. If he broke the lash of his father's gig-whip by lashing the gate, he couldn't help it – the whip shouldn't have got caught in the hinge. If Tom Tulliver whipped a gate, he was convinced, not that the whipping of gates by all boys was a justifiable act, but that he, Tom Tulliver, was justifiable in whipping that particular gate, and he wasn't going to be sorry. But Maggie, as she stood crying before the glass, felt it impossible that she should go down to dinner and endure the severe eyes and severe words of her aunts, while Tom, and Lucy, and Martha, who waited at table, and perhaps her father and her uncles, would laugh at her, – for if Tom had laughed at her, of course everyone else would; and if she had only let her hair alone, she could have sat with Tom and Lucy, and had the apricot pudding and the custard! What could she do but sob? She sat as helpless and despairing among her black locks as Ajax among the slaughtered sheep. Very trivial, perhaps, this anguish seems to weather-worn mortals who have to think of Christmas bills, dead loves, and broken friendships; but it was not less bitter to Maggie – perhaps it was even more bitter – than what we are fond of calling antithetically the real troubles of mature life. 'Ah, my child, you will have real troubles to fret about by and by,' is the consolation we have almost all of us had administered to us in our childhood, and have repeated to other children since we have been grown up. We have all of us sobbed so piteously, standing with tiny bare legs above our little socks, when we lost sight of our mother or nurse in some strange place; but we can no longer recall the poignancy of that moment and weep over it, as we do over the remembered sufferings of five or ten years ago. Every one of those keen moments has left its trace, and lives in us still, but such traces have blent themselves irrecoverably with the firmer texture of our youth and manhood; and so it comes that we can look on at the troubles of our children with a smiling disbelief in the reality of their pain. Is there anyone who can recover the experience of his childhood, not merely with a memory of what he did and what happened to him, of what he liked and disliked when he was in frock and trousers, but with an intimate penetration, a revived consciousness of what he felt then – when it was so long from one Midsummer to another? what he felt when his schoolfellows shut him out of their game because he would pitch the ball wrong out of mere wilfulness; or on a rainy day in the holidays, when he didn't know how to amuse himself, and fell from idleness into mischief, from mischief into defiance, and from defiance into sulkiness; or when his mother absolutely refused to let him have a tailed coat that 'half', although every other boy of his age had gone into tails already? Surely if we could recall that early bitterness, and the dim guesses, the strangely perspectiveless conception of life that gave the bitterness its intensity, we should not pooh-pooh the griefs of our children.

'Miss Maggie, you're to come down this minute,' said Kezia, entering the room hurriedly. 'Lawks! what have you been adoing? I niver *see* such a fright.'

'Don't, Kezia,' said Maggie, angrily. 'Go away!'

'But I tell you, you're to come down, Miss, this minute: your mother says so,' said Kezia, going up to Maggie and taking her by the hand to raise her from the floor.

'Get away, Kezia; I don't want any dinner,' said Maggie, resisting Kezia's arm. 'I shan't come.'

'O, well, I can't stay. I've got to wait at dinner,' said Kezia, going out again.

'Maggie, you little silly,' said Tom, peeping into the room ten minutes after, 'why don't you come and have your dinner? There's lots o' goodies, and mother says you're to come. What are you crying for, you little spooney?'

O, it was dreadful! Tom was so hard and unconcerned; if *he* had been crying on the floor, Maggie would have cried too. And there was the dinner, so nice; and she was *so* hungry. It was very bitter.

But Tom was not altogether hard. He was not inclined to cry, and did not feel that Maggie's grief spoiled his prospect of the sweets; but he went and put his head near her, and said in a lower, comforting tone, 'Won't you come, then, Magsie? Shall I bring you a bit o' pudding when I've had mine?. . . and a custard and things?'

'Ye-e-es,' said Maggie, beginning to feel life a little more tolerable.

'Very well,' said Tom, going away. But he turned again at the door and said, 'But you'd better come, you know. There's the dessert – nuts, you know – and cowslip wine.'

Maggie's tears had ceased, and she looked reflective as Tom left her. His good nature had taken off the keenest edge of her suffering, and nuts with cowslip wine began to assert their legitimate influence.

Slowly she rose from amongst her scattered locks, and slowly she made her way downstairs. Then she stood leaning with one shoulder against the frame of the dining-parlour door, peeping in when it was ajar. She saw Tom and Lucy with an empty chair between them, and there were the custards on a side-table – it was too much. She slipped in and went towards the empty chair. But she had no sooner sat down than she repented, and wished herself back again.

Mrs Tulliver gave a little scream as she saw her, and felt such a 'turn' that she dropped the large gravy-spoon into the dish with the most serious results to the tablecloth. For Kezia had not betrayed the reason of Maggie's refusal to come down, not liking to give her mistress a shock in the moment of carving, and Mrs Tulliver thought there was nothing worse in question than a fit of perverseness, which was inflicting its own punishment by depriving Maggie of half her dinner.

Mrs Tulliver's scream made all eyes turn towards the same point as her own, and Maggie's cheeks and ears began to burn, while uncle Glegg, a kind-looking, white-haired old gentleman, said, 'Heyday! what little gell's this – why, I don't know her. Is it some little gell you've picked up in the road, Kezia?'

'Why, she's gone and cut her hair herself,' said Mr Tulliver in an undertone to Mr Deane, laughing with much enjoyment. 'Did you ever know such a little hussy as it is?'

'Why, little miss, you've made yourself look very funny,' said uncle Pullet, and perhaps he never in his life made an observation which was felt to be so lacerating.

'Fie, for shame!' said aunt Glegg, in her loudest, severest tone of reproof. 'Little gells as cut their own hair should be whipped and fed on bread-and-water – not come and sit down with their aunts and uncles.'

'Ay, ay,' said uncle Glegg, meaning to give a playful turn to this denunciation, 'she must be sent to gaol, I think, and they'll cut the rest of her hair off there, and make it all even.'

'She's more like a gypsy nor ever,' said aunt Pullet, in a pitying tone; 'it's very bad luck, sister, as the gell should be so brown – the boy's fair enough. I doubt it'll stand in her way i' life to be so brown.'

'She's a naughty child, as 'll break her mother's heart,' said Mrs Tulliver, with the tears in her eyes.

Maggie seemed to be listening to a chorus of reproach and derision. Her first flush came from anger, which gave her a transient power of defiance, and Tom thought she was braving it out, supported by the recent appearance of the pudding and custard. Under this impression, he whispered, 'Oh, my! Maggie, I told you you'd catch it.' He meant to be friendly, but Maggie felt convinced that Tom was rejoicing in her ignominy. Her feeble power of defiance left her in an instant, her heart swelled, and, getting up from her chair, she ran to her father, hid her face on his shoulder, and burst out into loud sobbing.

'Come, come, my wench,' said her father soothingly, putting his arm round her, 'never mind; you was i' the right to cut it off if it plagued you; give over crying: father'll take your part.'

Delicious words of tenderness! Maggie never forgot any of these moments when her father 'took her part ;' she kept them in her heart, and thought of them long years after, when everyone else said that her father had done very ill by his children.

'How your husband does spoil that child, Bessy!' said Mrs Glegg, in a loud 'aside,' to Mrs Tulliver. 'It'll be the ruin of her, if you don't take care. *My* father niver brought his children up so, else we should ha' been a different sort o' family to what we are.'

Mrs Tulliver's domestic sorrows seemed at this moment to have reached the point at which insensibility begins. She took no notice of her sister's remark, but threw back her cap-strings and dispensed the pudding, in mute resignation.

With the dessert there came entire deliverance for Maggie, for the children were told they might have their nuts and wine in the summerhouse, since the day was so mild, and they scampered out among the budding bushes of the garden with the alacrity of small animals getting from under a burning-glass.

Mrs Tulliver had her special reason for this permission: now the dinner was despatched, and everyone's mind disengaged, it was the right moment to communicate Mr Tulliver's intention concerning Tom, and it would be as well for Tom himself to be absent. The children were used to hear themselves talked of as freely as if they were birds, and could understand nothing, however they might stretch their necks and listen; but on this occasion Mrs Tulliver manifested an unusual discretion, because she had recently had evidence that the going to school to a clergyman was a sore point with Tom, who looked at it as very much on a par with going to school to a constable. Mrs Tulliver had a sighing sense that her husband would do as he liked, whatever sister Glegg said, or sister Pullet either, but at least they would not be able to say, if the thing turned out ill, that Bessy had fallen in with her husband's folly without letting her own friends know a word about it.

'Mr Tulliver,' she said, interrupting her husband in his talk with Mr Deane, 'it's time now to tell the children's aunts and uncles what you're thinking of doing with Tom, isn't it?'

'Very well,' said Mr Tulliver, rather sharply, 'I've no objections to tell anybody what I mean to do with him. I've settled,' he added, looking towards Mr Glegg and Mr Deane – 'I've settled to send him to a Mr Stelling, a parson, down at King's Lorton, there – an uncommon clever fellow, I understand – as'll put him up to most things.'

There was a rustling demonstration of surprise in the company, such as you may have observed in a country congregation when they hear an allusion to their weekday affairs from the pulpit. It was equally astonishing to the aunts and uncles to find a parson introduced into Mr Tulliver's family arrangements. As for uncle Pullet, he could hardly have been more thoroughly obfuscated if Mr Tulliver had said that he was going to send Tom to the Lord Chancellor: for uncle Pullet belonged to that extinct class of British yeomen who, dressed in good broadcloth, paid high rates and taxes, went to church, and ate a particularly good dinner on Sunday, without dreaming that the British constitution in Church and State had a traceable origin any more than the solar system and the fixed stars. It is melancholy, but true, that Mr Pullet had the most confused idea of a bishop as a sort of a baronet, who might or might not be a clergyman; and as the rector of his own parish was a man of high family and fortune, the idea that a clergyman could be a schoolmaster was too remote from Mr Pullet's experience to be readily conceivable. I know it is difficult for people in these instructed times to believe in uncle Pullet's ignorance; but let them reflect on the remarkable results of a great natural faculty under favouring circumstances. And uncle Pullet had a great natural faculty for ignorance. He was the first to give utterance to his astonishment.

'Why, what can you be going to send him to a parson for?' he said, with an amazed twinkling in his eyes, looking at Mr Glegg and Mr Deane, to see if they showed any signs of comprehension.

'Why, because the parsons are the best schoolmasters, by what I can make out,' said poor Mr Tulliver, who, in the maze of this puzzling world, laid hold of any clue with great readiness and tenacity. 'Jacobs at th'academy's no parson, and he's done very bad by the boy; and I made up my mind, if I sent him to school again, it should be to somebody different to Jacobs. And this Mr Stelling, by what I can make out, is the sort o' man I want. And I mean my boy to go to him at Midsummer,' he concluded, in a tone of decision, tapping his snuffbox and taking a pinch.

'You'll have to pay a swinging half-yearly bill, then, eh, Tulliver? The clergymen have highish notions, in general,' said Mr Deane, taking snuff vigorously, as he always did when wishing to maintain a neutral position.

'What! do you think the parson'll teach him to know a good sample o' wheat when he sees it, neighbour Tulliver?' said Mr Glegg, who was fond of his jest; and, having retired from business, felt that it was not only allowable but becoming in him to take a playful view of things.

'Why, you see, I've got a plan i' my head about Tom,' said Mr Tulliver, pausing after that statement and lifting up his glass.

'Well, if I may be allowed to speak, and it's seldom as I am,' said Mrs Glegg, with a tone of bitter meaning, 'I should like to know what good is to come to the boy, by bringin' him up above his fortin.'

'Why,' said Mr Tulliver, not looking at Mrs Glegg, but at the male part of his audience, 'you see, I've made up my mind not to bring Tom up to my own business. I've had my thoughts about it all along, and I made up my mind by what I saw with Garnett and *his* son. I mean to put him to some business, as he can go into without capital, and I want to give him an eddication as he'll be even wi' the lawyers and folks, and put me up to a notion now an' then.'

Mrs Glegg emitted a long sort of guttural sound with closed lips, that smiled in mingled pity and scorn.

'It 'ud be a fine deal better for some people,' she said, after that introductory note, 'if they'd let the lawyers alone.'

'Is he at the head of a grammar school, then, this clergyman – such as that at Market Bewley?' said Mr Deane.

'No – nothing o' that,' said Mr Tulliver. 'He won't take more than two or three pupils – and so he'll have the more time to attend to 'em, you know.'

'Ah, and get his eddication done the sooner: they can't learn much at a time when there's so many of 'em,' said uncle Pullet, feeling that he was getting quite an insight into this difficult matter.

'But he'll want the more pay, I doubt,' said Mr Glegg.

'Ay, ay, a cool hundred a-year – that's all,' said Mr Tulliver, with some pride at his own spirited course. 'But then, you know, it's an investment; Tom's eddication 'ull be so much capital to him.'

'Ay, there's something in that,' said Mr Glegg. 'Well, well, neighbour Tulliver, you may be right, you may be right:

> When land is gone and money's spent,
> Then learning is most excellent.

I remember seeing those two lines wrote on a window at Buxton. But us that have got no learning had better keep our money, eh, neighbour Pullet?' Mr Glegg rubbed his knees and looked very pleasant.

'Mr Glegg, I wonder *at* you,' said his wife. 'It's very unbecoming in a man o' your age and belongings.'

'What's unbecoming, Mrs G.?' said Mr Glegg, winking pleasantly at the company. 'My new blue coat as I've got on?'

'I pity your weakness, Mr Glegg. I say it's unbecoming to be making a joke when you see your own kin going headlongs to ruin.'

'If you mean me by that,' said Mr Tulliver, considerably nettled, 'you needn't trouble yourself to fret about me. I can manage my own affairs without troubling other folks.'

'Bless me,' said Mr Deane, judiciously introducing a new idea, 'why, now I come to think of it, somebody said Wakem was going to send *his* son – the deformed lad – to a clergyman, didn't they, Susan?' (appealing to his wife).

'I can give no account of it, I'm sure,' said Mrs Deane, closing her lips very tightly again. Mrs Deane was not a woman to take part in a scene where missiles were flying.

'Well,' said Mr Tulliver, speaking all the more cheerfully, that Mrs Glegg might see he didn't mind her, 'if Wakem thinks o' sending his son to a clergyman, depend on it I shall make no mistake i' sending Tom to one. Wakem's as big a scoundrel as Old Harry ever made, but he knows the length of every man's foot he's got to deal with. Ay, ay, tell me who's Wakem's butcher, and I'll tell you where to get your meat.'

'But sawyer Wakem's son's got a humpback,' said Mrs Pullet, who felt as if the whole business had a funereal aspect; 'it's more nat'ral to send *him* to a clergyman.'

'Yes,' said Mr Glegg, interpreting Mrs Pullet's observation with erroneous plausibility, 'you must consider that, neighbour Tulliver; Wakem's son isn't likely to follow any business. Wakem 'ull make a gentleman of him, poor fellow.'

'Mr Glegg,' said Mrs G., in a tone which implied that her indignation would fizz and ooze a little, though she was determined to keep it corked up, 'you'd far better hold your tongue. Mr Tulliver doesn't want to know your opinion nor mine neither. There's folks in the world as know better than everybody else.'

'Why, I should think that's you, if we're to trust your own tale,' said Mr Tulliver, beginning to boil up again.

'O, *I* say nothing,' said Mrs Glegg, sarcastically. 'My advice has never been asked, and I don't give it.'

'It'll be the first time, then,' said Mr Tulliver. 'It's the only thing you're over-ready at giving.'

'I've been over-ready at lending, then, if I haven't been over ready at giving,' said Mrs Glegg. 'There's folks I've lent money to, as perhaps I shall repent o' lending money to kin.'

'Come, come, come,' said Mr Glegg, soothingly. But Mr Tulliver was not to be hindered of his retort.

'You've got a bond for it, I reckon,' he said; 'and you've had your five per cent, kin or no kin.'

'Sister,' said Mrs Tulliver, pleadingly, 'drink your wine and let me give you some almonds and raisins.'

'Bessy, I'm sorry for you,' said Mrs Glegg, very much with the feeling of a cur that seizes the opportunity of diverting his bark towards the man who carries no stick. 'It's poor work, talking o' almonds and raisins.'

'Lors, sister Glegg, don't be so quarrelsome,' said Mrs Pullet, beginning to cry a little. 'You may be struck with a fit, getting so red in the face after dinner, and we are but just out o' mourning, all of us – and all wi' gowns craped alike and just put by – it's very bad among sisters.'

'I should think it *is* bad,' said Mrs Glegg. 'Things are come to a fine pass when one sister invites the other to her house o' purpose to quarrel with her and abuse her.'

'Softly, softly, Jane – be reasonable – be reasonable,' said Mr Glegg.

But while he was speaking, Mr Tulliver, who had by no means said enough to satisfy his anger, burst out again.

'Who wants to quarrel with you?' he said. 'It's you as can't let people alone, but must be gnawing at 'em for ever. *I* should never want to quarrel with any woman, if she kept her place.'

'My place, indeed!' said Mrs Glegg, getting rather more shrill. 'There's your betters, Mr Tulliver, as are dead and in their grave, treated me with a different sort o' respect to what you do – *though* I've got a husband as'll sit by and see me abused by them as 'ud never ha' had the chance if there hadn't been them in our family as married worse than they might ha' done.'

'If you talk o' that,' said Mr Tulliver, 'my family's as good as yours – and better, for it hasn't got a damned ill-tempered woman in it.'

'Well!' said Mrs Glegg, rising from her chair, 'I don't know whether you think it's a fine thing to sit by and hear me swore at, Mr Glegg; but I'm not going to stay a minute longer in this house. You can stay behind, and come home with the gig – and I'll walk home.'

'Dear heart, dear heart!' said Mr Glegg in a melancholy tone, as he followed his wife out of the room.

'Mr Tulliver, how could you talk so?' said Mrs Tulliver, with the tears in her eyes.

'Let her go,' said Mr Tulliver, too hot to be damped by any amount of tears. 'Let her go, and the sooner the better: she won't be trying to domineer over *me* again in a hurry.'

'Sister Pullet,' said Mrs Tulliver helplessly, 'do you think it 'ud be any use for you to go after her and try to pacify her?'

'Better not, better not,' said Mr Deane. 'You'll make it up another day.'

'Then, sisters, shall we go and look at the children?' said Mrs Tulliver, drying her eyes.

No proposition could have been more seasonable. Mr Tulliver felt very much as if the air had been cleared of obtrusive flies now the women were out of the room. There were few things he liked better than a chat with Mr Deane, whose close application to business allowed the pleasure very rarely. Mr Deane, he considered, was the 'knowingest' man of his acquaintance, and he had besides a ready causticity of tongue that made an agreeable supplement to Mr Tulliver's own tendency that way, which had remained in rather an inarticulate condition. And now the women were gone, they could carry on their serious talk without frivolous interruption. They could exchange their views concerning the Duke of Wellington, whose conduct in the Catholic Question had thrown such an entirely new light on his character; and speak slightingly of his conduct at the battle of Waterloo, which he would never have won if there hadn't been a great many Englishmen at his back, not to speak of Blucher and the Prussians who, as Mr Tulliver had heard from a person of particular knowledge in that matter, had come up in the very nick of time; though here there was a slight dissidence, Mr Deane remarking that he was not disposed to give much credit to the Prussians – the build of their vessels, together with the unsatisfactory character of transactions in Dantzic beer, inclining him to form rather a low view of Prussian pluck generally. Rather beaten on this ground, Mr Tulliver proceeded to express his fears that the country could never again be what it used to be; but Mr Deane, attached to a firm of which the returns were on the increase, naturally took a more lively view of the present; and had some details to give concerning the state of the imports, especially in hides and spelter, which soothed Mr Tulliver's imagination by throwing into more distant perspective the period when the country would become utterly the prey of Papists and Radicals, and there would be no more chance for honest men.

Uncle Pullet sat by and listened with twinkling eyes to these high matters. He didn't understand politics himself – thought they were a natural gift – but by what he could make out, this Duke of Wellington was no better than he should be.

CHAPTER 8

Mr Tulliver Shows His Weaker Side

'Suppose sister Glegg should call her money in – it'ud be very awkward for you to have to raise five hundred pounds now,' said Mrs Tulliver to her husband that evening, as she took a plaintive review of the day.

Mrs Tulliver had lived thirteen years with her husband, yet she retained in all the freshness of her early married life a facility of saying things which drove him in the opposite direction to the one she desired. Some minds are wonderful for keeping their bloom in this way, as a patriarchal goldfish apparently retains to the last its youthful illusion that it can swim in a straight line beyond the encircling glass. Mrs Tulliver was an amiable fish of this kind, and, after running her head against the same resisting medium for thirteen years, would go at it again today with undulled alacrity.

This observation of hers tended directly to convince Mr Tulliver that it would not be at all awkward for him to raise five hundred pounds; and when Mrs Tulliver became rather pressing to know *how* he would raise it without mortgaging the mill and the house, which he had said he never *would* mortgage, since nowadays people were none so ready to lend money without security, Mr Tulliver, getting warm, declared that Mrs Glegg might do as she liked about calling in her money – he should pay it in, whether or not. He was not going to be beholding to his wife's sisters. When a man had married into a family where there was a whole litter of women, he might have plenty to put up with if he chose. But Mr Tulliver did *not* choose.

Mrs Tulliver cried a little in a trickling, quiet way as she put on her nightcap; but presently sank into a comfortable sleep, lulled by the thought that she would talk everything over with her sister Pullet tomorrow, when she was to take the children to Garum Firs to tea. Not that she looked forward to any distinct issue from that talk; but it seemed impossible that past events should be so obstinate as to remain unmodified when they were complained against.

Her husband lay awake rather longer, for he too was thinking of a visit he would pay on the morrow, and his ideas on the subject were not of so vague and soothing a kind as those of his amiable partner.

Mr Tulliver, when under the influence of a strong feeling, had a promptitude in action that may seem inconsistent with that painful sense of the complicated puzzling nature of human affairs under which his more dispassionate deliberations were conducted; but it is really not improbable that there was a direct relation between these apparently contradictory phenomena, since I have observed that for getting a strong impression that a skein is tangled, there is nothing like snatching hastily at a single thread. It was owing to this promptitude that Mr Tulliver was on horseback soon after dinner the next day (he was not dyspeptic) on his way to Basset to see his sister Moss and her husband. For having made up his mind irrevocably that he would pay Mrs Glegg her loan of five hundred pounds, it naturally occurred to him that he had a promissory note for three hundred pounds lent to his brother-in-law Moss, and if said brother-in-law could manage to pay in the money within a given time, it would go far to lessen the fallacious air of inconvenience which Mr Tulliver's spirited step might have worn in the eyes of weak people who require to know precisely how a thing is to be done before they are strongly confident that it will be easy.

For Mr Tulliver was in a position neither new nor striking, but, like other everyday things, sure to have a cumulative effect that will be felt in the long run: he was held to be a much more substantial man than he really was. And as we are all apt to believe what the world believes about us, it was his habit to think of failure and ruin with the same sort of remote pity with which a spare long-necked man hears that his plethoric short-necked neighbour is stricken with apoplexy. He had been always used to hear pleasant jokes about his advantages as a man who worked his own mill, and owned a pretty bit of land; and these jokes naturally kept up his sense that he was a man of considerable substance. They gave a pleasant flavour to his glass on a market-day, and if it had not been for the recurrence of half-yearly payments, Mr Tulliver would really have forgotten that there was a mortgage of two thousand pounds on his very desirable freehold. That was not altogether his own fault, since one of the thousand pounds was his sister's fortune, which he had had to pay on her marriage; and a man who has neighbours that *will* go to law with him, is not likely to pay off his mortgages, especially if he enjoys the good opinion of acquaintances who want to borrow a hundred pounds on security too lofty to be represented by parchment. Our friend Mr Tulliver had a good-natured fibre in him, and did not like to give harsh refusals even to a sister, who had not only come into the world in that superfluous way characteristic of sisters, creating a necessity for mortgages, but had quite thrown herself away in marriage, and had crowned her mistakes by having an eighth baby. On this point Mr Tulliver was conscious of being a little weak; but he apologised to himself by saying that poor Gritty had been a good-looking wench before she married Moss – he would sometimes say this even with a slight tremulousness in his voice. But this morning he was in a mood more becoming a man of business, and in the course of his ride along the Basset lanes, with their deep ruts, – lying so far away from a market-town that the labour of drawing produce and manure was enough to take away the best part of the profits on such poor land as that parish was made of, – he got up a due amount of irritation against Moss as a man without capital, who, if murrain and blight were abroad, was sure to have his share of them, and who, the more you tried to help him out of the mud, would sink the farther in. It would do him good rather than harm, now, if he were obliged to raise this three hundred pounds: it would make him look about him better, and not act so foolishly about his wool this year as he did the last: in fact, Mr Tulliver had been too easy with his brother-in-law, and because he had let the interest run on for two years, Moss was likely enough to think that he should never be troubled about the principal. But Mr Tulliver was determined not to encourage such shuffling people any longer; and a ride along the Basset lanes was not likely to enervate a man's resolution by softening his temper. The deep-trodden hoof-marks, made in the muddiest days of winter, gave him a shake now and then which suggested a rash but stimulating snarl at the father of lawyers, who, whether by means of his hoof or otherwise, had doubtless something to do with this state of the roads; and the abundance of foul land and neglected fences that met his eye, though they made no part of his brother Moss's farm, strongly contributed to his dissatisfaction with that unlucky agriculturist. If this wasn't Moss's fallow, it might have been: Basset was all alike; it was a beggarly parish in Mr Tulliver's opinion, and his opinion was certainly not groundless. Basset had a poor soil, poor roads, a poor non-resident landlord, a poor nonresident vicar, and rather less than half a curate, also poor. If anyone strongly impressed with the power of the human mind to triumph over circumstances, will contend that the parishioners of Basset might nevertheless have been a very superior class of people, I have nothing to urge against that abstract proposition; I only know that, in point of fact, the Basset mind was in strict keeping with its circumstances. The muddy lanes, green or clayey, that seemed to the unaccustomed eye to lead nowhere but into each other, did really lead, with patience, to a distant highroad; but there were many feet in Basset which they led more frequently to a centre of dissipation, spoken of formally as the 'Markis o' Granby,' but among intimates as 'Dickison's.' A large low room with a sanded floor, a cold scent of tobacco, modified by undetected beer-dregs, Mr Dickison leaning against the doorpost with a melancholy pimpled face, looking as irrelevant to the daylight as a last night's guttered candle – all this may not seem a very seductive form of temptation; but the majority of men in Basset found it fatally alluring when encountered on their road towards four o'clock on a wintry afternoon; and if any wife in Basset wished to indicate that her husband was not a pleasure-seeking man, she could hardly do it more emphatically than by saying that he didn't spend a shilling at Dickison's from one Whitsuntide to another. Mrs Moss had said so of *her* husband more than once, when her brother was in a mood to find fault with him, as he certainly was today. And nothing could be less pacifying to Mr Tulliver than the behaviour of the farmyard gate, which he had no sooner attempted to push open with his riding-stick, than it acted as gates without the upper hinge are known to do, to the peril of shins, whether equine or human. He was about to get down and lead his horse through the damp dirt of the hollow farmyard, shadowed drearily by the large half-timbered buildings, up to the long line of tumbledown dwelling-houses standing on a raised causeway; but the timely appearance of a cowboy saved him that frustration of a plan he had determined on – namely, not to get down from his horse during this visit. If a man means to be hard, let him keep in his saddle and speak from that height, above the level of pleading eyes, and with the command of a distant horizon. Mrs Moss heard the sound of the horse's feet, and, when her brother rode up, was already outside the kitchen door, with a half-weary smile on her face, and a black-eyed baby in her arms. Mrs Moss's face bore a faded resemblance to her brother's; baby's little fat hand, pressed against her cheek, seemed to show more strikingly that the cheek was faded.

'Brother, I'm glad to see you,' she said, in an affectionate tone. 'I didn't look for you today. How do you do?'

'Oh . . . pretty well, Mrs Moss . . . pretty well,' answered the brother, with cool deliberation, as if it were rather too forward of her to ask that question. She knew at once that her brother was not in a good humour: he never called her Mrs Moss except when he was angry, and when they were in company. But she thought it was in the order of nature that people who were poorly off should be snubbed. Mrs Moss did not take her stand on the equality of the human race: she was a patient, prolific, loving-hearted woman.

'Your husband isn't in the house, I suppose?' added Mr Tulliver, after a grave pause, during which four children had run out, like chickens whose mother has been suddenly in eclipse behind the hencoop.

'No,' said Mrs Moss, 'but he's only in the potato-field yonders. Georgy, run to the Far Close in a minute, and tell father your uncle's come. You'll get down, brother, won't you, and take something?'

'No, no; I can't get down. I must be going home again directly,' said Mr Tulliver, looking at the distance.

'And how's Mrs Tulliver and the children?' said Mrs Moss, humbly, not daring to press her invitation.

'Oh . . . pretty well. Tom's going to a new school at Midsummer – a deal of expense to me. It's bad work for me, lying out o' my money.'

'I wish you'd be so good as let the children come and see their cousins someday. My little uns want to see their cousin Maggie, so as never was. And me her godmother, and so fond of her – there's nobody 'ud make a bigger fuss with her, according to what they've got. And I know she likes to come, for she's a loving child, and how quick and clever she is, to be sure!'

If Mrs Moss had been one of the most astute women in the world, instead of being one of the simplest, she could have thought of nothing more likely to propitiate her brother than this praise of Maggie. He seldom found anyone volunteering praise of 'the little wench:' it was usually left entirely to himself to insist on her merits. But Maggie always appeared in the most amiable light at her aunt Moss's: it was her Alsatia, where she was out of the reach of law – if she upset anything, dirtied her shoes, or tore her frock, these things were matters of course at her aunt Moss's. In spite of himself, Mr Tulliver's eyes got milder, and he did not look away from his sister, as he said,

'Ay: she's fonder o' you than o' the other aunts, I think. She takes after our family: not a bit of her mother's in her.'

'Moss says she's just like what I used to be,' said Mrs Moss, 'though I was never so quick and fond o' the books. But I think my Lizzy's like her – *she's* sharp. Come here, Lizzy, my dear, and let your uncle see you; he hardly knows you, you grow so fast.'

Lizzy, a black-eyed child of seven, looked very shy when her mother drew her forward, for the small Mosses were much in awe of their uncle from Dorlcote Mill. She was inferior enough to Maggie in fire and strength of expression, to make the resemblance between the two entirely flattering to Mr Tulliver's fatherly love.

'Ay, they're a bit alike,' he said, looking kindly at the little figure in the soiled pinafore. 'They both take after our mother. You've got enough o' gells, Gritty,' he added, in a tone half compassionate, half reproachful.

'Four of 'em, bless 'em,' said Mrs Moss, with a sigh, stroking Lizzy's hair on each side of her forehead; 'as many as there's boys. They've got a brother apiece.'

'Ah, but they must turn out and fend for themselves,' said Mr Tulliver, feeling that his severity was relaxing, and trying to brace it by throwing out a wholesome hint. 'They mustn't look to hanging on their brothers.'

'No: but I hope their brothers 'ull love the poor things, and remember they came o' one father and mother: the lads 'ull never be the poorer for that,' said Mrs Moss, flashing out with hurried timidity, like a half-smothered fire.

Mr Tulliver gave his horse a little stroke on the flank, then checked it, and said, angrily, 'Stand still with you!' much to the astonishment of that innocent animal.

'And the more there is of 'em, the more they must love one another,' Mrs Moss went on, looking at her children with a didactic purpose. But she turned towards her brother again to say, 'Not but what I hope your boy 'ull allays be good to his sister, though there's but two of 'em, like you and me, brother.'

That arrow went straight to Mr Tulliver's heart. He had not a rapid imagination, but the thought of Maggie was very near to him, and he was not long in seeing his relation to his own sister side by side with Tom's relation to Maggie. Would the little wench ever be poorly off, and Tom rather hard upon her?

'Ay, ay, Gritty,' said the miller, with a new softness in his tone; 'but I've allays done what I could for you,' he added, as if vindicating himself from a reproach.

'I'm not denying that, brother, and I'm no ways ungrateful,' said poor Mrs Moss, too ragged by toil and children to have strength left for any pride. 'But here's the father. What a while you've been, Moss!'

'While, do you call it?' said Mr Moss, feeling out of breath and injured. 'I've been running all the way. Won't you light, Mr Tulliver?'

'Well, I'll just get down and have a bit o' talk with you in the garden,' said Mr Tulliver, thinking that he should be more likely to show a due spirit of resolve if his sister were not present.

He got down, and passed with Mr Moss into the garden, towards an old yew-tree arbour, while his sister stood tapping her baby on the back, and looking wistfully after them.

Their entrance into the yew-tree arbour surprised several fowls that were recreating themselves by scratching deep holes in the dusty ground, and at once took flight with much pother and cackling. Mr Tulliver sat down on the bench, and tapping the ground curiously here and there with his stick, as if he suspected some hollowness, opened the conversation by observing, with something like a snarl in his tone, 'Why, you've got wheat again in that Corner Close, I see; and never a bit o' dressing on it. You'll do no good with it this year.'

Mr Moss, who, when he married Miss Tulliver, had been regarded as the buck of Basset, now wore a beard nearly a week old, and had the depressed, unexpectant air of a machine-horse. He answered in a patient-grumbling tone, 'Why, poor farmers like me must do as they can: they must leave it to them as have got money to play with, to put half as much into the ground as they mean to get out of it.'

'I don't know who should have money to play with, if it isn't them as can borrow money without paying interest,' said Mr Tulliver, who wished to get into a slight quarrel; it was the most natural and easy introduction to calling in money.

'I know I'm behind with the interest,' said Mr Moss, 'but I was so unlucky wi' the wool last year; and what with the Missis being laid up so, things have gone awk'arder nor usual.'

'Ay,' snarled Mr Tulliver, 'there's folks as things 'ull allays go awk'ard with: empty sacks 'ull never stand upright.'

'Well, I don't know what fault you've got to find wi' me, Mr Tulliver,' said Mr Moss, deprecatingly; 'I know there isn't a day-labourer works harder.'

'What's the use o' that,' said Mr Tulliver, sharply, 'when a man marries, and's got no capital to work his farm but his wife's bit o' fortin? I was against it from the first; but you'd neither of you listen to me. And I can't lie out o' my money any longer, for I've got to pay five hundred o' Mrs Glegg's, and there 'ull be Tom an expense to me – I should find myself short, even saying I'd got back all as is my own. You must look about and see how you can pay me the three hundred pound.'

'Well, if that's what you mean,' said Mr Moss, looking blankly before him, 'we'd better be sold up, an' ha' done with it; I must part wi' every head o' stock I've got, to pay you and the landlord too.'

Poor relations are undeniably irritating – their existence is so entirely uncalled for on our part, and they are almost always very faulty people. Mr Tulliver had succeeded in getting quite as much irritated with Mr Moss as he had desired, and he was able to say angrily, rising from his seat, 'Well, you must do as you can. I can't find money for everybody else as well as myself. I must look to my own business and my own family. I can't lie out o' my money any longer. You must raise it as quick as you can.'

Mr Tulliver walked abruptly out of the arbour as he uttered the last sentence, and, without looking round at Mr Moss, went on to the kitchen-door, where the eldest boy was holding his horse, and his sister was waiting in a state of wondering alarm, which was not without its alleviations, for baby was making pleasant gurgling sounds, and performing a great deal of finger practice on the faded face. Mrs Moss had eight children, but could never overcome her regret that the twins had not lived. Mr Moss thought their removal was not without its consolations. 'Won't you come in, brother?' she said, looking anxiously at her husband, who was walking slowly up, while Mr Tulliver had his foot already in the stirrup.

'No, no; goodbye,' said he, turning his horse's head, and riding away.

No man could feel more resolute till he got outside the yard-gate, and a little way along the deep-rutted lane; but before he reached the next turning, which would take him out of sight of the dilapidated farm-buildings, he appeared to be smitten by some sudden thought. He checked his horse, and made it stand still in the same spot for two or three minutes, during which he turned his head from side to side in a melancholy way, as if he were looking at some painful object on more sides than one. Evidently, after his fit of promptitude, Mr Tulliver was relapsing into the sense that this is a puzzling world. He turned his horse, and rode slowly back, giving vent to the climax of feeling which had determined this movement by saying aloud, as he struck his horse, 'Poor little wench! she'll have nobody but Tom, belike, when I'm gone.'

Mr Tulliver's return into the yard was descried by several young Mosses, who immediately ran in with the exciting news to their mother, so that Mrs Moss was again on the doorstep when her brother rode up. She had been crying, but was rocking baby to sleep in her arms now, and made no ostentatious show of sorrow as her brother looked at her, but merely said, 'The father's gone to the field again, if you want him, brother.'

'No, Gritty, no,' said Mr Tulliver, in a gentle tone. 'Don't you fret – that's all – I'll make a shift without the money a bit – only you must be as cliver and contriving as you can.'

Mrs Moss's tears came again at this unexpected kindness, and she could say nothing.

'Come, come! – the little wench shall come and see you. I'll bring her and Tom someday before he goes to school. You mustn't fret . . . I'll always be a good brother to you.'

'Thank you for that word, brother,' said Mrs Moss, drying her tears; then turning to Lizzy, she said, 'Run now, and fetch the coloured egg for cousin Maggie.' Lizzy ran in, and quickly reappeared with a small paper parcel.

'It's boiled hard, brother, and coloured with thrums – very pretty: it was done o' purpose for Maggie. Will you please to carry it in your pocket?'

'Ay, ay,' said Mr Tulliver, putting it carefully in his side pocket. 'Goodbye.'

And so the respectable miller returned along the Basset lanes rather more puzzled than before as to ways and means, but still with the sense of a danger escaped. It had come across his mind that if he were hard upon his sister, it might somehow tend to make Tom hard upon Maggie at some distant day, when her father was no longer there to take her part; for simple people, like our friend Mr Tulliver, are apt to clothe unimpeachable feelings in erroneous ideas, and this was his confused way of explaining to himself that his love and anxiety for 'the little wench' had given him a new sensibility towards his sister.

CHAPTER 9

To Garum Firs

While the possible troubles of Maggie's future were occupying her father's mind, she herself was tasting only the bitterness of the present. Childhood has no forebodings; but then, it is soothed by no memories of outlived sorrow.

The fact was, the day had begun ill with Maggie. The pleasure of having Lucy to look at, and the prospect of the afternoon visit to Garum Firs, where she would hear uncle Pullet's musical box, had been marred as early as eleven o'clock by the advent of the hairdresser from St Ogg's, who had spoken in the severest terms of the condition in which he had found her hair, holding up one jagged lock after another and saying. 'See here! tut – tut – tut! in a tone of mingled disgust and pity, which to Maggie's imagination was equivalent to the strongest expression of public opinion. Mr Rappit, the hairdresser, with his well-anointed coronal locks tending wavily upward, like the simulated pyramid of flame on a monumental urn, seemed to her at that moment the most formidable of her contemporaries, into whose street at St Ogg's she would carefully refrain from entering through the rest of her life.

Moreover, the preparation for a visit being always a serious affair in the Dodson family, Martha was enjoined to have Mrs Tulliver's room ready an hour earlier than usual, that the laying-out of the best clothes might not be deferred till the last moment, as was sometimes the case in families of lax views, where the ribbon-strings were never rolled up, where there was little or no wrapping in silver paper, and where the sense that the Sunday clothes could be got at quite easily produced no shock to the mind. Already, at twelve o'clock, Mrs Tulliver had on her visiting costume, with a protective apparatus of brown holland, as if she had been a piece of satin furniture in danger of flies; Maggie was frowning and twisting her shoulders, that she might if possible shrink away from the prickliest of tuckers, while her mother was remonstrating, 'Don't, Maggie, my dear – don't look so ugly!' and Tom's cheeks were looking particularly brilliant as a relief to his best blue suit, which he wore with becoming calmness; having, after a little wrangling, effected what was always the one point of interest to him in his toilet – he had transferred all the contents of his everyday pockets to those actually in wear.

As for Lucy, she was just as pretty and neat as she had been yesterday: no accidents ever happened to her clothes, and she was never uncomfortable in them, so that she looked with wondering pity at Maggie pouting and writhing under the exasperating tucker. Maggie would certainly have torn it off, if she had not been checked by the remembrance of her recent humiliation about her hair: as it was, she confined herself to fretting and twisting, and behaving peevishly about the card-houses which they were allowed to build till dinner, as a suitable amusement for boys and girls in their best clothes. Tom could build perfect pyramids of houses; but Maggie's would never bear the laying on of the roof: it was always so with the things that Maggie made; and Tom had deduced the conclusion that no girls could ever make anything. But it happened that Lucy proved wonderfully clever at building: she handled the cards so lightly, and moved so gently, that Tom condescended to admire her houses as well as his own, the more readily because she had asked him to teach her. Maggie, too, would have admired Lucy's houses, and would have given up her own unsuccessful building to contemplate them, without ill-temper, if her tucker had not made her peevish, and if Tom had not inconsiderately laughed when her houses fell, and told her she was 'a stupid.'

'Don't laugh at me, Tom!' she burst out, angrily; 'I'm not a stupid. I know a great many things you don't.'

'Oh, I dare say, Miss Spitfire! I'd never be such a cross thing as you – making faces like that. Lucy doesn't do so. I like Lucy better than you: *I* wish Lucy was *my* sister.'

'Then it's very wicked and cruel of you to wish so,' said Maggie, starting up hurriedly from her place on the floor, and upsetting Tom's wonderful pagoda. She really did not mean it, but the circumstantial evidence was against her, and Tom turned white with anger, but said nothing: he would have struck her, only he knew it was cowardly to strike a girl, and Tom Tulliver was quite determined he would never do anything cowardly.

Maggie stood in dismay and terror, while Tom got up from the floor and walked away, pale, from the scattered ruins of his pagoda, and Lucy looked on mutely, like a kitten pausing from its lapping.

'Oh, Tom,' said Maggie, at last, going halfway towards him, 'I didn't mean to knock it down – indeed, indeed I didn't.'

Tom took no notice of her, but took, instead, two or three hard peas out of his pocket, and shot them with his thumbnail against the window – vaguely at first, but presently with the distinct aim of hitting a superannuated bluebottle which was exposing its imbecility in the spring sunshine, clearly against the views of Nature, who had provided Tom and the peas for the speedy destruction of this weak individual.

Thus the morning had been made heavy to Maggie, and Tom's persistent coldness to her all through their walk spoiled the fresh air and sunshine for her. He called Lucy to look at the half-built bird's nest without caring to show it Maggie, and peeled a willow switch for Lucy and himself, without offering one to Maggie. Lucy had said, 'Maggie, shouldn't *you* like one?' but Tom was deaf.

Still the sight of the peacock opportunely spreading his tail on the stackyard wall, just as they reached Garum Firs, was enough to divert the mind temporarily from personal grievances. And this was only the beginning of beautiful sights at Garum Firs. All the farmyard life was wonderful there – bantams, speckled and top-knotted; Friesland hens, with their feathers all turned the wrong way; guinea-fowls that flew and screamed and dropped their pretty-spotted feathers; pouter-pigeons and a tame magpie; nay, a goat, and a wonderful brindled dog, half mastiff, half bulldog, as large as a lion. Then there were white railings and white gates all about, and glittering weathercocks of various design, and garden-walks paved with pebbles in beautiful patterns – nothing was quite common at Garum Firs: and Tom thought that the unusual size of the toads there was simply due to the general unusualness which characterised uncle Pullet's possessions as a gentleman farmer. Toads who paid rent were naturally leaner. As for the house, it was not less remarkable: it had a receding centre, and two wings with battlemented turrets, and was covered with glittering white stucco.

Uncle Pullet had seen the expected party approaching from the window, and made haste to unbar and unchain the front door, kept always in this fortified condition from fear of tramps, who might be supposed to know of the glass-case of stuffed birds in the hall, and to contemplate rushing in and carrying it away on their heads. Aunt Pullet, too, appeared at the doorway, and as soon as her sister was within hearing said, 'Stop the children, for God's sake, Bessy, – don't let 'em come up the doorsteps: Sally's bringing the old mat and the duster, to rub their shoes.'

Mrs Pullet's front-door mats were by no means intended to wipe shoes on: the very scraper had a deputy to do its dirty work. Tom rebelled particularly against this shoe-wiping, which he always considered in the light of an indignity to his sex. He felt it as the beginning of the disagreeables incident to a visit at aunt Pullet's, where he had once been compelled to sit with towels wrapped round his boots; a fact which may serve to correct the too hasty conclusion that a visit to Garum Firs must have been a great treat to a young gentleman fond of animals – fond, that is, of throwing stones at them.

The next disagreeable was confined to his feminine companions: it was the mounting of the polished oak stairs, which had very handsome carpets rolled up and laid by in a spare bedroom, so that the ascent of these glossy steps might have served, in barbarous times, as a trial by ordeal from which none but the most spotless virtue could have come off with unbroken limbs. Sophy's weakness about these polished stairs was always a subject of bitter remonstrance on Mrs Glegg's part; but Mrs Tulliver ventured on no comment, only thinking to herself it was a mercy when she and the children were safe on the landing.

'Mrs Gray has sent home my new bonnet, Bessy,' said Mrs Pullet, in a pathetic tone, as Mrs Tulliver adjusted her cap.

'Has she, sister?' said Mrs Tulliver, with an air of much interest. 'And how do you like it?'

'It's apt to make a mess with clothes, taking 'em out and putting 'em in again,' said Mrs Pullet, drawing a bunch of keys from her pocket and looking at them earnestly, 'but it 'ud be a pity for you to go away without seeing it. There's no knowing what may happen.'

Mrs Pullet shook her head slowly at this last serious consideration, which determined her to single out a particular key.

'I'm afraid it'll be troublesome to you getting it out, sister,' said Mrs Tulliver, 'but I *should* like to see what sort of a crown she's made you.'

Mrs Pullet rose with a melancholy air and unlocked one wing of a very bright wardrobe, where you may have hastily supposed she would find the new bonnet. Not at all. Such a supposition could only have arisen from a too superficial acquaintance with the habits of the Dodson family. In this wardrobe Mrs Pullet was seeking something small enough to be hidden among layers of linen – it was a door-key.

'You must come with me into the best room,' said Mrs Pullet.

'May the children come too, sister?' enquired Mrs Tulliver, who saw that Maggie and Lucy were looking rather eager.

'Well,' said aunt Pullet, reflectively, 'it'll perhaps be safer for 'em to come – they'll be touching something if we leave 'em behind.'

So they went in procession along the bright and slippery corridor, dimly lighted by the semi-lunar top of the window which rose above the closed shutter: it was really quite solemn. Aunt Pullet paused and unlocked a door which opened on something still more solemn than the passage: a darkened room, in which the outer light, entering feebly, showed what looked like the corpses of furniture in white shrouds. Everything that was not shrouded stood with its legs upwards. Lucy laid hold of Maggie's frock, and Maggie's heart beat rapidly.

Aunt Pullet half-opened the shutter and then unlocked the wardrobe, with a melancholy deliberateness which was quite in keeping with the funereal solemnity of the scene. The delicious scent of rose-leaves that issued from the wardrobe made the process of taking out sheet after sheet of silver-paper quite pleasant to assist at, though the sight of the bonnet at last was an anticlimax to Maggie, who would have preferred something more strikingly preternatural. But few things could have been more impressive to Mrs Tulliver. She looked all round it in silence for some moments, and then said emphatically, 'Well sister, I'll never speak against the full crowns again!'

It was a great concession, and Mrs Pullet felt it: she felt something was due to it.

'You'd like to see it on, sister?' she said, sadly. 'I'll open the shutter a bit further.'

'Well, if you don't mind taking off your cap, sister,' said Mrs Tulliver.

Mrs Pullet took off her cap, displaying the brown silk scalp with a jutting promontory of curls which was common to the more mature and judicious women of those times, and, placing the bonnet on her head, turned slowly round, like a draper's lay-figure, that Mrs Tulliver might miss no point of view.

'I've sometimes thought there's a loop too much o' ribbon on this left side; what do you think?' said Mrs Pullet.

Mrs Tulliver looked earnestly at the point indicated, and turned her head on one side. 'Well, I think it's best as it is; if you meddled with it, sister, you might repent.'

'That's true,' said aunt Pullet, taking off the bonnet and looking at it contemplatively.

'How much might she charge you for that bonnet, sister?' said Mrs Tulliver, whose mind was actively engaged on the possibility of getting a humble imitation of this *chef-d'oeuvre* made from a piece of silk she had at home.

Mrs Pullet screwed up her mouth and shook her head, and then whispered, 'Pullet pays for it; he said I was to have the best bonnet at Garum Church, let the next best be whose it would.'

She began slowly to adjust the trimmings in preparation for returning it to its place in the wardrobe, and her thoughts seemed to have taken a melancholy turn, for she shook her head.

'Ah,' she said at last, 'I may never wear it twice, sister; who knows?'

'Don't talk o' that, sister,' answered Mrs Tulliver. 'I hope you'll have your health this summer.'

'Ah! but there may come a death in the family, as there did soon after I had my green satin bonnet. Cousin Abbott may go and we can't think o' wearing crape less nor half a year for him.'

'That *would* be unlucky,' said Mrs Tulliver, entering thoroughly into the possibility of an inopportune decease. 'There's never so much pleasure i' wearing a bonnet the second year, especially when the crowns are so chancy – never two summers alike.'

'Ah, it's the way i' this world,' said Mrs Pullet, returning the bonnet to the wardrobe and locking it up. She maintained a silence characterised by head-shaking, until they had all issued from the solemn chamber and were in her own room again. Then, beginning to cry, she said, 'Sister, if you should never see that bonnet again till I'm dead and gone, you'll remember I showed it you this day.'

Mrs Tulliver felt that she ought to be affected, but she was a woman of sparse tears, stout and healthy – she couldn't cry so much as her sister Pullet did, and had often felt her deficiency at funerals. Her effort to bring tears into her eyes issued in an odd contraction of her face. Maggie, looking on attentively, felt that there was some painful mystery about her aunt's bonnet which she was con-sidered too young to understand; indignantly conscious, all the while, that she could have understood that, as well as everything else, if she had been taken into confidence.

When they went down, uncle Pullet observed with some acumen, that he reckoned the missis had been showing her bonnet – that was what had made them so long upstairs. With Tom the interval had seemed still longer, for he had been seated in irksome constraint on the edge of a sofa directly opposite his uncle Pullet, who regarded him with twinkling grey eyes, and occasionally addressed him as 'Young sir.'

'Well, young sir, what do you learn at school?' was a standing question with uncle Pullet; whereupon Tom always looked sheepish, rubbed his hands across his face and answered, 'I don't know.' It was altogether so embarrassing to be seated *tête-à-tête* with uncle Pullet, that Tom could not even look at the prints on the walls, or the fly-cages, or the wonderful flowerpots; he saw nothing but his uncle's gaiters. Not that Tom was in awe of his uncle's mental superiority; indeed, he had made up his mind that he didn't want to be a gentleman farmer, because he shouldn't like to be such a thin-legged silly fellow as his uncle Pullet – a molly-coddle, in fact. A boy's sheepishness is by no means a sign of overmastering reverence; and while you are making encouraging advances to him under the idea that he is overwhelmed by a sense of your age and wisdom, ten to one he is thinking you extremely queer. The only consolation I can suggest to you is, that the Greek boys probably thought the same of Aristotle. It is only when you have mastered a restive horse, or thrashed a drayman, or have got a gun in your hand, that these shy juniors feel you to be a truly admirable and enviable character. At least, I am quite sure of Tom Tulliver's sentiments on these points. In very tender years, when he still wore a lace border under his outdoor cap, he was often observed peeping through the bars of a gate and making minatory gestures with his small forefinger while he scolded the sheep with an inarticulate burr, intended to strike terror into their astonished minds; indicating thus early that desire for mastery over the inferior animals, wild and domestic, including cockchafers, neighbours' dogs, and small sisters, which in all ages has been an attribute of so much promise for the fortunes of our race. Now Mr Pullet never rode anything taller than a low pony, and was the least predatory of men, considering firearms dangerous, as apt to go off of themselves by nobody's particular desire. So that Tom was not without strong reasons when, in confidential talk with a chum, he had described uncle Pullet as a nincompoop, taking care at the same time to observe that he was a very 'rich fellow'.

The only alleviating circumstance in a *tête-à-tête* with uncle Pullet was that he kept a variety of lozenges and peppermint drops about his person, and when at a loss for conversation, he filled up the void by proposing a mutual solace of this kind.

'Do you like peppermints, young sir?' required only a tacit answer when it was accompanied by a presentation of the article in question.

The appearance of the little girls suggested to uncle Pullet the further solace of small sweet-cakes, of which he also kept a stock under lock and key for his own private eating on wet days; but the three children had no sooner got the tempting delicacy between their fingers, than aunt Pullet desired them to abstain from eating it till the tray and the plates came, since with those crisp cakes they would make the floor 'all over' crumbs. Lucy didn't mind that much, for the cake was so pretty, she thought it was rather a pity to eat it; but Tom, watching his opportunity while the elders were talking, hastily stowed it in his mouth at two bites, and chewed it furtively. As for Maggie, becoming fascinated, as usual, by a print of Ulysses and Nausicaa, which uncle Pullet had bought as a 'pretty Scripture thing', she presently let fall her cake, and in an unlucky movement crushed it beneath her foot – a source of so much agitation to aunt Pullet and conscious disgrace to Maggie, that she began to despair of hearing the musical snuffbox today, till, after some reflection, it occurred to her that Lucy was in high favour enough to venture on asking for a tune. So she whispered to Lucy, and Lucy, who always did what she was desired to do, went up quietly to her uncle's knee, and, blushing all over her neck while she fingered her necklace, said, 'Will you please play us a tune, uncle?'

Lucy thought it was by reason of some exceptional talent in uncle Pullet that the snuffbox played such beautiful tunes, and indeed the thing was viewed in that light by the majority of his neighbours in Garum. Mr Pullet had *bought* the box, to begin with, and he understood winding it up, and knew which tune it was going to play beforehand; altogether, the possession of this unique 'piece of music' was a proof that Mr Pullet's character was not of that entire nullity which might otherwise have been attributed to it. But uncle Pullet, when entreated to exhibit his accomplishment, never depreciated it by a too ready consent. 'We'll see about it,' was the answer he always gave, carefully abstaining from any sign of compliance till a suitable number of minutes had passed. Uncle Pullet had a programme for all great social occasions, and in this way fenced himself in from much painful confusion and perplexing freedom of will.

Perhaps the suspense did heighten Maggie's enjoyment when the fairy tune began: for the first time she quite forgot that she had a load on her mind – that Tom was angry with her; and by the time 'Hush, ye pretty warbling choir,' had been played, her face wore that bright look of happiness, while she sat immovable with her hands clasped, which sometimes comforted her mother with the sense that Maggie could look pretty now and then, in spite of her brown skin. But when the magic music ceased, she jumped up, and, running towards Tom, put her arm round his neck and said, 'O, Tom, isn't it pretty?'

Lest you should think it showed a revolting insensibility in Tom that he felt any new anger towards Maggie for this uncalled-for and, to him, inexplicable caress, I must tell you that he had his glass of cowslip wine in his hand, and that she jerked him so as to make him spill half of it. He must have been an extreme milksop not to say angrily, 'Look there, now!' especially when his resentment was sanctioned, as it was, by general disapprobation of Maggie's behaviour.

'Why don't you sit still, Maggie?' her mother said, peevishly.

'Little gells mustn't come to see me if they behave in that way,' said aunt Pullet.

'Why, you're too rough, little miss,' said uncle Pullet.

Poor Maggie sat down again, with the music all chased out of her soul, and the seven small demons all in again.

Mrs Tulliver, foreseeing nothing but misbehaviour while the children remained indoors, took an early opportunity of suggesting that, now they were rested after their walk, they might go and play out of doors; and aunt Pullet gave permission, only enjoining them not to go off the paved walks in the garden, and if they wanted to see the poultry fed, to view them from a distance on the horse-block; a restriction which had been imposed ever since Tom had been found guilty of running after the peacock, with an illusory idea that flight would make one of its feathers drop off.

Mrs Tulliver's thoughts had been temporarily diverted from the quarrel with Mrs Glegg by millinery and maternal cares, but now the great theme of the bonnet was thrown into perspective, and the children were out of the way, yesterday's anxieties recurred.

'It weighs on my mind so as never was,' she said, by way of opening the subject, 'sister Glegg's leaving the house in that way. I'm sure I'd no wish t'offend a sister.'

'Ah,' said aunt Pullet, 'there's no accounting for what Jane 'ull do. I wouldn't speak of it out o' the family – if it wasn't to Dr Turnbull; but it's my belief Jane lives too low. I've said so to Pullet often and often, and he knows it.'

'Why, you said so last Monday was a week, when we came away from drinking tea with 'em,' said Mr Pullet, beginning to nurse his knee and shelter it with his pocket-handkerchief, as was his way when the conversation took an interesting turn.

'Very like I did,' said Mrs Pullet, 'for you remember when I said things, better than I can remember myself. He's got a wonderful memory, Pullet has,' she continued, looking pathetically at her sister. 'I should be poorly off if he was to have a stroke, for he always remembers when I've got to take my doctor's stuff – and I'm taking three sorts now.'

'There's the "pills as before" every other night, and the new drops at eleven and four, and the 'fervescing mixture "when agreeable," ' rehearsed Mr Pullet, with a punctuation determined by a lozenge on his tongue.

'Ah, perhaps it 'ud be better for sister Glegg, if *she'd* go to the doctor some-times, instead o' chewing Turkey rhubarb whenever there's anything the matter with her,' said Mrs Tulliver, who naturally saw the wide subject of medicine chiefly in relation to Mrs Glegg.

'It's dreadful to think on,' said aunt Pullet, raising her hands and letting them fall again, 'people playing with their own insides in that way! And it's flying i' the face o' Providence; for what are the doctors for, if we aren't to call 'em in? And when folks have got the money to pay for a doctor, it isn't respectable, as I've told Jane many a time. I'm ashamed of acquaintance knowing it.'

'Well, we've no call to be ashamed,' said Mr Pullet, 'for Dr Turnbull hasn't got such another patient as you i' this parish, now old Mrs Sutton's gone.'

'Pullet keeps all my physic-bottles – did you know, Bessy?' said Mrs Pullet. 'He won't have one sold. He says it's nothing but right folks should see 'em when I'm gone. They fill two o' the long storeroom shelves a'ready – but,' she added, beginning to cry a little, 'it's well if they ever fill three. I may go before I've made up the dozen o' these last sizes. The pill-boxes are in the closet in my room – you'll remember that, sister – but there's nothing to show for the boluses, if it isn't the bills.'

'Don't talk o' your going, sister,' said Mrs Tulliver: 'I should have nobody to stand between me and sister Glegg if you was gone. And there's nobody but you can get her to make it up with Mr Tulliver, for sister Deane's never o' my side, and if she was, it's not to be looked for as she can speak like them as have got an independent fortin.'

'Well, your husband *is* awk'ard, you know, Bessy,' said Mrs Pullet, good-naturedly ready to use her deep depression on her sister's account as well as her own. 'He's never behaved quite so pretty to our family as he should do, and the children take after him – the boy's very mischievous, and runs away from his aunts and uncles, and the gell's rude and brown. It's your bad luck, and I'm sorry for you, Bessy; for you was allays my favourite sister, and we allays liked the same patterns.'

'I know Tulliver's hasty, and says odd things,' said Mrs Tulliver, wiping away one small tear from the corner of her eye, 'but I'm sure he's never been the man, since he married me, to object to my making the friends o' my side o' the family welcome to the house.'

'*I* don't want to make the worst of you, Bessy,' said Mrs Pullet, compassion-ately, 'for I doubt you'll have trouble enough without that; and your husband's got that poor sister and her children hanging on him, – and so given to lawing, they say. I doubt he'll leave you poorly off when he dies. Not as I'd have it said out o' the family.'

This view of her position was naturally far from cheering to Mrs Tulliver. Her imagination was not easily acted on, but she could not help thinking that her case was a hard one, since it appeared that other people thought it hard.

'I'm sure, sister, I can't help myself,' she said, urged by the fear lest her anticipated misfortunes might be held retributive, to take a comprehensive review of her past conduct. 'There's no woman strives more for her children; and I'm sure, at scouring-time this Ladyday as I've had all the bed-hangings taken down, I did as much as the two gells put together; and there's this last elder-flower wine I've made – beautiful! I allays offer it along with the sherry, though sister Glegg will have it I'm so extravagant; and as for liking to have my clothes tidy, and not go a fright about the house, there's nobody in the parish can say anything against me in respect o' backbiting and making mischief, for I don't wish anybody any harm; and nobody loses by sending me a pork-pie, for my pies are fit to show with the best o' my neighbours'; and the linen's so in order, as if I was to die tomorrow I shouldn't be ashamed. A woman can do no more nor she can.'

'But it's all o' no use, you know, Bessy,' said Mrs Pullet, holding her head on one side, and fixing her eyes pathetically on her sister, 'if your husband makes away with his money. Not but what if you was sold up, and other folks bought your furniture, it's a comfort to think as you've kept it well rubbed. And there's the linen, with your maiden mark on, might go all over the country. It 'ud be a sad pity for our family.' Mrs Pullet shook her head slowly.

'But what can I do, sister?' said Mrs Tulliver. 'Mr Tulliver's not a man to be dictated to – not if I was to go to the parson, and get by heart what I should tell my husband for the best. And I'm sure I don't pretend to know anything about putting out money and all that. I could never see into men's business as sister Glegg does.'

'Well, you're like me in that, Bessy,' said Mrs Pullet; 'and I think it 'ud be a deal more becoming o' Jane if she'd have that pier-glass rubbed oftener – there was ever so many spots on it last week – instead o' dictating to folks as have more comings in than she ever had, and telling 'em what they've to do with their money. But Jane and me were allays contrairy: she *would* have striped things, and I like spots. You like a spot too, Bessy: we allays hung together i' that.'

Mrs Pullet, affected by this last reminiscence, looked at her sister pathetically.

'Yes, Sophy,' said Mrs Tulliver, 'I remember our having a blue ground with a white spot both alike – I've got a bit in a bed-quilt now; and if you would but go and see sister Glegg, and persuade her to make it up with Tulliver, I should take it very kind of you. You was allays a good sister to me.'

'But the right thing 'ud be for Tulliver to go and make it up with her himself, and say he was sorry for speaking so rash. If he's borrowed money of her, he shouldn't be above that,' said Mrs Pullet, whose partiality did not blind her to principles: she did not forget what was due to people of independent fortune.

'It's no use talking o' that,' said poor Mrs Tulliver, almost peevishly. 'If I was to go down on my bare knees on the gravel to Tulliver, he'd never humble himself.'

'Well, you can't expect me to persuade *Jane* to beg pardon,' said Mrs Pullet. 'Her temper's beyond everything; it's well if it doesn't carry her off her mind, though there never *was* any of our family went to a madhouse.'

'I'm not thinking of her begging pardon,' said Mrs Tulliver. 'But if she'd just take no notice, and not call her money in; as it's not so much for one sister to ask of another; time 'ud mend things, and Tulliver 'ud forget all about it, and they'd be friends again.'

Mrs Tulliver, you perceive, was not aware of her husband's irrevocable determination to pay in the five hundred pounds; at least such a determination exceeded her powers of belief.

'Well, Bessy,' said Mrs Pullet, mournfully, '*I* don't want to help you on to ruin. I won't be behindhand i' doing you a good turn, if it is to be done. And I don't like it said among acquaintance as we've got quarrels in the family. I shall tell Jane that; and I don't mind driving to Jane's tomorrow, if Pullet doesn't mind. What do you say, Mr Pullet?'

'I've no objections,' said Mr Pullet, who was perfectly contented with any course the quarrel might take, so that Mr Tulliver did not apply to *him* for money. Mr Pullet was nervous about his investments, and did not see how a man could have any security for his money unless he turned it into land.

After a little further discussion as to whether it would not be better for Mrs Tulliver to accompany them on a visit to sister Glegg, Mrs Pullet, observing that it was teatime, turned to reach from a drawer a delicate damask napkin, which she pinned before her in the fashion of an apron. The door did, in fact, soon open, but instead of the tea-tray, Sally introduced an object so startling that both Mrs Pullet and Mrs Tulliver gave a scream, causing uncle Pullet to swallow his lozenge – for the fifth time in his life, as he afterwards noted.

CHAPTER 10

Maggie Behaves Worse than She Expected

The startling object which thus made an epoch for uncle Pullet was no other than little Lucy, with one side of her person, from her small foot to her bonnet-crown, wet and discoloured with mud, holding out two tiny blackened hands, and making a very piteous face. To account for this unprecedented apparition in aunt Pullet's parlour, we must return to the moment when the three children went to play out of doors, and the small demons who had taken possession of Maggie's soul at an early period of the day had returned in all the greater force after a temporary absence. All the disagreeable recollections of the morning were thick upon her, when Tom, whose displeasure towards her had been considerably refreshed by her foolish trick of causing him to upset his cowslip wine, said, 'Here, Lucy, you come along with me,' and walked off to the area where the toads were, as if there were no Maggie in existence. Seeing this, Maggie lingered at a distance, looking like a small Medusa with her snakes cropped. Lucy was naturally pleased that cousin Tom was so good to her, and it was very amusing to see him tickling a fat toad with a piece of string when the toad was safe down the area, with an iron grating over him. Still Lucy wished Maggie to enjoy the spectacle also, especially as she would doubtless find a name for the toad; and say what had been his past history; for Lucy had a delighted semi-belief in Maggie's stories about the live things they came upon

by accident – how Mrs Earwig had a wash at home, and one of her children had
fallen into the hot copper, for which reason she was running so fast to fetch the
doctor. Tom had a profound contempt for this nonsense of Maggie's, smashing
the earwig at once as a superfluous yet easy means of proving the entire unreality
of such a story; but Lucy, for the life of her, could not help fancying there was
something in it, and at all events thought it was very pretty make-believe. So now
the desire to know the history of a very portly toad, added to her habitual
affectionateness, made her run back to Maggie and say, 'O, there is such a big,
funny toad, Maggie! Do come and see.'

Maggie said nothing, but turned away from her with a deeper frown. As long
as Tom seemed to prefer Lucy to her, Lucy made part of his unkindness.
Maggie would have thought a little while ago that she could never be cross with
pretty little Lucy, any more than she could be cruel to a little white mouse: but
then, Tom had always been quite indifferent to Lucy before, and it had been left
to Maggie to pet and make much of her. As it was, she was actually beginning to
think that she should like to make Lucy cry, by slapping or pinching her,
especially as it might vex Tom, whom it was of no use to slap, even if she dared,
because he didn't mind it. And if Lucy hadn't been there, Maggie was sure he
would have got friends with her sooner.

Tickling a fat toad who is not highly sensitive is an amusement that it is
possible to exhaust, and Tom by and by began to look round for some other
mode of passing the time. But in so prim a garden, where they were not to go off
the paved walks, there was not a great choice of sport. The only pleasure such a
restriction suggested was the pleasure of breaking it, and Tom began to meditate
an insurrectionary visit to the pond, about a field's length beyond the garden.

'I say, Lucy,' he began, nodding his head up and down with great significance,
as he coiled up his string again, 'what do you think I mean to do?'

'What, Tom?' said Lucy, with curiosity.

'I mean to go to the pond, and look at the pike. You may go with me if you
like,' said the young sultan.

'Oh, Tom, *dare* you?' said Lucy. 'Aunt said we musn't go out of the garden.'

'Oh, I shall go out at the other end of the garden,' said Tom. 'Nobody 'ull see
us. Besides, I don't care if they do – I'll run off home.'

'But *I* couldn't run,' said Lucy, who had never before been exposed to such
severe temptation.

'Oh, never mind – they won't be cross with *you*,' said Tom. 'You say I took you.'

Tom walked along, and Lucy trotted by his side, timidly enjoying the rare treat
of doing something naughty – excited also by the mention of that celebrity, the
pike, about which she was quite uncertain whether it was a fish or a fowl. Maggie
saw them leaving the garden, and could not resist the impulse to follow. Anger
and jealousy can no more bear to lose sight of their objects than love, and that
Tom and Lucy should do or see anything of which she was ignorant would
have been an intolerable idea to Maggie. So she kept a few yards behind them,
unobserved by Tom, who was presently absorbed in watching for the pike – a
highly interesting monster; he was said to be so very old, so very large, and to have
such a remarkable appetite. The pike, like other celebrities, did not show when he

was watched for, but Tom caught sight of something in rapid movement in the water, which attracted him to another spot on the brink of the pond.

'Here, Lucy!' he said in a loud whisper, 'come here! take care! keep on the grass – don't step where the cows have been!' he added, pointing to a peninsula of dry grass, with trodden mud on each side of it; for Tom's contemptuous conception of a girl included the attribute of being unfit to walk in dirty places.

Lucy came carefully as she was bidden, and bent down to look at what seemed a golden arrowhead darting through the water. It was a water-snake, Tom told her, and Lucy at last could see the serpentine wave of its body, very much wondering that a snake could swim. Maggie had drawn nearer and nearer – she *must* see it too, though it was bitter to her like everything else, since Tom did not care about her seeing it. At last, she was close by Lucy, and Tom, who had been aware of her approach, but would not notice it till he was obliged, turned round and said, 'Now, get away, Maggie; there's no room for you on the grass here. Nobody asked *you* to come.'

There were passions at war in Maggie at that moment to have made a tragedy, if tragedies were made by passion only; but the essential τί μέγεθοδ which was present in the passion was wanting to the action: the utmost Maggie could do, with a fierce thrust of her small brown arm, was to push poor little pink-and-white Lucy into the cow-trodden mud.

Then Tom could not restrain himself, and gave Maggie two smart slaps on the arm as he ran to pick up Lucy, who lay crying helplessly. Maggie retreated to the roots of a tree a few yards off, and looked on impenitently. Usually her repentance came quickly after one rash deed, but now Tom and Lucy had made her so miserable, she was glad to spoil their happiness – glad to make everybody uncomfortable. Why should she be sorry? Tom was very slow to forgive *her*, however sorry she might have been.

'I shall tell mother, you know, Miss Mag,' said Tom, loudly and emphatically, as soon as Lucy was up and ready to walk away. It was not Tom's practice to 'tell,' but here justice clearly demanded that Maggie should be visited with the utmost punishment: not that Tom had learned to put his views in that abstract form; he never mentioned 'justice', and had no idea that his desire to punish might be called by that fine name. Lucy was too entirely absorbed by the evil that had befallen her – the spoiling of her pretty best clothes, and the discomfort of being wet and dirty – to think much of the cause, which was entirely mysterious to her. She could never have guessed what she had done to make Maggie angry with her; but she felt that Maggie was very unkind and disagreeable, and made no magnanimous entreaties to Tom that he would not 'tell', only running along by his side and crying piteously, while Maggie sat on the roots of the tree and looked after them with her small Medusa face.

'Sally,' said Tom, when they reached the kitchen door, and Sally looked at them in speechless amaze, with a piece of bread-and-butter in her mouth and a toasting-fork in her hand – 'Sally, tell mother it was Maggie pushed Lucy into the mud.'

'But Lors ha' massy, how did you get near such mud as that?' said Sally, making a wry face, as she stooped down and examined the *corpus delicti*.

Tom's imagination had not been rapid and capacious enough to include this question among the foreseen consequences, but it was no sooner put than he foresaw whither it tended, and that Maggie would not be considered the only culprit in the case. He walked quietly away from the kitchen door, leaving Sally to that pleasure of guessing which active minds notoriously prefer to ready-made knowledge.

Sally, as you are aware, lost no time in presenting Lucy at the parlour door, for to have so dirty an object introduced into the house at Garum Firs was too great a weight to be sustained by a single mind.

'Goodness gracious!' aunt Pullet exclaimed, after preluding by an inarticulate scream; 'keep her at the door, Sally! Don't bring her off the oil-cloth, whatever you do.'

'Why, she's tumbled into some nasty mud,' said Mrs Tulliver, going up to Lucy to examine into the amount of damage to clothes for which she felt herself responsible to her sister Deane.

'If you please, 'um, it was Miss Maggie as pushed her in,' said Sally; 'Master Tom's been and said so, and they must ha' been to the pond, for it's only there they could ha' got into such dirt.'

'There it is, Bessy; it's what I've been telling you,' said Mrs Pullet, in a tone of prophetic sadness: 'it's your children – there's no knowing what they'll come to.'

Mrs Tulliver was mute, feeling herself a truly wretched mother. As usual, the thought pressed upon her that people would think she had done something wicked to deserve her maternal troubles, while Mrs Pullet began to give elaborate directions to Sally how to guard the premises from serious injury in the course of removing the dirt. Meantime tea was to be brought in by the cook, and the two naughty children were to have theirs in an ignominious manner in the kitchen. Mrs Tulliver went out to speak to these naughty children, supposing them to be close at hand; but it was not until after some search that she found Tom leaning with rather a hardened careless air against the white paling of the poultry-yard, and lowering his piece of string on the other side as a means of exasperating the turkey-cock.

'Tom, you naughty boy, where's your sister?' said Mrs Tulliver, in a distressed voice.

'I don't know,' said Tom; his eagerness for justice on Maggie had diminished since he had seen clearly that it could hardly be brought about without the injustice of some blame on his own conduct.

'Why, where did you leave her?' said his mother, looking round.

'Sitting under the tree against the pond,' said Tom, apparently indifferent to everything but the string and the turkey-cock.

'Then go and fetch her in this minute, you naughty boy. And how could you think o' going to the pond, and taking your sister where there was dirt? You know she'll do mischief, if there's mischief to be done.'

It was Mrs Tulliver's way, if she blamed Tom, to refer his misdemeanour, somehow or other, to Maggie.

The idea of Maggie sitting alone by the pond, roused an habitual fear in Mrs Tulliver's mind, and she mounted the horse-block to satisfy herself by a sight of that fatal child, while Tom walked – not very quickly – on his way towards her.

'They're such children for the water, mine are,' she said aloud, without reflecting that there was no one to hear her; 'they'll be brought in dead and drownded someday. I wish that river was far enough.'

But when she not only failed to discern Maggie, but presently saw Tom returning from the pool alone, this hovering fear entered and took complete possession of her, and she hurried to meet him.

'Maggie's nowhere about the pond, mother,' said Tom; 'she's gone away.'

You may conceive the terrified search for Maggie, and the difficulty of convincing her mother that she was not in the pond. Mrs Pullet observed that the child might come to a worse end if she lived – there was no knowing; and Mr Pullet, confused and overwhelmed by this revolutionary aspect of things – the tea deferred and the poultry alarmed by the unusual running to and fro – took up his spud as an instrument of search, and reached down a key to unlock the goose-pen, as a likely place for Maggie to lie concealed in.

Tom, after a while, started the idea that Maggie was gone home (without thinking it necessary to state that it was what he should have done himself under the circumstances), and the suggestion was seized as a comfort by his mother.

'Sister, for goodness' sake let 'em put the horse in the carriage and take me home – we shall perhaps find her on the road. Lucy can't walk in her dirty clothes,' she said, looking at that innocent victim, who was wrapped up in a shawl, and sitting with naked feet on the sofa.

Aunt Pullet was quite willing to take the shortest means of restoring her premises to order and quiet, and it was not long before Mrs Tulliver was in the chaise looking anxiously at the most distant point before her. What the father would say if Maggie was lost? was a question that predominated over every other.

CHAPTER 11

Maggie Tries to Run Away From Her Shadow

Maggie's intentions, as usual, were on a larger scale than Tom had imagined. The resolution that gathered in her mind, after Tom and Lucy had walked away, was not so simple as that of going home. No! she would run away and go to the gypsies, and Tom should never see her any more. That was by no means a new idea to Maggie; she had been so often told she was like a gypsy, and 'half wild', that when she was miserable it seemed to her the only way of escaping opprobrium, and being entirely in harmony with circumstances, would be to live in a little brown tent on the commons; the gypsies, she considered, would gladly receive her, and pay her much respect on account of her superior knowledge. She had once mentioned her views on this point to Tom, and suggested that he should stain his face brown, and they should run away together; but Tom rejected the scheme with contempt, observing that gypsies were thieves, and hardly got anything to eat, and had nothing to drive but a donkey. Today, however, Maggie thought her misery had reached a pitch at which gypsydom was her only refuge, and she rose from her seat on the roots of the tree with the sense that this was a great crisis in her life; she would run straight away till she came to Dunlow Common, where there would certainly be gypsies; and cruel Tom, and the rest of her relations who found fault with her, should never see her any more. She thought of her father as she ran along, but she reconciled herself to the idea of parting with him, by determining that she would secretly send him a letter by a small gypsy, who would run away without telling where she was, and just let him know that she was well and happy, and always loved him very much.

Maggie soon got out of breath with running, but by the time Tom got to the pond again, she was at the distance of three long fields, and was on the edge of the lane leading to the highroad. She stopped to pant a little, reflecting that running away was not a pleasant thing until one had got quite to the common where the gypsies were, but her resolution had not abated: she presently passed through the gate into the lane, not knowing where it would lead her, for it was not this way that they came from Dorlcote Mill to Garum Firs, and she felt all the safer for that, because there was no chance of her being overtaken. But she was soon aware, not without trembling, that there were two men coming along the lane in front of her: she had not thought of meeting strangers – she had been too much occupied with the idea of her friends coming after her. The formidable strangers were two shabby-looking men with flushed faces, one of them carrying a bundle on a stick over his shoulder: but to her surprise, while she was dreading their disapprobation as a runaway, the man with the bundle stopped, and in a half-whining half-coaxing tone asked her if she had a copper to give a poor man. Maggie had a sixpence in her pocket – her uncle Glegg's present – which she immediately drew out and gave this poor man with a polite smile, hoping he would feel very kindly towards her as a generous person. 'That's the only money I've got,' she said, apologetically. 'Thank you, little miss,' said the man in a less respectful and grateful tone than Maggie anticipated, and she even observed that he smiled and winked at his companion. She walked on hurriedly, but was aware that the two men were standing still, probably to look after her, and she presently heard them laughing loudly. Suddenly it occurred to her that they might think she was an idiot: Tom had said that her cropped hair made her look like an idiot, and it was too painful an idea to be readily forgotten. Besides, she had no sleeves on – only a cape and a bonnet. It was clear that she was not likely to make a favourable impression on passengers, and she thought she would turn into the fields again; but not on the same side of the lane as before, lest they should still be uncle Pullet's fields. She turned through the first gate that was not locked, and felt a delightful sense of privacy in creeping along by the hedgerows, after her recent humiliating encounter. She was used to wandering about the fields by herself, and was less timid there than on the highroad. Sometimes she had to climb over high gates, but that was a small evil; she was getting out of reach very fast, and she should probably soon come within sight of Dunlow Common, or at least of some other common, for she had heard her father say that you couldn't go very far without coming to a common. She hoped so, for she was getting rather tired and hungry, and until she reached the gypsies there was no definite prospect of bread-and-butter. It was still broad daylight, for aunt Pullet, retaining the early habits of the Dodson family, took tea at half-past four by the sun, and at five by the kitchen clock; so, though it was nearly an hour since Maggie started, there was no gathering gloom on the fields to remind her that the night would come. Still, it seemed to her that she had been walking a very great distance indeed, and it was really surprising that the common did not come within sight. Hitherto she had been in the rich parish of Garum, where there was a great deal of pasture-land, and she had only seen one labourer at a distance. That was fortunate in some respects, as labourers might be too ignorant to understand the propriety of her wanting to go to Dunlow Common; yet it would have been better if she could have met someone who would tell her the way without wanting to know anything about her private business. At last, however, the green fields came to an end, and Maggie found herself looking through the bars of a gate into a lane with a wide margin of grass on each side of it. She had never seen such a wide lane before, and without her knowing why, it gave her the impression that the common could not be far off; perhaps it was because she saw a donkey with a log to his foot feeding on the grassy margin, for she had seen a donkey with that pitiable encumbrance on Dunlow Common when she had been across it in her father's gig. She crept through the bars of the gate and walked on with new spirit, though not without haunting images of Apollyon, and a highwayman with a pistol, and a blinking dwarf in yellow, with a mouth from ear to ear, and other miscellaneous dangers. For poor little Maggie had at once the timidity of an active imagination and the daring that comes from overmastering impulse. She had rushed into the adventure of seeking her unknown kindred, the gypsies; and now she was in this strange lane, she hardly dared look on one side of her, lest she should see the diabolical blacksmith in his leathern apron grinning at her with arms akimbo. It was not without a leaping of the heart that she caught sight of a small pair of bare legs sticking up, feet uppermost, by the side of a hillock; they seemed something hideously preternatural – a diabolical kind of fungus; for she was too much agitated at the first glance to see the ragged clothes and the dark shaggy head attached to them. It was a boy asleep, and Maggie trotted along faster and more lightly, lest she should wake him: it did not occur to her that he was one of her friends the gypsies, who in all probability would have very genial manners. But the fact was so, for at the next bend in the lane, Maggie actually saw the little semicircular black tent with the blue smoke rising before it, which was to be her refuge from all the blighting obloquy that had pursued her in civilised life. She even saw a tall female figure by the column of smoke – doubtless the gypsy-mother, who provided the tea and other groceries; it was astonishing to herself that she did not feel more delighted. But it was startling to find the gypsies in a lane, after all, and not on a common; indeed, it was rather disappointing; for a mysterious illimitable common, where there were sand-pits to hide in, and one was out of everybody's reach, had always made part of Maggie's picture of gypsy life. She went on, however, and thought with some comfort that gypsies most likely knew nothing about idiots, so there was no danger of their falling into the mistake of setting her down at the first glance as an idiot. It was plain she had attracted attention; for the tall figure, who proved to be a young woman with a baby on her arm, walked slowly to meet her. Maggie looked up in the new face rather tremblingly as it approached, and was reassured by the thought that her aunt Pullet and the rest were right when they called her a gypsy, for this face, with the bright dark eyes and the long hair, was really something like what she used to see in the glass before she cut her hair off.

'My little lady, where are you going to?' the gypsy said, in a tone of coaxing deference.

It was delightful, and just what Maggie expected: the gypsies saw at once that she was a little lady, and were prepared to treat her accordingly.

'Not any farther,' said Maggie, feeling as if she were saying what she had rehearsed in a dream. 'I'm come to stay with *you*, please.'

'That's pritty; come, then. Why, what a nice little lady you are, to be sure,' said the gypsy, taking her by the hand. Maggie thought her very agreeable, but wished she had not been so dirty.

There was quite a group round the fire when they reached it. An old gypsy woman was seated on the ground nursing her knees, and occasionally poking a skewer into the round kettle that sent forth an odorous steam: two small shock-headed children were lying prone and resting on their elbows something like small sphinxes; and a placid donkey was bending his head over a tall girl, who, lying on her back, was scratching his nose and indulging him with a bite of excellent stolen hay. The slanting sunlight fell kindly upon them, and the scene was really very pretty and comfortable, Maggie thought, only she hoped they would soon set out the teacups. Everything would be quite charming when she had taught the gypsies to use a washing-basin, and to feel an interest in books. It was a little confusing, though, that the young woman began to speak to the old one in a language which Maggie did not understand, while the tall girl, who was feeding the donkey, sat up and stared at her without offering any salutation. At last the old woman said, 'What, my pretty lady, are you come to stay with us? Sit ye down and tell us where ye come from.'

It was just like a story: Maggie liked to be called pretty lady and treated in this way. She sat down and said, 'I'm come from home because I'm unhappy, and I mean to be a gypsy. I'll live with you, if you like, and I can teach you a great many things.'

'Such a clever little lady,' said the woman with the baby, sitting down by Maggie, and allowing baby to crawl; 'and such a pritty bonnet and frock,' she added, taking off Maggie's bonnet and looking at it while she made an observation to the old woman, in the unknown language. The tall girl snatched the bonnet and put it on her own head hind-foremost with a grin; but Maggie was determined not to show any weakness on this subject, as if she were susceptible about her bonnet.

'I don't want to wear a bonnet,' she said, 'I'd rather wear a red handerkerchief, like yours' (looking at her friend by her side); my hair was quite long till yester-day, when I cut it off: but I dare say it will grow again very soon,' she added apologetically, thinking it probable the gypsies had a strong prejudice in favour of long hair. And Maggie had forgotten even her hunger at that moment in the desire to conciliate gypsy opinion.

'O what a nice little lady! – and rich, I'm sure,' said the old woman. 'Didn't you live in a beautiful house at home?'

'Yes, my home is pretty, and I'm very fond of the river, where we go fishing – but I'm often very unhappy. I should have liked to bring my books with me, but I came away in a hurry, you know. But I can tell you almost everything there is in my books, I've read them so many times – and that will amuse you. And I can tell you something about Geography too – that's about the world we live in – very useful and interesting. Did you ever hear about Columbus?'

Maggie's eyes had begun to sparkle and her cheeks to flush – she was really beginning to instruct the gypsies, and gaining great influence over them. The gypsies themselves were not without amazement at this talk, though their attention was divided by the contents of Maggie's pocket, which the friend at her right hand had by this time emptied without attracting her notice.

'Is that where you live, my little lady?' said the old woman, at the mention of Columbus.

'Oh, no!' said Maggie, with some pity; 'Columbus was a very wonderful man, who found out half the world, and they put chains on him and treated him very badly, you know – it's in my Catechism of Geography – but perhaps it's rather too long to tell before tea . . . I want my tea so.'

The last words burst from Maggie, in spite of herself, with a sudden drop from patronising instruction to simple peevishness.

'Why, she's hungry, poor little lady,' said the younger woman. 'Give her some o' the cold victual. You've been walking a good way, I'll be bound, my dear. Where's your home?'

'It's Dorlcote Mill, a good way off,' said Maggie. 'My father is Mr Tulliver, but we mustn't let him know where I am, else he'll fetch me home again. Where does the queen of the gypsies live?'

'What! do you want to go to her, my little lady?' said the younger woman. The tall girl meanwhile was constantly staring at Maggie and grinning. Her manners were certainly not agreeable.

'No,' said Maggie, 'I'm only thinking that if she isn't a very good queen you might be glad when she died, and you could choose another. If I was a queen, I'd be a very good queen, and kind to everybody.'

'Here's a bit o' nice victual, then,' said the old woman, handing to Maggie a lump of dry bread, which she had taken from a bag of scraps, and a piece of cold bacon.

'Thank you,' said Maggie, looking at the food without taking it; 'but will you give me some bread-and-butter and tea instead? l don't like bacon.'

'We've got no tea or butter,' said the old woman with something like a scowl, as if she were getting tired of coaxing.

'O, a little bread and treacle would do,' said Maggie.

'We han't got no treacle,' said the old woman crossly, whereupon there followed a sharp dialogue between the two women in their unknown tongue, and one of the small sphinxes snatched at the bread-and-bacon, and began to eat it. At this moment the tall girl, who had gone a few yards off, came back, and said something which produced a strong effect. The old woman, seeming to forget Maggie's hunger, poked the skewer into the pot with new vigour, and the younger crept under the tent, and reached out some platters and spoons. Maggie trembled a little, and was afraid the tears would come into her eyes. Meanwhile the tall girl gave a shrill cry, and presently came running up the boy whom Maggie had passed as he was sleeping – a rough urchin about the age of Tom. He stared at Maggie, and there ensued much incomprehensible chattering. She felt very lonely, and was quite sure she should begin to cry before long: the gypsies didn't seem to mind her at all, and she felt quite weak among them. But the springing tears were checked by a new terror, when two men came up, whose approach had been the cause of the sudden excitement. The elder of the two carried a bag, which he flung down, addressing the women in a loud and scolding tone, which they answered by a shower of treble sauciness; while a black cur ran barking up to Maggie, and threw her into a tremor that only found a new cause in the curses with which the younger man called the dog off, and gave him a rap with a great stick he held in his hand.

Maggie felt that it was impossible she should ever be queen of these people, or ever communicate to them amusing and useful knowledge.

Both the men now seemed to be enquiring about Maggie, for they looked at her, and the tone of the conversation became of that pacific kind which implies curiosity on one side and the power of satisfying it on the other. At last the younger woman said in her previous deferential coaxing tone, 'This nice little lady's come to live with us: aren't you glad?'

'Ay, very glad,' said the younger man, who was looking at Maggie's silver thimble and other small matters that had been taken from her pocket. He returned them all except the thimble to the younger woman, with some observation, and she immediately restored them to Maggie's pocket, while the men seated themselves, and began to attack the contents of the kettle – a stew of meat and potatoes – which had been taken off the fire and turned out into a yellow platter.

Maggie began to think that Tom must be right about the gypsies – they must certainly be thieves, unless the man meant to return her thimble by and by. She would willingly have given it to him, for she was not at all attached to her thimble; but the idea that she was among thieves prevented her from feeling any comfort in the revival of deference and attention towards her – all thieves, except Robin Hood, were wicked people. The women saw she was frightened.

'We've got nothing nice for a lady to eat,' said the old woman, in her coaxing tone. 'And she's so hungry, sweet little lady.'

'Here, my dear, try if you can eat a bit o' this,' said the younger woman, handing some of the stew on a brown dish with an iron spoon to Maggie, who, remembering that the old woman had seemed angry with her for not liking the bread-and-bacon, dared not refuse the stew, though fear had chased away her appetite. If her father would come by in the gig and take her up! Or even if Jack the Giantkiller, or Mr Greatheart, or St George who slew the dragon on the halfpennies, would happen to pass that way! But Maggie thought with a sinking heart that these heroes were never seen in the neighbourhood of St Ogg's – nothing very wonderful ever came there.

Maggie Tulliver, you perceive, was by no means that well-trained, well-informed young person that a small female of eight or nine necessarily is in these days: she had only been to school a year at St Ogg's, and had so few books that she sometimes read the dictionary; so that in travelling over her small mind you would have found the most unexpected ignorance as well as unexpected knowledge. She could have informed you that there was such a word as 'polygamy,' and being also acquainted with 'polysyllable,' she had deduced the conclusion that 'poly' meant 'many'; but she had had no idea that gypsies were not well supplied with groceries, and her thoughts generally were the oddest mixture of clear-eyed acumen and blind dreams.

Her ideas about the gypsies had undergone a rapid modification in the last five minutes. From having considered them very respectful companions, amenable to instruction, she had begun to think that they meant perhaps to kill her as soon as it was dark, and cut up her body for gradual cooking: the suspicion crossed her that the fierce-eyed old man was in fact the devil, who might drop that transparent disguise at any moment, and turn either into the grinning blacksmith or else a fiery-eyed monster with dragon's wings. It was no use trying to eat the stew, and yet the thing she most dreaded was to offend the gypsies, by betraying her extremely unfavourable opinion of them, and she wondered, with a keenness of interest that no theologian could have exceeded, whether, if the devil were really present, he would know her thoughts.

'What! you don't like the smell of it, my dear,' said the young woman, observing that Maggie did not even take a spoonful of the stew. 'Try a bit – come.'

'No, thank you,' said Maggie, summoning all her force for a desperate effort, and trying to smile in a friendly way. 'I haven't time, I think – it seems getting darker. I think I must go home now, and come again another day, and then I can bring you a basket with some jam-tarts and things.'

Maggie rose from her seat as she threw out this illusory prospect, devoutly hoping that Apollyon was gullible; but her hope sank when the old gypsy-woman said, 'Stop a bit, stop a bit, little lady – we'll take you home, all safe, when we've done supper: you shall ride home, like a lady.'

Maggie sat down again, with little faith in this promise, though she presently saw the tall girl putting a bridle on the donkey, and throwing a couple of bags on his back.

'Now, then, little missis,' said the younger man, rising, and leading the donkey forward, 'tell us where you live – what's the name o' the place?'

'Dorlcote Mill is my home,' said Maggie, eagerly. 'My father is Mr Tulliver – he lives there.'

'What! a big mill a little way this side o' St Ogg's?'

'Yes,' said Maggie. 'Is it far off? I think I should like to walk there, if you please.'

'No, no, it'll be getting dark, we must make haste. And the donkey 'll carry you as nice as can be – you'll see.'

He lifted Maggie as he spoke, and set her on the donkey. She felt relieved that it was not the old man who seemed to be going with her, but she had only a trembling hope that she was really going home.

'Here's your pretty bonnet,' said the younger woman, putting that recently-despised but now welcome article of costume on Maggie's head: 'and you'll say we've been very good to you, won't you? and what a nice little lady we said you was.'

'Oh, yes, thank you,' said Maggie, 'I'm very much obliged to you. But I wish you'd go with me too.' She thought anything was better than going with one of the dreadful men alone: it would be more cheerful to be murdered by a larger party.

'Ah, you're fondest o' me, aren't you?' said the woman. 'But I can't go – you'll go too fast for me.'

It now appeared that the man also was to be seated on the donkey, holding Maggie before him, and she was as incapable of remonstrating against this arrangement as the donkey himself, though no nightmare had ever seemed to her more horrible. When the woman had patted her on the back, and said 'Goodbye,' the donkey, at a strong hint from the man's stick, set off at a rapid walk along the lane towards the point Maggie had come from an hour ago, while the tall girl and the rough urchin, also furnished with sticks, obligingly escorted them for the first hundred yards, with much screaming and thwacking.

Not Leonore, in that preternatural midnight excursion with her phantom lover, was more terrified than poor Maggie in this entirely natural ride on a short-paced donkey, with a gypsy behind her, who considered that he was earning half a crown. The red light of the setting sun seemed to have a portentous meaning, with which the alarming bray of the second donkey with the log on its foot must surely have some connexion. Two low thatched cottages – the only houses they passed in this lane – seemed to add to its dreariness: they had no windows to speak of, and the doors were closed: it was probable that they were inhabited by witches, and it was a relief to find that the donkey did not stop there.

At last – oh, sight of joy! – this lane, the longest in the world, was coming to an end, was opening on a broad highroad, where there was actually a coach passing! And there was a finger-post at the corner: she had surely seen that finger-post before – 'To St Ogg's, 2 miles.' The gypsy really meant to take her home, then: he was probably a good man, after all, and might have been rather hurt at the thought that she didn't like coming with him alone. This idea became stronger as she felt more and more certain that she knew the road quite well, and she was considering how she might open a conversation with the injured gypsy, and not only gratify his feelings but efface the impression of her own cowardice, when, as they reached a cross-road, Maggie caught sight of someone coming on a white-faced horse.

'Oh, stop, stop!' she cried out. 'There's my father! Oh, father, father!'

The sudden joy was almost painful, and before her father reached her, she was sobbing. Great was Mr Tulliver's wonder, for he had made a round from Basset, and had not yet been home.

'Why, what's the meaning o' this?' he said, checking his horse, while Maggie slipped from the donkey and ran to her father's stirrup.

'The little miss lost herself, I reckon,' said the gypsy. 'She'd come to our tent at the far end o' Dunlow Lane, and I was bringing her where she said her home was. It's a good way to come arter being on the tramp all day.'

'Oh, yes, father, he's been very good to bring me home,' said Maggie. 'A very kind, good man!'

'Here, then, my man,' said Mr Tulliver, taking out five shillings. 'It's the best day's work *you* ever did. I couldn't afford to lose the little wench: here, lift her up before me.'

'Why, Maggie, how's this, how's this?' he said, as they rode along, while she laid her head against her father, and sobbed. 'How came you to be rambling about and lose yourself?'

'Oh, father,' sobbed Maggie, 'I ran away because I was so unhappy – Tom was so angry with me. I couldn't bear it.'

'Pooh, pooh,' said Mr Tulliver, soothingly, 'you mustn't think o' running away from father. What 'ud father do without his little wench?'

'O no, I never will again, father – never.'

Mr Tulliver spoke his mind very strongly when he reached home that evening, and the effect was seen in the remarkable fact, that Maggie never heard one reproach from her mother, or one taunt from Tom, about this foolish business of her running away to the gypsies. Maggie was rather awe-stricken by this unusual treatment, and sometimes thought that her conduct had been too wicked to be alluded to.

CHAPTER 12

Mr and Mrs Glegg at Home

In order to see Mr and Mrs Glegg at home, we must enter the town of St Ogg's – that venerable town with the red-fluted roofs and the broad warehouse gables, where the black ships unlade themselves of their burthens from the far north, and carry away, in exchange, the precious inland products, the well-crushed cheese and the soft fleeces, which my refined readers have doubtless become acquainted with through the medium of the best classic pastorals.

It is one of those old, old towns which impress one as a continuation and outgrowth of nature, as much as the nests of the bower-birds or the winding galleries of the white ants: a town which carries the traces of its long growth and history like a millennial tree, and has sprung up and developed in the same spot between the river and the low hill from the time when the Roman legions turned their backs on it from the camp on the hillside, and the long-haired sea-kings came up the river and looked with fierce, eager eyes at the fatness of the land. It is a town 'familiar with forgotten years'. The shadow of the Saxon hero-king still walks there fitfully, reviewing the scenes of his youth and love-time, and is met by the gloomier shadow of the dreadful heathen Dane, who was stabbed in the midst of his warriors by the sword of an invisible avenger, and who rises on autumn evenings like a white mist from his tumulus on the hill, and hovers in the court of the old hall by the riverside – the spot where he was thus miraculously slain in the days before the old hall was built. It was the Normans who began to build that fine old hall, which is like the town, telling of the thoughts and hands of widely-sundered generations; but it is all so old that we look with loving pardon at its inconsistencies, and are well content that they who built the stone oriel, and they who built the Gothic façade and towers of finest small brickwork with the trefoil ornament, and the windows and battlements defined with stone, did not sacrilegiously pull down the ancient half-timbered body with its oak-roofed banqueting-hall.

But older even than this old hall is perhaps the bit of wall now built into the belfry of the parish church, and said to be a remnant of the original chapel dedicated to St Ogg, the patron saint of this ancient town, of whose history I possess several manuscript versions. I incline to the briefest, since, if it should not be wholly true, it is at least likely to contain the least falsehood. 'Ogg the son of Beorl,' says my private hagiographer, 'was a boatman who gained a scanty living by ferrying passengers across the river Floss. And it came to pass, one evening when the winds were high, that there sat moaning by the brink of the river a woman with a child in her arms; and she was clad in rags, and had a worn and withered look, and she craved to be rowed across the river. And the men thereabout questioned her, and said, 'Wherefore dost thou desire to cross the river? Tarry till the morning, and take shelter here for the night: so shalt thou be wise, and not foolish.' Still she went on to mourn and crave. But Ogg the son of Beorl came up and said, 'I will ferry thee across: it is enough that thy heart needs it.' And he ferried her across. And it came to pass, when she stepped ashore, that her rags were turned into robes of flowing white, and her face became bright with exceeding beauty, and there was a glory around it, so that she shed a light on the water like the moon in its brightness. And she said – 'Ogg the son of Beorl, thou art blessed in that thou didst not question and wrangle with the heart's need, but wast smitten with pity, and didst straightway relieve the same. And from henceforth who so steps into thy boat shall be in no peril from the storm; and whenever it puts forth to the rescue, it shall save the lives both of men and beasts.' And when the floods came, many were saved by reason of that blessing on the boat. But when Ogg the son of Beorl died, behold, in the parting of his soul, the boat loosed itself from its moorings, and was floated with the ebbing tide in great swiftness to the ocean, and was seen no more. Yet it was witnessed in the floods of aftertime, that at the coming on of eventide, Ogg the son of Beorl was always seen with his boat upon the wide-spreading waters, and the Blessed Virgin sat in the prow, shedding a light around as of the moon in its brightness, so that the rowers in the gathering darkness took heart and pulled anew.'

This legend, one sees, reflects from a far-off time the visitation of the floods, which, even when they left human life untouched, were widely fatal to the helpless cattle, and swept as sudden death over all smaller living things. But the town knew worse troubles even than the floods – troubles of the civil wars, when it was a continual fighting-place, where first Puritans thanked God for the blood of the Loyalists, and then Loyalists thanked God for the blood of the Puritans. Many honest citizens lost all their possessions for conscience' sake in those times, and went forth beggared from their native town. Doubtless there are many houses standing now on which those honest citizens turned their backs in sorrow: quaint-gabled houses looking on the river, jammed between newer warehouses, and penetrated by surprising passages, which turn and turn at sharp angles till they lead you out on a muddy strand overflowed continually by the rushing tide. Everywhere the brick houses have a mellow look, and in Mrs Glegg's day there was no incongruous new-fashioned smartness, no plate-glass in shop windows, no fresh stucco-facing or other fallacious attempt to make fine old red St Ogg's wear the air of a town that sprang up yesterday. The shop windows were small and unpretending; for the farmers' wives and daughters who came to do their shopping on market-days were not to be withdrawn from their regular, well-known shops; and the tradesmen had no wares intended for customers who would go on their way and be seen no more. Ah! even Mrs Glegg's day seems far back in the past now, separated from us by changes that widen the years. War and the rumour of war had then died out from the minds of men, and if they were ever thought of by the farmers in drab greatcoats, who shook the grain out of their sample-bags and buzzed over it in the full market-place, it was as a state of things that belonged to a past golden age, when prices were high. Surely the time was gone for ever when the broad river could bring up unwelcome ships: Russia was only the place where the linseed came from – the more the better – making grist for the great vertical millstones with their scythe-like arms, roaring and grinding and carefully sweeping as if an informing soul were in them. The Catholics, bad harvests, and the mysterious fluctuations of trade, were the three evils mankind had to fear: even the floods had not been great of late years. The mind of St Ogg's did not look extensively before or after. It inherited a long past without thinking of it, and had no eyes for the spirits that walked the streets. Since the centuries when St Ogg with his boat and the Virgin Mother at the prow had been seen on the wide water, so many memories had been left behind, and had gradually vanished like the receding hilltops! And the present time was like the level plain where men lose their belief in volcanoes and earthquakes, thinking tomorrow will be as yesterday, and the giant forces that used to shake the earth are for ever laid to sleep. The days were gone when people could be greatly wrought upon by their faith, still less change it: the Catholics were formidable because they would lay hold of government and property, and burn men alive: not because any sane and honest parishioner of St Ogg's could be brought to believe in the Pope. One aged person remembered how a rude multitude had been swayed when John Wesley preached in the cattle-market; but for a long while it had not been expected of preachers that they should shake the souls of men. An occasional burst of fervour, in Dissenting pulpits, on the subject of infant baptism, was the only symptom of a zeal unsuited to sober times when men had done with change. Protestantism sat at ease, unmindful of schisms, careless of proselytism: Dissent was an inheritance along with a superior pew and a business connection; and Churchmanship only wondered contemptuously at Dissent as a foolish habit that clung greatly to families in the grocery and chandlering lines, though not incompatible with prosperous wholesale dealing. But with the Catholic Question had come a slight wind of controversy to break the calm: the elderly rector had become occasionally historical and argumentative, and Mr Spray, the Independent minister, had begun to preach political sermons, in which he distinguished with much subtlety between his fervent belief in the right of the Catholics to the franchise and his fervent belief in their eternal perdition. Most of Mr Spray's hearers, however, were incapable of following his subtleties, and many old-fashioned Dissenters were much pained by his 'siding with the Catholics;' while others thought he had better let politics alone. Public spirit was not held in high esteem at St Ogg's, and men who busied themselves with political questions were regarded with some suspicion, as dangerous characters: they were usually persons who had little or no business of their own to manage, or, if they had, were likely enough to become insolvent.

This was the general aspect of things at St Ogg's in Mrs Glegg's day, and at that particular period in her family history when she had her quarrel with Mr Tulliver. It was a time when ignorance was much more comfortable than at present, and was received with all the honours in very good society, without being obliged to dress itself in an elaborate costume of knowledge; a time when cheap periodicals were not, and when country surgeons never thought of asking their female patients if they were fond of reading, but simply took it for granted that they preferred gossip; a time when ladies in rich silk gowns wore large pockets, in which they carried a mutton-bone to secure them against cramp. Mrs Glegg carried such a bone, which she had inherited from her grandmother with a brocaded gown that would stand up empty, like a suit of armour, and a silver-headed walking-stick; for the Dodson family had been respectable for many generations.

Mrs Glegg had both a front and a back parlour in her excellent house at St Ogg's, so that she had two points of view from which she could observe the weaknesses of her fellow-beings, and reinforce her thankfulness for her own exceptional strength of mind. From her front windows she could look down the Tofton Road, leading out of St Ogg's and note the growing tendency to 'gadding about' in the wives of men not retired from business, together with a practice of wearing woven cotton stockings, which opened a dreary prospect for the coming generation; and from her back windows she could look down the pleasant garden and orchard which stretched to the river, and observe the folly of Mr Glegg in spending his time among 'them flowers and vegetables.' For Mr Glegg, having retired from active business as a wool-stapler, for the purpose of enjoying himself through the rest of his life, had found this last occupation so much more severe than his business, that he had been driven into amateur hard labour as a dissipation, and habitually relaxed by doing the work of two ordinary gardeners. The economising of a gardener's wages might perhaps have induced Mrs Glegg to wink at this folly, if it were possible for a healthy female mind even to simulate respect for a husband's hobby. But it is well known that this conjugal complacency belongs only to the weaker portion of the sex, who are scarcely alive to the responsibilities of a wife as a constituted check on her husband's pleasures, which are hardly ever of a rational or commendable kind.

Mr Glegg on his side, too, had a double source of mental occupation, which gave every promise of being inexhaustible. On the one hand, he surprised himself by his discoveries in natural history, finding that his piece of garden-ground contained wonderful caterpillars, slugs, and insects, which, so far as he had heard, had never before attracted human observation: and he noticed remarkable coincidences between these zoological phenomena and the great events of that time, – as, for example, that before the burning of York Minster there had been mysterious serpentine marks on the leaves of the rose trees, together with an unusual prevalence of slugs, which he had been puzzled to know the meaning of, until it flashed upon him with this melancholy conflagration. (Mr Glegg had an unusual amount of mental activity, which, when disengaged from the wool business, naturally made itself a pathway in other directions.) And his second subject of meditation was the 'contrariness' of the female mind, as typically exhibited in Mrs Glegg. That a creature made – in a genealogical sense – out of a man's rib, and in this particular case maintained in the highest respectability without any trouble of her own, should be normally in a state of contradiction to the blandest propositions and even to the most accommodating concessions, was a mystery in the scheme of things to which he had often in vain sought a clue in the early chapters of Genesis. Mr Glegg had chosen the eldest Miss Dodson as a handsome embodiment of female prudence and thrift, and being himself of a money-getting, money-keeping turn, had calculated on much conjugal harmony. But in that curious compound, the feminine character, it may easily happen that the flavour is unpleasant in spite of excellent ingredients; and a fine systematic stinginess may be accompanied with a seasoning that quite spoils its relish. Now, good Mr Glegg himself was stingy in the most amiable manner: his neighbours called him 'near,' which always means that the person in question is a lovable skinflint. If you expressed a preference for cheese-parings, Mr Glegg would remember to save them for you, with a good-natured delight in gratifying your palate, and he was given to pet all animals which required no appreciable keep. There was no humbug or hypocrisy about Mr Glegg: his eyes would have watered with true feeling over the sale of a widow's furniture, which a five-pound note from his side-pocket would have prevented; but a donation of five pounds to a person 'in a small way of life' would have seemed to him a mad kind of lavishness rather than 'charity,' which had always presented itself to him as a contribution of small aids, not a neutralising of misfortune. And Mr Glegg was just as fond of saving other people's money as his own: he would have ridden as far round to avoid a turnpike when his expenses were to be paid for him, as when they were to come out of his own pocket, and was quite zealous in trying to induce indifferent acquaintances to adopt a cheap substitute for blacking. This inalienable habit of saving, as an end in itself, belonged to the industrious men of business of a former generation, who made their fortunes slowly, almost as the tracking of the fox belongs to the harrier – it constituted them a 'race,' which is nearly lost in these days of rapid money-getting, when lavishness comes close on the back of want. In old-fashioned times, an 'independence' was hardly ever made without a little miserliness as a condition, and you would have found that quality in every provincial district, combined with characters as various as the fruits from which we can extract acid. The true Harpagons were always marked and exceptional characters: not so the worthy taxpayers, who, having once pinched from real necessity, retained even in the midst of their comfortable retirement, with their wall-fruit and wine-bins, the habit of regarding life as an ingenious process of nibbling out one's liveli-hood without leaving any perceptible deficit, and who would have been as immediately prompted to give up a newly-taxed luxury when they had their clear five hundred a-year, as when they had only five hundred pounds of capital. Mr Glegg was one of these men, found so impracticable by chancellors of the exchequer; and knowing this, you will be the better able to understand why he had not swerved from the conviction that he had made an eligible marriage, in spite of the too pungent seasoning that nature had given to the eldest Miss Dodson's virtues. A man with an affectionate disposition, who finds a wife to concur with his fundamental idea of life, easily comes to persuade himself that no other woman would have suited him so well, and does a little daily snapping and quarrelling without any sense of alienation. Mr Glegg, being of a reflective turn, and no longer occupied with wool, had much wondering meditation on the peculiar constitution of the female mind as unfolded to him in his domestic life; and yet he thought Mrs Glegg's household ways a model for her sex: it struck him as a pitiable irregularity in other women if they did not roll up their table-napkins with the same tightness and emphasis as Mrs Glegg did, if their pastry had a less leathery consistence, and their damson cheese a less venerable hardness than hers: nay, even the peculiar combination of grocery and drug-like odours in Mrs Glegg's private cupboard impressed him as the only right thing in the way of cupboard smells. I am not sure that he would not have longed for the quarrelling again, if it had ceased for an entire week; and it is certain that an acquiescent mild wife would have left his meditations comparatively jejune and barren of mystery.

Mr Glegg's unmistakable kind-heartedness was shown in this, that it pained him more to see his wife at variance with others – even with Dolly, the servant – than to be in a state of cavil with her himself; and the quarrel between her and Mr Tulliver vexed him so much that it quite nullified the pleasure he would otherwise have had in the state of his early cabbages, as he walked in his garden before breakfast the next morning. Still he went in to breakfast with some slight hope that, now Mrs Glegg had 'slept upon it,' her anger might be subdued enough to give way to her usually strong sense of family decorum. She had been used to boast that there had never been any of those deadly quarrels among the Dodsons which had disgraced other families; that no Dodson had ever been 'cut off with a shilling,' and no cousin of the Dodsons disowned; as, indeed, why should they be? for they had no cousins who had not money out at use, or some houses of their own, at the very least.

There was one evening-cloud which had always disappeared from Mrs Glegg's brow when she sat at the breakfast-table: it was her fuzzy front of curls; for as she occupied herself in household matters in the morning, it would have been a mere extravagance to put on anything so superfluous to the making of leathery pastry as a fuzzy curled front. By half-past ten decorum demanded the front: until then Mrs Glegg could economise it, and society would never be any the wiser. But the absence of that cloud only left it more apparent that the cloud of severity remained; and Mr Glegg, perceiving this, as he sat down to his milk-porridge, which it was his old frugal habit to stem his morning hunger with, prudently resolved to leave the first remark to Mrs Glegg, lest, to so delicate an article as a lady's temper, the slightest touch should do mischief. People who seem to enjoy their ill-temper have a way of keeping it in fine condition by inflicting privations on themselves. That was Mrs Glegg's way; she made her tea weaker than usual this morning, and declined butter. It was a hard case that a vigorous mood for quarrelling, so highly capable of using any opportunity, should not meet with a single remark from Mr Glegg on which to exercise itself. But by and by it appeared that his silence would answer the purpose, for he heard himself apostrophised at last in that tone peculiar to the wife of one's bosom.

'Well, Mr Glegg! it's a poor return I get for making you the wife I've made you all these years. If this is the way I'm to be treated, I'd better ha' known it before my poor father died, and then, when I'd wanted a home, I should ha' gone elsewhere – as the choice was offered me.'

Mr Glegg paused from his porridge and looked up – not with any new amazement, but simply with that quiet, habitual wonder with which we regard constant mysteries.

'Why, Mrs G., what have I done now?'

'Done now, Mr Glegg? *done now?* . . . I'm sorry for you.'

Not seeing his way to any pertinent answer, Mr Glegg reverted to his porridge.

'There's husbands in the world,' continued Mrs Glegg, after a pause, 'as 'ud have known how to do something different to siding with everybody else against their own wives. Perhaps I'm wrong, and you can teach me better – but I've allays heard as it's the husband's place to stand by the wife, instead o' rejoicing and triumphing when folks insult her.'

'Now, what call have you to say that?' said Mr Glegg, rather warmly, for though a kind man, he was not as meek as Moses. 'When did I rejoice or triumph over you?'

'There's ways o'doing things worse than speaking out plain, Mr Glegg. I'd sooner you'd tell me to my face as you make light of me, than try to make out everybody's in the right but me, and come to your breakfast in the morning, as I've hardly slept an hour this night, and sulk at me as if I was the dirt under your feet.'

'Sulk at you?' said Mr Glegg, in a tone of angry facetiousness. 'You're like a tipsy man as thinks everybody's had too much but himself.'

'Don't lower yourself with using coarse language to *me*, Mr Glegg! It makes you look very small, though you can't see yourself,' said Mrs Glegg, in a tone of energetic compassion. 'A man in your place should set an example, and talk more sensible.'

'Yes; but will you listen to sense?' retorted Mr Glegg, sharply. 'The best sense I can talk to you is what I said last night – as you're i' the wrong to think o' calling in your money, when it's safe enough if you'd let it alone, all because of a bit of a tiff, and I was in hopes you'd ha' altered your mind this morning. But if you'd like to call it in, don't do it in a hurry now, and breed more enmity in the family – but wait till there's a pretty mortgage to be had without any trouble. You'd have to set the lawyer to work now to find an investment, and make no end o' expense.'

Mrs Glegg felt there was really something in this, but she tossed her head and emitted a guttural interjection to indicate that her silence was only an armistice, not a peace. And, in fact, hostilities soon broke out again.

'I'll thank you for my cup o' tea, now, Mrs G.' said Mr Glegg, seeing that she did not proceed to give it him as usual, when he had finished his porridge. She lifted the teapot with a slight toss of the head, and said,

'I'm glad to hear you'll *thank* me, Mr Glegg. It's little thanks *I* get for what I do for folks i' this world. Though there's never a woman o' *your* side o' the family, Mr Glegg, as is fit to stand up with me, and I'd say it if I was on my dying bed. Not but what I've allays conducted myself civil to your kin, and there isn't one of 'em can say the contrary, though my equils they aren't, and nobody shall make me say it.'

'You'd better leave finding fault wi' my kin till you've left off quarrelling with your own, Mrs G.,' said Mr Glegg, with angry sarcasm. 'I'll trouble you for the milk-jug.'

'That's as false a word as ever you spoke, Mr Glegg,' said the lady, pouring out the milk with unusual profuseness, as much as to say, if he wanted milk he should have it with a vengeance. 'And you know it's false. I'm not the woman to quarrel with my own kin: *you* may, for I've known you do it.'

'Why, what did you call it yesterday, then, leaving your sister's house in a tantrum?'

'I'd no quarrel wi' my sister, Mr Glegg, and it's false to say it. Mr Tulliver's none o' my blood, and it was him quarrelled with me, and drove me out o' the house. But perhaps you'd have had me stay and be swore at, Mr Glegg: perhaps you was vexed not to hear more abuse and foul language poured out upo' your own wife. But, let me tell you, it's *your* disgrace.'

'Did ever anybody hear the like i' this parish?' said Mr Glegg, getting hot. 'A woman, with everything provided for her, and allowed to keep her own money the same as if it was settled on her, and with a gig new stuffed and lined at no end o' expense, and provided for when I die beyond anything she could expect . . . to go on i' this way, biting and snapping like a mad dog! It's beyond everything, as God A'mighty should ha' made women *so*.' (These last words were uttered in a tone of sorrowful agitation. Mr Glegg pushed his tea from him, and tapped the table with both his hands.)

'Well, Mr Glegg! if those are your feelings, it's best they should be known,' said Mrs Glegg, taking off her napkin, and folding it in an excited manner. 'But if you' talk o' my being provided for beyond what I could expect, I beg leave to tell you as I'd a right to expect a many things as I don't find. And as to my being like a mad dog, it's well if you're not cried shame on by the county for your treatment of me, for it's what I can't bear, and I won't bear'. . . .

Here Mrs Glegg's voice intimated that she was going to cry, and, breaking off from speech, she rang the bell violently.

'Sally,' she said, rising from her chair, and speaking in rather a choked voice, 'light a fire upstairs, and put the blinds down. Mr Glegg, you'll please to order what you'd like for dinner. I shall have gruel.'

Mrs Glegg walked across the room to the small bookcase, and took down Baxter's 'Saints' Everlasting Rest,' which she carried with her upstairs. It was the book she was accustomed to lay open before her on special occasions: on wet Sunday mornings, or when she heard of a death in the family, or when, as in this case, her quarrel with Mr Glegg had been set an octave higher than usual.

But Mrs Glegg carried something else upstairs with her, which together with the 'Saints' Rest' and the gruel, may have had some influence in gradually calming her feelings, and making it possible for her to endure existence on the ground-floor shortly before teatime. This was, partly, Mr Glegg's suggestion, that she would do well to let her five hundred lie still until a good investment turned up; and, further, his parenthetic hint at his handsome provision for her in case of his death. Mr Glegg, like all men of his stamp, was extremely reticent about his will; and Mrs Glegg, in her gloomier moments, had forebodings that, like other husbands of whom she had heard, he might cherish the mean project of heightening her grief at his death by leaving her poorly off, in which case she was firmly resolved that she would have scarcely any weeper on her bonnet, and would cry no more than if he had been a second husband. But if he had really shown her any testamentary tenderness, it would be affecting to think of him, poor man, when he was gone; and even his foolish fuss about the flowers and garden-stuff, and his insistence on the subject of snails, would be touching when it was once fairly at an end. To survive Mr Glegg, and talk eulogistically of him as a man who might have his weaknesses, but who had done the right thing by her, notwithstanding his numerous poor relations – to have sums of interest coming in more frequently, and secrete it in various corners, baffling to the most ingenious of thieves (for, to Mrs Glegg's mind, banks and strong-boxes would have nullified the pleasure of property – she might as well have taken her food in capsules) – finally, to be looked up to by her own family and the neighbourhood, so as no woman can ever hope to be who has not the praeterite and present dignity comprised in being a 'widow well left' – all this made a flattering and conciliatory view of the future. So that when good Mr Glegg, restored to good-humour by much hoeing, and moved by the sight of his wife's empty chair, with her knitting rolled up in the corner, went upstairs to her, and observed that the bell had been tolling for poor Mr Morton, Mrs Glegg answered magnanimously, quite as if she had been an uninjured woman, 'Ah! then, there'll be a good business for somebody to take to.'

Baxter had been open at least eight hours by this time, for it was nearly five o'clock; and if people are to quarrel often, it follows as a corollary that their quarrels cannot be protracted beyond certain limits.

Mr and Mrs Glegg talked quite amicably about the Tullivers that evening. Mr Glegg went the length of admitting that Tulliver was a sad man for getting into hot water, and was like enough to run through his property; and Mrs Glegg, meeting this acknowledgment halfway, declared that it was beneath her to take notice of such a man's conduct, and that, for her sister's sake, she would let him keep the five hundred a while longer, for when she put it out on a mortgage she should only get four per cent.

CHAPTER 13

Mr Tulliver Further Entangles the Skein of Life

Owing to this new adjustment of Mrs Glegg's thoughts, Mrs Pullet found her task of mediation the next day surprisingly easy. Mrs Glegg, indeed, checked her rather sharply for thinking it would be necessary to tell her elder sister what was the right mode of behaviour in family matters. Mrs Pullet's argument, that it would look ill in the neighbourhood if people should have it in their power to say that there was a quarrel in the family, was particularly offensive. If the family name never suffered except through Mrs Glegg, Mrs Pullet might lay her head on her pillow in perfect confidence.

'It's not to be expected, I suppose,' observed Mrs Glegg, by way of winding up the subject, 'as I shall go to the mill again before Bessy comes to see me, or as I shall go and fall down o' my knees to Mr Tulliver, and ask his pardon for showing him favours: but I shall bear no malice, and when Mr Tulliver speaks civil to me, I'll speak civil to him. Nobody has any call to tell me what's becoming.'

Finding it unnecessary to plead for the Tullivers, it was natural that aunt Pullet should relax a little in her anxiety for them, and recur to the annoyance she had suffered yesterday from the offspring of that apparently ill-fated house. Mrs Glegg heard a circumstantial narrative, to which Mr Pullet's remarkable memory furnished some items; and while aunt Pullet pitied poor Bessy's bad-luck with her children, and expressed a half-formed project of paying for Maggie's being sent to a distant boarding-school, which would not prevent her being so brown, but might tend to subdue some other vices in her, aunt Glegg blamed Bessy for her weakness, and appealed to all witnesses who should be living when the Tulliver children had turned out ill, that she, Mrs Glegg, had always said how it would be from the very first, observing that it was wonderful to herself how all her words came true.

'Then I may call and tell Bessy you'll bear no malice, and everything be as it was before?' Mrs Pullet said, just before parting.

'Yes, you may, Sophy,' said Mrs Glegg; 'you may tell Mr Tulliver, and Bessy too, as I'm not going to behave ill because folks behave ill to me: *I* know it's my place, as the eldest, to set an example in every respect, and I do it. Nobody can say different of me, if they'll keep to the truth.'

Mrs Glegg being in this state of satisfaction in her own lofty magnanimity, I leave you to judge what effect was produced on her by the reception of a short letter from Mr Tulliver, that very evening, after Mrs Pullet's departure, informing her that she needn't trouble her mind about her five hundred pounds, for it should be paid back to her in the course of the next month at farthest, together with the interest due thereon until the time of payment. And furthermore, that Mr Tulliver had no wish to behave uncivilly to Mrs Glegg, and she was welcome to his house whenever she liked to come, but he desired no favours from her, either for himself or his children.

It was poor Mrs Tulliver who had hastened this catastrophe, entirely through that irrepressible hopefulness of hers which led her to expect that similar causes may at any time produce different results. It had very often occurred in her experience that Mr Tulliver had done something because other people had said he was not able to do it, or had pitied him for his supposed inability, or in any other way piqued his pride; still, she thought today, if she told him when he came in to tea that sister Pullet was gone to try and make everything up with sister Glegg, so that he needn't think about paying in the money, it would give a cheerful effect to the meal. Mr Tulliver had never slackened in his resolve to raise the money, but now he at once determined to write a letter to Mrs Glegg which should cut off all possibility of mistake. Mrs Pullet gone to beg and pray for *him* indeed! Mr Tulliver did not willingly write a letter, and found the relation between spoken and written language, briefly known as spelling, one of the most puzzling things in this puzzling world. Nevertheless, like all fervid writing, the task was done in less time than usual, and if the spelling differed from Mrs Glegg's – why she belonged, like himself, to a generation with whom spelling was a matter of private judgement.

Mrs Glegg did not alter her will in consequence of this letter, and cut off the Tulliver children from their sixth and seventh share in her thousand pounds; for she had her principles. No one must be able to say of her when she was dead that she had not divided her money with perfect fairness among her own kin: in the matter of wills, personal qualities were subordinate to the great fundamental fact of blood; and to be determined in the distribution of your property by caprice, and not make your legacies bear a direct ratio to degrees of kinship, was a prospective disgrace that would have embittered her life. This had always been a principle in the Dodson family; it was one form of that sense of honour and rectitude which was a proud tradition in such families – a tradition which has been the salt of our provincial society.

But though the letter could not shake Mrs Glegg's principles, it made the family breach much more difficult to mend; and as to the effect it produced on Mrs Glegg's opinion of Mr Tulliver – she begged to be understood from that time forth that she had nothing whatever to say about him: his state of mind, apparently, was too corrupt for her to contemplate it for a moment. It was not until the evening before Tom went to school, at the beginning of August, that Mrs Glegg paid a visit to her sister Tulliver, sitting in her gig all the while, and showing her displeasure by markedly abstaining from all advice and criticism, for, as she observed to her sister Deane, 'Bessy must bear the consequences o' having such a husband, though I'm sorry for her,' and Mrs Deane agreed that Bessy was pitiable.

That evening Tom observed to Maggie, 'O my! Maggie, aunt Glegg's beginning to come again; I'm glad I'm going to school. *You'll* catch it all now!'

Maggie was already so full of sorrow at the thought of Tom's going away from her, that this playful exultation of his seemed very unkind, and she cried herself to sleep that night.

Mr Tulliver's prompt procedure entailed on him further promptitude in finding the convenient person who was desirous of lending five hundred pounds on bond. 'It must be no client of Wakem's,' he said to himself; and yet at the end of a fortnight it turned out to the contrary; not because Mr Tulliver's will was feeble, but because external fact was stronger. Wakem's client was the only convenient person to be found. Mr Tulliver had a destiny as well as Oedipus, and in this case he might plead, like Oedipus, that his deed was inflicted on him rather than committed by him.

BOOK SECOND

School-Time

CHAPTER I

Tom's 'First Half'

Tom Tulliver's sufferings during the first quarter he was at King's Lorton, under the distinguished care of the Revd Walter Stelling, were rather severe. At Mr Jacobs' academy, life had not presented itself to him as a difficult problem: there were plenty of fellows to play with, and Tom being good at all active games – fighting especially – had that precedence among them which appeared to him inseparable from the personality of Tom Tulliver. Mr Jacobs himself, familiarly known as Old Goggles, from his habit of wearing spectacles, imposed no painful awe; and if it was the property of snuffy old hypocrites like him to write like copperplate and surround their signatures with arabesques, to spell without forethought, and to spout 'My name is Norval' without bungling, Tom, for his part, was rather glad he was not in danger of those mean accomplishments. He was not going to be a snuffy schoolmaster – he; but a substantial man, like his father, who used to go hunting when he was younger, and rode a capital black mare – as pretty a bit of horseflesh as ever you saw: Tom had heard what her points were a hundred times. *He* meant to go hunting too, and to be generally respected. When people were grown up, he considered, nobody enquired about their writing and spelling: when he was a man, he should be master of everything, and do just as he liked. It had been very difficult for him to reconcile himself to the idea that his school-time was to be prolonged, and that he was not to be brought up to his father's business, which he had always thought extremely pleasant, for it was nothing but riding about, giving orders, and going to market; and he thought that a clergyman would give him a great many Scripture lessons, and probably make him learn the Gospel and Epistle on a Sunday as well as the Collect. But in the absence of specific information, it was impossible for him to imagine that school and a schoolmaster would be something entirely different from the academy of Mr Jacobs. So, not to be at a deficiency, in case of his finding genial companions, he had taken care to carry with him a small box of percussion-caps; not that there was anything particular to be done with them, but they would serve to impress strange boys with a sense of his familiarity with guns. Thus poor Tom, though he saw very clearly through Maggie's illusions, was not without illusions of his own, which were to be cruelly dissipated by his enlarged experience at King's Lorton.

He had not been there a fortnight before it was evident to him that life, complicated not only with the Latin grammar but with a new standard of

English pronunciation, was a very difficult business, made all the more obscure by a thick mist of bashfulness. Tom, as you have observed, was never an exception among boys for ease of address; but the difficulty of enunciating a monosyllable in reply to Mr or Mrs Stelling was so great, that he even dreaded to be asked at table whether he would have more pudding. As to the percussion-caps, he had almost resolved, in the bitterness of his heart, that he would throw them into a neighbouring pond; for not only was he the solitary pupil, but he began even to have a certain scepticism about guns, and a general sense that his theory of life was undermined. For Mr Stelling thought nothing of guns, or horses either, apparently; and yet it was impossible for Tom to despise Mr Stelling as he had despised Old Goggles. If there were anything that was not thoroughly genuine about Mr Stelling, it lay quite beyond Tom's power to detect it: it is only by a wide comparison of facts that the wisest full-grown man can distinguish well-rolled barrels from more supernal thunder.

Mr Stelling was a well-sized, broad-chested man, not yet thirty, with flaxen hair standing erect, and large lightish-grey eyes, which were always very wide open; he had a sonorous bass voice, and an air of defiant self-confidence inclining to brazenness. He had entered on his career with great vigour, and intended to make a considerable impression on his fellow-men. The Revd Walter Stelling was not a man who would remain among the 'inferior clergy' all his life. He had a true British determination to push his way in the world. As a schoolmaster, in the first place; for there were capital masterships of grammar-schools to be had, and Mr Stelling meant to have one of them. But as a preacher also, for he meant always to preach in a striking manner, so as to have his congregation swelled by admirers from neighbouring parishes, and to produce a great sensation whenever he took occasional duty for a brother clergyman of minor gifts. The style of preaching he had chosen was the extemporaneous, which was held little short of the miraculous in rural parishes like King's Lorton. Some passages of Massilion and Bourdaloue, which he knew by heart, were really very effective when rolled out in Mr Stelling's deepest tones; but as comparatively feeble appeals of his own were delivered in the same loud and impressive manner, they were often thought quite as striking by his hearers. Mr Stelling's doctrine was of no particular school; if anything, it had a tinge of evangelicalism, for that was 'the telling thing' just then in the diocese to which King's Lorton belonged. In short, Mr Stelling was a man who meant to rise in his profession, and to rise by merit, clearly, since he had no interest beyond what might be promised by a problematic relationship to a great lawyer who had not yet become Lord Chancellor. A clergyman who has such vigorous intentions naturally gets a little into debt at starting; it is not to be expected that he will live in the meagre style of a man who means to be a poor curate all his life, and if the few hundreds Mr Timpson advanced towards his daughter's fortune did not suffice for the purchase of handsome furniture, together with a stock of wine, a grand piano, and the laying-out of a superior flower-garden, it followed in the most rigorous manner, either that these things must be procured by some other means, or else that the Revd Mr Stelling must go without them – which last alternative would be an absurd procrastination of the fruits of success, where success was certain. Mr Stelling was so broad-chested and resolute that he felt equal to anything; he would become celebrated by shaking the consciences of his hearers, and he would by and by edit a Greek play, and invent several new readings. He had not yet selected the play, for having been married little more than two years, his leisure time had been much occupied with attentions to Mrs Stelling; but he had told that fine woman what he meant to do someday, and she felt great confidence in her husband, as a man who understood everything of that sort.

But the immediate step to future success was to bring on Tom Tulliver during this first half-year; for, by a singular coincidence, there had been some negotiation concerning another pupil from the same neighbourhood, and it might further a decision in Mr Stelling's favour, if it were understood that young Tulliver, who, Mr Stelling observed in conjugal privacy, was rather a rough cub, had made prodigious progress in a short time. It was on this ground that he was severe with Tom about his lessons: he was clearly a boy whose powers would never be developed through the medium of the Latin grammar, without the application of some sternness. Not that Mr Stelling was a harsh-tempered or unkind man – quite the contrary: he was jocose with Tom at table, and corrected his provincialisms and his deportment in most playful manner; but Tom was only the more cowed and confused by this double novelty, for he had never been used to jokes at all like Mr Stelling's; and for the first time in his life he had a painful sense that he was all wrong somehow. When Mr Stelling said, as the roast-beef was being uncovered, 'Now, Tulliver! which would you rather decline, roast-beef or the Latin for it?' – Tom, to whom in his coolest moments a pun would have been a hard nut, was thrown into a state of embarrassed alarm that made everything dim to him except the feeling that he would rather not have anything to do with Latin: of course he answered, 'Roast-beef,' whereupon there followed much laughter and some practical joking with the plates, from which Tom gathered that he had in some mysterious way refused beef, and, in fact, made himself appear 'a silly.' If he could have seen a fellow-pupil undergo these painful operations and survive them in good spirits, he might sooner have taken them as a matter of course. But there are two expensive forms of education, either which a parent may procure for his son by sending him as solitary pupil to a clergyman: one is, the enjoyment of the reverend gentleman's undivided neglect; the other is, the endurance of the reverend gentleman's undivided attention. It was the latter privilege for which Mr Tulliver paid a high price in Tom's initiatory months at King's Lorton.

That respectable miller and maltster had left Tom behind, and driven home-ward in a state of great mental satisfaction. He considered that it was a happy moment for him when he had thought of asking Riley's advice about a tutor for Tom. Mr Stelling's eyes were so wide open, and he talked in such an offhand, matter-of-fact way – answering every difficult slow remark of Mr Tulliver's with, 'I see, my good sir, I see;' 'To be sure, to be sure;' 'You want your son to be a man who will make his way in the world,' – that Mr Tulliver was delighted to find in him a clergyman whose knowledge was so applicable to the everyday affairs of this life. Except Counsellor Wylde, whom he had heard at the last sessions, Mr Tulliver thought the Revd Mr Stelling was the shrewdest fellow he had ever met with – not unlike Wylde, in fact: he had the same way of sticking his thumbs in the armholes of his waistcoat. Mr Tulliver was not by any means an exception in mistaking brazenness for shrewdness: most laymen thought Stelling shrewd, and a man of remarkable powers generally: it was chiefly by his clerical brethren that he was considered rather a dull fellow. But he told Mr Tulliver several stories about 'swing' and incendiarism, and asked his advice about feeding pigs in so thoroughly secular and judicious a manner, with so much polished glibness of tongue, that the miller thought, here was the very thing he wanted for Tom. He had no doubt this first-rate man was acquainted with every branch of information, and knew exactly what Tom must learn in order to become a match for the lawyers – which poor Mr Tulliver himself did *not* know, and so was necessarily thrown for self-direction on this wide kind of inference. It is hardly fair to laugh at him, for I have known much more highly-instructed persons than he make inferences quite as wide, and not at all wiser.

As for Mrs Tulliver – finding that Mrs Stelling's views as to the airing of linen and the frequent recurrence of hunger in a growing boy, entirely coincided with her own; moreover, that Mrs Stelling, though so young a woman, and only anticipating her second confinement, had gone through very nearly the same experience as herself with regard to the behaviour and fundamental character of the monthly nurse – she expressed great contentment to her husband, when they drove away, at leaving Tom with a woman who, in spite of her youth, seemed quite sensible and motherly, and asked advice as prettily as could be.

'They must be very well off, though,' said Mrs Tulliver, 'for everything's as nice as can be all over the house, and that watered-silk she had on cost a pretty penny. Sister Pullet has got one like it.'

'Ah,' said Mr Tulliver, 'he's got some income besides the curacy, I reckon. Perhaps her father allows 'em something. There's Tom 'ull be another hundred to him, and not much trouble either, by his own account: he says teaching comes natural to him. That's wonderful, now,' added Mr Tulliver, turning his head on one side, and giving his horse a meditative tickling on the flank.

Perhaps it was because teaching came naturally to Mr Stelling, that he set about it with that uniformity of method and independence of circumstances, which distinguish the actions of animals understood to be under the immediate teaching of nature. Mr Broderip's amiable beaver, as that charming naturalist tells us, busied himself as earnestly in constructing a dam, in a room up three pair of stairs in London, as if he had been laying his foundation in a stream or lake in Upper Canada. It was 'Binny's' function to build: the absence of water or of possible progeny was an accident for which he was not accountable. With the same unerring instinct Mr Stelling set to work at his natural method of instilling the Eton Grammar and Euclid into the mind of Tom Tulliver. This, he considered, was the only basis of solid instruction: all other means of education were mere charlatanism, and could produce nothing better than smatterers. Fixed on this firm basis, a man might observe the display of various or special knowledge made by irregularly educated people with a pitying smile: all that sort of thing was very well, but it was impossible these people could form sound opinions. In holding this conviction Mr Stelling was not biased, as some tutors have been, by the excessive accuracy or extent of his own scholarship; and as to his views about Euclid, no opinion could have been freer from personal partiality. Mr Stelling was very far from being led astray by enthusiasm, either religious or intellectual: on the other hand, he had no secret belief that everything was humbug. He thought religion was a very excellent thing, and Aristotle a great authority, and deaneries and prebends useful institutions, and Great Britain the providential bulwark of Protestantism, and faith in the unseen a great support to afflicted minds: he believed in all these things, as a Swiss hotel keeper believes in the beauty of the scenery around him, and in the pleasure it gives to artistic visitors. And in the same way Mr Stelling believed in his method of education: he had no doubt that he was doing the very best thing for Mr Tulliver's boy. Of course, when the miller talked of 'mapping' and 'summing,' in a vague and diffident manner, Mr Stelling had set his mind at rest by an assurance that he understood what was wanted; for how was it possible the good man could form any reasonable judgement about the matter? Mr Stelling's duty was to teach the lad in the only right way – indeed, he knew no other: he had not wasted his time in the acquirement of anything abnormal.

He very soon set down poor Tom as a thoroughly stupid lad; for though by hard labour he could get particular declensions into his brain, anything so abstract as the relation between cases and terminations could by no means get such a lodgment there as to enable him to recognise a chance genitive or dative. This struck Mr Stelling as something more than natural stupidity: he suspected obstinacy, or at any rate, indifference; and lectured Tom severely on his want of thorough application. 'You feel no interest in what you're doing, sir,' Mr Stelling would say, and the reproach was painfully true. Tom had never found any difficulty in discerning a pointer from a setter, when once he had been told the distinction, and his perceptive powers were not at all deficient. I fancy they were quite as strong as those of the Revd Mr Stelling; for Tom could predict with accuracy what number of horses were cantering behind him, he could throw a stone right into the centre of a given ripple, he could guess to a fraction how many lengths of his stick it would take to reach across the playground, and could draw almost perfect squares on his slate without any measurement. But Mr Stelling took no note of these things: he only observed that Tom's faculties failed him before the abstractions hideously symbolised to him in the pages of the Eton Grammar, and that he was in a state bordering on idiocy with regard to the demonstration that two given triangles must be equal – though he could discern with great promptitude and certainty the fact that they *were* equal. Whence Mr Stelling concluded that Tom's brain, being peculiarly impervious to etymology and demonstrations, was peculiarly in need of being ploughed and harrowed by these patent implements: it was his favourite metaphor, that the classics and geometry constituted that culture of the mind which prepared it for the reception of any subsequent crop. I say nothing against Mr Stelling's theory: if we are to have one regimen for all minds, his seems to me as good as any other. I only know it turned out as uncomfortably for Tom Tulliver as if he had been plied with cheese in order to remedy a gastric weakness which prevented him from digesting it. It is astonishing what a different result one gets by changing the metaphor! Once call the brain an intellectual stomach, and one's ingenious conception of the classics and geometry as ploughs and harrows seems to settle nothing. But then it is open to someone else to follow great authorities, and call the mind a sheet of white paper or a mirror, in which case one's knowledge of the digestive process becomes quite irrelevant. It was doubtless an ingenious idea to call the camel the ship of the desert, but it would hardly lead one far in training that useful beast. O Aristotle! if you had had the advantage of being 'the freshest modern' instead of the greatest ancient, would you not have mingled your praise of metaphorical speech, as a sign of high intelligence, with a lamentation that intelligence so rarely shows itself in speech without metaphor – that we can so seldom declare what a thing is, except by saying it is something else?

Tom Tulliver, being abundant in no form of speech, did not use any metaphor to declare his views as to the nature of Latin: he never called it an instrument of torture; and it was not until he had got on some way in the next half-year, and in the Delectus, that he was advanced enough to call it a 'bore' and 'beastly stuff'. At present, in relation to this demand that he should learn Latin declensions and conjugations, Tom was in a state of as blank unimaginativeness concerning the cause and tendency of his sufferings, as if he had been an innocent shrew-mouse imprisoned in the split trunk of an ash tree in order to cure lameness in cattle. It is doubtless almost incredible to instructed minds of the present day that a boy of twelve, not belonging strictly to 'the masses,' who are now understood to have the monopoly of mental darkness, should have had no distinct idea how there came to be such a thing as Latin on this earth: yet so it was with Tom. It would have taken a long while to make conceivable to him that there ever existed a people who bought and sold sheep and oxen, and transacted the everyday affairs of life, through the medium of this language, and still longer to make him understand why he should be called upon to learn it, when its connection with those affairs had become entirely latent. So far as Tom had gained any acquaintance with the Romans at Mr Jacobs's academy, his knowledge was strictly correct, but it went no farther than the fact that they were 'in the New Testament;' and Mr Stelling was not the man to enfeeble and emasculate his pupil's mind by simplifying and explaining, or to reduce the tonic effect of etymology by mixing it with smattering, extraneous information, such as is given to girls.

Yet, strange to say, under this vigorous treatment Tom became more like a girl than he had ever been in his life before. He had a large share of pride, which had hitherto found itself very comfortable in the world, despising Old Goggles, and reposing in the sense of unquestioned rights; but now this same pride met with nothing but bruises and crushings. Tom was too clear-sighted not to be aware that Mr Stelling's standard of things was quite different, was certainly something higher in the eyes of the world than that of the people he had been living amongst, and that, brought in contact with it, he, Tom Tulliver, appeared uncouth and stupid: he was by no means indifferent to this, and his pride got into an uneasy condition which quite nullified his boyish self-satisfaction, and gave him something of the girl's susceptibility. He was of a very firm, not to say obstinate disposition, but there was no brute-like rebellion and recklessness in his nature: the human sensibilities predominated, and if it had occurred to him that he could enable himself to show some quickness at his lessons, and so acquire Mr Stelling's approbation, by standing on one leg for an inconvenient length of time, or rapping his head moderately against the wall, or any voluntary action of that sort, he would certainly have tried it. But no – Tom had never heard that these measures would brighten the understanding, or strengthen the verbal memory; and he was not given to hypothesis and experiment. It did occur to him that he could perhaps get some help by praying for it; but as the prayers he said every evening were forms learned by heart, he rather shrank from the novelty and irregularity of introducing an extempore passage on a topic of petition for which he was not aware of any precedent. But one day when he had broken down, for the fifth time, in the supines of the third conjugation, and Mr Stelling, convinced that this must be carelessness, since it transcended the bounds of possible stupidity, had lectured him very seriously, pointing out that if he failed to seize the present golden opportunity of learning supines, he would have to regret it when he became a man – Tom, more miserable than usual, determined to try his sole resource; and that evening, after his usual form of prayer for his parents and 'little sister' (he had begun to pray for Maggie when she was a baby), and that he might be able always to keep God's commandments, he added, in the same low whisper, 'and please to make me always remember my Latin.' He paused a little to consider how he should pray about Euclid – whether he should ask to see what it meant, or whether there was any other mental state which would be more applicable to the case. But at last he added – 'And make Mr Stelling say I shan't do Euclid any more. Amen.'

The fact that he got through his supines without mistake the next day, encouraged him to persevere in this appendix to his prayers, and neutralised any scepticism that might have arisen from Mr Stelling's continued demand for Euclid. But his faith broke down under the apparent absence of all help when he got into the irregular verbs. It seemed clear that Tom's despair under the caprices of the present tense did not constitute a *nodus* worthy of interference, and since this was the climax of his difficulties, where was the use of praying for help any longer? He made up his mind to this conclusion in one of his dull, lonely evenings, which he spent in the study, preparing his lessons for the morrow. His eyes were apt to get dim over the page – though he hated crying, and was ashamed of it: he couldn't help thinking with some affection even of Spouncer, whom he used to fight and quarrel with; he would have felt at home with Spouncer, and in a condition of superiority. And then the mill, and the river, and Yap pricking up his ears, ready to obey the least sign when Tom said 'Hoigh!' would all come before him in a sort of calenture, when his fingers played absently in his pocket with his great knife and his coil of whip-cord, and other relics of the past. Tom, as I said, had never been so much like a girl in his life before, and at that epoch of irregular verbs his spirit was further depressed by a new means of mental development, which had been thought of for him out of school hours. Mrs Stelling had lately had her second baby, and as nothing could be more salutary for a boy than to feel himself useful, Mrs Stelling considered she was doing Tom a service by setting him to watch the little cherub Laura while the nurse was occupied with the sickly baby. It was quite a pretty employment for Tom to take little Laura out in the sunniest hour of the autumn day – it would help to make him feel that Lorton Parsonage was a home for him, and that he was one of the family. The little cherub Laura, not being an accomplished walker at present, had a ribbon fastened round her waist, by which Tom held her as if she had been a little dog during the minutes in which she chose to walk; but as these were rare, he was for the most part carrying this fine child round and round the garden, within sight of Mrs Stelling's window – according to orders. If anyone considers this unfair and even oppressive towards Tom, I beg him to consider that there are feminine virtues which are with difficulty combined, even if they are not incompatible. When the wife of a poor curate contrives, under all her disadvantages, to dress extremely well, and to have a style of coiffure which requires that her nurse shall occasionally officiate as lady's-maid, – when, moreover, her dinner-parties and her drawing-room show that effort at elegance and completeness of appointment to which ordinary women might imagine a large income necessary, it would be unreasonable to expect of her that she should employ a second nurse, or even act as a nurse herself. Mr Stelling knew better: he saw that his wife did wonders already, and was proud of her: it was certainly not the best thing in the world for young Tulliver's gait to carry a heavy child, but he had plenty of exercise in long walks with himself, and next half-year Mr Stelling would see about having a drilling-master. Among the many means whereby Mr Stelling intended to be more fortunate than the bulk of his fellow-men, he had entirely given up that of having his own way in his own house. What then? he had married 'as kind a little soul as ever breathed,' according to Mr Riley, who had been acquainted with Mrs Stelling's blond ringlets and smiling demeanour throughout her maiden life, and on the strength of that knowledge would have been ready any day to pronounce that whatever domestic differences might arise in her married life must be entirely Mr Stelling's fault.

If Tom had had a worse disposition, he would certainly have hated the little cherub Laura, but he was too kind-hearted a lad for that – there was too much in him of the fibre that turns to true manliness, and to protecting pity for the weak. I am afraid he hated Mrs Stelling, and contracted a lasting dislike to pale blond ringlets and broad plaits, as directly associated with haughtiness of manner, and a frequent reference to other people's 'duty.' But he couldn't help playing with little Laura, and liking to amuse her: he even sacrificed his percussion-caps for her sake, in despair of their ever serving a greater purpose – thinking the small flash and bang would delight her, and thereby drawing down on himself a rebuke from Mrs Stelling for teaching her child to play with fire. Laura was a sort of playfellow – and oh, how Tom longed for playfellows! In his secret heart he yearned to have Maggie with him, and was almost ready to dote on her exasperating acts of forgetfulness; though, when he was at home, he always represented it as a great favour on his part to let Maggie trot by his side on his pleasure excursions.

And before this dreary half-year was ended, Maggie actually came. Mrs Stelling had given a general invitation for the little girl to come and stay with her brother: so when Mr Tulliver drove over to King's Lorton late in October, Maggie came too, with the sense that she was taking a great journey, and beginning to see the world. It was Mr Tulliver's first visit to see Tom, for the lad must learn not to think too much about home.

'Well, my lad,' he said to Tom, when Mr Stelling had left the room to announce the arrival to his wife, and Maggie had begun to kiss Tom freely, 'you look rarely! School agrees with you.'

Tom wished he had looked rather ill.

'I don't think I *am* well, father,' said Tom; 'I wish you'd ask Mr Stelling not to let me do Euclid – it brings on the toothache, I think.'

(The toothache was the only malady to which Tom had ever been subject.)

'Euclid, my lad – why, what's that?' said Mr Tulliver.

'Oh, I don't know: it's definitions, and axioms, and triangles, and things. It's a book I've got to learn in – there's no sense in it.'

'Go, go!' said Mr Tulliver, reprovingly, 'you mustn't say so. You must learn what your master tells you. He knows what it's right for you to learn.'

'*I'll* help you now, Tom,' said Maggie, with a little air of patronising consolation. 'I'm come to stay ever so long, if Mrs Stelling asks me. I've brought my box and my pinafores, haven't I, father?'

'*You* help me, you silly little thing!' said Tom, in such high spirits at this announcement that he quite enjoyed the idea of confounding Maggie by showing her a page of Euclid. 'I should like to see you doing one of *my* lessons! Why, I learn Latin too! Girls never learn such things. They're too silly.'

'I know what Latin is very well,' said Maggie, confidently. 'Latin's a language. There are Latin words in the Dictionary. There's bonus, a gift.'

'Now, you're just wrong there, Miss Maggie!' said Tom, secretly astonished. 'You think you're very wise! But 'bonus' means 'good,' as it happens – bonus, bona, bonum.'

'Well, that's no reason why it shouldn't mean "gift" ' said Maggie, stoutly. 'It may mean several things – almost every word does. There's "lawn," – it means the grass-plot, as well as the stuff pocket-handkerchiefs are made of.'

'Well done, little 'un,' said Mr Tulliver, laughing, while Tom felt rather disgusted with Maggie's knowingness, though beyond measure cheerful at the thought that she was going to stay with him. Her conceit would soon be overawed by the actual inspection of his books.

Mrs Stelling, in her pressing invitation, did not mention a longer time than a week for Maggie's stay; but Mr Stelling, who took her between his knees, and asked where she stole her dark eyes from, insisted that she must stay a fortnight. Maggie thought Mr Stelling was a charming man, and Mr Tulliver was quite proud to leave his little wench where she would have an opportunity of showing her cleverness to appreciating strangers. So it was agreed that she should not be fetched home till the end of the fortnight.

'Now, then, come with me into the study, Maggie,' said Tom, as their father drove away. 'What do you shake and toss your head now for, you silly?' he continued; for though her hair was now under a new dispensation, and was brushed smoothly behind her ears, she seemed still in imagination to be tossing it out of her eyes. 'It makes you look as if you were crazy.'

'Oh, I can't help it,' said Maggie, impatiently. 'Don't tease me, Tom. Oh, what books!' she exclaimed, as she saw the bookcases in the study. 'How I should like to have as many books as that!'

'Why, you couldn't read one of 'em,' said Tom, triumphantly. 'They're all Latin.'

'No, they aren't,' said Maggie. 'I can read the back of this . . . *History of the Decline and Fall of the Roman Empire.*'

'Well, what does that mean? *You* don't know,' said Tom, wagging his head.

'But I could soon find out,' said Maggie, scornfully.

'Why, how?'

'I should look inside, and see what it was about.'

'You'd better not, Miss Maggie,' said Tom, seeing her hand on the volume. 'Mr Stelling lets nobody touch his books without leave, and *I* shall catch it, if you take it out.'

'O, very well! Let me see all *your* books, then,' said Maggie, turning to throw her arms round Tom's neck, and rub his cheek with her small round nose.

Tom, in the gladness of his heart at having dear old Maggie to dispute with and crow over again, seized her round the waist, and began to jump with her round the large library table. Away they jumped with more and more vigour, till Maggie's hair flew from behind her ears, and twirled about like an animated mop. But the revolutions round the table became more and more irregular in their sweep, till at last reaching Mr Stelling's reading-stand, they sent it thundering down with its heavy lexicons to the floor. Happily it was the ground-floor, and the study was a one-storeyed wing to the house, so that the downfall made no alarming resonance, though Tom stood dizzy and aghast for a few minutes, dreading the appearance of Mr or Mrs Stelling.

'Oh, I say, Maggie,' said Tom at last, lifting up the stand, 'we must keep quiet here, you know. If we break anything, Mrs Stelling'll make us cry *peccavi.*'

'What's that?' said Maggie.

'Oh, it's the Latin for a good scolding,' said Tom, not without some pride in his knowledge.

'Is she a cross woman?' said Maggie.

'I believe you!' said Tom, with an emphatic nod.

'I think all women are crosser than men,' said Maggie. 'Aunt Glegg's a great deal crosser than uncle Glegg, and mother scolds me more than father does.'

'Well, *you'll* be a woman someday,' said Tom, 'so *you* needn't talk.'

'But I shall be a *clever* woman,' said Maggie, with a toss.

'Oh, I dare say, and a nasty conceited thing. Everybody'll hate you.'

'But you oughtn't to hate me, Tom: it'll be very wicked of you, for I shall be your sister.'

'Yes, but if you're a nasty disagreeable thing, I *shall* hate you.'

'Oh, but Tom, you won't! I shan't be disagreeable. I shall be very good to you – and I shall be good to everybody. You won't hate me really, will you, Tom?'

'Oh, bother! never mind! Come, it's time for me to learn my lessons. See here! what I've got to do,' said Tom, drawing Maggie towards him and showing her his theorem, while she pushed her hair behind her ears, and prepared herself to prove her capability of helping him in Euclid. She began to read with full confidence in her own powers, but presently, becoming quite bewildered, her face flushed with irritation. It was unavoidable – she must confess her incompetency, and she was not fond of humiliation.

'It's nonsense!' she said, 'and very ugly stuff – nobody need want to make it out.'

'Ah, there now, Miss Maggie!' said Tom, drawing the book away, and wagging his head at her, 'you see you're not so clever as you thought you were.'

'Oh,' said Maggie, pouting, 'I dare say I could make it out, if I'd learned what goes before, as you have.'

'But that's what you just couldn't, Miss Wisdom,' said Tom. 'For it's all the harder when you know what goes before: for then you've got to say what definition 3 is and what axiom V is. But get along with you now: I must go on with this. Here's the Latin Grammar. See what you can make of that.'

Maggie found the Latin Grammar quite soothing after her mathematical mortification; for she delighted in new words, and quickly found that there was an English Key at the end, which would make her very wise about Latin, at slight expense. She presently made up her mind to skip the rules in the Syntax – the examples became so absorbing. The mysterious sentences, snatched from an unknown context – like strange horns of beasts, and leaves of unknown plants, brought from some far-off region – gave boundless scope to her imagination, and were all the more fascinating because they were in a peculiar tongue of their own, which she could learn to interpret. It was really interesting – the Latin Grammar that Tom had said no girls could learn: and she was proud because she found it interesting. The most fragmentary examples were her favourites. *Mors omnibus est communis* would have been jejune, only she liked to know the Latin; but the fortunate gentleman whom everyone congratulated because he had a son 'endowed with *such a* disposition' afforded her a great deal of pleasant conjecture, and she was quite lost in the 'thick grove penetrable by no star,' when Tom called out, 'Now, then, Magsie, give us the Grammar!'

'Oh, Tom, it's such a pretty book!' she said, as she jumped out of the large armchair to give it him; 'it's much prettier than the Dictionary. I could learn Latin very soon. I don't think it's at all hard.'

'Oh, I know what you've been doing,' said Tom; 'you've been reading the English at the end. Any donkey can do that.'

Tom seized the book and opened it with a determined and businesslike air, as much as to say that he had a lesson to learn which no donkeys would find themselves equal to. Maggie, rather piqued, turned to the bookcases to amuse herself with puzzling out the titles.

Presently Tom called to her: 'Here, Magsie, come and hear if I can say this. Stand at the end of the table, where Mr Stelling sits when he hears me.'

Maggie obeyed, and took the open book.

'Where do you begin, Tom?'

'Oh, I begin at *'Appellativa arborum,'* because I say all over again what I've been learning this week.'

Tom sailed along pretty well for three lines; and Maggie was beginning to forget her office of prompter in speculating as to what *mas* could mean, which came twice over, when he stuck fast at *Sunt etiam volucrum*.

'Don't tell me, Maggie; *Sunt etiam volucrum* . . . *Sunt etiam volucrum* . . . *ut ostrea, cetus* . . .'

'No,' said Maggie, opening her mouth and shaking her head.

'*Sunt etiam volucrum,*' said Tom, very slowly, as if the next words might be expected to come sooner when he gave them this strong hint that they were waited for.

'C, e, u,' said Maggie, getting impatient.

'Oh, I know – hold your tongue,' said Tom. '*Ceu passer, hirundo; Ferarum* . . . *ferarum* . . .' Tom took his pencil and made several hard dots with it on his book cover . . . '*ferarum*. . .'

'Oh dear, Oh dear, Tom' said Maggie, 'what a time you are! *Ut* . . . '

'Ut, ostrea . . . '

'No, no,' said Maggie, '*ut, tigris* . . .'

'Oh yes, now I can do,' said Tom; 'it was *tigris, vulpes,* I'd forgotten: *ut tigris, vulpes, et Piscium.*'

With some further stammering and repetition, Tom got through the next few lines.

'Now, then,' he said, 'the next is what I've just learned for tomorrow. Give me hold of the book a minute.'

After some whispered gabbling, assisted by the beating of his fist on the table, Tom returned the book.

'*Mascula nomina in a,*' he began.

'No, Tom,' said Maggie, 'that doesn't come next. It's *Nomen non creskens genittivo* . . . '

'*Creskens genittivo,*' exclaimed Tom, with a derisive laugh, for Tom had learned this omitted passage for his yesterday's lesson, and a young gentleman does not require an intimate or extensive acquaintance with Latin before he can feel the pitiable absurdity of a false quantity. '*Creskens genittivo!* What a silly you are, Maggie!'

'Well, you needn't laugh, Tom, for you didn't remember it at all. I'm sure it's spelt so; how was I to know?'

'Phee-e-e-h! I told you girls couldn't learn Latin. It's *Nommen non crescens genitivo.*'

'Very well, then,' said Maggie, pouting. 'I can say that as well as you can. And you don't mind your stops. For you ought to stop twice as long at a semicolon as you do at a comma, and you make the longest stops where there ought to be no stop at all.'

'Oh, well, don't chatter. Let me go on.'

They were presently fetched to spend the rest of the evening in the drawing-room, and Maggie became so animated with Mr Stelling, who, she felt sure, admired her cleverness, that Tom was rather amazed and alarmed at her audacity. But she was suddenly subdued by Mr Stelling's alluding to a little girl of whom he had heard that she once ran away to the gypsies.

'What a very odd little girl that must be!' said Mrs Stelling, meaning to be playful – but a playfulness that turned on her supposed oddity was not at all to Maggie's taste. She feared that Mr Stelling, after all, did not think much of her, and went to bed in rather low spirits. Mrs Stelling, she felt, looked at her as if she thought her hair was very ugly because it hung down straight behind.

Nevertheless it was a very happy fortnight to Maggie, this visit to Tom. She was allowed to be in the study while he had his lessons, and in her various readings got very deep into the examples in the Latin Grammar. The astronomer who hated women generally, caused her so much puzzling speculation that she one day asked Mr Stelling if all astronomers hated women, or whether it was only this particular astronomer. But, forestalling his answer, she said,

'I suppose it's all astronomers: because, you know, they live up in high towers, and if the women came there, they might talk and hinder them from looking at the stars.'

Mr Stelling liked her prattle immensely, and they were on the best terms. She told Tom she should like to go to school to Mr Stelling, as he did, and learn just the same things. She knew she could do Euclid, for she had looked into it again, and she saw what A B C meant: they were the names of the lines.

'I'm sure you couldn't do it, now,' said Tom; 'and I'll just ask Mr Stelling if you could.'

'I don't mind,' said the little conceited minx. 'I'll ask him myself.'

'Mr Stelling,' she said, that same evening when they were in the drawing-room, 'couldn't I do Euclid, and all Tom's lessons, if you were to teach me instead of him?'

'No; you couldn't,' said Tom, indignantly. 'Girls can't do Euclid: can they, sir?'

'They can pick up a little of everything, I dare say,' said Mr Stelling. 'They've a great deal of superficial cleverness; but they couldn't go far into anything. They're quick and shallow.'

Tom, delighted with this verdict, telegraphed his triumph by wagging his head at Maggie behind Mr Stelling's chair. As for Maggie, she had hardly ever been so mortified. She had been so proud to be called 'quick' all her little life, and now it appeared that this quickness was the brand of inferiority. It would have been better to be slow, like Tom.

'Ha, ha! Miss Maggie!' said Tom, when they were alone; 'you see it's not such a fine thing to be quick. You'll never go far into anything, you know.'

And Maggie was so oppressed by this dreadful destiny that she had no spirit for a retort.

But when this small apparatus of shallow quickness was fetched away in the gig by Luke, and the study was once more quite lonely for Tom, he missed her grievously. He had really been brighter, and had got through his lessons better, since she had been there; and she had asked Mr Stelling so many questions about the Roman Empire, and whether there really ever was a man who said, in Latin, 'I would not buy it for a farthing or a rotten nut,' or whether that had only been turned into Latin, that Tom had actually come to a dim understanding of the fact that there had once been people upon the earth who were so fortunate as to know Latin without learning it through the medium of the Eton Grammar. This luminous idea was a great addition to his historical acquirements during this half-year, which were otherwise confined to an epitomised history of the Jews.

But the dreary half-year *did* come to an end. How glad Tom was to see the last yellow leaves fluttering before the cold wind! The dark afternoons, and the first December snow, seemed to him far livelier than the August sunshine: and that he might make himself the surer about the flight of the days that were carrying him homeward, he stuck twenty-one sticks deep in a corner of the garden, when he was three weeks from the holidays, and pulled one up every day with a great wrench, throwing it to a distance with a vigour of will which would have carried it to limbo, if it had been in the nature of sticks to travel so far.

But it was worth purchasing, even at the heavy price of the Latin Grammar – the happiness of seeing the bright light in the parlour at home, as the gig passed noiselessly over the snow-covered bridge: the happiness of passing from the cold air to the warmth, and the kisses and the smiles of that familiar hearth, where the pattern of the rug and the grate and the fire-irons were 'first ideas' that it was no more possible to criticise than the solidity and extension of matter. There is no sense of ease like the ease we felt in those scenes where we were born, where objects became dear to us before we had known the labour of choice, and where the outer world seemed only an extension of our personality: we accepted and loved it as we accepted our own sense of existence and our own limbs. Very commonplace, even ugly, that furniture of our early home might look if it were put up to auction; an improved taste in upholstery scorns it; and is not the striving after something better and better in our surroundings, the grand characteristic that distinguishes man from the brute – or, to satisfy a scrupulous accuracy of definition, that distinguishes the British man from the foreign brute? But heaven knows where that striving might lead us, if our affections had not a trick of twining round those old inferior things – if the loves and sanctities of our life had no deep immovable roots in memory. One's delight in an elderberry bush overhanging the confused leafage of a hedgerow bank, as a more gladdening sight than the finest cistus or fuchsia spreading itself on the softest undulating turf, is an entirely unjustifable preference to a landscape-gardener, or to any of those severely regulated minds who are free from the weakness of any attachment that does not rest on a demonstrable superiority of qualities. And there is no better reason for preferring this elderberry bush than that it stirs an early memory – that it is no novelty in my life, speaking to me merely through my present sensibilities to form and colour, but the long companion of my existence, that wove itself into my joys when joys were vivid.

CHAPTER 2

The Christmas Holidays

Fine old Christmas, with the snowy hair and ruddy face, had done his duty that year in the noblest fashion, and had set off his rich gifts of warmth and colour with all the heightening contrast of frost and snow.

Snow lay on the croft and river-bank in undulations softer than the limbs of infancy; it lay with the neatliest finished border on every sloping roof, making the dark-red gables stand out with a new depth of colour; it weighed heavily on the laurels and fir trees, till it fell from them with a shuddering sound; it clothed the rough turnip-field with whiteness, and made the sheep look like dark blotches; the gates were all blocked up with the sloping drifts, and here and there a disregarded four-footed beast stood as if petrified 'in unrecumbent sadness'; there was no gleam, no shadow, for the heavens, too, were one still, pale cloud – no sound or motion in anything but the dark river, that flowed and moaned like an unresting sorrow. But old Christmas smiled as he laid this cruel-seeming spell on the outdoor world, for he meant to light up home with new brightness, to deepen all the richness of indoor colour, and give a keener edge of delight to the warm fragrance of food: he meant to prepare a sweet imprisonment that would strengthen the primitive fellowship of kindred, and make the sunshine of familiar human faces as welcome as the hidden day-star. His kindness fell but hardly on the homeless – fell but hardly on the homes where the hearth was not very warm, and where the food had little fragrance; where the human faces had no sunshine in them, but rather the leaden, blank-eyed gaze of unexpectant want. But the fine old season meant well; and if he has not learnt the secret how to bless men impartially, it is because his father Time, with ever-unrelenting purpose, still hides that secret in his own mighty, slow-beating heart.

And yet this Christmas day, in spite of Tom's fresh delight in home, was not, he thought, somehow or other, quite so happy as it had always been before. The red berries were just as abundant on the holly, and he and Maggie had dressed all the windows and mantelpieces and picture-frames on Christmas eve with as much taste as ever, wedding the thick-set scarlet clusters with branches of the black-berried ivy. There had been singing under the windows after midnight – supernatural singing, Maggie always felt, in spite of Tom's contemptuous insistence that the singers were old Patch, the parish clerk, and the rest of the church choir: she trembled with awe when their caroling broke in upon her dreams, and the image of men in fustian clothes was always thrust away by the vision of angels resting on the parted cloud. The midnight chant had helped as usual to lift the morning above the level of common days; and then there was the smell of hot toast and ale from the kitchen, at the breakfast hour; the favourite anthem, the green boughs, and the short sermon, gave the appropriate festal character to the church-going; and aunt and uncle Moss, with all their seven children, were looking like so many reflectors of the bright parlour-fire, when the churchgoers came back, stamping the snow from their feet. The plum-pudding was of the same handsome roundness as ever, and came in with the symbolic blue flames around it, as if it had been heroically snatched from the nether fires into which it had been thrown by dyspeptic Puritans; the dessert was as splendid as ever, with its golden oranges, brown nuts, and the crystalline light and dark of apple jelly and damson cheese: in all these things Christmas was as it had always been since Tom could remember; it was only distinguished, if by anything, by superior sliding and snowballs.

Christmas was cheery, but not so Mr Tulliver. He was irate and defiant, and Tom, though he espoused his father's quarrels and shared his father's sense of injury, was not without some of the feeling that oppressed Maggie when Mr Tulliver got louder and more angry in narration and assertion with the increased leisure of dessert. The attention that Tom might have concentrated on his nuts and wine was distracted by a sense that there were rascally enemies in the world, and that the business of grown-up life could hardly be conducted without a good deal of quarrelling. Now Tom was not fond of quarrelling, unless it could soon be put an end to by a fair stand-up fight with an adversary whom he had every chance of thrashing; and his father's irritable talk made him uncomfortable, though he never accounted to himself for the feeling, or conceived the notion that his father was faulty in this respect.

The particular embodiment of the evil principle now exciting Mr Tulliver's determined resistance was Mr Pivart, who, having lands higher up the Ripple, was taking measures for their irrigation, which either were, or would be, or were bound to be (on the principle that water was water), an infringement on Mr Tulliver's legitimate share of water-power. Dix, who had a mill on the stream, was a feeble auxiliary of Old Harry compared with Pivart. Dix had been brought to his senses by arbitration, and Wakem's advice had not carried *him* far; no: Dix, Mr Tulliver considered, had been as good as nowhere in point of law; and in the intensity of his indignation against Pivart, his contempt for a baffled adversary like Dix began to wear the air of a friendly attachment. He had no male audience today except Mr Moss, who knew nothing, as he said, of the 'natur' o' mills,' and could only assent to Mr Tulliver's arguments on the *a priori* ground of family relationship and monetary obligation; but Mr Tulliver did not talk with the futile intention of convincing his audience – he talked to relieve himself; while good Mr Moss made strong efforts to keep his eyes wide open, in spite of the sleepiness which an unusually good dinner produced in his hard-worked frame. Mrs Moss, more alive to the subject, and interested in everything that affected her brother, listened and put in a word as often as maternal preoccupations allowed.

'Why, Pivart's a new name hereabout, brother, isn't it?' she said: 'he didn't own the land in father's time, nor yours either, before I was married.'

'New name? Yes – I should think it is a new name,' said Mr Tulliver, with angry emphasis. 'Dorlcote Mill's been in our family a hundred year and better, and nobody ever heard of a Pivart meddling with the river, till this fellow came and bought Bincome's farm out of hand, before anybody else could so much as say "snap". But I'll *Pivart* him!' added Mr Tulliver, lifting his glass with a sense that he had defined his resolution in an unmistakable manner.

'You won't be forced to go to law with him, I hope, brother?' said Mrs Moss, with some anxiety.

'I don't know what I shall be forced to; but I know what I shall force *him* to, with his dykes and erigations, if there's any law to be brought to bear o' the right side. I know well enough who's at the bottom of it; he's got Wakem to back him and egg him on. I know Wakem tells him the law can't touch him for it, but there's folks can handle the law besides Wakem. It takes a big raskill to beat him; but there's bigger to be found, as know more o' th' ins and outs o' the law, else how came Wakem to lose Brumley's suit for him?'

Mr Tulliver was a strictly honest man, and proud of being honest, but he considered that in law the ends of justice could only be achieved by employing a stronger knave to frustrate a weaker. Law was a sort of cock-fight, in which it was the business of injured honesty to get a game bird with the best pluck and the strongest spurs.

'Gore's no fool – you needn't tell me that,' he observed presently in a pugnacious tone, as if poor Gritty had been urging that lawyer's capabilities; 'but, you see, he isn't up to the law as Wakem is. And water's a very particular thing – you can't pick it up with a pitchfork. That's why it's been nuts to Old Harry and the lawyers. It's plain enough what's the rights and the wrongs of water, if you look at it straightforrard; for a river's a river, and if you've got a mill, you must have water to turn it; and it's no use telling me, Pivart's erigation and nonsense won't stop my wheel: I know what belongs to water better than that. Talk to me o' what th' engineers say! I say it's common sense, as Pivart's dykes must do me an injury. But if that's their engineering, I'll put Tom to it by and by, and he shall see if he can't find a bit more sense in th' engineering business than what *that* comes to.'

Tom, looking round with some anxiety at this announcement of his prospects, unthinkingly withdrew a small rattle he was amusing Baby Moss with, whereupon she, being a baby that knew her own mind with remarkable clearness, instantaneously expressed her sentiments in a piercing yell, and was not to be appeased even by the restoration of the rattle, feeling apparently that the original wrong of having it taken from her remained in all its force. Mrs Moss hurried away with her into another room, and expressed to Mrs Tulliver, who accompanied her, the conviction that the dear child had good reasons for crying; implying that if it was supposed to be the rattle that baby clamoured for, she was a misunderstood baby. The thoroughly justifiable yell being quieted, Mrs Moss looked at her sister-in-law and said, 'I'm sorry to see brother so put out about this water work.'

'It's your brother's way, Mrs Moss; I'd never anything o' that sort before I was married,' said Mrs Tulliver, with a half-implied reproach. She always spoke of her husband as 'your brother' to Mrs Moss in any case when his line of conduct was not matter of pure admiration. Amiable Mrs Tulliver, who was never angry in her life, had yet her mild share of that spirit without which she could hardly have been at once a Dodson and a woman. Being always on the defensive towards her own sisters, it was natural that she should be keenly conscious of her superiority, even as the weakest Dodson, over a husband's sister, who, besides being poorly off, and inclined to 'hang on' her brother, had the good-natured submissiveness of a large, easy-tempered, untidy, prolific woman, with affection enough in her not only for her own husband and abundant children, but for any number of collateral relations.

'I hope and pray he won't go to law,' said Mrs Moss, 'for there's never any knowing where that'll end. And the right doesn't allays win. This Mr Pivart's a rich man, by what I can make out, and the rich mostly get things their own way.'

'As to that,' said Mrs Tulliver, stroking her dress down, 'I've seen what riches are in my own family; for my sisters have got husbands as can afford to do pretty much what they like. But I think sometimes I shall be drove off my head with the talk about this law and erigation; and my sisters lay all the fault to me, for they don't know what it is to marry a man like your brother – how should they? Sister Pullet has her own way from morning till night.'

'Well,' said Mrs Moss, 'I don't think I should like my husband if he hadn't got any wits of his own, and I had to find head-piece for him. It's a deal easier to do what pleases one's husband than to be puzzling what else one should do.'

'If people come to talk o' doing what pleases their husbands,' said Mrs Tulliver, with a faint imitation of her sister Glegg, 'I'm sure your brother might have waited a long while before he'd have found a wife that 'ud have let him have his say in everything, as I do. It's nothing but law and erigation now, from when we first get up in the morning till we go to bed at night; and I niver contradict him; I only say – "Well, Mr Tulliver, do as you like, but whativer you do, don't go to law.' "

Mrs Tulliver, as we have seen, was not without influence over her husband. No woman is; she can always incline him to do either what she wishes, or the reverse, and on the composite impulses that were threatening to hurry Mr Tulliver into 'law,' Mrs Tulliver's monotonous pleading had doubtless its share of force; it might even be comparable to that proverbial feather which has the credit or discredit of breaking the camel's back, though, on a strictly impartial view, the blame ought rather to lie with the previous weight of feathers which had already placed the back in such imminent peril, that an otherwise innocent feather could not settle on it without mischief. Not that Mrs Tulliver's feeble beseeching could have had this feather's weight in virtue of her single personality; but whenever she departed from entire assent to her husband, he saw in her the representative of the Dodson family; and it was a guiding principle with Mr Tulliver, to let the Dodsons know that they were not to domineer over *him*, or – more specifically – that a male Tulliver was far more than equal to four female Dodsons, even though one of them was Mrs Glegg.

But not even a direct argument from that typical Dodson female herself against his going to law, could have heightened his disposition towards it so much as the mere thought of Wakem, continually freshened by the sight of the too able attorney on market-days. Wakem, to his certain knowledge, was (metaphorically speaking) at the bottom of Pivart's irrigation: Wakem had tried to make Dix stand out, and go to law about the dam: it was unquestionably Wakem who had caused Mr Tulliver to lose the suit about the right of road and the bridge that made a thoroughfare of his land for every vagabond who preferred an opportunity of damaging private property to walking like an honest man along the highroad: all lawyers were more or less rascals, but Wakem's rascality was of that peculiarly aggravated kind which placed itself in opposition to that form of right embodied in Mr Tulliver's interests and opinions. And as an extra touch of bitterness, the injured miller had recently, in borrowing the five hundred pounds, been obliged to carry a little business to Wakem's office on his own account. A hook-nosed glib fellow! as cool as a cucumber – always looking so sure of his game! And it was vexatious that Lawyer Gore was not more like him, but was a bald, round-featured man, with bland manners and fat hands; a game-cock that you would be rash to bet upon against Wakem. Gore was a sly fellow; his weakness did not lie on the side of scrupulosity: but the largest amount of winking, however significant, is not equivalent to seeing through a stone wall; and confident as Mr Tulliver was in his principle that water was water, and in the direct inference that Pivart had not a leg to stand on in this affair of irrigation, he had an uncomfortable suspicion that Wakem had more law to show against this (rationally) irrefragable inference, than Gore could show for it. But then, if they went to law, there was a chance for Mr Tulliver to employ Counsellor Wylde on his side, instead of having that admiable bully against him; and the prospect of seeing a witness of Wakem's made to perspire and become confounded, as Mr Tulliver's witness had once been, was alluring to the love of retributive justice.

Much rumination had Mr Tulliver on these puzzling subjects during his rides on the grey horse – much turning of the head from side to side, as the scales dipped alternately; but the probable result was still out of sight, only to be reached through much hot argument and iteration in domestic and social life. That initial stage of the dispute which consisted in the narration of the case and the enforcement of Mr Tulliver's views concerning it throughout the entire circle of his connections would necessarily take time, and at the beginning of February, when Tom was going to school again, there were scarcely any new items to be detected in his father's statement of the case against Pivart, or any more specific indication of the measures he was bent on taking against that rash contravener of the principle that water was water. Iteration, like friction, is likely to generate heat instead of progress, and Mr Tulliver's heat was certainly more and more palpable. If there had been no new evidence on any other point, there had been new evidence that Pivart was as 'thick as mud' with Wakem.

'Father,' said Tom, one evening near the end of the holidays, 'uncle Glegg says Lawyer Wakem *is* going to send his son to Mr Stelling. It isn't true – what they said about his going to be sent to France. You won't like me to go to school with Wakem's son, shall you?'

'It's no matter for that, my boy,' said Mr Tulliver; 'don't you learn anything bad of him, that's all. The lad's a poor deformed creatur, and takes after his mother in the face: I think there isn't much of his father in him. It's a sign Wakem thinks high o' Mr Stelling, as he sends his son to him, and Wakem knows meal from bran.'

Mr Tulliver in his heart was rather proud of the fact that his son was to have the same advantages as Wakem's: but Tom was not at all easy on the point; it would have been much clearer if the lawyer's son had not been deformed, for then Tom would have had the prospect of pitching into him with all that freedom which is derived from a high moral sanction.

CHAPTER 3

The New Schoolfellow

It was a cold, wet February day on which Tom went back to school: a day quite in keeping with this severe phase of his destiny. If he had not carried in his pocket a parcel of sugar-candy and a small Dutch doll for little Laura, there would have been no ray of expected pleasure to enliven the general gloom. But he liked to think how Laura would put out her lips and her tiny hands for the bits of sugar-candy; and, to give the greater keenness to these pleasures of imagination, he took out the parcel, made a small hole in the paper, and bit off a crystal or two, which had so solacing an effect under the confined prospect and damp odours of the gig-umbrella, that he repeated the process more than once on his way.

'Well, Tulliver, we're glad to see you again,' said Mr Stelling, heartily. 'Take off your wrappings and come into the study till dinner. You'll find a bright fire there, and a new companion.'

Tom felt in an uncomfortable flutter as he took off his woollen comforter and other wrappings. He had seen Philip Wakem at St Ogg's, but had always turned his eyes away from him as quickly as possible. He would have disliked having a deformed boy for his companion, even if Philip had not been the son of a bad man. And Tom did not see how a bad man's son could be very good. His own father was a good man, and he would readily have fought anyone who said the contrary. He was in a state of mingled embarrassment and defiance as he followed Mr Stelling to the study.

'Here is a new companion for you to shake hands with, Tulliver,' said that gentleman on entering the study – 'Master Philip Wakem. I shall leave you to make acquaintance by yourselves. You already know something of each other, I imagine; for you are neighbours at home.'

Tom looked confused and awkward, while Philip rose and glanced at him timidly. Tom did not like to go up and put out his hand, and he was not prepared to say, 'How do you do?' on so short a notice.

Mr Stelling wisely turned away, and closed the door behind him: boys' shyness only wears off in the absence of their elders.

Philip was at once too proud and too timid to walk towards Tom. He thought, or rather felt, that Tom had an aversion to looking at him: everyone, almost, disliked looking at him; and his deformity was more conspicuous when he walked. So they remained without shaking hands or even speaking, while Tom went to the fire and warmed himself, every now and then casting furtive glances at Philip, who seemed to be drawing absently first one object and then another on a piece of paper he had before him. He had seated himself again, and as he drew, was thinking what he could say to Tom, and trying to overcome his own repugnance to making the first advances.

Tom began to look oftener and longer at Philip's face, for he could see it without noticing the hump, and it was really not a disagreeable face – very old-looking, Tom thought. He wondered how much older Philip was than himself. An anatomist – even a mere physiognomist – would have seen that the deformity of Philip's spine was not a congenital hump, but the result of an accident in infancy; but you do not expect from Tom any acquaintance with such distinctions: to him, Philip was simply a humpback. He had a vague notion that the deformity of Wakem's son had some relation to the lawyer's rascality, of which he had so often heard his father talk with hot emphasis; and he felt, too, a half-admitted fear of him as probably a spiteful fellow, who, not being able to fight you, had cunning ways of doing you a mischief by the sly. There was a humpbacked tailor in the neighbourhood of Mr Jacobs's academy, who was considered a very unamiable character, and was much hooted after by public-spirited boys solely on the ground of his unsatisfactory moral qualities; so that Tom was not without a basis of fact to go upon. Still, no face could be more unlike that ugly tailor's than this melancholy boy's face; the brown hair round it waved and curled at the ends like a girl's: Tom thought that truly pitiable. This Wakem was a pale, puny fellow, and it was quite clear he would not be able to play at anything worth speaking of: but he handled his pencil in an enviable manner, and was apparently making one thing after another without any trouble. What was he drawing? Tom was quite warm now, and wanted something new to be going forward. It was certainly more agreeable to have an ill-natured hump-back as a companion than to stand looking out of the study window at the rain, and kicking his foot against the washboard in solitude; something would happen every day – 'a quarrel or something'; and Tom thought he should rather like to show Philip that he had better not try his spiteful tricks on *him*. He suddenly walked across the hearth, and looked over Philip's paper.

'Why, that's a donkey with panniers – and a spaniel, and partridges in the corn!' he exclaimed, his tongue being completely loosed by surprise and admiration. 'O my buttons! I wish I could draw like that. I'm to learn drawing this half – I wonder if I shall learn to make dogs and donkeys!'

'Oh, you can do them without learning,' said Philip; 'I never learned drawing.'

'Never learned?' said Tom, in amazement. 'Why, when I make dogs and horses, and those things, the heads and the legs won't come right; though I can see how they ought to be very well. I can make houses, and all sorts of chimneys – chimneys going all down the wall, and windows in the roof, and all that. But I dare say I could do dogs and horses if I was to try more,' he added, reflecting that Philip might falsely suppose that he was going to 'knock under,' if he were too frank about the imperfection of his accomplishments.

'Oh yes,' said Philip, 'it's very easy. You've only to look well at things, and draw them over and over again. What you do wrong once, you can alter the next time.'

'But haven't you been taught *anything*?' said Tom, beginning to have a puzzled suspicion that Philip's crooked back might be the source of remarkable faculties. 'I thought you'd been to school a long while.'

'Yes,' said Philip, smiling, 'I've been taught Latin, and Greek, and mathematics – and writing, and such things.'

'Oh, but, I say, you don't like Latin, though, do you?' said Tom, lowering his voice confidentially.

'Pretty well; I don't care much about it,' said Philip.

'Ah, but perhaps you haven't got into the *Propria quae maribus*,' said Tom, nodding his head sideways, as much as to say, 'That was the test: it was easy talking till you came to *that*.'

Philip felt some bitter complacency in the promising stupidity of this well-made active-looking boy; but made polite by his own extreme sensitiveness, as well as by his desire to conciliate, he checked his inclination to laugh, and said, quietly, 'I've done with the grammar; I don't learn that any more.'

'Then you won't have the same lessons as I shall?' said Tom, with a sense of disappointment.

'No; but I dare say I can help you. I shall be very glad to help you if I can.'

Tom did not say, 'Thank you,' for he was quite absorbed in the thought that Wakem's son did not seem so spiteful a fellow as might have been expected.

'I say,' he said presently, 'do you love your father?'

'Yes,' said Philip, colouring deeply; 'don't you love yours?'

'O yes . . . I only wanted to know,' said Tom, rather ashamed of himself, now he saw Philip colouring and looking uncomfortable. He found much difficulty in adjusting his attitude of mind towards the son of Lawyer Wakem, and it had occurred to him that if Philip disliked his father, that fact might go some way towards clearing up his perplexity.

'Shall you learn drawing now?' he said, by way of changing the subject.

'No,' said Philip. 'My father wishes me to give all my time to other things now.'

'What! Latin, and Euclid, and those things?' said Tom.

'Yes,' said Philip, who had left off using his pencil, and was resting his head on one hand, while Tom was leaning forward on both elbows, and looking with increasing admiration at the dog and the donkey.

'And you don't mind that?' said Tom, with strong curiosity.

'No: I like to know what everybody else knows. I can study what I like by and by.'

'I can't think why anybody should learn Latin,' said Tom. 'It's no good.'

'It's part of the education of a gentleman,' said Philip. 'All gentlemen learn the same things.'

'What! do you think Sir John Crake, the master of the harriers, knows Latin?' said Tom, who had often thought he should like to resemble Sir John Crake.

'He learned it when he was a boy, of course,' said Philip. 'But I dare say he's forgotten it.'

'Oh, well, I can do that, then,' said Tom, not with any epigrammatic intention, but with serious satisfaction at the idea that, as far as Latin was concerned, there was no hindrance to his resembling Sir John Crake. 'Only you're obliged to remember it while you're at school, else you've got to learn ever so many lines of "Speaker". Mr Stelling's very particular – did you know? He'll have you up ten times if you say "nam" for "jam" . . . he won't let you go a letter wrong, I can tell you.'

'Oh, I don't mind,' said Philip, unable to choke a laugh; 'I can remember things easily. And there are some lessons I'm very fond of. I'm very fond of Greek history and everything about the Greeks. I should like to have been a Greek and fought the Persians, and then have come home and have written tragedies, or else have been listened to by everybody for my wisdom, like Socrates, and have died a grand death.' (Philip, you perceive, was not without a wish to impress the well-made barbarian with a sense of his mental superiority.)

'Why, were the Greeks great fighters?' said Tom, who saw a vista in this direction. 'Is there anything like David, and Goliath, and Samson, in the Greek history? Those are the only bits I like in the history of the Jews.'

'Oh, there are very fine stories of that sort about the Greeks – about the heroes of early times who killed the wild beasts, as Samson did. And in the *Odyssey* – that's a beautiful poem – there's a more wonderful giant than Goliath – Polypheme, who had only one eye in the middle of his forehead; and Ulysses, a little fellow, but very wise and cunning, got a red-hot pine tree and stuck it into this one eye, and made him roar like a thousand bulls.'

'Oh, what fun!' said Tom, jumping away from the table, and stamping first with one leg and then the other. 'I say, can you tell me all about those stories? Because I shan't learn Greek you know . . . Shall I?' he added, pausing in his stamping with a sudden alarm, lest the contrary might be possible. 'Does every gentleman learn Greek? . . . Will Mr Stelling make me begin with it, do you think?'

'No, I should think not – very likely not,' said Philip. 'But you may read those stories without knowing Greek. I've got them in English.'

'Oh, but I don't like reading; I'd sooner have you tell them me. But only the fighting ones, you know. My sister Maggie is always wanting to tell me stories – but they're stupid things. Girls' stories always are. Can you tell a good many fighting stories?'

'Oh, yes,' said Philip; 'lots of them besides the Greek stories. I can tell you about Richard Coeur-de-Lion and Saladin, and about William Wallace, and Robert Bruce, and James Douglas – I know no end.'

'You're older than I am, aren't you?' said Tom.

'Why, how old are *you*? I'm fifteen.'

'I'm only going in fourteen,' said Tom. 'But I thrashed all the fellows at Jacobs's – that's where I was before I came here. And I beat 'em all at bandy and climbing. And I wish Mr Stelling would let us go fishing. *I* could show you how to fish. You *could* fish, couldn't you? It's only standing, and sitting still, you know.'

Tom, in his turn, wished to make the balance dip in his favour. This hunch-back must not suppose that his acquaintance with fighting stories put him on a par with an actual fighting hero, like Tom Tulliver. Philip winced under this allusion to his unfitness for active sports, and he answered almost peevishly, 'I can't bear fishing. I think people look like fools sitting watching a line hour after hour – or else throwing and throwing, and catching nothing.'

'Ah, but you wouldn't say they looked like fools when they landed a big pike, I can tell you,' said Tom, who had never caught anything that was 'big' in his life, but whose imagination was on the stretch with indignant zeal for the honour of sport. Wakem's son, it was plain, had his disagreeable points, and must be kept in due check. Happily for the harmony of this first interview, they were now called to dinner, and Philip was not allowed to develop farther his unsound views on the subject of fishing. But Tom said to himself, that was just what he should have expected from a hunchback.

CHAPTER 4

'The Young Idea'

The alternations of feeling in that first dialogue between Tom and Philip continued to mark their intercourse even after many weeks of schoolboy intimacy. Tom never quite lost the feeling that Philip, being the son of a 'rascal', was his natural enemy, never thoroughly overcame his repulsion to Philip's deformity: he was a boy who adhered tenaciously to impressions once received: as with all minds in which mere perception predominates over thought and emotion, the external remained to him rigidly what it was in the first instance. But then, it was impossible not to like Philip's company when he was in a good humour; he could help one so well in one's Latin exercises, which Tom regarded as a kind of puzzle that could only be found out by a lucky chance; and he could tell such wonderful fighting stories about Hal of the Wynd, for example, and other heroes who were especial favourites with Tom, because they laid about them with heavy strokes. He had small opinion of Saladin, whose scimitar could cut a cushion in two in an instant: who wanted to cut cushions? That was a stupid story, and he didn't care to hear it again. But when Robert Bruce, on the black pony, rose in his stirrups, and, lifting his good battle-axe, cracked at once the helmet and the skull of the too-hasty knight at Bannockburn, then Tom felt all the exaltation of sympathy, and if he had had a coconut at hand, he would have cracked it at once with the poker. Philip in his happier moods, indulged Tom to the top of his bent, heightening the crash and bang and fury of every fight with all the artillery of epithets and similes at his command. But he was not always in a good humour or happy mood. The slight spurt of peevish susceptibility which had escaped him in their first interview, was a symptom of a perpetually-recurring mental ailment – half of it nervous irritability, half of it the heart-bitterness produced by the sense of his deformity. In these fits of susceptibility every glance seemed to him to be charged either with offensive pity or with ill-repressed disgust – at the very least it was an indifferent glance, and Philip felt indifference as a child of the south feels the chill air of a northern spring. Poor Tom's blundering patronage when they were out of doors together would sometimes make him turn upon the well-meaning lad quite savagely: and his eyes, usually sad and quiet, would flash with anything but playful lightning. No wonder Tom retained his suspicions of the hunchback.

But Philip's self-taught skill in drawing was another link between them: for Tom found, to his disgust, that his new drawing-master gave him no dogs and donkeys to draw, but brooks and rustic bridges and ruins, all with a general softness of black-lead surface, indicating that nature, if anything, was rather satiny; and as Tom's feeling for the picturesque in landscape was at present quite latent, it is not surprising that Mr Goodrich's productions seemed to him an uninteresting form of art. Mr Tulliver, having a vague intention that Tom should be put to some business which included the drawing out of plans and maps, had complained to Mr Riley, when he saw him at Mudport, that Tom seemed to be learning nothing of that sort; whereupon that obliging adviser had suggested that Tom should have drawing-lessons. Mr Tulliver must not mind paying extra for drawing: let Tom be made a good draughtsman, and he would be able to turn his pencil to any purpose. So it was ordered that Tom should have drawing-lessons: and whom should Mr Stelling have selected as a master if not Mr Goodrich, who was considered quite at the head of his profession within a circuit of twelve miles round King's Lorton? By which means Tom learned to make an extremely fine point to his pencil, and to represent landscape with a 'broad generality', which, doubtless from a narrow tendency in his mind to details, he thought extremely dull.

All this, you remember, happened in those dark ages when there were no schools of design – before schoolmasters were invariably men of scrupulous integrity, and before the clergy were all men of enlarged minds and varied culture. In those less-favoured days, it is no fable that there were other clergy-men besides Mr Stelling who had narrow intellects and large wants, and whose income, by a logical confusion to which Fortune, being a female as well as blindfold, is peculiarly liable, was proportioned not to their wants but to their intellect – with which income has clearly no inherent relation. The problem these gentlemen had to solve was to readjust the proportion between their wants and their income; and since wants are not easily starved to death, the simpler method appeared to be – to raise their income. There was but one way of doing this: any of those low callings in which men are obliged to do good work at a low price were forbidden to clergymen: was it their fault if their only resource was to turn out very poor work at a high price? Besides, how should Mr Stelling be expected to know that education was a delicate and difficult business? any more than an animal endowed with a power of boring a hole through a rock should be expected to have wide views of excavation. Mr Stelling's faculties had been early trained to boring in a straight line, and he had no faculty to spare. But among Tom's contemporaries, whose fathers cast their sons on clerical instruction to find them ignorant after many days, there were many far less lucky than Tom Tulliver. Education was almost entirely a matter of luck – usually of ill-luck – in those distant days. The state of mind in which you take a billiard-cue or a dice-box in your hand is one of sober certainty compared with that of old-fashioned fathers, like Mr Tulliver, when they selected a school or a tutor for their sons. Excellent men, who had been forced all their lives to spell on an impromptu-phonetic system, and having carried on a successful business in spite of this disadvantage, had acquired money enough to give their sons a better start in life than they had had themselves, must necessarily take their chance as to the conscience and the competence of the schoolmaster whose circular fell in their way, and appeared to promise so much more than they would ever have thought of asking for, including the return of linen, fork, and spoon. It was happy for them if some ambitious draper of their acquaintance had not brought up his son to the Church, and if that young gentleman, at the age of four-and-twenty, had not closed his college dissipations by an imprudent marriage; otherwise, these innocent fathers, desirous of doing the best for their offspring, could only escape the draper's son by happening to be on the foundation of a grammar-school as yet unvisited by commissioners, where two or three boys could have, all to themselves, the advantages of a large and lofty building, together with a head-master, toothless, dim-eyed, and deaf, whose erudite indistinctness and inattention were engrossed by them at the rate of three hundred pounds ahead – a ripe scholar, doubtless, when first appointed; but all ripeness beneath the sun has a further stage less esteemed in the market.

Tom Tulliver, then, compared with many other British youths of his time, who have since had to scramble through life with some fragments of more or less relevant knowledge, and a great deal of strictly relevant ignorance, was not so very unlucky. Mr Stelling was a broad-chested healthy man, with the bearing of a gentleman, a conviction that a growing boy required a sufficiency of beef, and a certain hearty kindness in him that made him like to see Tom looking well and enjoying his dinner; not a man of refined conscience, or with any deep sense of the infinite issues belonging to everyday duties; not quite competent to his high offices; but incompetent gentlemen must live, and without private fortune it is difficult to see how they could all live genteelly if they had nothing to do with education or government. Besides, it was the fault of Tom's mental constitution that his faculties could not be nourished on the sort of knowledge Mr Stelling had to communicate. A boy born with a deficient power of appre-hending signs and abstractions must suffer the penalty of his congenital deficiency, just as if he had been born with one leg shorter than the other. A method of education sanctioned by the long practice of our venerable ancestors was not to give way before the exceptional dulness of a boy who was merely living at the time then present. And Mr Stelling was convinced that a boy so stupid at signs and abstractions must be stupid at everything else, even if that reverend gentleman could have taught him everything else. It was the practice of our venerable ancestors to apply that ingenious instrument the thumbscrew, and to tighten and tighten it in order to elicit non-existent facts; they had a fixed opinion to begin with, that the facts were existent, and what had they to do but to tighten the thumbscrew? In like manner, Mr Stelling had a fixed opinion that all boys with any capacity could learn what it was the only regular thing to teach: if they were slow, the thumbscrew must be tightened – the exercises must be insisted on with increased severity, and a page of Virgil be awarded as a penalty, to encourage and stimulate a too languid inclination to Latin verse.

Nevertheless the thumbscrew was relaxed a little during this second half-year. Philip was so advanced in his studies, and so apt, that Mr Stelling could obtain credit by his facility, which required little help, much more easily than by the troublesome process of overcoming Tom's dulness. Gentlemen with broad chests and ambitious intentions do sometimes disappoint their friends by failing to carry the world before them. Perhaps it is, that high achievements demand some other unusual qualification besides an unusual desire for high prizes; perhaps it is that these stalwart gentlemen are rather indolent, their *divinae particulam aurae* being obstructed from soaring by a too hearty appetite. Some reason or other there was why Mr Stelling deferred the execution of many spirited projects – why he did not begin the editing of his Greek play, or any other work of scholarship, in his leisure hours, but, after turning the key of his private study with much resolution, sat down to one of Theodore Hook's novels. Tom was gradually allowed to shuffle through his lessons with less rigour, and having Philip to help him, he was able to make some show of having applied his mind in a confused and blundering way, without being cross-examined into a betrayal that his mind had been entirely neutral in the matter. He thought school much more bearable under this modification of circumstances; and he went on contentedly enough, picking up a promiscuous education chiefly from things that were not intended as education at all. What was understood to be his education, was simply the practice of reading, writing, and spelling, carried on by an elaborate appliance of unintelligible ideas, and by much failure in the effort to learn by rote.

Nevertheless, there was a visible improvement in Tom under this training; perhaps because he was not a boy in the abstract, existing solely to illustrate the evils of a mistaken education, but a boy made of flesh and blood, with dispositions not entirely at the mercy of circumstances.

There was a great improvement in his bearing, for example, and some credit on this score was due to Mr Poulter, the village schoolmaster, who, being an old Peninsular soldier, was employed to drill Tom – a source of high mutual pleasure. Mr Poulter, who was understood by the company at the Black Swan to have once struck terror into the hearts of the French, was no longer personally formidable. He had rather a shrunken appearance, and was tremulous in the mornings, not from age, but from the extreme perversity of the King's Lorton boys, which nothing but gin could enable him to sustain with any firmness. Still, he carried himself with martial erectness, had his clothes scrupulously brushed, and his trousers tightly strapped; and on the Wednesday and Saturday afternoons, when he came to Tom, he was always inspired with gin and old memories, which gave him an exceptionally spirited air, as of a superannuated charger who hears the drum. The drilling-lessons were always protracted by episodes of warlike narrative, much more interesting to Tom than Philip's stories out of the *Iliad;* for there were no cannon in the *Iliad,* and, besides, Tom had felt some disgust on learning that Hector and Achilles might possibly never have existed. But the Duke of Wellington was really alive, and Bony had not been long dead – therefore Mr Poulter's reminiscences of the Peninsular War were removed from all suspicion of being mythical. Mr Poulter, it appeared, had been a conspicuous figure at Talavera, and had contributed not a little to the peculiar terror with which his regiment of infantry was regarded by the enemy.

On afternoons, when his memory was more stimulated than usual, he remembered that the Duke of Wellington had (in strict privacy, lest jealousies should be awakened) expressed his esteem for that fine fellow Poulter. The very surgeon who attended him in the hospital after he had received his gunshot wound, had been profoundly impressed with the superiority of Mr Poulter's flesh: no other flesh would have healed in anything like the same time. On less personal matters connected with the important warfare in which he had been engaged, Mr Poulter was more reticent, only taking care not to give the weight of his authority to any loose notions concerning military history. Anyone who pretended to a knowledge of what occurred at the siege of Badajos, was especially an object of silent pity to Mr Poulter; he wished that prating person had been run down, and had the breath trampled out of him at the first go-off, as he himself had – he might talk about the siege of Badajos then! Tom did not escape irritating his drilling-master occasionally, by his curiosity concerning other military matters than Mr Poulter's personal experience.

'And General Wolfe, Mr Poulter? wasn't he a wonderful fighter?' said Tom, who held the notion that all martial heroes commemorated in the public-house signs were engaged in the war with Bony.

'Not at all!' said Mr Poulter, contemptuously. 'Nothing o' the sort! . . . Heads up!' he added, in a tone of stern command, which delighted Tom, and made him feel as if he were a regiment in his own person.

'No, no!' Mr Poulter would continue, on coming to a pause in his discipline. 'They better not talk to me about General Wolfe. He did nothing but die of his wound; that's a poor haction, I consider. Any other man 'ud have died o' the wounds I've had . . . One of my sword-cuts 'ud ha' killed a fellow like General Wolfe.'

'Mr Poulter,' Tom would say, at any allusion to the sword, 'I wish you'd bring your sword and do the sword-exercise!'

For a long while Mr Poulter only shook his head in a significant manner at this request, and smiled patronisingly, as Jupiter may have done when Semele urged her too ambitious request. But one afternoon, when a sudden shower of heavy rain had detained Mr Poulter twenty minutes longer than usual at the Black Swan, the sword was brought – just for Tom to look at.

'And this is the real sword you fought with in all the battles, Mr Poulter?' said Tom, handling the hilt. 'Has it ever cut a Frenchman's head off?'

'Head off? Ah! and would, if he'd had three heads.'

'But you had a gun and bayonet besides?' said Tom. 'I should like the gun and bayonet best, because you could shoot 'em first and spear 'em after. Bang! Ps-s-s-s!' Tom gave the requisite pantomime to indicate the double enjoyment of pulling the trigger and thrusting the spear.

'Ah, but the sword's the thing when you come to close fighting,' said Mr Poulter, involuntarily falling in with Tom's enthusiasm, and drawing the sword so suddenly that Tom leaped back with much agility.

'Oh, but, Mr Poulter, if you're going to do the exercise,' said Tom, a little conscious that he had not stood his ground as became an Englishman, 'let me go and call Philip. He'll like to see you, you know.'

'What! the humpbacked lad?' said Mr Poulter, contemptuously. 'What's the use of his looking on?'

'O but he knows a great deal about fighting,' said Tom, 'and how they used to fight with bows and arrows, and battle-axes.'

'Let him come then. I'll show him something different from his bows and arrows,' said Mr Poulter, coughing, and drawing himself up, while he gave a little preliminary play to his wrist.

Tom ran in to Philip, who was enjoying his afternoon's holiday at the piano, in the drawing-room, picking out tunes for himself and singing them. He was supremely happy, perched like an amorphous bundle on the high stool, with his head thrown back, his eyes fixed on the opposite cornice, and his lips wide open, sending forth, with all his might, impromptu syllables to a tune of Arne's, which had hit his fancy.

'Come, Philip,' said Tom, bursting in; 'don't stay roaring "la la" there – come and see old Poulter do his sword-exercise in the carriage-house!'

The jar of this interruption – the discord of Tom's tones coming across the notes to which Philip was vibrating in soul and body, would have been enough to unhinge his temper, even if there had been no question of Poulter the drilling-master; and Tom, in the hurry of seizing something to say to prevent Mr Poulter from thinking he was afraid of the sword when he sprang away from it, had alighted on this proposition to fetch Philip – though he knew well enough that Philip hated to hear him mention his drilling-lessons. Tom would never have done so inconsiderate a thing except under the severe stress of his personal pride.

Philip shuddered visibly as he paused from his music. Then turning red, he said, with violent passion, 'Get away, you lumbering idiot! Don't come bellowing at me – you're not fit to speak to anything but a cart-horse!'

It was not the first time Philip had been made angry by him, but Tom had never before been assailed with verbal missiles that he understood so well.

'I'm fit to speak to something better than you – you poor-spirited imp!' said Tom, lighting up immediately at Philip's fire. 'You know I won't hit you, because you're no better than a girl. But I'm an honest man's son, and *your* father's a rogue – everybody says so!'

Tom flung out of the room, and slammed the door after him, made strangely heedless by his anger; for to slam doors within the hearing of Mrs Stelling, who was probably not far off, was an offence only to be wiped out by twenty lines of Virgil. In fact, that lady did presently descend from her room, in double wonder at the noise and the subsequent cessation of Philip's music. She found him sitting in a heap on the hassock, and crying bitterly.

'What's the matter, Wakem? What was that noise about? Who slammed the door?'

Philip looked up, and hastily dried his eyes. 'It was Tulliver who came in . . . to ask me to go out with him.'

'And what are you in trouble about?' said Mrs Stelling.

Philip was not her favourite of the two pupils; he was less obliging than Tom, who was made useful in many ways. Still his father paid more than Mr Tulliver did, and she meant him to feel that she behaved exceedingly well to him. Philip, however, met her advances towards a good understanding very much as a caressed mollusc meets an invitation to show himself out of his shell. Mrs Stelling was not a loving, tender-hearted woman: she was a woman whose skirt sat well, who adjusted her waist and patted her curls with a preoccupied air when she enquired after your welfare. These things, doubtless, represent a great social power, but it is not the power of love – and no other power could win Philip from his personal reserve.

He said, in answer to her question, 'My toothache came on, and made me hysterical again.'

This had been the fact once, and Philip was glad of the recollection – it was like an inspiration to enable him to excuse his crying. He had to accept eau-de-Cologne, and to refuse creosote in consequence: but that was easy.

Meanwhile Tom, who had for the first time sent a poisoned arrow into Philip's heart, had returned to the carriage-house, where he found Mr Poulter, with a fixed and earnest eye, wasting the perfections of his sword-exercise on probably observant but inappreciative rats. But Mr Poulter was a host in himself; that is to say, he admired himself more than a whole army of spectators could have admired him. He took no notice of Tom's return, being too entirely absorbed in the cut and thrust – the solemn one, two, three, four; and Tom, not without a slight feeling of alarm at Mr Poulter's fixed eye and hungry-looking sword, which seemed impatient for something else to cut besides the air, admired the performance from as great a distance as possible. It was not until Mr Poulter paused and wiped the perspiration from his forehead, that Tom felt the full charm of the sword-exercise, and wished it to be repeated.

'Mr Poulter,' said Tom, when the sword was being finally sheathed, 'I wish you'd lend me your sword a little while to keep.'

'No, no, young gentleman,' said Mr Poulter, shaking his head decidedly, 'you might do yourself some mischief with it.'

'No, I'm sure I wouldn't – I'm sure I'd take care and not hurt myself. I shouldn't take it out of the sheath much, but I could ground arms with it, and all that.'

'No, no, it won't do, I tell you; it won't do,' said Mr Poulter, preparing to depart. 'What 'ud Mr Stelling say to me?'

'Oh, I say, do, Mr Poulter! I'd give you my five-shilling piece if you'd let me keep the sword a week. Look here!' said Tom, reaching out the attractively large round of silver. The young dog calculated the effect as well as if he had been a philosopher.

'Well,' said Mr Poulter, with still deeper gravity, 'you must keep it out of sight, you know.'

'Oh, yes, I'll keep it under the bed,' said Tom, eagerly, 'or else at the bottom of my large box.'

'And let me see, now, whether you can draw it out of the sheath without hurting yourself.'

That process having been gone through more than once, Mr Poulter felt that he had acted with scrupulous conscientiousness, and said, 'Well, now, Master

Tulliver, if I take the crown-piece, it is to make sure as you'll do no mischief with the sword.'

'Oh, no, indeed, Mr Poulter,' said Tom, delightedly handing him the crown-piece, and grasping the sword, which, he thought, might have been lighter with advantage.

'But if Mr Stelling catches you carrying it?' said Mr Poulter, pocketing the crown-piece provisionally while he raised this new doubt.

'Oh, he always keeps in his upstairs study on Saturday afternoons,' said Tom, who disliked anything sneaking, but was not disinclined to a little stratagem in a worthy cause. So he carried off the sword in triumph, mixed with dread – dread that he might encounter Mr or Mrs Stelling – to his bedroom, where, after some consideration, he hid it in the closet behind some hanging clothes. That night he fell asleep in the thought that he would astonish Maggie with it when she came – tie it round his waist with his red comforter, and make her believe that the sword was his own, and that he was going to be a soldier. There was nobody but Maggie who would be silly enough to believe him, or whom he dared allow to know that he had a sword; and Maggie was really coming next week to see Tom, before she went to a boarding-school with Lucy.

If you think a lad of thirteen would not have been so childish, you must be an exceptionally wise man, who, although you are devoted to a civil calling, requiring you to look bland rather than formidable, yet never, since you had a beard, threw yourself into a martial attitude, and frowned before the looking-glass. It is doubtful whether our soldiers would be maintained if there were not pacific people at home who like to fancy themselves soldiers. War, like other dramatic spectacles, might possibly cease for want of a 'public'.

CHAPTER 5

Maggie's Second Visit

This last breach between the two lads was not readily mended, and for some time they spoke to each other no more than was necessary. Their natural anti-pathy of temperament made resentment an easy passage to hatred, and in Philip the transition seemed to have begun: there was no malignity in his disposition, but there was a susceptibility that made him peculiarly liable to a strong sense of repulsion. The ox – we may venture to assert it on the authority of a great classic – is not given to use his teeth as an instrument of attack; and Tom was an excellent bovine lad, who ran at questionable objects in a truly ingenuous bovine manner; but he had blundered on Philip's tenderest point, and had caused him as much acute pain as if he had studied the means with the nicest precision and the most envenomed spite. Tom saw no reason why they should not make up this quarrel as they had done many others, by behaving as if nothing had happened; for though he had never before said to Philip that his father was a rogue, this idea had so habitually made part of his feeling as to the relation between himself and his dubious schoolfellow, whom he could neither like nor dislike, that the mere utterance did not make such an epoch to him as it did to Philip. And he had a right to say so, when Philip hectored over *him*, and called him names. But perceiving that his first advances towards amity were not met, he relapsed into his least favourable disposition towards Philip, and resolved never to appeal to him either about drawing or exercises again. They were only so far civil to each other as was necessary to prevent their state of feud from being observed by Mr Stelling, who would have 'put down' such nonsense with great vigour.

When Maggie came, however, she could not help looking with growing interest at the new schoolfellow, although he was the son of that wicked Lawyer Wakem, who made her father so angry. She had arrived in the middle of school-hours, and had sat by while Philip went through his lessons with Mr Stelling. Tom, some weeks ago, had sent her word that Philip knew no end of stories – not stupid stories like hers; and she was convinced now from her own observation that he must be very clever: she hoped he would think *her* rather clever too, when she came to talk to him. Maggie, moreover, had rather a tenderness for deformed things; she preferred the wry-necked lambs, because it seemed to her that the lambs which were quite strong and well made wouldn't mind so much about being petted; and she was especially fond of petting objects that would think it very delightful to be petted by her. She loved Tom very dearly, but she often wished that he *cared* more about her loving him.

'I think Philip Wakem seems a nice boy, Tom,' she said, when they went out of the study together into the garden, to pass the interval before dinner. 'He couldn't choose his father, you know; and I've read of very bad men who had good sons, as well as good parents who had bad children. And if Philip is good, I think we ought to be the more sorry for him because his father is not a good man. *You* like him, don't you?'

'Oh, he's a queer fellow,' said Tom, curtly, 'and he's as sulky as can be with me, because I told him his father was a rogue. And I'd a right to tell him so, for it was true – and he began it, with calling me names. But you stop here by yourself a bit, Magsie, will you ? I've got something I want to do upstairs.'

'Can't I go too?' said Maggie, who, in this first day of meeting again, loved Tom's shadow.

'No, it's something I'll tell you about by and by – not yet,' said Tom, skipping away.

In the afternoon the boys were at their books in the study, preparing the morrow's lessons, that they might have a holiday in the evening in honour of Maggie's arrival. Tom was hanging over his Latin grammar, moving his lips inaudibly like a strict but impatient Catholic repeating his tale of paternosters; and Philip, at the other end of the room, was busy with two volumes, with a look of contented diligence that excited Maggie's curiosity; he did not look at all as if he were learning a lesson. She sat on a low stool at nearly a right angle with the two boys, watching first one and then the other; and Philip, looking off his book once towards the fireplace, caught the pair of questioning dark eyes fixed upon him. He thought this sister of Tulliver's seemed a nice little thing, quite unlike her brother; he wished *he* had a little sister. What was it, he wondered, that made Maggie's dark eyes remind him of the stories about princesses being turned into animals? . . . I think it was that her eyes were full of unsatisfied intelligence, and unsatisfied, beseeching affection.

'I say, Magsie,' said Tom at last, shutting his books and putting them away with the energy and decision of a perfect master in the art of leaving off, 'I've done my lessons now. Come upstairs with me.'

'What is it?' said Maggie, when they were outside the door, a slight suspicion crossing her mind as she remembered Tom's preliminary visit upstairs. 'It isn't a trick you're going to play me, now?'

'No, no, Maggie,' said Tom, in his most coaxing tone; 'it's something you'll like *ever so.*'

He put his arm round her neck, and she put hers round his waist, and, twined together in this way, they went upstairs.

'I say, Magsie, you must not tell anybody, you know,' said Tom, 'else I shall get fifty lines.'

'Is it alive?' said Maggie, whose imagination had settled for the moment on the idea that Tom kept a ferret clandestinely.

'Oh, I shan't tell you,' said he. 'Now you go into that corner and hide your face, while I reach it out,' he added, as he locked the bedroom door behind them. 'I'll tell you when to turn round. You mustn't squeal out, you know.'

'Oh, but if you frighten me, I shall,' said Maggie, beginning to look rather serious.

'You won't be frightened, you silly thing,' said Tom. 'Go and hide your face, and mind you don't peep.'

'Of course I shan't peep,' said Maggie, disdainfully; and she buried her face in the pillow like a person of strict honour.

But Torn looked round warily as he walked to the closet; then he stepped into the narrow space, and almost closed the door. Maggie kept her face buried without the aid of principle, for in that dream-suggestive attitude she had soon forgotten where she was, and her thoughts were busy with the poor deformed boy, who was so clever, when Tom called out, 'Now then, Magsie!'

Nothing but long meditation and preconcerted arrangement of effects could have enabled Tom to present so striking a figure as he did to Maggie when she looked up. Dissatisfied with the pacific aspect of a face which had no more than the faintest hint of flaxen eyebrow, together with a pair of amiable blue-grey eyes and round pink cheeks that refused to look formidable, let him frown as he would before the looking-glass – (Philip had once told him of a man who had a horseshoe frown, and Tom had tried with all his frowning-might to make a horseshoe on his forehead) – he had had recourse to that unfailing source of the terrible, burnt cork, and had made himself a pair of black eyebrows that met in a satisfactory manner over his nose, and were matched by a less carefully adjusted blackness about the chin. He had wound a red handkerchief round his cloth cap to give it the air of a turban, and his red comforter across his breast as a scarf – an amount of red which, with the tremendous frown on his brow, and the decision with which he grasped the sword, as he held it with its point resting on the ground, would suffice to convey an approximate idea of his fierce and blood-thirsty disposition.

Maggie looked bewildered for a moment, and Tom enjoyed that moment keenly; but in the next, she laughed, clapped her hands together, and said, 'Oh, Tom, you've made yourself like Bluebeard at the show.'

It was clear she had not been struck with the presence of the sword – it was not unsheathed. Her frivolous mind required a more direct appeal to its sense of the terrible, and Tom prepared for his master-stroke. Frowning with a double amount of intention, if not of corrugation, he (carefully) drew the sword from its sheath and pointed it at Maggie.

'Oh, Tom, please don't,' exclaimed Maggie, in a tone of suppressed dread, shrinking away From him into the opposite corner. 'I *shall* scream – I'm sure I shall! Oh, don't. I wish I'd never come upstairs!'

The corners of Tom's mouth showed an inclination to a smile of complacency that was immediately checked as inconsistent with the severity of a great warrior. Slowly he let down the scabbard on the floor, lest it should make too much noise, and then said, sternly, 'I'm the Duke of Wellington! March!' stamping forward with the right leg a little bent, and the sword still pointing towards Maggie, who, trembling, and with tear-filled eyes, got upon the bed, as the only means of widening the space between them.

Tom, happy in this spectator of his military performances, even though the spectator was only Maggie, proceeded, with the utmost exertion of his force, to such an exhibition of the cut and thrust as would necessarily be expected of the Duke of Wellington.

'Tom, I *will not* bear it – I *will* scream,' said Maggie, at the first movement of the sword. 'You'll hurt yourself; you'll cut your head off!'

'One – two,' said Tom, resolutely, though at 'two' his wrist trembled a little. 'Three,' came more slowly, and with it the sword swung downwards, and Maggie gave a loud shriek. The sword had fallen, with its edge on Tom's foot, and in a moment after, he had fallen too. Maggie leaped from the bed, still shrieking, and immediately there was a rush of footsteps towards the room. Mr Stelling, from his upstairs study, was the first to enter. He found both the children on the floor. Tom had fainted, and Maggie was shaking him by the collar of his jacket, screaming, with wild eyes. She thought he was dead, poor child! and yet she shook him, as if that would bring him back to life. In another minute she was sobbing with joy because Tom had opened his eyes: she couldn't sorrow yet that he had hurt his foot – it seemed as if all happiness lay in his being alive.

CHAPTER 6

A Love Scene

Poor Tom bore his severe pain heroically, and was resolute in not 'telling' of Mr Poulter more than was unavoidable: the five-shilling piece remained a secret even to Maggie. But there was a terrible dread weighing on his mind – so terrible that he dared not even ask the question which might bring the fatal 'yes' – he dared not ask the surgeon or Mr Stelling, 'Shall I be lame, sir?' He mastered himself so as not to cry out at the pain, but when his foot had been dressed, and he was left alone with Maggie seated by his bedside, the children sobbed together with their heads laid on the same pillow. Tom was thinking of himself walking about on crutches, like the wheelwright's son; and Maggie, who did not guess what was in his mind, sobbed for company. It had not occurred to the surgeon or to Mr Stelling to anticipate this dread in Tom's mind, and to reassure him by hopeful words. But Philip watched the surgeon out of the house, and waylaid Mr Stelling to ask the very question that Tom had not dared to ask for himself.

'I beg your pardon, sir – but does Mr Askern say Tulliver will be lame?'

'Oh no, oh no,' said Mr Stelling, 'not permanently, only for a little while.'

'Did he tell Tulliver so, sir, do you think?'

'No: nothing was said to him on the subject.'

'Then may I go and tell him, sir?'

'Yes, to be sure: now you mention it, I dare say he may be troubling about that. Go to his bedroom, but be very quiet at present.'

It had been Philip's first thought when he heard of the accident – 'Will Tulliver be lame? It will be very hard for him if he is' – and Tom's hitherto unforgiven offences were washed out by that pity. Philip felt that they were no longer in a state of repulsion, but were being drawn into a common current of suffering and sad privation. His imagination did not dwell on the outward calamity and its future effect on Tom's life, but it made vividly present to him the probable state of Tom's feelings: he had only lived fourteen years, but those years had, most of them, been steeped in the sense of a lot irremediably hard.

'Mr Askern says you'll soon be all right again, Tulliver, did you know?' he said, rather timidly, as he stepped gently up to Tom's bed. 'I've just been to ask Mr Stelling, and he says you'll walk as well as ever again, by and by.'

Tom looked up with that momentary stopping of the breath which comes with a sudden joy; then he gave a long sigh, and turned his blue-grey eyes straight on Philip's face, as he had not done for a fortnight or more. As for Maggie, this intimation of a possibility she had not thought of before, affected her as a new trouble; the bare idea of Tom's being always lame overpowered the assurance that such a misfortune was not likely to befall him, and she clung to him and cried afresh.

'Don't be a little silly, Magsie,' said Tom, tenderly, feeling very brave now. 'I shall soon get well.'

'Goodbye, Tulliver,' said Philip, putting out his small, delicate hand, which Tom clasped immediately with his more substantial fingers.

'I say,' said Tom, 'ask Mr Stelling to let you come and sit with me sometimes, till I get up again, Wakem – and tell me about Robert Bruce, you know.'

After that, Philip spent all his time out of school-hours with Tom and Maggie. Tom liked to hear fighting stories as much as ever, but he insisted strongly on the fact that those great fighters, who did so many wonderful things and came off unhurt, wore excellent armour from head to foot, which made fighting easy work, he considered. He should not have hurt his foot if he had had an iron shoe on. He listened with great interest to a new story of Philip's about a man who had a very bad wound in his foot, and cried out so dreadfully with the pain that his friends could bear with him no longer, but put him ashore on a desert island, with nothing but some wonderful poisoned arrows to kill animals with for food.

'I didn't roar out a bit, you know,' Tom said, 'and I dare say my foot was as bad as his. It's cowardly to roar.'

But Maggie would have it that when anything hurt you very much, it was quite permissible to cry out, and it was cruel of people not to bear it. She wanted to know if Philoctetes had a sister, and why *she* didn't go with him on the desert island and take care of him.

One day, soon after Philip had told this story, he and Maggie were in the study alone together while Tom's foot was being dressed. Philip was at his books, and Maggie, after sauntering idly round the room, not caring to do anything in particular, because she would soon go to Tom again, went and leaned on the table near Philip to see what he was doing, for they were quite old friends now, and perfectly at home with each other.

'What are you reading about in Greek?' she said. 'It's poetry – I can see that, because the lines are so short.'

'It's about Philoctetes – the lame man I was telling you of yesterday,' he answered, resting his head on his hand, and looking at her, as if he were not at all sorry to be interrupted. Maggie, in her absent way, continued to lean forward, resting on her arms and moving her feet about, while her dark eyes got more and more fixed and vacant, as if she had quite forgotten Philip and his book.

'Maggie,' said Philip, after a minute or two, still leaning on his elbow and looking at her, 'if you had had a brother like me, do you think you should have loved him as well as Tom?'

Maggie started a little on being roused from her reverie, and said, 'What?' Philip repeated his question.

'O yes, better,' she answered, immediately. 'No, not better; because I don't think I *could* love you better than Tom. But I should be so sorry – *so sorry* for you.'

Philip coloured: he had meant to imply, would she love him as well in spite of his deformity, and yet when she alluded to it so plainly, he winced under her pity. Maggie, young as she was, felt her mistake. Hitherto she had instinctively behaved as if she were quite unconscious of Philip's deformity: her own keen sensitiveness and experience under family criticism sufficed to teach her this as well as if she had been directed by the most finished breeding.

'But you are so very clever, Philip, and you can play and sing,' she added, quickly. 'I wish you *were* my brother. I'm very fond of you. And you would stay at home with me when Tom went out, and you would teach me everything – wouldn't you ? Greek and everything?'

'But you'll go away soon, and go to school, Maggie,' said Philip, 'and then you'll forget all about me, and not care for me any more. And then I shall see you when you're grown up, and you'll hardly take any notice of me.'

'O no, I shan't forget you, I'm sure,' said Maggie, shaking her head very seriously. 'I never forget anything, and I think about everybody when I'm away from them. I think about poor Yap – he's got a lump in his throat, and Luke says he'll die. Only don't you tell Tom, because it will vex him so. You never saw Yap: he's a queer little dog – nobody cares about him but Tom and me.'

'Do you care as much about me as you do about Yap, Maggie?' said Philip, smiling rather sadly.

'Oh, yes, I should think so,' said Maggie, laughing.

'I'm very fond of *you*, Maggie; I shall never forget *you*,' said Philip, 'and when I'm very unhappy, I shall always think of you, and wish I had a sister with dark eyes, just like yours.'

'Why do you like my eyes?' said Maggie, well pleased. She had never heard anyone but her father speak of her eyes as if they had merit.

'I don't know,' said Philip. 'They're not like any other eyes. They seem trying to speak – trying to speak kindly. I don't like other people to look at me much, but I like you to look at me, Maggie.'

'Why, I think you're fonder of me than Tom is,' said Maggie, rather sorrowfully. Then, wondering how she could convince Philip that she could like him just as well, although he was crooked, she said,

'Should you like me to kiss you, as I do Tom? I will, if you like.'

'Yes, very much: nobody kisses me.'

Maggie put her arm round his neck and kissed him quite earnestly.

'There now,' she said, 'I shall always remember you, and kiss you when I see you again, if it's ever so long. But I'll go now, because I think Mr Askern's done with Tom's foot.'

When their father came the second time, Maggie said to him, 'Oh, father, Philip Wakem is so very good to Tom – he is such a clever boy, and I *do* love him. And you love him too, Tom, don't you! *Say* you love him,' she added, entreatingly.

Tom coloured a little as he looked at his father, and said, 'I shan't be friends with him when I leave school, father; but we've made it up now, since my foot has been bad, and he's taught me to play at draughts, and I can beat him.'

'Well, well,' said Mr Tulliver, 'if he's good to you, try and make him amends, and be good to *him*. He's a poor crooked creatur, and takes after his dead mother. But don't you be getting too thick with him – he's got his father's blood in him too. Ay, ay, the grey colt may chance to kick like his black sire.'

The jarring natures of the two boys effected what Mr Tulliver's admonition alone might have failed to effect: in spite of Philip's new kindness, and Tom's answering regard in this time of his trouble, they never became close friends. When Maggie was gone, and when Tom by and by began to walk about as usual, the friendly warmth that had been kindled by pity and gratitude died out by degrees, and left them in their old relation to each other. Philip was often peevish and contemptuous; and Tom's more specific and kindly impressions gradually melted into the old background of suspicion and dislike towards him as a queer fellow, a humpback, and the son of a rogue. If boys and men are to be welded together in the glow of transient feeling, they must be made of metal that will mix, else they inevitably fall asunder when the heat dies out.

CHAPTER 7

The Golden Gates are Passed

So Tom went on even to the fifth half-year – till he was turned sixteen – at King's Lorton, while Maggie was growing, with a rapidity which her aunts considered highly reprehensible, at Miss Firniss's boarding-school in the ancient town of Laceham on the Floss, with cousin Lucy for her companion. In her early letters to Tom she had always sent her love to Philip, and asked many questions about him, which were answered by brief sentences about Tom's toothache, and a turf-house which he was helping to build in the garden, with other items of that kind. She was pained to hear Tom say in the holidays that Philip was as queer as ever again, and often cross: they were no longer very good friends, she perceived; and when she reminded Tom that he ought always to love Philip for being so good to him when his foot was bad, he answered, 'Well, it isn't my fault: *I* don't do anything to him.' She hardly ever saw Philip during the remainder of their school-life; in the Midsummer holidays he was always away at the seaside, and at Christmas she could only meet him at long intervals in the streets of St Ogg's. When they did meet, she remembered her promise to kiss him, but, as a young lady who had been at a boarding-school, she knew now that such a greeting was out of the question, and Philip would not expect it. This promise was void, like so many other sweet, illusory promises of our childhood; void as promises made in Eden before the seasons were divided, and when the starry blossoms grew side by side with the ripening peach – impossible to be fulfilled when the golden gates had been passed.

But when their father was actually engaged in the long-threatened lawsuit, and Wakem, as the agent at once of Pivart and Old Harry, was acting against him, even Maggie felt, with some sadness, that they were not likely ever to have any intimacy with Philip again: the very name of Wakem made her father angry, and she had once heard him say, that if that crook-backed son lived to inherit his father's ill-gotten gains, there would be a curse upon him. 'Have as little to do with him at school as you can, my lad,' he said to Tom; and the command was obeyed the more easily because Mr Stelling by this time had two additional pupils; for though this gentleman's rise in the world was not of that meteor-like rapidity which the admirers of his extemporaneous eloquence had expected for a preacher whose voice demanded so wide a sphere, he had yet enough of growing prosperity to enable him to increase his expenditure in continued disproportion to his income.

As for Tom's school course, it went on with mill-like monotony, his mind continuing to move with a slow, half-stifled pulse in a medium of uninteresting or unintelligible ideas. But each vacation he brought home larger and larger drawings with the satiny rendering of landscape, and watercolours in vivid greens, together with manuscript books full of exercises and problems, in which the handwriting was all the finer because he gave his whole mind to it. Each vacation he brought home a new book or two, indicating his progress through different stages of history, Christian doctrine, and Latin literature; and that passage was not entirely without result, besides the possession of the books. Tom's ear and tongue had become accustomed to a great many words and phrases which are understood to be signs of an educated condition; and though he had never really applied his mind to any one of his lessons, the lessons had left a deposit of vague, fragmentary, ineffectual notions. Mr Tulliver, seeing signs of acquirement beyond the reach of his own criticism, thought it was probably all right with Tom's education: he observed, indeed, that there were no maps, and not enough 'summing'; but he made no formal complaint to Mr Stelling. It was a puzzling business, this schooling; and if he took Tom away, where could he send him with better effect?

By the time Tom had reached his last quarter at King's Lorton, the years had made striking changes in him since the day we saw him returning from Mr Jacobs's academy. He was a tall youth now, carrying himself without the least awkwardness, and speaking without more shyness than was a becoming symptom of blended diffidence and pride: he wore his tail-coat and his stand-up collars, and watched the down on his lip with eager impatience, looking every day at his virgin razor, with which he had provided himself in the last holidays. Philip had already left – at the autumn quarter – that he might go to the south for the winter, for the sake of his health; and this change helped to give Tom the unsettled, exultant feeling that usually belongs to the last months before leaving school. This quarter, too, there was some hope of his father's lawsuit being decided: *that* made the prospect of home more entirely pleasurable. For Tom, who had gathered his view of the case from his father's conversation, had no doubt that Pivart would be beaten.

Tom had not heard anything from home for some weeks – a fact which did not surprise him, for his father and mother were not apt to manifest their affection in unnecessary letters – when, to his great surprise, on the morning of a dark cold day near the end of November, he was told, soon after entering the study at nine o'clock, that his sister was in the drawing-room. It was Mrs Stelling who had come into the study to tell him, and she left him to enter the drawing-room alone.

Maggie, too, was tall now, with braided and coiled hair: she was almost as tall as Tom, though she was only thirteen; and she really looked older than he did at that moment. She had thrown off her bonnet, her heavy braids were pushed back from her forehead, as if it would not bear that extra load, and her young face had a strangely worn look, as her eyes turned anxiously towards the door. When Tom entered she did not speak, but only went up to him, put her arms round his neck, and kissed him earnestly. He was used to various moods of hers, and felt no alarm at the unusual seriousness of her greeting.

'Why, how is it you're come so early this cold morning, Maggie? Did you come in the gig?' said Tom, as she backed towards the sofa, and drew him to her side.

'No, I came by the coach. I've walked from the turnpike.'

'But how is it you're not at school? The holidays have not begun yet?'

'Father wanted me at home,' said Maggie, with a slight trembling of the lip. 'I came home three or four days ago.'

'Isn't my father well?' said Tom, rather anxiously.

'Not quite,' said Maggie. 'He's very unhappy, Tom. The lawsuit is ended, and I came to tell you, because I thought it would be better for you to know it before you came home, and I didn't like only to send you a letter.'

'My father hasn't lost?' said Tom, hastily, springing from the sofa, and standing before Maggie with his hands suddenly thrust in his pockets.

'Yes, dear Tom,' said Maggie, looking up at him with trembling.

Tom was silent a minute or two, with his eyes fixed on the floor. Then he said, 'My father will have to pay a good deal of money, then?'

'Yes,' said Maggie, rather faintly.

'Well, it can't be helped,' said Tom, bravely, not translating the loss of a large sum of money into any tangible results. 'But my father's very much vexed, I dare say?' he added, looking at Maggie, and thinking that her agitated face was only part of her girlish way of taking things.

'Yes,' said Maggie, again faintly. Then, urged to fuller speech by Tom's freedom from apprehension, she said loudly and rapidly, as if the words *would* burst from her, 'Oh, Tom, he will lose the mill and the land, and everything; he will have nothing left.'

Tom's eyes flashed out one look of surprise at her, before he turned pale, and trembled visibly. He said nothing, but sat down on the sofa again, looking vaguely out of the opposite window.

Anxiety about the future had never entered Tom's mind. His father had always ridden a good horse, kept a good house, and had the cheerful, confident air of a man who has plenty of property to fall back upon. Tom had never dreamed that his father would 'fail'; *that* was a form of misfortune which he had always heard spoken of as a deep disgrace, and disgrace was an idea that he could not associate with any of his relations, least of all with his father. A proud sense of family respectability was part of the very air Tom had been born and brought up in. He knew there were people in St Ogg's who made a show without money to support it, and he had always heard such people spoken of by his own friends with contempt and reprobation. He had a strong belief, which was a life-long habit, and required no definite evidence to rest on, that his father could spend a great deal of money if he chose; and since his education at Mr Stelling's had given him a more expensive view of life, he had often thought that when he got older he would make a figure in the world with his horse and dogs and saddle, and other accoutrements of a fine young man, and show himself equal to any of his contemporaries at St Ogg's, who might consider themselves a grade above him in society, because their fathers were professional men, or had large oil-mills. As to the prognostics and head shaking of his aunts and uncles, they had never produced the least effect on him, except to make him think that aunts and uncles were disagreeable society: he had heard them find fault in much the same way as long as he could remember. His father knew better than they did.

The down had come on Tom's lip, yet his thoughts and expectations had been hitherto only the reproduction, in changed forms, of the boyish dreams in which he had lived three years ago. He was awakened now with a violent shock.

Maggie was frightened at Tom's pale, trembling silence. There was some-thing else to tell him – something worse. She threw her arms round him at last, with a half sob, 'Oh, Tom – dear, dear Tom, don't fret too much – try and bear it well.'

Tom turned his cheek passively to meet her entreating kisses, and there gathered a moisture in his eyes, which he just rubbed away with his hand. The action seemed to rouse him, for he shook himself and said, 'I shall go home with you, Maggie. Didn't my father say I was to go?'

'No, Tom, father didn't wish it,' said Maggie, her anxiety about his feeling helping her to master her agitation. What *would* he do when she told him all? 'But mother wants you to come – poor mother! – she cries so. Oh, Tom, it's very dreadful at home.'

Maggie's lips grew whiter, and she began to tremble almost as Tom had done. The two poor things clung closer to each other – both trembling – the one at an unshapen fear, the other at the image of a terrible certainty. When Maggie spoke, it was hardly above a whisper.

'And . . . and . . . poor father . . . '

Maggie could not utter it. But the suspense was intolerable to Tom. A vague idea of going to prison, as a consequence of debt, was the shape his fears had begun to take.

'Where's my father?' he said, impatiently. '*Tell* me, Maggie.'

'He's at home,' said Maggie, finding it easier to reply to that question. 'But,' she added, after a pause, 'not himself . . . He fell off his horse . . . He has known nobody but me ever since . . . He seems to have lost his senses . . . O, father, father . . . '

With these last words, Maggie's sobs burst forth with the more violence for the previous struggle against them. Tom felt that pressure of the heart which forbids tears: he had no distinct vision of their troubles as Maggie had, who had been at home; he only felt the crushing weight of what seemed unmitigated misfortune. He tightened his arm almost convulsively round Maggie as she sobbed, but his face looked rigid and tearless – his eyes blank – as if a black curtain of cloud had suddenly fallen on his path.

But Maggie soon checked herself abruptly: a single thought had acted on her like a startling sound.

'We must set out, Tom – we must not stay – father will miss me – we must be at the turnpike at ten to meet the coach.' She said this with hasty decision, rubbing her eyes, and rising to seize her bonnet.

Tom at once felt the same impulse, and rose too. 'Wait a minute, Maggie,' he said. 'I must speak to Mr Stelling, and then we'll go.'

He thought he must go to the study where the pupils were, but on his way he met Mr Stelling, who had heard from his wife that Maggie appeared to be in trouble when she asked for her brother; and, now that he thought the brother and sister had been alone long enough, was coming to enquire and offer his sympathy.

'Please, sir, I must go home,' Tom said, abruptly, as he met Mr Stelling in the passage. 'I must go back with my sister directly. My father's lost his lawsuit – he's lost all his property – and he's very ill.'

Mr Stelling felt like a kind-hearted man; he foresaw a probable money loss for himself, but this had no appreciable share in his feeling, while he looked with grave pity at the brother and sister for whom youth and sorrow had begun together. When he knew how Maggie had come, and how eager she was to get home again, he hurried their departure, only whispering something to Mrs Stelling, who had followed him, and who immediately left the room.

Tom and Maggie were standing on the doorstep, ready to set out, when Mrs Stelling came with a little basket, which she hung on Maggie's arm, saying, 'Do remember to eat something on the way, dear.' Maggie's heart went out towards this woman whom she had never liked, and she kissed her silently. It was the first sign within the poor child of that new sense which is the gift of sorrow – that susceptibility to the bare offices of humanity which raises them into a bond of loving fellowship, as to haggard men among the icebergs the mere presence of an ordinary comrade stirs the deep fountains of affection.

Mr Stelling put his hand on Tom's shoulder and said, 'God bless you, my boy: let me know how you get on.' Then he pressed Maggie's hand; but there were no audible goodbyes. Tom had so often thought how joyful he should be the day he left school 'for good!' And now his school years seemed like a holiday that had come to an end.

The two slight youthful figures soon grew indistinct on the distant road – were soon lost behind the projecting hedgerow.

They had gone forth together into their new life of sorrow, and they would never more see the sunshine undimmed by remembered cares. They had entered the thorny wilderness, and the golden gates of their childhood had for ever closed behind them.

BOOK THIRD

The Downfall

CHAPTER I

What Had Happened at Home

When Mr Tulliver first knew the fact that the lawsuit was decided against him, and that Pivart and Wakem were triumphant, everyone who happened to observe him at the time thought that, for so confident and hot-tempered a man, he bore the blow remarkably well. He thought so himself: he thought he was going to show that if Wakem or anybody else considered him crushed, they would find themselves mistaken. He could not refuse to see that the costs of this protracted suit would take more than he possessed to pay them; but he appeared to himself to be full of expedients by which he could ward off any results but such as were tolerable, and could avoid the appearance of breaking down in the world. All the obstinacy and defiance of his nature, driven out of their old channel, found a vent for themselves in the immediate formation of plans by which he would meet his difficulties, and remain Mr Tulliver of Dorlcote Mill in spite of them. There was such a rush of projects in his brain, that it was no wonder his face was flushed when he came away from his talk with his attorney, Mr Gore, and mounted his horse to ride home from Lindum. There was Furley, who held the mortgage on the land – a reasonable fellow, who would see his own interest, Mr Tulliver was convinced, and would be glad not only to purchase the whole estate, including the mill and homestead, but would accept Mr Tulliver as tenant, and be willing to advance money to be repaid with high interest out of the profits of the business, which would be made over to him, Mr Tulliver only taking enough barely to maintain himself and his family. Who would neglect such a profitable investment? Certainly not Furley, for Mr Tulliver had determined that Furley should meet his plans with the utmost alacrity; and there are men whose brains have not yet been dangerously heated by the loss of a lawsuit who are apt to see in their own interest or desires a motive for other men's actions. There was no doubt (in the miller's mind) that Furley would do just what was desirable; and if he did – why, things would not be so very much worse. Mr Tulliver and his family must live more meagrely and humbly, but it would only be till the profits of the business had paid off Furley's advances, and that might be while Mr Tulliver had still a good many years of life before him. It was clear that the costs of the suit could be paid without his being obliged to turn out of his old place, and look like a ruined man. It was certainly an awkward moment in his affairs. There was that suretyship for poor Riley, who had died suddenly last April, and left his friend saddled with a debt of two hundred and fifty pounds – a fact which had helped to make Mr Tulliver's banking book less pleasant reading than a man might desire towards Christmas. Well! he had never been one of those poor-spirited sneaks who would refuse to give a helping hand to a fellow-traveller in this puzzling world. The really vexatious business was the fact that some months ago the creditor who had lent him the five hundred pounds to repay Mrs Glegg, had become uneasy about his money (set on by Wakem, of course), and Mr Tulliver, still confident that he should gain his suit, and finding it eminently inconvenient to raise the said sum until that desirable issue had taken place, had rashly acceded to the demand that he should give a bill of sale on his household furniture, and some other effects, as security in lieu of the bond. It was all one, he had said to himself: he should soon pay off the money, and there was no harm in giving that security any more than another. But now the consequences of this bill of sale occurred to him in a new light, and he remembered that the time was close at hand, when it would be enforced unless the money were repaid. Two months ago he would have declared stoutly that he would never be beholden to his wife's friends; but now he told himself as stoutly that it was nothing but right and natural that Bessy should go to the Pullets and explain the thing to them: they would hardly let Bessy's furniture be sold, and it might be security to Pullet if he advanced the money – there would, after all, be no gift or favour in the matter. Mr Tulliver would never have asked for anything from so poor-spirited a fellow for himself, but Bessy might do so if she liked.

It is precisely the proudest and most obstinate men who are the most liable to shift their position and contradict themselves in this sudden manner: everything is easier to them than to face the simple fact that they have been thoroughly defeated, and must begin life anew. And Mr Tulliver, you perceive, though nothing more than a superior miller and maltster, was as proud and obstinate as if he had been a very lofty personage, in whom such dispositions might be a source of that conspicuous, far-echoing tragedy, which sweeps the stage in regal robes and makes the dullest chronicler sublime. The pride and obstinacy of millers, and other insignificant people, whom you pass unnoticingly on the road every day, have their tragedy too; but it is of that unwept, hidden sort, that goes on from generation to generation, and leaves no record – such tragedy, perhaps, as lies in the conflicts of young souls, hungry for joy, under a lot made suddenly hard to them, under the dreariness of a home where the morning brings no promise with it, and where the unexpectant discontent of worn and disappointed parents weighs on the children like a damp, thick air, in which all the functions of life are depressed; or such tragedy as lies in the slow or sudden death that follows on a bruised passion, though it may be a death that finds only a parish funeral. There are certain animals to which tenacity of position is a law of life – they can never flourish again, after a single wrench: and there are certain human beings to whom predominance is a law of life – they can only sustain humiliation so long as they can refuse to believe in it, and, in their own conception, predominate still.

Mr Tulliver was still predominating in his own imagination as he approached St Ogg's, through which he had to pass on his way homeward. But what was it that suggested to him, as he saw the Laceham coach entering the town, to follow it to the coach-office, and get the clerk there to write a letter, requiring Maggie to come home the very next day? Mr Tulliver's own hand shook too much under his excitement for him to write himself, and he wanted the letter to be given to the coachman to deliver at Miss Firniss's school in the morning. There was a craving which he would not account for to himself, to have Maggie near him – without delay – she must come back by the coach tomorrow.

To Mrs Tulliver, when he got home, he would admit no difficulties, and scolded down her burst of grief on hearing that the lawsuit was lost, by angry assertions that there was nothing to grieve about. He said nothing to her that night about the bill of sale, and the application to Mrs Pullet, for he had kept her in ignorance of the nature of that transaction, and had explained the necessity for taking an inventory of the goods as a matter connected with his will. The possession of a wife conspicuously one's inferior in intellect, is, like other high privileges, attended with a few inconveniences, and, among the rest, with the occasional necessity for using a little deception.

The next day Mr Tulliver was again on horseback in the afternoon, on his way to Mr Gore's office at St Ogg's. Gore was to have seen Furley in the morning, and to have sounded him in relation to Mr Tulliver's affairs. But he had not gone halfway when he met a clerk from Mr Gore's office, who was bringing a letter to Mr Tulliver. Mr Gore had been prevented by a sudden call of business from waiting at his office to see Mr Tulliver, according to appointment, but would be at his office at eleven tomorrow morning, and meanwhile had sent some important information by letter.

'Oh!' said Mr Tulliver, taking the letter, but not opening it. 'Then tell Gore I'll see him tomorrow at eleven;' and he turned his horse.

The clerk, struck with Mr Tulliver's glistening excited glance looked after him for a few moments, and then rode away. The reading of a letter was not the affair of an instant to Mr Tulliver; he took in the sense of a statement very slowly through the medium of written or even printed characters; so he had put the letter in his pocket, thinking he would open it in his armchair at home. But by and by it occurred to him that there might be something in the letter Mrs Tulliver must not know about, and if so, it would be better to keep it out of her sight altogether. He stopped his horse, took out the letter, and read it. It was only a short letter; the substance was, that Mr Gore had ascertained, on secret but sure authority, that Furley had been lately much straitened for money, and had parted with his securities – among the rest, the mortgage on Mr Tulliver's property, which he had transferred to – Wakem.

In half an hour after this, Mr Tulliver's own waggoner found him lying by the roadside insensible, with an open letter near him, and his grey horse snuffing uneasily about him.

When Maggie reached home that evening, in obedience to her father's call, he was no longer insensible. About an hour before, he had become conscious, and after vague, vacant looks around him, had muttered something about 'a letter,' which he presently repeated impatiently. At the instance of Mr Turnbull, the medical man, Gore's letter was brought and laid on the bed, and the previous impatience seemed to be allayed. The stricken man lay for some time with his eyes fixed on the letter, as if he were trying to knit up his thoughts by its help. But presently a new wave of memory seemed to have come and swept the other away; he turned his eyes from the letter to the door, and after looking uneasily, as if striving to see something his eyes were too dim for, he said, 'The little wench.'

He repeated the words impatiently from time to time, appearing entirely unconscious of everything except this one importunate want, and giving no sign of knowing his wife or anyone else; and poor Mrs Tulliver, her feeble faculties almost paralysed by this sudden accumulation of troubles, went backwards and forwards to the gate to see if the Laceham coach were coming, though it was not yet time.

But it came at last, and set down the poor anxious girl, no longer the 'little wench,' except to her father's fond memory.

'Oh, mother, what is the matter?' Maggie said, with pale lips, as her mother came towards her crying. She didn't think her father was ill, because the letter had come at his dictation from the office at St Ogg's.

But Mr Turnbull came now to meet her: a medical man is the good angel of the troubled house, and Maggie ran towards the kind old friend, whom she remembered as long as she could remember anything, with a trembling, questioning look.

'Don't alarm yourself too much, my dear,' he said, taking her hand. 'Your father has had a sudden attack, and has not quite recovered his memory. But he has been asking for you, and it will do him good to see you. Keep as quiet as you can; take off your things, and come upstairs with me.'

Maggie obeyed, with that terrible beating of the heart which makes existence seem simply a painful pulsation. The very quietness with which Mr Turnbull spoke had frightened her susceptible imagination. Her father's eyes were still turned uneasily towards the door when she entered and met the strange, yearning, helpless look that had been seeking her in vain. With a sudden flash and movement, he raised himself in the bed – she rushed towards him, and clasped him with agonised kisses.

Poor child! it was very early for her to know one of those supreme moments in life when all we have hoped or delighted in, all we can dread or endure, falls away from our regard as insignificant – is lost, like a trivial memory, in that simple, primitive love which knits us to the beings who have been nearest to us, in their times of helplessness or of anguish.

But that flash of recognition had been too great a strain on the father's bruised, enfeebled powers. He sank back again in renewed insensibility and rigidity, which lasted for many hours, and was only broken by a flickering return of consciousness, in which he took passively everything that was given to him, and seemed to have a sort of infantine satisfaction in Maggie's near presence – such satisfaction as a baby has when it is returned to the nurse's lap.

Mrs Tulliver sent for her sisters, and there was much wailing and lifting up of hands below stairs: both uncles and aunts saw that the ruin of Bessy and her family was as complete as they had ever foreboded it, and there was a general family sense that a judgement had fallen on Mr Tulliver, which it would be an impiety to counteract by too much kindness. But Maggie heard little of this, scarcely ever leaving her father's bedside, where she sat opposite him with her hand on his. Mrs Tulliver wanted to have Tom fetched home, and seemed to be thinking more of her boy even than of her husband; but the aunts and uncles opposed this. Tom was better at school, since Mr Turnbull said there was no immediate danger, he believed. But at the end of the second day, when Maggie had become more accustomed to her father's fits of insensibility, and to the expectation that he would revive from them, the thought of Tom had become urgent with *her* too; and when her mother sat crying at night and saying, 'My poor lad . . . it's nothing but right he should come home.' Maggie said, 'Let me go for him, and tell him, mother: I'll go tomorrow morning if father doesn't know me and want me. It would be so hard for Tom to come home and not know anything about it beforehand.'

And the next morning Maggie went, as we have seen. Sitting on the coach on their way home, the brother and sister talked to each other in sad, interrupted whispers.

'They say Mr Wakem has got a mortgage or something on the land, Tom,' said Maggie. 'It was the letter with that news in it that made father ill, they think.'

'I believe that scoundrel's been planning all along to ruin my father,' said Tom, leaping from the vaguest impressions to a definite conclusion. 'I'll make him feel for it when I'm a man. Mind you never speak to Philip again.'

'Oh, Tom!' said Maggie, in a tone of sad remonstrance; but she had no spirit to dispute anything then, still less to vex Tom by opposing him.

CHAPTER 2

Mrs Tulliver's Teraphim, or Household Gods

When the coach set down Tom and Maggie, it was five hours since she had started from home, and she was thinking with some trembling that her father had perhaps missed her, and asked for 'the little wench' in vain. She thought of no other change that might have happened.

She hurried along the gravel-walk and entered the house before Tom; but in the entrance she was startled by a strong smell of tobacco. The parlour door was ajar – that was where the smell came from. It was very strange: could any visitor be smoking at a time like this? Was her mother there? If so she must be told that Tom was come. Maggie, after this pause of surprise, was only in the act of opening the door when Tom came up, and they both looked into the parlour together. There was a coarse, dingy man, of whose face Tom had some vague recollection, sitting in his father's chair, smoking, with a jug and glass beside him.

The truth flashed on Tom's mind in an instant. To 'have the bailiff in the house', and 'to be sold up', were phrases which he had been used to, even as a little boy: they were part of the disgrace and misery of 'failing', of losing all one's money, and being ruined – sinking into the condition of poor working people. It seemed only natural this should happen, since his father had lost all his property, and he thought of no more special cause for this particular form of misfortune than the loss of the lawsuit. But the immediate presence of this disgrace was so much keener an experience to Tom than the worst form of apprehension, that he felt at this moment as if his real trouble had only just begun: it was a touch on the irritated nerve compared with its spontaneous dull aching.

'How do you do, sir?' said the man, taking the pipe out of his mouth, with rough, embarrassed civility. The two young startled faces made him a little uncomfortable.

But Tom turned away hastily without speaking: the sight was too hateful. Maggie had not understood the appearance of this stranger, as Tom had. She followed him, whispering, 'Who can it be, Tom? – what is the matter?' Then, with a sudden undefined dread lest this stranger might have something to do with a change in her father, she rushed upstairs, checking herself at the bedroom door to throw off her bonnet, and enter on tiptoe. All was silent there: her father was lying, heedless of everything around him, with his eyes closed as when she had left him. A servant was there, but not her mother.

'Where's my mother?' she whispered. The servant did not know.

Maggie hastened out, and said to Tom, 'Father is lying quiet: let us go and look for my mother. I wonder where she is.'

Mrs Tulliver was not downstairs – not in any of the bedrooms. There was but one room below the attic which Maggie had left unsearched: it was the storeroom, where her mother kept all her linen and all the precious 'best things' that were only unwrapped and brought out on special occasions. Tom, preceding Maggie as they returned along the passage, opened the door of this room, and immediately said, 'Mother!'

Mrs Tulliver was seated there with all her laid-up treasures. One of the linen-chests was open: the silver teapot was unwrapped from its many folds of paper, and the best china was laid out on the top of the closed linen-chest; spoons and skewers and ladles were spread in rows on the shelves; and the poor woman was shaking her head and weeping, with a bitter tension of the mouth, over the mark, 'Elizabeth Dodson,' on the corner of some tablecloths she held in her lap.

She dropped them, and started up as Tom spoke.

'O my boy, my boy!' she said, clasping him round the neck. 'To think as I should live to see this day! We're ruined . . . everything's going to be sold up . . . to think as your father should ha' married me to bring me to this! We've got nothing . . . we shall be beggars . . . we must go to the work-house . . .

She kissed him, then seated herself again, and took another tablecloth on her lap, unfolding it a little way to look at the pattern, while the children stood by in mute wretchedness – their minds quite filled for the moment with the words 'beggars' and 'workhouse.'

'To think o' these cloths as I spun myself,' she went on, lifting things out and turning them over with an excitement all the more strange and piteous because the stout blond woman was usually so passive: if she had been ruffled before, it was at the surface merely: 'and Job Haxey wove 'em, and brought the piece home on his back, as I remember standing at the door and seeing him come, before I ever thought o' marrying your father! And the pattern as I chose myself – and bleached so beautiful, and I marked 'em so as nobody ever saw such marking – they must cut the cloth to get it out, for it's a particular stitch. And they're all to be sold – and go into strange people's houses, and perhaps be cut with the knives, and wore out before I'm dead. You'll never have one of 'em, my boy,' she said, looking up at Tom with her eyes full of tears, 'and I meant 'em for you. I wanted you to have all o' this pattern. Maggie could have had the large check – it never shows so well when the dishes are on it.'

Tom was touched to the quick, but there was an angry reaction immediately. His face flushed as he said, 'But will my aunts let them be sold, mother? Do they know about it? They'll never let your linen go, will they? Haven't you sent to them?'

'Yes, I sent Luke directly they'd put the bailies in, and your aunt Pullet's been – and, oh dear, oh dear, she cries so, and says your father's disgraced my family and made it the talk o' the country; and she'll buy the spotted cloths for herself, because she's never had so many as she wanted o' that pattern, and they shan't go to strangers, but she's got more checks a'ready nor she can do with.' (Here Mrs Tulliver began to lay back the tablecloths in the chest, folding and stroking them automatically.) 'And your uncle Glegg's been too, and he says things must be bought in for us to lie down on, but he must talk to your aunt; and they're all coming to consult . . . But I know they'll none of 'em take my chany,' she added, turning towards the cups and saucers – 'for they all found fault with 'em when I bought 'em, 'cause o' the small gold sprig all over 'em, between the flowers. But there's none of 'em got better chany, not even your aunt Pullet herself, – and I bought it wi' my own money as I'd saved ever since I was turned fifteen; and the silver teapot, too – your father never paid for 'em. And to think as he should ha' married me, and brought me to this.'

Mrs Tulliver burst out crying afresh, and she sobbed with her handkerchief at her eyes a few moments, but then removing it, she said in a deprecating way, still half-sobbing, as if she were called upon to speak before she could command her voice, 'And I *did* say to him times and times, "Whativer you do, don't go to law" – and what more could I do? I've had to sit by while my own fortin's been spent, and what should ha' been my children's, too. You'll have niver a penny, my boy . . . but it isn't your poor mother's fault.'

She put out one arm towards Tom, looking up at him piteously with her helpless, childish blue eyes. The poor lad went to her and kissed her, and she clung to him. For the first time Tom thought of his father with some reproach. His natural inclination to blame, hitherto kept entirely in abeyance towards his father by the predisposition to think him always right, simply on the ground that he was Tom Tulliver's father – was turned into this channel by his mother's plaints, and with his indignation against Wakem there began to mingle some indignation of another sort. Perhaps his father might have helped bringing them all down in the world, and making people talk of them with contempt; but no one should talk long of Tom Tulliver with contempt. The natural strength and firmness of his nature was beginning to assert itself, urged by the double stimulus of resentment against his aunts, and the sense that he must behave like a man and take care of his mother.

'Don't fret, mother,' he said tenderly. 'I shall soon be able to get money: I'll get a situation of some sort.'

'Bless you, my boy!' said Mrs Tulliver, a little soothed. Then, looking round sadly, 'But I shouldn't ha' minded so much if we could ha' kept the things wi' my name on 'em.'

Maggie had witnessed this scene with gathering anger. The implied reproaches against her father – her father, who was lying there in a sort of living death – neutralised all her pity for griefs about tablecloths and china; and her anger on her father's account was heightened by some egoistic resentment at Tom's silent concurrence with her mother in shutting her out from the common calamity. She had become almost indifferent to her mother's habitual depreciation of her, but she was keenly alive to any sanction of it, however passive, that she might suspect in Tom. Poor Maggie was by no means made up of unalloyed devotedness, but put forth large claims for herself where she loved strongly. She burst out at last in an agitated, almost violent tone, 'Mother, how can you talk so? as if you cared only for things with *your* name on, and not for what has my father's name too – and to care about anything but dear father himself! – when he's lying there, and may never speak to us again. Tom, you ought to say so too – you ought not to let anyone find fault with my father.'

Maggie, almost choked with mingled grief and anger, left the room, and took her old place on her father's bed. Her heart went out to him with a stronger movement than ever, at the thought that people would blame him. Maggie hated blame: she had been blamed all her life, and nothing had come of it but evil tempers. Her father had always defended and excused her, and her loving remembrance of his tenderness was a force within her that would enable her to do or bear anything for his sake.

Tom was a little shocked at Maggie's outburst – telling *him* as well as his mother what it was right to do! She ought to have learned better than have those hectoring, assuming manners, by this time. But he presently went into his father's room, and the sight there touched him in a way that effaced the slighter impressions of the previous hour. When Maggie saw how he was moved, she went to him and put her arm round his neck as he sat by the bed, and the two children forgot everything else in the sense that they had one father and one sorrow.

CHAPTER 3

The Family Council

It was at eleven o'clock the next morning that the aunts and uncles came to hold their consultation. The fire was lighted in the large parlour, and poor Mrs Tulliver, with a confused impression that it was a great occasion, like a funeral, unbagged the bell-rope tassels, and unpinned the curtains, adjusting them in proper folds – looking round and shaking her head sadly at the polished tops and legs of the tables, which sister Pullet herself could not accuse of insufficient brightness.

Mr Deane was not coming – he was away on business; but Mrs Deane appeared punctually in that handsome new gig with the head to it, and the livery-servant driving it, which had thrown so clear a light on several traits in her character to some of her female friends in St Ogg's. Mr Deane had been advancing in the world as rapidly as Mr Tulliver had been going down in it; and in Mrs Deane's house the Dodson linen and plate were beginning to hold quite a subordinate position, as a mere supplement to the handsomer articles of the same kind, purchased in recent years: a change which had caused an occasional coolness in the sisterly intercourse between her and Mrs Glegg, who felt that Susan was getting 'like the rest,' and there would soon be little of the true Dodson spirit surviving except in herself, and, it might be hoped, in those nephews who supported the Dodson name on the family land, far away in the Wolds. People who live at a distance are naturally less faulty than those immediately under our own eyes; and it seems superfluous, when we consider the remote geographical position of the Ethiopians, and how very little the Greeks had to do with them, to enquire further why Homer calls them 'blameless.'

Mrs Deane was the first to arrive; and when she had taken her seat in the large parlour, Mrs Tulliver came down to her with her comely face a little distorted, nearly as it would have been if she had been crying: she was not a woman who could shed abundant tears, except in moments when the prospect of losing her furniture became unusually vivid, but she felt how unfitting it was to be quite calm under present circumstances.

'Oh, sister, what a world this is!' she exclaimed as she entered; 'what trouble, oh, dear!'

Mrs Deane was a thin-lipped woman, who made small well-considered speeches on peculiar occasions, repeating them afterwards to her husband, and asking him if she had not spoken very properly.

'Yes, sister,' she said, deliberately, 'this is a changing world, and we don't know today what may happen tomorrow. But its right to be prepared for all things, and if trouble's sent, to remember as it isn't sent without a cause. I'm very sorry for you as a sister, and if the doctor orders jelly for Mr Tulliver, I hope you'll let me know: I'll send it willingly. For it is but right he should have proper attendance while he's ill.'

'Thank you, Susan,' said Mrs Tulliver, rather faintly, withdrawing her fat hand from her sister's thin one. 'But there's been no talk o' jelly yet.' Then after a moment's pause she added, 'There's a dozen o' cut jelly-glasses upstairs . . . I shall niver put jelly into 'em no more.'

Her voice was rather agitated as she uttered the last words, but the sound of wheels diverted her thoughts. Mr and Mrs Glegg were come, and were almost immediately followed by Mr and Mrs Pullet.

Mrs Pullet entered crying, as a compendious mode, at all times, of expressing what were her views of life in general, and what, in brief, were the opinions she held concerning the particular case before her.

Mrs Glegg had on her fuzziest front, and garments which appeared to have had a recent resurrection from rather a creasy form of burial; a costume selected with the high moral purpose of instilling perfect humility into Bessy and her children.

'Mrs G., won't you come nearer the fire?' said her husband, unwilling to take the more comfortable seat without offering it to her.

'You see I've seated myself here, Mr Glegg,' returned this superior woman; '*you* can roast yourself, if you like.'

'Well,' said Mr Glegg, seating himself good-humouredly, 'and how's the poor man upstairs?'

'Dr Turnbull thought him a deal better this morning,' said Mrs Tulliver; 'he took more notice, and spoke to me; but he's never known Tom yet – looks at the poor lad as if he was a stranger, though he said something once about Tom and the pony. The doctor says his memory's gone a long way back, and he doesn't know Tom because he's thinking of him when he was little. Eh dear, eh dear!'

'I doubt it's the water got on his brain,' said aunt Pullet, turning round from adjusting her cap in a melancholy way at the pier-glass. 'It's much if he ever gets up again; and if he does, he'll most like be childish, as Mr Carr was, poor man! They fed him with a spoon as if he'd been a babby for three year. He'd quite lost the use of his limbs; but then he'd got a Bath chair, and somebody to draw him; and that's what you won't have, I doubt, Bessy.'

'Sister Pullet,' said Mrs Glegg, severely, 'if I understand right, we've come together this morning to advise and consult about what's to be done in this disgrace as has fallen upon the family and not to talk o' people as don't belong to us. Mr Carr was none of our blood, nor no ways connected with us, as I've ever heared.'

'Sister Glegg,' said Mrs Pullet, in a pleading tone, drawing on her gloves again, and stroking the fingers in an agitated manner, 'if you've got anything disrespectful to say o' Mr Carr, I do beg of you as you won't say it to me. *I* know what he was,' she added, with a sigh; 'his breath was short to that degree as you could hear him two rooms off.'

'Sophy!' said Mrs Glegg, with indignant disgust, 'you *do* talk o' people's complaints till it's quite undecent. But I say again, as I said before, I didn't come away from home to talk about acquaintance, whether they'd short breath or long. If we aren't come together for one to hear what the other 'ull do to save a sister and her children from the parish, I shall go back. *One* can't act without the other, I suppose; it isn't to be expected as *I* should do everything.'

'Well, Jane,' said Mrs Pullet, 'I don't see as you've been so very forrard at doing. So far as I know, this is the first time as here you've been, since it's been known as the bailiff's in the house; and I was here yesterday, and looked at all Bessy's linen and things, and I told her I'd buy in the spotted tablecloths. I couldn't speak fairer; for as for the teapot as she doesn't want to go out o' the family, it stands to sense I can't do with two silver teapots, not if it *hadn't* a straight spout – but the spotted damask I was allays fond on.'

'I wish it could be managed so as my teapot and chany and the best castors needn't be put up for sale,' said poor Mrs Tulliver, beseechingly, 'and the sugar-tongs, the first things ever I bought.'

'But that can't be helped, you know,' said Mr Glegg. 'If one o' the family chooses to buy 'em in, they can, but one thing must be bid for as well as another.'

'And it isn't to be looked for,' said uncle Pullet, with unwonted independence of idea, 'as your own family should pay more for things nor they'll fetch. They may go for an old song by auction.'

'Oh dear, oh dear,' said Mrs Tulliver, 'to think o' my chany being sold i' that way – and I bought it when I was married, just as you did yours, Jane and Sophy: and I know you didn't like mine, because o' the sprig, but I was fond of it; and there's never been a bit broke, for I've washed it myself – and there's the tulips on the cups, and the roses, as anybody might go and look at 'em for pleasure. You wouldn't like *your* chany to go for an old song and be broke to pieces, though yours has got no colour in it, Jane – it's all white and fluted, and didn't cost so much as mine. And there's the castors – sister Deane, I can't think but you'd like to have the castors, for I've heard you say they're pretty.'

'Well, I've no objection to buy some of the best things,' said Mrs Deane, rather loftily; 'we can do with extra things in our house.'

'Best things!' exclaimed Mrs Glegg with severity, which had gathered intensity from her long silence. 'It drives me past patience to hear you all talking o' best things, and buying in this, that, and the other, such as silver and chany. You must bring your mind to your circumstances, Bessy, and not be thinking o' silver and chany; but whether you shall get so much as a flock bed to lie on, and a blanket to cover you, and a stool to sit on. You must remember, if you get 'em, it'll be because your friends have bought 'em for you, for you're dependent upon *them* for everything; for your husband lies there helpless, and hasn't got a penny i' the world to call his own. And it's for your own good I say this, for it's right you should feel what your state is, and what disgrace your husband's brought on your own family, as you've got to look to for everything – and be humble in your mind.'

Mrs Glegg paused, for speaking with much energy for the good of others is naturally exhausting. Mrs Tulliver, always borne down by the family pre-dominance of sister Jane, who had made her wear the yoke of a younger sister in very tender years, said pleadingly, 'I'm sure, sister, I've never asked anybody to do anything, only buy things as it 'ud be a pleasure to 'em to have, so as they mightn't go and be spoiled i' strange houses. I never asked anybody to buy the things in for me and my children; though there's the linen I spun, and I thought when Tom was born – I thought one o' the first things when he was lying i' the cradle, as all the things I'd bought wi' my own money, and been so careful of, 'ud go to him. But I've said nothing as I wanted my sisters to pay their money for me. What my husband has done for *his* sister's unknown, and we should ha' been better off this day if it hadn't been as he's lent money and never asked for it again.'

'Come, come,' said Mr Glegg, kindly, 'don't let us make things too dark. What's done can't be undone. We shall make a shift among us to buy what's sufficient for you; though, as Mrs G. says, they must be useful, plain things. We mustn't be thinking o' what's unnecessary. A table, and a chair or two, and kitchen things, and a good bed, and suchlike. Why, I've seen the day when I shouldn't ha' known myself if I'd lain on sacking i'stead o' the floor. We get a deal o' useless things about us, only because we've got the money to spend.'

'Mr Glegg,' said Mrs G., 'if you'll be kind enough to let me speak, i'stead o' taking the words out o' my mouth – I was going to say, Bessy, as it's fine for you to say as you've never asked us to buy anything for you; let me tell you, you *ought* to have asked us. Pray, how are you to be purvided for, if your own family don't help you? You must go to the parish, if they didn't. And you ought to know that, and keep it in mind, and ask us humble to do what we can for you, i'stead o' saying, and making a boast, as you've never asked us for anything.'

'You talked o' the Mosses, and what Mr Tulliver's done for 'em,' said uncle Pullet, who became unusually suggestive where advances of money were concerned. 'Haven't *they* been a-near you? They ought to do something, as well as other folks; and if he's lent 'em money, they ought to be made to pay it back.'

'Yes, to be sure,' said Mrs Deane; 'I've been thinking so. How is it Mr and Mrs Moss aren't here to meet us? It is but right they should do their share.'

'Oh dear!' said Mrs Tulliver, 'I never sent 'em word about Mr Tulliver, and they live so back'ard among the lanes at Basset, they niver hear anything only when Mr Moss comes to market. But I niver gave 'em a thought. I wonder Maggie didn't, though, for she was allays so fond of her aunt Moss.'

'Why don't your children come in, Bessy?' said Mrs Pullet, at the mention of Maggie. 'They should hear what their aunts and uncles have got to say: and Maggie – when it's me as have paid for half her schooling, she ought to think more of her aunt Pullet than of aunt Mosses. I may go off sudden when I get home today – there's no telling.'

'If I'd had *my* way,' said Mrs Glegg, 'the children 'ud ha' been in the room from the first. It's time they knew who they've to look to, and it's right as *somebody* should talk to 'em, and let 'em know their condition i' life, and what they're come down to, and make 'em feel as they've got to suffer for their father's faults.'

'Well, I'll go and fetch 'em, sister,' said Mrs Tulliver, resignedly. She was quite crushed now, and thought of the treasures in the storeroom with no other feeling than blank despair.

She went upstairs to fetch Tom and Maggie, who were both in their father's room, and was on her way down again, when the sight of the storeroom door suggested a new thought to her. She went towards it, and left the children to go down by themselves.

The aunts and uncles appeared to have been in warm discussion when the brother and sister entered – both with shrinking reluctance; for though Tom, with a practical sagacity which had been roused into activity by the strong stimulus of the new emotions he had undergone since yesterday, had been turning over in his mind a plan which he meant to propose to one of his aunts or uncles, he felt by no means amicably towards them, and dreaded meeting them all at once as he would have dreaded a large dose of concentrated physic, which was but just endurable in small draughts. As for Maggie, she was peculiarly depressed this morning: she had been called up, after brief rest, at three o'clock, and had that strange dreamy weariness which comes from watching in a sick-room through the chill hours of early twilight and breaking day – in which the outside daylight life seems to have no importance, and to be a mere margin to the hours in the darkened chamber. Their entrance interrupted the conversation. The shaking of hands was a melancholy and silent ceremony, till uncle Pullet observed, as Tom approached him, 'Well, young sir, we've been talking as we should want your pen and ink; you can write rarely now, after all your schooling, I should think.'

'Ay, ay,' said uncle Glegg, with admonition which he meant to be kind, 'we must look to see the good of all this schooling, as your father's sunk so much money in, now –

> When land is gone and money's spent,
> Then learning is most excellent.

Now's the time, Tom, to let us see the good o' your learning. Let us see whether you can do better than I can, as have made my fortin without it. But I began wi' doing with little, you see: I could live on a basin o' porridge and a crust o' bread-and-cheese. But I doubt high living and high learning 'ull make it harder for you, young man, nor it was for me.'

'But he must do it,' interposed aunt Glegg, energetically, 'whether it's hard or no. He hasn't got to consider what's hard; he must consider as he isn't to trusten to his friends to keep him in idleness and luxury: he's got to bear the fruits of his father's misconduct, and bring his mind to fare hard and to work hard. And he must be humble and grateful to his aunts and uncles for what they're doing for his mother and father, as must be turned out into the streets and go to the workhouse if they didn't help 'em. And his sister, too,' continued Mrs Glegg, looking severely at Maggie, who had sat down on the sofa by her aunt Deane, drawn to her by the sense that she was Lucy's mother, 'she must make up her mind to be humble and work; for there'll be no servants to wait on her any more – she must remember that. She must do the work o' the house, and she must respect and love her aunts as have done so much for her, and saved their money to leave to their nepheys and nieces.'

Tom was still standing before the table in the centre of the group. There was a heightened colour in his face, and he was very far from looking humbled, but he was preparing to say, in a respectful tone, something he had previously meditated, when the door opened and his mother re-entered.

Poor Mrs Tulliver had in her hands a small tray, on which she had placed her silver teapot, a specimen teacup and saucer, the castors, and sugar-tongs.

'See here, sister,' she said, looking at Mrs Deane, as she set the tray on the table, 'I thought, perhaps, if you looked at the teapot again – it's a good while since you saw it – you might like the pattern better: it makes beautiful tea, and there's a stand and everything: you might use it for everyday, or else lay it by for Lucy when she goes to housekeeping. I should be so loth for 'em to buy it at the Golden Lion,' said the poor woman, her heart swelling, and the tears coming, 'my teapot as I bought when I was married, and to think of its being scratched, and set before the travellers and folks, and my letters on it – see here, E.D. – and everybody to see 'em.'

'Ah, dear, dear!' said aunt Pullet, shaking her head with deep sadness, 'it's very bad – to think o' the family initials going about everywhere – it niver was so before: you're a very unlucky sister, Bessy. But what's the use o' buying the teapot, when there's the linen and spoons and everything to go, and some of 'em with your full name – and when it's got that straight spout, too.'

'As to disgrace o' the family,' said Mrs Glegg, 'that can't be helped wi' buying teapots. The disgrace is, for one o' the family to ha' married a man as has brought her to beggary. The disgrace is, as they're to be sold up. We can't hinder the country from knowing that.'

Maggie had started up from the sofa at the allusion to her father, but Tom saw her action and flushed face in time to prevent her from speaking. 'Be quiet, Maggie,' he said, authoritatively, pushing her aside. It was a remarkable manifestation of self-command and practical judgement in a lad of fifteen, that when his aunt Glegg ceased, he began to speak in a quiet and respectful manner, though with a good deal of trembling in his voice; for his mother's words had cut him to the quick.

'Then, aunt,' he said, looking straight at Mrs Glegg, 'if you think it's a disgrace to the family that we should be sold up, wouldn't it be better to prevent it altogether? And if you and my aunt Pullet,' he continued, looking at the latter, 'think of leaving any money to me and Maggie, wouldn't it be better to give it now, and pay the debt we're going to be sold up for, and save my mother from parting with her furniture?'

There was silence for a few moments, for everyone, including Maggie, was astonished at Tom's sudden manliness of tone. Uncle Glegg was the first to speak.

'Ay, ay, young man – come now! You show some notion o' things. But there's the interest, you must remember; your aunts get five per cent on their money, and they'd lose that if they advanced it – you haven't thought o' that.'

'I could work and pay that every year,' said Tom, promptly. 'I'd do anything to save my mother from parting with her things.'

'Well done!' said uncle Glegg, admiringly. He had been drawing Tom out, rather than reflecting on the practicability of his proposal. But he had produced the unfortunate result of irritating his wife.

'Yes, Mr Glegg!' said that lady, with angry sarcasm. 'It's pleasant work for you to be giving my money away, as you've pretended to leave at my own disposal. And my money, as was my own father's gift, and not yours, Mr Glegg; and I've saved it, and added to it myself, and had more to put out almost every year, and it's to go and be sunk in other folks' furniture, and encourage 'em in luxury and extravagance as they've no means of supporting; and I'm to alter my will, or have a codicil made, and leave two or three hundred less behind me when I die – me as have allays done right and been careful, and the eldest o' the family; and my money's to go and be squandered on them as have had the same chance as me, only they've been wicked and wasteful. Sister Pullet, *you* may do as you like, and you may let your husband rob you back again o' the money he's given you, but that isn't *my* sperrit.'

'La, Jane, how fiery you are!' said Mrs Pullet. 'I'm sure you'll have the blood in your head, and have to be cupped. I'm sorry for Bessy and her children – I'm sure I think of 'em o' nights dreadful, for I sleep very bad wi' this new medicine:

but it's no use for me to think o' doing anything, if you won't meet me halfway.'

'Why, there's this to be considered,' said Mr Glegg. 'It's no use to pay off this debt and save the furniture, when there's all the law debts behind, as 'ud take every shilling, and more than could be made out o' land and stock, for I've made that out from Lawyer Gore. We'd need save our money to keep the poor man with, instead o' spending it on furniture as he can neither eat nor drink. You *will* be so hasty, Jane, as if I didn't know what was reasonable.'

'Then speak accordingly, Mr Glegg!' said his wife, with slow, loud emphasis, bending her head towards him significantly.

Tom's countenance had fallen during this conversation, and his lip quivered; but he was determined not to give way. He would behave like a man. Maggie, on the contrary, after her momentary delight in Tom's speech, had relapsed into her state of trembling indignation. Her mother had been standing close by Tom's side, and had been clinging to his arm ever since he had last spoken: Maggie suddenly started up and stood in front of them, her eyes flashing like the eyes of a young lioness.

'Why do you come, then,' she burst out, 'talking and interfering with us and scolding us, if you don't mean to do anything to help my poor mother – your own sister – if you've no feeling for her when she's in trouble, and won't part with anything, though you would never miss it, to save her from pain? Keep away from us then, and don't come to find fault with my father – he was better than any of you – he was kind – he would have helped *you*, if you had been in trouble. Tom and I don't ever want to have any of your money, if you won't help my mother. We'd rather not have it! we'll do without you.'

Maggie, having hurled her defiance at aunts and uncles in this way, stood still, with her large dark eyes glaring at them, as if she were ready to await all consequences.

Mrs Tulliver was frightened; there was something portentous in this mad outbreak; she did not see how life could go on after it. Tom was vexed; it was no *use* to talk so. The aunts were silent with surprise for some moments. At length, in a case of aberration such as this, comment presented itself as more expedient than any answer.

'You haven't seen the end o' your trouble wi' that child, Bessy,' said Mrs Pullet; 'she's beyond everything for boldness and unthankfulness. It's dreadful. I might ha' let alone paying for her schooling, for she's worse nor ever.'

'It's no more than what I've allays said,' followed Mrs Glegg. 'Other folks may be surprised, but I'm not. I've said over and over again – years ago I've said – "Mark my words; that child 'ull come to no good: there isn't a bit of our family in her." And as for her having so much schooling, I never thought well o' that. I'd my reasons when I said *I* wouldn't pay anything towards it.'

'Come, come,' said Mr Glegg, 'let's waste no more time in talking – let's go to business. Tom now, get the pen and ink –'

While Mr Glegg was speaking, a tall dark figure was seen hurrying past the window.

'Why, there's Mrs Moss,' said Mrs Tulliver. 'The bad news must ha' reached her, then;' and she went out to open the door, Maggie eagerly following her.

'That's fortunate,' said Mrs Glegg. 'She can agree to the list o' things to be bought in. It's but right she should do her share when it's her own brother.'

Mrs Moss was in too much agitation to resist Mrs Tulliver's movement, as she drew her into the parlour, automatically, without reflecting that it was hardly kind to take her among so many persons in the first painful moment of arrival. The tall, worn, dark-haired woman was a strong contrast to the Dodson sisters as she entered in her shabby dress, with her shawl and bonnet looking as if they had been hastily huddled on, and with that entire absence of self-consciousness which belongs to keenly-felt trouble. Maggie was clinging to her arm; and Mrs Moss seemed to notice no one else except Tom, whom she went straight up to and took by the hand.

'Oh, my dear children,' she burst out, 'you've no call to think well o' me; I'm a poor aunt to you, for I'm one o' them as take all and give nothing. How's my poor brother?'

'Mr Turnbull thinks he'll get better,' said Maggie. 'sit down, aunt Gritty. Don't fret.'

'Oh, my sweet child, I feel torn i' two,' said Mrs Moss, allowing Maggie to lead her to the sofa, but still not seeming to notice the presence of the rest. 'We've three hundred pounds o' my brother's money, and now he wants it, and you all want it, poor things! – and yet we must be sold up to pay it, and there's my poor children – eight of 'em, and the little un of all can't speak plain. And I feel as is I was a robber. But I'm sure I'd no thought as my brother . . .'

The poor woman was interrupted by a rising sob.

'Three hundred pounds! Oh, dear, dear,' said Mrs Tulliver, who, when she had said that her husband had done 'unknown' things for his sister, had not had any particular sum in her mind, and felt a wife's irritation at having been kept in the dark.

'What madness, to be sure!' said Mrs Glegg. 'A man with a family! He'd no right to lend his money i' that way; and without security, I'll be bound, if the truth was known.'

Mrs Glegg's voice had arrested Mrs Moss's attention, and, looking up, she said, 'Yes, there *was* security: my husband gave a note for it. We're not that sort o' people, neither of us, as 'ud rob my brother's children; and we looked to paying back the money, when the times got a bit better.'

'Well, but now,' said Mr Glegg, gently, 'hasn't your husband no way o' raising this money? Because it 'ud be a little fortin, like, for these folks, if we can do without Tulliver's being made a bankrupt. Your husband's got stock: it is but right he should raise the money, as it seems to me – not but what I'm sorry for you, Mrs Moss.'

'Oh, sir, you don't know what bad luck my husband's had with his stock. The farm's suffering so as never was for want o' stock; and we've sold all the wheat, and we're behind with our rent . . . not but what we'd like to do what's right, and I'd sit up and work half the night, if it 'ud be any good . . . but there's them poor children . . . four of 'em such little uns . . . '

'Don't cry so, aunt – don't fret,' whispered Maggie, who had kept hold of Mrs Moss's hand.

'Did Mr Tulliver let you have the money all at once?' said Mrs Tulliver, still lost in the conception of things which had been 'going on' without her knowledge.

'No; at twice,' said Mrs Moss, rubbing her eyes and making an effort to restrain her tears. 'The last was after my bad illness, four years ago, as everything went wrong, and there was a new note made then. What with illness and bad luck, I've been nothing but cumber all my life.'

'Yes, Mrs Moss,' said Mrs Glegg, with decision. 'Yours is a very unlucky family; the more's the pity for *my* sister.'

'I set off in the cart as soon as ever I heard o' what had happened,' said Mrs Moss, looking at Mrs Tulliver. 'I should never ha' stayed away all this while, if you'd thought well to let me know. And it isn't as I'm thinking all about ourselves, and nothing about my brother – only the money was so on my mind, I couldn't help speaking about it. And my husband and me desire to do the right thing, sir,' she added, looking at Mr Glegg, 'and we'll make shift and pay the money, come what will, if that's all my brother's got to trust to. We've been used to trouble, and don't look for much else. It's only the thought o' my poor children pulls me i' two.'

'Why, there's this to be thought on, Mrs Moss,' said Mr Glegg, 'and it's right to warn you – if Tulliver's made a bankrupt, and he's got a note-of-hand of your husband's for three hundred pounds, you'll be obliged to pay it: th' assignees 'ull come on you for it.'

'Oh dear, oh dear!' said Mrs Tulliver, thinking of the bankruptcy, and not of Mrs Moss's concern in it. Poor Mrs Moss herself listened in trembling submission, while Maggie looked with bewildered distress at Tom to see if *he* showed any signs of understanding this trouble, and caring about poor aunt Moss. Tom was only looking thoughtful, with his eyes on the tablecloth.

'And if he isn't made bankrupt,' continued Mr Glegg, 'as I said before, three hundred pounds 'ud be a little fortin for him, poor man. We don't know but what he may be partly helpless, if he ever gets up again. I'm very sorry if it goes hard with you, Mrs Moss – but my opinion is, looking at it one way, it'll be right for you to raise the money; and looking at it th' other way, you'll be obliged to pay it. You won't think ill o' me for speaking the truth?'

'Uncle,' said Tom, looking up suddenly from his meditative view of the tablecloth, 'I don't think it would be right for my aunt Moss to pay the money, if it would be against my father's will for her to pay it; would it?'

Mr Glegg looked surprised for a moment or two before he said, 'Why, no, perhaps not, Tom; but then he'd ha' destroyed the note, you know. We must look for the note. What makes you think it 'ud be against his will?'

'Why,' said Tom, colouring, but trying to speak firmly, in spite of a boyish tremor, 'I remember quite well, before I went to school to Mr Stelling, my father said to me one night, when we were sitting by the fire together, and no one else was in the room . . . '

Tom hesitated a little, and then went on.

'He said something to me about Maggie, and then he said, "I've always been good to my sister, though she married against my will – and I've lent Moss money; but I shall never think of distressing him to pay it: I'd rather lose it. My children must not mind being the poorer for that." And now my father's ill, and not able to speak for himself, I shouldn't like anything to be done contrary to what he said to me.'

'Well, but then, my boy,' said uncle Glegg, whose good feeling led him to enter into Tom's wish, but who could not at once shake off his habitual abhorrence of such recklessness as destroying securities, or alienating anything important enough to make an appreciable difference in a man's property, 'we should have to make away wi' the note, you know, if we're to guard against what may happen, supposing your father's made bankrupt . . .'

'Mr Glegg,' interrupted his wife, severely, 'mind what you're saying. You're putting yourself very forrard in other folks's business. If you speak rash, don't say it was my fault.'

'That's such a thing as I never heared of before,' said uncle Pullet, who had been making haste with his lozenge in order to express his amazement; 'making away with a note! I should think anybody could set the constable on you for it.'

'Well, but,' said Mrs Tulliver, 'if the note's worth all that money, why can't we pay it away, and save my things from going away? We've no call to meddle with your uncle and aunt Moss, Tom, if you think your father 'ud be angry when he gets well.'

Mrs Tulliver had not studied the question of exchange, and was straining her mind after original ideas on the subject.

'Pooh, pooh, pooh! you women don't understand these things,' said uncle Glegg. 'there's no way o' making it safe for Mr and Mrs Moss but destroying the note.'

'Then I hope you'll help me to do it, uncle,' said Tom, earnestly. 'If my father shouldn't get well, I should be very unhappy to think anything had been done against his will, that I could hinder. And I'm sure he meant me to remember what he said that evening. I ought to obey my father's wish about his property.'

Even Mrs Glegg could not withhold her approval from Tom's words: she felt that the Dodson blood was certainly speaking in him, though, if his father had been a Dodson, there would never have been this wicked alienation of money. Maggie would hardly have restrained herself from leaping on Tom's neck, if her aunt Moss had not prevented her by herself rising and taking Tom's hand, while she said, with rather a choked voice, 'You'll never be the poorer for this, my dear boy, if there's a God above; and if the money's wanted for your father, Moss and me 'ull pay it, the same as if there was ever such security. We'll do as we'd be done by; for if my children have got no other luck, they've got an honest father and mother.'

'Well,' said Mr Glegg, who had been meditating after Tom's words, 'we shouldn't be doing any wrong by the creditors, supposing your father *was* bankrupt. I've been thinking o' that, for I've been a creditor myself, and seen no end o' cheating. If he meant to give your aunt the money before ever he got into this sad work o' lawing, it's the same as if he'd made away with the note himself; for he'd made up his mind to be that much poorer. But there's a deal o' things to be considered, young man,' Mr Glegg added, looking admonishingly at Tom, 'when you come to money business, and you may be taking one man's dinner away to make another man's breakfast. You don't understand that, I doubt?'

'Yes, I do,' said Tom, decidedly. 'I know if I owe money to one man, I've no right to give it to another. But if my father had made up his mind to give my aunt the money before he was in debt, he had a right to do it.'

'Well done, young man! I didn't think you'd been so sharp,' said uncle Glegg, with much candour. 'But perhaps your father *did* make away with the note. Let us go and see if we can find it in the chest.'

'It's in my father's room. Let us go too, aunt Gritty,' whispered Maggie.

CHAPTER 4

A Vanishing Gleam

Mr Tulliver, even between the fits of spasmodic rigidity which had recurred at intervals ever since he had been found fallen from his horse, was usually in so apathetic a condition that the exits and entrances into his room were not felt to be of great importance. He had lain so still, with his eyes closed, all this morning, that Maggie told her aunt Moss she must not expect her father to take any notice of them.

They entered very quietly, and Mrs Moss took her seat near the head of the bed, while Maggie sat in her old place on the bed, and put her hand on her father's, without causing any change in his face.

Mr Glegg and Tom had also entered, treading softly, and were busy selecting the key of the old oak chest from the bunch which Tom had brought from his father's bureau. They succeeded in opening the chest – which stood opposite the foot of Mr Tulliver's bed – and propping the lid with the iron holder, without much noise.

'There's a tin box,' whispered Mr Glegg; 'he'd most like put a small thing like a note in there. Lift it out, Tom; but I'll just lift up these deeds – they're the deeds o' the house and mill, I suppose – and see what there is under 'em.'

Mr Glegg had lifted out the parchments, and had fortunately drawn back a little when the iron holder gave way, and the heavy lid fell with a loud bang, that resounded over the house.

Perhaps there was something in that sound more than the mere fact of the strong vibration that produced the instantaneous effect on the frame of the prostrate man, and for the time completely shook off the obstruction of paralysis. The chest had belonged to his father and his father's father, and it had always been rather a solemn business to visit it. All long-known objects, even a mere window fastening or a particular door-latch, have sounds which are a sort of recognised voice to us – a voice that will thrill and awaken, when it has been used to touch deep-lying fibres. In the same moment when all the eyes in the room were turned upon him, he started up and looked at the chest, the parchments in Mr Glegg's hand, and Tom holding the tin box, with a glance of perfect consciousness and recognition.

'What are you going to do with those deeds?' he said, in his ordinary tone of sharp questioning whenever he was irritated. 'Come here, Tom. What do you do, going to my chest?'

Tom obeyed, with some trembling: it was the first time his father had recognised him. But instead of saying anything more to him, his father continued to look with a growing distinctness of suspicion at Mr Glegg and the deeds.

'What's been happening, then?' he said, sharply. 'What are you meddling with my deeds for? Is Wakem laying hold of everything? . . . Why don't you tell me what you've been adoing?' he added, impatiently, as Mr Glegg advanced to the foot of the bed before speaking.

'No, no, friend Tulliver,' said Mr Glegg, in a soothing tone. 'Nobody's getting hold of anything as yet. We only came to look and see what was in the chest. You've been ill, you know, and we've had to look after things a bit. But let's hope you'll soon be well enough to attend to everything yourself.'

Mr Tulliver looked round him meditatively – at Tom, at Mr Glegg, and at Maggie; then suddenly appearing aware that someone was seated by his side at the head of the bed, he turned sharply round and saw his sister.

'Eh, Gritty!' he said, in the half-sad, affectionate tone in which he had been wont to speak to her. 'What! you're there, are you? How could you manage to leave the children?'

'Oh, brother!' said good Mrs Moss, too impulsive to be prudent, 'I'm thankful I'm come now to see you yourself again – I thought you'd never know us any more.'

'What! have I had a stroke?' said Mr Tulliver, anxiously, looking at Mr Glegg.

'A fall from your horse – shook you a bit – that's all, I think,' said Mr Glegg. 'But you'll soon get over it, let's hope.'

Mr Tulliver fixed his eyes on the bedclothes, and remained silent for two or three minutes. A new shadow came over his face. He looked up at Maggie first, and said in a lower tone, 'You got the letter, then, my wench?'

'Yes, father,' she said, kissing him with a full heart. She felt as if her father were come back to her from the dead, and her yearning to show him how she had always loved him could be fulfilled.

'Where's your mother?' he said, so preoccupied that he received the kiss as passively as some quiet animal might have received it.

'She's downstairs with my aunts, father: shall I fetch her?'

'Ay, ay: poor Bessy!' and his eyes turned towards Tom as Maggie left the room.

'You'll have to take care of 'em both if I die, you know, Tom. You'll be badly off, I doubt. But you must see and pay everybody. And mind – there's fifty pound o' Luke's as I put into the business – he gave it me a bit at a time, and he's got nothing to show for it. You must pay him first thing.'

Uncle Glegg involuntarily shook his head, and looked more concerned then ever, but Tom said firmly, 'Yes, father. And haven't you a note from my uncle Moss for three hundred pounds? We came to look for that. What do you wish to be done about it, father?'

'Ah! I'm glad you thought o' that my lad,' said Mr Tulliver. 'I allays meant to be easy about that money, because o' your aunt. You mustn't mind losing the money, if they can't pay it – and it's like enough they can't. The note's in that box, mind! allays meant to be good to you, Gritty,' said Mr Tulliver, turning to his sister; 'but, you know, you aggravated me when you would have Moss.'

At this moment Maggie re-entered with her mother, who came in much agitated by the news that her husband was quite himself again.

'Well, Bessy,' he said, as she kissed him, 'you must forgive me if you're worse off than you ever expected to be. But it's the fault o' the law – it's none o' mine,' he added, angrily. 'It's the fault o' raskills! Tom – you mind this: if ever you've got the chance, you make Wakem smart. If you don't, you're a good-for-nothing son. You might horse-whip him – but he'd set the law on you – the law's made to take care o' raskills.'

Mr Tulliver was getting excited, and an alarming flush was on his face. Mr Glegg wanted to say something soothing, but he was prevented by Mr Tulliver's speaking again to his wife. 'They'll make a shift to pay everything, Bessy,' he said, 'and yet leave you your furniture; and your sisters'll do something for you . . . and Tom'll grow up . . . though what he's to be I don't know. . . I've done what I could . . . I've given him a eddication . . . and there's the little wench, she'll get married . . . but it's a poor tale . . . '

The sanative effect of the strong vibration was exhausted, and with the last words the poor man fell again, rigid and insensible. Though this was only a recurrence of what had happened before, it struck all present as if it had been death, not only from its contrast with the completeness of the revival, but because his words had all had reference to the possibility that his death was near. But with poor Tulliver death was not to be a leap: it was to be a long descent under thickening shadows.

Mr Turnbull was sent for; but when he heard what had passed, he said this complete restoration, though only temporary, was a hopeful sign, proving that there was no permanent lesion to prevent ultimate recovery.

Among the threads of the past which the stricken man had gathered up, he had omitted the bill of sale; the flash of memory had only lit up prominent ideas, and he sank into forgetfulness again with half his humiliation unlearned.

But Tom was clear upon two points – that his uncle Moss's note must be destroyed, and that Luke's money must be paid, if in no other way, out of his own and Maggie's money now in the savings bank. There were subjects, you perceive, on which Tom was much quicker than on the niceties of classical construction, or the relations of a mathematical demonstration.

CHAPTER 5

Tom Applies his Knife to the Oyster

The next day, at ten o'clock, Tom was on his way to St Ogg's, to see his uncle Deane, who was to come home last night, his aunt had said; and Tom had made up his mind that his uncle Deane was the right person to ask for advice about getting some employment. He was in a great way of business; he had not the narrow notions of uncle Glegg; and he had risen in the world on a scale of advancement which accorded with Tom's ambition.

It was a dark, chill, misty morning, likely to end in rain – one of those mornings when even happy people take refuge in their hopes. And Tom was very unhappy: he felt the humiliation as well as the prospective hardships of his lot with all the keenness of a proud nature; and with all his resolute dutifulness towards his father there mingled an irrepressible indignation against him which gave misfortune the less endurable aspect of a wrong. Since these were the consequences of going to law, his father was really blamable, as his aunts and uncles had always said he was; and it was a significant indication of Tom's character, that though he thought his aunts ought to do something more for his mother, he felt nothing like Maggie's violent resentment against them for showing no eager tenderness and generosity. There were no impulses in Tom that led him to expect what did not present itself to him as a right to be demanded. Why should people give away their money plentifully to those who had not taken care of their own money? Tom saw some justice in severity; and all the more, because he had confidence in himself that he should never deserve that just severity. It was very hard upon him that he should be put at this disadvantage in life by his father's want of prudence; but he was not going to complain and to find fault with people because they did not make everything easy for him. He would ask no one to help him, more than to give him work and pay him for it. Poor Tom was not without his hopes to take refuge in under the chill damp imprisonment of the December fog which seemed only like a part of his home troubles. At sixteen, the mind that has the strongest affinity for fact cannot escape illusion and self-flattery; and Tom, in sketching his future, had no other guide in arranging his facts than the suggestions of his own brave self-reliance. Both Mr Glegg and Mr Deane, he knew, had been very poor once: he did not want to save money slowly and retire on a moderate fortune like his uncle Glegg, but he would be like his uncle Deane – get a situation in some great house of business and rise fast. He had scarcely seen anything of his uncle Deane for the last three years – the two families had been getting wider apart; but for this very reason Tom was the more hopeful about applying to him. His uncle Glegg, he felt sure, would never encourage any spirited project, but he had a vague imposing idea of the resources at his uncle Deane's command. He had heard his father say, long ago, how Deane had made himself so valuable to Guest & Co. that they were glad enough to offer him a share in the business:

that was what Tom resolved he would do. It was intolerable to think of being poor and looked down upon all one's life. He would provide for his mother and sister, and make everyone say that he was a man of high character. He leaped over the years in this way, and in the haste of strong purpose and strong desire, did not see how they would be made up of slow days, hours, and minutes.

By the time he had crossed the stone bridge over the Floss and was entering St Ogg's, he was thinking that he would buy his father's mill and land again when he was rich enough, and improve the house and live there: he should prefer it to any smarter, newer place, and he could keep as many horses and dogs as he liked.

Walking along the street with a firm, rapid step, at this point in his reverie he was startled by someone who had crossed without his notice, and who said to him in a rough, familiar voice, 'Why, Master Tom, how's your father this morning?' It was a publican of St Ogg's – one of his father's customers.

Tom disliked being spoken to just then; but he said civilly, 'He's still very ill, thank you.'

'Ay, it's been a sore chance for you, young man, hasn't it? this lawsuit turning out against him,' said the publican, with a confused beery idea of being good-natured.

Tom reddened and passed on: he would have felt it like the handling of a bruise, even if there had been the most polite and delicate reference to his position.

'That's Tulliver's son,' said the publican to a grocer standing on the adjacent doorstep.

'Ah!' said the grocer, 'I thought I knew his features. He takes after his mother's family: she was a Dodson. He's a fine, straight youth: what's he been brought up to?'

'Oh! to turn up his nose at his father's customers, and be a fine gentleman – not much else, I think.'

Tom, roused from his dream of the future to a thorough consciousness of the present, made all the greater haste to reach the warehouse offices of Guest & Co., where he expected to find his uncle Deane. But this was Mr Deane's morning at the bank, a clerk told him, with some contempt for his ignorance: Mr Deane was not to be found in River Street on a Thursday morning.

At the bank Tom was admitted into the private room where his uncle was, immediately after sending in his name. Mr Deane was auditing accounts; but he looked up as Tom entered, and, putting out his hand, said, 'Well, Tom, nothing fresh the matter at home, I hope? How's your father?'

'Much the same, thank you, uncle,' said Tom, feeling nervous. 'But I want to speak to you, please, when you're at liberty.'

'Sit down, sit down,' said Mr Deane, relapsing into his accounts, in which he and the managing-clerk remained so absorbed for the next half-hour that Tom began to wonder whether he should have to sit in this way till the bank closed – there seemed so little tendency towards a conclusion in the quiet monotonous procedure of these sleek, prosperous men of business. Would his uncle give him a place in the bank? it would be very dull, prosy work, he thought, writing there for ever to the loud ticking of a time-piece. He preferred some other way of getting rich. But at last there was a change: his uncle took a pen and wrote something with a flourish at the end.

'You'll just step up to Torry's now, Mr Spence, will you?' said Mr Deane, and the clock suddenly became less loud and deliberate in Tom's ears.

'Well, Tom,' said Mr Deane, when they were alone, turning his substantial person a little in his chair, and taking out his snuffbox, 'what's the business, my boy – what's the business?' Mr Deane, who had heard from his wife what had passed the day before, thought Tom was come to him for some means of averting the sale.

'I hope you'll excuse me for troubling you, uncle,' said Tom, colouring, but speaking in a tone which, though tremulous, had a certain proud independence in it; 'but I thought you were the best person to advise me what to do.'

'Ah!' said Mr Deane, reserving his pinch of snuff, and looking at Tom with new attention, 'let us hear.'

'I want to get a situation, uncle, so that I may earn some money,' said Tom, who never fell into circumlocution.

'A situation?' said Mr Deane, and then took his pinch of snuff with elaborate justice to each nostril. Tom thought snuff-taking a most provoking habit.

'Why, let me see, how old are you?' said Mr Deane, as he threw himself backward again.

'Sixteen – I mean, I am going in seventeen,' said Tom, hoping his uncle noticed how much beard he had.

'Let me see – your father had some notion of making you an engineer, I think?'

'But I don't think I could get any money at that for a long while, could I?'

'That's true; but people don't get much money at anything, my boy, when they're only sixteen. You've had a good deal of schooling, however: I suppose you're pretty well up in accounts, eh? You understand bookkeeping?'

'No', said Tom, rather falteringly. 'I was in Practice. But Mr Stelling says I write a good hand, uncle. That's my writing,' added Tom, laying on the table a copy of the list he had made yesterday.

'Ah! that's good, that's good. But, you see, the best hand in the world'll not get you a better place than a copying-clerk's, if you know nothing of bookkeeping – nothing of accounts. And a copying-clerk's a cheap article. But what have you been learning at school, then?'

Mr Deane had not occupied himself with methods of education, and had no precise conception of what went forward in expensive schools.

'We learned Latin,' said Tom, pausing a little between each item, as if he were turning over the books in his school-desk to assist his memory – 'a good deal of Latin; and the last year I did Themes, one week in Latin and one in English; and Greek and Roman History; and Euclid; and I began Algebra, but I left it off again; and we had one day every week for Arithmetic. Then I used to have drawing-lessons; and there were several other books we either read or learned out of, *English Poetry*, and *Horae Paulinae*, and Blair's *Rhetoric*, the last half.'

Mr Deane tapped his snuffbox again, and screwed up his mouth: he felt in the position of many estimable persons when they had read the New Tariff, and found how many commodities were imported of which they knew nothing: like a cautious man of business, he was not going to speak rashly of a raw material in which he had had no experience. But the presumption was, that if it had been good for anything, so successful a man as himself would hardly have been ignorant of it. About Latin he had an opinion, and thought that in case of another war, since people would no longer wear hair-powder, it would be well to put a tax upon Latin, as a luxury much run upon by the higher classes, and not telling at all on the ship-owning department. But, for what he knew, the Horae Paulinae might be something less neutral. On the whole, this list of acquirements gave him a sort of repulsion towards poor Tom.

'Well,' he said, at last, in rather a cold, sardonic tone, 'you've had three years at these things – you must be pretty strong in 'em. Hadn't you better take up some line where they'll come in handy?'

Tom coloured, and burst out, with new energy, 'I'd rather not have any employment of that sort, uncle. I don't like Latin and those things. I don't know what I could do with them unless I went as usher in a school; and I don't know them well enough for that: besides, I would as soon carry a pair of panniers. I don't want to be that sort of person. I should like to enter into some business where I can get on – a manly business, where I should have to look after things, and get credit for what! I did. And I shall want to keep my mother and sister.'

'Ah, young gentleman,' said Mr Deane, with that tendency to repress youthful hopes which stout and successful men of fifty find one of their easiest duties, 'that's sooner said than done – sooner said than done.'

'But didn't *you* get on in that way, uncle?' said Tom, a little irritated that Mr Deane did not enter more rapidly into his views. 'I mean, didn't you rise from one place to another through your abilities and good conduct?'

'Ay, ay, sir,' said Mr Deane, spreading himself in his chair a little, and entering with great readiness into a retrospect of his own career. 'But I'll tell you how I got on. It wasn't by getting astride a stick, and thinking it would turn into a horse if I sat on it long enough. I kept my eyes and ears open, sir, and I wasn't too fond of my own back, and I made my master's interest my own. Why, with only looking into what went on in the mill, I found out how there was a waste of five hundred a-year that might be hindered. Why, sir, I hadn't more schooling to begin with than a charity boy; but I saw pretty soon that I couldn't get on far without mastering accounts, and I learned 'em between working hours, after I'd been unlading. Look here.' Mr Deane opened a book, and pointed to the page. 'I write a good hand enough, and I'll match anybody at all sorts of reckoning by the head, and I got it all by hard work, and paid for it out of my own earnings – often out of my own dinner and supper. And I looked into the nature of all the things we had to do with in the business, and picked up knowledge as I went about my work, and turned it over in my head. Why, I'm no mechanic – I never pretended to be – but I've thought of a thing or two that the mechanics never thought of, and it's made a fine difference in our returns. And there isn't an article shipped or unshipped at our wharf but I know the quality of it. If I got places, sir, it was because I made myself fit for 'em. If you want to slip into a round hole, you must make a ball of yourself – that's where it is.'

Mr Deane tapped his box again. He had been led on by pure enthusiasm in his subject, and had really forgotten what bearing this retrospective survey had on his listener. He had found occasion for saying the same thing more than once before, and was not distinctly aware that he had not his port-wine before him.

'Well, uncle,' said Tom, with a slight complaint in his tone, 'that's what I should like to do. Can't *I* get on in the same way?'

'In the same way?' said Mr Deane, eyeing Tom with quiet deliberation. 'There go two or three questions to that, Master Tom. That depends on what sort of material you are, to begin with, and whether you've been put into the right mill. But I'll tell you what it is. Your poor father went the wrong way to work in giving you an education. It wasn't my business, and I didn't interfere: but it is as I thought it would be. You've had a sort of learning that's all very well for a young fellow like our Mr Stephen Guest, who'll have nothing to do but sign cheques all his life, and may as well have Latin inside his head as any other sort of stuffing.'

'But, uncle,' said Tom, earnestly, 'I don't see why the Latin need hinder me from getting on in business. I shall soon forget it all: it makes no difference to me. I had to do my lessons at school; but I always thought they'd never be of any use to me afterwards – I didn't care about them.'

'Ay, ay, that's all very well,' said Mr Deane; 'But it doesn't alter what I was going to say. Your Latin and rigmarole may soon dry off you, but you'll be but a bare stick after that. Besides, it's whitened your hands and taken the rough work out of you. And what do you know? Why, you know nothing about bookkeeping, to begin with, and not so much of reckoning as a common shopman. You'll have to begin at a low round of the ladder, let me tell you, if you mean to get on in life. It's no use forgetting the education your father's been paying for, if you don't give yourself a new un.'

Tom bit his lips hard; he felt as if the tears were rising, and he would rather die than let them.

'You want me to help you to a situation,' Mr Deane went on; 'well, I've no fault to find with that. I'm willing to do something for you. But you youngsters nowadays think you're to begin with living well and working easy: you've no notion of running afoot before you get on horseback. Now, you must remember what you are – you're a lad of sixteen, trained to nothing particular. There's heaps of your sort, like so many pebbles, made to fit in nowhere. Well, you might be apprenticed to some business – a chemist's and druggist's perhaps: your Latin might come in a bit there . . .'

Tom was going to speak, but Mr Deane put up his hand and said, 'Stop! hear what I've got to say. You don't want to be a 'prentice – I know, I know – you want to make more haste – and you don't want to stand behind a counter. But if you're a copying-clerk, you'll have to stand behind a desk, and stare at your ink and paper all day: there isn't much out-look there, and you won't be much wiser at the end of the year than at the beginning. The world isn't made of pen, ink, and paper, and if you're to get on in the world, young man, you must know what the world's made of. Now the best chance for you 'ud be to have a place on a wharf, or in a warehouse, where you'd learn the smell of things – but you wouldn't like that, I'll be bound; you'd have to stand cold and wet, and be shouldered about by rough fellows. You're too fine a gentleman for that.'

Mr Deane paused and looked hard at Tom, who certainly felt some inward struggle before he could reply.

'I would rather do what will be best for me in the end, sir: I would put up with what was disagreeable.'

'That's well, if you can carry it out. But you must remember it isn't only laying hold of a rope – you must go on pulling. It's the mistake you lads make that have got nothing either in your brains or your pocket, to think you've got a better start in the world if you stick yourself in a place where you can keep your coats clean, and have the shop-wenches take you for fine gentlemen. That wasn't the way *I* started, young man: when I was sixteen, my jacket smelt of tar, and I wasn't afraid of handling cheeses. That's the reason I can wear good broadcloth now, and have my legs under the same table with the heads of the best firms in St Ogg's.'

Uncle Deane tapped his box, and seemed to expand a little under his waistcoat and gold chain, as he squared his shoulders in the chair.

'Is there any place at liberty that you know of now, uncle, that I should do for? I should like to set to work at once,' said Tom, with a slight tremor in his voice.

'Stop a bit, stop a bit; we mustn't be in too great a hurry. You must bear in mind, if I put you in a place you're a bit young for, because you happen to be my nephew, I shall be responsible for you. And there's no better reason, you know, than your being my nephew; because it remains to be seen whether you're good for anything.'

'I hope I should never do you any discredit, uncle,' said Tom, hurt, as all boys are at the statement of the unpleasant truth that people feel no ground for trusting them. 'I care about my own credit too much for that.'

'Well done, Tom, well done! That's the right spirit, and I never refuse to help anybody if they've a mind to do themselves justice. There's a young man of two-and-twenty I've got my eye on now. I shall do what I can for that young man – he's got some pith in him. But then, you see, he's made good use of his time – a first-rate calculator – can tell you the cubic contents of anything in no time, and put me up the other day to a new market for Swedish bark; he's uncommonly knowing in manufactures, that young fellow.'

'I'd better set about learning bookkeeping, hadn't I, uncle?' said Tom, anxious to prove his readiness to exert himself.

'Yes, yes, you can't do amiss there. But . . . ah, Spence, you're back again. Well, Tom, there's nothing more to be said just now, I think, and I must go to business again. Goodbye. Remember me to your mother.'

Mr Deane put out his hand, with an air of friendly dismissal, and Tom had not courage to ask another question, especially in the presence of Mr Spence. So he went out again into the cold damp air. He had to call at his uncle Glegg's about the money in the savings bank, and by the time he set out again, the mist had thickened, and he could not see very far before him; but going along River Street again, he was startled, when he was within two yards of the projecting side of a shop-window, by the words 'Dorlcote Mill' in large letters on a handbill, placed as if on purpose to stare at him. It was the catalogue of the sale to take place the next week – it was a reason for hurrying faster out of the town.

Poor Tom formed no visions of the distant future as he made his way homeward; he only felt that the present was very hard. It seemed a wrong towards him that his uncle Deane had no confidence in him – did not see at once that he should acquit himself well, which Tom himself was as certain of as of the daylight. Apparently he, Tom Tulliver, was likely to be held of small account in the world, and for the first time he felt a sinking of heart under the sense that he really was very ignorant, and could do very little. Who was that enviable young man, that could tell the cubic contents of things in no time, and make suggestions about Swedish bark? Swedish bark! Tom had been used to be so entirely satisfied with himself in spite of his breaking down in a demonstration, and construing *nunc illas promite vires*, as 'now promise those men'; but now he suddenly felt at a disadvantage, because he knew less than someone else knew. There must be a world of things connected with that Swedish bark, which, if he only knew them, might have helped him to get on. It would have been much easier to make a figure with a spirited horse and a new saddle.

Two hours ago, as Tom was walking to St Ogg's, he saw the distant future before him, as he might have seen a tempting stretch of smooth sandy beach beyond a belt of flinty shingles; he was on the grassy bank then, and thought the shingles might soon be passed. But now his feet were on the sharp stones; the belt of shingles had widened, and the stretch of sand had dwindled into narrowness.

'What did my uncle Deane say, Tom?' said Maggie, putting her arm through Tom's as he was warming himself rather drearily by the kitchen fire. 'Did he say he would give you a situation?'

'No, he didn't say that. He didn't quite promise me anything; he seemed to think I couldn't have a very good situation. I'm too young.'

'But didn't he speak kindly, Tom?'

'Kindly? Pooh! what's the use of talking about that? I wouldn't care about his speaking kindly, if I could get a situation. But it's such a nuisance and bother – I've been at school all this while learning Latin and things – not a bit of good to me – and now my uncle says, I must set about learning bookkeeping and calculation, and those things. He seems to make out I'm good for nothing.'

Tom's mouth twitched with a bitter expression as he looked at the fire.

'Oh, what a pity we haven't got Dominie Sampson,' said Maggie, who couldn't help mingling some gaiety with their sadness. 'If he had taught me bookkeeping by double entry and after the Italian method, as he did Lucy Bertram, I could teach you, Tom.'

'*You* teach! Yes, I dare say. That's always the tone you take,' said Tom.

'Dear Tom! I was only joking,' said Maggie, putting her cheek against his coat-sleeve.

'But it's always the same, Maggie,' said Tom, with the little frown he put on when he was about to be justifiably severe. 'You're always setting yourself up above me and everyone else, and I've wanted to tell you about it several times. You ought not to have spoken as you did to my uncles and aunts – you should

THE MILL ON THE FLOSS

leave it to me to take care of my mother and you, and not put yourself forward. You think you know better than anyone, but you're almost always wrong. I can judge better than you can.'

Poor Tom! he had just come from being lectured and made to feel his inferiority: the reaction of his strong, self-asserting nature must take place somehow; and here was a case in which he could justly show himself dominant. Maggie's cheek flushed and her lip quivered with conflicting resentment and affection, and a certain awe as well as admiration of Tom's firmer and more effective character. She did not answer immediately; very angry words rose to her lips, but they were driven back again, and she said at last, 'You often think I'm conceited, Tom, when I don't mean what I say at all in that way. I don't mean to put myself above you – I know you behaved better than I did yesterday. But you are always so harsh to me, Tom.'

With the last words the resentment was rising again.

'No, I'm not harsh,' said Tom, with severe decision. 'I'm always kind to you; and so I shall be: I shall always take care of you. But you must mind what I say.'

Their mother came in now, and Maggie rushed away, that her burst of tears, which she felt must come, might not happen till she was safe upstairs. They were very bitter tears: everybody in the world seemed so hard and unkind to Maggie: there was no indulgence, no fondness, such as she imagined when she fashioned the world afresh in her own thoughts. In books there were people who were always agreeable or tender, and delighted to do things that made one happy, and who did not show their kindness by finding fault. The world outside the books was not a happy one, Maggie felt: it seemed to be a world where people behaved the best to those they did not pretend to love, and that did not belong to them. And if life had no love in it, what else was there for Maggie? Nothing but poverty and the companionship of her mother's narrow griefs – perhaps of her father's heart-cutting childish dependence. There is no hopelessness so sad as that of early youth, when the soul is made up of wants, and has no long memories, no super-added life in the life of others; though we who look on think lightly of such premature despair, as if our vision of the future lightened the blind sufferer's present.

Maggie in her brown frock, with her eyes reddened and her heavy hair pushed back, looking from the bed where her father lay, to the dull walls of this sad chamber which was the centre of her world, was a creature full of eager, passionate longings for all that was beautiful and glad; thirsty for all knowledge; with an ear straining after dreamy music that died away and would not come near to her; with a blind, unconscious yearning for something that would link together the wonderful impressions of this mysterious life, and give her soul a sense of home in it.

No wonder, when there is this contrast between the outward and the inward, that painful collisions come of it.

CHAPTER 6

*Tending to Refute the Popular Prejudice
against the Present of a Pocket-Knife*

In that dark time of December, the sale of the household furniture lasted
beyond the middle of the second day. Mr Tulliver, who had begun, in his
intervals of consciousness, to manifest an irritability which often appeared to
have as a direct effect the recurrence of spasmodic rigidity and insensibility, had
lain in this living death throughout the critical hours when the noise of the sale
came nearest to his chamber. Mr Turnbull had decided that it would be a less
risk to let him remain where he was, than to move him to Luke's cottage – a plan
which the good Luke had proposed to Mrs Tulliver, thinking it would be very
bad if the master were 'to waken up' at the noise of the sale; and the wife and
children had sat imprisoned in the silent chamber, watching the large prostrate
figure on the bed, and trembling lest the blank face should suddenly show some
response to the sounds which fell on their own ears with such obstinate, painful
repetition.

But it was over at last – that time of importunate certainty and eye-straining
suspense. The sharp sound of a voice, almost as metallic as the rap that followed
it, had ceased: the tramping of footsteps on the gravel had died out. Mrs
Tulliver's blond face seemed aged ten years by the last thirty hours: the poor
woman's mind had been busy divining when her favourite things were being
knocked down by the terrible hammer; her heart had been fluttering at the
thought that first one thing and then another had gone to be identified as hers in
the hateful publicity of the Golden Lion; and all the while she had to sit and
make no sign of this inward agitation. Such things bring lines in well-rounded
faces, and broaden the streaks of white among the hairs that once looked as if
they had been dipped in pure sunshine. Already, at three o'clock, Kezia, the
good-hearted, bad-tempered housemaid, who regarded all people that came to
the sale as her personal enemies, the dirt on whose feet was of a peculiarly vile
quality, had begun to scrub and swill with an energy much assisted by a
continual low muttering against 'folks as came to buy up other folks's things,'
and made light of 'scrazing' the tops of mahogany tables over which better folks
than themselves had had to suffer a waste of tissue through evaporation. She was
not scrubbing indiscriminately, for there would be further dirt of the same
atrocious kind made by people who had still to fetch away their purchases: but
she was bent on bringing the parlour, where that 'pipe-smoking pig' the bailiff
had sat, to such an appearance of scant comfort as could be given to it by
cleanliness, and the few articles of furniture bought in for the family. Her
mistress and the young folks should have their tea in it that night, Kezia was
determined.

It was between five and six o'clock, near the usual teatime, when she came
upstairs and said that Master Tom was wanted. The person who wanted him

was in the kitchen, and in the first moments, by the imperfect fire and candle-light, Tom had not even an indefinite sense of any acquaintance with the rather broad-set but active figure, perhaps two years older than himself, that looked at him with a pair of blue eyes set in a disc of freckles, and pulled some curly red locks with a strong intention of respect. A low-crowned, oilskin-covered hat, and a certain shiny deposit of dirt on the rest of the costume, as of tablets prepared for writing upon, suggested a calling that had to do with boats; but this did not help Tom's memory.

'Sarvant, Mister Tom,' said he of the red locks, with a smile which seemed to break through a self-imposed air of melancholy. 'You don't know me again, I doubt,' he went on, as Tom continued to look at him enquiringly; 'but I'd like to talk to you by yourself a bit, please.'

'There's a fire i' the parlour, Master Tom,' said Kezia, who objected to leaving the kitchen in the crisis of toasting.

'Come this way, then,' said Tom, wondering if this young fellow belonged to Guest & Co.'s wharf; for his imagination ran continually towards that particular spot, and uncle Deane might any time be sending for him to say that there was a situation at liberty.

The bright fire in the parlour was the only light that showed the few chairs, the bureau, the carpetless floor, and the one table – no, not the *one* table: there was a second table, in a corner, with a large Bible and a few other books upon it. It was this new strange bareness that Tom felt first, before he thought of looking again at the face which was also lit up by the fire, and which stole a half-shy, questioning glance at him as the entirely strange voice said, 'Why! you don't remember Bob, then, as you gen the pocketknife to, Mr Tom?'

The rough-handled pocketknife was taken out in the same moment, and the largest blade opened by way of irresistible demonstration.

'What! Bob Jakin?' said Tom – not with any cordial delight, for he felt a little ashamed of that early intimacy symbolised by the pocketknife, and was not at all sure that Bob's motives for recalling it were entirely admirable.

'Ay, ay, Bob Jakin – if Jakin it must be, 'cause there's so many Bobs as you went arter the squerrils with, that day as I plumped right down from the bough, and bruised my shins a good un – but I got the squerril tight for all that, an' a scratter it was. An' this littlish blade's broke, you see, but I wouldn't hev a new un put in, 'cause they might be cheatin' me an givin' me another knife istid, for there isn't such a blade i' the country – it's got used to my hand, like. An' there was niver nobody else gen me nothin' but what I got by my own sharpness, only you, Mr Tom; if it wasn't Bill Fawks as gen me the terrier pup istid o' drowndin' it, an' I had to jaw him a good un afore he'd give it me,'

Bob spoke with a sharp and rather treble volubility, and got through his long speech with surprising despatch, giving the blade of his knife an affectionate rub on his sleeve when he had finished.

'Well, Bob,' said Tom, with a slight air of patronage, the foregoing reminiscences having disposed him to be as friendly as was becoming, though there was no part of his acquaintance with Bob that he remembered better than the cause of their parting quarrel; 'is there anything I can do for you?'

'Why, no, Mr Tom,' answered Bob, shutting up his knife with a click and returning it to his pocket, where he seemed to be feeling for something else. 'I shouldn't ha' come back upon you now ye're i' trouble, an' folks say as the master, as I used to frighten the birds for, an' he flogged me a bit for fun when he catched me eatin' the turnip, as they say he'll niver lift up his yead no more – I shouldn't ha' come now to ax you to gi' me another knife, 'cause you gen me one afore. If a chap gives me one black eye, that's enough for me: I shan't ax him for another afore I sarve him out; an' a good turn's worth as much as a bad un, anyhow. I shall niver grow down'ards again, Mr Tom, an' you war the little chap as I liked the best when *I* war a little chap, for all you leathered me, and wouldn't look at me again. There's Dick Brumby, there, I could leather him as much as I'd a mind; but lors! you get tired o' leatherin' a chap when you can niver make him see what you want him to shy at. I'n seen chaps as' ud stand starin' at a bough till their eyes shot out, afore they'd see as a bird's tail warn't a leaf. It's poor work goin' wi' such raff – but you war allays a rare un at shying, Mr Tom, an'I could trusten to you for droppin' down wi' your stick in the nick o' time at a runnin' rat, or a stoat, or that, when I war a-beatin' the bushes.'

Bob had drawn out a dirty canvas bag, and would perhaps not have paused just then if Maggie had not entered the room and darted a look of surprise and curiosity at him, whereupon he pulled his red locks again with due respect. But the next moment the sense of the altered room came upon Maggie with a force that overpowered the thought of Bob's presence. Her eyes immediately glanced from him to the place where the bookcase had hung; there was nothing now but the oblong unfaded space on the wall, and below it the small table with the Bible and the few other books.

'Oh, Tom,' she burst out, clasping her hands, 'where are the books? I thought my uncle Glegg said he would buy them – didn't he? – are those all they've left us?'

'I suppose so,' said Tom, with a sort of desperate indifference. 'Why should they buy many books when they bought so little furniture?'

'Oh but, Tom', said Maggie, her eyes filling with tears, as she rushed up to the table to see what books had been rescued. 'Our dear old Pilgrim's Progress that you coloured with your little paints and that picture of Pilgrim with a mantle on, looking just like a turtle – oh dear!' Maggie went on, half sobbing as she turned over the few books. 'I thought we should never part with that while we lived – everything is going away from us – the end of our lives will have nothing in it like the beginning!'

Maggie turned away from the table and threw herself into a chair, with the big tears ready to roll down her cheeks – quite blinded to the presence of Bob, who was looking at her with the pursuant gaze of an intelligent dumb animal, with perceptions more perfect than his comprehension.

'Well, Bob,' said Tom, feeling that the subject of the books was unseasonable, 'I suppose you just came to see me because we're in trouble? That was very good-natured of you.'

'I'll tell you how it is, Master Tom,' said Bob, beginning to untwist his canvas bag. 'You see, I'n been with a barge this two 'ear – that's how I'n been gettin' my livin' – if it wasn't when I was tentin' the furnace, between whiles, at Torry's mill. But a fortni't ago I'd a rare bit o' luck – I allays thought I was a lucky chap, for I niver set a trap but what I catched something; but this wasn't a trap, it was a fire i' Torry's mill, an' I doused it, else it 'ud ha' set th' oil alight, an' the genelman gen me ten suvreigns – he gen me 'em himself last week. An' he said first, I was a sperrited chap – but I knowed that afore – but then he outs wi' the ten suvreigns, an' that war summat new. Here they are – all but one!' Here Bob emptied the canvas bag on the table. 'An' when I'd got 'em, my head was all of a boil like a kettle o' broth, thinkin' what sort o' life I should take to – for there war a many trades I'd thought on; for as for the barge, I'm clean tired out wi't, for it pulls the days out till they're as long as pigs' chitterlings. An' I thought first I'd ha' ferrets an' dogs, an' be a rat-catcher; an' then I thought as I should like a bigger way o' life, as I didn't know so well; for I'n seen to the bottom o' rat-catching; an' I thought, an' thought, till at last I settled I'd be a packman, for they're knowin' fellers, the packmen are – an' I'd carry the lightest things I could i' my pack – an' there'd be a use for a feller's tongue, as is no use neither wi' rats nor barges. An' I should go about the country far an' wide, an' come round the women wi' my tongue, an' get my dinner hot at the public – lors! it 'ud be a lovely life!'

Bob paused, and then said, with defiant decision, as if resolutely turning his back on that paradisaic picture, 'But I don't mind about it – not a chip! An' I'n changed one o' the suvreigns to buy my mother a goose for dinner, an' I'n bought a blue plush wescoat, an' a sealskin cap – for if I meant to be a packman, I'd do it respectable. But I don't mind about it – not a chip! My yead isn't a turnip, an' I shall p'r'aps have a chance o' dousing another fire afore long. I'm a lucky chap. So I'll thank you to take the nine suvreigns, Mr Tom, and set yoursen up with 'em somehow – if it's true as the master's broke. They mayn't go fur enough – but they'll help.'

Tom was touched keenly enough to forget his pride and suspicion.

'You're a very kind fellow, Bob,' he said, colouring, with that little diffident tremor in his voice, which gave a certain charm even to Tom's pride and severity, 'and I shan't forget you again, though I didn't know you this evening. But I can't take the nine sovereigns: I should be taking your little fortune from you, and they wouldn't do me much good either.'

'Wouldn't they, Mr Tom?' said Bob, regretfully. 'Now don't say so 'cause you think I want 'em. I aren't a poor chap. My mother gets a good penn'orth wi' picking feathers an' things; an' if she eats nothin' but bread an' water, it runs to fat. An' I'm such a lucky chap: an' I doubt you aren't quite so lucky, Mr Tom – th' old master isn't, anyhow – an' so you might take a slice o' my luck, an' no harm done. Lors! I found a leg o' pork i' the river one day: it had tumbled out o' one o' them round-sterned Dutchmen, I'll be bound. Come, think better on it, Mr Tom, for old 'quinetance sake – else I shall think you bear me a grudge.'

Bob pushed the sovereigns forward, but before Tom could speak, Maggie, clasping her hands, and looking penitently at Bob, said – 'Oh, I'm so sorry, Bob – I never thought you were so good. Why, I think you're the kindest person in the world!'

Bob had not been aware of the injurious opinion for which Maggie was performing an inward act of penitence, but he smiled with pleasure at this handsome eulogy – especially from a young lass who, as he informed his mother that evening, had 'such uncommon eyes, they looked somehow as they made him feel no how.'

'No indeed, Bob, I can't take them,' said Tom; 'But don't think I feel your kindness less because I say no. I don't want to take anything from anybody, but to work my own way. And those sovereigns wouldn't help me much – they wouldn't, really – if I were to take them. Let me shake hands with you instead.'

Tom put out his pink palm, and Bob was not slow to place his hard, grimy hand within it.

'Let me put the sovereigns in the bag again,' said Maggie; 'and you'll come and see us when you've bought your pack, Bob.'

'It's like as if I'd come out o' make-believe, o' purpose to show 'em you,' said Bob, with an air of discontent, as Maggie gave him the bag again, 'a-taking 'em back i' this way. I *am* a bit of a Do, you know; but it isn't that sort o' Do: it's on'y when a feller's a big rogue, or a big flat, I like to let him in a bit, that's all.'

'Now, don't you be up to any tricks, Bob,' said Tom, 'else you'll get transported someday.'

'No, no; not me, Mr Tom,' said Bob, with an air of cheerful confidence. 'There's no law again' fleabites. If I wasn't to take a fool in now and then, he'd niver get any wiser. But, lors! hev a suvreign to buy you and Miss summat, on'y for a token – just to match my pocketknife.'

While Bob was speaking he laid down the sovereign, and resolutely twisted up his bag again. Tom pushed back the gold, and said, 'No, indeed, Bob; thank you heartily; but I can't take it.' And Maggie, taking it between her fingers, held it up to Bob, and said, more persuasively, 'Not now – but perhaps another time. If ever Tom or my father wants help that you can give, we'll let you know – won't we, Tom? That's what you would like – to have us always depend on you as a friend that we can go to – isn't it, Bob?'

'Yes, Miss, and thank you,' said Bob, reluctantly taking the money; 'that's what I'd like – anything as you like. An' I wish you goodbye, Miss, and good-luck, Mr Tom, and thank you for shaking hands wi' me, *though* you wouldn't take the money.'

Kezia's entrance, with very black looks, to enquire if she shouldn't bring in the tea now, or whether the toast was to get hardened to a brick, was a seasonable check on Bob's flux of words, and hastened his parting bow.

CHAPTER 7

How a Hen Takes to Stratagem

The days passed, and Mr Tulliver showed, at least to the eyes of the medical man, stronger and stronger symptoms of a gradual return to his normal condition: the paralytic obstruction was, little by little, losing its tenacity, and the mind was rising from under it with fitful struggles, like a living creature making its way from under a great snowdrift, that slides and slides again, and shuts up the newly-made opening.

Time would have seemed to creep to the watchers by the bed, if it had only been measured by the doubtful distant hope which kept count of the moments within the chamber; but it was measured for them by a fast-approaching dread which made the nights come too quickly. While Mr Tulliver was slowly becoming himself again, his lot was hastening towards its moment of most palpable change. The taxing-masters had done their work like any respectable gunsmith conscientiously preparing the musket, that, duly pointed by a brave arm, will spoil a life or two. Allocaturs, filing of bills in Chancery, decrees of sale, are legal chain-shot or bombshells that can never hit a solitary mark, but must fall with widespread shattering. So deeply inherent is it in this life of ours that men have to suffer for each other's sins, so inevitably diffusive is human suffering, that even justice makes its victims, and we can conceive no retribution that does not spread beyond its mark in pulsations of unmerited pain.

By the beginning of the second week in January the bills were out advertising the sale, under a decree of Chancery, of Mr Tulliver's farming and other stock, to be followed by a sale of the mill and land, held in the proper after-dinner hour at the Golden Lion. The miller himself, unaware of the lapse of time, fancied himself still in that first stage of his misfortunes when expedients might be thought of; and often in his conscious hours talked in a feeble, disjointed manner, of plans he would carry out when he 'got well.' The wife and children were not without hope of an issue that would at least save Mr Tulliver from leaving the old spot, and seeking an entirely strange life. For uncle Deane had been induced to interest himself in this stage of the business. It would not, he acknowledged, be a bad speculation for Guest & Co. to buy Dorlcote Mill, and carry on the business, which was a good one, and might be increased by the addition of steam-power; in which case Tulliver might be retained as manager. Still Mr Deane would say nothing decided about the matter: the fact that Wakem held the mortgage on the land might put it into his head to bid for the whole estate, and further, to outbid the cautious firm of Guest & Co., who did not carry on business on sentimental grounds. Mr Deane was obliged to tell Mrs Tulliver something to that effect, when he rode over to the mill to inspect the books in company with Mr Glegg: for she had observed that 'if Guest & Co. would only think about it, Mr Tulliver's father and grandfather had been carrying on Dorlcote Mill long before the oil-mill of that firm had been so much as thought of.' Mr Deane, in reply, doubted whether that was precisely the relation between the two mills which would determine their value as investments. As for uncle Glegg, the thing lay quite beyond his imagination; the good-natured man felt sincere pity for the Tulliver family, but his money was all locked up in excellent mortgages, and he could run no risk; that would be unfair to his own relatives; but he had made up his mind that Tulliver should have some new flannel waistcoats which he had himself renounced in favour of a more elastic commodity, and that he would buy Mrs Tulliver a pound of tea now and then; it would be a journey which his benevolence delighted in beforehand, to carry the tea, and see her pleasure on being assured it was the best black.

Still, it was clear that Mr Deane was kindly disposed towards the Tullivers. One day he had brought Lucy, who was come home for the Christmas holidays, and the little blond angel-head had pressed itself against Maggie's darker cheek with many kisses and some tears. These fair slim daughters keep up a tender spot in the heart of many a respectable partner in a respectable firm, and perhaps Lucy's anxious pitying questions about her poor cousins helped to make uncle Deane more prompt in finding Tom a temporary place in the warehouse, and in putting him in the way of getting evening lessons in bookkeeping and calculation.

That might have cheered the lad and fed his hopes a little, if there had not come at the same time the much-dreaded blow of finding that his father must be a bankrupt, after all; at least, the creditors must be asked to take less than their due, which to Tom's untechnical mind was the same thing as bankruptcy. His father must not only be said to have 'lost his property,' but to have 'failed' – the word that carried the worst obloquy to Tom's mind. For when the defendant's claim for costs had been satisfied, there would remain the friendly bill of Mr Gore, and the deficiency at the bank, as well as the other debts, which would make the assets shrink into unequivocal disproportion: 'not more than ten or twelve shillings in the pound,' predicted Mr Deane, in a decided tone, tightening his lips; and the words fell on Tom like a scalding liquid, leaving a continual smart.

He was sadly in want of something to keep up his spirits a little in the unpleasant newness of his position – suddenly transported from the easy carpeted ennui of study-hours at Mr Stelling's, and the busy idleness of castle-building in a 'last-half' at school, to the companionship of sacks and hides, and bawling men thundering down heavy weights at his elbow. The first step towards getting on in the world was a chill, dusty, noisy affair, and implied going without one's tea in order to stay in St Ogg's and have an evening lesson from a one-armed elderly clerk, in a room smelling strongly of bad tobacco. Tom's young pink-and-white face had its colours very much deadened by the time he took off his hat at home, and sat down with keen hunger to his supper. No wonder he was a little cross if his mother or Maggie spoke to him.

But all this while Mrs Tulliver was brooding over a scheme by which she, and no one else, would avert the result most to be dreaded, and prevent Wakem from entertaining the purpose of bidding for the mill. Imagine a truly respectable and amiable hen, by some portentous anomaly, taking to reflection and inventing combinations by which she might prevail on Hodge not to wring her neck, or send her and her chicks to market: the result could hardly be other than much cackling and fluttering. Mrs Tulliver, seeing that everything had gone wrong, had begun to think that she had been too passive in life; and that, if she had applied her mind to business, and taken a strong resolution now and then, it would have been all the better for her and her family. Nobody, it appeared, had thought of going to speak to Wakem on this business of the mill; and yet, Mrs Tulliver reflected, it would have been quite the shortest method of securing the right end. It would have been of no use, to be sure, for Mr Tulliver to go – even if he had been able and willing – for he had been 'going to law against Wakem' and abusing him for the last ten years; Wakem was always likely to have a spite against him. And now that Mrs Tulliver had come to the conclusion that her husband was very much in the wrong to bring her into this trouble, she was inclined to think that his opinion of Wakem was wrong too. To be sure, Wakem had 'put the bailies in the house, and sold them up'; but she supposed he did that to please the man that lent Mr Tulliver the money, for a lawyer had more folks to please than one, and he wasn't likely to put Mr Tulliver, who had gone to law with him, above everybody else in the world. The attorney might be a very reasonable man – why not? He had married a Miss Clint, and at the time Mrs Tulliver had heard of that marriage, the summer when she wore her blue satin spencer, and had not yet any thoughts of Mr Tulliver, she knew no harm of Wakem. And certainly towards herself whom he knew to have been a Miss Dodson – it was out of all possibility that he could entertain anything but good-will, when it was once brought home to his observation that she, for her part, had never wanted to go to law, and indeed was at present disposed to take Mr Wakem's view of all subjects rather than her husband's. In fact, if that attorney saw a respectable matron like herself disposed 'to give him good words', why shouldn't he listen to her representations? For she would put the matter clearly before him, which had never been done yet. And he would never go and bid for the mill on purpose to spite her, an innocent woman, who thought it likely enough that she had danced with him in their youth at Squire Darleigh's, for at those big dances she had often and often danced with young men whose names she had forgotten.

Mrs Tulliver hid these reasonings in her own bosom; for when she had thrown out a hint to Mr Deane and Mr Glegg, that she wouldn't mind going to speak to Wakem herself, they had said, 'No, no, no,' and 'Pooh, pooh,' and 'Let Wakem alone,' in the tone of men who were not likely to give a candid attention to a more definite exposition of her project; still less dared she mention the plan to Tom and Maggie, for 'the children were always so against everything their mother said'; and Tom, she observed, was almost as much set against Wakem as his father was. But this unusual concentration of thought naturally gave Mrs Tulliver an unusual power of device and determination; and a day or two before the sale, to be held at the Golden Lion, when there was no longer any time to be lost, she carried out her plan by a stratagem. There were pickles in question – a large stock of pickles and ketchup which Mrs Tulliver possessed, and which Mr Hyndmarsh the grower would certainly purchase if she could transact the business in a personal interview, so she would walk with Tom to St Ogg's that morning: and when Tom urged that she might let the pickles be, at present – he didn't like her to go about just yet – she appeared so hurt at this conduct in her son, contradicting her about pickles which she had made after the family receipts inherited from his own grandmother, who had died when his mother was a little girl, that he gave way, and they walked together until she turned towards Danish Street, where Mr Hyndmarsh retailed his grocery, not far from the offices of Mr Wakem.

That gentleman was not yet come to his office: would Mrs Tulliver sit down by the fire in his private room and wait for him? She had not long to wait before the punctual attorney entered, knitting his brow with an examining glance at the stout blond woman who rose, curtsying deferentially: – a tallish man, with an aquiline nose and abundant iron-grey hair. You have never seen Mr Wakem before, and are possibly wondering whether he was really as eminent a rascal, and as crafty, bitter an enemy of honest humanity in general, and of Mr Tulliver in particular, as he is represented to be in that eidolon or portrait of him which we have seen to exist in the miller's mind.

It is clear that the irascible miller was a man to interpret any chance-shot that grazed him as an attempt on his own life and was liable to entanglements in this puzzling world, which, due consideration had to his own infallibility, required the hypothesis of a very active diabolical agency to explain them. It is still possible to believe that the attorney was not more guilty towards him, than an ingenious machine, which performs its work with much regularity, is guilty towards the rash man who, venturing too near it, is caught up by some flywheel or other, and suddenly converted into unexpected mincemeat.

But it is really impossible to decide this question by a glance at his person: the lines and lights of the human countenance are like other symbols – not always easy to read with a key. On an *a priori* view of Wakem's aquiline nose, which offended Mr Tulliver, there was not more rascality than in the shape of his stiff shirt-collar, though this too, along with his nose, might have become fraught with damnatory meaning when once the rascality was ascertained.

'Mrs Tulliver, I think?' said Mr Wakem.

'Yes, sir. Miss Elizabeth Dodson as was.'

'Pray be seated. You have some business with me?'

'Well, sir, yes,' said Mrs Tulliver, beginning to feel alarmed at her own courage, now she was really in presence of the formidable man, and reflecting that she had not settled with herself how she should begin. Mr Wakem felt in his waistcoat pockets, and looked at her in silence.

'I hope, sir,' she began at last – 'I hope, sir, you're not a thinking as *I* bear you any ill-will because o' my husband's losing his lawsuit, and the bailies being put in, and the linen being sold – oh dear! . . . for I wasn't brought up in that way. I'm sure you remember my father, sir, for he was close friends with Squire Darleigh, and we allays went to the dances there – the Miss Dodsons – nobody could be more looked on – and justly, for there was four of us, and you're quite aware as Mrs Glegg and Mrs Deane are my sisters. And as for going to law, and losing money, and having sales before you're dead, I never saw anything o' that before I was married, nor for a long while after. And I'm not to be answerable for my bad luck i' marrying out o' my own family into one where the goings-on was different. And as for being drawn in t' abuse you as other folks abuse you, sir, *that* I niver was, and nobody can say it of me.'

Mrs Tulliver shook her head a little, and looked at the hem of her pocket-handkerchief.

'I've no doubt of what you say, Mrs Tulliver,' said Mr Wakem, with cold politeness. 'But you have some question to ask me?'

'Well, sir, yes. But that's what I've said to myself – I've said you'd have some nat'ral feeling; and as for my husband, as hasn't been himself for this two months, I'm not a-defending him, in no way, for being so hot about th' erigation – not but what there's worse men, for he never wronged nobody of a shilling nor a penny, not willingly – and as for his fieriness and lawing, what could I do? And him struck as if it was with death when he got the letter as said you'd the hold upo' the land. But I can't believe but what you'll behave as a gentleman.'

'What does all this mean, Mrs Tulliver?' said Mr Wakem, rather sharply. 'What do you want to ask me?'

'Why, sir, if you'll be so good,' said Mrs Tulliver, starting a little, and speaking more hurriedly, 'if you'll be so good not to buy the mill an' the land – the land wouldn't so much matter, only my husband 'ull be like mad at your having it.'

Something like a new thought flashed across Mr Wakem's face as he said, 'Who told you I meant to buy it?'

'Why, sir, it's none o' my inventing; and I should never ha' thought of it, for my husband, as ought to know about the law, he allays used to say as lawyers had never no call to buy anything – either lands or houses – for they allays got 'em into their hands other ways. An' I should think that 'ud be the way with you, sir; and I niver said as you'd be the man to do contrairy to that.'

'Ah, well, who was it that *did* say so?' said Wakem, opening his desk, and moving things about, with the accompaniment of an almost inaudible whistle.

'Why, sir, it was Mr Glegg and Mr Deane, as have all the management: and Mr Deane thinks as Guest & Co. 'ud buy the mill and let Mr Tulliver work it for 'em, if you didn't bid for it and raise the price. And it 'ud be such a thing for my husband to stay where he is, if he could get his living: for it was his father's before him, the mill was, and his grandfather built it, though I wasn't fond o' the noise of it, when first I was married, for there was no mills in our family – not the Dodsons' – and if I'd known as the mills had so much to do with the law, it wouldn't have been me as 'ud have been the first Dodson to marry one; but I went into it blindfold, that I did, erigation and everything.'

'What! Guest & Co. would keep the mill in their own hands, I suppose, and pay your husband wages?'

'Oh dear, sir, it's hard to think of,' said poor Mrs Tulliver, a little tear making its way, 'as my husband should take wage. But it 'ud look more like what used to be, to stay at the mill than to go anywhere else: and if you'll only think – if you was to bid for the mill and buy it, my husband might be struck worse than he was before, and niver get better again as he's getting now.'

'Well, but if I bought the mill, and allowed your husband to act as my manager in the same way, how then?' said Mr Wakem.

'Oh, sir, I doubt he could niver be got to do it, not if the very mill stood still to beg and pray of him. For your name's like poison to him, it's so as never was; and he looks upon it as you've been the ruin of him all along, ever since you set the law on him about the road through the meadow – that's eight year ago, and he's been going on ever since – as I've allays told him he was wrong . . . '

'He's a pig-headed, foul-mouthed fool!' burst out Mr Wakem, forgetting himself.

'Oh dear, sir!' said Mrs Tulliver, frightened at a result so different from the one she had fixed her mind on: 'I wouldn't wish to contradict you, but it's like enough he's changed his mind with this illness – he's forgot a many things he used to talk about. And you wouldn't like to have a corpse on your mind, if he was to die; and they *do* say as it's allays unlucky when Dorlcote Mill changes hands, and the water might all run away, and *then* . . . not as I'm wishing you any ill-luck, sir, for I forgot to tell you as I remember your wedding as if it was yesterday – Mrs Wakem was a Miss Clint, I know *that* – and my boy, as there isn't a nicer, handsomer, straighter boy nowhere, went to school with your son . . . '

Mr Wakem rose, opened the door, and called to one of his clerks.

'You must excuse me for interrupting you, Mrs Tulliver; I have business that must be attended to; and I think there is nothing more necessary to be said.'

'But if you *would* bear it in mind, sir,' said Mrs Tulliver, rising, 'and not run against me and my children; and I'm not denying Mr Tulliver's been in the wrong, but he's been punished enough, and there's worse men, for it's been giving to other folks has been his fault. He's done nobody any harm but himself and his family – the more's the pity – and I go and look at the bare shelves every day, and think where all my things used to stand.'

'Yes, yes, I'll bear it in mind,' said Mr Wakem, hastily, looking towards the open door.

'And if you'd please not to say as I've been to speak to you, for my son 'ud be very angry with me for demeaning myself, I know he would, and I've trouble enough without being scolded by my children.'

Poor Mrs Tulliver's voice trembled a little, and she could make no answer to the attorney's 'good morning,' but curtsied and walked out in silence.

'Which day is it that Dorlcote Mill is to be sold? Where's the bill?' said Mr Wakem to his clerk when they were alone.

'Next Friday is the day: Friday, at six o'clock.'

'Oh! just run to Winship's the auctioneer, and see if he's at home. I have some business for him: ask him to come up.'

Although, when Mr Wakem entered his office that morning, he had had no intention of purchasing Dorlcote Mill, his mind was already made up: Mrs Tulliver had suggested to him several determining motives, and his mental glance was very rapid: he was one of those men who can be prompt without being rash, because their motives run in fixed tracks, and they have no need to reconcile conflicting aims.

To suppose that Wakem had the same sort of inveterate hatred towards

Tulliver, that Tulliver had towards him, would be like supposing that a pike and a roach can look at each other from a similar point of view. The roach necessarily abhors the mode in which the pike gets his living, and the pike is likely to think nothing further even of the most indignant roach than that he is excellent good eating; it could only be when the roach choked him that the pike could entertain a strong personal animosity. If Mr Tulliver had ever seriously injured or thwarted the attorney, Wakem would not have refused him the distinction of being a special object of his vindictiveness. But when Mr Tulliver called Wakem a rascal at the market dinner-table, the attorney's clients were not a whit inclined to withdraw their business from him; and if, when Wakem himself happened to be present, some jocose cattle-feeder, stimulated by opportunity and brandy, made a thrust at him by alluding to old ladies' wills, he maintained perfect *sang froid*, and knew quite well that the majority of substantial men then present were perfectly contented with the fact that 'Wakem was Wakem ;' that is to say, a man who always knew the stepping-stones that would carry him through very muddy bits of practice. A man who had made a large fortune, had a handsome house among the trees at Tofton, and decidedly the finest stock of port-wine in the neighbourhood of St Ogg's, was likely to feel himself on a level with public opinion. And I am not sure that even honest Mr Tulliver himself, with his general view of law as a cockpit, might not, under opposite circumstances, have seen a fine appropriateness in the truth that 'Wakem was Wakem;' since I have understood from persons versed in history, that mankind is not disposed to look narrowly into the conduct of great victors when their victory is on the right side. Tulliver, then, could be no obstruction to Wakem; on the contrary, he was a poor devil whom the lawyer had defeated several times – a hot-tempered fellow, who would always give you a handle against him. Wakem's conscience was not uneasy because he had used a few tricks against the miller: why should he hate that unsuccessful plaintiff – that pitiable, furious bull entangled in the meshes of a net?

Still, among the various excesses to which human nature is subject, moralists have never numbered that of being too fond of the people who openly revile us. The successful Yellow candidate for the borough of Old Topping, perhaps, feels no pursuant meditative hatred towards the Blue editor who consoles his subscribers with vituperative rhetoric against Yellow men who sell their country, and are the demons of private life; but he might not be sorry, if law and opportunity favoured, to kick that Blue editor to a deeper shade of his favourite colour. Prosperous men take a little vengeance now and then, as they take a diversion, when it comes easily in their way, and is no hindrance to business; and such small unimpassioned revenges have an enormous effect in life, running through all degrees of pleasant infliction, blocking the fit men out of places, and blackening characters in unpremeditated talk. Still more, to see people who have been only insignificantly offensive to us, reduced in life and humiliated without any special efforts of ours, is apt to have a soothing, flattering influence: Providence, or some other prince of this world, it appears, has undertaken the task of retribution for us; and really, by an agreeable constitution of things, our enemies somehow *don't* prosper.

Wakem was not without this parenthetic vindictiveness towards the uncom-plimentary miller; and now Mrs Tulliver had put the notion into his head, it presented itself to him as a pleasure to do the very thing that would cause Mr Tulliver the most deadly mortification – and a pleasure of a complex kind, not made up of crude malice, but mingling with it the relish of self-approbation. To see an enemy humiliated gives a certain contentment, but this is jejune compared with the highly blent satisfaction of seeing him humiliated by your benevolent action or concession on his behalf. That is a sort of revenge which fills into the scale of virtue, and Wakem was not without an intention of keeping that scale respectably filled. He had once had the pleasure of putting an old enemy of his into one of the St Ogg's alms-houses, to the rebuilding of which he had given a large subscription; and here was an opportunity of providing for another by making him his own servant. Such things give a completeness to prosperity, and contribute elements of agreeable consciousness that are not dreamed of by that short-sighted, over-heated vindictiveness, which goes out of its way to wreak itself in direct injury. And Tulliver, with his rough tongue filed by a sense of obligation, would make a better servant than any chance-fellow who was cap-in-hand for a situation. Tulliver was known to be a man of proud honesty, and Wakem was too acute not to believe in the existence of honesty. He was given to observing individuals, not to judging of them according to maxims, and no one knew better than he that all men were not like himself. Besides, he intended to overlook the whole business of land and mill pretty closely: he was fond of these practical rural matters. But there were good reasons for purchasing Dorlcote Mill, quite apart from any benevolent vengeance on the miller. It was really a capital investment; besides, Guest & Co. were going to bid for it. Mr Guest and Mr Wakem were on friendly dining terms, and the attorney liked to pre-dominate over a ship-owner and mill-owner who was a little too loud in the town affairs as well as in his table-talk. For Wakem was not a mere man of business: he was considered a pleasant fellow in the upper circles of St Ogg's – chatted amusingly over his port-wine, did a little amateur farming, and had certainly been an excellent husband and father: at church, when he went there, he sat under the handsomest of mural monuments erected to the memory of his wife. Most men would have married again under his circumstances, but he was said to be more tender to his deformed son than most men were to their best-shapen offspring. Not that Mr Wakem had not other sons besides Philip; but towards them he held only a chiaroscuro parentage, and provided for them in a grade of life duly beneath his own. In this fact, indeed, there lay the clenching motive to the purchase of Dorlcote Mill. While Mrs Tulliver was talking, it had occurred to the rapid-minded lawyer, among all the other circumstances of the case, that this purchase would, in a few years to come, furnish a highly suitable position for a certain favourite lad whom he meant to bring on in the world.

These were the mental conditions on which Mrs Tulliver had undertaken to act persuasively, and had failed: a fact which may receive some illustration from the remark of a great philosopher, that fly-fishers fail in preparing their bait so as to make it alluring in the right quarter, for want of a due acquaintance with the subjectivity of fishes.

CHAPTER 8

Daylight on the Wreck

It was a clear frosty January day on which Mr Tulliver first came downstairs: the bright sun on the chestnut boughs and the roofs opposite his window had made him impatiently declare that he would be caged up no longer: he thought everywhere would be more cheery under this sunshine than his bedroom; for he knew nothing of the bareness below, which made the flood of sunshine importunate, as if it had an unfeeling pleasure in showing the empty places, and the marks where well-known objects once had been. The impression on his mind that it was but yesterday when he received the letter from Mr Gore was so continually implied in his talk, and the attempts to convey to him the idea that many weeks had passed and much had happened since then, had been so soon swept away by recurrent forgetfulness, that even Mr Turnbull had begun to despair of preparing him to meet the facts by previous knowledge. The full sense of the present could only be imparted gradually by new experience – not by mere words, which must remain weaker than the impressions left by the *old* experience. This resolution to come downstairs was heard with trembling by the wife and children. Mrs Tulliver said Tom must not go to St Ogg's at the usual hour – he must wait and see his father downstairs: and Tom complied, though with an intense inward shrinking from the painful scene. The hearts of all three had been more deeply dejected than ever during the last few days. For Guest & Co. had not bought the mill: both mill and land had been knocked down to Wakem, who had been over the premises, and had laid before Mr Deane and Mr Glegg, in Mrs Tulliver's presence, his willingness to employ Mr Tulliver, in case of his recovery, as a manager of the business. This proposition had occasioned much family debating. Uncles and aunts were almost unanimously of opinion that such an offer ought not to be rejected when there was nothing in the way but a feeling in Mr Tulliver's mind, which, as neither aunts nor uncles shared it, was regarded as entirely unreasonable and childish – indeed, as a transferring towards Wakem of that indignation and hatred which Mr Tulliver ought properly to have directed against himself for his general quarrelsomeness, and his special exhibition of it in going to law. Here was an opportunity for Mr Tulliver to provide for his wife and daughter without any assistance from his wife's relations, and without that too evident descent into pauperism which makes it annoying to respectable people to meet the degraded member of the family by the wayside. Mr Tulliver, Mrs Glegg considered, must be made to feel, when he came to his right mind, that he could never humble himself enough; for *that* had come which she had always foreseen would come of his insolence in time past 'to them as were the best friends he'd got to look to.' Mr Glegg and Mr Deane were less stern in their views, but they both of them thought Tulliver had done enough harm by his hot-tempered crochets, and ought to put them out of the question when a livelihood was offered him:

Wakem showed a right feeling about the matter – *he* had no grudge against Tulliver. Tom had protested against entertaining the proposition: he shouldn't like his father to be under Wakem; he thought it would look mean-spirited; but his mother's main distress was the utter impossibility of ever 'turning Mr Tulliver round about Wakem', or getting him to hear reason – no, they would all have to go and live in a pigsty on purpose to spite Wakem, who spoke 'so as nobody could be fairer'. Indeed, Mrs Tulliver's mind was reduced to such confusion by living in this strange medium of unaccountable sorrow, against which she continually appealed by asking, 'Oh dear, what *have* I done to deserve worse than other women?' that Maggie began to suspect her poor mother's wits were quite going.

'Tom,' she said, when they were out of their father's room together, 'we *must* try to make father understand a little of what has happened before he goes downstairs. But we must get my mother away. She will say something that will do harm. Ask Kezia to fetch her down, and keep her engaged with something in the kitchen.'

Kezia was equal to the task. Having declared her intention of staying till the master could get about again, 'wage or no wage', she had found a certain recompense in keeping a strong hand over her mistress, scolding her for 'moithering' herself, and going about all day without changing her cap, and looking as if she was 'mushed'. Altogether, this time of trouble was rather a Saturnalian time to Kezia: she could scold her betters with unreproved freedom. On this particular occasion there were drying clothes to be fetched in: she wished to know if one pair of hands could do everything indoors and out, and observed that *she* should have thought it would be good for Mrs Tulliver to put on her bonnet, and get a breath of fresh air by doing that needful piece of work. Poor Mrs Tulliver went submissively downstairs: to be ordered about by a servant was the last remnant of her household dignities – she would soon have no servant to scold her.

Mr Tulliver was resting in his chair a little after the fatigue of dressing, and Maggie and Tom were seated near him, when Luke entered to ask if he should help master downstairs.

'Ay, ay, Luke, stop a bit, sit down,' said Mr Tulliver, pointing his stick towards a chair, and looking at him with that pursuant gaze which convalescent persons often have for those who have tended them, reminding one of an infant gazing about after its nurse. For Luke had been a constant night-watcher by his master's bed.

'How's the water now, eh, Luke?' said Mr Tulliver. 'Dix hasn't been choking you up again, eh?'

'No, sir, it's all right.'

'Ay, I thought not: he won't be in a hurry at that again, now Riley's been to settle him. That was what I said to Riley yesterday . . . I said . . .'

Mr Tulliver leaned forward, resting his elbows on the armchair and looking on the ground as if in search of something – striving after vanishing images like a man struggling against a doze. Maggie looked at Tom in mute distress – their father's mind was so far off the present, which would by and by thrust itself on his wandering consciousness. Tom was almost ready to rush away, with that impatience of painful emotion which makes one of the differences between youth and maiden, man and woman.

'Father,' said Maggie, laying her hand on his, 'don't you remember that Mr Riley is dead?'

'Dead?' said Mr Tulliver, sharply, looking in her face with a strange, examining glance.

'Yes, he died of apoplexy nearly a year ago; I remember hearing you say you had to pay money for him; and he left his daughters badly off – one of them is under-teacher at Miss Firniss's, where I've been to school, you know . . . '

'Ah?' said her father, doubtfully, still looking in her face. But as soon as Tom began to speak he turned to look at *him* with the same enquiring glances, as if he were rather surprised at the presence of these two young people. Whenever his mind was wandering in the far past, he fell into this oblivion of their actual faces: they were not those of the lad and the little wench who belonged to that past.

'It's a long while since you had the dispute with Dix, father,' said Tom. 'I remember your talking about it three years ago, before I went to school at Mr Stelling's. I've been at school there three years; don't you remember?'

Mr Tulliver threw himself backward again, losing the childlike outward glance under a rush of new ideas, which diverted him from external impressions.

'Ay, ay,' he said, after a minute or two, 'I've paid a deal o' money . . . I was determined my son should have a good eddication: I'd none myself, and I've felt the miss of it. And he'll want no other fortin: that's what I say . . . if Wakem was to get the better of me again . . . '

The thought of Wakem roused new vibrations, and after a moment's pause he began to look at the coat he had on, and to feel in his side-pocket. Then he turned to Tom, and said, in his old sharp way, 'Where have they put Gore's letter?'

It was close at hand in a drawer, for he had often asked for it before.

'You know what there is in the letter, father?' said Tom, as he gave it to him.

'To be sure I do,' said Mr Tulliver, rather angrily. 'What o' that? If Furley can't take to the property, somebody else can: there's plenty o' people in the world besides Furley. But it's hindering – my not being well – go and tell 'em to get the horse in the gig, Luke: I can get down to St Ogg's well enough – Gore's expecting me.'

'No, dear father!' Maggie burst out entreatingly, 'it's a very long while since all that: you've been ill a great many weeks – more than two months – everything is changed.'

Mr Tulliver looked at them all three alternately with a startled gaze: the idea that much had happened of which he knew nothing had often transiently arrested him before, but it came upon him now with entire novelty.

'Yes, father,' said Tom, in answer to the gaze. 'You needn't trouble your mind about business until you are quite well: everything is settled about that for the present – about the mill and the land and the debts.'

'What's settled, then?' said his father, angrily.

'Don't you take on too much about it, sir,' said Luke. 'You'd ha' paid iverybody if you could – that's what I said to Master Tom – I said you'd ha' paid iverybody if you could.'

Good Luke felt, after the manner of contented hard-working men whose lives have been spent in servitude, that sense of natural fitness in rank which made his master's downfall a tragedy to him. He was urged, in his slow way, to say something that would express his share in the family sorrow, and these words, which he had used over and over again to Tom when he wanted to decline the full payment of his fifty pounds out of the children's money, were the most ready to his tongue. They were just the words to lay the most painful hold on his master's bewildered mind.

'Paid everybody?' he said, with vehement agitation, his face flushing, and his eye lighting up. 'Why . . . what . . . have they made me a *bankrupt?*'

'O father, dear father!' said Maggie, who thought that terrible word really represented the fact; 'bear it well – because we love you – your children will always love you. Tom will pay them all; he says he will, when he's a man.'

She felt her father beginning to tremble – his voice trembled too, as he said, after a few moments, 'Ay, my little wench, but I shall never live twice o'er.'

'But perhaps you will live to see me pay everybody, father,' said Tom, speaking with a great effort.

'Ah, my lad,' said Mr Tulliver, shaking his head slowly, 'but what's broke can never be whole again: it 'ud be your doing, not mine.' Then, looking up at him, 'You're only sixteen – it's an uphill fight for you – but you mustn't throw it at your father; the raskills have been too many for him. I've given you a good eddication – that'll start you.'

Something in his throat half-choked the last words; the flush which had alarmed his children because it had so often preceded a recurrence of paralysis, had subsided, and his face looked pale and tremulous. Tom said nothing: he was still struggling against his inclination to rush away. His father remained quiet a minute or two, but his mind did not seem to be wandering again.

'Have they sold me up, then?' he said, more calmly, as if he were possessed simply by the desire to know what had happened.

'Everything is sold, father; but we don't know all about the mill and the land yet,' said Tom, anxious to ward off any question leading to the fact that Wakem was the purchaser.

'You must not be surprised to see the room look very bare downstairs, father,' said Maggie; 'but there's your chair and the bureau – *they're* not gone.'

'Let us go – help me down, Luke – I'll go and see everything,' said Mr Tulliver, leaning on his stick, and stretching out his other hand towards Luke.

'Ay, sir,' said Luke, as he gave his arm to his master, 'you'll make up your mind to't a bit better when you've seen iverything: you'll get used to't. That's what my mother says about her shortness o' breath – she says she's made friends wi't now, though she fought again' it sore when it fust come on.'

Maggie ran on before to see that all was right in the dreary parlour, where the fire, dulled by the frosty sunshine, seemed part of the general shabbiness. She turned her father's chair, and pushed aside the table to make an easy way for him, and then stood with a beating heart to see him enter and look round for the first time. Tom advanced before him, carrying the leg-rest, and stood beside Maggie on the hearth. Of those two young hearts Tom's suffered the most unmixed pain, for Maggie, with all her keen susceptibility, yet felt as if the sorrow made larger room for her love to flow in, and gave breathing-space to her passionate nature. No true boy feels that: he would rather go and slay the Nemean lion, or perform any round of heroic labours, than endure perpetual appeals to his pity, for evils over which he can make no conquest.

Mr Tulliver paused just inside the door, resting on Luke, and looking round him at all the bare places, which for him were filled with the shadows of departed objects – the daily companions of his life. His faculties seemed to be renewing their strength from getting a footing on this demonstration of the senses.

'Ah!' he said, slowly, moving towards his chair, 'they've sold me up . . . they've sold me up.'

Then seating himself, and laying down his stick, while Luke left the room, he looked round again.

'They've left the big Bible,' he said. 'It's got everything in – when I was born and married – bring it me, Tom.'

The quarto Bible was laid open before him at the fly-leaf, and while he was reading with slowly-travelling eyes, Mrs Tulliver entered the room, but stood in mute surprise to find her husband down already, and with the great Bible before him.

'Ah,' he said, looking at a spot where his finger rested, 'my mother was Margaret Beaton – she died when she was forty-seven: hers wasn't a long-lived family – we're our mother's children – Gritty and me are – we shall go to our last bed before long.'

He seemed to be pausing over the record of his sister's birth and marriage, as if it were suggesting new thoughts to him: then he suddenly looked up at Tom, and said, in a sharp tone of alarm, 'They haven't come upo' Moss for the money as I lent him, have they?'

'No, father,' said Tom; 'the note was burnt.'

Mr Tulliver turned his eyes on the page again, and presently said, 'Ah . . . Elizabeth Dodson . . . it's eighteen year since I married her . . . '

'Come next Ladyday,' said Mrs Tulliver, going up to his side and looking at the page.

Her husband fixed his eyes earnestly on her face.

'Poor Bessy,' he said, 'you was a pretty lass then – everybody said so – and I used to think you kept your good looks rarely. But you're sorely aged . . . don't you bear me ill-will . . . I meant to do well by you . . . we promised one another for better or for worse . . . '

'But I never thought it 'ud be so for worse as this,' said poor Mrs Tulliver, with the strange scared look that had come over her of late; 'and my poor father gave me away . . . and to come on so all at once . . . '

'Oh, mother,' said Maggie, 'don't talk in that way.'

'No, I know you won't let your poor mother speak . . . that's been the way all my life . . . your father never minded what I said . . . it 'ud have been o' no use for me to beg and pray . . . and it 'ud be no use now, if I was to go down o' my hands and knees . . . '

'Don't say so, Bessy,' said Mr Tulliver, whose pride, in these first moments of humiliation, was in abeyance to the sense of some justice in his wife's reproach. 'If there's anything left as I could do to make you amends, I wouldn't say you nay.'

'Then we might stay here and get a living, and I might keep among my own sisters . . . and me been such a good wife to you, and never crossed you from week's end to week's end . . . and they all say so . . . they say it 'ud be nothing but right . . . only you're so turned against Wakem.'

'Mother,' said Tom, severely, 'this is not the time to talk about that.'

'Let her be,' said Mr Tulliver. 'Say what you mean, Bessy.'

'Why, now the mill and the land's all Wakem's, and he's got everything in his hands, what's the use o' setting your face against him? – when he says you may stay here, and speaks as fair as can be, and says you may manage the business, and have thirty shillings a-week, and a horse to ride about to market? And where have we got to put our heads? We must go into one o' the cottages in the village . . . and me and my children brought down to that . . . and all because you must set your mind against folks till there's no turning you.'

Mr Tulliver had sunk back in his chair trembling.

'You may do as you like wi' me, Bessy,' he said, in a low voice; 'I've been the bringing of you to poverty . . . this world's too many for me . . . I'm nought but a bankrupt – it's no use standing up for anything now.'

'Father,' said Tom, 'I don't agree with my mother or my uncles, and I don't think you ought to submit to be under Wakem. I get a pound a-week now, and you can find something else to do when you get well.'

'Say no more, Tom, say no more: I've had enough for this day. Give me a kiss, Bessy, and let us bear one another no ill-will: we shall never be young again . . . This world's been too many for me.'

CHAPTER 9

An Item Added to the Family Register

That first moment of renunciation and submission was followed by days of violent struggle in the miller's mind, as the gradual access of bodily strength brought with it increasing ability to embrace in one view all the conflicting conditions under which he found himself. Feeble limbs easily resign themselves to be tethered, and when we are subdued by sickness it seems possible to us to fulfil pledges which the old vigour comes back and breaks. There were times when poor Tulliver thought the fulfilment of his promise to Bessy was some-thing quite too hard for human nature: he had promised her without knowing what she was going to say – she might as well have asked him to carry a ton weight on his back. But again, there were many feelings arguing on her side, besides the sense that life had been made hard to her by having married him. He saw a possibility, by much pinching, of saving money out of his salary towards paying a second dividend to his creditors, and it would not be easy elsewhere to get a situation such as he could fill. He had led an easy life, ordering much and working little, and had no aptitude for any new business. He must perhaps take to day-labour, and his wife must have help from her sisters – a prospect doubly bitter to him, now they had let all Bessy's precious things be sold, probably because they liked to set her against him, by making her feel that he had brought her to that pass. He listened to their admonitory talk, when they came to urge on him what he was bound to do for poor Bessy's sake, with averted eyes, that every now and then flashed on them furtively when their backs were turned. Nothing but the dread of needing their help could have made it an easier alternative to take their advice.

But the strongest influence of all was the love of the old premises where he had run about when he was a boy, just as Tom had done after him. The Tullivers had lived on this spot for generations, and he had sat listening on a low stool on winter evenings while his father talked of the old half-timbered mill that had been there before the last great floods which damaged it so that his grandfather pulled it down and built the new one. It was when he got able to walk about and look at all the old objects, that he felt the strain of this clinging affection for the old home as part of his life, part of himself. He couldn't bear to think of himself living on any other spot than this, where he knew the sound of every gate and door, and felt that the shape and colour of every roof and weather-stain and broken hillock was good, because his growing senses had been fed on them. Our instructed vagrancy, which has hardly time to linger by the hedgerows, but runs away early to the tropics, and is at home with palms and banyans – which is nourished on books of travel, and stretches the theatre of its imagination to the Zambesi – can hardly get a dim notion of what an old-fashioned man like Tulliver felt for this spot, where all his memories centred, and where life seemed like a familiar smooth-handled tool that the fingers clutch with loving ease. And just now he was living in that freshened memory of the far-off time which comes to us in the passive hours of recovery from sickness.

'Ay, Luke,' he said, one afternoon, as he stood looking over the orchard gate, 'I remember the day they planted those apple trees. My father was a huge man for planting – it was like a merrymaking to him to get a cart full o' young trees – and I used to stand i' the cold with him, and follow him about like a dog.'

Then he turned round, and, leaning against the gatepost, looked at the opposite buildings.

'The old mill 'ud miss me, I think, Luke. There's a story as when the mill changes hands, the river's angry – I've heard my father say it many a time. There's no telling whether there mayn't be summat *in* the story, for this is a puzzling world, and Old Harry's got a finger in it – it's been too many for me, I know.'

'Ay, sir,' said Luke, with soothing sympathy, 'what wi' the rust on the wheat, an' the firin' o' the ricks an' that, as I've seen i' my time – things often looks comical: there's the bacon fat wi' our last pig runs away like butter – it leaves nought but a scratchin'.'

'It's just as if it was yesterday, now,' Mr Tulliver went on, 'when my father began the malting. I remember, the day they finished the malt-house, I thought summat great was to come of it; for we'd a plum-pudding that day and a bit of a feast, and I said to my mother – she was a fine dark-eyed woman, my mother was – the little wench 'ull be as like her as two peas.' – Here Mr Tulliver put his stick between his legs, and took out his snuffbox, for the greater enjoyment of this anecdote, which dropped from him in fragments, as if he every other moment lost narration in vision. 'I was a little chap no higher much than my mother's knee – she was sore fond of us children, Gritty and me – and so I said to her, 'Mother,' I said, 'shall we have plum-pudding *every* day because o' the malt-house?' She used to tell me o' that till her dying day. She was but a young woman when she died, my mother was. But it's forty good year since they finished the malt-house, and it isn't many days out of 'em all, as I haven't looked out into the yard there, the first thing in the morning – all weathers, from year's end to year's end. I should go off my head in a new place. I should be like as if I'd lost my way. It's all hard, whichever way I look at it – the harness 'ull gall me – but it 'ud be summat to draw along the old road, instead of a new un.'

'Ay, sir,' said Luke. 'you'd be a deal better here nor in some new place. I can't abide new places mysen: things is allays awk'ard – narrow-wheeled waggins, belike, and the stiles all another sort, an' oatcake i' some places, tow'rt th' head o' the Floss, there. It's poor work, changing your countryside.'

'But I doubt, Luke, they'll be for getting rid o' Ben, and making you do with a lad – and I must help a bit wi' the mill. You'll have a worse place.'

'Ne'er mind, sir,' said Luke, 'I shan't plague mysen. I'n been wi' you twenty year, an' you can't get twenty year wi' whistlin' for 'em, no more nor you can make the trees grow: you mun wait till God A'mighty sends 'em. I can't abide new victual nor new faces, *I* can't – you niver know but what they'll gripe you.'

The walk was finished in silence after this, for Luke had disburthened himself of thoughts to an extent that left his conversational resources quite barren, and Mr Tulliver had relapsed from his recollections into a painful meditation on the choice of hardships before him. Maggie noticed that he was unusually absent that evening at tea; and afterwards he sat leaning forward in his chair, looking at the ground, moving his lips, and shaking his head from time to time. Then he looked hard at Mrs Tulliver, who was knitting opposite him, then at Maggie, who, as she bent over her sewing, was intensely conscious of some drama going forward in her father's mind. Suddenly he took up the poker and broke the large coal fiercely.

'Dear heart, Mr Tulliver, what can you be thinking of?' said his wife, looking up in alarm: 'it's very wasteful, breaking the coal, and we've got hardly any large coal left, and I don't know where the rest is to come from.'

'I don't think you're quite so well tonight, are you, father?' said Maggie; 'you seem uneasy.'

'Why, how is it Tom doesn't come?' said Mr Tulliver, impatiently.

'Dear heart! is it time? I must go and get his supper,' said Mrs Tulliver, laying down her knitting, and leaving the room.

'It's nigh upon half-past eight,' said Mr Tulliver. 'He'll be here soon. Go, go and get the big Bible, and open it at the beginning, where everything's set down. And get the pen and ink.'

Maggie obeyed, wondering: but her father gave no further orders, and only sat listening for Tom's footfall on the gravel, apparently irritated by the wind, which had risen, and was roaring so as to drown all other sounds. There was a strange light in his eyes that rather frightened Maggie: she began to wish that Tom would come, too.

'There he is, then,' said Mr Tulliver, in an excited way, when the knock came at last. Maggie went to open the door, but her mother came out of the kitchen, hurriedly, saying, 'Stop a bit, Maggie; I'll open it.'

Mrs Tulliver had begun to be a little frightened at her boy, but she was jealous of every office others did for him.

'Your supper's ready by the kitchen-fire, my boy,' she said, as he took off his hat and coat. 'You shall have it by yourself, just as you like, and I won't speak to you.'

'I think my father wants Tom, mother,' said Maggie; 'he must come into the parlour first.'

Tom entered with his usual saddened evening face, but his eyes fell immediately on the open Bible and the inkstand, and he glanced with a look of anxious surprise at his father, who was saying, 'Come, come, you're late – I want you.'

'Is there anything the matter, father?' said Tom.

'You sit down – all of you,' said Mr Tulliver, peremptorily. 'And, Tom, sit down here; I've got something for you to write i' the Bible.'

They all three sat down, looking at him. He began to speak, slowly, looking first at his wife.

'I've made up my mind, Bessy, and I'll be as good as my word to you. There'll be the same grave made for us to lie down in, and we mustn't be bearing one another ill-will. I'll stop in the old place, and I'll serve under Wakem – and I'll serve him like an honest man: there's no Tulliver but what's honest, mind that, Tom' – here his voice rose: 'they'll have it to throw up against me as I paid a dividend – but it wasn't my fault – it was because there's raskills in the world. They've been too many for me, and I must give in. I'll put my neck in harness – for you've a right to say as I've brought you into trouble, Bessy – and I'll serve him as honest as if he was no raskill: I'm an honest man, though I shall never hold my head up no more – I'm a tree as is broke – a tree as is broke.'

He paused, and looked on the ground. Then suddenly raising his head, he said, in a louder yet deeper tone, 'But I won't forgive him! I know what they say – he never meant me any harm – that's the way Old Harry props up the raskills – he's been at the bottom of everything – but he's a fine gentleman – I know, I know. I shouldn't ha' gone to law, they say. But who made it so as there was no arbitratin', and no justice to be got? It signifies nothing to him – I know that; he's one o' them fine gentlemen as get money by doing business for poorer folks, and when he's made beggars of 'em he'll give 'em charity. I won't forgive him! I wish he might be punished with shame till his own son 'ud like to forget him. I wish he may do summat as they'd make him work at the treadmill! But he won't – he's too big a raskill to let the law lay hold on him. And you mind this,

Tom – you never forgive him, neither if you mean to be my son. There'll maybe come a time when you may make him feel – it'll never come to me – I'n got my head under the yoke. Now write – write it i' the Bible.'

'Oh, father, what?' said Maggie, sinking down by his knee, pale and trembling. 'It's wicked to curse and bear malice.'

'It isn't wicked, I tell you,' said her father, fiercely. 'It's wicked as the raskills should prosper – it's the devil's doing. Do as I tell you, Tom. Write.'

'What am I to write, father?' said Tom, with gloomy submission.

'Write as your father, Edward Tulliver, took service under John Wakem, the man as had helped to ruin him, because I'd promised my wife to make her what amends I could for her trouble, and because I wanted to die in th' old place, where I was born and my father was born. Put that i' the right words – you know how – and then write, as I don't forgive Wakem, for all that: and for all I'll serve him honest, I wish evil may befall him. Write that.'

There was a dead silence as Tom's pen moved along the paper: Mrs Tulliver looked scared, and Maggie trembled like a leaf.

'Now let me hear what you've wrote,' said Mr Tulliver. Tom read aloud, slowly.

'Now write – write as you'll remember what Wakem's done to your father, and you'll make him and his feel it, if ever the day comes. And sign your name Thomas Tulliver.'

'Oh, no, father, dear father!' said Maggie, almost choked with fear. 'You shouldn't make Tom write that.'

'Be quiet, Maggie!' said Tom. 'I *shall* write it.'

BOOK FOURTH

The Valley of Humiliation

CHAPTER I

A Variation of Protestantism Unknown to Bossuet

Journeying down the Rhone on a summer's day, you have perhaps felt the sunshine made dreary by those ruined villages which stud the banks in certain parts of its course, telling how the swift river once rose, like an angry, destroying god, sweeping down the feeble generations whose breath is in their nostrils, and making their dwellings a desolation. Strange contrast, you may have thought, between the effect produced on us by these dismal remnants of commonplace houses, which in their best days were but the sign of a sordid life, belonging in all its details to our own vulgar era; and the effect produced by those ruins on the castled Rhine, which have crumbled and mellowed into such harmony with the green and rocky steeps, that they seem to have a natural fitness, like the mountain-pine: nay, even in the day when they were built they must have had this fitness, as if they had been raised by an earth-born race, who had inherited from their mighty parent a sublime instinct of form. And that was a day of romance! If those robber-barons were somewhat grim and drunken ogres, they had a certain grandeur of the wild beast in them – they were forest boars with tusks, tearing and rending, not the ordinary domestic grunter; they represented the demon forces for ever in collision with beauty, virtue, and the gentle uses of life; they made a fine contrast in the picture with the wandering minstrel, the soft-lipped princess, the pious recluse, and the timid Israelite. That was a time of colour, when the sunlight fell on glancing steel and floating banners; a time of adventure and fierce struggle – nay, of living, religious art and religious enthusiasm; for were not cathedrals built in those days and did not great emperors leave their Western palaces to die before the infidel strongholds in the sacred East? Therefore it is that these Rhine castles thrill me with a sense of poetry: they belong to the grand historic life of humanity and raise up for me the vision of an epoch. But these dead-tinted hollow-eyed, angular skeletons of villages on the Rhone oppress me with the feeling that human life – very much of it – is a narrow, ugly grovelling existence, which even calamity does not elevate, but rather tends to exhibit in all its bare vulgarity of conception; and I have a cruel conviction that the lives these ruins are the traces of, were part of a gross sum of obscure vitality, that will be swept into the same oblivion with the generations of ants and beavers.

Perhaps something akin to this oppressive feeling may have weighed upon you in watching this old-fashioned family life on the banks of the Floss, which even sorrow hardly suffices to lift above the level of the tragi-comic. It is a sordid life, you say, this of the Tullivers and Dodsons – irradiated by no sublime principles, no romantic visions, no active, self-renouncing faith – moved by none of those wild, uncontrollable passions which create the dark shadows of misery and crime – without that primitive rough simplicity of wants, that hard, submissive, ill-paid toil, that childlike spelling-out of what nature has written, which gives its poetry to peasant life. Here, one has conventional worldly notions and habits without instruction and without polish – surely the most prosaic form of human life: proud respectability in a gig of unfashionable build: worldliness without side-dishes. Observing these people narrowly, even when the iron hand of misfortune has shaken them from their unquestioning hold on the world, one sees little trace of religion, still less of a distinctively Christian creed. Their belief in the Unseen, so far as it manifests itself at all, seems to be rather of a pagan kind; their moral notions, though held with strong tenacity, seem to have no standard beyond hereditary custom. You could not live among such people; you are stifled for want of an outlet towards something beautiful, great, or noble; you are irritated with these dull men and women, as a kind of population out of keeping with the earth on which they live – with this rich plain where the great river flows for ever onward, and links the small pulse of the old English town with the beatings of the world's mighty heart. A vigorous superstition, that lashes its gods or lashes its own back, seems to be more congruous with the mystery of the human lot, than the mental condition of these emmet-like Dodsons and Tullivers.

I share with you this sense of oppressive narrowness; but it is necessary that we should feel it, if we care to understand how it acted on the lives of Tom and Maggie – how it has acted on young natures in many generations, that in the onward tendency of human things have risen above the mental level of the generation before them, to which they have been nevertheless tied by the strongest fibres of their hearts. The suffering, whether of martyr or victim, which belongs to every historical advance of mankind, is represented in this way in every town, and by hundreds of obscure hearths; and we need not shrink from this comparison of small things with great; for does not science tell us that its highest striving is after the ascertainment of a unity which shall bind the smallest things with the greatest? In natural science, I have understood, there is nothing petty to the mind that has a large vision of relations, and to which every single object suggests a vast sum of conditions. It is surely the same with the observation of human life.

Certainly the religious and moral ideas of the Dodsons and Tullivers were of too specific a kind to be arrived at deductively, from the statement that they were part of the Protestant population of Great Britain. Their theory of life had its core of soundness, as all theories must have on which decent and prosperous families have been reared and have flourished; but it had the very slightest tincture of theology. If, in the maiden days of the Dodson sisters, their Bibles opened more easily at some parts than others, it was because of dried tulip-petals, which had been distributed quite impartially, without preference for the historical, devotional, or doctrinal. Their religion was of a simple, semi-pagan kind, but there was no heresy in it – if heresy properly means choice – for they didn't know there was any other religion, except that of chapel-goers, which appeared to run in families, like asthma. How *should* they know? The vicar of their pleasant rural parish was not a controversialist, but a good hand at whist, and one who had a joke always ready for a blooming female parishioner. The religion of the Dodsons consisted in revering whatever was customary and respectable: it was necessary to be baptised, else one could not be buried in the churchyard, and to take the sacrament before death as a security against more dimly understood perils; but it was of equal necessity to have the proper pall-bearers and well-cured hams at one's funeral, and to leave an unimpeachable will. A Dodson would not be taxed with the omission of anything that was becoming, or that belonged to that eternal fitness of things which was plainly indicated in the practice of the most substantial parishioners, and in the family traditions – such as, obedience to parents, faithfulness to kindred, industry, rigid honesty, thrift, the thorough scouring of wooden and copper utensils, the hoarding of coins likely to disappear from the currency, the production of first-rate commodities for the market, and the general preference for whatever was home-made. The Dodsons were a very proud race, and their pride lay in the utter frustration of all desire to tax them with a breach of traditional duty or propriety. A wholesome pride in many respects, since it identified honour with perfect integrity, thoroughness of work, and faithfulness to admitted rules: and society owes some worthy qualities in many of her members to mothers of the Dodson class, who made their butter and their fromenty well, and would have felt disgraced to make it otherwise. To be honest and poor was never a Dodson motto, still less to seem rich though being poor; rather, the family badge was to be honest and rich; and not only rich, but richer than was supposed. To live respected, and have the proper bearers at your funeral, was an achievement of the ends of existence that would be entirely nullified if, on the reading of your will, you sank in the opinion of your fellow-men, either by turning out to be poorer than they expected, or by leaving your money in a capricious manner, without strict regard to degrees of kin. The right thing must always be done towards kindred. The right thing was to correct them severely, if they were other than a credit to the family, but still not to alienate from them the smallest rightful share in the family shoe-buckles and other property. A conspicuous quality in the Dodson character was its genuineness: its vices and virtues alike were phases of a proud, honest egoism, which had a hearty dislike to whatever made against its own credit and interest, and would be frankly hard of speech to inconvenient 'kin', but would never forsake or ignore them – would not let them want bread, but only require them to eat it with bitter herbs.

The same sort of traditional belief ran in the Tulliver veins, but it was carried in richer blood, having elements of generous imprudence, warm affection, and hot-tempered rashness. Mr Tulliver's grandfather had been heard to say that he was descended from one Ralph Tulliver, a wonderfully clever fellow, who had ruined himself. It is likely enough that the clever Ralph was a high liver, rode spirited horses, and was very decidedly of his own opinion. On the other hand, nobody had ever heard of a Dodson who had ruined himself: it was not the way of that family.

If such were the views of life on which the Dodsons and Tullivers had been reared in the praiseworthy past of Pitt and high prices, you will infer from what you already know concerning the state of society in St Ogg's, that there had been no highly modifying influence to act on them in their mature life. It was still possible, even in that later time of anti-Catholic preaching, for people to hold many pagan ideas, and believe themselves good church-people notwithstanding; so we need hardly feel any surprise at the fact that Mr Tulliver, though a regular church-goer, recorded his vindictiveness on the fly-leaf of his Bible. It was not that any harm could be said concerning the vicar of that charming rural parish to which Dorlcote Mill belonged: he was a man of excellent family, an irreproachable bachelor, of elegant pursuits – had taken honours, and held a fellowship. Mr Tulliver regarded him with dutiful respect, as he did everything else belonging to the church-service; but he considered that church was one thing and common-sense another, and he wanted nobody to tell *him* what common-sense was. Certain seeds which are required to find a nidus for themselves under unfavourable circumstances, have been supplied by nature with an apparatus of hooks, so that they will get a hold on very unreceptive surfaces. The spiritual seed which had been scattered over Mr Tulliver had apparently been destitute of any corresponding provision, and had slipped off to the winds again, from a total absence of hooks.

CHAPTER 2

The Torn Nest is Pierced by the Thorns

There is something sustaining in the very agitation that accompanies the first shocks of trouble, just as an acute pain is often a stimulus, and produces an excitement which is transient strength. It is in the slow, changed life that follows – in the time when sorrow has become stale, and has no longer an emotive intensity that counteracts its pain – in the time when day follows day in dull unexpectant sameness, and trial is a dreary routine – it is then that despair threatens; it is then that the peremptory hunger of the soul is felt, and eye and ear are strained after some unlearned secret of our existence, which shall give to endurance the nature of satisfaction.

This time of utmost need was come to Maggie, with her short span of thirteen years. To the usual precocity of the girl, she added that early experience of struggle, of conflict between the inward impulse and outward fact, which is the lot of every imaginative and passionate nature; and the years since she hammered the nails into her wooden Fetish among the worm-eaten shelves of the attic, had been filled with so eager a life in the triple world of Reality, Books, and Waking Dreams, that Maggie was strangely old for her years in everything except in her entire want of that prudence and self-command which were the qualities that made Tom manly in the midst of his intellectual boyishness. And now her lot was beginning to have a still, sad monotony, which threw her more than ever on her inward self. Her father was able to attend to business again, his affairs were settled, and he was acting as Wakem's manager on the old spot. Tom went to and fro every morning and evening, and became more and more silent in the short intervals at home: what was there to say? One day was like another, and Tom's interest in life, driven back and crushed on every other side, was concentrating itself into the one channel of ambitious resistance to misfortune. The peculiarities of his father and mother were very irksome to him, now they were laid bare of all the softening accompaniments of an easy prosperous home; for Tom had very clear prosaic eyes, not apt to be dimmed by mists of feeling or imagination. Poor Mrs Tulliver, it seemed, would never recover her old self – her placid household activity: how could she? The objects among which her mind had moved complacently were all gone – all the little hopes, and schemes, and speculations, all the pleasant little cares about her treasures which had made the world quite comprehensible to her for a quarter of a century, since she had made her first purchase of the sugar-tongs, had been suddenly snatched away from her, and she remained bewildered in this empty life. Why that should have happened to her which had not happened to other women, remained an insoluble question by which she expressed her perpetual ruminating comparison of the past with the present. It was piteous to see the comely woman getting thinner and more worn under a bodily as well as mental restlessness, which made her often wander about the empty house after her work was done, until Maggie, becoming alarmed about her, would seek her, and bring her down by telling her how it vexed Tom that she was injuring her health by never sitting down and resting herself. Yet amidst this helpless imbecility there was a touching trait of humble self-devoting maternity, which made Maggie feel tenderly towards her poor mother amidst all the little wearing griefs caused by her mental feebleness. She would let Maggie do none of the work that was heaviest and most soiling to the hands, and was quite peevish when Maggie attempted to relieve her from her grate-brushing and scouring: 'Let it alone, my dear; your hands 'ull get as hard as hard,' she would say: 'it's your mother's place to do that. I can't do the sewing – my eyes fail me.' And she would still brush and carefully tend Maggie's hair, which she had become reconciled to, in spite of its refusal to curl, now it was so long and massy. Maggie was not her pet child, and, in general, would have been much better if she had been quite different; yet the womanly heart, so bruised in its small personal desires, found a future to rest on in the life of this young thing, and the mother pleased herself with wearing out her own hands to save the hands that had so much more life in them.

But the constant presence of her mother's regretful bewilderment was less painful to Maggie than that of her father's sullen incommunicative depression. As long as the paralysis was upon him, and it seemed as if he might always be in a childlike condition of dependence – as long as he was still only half-awakened to his trouble, Maggie had felt the strong tide of pitying love almost as an inspiration, a new power, that would make the most difficult life easy for his sake; but now, instead of childlike dependence there had come a taciturn hard concentration of purpose, in strange contrast with his old vehement communicativeness and high spirit; and this lasted from day to day, and from week to week, the dull eye never brightening with any eagerness or any joy. It is something cruelly incomprehensible to youthful natures, this sombre sameness in middle-aged and elderly people, whose life has resulted in disappointment and discontent, to whose faces a smile becomes so strange that the sad lines all about the lips and brow seem to take no notice of it, and it hurries away again for want of a welcome. 'Why will they not kindle up and be glad sometimes?' thinks young elasticity. 'It would be so easy if they only liked to do it.' And these leaden clouds that never part are apt to create impatience even in the filial affection that streams forth in nothing but tenderness and pity in the time of more obvious affliction.

Mr Tulliver lingered nowhere away from home: he hurried away from market, he refused all invitations to stay and chat, as in old times, in the houses where he called on business. He could not be reconciled with his lot: there was no attitude in which his pride did not feel its bruises; and in all behaviour towards him, whether kind or cold, he detected an allusion to the change in his circumstances. Even the days on which Wakem came to ride round the land and enquire into the business, were not so black to him as those market-days on which he had met several creditors who had accepted a composition from him. To save something towards the repayment of those creditors was the object towards which he was now bending all his thoughts and efforts; and under the influence of this all-compelling demand of his nature, the somewhat profuse man, who hated to be stinted or to stint anyone else in his own house, was gradually metamorphosed into the keen-eyed grudger of morsels. Mrs Tulliver could not economise enough to satisfy him, in their food and firing; and he would eat nothing himself but what was of the coarsest quality. Tom, though depressed and strongly repelled by his father's sullenness, and the dreariness of home, entered thoroughly into his father's feelings about paying the creditors; and the poor lad brought his first quarter's money, with a delicious sense of achievement, and gave it to his father to put into the tin box which held the savings. The little store of sovereigns in the tin box seemed to be the only sight that brought a faint beam of pleasure into the miller's eyes – faint and transient, for it was soon dispelled by the thought that the time would be long – perhaps longer than his life – before the narrow savings could remove the hateful incubus of debt. A deficit of more than five hundred pounds, with the accumulating interest, seemed a deep pit to fill with the savings from thirty shillings a-week, even when Tom's probable savings were to be added. On this one point there was entire community of feeling in the four widely differing beings who sat round the dying fire of sticks, which made a cheap warmth for them on the verge of bedtime. Mrs Tulliver carried the proud integrity of the Dodsons in her blood, and had been brought up to think that to wrong people of their money, which was another phrase for debt, was a sort of moral pillory: it would have been wickedness, to her mind, to have run counter to her husband's desire to 'do the right thing,' and retrieve his name. She had a confused dreamy notion that, if the creditors were all paid, her plate and linen ought to come back to her; but she had an inbred perception that while people owed money they were unable to pay, they couldn't rightly call anything their own. She murmured a little that Mr Tulliver so peremptorily refused to receive anything in repayment from Mr and Mrs Moss; but to all his requirements of household economy she was submissive to the point of denying herself the cheapest indulgences of mere flavour: her only rebellion was to smuggle into the kitchen something that would make rather a better supper than usual for Tom.

These narrow notions about debt, held by the old-fashioned Tullivers, may perhaps excite a smile on the faces of many readers in these days of wide commercial views and wide philosophy, according to which everything rights itself without any trouble of ours: the fact that my tradesman is out of pocket by me, is to be looked at through the serene certainty that somebody else's tradesman is in pocket by somebody else; and since there must be bad debts in the world, why, it is mere egoism not to like that we in particular should make them instead of our fellow-citizens. I am telling the history of very simple people, who had never had any illuminating doubts as to personal integrity and honour.

Under all this grim melancholy and narrowing concentration of desire, Mr Tulliver retained the feeling towards his 'little wench' which made her presence a need to him, though it would not suffice to cheer him. She was still the desire of his eyes; but the sweet spring of fatherly love was now mingled with bitterness, like everything else. When Maggie laid down her work at night, it was her habit to get a low stool and sit by her father's knee, leaning her cheek against it. How she wished he would stroke her head, or give some sign that he was soothed by the sense that he had a daughter who loved him! But now she got no answer to her little caresses, either from her father or from Tom – the two idols of her life. Tom was weary and abstracted in the short intervals when he was at home, and her father was bitterly preoccupied with the thought that the girl was growing up – was shooting up into a woman; and how was she to do well in life? She had a poor chance for marrying, down in the world as they were. And he hated the thought of her marrying poorly, as her aunt Gritty had done: *that* would be a thing to make him turn in his grave – the little wench so pulled down by children and toil, as her aunt Moss was. When uncultured minds, confined to a narrow range of personal experience, are under the pressure of continued misfortune, their inward life is apt to become a perpetually repeated round of sad and bitter thoughts: the same words, the same scenes are revolved over and over again, the same mood accompanies them – the end of the year finds them as much what they were at the beginning as if they were machines set to a recurrent series of movements.

The sameness of the days was broken by few visitors. Uncles and aunts paid only short visits now: of course, they could not stay to meals, and the constraint caused by Mr Tulliver's savage silence, which seemed to add to the hollow resonance of the bare uncarpeted room when the aunts were talking, heightened the unpleasantness of these family visits on all sides, and tended to make them rare. As for other acquaintances – there is a chill air surrounding those who are down in the world, and people are glad to get away from them, as from a cold room: human beings, mere men and women, without furniture, without anything to offer you, who have ceased to count as anybody, present an embarrassing negation of reasons for wishing to see them, or of subjects on which to converse with them. At that distant day, there was a dreary isolation in the civilised Christian society of these realms for families that had dropped below their original level, unless they belonged to a sectarian church, which gets some warmth of brotherhood by walling in the sacred fire.

CHAPTER 3

A Voice from the Past

One afternoon, when the chestnuts were coming into flower, Maggie had brought her chair outside the front door, and was seated there with a book on her knees. Her dark eyes had wandered from the book, but they did not seem to be enjoying the sunshine which pierced the screen of jasmine on the projecting porch at her right, and threw leafy shadows on her pale round cheek; they seemed rather to be searching for something that was not disclosed by the sunshine. It had been a more miserable day than usual: her father, after a visit of Wakem's, had had a paroxysm of rage, in which for some trifling fault he had beaten the boy who served in the mill. Once before, since his illness, he had had a similar paroxysm, in which he had beaten his horse, and the scene had left a lasting terror in Maggie's mind. The thought had risen, that some time or other he might beat her mother if she happened to speak in her feeble way at the wrong moment. The keenest of all dread with her was, lest her father should add to his present misfortune the wretchedness of doing something irretrievably disgraceful. The battered schoolbook of Tom's which she held on her knees could give her no fortitude under the pressure of that dread, and again and again her eyes had filled with tears, as they wandered vaguely, seeing neither the chestnut trees nor the distant horizon, but only future scenes of home-sorrow.

Suddenly she was roused by the sound of the opening gate and of footsteps on the gravel. It was not Tom who was entering, but a man in a seal-skin cap and a blue plush waistcoat, carrying a pack on his back, and followed closely by a bull-terrier of brindled coat and defiant aspect.

'Oh Bob, it's you!' said Maggie, starting up with a smile of pleased recognition, for there had been no abundance of kind acts to efface the recollection of Bob's generosity; 'I'm so glad to see you.'

'Thank you, Miss,' said Bob, lifting his cap and showing a delighted face, but immediately relieving himself of some accompanying embarrassment by looking down at his dog, and saying in a tone of disgust, 'Get out wi' you, you thunderin' sawney!'

'My brother is not at home yet, Bob,' said Maggie; 'he is always at St Ogg's in the daytime.'

'Well, Miss,' said Bob, 'I should be glad to see Mr Tom – but that isn't just what I'm come for – look here!'

Bob was in the act of depositing his pack on the doorstep, and with it a row of small books fastened together with string. Apparently, however, they were not the object to which he wished to call Maggie's attention, but rather something which he had carried under his arm, wrapped in a red handkerchief.

'See here!' he said again, laying the red parcel on the others and unfolding it; 'you won't think I'm a-makin' too free, Miss, I hope, but I lighted on these books, and I thought they might make up to you a bit for them as you've lost; for I heared you speak o' picturs – an' as for picturs, *look* here!'

The opening of the red handkerchief had disclosed a superannuated *Keepsake* and six or seven numbers of *A Portrait Gallery*, in royal octavo; and the emphatic request to look referred to a portrait of George the Fourth in all the majesty of his depressed cranium and voluminous neckcloth.

'There's all sorts o' genelmen here,' Bob went on, turning over the leaves with some excitement, 'wi' all sorts o' noses – an' some bald an' some wi' wigs – Parlament genelmen, I reckon. An' here,' he added, opening the *Keepsake*, 'here's ladies for you, some wi' curly hair and some wi' smooth, an' some a-smiling wi' their heads o' one side, an' some as if they was goin' to cry – look here – a-sittin' on the ground out o' door, dressed like the ladies I'n seen get out o' the carriages at the balls in th' Old Hall there. My eyes, I wonder what the chaps wear as go a-courtin' em! I sot up till the clock was gone twelve last night a-lookin' at 'em – I did – till they stared at me out o' the picturs as if they'd know when I spoke to 'em. But, lors! I shouldn't know what to say to 'em. They'll be more fittin' company for you, Miss; and the man at the bookstall, he said they banged iverything for picturs – he said they was a fust-rate article.'

'And you've bought them for me, Bob?' said Maggie, deeply touched by this simple kindness. 'How very, very, good of you! But I'm afraid you gave a great deal of money for them.'

'Not me!' said Bob. 'I'd ha' gev three times the money if they'll make up to you a bit for them as was sold away from you, Miss. For I'n niver forgot how you looked when you fretted about the books bein' gone – it's stuck by me as if it was a pictur hingin' before me. An' when I see'd the book open upo' the stall, wi' the lady lookin' out of it wi' eyes a bit like your'n when you was frettin' – you'll excuse my takin' the liberty, Miss – I thought I'd make free to buy it for you, an' then I bought the books full o' genelmen to match – an' then' – here Bob took up the small stringed packet of books – 'I thought you might like a bit more print as well as the picturs, an' I got these for a say-so – they're cram-full o' print, an' I thought they'd do no harm comin' along wi' these better-most books. An' I hope you won't say me nay, an' tell me as you won't have 'em, like Mr Tom did wi' the suvreigns.'

'No, indeed, Bob,' said Maggie, 'I'm very thankful to you for thinking of me, and being so good to me and Tom. I don't think anyone ever did such a kind thing for me before. I haven't many friends who care for me.'

'Hev a dog, Miss! – they're better friends nor any Christian,' said Bob, laying down his pack again, which he had taken up with the intention of hurrying away; for he felt considerable shyness in talking to a young lass like Maggie, though, as he usually said of himself, 'his tongue overrun him' when he began to speak. 'I can't give you Mumps, 'cause he'd break his heart to go away from me – eh, Mumps, what do you say, you riff-raff?' – (Mumps declined to express himself more diffusely than by a single affirmative movement of his tail.) 'But I'd get you a pup, Miss, an' welcome.'

'No, thank you, Bob. We have a yard dog, and I mayn't keep a dog of my own.'

'Eh, that's a pity: else there's a pup – if you didn't mind about it not bein' thoroughbred: its mother acts in the Punch show – an uncommon sensable bitch – she means more sense wi' her bark nor half the chaps can put into their talk from breakfast to sundown. There's one chap carries pots – a poor low trade as any on the road – he says, "Why, Toby's nought but a mongrel – there's nought to look at in her." But I says to him, "Why, what are you yoursen but a mongrel? There wasn't much pickin' o' *your* feyther an' mother, to look at you." Not but what I like a bit o' breed myself, but I can't abide to see one cur grinnin' at another. I wish you good-evenin', Miss,' added Bob, abruptly taking up his pack again, under the consciousness that his tongue was acting in an undisciplined manner.

'Won't you come in the evening sometime, and see my brother, Bob?' said Maggie.

'Yes, Miss, thank you – another time. You'll give my duty to him, if you please. Eh, he's a fine growed chap. Mr Tom is; he took to growin' i' the legs, and' *I* didn't.'

The pack was down again, now – the hook of the stick having somehow gone wrong.

'You don't call Mumps a cur, I suppose?' said Maggie, divining that any interest she showed in Mumps would be gratifying to his master.

'No, Miss, a fine way off that,' said Bob, with a pitying smile; 'Mumps is as fine a cross as you'll see anywhere along the Floss, an' I'n been up it wi' the barge times enow. Why, the gentry stops to look at him; but you won't catch Mumps a-looking at the gentry much – he minds his own business, he does.'

The expression of Mumps's face, which seemed to be tolerating the super-fluous existence of objects in general, was strongly confirmatory of this high praise.

'He looks dreadfully surly,' said Maggie. 'Would he let me pat him?'

'Ay, that would he, and thank you. He knows his company, Mumps does. He isn't a dog as 'ull be caught wi' gingerbread: he'd smell a thief a good deal stronger nor the gingerbread – he would. Lors, I talk to him by th' hour together, when I'm walking i' lone places, and if I'n done a bit o' mischief, I allays tell him. I'n got no secrets but what Mumps knows 'em. He knows about my big thumb, he does.'

'Your big thumb – what's that, Bob?' said Maggie.

'That's what it is, Miss,' said Bob, quickly, exhibiting a singularly broad specimen of that difference between the man and the monkey. 'It tells i' measuring out the flannel, you see. I carry flannel, 'cause it's light for my pack, an' it's dear stuff, you see, so a big thumb tells. I clap my thumb at the end o' the yard and cut o' the hither side of it, and the old women aren't up to't.'

'But, Bob,' said Maggie, looking serious, 'that's cheating: I don't like to hear you say that.'

'Don't you, Miss?' said Bob, regretfully, 'Then I'm sorry I said it. But I'm so used to talking to Mumps, an' he doesn't mind a bit o' cheating, when it's them skinflint women, as haggle an' haggle, an' 'ud like to get their flannel for nothing, an' 'ud niver ask theirselves how I got my dinner out on't. I niver cheat anybody as doesn't want to cheat me, Miss – lors, I'm a honest chap, I am; only I must hev a bit o' sport, an' now I don't go wi' the ferrets, I'n got no varmint to come over but them haggling women. I wish you good-evening, Miss.'

'Goodbye, Bob. Thank you very much for bringing me the books. And come again to see Tom.'

'Yes, Miss,' said Bob, moving on a few steps; then turning half round, he said, 'I'll leave off that trick wi' my big thumb, if you don't think well of me for it, Miss – but it 'ud be a pity, it would. I couldn't find another trick so good – an' what 'ud be the use o' havin' a big thumb? It might as well ha' been narrow.'

Maggie, thus exalted into Bob's directing Madonna, laughed in spite of herself; at which her worshipper's blue eyes twinkled too, and under these favouring auspices he touched his cap and walked away.

The days of chivalry are not gone, notwithstanding Burke's grand dirge over them: they live still in that far-off worship paid by many a youth and man to the woman of whom he never dreams that he shall touch so much as her little finger or the hem of her robe. Bob, with the pack on his back, had as respectful an adoration for this dark-eyed maiden as if he had been a knight in armour calling aloud on her name as he pricked on to the fight.

That gleam of merriment soon died away from Maggie's face, and perhaps only made the returning gloom deeper by contrast. She was too dispirited even to like answering questions about Bob's present of books, and she carried them away to her bedroom, laying them down there and seating herself on her one stool, without caring to look at them just yet. She leaned her cheek against the window-frame, and thought that the light-hearted Bob had a lot much happier than hers.

Maggie's sense of loneliness, and utter privation of joy, had deepened with the brightness of advancing spring. All the favourite outdoor nooks about home, which seemed to have done their part with her parents in nurturing and cherishing her, were now mixed up with the home-sadness, and gathered no smile from the sunshine. Every affection, every delight the poor child had had, was like an aching nerve to her. There was no music for her any more – no piano, no harmonised voices, no delicious stringed instruments, with their passionate cries of imprisoned spirits sending a strange vibration through her frame. And of all her school-life there was nothing left her now but her little collection of schoolbooks, which she turned over with a sickening sense that she knew them all, and they were all barren of comfort. Even at school she had often wished for books with *more* in them: everything she learned there seemed like the ends of long threads that snapped immediately. And now – without the indirect charm of school-emulation – Télémaque was mere bran; so were the hard dry questions on Christian Doctrine: there was no flavour in them – no strength. Sometimes Maggie thought she could have been contented with absorbing fancies; if she could have had all Scott's novels and all Byron's poems! – then, perhaps, she might have found happiness enough to dull her sensibility to her actual daily life. And yet . . . they were hardly what she wanted. She could make dream-worlds of her own – but no dream-world would satisfy her now. She wanted some explanation of this hard, real life: the unhappy-looking father, seated at the dull breakfast-table; the childish, bewildered mother; the little sordid tasks that filled the hours, or the more oppressive emptiness of weary, joyless leisure; the need of some tender, demonstrative love; the cruel sense that Tom didn't mind what she thought or felt, and that they were no longer playfellows together; the privation of all pleasant things that had come to *her* more than to others: she wanted some key that would enable her to understand, and, in understanding, endure, the heavy weight that had fallen on her young heart. If she had been taught 'real learning and wisdom, such as great men knew,' she thought she should have held the secrets of life; if she had only books, that she might learn for herself what wise men knew! Saints and martyrs had never interested Maggie so much as sages and poets. She knew little of saints and martyrs, and had gathered, as a general result of her teaching, that they were a temporary provision against the spread of Catholicism, and had all died at Smithfield.

In one of these meditations it occurred to her that she had forgotten Tom's schoolbooks, which had been sent home in his trunk. But she found the stock unaccountably shrunk down to the few old ones which had been well thumbed – the Latin Dictionary and Grammar, a Delectus, a torn Eutropius, the well-worn Virgil, Aldrich's Logic, and the exasperating Euclid. Still, Latin, Euclid, and Logic would surely be a considerable step in masculine wisdom – in that knowledge which made men contented, and even glad to live. Not that the yearning for effectual wisdom was quite unmixed: a certain mirage would now and then rise on the desert of the future, in which she seemed to see herself honoured for her surprising attainments. And so the poor child, with her soul's hunger and her illusions of self-flattery, began to nibble at this thick-rinded fruit of the tree of knowledge, filling her vacant hours with Latin, geometry, and the forms of the syllogism, and feeling a gleam of triumph now and then that her understanding was quite equal to these peculiarly masculine studies. For a week or two she went on resolutely enough, though with an occasional sinking of heart, as if she had set out towards the Promised Land alone, and found it a thirsty, trackless, uncertain journey. In the severity of her early resolution, she would take Aldrich out into the fields, and then look off her book towards the sky, where the lark was twinkling, or to the reeds and bushes by the river, from which the water-fowl rustled forth on its anxious, awkward flight – with a startled sense that the relation between Aldrich and this living world was extremely remote for her. The discouragement deepened as the days went on, and the eager heart gained faster and faster on the patient mind. Somehow, when she sat at the window with her book, her eyes *would* fix themselves blankly on the outdoor sunshine; then they would fill with tears, and sometimes, if her mother was not in the room, the studies would all end in sobbing. She rebelled against her lot, she fainted under its loneliness, and fits even of anger and hatred towards her father and mother, who were so unlike what she would have them to be – towards Tom, who checked her, and met her thought or feeling always by some thwarting difference – would flow out over her affections and conscience like a lava stream, and frighten her with a sense that it was not difficult for her to become a demon. Then her brain would be busy with wild romances of a flight from home in search of something less sordid and dreary: she would go to some great man – Walter Scott, perhaps – and tell him how wretched and how clever she was, and he would surely do something for her. But, in the middle of her vision, her father would perhaps enter the room for the evening, and, surprised that she sat still without noticing him, would say, complainingly, 'Come, am I to fetch my slippers myself?' The voice pierced through Maggie like a sword: there was another sadness besides her own, and she had been thinking of turning her back on it and forsaking it.

This afternoon, the sight of Bob's cheerful freckled face had given her discontent a new direction. She thought it was part of the hardship of her life that there was laid upon her the burthen of larger wants than others seemed to feel – that she had to endure this wide hopeless yearning for that something, whatever it was, that was greatest and best on this earth. She wished she could have been like Bob, with his easily satisfied ignorance, or like Tom, who had something to do on which he could fix his mind with a steady purpose, and disregard everything else. Poor child! as she leaned her head against the window-frame, with her hands clasped tighter and tighter, and her foot beating the ground, she was as lonely in her trouble as if she had been the only girl in the civilised world of that day who had come out of her school-life with a soul untrained for inevitable struggles – with no other part of her inherited share in the hard-won treasures of thought, which generations of painful toil have laid up for the race of men, than shreds and patches of feeble literature and false history – with much futile information about Saxon and other kings of doubtful example – but unhappily quite without that knowledge of the irreversible laws within and without her, which, governing the habits, becomes morality, and, developing the feelings of submission and dependence, becomes religion: – as lonely in her trouble as if every other girl besides herself had been cherished and watched over by elder minds, not forgetful of their own early time, when need was keen and impulse strong.

At last Maggie's eyes glanced down on the books that lay on the window-shelf, and she half forsook her reverie to turn over listlessly the leaves of the 'Portrait Gallery', but she soon pushed this aside to examine the little row of books tied together with string. *Beauties of the Spectator*, *Rasselas*, *Economy of Human Life*, Gregory's *Letters* – she knew the sort of matter that was inside all these: the *Christian Year* – that seemed to be a hymn-book, and she laid it down again; but *Thomas à Kempis?* – the name had come across her in her reading, and she felt the satisfaction, which everyone knows, of getting some ideas to attach to a name that strays solitary in the memory. She took up the little, old, clumsy book with some curiosity: it had the corners turned down in many places, and some hand, now for ever quiet, had made at certain passages strong pen-and-ink marks, long since browned by time. Maggie turned from leaf to leaf, and read where the quiet hand pointed . . .

Know that the love of thyself doth hurt thee more than anything in the world . . . If thou seekest this or that, and wouldst be here or there to enjoy thy own will and pleasure, thou shalt never be quiet nor free from care: for in everything somewhat will be wanting, and in every place there will be some that will cross thee . . . Both above and below, which way soever thou dost turn thee, everywhere thou shalt find the Cross: and everywhere of necessity thou must have patience, if thou wilt have inward peace, and enjoy an everlasting crown . . . If thou desire to mount unto this height, thou must set out courageously, and lay the axe to the root, that thou mayst pluck up and destroy that hidden inordinate inclination to thyself, and unto all private and earthly good. On this sin, that a man inordinately loveth himself, almost all dependeth, whatsoever is thoroughly to be overcome; which evil being once overcome and subdued, there will presently ensue great peace and tranquillity . . . It is but little thou sufferest in comparison of them that have suffered so much, were so strongly tempted, so grievously afflicted, so many ways tried and exercised. Thou oughtest therefore to call to mind the more heavy sufferings of others, that thou mayest the easier bear thy little adversities. And if they seem not little unto thee, beware lest thy impatience be the cause thereof . . . . Blessed are those ears that receive the whispers of the divine voice, and listen not to the whisperings of the world. Blessed are those ears which hearken not unto the voice which soundeth outwardly, but unto the Truth, which teacheth inwardly . . .

A strange thrill of awe passed through Maggie while she read, as if she had been wakened in the night by a strain of solemn music, telling of beings whose souls had been astir while hers was in stupor. She went on from one brown mark to another, where the quiet hand seemed to point, hardly conscious that she was reading – seeming rather to listen while a low voice said :

'Why dost thou here gaze about, since this is not the place of thy rest? In heaven ought to be thy dwelling, and all earthly things are to be looked on as they forward thy journey thither. All things pass away, and thou together with them. Beware thou cleave not unto them, lest thou be entangled and perish . . . If a man should give all his substance, yet it is as nothing. And if he should do great penances, yet are they but little. And if he should attain to all knowledge, he is yet far off. And if he should be of great virtue, and very fervent devotion, yet is there much wanting; to wit, one thing, which is most necessary for him. What is that? That having left all, he leave himself, and go wholly out of himself, and retain nothing of self-love . . . I have often said unto thee, and now again I say the same, forsake thyself, resign thyself, and thou shalt enjoy much inward peace . . . Then shall all vain imaginations, evil perturbations, and superfluous cares fly away; then shall immoderate fear leave thee, and inordinate love shall die.'

Maggie drew a long breath and pushed her heavy hair back, as if to see a sudden vision more clearly. Here, then, was a secret of life that would enable her to renounce all other secrets – here was a sublime height to be reached without the help of outward things – here was insight, and strength, and conquest, to be won by means entirely within her own soul, where a supreme Teacher was waiting to be heard. It flashed through her like the suddenly apprehended solution of a problem, that all the miseries of her young life had come from fixing her heart on her own pleasure, as if that were the central necessity of the universe; and for the first time she saw the possibility of shifting the position from which she looked at the gratification of her own desires – of taking her stand out of herself, and looking at her own life as an insignificant part of a divinely-guided whole. She read on and on in the old book, devouring eagerly the dialogues with the invisible Teacher, the pattern of sorrow, the source of all strength; returning to it after she had been called away, and reading till the sun went down behind the willows. With all the hurry of an imagination that could never rest in the present, she sat in the deepening twilight forming plans of self-humiliation and entire devotedness; and, in the ardour of first discovery, renunciation seemed to her the entrance into that satisfaction which she had so long been craving in vain. She had not perceived – how could she until she had lived longer? – the inmost truth of the old monk's outpourings, that renunciation remains sorrow, though a sorrow borne willingly. Maggie was still panting for happiness, and was in ecstasy because she had found the key to it. She knew nothing of doctrines and systems – of mysticism or quietism; but this voice out of the far-off Middle Ages was the direct communication of a human soul's belief and experience, and came to Maggie as an unquestioned message.

I suppose that is the reason why the small old-fashioned book, for which you need only pay sixpence at a bookstall, works miracles to this day, turning bitter waters into sweetness: while expensive sermons and treatises, newly issued, leave all things as they were before. It was written down by a hand that waited for the heart's prompting; it is the chronicle of a solitary, hidden anguish, struggle, trust and triumph – not written on velvet cushions to teach endurance to those who are treading with bleeding feet on the stones. And so it remains to all time a lasting record of human needs and human consolations: the voice of a brother who, ages ago, felt and suffered and renounced – in the cloister, perhaps, with serge gown and tonsured head, with much chanting and long fasts, and with a fashion of speech different from ours – but under the same silent far-off heavens, and with the same passionate desires, the same strivings, the same failures, the same weariness.

In writing the history of unfashionable families, one is apt to fall into a tone of emphasis which is very far from being the tone of good society, where principles and beliefs are not only of an extremely moderate kind, but are always pre-supposed, no subjects being eligible but such as can be touched with a light and graceful irony. But then, good society has its claret and its velvet-carpets, its dinner-engagements six weeks deep, its opera and its faery ballrooms; rides off its ennui on thoroughbred horses, lounges at the club, has to keep clear of crinoline vortices, gets its science done by Faraday, and its religion by the superior clergy who are to be met in the best houses: how should it have time or need for belief and emphasis? But good society, floated on gossamer wings of light irony, is of very expensive production; requiring nothing less than a wide and arduous national life condensed in unfragrant deafening factories, cramping itself in mines, sweating at furnaces, grinding, hammering, weaving under more or less oppression of carbonic acid – or else, spread over sheepwalks, and scattered in lonely houses and huts on the clayey or chalky corn-lands, where the rainy days look dreary. This wide national life is based entirely on emphasis – the emphasis of want, which urges it into all the activities necessary for the maintenance of good society and light irony: it spends its heavy years often in a chill, uncarpeted fashion, amidst family discord unsoftened by long corridors. Under such circumstances, there are many among its myriads of souls who have absolutely needed an emphatic belief: life in this unpleasurable shape demanding some solution even to unspeculative minds; just as you enquire into the stuffing of your couch when anything galls you there, whereas eiderdown and perfect French springs excite no question. Some have an emphatic belief in alcohol, and seek their *ekstasis* or outside standing-ground in gin; but the rest require something that good society calls 'enthusiasm,' something that will present motives in an entire absence of high prizes, something that will give patience and feed human love when the limbs ache with weariness, and human looks are hard upon us – something, clearly, that lies outside personal desires, that includes resignation for ourselves and active love for what is not ourselves. Now and then, that sort of enthusiasm finds a far-echoing voice that comes from an experience springing out of the deepest need. And it was by being brought within the long lingering vibrations of such a voice that Maggie, with her girl's face and unnoted sorrows, found an effort and a hope that helped her through years of loneliness, making out a faith for herself without the aid of established authorities and appointed guides – for they were not at hand, and her need was pressing. From what you know of her, you will not be surprised that she threw some exaggeration and wilfulness, some pride and impetuosity, even into her self-renunciation: her own life was still a drama for her, in which she demanded of herself that her part should be played with intensity. And so it came to pass that she often lost the spirit of humility by being excessive in the outward act; she often strove after too high a flight, and came down with her poor little half-fledged wings dabbled in the mud. For example, she not only determined to work at plain sewing, that she might contribute something towards the fund in the tin box, but she went, in the first instance, in her zeal of self-mortification, to ask for it at a linen-shop in St Oggs, instead of getting it in a more quiet and indirect way; and could see nothing but what was entirely wrong and unkind, nay, persecuting, in Tom's reproof of her for this unnecessary act. 'I don't like *my* sister to do such things,' said Tom; 'I'll take care that the debts are paid, without your lowering yourself in that way.' Surely there was some tenderness and bravery mingled with the worldliness and self-assertion of that little speech; but Maggie held it as dross, overlooking the grains of gold, and took Tom's rebuke as one of her outward crosses. Tom was very hard to her, she used to think, in her long night-watchings – to her who had always loved him so; and then she strove to be contented with that hardness, and to require nothing. That is the path we all like when we set out on our abandonment of egoism – the path of martyrdom and endurance, where the palm-branches grow, rather than the steep highway of tolerance, just allowance, and self-blame, where there are no leafy honours to be gathered and worn.

The old books, Virgil, Euclid, and Aldrich – that wrinkled fruit of the tree of knowledge – had been all laid by; for Maggie had turned her back on the vain ambition to share the thoughts of the wise. In her first ardour she flung away the books with a sort of triumph that she had risen above the need of them; and if they had been her own, she would have burned them, believing that she would never repent. She read so eagerly and constantly in her three books, the Bible, Thomas à Kempis, and the 'Christian Year' (no longer rejected as a 'hymn-book'), that they filled her mind with a continual stream of rhythmic memories; and she was too ardently learning to see all nature and life in the light of her new faith, to need any other material for her mind to work on, as she sat with her well-plied needle, making shirts and other complicated stitchings, falsely called 'plain' – by no means plain to Maggie, since wristband and sleeve and the like had a capability of being sewed in wrong side outwards in moments of mental wandering.

Hanging diligently over her sewing, Maggie was a sight anyone might have been pleased to look at. That new inward life of hers, notwithstanding some volcanic upheavings of imprisoned passions, yet shone out in her face with a tender soft light that mingled itself as added loveliness with the gradually enriched colour and outline of her blossoming youth. Her mother felt the change in her with a sort of puzzled wonder that Maggie should be 'growing up so good;' it was amazing that this once 'contrairy' child was become so submissive, so backward to assert her own will. Maggie used to look up from her work and find her mother's eyes fixed upon her: they were watching and waiting for the large young glance, as if her elder frame got some needful warmth from it. The mother was getting fond of her tall, brown girl, the only bit of furniture now on which she could bestow her anxiety and pride; and Maggie, in spite of her own ascetic wish to have no personal adornment, was obliged to give way to her mother about her hair, and submit to have the abundant black locks plaited into a coronet on the summit of her head, after the pitiable fashion of those antiquated times.

'Let your mother have that bit o' pleasure, my dear,' said Mrs Tulliver; 'I'd trouble enough with your hair once.'

So Maggie, glad of anything that would soothe her mother, and cheer their long day together, consented to the vain decoration, and showed a queenly head above her old frocks – steadily refusing, however, to look at herself in the glass. Mrs Tulliver liked to call the father's attention to Maggie's hair and other unexpected virtues, but he had a brusque reply to give.

'I knew well enough what she'd be, before now – it's nothing new to me. But it's a pity she isn't made o' commoner stuff – she'll be thrown away, I doubt: there'll be nobody to marry her as is fit for her.'

And Maggie's graces of mind and body fed his gloom. He sat patiently enough while she read him a chapter, or said something timidly when they were alone together about trouble being turned into a blessing. He took it all as part of his daughter's goodness, which made his misfortunes the sadder to him because they damaged her chance in life. In a mind charged with an eager purpose and an unsatisfied vindictiveness, there is no room for new feelings: Mr Tulliver did not want spiritual consolation – he wanted to shake off the degradation of debt, and to have his revenge.

BOOK FIFTH

Wheat and Tares

CHAPTER I

In the Red Deeps

The family sitting-room was a long room with a window at each end; one looking towards the croft and along the Ripple to the banks of the Floss, the other into the mill-yard. Maggie was sitting with her work against the latter window when she saw Mr Wakem entering the yard, as usual, on his fine black horse; but not alone, as usual. Someone was with him – a figure in a cloak, on a handsome pony. Maggie had hardly time to feel that it was Philip come back, before they were in front of the window, and he was raising his hat to her; while his father, catching the movement by a side-glance, looked sharply round at them both.

   Maggie hurried away from the window and carried her work upstairs; for Mr Wakem sometimes came in and inspected the books, and Maggie felt that the meeting with Philip would be robbed of all pleasure in the presence of the two fathers. Someday, perhaps, she should see him when they could just shake hands, and she could tell him that she remembered his goodness to Tom, and the things he had said to her in the old days, though they could never be friends any more. It was not at all agitating to Maggie to see Philip again: she retained her childish gratitude and pity towards him, and remembered his cleverness; and in the early weeks of her loneliness she had continually recalled the image of him among the people who had been kind to her in life; often wishing she had him for a brother and a teacher, as they had fancied it might have been, in their talk together. But that sort of wishing had been banished along with other dreams that savoured of seeking her own will; and she thought, besides, that Philip might be altered by his life abroad – he might have become worldly, and really not care about her saying anything to him now. And yet, his face was wonderfully little altered – it was only a larger, more manly copy of the pale small-featured boy's face, with the grey eyes and the longish waving brown hair: there was the old deformity to awaken the old pity; and after all her meditations, Maggie felt that she really *should* like to say a few words to him. He might still be melancholy, as he always used to be, and like her to look at him kindly. She wondered if he remembered how he used to like her eyes; with that thought Maggie glanced towards the square looking-glass which was condemned to hang with its face towards the wall, and she half-started from her seat to reach it down; but she checked herself and snatched up her work, trying to repress the rising wishes by forcing her memory to recall snatches of hymns, until she saw Philip and his father returning along the road, and she could go down again.

It was far on in June now, and Maggie was inclined to lengthen the daily walk which was her one indulgence; but this day and the following she was so busy with work which must be finished that she never went beyond the gate, and satisfied her need of the open air by sitting out of doors. One of her frequent walks, when she was not obliged to go to St Ogg's, was to a spot that lay beyond what was called the 'Hill' – an insignificant rise of ground crowned by trees, lying along the side of the road which ran by the gates of Dorlcote Mill. Insignificant I call it, because in height it was hardly more than a bank; but there may come moments when Nature makes a mere bank a means towards a fateful result, and that is why I ask you to imagine this high bank crowned with trees, making an uneven wall for some quarter of a mile along the left side of Dorlcote Mill and the pleasant fields behind it, bounded by the murmuring Ripple. Just where this line of bank sloped down again to the level, a by-road turned off and led to the other side of the rise, where it was broken into very capricious hollows and mounds by the working of an exhausted stone-quarry – so long exhausted that both mounds and hollows were now clothed with brambles and trees, and here and there by a stretch of grass which a few sheep kept close-nibbled. In her childish days Maggie held this place, called the Red Deeps, in very great awe, and needed all her confidence in Tom's bravery to reconcile her to an excursion thither – visions of robbers and fierce animals haunting every hollow. But now it had the charm for her which any broken ground, any mimic rock and ravine, have for the eyes that rest habitually on the level; especially in summer, when she could sit in a grassy hollow under the shadow of a branching ash, stooping aslant from the steep above her, and listen to the hum of insects, like tiniest bells on the garment of Silence, or see the sunlight piercing the distant boughs, as if to chase and drive home the truant heavenly blue of the wild hyacinths. In this June time too, the dog-roses were in their glory, and that was an additional reason why Maggie should direct her walk to the Red Deeps, rather than to any other spot, on the first day she was free to wander at her will – a pleasure she loved so well, that sometimes, in her ardours of renunciation, she thought she ought to deny herself the frequent indulgence in it.

You may see her now, as she walks down the favourite turning, and enters the Deeps by a narrow path through a group of Scotch firs – her tall figure and old lavender gown visible through the hereditary black silk shawl of some wide-meshed net-like material; and now she is sure of being unseen, she takes off her bonnet and ties it over her arm. One would certainly suppose her to be farther on in life than her seventeenth year – perhaps because of the slow resigned sadness of the glance, from which all search and unrest seem to have departed, perhaps because her broad-chested figure has the mould of early womanhood. Youth and health have withstood well the involuntary and voluntary hardships of her lot, and the nights in which she has lain on the hard floor for a penance have left no obvious trace; the eyes are liquid, the brown cheek is firm and rounded, the full lips are red. With her dark colouring and jet crown surmounting her tall figure, she seems to have a sort of kinship with the grand Scotch firs, at which she is looking up as if she loved them well. Yet one has a sense of uneasiness in looking at her – a sense of opposing elements, of which a fierce collision is imminent: surely there is a hushed expression, such as one often sees in older faces under borderless caps, out of keeping with the resistant youth, which one expects to flash out in a sudden, passionate glance, that will dissipate all the quietude, like a damp fire leaping out again when all seemed safe.

But Maggie herself was not uneasy at this moment. She was calmly enjoying the free air, while she looked up at the old fir trees, and thought that those broken ends of branches were the records of past storms, which had only made the red stems soar higher. But while her eyes were still turned upward, she became conscious of a moving shadow cast by the evening sun on the grassy path before her, and looked down with a startled gesture to see Philip Wakem, who first raised his hat, and then, blushing deeply, came forward to her and put out his hand. Maggie, too, coloured with surprise, which soon gave way to pleasure. She put out her hand and looked down at the deformed figure before her with frank eyes, filled for the moment with nothing but the memory of her child's feelings – a memory that was always strong in her. She was the first to speak.

'You startled me,' she said, smiling faintly; 'I never meet anyone here. How came you to be walking here? Did you come to meet *me?*'

It was impossible not to perceive that Maggie felt herself a child again.

'Yes, I did.' said Philip, still embarrassed: 'I wished to see you very much. I watched a long while yesterday on the bank near your house to see if you would come out, but you never came. Then I watched again today, and when I saw the way you took, I kept you in sight and came down the bank, behind there. I hope you will not be displeased with me.'

'No,' said Maggie, with simple seriousness, walking on, as if she meant Philip to accompany her, 'I'm very glad you came, for I wished very much to have an opportunity of speaking to you. I've never forgotten how good you were long ago to Tom, and me too; but I was not sure that you would remember us so well. Tom and I have had a great deal of trouble since then, and I think *that* makes one think more of what happened before the trouble came.'

'I can't believe that you have thought of me so much as I have thought of you,' said Philip, timidly. 'Do you know, when I was away, I made a picture of you as you looked that morning in the study when you said you would not forget me.'

Philip drew a large miniature-case from his pocket, and opened it. Maggie saw her old self leaning on a table, with her black locks hanging down behind her ears, looking into space with strange, dreamy eyes. It was a watercolour sketch, of real merit as a portrait.

'Oh dear,' said Maggie, smiling, and flushed with pleasure, 'what a queer little girl I was! I remember myself with my hair in that way, in that pink frock. I really *was* like a gypsy. I dare say I am now,' she added, after a little pause; 'am I like what you expected me to be?'

The words might have been those of a coquette, but the full bright glance Maggie turned on Philip was not that of a coquette. She really did hope he liked her face as it was now, but it was simply the rising again of her innate delight in admiration and love. Philip met her eyes and looked at her in silence for a long moment, before he said, quietly, 'No, Maggie.'

The light died out a little from Maggie's face, and there was a slight trembling of the lip. Her eyelids fell lower, but she did not turn away her head, and Philip continued to look at her. Then he said, slowly, 'You are very much more beautiful than I thought you would be.'

'Am I?' said Maggie, the pleasure returning in a deeper flush. She turned her face away from him and took some steps, looking straight before her in silence, as if she were adjusting her consciousness to this new idea. Girls are so accustomed to think of dress as the main ground of vanity, that, in abstaining from the looking-glass, Maggie had thought more of abandoning all care for adornment than of renouncing the contemplation of her face. Comparing herself with elegant, wealthy young ladies, it had not occurred to her that she could produce any effect with her person. Philip seemed to like the silence well. He walked by her side, watching her face, as if that sight left no room for any other wish. They had passed from among the fir trees, and had now come to a green hollow almost surrounded by an amphitheatre of the pale pink dog-roses. But as the light about them had brightened, Maggie's face had lost its glow. She stood still when they were in the hollows, and, looking at Philip again, she said, in a serious, sad voice, 'I wish we could have been friends – I mean, if it would have been good and right for us. But that is the trial I have to bear in everything: I may not keep anything I used to love when I was little. The old books went; and Tom is different – and my father. It is like death. I must part with everything I cared for when I was a child. And I must part with you: we must never take any notice of each other again. That was what I wanted to speak to you for. I wanted to let you know that Tom and I can't do as we like about such things, and that if I behave as if I had forgotten all about you, it is not out of envy or pride – or – or any bad feeling.'

Maggie spoke with more and more sorrowful gentleness as she went on, and her eyes began to fill with tears. The deepening expression of pain on Philip's face gave him a stronger resemblance to his boyish self, and made the deformity appeal more strongly to her pity.

'I know – I see all that you mean,' he said, in a voice that had become feebler from discouragement: 'I know what there is to keep us apart on both sides. But it is not right, Maggie – don't you be angry with me, I am so used to call you Maggie in my thoughts – it is not right to sacrifice everything to other people's unreasonable feelings. I would give up a great deal for *my* father; but I would not give up a friendship or – or an attachment of any sort, in obedience to any wish of his that I didn't recognise as right.'

'I don't know,' said Maggie, musingly. 'Often, when I have been angry and discontented, it has seemed to me that I was not bound to give up anything; and I have gone on thinking till it has seemed to me that I could think away all my duty. But no good has ever come of that – it was an evil state of mind. I'm quite sure that whatever I might do, I should wish in the end that I had gone without anything for myself, rather than have made my father's life harder to him.'

'But would it make his life harder if we were to see each other sometimes?' said Philip. He was going to say something else, but checked himself.

'Oh, I'm sure he wouldn't like it. Don't ask me why, or anything about it,' said

Maggie, in a distressed tone. 'My father feels so strongly about some things. He is not at all happy.'

'No more am I,' said Philip, impetuously: '*I* am not happy.'

'Why?' said Maggie, gently. 'At least – I ought not to ask – but I'm very, very sorry.'

Philip turned to walk on, as if he had not patience to stand still any longer, and they went out of the hollow, winding amongst the trees and bushes in silence. After that last word of Philip's, Maggie could not bear to insist immediately on their parting.

'I've been a great deal happier,' she said at last, timidly, 'since I have given up thinking about what is easy and pleasant, and being discontented because I couldn't have my own will. Our life is determined for us – and it makes the mind very free when we give up wishing, and only think of bearing what is laid upon us, and doing what is given us to do.'

'But I can't give up wishing,' said Philip, impatiently. 'It seems to me we can never give up longing and wishing while we are thoroughly alive. There are certain things we feel to be beautiful and good, and we *must* hunger after them. How can we ever be satisfied without them until our feelings are deadened? I delight in fine pictures – I long to be able to paint such. I strive and strive, and can't produce what I want. That is pain to me, and always *will* be pain, until my faculties lose their keenness, like aged eyes. Then there are many other things I long for' – here Philip hesitated a little, and then said – 'things that other men have, and that will always be denied me. My life will have nothing great or beautiful in it; I would rather not have lived.'

'O, Philip,' said Maggie, 'I wish you didn't feel so.' But her heart began to beat with something of Philip's discontent.

'Well then,' said he, turning quickly round and fixing his grey eyes entreatingly on her face, 'I should be contented to live, if you would let me see you sometimes.' Then, checked by a fear which her face suggested, he looked away again, and said, more calmly, 'I have no friend to whom I can tell everything – no one who cares enough about me; and if I could only see you now and then, and you would let me talk to you a little, and show me that you cared for me – and that we may always be friends in heart, and help each other ~ then I might come to be glad of life.'

'But how can I see you, Philip?' said Maggie, falteringly. (Could she really do him good? It would be very hard to say 'goodbye' this day, and not speak to him again. Here was a new interest to vary the days – it was so much easier to renounce the interest before it came.)

'If you would let me see you here sometimes – walk with you here – I would be contented if it were only once or twice in a month. *That* could injure no one's happiness, and it would sweeten my life. Besides,' Philip went on, with all the inventive astuteness of love at one-and-twenty, 'if there is any enmity between those who belong to us, we ought all the more to try and quench it by our friendship – I mean, that by our influence on both sides we might bring about a healing of the wounds that have been made in the past, if I could know everything about them. And I don't believe there is any enmity in my own father's mind: I think he has proved the contrary.'

Maggie shook her head slowly, and was silent, under conflicting thoughts. It seemed to her inclination, that to see Philip now and then, and keep up the bond of friendship with him, was something not only innocent, but good: perhaps she might really help him to find contentment as she had found it. The voice that said this made sweet music to Maggie; but athwart it there came an urgent monotonous warning from another voice which she had been learning to obey: the warning that such interviews implied secrecy – implied doing something she would dread to be discovered in – something that, if discovered, must cause anger and pain; and that the admission of anything so near doubleness would act as a spiritual blight. Yet the music would swell out again, like chimes borne onward by a recurrent breeze, persuading her that the wrong lay all in the faults and weaknesses of others, and that there was such a thing as futile sacrifice for one to the injury of another. It was very cruel for Philip that he should be shrunk from, because of an unjustifiable vindictiveness towards his father – poor Philip, whom some people would shrink from only because he was deformed. The idea that he might become her lover, or that her meeting him could cause disapproval in that light, had not occurred to her; and Philip saw the absence of this idea clearly enough – saw it with a certain pang, although it made her consent to his request the less unlikely. There was bitterness to him in the perception that Maggie was almost as frank and unconstrained towards him as when she was a child.

'I can't say either yes or no,' she said at last, turning round and walking towards the way she had come; 'I must wait, lest I should decide wrongly. I must seek for guidance.'

'May I come again, then – tomorrow – or the next day – or next week?'

'I think I had better write,' said Maggie, faltering again. 'I have to go to St Ogg's sometimes, and I can put the letter in the post.'

'Oh, no,' said Philip, eagerly; 'that would not be so well. My father might see the letter – and – he has not any enmity, I believe, but he views things differently from me: he thinks a great deal about wealth and position. Pray let me come here once more. *Tell* me when it shall be; or if you can't tell me, I will come as often as I can till I do see you.'

'I think it must be so, then,' said Maggie, 'for I can't be quite certain of coming here any particular evening.'

Maggie felt a great relief in adjourning the decision. She was free now to enjoy the minutes of companionship; she almost thought she might linger a little; the next time they met she should have to pain Philip by telling him her determination.

'I can't help thinking,' she said, looking smilingly at him, after a few moments of silence, 'how strange it is that we should have met and talked to each other, just as if it had been only yesterday when we parted at Lorton. And yet we must both be very much altered in those five years – I think it is five years. How was it you seemed to have a sort of feeling that I was the same Maggie? – I was not quite so sure that you would be the same: I know you are so clever, and you must have seen and learned so much to fill your mind: I was not quite sure you would care about me now.'

'I have never had any doubt that you would be the same, whenever I might see you,' said Philip. 'I mean, the same in everything that made me like you better than anyone else. I don't want to explain that: I don't think any of the strongest effects our natures are susceptible of can ever be explained. We can neither detect the process by which they are arrived at, nor the mode in which they act on us. The greatest of painters only once painted a mysteriously divine child; he couldn't have told how he did it, and we can't tell why we feel it to be divine. I think there are stores laid up in our human nature that our understandings can make no complete inventory of. Certain strains of music affect me so strangely – I can never hear them without their changing my whole attitude of mind for a time, and if the effect would last, I might be capable of heroisms.'

'Ah! I know what you mean about music – *I* feel so,' said Maggie, clasping her hands with her old impetuosity. 'At least,' she added, in a saddened tone, 'I used to feel so when I had any music: I never have any now except the organ at church.'

'And you long for it, Maggie?' said Philip, looking at her with affectionate pity. 'Ah, you can have very little that is beautiful in your life. Have you many books? You were so fond of them when you were a little girl.'

They were come back to the hollow, round which the dog-roses grew, and they both paused under the charm of the faëry evening light, reflected from the pale pink clusters.

'No, I have given up books,' said Maggie, quietly, 'except a very, very few.'

Philip had already taken from his pocket a small volume, and was looking at the back, as he said, 'Ah, this is the second volume, I see, else you might have liked to take it home with you. I put it in my pocket because I am studying a scene for a picture.'

Maggie had looked at the back too, and saw the title: it revived an old impression with overmastering force.

'*The Pirate*,' she said, taking the book from Philip's hands. 'Oh, I began that once; I read to where Minna is walking with Cleveland, and I could never get to read the rest. I went on with it in my own head, and I made several endings; but they were all unhappy. I could never make a happy ending out of that beginning. Poor Minna! I wonder what is the real end. For a long while I couldn't get my mind away from the Shetland Isles – I used to feel the wind blowing on me from the rough sea.'

Maggie spoke rapidly, with glistening eyes.

'Take that volume home with you, Maggie,' said Philip, watching her with delight. 'I don't want it now. I shall make a picture of you instead – you, among the Scotch firs and the slanting shadows.'

Maggie had not heard a word he had said: she was absorbed in a page at which she had opened. But suddenly she closed the book, and gave it back to Philip, shaking her head with a backward movement, as if to say 'avaunt' to floating visions.

'Do keep it, Maggie,' said Philip, entreatingly; 'it will give you pleasure.'

'No, thank you,' said Maggie, putting it aside with her hand and walking on. 'It would make me in love with this world again, as I used to be – it would make me long to see and know many things – it would make me long for a full life.'

'But you will not always be shut up in your present lot: why should you starve your mind in that way? It is narrow asceticism – I don't like to see you persisting in it, Maggie. Poetry and art and knowledge are sacred and pure.'

'But not for me – not for me,' said Maggie, walking more hurriedly. 'Because I should want too much. I must wait – this life will not last long.'

'Don't hurry away from me without saying "goodbye," Maggie,' said Philip, as they reached the group of Scotch firs, and she continued still to walk along without speaking. 'I must not go any farther, I think, must I?'

'Oh no, I forgot; goodbye,' said Maggie, pausing, and putting out her hand to him. The action brought her feeling back in a strong current to Philip; and after they had stood looking at each other in silence for a few moments, with their hands clasped, she said, withdrawing her hand, 'I'm very grateful to you for thinking of me all those years. It is very sweet to have people love us. What a wonderful, beautiful thing it seems that God should have made your heart so that you could care about a queer little girl whom you only knew for a few weeks! I remember saying to you, that I thought you cared for me more than Tom did.'

'Ah, Maggie,' said Philip, almost fretfully, 'you would never love me so well as you love your brother.'

'Perhaps not,' said Maggie, simply; 'but then, you know, the first thing I ever remember in my life is standing with Tom by the side of the Floss, while he held my hand: everything before that is dark to me. But I shall never forget you – though we must keep apart.'

'Don't say so, Maggie,' said Philip. 'If I kept that little girl in my mind for five years, didn't I earn some part in her? She ought not to take herself quite away from me.'

'Not if I were free,' said Maggie; 'but I am not – I must submit.' She hesitated a moment, and then added, 'And I wanted to say to you, that you had better not take more notice of my brother than just bowing to him. He once told me not to speak to you again, and he doesn't change his mind . . . Oh dear, the sun is set. I am too long away. Goodbye.' She gave him her hand once more.

'I shall come here as often as I can, till I see you again, Maggie. Have some feeling for *me* as well as for others.'

'Yes, yes, I have,' said Maggie, hurrying away, and quickly disappearing behind the last fir tree; though Philip's gaze after her remained immovable for minutes as if he saw her still.

Maggie went home, with an inward conflict already begun; Philip went home to do nothing but remember and hope. You can hardly help blaming him severely. He was four or five years older than Maggie, and had a full consciousness of his feeling towards her to aid him in foreseeing the character his contemplated interviews with her would bear in the opinion of a third person. But you must not suppose that he was capable of a gross selfishness, or that he could have been satisfied without persuading himself that he was seeking to infuse some happiness into Maggie's life – seeking this even more than any direct ends for himself. He could give her sympathy – he could give her help. There was not the slightest promise of love towards him in her manner; it was nothing more than the sweet girlish tenderness she had shown him when she was twelve; perhaps she would never love him – perhaps no woman ever *could* love him: well, then, he would endure that; he should at least have the happiness of seeing her – of feeling some nearness to her. And he clutched passionately the possibility that she *might* love him: perhaps the feeling would grow, if she could come to associate him with that watchful tenderness which her nature would be so keenly alive to. If any woman could love him, surely Maggie was that woman: there was such wealth of love in her, and there was no one to claim it all. Then – the pity of it, that a mind like hers should be withering in its very youth, like a young forest tree, for want of the light and space it was formed to flourish in! Could he not hinder that, by persuading her out of her system of privation? He would be her guardian angel; he would do anything, bear anything, for her sake – except not seeing her.

CHAPTER 2

Aunt Glegg Learns the Breadth of Bob's Thumb

While Maggie's life-struggles had lain almost entirely within her own soul, one shadowy army fighting another, and the slain shadows for ever rising again, Tom was engaged in a dustier, noisier warfare, grappling with more substantial obstacles, and gaining more definite conquests. So it has been since the days of Hecuba, and of Hector, Tamer of horses: inside the gates, the women with streaming hair and uplifted hands offering prayers, watching the world's combat from afar, filling their long, empty days with memories and fears: outside, the men, in fierce struggle with things divine and human, quenching memory in the stronger light of purpose, losing the sense of dread and even of wounds in the hurrying ardour of action.

From what you have seen of Tom, I think he is not a youth of whom you would prophesy failure in anything he had thoroughly wished: the wagers are likely to be on his side, notwithstanding his small success in the classics. For Tom had never desired success in this field of enterprise; and for getting a fine flourishing growth of stupidity there is nothing like pouring out on a mind a good amount of subjects in which it feels no interest. But now Tom's strong will bound together his integrity, his pride, his family regrets, and his personal ambition, and made them one force, concentrating his efforts and surmounting discouragements. His uncle Deane, who watched him closely, soon began to conceive hopes of him, and to be rather proud that he had brought into the employment of the firm a nephew who appeared to be made of such good commercial stuff. The real kindness of placing him in the warehouse first was soon evident to Tom, in the hints his uncle began to throw out, that after a time he might perhaps be trusted to travel at certain seasons, and buy in for the firm various vulgar commodities with which I need not shock refined ears in this place; and it was doubtless with a view to this result that Mr Deane, when he expected to take his wine alone, would tell Tom to step in and sit with him an hour, and would pass that hour in much lecturing and catechising concerning articles of export and import, with an occasional excursus of more indirect utility on the relative advantages to the merchants of St Ogg's of having goods brought in their own and in foreign bottoms – a subject on which Mr Deane, as a shipowner, naturally threw off a few sparks when he got warmed with talk and wine. Already, in the second year, Tom's salary was raised; but all, except the price of his dinner and clothes, went home into the tin box; and he shunned comradeship, lest it should lead him into expenses in spite of himself. Not that Tom was moulded on the spooney type of the Industrious Apprentice; he had a very strong appetite for pleasure – would have liked to be a Tamer of horses, and to make a distinguished figure in all neighbouring eyes, dispensing treats and benefits to others with well-judged liberality, and being pronounced one of the finest young fellows of those parts; nay, he determined to achieve these things sooner or later; but his practical shrewdness told him that the means to such achievements could only lie for him in present abstinence and self-denial: there were certain milestones to be passed, and one of the first was the payment of his father's debts. Having made up his mind on that point, he strode along without swerving, contracting some rather saturnine sternness, as a young man is likely to do who has a premature call upon him for self-reliance. Tom felt intensely that common cause with his father which springs from family pride, and was bent on being irreproachable as a son; but his growing experience caused him to pass much silent criticism on the rashness and imprudence of his father's past conduct: their dispositions were not in sympathy, and Tom's face showed little radiance during his few home hours. Maggie had an awe of him, against which she struggled as something unfair to her consciousness of wider thoughts and deeper motives; but it was of no use to struggle. A character at unity with itself – that performs what it intends, subdues every counteracting impulse, and has no visions beyond the distinctly possible – is strong by its very negations.

You may imagine that Tom's more and more obvious unlikeness to his father was well fitted to conciliate the maternal aunts and uncles; and Mr Deane's favourable reports and predictions to Mr Glegg concerning Tom's qualifications for business, began to be discussed amongst them with various acceptance. He was likely, it appeared, to do the family credit, without causing it any expense and trouble. Mrs Pullet had always thought it strange if Tom's excellent complexion, so entirely that of the Dodsons, did not argue a certainty that he would turn out well, his juvenile errors of running down the peacock, and general disrespect to his aunts, only indicating a tinge of Tulliver blood which he had doubtless outgrown. Mr Glegg, who had contracted a cautious liking for Tom ever since his spirited and sensible behaviour when the execution was in the house, was now warming into a resolution to further his prospects actively – some time, when an opportunity offered of doing so in a prudent manner, without ultimate loss; but Mrs Glegg observed that she was not given to speak without book, as some people were; that those who said least were most likely to find their words made good; and that when the right moment came, it would be seen who could do something better than talk. Uncle Pullet, after silent meditation for a period of several lozenges, came distinctly to the conclusion, that when a young man was likely to do well, it was better not to meddle with him.

Tom, meanwhile, had shown no disposition to rely on anyone but himself, though, with a natural sensitiveness towards all indications of favourable opinion, he was glad to see his uncle Glegg look in on him sometimes in a friendly way during business hours, and glad to be invited to dine at his house, though he usually preferred declining on the ground that he was not sure of being punctual. But about a year ago, something had occurred which induced Tom to test his uncle Glegg's friendly disposition.

Bob Jakin, who rarely returned from one of his rounds without seeing Tom and Maggie, awaited him on the bridge as he was coming home from St Ogg's one evening, that they might have a little private talk. He took the liberty of asking if Mr Tom had ever thought of making money by trading a bit on his own account. Trading, how? Tom wished to know. Why, by sending out a bit of a cargo to foreign ports; because Bob had a particular friend who had offered to do a little business for him in that way in Laceham goods, and would be glad to serve Mr Tom on the same footing. Tom was interested at once, and begged for full explanation, wondering he had not thought of this plan before. He was so well pleased with the prospect of a speculation that might change the slow process of addition into multiplication, that he at once determined to mention the matter to his father, and get his consent to appropriate some of the savings in the tin box to the purchase of a small cargo. He would rather not have consulted his father, but he had just paid his last quarter's money into the tin box, and there was no other resource. All the savings were there; for Mr Tulliver would not consent to put the money out at interest lest he should lose it. Since he had speculated in the purchase of some corn, and had lost by it, he could not be easy without keeping the money under his eye.

Tom approached the subject carefully, as he was seated on the hearth with his father that evening, and Mr Tulliver listened, leaning forward in his armchair and looking up in Tom's face with a sceptical glance. His first impulse was to give a positive refusal, but he was in some awe of Tom's wishes, and since he had had the sense of being an 'unlucky' father, he had lost some of his old peremptoriness and determination to be master. He took the key of the bureau from his pocket, got out the key of the large chest, and fetched down the tin box – slowly, as if he were trying to defer the moment of a painful parting. Then he seated himself against the table, and opened the box with that little padlock key which he fingered in his waistcoat pocket in all vacant moments. There they were, the dingy bank-notes and the bright sovereigns, and he counted them out on the table – only a hundred and sixteen pounds in two years, after all the pinching.

'How much do you want, then?' he said, speaking as if the words burnt his lips.

'Suppose I begin with the thirty-six pounds, father?' said Tom.

Mr Tulliver separated this sum from the rest, and, keeping his hand over it, said, 'It's as much as I can save out o' my pay in a year.'

'Yes, father: it is such slow work – saving out of the little money we get. And in this way we might double our savings.'

'Ay, my lad,' said the father, keeping his hand on the money, 'but you might lose it – you might lose a year o' my life – and I haven't got many.'

Tom was silent.

'And you know I wouldn't pay a dividend with the first hundred, because I wanted to see it all in a lump – and when I see it, I'm sure on't. If you trust to luck, it's sure to be against me. It's Old Harry's got the luck in his hands; and if I lose one year, I shall never pick it up again – death 'ull o'ertake me.'

Mr Tulliver's voice trembled, and Tom was silent for a few minutes before he said, 'I'll give it up, father, since you object to it so strongly.'

But, unwilling to abandon the scheme altogether, he determined to ask his uncle Glegg to venture twenty pounds, on condition of receiving five per cent of the profits. That was really a very small thing to ask. So when Bob called the next day at the wharf to know the decision, Tom proposed that they should go together to his uncle Glegg's to open the business; for his diffident pride clung to him, and made him feel that Bob's tongue would relieve him from some embarrassment.

Mr Glegg, at the pleasant hour of four in the afternoon of a hot August day, was naturally counting his wall-fruit to assure himself that the sum total had not varied since yesterday. To him entered Tom, in what appeared to Mr Glegg very questionable companionship: that of a man with a pack on his back – for Bob was equipped for a new journey – and of a huge brindled bull-terrier, who walked with a slow swaying movement from side to side, and glanced from under his eyelids with a surly indifference which might after all be a cover to the most offensive designs. Mr Glegg's spectacles, which had been assisting him in counting the fruit, made these suspicious details alarmingly evident to him.

'Heigh! heigh! keep that dog back, will you?' he shouted, snatching up a stake and holding it before him as a shield when the visitors were within three yards of him.

'Get out wi' you, Mumps,' said Bob, with a kick. 'He's as quiet as a lamb, sir,' – an observation which Mumps corroborated by a low growl as he retreated behind his master's legs.

'Why, whatever does this mean, Tom?' said Mr Glegg. 'Have you brought information about the scoundrels as cut my trees?' If Bob came in the character of 'information,' Mr Glegg saw reasons for tolerating some irregularity.

'No, sir,' said Tom: 'I came to speak to you about a little matter of business of my own.'

'Ay – well; but what has this dog got to do with it?' said the old gentleman, getting mild again.

'It's my dog, sir,' said the ready Bob. 'An' it's me as put Mr Tom up to the bit o' business; for Mr Tom's been a friend o' mine iver since I was a little chap: fust thing iver I did was frightenin' the birds for th' old master. An' if a bit a o' luck turns up, I'm allays thinkin' if I can let Mr Tom have a pull at it. An' it's a downright roarin' shame, as when he's got the chance o' making a bit o' money wi' sending goods out – ten or twelve per zent clear, when freight an' commission's paid – as he shouldn't lay hold o' the chance for want o' money. An' when there's the Laceham goods – lors! they're made o' purpose for folks as want to send out a little carguy;

light, an' take up no room – you may pack twenty pound so as you can't see the passill: an' they're manifacturs as please fools, so I reckon they aren't like to want a market. An' I'd go to Laceham an' buy in the goods for Mr Tom along wi' my own. An' there's the shuper-cargo o' the bit of a vessel as is goin' to take 'em out. I know him partic'lar; he's a solid man, an' got a family i' the town here. Salt, his name is – an' a briny chap he is too – an' if you don't believe me, I can take you to him.'

Uncle Glegg stood open-mouthed with astonishment at this unembarrassed loquacity, with which his understanding could hardly keep pace. He looked at Bob, first over his spectacles, then through them, then over them again; while Tom, doubtful of his uncle's impression, began to wish he had not brought this singular Aaron or mouthpiece: Bob's talk appeared less seemly, now someone beside himself was listening to it.

'You seem to be a knowing fellow,' said Mr Glegg, at last.

'Ay, sir, you say true,' returned Bob, nodding his head aside; 'I think my head's all alive inside like an old cheese, for I'm so full o' plans, one knocks another over. If I hadn't Mumps to talk to, I should get top-heavy an' tumble in a fit. I suppose it's because I niver went to school much. That's what I jaw my old mother for. I says, "You should ha' sent me to school a bit more," I says – "an then I could ha' read i' the books like fun, an' kep' my head cool an' empty." Lors, she's fine an' comfor'ble now, my old mother is: she ates her baked meat an' taters as often as she likes. For I'm gettin' so full o' money, I must hev a wife to spend it for me. But it's botherin', a wife is – and Mumps mightn't like her.'

Uncle Glegg, who regarded himself as a jocose man since he had retired from business, was beginning to find Bob amusing, but he had still a disapproving observation to make, which kept his face serious.

'Ah,' he said, 'I should think you're at a loss for ways o' spending your money, else you wouldn't keep that big dog, to eat as much as two Christians. It's shameful – shameful!' But he spoke more in sorrow than in anger, and quickly added, 'But, come now, let's hear more about this business, Tom. I suppose you want a little sum to make a venture with. But where's all your own money? You don't spend it all – eh?'

'No, sir,' said Tom, colouring; 'but my father is unwilling to risk it, and I don't like to press him. If I could get twenty or thirty pounds to begin with, I could pay five per cent for it, and then I could gradually make a little capital of my own, and do without a loan.'

'Ay . . . ay,' said Mr Glegg, in an approving tone; 'that's not a bad notion, and I won't say as I wouldn't be your man. But it 'ull be as well for me to see this Salt, as you talk on. And then . . . here's this friend o' yours offers to buy the goods for you. Perhaps you've got somebody to stand surety for you if the money's put into your hands?' added the cautious old gentleman, looking over his spectacles at Bob.

'I don't think that's necessary, uncle,' said Tom. 'At least, I mean it would not be necessary for me, because I know Bob well; but perhaps it would be right for you to have some security.'

'You get your percentage out o' the purchase, I suppose?' said Mr Glegg, looking at Bob.

'No, sir,' said Bob, rather indignantly; 'I didn't offer to get a apple for Mr

Tom, o' purpose to hev a bite out of it myself. When I play folks tricks there'll be more fun in 'em nor that.'

'Well, but it's nothing but right you should have a small percentage,' said Mr Glegg. 'I've no opinion o' transactions where folks do things for nothing. It allays looks bad.'

'Well, then,' said Bob, whose keenness saw at once what was implied, 'I'll tell you what I get by't, an' it's money in my pocket in the end: – I make myself look big, wi' makin' a bigger purchase. That's what I'm thinking on. Lors! I'm a 'cute chap – I am.'

'Mr Glegg, Mr Glegg,' said a severe voice from the open parlour window, 'pray are you coming in to tea? – or are you going to stand talking with packmen till you get murdered in the open daylight?'

'Murdered?' said Mr Glegg; 'what's the woman talking of? Here's your nephey Tom come about a bit o' business.'

'Murdered – yes – it isn't many 'sizes ago since a packman murdered a young woman in a lone place, and stole her thimble, and threw her body into a ditch.'

'Nay, nay,' said Mr Glegg, soothingly, 'you're thinking o' the man wi' no legs, as drove a dog-cart.'

'Well, it's the same thing, Mr Glegg – only you're fond o' contradicting what I say; and if my nephey's come about business, it 'ud be more fitting if you'd bring him into the house, and let his aunt know about it, instead o' whispering in corners, in that plotting, underminding way.'

'Well, well,' said Mr Glegg, 'we'll come in now.'

'You needn't stay here,' said the lady to Bob, in a loud voice, adapted to the moral not the physical distance between them. 'We don't want anything. I don't deal wi' packmen. Mind you shut the gate after you.'

'Stop a bit; not so fast,' said Mr Glegg: 'I haven't done with this young man yet. Come in, Tom; come in,' he added, stepping in at the French window.

'Mr Glegg,' said Mrs G., in a fatal tone, 'if you're going to let that man and his dog in on my carpet, before my very face, be so good as to let me know. A wife's got a right to ask that, I hope.'

'Don't you be uneasy, mum,' said Bob, touching his cap. He saw at once that Mrs Glegg was a bit of game worth running down, and longed to be at the sport; 'we'll stay out upo' the gravel here – Mumps and me will. Mumps knows his company – he does. I might hish at him by th' hour together, before he'd fly at a real gentleman like you. It's wonderful how he knows which is the good-looking ladies – and's partic'lar fond of 'em when they've good shapes. Lors!' added Bob, laying down his pack on the gravel, 'it's a thousand pities such a lady as you shouldn't deal with a packman, i'stead o' goin' into these new-fangled shops, where there's half a dozen fine gents wi' their chins propped up wi'a stiff stock, a-looking like bottles wi' ornamental stoppers, an' all got to get their dinner out of a bit o' calico: it stan's to reason you must pay three times the price you pay a packman, as is the nat'ral way o' gettin' goods – an' pays no rent, an' isn't forced to throttle himself till the lies are squeezed out on him, whether he will or no. But lors! mum, you know what it is better nor I do – *you* can see through them shopmen, I'll be bound.'

'Yes, I reckon I can, and through the packmen, too,' observed Mrs Glegg, intending to imply that Bob's flattery had produced no effect on *her*; while her husband, standing behind her with his hands, in his pockets and legs apart, winked and smiled with conjugal delight at the probability of his wife's being circumvented.

'Ay, to be sure, mum,' said Bob. 'Why, you must ha' dealt wi' no end o' packmen when you war a young lass – before the master here had the luck to set eyes on you. I know where you lived, I do – seen th' house many a time – close upon Squire Darleigh's – a stone house wi' steps . . .'

'Ah, that it had,' said Mrs Glegg, pouring out the tea. 'You know something o' my family then . . . are you akin to that packman with a squint in his eye, as used to bring th' Irish linen?'

'Look you there now!' said Bob, evasively. 'Didn't I know as you'd remember the best bargains you've made in your life was made wi' packmen? Why, you see, even a squintin' packman's better nor a shopman as can see straight. Lors! if I'd the luck to call at the stone house wi' my pack, as lies here,' – stooping and thumping the bundle emphatically with his fist, – 'an' th' handsome young lasses all stannin' out on the stone steps, it 'ud ha' been summat like openin' a pack – that would. It's on'y the poor houses now as a packman calls on, if it isn't for the sake o' the sarvant-maids. They're paltry times – these are. Why, mum, look at the printed cottons now, an' what they was when you wore 'em – why, you wouldn't put such a thing on now, I can see. It must be first-rate quality – the manifactur as you'd buy – summat as 'ud wear as well as your own faitures.'

'Yes, better quality nor any you're like to carry: you've got nothing first-rate but brazenness, I'll be bound,' said Mrs Glegg, with a triumphant sense of her insurmountable sagacity. 'Mr Glegg, are you going ever to sit down to your tea? Tom, there's a cup for you.'

'You speak true there, mum,' said Bob. 'My pack isn't for ladies like you. The time's gone by for that. Bargains picked up dirt cheap! A bit o' damage here an' there, as can be cut out, or else niver seen i' the wearin'; but not fit to offer to rich folks as can pay for the look o' things as nobody sees. I'm not the man as 'ud offer t' open my pack to *you*, mum: no, no; I'm a imperent chap, as you say – these times makes folks imperent – but I'm not up to the mark o' that.'

'Why, what goods do you carry in your pack?' said Mrs Glegg. 'Fine-coloured things, I suppose – shawls an' that?'

'All sorts, mum, all sorts,' said Bob, thumping his bundle; 'but let us say no more about that, if *you* please. I'm here upo' Mr Tom's business, an' I'm not the man to take up the time wi' my own.'

'And pray, what *is* this business as is to be kept from me?' said Mrs Glegg, who, solicited by a double curiosity, was obliged to let the one-half wait.

'A little plan o' nephey Tom's here,' said good-natured Mr Glegg; 'and not altogether a bad un, I think. A little plan for making money: that's the right sort o' plan for young folks as have got their fortin to make, eh, Jane?'

'But I hope it isn't a plan where he expects iverything to be done for him by his friends: that's what the young folks think of mostly nowadays. And pray, what has this packman got to do wi' what goes on in our family? Can't you speak for yourself, Tom, and let your aunt know things, as a nephey should?'

'This is Bob Jakin, aunt,' said Tom, bridling the irritation that aunt Glegg's voice always produced. 'I've known him ever since we were little boys. He's a very good fellow, and always ready to do me a kindness. And he has had some experience in sending goods out – a small part of a cargo as a private speculation; and he thinks, if I could begin to do a little in the same way, I might make some money. A large interest is got in that way.'

'Large int'rest?' said Aunt Glegg, with eagerness; 'and what do you call large int'rest?'

'Ten or twelve per cent, Bob says, after expenses are paid.'

'Then why wasn't I let to know o' such things before, Mr Glegg?' said Mrs Glegg, turning to her husband, with a deep grating tone of reproach. 'Haven't you allays told me as there was no getting more nor five per cent?'

'Pooh, pooh, nonsense, my good woman,' said Mr Glegg. 'You couldn't go into trade, could you? You can't get more than five per cent with security.'

'But I can turn a bit o' money for you, an' welcome, mum,' said Bob, 'if you'd like to risk it – not as there's any risk to speak on. But if you'd a mind to lend a bit o' money to Mr Tom, he'd pay you six or seven per zent, an' get a trifle for himself as well; an' a good-natur'd lady like you 'ud like the feel o' the money better if your nephey took part on it.'

'What do you say, Mrs G.?' said Mr Glegg. 'I've a notion, when I've made a bit more enquiry, as I shall perhaps start Tom here with a bit of a nest-egg – he'll pay me int'rest, you know – an' if you've got some little sums lyin' idle twisted up in a stockin' toe, or that . . .'

'Mr Glegg, it's beyond iverything! You'll go and give information to the tramps next, as they may come and rob me.'

'Well, well, as I was sayin', if you like to join me wi' twenty pounds, you can – I'll make it fifty. That'll be a pretty good nest-egg – eh, Tom?'

'You're not counting on me, Mr Glegg, I hope,' said his wife. 'You could do fine things wi' my money, I don't doubt.'

'Very well,' said Mr Glegg, rather snappishly, 'then we'll do without you. I shall go with you to see this Salt,' he added, turning to Bob.

'And now, I suppose, you'll go all the other way, Mr Glegg,' said Mrs G. 'and want to shut me out o' my own nephey's business. I never said I wouldn't put money into it – I don't say as it shall be twenty pounds, though you're so ready to say it for me – but he'll see someday as his aunt's in the right not to risk the money she's saved for him till it's proved as it won't be lost.'

'Ay, that's a pleasant sort o' risk, that is,' said Mr Glegg, indiscreetly winking at Tom, who couldn't avoid smiling. But Bob stemmed the injured lady's outburst.

'Ay, mum,' he said admiringly, 'you know what's what – you do. An' its nothing but fair. *You* see how the first bit of a job answers, an' then you'll come down handsome. Lors, it's a fine thing to hev good kin. I got my bit of a nest-egg, as the master calls it, all by my own sharpness – ten suvreigns it was – wi' dousing the fire at Torry's mill, an' it's growed an' growed by a bit an' a bit, till I'n got a matter o' thirty pound to lay out, besides makin' my mother comfor'ble. I should get more, on'y I'm such a soft wi' the women – I can't help lettin' 'em hev such good bargains. There's this bundle, now' (thumping it lustily), 'any other chap 'ud make a pretty penny out on it. But me! . . . lors, I shall sell 'em for pretty near what I paid for 'em.'

'Have you got a bit of good net, now?' said Mrs Glegg, in a patronising tone, moving from the tea-table, and folding her napkin.

'Eh, mum, not what you'd think it worth your while to look at. I'd scorn to show it you. It 'ud be an insult to you.'

'But let me see,' said Mrs Glegg, still patronising. 'If they're damaged goods, they're like enough to be a bit the better quality.'

'No, mum. I know my place,' said Bob, lifting up his pack and shouldering it. 'I'm not going t' expose the lowness o' my trade to a lady like you. Packs is come down i' the world: it 'ud cut you to th' heart to see the difference. I'm at your sarvice, sir, when you've a mind to go and see Salt.'

'All in good time,' said Mr Glegg, really unwilling to cut short the dialogue. 'Are you wanted at the wharf, Tom?'

'No, sir; I left Stowe in my place.'

'Come, put down your pack, and let me see,' said Mrs Glegg, drawing a chair to the window, and seating herself with much dignity.

'Don't you ask it, mum,' said Bob, entreatingly.

'Make no more words,' said Mrs Glegg, severely, 'but do as I tell you.'

'Eh, mum, I'm loath – that I am,' said Bob, slowly depositing his pack on the step, and beginning to untie it with unwilling fingers. 'But what you order shall be done' (much fumbling in pauses between the sentences). 'It's not as you'll buy a single thing on me . . . I'd be sorry for you to do it . . . for think o' them poor women up i' the villages there, as niver stir a hundred yards from home . . . it 'ud be a pity for anybody to buy up their bargains. Lors, it's as good as a junketing to 'em when they see me wi' my pack . . . an' I shall niver pick up such bargains for 'em again. Least ways, I've no time now, for I'm off to Laceham. See here, now,' Bob went on, becoming rapid again, and holding up a scarlet woollen kerchief with an embroidered wreath in the corner; 'here's a thing to make a lass's mouth water, an' on'y two shillin' – an' why? Why, 'cause there's a bit of a moth-hole i' this plain end. Lors, I think the moths an' the mildew was sent by Providence o' purpose to cheapen the goods a bit for the good-lookin' women as han't got much money. If it hadn't been for the moths, now, every hankicher on 'em 'ud ha' gone to the rich handsome ladies, like you, mum, at five shillin' apiece – not a farthin' less; but what does the moth do? Why, it nibbles off three shillin' o' the price i' no time, an' then a packman like me can carry't to the poor lasses as live under the dark thack, to make a bit of a blaze for 'em. Lors, it's as good as a fire, to look at such a hankicher!'

Bob held it at a distance for admiration, but Mrs Glegg said sharply, 'Yes, but nobody wants a fire this time o' year. Put these coloured things by – let me look at your nets, if you've got 'em.'

'Eh, mum, I told you how it 'ud be,' said Bob, flinging aside the coloured things with an air of desperation. 'I knowed it 'ud turn again' you to look at such paltry articles as I carry. Here's a piece o' figured muslin now – what's the use o' you lookin' at it? You might as well look at poor folks's victual, mum – it 'ud only take away your appetite. There's a yard i' the middle on't as the pattern's all missed – lors, why it's a muslin as the Princess Victoree might ha' wore – but,' added Bob, flinging it behind him on to the turf, as if to save Mrs Glegg's eyes, 'it'll be bought up by the huckster's wife at Fibb's End – that's where *it*'ll go – ten shillin' for the whole lot – ten yards, countin' the damaged un – five-an'-twenty shillin' 'ud ha' been the price – not a penny less. But I'll say no more, mum; it's nothing to you – **a** piece o' muslin like that; you can afford to pay three times the money for a thing as isn't half so good. It's nets *you* talked on; well, I've got a piece as 'ull serve you to make fun on . . . '

'Bring me that muslin,' said Mrs Glegg: 'it's a buff – I'm partial to buff.'

'Eh, but a *damaged* thing,' said Bob, in a tone of deprecating disgust. 'You'd do nothing with it, mum – you'd give it to the cook, I know you would – an' it 'ud be a pity – she'd look too much like a lady in it – it's unbecoming for servants.'

'Fetch it, and let me see you measure it,' said Mrs Glegg, authoritatively.

Bob obeyed with ostentatious reluctance.

'See what there is over measure!' he said, holding forth the extra half-yard, while Mrs Glegg was busy examining the damaged yard, and throwing her head back to see how far the fault would be lost on a distant view.

'I'll give you six shilling for it,' she said, throwing it down with the air of a person who mentions an ultimatum.

'Didn't I tell you now, mum, as it 'ud turn your feelings to look at my pack? That damaged bit's turned your stomach now – I see it has,' said Bob, wrapping the muslin up with the utmost quickness, and apparently about to fasten up his pack. 'You're used to seein' a different sort o' article carried by packmen, when you lived at the stone house. Packs is come down i' the world; I told you that; *my* goods are for common folks. Mrs Pepper 'ull give me ten shillin' for that muslin, an' be sorry as I didn't ask her more. Such articles answer i' the wearin' – they keep their colour till the threads melt away i' the washtub, an' that won't be while I'm a young un.'

'Well, seven shilling,' said Mrs Glegg.

'Put it out o' your mind, mum, now do,' said Bob. 'Here's a bit o' net, then, for you to look at before I tie up my pack: just for you to see what my trade's come to: spotted and sprigged, you see, beautiful, but yallow – 's been lyin' by an' got the wrong colour. I could niver ha' bought such net, if it hadn't been yallow. Lors, it's took me a deal o' study to know the vally o' such articles; when I begun to carry a pack, I was as ignirant as a pig – net or calico was all the same to me. I thought them things the most vally as was the thickest. I was took in dreadful – for I'm a straightforrard chap – up to no tricks, mum. I can on'y say my nose is my own, for if I went beyond, I should lose myself pretty quick. An' I gev five-an'-eightpence for that piece o' net – if I was to tell y' anything else I should be tellin' you fibs: an' five-an'-eightpence I shall ask for it – not a penny more – for it's a woman's article, an' I like to 'commodate the women. Five-an'-eightpence for six yards – as cheap as if it was only the dirt on it as was paid for.'

'I don't mind having three yards of it,' said Mrs Glegg.

'Why, there's but six altogether,' said Bob. 'No, mum, it isn't worth your while; you can go to the shop tomorrow an' get the same pattern ready whitened. It's on'y three times the money – what's that to a lady like you?' He gave an emphatic tie to his bundle.

'Come, lay me out that muslin,' said Mrs Glegg. 'Here's eight shilling for it.'

'You *will* be jokin', mum,' said Bob, looking up with a laughing face; 'I see'd you was a pleasant lady when I fust come to the winder.'

'Well, put it me out,' said Mrs Glegg, peremptorily.

'But if I let you have it for ten shillin', mum, you'll be so good as not tell nobody. I should be a laughin'-stock – the trade 'ud hoot me, if they knowed it. I'm obliged to make believe as I ask more nor I do for my goods, else they'd find out I was a flat. I'm glad you don't insist upo' buyin' the net, for then I should ha' lost my two best bargains for Mrs Pepper o' Fibb's End – an' she's a rare customer.'

'Let me look at the net again,' said Mrs Glegg, yearning after the cheap spots and sprigs, now they were vanishing.

'Well, I can't deny *you*, mum,' said Bob, handing it out. 'Eh! see what a pattern now! Real Laceham goods. Now, this is the sort o' article I'm recommendin' Mr Tom to send out. Lors, it's a fine thing for anybody as has got a bit o' money – these Laceham goods 'ud make it breed like maggits. If I was a lady wi' a bit o' money! – why, I know one as put thirty pound into them goods – a lady wi' a cork leg; but as sharp – you wouldn't catch *her* runnin' her head into a sack; *she'd* see her way clear out o' anything afore she'd be in a hurry to start. Well, she let out thirty pound to a young man in the drapering line, and he laid it out i' Laceham goods, an' a shuper-cargo o' my acquintance (not Salt) took 'em out, an' she got her eight per zent fust go off – an' now you can't hold her but she must be sendin' out carguies wi' every ship, till she's gettin' as rich as a Jew. Bucks her name is – she doesn't live i' this town. Now then, mum, if you'll please to give me the net . . .'

'Here's fifteen shilling, then, for the two,' said Mrs Glegg. 'But it's a shameful price.'

'Nay, mum, you'll niver say that when you're upo' your knees i' church i' five years' time. I'm makin' you a present o' th' articles – I am, indeed. That eight-pence shaves off my profit as clean as a razor. Now then, sir,' continued Bob, shouldering his pack, 'if you please, I'll be glad to go and see about makin' Mr Tom's fortin. Eh, I wish I'd got another twenty pound to lay out for *my*sen: I shouldn't stay to say my Catechism afore I knowed what to do wi't.'

'Stop a bit, Mr Glegg,' said the lady, as her husband took his hat, 'you never *will* give me the chance o' speaking. You'll go away now, and finish everything about this business, and come back and tell me it's too late for me to speak. As if I wasn't my nephey's own aunt, and th' head o' the family on his mother's side! and laid by guineas, all full weight, for him – as he'll know who to respect when I'm laid in my coffin.'

'Well, Mrs G. say what you mean,' said Mr G., hastily.

'Well, then, I desire as nothing may be done without my knowing. I don't say as I shan't venture twenty pounds, if you make out as everything's right and safe. And if I do, Tom,' concluded Mrs Glegg, turning impressively to her nephew, 'I hope you'll allays bear it in mind and be grateful for such an aunt. I mean you to pay me interest, you know – I don't approve o' giving; we niver looked for that in *my* family.'

'Thank you, aunt,' said Tom, rather proudly. 'I prefer having the money only lent to me.'

'Very well: that's the Dodson sperrit,' said Mrs Glegg, rising to get her knitting with the sense that any further remark after this would be bathos.

Salt – that eminently 'briny chap' – having been discovered in a cloud of tobacco-smoke at the Anchor Tavern, Mr Glegg commenced enquiries which turned out satisfactorily enough to warrant the advance of the 'nest-egg,' to which aunt Glegg contributed twenty pounds; and in this modest beginning you see the ground of a fact which might otherwise surprise you – namely, Tom's accumulation of a fund, unknown to his father, that promised in no very long time to meet the more tardy process of saving, and quite cover the deficit. When once his attention had been turned to this source of gain, Tom determined to make the most of it, and lost no opportunity of obtaining information and extending his small enterprises. In not telling his father, he was influenced by that strange mixture of opposite feelings which often gives equal truth to those who blame an action and those who admire it: partly, it was that disinclination to confidence which is seen between near kindred – that family repulsion which spoils the most sacred relations of our lives; partly, it was the desire to surprise his father with a great joy. He did not see that it would have been better to soothe the interval with a new hope, and prevent the delirium of a too sudden elation.

At the time of Maggie's first meeting with Philip, Tom had already nearly a hundred and fifty pounds of his own capital; and while they were walking by the evening light in the Red Deeps, he, by the same evening light, was riding into Laceham; proud of being on his first journey on behalf of Guest & Co., and revolving in his mind all the chances that by the end of another year he should have doubled his gains, lifted off the obloquy of debt from his father's name, and perhaps – for he should be twenty-one – have got a new start for himself, on a higher platform of employment. Did he not deserve it? He was quite sure that he did.

CHAPTER 3

The Wavering Balance

I said that Maggie went home that evening from the Red Deeps with a mental conflict already begun. You have seen clearly enough, in her interview with Philip, what that conflict was. Here suddenly was an opening in the rocky wall which shut in the narrow valley of humiliation, where all her prospect was the remote unfathomed sky; and some of the memory-haunting earthly delights were no longer out of her reach. She might have books, converse, affection – she might hear tidings of the world from which her mind had not yet lost its sense of exile; and it would be a kindness to Philip too, who was pitiable – clearly not happy; and perhaps here was an opportunity indicated for making her mind more worthy of its highest service – perhaps the noblest, completest devoutness could hardly exist without some width of knowledge: *must* she always live in this resigned imprisonment? It was so blameless, so good a thing that there should be friendship between her and Philip; the motives that forbade it were so unreasonable – so unchristian! But the severe monotonous warning came again and again – that she was losing the simplicity and clearness of her life by admitting a ground of concealment, and that, by forsaking the simple rule of renunciation, she was throwing herself under the seductive guidance of illimitable wants. She thought she had won strength to obey the warning before she allowed herself the next week to turn her steps in the evening to the Red Deeps. But while she was resolved to say an affectionate farewell to Philip, how she looked forward to that evening walk in the still, fleckered shade of the hollows, away from all that was harsh and unlovely; to the affectionate admiring looks that would meet her; to the sense of comradeship that childish memories would give to wiser, older talk; to the certainty that Philip would care to hear everything she said, which no one else cared for! It was a half-hour that it would be very hard to turn her back upon, with the sense that there would be no other like it. Yet she said what she meant to say; she looked firm as well as sad.

'Philip, I have made up my mind – it is right that we should give each other up, in everything but memory. I could not see you without concealment – stay, I know what you are going to say – it is other people's wrong feelings that make concealment necessary; but concealment is bad, however it may be caused. I feel that it would be bad for me, for us both. And then, if our secret were discovered, there would be nothing but misery – dreadful anger; and then we must part after all, and it would be harder, when we were used to seeing each other.'

Philip's face had flushed, and there was a momentary eagerness of expression, as if he had been about to resist this decision with all his might. But he controlled himself, and said, with assumed calmness, 'Well, Maggie, if we must part, let us try and forget it for one half-hour: let us talk together a little while – for the last time.'

He took her hand, and Maggie felt no reason to withdraw it: his quietness made her all the more sure she had given him great pain, and she wanted to show him how unwillingly she had given it. They walked together hand in hand in silence.

'Let us sit down in the hollow,' said Philip, 'where we stood the last time. See how the dog-roses have strewed the ground, and spread their opal petals over it!'

They sat down at the roots of the slanting ash.

'I've begun my picture of you among the Scotch firs, Maggie,' said Philip, 'so you must let me study your face a little, while you stay – since I am not to see it again. Please, turn your head this way.'

This was said in an entreating voice, and it would have been very hard of Maggie to refuse. The full lustrous face, with the bright black coronet, looked down like that of a divinity well pleased to be worshipped, on the pale-hued, small-featured face that was turned up to it.

'I shall be sitting for my second portrait then,' she said, smiling. 'Will it be larger than the other?'

'Oh, yes, much larger. It is an oil-painting. You will look like a tall Hamadryad, dark and strong and noble, just issued from one of the fir trees, when the stems are casting their afternoon shadows on the grass.'

'You seem to think more of painting than of anything now, Philip?'

'Perhaps I do,' said Philip, rather sadly; 'but I think of too many things – sow all sorts of seeds, and get no great harvest from any one of them. I'm cursed with susceptibility in every direction, and effective faculty in none. I care for painting and music; I care for classic literature, and mediaeval literature, and modern literature: I flutter all ways, and fly in none.'

'But surely that is a happiness to have so many tastes – to enjoy so many beautiful things – when they are within your reach,' said Maggie, musingly. 'It always seemed to me a sort of clever stupidity only to have one sort of talent – almost like a carrier-pigeon.'

'It might be a happiness to have many tastes if I were like other men,' said Philip, bitterly. 'I might get some power and distinction by mere mediocrity, as they do; at least I should get those middling satisfactions which make men contented to do without great ones. I might think society at St Ogg's agreeable then. But nothing could make life worth the purchase-money of pain to me, but some faculty that would lift me above the dead level of provincial existence. Yes – there is one thing: a passion answers as well as a faculty.'

Maggie did not hear the last words: she was struggling against the consciousness that Philip's words had set her own discontent vibrating again as it used to do.

'I understand what you mean,' she said, 'though I know so much less than you do. I used to think I could never bear life if it kept on being the same every day, and I must always be doing things of no consequence, and never know anything greater. But, dear Philip, I think we are only like children, that someone who is wiser is taking care of. Is it not right to resign ourselves entirely, whatever may be denied us? I have found great peace in that for the last two or three years – even joy in subduing my own will.'

'Yes, Maggie,' said Philip, vehemently; 'and you are shutting yourself up in a narrow self-delusive fanaticism, which is only a way of escaping pain by starving into dulness all the highest powers of your nature. Joy and peace are not resignation: resignation is the willing endurance of a pain that is not allayed – that you don't expect to be allayed. Stupefaction is not resignation: and it is stupefaction to remain in ignorance – to shut up all the avenues by which the life of your fellow-men might become known to you. I am not resigned: I am not sure that life is long enough to learn that lesson. *You* are not resigned: you are only trying to stupefy yourself.'

Maggie's lips trembled; she felt there was some truth in what Philip said, and yet there was a deeper consciousness that, for any immediate application it had to her conduct, it was no better than falsity. Her double impression corresponded to the double impulse of the speaker. Philip seriously believed what he said, but he said it with vehemence because it made an argument against the resolution that opposed his wishes. But Maggie's face, made more childlike by the gathering tears, touched him with a tenderer, less egoistic feeling. He took her hand and said gently, 'Don't let us think of such things in this short half-hour, Maggie. Let us only care about being together . . . We shall be friends in spite of separation . . . We shall always think of each other. I shall be glad to live as long as you are alive, because I shall think there may always come a time when I can – when you will let me help you in some way.'

'What a dear, good brother you would have been, Philip,' said Maggie, smiling through the haze of tears. 'I think you would have made as much fuss about me, and been as pleased for me to love you, as would have satisfied even me. You would have loved me well enough to bear with me, and forgive me everything. That was what I always longed that Tom should do. I was never satisfied with a *little* of anything. That is why it is better for me to do without earthly happiness altogether . . . I never felt that I had enough music – I wanted more instruments playing together – I wanted voices to be fuller and deeper. Do you ever sing now, Philip?' she added abruptly, as if she had forgotten what went before.

'Yes,' he said, 'every day, almost. But my voice is only middling – like everything else in me.'

'Oh, sing me something – just one song. I *may* listen to that before I go – something you used to sing at Lorton on a Saturday afternoon, when we had the drawing-room all to ourselves, and I put my apron over my head to listen.'

'I know,' said Philip, and Maggie buried her face in her hands, while he sang *sotto voce*, 'Love in her eyes sits playing;' and then said, 'That's it, isn't it?'

'Oh, no, I won't stay,' said Maggie, starting up. 'It will only haunt me. Let us walk, Philip. I must go home.'

She moved away, so that he was obliged to rise and follow her.

'Maggie,' he said, in a tone of remonstrance, 'don't persist in this wilful, senseless privation. It makes me wretched to see you benumbing and cramping your nature in this way. You were so full of life when you were a child: I thought you would be a brilliant woman – all wit and bright imagination. And it flashes out in your face still, until you draw that veil of dull quiescence over it.'

'Why do you speak so bitterly to me, Philip?' said Maggie.

'Because I foresee it will not end well: you can never carry on this self-torture.'

'I shall have strength given me,' said Maggie, tremulously.

'No, you will not, Maggie: no one has strength given to do what is unnatural. It is mere cowardice to seek safety in negations. No character becomes strong in that way. You will be thrown into the world someday, and then every rational satisfaction of your nature that you deny now, will assault you like a savage appetite.'

Maggie started and paused, looking at Philip with alarm in her face.

'Philip, how dare you shake me in this way? You are a tempter.'

'No, I am not; but love gives insight, Maggie, and insight often gives foreboding. *Listen* to me – *let* me supply you with books; do let me see you sometimes – be your brother and teacher, as you said at Lorton. It is less wrong that you should see me than that you should be committing this long suicide.'

Maggie felt unable to speak. She shook her head and walked on in silence, till they came to the end of the Scotch firs, and she put out her hand in sign of parting.

'Do you banish me from this place for ever, then, Maggie? Surely I may come and walk in it sometimes? If I meet you by chance, there is no concealment in that?'

It is the moment when our resolution seems about to become irrevocable – when the fatal iron gates are about to close upon us – that tests our strength. Then, after hours of clear reasoning and firm conviction, we snatch at any sophistry that will nullify our long struggles, and bring us the defeat that we love better than victory.

Maggie felt her heart leap at this subterfuge of Philip's, and there passed over her face that almost imperceptible shock which accompanies any relief. He saw it, and they parted in silence.

Philip's sense of the situation was too complete for him not to be visited with glancing fears lest he had been intervening too presumptuously in the action of Maggie's conscience – perhaps for a selfish end. But no! – he persuaded himself his end was not selfish. He had little hope that Maggie would ever return the strong feeling he had for her; and it must be better for Maggie's future life, when these petty family obstacles to her freedom had disappeared, that the present should not be entirely sacrificed, and that she should have some opportunity of culture – some interchange with a mind above the vulgar level of those she was now condemned to live with. If we only look far enough off for the consequences of our actions, we can always find some point in the combination of results by which those actions can be justified: by adopting the point of view of a Providence who arranges results, or of a philosopher who traces them, we shall find it possible to obtain perfect complacency in choosing to do what is most agreeable to us in the present moment. And it was in this way that Philip justified his subtle efforts to overcome Maggie's true prompting against a concealment that would introduce doubleness into her own mind, and might cause new misery to those who had the primary natural claim on her. But there was a surplus of passion in him that made him half independent of justifying motives. His longing to see Maggie, and make an element in her life, had in it some of that savage impulse to snatch an offered joy, which springs from a life in which the mental and bodily constitution have made pain predominate. He had not his full share in the common good of men: he could not even pass muster with the insignificant, but must be singled out for pity, and excepted from what was a matter of course with others. Even to Maggie he was an exception: it was clear that the thought of his being her lover had never entered her mind.

Do not think too hardly of Philip. Ugly and deformed people have great need of unusual virtues, because they are likely to be extremely uncomfortable without them: but the theory that unusual virtues spring by a direct consequence out of personal disadvantages, as animals get thicker wool in severe climates, is perhaps a little over-strained. The temptations of beauty are much dwelt upon, but I fancy they only bear the same relation to those of ugliness, as the temptation to excess at a feast, where the delights are varied for eye and ear as well as palate, bears to the temptations that assail the desperation of hunger. Does not the Hunger Tower stand as the type of the utmost trial to what is human in us?

Philip had never been soothed by that mother's love which flows out to us in the greater abundance because our need is greater, which clings to us the more tenderly because we are the less likely to be winners in the game of life; and the sense of his father's affection and indulgence towards him was marred by the keener perception of his father's faults. Kept aloof from all practical life as Philip had been, and by nature half feminine in sensitiveness, he had some of the woman's intolerant repulsion towards worldliness and the deliberate pursuit of sensual enjoyment; and this one strong natural tie in his life – his relation as a son – was like an aching limb to him. Perhaps there is inevitably something morbid in a human being who is in any way unfavourably excepted from ordinary conditions, until the good force has had time to triumph; and it has rarely had time for that at two-and-twenty. That force was present in Philip in much strength, but the sun himself looks feeble through the morning mists.

CHAPTER 4

Another Love Scene

Early in the following April, nearly a year after that dubious parting you have just witnessed, you may, if you like, again see Maggie entering the Red Deeps through the group of Scotch firs. But it is early afternoon and not evening, and the edge of sharpness in the spring air makes her draw her large shawl close about her and trip along rather quickly; though she looks round, as usual, that she may take in the sight of her beloved trees. There is a more eager, enquiring look in her eyes than there was last June, and a smile is hovering about her lips, as if some playful speech were awaiting the right hearer. The hearer was not long in appearing.

'Take back your *Corinne*,' said Maggie, drawing a book from under her shawl. 'You were right in telling me she would do me no good; but you were wrong in thinking I should wish to be like her.'

'Wouldn't you really like to be a tenth Muse, then, Maggie?' said Philip, looking up in her face as we look at a first parting in the clouds that promises us a bright heaven once more.

'Not at all,' said Maggie, laughing. 'The Muses were uncomfortable goddesses, I think – obliged always to carry rolls and musical instruments about with them. If I carried a harp in this climate, you know, I must have a green baize cover for it – and I should be sure to leave it behind me by mistake.'

'You agree with me in not liking *Corinne*, then?'

'I didn't finish the book,' said Maggie. 'As soon as I came to the blond-haired young lady reading in the park, I shut it up, and determined to read no further. I foresaw that that light-complexioned girl would win away all the love from Corinne and make her miserable. I'm determined to read no more books where the blond-haired women carry away all the happiness. I should begin to have a prejudice against them. If you could give me some story, now, where the dark woman triumphs, it would restore the balance. I want to avenge Rebecca and Flora MacIvor, and Minna and all the rest of the dark unhappy ones. Since you are my tutor, you ought to preserve my mind from prejudices – you are always arguing against prejudices.'

'Well, perhaps you will avenge the dark women in your own person, and carry away all the love from your cousin Lucy. She is sure to have some handsome young man of St Ogg's at her feet now: and you have only to shine upon him – your fair little cousin will be quite quenched in your beams.'

'Philip, that is not pretty of you, to apply my nonsense to anything real,' said Maggie, looking hurt. 'As if I, with my old gowns and want of all accomplishments, could be a rival of dear little Lucy, who knows and does all sorts of charming things, and is ten times prettier than I am – even if I were odious and base enough to wish to be her rival. Besides, I never go to aunt Deane's when anyone is there: it is only because dear Lucy is good, and loves me, that she comes to see me, and will have me go to see her sometimes.'

'Maggie,' said Philip, with surprise, 'it is not like you to take playfulness literally. You must have been in St Ogg's this morning, and brought away a slight infection of dulness.'

'Well,' said Maggie, smiling, 'if you meant that for a joke, it was a poor one; but I thought it was a very good reproof. I thought you wanted to remind me that I am vain, and wish everyone to admire me most. But it isn't for that, that I'm jealous for the dark women – not because I'm dark myself. It's because I always care the most about the unhappy people: if the blond girl were forsaken, I should like *her* best. I always take the side of the rejected lover in the stories.'

'Then you would never have the heart to reject one yourself – should you, Maggie?' said Philip, flushing a little.

'I don't know,' said Maggie, hesitatingly. Then with a bright smile – 'I think perhaps I could if he were very conceited; and yet if he got extremely humiliated afterwards, I should relent.'

'I've often wondered, Maggie,' Philip said, with some effort, 'whether you wouldn't really be more likely to love a man that other women were not likely to love.'

'That would depend on what they didn't like him for,' said Maggie, laughing. 'He might be very disagreeable. He, might look at me through an eye-glass stuck in his eye, making a hideous face, as young Torry does. I should think other women are not fond of that; but I never felt any pity for young Torry. I've never any pity for conceited people, because I think they carry their comfort about with them.'

'But suppose, Maggie – suppose it was a man who was not conceited – who felt he had nothing to be conceited about – who had been marked from child-hood for a peculiar kind of suffering – and to whom you were the day-star of his life – who loved you, worshipped you, so entirely that he felt it happiness enough for him if you would let him see you at rare, moments . . . '

Philip paused with a pang of dread lest his confession should cut short this very happiness – a pang of the same dread that had kept his love mute through long months. A rush of self-consciousness told him that he was besotted to have said all this. Maggie's manner this afternoon had been as unconstrained and indifferent as ever.

But she was not looking indifferent now. Struck with the unusual emotion in Philip's tone, she had turned quickly to look at him, and as he went on speaking, a great change came over her face – a flush and slight spasm of the features such as we see in people who hear some news that will require them to readjust their conceptions of the past. She was quite silent, and, walking on towards the trunk of a fallen tree, she sat down, as if she had no strength to spare for her muscles. She was trembling.

'Maggie,' said Philip, getting more and more alarmed in every fresh moment of silence. 'I was a fool to say it – forget that I've said it. I shall be contented if things can be as they were.'

The distress with which he spoke urged Maggie to say something. 'I am so surprised, Philip – I had not thought of it.' And the effort to say this brought the tears down too.

'Has it made you hate me, Maggie?' said Philip, impetuously. 'Do you think I'm a presumptuous fool?'

'Oh, Philip!' said Maggie, 'how can you think I have such feelings? – as if I were not grateful for *any* love. But . . . but I had never thought of your being my lover. It seemed so far off – like a dream – only like one of the stories one imagines – that I should ever have a lover.'

'Then can you bear to think of me as your lover, Maggie?' said Philip, seating himself by her, and taking her hand, in the elation of a sudden hope. 'Do you love me?'

Maggie turned rather pale: this direct question seemed .not easy to answer. But her eyes met Philip's, which were in this moment liquid and beautiful with beseeching love. She spoke with hesitation, yet with sweet, simple, girlish tenderness.

'I think I could hardly love anyone better: there is nothing but what I love you for.' She paused a little while, and then added, 'But it will be better for us not to say any more about it – won't it, dear Philip? You know we couldn't even be friends, if our friendship were discovered. I have never felt that I was right in giving way about seeing you – though it has been so precious to me in some ways; and now the fear comes upon me strongly again, that it will lead to evil.'

'But no evil has come, Maggie; and if you had been guided by that fear before, you would only have lived through another dreary benumbing year, instead of reviving into your real self.'

Maggie shook her head. 'It has been very sweet, I know – all the talking together, and the books, and the feeling that I had the walk to look forward to, when I could tell you the thoughts that had come into my head while I was away from you. But it has made me restless: it has made me think a great deal about the world; and I have impatient thoughts again – I get weary of my home – and then it cuts me to the heart afterwards, that I should ever have felt weary of my father and mother. I think what you call being benumbed was better – better for me – for then my selfish desires were benumbed.'

Philip had risen again, and was walking backwards and forwards impatiently.

'No, Maggie, you have wrong ideas of self-conquest, as I've often told you. What you call self-conquest – blinding and deafening yourself to all but one train of impression – is only the culture of monomania in a nature like yours.'

He had spoken with some irritation, but now he sat down by her again, and took her hand.

'Don't think of the past now, Maggie; think only of our love. If you can really cling to me with all your heart, every obstacle will be overcome in time: we need only wait. I can live on hope. Look at me, Maggie; tell me again, it is possible for you to love me. Don't look away from me to that cloven tree; it is a bad omen.'

She turned her large dark glance upon him with a sad smile.

'Come, Maggie, say one kind word, or else you were better to me at Lorton. You asked me if I should like you to kiss me – don't you remember? – and you promised to kiss me when you met me again. You never kept the promise.'

The recollection of that childish time came as a sweet relief to Maggie. It made the present moment less strange to her. She kissed him almost as simply and quietly as she had done when she was twelve years old. Philip's eyes flashed with delight, but his next words were words of discontent.

'You don't seem happy enough, Maggie: you are forcing yourself to say you love me, out of pity.'

'No, Philip,' said Maggie, shaking her head, in her old childish way; 'I'm telling you the truth. It is all new and strange to me; but I don't think I could love anyone better than I love you. I should like always to live with you – to make you happy. I have always been happy when I have been with you. There is only one thing I will not do for your sake; I will never do anything to wound my father. You must never ask that from me.'

'No, Maggie: I will ask nothing – I will bear everything – I'll wait another year only for a kiss, if you will only give me the first place in your heart.'

'No,' said Maggie, smiling, 'I won't make you wait so long as that.' But then, looking serious again, she added, as she rose from her seat, 'But what would your own father say, Philip? Oh, it is quite impossible we can ever be more than friends – brother and sister in secret, as we have been. Let us give up thinking of everything else.'

'No, Maggie, I can't give you up – unless you are deceiving me – unless you really only care for me as if I were your brother. Tell me the truth.'

'Indeed, I do, Philip. What happiness have I ever had so great as being with you? – since I was a little girl – the days Tom was good to me. And your mind is a sort of world to me: you can tell me all I want to know. I think I should never be tired of being with you.'

They were walking hand in hand, looking at each other; Maggie, indeed, was hurrying along, for she felt it time to be gone. But the sense that their parting was near, made her more anxious lest she should have unintentionally left some painful impression on Philip's mind. It was one of those dangerous moments when speech is at once sincere and deceptive – when feeling, rising high above its average depth, leaves flood-marks which are never reached again.

They stopped to part among the Scotch firs.

'Then my life will be filled with hope, Maggie – and I shall be happier than other men, in spite of all? We *do* belong to each other – for always – whether we are apart or together?'

'Yes, Philip: I should like never to part: I should like to make your life very happy.'

'I am waiting for something else – I wonder whether it will come.'

Maggie smiled, with glistening tears, and then stooped her tall head to kiss the pale face that was full of pleading, timid love – like a woman's.

She had a moment of real happiness then – a moment of belief that, if there were sacrifices in this love, it was all the richer and more satisfying.

She turned away and hurried home, feeling that in the hour since she had trodden this road before, a new era had begun for her. The tissue of vague dreams must now get narrower and narrower, and all the threads of thought and emotion be gradually absorbed in the woof of her actual daily life.

CHAPTER 5

The Cloven Tree

Secrets are rarely betrayed or discovered according to any programme our fear has sketched out. Fear is almost always haunted by terrible dramatic scenes, which recur in spite of the best-argued probabilities against them; and during a year that Maggie had had the burthen of concealment on her mind, the possibility of discovery had continually presented itself under the form of a sudden meeting with her father or Tom when she was walking with Philip in the Red Deeps. She was aware that this was not one of the most likely events; but it was the scene that most completely symbolised her inward dread. Those slight indirect suggestions which are dependent on apparently trivial coincidences and incalculable states of mind, are the favourite machinery of Fact, but are not the stuff in which imagination is apt to work.

Certainly one of the persons about whom Maggie's fears were farthest from troubling themselves was her aunt Pullet, on whom, seeing that she did not live in St Ogg's, and was neither sharp-eyed nor sharp-tempered, it would surely have been quite whimsical of them to fix rather than on aunt Glegg. And yet the channel of fatality – the pathway of the lightning – was no other than aunt Pullet. She did not live at St Ogg's, but the road from Garum Firs lay by the Red Deeps, at the end opposite that by which Maggie entered.

The day after Maggie's last meeting with Philip, being a Sunday on which Mr Pullet was bound to appear in funeral hatband and scarf at St Ogg's church, Mrs Pullet made this the occasion of dining with sister Glegg, and taking tea with poor sister Tulliver. Sunday was the one day in the week on which Tom was at home in the afternoon; and today the brighter spirits he had been in of late had flowed over in unusually cheerful open chat with his father, and in the invitation, 'Come, Magsie, you come too!' when he strolled out with his mother in the garden to see the advancing cherry-blossoms. He had been better pleased with Maggie since she had been less odd and ascetic; he was even getting rather proud of her: several persons had remarked in his hearing that his sister was a very fine girl. Today there was a peculiar brightness in her face, due in reality to an undercurrent of excitement, which had as much doubt and pain as pleasure in it; but it might pass for a sign of happiness.

'You look very well, my dear,' said aunt Pullet, shaking her head sadly, as they sat round the tea-table. 'I niver thought your girl 'ud be so good-looking, Bessy. But you must wear pink, my dear: that blue thing as your aunt Glegg gave you turns you into a crowflower. Jane never *was* tasty. Why don't you wear that gown o' mine?'

'It is so pretty and so smart, aunt. I think it's too showy for me – at least for my other clothes, that I must wear with it.'

'To be sure, it 'ud be unbecoming if it wasn't well known you've got them belonging to you as can afford to give you such things when they've done with 'em themselves. It stands to reason I must give my own niece clothes now and then – such things as *I* buy every year, and never wear anything out. And as for Lucy, there's no giving to her, for she's got everything o' the choicest; sister Deane may well hold her head up, though she looks dreadful yallow, poor thing – I doubt this liver complaint 'ull carry her off. That's what this new vicar, this Dr Kenn, said in the funeral sermon today.'

'Ah, he's a wonderful preacher, by all account – isn't he, Sophy?' said Mrs Tulliver.

'Why, Lucy had got a collar on this blessed day,' continued Mrs Pullet, with her eyes fixed in a ruminating manner, 'as I don't say I haven't got as good, but I must look out my best to match it.'

'Miss Lucy's called the bell o' St Ogg's, they say: that's a cur'ous word,' observed Mr Pullet, on whom the mysteries of etymology sometimes fell with an oppressive weight.

'Pooh!' said Mr Tulliver, jealous for Maggie, 'she's a small thing, not much of a figure. But fine feathers make fine birds. I see nothing to admire so much in those diminitive women; they look silly by the side o' the men – out o' proportion. When I chose my wife, I chose her the right size – neither too little nor too big.'

The poor wife, with her withered beauty, smiled complacently.

'But the men aren't *all* big,' said uncle Pullet, not without some self-reference; 'a young fellow may be good-looking and yet not be a six-foot, like Master Tom here.'

'Ah, it's poor talking about littleness and bigness – anybody may think it's a mercy they're straight,' said aunt Pullet. 'There's that mismade son o' Lawyer Wakem's – I saw him at church today. Dear, dear! to think o' the property he's like to have; and they say he's very queer and lonely – doesn't like much company. I shouldn't wonder if he goes out of his mind; for we never come along the road but he's a-scrambling out o' the trees and brambles at the Red Deeps.'

This wide statement, by which Mrs Pullet represented the fact that she had twice seen Philip at the spot indicated, produced an effect on Maggie which was all the stronger because Tom sat opposite her, and she was intensely anxious to look indifferent. At Philip's name she had blushed, and the blush deepened every instant from consciousness, until the mention of the Red Deeps made her feel as if the whole secret were betrayed, and she dared not even hold her teaspoon lest she should show how she trembled. She sat with her hands clasped under the table, not daring to look round. Happily, her father was seated on the same side with herself, beyond her uncle Pullet, and could not see her face without stooping forward. Her mother's voice brought the first relief – turning the conversation; for Mrs Tulliver was always alarmed when the name of Wakem was mentioned in her husband's presence. Gradually Maggie recovered composure enough to look up; her eyes met Tom's, but he turned away his head immediately; and she went to bed that night wondering if he had gathered any suspicion from her confusion. Perhaps not: perhaps he would think it was only her alarm at her aunt's mention of Wakem before her father: that was the interpretation her mother had put on it. To her father, Wakem was like a disfiguring disease, of which he was obliged to endure the consciousness, but was exasperated to have the existence recognised by others; and no amount of sensitiveness in her about her father could be surprising, Maggie thought.

But Tom was too keen-sighted to rest satisfied with such an interpretation: he had seen clearly enough that there was something distinct from anxiety about her father in Maggie's excessive confusion. In trying to recall all the details that could give shape to his suspicions, he remembered only lately hearing his mother scold Maggie for walking in the Red Deeps when the ground was wet, and bringing home shoes clogged with red soil: still Tom, retaining all his old repulsion for Philip's deformity, shrank from attributing to his sister the probability of feeling more than a friendly interest in such an unfortunate exception to the common run of men. Tom's was a nature which had a sort of superstitious repugnance to everything exceptional. A love for a deformed man would be odious in any woman – in a sister intolerable. But if she had been carrying on any kind of intercourse whatever with Philip, a stop must be put to it at once: she was disobeying her father's strongest feelings and her brother's express commands, besides compromising herself by secret meetings. He left home the next morning in that watchful state of mind which turns the most ordinary course of things into pregnant coincidences.

That afternoon, about half-past three o'clock, Tom was standing on the wharf, talking with Bob Jakin about the probability of the good ship Adelaide coming in, in a day or two, with results highly important to both of them.

'Eh,' said Bob, parenthetically, as he looked over the fields on the other side of the river, 'there goes that crooked young Wakem. I know him or his shadder as far off as I can see 'em; I'm allays lighting on him o' that side the river.'

A sudden thought seemed to have darted through Tom's mind. 'I must go, Bob,' he said. 'I've something to attend to,' hurrying off to the warehouse, where he left notice for someone to take his place – he was called away home on peremptory business.

The swiftest pace and the shortest road took him to the gate, and he was pausing to open it deliberately, that he might walk into the house with an appearance of perfect composure, when Maggie came out at the front door in bonnet and shawl. His conjecture was fulfilled, and he waited for her at the gate. She started violently when she saw him.

'Tom, how is it you are come home? Is there anything the matter?' Maggie spoke in a low tremulous voice.

'I'm come to walk with you to the Red Deeps and meet Philip Wakem,' said Tom, the central fold in his brow, which had become habitual with him, deepening as he spoke.

Maggie stood helpless – pale and cold. By some means, then, Tom knew everything. At last she said, 'I'm not going,' and turned round.

'Yes, you are; but I want to speak to you first. Where is my father?'

'Out on horseback.'

'And my mother?'

'In the yard, I think, with the poultry.'

'I can go in, then, without her seeing me?'.

They walked in together, and Tom, entering the parlour, said to Maggie, 'Come in here.'

She obeyed, and he closed the door behind her.

'Now, Maggie, tell me this instant everything that has passed between you and Philip Wakem.'

'Does my father know anything?' said Maggie, still trembling.

'No,' said Tom, indignantly. 'But he *shall* know, if you attempt to use deceit towards me any further.'

'I don't wish to use deceit,' said Maggie, flushing into resentment at hearing this word applied to her conduct.

'Tell me the whole truth then.'

'Perhaps you know it.'

'Never mind whether I know it or not. Tell me exactly what has happened, or my Father shall know everything.'

'I tell it for my father's sake, then.'

'Yes, it becomes you to profess affection for your father, when you have despised his strongest feelings.'

'You never do wrong, Tom,' said Maggie, tauntingly.

'Not if I know it,' answered Tom, with proud sincerity. 'But I have nothing to say to you, beyond this: tell me what has passed between you and Philip Wakem. When did you first meet him in the Red Deeps?'

'A year ago,' said Maggie, quietly. Tom's severity gave her a certain fund of defiance, and kept her sense of error in abeyance. 'You need ask me no more questions. We have been friendly a year. We have met and walked together often. He has lent me books.'

'Is that all?' said Tom, looking straight at her with his frown.

Maggie paused a moment; then, determined to make an end of Tom's right to accuse her of deceit, she said, haughtily, 'No, not quite all. On Saturday he told me that he loved me. I didn't think of it before then – I had only thought of him as an old friend.'

'And you *encouraged* him?' said Tom, with an expression of disgust.

'I told him that I loved him too.'

Tom was silent a few moments, looking on the ground and frowning, with his hands in his pockets. At last, he looked up, and said, coldly, 'Now, then, Maggie, there are but two courses for you to take; either you vow solemnly to me, with your hand on my father's Bible, that you will never have another meeting or speak another word in private with Philip Wakem, or you refuse, and I tell my father everything; and this month, when by my exertions he might be made happy once more, you will cause him the blow of knowing that you are a disobedient, deceitful daughter, who throws away her own respectability by clandestine meetings with the son of a man that has helped to ruin her father. Choose!' Tom ended with cold decision, going up to the large Bible, drawing it forward, and opening it at the fly-leaf, where the writing was.

It was a crushing alternative to Maggie.

'Tom,' she said, urged out of pride into pleading, 'don't ask me that. I will promise you to give up all intercourse with Philip, if you will let me see him once, or even only write to him and explain everything – to give it up as long as it would ever cause any pain to my father . . . I feel something for Philip too. *He* is not happy.'

'I don't wish to hear anything of your feelings; I have said exactly what I mean: choose – and quickly, lest my mother should come in.'

'If I give you my word, that will be as strong a bond to me as if I laid my hand on the Bible. I don't require that to bind me.'

'Do what *I* require,' said Tom. 'I can't trust you, Maggie. There is no consistency in you. Put your hand on this Bible, and say, "I renounce all private speech and intercourse with Philip Wakem from this time forth." Else you will bring shame on us all, and grief on my father; and what is the use of my exerting myself and giving up everything else for the sake of paying my father's debts, if you are to bring madness and vexation on him, just when he might be easy and hold up his head once more?'

'Oh, Tom – *will* the debts be paid soon?' said Maggie, clasping her hands, with a sudden flash of joy across her wretchedness.

'If things turn out as I expect,' said Tom. 'But,' he added, his voice trembling with indignation, 'while I have been contriving and working that my father may have some peace of mind before he dies – working for the respectability of our family – you have done all you can to destroy both.'

Maggie felt a deep movement of compunction: for the moment, her mind ceased to contend against what she felt to be cruel and unreasonable, and in her self-blame she justified her brother.

'Tom,' she said, in a low voice, 'it was wrong of me – but I was so lonely – and I was sorry for Philip. And I think enmity and hatred are wicked.'

'Nonsense!' said Tom. 'Your duty was clear enough. Say no more; but promise, in the words I told you.'

'I *must* speak to Philip once more.'

'You will go with me now and speak to him.'

'I give you my word not to meet him or write to him again without your knowledge. That is the only thing I will say. I will put my hand on the Bible if you like.'

'Say it, then.'

Maggie laid her hand on the page of manuscript and repeated the promise. Tom closed the book, and said, 'Now, let us go.'

Not a word was spoken as they walked along. Maggie was suffering in anticipation of what Philip was about to suffer, and dreading the galling words that would fall on him from Tom's lips; but she felt it was in vain to attempt anything but submission. Tom had his terrible clutch on her conscience and her deepest dread; she writhed under the demonstrable truth of the character he had given to her conduct, and yet her whole soul rebelled against it as unfair from its incompleteness. He, meanwhile, felt the impetus of his indignation diverted towards Philip. He did not know how much of an old boyish repulsion and of mere personal pride and animosity was concerned in the bitter severity of the words by which he meant to do the duty of a son and a brother. Tom was not given to enquire subtly into his own motives, any more than into other matters of an intangible kind; he was quite sure that his own motives as well as actions were good, else he would have had nothing to do with them.

Maggie's only hope was that something might, for the first time, have prevented Philip from coming. Then there would be delay – then she might get Tom's permission to write to him. Her heart beat with double violence when they got under the Scotch firs. It was the last moment of suspense, she thought; Philip always met her soon after she got beyond them. But they passed across the more open green space, and entered the narrow bushy path by the mound. Another turning, and they came so close upon him that both Tom and Philip stopped suddenly within a yard of each other. There was a moment's silence, in which Philip darted a look of enquiry at Maggie's face. He saw an answer there, in the pale parted lips, and the terrified tension of the large eyes. Her imagination, always rushing extravagantly beyond an immediate impression, saw her tall strong brother grasping the feeble Philip bodily, crushing him and trampling on him.

'Do you call this acting the part of a man and a gentleman, sir?' Tom said, in a voice of harsh scorn, as soon as Philip's eyes were turned on him again.

'What do you mean?' answered Philip, haughtily.

'Mean? Stand farther from me, lest I should lay hands on you, and I'll tell you what I mean. I mean, taking advantage of a young girl's foolishness and ignorance to get her to have secret meetings with you. I mean, daring to trifle with the respectability of a family that has a good and honest name to support.'

'I deny that,' interrupted Philip, impetuously. 'I could never trifle with any-thing that affected your sister's happiness. She is dearer to me than she is to you; I honour her more than you can ever honour her; I would give up my life to her.'

'Don't talk high-flown nonsense to me, sir! Do you mean to pretend that you didn't know it would be injurious to her to meet you here week after week? Do you pretend you had any right to make professions of love to her, even if you had been a fit husband for her, when neither her father nor your father would ever consent to a marriage between you? And *you* – *you* to try and worm yourself into the affections of a handsome girl who is not eighteen, and has been shut out from the world by her father's misfortunes! That's your crooked notion of honour, is it? I call it base treachery – I call it taking advantage of circumstances to win what's too good for you – what you'd never get by fair means.'

'It is manly of you to talk in this way to *me*,' said Philip, bitterly, his whole frame shaken by violent emotions. 'Giants have an immemorial right to stupidity and insolent abuse. You are incapable even of understanding what I feel for your sister. I feel so much for her that I could even desire to be at friendship with *you*.'

'I should be very sorry to understand your feelings,' said Tom, with scorching contempt. 'What I wish is that you should understand *me* – that I shall take care of *my* sister, and that if you dare to make the least attempt to come near her, or to write to her, or to keep the slightest hold on her mind, your puny, miserable body, that ought to have put some modesty into your mind, shall not protect you. I'll thrash you – I'll hold you up to public scorn. Who wouldn't laugh at the idea of *your* turning lover to a fine girl?'

'Tom, I will not bear it – I will listen no longer,' Maggie burst out, in a convulsed voice.

'Stay, Maggie!' said Philip, making a strong effort to speak. Then, looking at Tom, 'You have dragged your sister here, I suppose, that she may stand by while you threaten and insult me. These naturally seemed to you the right means to influence me. But you are mistaken. Let your sister speak. If she says she is bound to give me up, I shall abide by her wishes to the slightest word.'

'It was for my father's sake, Philip,' said Maggie, imploringly. 'Tom threatens to tell my father – and he couldn't bear it: I have promised, I have vowed solemnly, that we will not have any intercourse without my brother's knowledge.'

'It is enough, Maggie. *I* shall not change; but I wish you to hold yourself entirely free. But trust me – remember that I can never seek for anything but good to what belongs to you.'

'Yes,' said Tom, exasperated by this attitude of Philip's, 'you can talk of seeking good for her and what belongs to her now: did you seek her good before?'

'I did – at some risk, perhaps. But I wished her to have a friend for life – who would cherish her, who would do her more justice than a coarse and narrow-minded brother, that she has always lavished her affections on.'

'Yes, my way of befriending her is different from yours; and I'll tell you what is my way. I'll save her from disobeying and disgracing her father: I'll save her from throwing herself away on you – from making herself a laughing-stock – from being flouted by a man like *your* father, because she's not good enough for his son. You know well enough what sort of justice and cherishing you were preparing for her. I'm not to be imposed upon by fine words: I can see what actions mean. Come away, Maggie.'

He seized Maggie's right wrist as he spoke, and she put out her left hand. Philip clasped it an instant, with one eager look, and then turned away.

Tom and Maggie walked on in silence for some yards. He was still holding her wrist tightly, as if he were compelling a culprit from the scene of action. At last Maggie, with a violent snatch, drew her hand away, and her pent-up, long-gathered irritation burst into utterance.

'Don't suppose that I think you are right, Tom, or that I bow to your will. I despise the feelings you have shown in speaking to Philip: I detest your insulting unmanly allusions to his deformity. You have been reproaching other people all your life – you have been always sure you yourself are right: it is because you have not a mind large enough to see that there is anything better than your own conduct and your own petty aims.'

'Certainly,' said Tom, coolly. 'I don't see that your conduct is better, or your aims either. If your conduct, and Philip Wakem's conduct, has been right, why are you ashamed of its being known? Answer me that. I know what I have aimed at in my conduct, and I've succeeded: pray, what good has your conduct brought to you or anyone else?'

'I don't want to defend myself,' said Maggie, still with vehemence: 'I know I've been wrong – often, continually. But yet, sometimes when I have done wrong, it has been because I have feelings that you would be the better for, if you had them. If *you* were in fault ever – if you had done anything very wrong, I should be sorry for the pain it brought you; I should not want punishment to be heaped on you. But you have always enjoyed punishing me – you have always been hard and cruel to me: even when I was a little girl, and always loved you better than anyone else in the world, you would let me go crying to bed without forgiving me. You have no pity: you have no sense of your own imperfection and your own sins. It is a sin to be hard; it is not fitting for a mortal – for a Christian. You are nothing but a Pharisee. You thank God for nothing but your own virtues – you think they are great enough to win you everything else. You have not even a vision of feelings by the side of which your shining virtues are mere darkness!'

'Well,' said Tom, with cold scorn, 'if your feelings are so much better than mine, let me see you show them in some other way than by conduct that's likely to disgrace us all – than by ridiculous flights first into one extreme and then into another. Pray, how have you shown your love, that you talk of, either to me or my father? By disobeying and deceiving us. I have a different way of showing my affection.'

'Because you are a man, Tom, and have power, and can do something in the world.'

'Then, if you can do nothing, submit to those that can.'

'So I *will* submit to what I acknowledge and feel to be right. I will submit even to what is unreasonable from my father, but I will not submit to it from you. You boast of your virtues as if they purchased you a right to be cruel and unmanly as you've been today. Don't suppose I would give up Philip Wakem in obedience to you. The deformity you insult would make me cling to him and care for him the more.'

'Very well – that is your view of things,' said Tom, more coldly than ever; 'you need say no more to show me what a wide distance there is between us. Let us remember that in future, and be silent.'

Tom went back to St Ogg's, to fulfil an appointment with his uncle Deane, and receive directions about a journey on which he was to set out the next morning.

Maggie went up to her own room to pour out all that indignant remonstrance, against which Tom's mind was close barred, in bitter tears. Then, when the first burst of unsatisfied anger was gone by, came the recollection of that quiet time before the pleasure which had ended in today's misery had perturbed the clearness and simplicity of her life. She used to think in that time that she had made great conquests, and won a lasting stand on serene heights above worldly temptations and conflict. And here she was down again in the thick of a hot strife with her own and others' passions. Life was not so short, then, and perfect rest was not so near as she had dreamed when she was two years younger. There was more struggle for her – perhaps more falling. If she had felt that she was entirely wrong, and that Tom had been entirely right, she could sooner have recovered more inward harmony; but now her penitence and submission were constantly obstructed by resentment that would present itself to her no otherwise than as a just indignation. Her heart bled for Philip: she went on recalling the insults that had been flung at him with so vivid a conception of what he had felt under them, that it was almost like a sharp bodily pain to her, making her beat the floor with her foot, and tighten her fingers on her palm.

And yet, how was it that she was now and then conscious of a certain dim background of relief in the forced separation from Philip? Surely it was only because the sense of a deliverance from concealment was welcome at any cost?

CHAPTER 6

The Hard-Won Triumph

Three weeks later, when Dorlcote Mill was at its prettiest moment in all the year – the great chestnuts in blossom, and the grass all deep and daisied – Tom Tulliver came home to it earlier than usual in the evening, and as he passed over the bridge, he looked with the old deep-rooted affection at the respectable red brick house, which always seemed cheerful and inviting outside, let the rooms be as bare and the hearts as sad as they might, inside. There is a very pleasant light in Tom's blue-grey eyes as he glances at the house-windows: that fold in his brow never disappears, but it is not unbecoming; it seems to imply a strength of will that may possibly be without harshness, when the eyes and mouth have their gentlest expression. His firm step becomes quicker, and the corners of his mouth rebel against the compression which is meant to forbid a smile.

The eyes in the parlour were not turned towards the bridge just then, and the group there was sitting in unexpectant silence – Mr Tulliver in his armchair, tired with a long ride, and ruminating with a worn look, fixed chiefly on Maggie, who was bending over her sewing while her mother was making the tea.

They all looked up with surprise when they heard the well-known foot.

'Why, what's up now, Tom?' said his father. 'You're a bit earlier than usual.'

'Oh, there was nothing more for me to do, so I came away. Well, mother!'

Tom went up to his mother and kissed her, a sign of unusual good-humour with him. Hardly a word or look had passed between him and Maggie in all the three weeks; but his usual incommunicativeness at home prevented this from being noticeable to their parents.

'Father,' said Tom, when they had finished tea, 'do you know exactly how much money there is in the tin box?'

'Only a hundred and ninety-three pound,' said Mr Tulliver, 'You've brought less o' late – but young fellows like to have their own way with their money.

Though I didn't do as I liked before *I* was of age.' He spoke with rather timid discontent.

'Are you quite sure that's the sum, father?' said Tom: 'I wish you would take the trouble to fetch the tin box down. I think you have perhaps made a mistake.'

'How should I make a mistake?' said his father, sharply. 'I've counted it often enough; but I can fetch it, if you won't believe me.'

It was always an incident Mr Tulliver liked, in his gloomy life, to fetch the tin box and count the money.

'Don't go out of the room, mother,' said Tom, as he saw her moving when his father was gone upstairs.

'And isn't Maggie to go?' said Mrs Tulliver; 'because somebody must take away the things.'

'Just as she likes,' said Tom, indifferently.

That was a cutting word to Maggie. Her heart had leaped with the sudden conviction that Tom was going to tell their father the debts could be paid – and Tom would have let her be absent when that news was told! But she carried away the tray, and came back immediately. The feeling of injury on her own behalf could not predominate at that moment.

Tom drew to the corner of the table near his father when the tin box was set down and opened, and the red evening light falling on them made conspicuous the worn, sour gloom of the dark-eyed father and the suppressed joy in the face of the fair-complexioned son. The mother and Maggie sat at the other end of the table, the one in blank patience, the other in palpitating expectation.

Mr Tulliver counted out the money, setting it in order on the table, and then said, glancing sharply at Tom, 'There now! you see I was right enough.'

He paused, looking at the money with bitter despondency.

'There's more nor three hundred wanting – it'll be a fine while before I can save that. Losing that forty-two pound wi' the corn was a sore job. This world's been too many for me. It's took four year to lay *this* by – it's much if I'm above ground for another four year . . . I must trusten to you to pay 'em,' he went on, with a trembling voice, 'if you keep i' the same mind now you're coming o' age . . . But you're like enough to bury me first.'

He looked up in Tom's face with a querulous desire for some assurance.

'No, father,' said Tom, speaking with energetic decision, though there was tremor discernible in his voice too, 'you will live to see the debts all paid. You shall pay them with your own hand.'

His tone implied something more than mere hopefulness or resolution. A slight electric shock seemed to pass through Mr Tulliver, and he kept his eyes fixed on Tom with a look of eager enquiry, while Maggie, unable to restrain herself, rushed to her father's side and knelt down by him. Tom was silent a little while before he went on.

'A good while ago, my uncle Glegg lent me a little money to trade with, and that has answered. I have three hundred and twenty pounds in the bank.'

His mother's arms were round his neck as soon as the last words were uttered, and she said, half-crying: 'O, my boy, I knew you'd make iverything right again, when you got a man.'

But his father was silent: the flood of emotion hemmed in all power of speech. Both Tom and Maggie were struck with fear lest the shock of joy might even be fatal. But the blessed relief of tears came. The broad chest heaved, the muscles of the face gave way, and the grey-haired man burst into loud sobs. The fit of weeping gradually subsided, and he sat quiet, recovering the regularity of his breathing. At last he looked up at his wife and said, in a gentle tone: 'Bessy, you must come and kiss me now – the lad has made you amends. You'll see a bit o' comfort again, belike.'

When she had kissed him, and he had held her hand a minute, his thoughts went back to the money.

'I wish you'd brought me the money to look at, Tom,' he said, fingering the sovereigns on the table; 'I should ha' felt surer.'

'You shall see it tomorrow, father,' said Tom. 'My uncle Deane has appointed the creditors to meet tomorrow at the Golden Lion, and he has ordered a dinner for them at two o'clock. My uncle Glegg and he will both be there. It was advertised in the *Messenger* on Saturday.'

'Then Wakem knows on't!' said Mr Tulliver, his eye kindling with triumphant fire. 'Ah!' he went on, with a long-drawn guttural enunciation, taking out his snuffbox, the only luxury he had left himself, and tapping it with something of his old air of defiance – 'I'll get from under *his* thumb now – though I *must* leave th' old mill. I thought I could ha' held out to die here – but I can't . . . We've got a glass o' nothing in the house, have we, Bessy?'

'Yes,' said Mrs Tulliver, drawing out her much-reduced bunch of keys, 'there's some brandy sister Deane brought me when I was ill.'

'Get it me, then, get it me. I feel a bit weak.'

'Tom, my lad,' he said, in a stronger voice, when he had taken some brandy-and-water, 'you shall make a speech to 'em. I'll tell 'em it's you as got the best part o' the money. They'll see I'm honest at last, and ha' got an honest son. Ah! Wakem 'ud be fine and glad to have a son like mine – a fine straight fellow – i'stead o' that poor crooked creatur! You'll prosper i' the world, my lad; you'll maybe see the day when Wakem and his son 'ull be a round or two below you. You'll like enough be ta'en into partnership, as your uncle Deane was before you – you're in the right way for't; and then there's nothing to hinder your getting rich . . . And if ever you're rich enough – mind this – try and get th' old mill again.'

Mr Tulliver threw himself back in his chair: his mind, which had so long been the home of nothing but bitter discontent and foreboding, suddenly filled, by the magic of joy, with visions of good fortune. But some subtle influence prevented him from foreseeing the good fortune as happening to himself.

'Shake hands wi' me, my lad,' he said, suddenly putting out his hand. 'It's a great thing when a man can be proud as he's got a good son. I've had *that* luck.'

Tom never lived to taste another moment so delicious as that; and Maggie couldn't help forgetting her own grievances. Tom *was* good; and in the sweet humility that springs in us all in moments of true admiration and gratitude, she felt that the faults he had to pardon in her had never been redeemed, as his faults were. She felt no jealousy this evening that, for the first time, she seemed to be thrown into the background in her father's mind.

There was much more talk before bedtime. Mr Tulliver naturally wanted to hear all the particulars of Tom's trading adventures, and he listened with growing excitement and delight. He was curious to know what had been said on every occasion – if possible, what had been thought; and Bob Jakin's part in the business threw him into peculiar outbursts of sympathy with the triumphant knowingness of that remarkable packman. Bob's juvenile history, so far as it had come under Mr Tulliver's knowledge, was recalled with that sense of astonishing promise it displayed, which is observable in all reminiscences of the childhood of great men.

It was well that there was this interest of narrative to keep under the vague but fierce sense of triumph over Wakem, which would otherwise have been the channel his joy would have rushed into with dangerous force. Even as it was, that feeling from time to time gave threats of its ultimate mastery, in sudden bursts of irrelevant exclamation.

It was long before Mr Tulliver got to sleep that night, and the sleep, when it came, was filled with vivid dreams. At half-past five o'clock in the morning, when Mrs Tulliver was already rising, he alarmed her by starting up with a sort of smothered shout, and looking round in a bewildered way at the walls of the bedroom.

'What's the matter, Mr Tulliver?' said his wife. He looked at her, still with a puzzled expression, and said at last, 'Ah! – I was dreaming . . . did I make a noise? . . . I thought I'd got hold of him.'

CHAPTER 7

A Day of Reckoning

Mr Tulliver was an essentially sober man – able to take his glass and not averse to it, but never exceeding the bounds of moderation. He had naturally an active Hotspur temperament, which did not crave liquid fire to set it a-glow; his impetuosity was usually equal to an exciting occasion without any such reinforcements; and his desire for the brandy-and-water implied that the too sudden joy had fallen with a dangerous shock on a frame depressed by four years of gloom and unaccustomed hard fare. But that first doubtful tottering moment passed, he seemed to gather strength with his gathering excitement; and the next day, when he was seated at table with his creditors, his eye kindling and his cheek flushed with the consciousness that he was about to make an honourable figure once more, he looked more like the proud, confident, warm-hearted and warm-tempered Tulliver of old times, than might have seemed possible to anyone who had met him a week before, riding along as had been his wont for the last four years since the sense of failure and debt had been upon him – with his head hanging down, casting brief, unwilling looks on those who forced themselves on his notice. He made his speech, asserting his honest principles with his old confident eagerness, alluding to the rascals and the luck that had been against him, but that he had triumphed over, to some extent, by hard efforts and the aid of a good son; and winding up with the story of how Tom had got the best part of the needful money. But the streak of irritation and hostile triumph seemed to melt for a little while into purer fatherly pride and pleasure when, Tom's health having been proposed, and uncle Deane having taken occasion to say a few words of eulogy on his general character and conduct, Tom himself got up and made the single speech of his life. It could hardly have been briefer: he thanked the gentlemen for the honour they had done him. He was glad that he had been able to help his father in proving his integrity and regaining his honest name; and, for his own part, he hoped he should never undo that work and disgrace that name. But the applause that followed was so great, and Tom looked so gentlemanly as well as tall and straight, that Mr Tulliver remarked, in an explanatory manner, to his friends on his right and left, that he had spent a deal of money on his son's education.

The party broke up in very sober fashion at five o'clock. Tom remained in St Ogg's to attend to some business, and Mr Tulliver mounted his horse to go home, and describe the memorable things that had been said and done, to 'poor Bessy and the little wench.' The air of excitement that hung about him was but faintly due to good cheer or any stimulus but the potent wine of triumphant joy. He did not choose any back street today, but rode slowly, with uplifted head and free glances, along the principal street all the way to the bridge. Why did he not happen to meet Wakem? The want of that coincidence vexed him, and set his mind at work in an irritating way. Perhaps Wakem was gone out of town today on purpose to avoid seeing or hearing anything of an honourable action, which might well cause him some unpleasant twinges. If Wakem were to meet him then, Mr Tulliver would look straight at him, and the rascal would perhaps be forsaken a little by his cool domineering impudence. He would know by and by that an honest man was not going to serve *him* any longer, and lend his honesty to fill a pocket already over-full of dishonest gains. Perhaps the luck was beginning to turn; perhaps the devil didn't always hold the best cards in this world.

Simmering in this way, Mr Tulliver approached the yard-gates of Dorlcote Mill, near enough to see a well-known figure coming out of them on a fine black horse. They met about fifty yards from the gates, between the great chestnuts and elms and the high bank.

'Tulliver,' said Wakem, abruptly, in a haughtier tone than usual, 'what a fool's trick you did – spreading those hard lumps on that Far Close. I told you how it would be; but you men never learn to farm with any method.'

'Oh!' said Tulliver, suddenly boiling up. 'Get somebody else to farm for you, then, as'll ask *you* to teach him.'

'You have been drinking, I suppose,' said Wakem, really believing that this was the meaning of Tulliver's flushed face and sparkling eyes.

'No, I've not been drinking,' said Tulliver; 'I want no drinking to help me make up my mind as I'll serve no longer under a scoundrel.'

'Very well! you may leave my premises tomorrow, then: hold your insolent tongue and let me pass.' (Tulliver was backing his horse across the road to hem Wakem in.)

'No, I *shan't* let you pass,' said Tulliver, getting fiercer. 'I shall tell you what I think of you first. You're too big a raskill to get hanged – you're . . .'

'Let me pass, you ignorant brute, or I'll ride over you.'

Mr Tulliver, spurring his horse and raising his whip, made a rush forward, and Wakem's horse, rearing and staggering backward, threw his rider from the saddle and sent him sideways on the ground. Wakem had had the presence of mind to loose the bridle at once, and as the horse only staggered a few paces and then stood still, he might have risen and remounted without more inconvenience than a bruise and a shake. But before he could rise, Tulliver was off his horse too. The sight of the long-hated predominant man down and in his power, threw him into a frenzy of triumphant vengeance, which seemed to give him preternatural agility and strength. He rushed on Wakem, who was in the act of trying to recover his feet, grasped him by the left arm so as to press Wakem's whole weight on the right arm, which rested on the ground, and flogged him fiercely across the back with his riding-whip. Wakem shouted for help, but no help came, until a woman's scream was heard, and the cry of 'Father, father!'

Suddenly, Wakem felt, something had arrested Mr Tulliver's arm; for the flogging ceased, and the grasp on his own arm was relaxed.

'Get away with you – go!' said Tulliver, angrily. But it was not to Wakem that he spoke. Slowly the lawyer rose, and, as he turned his head, saw that Tulliver's arms were being held by a girl – rather by the fear of hurting the girl that clung to him with all her young might.

'O Luke – mother – come and help Mr Wakem!' Maggie cried, as she heard the longed-for footsteps.

'Help me on to that low horse,' said Wakem to Luke, 'then I shall perhaps manage: though – confound it – I think this arm is sprained.'

With some difficulty, Wakem was heaved on to Tulliver's horse. Then he turned towards the miller and said, with white rage. 'You'll suffer for this, sir. Your daughter is a witness that you've assaulted me.'

'I don't care,' said Mr Tulliver, in a thick, fierce voice; 'go and show your back, and tell 'em I thrashed you. Tell 'em I've made things a bit more even i' the world.'

'Ride my horse home with me,' said Wakem to Luke. 'By the Tofton Ferry – not through the town.'

'Father, come in!' said Maggie, imploringly. Then, seeing that Wakem had ridden off, and that no further violence was possible, she slackened her hold and burst into hysteric sobs, while poor Mrs Tulliver stood by in silence, quivering with fear. But Maggie became conscious that as she was slackening her hold, her father was beginning to grasp her and lean on her. The surprise checked her sobs.

'I feel ill – faintish,' he said. 'Help me in, Bessy – I'm giddy – I've a pain i' the head.'

He walked in slowly, propped by his wife and daughter, and tottered into his armchair. The almost purple flush had given way to paleness, and his hand was cold.

'Hadn't we better send for the doctor?' said Mrs Tulliver.

He seemed to be too faint and suffering to hear her; but presently, when she said to Maggie, 'Go and see for somebody to fetch the doctor,' he looked up at her with full comprehension, and said, 'Doctor? no – no doctor. It's my head – that's all. Help me to bed.'

Sad ending to the day that had risen on them all like a beginning of better times! But mingled seed must bear a mingled crop.

In half an hour after his father had lain down Tom came home. Bob Jakin was with him – come to congratulate 'the old master,' not without some excusable pride that he had had his share in bringing about Mr Tom's good-luck; and Tom had thought his father would like nothing better, as a finish to the day, than a talk with Bob. But now Tom could only spend the evening in gloomy expectation of the unpleasant consequences that must follow on this mad outbreak of his father's long-smothered hate. After the painful news had been told, he sat in silence: he had not spirit or inclination to tell his mother and sister anything about the dinner – they hardly cared to ask it. Apparently the mingled thread in the web of their life was so curiously twisted together, that there could be no joy without a sorrow coming close upon it. Tom was dejected by the thought that his exemplary effort must always be baffled by the wrongdoing of others: Maggie was living through, over and over again, the agony of the moment in which she had rushed to throw herself on her father's arm – with a vague, shuddering foreboding of wretched scenes to come. Not one of the three felt any particular alarm about Mr Tulliver's health: the symptoms did not recall his former dangerous attack, and it seemed only a necessary consequence that his violent passion and effort of strength, after many hours of unusual excitement, should have made him feel ill. Rest would probably cure him.

Tom, tired out by his active day, fell asleep soon, and slept soundly: it seemed to him as if he had only just come to bed, when he waked to see his mother standing by him in the grey light of early morning.

'My boy, you must get up this minute: I've sent for the doctor, and your father wants you and Maggie to come to him.'

'Is he worse, mother?'

'He's been very ill all night with his head, but he doesn't say it's worse – he only said sudden, "Bessy, fetch the boy and girl. Tell 'em to make haste."'

Maggie and Tom threw on their clothes hastily in the chill grey light, and reached their father's room almost at the same moment. He was watching for them with an expression of pain on his brow, but with sharpened anxious consciousness in his eyes. Mrs Tulliver stood at the foot of the bed, frightened and trembling, looking worn and aged from disturbed rest. Maggie was at the bedside first, but her father's glance was towards Tom, who came and stood next to her.

'Tom, my lad, it's come upon me as I shan't get up again . . . This world's been too many for me, my lad, but you've done what you could to make things a bit even. Shake hands wi' me again, my lad, before I go away from you.'

The father and son clasped hands and looked at each other an instant. Then Tom said, trying to speak firmly, 'Have you any wish, father – that I can fulfil, when . . .'

'Ay, my lad . . . you'll try and get the old mill back.'

'Yes, father.'

'And there's your mother – you'll try and make her amends, all you can, for my bad luck . . . and there's the little wench . . . '

The father turned his eyes on Maggie with a still more eager look, while she, with a bursting heart, sank on her knees, to be closer to the dear, time-worn face which had been present with her through long years, as the sign of her deepest love and hardest trial.

'You must take care of her, Tom . . . don't you fret, my wench . . . there'll come somebody as'll love you and take your part . . . and you must be good to her, my lad. I was good to *my* sister. Kiss me, Maggie . . . Come, Bessy . . . You'll manage to pay for a brick grave, Tom, so as your mother and me can lie together.'

He looked away from them all when he had said this, and lay silent for some minutes, while they stood watching him, not daring to move. The morning light was growing clearer for them, and they could see the heaviness gathering in his face, and the dulness in his eyes. But at last he looked towards Tom and said, 'I had my turn – I beat him. That was nothing but fair. I never wanted anything but what was fair.'

'But, father, dear father,' said Maggie, an unspeakable anxiety predominating over her grief, 'you forgive him – you forgive everyone now?'

He did not move his eyes to look at her, but he said, 'No, my wench. I don't forgive him . . . What's forgiving to do? I can't love a raskill . . . '

His voice had become thicker; but he wanted to say more, and moved his lips again and again, struggling in vain to speak. At length the words forced their way.

'Does God forgive raskills? . . . but if He does, He won't be hard wi' me.'

His hands moved uneasily, as if he wanted them to remove some obstruction that weighed upon him. Two or three times there fell from him some broken words, 'This world's . . . too many . . . honest man . . . puzzling . . . '

Soon they merged into mere mutterings; the eyes had ceased to discern; and then came the final silence.

But not of death. For an hour or more the chest heaved, the loud hard breathing continued, getting gradually slower, as the cold dews gathered on the brow.

At last there was total stillness, and poor Tulliver's dimly lighted soul had for ever ceased to be vexed with the painful riddle of this world.

Help was come now: Luke and his wife were there, and Mr Turnbull had arrived, too late for everything but to say, 'This is death.'

Tom and Maggie went downstairs together into the room where their father's place was empty. Their eyes turned to the same spot, and Maggie spoke:

'Tom, forgive me – let us always love each other;' and they clung and wept together.

BOOK SIXTH

The Great Temptation

CHAPTER I

A Duet in Paradise

The well-furnished drawing-room, with the open grand piano, and the pleasant outlook down a sloping garden to a boat-house by the side of the Floss, is Mr Deane's. The neat little lady in mourning, whose light-brown ringlets are falling over the coloured embroidery with which her fingers are busy, is of course Lucy Deane; and the fine young man who is leaning down from his chair to snap the scissors in the extremely abbreviated face of the 'King Charles' lying on the young lady's feet, is no other than Mr Stephen Guest, whose diamond ring, attar of roses, and air of nonchalant leisure, at twelve o'clock in the day, are the graceful and odoriferous result of the largest oil-mill and the most extensive wharf in St Ogg's. There is an apparent triviality in the action with the scissors, but your discernment perceives at once that there is a design in it which makes it eminently worthy of a large-headed, long-limbed young man; for you see that Lucy wants the scissors, and is compelled, reluctant as she may be, to shake her ringlets back, raise her soft hazel eyes, smile playfully down on the face that is so very nearly on a level with her knee, and, holding out her little shell-pink palm, to say, 'My scissors, please, if you can renounce the great pleasure of persecuting my poor Minny.'

The foolish scissors have slipped too far over the knuckles, it seems, and Hercules holds out his entrapped fingers hopelessly.

'Confound the scissors! The oval lies the wrong way. Please, draw them off for me.'

'Draw them off with your other hand,' says Miss Lucy, roguishly.

'O, but that's my left hand: I'm not left-handed.' Lucy laughs, and the scissors are drawn off with gentle touches from tiny tips, which naturally dispose Mr Stephen for a repetition *da capo*. Accordingly, he watches for the release of the scissors, that he may get them into his possession again.

'No, no,' said Lucy, sticking them in her band, 'you shall not have my scissors again – you have strained them already. Now don't set Minny growling again. Sit up and behave properly, and then I will tell you some news.'

'What is that?' said Stephen, throwing himself back and hanging his right arm over the corner of his chair. He might have been sitting for his portrait, which would have represented a rather striking young man of five-and-twenty, with a square forehead, short dark-brown hair standing erect, with a slight wave at the end, like a thick crop of corn, and a half-ardent, half-sarcastic glance from under his well-marked horizontal eyebrows. 'Is it very important news?'

'Yes – very. Guess.'

'You are going to change Minny's diet, and give him three ratafias soaked in a dessert-spoonful of cream daily?

'Quite wrong.'

'Well, then, Dr Kenn has been preaching against buckram, and you ladies have all been sending him a round-robin, saying – 'This is a hard doctrine; who can bear it?'

'For shame!' said Lucy, adjusting her little mouth gravely. 'It is rather dull of you not to guess my news, because it is about something I mentioned to you not very long ago.'

'But .you have mentioned many things to me not long ago. Does your feminine tyranny require that when you say the thing you mean is one of several things, I should know it immediately by that mark?'

'Yes, I know you think I am silly.'

'I think you are perfectly charming.'

'And my silliness is part of my charm?'

'I didn't say *that.*'

'But I know you like women to be rather insipid. Philip Wakem betrayed you: he said so one day when you were not here.'

'Oh, I know Phil is fierce on that point; he makes it quite a personal matter. I think he must be love-sick for some unknown lady – some exalted Beatrice whom he met abroad.'

'By the by!' said Lucy, pausing in her work, 'it has just occurred to me that I have never found out whether my cousin Maggie will object to see Philip, as her brother does. Tom will not enter a room where Philip is, if he knows it: perhaps Maggie may be the same, and then we shan't be able to sing our glees – shall we?'

'What! is your cousin coming to stay with you?' said Stephen, with a look of slight annoyance . . .

'Yes; that was my news, which you have forgotten. She's going to leave her situation, where she has been nearly two years, poor thing – ever since her father's death; and she will stay with me a month or two – many months, I hope.'

'And am *I* bound to be pleased at that news?'

'Oh, no, not at all,' said Lucy, with a little air of pique. 'I am pleased, but that, of course, is no reason why *you* should be pleased. There is no girl in the world I love so well as my cousin Maggie.'

'And you will be inseparable, I suppose, when she comes. There will be no possibility of a *tête-à-tête* with you any more, unless you can find an admirer for her, who will pair off with her occasionally. What is the ground of dislike to Philip? He might have been a resource.'

'It is a family quarrel with Philip's father. There were very painful circumstances, I believe. I never quite understood them, or knew them all. My uncle Tulliver was unfortunate and lost all his property, and I think he considered Mr Wakem was somehow the cause of it. Mr Wakem bought Dorlcote Mill, my uncle's old place, where he always lived. You must remember my uncle Tulliver, don't you?'

THE MILL ON THE FLOSS

'No,' said Stephen, with rather supercilious indifference. 'I've always known the name, and I dare say I knew the man by sight, apart from his name. I know half the names and faces in the neighbourhood in that detached, disjointed way.'

'He was a very hot-tempered man. I remember, when I was a little girl, and used to go to see my cousins, he often frightened me by talking as if he were angry. Papa told me there was a dreadful quarrel, the very day before my uncle's death, between him and Mr Wakem, but it was hushed up. That was when you were in London. Papa says my uncle was quite mistaken in many ways: his mind had become embittered. But Tom and Maggie must naturally feel it very painful to be reminded of these things. They have had so much – so very much trouble. Maggie was at school with me six years ago, when she was fetched away because of her father's misfortunes, and she has hardly had any pleasure since, I think. She has been in a dreary situation in a school since uncle's death, because she is determined to be independent, and not live with aunt Pullet; and I could hardly wish her to come to me then, because dear mamma was ill, and everything was so sad. That is why I want her to come to me now, and have a long, long holiday.'

'Very sweet and angelic of you,' said Stephen, looking at her with an admiring smile; 'and all the more so if she has the conversational qualities of her mother.'

'Poor aunty! You are cruel to ridicule her. She is very valuable to *me*, I know. She manages the house beautifully – much better than any stranger would – and she was a great comfort to me in mamma's illness.'

'Yes, but in point of companionship, one would prefer that she should be represented by her brandy-cherries and cream-cakes. I think with a shudder that her daughter will always be present in person, and have no agreeable proxies of that kind – a fat, blond girl, with round blue eyes, who will stare at us silently.'

'Oh, yes!' exclaimed Lucy, laughing wickedly and clapping her hands, 'that is just my cousin Maggie. You must have seen her!'

'No, indeed: I'm only guessing what Mrs Tulliver's daughter must be; and then if she is to banish Philip, our only apology for a tenor, that will be an additional bore.'

'But I hope that may not be. I think I will ask you to call on Philip and tell him Maggie is coming tomorrow. He is quite aware of Tom's feeling, and always keeps out of his way; so he will understand, if you tell him, that I asked you to warn him not to come until I write to ask him.'

'I think you had better write a pretty note for me to take: Phil is so sensitive, you know, the least thing might frighten him off coming at all, and we had hard work to get him. I can never induce him to come to the Park: he doesn't like my sisters, I think. It is only your faëry touch that can lay his ruffled feathers.'

Stephen mastered the little hand that was straying towards the table, and touched it lightly with his lips. Little Lucy felt very proud and happy. She and Stephen were in that stage of courtship which makes the most exquisite moment of youth, the freshest blossom-time of passion – when each is sure of the other's love, but no formal declaration has been made, and all is mutual divination, exalting the most trivial word, the lightest gesture, into thrills delicate and delicious as wafted jasmine scent. The explicitness of an engagement wears off this finest edge of susceptibility: it is jasmine gathered and presented in a large bouquet.

'But it is really odd that you should have hit so exactly on Maggie's appearance and manners,' said the cunning Lucy, moving to reach her desk, 'because she might have been like her brother, you know; and Tom has not round eyes; and he is as far as possible from staring at people.'

'Oh, I suppose he is like the father: he seems to be as proud as Lucifer. Not a brilliant companion, though, I should think.'

'I like Tom. He gave me my Minny when I lost Lolo; and papa is very fond of him: he says Tom has excellent principles. It was through him that his father was able to pay all his debts before he died.'

'Oh, ah; I've heard about that. I heard your father and mine talking about it a little while ago, after dinner, in one of their interminable discussions about business. They think of doing something for young Tulliver: he saved them from a considerable loss by riding home in some marvellous way, like Turpin, to bring them news about the stoppage of a bank, or something of that sort. But I was rather drowsy at the time.'

Stephen rose from his seat, and sauntered to the piano, humming in falsetto, 'Graceful Consort,' as he turned over the volume of 'The Creation,' which stood open on the desk.

'Come and sing this,' he said, when he saw Lucy rising.

'What! 'Graceful Consort?' I don't think it suits your voice.'

'Never mind; it exactly suits my feeling, which, Philip will have it, is the grand element of good singing. I notice men with indifferent voices are usually of that opinion.'

'Philip burst into one of his invectives against 'The Creation' the other day,' said Lucy, seating herself at the piano. 'He says it has a sort of sugared complacency and flattering make-believe in it, as if it were written for the birthday fête of a German Grand-Duke.'

'Oh, pooh! He is the fallen Adam with a soured temper. We are Adam and Eve unfallen, in paradise. Now, then – the recitative, for the sake of the moral. You will sing the whole duty of woman – "And from obedience grows my pride and happiness." '

'Oh, no, I shall not respect an Adam who drags the tempo, as you will,' said Lucy, beginning to play the duet.

Surely the only courtship unshaken by doubts and fears, must be that in which the lovers can sing together. The sense of mutual fitness that springs from the two deep notes fulfilling expectation just at the right moment between the notes of the silvery soprano, from the perfect accord of descending thirds and fifths, from preconcerted loving chase of a fugue, is likely enough to supersede any immediate demand for less impassioned forms of agreement. The contralto will not care to catechise the bass; the tenor will foresee no embarrassing dearth of remark in evenings spent with the lovely soprano. In the provinces, too, where music was so scarce in that remote time, how could the musical people avoid falling in love with each other? Even political principle must have been in danger of relaxation under such circumstances; and the violin, faithful to rotten boroughs, must have been tempted to fraternise in a demoralising way with a reforming violoncello. In this case, the linnet-throated soprano, and the full-toned bass, singing,

> 'With thee delight is ever new,
> With thee is life incessant bliss,'

believed what they sang all the more *because* they sang it.

'Now for Raphael's great song,' said Lucy, when they had finished the duet. 'You do the "heavy beasts" to perfection.'

'That sounds complimentary,' said Stephen, looking at his watch. 'By Jove, it's nearly half-past one. Well, I can just sing this.'

Stephen delivered with admirable ease the deep notes representing the tread of the heavy beasts: but when a singer has an audience of two, there is room for divided sentiments. Minny's mistress was charmed; but Minny, who had intrenched himself, trembling, in his basket as soon as the music began, found this thunder so little to his taste that he leaped out and scampered under the remotest *chiffonière*, as the most eligible place in which a small dog could await the crack of doom.

'Adieu, "graceful consort",' said Stephen, buttoning his coat across when he had done singing, and smiling down from his tall height, with the air of rather a patronising lover, at the little lady on the music-stool. 'My bliss is not incessant, for I must gallop home. I promised to be there at lunch.'

'You will not be able to call on Philip, then? It is of no consequence: I have said everything in my note.'

'You will be engaged with your cousin tomorrow, I suppose?'

'Yes, we are going to have a little family-party. My cousin Tom will dine with us; and poor aunty will have her two children together for the first time. It will be very pretty; I think a great deal about it.'

'But I may come the next day?'

'Oh, yes! Come and be introduced to my cousin Maggie – though you can hardly be said not to have seen her, you have described her so well.'

'Goodbye, then.' And there was that slight pressure of the hands, and momentary meeting of the eyes, which will often leave a little lady with a slight flush and smile on her face that do not subside immediately when the door is closed, and with an inclination to walk up and down the room rather than to seat herself quietly at her embroidery, or other rational and improving occupation. At least this was the effect on Lucy; and you will not, I hope, consider it an indication of vanity predominating over more tender impulses, that she just glanced in the chimney-glass as her walk brought her near it. The desire to know that one has not looked an absolute fright during a few hours of conversation, may be construed as lying within the bonds of a laudable benevolent consideration for others. And Lucy had so much of this benevolence in her nature that I am inclined to think her small egoisms were impregnated with it, just as there are people not altogether unknown to you, whose small benevolences have a predominant and somewhat rank odour of egoism. Even now, that she is walking up and down with a little triumphant flutter of her girlish heart at the sense that she is loved by the person of chief consequence in her small world, you may see in her hazel eyes an ever-present sunny benignity, in which the momentary harmless flashes of personal vanity are quite lost; and if she is happy in thinking of her lover, it is because the thought of him mingles readily with all the gentle affections and good-natured offices with which she fills her peaceful days. Even now, her mind, with the instantaneous alteration which makes two currents of feeling or imagination seem simultaneous, is glancing continually from Stephen to the preparations she has only half finished in Maggie's room. Cousin Maggie should be treated as well as the grandest lady-visitor – nay, better, for she should have Lucy's best prints and drawings in her bedroom, and the very finest bouquet of spring flowers on her table. Maggie would enjoy all that – she was so fond of pretty things! And there was poor aunt Tulliver, that no one made any account of – she was to be surprised with the present of a cap of superlative quality, and to have her health drunk in a gratifying manner, for which Lucy was going to lay a plot with her father this evening. Clearly, she had not time to indulge in long reveries about her own happy love-affairs. With this thought she walked towards the door, but paused there.

'What's the matter, then, Minny?' she said, stooping in answer to some whimpering of that small quadruped, and lifting his glossy head against her pink cheek. 'Did you think I was going without you? Come then, let us go and see Sindbad.'

Sindbad was Lucy's chestnut horse, that she always fed with her own hand when he was turned out in the paddock. She was fond of feeding dependent creatures, and knew the private tastes of all the animals about the house, delighting in the little rippling sounds of her canaries when their beaks were busy with fresh seed, and in the small nibbling pleasures of certain animals which, lest she should appear too trivial, I will here call 'the more familiar rodents'.

Was not Stephen Guest right in his decided opinion that this slim maiden of eighteen was quite the sort of wife a man would not be likely to repent of marrying? – a woman who was loving and thoughtful for other women, not giving them Judas-kisses with eyes askance on their welcome defects, but with real care and vision for their half-hidden pains and mortifications, with long ruminating enjoyment of little pleasures prepared for them? Perhaps the emphasis of his admiration did not fall precisely on this rarest quality in her – perhaps he approved his own choice of her chiefly because she did not strike him as a remarkable rarity. A man likes his wife to be pretty: well, Lucy was pretty, but not to a maddening extent. A man likes his wife to be accomplished, gentle, affectionate, and not stupid; and Lucy had all these qualifications. Stephen was not surprised to find himself in love with her, and was conscious of excellent judgement in preferring her to Miss Leyburn, the daughter of the county member, although Lucy was only the daughter of his father's subordinate partner; besides, he had had to defy and overcome a slight unwillingness and disappointment in his father and sisters – a circumstance which gives a young man an agreeable consciousness of his own dignity. Stephen was aware that he had sense and independence enough to choose the wife who was likely to make him happy, unbiassed by any indirect considerations. He meant to choose Lucy: she was a little darling, and exactly the sort of woman he had always most admired.

CHAPTER 2

First Impressions

'He is very clever, Maggie,' said Lucy. She was kneeling on a footstool at Maggie's feet, after placing that dark lady in the large crimson-velvet chair. 'I feel sure you will like him. I hope you will.'

'I shall be very difficult to please,' said Maggie, smiling, and holding up one of Lucy's long curls, that the sunlight might shine through it. 'A gentleman who thinks he is good enough for Lucy must expect to be sharply criticised.'

'Indeed, he's a great deal too good for me. And sometimes, when he is away, I almost think it can't really be that he loves me. But I can never doubt it when he is with me – though I couldn't bear anyone but you to know that I feel in that way, Maggie.'

'Oh, then, if I disapprove of him you can give him up, since you are not engaged,' said Maggie, with playful gravity.

'I would rather not be engaged. When people are engaged, they begin to think of being married soon,' said Lucy, too thoroughly preoccupied to notice Maggie's joke; 'and I should like everything to go on for a long while just as it is. Sometimes I am quite frightened lest Stephen should say that he has spoken to papa; and from something that fell from papa the other day, I feel sure he and Mr Guest are expecting that. And Stephen's sisters are very civil to me now. At first, I think they didn't like his paying me attention; and that was natural. It *does* seem out of keeping that I should ever live in a great place like the Park House – such a little insignificant thing as I am.'

'But people are not expected to be large in proportion to the houses they live in, like snails,' said Maggie, laughing. 'Pray, are Mr Guest's sisters giantesses?'

'Oh, no; and not handsome – that is, not very,' said Lucy, half-penitent at this uncharitable remark. 'But *he* is – at least he is generally considered very handsome.'

'Though you are unable to share that opinion?'

'Oh, I don't know,' said Lucy, blushing pink over brow and neck. 'It is a bad plan to raise expectation; you will perhaps be disappointed. But I have prepared a charming surprise for him; I shall have a glorious laugh against him. I shall not tell you what it is, though.'

Lucy rose from her knees and went to a little distance, holding her pretty head on one side, as if she had been arranging Maggie for a portrait, and wished to judge of the general effect.

'Stand up a moment, Maggie.'

'What is your pleasure now?' said Maggie, smiling languidly as she rose from her chair and looked down on her slight, aerial cousin, whose figure was quite subordinate to her faultless drapery of silk and crape.

Lucy kept her contemplative attitude a moment or two in silence, and then said, 'I can't think what witchery it is in you, Maggie, that makes you look best in shabby clothes; though you really must have a new dress now. But do you know, last night I was trying to fancy you in a handsome fashionable dress, and do what I would, that old limp merino would come back as the only right thing for you. I wonder if Marie Antoinette looked all the grander when her gown was darned at the elbows. Now, if *I* were to put anything shabby on, I should be quite unnoticeable – I should be a mere rag.'

'Oh, quite,' said Maggie, with mock gravity. 'You would be liable to be swept out of the room with the cobwebs and carpet-dust, and to find yourself under the grate, like Cinderella. Mayn't I sit down now?'

'Yes, now you may,' said Lucy, laughing. Then, with an air of serious reflection, unfastening her large jet brooch, 'But you must change brooches, Maggie; that little butterfly looks silly on you.'

'But won't that mar the charming effect of my consistent shabbiness?' said Maggie, seating herself submissively, while Lucy knelt again and unfastened the contemptible butterfly. 'I wish my mother were of your opinion, for she was fretting last night because this is my best frock. I've been saving my money to pay for some lessons: I shall never get a better situation without more accomplishments.'

Maggie gave a little sigh.

'Now, don't put on that sad look again,' said Lucy, pinning the large brooch below Maggie's fine throat. 'You're forgetting that you've left that dreary school-room behind you, and have no little girls' clothes to mend.'

'Yes,' said Maggie. 'It is with me as I used to think it would be with the poor uneasy white bear I saw at the show. I thought he must have got so stupid with the habit of turning backwards and forwards in that narrow space, that he would keep doing it if they set him free. One gets a bad habit of being unhappy.'

'But I shall put you under a discipline of pleasure that will make you lose that bad habit,' said Lucy, sticking the black butterfly absently in her own collar, while her eyes met Maggie's affectionately.

'You dear, tiny thing,' said Maggie, in one of her bursts of loving admiration, 'you enjoy other people's happiness so much, I believe you would do without any of your own. I wish I were like you.'

'I've never been tried in that way,' said Lucy. 'I've always been so happy. I don't know whether I could bear much trouble; I never had any but poor mamma's death. You *have* been tried, Maggie; and I'm sure you feel for other people quite as much as I do.'

'No, Lucy,' said Maggie, shaking her head slowly, 'I don't enjoy their happiness as you do – else I should be more contented. I do feel for them when they are in trouble; I don't think I could ever bear to make anyone *un*happy; and yet I often hate myself, because I get angry sometimes at the sight of happy people. I think I get worse as I get older – more selfish. That seems very dreadful.'

'Now, Maggie!' said Lucy, in a tone of remonstrance, 'I don't believe a word of that. It is all a gloomy fancy – just because you are depressed by a dull, wearisome life.'

'Well, perhaps it is,' said Maggie, resolutely clearing away the clouds from her face with a bright smile, and throwing herself backward in her chair. 'Perhaps it comes from the school diet – watery rice-pudding spiced with Pinnock. Let us hope it will give way before my mother's custards and this charming Geoffrey Crayon.'

Maggie took up the 'Sketch Book,' which lay by her on the table.

'Do I look fit to be seen with this little brooch?' said Lucy, going to survey the effect in the chimney-glass.

'Oh, no, Mr Guest will be obliged to go out of the room again if he sees you in it. Pray make haste and put another on.'

Lucy hurried out of the room, but Maggie did not take the opportunity of opening her book: she let it fall on her knees, while her eyes wandered to the window, where she could see the sunshine falling on the rich clumps of spring flowers and on the long hedge of laurels – and beyond, the silvery breadth of the dear old Floss, that at this distance seemed to be sleeping in a morning holiday. The sweet fresh garden-scent came through the open window, and the birds were busy flitting and alighting, gurgling and singing. Yet Maggie's eyes began to fill with tears. The sight of the old scenes had made the rush of memories so painful, that even yesterday she had only been able to rejoice in her mother's restored comfort and Tom's brotherly friendliness as we rejoice in good news of friends at a distance, rather than in the presence of a happiness which we share. Memory and imagination urged upon her a sense of privation too keen to let her taste what was offered in the transient present: her future, she thought, was likely to be worse than her past, for after her years of contented renunciation, she had slipped back into desire and longing: she found joyless days of distasteful occupation harder and harder – she found the image of the intense and varied life she yearned for, and despaired of, becoming more and more importunate. The sound of the opening door roused her, and, hastily wiping away her tears, she began to turn over the leaves of her book.

'There is one pleasure, I know, Maggie, that your deepest dismalness will never resist,' said Lucy, beginning to speak as soon as she entered the room. 'That is music, and I mean you to have quite a riotous feast of it. I mean you to get up your playing again, which used to be so much better than mine, when we were at Laceham.'

'You would have laughed to see me playing the little girls' tunes over and over to them, when I took them to practice,' said Maggie, 'just for the sake of fingering the dear keys again. But I don't know whether I could play anything more difficult now than "Begone, dull care!" '

'I know what a wild state of joy you used to be in when the glee-men came round,' said Lucy, taking up her embroidery, 'and we might have all those old glees that you used to love so, if I were certain that you don't feel exactly as Tom does about some things.'

'I should have thought there was nothing you might be more certain of,' said Maggie, smiling.

'I ought rather to have said, one particular thing. Because if you feel just as he does about that, we shall want our third voice. St Ogg's is so miserably provided with musical gentlemen. There are really only Stephen and Philip Wakem who have any knowledge of music, so as to be able to sing a part.'

Lucy had looked up from her work as she uttered the last sentence, and saw that there was a change in Maggie's face.

'Does it hurt you to hear the name mentioned, Maggie? If it does, I will not speak of him again. I know Tom will not see him if he can avoid it.'

'I don't feel at all as Tom does on that subject,' said Maggie, rising and going to the window as if she wanted to see more of the landscape. 'I've always liked Philip Wakem ever since I was a little girl, and saw him at Lorton. He was so good when Tom hurt his foot.'

'Oh, I'm so glad!' said Lucy. 'Then you won't mind his coming sometimes, and we can have much more music than we could without him. I'm very fond of poor Philip, only I wish he were not so morbid about his deformity. I suppose it's his deformity that makes him so sad – and sometimes bitter. It is certainly very piteous to see his poor little crooked body and pale face among great strong people.'

'But, Lucy,' said Maggie, trying to arrest the prattling stream . . .

'Ah, there is the door-bell. That must be Stephen,' Lucy went on, not noticing Maggie's faint effort to speak. 'One of the things I most admire in Stephen is, that he makes a greater friend of Philip than anyone.'

It was too late for Maggie to speak now: the drawing-room door was opening, and Minny was already growling in a small way at the entrance of a tall gentleman, who went up to Lucy and took her hand with a half-polite, half-tender glance and tone of enquiry, which seemed to indicate that he was unconscious of any other presence.

'Let me introduce you to my cousin, Miss Tulliver,' said Lucy, turning with wicked enjoyment towards Maggie, who now approached from the farther window. 'This is Mr Stephen Guest.'

For one instant Stephen could not conceal his astonishment at the sight of this tall, dark-eyed nymph with her jet-black coronet of hair; the next, Maggie felt herself, for the first time in her life, receiving the tribute of a very deep blush and a very deep bow from a person towards whom she herself was conscious of timidity. This new experience was very agreeable to her – so agreeable, that it almost effaced her previous emotion about Philip. There was a new brightness in her eyes, and a very becoming flush on her cheek, as she seated herself.

'I hope you perceive what a striking likeness you drew the day before yesterday,' said Lucy, with a pretty laugh of triumph. She enjoyed her lover's confusion – the advantage was usually on his side.

'This designing cousin of yours quite deceived me, Miss Tulliver,' said Stephen, seating himself by Lucy, and stooping to play with Minny – only looking at Maggie furtively. 'She said you had light hair and blue eyes.'

'Nay, it was you who said so,' remonstrated Lucy. 'I only refrained from destroying your confidence in your own second-sight.'

'I wish I could always err in the same way,' said Stephen, 'and find reality so much more beautiful than my preconceptions.'

'Now you have proved yourself equal to the occasion,' said Maggie, 'and said what it was incumbent on you to say under the circumstances.'

She flashed a slightly defiant look at him: it was clear to her that he had been drawing a satirical portrait of her beforehand. Lucy had said he was inclined to be satirical, and Maggie had mentally supplied the addition – 'and rather conceited.'

'An alarming amount of devil there,' was Stephen's first thought. The second, when she had bent over her work, was, 'I wish she would look at me again.' The next was to answer:

'I suppose all phrases of mere compliment have their turn to be true. A man is occasionally grateful when he says "thank you." It's rather hard upon him that he must use the same words with which all the world declines a disagreeable invitation – don't you think so, Miss Tulliver?'

'No,' said Maggie, looking at him with her direct glance; 'if we use common words on a great occasion, they are the more striking, because they are felt at once to have a particular meaning, like old banners, or everyday clothes, hung up in a sacred place.'

'Then my compliment ought to be eloquent,' said Stephen, really not quite knowing what he said while Maggie looked at him, 'seeing that the words were so far beneath the occasion.'

'No compliment can be eloquent, except as an expression of indifference,' said Maggie, flushing a little.

Lucy was rather alarmed: she thought Stephen and Maggie were not going to like each other. She had always feared lest Maggie should appear too odd and clever to please that critical gentleman. 'Why, dear Maggie,' she interposed, 'you have always pretended that you are too fond of being admired; and now, I think, you are angry because someone ventures to admire you.'

'Not at all,' said Maggie; 'I like too well to feel that I am admired, but compliments never make me feel that.'

'I will never pay you a compliment again, Miss Tulliver,' said Stephen.

'Thank you; that will be a proof of respect.'

Poor Maggie! She was so unused to society that she could take nothing as a matter of course, and had never in her life spoken from the lips merely, so that she must necessarily appear absurd to more experienced ladies, from the excessive feeling she was apt to throw into very trivial incidents. But she was even conscious herself of a little absurdity in this instance. It was true she had a theoretic objection to compliments, and had once said impatiently to Philip, that she didn't see why women were to be told with a simper that they were beautiful, any more than old men were to be told that they were venerable: still, to be so irritated by a common practice in the case of a stranger like Mr Stephen Guest, and to care about his having spoken slightingly of her before he had seen her, was certainly unreasonable, and as soon as she was silent she began to be ashamed of herself. It did not occur to her that her irritation was due to the pleasanter emotion which preceded it, just as when we are satisfied with a sense of glowing warmth, an innocent drop of cold water may fall upon us as a sudden smart.

Stephen was too well-bred not to seem unaware that the previous conversation could have been felt embarrassing, and at once began to talk of impersonal matters, asking Lucy if she knew when the bazaar was at length to take place, so that there might be some hope of seeing her rain the influence of her eyes on objects more grateful than those worsted flowers that were growing under her fingers.

'Some day next month, I believe,' said Lucy. 'But your sisters are doing more for it than I am: they are to have the largest stall.'

'Ah, yes; but they carry on their manufactures in their own sitting-room, where I don't intrude on them. I see you are not addicted to the fashionable vice of fancy-work, Miss Tulliver,' said Stephen, looking at Maggie's plain hemming.

'No,' said Maggie, 'I can do nothing more difficult or more elegant than shirt-making.'

'And your plain sewing is so beautiful, Maggie,' said Lucy, 'that I think I shall beg a few specimens of you to show as fancy-work. Your exquisite sewing is quite a mystery to me – you used to dislike that sort of work so much in old days.'

'It is a mystery easily explained, dear,' said Maggie, looking up quietly. 'Plain sewing was the only thing I could get money by; so I was obliged to try and do it well.'

Lucy, good and simple as she was, could not help blushing a little: she did not quite like that Stephen should know that – Maggie need not have mentioned it. Perhaps there was some pride in the confession: the pride of poverty that will not be ashamed of itself. But if Maggie had been the queen of coquettes she could hardly have invented a means of giving greater piquancy to her beauty in Stephen's eyes: I am not sure that the quiet admission of plain sewing and poverty would have done alone, but assisted by the beauty, they made Maggie more unlike other women even than she had seemed at first.

'But I can knit, Lucy,' Maggie went on, 'if that will be of any use for your bazaar.'

'Oh, yes, of infinite use. I shall set you to work with scarlet wool tomorrow. But your sister is the most enviable person,' continued Lucy, turning to Stephen, 'to have the talent of modelling. She is doing a wonderful bust of Dr Kenn entirely from memory.'

'Why, if she can remember to put the eyes very near together, and the corners of the mouth very far apart, the likeness can hardly fail to be striking in St Ogg's.'

'Now that is very wicked of you,' said Lucy, looking rather hurt. 'I didn't think you would speak disrespectfully of Dr Kenn.'

'I say anything disrespectful of Dr Kenn? Heaven forbid! But I am not bound to respect a libellous bust of him. I think Kenn one of the finest fellows in the world. I don't care much about the tall candlesticks he has put on the communion-table, and I shouldn't like to spoil my temper by getting up to early prayers every morning. But he's the only man I ever knew personally who seems to me to have anything of the real apostle in him – a man who has eight hundred a-year, and is contented with deal furniture and boiled beef because he gives away two-thirds of his income. That was a very fine thing of him – taking into his house that poor lad Grattan who shot his mother by accident. He sacrifices more time than a less busy man could spare, to save the poor fellow from getting into a morbid state of mind about it. He takes the lad out with him constantly, I see.'

'That is beautiful,' said Maggie, who had let her work fall, and was listening with keen interest. 'I never knew anyone who did such things.'

'And one admires that sort of action in Kenn all the more,' said Stephen, 'because his manners in general are rather cold and severe. There's nothing sugary and maudlin about him.'

'Oh, I think he's a perfect character!' said Lucy, with pretty enthusiasm.

'No; there I can't agree with you,' said Stephen, shaking his head with sarcastic gravity.

'Now, what fault can you point out in him?'

'He's an Anglican.'

'Well, those are the right views, I think,' said Lucy, gravely.

'That settles the question in the abstract,' said Stephen, 'but not from a parliamentary point of view. He has set the Dissenters and the Church people by the ears; and a rising senator like myself, of whose services the country is very much in need, will find it inconvenient when he puts up for the honour of representing St Ogg's in Parliament.'

'Do you really think of that?' said Lucy, her eyes brightening with a proud pleasure that made her neglect the argumentative interests of Anglicanism.

'Decidedly – whenever old Mr Leyburn's public spirit and gout induce him to give way. My father's heart is set on it; and gifts like mine, you know' – here Stephen drew himself up, and rubbed his large white hands over his hair with playful self-admiration – 'gifts like mine involve great responsibilities. Don't you think so, Miss Tulliver?'

'Yes,' said Maggie, smiling, but not looking up; 'so much fluency and self-possession should not be wasted entirely on private occasions.'

'Ah, I see how much penetration you have,' said Stephen. 'You have discovered already that I am talkative and impudent. Now superficial people never discern that – owing to my manner, I suppose.'

'She doesn't look at me when I talk of myself,' he thought, while his listeners were laughing. 'I must try other subjects.'

Did Lucy intend to be present at the meeting of the Book Club next week? was the next question. Then followed the recommendation to choose Southey's *Life of Cowper*, unless she were inclined to be philosophical, and startle the ladies of St Ogg's by voting for one of the Bridgewater Treatises. Of course Lucy wished to know what these alarmingly learned books were; and as it is always pleasant to improve the minds of ladies by talking to them at ease on subjects of which they know nothing, Stephen became quite brilliant in an account of Buckland's Treatise, which he had just been reading. He was rewarded by seeing Maggie let her work fall, and gradually get so absorbed in his wonderful geological story that she sat looking at him, leaning forward with crossed arms, and with an entire absence of self-consciousness, as if he had been the snuffiest of old professors, and she a downy-lipped alumnus. He was so fascinated by this clear, large gaze, that at last he forgot to look away from it occasionally towards Lucy; but she, sweet child, was only rejoicing that Stephen was proving to Maggie how clever he was, and that they would certainly be good friends after all.

'I will bring you the book, shall I, Miss Tulliver?' said Stephen when he found the stream of his recollections running rather shallow. 'There are many illustrations in it that you will like to see.'

'Oh, thank you,' said Maggie, blushing with returning self-consciousness at this direct address, and taking up her work again.

'No, no,' Lucy interposed. 'I must forbid your plunging Maggie in books. I shall never get her away from them; and I want her to have delicious do-nothing days, filled with boating, and chatting, and riding, and driving: that is the holiday she needs.'

'Apropos!' said Stephen, looking at his watch. 'Shall we go out for a row on the river now? The tide will suit for us to go the Tofton way, and we can walk back.'

That was a delightful proposition to Maggie, for it was years since she had been on the river. When she was gone to put on her bonnet, Lucy lingered to give an order to the servant, and took the opportunity of telling Stephen that Maggie had no objection to seeing Philip, so that it was a pity she had sent that note the day before yesterday. But she would write another tomorrow and invite him.

'I'll call and beat him up tomorrow,' said Stephen, 'and bring him with me in the evening, shall I? My sisters will want to call on you when I tell them your cousin is with you. I must leave the field clear for them in the morning.'

'Oh yes, pray bring him,' said Lucy. 'And you will like Maggie, shan't you?' she added, in a beseeching tone. 'Isn't she a dear, noble-looking creature?'

'Too tall,' said Stephen, smiling down upon her, 'and a little too fiery. She is not my type of woman, you know.'

Gentlemen, you are aware, are apt to impart these imprudent confidences to ladies concerning their unfavourable opinion of sister fair ones. That is why so many women have the advantage of knowing that they are secretly repulsive to men who have self-denyingly made ardent love to them. And hardly anything could be more distinctively characteristic of Lucy, than that she both implicitly believed what Stephen said, and was determined that Maggie should not know it. But you, who have a higher logic than the verbal to guide you, have already foreseen, as the direct sequence to that unfavourable opinion of Stephen's, that he walked down to the boat-house calculating, by the aid of a vivid imagination, that Maggie must give him her hand at least twice in consequence of this pleasant boating plan, and that a gentleman who wishes ladies to look at him is advantageously situated when he is rowing them in a boat. What then? Had he fallen in love with this surprising daughter of Mrs Tulliver at first sight? Certainly not. Such passions are never heard of in real life. Besides, he was in love already, and half-engaged to the dearest little creature in the world; and he was not a man to make a fool of himself in any way. But when one is five-

and-twenty, one has not chalk-stones at one's finger-ends that the touch of a handsome girl should be entirely indifferent. It was perfectly natural and safe to admire beauty and enjoy looking at it – at least under such circumstances as the present. And there was really something very interesting about this girl, with her poverty and troubles: it was gratifying to see the friendship between the two cousins. Generally, Stephen admitted, he was not fond of women who had any peculiarity of character – but here the peculiarity seemed really of a superior kind; and provided one is not obliged to marry such women, why, they certainly make a variety in social intercourse.

Maggie did not fulfil Stephen's hope by looking at him during the first quarter of an hour: her eyes were too full of the old banks that she knew so well. She felt lonely, cut off from Philip – the only person who had ever seemed to love her devotedly, as she had always longed to be loved. But presently the rhythmic movement of the oars attracted her, and she thought she should like to learn how to row. This roused her from her reverie, and she asked if she might take an oar. It appeared that she required much teaching, and she became ambitious. The exercise brought the warm blood into her cheeks, and made her inclined to take her lesson merrily.

'I shall not be satisfied until I can manage both oars, and row you and Lucy,' she said, looking very bright as she stepped out of the boat. Maggie, we know, was apt to forget the thing she was doing, and she had chosen an inopportune moment for her remark: her foot slipped, but happily Mr Stephen Guest held her hand, and kept her up with a firm grasp.

'You have not hurt yourself at all, I hope?' he said, bending to look in her face with anxiety. It was very charming to be taken care of in that kind graceful manner by someone taller and stronger than oneself. Maggie had never felt just in the same way before.

When they reached home again, they found uncle and aunt Pullet seated with Mrs Tulliver in the drawing-room, and Stephen hurried away, asking leave to come again in the evening.

'And pray bring with you the volume of Purcell that you took away,' said Lucy. 'I want Maggie to hear your best songs.'

Aunt Pullet, under the certainty that Maggie would be invited to go out with Lucy, probably to Park House, was much shocked at the shabbiness of her clothes, which, when witnessed by the higher society of St Ogg's, would be a discredit to the family, that demanded a strong and prompt remedy; and the consultation as to what would be most suitable to this end from among the superfluities of Mrs Pullet's wardrobe, was one that Lucy as well as Mrs Tulliver entered into with some zeal. Maggie must really have an evening-dress as soon as possible, and she was about the same height as aunt Pullet.

'But she's so much broader across the shoulders than I am – it's very ill-convenient,' said Mrs Pullet, 'else she might wear that beautiful black brocade o' mine without any alteration; and her arms are beyond everything,' added Mrs Pullet, sorrowfully, as she lifted Maggie's large round arm. 'She'd never get my sleeves on.'

'O never mind that, aunt: pray send us the dress,' said Lucy. 'I don't mean

Maggie to have long sleeves, and I have abundance of black lace for trimming. Her arms will look beautiful.'

'Maggie's arms *are* a pretty shape,' said Mrs Tulliver. 'They're like mine used to be – only mine was never brown. I wish she'd had *our* family skin.'

'Nonsense, aunty!' said Lucy, patting her aunt Tulliver's shoulder, 'you don't understand those things. A painter would think Maggie's complexion beautiful.'

'May be, my dear,' said Mrs Tulliver, submissively. 'You know better than I do. Only when I was young a brown skin wasn't thought well on among respectable folks.'

'No,' said uncle Pullet, who took intense interest in the ladies' conversation as he sucked his lozenges. 'Though there was a song about the 'Nut-brown Maid,' too; I think she was crazy – crazy Kate – but I can't justly remember.'

'Oh, dear, dear!' said Maggie, laughing, but impatient; 'I think that will be the end of *my* brown skin, if it is always to be talked about so much.'

CHAPTER 3

Confidential Moments

When Maggie went up to her bedroom that night, it appeared that she was not at all inclined to undress. She set down her candle on the first table that presented itself, and began to walk up and down her room, which was a large one, with a firm, regular, and rather rapid step, which showed that the exercise was the instinctive vent of strong excitement. Her eyes and cheeks had an almost feverish brilliancy; her head was thrown backward, and her hands were clasped with the palms outward, and with that tension of the arms which is apt to accompany mental absorption.

Had anything remarkable happened?

Nothing that you are not likely to consider in the highest degree unimportant. She had been hearing some fine music sung by a fine bass voice – but then it was sung in a provincial, amateur fashion, such as would have left a critical ear much to desire. And she was conscious of having been looked at a great deal, in rather a furtive manner, from beneath a pair of well-marked horizontal eyebrows, with a glance that seemed somehow to have caught the vibratory influence of the voice. Such things could have had no perceptible effect on a thoroughly well-educated young lady, with a perfectly balanced mind, who had had all the advantages of fortune, training, and refined society. But if Maggie had been that young lady, you would probably have known nothing about her; her life would have had so few vicissitudes that it could hardly have been written; for the happiest women, like the happiest nations, have no history.

In poor Maggie's highly-strung, hungry nature – just come away from a third-rate schoolroom, with all its jarring sounds and petty round of tasks – these apparently trivial causes had the effect of rousing and exalting her imagination in a way that was mysterious to herself. It was not that she thought distinctly of Mr Stephen Guest, or dwelt on the indications that he looked at her with admiration; it was rather that she felt the half-remote presence of a world of love and beauty and delight, made up of vague, mingled images from all the poetry and romance she had ever read, or had ever woven in her dreamy reveries. Her mind glanced back once or twice to the time when she had courted privation, when she had thought all longing, all impatience was subdued; but that condition seemed irrecoverably gone, and she recoiled from the remembrance of it. No prayer, no striving now, would bring back that negative peace: the battle of her life, it seemed, was not to be decided in that short and easy way – by perfect renunciation at the very threshold of her youth. The music was vibrating in her still – Purcell's music, with its wild passion and fancy – and she could not stay in the recollection of that bare, lonely past. She was in her brighter aerial world again, when a little tap came at the door: of course it was her cousin, who entered in ample white dressing-gown.

'Why, Maggie, you naughty child, haven't you begun to undress?' said Lucy in astonishment. 'I promised not to come and talk to you, because I thought you must be tired. But here you are, looking as if you were ready to dress for a ball. Come, come, get on your dressing-gown, and unplait your hair.'

'Well, *you* are not very forward,' retorted Maggie, hastily reaching her own pink cotton gown, and looking at Lucy's light-brown hair brushed back in curly disorder.

'Oh, I have not much to do. I shall sit down and talk to you till I see you are really on the way to bed.'

While Maggie stood and unplaited her long black hair over her pink drapery, Lucy sat down near the toilette-table, watching her with affectionate eyes, and head a little aside, like a pretty spaniel. If it appears to you at all incredible that young ladies should be led on to talk confidentially in a situation of this kind, I will beg you to remember that human life furnishes many exceptional cases.

'You really *have* enjoyed the music tonight, haven't you, Maggie?'

'Oh, yes, that is what prevents me from feeling sleepy. I think I should have no other mortal wants, if I could always have plenty of music. It seems to infuse strength into my limbs, and ideas into my brain. Life seems to go on without effort, when I am filled with music. At other times one is conscious of carrying a weight.'

'And Stephen has a splendid voice, hasn't he?'

'Well, perhaps we are neither of us judges of that,' said Maggie, laughing, as she seated herself and tossed her long hair back. 'You are not impartial, and *I* think any barrel-organ splendid.'

'But tell me what you think of him, now. Tell me exactly – good and bad too.'

'O, I think you should humiliate him a little. A lover should not be so much at ease, and so self-confident. He ought to tremble more.'

'Nonsense, Maggie! As if anyone could tremble at me! You think he is conceited – I see that. But you don't dislike him, do you?'

'Dislike him! No. Am I in the habit of seeing such charming people, that I should be very difficult to please? Besides, how could I dislike anyone that promised to make you happy, you dear thing!' Maggie pinched Lucy's dimpled chin.

'We shall have more music tomorrow evening,' said Lucy, looking happy already, 'for Stephen will bring Philip Wakem with him.'

'Oh, Lucy, I can't see him,' said Maggie, turning pale. 'At least, I could not see him without Tom's leave.'

'Is Tom such a tyrant as that?' said Lucy, surprised. 'I'll take the responsibility, then – tell him it was my fault.'

'But, dear,' said Maggie, falteringly, 'I promised Tom very solemnly – before my father's death – I promised him I would not speak to Philip without his knowledge and consent. And I have a great dread of opening the subject with Tom – of getting into a quarrel with him again.'

'But I never heard of anything so strange and unreasonable. What harm can poor Philip have done? May I speak to Tom about it?'

'Oh, no, pray don't, dear,' said Maggie. 'I'll go to him myself tomorrow, and tell him that you wish Philip to come. I've thought before of asking him to absolve me from my promise, but I've not had the courage to determine on it.'

They were both silent for some moments, and then Lucy said, 'Maggie, you have secrets from me, and I have none from you.'

Maggie looked meditatively away from Lucy. Then she turned to her and said, 'I should like to tell you about Philip. But, Lucy, you must not betray that you know it to anyone – least of all to Philip himself, or to Mr Stephen Guest.'

The narrative lasted long, for Maggie had never before known the relief of such an outpouring: she had never before told Lucy anything of her inmost life; and the sweet face bent towards her with sympathetic interest, and the little hand pressing hers, encouraged her to speak on. On two points only she was not expansive. She did not betray fully what still rankled in her mind as Tom's great offence – the insults he had heaped on Philip. Angry as the remembrance still made her, she could not bear that anyone else should know it all – both for Tom's sake and Philip's. And she could not bear to tell Lucy of the last scene between her father and Wakem, though it was this scene which she had ever since felt to be a new barrier between herself and Philip. She merely said, she saw now that Tom was, on the whole, right in regarding any prospect of love and marriage between her and Philip as put out of the question by the relation of the two families. Of course Philip's father would never consent.

'There, Lucy, you have had my story,' said Maggie, smiling, with the tears in her eyes. 'You see I am like Sir Andrew Aguecheek – I was adored once.'

'Ah, now I see how it is you know Shakespeare and everything, and have learned so much since you left school; which always seemed to me witchcraft before – part of your general uncanniness,' said Lucy.

She mused a little with her eyes downward, and then added, looking at Maggie, 'It is very beautiful that you should love Philip: I never thought such a happiness would befall him. And in my opinion, you ought not to give him up. There are obstacles now; but they may be done away with in time.'

Maggie shook her head.

'Yes, yes,' persisted Lucy; 'I can't help being hopeful about it. There is something romantic in it – out of the common way – just what everything that happens to you ought to be. And Philip will adore you like a husband in a fairy tale. Oh, I shall puzzle my small brain to contrive some plot that will bring everybody into the right mind, so that you may marry Philip, when I marry – somebody else. Wouldn't that be a pretty ending to all my poor, poor Maggie's troubles?'

Maggie tried to smile, but shivered, as if she felt a sudden chill.

'Ah, dear, you are cold,' said Lucy. 'You must go to bed; and so must I. I dare not think what time it is.'

They kissed each other, and Lucy went away – possessed of a confidence which had a strong influence over her subsequent impressions. Maggie had been thoroughly sincere: her nature had never found it easy to be otherwise. But confidences are sometimes blinding, even when they are sincere.

CHAPTER 4

Brother and Sister

Maggie was obliged to go to Tom's lodgings in the middle of the day, when he would be coming in to dinner, else she would not have found him at home. He was not lodging with entire strangers. Our friend Bob Jakin had, with Mumps's tacit consent, taken not only a wife about eight months ago, but also one of those queer old houses pierced with surprising passages, by the waterside, where, as he observed, his wife and mother could keep themselves out of mischief by letting out two 'pleasure-boats,' in which he had invested some of his savings, and by taking in a lodger for the parlour and spare bedroom. Under these circumstances, what could be better for the interests of all parties, sanitary considerations apart, than that the lodger should be Mr Tom?

It was Bob's wife who opened the door to Maggie. She was a tiny woman, with the general physiognomy of a Dutch doll, looking, in comparison with Bob's mother, who filled up the passage in the rear, very much like one of those human figures which the artist finds conveniently standing near a colossal statue to show the proportions. The tiny woman curtsied and looked up at Maggie with some awe as soon as she had opened the door; but the words, 'Is my brother at home?' which Maggie uttered smilingly, made her turn round with sudden excitement, and say, 'Eh, mother, mother – tell Bob! – it's Miss Maggie! Come in, Miss, for goodness do,' she went on, opening a side door, and endeavouring to flatten her person against the wall to make the utmost space for the visitor.

Sad recollections crowded on Maggie as she entered the small parlour, which was now all that poor Tom had to call by the name of 'home' – that name which had once, so many years ago, meant for both of them the same sum of dear familiar objects. But everything was not strange to her in this new room: the first thing her eyes dwelt on was the large old Bible, and the sight was not likely to disperse the old memories. She stood without speaking.

'If you please to take the privilege o' sitting down, Miss,' said Mrs Jakin, rubbing her apron over a perfectly clean chair, and then lifting up the corner of that garment and holding it to her face with an air of embarrassment, as she looked wonderingly at Maggie.

'Bob is at home, then?' said Maggie, recovering herself, and smiling at the bashful Dutch doll.

'Yes, Miss; but I think he must be washing and dressing himself – I'll go and see,' said Mrs Jakin, disappearing.

But she presently came back walking with new courage a little way behind her husband, who showed the brilliancy of his blue eyes and regular white teeth in the doorway, bowing respectfully.

'How do you do, Bob?' said Maggie, coming forward and putting out her hand to him; 'I always meant to pay your wife a visit, and I shall come another day on purpose for that, if she will let me. But I was obliged to come today, to speak to my brother.'

'He'll be in before long, Miss. He's doin' finely, Mr Tom is: he'll be one o' the first men hereabouts – you'll see that.'

'Well, Bob, I'm sure he'll be indebted to you, whatever he becomes: he said so himself only the other night, when he was talking of you.'

'Eh, Miss, that's his way o' takin' it. But I think the more on't when he says a thing, because his tongue doesn't overshoot him as mine does. Lors! I'm no better nor a tilted bottle, I arn't – I can't stop mysen when once I begin. But you look rarely, Miss – it does me good to see you. What do you say now, Prissy?' – here Bob turned to his wife. 'Isn't it all come true as I said? Though there isn't many sorts o' goods as I can't over-praise when I set my tongue to't.'

Mrs Bob's small nose seemed to be following the example of her eyes in turning up reverentially towards Maggie, but she was able now to smile and curtsy, and say, 'I'd looked forrard like aenything to seein' you, Miss, for my husband's tongue's been runnin' on you, like as if he was light-headed, iver since first he come a-courtin' on me.'

'Well, well,' said Bob, looking rather silly. 'Go an' see after the taters, else Mr Tom 'ull have to wait for 'em.'

'I hope Mumps is friendly with Mrs Jakin, Bob,' said Maggie, smiling. 'I remember you used to say, he wouldn't like your marrying.'

'Eh, Miss,' said Bob, grinning, 'he made up his mind to't when he see'd what a little un she was. He pretends not to see her mostly, or else to think as she isn't full-growed. But about Mr Tom, Miss,' said Bob, speaking lower and looking serious, 'he's as close as a iron biler, he is; but I'm a 'cutish chap, an' when I've left off carrying my pack, an' am at a loose end, I've got more brains nor I know what to do wi', an' I'm forced to busy myself wi' other folks's insides. An' it worrets me as Mr Tom 'ull sit by himself so glumpish, a-knittin' his brow, an' a-lookin' at the fire of a night. He should be a bit livelier now – a fine young fellow like him. My wife says, when she goes in sometimes, an' he takes no notice of her, he sits lookin' into the fire, and frownin' as if he was watchin' folks at work in it.'

'He thinks so much about business,' said Maggie.

'Ay,' said Bob, speaking lower; 'but do you think it's nothin' else, Miss? He's close, Mr Tom is; but I'm a 'cute chap, I am, an' I thought tow'rt last Christmas as I'd found out a soft place in him. It was about a little black spaniel – a rare bit o' breed – as he made a fuss to get. But since then summat's come over him, as he's set his teeth again' things more nor iver, for all he's had such good-luck. An' I wanted to tell *you*, Miss, 'cause I thought you might work it out of him a bit, now you're come. He's a deal too lonely, and doesn't go into company enough.'

'I'm afraid I have very little power over him, Bob,' said Maggie, a good deal moved by Bob's suggestion. It was a totally new idea to her mind, that Tom could have his love troubles. Poor fellow! – and in love with Lucy too! But it was perhaps a mere fancy of Bob's too officious brain. The present of the dog meant nothing more than cousinship and gratitude. But Bob had already said, 'Here's Mr Tom,' and the outer door was opening.

'There's no time to spare, Tom,' said Maggie, as soon as Bob had left the room. 'I must tell you at once what I came about, else I shall be hindering you from taking your dinner.'

Tom stood with his back against the chimney-piece, and Maggie was seated opposite the light. He noticed that she was tremulous, and he had a presentiment of the subject she was going to speak about. The presentiment made his voice colder and harder as he said, 'What is it?'

This tone roused a spirit of resistance in Maggie, and she put her request in quite a different form from the one she had predetermined on. She rose from her seat, and, looking straight at Tom, said, 'I want you to absolve me from my promise about Philip Wakem. Or rather, I promised you not see him without telling you. I am come to tell you that I wish to see him.'

'Very well,' said Tom, still more coldly.

But Maggie had hardly finished speaking in that chill, defiant manner, before she repented, and felt the dread of alienation from her brother.

'Not for myself, dear Tom. Don't be angry. I shouldn't have asked it, only that Philip, you know, is a friend of Lucy's and she wishes him to come – has invited him to come this evening; and I told her I couldn't see him without telling you. I shall only see him in the presence of other people. There will never be anything secret between us again.'

Tom looked away from Maggie, knitting his brow more strongly for a little while. Then he turned to her and said, slowly and emphatically, 'You know what is my feeling on that subject, Maggie. There is no need for my repeating anything I said a year ago. While my father was living, I felt bound to use the utmost power over you, to prevent you from disgracing him as well as yourself, and all of us. But now I must leave you to your own choice. You wish to be independent – you told me so after my father's death. My opinion is not changed. If you think of Philip Wakem as a lover again, you must give up me.'

'I don't wish it, dear Tom – at least as things are: I see that it would lead to misery. But I shall soon go away to another situation, and I should like to be friends with him again while I am here. Lucy wishes it.'

The severity of Tom's face relaxed a little.

'I shouldn't mind your seeing him occasionally at my uncle's – I don't want you to make a fuss on the subject. But I have no confidence in you, Maggie. You would be led away to do anything.'

That was a cruel word. Maggie's lip began to tremble.

'Why will you say that, Tom? It is very hard of you. Have I not done and borne everything as well as I could? And I have kept my word to you – when – when . . . My life has not been a happy one, any more than yours.'

She was obliged to be childish – the tears would come. When Maggie was not angry, she was as dependent on kind or cold words as a daisy on the sunshine or the cloud: the need of being loved would always subdue her, as, in old days, it subdued her in the worm-eaten attic. The brother's goodness came uppermost at this appeal, but it could only show itself in Tom's fashion. He put his hand gently on her arm, and said, in the tone of a kind pedagogue, 'Now listen to me, Maggie. I'll tell you what I mean. You're always in extremes – you have no judgement and self-command; and yet you think you know best, and will not submit to be guided. You know I didn't wish you to take a situation. My aunt Pullet was willing to give you a good home, and you might have lived respectably amongst your relations, until I could have provided a home for you with my mother. And that is what I should like to do. I wished my sister to be a lady, and I would always have taken care of you, as my father desired, until you were well married. But your ideas and mine never accord, and you will not give way. Yet you might have sense enough to see that a brother, who goes out into the world and mixes with men, necessarily knows better what is right and respectable for his sister than she can know herself. You think I am not kind; but my kindness can only be directed by what I believe to be good for you.'

'Yes – I know – dear Tom,' said Maggie, still half-sobbing, but trying to control her tears. 'I know you would do a great deal for me: I know how you work, and don't spare yourself. I am grateful to you. But, indeed, you can't quite judge for me – our natures are very different. You don't know how differently things affect me from what they do you.'

'Yes, I *do* know: I know it too well. I know how differently you must feel about all that affects our family, and your own dignity as a young woman, before you could think of receiving secret addresses from Philip Wakem. If it was not disgusting to me in every other way, I should object to my sister's name being associated for a moment with that of a young man whose father must hate the very thought of us all, and would spurn you. With anyone but you, I should think it quite certain that what you witnessed just before my father's death would secure you from ever thinking again of Philip Wakem as a lover. But I don't feel certain of it with you – I never feel certain about anything with *you*. At one time you take pleasure in a sort of perverse self-denial, and at another you have not resolution to resist a thing that you know to be wrong.'

There was a terrible cutting truth in Tom's words – that hard rind of truth which is discerned by unimaginative, unsympathetic minds. Maggie always writhed under this judgement of Tom's: she rebelled and was humiliated in the same moment: it seemed as if he held a glass before her to show her her own folly and weakness – as if he were a prophetic voice predicting her future fallings – and yet, all the while, she judged him in return: she said inwardly that he was narrow and unjust, that he was below feeling those mental needs which were often the source of the wrong-doing or absurdity that made her life a planless riddle to him.

She did not answer directly: her heart was too full, and she sat down, leaning her arm on the table. It was no use trying to make Tom feel that she was near to him. He always repelled her. Her feeling under his words was complicated by the allusion to the last scene between her father and Wakem; and at length that painful, solemn memory surmounted the immediate grievance. No! She did not think of such things with frivolous indifference, and Tom must not accuse her of that. She looked up at him with a grave, earnest gaze, and said, 'I can't make you think better of me, Tom, by anything I can say. But I am not so shut out from all your feelings as you believe me to be. I see as well as you do, that from our position with regard to Philip's father – not on other grounds – it would be unreasonable – it would be wrong for us to entertain the idea of marriage; and I have given up thinking of him as a lover . . . I am telling you the truth, and you have no right to disbelieve me: I have kept my word to you, and you have never detected me in a falsehood. I should not only not encourage, I should carefully avoid, any intercourse with Philip on any other footing than that of quiet friendship. You may think that I am unable to keep any resolutions; but at least you ought not to treat me with hard contempt on the ground of faults that I have not committed yet.'

'Well, Maggie,' said Tom, softening under this appeal, 'I don't want to over-strain matters. I think, all things considered, it will be best for you to see Philip Wakem, if Lucy wishes him to come to the house. I believe what you say – at least you believe it yourself, I know: I can only warn you. I wish to be as good a brother to you as you will let me.'

There was a little tremor in Tom's voice as he uttered the last words, and Maggie's ready affection came back with as sudden a glow as when they were children, and bit their cake together as a sacrament of conciliation. She rose and laid her hand on Tom's shoulder.

'Dear Tom, I know you mean to be good. I know you have had a great deal to bear, and have done a great deal. I should like to be a comfort to you – not to vex you. You don't think I'm altogether naughty, now, do you?'

Tom smiled at the eager face: his smiles were very pleasant to see when they did come, for the grey eyes could be tender underneath the frown.

'No, Maggie.'

'I may turn out better than you expect.'

'I hope you will.'

'And may I come someday and make tea for you, and see this extremely small wife of Bob's again?'

'Yes, but trot away now, for I've no more time to spare,' said Tom, looking at his watch.

'Not to give me a kiss?'

Tom bent to kiss her cheek, and then said –

'There! Be a good girl. I've got a great deal to think of today. I'm going to have a long consultation with my uncle Deane this afternoon.'

'You'll come to aunt Glegg's tomorrow? We're going all to dine early, that we may go there to tea. You *must* come: Lucy told me to say so.'

'Oh, pooh! I've plenty else to do,' said Tom, pulling his bell violently, and bringing down the small bell-rope.

'I'm frightened – I shall run away,' said Maggie, making a laughing retreat; while Tom, with masculine philosophy, flung the bell-rope to the farther end of the room – not very far either: a touch of human experience which I flatter myself will come home to the bosoms of not a few substantial or distinguished men who were once at an early stage of their rise in the world, and were cherishing very large hopes in very small lodgings.

CHAPTER 5

Showing that Tom had Opened the Oyster

'And now we've settled this Newcastle business, Tom,' said Mr Deane, that same afternoon, as they were seated in the private room at the bank together, 'there's another matter I want to talk to you about. Since you're likely to have rather a smoky, unpleasant time of it at Newcastle for the next few weeks, you'll want a good prospect of some sort to keep up your spirits.'

Tom waited less nervously than he had done on a former occasion in this apartment, while his uncle took out his snuffbox and gratified each nostril with deliberate impartiality.

'You see, Tom,' said Mr Deane, at last, throwing himself backward, 'the world goes on at a smarter pace now than it did when I was a young fellow. Why, sir, forty years ago, when I was much such a strapping youngster as you, a man expected to pull between the shafts the best part of his life, before he got the whip in his hand. The looms went slowish, and fashions didn't alter quite so fast: I'd a best suit that lasted me six years. Everything was on a lower scale, sir – in point of expenditure, I mean. It's this steam, you see, that has made a difference: it drives on every wheel double pace, and the wheel of fortune along with 'em, as our Mr Stephen Guest said at the anniversary dinner (he hits these things off wonderfully, considering he's seen nothing of business). I don't find fault with the change, as some people do. Trade, sir, opens a man's eyes; and if the population is to get thicker upon the ground, as it's doing, the world must use its wits at inventions of one sort or other. I know I've done my share as an ordinary man of business. Somebody has said it's a fine thing to make two ears of corn grow where only one grew before; but, sir it's a fine thing, too, to further the exchange of commodities, and bring the grains of corn to the mouths that are hungry. And that's our line of business; and I consider it as honourable a position as a man can hold, to be connected with it.'

Tom knew that the affair his uncle had to speak of was not urgent; Mr Deane was too shrewd and practical a man to allow either his reminiscences or his snuff to impede the progress of trade. Indeed, for the last month or two, there had been hints thrown out to Tom which enabled him to guess that he was going to hear some proposition for his own benefit. With the beginning of the last speech he had stretched out his legs, thrust his hands in his pockets, and prepared himself for some introductory diffuseness, tending to show that Mr Deane had succeeded by his own merit, and that what he had to say to young men in general

THE MILL ON THE FLOSS

was, that if they didn't succeed too, it was because of their own demerit. He was rather surprised, then, when his uncle put a direct question to him.

'Let me see – it's going on for seven years now since you applied to me for a situation – eh, Tom?'

'Yes, sir; I'm three-and-twenty now,' said Tom.

'Ah – it's as well not to say that, though: for you'd pass for a good deal older, and age tells well in business. I remember your coming very well: I remember I saw there was some pluck in you, and that was what made me give you encouragement. And I'm happy to say, I was right – I'm not often deceived. I was naturally a little shy at pushing my nephew, but I'm happy to say you've done me credit, sir; and if I'd had a son o' my own, I shouldn't have been sorry to see him like you.'

Mr Deane tapped his box and opened it again, repeating in a tone of some feeling – 'No, I shouldn't have been sorry to see him like you.'

'I'm very glad I've given you satisfaction, sir; I've done my best,' said Tom, in his proud, independent way.

'Yes, Tom, you've given me satisfaction. I don't speak of your conduct as a son; though that weighs with me in my opinion of you. But what I have to do with, as a partner in our firm, is the qualities you've shown as a man o' business. Ours is a fine business – a splendid concern, sir – and there's no reason why it shouldn't go on growing: there's a growing capital, and growing outlets for it; but there's another thing that's wanted for the prosperity of every concern, large or small, and that's men to conduct it – men of the right habits; none o' your flashy fellows, but such as are to be depended on. Now this is what Mr Guest and I see clear enough. Three years ago, we took Gell into the concern: we gave him a share in the oil-mill. And why? Why, because Gell was a fellow whose services were worth a premium. So it will always be, sir. So it was with me. And though Gell is pretty near ten years older than you, there are other points in your favour.'

Tom was getting a little nervous as Mr Deane went on speaking; he was conscious of something he had in his mind to say, which might not be agreeable to his uncle, simply because it was a new suggestion rather than an acceptance of the proposition he foresaw.

'It stands to reason,' Mr Deane went on, when he had finished his new pinch, 'that your being my nephew weighs in your favour; but I don't deny that if you'd been no relation of mine at all, your conduct in that affair of Pelley's bank would have led Mr Guest and myself to make some acknowledgment of the service you've been to us; and, backed by your general conduct and business ability, it has made us determine on giving you a share in the business – a share which we shall be glad to increase as the years go on. We think that'll be better, on all grounds, than raising your salary. It'll give you more importance, and prepare you better for taking some of the anxiety off my shoulders by and by. I'm equal to a good deal o' work at present, thank God; but I'm getting older – there's no denying that. I told Mr Guest I would open the subject to you; and when you come back from this northern business, we can go into particulars. This is a great stride for a young fellow of three-and-twenty, but I'm bound to say you've deserved it.'

'I'm very grateful to Mr Guest and you, sir; of course I feel the most indebted to *you*, who first took me into the business, and have taken a good deal of pains with me since.'

Tom spoke with a slight tremor, and paused after he had said this.

'Yes, yes,' said Mr Deane. 'I don't spare pains when I see they'll be of any use. I gave myself some trouble with Gell – else he wouldn't have been what he is.'

'But there's one thing I should like to mention to you, uncle. I've never spoken to you of it before. If you remember, at the time my father's property was sold, there was some thought of your firm buying the mill: I know you thought it would be a very good investment, especially if steam were applied.'

'To be sure, to be sure. But Wakem outbid us – he'd made up his mind to that. He's rather fond of carrying everything over other people's heads.'

'Perhaps it's of no use my mentioning it at present,' Tom went on, 'but I wish you to know what I have in my mind about the mill. I've a strong feeling about it. It was my father's dying wish that I should try and get it back again whenever I could: it was in his family for five generations. I promised my father; and besides that, I'm attached to the place. I shall never like any other so well. And if it should ever suit your views to buy it for the firm, I should have a better chance of fulfilling my father's wish. I shouldn't have liked to mention the thing to you, only you've been kind enough to say my services have been of some value. And I'd give up a much greater chance in life for the sake of having the mill again – I mean, having it in my own hands, and gradually working off the price.'

Mr Deane had listened attentively, and now looked thoughtful.

'I see, I see,' he said, after a while; 'the thing would be possible, if there were any chance of Wakem's parting with the property. But that I *don't* see. He's put that young Jetsome in the place; and he had his reasons when he bought it, I'll be bound.'

'He's a loose fish, that young Jetsome,' said Tom. 'He's taking to drinking, and they say he's letting the business go down. Luke told me about it – our old miller. He says, he shan't stay unless there's an alteration. I was thinking, if things went on in that way, Wakem might be more willing to part with the mill. Luke says he's getting very sour about the way things are going on.'

'Well, I'll turn it over, Tom. I must enquire into the matter, and go into it with Mr Guest. But, you see, it's rather striking out a new branch, and putting you to that, instead of keeping you where you are, which was what we'd wanted.'

'I should be able to manage more than the mill when things were once set properly going, sir. I want to have plenty of work. There's nothing else I care about much.'

There was something rather sad in that speech from a young man of three-and-twenty, even in uncle Deane's business-loving ears.

'Pooh, pooh! you'll be having a wife to care about one of these days, if you get on at this pace in the world. But as to this mill, we mustn't reckon on our chickens too early. However, I promise you to bear it in mind, and when you come back we'll talk of it again. I am going to dinner now. Come and breakfast with us tomorrow morning, and say goodbye to your mother and sister before you start.'

CHAPTER 6

Illustrating the Laws of Attraction

It is evident to you now that Maggie had arrived at a moment in her life which must be considered by all prudent persons as a great opportunity for a young woman. Launched into the higher society of St Ogg's, with a striking person, which had the advantage of being quite unfamiliar to the majority of beholders, and with such moderate assistance of costume as you have seen foreshadowed in Lucy's anxious colloquy with aunt Pullet, Maggie was certainly at a new starting-point in life. At Lucy's first evening-party, young Torry fatigued his facial muscles more than usual in order that 'the dark-eyed girl there, in the corner', might see him in all the additional style conferred by his eye-glass; and several young ladies went home intending to have short sleeves with black lace, and to plait their hair in a broad coronet at the back of their head – 'That cousin of Miss Deane's looked so very well.' In fact, poor Maggie, with all her inward consciousness of a painful past and her presentiment of a troublous future, was on the way to become an object of some envy – a topic of discussion in the newly-established billiard-room, and between fair friends who had no secrets from each other on the subject of trimmings. The Miss Guests, who associated chiefly on terms of condescension with the families of St Ogg's, and were the glass of fashion there, took some exception to Maggie's manners. She had a way of not assenting at once to the observations current in good society, and of saying that she didn't know whether those observations were true or not, which gave her an air of *gaucherie*, and impeded the even flow of conversation; but it is a fact capable of an amiable interpretation, that ladies are not the worse disposed towards a new acquaintance of their own sex because she has points of inferiority. And Maggie was so entirely without those pretty airs of coquetry which have the traditional reputation of driving gentlemen to despair, that she won some feminine pity for being so ineffective in spite of her beauty. She had not had many advantages, poor thing! and it must be admitted there was no pretension about her: her abruptness and unevenness of manner were plainly the result of her secluded and lowly circumstances. It was only a wonder that there was no tinge of vulgarity about her, considering what the rest of poor Lucy's relations were: an allusion which always made the Miss Guests shudder a little. It was not agreeable to think of any connection by marriage with such people as the Gleggs and the Pullets; but it was of no use to contradict Stephen, when once he had set his mind on anything, and certainly there was no possible objection to Lucy in herself – no one could help liking her. She would naturally desire that the Miss Guests should behave kindly to this cousin of whom she was so fond, and Stephen would make a great fuss if they were deficient in civility. Under these circumstances the invitations to Park House were not wanting; and else-where, also, Miss Deane was too popular and too distinguished a member of society in St Ogg's for any attention towards her to be neglected.

Thus Maggie was introduced for the first time to the young lady's life, and knew what it was to get up in the morning without any imperative reason for doing one thing more than another. This new sense of leisure and unchecked enjoyment amidst the soft-breathing airs and garden-scents of advancing spring – amidst the new abundance of music, and lingering strolls in the sunshine, and the delicious dreaminess of gliding on the river – could hardly be without some intoxicating effect on her, after her years of privation; and even in the first week Maggie began to be less haunted by her sad memories and anticipations. Life was certainly very pleasant just now: it was becoming very pleasant to dress in the evening, and to feel that she was one of the beautiful things of this springtime. And there were admiring eyes always awaiting her now; she was no longer an unheeded person, liable to be chid, from whom attention was continually claimed, and on whom no one felt bound to confer any. It was pleasant, too, when Stephen and Lucy were gone out riding, to sit down at the piano alone, and find that the old fitness between her fingers and the keys remained, and revived, like a sympathetic kinship not to be worn out by separation – to get the tunes she had heard the evening before, and repeat them again and again until she had found out a way of producing them so as to make them a more pregnant, passionate language to her. The mere concord of octaves was a delight to Maggie, and she would often take up a book of studies rather than any melody, that she might taste more keenly by abstraction the more primitive sensation of intervals. Not that her enjoyment of music was of the kind that indicates a great specific talent; it was rather that her sensibility to the supreme excitement of music was only one form of that passionate sensibility which belonged to her whole nature, and made her faults and virtues all merge in each other – made her affections sometimes an impatient demand, but also prevented her vanity from taking the form of mere feminine coquetry and device, and gave it the poetry of ambition. But you have known Maggie a long while, and need to be told, not her characteristics, but her history, which is a thing hardly to be predicted even from the completest knowledge of characteristics. For the tragedy of our lives is not created entirely from within. 'Character,' says Novalis, in one of his questionable aphorisms, 'character is destiny.' But not the whole of our destiny. Hamlet, Prince of Denmark, was speculative and irresolute, and we have a great tragedy in con-sequence. But if his father had lived to a good old age, and his uncle had died an early death, we can conceive Hamlet's having married Ophelia, and got through life with a reputation of sanity notwithstanding many soliloquies, and some moody sarcasms towards the fair daughter of Polonius, to say nothing of the frankest incivility to his father-in-law.

Maggie's destiny, then, is at present hidden, and we must wait for it to reveal itself like the course of an unmapped river: we only know that the river is full and rapid, and that for all rivers there is the same final home. Under the charm of her new pleasures, Maggie herself was ceasing to think, with her eager prefiguring imagination, of her future lot; and her anxiety about her first interview with Philip was losing its predominance: perhaps, unconsciously to herself, she was not sorry that the interview had been deferred.

For Philip had not come the evening he was expected, and Mr Stephen Guest brought word that he was gone to the coast – probably, he thought, on a sketching expedition; but it was not certain when he would return. It was just like Philip – to go off in that way without telling anyone. It was not until the twelfth day that he returned, to find both Lucy's notes awaiting him: he had left before he knew of Maggie's arrival.

Perhaps one had need be nineteen again to be quite convinced of the feelings that were crowded for Maggie into those twelve days – of the length to which they were stretched for her by the novelty of her experience in them, and the varying attitudes of her mind. The early days of an acquaintance almost always have this importance for us, and fill up a larger space in our memory than longer subsequent periods, which have been less filled with discovery and new impressions. There were not many hours in those ten days in which Mr Stephen Guest was not seated by Lucy's side, or standing near her at the piano, or accompanying her on some outdoor excursion: his attentions were clearly becoming more assiduous; and that was what everyone had expected. Lucy was very happy: all the happier because Stephen's society seemed to have become much more interesting and amusing since Maggie had been there. Playful discussions – sometimes serious ones – were going forward, in which both Stephen and Maggie revealed themselves, to the admiration of the gentle unobtrusive Lucy; and it more than once crossed her mind what charming quartet they should have through life when Maggie married Philip. Is it an inexplicable thing that a girl should enjoy her lover's society the more for the presence of a third person, and be without the slightest spasm of jealousy that the third person had the conversation habitually directed to her? Not when that girl is as tranquil-hearted as Lucy, thoroughly possessed with a belief that she knows the state of her companions' affections, and not prone to the feelings which shake such a belief in the absence of positive evidence against it. Besides, it was Lucy by whom Stephen sat, to whom he gave his arm, to whom he appealed as the person sure to agree with him; and every day there was the same tender politeness towards her, the same consciousness of her wants and care to supply them. Was there really the same? – it seemed to Lucy that there was more; and it was no wonder that the real significance of the change escaped her. It was a subtle act of conscience in Stephen that even he himself was not aware of. His personal attentions to Maggie were comparatively slight, and there had even sprung up an apparent distance between them, that prevented the renewal of that faint resemblance to gallantry into which he had fallen the first day in the boat. If Stephen came in when Lucy was out of the room – if Lucy left them together, they never spoke to each other: Stephen, perhaps, seemed to be examining books or music, and Maggie bent her head assiduously over her work. Each was oppressively conscious of the other's presence, even to the finger-ends. Yet each looked and longed for the same thing to happen the next day. Neither of them had begun to reflect on the matter, or silently to ask, 'To what does all this tend?' Maggie only felt that life was revealing something quite new to her; and she was absorbed in the direct, immediate experience, without any energy left for taking account of it, and reasoning about it. Stephen wilfully abstained from self-questioning, and would not admit to himself that he felt an influence which was to have any determining effect on his conduct. And when Lucy came into the room again, they were once more unconstrained: Maggie could contradict Stephen and laugh at him, and he could recommend to her consideration the example of that most charming heroine, Miss Sophia Western, who had a great 'respect for the understandings of men.' Maggie could look at Stephen – which, for some reason or other, she always avoided when they were alone; and he could even ask her to play his accompaniment for him, since Lucy's fingers were so busy with that bazaar-work; and lecture her on hurrying the *tempo*, which was certainly Maggie's weak point.

One day – it was the day of Philip's return – Lucy had formed a sudden engagement to spend the evening with Mrs Kenn, whose delicate state of health, threatening to become confirmed illness through an attack of bronchitis, obliged her to resign her functions at the coming bazaar into the hands of the other ladies, of whom she wished Lucy to be one. The engagement had been formed in Stephen's presence, and he had heard Lucy promise to dine early and call at six o'clock for Miss Torry, who brought Mrs Kenn's request.

'Here is another of the moral results of this idiotic bazaar,' Stephen burst forth, as soon as Miss Torry had left the room, 'taking young ladies from the duties of the domestic hearth into scenes of dissipation among urn-rugs and embroidered reticules! I should like to know what is the proper function of women, if it is not to make reasons for husbands to stay at home, and still stronger reasons for bachelors to go out. If this goes on much longer, the bonds of society will be dissolved.'

'Well, it will not go on much longer,' said Lucy, laughing, 'for the bazaar is to take place on Monday week.'

'Thank heaven!' said Stephen. 'Kenn himself said the other day, that he didn't like this plan of making vanity do the work of charity; but just as the British public is not reasonable enough to bear direct taxation, so St Ogg's has not got force of motive enough to build and endow schools without calling in the force of folly.'

'Did he say so?' said little Lucy, her hazel eyes opening wide with anxiety. 'I never heard him say anything of that kind: I thought he approved of what we were doing.'

'I'm sure he approves *you*,' said Stephen, smiling at her affectionately; 'your conduct in going out tonight looks vicious, I own, but I know there is benevolence at the bottom of it.'

'Oh, you think too well of me,' said Lucy, shaking her head, with a pretty blush, and there the subject ended. But it was tacitly understood that Stephen would not come in the evening, and on the strength of that tacit understanding he made his morning visit the longer, not saying goodbye until after four.

Maggie was seated in the drawing-room alone, shortly after dinner, with Minny on her lap, having left her uncle to his wine and his nap, and her mother to the compromise between knitting and nodding, which, when there was no company, she always carried on in the dining-room till teatime. Maggie was stooping to caress the tiny silken pet, and comforting him for his mistress's absence, when the sound of a footstep on the gravel made her look up, and she saw Mr Stephen Guest walking up the garden, as if he had come straight from the river. It was very unusual to see him so soon after dinner! He often complained that their dinner-hour was late at Park House. Nevertheless, there he was, in his black dress: he had evidently been home, and must have come again by the river. Maggie felt her cheeks glowing and her heart beating: it was natural she should be nervous, for she was not accustomed to receive visitors alone. He had seen her look up through the open window, and raised his hat as he walked towards it, to enter that way instead of by the door. He blushed too, and certainly looked as foolish as a young man of some wit and self-possession can be expected to look, as he walked in with a roll of music in his hand, and said, with an air of hesitating improvisation, 'You are surprised to see me again, Miss Tulliver – I ought to apologise for coming upon you by surprise, but I wanted to come into the town, and I got our man to row me; so I thought I would bring these things from the "Maid of Artois" for your cousin: I forgot them this morning. Will you give them to her?'

'Yes,' said Maggie, who had risen confusedly with Minny in her arms, and now, not quite knowing what else to do, sat down again.

Stephen laid down his hat, with the music, which rolled on the floor, and sat down in the chair close by her. He had never done so before, and both he and Maggie were quite aware that it was an entirely new position.

'Well, you pampered minion!' said Stephen, leaning to pull the long curly ears that drooped over Maggie's arm. It was not a suggestive remark, and as the speaker did not follow it up by further development, it naturally left the conversation at a standstill. It seemed to Stephen like some action in a dream, that he was obliged to do, and wonder at himself all the while – to go on stroking Minny's head. Yet it was very pleasant: he only wished he dared look at Maggie, and that she would look at him – let him have one long look into those deep strange eyes of hers, and then he would be satisfied, and quite reasonable after that. He thought it was becoming a sort of monomania with him, to want that long look from Maggie; and he was racking his invention continually to find out some means by which he could have it without its appearing singular and entailing subsequent embarrassment. As for Maggie, she had no distinct thought – only the sense of a presence like that of a closely-hovering broad-winged bird in the darkness, for she was unable to look up, and saw nothing but Minny's black wavy coat.

But this must end sometime – perhaps it ended very soon, and only seemed long, as a minute's dream does. Stephen at last sat upright sideways in his chair, leaning one hand and arm over the back and looking at Maggie. What should he say?

'We shall have a splendid sunset, I think; shan't you go out and see it?'

'I don't know,' said Maggie. Then, courageously raising her eyes and looking out of the window, 'If I'm not playing cribbage with my uncle.'

A pause: during which Minny is stroked again, but has sufficient insight not to be grateful for it – to growl rather.

'Do you like sitting alone?'

A rather arch look came over Maggie's face, and, just glancing at Stephen, she said, 'Would it be quite civil to say "yes"?'

'It was rather a dangerous question for an intruder to ask,' said Stephen, delighted with that glance, and getting determined to stay for another. 'But you will have more than half an hour to yourself after I am gone,' he added, taking out his watch. 'I know Mr Deane never comes in till half-past seven.'

Another pause, during which Maggie looked steadily out of the window, till by a great effort she moved her head to look down at Minny's back again, and said, 'I wish Lucy had not been obliged to go out. We lose our music.

'We shall have a new voice tomorrow night,' said Stephen. 'Will you tell your cousin that our friend Philip Wakem is come back? I saw him as I went home.'

Maggie gave a little start – it seemed hardly more than a vibration that passed from head to foot in an instant. But the new images summoned by Philip's name, dispersed half the oppressive spell she had been under. She rose from her chair with a sudden resolution, and, laying Minny on his cushion, went to reach Lucy's large work-basket from its corner. Stephen was vexed and disappointed: he thought, perhaps Maggie didn't like the name of Wakem to be mentioned to her in that abrupt way – for he now recalled what Lucy had told him of the family quarrel. It was of no use to stay any longer. Maggie was seating herself at the table with her work, and looking chill and proud; and he – he looked like a simpleton for having come. A gratuitous, entirely superfluous visit of that sort was sure to make a man disagreeable and ridiculous. Of course it was palpable to Maggie's thinking, that he had dined hastily in his own room for the sake of setting off again and finding her alone.

A boyish state of mind for an accomplished young gentleman of five-and-twenty, not without legal knowledge! But a reference to history, perhaps, may make it not incredible.

At this moment Maggie's ball of knitting-wool rolled along the ground, and she started up to reach it. Stephen rose too, and, picking up the ball, met her with a vexed complaining look that gave his eyes quite a new expression to Maggie, whose own eyes met them as he presented the ball to her.

'Goodbye,' said Stephen, in a tone that had the same beseeching discontent as his eyes. He dared not put out his hand – he thrust both hands into his tail-pockets as he spoke. Maggie thought she had perhaps been rude.

'Won't you stay?' she said timidly, not looking away, for that would have seemed rude again.

'No, thank you,' said Stephen, looking still into the half-unwilling, half-fascinated eyes, as a thirsty man looks towards the track of the distant brook. 'The boat is waiting for me . . . You'll tell your cousin?'

'Yes.'

'That I brought the music, I mean?'

'Yes.'

'And that Philip is come back ?'

'Yes.' (Maggie did not notice Philip's name this time.)

'Won't you come out a little way into the garden?' said Stephen, in a still gentler tone; but the next moment he was vexed that she did not say 'No,' for she moved away now towards the open window, and he was obliged to take his hat and walk by her side. But he thought of something to make him amends.

'Do take my arm,' he said, in a low tone, as if it were a secret.

There is something strangely winning to most women in that offer of the firm arm: the help is not wanted physically at that moment, but the sense of help – the presence of strength that is outside them and yet theirs – meets a continual want of the imagination. Either on that ground or some other, Maggie took the arm. And they walked together round the grass plot and under the drooping green of the laburnums, in the same dim dreamy state as they had been in a quarter of an hour before; only that Stephen had had the look he longed for, without yet perceiving in himself the symptoms of returning reasonableness, and Maggie had darting thoughts across the dimness: – how came she to be there? – why had she come out? Not a word was spoken. If it had been, each would have been less intensely conscious of the other.

'Take care of this step,' said Stephen, at last.

'Oh, I will go in now,' said Maggie, feeling that the step had come like a rescue. 'Good evening.'

In an instant she had withdrawn her arm, and was running back to the house. She did not reflect that this sudden action would only add to the embarrassing recollections of the last half-hour. She had no thought left for that. She only threw herself into the low armchair, and burst into tears.

'Oh, Philip, Philip, I wish we were together again – so quietly – in the Red Deeps.'

Stephen looked after her a moment, then went on to the boat, and was soon landed at the wharf. He spent the evening in the billiard-room, smoking one cigar after another, and losing 'lives' at pool. But he would not leave off. He was determined not to think – not to admit any more distinct remembrance than was urged upon him by the perpetual presence of Maggie. He was looking at her, and she was on his arm.

But there came the necessity of walking home in the cool starlight, and with it the necessity of cursing his own folly, and bitterly determining that he would never trust himself alone with Maggie again. It was all madness: he was in love, thoroughly attached to Lucy, and engaged – engaged as strongly as an honourable man need be. He wished he had never seen this Maggie Tulliver, to be thrown into a fever by her in this way: she would make a sweet, strange, troublesome, adorable wife to some man or other, but he would never have chosen her himself. Did she feel as he did? He hoped she did – not. He ought not to have gone. He would master himself in future. He would make himself disagreeable to her – quarrel with her perhaps. Quarrel with her? Was it possible to quarrel with a creature who had such eyes – defying and deprecating, contradicting and clinging, imperious and beseeching – full of delicious opposites? To see such a creature subdued by love for one would be a lot worth having – to another man.

There was a muttered exclamation which ended this inward soliloquy, as Stephen threw away the end of his last cigar, and, thrusting his hands into his pockets, stalked along at a quieter pace through the shrubbery. It was not of a benedictory kind.

CHAPTER 7

Philip Re-enters

The next morning was very wet: the sort of morning on which male neighbours who have no imperative occupation at home are likely to pay their fair friends an illimitable visit. The rain, which has been endurable enough for the walk or ride one way, is sure to become so heavy, and at the same time so certain to clear up by and by, that nothing but an open quarrel can abbreviate the visit: latent detestation will not do at all. And if people happen to be lovers, what can be so delightful, in England, as a rainy morning? English sunshine is dubious; bonnets are never quite secure; and if you sit down on the grass it may lead to catarrhs. But the rain is to be depended on. You gallop through it in a mackintosh, and presently find yourself in the seat you like best – a little above or a little below the one on which your goddess sits (it is the same thing to the metaphysical mind, and that is the reason why women are at once worshipped and looked down upon), with a satisfactory confidence that there will be no lady-callers.

'Stephen will come earlier this morning, I know,' said Lucy: 'he always does when it's rainy.'

Maggie made no answer. She was angry with Stephen: she began to think she should dislike him; and if it had not been for the rain, she would have gone to her aunt Glegg's this morning, and so have avoided him altogether. As it was, she must find some reason for remaining out of the room with her mother.

But Stephen did not come earlier, and there was another visitor – a nearer neighbour – who preceded him. When Philip entered the room, he was going merely to bow to Maggie, feeling that their acquaintance was a secret which he was bound not to betray; but when she advanced towards him and put out her hand, he guessed at once that Lucy had been taken into her confidence. It was a moment of some agitation to both, though Philip had spent many hours in preparing for it; but like all persons who have passed through life with little expectation of sympathy, he seldom lost his self-control and shrank with the most sensitive pride from any noticeable betrayal of emotion. A little extra paleness, a little tension of the nostril when he spoke, and the voice pitched in rather a higher key, that to strangers would seem expressive of cold indifference, were all the signs Philip usually gave of an inward drama that was not without its fierceness. But Maggie, who had little more power of concealing the impressions made upon her than if she had been constructed of musical strings, felt her eyes getting larger with tears as they took each other's hands in silence. They were not painful tears: they had rather something of the same origin as the tears women and children shed when they have found some protection to cling to, and look back on the threatened danger. For Philip, who a little while ago was associated continually in Maggie's mind with the sense that Tom might reproach her with some justice, had now, in this short space, become a sort of outward conscience to her, that she might fly to for rescue and strength. Her tranquil, tender affection for Philip, with its root deep down in her childhood, and its memories of long quiet talk confirming by distinct successive impressions the first instinctive bias – the fact that in him the appeal was more strongly to her pity and womanly devotedness than to her vanity or other egoistic excitability of her nature, seemed now to make a sort of sacred place, a sanctuary where she could find refuge from an alluring influence which the best part of herself must resist, which must bring horrible tumult within, wretchedness without. This new sense of her relation to Philip nullified the anxious scruples she would otherwise have felt, lest she should over-step the limit of intercourse with him that Tom would sanction; and she put out her hand to him, and felt the tears in her eyes without any consciousness of an inward check. The scene was just what Lucy expected, and her kind heart delighted in bringing Philip and Maggie together again; though, even with all *her* regard for Philip, she could not resist the impression that her cousin Tom had some excuse for feeling shocked at the physical incongruity between the two – a prosaic person like cousin Tom, who didn't like poetry and fairy tales. But she began to speak as soon as possible, to set them at ease.

'This was very good and virtuous of you,' she said, in her pretty treble, like the low conversational notes of little birds, 'to come so soon after your arrival. And as it is, I think I will pardon you for running away in an inopportune manner, and giving your friends no notice. Come and sit down here,' she went on, placing the chair that would suit him best, 'and you shall find yourself treated mercifully.'

'You will never govern well, Miss Deane,' said Philip as he seated himself, 'because no one will ever believe in your severity. People will always encourage themselves in misdemeanours by the certainty that you will be indulgent.'

Lucy gave some playful contradictions, but Philip did not hear what it was, for he had naturally turned towards Maggie, and she was looking at him with that open, affectionate scrutiny, which we give to a friend from whom we have been long separated. What a moment their parting had been! And Philip felt as if he were only in the morrow of it. He felt this so keenly – with such intense, detailed remembrance – with such passionate revival of all that had been said and looked in their last conversation – that with that jealousy and distrust which in diffident natures is almost inevitably linked with a strong feeling, he thought he read in Maggie's glance and manner the evidence of a change. The very fact that he feared and half expected it, would be sure to make this thought rush in, in the absence of positive proof to the contrary.

'I am having a great holiday, am I not?' said Maggie. 'Lucy is like a fairy godmother: she has turned me from a drudge into a princess in no time. I do nothing but indulge myself all day long, and she always finds out what I want before I know it myself.'

'I'm sure she is the happier for having you, then,' said Philip. 'You must be better than a whole menagerie of pets to her. And you look well – you are benefiting by the change.'

Artificial conversation of this sort went on a little while, till Lucy, determined to put an end to it, exclaimed, with a good imitation of annoyance, that she had forgotten something, and was quickly out of the room.

In a moment Maggie and Philip leaned forward, and the hands were clasped again, with a look of sad contentment like that of friends who meet in the memory of recent sorrow.

'I told my brother I wished to see you, Philip – I asked him to release me from my promise, and he consented.'

Maggie, in her impulsiveness, wanted Philip to know at once the position they must hold towards each other; but she checked herself. The things that had happened since he had spoken of his love for her were so painful that she shrank from being the first to allude to them. It seemed almost like an injury towards Philip even to mention her brother – her brother who had insulted him. But he was thinking too entirely of her to be sensitive on any other point at that moment.

'Then we can at least be friends, Maggie? There is nothing to hinder that now?'

'Will not your father object?' said Maggie, withdrawing her hand.

'I should not give you up on any ground but your own wish, Maggie,' said Philip, colouring. 'There are points on which I should always resist my father, as I used to tell you. *That* is one.'

'Then there is nothing to hinder our being friends, Philip – seeing each other and talking to each other while I am here: I shall soon go away again. I mean to go very soon – to a new situation.'

'Is that inevitable, Maggie?'

'Yes: I must not stay here long. It would unfit me for the life I must begin again at last. I can't live in dependence – I can't live with my brother – though he is very good to me. He would like to provide for me; but that would be intolerable to me.'

Philip was silent a few moments, and then said, in that high, feeble voice which with him indicated the resolute suppression of emotion, 'Is there no other alternative, Maggie? Is that life, away from those who love you, the only one you will allow yourself to look forward to?'

'Yes, Philip,' she said, looking at him pleadingly, as if she entreated him to believe that she was compelled to this course. 'At least, as things are; I don't know what may be in years to come. But I begin to think there can never come much happiness to me from loving: I have always had so much pain mingled with it. I wish I could make myself a world outside it, as men do.'

'Now, you are returning to your old thought in a new form, Maggie – the thought I used to combat,' said Philip, with a slight tinge of bitterness. 'You want to find out a mode of renunciation that will be an escape from pain. I tell you again, there is no such escape possible except by perverting or mutilating one's nature. What would become of me, if I tried to escape from pain? Scorn and cynicism would be my only opium; unless I could fall into some kind of conceited madness, and fancy myself a favourite of Heaven because I am not a favourite with men.'

The bitterness had taken on some impetuosity as Philip went on speaking: the words were evidently an outlet for some immediate feeling of his own, as well as an answer to Maggie. There was a pain pressing on him at that moment. He shrank with proud delicacy from the faintest allusion to the words of love – of plighted love that had passed between them. It would have seemed to him like reminding Maggie of a promise; it would have had for him something of the baseness of compulsion. He could not dwell on the fact that he himself had not changed; for that too would have had the air of an appeal. His love for Maggie was stamped, even more than the rest of his experience, with the exaggerated sense that he was an exception – that she, that everyone, saw him in the light of an exception.

But Maggie was conscience-stricken.

'Yes, Philip,' she said, with her childish contrition when he used to chide her, 'you are right, I know. I do always think too much of my own feelings, and not enough of others' – not enough of yours. I had need have you always to find fault with me and teach me: so many things have come true that you used to tell me.'

Maggie was resting her elbow on the table, leaning her head on her hand and looking at Philip with half-penitent dependent affection, as she said this; while he was returning her gaze with an expression that, to her consciousness, gradually became less vague – became charged with a specific recollection. Had his mind flown back to something that *she* now remembered? – something about a lover of Lucy's? It was a thought that made her shudder: it gave new definiteness to her present position, and to the tendency of what had happened the evening before. She moved her arm from the table, urged to change her position by that positive physical oppression at the heart that sometimes accompanies a sudden mental pang.

'What is the matter, Maggie? Has something happened?' Philip said, in inexpressible anxiety – his imagination being only too ready to weave everything that was fatal to them both.

'No – nothing,' said Maggie, rousing her latent will. Philip must not have that odious thought in his mind: she would banish it from her own. 'Nothing,' she repeated, 'except in my own mind. You used to say I should feel the effect of my starved life, as you called it, and I do. I am too eager in my enjoyment of music and all luxuries, now they are come to me.'

She took up her work and occupied herself resolutely, while Philip watched her, really in doubt whether she had anything more than this general allusion in her mind. It was quite in Maggie's character to be agitated by vague self-reproach. But soon there came a violent well-known ring at the door-bell resounding through the house.

'Oh, what a startling announcement!' said Maggie, quite mistress of herself, though not without some inward flutter. 'I wonder where Lucy is.'

Lucy had not been deaf to the signal, and after an interval long enough for a few solicitous but not hurried enquiries, she herself ushered Stephen in.

'Well, old fellow,' he said, going straight up to Philip and shaking him heartily by the hand, bowing to Maggie in passing, 'it's glorious to have you back again; only I wish you'd conduct yourself a little less like a sparrow with a residence on the house-top, and not go in and out constantly without letting the servants know. This is about the twentieth time I've had to scamper up those countless stairs to that painting-room of yours, all to no purpose, because your people thought you were at home. Such incidents embitter friendship.'

'I've so few visitors – it seems hardly worth while to leave notice of my exits and entrances,' said Philip, feeling rather oppressed just then by Stephen's bright strong presence and strong voice.

'Are you quite well this morning, Miss Tulliver?' said Stephen, turning to Maggie with stiff politeness, and putting out his hand with the air of fulfilling a social duty.

Maggie gave the tips of her fingers, and said, 'Quite well, thank you,' in a tone of proud indifference. Philip's eyes were watching them keenly; but Lucy was used to seeing variations in their manner to each other, and only thought with regret that there was some natural antipathy which every now and then surmounted their mutual goodwill. 'Maggie is not the sort of woman Stephen admires, and she is irritated by something in him which she interprets as conceit,' was the silent observation that accounted for everything to guileless Lucy. Stephen and Maggie had no sooner completed this studied greeting than each felt hurt by the other's coldness. And Stephen, while rattling on in questions to Philip about his recent sketching expedition, was thinking all the more about Maggie because he was not drawing her into the conversation as he had invariably done before. 'Maggie and Philip are not looking happy,' thought Lucy: 'this first interview has been saddening to them.'

'I think we people who have not been galloping,' she said to Stephen, 'are all a little damped by the rain. Let us have some music. We ought to take advantage of having Philip and you together. Give us the duet in "Masaniello": Maggie has not heard that, and I know it will suit her.'

'Come, then,' said Stephen, going towards the piano, and giving a foretaste of the tune in his deep 'brum-brum', very pleasant to hear.

'You, please, Philip – you play the accompaniment,' said Lucy, 'and then I can go on with my work. You will like to play, shan't you?' she added, with a pretty enquiring look, anxious, as usual lest she should have proposed what was not pleasant to another; but with yearnings towards her unfinished embroidery.

Philip had brightened at the proposition, for there is no feeling, perhaps, except the extremes of fear and grief, that does not find relief in music – that does not make a man sing or play the better; and Philip had an abundance of pent-up feeling at this moment, as complex as any trio or quartet that was ever meant to express love and jealousy, and resignation and fierce suspicion, all at the same time.

'Oh, yes,' he said, seating himself at the piano, 'it is a way of eking out one's imperfect life and being three people at once – to sing and make the piano sing, and hear them both all the while – or else to sing and paint.'

'Ah, there you are an enviable fellow. I can do nothing with my hands,' said Stephen. 'That has generally been observed in men of great administrative capacity, I believe. A tendency to predominance of the reflective powers in me! – haven't you observed that, Miss Tulliver?'

Stephen had fallen by mistake into his habit of playful appeal to Maggie, and she could not repress the answering flush and epigram.

'I *have* observed a tendency to predominance,' she said, smiling; and Philip at that moment devoutly hoped that she found the tendency disagreeable.

'Come, come,' said Lucy; 'music, music! We will discuss each other's qualities another time.'

Maggie always tried in vain to go on with her work when music began. She tried harder than ever today; for the thought that Stephen knew how much she cared for his singing was one that no longer roused a merely playful resistance; and she knew, too, that it was his habit always to stand so that he could look at her. But it was of no use: she soon threw her work down, and all her intentions were lost in the vague state of emotion produced by the inspiring duet – emotion that seemed to make her at once strong and weak: strong for all enjoyment, weak for all resistance. When the strain passed into the minor, she half-started from her seat with the sudden thrill of that change. Poor Maggie! She looked very beautiful when her soul was being played on in this way by the inexorable power of sound. You might have seen the slightest perceptible quivering through her whole frame as she leaned a little forward, clasping her hands as if to steady herself; while her eyes dilated and brightened into that wide-open, childish expression of wondering delight, which always came back in her happiest moments. Lucy, who at other times had always been at the piano when Maggie was looking in this way, could not resist the impulse to steal up to her and kiss her. Philip, too, caught a glimpse of her now and then round the open book on the desk, and felt that he had never before seen her under so strong an influence.

'More, more!' said Lucy, when the duet had been encored. 'Something spirited again. Maggie always says she likes a great rush of sound.'

'It must be "Let us take the road," then,' said Stephen – 'so suitable for a wet morning. But are you prepared to abandon the most sacred duties of life, and come and sing with us?'

'Oh, yes,' said Lucy, laughing. 'If you will look out the "Beggar's Opera" from the large canterbury. It has a dingy cover.'

'That is a great clue, considering there are about a score covers here of rival dinginess,' said Stephen, drawing out the canterbury.

'Oh, play something the while, Philip,' said Lucy, noticing that his fingers were wandering over the keys. 'What is that you are falling into? – something delicious that I don't know.'

'Don't you know that?' said Philip, bringing out the tune more definitely. 'It's from the *Somnambula* – "Ah! perchè non posso odiarti." I don't know the opera, but it appears the tenor is telling the heroine that he shall always love her though she may forsake him. You've heard me sing it to the English words, "I love thee still."'

It was not quite unintentionally that Philip had wandered into this song, which might be an indirect expression to Maggie of what he could not prevail on himself to say to her directly. Her ears had been open to what he was saying, and when he began to sing, she understood the plaintive passion of the music. That pleading tenor had no very fine qualities as a voice, but it was not quite new to her: it had sung to her by snatches, in a subdued way, among the grassy walks and hollows, and underneath the leaning ash tree in the Red Deeps. There seemed to be some reproach in the words – did Philip mean that? She wished she had assured him more distinctly in their conversation that she desired not to renew the hope of love between them, only because it clashed with her inevitable circumstances. She was touched, not thrilled by the song: it suggested distinct memories and thoughts, and brought quiet regret in the place of excitement.

'That's the way with you tenors,' said Stephen, who was waiting with music in his hand while Philip finished the song. 'You demoralise the fair sex by warbling your sentimental love and constancy under all sorts of vile treatment. Nothing short of having your heads served up in a dish like that mediaeval tenor or troubadour, would prevent you from expressing your entire resignation. I must administer an antidote, while Miss Deane prepares to tear herself away from her bobbins.'

Stephen rolled out, with saucy energy –

> 'Shall I, wasting in despair,
> Die because a woman's fair?'

and seemed to make all the air in the room alive with a new influence. Lucy, always proud of what Stephen did, went towards the piano with laughing, admiring looks at him; and Maggie, in spite of her resistance to the spirit of the song and to the singer, was taken hold of and shaken by the invisible influence – was borne along by a wave too strong for her.

But, angrily resolved not to betray herself, she seized her work, and went on making false stitches and pricking her fingers with much perseverance, not looking up or taking notice of what was going forward, until all the three voices united in 'Let us take the road.'

I am afraid there would have been a subtle, stealing gratification in her mind if she had known how entirely this saucy, defiant Stephen was occupied with her: how he was passing rapidly from a determination to treat her with ostentatious indifference to an irritating desire for some sign of inclination from her – some interchange of subdued word or look with her. It was not long before he found an opportunity, when they had passed to the music of *The Tempest*. Maggie, feeling the need of a footstool, was walking across the room to get one, when Stephen, who was not singing just then, and was conscious of all her movements, guessed her want, and flew to anticipate her, lifting the footstool with an entreating look at her, which made it impossible not to return a glance of gratitude. And then, to have the footstool placed carefully by a too self-confident personage – not *any* self-confident personage, but one in particular, who suddenly looks humble and anxious, and lingers, bending still, to ask if there is not some draught in that position between the window and the fire-place, and if he may not be allowed to move the work-table to her – these things will summon a little of the too-ready, traitorous tenderness into a woman's eyes, compelled as she is in her girlish time to learn her life-lessons in very trivial language. And to Maggie such things had not been everyday incidents, but were a new element in her life, and found her keen appetite for homage quite fresh. That tone of gentle solicitude obliged her to look at the face that was bent towards her, and to say, 'No, thank you ;' and nothing could prevent that mutual glance from being delicious to both, as it had been the evening before.

It was but an ordinary act of politeness in Stephen; it had hardly taken two minutes; and Lucy, who was singing, scarcely noticed it. But to Philip's mind, filled already with a vague anxiety that was likely to find a definite ground for itself in any trivial incident, this sudden eagerness in Stephen, and the change in Maggie's face, which was plainly reflecting a beam from his, seemed so strong a contrast with the previous overwrought signs of indifference, as to be charged with painful meaning. Stephen's voice, pouring in again, jarred upon his nervous susceptibility as if it had been the clang of sheet-iron, and he felt inclined to make the piano shriek in utter discord. He had really seen no communicable ground for suspecting any unusual feeling between Stephen and Maggie: his own reason told him so, and he wanted to go home at once that he might reflect coolly on these false images, till he had convinced himself of their nullity. But then, again, he wanted to stay as long as Stephen stayed – always to be present when Stephen was with Maggie. It seemed to poor Philip so natural, nay, inevitable, that any man who was near Maggie should fall in love with her! There was no promise of happiness for her if she were beguiled into loving Stephen Guest; and this thought emboldened Philip to view his own love for her in the light of a less unequal offering. He was beginning to play very falsely under this deafening inward tumult, and Lucy was looking at him in astonishment, when Mrs Tulliver's entrance to summon them to lunch came as an excuse for abruptly breaking off the music.

'Ah, Mr Philip,' said Mr Deane, when they entered the dining-room, 'I've not seen you for a long while. Your father's not at home, I think, is he? I went after him to the office the other day, and they said he was out of town.'

'He's been to Mudport on business for several days,' said Philip; 'but he's come back now.'

'As fond of his farming hobby as ever, eh?'

'I believe so,' said Philip, rather wondering at this sudden interest in his father's pursuits.

'Ah?' said Mr Deane, 'he's got some land in his own hands on this side the river as well as the other, I think?'

'Yes, he has.'

'Ah!' continued Mr Deane, as he dispensed the pigeon-pie; 'he must find farming a heavy item – an expensive hobby. I never had a hobby myself – never would give in to that. And the worst of all hobbies are those that people think they can get money at. They shoot their money down like corn out of a sack then.'

Lucy felt a little nervous under her father's apparently gratuitous criticism of Mr Wakem's expenditure. But it ceased there, and Mr Deane became unusually silent and meditative during his luncheon. Lucy, accustomed to watch all indications in her father, and having reasons, which had recently become strong, for an extra interest in what referred to the Wakems, felt an unusual curiosity to know what had prompted her father's questions. His subsequent silence made her suspect there had been some special reason for them in his mind.

With this idea in her head, she resorted to her usual plan when she wanted to tell or ask her father anything particular: she found a reason for her aunt

Tulliver to leave the dining-room after dinner, and seated herself on a small stool at her father's knee. Mr Deane, under those circumstances, considered that he tasted some of the most agreeable moments his merits had purchased him in life, notwithstanding that Lucy, disliking to have her hair powdered with snuff, usually began by mastering his snuffbox on such occasions.

'You don't want to go to sleep yet, papa, *do* you?' she said, as she brought up her stool and opened the large fingers that clutched the snuffbox.

'Not yet,' said Mr Deane, glancing at the reward of merit in the decanter. 'But what do *you* want?' he added, pinching the dimpled chin fondly. 'To coax some more sovereigns out of my pocket for your bazaar? Eh?'

'No, I have no base motives at all today. I only want to talk, not to beg. I want to know what made you ask Philip Wakem about his father's farming today, papa? It seemed rather odd, because you never hardly say anything to him about his father; and why should you care about Mr Wakem's losing money by his hobby?'

'Something to do with business,' said Mr Deane, waving his hands, as if to repel intrusion into that mystery.

'But, papa, you always say Mr Wakem has brought Philip up like a girl: how came you to think you should get any business knowledge out of him? Those abrupt questions sounded rather oddly. Philip thought them queer.'

'Nonsense, child!' said Mr Deane, willing to justify his social demeanour, with which he had taken some pains in his upward progress. 'There's a report that Wakem's mill and farm on the other side of the river – Dorlcote Mill, your uncle Tulliver's, you know – isn't answering so well as it did. I wanted to see if your friend Philip would let anything out about his father's being tired of farming.'

'Why? Would you buy the mill, papa, if he would part with it?' said Lucy, eagerly. 'Oh, tell me everything – here, you shall have your snuffbox if you'll tell me. Because Maggie says all their hearts are set on Tom's getting back the mill sometime. It was one of the last things her father said to Tom, that he must get back the mill.'

'Hush, you little puss,' said Mr Deane, availing himself of the restored snuffbox. 'You must not say a word about this thing – do you hear? There's very little chance of their getting the mill, or of anybody's getting it out of Wakem's hands. And if he knew that we wanted it with a view to the Tullivers getting it again, he'd be the less likely to part with it. It's natural, after what happened. He behaved well enough to Tulliver before; but a horse-whipping is not likely to be paid for with sugar-plums.'

'Now, papa,' said Lucy, with a little air of solemnity, 'will you trust me? You must not ask me all my reasons for what I'm going to say – but I have very strong reasons. And I'm very cautious – I am, indeed.'

'Well, let us hear.'

'Why, I believe, if you will let me take Philip Wakem into our confidence – let me tell him all about your wish to buy, and what it's for – that my cousins wish to have it, and why they wish to have it – I believe Philip would help to bring it about. I know he would desire to do it.'

'I don't see how that can be, child,' said Mr Deane, looking puzzled. 'Why should *he* care?' – then, with a sudden penetrating look at his daughter, 'You don't think the poor lad's fond of you, and so you can make him do what you like?' (Mr Deane felt quite safe about his daughter's affections.)

'No, papa; he cares very little about me – not so much as I care about him. But I have a reason for being quite sure of what I say. Don't you ask me. And if you ever guess, don't tell me. Only give me leave to do as I think fit about it.'

Lucy rose from her stool to seat herself on her father's knee, and kissed him with that last request.

'Are you sure you won't do mischief, now?' he said, looking at her with delight.

'Yes, papa, quite sure. I'm very wise; I've got all your business talents. Didn't you admire my accompt-book, now, when I showed it you?'

'Well, well, if this youngster will keep his counsel, there won't be much harm done. And to tell the truth, I think there's not much chance for us any way. Now, let me go off to sleep.'

CHAPTER 8

Wakem in a New Light

Before three days had passed after the conversation you have just overheard between Lucy and her father, she had contrived to have a private interview with Philip during a visit of Maggie's to her aunt Glegg. For a day and a night Philip turned over in his mind with restless agitation all that Lucy had told him in that interview, till he had thoroughly resolved on a course of action. He thought he saw before him now a possibility of altering his position with respect to Maggie, and removing at least one obstacle between them. He laid his plan and calculated all his moves with the fervid deliberation of a chess-player in the days of his first ardour, and was amazed himself at his sudden genius as a tactician. His plan was as bold as it was thoroughly calculated. Having watched for a moment when his father had nothing more urgent on his hands than the newspaper, he went behind him, laid a hand on his shoulder, and said, 'Father, will you come into my sanctum, and look at my new sketches? I've arranged them now,'

'I'm getting terribly stiff in the joints, Phil, for climbing those stairs of yours,' said Wakem, looking kindly at his son as he laid down his paper. 'But come along, then.'

'This is a nice place for you, isn't it, Phil? – a capital light that from the roof, eh?' was, as usual, the first thing he said on entering the painting-room. He liked to remind himself and his son too that his fatherly indulgence had provided the accommodation. He had been a good father. Emily would have nothing to reproach him with there, if she came back again from her grave.

'Come, come,' he said, putting his double eye-glass over his nose, and seating himself to take a general view while he rested, 'you've got a famous show here. Upon my word, I don't see that your things aren't as good as that London artist's – what's his name – that Leyburn gave so much money for.'

Philip shook his head and smiled. He had seated himself on his painting-stool, and had taken a lead pencil in his hand, with which he was making strong marks to counteract the sense of tremulousness. He watched his father get up, and walk slowly round, good-naturedly dwelling on the pictures much longer than his amount of genuine taste for landscape would have prompted, till he stopped before a stand on which two pictures were placed – one much larger than the other – the smaller one in a leather case.

'Bless me! what have you here?' said Wakem, startled by a sudden transition from landscape to portrait. 'I thought you'd left off figures. Who are these?'

'They are the same person,' said Philip, with calm promptness, 'at different ages.'

'And what person?' said Wakem sharply, fixing his eyes with a growing look of suspicion on the larger picture.

'Miss Tulliver. The small one is something like she was when I was at school with her brother at King's Lorton: the larger one is not quite so good a likeness of what she was when I came from abroad.'

Wakem turned round fiercely, with a flushed face, letting his eye-glass fall, and looking at his son with a savage expression for a moment, as if he was ready to strike that daring feebleness from the stool. But he threw himself into the armchair again, and thrust his hands into his trouser-pockets, still looking angrily at his son, however Philip did not return the look but sat quietly watching the point of his pencil.

'And do you mean to say, then, that you have had any acquaintance with her since you came from abroad?' said Wakem, at last, with that vain effort which rage always makes to throw as much punishment as it desires to inflict into words and tones, since blows are forbidden.

'Yes: I saw a great deal of her for a whole year before her father's death. We met often in that thicket – the Red Deeps – near Dorlcote Mill. I love her dearly: I shall never love any other woman. I have thought of her ever since she was a little girl.'

'Go on, sir! – and you have corresponded with her all this while?'

'No. I never told her I loved her till just before we parted, and she promised her brother not to see me again or to correspond with me. I am not sure that she loves me, or would consent to marry me. But if she would consent – if she *did* love me well enough – I should marry her.'

'And this is the return you make me for all the indulgences I've heaped on you?' said Wakem, getting white, and beginning to tremble under an enraged sense of impotence before Philip's calm defiance and concentration of purpose.

'No, father,' said Philip, looking up at him for the first time. 'I don't regard it as a return. You have been an indulgent father to me; but I have always felt that it was because you had an affectionate wish to give me as much happiness as my unfortunate lot would admit of – not that it was a debt you expected me to pay by sacrificing all my chance of happiness to satisfy feelings of yours, which I can never share.'

'I think most sons would share their father's feelings in this case,' said Wakem, bitterly. 'The girl's father was an ignorant mad brute, who was within an inch of murdering me. The whole town knows it. And the brother is just as insolent, only in a cooler way. He forbade her seeing you, you say; he'll break every bone in your body, for your greater happiness, if you don't take care. But you seem to have made up your mind: you have counted the consequences, I suppose. Of course you are independent of me: you can marry this girl tomorrow, if you like: you are a man of five-and-twenty – you can go your way, and I can go mine. We need have no more to do with each other.'

Wakem rose and walked towards the door, but something held him back, and instead of leaving the room, he walked up and down it. Philip was slow to reply, and when he spoke, his tone had a more incisive quietness and clearness than ever.

'No: I can't marry Miss Tulliver, even if she would have me – if I have only my own resources to maintain her with: I have been brought up to no profession. I can't offer her poverty as well as deformity.'

'Ah, *there* is a reason for your clinging to me, doubtless,' said Wakem, still bitterly, though Philip's last words had given him a pang: they had stirred a feeling which had been a habit for a quarter of a century. He threw himself into the chair again.

'I expected all this,' said Philip. 'I know these scenes are often happening between father and son. If I were like other men of my age, I might answer your angry words by still angrier – we might part – I should marry the woman I love, and have a chance of being as happy as the rest. But if it will be a satisfaction to you to annihilate the very object of everything you've done for me, you have an advantage over most fathers: you can completely deprive me of the only thing that would make my life worth having.'

Philip paused, but his father was silent.

'You know best what satisfaction you would have, beyond that of gratifying a ridiculous rancour worthy only of wandering savages.'

'Ridiculous rancour!' Wakem burst out. 'What do you mean? Damn it! is a man to be horsewhipped by a boor and love him for it? Besides, there's that cold, proud devil of a son, who said a word to me I shall not forget when we had the settling. He would be as pleasant a mark for a bullet as I know – if he were worth the expense.'

'I don't mean your resentment towards them,' said Philip, who had his reasons for some sympathy with this view of Tom, 'though a feeling of revenge is not worth much, that you should care to keep it. I mean your extending the enmity to a helpless girl, who has too much sense and goodness to share their narrow prejudices. *She* has never entered into the family quarrels.'

'What does that signify? We don't ask what a woman does – we ask whom she belongs to. It's altogether a degrading thing to you – to think of marrying old Tulliver's daughter.'

For the first time in the dialogue, Philip lost some of his self-control, and coloured with anger.

'Miss Tulliver,' he said, with bitter incisiveness, 'has the only grounds of rank that anything but vulgar folly can suppose to belong to the middle class: she is thoroughly refined, and her friends, whatever else they may be, are respected for irreproachable honour and integrity. All St Ogg's, I fancy, would pronounce her to be more than my equal.'

Wakem darted a glance of fierce question at his son; but Philip was not looking at him, and with a certain penitent consciousness went on, in a few moments, as if in amplification of his last words, 'Find a single person in St Oggs's who will not tell you that a beautiful creature like her would be throwing herself away on a pitiable object like me.'

'Not she!' said Wakem, rising again, and forgetting everything else in a burst of resentful pride, half fatherly, half personal. 'It would be a deuced fine match for her. It's all stuff about an accidental deformity, when a girl's really attached to a man.'

'But girls are not apt to get attached under those circumstances,' said Philip.

'Well, then,' said Wakem, rather brutally, trying to recover his previous position, 'if she doesn't care for you, you might have spared yourself the trouble of talking to me about her – and you might have spared me the trouble of refusing my consent to what was never likely to happen.'

Wakem strode to the door, and, without looking round again, banged it after him.

Philip was not without confidence that his father would be ultimately wrought upon as he had expected, by what had passed; but the scene had jarred upon his nerves, which were as sensitive as a woman's. He determined not to go down to dinner: he couldn't meet his father again that day. It was Wakem's habit, when he had no company at home, to go out in the evening – often as early as half-past seven; and as it was far on in the afternoon now, Philip locked up his room and went out for a long ramble, thinking he would not return until his father was out of the house again. He got into a boat, and went down the river to a favourite village, where he dined, and lingered till it was late enough for him to return. He had never had any sort of quarrel with his father before, and had a sickening fear that this contest, just begun, might go on for weeks – and what might not happen in that time? He would not allow himself to define what that involuntary question meant. But if he could once be in the position of Maggie's accepted, acknowledged lover, there would be less room for vague dread. He went up to his painting-room again, and threw himself, with a sense of fatigue, into the armchair, looking round absently at the views of water and rock that were ranged around, till he fell into a doze, in which he fancied Maggie was slipping down a glistening, green, slimy channel of a waterfall, and he was looking on helpless, till he was awakened by what seemed a sudden, awful crash.

.It was the opening of the door, and he could hardly have dozed more than a few moments, for there was no perceptible change in the evening light. It was his father who entered, and when Philip moved to vacate the chair for him, he said, 'Sit still. I'd rather walk about.'

He stalked up and down the room once or twice, and then, standing opposite Philip with his hands thrust in his side-pockets, he said, as if continuing a conversation that had not been broken off, 'But this girl seems to have been fond of you, Phil, else she wouldn't have met you in that way.'

Philip's heart was beating rapidly, and a transient flush passed over his face like a gleam. It was not quite easy to speak at once.

'She liked me at King's Lorton, when she was a little girl, because I used to sit with her brother a great deal when he had hurt his foot. She had kept that in her memory, and thought of me as a friend of a long while ago. She didn't think of me as a lover, when she met me.'

'Well, but you made love to her at last. What did she say then?' said Wakem, walking about again.

'She said she *did* love me then.'

'Confound it, then, what else do you want? Is she a jilt?'

'She was very young then,' said Philip, hesitatingly. 'I'm afraid she hardly knew what she felt. I'm afraid our long separation, and the idea that events must always divide us, may have made a difference.'

'But she's in the town. I've seen her at church. Haven't you spoken to her since you came back?'

'Yes, at Mr Deane's. But I couldn't renew my proposals to her on several grounds. One obstacle would be removed if you would give your consent – if you would be willing to think of her as a daughter-in-law.'

Wakem was silent a little while, pausing before Maggie's picture.

'She's not the sort of woman your mother was, though, Phil,' he said, at last. 'I saw her at church – she's handsomer than this – deuced fine eyes and fine figure, I saw; but rather dangerous and unmanageable, eh?'

'She's very tender and affectionate; and so simple – without the airs and petty contrivances other women have.'

'Ah?' said Wakem. Then looking round at his son, 'But your mother looked gentler: she had that brown wavy hair and grey eyes, like yours. You can't remember her very well. It was a thousand pities I'd no likeness of her.'

'Then, shouldn't you be glad for me to have the same sort of happiness, father, to sweeten my life for me? There can never be another tie so strong to you as that which began eight-and-twenty years ago, when you married my mother, and you have been tightening it ever since.'

'Ah, Phil – you're the only fellow that knows the best of me,' said Wakem, giving his hand to his son. 'We must keep together if we can. And now, what am I to do? You must come downstairs and tell me. Am I to go and call on this dark-eyed damsel?'

The barrier once thrown down in this way, Philip could talk freely to his father of the entire relation with the Tullivers – of the desire to get the mill and land back into the family – and of its transfer to Guest & Co. as an intermediate step. He could venture now to be persuasive and urgent, and his father yielded with more readiness than he had calculated on.

'I don't care about the mill,' he said at last, with a sort of angry compliance. 'I've had an infernal deal of bother lately about the mill. Let them pay me for my improvements, that's all. But there's one thing you needn't ask me. I shall have no direct transactions with young Tulliver. If you like to swallow him, for his sister's sake, you may; but I've no sauce that will make him go down.'

I leave you to imagine the agreeable feelings with which Philip went to Mr

Deane the next day, to say that Mr Wakem was ready to open the negotiations, and Lucy's pretty triumph as she appealed to her father whether she had not proved her great business abilities. Mr Deane was rather puzzled, and suspected that there had been something 'going on' among the young people to which he wanted a clue. But to men of Mr Deane's stamp, what goes on among the young people is as extraneous to the real business of life as what goes on among the birds and butterflies – until it can be shown to have a malign bearing on monetary affairs. And in this case the bearing appeared to be entirely propitious.

CHAPTER 9

Charity in Full-Dress

The culmination of Maggie's career as an admired member of society in St Ogg's was certainly the day of the bazaar, when her simple, noble beauty, clad in a white muslin of some soft-floating kind, which I suspect must have come from the stores of aunt Pullet's wardrobe, appeared with marked distinction among the more adorned and conventional women around her. We perhaps never detect how much of our social demeanour is made up of artificial airs, until we see a person who is at once beautiful and simple: without the beauty, we are apt to call simplicity awkwardness. The Miss Guests were much too well-bred to have any of the grimaces and affected tones that belong to pretentious vulgarity; but their stall being next to the one where Maggie sat, it seemed newly obvious today that Miss Guest held her chin too high, and that Miss Laura spoke and moved continually with a view to effect.

All well-dressed St Ogg's and its neighbourhood were there; and it would have been worth while to come, even from a distance, to see the fine old hall, with its open roof and carved oaken rafters, and great oaken folding-doors, and light shed down from a height on the many-coloured show beneath: a very quaint place, with broad faded stripes painted on the walls, and here and there a show of heraldic animals of a bristly, long-snouted character, the cherished emblems of a noble family once the seigniors of this now civic hall. A grand arch, cut in the upper wall at one end, surmounted an oaken orchestra, with an open room behind it, where hothouse plants and stalls for refreshments were disposed: an agreeable resort for gentlemen disposed to loiter, and yet to exchange the occasional crush down below for a more commodious point of view. In fact, the perfect fitness of this ancient building for an admirable modern purpose, that made charity truly elegant, and led through vanity up to the supply of a deficit, was so striking that hardly a person entered the room without exchanging the remark more than once. Near the great arch over the orchestra was the stone oriel with painted glass, which was one of the venerable inconsistencies of the old hall; and it was close by this that Lucy had her stall, for the convenience of certain large plain articles which she had taken charge of for Mrs Kenn. Maggie had begged to sit at the open end of the stall, and to have the sale of these articles rather than of bead-mats and other elaborate products of which she had but a dim understanding. But it soon appeared that the gentlemen's dressing-gowns, which were among her commodities, were objects of such general attention and enquiry, and excited so troublesome a curiosity as to their lining and comparative merits, together with a determination to test them by trying on, as to make her post a very conspicuous one. The ladies who had commodities of their own to sell, and did not want dressing-gowns, saw at once the frivolity and bad taste of this masculine preference for goods which any tailor could furnish; and it is possible that the emphatic notice of various kinds which was drawn towards Miss Tulliver on this public occasion, threw a very strong and unmistakable light on her subsequent conduct in many minds then present. Not that anger, on account of spurned beauty, can dwell in the celestial breasts of charitable ladies, but rather, that the errors of persons who have once been much admired necessarily take a deeper tinge from the mere force of contrast; and also, that today Maggie's conspicuous position, for the first time, made evident certain characteristics which were subsequently felt to have an explanatory bearing. There was something rather bold in Miss Tulliver's direct gaze, and something undefinably coarse in the style of her beauty, which placed her, in the opinion of all feminine judges, far below her cousin Miss Deane; for the ladies of St Ogg's had now completely ceded to Lucy their hypothetic claims on the admiration of Mr Stephen Guest.

As for dear little Lucy herself, her late benevolent triumph about the mill, and all the affectionate projects she was cherishing for Maggie and Philip, helped to give her the highest spirits today, and she felt nothing but pleasure in the evidence of Maggie's attractiveness. It is true, she was looking very charming herself, and Stephen was paying her the utmost attention on this public occasion; jealously buying up the articles he had seen under her fingers in the process of making, and gaily helping her to cajole the male customers into the purchase of the most effeminate futilities. He chose to lay aside his hat and wear a scarlet fez of her embroidering; but by superficial observers this was necessarily liable to be interpreted less as a compliment to Lucy than as a mark of coxcombry. 'Guest is a great coxcomb,' young Torry observed; 'but then he is a privileged person in St Ogg's – he carries all before him: if another fellow did such things, everybody would say he made a fool of himself.'

And Stephen purchased absolutely nothing from Maggie, until Lucy said, in rather a vexed undertone, 'See, now; all the things of Maggie's knitting will be gone, and you will not have bought one. There are those deliciously soft warm things for the wrists – do buy them.'

'Oh, no,' said Stephen, 'they must be intended for imaginative persons, who can chill themselves on this warm day by thinking of the frosty Caucasus. Stern reason is my forte, you know. You must get Philip to buy those. By the way, why doesn't he come?'

'He never likes going where there are many people, though I enjoined him to come. He said he would buy up any of my goods that the rest of the world rejected. But now, do go and buy something of Maggie.'

'No, no – see – she has got a customer: there is old Wakem himself just coming up.'

Lucy's eyes turned with anxious interest towards Maggie, to see how she went through this first interview, since a sadly memorable time, with a man towards whom she must have so strange a mixture of feelings; but she was pleased to notice that Wakem had tact enough to enter at once into talk about the bazaar wares, and appear interested in purchasing, smiling now and then kindly at Maggie, and not calling on her to speak much, as if he observed that she was rather pale and tremulous.

"Why, Wakem is making himself particularly amiable to your cousin,' said Stephen, in an undertone to Lucy; 'is it pure magnanamity? You talked of a family quarrel.'

'Oh, that will soon be quite healed, I hope,' said Lucy, becoming a little indiscreet in her satisfaction, and speaking with an air of significance. But Stephen did not appear to notice this, and as some lady-purchasers came up, he lounged on towards Maggie's end, handling trifles and standing aloof until Wakem, who had taken out his purse, had finished his transactions.

'My son came with me,' he overheard Wakem saying, 'but he has vanished into some other part of the building, and has left all these charitable gallantries to me. I hope you'll reproach him for his shabby conduct.'

She returned his smile and bow without speaking, and he turned away, only then observing Stephen, and nodding to him. Maggie, conscious that Stephen was still there, busied herself with counting money, and avoided looking up. She had been well pleased that he had devoted himself to Lucy today, and had not come near her. They had begun the morning with an indifferent salutation, and both had rejoiced in being aloof from each other, like a patient who has actually done without his opium, in spite of former failures in resolution. And during the last few days they had even been making up their minds to failures, looking to the outward events that must soon come to separate them, as a reason for dispensing with self-conquest in detail.

Stephen moved step by step as if he were being unwillingly dragged, until he had got round the open end of the stall, and was half hidden by a screen of draperies. Maggie went on counting her money till she suddenly heard a deep gentle voice saying, 'Aren't you very tired? Do let me bring you something – some fruit or jelly – mayn't I?'

The unexpected tones shook her like a sudden accidental vibration of a harp close by her.

'Oh, no, thank you,' she said, faintly, and only half looking up for an instant.

'You look so pale,' Stephen insisted, in a more entreating tone. 'I'm sure you're exhausted. I must disobey you, and bring something.'

'No, indeed, I couldn't take it.'

'Are you angry with me? What have I done? *Do* look at me.'

Pray, go away,' said Maggie, looking at him hopelessly, her eyes glancing immediately from him to the opposite corner of the orchestra, which was half hidden by the folds of the old faded green curtain. Maggie had no sooner uttered this entreaty than she was wretched at the admission it implied; but Stephen turned away at once, and, following her upward glance, he saw Philip Wakem seated in the half-hidden corner, so that he could command little more than that angle of the hall in which Maggie sat. An entirely new thought occurred to

Stephen, and, linking itself with what he had observed of Wakem's manner, and with Lucy's reply to his observation, it convinced him that there had been some former relation between Philip and Maggie beyond that childish one of which he had heard. More than one impulse made him immediately leave the hall and go upstairs to the refreshment-room, where, walking up to Philip, he sat down behind him, and put his hand on his shoulder.

'Are you studying for a portrait, Phil,' he said, 'or for a sketch of that oriel window? By George! it makes a capital bit from this dark corner, with the curtain just marking it off.'

'I have been studying expression,' said Philip, curtly.

'What! Miss Tulliver's? It's rather of the savage-moody order today, I think – something of the fallen princess serving behind a counter. Her cousin sent me to her with a civil offer to get her some refreshment, but I have been snubbed, as usual. There's a natural antipathy between us, I suppose: I have seldom the honour to please her.'

'What a hypocrite you are! said Philip, flushing angrily.

'What! because experience must have told me that I'm universally pleasing? I admit the law, but there's some disturbing force here.'

'I am going,' said Philip, rising abruptly.

'So am I – to get a breath of fresh air; this place gets oppressive. I think I have done suit and service long enough.'

The two friends walked downstairs together without speaking. Philip turned through the outer door into the courtyard, but Stephen, saying, 'Oh, by the by, I must call in here,' went on along the passage to one of the rooms at the other end of the building, which were appropriated to the town library. He had the room all to himself, and a man requires nothing less than this, when he wants to dash his cap on the table, throw himself astride a chair, and stare at a high brick wall with a frown which would not have been beneath the occasion if he had been slaying 'the giant Python.' The conduct that issues from a moral conflict has often so close a resemblance to vice, that the distinction escapes all outward judgements, rounded on a mere comparison of actions. It is clear to you, I hope, that Stephen was not a hypocrite – capable of deliberate doubleness for a selfish end; and yet his fluctuations between the indulgence of a feeling and the systematic concealment of it, might have made a good case in support of Philip's accusation.

Meanwhile, Maggie sat at her stall cold and trembling, with that painful sensation in the eyes which comes from resolutely repressed tears. Was her life to be always like this? – always bringing some new source of inward strife? She heard confusedly the busy indifferent voices around her, and wished her mind could flow into that easy, babbling current. It was at this moment that Dr Kenn, who had quite lately come into the hall, and was now walking down the middle with his hands behind him, taking a general view, fixed his eyes on Maggie for the first time, and was struck with the expression of pain on her beautiful face. She was sitting quite still, for the stream of customers had lessened at this late hour in the afternoon: the gentlemen had chiefly chosen the middle of the day, and Maggie's stall was looking rather bare. This, with her absent, pained expression, finished the contrast between her and her companions, who were all bright, eager, and busy. He was strongly arrested. Her face had naturally drawn his attention as a new and striking one at church, and he had been introduced to her during a short call on business at Mr Deane's, but he had never spoken more than three words to her. He walked towards her now, and Maggie, perceiving someone approaching, roused herself to look up and be prepared to speak. She felt a childlike, instinctive relief from the sense of uneasiness in this exertion, when she saw it was Dr Kenn's face that was looking at her: that plain, middle-aged face, with a grave, penetrating kindness in it, seeming to tell of a human being who had reached a firm, safe strand, but was looking with helpful pity towards the strugglers still tossed by the waves, had an effect on Maggie at this moment which was afterwards remembered by her as if it had been a promise. The middle-aged, who have lived through their strongest emotions, but are yet in the time when memory is still half passionate and not merely contemplative, should surely be a sort of natural priesthood, whom life has disciplined and consecrated to be the refuge and rescue of early stumblers and victims of self-despair. Most of us, at some moment in our young lives, would have welcomed a priest of that natural order in any sort of canonicals or uncanonicals, but had to scramble upwards into all the difficulties of nineteen entirely without such aid, as Maggie did.

'You find your office rather a fatiguing one, I fear, Miss Tulliver?' said Dr Kenn.

'It is, rather,' said Maggie, simply, not being accustomed to simper amiable denials of obvious facts.

'But I can tell Mrs Kenn that you have disposed of her goods very quickly,' he added; 'she will be very much obliged to you.'

'Oh, I have done nothing: the gentlemen came very fast to buy the dressing-gowns and embroidered waistcoats, but I think any of the other ladies would have sold more: I didn't know what to say about them.'

Dr Kenn smiled. 'I hope I'm going to have you as a permanent parishioner now, Miss Tulliver – am I? You have been at a distance from us hitherto.'

'I have been a teacher in a school, and I'm going into another situation of the same kind very soon.'

'Ah? I was hoping you would remain among your friends, who are all in this neighbourhood, I believe.'

'Oh, *I must go*,' said Maggie, earnestly, looking at Dr Kenn with an expression of reliance, as if she had told him her history in those three words. It was one of those moments of implicit revelation which will sometimes happen even between people who meet quite transiently – on a mile's journey, perhaps, or when resting by the wayside. There is always this possibility of a word or look from a stranger to keep alive the sense of human brotherhood.

Dr Kenn's ear and eye took in all the signs that this brief confidence of Maggie's was charged with meaning.

'I understand,' he said; 'you feel it right to go. But that will not prevent our meeting again, I hope: it will not prevent my knowing you better, if I can be of any service to you.'

He put out his hand and pressed hers kindly before he turned away.

'She has some trouble or other at heart,' he thought. 'Poor child! she looks as if she might turn out to be one of

> The souls by nature pitched too high,
> By suffering plunged too low.

There's something wonderfully honest in those beautiful eyes.'

It may be surprising that Maggie, among whose many imperfections an excessive delight in admiration and acknowledged supremacy were not absent now, any more than when she was instructing the gypsies with a view towards achieving a royal position among them, was not more elated on a day when she had had the tribute of so many looks and smiles, together with that satisfactory consciousness which had necessarily come from being taken before Lucy's cheval-glass, and made to look at the full length of her tall beauty, crowned by the night of her massy hair. Maggie had smiled at herself then, and for the moment had forgotten everything in the sense of her own beauty. If that state of mind could have lasted, her choice would have been to have Stephen Guest at her feet, offering her a life filled with all luxuries, with daily incense of adoration near and distant, and with all possibilities of culture at her command. But there were things in her stronger than vanity – passion, and affection, and long deep memories of early discipline and effort, of early claims on her love and pity; and the stream of vanity was soon swept along and mingled imperceptibly with that wider current which was at its highest force today, under the double urgency of the events and inward impulses brought by the last week.

Philip had not spoken to her himself about the removal of obstacles between them on his father's side – he shrank from that; but he had told everything to Lucy, with the hope that Maggie, being informed through her, might give him some encouraging sign that their being brought thus much nearer to each other was a happiness to her. The rush of conflicting feelings was too great for Maggie to say much when Lucy, with a face breathing playful joy, like one of Correggio's cherubs, poured forth her triumphant revelation; and Lucy could hardly be surprised that she could do little more than cry with gladness at the thought of her father's wish being fulfilled, and of Tom's getting the mill again in reward for all his hard striving. The details of preparation for the bazaar had then come to usurp Lucy's attention for the next few days, and nothing had been said by the cousins on subjects that were likely to rouse deeper feelings. Philip had been to the house more than once, but Maggie had had no private conversation with him, and thus she had been left to fight her inward battle without interference.

But when the bazaar was fairly ended, and the cousins were alone again, resting together at home, Lucy said, 'You must give up going to stay with your aunt Moss the day after tomorrow, Maggie: write a note to her, and tell her you have put it off at my request, and I'll send the man with it. She won't be displeased; you'll have plenty of time to go by and by; and I don't want you to go out of the way just now.'

'Yes, indeed I must go, dear; I can't put it off. I wouldn't leave aunt Gritty out for the world. And I shall have very little time, for I'm going away to a new situation on the 25th of June.'

'Maggie!' said Lucy, almost white with astonishment.

'I didn't tell you, dear,' said Maggie, making a great effort to command herself, 'because you've been so busy. But some time ago I wrote to our old governess, Miss Firniss, to ask her to let me know if she met with any situation that I could fill, and the other day I had a letter from her telling me that I could take three orphan pupils of hers to the coast during the holidays, and then make trial of a situation with her as teacher. I wrote yesterday to accept the offer.'

Lucy felt so hurt that for some moments she was unable to speak.

'Maggie,' she said at last, 'how could you be so unkind to me – not to tell me – to take *such* a step – and now!' She hesitated a little, and then added – 'And Philip? I thought everything was going to be so happy. Oh, Maggie – what is the reason? Give it up; let me write. There is nothing now to keep you and Philip apart.'

'Yes,' said Maggie, faintly. 'There is Tom's feeling. He said I must give him up if I married Philip. And I know he would not change – at least not for a long while – unless something happened to soften him.'

'But I will talk to him: he's coming back this week. And this good news about the mill will soften him. And I'll talk to him about Philip. Tom's always very compliant to me: I don't think he's so obstinate.'

'But I must go,' said Maggie, in a distressed voice. 'I must leave some time to pass. Don't press me to stay, dear Lucy.'

Lucy was silent for two or three minutes, looking away and ruminating. At length she knelt down by her cousin, and, looking up in her face with anxious seriousness, said, 'Maggie, is it that you don't love Philip well enough to marry him? – tell me – trust me.'

Maggie held Lucy's hands tightly in silence a little while. Her own hands were quite cold. But when she spoke, her voice was quite clear and distinct.

'Yes, Lucy, I would choose to marry him. I think it would be the best and highest lot for me – to make his life happy. He loved me first. No one else could be quite what he is to me. But I can't divide myself from my brother for life. I must go away, and wait. Pray, don't speak to me again about it.'

Lucy obeyed in pain and wonder. The next word she said was, 'Well, dear Maggie, at least you will go to the dance at Park House tomorrow, and have some music and brightness, before you go to pay these dull, dutiful visits. Ah! here come aunty and the tea.'

CHAPTER 10

The Spell Seems Broken

The suite of rooms opening into each other at Park House looked duly brilliant with lights and flowers and the personal splendours of sixteen couples, with attendant parents and guardians. The focus of brilliancy was the long drawing-room, where the dancing went forward, under the inspiration of the grand piano; the library, into which it opened at one end, had the more sober illumination of maturity, with caps and cards; and at the other end, the pretty sitting-room with a conservatory attached, was left as an occasional cool retreat. Lucy, who had laid aside her black for the first time, and had her pretty slimness set off by an abundant dress of white crape, was the acknowledged queen of the occasion; for this was one of the Miss Guests' thoroughly condescending parties, including no member of any aristocracy higher than that of St Ogg's, and stretching to the extreme limits of commercial and professional gentility.

Maggie at first refused to dance, saying that she had forgotten all the figures – it was so many years since she had danced at school; and she was glad to have that excuse, for it is ill dancing with a heavy heart. But at length the music wrought in her young limbs, and the longing came; even though it was the horrible young Torry, who walked up a second time to try and persuade her. She warned him that she could not dance anything but a country-dance; but he, of course, was willing to wait for that high felicity, meaning only to be complimentary when he assured her at several intervals that it was a 'great bore' that she couldn't waltz – he would have liked so much to waltz with her. But at last it was the turn of the good old-fashioned dance, which has the least of vanity and the most of merriment in it, and Maggie quite forgot her troublous life in a childlike enjoyment of that half-rustic rhythm which seems to banish pretentious etiquette. She felt quite charitably towards young Torry, as his hand bore her along and held her up in the dance; her eyes and cheeks had that fire of young joy in them which will flame out if it can find the least breath to fan it; and her simple black dress, with its bit of black lace, seemed like the dim setting of a jewel.

Stephen had not yet asked her to dance – had not yet paid her more than a passing civility. Since yesterday, that inward vision of her which perpetually made part of his consciousness, had been half-screened by the image of Philip Wakem, which came across it like a blot: there was some attachment between her and Philip; at least there was an attachment on his side which made her feel in some bondage. Here then, Stephen told himself, was another claim of honour which called on him to resist the attraction that was continually threatening to overpower him. He told himself so; and yet he had once or twice felt a certain savage resistance, and at another moment a shuddering repugnance, to this intrusion of Philip's image, which almost made it a new incitement to rush towards Maggie and claim her for himself. Nevertheless he had done what he meant to do this evening: he had kept aloof from her; he had hardly looked at her; and he had been gaily assiduous to Lucy. But now his eyes were devouring Maggie: he felt inclined to kick young Torry out of the dance, and take his place. Then he wanted the dance to end that he might get rid of his partner. The possibility that he too should dance with Maggie, and have her hand in his so long, was beginning to possess him like a thirst. But even now their hands were meeting in the dance – were meeting still to the very end of it, though they were far off each other.

Stephen hardly knew what happened, or in what automatic way he got through the duties of politeness in the interval, until he was free and saw Maggie seated alone again, at the farther end of the room. He made his way towards her round the couples that were forming for the waltz, and when Maggie became conscious that she was the person he sought, she felt, in spite of all the thoughts that had gone before, a glowing gladness at heart. Her eyes and cheeks were still brightened with her childlike enthusiasm in the dance; her whole frame was set to joy and tenderness; even the coming pain could not seem bitter – she was ready to welcome it as a part of life, for life at this moment seemed a keen vibrating consciousness poised above pleasure or pain. This one, this last night, she might expand unrestrainedly in the warmth of the present, without those chill eating thoughts of the past and the future.

'They're going to waltz again,' said Stephen, bending to speak to her, with that glance and tone of subdued tenderness which young dreams create to themselves in the summer woods when low cooing voices fill the air. Such glances and tones bring the breath of poetry with them into a room that is half-stifling with glaring gas and hard flirtation.

'They are going to waltz again: it is rather dizzy work to look on, and the room is very warm. Shall we walk about a little?'

He took her hand and placed it within his arm, and they walked on into the sitting-room, where the tables were strewn with engravings for the accommodation of visitors who would not want to look at them. But no visitors were here at this moment. They passed on into the conservatory.

'How strange and unreal the trees and flowers look with the lights among them,' said Maggie, in a low voice. 'They look as if they belonged to an enchanted land, and would never fade away – I could fancy they were all made of jewels.'

She was looking at the tier of geraniums as she spoke, and Stephen made no answer: but he was looking at her – and does not a supreme poet blend light and sound into one, calling darkness mute, and light eloquent? Something strangely powerful there was in the light of Stephen's long gaze, for it made Maggie's face turn towards it and look upwards at it – slowly, like a flower at the ascending brightness. And they walked unsteadily on, without feeling that they were walking – without feeling anything but that long grave mutual gaze which has the solemnity belonging to all deep human passion. The hovering thought that they must and would renounce each other made this moment of mute confession more intense in its rapture.

But they had reached the end of the conservatory, and were obliged to pause and turn. The change of movement brought a new consciousness to Maggie: she blushed deeply, turned away her head, and drew her arm from Stephen's, going up to some flowers to smell them. Stephen stood motionless, and still pale.

'Oh, may I get this rose?' said Maggie, making a great effort to say something, and dissipate the burning sense of irretrievable confession. 'I think I am quite wicked with roses – I like to gather them and smell them till they have no scent left.'

Stephen was mute; he was incapable of putting a sentence together, and Maggie bent her arm a little upward towards the large half-opened rose that had attracted her. Who has not felt the beauty of a woman's arm? – the unspeakable suggestions of tenderness that lie in the dimpled elbow, and all the varied gently-lessening curves down to the delicate wrist, with its tiniest, almost imperceptible nicks in the firm softness. A woman's arm touched the soul of a great sculptor two thousand years ago, so that he wrought an image of it for the Parthenon which moves us still as it clasps lovingly the time-worn marble of a headless trunk. Maggie's was such an arm as that – and it had the warm tints of life.

A mad impulse seized on Stephen; he darted towards the arm, and showered kisses on it, clasping the wrist.

But the next moment Maggie snatched it from him, and glared at him like a wounded war-goddess, quivering with rage and humiliation.

'How dare you?' – she spoke in a deeply-shaken, half-smothered voice. 'What right have I given you to insult me?'

She darted from him to the adjoining room, and threw herself on the sofa, panting and trembling.

A horrible punishment was come upon her for the sin of allowing a moment's happiness that was treachery to Lucy, to Philip – to her own better soul. That momentary happiness had been smitten with a blight – a leprosy: Stephen thought more lightly of *her* than he did of Lucy.

As for Stephen, he leaned back against the framework of the conservatory, dizzy with the conflict of passion – love, rage, and confused despair: despair at his want of self-mastery, and despair that he had offended Maggie.

The last feeling surmounted every other: to be by her side again and entreat forgiveness was the only thing that had the force of a motive for him, and she had not been seated more than a few minutes when he came and stood humbly before her. But Maggie's bitter rage was unspent.

'Leave me to myself, if you please,' she said, with impetuous haughtiness, 'and for the future avoid me.'

Stephen turned away, and walked backwards and forwards at the other end of the room. There was the dire necessity of going back into the dancing-room again, and he was beginning to be conscious of that. They had been absent so short a time, that when he went in again the waltz was not ended.

Maggie, too, was not long before she re-entered. All the pride of her nature was stung into activity: the hateful weakness which had dragged her within reach of this wound to her self-respect, had at least wrought its own cure. The thoughts and temptations of the last month should all be flung away into an unvisited chamber of memory: there was nothing to allure her now; duty would be easy, and all the old calm purposes would reign peacefully once more. She re-entered the drawing-room still with some excited brightness in her face, but with a sense of proud self-command that defied anything to agitate her. She refused to dance again, but she talked quite readily and calmly with everyone who addressed her. And when they got home that night, she kissed Lucy with a free heart, almost exulting in this scorching moment, which had delivered her from the possibility of another word or look that would have the stamp of treachery towards that gentle, unsuspicious sister.

The next morning Maggie did not set off to Basset quite so soon as she had expected. Her mother was to accompany her in the carriage, and household business could not be despatched hastily by Mrs Tulliver. So Maggie, who had been in a hurry to prepare herself, had to sit waiting, equipped for the drive, in the garden. Lucy was busy in the house wrapping up some bazaar presents for the younger ones at Basset, and when there was a loud ring at the door-bell, Maggie felt some alarm lest Lucy should bring out Stephen to her: it was sure to be Stephen.

But presently the visitor came out into the garden alone, and seated himself by her on the garden-chair. It was not Stephen.

'We can just catch the tips of the Scotch firs, Maggie, from this seat,' said Philip.

They had taken each other's hands in silence, but Maggie had looked at him with a more complete revival of the old childlike affectionate smile than he had seen before, and he felt encouraged.

'Yes,' she said, 'I often look at them, and wish I could see the low sunlight on the stems again. But I have never been that way but once – to the churchyard, with my mother.'

'I have been there – I go there – continually,' said Philip. 'I have nothing but the past to live upon.'

A keen remembrance and keen pity impelled Maggie to put her hand in Philip's. They had so often walked hand-in-hand!

'I remember all the spots,' she said – 'just where you told me of particular things – beautiful stories that I had never heard of before.'

'You will go there again soon – won't you, Maggie?' said Philip, getting timid. 'The mill will soon be your brother's home again.'

'Yes; but I shall not be there,' said Maggie. 'I shall only hear of that happiness. I am going away again – Lucy has not told you, perhaps?'

'Then the future will never join on to the past again, Maggie? That book is quite closed?'

The grey eyes that had so often looked up at her with entreating worship, looked up at her now, with a last struggling ray of hope in them, and Maggie met them with her large sincere gaze.

'That book never will be closed, Philip,' she said, with grave sadness; 'I desire no future that will break the ties of the past. But the tie to my brother is one of the strongest. I can do nothing willingly that will divide me always from him.'

'Is that the only reason that would keep us apart for ever, Maggie?' said Philip, with a desperate determination to have a definite answer.

'The only reason,' said Maggie, with calm decision. And she believed it. At that moment she felt as if the enchanted cup had been dashed to the ground. The reactionary excitement that gave her a proud self-mastery had not subsided, and she looked at the future with a sense of calm choice.

They sat hand-in-hand without looking at each other or speaking for a few minutes: in Maggie's mind the first scenes of love and parting were more present than the actual moment, and she was looking at Philip in the Red Deeps.

Philip felt that he ought to have been thoroughly happy in that answer of hers: she was as open and transparent as a rockpool. Why was he not thoroughly happy? Jealousy is never satisfied with anything short of an omniscience that would detect the subtlest fold of the heart.

CHAPTER 11

In the Lane

Maggie had been four days at her aunt Moss's, giving the early June sunshine quite a new brightness in the care-dimmed eyes of that affectionate woman, and making an epoch for her cousins great and small, who were learning her words and actions by heart, as if she had been a transient avatar of perfect wisdom and beauty.

She was standing on the causeway with her aunt and a group of cousins feeding the chickens, at that quiet moment in the life of the farmyard before the afternoon milking-time. The great buildings round the hollow yard were as dreary and tumbledown as ever, but over the garden-wall the straggling rose-bushes were beginning to toss their summer weight, and the grey wood and old bricks of the house, on its higher level, had a look of sleepy age in the broad afternoon sunlight, that suited the quiescent time. Maggie, with her bonnet over her arm, was smiling down at the hatch of small fluffy chickens, when her aunt exclaimed, 'Goodness me! who is that gentleman coming in at the gate?'

It was a gentleman on a tall bay horse; and the flanks and neck of the horse were streaked black with fast riding. Maggie felt a beating at head and heart – horrible as the sudden leaping to life of a savage enemy who had feigned death.

'Who is it, my dear?' said Mrs Moss, seeing in Maggie's face the evidence that she knew.

'It is Mr Stephen Guest,' said Maggie, rather faintly. 'My cousin Lucy's – a gentleman who is very intimate at my cousin's.'

Stephen was already close to them, had jumped off his horse, and now raised his hat as he advanced.

'Hold the horse, Willy,' said Mrs Moss to the twelve-year-old boy.

'No, thank you,' said Stephen, pulling at the horse's impatiently tossing head. 'I must be going again immediately. I have a message to deliver to you, Miss Tulliver – on private business. May I take the liberty of asking you to walk a few yards with me?'

He had a half-jaded, half-irritated look, such as a man gets when he has been dogged by some care or annoyance that makes his bed and his dinner of little use to him. He spoke almost abruptly, as if his errand were too pressing for him to trouble himself about what would be thought by Mrs Moss of his visit and request. Good Mrs Moss, rather nervous in the presence of this apparently haughty gentleman, was inwardly wondering whether she would be doing right or wrong to invite him again to leave his horse and walk in, when Maggie, feeling all the embarrassment of the situation, and unable to say anything, put on her bonnet, and turned to walk towards the gate.

Stephen turned too, and walked by her side, leading his horse.

Not a word was spoken till they were out in the lane, and had walked four or five yards, when Maggie, who had been looking straight before her all the while, turned again to walk back, saying, with haughty resentment, 'There is no need for me to go any farther. I don't know whether you consider it gentlemanly and delicate conduct to place me in a position that forced me to come out with you – or whether you wished to insult me still further by thrusting an interview upon me in this way.'

'Of course you are angry with me for coming,' said Stephen, bitterly. 'Of course it is of no consequence what a man has to suffer – it is only your woman's dignity that you care about.'

Maggie gave a slight start, such as might have come from the slightest possible electric shock.

'As if it were not enough that I'm entangled in this way – that I'm mad with love for you – that I resist the strongest passion a man can feel, because I try to be true to other claims – but you must treat me as if I were a coarse brute, who would willingly offend you. And when, if I had my own choice, I should ask you to take my hand, and my fortune, and my whole life, and do what you like with them! I know I forgot myself. I took an unwarrantable liberty. I hate myself for having done it. But I repented immediately – I've been repenting ever since. You ought not to think it unpardonable: a man who loves with his whole soul, as I do you, is liable to be mastered by his feelings for a moment; but you know – you must believe – that the worst pain I could have is to have pained you – that I would give the world to recall the error.'

Maggie dared not speak – dared not turn her head. The strength that had come from resentment was all gone, and her lips were quivering visibly. She could not trust herself to utter the full forgiveness that rose in answer to that confession.

They were come nearly in front of the gate again, and she paused, trembling.

'You must not say these things – I must not hear them,' she said, looking down in misery, as Stephen came in front of her, to prevent her from going farther towards the gate. 'I'm very sorry for any pain you have to go through; but it is of no use to speak.'

'Yes, it *is* of use,' said Stephen, impetuously. 'It would be of use if you would treat me with some sort of pity and consideration, instead of doing me vile injustice in your mind. I could bear everything more quietly if I knew you didn't hate me for an insolent coxcomb. Look at me – see what a hunted devil I am: I've been riding thirty miles every day to get away from the thought of you.'

Maggie did not – dared not look. She had already seen the harassed face. But she said, gently, 'I don't think any evil of you.'

'Then, dearest, look at me,' said Stephen, in deepest, tenderest tones of entreaty. 'Don't go away from me yet. Give me a moment's happiness – make me feel you've forgiven me.'

'Yes, I do forgive you,' said Maggie, shaken by those tones, and all the more frightened at herself. 'But pray let me go in again. Pray go away.'

A great tear fell from under her lowered eyelids.

'I can't go away from you – I can't leave you,' said Stephen, with still more passionate pleading. 'I shall come back again if you send me away with this coldness – I can't answer for myself. But if you will go with me only a little way,

I can live on that. You see plainly enough that your anger has only made me ten times more unreasonable.'

Maggie turned. But Tancred, the bay horse, began to make such spirited remonstrances against this frequent change of direction, that Stephen, catching sight of Willy Moss peeping through the gate, called out, 'Here! just come and hold my horse for five minutes.'

'Oh, no,' said Maggie, hurriedly, 'my aunt will think it so strange.'

'Never mind,' Stephen answered, impatiently; 'they don't know the people at St Ogg's. Lead him up and down just here, for five minutes,' he added to Willy, who was now close to them; and then he turned to Maggie's side, and they walked on. It was clear that she *must* go on now.

'Take my arm,' said Stephen, entreatingly; and she took it, feeling all the while as if she were sliding downwards in a nightmare.

'There is no end to this misery,' she began, struggling to repel the influence by speech. 'It is wicked – base – ever allowing a word or look that Lucy – that others might not have seen. Think of Lucy.'

'I do think of her – bless her. If I didn't – ' Stephen had laid his hand on Maggie's that rested on his arm, and they both felt it difficult to speak.

'And I have other ties,' Maggie went on, at last, with a desperate effort, 'even if Lucy did not exist.'

'You are engaged to Philip Wakem?' said Stephen, hastily. 'Is it so?'

'I consider myself engaged to him – I don't mean to marry anyone else.'

Stephen was silent again until they had turned out of the sun into a side lane, all grassy and sheltered. Then he burst out impetuously, 'It is unnatural – it is horrible. Maggie, if you loved me as I love you, we should throw everything else to the winds for the sake of belonging to each other. We should break all these mistaken ties that were made in blindness, and determine to marry each other.'

'I would rather die than fall into that temptation,' said Maggie, with deep, slow distinctness – all the gathered spiritual force of painful years coming to her aid in this extremity. She drew her arm from his as she spoke.

'Tell me, then, that you don't care for me,' he said, almost violently. 'Tell me that you love someone else better.'

It darted through Maggie's mind that here was a mode of releasing herself from outward struggle – to tell Stephen that her whole heart was Philip's. But her lips would not utter that, and she was silent.

'If you do love me, dearest,' said Stephen, gently, taking up her hand again and laying it within his arm, 'it is better – it is right that we should marry each other. We can't help the pain it will give. It is come upon us without our seeking: it is natural – it has taken hold of me in spite of every effort I have made to resist it. God knows, I've been trying to be faithful to tacit engagements, and I've only made things worse – I'd better have given way at first.'

Maggie was silent. If it were *not* wrong – if she were once convinced of that, and need no longer beat and struggle against this current, soft and yet strong as the summer stream!

'Say "Yes," dearest,' said Stephen, leaning to look entreatingly in her face. 'What could we care about in the whole world beside, if we belong to each other?'

Her breath was on his face – his lips were very near hers – but there was a great dread dwelling in his love for her.

Her lips and eyelids quivered; she opened her eyes full on his for an instant, like a lovely wild animal timid and struggling under caresses, and then turned sharp round towards home again.

'And after all,' he went on, in an impatient tone, trying to defeat his own scruples as well as hers, 'I am breaking no positive engagement: if Lucy's affections had been withdrawn from me and given to someone else, I should have felt no right to assert a claim on her. If you are not absolutely pledged to Philip, we are neither of us bound.'

'You don't believe that – it is not your real feeling,' said Maggie, earnestly. 'You feel, as I do, that the real tie lies in the feelings and expectations we have raised in other minds. Else all pledges might be broken, when there was no outward penalty. There would be no such thing as faithfulness.'

Stephen was silent: he could not pursue that argument; the opposite conviction had wrought in him too strongly through his previous time of struggle. But it soon presented itself in a new form.

'The pledge *can't* be fulfilled,' he said, with impetuous insistence. 'It is unnatural: we can only pretend to give ourselves to anyone else. There is wrong in that too – there may be misery in it for *them* as well as for us. Maggie, you must see that – you do see that.'

He was looking eagerly at her face for the least sign of compliance; his large, firm, gentle grasp was on her hand. She was silent for a few moments, with her eyes fixed on the ground; then she drew a deep breath, and, said looking up at him with solemn sadness, 'Oh, it is difficult – life is very difficult! It seems right to me sometimes that we should follow our strongest feeling; but then, such feelings continually come across the ties that all our former life has made for us – the ties that have made others dependent on us – and would cut them in two. If life were quite easy and simple, as it might have been in Paradise, and we could always see that one being first towards whom . . . I mean, if life did not make duties for us before love comes – love would be a sign that two people ought to belong to each other. But I see – I feel it is not so now: there are things we must renounce in life; some of us must resign love. Many things are difficult and dark to me; but I see one thing quite clearly – that I must not, cannot, seek my own happiness by sacrificing others. Love is natural; but surely pity and faithfulness and memory are natural too. And they would live in me still, and punish me if I did not obey them. I should be haunted by the suffering I had caused. Our love would be poisoned. Don't urge me; help me – help me, *because* I love you.'

Maggie had become more and more earnest as she went on; her face had become flushed, and her eyes fuller and fuller of appealing love. Stephen had the fibre of nobleness in him that vibrated to her appeal: but in the same moment – how could it be otherwise? – that pleading beauty gained new power over him.

'Dearest,' he said, in scarcely more than a whisper, while his arm stole round her, 'I'll do, I'll bear anything you wish. But – one kiss – one – the last – before we part.'

One kiss – and then a long look – until Maggie said tremulously, 'Let me go – let us make haste back.'

She hurried along, and not another word was spoken. Stephen stood still and beckoned when they came within sight of Willy and the horse, and Maggie went on through the gate. Mrs Moss was standing alone at the door of the old porch: she had sent all the cousins in, with kind thoughtfulness. It might be a joyful thing that Maggie had a rich and handsome lover, but she would naturally feel embarrassed at coming in again: – and it might *not* be joyful. In either case, Mrs Moss waited anxiously to receive Maggie by herself. The speaking face told plainly enough that, if there was joy, it was of a very agitating, dubious sort.

'Sit down here a bit, my dear.' She drew Maggie into the porch, and sat down on the bench by her: there was no privacy in the house.

'Oh, Aunt Gritty, I'm very wretched. I wish I could have died when I was fifteen. It seemed so easy to give things up then – it is so hard now.'

The poor child threw her arms round her aunt's neck, and fell into long, deep sobs.

CHAPTER 12

A Family Party

Maggie left her good aunt Gritty at the end of the week, and went to Garum Firs to pay her visit to aunt Pullet according to agreement. In the meantime very unexpected things had happened, and there was to be a family party at Garum to discuss and celebrate a change in the fortunes of the Tullivers, which was likely finally to carry away the shadow of their demerits like the last limb of an eclipse, and cause their hitherto obscured virtues to shine forth in full-rounded splendour. It is pleasant to know that a new ministry just come into office are not the only fellow-men who enjoy a period of high appreciation and full-blown eulogy: in many respectable families throughout this realm, relatives becoming creditable meet with a similar cordiality of recognition, which, in its fine freedom from the coercion of any antecedents, suggests the hopeful possibility that we may someday without any notice find ourselves in full millennium, with cockatrices who have ceased to bite, and wolves that no longer show their teeth with any but the blandest intentions.

Lucy came so early as to have the start even of aunt Glegg; for she longed to have some undisturbed talk with Maggie about the wonderful news. It seemed – did it not? said Lucy, with her prettiest air of wisdom – as if everything, even other people's misfortunes (poor creatures!) were conspiring now to make poor dear aunt Tulliver, and cousin Tom, and naughty Maggie too, if she were not obstinately bent on the contrary, as happy as they deserved to be after all their troubles. To think that the very day – the *very day* – after Tom had come back from Newcastle, that unfortunate young Jetsome, whom Mr Wakem had placed at the mill, had been pitched off his horse in a drunken fit, and was lying at St Ogg's in a dangerous state, so that Wakem had signified his wish that the new purchasers should enter on the premises at once! It was very dreadful for that unhappy young man, but it did seem as if the misfortune had happened then, rather than at any other time, in order that cousin Tom might all the sooner have the fit reward of his exemplary conduct – papa thought so very highly of him. Aunt Tulliver must certainly go to the mill now, and keep house for Tom: that was rather a loss to Lucy in the matter of household comfort; but then, to think of poor aunty being in her old place again, and gradually getting comforts about her there!

On this last point Lucy had her cunning projects, and when she and Maggie had made their dangerous way down the bright stairs into the handsome parlour, where the very sunbeams seemed cleaner than elsewhere, she directed her manoeuvres, as any other great tactician would have done, against the weaker side of the enemy.

'Aunt Pullet,' she said, seating herself on the sofa, and caressingly adjusting that lady's floating cap-string, 'I want you to make up your mind what linen and things you will give Tom towards housekeeping; because you're always so generous – you give such nice things, you know; and if you set the example, aunt Glegg will follow.'

'That she niver can, my dear,' said Mrs Pullet, with unusual vigour, 'for she hasn't got the linen to follow suit wi' mine, I can tell you. She'd niver the taste, not if she'd spend the money. Big checks and live things, like stags and foxes, all her table-linen is – not a spot nor a diamont among 'em. But it's poor work, dividing one's linen before one dies – I niver thought to ha' done that, Bessy,' Mrs Pullet continued, shaking her head and looking at her sister Tulliver, 'when you and me chose the double diamont, the first flax iver we'd spun – and the Lord knows where yours is gone.'

'I'd no choice, I'm sure, sister,' said poor Mrs Tulliver, accustomed to consider herself in the light of an accused person. 'I'm sure it was no wish o' mine, iver, as I should lie awake o' nights thinking o' my best bleached linen all over the country.'

'Take a peppermint, Mrs Tulliver,' said uncle Pullet, feeling that he was offering a cheap and wholesome form of comfort, which he was recommending by example.

'Oh, but, aunt Pullet,' said Lucy, 'you've so much beautiful linen. And suppose you had had daughters! Then you must have divided it, when they were married.'

'Well, I don't say as I won't do it,' said Mrs Pullet, 'for now Tom's so lucky, it's nothing but right his friends should look on him and help him. There's the tablecloths I bought at your sale, Bessy; it was nothing but good natur' o' me to buy 'em, for they've been lying in the chest ever since. But I'm not going to give Maggie any more o' my Indy muslin and things, if she's to go into service again, when she might stay and keep me company, and do my sewing for me, if she wasn't wanted at her brother's.'

'Going into service,' was the expression by which the Dodson mind represented to itself the position of teacher or governess, and Maggie's return to that menial condition, now circumstances offered her more eligible prospects, was likely to be a sore point with all her relatives, besides Lucy. Maggie in her crude form, with her hair down her back, and altogether in a state of dubious promise, was a most undesirable niece; but now she was capable of being at once ornamental and useful. The subject was revived in aunt and uncle Glegg's presence, over the tea and muffins.

'Hegh, hegh!' said Mr Glegg, good-naturedly patting Maggie on the back, 'nonsense, nonsense! Don't let us hear of you taking a place again, Maggie. Why, you must ha' picked up half a dozen sweethearts at the bazaar: isn't there one of 'em the right sort of article? Come, now?'

'Mr Glegg,' said his wife, with that shade of increased politeness in her severity which she always put on with her crisper fronts, 'you'll excuse me, but you're far too light for a man of your years. It's respect and duty to her aunts, and the rest of her kin as are so good to her, should have kept my niece from fixing about going away again without consulting us – not sweethearts, if I'm to use such a word, though it was never heard in *my* family.'

'Why, what did they call us, when we went to see 'em, then, eh, neighbour Pullet? They thought us sweet enough then,' said Mr Glegg, winking pleasantly, while Mr Pullet, at the suggestion of sweetness, took a little more sugar.

'Mr Glegg,' said Mrs G., 'if you're going to be undelicate, let me know.'

'La, Jane, your husband's only joking,' said Mrs Pullet; 'let him joke while he's got health and strength. There's poor Mr Tilt got his mouth drawn all o' one side, and couldn't laugh if he was to try.'

'I'll trouble you for the muffineer, then, Mr Glegg,' said Mrs G., 'if I may be so bold to interrupt your joking. Though it's other people must see the joke in a niece's putting a slight on her mother's eldest sister, as is the head o' the family; and only coming in and out on short visits, all the time she's been in the town, and then settling to go away without my knowledge – as I'd laid caps out on purpose for her to make 'em up for me, and me as have divided my money so equal – '

'Sister,' Mrs Tulliver broke in, anxiously, 'I'm sure Maggie never thought o' going away without staying at your house as well as the others. Not as it's my wish she should go away at all – but quite contrairy. I'm sure I'm innocent. I've said over and over again, "My dear, you've no call to go away." But there's ten days or a fortnight Maggie 'll have before she's fixed to go: she can stay at your house just as well, and I'll step in when I can, and so will Lucy.'

'Bessy,' said Mrs Glegg, 'if you'd exercise a little more thought, you might know I should hardly think it was worth while to unpin a bed, and go to all that trouble now, just at the end o' the time, when our house isn't above a quarter of an hour's walk from Mr Deane's. She can come the first thing in the morning, and go back the last at night, and be thankful she's got a good aunt so close to her to come and sit with. I know I should, when I was her age.'

'La, Jane,' said Mrs Pullet, 'it 'ud do your beds good to have somebody to sleep in 'em. There's that striped room smells dreadful mouldy, and the glass mildewed like anything. I'm sure I thought I should be struck with death when you took me in.'

'Oh, there is Tom!' exclaimed Lucy, clapping her hands. 'He's come on Sindbad, as I told him. I was afraid he was not going to keep his promise.'

Maggie jumped up to kiss Tom as he entered, with strong feeling, at this first meeting since the prospect of returning to the mill had been opened to him; and she kept his hand, leading him to the chair by her side. To have no cloud between herself and Tom was still a perpetual yearning in her, that had its root deeper than all change. He smiled at her very kindly this evening, and said, 'Well, Magsie, how's aunt Moss?'

'Come, come, sir,' said Mr Glegg, putting out his hand. 'Why, you're such a big man, you carry all before you, it seems. You're come into your luck a good deal earlier than us old folks did – but I wish you joy, I wish you joy. You'll get the mill all for your own again, someday, I'll be bound. You won't stop halfway up the hill.'

'But I hope he'll bear in mind as it's his mother's family as he owes it to,' said Mrs Glegg. 'If he hadn't had them to take after, he'd ha' been poorly off. There was never failures, nor lawing, nor wastefulness in our family – nor dying without wills – '

'No, nor sudden deaths,' said aunt Pullet: 'allays the doctor called in. But Tom had the Dodson skin: I said that from the first. And I don't know what *you* mean to do, sister Glegg, but I mean to give him a tablecloth of all my three biggest sizes but one, besides sheets. I don't say what more I shall do; but *that* I shall do, and if I should die tomorrow, Mr Pullet, you'll bear it in mind – though you'll be blundering with the keys, and never remember as that on the third shelf o' the left-hand wardrobe, behind the nightcaps with the broad ties – not the narrow-frilled uns – is the key o' the drawer in the Blue Room, where the key o' the Blue Closet is. You'll make a mistake, and I shall niver be worthy to know it. You've a memory for my pills and draughts, wonderful – I'll allays say that of you – but you're lost among the keys.' This gloomy prospect of the confusion that would ensue on her decease, was very affecting to Mrs Pullet.

'You carry it too far, Sophy – that locking in and out,' said Mrs Glegg, in a tone of some disgust at this folly. 'You go beyond your own family. There's nobody can say I don't lock up; but I do what's reasonable, and no more. And as for the linen, I shall look out what's serviceable, to make a present of to my nephey: I've got cloth as has never been whitened, better worth having than other people's fine holland; and I hope he'll lie down in it and think of his aunt.'

Tom thanked Mrs Glegg, but evaded any promise to meditate nightly on her virtues; and Mr Glegg effected a diversion for him by asking about Mr Deane's intentions concerning steam.

Lucy had had her far-sighted views in begging Tom to come on Sindbad. It appeared, when it was time to go home, that the manservant was to ride the horse, and cousin Tom was to drive home his mother and Lucy. 'You must sit by yourself, aunty,' said that contriving young lady, 'because I must sit by Tom; I've a great deal to say to him.'

In the eagerness of her affectionate anxiety for Maggie, Lucy could not persuade herself to defer a conversation about her with Tom, who, she thought, with such a cup of joy before him as this rapid fulfilment of his wish about the mill, must become pliant and flexible. Her nature supplied her with no key to Tom's; and she was puzzled as well as pained to notice the unpleasant change on his countenance when she gave the history of the way in which Philip had used his influence with his father. She had counted on this revelation as a great stroke of policy, which was to turn Tom's heart towards Philip at once, and, besides that, prove that the elder Wakem was ready to receive Maggie with all the honours of a daughter-in-law. Nothing was wanted, then, but for dear Tom, who always had that pleasant smile when he looked at cousin Lucy, to turn completely round, say the opposite of what he had always said before, and declare that he, for his part, was delighted that all the old grievances should be healed, and that Maggie should have Philip with all suitable despatch: in cousin Lucy's opinion nothing could be easier.

But to minds strongly marked by the positive and negative qualities that create severity – strength of will, conscious rectitude of purpose, narrowness of imagination and intellect, great power of self-control, and a disposition to exert control over others – prejudices come as the natural food of tendencies which can get no sustenance out of that complex, fragmentary, doubt-provoking knowledge which we call truth. Let a prejudice be bequeathed, carried in the air, adopted by hearsay, caught in through the eye – however it may come, these minds will give it a habitation: it is something to assert strongly and bravely, something to fill up the void of spontaneous ideas, something to impose on others with the authority of conscious right: it is at once a staff and a baton. Every prejudice that will answer these purposes is self-evident. Our good upright Tom Tulliver's mind was of this class: his inward criticism of his father's faults did not prevent him from adopting his father's prejudice; it was a prejudice against a man of lax principle and lax life, and it was a meeting-point for all the disappointed feelings of family and personal pride. Other feelings added their force to produce Tom's bitter repugnance to Philip, and to Maggie's union with him; and notwithstanding Lucy's power over her strong-willed cousin, she got nothing but a cold refusal ever to sanction such a marriage: 'but of course Maggie could do as she liked – she had declared her determination to be independent.' For Tom's part, he held himself bound by his duty to his father's memory, and by every manly feeling, never to consent to any relation with the Wakems.

Thus, all that Lucy had effected by her zealous mediation was to fill Tom's mind with the expectation that Maggie's perverse resolve to go into a situation again, would presently metamorphose itself, as her resolves were apt to do, into something equally perverse, but entirely different – a marriage with Philip Wakem.

CHAPTER 13

Borne Along by the Tide

In less than a week Maggie was at St Ogg's again – outwardly in much the same position as when her visit there had just begun. It was easy for her to fill her mornings apart from Lucy without any obvious effort; for she had her promised visits to pay to her aunt Glegg, and it was natural that she should give her mother more than usual of her companionship in these last weeks, especially as there were preparations to be thought of for Tom's housekeeping. But Lucy would hear of no pretext for her remaining away in the evenings: she must always come from aunt Glegg's before dinner – 'Else what shall I have of you?' said Lucy, with a tearful pout that could not be resisted. And Mr Stephen Guest had unaccountably taken to dining at Mr Deane's as often as possible, instead of avoiding that, as he used to do. At first he began his mornings with a resolution that he would not dine there – not even go in the evening, till Maggie was away. He had even devised a plan of starting off on a journey in this agreeable June weather: the headaches which he had constantly been alleging as a ground for stupidity and silence were a sufficient ostensible motive. But the journey was not taken, and by the fourth morning no distinct resolution was formed about the evenings: they were only foreseen as times when Maggie would still be present for a little while – when one more touch, one more glance, might be snatched. For, why not? There was nothing to conceal between them: they knew – they had confessed their love, and they had renounced each other: they were going to part. Honour and conscience were going to divide them: Maggie, with that appeal from her inmost soul, had decided it; but surely they might cast a lingering look at each other across the gulf, before they turned away never to look again till that strange light had for ever faded out of their eyes.

Maggie, all this time, moved about with a quiescence and even torpor of manner, so contrasted with her usual fitful brightness and ardour, that Lucy would have had to seek some other cause for such a change, if she had not been convinced that the position in which Maggie stood between Philip and her brother, and the prospect of her self-imposed wearisome banishment, were quite enough to account for a large amount of depression. But under this torpor there was a fierce battle of emotions, such as Maggie in all her life of struggle had never known or foreboded: it seemed to her as if all the worst evil in her had lain in ambush till now, and had suddenly started up full-armed, with hideous, overpowering strength! There were moments in which a cruel selfish-ness seemed to be getting possession of her; why should not Lucy – why should not Philip suffer? *She* had had to suffer through many years of her life; and who had renounced anything for her? And when something like that fullness of existence – love, wealth, ease, refinement, all that her nature craved – was brought within her reach, why was she to forego it, that another might have it – another, who perhaps needed it less? But amidst all this new passionate tumult there were the old voices making themselves heard with rising power, till, from time to time, the tumult seemed quelled. Was that existence which tempted her the full existence she dreamed? Where, then, would be all the memories of early striving – all the deep pity for another's pain, which had been nurtured in her through years of affection and hardship – all the divine presentiment of something higher than mere personal enjoyment, which had made the sacredness of life? She might as well hope to enjoy walking by maiming her feet, as hope to enjoy an existence in which she set out by maiming the faith and sympathy that were the best organs of her soul. And then, if pain were so hard to *her*, what was it to others? – 'Ah, God! preserve me from inflicting – give me strength to bear it.' – How had she sunk into this struggle with a temptation that she would once have thought herself as secure from, as from deliberate crime? When was that first hateful moment in which she had been conscious of a feeling that clashed with her truth, affection, and gratitude, and had not shaken it from her with horror, as if it had been a loathsome thing? – And yet, since this strange, sweet, subduing influence did not, should not, conquer her – since it was to remain simply her own suffering . . . her mind was meeting Stephen's in that thought of his, that they might still snatch moments of mute confession before the parting came. For was not he suffering too? She saw it daily – saw it in the sickened look of fatigue with which, as soon as he was not compelled to exert himself, he relapsed into indifference towards everything but the possibility of watching her. Could she refuse sometimes to answer that beseeching look which she felt to be following her like a low murmur of love and pain? She refused it less and less, till at last the evening for them both was sometimes made of a moment's mutual gaze: they thought of it till it came, and when it had come, they thought of nothing else. One other thing Stephen seemed now and then to care for, and that was, to sing: it was a way of speaking to Maggie. Perhaps he was not distinctly conscious that he was impelled to it by a secret longing – running counter to all his self-confessed resolves – to deepen the hold he had on her. Watch your own speech, and notice how it is guided by your less conscious purposes, and you will understand that contradiction in Stephen.

Philip Wakem was a less frequent visitor, but he came occasionally in the evening, and it happened that he was there when Lucy said, as they sat out on the lawn, near sunset, 'Now Maggie's tale of visits to aunt Glegg is completed, I mean that we shall go out boating every day until she goes. She has not had half enough boating, because of these tiresome visits, and she likes it better than anything. Don't you, Maggie?'

'Better than any sort of locomotion, I hope you mean,' said Philip, smiling at Maggie, who was lolling backward in a low garden-chair, 'else she will be selling her soul to that ghostly boatman who haunts the Floss – only for the sake of being drifted in a boat for ever.'

'Should you like to be her boatman?' said Lucy. 'Because, if you would, you can come with us and take an oar. If the Floss were but a quiet lake instead of a river, we should be independent of any gentleman, for Maggie can row splendidly. As it is, we are reduced to ask services of knights and squires, who do not seem to offer them with great alacrity.'

She looked playful reproach at Stephen, who was sauntering up and down, and was just singing in pianissimo falsetto –

> 'The thirst that from the soul doth rise,
> Doth ask a drink divine.'

He took no notice, but still kept aloof: he had done so frequently during Philip's recent visits.

'You don't seem inclined for boating,' said Lucy, when he came to sit down by her on the bench. 'Doesn't rowing suit you now?'

'Oh, I hate a large party in a boat,' he said, almost irritably, 'I'll come when you have no one else.'

Lucy coloured, fearing that Philip would be hurt: it was quite a new thing for Stephen to speak in that way; but he had certainly not been well of late. Philip coloured too, but less from a feeling of personal offence than from a vague suspicion that Stephen's moodiness had some relation to Maggie, who had started up from her chair as he spoke, and had walked towards the hedge of laurels to look at the descending sunlight on the river.

'As Miss Deane didn't know she was excluding others by inviting me,' said Philip, 'I am bound to resign.'

'No, indeed, you shall not,' said Lucy, much vexed. 'I particularly wish for your company tomorrow. The tide will suit at half-past ten: it will be a delicious time for a couple of hours to row to Luckreth and walk back, before the sun gets too hot. And how can you object to four people in a boat?' she added, looking at Stephen.

'I don't object to the people, but the number,' said Stephen, who had recovered himself, and was rather ashamed of his rudeness. 'If I voted for a fourth at all, of course it would be you, Phil. But we won't divide the pleasure of escorting the ladies; we'll take it alternately. I'll go the next day.'

This incident had the effect of drawing Philip's attention with freshened solicitude towards Stephen and Maggie; but when they re-entered the house, music was proposed, and Mrs Tulliver and Mr Deane being occupied with cribbage, Maggie sat apart near the table where the books and work were placed – doing nothing, however, but listening abstractedly to the music. Stephen presently turned to a duet which he insisted that Lucy and Philip should sing: he had often done the same thing before; but this evening Philip thought he divined some double intention in every word and look of Stephen's, and watched him keenly – angry with himself all the while for this clinging suspicion. For had not Maggie virtually denied any ground for his doubts on her side? and she was truth itself: it was impossible not to believe her word and glance when they had last spoken together in the garden. Stephen might be strongly fascinated by her (what was more natural?), but Philip felt himself rather base for intruding on what must be his friend's painful secret. Still, he watched. Stephen, moving away from the piano, sauntered slowly towards the table near which Maggie sat, and turned over the newspapers, apparently in mere idleness. Then he seated himself with his back to the piano, dragging a newspaper under his elbow, and thrusting his hand through his hair, as if he had been attracted by some bit of local news in the *Laceham Courier*. He was in reality looking at Maggie, who had not taken the slightest notice of his approach. She had always additional strength of resistance when Philip was present, just as we can restrain our speech better in a spot that we feel to be hallowed. But at last she heard the word 'dearest' uttered in the softest tone of pained entreaty, like that of a patient who asks for something that ought to have been given without asking. She had never heard that word since the moments in the lane at Basset, when it had come from Stephen again and again, almost as involuntarily as if it had been an inarticulate cry. Philip could hear no word, but he had moved to the opposite side of the piano, and could see Maggie start and blush, raise her eyes an instant towards Stephen's face, but immediately look apprehensively towards himself. It was not evident to her that Philip had observed her; but a pang of shame, under the sense of this concealment, made her move from her chair and walk to her mother's side to watch the game at cribbage.

Philip went home soon after in a state of hideous doubt mingled with wretched certainty. It was impossible for him now to resist the conviction that there was some mutual consciousness between Stephen and Maggie; and for half the night his irritable, susceptible nerves were pressed upon almost to frenzy by that one wretched fact: he could attempt no explanation that would reconcile it with her words and actions. When, at last, the need for belief in Maggie rose to its habitual predominance, he was not long in imagining the truth: – she was struggling, she was banishing herself – this was the clue to all he had seen since his return. But athwart that belief there came other possibilities that would not be driven out of sight. His imagination wrought out the whole story: Stephen was madly in love with her; he must have told her so; she had rejected him, and was hurrying away. But would he give her up, knowing – Philip felt the fact with heart-crushing despair – that she was made half helpless by her feeling towards him?

When the morning came, Philip was too ill to think of keeping his engagement to go in the boat. In his present agitation he could decide on nothing: he could only alternate between contradictory intentions. First, he thought he must have an interview with Maggie, and entreat her to confide in him; then again, he distrusted his own interference. Had he not been thrusting himself on Maggie all along? She had uttered words long ago in her young ignorance; it was enough to make her hate him that these should be continually present with her as a bond. And had he any right to ask her for a revelation of feelings which she had evidently intended to withhold from him? He would not trust himself to see her, till he had assured himself that he could act from pure anxiety for her, and not from egoistic irritation. He wrote a brief note to Stephen, and sent it early by the servant, saying that he was not well enough to fulfil his engagement to Miss Deane. Would Stephen take his excuse, and fill his place?

Lucy had arranged a charming plan, which had made her quite content with Stephen's refusal to go in the boat. She discovered that her father was to drive to Lindum this morning at ten: Lindum was the very place she wanted to go to, to make purchases – important purchases, which must by no means be put off to another opportunity; and aunt Tulliver must go too, because she was concerned in some of the purchases.

'You will have your row in the boat just the same, you know,' she said to Maggie when they went out of the breakfast-room and upstairs together; 'Philip will be here at half-past ten, and it is a delicious morning. Now, don't say a word against it, you dear dolorous thing. What is the use of my being a fairy godmother, if you set your face against all the wonders I work for you? Don't think of awful cousin Tom: you may disobey him a little.'

Maggie did not persist in objecting. She was almost glad of the plan; for perhaps it would bring her some strength and calmness to be alone with Philip again: it was like revisiting the scene of a quieter life, in which the very struggles were repose, compared with the daily tumult of the present. She prepared herself for the boat, and at haft-past ten sat waiting in the drawing-room.

The ring of the door-bell was punctual, and she was thinking with half-sad, affectionate pleasure of the surprise Philip would have in finding that he was to be with her alone, when she distinguished a firm rapid step across the hall, that was certainly not Philip's: the door opened, and Stephen Guest entered.

In the first moment they were both too much agitated to speak; for Stephen had learned from the servant that the others were gone out. Maggie had started up and sat down again, with her heart beating violently; and Stephen, throwing down his cap and gloves, came and sat by her in silence. She thought Philip would be coming soon; and with great effort – for she trembled visibly – she rose to go to a distant chair.

'He is not coming,' said Stephen, in a low tone. '*I* am going in the boat.'

'Oh, we can't go,' said Maggie, sinking into her chair again. 'Lucy did not expect – she would be hurt. Why is not Philip come?'

'He is not well; he asked me to come instead.'

'Lucy is gone to Lindum,' said Maggie, taking off her bonnet, with hurried, trembling fingers. 'We must not go.'

'Very well,' said Stephen, dreamily, looking at her, as he rested his arm on the back of his chair. 'Then we'll stay here.'

He was looking into her deep, deep eyes – far-off and mysterious as the starlit blackness, and yet very near, and timidly loving. Maggie sat perfectly still – perhaps for moments, perhaps for minutes – until the helpless trembling had ceased, and there was a warm glow on her cheek.

'The man is waiting – he has taken the cushions,' she said. 'Will you go and tell him?'

'What shall I tell him?' said Stephen, almost in a whisper. He was looking at the lips now.

Maggie made no answer.

'Let us go,' Stephen murmured, entreatingly, rising, and taking her hand to raise her too. 'We shall not be long together.'

And they went. Maggie felt that she was being led down the garden among the roses, being helped with firm tender care into the boat, having the cushion and cloak arranged for her feet, and her parasol opened for her (which she had forgotten) – all by this stronger presence that seemed to bear her along without any act of her own will, like the added self which comes with the sudden exalting influence of a strong tonic – and she felt nothing else. Memory was excluded.

They glided rapidly along, Stephen rowing, helped by the backward-flowing tide, past the Tofton trees and houses – on between the silent sunny fields and pastures, which seemed filled with a natural joy that had no reproach for theirs. The breath of the young, unwearied day, the delicious rhythmic dip of the oars, the fragmentary song of a passing bird heard now and then, as if it were only the overflowing of brim-full gladness, the sweet solitude of a twofold consciousness that was mingled into one by that grave untiring gaze which need not be averted – what else could there be in their minds for the first hour? Some low, subdued, languid exclamation of love came from Stephen from time to time, as he went on rowing idly, half automatically: otherwise, they spoke no word; for what could words have been but an inlet to thought? and thought did not belong to that enchanted haze in which they were enveloped – it belonged to the past and the future that lay outside the haze. Maggie was only dimly conscious of the banks, as they passed them, and dwelt with no recognition on the villages: she knew there were several to be passed before they reached Luckreth, where they always stopped and left the boat. At all times she was so liable to fits of absence, that she was likely enough to let her way-marks pass unnoticed.

But at last Stephen, who had been rowing more and more idly, ceased to row, laid down the oars, folded his arms, and looked down on the water as if watching the pace at which the boat glided without his help. This sudden change roused Maggie. She looked at the far-stretching fields – at the banks close by – and felt that they were entirely strange to her. A terrible alarm took possession of her.

'Oh, have we passed Luckreth – where we were to stop?' she exclaimed, looking back to see if the place were out of sight. No village was to be seen. She turned round again, with a look of distressed questioning at Stephen.

He went on watching the water, and said, in a strange, dreamy, absent tone, 'Yes – a long way.'

'Oh, what shall I do?' cried Maggie, in an agony. 'We shall not get home for hours – and Lucy – O God, help me!'

She clasped her hands and broke into a sob, like a frightened child: she thought of nothing but of meeting Lucy, and seeing her look of pained surprise and doubt – perhaps of just upbraiding.

Stephen moved and sat near her, and gently drew down the clasped hands.

'Maggie,' he said, in a deep tone of slow decision, 'let us never go home again – till no one can part us – till we are married.'

The unusual tone, the startling words, arrested Maggie's sob, and she sat quite still – wondering: as if Stephen might have seen some possibilities that would alter everything, and annul the wretched facts.

'See, Maggie, how everything has come without our seeking – in spite of all our efforts. We never thought of being alone together again: it has all been done by others. See how the tide is carrying us out – away from all those unnatural bonds that we have been trying to make faster round us – and trying in vain. It will carry us on to Torby, and we can land there, and get some carriage, and hurry on to York, and then to Scotland – and never pause a moment till we are bound to each other, so that only death can part us. It is the only right thing, dearest: it is the only way of escaping from this wretched entanglement.

Everything has concurred to point it out to us. We have contrived nothing, we have thought of nothing ourselves.'

Stephen spoke with deep, earnest pleading. Maggie listened – passing from her startled wonderment to the yearning after that belief, that the tide was doing it all – that she might glide along with the swift, silent stream, and not struggle any more. But across that stealing influence came the terrible shadow of past thoughts; and the sudden horror lest now, at last, the moment of fatal intoxication was close upon her, called up feelings of angry resistance towards Stephen.

'Let me go!' she said, in an agitated tone, flashing an indignant look at him, and trying to get her hands free. 'You have wanted to deprive me of any choice. You knew we were come too far – you have dared to take advantage of my thoughtlessness. It is unmanly to bring me into such a position.'

Stung by this reproach, he released her hands, moved back to his former place, and folded his arms, in a sort of desperation at the difficulty Maggie's words had made present to him. If she would not consent to go on, he must curse himself for the embarrassment he had led her into. But the reproach was the unendurable thing: the one thing worse than parting with her was, that she should feel he had acted unworthily towards her. At last he said, in a tone of suppressed rage –

'I didn't notice that we had passed Luckreth till we had got to the next village; and then it came into my mind that we would go on. I can't justify it: I ought to have told you. It is enough to make you hate me – since you don't love me well enough to make everything else indifferent to you, as I do you. Shall I stop the boat, and try to get you out here? I'll tell Lucy that I was mad – and that you hate me – and you shall be clear of me for ever. No one can blame you, because I have behaved unpardonably to you.'

Maggie was paralysed: it was easier to resist Stephen's pleading, than this picture he had called up of himself suffering while she was vindicated – easier even to turn away from his look of tenderness than from this look of angry misery, that seemed to place her in selfish isolation from him. He had called up a state of feeling in which the reasons which had acted on her conscience seemed to be transmuted into mere self-regard. The indignant fire in her eyes was quenched, and she began to look at him with timid distress. She had reproached him for being hurried into irrevocable trespass – she, who had been so weak herself.

'As if I shouldn't feel what happened to you – just the same,' she said, with reproach of another kind – the reproach of love, asking for more trust. This yielding to the idea of Stephen's suffering was more fatal than the other yielding, because it was less distinguishable from that sense of others' claims which was the moral basis of her resistance.

He felt all the relenting in her look and tone – it was heaven opening again. He moved to her side, and took her hand, leaning his elbow on the back of the boat, and saying nothing. He dreaded to utter another word, he dreaded to make another movement, that might provoke reproach or denial from her. Life hung on her consent: everything else was hopeless, confused, sickening misery. They glided along in this way, both resting in that silence as in a haven, both dreading lest their feeling should be divided again – till they became aware that the clouds had gathered, and that the slightest perceptible freshening of the breeze was growing and growing, so that the whole character of the day was altered.

'You will be chilly, Maggie, in this thin dress. Let me raise the cloak over your shoulders. Get up an instant, dearest.'

Maggie obeyed: there was an unspeakable charm in being told what to do, and having everything decided for her. She sat down again, covered with the cloak, and Stephen took to his oars again, making haste; for they must try to get to Torby as fast as they could. Maggie was hardly conscious of having said or done anything decisive. All yielding is attended with a less vivid consciousness than resistance; it is the partial sleep of thought; it is the submergence of our own personality by another. Every influence tended to lull her into acquiescence: that dreamy gliding in the boat, which had lasted for four hours, and had brought some weariness and exhaustion – the recoil of her fatigued sensations from the impracticable difficulty of getting out of the boat at this unknown distance from home, and walking for long miles – all helped to bring her into more complete subjection to that strong mysterious charm which made a last parting from Stephen seem the death of all joy – which made the thought of wounding him like the first touch of the torturing iron before which resolution shrank. And then there was the present happiness of being with him, which was enough to absorb all her languid energy.

Presently Stephen observed a vessel coming after them. Several vessels, among them the steamer to Mudport, had passed them with the early tide, but for the last hour they had seen none. He looked more and more eagerly at this vessel, as if a new thought had come into his mind along with it, and then he looked at Maggie, hesitatingly.

'Maggie, dearest,' he said, at last, 'if this vessel should be going to Mudport, or to any convenient place on the coast northward, it would be our best plan to get them to take us on board. You are fatigued – and it may soon rain – it may be a wretched business, getting to Torby in this boat. It's only a trading-vessel, but I dare say you can be made tolerably comfortable. We'll take the cushions out of the boat. It is really our best plan. They'll be glad enough to take us: I've got plenty of money about me; I can pay them well.'

Maggie's heart began to beat with reawakened alarm at this new proposition; but she was silent – one course seemed as difficult as another.

Stephen hailed the vessel. It was a Dutch vessel going to Mudport, the English mate informed him, and, if this wind held, would be there in less than two days.

'We had got out too far with our boat,' said Stephen. 'I was trying to make for Torby. But I'm afraid of the weather; and this lady – my wife – will be exhausted with fatigue and hunger. Take us on board – will you? and haul up the boat. I'll pay you well.'

Maggie, now really faint and trembling with fear, was taken on board, making an interesting object of contemplation to admiring Dutchmen. The mate feared the lady would have a poor time of it on board, for they had no accommodation for such entirely unlooked-for passengers – no private cabin larger than an old fashioned church-pew. But at least they had Dutch cleanliness, which makes all other inconveniences tolerable; and the boat-cushions were spread into a couch for Maggie on the poop with all alacrity. But to pace up and down the deck leaning on Stephen – being upheld by his strength – was the first change that she needed: then came food, and then quiet reclining on the cushions, with the sense that no new resolution *could* be taken that day. Everything must wait till tomorrow. Stephen sat beside her with her hand in his; they could only speak to each other in low tones; only look at each other now and then, for it would take a long while to dull the curiosity of the five men on board, and reduce these handsome young strangers to that minor degree of interest, which belongs, in a sailor's regard, to all objects nearer than the horizon. But Stephen was triumphantly happy. Every other thought or care was thrown into unmarked perspective by the certainty that Maggie must be his. The leap had been taken now: he had been tortured by scruples, he had fought fiercely with over-mastering inclination, he had hesitated: but repentance was impossible. He murmured forth in fragmentary sentences his happiness – his adoration – his tenderness – his belief that their life together must be heaven – that her presence with him would give rapture to every common day – that to satisfy her lightest wish was dearer to him than all other bliss – that everything was easy for her sake, except to part with her; and now they never *would* part; he would belong to her for ever, and all that was his was hers – had no value for him except as it was hers. Such things, uttered in low broken tones by the one voice that has first stirred the fibre of young passion, have only a feeble effect – on experienced minds at a distance from them. To poor Maggie they were very near: they were like nectar held close to thirsty lips: there was, there *must* be, then, a life for mortals here below which was not hard and chill – in which affection would no longer be self-sacrifice. Stephen's passionate words made the vision of such a life more fully present to her than it had ever been before; and the vision for the time excluded all realities – all except the returning sun-gleams which broke out on the waters as the evening approached, and mingled with the visionary sun-light of promised happiness – all except the hand that pressed hers, and the voice that spoke to her, and the eyes that looked at her with grave, unspeakable love.

There was to be no rain, after all; the clouds rolled off to the horizon again, making the great purple rampart and long purple isles of that wondrous land which reveals itself to us when the sun goes down – the land that the evening star watches over. Maggie was to sleep all night on the poop; it was better than going below; and she was covered with the warmest wrappings the ship could furnish. It was still early, when the fatigues of the day brought on a drowsy longing for perfect rest, and she laid down her head, looking at the faint dying flush in the west, where the one golden lamp was getting brighter and brighter. Then she looked up at Stephen, who was still seated by her, hanging over her as he leaned his arm against the vessel's side. Behind all the delicious visions of these last hours, which had flowed over her like a soft stream, and made her entirely passive, there was the dim consciousness that the condition was a transient one, and that the morrow must bring back the old life of struggle – that there were thoughts which would presently avenge themselves for this oblivion. But now nothing was distinct to her: she was being lulled to sleep with that soft stream still flowing over her, with those delicious visions melting and fading like a wondrous aerial land of the west.

CHAPTER 14

Waking

When Maggie was gone to sleep, Stephen, weary too with his unaccustomed amount of rowing, and with the intense inward life of the last twelve hours, but too restless to sleep, walked and lounged about the deck, with his cigar, far on into midnight, not seeing the dark water – hardly conscious that there were stars – living only in the near and distant future. At last fatigue conquered restlessness, and he rolled himself up in a piece of tarpauling on the deck near Maggie's feet.

She had fallen asleep before nine, and had been sleeping for six hours before the faintest hint of a midsummer daybreak was discernible. She awoke from that vivid dreaming which makes the margin of our deeper rest: she was in a boat on the wide water with Stephen, and in the gathering darkness something like a star appeared, that grew and grew till they saw it was the Virgin seated in St Ogg's boat, and it came nearer and nearer, till they saw the Virgin was Lucy and the boatman was Philip – no, not Philip, but her brother, who rowed past without looking at her; and she rose to stretch out her arms and call to him, and their own boat turned over with the movement, and they began to sink, till with one spasm of dread she seemed to awake, and find she was a child again in the parlour at evening twilight, and Tom was not really angry. From the soothed sense of that false waking she passed to the real waking – to the splash of water against the vessel, and the sound of a footstep on the deck, and the awful starlit sky. There was a moment of utter bewilderment before her mind could get disentangled from the confused web of dreams; but soon the whole terrible truth urged itself upon her. Stephen was not by her now: she was alone with her own memory and her own dread. The irrevocable wrong that must blot her life had been committed: she had brought sorrow into the lives of others – into the lives that were knit up with hers by trust and love. The feeling of a few short weeks had hurried her into the sins her nature had most recoiled from – breach of faith and cruel selfishness; she had rent the ties that had given meaning to duty, and had made herself an outlawed soul, with no guide but the wayward choice of her own passion. And where would that lead her? – where had it led her now? She had said she would rather die than fall into that temptation. She felt it now – now that the consequences of such a fall had come before the outward act was completed. There was at least this fruit from all her years of striving after the highest and best – that her soul, though betrayed, beguiled, ensnared, could never deliberately consent to a choice of the lower. And a choice of what? O God – not a choice of joy, but of conscious cruelty and hardness; for could she ever cease to see before her Lucy and Philip, with their murdered trust and hopes? Her life with Stephen could have no sacredness: she must for ever sink and wander vaguely, driven by uncertain impulse; for she had let go the clue of life – that clue which once in the far-off years her young need had clutched so strongly. She had renounced all delights then, before she knew them, before they had come within her reach. Philip had been right when he told her that she knew nothing of renunciation: she had thought it was quiet ecstasy; she saw it face to face now – that sad patient loving strength which holds the clue of life – and saw that the thorns were for ever pressing on its brow. The yesterday, which could never be revoked – if she could have changed it now for any length of inward silent endurance, she would have bowed beneath that cross with a sense of rest.

Daybreak came and the reddening eastern light, while her past life was grasping her in this way, with the tightening clutch which comes in the last moments of possible rescue. She could see Stephen now lying on the deck still fast asleep, and with the sight of him there came a wave of anguish that found its way in a long-suppressed sob. The worst bitterness of parting – the thought that urged the sharpest inward cry for help, was the pain it must give to *him*. But surmounting everything was the horror at her own possible failure, the dread lest her conscience should be benumbed again, and not rise to energy till it was too late. Too late! It was too late already not to have caused misery: too late for everything, perhaps, but to rush away from the last act of baseness – the tasting of joys that were wrung from crushed hearts.

The sun was rising now, and Maggie started up with the sense that a day of resistance was beginning for her. Her eyelashes were still wet with tears, as with her shawl over head, she sat looking at the slowly-rounding sun. Something roused Stephen too, and, getting up from his hard bed, he came to sit beside her. The sharp instinct of anxious love saw something to give him alarm in the very first glance. He had a hovering dread of some resistance in Maggie's nature that he would be unable to overcome. He had the uneasy consciousness that he had robbed her of perfect freedom yesterday: there was too much native honour in him, for him not to feel that, if her will should recoil, his conduct would have been odious, and she would have a right to reproach him.

But Maggie did not feel that right: she was too conscious of fatal weakness in herself – too full of the tenderness that comes with the foreseen need for inflicting a wound. She let him take her hand when he came to sit down beside her, and smiled at him – only with rather a sad glance: she could say nothing to pain him till the moment of possible parting was nearer. And so they drank their cup of coffee together, and walked about the deck, and heard the captain's assurance that they should be in at Mudport by five o' clock, each with an inward burthen, but in him it was an undefined fear, which he trusted to the coming hours to dissipate; in her it was a definite resolve on which she was trying silently to tighten her hold. Stephen was continually, through the morning, expressing his anxiety at the fatigue and discomfort she was suffering, and alluded to landing and to the change of motion and repose she would have in a carriage, wanting to assure himself more completely by presupposing that everything would be as he had arranged it. For a long while Maggie contented herself with assuring him that she had had a good night's rest, and that she didn't mind about being on the vessel – it was not like being on the open sea – it was only a little less pleasant than being in a boat on the Floss. But a suppressed resolve will betray itself in the eyes, and Stephen became more and more uneasy as the day advanced, under the sense that Maggie had entirely lost her passiveness. He longed, but did not dare, to speak of their marriage – of where they would go after it, and the steps he would take to inform his father, and the rest, of what had happened. He longed to assure himself of a tacit assent from her. But each time he looked at her, he gathered a stronger dread of the new, quiet sadness with which she met his eyes. And they were more and more silent.

'Here we are in sight of Mudport,' he said, at last. 'Now dearest,' he added, turning towards her with a look that was half beseeching, 'the worst part of your fatigue is over. On the land we can command swiftness. In another hour and a half we shall be in a chaise together – and that will seem rest to you after this.'

Maggie felt it was time to speak: it would only be unkind now to assent by silence. She spoke in the lowest tone, as he had done, but with distinct decision.

'We shall not be together – we shall have parted.'

The blood rushed to Stephen's face.

'We shall not,' he said. 'I'll die first.'

It was as he had dreaded – there was a struggle coming. But neither of them dared to say another word, till the boat was let down, and they were taken to the landing-place. Here there was a cluster of gazers and passengers awaiting the departure of the steamboat to St Ogg's. Maggie had a dim sense, when she had landed, and Stephen was hurrying her along on his arm, that someone had advanced towards her from that cluster as if he were coming to speak to her. But she was hurried along, and was indifferent to everything but the coming trial.

A porter guided them to the nearest inn and posting-house, and Stephen gave the order for the chaise as they passed through the yard. Maggie took no notice of this, and only said, 'Ask them to show us into a room where we can sit down.'

When they entered, Maggie did not sit down, and Stephen, whose face had a desperate determination in it, was about to ring the bell, when she said, in a firm voice, 'I'm not going: we must part here.'

'Maggie,' he said, turning round towards her, and speaking in the tones of a man who feels a process of torture beginning, 'do you mean to kill me? What is the use of it now? The whole thing is done.'

'No, it is not done,' said Maggie. 'Too much is done – more than we can ever remove the trace of. But I will go no farther. Don't try to prevail with me again. I couldn't choose yesterday.'

What was he to do? He dared not go near her – her anger might leap out, and make a new barrier. He walked backwards and forwards in maddening perplexity.

'Maggie,' he said at last, pausing before her, and speaking in a tone of imploring wretchedness, 'have some pity – hear me – forgive me for what I did yesterday. I will obey you now – I will do nothing without your full consent. But don't blight our lives for ever by a rash perversity that can answer no good purpose to anyone – that can only create new evils. Sit down, dearest; wait – think what you are going to do. Don't treat me as if you couldn't trust me.'

He had chosen the most effective appeal; but Maggie's will was fixed unswervingly on the coming wrench. She had made up her mind to suffer.

'We must not wait,' she said, in a low but distinct voice; 'we must part at once.'

'We *can't* part, Maggie,' said Stephen, more impetuously. 'I can't bear it. What is the use of inflicting that misery on me? The blow – whatever it may have been – has been struck now. Will it help anyone else that you should drive me mad?'

'I will not begin any future, even for you,' said Maggie, tremulously, 'with a deliberate consent to what ought not to have been. What I told you at Basset I feel now: I would rather have died than fall into this temptation. It would have been better if we had parted for ever then. But we must part now.'

'We will *not* part,' Stephen burst out, instinctively placing his back against the door – forgetting everything he had said a few moments before; 'I will not endure it. You'll make me desperate – I shan't know what I do.'

Maggie trembled. She felt that the parting could not be effected suddenly. She must rely on a slower appeal to Stephen's better self – she must be prepared for a harder task than that of rushing away while resolution was fresh. She sat down. Stephen, watching her with that look of desperation which had come over him like a lurid light, approached slowly from the door, seated himself close beside her, and grasped her hand. Her heart beat like the heart of a frightened bird; but this direct opposition helped her. She felt her determination growing stronger.

'Remember what you felt weeks ago,' she began, with beseeching earnestness – 'remember what we both felt – that we owed ourselves to others, and must conquer every inclination which could make us false to that debt. We have failed to keep our resolutions; but the wrong remains the same.'

'No, it does *not* remain the same,' said Stephen. 'We have proved that it was impossible to keep our resolutions. We have proved that the feeling which draws us towards each other is too strong to be overcome: that natural law surmounts every other; we can't help what it clashes with.'

'It is not so, Stephen – I'm quite sure that is wrong. I have tried to think it again and again; but I see, if we judged in that way, there would be a warrant for all treachery and cruelty – we should justify breaking the most sacred ties that can ever be formed on earth. If the past is not to bind us, where can duty lie? We should have no law but the inclination of the moment.'

'But there are ties that can't be kept by mere resolution,' said Stephen, starting up and walking about again. 'What is outward faithfulness? Would they have thanked us for anything so hollow as constancy without love?'

Maggie did not answer immediately. She was undergoing an inward as well as an outward contest. At last she said, with passionate assertion of her conviction, as much against herself as against him, 'That seems right – at first; but when I look further, I'm sure it is *not* right. Faithfulness and constancy mean something else besides doing what is easiest and pleasantest to ourselves. They mean renouncing whatever is opposed to the reliance others have in us – whatever would cause misery to those whom the course of our lives has made dependent on us. If we – if I had been better, nobler, those claims would have been so strongly present with me – I should have felt them pressing on my heart so continually, just as they do now in the moments when my conscience is awake – that the opposite feeling would never have grown in me, as it has done: it would have been quenched at once – I should have prayed for help so earnestly – I should have rushed away as we rush from hideous danger. I feel no excuse for myself – none. I should never have failed towards Lucy and Philip as I have done, if I had not been weak, selfish, and hard – able to think of their pain without a pain to myself that would have destroyed all temptation. Oh, what is Lucy feeling now? She believed in me – she loved me – she was so good to me. Think of her . . .'

Maggie's voice was getting choked as she uttered these last words.

'I *can't* think of her,' said Stephen, stamping as if with pain. 'I can think of nothing but you, Maggie. You demand of a man what is impossible. I felt that once; but I can't go back to it now. And where is the use of *your* thinking of it, except to torture me? You can't save them from pain now; you can only tear yourself from me, and make my life worthless to me. And even if we could go back, and both fulfil our engagements – if that were possible now – it would be hateful – horrible, to think of your ever being Philip's wife – of your ever being the wife of a man you didn't love. We have both been rescued from a mistake.'

A deep flush came over Maggie's face, and she couldn't speak. Stephen saw this. He sat down again, taking her hand in his, and looking at her with passionate entreaty.

'Maggie! Dearest! If you love me, you are mine. Who can have so great a claim on you as I have? My life is bound up in your love. There is nothing in the past that can annul our right to each other: it is the first time we have either of us loved with our whole heart and soul.'

Maggie was still silent for a little while – looking down. Stephen was in a flutter of new hope: he was going to triumph. But she raised her eyes and met his with a glance that was filled with the anguish of regret – not with yielding.

'No – not with my whole heart and soul, Stephen,' she said, with timid resolution. 'I have never consented to it with my whole mind. There are memories, and affections, and longing after perfect goodness, that have such a strong hold on me; they would never quit me for long; they would come back and be pain to me – repentance. I couldn't live in peace if I put the shadow of a wilful sin between myself and God. I have caused sorrow already – I know – I feel it; but I have never deliberately consented to it: I have never said, "They shall suffer, that I may have joy." It has never been my will to marry you: if you were to win consent from the momentary triumph of my feeling for you, you would not have my whole soul. If I could wake back again into the time before yesterday, I would choose to be true to my calmer affections, and live without the joy of love.'

Stephen loosed her hand, and, rising impatiently, walked up and down the room in suppressed rage.

'Good God!' he burst out, at last, 'what a miserable thing a woman's love is to a man's! I could commit crimes for you – and you can balance and choose in that way. But you *don't* love me: if you had a tithe of the feeling for me that I have for you, it would be impossible to you to think for a moment of sacrificing me. But it weighs nothing with you that you are robbing me of *my* life's happiness.'

Maggie pressed her fingers together almost convulsively as she held them clasped on her lap. A great terror was upon her, as if she were ever and anon seeing where she stood by great flashes of lightning, and then again stretched forth her hands in the darkness.

'No – I don't sacrifice you – I couldn't sacrifice you,' she said, as soon as she could speak again; 'but I can't believe in a good for you, that I feel – that we both feel is a wrong towards others. We can't choose happiness either for ourselves or for another: we can't tell where that will lie. We can only choose whether we will indulge ourselves in the present moment, or whether we will renounce that, for the sake of obeying the divine voice within us – for the sake of being true to all the motives that sanctify our lives. I know this belief is hard: it has slipped away from me again and again; but I have felt that if I let it go for ever, I should have no light through the darkness of this life.'

'But, Maggie,' said Stephen, seating himself by her again, 'is it possible you don't see that what happened yesterday has altered the whole position of things? What infatuation is it – what obstinate prepossession that blinds you to that? It is too late to say what we might have done or what we ought to have done. Admitting the very worst view of what has been done, it is a fact we must act on now; our position is altered; the right course is no longer what it was before. We must accept our own actions and start afresh from them. Suppose we had been married yesterday? It is nearly the same thing. The effect on others would not have been different. It would only have made this difference to ourselves,' Stephen added, bitterly 'that you might have acknowledged then that your tie to me was stronger than to others.'

Again a deep flush came over Maggie's face, and she was silent. Stephen thought again that he was beginning to prevail – he had never yet believed that he should *not* prevail: there are possibilities which our minds shrink from too completely for us to fear them.

'Dearest,' he said, in his deepest, tenderest tone, leaning towards her, and putting his arm round her, 'you *are* mine now – the world believes it – duty must spring out of that now: in a few hours you will be legally mine, and those who had claims on us will submit – they will see that there was a force which declared against their claims.'

Maggie's eyes opened wide in one terrified look at the face that was close to hers, and she started up – pale again.

'Oh, I can't do it,' she said, in a voice almost of agony – 'Stephen – don't ask me – don't urge me. I can't argue any longer – I don't know what is wise; but my heart will not let me do it. I see – I feel their trouble now: it is as if it were branded on my mind. *I* have suffered, and had no one to pity me; and now I have made others suffer. It would never leave me; it would embitter your love to me. I *do* care for Philip – in a different way: I remember all we said to each other; I know how he thought of me as the one promise of his life. He was given to me that I might make his lot less hard; and I have forsaken him. And Lucy – she has been deceived – she who trusted me more than anyone. I cannot marry you: I cannot take a good for myself that has been wrung out of their misery. It is not the force that ought to rule us – this that we feel for each other; it would rend me away from all that my past life has made dear and holy to me. I can't set out on a fresh life, and forget that: I must go back to it, and cling to it, else I shall feel as if there were nothing firm beneath my feet.'

'Good God, Maggie !' said Stephen, rising too and grasping her arm, 'you rave. How can you go back without marrying me? You don't know what will be said, dearest. You see nothing as it really is.'

'Yes, I do. But they will believe me. I will confess everything. Lucy will believe me – she will forgive you, and – and – oh, *some* good will come by clinging to the right. Dear, dear Stephen, let me go! – don't drag me into deeper remorse. My whole soul has never consented – it does not consent now.'

Stephen let go her arm, and sank back on his chair, half stunned by despairing rage. He was silent a few moments, not looking at her; while her eyes were turned towards him yearningly, in alarm at this sudden change. At last he said, still without looking at her, 'Go, then – leave me – don't torture me any longer – I can't bear it.'

Involuntarily she leaned towards him and put out her hand to touch his. But he shrank from it as if it had been burning iron, and said again, 'Leave me.'

Maggie was not conscious of a decision as she turned away from that gloomy averted face, and walked out of the room: it was like an automatic action that fulfils a forgotten intention. What came after? A sense of stairs descended as if in a dream – of flagstones – of a chaise and horses standing – then a street, and a turning into another street where a stagecoach was standing, taking in passengers – and the darting thought that that coach would take her away, perhaps towards home. But she could ask nothing yet; she only got into the coach.

Home – where her mother and brother were – Philip – Lucy – the scene of her very cares and trials – was the haven towards which her mind tended – the sanctuary where sacred relics lay – where she would be rescued from more falling. The thought of Stephen was like a horrible throbbing pain, which yet, as such pains do, seemed to urge all other thoughts into activity. But among her thoughts, what others would say and think of her conduct was hardly present. Love and deep pity and remorseful anguish left no room for that.

The coach was taking her to York – farther away from home; but she did not learn that until she was set down in the old city at midnight. It was no matter: she could sleep there, and start home the next day. She had her purse in her pocket, with all her money in it – a bank-note and a sovereign: she had kept it in her pocket from forgetfulness, after going out to make purchases the day before yesterday.

Did she lie down in the gloomy bedroom of the old inn that night with her will bent unwaveringly on a path of penitent sacrifice? The great struggles of life are not so easy as that; the great problems of life are not so clear. In the darkness of that night she saw Stephen's face turned towards her in passionate, reproachful misery, she lived through again all the tremulous delights of his presence with her that made existence an easy floating in a stream of joy, instead of a quiet resolved endurance and effort. The love she had renounced came back upon her with a cruel charm, she felt herself opening her arms to receive it once more and then it seemed to slip away and fade and vanish, leaving only the dying sound of a deep thrilling voice that said, 'Gone – for ever gone.'

BOOK SEVENTH

The Final Rescue

CHAPTER I

The Return to the Mill

Between four and five o'clock on the afternoon of the fifth day from that on which Stephen and Maggie had left St Ogg's, Tom Tulliver was standing on the gravel-walk outside the old house at Dorlcote Mill. He was master there now: he had half-fulfilled his father's dying wish, and by years of steady self-government and energetic work he had brought himself near to the attainment of more than the old respectability which had been the proud inheritance of the Dodsons and Tullivers.

But Tom's face, as he stood in the hot still sunshine of that summer afternoon, had no gladness, no triumph in it. His mouth wore its bitterest expression, his severe brow its hardest and deepest fold, as he drew down his hat farther over his eyes to shelter them from the sun, and, thrusting his hands deep into his pockets, began to walk up and down the gravel. No news of his sister had been heard since Bob Jakin had come back in the steamer from Mudport, and put an end to all improbable suppositions of an accident on the water by stating that he had seen her land from a vessel with Mr Stephen Guest. Would the next news be that she was married – or what? Probably that she was not married: Tom's mind was set to the expectation of the worst that could happen – not death, but disgrace.

As he was walking with his back towards the entrance gate, and his face towards the rushing millstream, a tall dark-eyed figure, that we know well, approached the gate, and paused to look at him, with a fast-beating heart. Her brother was the human being of whom she had been most afraid, from her childhood upwards: afraid with that fear which springs in us when we love one who is inexorable, unbending, unmodifiable – with a mind that we can never mould ourselves upon, and yet that we cannot endure to alienate from us. That deep-rooted fear was shaking Maggie now; but her mind was unswervingly bent on returning to her brother, as the natural refuge that had been given her. In her deep humiliation under the retrospect of her own weakness – in her anguish at the injury she had inflicted – she almost desired to endure the severity of Tom's reproof, to submit in patient silence to that harsh disapproving judgement against which she had so often rebelled: it seemed no more than just to her now – who was weaker than she was? She craved that outward help to her better purpose which would come from complete, submissive confession – from being in the presence of those whose looks and words would be a reflection of her own conscience.

Maggie had been kept on her bed at York for a day with that prostrating headache which was likely to follow on the terrible strain of the previous day and night. There was an expression of physical pain still about her brow and eyes, and her whole appearance, with her dress so long unchanged, was worn and distressed. She lifted the latch of the gate and walked in – slowly. Tom did not hear the gate; he was just then close upon the roaring dam; but he presently turned, and, lifting up his eyes, saw the figure whose worn look and loneliness seemed to him a confirmation of his worst conjectures. He paused, trembling and white with disgust and indignation.

Maggie paused too – three yards before him. She felt the hatred in his face: felt it rushing through her fibres; but she must speak.

'Tom,' she began, faintly, 'I am come back to you – I am come back home – for refuge – to tell you everything.'

'You will find no home with me,' he answered, with tremulous rage. 'You have disgraced us all. You have disgraced my father's name. You have been a curse to your best friends. You have been base – deceitful; no motives are strong enough to restrain you. I wash my hands of you for ever. You don't belong to me.'

Their mother had come to the door now. She stood paralysed by the double shock of seeing Maggie and hearing Tom's words.

'Tom,' said Maggie, with more courage, 'I am perhaps not so guilty as you believe me to be. I never meant to give way to my feelings. I struggled against them. I was carried too far in the boat to come back on Tuesday. I came back as soon as I could.'

'I can't believe in you any more,' said Tom, gradually passing from the tremulous excitement of the first moment to cold inflexibility. 'You have been carrying on a clandestine relation with Stephen Guest – as you did before with another. He went to see you at my aunt Moss's; you walked alone with him in the lanes; you must have behaved as no modest girl would have done to her cousin's lover, else that could never have happened. The people at Luckreth saw you pass – you passed all the other places; you knew what you were doing. You have been using Philip Wakem as a screen to deceive Lucy – the kindest friend you ever had. Go and see the return you have made her: she's ill – unable to speak – my mother can't go near her, lest she should remind her of *you*.'

Maggie was half stunned – too heavily pressed upon by her anguish even to discern any difference between her actual guilt and her brother's accusations, still less to vindicate herself.

'Tom,' she said, crushing her hands together under her cloak, in the effort to speak again. 'Whatever I have done, I repent it bitterly. I want to make amends. I will endure anything. I want to be kept from doing wrong again.'

'What *will* keep you?' said Tom, with cruel bitterness. 'Not religion; not your natural feelings of gratitude and honour. And he – he would deserve to be shot, if it were not – But you are ten times worse than he is. I loathe your character and your conduct. You struggled with your feelings, you say. Yes! *I* have had feelings to struggle with; but I conquered them. I have had a harder life than you have had: but I have found *my* comfort in doing my duty. But I will sanction no such character as yours: the world shall know that I feel the difference between right and wrong. If you are in want, I will provide for you – let my mother know. But you shall not come under my roof. It is enough that I have to bear the thought of your disgrace: the sight of you is hateful to me.'

Slowly Maggie was turning away with despair in her heart. But the poor frightened mother's love leaped out now, stronger than all dread.

'My child! I'll go with you. You've got a mother.'

Oh, the sweet rest of that embrace to the heart-stricken Maggie! More helpful than all wisdom is one draught of simple human pity that will not forsake us.

Tom turned and walked into the house.

'Come in, my child,' Mrs Tulliver whispered. 'He'll let you stay and sleep in my bed. He won't deny that, if I ask him.'

'No mother,' said Maggie, in a low tone, like a moan. 'I will never go in.'

'Then wait for me outside. I'll get ready and come with you.'

When his mother appeared with her bonnet on, Tom came out to her in the passage, and put money into her hands.

'My house is yours, mother, always,' he said. 'You will come and let me know everything you want – you will come back to me.'

Poor Mrs Tulliver took the money, too frightened to say anything. The only thing clear to her was the mother's instinct, that she would go with her unhappy child.

Maggie was waiting outside the gate; she took her mother's hand, and they walked a little way in silence.

'Mother,' said Maggie, at last, 'we will go to Luke's cottage. Luke will take me in. He was very good to me when I was a little girl.'

'He's got no room for us, my dear, now; his wife's got so many children. I don't know where to go, if it isn't to one o' your aunts; and I hardly durst,' said poor Mrs Tulliver, quite destitute of mental resources in this extremity.

Maggie was silent a little while, and then said, 'Let us go to Bob Jakin's, mother: his wife will have room for us, if they have no other lodger.'

So they went on their way to St Ogg's – to the old house by the riverside.

Bob himself was at home, with a heaviness at heart which resisted even the new joy and pride of possessing a two months' old baby – quite the liveliest of its age that had ever been born to prince or packman. He would perhaps not so thoroughly have understood all the dubiousness of Maggie's appearance with Mr Stephen Guest on the quay at Mudport, if he had not witnessed the effect it produced on Tom when he went to report it; and since then, the circumstances which in any case gave a disastrous character to her elopement, had passed beyond the more polite circles of St Ogg's, and had become matter of common talk, accessible to the grooms and errand-boys. So that when he opened the door and saw Maggie standing before him in her sorrow and weariness, he had no questions to ask, except one, which he dared only ask himself – where was Mr Stephen Guest? Bob, for his part, hoped he might be in the warmest department of an asylum understood to exist in the other world for gentlemen who are likely to be in fallen circumstances there.

The lodgings were vacant, and both Mrs Jakin the larger and Mrs Jakin the less were commanded to make all things comfortable for 'the old Missis and the young Miss' – alas! that she was still 'Miss'. The ingenious Bob was sorely perplexed as to how this result could have come about – how Mr Stephen Guest could have gone away from her, or could have let her go away from him, when he had the chance of keeping her with him. But he was silent, and would not allow his wife to ask him a question: would not present himself in the room, lest it should appear like intrusion and a wish to pry; having the same chivalry towards dark-eyed Maggie, as in the days when he had bought her the memorable present of books.

But after a day or two Mrs Tulliver was gone to the mill again for a few hours to see to Tom's household matters. Maggie had wished this: after the first violent outburst of feeling, which came as soon as she had no longer any active purpose to fulfil, she was less in need of her mother's presence; she even desired to be alone with her grief. But she had been solitary only a little while in the old sitting-room that looked on the river, when there came a tap at the door, and turning round her sad face as she said, 'Come in,' she saw Bob enter with the baby in his arms and Mumps at his heels.

'We'll go back, if it disturbs you, Miss,' said Bob.

'No,' said Maggie, in a low voice, wishing she could smile.

Bob, closing the door behind him, came and stood before her.

'You see, we've got a little un, Miss, an' I wanted you to look at it, an' take it i' your arms, if you'd be so good. For we made free to name it after you, an' it 'ud be better for your takin' a bit o' notice on it.'

Maggie could not speak, but she put out her arms to receive the tiny baby, while Mumps snuffed at it anxiously, to ascertain that this transference was all right. Maggie's heart had swelled at this action and speech of Bob's: she knew well enough that it was a way he had chosen to show his sympathy and respect.

'Sit down, Bob,' she said presently, and he sat down in silence, finding his tongue unmanageable in quite a new fashion, refusing to say what he wanted it to say.

'Bob,' she said, after a few moments, looking down at the baby, and holding it anxiously, as if she feared it might slip from her mind and her fingers, 'I have a favour to ask of you.'

'Don't you speak so, Miss,' said Bob, grasping the skin of Mumps's neck; 'if there's anything I can do for you, I should look upon it as a day's earnings.'

'I want you to go to Dr Kenn's, and ask to speak to him, and tell him that I am here, and should be very grateful if he would come to me while my mother is away. She will not come back till evening.'

'Eh, Miss – I'd do it in a minute – it is but a step; but Dr Kenn's wife lies dead – she's to be buried tomorrow – died the day I come from Mudport. It's all the more pity she should ha' died just now, if you want him. I hardly like to go a-nigh him yet.'

'Oh, no, Bob,' said Maggie, 'we must let it be – till after a few days, perhaps – when you hear that he is going about again. But perhaps he may be going out of town – to a distance,' she added, with a new sense of despondency at this idea.

'Not he, Miss,' said Bob. 'He'll none go away. He isn't one o' them gentlefolks as go to cry at waterin'-places when their wives die: he's got summat else to do. He looks fine an' sharp after the parish – he does. He christened the little un; he was at me to know what I did of a Sunday, as I didn't come to church. But I told him I was upo' the travel three parts o' the Sundays – an' then I'm so used to being on my legs, I can't sit so long on end – "an' lors, sir," says I, "a packman can do wi' a small 'lowance o' church: it tastes strong," says I; "there's no call to lay it on thick." Eh, Miss, how good the little un is wi' you! It's like as if it knowed you: it partly does, I'll be bound – like the birds know the mornin'.'

Bob's tongue was now evidently loosed from its unwonted bondage, and might even be in danger of doing more work than was required of it. But the subjects on which he longed to be informed were so steep and difficult of approach, that his tongue was likely to run on along the level rather than to carry him on that unbeaten road. He felt this, and was silent again for a little while, ruminating much on the possible forms in which he might put a question. At last he said, in a more timid voice than usual, 'Will you give me leave to ask you only one thing, Miss?'

Maggie was rather startled, but she answered, 'Yes, Bob, if it is about myself – not about anyone else.'

'Well, Miss, it's this: *Do* you owe anybody a grudge?'

'No, not anyone,' said Maggie, looking up at him enquiringly. 'Why?'

'Oh, lors, Miss,' said Bob, pinching Mumps's neck harder then ever, 'I wish you did – an' 'ud tell me – I'd leather him till I couldn't see – I would – an' the Justice might do what he liked to me after.'

'Oh, Bob,' said Maggie, smiling faintly, 'you're a very good friend to me. But I shouldn't like to punish anyone, even if they'd done me wrong; I've done wrong myself too often.'

This view of things was puzzling to Bob, and threw more obscurity than ever over what could possibly have happened between Stephen and Maggie. But further questions would have been too intrusive, even if he could have framed them suitably, and he was obliged to carry baby away to an expectant mother.

'Happen you'd like Mumps for company, Miss,' he said when he had taken the baby again. 'He's rare company – Mumps is – he knows iverything, an' makes no bother about it. If I tell him, he'll lie before you an' watch you – as still – just as he watches my pack. You'd better let me leave him a bit; he'll get fond on you. Lors, it's a fine thing to hev a dumb brute fond on you; it'll stick to you, an' make no jaw.'

'Yes, do leave him, please,' said Maggie. 'I think I should like to have Mumps for a friend.'

'Mumps, lie down there,' said Bob, pointing to a place in front of Maggie, 'an' niver do you stir till you're spoke to.'

Mumps lay down at once, and made no sign of restlessness when his master left the room.

CHAPTER 2

St Ogg's Passes Judgement

It was soon known throughout St Ogg's that Miss Tulliver was come back: she had not, then, eloped in order to be married to Mr Stephen Guest – at all events, Mr Stephen Guest had not married her – which came to the same thing, so far as her culpability was concerned. We judge others according to results; how else? – not knowing the processes by which results are arrived at. If Miss Tulliver, after a few months of well-chosen travel, had returned as Mrs Stephen Guest – with a post-marital *trousseau*, and all the advantages possessed even by the most unwelcome wife of an only son, public opinion, which at St Ogg's, as elsewhere, always knew what to think, would have judged in strict consistency with those results. Public opinion, in these cases, is always of the feminine gender – not the world, but the world's wife; and she would have seen, that two handsome young people – the gentleman of quite the first family in St Ogg's – having found themselves in a false position, had been led into a course which, to say the least of it, was highly injudicious, and productive of sad pain and disappointment, especially to that sweet young thing, Miss Deane. Mr Stephen Guest had certainly not behaved well; but then, young men were liable to those sudden infatuated attachments; and bad as it might seem in Mrs Stephen Guest to admit the faintest advances from her cousin's lover (indeed it *had* been said that she was actually engaged to young Wakem – old Wakem himself had mentioned it), still she was very young – 'and a deformed young man, you know! – and young Guest so very fascinating; and, they say, he positively worships her (to be sure, that can't last!) and he ran away with her in the boat quite against her will – and what could she do? She couldn't come back then: no one would have spoken to her; and how very well that maize-coloured satinette becomes her complexion! It seems as if the folds in front were quite come in; several of her dresses are made so; – they say he thinks nothing too handsome to buy for her. Poor Miss Deane! She is very pitiable; but then, there was no positive engagement; and the air at the coast will do her good. After all, if young Guest felt no more for her than *that*, it was better for her not to marry him. What a wonderful marriage for a girl like Miss Tulliver – quite romantic! Why, young Guest will put up for the borough at the next election. Nothing like commerce nowadays! That young Wakem nearly went out of his mind – he always *was* rather queer; but he's gone abroad again to be out of the way – quite the best thing for a deformed young man. Miss Unit declares she will never visit Mr and Mrs Stephen Guest – such nonsense! pretending to be better than other people. Society couldn't be carried on if we enquired into private conduct in that way – and Christianity tells us to think no evil – and my belief is, that Miss Unit had no cards sent her.'

But the results, we know, were not of a kind to warrant this extenuation of the past. Maggie had returned without a *trousseau*, without a husband – in that

degraded and outcast condition to which error is well known to lead; and the
world's wife, with that fine instinct which is given her for the preservation
of Society, saw at once that Miss Tulliver's conduct had been of the most
aggravated kind. Could anything be more detestable? A girl so much indebted
to her friends – whose mother as well as herself had received so much kindness
from the Deanes – to lay the design of winning a young man's affections away
from her own cousin, who had behaved like a sister to her! Winning his
affections? That was not the phrase for such a girl as Miss Tulliver: it would
have been more correct to say that she had been actuated by mere unwomanly
boldness and unbridled passion. There was always something questionable
about her. That connection with young Wakem, which, they said, had been
carried on for years, looked very ill – disgusting, in fact! But with a girl of that
disposition! – To the world's wife there had always been something in Miss
Tulliver's very physique that a refined instinct felt to be prophetic of harm. As
for poor Mr Stephen Guest, he was rather pitiable than otherwise: a young man
of five-and-twenty is not to be too severely judged in these cases – he is really
very much at the mercy of a designing bold girl. And it was clear that he had
given way in spite of himself: he had shaken her off as soon as he could; indeed,
their having parted so soon looked very black indeed – *for her*. To be sure, he
had written a letter, laying all the blame on himself, and telling the story in a
romantic fashion so as to try and make her appear quite innocent: of course he
would do that! But the refined instinct of the world's wife was not to be
deceived: providentially! – else what would become of Society? Why – her own
brother had turned her from his door: he had seen enough, you might be sure,
before he would do that. A truly respectable young man – Mr Tom Tulliver:
quite likely to rise in the world! His sister's disgrace was naturally a heavy blow
to him. It was to be hoped that she would go out of the neighbourhood – to
America, or anywhere – so as to purify the air of St Ogg's from the taint of her
presence, extremely dangerous to daughters there! No good could happen to
her: it was only to be hoped she would repent, and that God would have mercy
on her: He had not the care of Society on His hands – as the world's wife had.

It required nearly a fortnight for fine instinct to assure itself of these
inspirations; indeed, it was a whole week before Stephen's letter came, telling
his father the facts, and adding that he was gone across to Holland – had drawn
upon the agent at Mudport for money – was incapable of any resolution at
present.

Maggie, all this while, was too entirely filled with a more agonising anxiety to
spend any thought on the view that was being taken of her conduct by the world
of St Ogg's: anxiety about Stephen – Lucy – Philip – beat on her poor heart in a
hard, driving, ceaseless storm of mingled love, remorse, and pity. If she had
thought of rejection and injustice at all, it would have seemed to her that
they had done their worst – that she could hardly feel any stroke from them
intolerable since the words she had heard from her brother's lips. Across all her
anxiety for the loved and the injured, those words shot again and again, like a
horrible pang that would have brought misery and dread even into a heaven of
delights. The idea of ever recovering happiness never glimmered in her mind

for a moment; it seemed as if every sensitive fibre in her were too entirely preoccupied by pain ever to vibrate again to another influence. Life stretched before her as one act of penitence, and all she craved, as she dwelt on her future lot, was something to guarantee her from more falling: her own weakness haunted her like a vision of hideous possibilities, that made no peace conceivable except such as lay in the sense of a sure refuge.

But she was not without practical intentions: the love of independence was too strong an inheritance and a habit for her not to remember that she must get her bread; and when other projects looked vague, she fell back on that of returning to her plain sewing, and so getting enough to pay for her lodging at Bob's. She meant to persuade her mother to return to the mill by and by, and live with Tom again; and somehow or other she would maintain herself at St Ogg's. Dr Kenn would perhaps help her and advise her. She remembered his parting words at the bazaar. She remembered the momentary feeling of reliance that had sprung in her when he was talking with her, and she waited with yearning expectation for the opportunity of confiding everything to him. Her mother called every day at Mr Deane's to learn how Lucy was: the report was always sad – nothing had yet roused her from the feeble passivity which had come on with the first shock. But of Philip, Mrs Tulliver had learned nothing: naturally, no one whom she met would speak to her about what related to her daughter. But at last she summoned courage to go and see sister Glegg, who of course would know everything, and had even been to see Tom at the mill in Mrs Tulliver's absence, though he had said nothing of what had passed on the occasion.

As soon as her mother was gone, Maggie put on her bonnet. She had resolved on walking to the Rectory and asking to see Dr Kenn: he was in deep grief – but the grief of another does not jar upon us in such circumstances. It was the first time she had been beyond the door since her return; nevertheless her mind was so bent on the purpose of her walk, that the unpleasantness of meeting people on the way, and being stared at, did not occur to her. But she had no sooner passed beyond the narrower streets which she had to thread from Bob's dwelling, than she became aware of unusual glances cast at her; and this consciousness made her hurry along nervously, afraid to look to right or left. Presently, however, she came full on Mrs and Miss Turnbull, old acquaintances of her family; they both looked at her strangely, and turned a little aside without speaking. All hard looks were pain to Maggie, but her self-reproach was too strong for resentment: no wonder they will not speak to me, she thought – they are very fond of Lucy. But now she knew that she was about to pass a group of gentlemen, who were standing at the door of the billiard-rooms, and she could not help seeing young Torry step out a little with his glass at his eye, and bow to her with that air of nonchalance which he might have bestowed on a friendly barmaid. Maggie's pride was too intense for her not to feel that sting, even in the midst of her sorrow; and for the first time the thought took strong hold of her that she would have other obloquy cast on her besides that which was felt to be due to her breach of faith towards Lucy. But she was at the Rectory now; there, perhaps, she would find something else than retribution. Retribution may come from any voice: the hardest, cruelest, most imbruted urchin at the street-corner can inflict it: surely help and pity are rarer things – more needful for the righteous to bestow.

She was shown up at once, after being announced, into Dr Kenn's study, where he sat amongst piled-up books, for which he had little appetite, leaning his cheek against the head of his youngest child, a girl of three. The child was sent away with the servant, and when the door was closed, Dr Kenn said, placing a chair for Maggie,, 'I was coming to see you, Miss Tulliver; you have anticipated me; I am glad you did.'

Maggie looked at him with her childlike directness as she had done at the bazaar, and said, 'I want to tell you everything.' But her eyes filled fast with tears as she said it, and all the pent-up excitement of her humiliating walk would have its vent before she could say more.

'Do tell me everything,' Dr Kenn said, with quiet kindness in his grave firm voice. 'Think of me as one to whom a long experience has been granted, which may enable him to help you.'

In rather broken sentences, and with some effort at first, but soon with the greater ease that came from a sense of relief in the confidence, Maggie told the brief story of a struggle that must be the beginning of a long sorrow. Only the day before, Dr Kenn had been made acquainted with the contents of Stephen's letter, and he had believed them at once, without the confirmation of Maggie's statement. That involuntary plaint of hers, *'Oh, I must go,'* had remained with him as the sign that she was undergoing some inward conflict.

Maggie dwelt the longest on the feeling which had made her come back to her mother and brother, which made her cling to all the memories of the past. When she had ended, Dr Kenn was silent for some minutes: there was a difficulty on his mind. He rose, and walked up and down the hearth with his hands behind him. At last he seated himself again, and said, looking at Maggie, 'Your prompting to go to your nearest friends – to remain where all the ties of your life have been formed – is a true prompting, to which the Church in its original constitution and discipline responds – opening its arms to the penitent – watching over its children to the last – never abandoning them until they are hopelessly reprobate. And the Church ought to represent the feeling of the community, so that every parish should be a family knit together by Christian brotherhood under a spiritual father. But the ideas of discipline and Christian fraternity are entirely relaxed – they can hardly be said to exist in the public mind: they hardly survive except in the partial, contradictory form they have taken in the narrow communities of schismatics: and if I were not supported by the firm faith that the Church must ultimately recover the full force of that constitution which is alone fitted to human needs, I should often lose heart at observing the want of fellowship and sense of mutual responsibility among my own flock. At present everything seems tending towards the relaxation of ties – towards the substitution of wayward choice for the adherence to obligation, which has its roots in the past. Your conscience and your heart have given you true light on this point, Miss Tulliver; and I have said all this that you may know what my wish about you – what my advice to you –

would be, if they sprang from my own feeling and opinion unmodified by counteracting circumstances.'

Dr Kenn paused a little while. There was an entire absence of effusive benevolence in his manner; there was something almost cold in the gravity of his look and voice. If Maggie had not known that his benevolence was persevering in proportion to its reserve, she might have been chilled and frightened. As it was, she listened expectantly, quite sure that there would be some effective help in his words. He went on.

'Your inexperience of the world, Miss Tulliver, prevents you from anticipating the very unjust conceptions that will probably be formed concerning your conduct – conceptions which will have a baneful effect, even in spite of known evidence to disprove them.'

'Oh, I do – I begin to see,' said Maggie, unable to repress this utterance other recent pain. 'I know I shall be insulted: I shall be thought worse than I am.'

'You perhaps do not yet know,' said Dr Kenn, with a touch of more personal pity, 'that a letter is come which ought to satisfy everyone who has known anything of you, that you chose the steep and difficult path of a return to the right, at the moment when that return was most of all difficult.'

'Oh – where is he?' said poor Maggie, with a flush and tremor that no presence could have hindered.

'He is gone abroad: he has written of all that passed to his father. He has vindicated you to the utmost; and I hope the communication of that letter to your cousin will have a beneficial effect on her.'

Dr Kenn waited for her to get calm before he went on.

'That letter, as I said, ought to suffice to prevent false impressions concerning you. But I am bound to tell you, Miss Tulliver, that not only the experience of my whole life, but my observation within the last three days, makes me fear that there is hardly any evidence which will save you from the painful effect of false imputations. The persons who are the most incapable of a conscientious struggle such as yours, are precisely those who will be likely to shrink from you; because they will not believe in your struggle. I fear your life here will be attended not only with much pain, but with many obstructions. For this reason – and for this only – I ask you to consider whether it will not perhaps be better for you to take a situation at a distance, according to your former intention. I will exert myself at once to obtain one for you.'

'Oh, if I could but stop here!' said Maggie. 'I have no heart to begin a strange life again. I should have no stay. I should feel like a lonely wanderer – cut off from the past. I have written to the lady who offered me a situation to excuse myself. If I remained here, I could perhaps atone in some way to Lucy – to others: I could convince them that I'm sorry. And,' she added, with some of the old proud fire flashing out, 'I will not go away because people say false things of me. They shall learn to retract them. If I must go away at last, because – because others wish it, I will not go now.'

'Well,' said Dr Kenn, after some consideration, 'if you determine on that, Miss Tulliver, you may rely on all the influence my position gives me. I am bound to aid and countenance you by the very duties of my office as a parish priest. I will add, that personally I have a deep interest in your peace of mind and welfare.'

'The only thing I want is some occupation that will enable me to get my bread and be independent,' said Maggie. 'I shall not want much. I can go on lodging where I am.'

'I must think over the subject maturely,' said Dr Kenn, 'and in a few days I shall be better able to ascertain the general feeling. I shall come to see you: I shall bear you constantly in mind.'

When Maggie had left him, Dr Kenn stood ruminating with his hands behind him, and his eyes fixed on the carpet, under a painful sense of doubt and difficulty. The tone of Stephen's letter, which he had read, and the actual relations of all the persons concerned, forced upon him powerfully the idea of an ultimate marriage between Stephen and Maggie as the least evil; and the impossibility of their proximity in St Ogg's on any other supposition, until after years of separation, threw an insurmountable prospective difficulty over Maggie's stay there. On the other hand, he entered with all the comprehension of a man who had known spiritual conflict, and lived through years of devoted service to his fellow-men, into that state of Maggie's heart and conscience which made the consent to the marriage a desecration to her: her conscience must not be tampered with: the principle on which she had acted was a safer guide than any balancing of consequences. His experience told him that intervention was too dubious a responsibility to be lightly incurred: the possible issue either of an endeavour to restore the former relations with Lucy and Philip, or of counselling submission to this irruption of a new feeling, was hidden in a darkness all the more impenetrable because each immediate step was clogged with evil.

The great problem of the shifting relation between passion and duty is clear to no man who is capable of apprehending it: the question, whether the moment has come in which a man has fallen below the possibility of a renunciation that will carry any efficacy, and must accept the sway of a passion against which he had struggled as a trespass, is one for which we have no masterkey that will fit all cases. The casuists have become a byword of reproach; but their perverted spirit of minute discrimination was the shadow of a truth to which eyes and hearts are too often fatally sealed – the truth, that moral judgements must remain false and hollow, unless they are checked and enlightened by a perpetual reference to the special circumstances that mark the individual lot.

All people of broad, strong sense have an instinctive repugnance to the men of maxims; because such people early discern that the mysterious complexity of our life is not to be embraced by maxims, and that to lace ourselves up in formulas of that sort is to repress all the divine promptings and inspirations that spring from growing insight and sympathy. And the man of maxims is the popular representative of the minds that are guided in their moral judgement solely by general rules, thinking that these will lead them to justice by a ready-made patent method, without the trouble of exerting patience, discrimination, impartiality – without any care to assure themselves whether they have the insight that comes from a hardly-earned estimate of temptation, or from a life vivid and intense enough to have created a wide fellow-feeling with all that is human.

CHAPTER 3

Showing that Old Acquaintances are Capable of Surprising Us

When Maggie was at home again, her mother brought her news of an unexpected line of conduct in aunt Glegg. As long as Maggie had not been heard of, Mrs Glegg had half-closed her shutters and drawn down her blinds: she felt assured that Maggie was drowned: that was far more probable than that her niece and legatee should have done anything to wound the family honour in the tenderest point. When, at last, she learned from Tom that Maggie had come home, and gathered from him what was her explanation of her absence, she burst forth in severe reproof of Tom for admitting the worst of his sister until he was compelled. If you were not to stand by your 'kin' as long as there was a shred of honour attributable to them, pray what were you to stand by? Lightly to admit conduct in one of your own family that would force you to alter your will, had never been the way of the Dodsons; and though Mrs Glegg had always augured ill of Maggie's future at a time when other people were perhaps less clear-sighted, yet fair-play was a jewel, and it was not for her own friends to help to rob the girl of her fair fame, and to cast her out from family shelter to the scorn of the outer world, until she had become unequivocally a family disgrace. The circumstances were unprecedented in Mrs Glegg's experience – nothing of that kind had happened among the Dodsons before; but it was a case in which her hereditary rectitude and personal strength of character found a common channel along with her fundamental idea of clanship, as they did in her life-long regard to equity in money matters. She quarrelled with Mr Glegg, whose kindness, flowing entirely into compassion for Lucy, made him as hard in his judgement of Maggie as Mr Deane himself was; and, fuming against her sister Tulliver because she did not at once come to her for advice and help, shut herself up in her own room with Baxter's 'Saints' Rest' from morning till night, denying herself to all visitors, till Mr Glegg brought from Mr Deane the news of Stephen's letter. Then Mrs Glegg felt that she had adequate fighting-ground – then she laid aside Baxter, and was ready to meet all comers. While Mrs Pullet could do nothing but shake her head and cry, and wish that cousin Abbott had died, or any number of funerals had happened rather than this, which had never happened before, so that there was no knowing how to act, and Mrs Pullet could never enter St Ogg's again, because 'acquaintances' knew of it all – Mrs Glegg only hoped that Mrs Wooll, or anyone else, would come to her with their false tales about her own niece, and she would know what to say to that ill-advised person!

Again she had a scene of remonstrance with Tom, all the more severe in proportion to the greater strength of her present position. But Tom, like other immovable things, seemed only the more rigidly fixed under that attempt to shake him. Poor Tom! he judged by what he had been able to see; and the judgement was painful enough to himself. He thought he had the demonstration of facts observed through years by his own eyes which gave no warning of their imperfection, that Maggie's nature was utterly untrustworthy, and too strongly marked with evil tendencies to be safely treated with leniency: he would act on that demonstration at any cost; but the thought of it made his days bitter to him. Tom, like every one of us, was imprisoned within the limits of his own nature, and his education had simply glided over him, leaving a slight deposit of polish: if you are inclined to be severe on his severity, remember that the responsibility of tolerance lies with those who have the wider vision. There had arisen in Tom a repulsion towards Maggie that derived its very intensity from their early childish love in the time when they had clasped tiny fingers together, and their later sense of nearness in a common duty and a common sorrow: the sight of her, as he had told her, was hateful to him. In this branch of the Dodson family aunt Glegg found a stronger nature than her own – a nature in which family feeling had lost the character of clanship, in taking on a doubly deep dye of personal pride. Mrs Glegg allowed that Maggie ought to be punished – she was not a woman to deny that – she knew what conduct was; but punished in proportion to the misdeeds proved against her, not to those which were cast upon her by people outside her own family, who might wish to show that their own kin were better.

'Your aunt Glegg scolded me so as niver was, my dear,' said poor Mrs Tulliver, when she came back to Maggie, 'as I didn't go to her before – she said it wasn't for her to come to me first. But she spoke like a sister, too: *having* she allays was, and hard to please – oh dear! – but she's said the kindest word as has ever been spoke by you yet, my child. For she says, for all she's been so set again' having one extry in the house, and making extry spoons and things, and putting her about in her ways, you shall have a shelter in her house, if you'll go to her dutiful, and she'll uphold you against folks as say harm of you when they've no call. And I told her I thought you couldn't bear to see anybody but me, you were so beat down with trouble: but she said, "*I* won't throw ill words at her – there's them out o' the' family 'ull be ready enough to do that. But I'll give her good advice; an' she must be humble." It's wonderful o' Jane; for I'm sure she used to throw everything I did wrong at me – if it was the raisin wine as turned out bad, or the pies too hot – or whativer it was.'

'Oh, mother,' said poor Maggie, shrinking from the thought of all the contact her bruised mind would have to bear, 'tell her I'm very grateful – I'll go to see her as soon as I can; but I can't see anyone just yet, except Dr Kenn. I've been to him – he will advise me, and help me to get some occupation. I can't live with anyone, or be dependent on them, tell aunt Glegg: I must get my own bread. But did you hear nothing of Philip – Philip Wakem? Have you never seen anyone that has mentioned him?'

'No, my dear: but I've been to Lucy's, and I saw your uncle, and he says they got her to listen to the letter, and she took notice o' Miss Guest, and asked questions, and the doctor thinks she's on the turn to be better. What a world this is – what trouble, oh dear! The law was the first beginning, an' it's gone from bad to worse, all of a sudden, just when the luck seemed on the turn.' This was the first lamentation that Mrs Tulliver had let slip to Maggie, but old habit had been revived by the interview with sister Glegg.

'My poor, poor mother!' Maggie burst out, cut to the heart with pity and compunction, and throwing her arms round her mother's neck, 'I was always naughty and troublesome to you. And now you might have been happy if it hadn't been for me.'

'Eh, my dear,' said Mrs Tulliver, leaning towards the warm young cheek; 'I must put up wi' my children – I shall never have no more; and if they bring me bad luck, I must be fond on it – there's nothing else much to be fond on, for my furnitur' went long ago. And you'd got to be very good once; I can't think how it's turned out the wrong way so!'

Still two or three more days passed, and Maggie heard nothing of Philip; anxiety about him was becoming her predominant trouble, and she summoned courage at last to enquire about him of Dr Kenn, on his next visit to her. He did not even know if Philip was at home. The elder Wakem was made moody by an accumulation of annoyance: the disappointment in this young Jetsome, to whom, apparently, he was a good deal attached, had been followed close by the catastrophe to his son's hopes after he had conceded his feelings to them, and incautiously mentioned this concession in St Ogg's – and he was almost fierce in his brusqueness when anyone asked him a question about his son. But Philip could hardly have been ill, or it would have been known through the calling in of the medical man; it was probable that he was gone out of the town for a little while. Maggie sickened under this suspense, and her imagination began to live more and more persistently in what Philip was enduring. What did he believe about her?

At last Bob brought her a letter, without a postmark, directed in a hand which she knew familiarly in the letters of her own name – a hand in which her name had been written long ago, in a pocket Shakespeare which she possessed. Her mother was in the room, and Maggie, in violent agitation, hurried upstairs that she might read the letter in solitude. She read it with a throbbing brow.

MAGGIE – I believe in you – I know you never meant to deceive me – I know you tried to keep faith to me, and to all. I believed this before I had any other evidence of it than your own nature. The night after I last parted from you I suffered torments. I had seen what convinced me that you were not free; that there was another whose presence had a power over you which mine never possessed; but through all the suggestions – almost murderous suggestions – of rage and jealousy, my mind made its way to belief in your truthfulness. I was sure that you meant to cleave to me, as you had said; that you had rejected him; that you struggled to renounce him, for Lucy's sake and for mine. But I could see no issue that was not fatal for you; and that dread shut out the very thought of resignation. I foresaw that he would not relinquish you, and I believed then, as I believe now, that the strong attraction which drew you together proceeded only from one side of your characters, and belonged to that partial, divided action of our nature which makes half the tragedy of the human lot. I have felt the vibration of chords in your nature that I have continually felt the want of in his. But perhaps I am wrong; perhaps I feel about you as the artist does about the scene over which his soul has brooded with love: he would tremble to see it confided to other hands; he would never believe that it could bear for another all the meaning and the beauty it bears for him.

I dared not trust myself to see you that morning; I was filled with selfish passion: I was shattered by a night of conscious delirium. I told you long ago that I had never been resigned even to the mediocrity of my powers: how could I be resigned to the loss of the one thing which had ever come to me on earth, with the promise of such deep joy as would give a new and blessed meaning to the foregoing pain – the promise of another self that would lift my aching affection into the divine rapture of an ever-springing, ever-satisfied want?

But the miseries of that night had prepared me for what came before the next. It was no surprise to me. I was certain that he had prevailed on you to sacrifice everything to him, and I waited with equal certainty to hear of your marriage. I measured your love and his by my own. But I was wrong, Maggie. There is something stronger in you than your love for him.

I will not tell you what I went through in that interval. But even in its utmost agony – even in those terrible throes that love must suffer before it can be disembodied of selfish desire – my love for you sufficed to withhold me from suicide, without the aid of any other motive. In the midst of my egoism, I yet could not bear to come like a death-shadow across the feast of your joy. I could not bear to forsake the world in which you still lived and might need me; it was part of the faith I had vowed to you – to wait and endure. Maggie, that is a proof of what I write now to assure you of – that no anguish I have had to bear on your account has been too heavy a price to pay for the new life into which I have entered in loving you. I want you to put aside all grief because of the grief you have caused me. I was nurtured in the sense of privation; I never expected happiness; and in knowing you, in loving you, I have had, and still have, what reconciles me to life. You have been to my affections what light, what colour is to my eyes – what music is to the inward ear; you have raised a dim unrest into a vivid consciousness. The new life I have found in caring for your joy and sorrow more than for what is directly my own, has transformed the spirit of rebellious murmuring into that willing endurance which is the birth of strong sympathy. I think nothing but such complete and intense love could have initiated me into that enlarged life which grows and grows by appropriating the life of others; for before, I was always dragged back from it by ever-present painful self-consciousness. I even think sometimes that this gift of transferred life which has come to me in loving you, may be a new power to me.

Then – dear one – in spite of all, you have been the blessing of my life. Let no self-reproach weigh on you because of me. It is I who should rather reproach myself for having urged my feelings upon you, and hurried you into words that you have felt as fetters. You meant to be true to those words; you have been true. I can measure your sacrifice by what I have known in only one half-hour of your presence with me, when I dreamed that you might love me best. But, Maggie, I have no just claim on you for more than affectionate remembrance.

For some time I have shrunk from writing to you, because I have shrunk even from the appearance of wishing to thrust myself before you, and so repeating my original error. But you will not misconstrue me. I know that we must keep apart for a long while; cruel tongues would force us apart, if nothing else did. But I shall not go away. The place where you are is the one where my mind must live, wherever I might travel. And remember that I am unchangeably yours: yours – not with selfish wishes, but with a devotion that excludes such wishes.

God comfort you – my loving, large-souled Maggie. If everyone else has misconceived you, remember that you have never been doubted by him whose heart recognised you ten years ago.

Do not believe anyone who says I am ill, because I am not seen out of doors. I have only had nervous headaches – no worse than I have sometimes had them before. But the overpowering heat inclines me to be perfectly quiescent in the daytime. I am strong enough to obey any word which shall tell me that I can serve you by word or deed.

Yours, to the last,

PHILIP WAKEM

As Maggie knelt by the bed sobbing, with that letter pressed under her, her feelings again and again gathered themselves in a whispered cry, always in the same words: 'O God, is there any happiness in love that could make me forget *their* pain?'

CHAPTER 4

Maggie and Lucy

By the end of the week Dr Kenn had made up his mind that there was only one way in which he could secure to Maggie a suitable living at St Ogg's. Even with his twenty years' experience as a parish priest, he was aghast at the obstinate continuance of imputations against her in the face of evidence. Hitherto he had been rather more adored and appealed to than was quite agreeable to him; but now, in attempting to open the ears of women to reason, and their consciences to justice, on behalf of Maggie Tulliver, he suddenly found himself as powerless as he was aware he would have been if he had attempted to influence the shape of bonnets. Dr Kenn could not be contradicted; he was listened to in silence; but when he left the room, a comparison of opinions among his hearers yielded much the same result as before. Miss Tulliver had undeniably acted in a blamable manner; even Dr Kenn did not deny that: how, then, could he think so lightly of her as to put that favourable interpretation on everything she had done? Even on the supposition that required the utmost stretch of belief – namely, that none of the things said about Miss Tulliver were true – still, since they *had* been said about her, they had cast an odour round her which must cause her to be shrunk from by every woman who had to take care of her own reputation – and of Society. To have taken Maggie by the hand and said, 'I will not believe unproved evil of you: my lips shall not utter it; my ears shall be closed against it; I, too, am an erring mortal, liable to stumble, apt to come short of my most earnest efforts; your lot has been harder than mine, your temptation greater; let us help each other to stand and walk without more falling;' – to have done this would have demanded courage, deep pity, self-knowledge, generous trust – would have demanded a mind that tasted no piquancy in evil-speaking, that felt no self-exaltation in condemning, that cheated itself with no large words into the belief that life can have any moral end, any high religion, which excludes the striving after perfect truth, justice, and love towards the individual men and women who come across our own path. The ladies of St Ogg's were not beguiled by any wide speculative conceptions; but they had their favourite abstraction, called Society, which served to make their consciences perfectly easy in doing what satisfied their own egoism – thinking and speaking the worst of Maggie Tulliver, and turning their backs upon her. It was naturally disappointing to Dr Kenn, after two years of superfluous incense from his feminine parishioners, to find them suddenly maintaining their views in opposition to his; but then, they maintained them in opposition to a Higher Authority, which they had venerated longer. That Authority had furnished a very explicit answer to persons who might enquire where their social duties began, and might be inclined to take wide views as to the starting-point. The answer had not turned on the ultimate good of Society, but on 'a certain man' who was found in trouble by the wayside.

Not that St Ogg's was empty of women with some tenderness of heart and conscience: probably it had as fair a proportion of human goodness in it as any other small trading town of that day. But until every good man is brave, we must expect to find many good women timid: too timid even to believe in the correctness of their own best promptings, when these would place them in a minority. And the men at St Ogg's were not all brave by any means: some of them were even fond of scandal – and to an extent that might have given their conversation an effeminate character, if it had not been distinguished by masculine jokes, and by an occasional shrug of the shoulders at the mutual hatred of women. It was the general feeling of the masculine mind at St Ogg's that women were not to be interfered with in their treatment of each other.

And thus every direction in which Dr Kenn had turned in the hope of procuring some kind recognition and some employment for Maggie, proved a disappointment to him. Mrs James Torry could not think of taking Maggie as a nursery governess, even temporarily – a young woman about whom 'such things had been said', and about whom 'gentlemen joked'; and Miss Kirke, who had a spinal complaint, and wanted a reader and companion, felt quite sure that Maggie's mind must be of a quality with which she, for her part, could not risk *any* contact. Why did not Miss Tulliver accept the shelter offered her by her aunt Glegg? – it did not become a girl like her to refuse it. Or else, why did she not go out of the neighbourhood, and get a situation where she was not known? (It was not, apparently, of so much importance that she should carry her dangerous tendencies into strange families unknown at St Ogg's.) She must be very bold and hardened to wish to stay in a parish where she was so much stared at and whispered about.

Dr Kenn, having great natural firmness, began, in the presence of this opposition, as every firm man would have done, to contract a certain strength of determination over and above what would have been called forth by the end in view. He himself wanted a daily governess for his younger children; and though he had hesitated in the first instance to offer this position to Maggie, the resolution to protest with the utmost force of his personal and priestly character against her being crushed and driven away by slander, was now decisive. Maggie gratefully accepted an employment that gave her duties as well as a support: her days would be filled now, and solitary evenings would be a welcome rest. She no longer needed the sacrifice her mother made in staying with her, and Mrs Tulliver was persuaded to go back to the mill.

But now it began to be discovered that Dr Kenn, exemplary as he had hitherto appeared, had his crotchets – possibly his weaknesses. The masculine mind of St Ogg's smiled pleasantly, and did not wonder that Kenn liked to see a fine pair of eyes daily, or that he was inclined to take so lenient a view of the past; the feminine mind, regarded at that period as less powerful, took a more melancholy view of the case. If Dr Kenn should be beguiled into marrying that Miss Tulliver! It was not safe to be too confident, even about the best of men: an apostle had fallen, and wept bitterly afterwards; and though Peter's denial was not a close precedent, his repentance was likely to be.

Maggie had not taken her daily walks to the Rectory for many weeks, before the dreadful possibility of her sometime or other becoming the Rector's wife had been talked of so often in confidence, that ladies were beginning to discuss how they should behave to her in that position. For Dr Kenn, it had been understood, had sat in the schoolroom half an hour one morning, when Miss Tulliver was giving her lessons; nay, he had sat there every morning: he had once walked home with her – he almost *always* walked home with her – and if not, he went to see her in the evening. What an artful creature she was! What a *mother* for those children! It was enough to make poor Mrs Kenn turn in her grave, that they should be put under the care of this girl only a few weeks after her death. Would he be so lost to propriety as to marry her before the year was out? The masculine mind was sarcastic, and thought *not*.

The Miss Guests saw an alleviation to the sorrow of witnessing a folly in their Rector: at least their brother would be safe; and their knowledge of Stephen's tenacity was a constant ground of alarm to them, lest he should come back and marry Maggie. They were not among those who disbelieved their brother's letter; but they had no confidence in Maggie's adherence to her renunciation of him; they suspected that she had shrunk rather from the elopement than from the marriage, and that she lingered in St Ogg's, relying on his return to her. They had always thought her disagreeable; they now thought her artful and proud; having quite as good grounds for that judgement as you and I probably have for many strong opinions of the same kind. Formerly they had not altogether delighted in the contemplated match with Lucy, but now their dread of a marriage between Stephen and Maggie added its momentum to their genuine pity and indignation on behalf of the gentle forsaken girl, in making them desire that he should return to her. As soon as Lucy was able to leave home, she was to seek relief from the oppressive heat of this August by going to the coast with the Miss Guests; and it was in their plans that Stephen should be induced to join them. On the very first hint of gossip concerning Maggie and Dr Kenn, the report was conveyed in Miss Guest's letter to her brother.

Maggie had frequent tidings through her mother, or aunt Glegg, or Dr Kenn, of Lucy's gradual progress towards recovery, and her thoughts tended continually towards her uncle Deane's house: she hungered for an interview with Lucy, if it were only for five minutes – to utter a word of penitence, to be assured by Lucy's own eyes and lips that she did not believe in the willing treachery of those whom she had loved and trusted. But she knew that even if her uncle's indignation had not closed his house against her, the agitation of such an interview would have been forbidden to Lucy. Only to have seen her without speaking, would have been some relief; for Maggie was haunted by a face cruel in its very gentleness: a face that had been turned on hers with glad sweet looks of trust and love from the twilight time of memory; changed now to a sad and weary face by a first heart-stroke. And as the days passed on, that pale image became more and more distinct; the picture grew and grew into more speaking definiteness under the avenging hand of remorse; the soft hazel eyes, in their look of pain, were bent for ever on Maggie, and pierced her the more because she could see no anger in them. But Lucy was not yet able to go to church, or any place where Maggie could see her; and even the hope of that departed, when the news was told her by aunt Glegg, that Lucy was really going away in a few days to Scarborough with the Miss Guests, who had been heard to say that they expected their brother to meet them there.

Only those who have known what hardest inward conflict is, can know what Maggie felt as she sat in her loneliness the evening after hearing that news from Mrs Glegg – only those who have known what it is to dread their own selfish desires as the watching mother would dread the sleeping-potion that was to still her own pain.

She sat without candle in the twilight, with the window wide open towards the river; the sense of oppressive heat adding itself undistinguishably to the burthen of her lot. Seated on a chair against the window, with her arm on the window-sill, she was looking blankly at the flowing river, swift with the advancing rushing tide – struggling to see still the sweet face in its unreproaching sadness, that seemed now from moment to moment to sink away and be hidden behind a form that thrust itself between, and made darkness. Hearing the door open, she thought Mrs Jakin was coming in with her supper, as usual; and with that repugnance to trivial speech which comes with langour and wretchedness, she shrank from turning round and saying she wanted nothing: good little Mrs Jakin would be sure to make some well-meant remarks. But the next moment, without her having discerned the sound of a footstep, she felt a light hand on her shoulder, and heard a voice close to her saying, 'Maggie!'

The face was there – changed, but all the sweeter: the hazel eyes were there, with their heart-piercing tenderness.

'Maggie!' the soft voice said. 'Lucy!' answered a voice with a sharp ring of anguish in it; and Lucy threw her arms round Maggie's neck, and leaned her pale cheek against the burning brow.

'I stole out,' said Lucy, almost in a whisper, while she sat down close to Maggie and held her hand, 'when papa and the rest were away. Alice is come with me. I asked her to help me. But I must only stay a little while, because it is so late.'

It was easier to say that at first than to say anything else. They sat looking at each other. It seemed as if the interview must end without more speech, for speech was very difficult. Each felt that there would be something scorching in the words that would recall the irretrievable wrong. But soon, as Maggie looked, every distinct thought began to be overflowed by a wave of loving penitence, and words burst forth with a sob.

'God bless you For coming, Lucy.'

The sobs came thick on each other after that.

'Maggie, dear, be comforted,' said Lucy now, putting her cheek against Maggie's again. 'Don't grieve.' And she sat still, hoping to soothe Maggie with that gentle caress.

'I didn't mean to deceive you, Lucy,' said Maggie, as soon as she could speak. 'It always made me wretched that I felt what I didn't like you to know . . . It was because I thought it would all be conquered, and you might never see anything to wound you.'

'I know, dear,' said Lucy. 'I know you never meant to make me unhappy . . . It is a trouble that has come on us all: you have more to bear than I have – and you gave him up, when . . . you did what it must have been very hard to do.'

They were silent again a little while, sitting with clasped hands, and cheeks leaned together.

'Lucy,' Maggie began again, '*he* struggled too. He wanted to be true to you. He will come back to you. Forgive him – he will be happy then . . . '

These words were wrung forth from Maggie's deepest soul, with an effort like the convulsed clutch of a drowning man. Lucy trembled and was silent.

A gentle knock came at the door. It was Alice, the maid, who entered and said, 'I daren't stay any longer, Miss Deane. They'll find it out, and there'll be such anger at your coming out so late.'

Lucy rose and said, 'Very well, Alice – in a minute.'

'I'm to go away on Friday, Maggie,' she added, when Alice had closed the door again. 'When I come back, and am strong, they will let me do as I like. I shall come to you when I please then.'

'Lucy,' said Maggie, with another great effort, 'I pray to God continually that I may never be the cause of sorrow to you any more.'

She pressed the little hand that she held between hers, and looked up into the face that was bent over hers. Lucy never forgot that look.

'Maggie,' she said, in a low voice, that had the solemnity of confession in it, 'you are better than I am. I can't . . . '

She broke off there, and said no more. But they clasped each other again in a last embrace.

CHAPTER 5

The Last Conflict

In the second week of September, Maggie was again sitting in her lonely room, battling with the old shadowy enemies that were for ever slain and rising again. It was past midnight, and the rain was beating heavily against the window, driven with fitful force by the rushing, loud-moaning wind. For, the day after Lucy's visit, there had been a sudden change in the weather: the heat and drought had given way to cold variable winds, and heavy falls of rain at intervals; and she had been forbidden to risk the contemplated journey until the weather should become more settled. In the counties higher up the Floss, the rains had been continuous, and the completion of the harvest had been arrested. And now, for the last two days, the rains on this lower course of the river had been incessant, so that the old men had shaken their heads and talked of sixty years ago, when the same sort of weather, happening about the equinox, brought on the great floods, which swept the bridge away, and reduced the town to great misery. But the younger generation who had seen several small floods, thought lightly of these sombre recollections and forebodings; and Bob Jakin, naturally prone to take a hopeful view of his own luck, laughed at his mother when she regretted their having taken a house by the riverside; observing that but for that they would have had no boats, which were the most lucky of possessions in case of a flood that obliged them to go to a distance for food.

But the careless and the fearful were alike sleeping in their beds now. There was hope that the rain would abate by the morrow; threatenings of a worse kind, from sudden thaws after falls of snow, had often passed off in the experience of the younger ones; and at the very worst, the banks would be sure to break lower down the river when the tide came in with violence, and so the waters would be carried off, without causing more than temporary inconvenience, and losses that would be felt only by the poorer sort, whom charity would relieve.

All were in their beds now, for it was past midnight: all, except some solitary watchers such as Maggie. She was seated in her little parlour towards the river with one candle, that left everything dim in the room, except a letter which lay before her on the table. That letter, which had come to her today, was one of the causes that had kept her up far on into the night – unconscious how the hours were going – careless of seeking rest – with no image of rest coming across her mind, except of that far, far off rest, from which there would be no more waking for her into this struggling earthly life.

Two days before Maggie received that letter she had been to the Rectory for the last time. The heavy rain would have prevented her from going since; but there was another reason. Dr Kenn, at first enlightened only by a few hints as to the new turn which gossip and slander had taken in relation to Maggie, had recently been made more fully aware of it by an earnest remonstrance from one of his male parishioners against the indiscretion of persisting in the attempt to

overcome the prevalent feeling in the parish by a course of resistance. Dr
Kenn, having a conscience void of offence in the matter, was still inclined to
persevere – was still averse to give way before a public sentiment that was odious
and contemptible; but he was finally wrought upon by the consideration of the
peculiar responsibility attached to his office, of avoiding the appearance of evil –
an 'appearance' that is always dependent on the average quality of surrounding
minds. Where these minds are low and gross, the area of that 'appearance' is
proportionately widened. Perhaps he was in danger of acting from obstinacy;
perhaps it was his duty to succumb: conscientious people are apt to see their
duty in that which is the most painful course; and to recede was always painful to
Dr Kenn. He made up his mind that he must advise Maggie to go away from St
Ogg's for a time; and he performed that difficult task with as much delicacy as
he could, only stating in vague terms that he found his attempt to countenance
her stay was a source of discord between himself and his parishioners, that was
likely to obstruct his usefulness as a clergyman. He begged her to allow him to
write to a clerical friend of his, who might possibly take her into his own family
as governess; and, if not, would probably know of some other available position
for a young woman in whose welfare Dr Kenn felt a strong interest.

Poor Maggie listened with a trembling lip: she could say nothing but a faint
'thank you – I shall be grateful'; and she walked back to her lodgings, through
the driving rain, with a new sense of desolation. She must be a lonely wanderer;
she must go out among fresh faces, that would look at her wonderingly, because
the days did not seem joyful to her; she must begin a new life, in which
she would have to rouse herself to receive new impressions – and she was so
unspeakably, sickeningly weary! There was no home, no help for the erring:
even those who pitied were constrained to hardness. But ought she to complain?
Ought she to shrink in this way from the long penance of life, which was all
the possibility she had of lightening the load to some other sufferers, and so
changing that passionate error into a new force of unselfish human love? All the
next day she sat in her lonely room, with a window darkened by the cloud and
the driving rain, thinking of that future, and wrestling for patience: – for what
repose could poor Maggie ever win except by wrestling?

And on the third day – this day of which she had just sat out the close – the
letter had come which was lying on the table before her.

The letter was from Stephen. He was come back from Holland: he was at
Mudport again, unknown to any of his friends; and had written to her from that
place, enclosing the letter to a person whom he trusted in St Ogg's. From
beginning to end it was a passionate cry of reproach: an appeal against her
useless sacrifice of him – of herself: against that perverted notion of right which
led her to crush all his hopes, for the sake of a mere idea, and not any substantial
good – *his* hopes, whom she loved, and who loved her with that single overpowering passion, that worship, which a man never gives to a woman more than
once in his life.

'They have written to me that you are to marry Kenn. As if I should believe
that! Perhaps they have told you some such fables about me. Perhaps they tell
you I have been "travelling", My body has been dragged about somewhere; but

I have never travelled from the hideous place where you left me – where I started up from the stupor of helpless rage to find you gone.

'Maggie! whose pain can have been like mine? Whose injury is like mine? Who besides me has met that long look of love that has burnt itself into my soul, so that no other image can come there? Maggie, call me back to you! – call me back to life and goodness! I am banished from both now. I have no motives: I am indifferent to everything. Two months have only deepened the certainty that I can never care for life without you. Write me one word – say "Come!" In two days I should be with you. Maggie – have you forgotten what it was to be together? – to be within reach of a look – to be within hearing of each other's voice?'

When Maggie first read this letter she felt as if her real temptation had only just begun. At the entrance of the chill dark cavern, we turn with unworn courage from the warm light; but how, when we have trodden far in the damp darkness, and have begun to be faint and weary – how, if there is a sudden opening above us, and we are invited back again to the life-nourishing day? The leap of natural longing from under the pressure of pain is so strong, that all less immediate motives are likely to be forgotten – till the pain has been escaped from.

For hours Maggie felt as if her struggle had been in vain. For hours every other thought that she strove to summon was thrust aside by the image of Stephen waiting for the single word that would bring him to her. She did not *read* the letter: she heard him uttering it, and the voice shook her with its old strange power. All the day before she had been filled with the vision of a lonely future through which she must carry the burthen of regret, upheld only by clinging faith. And here – close within her reach – urging itself upon her even as a claim – was another future, in which hard endurance and effort were to be exchanged for easy delicious leaning on another's loving strength! And yet that promise of joy in the place of sadness did not make the dire force of the temptation to Maggie. It was Stephen's tone of misery, it was the doubt in the justice of her own resolve, that made the balance tremble, and made her once start from her seat to reach the pen and paper, and write 'Come!'

But close upon that decisive act, her mind recoiled; and the sense of contradiction with her past self in her moments of strength and clearness, came upon her like a pang of conscious degradation. No – she must wait – she must pray – the light that had forsaken her would come again: she should feel again what she had felt, when she had fled away, under an inspiration strong enough to conquer agony – to conquer love: she should feel again what she had felt when Lucy stood by her, when Philip's letter had stirred all the fibres that bound her to the calmer past.

She sat quite still, far on into the night: with no impulse to change her attitude, without active force enough even for the mental act of prayer: only waiting for the light that would surely come again. It came with the memories that no passion could long quench: the long past came back to her, and with it the fountains of self-renouncing pity and affection, of faithfulness and resolve. The words that were marked by the quiet hand in the little old book that she had long ago learned by heart, rushed even to her lips, and found a vent for themselves in a low murmur that was quite lost in the loud driving of the rain against the window and the loud moan and roar of the wind: 'I have received the Cross, I have received it from Thy hand; I will bear it, and bear it till death, as Thou hast laid it upon me.'

But soon other words rose that could find no utterance but in a sob: 'Forgive me, Stephen! It will pass away. You will come back to her.'

She took up the letter, held it to the candle, and let it burn slowly on the hearth. Tomorrow she would write to him the last word of parting.

'I will bear it, and bear it till death . . . But how long it will be before death comes! I am so young, so healthy. How shall I have patience and strength? Am I to struggle and fall and repent again? – has life other trials as hard for me still?' With that cry of self-despair, Maggie fell on her knees against the table, and buried her sorrow-stricken face. Her soul went out to the Unseen Pity that would be with her to the end. Surely there was something taught her by this experience of great need; and she must be learning a secret of human tenderness and long-suffering, that the less erring could hardly know? 'O God, if my life is to be long, let me live to bless and comfort', At that moment Maggie felt a startling sensation of sudden cold about her knees and feet: it was water flowing under her. She started up: the stream was flowing under the door that led into the passage. She was not bewildered for an instant – she knew it was the flood!

The tumult of emotion she had been enduring for the last twelve hours seemed to have left a great calm in her: without screaming, she hurried with the candle upstairs to Bob Jakin's bedroom. The door was ajar; she went in and shook him by the shoulder.

'Bob, the flood is come! it is in the house! let us see if we can make the boats safe.'

She lighted his candle, while the poor wife, snatching up her baby, burst into screams; and then she hurried down again to see if the waters were rising fast. There was a step down into the room at the door leading from the staircase; she saw that the water was already on a level with the step. While she was looking, something came with a tremendous crash against the window, and sent the leaded panes and the old wooden framework inwards in shivers – the water pouring in after it.

'It is the boat!' cried Maggie. 'Bob, come down to get the boats!'

And without a moment's shudder of fear, she plunged through the water, which was rising fast to her knees, and by the glimmering light of the candle she had left on the stairs, she mounted on to the window-sill, and crept into the boat, which was left with the prow lodging and protruding through the window. Bob was not long after her, hurrying without shoes or stockings, but with the lanthorn in his hand.

'Why, they're both here – both the boats,' said Bob, as he got into the one where Maggie was. 'It's wonderful this fastening isn't broke too, as well as the mooring.'

In the excitement of getting into the other boat, unfastening it, and mastering an oar, Bob was not struck with the danger Maggie incurred. We are not apt to fear for the fearless, when we are companions in their danger, and Bob's mind was absorbed in possible expedients for the safety of the helpless indoors. The fact that Maggie had been up, had waked him, and had taken the lead in activity, gave Bob a vague impression of her as one who would help to protect, not need to be protected. She too had got possession of an oar, and had pushed off, so as to release the boat from the overhanging window-frame.

'The water's rising so fast,' said Bob, 'I doubt it'll be in at the chambers before long – th' house is so low. I've more mind to get Prissy and the child and the mother into the boat, if I could, and trusten to the water – for th' old house is none so safe. And I let go the boat . . . but *you*,' he exclaimed, suddenly lifting the light of his lanthorn on Maggie, as she stood in the rain with the oar in her hand and her black hair streaming.

Maggie had no time to answer, for a new tidal current swept along the line of the houses, and drove both the boats out on the wide water, with a force that carried them far past the meeting current of the river.

In the first moments Maggie felt nothing, thought of nothing, but that she had suddenly passed away from that life which she had been dreading: it was the transition of death, without its agony – and she was alone in the darkness with God.

The whole thing had been so rapid – so dream-like – that the threads of ordinary association were broken: she sank down on the seat clutching the oar mechanically, and for a long while had no distinct conception of her position. The first thing that waked her to fuller consciousness was the cessation of the rain, and a perception that the darkness was divided by the faintest light, which parted the overhanging gloom from the immeasurable watery level below. She was driven out upon the flood – that awful visitation of God which her father used to talk of – which had made the nightmare of her childish dreams. And with that thought there rushed in the vision of the old home – and Tom – and her mother – they had all listened together.

'O God, where am I? Which is the way home?' she cried out, in the dim loneliness.

What was happening to them at the mill? The flood had once nearly destroyed it. They might be in danger – in distress: her mother and her brother, alone there, beyond reach of help! Her whole soul was strained now on that thought; and she saw the long-loved faces looking for help into the darkness, and finding none.

She was floating in smooth water now – perhaps far on the over-flooded fields. There was no sense of present danger to check the outgoing of her mind to the old home; and she strained her eyes against the curtain of gloom that she might seize the first sight of her whereabouts – that she might catch some faint suggestion of the spot towards which all her anxieties tended.

Oh, how welcome, the widening of that dismal watery level – the gradual uplifting of the cloudy firmament – the slowly defining blackness of objects above the glassy dark! Yes – she must be out on the fields – those were the tops of hedgerow trees. Which way did the river lie? Looking behind her, she saw the lines of black trees: looking before her, there were none: then, the river lay before her. She seized an oar and began to paddle the boat forward with the energy of wakening hope: the dawning seemed to advance more swiftly, now she was in action; and she could soon see the poor dumb beasts crowding piteously on a mound where they had taken refuge. Onward she paddled and rowed by turns in the growing twilight: her wet clothes clung round her, and her streaming hair was dashed about by the wind, but she was hardly conscious of any bodily sensations – except a sensation of strength, inspired by mighty emotion. Along with the sense of danger and possible rescue for those long-remembered beings at the old home, there was an undefined sense of reconcilement with her brother: what quarrel, what harshness, what unbelief in each other can subsist in the presence of a great calamity, when all the artificial vesture of our life is gone, and we are all one with each other in primitive mortal needs? Vaguely, Maggie felt this – in the strong resurgent love towards her brother that swept away all the later impressions of hard, cruel offence and misunderstanding, and left only the deep, underlying, unshakable memories of early union.

But now there was a large dark mass in the distance, and near to her Maggie could discern the current of the river. The dark mass must be – yes, it was – St Ogg's. Ah, now she knew which way to look for the first glimpse of the well-known trees – the grey willows, the now yellowing chestnuts – and above them the old roof! But there was no colour, no shape yet: all was faint and dim. More and more strongly the energies seemed to come and put themselves forth, as if her life were a stored-up force that was being spent in this hour, unneeded for any future.

She must get her boat into the current of the Floss, else she would never be able to pass the Ripple and approach the house: this was the thought that occurred to her, as she imagined with more and more vividness the state of things round the old home. But then she might be carried very far down, and be unable to guide her boat out of the current again. For the first time distinct ideas of danger began to press upon her; but there was no choice of courses, no room for hesitation, and she floated into the current. Swiftly she went now, without effort; more and more clearly in the lessening distance and the growing light she began to discern the objects that she knew must be the well-known trees and roofs; nay she was not far off a rushing muddy current that must be the strangely altered Ripple.

Great God! there were floating masses in it, that might dash against her boat as she passed, and cause her to perish too soon. What were those masses?

For the first time Maggie's heart began to beat in an agony of dread. She sat helpless – dimly conscious that she was being floated along – more intensely conscious of the anticipated clash. But the horror was transient: it passed away before the oncoming warehouses of St Ogg's: she had passed the mouth of the Ripple, then: *now*, she must use all her skill and power to manage the boat and get it if possible out of the current. She could see now that the bridge was broken down: she could see the masts of a stranded vessel far out over the watery field. But no boats were to be seen moving on the river – such as had been laid hands on were employed in the flooded streets.

With new resolution, Maggie seized her oar, and stood up again to paddle; but the now ebbing tide added to the swiftness of the river, and she was carried along beyond the bridge. She could hear shouts from the windows overlooking the river, as if the people there were calling to her. It was not till she had passed on nearly to Tofton that she could get the boat clear of the current. Then with one yearning look towards her uncle Deane's house that lay further down the river, she took to both her oars and rowed with all her might across the watery fields, back towards the mill. Colour was beginning to awake now, and as she approached the Dorlcote fields, she could discern the tints of the trees – could see the old Scotch firs far to the right, and the home chestnuts – Oh! how deep they lay in the water: deeper than the trees on this side the hill. And the roof of the mill – where was it? Those heavy fragments hurrying down the Ripple – what had they meant? But it was not the house – the house stood firm; drowned up to the first storey, but still firm – or was it broken in at the end towards the mill?

With panting joy that she was there at last – joy that overcame all distress – Maggie neared the front of the house. At first she heard no sound: she saw no object moving. Her boat was on a level with the upstairs windows. She called out in a loud piercing voice.

'Tom, where are you? Mother, where are you? Here is Maggie!'

Soon, from the window of the attic in the central gable, she heard Tom's voice:

'Who is it? Have you brought a boat?'

'It is I, Tom – Maggie. Where is mother?'

'She is not here: she went to Garum, the day before yesterday. I'll come down to the lower window.'

'Alone, Maggie?' said Tom, in a voice of deep astonishment, as he opened the middle window on a level with the boat.

'Yes, Tom: God has taken care of me, to bring me to you. Get in quickly. Is there no one else?'

'No,' said Tom, stepping into the boat, 'I fear the man is drowned: he was carried down the Ripple, I think, when part of the mill fell with the crash of trees and stones against it: I've shouted again and again, and there has been no answer. Give me the oars, Maggie.'

It was not till Tom had pushed off and they were on the wide water – he face to face with Maggie – that the full meaning of what had happened rushed upon his mind. It came with so overpowering a force – it was such a new revelation to his spirit, of the depths in life that had lain beyond his vision, which he had fancied so keen and clear – that he was unable to ask a question. They sat mutely gazing at each other: Maggie with eyes of intense life looking out from a weary, beaten face – Tom pale with a certain awe and humiliation. Thought was busy though the lips were silent: and though he could ask no question, he guessed a story of almost miraculous divinely-protected effort. But at last a mist gathered over the blue-grey eyes, and the lips found a word they could utter: the old childish – 'Magsie!'

Maggie could make no answer but a long deep sob of that mysterious wondrous happiness that is one with pain.

As soon as she could speak, she said, 'We will go to Lucy, Tom: we'll go and see if she is safe, and then we can help the rest.'

Tom rowed with untired vigour, and with a different speed from poor Maggie's. The boat was soon in the current of the river again, and soon they would be at Tofton.

'Park House stands high up out of the flood,' said Maggie. 'Perhaps they have got Lucy there.'

Nothing else was said; a new danger was being carried towards them by the river. Some wooden machinery had just given way on one of the wharves, and huge fragments were being floated along. The sun was rising now, and the wide area of watery desolation was spread out in dreadful clearness around them – in dreadful clearness floated onwards the hurrying, threatening masses. A large company in a boat that was working its way along under the Tofton houses, observed their danger, and shouted, 'Get out of the current!'

But that could not be done at once, and Tom, looking before him, saw death rushing on them. Huge fragments, clinging together in fatal fellowship, made one wide mass across the stream.

'It is coming, Maggie!' Tom said, in a deep hoarse voice, loosing the oars, and clasping her.

The next instant the boat was no longer seen upon the water – and the huge mass was hurrying on in hideous triumph.

But soon the keel of the boat reappeared, a black speck on the golden water.

The boat reappeared – but brother and sister had gone down in an embrace never to be parted: living through again in one supreme moment, the days when they had clasped their little hands in love, and roamed the daisied fields together.

Conclusion

Nature repairs her ravages – repairs them with her sunshine, and with human labour. The desolation wrought by that flood, had left little visible trace on the face of the earth, five years after. The fifth autumn was rich in golden corn-stacks, rising in thick clusters among the distant hedgerows; the wharves and warehouses on the Floss were busy again, with echoes of eager voices, with hopeful lading and unlading.

And every man and woman mentioned in this history was still living – except those whose end we know.

Nature repairs her ravages – but not all. The uptorn trees are not rooted again; the parted hills are left scarred: if there is a new growth, the trees are not the same as the old, and the hills underneath their green vesture bear the marks of the past rending. To the eyes that have dwelt on the past, there is no thorough repair.

Dorlcote Mill was rebuilt. And Dorlcote churchyard – where the brick grave that held a father whom we know, was found with the stone laid prostrate upon it after the flood – had recovered all its grassy order and decent quiet.

Near that brick grave there was a tomb erected, very soon after the flood, for two bodies that were found in close embrace; and it was visited at different moments by two men who both felt that their keenest joy and keenest sorrow were for ever buried there.

One of them visited the tomb again with a sweet face beside him – but that was years after.

The other was always solitary. His great companionship was among the trees of the Red Deeps, where the buried joy seemed still to hover – like a revisiting spirit.

The tomb bore the names of Tom and Maggie Tulliver, and below the names it was written –

IN THEIR DEATH THEY WERE NOT DIVIDED.

SILAS MARNER

Silas Marner

A novel by
GEORGE ELIOT
first published in 1861

PART ONE

Chapter 1

In the days when the spinning-wheels hummed busily in the farmhouses – and even great ladies, clothed in silk and thread-lace, had their toy spinning-wheels of polished oak – there might be seen, in districts far away among the lanes, or deep in the bosom of the hills, certain pallid undersized men, who, by the side of the brawny country-folk, looked like the remnants of a disinherited race. The shepherd's dog barked fiercely when one of these alien-looking men appeared on the upland, dark against the early winter sunset; for what dog likes a figure bent under a heavy bag? – and these pale men rarely stirred abroad without that mysterious burden. The shepherd himself, though he had good reason to believe that the bag held nothing but flaxen thread, or else the long rolls of strong linen spun from that thread, was not quite sure that this trade of weaving, indispensable though it was, could be carried on entirely without the help of the Evil One. In that far-off time superstition clung easily round every person or thing that was at all unwonted, or even intermittent and occasional merely, like the visits of the pedlar or the knife-grinder. No one knew where wandering men had their homes or their origin; and how was a man to be explained unless you at least knew somebody who knew his father and mother? To the peasants of old times, the world outside their own direct experience was a region of vagueness and mystery: to their untravelled thought a state of wandering was a conception as dim as the winter life of the swallows that came back with the spring; and even a settler, if he came from distant parts, hardly ever ceased to be viewed with a remnant of distrust, which would have prevented any surprise if a long course of inoffensive conduct on his part had ended in the commission of a crime; especially if he had any reputation for knowledge, or showed any skill in handicraft. All cleverness, whether in the rapid use of that difficult instrument the tongue, or in some other art unfamiliar to villagers, was in itself suspicious: honest folks, born and bred in a visible manner, were mostly not over-wise or clever – at least, not beyond such a matter as knowing the signs of the weather; and the process by which rapidity and dexterity of any kind were acquired was so wholly hidden, that they partook of the nature of conjuring. In this way it came to pass that those scattered linen-weavers – emigrants from the town into the country – were to the last regarded as aliens by their rustic neighbours, and usually contracted the eccentric habits which belong to a state of loneliness.

In the early years of this century, such a linen-weaver, named Silas Marner, worked at his vocation in a stone cottage that stood among the nutty hedgerows near the village of Raveloe, and not far from the edge of a deserted stone-pit. The questionable sound of Silas's loom, so unlike the natural cheerful trotting of the winnowing machine, or the simpler rhythm of the flail, had a half-fearful fascination for the Raveloe boys, who would often leave off their nutting or birds'-nesting to peep in at the window of the stone cottage, counterbalancing a certain awe at the mysterious action of the loom, by a pleasant sense of scornful superiority, drawn from the mockery of its alternating noises, along with the bent, treadmill attitude of the weaver. But sometimes it happened that Marner, pausing to adjust an irregularity in his thread, became aware of the small scoundrels, and, though chary of his time, he liked their intrusion so ill that he would descend from his loom, and, opening the door, would fix on them a gaze that was always enough to make them take to their legs in terror. For how was it possible to believe that those large brown protuberant eyes in Silas Marner's pale face really saw nothing very distinctly that was not close to them, and not rather that their dreadful stare could dart cramp, or rickets, or a wry mouth at any boy who happened to be in the rear? They had, perhaps, heard their fathers and mothers hint that Silas Marner could cure folks' rheumatism if he had a mind, and add, still more darkly, that if you could only speak the devil fair enough, he might save you the cost of the doctor. Such strange lingering echoes of the old demon-worship might perhaps even now be caught by the diligent listener among the grey-haired peasantry; for the rude mind with difficulty associates the idea of power and benignity. A shadowy conception of power that by much persuasion can be induced to refrain from inflicting harm, is the shape most easily taken by the sense of the Invisible in the minds of men who have always been pressed close by primitive wants, and to whom a life of hard toil has never been illuminated by any enthusiastic religious faith. To them pain and mishap present a far wider range of possibilities than gladness and enjoyment: their imagination is almost barren of the images that feed desire and hope, but is all overgrown by recollections that are a perpetual pasture to fear. 'Is there anything you can fancy that you would like to eat?' I once said to an old labouring man, who was in his last illness, and who had refused all the food his wife had offered him. 'No,' he answered, 'I've never been used to nothing but common victual, and I can't eat that.' Experience had bred no fancies in him that could raise the phantasm of appetite.

And Raveloe was a village where many of the old echoes lingered, undrowned by new voices. Not that it was one of those barren parishes lying on the outskirts of civilisation – inhabited by meagre sheep and thinly-scattered shepherds: on the contrary, it lay in the rich central plain of what we are pleased to call Merry England, and held farms which, speaking from a spiritual point of view, paid highly-desirable tithes. But it was nestled in a snug well-wooded hollow, quite an hour's journey on horseback from any turnpike, where it was never reached by the vibrations of the coach-horn, or of public opinion. It was an important-looking village, with a fine old church and large churchyard in the heart of it, and two or three large brick-and-stone homesteads, with well-walled orchards and ornamental weathercocks, standing close upon the road, and lifting more imposing fronts than the rectory, which peeped from among the trees on the other side of the churchyard; – a village which showed at once the summits of its social life, and told the practised eye that there was no great park and manor-house in the vicinity, but that there were several chiefs in Raveloe who could farm badly quite at their ease, drawing enough money from their bad farming, in those war times, to live in a rollicking fashion, and keep a jolly Christmas, Whitsun, and Easter tide.

It was fifteen years since Silas Marner had first come to Raveloe; he was then simply a pallid young man, with prominent, short-sighted brown eyes, whose appearance would have had nothing strange for people of average culture and experience, but for the villagers near whom he had come to settle it had mysterious peculiarities which corresponded with the exceptional nature of his occupation, and his advent from an unknown region called 'North'ard'. So had his way of life – he invited no comer to step across his door-sill, and he never strolled into the village to drink a pint at the Rainbow, or to gossip at the wheelwrights: he sought no man or woman, save for the purposes of his calling, or in order to supply himself with necessaries; and it was soon clear to the Raveloe lasses that he would never urge one of them to accept him against her will – quite as if he had heard them declare that they would never marry a dead man come to life again. This view of Marner's personality was not without another ground than his pale face and unexampled eyes, for Jem Rodney, the mole-catcher, averred that, one evening as he was returning homeward, he saw Silas Marner leaning against a stile with a heavy bag on his back, instead of resting the bag on the stile as a man in his senses would have done; and that, on coming up to him, he saw that Marner's eyes were set like a dead man's, and he spoke to him, and shook him, and his limbs were stiff, and his hands clutched the bag as if they'd been made of iron; but just as he had made up his mind that the weaver was dead, he came all right again, like, as you might say, in the winking of an eye, and said 'Good-night', and walked off. All this Jem swore he had seen, more by token, that it was the very day he had been mole-catching on Squire Cass's land, down by the old saw-pit. Some said Marner must have been in a 'fit', a word which seemed to explain things otherwise incredible; but the argumentative Mr Macey, clerk of the parish, shook his head, and asked if anybody was ever known to go off in a fit and not fall down. A fit was a stroke, wasn't it? and it was in the nature of a stroke to partly take away the use of a man's limbs and throw him on the parish, if he'd got no children to look to. No, no; it was no stroke that would let a man stand on his legs, like a horse between the shafts, and then walk off as soon as you can say 'Gee!' But there might be such a thing as a man's soul being loose from his body, and going out and in, like a bird out of its nest and back; and that was how folks got over-wise, for they went to school in this shell-less state to those who could teach them more than their neighbours could learn with their five senses and the parson. And where did Master Marner get his knowledge of herbs from – and charms, too, if he liked to give them away? Jem Rodney's story was no more than what might have been expected by anybody who had seen how Marner had cured Sally Oates, and made her sleep like a baby, when her heart had been beating enough to burst her body, for two months and more, while she had been under the doctor's care. He might cure more folks if he would; but he was worth speaking fair, if it was only to keep him from doing you a mischief.

It was partly to this vague fear that Marner was indebted for protecting him from the persecution that his singularities might have drawn upon him, but still more to the fact that, the old linen-weaver in the neighbouring parish of Tarley being dead, his handicraft made him a highly welcome settler to the richer housewives of the district, and even to the more provident cottagers, who had their little stock of yarn at the year's end; and their sense of his usefulness would have counteracted any repugnance or suspicion which was not confirmed by a deficiency in the quality or the tale of the cloth he wove for them. And the years had rolled on without producing any change in the impressions of the neighbours concerning Marner, except the change from novelty to habit. At the end of fifteen years the Raveloe men said just the same things about Silas Marner as at the beginning: they did not say them quite so often, but they believed them much more strongly when they did say them. There was only one important addition which the years had brought: it was, that Master Marner had laid by a fine sight of money somewhere, and that he could buy up 'bigger men' than himself.

But while opinion concerning him had remained nearly stationary, and his daily habits had presented scarcely any visible change, Marner's inward life had been a history and a metamorphosis, as that of every fervid nature must be when it has fled, or been condemned, to solitude. His life, before he came to Raveloe, had been filled with the movement, the mental activity, and the close fellowship, which, in that day as in this, marked the life of an artisan early incorporated in a narrow religious sect, where the poorest layman has the chance of distinguishing himself by gifts of speech, and has, at the very least, the weight of a silent voter in the government of his community. Marner was highly thought of in that little hidden world, known to itself as the church assembling in Lantern Yard; he was believed to be a young man of exemplary life and ardent faith; and a peculiar interest had been centred in him ever since he had fallen, at a prayer-meeting, into a mysterious rigidity and suspension of consciousness, which, lasting for an hour or more, had been mistaken for death. To have sought a medical explanation for this phenomenon would have been held by Silas himself, as well as by his minister and fellow-members, a wilful self-exclusion from the spiritual significance that might lie therein. Silas was evidently a brother selected for a peculiar discipline, and though the effort to interpret this discipline was discouraged by the absence, on his part, of any spiritual vision during his outward trance, yet it was believed by himself and others that its effect was seen in an accession of light and fervour. A less truthful man than he might have been tempted into the subsequent creation of a vision in the form of resurgent memory; a less sane man might have believed in such a creation; but Silas was both sane and honest, though, as with many honest and fervent men, culture had not defined any channels for his sense of mystery, and so it spread itself over the proper pathway of enquiry and knowledge. He had inherited from his mother some acquaintance with medicinal herbs and their preparation – a little store of wisdom which she had imparted to him as a solemn bequest – but of late years he had had doubts about the lawfulness of applying this knowledge, believing that herbs could have no efficacy without prayer, and that prayer might suffice without herbs; so that the inherited delight he had in wandering in the fields in search of foxglove and dandelion and coltsfoot, began to wear to him the character of a temptation.

Among the members of his church there was one young man, a little older than himself, with whom he had long lived in such close friendship that it was the custom of their Lantern Yard brethren to call them David and Jonathan. The real name of the friend was William Dane, and he, too, was regarded as a shining instance of youthful piety, though somewhat given to over-severity towards weaker brethren, and to be so dazzled by his own light as to hold himself wiser than his teachers. But whatever blemishes others might discern in William, to his friend's mind he was faultless; for Marner had one of those impressible self-doubting natures which, at an inexperienced age, admire imperativeness and lean on contradiction. The expression of trusting simplicity in Marner's face, heightened by that absence of special observation, that defenceless, deer-like gaze which belongs to large prominent eyes, was strongly contrasted by the self-complacent suppression of inward triumph that lurked in the narrow slanting eyes and compressed lips of William Dane. One of the most frequent topics of conversation between the two friends was Assurance of salvation: Silas confessed that he could never arrive at anything higher than hope mingled with fear, and listened with longing wonder when William declared that he had possessed unshaken assurance ever since, in the period of his conversion, he had dreamed that he saw the words 'calling and election sure' standing by themselves on a white page in the open Bible. Such colloquies have occupied many a pair of pale-faced weavers, whose unnurtured souls have been like young winged things, fluttering forsaken in the twilight.

It had seemed to the unsuspecting Silas that the friendship had suffered no chill even from his formation of another attachment of a closer kind. For some months he had been engaged to a young servant-woman, waiting only for a little increase to their mutual savings in order to their marriage; and it was a great delight to him that Sarah did not object to William's occasional presence in their Sunday interviews. It was at this point in their history that Silas's cataleptic fit occurred during the prayer-meeting; and amidst the various queries and expressions of interest addressed to him by his fellow-members, William's suggestion alone jarred with the general sympathy towards a brother thus singled out for special dealings. He observed that, to him, this trance looked more like a visitation of Satan than a proof of divine favour, and exhorted his friend to see that he hid no accursed thing within his soul. Silas, feeling bound to accept rebuke and admonition as a brotherly office, felt no resentment, but only pain, at his friend's doubts concerning him; and to this was soon added some anxiety at the perception that Sarah's manner towards him began to exhibit a strange fluctuation between an effort at an increased manifestation of regard and involuntary signs of shrinking and dislike. He asked her if she wished to break off their engagement; but she denied this: their engagement was known to the church, and had been recognised in the prayer-meetings; it could not be broken off without strict investigation, and Sarah could render no reason that would be sanctioned by the feeling of the community. At this time the senior deacon was taken dangerously ill, and, being a childless widower, he was tended night and day by some of the younger brethren or sisters. Silas frequently took his turn in the night-watching with William, the one relieving the other at two in the morning. The old man, contrary to expectation, seemed to be on the way to recovery, when one night Silas, sitting up by his bedside, observed that his usually audible breathing had ceased. The candle was burning low, and he had to lift it to see the patient's face distinctly. Examination convinced him that the deacon was dead – had been dead some time, for the limbs were rigid. Silas asked himself if he had been asleep, and looked at the clock: it was already four in the morning. How was it that William had not come? In much anxiety he went to seek for help, and soon there were several friends assembled in the house, the minister among them, while Silas went away to his work, wishing he could have met William to know the reason of his non-appearance. But at six o'clock, as he was thinking of going to seek his friend, William came, and with him the minister. They came to summon him to Lantern Yard, to meet the church members there; and to his enquiry concerning the cause of the summons the only reply was, 'You will hear.' Nothing further was said until Silas was seated in the vestry, in front of the minister, with the eyes of those who to him represented God's people fixed solemnly upon him. Then the minister, taking out a pocketknife, showed it to Silas, and asked him if he knew where he had left that knife? Silas said, he did not know that he had left it anywhere out of his own pocket – but he was trembling at this strange interrogation. He was then exhorted not to hide his sin, but to confess and repent. The knife had been found in the bureau by the departed deacon's bedside – found in the place where the little bag of church money had lain, which the minister himself had seen the day before. Some hand had removed that bag; and whose hand could it be, if not that of the man to whom the knife belonged? For some time Silas was mute with astonishment: then he said, 'God will clear me: I know nothing about the knife being there, or the money being gone. Search me and my dwelling: you will find nothing but three pound five of my own savings, which William Dane knows I have had these six months.' At this William groaned, but the minister said, 'The proof is heavy against you, brother Marner. The money was taken in the night last past, and no man was with our departed brother but you, for William Dane declares to us that he was hindered by sudden sickness from going to take his place as usual, and you yourself said that he had not come; and, moreover, you neglected the dead body.'

'I must have slept,' said Silas. Then, after a pause, he added, 'Or I must have had another visitation like that which you have all seen me under, so that the thief must have come and gone while I was not in the body, but out of the body. But, I say again, search me and my dwelling, for I have been nowhere else.'

The search was made, and it ended – in William Dane's finding the well-known bag, empty, tucked behind the chest of drawers in Silas's chamber! On this William exhorted his friend to confess, and not to hide his sin any longer. Silas turned a look of keen reproach on him, and said, 'William, for nine years that we have gone in and out together, have you ever known me tell a lie? But God will clear me.'

'Brother,' said William, 'how do I know what you may have done in the secret chambers of your heart, to give Satan an advantage over you?'

Silas was still looking at his friend. Suddenly a deep flush came over his face, and he was about to speak impetuously, when he seemed checked again by some inward shock, that sent the flush back and made him tremble. But at last he spoke feebly, looking at William.

'I remember now – the knife wasn't in my pocket.'

William said, 'I know nothing of what you mean.' The other persons present, however, began to enquire where Silas meant to say that the knife was, but he would give no further explanation: he only said, 'I am sore stricken; I can say nothing. God will clear me.'

On their return to the vestry there was further deliberation. Any resort to legal measures for ascertaining the culprit was contrary to the principles of the Church: prosecution was held by them to be forbidden to Christians, even if it had been a case in which there was no scandal to the community. But they were bound to take other measures for finding out the truth, and they resolved on praying and drawing lots. This resolution can be a ground of surprise only to those who are unacquainted with that obscure religious life which has gone on in the alleys of our towns. Silas knelt with his brethren, relying on his own innocence being certified by immediate divine interference, but feeling that there was sorrow and mourning behind for him even then – that his trust in man had been cruelly bruised. *The lots declared that Silas Marner was guilty.* He was solemnly suspended from church-membership, and called upon to render up the stolen money: only on confession, as the sign of repentance, could he be received once more within the fold of the church. Marner listened in silence. At last, when everyone rose to depart, he went towards William Dane and said, in a voice shaken by agitation – 'The last time I remember using my knife, was when I took it out to cut a strap for you. I don't remember putting it in my pocket again. *You* stole the money, and you have woven a plot to lay the sin at my door. But you may prosper, for all that: there is no just God that governs the earth righteously, but a God of lies, that bears witness against the innocent.'

There was a general shudder at this blasphemy.

William said meekly, 'I leave our brethren to judge whether this is the voice of Satan or not. I can do nothing but pray for you, Silas.'

Poor Marner went out with that despair in his soul – that shaken trust in God and man, which is little short of madness to a loving nature. In the bitterness of his wounded spirit, he said to himself, '*She* will cast me off too.' And he reflected that, if she did not believe the testimony against him, her whole faith must be upset, as his was. To people accustomed to reason about the forms in which their religious feeling has incorporated itself, it is difficult to enter into that simple, untaught state of mind in which the form and the feeling have never been severed by an act of reflection. We are apt to think it inevitable that a man in Marner's position should have begun to question the validity of an appeal to the divine judgement by drawing lots; but to him this would have been an effort of independent thought such as he had never known; and he must have made the effort at a moment when all his energies were turned into the anguish of disappointed faith. If there is an angel who records the sorrows of men as well as their sins, he knows how many and deep are the sorrows that spring from false ideas for which no man is culpable.

Marner went home, and for a whole day sat alone, stunned by despair, without any impulse to go to Sarah and attempt to win her belief in his innocence. The second day he took refuge from benumbing unbelief, by getting into his loom and working away as usual; and before many hours were past, the minister and one of the deacons came to him with the message from Sarah, that she held her engagement to him at an end. Silas received the message mutely, and then turned away from the messengers to work at his loom again. In little more than a month from that time, Sarah was married to William Dane; and not long afterwards it was known to the brethren in Lantern Yard that Silas Marner had departed from the town.

Chapter 2

Even people whose lives have been made various by learning, sometimes find it hard to keep a fast hold on their habitual views of life, on their faith in the Invisible – nay, on the sense that their past joys and sorrows are a real experience, when they are suddenly transported to a new land, where the beings around them know nothing of their history, and share none of their ideas – where their mother earth shows another lap, and human life has other forms than those on which their souls have been nourished. Minds that have been unhinged from their old faith and love, have perhaps sought this Lethean influence of exile, in which the past becomes dreamy because its symbols have all vanished, and the present too is dreamy because it is linked with no memories. But even *their* experience may hardly enable them thoroughly to imagine what was the effect on a simple weaver like Silas Marner, when he left his own country and people and came to settle in Raveloe. Nothing could be more unlike his native town, set within sight of the wide-spread hillsides than this low, wooded region, where he felt hidden even from the heavens by the screening trees and hedgerows. There was nothing here, when he rose in the deep morning quiet and looked out on the dewy brambles and rank tufted grass, that seemed to have any relation with that life centring in Lantern Yard, which had once been to him the altar-place of high dispensations. The whitewashed walls; the little pews where well-known figures entered with a subdued rustling, and where first one well-known voice and then another, pitched in a peculiar key of petition, uttered phrases at once occult and familiar, like the amulet worn on the heart; the pulpit where the minister delivered unquestioned doctrine, and swayed to and fro, and handled the book in a long-accustomed manner; the very pauses between the couplets of the hymn, as it was given out, and the recurrent swell of voices in song: these things had been the channel of divine influences to Marner – they were the fostering home of his religious emotions – they were Christianity and God's kingdom upon earth. A weaver who finds hard words in his hymn-book knows nothing of abstractions; as the little child knows nothing of parental love, but only knows one face and one lap towards which it stretches its arms for refuge and nurture.

And what could be more unlike that Lantern Yard world than the world in Raveloe? – orchards looking lazy with neglected plenty; the large church in the wide churchyard, which men gazed at lounging at their own doors in service-time; the purple-faced farmers, jogging along the lanes or turning in at the Rainbow; homesteads, where men supped heavily and slept in the light of the evening hearth, and where women seemed to be laying up a stock of linen for the life to come. There were no lips in Raveloe from which a word could fall that would stir Silas Marner's benumbed faith to a sense of pain. In the early ages of the world, we know, it was believed that each territory was inhabited and ruled by its own divinities, so that a man could cross the bordering heights and be out of the reach of his native gods, whose presence was confined to the streams and the groves and the hills among which he had lived from his birth. And poor Silas was vaguely conscious of something not unlike the feeling of primitive men, when they fled thus, in fear or in sullenness, from the face of an unpropitious deity. It seemed to him that the Power in which he had vainly trusted among the streets and in the prayer-meetings, was very far away from this land in which he had taken refuge, where men lived in careless abundance, knowing and needing nothing of that trust, which, for him, had been turned to bitterness. The little light he possessed spread its beams so narrowly, that frustrated belief was a curtain broad enough to create for him the blackness of night.

His first movement after the shock had been to work in his loom; and he went on with this unremittingly, never asking himself why, now he was come to Raveloe, he worked far on into the night to finish the tale of Mrs Osgood's table-linen sooner than she expected – without contemplating beforehand the money she would put into his hand for the work. He seemed to weave, like the spider, from pure impulse, without reflection. Every man's work, pursued steadily, tends in this way to become an end in itself, and so to bridge over the loveless chasms of his life. Silas's hand satisfied itself with throwing the shuttle, and his eye with seeing the little squares in the cloth complete themselves under his effort. Then there were the calls of hunger; and Silas, in his solitude, had to provide his own breakfast, dinner, and supper, to fetch his own water from the well, and put his own kettle on the fire; and all these immediate promptings helped, along with the weaving, to reduce his life to the unquestioning activity of a spinning insect. He hated the thought of the past; there was nothing that called out his love and fellowship toward the strangers he had come amongst; and the future was all dark, for there was no Unseen Love that cared for him. Thought was arrested by utter bewilderment, now its old narrow pathway was closed, and affection seemed to have died under the bruise that had fallen on its keenest nerves.

But at last Mrs Osgood's table-linen was finished, and Silas was paid in gold. His earnings in his native town, where he worked for a wholesale dealer, had been after a lower rate; he had been paid weekly, and of his weekly earnings a large proportion had gone to objects of piety and charity. Now, for the first time in his life, he had five bright guineas put into his hand; no man expected a share of them, and he loved no man that he should offer him a share. But what were the guineas to him who saw no vista beyond countless days of weaving? It was needless for him to ask that, for it was pleasant to him to feel them in his palm, and look at their bright faces, which were all his own: it was another element of life, like the weaving and the satisfaction of hunger, subsisting quite aloof from the life of belief and love from which he had been cut off. The weaver's hand had known the touch of hard-won money even before the palm had grown to its full breadth; for twenty years, mysterious money had stood to him as the symbol of earthly good, and the immediate object of toil. He had seemed to love it little in the years when every penny had its purpose for him; for he loved the *purpose* then. But now, when all purpose was gone, that habit of looking towards the money and grasping it with a sense of fulfilled effort made a loam that was deep enough for the seeds of desire; and as Silas walked homeward across the fields in the twilight, he drew out the money, and thought it was brighter in the gathering gloom.

About this time an incident happened which seemed to open a possibility of some fellowship with his neighbours. One day, taking a pair of shoes to be mended, he saw the cobbler's wife seated by the fire, suffering from the terrible symptoms of heart-disease and dropsy, which he had witnessed as the precursors of his mother's death. He felt a rush of pity at the mingled sight and remembrance, and, recalling the relief his mother had found from a simple preparation of foxglove, he promised Sally Oates to bring her something that would ease her, since the doctor did her no good. In this office of charity, Silas felt, for the first time since he had come to Raveloe, a sense of unity between his past and present life, which might have been the beginning of his rescue from the insect-like existence into which his nature had shrunk. But Sally Oates's disease had raised her into a personage of much interest and importance among the neighbours, and the fact of her having found relief from drinking Silas Marner's 'stuff' became a matter of general discourse. When Dr Kimble gave physic, it was natural that it should have an effect; but when a weaver, who came from nobody knew where, worked wonders with a bottle of brown waters, the occult character of the process was evident. Such a sort of thing had not been known since the Wise Woman at Tarley died; and she had charms as well as 'stuff': everybody went to her when their children had fits. Silas Marner must be a person of the same sort, for how did he know what would bring back Sally Oates's breath, if he didn't know a fine sight more than that? The Wise Woman had words that she muttered to herself, so that you couldn't hear what they were, and if she tied a bit of red thread round the child's toe the while, it would keep off the water in the head. There were women in Raveloe, at that present time, who had worn one of the Wise Woman's little bags round their necks, and, in consequence, had never had an idiot child, as Ann Coulter had. Silas Marner could very likely do as much, and more; and now it was all clear how he should have come from unknown parts, and be so 'comical-looking.' But Sally Oates must mind and not tell the doctor, for he would be sure to set his face against Marner: he was always angry about the Wise Woman, and used to threaten those who went to her that they should have none of his help any more.

Silas now found himself and his cottage suddenly beset by mothers who wanted him to charm away the hooping-cough, or bring back the milk, and by men who wanted stuff against the rheumatics or the knots in the hands; and, to secure themselves against a refusal, the applicants brought silver in their palms. Silas might have driven a profitable trade in charms as well as in his small list of drugs; but money on this condition was no temptation to him: he had never known an impulse towards falsity, and he drove one after another away with growing irritation, for the news of him as a wise man had spread even to Tarley, and it was long before people ceased to take long walks for the sake of asking his aid. But the hope in his wisdom was at length changed into dread, for no one believed him when he said he knew no charms and could work no cures, and every man and woman who had an accident or a new attack after applying to him, set the misfortune down to Master Marner's ill-will and irritated glances. Thus it came to pass that his movement of pity towards Sally Oates, which had given him a transient sense of brotherhood, heightened the repulsion between him and his neighbours, and made his isolation more complete.

Gradually the guineas, the crowns, and the half-crowns, grew to a heap, and Marner drew less and less for his own wants, trying to solve the problem of keeping himself strong enough to work sixteen hours a-day on as small an outlay as possible. Have not men, shut up in solitary imprisonment, found an interest in marking the moments by straight strokes of a certain length on the wall, until the growth of the sum of straight strokes, arranged in triangles, has become a mastering purpose? Do we not wile away moments of inanity or fatigued waiting by repeating some trivial movement or sound, until the repetition has bred a want, which is incipient habit? That will help us to understand how the love of accumulating money grows an absorbing passion in men whose imaginations, even in the very beginning of their hoard, showed them no purpose beyond it. Marner wanted the heaps of ten to grow into a square, and then into a larger square; and every added guinea, while it was itself a satisfaction, bred a new desire. In this strange world, made a hopeless riddle to him, he might, if he had had a less intense nature, have sat weaving, weaving – looking towards the end of his pattern, or towards the end of his web, till he forgot the riddle, and everything else but his immediate sensations; but the money had come to mark off his weaving into periods, and the money not only grew, but it remained with him. He began to think it was conscious of him, as his loom was, and he would on no account have exchanged those coins, which had become his familiars, for other coins with unknown faces. He handled them, he counted them, till their form and colour were like the satisfaction of a thirst to him; but it was only in the night, when his work was done, that he drew them out to enjoy their companionship. He had taken up some bricks in his floor underneath his loom, and here he had made a hole in which he set the iron pot that contained his guineas and silver coins, covering the bricks with sand whenever he replaced them. Not that the idea of being robbed presented itself often or strongly to his mind: hoarding was common in country districts in those days; there were old labourers in the parish of Raveloe who were known to have their savings by them, probably inside their flock-beds; but their rustic neighbours, though not all of them as honest as their ancestors in the days of King Alfred, had not imaginations bold enough to lay a plan of burglary. How could they have spent the money in their own village without betraying themselves? They would be obliged to 'run away' – a course as dark and dubious as a balloon journey.

So, year after year, Silas Marner had lived in this solitude, his guineas rising in the iron pot, and his life narrowing and hardening itself more and more into a mere pulsation of desire and satisfaction that had no relation to any other being. His life had reduced itself to the mere functions of weaving and hoarding, without any contemplation of an end towards which the functions tended. The same sort of process has perhaps been undergone by wiser men, when they have been cut off from faith and love – only, instead of a loom and a heap of guineas, they have had some erudite research, some ingenious project, or some well-knit theory. Strangely Marner's face and figure shrank and bent themselves into a constant mechanical relation to the objects of his life, so that he produced the same sort of impression as a handle or a crooked tube, which has no meaning standing apart. The prominent eyes that used to look trusting and dreamy, now looked as if they had been made to see only one kind of thing that was very small, like tiny grain, for which they hunted everywhere: and he was so withered and yellow, that, though he was not yet forty, the children always called him 'Old Master Marner'.

Yet even in this stage of withering a little incident happened, which showed that the sap of affection was not all gone. It was one of his daily tasks to fetch his water from a well a couple of fields off, and for this purpose, ever since he came to Raveloe, he had had a brown earthenware pot, which he held as his most precious utensil, among the very few conveniences he had granted himself. It had been his companion for twelve years, always standing on the same spot, always lending its handle to him in the early morning, so that its form had an expression for him of willing helpfulness, and the impress of its handle on his palm gave a satisfaction mingled with that of having the fresh clear water. One day as he was returning from the well, he stumbled against the step of the stile, and his brown pot, falling with force against the stones that over-arched the ditch below him, was broken in three pieces. Silas picked up the pieces and carried them home with grief in his heart. The brown pot could never be of use to him any more, but he stuck the bits together and propped the ruin in its old place for a memorial.

This is the history of Silas Marner until the fifteenth year after he came to Raveloe. The livelong day he sat in his loom, his ear filled with its monotony, his eyes bent close down on the slow growth of sameness in the brownish web, his muscles moving with such even repetition that their pause seemed almost as much a constraint as the holding of his breath. But at night came his revelry: at night he closed his shutters, and made fast his doors, and drew out his gold. Long ago the heap of coins had become too large for the iron pot to hold them, and he had made for them two thick leather bags, which wasted no room in their resting-place, but lent themselves flexibly to every corner. How the guineas shone as they came pouring out of the dark leather mouths! The silver bore no large proportion in amount to the gold, because the long pieces of linen which formed his chief work were always partly paid for in gold, and out of the silver he supplied his own bodily wants, choosing always the shillings and sixpences to spend in this way. He loved the guineas best, but he would not change the silver – the crowns and half-crowns that were his own earnings, begotten by his labour; he loved them all. He spread them out in heaps and bathed his hands in them; then he counted them and set them up in regular piles, and felt their rounded outline between his thumb and fingers, and thought fondly of the guineas that were only half-earned by the work in his loom, as if they had been unborn children – thought of the guineas that were coming slowly through the coming years, through all his life, which spread far away before him, the end quite hidden by countless days of weaving. No wonder his thoughts were still with his loom and his money when he made his journeys through the fields and the lanes to fetch and carry home his work, so that his steps never wandered to the hedge-banks and the lane-side in search of the once familiar herbs: these too belonged to the past, from which his life had shrunk away, like a rivulet that has sunk far down from the grassy fringe of its old breadth into a little shivering thread, that cuts a groove for itself in the barren sand.

But about the Christmas of that fifteenth year, a second great change came over Marner's life, and his history became blent in a singular manner with the life of his neighbours.

Chapter 3

The greatest man in Raveloe was Squire Cass, who lived in the large red house, with the handsome flight of stone steps in front and the high stables behind it, nearly opposite the church. He was only one among several landed parishioners, but he alone was honoured with the title of Squire; for though Mr Osgood's family was also understood to be of timeless origin – the Raveloe imagination having never ventured back to that fearful blank when there were no Osgoods – still, he merely owned the farm he occupied; whereas Squire Cass had a tenant or two, who complained of the game to him quite as if he had been a lord.

It was still that glorious wartime which was felt to be a peculiar favour of Providence towards the landed interest, and the fall of prices had not yet come to carry the race of small squires and yeomen down that road to ruin for which extravagant habits and bad husbandry were plentifully anointing their wheels. I am speaking now in relation to Raveloe and the parishes that resembled it; for our old-fashioned country life had many different aspects, as all life must have when it is spread over a various surface, and breathed on variously by multitudinous currents, from the winds of heaven to the thoughts of men, which are for ever moving and crossing each other, with incalculable results. Raveloe lay low among the bushy trees and the rutted lanes, aloof from the currents of industrial energy and Puritan earnestness: the rich ate and drank freely, and accepted gout and apoplexy as things that ran mysteriously in respectable families, and the poor thought that the rich were entirely in the right of it to lead a jolly life; besides, their feasting caused a multiplication of orts, which were the heirlooms of the poor. Betty Jay scented the boiling of Squire Cass's hams, but her longing was arrested by the unctuous liquor in which they were boiled; and when the seasons brought round the great merry-makings, they were regarded on all hands as a fine thing for the poor. For the Raveloe feasts were like the rounds of beef and the barrels of ale – they were on a large scale, and lasted a good while, especially in the wintertime. When ladies had packed up their best gowns and topknots in bandboxes, and had incurred the risk of fording streams on pillions with the precious burden in rainy or snowy weather, when there was no knowing how high the water would rise, it was not to be supposed that they looked forward to a brief pleasure. On this ground it was always contrived in the dark seasons, when there was little work to be done, and the hours were long, that several neighbours should keep open house in succession. When Squire Cass's standing dishes diminished in plenty and freshness, his guests had nothing to do but to walk a little higher up the village to Mr Osgood's, at the Orchards, and they found hams and chines uncut, pork-pies with the scent of the fire in them, spun butter in all its freshness – everything, in fact, that appetites at leisure could desire, in perhaps greater perfection, though not in greater abundance, than at Squire Cass's.

For the Squire's wife had died long ago, and the Red House was without that presence of the wife and mother which is the fountain of wholesome love and fear in parlour and kitchen; and this helped to account not only for there being more profusion than finished excellence in the holiday provisions, but also for the frequency with which the proud Squire condescended to preside in the parlour of the Rainbow rather than under the shadow of his own dark wainscot; perhaps, also, for the fact that his sons had turned out rather ill. Raveloe was not a place where moral censure was severe, but it was thought a weakness in the Squire that he had kept all his sons at home in idleness; and though some licence was to be allowed to young men whose fathers could afford it, people shook their heads at the courses of the second son, Dunstan, commonly called Dunsey Cass, whose taste for swopping and betting might turn out to be a sowing of something worse than wild oats. To be sure, the neighbours said, it was no matter what became of Dunsey – a spiteful jeering fellow, who seemed to enjoy his drink the more when other people went dry – always provided that his doings did not bring trouble on a family like Squire Cass's, with a monument in the church, and tankards older than King George. But it would be a thousand pities if Mr Godfrey, the eldest, a fine, open-faced, good-natured young man, who was to come into the land someday, should take to going along the same road as his brother, as he had seemed to do of late. If he went on in that way, he would lose Miss Nancy Lammeter; for it was well known that she had looked very shyly on him ever since last Whitsuntide twelvemonth, when there was so much talk about his being away from home days and days together. There was something wrong, more than common – that was quite clear; for Mr Godfrey didn't look half so fresh-coloured and open as he used to do. At one time everybody was saying what a handsome couple he and Miss Nancy Lammeter would make! and if she could come to be mistress at the Red House, there would be a fine change, for the Lammeters had been brought up in that way, that they never suffered a pinch of salt to be wasted, and yet everybody in their household had of the best, according to his place. Such a daughter-in-law would be a saving to the old Squire, if she never brought a penny to her fortune, for it was to be feared that, notwithstanding his incomings, there were more holes in his pocket than the one where he put his own hand in. But if Mr Godfrey didn't turn over a new leaf, he might say 'Goodbye' to Miss Nancy Lammeter.

It was the once hopeful Godfrey who was standing, with his hands in his side-pockets and his back to the fire, in the dark wainscoted parlour, one late November afternoon, in that fifteenth year of Silas Marner's life at Raveloe. The fading grey light fell dimly on the walls decorated with guns, whips, and foxes' brushes, on coats and hats flung on the chairs, on tankards sending forth a scent of flat ale, and on a half-choked fire, with pipes propped up in the chimney-corners: signs of a domestic life destitute of any hallowing charm, with which the look of gloomy vexation on Godfrey's blonde face was in sad accordance. He seemed to be waiting and listening for someone's approach, and presently the sound of a heavy step, with an accompanying whistle, was heard across the large empty entrance-hall.

The door opened, and a thick-set, heavy-looking young man entered, with the flushed face and the gratuitously elated bearing which mark the first stage of intoxication. It was Dunsey, and at the sight of him Godfrey's face parted with some of its gloom to take on the more active expression of hatred. The handsome brown spaniel that lay on the hearth retreated under the chair in the chimney-corner.

'Well, Master Godfrey, what do you want with me?' said Dunsey, in a mocking tone. 'You're my elders and betters, you know; I was obliged to come when you sent for me.'

'Why, this is what I want – and just shake yourself sober and listen, will you?' said Godfrey, savagely. He had himself been drinking more than was good for him, trying to turn his gloom into uncalculating anger. 'I want to tell you, I must hand over that rent of Fowler's to the Squire, or else tell him I gave it you; for he's threatening to distrain for it, and it'll all be out soon, whether I tell him or not. He said, just now, before he went out, he should send word to Cox to distrain, if Fowler didn't come and pay up his arrears this week. The Squire's short o' cash, and in no humour to stand any nonsense; and you know what he threatened, if ever he found you making away with his money again. So, see and get the money, and pretty quickly, will you?'

'Oh!' said Dunsey, sneeringly, coming nearer to his brother and looking in his face. 'Suppose, now, you get the money yourself, and save me the trouble, eh? Since you was so kind as to hand it over to me, you'll not refuse me the kindness to pay it back for me: it was your brotherly love made you do it, you know.'

Godfrey bit his lips and clenched his fist. 'Don't come near me with that look, else I'll knock you down.'

'O no, you won't,' said Dunsey, turning away on his heel, however. 'Because

I'm such a good-natured brother, you know. I might get you turned out of house and home, and cut off with a shilling any day. I might tell the Squire how his handsome son was married to that nice young woman, Molly Farren, and was very unhappy because he couldn't live with his drunken wife, and I should slip into your place as comfortable as could be. But, you see, I don't do it – I'm so easy and good-natured. You'll take any trouble for me. You'll get the hundred pounds for me – I know you will.'

'How can I get the money?' said Godfrey, quivering. 'I haven't a shilling to bless myself with. And it's a lie that you'd slip into my place: you'd get yourself turned out too, that's all. For if you begin telling tales, I'll follow. Bob's my father's favourite – you know that very well. He'd only think himself well rid of you.'

'Never mind,' said Dunsey, nodding his head sideways as he looked out of the window. 'It 'ud be very pleasant to me to go in your company – you're such a handsome brother, and we've always been so fond of quarrelling with one another, I shouldn't know what to do without you. But you'd like better for us both to stay at home together; I know you would. So you'll manage to get that little sum o' money, and I'll bid you goodbye, though I'm sorry to part.'

Dunstan was moving off, but Godfrey rushed after him and seized him by the arm, saying, with an oath,

'I tell you, I have no money: I can get no money.'

'Borrow of old Kimble.'

'I tell you, he won't lend me any more, and I shan't ask him.'

'Well then, sell Wildfire.'

'Yes, that's easy talking. I must have the money directly.'

'Well, you've only got to ride him to the hunt tomorrow. There'll be Bryce and Keating there, for sure. You'll get more bids than one.'

'I dare say, and get back home at eight o'clock, splashed up to the chin. I'm going to Mrs Osgood's birthday dance.'

'Oho!' said Dunsey, turning his head on one side, and trying to speak in a small mincing treble. 'And there's sweet Miss Nancy coming; and we shall dance with her, and promise never to be naughty again, and be taken into favour, and – '

'Hold your tongue about Miss Nancy, you fool,' said Godfrey, turning red, 'else I'll throttle you.'

'What for?' said Dunsey, still in an artificial tone, but taking a whip from the table and beating the butt-end of it on his palm. 'You've a very good chance. I'd advise you to creep up her sleeve again: it 'ud be saving time, if Molly should happen to take a drop too much laudanum someday, and make a widower of you. Miss Nancy wouldn't mind being a second, if she didn't know it. And you've got a good-natured brother, who'll keep your secret well, because you'll be so very obliging to him.'

'I'll tell you what it is,' said Godfrey, quivering, and pale again. 'My patience is pretty near at an end. If you'd a little more sharpness in you, you might know that you may urge a man a bit too far, and make one leap as easy as another. I don't know but what it is so now: I may as well tell the Squire everything myself – I should get you off my back, if I got nothing else. And, after all, he'll know sometime. She's been threatening to come herself and tell him. So, don't flatter yourself that your secrecy's worth any price you choose to ask. You drain me of money till I've got nothing to pacify *her* with, and she'll do as she threatens someday. It's all one. I'll tell my father everything myself, and you may go to the devil.'

Dunsey perceived that he had overshot his mark, and that there was a point at which even the hesitating Godfrey might be driven into decision. But he said, with an air of unconcern,

'As you please; but I'll have a draught of ale first.' And ringing the bell, he threw himself across two chairs, and began to rap the window-seat with the handle of his whip.

Godfrey stood, still with his back to the fire, uneasily moving his fingers among the contents of his side-pockets, and looking at the floor. That big muscular frame of his held plenty of animal courage, but helped him to no decision when the dangers to be braved were such as could neither be knocked down nor throttled. His natural irresolution and moral cowardice were exaggerated by a position in which dreaded consequences seemed to press equally on all sides, and his irritation had no sooner provoked him to defy Dunstan and anticipate all possible betrayals, than the miseries he must bring on himself by such a step seemed more unendurable to him than the present evil. The results of confession were not contingent, they were certain; whereas betrayal was not certain. From the near vision of that certainty he fell back on suspense and vacillation with a sense of repose. The disinherited son of a small squire, equally disinclined to dig and to beg, was almost as helpless as an uprooted tree, which, by the favour of earth and sky, has grown to a handsome bulk on the spot where it first shot upward. Perhaps it would have been possible to think of digging with some cheerfulness if Nancy Lammeter were to be won on those terms; but, since he must irrevocably lose *her* as well as the inheritance, and must break every tie but the one that degraded him and left him without motive for trying to recover his better self, he could imagine no future for himself on the other side of confession but that of ' 'listing for a soldier' – the most desperate step, short of suicide, in the eyes of respectable families. No! he would rather trust to casualties than to his own resolve – rather go on sitting at the feast and sipping the wine he loved, though with the sword hanging over him and terror in his heart, than rush away into the cold darkness where there was no pleasure left. The utmost concession to Dunstan about the horse began to seem easy, compared with the fulfilment of his own threat. But his pride would not let him recommence the conversation otherwise than by continuing the quarrel. Dunstan was waiting for this, and took his ale in shorter draughts than usual.

'It's just like you,' Godfrey burst out, in a bitter tone, 'to talk about my selling Wildfire in that cool way – the last thing I've got to call my own, and the best bit of horseflesh I ever had in my life. And if you'd got a spark of pride in you, you'd be ashamed to see the stables emptied, and everybody sneering about it. But it's my belief you'd sell yourself, if it was only for the pleasure of making somebody feel he'd got a bad bargain.'

'Ay, ay,' said Dunstan, very placably, 'you do me justice, I see. You know I'm a jewel for 'ticing people into bargains. For which reason I advise you to let *me* sell Wildfire. I'd ride him to the hunt tomorrow for you, with pleasure. I shouldn't look so handsome as you in the saddle, but it's the horse they'll bid for, and not the rider.'

'Yes, I dare say – trust my horse to you!'

'As you please,' said Dunstan, rapping the window-seat again with an air of great unconcern. 'It's *you* have got to pay Fowler's money; it's none of my business. You received the money from him when you went to Bramcote, and *you* told the Squire it wasn't paid. I'd nothing to do with that; you chose to be so obliging as give it me, that was all. If you don't want to pay the money, let it alone; it's all one to me. But I was willing to accommodate you by undertaking to sell the horse, seeing it's not convenient to you to go so far tomorrow.'

Godfrey was silent for some moments. He would have liked to spring on Dunstan, wrench the whip from his hand, and flog him to within an inch of his life; and no bodily fear could have deterred him; but he was mastered by another sort of fear, which was fed by feelings stronger even than his resentment. When he spoke again, it was in a half-conciliatory tone.

'Well, you mean no nonsense about the horse, eh? You'll sell him all fair, and hand over the money? If you don't, you know, everything'll go to smash, for I've got nothing else to trust to. And you'll have less pleasure in pulling the house over my head, when your own skull's to be broken too.'

'Ay, ay,' said Dunstan, rising, 'all right. I thought you'd come round. I'm the fellow to bring old Bryce up to the scratch. I'll get you a hundred and twenty for him, if I get you a penny.'

'But it'll perhaps rain cats and dogs tomorrow, as it did yesterday, and then you can't go,' said Godfrey, hardly knowing whether he wished for that obstacle or not.

'Not *it*,' said Dunstan. 'I'm always lucky in my weather. It might rain if you wanted to go yourself. You never hold trumps, you know – I always do. You've got the beauty, you see, and I've got the luck, so you must keep me by you for your crooked sixpence; you'll *ne*–ver get along without me.'

'Confound you, hold your tongue,' said Godfrey, impetuously. 'And take care to keep sober tomorrow, else you'll get pitched on your head coming home, and Wildfire might be the worse for it.'

'Make your tender heart easy,' said Dunstan, opening the door. 'You never knew me see double when I'd got a bargain to make; it 'ud spoil the fun. Besides, whenever I fall, I'm warranted to fall on my legs.'

With that, Dunstan slammed the door behind him, and left Godfrey to that bitter rumination on his personal circumstances which was now unbroken from day to day save by the excitement of sporting, drinking, card-playing, or the rarer and less oblivious pleasure of seeing Miss Nancy Lammeter. The subtle and varied pains springing from the higher sensibility that accompanies higher culture, are perhaps less pitiable than that dreary absence of impersonal enjoyment and consolation which leaves ruder minds to the perpetual urgent companionship of their own griefs and discontents. The lives of those rural forefathers, whom we are apt to think very prosaic figures – men whose only work was to ride round their land, getting heavier and heavier in their saddles, and who passed the rest of their days in the half-listless gratification of senses dulled by monotony – had a certain pathos in them nevertheless. Calamities came to *them* too, and their early errors carried hard consequences: perhaps the love of some sweet maiden, the image of purity, order, and calm, had opened their eyes to the vision of a life in which the days would not seem too long, even without rioting; but the maiden was lost, and the vision passed away, and then what was left to them, especially when they had become too heavy for the hunt, or for carrying a gun over the furrows, but to drink and get merry, or to drink and get angry, so that they might be independent of variety, and say over again with eager emphasis the things they had said already any time that twelvemonth? Assuredly, among these flushed and dull-eyed men there were some whom – thanks to their native human-kindness – even riot could never drive into brutality; men who, when their cheeks were fresh, had felt the keen point of sorrow or remorse, had been pierced by the reeds they leaned on, or had lightly put their limbs in fetters from which no struggle could loose them; and under these sad circumstances, common to us all, their thoughts could find no resting-place outside the ever-trodden round of their own petty history.

That, at least, was the condition of Godfrey Cass in this six-and-twentieth year of his life. A movement of compunction, helped by those small indefinable influences which every personal relation exerts on a pliant nature, had urged him into a secret marriage, which was a blight on his life. It was an ugly story of low passion, delusion, and waking from delusion, which needs not to be dragged from the privacy of Godfrey's bitter memory. He had long known that the delusion was partly due to a trap laid for him by Dunstan, who saw in his brother's degrading marriage the means of gratifying at once his jealous hate and his cupidity. And if Godfrey could have felt himself simply a victim, the iron bit that destiny had put into his mouth would have chafed him less intolerably. If the curses he muttered half aloud when he was alone had had no other object than Dunstan's diabolical cunning, he might have shrunk less from the con-sequences of avowal. But he had something else to curse – his own vicious folly, which now seemed as mad and unaccountable to him as almost all our follies and vices do when their promptings have long passed away. For four years he had thought of Nancy Lammeter, and wooed her with tacit patient worship, as the woman who made him think of the future with joy: she would be his wife, and would make home lovely to him, as his father's home had never been; and it would be easy, when she was always near, to shake off those foolish habits that were no pleasures, but only a feverish way of annulling vacancy. Godfrey's was an essentially domestic nature, bred up in a home where the hearth had no smiles, and where the daily habits were not chastised by the presence of household order; his easy disposition made him fall in unresistingly with the family courses, but the need of some tender permanent affection, the longing for some influence that would make the good he preferred easy to pursue, caused the neatness, purity, and liberal orderliness of the Lammeter household, sunned by the smile of Nancy, to seem like those fresh bright hours of the morning, when temptations go to sleep, and leave the ear open to the voice of the good angel, inviting to industry, sobriety, and peace. And yet the hope of this paradise had not been enough to save him from a course which shut him out of it for ever. Instead of keeping fast hold of the strong silken rope by which Nancy would have drawn him safe to the green banks, where it was easy to step firmly, he had let himself be dragged back into mud and slime, in which it was useless to struggle. He had made ties for himself which robbed him of all wholesome motives, and were a constant exasperation.

Still, there was one position worse than the present: it was the position he would be in when the ugly secret was disclosed; and the desire that continually triumphed over every other was that of warding off the evil day, when he would have to bear the consequences of his father's violent resentment for the wound inflicted on his family pride – would have, perhaps, to turn his back on that hereditary ease and dignity which, after all, was a sort of reason for living, and would carry with him the certainty that he was banished for ever from the sight and esteem of Nancy Lammeter. The longer the interval, the more chance there was of deliverance from some, at least, of the hateful consequences to which he had sold himself – the more opportunities remained for him to snatch the strange gratification of seeing Nancy, and gathering some faint indications of her lingering regard. Towards this gratification he was impelled, fitfully every now and then, after having passed weeks in which he had avoided her as the far-off, bright-winged prize, that only made him spring forward, and find his chain all the more galling. One of those fits of yearning was on him now, and it would have been strong enough to have persuaded him to trust Wildfire to Dunstan rather than disappoint the yearning, even if he had not had another reason for his disinclination towards the morrow's hunt. That other reason was the fact that the morning's meet was near Batherley, the market-town where the unhappy woman lived, whose image became more odious to him every day; and to his thought the whole vicinage was haunted by her. The yoke a man creates for himself by wrong-doing will breed hate in the kindliest nature; and the good-humoured, affectionate-hearted Godfrey Cass, was fast becoming a bitter man, visited by cruel wishes, that seemed to enter, and depart, and enter again, like demons who had found in him a ready-garnished home.

What was he to do this evening to pass the time? He might as well go to the Rainbow, and hear the talk about the cock-fighting: everybody was there, and what else was there to be done? Though, for his own part, he did not care a button for cock-fighting. Snuff, the brown spaniel, who had placed herself in front of him, and had been watching him for some time, now jumped up in impatience for the expected caress. But Godfrey thrust her away without looking at her, and left the room, followed humbly by the unresenting Snuff – perhaps because she saw no other career open to her.

Chapter 4

Dunstan Cass, setting off in the raw morning, at the judiciously quiet pace of a man who is obliged to ride to cover on his hunter, had to take his way along the lane, which, at its farther extremity, passed by the piece of unenclosed ground called the Stonepit, where stood the cottage, once a stone-cutter's shed, now for fifteen years inhabited by Silas Marner. The spot looked very dreary at this season, with the moist trodden clay about it, and the red, muddy water high up in the deserted quarry. That was Dunstan's first thought as he approached it; the second was, that the old fool of a weaver, whose loom he heard rattling already, had a great deal of money hidden somewhere. How was it that he, Dunstan Cass, who had often heard talk of Marner's miserliness, had never thought of suggesting to Godfrey that he should frighten or persuade the old fellow into lending the money on the excellent security of the young Squire's prospects? The resource occurred to him now as so easy and agreeable, especially as Marner's hoard was likely to be large enough to leave Godfrey a handsome surplus beyond his immediate needs, and enable him to accommodate his faithful brother, that he had almost turned the horse's head towards home again. Godfrey would be ready enough to accept the suggestion: he would snatch eagerly at a plan that might save him from parting with Wildfire. But when Dunstan's meditation reached this point, the inclination to go on grew strong and prevailed. He didn't want to give Godfrey that pleasure: he preferred that Master Godfrey should be vexed. Moreover, Dunstan enjoyed the self-important consciousness of having a horse to sell, and the opportunity of driving a bargain, swaggering, and, possibly, taking somebody in. He might have all the satisfaction attendant on selling his brother's horse, and not the less have the further satisfaction of setting Godfrey to borrow Marner's money. So he rode on to cover.

Bryce and Keating were there, as Dunstan was quite sure they would be – he was such a lucky fellow.

'Hey-day,' said Bryce, who had long had his eye on Wildfire, 'you're on your brother's horse today: how's that?'

'O, I've swopped with him,' said Dunstan, whose delight in lying, grandly independent of utility, was not to be diminished by the likelihood that his hearer would not believe him – 'Wildfire's mine now.'

'What! has he swopped with you for that big-boned hack of yours?' said Bryce, quite aware that he should get another lie in answer.

'O, there was a little account between us,' said Dunsey, carelessly, 'and Wildfire made it even. I accommodated him by taking the horse, though it was against my will, for I'd got an itch for a mare o' Jortin's – as rare a bit o' blood as ever you threw your leg across. But I shall keep Wildfire, now I've got him; though I'd a bid of a hundred and fifty for him the other day, from a man over at Flitton – he's buying for Lord Cromleck – a fellow with a cast in his eye, and a green waistcoat. But I mean to stick to Wildfire: I shan't get a better at a fence in a hurry. The mare's got more blood, but she's a bit too weak in the hindquarters.'

Bryce of course divined that Dunstan wanted to sell the horse, and Dunstan knew that he divined it (horse-dealing is only one of many human transactions carried on in this ingenious manner); and they both considered that the bargain was in its first stage, when Bryce replied ironically – 'I wonder at that now; I wonder you mean to keep him; for I never heard of a man who didn't want to sell his horse getting a bid of half as much again as the horse was worth. You'll be lucky if you get a hundred.'

Keating rode up now, and the transaction became more complicated. It ended in the purchase of the horse by Bryce for a hundred and twenty, to be paid on the delivery of Wildfire, safe and sound, at the Batherley stables. It did occur to Dunsey that it might be wise for him to give up the day's hunting, proceed at once to Batherley, and, having waited for Bryce's return, hire a horse to carry him home with the money in his pocket. But the inclination for a run, encouraged by confidence in his luck, and by a draught of brandy from his pocket-pistol at the conclusion of the bargain, was not easy to overcome, especially with a horse under him that would take the fences to the admiration of the field. Dunstan, however, took one fence too many, and 'staked' his horse. His own ill-favoured person, which was quite unmarketable, escaped without injury, but poor Wildfire, unconscious of his price, turned on his flank, and painfully panted his last. It happened that Dunstan, a short time before, having had to get down to arrange his stirrup, had muttered a good many curses at this interruption, which had thrown him in the rear of the hunt near the moment of glory, and under this exasperation had taken the fences more blindly. He would soon have been up with the hounds again, when the fatal accident happened; and hence he was between eager riders in advance, not troubling themselves about what happened behind them, and far-off stragglers, who were as likely as not to pass quite aloof from the line of road in which Wildfire had fallen. Dunstan, whose nature it was to care more for immediate annoyances than for remote consequences, no sooner recovered his legs, and saw that it was all over with Wildfire, than he felt a satisfaction at the absence of witnesses to a position which no swaggering could make enviable. Reinforcing himself, after his shake, with a little brandy and much swearing, he walked as fast as he could to a coppice on his right hand, through which it occurred to him that he could make his way to Batherley without danger of encountering any member of the hunt. His first intention was to hire a horse there and ride home forthwith, for to walk many miles without a gun in his hand, and along an ordinary road, was as much out of the question to him as to other spirited young men of his kind. He did not much mind about taking the bad news to Godfrey, for he had to offer him at the same time the resource of Marner's money; and if Godfrey kicked, as he always did, at the notion of making a fresh debt, from which he himself got the smallest share of advantage, why, he wouldn't kick long: Dunstan felt sure he could worry Godfrey into anything. The idea of Marner's money kept growing in vividness, now the want of it had become immediate; the prospect of having to make his appearance with the muddy boots of a pedestrian at Batherley, and encounter the grinning queries of stablemen, stood unpleasantly in the way of his impatience to be back at Raveloe and carry out his felicitous plan; and a casual visitation of his waistcoat-pocket, as he was ruminating, awakened his memory to the fact the two or three small coins his forefinger encountered there were of too pale a colour to cover that small debt, without payment of which Jennings had declared he would never do any more business with Dunsey Cass. After all, according to the direction in which the run had brought him, he was not so very much farther from home than he was from Batherley; but Dunsey, not being remarkable for clearness of head, was only led to this conclusion by the gradual perception that there were other reasons for choosing the unprecedented course of walking home. It was now nearly four o'clock, and a mist was gathering: the sooner he got into the road the better. He remembered having crossed the road and seen the finger-post only a little while before Wildfire broke down; so, buttoning his coat, twisting the lash of his hunting-whip compactly round the handle, and rapping the tops of his boots with a self-possessed air, as if to assure himself that he was not at all taken by surprise, he set off with the sense that he was undertaking a remarkable feat of bodily exertion, which somehow, and at sometime, he should be able to dress up and magnify to the admiration of a select circle at the Rainbow. When a young gentleman like Dunsey is reduced to so exceptional a mode of locomotion as walking, a whip in his hand is a desirable corrective to a too bewildering dreamy sense of unwontedness in his position; and Dunstan, as he went along through the gathering mist, was always rapping his whip somewhere. It was Godfrey's whip, which he had chosen to take without leave because it had a gold handle; of course no one could see, when Dunstan held it, that the name *Godfrey Cass* was cut in deep letters on that gold handle – they could only see that it was a very handsome whip. Dunsey was not without fear that he might meet some acquaintance in whose eyes he would cut a pitiable figure, for mist is no screen when people get close to each other; but when he at last found himself in the well-known Raveloe lanes without having met a soul, he silently remarked that that was part of his usual good-luck. But now the mist, helped by the evening darkness, was more of a screen than he desired, for it hid the ruts into which his feet were liable to slip – hid everything, so that he had to guide his steps by dragging his whip along the low bushes in advance of the hedgerow. He must soon, he thought, be getting near the opening at the Stone-pits: he should find it out by the break in the hedgerow. He found it out, however, by another circum-stance which he had not expected – namely, by certain gleams of light, which he presently guessed to proceed from Silas Marner's cottage. That cottage and the money hidden within it had been in his mind continually during his walk, and he had been imagining ways of cajoling and tempting the weaver to part with the immediate possession of his money for the sake of receiving interest. Dunstan felt as if there must be a little frightening added to the cajolery, for his own arithmetical convictions were not clear enough to afford him any forcible demonstration as to the advantages of interest; and as for security, he regarded it vaguely as a means of cheating a man, by making him believe that he would be paid. Altogether, the operation on the miser's mind was a task that Godfrey would be sure to hand over to his more daring and cunning brother: Dunstan had made up his mind to that; and by the time he saw the light gleaming through the chinks of Marner's shutters, the idea of a dialogue with the weaver had become so familiar to him, that it occurred to him as quite a natural thing to make the acquaintance forthwith. There might be several conveniences attending this course: the weaver had possibly got a lantern, and Dunstan was tired of feeling his way. He was still nearly three-quarters of a mile from home, and the lane was becoming unpleasantly slippery, for the mist was passing into rain. He turned up the bank, not without some fear lest he might miss the right way, since he was not certain whether the light were in front or on the side of the cottage. But he felt the ground before him cautiously with his whip-handle, and at last arrived safely at the door. He knocked loudly, rather enjoying the idea that the old fellow would be frightened at the sudden noise. He heard no movement in reply: all was silence in the cottage. Was the weaver gone to bed, then? If so, why had he left a light? That was a strange forgetfulness in a miser. Dunstan knocked still more loudly, and, without pausing for a reply, pushed his fingers through the latch-hole, intending to shake the door and pull the latch-string up and down, not doubting that the door was fastened. But, to his surprise, at this double motion the door opened, and he found himself in front of a bright fire, which lit up every corner of the cottage – the bed, the loom, the three chairs, and the table – and showed him that Marner was not there.

Nothing at that moment could be much more inviting to Dunsey than the bright fire on the brick hearth: he walked in and seated himself by it at once. There was something in front of the fire, too, that would have been inviting to a hungry man, if it had been in a different stage of cooking. It was a small bit of pork suspended from the kettle-hanger by a string passed through a large door-key, in a way known to primitive housekeepers unpossessed of jacks. But the pork had been hung at the farthest extremity of the hanger, apparently to prevent the roasting from proceeding too rapidly during the owner's absence. The old staring simpleton had hot meat for his supper, then? thought Dunstan. People had always said he lived on mouldy bread, on purpose to check his appetite. But where could he be at this time, and on such an evening, leaving his supper in this stage of preparation, and his door unfastened? Dunstan's own recent difficulty in making his way suggested to him that the weaver had perhaps gone outside his cottage to fetch in fuel, or for some such brief purpose, and had slipped into the Stone-pit. That was an interesting idea to Dunstan, carrying consequences of entire novelty. If the weaver was dead, who had a right to his money? Who would know where his money was hidden? *Who would know that anybody had come to take it away?* He went no farther into the subtleties of evidence: the pressing question, 'Where *is* the money?' now took such entire possession of him as to make him quite forget that the weaver's death was not a certainty. A dull mind, once arriving at an inference that flatters a desire, is rarely able to retain the impression that the notion from which the inference started was purely problematic. And Dunstan's mind was as dull as the mind of a possible felon usually is. There were only three hiding-places where he had ever heard of cottagers' hoards being found: the thatch, the bed, and a hole in the floor. Marner's cottage had no thatch; and Dunstan's first act, after a train of thought made rapid by the stimulus of cupidity, was to go up to the bed; but while he did so, his eyes travelled eagerly over the floor, where the bricks, distinct in the fire-light, were discernible under the sprinkling of sand. But not everywhere; for there was one spot, and one only, which was quite covered with sand, and sand showing the marks of fingers which had apparently been careful to spread it over a given space. It was near the treddles of the loom. In an instant Dunstan darted to that spot, swept away the sand with his whip, and, inserting the thin end of the hook between the bricks, found that they were loose. In haste he lifted up two bricks, and saw what he had no doubt was the object of his search; for what could there be but money in those two leathern bags? And, from their weight, they must be filled with guineas. Dunstan felt round the hole, to be certain that it held no more; then hastily replaced the bricks, and spread the sand over them. Hardly more than five minutes had passed since he entered the cottage, but it seemed to Dunstan like a long while; and though he was without any distinct recognition of the possibility that Marner might be alive, and might re-enter the cottage at any moment, he felt an undefinable dread laying hold on him, as he rose to his feet with the bags in his hand. He would hasten out into the darkness, and then consider what he should do with the bags. He closed the door behind him immediately, that he might shut in the stream of light: a few steps would be enough to carry him beyond betrayal by the gleams from the shutter-chinks and the latch-hole. The rain and darkness had got thicker, and he was glad of it; though it was awkward walking with both hands filled, so that it was as much as he could do to grasp his whip along with one of the bags. But when he had gone a yard or two, he might take his time. So he stepped forward into the darkness.

Chapter 5

When Dunstan Cass turned his back on the cottage, Silas Marner was not more than a hundred yards away from it, plodding along from the village with a sack thrown round his shoulders as an overcoat, and with a horn lantern in his hand. His legs were weary, but his mind was at ease, free from the presentiment of change. The sense of security more frequently springs from habit than from conviction, and for this reason it often subsists after such a change in the conditions as might have been expected to suggest alarm. The lapse of time during which a given event has not happened, is, in this logic of habit, constantly alleged as a reason why the event should never happen, even when the lapse of time is precisely the added condition which makes the event imminent. A man will tell you that he has worked in a mine for forty years unhurt by an accident, as a reason why he should apprehend no danger, though the roof is beginning to sink; and it is often observable, that the older a man gets, the more difficult it is to him to retain a believing conception of his own death. This influence of habit was necessarily strong in a man whose life was so monotonous as Marner's – who saw no new people and heard of no new events to keep alive in him the idea of the unexpected and the changeful; and it explains, simply enough, why his mind could be at ease, though he had left his house and his treasure more defenceless than usual. Silas was thinking with double complacency of his supper: first, because it would be hot and savoury; and, secondly, because it would cost him nothing. For the little bit of pork was a present from that excellent housewife, Miss Priscilla Lammeter, to whom he had this day carried home a handsome piece of linen; and it was only on occasion of a present like this, that Silas indulged himself with roast-meat. Supper was his favourite meal, because it came at his time of revelry, when his heart warmed over his gold; whenever he had roast-meat, he always chose to have it for supper. But this evening, he had no sooner ingeniously knotted his string fast round his bit of pork, twisted the string according to rule over his door-key, passed it through the handle, and made it fast on the hanger, than he remembered that a piece of very fine twine was indispensable to his 'setting up' a new piece of work in his loom early in the morning. It had slipped his memory, because, in coming from Mr Lammeter's, he had not had to pass through the village; but to lose time by going on errands in the morning was out of the question. It was a nasty fog to turn out into, but there were things Silas loved better than his own comfort; so, drawing his pork to the extremity of the hanger, and arming himself with his lantern and his old sack, he set out on what, in ordinary weather, would have been a twenty minutes' errand. He could not have locked his door without undoing his well-knotted string and retarding his supper; it was not worth his while to make that sacrifice. What thief would find his way to the Stone-pits on such a night as this? and why should he come on this particular night, when he had never come through all the twelve years before? These questions were not distinctly present in Silas's mind; they merely serve to represent the vaguely-felt foundation of his freedom from anxiety.

He reached his door in much satisfaction that his errand was done: he opened it, and to his short-sighted eyes everything remained as he had left it, except that the fire sent out a welcome increase of heat. He trod about the floor while putting by his lantern and throwing aside his hat and sack, so as to merge the marks of Dunstan's feet on the sand in the marks of his own nailed boots. Then he moved his pork nearer to the fire, and sat down to the agreeable business of tending the meat and warming himself at the same time.

Anyone who had looked at him as the red light shone upon his pale face, strange straining eyes, and meagre form, would perhaps have understood the mixture of contemptuous pity, dread, and suspicion with which he was regarded by his neighbours in Raveloe. Yet few men could be more harmless than poor Marner. In his truthful simple soul, not even the growing greed and worship of gold could beget any vice directly injurious to others. The light of his faith quite put out, and his affections made desolate, he had clung with all the force of his nature to his work and his money; and like all objects to which a man devotes himself, they had fashioned him into correspondence with themselves. His loom, as he wrought in it without ceasing, had in its turn wrought on him, and confirmed more and more the monotonous craving for its monotonous response. His gold, as he hung over it and saw it grow, gathered his power of loving together into a hard isolation like its own.

As soon as he was warm he began to think it would be a long while to wait till after supper before he drew out his guineas, and it would be pleasant to see them on the table before him as he ate his unwonted feast. For joy is the best of wine, and Silas's guineas were a golden wine of that sort.

He rose and placed his candle unsuspectingly on the floor near his loom, swept away the sand without noticing any change, and removed the bricks. The sight of the empty hole made his heart leap violently, but the belief that his gold was gone could not come at once – only terror, and the eager effort to put an end to the terror. He passed his trembling hand all about the hole, trying to think it possible that his eyes had deceived him; then he held the candle in the hole and examined it curiously, trembling more and more. At last he shook so violently that he let fall the candle, and lifted his hands to his head, trying to steady himself, that he might think. Had he put his gold somewhere else, by a sudden resolution last night, and then forgotten it? A man falling into dark water seeks a momentary footing even on sliding stones; and Silas, by acting as if he believed in false hopes, warded off the moment of despair. He searched in every corner, he turned his bed over, and shook it, and kneaded it; he looked in his brick oven where he laid his sticks. When there was no other place to be searched, he kneeled down again and felt once more all round the hole. There was no untried refuge left for a moment's shelter from the terrible truth.

Yes, there was a sort of refuge which always comes with the prostration of thought under an overpowering passion: it was that expectation of impossibilities, that belief in contradictory images, which is still distinct from madness, because it is capable of being dissipated by the external fact. Silas got up from his knees trembling, and looked round at the table: didn't the gold lie there after all? The table was bare. Then he turned and looked behind him – looked all round his dwelling, seeming to strain his brown eyes after some possible appearance of the bags where he had already sought them in vain. He could see every object in his cottage – and his gold was not there.

Again he put his trembling hands to his head, and gave a wild ringing scream, the cry of desolation. For a few moments after, he stood motionless; but the cry had relieved him from the first maddening pressure of the truth. He turned, and tottered towards his loom, and got into the seat where he worked, instinctively seeking this as the strongest assurance of reality.

And now that all the false hopes had vanished, and the first shock of certainty was past, the idea of a thief began to present itself, and he entertained it eagerly, because a thief might be caught and made to restore the gold. The thought brought some new strength with it, and he started from his loom to the door. As he opened it the rain beat in upon him, for it was falling more and more heavily. There were no footsteps to be tracked on such a night – footsteps? When had the thief come? During Silas's absence in the daytime the door had been locked, and there had been no marks of any inroad on his return by daylight. And in the evening, too, he said to himself, everything was the same as when he had left it. The sand and bricks looked as if they had not been moved. *Was* it a thief who had taken the bags? or was it a cruel power that no hands could reach, which had delighted in making him a second time desolate? He shrank from this vaguer dread, and fixed his mind with struggling effort on the robber with hands, who could be reached by hands. His thoughts glanced at all the neighbours who had made any remarks, or asked any questions which he might now regard as a ground of suspicion. There was Jem Rodney, a known poacher, and otherwise disreputable: he had often met Marner in his journeys across the fields, and had said something jestingly about the weaver's money; nay, he had once irritated Marner, by lingering at the fire when he called to light his pipe, instead of going about his business. Jem Rodney was the man – there was ease in the thought. Jem could be found and made to restore the money: Marner did not want to punish him, but only to get back his gold which had gone from him, and left his soul like a forlorn traveller on an unknown desert. The robber must be laid hold of Marner's ideas of legal authority were confused, but he felt that he must go and proclaim his loss; and the great people in the village – the clergyman, the constable, and Squire Cass – would make Jem Rodney, or somebody else, deliver up the stolen money. He rushed out in the rain, under the stimulus of this hope, forgetting to cover his head, not caring to fasten his door; for he felt as if he had nothing left to lose. He ran swiftly till want of breath compelled him to slacken his pace as he was entering the village at the turning close to the Rainbow.

The Rainbow, in Marner's view, was a place of luxurious resort for rich and stout husbands, whose wives had superfluous stores of linen; it was the place where he was likely to find the powers and dignities of Raveloe, and where he could most speedily make his loss public. He lifted the latch, and turned into the bright bar or kitchen on the right hand, where the less lofty customers of the house were in the habit of assembling, the parlour on the left being reserved for the more select society in which Squire Cass frequently enjoyed the double pleasure of conviviality and condescension. But the parlour was dark tonight, the chief personages who ornamented its circle being all at Mrs Osgood's birthday dance, as Godfrey Cass was. And in consequence of this, the party on the high-screened seats in the kitchen was more numerous than usual; several personages, who would otherwise have been admitted into the parlour and enlarged the opportunity of hectoring and condescension for their betters, being content this evening to vary their enjoyment by taking their spirits-and-water where they could themselves hector and condescend in company that called for beer.

Chapter 6

The conversation, which was at a high pitch of animation when Silas approached the door of the Rainbow, had, as usual, been slow and intermittent when the company first assembled. The pipes began to be puffed in a silence which had an air of severity; the more important customers, who drank spirits and sat nearest the fire, staring at each other as if a bet were depending on the first man who winked; while the beer-drinkers, chiefly men in fustian jackets and smock-frocks, kept their eyelids down and rubbed their hands across their mouths, as if their draughts of beer were a funereal duty attended with embarrassing sadness. At last, Mr Snell, the landlord, a man of a neutral disposition, accustomed to stand aloof from human differences as those of beings who were all alike in need of liquor, broke silence, by saying in a doubtful tone to his cousin the butcher: 'Some folks 'ud say that was a fine beast you druv in yesterday, Bob?'

The butcher, a jolly, smiling, red-haired man, was not disposed to answer rashly. He gave a few puffs before he spat and replied, 'And they wouldn't be fur wrong, John.'

After this feeble delusive thaw, the silence set in as severely as before.

'Was it a red Durham?' said the farrier, taking up the thread of discourse after the lapse of a few minutes.

The farrier looked at the landlord, and the landlord looked at the butcher, as the person who must take the responsibility of answering.

'Red it was,' said the butcher, in his good-humoured husky treble – 'and a Durham it was.'

'Then you needn't tell *me* who you bought it of,' said the farrier, looking round with some triumph; 'I know who it is has got the red Durhams o' this countryside. And she'd a white star on her brow, I'll bet a penny?' The farrier leaned forward with his hands on his knees as he put this question, and his eyes twinkled knowingly.

'Well; yes – she might,' said the butcher, slowly, considering that he was giving a decided affirmative. 'I don't say contrairy.'

'I knew that very well,' said the farrier, throwing himself backward again, and speaking defiantly; 'if *I* don't know Mr Lammeter's cows, I should like to know who does – that's all. And as for the cow you've bought, bargain or no bargain, I've been at the drenching of her – contradick me who will.'

The farrier looked fierce, and the mild butcher's conversational spirit was roused a little.

'I'm not for contradicking no man,' he said; 'I'm for peace and quietness. Some are for cutting long ribs – I'm for cutting 'em short, myself; but *I* don't quarrel with 'em. All I say is, it's a lovely carkiss – and anybody as was reasonable, it 'ud bring tears into their eyes to look at it.'

'Well, it's the cow as I drenched, whatever it is,' pursued the farrier, angrily; 'and it was Mr Lammeter's cow, else you told a lie when you said it was a red Durham.'

'I tell no lies,' said the butcher, with the same mild huskiness as before; 'and I contradick none – not if a man was to swear himself black: he's no meat o' mine, nor none o' my bargains. All I say is, it's a lovely carkiss. And what I say, I'll stick to; but I'll quarrel wi' no man.'

'No,' said the farrier, with bitter sarcasm, looking at the company generally; 'and p'rhaps you aren't pig-headed; and p'rhaps you didn't say the cow was a red Durham; and p'rhaps you didn't say she'd got a star on her brow – stick to that, now you're at it.'

'Come, come,' said the landlord; 'let the cow alone. The truth lies atween you: you're both right and both wrong, as I allays say. And as for the cow's being Mr Lammeter's, I say nothing to that; but this I say, as the Rainbow's the Rainbow.

And for the matter o' that, if the talk is to be o' the Lammeters, *you* know the most upo' that head, eh, Mr Macey? You remember when first Mr Lammeter's father come into these parts, and took the Warrens?'

Mr Macey, tailor and parish-clerk, the latter of which functions rheumatism had of late obliged him to share with a small-featured young man who sat opposite him, held his white head on one side, and twirled his thumbs with an air of complacency, slightly seasoned with criticism. He smiled pityingly, in answer to the landlord's appeal, and said: 'Ay, ay; I know, I know; but I let other folks talk. I've laid by now, and gev up to the young uns. Ask them as have been to school at Tarley: they've learnt pernouncing; that's come up since my day.'

'If you're pointing at me, Mr Macey,' said the deputy-clerk, with an air of anxious propriety, 'I'm nowise a man to speak out of my place. As the psalm says –

> I know what's right, nor only so,
> But also practise what I know.'

'Well, then, I wish you'd keep hold o' the tune when it's set for you; if you're for prac*tis*ing, I wish you'd prac*tise* that,' said a large jocose-looking man, an excellent wheelwright in his weekday capacity, but on Sundays leader of the choir. He winked, as he spoke, at two of the company, who were known officially as the 'bassoon' and 'the key-bugle,' in the confidence that he was expressing the sense of the musical profession in Raveloe.

Mr Tookey, the deputy-clerk, who shared the unpopularity common to deputies, turned very red, but replied, with careful moderation – 'Mr Winthrop, if you'll bring me any proof as I'm in the wrong, I'm not the man to say I won't alter. But there's people set up their own ears for a standard, and expect the whole choir to follow 'em. There may be two opinions, I hope.'

'Ay, ay,' said Mr Macey, who felt very well satisfied with this attack on youthful presumption: 'you're right there, Tookey: there's allays two 'pinions; there's the 'pinion a man has of himsen, and there's the 'pinion other folks have on him. There'd be two 'pinions about a cracked bell, if the bell could hear itself.'

'Well, Mr Macey,' said poor Tookey, serious amidst the general laughter, 'I undertook to partially fill up the office of parish-clerk by Mr Crackenthorp's desire, whenever your infirmities should make you unfitting; and it's one of the rights thereof to sing in the choir – else why have you done the same yourself?'

'Ah! but the old gentleman and you are two folks,' said Ben Winthrop. 'The old gentleman's got a gift. Why, the Squire used to invite him to take a glass, only to hear him sing the "Red Rovier"; didn't he, Mr Macey? It's a nat'ral gift. There's my little lad Aaron, he's got a gift – he can sing a tune off straight, like a throstle. But as for you, Master Tookey, you'd better stick to your "Amens:" your voice is well enough when you keep it up in your nose. It's your inside as isn't right made for music: it's no better nor a hollow stalk.'

This kind of unflinching frankness was the most piquant form of joke to the company at the Rainbow, and Ben Winthrop's insult was felt by everybody to have capped Mr Macey's epigram.

'I see what it is plain enough,' said Mr Tookey, unable to keep cool any longer. 'There's a conspiracy to turn me out o' the choir, as I shouldn't share the Christmas money – that's where it is. But I shall speak to Mr Crackenthorp; I'll not be put upon by no man.'

'Nay, nay, Tookey,' said Ben Winthrop. 'We'll pay you your share to keep out of it – that's what we'll do. There's things folks 'ud pay to be rid on, besides varmin.'

'Come, come,' said the landlord, who felt that paying people for their absence was a principle dangerous to society; 'a joke's a joke. We're all good friends here, I hope. We must give and take. You're both right and you're both wrong, as I say. I agree wi' Mr Macey here, as there's two opinions; and if mine was asked, I should say they're both right. Tookey's right and Winthrop's right, and they've only got to split the difference and make themselves even.'

The farrier was puffing his pipe rather fiercely, in some contempt at this trivial discussion. He had no ear for music himself, and never went to church, as being of the medical profession, and likely to be in requisition for delicate cows. But the butcher, having music in his soul, had listened with a divided desire for Tookey's defeat, and for the preservation of the peace.

'To be sure,' he said, following up the landlord's conciliatory view, 'we're fond of our old clerk; it's nat'ral, and him used to be such a singer, and got a brother as is known for the first fiddler in this countryside. Eh, it's a pity but what Solomon lived in our village, and could give us a tune when we liked; eh, Mr Macey? I'd keep him in liver and lights for nothing – that I would.'

'Ay, ay,' said Mr Macey, in the height of complacency; 'our family's been known for musicianers as far back as anybody can tell. But them things are dying out, as I tell Solomon every time he comes round; there's no voices like what there used to be, and there's nobody remembers what we remember, if it isn't the old crows.'

'Ay, you remember when first Mr Lammeter's father came into these parts, don't you, Mr Macey?' said the landlord.

'I should think I did,' said the old man, who had now gone through that complimentary process necessary to bring him up to the point of narration; 'and a fine old gentleman he was – as fine, and finer nor the Mr Lammeter as now is. He came from a bit north'ard, so far as I could ever make out. But there's nobody rightly knows about those parts: only it couldn't be far north'ard, nor much different from this country, for he brought a fine breed o' sheep with him, so there must be pastures there, and everything reasonable. We heared tell as he'd sold his own land to come and take the Warrens, and that seemed odd for a man as had land of his own, to come and rent a farm in a strange place. But they said it was along of his wife's dying; though there's reasons in things as nobody knows on – that's pretty much what I've made out; though some folks are so wise, they'll find you fifty reasons straight off, and all the while the real reason's winking at 'em in the corner, and they niver see't. Howsomever, it was soon seen as we'd got a new parish'ner as know'd the rights and customs o' things, and kep a good house, and was well looked on by everybody. And the young man – that's the Mr Lammeter as now is, for he'd niver a sister – soon begun to court Miss Osgood, that's the sister o' the Mr Osgood as now is, and a fine handsome lass she was – eh, you can't think – they pretend this young lass is like her, but that's the way wi' people as don't know what come before 'em. *I* should know, for I helped the old rector, Mr Drumlow as was, I helped him marry 'em.'

Here Mr Macey paused; he always gave his narrative in instalments, expecting to be questioned according to precedent.

'Ay, and a partic'lar thing happened, didn't it, Mr Macey, so as you were likely to remember that marriage?' said the landlord, in a congratulatory tone.

'I should think there did – a *very* partic'lar thing,' said Mr Macey, nodding sideways. 'Mr Drumlow – poor old gentleman, I was fond on him, though he'd got a bit confused in his head, what wi' age and wi' taking a drop o' summat warm when the service come of a cold morning. And young Mr Lammeter, he'd have no way but he must be married in Janiwary, which, to be sure's an unreasonable time to be married in, for it isn't like a christening or a burying, as you can't help; and so Mr Drumlow – poor old gentleman, I was fond on him – but when he come to put the questions, he put 'em by the rule o' contrairy, like, and he says, "Wilt thou have this man to thy wedded wife?" says he, and then he says, "Wilt thou have this woman to thy wedded husband?" says he. But the partic'larest thing of all is, as nobody took any notice on it but me, and they answered straight off "yes", like as if it had been me saying "Amen" i' the right place, without listening to what went before.'

'But *you* knew what was going on well enough, didn't you, Mr Macey? You were live enough, eh?' said the butcher.

'Lor bless you!' said Mr Macey, pausing, and smiling in pity at the impotence of his hearers' imagination – 'why, I was all of a tremble: it was as if I'd been a coat pulled by the two tails, like; for I couldn't stop the parson, I couldn't take upon me to do that; and yet I said to myself, I says, "Suppose they shouldn't be fast married, 'cause the words are contrairy?" and my head went working like a mill, for I was allays uncommon for turning things over and seeing all round 'em; and I says to myself, "Is't the meanin' or the words as makes folks fast i' wedlock?" For the parson meant right, and the bride and bridegroom meant right. But then, when I come to think on it, meanin' goes but a little way i' most things, for you may mean to stick things together and your glue may be bad, and then where are you? And so I says to mysen, "It isn't the meanin', it's the glue." And I was worreted as if I'd got three bells to pull at once, when we went into the vestry, and they begun to sign their names. But where's the use o' talking? – you can't think what goes on in a 'cute man's inside.'

'But you held in for all that, didn't you, Mr Macey?' said the landlord.

'Ay, I held in tight till I was by mysen wi' Mr Drumlow, and then I out wi' everything, but respectful, as I allays did. And he made light on it, and he says, "Pooh, pooh, Macey, make yourself easy," he says, "it's neither the meaning nor the words – it's the re*ges*ter does it – that's the glue." So you see he settled it easy; for parsons and doctors know everything by heart, like, so as they aren't worreted wi' thinking what's the rights and wrongs o' things, as I'n been many and many's the time. And sure enough the wedding turned out all right, on'y poor Mrs Lammeter – that's Miss Osgood as was – died afore the lasses were growed up; but for prosperity and everything respectable, there's no family more looked on.'

Every one of Mr Macey's audience had heard this story many times, but it was listened to as if it had been a favourite tune, and at certain points the puffing of the pipes was momentarily suspended, that the listeners might give their whole minds to the expected words. But there was more to come; and Mr Snell, the landlord, duly put the leading question.

'Why, old Mr Lammeter had a pretty fortin, didn't they say, when he come into these parts?'

'Well, yes,' said Mr Macey; 'but I dare say it's as much as this Mr Lammeter's done to keep it whole. For there was allays a talk as nobody could get rich on the Warrens: though he holds it cheap, for it's what they call Charity Land.'

'Ay, and there's few folks know so well as you how it come to be Charity Land, eh, Mr Macey?' said the butcher.

'How should they?' said the old clerk, with some contempt. 'Why, my grandfather made the grooms' livery for that Mr Cliff as came and built the big stables at the Warrens. Why, they're stables four times as big as Squire Cass's, for he thought o' nothing but hosses and hunting, Cliff didn't – a Lunnon tailor, some folks said, as had gone mad wi' cheating. For he couldn't ride; lor bless you! they said he'd got no more grip o' the hoss than if his legs had been cross-sticks: my grandfather heared old Squire Cass say so many and many a time. But ride he would, as if old Harry had been a-driving him; and he'd a son, a lad o' sixteen; and nothing would his father have him do, but he must ride and ride – though the lad was frighted, they said. And it was a common saying as the father wanted to ride the tailor out o' the lad, and make a gentleman on him – not but what I'm a tailor myself, but in respect as God made me such, I'm proud on it, for "Macey, tailor" 's been wrote up over our door since afore the Queen's heads went out on the shillings. But Cliff, he was ashamed o' being called a tailor, and he was sore vexed as his riding was laughed at, and nobody o' the gentlefolks hereabout could abide him. Howsomever, the poor lad got sickly and died, and the father didn't live long after him, for he got queerer nor ever, and they said he used to go out i' the dead o' the night, wi' a lantern in his hand, to the stables, and set a lot o' lights burning, for he got as he couldn't sleep; and there he'd stand, cracking his whip and looking at his hosses; and they said it was a mercy as the stables didn't get burnt down wi' the poor dumb creaturs in 'em. But at last he died raving, and they found as he'd left all his property, Warrens and all, to a Lunnon Charity, and that's how the Warrens come to be Charity land; though, as for the stables, Mr Lammeter never uses 'em – they're out o' all charicter – lor bless you! if you was to set the doors a-banging in 'em, it 'ud sound like thunder half o'er the parish.'

'Ay, but there's more going on in the stables than what folks see by daylight, eh, Mr Macey?' said the landlord.

'Ay, ay; go that way of a dark night, that's all,' said Mr Macey, winking mysteriously, 'and then make believe, if you like, as you didn't see lights i' the stables, nor hear the stamping o' the hosses, nor the cracking o' the whips, and howling, too, if it's tow'rt daybreak. "Cliff's Holiday" has been the name of it ever sin' I were a boy; that's to say, some said as it was the holiday Old Harry gev him from roasting, like. That's what my father told me, and he was a reasonable man, though there's folks nowadays know what happened afore they were born better nor they know their own business.'

'What do you say to that, eh, Dowlas?' said the landlord, turning to the farrier, who was swelling with impatience for his cue. 'There's a nut for *you* to crack.'

Mr Dowlas was the negative spirit in the company, and was proud of his position.

'Say? I say what a man *should* say as doesn't shut his eyes to look at a finger-post. I say, as I'm ready to wager any man ten pound, if he'll stand out wi' me any dry night in the pasture before the Warren stables, as we shall neither see lights nor hear noises, if it isn't the blowing of our own noses. That's what I say, and I've said it many a time; but there's nobody 'ull ventur a ten-pun' note on their ghos'es as they make so sure of.'

'Why, Dowlas, that's easy betting, that is,' said Ben Winthrop. 'You might as well bet a man as he wouldn't catch the rheumatise if he stood up to 's neck in the pool of a frosty night. It 'ud be fine fun for a man to win his bet as he'd catch the rheumatise. Folks as believe in Cliff's Holiday aren't a-going to ventur near it for a matter o' ten pound.'

'If Master Dowlas wants to know the truth on it,' said Mr Macey, with a sarcastic smile, tapping his thumbs together, 'he's no call to lay any bet – let him go and stan' by himself – there's nobody 'ull hinder him; and then he can let the parish'ners know if they're wrong.'

'Thank you! I'm obliged to you, 'said the farrier, with a snort of scorn. 'If folks are fools, it's no business o' mine. *I* don't want to make out the truth about ghos'es: I know it a'ready. But I'm not against a bet – everything fair and open. Let any man bet me ten pound as I shall see Cliff's Holiday, and I'll go and stand by myself. I want no company. I'd as lief do it as I'd fill this pipe.'

'Ah, but who's to watch you, Dowlas, and see you do it? That's no fair bet,' said the butcher.

'No fair bet?' replied Mr Dowlas, angrily. 'I should like to hear any man stand up and say I want to bet unfair. Come now, Master Lundy, I should like to hear you say it.'

'Very like you would,' said the butcher. 'But it's no business o' mine. You're none o' my bargains, and I aren't a-going to try and 'bate your price. If anybody 'll bid for you at your own vallying, let him. I'm for peace and quietness, I am.'

'Yes, that's what every yapping cur is, when you hold a stick up at him,' said the farrier. 'But I'm afraid o' neither man nor ghost, and I'm ready to lay a fair bet – *I* aren't a turn-tail cur.'

'Ay, but there's this in it, Dowlas,' said the landlord, speaking in a tone of much candour and tolerance. 'There's folks, i' my opinion, they can't see ghos'es, not if they stood as plain as a pike-staff before 'em. And there's reason i' that. For there's my wife, now, can't smell, not if she'd the strongest o' cheese under her nose. I never see'd a ghost myself, but then I says to myself, "Very like I haven't got the smell for 'em." I mean, putting a ghost for a smell, or else contrairiways. And so, I'm for holding with both sides; for, as I say, the truth lies between 'em. And if Dowlas was to go and stand, and say he'd never seen a wink o' Cliff's

Holiday all the night through, I'd back him; and if anybody said as Cliff's Holiday was certain sure, for all that, I'd back *him* too. For the smell's what I go by.'

The landlord's analogical argument was not well received by the farrier – a man intensely opposed to compromise.

'Tut, tut,' he said, setting down his glass with refreshed irritation; 'what's the smell got to do with it? Did ever a ghost give a man a black eye? That's what I should like to know. If ghos'es want me to believe in 'em, let 'em leave off skulking i' the dark and i' lone places – let 'em come where there's company and candles.'

'As if ghos'es 'ud want to be believed in by anybody so ignirant!' said Mr Macey, in deep disgust at the farrier's crass incompetence to apprehend the conditions of ghostly phenomena.

Chapter 7

Yet the next moment there seemed to be some evidence that ghosts had a more condescending disposition than Mr Macey attributed to them; for the pale thin figure of Silas Marner was suddenly seen standing in the warm light, uttering no word, but looking round at the company with his strange unearthly eyes. The long pipes gave a simultaneous movement, like the antennae of startled insects, and every man present, not excepting even the sceptical farrier, had an impression that he saw, not Silas Marner in the flesh, but an apparition; for the door by which Silas had entered was hidden by the high-screened seats, and no one had noticed his approach. Mr Macey, sitting a long way off the ghost, might be supposed to have felt an argumentative triumph, which would tend to neutralise his share of the general alarm. Had he not always said that when Silas Marner was in that strange trance of his, his soul went loose from his body? Here was the demonstration: nevertheless, on the whole, he would have been as well contented without it. For a few moments there was a dead silence, Marner's want of breath and agitation not allowing him to speak. The landlord, under the habitual sense that he was bound to keep his house open to all company, and confident in the protection of his unbroken neutrality, at last took on himself the task of adjuring the ghost.

'Master Marner,' he said, in a conciliatory tone, 'what's lacking to you? What's your business here?'

'Robbed!' said Silas, gaspingly. 'I've been robbed! I want the constable and the Justice – and Squire Cass – and Mr Crackenthorp.'

'Lay hold on him, Jem Rodney,' said the landlord, the idea of a ghost subsiding; 'he's off his head, I doubt. He's wet through.'

Jem Rodney was the outermost man, and sat conveniently near Marner's standing-place; but he declined to give his services.

'Come and lay hold on him yourself, Mr Snell, if you've a mind,' said Jem, rather sullenly. 'He's been robbed, and murdered too, for what I know,' he added, in a muttering tone.

'Jem Rodney!' said Silas, turning and fixing his strange eyes on the suspected man.

'Ay, Master Marner, what do you want wi' me?' said Jem, trembling a little, and seizing his drinking-can as a defensive weapon.

'If it was you stole my money,' said Silas, clasping his hands entreatingly, and raising his voice to a cry, 'give it me back – and I won't meddle with you. I won't set the constable on you. Give it me back, and I'll let you – I'll let you have a guinea.'

'Me stole your money!' said Jem, angrily. 'I'll pitch this can at your eye if you talk o' *my* stealing your money.'

'Come, come, Master Marner,' said the landlord, now rising resolutely, and seizing Marner by the shoulder, 'if you've got any information to lay, speak it out sensible, and show as you're in your right mind, if you expect anybody to listen to you. You're as wet as a drownded rat. Sit down and dry yourself and speak straight forrard.'

'Ah, to be sure, man,' said the farrier, who began to feel that he had not been quite on a par with himself and the occasion. 'Let's have no more staring and screaming, else we'll have you strapped for a madman. That was why I didn't speak at the first – thinks I, the man's run mad.'

'Ay, ay, make him sit down,' said several voices at once, well pleased that the reality of ghosts remained still an open question.

The landlord forced Marner to take off his coat, and then to sit down on a chair aloof from everyone else, in the centre of the circle, and in the direct rays of the fire. The weaver, too feeble to have any distinct purpose beyond that of getting help to recover his money, submitted unresistingly. The transient fears of the company were now forgotten in their strong curiosity, and all faces were turned towards Silas, when the landlord, having seated himself again, said: 'Now then, Master Marner, what's this you've got to say, as you've been robbed? speak out.'

'He'd better not say again as it was me robbed him,' cried Jem Rodney, hastily. 'What could I ha' done with his money? I could as easy steal the parson's surplice, and wear it.'

'Hold your tongue, Jem, and let's hear what he's got to say,' said the landlord. 'Now then, Master Marner.'

Silas now told his story under frequent questioning, as the mysterious character of the robbery became evident.

This strangely novel situation of opening his trouble to his Raveloe neighbours, of sitting in the warmth of a hearth not his own, and feeling the presence of faces and voices which were his nearest promise of help, had doubtless its influence on Marner, in spite of his passionate preoccupation with his loss. Our consciousness rarely registers the beginning of a growth within us any more than without us: there have been many circulations of the sap before we detect the smallest sign of the bud.

The slight suspicion with which his hearers at first listened to him, gradually melted away before the convincing simplicity of his distress: it was impossible for the neighbours to doubt that Marner was telling the truth, not because they were capable of arguing at once from the nature of his statements to the absence of any motive for making them falsely, but because, as Mr Macey observed, 'Folks as had the devil to back 'em were not likely to be so mushed 'as poor Silas was. Rather, from the strange fact that the robber had left no traces, and had happened to know the nick of time, utterly incalculable by mortal agents, when Silas would go away from home without locking his door, the more probable conclusion seemed to be, that his disreputable intimacy in that quarter, if it ever existed, had been broken up, and that, in consequence, this ill turn had been done to Marner by somebody it was quite in vain to set the constable after. Why this preternatural felon should be obliged to wait till the door was left unlocked, was a question which did not present itself.

'It isn't Jem Rodney as has done this work, Master Marner,' said the landlord. 'You mustn't be a-casting your eye at poor Jem. There may be a bit of a reckoning against Jem for the matter of a hare or so, if anybody was bound to keep their eyes staring open, and niver to wink – but Jem's been a-sitting here drinking his can, like the decentest man i' the parish, since before you left your house, Master Marner, by your own account.'

'Ay, ay,' said Mr Macey; 'let's have no accusing o' the innicent. That isn't the law. There must be folks to swear again' a man before he can be ta'en up. Let's have no accusing o' the innicent, Master Marner.'

Memory was not so utterly torpid in Silas that it could not be wakened by these words. With a movement of compunction, as new and strange to him as everything else within the last hour, he started from his chair and went close up to Jem, looking at him as if he wanted to assure himself of the expression in his face.

'I was wrong,' he said – 'yes, yes – I ought to have thought. There's nothing to witness against you, Jem. Only you'd been into my house oftener than anybody else, and so you came into my head. I don't accuse you – I won't accuse anybody – only,' he added, lifting up his hands to his head, and turning away with bewildered misery, 'I try – I try to think where my money can be.'

'Ay, ay, they're gone where it's hot enough to melt 'em, I doubt,' said Mr Macey.

'Tchuh!' said the farrier. And then he asked, with a cross-examining air, 'How much money might there be in the bags, Master Marner?'

'Two hundred and seventy-two pounds, twelve and sixpence, last night when I counted it,' said Silas, seating himself again, with a groan.

'Pooh! why, they'd be none so heavy to carry. Some tramp's been in, that's all; and as for the no footmarks, and the bricks and the sand being all right – why, your eyes are pretty much like a insect's, Master Marner; they're obliged to look so close, you can't see much at a time. It's my opinion as, if I'd been you, or you'd been me for it comes to the same thing – you wouldn't have thought you'd found everything as you left it. But what I vote is, as two of the sensiblest o' the company should go with you to Master Kench, the constable's – he's ill i' bed, I know that much – and get him to appoint one of us his deppity; for that's the law, and I don't think anybody 'ull take upon him to contradick me there. It isn't much of a walk to Kench's; and then, if it's me as is deppity, I'll go back with you, Master Marner, and examine your primises; and if anybody's got any fault to find with that, I'll thank him to stand up and say it out like a man.'

By this pregnant speech the farrier had re-established his self-complacency, and waited with confidence to hear himself named as one of the superlatively sensible men.

'Let us see how the night is, though,' said the landlord, who also considered himself personally concerned in this proposition. 'Why, it rains heavy still,' he said, returning from the door.

'Well, I'm not the man to be afraid o' the rain,' said the farrier. 'For it 'll look bad when Justice Malam hears as respectable men like us had a information laid before 'em and took no steps.'

The landlord agreed with this view, and after taking the sense of the company, and duly rehearsing a small ceremony known in high ecclesiastical life as the *nolo episcopari*, he consented to take on himself the chill dignity of going to Kench's. But to the farrier's strong disgust, Mr Macey now started an objection to his proposing himself as a deputy-constable; for that oracular old gentleman, claiming to know the law, stated, as a fact delivered to him by his father, that no doctor could be a constable.

'And you're a doctor, I reckon, though you're only a cow-doctor – for a fly's a fly, though it may be a hoss-fly,' concluded Mr Macey, wondering a little at his own ' 'cuteness.'

There was a hot debate upon this, the farrier being of course indisposed to renounce the quality of doctor, but contending that a doctor could be a constable if he liked – the law meant, he needn't be one if he didn't like. Mr Macey thought this was nonsense, since the law was not likely to be fonder of doctors than of other folks. Moreover, if it was in the nature of doctors more than of other men not to like being constables, how came Mr Dowlas to be so eager to act in that capacity?

'*I* don't want to act the constable,' said the farrier, driven into a corner by this merciless reasoning; 'and there's no man can say it of me, if he'd tell the truth. But if there's to be any jealousy and envying about going to Kench's in the rain, let them go as like it – you won't get me to go, I can tell you.'

By the landlord's intervention, however, the dispute was accommodated. Mr Dowlas consented to go as a second person disinclined to act officially; and so poor Silas, furnished with some old coverings, turned out with his two companions into the rain again, thinking of the long night-hours before him, not as those do who long to rest, but as those who expect to 'watch for the morning'.

Chapter 8

When Godfrey Cass returned from Mrs Osgood's party at midnight, he was not much surprised to learn that Dunsey had not come home. Perhaps he had not sold Wildfire, and was waiting for another chance – perhaps, on that foggy afternoon, he had preferred housing himself at the Red Lion at Batherley for the night, if the run had kept him in that neighbourhood; for he was not likely to feel much concern about leaving his brother in suspense. Godfrey's mind was too full of Nancy Lammeter's looks and behaviour, too full of the exasperation against himself and his lot, which the sight of her always produced in him, for him to give much thought to Wildfire or to the probabilities of Dunstan's conduct.

The next morning the whole village was excited by the story of the robbery, and Godfrey, like everyone else, was occupied in gathering and discussing news about it, and in visiting the Stone-pits. The rain had washed away all possibility of distinguishing footmarks, but a close investigation of the spot had disclosed, in the direction opposite to the village, a tinderbox, with a flint and steel, half sunk in the mud. It was not Silas's tinderbox, for the only one he had ever had was still standing on his shelf; and the inference generally accepted was, that the tinderbox in the ditch was somehow connected with the robbery. A small minority shook their heads, and intimated their opinion that it was not a robbery to have much light thrown on it by tinderboxes, that Master Marner's tale had a queer look with it, and that such things had been known as a man's doing himself a mischief, and then setting the justice to look for the doer. But when questioned closely as to their grounds for this opinion, and what Master Marner had to gain by such false pretences, they only shook their heads as before, and observed that there was no knowing what some folks counted gain; moreover, that everybody had a right to their own opinions, grounds or no grounds, and that the weaver, as everybody knew, was partly crazy. Mr Macey, though he joined in the defence of Marner against all suspicions of deceit, also pooh-poohed the tinderbox; indeed, repudiated it as a rather impious suggestion, tending to imply that everything must be done by human hands, and that there was no power which could make away with the guineas without moving the bricks. Nevertheless, he turned round rather sharply on Mr Tookey, when the zealous deputy, feeling that this was a view of the case peculiarly suited to a parish-clerk, carried it still farther, and doubted whether it was right to enquire into a robbery at all when the circumstances were so mysterious.

'As if,' concluded Mr Tookey – 'as if there was nothing but what could be made out by justices and constables.'

'Now, don't you be for overshooting the mark, Tookey,' said Mr Macey, nodding his head aside, admonishingly. 'That's what you're allays at; if I throw a stone and hit, you think there's summat better than hitting, and you try to throw a stone beyond. What I said was against the tinderbox: I said nothing against justices and constables, for they're o' King George's making, and it 'ud be ill-becoming a man in a parish office to fly out again' King George.'

While these discussions were going on amongst the group outside the Rainbow, a higher consultation was being carried on within, under the presidency of Mr Crackenthorp, the rector, assisted by Squire Cass and other substantial parishioners. It had just occurred to Mr Snell, the landlord – he being, as he observed, a man accustomed to put two and two together – to connect with the tinderbox which, as deputy-constable, he himself had had the honourable distinction of finding, certain recollections of a pedlar who had called to drink at the house about a month before, and had actually stated that he carried a tinderbox about with him to light his pipe. Here, surely, was a clue to be followed out. And as memory, when duly impregnated with ascertained facts, is sometimes surprisingly fertile, Mr Snell gradually recovered a vivid impression of the effect produced on him by the pedlar's countenance and conversation. He had a 'look with his eye' which fell unpleasantly on Mr Snell's sensitive organism. To be sure, he didn't say anything particular – no, except that about the tinderbox – but it isn't what a man says, it's the way he says it. Moreover, he had a swarthy foreignness of complexion which boded little honesty.

'Did he wear ear-rings?' Mr Crackenthorp wished to know, having some acquaintance with foreign customs.

'Well – stay – let me see,' said Mr Snell, like a docile clairvoyante, who would really not make a mistake if she could help it. After stretching the corners of his mouth and contracting his eyes, as if he were trying to see the ear-rings, he appeared to give up the effort, and said, 'Well, he'd got ear-rings in his box to sell, so it's nat'ral to suppose he might wear 'em. But he called at every house, a'most, in the village: there's somebody else, mayhap, saw 'em in his ears, though I can't take upon me rightly to say.'

Mr Snell was correct in his surmise, that somebody else would remember the pedlar's ear-rings. For, on the spread of enquiry among the villagers, it was stated with gathering emphasis, that the parson had wanted to know whether the pedlar wore ear-rings in his ears, and an impression was created that a great deal depended on the eliciting of this fact. Of course everyone who heard the question, not having any distinct image of the pedlar as *without* ear-rings, immediately had an image of him *with* ear-rings, larger or smaller, as the case might be; and the image was presently taken for a vivid recollection, so that the glazier's wife, a well-intentioned woman, not given to lying, and whose house was among the cleanest in the village, was ready to declare, as sure as ever she meant to take the sacrament, the very next Christmas that was ever coming, that she had seen big ear-rings, in the shape of the young moon, in the pedlar's two ears; while Jinny Oates, the cobbler's daughter, being a more imaginative person, stated not only that she had seen them too, but that they had made her blood creep, as it did at that very moment while there she stood.

Also, by way of throwing further light on this clue of the tinderbox, a collection was made of all the articles purchased from the pedlar at various houses, and carried to the Rainbow to be exhibited there. In fact, there was a general feeling in the village, that for the clearing-up of this robbery there must be a great deal done at the Rainbow, and that no man need offer his wife an excuse for going there while it was the scene of severe public duties.

Some disappointment was felt, and perhaps a little indignation also, when it became known that Silas Marner, on being questioned by the Squire and the parson, had retained no other recollection of the pedlar than that he had called at his door, but had not entered his house, having turned away at once when Silas, holding the door ajar, had said that he wanted nothing. This had been Silas's testimony, though he clutched strongly at the idea of the pedlar's being the culprit, if only because it gave him a definite image of a whereabouts for his gold, after it had been taken away from its hiding-place: he could see it now in the pedlar's box. But it was observed with some irritation in the village, that anybody but a 'blind creatur' like Marner would have seen the man prowling about, for how came he to leave his tinderbox in the ditch close by, if he hadn't been lingering there? Doubtless, he had made his observations when he saw Marner at the door. Anybody might know – and only look at him – that the weaver was a half-crazy miser. It was a wonder the pedlar hadn't murdered him; men of that sort, with rings in their ears, had been known for murderers often and often; there had been one tried at the 'sizes, not so long ago but what there were people living who remembered it.

Godfrey Cass, indeed, entering the Rainbow during one of Mr Snell's frequently repeated recitals of his testimony, had treated it lightly, stating that he himself had bought a penknife of the pedlar, and thought him a merry grinning fellow enough; it was all nonsense, he said, about the man's evil looks. But this was spoken of in the village as the random talk of youth, 'as if it was only Mr Snell who had seen something odd about the pedlar!' On the contrary, there were at least half a dozen who were ready to go before Justice Malam, and give in much more striking testimony than any the landlord could furnish. It was to be hoped Mr Godfrey would not go to Tarley and throw cold water on what Mr Snell said there, and so prevent the justice from drawing up a warrant. He was suspected of intending this, when, after midday, he was seen setting off on horseback in the direction of Tarley.

But by this time Godfrey's interest in the robbery had faded before his growing anxiety about Dunstan and Wildfire, and he was going, not to Tarley, but to Batherley, unable to rest in uncertainty about them any longer. The possibility that Dunstan had played him the ugly trick of riding away with Wildfire, to return at the end of a month, when he had gambled away or otherwise squandered the price of the horse, was a fear that urged itself upon him more, even, than the thought of an accidental injury; and now that the dance at Mrs Osgood's was past, he was irritated with himself that he had trusted his horse to Dunstan. Instead of trying to still his fears, he encouraged them, with that superstitious impression which clings to us all, that if we expect evil very strongly it is the less likely to come; and when he heard a horse approaching at a trot, and saw a hat rising above a hedge beyond an angle of the lane, he felt as if his conjuration had succeeded. But no sooner did the horse come within sight, than his heart sank again. It was not Wildfire; and in a few moments more he discerned that the rider was not Dunstan, but Bryce, who pulled up to speak, with a face that implied something disagreeable.

'Well Mr Godfrey, that's a lucky brother of yours, that Master Dunsey, isn't he?'

'What do you mean?' said Godfrey, hastily.

'Why, hasn't he been home yet?' said Bryce.

'Home? no. What has happened? Be quick. What has he done with my horse?'

'Ah, I thought it was yours, though he pretended you had parted with it to him.'

'Has he thrown him down and broken his knees?' said Godfrey, flushed with exasperation.

'Worse than that,' said Bryce. 'You see, I'd made a bargain with him to buy the horse for a hundred and twenty – a swinging price, but I always liked the horse. And what does he do but go and stake him – fly at a hedge with stakes in it, atop of a bank with a ditch before it. The horse had been dead a pretty good while when he was found. So he hasn't been home since, has he?'

'Home? no,' said Godfrey, 'and he'd better keep away. Confound me for a fool! I might have known this would be the end of it.'

'Well, to tell you the truth,' said Bryce, 'after I'd bargained for the horse, it did come into my head that he might be riding and selling the horse without your knowledge, for I didn't believe it was his own. I knew Master Dunsey was up to his tricks sometimes. But where can he be gone? He's never been seen at Batherley. He couldn't have been hurt, for he must have walked off.'

'Hurt?' said Godfrey, bitterly. 'He'll never be hurt – he's made to hurt other people.'

'And so you *did* give him leave to sell the horse, eh?' said Bryce.

'Yes; I wanted to part with the horse – he was always a little too hard in the mouth for me,' said Godfrey; his pride making him wince under the idea that Bryce guessed the sale to be a matter of necessity. 'I was going to see after him – I thought some mischief had happened. I'll go back now,' he added, turning the horse's head, and wishing he could get rid of Bryce; for he felt that the long-dreaded crisis in his life was close upon him. 'You're coming on to Raveloe, aren't you?'

'Well, no, not now,' said Bryce. 'I *was* coming round there, for I had to go to Flitton, and I thought I might as well take you in my way, and just let you know all I knew myself about the horse. I suppose Master Dunsey didn't like to show himself till the ill news had blown over a bit. He's perhaps gone to pay a visit at the Three Crowns, by Whitbridge – I know he's fond of the house.'

'Perhaps he is,' said Godfrey, rather absently. Then rousing himself, he said, with an effort at carelessness, 'We shall hear of him soon enough, I'll be bound.'

'Well, here's my turning,' said Bryce, not surprised to perceive that Godfrey was rather 'down;' 'so I'll bid you good-day, and wish I may bring you better news another time.'

Godfrey rode along slowly, representing to himself the scene of confession to his father from which he felt that there was now no longer any escape. The revelation about the money must be made the very next morning; and if he withheld the rest, Dunstan would be sure to come back shortly, and finding that he must bear the brunt of his father's anger, would tell the whole story out of spite, even though he had nothing to gain by it. There was one step, perhaps, by which he might still win Dunstan's silence and put off the evil day: he might tell his father that he had himself spent the money paid to him by Fowler; and as he had never been guilty of such an offence before, the affair would blow over after a little storming. But Godfrey could not bend himself to this. He felt that in letting Dunstan have the money, he had already been guilty of a breach of trust hardly less culpable than that of spending the money directly for his own behoof; and yet there was a distinction between the two acts which made him feel that the one was so much more blackening than the other as to be intolerable to him.

'I don't pretend to be a good fellow,' he said to himself; 'but I'm not a scoundrel – at least, I'll stop short somewhere. I'll bear the consequences of what I *have* done sooner than make believe I've done what I never would have done. I'd never have spent the money for my own pleasure – I was tortured into it.'

Through the remainder of this day Godfrey, with only occasional fluctuations, kept his will bent in the direction of a complete avowal to his father, and he withheld the story of Wildfire's loss till the next morning, that it might serve him as an introduction to heavier matter. The old Squire was accustomed to his son's frequent absence from home, and thought neither Dunstan's nor Wildfire's non-appearance a matter calling for remark. Godfrey said to himself again and again, that if he let slip this one opportunity of confession, he might never have another; the revelation might be made even in a more odious way than by Dunstan's malignity: *she* might come, as she had threatened to do. And then he tried to make the scene easier to himself by rehearsal: he made up his mind how he would pass from the admission of his weakness in letting Dunstan have the money to the fact that Dunstan had a hold on him which he had been unable to shake off, and how he would work up his father to expect something very bad before he told him the fact. The old Squire was an implacable man: he made resolutions in violent anger, but he was not to be moved from them after his anger had subsided – as fiery volcanic matters cool and harden into rock. Like many violent and implacable men, he allowed evils to grow under favour of his own heedlessness, till they pressed upon him with exasperating force, and then he turned round with fierce severity and became unrelentingly hard. This was his system with his tenants: he allowed them to get into arrears, neglect their fences, reduce their stock, sell their straw, and otherwise go the wrong way, – and then, when he became short of money in consequence of this indulgence, he took the hardest measures and would listen to no appeal. Godfrey knew all this, and felt it with the greater force because he had constantly suffered annoyance from witnessing his father's sudden fits of unrelentingness, for which his own habitual irresolution deprived him of all sympathy. (He was not critical on the faulty indulgence which preceded these fits; *that* seemed to him natural enough.) Still there was just the chance, Godfrey thought, that his father's pride might see this marriage in a light that would induce him to hush it up, rather than turn his son out and make the family the talk of the country for ten miles round.

This was the view of the case that Godfrey managed to keep before him pretty closely till midnight, and he went to sleep thinking that he had done with inward debating. But when he awoke in the still morning darkness he found it impossible to reawaken his evening thoughts; it was as if they had been tired out and were not to be roused to further work. Instead of arguments for confession, he could now feel the presence of nothing but its evil consequences: the old dread of disgrace came back – the old shrinking from the thought of raising a hopeless barrier between himself and Nancy – the old disposition to rely on chances which might be favourable to him, and save him from betrayal. Why, after all, should he cut off the hope of them by his own act? He had seen the matter in a wrong light yesterday. He had been in a rage with Dunstan, and had thought of nothing but a thorough break-up of their mutual understanding; but what it would be really wisest for him to do, was to try and soften his father's anger against Dunsey, and keep things as nearly as possible in their old condition. If Dunsey did not come back for a few days (and Godfrey did not know but that the rascal had enough money in his pocket to enable him to keep away still longer), everything might blow over.

Chapter 9

Godfrey rose and took his own breakfast earlier than usual, but lingered in the wainscoted parlour till his younger brothers had finished their meal and gone out, awaiting his father, who always went out and had a walk with his managing-man before breakfast. Everyone breakfasted at a different hour in the Red House, and the Squire was always the latest, giving a long chance to a rather feeble morning appetite before he tried it. The table had been spread with substantial eatables nearly two hours before he presented himself – a tall, stout man of sixty, with a face in which the knit brow and rather hard glance seemed contradicted by the slack and feeble mouth. His person showed marks of habitual neglect, his dress was slovenly; and yet there was something in the presence of the old Squire distinguishable from that of the ordinary farmers in the parish, who were perhaps every whit as refined as he, but, having slouched their way through life with a consciousness of being in the vicinity of their 'betters,' wanted that self-possession and authoritativeness of voice and carriage which belonged to a man who thought of superiors as remote existences, with whom he had personally little more to do than with America or the stars. The Squire had been used to parish homage all his life, used to the presupposition that his family, his tankards, and everything that was his, were the oldest and best; and as he never associated with any gentry higher than himself, his opinion was not disturbed by comparison.

He glanced at his son as he entered the room, and said, 'What, sir! haven't *you* had your breakfast yet?' but there was no pleasant morning greeting between them; not because of any unfriendliness, but because the sweet flower of courtesy is not a growth of such homes as the Red House.

'Yes, sir,' said Godfrey, 'I've had my breakfast, but I was waiting to speak to you.'

'Ah! well,' said the Squire, throwing himself indifferently into his chair, and speaking in a ponderous coughing fashion, which was felt in Raveloe to be a sort of privilege of his rank, while he cut a piece of beef, and held it up before the deerhound that had come in with him, 'Ring the bell for my ale, will you? You youngsters' business is your own pleasure, mostly. There's no hurry about it for anybody but yourselves.'

The Squire's life was quite as idle as his sons', but it was a fiction kept up by himself and his contemporaries in Raveloe that youth was exclusively the period of folly, and that their aged wisdom was constantly in a state of endurance mitigated by sarcasm. Godfrey waited, before he spoke again, until the ale had been brought and the door closed – an interval during which Fleet, the deerhound, had consumed enough bits of beef to make a poor man's holiday dinner.

'There's been a cursed piece of ill-luck with Wildfire,' he began; 'happened the day before yesterday.'

'What! broke his knees?' said the Squire, after taking a draught of ale. 'I thought you knew how to ride better than that, sir. I never threw a horse down in my life. If I had, I might ha' whistled for another, for *my* father wasn't quite so ready to unstring as some other fathers I know of. But they must turn over a new leaf – *they* must. What with mortgages and arrears, I'm as short o' cash as a roadside pauper. And that fool Kimble says the newspaper's talking about peace. Why, the country wouldn't have a leg to stand on. Prices 'ud run down like a jack, and I should never get my arrears, not if I sold all the fellows up. And there's that damned Fowler, I won't put up with him any longer; I've told Winthrop to go to Cox this very day. The lying scoundrel told me he'd be sure to pay me a hundred last month. He takes advantage because he's on that outlying farm, and thinks I shall forget him.'

The Squire had delivered this speech in a coughing and interrupted manner, but with no pause long enough for Godfrey to make it a pretext for taking up the word again. He felt that his father meant to ward off any request for money on the ground of the misfortune with Wildfire, and that the emphasis he had thus been led to lay on his shortness of cash and his arrears was likely to produce an attitude of mind the most unfavourable for his own disclosure. But he must go on, now he had begun.

'It's worse than breaking the horse's knees – he's been staked and killed,' he said, as soon as his father was silent, and had begun to cut his meat. 'But I wasn't thinking of asking you to buy me another horse; I was only thinking I'd lost the means of paying you with the price of Wildfire, as I'd meant to do. Dunsey took him to the hunt to sell him for me the other day, and after he'd made a bargain for a hundred and twenty with Bryce, he went after the hounds, and took some fool's leap or other, that did for the horse at once. If it hadn't been for that, I should have paid you a hundred pounds this morning.'

The Squire had laid down his knife and fork, and was staring at his son in amazement, not being sufficiently quick of brain to form a probable guess as to what could have caused so strange an inversion of the paternal and filial relations as this proposition of his son to pay him a hundred pounds.

'The truth is, sir – I'm very sorry – I was quite to blame,' said Godfrey. 'Fowler did pay that hundred pounds. He paid it to me, when I was over there one day last month. And Dunsey bothered me for the money, and I let him have it, because I hoped I should be able to pay it you before this.'

The Squire was purple with anger before his son had done speaking, and found utterance difficult. 'You let Dunsey have it, sir? And how long have you been so thick with Dunsey that you must *collogue* with him to embezzle my money? Are you turning out a scamp? I tell you, I won't have it. I'll turn the whole pack of you out of the house together, and marry again. I'd have you to remember, sir, my property's got no entail on it; – since my grandfather's time the Casses can do as they like with their land. Remember that, sir. Let Dunsey have the money! Why should you let Dunsey have the money? There's some lie at the bottom of it.'

'There's no lie, sir,' said Godfrey. 'I wouldn't have spent the money myself, but Dunsey bothered me, and I was a fool and let him have it. But I meant to pay it, whether he did or not. That's the whole story. I never meant to embezzle money, and I'm not the man to do it. You never knew me do a dishonest trick, sir.'

'Where's Dunsey, then? What do you stand talking there for? Go and fetch Dunsey, as I tell you, and let him give account of what he wanted the money for, and what he's done with it. He shall repent it. I'll turn him out. I said I would, and I'll do it. He shan't brave me. Go and fetch him.'

'Dunsey isn't come back, sir.'

'What! did he break his own neck then?' said the Squire, with some disgust at the idea that, in that case, he could not fulfil his threat.

'No, he wasn't hurt, I believe, for the horse was found dead, and Dunsey must have walked off. I dare say we shall see him again by and by. I don't know where he is.'

'And what must you be letting him have my money for? Answer me that,' said the Squire, attacking Godfrey again, since Dunsey was not within reach.

'Well, sir, I don't know,' said Godfrey, hesitatingly. That was a feeble evasion, but Godfrey was not fond of lying, and, not being sufficiently aware that no sort of duplicity can long flourish without the help of vocal falsehoods, he was quite unprepared with invented motives.

'You don't know? I tell you what it is, sir. You've been up to some trick, and you've been bribing him not to tell,' said the Squire, with a sudden acuteness which startled Godfrey, who felt his heart beat violently at the nearness of his father's guess. The sudden alarm pushed him on to take the next step – a very slight impulse suffices for that on a downward road.

'Why, sir,' he said, trying to speak with careless ease, 'it was a little affair between me and Dunsey; it's no matter to anybody else. It's hardly worth while to pry into young men's fooleries: it wouldn't have made any difference to you, sir, if I'd not had the bad luck to lose Wildfire. I should have paid you the money.'

'Fooleries! Pshaw! it's time you'd done with fooleries. And I'd have you know, sir, you *must* ha' done with 'em,' said the Squire, frowning and casting an angry glance at his son. 'Your goings-on are not what I shall find money for any longer. There's my grandfather had his stables full o' horses, and kept a good house too, and in worse times, by what I can make out; and so might I, if I hadn't four good-for-nothing fellows to hang on me like horse-leeches. I've been too good a father to you all – that's what it is. But I shall pull up, sir.'

Godfrey was silent. He was not likely to be very penetrating in his judgments, but he had always had a sense that his father's indulgence had not been kindness, and had had a vague longing for some discipline that would have checked his own errant weakness, and helped his better will. The Squire ate his bread and meat hastily, took a deep draught of ale, then turned his chair from the table, and began to speak again.

'It'll be all the worse for you, you know – you'd need try and help me keep things together.'

'Well, sir, I've often offered to take the management of things, but you know you've taken it ill always, and seemed to think I wanted to push you out of your place.'

'I know nothing o' your offering or o' my taking it ill,' said the Squire, whose memory consisted in certain strong impressions unmodified by detail; 'but I know, one while you seemed to be thinking o' marrying, and I didn't offer to put any obstacles in your way, as some fathers would. I'd as lieve you married Lammeter's daughter as anybody. I suppose, if I'd said you nay, you'd ha' kept on with it; but, for want o' contradiction, you've changed your mind. You're a shilly-shally fellow: you take after your poor mother. She never had a will of her own; a woman has no call for one, if she's got a proper man for her husband. But *your* wife had need have one, for you hardly know your own mind enough to make both your legs walk one way. The lass hasn't said downright she won't have you, has she?'

'No,' said Godfrey, feeling very hot and uncomfortable; 'but I don't think she will.'

'Think! why, haven't you the courage to ask her? Do you stick to it, you want to have *her* – that's the thing?'

'There's no other woman I want to marry,' said Godfrey, evasively.

'Well, then, let me make the offer for you, that's all, if you haven't the pluck to do it yourself. Lammeter isn't likely to be loth for his daughter to marry into *my* family, I should think. And as for the pretty lass, she wouldn't have her cousin – and there's nobody else, as I see, could ha' stood in your way.'

'I'd rather let it be, please sir, at present,' said Godfrey, in alarm. 'I think she's a little offended with me just now, and I should like to speak for myself. A man must manage these things for himself.'

'Well, speak then and manage it, and see if you can't turn over a new leaf. That's what a man must do when he thinks o' marrying.'

'I don't see how I can think of it at present, sir. You wouldn't like to settle me on one of the farms, I suppose, and I don't think she'd come to live in this house with all my brothers. It's a different sort of life to what she's been used to.'

'Not come to live in this house? Don't tell me. You ask her, that's all,' said the Squire, with a short, scornful laugh.

'I'd rather let the thing be, at present, sir,' said Godfrey. 'I hope you won't try to hurry it on by saying anything.'

'I shall do what I choose,' said the Squire, 'and I shall let you know I'm master; else you may turn out and find an estate to drop into somewhere else. Go out and tell Winthrop not to go to Cox's, but wait for me. And tell 'em to get my horse saddled. And stop: look out and get that hack o' Dunsey's sold, and hand me the money, will you? He'll keep no more hacks at my expense. And if you know where he's sneaking – I dare say you do – you may tell him to spare himself the journey o' coming back home. Let him turn ostler, and keep himself. He shan't hang on me any more.'

'I don't know where he is, sir; and if I did, it isn't my place to tell him to keep away,' said Godfrey, moving towards the door.

'Confound it, sir, don't stay arguing, but go and order my horse,' said the Squire, taking up a pipe.

Godfrey left the room, hardly knowing whether he were more relieved by the sense that the interview was ended without having made any change in his position, or more uneasy that he had entangled himself still further in prevarication and deceit. What had passed about his proposing to Nancy had raised a new alarm, lest by some after-dinner words of his father's to Mr Lammeter he should be thrown into the embarrassment of being obliged absolutely to decline her when she seemed to be within his reach. He fled to his usual refuge, that of hoping for some unforeseen turn of fortune, some favourable chance which would save him from unpleasant consequences – perhaps even justify his insincerity by manifesting its prudence. And in this point of trusting to some throw of fortune's dice, Godfrey can hardly be called specially old-fashioned. Favourable Chance, I fancy, is the god of all men who follow their own devices instead of obeying a law they believe in. Let even a polished man of these days get into a position he is ashamed to avow, and his mind will be bent on all the possible issues that may deliver him from the calculable results of that position. Let him live outside his income, or shirk the resolute honest work that brings wages, and he will presently find himself dreaming of a possible benefactor, a possible simpleton who may be cajoled into using his interest, a possible state of mind in some possible person not yet forthcoming. Let him neglect the responsibilities of his office, and he will inevitably anchor himself on the chance, that the thing left undone may turn out not to be of the supposed importance. Let him betray his friend's confidence, and he will adore that same cunning complexity called Chance, which gives him the hope that his friend will never know; let him forsake a decent craft that he may pursue the gentilities of a profession to which nature never called him, and his religion will infallibly be the worship of blessed Chance, which he will believe in as the mighty creator of success. The evil principle deprecated in that religion, is the orderly sequence by which the seed brings forth a crop after its kind.

Chapter 10

Justice Malam was naturally regarded in Tarley and Raveloe as a man of capacious mind, seeing that he could draw much wider conclusions without evidence than could be expected of his neighbours who were not on the Commission of the Peace. Such a man was not likely to neglect the clue of the tinderbox, and an enquiry was set on foot concerning a pedlar, name unknown, with curly black hair and a foreign complexion, carrying a box of cutlery and jewellery, and wearing large rings in his ears. But either because enquiry was too slow-footed to overtake him, or because the description applied to so many pedlars that enquiry did not know how to choose among them, weeks passed away, and there was no other result concerning the robbery than a gradual cessation of the excitement it had caused in Raveloe. Dunstan Cass's absence was hardly a subject of remark: he had once before had a quarrel with his father, and had gone off, nobody knew whither, to return at the end of six weeks, take up his old quarters unforbidden, and swagger as usual. His own family, who equally expected this issue, with the sole difference that the Squire was determined this time to forbid him the old quarters, never mentioned his absence; and when his uncle Kimble or Mr Osgood noticed it, the story of his having killed Wildfire, and committed some offence against his father, was enough to prevent surprise. To connect the fact of Dunsey's disappearance with that of the robbery occurring on the same day, lay quite away from the track of everyone's thought – even Godfrey's, who had better reason than anyone else to know what his brother was capable of. He remembered no mention of the weaver between them since the time, twelve years ago, when it was their boyish sport to deride him; and, besides, his imagination constantly created an *alibi* for Dunstan: he saw him continually in some congenial haunt, to which he had walked off on leaving Wildfire – saw him sponging on chance acquaintances, and meditating a return home to the old amusement of tormenting his elder brother. Even if any brain in Raveloe had put the said two facts together, I doubt whether a combination so injurious to the prescriptive respectability of a family with a mural monument and venerable tankards, would not have been suppressed as of unsound tendency. But Christmas puddings, brawn, and abundance of spirituous liquors, throwing the mental originality into the channel of nightmare, are great preservatives against a dangerous spontaneity of waking thought.

When the robbery was talked of at the Rainbow and elsewhere, in good company, the balance continued to waver between the rational explanation founded on the tinderbox, and the theory of an impenetrable mystery that mocked investigation. The advocates of the tinder-box-and-pedlar view considered the other side a muddle-headed and credulous set, who, because they themselves were wall-eyed, supposed everybody else to have the same blank outlook; and the adherents of the inexplicable, more than hinted that their antagonists were animals inclined to crow before they had found any corn – mere skimming-dishes in point of depth – whose clear-sightedness consisted in supposing there was nothing behind a barn-door because they couldn't see through it; so that, though their controversy did not serve to elicit the fact concerning the robbery, it elicited some true opinions of collateral importance.

But while poor Silas's loss served thus to brush the slow current of Raveloe conversation, Silas himself was feeling the withering desolation of that bereavement, about which his neighbours were arguing at their ease. To anyone who had observed him before he lost his gold, it might have seemed that so withered and shrunken a life as his could hardly be susceptible of a bruise, could hardly endure any subtraction but such as would put an end to it altogether. But in reality it had been an eager life, filled with immediate purpose, which fenced him in from the wide, cheerless unknown. It had been a clinging life; and though the object round which its fibres had clung was a dead disrupted thing, it satisfied the need for clinging. But now the fence was broken down – the support was snatched away. Marner's thoughts could no longer move in their old round, and were baffled by a blank like that which meets a plodding ant when the earth has broken away on its homeward path. The loom was there, and the weaving, and the growing pattern in the cloth; but the bright treasure in the hole under his feet was gone; the prospect of handling and counting it was gone: the evening had no phantasm of delight to still the poor soul's craving. The thought of the money he would get by his actual work could bring no joy, for its meagre image was only a fresh reminder of his loss; and hope was too heavily crushed by the sudden blow for his imagination to dwell on the growth of a new hoard from that small beginning.

He filled up the blank with grief. As he sat weaving, he every now and then moaned low, like one in pain: it was the sign that his thoughts had come round again to the sudden chasm – to the empty evening-time. And all the evening, as he sat in his loneliness by his dull fire, he leaned his elbows on his knees, and clasped his head with his hands, and moaned very low – not as one who seeks to be heard.

And yet he was not utterly forsaken in his trouble. The repulsion Marner had always created in his neighbours was partly dissipated by the new light in which this misfortune had shown him. Instead of a man who had more cunning than honest folks could come by, and, what was worse, had not the inclination to use that cunning in a neighbourly way, it was now apparent that Silas had not cunning enough to keep his own. He was generally spoken of as a 'poor mushed creatur'; and that avoidance of his neighbours, which had before been referred to his ill-will, and to a probable addiction to worse company, was now considered mere craziness.

This change to a kindlier feeling was shown in various ways. The odour of Christmas cooking being on the wind, it was the season when superfluous pork and black puddings are suggestive of charity in well-to-do families; and Silas's misfortune had brought him uppermost in the memory of housekeepers like Mrs Osgood. Mr Crackenthorp, too, while he admonished Silas that his money had probably been taken from him because he thought too much of it, and never came to church, enforced the doctrine by a present of pigs' pettitoes, well calculated to dissipate unfounded prejudices against the clerical character. Neighbours, who had nothing but verbal consolation to give, showed a disposition not only to greet Silas, and discuss his misfortune at some length when they encountered him in the village; but also to take the trouble of calling at his cottage, and getting him to repeat all the details on the very spot; and then they would try to cheer him by saying, 'Well, Master Marner, you're no worse off nor other poor folks, after all; and if you was to be crippled, the parish 'ud give you a 'lowance.'

I suppose one reason why we are seldom able to comfort our neighbours with our words is, that our goodwill gets adulterated, in spite of ourselves, before it can pass our lips. We can send black puddings and pettitoes without giving them a flavour of our own egoism; but language is a stream that is almost sure to smack of a mingled soil. There was a fair proportion of kindness in Raveloe; but it was often of a beery and bungling sort, and took the shape least allied to the complimentary and hypocritical.

Mr Macey, for example, coming one evening expressly to let Silas know that recent events had given him the advantage of standing more favourably in the opinion of a man whose judgement was not formed lightly, opened the conversation by saying, as soon as he had seated himself and adjusted his thumbs: 'Come, Master Marner, why, you've no call to sit a-moaning. You're a deal better off to ha' lost your money, nor to ha' kep it by foul means. I used to think, when you first come into these parts, as you were no better nor you should be; you were younger a deal than what you are now; but you were allays a staring, white-faced creatur, partly like a bald-faced calf, as I may say. But there's no knowing: it isn't every queer-looksed thing as Old Harry's had the making of – I mean, speaking o' toads and such; for they're often harmless, like, and useful against varmin. And it's pretty much the same wi' you, as fur as I can see. Though as to the yarbs and stuff to cure the breathing, if you brought that sort o' knowledge from distant parts, you might ha' been a bit freer of it. And if the knowledge wasn't well come by, why, you might ha' made up for it by coming to church reg'lar; for, as for the children as the Wise Woman charmed, I've been at the christening of 'em again and again, and they took the water just as well. And that's reasonable; for if Old Harry's a mind to do a bit o' kindness for a holiday, like, who's got anything against it? That's my thinking; and I've been clerk o' this parish forty year, and I know, when the parson and me does the cussing of a Ash-Wednesday, there's no cussing o' folks as have a mind to be cured without a doctor, let Kimble say what he will. And so, Master Marner, as I was saying – for there's windings i' things as they may carry you to the fur end o' the prayer-book afore you get back to 'em – my advice is, as you keep up your sperrits; for as for thinking you're a deep un, and ha' got more inside you nor 'ull bear daylight, I'm not o' that opinion at all, and so I tell the neighbours. For, says I, you talk o' Master Marner making out a tale – why, its nonsense, that is: it 'ud take a 'cute man to make a tale like that; and, says I, he looked as scared as a rabbit.'

During this discursive address Silas had continued motionless in his previous attitude, leaning his elbows on his knees, and pressing his hands against his head. Mr Macey, not doubting that he had been listened to, paused, in the expectation of some appreciatory reply, but Marner remained silent. He had a sense that the old man meant to be good-natured and neighbourly; but the kindness fell on him as sunshine falls on the wretched – he had no heart to taste it, and felt that it was very far off him.

'Come, Master Marner, have you got nothing to say to that?' said Mr Macey at last, with a slight accent of impatience.

'Oh,' said Marner, slowly, shaking his head between his hands, 'I thank you – thank you – kindly.'

'Ay, ay, to be sure: I thought you would,' said Mr Macey; 'and my advice is – have you got a Sunday suit?'

'No,' said Marner.

'I doubted it was so,' said Mr Macey. 'Now, let me advise you to get a Sunday suit: there's Tookey, he's a poor creatur, but he's got my tailoring business, and some o' my money in it, and he shall make a suit at a low price, and give you trust, and then you can come to church, and be a bit neighbourly. Why you've never heared me say "Amen" since you come into these parts, and I recommend you to lose no time, for it'll be poor work when Tookey has it all to himself, for I mayn't be equil to stand i' the desk at all, come another winter.' Here Mr

Macey paused, perhaps expecting some sign of emotion in his hearer; but not observing any, he went on. 'And as for the money for the suit o' clothes, why, you get a matter of a pound a-week at your weaving, Master Marner, and you're a young man, eh, for all you look so mushed. Why, you couldn't ha' been five-and-twenty when you come into these parts, eh?'

Silas started a little at the change to a questioning tone, and answered mildly, 'I don't know; I can't rightly say – it's a long while since.'

After receiving such an answer as this, it is not surprising that Mr Macey observed, later on in the evening at the Rainbow, that Marner's head was 'all of a muddle,' and that it was to be doubted if he ever knew when Sunday came round, which showed him a worse heathen than many a dog.

Another of Silas's comforters, besides Mr Macey, came to him with a mind highly charged on the same topic. This was Mrs Winthrop, the wheelwright's wife. The inhabitants of Raveloe were not severely regular in their church-going, and perhaps there was hardly a person in the parish who would not have held that to go to church every Sunday in the calendar would have shown a greedy desire to stand well with Heaven, and get an undue advantage over their neighbours – a wish to be better than the 'common run,' that would have implied a reflection on those who had had godfathers and godmothers as well as themselves, and had an equal right to the burying-service. At the same time, it was understood to be requisite for all who were not household servants, or young men, to take the sacrament at one of the great festivals: Squire Cass himself took it on Christmas-day; while those who were held to be 'good livers' went to church with greater, though still with moderate frequency.

Mrs Winthrop was one of these: she was in all respects a woman of scrupulous conscience, so eager for duties, that life seemed to offer them too scantily unless she rose at half-past four, though this threw a scarcity of work over the more advanced hours of the morning, which it was a constant problem with her to remove. Yet she had not the vixenish temper which is sometimes supposed to be a necessary condition of such habits: she was a very mild, patient woman, whose nature it was to seek out all the sadder and more serious elements of life, and pasture her mind upon them. She was the person always first thought of in Raveloe when there was illness or death in a family, when leeches were to be applied, or there was a sudden disappointment in a monthly nurse. She was a 'comfortable woman' – good-looking, fresh-complexioned, having her lips always slightly screwed, as if she felt herself in a sickroom with the doctor or the clergyman present. But she was never whimpering; no one had seen her shed tears; she was simply grave and inclined to shake her head and sigh, almost imperceptibly, like a funereal mourner who is not a relation. It seemed surprising that Ben Winthrop, who loved his quart-pot and his joke, got along so well with Dolly; but she took her husband's jokes and joviality as patiently as everything else, considering that 'men *would* be so', and viewing the stronger sex in the light of animals whom it had pleased Heaven to make naturally troublesome, like bulls and turkey-cocks.

This good wholesome woman could hardly fail to have her mind drawn strongly towards Silas Marner, now that he appeared in the light of a sufferer;

and one Sunday afternoon she took her little boy Aaron with her, and went to call on Silas, carrying in her hand some small lard-cakes, flat paste-like articles, much esteemed in Raveloe. Aaron, an apple-cheeked youngster of seven, with a clean starched frill, which looked like a plate for the apples, needed all his adventurous curiosity to embolden him against the possibility that the big-eyed weaver might do him some bodily injury; and his dubiety was much increased when, on arriving at the Stone-pits, they heard the mysterious sound of the loom.

'Ah, it is as I thought,' said Mrs Winthrop, sadly.

They had to knock loudly before Silas heard them; but when he did come to the door, he showed no impatience, as he would once have done, at a visit that had been unasked for and unexpected. Formerly, his heart had been as a locked casket with its treasure inside; but now the casket was empty, and the lock was broken. Left groping in darkness, with his prop utterly gone, Silas had inevitably a sense, though a dull and half-despairing one, that if any help came to him it must come from without; and there was a slight stirring of expectation at the sight of his fellow-men, a faint consciousness of dependence on their goodwill. He opened the door wide to admit Dolly, but without otherwise returning her greeting than by moving the armchair a few inches as a sign that she was to sit down in it. Dolly, as soon as she was seated, removed the white cloth that covered her lard-cakes, and said in her gravest way: 'I'd a baking yisterday, Master Marner, and the lard-cakes turned out better nor common, and I'd ha' asked you to accept some, if you'd thought well. I don't eat such things myself, for a bit o' bread's what I like from one year's end to the other; but men's stomichs are made so comical, they want a change – they do, I know, God help 'em.'

Dolly sighed gently as she held out the cakes to Silas, who thanked her kindly, and looked very close at them, absently, being accustomed to look so at everything he took into his hand – eyed all the while by the wondering bright orbs of the small Aaron, who had made an outwork of his mother's chair, and was peeping round from behind it.

'There's letters pricked on 'em,' said Dolly. 'I can't read 'em myself, and there's nobody, not Mr Macey himself, rightly knows what they mean; but they've a good meaning, for they're the same as is on the pulpit-cloth at church. What are they, Aaron, my dear?'

Aaron retreated completely behind his outwork.

'O go, that's naughty,' said his mother, mildly. 'Well, what-iver the letters are, they've a good meaning; and it's a stamp as has been in our house, Ben says, ever since he was a little un, and his mother used to put it on the cakes, and I've allays put it on too; for if there's any good, we've need of it i' this world.'

'It's I. H. S.,' said Silas, at which proof of learning Aaron peeped round the chair again.

'Well, to be sure, you can read 'em off,' said Dolly. 'Ben's read 'em to me many and many a time, but they slip out o' my mind again; the more's the pity, for they're good letters, else they wouldn't be in the church; and so I prick 'em on all the loaves and all the cakes, though sometimes they won't hold, because o' the rising – for, as I said, if there's any good to be got, we've need on it i' this world – that we have; and I hope they'll bring good to you, Master Marner, for it's wi' that will I brought you the cakes; and you see the letters have held better nor common.'

Silas was as unable to interpret the letters as Dolly, but there was no possibility of misunderstanding the desire to give comfort that made itself heard in her quiet tones. He said, with more feeling than before – 'Thank you – thank you kindly.' But he laid down the cake and seated himself absently – drearily unconscious of any distinct benefit towards which the cake and the letters, or even Dolly's kindness, could tend for him.

'Ah, if there's good anywhere, we've need of it,' repeated Dolly, who did not lightly forsake a serviceable phrase. She looked at Silas pityingly as she went on. 'But you didn't hear the church-bells this morning, Master Marner. I doubt you didn't know it was Sunday. Living so lone here, you lose your count, I dare say; and then, when your loom makes a noise, you can't hear the bells, more partic'lar now the frost kills the sound.'

'Yes, I did; I heard 'em,' said Silas, to whom Sunday bells were a mere accident of the day, and not part of its sacredness. There had been no bells in Lantern Yard.

'Dear heart!' said Dolly, pausing before she spoke again. 'But what a pity it is you should work of a Sunday, and not clean yourself – if you *didn't* go to church; for if you'd a roasting bit, it might be as you couldn't leave it, being a lone man. But there's the bakehus, if you could make up your mind to spend a twopence on the oven now and then, – not every week, in course – I shouldn't like to do that myself, – you might carry your bit o' dinner there, for it's nothing but right to have a bit o' summat hot of a Sunday, and not to make it as you can't know your dinner from Saturday. But now, upo' Christmasday, this blessed Christmas as is ever coming, if you was to take your dinner to the bakehus, and go to church, and see the holly and the yew, and hear the anthim, and then take the sacramen', you'd be a deal the better, and you'd know which end you stood on, and you could put your trust i' Them as knows better nor we do, seein' you'd ha' done what it lies on us all to do.'

Dolly's exhortation, which was an unusually long effort of speech for her, was uttered in the soothing persuasive tone with which she would have tried to prevail on a sick man to take his medicine, or a basin of gruel for which he had no appetite. Silas had never before been closely urged on the point of his absence from church, which had only been thought of as a part of his general queerness; and he was too direct and simple to evade Dolly's appeal.

'Nay, nay,' he said, 'I know nothing o' church. I've never been to church.'

'No!' said Dolly, in a low tone of wonderment. Then bethinking herself of Silas's advent from an unknown country, she said, 'Could it ha' been as they'd no church where you was born?'

'O yes,' said Silas, meditatively, sitting in his usual posture of leaning on his knees, and supporting his head. 'There was churches – a many – it was a big town. But I knew nothing of 'em – I went to chapel.'

Dolly was much puzzled at this new word, but she was rather afraid of enquiring further, lest 'chapel' might mean some haunt of wickedness. After a little thought, she said, 'Well, Master Marner, it's niver too late to turn over a new leaf, and if you've niver had no church, there's no telling the good it 'll do you. For I feel so set up and comfortable as niver was, when I've been and heard the prayers, and the singing to the praise and glory o' God, as Mr Macey gives out – and Mr Crackenthorp saying good words, and more partic'lar on Sacramen' Day; and if a bit o' trouble comes, I feel as I can put up wi' it, for I've looked for help i' the right quarter, and gev myself up to Them as we must all give ourselves up to at the last; and if we'n done our part, it isn't to be believed as Them as are above us 'ull be worse nor we are, and come short o' Their'n.'

Poor Dolly's exposition of her simple Raveloe theology fell rather unmeaningly on Silas's ears, for there was no word in it that could rouse a memory of what he had known as religion, and his comprehension was quite baffled by the plural pronoun, which was no heresy of Dolly's, but only her way of avoiding a pre-sumptuous familiarity. He remained silent, not feeling inclined to assent to the part of Dolly's speech which he fully understood – her recommendation that he should go to church. Indeed, Silas was so unaccustomed to talk beyond the brief questions and answers necessary for the transaction of his simple business, that words did not easily come to him without the urgency of a distinct purpose.

But now, little Aaron, having become used to the weaver's awful presence, had advanced to his mother's side, and Silas, seeming to notice him for the first time, tried to return Dolly's signs of goodwill by offering the lad a bit of lard-cake. Aaron shrank back a little, and rubbed his head against his mother's shoulder, but still thought the piece of cake worth the risk of putting his hand out for it.

'O, for shame, Aaron,' said his mother, taking him on her lap, however; 'why, you don't want cake again yet awhile. He's wonderfully hearty,' she went on, with a little sigh – 'that he is, God knows. He's my youngest, and we spoil him sadly, for either me or the father must allays hev him in our sight – that we must.'

She stroked Aaron's brown head, and thought it must do Master Marner good to see such a 'pictur of a child.' But Marner, on the other side of the hearth, saw the neat-featured rosy face as a mere dim round, with two dark spots in it.

'And he's got a voice like a bird – you wouldn't think,' Dolly went on; 'he can sing a Christmas carril as his father's taught him; and I take it for a token as he'll come to good, as he can learn the good tunes so quick. Come, Aaron, stan' up and sing the carril to Master Marner, come.'

Aaron replied by rubbing his forehead against his mother's shoulder.

'O, that's naughty,' said Dolly, gently. 'Stan' up, when mother tells you, and let me hold the cake till you've done.'

Aaron was not indisposed to display his talents, even to an ogre, under protecting circumstances; and after a few more signs of coyness, consisting chiefly in rubbing the backs of his hands over his eyes, and then peeping between them at Master Marner, to see if he looked anxious for the 'carril', he at length allowed his head to be duly adjusted, and standing behind the table, which let him appear above it only as far as his broad frill, so that he looked like a cherubic head untroubled with a body, he began with a clear chirp, and in a melody that had the rhythm of an industrious hammer,

> God rest you merry, gentlemen,
> Let nothing you dismay.
> For Jesus Christ our Saviour
> Was born on Christmas-day.

Dolly listened with a devout look, glancing at Marner in some confidence that this strain would help to allure him to church.

'That's Christmas music,' she said, when Aaron had ended, and had secured his piece of cake again. 'There's no other music equil to the Christmas music – "Hark the erol angils sing". And you may judge what it is at church, Master Marner, with the bassoon and the voices, as you can't help thinking you've got to a better place a'ready – for I wouldn't speak ill o' this world, seeing as Them put us in it as knows best; but what wi' the drink, and the quarrelling, and the bad illnesses, and the hard dying, as I've seen times and times, one's thankful to hear of a better. The boy sings pretty, don't he, Master Marner?'

'Yes,' said Silas, absently, 'very pretty.'

The Christmas carol, with its hammer-like rhythm, had fallen on his ears as strange music, quite unlike a hymn, and could have none of the effect Dolly contemplated. But he wanted to show her that he was grateful, and the only mode that occurred to him was to offer Aaron a bit more cake.

'O, no, thank you, Master Marner,' said Dolly, holding down Aaron's willing hands. 'We must be going home now. And so I wish you goodbye, Master Marner; and if you ever feel anyways bad in your inside, as you can't fend for yourself, I'll come and clean up for you, and get you a bit o' victual, and willing. But I beg and pray of you to leave off weaving of a Sunday, for it's bad for soul and body – and the money as comes i' that way 'ull be a bad bed to lie down on at the last, if it doesn't fly away, nobody knows where, like the white frost. And you'll excuse me being that free with you, Master Marner, for I wish you well – I do. Make your bow, Aaron.'

Silas said 'Goodbye, and thank you, kindly,' as he opened the door for Dolly, but he couldn't help feeling relieved when she was gone – relieved that he might weave again and moan at his ease. Her simple view of life and its comforts, by which she had tried to cheer him, was only like a report of unknown objects, which his imagination could not fashion. The fountains of human love and divine faith had not yet been unlocked, and his soul was still the shrunken rivulet, with only this difference, that its little groove of sand was blocked up, and it wandered confusedly against dark obstruction.

And so, notwithstanding the honest persuasions of Mr Macey and Dolly Winthrop, Silas spent his Christmas-day in loneliness, eating his meat in sadness of heart, though the meat had come to him as a neighbourly present. In the morning he looked out on the black frost that seemed to press cruelly on every blade of grass, while the half-icy red pool shivered under the bitter wind; but towards evening the snow began to fall, and curtained from him even that dreary outlook, shutting him close up with his narrow grief. And he sat in his robbed home through the livelong evening, not caring to close his shutters or lock his door, pressing his head between his hands and moaning, till the cold grasped him and told him that his fire was grey.

Nobody in this world but himself knew that he was the same Silas Marner who had once loved his fellow with tender love, and trusted in an unseen goodness. Even to himself that past experience had become dim.

But in Raveloe village the bells rang merrily, and the church was fuller than all through the rest of the year, with red faces among the abundant dark-green boughs – faces prepared for a longer service than usual by an odorous breakfast of toast and ale. Those green boughs, the hymn and anthem never heard but at Christmas – even the Athanasian Creed, which was discriminated from the others only as being longer and of exceptional virtue, since it was only read on rare occasions – brought a vague exulting sense, for which the grown men could as little have found words as the children, that something great and mysterious had been done for them in heaven above, and in earth below, which they were appropriating by their presence. And then the red faces made their way through the black biting frost to their own homes, feeling themselves free for the rest of the day to eat, drink, and be merry, and using that Christian freedom without diffidence.

At Squire Cass's family party that day nobody mentioned Dunstan – nobody was sorry for his absence, or feared it would be too long. The doctor and his wife, uncle and aunt Kimble, were there, and the annual Christmas talk was carried through without any omissions, rising to the climax of Mr Kimble's experience when he walked the London hospitals thirty years back, together with striking professional anecdotes then gathered. Whereupon cards followed, with aunt Kimble's annual failure to follow suit, and uncle Kimble's irascibility concerning the odd trick which was rarely explicable to him, when it was not on his side, without a general visitation of tricks to see that they were formed on sound principles: the whole being accompanied by a strong steaming odour of spirits-and-water.

But the party on Christmas-day, being a strictly family party, was not the pre-eminently brilliant celebration of the season at the Red House. It was the great dance on New Year's Eve that made the glory of Squire Cass's hospitality, as of his forefathers', time out of mind. This was the occasion when all the society of Raveloe and Tarley, whether old acquaintances separated by long rutty distances, or cooled acquaintances separated by misunderstandings concerning runaway calves, or acquaintances founded on intermittent condescension, counted on meeting and on comporting themselves with mutual appropriateness. This was the occasion on which fair dames who came on pillions sent their bandboxes before them, supplied with more than their evening costume; for the feast was not to end with a single evening, like a paltry town entertainment, where the whole supply of eatables is put on the table at once, and bedding is scanty. The Red House was provisioned as if for a siege; and as for the spare featherbeds ready to be laid on floors, they were as plentiful as might naturally be expected in a family that had killed its own geese for many generations.

Godfrey Cass was looking forward to this New Year's Eve with a foolish reckless longing, that made him half deaf to his importunate companion, Anxiety.

'Dunsey will be coming home soon: there will be a great blow-up, and how will you bribe his spite to silence?' said Anxiety.

'O, he won't come home before New Year's Eve, perhaps,' said Godfrey; 'and I shall sit by Nancy then, and dance with her, and get a kind look from her in spite of herself.'

'But money is wanted in another quarter,' said Anxiety, in a louder voice, 'and how will you get it without selling your mother's diamond pin? And if you don't get it . . . ?'

'Well, but something may happen to make things easier. At any rate, there's one pleasure for me close at hand: Nancy is coming.'

'Yes, and suppose your father should bring matters to a pass that will oblige you to decline marrying her – and to give your reasons?'

'Hold your tongue, and don't worry me. I can see Nancy's eyes, just as they will look at me, and feel her hand in mine already.'

But Anxiety went on, though in noisy Christmas company; refusing to be utterly quieted even by much drinking.

Chapter 11

Some women, I grant, would not appear to advantage seated on a pillion, and attired in a drab joseph and a drab beaver-bonnet, with a crown resembling a small stew-pan; for a garment suggesting a coachman's greatcoat, cut out under an exiguity of cloth that would only allow of miniature capes, is not well adapted to conceal deficiencies of contour, nor is drab a colour that will throw sallow cheeks into lively contrast. It was all the greater triumph to Miss Nancy Lammeter's beauty that she looked thoroughly bewitching in that costume, as seated on the pillion behind her tall, erect father, she held one arm round him, and looked down, with open-eyed anxiety, at the treacherous snow-covered pools and puddles, which sent up formidable splashings of mud under the stamp of Dobbin's foot. A painter would, perhaps, have preferred her in those moments when she was free from self-consciousness; but certainly the bloom on her cheeks was at its highest point of contrast with the surrounding drab when she arrived at the door of the Red House, and saw Mr Godfrey Cass ready to lift her from the pillion. She wished her sister Priscilla had come up at the same time with the servant, for then she would have contrived that Mr Godfrey should have lifted off Priscilla first, and, in the mean time, she would have persuaded her father to go round to the horse-block instead of alighting at the doorsteps. It was very painful, when you had made it quite clear to a young man that you were determined not to marry him, however much he might wish it, that he would still continue to pay you marked attentions; besides, why didn't he always show the same attentions, if he meant them sincerely, instead of being so strange as Mr Godfrey Cass was, sometimes behaving as if he didn't want to speak to her, and taking no notice of her for weeks and weeks, and then, all on a sudden, almost making love again? Moreover, it was quite plain he had no real love for her, else he would not let people have *that* to say of him which they did say. Did he suppose that Miss Nancy Lammeter was to be won by any man, squire or no squire, who led a bad life? That was not what she had been used to see in her own father, who was the soberest and best man in that countryside, only a little hot and hasty now and then, if things were not done to the minute.

All these thoughts rushed through Miss Nancy's mind, in their habitual succession, in the moments between her first sight of Mr Godfrey Cass standing at the door and her own arrival there. Happily, the Squire came out too, and gave a loud greeting to her father, so that, somehow, under cover of this noise, she seemed to find concealment for her confusion and neglect of any suitably formal behaviour, while she was being lifted from the pillion by strong arms, which seemed to find her ridiculously small and light. And there was the best reason for hastening into the house at once, since the snow was beginning to fall again, threatening an unpleasant journey for such guests as were still on the road. These were a small minority; for already the afternoon was beginning to decline, and there would not be too much time for the ladies who came from a distance to attire themselves in readiness for the early tea which was to inspirit them for the dance.

There was a buzz of voices through the house, as Miss Nancy entered, mingled with the scrape of a fiddle preluding in the kitchen; but the Lammeters were guests whose arrival had evidently been thought of so much that it had been watched for from the windows, for Mrs Kimble, who did the honours at the Red House on these great occasions, came forward to meet Miss Nancy in the hall, and conduct her upstairs. Mrs Kimble was the Squire's sister, as well as the doctor's wife – a double dignity, with which her diameter was in direct proportion; so that, a journey upstairs being rather fatiguing to her, she did not oppose Miss Nancy's request to be allowed to find her way alone to the Blue Room, where the Miss Lammeters' bandboxes had been deposited on their arrival in the morning.

There was hardly a bedroom in the house where feminine compliments were not passing and feminine toilettes going forward, in various stages, in space made scanty by extra beds spread upon the floor; and Miss Nancy, as she entered the Blue Room, had to make her little formal curtsy to a group of six. On the one hand, there were ladies no less important than the two Miss Gunns, the wine merchant's daughters from Lytherly, dressed in the height of fashion, with the tightest skirts and the shortest waists, and gazed at by Miss Ladbrook (of the Old Pastures) with a shyness not unsustained by inward criticism. Partly, Miss Ladbrook felt that her own skirt must be regarded as unduly lax by the Miss Gunns, and partly, that it was a pity the Miss Gunns did not show that judgement which she herself would show if she were in their place, by stopping a little on this side of the fashion. On the other hand, Mrs Ladbrook was standing in skullcap and front, with her turban in her hand, curtsying and smiling blandly and saying 'After you, ma'am' to another lady in similar circumstances, who had politely offered the precedence at the looking-glass.

But Miss Nancy had no sooner made her curtsy than an elderly lady came forward, whose full white muslin kerchief, and mob-cap round her curls of smooth grey hair, were in daring contrast with the puffed yellow satins and top-knotted caps of her neighbours. She approached Miss Nancy with much primness, and said, with a slow, treble suavity: 'Niece, I hope I see you well in health.' Miss Nancy kissed her aunt's cheek dutifully, and answered, with the same sort of amiable primness, 'Quite well, I thank you, aunt, and I hope I see you the same.'

'Thank you, niece, I keep my health for the present. And how is my brother-in-law?'

These dutiful questions and answers were continued until it was ascertained in detail that the Lammeters were all as well as usual, and the Osgoods likewise, also that niece Priscilla must certainly arrive shortly, and that travelling on pillions in snowy weather was unpleasant, though a joseph was a great protection. Then Nancy was formally introduced to her aunt's visitors, the Miss Gunns, as being the daughters of a mother known to *their* mother, though now for the first time induced to make a journey into these parts; and these ladies were so taken by surprise at finding such a lovely face and figure in an out-of-the-way country place, that they began to feel some curiosity about the dress she would put on when she took off her joseph. Miss Nancy, whose thoughts were always conducted with the propriety and moderation conspicuous in her manners, remarked to herself that the Miss Gunns were rather hard-featured than otherwise, and that such very low dresses as they wore might have been attributed to vanity if their shoulders had been pretty, but that, being as they were, it was not reasonable to suppose that they showed their necks from a love of display, but rather from some obligation not inconsistent with sense and modesty. She felt convinced, as she opened her box, that this must be her aunt Osgood's opinion, for Miss Nancy's mind resembled her aunt's to a degree that everybody said was surprising, considering the kinship was on Mr Osgood's side; and though you might not have supposed it from the formality of their greeting, there was a devoted attachment and mutual admiration between aunt and niece. Even Miss Nancy's refusal of her cousin Gilbert Osgood (on the ground solely that he was her cousin), though it had grieved her aunt greatly, had not in the least cooled the preference which had determined her to leave Nancy several of her hereditary ornaments, let Gilbert's future wife be whom she might.

Three of the ladies quickly retired, but the Miss Gunns were quite content that Mrs Osgood's inclination to remain with her niece gave them also a reason for staying to see the rustic beauty's toilette. And it was really a pleasure – from the first opening of the bandbox, where everything smelt of lavender and rose-leaves, to the clasping of the small coral necklace that fitted closely round her little white neck. Everything belonging to Miss Nancy was of delicate purity and nattiness: not a crease was where it had no business to be, not a bit of her linen professed whiteness without fulfilling its profession; the very pins on her pin-cushion were stuck in after a pattern from which she was careful to allow no aberration; and as for her own person, it gave the same idea of perfect unvarying

neatness as the body of a little bird. It is true that her light-brown hair was
cropped behind like a boy's, and was dressed in front in a number of flat rings,
that lay quite away from her face; but there was no sort of coiffure that could
make Miss Nancy's cheek and neck look otherwise than pretty; and when at last
she stood complete in her silvery twilled silk, her lace tucker, her coral necklace,
and coral ear-drops, the Miss Gunns could see nothing to criticise except her
hands, which bore the traces of butter-making, cheese-crushing, and even still
coarser work. But Miss Nancy was not ashamed of that, for even while she was
dressing she narrated to her aunt how she and Priscilla had packed their boxes
yesterday, because this morning was baking morning, and since they were leaving
home, it was desirable to make a good supply of meat pies for the kitchen; and as
she concluded this judicious remark, she turned to the Miss Gunns that she
might not commit the rudeness of not including them in the conversation. The
Miss Gunns smiled stiffly, and thought what a pity it was that these rich country
people, who could afford to buy such good clothes (really Miss Nancy's lace and
silk were very costly), should be brought up in utter ignorance and vulgarity.
She actually said 'mate' for 'meat', ' 'appen' for 'perhaps', and 'oss' for 'horse',
which, to young ladies living in good Lytherly society, who habitually said 'orse,
even in domestic privacy, and only said 'appen on the right occasions, was
necessarily shocking. Miss Nancy, indeed, had never been to any school higher
than Dame Tedman's: her acquaintance with profane literature hardly went
beyond the rhymes she had worked in her large sampler under the lamb and the
shepherdess; and in order to balance an account, she was obliged to effect her
subtraction by removing visible metallic shillings and sixpences from a visible
metallic total. There is hardly a servant-maid in these days who is not better
informed than Miss Nancy; yet she had the essential attributes of a lady – high
veracity, delicate honour in her dealings, deference to others, and refined
personal habits, – and lest these should not suffice to convince grammatical fair
ones that her feelings can at all resemble theirs, I will add that she was slightly
proud and exacting, and as constant in her affection towards a baseless opinion
as towards an erring lover.

   The anxiety about sister Priscilla, which had grown rather active by the
time the coral necklace was clasped, was happily ended by the entrance of that
cheerful-looking lady herself, with a face made blowsy by cold and damp. After
the first questions and greetings, she turned to Nancy, and surveyed her from
head to foot – then wheeled her round, to ascertain that the back view was
equally faultless.

   'What do you think o' *these* gowns, aunt Osgood?' said Priscilla, while Nancy
helped her to unrobe.

   'Very handsome indeed, niece,' said Mrs Osgood, with a slight increase of
formality. She always thought niece Priscilla too rough.

   'I'm obliged to have the same as Nancy, you know, for all I'm five years older
and it makes me look yellow; for she never *will* have anything without I have
mine just like it, because she wants us to look like sisters. And I tell her folks 'ull
think it's my weakness makes me fancy as I shall look pretty in what she looks
pretty in. For I *am* ugly – there's no denying that: I feature my father's family.

But, law! I don't mind, do you?' Priscilla here turned to the Miss Gunns, rattling on in too much preoccupation with the delight of talking, to notice that her candour was not appreciated. 'The pretty uns do for fly-catchers – they keep the men off us. I've no opinion o' the men, Miss Gunn – I don't know what *you* have. And as for fretting and stewing about what *they'll* think of you from morning till night, and making your life uneasy about what they're doing when they're out o' your sight – as I tell Nancy, it's a folly no woman need be guilty of, if she's got a good father and a good home: let her leave it to them as have got no fortin, and can't help themselves. As I say, Mr Have-your-own-way is the best husband, and the only one I'd ever promise to obey. I know it isn't pleasant, when you've been used to living in a big way, and managing hogsheads and all that, to go and put your nose in by somebody else's fireside, or to sit down by yourself to a scrag or a knuckle; but, thank God! my father's a sober man and likely to live; and if you've got a man by the chimney-corner, it doesn't matter if he's childish – the business needn't be broke up.'

The delicate process of getting her narrow gown over her head without injury to her smooth curls, obliged Miss Priscilla to pause in this rapid survey of life, and Mrs Osgood seized the opportunity of rising and saying, 'Well, niece, you'll follow us. The Miss Gunns will like to go down.'

'Sister,' said Nancy, when they were alone, 'you've offended the Miss Gunns, I'm sure.'

'What have I done, child?' said Priscilla, in some alarm.

'Why, you asked them if they minded about being ugly – you're so very blunt.'

'Law, did I? Well, it popped out: it's a mercy I said no more, for I'm a bad un to live with folks when they don't like the truth. But as for being ugly, look at me, child, in this silver-coloured silk – I told you how it 'ud be – I look as yellow as a daffodil. Anybody 'ud say you wanted to make a mawkin of me.'

'No, Priscy, don't say so. I begged and prayed of you not to let us have this silk if you'd like another better. I was willing to have *your* choice, you know I was,' said Nancy, in anxious self-vindication.

'Nonsense, child, you know you'd set your heart on this; and reason good, for you're the colour o' cream. It 'ud be fine doings for you to dress yourself to suit *my* skin. What I find fault with, is that notion o' yours as I must dress myself just like you. But you do as you like with me – you always did, from when first you began to walk. If you wanted to go the field's length, the field's length you'd go; and there was no whipping you, for you looked as prim and innicent as a daisy all the while.'

'Priscy,' said Nancy, gently, as she fastened a coral necklace, exactly like her own, round Priscilla's neck, which was very far from being like her own, 'I'm sure I'm willing to give way as far as is right, but who shouldn't dress alike if it isn't sisters? Would you have us go about looking as if we were no kin to one another – us that have got no mother and not another sister in the world? I'd do what was right, if I dressed in a gown dyed with cheese-colouring; and I'd rather you'd choose, and let me wear what pleases you.'

'There you go again! You'd come round to the same thing if one talked to you from Saturday night till Saturday morning. It'll be fine fun to see how you'll master your husband and never raise your voice above the singing o' the kettle all the while. I like to see the men mastered!'

'Don't talk *so*, Priscy,' said Nancy, blushing. 'You know I don't mean ever to be married.'

'O, you never mean a fiddlestick's end!' said Priscilla, as she arranged her discarded dress, and closed her bandbox. 'Who shall *I* have to work for when father's gone, if you are to go and take notions in your head and be an old maid, because some folks are no better than they should be? I haven't a bit o' patience with you – sitting on an addled egg for ever, as if there was never a fresh un in the world. One old maid's enough out o' two sisters; and I shall do credit to a single life, for God A'mighty meant me for it. Come, we can go down now. I'm as ready as a mawkin *can* be – there's nothing a-wanting to frighten the crows, now I've got my ear-droppers in.'

As the two Miss Lammeters walked into the large parlour together, anyone who did not know the character of both, might certainly have supposed that the reason why the square-shouldered, clumsy, high-featured Priscilla wore a dress the facsimile of her pretty sister's, was either the mistaken vanity of the one, or the malicious contrivance of the other in order to set off her own rare beauty. But the good-natured self-forgetful cheeriness and common sense of Priscilla would soon have dissipated the one suspicion; and the modest calm of Nancy's speech and manners told clearly of a mind free from all disavowed devices.

Places of honour had been kept for the Miss Lammeters near the head of the principal tea-table in the wainscoted parlour, now looking fresh and pleasant with handsome branches of holly, yew, and laurel, from the abundant growths of the old garden; and Nancy felt an inward flutter, that no firmness of purpose could prevent, when she saw Mr Godfrey Cass advancing to lead her to a seat between himself and Mr Crackenthorp, while Priscilla was called to the opposite side between her father and the Squire. It certainly did make some difference to Nancy that the lover she had given up was the young man of quite the highest consequence in the parish – at home in a venerable and unique parlour, which was the extremity of grandeur in her experience, a parlour where *she* might one day have been mistress, with the consciousness that she was spoken of as 'Madam Cass,' the Squire's wife. These circumstances exalted her inward drama in her own eyes, and deepened the emphasis with which she declared to herself that not the most dazzling rank should induce her to marry a man whose conduct showed him careless of his character, but that, 'love once, love always,' was the motto of a true and pure woman, and no man should ever have any right over her which would be a call on her to destroy the dried flowers that she treasured, and always would treasure, for Godfrey Cass's sake. And Nancy was capable of keeping her word to herself under very trying conditions. Nothing but a becoming blush betrayed the moving thoughts that urged themselves upon her as she accepted the seat next to Mr Crackenthorp; for she was so instinctively neat and adroit in all her actions, and her pretty lips met each other with such quiet firmness, that it would have been difficult for her to appear agitated.

It was not the rector's practice to let a charming blush pass without an appropriate compliment. He was not in the least lofty or aristocratic, but simply a merry-eyed, small-featured, grey-haired man, with his chin propped by an ample, many-creased white neckcloth, which seemed to predominate over every other point in his person, and somehow to impress its peculiar character on his remarks; so that to have considered his amenities apart from his cravat, would have been a severe, and perhaps a dangerous, effort of abstraction.

'Ha, Miss Nancy,' he said, turning his head within his cravat, and smiling down pleasantly upon her, 'when anybody pretends this has been a severe winter, I shall tell them I saw the roses blooming on New Year's Eve – eh, Godfrey, what do *you* say?'

Godfrey made no reply, and avoided looking at Nancy very markedly; for though these complimentary personalities were held to be in excellent taste in old-fashioned Raveloe society, reverent love has a politeness of its own which it teaches to men otherwise of small schooling. But the Squire was rather impatient at Godfrey's showing himself a dull spark in this way. By this advanced hour of the day, the Squire was always in higher spirits than we have seen him in at the breakfast-table, and felt it quite pleasant to fulfil the hereditary duty of being noisily jovial and patronising: the large silver snuffbox was in active service, and was offered without fail to all neighbours from time to time, however often they might have declined the favour. At present, the Squire had only given an express welcome to the heads of families as they appeared; but always as the evening deepened, his hospitality rayed out more widely, till he had tapped the youngest guests on the back and shown a peculiar fondness for their presence, in the full belief that they must feel their lives made happy by their belonging to a parish where there was such a hearty man as Squire Cass to invite them and wish them well. Even in this early stage of the jovial mood, it was natural that he should wish to supply his son's deficiencies by looking and speaking for him.

'Ay, ay,' he began, offering his snuffbox to Mr Lammeter, who for the second time bowed his head and waved his hand in stiff rejection of the offer, 'us old fellows may wish ourselves young tonight, when we see the mistletoe-bough in the White Parlour. It's true, most things are gone back'ard in these last thirty years – the country's going down since the old king fell ill. But when I look at Miss Nancy here, I begin to think the lasses keep up their quality; – ding me if I remember a sample to match her, not when I was a fine young fellow, and thought a deal about my pigtail. No offence, to you, madam,' he added, bending to Mrs Crackenthorp, who sat by him, 'I didn't know you when you were as young as Miss Nancy here.'

Mrs Crackenthorp – a small blinking woman, who fidgeted incessantly with her lace, ribbons, and gold chain, turning her head about and making subdued noises, very much like a guinea-pig, that twitches its nose and soliloquises in all company indiscriminately – now blinked and fidgeted towards the Squire, and said, 'O no – no offence.'

This emphatic compliment of the Squire's to Nancy was felt by others besides Godfrey to have a diplomatic significance; and her father gave a slight additional erectness to his back, as he looked across the table at her with complacent gravity. That grave and orderly senior was not going to bate a jot of his dignity by seeming elated at the notion of a match between his family and the Squire's:

he was gratified by any honour paid to his daughter; but he must see an alteration in several ways before his consent would be vouchsafed. His spare but healthy person, and high-featured firm face, that looked as if it had never been flushed by excess, was in strong contrast, not only with the Squire's, but with the appearance of the Raveloe farmers generally – in accordance with a favourite saying of his own, that 'breed was stronger than pasture.'

'Miss Nancy's wonderful like what her mother was, though; isn't she, Kimble?' said the stout lady of that name, looking round for her husband.

But Dr Kimble (county apothecaries in old days enjoyed that title without authority of diploma), being a thin and agile man, was flitting about the room with his hands in his pockets, making himself agreeable to his feminine patients, with medical impartiality, and being welcomed everywhere as a doctor by hereditary right – not one of those miserable apothecaries who canvass for practice in strange neighbourhoods, and spend all their income in starving their one horse, but a man of substance, able to keep an extravagant table like the best of his patients. Time out of mind the Raveloe doctor had been a Kimble; Kimble was inherently a doctor's name; and it was difficult to contemplate firmly the melancholy fact that the actual Kimble had no son, so that his practice might one day be handed over to a successor, with the incongruous name of Taylor or Johnson. But in that case the wiser people in Raveloe would employ Dr Blick of Flitton – as less unnatural.

'Did you speak to me, my dear?' said the authentic doctor, coming quickly to his wife's side; but, as if foreseeing that she would be too much out of breath to repeat her remark, he went on immediately – 'Ha, Miss Priscilla, the sight of you revives the taste of that super-excellent pork-pie. I hope the batch isn't near an end.'

'Yes, indeed, it is, doctor,' said Priscilla; 'but I'll answer for it the next shall be as good. My pork-pies don't turn out well by chance.'

'Not as your doctoring does, eh, Kimble? – because folks forget to take your physic, eh?' said the Squire, who regarded physic and doctors as many loyal churchmen regard the church and the clergy – tasting a joke against them when he was in health, but impatiently eager for their aid when anything was the matter with him. He tapped his box, and looked round with a triumphant laugh.

'Ah, she has a quick wit, my friend Priscilla has,' said the doctor, choosing to attribute the epigram to the lady rather than allow a brother-in-law that advantage over him. 'She saves a little pepper to sprinkle over her talk – that's the reason why she never puts too much into her pies. There's my wife, now, she never has an answer at her tongue's end; but if I offend her, she's sure to scarify my throat with black pepper the next day, or else give me the colic with watery greens. That's an awful tit-for-tat.' Here the vivacious doctor made a pathetic grimace.

'Did you ever hear the like?' said Mrs Kimble, laughing above her double chin with much good-humour, aside to Mrs Crackenthorp, who blinked and nodded, and seemed to intend a smile, which, by the correlation of forces, went off in small twitchings and noises.

'I suppose that's the sort of tit-for-tat adopted in your profession, Kimble, if you've a grudge against a patient,' said the Rector.

'Never do have a grudge against our patients,' said Mr Kimble, 'except when they leave us: and then, you see, we haven't the chance of prescribing for 'em. Ha, Miss Nancy,' he continued, suddenly skipping to Nancy's side, 'you won't forget your promise? You're to save a dance for me, you know.' 'Come, come, Kimble, don't you be too for'ard,' said the Squire. 'Give the young uns fair-play. There's my son Godfrey'll be wanting to have a round with you if you run off with Miss Nancy. He's bespoke her for the first dance, I'll be bound. Eh, sir! what do you say?' he continued, throwing himself backward, and looking at Godfrey. 'Haven't you asked Miss Nancy to open the dance with you?'

Godfrey, sorely uncomfortable under this significant insistance about Nancy, and afraid to think where it would end by the time his father had set his usual hospitable example of drinking before and after supper, saw no course open but to turn to Nancy and say, with as little awkwardness as possible: 'No; I've not asked her yet, but I hope she'll consent – if somebody else hasn't been before me.'

'No, I've not engaged myself,' said Nancy, quietly, though blushingly. (If Mr Godfrey founded any hopes on her consenting to dance with him, he would soon be undeceived; but there was no need for her to be uncivil.)

'Then I hope you've no objections to dancing with me,' said Godfrey, beginning to lose the sense that there was anything uncomfortable in this arrangement.

'No, no objections,' said Nancy, in a cold tone.

'Ah, well, you're a lucky fellow, Godfrey,' said uncle Kimble; 'but you're my godson, so I won't stand in your way. Else I'm not so very old, eh, my dear?' he went on, skipping to his wife's side again. 'You wouldn't mind my having a second after you were gone – not if I cried a good deal first?'

'Come, come, take a cup o' tea and stop your tongue, do,' said good-humoured Mrs Kimble, feeling some pride in a husband who must be regarded as so clever and amusing by the company generally. If he had only not been irritable at cards!

While safe, well-tested personalities were enlivening the tea in this way, the sound of the fiddle approaching within a distance at which it could be heard distinctly, made the young people look at each other with sympathetic impatience for the end of the meal.

'Why, there's Solomon in the hall,' said the Squire, 'and playing my fav'rite tune, I believe – "The flaxen-headed ploughboy" – he's for giving us a hint as we aren't enough in a hurry to hear him play. Bob,' he called out to his third long-legged son, who was at the other end of the room, 'open the door, and tell Solomon to come in. He shall give us a tune here.'

Bob obeyed, and Solomon walked in, fiddling as he walked, for he would on no account break off in the middle of a tune.

'Here, Solomon,' said the Squire, with loud patronage. 'Round here, my man. Ah, I knew it was "The flaxen-headed ploughboy": there's no finer tune.'

Solomon Macey, a small hale old man with an abundant crop of long white hair reaching nearly to his shoulders, advanced to the indicated spot, bowing reverently while he fiddled, as much as to say that he respected the company, though he respected the key-note more. As soon as he had repeated the tune and lowered his fiddle, he bowed again to the Squire and the Rector, and said, 'I hope I see your honour and your reverence well, and wishing you health and long life and a happy New Year. And wishing the same to you, Mr Lammeter, sir; and to the other gentlemen, and the madams, and the young lasses.'

As Solomon uttered the last words, he bowed in all directions solicitously, lest he should be wanting in due respect. But thereupon he immediately began to prelude, and fell into the tune which he knew would be taken as a special compliment by Mr Lammeter.

'Thank ye, Solomon, thank ye,' said Mr Lammeter, when the fiddle paused again. 'That's "Over the hills and far away", that is. My father used to say to me, whenever we heard that tune, "Ah, lad, *I* come from over the hills and far away." There's a many tunes I don't make head or tail of; but that speaks to me like the blackbird's whistle. I suppose it's the name: there's a deal in the name of a tune.'

But Solomon was already impatient to prelude again, and presently broke with much spirit into 'Sir Roger de Coverley', at which there was a sound of chairs pushed back, and laughing voices.

'Ay, ay, Solomon, we know what that means,' said the Squire, rising. 'It's time to begin the dance, eh? Lead the way, then, and we'll all follow you.'

So Solomon, holding his white head on one side, and playing vigorously, marched forward at the head of the gay procession into the White Parlour, where the mistletoe-bough was hung, and multitudinous tallow candles made rather a brilliant effect, gleaming from among the berried holly-boughs, and reflected in the old-fashioned oval mirrors fastened in the panels of the white wainscot. A quaint procession! Old Solomon, in his seedy clothes and long white locks, seemed to be luring that decent company by the magic scream of his fiddle – luring discreet matrons in turban-shaped caps, nay, Mrs Cracken-thorp herself, the summit of whose perpendicular feather was on a level with the Squire's shoulder – luring fair lasses complacently conscious of very short waists and skirts blameless of front-folds – luring fathers, in large variegated waist-coats, and ruddy sons, for the most part shy and sheepish, in short nether garments and very long coat-tails.

Already, Mr Macey and a few other privileged villagers, who were allowed to be spectators on these great occasions, were seated on benches placed for them near the door; and great was the admiration and satisfaction in that quarter when the couples had formed themselves for the dance, and the Squire led off with Mrs Crackenthorp, joining hands with the Rector and Mrs Osgood. That was as it should be – that was what everybody had been used to – and the charter of Raveloe seemed to be renewed by the ceremony. It was not thought of as an unbecoming levity for the old and middle-aged people to dance a little before sitting down to cards, but rather as part of their social duties. For what were these if not to be merry at appropriate times, interchanging visits and poultry with due frequency, paying each other old-established compliments in sound traditional phrases, passing well-tried personal jokes, urging your guests to eat and drink too much out of hospitality, and eating and drinking too much in your neighbour's house to show that you liked your cheer? And the parson naturally set an example in these social duties. For it would not have been possible for the Raveloe mind, without a peculiar revelation, to know that a clergyman should be a pale-faced memento of solemnities, instead of a reasonably faulty man, whose exclusive authority to read prayers and preach, to christen, marry, and bury you, necessarily co-existed with the right to sell you the ground to be buried in, and to take tithe in kind; on which last point, of course, there was a little grumbling, but not to the extent of irreligion – not beyond the grumbling at the rain, which was by no means accompanied with a spirit of impious defiance, but with a desire that the prayer for fine weather might be read forthwith.

There was no reason, then, why the Rector's dancing should not be received as part of the fitness of things quite as much as the Squire's, or why, on the other hand, Mr Macey's official respect should restrain him from subjecting the parson's performance to that criticism with which minds of extraordinary acuteness must necessarily contemplate the doings of their fallible fellow-men.

'The Squire's pretty springe, considering his weight,' said Mr Macey, 'and he stamps uncommon well. But Mr Lammeter beats 'em all for shapes: you see, he holds his head like a sodger, and he isn't so cushiony as most o' the oldish gentlefolks – they run fat in general; and he's got a fine leg. The parson's nimble enough, but he hasn't got much of a leg: it's a bit too thick down'ard, and his knees might be a bit nearer wi'out damage; but he might do worse, he might do worse. Though he hasn't that grand way o' waving his hand as the Squire has.'

'Talk o' nimbleness, look at Mrs Osgood,' said Ben Winthrop, who was holding his son Aaron between his knees. 'She trips along with her little steps, so as nobody can see how she goes – it's like as if she had little wheels to her feet. She doesn't look a day older nor last year: she's the finest-made woman as is, let the next be where she will.'

'I don't heed how the women are made,' said Mr Macey, with some contempt. 'They wear nayther coat nor breeches: you can't make much out o' their shapes.'

'Fayder,' said Aaron, whose feet were busy beating out the tune, 'how does that big cock's-feather stick in Mrs Crackenthorp's yead? Is there a little hole for it, like in my shuttlecock?'

'Hush, lad, hush; that's the way the ladies dress theirselves, that is,' said the father, adding, however, in an undertone to Mr Macey, 'It does make her look funny, though – partly like a short-necked bottle wi' a long quill in it. Hey, by jingo, there's the young Squire leading off now, wi' Miss Nancy for partners. There's a lass for you! – like a pink-and-white posy – there's nobody 'ud think as anybody could be so pritty. I shouldn't wonder if she's Madam Cass someday, arter all – and nobody more rightfuller, for they'd make a fine match. You can find nothing against Master Godfrey's shapes, Macey, I'll bet a penny.'

Mr Macey screwed up his mouth, leaned his head further on one side, and twirled his thumbs with a presto movement as his eyes followed Godfrey up the dance. At last he summed up his opinion.

'Pretty well down'ard, but a bit too round i' the shoulder-blades. And as for them coats as he gets from the Flitton tailor, they're a poor cut to pay double money for.'

'Ah, Mr Macey, you and me are two folks,' said Ben, slightly indignant at this carping. 'When I've got a pot o' good ale, I like to swaller it, and do my inside good, i'stead o' smelling and staring at it to see if I can't find faut wi' the brewing. I should like you to pick me out a finer-limbed young fellow nor Master Godfrey – one as 'ud knock you down easier, or's more pleasanter-looksed when he's piert and merry.'

'Tchuh!' said Mr Macey, provoked to increased severity, 'he isn't come to his right colour yet: he's partly like a slack-baked pie. And I doubt he's got a soft place in his head, else why should he be turned round the finger by that offal Dunsey as nobody's seen o' late, and let him kill that fine hunting hoss as was the talk o' the country? And one while he was allays after Miss Nancy, and then it all went off again, like a smell o' hot porridge, as I may say. That wasn't my way, when *I* went a-coorting.'

'Ah, but mayhap Miss Nancy hung off, like, and your lass didn't,' said Ben.

'I should say she didn't,' said Mr Macey, significantly. 'Before I said "sniff", I took care to know as she'd say "snaff", and pretty quick too. I wasn't a-going to open *my* mouth, like a dog at a fly, and snap it to again, wi' nothing to swaller.'

'Well, I think Miss Nancy's a-coming round again,' said Ben, 'for Master Godfrey doesn't look so down-hearted tonight. And I see he's for taking her away to sit down, now they're at the end o' the dance: that looks like sweet-hearting, that does.'

The reason why Godfrey and Nancy had left the dance was not so tender as Ben imagined. In the close press of couples a slight accident had happened to Nancy's dress, which, while it was short enough to show her neat ankle in front, was long enough behind to be caught under the stately stamp of the Squire's foot, so as to rend certain stitches at the waist, and cause much sisterly agitation in Priscilla's mind, as well as serious concern in Nancy's. One's thoughts may be much occupied with love-struggles, but hardly so as to be insensible to a disorder in the general framework of things. Nancy had no sooner completed her duty in the figure they were dancing than she said to Godfrey, with a deep blush, that she must go and sit down till Priscilla could come to her; for the sisters had already exchanged a short whisper and an open-eyed glance full of meaning. No reason less urgent than this could have prevailed on Nancy to give Godfrey this opportunity of sitting apart with her. As for Godfrey, he was feeling so happy and oblivious under the long charm of the country-dance with Nancy, that he got rather bold on the strength of her confusion, and was capable of leading her straight away, without leave asked, into the adjoining small parlour, where the card-tables were set.

'O no, thank you,' said Nancy, coldly, as soon as she perceived where he was going, 'not in there. I'll wait here till Priscilla's ready to come to me. I'm sorry to bring you out of the dance and make myself troublesome.'

'Why, you'll be more comfortable here by yourself,' said the artful Godfrey; 'I'll leave you here till your sister can come.' He spoke in an indifferent tone.

That was an agreeable proposition, and just what Nancy desired; why, then, was she a little hurt that Mr Godfrey should make it? They entered, and she seated herself on a chair against one of the card-tables, as the stiffest and most unapproachable position she could choose.

'Thank you, sir,' she said immediately. 'I needn't give you any more trouble. I'm sorry you've had such an unlucky partner.'

'That's very ill-natured of you,' said Godfrey, standing by her without any sign of intended departure, 'to be sorry you've danced with me.'

'Oh, no, sir, I don't mean to say what's ill-natured at all,' said Nancy, looking distractingly prim and pretty. 'When gentlemen have so many pleasures, one dance can matter but very little.'

'You know that isn't true. You know one dance with you matters more to me than all the other pleasures in the world.'

It was a long, long while since Godfrey had said anything so direct as that, and Nancy was startled. But her instinctive dignity and repugnance to any show of emotion made her sit perfectly still, and only throw a little more decision into her voice as she said: 'No, indeed, Mr Godfrey, that's not known to me, and I have very good reasons for thinking different. But if it's true, I don't wish to hear it.'

'Would you never forgive me, then, Nancy – never think well of me, let what would happen – would you never think the present made amends for the past? Not if I turned a good fellow, and gave up everything you didn't like?'

Godfrey was half conscious that this sudden opportunity of speaking to Nancy alone had driven him beside himself; but blind feeling had got the mastery of his tongue. Nancy really felt much agitated by the possibility Godfrey's words suggested, but this very pressure of emotion that she was in danger of finding too strong for her, roused all her power of self-command.

'I should be glad to see a good change in anybody, Mr Godfrey,' she answered, with the slightest discernible difference of tone, 'but it 'ud be better if no change was wanted.'

'You're very hard-hearted, Nancy,' said Godfrey, pettishly. 'You might encourage me to be a better fellow. I'm very miserable – but you've no feeling.'

'I think those have the least feeling that act wrong to begin with,' said Nancy, sending out a flash in spite of herself. Godfrey was delighted with that little flash, and would have liked to go on and make her quarrel with him; Nancy was so exasperatingly quiet and firm. She was not indifferent to him *yet* though.

The entrance of Priscilla, bustling forward and saying, 'Dear heart alive, child, let us look at this gown,' cut off Godfrey's hopes of a quarrel.

'I suppose I must go now,' he said to Priscilla.

'It's no matter to me whether you go or stay,' said that frank lady, searching for something in her pocket, with a preoccupied brow.

'Do *you* want me to go?' said Godfrey, looking at Nancy, who was now standing up by Priscilla's order.

'As you like,' said Nancy, trying to recover all her former coldness, and looking down carefully at the hem of her gown.

'Then I like to stay,' said Godfrey, with a reckless determination to get as much of this joy as he could tonight, and think nothing of the morrow.

Chapter 12

While Godfrey Cass was taking draughts of forgetfulness from the sweet presence of Nancy, willingly losing all sense of that hidden bond which at other moments galled and fretted him so as to mingle irritation with the very sunshine, Godfrey's wife was walking with slow uncertain steps through the snow-covered Raveloe lanes, carrying her child in her arms.

This journey on New Year's Eve was a premeditated act of vengeance which she had kept in her heart ever since Godfrey, in a fit of passion, had told her he would sooner die than acknowledge her as his wife. There would be a great party at the Red House on New Year's Eve, she knew: her husband would be smiling and smiled upon, hiding *her* existence in the darkest corner of his heart. But she would mar his pleasure: she would go in her dingy rags, with her faded face, once as handsome as the best, with her little child that had its father's hair and eyes, and disclose herself to the Squire as his eldest son's wife. It is seldom that the miserable can help regarding their misery as a wrong inflicted by those who are less miserable. Molly knew that the cause of her dingy rags was not her husband's neglect, but the demon Opium to whom she was enslaved, body and soul, except in the lingering mother's tenderness that refused to give him her hungry child. She knew this well; and yet, in the moments of wretched unbenumbed consciousness, the sense of her want and degradation transformed itself continually into bitterness towards Godfrey. *He* was well off; and if she had her rights she would be well off too. The belief that he repented his marriage, and suffered from it, only aggravated her vindictiveness. Just and self-reproving thoughts do not come to us too thickly, even in the purest air, and with the best lessons of heaven and earth; how should those white-winged delicate messengers make their way to Molly's poisoned chamber, inhabited by no higher memories than those of a barmaids paradise of pink ribbons and gentlemen's jokes?

She had set out at an early hour, but had lingered on the road, inclined by her indolence to believe that if she waited under a warm shed the snow would cease to fall. She had waited longer than she knew, and now that she found herself belated in the snow-hidden ruggedness of the long lanes, even the animation of a vindictive purpose could not keep her spirit from failing. It was seven o'clock, and by this time she was not very far from Raveloe, but she was not familiar enough with those monotonous lanes to know how near she was to her journey's end. She needed comfort, and she knew but one comforter – the familiar demon in her bosom; but she hesitated a moment, after drawing out the black remnant, before she raised it to her lips. In that moment the mother's love pleaded for painful consciousness rather than oblivion – pleaded to be left in aching weariness, rather than to have the encircling arms benumbed so that they could not feel the dear burden. In another moment Molly had flung something away, but it was not the black remnant – it was an empty phial. And she walked on again under the breaking cloud, from which there came now and then the light of a quickly-veiled star, for a freezing wind had sprung up since the snowing had ceased. But she walked always more and more drowsily, and clutched more and more automatically the sleeping child at her bosom.

Slowly the demon was working his will, and cold and weariness were his helpers. Soon she felt nothing but a supreme immediate longing that curtained off all futurity – the longing to lie down and sleep. She had arrived at a spot where her footsteps were no longer checked by a hedgerow, and she had wandered vaguely, unable to distinguish any objects, notwithstanding the wide whiteness around her, and the growing starlight. She sank down against a straggling furze bush, an easy pillow enough; and the bed of snow, too, was soft. She did not feel that the bed was cold, and did not heed whether the child would wake and cry for her. But her arms did not yet relax their instinctive clutch; and the little one slumbered on as gently as if it had been rocked in a lace-trimmed cradle.

But the complete torpor came at last: the fingers lost their tension, the arms unbent; then the little head fell away from the bosom, and the blue eyes opened wide on the cold starlight. At first there was a little peevish cry of 'mammy', and an effort to regain the pillowing arm and bosom; but mammy's ear was deaf, and the pillow seemed to be slipping away backward. Suddenly, as the child rolled downward on its mother's knees, all wet with snow, its eyes were caught by a bright glancing light on the white ground, and, with the ready transition of infancy, it was immediately absorbed in watching the bright living thing running towards it, yet never arriving. That bright living thing must be caught; and in an instant, the child had slipped on all-fours, and held out one little hand to catch the gleam. But the gleam would not be caught in that way, and now the head was held up to see where the cunning gleam came from. It came from a very bright place; and the little one, rising on its legs, toddled through the snow, the old grimy shawl in which it was wrapped trailing behind it, and the queer little bonnet dangling at its back – toddled on to the open door of Silas Marner's cottage, and right up to the warm hearth, where there was a bright fire of logs and sticks, which had thoroughly warmed the old sack (Silas's greatcoat) spread out on the bricks to dry. The little one, accustomed to be left to itself for long hours without notice from its mother, squatted down on the sack, and spread its tiny hands towards the blaze, in perfect contentment, gurgling and making many inarticulate communications to the cheerful fire, like a new-hatched gosling beginning to find itself comfortable. But presently the warmth had a lulling effect, and the little golden head sank down on the old sack, and the blue eyes were veiled by their delicate half-transparent lids.

But where was Silas Marner while this stranger-visitor had come to his hearth? He was in the cottage, but he did not see the child. During the last few weeks, since he had lost his money, he had contracted the habit of opening his door and looking out from time to time, as if he thought that his money might be somehow coming back to him, or that some trace, some news of it, might be mysteriously on the road, and be caught by the listening ear or the straining eye. It was chiefly at night, when he was not occupied in his loom, that he fell into this repetition of an act for which he could have assigned no definite purpose, and which can hardly be understood except by those who have undergone a bewildering separation from a supremely loved object. In the evening twilight, and later whenever the night was not dark, Silas looked out on that narrow prospect round the Stone-pits, listening and gazing, not with hope, but with mere yearning and unrest.

This morning he had been told by some of his neighbours that it was New Year's Eve, and that he must sit up and hear the old year rung out and the new rung in, because that was good luck, and might bring his money back again. This was only a friendly Raveloe-way of jesting with the half-crazy oddities of a miser, but it had perhaps helped to throw Silas into a more than usually excited state. Since the on-coming of twilight he had opened his door again and again, though only to shut it immediately at seeing all distance veiled by the falling snow. But the last time he opened it the snow had ceased, and the clouds were parting here and there. He stood and listened, and gazed for a long while – there was really something on the road coming towards him then, but he caught no sign of it; and the stillness and the wide trackless snow seemed to narrow his solitude, and touched his yearning with the chill of despair. He went in again, and put his right hand on the latch of the door to close it – but he did not close it: he was arrested, as he had been already since his loss, by the invisible wand of catalepsy, and stood like a graven image, with wide but sightless eyes, holding open his door, powerless to resist either the good or evil that might enter there.

When Marner's sensibility returned, he continued the action which had been arrested, and closed his door, unaware of the chasm in his consciousness, unaware of any intermediate change, except that the light had grown dim, and that he was chilled and faint. He thought he had been too long standing at the door and looking out. Turning towards the hearth, where the two logs had fallen apart, and sent forth only a red uncertain glimmer, he seated himself on his fireside chair, and was stooping to push his logs together, when, to his blurred vision, it seemed as if there were gold on the floor in front of the hearth. Gold! – his own gold – brought back to him as mysteriously as it had been taken away! He felt his heart begin to beat violently, and for a few moments he was unable to stretch out his hand and grasp the restored treasure. The heap of gold seemed to glow and get larger beneath his agitated gaze. He leaned forward at last, and stretched forth his hand; but instead of the hard coin with the familiar resisting outline, his fingers encountered soft warm curls. In utter amazement, Silas fell on his knees and bent his head low to examine the marvel: it was a sleeping child – a round, fair thing, with soft yellow rings all over its head. Could this be his little sister come back to him in a dream – his little sister whom he had carried about in his arms for a year before she died, when he was a small boy without shoes or stockings? That was the first thought that darted across Silas's blank wonderment. *Was* it a dream? He rose to his feet again, pushed his logs together, and, throwing on some dried leaves and sticks, raised a flame; but the flame did not disperse the vision – it only lit up more distinctly the little round form of the child and its shabby clothing. It was very much like his little sister. Silas sank into his chair powerless, under the double presence of an inexplicable surprise and a hurrying influx of memories. How and when had the child come in without his knowledge? He had never been beyond the door. But along with that question, and almost thrusting it away, there was a vision of the old home and the old streets leading to Lantern Yard – and within that vision another, of the thoughts which had been present with him in those far-off scenes. The thoughts were strange to him now, like old friendships impossible to revive; and yet he had a dreamy feeling that this child was somehow a message come to him from that far-off life: it stirred fibres that had never been moved in Raveloe – old quiverings of tenderness – old impressions of awe at the presentiment of some Power presiding over his life; for his imagination had not yet extricated itself from the sense of mystery in the child's sudden presence, and had formed no conjectures of ordinary natural means by which the event could have been brought about.

But there was a cry on the hearth: the child had awaked, and Marner stooped to lift it on his knee. It clung round his neck, and burst louder and louder into that mingling of inarticulate cries with 'mammy' by which little children express the bewilderment of waking. Silas pressed it to him, and almost unconsciously uttered sounds of hushing tenderness, while he bethought himself that some of his porridge, which had got cool by the dying fire, would do to feed the child with if it were only warmed up a little.

He had plenty to do through the next hour. The porridge, sweetened with some dry brown sugar from an old store which he had refrained from using for himself, stopped the cries of the little one, and made her lift her blue eyes with a wide quiet gaze at Silas, as he put the spoon into her mouth. Presently she slipped from his knee and began to toddle about, but with a pretty stagger that made Silas jump up and follow her lest she should fall against anything that would hurt her. But she only fell in a sitting posture on the ground, and began to pull at her boots, looking up at him with a crying face as if the boots hurt her. He took her on his knee again, but it was some time before it occurred to Silas's dull bachelor mind that the wet boots were the grievance, pressing on her warm ankles. He got them off with difficulty, and baby was at once happily occupied with the primary mystery of her own toes, inviting Silas, with much chuckling, to consider the mystery too. But the wet boots had at last suggested to Silas that the child had been walking on the snow, and this roused him from his entire oblivion of any ordinary means by which it could have entered or been brought into his house. Under the prompting of this new idea, and without waiting to form conjectures, he raised the child in his arms, and went to the door. As soon as he had opened it, there was the cry of 'mammy' again, which Silas had not heard since the child's first hungry waking. Bending forward, he could just discern the marks made by the little feet on the virgin snow, and he followed their track to the furze bushes. 'Mammy!' the little one cried again and again, stretching itself forward so as almost to escape from Silas's arms, before he himself was aware that there was something more than the bush before him – that there was a human body, with the head sunk low in the furze, and half-covered with the shaken snow.

Chapter 13

It was after the early supper-time at the Red House, and the entertainment was in that stage when bashfulness itself had passed into easy jollity, when gentlemen, conscious of unusual accomplishments, could at length be prevailed on to dance a hornpipe, and when the Squire preferred talking loudly, scattering snuff, and patting his visitors' backs, to sitting longer at the whist-table – a choice exasperating to uncle Kimble, who, being always volatile in sober business hours, became intense and bitter over cards and brandy, shuffled before his adversary's deal with a glare of suspicion, and turned up a mean trump-card with an air of inexpressible disgust, as if in a world where such things could happen one might as well enter on a course of reckless profligacy. When the evening had advanced to this pitch of freedom and enjoyment, it was usual for the servants, the heavy duties of supper being well over, to get their share of amusement by coming to look on at the dancing; so that the back regions of the house were left in solitude.

There were two doors by which the White Parlour was entered from the hall, and they were both standing open for the sake of air; but the lower one was crowded with the servants and villagers, and only the upper doorway was left free. Bob Cass was figuring in a hornpipe, and his father, very proud of this lithe son, whom he repeatedly declared to be just like himself in his young days, in a tone that implied this to be the very highest stamp of juvenile merit, was the centre of a group who had placed themselves opposite the performer, not far from the upper door. Godfrey was standing a little way off, not to admire his brother's dancing, but to keep sight of Nancy, who was seated in the group, near her father. He stood aloof, because he wished to avoid suggesting himself as a subject for the Squire's fatherly jokes in connection with matrimony and Miss Nancy Lammeter's beauty, which were likely to become more and more explicit. But he had the prospect of dancing with her again when the hornpipe was concluded, and in the meanwhile it was very pleasant to get long glances at her quite unobserved.

But when Godfrey was lifting his eyes from one of those long glances, they encountered an object as startling to him at that moment as if it had been an apparition from the dead. It *was* an apparition from that hidden life which lies, like a dark by-street, behind the goodly ornamented façade that meets the sunlight and the gaze of respectable admirers. It was his own child, carried in Silas Marner's arms. That was his instantaneous impression, unaccompanied by doubt, though he had not seen the child for months past; and when the hope was rising that he might possibly be mistaken, Mr Crackenthorp and Mr Lammeter had already advanced to Silas, in astonishment at this strange advent. Godfrey joined them immediately, unable to rest without hearing every word – trying to control himself, but conscious that if anyone noticed him, they must see that he was white-lipped and trembling.

But now all eyes at that end of the room were bent on Silas Marner; the Squire himself had risen, and asked angrily, 'How's this? – what's this? – what do you do coming in here in this way?'

'I'm come for the doctor – I want the doctor,' Silas had said, in the first moment, to Mr Crackenthorp.

'Why, what's the matter, Marner?' said the Rector. 'The doctor's here; but say quietly what you want him for.'

'It's a woman,' said Silas, speaking low, and half-breathlessly, just as Godfrey came up. 'She's dead, I think – dead in the snow at the Stone-pits – not far from my door.'

Godfrey felt a great throb: there was one terror in his mind at that moment: it was, that the woman might *not* be dead. That was an evil terror – an ugly inmate to have found a nestling-place in Godfrey's kindly disposition; but no disposition is a security from evil wishes to a man whose happiness hangs on duplicity.

'Hush, hush!' said Mr Crackenthorp. 'Go out into the hall there. I'll fetch the doctor to you. Found a woman in the snow – and thinks she's dead,' he added, speaking low to the Squire. 'Better say as little about it as possible: it will shock the ladies. Just tell them a poor woman is ill from cold and hunger. I'll go and fetch Kimble.'

By this time, however, the ladies had pressed forward, curious to know what could have brought the solitary linen-weaver there under such strange circumstances, and interested in the pretty child, who, half alarmed and half attracted by the brightness and the numerous company, now frowned and hid her face, now lifted up her head again and looked round placably, until a touch or a coaxing word brought back the frown, and made her bury her face with new determination.

'What child is it?' said several ladies at once, and, among the rest, Nancy Lammeter, addressing Godfrey.

'I don't know – some poor woman's who has been found in the snow, I believe,' was the answer Godfrey wrung from himself with a terrible effort. ('After all, *am* I certain?' he hastened to add, silently, in anticipation of his own conscience.)

'Why, you'd better leave the child here, then, Master Marner,' said good-natured Mrs Kimble, hesitating, however, to take those dingy clothes into contact with her own ornamented satin bodice. 'I'll tell one o' the girls to fetch it.'

'No – no – I can't part with it, I can't let it go,' said Silas, abruptly. 'It's come to me – I've a right to keep it.'

The proposition to take the child from him had come to Silas quite unexpectedly, and his speech, uttered under a strong sudden impulse, was almost like a revelation to himself: a minute before, he had no distinct intention about the child.

'Did you ever hear the like?' said Mrs Kimble, in mild surprise, to her neighbour.

'Now, ladies, I must trouble you to stand aside,' said Mr Kimble, coming from the cardroom, in some bitterness at the interruption, but drilled by the long habit of his profession into obedience to unpleasant calls, even when he was hardly sober.

'It's a nasty business turning out now, eh, Kimble?' said the Squire. 'He might ha' gone for your young fellow – the 'prentice, there – what's his name?'

'Might? ay – what's the use of talking about might?' growled uncle Kimble, hastening out with Marner, and followed by Mr Crackenthorp and Godfrey. 'Get me a pair of thick boots, Godfrey, will you? And stay, let somebody run to Winthrop's and fetch Dolly – she's the best woman to get. Ben was here himself before supper; is he gone?'

'Yes, sir, I met him,' said Marner; 'but I couldn't stop to tell him anything, only I said I was going for the doctor, and he said the doctor was at the Squire's. And I made haste and ran, and there was nobody to be seen at the back o' the house, and so I went in to where the company was.'

The child, no longer distracted by the bright light and the smiling women's faces, began to cry and call for 'mammy', though always clinging to Marner, who had apparently won her thorough confidence. Godfrey had come back with the boots, and felt the cry as if some fibre were drawn tight within him.

'I'll go,' he said, hastily, eager for some movement; 'I'll go and fetch the woman – Mrs Winthrop.'

'O, pooh – send somebody else,' said uncle Kimble, hurrying away with Marner.

'You'll let me know if I can be of any use, Kimble,' said Mr Crackenthorp. But the doctor was out of hearing.

Godfrey, too, had disappeared: he was gone to snatch his hat and coat, having just reflection enough to remember that he must not look like a madman; but he rushed out of the house into the snow without heeding his thin shoes.

In a few minutes he was on his rapid way to the Stone-pits by the side of Dolly, who, though feeling that she was entirely in her place in encountering cold and snow on an errand of mercy, was much concerned at a young gentleman's getting his feet wet under a like impulse.

'You'd a deal better go back, sir,' said Dolly, with respectful compassion. 'You've no call to catch cold; and I'd ask you if you'd be so good as tell my husband to come, on your way back – he's at the Rainbow, I doubt – if you found him anyway sober enough to be o' use. Or else, there's Mrs Snell 'ud happen send the boy up to fetch and carry, for there may be things wanted from the doctor's.'

'No, I'll stay, now I'm once out – I'll stay outside here,' said Godfrey, when they came opposite Marner's cottage. 'You can come and tell me if I can do anything.'

'Well, sir, you're very good: you've a tender heart,' said Dolly, going to the door.

Godfrey was too painfully preoccupied to feel a twinge of self-reproach at this undeserved praise. He walked up and down, unconscious that he was plunging ankle-deep in snow, unconscious of everything but trembling suspense about what was going on in the cottage, and the effect of each alternative on his future lot. No, not quite unconscious of everything else. Deeper down, and half-smothered by passionate desire and dread, there was the sense that he ought not to be waiting on these alternatives; that he ought to accept the consequences of his deeds, own the miserable wife, and fulfil the claims of the helpless child. But he had not moral courage enough to contemplate that active renunciation of

Nancy as possible for him: he had only conscience and heart enough to make him for ever uneasy under the weakness that forbade the renunciation. And at this moment his mind leaped away from all restraint toward the sudden prospect of deliverance from his long bondage.

'Is she dead?' said the voice that predominated over every other within him. 'If she is, I may marry Nancy; and then I shall be a good fellow in future, and have no secrets, and the child – shall be taken care of somehow.' But across that vision came the other possibility – 'She may live, and then it's all up with me.'

Godfrey never knew how long it was before the door of the cottage opened and Mr Kimble came out. He went forward to meet his uncle, prepared to suppress the agitation he must feel, whatever news he was to hear.

'I waited for you, as I'd come so far,' he said, speaking first.

'Pooh, it was nonsense for you to come out: why didn't you send one of the men? There's nothing to be done. She's dead – has been dead for hours, I should say.'

'What sort of woman is she?' said Godfrey, feeling the blood rush to his face.

'A young woman, but emaciated, with long black hair. Some vagrant – quite in rags. She's got a wedding-ring on, however. They must fetch her away to the workhouse tomorrow. Come, come along.'

'I want to look at her,' said Godfrey. 'I think I saw such a woman yesterday. I'll overtake you in a minute or two.'

Mr Kimble went on, and Godfrey turned back to the cottage. He cast only one glance at the dead face on the pillow, which Dolly had smoothed with decent care; but he remembered that last look at his unhappy hated wife so well, that at the end of sixteen years every line in the worn face was present to him when he told the full story of this night.

He turned immediately towards the hearth where Silas Marner sat lulling the child. She was perfectly quiet now, but not asleep – only soothed by sweet porridge and warmth into that wide-gazing calm which makes us older human beings, with our inward turmoil, feel a certain awe in the presence of a little child, such as we feel before some quiet majesty or beauty in the earth or sky – before a steady-glowing planet, or a full-flowered eglantine, or the bending trees over a silent pathway. The wide-open blue eyes looked up at Godfrey's without any uneasiness or sign of recognition: the child could make no visible audible claim on its father; and the father felt a strange mixture of feelings, a conflict of regret and joy, that the pulse of that little heart had no response for the half-jealous yearning in his own, when the blue eyes turned away from him slowly, and fixed themselves on the weaver's queer face, which was bent low down to look at them, while the small hand began to pull Marner's withered cheek with loving disfiguration.

'You'll take the child to the parish tomorrow?' asked Godfrey, speaking as indifferently as he could.

'Who says so?' said Marner, sharply. 'Will they make me take her?'

'Why, you wouldn't like to keep her, should you – an old bachelor like you?'

'Till anybody shows they've a right to take her away from me,' said Marner. 'The mother's dead, and I reckon it's got no father: it's a lone thing – and I'm a lone thing. My money's gone, I don't know where – and this is come from I don't know where. I know nothing – I'm partly mazed.'

'Poor little thing!' said Godfrey. 'Let me give something towards finding it clothes.'

He had put his hand in his pocket and found half a guinea, and, thrusting it into Silas's hand, he hurried out of the cottage to overtake Mr Kimble.

'Ah, I see it's not the same woman I saw,' he said, as he came up. 'It's a pretty little child: the old fellow seems to want to keep it; that's strange for a miser like him. But I gave him a trifle to help him out: the parish isn't likely to quarrel with him for the right to keep the child.'

'No; but I've seen the time when I might have quarrelled with him for it myself. It's too late now, though. If the child ran into the fire, your aunt's too fat to overtake it: she could only sit, and grunt like an alarmed sow. But what a fool you are, Godfrey, to come out in your dancing shoes and stockings in this way – and you one of the beaux of the evening, and at your own house! What do you mean by such freaks, young fellow? Has Miss Nancy been cruel, and do you want to spite her by spoiling your pumps?'

'O, everything has been disagreeable tonight. I was tired to death of jigging and gallanting, and that bother about the hornpipes. And I'd got to dance with the other Miss Gunn,' said Godfrey, glad of the subterfuge his uncle had suggested to him.

The prevarication and white lies which a mind that keeps itself ambitiously pure is as uneasy under as a great artist under the false touches that no eye detects but his own, are worn as lightly as mere trimmings when once the actions have become a lie.

Godfrey reappeared in the White Parlour with dry feet, and, since the truth must be told, with a sense of relief and gladness that was too strong for painful thoughts to struggle with. For could he not venture now, whenever opportunity offered, to say the tenderest things to Nancy Lammeter – to promise her and himself that he would always be just what she would desire to see him? There was no danger that his dead wife would be recognised: those were not days of active enquiry and wide report; and as for the registry of their marriage, that was a long way off, buried in unturned pages, away from everyone's interest but his own. Dunsey might betray him if he came back; but Dunsey might be won to silence.

And when events turn out so much better for a man than he has had reason to dread, is it not a proof that his conduct has been less foolish and blameworthy than it might otherwise have appeared? When we are treated well, we naturally begin to think that we are not altogether unmeritorious, and that it is only just we should treat ourselves well, and not mar our own good fortune. Where, after all, would be the use of his confessing the past to Nancy Lammeter, and throwing away his happiness? – nay, hers? for he felt some confidence that she loved him. As for the child, he would see that it was cared for: he would never forsake it; he would do everything but own it. Perhaps it would be just as happy in life without being owned by its father, seeing that nobody could tell how things would turn out, and that – is there any other reason wanted? – well, then, that the father would be much happier without owning the child.

There was a pauper's burial that week in Raveloe, and up Kench Yard at Batherley it was known that the dark-haired woman with the fair child, who had lately come to lodge there, was gone away again. That was all the express note taken that Molly had disappeared from the eyes of men. But the unwept death which, to the general lot, seemed as trivial as the summer-shed leaf, was charged with the force of destiny to certain human lives that we know of, shaping their joys and sorrows even to the end.

Silas Marner's determination to keep the 'tramp's child' was matter of hardly less surprising and iterated talk in the village than the robbery of his money. That softening of feeling towards him which dated from his misfortune, that merging of suspicion and dislike in a rather contemptuous pity for him as lone and crazy, was now accompanied with a more active sympathy, especially amongst the women. Notable mothers, who knew what it was to keep children 'whole and sweet'; lazy mothers, who knew what it was to be interrupted in folding their arms and scratching their elbows by the mischievous propensities of children just firm on their legs, were equally interested in conjecturing how a lone man would manage with a two-year-old child on his hands, and were equally ready with their suggestions: the notable chiefly telling him what he had better do, and the lazy ones being emphatic in telling him what he would never be able to do.

Among the notable mothers, Dolly Winthrop was the one whose neighbourly offices were the most acceptable to Marner, for they were rendered without any show of bustling instruction. Silas had shown her the half-guinea given to him by Godfrey, and had asked her what he should do about getting some clothes for the child.

'Eh, Master Marner,' said Dolly, 'there's no call to buy, no more nor a pair o' shoes; for I've got the little petticoats as Aaron wore five years ago, and it's ill spending the money on them baby-clothes, for the child 'ull grow like grass i' May, bless it – that it will.'

And the same day Dolly brought her bundle, and displayed to Marner, one by one, the tiny garments in their due order of succession, most of them patched and darned, but clean and neat as fresh-sprung herbs. This was the introduction to a great ceremony with soap and water, from which baby came out in new beauty, and sat on Dolly's knee, handling her toes and chuckling and patting her palms together with an air of having made several discoveries about herself, which she communicated by alternate sounds of 'gug-gug-gug' and 'mammy'. The 'mammy' was not a cry of need or uneasiness: Baby had been used to utter it without expecting either tender sound or touch to follow.

'Anybody 'ud think the angils in heaven couldn't be prettier,' said Dolly, rubbing the golden curls and kissing them. 'And to think of its being covered wi' them dirty rags – and the poor mother – froze to death; but there's Them as took care of it, and brought it to your door, Master Marner. The door was open, and it walked in over the snow, like as if it had been a little starved robin. Didn't you say the door was open?'

'Yes,' said Silas, meditatively. 'Yes – the door was open. The money's gone I don't know where, and this is come from I don't know where.'

He had not mentioned to anyone his unconsciousness of the child's entrance, shrinking from questions which might lead to the fact he himself suspected – namely, that he had been in one of his trances.

'Ah,' said Dolly, with soothing gravity, 'it's like the night and the morning, and the sleeping and the waking, and the rain and the harvest – one goes and the other comes, and we know nothing how nor where. We may strive and scrat and fend, but it's little we can do arter all – the big things come and go wi' no striving o' our'n – they do, that they do; and I think you're in the right on it to keep the little un, Master Marner, seeing as it's been sent to you, though there's folks as thinks different. You'll happen be a bit moithered with it while it's so little; but I'll come, and welcome, and see to it for you: I've a bit o' time to spare most days, for when one gets up betimes i' the morning, the clock seems to stan' still tow'rt ten, afore it's time to go about the victual. So, as I say, I'll come and see to the child for you, and welcome.'

'Thank you . . . kindly,' said Silas, hesitating a little. 'I'll be glad if you'll tell me things. But,' he added, uneasily, leaning forward to look at Baby with some jealousy, as she was resting her head backward against Dolly's arm, and eyeing him contentedly from a distance – 'But I want to do things for it myself, else it may get fond o' somebody else, and not fond o' me. I've been used to fending for myself in the house – I can learn, I can learn.'

'Eh, to be sure,' said Dolly, gently. 'I've seen men as are wonderful handy wi' children. The men are awk'ard and contrairy mostly, God help 'em – but when the drink's out of 'em, they aren't unsensible, though they're bad for leeching and bandaging – so fiery and unpatient. You see this goes first, next the skin,' proceeded Dolly, taking up the little shirt, and putting it on.

'Yes,' said Marner, docilely, bringing his eyes very close, that they might be initiated in the mysteries; whereupon Baby seized his head with both her small arms, and put her lips against his face with purring noises.

'See there,' said Dolly, with a woman's tender tact, 'she's fondest o' you. She wants to go o' your lap, I'll be bound. Go, then: take her, Master Marner; you can put the things on, and then you can say as you've done for her from the first of her coming to you.'

Marner took her on his lap, trembling with an emotion mysterious to himself, at something unknown dawning on his life. Thought and feeling were so confused within him, that if he had tried to give them utterance, he could only have said that the child was come instead of the gold – that the gold had turned into the child. He took the garments from Dolly, and put them on under her teaching; interrupted, of course, by Baby's gymnastics.

'There, then! why, you take to it quite easy, Master Marner,' said Dolly; 'but what shall you do when you're forced to sit in your loom? For she'll get busier and mischievouser every day – she will, bless her. It's lucky as you've got that high hearth i'stead of a grate, for that keeps the fire more out of her reach; but if you've got anything as can be spilt or broke, or as is fit to cut her fingers off, she'll be at it – and it is but right you should know.'

Silas meditated a little while in some perplexity. 'I'll tie her to the leg o' the loom,' he said at last – 'tie her with a good long strip o' something.'

'Well, mayhap that'll do, as it's a little gell, for they're easier persuaded to sit i' one place nor the lads. I know what the lads are; for I've had four – four I've had, God knows – and if you was to take and tie 'em up, they'd make a fighting and a crying as if you was ringing pigs. But I'll bring you my little chair, and some bits o' red rag and things for her to play wi'; an' she'll sit and chatter to 'em as if they was alive. Eh, if it wasn't a sin to the lads to wish 'em made different, bless 'em, I should ha' been glad for one of 'em to be a little gell; and to think as I could ha' taught her to scour, and mend, and the knitting, and everything. But I can teach 'em this little un, Master Marner, when she gets old enough.'

'But she'll be *my* little un,' said Marner, rather hastily. 'She'll be nobody else's.'

'No, to be sure; you'll have a right to her if you're a father to her, and bring her up according. But,' added Dolly, coming to a point which she had determined beforehand to touch upon, 'you must bring her up like christened folks's children, and take her to church, and let her learn her catechise, as my little Aaron can say off – the "I believe", and everything, and "hurt nobody by word or deed" – as well as if he was the clerk. That's what you must do, Master Marner, if you'd do the right thing by the orphin child.'

Marner's pale face flushed suddenly under a new anxiety. His mind was too busy trying to give some definite bearing to Dolly's words for him to think of answering her.

'And it's my belief,' she went on, 'as the poor little creatur has never been christened, and it's nothing but right as the parson should be spoke to; and if you was no ways unwilling, I'd talk to Mr Macey about it this very day. For if the child ever went anyways wrong, and you hadn't done your part by it, Master Marner – 'noculation, and everything to save it from harm – it 'ud be a thorn i' your bed for ever o' this side the grave; and I can't think as it 'ud be easy lying down for anybody when they'd got to another world, if they hadn't done their part by the helpless children as come wi'out their own asking.'

Dolly herself was disposed to be silent for some time now, for she had spoken from the depths of her own simple belief, and was much concerned to know whether her words would produce the desired effect on Silas. He was puzzled and anxious, for Dolly's word 'christened' conveyed no distinct meaning to him. He had only heard of baptism, and had only seen the baptism of grown-up men and women.

'What is it as you mean by "christened"?' he said at last, timidly. 'Won't folks be good to her without it?'

'Dear, dear! Master Marner,' said Dolly, with gentle distress and compassion. 'Had you never no father nor mother as taught you to say your prayers, and as there's good words and good things to keep us from harm?'

'Yes,' said Silas, in a low voice; 'I know a deal about that – used to, used to. But your ways are different: my country was a good way off.' He paused a few moments, and then added, more decidedly, 'But I want to do everything as can be done for the child. And whatever's right for it i' this country, and you think 'ull do it good, I'll act according, if you'll tell me.'

'Well, then, Master Marner,' said Dolly, inwardly rejoiced, 'I'll ask Mr Macey to speak to the parson about it; and you must fix on a name for it, because it must have a name giv' it when it's christened.'

'My mother's name was Hephzibah,' said Silas, 'and my little sister was named after her.'

'Eh, that's a hard name,' said Dolly. 'I partly think it isn't a christened name.'

'It's a Bible name,' said Silas, old ideas recurring.

'Then I've no call to speak again' it,' said Dolly, rather startled by Silas's knowledge on this head; 'but you see I'm no scholard, and I'm slow at catching the words. My husband says I'm allays like as if I was putting the haft for the handle – that's what he says – for he's very sharp, God help him. But it was awk'ard calling your little sister by such a hard name, when you'd got nothing big to say, like – wasn't it, Master Marner?'

'We called her Eppie,' said Silas.

'Well, if it was no ways wrong to shorten the name, it 'ud be a deal handier. And so I'll go now, Master Marner, and I'll speak about the christening afore dark; and I wish you the best o' luck, and it's my belief as it'll come to you, if you do what's right by the orphin child; – and there's the 'noculation to be seen to; and as to washing its bits o' things, you need look to nobody but me, for I can do 'em wi' one hand when I've got my suds about. Eh, the blessed angil! You'll let me bring my Aaron one o' these days, and he'll show her his little cart as his father's made for him, and the black-and-white pup as he's got a-rearing.'

Baby *was* christened, the rector deciding that a double baptism was the lesser risk to incur; and on this occasion Silas, making himself as clean and tidy as he could, appeared for the first time within the church, and shared in the observances held sacred by his neighbours. He was quite unable, by means of anything he heard or saw, to identify the Raveloe religion with his old faith: if he could at any time in his previous life have done so, it must have been by the aid of a strong feeling ready to vibrate with sympathy, rather than by a comparison of phrases and ideas; and now for long years that feeling had been dormant. He had no distinct idea about the baptism and the church-going, except that Dolly had said it was for the good of the child; and in this way, as the weeks grew to months, the child created fresh and fresh links between his life and the lives from which he had hitherto shrunk continually into narrower isolation. Unlike the gold which needed nothing, and must be worshipped in close-locked solitude – which was hidden away from the daylight, was deaf to the song of birds, and started to no human tones – Eppie was a creature of endless claims and ever-growing desires, seeking and loving sunshine, and living sounds, and living movements; making trial of everything, with trust in new joy, and stirring the human kindness in all eyes that looked on her. The gold had kept his thoughts in an ever-repeated circle, leading to nothing beyond itself; but Eppie was an object compacted of changes and hopes that forced his thoughts onward, and carried them far away from their old eager pacing towards the same blank limit – carried them away to the new things that would come with the coming years, when Eppie would have learned to understand how her father Silas cared for her; and made him look for images of that time in the ties and charities that bound together the families of his neighbours. The gold had asked that he should sit weaving longer and longer, deafened and blinded more and more to all things except the monotony of his loom and the repetition of his web; but Eppie called him away from his weaving, and made him think all its pauses a holiday, reawakening his senses with her fresh life, even to the old winter-flies that came crawling forth in the early spring sunshine, and warming him into joy because *she* had joy.

And when the sunshine grew strong and lasting, so that the buttercups were thick in the meadows, Silas might be seen in the sunny midday, or in the late afternoon when the shadows were lengthening under the hedgerows, strolling out with uncovered head to carry Eppie beyond the Stone-pits to where the flowers grew, till they reached some favourite bank where he could sit down, while Eppie toddled to pluck the flowers, and make remarks to the winged things that murmured happily above the bright petals, calling 'Dad-dad's' attention continually by bringing him the flowers. Then she would turn her ear to some sudden bird-note, and Silas learned to please her by making signs of hushed stillness, that they might listen for the note to come again: so that when it came, she set up her small back and laughed with gurgling triumph. Sitting on the banks in this way, Silas began to look for the once familiar herbs again; and as the leaves, with their unchanged outline and markings, lay on his palm, there was a sense of crowding remembrances from which he turned away timidly, taking refuge in Eppie's little world, that lay lightly on his enfeebled spirit.

As the child's mind was growing into knowledge, his mind was growing into memory: as her life unfolded, his soul, long stupefied in a cold narrow prison, was unfolding too, and trembling gradually into full consciousness.

It was an influence which must gather force with every new year: the tones that stirred Silas's heart grew articulate, and called for more distinct answers; shapes and sounds grew clearer for Eppie's eyes and ears, and there was more that 'Dad-dad' was imperatively required to notice and account for. Also, by the time Eppie was three years old, she developed a fine capacity for mischief, and for devising ingenious ways of being troublesome, which found much exercise, not only for Silas's patience, but for his watchfulness and penetration. Sorely was poor Silas puzzled on such occasions by the incompatible demands of love. Dolly Winthrop told him punishment was good for Eppie, and that, as for rearing a child without making it tingle a little in soft and safe places now and then, it was not to be done.

'To be sure, there's another thing you might do, Master Marner,' added Dolly, meditatively: 'you might shut her up once i' the coal-hole. That was what I did wi' Aaron; for I was that silly wi' the youngest lad, as I could never bear to smack him. Not as I could find i' my heart to let him stay i' the coal-hole more nor a minute, but it was enough to colly him all over, so as he must be new washed and dressed, and it was as good as a rod to him – that was. But I put it upo' your conscience, Master Marner, as there's one of 'em you must choose –

ayther smacking or the coal-hole – else she'll get so masterful, there'll be no holding her.'

Silas was impressed with the melancholy truth of this last remark; but his force of mind failed before the only two penal methods open to him, not only because it was painful to him to hurt Eppie, but because he trembled at a moment's contention with her, lest she should love him the less for it. Let even an affectionate Goliath get himself tied to a small tender thing, dreading to hurt it by pulling, and dreading still more to snap the cord, and which of the two, pray, will be master? It was clear that Eppie, with her short toddling steps, must lead father Silas a pretty dance on any fine morning when circumstances favoured mischief.

For example. He had wisely chosen a broad strip of linen as a means of fastening her to his loom when he was busy: it made a broad belt round her waist, and was long enough to allow of her reaching the truckle-bed and sitting down on it, but not long enough for her to attempt any dangerous climbing. One bright summer's morning Silas had been more engrossed than usual in 'setting up' a new piece of work, an occasion on which his scissors were in requisition. These scissors, owing to an especial warning of Dolly's, had been kept carefully out of Eppie's reach; but the click of them had had a peculiar attraction for her ear, and, watching the results of that click, she had derived the philosophic lesson that the same cause would produce the same effect. Silas had seated himself in his loom, and the noise of weaving had begun; but he had left his scissors on a ledge which Eppie's arm was long enough to reach; and now, like a small mouse, watching her opportunity, she stole quietly from her corner, secured the scissors, and toddled to the bed again, setting up her back as a mode of concealing the fact. She had a distinct intention as to the use of the scissors; and having cut the linen strip in a jagged but effectual manner, in two moments she had run out at the open door where the sunshine was inviting her, while poor Silas believed her to be a better child than usual. It was not until he happened to need his scissors that the terrible fact burst upon him: Eppie had run out by herself – had perhaps fallen into the Stone-pit. Silas, shaken by the worst fear that could have befallen him, rushed out, calling 'Eppie!' and ran eagerly about the unenclosed space, exploring the dry cavities into which she might have fallen, and then gazing with questioning dread at the smooth red surface of the water. The cold drops stood on his brow. How long had she been out? There was one hope – that she had crept through the stile and got into the fields where he habitually took her to stroll. But the grass was high in the meadow, and there was no descrying her, if she were there, except by a close search that would be a trespass on Mr Osgood's crop. Still, that misdemeanour must be committed; and poor Silas, after peering all round the hedgerows, traversed the grass, beginning with perturbed vision to see Eppie behind every group of red sorrel, and to see her moving always farther off as he approached. The meadow was searched in vain; and he got over the stile into the next field, looking with dying hope towards a small pond which was now reduced to its summer shallowness, so as to leave a wide margin of good adhesive mud. Here, however, sat Eppie, discoursing cheerfully to her own small boot, which she was using as a bucket to convey the water into a deep hoof-mark, while her little naked foot was planted comfortably on a cushion of olive-green mud. A red-headed calf was observing her with alarmed doubt through the opposite hedge.

Here was clearly a case of aberration in a christened child which demanded severe treatment; but Silas, overcome with convulsive joy at finding his treasure again, could do nothing but snatch her up, and cover her with half-sobbing kisses. It was not until he had carried her home, and had begun to think of the necessary washing, that he recollected the need that he should punish Eppie, and 'make her remember.' The idea that she might run away again and come to harm, gave him unusual resolution, and for the first time he determined to try the coal-hole – a small closet near the hearth.

'Naughty, naughty Eppie,' he suddenly began, holding her on his knee, and pointing to her muddy feet and clothes – 'naughty to cut with the scissors, and run away. Eppie must go into the coal-hole for being naughty. Daddy must put her in the coal-hole.'

He half expected that this would be shock enough, and that Eppie would begin to cry. But instead of that, she began to shake herself on his knee, as if the proposition opened a pleasing novelty. Seeing that he must proceed to extremities, he put her into the coal-hole, and held the door closed, with a trembling sense that he was using a strong measure. For a moment there was silence, but then came a little cry, 'Opy, opy!' and Silas let her out again, saying, 'Now Eppie 'ull never be naughty again, else she must go in the coal-hole – a black naughty place.'

The weaving must stand still a long while this morning, for now Eppie must be washed and have clean clothes on; but it was to be hoped that this punishment would have a lasting effect, and save time in future – though, perhaps, it would have been better if Eppie had cried more.

In half an hour she was clean again, and Silas having turned his back to see what he could do with the linen band, threw it down again, with the reflection that Eppie would be good without fastening for the rest of the morning. He turned round again, and was going to place her in her little chair near the loom, when she peeped out at him with black face and hands again, and said, 'Eppie in de toal-hole!'

This total failure of the coal-hole discipline shook Silas's belief in the efficacy of punishment. 'She'd take it all for fun,' he observed to Dolly, 'if I didn't hurt her, and that I can't do, Mrs Winthrop. If she makes me a bit o' trouble, I can bear it. And she's got no tricks but what she'll grow out of.'

'Well, that's partly true, Master Marner,' said Dolly, sympathetically; 'and if you can't bring your mind to frighten her off touching things, you must do what you can to keep 'em out of her way. That's what I do wi' the pups as the lads are allays a-rearing. They *will* worry and gnaw – worry and gnaw they will, if it was one's Sunday cap as hung anywhere so as they could drag it. They know no difference, God help 'em: it's the pushing o' the teeth as sets them on, that's what it is.'

So Eppie was reared without punishment, the burden of her misdeeds being borne vicariously by father Silas. The stone hut was made a soft nest for her, lined with downy patience: and also in the world that lay beyond the stone hut for her, she knew nothing of frowns and denials.

Notwithstanding the difficulty of carrying her and his yarn or linen at the same time, Silas took her with him in most of his journeys to the farmhouses, unwilling to leave her behind at Dolly Winthrop's, who was always ready to take care of her; and little curly-headed Eppie, the weaver's child, became an object of interest at several out-lying homesteads, as well as in the village. Hitherto he had been treated very much as if he had been a useful gnome or brownie – a queer and unaccountable creature, who must necessarily be looked at with wondering curiosity and repulsion, and with whom one would be glad to make all greetings and bargains as brief as possible, but who must be dealt with in a propitiatory way, and occasionally have a present of pork or garden-stuff to carry home with him, seeing that without him there was no getting the yarn woven. But now Silas met with open smiling faces and cheerful questioning, as a person whose satisfactions and difficulties could be understood. Everywhere he must sit a little and talk about the child, and words of interest were always ready for him: 'Ah, Master Marner, you'll be lucky if she takes the measles soon and easy!' – or, 'Why, there isn't many lone men 'ud ha' been wishing to take up with a little un like that: but I reckon the weaving makes you handier than men as do outdoor work – you're partly as handy as a woman, for weaving comes next to spinning.' Elderly masters and mistresses, seated observantly in large kitchen armchairs, shook their heads over the difficulties attendant on rearing children, felt Eppie's round arms and legs, and pronounced them remarkably firm, and told Silas that, if she turned out well (which, however, there was no telling), it would be a fine thing for him to have a steady lass to do for him when he got helpless. Servant maidens were fond of carrying her out to look at the hens and chickens, or to see if any cherries could be shaken down in the orchard; and the small boys and girls approached her slowly, with cautious movement and steady gaze, like little dogs face to face with one of their own kind, till attraction had reached the point at which the soft lips were put out for a kiss. No child was afraid of approaching Silas when Eppie was near him: there was no repulsion around him now, either for young or old; for the little child had come to link him once more with the whole world. There was love between him and the child that blent them into one, and there was love between the child and the world – from men and women with parental looks and tones, to the red ladybirds and the round pebbles.

Silas began now to think of Raveloe life entirely in relation to Eppie: she must have everything that was a good in Raveloe; and he listened docilely, that he might come to understand better what this life was, from which, for fifteen years, he had stood aloof as from a strange thing, with which he could have no communion: as some man who has a precious plant to which he would give a nurturing home in a new soil, thinks of the rain and sunshine, and all influences, in relation to his nursling, and asks industriously for all knowledge that will help him to satisfy the wants of the searching roots, or to guard leaf and bud from invading harm. The disposition to hoard had been utterly crushed at the very first by the loss of his long-stored gold: the coins he earned afterwards seemed as irrelevant as stones brought to complete a house suddenly buried by an earth-quake; the sense of bereavement was too heavy upon him for the old thrill of satisfaction to arise again at the touch of the newly-earned coin. And now something had come to replace his hoard which gave a growing purpose to the earnings, drawing his hope and joy continually onward beyond the money.

In old days there were angels who came and took men by the hand and led them away from the city of destruction. We see no white-winged angels now. But yet men are led away from threatening destruction: a hand is put into theirs, which leads them forth gently towards a calm and bright land, so that they look no more backward; and the hand may be a little child's.

Chapter 15

There was one person, as you will believe, who watched with keener though more hidden interest than any other, the prosperous growth of Eppie under the weaver's care. He dared not do anything that would imply a stronger interest in a poor man's adopted child than could be expected from the kindliness of the young Squire, when a chance meeting suggested a little present to a simple old fellow whom others noticed with goodwill; but he told himself that the time would come when he might do something towards furthering the welfare of his daughter without incurring suspicions. Was he very uneasy in the mean time at his inability to give his daughter her birthright? I cannot say that he was. The child was being taken care of, and would very likely be happy, as people in humble stations often were – happier, perhaps, than those who are brought up in luxury.

That famous ring that pricked its owner when he forgot duty and followed desire – I wonder if it pricked very hard when he set out on the chase, or whether it pricked but lightly then, and only pierced to the quick when the chase had long been ended, and hope, folding her wings, looked backward and became regret?

Godfrey Cass's cheek and eye were brighter than ever now. He was so undivided in his aims, that he seemed like a man of firmness. No Dunsey had come back: people had made up their minds that he was gone for a soldier, or gone 'out of the country,' and no one cared to be specific in their enquiries on a subject delicate to a respectable family. Godfrey had ceased to see the shadow of Dunsey across his path; and the path now lay straight forward to the accomplishment of his best, longest-cherished wishes. Everybody said Mr Godfrey had taken the right turn; and it was pretty clear what would be the end of things, for there were not many days in the week that he was not seen riding to the Warrens. Godfrey himself, when he was asked jocosely if the day had been fixed, smiled with the pleasant consciousness of a lover who could say 'yes,' if he liked. He felt a reformed man, delivered from temptation; and the vision of his future life seemed to him as a promised land for which he had no cause to fight. He saw himself with all his happiness centred on his own hearth, where Nancy would smile on him as he played with the children.

And that other child – not on the hearth – he would not forget it; he would see that it was well provided for. That was a father's duty.

PART TWO

Chapter 16

It was a bright autumn Sunday, sixteen years after Silas Marner had found his new treasure on the hearth. The bells of the old Raveloe church were ringing the cheerful peal which told that the morning service was ended; and out of the arched doorway in the tower came slowly, retarded by friendly greetings and questions, the richer parishioners who had chosen this bright Sunday morning as eligible for church-going. It was the rural fashion of that time for the more important members of the congregation to depart first, while their humbler neighbours waited and looked on, stroking their bent heads or dropping their curtsies to any large ratepayer who turned to notice them.

Foremost among these advancing groups of well-clad people, there are some whom we shall recognise, in spite of Time, who has laid his hand on them all. The tall blonde man of forty is not much changed in feature from the Godfrey Cass of six-and-twenty: he is only fuller in flesh, and has only lost the indefinable look of youth – a loss which is marked even when the eye is undulled and the wrinkles are not yet come. Perhaps the pretty woman, not much younger than he, who is leaning on his arm, is more changed than her husband: the lovely bloom that used to be always on her cheek now comes but fitfully, with the fresh morning air or with some strong surprise; yet to all who love human faces best for what they tell of human experience, Nancy's beauty has a heightened interest. Often the soul is ripened into fuller goodness while age has spread an ugly film, so that mere glances can never divine the preciousness of the fruit. But the years have not been so cruel to Nancy. The firm yet placid mouth, the clear veracious glance of the brown eyes, speak now of a nature that has been tested and has kept its highest qualities; and even the costume, with its dainty neatness and purity, has more significance now the coquetries of youth can have nothing to do with it.

Mr and Mrs Godfrey Cass (any higher title has died away from Raveloe lips since the old Squire was gathered to his fathers, and his inheritance was divided) have turned round to look for the tall aged man and the plainly-dressed woman who are a little behind – Nancy having observed that they must wait for 'father and Priscilla' – and now they all turn into a narrower path leading across the churchyard to a small gate opposite the Red House. We will not follow them now; for may there not be some others in this departing congregation whom we should like to see again – some of those who are not likely to be handsomely clad, and whom we may not recognise so easily as the master and mistress of the Red House?

But it is impossible to mistake Silas Marner. His large brown eyes seem to have gathered a longer vision, as is the way with eyes that have been short-

sighted in early life, and they have a less vague, a more answering look; but in everything else one sees signs of a frame much enfeebled by the lapse of the sixteen years. The weaver's bent shoulders and white hair give him almost the look of advanced age, though he is not more than five-and-fifty; but there is the freshest blossom of youth close by his side – a blonde dimpled girl of eighteen, who has vainly tried to chastise her curly auburn hair into smoothness under her brown bonnet: the hair ripples as obstinately as a brooklet under the March breeze, and the little ringlets burst away from the restraining comb behind and show themselves below the bonnet-crown. Eppie cannot help being rather vexed about her hair, for there is no other girl in Raveloe who has hair at all like it, and she thinks hair ought to be smooth. She does not like to be blameworthy even in small things: you see how neatly her prayer-book is folded in her spotted handkerchief.

That good-looking young fellow, in a new fustian suit, who walks behind her, is not quite sure upon the question of hair in the abstract, when Eppie puts it to him, and thinks that perhaps straight hair is the best in general, but he doesn't want Eppie's hair to be different. She surely divines that there is someone behind her who is thinking about her very particularly, and mustering courage to come to her side as soon as they are out in the lane, else why should she look rather shy, and take care not to turn away her head from her father Silas, to whom she keeps murmuring little sentences as to who was at church and who was not at church, and how pretty the red mountain-ash is over the Rectory wall?

'I wish *we* had a little garden, father, with double daisies in, like Mrs Winthrop's,' said Eppie, when they were out in the lane; 'only they say it 'ud take a deal of digging and bringing fresh soil – and you couldn't do that, could you, father? Anyhow, I shouldn't like you to do it, for it 'ud be too hard work for you.'

'Yes, I could do it, child, if you want a bit o' garden: these long evenings, I could work at taking in a little bit o' the waste, just enough for a root or two o' flowers for you; and again, i' the morning, I could have a turn wi' the spade before I sat down to the loom. Why didn't you tell me before as you wanted a bit o' garden?'

'*I* can dig it for you, Master Marner,' said the young man in fustian, who was now by Eppie's side, entering into the conversation without the trouble of formalities. 'It'll be play to me after I've done my day's work, or any odd bits o' time when the work's slack. And I'll bring you some soil from Mr Cass's garden – he'll let me, and willing.'

'Eh, Aaron, my lad, are you there?' said Silas; 'I wasn't aware of you; for when Eppie's talking o' things, I see nothing but what she's a-saying. Well, if you could help me with the digging, we might get her a bit o' garden all the sooner.'

'Then, if you think well and good,' said Aaron, 'I'll come to the Stone-pits this afternoon, and we'll settle what land's to be taken in, and I'll get up an hour earlier i' the morning, and begin on it.'

'But not if you don't promise me not to work at the hard digging, father,' said Eppie. 'For I shouldn't ha' said anything about it,' she added, half-bashfully half-roguishly, 'only Mrs Winthrop said as Aaron 'ud be so good, and – '

'And you might ha' known it without mother telling you,' said Aaron. 'And

Master Marner knows too, I hope, as I'm able and willing to do a turn o' work for him, and he won't do me the unkindness to anyways take it out o' my hands.'

'There, now, father, you won't work in it till it's all easy,' said Eppie, 'and you and me can mark out the beds, and make holes and plant the roots. It'll be a deal livelier at the Stone-pits when we've got some flowers, for I always think the flowers can see us and know what we're talking about. And I'll have a bit o' rosemary, and bergamot, and thyme, because they're so sweet-smelling; but there's no lavender only in the gentlefolks' gardens, I think.'

'That's no reason why you shouldn't have some,' said Aaron, 'for I can bring you slips of anything; I'm forced to cut no end of 'em when I'm gardening, and throw 'em away mostly. There's a big bed o' lavender at the Red House: the missis is very fond of it.'

'Well,' said Silas, gravely, 'so as you don't make free for us, or ask for anything as is worth much at the Red House: for Mr Cass's been so good to us, and built us up the new end o' the cottage, and given us beds and things, as I couldn't abide to be imposin' for garden-stuff or anything else.'

'No, no, there's no imposin',' said Aaron; 'there's never a garden in all the parish but what there's endless waste in it for want o' somebody as could use everything up. It's what I think to myself sometimes, as there need nobody run short o' victuals if the land was made the most on, and there was never a morsel but what could find its way to a mouth. It sets one thinking o' that – gardening does. But I must go back now, else mother 'ull be in trouble as I aren't there.'

'Bring her with you this afternoon, Aaron,' said Eppie; 'I shouldn't like to fix about the garden, and her not know everything from the first – should *you*, father?'

'Ay, bring her if you can, Aaron,' said Silas; 'she's sure to have a word to say as'll help us to set things on their right end.'

Aaron turned back up the village, while Silas and Eppie went on up the lonely sheltered lane.

'O daddy!' she began, when they were in privacy, clasping and squeezing Silas's arm, and skipping round to give him an energetic kiss. 'My little old daddy! I'm so glad. I don't think I shall want anything else when we've got a little garden; and I knew Aaron would dig it for us,' she went on with roguish triumph – 'I knew that very well.'

'You're a deep little puss, you are,' said Silas, with the mild passive happiness of love-crowned age in his face; 'but you'll make yourself fine and beholden to Aaron.'

'O no, I shan't,' said Eppie, laughing and frisking; 'he likes it.'

'Come, come, let me carry your prayer-book, else you'll be dropping it, jumping i' that way.'

Eppie was now aware that her behaviour was under observation, but it was only the observation of a friendly donkey, browsing with a log fastened to his foot – a meek donkey, not scornfully critical of human trivialities, but thankful to share in them, if possible, by getting his nose scratched; and Eppie did not fail to gratify him with her usual notice, though it was attended with the inconvenience of his following them, painfully, up to the very door of their home.

But the sound of a sharp bark inside, as Eppie put the key in the door, modified the donkey's views, and he limped away again without bidding. The sharp bark was the sign of an excited welcome that was awaiting them from a knowing brown terrier, who, after dancing at their legs in a hysterical manner, rushed with a worrying noise at a tortoiseshell kitten under the loom, and then rushed back with a sharp bark again, as much as to say, 'I have done my duty by this feeble creature, you perceive;' while the lady-mother of the kitten sat sunning her white bosom in the window, and looked round with a sleepy air of expecting caresses, though she was not going to take any trouble for them.

The presence of this happy animal life was not the only change which had come over this interior of the stone cottage. There was no bed now in the living-room, and the small space was well filled with decent furniture, all bright and clean enough to satisfy Dolly Winthrop's eye. The oaken table and three-cornered oaken chair were hardly what was likely to be seen in so poor a cottage: they had come, with the beds and other things, from the Red House; for Mr Godfrey Cass, as everyone said in the village, did very kindly by the weaver; and it was nothing but right a man should be looked on and helped by those who could afford it, when he had brought up an orphan child, and been father and mother to her – and had lost his money too, so as he had nothing but what he worked for week by week, and when the weaving was going down too – for there was less and less flax spun – and Master Marner was none so young. Nobody was jealous of the weaver, for he was regarded as an exceptional person, whose claims on neighbourly help were not to be matched in Raveloe. Any superstition that remained concerning him had taken an entirely new colour; and Mr Macey, now a very feeble old man of fourscore and six, never seen except in his chimney-corner or sitting in the sunshine at his door-sill, was of opinion that when a man had done what Silas had done by an orphan child, it was a sign that his money would come to light again, or leastwise that the robber would be made to answer for it – for, as Mr Macey observed of himself, his faculties were as strong as ever.

Silas sat down now and watched Eppie with a satisfied gaze as she spread the clean cloth, and set on it the potato-pie, warmed up slowly in a safe Sunday fashion, by being put into a dry pot over a slowly-dying fire, as the best substitute for an oven. For Silas would not consent to have a grate and oven added to his conveniences: he loved the old brick hearth as he had loved his brown pot – and was it not there when he had found Eppie? The gods of the hearth exist for us still; and let all new faith be tolerant of that fetishism, lest it bruise its own roots.

Silas ate his dinner more silently than usual, soon laying down his knife and fork, and watching half-abstractedly Eppie's play with Snap and the cat, by which her own dining was made rather a lengthy business. Yet it was a sight that might well arrest wandering thoughts: Eppie, with the rippling radiance of her hair and the whiteness of her rounded chin and throat set off by the dark-blue cotton gown, laughing merrily as the kitten held on with her four claws to one shoulder, like a design for a jug-handle, while Snap on the right hand and Puss on the other put up their paws towards a morsel which she held out of the reach of both – Snap occasionally desisting in order to remonstrate with the cat by a cogent worrying growl on the greediness and futility of her conduct; till Eppie relented, caressed them both, and divided the morsel between them.

But at last Eppie, glancing at the clock, checked the play, and said, 'O daddy, you're wanting to go into the sunshine to smoke your pipe. But I must clear away first, so as the house may be tidy when godmother comes. I'll make haste – I won't be long.'

Silas had taken to smoking a pipe daily during the last two years, having been strongly urged to it by the sages of Raveloe, as a practice 'good for the fits;' and this advice was sanctioned by Dr Kimble, on the ground that it was as well to try what could do no harm – a principle which was made to answer for a great deal of work in that gentleman's medical practice. Silas did not highly enjoy smoking, and often wondered how his neighbours could be so fond of it; but a humble sort of acquiescence in what was held to be good, had become a strong habit of that new self which had been developed in him since he had found Eppie on his hearth: it had been the only clue his bewildered mind could hold by in cherishing this young life that had been sent to him out of the darkness into which his gold had departed. By seeking what was needful for Eppie, by sharing the effect that everything produced on her, he had himself come to appropriate the forms of custom and belief which were the mould of Raveloe life; and as, with reawakening sensibilities, memory also reawakened, he had begun to ponder over the elements of his old faith, and blend them with his new impressions, till he recovered a consciousness of unity between his past and present. The sense of presiding goodness and the human trust which come with all pure peace and joy, had given him a dim impression that there had been some error, some mistake, which had thrown that dark shadow over the days of his best years; and as it grew more and more easy to him to open his mind to Dolly Winthrop, he gradually communicated to her all he could describe of his early life. The communication was necessarily a slow and difficult process, for Silas's meagre power of explanation was not aided by any readiness of interpretation in Dolly, whose narrow outward experience gave her no key to strange customs, and made every novelty a source of wonder that arrested them at every step of the narrative. It was only by fragments, and at intervals which left Dolly time to revolve what she had heard till it acquired some familiarity for her, that Silas at last arrived at the climax of the sad story – the drawing of lots, and its false testimony concerning him; and this had to be repeated in several interviews, under new questions on her part as to the nature of this plan for detecting the guilty and clearing the innocent.

'And yourn's the same Bible, you're sure o' that, Master Marner – the Bible as you brought wi' you from that country – it's the same as what they've got at church, and what Eppie's a-learning to read in?'

'Yes,' said Silas, 'every bit the same; and there's drawing o' lots in the Bible, mind you,' he added, in a lower tone.

'O dear, dear,' said Dolly, in a grieved voice, as if she were hearing an un-favourable report of a sick man's case. She was silent for some minutes; at last she said, 'There's wise folks, happen, as know how it all is; the parson knows, I'll be bound; but it takes big words to tell them things, and such as poor folks can't make much out on. I can never rightly know the meaning o' what I hear at church, only a bit here and there, but I know it's good words – I do. But what lies upo' your mind – it's this, Master Marner: as, if Them above had done the right thing by you, They'd never ha' let you be turned out for a wicked thief when you was innicent.'

'Ah!' said Silas, who had now come to understand Dolly's phraseology, 'that was what fell on me like as if it had been red-hot iron; because, you see, there was nobody as cared for me or clave to me above nor below. And him as I'd gone out and in wi' for ten year and more, since when we was lads and went halves – mine own famil'ar friend, in whom I trusted, had lifted up his heel again' me, and worked to ruin me.'

'Eh, but he was a bad un – I can't think as there's another such,' said Dolly. 'But I'm o'ercome, Master Marner; I'm like as if I'd waked and didn't know whether it was night or morning. I feel somehow as sure as I do when I've laid something up though I can't justly put my hand on it, as there was a right in what happened to you, if one could but make it out; and you'd no call to lose heart as you did. But we'll talk on it again; for sometimes things come into my head when I'm leeching or poulticing, or such, as I could never think on when I was sitting still.'

Dolly was too useful a woman not to have many opportunities of illumination of the kind she alluded to, and she was not long before she recurred to the subject.

'Master Marner,' she said, one day that she came to bring home Eppie's washing, 'I've been sore puzzled for a good bit wi' that trouble o' yourn and the drawing o' lots; and it got twisted back'ards and for'ards, as I didn't know which end to lay hold on. But it come to me all clear like, that night when I was sitting up wi' poor Bessy Fawkes, as is dead and left her children behind, God help 'em – it come to me as clear as daylight; but whether I've got hold on it now, or can anyways bring it to my tongue's end, that I don't know. For I've often a deal inside me as 'll niver come out; and for what you talk o' your folks in your old country niver saying prayers by heart nor saying 'em out of a book, they must be wonderful cliver; for if I didn't know "Our Father", and little bits o' good words as I can carry out o' church wi' me, I might down o' my knees every night, but nothing could I say.'

'But you can mostly say something as I can make sense on, Mrs Winthrop,' said Silas.

'Well, then, Master Marner, it come to me summat like this: I can make nothing o' the drawing o' lots and the answer coming wrong; it 'ud mayhap take the parson to tell that, and he could only tell us i' big words. But what come to me as clear as the daylight, it was when I was troubling over poor Bessy Fawkes, and it allays comes into my head when I'm sorry for folks, and feel as I can't do a power to help 'em, not if I was to get up i' the middle o' the night – it comes into my head as Them above has got a deal tenderer heart nor what I've got – for I can't be anyways better nor Them as made me, and if anything looks hard to me, it's because there's things I don't know on; and for the matter o' that, there may be plenty o' things I don't know on, for it's little as I know – that it is. And so, while I was thinking o' that, you come into my mind, Master Marner, and it all come pouring in: – if *I* felt i' my inside what was the right and just thing by you, and them as prayed and drawed the lots, all but that wicked un, if *they*'d ha' done the right thing by you if they could, isn't there Them as was at the making on us, and knows better and has a better will? And that's all as ever I can be sure on, and everything else is a big puzzle to me when I think on it. For there was the fever come and took off them as were full-growed, and left the helpless children; and there's the breaking o' limbs; and them as 'ud do right and be sober have to suffer by them as are contrary – eh, there's trouble i' this world, and there's things as we can niver make out the rights on. And all as we've got to do is to trusten, Master Marner – to do the right thing as fur as we know, and to trusten. For if us as knows so little can see a bit o' good and rights, we may be sure as there's a good and a rights bigger nor what we can know – I feel it i' my own inside as it must be so. And if you could but ha' gone on trustening, Master Marner, you wouldn't ha' run away from your fellow-creaturs and been so lone.'

'Ah, but that 'ud ha' been hard,' said Silas, in an undertone; 'it 'ud ha' been hard to trusten then.'

'And so it would,' said Dolly, almost with compunction; 'them things are easier said nor done; and I'm partly ashamed o' talking.'

'Nay, nay,' said Silas, 'you're i' the right, Mrs Winthrop – you're i' the right. There's good i' this world – I've a feeling o' that now; and it makes a man feel as there's a good more nor he can see, i' spite o' the trouble and the wickedness. That drawing o' the lots is dark; but the child was sent to me: there's dealings with us – there's dealings.'

This dialogue took place in Eppie's earlier years, when Silas had to part with her for two hours every day, that she might learn to read at the dame school, after he had vainly tried himself to guide her in that first step to learning. Now that she was grown up, Silas had often been led, in those moments of quiet outpouring which come to people who live together in perfect love, to talk with *her* too of the past, and how and why he had lived a lonely man until she had been sent to him. For it would have been impossible for him to hide from Eppie that she was not his own child: even if the most delicate reticence on the point could have been expected from Raveloe gossips in her presence, her own questions about her mother could not have been parried, as she grew up, without that complete shrouding of the past which would have made a painful barrier between their minds. So Eppie had long known how her mother had died on the snowy ground, and how she herself had been found on the hearth by father Silas, who had taken her golden curls for his lost guineas brought back to him. The tender and peculiar love with which Silas had reared her in almost inseparable companionship with himself, aided by the seclusion of their dwelling, had preserved her from the lowering influences of the village talk and habits, and had kept her mind in that freshness which is sometimes falsely supposed to be an invariable attribute of rusticity. Perfect love has a breath of poetry which can exalt the relations of the least instructed human beings; and this breath of poetry had surrounded Eppie from the time when she had followed the bright gleam that beckoned her to

Silas's hearth; so that it is not surprising if, in other things besides her delicate prettiness, she was not quite a common village maiden, but had a touch of refinement and fervour which came from no other teaching than that of tenderly-nurtured unvitiated feeling. She was too childish and simple for her imagination to rove into questions about her unknown father; for a long while it did not even occur to her that she must have had a father; and the first time that the idea of her mother having had a husband presented itself to her, was when Silas showed her the wedding-ring which had been taken from the wasted finger, and had been carefully preserved by him in a little lacquered box shaped like a shoe. He delivered this box into Eppie's charge when she had grown up, and she often opened it to look at the ring; but still she thought hardly at all about the father of whom it was the symbol. Had she not a father very close to her, who loved her better than any real fathers in the village seemed to love their daughters? On the contrary, who her mother was, and how she came to die in that forlornness, were questions that often pressed on Eppie's mind. Her knowledge of Mrs Winthrop, who was her nearest friend next to Silas, made her feel that a mother must be very precious; and she had again and again asked Silas to tell her how her mother looked, whom she was like, and how he had found her against the furze bush, led towards it by the little footsteps and the outstretched arms. The furze bush was there still; and this afternoon, when Eppie came out with Silas into the sunshine, it was the first object that arrested her eyes and thoughts.

'Father,' she said, in a tone of gentle gravity, which sometimes came like a sadder, slower cadence across her playfulness, 'we shall take the furze bush into the garden; it'll come into the corner, and just against it I'll put snowdrops and crocuses, 'cause Aaron says they won't die out, but 'll always get more and more.'

'Ah, child,' said Silas, always ready to talk when he had his pipe in his hand, apparently enjoying the pauses more than the puffs, 'it wouldn't do to leave out the furze bush; and there's nothing prettier, to my thinking, when it's yellow with flowers. But it's just come into my head what we're to do for a fence – mayhap Aaron can help us to a thought; but a fence we must have, else the donkeys and things 'ull come and trample everything down. And fencing's hard to be got at, by what I can make out.'

'O, I'll tell you, daddy,' said Eppie, clasping her hands suddenly, after a minute's thought. 'There's lots o' loose stones about, some of 'em not big, and we might lay 'em atop of one another and make a wall. You and me could carry the smallest, and Aaron 'ud carry the rest – I know he would.'

'Eh, my precious un,' said Silas, 'there isn't enough stones to go all round; and as for you carrying, why, wi' your little arms you couldn't carry a stone no bigger than a turnip. You're dilicate made, my dear,' he added, with a tender intonation – 'that's what Mrs Winthrop says.'

'O, I'm stronger than you think, daddy,' said Eppie; 'and if there wasn't stones enough to go all round, why they'll go part o' the way, and then it'll be easier to get sticks and things for the rest. See here, round the big pit, what a many stones!'

She skipped forward to the pit, meaning to lift one of the stones and exhibit her strength, but she started back in surprise.

'O, father, just come and look here,' she exclaimed – 'come and see how the water's gone down since yesterday. Why, yesterday the pit was ever so full!'

'Well, to be sure,' said Silas, coming to her side. 'Why, that's the draining they've begun on, since harvest, i' Mr Osgood's fields, I reckon. The foreman said to me the other day, when I passed by 'em, "Master Marner," he said, "I shouldn't wonder if we lay your bit o' waste as dry as a bone." It was Mr Godfrey Cass, he said, had gone into the draining: he'd been taking these fields o' Mr Osgood.'

'How odd it 'll seem to have the old pit dried up,' said Eppie, turning away, and stooping to lift rather a large stone. 'See, daddy, I can carry this quite well,' she said, going along with much energy for a few steps, but presently letting it fall.

'Ah, you're fine and strong, arn't you?' said Silas, while Eppie shook her aching arms and laughed. 'Come, come, let us go and sit down on the bank against the stile there, and have no more lifting. You might hurt yourself, child. You'd need have somebody to work for you – and my arm isn't over strong.'

Silas uttered the last sentence slowly, as if it implied more than met the ear; and Eppie, when they sat down on the bank, nestled close to his side, and, taking hold caressingly of the arm that was not over strong, held it on her lap, while Silas puffed again dutifully at the pipe, which occupied his other arm. An ash in the hedgerow behind made a fretted screen from the sun, and threw happy playful shadows all about them.

'Father,' said Eppie, very gently, after they had been sitting in silence a little while, 'if I was to be married, ought I to be married with my mother's ring?'

Silas gave an almost imperceptible start, though the question fell in with the undercurrent of thought in his own mind, and then said, in a subdued tone, 'Why, Eppie, have you been a-thinking on it?'

'Only this last week, father,' said Eppie, ingenuously, 'since Aaron talked to me about it.'

'And what did he say?' said Silas, still in the same subdued way, as if he were anxious lest he should fall into the slightest tone that was not for Eppie's good.

'He said he should like to be married, because he was a-going in four-and-twenty, and had got a deal of gardening work, now Mr Mott's given up; and he goes twice a-week regular to Mr Cass's, and once to Mr Osgood's, and they're going to take him on at the Rectory.'

'And who is it as he's wanting to marry?' said Silas, with rather a sad smile.

'Why, me, to be sure, daddy,' said Eppie, with dimpling laughter, kissing her father's cheek; 'as if he'd want to marry anybody else!'

'And you mean to have him, do you?' said Silas.

'Yes, sometime,' said Eppie, 'I don't know when. Everybody's married some-time, Aaron says. But I told him that wasn't true: for, I said, look at father – he's never been married.'

'No, child,' said Silas, 'your father was a lone man till you was sent to him.'

'But you'll never be lone again, father,' said Eppie, tenderly. 'That was what

Aaron said – "I could never think o' taking you away from Master Marner, Eppie." And I said, "It 'ud be no use if you did, Aaron." And he wants us all to live together, so as you needn't work a bit, father, only what's for your own pleasure; and he'd be as good as a son to you – that was what he said.'

'And should you like that, Eppie?' said Silas, looking at her.

'I shouldn't mind it, father,' said Eppie, quite simply. 'And I should like things to be so as you needn't work much. But if it wasn't for that, I'd sooner things didn't change. I'm very happy: I like Aaron to be fond of me, and come and see us often, and behave pretty to you – he always *does* behave pretty to you, doesn't he, father?'

'Yes, child, nobody could behave better,' said Silas, emphatically. 'He's his mother's lad.'

'But I don't want any change,' said Eppie. 'I should like to go on a long, long while, just as we are. Only Aaron does want a change; and he made me cry a bit – only a bit – because he said I didn't care for him, for if I cared for him I should want us to be married, as he did.'

'Eh, my blessed child,' said Silas, laying down his pipe as if it were useless to pretend to smoke any longer, 'you're o'er young to be married. We'll ask Mrs Winthrop – we'll ask Aaron's mother what *she* thinks: if there's a right thing to do, she'll come at it. But there's this to be thought on, Eppie: things *will* change, whether we like it or not; things won't go on for a long while just as they are and no difference. I shall get older and helplesser, and be a burden on you, belike, if I don't go away from you altogether. Not as I mean you'd think me a burden – I know you wouldn't – but it 'ud be hard upon you; and when I look for'ard to that, I like to think as you'd have somebody else besides me – somebody young and strong, as'll outlast your own life, and take care on you to the end.' Silas paused, and, resting his wrists on his knees, lifted his hands up and down meditatively as he looked on the ground.

'Then, would you like me to be married, father?' said Eppie, with a little trembling in her voice.

'I'll not be the man to say no, Eppie,' said Silas, emphatically; 'but we'll ask your godmother. She'll wish the right thing by you and her son too.'

'There they come then,' said Eppie. 'Let us go and meet 'em. O the pipe! won't you have it lit again, father?' said Eppie, lifting that medicinal appliance from the ground.

'Nay, child,' said Silas, 'I've done enough for today. I think, mayhap, a little of it does me more good than so much at once.'

Chapter 17

While Silas and Eppie were seated on the bank discoursing in the fleckered shade of the ash tree, Miss Priscilla Lammeter was resisting her sister's arguments, that it would be better to take tea at the Red House, and let her father have a long nap, than drive home to the Warrens so soon after dinner. The family party (of four only) were seated round the table in the dark wainscoted parlour, with the

Sunday dessert before them, of fresh filberts, apples, and pears, duly ornamented with leaves by Nancy's own hand before the bells had rung for church.

A great change has come over the dark wainscoted parlour since we saw it in Godfrey's bachelor days, and under the wifeless reign of the old Squire. Now all is polish, on which no yesterday's dust is ever allowed to settle, from the yard's width of oaken boards round the carpet, to the old Squire's gun and whips and walking-sticks, ranged on the stag's antlers above the mantelpiece. All other signs of sporting and outdoor occupation Nancy has removed to another room; but she has brought into the Red House the habit of filial reverence, and preserves sacredly in a place of honour these relics of her husband's departed father. The tankards are on the side-table still, but the bossed silver is undimmed by handling, and there are no dregs to send forth unpleasant suggestions: the only prevailing scent is of the lavender and rose-leaves that fill the vases of Derbyshire spar. All is purity and order in this once dreary room, for, fifteen years ago, it was entered by a new presiding spirit.

'Now, father,' said Nancy, '*is* there any call for you to go home to tea? Mayn't you just as well stay with us? – such a beautiful evening as it's likely to be.'

The old gentleman had been talking with Godfrey about the increasing poor-rate and the ruinous times, and had not heard the dialogue between his daughters.

'My dear, you must ask Priscilla,' he said, in the once firm voice, now become rather broken. 'She manages me and the farm too.'

'And reason good as I should manage you, father,' said Priscilla, 'else you'd be giving yourself your death with rheumatism. And as for the farm, if anything turns out wrong, as it can't but do in these times, there's nothing kills a man so soon as having nobody to find fault with but himself. It's a deal the best way o' being master, to let somebody else do the ordering, and keep the blaming in your own hands. It 'ud save many a man a stroke, *I* believe.'

'Well, well, my dear,' said her father, with a quiet laugh, 'I didn't say you don't manage for everybody's good.'

'Then manage so as you may stay tea, Priscilla,' said Nancy, putting her hand on her sister's arm affectionately. 'Come now; and we'll go round the garden while father has his nap.'

'My dear child, he'll have a beautiful nap in the gig, for I shall drive. And as for staying tea, I can't hear of it; for there's this dairymaid, now she knows she's to be married, turned Michaelmas, she'd as like pour the new milk into the pig-trough as into the pans. That's the way with 'em all: it's as if they thought the world 'ud be new-made because they're to be married. So come and let me put my bonnet on, and there'll be time for us to walk round the garden while the horse is being put in.'

When the sisters were treading the neatly-swept garden-walks, between the bright turf that contrasted pleasantly with the dark cones and arches and wall-like hedges of yew, Priscilla said, 'I'm as glad as anything at your husband's making that exchange o' land with cousin Osgood, and beginning the dairying. It's a thousand pities you didn't do it before; for it'll give you something to fill your mind. There's nothing like a dairy if folks want a bit o' worrit to make the days pass. For as for rubbing furniture, when you can once see your face in a table there's nothing else to look for; but there's always something fresh with the dairy; for even in the depths o' winter there's some pleasure in conquering the butter, and making it come whether or no. My dear,' added Priscilla, pressing her sister's hand affectionately as they walked side by side, 'you'll never be low when you've got a dairy.'

'Ah, Priscilla,' said Nancy, returning the pressure with a grateful glance of her clear eyes, 'but it won't make up to Godfrey: a dairy's not so much to a man. And it's only what he cares for that ever makes me low. I'm contented with the blessings we have, if he could be contented.'

'It drives me past patience,' said Priscilla, impetuously, 'that way o' the men – always wanting and wanting, and never easy with what they've got: they can't sit comfortable in their chairs when they've neither ache nor pain, but either they must stick a pipe in their mouths, to make 'em better than well, or else they must be swallowing something strong, though they're forced to make haste before the next meal comes in. But, joyful be it spoken, our father was never that sort o' man. And if it had pleased God to make you ugly, like me, so as the men wouldn't ha' run after you, we might have kept to our own family, and had nothing to do with folks as have got uneasy blood in their veins.'

'O don't say so, Priscilla,' said Nancy, repenting that she had called forth this outburst; 'nobody has any occasion to find fault with Godfrey. It's natural he should be disappointed at not having any children: every man likes to have somebody to work for and lay by for, and he always counted so on making a fuss with 'em when they were little. There's many another man 'ud hanker more than he does. He's the best of husbands.'

'O, I know,' said Priscilla, smiling sarcastically, 'I know the way o' wives; they set one on to abuse their husbands, and then they turn round on one and praise 'em as if they wanted to sell 'em. But father'll be waiting for me; we must turn now.'

The large gig with the steady old grey was at the front door, and Mr Lammeter was already on the stone steps, passing the time in recalling to Godfrey what very fine points Speckle had when his master used to ride him.

'I always *would* have a good horse, you know,' said the old gentleman, not liking that spirited time to be quite effaced from the memory of his juniors.

'Mind you bring Nancy to the Warrens before the week's out, Mr Cass,' was Priscilla's parting injunction, as she took the reins, and shook them gently, by way of friendly incitement to Speckle.

'I shall just take a turn to the fields against the Stone-pits, Nancy, and look at the draining,' said Godfrey.

'You'll be in again by teatime, dear?'

'O yes, I shall be back in an hour.'

It was Godfrey's custom on a Sunday afternoon to do a little contemplative farming in a leisurely walk. Nancy seldom accompanied him; for the women of her generation – unless, like Priscilla, they took to outdoor management – were not given to much walking beyond their own house and garden, finding sufficient exercise in domestic duties. So, when Priscilla was not with her, she usually sat with Mant's Bible before her, and after following the text with her eyes for a little while, she would gradually permit them to wander as her thoughts had already insisted on wandering.

But Nancy's Sunday thoughts were rarely quite out of keeping with the devout and reverential intention implied by the book spread open before her. She was not theologically instructed enough to discern very clearly the relation between the sacred documents of the past which she opened without method, and her own obscure, simple life; but the spirit of rectitude, and the sense of responsibility for the effect of her conduct on others, which were strong elements in Nancy's character, had made it a habit with her to scrutinise her past feelings and actions with self-questioning solicitude. Her mind not being courted by a great variety of subjects, she filled the vacant moments by living inwardly, again and again, through all her remembered experience, especially through the fifteen years of her married time, in which her life and its significance had been doubled. She recalled the small details, the words, tones, and looks, in the critical scenes which had opened a new epoch for her, by giving her a deeper insight into the relations and trials of life, or which had called on her for some little effort of forbearance, or of painful adherence to an imagined or real duty – asking herself continually whether she had been in any respect blamable. This excessive rumination and self-questioning is perhaps a morbid habit inevitable to a mind of much moral sensibility when shut out from its due share of outward activity and of practical claims on its affections – inevitable to a noble-hearted, childless woman, when her lot is narrow. 'I can do so little – have I done it all well?' is the perpetually recurring thought; and there are no voices calling her away from that soliloquy, no peremptory demands to divert energy from vain regret or superfluous scruple.

There was one main thread of painful experience in Nancy's married life, and on it hung certain deeply-felt scenes, which were the oftenest revived in retrospect. The short dialogue with Priscilla in the garden had determined the current of retrospect in that frequent direction this particular Sunday afternoon. The first wandering of her thought from the text, which she still attempted dutifully to follow with her eyes and silent lips, was into an imaginary enlargement of the defence she had set up for her husband against Priscilla's implied blame. The vindication of the loved object is the best balm affection can find for its wounds: – 'A man must have so much on his mind,' is the belief by which a wife often supports a cheerful face under rough answers and unfeeling words. And Nancy's deepest wounds had all come from the perception that the absence of children from their hearth was dwelt on in her husband's mind as a privation to which he could not reconcile himself.

Yet sweet Nancy might have been expected to feel still more keenly the denial of a blessing to which she had looked forward with all the varied expectations and preparations, solemn and prettily trivial, which fill the mind of a loving woman when she expects to become a mother. Was there not a drawer filled with the neat work of her hands, all unworn and untouched, just as she had arranged it there fourteen years ago – just, but for one little dress, which had been made the burial-dress? But under this immediate personal trial Nancy was so firmly unmurmuring, that years ago she had suddenly renounced the habit of visiting this drawer, lest she should in this way be cherishing a longing for what was not given.

Perhaps it was this very severity towards any indulgence of what she held to be sinful regret in herself, that made her shrink from applying her own standard to her husband. 'It was very different – it was much worse for a man to be disappointed in that way: a woman could always be satisfied with devoting herself to her husband, but a man wanted something that would make him look forward more – and sitting by the fire was so much duller to him than to a woman.' And always, when Nancy reached this point in her meditations – trying, with predetermined sympathy, to see everything as Godfrey saw it – there came a renewal of self-questioning. *Had* she done everything in her power to lighten Godfrey's privation? Had she really been right in the resistance which had cost her so much pain six years ago, and again four years ago – the resistance to her husband's wish that they should adopt a child? Adoption was more remote from the ideas and habits of that time than of our own; still Nancy had her opinion on it. It was as necessary to her mind to have an opinion on all topics, not exclusively masculine, that had come under her notice, as for her to have a precisely marked place for every article of her personal property: and her opinions were always principles, to be unwaveringly acted on. They were firm, not because of their basis, but because she held them with a tenacity inseparable from her mental action. On all the duties and proprieties of life, from filial behaviour to the arrangement of the evening toilette, pretty Nancy Lammeter, by the time she was three-and-twenty, had her unalterable little code, and had formed every one of her habits in strict accordance with that code. She carried these decided judgements within her in the most unobtrusive way: they rooted themselves in her mind, and grew there as quietly as grass. Years ago, we know, she insisted on dressing like Priscilla, because 'it was right for sisters to dress alike,' and because 'she would do what was right if she wore a gown dyed with cheese-colouring.' That was a trivial but typical instance of the mode in which Nancy's life was regulated.

It was one of those rigid principles, and no petty egoistic feeling, which had been the ground of Nancy's difficult resistance to her husband's wish. To adopt a child, because children of your own had been denied you, was to try and choose your lot in spite of Providence: the adopted child, she was convinced, would never turn out well, and would be a curse to those who had wilfully and rebelliously sought what it was clear that, for some high reason, they were better without. When you saw a thing was not meant to be, said Nancy, it was a bounden duty to leave off so much as wishing for it. And so far, perhaps, the wisest of men could scarcely make more than a verbal improvement in her principle. But the conditions under which she held it apparent that a thing was not meant to be, depended on a more peculiar mode of thinking. She would have given up making a purchase at a particular place if, on three successive times, rain, or some other cause of Heaven's sending, had formed an obstacle; and she would have anticipated a broken limb or other heavy misfortune to anyone who persisted in spite of such indications.

'But why should you think the child would turn out ill?' said Godfrey, in his remonstrances. 'She has thriven as well as child can do with the weaver; and *he* adopted her. There isn't such a pretty little girl anywhere else in the parish, or one fitter for the station we could give her. Where can be the likelihood of her being a curse to anybody?'

'Yes, my dear Godfrey,' said Nancy, who was sitting with her hands tightly clasped together, with yearning, regretful affection in her eyes. 'The child may not turn out ill with the weaver. But, then, he didn't go to seek her, as we should be doing. It will be wrong: I feel sure it will. Don't you remember what that lady we met at the Royston Baths told us about the child her sister adopted? That was the only adopting I ever heard of: and the child was transported when it was twenty-three. Dear Godfrey, don't ask me to do what I know is wrong: I should never be happy again. I know it's very hard for *you* – it's easier for me – but it's the will of Providence.'

It might seem singular that Nancy – with her religious theory pieced together out of narrow social traditions, fragments of church doctrine imperfectly under-stood, and girlish reasonings on her small experience – should have arrived by herself at a way of thinking so nearly akin to that of many devout people, whose beliefs are held in the shape of a system quite remote from her knowledge – singular, if we did not know that human beliefs, like all other natural growths, elude the barriers of system.

Godfrey had from the first specified Eppie, then about twelve years old, as a child suitable for them to adopt. It had never occurred to him that Silas would rather part with his life than with Eppie. Surely the weaver would wish the best to the child he had taken so much trouble with, and would be glad that such good fortune should happen to her: she would always be very grateful to him, and he would be well provided for to the end of his life – provided for as the excellent part he had done by the child deserved. Was it not an appropriate thing for people in a higher station to take a charge off the hands of a man in a lower? It seemed an eminently appropriate thing to Godfrey, for reasons that were known only to himself; and by a common fallacy, he imagined the measure would be easy because he had private motives for desiring it. This was rather a coarse mode of estimating Silas's relation to Eppie; but we must remember that many of the impressions which Godfrey was likely to gather concerning the labouring people around him would favour the idea that deep affections can hardly go along with callous palms and scant means; and he had not had the opportunity, even if he had had the power, of entering intimately into all that was exceptional in the weaver's experience. It was only the want of adequate knowledge that could have made it possible for Godfrey deliberately to entertain an unfeeling project: his natural kindness had outlived that blighting time of cruel wishes, and Nancy's praise of him as a husband was not founded entirely on a wilful illusion.

'I was right,' she said to herself, when she had recalled all their scenes of discussion – 'I feel I was right to say him nay, though it hurt me more than anything; but how good Godfrey has been about it! Many men would have been very angry with me for standing out against their wishes; and they might have thrown out that they'd had ill-luck in marrying me; but Godfrey has never been the man to say me an unkind word. It's only what he can't hide: everything seems so blank to him, I know; and the land – what a difference it 'ud make to him, when he goes to see after things, if he'd children growing up that he was doing it all for! But I won't murmur; and perhaps if he'd married a woman who'd have had children, she'd have vexed him in other ways.'

This possibility was Nancy's chief comfort; and to give it greater strength, she laboured to make it impossible that any other wife should have had more perfect tenderness. She had been *forced* to vex him by that one denial. Godfrey was not insensible to her loving effort, and did Nancy no injustice as to the motives of her obstinacy. It was impossible to have lived with her fifteen years and not be aware that an unselfish clinging to the right, and a sincerity clear as the flower-born dew, were her main characteristics; indeed, Godfrey felt this so strongly, that his own more wavering nature, too averse to facing difficulty to be unvaryingly simple and truthful, was kept in a certain awe of this gentle wife who watched his looks with a yearning to obey them. It seemed to him impossible that he should ever confess to her the truth about Eppie: she would never recover from the repulsion the story of his earlier marriage would create, told to her now, after that long concealment. And the child, too, he thought, must become an object of repulsion: the very sight of her would be painful. The shock to Nancy's mingled pride and ignorance of the world's evil might even be too much for her delicate frame. Since he had married her with that secret on his heart, he must keep it there to the last. Whatever else he did, he could not make an irreparable breach between himself and this long-loved wife.

Meanwhile, why could he not make up his mind to the absence of children from a hearth brightened by such a wife? Why did his mind fly uneasily to that void, as if it were the sole reason why life was not thoroughly joyous to him? I suppose it is the way with all men and women who reach middle age without the clear perception that life never *can* be thoroughly joyous: under the vague dulness of the grey hours, dissatisfaction seeks a definite object, and finds it in the privation of an untried good. Dissatisfaction, seated musingly on a childless hearth, thinks with envy of the father whose return is greeted by young voices – seated at the meal where the little heads rise one above another like nursery plants, it sees a black care hovering behind every one of them, and thinks the impulses by which men abandon freedom, and seek for ties, are surely nothing but a brief madness. In Godfrey's case there were further reasons why his thoughts should be continually solicited by this one point in his lot: his conscience, never thoroughly easy about Eppie, now gave his childless home the aspect of a retribution; and as the time passed on, under Nancy's refusal to adopt her, any retrieval of his error became more and more difficult.

On this Sunday afternoon it was already four years since there had been any allusion to the subject between them, and Nancy supposed that it was for ever buried.

'I wonder if he'll mind it less or more as he gets older,' she thought; 'I'm afraid more. Aged people feel the miss of children: what would father do without Priscilla? And if I die, Godfrey will be very lonely – not holding together with his brothers much. But I won't be over-anxious, and trying to make things out beforehand: I must do my best for the present.'

With that last thought Nancy roused herself from her reverie, and turned her eyes again towards the forsaken page. It had been forsaken longer than she imagined, for she was presently surprised by the appearance of the servant with the tea-things. It was, in fact, a little before the usual time for tea; but Jane had her reasons.

'Is your master come into the yard, Jane?'

'No 'm, he isn't,' said Jane, with a slight emphasis, of which, however, her mistress took no notice.

'I don't know whether you've seen 'em, 'm,' continued Jane, after a pause, 'but there's folks making haste all one way, afore the front window. I doubt something's happened. There's niver a man to be seen i' the yard, else I'd send and see. I've been up into the top attic, but there's no seeing anything for trees. I hope nobody's hurt, that's all.'

'O, no, I dare say there's nothing much the matter,' said Nancy. 'It's perhaps Mr Snell's bull got out again, as he did before.'

'I wish he mayn't gore anybody, then, that's all,' said Jane, not altogether despising a hypothesis which covered a few imaginary calamities.

'That girl is always terrifying me,' thought Nancy; 'I wish Godfrey would come in.'

She went to the front window and looked as far as she could see along the road, with an uneasiness which she felt to be childish, for there were now no such signs of excitement as Jane had spoken of, and Godfrey would not be likely to return by the village road, but by the fields.

She continued to stand, however, looking at the placid churchyard with the long shadows of the gravestones across the bright green hillocks, and at the glowing autumn colours of the Rectory trees beyond. Before such calm external beauty the presence of a vague fear is more distinctly felt – like a raven flapping its slow wing across the sunny air. Nancy wished more and more that Godfrey would come in.

Chapter 18

Someone opened the door at the other end of the room, and Nancy felt that it was her husband. She turned from the window with gladness in her eyes, for the wife's chief dread was stilled.

'Dear, I'm so thankful you're come,' she said, going towards him. 'I began to get . . .'

She paused abruptly, for Godfrey was laying down his hat with trembling hands, and turned towards her with a pale face and a strange unanswering glance, as if he saw her indeed, but saw her as part of a scene invisible to herself. She laid her hand on his arm, not daring to speak again; but he left the touch unnoticed, and threw himself into his chair.

Jane was already at the door with the hissing urn. 'Tell her to keep away, will you?' said Godfrey; and when the door was closed again he exerted himself to speak more distinctly.

'Sit down, Nancy – there,' he said, pointing to a chair opposite him. 'I came back as soon as I could, to hinder anybody's telling you but me. I've had a great shock – but I care most about the shock it'll be to you.'

'It isn't father and Priscilla?' said Nancy, with quivering lips, clasping her hands together tightly on her lap.

'No, it's nobody living,' said Godfrey, unequal to the considerate skill with which he would have wished to make his revelation. 'It's Dunstan – my brother Dunstan, that we lost sight of sixteen years ago. We've found him – found his body – his skeleton.'

The deep dread Godfrey's look had created in Nancy made her feel these words a relief. She sat in comparative calmness to hear what else he had to tell. He went on: 'The Stone-pit has gone dry suddenly – from the draining, I suppose; and there he lies – has lain for sixteen years, wedged between two great stones. There's his watch and seals, and there's my gold-handled hunting-whip, with my name on: he took it away, without my knowing, the day he went hunting on Wildfire, the last time he was seen.'

Godfrey paused: it was not so easy to say what came next. 'Do you think he drowned himself?' said Nancy, almost wondering that her husband should be so deeply shaken by what had happened all those years ago to an unloved brother, of whom worse things had been augured.

'No, he fell in,' said Godfrey, in a low but distinct voice, as if he felt some deep meaning in the fact. Presently he added: 'Dunstan was the man that robbed Silas Marner.'

The blood rushed to Nancy's face and neck at this surprise and shame, for she had been bred up to regard even a distant kinship with crime as a dishonour.

'O Godfrey!' she said, with compassion in her tone, for she had immediately reflected that the dishonour must be felt still more keenly by her husband.

'There was the money in the pit,' he continued – 'all the weaver's money. Everything's being gathered up, and they're taking the skeleton to the Rainbow. But I came back to tell you: there was no hindering it; you must know.'

He was silent, looking on the ground for two long minutes. Nancy would have said some words of comfort under this disgrace, but she refrained, from an instinctive sense that there was something behind – that Godfrey had something else to tell her. Presently he lifted his eyes to her face, and kept them fixed on her, as he said: 'Everything comes to light, Nancy, sooner or later. When God Almighty wills it, our secrets are found out. I've lived with a secret on my mind, but I'll keep it from you no longer. I wouldn't have you know it by somebody else, and not by me – I wouldn't have you find it out after I'm dead. I'll tell you now. It's been "I will" and "I won't" with me all my life – I'll make sure of myself now.'

Nancy's utmost dread had returned. The eyes of the husband and wife met with awe in them, as at a crisis which suspended affection.

'Nancy,' said Godfrey, slowly, 'when I married you, I hid something from you – something I ought to have told you. That woman Marner found dead in the snow – Eppie's mother – that wretched woman – was my wife: Eppie is my child.'

He paused, dreading the effect of his confession. But Nancy sat quite still, only that her eyes dropped and ceased to meet his. She was pale and quiet as a meditative statue, clasping her hands on her lap.

'You'll never think the same of me again,' said Godfrey, after a little while, with some tremor in his voice.

She was silent.

'I oughtn't to have left the child unowned: I oughtn't to have kept it from you. But I couldn't bear to give you up, Nancy. I was led away into marrying her – I suffered for it.'

Still Nancy was silent, looking down; and he almost expected that she would presently get up and say she would go to her father's. How could she have any mercy for faults that must seem so black to her, with her simple, severe notions?

But at last she lifted up her eyes to his again and spoke. There was no indignation in her voice – only deep regret.

'Godfrey, if you had but told me this six years ago, we could have done some of our duty by the child. Do you think I'd have refused to take her in, if I'd known she was yours?'

At that moment Godfrey felt all the bitterness of an error that was not simply futile, but had defeated its own end. He had not measured this wife with whom he had lived so long. But she spoke again, with more agitation.

'And – O, Godfrey – if we'd had her from the first, if you'd taken to her as you ought, she'd have loved me for her mother – and you'd have been happier with me: I could better have bore my little baby dying, and our life might have been more like what we used to think it 'ud be.'

The tears fell, and Nancy ceased to speak.

'But you wouldn't have married me then, Nancy, if I'd told you,' said Godfrey, urged, in the bitterness of his self-reproach, to prove to himself that his conduct had not been utter folly. 'You may think you would now, but you wouldn't then. With your pride and your father's, you'd have hated having anything to do with me after the talk there'd have been.'

'I can't say what I should have done about that, Godfrey. I should never have married anybody else. But I wasn't worth doing wrong for – nothing is in this world. Nothing is so good as it seems beforehand – not even our marrying wasn't, you see.' There was a faint sad smile on Nancy's face as she said the last words.

'I'm a worse man than you thought I was, Nancy,' said Godfrey, rather tremulously. 'Can you forgive me ever?'

'The wrong to me is but little, Godfrey: you've made it up to me – you've been good to me for fifteen years. It's another you did the wrong to; and I doubt it can never be all made up for.'

'But we can take Eppie now,' said Godfrey. 'I won't mind the world knowing at last. I'll be plain and open for the rest o' my life.'

'It'll be different coming to us, now she's grown up,' said Nancy, shaking her head sadly. 'But it's your duty to acknowledge her and provide for her; and I'll do my part by her, and pray to God Almighty to make her love me.'

'Then we'll go together to Silas Marner's this very night, as soon as every- thing's quiet at the Stone-pits.'

Between eight and nine o'clock that evening, Eppie and Silas were seated alone in the cottage. After the great excitement the weaver had undergone from the events of the afternoon, he had felt a longing for this quietude, and had even begged Mrs Winthrop and Aaron, who had naturally lingered behind everyone else, to leave him alone with his child. The excitement had not passed away: it had only reached that stage when the keenness of the susceptibility makes external stimulus intolerable – when there is no sense of weariness, but rather an intensity of inward life, under which sleep is an impossibility. Anyone who has watched such moments in other men remembers the brightness of the eyes and the strange definiteness that comes over coarse features from that transient influence. It is as if a new fineness of ear for all spiritual voices had sent wonder-working vibrations through the heavy mortal frame – as if 'beauty born of murmuring sound' had passed into the face of the listener.

Silas's face showed that sort of transfiguration, as he sat in his armchair and looked at Eppie. She had drawn her own chair towards his knees, and leaned forward, holding both his hands, while she looked up at him. On the table near them, lit by a candle, lay the recovered gold – the old long-loved gold, ranged in orderly heaps, as Silas used to range it in the days when it was his only joy. He had been telling her how he used to count it every night, and how his soul was utterly desolate till she was sent to him.

'At first, I'd a sort o' feeling come across me now and then,' he was saying in a subdued tone, 'as if you might be changed into the gold again; for sometimes, turn my head which way I would, I seemed to see the gold; and I thought I should be glad if I could feel it, and find it was come back. But that didn't last long. After a bit, I should have thought it was a curse come again, if it had drove you from me, for I'd got to feel the need o' your looks and your voice and the touch o' your little fingers. You didn't know then, Eppie, when you were such a little un – you didn't know what your old father Silas felt for you.'

'But I know now, father,' said Eppie. 'If it hadn't been for you, they'd have taken me to the workhouse, and there'd have been nobody to love me.'

'Eh, my precious child, the blessing was mine. If you hadn't been sent to save me, I should ha' gone to the grave in my misery. The money was taken away from me in time; and you see it's been kept – kept till it was wanted for you. It's wonderful – our life is wonderful.'

Silas sat in silence a few minutes, looking at the money. 'It takes no hold of me now,' he said, ponderingly – 'the money doesn't. I wonder if it ever could again – I doubt it might, if I lost you, Eppie. I might come to think I was forsaken again, and lose the feeling that God was good to me.'

At that moment there was a knocking at the door; and Eppie was obliged to rise without answering Silas. Beautiful she looked, with the tenderness of gathering tears in her eyes and a slight flush on her cheeks, as she stepped to open the door. The flush deepened when she saw Mr and Mrs Godfrey Cass.

She made her little rustic curtsy, and held the door wide for them to enter.

'We're disturbing you very late, my dear,' said Mrs Cass, taking Eppie's hand, and looking in her face with an expression of anxious interest and admiration. Nancy herself was pale and tremulous.

Eppie, after placing chairs for Mr and Mrs Cass, went to stand against Silas, opposite to them.

'Well, Marner,' said Godfrey, trying to speak with perfect firmness, 'it's a great comfort to me to see you with your money again, that you've been deprived of so many years. It was one of my family did you the wrong – the more grief to me – and I feel bound to make up to you for it in every way. Whatever I can do for you will be nothing but paying a debt, even if I looked no farther than the robbery. But there are other things I'm beholden – shall be beholden to you for, Marner.'

Godfrey checked himself. It had been agreed between him and his wife that the subject of his fatherhood should be approached very carefully, and that, if possible, the disclosure should be reserved for the future, so that it might be made to Eppie gradually. Nancy had urged this, because she felt strongly the painful light in which Eppie must inevitably see the relation between her father and mother.

Silas, always ill at ease when he was being spoken to by 'betters,' such as Mr Cass – tall, powerful, florid men, seen chiefly on horseback – answered with some constraint: 'Sir, I've a deal to thank you for a'ready. As for the robbery, I count it no loss to me. And if I did, you couldn't help it: you aren't answerable for it.'

'You may look at it in that way, Marner, but I never can; and I hope you'll let me act according to my own feeling of what's just. I know you're easily contented: you've been a hard-working man all your life.'

'Yes, sir, yes,' said Marner, meditatively. 'I should ha' been bad off without my work: it was what I held by when everything else was gone from me.'

'Ah,' said Godfrey, applying Marner's words simply to his bodily wants, 'it was a good trade for you in this country, because there's been a great deal of linen-weaving to be done. But you're getting rather past such close work, Marner: it's time you laid by and had some rest. You look a good deal pulled down, though you're not an old man, *are* you?'

'Fifty-five, as near as I can say, sir,' said Silas.

'O, why, you may live thirty years longer – look at old Macey! And that money on the table, after all, is but little. It won't go far either way – whether it's put out to interest, or you were to live on it as long as it would last: it wouldn't go far if you'd nobody to keep but yourself, and you've had two to keep for a good many years now.'

'Eh, sir,' said Silas, unaffected by anything Godfrey was saying, 'I'm in no fear o' want. We shall do very well – Eppie and me 'ull do well enough. There's few working-folks have got so much laid by as that. I don't know what it is to gentlefolks, but I look upon it as a deal – almost too much. And as for us, it's little we want.'

'Only the garden, father,' said Eppie, blushing up to the ears the moment after.

'You love a garden, do you, my dear?' said Nancy, thinking that this turn in the point of view might help her husband. 'We should agree in that: I give a deal of time to the garden.'

'Ah, there's plenty of gardening at the Red House,' said Godfrey, surprised at the difficulty he found in approaching a proposition which had seemed so easy to him in the distance. 'You've done a good part by Eppie, Marner, for sixteen years. It 'ud be a great comfort to you to see her well provided for, wouldn't it? She looks blooming and healthy, but not fit for any hardships: she doesn't look like a strapping girl come of working parents. You'd like to see her taken care of by those who can leave her well off, and make a lady of her; she's more fit for it than for a rough life, such as she might come to have in a few years' time.'

A slight flush came over Marner's face, and disappeared, like a passing gleam. Eppie was simply wondering Mr Cass should talk so about things that seemed to have nothing to do with reality; but Silas was hurt and uneasy.

'I don't take your meaning, sir,' he answered, not having words at command to express the mingled feelings with which he had heard Mr Cass's words.

'Well, my meaning is this, Marner,' said Godfrey, determined to come to the point. 'Mrs Cass and I, you know, have no children – nobody to benefit by our good home and everything else we have – more than enough for ourselves. And we should like to have somebody in the place of a daughter to us – we should like to have Eppie, and treat her in every way as our own child. It would be a great comfort to you in your old age, I hope, to see her fortune made in that way, after you have been at the trouble of bringing her up so well. And it's right you should have every reward for that. And Eppie, I'm sure, will always love you and be grateful to you: she'd come and see you very often, and we should all be on the look-out to do everything we could towards making you comfortable.'

A plain man like Godfrey Cass, speaking under some embarrassment, necessarily blunders on words that are coarser than his intentions, and that are likely to fall gratingly on susceptible feelings. While he had been speaking, Eppie had quietly passed her arm behind Silas's head, and let her hand rest against it caressingly: she felt him trembling violently. He was silent for some moments when Mr Cass had ended – powerless under the conflict of emotions, all alike painful. Eppie's heart was swelling at the sense that her father was in distress; and she was just going to lean down and speak to him, when one struggling dread at last gained the mastery over every other in Silas, and he said, faintly: 'Eppie, my child, speak. I won't stand in your way. Thank Mr and Mrs Cass.'

Eppie took her hand from her father's head, and came forward a step. Her cheeks were flushed, but not with shyness this time: the sense that her father was in doubt and suffering banished that sort of self-consciousness. She dropped a low curtsy, first to Mrs Cass and then to Mr Cass, and said: 'Thank you, ma'am – thank you, sir. But I can't leave my father, nor own anybody nearer than him. And I don't want to be a lady – thank you all the same' (here Eppie dropped another curtsy). 'I couldn't give up the folks I've been used to.'

Eppie's lip began to tremble a little at the last words. She retreated to her father's chair again, and held him round the neck; while Silas, with a subdued sob, put up his hand to grasp hers.

The tears were in Nancy's eyes, but her sympathy with Eppie was, naturally, divided with distress on her husband's account. She dared not speak, wondering what was going on in her husband's mind.

Godfrey felt an irritation inevitable to almost all of us when we encounter an unexpected obstacle. He had been full of his own penitence and resolution to retrieve his error as far as the time was left to him; he was possessed with all-important feelings, that were to lead to a predetermined course of action which he had fixed on as the right, and he was not prepared to enter with lively appreciation into other people's feelings counteracting his virtuous resolves. The agitation with which he spoke again was not quite unmixed with anger.

'But I have a claim on you, Eppie – the strongest of all claims. It is my duty, Marner, to own Eppie as my child, and provide for her. She is my own child – her mother was my wife. I have a natural claim on her that must stand before every other.'

Eppie had given a violent start, and turned quite pale. Silas, on the contrary, who had been relieved, by Eppie's answer, from the dread lest his mind should be in opposition to hers, felt the spirit of resistance in him set free, not without a touch of parental fierceness. 'Then, sir,' he answered, with an accent of bitterness that had been silent in him since the memorable day when his youthful hope had perished – 'then, sir, why didn't you say so sixteen year ago, and claim her before I'd come to love her, i'stead o' coming to take her from me now, when you might as well take the heart out o' my body? God gave her to me because you turned your back upon her, and He looks upon her as mine: you've no right to her! When a man turns a blessing from his door, it falls to them as take it in.'

'I know that, Marner. I was wrong. I've repented of my conduct in that matter,' said Godfrey, who could not help feeling the edge of Silas's words.

'I'm glad to hear it, sir,' said Marner, with gathering excitement; 'but repentance doesn't alter what's been going on for sixteen year. Your coming now and saying "I'm her father" doesn't alter the feelings inside us. It's me she's been calling her father ever since she could say the word.'

'But I think you might look at the thing more reasonably, Marner,' said Godfrey, unexpectedly awed by the weaver's direct truth-speaking. 'It isn't as if she was to be taken quite away from you, so that you'd never see her again. She'll be very near you, and come to see you very often. She'll feel just the same towards you.'

'Just the same?' said Marner, more bitterly than ever. 'How'll she feel just the same for me as she does now, when we eat o' the same bit, and drink o' the same cup, and think o' the same things from one day's end to another? Just the same? that's idle talk. You'd cut us i' two.'

Godfrey, unqualified by experience to discern the pregnancy of Marner's simple words, felt rather angry again. It seemed to him that the weaver was very selfish (a judgement readily passed by those who have never tested their own power of sacrifice) to oppose what was undoubtedly for Eppie's welfare; and he felt himself called upon, for her sake, to assert his authority.

'I should have thought, Marner,' he said, severely – 'I should have thought your affection for Eppie would have made you rejoice in what was for her good, even if it did call upon you to give up something. You ought to remember that your own life is uncertain, and that she's at an age now when her lot may soon be fixed in a way very different from what it would be in her father's home: she may marry some low working-man, and then, whatever I might do for her, I couldn't make her well-off. You're putting yourself in the way of her welfare; and though I'm sorry to hurt you after what you've done, and what I've left undone, I feel now it's my duty to insist on taking care of my own daughter. I want to do my duty.'

It would be difficult to say whether it were Silas or Eppie that was most deeply stirred by this last speech of Godfrey's. Thought had been very busy in Eppie as she listened to the contest between her old long-loved father and this new unfamiliar father who had suddenly come to fill the place of that black feature-less shadow which had held the ring and placed it on her mother's finger. Her imagination had darted backward in conjectures, and forward in previsions, of what this revealed fatherhood implied; and there were words in Godfrey's last speech which helped to make the previsions especially definite. Not that these thoughts, either of past or future, determined her resolution – that was determined by the feelings which vibrated to every word Silas had uttered; but they raised, even apart from these feeling, a repulsion towards the offered lot and the newly-revealed father.

Silas, on the other hand, was again stricken in conscience, and alarmed lest Godfrey's accusation should be true – lest he should be raising his own will as an obstacle to Eppie's good. For many moments he was mute, struggling for the self-conquest necessary to the uttering of the difficult words. They came out tremulously.

'I'll say no more. Let it be as you will. Speak to the child. I'll hinder nothing.'

Even Nancy, with all the acute sensibility of her own affections, shared her husband's view, that Marner was not justifiable in his wish to retain Eppie, after her real father had avowed himself. She felt that it was a very hard trial for the poor weaver, but her code allowed no question that a father by blood must have a claim above that of any foster-father. Besides, Nancy, used all her life to plenteous circumstances and the privileges of 'respectability', could not enter into the pleasures which early nurture and habit connect with all the little aims and efforts of the poor who are born poor: to her mind, Eppie, in being restored to her birthright, was entering on a too long withheld but unquestionable good. Hence she heard Silas's last words with relief, and thought, as Godfrey did, that their wish was achieved.

'Eppie, my dear,' said Godfrey, looking at his daughter, not without some embarrassment, under the sense that she was old enough to judge him, 'it'll always be our wish that you should show your love and gratitude to one who's been a father to you so many years, and we shall want to help you to make him comfortable in every way. But we hope you'll come to love us as well; and though I haven't been what a father should have been to you all these years, I wish to do the utmost in my power for you for the rest of my life, and provide for you as my only child. And you'll have the best of mothers in my wife – that'll be a blessing you haven't known since you were old enough to know it.'

'My dear, you'll be a treasure to me,' said Nancy, in her gentle voice. 'We shall want for nothing when we have our daughter.'

Eppie did not come forward and curtsy, as she had done before. She held Silas's hand in hers, and grasped it firmly – it was a weaver's hand, with a palm and fingertips that were sensitive to such pressure – while she spoke with colder decision than before.

'Thank you, ma'am – thank you, sir, for your offers – they're very great, and far above my wish. For I should have no delight i' life any more if I was forced to go away from my father, and knew he was sitting at home, a-thinking of me and feeling lone. We've been used to be happy together every day, and I can't think o' no happiness without him. And he says he'd nobody i' the world till I was sent to him, and he'd have nothing when I was gone. And he's took care of me and loved me from the first, and I'll cleave to him as long as he lives, and nobody shall ever come between him and me.'

'But you must make sure, Eppie,' said Silas, in a low voice – 'you must make sure as you won't ever be sorry, because you've made your choice to stay among poor folks, and with poor clothes and things, when you might ha' had everything o' the best.'

His sensitiveness on this point had increased as he listened to Eppie's words of faithful affection.

'I can never be sorry, father,' said Eppie. 'I shouldn't know what to think on or to wish for with fine things about me, as I haven't been used to. And it 'ud be poor work for me to put on things, and ride in a gig, and sit in a place at church, as 'ud make them as I'm fond of think me unfitting company for 'em. What could *I* care for then?'

Nancy looked at Godfrey with a pained questioning glance. But his eyes were fixed on the floor, where he was moving the end of his stick, as if he were pondering on something absently. She thought there was a word which might perhaps come better from her lips than from his.

'What you say is natural, my dear child – it's natural you should cling to those who've brought you up,' she said, mildly; 'but there's a duty you owe to your lawful father. There's perhaps something to be given up on more sides than one. When your father opens his home to you, I think it's right you shouldn't turn your back on it.'

'I can't feel as I've got any father but one,' said Eppie, impetuously, while the tears gathered. 'I've always thought of a little home where he'd sit i' the corner, and I should fend and do everything for him: I can't think o' no other home. I wasn't brought up to be a lady, and I can't turn my mind to it. I like the working folks, and their houses, and their ways. And,' she ended passionately, while the tears fell, 'I'm promised to marry a working man, as 'll live with father, and help me to take care of him.'

Godfrey looked up at Nancy with a flushed face and a smarting dilation of the eyes. This frustration of a purpose towards which he had set out under the exalted consciousness that he was about to compensate in some degree for the greatest demerit of his life, made him feel the air of the room stifling.

'Let us go,' he said, in an undertone.

'We won't talk of this any longer now,' said Nancy, rising. 'We're your well-wishers, my dear – and yours too, Marner. We shall come and see you again. It's getting late now.'

In this way she covered her husband's abrupt departure, for Godfrey had gone straight to the door, unable to say more.

Chapter 20

Nancy and Godfrey walked home under the starlight in silence. When they entered the oaken parlour, Godfrey threw himself into his chair, while Nancy laid down her bonnet and shawl, and stood on the hearth near her husband, unwilling to leave him even for a few minutes, and yet fearing to utter any word lest it might jar on his feeling. At last Godfrey turned his head towards her, and their eyes met, dwelling in that meeting without any movement on either side. That quiet mutual gaze of a trusting husband and wife is like the first moment of rest or refuge from a great weariness or a great danger – not to be interfered with by speech or action which would distract the sensations from the fresh enjoyment of repose.

But presently he put out his hand, and as Nancy placed hers within it, he drew her towards him, and said: 'That's ended!'

She bent to kiss him, and then said, as she stood by his side, 'Yes, I'm afraid we must give up the hope of having her for a daughter. It wouldn't be right to want to force her to come to us against her will. We can't alter her bringing up and what's come of it.'

'No,' said Godfrey, with a keen decisiveness of tone, in contrast with his usually careless and unemphatic speech – 'there's debts we can't pay like money debts, by paying extra for the years that have slipped by. While I've been putting off and putting off, the trees have been growing – it's too late now. Marner was in the right in what he said about a man's turning away a blessing from his door: it falls to somebody else. I wanted to pass for childless once, Nancy – I shall pass for childless now against my wish.'

Nancy did not speak immediately, but after a little while she asked – 'You won't make it known, then, about Eppie's being your daughter?'

'No – where would be the good to anybody? – only harm. I must do what I can for her in the state of life she chooses. I must see who it is she's thinking of marrying.'

'If it won't do any good to make the thing known,' said Nancy, who thought she might now allow herself the relief of entertaining a feeling which she had tried to silence before, 'I should be very thankful for father and Priscilla never to be troubled with knowing what was done in the past, more than about Dunsey: it can't be helped, their knowing that.'

'I shall put it in my will – I think I shall put it in my will. I shouldn't like to leave anything to be found out, like this of Dunsey,' said Godfrey, meditatively. 'But I can't see anything but difficulties that 'ud come from telling it now. I must do what I can to make her happy in her own way. I've a notion,' he added, after a moment's pause, 'it's Aaron Winthrop she meant she was engaged to. I remember seeing him with her and Marner going away from church.'

'Well, he's very sober and industrious,' said Nancy, trying to view the matter as cheerfully as possible.

Godfrey fell into thoughtfulness again. Presently he looked up at Nancy sorrowfully, and said: 'She's a very pretty, nice girl, isn't she, Nancy?'

'Yes, dear; and with just your hair and eyes: I wondered it had never struck me before.'

'I think she took a dislike to me at the thought of my being her father: I could see a change in her manner after that.'

'She couldn't bear to think of not looking on Marner as her father,' said Nancy, not wishing to confirm her husband's painful impression.

'She thinks I did wrong by her mother as well as by her. She thinks me worse than I am. But she *must* think it: she can never know all. It's part of my punishment, Nancy, for my daughter to dislike me. I should never have got into that trouble if I'd been true to you – if I hadn't been a fool. I'd no right to expect anything but evil could come of that marriage – and when I shirked doing a father's part too.'

Nancy was silent: her spirit of rectitude would not let her try to soften the edge of what she felt to be a just compunction. He spoke again after a little while, but the tone was rather changed: there was tenderness mingled with the previous self-reproach.

'And I got *you*, Nancy, in spite of all; and yet I've been grumbling and uneasy because I hadn't something else – as if I deserved it.'

'You've never been wanting to me, Godfrey,' said Nancy, with quiet sincerity. 'My only trouble would be gone if you resigned yourself to the lot that's been given us.'

'Well, perhaps it isn't too late to mend a bit there. Though it *is* too late to mend some things, say what they will.'

Chapter 21

The next morning, when Silas and Eppie were seated at their breakfast, he said to her: 'Eppie, there's a thing I've had on my mind to do this two year, and now the money's been brought back to us, we can do it. I've been turning it over and over in the night, and I think we'll set out tomorrow, while the fine days last. We'll leave the house and everything for your godmother to take care on, and we'll make a little bundle o' things and set out.'

'Where to go, daddy?' said Eppie, in much surprise.

'To my old country – to the town where I was born – up Lantern Yard. I want to see Mr Paston, the minister: something may ha' come out to make 'em know I was innicent o' the robbery. And Mr Paston was a man with a deal o' light – I want to speak to him about the drawing o' the lots. And I should like to talk to him about the religion o' this countryside, for I partly think he doesn't know on it.'

Eppie was very joyful, for there was the prospect not only of wonder and delight at seeing a strange country, but also of coming back to tell Aaron all about it. Aaron was so much wiser than she was about most things – it would be rather pleasant to have this little advantage over him. Mrs Winthrop, though possessed with a dim fear of dangers attendant on so long a journey, and requiring many assurances that it would not take them out of the region of carriers' carts and slow waggons, was nevertheless well pleased that Silas should revisit his own country, and find out if he had been cleared from that false accusation.

'You'd be easier in your mind for the rest o' your life, Master Marner,' said Dolly – 'that you would. And if there's any light to be got up the yard as you talk on, we've need of it i' this world, and I'd be glad on it myself, if you could bring it back.'

So, on the fourth day from that time, Silas and Eppie, in their Sunday clothes, with a small bundle tied in a blue linen handkerchief, were making their way through the streets of a great manufacturing town. Silas, bewildered by the changes thirty years had brought over his native place, had stopped several persons in succession to ask them the name of this town, that he might be sure he was not under a mistake about it.

'Ask for Lantern Yard, father – ask this gentleman with the tassels on his shoulders a-standing at the shop-door; he isn't in a hurry like the rest,' said Eppie, in some distress at her father's bewilderment, and ill at ease, besides, amidst the noise, the movement, and the multitude of strange indifferent faces.

'Eh, my child, he won't know anything about it,' said Silas; 'gentlefolks didn't ever go up the Yard. But happen somebody can tell me which is the way to Prison Street, where the jail is. I know the way out o' that as if I'd seen it yesterday.'

With some difficulty, after many turnings and new enquiries, they reached Prison Street; and the grim walls of the jail, the first object that answered to any image in Silas's memory, cheered him with the certitude, which no assurance of the town's name had hitherto given him, that he was in his native place.

'Ah,' he said, drawing a long breath, 'there's the jail, Eppie; that's just the same: I aren't afraid now. It's the third turning on the left hand from the jail doors, that's the way we must go.'

'O, what a dark ugly place!' said Eppie. 'How it hides the sky! It's worse than the Workhouse. I'm glad you don't live in this town now, father. Is Lantern Yard like this street?'

'My precious child,' said Silas, smiling, 'it isn't a big street like this. I never was easy i' this street myself, but I was fond o' Lantern Yard. The shops here are all altered, I think – I can't make 'em out; but I shall know the turning, because it's the third.'

'Here it is,' he said, in a tone of satisfaction, as they came to a narrow alley. 'And then we must go to the left again, and then straight for'ard for a bit, up Shoe Lane; and then we shall be at the entry next to the o'erhanging window, where there's the nick in the road for the water to run. Eh, I can see it all.'

'O father, I'm like as if I was stifled,' said Eppie. 'I couldn't ha' thought as any folks lived i' this way, so close together. How pretty the Stone-pits 'ull look when we get back!'

'It looks comical to *me*, child, now – and smells bad. I can't think as it usened to smell so.'

Here and there a sallow, begrimed face looked out from a gloomy doorway at the strangers, and increased Eppie's uneasiness, so that it was a longed-for relief when they issued from the alleys into Shoe Lane, where there was a broader strip of sky.

'Dear heart!' said Silas, 'why, there's people coming out o' the Yard as if they'd been to chapel at this time o' day – a weekday noon!'

Suddenly he started and stood still with a look of distressed amazement, that alarmed Eppie. They were before an opening in front of a large factory, from which men and women were streaming for their midday meal.

'Father,' said Eppie, clasping his arm, 'what's the matter?'

But she had to speak again and again before Silas could answer her.

'It's gone, child,' he said, at last, in strong agitation – 'Lantern Yard's gone. It must ha' been here, because here's the house with the o'erhanging window – I know that – it's just the same; but they've made this new opening; and see that big factory! It's all gone – chapel and all.'

'Come into that little brush-shop and sit down, father – they'll let you sit down,' said Eppie, always on the watch lest one of her father's strange attacks should come on. 'Perhaps the people can tell you all about it.'

But neither from the brush-maker, who had come to Shoe Lane only ten years ago, when the factory was already built, nor from any other source within his reach, could Silas learn anything of the old Lantern Yard friends, or of Mr Paston, the minister.

'The old place is all swep' away,' Silas said to Dolly Winthrop on the night of his return – 'the little graveyard and everything. The old home's gone; I've no home but this now. I shall never know whether they got at the truth o' the robbery, nor whether Mr Paston could ha' given me any light about the drawing o' the lots. It's dark to me, Mrs Winthrop, that is; I doubt it'll be dark to the last.'

'Well, yes, Master Marner,' said Dolly, who sat with a placid listening face, now bordered by grey hairs; 'I doubt it may. It's the will o' Them above as a many things should be dark to us; but there's some things as I've never felt i' the dark about, and they're mostly what comes i' the day's work. You were hard done by that once, Master Marner, and it seems as you'll never know the rights of it; but that doesn't hinder there *being* a rights, Master Marner, for all it's dark to you and me.'

'No,' said Silas, 'no; that doesn't hinder. Since the time the child was sent to me and I've come to love her as myself, I've had light enough to trusten by; and, now she says she'll never leave me, I think I shall trusten till I die.'

Conclusion

There was one time of the year which was held in Raveloe to be especially suitable for a wedding. It was when the great lilacs and laburnums in the old-fashioned gardens showed their golden and purple wealth above the lichen-tinted walls, and when there were calves still young enough to want bucketfuls of fragrant milk. People were not so busy then as they must become when the full cheese-making and the mowing had set in; and besides, it was a time when a light bridal dress could be worn with comfort and seen to advantage.

Happily the sunshine fell more warmly than usual on the lilac tufts the morning that Eppie was married, for her dress was a very light one. She had often thought, though with a feeling of renunciation, that the perfection of a wedding-dress would be a white cotton, with the tiniest pink sprig at wide intervals; so that when Mrs Godfrey Cass begged to provide one, and asked Eppie to choose what it should be, previous meditation had enabled her to give a decided answer at once.

Seen at a little distance as she walked across the churchyard and down the village, she seemed to be attired in pure white, and her hair looked like the dash of gold on a lily. One hand was on her husband's arm, and with the other she clasped the hand of her father Silas.

'You won't be giving me away, father,' she had said before they went to church; 'you'll only be taking Aaron to be a son to you.'

Dolly Winthrop walked behind with her husband; and there ended the little bridal procession.

There were many eyes to look at it, and Miss Priscilla Lammeter was glad that she and her father had happened to drive up to the door of the Red House just in time to see this pretty sight. They had come to keep Nancy company today, because Mr Cass had had to go away to Lytherley, for special reasons. That seemed to be a pity, for otherwise he might have gone, as Mr Crackenthorp and Mr Osgood certainly would, to look on at the wedding-feast which he had ordered at the Rainbow, naturally feeling a great interest in the weaver who had been wronged by one of his own family.

'I could ha' wished Nancy had had the luck to find a child like that and bring her up,' said Priscilla to her father, as they sat in the gig; 'I should ha' had something young to think of then, besides the lambs and the calves.'

'Yes, my dear, yes,' said Mr Lammeter; 'one feels that as one gets older. Things look dim to old folks: they'd need have some young eyes about 'em, to let 'em know the world's the same as it used to be.'

Nancy came out now to welcome her father and sister; and the wedding group had passed on beyond the Red House to the humbler part of the village.

Dolly Winthrop was the first to divine that old Mr Macey, who had been set in his armchair outside his own door, would expect some special notice as they passed, since he was too old to be at the wedding-feast.

'Mr Macey's looking for a word from us,' said Dolly; 'he'll be hurt if we pass him and say nothing – and him so racked with rheumatiz.'

So they turned aside to shake hands with the old man. He had looked forward to the occasion, and had his premeditated speech.

'Well, Master Marner,' he said, in a voice that quavered a good deal, 'I've lived to see my words come true. I was the first to say there was no harm in you, though your looks might be again' you; and I was the first to say you'd get your money back. And its nothing but rightful as you should. And I'd ha' said the "Amens", and willing, at the holy matrimony; but Tookey's done it a good while now, and I hope you'll have none the worse luck.'

In the open yard before the Rainbow, the party of guests were already assembled, though it was still nearly an hour before the appointed feast-time. But by this means they could not only enjoy the slow advent of their pleasure; they had also ample leisure to talk of Silas Marner's strange history, and arrive by due degrees at the conclusion that he had brought a blessing on himself by acting like a father to a lone motherless child. Even the farrier did not negative this sentiment: on the contrary, he took it up as peculiarly his own, and invited any hardy person present to contradict him. But he met with no contradiction; and all differences among the company were merged in a general agreement with Mr Snell's sentiment, that when a man had deserved his good luck, it was the part of his neighbours to wish him joy.

As the bridal group approached, a hearty cheer was raised in the Rainbow yard; and Ben Winthrop, whose jokes had retained their acceptable flavour, found it agreeable to turn in there and receive congratulations; not requiring the proposed interval of quiet at the Stone-pits before joining the company.

Eppie had a larger garden than she had ever expected there now; and in other ways there had been alterations at the expense of Mr Cass, the landlord, to suit Silas's larger family. For he and Eppie had declared that they would rather stay at the Stone-pits than go to any new home. The garden was fenced with stones on two sides, but in front there was an open fence, through which the flowers shone with answering gladness, as the four united people came within sight of them.

'O father,' said Eppie, 'what a pretty home ours is! I think nobody could be happier than we are.'